Historical Manuscripts Commission

Fifth Report of the Royal Commission on Historical Manuscripts

Historical Manuscripts Commission

Fifth Report of the Royal Commission on Historical Manuscripts

ISBN/EAN: 9783742809353

Manufactured in Europe, USA, Canada, Australia, Japa

Cover: Foto ©Andreas Hilbeck / pixelio.de

Manufactured and distributed by brebook publishing software
(www.brebook.com)

Historical Manuscripts Commission

Fifth Report of the Royal Commission on Historical Manuscripts

CONTENTS.

COMMISSION.

VICTORIA R.

Victoria, by the Grace of God of the United Kingdom of Great Britain and Ireland Queen, Defender of the Faith.

To our right trusty and well-beloved Councillor Sir George Jessel, Knight, Master or Keeper of the Rolls and Records in Chancery; Our right trusty and entirely-beloved Cousin and Councillor Robert Arthur Talbot, Marquess of Salisbury; Our right trusty and right well-beloved Cousin David Graham Drummond, Earl of Airlie, Knight of Our Most Ancient and Most Noble Order of the Thistle; Our right trusty and right well-beloved Cousin Philip Henry, Earl Stanhope; Our trusty and well-beloved Edmond George Fitzmaurice, Esq. (commonly called Lord Edmond George Fitzmaurice); the Right Reverend Father in God Charles Bishop of Limerick, Ardfert, and Aghadoe; Our right trusty and well-beloved James, Baron Talbot de Malahide; Our right trusty and well-beloved Richard Monckton, Baron Houghton; Our right trusty and well-beloved John Emerich Edward, Baron Acton; Our trusty and well-beloved Sir William Stirling Maxwell, Baronet; Our trusty and well-beloved Sir Thomas Duffus Hardy, Knight, Deputy Keeper of the Records; Our trusty and well-beloved Charles William Russell, Doctor in Divinity, President of the College of St. Patrick, Maynooth; and Our trusty and well-beloved George Webbe Dasent, Doctor of Civil Law, greeting.

Whereas We did, by Warrant under Our Royal Sign Manual bearing date the second day of April one thousand eight hundred and sixty-nine, and by subsequent Warrants, authorise and appoint Our right trusty and well-beloved Councillor John, Baron Romilly (since deceased), together with the several noblemen and gentlemen therein named, or any three or more of them, to be Our Commissioners to make inquiry into the places in which Documents illustrative of History or General Public Interest belonging to private persons are deposited, and to consider whether, with the consent of the owners, means might not be taken to render such Documents available for public reference, as by the tenor of the first-recited Warrant under Our Sign Manual, dated the second day of April one thousand eight hundred and sixty-nine, does more fully and at large appear:

Now know ye, that We have revoked and determined, and do by these Presents revoke and determine, the said several Warrants and every matter and thing therein contained:

And whereas We have deemed it expedient that a new Commission should issue for the purposes specified in such Warrant of second day of April one thousand eight hundred and sixty-nine:

Commission appointing Commissioners to make inquiry as to the places in which Documents illustrative of History or General Public Interest belonging to private persons are deposited, and to consider whether, with the consent of the owners, means might not be taken to render such Documents available for public reference.

34961.

a 2

Further know ye that We, reposing great trust and confidence in your ability and discretion, have appointed, and do by these Presents nominate, constitute, and appoint, you the said Sir George Jessel; Robert Arthur Talbot, Marquess of Salisbury; David Graham Drummond, Earl of Airlie; Philip Henry, Earl Stanhope; Edmond George Fitzmaurice (commonly called Lord Edmond George Fitzmaurice); Charles, Bishop of Limerick, Ardfert, and Aghadoe; James, Baron Talbot de Malahide; Richard Monckton, Baron Houghton; John Emerich Edward, Baron Acton; Sir William Stirling Maxwell; Sir Thomas Duffus Hardy; Charles William Russell; and George Webbe Dasent, to be Our Commissioners to make inquiry as to the places in which such Papers and Manuscripts are deposited, and for any of the purposes set forth in the original Warrant under Our Sign Manual, dated second day of April one thousand eight hundred and sixty-nine:

And for the purpose of carrying out the said inquiry We do hereby authorise you to call in the aid and co-operation of all possessors of Manuscripts and Papers, inviting them to assist you in furthering the object of this Commission, and to give them full assurance that no information is sought except such as relates to Public Affairs, and that no knowledge or information which may be obtained from their collections shall be promulgated without their full license and consent:

And We do further by these Presents authorise you, with the consent of the owners of such Manuscripts, to make abstracts and catalogues of such Manuscripts:

And We do hereby direct that you, or any three or more of you, shall form a quorum, and that you, or any three or more of you, shall have power to invite the possessors of such Papers and Records as you may deem it desirable to inspect, and to produce them before you.

And Our further will and pleasure is that you Our said Commissioners, or any three or more of you, do report to Us from time to time in writing under your hands and seals all and every your proceedings under and by virtue of these Presents:

And for the better enabling you to execute these Presents We do hereby nominate, constitute, and appoint Our trusty and well-beloved John Romilly, Esquire, Barister-at-Law, as the Secretary to this Our Commission to attend you, whose services and assistance We require you to use from time to time as occasion may require.

Given at Our Court at St. James's, the Seventh day of December one thousand eight hundred and seventy-five, in the Thirty-ninth Year of Our Reign.

By Her Majesty's Command.

RICHD. ASSHETON CROSS.

FIFTH REPORT

ROYAL COMMISSION ON HISTORICAL MANUSCRIPTS.

TO THE QUEEN'S MOST EXCELLENT MAJESTY.

MAY IT PLEASE YOUR MAJESTY,

WE, Your Majesty's Commissioners appointed by Your Royal Warrant bearing date the 7th of December 1875, to inquire what papers and manuscripts belonging to private families would be useful in illustrating constitutional Law, Science, and General History of this country, and to which their respective possessors would be willing to give access, respectfully beg leave to submit this our Report, to Your Majesty.

Your Majesty, by Royal Warrant, dated the 2nd of April 1869, and by subsequent Warrants, did authorise and appoint the late John Baron Romilly, together with the several other noblemen and gentlemen therein named, to be Your Majesty's Commissioners, to make inquiry as to the places in which documents illustrative of History or of general public interest, belonging to private persons, are deposited, and to consider whether, with the consent of the owners thereof, means might not be taken to render such documents available for public reference; and Your Majesty's Commissioners, pursuant to such instructions in Your Majesty's Royal Warrants, did make such inquiries as they were thereby authorised and instructed to make, and did accordingly make four several Reports to Your Majesty, giving a detailed account of their proceedings therein.

Your Majesty's Commissioners also did further pursue their instructions and collect materials for a Fifth Report to Your Majesty of their proceedings therein, but, owing to certain unforeseen occurrences, were not able to complete the same; foremost among them being the unexpected and lamented death of Baron Romilly, the late Master of the Rolls, who had taken great interest and an active and prominent part in the management of the business of the said Commission; the illness and consequent incapacity of one of the gentlemen appointed by the Commission to act as Inspector of Manuscripts in Ireland, and the prolonged illness and ultimate death of their Assistant Secretary. In consequence of these untoward and most unfortunate occurrences, it was deemed advisable by Your Majesty to revoke and determine Your Majesty's previous Warrants, and, by another Warrant, in substitution thereof to issue a new Commission, appointing thereby the same noblemen and gentlemen (with the exception of Baron Romilly, now deceased), of whom three or more were to form a quorum, to perform the same duties as had been entrusted to them by Your Majesty's previous Warrants. In conformity with the duties so devolving upon them by virtue thereof Your Majesty's Commissioners, with the aid of the materials collected by the Commissioners under the late Commission for their intended Fifth Report, and by adopting the substance of that intended Report, are enabled to present and now have the honour of presenting to Your Majesty the following as their Report (herein called the Fifth Report).

The work of inspection during the past year has been carried on by Mr. Alfred J. Horwood, Mr. H. T. Riley, and Mr. J. C. Jeaffreson for England; Dr. Stuart and Mr. Fraser for Scotland; and Mr. Gilbert for Ireland. In addition to which, Professor Brewer has continued his examination of the Cecil documents in the possession of the Marquis of Salisbury. The Rev. Canon J. C. Robertson (assisted by Mr. J. B. Sheppard) has furnished a report on the manuscripts preserved in Canterbury Cathedral.

In accordance with the original circular of the Commission, the Report of every Inspector has been submitted to the owner of the papers to which his Report refers; and no Report has been published of any manuscripts until consent for its publication has first been obtained from the owner of them.

In the course of the past year 70 additional Collections have been examined, and about 60 Reports have been prepared; and your Commissioners have the gratification

5.

b

of assuring Your Majesty that since the issue of Your Majesty's Royal Warrant of 2d April 1869 more than 420 different collections of manuscripts have thus been examined. Besides which, numerous applications have been spontaneously made for the services of the Inspectors, and the utmost willingness has been evinced by many noblemen and gentlemen to assist the work of the Commission.

The Reports of the Inspectors, printed in the Appendix, pp. 1–665, embrace the following collections :—

In England and Wales.—Of the House of Lords; the Duke of Sutherland; the Marquis of Lansdowne; the Marquis of Salisbury; the Marquis of Ripon; Lord Hatherton; Sir Edmund Lechmere; Sir John Maryon Wilson; Sir John Lawson; Sir Henry Mildmay; Sir Alexander Malet; Sir Gerald Fitzgerald; Lewis Majendie, Esq., M.P.; Rev. H. T. Ellacombe; Walter Charles Strickland, Esq.; Reginald Cholmondeley, Esq.; A. C. Ranyard, Esq.; Stanhope Grove, Esq., Commander R.N.; Evelyn Philip Shirley, Esq.; J. R. Pine Coffin, Esq.; Rev. Edmund Field; Miss Conway Griffith; Robert M. Prideaux, Esq.; Canterbury Cathedral; Catholic Chapter of Westminster, Spanish Place; Cardinal Manning; University College, Oxford; Wadham College, Oxford; Magdalene College, Cambridge; Pembroke College, Cambridge; Parish of Alwington, North Devon; Corporation of Rye; Corporation of New Romney; Corporation of Lydd, Kent; Corporation of Folkestone; Corporation of Dartmouth; Weymouth and Melcombe Regis; High Wycombe, or Chipping Wycombe, Bucks; Corporation of St. Albans; Corporation of Sandwich; Parish of Hartland, North Devon; Corporation of Fordwich, Kent; Mendlesham, Suffolk.

In Scotland.—Of the Marquis of Ailsa; the Marquis of Bute; the Earl of Aberdeen; the Earl of Lauderdale; Lord Kinnaird; Lord Wharncliffe; Sir William Forbes; Sir John Bethune of Kilconquhar; Mrs. Barclay-Allardice; A. D. R. Baillie Cochrane. Esq., M.P.; William Cosmo Gordon, Esq.; A. J. W. H. K. Erskine of Dun; Mrs. D. M. Maxwell Witham, and R. Maxwell Witham, Esq.; Miss M. E. Stirling of Renton; Royal Burgh of Perth.

House of Lords.—Messrs. Monro and Thoms have continued their labours on the manuscripts of the House of Lords, and had at the date of the present Report carried the Calendar to the end of the year 1643. In their Report (App., p. 1) they call special attention to the Minute Books, or rough Journal, kept by one of the Clerks of the Table, and more particularly to the volume containing a record of the Earl of Strafford's trial; which, however, unfortunately ends on the very day that the Bill of Attainder was read a first time in the House of Commons. Many letters have come to light respecting the different incidents in the Civil War, and the most eminent agents who figured in them; also numerous papers referring to the Irish rebellion; letters from Laud, during his imprisonment in the Tower, showing the needless hardships to which he was subjected, and many papers which illustrate the violence of the religious parties of the period. Under the date of Aug. 17, 1643, appears a petition from three messengers, asking for some reward for the number of Papists they have been the means of bringing to trial. In a list of the victims annexed, it appears that six were executed, eight reprieved by the King, while others were outlawed or effected their escape. The outrages committed in Canterbury Cathedral are graphically described in a letter from Dr. Paske dated Aug. 30, 1642, from whose account it appears that the soldiers overthrew the communion table, defaced the screen, violated the monuments of the dead, spoiled the organs, broke down the rails, and destroyed the surplices and prayer books, strewing them all over the pavement. From these and other particulars, it will be seen that the researches of Messrs. Monro and Thoms are of considerable value.

The Duke of Sutherland.—The Duke of Sutherland has at Trentham a collection of several hundred letters which he most courteously sent to London for the use of the Commission. They extend over a period of two centuries, and extracts have been made by Mr. Horwood from such of them as deal with public events. The series opens with the correspondence of Admiral Sir Richard Leveson and his cousin Sir John Leveson. Sir Richard was concerned towards the end of the reign of Queen Elizabeth in taking one of the Spanish carracks, and many difficulties had to be surmounted before the matter of his rich prize could be settled. Sir Richard Leveson, who was present at the siege of Kinsale in 1601, describes how the town was garrisoned by Spaniards, and the defeat of Tyrone and O'Donnell by the English forces. The collection also comprises letters addressed to Lord Cobham, Lord Warden of the Cinque Ports, in the latter years of the same reign. The letters relating to the Civil War and the Commonwealth contain news of interest. In the correspondence of Francis Newport, M.P. for Shrewsbury, evidence is given of the moderate demand made by Charles I. of Sir John Hotham before Hull. The apprehensions of the

Protector Oliver Cromwell and the design to make him a king are here noticed, as also the wedding feast of one of Oliver's daughters, where he drank well, and came out of his chamber in *déshabille* to answer a petition. The statements in a letter of news at p. 143 respecting Oliver and Lady Claypole, and at p. 150 of the attempt of Heveningham to escape prosecution by throwing on Bradshaw the blame of his attendance during the trial of King Charles, will be read with interest. The various speculations at the Restoration regarding the future Queen are detailed in these papers. These speculations raised the hopes of foreign countries, and eventually ended in a fight between the King's French cook and the cooks of three noblemen (p. 160). The letters from Stephen Charlton are numerous and full of news of the day. He gives instances of the irresolution and yet tyrannical conduct of the Protector in the last years of his life, and of the great dissatisfaction of the people. He mentions an attempt to assassinate Oliver's eldest son Richard (p. 166). In the letters of Sir Richard Temple an account is given of what took took place at Whitehall among the officers of the army a few weeks after the death of Oliver (p. 172). The sixteen letters by Dugdale are valuable both for their notices of public affairs and for their allusions to Dugdale's literary labours. The rejoicings at the Restoration, the presents to Charles II., the punishment of the Regicides, his favour to the Presbyterians and neglect of the Cavaliers, are fully related by various writers. Notices are also preserved of the public curiosity regarding Anne Hyde, and of the Duke of York's vexation at her declaration of their marriage. Sir Thomas Gower's two long letters of January 1650 relating to military affairs in the North will be read with interest. A few particulars for theatrical history may be gathered from the letters of Lord Granville (p. 197) and Edward Gower (p. 200). The letters of Lord North, in the last century, show his views with regard to our American colonies at the beginning of the war. Lord Thurlow's letters are very characteristic; and his account of what ensued on the death of Lord Rockingham is curious. His letters on the education which he recommends for a boy are marked by his usual good sense. This collection is extremely valuable for the abundant illustration which it affords for the middle of the 17th century.

The Duke of Marlborough.—The value of the collection at Blenheim is well known to the world at large; and it is with no small satisfaction that Your Majesty's Commissioners announce that his Grace has, in a most liberal spirit, offered to the Commissioners every possible facility for the publication of a detailed account of its priceless contents.

The Marquis of Salisbury.—The list of the Marquis of Salisbury's papers extends from 1588 to the close of 1597. As the first earl entered more into public business, these papers become more numerous and important, increasing in bulk and volume as they proceed. These letters bring to light many facts connected with the history of England, for which the papers either at the Public Record Office or at the British Museum will be searched in vain. As much of this correspondence is connected with Sir Robert Cecil in his private as well as in his official capacity, they afford a closer view of his opinions and those of his contemporaries, and more secret information than can be derived from any other source. When the series is brought down to the close of the reign of Elizabeth, it will add much to the materials for illustrating a period of English history now very imperfectly known.

The Marquis of Lansdowne.—Lord Edmond Fitzmaurice has continued his report (p. 215) on the papers at Lansdowne House. The greater part of it relates to colonial affairs and the peace with America. The most important of these papers will be printed in the concluding volumes of the Life of Lord Shelburne. Several of those at Lansdowne House mentioned in the previous Reports of the late Commissioners have already appeared in the first volume of that work. The few papers at Lansdowne House which still remain to be noticed relate to Irish and Indian affairs, and will be reported on in the future Reports of the Commissioners.

The Marquis of Ripon.—The Marquis of Ripon sent a very early copy of a Latin work on Medicine compiled by Bernard de Gordon, of the celebrated School of Medicine at Montpelier. The volume was once part of the Library of Fountains Abbey. It is described at p. 294 of the Appendix.

Lord Hatherton.—Lord Hatherton's collection is described at p. 294. A deed executed by Justice Littleton, author of the well known book on Tenures, shows his large landed property. Among the autograph signatures is the rare one of King Edward IV.; and there are holograph letters by John Churchill, John Locke, Dean Swift, and George Washington. Portrait collectors will be interested in knowing that an engraving made in Dublin in or before 1726, was thought by the Dean to be the best likeness of himself. Evidence is found among these papers that the translation of Juvenal's Satires, which goes under the name of Dryden, was not wholly made by him. The translation of the eighth satire, which was corrected by Dryden, is due to George Stepney. A note by Pope on Stepney's MS. translation shows how well he appreciated Dryden's talents.

Sir Edmund Lechmere.—Among the manuscripts of Sir Edmund Lechmere the most important is the Taxation Roll for the county of Worcester in the reign of Edward I. From this long and beautifully written document, the names of holders of houses or land in the town of Worcester and in a multitude of manors and villages, and their relative status, can be ascertained. The deeds of the 12th and 13th and 14th centuries relating to the Priory of Worcester are very important. In one of them reference is made to the settlement of a lease by duel. Another describes the furniture and fittings of a chantry in the reign of Edward II. In the reign of Henry V. the Earl of Worcester awards penance to be done by Nicolas Burdet for an offence committed in Worcester Cathedral. (See App., p. 299.)

Sir John Wilson.—Sir John Maryon Wilson, Bart., possesses an early manuscript on parchment of the Code of Iceland Laws known as *Ionsbok*. Such MSS. are not common. Among his papers is also the diploma, from the University of Ferrara, granting the degree of Doctor of Laws to Sir Thomas Wilson, afterwards secretary to Queen Elizabeth; and a certificate by Gustavus Adolphus, on the occasion of his being made Knight of the Garter. (See App., p. 304.)

Sir John Lawson.—The York Ritual mentioned in the last Report of the late Commissioners as belonging to Sir John Lawson, Bart., has been found and sent by him to London. Mr. Horwood has described it at p. 305 of the Appendix. It is of the 14th century, and believed to be the only copy known. The long passages in English contained in it were thought worthy of transcription.

Sir Henry Mildmay.—Sir Henry Mildmay possesses the original Order in Council signed by Oliver Cromwell (three weeks after the death of King Charles) for the arms and designs "thenceforth to be used on the ships and flags of the Navy;" and a large portion of the original MS. of "The Light of Nature," by Abraham Tucker.

Sir A. Malet.—The remarkably fine collection of Sir A. Malet has been described by Mr. Horwood at p. 308. By reason of Sir Alexander's expression of an intention some day to publish a work in which his MSS. would be used, the extracts in the Appendix are few compared with the importance of the documents. The contents of the letters from Brussels of Sir Thos. Boleyn and Sir Thomas Spinelly to King Henry VIII. are for the present reserved. In Scotch affairs the King roundly accuses Cardinal Beaton of having "powdered his speech with lies." Long letters by Sir Thomas Wharton to the Earl of Hertford relate his ravages in Scotland. In relation to Mary Queen of Scots, the documents are very interesting. Among them is an original letter, in 1567, from the confederate lords to Lord Grey for the deliverance of Mary from her thraldom; a copy of Morton's declaration in 1568 regarding the silver casket; original depositions by Lord Hume and W. Kircaldy touching the death of Darnley; a letter by the Earl of Leicester to the Regent Murray in 1567. In 1561 the Regent writes in strong terms to dissuade his sister Queen Mary from interfering in matters of religion, and in the same year is a letter from him to Mr. Wood at the Court of England. In 1562 a letter from Maitland comments on the execution of Chastelard, and another discusses the proposed meeting between the English and Scottish Queens. In 1567 is a holograph letter by Cecil to Randolph against the proposed marriage of Mary with a Spanish Prince. A letter from King James, in 1582, asks that Archibald Douglas, one of Darnley's murderers, may be given up; and there is an extraordinary letter by him to the Earl of Leicester, a few weeks before his mother was beheaded, showing his indifference to her fate. Other writers are Grindal, Bishop of London and Archbishop of York; Sir John Perrot and Sir Francis Knollys on Irish affairs; Walsingham and the Archbishop of Canterbury, and some bishops in 1582 and 1583 on the proposed alteration of the calendar. In July 1588 a letter from the Council orders the clergy to offer up prayers against the Spaniards. In the time of King James I. there is a pathetic petition by Lady Arabella Stuart (Seymour) to the King, and an original letter asking the Earl of Northampton to interfere with the King on her behalf. A letter from Sir Theodore Mayerne to the King mentions De Thou's desire that Sir R. Cotton should write a continuation of his Memoirs; so that De Thou might have the benefit of them for his great History. In the time of Charles I. there are several original letters by John Selden, and notice of a volume containing upwards of 200 letters addressed to him; also letters by Secretary Windebank to Sir Arthur Hopton in Spain. There are several letters to Whitelock in the time of the Commonwealth. From other papers in Sir Alexander's possession it appears that Brian Walton had a loan of the Codex Alexandrinus in 1653; and there is an approbation by the Archbishop of Armagh and Selden of a proof of Walton's Polyglot. Portions remain of a draft of a project by Cromwell for founding a new College at Oxford. There also is a proposition by James Howell for a new treatise on the sovereignty of the seas. To these must be added original documents signed by King Charles II. in 1652 and the two following years; a letter by Algernon Sydney at Elsinore shortly before the Restoration; a long Latin address by Henry Earl of Rochester to the Emperor urging him to use his influence with the Dutch and the Pope in favour of King Charles. There are also letters by Prince Rupert, the Duke of Albemarle, Sir W. Coventry, the Duke of Ormond, Bishop Burnet, Pepys, and Clifford. There are several letters by Lord Clarendon to Henry Coventry at Breda; also many papers and letters on Navy and Scotch affairs in the reign of Charles II.; a number of letters to the Duke of Lauderdale, some of which relate to the murder of the Archbishop of St. Andrews. There is a series of letters from Sir Thomas Higgons the King's Envoy at Vienna in 1674 and the two following years. One of the documents appears to be the original note which Charles II. wrote to the Duke of York advising or rather directing him to go beyond sea; it is dated Feb. 28th, 1679. The King's religious proclivities brought him up several Christmas and the New Years' congratulations from Cardinals at Rome. There is a letter from Rushworth stating the cause of certain omissions from his well known Historical Collections. In 1688 there are letters by the Duke of Tyrconnel and the Marquis d'Albeville to King James II. chiefly on the question of religion; and an account of the capture of King James at Faversham. Two of Bishop Atterbury's letters mention Mr. Bedford, the person who was imprisoned as the supposed author of a Jacobite book called "The Hereditary Right of the Crown of England asserted." The doubt as to the authorship of that book has been quite set at rest by the recent discovery of the original manuscript in the handwriting of Dr. George Harbin to whom Atterbury's letters were addressed.

Mr. Majendie.—The manuscripts of Mr. Majendie, M.P., comprise among other things a very remarkable Bede roll of the end of the 12th century; which shows the answers of 120 churches in various parts of the kingdom to the request of the prioress of Hedingham for prayers for the soul of her predecessor Lucy Countess of Oxford. The various specimens of writing in the roll render it very valuable for palæographical purposes. A careful survey made for Lord Burghley shows the extent and parcels of the honour and manor of Castle Hedingham in the time of Queen Elizabeth. In the middle of the last century Mr. J. J. Majendie exerted himself much in obtaining assistance for Protestants abroad; and there are at Hedingham Castle many letters to him from Herring and Secker, successively Archbishops of Canterbury, on the subject. (See App., p. 321.)

Mr. Ellacombe.—Much information as to the early topography of Bristol and the names of its civil officers and residents is furnished by the charters in the collection of the Rev. H. T. Ellacombe, described at p. 323 of the Appendix. The danger of joining a mob merely as a spectator is well shown by the papers relating to Francis Creswick, whose curiosity to know what was going on when the Duke of Monmouth came to Keynsham caused his imprisonment, and (in those days) risked his life. By one of the letters we learn that when Lord Chancellor Jeffreys was captured he had in his possession 35,000 guineas and much silver. Most of the papers and documents mentioned in the report are portions of the family papers of Newton of Barrs Court, in the county of Gloucester, which are very numerous, but chiefly of private interest.

Mr. Strickland.—Mr. Strickland, of Sizergh Castle (whose collection is noticed at p. 329), possesses a series of charters from the 12th century relating to the estates which he and his ancestors have held so long. Among the miscellaneous documents at the Castle, is a portion of a cartulary of the Abbey of Cokersand. One of the very early deeds has for witness William de Daker, Sheriff of Westmoreland, a name not hitherto placed in the list of sheriffs for that county, and in another deed John De Bellocampo is called Sheriff of Appleby. There is a deed of the time of Henry VI. which shows the terms on which the Strickland of that time took service with a great noble and soldier; among other stipulations is one by which when a man of rank was captured by a Strickland the ransom would go to the Earl, he paying a portion to the captor. The Strickland of Henry VIII.'s time was capable of raising from his tenants and servants a troop of 280 armed men. There are a few letters and papers during the Civil War, in which the then Strickland fought for the King. The King's letter to the

Yorkshire gentlemen (in 1640) rebukes them for troubling him before they had applied to the Lord Lieutenant, whom they were desired to consider as their Sovereign.

Mr. Cholmondely.—The manuscripts of Mr. Cholmondely, of Condover Hall (described by Mr. Horwood at p. 333), are of much interest. The register of Kingswood Abbey (once in that collection) has yet to be discovered; in the meantime its place is partly supplied by a series of early charters to that house, now at Condover Hall. There are large collections for the history of Cheshire and its families, also for the history of Lancashire and the Isle of Man; also personal memorials of the Earl of Derby and his Countess, the defender of Latham House, and a copy signed by her of the articles for the surrender of Castle Rushen and Peel Castle. The illustrations for the county of Gloucester are numerous. There is a list of nearly all the able-bodied men in the county in 1608; valuable memoranda for the history of domestic life in the rules for the household of Sir Thomas Berkeley and his wife in the times of Queen Elizabeth and King James I. Among the original letters and papers relating to the siege of Berkeley Castle, are the original articles for its surrender to the Parliament. Many letters relate to the transport of troops to Ireland by way of Chester; and in 1642 there is a long letter giving an account of the fighting in Ireland. When the Five Members fled for fear of the King, it was supposed that they would leave the kingdom, and the King's letter to the Mayor of Chester telling him to stay them if they came that way is in this collection, as is also a letter signed by Queen Mary denouncing Lady Jane Grey and her husband. A letter of 1684 under the hand of King Charles II. shows that he expended a large sum from his private purse towards founding Chelsea Hospital. There is a letter by Alexander Pope; and another by Hume shows how gracefully a philosopher could receive correction of an error from a fellow labourer in the field of History.

Mr. Ranyard.—Mr. Ranyard, of Lincoln's Inn, sent his collection of MSS. (described at p. 404) among which is an early copy of one of the Chronicles of the Crusades; also the original certificate of admission to deacon's orders of the celebrated George Whitefield, and the original certificate of his being made a burgess of Glasgow.

· *Commander Grove.*—Commander Grove's papers consist of letters by Monck and other Commonwealth authorities to his ancestor Colonel Pury who held command in Gloucestershire for Cromwell. One of the letters offers a reward of 100*l.* to any officer or soldier who shall capture Lambert, just then escaped from the Tower.

Mr. Shirley.—Mr. Shirley's collection of manuscripts (described at p. 362) is rich in heraldic and genealogical works. The volume presented to Queen Elizabeth is particularly noticeable. There are some interesting papers relating to the unfortunate Robert Devereux, Earl of Essex; original correspondence of James Stanhope, afterwards Earl Stanhope, with Lord Treasurer Godolphin, and numerous original compositions of the second Earl of Chesterfield. Among these papers are the originals of the celebrated *Characters*, published by the late Earl Stanhope in his edition of the fourth earl's letters; also a tract by Bishop Morley on Transubstantiation supposed to be yet unprinted. A letter of advice by Lord Chesterfield to his godson and heir is remarkable for the strong terms in which he commends to his care Dr. Dodd, who afterwards came to an untimely end. A 16th century volume contains copies of many letters by Roger Marbeck, the compiler of the first printed English Concordance to the Bible. Among the copies of University documents, is a decree appointing what authors were to be read by students and Bachelors of Arts in the University of Oxford, belonging to the house of King Henry VIII. In old times when the King pardoned a man who had slain another he could not thereby abrogate with the private right of the relatives of the slain, and the pardon used to contain words which reserved that right. This rule is well illustrated by the pardon of King Edward III. (among Mr. Shirley's deeds), and the deed following, showing that the slayer paid money to the widow of the dead man in satisfaction of her right to appeal him for the death of her husband.

Mr. Bacon Frank.—The report on the collection of Mr. Bacon Frank, of Campsall Hall, Yorkshire, is completed, but will be reserved for a future Report. It comprises the large collections for Yorkshire history made by Dr. Nathaniel Johnston of Pontefract, in the 17th century, and by Mr. R. Frank in the last century. Dr. Johnston's papers contain original documents obtained by him from Sheffield Castle and valuable letters, including one by Sir Walter Raleigh. Mr. Frank has a fine MS. of Chaucer's " Troilus and Cressida."

Sir Henry Ingilby.—The report on the collection of Sir Henry Ingilby, of Ripley Castle, has also been completed. In it will be found noticed several ancient volumes formerly part of the library of Fountains Abbey, books of accounts and rentals of the abbey, and a very early copy of Ralph de Diceto's Annals. Two volumes contain

letters to and from Sir Robert Paston, Viscount Yarmouth, in the 17th century, and
from these large extracts have been taken.

Sir Alexander Hood.—The collection of Sir Alexander Hood, of St. Audries, in Somersetshire, has been examined. It contains, among other things, a fine Wickliffe Bible,
a 15th century translation into English of Trivet's French Chronicle with a continuation.

Duke of Northumberland.—The Duke of Northumberland very kindly opened to Your
Commissioners his evidence room at Syon House. Most of the letters once preserved
there have been removed to Alnwick and are described in the Appendix to the Third
Report there made by Your Majesty's late Commissioners. Among other MSS. of
interest a register of Tynemouth Priory and upwards of a hundred rolls of account of
the 16th and 17th centuries are still preserved at Syon House; and from the latter Mr.
Horwood has made extracts, many of which illustrate the life of Henry the ninth Earl
of Northumberland while in the Tower, and give some account of the Earl's pursuits
during his imprisonment. There are also notices of Sir Walter Raleigh, Thomas
Hariot the mathematician, and George Peele the poet.

Sir Reginald Graham.—Sir Reginald Graham has sent a very large collection of
papers, nearly all relating to the 17th century. These have been examined and a selection has been made, a notice of which will be given in the next Report. There are many
accounts of the expenses of the first George Villiers, Duke of Buckingham; several
Council letters from Scotland with the signature of King Charles I. impressed by
means of a stamp; and many papers on Mint affairs while Sir Henry Slingsby was
Master.

Sir Frederick Graham.—The examination of the manuscripts of Sir Frederick
Graham, of Netherby, is now in hand. They comprise the letter books and original
papers of Viscount Preston while Ambassador in Paris at the end of the reign of
King Charles II. and afterwards, and these alone will furnish matter for a large and
interesting report. Your Commissioners cannot but think it a matter of congratulation
that the examination of Sir Frederick Graham's papers by Mr. Horwood has been the
means of discovering and identifying a commonplace book, the greater part of which is
in the handwriting of John Milton the poet. A full description of it will be contained
in the report on Sir Frederick Graham's MSS.

Mr. Lowndes.—The manuscripts of Mr. Lowndes, of Barrington Hall, in Essex, are
now under examination. They comprise many hundred original letters chiefly of the
17th century; among the writers may be mentioned Oliver Cromwell, John Hampden,
and John Pym. The affairs of the county of Essex during the Civil War are largely
illustrated. There are upwards of 300 early charters to the Priory of Hatfield Regis,
a valuable contribution to monastic history, as no cartulary of that house seems to be
known.

Lord Leconfield.—Lord Leconfield's manuscripts, at Petworth, have been examined :
many of the volumes there belonged to Henry ninth Earl of Northumberland. His
Lordship possesses the MS. of Chaucer's Canterbury Tales, now being printed for the
Chaucer Society ; a very interesting register of Ely Priory ; a copy of the Black Book
of the Admiralty, and some state papers of the last century. The report on these
manuscripts is nearly completed.

Miss C. Griffith.—Among the Carreglwyd MSS. (for which Miss Conway Griffith,
of Carreglwyd, Anglesey, North Wales, is chiefly indebted to her ancestor, John Griffith,
Esq., a lawyer of Gray's Inn, who was for several years private secretary to Henry
Earl of Northampton, Lord Privy Seal to James I.) will be found a collection of
protestations of loyalty to Queen Elizabeth, signed by Catholic gentlemen imprisoned
in Ely Palace, 1588-1590 ;—a list of the captains cashiered by the Earl of Essex in
Ireland ;—a survey and description of Romney Marsh, temp. Eliz. ;—a copy of Sir
Robert Naunton's Fragmenta Regalia ;—the patent of a grant (Mar. 12, 1604) of lands,
containing minute particulars of the topography of the purlieus of Whitehall and
Westminster Palace ;—a list of the officers who attended the Earl of Nottingham
to Spain (1605) ;—a list of the lords and gentlemen who attended Lord Hertford on
his embassy to the Archduke the same year ;—a tract on the abuses of wainage (temp.
Eliz. and Jac. I.) written for the information of the Earl of Northampton, Lord Privy Seal,
by the King's yeoman-cart-taker ;—a declaration of the quarrel between Lord Walden
and Sir Edward Herbert ;—papers relating to the foundation and early government of
Lord Northampton's charitable colleges at Castle Rising, Clunn, and Greenwich ;—the
Earl of Northampton's last testament ;—a letter from the Earl of Arundel to the Lord
Keeper, Sir Francis Bacon ;—two sets of verses written by James I. ;—orders respecting
the funeral of James I. and liveries of mourning from the Great Wardrobe ;—the Earl
of Oxford's letter (15th May 1625) to his Countess from Gertruydenberg ;—a letter

(7th Feb. 1626) from Lewes, Bishop of Bangor, describing Charles I.'s coronation and the life of his court ;—a list of the persons slain at the Isle of Rhé ;—a Narrative, by an eye-witness, of the naval and military operations attending the army's landing in the Isle of Rhé ;—a Latin letter describing Van Tromp's victories over the Spanish fleets off the Downs ;—a copy (made from the original draft) of the speech which the Earl of Strafford intended to deliver on the scaffold ;—a set of verses lampooning Sir John Suckling, with his reply ;—satirical verses on the Westminster Assembly of Divines ;—satirical verses on Presbytery and Parliament ;—muster-rolls and warrants exhibiting the strength, equipment, and discipline of the trained bands in Anglesey in the 17th century ;—a curious marriage-settlement (20th Aug. 1612) illustrative of manners in North Wales ;—James I.'s licence exempting the Bishop of Bangor from attendance in Parliament ;—bills illustrative of the price of labour and materials for building in North Wales, temp. Car. I. ;—correspondence and papers, exhibiting the attitude and action of the adherents of Charles I., and the supporters of the Parliament in North Wales during the Civil War. (See App., p. 405.)

Cardinal Manning.—The historical MSS. in the official custody of Cardinal Manning have been found upon examination to be more important and more numerous than had been anticipated. They relate for the most part to the fortunes of the Catholics in England from the close of the reign of Elizabeth to the Revolution of 1688 and a little later. There is a long series of original letters consisting of correspondence between England and Rome, of which the longer portion is addressed to the agent of the English Catholic clergy resident in the Papal court. The correspondence is by no means purely official. The writers supplied their agent with such notices of English affairs as were, politically as well as religiously, interesting. Besides these details much light is thrown upon the origin and history of the English Colleges at Rome, Douai, Rheims, &c., as well as upon the monasteries and convents founded in France, Belgium, Spain, and Germany. (See App., p. 470.)

The portion of these MSS. here catalogued forms about one half of the entire collection. Many of these papers are well worthy of a more minute description, especially the correspondence. Nearly identical with the above, and extending over the same period, is the collection of papers now in the custody of Provost Hunt, belonging to the Catholic Chapter of Westminster, in Spanish Place, Manchester Square.

Dodd's Historical Dictionary of eminent Catholics, which has strayed from its fellows in Spanish Place, is safely deposited in the library of St. Mary's College, Oscott, already described in the Appendix to the First Report, p. 89.

Rev. E. Field.—The MSS. in the possession of the Reverend Edmund Field of Lancing College, Sussex, generally reflect the commercial derangement and social inconveniences attending the conflict of the Crown and Parliament in the 17th century. Sir Abel Barker's private letter-book (1642–1665) is a remarkable record of a Rutland squire's doings in business, politics, and society during the busiest period of a long and fully occupied life ; his private account book (1665–1677) affords precise information respecting the interests and engagements of his closing years. Another division of the collection consists chiefly of letters written to him by his second wife, his brothers, and others of his domestic circle. There are also documents relating to taxation and public affairs in Rutland, and the adjoining counties, in the times of Charles I., the Commonwealth, and Charles II., writs, ordinary and extra-ordinary, for the levying of ship-money, receipts for money, horses, cattle, provender for animals and other goods, supplied by Mr. (afterwards Sir) Abel Barker, in sub-mission to military requisitions, for the service of the King and Parliament ; General Ireton's order to the army in Rutland ; letters of instruction for drilling the trained bands in the same county. Amongst the more recent papers of Mr. Field's collection appear the correspondence of William Whiston, the mathematician, with his children and scientific friends ; the register of the minutes of William Whiston's Society for the promotion of Primitive Christianity ; and letters by Gilbert White, of Selborne, and his brothers. (See App., p. 387.)

Dean and Chapter of Canterbury.—These archives contain, at least, five thousand original MSS., exclusive of the registers in which are recorded the domestic trans-actions of the Prior and Chapter of Christ Church, *sede plena,* and their authoritative acts as custodians of the spiritualities of the archbishopric, *sede vacante.* Up to the date of this present Report the detached MSS. of the Chartæ Antiquæ only have been examined ; the registers are left for another occasion. Almost every chapter in the history of the See of Canterbury is here indicated by contemporary charters and other documents, which are so abundant that from very early days they have furnished the sources from which the ancient chroniclers and church historians afterwards drew much of their materials. Thorne is especially indebted to these documents. One is copied into the MS. of William of Canterbury, and more lately many have appeared in Kemble's "Codex Diplomaticus." Abundant supplies are here found for a domestic history of the great Benedictine Convent of Canterbury, beginning with the narratives of the elections of the Priors, who were summoned to attend the King as Lords of Parliament, and descending through the yearly accounts of the several monastic officers to the small bills paid by the cook for sundries used in his department. Under the title *sede vacante* is found a large number of MSS. which illustrate the position of the Prior, promoted almost to an Archbishopric, whenever the Metropolitan chair became vacant. Several important papers contain remonstrances and "Articuli Cleri" propounded by the clergy assembled in Synod. There are a few original Papal Bulls, and Apostolical Letters, but the number is not so great as might have been expected. The records of the consecrations of suffragan bishops, with their professions of canonical obedience to the Church of Canterbury, are found in a long continued series, accompanied by letters of "Alibi Consecrari" issued to them by the Prior in those cases in which, by his permission, they were consecrated elsewhere than in the Metropolitan Cathedral. The monopoly referred to was enjoyed by the Priory by virtue of a charter of Archbishop Becket, of which a copy still exists. The dispute as to the precedence and insignia of the Archbishop of York whilst a sojourner in the southern province, was a cause of much debate from the time of William the Conqueror, whose autograph corroborates a composition made between the Archbishops of his day, to the period when Robert Winchelsey, by sheer force of character, almost crushed the northern Archbishop in the province of Canterbury, whilst he himself triumphantly marched through that of York with his cross carried erect before him. The licenses granted on the special occasion, when the Statute of Mortmain was suspended in favour of the Priory, are evidence of the frequency of this indulgence. There are progressive examples of the English tongue from ante-Norman times up to the 16th century. Many of the earliest of these specimens have been printed. For obvious reasons, very few direct allusions to Archbishop Becket remain among these Chartæ Antiquæ, and his charters and letters have all been suppressed, but there still exist a few writs of Henry II. which were attested, and possibly written, by "Tom. Canc." The Archbishop's family—"Consanguinei" and "Nepotes"—are mentioned during a space of fifty years after his death, and always as recipients of alms, or incumbents of small ecclesiastical benefices. One of the four murderers, William De Tracy, made some atonement for his offence by giving the manor of Doccumbe to the convent of which the murdered Archbishop was a protector during his life, and more than a patron after his death. A few papers remain which go to prove how nearly Archbishop Winchelsey, by the zeal of Earl Thomas of Lancaster, attained the honours of canonization. A mortuary roll sent round from Ely, after the death of Bishop Hotham, to all the monasteries which had entered into the bond of "mutual society" with the convent of Ely, heads a considerable number of notices and letters, all relating to the brotherly offices which monks and friars of different houses and orders undertook on behalf of those who were linked with them in the same spiritual tie. Notices of Sandwich and Fordwich, at which ports Christ Church and St. Augustine's respectively landed their imports, afford a glimpse of the commerce of the Middle Ages ; and a correspondence between Henry IV. and the Hanseatic League exhibits commercial and international law in its cradle. An interesting series of charters, many of them carrying the great seals of the kings of France, relate how Louis VII. on his pilgrimage gave to the monks of Canterbury a hundred muids of wine, which gift his successors from time to time renewed, the French nobility at the same time allowing a free passage through such of their lands as lay between the vineyards and the sea. The foundation by Archbishop Islip, and the restoration by Prior Chillenden, of Canterbury College in Oxford, are chronicled in the deeds of foundation and endowment, and in the bills for work and materials paid at the time of the rebuilding. The deed of endowment by Henry VII. of a chantry in Canterbury Cathedral is contained in a parchment volume sumptuously bound in blue velvet and decorated with the king's badges of the Rose and Portcullis. The period of the dissolution of monasteries is marked by an inventory of plate, by a deed providing for some of the disestablished monks, and by a complete list of all the real estate of the "late monastery of Christ Church in Canterbury" made in 1540. (See App., p. 427.)

Your Majesty's Commissioners are indebted for the Report on the MSS. of this cathedral to Mr. J. B. Sheppard, of Canterbury, who was recommended to them by the Rev. Canon Robertson as one "who had for many months been employed in the study of these documents." Mr. Sheppard has rendered the Chapter of Canterbury great service by his labours in connexion with their muniments.

Mr. Pine-Coffin.—In continuation of the account given in the Fourth Report of the documents in the possession of J. R. Pine-Coffin, Esq., preserved at Portledge in North Devon, three deeds of the 16th century are noticed by Mr. Riley in the Appendix, containing the names of John Gaye, Thomas Gaye, and a second John Gaye, of Gulworthy (now Goldsworthy) in North Devon, ancestors of John Gay the poet ; with those of several of the family of Risdon, also of Goldsworthy, to which Tristram Rysdon (named in the preceding Report), a writer on the laws of England, belonged. From the letters and miscellaneous papers, 600 in number, large extracts have been made. (See App., p. 370.)

The letters are mostly addressed to Mr. Richard Coffin, of Portledge, who was Sheriff of Devon in the eventful year 1685. Among the miscellaneous letters, is one addressed by Edmund Prideaux, of Padstowe, (father of Humphrey, Dean of Norwich), to Ann, his daughter, second wife of Richard Coffin, referring to the Popish Plot ; another, addressed to Richard Coffin, as to "the bookes bought for mee at the auction of " Dr. Heinsius in Holland ; " a letter from the Mayor of Taunton to the Mayor of Exeter, sent to Richard Coffin, as High Sheriff for the county of Devon, giving an account of disturbances near Taunton, nearly a fortnight in advance of the Duke of Monmouth's landing at Lyme Regis in Dorset ; a letter written to Richard Coffin by John Prince, still remembered as the author of the "Worthies of Devon " (1701), a work which at this date (1686) he seems to have been inclined to press Richard Coffin to undertake ; a long paper, beautifully written, headed " Reasons humbly offered to " the Duke of Albemarle against his going Governor of Jamaica." The Duke had not shown the requisite aptitude or courage on the occasion of Monmouth's landing in the West ; hence perhaps his desire to accept the Governorship of so remote a place as the Island of Jamaica. It is not improbable that Richard Coffin was the author of this Expostulation, from which some extracts are given in the Appendix. Mr. Thomas Northmore, of Exeter, was Deputy-Assistant Sheriff to Richard Coffin during his year of office in 1685 ; out of his twenty letters extracts from nine are given. They mostly refer to the progress and termination of Monmouth's rebellion, the preparations for opposing it, and the arrangements ultimately made for the punishment of the rebels. The whippings and executions, the boiling and tarring of the quarters, and their proposed transmission to various towns, are noticed without a single expression of pity. From 1683 to within a year or two before the death of Mr. Richard Coffin (in 1699) a correspondence was kept up between him and his brother-in-law, Dr. Humphrey Prideaux, Prebendary, and afterwards Dean, of Norwich. Most of the Dean's letters have probably perished, but selections are given from eleven out of the twelve remaining. In them the politics of the day and the religious aspect of the times are discussed ; the characters respectively of the Universities come under review, the Doctor in general giving a very disparaging account of Oxford. He looks upon Wadham as the "best governed" College in the University ; of Christ Church he speaks with very faint praise ; while in Exeter College he "never knew anything . . . but drinking " and duncery." In more than one of his letters the Doctor alludes to his *Life of Mahomet*, and says that he is "sorry the wickedness of the present age makes us " soe much need such bookes." A constant correspondence was also maintained between Dr. Prideaux and his sister, Mrs. Ann Coffin, from 1673 to 1705 probably, the year of her death. Of these letters extracts are given from 27 out of the 66 which still remain. In the first that is quoted (November 1673), he gives a very unfavourable account of " the new Dutchesse of York," Mary of Modena. She is "hunch-back'd," he says, "and " ugly, and the daughter of a poor beggarly Prince." In another letter he tells his sister " You are soe much in love with your Mons. Jureu [Jurieu] that I believe if my " brother were dead you would make him your second husband." In another letter, the Doctor returns to the charge :—"Exeter College is totally spoyld, and soe is " Christ Church, and for that reason when lately chosen Canon of Christ Church " and Professor of the Oriental languages in Dr. Pocock's place, I refused to goe." Walter Moyle, a kinsman of Dr. Prideaux, and still remembered in literature as one of the wits of the day, comes under the lash of his censure more than once. In 1698 it was the Doctor's opinion of the progress made by the Jesuits in China, that they had done nothing more than to "get the Chinese to worship Jesus " Christ, the Virgin Mary, and St. Peter, amongst the rest of their heathen " gods." Upon the Greek Church and its liturgy he is inclined to be severe, and in reference to the Dissenters of his day he says, "I think, never any church was " better established than ours, ... the toleration which is now allowed them that " doe oppose it, makes only way for the driving of Christianity out of the land, for

" the only sect that grows upon it are the Quakers, who are noe Christians. All sects
" besides begin to dwindle to nothing; I am sure they do so where I am concerned."
Within six months after he had lost his wife, Bridget Bokenham, he writes to his sister,
" I am mightily pressed to marry again, with abundance of offers and very valuable
" ones, but considering all things I shall think of making no more changes till I
" make my great change of this life, as I hope for a better, and I have some reason to
" apprehend that I am at no great distance from it." Though, probably even then
threatened with the stone, he survived no less than 23 years.

From 1683 to 1697 Mr. Richard Lapthorne, residing in Hatton Garden, was Richard
Coffin's London agent, purchasing books for the library he was then forming at Portledge, and sending him letters of news every Saturday. Of these letters, no less than 409
have survived. They have been all examined for the purposes of this Report, and extracts
of a miscellaneous description are given from 139. In one of them mention is made of
four manuscripts of the works of Wyclif, which had been recently bought (1687) at an
auction by the Earl of Kent for 21l., " od money." Mr. Lapthorne " could have
" almost have wished he had bought them himself at that price." The crimes, accidents, and offences of the time, figure largely in Lapthorne's communications. An
account is given (14 July 1688) of the great rejoicings in London on the birth of the
unfortunate Prince, afterwards known as the Old Pretender. In the same year
the Mayor of Scarborough is represented as going to Windsor to complain about a
Captain who had tossed him in a blanket, though at this date (Sept. 1688) the Court at
Windsor would have something more serious to think of. The people of London,
however, in these letters are represented as showing no concern under the impending
menace of an invasion. In 1689 mention is made of John Bagford, afterwards well
known as a typographical antiquary, and whose collections are now in the British
Museum. Of a "gentlewoman in Duke Street near Covent Garden," the following
account is given (Feb. 1691):—"There have bin a College of Theologists to make
" their observations on her; and in order to consult about a way to restore her, (viz.)
" Dr. Hornick and others. . .Sometimes sitting in her chayre she will be visibly lifted
" up, together with her chayre, a great distance from the ground, no one touching
" the same that can be perceived." The fire is described (11 Apr. 1691) which so
nearly brought to an end all the glories of the Palace at Whitehall, as originating in
the laziness of "a mayd's burning off a single candle from the pound, instead of
" cutting it with a knife." An account is also given of the Cottonian Library at Westminster as it appeared in 1692, and some few of its more striking curiosities are
described. A short account of Slingsby Bethell, Sheriff of London, forms an item in
the latest portion of this correspondence.

University College, Oxford.—From such of the early archives of University College
as have survived, comparatively few in number, may be gathered various particulars in reference to the halls and other buildings of Oxford in the 14th century.
About the year 1400 several of the "Schools" of Oxford are mentioned. Among
the visitors entertained from time to time by this College will be found at least one or
two names of interest. Most, if not all, of the ancient deeds in the possession of the
College, which are very numerous, were transcribed, about the close of the 17th century
into a series of quarto volumes by William Smith, Senior Fellow, and afterwards rector
of Melsonby, in Yorkshire. He was the author also of a book intituled, "The Annals
" of University College, proving William of Durham the true founder, and answering
" all their arguments who ascribe it to King Alfred (1727)." In the earliest Bursar's
accounts the house is styled, "The College of Master William de Durham, commonly
" named Universite Hall." These accounts contain many curious particulars of the
ancient buildings of the College at the close of the 14th century. A service is mentioned in the Report, at considerable length, as having been instituted in this College
in 1493 "for the health and wele of the soul" of Ann, Countess of Warwick, deceased.
She was the widow of Richard Neville, known in history as "the Kingmaker," who
closed his restless career at the Battle of Barnet in 1471. (See App., p. 477.)

Wadham College, Oxford.—The only article that deserves especial notice among
the comparatively few archives of Wadham, is a deed, under the seal of the Dean and
Chapter of St. Paul's, London, whereby the Dean and Chapter ratify a grant to Adam
Fitz Nicholas by William de St. Mary Church, Bishop of London, of 30 acres of land
in the park of Orundene. It bears date about A.D. 1198, and is a beautiful specimen
of penmanship, but its main interest lies in the fact that Peter of Blois, the eminent
scholar, is mentioned among the attesting witnesses. (See App., p. 479.)

Magdalene College, Cambridge.—In the account given of the archives of this
College, some notice will be found of the college career of Samuel Pepys, the Diarist.
The names of Samuel Morland, afterwards known as an experimental philosopher, and

c 2

Orlando Bridgeman (afterwards Keeper of the Great Seal), both Fellows of the same College, are also mentioned. In a letter signed by Queen Elizabeth in the second year of her reign, she signifies her desire that John Dawbney, B.A., and Ciprian Valerie, a Spaniard, then a student in the College, should be admitted to the "King's Fellowships" then vacant. An interesting passage will be found in this Report in reference to College manners and discipline in the year 1679. (See App., p. 481.)

Pembroke College, Cambridge.—(Second Report.)—In a portfolio in the possession of the College, which has been lately brought to light after it had been probably overlooked for many years, a number of letters have been found reaching as far back as the 15th century. A selection has been made from them, and will be found in the Appendix. Among them may be mentioned, letters from Sir John Fastolf, of Caistor, in reference to the ransom and exchange of prisoners taken in France; from Lord Scales, as it is supposed, afterwards Earl Rivers, who was beheaded by order of Richard III.; Thomas Howard, Earl of Surrey, who commanded at Flodden Field (1513); John de Vere, Earl of Oxford (1530), and Anne de Vere, his widow; a warrant signed by the Ministers for the imprisonment of Sir Anthony Kingston, December 1555, accused of conspiring against Queen Mary, for the purpose of putting the Princess Elizabeth on the throne; a receipt signed by Sir Horatio Palavicini, an active man in the reign of Queen Elizabeth, who from being a Papal emissary became a convert to the Protestant faith; a letter to Sir Edward Coke from John Coke, his offending and penitent son; a letter from Francis Walsingham, Secretary of Queen Elizabeth, soliciting a next presentation; also from Sir Edward Coke to Sir Thomas Knevet; with several letters from Archbishop Whitgift and Bishop Bancroft. There is also a letter of some interest written by Sir Thomas Browne, in 1657, to Mr. (afterwards Sir) William Dugdale, making allusion, among other things, to the progress of the Monasticon; also a letter, in somewhat indignant terms, written by Ralph Cudworth. An interesting notice will also be found in the same Report in reference to Dr. Samuel Parker, intended by James II. to be forced on Magdalen College, Oxford, as President; and afterwards promoted to the See of Oxford. (See App., p. 484.)

Dartmouth.—Many particulars are given in this Report in reference to the remote history of the inhabitants and localities of Dartmouth. Some deeds are transcribed, executed by various members of the family of Haule, or Hauley, whose fame was widely extended in the 14th century, as singularly opulent merchants of this place. Mention also will be found of the family of Raleghe in the 14th century, from which, or one of its collateral branches, Sir Walter Raleigh probably sprang. The name also of Guido de Brienne, the powerful Lord of Dartmouth and Lord of Stokenham, in the 14th century, occurs more than once. Several deeds are here transcribed which throw light upon the localities of Exeter as early as the reign of Henry III.; while other deeds preserved in the Corporation chest are noticed, as bearing reference to Blandford in Dorset, and Totnes. A deed of grant by William Fitz-Stephen to Torre Abbey, bears date prior to the year 1208, and another deed to the same abbey, of like purport, is executed by William Briwere, Bishop of Exeter, A.D. 1224 to 1244. Descending to a much more recent date, a map of the time of Charles I. sets forth a description of "the lands that are set out unto the Corporation of Dartmouth, being "the first lot of the Second Quarter of the Barony of Rathconrath in the County of "Westmeath." (See App., p. 597.)

Folkestone.—The papers belonging to the Corporation of Folkestone that have been examined for the purpose of this Report are few in number, and refer to the contest that took place, in the reign of Edward IV. (A.D. 1463), between Thomas Banns, or Banes, and Henry Ferrers, brother of the Earl Ferrers, for the office of Prior of the Benedictine Priory of Folkestone. Banns, to all appearance, was a man of singularly evil character; but having secured the interest of the Sovereign, of the Archbishop of York, and of Cecily, Duchess of York, the King's mother, in his behalf, he ultimately prevailed against his antagonist, and retained the office for 30 years, at the end of which he was removed for dilapidating the property of the house. (See App., p. 590.)

The Parish of Alwington, North Devon.—The Church Books of this parish, though beginning with entries as far back as 1550, are singularly destitute of interest. The earliest Church Rate book now extant begins in 1767, and comes down to 1824. The most noteworthy passages in it probably are the items of payment by the Church-wardens for the killing of foxes. The tariff is at first 2s., but at a later date 5s., per head. In this century "fox ale" came to be substituted for payments in money, and 15s. is an item of payment for "fox ale" as recently as 1816. (See App., p. 597.)

Parish of Hartland, North Devon.—The Churchwardens' Account books of the parish of Hartland, belonging to the period extending from the close of the 16th to the early part of the 18th century, though in a much neglected condition, contain many passages deserving notice, in reference to the usages of those times. In the early part of the 17th century, the "Church Armour," consisting of calivers, muskets, pikes, daggers, corslets, and morions, is frequently referred to, and a chain is bought in 1613 for fastening up a work of Erasmus in the Church. The "dog " whipper " was an established officer of the Church throughout this century; and the man who held this office from 1647 to 1676 had the name of William Noy, in common with the more famous Attorney General of Charles I. Subscriptions are entered for redeeming persons in captivity from the Turks; and in 1610 there is an entry of eight shillings "given to two poor men being some time taken " captives by the Turks, and their tongues cut out." Such was the comfort of the seats in the Church in 1680, that "room" (such as " the southern middle room ") seems to have been considered the most appropriate name for them. In Hartland Church, down to the close of the 17th century, the women occupied seats and pews apart from the men. (See App., p. 571.)

High Wycombe.—The surviving records of the town of High Wycombe, so far as has been hitherto ascertained, appear to be few in number. In its earliest "Leger " Book," which commences in the latter half of the 15th century,|are to be found entries of considerable length in reference to church vestments and ornaments in the first and sixth years of King Edward VI. Extracts are also given in this book from a more ancient work, throwing some light upon the history of the town in the 14th century, its ancient buildings and its more influential inhabitants. (See App., p. 554.)

Lydd.—Lydd, now no more than a quiet country village in appearance, was in the 15th century a busy and important town, alike for the fact of it being a member of the Cinque Ports, and for its fishing station at Denge-Ness. A watch here seems to have been constantly kept upon the movements of the French. The " Boy " Bishop" repaired to Lydd from New Romney on St. Nicholas' Day in each year. Minstrels attached to the households of the nobility, and players from the towns and villages of East Kent, were continually welcomed by the townsfolk with feasting and pecuniary reward, one of the plays acted being that of St. George. A correspondence was continually kept up with the Lord Warden of the Cinque Ports at Dover, or his Lieutenant; but upon Jack Cade's insurrection (which commenced at Ashford or its vicinity) appearing to be a matter for serious consideration, a deputation from the town waited upon "the Captain," as he was called, and asked his acceptance of a porpoise. In the Wars of the Roses, the predilections of the people in this part of the country were evidently in favour of the Yorkists. Mention of the Earl of Warwick occurs more than once, and allusion is made to the town's contingent which fought on the Yorkists' side at the second battle of St. Alban's. In these Records, as also in those of New Romney and Rye, mention is made of a Thomas Caxton, who was Common Clerk of Lydd for about 10 years, from 1458 to 1467 or 1468, and, upon his resignation, became first Treasurer, and then Bailiff, of the town, in 1471 and 1472; after which he removed to Sandwich, where he acted as Common Clerk for several years, but in 1482 or 1483 he seems to have returned to Lydd. The "Custumall " of Lydd, transcribed by his hand from the original, then preserved at New Romney, still exists. Some reasons will be found stated in the Report for suggesting that he was a native of Tenterden, and not improbably closely related to William Caxton, our first printer, who speaks of himself as born in the Weald of Kent. That Thomas Caxton was a man of remarkable ability is shown beyond dispute, in the numerous extracts given from the Records above mentioned. (See App., p. 516.)

New Romney.—(Second Report.)—From the Report upon the archives of New Romney, many particulars hitherto lost to memory may be recovered, in reference to its former harbour, long since silted up, and the ancient course of the Rother, when it still existed as a river, at least in some degree, in its vicinity. The "Slow," or " Sluice," of this town, is a subject of repeated expenditure, but it is probably impossible at the present day to suggest even where it was situate. Several memoranda also occur, in reference to the coronations of our sovereigns in succession, and to that of Queen Isabella of France (the second wife of Richard II.) at the close of the 14th century; in all of which the Barons of the Cinque Ports played an important part. In these records " guns with six chambers " are alluded to at as early a date as 1456. Players from the neighbouring towns and villages are repeatedly mentioned as resorting to the town. Minstrels, as elsewhere in the vicinity, were welcomed with bounteous " reward," and the successful candidates in wrestling matches received their guerdon at the hands of the Corporate authorities. The Jurats and Commons of New Romney, we are told, had been wont from of old to choose Wardens "to have the play of Christ's

" Passion " represented, but in 1518 a mandate was sent by the Lord Warden to the
" Barons " of that place, informing them " that they ought not to play the play of the
" Passion of Christ until they had had the King's leave ; " the sovereign who seems to
have made objection thereto being Henry VIII. In 1408 John Hacche, then vicar, gave
to the Jurats of New Romney 3s. 4d. in free gift " on condition that they should not
" in future hold their session in his church (that of St. Nicholas) while Divine
" service is being celebrated." It is only at a recent date that the sittings of
the Jurats in the church, at other times than during Divine service, have been
discontinued. The Mayor, however, is still elected yearly in the Parish Church of
New Romney, while in its own Parish Church the Bailiff of Lydd is also elected ;
the election at each town taking place at the tomb of a member of the family of
Stuppeny, for some reason now unknown. (See App., p. 533.)

Mendlesham, Co. Suffolk.—The manuscripts of the parish of Mendlesham, Suffolk,
have been inspected. In the church chests, among other things, were found the wills
of the two earliest benefactors of the parish,—Robert Cake (temp. Edw. IV.) and
Henry Jesope (temp. Hen. VIII.). The Parish Accounts and Parish Registers give a
complete picture of the life of the parish for more than three centuries. One of the
registers, the " Boake for Registering " (1653–1659) contains records of all the civil
marriages performed, before Justices of the Peace, by parishioners of Mendlesham,
during the Commonwealth, in accordance with the Marriage Act of the Parliament of
1653. (See App., p. 593.)

Rye.—The greater part, probably, of the archives of Rye were destroyed, when the
place was attacked and burnt by the French in 1377, and again in 1448. A not inconsiderable number of documents has however survived, belonging to times even prior
to the former date. Until now these seem for several centuries to have been overlooked.
The printed list of the Mayors begins no earlier than 1396, whereas from a close
examination of the documents in question, the names of the Mayors have been restored
to light from the beginning of the 14th century down to 1380, in almost unbroken
succession. In the extracts from the archives of a latter date than 1448, several
references will be found to the Wars of the Roses, and the aid afforded by the town to
the Yorkist cause. Shortly before the second Battle of St. Albans, the Mayor and
Common Clerk, in obedience to a summons, set out for Canterbury, to meet the Earl of
March (afterwards Edward IV.) and the Earl of Warwick ; but by the time of their
arrival at Sittingbourne, the Earls had passed onward to the West ; they comforted
themselves, however, by sleeping at Leene ; and enjoyed there, not improbably for the
first time, the pleasure of sleeping on a bed made of something better than straw.
Apologizing, apparently, for the exorbitance of the sum they had paid for the accommodation, namely, one penny, they call attention to the fact that it was really " worth the
" money, for it was a feather bed they slept upon." In expectation of an attack
by the Lancastrian party, cartloads of stones were laid upon the town walls for
hurling down upon the foe. As in the archives of Lydd, allusion is made to
Jack Cade's insurrection, prior to this date. Here, as at those places, we find troops
of minstrels welcomed from time to time with money and feasting ; while the players
from the neighbouring towns acted their play not only in the Churchyard but in the
Church, Sunday being, sometimes at least, the day selected for the performance. The
people of Lydd, as appears by the records of that place, were treated to the sight of
a dromedary, passing through the town, while the " man with the baboon " did not
miss his reward from the Corporation of New Romney, on a like occasion : 2s. 1d.
being the remuneration given by Rye to the bear-ward of George, Duke of Clarence,
for treating its inhabitants to a " baytinge of the berys." (See App., p. 488.)

St. Albans.—The archives of the Corporation of St. Albans are comparatively few,
and of no great interest. The town only received its Charter of Incorporation as late
as the reign of Edward VI. Among the miscellaneous papers in the Corporation chest,
is a letter of request giving a description of the ruin that had been wrought by fire in
1583, at the town of Nampwicke (Nantwich) in Cheshire. Mention will be found in
the Appendix, p. 566, of a letter written by John Thomas (1583), Master of the Grammar
School of St. Albans, a native of Bois-le-Duc, in Holland ; with a suggestion, for the
reason there stated, that he may have been one of the instructors of Francis Bacon,
the particulars of whose early education are comparatively unknown.

Sandwich.—The most important contents of the more ancient among the archives
of Sandwich have been exhaustively described by the late Mr. W. Boys, a Jurat of the
town, in his *Collections for a History of Sandwich.* There are three portfolios filled
with miscellaneous documents, letters, and papers, belonging to the Corporation, which

he does not appear to have noticed. The more important of them will be found described in the Appendix, p. 568. The oldest among them are in a very mutilated condition. One of the most recent documents, probably also of the greatest interest, is a sheet of parchment, containing a list of those of the gentry who in that part of Kent also joined the association for the protection of King William III. from assassination, in 1696; the signatures in autograph are more than 100 in number. There are several charters, granted either to the town or to the Cinque Ports, by King Edward III., but they are mostly in fragments. A letter to the Honourable Leopold Finch, Esq., from John Tillotson, afterwards Archbishop of Canterbury, bears date 13 Sept. 1689. There are also several documents and letters in the handwriting of Roger Manwood, a lawyer of eminence in the time of Elizabeth, and letters from Edward, Lord Zouch, John Philipott, Somerset Herald, Secretary Edward Nicholas, and Algernon Sidney, are also to be found in the collection.

Weymouth and Melcombe Regis.—In the present Report, the names of some Mayors of Melcombe, in the 14th century, hitherto lost, have been brought to light. An information, shadowing forth the intended invasion of the Spanish Armada, more than two years before the event, deserves notice. Under the date of 1610 mention is made of a vessel called the "Mayflower," which it seems not improbable was the same vessel that in 1620 carried the Pilgrim Fathers to the coast of Massachusetts. Another paper gives an account of depredations committed, as late as 1636, by Algerine pirates in the Severn, and off the British coast. The account also of various high-handed proceedings in the town, when in the hands of the Parliamentary forces, under the command of Colonel Sydenham in 1646, is well deserving of attention. Members of the family of Pytte, from which the great Earl of Chatham was descended, are not unfrequently mentioned in these records. Few of the archives of ancient date belonging to these towns, seem now to be in existence. (See App., p. 575.)

Marquis of Bute.—The charters of the Marquis of Bute have already been reported on, and the present report is limited to a collection of letters at Mountstuart. The first portion of them consists of a miscellaneous Scotch correspondence ranging in date from 1683 to 1763, addressed to the Earls of Bute. Among the writers are the Duke of Hamilton, Lord Haddo, the Earl of Mar, Earl of Glasgow, the Duke of Argyll, and his brother Lord Islay. They relate to the intrigues and political arrangements of the time immediately before the Union, and also of that which followed on the rising of 1715. The second portion consists of a series of letters addressed by Lady Mary Wortley Montagu to her sister the Countess of Mar. Most of these have been printed in the last edition of Lady Mary's works. (See App., p. 617.)

The Marquis of Ailsa.—The charters of the Marquis of Ailsa form an extensive and interesting series. Among them is a set of documents almost unique relating to a privilege of the early Lords of Carrick, and their successors the Kennedys of Dunure, as head of their kin. The right was frequently confirmed by the Crown, and some of the Royal Charters define it in terms of which the precise purport has been lost. The collection of family muniments relating to their lands is unusually full, and is of great use in illustrating the history of the district. It has also a wider scope in its bearings on national history. Several muniments relate to the foundation and administration of a collegiate church at Maybole by the Laird of Dunure in 1371; others convey the office of heritable coroner of the Earldom of Carrick. Some of the papers throw light on the disputed claims to the abbacy of Glenluce about the time of the Reformation, and among the letters is a series from Queen Mary of Scotland to the Earl of Cassilis, ranging in date from 1562 to 1569. (See App., p. 613.)

The Earl of Aberdeen.—The records belonging to the Earl of Aberdeen consist of an extensive series of charters dating from the end of the 14th century, and a collection of political letters addressed to the first earl while Lord Chancellor of Scotland in the time of Charles II. Some of the charters relate to the church lands of Ellon in the 15th century, which were in the hands of tenants called Scolocs, and were held by a peculiar tenure of finding copes and surplices for certain clerks in the parish church, with wax candles for the perk before the high altar, and a smithy in the village. Among the writers of the letters are the leading public men of the day, and many of them discuss the questions which were then of prominent interest. In the library is a household book of King James V. of Scotland containing an account of the royal expenditure from September 1538 to September 1539, and a volume of the Lord Chancellor's personal expenses from 1682 to 1684. (See App., p. 608.)

The Earl of Lauderdale.—The records belonging to the Earl of Lauderdale comprise many of great age and considerable importance. One portion of them was buried in the ground at Balcarres for preservation after the battle of Dunbar in the year 1650, and were mostly destroyed ; but full inventories of them had been prepared with his own hand by the Earl of Lauderdale before they were placed in the ground, and such was the confidence in his integrity that after the Restoration it was ordered by an Act of the Scottish Parliament that the inventories should be of the same value as the original papers. These inventories being engrossed in the Act, the historical materials of the documents are still available. Besides this series of records there yet remains at Thirlestane a large collection, consisting of papers connected with public events in the time of Charles II., a large number of early charters of the barony of Hatton, and other lands in Midlothian, writs relating to the constabulary of Dundee, and grants to the Abbey of Dryburgh. (See App., p. 610.)

Lord Kinnaird.—Among the miscellaneous papers in Lord Kinnaird's possession is a document addressed to General Monk, a few months before the Restoration, containing some remarkable suggestions for the best method of securing the peace and welfare of Scotland. The bulk of this collection comprises family charters dating from the time of King William the Lion. (See App., p. 620.)

Lord Wharncliffe.—The collection of Lord Wharncliffe contains a series of fine charters of early date of lands in the counties of Forfar and Perth, and are remarkable for their illustrations of curious feudal tenures. Some court books of later date throw light on the administration of a barony and on agricultural arrangements. (See App., p. 621.)

Sir William Forbes.—Among the papers of Sir William Forbes at Fintray House are many charters and documents connected with the transmission of lands dating from the 15th century, mostly of local interest. There is also a series of letters addressed to various correspondents by Sir Andrew Mitchell, who was British ambassador at the court of Frederick the Great, with drafts and notes of his letters and dispatches while on his embassy, and also while he was Under Secretary of State for Scotland. Among the letters addressed to Sir Andrew, are some from Frederick himself. In the library is the original MS. diary of Dr. John Forbes, who was for some time Professor of Divinity in King's College, Aberdeen. It ranges in date from 1624 to 1647, and while mainly devoted to a record of what the author designates his spiritual exercises, it contains many historical notices illustrating the position of parties during the great Rebellion. (See App., p. 626.)

Mrs. Barclay Allardice.—The collection of Mrs. Barclay Allardice is very extensive and consists for the most part of the charters and papers relating to the baronies of Allardice and Ury in the Shire of Kincardine vested in the families represented by Mrs. Barclay Allardice.

Among the miscellaneous papers are copies of two letters from the Laird of Ury in 1713 to the Earls of Marr and Argyll, on the subject of a proposal to extend toleration to the Scotch Quakers. (See App., p. 629.)

Mr. Baillie Cochrane.—The collection of Mr. Baillie Cochrane of Lamingtoun consists exclusively of the title deeds of his various estates. The only papers of historical interest relate to a portion of the lands in the neighbourhood of the town of Lanark, which were held by the tenure of baking certain wafers for the king when he happened to reside there. (See App., p. 632.)

Mr. Cosmo Gordon.—In the charter room at Fyvie Castle, belonging to Mr. Gordon are many documents of great historical interest, the series beginning towards the end of the 14th century. There are also many state papers connected with the Earls of Dunfermline in the reigns of Charles I. and Charles II. (See App., p. 644.)

Maxwell of Kirkconnell.—The manuscripts of the ancient family of Maxwell of Kirkconnell, reported on by Mr. Fraser, are very important. Among the letters specially to be mentioned is one of King Henry VIII. of England to King James V. previous to his marriage, reciprocating the Scottish monarch's anxiety for the maintenance of amity between the two kingdoms. Eighteen articles of instruction signed by the Earl of Arran, as Governor of Scotland, to David Pantar, Bishop Elect of Ross and Scottish ambassador at the court of France, propose, among other things, a common catholic bond of union between France and England, and desire the French monarch to send to the Pope for a longer absolution than had previously been sent to the murderers of Cardinal Bethune. A volume preserved in the Kirkconnell library, deserving special attention is a copy, probably unique, of a work by King James II., consisting of 172 pages, entitled " A Collection of several of his late Majesties papers " of devotion copied exactly out of the original manuscripts left by his Majesty in his " own handwriting." The authenticity of the volume is placed beyond all doubt by an attestation in holograph of Mary of Modena, that the manuscript is a true copy of the original papers in her possession, and which when the king, her son, and herself had no more use of them, were to be deposited in the Scots College at Paris with the rest of the king's original papers conformably to his intention.

Another manuscript in the same library contains the two registers of the Scots College of Douay. They afford much varied information respecting the Roman Catholic seminary and its students for nearly two centuries. It is sufficient to state that the first, called in the Kirkconnell library the "Larger Register of Douay," contains the names of the alumni of the Scots College, which was successively established at Pont-a-Mousson, Douay, and Louvain, from 1581 to 1772, with short notes of the character and subsequent career of each student, and notices by the early professors relating to the foundation and history of the institution, its revenues and benefactors. The other called the "Smaller Douay Register," is an abridgment from the Larger of the alumni of the Scots College from 1581 to 1742. Many of the students were connected with distinguished Scottish families. (See App., p. 650.)

Sir John Bethune.—The collection of manuscripts in the possession of Sir John Bethune, of Kilconquhar, Bart., contains various documents of historical interest. Among the charters will be found one attributed to William the Lion, dated 1165, and two others granted between 1189 and 1192. They are of historical value from the names of the persons who were present as witnesses. Among the correspondence are 17 letters from James Sharpe, Archbishop of St. Andrews; three have been extracted *in extenso;* one of them is "for his much-honoured Patrick Lindsay, of Wormistoun, "to be communicated to the Elders of the Session of Craill," written from London in May 1661, whither Sharpe had gone for consecration after his appointment to be Archbishop of St. Andrews. It expresses his affectionate and pious concern that his former parishioners might be provided with a suitable pastor. Another of Sharpe's letters, dated Edinburgh, January 14, 1675, relates to the measures then adopted by the Privy Council of Scotland for the suppression of conventicles. (See App., p. 623.)

Erskines of Dun.—The muniments of the Erskines of Dun supply much biographical and historical information. The correspondence, extending from 1544 to 1753, embraces letters from Cardinal Bethune; Mary, Queen Dowager of Scotland; James, Earl of Murray, Regent of Scotland; King James the Sixth; David, Earl of Crawfurd; John, Earl of Montrose; John Erskine of Dun; Patrick Maule, of Panmure; King Charles I.; David Leslie, Lieutenant-General of the Forces in Scotland, and others. All these letters relate to the civil and ecclesiastical transactions of the period over which they extend. The same remark applies to the section of royal warrants and commissions, and miscellaneous papers of the Erskines of Dun from the year 1474. The letters and other papers relating to John Erskine of Dun, Superintendent of Angus and Mearns, coadjutor of John Knox the Scottish reformer, furnish varied materials bearing on the history of the times in which he lived.

The act of admission of James Erskine into the parsonage of Dun in 1570 by the superintendent furnishes a specimen of the form observed in such cases by the Reformed Church of Scotland.

The correspondence relates to the family of Riddell, of Haining, in the County of Selkirk, now at Dun, from the year 1674, and the royal commissions and other papers connected with the Scottish Borders from the year 1619. (See App., p. 633.)

The Homes of Renton.—The manuscripts of the family of Home of Renton in the County of Berwick, are mainly historical. From the connexion of the proprietors of Renton with the ancient Priory of Coldingham, many of the Charters relate to that religious house, and contain notices of Henry Belnavis of Halhill, James Kirkcaldy of Grange, Robert Logan of Restalrig, and Sir George Home afterwards Earl of Dunbar, the favourite minister of James VI. It appears by these Charters that James IV. and James V., bestowed the lands of the monasteries on their favourites, proceedings to which the priors or abbots judged it prudent to submit.

The letters in the Collection from James VI. and Charles II. vary in importance. Sir John Home of Renton in his petition to Charles II. after the Restoration, claims to have been the first who to the hazard of his life and estate publicly asserted the interests of that monarch and of his father, and to have constantly adhered to the royal cause through the whole period of the Rebellion. In reward for his faithful services and heavy losses, he was knighted, created a Privy Councillor, and made a Lord of Session and Justice Clerk. (See App., p. 646.)

Borough of Perth.—Among the muniments of the Royal Burgh of Perth, is a series of Royal Charters of incorporation and privilege, of great use for the early history and constitution of Scottish Burghs. They begin with a Charter from King William the

Lion which together with the subsequent Royal grants is engrossed in a charter to the Town by King James VI. dated in 1600. The Burgh Record which contains the acts of the Council begins in 1543. In this volume is engrossed a letter from King James I. written on the termination of his imprisonment in England in 1424, requesting pecuniary aid from the Burgh. (See App., p. 655.)

The Report of Mr. Gilbert, the Inspector of MSS. for Ireland, is unavoidably omitted owing to his long and severe indisposition.

In concluding this Report Your Majesty's Commissioners desire to call attention to the extent and literary value of the labours of the late Commission. The notices furnished of the numerous collections of valuable papers and documents in private hands cannot fail, they think, to preserve the knowledge of the existence of such collections and render them more accessible for the purposes of the historian.

Your Majesty's Commissioners have only to add the expression of a hope that their future labours may be attended with a like successful result.

G. JESSEL. (L.S.)   HOUGHTON. (L.S.)
SALISBURY. (L.S.)   ACTON. (L.S.)
AIRLIE. (L.S.)   WILLIAM STIRLING MAXWELL. (L.S.)
EDMOND FITZMAURICE. (L.S.)   T. DUFFUS HARDY. (L.S.)
CHARLES LIMERICK. (L.S.)   CHARLES WILLIAM RUSSELL. (L.S.)
TALBOT DE MALAHIDE. (L.S.)   GEORGE WEBBE DASENT. (L.S.)

JOHN ROMILLY,
Secretary.

APPENDIX.

The Manuscripts of the House of Lords.

Before noticing any of the papers in the portion of calendar printed below we wish again to call attention to the Minute books, or rough manuscript journal kept by one of the clerks of the House of Lords. Reference was made to these books in the third Report of the Commissioners, but they appear to us from further examination to require more particular mention.

The following is a list of the extant volumes so far as they have yet been discovered up to the abolition of the House of Lords in 1649 :—

1620-1, March 22 to May 18, 1621.
1623-4, February 12 to March 25, 1624.
1624, April 1 to March 15, 1624-5.
1625, May 17 to August 12, 1625.
1627-8, March 17 to October 20, 1628.
1640, April 13 to May 5, 1640.
1640-1, January 11 to April 10, 1641, numbered (2) outside.
1641, Nov. 29 to 26 March 1642, numbered (5).
1642, Dec.17 to 22 April 1643, numbered (8).
1643, April 24 to 4 Dec. 1643, numbered (9).
1644, July 22 to 3 March 1644-5, numbered (11).
1646, July 4 to 15 February 1646-7, numbered (14).

From 1660 there is an almost unbroken series of Minute books up to 1827.

From Mr. Horwood's report on Colonel Carew's MSS. (fourth Report of Commissioners, p. 369,) we learn that amongst them are seven folio volumes containing "scribbled" notes by Henry Elsynge, Clerk of the Parliaments, of proceedings in the House of Lords of the following dates :—

Vol. 1, 1621, 17 April to 18 May.
Vol. 2, 1621, 14 November to 8 February 1621-2.
Vol. 3, 1623-4, 12 February to 25 March 1624.
Vol. 4, 1624, 1 April to 29 May.
Vol. 5, 1625-6, 6 February to 29 April 1626.
Vol. 6, 1626, 1 May to 15 June.
Vol. 7, 1627-8, 17 March to 26 June 1628.

It will be seen that some of these volumes run over the same period as that to which those in the House of Lords relate. Mr. S. R. Gardiner, in the preface to the volume of these notes edited by him for the Camden Society in 1870, attributes those in Colonel Carew's collection to Henry Elsynge, Clerk of the Parliaments, and supposes those in the House of Lords to be the work of one of his clerks. The Minute book for the short Parliament, April 13 to May 5, 1640, is in the handwriting of John Browne, clerk of the Parliaments at that time.

We have felt it our duty to call attention to these volumes rather than to compare them with the Journals and other sources of information, which would have occupied much time, but a few instances of the information to be got from them alone will be useful.

We learn from the Journals that on Saturday the 2nd of May 1640, the Earl of Bristol on behalf of Lionel Cranfield, Earl of Middlesex, presented a petition stating that in consequence of the former censure of the House the Earl of Middlesex forbore to come and sit or send his proxy, though His Majesty had sent him a writ of summons to Parliament, and praying that he might be permitted to take his seat.

This petition was referred to the Grand Committee for privileges, "who on Monday next the first thing to be "handled"; the committee met and agreed to a report in favour of the Earl's petition, as we learn from the Minute book, and the Earl was actually present on Tuesday morning to have taken his seat, but that Tuesday was the fatal 5th of May on which the King dissolved Parliament before the House could proceed to business.

The following is the report* of the Committee for privileges, which is written in the Minute book after the notice of the dissolution.

The Reports of the Grand Committee for privileges

*There is a copy of this Report amongst the papers at Knole Park. See Hist. MSS. Commission, Fourth Report, p. 310 (Earl De La Warr's MSS.)

5.

for the Earle of Middlesex his admittaunce into the Parliament, being dated according to their Lopps meetinge and resolucōns in that buisines (viz'.)

Die Lunæ quarto die Maij 1640.

E. Middlesex. Upon a Peticōn of the Earle of Bristol on the behalfe of the Earle of Middlesex, that hee might bee restored to his voate and place in Parliament (as by the Peticōn it will more at large appeare, wᵗʰ by the Howse was ordered to be entered as of Record) The mocōn and peticon of the Earle of Bristol was referred unto the Grand Cōmittee for privileges, and they appointed to meete on Monday then next followeinge aboute it, as they did, accordingly. And after a serious debate then of the buisines, it was resolued by a vnanimous consent of the whole Cōmittee ; That they helde it fitt and honoᵇˡᵉ for the House to extende their Grace and favour vnto the Earle of Middlesex accordinge to the tenor of the Earle of Bristole's Peticon. And that the next morninge reports thereof should bee made unto the Howse by the Earle Marshall ; And the House being pleased to affirme the opinion and voate of the **E. Middlesex** Cōmittee, that the Earle of Middlesex should called in. bee called in, to his place, And then the flavour and Grace of the Howse should be declared vnto him by the Earle Marshall. And hee being admitted to his place, should make such humble and thankfull acknowledgement vnto the Howse for their favour and goodnes as hee should thinke fittinge. His lopp. (haveinge direccōns from yᵉ Comittee to attend the Howse that morninge) was then p'nte, to baue bine brought into that honᵇˡᵉ Court, according to the reporte of the said Cōmittee.

ARUNDELL & SURREY.
DORSETT.
BRISTOL.
WILL. PAGETT.

The matter seems to have been again brought up in the Long Parliament, but to have been deferred to make way for more important business, and though the Earl did not die till the 6th of August 1645, he does not appear to have ever taken his seat.

The Minute book for the earlier weeks of the Long Parliament has not been found, but at the end of the volume beginning the 11th January 1640-1, is given a list of peers present on the 3rd of November, the opening day of the Parliament; and the names of peers present each day are given in the Minute books, but are at this period altogether omitted from the Journals.

From the 11th January 1640-1, we have in the Minute book not only a record of all the proceedings on the Earl of Strafford's trial, but also notes of what was said by those who took any part in it, and also of the evidence given by the witnesses. This volume unfortunately ends on Saturday the 10th of April, when after long discussion the Lords decided that whatever favor as to production of fresh evidence was granted to the accusers must be extended also to the accused ; this decision was received by the Commons with a murmur of disapprobation, and on the same day the bill of attainder, under which the Earl was executed, was read a first time in the House of Commons. Search has been made, at present in vain, for the next volume of the Minute books, which would in all probability have contained a list of those who voted for and against the bill in the Upper House.

In the later volumes the numbers on each side in divisions of the House are often given, with the names of the tellers, when no mention is made of them in the Journals. Many other instances of the information to be obtained from these notes might be given, but enough has been said, for the present, to draw attention to their importance, and we trust that we may be able to say on some future occasion that the missing volumes have been recovered.

The calendar in the Appendix to the present report is carried up to the end of the year 1643, so we have now reached the period when there was an actual breach between the King and the Parliament, and every Act of State done by the latter was effected by an order or

A

ordinance of both Houses. Amongst the MSS. will be found an immense number of drafts of these orders and ordinances; many of them are given in extenso in the Journals, and these we have dismissed with the briefest possible notice, but some of them are interesting either as showing the amendments made on different stages, or because they were finally rejected, and do not therefore appear in the Journals. For instance, on the 19th of March 1641-2 the King's Counsel were directed to prepare a bill to secure such as have executed any power upon any commission of lieutenancy or array; the draft was prepared exonerating those who had acted upon such commissions, which it declares were in reality illegal; the bill was, however, never read even a first time. On the 22nd of March in the same year is a draft of a bill for asserting of some privileges of Parliament lately broken and to prevent the breaking thereof in time to come, but this vindication of the honour of Parliament against the attempted seizure of the five members did not reach the third reading. On the 9th of April 1642 is a draft of the petition of the two Houses to the King, in which they pray that the ammunition may be removed from Hull, and that the six condemned Roman Catholic priests may be executed. The draft shows that this last wish was an afterthought, for it is in the handwriting of John Browne, clerk of the Parliaments, added probably in the House to a much amended draft of the part about Hull, which is in a different hand.

There are many letters and other papers giving accounts of different incidents in the civil war. Amongst these may be mentioned—(16 Dec. 1642.) Copy of a letter from Colonels Fiennes and Goodwin to the Earl of Essex, Lord General, announcing the surrender of Winchester Castle by Lord Grandison. (17 Jan 1642-3.) A letter from Colonel Bulstrode and Thomas Tyrrill at Aylesbury, to the Earl of Essex, giving an account of a skirmish with the enemy near Brill. (7 Feb. 1642-3.) A letter from the Earl of Stamford at Plymouth, to the Speaker of the House of Lords concerning the proceedings in Devonshire. (21 March 1642-3.) A petition of poor prisoners in the Bridewell at Oxford who were taken at Marlborough, complaining of the harsh treatment they receive at the hands of their captors to compel them to take an oath, that the Earl of Essex and all his adherents are traitors, and that the war raised for the destruction of the Parliament is most just and necessary. (24 July 1643.) A letter from Col. Richard Brown about the taking of Tunbridge, and (7 Sept. 1643), a copy of a very entertaining letter, apparently from one of the soldiers under the Earl of Essex, giving an account of the march of the army from the rendezvous at Bayard's Green to the relief of Gloucester. Full abstracts of these papers will be found under their respective dates.

The following papers relating to the rebellion in Ireland deserve mention :—The examinations of Garrat Aylmer (14 March 1641-2), and Nicholas Dowdall (17 March 1641-2,), about the proceedings of the rebels near Drogheda, with accounts of their meetings on the famous hill of Tara and elsewhere. (11 May 1642.) Letter from the Lords Justices of Ireland to the Lord Keeper, stating that Lady Jepson and her son, Sir John Giffard, were upon the breaking out of the rebellion constrained to betake themselves to their castle of Jordan about 30 miles from Dublin; that they have been despoiled of everything they could not bring within the castle gates, and have been obliged to maintain their English tenants out of the little left to themselves; that they have now been long beleaguered, but that Sir John has made several sallies and slain many of the rebels; there is no possibility of their getting to Dublin without an army to protect them, and that Sir John's departure would much prejudice the public service and encourage the rebels. There are also numerous papers relating to the struggle with the rebels in the neighbourhood of Galway, and the submission of that town, under date 27 June 1642.

The following papers may be mentioned as interesting originals.

The letter from the nine lords at York (1642, June 5) excusing their not attending Parliament on the ground that the King had commanded them to remain with him.

Many petitions from Archbishop Laud, some of them in the handwriting of his secretary Dell, but for the most part in his own writing, and in the bold firm hand of earlier years. On the 27th of Oct. 1642 is one not mentioned in the Journals, in which he humbly prays that besides his two servants, which are to make his bed and do other things necessary for his age, going on with threescore and ten years of a weary life, their lordships would favorably allow him a butler and a cook, without which he knows not how to live, being not placed in any

house in the Tower, but in a solitary room destitute of all company and other help. Under the dates of 13, 14, and 24 April 1643 will be found three very interesting holograph petitions of the archbishop with reference to his right of presentation to the living of Chartham, Kent.

A paper (28 July 1642) from the Committee for the safety of the kingdom, desiring the Committee for the Irish adventurers to furnish 100,000l. by way of loan for the defence of the King, Parliament, and Kingdom, upon the public faith, to be repaid within so short a time that it shall not be diverted from the purpose for which it was intended. This paper is signed by the Earls of Essex, Bedford, Holland, and Pembroke and Montgomery, Lord Say and Seale, Denzell Hollis, Sir Philip Stapleton, Sir Wm. Waller, and John Hampden. It is dated at the top 18th July 1642, and noted at the bottom " read 31 July 1642 and assented." The '31st of July was Sunday. The journals also show that on Sunday the 8th of August 1641 both Houses sat in the morning and afternoon.

Another very interesting paper is a copy of the propositions to the King for a peace, dated 5th August 1643, which the Lords drew up and sent to the Commons for their approval. The Commons, on Saturday the 5th of August, agreed to the first of these propositions, but the next day, Sunday, Lord Mayor Pennington called a Common Council, at which a petition against these propositions, and a draft ordinance for prosecuting the war were prepared, and presented to the Commons on the morning of Monday, the 7th. The Commons thus influenced, proceeded with the consideration of the propositions, and finally rejected them, and appointed a Committee to prepare reasons to be given to the Lords for their so doing. These propositions and reasons are printed in extenso at page 98, as though often referred to they are not to be found, so far as we can discover, in any of the histories of the period.

The following papers bring the state of the times so vividly to light that they cannot be passed over without notice.

A petition (1643, Aug. 17) of three messengers desiring some reward for the number of papists they had been the means of bringing to trial; a list of their victims is annexed to the petition, showing in most cases their sentence and fate; six were executed, eight reprieved by His Majesty, of the rest some were outlawed, some effected their escape. On the 12th of October, upon a certificate of Mr. Recorder Glyn that the statements of these informers were true, the House recommends them to the Lord Mayor and court of aldermen for a speedy reward.

A petition of Michael Miller (1641-2, Feb. 19) is curious, though perhaps hardly a fair picture of the discipline of the trained bands. Miller, one of the captains, complains that though he has about 300 men under his command, he can only muster 32 to attend upon the House, and that the 32 protest, that they will never appear again unless some course be taken to enforce the attendance of the rest. Again, on the 5th of March he complains that a halbert, one of several bought with his own money for the officers of the company, had been pawned at a tavern by John Wayte, one of the soldiers, and that his offence having been in part condoned, Wayte and another soldier, John Bickers, made such base speeches and raised such a riot at the court of guard, that Miller was in danger of his life. A few days later, on the 8th of March, we have a petition of Wayte and Bickers stating that they had merely complained to their officers, and then to some members of the Commons, that Miller had allowed Allen Pricket, late a strong papist (though now a frequenter of the church) to remain in the company, though his wife was still a strong papist, and their son was being educated as such, and that for this they had been unworthily used by Miller, in blows, fearful oaths, and very uncivil language. The House seems to have thought that the soldiers had sufficient excuse for their insubordination, for on the 17th of March, on a report from the Earl of Holland, it was decided that the men were in no way faulty, and that Miller should pay the fees for their detention.

Under date of the 8th of November 1643 will be found a quaint example of the relations in matters of courtesy between the King and Parliament. George Kirk, master of His Majesty's robes, applies for a pass for John Daintrey one of the grooms in the office to go to Oxford with his servant with 4 dozen of gloves which are much . wanted by His Majesty, and " 4 yds. of taby, 2 ells and " ½ of tuffity to be a tennis suit, and 2 pair of garters " and roses with silk buttons and other necessaries for " the making up of the said suit." This application, though not mentioned in the Journals, is endorsed by the clerk "Exped.," and from the Minute book we learn, that though in open arms against the King, Parliament allowed his master of the robes to send him a tennis suit from London. The entry in the Minute book is "Ordered that John Daintrey shall have a pass to "Oxon with a servant to carry down some things for "the King's Majesty." See also 20 Dec. 1642 and 21 Feb. and 9 March 1642-3, on which dates warrants are granted for sending apothecary's staffs, wax lights, and gloves to Oxford, for His Majesty's use.

There are several papers graphically depicting the outrages committed in Canterbury Cathedral by the Parliamentarian troopers in August 1642; one a letter from Dr. Paske, dated August 30th, complaining that the soldiers had overthrown the Communion table, torn the cloth, defaced the screen, violated the monuments of the dead, spoiled the organs, broken down the ancient rails and seats, with the brazen eagle that did support the bible, forced open the cupboards of the singing men, rent some of their surplices, gowns and bibles, and carried away others, mangled all the service books and books of Common Prayer, bestrewing the whole pavement with the leaves; a miserable spectacle to every good eye; and further some few zealots exercised their malice on the arras hangings in the choir (representing the whole story of our Saviour) with horrible blasphemies wherever a representation of Christ appeared, and finding a statue of Christ in the frontispiece of the South gate, discharged more than 40 shots against it. We learn from a letter of Dr. Paske's of the 1st of September that Sir Michael Livesey, when he heard of these outrages, which had been committed without his knowledge, expressed the greatest regret, and withdrew his men as soon as possible, but some of the inferior officers justified their men. A certificate very numerously signed, confirming the statements made in Dr. Paske's first letter, will be found under date 17 Sept. 1642, and a further account of the proceedings of these troopers in other parts of Kent under the command of Colonel Sandys, Sir Michael Livesey, and others, under date of September 5, 1642.

At the end of the Calendar will be found a list of places, the returns from which, made under the order of Parliament for taking the protestation, have been preserved. The protestation runs as follows:—"I, A. B., "do, in the Presence of Almighty God, promise, vow, "and protest to maintain and defend, as far as law"fully I may, with my Life, Power, and Estate, the "true Reformed Protestant Religion, expressed in "the Doctrine of the Church of England, against all "Popery and Popish Innovations, within this Realm, "contrary to the same Doctrine, and according to the "Duty of my Allegiance, His Majesty's Royal Person, "Honour, and Estate, as also the Power and Privileges "of Parliaments, the lawful Rights and Liberties of "the Subjects, and every Person that maketh this "Protestation, in whatsoever he shall do in the lawful "Pursuance of the same; and to my power, and as "far as lawfully I may, I will oppose and by all good "Ways and Means endeavour to bring to condign "Punishment all such as shall, either by Force, Prac"tice, Counsels, Plots, Conspiracies, or otherwise, do "any Thing to the contrary of any Thing in this present "Protestation contained; and further, that I shall, in "all just and honourable Ways, endeavour to preserve "the Union and Peace betwixt the Three Kingdoms "of England, Scotland, and Ireland: and neither for "Hope, Fear, nor other Respect, shall relinquish this "Promise, Vow, and Protestation." L. J., IV. 234.

This protestation was reported and agreed to in the Commons, and ordered to be made by every member of that House on the 3rd of May 1641. It was agreed to by the Lords, and ordered to be made by every member of their House on the following day. On the 5th of May the Commons ordered the protestation and preamble to be printed, the copies to be attested by the clerk, and then sent by the members to their several counties and boroughs, with an intimation "with what "willingness the members of this House made this "protestation, and as they justify their taking of it in "themselves, so they cannot but approve it in them "that shall likewise take it." Subsequently it was resolved that the protestation is fit to be made by everyone, and that what person soever shall not make the protestation is unfit to bear office in the church or commonwealth, and that it is a "Shibboleth to discover "a true Israelite." In January 1641-2, the Speaker recommended by letter the making of the protestation to the sheriffs, mayors, and others in general. The returns of the names of those who had made the protestation appear to have come in rapidly after this, for on the 8th of March they are referred to a committee

instructed to receive them, and to consider what is fit to be done with those that refuse the protestation. The returns are for the most part dated February or March 1641-2, and contain in almost all cases the names of those persons who have subscribed the protestation, and sometimes also the names of any who have refused. In a few cases the minister of the parish certifies that all have subscribed without giving the names. The return from Oxford University is very interesting, and will be found at page 130.

We have again to acknowledge the assistance of Mr. G. Fulkes and Mr. A. Lowson; the former is now engaged in arranging in chronological order the papers belonging to the period from 1714 to 1760, and the latter has completed a list of them up to the time of the Restoration.

House of Lords,   ROBERT W. MONRO.
     20th August 1874.   MERTON A. THOMS.

CALENDAR OF HOUSE OF LORDS MANU-SCRIPTS.

Jan. 3. Copy of the King's Message touching Lord Kimbolton, and the Five Members. L. J., IV. 500. In extenso.

Jan. 3. Two other copies.

Jan. 3. Copy of the Articles of High Treason, and other High Misdemeanors against Lord Kimbolton, Mr. Denzill Holles, Sir Arthur Haslerigg, Mr. John Pym, Mr. John Hampden, and Mr. William Strode. L. J., IV. 501. In extenso.

Jan. 3. Two other copies.

Jan. 3. Petition of the Bishops, impeached by the House of Commons, to have certain Counsel assigned them. L. J., IV. 501. The petition is only signed by 11 Bishops, the Bishop of Ely not having signed it, though it is called in the Journals the Petition of the 12 Bishops.

Jan. 5. Draft order touching the meeting of the Bailiwick of Surrey in Windsor Forest. L. J., IV. 503. In extenso.

Jan. 6. Copy of the King's Warrant against the printing and publishing of seditious books and pamphlets. The warrant is addressed to Robert Barker, "our printer," and to the assignees of John Ball.

[Jan. 7.] Copy of the King's Answer to the Petition of the Mayor, Aldermen, and Common Council of the city of London, touching the five members, the Lieutenant of the Tower, and other matters. The petition and answer are printed in extenso in Rushworth, Part III., Vol. I., 480.

[Jan. 8.] Petition of George Bedford, prisoner in the King's Bench, praying for a hearing of his cause against Sir John Wostenholme, Katharine Fanshawe, and James Rivers, and that in the meantime he may have his liberty.

Jan. 11. Resolutions of the Committee of the Lords and Commons for Irish affairs. L. J., IV. 504.

Annexed:—

1. Resolutions of Committee of the Commons appointed to sit in London to consider of the safety of the Kingdom, and report from the sub-committee appointed to treat with the Committee of the Common Council. 8 Jan. 1641-2.

2. Resolution of the Lords Committee for Irish affairs. 10 Jan., 1641-2.

Jan. 11. Copy of the King's answer concerning a Guard for the Parliament. L. J., IV. 504. In extenso.

Annexed:—

1. Memorandum of proceedings of both Houses concerning the Guard.

Jan. 11. Draft order for hearing the cause between Lord Faucombridge and Thomas Harrison. L. J., IV. 505. In extenso.

Jan. 11. Engrossment of "An Act declaring that the "Lords and Commons may adjourn themselves re"spectively to any place." Brought from the Commons, L. J., IV. 505, passed both Houses, but did not receive the Royal assent.

Jan. 11. Message from the Commons for the Lords to join in an order for securing Hull, and for Sir John Hotham to put in a garrison there. L. J., IV. 505.

Jan. 11. Petition of the inhabitants of the County of Buckingham for the speedy perfecting of the work of reformation. L. J., IV. 506. In extenso.

Jan. 12. Petition of Edward Stacy. Was committed to Newgate about ten weeks since for some offence offered to Sir Jacob Ashley. Has made his submission and prays for his discharge. L. J., IV. 507.

Jan. 12. Engrossment of "An Act to restrain barge-"men, lightermen and others from labouring and "working on the Lord's day, commonly called Sun-"day." Brought from H.C. L. J., IV. 488, committed, 514, no further proceeding.

Annexed:—

1. List of the Committee on the Bill. 15 Jan.

Jan. 12. Joint order of Lords and Commons concerning the Tower of London. L. J., IV. 508. *In extenso.*

Jan. 12. Draft order that the Governor of Portsmouth shall not deliver up the town nor receive any forces into it, but by His Majesty's authority signified by both Houses of Parliament. L. J., IV. 509.

Jan. 12. Resolution that Sir John Byron, the Lieutenant of the Tower, be sent for as a delinquent. L. J., IV. 509.

[1641-2, Jan. 12.] Decision of the Justices assembled in quarter sessions at Chelmsford, that Mr. Thomas Stitch is not guilty of certain charges of recusancy brought against him.

Jan. 13. Draft order for hearing the cause Lake v. Lake. L. J., IV. 509.

Jan. 13. Draft order touching the sitting of the Common Council of London. L. J., IV. 510. *In extenso.*

Jan. 13. Message from the Commons for a conference touching the impeachment of the Five Members. L. J., IV. 511. *In extenso.*

Jan. 13. Copy of the Declaration of both Houses for putting the Kingdom into a posture of Defence. L. J., IV. 512. *In extenso.*

Jan. 14. Draft Resolution of both Houses enjoining the Marquis of Hertford to take care of the Prince lest he be conveyed out of the kingdom. L. J., IV. 513. *In extenso.*

Jan. 14. Copy of preceding.

Jan. 15. Draft order appointing a Committee to make enquiry touching the late tumults, and unlawful assemblies at Kingston-upon-Thames. L. J., IV. 515. *In extenso.*

Annexed:—

1. Form of oath to be ministered to the witnesses.

Jan. 15. Message from the Commons concerning the tumults about Kingston and Windsor. C. J., II. 380.

Jan. 15. Copy of the Resolutions of the Commons upon the propositions of the Scotch Commissioners touching the sending of men out of Scotland into Ireland. L. J., IV. 517. *In extenso.*

Jan. 15. Message from the Commons touching the impeachment of Lord Kimbolton, and the Five Members. L. J., IV. 517. *In extenso.*

Jan. 15. Draft order appointing a Committee to consider how to vindicate the breach of privilege, touching the impeachment of Lord Kimbolton and the Five Members. L. J., IV. 517.

Jan. 15. Copy of portion of preceding.

Jan. 15. Paper delivered by the Scotch Commissioners to the English Commissioners concerning the treaty about Ireland. L. J., IV. 520. *In extenso.*

Jan. 15. Draft order of Lords and Commons calling out the Trained Bands, and conferring the command upon Serjeant-Major General Skippon. See L. J., IV. 518, and C. J., II. 382.

Jan. 15. Petition of Peter Scott, one of the constables of St. Martin's-in-the-Fields to the Commons; was on duty at the time of the riot caused by Col. Lunsford's assault on the citizens at Westminster; tried to appease the 'prentices by promising to release their fellows detained prisoners in the Mermaid tavern; when approaching the door his fellow constable was thrust in the leg with a sword from within, on which the 'prentices were enraged and broke into the tavern, the keeper of which has since prosecuted petitioner for a riot; the hearing comes on this afternoon; prays for a stay of the trial, and for a hearing before a Committee of the House. See C. J., II. 382.

Jan. 17. Message from the Commons touching the removal of the ordnance, arms, and ammunition from Fawkes-hall into the City of London. L. J., IV. 518. *In extenso.*

Jan. 17. Message from the Commons touching the division between the King and the Parliament. L. J., IV. 518. *In extenso.*

Jan. 17. Copy of the order and declaration of the Lords and Commons in Parliament for the providing of guards and other necessary defence for the safety of His Majesty, the Parliament, and Kingdom. L. J., IV. 518. *In extenso.*

Jan. 17. Message from the Commons touching the Scotch propositions, contributions for Ireland, &c. L. J., IV. 520. *In extenso.*

Jan. 17. Draft order touching the power given to the Committee for Irish affairs at Grocers' Hall. L. J., IV. 520. *In extenso.*

Jan. 17. Petition of the Merchants and Goldsmiths,

traders to His Majesty's Mint with foreign bullion and coin, to the Commons, praying for the removal of Sir John Byron from the Lieutenancy of the Tower. C. J., II. 386. L. J., IV. 521. *In extenso.*

Jan. 17. Similar Petition to the House of Lords.

Jan. 17. Certificate of the Common Council of the City of London, in compliance with order of the 15th instant, that they do not find any stay or forbearing of bringing in of bullion into the Mint by reason of Sir John Byron's appointment. See L. J., IV. 515.

Jan. 17. Draft of proceedings this day upon the Impeachment of the 12 Bishops. L. J., IV. 521.

Jan. 17. Petition of the 12 Bishops praying for a speedy trial, and to be admitted to bail. L. J., IV. 522. *In extenso.*

Jan. 17. Draft of petition to the King to qualify the Lord President of Munster with power to make an equal levy on the county for payment of two troops of Horse, and that the arms for them may be had from the Tower.

Jan. 19. Draft of the letter to be sent by the Speaker of the House of Commons to the Sheriffs of Counties touching the taking of the Protestation, and on the same paper drafts of various orders of the House on the same subject. C. J., II. 389. *In extenso.*

Jan. 20. Petition of sundry of the knights, gentlemen, and inhabitants of the County of Essex, concerning the relief of Ireland, the safety of the Kingdom, &c. L. J., IV. 523. *In extenso.*

This petition and the following one to the Commons have an immense number of signatures attached to them.

Jan. 20. Copy of preceding.

Jan. 20. Petition of the knights, gentlemen, ministers, and other inhabitants of the County of Essex, to H. C.; thank the House for their endeavours to settle religion and peace, but apprehend a great stop to their endeavours in the way of reformation, if the designs of the papists and other ill-affected persons, already very insolent, and ready to act the parts of the savage bloodsuckers in Ireland, be not speedily prevented; designs which have already cast such a damp upon the farming and cloth working of the county, that many thousands are like to be brought to sudden want; petitioners, who can hope for no redress unless the Bishops and popish Lords be excluded from the Upper House, pray that their brethren in Ireland may be speedily relieved, the kingdom put into a posture of defence, and the Bishops and popish Lords excluded from Parliament. C. J., II. 387.

Jan. 20. Draft order of Lords and Commons for the indemnity of Serjeant-Major General Skippon. L. J. IV., 526. *In extenso.*

Jan. 20. Draft of Answer to the King's Message concerning the Peace of the Kingdom. L. J., IV. 527. *In extenso.*

Jan. 20. Order of Lords and Commons concerning arms for Ireland. L. J., IV. 527. *In extenso.*

Jan. 20. Heads of Conference with the Commons touching the Governorship of the Town of Hull. L. J., IV. 527.

Jan. 20. Copy of the petition of the Lords and Commons to the King, touching the Lord Kimbolton and the Five Members. L. J., IV. 528. *In extenso.*

Jan. 20. Draft of the Message to the Queen touching the Report that the House of Commons intended to accuse Her Majesty of Treason. L. J., IV. 528. *In extenso.*

Jan. 20. Copy of preceding.

Jan. 22. The Gentleman Usher's note of such things as were contained in the waggon of George Lord Digby at Mere, where the waggon was stayed. L. J., IV. 533. *In extenso.*

Jan. 24. Copy of the propositions of the Scotch Commissioners for sending 2,500 men into Ireland, &c., with the Resolutions of the Commons thereon, and the King's Answer. L. J., IV. 530. C. J., II. 399.

Jan. 24. The King's Answer to the Petition of both Houses concerning Lord Kimbolton and the Five Members. L. J., IV. 530. *In extenso.*

Jan. 25. Petition of the Mayor, Aldermen, and Common Council of London, for the relief of Ireland, the disarming Papists, &c. L. J., IV. 534. *In extenso.*

Annexed:—

1. Certificate of the Common Council that there is a forbearance of bringing bullion into the Tower, and that Sir John Byron, being Lieutenant, is the cause thereof. 19 Jan. 1641-2. L. J., IV. 535. *In extenso.*

Jan. 25. Petition of Knights, Gentlemen, Freeholders, and other Inhabitants of the County of Hertford, touching the State of the Nation. L. J., IV. 535. *In extenso.*

Jan. 25. Petition of the Mayor, Aldermen, and Common Council of the City of Exeter, for the preservation of true Religion, the maintenance of the Privilege of Parliament, the liberty of the subject, the disarming of papists, &c. L. J., IV. 536. *In extenso.*

Annexed:—

1. Petition of the Commons of the City of Exeter to the Mayor, Justices, and Common Council of Exeter, praying that their grievances may be represented to the King and the Parliament. This petition is referred to in preceding. *See* L. J., IV. 536.

2. Petition of the Mayor, Aldermen, Burgesses, and other Inhabitants of Totness, to the Justices of the Peace for the County of Devon; that their grievances may be represented to the King and the House of Commons; they complain of the decay of their trade in woollen drapery, caused by the granting of Letters Patent to several Companies, who under colour thereof exact intolerable taxes. They pray that the Bishops and all recusant Lords may be removed from the House of Peers.

3. Copy of petition of the Mayor, his brethren and the rest of the inhabitants of Clifton-Dartmouth-Hardnes, with the places adjacent, to the Justices of the Peace for the County of Devon. The petitioners, who are chiefly occupied in the New-foundland fisheries, complain that their trade is likely to be destroyed in consequence of the number of Turkish pirates from Algiers and Salles, the stagnation in trade owing to the rebellion in Ireland, and still more to the dread entertained of a popish rising: they pray that measures may be taken for redressing these grievances, and desire the removal of the popish Lords and Bishops from the Upper House.

Jan. 25. Draft Order for hearing the cause between the Inhabitants of Ramsey and the Earls of Bedford and Portland. *See* L. J., IV. 524.

Jan. 26. Petition and Answer of the Mayor, Aldermen, and the rest of the Common Council of the City of London to the Commons, concerning a loan of 100,000*l.* for levying forces for the suppression of the Rebellion in Ireland. L J., IV5. 37. *In extenso.*

Jan. 26. Petition of Gentlemen Freeholders and other Inhabitants of the County of Middlesex, distinct from the suburbs of London, touching the State of the Nation (numerously signed). L. J., IV. 539. *In extenso.*

Jan. 26. Petition of Daniel O'Neill, prisoner in the Gatehouse, praying that he may be allowed to go abroad to take the air for the sake of his health, or that he may be bailed. L. J., IV. 543.

Annexed:—

1. Certificate of Dr. Thomas Winston, that unless O'Neill is allowed the benefit of fresh air, it may prove dangerous to his life. 24 Jan. 1641-2.

Jan. 26. Draft order for the Earl of Stamford and the Lord Howard of Charleton to go to the States Ambassador to desire a definite answer to their Lordship's former message touching depredations by the Dutch. L. J., IV. 543. *In extenso.*

Jan. 26. Petition of Richard Malster and others, of Roxham in the County of Norfolk, praying for their discharge, having been committed to the custody of the Gentleman Usher for disobeying an order for the quieting the possession of the Prince's tenants of the improved lands at West Dereham and Roxham. L. J., IV. 544.

Jan. 26. Petition of Sir George Wentworth, Knt., concerning the Viscount Loftus' cause. L. J., IV. 545. *In extenso.*

Jan. 27. Resolutions of the Lords in answer to the Seven Propositions of the Scotch Commissioners. L. J., IV. 545. *In extenso.*

Jan. 27. Copy of preceding

Jan. 27. Draft Order concerning the carrying of provisions into Ireland. L. J., IV. 516. *In extenso.*

Jan. 27. Petition of Henry Ascough and others, defendants at the suit of Samuel Thomas, that they may have leave to return to their homes, and re-appear when called upon. *See* L. J., IV. 548.

Jan. 27. Draft Resolutions of the Commons' Committee for grievances concerning Privy Councillors and the Great Officers of State. *See* C. J., II. 433.

Jan. 27. Petition of Peter Smart, Senior Prebendary of Durham, for a speedy hearing of his cause, and that Richard Carre, George Leake, and others, may be sent for to answer for disobeying their Lordships' former order.

Jan. 27. Petition of Thomas Prichard, D.D., on behalf of the legatees of the last will and testament of Sir Thomas Canon, Knt., 60 in number, that the cause

between the legatees and Maurice Canon, concerning the said will, may be committed to the Judges Delegates.

Jan. 28. Letter from the King to the Lord Keeper Littleton, touching the 3rd Article of the Scotch Commissioners (signed by the King). L. J., IV. 547. *In extenso.*

Annexed:—

1. Message from the King on same subject. L. J., IV. 547. *In extenso.*
2. Copy of preceding message.

Jan. 28. Order concerning the payment of the fees to Officers of the House, upon charges of delinquency. L. J., IV., 548. *In extenso.*

Jan. 28. Copy of preceding.

Jan. 28. Draft of letter from the House of Commons to the Mayors of Bristol and Pembroke to stay the ships and goods of the merchants of Wexford, Ross, Kilkenny, and other towns in Ireland, and to cause the merchants to be apprehended and examined. C. J., II. 401.

Jan. 28. Order of the Commons for one of the ships prepared by the merchants, to be sent to Lough Royal for guarding the 2,500 men sent from Scotland into Ireland. C. J., II. 401.

Jan. 28. Certificate of Martyn Sandford, Sheriff of the County of Somerset. In accordance with their Lordships' order, caused search for arms to be made at the house of James Hanham, a popish recusant, at Hollewell, forwards list of arms found which have been removed to the town of Milbourne Port. *See* L. J., IV. 510.

Annexed:—

1. Particular of the arms which were taken and seized at the house of Mr. James Hanham, on the 21st of January 1641-2.
2. Certificate of Sir Henry Berkeley and Robert Harbyn, Esq., Justices of Somerset, who assisted at the search, as to the correctness of the list of arms. The following words are added to the certificate:—" Upon good information we did " also find that none of the said arms or am- " munition had been lately procured, but had " been there left by the ancestors of the said " Mr. James Hanham many years since. There " was also found in a trunk sundry popish " books."

Jan. 29. Petition of Lucie Lady Hastings, wife to the Right Honorable Lord Ferdinando Hastings, praying for a hearing of her suit against Francis Poulton touching the Rectory of Pirton in the County of Hertford. L. J., IV. 548.

Annexed:—

1. Statement of the case between Lady Hastings and Francis Poulton.

Jan. 29. Resolution of Lords and Commons for preventing Irish and Popish Commanders going to the Rebels, and for sending back Irish vagrants. L. J., IV., 549. *In extenso.*

Jan. 29. Copy of letter from the Justices of York to the Lord Chamberlain, informing him that Captain Thos. Frankland has been appointed to guard the magazine there, and desiring that the County may be put into a posture of defence.

Jan. 31. Commission for giving the Royal assent to the Bill for relief of distressed subjects in Ireland, and to the Bill for tonnage and poundage. Signed by the King. Seal wanting.

Jan. 31. Request of the Scots Commissioners that both Houses would go on in the Irish treaty, &c. without delay. L. J., IV. 554. *In extenso.*

Jan. 31. Petition of Sir George Garrett, and Sir George Clerke, Aldermen and Sheriffs of the City of London. The Lieutenant of the Tower refuses to permit them to carry out their Lordships' order of the 12th instant, concerning the guards about the Tower. Petitioners therefore pray some further order in the matter. L. J., IV. 555.

Jan. 31. Draft ordinance of Parliament concerning the Militia. C. J., II. 406. *In extenso.*

[Jan. .] Petition of Hugh Ross, Esq. Petitioner presented a petition on behalf of Jaques de Long, merchant, against Colonel Thomas Lunsford, and on the 1st of July an order was made for Colonel Lunsford to answer, and petitioner then lodged his papers with Mr. Browne, but no answer has been made, and Colonel Lunsford is now a prisoner in the Tower; petitioner, being for the present hopeless of relief, prays that his papers may be restored to him. *See* L. J., IV. 338, 509.

Annexed:—

1. Copy of order of 1st July mentioned in preceding.

[Jan.]. Application for a further order for quieting His Majesty's possessions in Lincolnshire, the order of the 17th April last having been disregarded. See L. J., IV., 559.

Annexed :—
1. Copy of order referred to in preceding, 17 April 1641. L. J., IV. 220.
2. Affidavit of Robert Richardson, that Nicholas Gardiner and others refusing to obey the order, 13 November 1641.
2. Affidavit of John Peacocke, 29 November 1641.
3. Affidavit of John Geddes, 31 December 1641.
4. Affidavit of Henry Dandyson, 7 Jan. 1641-2.
5. Affidavit of Philip Hix, 8 Jan. 1641-2.

[Jan. .]. Draft resolutions touching certain propositions of the Scotch Commissioners.

[Jan.]. Petition of Thomas Fletcher, merchant, committee of the body and estate of Ellyn Sperin, a lunatic, complaining that Meredith Madey has illegally obtained the custody and estate of the lunatic, and praying that he may be called upon to answer. See L. J., IV. 548.

Annexed :—
1. Copy of preceding.

Feb. 1. Copy of question put to the Judges in the Duke of Richmond's case respecting the examination of Mr. Scroope, servant to the Duke, with the answer thereto. L. J., IV. 555. In extenso.

Feb. 1. Petition of Daniel O'Neale; on his petition to be bailed or to be allowed liberty of some fresh air with a keeper, he was removed to the Tower, where he is at a charge which he is no way able to undergo, having by the troubles in Ireland lost all the means by which hitherto he subsisted, while the Commons have sequestered from him what pay was due to him for the time he served in His Majesty's late army in the North; the Lieutenant of the Tower will take no care of him without their Lordships' commands, and his physician will not come to him without their express license; prays that an allowance may be made to him, that their Lordships would mediate with the Commons for payment of the arrears due to him, and that his doctor and some of his friends may come to him without prejudice. L. J., IV. 556.

Annexed :—
1. Petition of same that the general order made on preceding petition, that he should have such good usage as befits a person of his quality, may be more particularly worded. (Undated).

Feb. 1. Copy of the petition of both Houses to the King concerning the Lord Kimbolton and the five members. L. J., IV. 556. In extenso.

Feb. 1. The Scots proposition for ammunition for Ulster. L. J., IV. 557. In extenso.

Feb. 1. Copy of preceding.

Feb. 1. Another copy.

Feb. 1. The King's answer to the petition of the Commons about the militia, Tower, and forts. L. J., IV. 557. In extenso.

Feb. 1. Copy of order of the Commons for Maurice Thompson and Wm. Benoice to have powder and arms for Ireland. C. J., II. 408. In extenso.

Feb. 1. Petition of many poor distressed women in and about London; after detailing their miseries from the interruption of trade, in consequence of the government of the church by Bishops, the fears caused by the Irish rebellion, and the rumours of foreign invasion, they pray that the church may be reformed, the papists disarmed, and the kingdom put into a posture of defence, &c.

Feb. 2. Draft of petition from both Houses to the King concerning the militia, forts, &c. L. J., IV. 559. In extenso.

Feb. 2. Draft of letter sent from both Houses to the Mayor and Aldermen of Hull. L. J., IV. 561. In extenso.

Feb. 2. Affidavit of Humphrey Clarke, that the witnesses and parties cannot be ready by the 10th inst. for the trial of Lord Morley and Captain Lewis Kirke, for the murdering of Captain Peter Clarke. See L. J., IV. 565.

Feb. 3. Commission for giving the royal assent to the Bill for pressing of mariners. Read in H. L. on the 4th of Feb. L. J., IV. 561. Signed by the King. Seal wanting.

Feb. 4. Petition of Sir Thos. Cary, Knt.; prays that his cause against the Bishop of Ardagh, for reversal of an order of the Council Board in Ireland concerning certain lands and tithes worth 150l. per annum, formerly recommended to both Houses in Ireland, may be referred to two or three of the spiritual or temporal Lords now in London to end the same by consent, or otherwise to

certify the true state thereof to the House. L. J., IV. 561.

Annexed :—
1. Statement of the case.
2. Petition of Sir Thomas Cary, that a day may be appointed for the hearing of his cause, and that the Bishop of Ardagh may be ordered to attend and produce certain deeds. (Undated.)

Feb. 4. Petition of Arthur Magneiss (or Magennis), that competent maintenance may be allowed him whilst he remains prisoner in the Tower. L. J., IV. 561.

Feb. 4. Draft order of both Houses concerning Serjeant-Major General Skippon, approving his conduct as Captain of the forces guarding the Houses of Parliament, &c. L. J., IV. 562.

Feb. 4. Petition of knights, gentlemen, freeholders and others, inhabitants of the county of Surrey : for a union of the two Houses in providing for the safety of the kingdom, the relief of Ireland, &c. L. J., IV. 563. In extenso.

Feb. 4. The King's answer to the petition of both Houses concerning the forts and militia : has received the message from both Houses and resolves to take it into his mature consideration, as the importance of the matter deserves, and will return a speedy answer by or before Saturday, if he can. C. J., II. 412.

Feb. 4. Petition of Alexander McDonnell : petitioner raised certain men in the North of Ireland to assist in the suppression of the rebellion there, and the better to proceed in that service, repaired to England hoping to obtain some employment; has spent his small means, and fears arrest for the debts of his brother the Earl of Antrim, with whom he stands bound for great sums of money ; prays for an allowance out of the Earl's estate in England, and for freedom from arrest until the Earl's debts are paid.

Annexed :—
1. Petition of the creditors of the Earl of Antrim and the Lady Duchess of Bucks, his wife; Archibald Stewart, John Traylman, and others, the sureties for the debts of the Earl and Duchess, cannot go free abroad or take steps for raising money for discharge of the debts, for fear of arrest by some few of the creditors, who will not join with the rest in granting the sureties this liberty : pray for a protection from Parliament for one year for Archibald Stewart and John Traylman. (Undated.)

Feb. 5. Affidavit of Wm. Pargiter concerning gunpowder sent to Mr. Draycott of Panesley (?) in Staffordshire. L. J., IV. 564. In extenso.

Feb. 6. Letter from the King to the Lord Keeper Littleton, read in the House on the 7th, signed by the King. L. J., IV. 566.

Encloses,—
1. His answer to the petitions of both Houses about the Militia and the Lord Kymbolton and the five Members. L. J., IV. 566. In extenso.
2. His answer concerning the Queen's going into Holland. L. J., IV. 566. In extenso.

Feb. 7. Draft order appointing two Lords to entreat His Majesty to pass with all convenient speed the bill for restraining persons in holy orders from exercising temporal jurisdiction. L. J., IV. 565.

Feb. 7. Draft of various resolutions of the Commons concerning the forts, &c. C. J., II. 418, 419.

[Feb. 7.] Petition of Martin Eldred to H. C. ; was committed to the Gatehouse by order of the House; humbly confesses his fault and prays for his enlargement. See C. J., II. 415.

Feb. 7. Accounts for copying petitions, orders, &c. of the House of Lords of various dates from 24th Feb. 1640-1 to 7th Feb. 1641-2.

Feb. 8. Eales v. Covell, in error. Transcript of record, &c., brought in this day. L. J., IV. 569.

Feb. 8. Petition of Dame Marie Carr, wife of Sir Robert Carr; some time past in consequence of the cruel conduct of her husband, petitioner was separated from him and forced to complain to the King, who referred the case to certain Lords of the Privy Council, they directed that a yearly sum should be paid into the hands of the Earl of Northumberland and other trustees for the maintenance of petitioner and her children; about Christmas last she was persuaded to return to her husband, but he had no sooner got her into his power than he treated her with even greater fury and violence than before, so that she has been again obliged to leave him ; prays for an order for her protection, for a hearing of her case, and for maintenance for herself and children until it be decided. L. J., IV. 569.

Feb. 8. Petition of the knights, gentlemen, ministers, freeholders, and other inhabitants of the county of Kent,

for a thorough reformation of the Church, &c. L. J.,
IV. 570. *In extenso.*

Feb. 8. Copy of order of the Commons for setting
forth 38 ships for guarding of the Narrow seas. C. J.,
II. 420. *In extenso.*

Feb. 9. Draft of "An ordinance of both Houses of
" Parliament for the ordering of the Militia of the
" Kingdom of England and dominion of Wales." L.
J., IV. 572. *In extenso.*

Annexed :—
1. Draft of portion of preceding.

Feb. 9. Three copies of preceding ordinance.

Feb. 9. Petition of divers gentlemen and others, inhabitants of the county of Suffolk, on the behalf of
themselves and many thousands of that county that
would have accompanied them, but have forborne in
obedience to a late order of the House of Commons;
pray for reformation of the Church, relief of Ireland,
&c. L. J., IV. 573. *In extenso.*

Feb. 9. Petition of Wm. Cox, gent. ; was arrested in
January last in the streets of Bristol by Edward
Bishop, a serjeant, at the suit of Richard Godwin, in
breach of privilege, for they knew that petitioner was
solicitor to the Lord Poulett; prays that he may be
freed from arrest. *Noted* ; Rejected.

Feb. 9. Affidavits of Richard Glover, Thos. Padmor,
and Wm. Simpson, porters, that certain barrels of gunpowder were sent down by carrier to Mr. Leigh of
Adlington in Cheshire, from the house of Parnell, a
tailor dwelling in an alley near Bow Church. *See* L.
J., IV. 576, &c.

Feb. 10. The King's answer concerning the bill for
levying of soldiers, and the bill for taking away Bishops' votes. L. J., IV. 574. *In extenso.*

Feb. 10. Petition of John Galping, clerk, enforced by
desperate extremity though against the late order of
restraining of private petitions for a time, humbly to
crave leave to implore the compassion of the House for
his relief. Petitioner is incumbent of Portisham in
the county of Dorset, a place of above 1,300 souls, a
vicarage worth 300*l.* per annum; the profits were for
many years detained by the patron and only 20 marks
paid to the vicar. Petitioner after spending all he had
in a suit against the patron, was forced to accept a
composition of 75*l.* per annum, and submit to a decree
in Chancery accordingly ; this decree only bound the
person of the patron, not his estate, and as he is already
in prison for debt he refuses to pay any part of the 75*l.*,
to the utter ruin of petitioner, his wife and children ;
prays for a hearing of the case and for sequestration of
the profits of the living. *Noted,* "To be retained until
" the Lords fall upon Petitions." L. J., IV. 574.

Feb. 10. Petition of the gentry, ministry and commonalty of Cleveland in the county of York, that they
may be secured, a happy reformation afforded, and the
laws of God and the King put in execution against
papists. L. J., IV. 574. *In extenso.* The petition
consists of a number of copies all numerously signed ;
to that signed at Ingleby Greenhow a certificate signed
by the minister and churchwardens is attached, that the
chief inhabitants that can write have subscribed the
petition, and that they who cannot write themselves have
willingly consented that their names should be subjoined to the same petition.

Feb. 10. Petition of the knights, gentlemen, freeholders, and subsidy men of the best rank and quality
in the county of Oxon ; for vindication of the privileges
of Parliament, removal of evil councillors, and abolishing of idolatry. L. J., IV. 575. *In extenso.*

Feb. 10. Petition of the knights, gentlemen and freeholders of the county of Northampton, for the removal
of evil councillors from the King, the restraint of recusants, securing of the ports, &c. L. J., IV. 575. *In
extenso.*

Feb. 11. Extracts from two letters of the 23rd of Jan.
and 1st of Feb. 1641-2, written from Antwerp to Sir
John [Reginer]: every one in Antwerp is afraid that
there will happen great mischiefs in England, and
that suddenly ; counsels him to withdraw from the
imminent dangers and to come thither, where he will
be welcome. *Endorsed,* "The extract of a letter
" written from Antwerp to a merchant in London,
" 11th Feb. 1641."

Feb. 11. Letter from Sir Edw. Rodes to the Right
Hon[ble]. Ferdinando, Lord Fairfax, and Henry Bellasis,
Esq., knights of Parliament for the county of York : the
inhabitants of the county are in even greater perplexity
than when they had two armies in the neighbourhood ;
they are specially apprehensive, who desire to see the
ordinances for disarming of recusants and securing the
magazines carried out : in obedience to these ordinances
the writer intreated the assistance of Mr. Wm. West,

J.P., having heard that Kellam Homer, armour dresser
to the Earl of Arundel, had sent for one Chapman to
dress arms, and that Homer had said that before May
day they should have such a peal rung in Sheffield as had
not been heard these hundred years ; meaning by the
papists against the town of Sheffield : and having heard
that Homer and others were papists, they thought it
right to make an inventory of the arms in his charge,
and to remove the offensive arms to the castle until the
pleasure of the House should be known. From York.
See C. J., II. 431. L. J., IV. 583.

Annexed :—
1. Petition of Kellam Homer ; is not guilty of the
words and matters in the preceding letter contained against him, hath all his life been a
protestant and never papist ; he and Chapman
are now in the messenger's house at great
charges ; prays that he may be dispatched according to the justice of his cause. (Undated.) *See*
L. J., IV. 645.

Feb. 11. Petition of Colonel Fitzwilliams : their
Lordships lately gave him license to transport three or
four hundred men into France as recruits to his regiment there : but with this clause that they should
consist only of Irish, which makes the order fruitless,
as it would be almost impossible at this time to transport any considerable number of that nation ; notwithstanding this, the French King will imagine the
order to be sufficient, and conceiving petitioner to be
backward in the charge he has undertaken, may ruin
him, by disbanding his regiment, the only means for
the present left to maintain him : prays to be allowed
to transport such of all nations as he may raise here to
the number aforesaid. *Noted,* "Exped. Nothing
"ordered." *See* L. J., IV. 554.

Feb. 12. Abstract of a letter from the Mayor of
Carlisle about the storing of provisions by private per-
sons, and the number of papists in that neighbourhood.
L. J., IV. 579. *In extenso.*

Feb. 12. Petition of inhabitants of the county of
Warwick and city of Coventry, here present in the behalf
of themselves and many others of the said county : pray
for thorough reformation of the church, punishment of
delinquents, vindication of the privileges of Parliament,
&c. L. J., IV. 579. *In extenso.*

Feb. 12. Information of Mr. Monyns, fellow of Peter-
house, Cambridge, against Francis Greene, a professed
Roman Catholic, for speaking scandalous words against
the Protestant religion : Greene was curate at Arundel
in Sussex and bred a Catholic, and was a scholar and
Master of Arts of Magdalen College, Oxford, in Dr.
Renold's time. *See* L. J., IV. 586.

[Feb. 12.] Copy of ordinance of both Houses appointing the Earl of Stamford, Lord Lieutenant for the county
of Leicester. *See* L. J., IV. 578. Earl of Stamford
nominated. *See* also ordinance for the Militia. L. J.
IV. 572.

Annexed :—
1. Copy of appointment of a deputy lieutenant by
the Earl of Stamford.

Feb. 12. Commission for giving the Royal Assent to
the "Act for disenabling persons in Holy Orders to
"exercise any temporal jurisdiction or authority,"
and to the "Act for the better raising and levying of
" soldiers for the present defence of the kingdom of
" England and Ireland." L. J., IV. 580. Signed by
the King. Seal wanting.

Feb. 12. Copy of examination of Henry McCartan,
major domo to Colonel Owen O'Neale, in Flanders, and
by him sent to Ireland with promises of support in
men and munitions for the rebels.

Feb. 13. Copy of license from the King to Francis
Lord Viscount Montague, with his lady and twelve
attendants, to travel beyond the seas. *See* L. J., IV.
599.

Feb. 14. Draft of the Lord Keeper's speech before
the passing of the bills for pressing of soldiers, and
for taking away the Bishops votes. L. J., IV. 580.
In extenso.

Feb. 14. Draft of the message of thanks to the King
for passing the bills for pressing of soldiers and for
taking away the Bishops votes. L. J., IV. 581. *In
extenso.*

Feb. 14. Informations respecting words spoken by
the Earl of Arundel, that he had advised Mr. Abden
not to stay in England. L. J., IV. 581. *In extenso.*

Feb. 14. Petition of Wolley Leigh, of Thorpe, in the
county of Surrey, Esq., to H. C. : about Easter term
last petitioner arrested Edward Maria Wingfield for
a debt of 2,000*l.*, but by virtue of a protection from the
Earl of Peterborough, Wingfield was commanded away

House of
Lords.
—
Calendar.
1641-2.

by the Earl, though not one of his menial servants. Petitioner has applied to the House of Lords in vain; hears that Wingfield intends to go to Ireland, and so defraud him; prays the Commons to mediate with the Lords, that the Earl of Peterborough may be enjoined to produce Mr. Wingfield, or give bail for his appearance. *See* C. J., II. 428. L. J., IV. 582.

Feb. 14. Copy of intercepted letter from Lord Digby, at Middleburgh, to Sir Lewes Dives, Jan. 20. Rushworth, Part III., Vol. I., p. 555. *In extenso.* Also copy of intercepted letter from same to Mr. Secretary Nicholas, dated Jan. 21; his sudden departure from England has given rise to many rumours against him, but his enemies were rancorous before his departure; desires his friends not to judge him rashly; has done nothing but what he considered best for the King's service. These letters were read in the House this day. L. J., IV. 583.

Feb. 14. Copy of intercepted letter from Lord Digby to the Queen, opened by order of the House this day. L. J., IV. 585. Rushworth, Part III., Vol. I., p. 554. *In extenso.*

Feb. 14. Order of both Houses of Parliament approving of all that Serjeant-Major Skippon has done for the security of the Tower.

This order, which is signed by Elsynge, was made by the Commons on the 12th, and agreed to by the Lords with a verbal addition on the 14th. L. J., IV. 584. *In extenso.*

Feb. 14. Answer of Sir Philip Mainwaring, Knight, His Majesty's principal Secretary of State within the realm of Ireland, to the transmission of the Commons upon the complaint of Adam Lord Viscount Loftus, of Ely, as also to a petition exhibited into this Honorable House by the said Lord Loftus. Conceives that he is in no way concerned in either the transmission or petition, except as a feoffee in trust of the lands of the Lord Loftus, under a decree of the Lord Deputy and Council of Ireland.

Feb. 15. Petition of Edward Watkins, Esq., and Thomas Aleway, searchers of His Majesty's Port of London: have made many seizures of popish books and reliques, and of gold and jewels, but have frequently been forced to give up the goods so seized through the action of the Archbishop of Canterbury and Mr. Endymion Porter, contrary to law, and have suffered loss and imprisonment in consequence of their activity in their office; about four years since the right of search at Gravesend (a member of the port of London), was unlawfully taken from them, and is still enjoyed by John Robinson and others under colour of letters patent which are void in law; but petitioners are unable to prove this, being restrained from legal proceedings by an injunction grounded upon a dormant bill in Chancery; upon complaint to the House the Commons voted that petitioners had been illegally imprisoned, but have since been too much occupied to proceed further in the business, while some of the popish party have set on one Atkinson, a decayed milliner, to seek the reversion of petitioners' office from the King, contrary to the statute of Edward the 6th; the patent is now waiting to be sealed; petitioners pray that the Lord Keeper may be ordered to make a stay of the grant until their rights are decided by the House of Commons. L. J., IV. 586.

Feb. 15. Petition of the knights, gentlemen, citizens, and other inhabitants within the county and city of York; for the relief of Ireland, &c. L. J., IV. 587. *In extenso.*

Feb. 15. Petition of John Edwards and Robert Thacker to the Commons; during the troubles with Scotland they were ordered to furnish 500 long pikes, and 1,000 musket rests monthly for the King's service, to be paid for as they delivered the goods; when peace was made they had only received 200l. and had delivered goods to that value; have a large stock on hand, and have become debtors for goods ordered by them; no pikes or rests have been bought from them since, though many foreign pikes which would never stand proof have been brought into His Majesty's stores; pray that their stock may be taken off their hands, and the importation of foreign pikes forbidden. C. J., II. 434.

Feb. 16. Petition of the inhabitants of the county of Leicester: for the punishment of the counsellors, contrivers, and actors of the late surpassing breach of Parliament privileges, &c. L. J., IV. 589. *In extenso.*

Feb. 16. Petition of the Lord Mayor and Court of Aldermen of the City of London: at a Court of Common Council a committee was appointed, in relation to several orders of the House of Commons, to take into their consideration what was still to be done touching the safety of the King, Parliament, and City, with intention that the committee should advise with the Lord Mayor and Court of Aldermen and not have sole power;

House of
Lords.
Calendar.
1641-2.

yet now the House of Commons intends to settle upon the committee the ordering of the militia which time out of mind has been under the rule of the Lord Mayor and Aldermen, as well in times of greatest danger as in peace: to put this power into new hands would bring the magistrates of the City into disesteem: pray that herein they may enjoy their wonted privileges: (Signed) Richard Gurney, Mayor, and others. L. J., IV. 590. The Minute Book says "The answer was "that they petitioned too late."

Feb. 16. Petition of Richard Mack Moyler and Edmund Moore: were by order of 6th November last committed to Newgate, and by order of the 15th of the same month ordered to be kept close prisoners for speaking scandalous words against the Earl of Holland; have made submission to him, and in consequence of their three months imprisonment have become so poor, that they must have starved, if the master keeper had not relieved them at his own charge: pray for enlargement. *See* L. J., IV. 418, 425, 620.

Annexed :—

   1. Petition of same : are Irishmen, and were serving abroad as soldiers when they heard of the war between England and Scotland: returned at once and served in the North under the King: pray that they may not be detained in prison, but allowed to enter His Majesty's service under the Earl of St. Alban's [Earl of Clanrickarde], or that they may be sent over into the Low Countries or elsewhere, where they may have some service.

   2. Petition of same : pray for an examination of the case between them and Lieutenant Trist, as they are soldiers of no settled force and cannot bear a long arrest without utter ruin.

Feb. 17. Petition of the High Sheriff, Knights, Esquires, gentlemen, ministers, freeholders, and inhabitants of the county of Sussex: that the protestation may be generally taken, the kingdom may be put into a posture of defence, &c. L. J., IV. 591. *In extenso.*

Feb. 17. Draft message from both Houses of Parliament to the Spanish Ambassador to take care that certain ships laden at Dunkirk with ammunition, &c. for Ireland be stopped. L. J., IV. 592.

Feb. 17. Draft of Petition of Lords and Commons to the King concerning the Lord Kimbolton and the Five Members. L. J., IV. 592. *In extenso.*

Feb. 18. The vote of the Lords and Commons upon the propositions for the speedy reducing of Ireland. L. J., IV. 593. *In extenso.*

Feb. 18. Petition of Henry Stewart, Esq., in behalf of himself and others who are interested in the same cause : has set forth in several petitions his sufferings in Ireland; attended (in hope) above a year on Parliament: returned to Ireland to his great hazard by their Lordships' directions to obtain writings, &c. to prove his complaints ; has now lost his wife, his house, and all his estate in Ireland by the rebels, some of his tenants have been killed and the rest enforced to flee away; his five children are now in the hands of the merciless enemy : has nothing wherewith to relieve either them or himself, by reason of his long attendance on Parliament, but is in danger of being cast in prison for debt ; prays their Lordships either speedily to right him, or else to supply his necessity until they have leisure to hear his case. *See* L. J., IV. 393, &c.

Feb. 18. Certificate of Justices Heath and Foster, recommending that the cause between Baud and Lane should be left to a trial at law.

Feb. 19. Petition of Michael Miller, Esq., one of the Captains of the trained bands of Middlesex : has 300 men or thereabouts under his command, and this day, as at other times, is come to do his duty in attending on the House, but with a very small appearance, not exceeding 32 men, on other occasions also he has wanted men to perform the duty, and those few men of his company, who have been constant appearers protest never to appear again, until some course be taken with the continual delinquents : prays that some course may be taken either by imposing fines or otherwise to inforce the delinquents to perform their duties, else petitioner will not be able to perform the service. L. J., IV. 596.

Feb. 19. Certificate of Thomas Crompton and George Cradock, that pursuant to their Lordships' order they searched the House of Mr. Philip Dracott of Painsley, but found only a little barrel containing about eight pounds of powder, bought (as he said) to kill hawks' meat, as he has in his house a cast and a half of long winged hawks : they likewise found arms for two lances or quirassiers, which he stands charged with in the list of the trained horse for the county, and besides a fowling-piece, and four other small pieces to kill birds and hawks' meat. L. J., IV. 596.

Feb. 19. Answer of both Houses to the King's message concerning Lord Digby's letter to the Queen. L. J., IV. 597. *In extenso.*

Feb. 21. The King's answer concerning the ordinance of Parliament touching the militia. L. J., IV. 509. *In extenso.*

Feb. 21. Copy of preceding.

Feb. 21. Petition of Henry Fisher: the writ of error which was brought in, in the cause between the petitioner and the Dean and Chapter of Christchurch, Oxford, and others, concerning the Castle there, having been affirmed, petitioner prays that a day may be appointed for the further hearing of the equity of his cause. L. J., IV. 599.

Feb. 21. Copy of order of the Commons for the Lord Admiral to give commissions to merchants to seize ships that belong to, or go to relieve the rebels of Ireland. C. J., II. 446. *In extenso.* Agreed to by the Lords, with an amendment. L. J., IV. 600.

Feb. 21. Message of both Houses to the King concerning the militia. L. J., IV. 600. *In extenso.*

Feb. 21. Order of the Commons concerning waggons to be sent from Hull to carry arms to Chester. C. J., II. 447. Agreed to by the Lords. L. J., IV. 600. *In extenso.*

Feb. 21. The King's answer to the Petition of both Houses concerning the Lord Kimbolton and the five members. L. J., IV. 600. *In extenso.*

Feb. 21. Petition of Lancelot Lake; as sole executor of his mother Dame Mary Lake, lately deceased, entered upon that part of her personal property, which was in her manor house of Cannons, Middx, intending to remove the same to London, but was interrupted by the servants and friends of Sir Thomas Lake in a hostile manner: prays for an order securing him free ingress and regress upon the lands of his late mother, and peaceable possession of her personal estate. L. J., IV. 601.

Feb. 21. Order for the Lord High Admiral to grant unto William and Ann Pawlett, and others, letters of marque by way of reprisal against the subjects of the States of the United Provinces. L. J., IV. 601.

Feb. 22. Names of those who have killed the King's deer in Windsor forest. *See* L. J., IV. 602.

Feb. 22. Answer of Sir Edward Herbert, Knt., His Majesty's Attorney General, to the impeachment exhibited against him by the House of Commons in this present Parliament assembled. L. J., IV. 603. *In extenso.*

Feb. 23. Letter from the King to Lord Mowbray and Maltravers, requesting him notwithstanding his former leave of absence to repair to London and give his personal attendance in Parliament. This letter is the same as that to the Earl of Berks, which is given *in extenso.* L. J., IV. 612.

Feb. 24. Petition of Charles Lord Stanhope, Baron of Harrington: Robert Knightley, a notorious recusant, has commenced an action in the Court of Common Pleas against Edward Chamberleyn, petitioner's tenant, for recovery of rent which he pretends to be issuing out of the Manor of Calcot [Caldecote] in the county of Warwick, which descended to petitioner free of any such incumbrances, as he conceives: prays for the benefit of privilege, and that the action may be stayed during the continuance of Parliament. L. J., IV. 607.

Feb. 24. The King's answer to the proposition concerning Ireland. L. J., IV. 607. *In extenso.*

Feb. 24. Copy of preceding.

Feb. 24. Petition of the Citizens of London whose names are underwritten: that the ordering the arms of the City may be left to the Lord Mayor and Court of Aldermen. L. J., IV. 609. *In extenso.*

Feb. 24. Copy of preceding: this copy was presented to the Commons unsigned, and sent out of the House for signature. C. J., II. 451. It is noted "This is a true "copy of a Petition subscribed with the names of many "citizens and now remaining in the hands of Walter "Long, Esq., a member of the honorable House of "Commons." *See* the Impeachment of Geo. Benyon. March 31. L. J., IV. 683.

Feb. 24. Another copy.

Feb. 24. Petition of John Robinson, Richard Ward, and Christopher Dighton, His Majesty's searchers at Gravesend: most seizures of goods prohibited and uncustomed, shipped at London, are made at Gravesend; the offices of searchers there are therefore very important, and have time past memory been distinct from those of London; about forty years since the searchers of London claimed to nominate the searchers of Gravesend to the Lord Treasurer, but Lord Treasurer Buckhurst, thinking this of dangerous consequence, disposed of them as separate offices, but allowed to the searchers of London a recom-

pense of 100*l.* per annum. Petitioners have held their offices for about nine years, and during that time have seized great quantities of gold, silver, and other prohibited and uncustomed goods, shipped at London, and escaped by the connivance or negligence of the searchers there; and have done many other acceptable services to the state, discovering of popish priests and Jesuits going out and coming into the kingdom, and preventing the transportation of divers young children of good birth to be educated in the Popish religion; and have lately seized a quantity of wool shipped at London as goat's hair. Edward Watkins and Thomas Aleway, the present searchers of the Port of London, have tried to oust petitioners from their offices, have molested them in the discharge of their duties, and have now presented a petition to the House on the subject; pray that the parties may be summoned, and petitioners peaceably settled in their offices. L. J., IV. 609.

Feb. 24. Message from the Commons respecting the proceedings against the twelve Bishops, &c. L. J., IV. 609.

Feb. 24. Order for securing payment to the merchants and others who set forth ships for the Summer Fleet. L. J., IV. 609. *In extenso.*

Feb. 24. Proclamation writ sent to the sheriffs of the several counties of England and Wales to summon George Lord Digby, accused of high treason, to appear. L. J., IV. 611. *In extenso.* Certificate of publication of notice in the County of Worcester attached.

Feb. 24. Similar proclamation writ, with certificate of publication in the County of [Hereford] attached.

Feb. 24. Similar proclamation writ, with certificate of publication in the County of Gloucester attached.

Feb. 24. Similar proclamation writ, with certificate of publication in the town of [Ross] attached.

Feb. 24. Petition of the Mayor, Aldermen, Gentlemen, Merchants, Citizens, and other inhabitants of the City of New Sarum, in the County of Wilts: that the Lords would co-operate with the Commons for a thorough reformation, &c. L. J., IV. 611. *In extenso.*

Feb. 25. The King's Answer to the petition of both Houses concerning the Militia. L. J., IV. 612. *In extenso.*

Feb. 25. Letter from Cambridgeshire, signed by Sir John Cutts and others, to Lord North, Lord Lieutenant of the County, desiring that the militia may be reviewed, and supplied with arms. L. J., IV. 612. *In extenso.*

Feb. 25. Petition of Edward Trelawny: twelve months since petitioner obtained a judgment in the King's Bench for 400*l.* against Thomas Babb, who to delay execution brought a writ of error into Parliament, which he has since never prosecuted. Prays that the cause may be remitted to the Judges of the King's Bench to proceed therein. L. J., IV. 614.

Annexed:—

1. Similar Petition of same (undated).

Feb. 25. The Lords Justices of Ireland to the Lord Keeper, concerning the Lord Loftus' cause, desiring that the answers of Robert Lord Dillon, Sir Adam Loftus, Vice-Treasurer and Treasurer at War in Ireland, and of Sir Paul Davys, Clerk of the Council, now sent, may be accepted without their personal attendance, as their services are much required in Ireland in these perilous times. This letter which was read in the House this day is dated 11th February 1641[-2]. L. J., IV. 613.

Feb. 26. The joint and several answers of Robert Lord Dillon, Sir Adam Loftus, Knt., His Majesty's Vice-Treasurer and Treasurer at War in Ireland, and Sir Paul Davys, Knt., Clerk of the Council in Ireland, to so much as concerns them of the criminal and civil part in the transmission mentioned in the order of the most honorable the Lords House of Parliament, in the kingdom of England, dated the 9th of December 1641, which concerns the right honorable the Lord Viscount Loftus: the Justices and Council in Ireland judge the attendance of the respondents on their duties in Ireland so necessary, that they think not fit to license their repairing to England to present their answer themselves. Robert Lord Dillon and Sir Robert Loftus only acted as trustees in the matter complained of, and are ready to obey any order the Lords may make, so that they be protected therein from action by the heir-general of Sir Robert Loftus. Sir Paul Davys only acted in obedience to the commands of the Council, his duty being to obey commands and not to examine their justice; if they have failed to answer with sufficient fulness, pray consideration in regard of the troubles in Ireland, which leave them hardly time to attend to any of their private affairs. L. J., IV. 614.

Feb. 26. Petition of James Lord Strange, Lieutenant

of the County of Chester. Peter Heywood (against whom petitioner has a suit), has printed and published a declaration against petitioner, and caused several bundles of papers to be printed here in London in the form of petitions in the name of the County of Lancaster, full of scandal against petitioner as unfit for his place, and reflecting upon Parliament for appointing him; prays for vindication of his honour. L. J., IV.

Annexed :—

1. Printed copy of declaration referred to in preceding.

2. The answer of Peter Heywood, gent., to the charge contained in the petition of James Lord Strange. 22 March 1641-2.

3. Petition of Peter Heywood, prays that he may be dismissed from any further attendance, and be discharged of the pretended scandal.

Feb. 26. Deposition of Richard Francklin, of scandalous words spoken by Henry Stanley against the Parliament. L. J., IV. 615. *In extenso.*

Feb. 26. Draft of letter agreed to by both Houses, to be sent to the Sheriffs of Counties concerning the propositions about Ireland. L. J., IV. 615. *In extenso.*

Feb. 26. Articles of Impeachment against George Lord Digby, by the Commons in this present Parliament assembled, in maintenance of their accusation whereby he standeth charged with High Treason in their name and in the name of all the Commons of England. L. J., IV. 616. *In extenso.* Attached is a memorandum dated 2 May 1642, that the Commons desired to add to the first article the words, " And did " levy war against the King." L. J., V. 37.

Feb. 26. Petition of Thomas Nettervill, Esq., son of the Lord Viscount Netervill, now a prisoner in the Compter in Wood Street. Was committed to the custody of Sheriff. Clerke by their Lordships until he should find security not to go into Ireland. The sheriff, having Justice Berkeley in his house and a large family of his own, pretended that he had no room for petitioner, and committed him to the Compter. Prays that he may be removed to some other place and have some allowance for his maintenance, as he has no friends or kindred in this kingdom to whom to apply. L. J., IV. 617.

Feb. 26. Petition of divers baronets, knights, esquires, gentlemen, yeomen, and others of the County of Derby, to H. C. : thank God for all that has been done in the way of Reformation, desire that the work may go on to perfection ; offenders in Church and Commonwealth may be punished ; papist lords and bishops removed from Parliament ; papists disarmed and their practices disappointed ; Ireland relieved, and England put into a posture of defence under persons, whom Parliament and the Kingdom can trust ; in support of all which petitioners will make good to the uttermost the protestation so wisely commanded by the House to be taken.

This petition consists of many copies very numerously signed, but no mention is made of it in the journals. It was no doubt presented to the House somewhat later than Feb. 26, on which day the inhabitants of Winshill are stated to have signed the petition.

Feb. 28. Copy of the resolutions of the House of Commons upon the King's answer to their petitions concerning the Prince and the Militia. C. J., II. 460. *In extenso.* Agreed to by the Lords on the afternoon of the same day. L. J., IV. 619. *In extenso.*

Feb. 28. Draft of preceding, chiefly in Rushworth's handwriting. (Three papers.)

Feb. 28. Petition of Sir George Clerke, knight, one of the Sheriffs of the City of London ; by their Lordship's order of the 9th inst., Mr. ‚Netterville was committed to his custody, but petitioner's family being large, he has only one spare room in which he has already, by order of the House, Mr. Justice Berkeley his prisoner, he therefore took special order with the keeper of Wood Street Compter for Mr. Nettervill to lodge there. Mr. Nettervill lately making moan to petitioner that he was destitute of means for his maintenance, he sent 40l. out of his own purse for his relief; has lately received an order commanding him to attend the House this day to give account why he has not obeyed the former order ; humbly conceives that he has not disobeyed, and desires the favourable opinion of the House. *See* L. J., IV. 617.

Feb. 28. Certificate for poll money for part of the Hundred of Offlow, in the county of Stafford, as also upon review thereof according to order, &c.—Aldridge, &c.

Feb. 28. Certificate for poll money for part of the Hundred of Offlow, in the county of Stafford, as also upon review thereof, according to order, &c.—Alrewas, &c.

[Feb. 28.] Certificate of what hath been done upon the poll money, as well upon the Act of poll money as upon the order of review of the same in the Hundred of Totmanslowe [Totmonslow], in the county of Stafford.

Feb. . Petition of Anthony Hooper and his creditors; the referees to whom were referred the differences between Hooper and his creditors were proceeding rapidly to a settlement, when one Philip Pascall, a Frenchman, pretending to be a creditor, charged Hooper in execution in the Poultry Compter, London, and is likely thereby to frustrate their Lordships' order and defraud the other creditors. Pray for an order for Hooper to attend the House with his keeper *de die in diem. See* L. J., IV. 329, &c.

Annexed :—

1. Certificate of referees in support of preceding.

March 1. Petition of the Bishop of Durham and the Bishop of Coventry and Lichfield. The House of Commons having voted free liberty unto them and the other Bishops to answer for themselves without counsel ; pray their Lordships' leave to present themselves before the House of Commons to manifest the truth of their cause. L. J., IV. 621.

March 1. Petition of Gilbert Fitch, one of the Marshals of His Majesty's Hall in Ordinary, to James, Duke of Richmond and Lennox, Lord Steward of His Majesty's Household. Was arrested at the suit of Ezechias Skarning contrary to privilege. Prays for his discharge, and that Skarning and others may be called upon to answer. L. J., IV. 621.

March 1. Petition of Archbald, Archbishop of Cassell, in Munster, in the behalf of Daniel MacCarthy. Signed by MacCarthy, for leave for him to return to Ireland lest he perish with hunger or be obliged to beg from door to door. *Noted.* To be sent to the Commons. *See* C. J., II. 462.

March 2. Message from the Commons touching the King's Message concerning the Militia. L. J., IV. 622. *In extenso.*

March 2. Order of Lords and Commons for the rigging of ships for the defence of the Kingdom. L. J., IV. 622. *In extenso.*

March 2. Petition of His Majesty's Attorney General touching the Counsel assigned to him. L. J., IV. 623. *In extenso.*

March 4. Petition of Allan Boteler, Esquire, Cupbearer to Her Sacred Majesty, praying for his discharge, having been arrested contrary to privilege. L. J., IV. 624.

Annexed :—

1. Copy of Order declaring that the Queen's servants are to enjoy the Privilege of Parliament. 6 August 1640.

March 4. Information of Sir John Lenthall and his son, Thomas Lenthall, concerning the riot in the King's Bench Prison. L. J., IV. 624. *In extenso.*

March 4. Letter from the King to Lord Keeper Littleton concerning the Attorney General. This letter was read in the House on the 8th of March. L. J., IV. 634. *In extenso.*

Annexed :—

1. Copy of the Articles of High Treason and other High Misdemeanours against the Lord Kimbolton, Mr. Denzill Holles, Sir Arthur Haslerig, Mr. John Pym, Mr. John Hampden, and Mr. William Strode. Enclosed in preceding. L. J., IV. 501. *In extenso.*

March 4. Acknowledgment by Christopher Elsinge of the receipt of 2l. from his brother Henry Elsinge.

March 4. Petition of Richard Delamain. Several rates of land in the four provinces of Ireland, with the rents reserved to the Crown, are lately published by order of Parliament for the information of such persons as shall be undertakers. Petitioner has prepared a table, whereby it may appear what number of acres will arise for any sum of money proposed. Prays that the table may be published by order of the House.

Annexed :—

1. Table shewing instantly by the eye the number of acres belonging to any sum of money, according to the rate settled by Parliament upon any of the lands within the four provinces of Ireland, or what sum of money is to be disbursed for any number of acres assigned, and what the yearly rent reserved for the King amounteth unto, for any number of acres in any of the four provinces. As also a table to reduce any number of Irish acres of 21 feet to the pole, unto Statute acres of 16½ feet to the pole, or any number of English acres proposed, to find what number of Irish

acres they make, all performed by an inspection of the table, calculated by Richard Delamain in the 14th year of his age, and dedicated to the high and honourable Court of Parliament. .

March 5. Engrossed ordinance of the Lords and Commons in Parliament, for the safety and defence of the kingdom of England and dominion of Wales. L. J., IV. 625. *In extenso.* (Parchment Collection.)

March 5. Draft of portion of preceding.

March 5. Petition of Michael Miller, Esquire, captain of one of the trained bands for the county of Middlesex, to the Earl of Holland, Lord-Lieutenant of the County, complaining of the boisterous and insolent behaviour of John Wayte and John Bickers, two of his company, when on guard at the Parliament House, and praying his Lordship's order in the matter. *See* L. J., IV. 628.

March 5. Petition of the high sheriff, knights, esquires, gentlemen, ministers, freeholders, and other inhabitants in the county of Berks, praying that the country may be put into a posture of defence. L. J., IV. 627. *In extenso.*

March 5. Petition of Colonel John Butler. Was with the King in Scotland when the rebellion in Ireland began, and disclaims all interest in rebellious designs and intentions. If their Lordships please to employ him, has great confidence that he shall persuade all the family of the Butlers to lay down their arms and assist in suppressing the rebels, and has no question that the Earl of Ormonde, his nephew, will be answerable for his misactions. Prays for his liberty, and if that cannot be granted, then that maintenance may be allotted to him. *See* L. J., IV. 533.

March 5. Draft resolutions of the Commons touching Commissions of Lieutenancy. C. J., II. 467. *In extenso.*

᠃ March 5. Copy of certificate of Lord Saville and Sir Peter Wich, that 918*l.* 5*s.* 7*d.* hath been spent for the diet and other expenses of the Lords in Parliament, from the 20th of March 1640-1 to the 31st December 1641, and requesting the Lords and officers of the Exchequer to take present order that this sum may be impressed to Mr. Cofferer.

March 7. Petition of Edward Sydenham, Esquire, praying for an order for quieting him in the possession of certain improved lands in the county of Derby. L. J., IV. 629.

March 7. Copy of the further declaration of both Houses presented to the King. L. J., IV. 629-633. *In extenso.*

March 7. Draft order of Lords and Commons, appointing receivers of the subscriptions for the speedy reducing of the rebels of Ireland. L. J., IV. 632. *In extenso.*

March 7. Petition of Lieutenant John Curtis to H. C. Petitioner, being an English protestant, settled in Ireland about seven years since, and gave a large sum as a fine for a lease of lands in the Queen's County, in Leinster. Has been despoiled by the rebels and forced to fly into this kingdom, where he has received the command of a lieutenant's place under the Lord General in the expedition into Ireland, whereby he may be enabled to regain his lost fortunes, but he has not yet received any pay, and is therefore in great distress. Prays for relief out of the monies contributed for the distressed protestants in Ireland. C. J., II. 469.

March 7. Petition of James Cocks, merchant, for relief against Thomas Seaman and others, upon whose suit concerning a bond, he is unjustly detained close prisoner in the Fleet.

March 7. Petition of William Wingfield, gent., with his wife, mother, two sisters, and three children. Their Lordships were pleased to grant passes to petitioners for their peaceable passage abroad. Being in extremity they were compelled to make their wants known to the resident clergy of certain parishes in Essex. Some were helpful to them until they came to Billericay, where they entreated Mr. Bridge, the minister, to recommend their distressed state to his parishioners; he not only refused to do this, but with the assistance of the officers of the town and one Hunter, intercepted and detained their passes, saying that they were hedge passes. Pray that Bridge, Hunter, and the officers of the town, may be called upon to answer.

March 8. Petition of John Waite, freeholder, and John Bickers, both of the Trained Bands under the command of Captain Michael Miller. Complain that Allen Prickott, late a strong papist, was allowed by Captain Miller to appear with part of his arms on Friday last at the Court of Guard, notwithstanding he had been discharged by the House of Commons upon Petitioner's complaint. They further complain of many wrongs

done to them by Captain Miller, and pray that the matter may be referred to the Lord Lieutenant, Deputy Lieutenants, and Knights of the County of Middlesex. L. J., IV. 634.

March 8. Petition of Edward Trelawny, Gent., for a speedy hearing of his cause against Babb. L. J., IV. 634.

March 8. Copy of Mr. Serjeant Wylde's speech in opening the proceedings of the House of Commons against Sir Edward Herbert, His Majesty's Attorney General, for exhibiting articles of High Treason against Lord Kimbolton and the five members. L. J., IV. 635. This paper is wrongly endorsed " Mr. Sergeant " Wyld"s opening of Mr. Benyon's charge."

March 8. Draft Order of the Commons touching the ᠂ Protestation. C. J., II. 471. *In extenso.*

March 9. Petition of Sir Philip Carteret with reference to the defence of the Island of Jersey. L. J., IV. 637. *In extenso.*

Annexed :—

1. Memorial of the state of the militia and forts in the Island of Jersey, the wants and defects, and means of defence. L. J., IV. 637. *In extenso.*

March 10. Petition of James, Earl of Suffolk. Theophilus, late Earl of Suffolk, was indebted to William Geeres, a silkman, for certain wares. Geeres understanding that Marmaduke Moore, a servant of the Earl, was feoffee for divers of the Earl's lands, got Moore to enter into bond to Thomas Masham, who pretended power to assign over debts to the King. Masham accordingly assigned the bond to the King, and not only extended such lands as Moore was feoffee in, but other lands of petitioner's wherein Moore had no colour of interest. Prays that the King's Remembrancer may be ordered to make no further process upon the extent until the abuses complained of have been examined into. L. J., IV. 640.

March 12. Petition of Thomas Gardiner, Knt., Recorder of London, now prisoner in the Tower by their Lordships' order. Acknowledges the justice of his imprisonment and prays for his discharge. L. J., IV. 642.

March 12. Similar Petition of Thomas Bedingfield, Knt., His Majesty's Attorney of the Duchy. L. J., IV. 642.

March 12. Draft Order for payment of 2,000*l.* to Mr. Nicholas Loftus, Deputy Treasurer at Wars for Ireland. C. J., II. 476. *In extenso.*

March 14. Copy of examination of Garrat Aylmer, of Balrath. At the beginning of the siege of Drogheda ho understood that all the Lords and many of the gentry of the County of Meath, met at the Hill of Crostie near Drogheda, with some of the chief of the Northern rebels, and there entered into an agreement with them. Soon after the Earl of Fingall, the Lord of Gormanston, and others, in truth, all or most of the gentry of the county, appeared at the Hill of Tarragh (Tara), summoned there by the Sheriff, by Lord Gormanston's direction; first, to give an answer to a proclamation touching the coming of the said Lords to Dublin to confer with the State (the answer was brought ready drawn by Lord Gormanston, and was agreed upon with little alteration): secondly, to provide victuals that the Northern rebels, that the spoil of the county might be prevented : thirdly, to; nominate a governor, (Lord Gormanston) and a Council to advise with him for the good and defence of the County. At the next meeting, examinant was absent, but heard that power was given to the Earl of Fingall and others to appoint captains out of every barony, and that it was determined to raise companies for them. The allowance of victual was a beef and a barrel of corn for every hundred men per diem, and the same for the Northern rebels. At another meeting at the Hill of Tarragh about a month ago, the Earl of Fingall proposed to raise horse throughout the County, and a list was accordingly drawn out, and proclamation made, that upon pain of death everyone named in the list should be ready with his horses at a certain day ; and accordingly his examinant sent a horse and horseman to the Hill of Tarragh on the day appointed. Being asked whether he was present at any meeting between the Lords and Gentry of the Pale and the Northern Rebels, says that when the shipping first went into the harbour for the relief of Drogheda, there being a general cry in the Country and the beacons lighted, he went to the Hill of Crostie, and there saw Sir Phelim O'Neale and other chiefs of the Northern rebels in consultation on horseback with Lord Gormanston, Lord Slane, and Lord Lowth. Examinant heard much shooting that night, and understood in the morning that a breach had been made in the wall of Drogheda ; the day after examinant was obliged to attend Lord Fingall to Plattin [Platten], where Lord Slane, Lord Gormanston, and many others met Sir Phelim O'Neale and others of the Irish rebels, when it was agreed that Sir Phelim should be governor of the forts about Drogheda. A short time after various meetings were called, and the inhabitants ordered to bring eight men for every plough land, but few brought any. The reasons for taking up arms were, according to report, liberty of religion, maintenance of the King's prerogative and freedom of the subjects. Lord Louth, Colonel Moore, and others, came more than once with troops to examinant's house, whilst the Irish army lay within two miles of it, and were every day robbing his and his neighbour's houses. He was forced to attend the meetings above mentioned by threats, that his house should be burnt and his head cut off if he failed : he also heard that Lord Gormanston wrote to Lord Mountgarrat and others in Munster to procure their assistance.

March 15. Message from the Commons concerning the equipping of a fleet under the command of the Earl of Warwick. L. J., IV. 645. *In extenso.*

March 15. Letter from the King to the Lord Keeper. Encloses :—

1. Message from the King concerning Ireland, and declaring against the validity of any Act or Ordinance that has not received the Royal Assent.

The Letter and Message were read on the 16th of March. L. J., IV. 646. *In extenso.*

March 16. Petition of the High Sheriff, Knights, Esquires, Gentlemen, Ministers, Freeholders, and Inhabitants of the County of Bedford, for the Reformation of the Government and Grievances of the Church and Commonwealth. L. J., IV. 647. *In extenso.*

March 16. Petition of the Merchant Strangers residing in Dover in the behalf of themselves and their principals, subjects to the King of Spain, and other Princes in amity with His Majesty. Petitioners' principals have of late forborne adventuring their estates hither in the same proportion as heretofore, out of apprehension of the present condition of the times. Pray that their bullion, goods, &c. may be secured against the violence of any people whatsoever, and that in case any breach of peace should happen between His Majesty and the King of Spain, or any other foreign Prince, petitioners may have six months respite for the transport of their persons and estates, according to the Articles agreed upon between His Majesty and the King of Spain. L. J., IV. 648.

March 16. Copy of the petition of the Knights, Esquires, Gentlemen, and Commons of the county of Cambridge, and Isle of Ely, for the removal of all unwarrantable orders and dignities, banishing Popish clergy, punishing delinquents, &c. L. J., IV. 648. *In extenso.*

March 16. Draft order in the cause Burrell v. Burrell.

March 16. Petition of parishioners of St. Leonard's, Foster Lane : William Warde, their late rector, was proved before the Committee for scandalous ministers to be innovating and scandalous, and forced to resign ; a Mr. Bevoies was presented, but shortly resigned ; and now owing to the delays of the Dean and Chapter of Westminster the right of presentation has lapsed to the Archbishop of Canterbury, though the petitioners had by direction of the Dean and Chapter selected Mr. Smith; pray for consideration. L. J., IV. 649.

March 17. Petition of Henry, Earl of Danby, concerning untrue reports made by Sir William Sant Ravie touching the Forest of Whichwood, Oxfordshire. L. J., V. 22. *In extenso.*

Annexed :—

1. Articles of complaint against Sir William Sant Ravie. L. J., V. 24. *In extenso.*

March 17. Petition of John Cooper and Daniel Wilgris that the hearing of their cause against Thomas Turner may be put off until next term. L. J., IV. 650.

March 17. Petition of George Benyon, citizen of London ; prays for discharge from the Tower. See L. J., IV. 653.

March 17. Copy of the examination of Nicholas Dowdall, of Brownestown, in the county of Meath, taken before the Chancellor of His Majesty's Court of Exchequer by direction of the Right Honorable the Lords Justices and Council. Examinant, who was Sheriff of Meath, gives an account of the meeting of the Earl of Fingall, Lord Gormanston, and many other noblemen and gentry of the county with the Northern rebels at the hill of Crostic. Lord Gormanston, in the names of the Lords and Gentry, demanded of the Rebels what were the grounds of their war, and the reason of their so coming

into the country in that hostile manner ? Unto which Roger Moore made answer, That their so doing was for their free exercise of the Catholic religion, the restoring of the King unto his prerogative, and the gaining unto the subjects of Ireland the like freedom that the subjects in England have. Lord Gormanston replied, that if those were the true grounds of their war, they likewise would join with them therein, but if they had any other ends they would not, whereupon Moore protested solemnly, that that was their only intention. Dowdall further describes other meetings, and the preparations made for raising men and supplying them with necessaries.

March 17. Commission for giving the Royal Assent to the bill for reducing the rebels in Ireland. See L. J., IV. 658.

March 18. Bragg v. Rosewoll in error. Transcript of record, &c., brought in this day. L. J., IV. 651.

March 18. Petition of John Bishop of Ardagh in Ireland, praying that he may be dismissed any longer attendance to answer the Petition of Sir Thomas Cary, and that the matter, which relates to tithes and lands of the See of Ardagh, may be left to the ordinary course of law. L. J., IV. 651.

Annexed :—

1. Copy of petition of the Bishop to the House of Lords in Ireland, complaining that Sir Thomas Cary has commenced a suit against him without leave of the House, and copy of the order of the House of Lords in Ireland for the Sergeant-at-Arms to arrest Sir Thomas Cary for his contempt in proceeding against a member of the House without license. 28 June 1641.

March 18. Petition of the Mayor, Aldermen, and the rest of the Common Council of the City of London, disavowing the petition of the Citizens of London presented on the 24th of February. L. J., IV. 651. *In extenso.*

Annexed :—

1. Answer of the Common Council to the Committee of Lords and Commons delivered in their name by the recorder, desiring that the proceedings upon the first petition presented in their name may be expunged from the journals, now that the second petition has been presented.

March 18. Message from the Commons touching the disposing of money come in upon the Act of Contribution, &c. L. J., IV. 652. *In extenso.*

March 18. Order for 200l. to be paid to Dr. Temple for Irish affairs. L. J., IV. 652. *In extenso.*

March 18. Petition of Daniel Fairfax and Isaac Legay; that certain tobacco may be ordered to be delivered up to them in accordance with the certificate of the referees, to whom the cause between petitioners and the creditors of Anthony Hooper was referred. L. J., IV. 653.

Annexed :—

1. Certificate mentioned in preceding, L. J. IV., 653.

March 18. Order for securing the bullion and coin of the Merchant Strangers. L. J., IV. 653. *In extenso.*

March 18. Draft of preceding.

March 19. Petition of George Benyon for his discharge. Duplicate of petition presented on the 17th March. L. J., IV. 653.

March 19. Petition of Katherine, wife of Henry Hughes, Dr. of Physic, that a writ ne exeat regno may be issued against Dr. Hughes. She obtained an order for alimony in the High Commission Court against him ; he has now sold his estate and is going beyond the seas. See L. J., IV. 653.

March 19. Draft of "An Act for the securing and " freeing all such persons as have executed any power " upon any Commission of Lieutenancy or Array." A Bill with this title was ordered to be prepared by the King's Counsel on this date, but does not appear to have been brought in. L. J., IV. 654.

March 19. Propositions of the Commons for an order of both Houses concerning Hull, &c. L. J., IV. 656. *In extenso.*

March 19. The names of the Lords Lieutenant who are to bring in their Commissions. See L. J., IV. 633, &c.

March 21. Petition of Joseph Atkinson, His Majesty's milliner, and John Dayntrie, gent. In January last His Majesty granted to petitioners the reversion of the office of searchers in the port of London, after the determination of the interest therein of Edward Watkins and Thomas Aleway. The sealing of the grant has been stayed in consequence of a scandalous petition presented by Watkins and Aleway. Pray that the Lord Keeper may be ordered to proceed with the sealing of the grant, and that Watkins and Aleway may be left to the due course of law for their remedy. L. J., IV. 659.

March 21. Petition of Thomas Lord Viscount Baltinglasse, complaining that the Sheriffs of London and the Keeper of the Wood Street Compter refuse to obey their Lordships' order for petitioner's release. See L. J., IV. 654, 660.

March 21. Commission for giving the Royal Assent to the " Act for the raising and levying of monies for the " necessary defence and great affairs of the Kingdom of " England and Ireland, and for the payment of debts " undertaken by the Parliament." See L. J., IV. 674. (Parchment Collection.)

March 21. Draft order of the Commons renewing former order concerning Lord Macguire and MacMahon. C. J., II. 489. On the back of this paper is a note from Rushworth to Throckmorton, requesting to know for Mr. Pym's information what has been done " in your " House concerning the inclosed."

March 21. Draft order for Lieutenant Broome to transport thirty recruits for Sir Ferdinando Knightley's Company.

[March 21.] Petition of George Benyon, Citizen of London. Their Lordships after giving order for his discharge have re-committed him to the Tower. Prays that he may receive a copy of the charge against him, if any there be, and that he may have his liberty to prepare his defence.

Annexed :—
1. Copy of Order for his re-commitment. 21 March 1641-2. L. J., IV. 659.

March 22. Petition of Thomas Bowghey, of Brockton, in the county of Stafford, complaining of the oppressions of Sir John Pearsall, a supposed recusant, who vexes petitioner with many unjust suits. Of late many hundreds of noted recusants have resorted to Sir John's house, and his servants have bought the greatest part of the provisions brought into any market near, much more than can be expended by his domestic family, and to the great want of the poor. Petitioner and his family have been beset and assaulted by Sir John's order, and now live in danger of their lives. Robert Low, one of the recusants, has threatened to bring an army of men and flay and salt petitioner and his wife. Prays for protection and that steps may be taken for suppressing the tumultuous meetings of these recusants. L. J., IV. 660.

March 22. Draft of " An Act for asserting of some " privileges of Parliament lately broken, and to prevent " the breaking thereof in the time to come." Recites that a great breach of privilege has been committed by Sir Edward Herbert, His Majesty's Attorney-General, in arresting a Peer of the Realm (Lord Kimbolton), and enacts that no peer during the continuance of this or any ensuing Parliament shall be brought to trial for any treason, felony, or capital offence, except in Parliament, and that by impeachment of the House of Commons. Read 1ª. L. J., IV. 660. Bill re-committed. L. J., IV. 665. No further proceeding.

Annexed :—
1. List of Committee, 23 March 1641-2. L. J., IV. 665. In extenso.

March 22. Petition of William Gaye, stationer, praying for his discharge, having been committed by their Lordships for printing a paper, intituled " Some passages " that happened the 9th of March between the King's " Majesty and the Committee of both Houses when the " Declaration was delivered to him." L. J., IV. 652, 660.

March 22. Copy of order of Lords and Commons concerning Hull. L. J., IV. 662. In extenso.

March 22. Petition of the Right Honorable John Earl of Peterborough and the Lady Elizabeth, his Countess, praying their Lordships to take the evidence of witnesses, some of whom are very aged, in their cause against the Lord Mounson touching certain lands, part of the manor of Reigate. The Lord Mounson having insisted upon his privilege as a member of the House of Commons, the Court of Wards forbears to proceed in the suit without the order of this House. L. J., IV. 663.

March 22. A relation of the sea and land forces, that are now preparing in Normandy, Brittany, and all along the Coast of France. Presented by the Lord High Admiral. L. J., IV. 662. In extenso.

March 22. Message from the Commons concerning deputy lieutenants, &c. C. J., II. 492. In extenso.

March 22. Petition of William San Ravy, Knt. The Earl of Danby has exhibited articles against petitioner, for the supposed publishing of false slanders; prays that the matter may be referred to a trial at common law, or that the Earl may be ordered to assign a certainty of

place and time, where and when, the supposed words were spoken, whereby petitioner may be enabled to apply his defence. See L. J., IV. 650.

March 22. Petition of the Mayors, Bailiffs, Jurats, freemen, and other inhabitants of the Cinque Ports, two ancients towns and their members, praying for the reformation of the government and grievances in the Church, State, and Commonwealth, and that their Lordships will by some good means obtain His Majesty's Royal person and presence near the Parliament with the Prince His Highness.

March 23. Copy of petition of the Admiralty of Amsterdam. A man-of-war belonging to petitioners was on the voyage from Portugal driven out of its course, and being very leaky was run ashore on the north coast of Wales. Pray leave to carry off their brass and iron ordnance (being 26 pieces) with the ammunition, sails, &c., and that Mr. Griffith, vice admiral of the said coast, may be ordered to receive fair recompence for salvage. L. J., IV. 665. Noted with order referring the matter to the Lord High Admiral.

March.23. Petition of Colonel John Butler, praying that he may have liberty to go abroad with a keeper to take the air for his health's sake. L. J., IV. 665.

March 23. Letter from the King at York to the Earl of Essex, Chamberlain of the household, desiring his attendance at York, where the King intends to keep both Easter, and St. George's Feast. This letter was read in the House on the 28th of March. L. J., IV. 675. In extenso.

March 23. Commission for giving the Royal Assent to the Act for granting a subsidy to the King of tonnage and poundage, and other sums of money payable upon merchandizes exported and imported. See L. J., IV. 679. (Parchment collection.) (Much mutilated.)

March 24. Petition of William Lord Archbishop of Canterbury. Was required by their Lordships' order of the 17th instant to give the presentation of St. Leonard's, Foster Lane, to Mr. George Smith, and has already caused the presentation to be drawn out and sealed. As he is bound by the duty he owes to the church and state to examine the sufficiency of those he presents to benefices, he prays that Mr. Smith may come to him in order that he may in some sort satisfy his own conscience and his duty to the public. The petition is written and signed by the Archbishop. L. J., IV. 666.

March 24. Petition of Sir John Bramston, Knt., Chief Justice of the King's Bench, Sir Humfrey Davenport, Knt., Chief Baron of the Exchequer, Sir Thomas Trevor, Knt., one of the Barons of the Exchequer, Sir Francis Crawley, Knt., one of the Justices of the Common Pleas, and Sir Richard Weston, Knt., one of the Barons of the Exchequer ; praying that they may have leave to make their several answers and defences to their impeachments by their counsel, and that certain counsel may be assigned to them. L. J., IV. 666.

March 24. Copy of the answers of the Marquis of Hertford and the Earl of Bridgewater respecting their commissions of lieutenancy. L. J., IV. 666.

March 24. The King's answer to the Declaration of both Houses against fears and jealousies and ill counsels. L. J., IV. 667. In extenso.

March 24. Draft letter from the clerk of the Parliaments to the Earl of Exeter, informing his Lordship that in the ordinance for settling the Militia he is nominated Lord Lieutenant for the county of Rutland. See L. J., IV. 625.

March 24. Affidavit of William Champnoll of Greenwich, that he served Jeremy Bagg and Francis Bristow with their Lordships' order of the 13th of May touching the making of glass, and that they treated the order with contempt. See L. J., IV. 669.

March 24. Affidavit of John Jenkins, that he was present when Bagg and Bristow were served with the order. See L. J., IV. 669.

March 25. Three drafts of the ordinance fixing the powers of Lords Lieutenant. L. J., IV. 670. In extenso.

March 25. Three drafts of the " deputations " to be given to Deputy Lieutenants. L. J., IV. 671. In extenso.

March 25. Petition of Frances Countess Dowager of Rutland, and William Willoughbby, Esquire; pray that John Earl of Rutland may be ordered to waive his privilege, and answer the Bill in Chancery exhibited against him by petitioners touching the devise of certain lands in the counties of Leicester and Warwick by George, late Earl of Rutland. See L. J., IV. 674.

March 25. The answer of Sir William San Ravy, Knight, to the petition and articles preferred against him by Henry Earl of Danby. L. J., V. 23. In extenso.

March 25. Reasons urged by Conyers Lord Darcy why their Lordships' order of the 23rd of June last made in his suit against Thomas and John Saville should stand as it now is. *See* L. J., IV. 670.

Annexed :—

1. Statement of the proceedings in the cause.

March 25. Petition of Richard Freshfield. Prays that an early day may be appointed for hearing his cause against the Mayor, Aldermen, and Council of the town of Colchester, and that in the meantime he may have protection from arrest by his creditors. L. J., IV. 670.

Annexed :—

1. Another petition of Freshfield, detailing at great length the particulars of his various suits against the Corporation of Colchester, and praying that all the parties may be called before their Lordships. (Undated.)

2. Copy of another petition of Freshfield, praying for redress for the wrongs and oppressions he has suffered at the hands of the Corporation of Colchester. (Undated.)

March 25. Order of the Commons to move the Lords to desire six demi-canon of His Majesty for the army in Ireland. C. J., II. 498. *In extenso.*

March 26. Petition of William Arundell, Esquire, that a writ ne exeat regno may be granted against Lord Baltimore, who is intending to depart the kingdom and go into Mary Land, where he hath a plantation. *See* L. J., IV. 671.

March 26. Draft order upon preceding petition. L. J., IV. 671.

March 26. Copy of order made upon Report from the Committee for the defence of the Kingdom upon the proposition of Sir Philip Carteret, Lieutenant Governor of the Isle of Jersey, for the safety and defence of that Island, and also upon the Remonstrance of some of the inhabitants of the Island. L. J., IV. 671. *In extenso.*

Annexed :—

1. The heads of such propositions as are humbly presented to the House of Peers by Sir Philip Carteret. L. J., IV. 671. *In extenso.*

2. Copy of preceding.

3. Petition of some of the inhabitants of the Isle of Jersey. Complain of the oppressions practised upon them by Sir Philip Carteret, and pray for a hearing of their complaints. The petition is signed David Bandinell, and Henry Dumaresq. *See* L. J., IV. 671.

4. " A word left by the way touching Sir Philip " Carteret, of the Isle of Jersey." An unsigned paper containing many charges against Sir Philip Carteret. Endorsed " Lybell."

5. Examination of William Lorting, of Liverpool, mariner. Came out of the River of Bordeaux about six weeks since in a vessel called the " George," of Liverpool, laden with wines, and being homeward bound, was driven into the River of Blewett (?), where he heard from one Mr. Morgan, an Irishman, but a protestant, that the friars who lived about Blewett had informed him, that there was a great fleet of shipping preparing by the French King to come to Ireland. Mr. Morgan also informed him that at Hamboore (?) proclamation was made, that all officers of shipping should repair aboard their several ships at Brest, where the French Fleet then lay. 17 Feb. 1641-2.

6. Examination of George Mason and others, Scotch merchants, at the Castle of Falmouth, the 8th of February 1641-2.

7. Letter from Walter Hungerford [at St. Malo] to Sir Philip Carteret. There are come to St. Malloes 4,000 soldiers, and 8,000 more are expected every day. Those of St. Malloes will not allow them to come into the Town, but have billetted them at Dennant [Dinan] and other Towns near. They write of 4,000 more to come to [St. Brewer], but of that I have no certainty. All our shipping are stayed for 5 or 6 days to transport these soldiers, but now, by the coming home of some shipping of their own, they are released. Some report they are to go to [Barcelona], others to Calais, or some port of Picardy. It behoves us to have a careful eye on these armies. The Commanders, Colonels, and Captains who are to go along with these soldiers are men of good experience, but they have in a quarrel killed the Captain of the Castle of St. Malloes. Knows not whether that will be an impediment to their intended employment. Believes the King is returned from his intended journey to Cattoloney [Catalonia], and

is marching towards Picardy. There is no more trust in the Cardinal than in the Devil. The small quantity of the King's wheat which the receiver hath received is intended to be put presently into the King's castles, but it is so small a quantity, that it will not maintain the ordinary garrison one month, nor can there be any assistance had hence.

March 26. Petition of George Benyon that counsel may be assigned to him in his cause against Lord St. John. L. J., IV. 673.

March 26. Petition of Sir Thomas Walsingham, Knight, and Robert Moulton, Esquire, that a day may be appointed for hearing their cause against Sir John Baker, Bart., touching their title to the Manor of Hunton, Kent. *See* L. J., IV. 674, &c.

March 26. Petition of Wolley Leigh, of Thorpe, in the County of Surrey. Prays that Edward Maria Wingfield, arrested at the suit of petitioner, and subsequently discharged by virtue of a protection from the Earl of Peterborough, and who has gained his name to be entered in the list to go over as a commander for Ireland, may not be allowed to depart this kingdom until he has given petitioner satisfaction for his just debt. L. J., IV. 674.

Annexed :—

1. Copy of petition presented by Leigh to the Commons, referred by them to the Lords. L. J., IV. 582.

2. Draft order appointing a Committee to consider the matter. 14 Feb. 1641. L. J., IV. 582. *In extenso.*

March 28. Petition of Cecil Lord Baltimore that the writ ne exeat regno, issued against him on the petition of William Arundell, may be stayed until he be heard by his counsel. L. J., IV. 675.

March 28. Affidavit of Lord Baltimore that he has no intention of suddenly leaving the Kingdom.

March 28. Information of Francis Jones concerning a petition of dangerous consequence read at the last assizes at Maidstone, Kent, which it is intended to present to both Houses of Parliament. L. J., IV. 675.

March 28. Copy of the petition of the Lords and Commons to the King that the Earl of Warwick may be appointed to the command of the Fleet. L. J., IV. 676. *In extenso.*

March 28. Copy of petition of the Gentry, Ministers, and Commonalty of the County of Kent, agreed upon at the General Assizes for that County. L. J., IV. 677. *In extenso.*

March 28. Affidavit of Peter Mackerell, servant to Daniel Farvacke, that he served Anthony Hooper with their Lordships' order of the 18th instant. *See* L. J., IV. 653, &c.

March 29. Reasons to be sent to the King for staying the Earls of Holland and Salisbury and Lord Savill from going to York. L. J., IV. 680. *In extenso.*

Annexed :—

1. Draft Resolutions concerning the staying of those Lords which are sent for to attend the King at York.

March 29. Petition of the High Sheriff, Knights, Esquires, Gentlemen, Ministers and others of good rank, within the County of Rutland; pray that the Kingdom may be put into a posture of defence, &c. L. J., IV. 680. *In extenso.*

Annexed :—

1. Copy of a Petition of " Your Majesties Loyal Subjects " in the county of Rutland to the King; pray his Majesty to return and vouchsafe his presence to the Parliament. Noted. This is a copy of the petition presented to His Majesty the 16th of this instant March, as he passed through the County towards York.

March 29. Copy of order in the cause between Sir Philip Vornatti and John Latch. L. J., IV. 682. *In extenso.*

Annexed :—

1. Copy of a previous order in the cause, 30 Jan. 1640-1.

2. Petition of Thomas Jenyns and others, sureties of John Latch : pray that the cause may be referred to certain arbitrators.

3. Order of referees to whom the matter was referred appointing a day for hearing, 11 May 1642.

4. Petition of Thomas Jenyns that Vernatti may be ordered to attend the referees, and that a writ ne exeat regno may be issued against him.

March 29. Copy of Ordinance for settling the Militia of London. L. J., IV. 682. *In extenso.*

March 29. Petition of Annekin Vanhoven, a Dutch woman and stranger. Petitioner's father being Captain of a troop of horse, served under one John Dalbier in Holland, under pay of the King's Majesty that now is, and did lay out in wages for his troop 511l., for which Dalbier gave bond, and received that sum and a far greater out of His Majesty's Exchequer at Westminster. Petitioner's father being slain in the Swedish war this debt was assigned to her as her portion. She was compelled to sue Dalbier upon his bond and obtained a verdict against him, but before execution could be had he procured a Writ of Error, and now has got employment beyond the seas under Sir William Belfore. Prays that a writ ne exeat regno may be issued against Dalbier, that he may not leave the Kingdom until he has satisfied petitioner's just debt. L. J., IV. 681.
Annexed :—
  1. Order upon preceding. L. J., IV. 681.
  2. Affidavit of Anne Vanhoven, that Dalbier intends to leave the Kingdom.
  3. Another petition of Annekin Vanhoven in the matter. (Undated.)

March 29. Copy of petition of a great number of distressed gentlewomen, lately come forth of Ireland, to H. C. Many of petitioners have lost their husbands, and all of them their estates; they have been compelled to fly hither for the safety of their lives; many are sick, and all like to perish for want of sustenance; pray that an order may be given to the Commissioners, appointed for the disposing of the charitable contributions of well disposed Christians, to pay to petitioners a portion of the same.

March 29. Petition of Christopher Harvey, to Sir Thomas Leigh and Sir William Boughton, two of His Majesty's Justices of the Peace in the County of Warwick; they have commended to him the protestation made by the House of Commons, in order that he should take it himself and tender it to his parishioners, but until certain doubts and scruples entertained by him are answered he cannot do this with a good conscience, these he is unwilling to state for fear they should raise doubts in others, and therefore sends a declaration of his fidelity to the doctrine of the church as contained in the 39 Articles, of his allegiance to the King, and his desire to maintain the privileges of Parliament, and the rights and liberties of the subject.

March 31. Draft order appointing the hearing of the cause between the Earl of Danby and Sir William San Ravy. L. J., IV. 683. In extenso.
Annexed :—
  1. Affidavit of Ralph Nowlson, servant to Lord Danby, that he served preceding order on Sir William San Ravy. 27 April 1642.

March 31. Articles of Impeachment against George Benyon. L. J., IV. 683. In extenso.

March 31. Report of the Conference touching the Impeachment of George Benyon. L. J., IV. 684.

March 31. Letter from John Fielder, High Sheriff of the County of Southampton, to [   ]. Has this day received two warrants signed with the King's own hand, for the publishing of certain books and messages in all the market towns of this County, the copies of which are herewith sent. Beseeches that the House may be made acquainted with them, and that he may receive directions in the matter. Encloses—
  1. Copy of the warrant from the King to the High Sheriff of Southampton, directing him to publish and disperse in the County all the printed books sent therewith, containing "Petitions and Mes-
  " sages from our Parliament concerning the Mili-
  " tia of the Kingdom, and our several and respec-
  " tive answers to the same." Royston. 5 March 1641-2.
  2. Copy of the warrant from the King to the same to publish and disperse in the County the printed copies therewith sent of "our gracious message
  " of the 15th of March, lately delivered in our
  " High Court of Parliament upon our removal to
  " the City of York." York. 19 March 1641-2.
  3. Printed copy of "The several petitions and mes-
  " sages of Parliament concerning the Militia of
  " the Kingdom, with His Majesty's answers there-
  " unto. Together with an Ordinance of Parlia-
  " ment concerning the same."
  4. Printed copy of "Divers Questions upon His
  " Majesty's last Answer concerning the Militia."
  " Resolved upon by both Houses of Parliament."
  5. Printed copy of "His Majesty's Message to
  " both Houses of Parliament upon his Removal
  " to the City of York."

March 31. Petition of the Vice-Chancellors of the University of Cambridge and such Heads of Colleges therein as have subscribed their names. By the Statutes all the Heads of Colleges ought to be divines, and the Masterships, except two, are of so small emolument that of themselves they cannot afford any competency of maintenance for persons of a degree and quality fitting for such employment. Most of the Heads of Colleges have hitherto held ecclesiastical livings, with their masterships, and have not been tied to a constant residence upon their livings. Petitioners pray that some provision may be made for them, as the taking of the Masters from their necessary residence in their Colleges, and not affording a sufficiency of means to them, will bring certain ruin to the whole University. The petition was no doubt directed against the "Bill
" against enjoying of Plurality of Benefices to Spiritual
" Persons and non-residency," at this time before the House.

March 31. Petition of John, Archbishop of York, and the rest of the Bishops now prisoners in the Tower, as likewise the two Bishops under the Black Rod. Pray that they may be admitted to bail, as the House of Commons has decided not to proceed against them by impeachment, as at first, but in another way. (Signed by all the Bishops.) L. J., IV. 685.

[1641-2.] March. Petition of John Raven, of the Inner Temple, London, "Utterbarister," for leave to proceed against Samuel Gookin for the recovery of a debt, notwithstanding that Gookin pretends to have a protection from the Earl of Dover.

April 1. Petition of William, Archbishop of Canterbury; prays for the approbation of the House upon the persons appointed by him to three livings now vacant and in his gift. L. J., IV. 686. The petition, which is in Dell's handwriting, is signed by the Archbishop.

April 1. The King's answer to the last message of both Houses. L. J., IV. 686. In extenso.

April 1. The answer of George Benyon to a petition exhibited before their Lordships by the right honorable Oliver Lord St. John. L. J., IV. 688. In extenso.

April 1. Declaration of the grievances and evils of the kingdom with the proposition of the remedies and cures. Imperfect. L. J., IV. 689–692.

April 2. Affidavit of William Kent in the case between William Walter and his wife. L. J., IV. 693.

April 2. Affidavit of David Bevon in the same case. L. J., IV. 693.

April 2. Order for the removal of the arms and magazine from Hull. L. J., IV. 694. In extenso.

April 2. Petition of Thomas Jenyns, Esq.: prays for a ne exeat regno against Sir Filibert Vernatti, whom he suspects of intending to depart beyond seas in order to avoid payment of his debts. L. J., IV. 694.

April 2. Draft order for borrowing 10,000l. for the service of Ireland. L. J., IV. 695.

April 2. Affidavit of service of an order of the 29th of March last upon John Dalbeere at the suit of Anne Vanhoven. L. J., IV. 694.

April 2. Petition of James Earl of Suffolke against the heirs of Sir Robert Hitcham and others about lands in Framlingham and Saxted [Saxtead], Suffolk. L. J., IV. 696. In extenso.

April 2. Copy of preceding.

April 2. Draft order referring preceding petition to a Committee. L. J., IV. 696. In extenso.

April 2. Affidavit of service of an order of the House of the 29th of March last upon Anthony Hooper at the suit of Isaac Legay and others.

April 4. Resolution of the Lords that they will support the Lord Admiral and the Earl of Warwick. L. J., IV. 697. In extenso.

April 4. Petition of Edward Maria Wingfield; Wolley Leigh having induced petitioner to become bound for a large sum of money has sued him upon the bond, and obtained a writ ne exeat regno against him. Petitioner has for his support procured himself to be listed as a commander in the expedition for Ireland; prays for discharge of the writ, which if executed will be his ruin. L. J., IV. 698.
Annexed :—
  1. List of bonds entered into by Wingfield.

April 4. Answer of George Benyon to the Impeachment preferred against him by the House of Commons. L. J., IV. 698. In extenso.

April 4. Petition of George Benyon, prisoner in the Tower; prays their Lordships to accept bail, that he may have liberty to attend to his domestic affairs, and prepare his defence to the impeachment of the House of Commons.

April 4. Draft order of the Commons for the Mayor and Aldermen of York to pay to the several persons mentioned the money received into the Chamber of York for the relief of the northern counties. C. J., II. 511. *In extenso.*

April 5. Petition of Edward, Earl of Sussex; petitioner has the sole right of fishing in Walfleet and the river of Burnham, in the county of Essex, but has been often injured by many of the adjoining inhabitants who pretend to have a right therein; and though this claim has been condemned by trial at law, yet they threaten to destroy the principal fishing in the river by taking the spat of oysters and other fish, and transporting the same to other oyster lanes, and breeding places of their own in other rivers, and to expel petitioner in a violent manner with sixty sail of great fishing boats; the design if executed is likely to be the cause of great tumults, and of serious loss to petitioner; prays that the Lord High Admiral may be directed to suppress all such disorders. L. J., IV. 699.

April 5. Petition of the Bishops in prison; thank the House for transmitting their former petition to the House of Commons, and pray for a comfortable answer thereto.

April 5. Draft of " An Act to prevent extortions for " burials : " fees to the value of two, three, four, five and sometimes six pounds or more are charged by ministers, churchwardens, and other officers for burying the dead, whereas no fee is due but one to the sexton for digging the grave; the Bill forbids all other fees. Read 1ª. C. J., II. 511. No further proceeding.

[April 5.] Draft order of the Committee appointed to consider of scandalous books and pamphlets, directing the gentleman usher to use his utmost endeavour for the apprehension of offenders. *See* L. J., IV. 700.

April 6. Petition of Thomas Bushell : petitioner by His Majesty's command, adventured his fortune in the recovery of the deserted mines in Cardiganshire, but, being much molested in the work by Sir Richard Price and others, obtained an order from their Lordships for securing his quiet possession; in spite of this order Sir Richard Price and the others have destroyed petitioner's engines and works, and refused him turf " to make into " charke " by a method of his own invention for the saving of wood, and in other ways molested him; prays that they may be convented to answer for their misdoings. L. J., IV. 700.

Annexed :—
1. Affidavit of Walter Barsbee, " Saye-master " of His Majesty's Mint, county of Cardigan.; 5 April 1642.
2. Affidavit of John Huson; when Mr. Nevell, who formerly worked the mines, heard that Bushell had bought the lease of them, he hired deponent and others to pull up the pumps, and inundated the mines, and stopped them up with rubbish.
3. Copy of the order referred to in Bushell's petition. 14 August 1641. L. J., IV. 364.
4. Another copy.
5. Letter from Sir Richard Price to Mr. Hevitoe; understands that he will interrupt the writer's workmen on the hill, would have him know that his interest is better there than that of any other.

April 6. Copy of order made on Bushell's petition for his protection. L. J., IV. 700. *In extenso.*

April 6. Charge presented by Thomas Bushell, Esq., against Sir Richard Price and others.

April 6. Petition of John Earl of Rutland ; is willing to waive his privilege and answer the Bill of the Countess Dowager of Rutland ; she has for her jointure certain woods near Belvoir, and under plea of cutting underwood is cutting timber trees ; petitioner has no remedy against her at law because of her privilege, and were she to waive this, she is very aged and not likely to live to see the issue of a suit; petitioner prays for an order enjoining her to forbear from further felling of timber trees. L. J., IV. 701.

Annexed :—
1. Affidavit of George Grundy in support of preceding.

April 6. Order for payment of 100*l.* to Mr. Vassall for corn for the poor of Londonderry. L. J., IV. 703. *In extenso.*

April 6. Copies of votes of the Commons concerning the impeached Bishops. C. J., II. 513 and 490.

[April 6.] Copy of letter from the Speaker of the House of Commons to the Lords Justices in Ireland. Thanks the Justices for the unwearied pains, constancy, and faithfulness they have shown in providing for the dangers and necessities of the kingdom, and opposing

the insolent attempts of the rebels. Assures their Lordships that it has not been any want of affection to the distressed English there, which has prevented the House sending more plentiful succours, but the manifold distresses caused by the malignant party in this kingdom, and the great burthens they have been consequently forced to lay upon the people. There is now direction given for the raising of 6,000 foot for the further supply of Ireland, and the House is in a hopeful course not only to maintain these and the other succours already agreed upon, but to make a further addition if there be cause. The House observes that the rebels in Ireland speak the same language with the malignant party here, making it one of their motives for taking up arms to vindicate His Majesty's privileges from the encroachments of Parliament. The rebellious Lords of the Pale in their instructions to Lord Dillon taxed the Justices of Ireland with adhering to the Parliament against the King, in which malignant slander the House observes a great congruity between the traitors there and the malignant party here, and as the House doubts not to make clear to the world their uprightness and integrity to His Majesty, so they hold it a great evidence of the sincerity of the Justices that such an imputation should be laid upon them. Prays the Justices to observe all such spirits, as are apt to ferment jealousies betwixt the King and his Parliament, as dangerous incendiaries of the State, enemies of the public peace, and unfit for any place of trust, and to endeavour to punish and suppress them. Desires their Lordships to take especial notice of all councillors and others employed in the service of the State, who stand well affected to the public good, and to give them thanks in the name of the House. Lastly, informs their Lordships that His Majesty has, at the humble desire of the Lords and Commons, granted a commission to divers members of both Houses for ordering and disposing all matters for the defence, relief, and recovery of Ireland. C. J., II. 513.

April 7. Informations and examinations concerning Sir William Willmer; of Peter Lord, John James, and Sir William Willmer. L. J., IV. 704. *In extenso.*

April 7. Resolution of the Commons that Sir William Willmer, High Sheriff of Northamptonshire, has broken the privileges of Parliament, and endeavoured to disturb the peace of the kingdom. C. J., II. 515.

April 7. Message from the Commons for the Earl of Bridgwater to deliver in the papers he has about the Isle of Anglesea. L. J., IV. 707.

April 7. Answer of Sir · George Wentworth, to the declaration or charge transmitted from the House of Commons on the behalf of Adam Viscount Loftus of Ely; hopes to prove that the decree and proceedings complained of, which were confirmed by the Privy Council in England, were according to justice; has himself no interest in the lands comprised in the decree, which are now in the hands of the rebels, for the lands belong to Ann Loftus, an infant of 14 years, to whom her grandmother Lady Jepson is guardian, and if the decree be declared void, Ann Loftus will not have one pennyworth of advancement either from her grandfather, Lord Loftus, or from her father; respondent believes that Lady Jepson and her son Sir John Gifford are now at Castle Jordan, Leinster, in such peril of the rebels, that they cannot appear or make their defence in this cause ; to those parts respondent is now going, at the hazard of his life, to attend to the duties conferred on him; all he did under the decree was done by good warrant, as he doubts not to prove, when the troubles and distractions of Ireland have been pacified, and time given for examination of proofs and witnesses. No mention is made of this answer in the journal.

April 7. Petition of John Earl of Bristol, prisoner in the Tower ; prays the House, if satisfied that he had no . hand in framing or procuring the petition from Kent, to be pleased to grant him enlargement.

April 8. Petition of John Earl of Bristol, prisoner in the Tower ; that for the sake of his health and for soliciting of his affairs he may have leave to go abroad, either upon his honour for true imprisonment, or with a keeper, a favour not denied him, when he was formerly a prisoner in the Tower under a high accusation. L. J., IV. 705.

April 8. Order of the Lords and Commons for reformation of the church. L. J., IV. 706. *In extenso.*

April 8. Declaration of the Lords and Commons for keeping a good correspondence with the Scots. L. J., IV. 707. *In extenso.*

April 8. Petition of Colonel Philip Hill; prays for the assistance of the House to make certain Irish, whom he has enlisted with their Lordships' permission, take ship for service in France. *See* L. J., IV. 709.

April 8. A true return of the names of all such Irish as are resident within the liberty of the Rolls in the county of Middlesex. The names of eleven persons are given, of whom only three are papists.

April 8. Petition of William Ward, clerk, rector of St. Leonard's, Foster Lane, London; petitioner agreed with Mr. Beauvoys, rector of Witheham [Withyham], Sussex, to exchange livings, and accordingly resigned St. Leonard's, and now Mr. Beauvoys refuses to perform his part, petitioner prays that no one else may be instituted to the rectory of St. Leonard's, and that his resignation may be cancelled.
Annexed :—
1. Affidavit of John Papworth and others in support of preceding.
April [8]. Three copies of a letter from J. Math. Palmer [to the Commissioners and Collectors of the county of Nottingham]; has received direction from the House of Commons to send up a return of what is in arrear of the six last subsidies; desires them therefore to meet him at Southwell, at widow Clarke's house, on Thursday the 14th instant, to give him an account, and meantime to collect as much as possible of the arrears.

April 9. Petition of John Wilson of St. Giles, Cripplegate, London, now a prisoner in the Gatehouse by their Lordships' commitment; his only crime is to have allowed his son part of his house to print such books, as lawfully he might, but not otherwise; prays for discharge. *See* L. J., IV. 708, &c.

April 9. Copy of the recognizance of Sir William Wilmer. *See* L. J., IV. 708.

April 9. Printed copy of the petition of the Lords and Commons to the King for leave to remove the magazine at Hull to the Tower of London, and also to take off the reprieve of the six condemned priests now in Newgate, together with His Majesty's answer thereunto. The petition is given *in extenso.* L. J., IV. 708. The King's answer, April 16. L. J., IV. 722.

April 9. Draft of preceding petition.

April 9. Order for the Earl of Bath to attend the House notwithstanding he has license from His Majesty to be absent. L. J., IV. 709. *In extenso.*

April 9. Motion for Henry Roseby and his wife to be sent for, for their contempt in continuing to build a house upon the King's ground, where the records of Parliament are kept, in defiance of their Lordships' order of the 6th of September last. *See* L. J., IV. 709 and 389.
Annexed :—
1. Letter from Mr. Serjeant Francis, Justice of the Peace, to Mr. Browne [clerk of the Parliaments]. Upon receipt of their Lordships' warrant went to Roseby's house and did there forbid the workmen then at work. Roseby said nothing, but his wife, who stood by, bid them go on, as she had spoken to some Lords and would speak to some more. Prays further directions. 11 March 1641-2.
2. Affidavit of Joseph Ware in the matter. 29 March 1642.

April 9. Copy of a petition of Allan Boteler, Esq., cup bearer to Her sacred Majesty, has been arrested contrary to privilege; prays for discharge. L. J., IV. 709.
Annexed :—
1. Petition of Allan Boteler; details the circumstances of his arrest at the instigation of Ann Brown and John Handford; prays for redress. (Undated.)

April 9. Petition of parishioners of Goudhurst in the county of Kent; have with the rest of the county enjoyed the fruition of the blessings for soul and body obtained by the sedulity of the House, "and heartily " desire one additament more to invest them with a " fulness of happiness," namely, that Mr. Edward Bright, a minister of godly life and conversation, may be appointed as lecturer there every Wednesday. C. J., II. 518.

April 9. Order of the Commons respecting the 6,000l. advanced by the county of Buckingham upon the Act of Contribution for the affairs of Ireland. C. J., II. 519.

April 11. Draft order for the Marquis of Hertford either to attend to his duties in Parliament, or still to continue his care of the Prince. L. J., IV. 711. *In extenso.*

April 11. Order of the Commons for payment of 4,000l. to Nicholas Loftus, deputy to the treasurer at war for Ireland. C. J., II. 521. *In extenso.*

April 11. Order of the Commons for payment of 500l. to Nicholas Loftus for shoes for the soldiers in Ireland. C. J., II. 521. *In extenso.*

April 12. Engrossment of " An Act to enable Sir " Christofer Wray, Knight, to sell the manor of Haw- " stead cum Buckenhams, alias Bucknams, and other

" things in the county of Suffolk." Brought from H. C. L. J., IV. 713. Passed both Houses, but did not recieve the Royal Assent.

April 12. Engrossment of " An Act for the making of " the town and chapelry of Holland, in the county of " Lancaster, a distinct parish from the parish of Wigan, " in the said county." Brought from the Commons. L. J., IV. 713. No further proceeding.

April 12. Petition of Frances, Countess Dowager of Rutland, and her answer to the petition of John, Earl of Rutland, presented on the 6th instant. L. J., IV. 714. *In extenso.*

April 13. Certificate by James Archbishop of Armagh [Usher] of the good character of Mr. William Howlett, proposed to be appointed by the Archbishop of Canterbury to the rectory of Lochenden [Latchingdon]. L. J., IV. 715.

April 14. Draft of " An Act for ratification of a par- " tition heretofore made by and between the late Phil- " lipp earl of Arundell and the Lady Anne his wife " of the one part, and the late Lord William Howard " and the Lady Elizabeth his wife of the other part." Read 1ᵃ. L. J., IV. 716. Read 2ᵃ, and committed, L. J., V. 10. No further proceeding.

April 14. Printed copy of " An Act to enable corpo- " rations and bodies politic to participate of the bene- " fit of an Act lately passed, intituled ' An Act for the " ' speedy and effectual reducing of the rebels in His " ' Majesty's kingdom of Ireland to their due obedi- " ' ence to His Majesty, and the Crown of England.' " Brought from H. C. L. J., IV. 716. Received the Royal Assent on the 22d April. L. J., V. 9. *See* Statutes, 8vo edition, 16 Car. I., c. 35.

April 14. Petition of the parishioners of St. Olave's in Southwark to H. C.; on the 2nd instant the petitioners chose churchwardens for the parish, three of the four old churchwardens being present; since which time about 20 parishioners met and chose other churchwardens, promoters of innovations in the worship of God, who intend to officiate by violence; petitioners pray for an examination of the legality of the election, that the poor may be provided for, and the public peace maintained.
Annexed :—
1. Return of the names of the churchwardens elected for the ensuing year. 31 March 1642.

April 14. Order of the Commons referring the preceding case to two justices of the peace. C. J., II. 527. *In extenso.*

April 14. Petition of Henry Stanley, prisoner in the Fleet; was accused by a waterman about two years since of speaking scandalous words against the Parliament, for which he was censured by the House; has since discovered that his servant was suborned to give false evidence; prays for liberty on bail that he may take steps to vindicate his innocency. *See* L. J., IV. 615.

April 15. Petition of John Pulford, His Majesty's servant, agent for the soliciting of the business against recusants: petitioner became bound with others for Sir Peregrine Bartue, deceased, and notwithstanding Lady Bartue's promises to pay, has been arrested: prays privilege of Parliament that he may be free to attend the great services expected of him. L. J., IV. 718.

April 15. Order for Pulford's release. L. J., IV. 718. *In extenso.*

April 15. The Lord Keeper's report of the conference with the House of Commons concerning the Earls of Essex and Holland, &c. (Two papers in Littleton's handwriting.) L. J., IV. 719, 720.
Annexed :—
1. Resolutions of the Commons respecting the Lord Chamberlain and the Earl of Holland, that their attendance on the House is no disobedience to the King's command. C. J., II. 525. Agreed to by the Lords this day. L. J., IV. 719. *In extenso.*
2. Resolutions of the Commons against the King's proposed journey to Ireland.
3. Another resolution on the same subject.

April 15. Message to the King from the Lords and Commons to dissuade him from going into Ireland. L. J., IV. 719. *In extenso.*

April 15. Note by Anthony Hooper of the receipt of two orders made by the Lords in Parliament about a parcel of tobacco in Guernsey. *See* L. J., IV. 721.

April 15. Petition of Allan Boteler, Esq., cup-bearer to Her gracious Majesty; has by command of many of their Lordships attended the House ever since the beginning of Parliament; has now been arrested contrary to privilege and prays for an order for enlargement.
Annexed :—
1. Certificate that Captain Allan Boteler is cup-bearer to Her Majesty and entitled to privilege. 13 Sept. 1630. (Signed by the Earl of Dorset.)

April 15. Copy of order for Boteler's discharge. L. J.,
IV. 722. *In extenso.*

April 15. The Answer of the Governor and Company
of Merchants trading the Levant seas, to a proposition
of the Committee for Trade of the House of Commons,
viz., whether the Turkey Company would go on buying
cloth and sending it to Turkey as formerly, in case they
were assured a fleet should not be sent against the
Turkish pirates of Algiers for two years next following?
The traders can do nothing until Sir Peter Wyche and Sir
Sackville Crow, who have unduly possessed themselves
of the company's duty, called Strangers Consulage, be
ordered to return it, and the company's charters be
further confirmed. C. J., II. 528.

April 16. Petition of Rebecca Owen, the wife of John
Owen; John Pulford, who became surety for a debt
due to petitioner's husband, was arrested on a judgment
given against him with his own consent. She hears
that he has obtained an order from the House for his
discharge without a hearing being given to her husband,
who is out of town on the King's business; prays that
Pulford may not be discharged until he has paid the
debt. L. J., IV. 722.

Annexed :—
1. Affidavit of George Owen respecting Pulford's
insolent conduct. 12 April 1642.
2. Petition of John Pulford that the order for his
discharge may be confirmed. [Undated.]

April 16. Two votes of the Commons concerning the
removing the magazine from Hull, and the indemnity of
Sir John Hotham. C. J., II. 531. *In extenso.*

April 18. Petition of Thomas Paramore, Esq. Was
appointed one of the collectors of the six subsidies, for
which there was an allowance granted to him, which
remains unpaid. Was also appointed collector of the
poll money to be paid by the nobility of England, but
for this there was no allowance. Prays that some satisfaction may be given to him for his services. L. J.,
V. 1.

April 18. Order of the Commons for payment of
6,000l. for Munster. C. J., II. 533.

April 18. Forms for a Colonel's commission, for a
Captain's commission of foot, and for a Captain's commission of horse. L. J., V. 4. (Three papers.)

Annexed :—
1. Draft of preceding.
2. Another draft.

April 18. The Sheriff of Pembrokeshire's account of
expenses incurred in the maintenance and convoy of
Captains Edward and George Darcie, and other Irish
prisoners. *See* C. J., II. 506.

April 19. Petition of Jane, the wife of Captain Edmond
Moore; her husband, on whose liberty her own and her
children's livelihood depends, has been seven months
prisoner in Newgate, on an imaginary supposition that
he was intending to join the rebels in Ireland; prays for
her husband's discharge on bail. L. J., V. 5.

April 19. Petition of John Archbishop of York; has
remained fifteen weeks a prisoner in the Tower, and all
that while, in a manner, continually sick; prays for
leave to go out with his keeper, returning to prison
every night. L. J., V. 6.

April 19. Propositions concerning adventurers by sea
for the relief of Ireland; some persons desirous to
further the conquest of Ireland, and the relief of their
brethren there, propose to fit out five, six, or seven
ships and pinnaces, with 500 soldiers, the expenses of
the adventurers to be repaid by an allotment of land
according to their several subscriptions; they desire a
commission securing them entire independence in their
proceedings, in division of spoil, &c. L. J., V. 6.

April 19. Petition of John Earl of Bristol, prisoner
in the Tower; prays for enlargement, as none of the
examinations have shown him to have had any hand in
promoting the petition of Kent. L. J., V. 6.

April 19. Petition of Nathaniel Burnand to H. C.;
has been chosen minister of Ovingham, in the county of
Northumberland, and because of the great want of
preaching there is willing, though to his great charge,
to accept the duty; but on account of the lamentable
ignorance and profaneness of those parts desires the
protection of the House. C. J., II. 535.

April 19. Commission for giving the Royal Assent to
the Bill for enabling corporations to have the benefit of
the Act of the adventure for Ireland. *See* L. J., V. 10.
Signed by the King. Seal wanting.

April 20. Petition of parishioners of Stisted, in the
county of Essex; that Mr. John Clarke, now curate,
may be appointed their minister. L. J., V. 6.

April 21. Heads for the conference about the Kentish
petition, &c. L. J., V. 7. *In extenso.*

April 21. Petition of William Lord Archbishop of

Canterbury; under a promise to Sir Thomas Rowe has
nominated Mr. Newsted, who was chaplain to Sir
Thomas for divers years in foreign parts, to the rectory
of Stisted; prays the House to confirm the nomination.
(Holograph.) *See* L. J., V. 6, &c.

April 21. Certificate of Mr. Justice Heath, in the
cause between Wolley Leigh and Edward Maria Wingfield, that Wingfield's lands at Keyston, Huntingdon-
shire are sufficient security for his debt. Read in H. L.,
May 3. L. J., V. 39.

Annexed :—
1. Copy of writ of extent. 24 March 1641-2.
2. Affidavit of Robert Hall respecting the value of
the lands.

April 21. Petition of Richard Mack Moyler [Mac-
miller]; was committed for the same offence as Edmond
Moore, and suffered seven months close imprisonment
with him in Newgate; Moore has been discharged;
prays for like favour to himself. *See* L. J., IV. 441,
&c.

April 22. Order for payment of 3,000l. for victuals
for Ireland. L. J., V. 9. *In extenso.*

April 22. Order for payment of 564l. 13s. 4d. for
caps and stockings for the soldiers in Ireland. L. J.,
V. 9. *In extenso.*

April 22. Petition of inhabitants of Broxbourne,
Herts, to H. C.; in Sept. 1641, the House made an
order that the parishioners of any parish might set
up a lecturer; petitioners in pursuance thereof chose
Mr. Daniel Evans, but the vicar, Mr. Parlet, will not
agree; locks the church and keeps the keys, and says
he will not let Evans preach without a direct order from
the House. C. J., II. 538.

April 22. Petition of Thomas Stanley, gent., mayor
of Maidstone; has attended for a whole week in accord
ance with the warrant of the House, but cannot learn
of what he is accused; prays to be discharged or bailed.
L. J., V. 9.

Annexed :—
1. Copy of warrant for attachment of Stanley and
his servant Skelton. 15 April 1642. L. J., IV.
721.

April 22. Petition of Robert Robins, of Penrhyn, in
the county of Cornwall. Complains that he was violently arrested by Captain Carter in the Island of Providence, banished from the island, robbed, and brutally
treated at sea, and finally landed at Bristol sick and
almost naked. Prays that his case may be referred to
any two of the company for the Island of Providence,
excepting the Earl of Warwick, whom he desires to call
as a witness. *See* L. J., V. 10.

April 22. Petition of knights, justices of the peace,
gentlemen, ministers, freeholders, and others of the
county of Cornwall. Thank the House for casting out
the bishops from sitting among them, &c. L. J., V. 10.
In extenso.

April 22. Printed copy of similar petition to H. C.
See C. J., II. 537.

April 22. Letter from Christian Prince of Anhalt at
Bernbourg to the gentlemen of the Parliaments of England
and Scotland. Doubts not that they have learnt from
other sources, and more particularly from Sir Thomas
Rowe, that the dowager Duchess of Mecklenburg, sister
to the writer, has been for six years cruelly treated by her
powerful adversary Duke Adolph Frederic of Mecklenburg, who has not only torn from her her only son, heir
to the principality of his father, Jean Albert, by whose
will she was named regent and guardian of the child,
but has forcibly detained the child, and kept the Duchess
herself like a captive, depriving her of servants, letters,
and even the necessaries of life, because she will not
cede her rights, which have been so fully assured to
her. Her unheard of sufferings, which are amply
proved and ought to be known, require to be met with
great firmness; while the writer and the rest of her
friends are so exhausted with the war, that they have
no resource, after God, but in seeking foreign assistance, and they therefore pray for the help of a good
sum of money from England and Scotland, to be spent
first in aiding the writer's sister, and secondly, in restoring the desolated churches, and assisting the widows,
orphans, and others reduced to the last extremity by
the calamities of war. If the money could be sent by
bills of exchange on Hamburgh ample acquittances and
grateful thanks would be given, and a return in kind
should England and Scotland ever require it, which
he prays may never happen. C. J., II. 633. This letter
was sent up to the Lords on the 20th of June 1642.
See L. J., V. 151.

April 22. Examinations of Thomas Roscarrock and
others respecting words spoken against the Lord Lieutenant of Ireland relative to the sale of a captain's commission. *See* L. J., V. 9.

April 22. Paper from the Privy Council of Scotland for conciliating matters between the King and Parliament, and for staying the King's journey to Ireland. Entered *in extenso* in the Journals. May 7. L. J., V., 53.

April 23. Draft preamble to the judgment against Sir Edward Herbert, Attorney-General, for impeaching the five members. L. J., V. 11. *In extenso.*

April 23. Petition of Francis Bristowe and Jeremy Bagge, glassmakers. Pray that the cause between them and Sir Robert Mansell may be referred to the House of Commons to be heard, or order given for their discharge. L. J., V. 12.

April 25. Draft of Commission for raising 10,000 volunteers for Ireland. L. J., V. 15. *In extenso.*

April 26. Petition of Colonel Fitzwilliam : has leave to transport 400 men to France, prays license to take his wife, children, horses, &c. L. J., V. 17.

April 26. Petition of Colonel Hill for leave to transport into France three horses for his own use. L. J., V. 20.

April 26. Notes of the conference respecting the removing the magazine from Hull, &c. L. J., V. 20.

April 26. Draft of the declaration of the Lords and Commons against stopping the passages between Hull and the Parliament. L. J., V. 21. *In extenso.*

April 26. Another draft.

April 26. Message from the Commons for Sir John Hales, Sir Thos. Darrell, and others, to be sent for as delinquents. L. J., V. 21.

April 28. List of witnesses sworn for the Earl of Danby in his cause against Sir William San Ravey. *See* L. J., V. 22.

April 28. Informations of John Hill and another, witnesses in preceding cause.

April 28. Petition of Herbert Finch, Esq. ; is sewer to Her Gracious Majesty, as appears by the annexed certificate : has been arrested contrary to privilege : prays for discharge. L. J., V. 25.

Annexed :—
1. Certificate that Finch is sworn sewer to Her Majesty, signed by the Earl of Dorset. 8 May 1635.

April 28. Petition of Isabella Baroness Dowager de Lawarr : complains that she was pulled out of her coach and violently arrested for a debt by one Reade and others contrary to privilege : prays that the suit against her may be stayed, and the offenders punished. L. J., V. 25.

April 28. Draft of the Instructions to the Committee of both Houses appointed to go to Hull. L. J., V. 27. *In extenso.*

April 28. Printed copy of "The order of assistance " given to the Committees of both Houses concerning " their going to Hull." L. J., V. 27. *In extenso.*

April 28. Copy of the King's warrant to Sir Richard Hutton to remain in the county of York.

April 28. Order of the Commons for issue of 2,000l. to Mr. Hotham, to pay the garrison at Hull. C. J., II. 545. *In extenso.*

April 29. Petition of John Hackett, Dr. of Divinity, to Robert Earl of Essex ; the King promised to support petitioner's claim to be elected a canon residentiary of St. Paul's, but some few days past Dr. Layfield has implored the King's patronage for the sake of his uncle, the Archbishop of Canterbury, and has obtained answer that the residentiaries shall be left to a liberty of election ; Dr. Montfort, one of the electors, is father-in-law to Dr. Layfield, and the King has written saying that a father and son-in-law ought not to be half a chapter in so great a foundation, and besides Dr. Layfield is obnoxious to Parliament as a scandalous innovator ; prays that the residentiaries may be directed to elect petitioner and not Dr. Layfield. L. J., V. 28.

April 29. Petition of John Feilder, High Sheriff of the county of Southampton, to H. C. ; having received an order of both Houses in March last to proclaim George Lord Digby a traitor in all market towns, petitioner sent Peter Ufman, a bailiff, and one Andrew Seaman to make proclamation at Portsmouth, but Mr. Winter, the deputy mayor there, and others, withstood the proclamation and committed the bailiff and Seaman to custody, and threatened to whip the latter, and said that they would have done as much for petitioner had he come himself ; he further complains that he received no assistance from the inhabitants of Andover in forwarding some Irish prisoners from the West towards London ; prays for consideration, lest the impunity of such contempts may encourage others to do the like. L. J., V. 28.

April 29. Order for appearance of Mr. Winter and others. L. J., V. 28. *In extenso.*

April 29. Copy of preceding.

April 29. Petition of Sir Edward Herbert, His Majesty's Attorney General ; for release from imprisonment, L. J., V..30. *In extenso.*

April 29. Petition of Robert Walsh, Esq. ; petitioner, a servant to the Queen, has been arrested for debt contrary to privilege ; prays for discharge. L. J., V. 30.

Annexed :—
1. Certificate of the Earl of Dorset that Walsh is a sworn servant to the Queen. 25 April 1642.

April 29. Petition of Anthony Etherington, gent., and Dorothy his wife ; Dorothy's only brother, a merchant at Lisbon, has made a large fortune, but having neither wife nor child is desirous of conferring the greater part of his means upon petitioners, if they will come and live with him ; petitioner Anthony is a younger son with small means ; pray that they may have leave with one servant to sail in a ship, which has already dropped down to Woolwich, and is only waiting for a fair wind. L. J., V. 30.

April 30. Interrogatories put to James Jackson, Dr. of Physic, concerning the madness of Sir Archibald Douglas, in the cause of Lady Lucy Hastings against Francis Poulton, with Dr. Jackson's answers attached. The examination was ordered to be published this day. L. J., V. 30.

Annexed :—
1. Copy of part of preceding.

April 30. Affidavit of Thomas Terrill, of Burnham, in the county of Essex ; that the fishermen, who claim the right of fishing for oysters, &c. in Walfleet and Burnham Water against the Earl of Sussex, threaten to fish there about the 25th inst. with 60 or 100 sail of boats, and to take away the spat, and breed of oysters, which will destroy the fishing for many years. L. J., V. 32.

April 30. Affidavit of same ; of his having found the fishermen fishing, as threatened, in a tumultuous manner, and that they laughed at the order of the House when read to them.

Annexed :—
1. Notes for an order for quieting the Earl's possession.

April 30. Order for discharge of Robert Walsh, servant to the Queen, from imprisonment. L. J., V. 32.

April 30. Petition of the Mayor and Aldermen of the town of Colchester ; the cause between petitioners and Richard Freshfield, a man of contentious and refractory spirit, is now ready for hearing in Chancery ; pray that the cause may be there remitted for decision, as Freshfield's petition to the House was only presented to annoy petitioners in order to force them to a composition, and is full of falsities. L. J., V. 33.

April 30. Petition of Elizabeth Clarke, widow of Captain Peter Clarke ; for appointment of a day certain for trial of her cause against Lord Morley and Mounteagle for killing her husband. *See* L. J., V. 33.

April 30. Petition of Richard Bruton against Sir John Lenthall ; complains of delay procured by Lenthall's potency, and prays that he may not be allowed to bring a second writ of error. L. J., V. 34.

April 30. Petition of Edmund Wingate, in behalf of the inhabitants of Ampthill, Bedfordshire ; by an order of the 23d of February 1640-1 (L. J., IV. 170), Hugh Reeve, late parson of Ampthill, for holding popish doctrines, was deprived of all his ecclesiastical livings, ordered to make recantation, and to leave the vicarage house, on doing this he was to receive 10l. per annum out of the parsonage, which a noble person of the parish freely offered to discharge ; Reeve still maintains two of the tenets that he recanted, converses with papists more than ever, and refuses to give up the vicarage house ; petitioner prays that the annuity may be transferred to the present incumbent, as it is unreasonable that Reeve should take any benefit under the order which he has contemned. L. J., V. 34.

Annexed :—
1. Affidavit of Edmund Wingate in support of preceding.

April 30. Draft order respecting the subscriptions of the adventurers for the additional forces by sea for Ireland. L. J., V. 34. *In extenso.*

April 30. Draft order appointing John Hotham, son of Sir John Hotham, governor of Hull in case of his father's death. L. J., V. 34. *In extenso.*

April 30. Another draft.

April 30. Draft of the declaration of the Lords and Commons, to be sent into Yorkshire, to prevent the raising of the militia by His Majesty for the purpose of taking possession of the town of Hull. L. J., V. 34. *In extenso.*

April 30. Copy of preceding.

April 30. Draft order for the Earl of Holland to attend the House, and for the sheriff of Berks to prevent riots, &c., in Windsor forest. L. J., V. 35. *In extenso.*

April 30. Petition of parishioners of Ackcliffe [Aycliffe]; about September last upon the death of Dr. Carr their late vicar, who was chaplain to the late Earl of Strafford, Mr. Daniel Carwardine was nominated by Mr. Smart, senior prebendary of Durham, according to custom, but the other prebendaries refused to confirm the nomination; the matter was brought before the House and the custom proved, but the grave affairs of the kingdom prevented any decision from being come to, whereupon Mr. Smart took institution himself, for fear of a lapse of his right, and appointed Mr. Carwardine his curate till the question should be determined; but Mr. Leke, a scandalous drunken man, who was curate under Dr. Carr, locked the pulpit door, violently broke into the vicarage, and expelled Mr. Carwardino; pray that Carwardino may be secured in possession till the matter be decided. L. J., V. 35.

April 30. Petition of parishioners of Pennard in the county of Glamorgan to H. C.; have never had more than four sermons a year in their parish church, and those by a man of a very scandalous life; pray for the nomination of Ambrose Mosten, as lecturer, a man of godly sort, and one who can preach in the Welsh and English tongues. C. J., II. 551.

April 30. Affidavit of Robert Parkins, that Captain Brough said that he heard 50*l.* was given for a company. *See* L. J., V. 9.

Annexed :—
1. Letter from Jerom Manwood at Maidenhead to Mr. Battiere, secretary to the Earl of Leicester, Lord Lieutenant of Ireland; denies the words imputed to him by Captain Brough. 23 April.

April 30. Warrant from the Speaker of the House of Commons directing all mayors, sheriffs, &c. to furnish Richard Eccleston with sufficient post horses, and an able guide to Hull and back. *See* C. J., II. 551.

[April .] Petition of Joseph Sanders, one of His Majesty's servants; has been arrested for debt contrary to privilege; prays for discharge. *See* L. J., V. 30.

[April .] Petition of Sir Philip Mainwaring; prays that the cause between him and the Lord Mountnorris, touching the right and possession of the office of one of His Majesty's principal Secretaries of State in Ireland, may be brought to a determination.

[April .] Petition of Sir William Middleton, His Majesty's sworn servant; complains of arrest at the suit of Sir Henry Garway, and others, contrary to privilege; prays that he may have the same protection that has been been lately accorded to Captain Butler, and Mr. Robert Welshe.

May 2. Petition of Alice Webb, alias Baker, a poor aged widow. In June last her petition to the House against the Bishop of Llandaff was referred to the Judge of Assize, who happened to be Timothy Turnor, an intimate friend of the bishop. The judge examined only three of petitioner's witnesses, pretending he had no time for more. She prays for a hearing before the House, where only she can expect justice, and that she may have a copy of the judge's certificate now in the clerk's hand. L. J., V. 35.

May 2. Affidavit of John Peacocke, under keeper of Newlodge Walk in the forest of Waltham, Essex, and of Richard Stocke. John Browne and others in April last assembled in a riotous manner in Waltham Forest, armed with guns, bills, pitchforks, and clubs, and killed and wounded many of the King's deer, saying they came for venison and venison they would have, for there was no law settled at this time, laughed at the warrant of the Earl of Carlisle, chief keeper of Newlodge Walk, threatened to kill bucks in Lowton Walk, and told deponents if they complained of offenders to complain of good store of them, that if they went to prison they might be merry together. *See* L. J., V. 37.

Annexed :—
1. Affidavit of same, that Mr. Russell, minister of Chingford, and others, daily assemble and kill the King's deer.

May 2. Petition of Isaac Legay and Daniel Farvack, merchants, praying for a writ ne exeat regno against Nicholas Phillipps, who is largely indebted to them, and who intends to leave the country for a two years' voyage. L. J., V. 37.

Annexed,
1. Affidavit in support of preceding.
2. Another affidavit.

May 2. Copy of an order that the former orders, staying proceedings in the cause between Dr. Featly

and Andrew Kirwin, should be taken off and the parties left to the ordinary course in law. L. J., V. 37. *In extenso.*

May 2. Another copy.

May 2. Another copy.

Annexed :—
1. Copy of petition of Kirwin, that the preceding order may be carried out. (Undated.)
2. Petition of Kirwin. Dr. Featly has obtained an injunction in equity to stay petitioner's proceedings at law, because the question in dispute is the title to a copyhold of the Prince's manor of Kennington. Prays that the court may be ordered to withdraw the injunction. (Undated.)
3. Similar petition of same. (Undated.)
4. Copy of petition of Daniel Featly, D.D., that their Lordships would explain whether their order of 2nd May referred to proceedings both in law and equity. (Undated.)

May 2. Petition of Esechias Scarning against Gilbert Fitch, one of the Marshals of the Hall, His Majesty's servant, to whom petitioner leased a house and lands in Wolvey, Warwickshire. Fitch not only failed to pay the rent, but has done great damage by cutting down trees. Petitioner applied to the officers of His Majesty's green cloth for leave to proceed against Fitch at law, unless he should show cause to the contrary within a specified time : after which petitioner caused him to be arrested, but by a false surmise he obtained an order from the House for his discharge on the ground of privilege. Petitioner prays for discharge of their Lordships' former order, and for leave to prosecute his suit at law. L. J., V. 38.

Annexed :—
1. Copy of order referred to in preceding. L. J., IV. 621.
2. Affidavit of service of the order made May 2 upon Fitch. 6 May.

May 2. Copy of an order for issuing arms from the Tower for Munster. L. J., V. 38. *In extenso.*

May 2. Two lists of the arms to be sent to Munster. L. J., V. 38. *In extenso.*

May 2. Resolution that the Committee of Lords and Commons, to whom the last messages concerning Hull were referred, be desired to expedite the answer to His Majesty, &c. *See* C. J., II. 553.

May 2. Petition of William, Lord Archbishop of Canterbury. In March last petitioner nominated Richard Howlett to the rectory of Lachynden [Latchingdon], Dr. Gandyn to the rectory of Bockyn [Bocking], and Mr. Newstead to the rectory of Stistead [Stisted]. Their Lordships approved of the first two, but recommended a Mr. Clarke instead of Mr. Newstead, in consequence of a petition of the parishioners of Stistead. Petitioner is under promise to Sir Thomas Roe for Mr. Newstead, his chaplain for many years. Prays that the nomination may be approved. *See* L. J., V. 38.

Annexed :—
1. Affidavit of William Isaacson, and others, that Mr. Christopher Newstead, Bachelor in Divinity, is an orthodox divine, a laborious preacher, and a man of civil life and conversation. 18 April

May 3. Draft resolutions, &c. in Lord Loftus' [Viscount Ely's] cause. L. J., V. 38. (Two papers.)

May 3. Petition of William Lord Viscount Grandison, and the Lady Mary his wife, Philip Lord Herbert and and the Lady Penelope, Viscountess of Bayninge of Sudbury, his wife, Francis, Lord Dacre, and the Lady Elizabeth his wife, and Sir Thomas Glemham, Knight; pray that while their cause concerning Sutton Marsh is depending before their Lordships, no division of the lands may be made amongst the commoners, and that the arrears of interest may be paid into the hands of some indifferent persons.

Annexed :—
1. Abstract of order made on preceding petition. L. J., V. 39.

May 3. Petition of Dr. John Scott, Dean of York, and Christopher Scott his brother, distressed prisoners in the King's Bench, against Ralph Cooke; pray that they may have copies of the evidence taken before the commission for examination of witnesses, and that a day may be appointed for hearing.

May 3. Copy of order for the publication of the depositions in the preceding cause. L. J., V. 40. *In extenso.*

Annexed :—
1. Petition of Christopher Scott, a poor prisoner in the King's Bench, administrator of the goods and

chattels of Dr. John Scott, late Dean of York, his brother, deceased; Bathurst and Cooke have received a large sum out of the late Dean's estate over and above the debt due to them, as has been proved before the commission for examination of witnesses, but petitioner still continues in prison; prays for an early day for hearing, and that meantime he may receive such rents and fines as still remain in the tenants' hands, and were due before the Dean's death. (Undated.)

2. Balance of account between the plaintiffs and defendants, certified by auditor Darell. 21 June 1642.

May 3. Petition of Sir Philip Mainwaring, Knight; petitioner has been summoned to answer a complaint of Henry Stewart concerning a sentence made in the Castle Chamber in Ireland. The sentence was passed by many of the Lords of the Council, and prime judges in Ireland, and petitioner prays that the case may be respited till the answers of all concerned are put in. L. J., V. 40.

May 3. Copy of order for the exercising and training of the trained bands of London. L. J., V. 41. *In extenso.*

May 3. Resolution of the Commons respecting Edward Lord Herbert's offer to advance money. C. J., II. 554. *In extenso.*

May 3. Affidavit of Richard Panton of Burnham, in the county of Essex, that George Asser, fisherman, of Barking, declared that he would fish for oysters in Burnham river and Wallfleet, in spite of their Lordships orders declaring the fishing to belong solely to the Earl of Sussex: that Asser and others have dredged there in a tumultuous manner and done great damage to the brood of oysters.

May 4. Petition of parishioners of St. Peter's in the Borough of St. Alban's; complain that for 60 years their vicars have not resided in the vicarage, and that the present vicar is non-resident, a pluralist, and accused of many crimes; he will now under the Act against pluralities have to give up one of his livings, which they hear will be St. Alban's, the patron is Matthew Wren, Bishop of Ely, a man charged in Parliament as a delinquent for many heinous crimes, who will, they fear, appoint some undeserving minister; petitioners pray that no presentation may be made unless approved by their Lordships. L. J., V. 41.

May 4. Statement that William Marsh, arrested at the suit of Thomas Harrison and Mrs. Stoiner, is a menial servant and receiver general to the Lord Marshal and Lord Mowbray; his discharge is desired. *See* L. J., V. 41.
Annexed:—
1. Certificate to the same effect, signed by Lord Mowbray and Maltravers.
2. Note from John Griffith to Throckmorton, for a copy of the order for Marsh's release.

May 4. Petition of Agmondesham Pickayes, servant to Robert Earl of Lindsey; his Lordship, on going into the North left petitioner to despatch his business in his absence; petitioner has been arrested by Kellam Smith, sergeant at mace, at the suit of Thomas Umfreville, and Smith has further charged him with two vexations actions for trespass at the suit of James Vickers, though petitioner told Smith that he was the Earl's servant; prays for discharge. L. J., V. 41.

May 4. Affidavit of Abell Pryor of Marson, in the county of Lincoln, that since the inclosure and division of the south fen of Balderton in the county of Nottingham, the inhabitants and many of the tenants have broken down the fences, and depastured their cattle there. Endorsed, "Queen's Tenants, Balderton Fens." *See* L. J., V. 42.

May 4. Engrossment of the Bill for the forfeiture of the lands and estates, and for the punishment of John Archbishop of York, and the other impeached bishops. Brought from H. C., and read 1ª this day. No further proceeding. L. J., V. 42, 43.

May 4. Paper from the Scottish Commissioners concerning the payment of "the brotherly assistance." The paper, which was read in the House this day, is dated, Westminster, 25 April 1642. L. J., V. 42. *In extenso.*

[May 4.] Petition of Edward Maria Wingfield to Robert Earl of Essex; prays him to cause Sir Robert Heath's report in the case between petitioner and Woolley Leigh to be read, that the ne exeat regno may be taken off, otherwise he and the sergeants, drummers, and others, whom he hath entertained for service in Ireland, will be cashiered. *See* L. J., V. 43.

May 5. Petition from the county of Kent to the Lords and Commons; disclaim a former petition presented in

the name of the county, and declare the determination of the petitioners to support the King, and the privileges of Parliament, according to their protestation. L. J., V. 44. *In extenso.* Endorsed, "1. Militia. 2. "14 days. 3. 6,000 hands and upwards and all Canterbury. 4. Many hundreds more have subscribed."

May 5. The Lord Keeper's answer, by direction of the House, to the gentlemen who brought the preceding petition. L. J., V. 44. *In extenso.*

May 5. Petition of John Archbishop of York, praying that he may be bailed. L. J., V. 44. *In extenso.*

May 5. Petition of the Bishops in restraint, praying that they may be bailed. L. J., V. 45. *In extenso.*

May 5. Order respecting the repayment of 20,000l. lent by the Merchant Adventurers. L. J., V. 46. *In extenso.*

May 5. Draft answer of Parliament to the King's messages about Sir John Hotham's refusal to admit him into Hull. L. J., V. 46. *In extenso.*

May 5. Draft instructions for the committees going to Yorkshire. L. J., V. 47. *In extenso.*

May 5. Copy of preceding.

May 5. Order of the Commons for the payment of 10,000l. for the service of Ireland. C. J., II. 559.

May 5. Petition of certain merchants and seamen; there are many causes in the Court of Admiralty long since ready for sentence, but stopped by rules from the King's Courts at Westminster: petitioners pray that until the House have time to determine the matters in dispute between the Admiralty and the other Courts, the Judge of the Admiralty may have leave to determine the causes there now depending. Endorsed, "Nothing done."

May 5. Copy of a warrant from the King to suppress the printing of his messages, &c., to Parliament.
Annexed:—
1. Another copy; and on the same paper a copy of warrant against printing libellous and seditious books. 6 Jan. 1641-2.

May 6. Message from the Commons requesting the Lords to issue a proclamation for the apprehension of Daniel O'Neale. L. J., V. 48.

April 6. Petition of Sir Edward Herbert, His Majesty's Attorney General: prays for enlargement from the Fleet, not so much on account of his health (wherein he is not free from suffering), as on account of the King's service, and his own sorrow to have incurred their Lordships' displeasure. *See* L. J., V. 58.

May 6. Order of the Commons respecting the removal of the magazine at Hull to the Tower of London. C. J., II. 562. *In extenso.*

May 7. Message from the Commons requesting the Lords to appoint a convenient place for the members appointed to manage the evidence at the trial of Mr. Justice Berkeley, &c. C. J., II. 562. *In extenso.*

May 7. Petition of Sir Richard Price, Richard Newell, Thomas Lloyd, James Vaughan, and John Fox: have been in custody since the 18th of April last; were yesterday brought up to appear before their Lordships, but could not be admitted because of the more weighty matters in hand. Pray to be dismissed from custody on bail. L. J., V. 53.
Annexed:—
1. Petition of Richard Newell and Thomas Lloyd, gentlemen, and John Fox: were with Sir Richard Price apprehended by a messenger, and brought from their homes 160 miles away, to answer a supposed contempt of an order of their Lordships procured by Thomas Bushell; petitioners were cleared of all such contempt on examination of the charge, but Newell and Lloyd have since been apprehended and detained until they should pay 35l. a piece for the messenger's fees; Newell has paid the fees, but Lloyd is still in custody. Pray for redress, and that Bushell may be ordered to satisfy the messenger. (Undated).

May 7. Petition of John Bromley, of Garsington, in the county of Oxford. George Melsam is now in custody of the sheriff of the county, by virtue of an outlawry from the King's Bench for riots and other misdemeanours. He and his brothers, Francis and John Melsam, have often been suspected of killing the King's deer, and petitioner, having lately got possession of a house which they had forcibly withheld from him, found venison in the house, and guns and other things "fit for destruction of a forest;" and hearing George Melsam boast that he had cut off the heads of 300 deer with his wood knife, petitioner scarched a well and found the bottom filled with stags' and other deers' heads. The Melsams pretend to be protected by the Earl of Lindsey, but without truth.

Petitioner prays that he may have liberty to proceed against them for recovery of 700l., for which sum they stand bound to him for nonperformance of covenants.

May 7. Copy of order upon preceding petition. L. J., V. 53. *In extenso.*

May 7. Letter from Henry Earl of Bath, at Mereworth Castle, in Kent, to the Lord Keeper Littleton. On account of the dangerous illness (suspected to be plague) of two of his servants, he has withdrawn himself to a house, borrowed from his brother, the Earl of Westmorland. Prays the Lord Keeper to move the House to excuse his absence, and to give him leave to be away for some time to recover his health impaired by long residence in London.

May 7. Warrant from the Speaker to all mayors, sheriffs, &c., to furnish Richard Eccleston, employed on special service from the Parliament, with post-horses and an able guide to any part of England and back again.

[May 7.] Petition of Anthony Hooper and his creditors; Nicholas Phillips, a correspondent of Hooper, was found by the referees in the case, to be indebted to Hooper in a large sum of money, and was arrested; but having procured his release on bail has left the country on a long and hazardous voyage. Pray that the bail may be ordered to deposit the money due in indifferent hands.

Annexed :—
1. Certificate of the referee in the cause.

May 9. Petition of John Hacket, Doctor of Divinity; prays that Dr. Montfort and Dr. Turner may be called upon to elect him a canon residentiary of St. Paul's, according to the King's and their Lordships' direction, before they go in progress to visit the lands of their church. L. J., V. 55.

May 9. Message from the Commons with an order for sending ordnance to Munster. L. J., V. 55.

May 9. Petition of Sir William Killegrew, Knight, Edward Heron, Esq., Richard Ligon, and other participants, with the Earl of Lindsey; complain that they have been turned out of their possessions in the Earl of Lindsey's level in Lincolnshire by a riotous multitude of people, who have destroyed works and drains that cost near 60,000l., have pulled down houses upon the tenants' heads, assaulted the sheriffs and others, who attempted to enforce their Lordships' former orders; and have appointed the 13th instant for completing the work of destruction. Pray their Lordships to take measures for preventing further mischief.

May 9. Copy of order on preceding petition. L. J., V. 55. *In extenso.*

May 9. Petition of Arthur Magneiss [Magennis]; prays that as their Lordships will not give him his liberty on the only security he can give, that is his oath not to go into Ireland or anywhere else to the prejudice of the Crown, they will direct the Lieutenant of the Tower to give order that he may have such allowance for his meat, clothes, and other necessaries, as other prisoners of his quality, condition, and distress. L. J., V. 56.

May 9. Report concerning Hull, &c. C. J., II. 564.

May 9. Copy of order of the Commons upon a petition of the Mayor and Aldermen of Bristol, for payment of money for the relief of the distressed protestants fled thither out of Ireland. C. J., II. 565. *In extenso.*

May 9. Petition of Sir John Conyers, Lieutenant of the Tower; Colonel Beeling, committed to his custody by warrant from their Lordships, is unable to maintain himself on account of his losses, and has ever since his commitment been supported with his servants by petitioner, who prays their Lordships to appoint him a competent maintenance.

Annexed :—
1. Petition of same for a competent allowance for the maintenance of Colonel Beeling, Mr. Arthur Mageinze [Magennis], and Henry Walker. (Undated.)

May 9. Petition of Henry Walker; has spent most part of his estate in prison about a petition touching the King's Majesty, for which he is heartily sorry. Prays for consideration of his deplorable condition and for enlargement.

May 10. Order for John Chaundler, English Consul at Lisbon, who, with his wife, is accused of being a papist, and seducing the King's subjects from their religion, to appear before Parliament and answer the charges against him. L. J., V. 57.

May 10. Report of the conference about removing the magazine from Monmouth, and for suppressing the growth of popery. L. J., II. 57. *In extenso.*

May 11. Petition of Sir Edward Herbert, His Majesty's Attorney-General. Prays for enlargement on the ground of daily growing ill-health. L. J., V. 58.

May 11. Notes of the Conference about the paper

from the Privy Council of Scotland, for conciliating matters between the King and the Parliament. L. J., V. 59.

May 11. Articles of Impeachment of Sir George Strode, Knight, by the Commons, for his share in promoting the petition from the county of Kent; voted seditious by them. L. J., V. 59. *See* the impeachment against Sir Edward Dering, which is given *in extenso.* L. J., V. 17.

Annexed :—
1. Copy of the petition referred to. L. J., IV. 677. *In extenso.*

May 11. Articles of Impeachment of Richard Spencer, Esq., by the Commons, for his share in promoting the petition from the county of Kent. L. J., V. 59.

Annexed :—
1. Copy of the petition.

May 11. Copy of the King's warrant to the officers at Hull, not to put any of the arms in the magazine there on board ship. L. J., V. 70. *In extenso.*

May 11. Motion in the cause of Henry Fisher against the Dean and Chapter of Christ Church, Oxford, Henry Thorpe, Gabriel Thorpe, John Steevens, and others: the defendants, who are tenants to the Dean and Chapter, have, in contempt of their Lordships' order of the 27th of July last, continued to commit waste upon the lands in question : it is requested that the defendants may be sent for as delinquents.

Annexed :—
1. Affidavit of Mathias Woods respecting words spoken by Gabriel Thorpe, in contempt of their Lordships' order. 2 June 1642.
2. Similar affidavit of Timothy Simpson. 15 June 1642.
3. Similar affidavit of Henry Fisher. 9 May 1642.

May 11. Letter from the Lords Justices of Ireland at Dublin Castle to the Lord Keeper: not long after the breaking out of the rebellion, Lady Jepson and her son Sir John Giffard were constrained to betake themselves to their Castle of Jordan, in the county of Meath, about 30 miles from Dublin; they have been despoiled of everything they could not bring within the castle gates, and have been obliged to receive and maintain their English tenants out of the little left to themselves; they have been long beleaguered, but Sir John has made frequent sallies, and slain divers of the rebels : the ways are so blocked with rebels that there would be no possibility for Lady Jepson or her son to come to Dublin without an army to guard them, while Sir John's departure would greatly prejudice the public service and encourage the rebels. Prays his Lordship to make these things known to the House. Endorsed, Lca. 4 Junii. L. J., V. 104.

May 12. Petition of John Hinton : is a doctor of physic and sworn physician to Her Majesty: has been arrested by one Osborne, a sergeant, in breach of privilege, though petitioner produced the Earl of Dorset's certificate of his appointment. Prays for protection. L. J., V. 60.

May 12. Copy of order against killing the King's deer within the limits of the forests of Windsor and Waltham. L. J., V. 61.

May 12. Another copy.

May 12. Petition of William Hawkes, a sergeant of the Mace, to Lady Isabella Delaware, praying for forgiveness for his rash act in arresting her ladyship, and for his discharge. Noted,—" 'Tis the sense of the House " that unless the petitioner do make an humble submis-" sion upon his knees to the Right Hon. the Lady Dela-" ware, as well as this his submission by petition, that he " shall be remanded to prison, and no ways from thence " released till he do so." L. J., V. 61.

Annexed :—
1. Petition of William Hawkes, prisoner in the Fleet : in arresting Lady Delaware he acted in ignorance of her privilege, confesses his error, and prays for release from prison without any corporal punishment or disgrace.
2. Duplicate of preceding.

May 12. Petition of Sir James Levingston : his petition to be restored to the possession of 1,016 acres in Sutton Marsh, has long been depending before their Lordships, if no decision be come to, the tenants will keep back their rent. Prays that they may be ordered to pay them into some safe hands. L. J., V. 61.

May 12. Votes to indemnify persons acting under the ordinance for the militia, &c. L. J., V. 63. *In extenso.*

May 12. " A note of their names that have received " the monies raised by the lottery." It is desired that an order be made that none of " the assurers about the " aqueduct" be released, until the money they have in their hands be brought in, and that a commission may be directed to Sir Robert Heath (who when Attorney-General drew the patents of the aqueduct and lottery), and to Sir John Wolstenholme for examination of the whole matter. *See* C. J., II. 567.

May 12. Letter from Lord Duddeley, at Duddeley Castle, to the Earl of Dorset; want of health preventing his personal attendance, he prays the Earl to move the House for the release of an old servant, Agmondesham Pickis, who has been arrested and laid in prison contrary to privilege. *See* L. J., V. 78.

Annexed:—

1. Petition of Agmondesham Pickayes : has for many years been a servant to Edward Lord Dudley, but has lately been arrested at the suit of James Vickers contrary to privilege. Prays for discharge. (Undated.)

May 12. Printed copy of His Majesty's speech to the gentry of the county of York attending His Majesty at the city of York this day. Parliamentary Register, X. 517. *In extenso.*

[May 12.] Petition of Elizabeth Clarke : implores justice against Lord Morley and Mounteagle for killing her husband, which was the ruin of herself and her children ; she has spent all her small means in prosecuting her case, and prays for a final determination of it on Saturday next. *See* L. J., V. 64.

May 13. Petition of Thomas Warren, clerk; was lately presented to the parsonage of St. Stephen's, Walbrook, by the Grocer's Company, the undoubted patrons, but some few of the parishioners refuse to receive him, and by locking the church doors and keeping the keys away, do hinder him of the enjoyment thereof. Prays for an order to put him in quiet possession. L. J., V. 62.

May 13. Petition of Sir George Strode, that Mr. Hackwell and others may be assigned him as counsel, that he may have a copy of the impeachment, &c. L. J., V. 62.

May 13. Similar petition of Richard Spencer. L. J., V. 62.

May 13. Note respecting the discharge of William Marsh, menial servant to the Lord Marshal. L. J., V. 62.

May 13. Petition of Elias Alleyn (or Allen), of the Strand, mathematical instrument maker. Edward Alleyn founded a college at Dulwich, to consist of one master, one warden, four fellows, six poor men, six poor women, and twelve poor boys, all single persons, and, in the statutes for the management of the college, directed that the master and warden for the future should be both single men of his blood and surname, and for want of such, of his surname only: the place of warden is now vacant, and one John Alleyn and one Edward Alleyn were competitors, but the former has been dismissed as a married man. On Monday last, the utmost day limited for the election, Edward Alleyn, to advance his cause, pretended that he was kinsman to the founder, but not being able to produce any evidence of this, time was granted for him to do so ; this petitioner believes to have been illegal, and that, now that the time for the college to elect is past, the power has fallen to the Archbishop of Canterbury, and by his suspension to their Lordships: petitioner, who is aged, of the surname of the founder, and single, prays that he may be appointed warden of the college, as his competitor is a young man and a soldier, and of no kin to the founder. L. J., V. 63.

May 13. Petition of Henry Bell, Scotsman, that a day may be appointed for the hearing of his case. *See* L. J., V. 63.

May 13. Draft order for grant of letters of reprisal to Huett Leat, son of Nicholas Leat, for recovery of losses suffered at the hands of the Spaniards. L. J., V. 63.

May 13. Petition of John Montfort and Thomas Turner, canons residentiary of St. Paul's, in answer to the orders recommending Dr. Hacket to them for the vacant residentiary's place in their church. They humbly state :—1. That they did not sooner answer because of their Lordships' order prohibiting further proceedings in private business, on account of the weighty matters in hand. 2. That the King when rightly informed of their customs was pleased to leave them full liberty of choice. 3. That they thereupon promised the place to another, before Dr. Hacket was a suitor for it. 4. That the King when informed was again pleased to leave them to their liberty of choice. Pray the House now rightly informed of the state of the case to imitate the King's example, and leave them to their former engagement.

May 14. Petition of Henry Stewart, Esq., and James Gray, merchant ; in 1639 petitioners, and the wife and two daughters of Henry Stewart, were sentenced by the Earl of Strafford and others of the Council in Ireland to pay fines amounting to 1,300*l.*, and to be imprisoned for life, for refusing to take an oath, proved afterwards on the Earl's trial to be illegal; petitioners were re-

leased from prison by the King's special order, and about fifteen months since came to London to seek redress for the wrongs they had suffered, and have presented divers petitions in the matter, while Henry Stewart has, at his great cost and in peril of his life, travelled to Ireland by their Lordships' direction to procure documents material to his case ; after long attendance the 29th of April was appointed for the hearing, but none of the defendants appeared except Sir Philip Mainwaring, some one pretending on behalf of the others that they had had no formal warning, and so the committee proceeded no further at that time, but on the following Monday reported, that the cause should be referred to the now Lord Lieutenant of Ireland; petitioner, however, despairs of his Lordship finding time for hearing of the cause ; petitioners' cause has been often recommended to their Lordships by the Scotch Parliament and their Commissioners in England ; pray their Lordships not to expose them to further misery, but to appoint a speedy day for the hearing, and determining of the matter. L. J., V. 65.

Annexed :—

1. Memorandum of the grievances of Henry Stewart and others.

May 14. Lord Capel's report from the committee appointed to consider the petition of Sir Thomas Cary against the Bishop of Ardagh. L. J., V. 65. *In extenso.*

May 14. Certificate of Mr. Justice Heath in the case between Woolley Leigh and Edward Maria Wingfield. *See* L. J., V. 75.

May 14. Letter from the Earl of Kingston to the Earl of Essex ; would gladly attend Parliament if his health would permit, but has now with other distempers a lameness in his leg, so that if he came to London he would have to come in a litter, and be fit for no place but his chamber when there ; prays the Earl of Essex to obtain leave from the House for him to stay in the country till his health permit him to come up. *See* L. J., V. 76.

May 16. Petition of Francis Bristowe and Jeremy Bagg, glassmakers : having been several times summoned to appear before their Lordships, have attended to their very great loss, and have suffered grievous wrongs and insults at the hands of Sir Robert Mansell, patentee for glass : pray that a day may be fixed for the hearing of their cause, or that they may be permitted to work till a day for hearing shall be appointed, or that they may be referred to the House of Commons, where they are also petitioners for relief. *See* L. J., V. 66.

May 16. Petition of Sir William Russell and of Richard George, and John George, and others, tenants of the manor of Eckington, in the county of Worcester. Petitioners claim a right of common of pasture in several lands in the parish of Eckington, and about 12 years since attempted to pasture their cattle upon them ; but Francis Hanford, Esq., obtained an injunction in Chancery, and not only so, but broke open lands of petitioners, claiming common of pasture, until he also was restrained by injunction ; the right of common was tried at law, when petitioners obtained three verdicts in their favour, but were defeated in Chancery and ordered to pay costs, as if they had claimed that which by law was not due to them ; they have no remedy in Chancery, but by bill of review "which in the formalities thereof will spend too much time and charge, "and yet the merits of the cause at the end of that way "be no riper for a determinate hearing than now." Pray their Lordships to recommend the cause to be fully heard before the Lord Keeper.

May 16. Petition of divers of the knights, esquires, gentlemen, ministers, freeholders, and other inhabitants of the county of Stafford, praying the House to present to the King their loyal and humble desires that he would settle the militia, that he would lean upon the hand and follow the counsels of Parliament, and that succour may speedily be sent to their brethren in Ireland. There are upwards of two thousand signatures. L. J., V. 66.

May 16. Petition of George Asser, Richard French, and William Thompson, of the county of Essex, fishermen. Time out of mind fishermen have had free liberty to take oysters in an arm of the sea called Burnham Water, but the Earl of Sussex has lately claimed the sole right of fishing there. Petitioners, who are in custody by their Lordships' order, pray that the charge against them may be heard, or that they may be released. L. J., V. 66.

May 16. Order for payment of 10,000*l.* for Dublin. L. J., V. 67. *In extenso.*

May 16. Petition of William Wheatley," mariner of Dover. As master of the "Willing Mind," of 120 tons

C 4

burthen, sailed in Dec. 1641, from Bilbao in Biscay, laden only with bags of wool, and anchored in the Downs on the 17th of Jan., waited there for advices till the 23rd, when he set sail for Rotterdam, but was carried out of his course by stress of weather, and seized by a Flemish frigate, the captain of which put a prize crew on board, and forced him and some of his men to serve on board the frigate. Petitioner took proceedings at Dunkirk against the captain and owners of the frigate, but is utterly unable to prosecute the suit. Prays that the Earl of Warwick may be ordered to stay Flemish ships and make satisfaction to petitioner, or that letters of marque may be granted to him.

May 17. Petition of George Benyon, prisoner in the Tower. In the cause between him and Lord St. John, he conceives he has just exceptions to some of the witnesses, and prays leave to except before the commission or before their Lordships at the hearing. L. J., V. 68.

May 17. Petition of Sir Filibert Vernatti, that no proceedings may be had upon the petition of Thomas Jennins, who is merely acting as substitute for his father-in-law, John Latch, until Latch shall have answered petitioner's bill against him.

May 17. Draft order upon preceding petition. L. J., V. 69. In extenso.

May 18. Examination of Ellis Nicholls, of Wiltsford, near Honiton, in the county of Devon; was arrested by Francis Bassett, Esq., Vice-Admiral of the north parts of the county of Cornwall, on account of his likeness to the description given by Parliament of O'Neale, lately escaped from the Tower, and because he had been travelling in Devonshire and in Wales without any apparent object, and without taking the shortest routes. L. J., V. 70.

May 18. Petition of Edward Stanford, of Puryhall, in the county of Stafford, for leave to go beyond seas with his wife and servants for recovery of his health. L. J., V. 71.

May 18. Copy of letter from the Parliament to Sir John Hotham at Hull, approving his conduct, &c. L. J., V. 71. In extenso.

May 18. Copy of the order to indemnify the captains of ships at Hull for removing the magazine. L. J., V. 72. In extenso.

May 18. Warrant from the Speaker to all mayors, sheriffs, &c., to furnish Richard Eccleston, employed on special service from the Parliament with post-horses, and an able guide to any part of England and back again.

May 19. Message from the Commons respecting the charge against the Recorder of London, &c. L. J., V. 72.

May 19. Draft list of the Committee appointed to join with a proportionable number of the House of Commons to consider of putting the militia of the kingdom into present execution. L. J., V. 73.

May 19. Another draft. Neither list agrees with that in the Journals.

May 19. Copy of order to the Commissioners appointed to treat with the Scots. L. J., V. 73. In extenso.

May 19. Draft order for punishment of delinquents. L. J., V. 75. In extenso.

May 20. Petition of inhabitants of Harlton [Harleton], in the county of Cambridge: petitioners have for a long time been destitute of a preaching minister, because there is a division amongst the patrons, the master and fellows of Jesus College, Cambridge; some wishing to appoint their Master, Dr. Sterne, a man complained of in the House of Commons, and a promoter of superstitious innovations, others wishing to appoint the senior fellow, who would add no more to petitioners' happiness than the Master. The right of presentation has now lapsed to the Bishop of Ely, suspended from exercising his power by their Lordships: pray that neither the master and fellows nor the Bishop may be permitted to put over them any man to whom it is not fit the souls of men should be committed, until the petitioners have offered a grave, learned, and orthodox divine for the approbation of the House. L. J., V. 76.

Annexed:—
1. Recommendation in favour of Mr. Ansell.

May 20. Order for payment of 10,000l. for the affairs of Ireland. L. J., V. 77. In extenso.

May 20. Copy of preceding, and of order for payment of 200l. for relief of the English in Bandonbrigg. L. J., V. 77. In extenso.

May 20. Order for attendance of witnesses in Mr. Justice Berkeley's case.

May 21. Petition of Edward Herbert, Baron of Cherbury and Castle Islands: prays for a benign interpretation of those words of his which gave offence, and for release. L. J., V. 77. In extenso.

May 21. Answer of Sir George Strode to the impeachment of the Commons; is accused of having hindered the execution of the ordinance concerning the militia on the 16th of March last, but did not then know of its existence; confesses to have signed a petition the same in effect with that sent up with the impeachment, but expected that the petition would have been brought to the next general quarter sessions for revision, when errors might have been corrected; he denies that he is guilty of the other offences with which he is charged.

May. 21. Similar answer of Richard Spencer, Esq.

May 21. Deposition of John Barnes, of Windlesham, in the county of Surrey, constable; having received warrant to apprehend certain persons for killing a stag in Swinley Walk, Berks, he went with assistance so to do, and meeting the men on the highway bade them surrender to his warrant, but they said they cared neither for King nor Parliament and made off, and as he was pursuing them on horseback one of them shot his horse under him, and has since been heard to make his brag in an alehouse at Chertsey, that they thereby escaped.

May 21. Deposition of Francis Beard, underkeeper of Swinley Walk, that he saw William Crockford and others shoot a stag there, and when he asked them how they durst do it, they threatened to shoot him too if he would not begone.

May 23. Petition of Thomas Bushell, farmer of his His Majesty's mines royal, in the county of Cardigan; is unable to fulfil his contracts with merchants for supply of lead, in consequence of the interference of Sir Richard Price; petitioner prays the House to mediate between him and the merchants, that they would give him further time for completion of his contracts, and for prosecuting his suit. L. J., V. 78.

May 23. Petition of John, Bishop of St. Asaph; prays that the time for his appearance before the House after notice given may be enlarged, as the present period of three days prevents his visiting his charge.

May 23. Order on preceding, extending the period to three weeks. L. J., V. 79.

May 23. Petition of Morgan Bishop of Llandaff, similar to that of the Bishop of St. Asaph.

May 23. Petition of Mathew, Bishop of Ely, in answer to their Lordships' order of the 20th instant, recommending him to institute Mr. Ansell to the parsonage of Harleton, the right of presentation having lapsed to him, the Bishop says that he had already restored the right of presentation to the Master and fellows of Jesus College, who have since made an unanimous election, and he is therefore unable to interfere further. L. J., V. 79.

May 23. Petition of George Benyon; prays for further liberty, and time to instruct counsel in the cause between him and Lord St. John. L. J., V. 79.

May 23. Copy of order for payment of 500l. for the relief of the distressed protestants come out of Ireland into the county of Devon. L. J., V. 79. In extenso.

May 23. Copy of order for payment of 150l. for the relief of the distressed protestants come out of Ireland to Exeter. L. J., V. 79. In extenso.

May 23. Order of the Commons for payment of 1,000l. to Captain Armstrong and 27 officers. C. J., II. 582. In extenso.

May 23. Ordinance for raising a thousand volunteers by beat of drum, to be employed in the reduction of Ireland. C. J., II. 583.

[May] 23. Warrant to all mayors, sheriffs, &c., to furnish the bearer, employed on the service of Parliament, with post-horses, a guide, &c. Signed by Henry Earl of Manchester, Speaker, pro tempore.

May 23. Copy of a letter from Sir Edward Nicholas, conveying the King's commands to the Lord High Admiral, to provide a ship to carry home the Portuguese Ambassador. Read at a conference, 4 July. L. J., V. 179. In extenso.

May 23. Petition of the undertakers and purchasers of the improved fen grounds in the Earl of Lindsey's level, in the county of Lincoln; notwithstanding their Lordships' orders for securing to petitioners quiet possession of their lands tumultuous multitudes, marching many hundreds in a troop after captains, continue to destroy the public drains, burn and pull down houses, and throw men and women into rivers intending to destroy them; pray their Lordships further consideration and assistance. See L. J., V. 82.

Annexed:—
1. Certificate of Sir Edward Heron, Knight, high sheriff of the county of Lincoln, and Humphrey Walrond, William Coney, and Edward Heron, Esqs., justices of the peace there; in March

last in pursuance of their Lordships' order they went to Little Hall Fen and turned out Christopher Quell, and other pretended commoners, and put Thomas Heron in possession, but Quell and the others returned the same day and forcibly entered on the lands; the same thing happened at Horbling and other places: in April last they went to Bullingbrooke [Bolingbroke], having heard of a riot there, and found John Pishey and others, to the number of 300, pulling down houses, and destroying the dikes and crops of cole, and rape seed; the rioters, who laughed at their Lordships' orders, continued the work of destruction, and were too many to be interfered with; the next day the sheriff and justices were at Boston to perfect the record of the riot, when Pishey and other rioters came in a braving and daring manner near the house, while the Mayor of Boston refused in any way to interfere; the sheriff however succeeded in arresting some of the rioters, upon which a mob of more than a thousand persons attacked the house where the sheriff and justices were, broke in the windows, and having procured from the church the instruments used to pull down houses in case of fire, threatened to pull the house down unless the prisoners were released, and further insulted the sheriff and justices as they rode away from the town; George Banfield was similarly turned out of possession of lands in Pinchbeck Fen, and when evidence was given in court to prove the indictment some of the jury said, that, whatever evidence might be given, they would not find a true Bill, for it was their own case; the rioting and destruction still continue, and the sheriff, justices, and their servants, though acting in obedience to their Lordships' order, have themselves been indicted for their conduct.

2. Copy of Sir Edward Heron's warrant for suppressing riot on Gedney Marsh.

May 24. Petition of Lucy Lady Hastings, wife to the Lord Ferdinando Hastings, on the behalf of her distressed mother, the Lady Elianor Douglas; petitioner lately exhibited a complaint to their Lordships on behalf of her mother against Francis Poulton, concerning the rectory of Purton [Pirton], Herts, her mother's jointure settled upon her by petitioner's father, Sir John Davis, and afterwards assigned for a long term by Sir Archibald Douglas, when not of sound mind or memory, and when Lady Elianor was under imprisonment; Poulton is now dead and petitioner cannot proceed in her suit until his will is proved; she herself is obliged to return to the country, but desires to represent her mother's distress to their Lordships, her jointure thus sold, her dower in Ireland possessed by the rebels, and petitioner unable to help her, as Lord Hastings has also lost the greater part of his estate by the rebellion in Ireland: prays that Sir Archibald Douglas, who has bought himself an annuity of 100l. with Lady Elianor's jointure, may be ordered to allow a portion to her. L. J., V. 80.

May 24. Copy of order of both Houses to their Committees, at York, to publish the votes and orders of Parliament. L. J., V. 83. *In extenso.*

May 24. Order of the Commons for payment of the 500l. loan from Middlesex into the hands of Sir Robert Pye and Mr. Wheeler. C. J., II. 584.

May 24. Petition of inhabitants of St. Olave's, in Southwark, to H. C.; a former petition respecting the election of churchwardens was referred to two neighbouring justices, who accordingly made certificate to the House, but since then some of the opposite party in the vestry have, contrary to their promise to wait the determination of the matter, officiated by violence as churchwardens at the distribution of the sacrament to the disturbance of the church; pray for a speedy determination of the matter. C. J., II. 585.

[May 24.] Babb v. Trelawney. Petition of defendant that the hearing of the cause may be postponed. *See* L. J., V. 83.

May 25. Petition of the Commissioners of the Prince His Highness revenue; notwithstanding their Lordships' order of the 6th April 1641, for securing them in the quiet possession of certain improvements on the Prince's manors of Berkhamstead, Mere, Fordington, and Stoake Clymsland [Stokeclimsland], the fences and hedges have again been pulled down at Berkhampstead and Mere; pray that till a legal determination can be had they may be secured in possession.

[May 26.] Petition of Joseph Hawes; in March 1638-9, Sir Henry Martin, late judge of the Admiralty Court,

certified that the "Elizabeth," bound for Virginia with passengers and merchandize, was taken by eleven sail of the Spanish West India Fleet, and that the damage was above 1,200l.; letters of State were thereupon sent to the ambassador in Spain, but no redress obtained; petitioner formerly arrested certain silver of the King of Spain's subjects in England, but by procurement of Roger Kilvert it was first bailed and then released; there are now in England several parcels of silver belonging to subjects of the King of Spain, but the judge of the Admiralty will not give order for their seizure without the leave of the House, for which petitioner (having been long a prisoner) prays, and for which he can show precedent. L. J., V. 84.

Annexed:—

1. Similar petition of same. (Undated.)

2. Petition of same; complains that Benjamin Newland, of the Isle of Wight, hath in his custody gunpowder, sails, &c., and eight pieces of brass ordnance, belonging to a ship called the "Angel," of the King of Spain, now adjudged to petitioner in the Court of Admiralty in part satisfaction of the great losses done to him by the Spaniards; Newland has got possession of these goods on pretence of satisfying a debt of far less value intending to defraud petitioner, who has no remedy against Newland at common law, and therefore prays that he may be allowed to join in the sale of the goods, in order that he may receive what remains after satisfaction of Newland's claim. (Undated.)

3. Similar petition of same. (Undated.)

May 26. Deposition of Francis Merlin [or Marley], that he served the Earl of Newport, the Earl of Lindsey, and the Lord Savile with the orders of the House, and was told by Secretary Nicholas that it was His Majesty's pleasure that none of the said Lords should depart the Court until His Majesty had justice upon Sir John Hotham, and when he served the Earl of Lindsey with the order, the Earl called to two or three of the King's guards to take deponent into custody. L. J., V. 85.

May 26. Petition of William Ebborne, William Cross, George Thacker, and George Reginalds, poor prisoners in the Fleet; were fetched up from Lincolnshire, and charged by Mr. Kirke and Mr. Walrond for casting down dikes, which they only did in a peaceable way to try their right, not knowing of their Lordships' order to stop such courses; have spent all their substance in prison and have wives and children dependent on them; pray for discharge. L. J., V. 85.

May 26. Order for the arms at Harwich to be restored to the county of Essex. L. J., V. 85.

May 26. Report of the conference about the King's intent to remove the term to York, &c. The report was made on the 27th. L. J., V. 85. *In extenso.*

May 27. Petition of Ralph Skipwith, Esq., His Majesty's servant in ordinary; complains of arrest, in breach of privilege, by order of Dame Bridgett Kingsman for pretended trespass, and prays for reparation. L. J., V. 86.

May 27. Certificate of Robert Phillips, that he summoned Sir Francis Wortley and others, to appear before their Lordships, pursuant to order of the 25th of April last. L. J., V. 86. *In extenso.*

May 30. Petition of Thomas and Symon Osbaldeston, His Majesty's sworn servants; have been arrested for pretended debts, contrary to privilege, by Thomas Bunting, of Greenwich, vintner, and others; pray for discharge. L. J., V. 92.

Annexed:—

1. Petition of David Ramsay, one of His Majesty's servants in ordinary; has been arrested by his creditors, and is now prisoner in the Gatehouse, though large arrears of pay are due to him from his Majesty; prays that he may have the like protection which has been granted to Osbaldeston and others. (Undated.)

May 30. Order for the appearance of the Lords who have gone to York. L. J., V. 92.

May 30. Petition of Edward Lord Littleton, Keeper of the Great Seal, expressing his inability to obey their Lordships' order for his return to London, on account of his ill health, and the King's command to the contrary. L. J., V. 93. *In extenso.*

Annexed:—

1. Certificate of Tobias Peaker, servant to the Lord Keeper, respecting his master's health. L. J., V. 93. *In extenso.*

May 30. Letter from the King to Algernon Earl of Northumberland, Lord High Admiral, to attend His

Majesty at York. . Entered *in extenso* on the 3rd of June. L. J., V. 101.

May 30. Letter from the King to Philip Earl of Pembroke and Montgomery to attend His Majesty at York. Similar to preceding. L. J., V. 101.

May 30. Letter from the King to Philip Earl of Pembroke and Montgomery giving him licence to be absent from Parliament. Similar to the licence to the Earl of Northumberland, which is entered *in extenso* on the 3rd of June. L. J., V. 101.

May 30. Interrogatories and depositions in the cause between Lord St. John and George Benyon. *See* L. J., V. 90, &c.

May 31. Petition of Sir Peter Osborne, Lieutenant-Governor of Guernsey ; two ministers have been chosen out of the island to attend the assembly of Divines ; the island, which has ten parishes, will then be left with but six ministers, the several parishioners every Sunday expecting two sermons, besides a constant lecture upon one of the week days ; petitioner prays that if both ministers cannot be forborne, then one of them may be chosen from Jersey, as the islanders are well content with the discipline of France so long enjoyed, and have not the curiosity to intermeddle in the government of other churches.

May 31. Copy of preceding.

May 31. Copy of order on preceding petition, dispensing with both ministers. L. J., V. 94. *In extenso*.

May 31. Petition of Edmund Harrington, Giles Johnson, and Thomas Marshall ; in consideration of the unjust oppression suffered by petitioners at the hands of Robert Taylcot and Thomas his son, their Lordships referred the case to two justices, who have made the annexed certificate ; pray that the case may be referred to a committee of their Lordships to settle. L. J., V. 94.

Annexed :—

1. Petition of Edmund Harrington and Elizabeth his wife, Giles Johnson and Grace his wife, Thomas Marshall and Anne his wife ; petitioners in right of their wives claim certain lands and tenements in Colchester, mortgaged in Queen Elizabeth's time, and afterwards fraudulently conveyed to Robert Taylcot ; a suit in the matter in Chancery was dismissed by Lord Coventry, but with a direction that Taylcot should pay petitioners 20l. for a release of their interest, the property in question being worth 2,000l. ; petitioners are thus cut off from relief except from their Lordships, whom they pray to grant them satisfaction. 22 May 1641. L. J., IV. 255.

2. Order referring preceding petition to two justices. 22 June 1641.

3. Certificate of the justices stating the facts of the case and exonerating Taylcot (mayor of Colchester) from fraud in the matter. 8 July 1641.

4. Affidavit of Thomas Rider that he served Taylcot with an order in the cause. 15 June 1642.

May 31. Draft order for raising a thousand men for service in Ireland. L. J., V. 95. *In extenso*.

Annexed :—

1. Amendments to preceding.

May 31. Petition of John Lord Balmerino ; King James in the first year of his reign granted to James Lord Balmerino, petitioner's father, the office of chief clerk or prothonotary of the King's Bench in reversion after the death of Sir John Roper, afterwards Lord Roper ; the said Lord Balmerino, by agreement with Mr., afterwards Sir, Robert Heath, in the fifth year of the late King's reign, surrendered the office to His Majesty, and obtained a new patent to himself and Sir Robert Heath for their lives, upon trust that Sir Robert should execute the office, and pay one moiety of the profits, amounting to at least 2,000l. per annum, to his Lordship ; but in the tenth year of the late King's reign Sir Robert made an entire surrender of the office without Lord Balmerino's will or knowledge, by which means petitioner, heir and executor to his father, has been deprived of the profits of the said moiety ever since the death of Lord Roper, twenty-six years ago ; petitioner can prove the truth of the premises by Sir Robert Heath's own handwriting, from whom he prays for satisfaction. L. J., V. 95.

May 31. Petition of Peter Smart, prebendary of Durham ; the great charge he has incurred in maintaining witnesses has quite ruined him in estate and credit ; prays that an early day may be appointed for the hearing of his case, or that the evidence of Nicholas Hobson, an old man of ninety-two, and of Robert King, who is

obliged to return to the country, may be taken down in writing and sealed up till the hearing. L. J., V. 95.

May 31. Petition of the churchwardens and parishioners of St. Mary Magdalen, Bermondsey ; Dr. Paske has for seventeen years been parson of their parish (being also Master of Clare Hall, Archdeacon of London, Prebendary of Canterbury, Prebendary of York, Parson of Great Hadham and of Little Hadham), he has scarce preached once a year, has always received the tithes but spent nothing for preaching or reading in church, or for a dwelling for a curate, the whole expense of which has fallen on the parish ; petitioners have lately bought the next presentation to the living, and have elected Mr. Whitakers, a godly minister, their lecturer for the time being, but he is much opposed by the present curate, Mr. Kenn, who is also parson of Little Chart, in Kent, and vicar of Low Leyton, in Essex : petitioners who were the more induced to elect Mr. Whitakers in the hope that pluralites would have been abolished by Parliament, pray that their choice may be confirmed. L. J., V. 95.

May 31. Petition of gentry of Chertsey ; that Mr. Boden may be ordered to preach there every market day, and also on Sunday when the minister of the parish preacheth not himself. C. J., II. 596.

May 31. Order of the Commons for 100l. to be paid to Lord Dungarvan for the relief of the distressed protestants of Youghal out of the contribution money collected at Dover. C. J., II. 596.

[May .] Request to Mr. Rushworth by some person not mentioned, that if there should be any proceedings in Parliament against Robert Hartpoole upon petition of Sir Edward Loftus, or others, that Mr. Rushworth would send word to Mr. Hussey, or write himself to Hartpoole by the ordinary post, " which is at Bartholo- " mew Lane, in backside of the old Exchange, a known " place from whence any one may send letters into Ire- " land." Hartpoole is stated had recovered certain lands in Ireland from Sir Edward Loftus, by petition to the Lord Deputy and Council in Ireland.

[May .] " List of the last ten ' Linares ' for Ireland, " 1642, set forth by the Parliament." The names of the ships are given.

[May .] Petition of John Squire, merchant, now prisoner in the King's Bench : in consequence of the protection granted by their Lordships to Edward Abbotts, and Agmondesham Pigars (Pickayes), debtors to petitioner, he has been unable to satisfy his creditors, and has been himself arrested ; prays for release and for liberty to prosecute his suit against Abbotts and Pigars. *See* L. J., V. 78.

Annexed :—

1. Similar petition of same.
2. Another petition.

June 1. Petition of Henry Lord Morley and Mounteagle ; by order (by consent) in a cause long depending in Chancery between petitioner and Sir George Strode and others, petitioner agreed to repay the purchase money of the manor of Martock, with interest, expecting Lord Pawlett (to whom the manor lay commodious) to find the money ; but now Lord Pawlett will have no dealings in the matter, and no one will purchase land in such distracted times ; petitioner prays the House to grant him the relief that cannot be had elsewhere. L. J., V. 95.

Annexed :—

1. Affidavit of John Harris of the Inner Temple, and others, in the matter. 3 May 1642.

June 1. Copy of order of both Houses about the sale of the crown jewels by the King. L. J., V. 96. *In extenso*.

June 1. Notes of the conference concerning the amendments in the propositions to the King, &c. L. J., V. 96.

June 1. Message from the Commons with resolutions of that House respecting an indemnity to those who have exercised the militia, &c. L. J., V. 97. *In extenso*. (Three papers.)

June 1. Copy of order to the committees at York respecting the presentation to the King of the petition from Parliament. L. J., V. 97. *In extenso*.

June 1. Draft of the 5th proposition respecting the marriage of any of the King's children contained in the petition of both Houses to the King. L. J., V. 98. *In extenso*.

June 1. Copy of information of Gilbert Yeildall and Francis Beard, keepers, charging Leonard Finch and Edward Barnard, of Warfield, with killing a stag on Warfield Heath.

[June 2.] Lord St. John v. George Benyon ; charge against Benyon of assigning his own private debts to

HOUSE OF
LORDS.

Calendar.
1642.

the King under colour of his receivership in order to recover them in that illegal way. L. J., V. 99.

Annexed :—

1. List of witnesses for Benyon.

2. Certificate of Thomas Brinley, one of the auditors of the Court of Exchequer, respecting the accounts between Lord St. John and Benyon.

June 2. Petition of George Rookes ; upon petitioner's complaint Robert Tookley was imprisoned for contempt in refusing to pay 145*l.* as ordered by their Lordships: prays for Tookley's discharge as they are now agreed. L. J., V. 100.

June 2. Letter from the Earl of Monmouth at York to the Lords now sitting in the House of Peers. I received your Lordships' order to appear on the 27th of this present month, to make answer to the impeachment of the House of Commons. I am infinitely sensible of my misfortune in being so impeached, though I doubt not, were it in my power to appear I could largely acquit myself, but I am kept here by the observance of the same allegiance which brought me hither, and not being able to appear, I am not so good a lawyer as to know what answer to make. I do further humbly beg your Lordships to believe that wheresoever I am, all my endeavours shall tend to the reconciling and bringing together again of our King and Parliament. June 3. Draft order as amended by the Lords to the officers of the ordnance to receive the arms and ammunition sent from Hull. L. J., V. 100.

June 3. Petition of Thomas Burwell ; stands impeached on pretence that he signed a warrant with the now Bishop of Durham, by which Mr. Smart was brought up prisoner to London in a cart ; the Bishop, the principal, was dismissed on transmission of the impeachment by the House of Commons, but Smart is now suing petitioner for the same imprisonment before the Barons of the Exchequer ; petitioner prays their Lordships to detain or dismiss the cause pending before them, that he may not be vexed in two courts at the same time. L. J., V. 101.

June 3. Order for the hearing of Henry Stewart's cause against Lord Cromwell and others of the Council in Ireland. L. J., V. 102.

Annexed :—

1. Petition of Fenton Parsons on the behalf of Sir William Parsons, Lord Justice of Ireland, and others, who by their counsel have often attended the hearing of the cause, in which they have been made defendants by Henry Stewart and James Gray, before the Committee for Petitions, but have never yet obtained a hearing though the cause has been reported to their Lordships, and 1,900*l.* damages is alleged to be due to Stewart and Gray ; the Lord Justice and the others pray to be heard by counsel at the Bar on the points of law that arise in the cause.

June 3. Draft letter from the Parliament to Lord Willoughby [of Parham] thanking him for his activity in putting the ordinance for the militia into execution in Lincolnshire. L. J., V. 103. *In extenso.*

June 3. Order of the Commons, upon the information of Mr. Nathan Wright and Mr. Jacob Fawrtree, respecting the payment of certain bills of exchange from Holland to Mr. Adrian May. C. J., II. 602. *In extenso.*

June 3. Petition of George Payler, late paymaster of the forces in garrison at Berwick, and of the works and fortifications there. C. J., II. 602. (Illegible from damp.)

June 3. Letter from Sir Thomas Stanley of Bickerstaffe to John Holcroft at Mr. Heywood's house near Westminster. Lord Strange is this day gone to York, Mr. Gerrard is come home, and is raising a troop of horse out of Lancashire and Cheshire to go to York ; would be glad to hear of the health of his friends. *See* L. J., V. 121.

June 4. Petition of Colonel John Butler : thanks the House with the utmost humility for continuing his commitment at the Lord Mayor's ; has no present means but what the House allows, and nothing in the future but what his own endeavours can procure ; prays for liberty and that the House would grant him such means as would bear his charges out of the kingdom, he giving security to depart and never to set foot in Ireland during the rebellion there. L. J., V. 103.

June 4. Ordinance for securing the sum of one hundred thousand pounds agreed to be lent to the Parliament by several companies, and citizens of the city of London, for the use of the kingdom. L. J., V. 105. *In extenso.*

June 4. Two copies of the order for the deputy lieu-

tenants to attend the musterings. L. J., V. 106. *In extenso.*

June 4. Three printed copies of preceding.

June 4. Depositions of John Loftus (May 31 and June 4) that he had several times waited upon Sir Philip Mainwaring, pursuant to their Lordships' order, with a reconveyance of the trusts conveyed to him by Lord Loftus, but Sir Philip had constantly made excuses of delay to avoid executing the same. L. J., V. 106.

June 4. Order to the Earl of Warwick and Lord Brook to stay, and search, all ships suspected of going to Ireland to relieve the rebels. L. J., V. 106. *In extenso.*

June 4. Petition of Mary Bagshaw, Margaret Wright, and Henry Bagshaw : pray for relief against their brother Thomas Bagshaw, who has not given them security for the payment of their portions, or for their present maintenance, pursuant to their Lordships' order of June last. L. J., V. 102.

Annexed :—

1. Motion to be made in the cause.

2. Abstract of the petition, &c.

June 4. List of Lords Committees added to the Commissioners for the Scotch affairs. *See* L. J., V. 103.

June 5. Letter from the nine Lords at York to the Speaker of the House of Lords, excusing their non-attendance. L. J., V. 115. *In extenso.*

June 6. Message from the Commons, with resolutions, declaring the Earl of Lindsey and Lord Savile to be enemies to the State. L. J., V. 109. *In extenso.*

June 6. Petition of the gentry, ministers, freeholders, and other inhabitants of the county of York, to the King's most excellent Majesty. One sheet of signatures. L. J., V. 109. *In extenso.*

June 6. Copy of petition of the gentry, ministers, freeholders, and other inhabitants of the county of York, assembled there at his Majesty's command, the third of June 1642, to both Houses of Parliament, respecting His Majesty's non-acceptance of a petition offered by them, &c. L. J., V. 110. *In extenso.*

June 6. Draft resolution of both Houses upon the preceding petitions. L. J., V. 111. *In extenso.*

June 6. Draft declaration of both Houses in answer to the King's proclamation forbidding the militia to assemble in obedience to the ordinance of Parliament. (Much amended.) L. J., V. 112. *In extenso.*

June 6. Petition of the greatest part of the parishioners of Hemel Hempstead, to H. C. ; that Mr. Philip Goodwin may be appointed lecturer to preach on Sunday afternoon and Thursday morning (market day) without hindrance from the vicar, John Taylor. C. J., II. 608.

Annexed :—

1. Petition of John Ashton of Hemel Hempstead, ironmonger, to H. C., for relief against several sentences of the High Commission Court, by which he has been fined and imprisoned at the suit of Mr. Taylor, the vicar, for playing at "Stoole" ball with the curate and others on a holiday, &c. Taylor having been proved to be a man of a scandalous life. (Undated.)

June 6. Proclamation writ to summon George Lord Digby, accused of high treason, to appear ; directed to the mayor, &c. of the city of Exeter, with certificate of publication attached. L. J., V. 37. *In extenso.* Returned this day.

June 7. Letter from the Portuguese Ambassador to the House of Lords on his departure from England. (Latin.) L. J., V. 114. *In extenso.*

June 7. Letter from Lord Willoughby [of Parham] to the Speaker of the House of Lords, thanking the House for their approbation of his conduct in executing the ordinance for the militia in Lincolnshire. This letter, which is dated the 6th, is entered *in extenso* on the 7th. L. J., V. 115.

Encloses :—

1. Letter from the King to Lord Willoughby of Parham : charging him to desist from mustering the trained bands of the county of Lincoln. 4 June. L. J., V. 115. *In extenso.*

2. Copy of Lord Willoughby's answer to preceding. L. J., V. 116. *In extenso.*

June 7. Answer of the officers of the ordnance at the Tower respecting the arms, &c. brought thither from Hull. L. J., V. 116. *In extenso.*

June 7. Draft order of the Commons for two pieces of "batterie," with their furniture, to be sent to Munster. C. J., II. 610. *In extenso.*

June 7. Draft order of the Commons for payment of 662*l.* 1*s.* 4*d.* to Mr. Loftus for Ireland. C. J., II. 610. *In extenso.*

HOUSE OF
LORDS.

Calendar.
1642.

June 7. Draft order of the Commons for repayment of the loan advanced by the gentlemen of Buckinghamshire. C. J., II. 611. *In extenso.*

June 7. Petition of Sir William Willmer, high sheriff of the county of Northampton; upon complaint to the Commons that petitioner had distributed some petitions of the House of Lords to the King, with the King's answer thereto, and that he had spoken certain words respecting the militia, he was apprehended, and has attended on bail, de die in diem, for almost three months; prays leave to go down into the country, the rather that he may expedite the sending up the contribution money delayed by his absence.

June 8. Message to the Commons in commendation of Lord Willoughby's conduct in raising the trained bands in Lincolnshire. L. J., V. 117. *In extenso.*

June 8. Draft of preceding.

June 8. Letter from the Earl of Warwick to his brother the Earl of Holland concerning the state of the militia in Essex. Dated 7th, entered 8th June. L. J., V. 117. *In extenso.*

Encloses:—
1. Petition of the Essex militia and volunteers to the Earl of Warwick, tendering their persons and estates for the support of Parliament. L. J., V. 118. *In extenso.*

June 8. Printed copy of petition of gentry, ministers, freeholders and other substantial inhabitants of the county of York; deplore the sufferings of their county on account of the late and present troubles, and pray the Parliament to give such assurances against tumult to His Majesty, that he may be allured to return to his great Council, and that Parliament would give such consideration to His Majesty's message of the 20th of January, as may give hopes of an effectual concurrence, and save petitioners from being distracted by contrary commands. "Imprinted at York and reprinted at "London for Richard Lownes, June 7, 1642." Lownes is ordered to appear before the House for re-printing this petition. L. J., V. 118.

June 8. Declaration of the Lords and Commons in commendation of the Essex petition. L. J., V. 119. *In extenso.*

June 8. Copy of preceding.

June 8. Draft resolution concerning the letter of the nine Lords who had withdrawn themselves to York. L. J., V. 119. *In extenso.*

June 8. Draft order for payment of 10,000l. to Mr. Loftus for Ireland. L. J., V. 119. *In extenso.*

June 8. Petition of Lady Elizabeth Sidley, to H. C.: on pretence of seeing pearls and hangings for sale at Madame Nurst's house, petitioner was drawn to a solitary house not inhabited, belonging, as she has since heard, to John Griffith the younger, a member of the House of Commons, where she was wickedly and violently assaulted by him to the endangering of her life and honour, but providentially escaped, whilst he, conscious of his foul attempt, has fled; prays liberty to prosecute him, and that order may be given to stay his departure from the country. C. J., II. 613.

June 8. Examination of Michael Shaw of Wapping, master of the "Lydia" of London, and Nicholas Cook of Rood Lane, respecting words spoken by Wm. Odoron, an Irishman, master of the "John and James" of Dover, who, in the tavern of Madam Sasanna at Rochelle, "when he had drunk too much, but was not drunk," said that there were no rebels in Ireland so great as the Parliament in England, and when rebuked came to blows with Shaw.

June 8. Examination of William Odoron, who denies that he said anything except that he was for the King, but confesses that he and Shaw came to blows.

June 9. Draft ordinance for bringing in plate, money, and horses for the service of Parliament. L. J., V. 121. *In extenso.*

June 9. Petition of divers of the inhabitants of Shepton Mallet, to the Commons. The parish is exceedingly populous, consisting of 2,000 communicants, but Mr. Cooth the parson does not preach in the afternoon on Sabbath days, and none preach for him. Petitioners pray that Mr. Robert Balsome, a pious and orthodox minister, for whom they are content to make a competent allowance out of their own purse, may be settled as their lecturer. C. J., II. 617.

June 9. Letter from [ ] to Samuel Vassall in London: has had occasion to go twice to Dunkirk in the last five weeks, has observed many youths and maidens brought over from England by every packet, the youths to St. Thomas' to the Jesuits, the maids to divers cloisters; Sir Richard Weston and others who come over

to Dunkirk vilify Parliament, terming the members roundheads, and hoping they will all soon be hanged; a frigate laden with powder for Limerick is lying at Dunkirk, but she is so watched by the Holland fleet of twenty-four sail, that her design of going to Ireland is for the present defeated.

[June 9.] Notes respecting certain votes this day.

June 10. Petition of Sir Philip Mainwaring; is ready to execute deeds of reconveyance to Lord Loftus of Ely pursuant to their Lordships' order, but expresses his exceptions to those tendered to him for signature as not giving him security from future actions, and prays that the deeds may be referred to such persons as their Lordships shall think fit for perfecting the same. L. J., V. 123.

June 10. Petition of Mr. Justice Heath: has received His Majesty's commands to attend him at York, hopes His Majesty will dismiss him in a few days, when he will with all speed wait on their Lordships. L. J., V. 124. *In extenso.*

June 11. Draft resolution of Lords and Commons that the departure of the nine Lords to York is an affront and contempt of both Houses of Parliament. L. J., V. 126. *In extenso.*

June 11. Another draft.

June 11. Order for stopping and staying of all arms, ammunition, powder, light horses, or horses for service in the wars, and great saddles, that are or shall be carried towards the north parts of England without the direction of one, or both Houses of Parliament. L. J., V. 126.

June 11. Copy of preceding.

June 11. Draft order of the Commons for departure of ships and pinnaces to guard the coasts of Ireland. C. J., II. 619. *In extenso.*

June 11. Draft of two orders of the Commons respecting the Committee appointed to receive the answers of the members who have not yet declared themselves. List of Committee, &c. C. J., II. 619, 620.

June 11. Notes of proceedings at the Committee appointed to consider of propositions for defence of the kingdom. Mr. Shughburgh declared that he hath horses in readiness to defend the King the Commonwealth, the laws, and the Parliament. Noted, Nihil. Sir Nicholas Slanning, that when the King and both Houses of Parliament shall command it he shall be ready to serve them with his life and fortune, till then he desires not to intermeddle. Noted, Nihil. Mr. Hayes, 100l. Mr. Gaudy, 50l. Sir John Price, two horses. Mr. Hodges, two horses, or one horse and 50l. Sir Nevil Pole, four horses, and his son, four horses.

June 12. Copy of the King's letter to the Commissioners of array for the county of Leicester, commanding them to execute the commission. Entered *in extenso* on the 18th instant. L. J., V. 148.

June 12. Johannes Fredericus Münsterus, Germanus, to the King and the Lords of Parliament, praying them well to consider the letters enclosed on the future judgment of the wicked. (Latin.) Letters wanting.

June 13. Particulars of a message from the Commons respecting instructions for the Committees going into Lincolnshire, &c. L. J., V. 127.

June 13. Instructions for the Committees going into Lancashire. L. J., V. 128. *In extenso.*

June 13. Subject of the conference concerning the departure of the Lord Lieutenant of Ireland for that kingdom. L. J., V. 129. *In extenso.*

June 13. Letter from William Savile at York to Mr. Holland, master of the "George" at Northampton; Mr. Neville, a friend of the writer's and servant to the King, who has had a horse stayed at Northampton, is desirous of recovering it by replevin, but cannot himself wait to prosecute the suit, the writer prays Holland to find Mr. Neville an honest attorney and two sureties, if necessary, as bail for the horse and for the prosecution of the suit, and if he can get the horse to send him by the bearer to Captain Neville at the "Talbot" in York.

June 13. Petition of John Van Haesdonck; notwithstanding their Lordships' orders for securing the quiet possession of lands in the fens, his crops are destroyed, his servants threatened, and their Lordships' orders treated with contempt; prays that the delinquents may be punished. *See* L. J., V. 101.

Annexed:—
1. Affidavit of Humphrey Kynnesman in support of preceding.

June 13. Examination of Bartholomew Gifford, owner of a ship called the "True Love," of Bristol, deposing that Stephen Welsh, merchant, owner of a ship called the "Peter" of Wexford, stayed at Holyhead by order of Parliament, said that the Irish were no rebels, &c.

[June 13.] Petition of Sir John Lenthall, Knight, marshal of the Marshalsea of the King's Bench; details certain proceedings in law and equity against him for the escape of one Morrett, a prisoner in execution at the suit of Richard Brewton; prays their Lordships to hear the whole case upon its merits, or else to stay a certain writ of error until the suit be decided in Chancery. *See* L. J., V. 128, &c.

June 14. Draft order for Sir John Wollaston and Wm. Gibbs to attend the service of the militia of London. L. J., V. 131. *In extenso.*

June 14. Order for the Scottish Commissioners to be informed that any towns or places taken in Ulster shall be kept by the English. L. J., V. 131. *In extenso.*

June 14. Affidavits of the following persons concerning the militia in Leicestershire. L. J., V. 132-133. *In extenso.*

 i. Thomas Clare.
 ii. William Browne.
 iii. William Gilbert.
 iv. Robert Creswell.
 v. John Mills.
 vi. Henry Whitaker.

June 14. Copy of resolution that Wolseley and others mentioned in preceding affidavits should be sent for as delinquents. L. J., V. 133. *In extenso.*

June 14. "Divers passages concerning the Lord " Keeper," showing how he had voted on several occasions in support of resolutions concerning the militia. L. J., V. 134. *In extenso.*

Annexed :—

 1. Various extracts from the Journals of resolutions concerning the militia, passed when the Lord Keeper was present in the House.

June 14. Instructions for Sir William Brereton and the Deputy Lieutenants for Chester. L. J., V. 134. *In extenso.*

June 14. Commission for giving the Royal Assent to " An Act for the further advancement of an effectual " and speedy reduction of the rebels in Ireland to the " obedience of his Majesty and the Crown of England." The Royal Assent was given on the 22d instant. *See* L. J., V. 154.

June 14. Petition of Robert Aylmore and Samuel Diglett, millers, to the Commons, on behalf of the fullers and millers of Essex and Suffolk, for leave to transport fullers earth from Rochester for use in their mills. C. J., II. 623.

June 15. Petition of Joseph Hawes; certain pieces of ordnance from the "Angel," a ship lately belonging to the King of Spain, were arrested by petitioner and one Bredcake, under order from the Court of Admiralty, in part satisfaction of great losses sustained by them ; but now Benjamin Newland is contriving with the Spanish Ambassador to send the said ordnance beyond seas ; petitioner prays their Lordships to recommend his case to the Court of Admiralty that he may have speedy justice. L. J., V. 136.

June 15. Draft order to the Justices, &c. of York not to deliver up any arms they have seized, " but by His " Majesty's command, signified by both Houses of " Parliament." L. J., V. 136. *In extenso.*

June 15. Copy of declaration of both Houses to the kingdom of Scotland, respecting the King's letter to the Privy Council of Scotland, and the petition of noblemen and others to the same. L. J., V. 136. *In extenso.*

June 15. Draft of the letter from the Parliament to the Committees at York to recall them from thence. L. J., V. 137. *In extenso.*

June 15. Another draft.

June 15. Copy of order for the Deputy Lieutenants of the county of Bucks to put the militia in execution in the absence of Lord Pagett. L. J., V. 137. *In extenso.*

June 15. Draft order of the Commons for the Lord Mayor, &c. of the city of London, to summon a meeting to consider of a loan to Parliament. C. J., II. 624. *In extenso.*

June 15. Petition of Samuel Thomas, Esq., and other undertakers in the fen lands north-east of the river of Witham, in Lincolnshire ; pray their Lordships to make a further order for securing petitioners in their possessions. *See* L. J., V. 79.

Annexed :—

 1. Similar petition of same. (Undated.)
 2. Draft of an order to the sheriff, &c., with the power of the county and failing that by force of arms with the assistance of friends and others,

to secure to the owners quiet enjoyment of their possessions in the fens.

3. Affidavit of Michael Broughton of Boston and Peter Taylor of Sibsey respecting the destruction of houses, drains, and crops upon the drained lands within the undertaking of the late Sir Anthony Thomas in Lincolnshire by a riotous multitude under the captaincy of John Hall.

June 15. Petition of his Majesty's late Commissioners for causes ecclesiastical ; now that the Commission under which they acted has been declared void by Act of this present Parliament, the Commissioners are liable to be vexed with suits for their judicial proceedings ; they pray that as they acted without fee or benefit to themselves, where no bribery or misdemeanour (other than the illegality of the Commission) can be proved against them, they may be protected from all actions or suits for their proceedings. Signed by Sir Nathaniel Brent.

June 16. Petition of James Halsall, servant to Thomas Worseley, clerk of the papers of Wood Street Compter ; petitioner's master is by his place bound to read all proclamations commanded by the Lord Mayor of London to be read, and petitioner, in his master's absence (who was not at that time, in town), was commanded by the Lord Mayor to read the late proclamation concerning the militia, and did so read it, and the common crier proclaimed the same without a thought of giving offence to Parliament ; for this petitioner was on the 10th instant committed to the Gatehouse, and there now remains to his great charge and almost ruin ; prays that as he was only obeying the Lord Mayor's command, in his master's absence, in ignorance of any inconvenience that might ensue, or distaste to their Lordships, they would accept of his humble submission and discharge him from prison. L. J., V. 139.

June 16. Instructions concerning the propositions for raising of plate, money, and horses. L. J., V. 140. *In extenso.*

June 16. Articles of impeachment against the nine Lords at York. L. J., V. 141. *In extenso.*

June 16. Order for the nine impeached Lords to answer. L. J., V. 141. *In extenso.*

June 16. Deposition of Richard Panton of Burnham, in the county of Essex ; that he read their Lordships' orders to Wm. Fowle, and others, forbidding the fishermen to dredge and take oyster spat in Walfleet and Burnham Water, but the fishermen, encouraged and protected by George Asser of Barking and his servants, persisted in dredging and fishing to the destruction of the oyster beds, and when deponent attempted to apprehend certain Kentish men so fishing they took refuge in a large boat of Asser's and made violent resistance.

June 16. Similar deposition of Francis Smith of Burnham.

June 17. Further deposition of same.

June 17. Similar deposition of John Bagglye of Burnham.

June 17. Draft order for the Earl of Exeter, Lord Lieutenant for the county of Rutland, to put the militia for that county in execution. L. J., V. 141. *In extenso.*

June 17. Resolution for putting in execution the propositions for raising horse. L. J., V. 142. *In extenso.*

June 17. The humble repromission and resolution of the captains and soldiers and other inhabitants of the county of Essex; are ready to spend their lives and fortunes in defence of liberty and religion, and pray that the arms lately taken out of the county may be restored to them. L. J., V. 143. *In extenso.*

June 17. Draft of the Lords' answer to preceding. L. J., V. 143. *In extenso.*

June 17. Draft letter from the Speaker of the House of Lords to Lord Dacres to attend the House in a fortnight. L. J., V. 143. *In extenso.*

June 17. Draft letter from the Speaker of the House of Lords to the Earl of Exeter, to put the militia in execution in the county of Rutland. L. J., V. 143. *In extenso.*

June 17. The original ordinance for the sea adventure to Ireland. L. J., V. 144. *In extenso.*

June 17. Draft of preceding.

June 17. An account of arms sold and bespoke from the Company of Gunmakers of London.

June 17. Petition of Richard Lovelace, Esq. to H. C. : was committed to the Gatehouse by order of the 30th of April last. Prays for discharge upon bail, in order that he may serve against the rebels in Ireland. C. J., II. 629.

June 18. Draft orders for Henry Hastings to be sent

for as a delinquent, and for Thomas Boughton to be a deputy lieutenant for the county of Warwick. L. J., V. 145. *In extenso.*

June 18. Order for the Earl of Antrim to be comitted to the Castle of Carrickfergus. L. J., V. 146.
Annexed :—
1. Draft of preceding.

June 18. Letter from Lord Grey de Ruthin and Sir Arthur Haslerig to the Speaker of the House of Commons, respecting their proceedings at Leicester in raising the trained bands, and Mr. Leicester's in publishing a Commission of Array from the King. Dated 16th. L. J., V. 147. *In extenso.*
Enclosing :—
1. Copy of warrant from the Commissioners of Array to the high sheriff of Leicestershire to call out the trained bands. L. J., V. 148. *In extenso.*
2. Copy of the Sheriff's warrant to the petty constables to put the commission of array in execution. L. J., V. 148. *In extenso.*

June 18. Draft declaration of the Parliament to the sheriff of Essex not to publish the King's proclamation against the militia. L. J., V. 149. *In extenso.*

June 18. Report from the Committee appointed to consider of Commissions of Array, declaring after a long examination of Statutes on the subject that the Commission of Array for the county of Leicester " is not " warranted by any Act of Parliament, is contrary to " the law and customs of the realm, destructive to the " liberty and property of the subject, contrary to the " petition of right and the Statute made this present " Parliament." (26 pp.) L. J., V. 150. Rushworth, Vol. I., Part III., p. 661. *In extenso.*
Annexed :—
1. Copy of the Statute of 5 Hen. 4., whereby the Commission of Array is supposed to be warranted.

June 18. Resolution that the Commission of Array for Leicestershire is illegal. L. J., V. 150. *In extenso.*

June 18. Order requiring the Lord Mayor not to publish the King's letter for staying the bringing in of money. L. J., V. 150. *In extenso.*

June 18. Order for the attachment of Mr. Henry Hastings, son of the Earl of Huntingdon, and others, for opposing the execution of the ordinance for the militia in Leicestershire. L. J., V. 150. *In extenso.*

June 18. Order of the Commons for the Chamberlain of London to pay 10,000l. to the treasurer of the Irish Adventure. C. J., II. 631. *In extenso.*

June 18. Petition of Thomas Carne, Lieutenant-Colonel to Sir John Merrick, to H. C. Petitioner was employed upon the late expedition in the North parts. Prays that he may receive the arrears of pay due unto him. C. J., II. 632.

June 18. Petition of Edmund Winstanley and Dorothy his wife : in July last their petition against Wm. Bullock was referred to the Lord Keeper, and after various delays the cause is now set down to be heard before him on the 27th of this instant June. Petitioners pray for an order directing the cause to be heard by such judge or judges, as shall sit in Chancery on that day.

June 18. Petition of Morgan, Bishop of Llandaff. Petitioner's charge and place of residence are distant above 130 miles ; he has been absent a long time and and cannot go thither, whilst he is bound to appear before their Lordships within three days after notice. Prays that this time may be extended.

June 18. " A computation and list of the equipage, " carriages, and horses necessary to a marching train " of the following ten pieces of ordnance, which we " humbly desire may be supplied out of the King's " store." Year uncertain.
[June 18.] Statement of the Lord Mayor of London respecting the King's letter to him and the aldermen and sheriffs, concerning the loans of money for the relief of Ireland. See L. J., V. 145.; C. J., II. 630.

June 20. Copy of the declaration of Parliament, in answer to the King's letter to the city of London, against the bringing in of money, plate, and horses. L. J., V. 153. *In extenso.*

June 20. Draft of preceding.

June 20. Last sheet of the King's proclamation respecting the lawfulness of the Commissions of Array. Rushworth, Part III., Vol. I., 659. *In extenso.*

June 20. Affidavit of John Venn, captain of the trained bands of Christ Church parish in the ward of Farringdon Within, that Exuperius Turner and others,

though summoned to do His Majesty and the Parliament service, have neglected to attend without showing cause for their absence. See L. J., V. 158.

June 21. List of officers of all grades chosen by the adventurers for Ireland, to serve under Philip Lord Wharton as Colonel General, with the alterations since the return of the list, names of other officers listed, and of the Beformado officers, and also a calculation of the charge per diem for horse and foot. See L. J., V. 153; C. J., II. 630. (14 pp.)

June 21. Draft letter from the Speaker of the House of Lords to the Mayor of Exeter, commending his conduct with regard to the militia. L. J., V. 154. *In extenso.*

June 22. Draft order for disposing of the arms, &c. brought from Hull. L. J., V. 155. *In extenso.*
Annexed :—
1. Paper of amendments.

June 22. Petition of the Lord Mackquire, Hugh MacMahowne, and Lieutenant Colonel Reade, now close prisoners in the Tower of London. Pray that they may be supplied with clothes and linen, and have necessary diet and attendance, as they are in extreme want and like to perish without relief from their Lordships. L. J., V. 155.
Annexed :—
1. Letter from Owen O'Connally to Hugh McMahowne. I wish you would have taken the advice I gave you at Lord Enniskillen's lodging last Friday, seeing the matter has been partly brought to light by me from no disaffection to you, or to the natives of this land, but out of conscience, and loyalty, and pity to the innocent who would have been cut off. I now offer my best assistance for your preservation and life, not remembering the danger I was in when I last left you. I desire to speak with you before I go into England, which will be speedily. Do not slight this advice, for I perceive that favour will be shown you by the Lords Justices at my suit. (Undated.)
2. Petition of Lieut.-Col. Reade to the Earl of Leicester, Lord Lieutenant of Ireland, &c.; though petitioner was a prisoner in the Castle of Dublin, he was not a close prisoner like those with whom he has come along ; if the Earl's pleasure is that he should be committed he desires that he may speak with him first. (Undated.)

June 22. Copy of Lord Willoughby's letter to the Speaker of the House of Lords about the Lincolnshire militia. Dated June 19th. L. J., V. 155. *In extenso.*
Encloses :—
1. Copy of declaration of the county. L. J., V. 155. *In extenso.*

June 22. Petition of George Benyon, a prisoner under their Lordships' order : understands that he is to be removed to Colchester, but on account of his wife's extreme sickness, and his necessary occasions to dispose of his estate, petitioner prays, that if what he has already suffered is not sufficient to expiate his offence, his removal from London may at least be dispensed with for a time, and that before judgment he may be further heard. See L. J., V. 155.
Annexed :—
1. Petition of same that the evidence of auditor Phelips may be received, and petitioner further heard before judgment be given in the cause between him and Lord St. John. (Undated.)
2. Certificate of Thomas Winton, Doctor of Physic, of the extreme illness of Benyon's wife. 21 June.

June 22. Warrant from Philip Lord Wharton, Speaker of the House of Lords *pro tempore*, to all mayors, sheriffs, &c., to furnish the bearer with post-horses and a guide to York or elsewhere.

June 23. Petition of Oliver Clobery, George Fletcher, and Henry Taverner to the Lords Commissioners for the affairs of the Kingdom of Scotland. Petitioners formerly exhibited a petition to the House of Commons complaining that the ship " Martha," of London, laden with tobacco from St. Christopher's, put into the river Clyde for relief, a little before the troubles began between England and Scotland, and was there with her lading seized and sold by the Scots, being worth upwards of 2,000l. Petitioners were by order of the House of Commons referred to their Lordships for redress, but have had none, though it is now almost three years since the seizure. Petitioners pray that they may have relief out of the money payable by Parliament to the Scottish nation. L. J., V. 156.

Annexed :—
1. Order of the Commons of 4th Aug. 1641, referring the matter to the English Commissioners for
Scottish affairs. C. J., II. 234.
June 23. List of Committee on the Bill for the settlement of an hospital of Fitzwilliam Coniaby at Hereford,
and of lands for the payment of his debts. L. J., V.
156.
June 23. Deposition of Henry Willis respecting words
spoken against the Parliament by John Escott of Launceston. L. J., V. 156. In extenso.
June 23. Petition of Sir Robert Heath, one of the
justices of the Court of King's Bench, for further time
to answer the petition of Lord Balmerino respecting the
office of prothonotary of the court. See L. J., V. 156.
Annexed :—
1. Affidavit of Sir Robert Heath, that he is by the
King's special command attending His Majesty
at York, who will not give him leave to come
to London, saying he might have need of his
counsel. 17 June.
2. Copy of a petition of Sir Robert Heath. Lord
Balmerino is now properly barred in the matter
by the Statute of Limitations, and might long
ago if he had had just cause have proceeded at
common law against petitioner, who could have
produced witnesses, since dead, to have proved
his case. It has never been the custom of the
House to interfere in any matter in which the
parties could obtain relief in law, when there has
been no failure of justice. Petitioner is now by
the King's special command, attending on His
Majesty at York, and therefore unable to produce
the proofs of his case which are in London.
Prays the acceptance of this answer, and that
the complainant may be left to his remedy in
law or equity.
June 23. Affidavit of Lewis Carre, that he served
Sir Robert Heath at York, with a copy of Lord Balmerino's petition and their Lordships' order in the
cause.
June 23. Copy of the King's order to the Lord Mayor,
&c., of London, to publish His Majesty's proclamations.
(Latin.)
June 24. Certificate of Mr. Justice Foster in the
cause between Lord Viscount Loftus and Sir Philip
Mainwaring, that Sir Philip is ready to execute the
deeds of reconveyance of the trust estates, if he be
saved harmless against the heirs of Sir Robert Loftus.
L. J., V. 157.
June 24. Petition of Gabriel Thorp, a poor distressed
servant, now prisoner in the Gatehouse by their Lordships' order. Stands committed upon misinformation
given by Henry Fisher. Petitioner never laid any
claim to the messuages and lands in dispute between
Fisher and the Dean and Chapter of Christchurch,
Oxford ; he has never used any words disrespectful
towards Parliament ; has already laid thirty-six days in
prison, and prays their Lordships to accept bail, until
they have leisure to hear the cause. L. J., V. 157.
Annexed :—
1. Affidavit of Thorp in support of preceding.
2. Order to one of the clerks of the Upper House to
send for Thorp, and take his own bond for his
appearance when summoned.
June 24. Petition of the captains, officers, and soldiers of the trained bands, and volunteers of the county
of Bucks, assembled at Aylesbury, June the·17th, praying for the appointment of ·a Lord Lieutenant in whom
they can confide. L. J., V. 159. In extenso.
June 24. Draft order for the issuing out of ordnance
for Ireland. L. J., V. 159. ·In extenso.
June 24. A list of such ordnance, ammunition, arms,
and necessaries, as are requisite for the train of artillery
to be sent into Ireland. L. J., V. 159. In extenso.
June 24. Letter from Mr. Alexander Rigby, at Manchester, to the Speaker of the House of Commons. On
the 20th about 5,000 persons met on Preston Moor at the
summons of the high sheriff, Sir John Girlington, who
was accompanied by Lord Strange and others, and who
read to the people the Commission of Array, and the
King's two last declarations, &c., but refused to read the
declarations of Parliament, or to deliver up the Commission of Array ; before the reading was ended the multitude, except about 700, went away ; the writer and
Mr. Shuttleworth, another deputy lieutenant, called
upon the sheriff to forbear the execution of the Commission of Array, but the sheriff and others cried out,
" All that are for the King follow us," and followed by
about 400 persons rode up and down the moor crying
out for the King, when the writer and Mr. Shuttleworth

explained the instructions of Parliament to those that
remained. They have heard that some powder was
secretly removed from Preston, but the quantity was
not large enough to justify them in seizing it by force.
They think that their conduct at Preston Moor tended
to the peace of the kingdom, but considering the
number and position of those opposed to them, they
pray for further support from Parliament. This letter
was read in the House on the 27th. L. J., V. 166.
June 24. Letter from Sir William Brereton, at Chester, to the Speaker of the House of Commons : since his
coming into these parts he has distributed the deputations, and instructions to the several deputy lieutenants,
and appointed them to meet on Monday next ; meantime
hears that the King is expected shortly ; that he has
issued a Commission of Array to Lord Strange and others,
which they will attempt to put in execution at the same
time as the ordinance for the militia ; desires more ample
instructions, as any attempt to apprehend persons persisting after warning in executing the Commission of
Array, cannot be effected without violence, which once
begun may not be easily composed, and cannot easily
be made good whilst the powder is in the hands of the
other side ; he will use his best endeavours for Parliament. This letter was read in the House on the 27th
of June. L. J., V. 167.
June 24. Letter from the Lords Justices and Council in
Ireland to the Speaker of the House of Lords, in answer
to their Lordships' order that Lord Cromwell, and others,
should appear before the Committee for Petitions on the
1st of July, to answer the petition of Henry Stewart and
James Gray, complaining of a sentence given in the
Court of Castle Chamber in Ireland. They state that
the persons complained of are almost all Privy Councillors, and were only doing their duty (for there is no
imputation of corruption) ; that the sentence was just
and necessary at the time it was made ; and that to
recognise such a complaint would cause great inconvenience in Ireland, and would infringe the privileges
of the Irish Parliament. L. J., V. 227. This letter is
almost identical with one of the 30th of July 1641. See
Calendar of that date.
June 24. Copy of preceding.
June 25. Petition of Benjamin Newland ; the ordnance
in.dispute between petitioner and Joseph Hawes was
mortgaged to petitioner long before Hawes made claim
to it, while his charge that petitioner is contriving with
the Spanish Ambassador to send the ordnance beyond
seas is untrue ; petitioner would have obtained a prohibition from the Court of Common Pleas preventing
the Court of Admiralty, an improper place for this trial,
from proceeding in the matter, had it not been for their
Lordships' order, and he now prays that he and Hawes
may be left to try the question at Common law. L. J.,
V. 160.
Annexed :—
1. Copy of order of Court of Common Pleas in the
cause.
June 25. Motion of the King's counsel that one Walker,
a prisoner in the Tower by order of the House, may be removed to Newgate, and that counsel may proceed against
him by indictment there, as the author and publisher
of a seditious libel against the peace. L. J., V. 160.
June 25. Petition of Richard Harding, gent., servant
to the Earl of Nottingham ; has been violently arrested
by William Dormer one of the Marshal's officers and
kept in custody though he produced his protection, and
though Mr. Browne, the clerk of the Parliaments, told
Dormer that he had received a letter from the Earl of
Nottingham certifying that petitioner was his servant,
and employed on his affairs ; prays for release on the
ground of privilege. L. J., V. 163.
Annexed :—
1. Petition of William Tull, Francis Adderley, and
John Barker ; Richard Harding, when arrested
for debt, pretended to have a protection from the
Earl of Nottingham, but could not produce it ; at
the time of the arrest he attempted to rescue
himself and so seriously wounded petitioner Tull
in the hand, that he cannot work at his craft ;
pray that Harding may be compelled to relinquish
his protection that petitioners may proceed against
him at law.
2. Petition of same to Robert Earl of Essex, praying
him to speed the reading of their petition before
the House.
June 25. Four drafts of the order of the Commons
for payment of arrears to the commanders in the North.
C. J., II. 640. In extenso.
June 25. Answer of William Bishop of Cork and Ross,
concerning the censure of Mr. Henry Stewart in the

Star Chamber in Ireland; defendant knew not where the Star Chamber of either kingdom stood, or the oath urged, or Mr. Henry Stewart, nor had any thought of intermeddling in anything of that nature, till about six o'clock overnight he received a peremptory command from the Lord Lieutenant to speak at nine o'clock the next morning in the cause, with a printed copy of the oath refused by Stewart; this command and other like expressions auguring the Lord Lieutenant's disaffection towards the defendant restrained him from daring to absent himself when so commanded; he conceives the Bishops were only to speak on the lawfulness of a promissory oath, and of that then urged, and not to censure, and this was all that he did.

June 25. Copy of warrant from the King to Mr. Henry Hastings, thanking him for his activity in the Commission of Array, declaring the opposition of the Earl of Stamford thereto to be treason, and authorising the Commissioners of Array to apprehend the Earl, and all arms, &c. intended for the supply of his followers.

June 25. Petition of James Wade and John Wentworth, Esquires : John Harwood and others make a practice of enticing young men of fortune, when they first come to town, selling them goods at exorbitant rates, inducing them to convey their lands upon secret trusts upon promise of easy redemption, and in other ways enrich themselves in an iniquitous manner, to the ruin of petitioners, and the great danger of all inexperienced young men ; pray for relief and for an example to be made of these evildoers.

[June 25.] Letter from Ralph Ashton, John Moore, and Alexander Rigby, at Manchester, to the Speaker of the House of Commons : the high sheriff of Lancashire having surprised the powder at Preston, they took immediate measures for securing that at Manchester, and succeeded in so doing, thereupon Lord Strange, who on Monday had seized a great quantity of powder at Liverpool, repaired to Bury with such a number of armed followers, that all the townsmen of Manchester put themselves in a posture of defence under the writers, and other deputy lieutenants, when, in order to prevent bloodshed, though the stronger party, they proposed some terms for surrender of the powder, which, however, came to nothing. Yesterday Lord Strange dismissed most of his followers, so the writers did the same; this morning they hear of new proclamations sent from York against their proceedings, and rumours that the King is coming with large forces. They have discovered a foul design from an intercepted letter, sent from Sir Edward Fitton, of Gawsworth, in Cheshire, to Sir Thomas Aston, which they have inclosed. Sir Edward came yesterday, and very uncivilly demanded the letter, and he and others threaten them for seizing it, while the high sheriff is always ready to oppose them, and an insurrection of malignant persons is daily to be expected, to prevent which they desire speedy assistance. This letter was read in the House on the 27th of June. L. J., V. 166.

Annexed :—

1. Letter from Sir Edward Fitton, at Gawsworth, to Sir Thomas Aston ; thanks him for his favour at York, and for his bringing him to kiss the hand of His Majesty, for whom he is ready to spend his life and fortune ; he and his fellow commissioners have met about the gathering of the subsidies, and have appointed collectors ; if there be any doubt about the money going the true way, he will do his utmost to stop it for His Majesty, if His Majesty will send him a commission for that purpose. Hears that Sir William Brereton will be at Chester on Saturday to settle the militia for the Parliament; he is so near his decoy that he may send out his ducks every way to fetch in others; feels sure that the major part of the hundred of Macclesfield will stand right; desires a brief answer by bearer. This letter was also read in the House on the 27th of June. L. J., V. 166.

June 27. Copy of the votes of both Houses concerning the canons made by the synod. These votes were made on the 12th June 1641 (L. J., IV. 273. *In extenso*), but were ordered to be printed and published this day. L. J., V. 163.

June 27. Petition of Edmond Harrington and Elizabeth his wife, Giles Johnson and Grace his wife, and Thomas Marshall and Anne his wife: petitioners' suit against Robert Taylcot was referred to Lord Stamford and others; Taylcot is dead, and his son Thomas, who now holds the property in question, refuses to appear before the referees on the ground that he has not been made a party ; pray that the order of reference may be revived against Thomas Taylcot. L. J., V. 164.

June 27. Draft order for Sir John Girlington, Sir George Middleton, and Sir Edward Fitton to be sent for as delinquents. L. J., V. 166. *In extenso*.

June 27. Resolutions respecting the surrender of Galway to the Earl of Clanrickard and St. Alban's. L. J., V. 166. *In extenso*.

June 27. Resolutions of the Commons that, when the town of Galway was in open rebellion, as appears by letters of the Lords Justices, by a declaration from Captain Willoughby, Governor of the fort, and by letters of the Earl of St. Alban's to the Lords Justices, the Earl of St. Alban's entered into treaty with the town, when the town in the name of the corporation and gentry presented seven propositions, the effect of which was, that they should have freedom of religion, be pardoned for all that was past, and be protected for the time to come in their lives, liberties, goods, and chattels, and so for all that should submit thereafter ; that the Earl of St. Alban's granted a protection accordingly until His Majesty's pleasure should be declared; that the House of Commons conceives this protection to be destructive of the Protestant religion, dishonourable to the Crown of England, and subversive of the Act for the speedy and effectual reducing the rebels of Ireland. These resolutions, with others on the same subject, were agreed to by the Lords this day. L. J., V. 167. *In extenso* :—

1. Letter from the Lords Justices of Ireland at Dublin Castle to the Lord Lieutenant. After the defection of Galway the rebels laid siege to the King's fort there, whilst the Earl of St. Alban's gave the place all the assistance he could ; by letters of the 19th of April we informed him that we doubted not soon to send forces enough to make the rebels repent their disloyalty, and finding by his letters of the 25th of April last that the rebels were treating for submission, we warned him not to engage himself by promising anything, but that they should be left in a condition to be dealt with according to His Majesty's justice ; but these letters were burnt by the messenger, when was intercepted by the rebels, and in any case they could not have reached the Earl in time to prevent the submission, for by letter of the 18th of May the Earl informed us that the Mayor of Galway made his public submission and delivered up the keys, that the young men laid down their arms, and that upon promise of their future loyalty, he then received them into His Majesty's protection until His Majesty's pleasure were further declared. The particulars of these proceedings will be found in the enclosed papers. We conceive the protection to be only till the King's pleasure be declared in Ireland or elsewhere. We wish that the Earl had provided that all arms and ammunition should have been put into the fort, and not left in the hands of the rebels ; that a garrison should have been placed in the town, and the hostages secured in the fort. We say this not to blame the Earl, but to acquit ourselves of any negligence, for we consider that the protection should only have been granted until our pleasure were known; but as the Earl has hitherto done good service against the rebels, and was, as it may seem from his letters, necessitated to grant those terms, we have not repudiated them, though we consider them destructive of the authority and honour of the Crown ; especially in the case of Galway, a harbour which lies open to Spain and France, and is the principal conduit of good or evil to the whole province of Connaught, and many other counties adjoining, and which might now be secured by placing a number of English there instead of the rebels. 9 June 1642.

2. Copy of the " Propositions made by the Right " Hon. Ullick, of Clanrickard and St. Alban's, " Lieutenant Governor for the county and the " town of Galway, and Captain Willoughby, " and consented unto by the town of Galway." 6 May 1642.

3. Copy of the submission of Galway. 6 May 1642.

4. Copy of the seven propositions made by the town of Galway, and of the protection granted to the inhabitants. 11 May 1642.

5. Copy of "Captain Willoughby's declaration of " the carriage of the town of Galway from the " 23rd of Feb. 1641-2." About that time a ship from St. Malo came with powder and arms, when the townsmen boarded her, and though

called back by a great shot from the fort, brought the goods on shore uncustomed. The next day came a ship from Rochelle, under Captain Clark, when the same thing happened, and when Captain Willoughby would have interfered the town gates were shut, and all egress or regress refused to the English, some of whom were kept prisoners in the town, and allowed to suffer the extremity of want. Meantime, intending revolt, the townsmen got up a declaration setting forth the loyalty of the town which by fraud or force they induced the English to sign, and this they intended to forward to the state, in order to prevent any forces or supplies being sent to the English. On the 19th of March they surprised Clark's ship, murdering two of the crew, after which they disarmed all the English and Protestants in the town, and suffered so many rogues of "Er Co-"naght" to be about, that the English were robbed and stripped at their very gates without interference; they kept much of the provision of the fort in the town, and yet made pretence of giving it up. On the 31st of March they sent for the rebels of the country under Sir Valentine Blake, and besieged the fort and used the town bell, usually rung when the gates were opened, to warn the rebels of any sally from the fort. On the 20th of April came a ship from France with powder and arms, which exchanged shots with an English pinnace which came two days after, upon which the townsmen also fired and raised a bulwark between the fort and the sea, from which they afterwards fired upon a boat coming from Captain Ashley's ship. 11 May 1642.

6. Copy of Captain Anthony Willoughby's letter to the Lords Justices. After thanking them for the timely assistance sent by Captain Ashley, he gives some account of the straits he and his small garrison had passed through, of the great support afforded him by the Earl of Clanrickard, and of his reasons for thinking the submission of the townsmen was not to be trusted; earnestly desires that further assistance may be sent, for certainly nothing will confirm the loyalty of the men of Galway but a good English army. 12 May 1642.

7. Copy of the Earl of Clanrickard's order to Nicholas More Linch, Alderman of Galway, to search for and take possession of all powder in the town. 14 May 1642.

8. Copy of letter from the Earl of Clanrickarde and St. Alban's to the Lords [Justices], reporting the surrender of the town of Galway, the state of feeling there, and the names of those who had done loyal service. 18 May 1642.

June 27. Message from the Commons, with resolutions respecting Sir Edward Fitton, &c. C. J., II. 642. *In extenso.*

June 27. Petition of parishioners of St. Mary Magdalen, Canterbury. Their parson, John Marston, a man of scandalous life, is known to persuade people to have an ill opinion of Parliament, and has caused many persons to forsake the church; pray that he may be removed, and an honest and sufficient man put in his place.

Annexed:—

1. Letter from William Bridge and others at Canterbury to Mr. Thomas Denn, at his chamber in Tanfield Court, in the Inner Temple. Besides all the former malignant practices of John Marston, their parson, he on last Lord's day in the afternoon read to all the congregation in the church His Majesty's answer to the declaration of the Lords and Commons; and when he had finished he said, I know some will question me what authority I had to publish this book, but I shall answer it well enough. Then he said, Here are a roll of books sent down to be read by the constable, which will take five or six hours to read (whereas when read they only took one hour and a half), but those who will not stay to bear them may depart. Whereupon some departed. When he had thus put the people off from hearing the books sent from the Parliament read, he exhorted them to take their Bibles and see if they could find any warrant for taking up arms against the King. P.S.—There are such divisions grown up between us and those that take his part, that we can hardly look one upon another in charity. 28 June 1642.

2. Affidavit of Thomas Bridge against John Marston for speaking scandalous words against Parliament. 24 June. L.J., V. 221. *In extenso.*

3. Affidavit of John Francklyn to the same effect. (Undated.)

June 28. Copy of order of both Houses to the Lord Mayor not to publish anything without acquainting Parliament. L. J., V. 168. *In extenso.*

June 28. Order for Captain Mayer's ship to stay at Hull, and for merchant ships to be hired to bring away the magazine. L. J., V. 168. *In extenso.*

June 28. Petition of Herbert Finch, common crier and serjeant-at-arms in the city of London. Was committed to the Gatehouse for proclaiming a proclamation concerning the militia. A former petition of petitioner for release was refused because the Lord Mayor, by whose order petitioner published the proclamation, had not been examined. This has now been done, and petitioner expressing sorrow for his offence prays for discharge. L. J., V. 168.

June 28. Petition of James Halsall, servant to Thomas Worseley, clerk of the papers in Wood Street Compter, committed to the Gatehouse for reading the proclamation concerning the militia. Similar to preceding. L. J., V. 168.

June 28. Petition of Edward Watkins and Thomas Alewey, Esqs. Petitioners are searchers of the port of London, with the members and creeks thereto belonging. Gravesend has been a member of the port of London for 300 years. About nine years ago Richard Ward and others procured a subsequent grant of the place at Gravesend, and have ever since molested petitioners by unjust suits and proceedings. Pray that the case may be heard at the bar, or referred to the judges of the King's Bench. L. J., V. 168.

June 28. Copy of a warrant from the King to Captain Phineas Pett, now at Chatham, or to any of the officers of the navy there, informing them that he has appointed Sir John Pennington to be Lord High Admiral of the Fleet in the room of the Earl of Northumberland, and directing them to send the standard and all necessaries for the fleet, as Sir John shall direct. *See* L. J., V. 179.

June 29. Copy of the King's warrant to Lord Mohun not to depart out of the county of Cornwall, but to keep himself ready to attend His Majesty's command. *See* L. J., V. 271.

June 30. Petition of John Lake and others. Having suffered imprisonment and extortion at the hands of various persons, petitioners brought actions against them, but these suits were stayed by an order of the House of 17th of March 1640–1 as detrimental to the Prince His Highness. This is not, in fact, the case, and petitioners pray that their suits may be referred to the Prince's attorney, that he may decide the point, that so they may have leave to proceed in law. L. J., V. 168.

June 30. Petition of the mayor and aldermen of the town of Colchester. A petition of Freshfield to the House was dismissed, when it was found that the matters in dispute were being tried in Chancery, and were ready for hearing there, but on the 31st of May last, in consequence of the absence of the Lord Keeper, the whole matter was referred to Mr. Justice Reeve, but as the petitioners were no parties to the suit in Chancery, and could not therefore under the order of reference appear before Mr. Justice Reeve, an order was made by consent that Freshfield should exhibit his bill de novo in Chancery, and make the petitioners parties, that they should at once answer and the cause be forthwith heard before Mr. Justice Reeve, whose decision should be final. Freshfield now refuses to abide by this order, and on the 16th instant presented a petition stating that Mr. Justice Reeve could not proceed, as he had no power to examine witnesses on oath. On this an order was made that the witnesses should be sworn in the House, and Mr. Justice Reeve be certified thereof, but he says that he cannot examine on such an oath except their Lordships be present, in regard all witnesses, as he alleges, were always examined before their Lordships, the judges being present. Pray for further directions, and for a determination of the matter which concerns all the magistrates of the corporation.

Annexed:—

1. Copy of order dismissing the cause to Chancery. 30 April 1642.

2. Copy of order referring the cause to Mr. Justice Reeve. 31 May 1642.

3. Copy of order for the witnesses to be sworn in the House. 16 June 1642.

4. Copy of the order by consent.

E

June 30. Draft order for payment of 5,030*l.* to the garrison at Portsmouth. L. J., V. 169. *In extenso.*

June 30. Affidavit of John Loftus, that he repaired to the lodgings of Sir Philip Mainwaring, and there learned that Sir Philip had gone out of town the Friday before. *See* L. J.. V. 169.

June 30, Letter from Francis Anderson, sheriff of Newcastle, to Mr. John Rushworth, at his chambers in Lincoln's Inn. The Lords of the Council of Scotland sent nine prisoners to Berwick, with a warrant for their conveyance to London. The Mayor of Berwick sent them to the High Sheriff of Northumberland, and he to the writer, who is forced to keep them to the great charge of the county, for the Sheriff of the bishopric of Durham refuses to receive them. The writer desires that the House of Commons may be informed, and order made for the Sheriff of the bishopric to receive the prisoners.

Annexed :—

1. Copy of letter from the Lords of the Council in Scotland to the Mayor of Berwick, sent with certain Irish prisoners, mentioned in preceding. 14 June 1642.

June 30. Petition of Thomas Batt, Thomas Frere, and William Leeke. One Robert Robins, by leave of the House, arrested William Jackson, who pretended to have a peer's protection, and who owed petitioners 4,000*l.*, whereupon Jackson petitioned the House to be relieved from the debt, but being left to the law petitioners laid process upon him. Jackson is now seeking to be discharged under his protection. Petitioners pray that they may be heard by counsel before his discharge is granted. Noted, Read, nothing done upon it. *See* L. J., V. 139.

Annexed :—

1. Similar petition of same. (Undated.)

[June 30.] Petition of Francis Poulton. George Benyon, lately adjudged to be imprisoned at Colchester (see L. J., V. 168), is a principal witness in the cause between petitioner and Lucy Lady Hastings. Prays that Benyon's examination may be taken before he is sent down to Colchester.

[June.] Draft order of the Commons for Sir Ambrose Browne and others to send up speedily all plate and money gathered in their several divisions. Year uncertain.

[June.] Draft message from the Commons desiring the Lords to expedite the instructions for the committee in Lincolnshire, &c. Year uncertain.

[June.] Two copies of petitions of Levant merchants for remission of customs. Year uncertain.

July 1. Abstract of some letters sent from Newcastle, dated the 22d and 23rd of June 1642. L. J., V. 170. *In extenso.*

Annexed :—

1. Copy of the Earl of Newcastle's warrant for raising the Durham militia to garrison Newcastle. L. J., V. 170. *In extenso.*
2. Reasons against bringing soldiers into Newcastle, &c., &c. (Three papers.) L. J., V 170. *In extenso.*

July 1. Declaration and resolution of the deputy lieutenants, colonels, captains, and officers, assented unto, and with great cheerfulness approved of by the soldiers of the trained bands within the county of Southampton, at the general musters begun the 21st day of this instant June, being to the number of above 5,000 men, besides a great many volunteers who then offered to serve in person. L. J., V. 172. *In extenso.*

July 1. Petition of the mayor and others of the town and county of Nottingham, to H. C., praying that measures may be taken for the security of the town and magazine there. L. J., V. 173. *In extenso.*

July 1. Petition of inhabitants of Watford, in the county of Hertford, to H. C. L. J., V. 173. *In extenso.*

Annexed :—

1. Propositions humbly offered by the petitioners. L. J., V. 173. *In extenso.*

July 1. Draft order upon preceding petition. L. J., V. 174. *In extenso.*

July 1. Message from the Commons, with an explanation to the propositions for raising of money and plate and horse, and some additions and instructions. L. J., V. 172, 175.

July 1. Draft order calling out the militia of Nottinghamshire. L. J., V. 173. *In extenso.*

July 1. Three draft orders for the Common Council of London to provide a place for the arms and ammunition brought from Hull. L. J., V. 174. *In extenso.*

July 1. Three drafts of the ordinance of Parliament conferring the chief command of the fleet upon the Earl of Warwick, the Earl of Northumberland having been

discharged by the King from being Lord High Admiral. L. J., V. 174. *In extenso.*

July 1. Draft order of the Commons for the payment of arrears due to Lieutenant Colonel Thomas Kirke. C. J., II. 647. *In extenso.*

July 2. Letter from Captain Jo. Burley to the Earl of Warwick. L. J., V. 179. *In extenso.*

July 3. Letter from Captain Robert Slingsby to the Earl of Warwick. Has been in hopes to receive some propositions whereby he might legally, and without breach of his allegiance, discharge himself of his ship. Has not yet heard that either His Majesty or the Parliament have declared any difference between themselves, and yet their several commands are directly opposite. Calls God to witness that his only desire is to do that which is just towards the King and the law of the land. If his Majesty will be pleased to join with the Parliament in their ordinance no man will obey his Lordship with greater alacrity than the writer, who will be ready to deliver up his ship to whomsoever His Majesty shall appoint. Would be contented, since his commission ceased with the Earl of Northumberland's, to deliver up the ship to the principal officers of the navy, whose commissions are derived from the King and are not disavowed by the Parliament; this may be readily done as Sir Henry Palmer is now here. Beseeches that those who serve in the ship, and whose conscience will not permit them to serve contrary to His Majesty's commands, may be discharged and paid at their departure, according to ancient custom, for the time they have served. Prays pardon for some roughness, which the incivility of those employed by his Lordship compelled the writer to, as he did not think fit to let every man that came on board use his own language. But there is nothing that the writer has received from his Lordship that he has not communicated to his men, particularly the last paper, directing the master and the rest of the men to turn the writer out of his ship. To show what confidence he has in this master, he has employed him to be the bearer of this letter. There is nothing he desires more than to serve his Lordship without breach of his allegiance to the King. At the end of this letter Captain Baldwin Wake adds that he has seen and perused Captain Slingsby's letter, and approves of each proposition in it. *See* L. J., V. 179, &c.

July 4. Order for the Lord Chief Justice of the King's Bench to examine Edmund Muschamp, prisoner in the Gatehouse, touching words spoken by him against the Earl of Northumberland. L. J., V. 176.

July 4. Declaration and protestation of divers of the knights, gentry, freeholders, and others of the counties of Lincoln and Lincolnshire, to Francis Lord Willoughby, Lord Lieutenant; in consequence of a malignant party endeavouring to breed jealousies between the King and his people, they are forced to express their desire and resolution to spend their lives and estates in defence of His Majesty's person, the true protestant religion, the peace of the realm, the maintenance of the rights and privileges of Parliament, the laws of the land, and the lawful liberties of the subject according to their late protestation against all those that attempt to separate His Majesty from Parliament, and to alienate his affection from his subjects. This document, which is numerously signed, is described in the Journal as a petition directed to the Lord Willoughby of Parham, and brought in by him from the county of Lincoln, when the thanks of the House were directed to be sent in a letter from the Speaker to the petitioners. L. J., V. 177.

July 4. Draft of various resolutions concerning the Earl of Warwick, &c. L. J., V. 178. *In extenso.*

July 4. Report of words spoken by Mr. William Elliott against the Parliament. L. J., V. 180. *In extenso.*

July 4. Report of scandalous words spoken by Mr. Windebank, senior, against Mr. Pym. L. J., V. 181. *In extenso.*

July 4. Letter from the Earl of Warwick to Mr. Pym, concerning the command of the fleet. L. J., V. 185. *In extenso.*

July 4. [   ] at Rotterdam, to Myles Corbett, Esquire. Details the preparations being made in Holland for transporting the Princes Rupert and Maurice, the Lords Danby and Digby, Sir Lewis Dives, and others, together with horses and arms, from Rotterdam to the Northern parts. This is no doubt a similar letter to that referred to the Journals of the House of Commons (see Vol II., 646), as the writer commences by stating that he has sent another letter to the same effect by a different hand. The signature is erased and the writer not named in the Journals, but referred to as "a private gentleman who wishes well to his country." See L. J., V. 171.

July 4. Order of the Commons for officers to be sent into Leicestershire to assist in putting the militia in execution. C. J., II. 649. *In extenso.*

July 4. Copy of order for the lord lieutenants and deputy lieutenants of different counties to assist one another upon occasions. C. J., II. 649. *In extenso.*

July 5. Petition of Elinor Winter, a poor distressed widow, praying for relief; her late husband, William Winter, a minister of God's word in Ireland, was despoiled of all his goods, and afterwards slain by the rebels. L. J., V. 181.
Annexed :—
1. Letter from Hen. Jones to [   ]. The name of petitioner was wrongly entered in the schedule as Devereux, instead of Winter.

July 5. Petition of the distressed ministers of Ireland. Pray for relief, as they have been despoiled of all their temporal and spiritual estates, and having a great charge of wives and children know not how to subsist. Endorsed. 5l. a piece, amounting to 50l. L. J., V. 181.

July 5. Draft order for the payment of 10,000l. to Mr. Loftus, Deputy Treasurer at War for the affairs of Ireland. L. J., V. 181. *In extenso.*

July 5. Another draft.

July 5. Draft message from the Commons, touching the impeachment of Sir Richard Gurney, Lord Mayor of London. L. J., V. 182.

July 5. Letter from the Committee at Hull to the Speaker of the House of Commons, respecting the arrival of the ship " Providence," from Holland, laden with powder and other ammunition. L. J., V. 182. *In extenso.*

July 5. Draft letter from the Speaker of the House of Lords to the Earl of Exeter, thanking him for his offer of 500l. for the raising of horse, &c. L. J., V. 185. *In extenso.*

July 5. Petition of the mayor, aldermen, assistants, common council, and free burgesses of Colchester, praying that the suit between them and Richard Freshfield may be dismissed. L. J., V. 182.
Annexed :—
1. Previous order in the cause. 30 April 1642.
2. Copy of order referring the matter to Mr. Justice Reeve, noted by him, appointing a day for hearing. 15 June 1642.
3. Copy of order referring the matter to a committee. 30 June 1642.

July 5. Letter from Secretary Nicholas, at York, to the Earl of Leicester, Lord Lieutenant of Ireland. Eugenio O'Neale is going for Ireland with 500 pair of arms. Your Lordship can well put in present exercise what may be most requisite to intercept this O'Neale. See L. J., V. 191.

July 5. Petition of Sara Richards. Petitioner's husband, Thomas Richards, servant and solicitor to the Lord Dudley, has been arrested by John Low, contrary to privilege. Prays for his discharge. See L. J., V. 184.
Annexed :—
1. Copy of certificate of Lord Dudley that Richards was his servant.

July 5. Draft order of the Commons, appointing days for putting the ordinance for the militia in execution. C. J., II. 654.

July 6. Petition of Ezechiel Johnson, clerk, praying that the Archbishop of Canterbury, Sir Nathaniel Brent, and others, may be called upon to answer for disobeying their Lordships' order, whereby petitioner was to have enjoyed the quiet possession of the parsonage of Paulerspury. L. J., V. 185.

July 6. Another petition of same to the like effect.

July 6. Message from the Commons, with two orders, for sending further assistance to Hull. L. J., V. 186. *In extenso.*

July 6. Four drafts of the ordinance for raising 2,000 men for the defence of Hull. L. J., V. 187. *In extenso.*

July 6. Petition of Thomas Wiseman, prisoner in the Fleet. Is heartily sorry for his offence and prays for his discharge. The petition does not mention the cause of his committal, but he appears by the Journals to have been concerned in the publication of proclamations respecting the militia. L. J., V. 187.
Annexed :—
1. Another petition of same to the like effect. (Undated.)

July 6. Copy of the letter from the Speaker of the House of Lords to the King, returning a letter from the King to the Queen, taken, with other papers, from Mr. Ashburnham. L. J., V. 187. *In extenso.*

July 6. Copy of petition of the deputy lieutenants, captains, officers, and soldiers of the trained bands, and volunteers of the county of Warwick, to Robert Lord Brooke, Lord Lieutenant of the county. L. J., V. 187. *In extenso.*

July 6. Draft of commission for captains in the newly raised forces for Hull. L. J., V. 188. *In extenso.*

July 6. The King's warrant to the Lord Mayor, &c. of London to publish His Majesty's " proclamation against " the forcible seizing or removing any of the magazine " or ammunition of any county. And concerning the " execution of the militia within this kingdom." See L. J., V. 227.
Annexed :—
Eighteen printed copies of the proclamation. Rushworth, Vol. I., Part III., p. 670. *In extenso.*

July 6. Examination of John Roper, boatswain's mate of H.M. ship "Guardland," taken before the Earl of Warwick, concerning the charges against Captain Slingsby. See L. J., V. 180, &c.
Annexed :—
1. Examination of John Herringam.
2. Report by Captain Harrison of a conversation with Captain Wake.
3. Deposition of Lieutenant Hugh Trefusis of the words spoken by Captain Wake when he was delivered into the custody of the Black Rod.
4. Examination of Roger Beale concerning Captain Wake.
5. Examination of Thomas Cooke, boatswain of the " Guardland."
6. Another deposition of John Roper.

July 6. Receipt to Mr. Justice Malet for sixteen parcels of writings, touching the Lord Maguire, Hugh MacMahun, and Lieutenant Colonel Reade, now prisoners in the Tower. (Unsigned.) See L. J., V. 182.

July 6. Draft order of the Commons, respecting Sir William Fenton. C. J., II. 656. *In extenso.*

July 6. Draft order for the stay of all proceedings against Tristram Whitcombe, Esquire, sovereign of Kinsale, indicted of treason by some ill-disposed persons in the city of Cork. C. J., II. 655. *In extenso.*
Annexed :—
1. Amendments proposed by the Lords to preceding order. See L. J., V.190.

July 7. Order conferring the command of the fleet upon the Earl of Warwick. L. J., V. 188. *In extenso.*

July 7. Copy of preceding.

July 7. Draft order for payment of 100l. for the education of two sons of the late Lord Cawfield, who was cruelly murdered during the rebellion in Ireland. L. J., V. 188. *In extenso.*

July 7. Order for the payment of 1,000l. to the Earl of Warwick for the service of Landguard Fort. L. J., V. 189. *In extenso.*

July 7. Copy of preceding.

July 7. Petition of Captain John Poyntz; petitioner, being recommended out of Ireland for raising a company in England, took ship at Dublin and landed at Minehead. On his passage he seized upon the body of Roger, Bishop of St. David's in a disguised habit, and took him before Thomas Luttrell, who committed him to the custody of a constable of Minehead where he now remains. Petitioner who has been put to great charge in the matter prays some reward for the great services he has done not only against the rebels in Ireland, but also in the taking of the said bishop. L. J., V. 189.
Annexed :—
1. Examinations of Captain Poyntz and the Bishop of St. David's. Taken the 14th June 1642.
2. Petition of Captain Poyntz to the Earl of Holland, praying his Lordship to move the House to send for and examine the Bishop, and to take petitioner's services into their favourable consideration.

July 7. Draft list of Committee appointed to consider the ordinances sent from the Commons touching the proclaiming of the Earl of Stamford, &c. The list does not agree with that given in the Journals. L. J., V. 189.

July 7. Another draft.

July 7. Letter from the Earl of Warwick to the Speaker of the House of Lords with regard to the fleet. L. J., V. 194. *In extenso.*

July 7. Copy of the King's warrant to the principal officers of the navy commanding them not to obey the orders of the Parliament. L. J., V. 224. *In extenso.*

July 7. Petition of divers common councilmen of the city of London, to H. C.; complain of many abuses in the government of the city of London by the Lord Mayor, Sir Richard Gurney, and certain aldermen siding with him, and pray that speedy steps may be taken for the redress of the grievances complained of. C. J., II. 658.

July 7. Draft order of the Commons authorising the committee for the defence of the kingdom to issue arms and ammunition from the Tower and public magazines. C. J., II. 657. In extenso.

July 7. Two drafts of order indemnifying the Earl of Stamford and others for the removal of the magazine of the county of Leicester. C. J., II. 658. In extenso.

July 7. Two drafts of order indemnifying subjects for not attending the King. C. J., II. 658. In extenso.

July 7. Draft order for payment of the troops raised for Munster out of the subscriptions for reducing Ireland. C. J., II. 658.

July 8. Petition of William Gregorie, under sheriff of the county of Leicester. Has been in custody for ten days by order of the House, prays that he may be ordered forthwith to put in his answer, or be discharged upon bail. L. J., V. 190.

July 8. Articles of impeachment of Henry Hastings, Esquire, second son of the Earl of Huntington, Sir Richard Hawford, Knight and Baronet, Sir John Bale, Knight, and John Pate, Esquire, by the Commons assembled in Parliament for high crimes and misdemeanours by them committed. L. J., V. 191. In extenso.

July 8. Message from the Commons with divers votes concerning the county of Bucks, &c. L. J., V. 193.

July 8. Two orders concerning the forces in the county of Bucks. L. J., V. 193. In extenso.

July 8. Order for the customers of Boston and Lynn to allow provisions to be sent to Hull without interruption. C. J., II. 660. In extenso.

July 8. Order for 100 tuns of beer to be sent to Hull. L. J., V. 193. In extenso.

July 8. Order for the indemnity of the Ashford men. L. J., V. 193. In extenso.

July 8. Draft of preceding.

July 8. Petition of Sir Thomas Cary, that his suit against the Bishop of Ardagh may be referred to four members of the House. See L. J., V. 195.

Annexed:—

1. Copy of preceding.
2. Another petition of Sir T. Cary. Was committed by the House of Lords in Ireland for contempt in bringing his suit against the Bishop without leave of that House. Prays for redress. (Undated.)
3. Copy of the order of the House of Lords in Ireland for the sergeant-at-arms to attach Sir T. Cary for his contempt. 28 July 1641.

July 8. Copy of warrant to the Gentleman Usher for the arrest of Thomas Awbrey, Chancellor of St. David's, and others.

Annexed:—

1. Petition of Edward Vaughan, clerk; by an order of the 25th of August 1641 the temporalities of Dr. Manwaringe, Bishop of St. David's, were seized into the King's hands. The vicarage of Llangafelach, Glamorganshire, in the donation of the Bishop, having become vacant in November last, petitioner was presented thereunto by the Lord Keeper. Thomas Awbrey, chancellor of the diocese, having sole power of institution, utterly refused to institute petitioner, and by unlawful combination with Walter Thomas and others, admitted Isaac Griffith into the said church. Petitioner prays that he may be instituted to the vicarage, and that the parties complained of may be called upon to answer for their contempt.
2. Statement of petitioner's grievances.
3. Copy of order referred to in petition. 25 August 1641. L. J., IV. 376.
4. Affidavit of Vaughan that on the 21st of January last, he tendered a presentation to the vicarage under the great seal to Awbrey, and that he utterly refused to institute him. 9 May 1642.
5. List of persons to be sent for. 9 July 1642.

July 8. Draft order respecting the payment of the officers sent into Leicestershire. C. J., II. 660. In extenso.

July 9. Petition of Isabella Massey, widow, praying that Alderman Corney and Richard Nowdigate may be ordered not to dispose of certain mortgaged lands until

petitioner's suit against William Rolfe is decided. L. J., V. 195.

Annexed:—

1. Petition of William Rolfe, a distressed prisoner in the Fleet; praying that Isabella Massey may be ordered to answer his bill in Chancery. (Undated.)

July 9. Petition of Edmond Muschamp. Was committed by the House on Friday last to the Gatehouse upon an information of his having spoken against the Earl of Northumberland. Denies the accusation and prays for his discharge. L. J., V. 195.

Annexed:—

1. Certificate of the vicar and many inhabitants of St. Leonard's, Shoreditch, that Muschamp is a man of good repute and a constant frequenter of the church.

July 9. Petition of Mary Bagshawe and Margaret Wright. Thomas Bagshawe, petitioners' brother, was, by their Lordships' order of 16th of June 1641, ordered to put in such security for the payment of their portions (according to the will of their late father) as Elize Wooderofe should approve; this he refuses to do. Pray that the order may be put in force. L. J., V. 195.

Annexed:—

1. Affidavit of Margaret Wright that her brother Thomas has failed to perform the order. 31 May 1642.
2. Copy of order referred to. 16 June 1641. L. J., IV. 273. In extenso.
3. Certificate of Elize Wooderofe in the matter. (Undated.)
4. Petition of Margaret Wright, on behalf of herself and her sister Mary Bagshawe, to the Viscount Kimbolton, praying his Lordship to be a means that the petition, order, certificate, and affidavit remaining in the custody of Mr. Throckmorton may be read.
4. Breviat of petitioners' case.

July 9. Draft order respecting the payment of the officers sent into Leicestershire, L. J., V. 195. In extenso.

July 9. Petition of Henry Wollaston, keeper of His Majesty's gaol of Newgate. Edward Moore and Richard Mackmiller were by order of the House committed prisoners to Newgate in November last, and discharged in April. On account of their poverty petitioner was obliged to supply them with meat and drink, and they have now left without paying one penny. Prays that the sheriffs of London and Middlesex may be ordered to allow him the costs to which he has been put in the matter. L. J., V. 195.

Annexed:—

1. Another petition of same, that satisfaction may be assigned to him out of the Exchequer, as formerly hath been done to his predecessors. (Undated.)

July 9. Order upon preceding. L. J., V. 195.

July 9. Petition of Paul Bennett, praying for relief, having been despoiled of all his estate by the rebels in Ireland. L. J., V. 195.

July 9. Draft of the propositions from the Lords and Commons to the city of London for raising 10,000 men, &c. L. J., V. 196. In extenso.

July 9. Report of a meeting of the Common Council concerning the disposal of the arms and ammunition brought from Hull. L. J., V. 197. In extenso.

Annexed:—

1. Copy of order for the Common Council to meet to consider the subject. 1 July 1642. C. J., II. 645.

July 9. Copy of the King's warrant for the arrest of William Watson, Alderman, and Ames, one of the sheriffs of Lincoln, for putting in execution the ordinance of Parliament concerning the militia. L. J., V. 216. In extenso.

July 9. Draft order of the Commons for the Lords to be moved to join in an order for apprehending the Earls of Northampton, Coventry, and Devon, for putting Commissions of Array in execution in their several counties. C. J., II.,,662. In extenso.

July 9. Resolution respecting the buying of arms. C. J., II. 663. In extenso.

July 11. Draft orders to the treasurers of the navy to pay 1,500l. to the Earl of Warwick, &c. L. J., V. 198. In extenso.

July 11. Draft order respecting Languard Fort. L. J., V. 198.

July 11. Order for the indemnity of the mayor of Northampton for staying horses, &c. L. J., V. 198. In extenso.

July 11. Further articles of impeachment against Sir Richard Gurney, Lord Mayor of London. L. J., V. 198.

July 11. List of persons to be sent for touching the riot in Windsor Forest. *See* L. J., V. 199.

July 11. Application from Sir Richard Gurney, Lord Mayor, praying the House to dispose of Colonel Butler, as the Lord Mayor is now away from his own house. L. J., V. 200.

July 11. Petition of Lady Lucy Hastings. Her suit respecting the rectory of Pirton, Herts, has become abated by the death of Francis Foulton ; prays that it may be revived in the names of his heir and executors. L. J., V. 200.

July 11. Eales v. Covell. Draft order for the plaintiff to assign errors. L. J., V. 200.

Annexed :—
1. Affidavit of Job Edmonds that he served their Lordships' order for the plaintiff to assign errors upon the clerk to Mr. Peregrine Herbert, attorney in the cause. (Undated.)

July 11. Draft order for payment of 10,000*l.* to the Committee for the defence of the kingdom. L. J., V. 200. *In extenso.*

July 11. Instructions for the Lord Ruthin and Sir Arthur Haselrigg, committees of the House of Commons assembled in Parliament, appointed to go into Leicestershire. L. J., V. 202. *In extenso.*

July 11. Order concerning subscriptions in the county of Essex. L. J., V. 203. *In extenso.*

July 11. Warrant for the apprehension of Richard Worrall, high constable of Bucklow, for summoning the inhabitants of his hundred to appear in arms at Knutsford in opposition to the King's proclamation, and contrary to the warrants issued by the Commissioners of Array for the county of Chester. L. J., V. 204. *In extenso.*

July 11. The King's warrant to the Lord Mayor, &c. of London to publish His Majesty's " Proclamation " declaring our purpose to go in our Royal Person to " Hull and the true occasion and end thereof." *See* L. J., V. 227.

Annexed :—
Thirty-eight printed copies of the proclamation. Rushworth, Vol. I., Part III., 601. *In extenso.*

July 11. Petition of Clement Spelman, to H. C. for his discharge upon bail. C. J., II. 666.

July 11. Petition of Peter Ingram, clerk, that he may have leave to attend a trial at Northampton assizes on Wednesday next touching the rectory of Paulerspury, to which he has been lawfully instituted, but is opposed in by Ezekiel Johnson, who, knowing the weakness of his case, hath under a false pretence procured an order enjoining petitioner to attend the House, to prevent his being present at the trial.

July 11. Petition of John Estcott, of Launceston, Cornwall ; petitioner has come 200 miles to answer a false charge of speaking scandalous words against the Parliament ; prays that the matter may be inquired into or that he may be discharged upon bail. *See* L. J., V. 156, &c.

July 12. Propositions of the Lieutenant of the Tower concerning the Lord Mayor now in his custody. L. J., V. 204. *In extenso.*

July 12. Draft orders for the Earl of Warwick to go with the fleet to the assistance of Hull, and for Sir John Hotham to deliver up the magazine. L. J., V. 205. *In extenso.*

July 12. Draft order for Sir Edward Stradling and others to be sent up in safe custody. L. J., V. 205. *In extenso.*

July 12. Order for the Lords Lieutenant to appoint officers to the troops newly raised in the several counties. L. J., V. 205. *In extenso.*

July 12. Copy of preceding.

July 12. Draft of petition of Lords and Commons to the King to compose differences. Much amended. L. J., V. 206. *In extenso.*

July 12. Affidavits of John Grigg and John Mathew, that they served their Lordships' order of the 3d of June last upon the several persons called upon to answer the petition of Henry Stewart and others. *See* L. J., V. 102.

July 12. Letter from Sir John Hotham at Hull to Sir Philip Stapleton, or in his absence to Mr. Hampden or Mr. Pym. L. J., V. 217. *In extenso.*

July 12. Petition of the grand jury of the county of Worcester to the justices of the peace of the county ; pray that the ordinance for the militia may be put in execution.

July 13. Draft order for 5,030*l.* to be paid to the garrison of Portsmouth. L. J., V. 210. *In extenso.*

July 13. Petition of inhabitants of Bridport, to H. C.

The town is now very populous containing 2,000 souls, but has but one parish church and one minister, petitioners pray for an order for settling Mr. Robert Tuchin, a godly and able minister, whom they have procured at their own charge, to be their lecturer. C. J., II. 670.

July 14. Order against the billeting of soldiers upon the inhabitants of Kings Lynn and Great Yarmouth. L. J., V. 210. *In extenso.*

July 14. Copy of preceding.

July 14. The Lord Mayor's answer to the message of the House of Lords that he should appoint a deputy for the government of the city during his absence. L. J., V. 210.

July 14. Draft order for the court of aldermen of the city of London to choose a locum tenens, the Lord Mayor being restrained of his liberty. L. J., V. 210. *In extenso.*

July 14. Orders respecting the presentation of the petition of both Houses to the King. L. J., V. 211. *In extenso.*

July 14. Petition of William Hall, sword-bearer to the Lord Mayor of the city of London. Prays for his discharge, having been committed about 20 days since for publishing the King's proclamation, which he did by command of the Lord Mayor. L. J., V. 211.

Annexed :—
1. Another petition of same to the like effect. (Undated.)

July 14. Petition of Richard Cholmeley, John Senior, John Farthing, and others. Pray that Sir John Brampston, and the referees to whom the petition of William Tanner was referred by their Lordships, may be ordered to certify whether upon examination it appears to them that Tanner has been wronged or oppressed by petitioners.

Annexed :—
1. Petition of William Tanner the elder ; complains of the oppressions he has suffered at the hands of John Farthing and others, respecting a debt, and prays that they may be called upon to answer. 10 Dec. 1640.

2. Another petition of Tanner to the same effect. (Undated.)

3. Copy of order referring the matter to Sir John Brampston and others. 24 Dec. 1640.

4. Petition of Tanner ; complains that he was arrested at the suit of John Senior when attending to make good his case before the referees. Prays that Senior and others may be sent for to answer for their contempt.

5. Affidavit of William Tanner the younger touching the arrest of his father. 5 May 1642.

6. Copy of order for the attendance of Senior and others to answer for their contempt in arresting Tanner. 3 June 1642. L. J., V. 101.

7. Further affidavit of William Tanner the younger. 7 June 1642.

July 14. Petition of William Gwatkin, to H. C. Prays that William Hill and others may be sent for to answer for their contempt in seizing his goods under colour of a pretended writ notwithstanding his protection as servant to Mr. Speaker Lenthall. C. J., II. 671.

July 14. Letter from Sir William Widdrington at Newcastle to Serjeant Major [Sibthorp]. Missed Lord Grandison at York, but will write to him to-morrow.

July 15. Petition of Dame Elizabeth Slingsby. Complains that Sir Faithful Fortescue has failed to obey their Lordships' order made in March last, and that he is about to leave for Ireland. Prays that his departure may be restrained until he shall give petitioner assurances to comply with the said order. L. J., V. 212.

Annexed :—
1. Affidavit of Dame Elizabeth Slingsby that Sir Faithful Fortescue declines to obey the order.

July 15. Petition of Nicholas Todd, Richard Giles, and George Hayward. Petitioners were, by virtue of an order of their Lordships of the 13th of June last, attached for contempt, pretended to have been committed by them in entering certain enclosed marsh lands in the county of Norfolk. Pray that they may be released upon bail. L. J., V. 212.

July 15. List of Committee on the Bill against innovations in churches and chapels. L. J., V. 212.

July 15. Order for victualling the navy. L. J., V. 212. *In extenso.*

July 15. Draft of preceding.

July 15. Order appointing a time for the election of a locum tenens during the Lord Mayor's confinement. L. J., V. 213. *In extenso.*

July 15. Depositions of witnesses in the cause of

Robert Partridge against William Grange and others. See L. J., IV. 304.

July 15. Letter from Sir William Russell, Navy office, London, to the Earl of Warwick enclosing money for the navy. L. J., V. 223. *In extenso.*

July 16. Petition of Sir John Conyers, Lieutenant of the Tower of London. William Felgate has recently erected a house upon a piece of ground between the ditch of the Tower and the Inner Tower Hill where the scaffold stands. The house is of such a height that the battlements of the Tower have lost the view of a great part of Tower Hill and the scaffold, and are made unserviceable in case any opposition should arise on that hill against the Tower, and the Tower itself is exposed to great danger both of fire and shot from the new building. Prays that an order may be issued for demolishing the house. L. J., V. 213.

Annexed:—
1. Petition of William Felgate. The late King James granted a lease for fourscore years of certain waste lands about the Tower with liberty to build. Petitioner, having a lease of a portion of the said lands, in April last commenced to build a small tenement thereon. Complains of the oppressions he has suffered in consequence at the hands of Sir John Conyers, who has broken into his promises, pulled down a portion of his tenement, ill-used his workmen, and kept petitioner a prisoner in the Tower. Prays that he may be allowed to continue his buildings without further molestation. (Undated.)

July 16. Order for Inigo Jones, the King's surveyor, to view and report upon the house referred to in preceding. L. J., V. 213.

July 16. Order for the indemnity of the Gloucestershire volunteers. L. J., V. 214. *In extenso.*

July 16. Petition of Thomas Tallcott. On the 28th of June their Lordships ordered petitioner to appear on the 19th of this instant July to answer the petition of Edmond Harrington. Prays that a further day may be appointed as petitioner is now sick of small-pox, and cannot attend without danger of his life.

Annexed:—
1. Affidavit of Robert Tallcott, that Thomas Tallcott has recently lost his wife and one child by small-pox, and that he himself, six of his children, and three of his servants are now visited with the same disease. 13 July 1642.
2. Copy of order referred to in petition. 28 June 1642.
3. Order postponing the cause until the 2nd of August. 16 July 1642.
4. Affidavit of James Le Febure, practitioner in physic, that Thomas Tallcott is suffering from small-pox, and cannot travel without danger to himself, and to those to whom he may apply for the management of his business. 25 July 1642.

July 16. Application for an order for the suppression of a riot in certain lands, in the county of Hereford, enclosed by the Earl of Essex.

July 16. Petition of divers of the aldermen and others of the town of Shrewsbury, to H. C. Many volunteers of Shrewsbury having entered themselves to be exercised in military discipline under the command of Thomas Hunt, the high sheriff of the county sent for Hunt and persuaded him to desist from that exercise, and discouraged the inhabitants from further training. Pray that the mayor may be enjoined to encourage such exercises and to join with petitioners for the better guarding of the town by warding, watching, and providing the arms necessary for its defence. C. J., II. 675.

July 16. Draft order referring the petition of William Townsend to Sir Thomas Bowes and the Mayor of Colchester.

July 17. Copy of the Earl of Warwick's letter to the Speaker of the House of Lords, complaining that he is proclaimed a traitor for obeying the Parliament, and desiring a supply of victuals for the fleet. L. J., V. 216. *In extenso ;* and on the same paper—
i. Copy of a letter from the Earl, on board the "James" in the Downs, to the King. Has received His Majesty's letter of dismission, and with it an ordinance of Parliament for his continuance in the employment. Beseeches His Majesty to consider the great straits he is in between these two commands. Hopes His Majesty hath been always as well assured of his fidelity as of that of Sir John Pennington or any other, and begs that he may not be divided between two commands. 5 July 1642.
ii. Copy of the answer of Sir Edward Nicholas, at Newark, to preceding letter. Has presented his Lordships' letter to the King, who was nothing satisfied with it, and commands him to signify that his Majesty conceived that nothing could have induced his Lordship to commit treason. Is sorry to be a messenger of such an answer. 13 July 1642.
iii. Copy of a letter from Lieutenant Watts [Waters] to Captain Slingsby, intercepted by the Earl of Warwick, and forwarded by him to the] Parliament. 12 July 1642. L. J., V. 216. *In extenso.*

July 17. Petition of Peregrine Herbert and Edward Saul, the one a clerk and the other an officer of the Lord Mayor of London. Pray for their discharge, having been committed for proclaiming the King's Proclamation, which they only did as servants by command of the Lord Mayor. *See* L. J., V. 209.

July 18. Drafts of various orders concerning Hull, &c. L. J., V. 217. *In extenso.*

July 18. Affidavit of Richard Capman, that he served the order of impeachment upon Sir John Bale and others. L. J., V. 218. *In extenso.*

July 18. Letter from the Earl of Warwick to the Speaker of the House of Lords, sending up Captains Slingsby and Wake as delinquents. L. J., V. 218. *In extenso.*

July 18. Letter from the Earl of Warwick, aboard "the James" in the Downs, to [   ]. I have this day received a petition from the officers of our fleet, which I beg your Lordship to present to the Parliament. The poor men are utterly undone for want of their pay, and many of their wives and children thrown out of doors by their landlords. The captain of the "Garland" tells me he has but 14 days' beer. I pray you to be a means to the House of Commons to send us speedily some victuals, and also powder and necessaries. All is stopt unto us at Chatham.

July 18. Letter from the Earl of Holland, at Beverley, to the Speaker of the House of Lords, concerning the delivery of the petition to the King. L. J., V. 224. *In extenso.*

July 18. Petition of the clothiers of the West Riding of York ; the cloth made by petitioners, who are too poor to go forward with their trade unless their stock is bought up weekly, so as to enable them to pay their workmen, is usually bought up by merchants, who, three times in the year, at March, at Midsummer, and Michaelmas, ship the cloth away to Germany ; but now a ship ready to start with cloth for Hamburgh from Hull has been stayed by Sir John Hotham, on the ground that he cannot spare any men from the town ; pray for consideration. C. J., II. 678.

July 19. Petition of Colonel John Butler. Prays that an allowance may be granted him for his maintenance. L. J., V. 219.

Annexed:—
1. Another petition of same. Prays that he may be released and furnished with funds for his passage out of the kingdom. (Undated.)

July 19. Examination of Edmund Muschamp, of Hoggesdon, in the county of Middlesex, touching threats used by him against the Earl of Northumberland. L. J., V. 220. *In extenso.*

Annexed:—
1. Information of Olive, wife of William Royston, in the same matter. L. J., V. 220. *In extenso.*
2. Affidavits of Thomas Wright, William Granwell, and Richard Pen, that the deponent, Olive Boyston, is a woman of bad fame and of ill life and behaviour. 14 July 1642.

July 19. Order for 1,000l. to be paid to Sir John Clotworthy. L. J., V. 221. *In extenso.*

July 19. Order for 10,000l. to be impressed unto Mr. Loftus, Deputy Treasurer at War for Ireland. L. J., V. 221. *In extenso.*

July 19. Answer of Sir Richard Gurney, Knight and Bart., Lord Mayor of the city of London, to the second impeachment exhibited against him by the House of Commons. L. J., V. 221. *In extenso.*

July 19. Draft of a general order for the indemnity of all volunteers. C. J., II. 680. *In extenso.*

July 19. Report of Inigo Jones, the King's surveyor, upon the new house built by William Felgate, close to the Tower. The house hinders the prospect of the most part of the hill from the Tower, and may be a prejudice to the safety thereof, and an evil precedent for the raising higher of many mean houses in the neighbourhood. *See* L. J., V. 213.

July 19. The answer of William Poulton, son and heir, and of Henry and Francis Poulton, executors of the late Francis Poulton, to the petition of Lady Lucy Hastings. *See* L. J., V. 200, &c.

House of
Lords.
———
Calendar.
1642.

Annexed:—
1. Another answer of same. (Undated.)

July 19. Petition of Francis Yong, Esq. Was appointed keeper of one of the walks in Windsor Park by the Earl of Holland, Constable of Windsor Castle, and has held the office for some years. On Monday last Mr. Edward Tyringham, one of the gentlemen of His Majesty's Privy Chamber, demanded possession of the lodge and walk under pretence that His Majesty had granted it to him by Letters Patent under the Great Seal. Prays that Mr. Tyringham may be ordered not to disturb petitioner in the performance of his service until the return of the Earl of Holland, who is now absent in the service of the Parliament. See L. J., V. 238.

July 20. Petition of Sir Filibert Vernatti. Has been arrested under a writ ne exeat regno by their Lordships' order. Some of his friends have tendered security for his appearance when called upon. Prays that some reasonable sum may be appointed, and that he may have his liberty to prosecute his cause. L. J., V. 222.

Annexed:—
1. Certificate of Sir Wm. Middleton and others, that they tender themselves as sureties for Sir Filibert Vernatti. 19 July 1642.
2. Copy of writ ne exeat regno. 19 July 1642.

July 20. Draft of the judgment against the nine Lords who went to York. L. J., V. 222.

July 20. Order concerning the proposition for raising horse, &c., for Somersetshire. L. J., V. 226. In extenso.

July 20. Certificate of the aldermen of London, concerning the election of a locum tenens during the Lord Mayor's confinement. L. J., V. 229. In extenso.

July 20. List of persons who have visited the Lord Mayor in the Tower between the 12th and 20th of July.

July 21. Petition of Captain Robert Slingsby and Captain Baldwyn Wake. Were kept prisoners by the Earl of Warwick for 17 days, and are now brought up to their Lordships' house. Pray that they may be discharged or speedily called upon to answer. L. J., V. 228.

July 21. Orders concerning the newly raised troops. L. J., V. 228. In extenso.

July 21. Two copies of the order for forces to be sent to the relief of the Earl of Thomond in Ireland, &c. L. J., V. 228. In extenso.

July 21. Order for the indemnity of the Boston volunteers. L. J., V. 228. In extenso.

July 21. Order for the town of Poole to raise and train volunteers. L. J., V. 229. In extenso.

July 21. Order for 20l. to be paid to Sir Rowland St. John, for the relief of the poor from Ireland. L. J., V. 229. In extenso.

July 21. Letter from the Earl of Warwick, aboard "the James" in the Downs, to the Speaker of the House of Lords. Will use his utmost vigilance in the command of the fleet. L. J., V. 232. In extenso.

July 21. Order of the Commons for certain wines, &c. belonging to the King and stayed by Sir John Hotham to be delivered up. C. J., II. 683. In extenso.

July 21. Letter from Henry Martin to Mr. Throckmorton. The commission granted to Captain John Holman is by mischance lost, I am therefore constrained on his behalf, or rather on my own, by whose negligence it was, to desire your attestation of a new commission.

Annexed:—
1. Copy of the form for a captain's commission in the forces raised for the relief of Hull. 6 July 1642. L. J., V. 187. In extenso. And on the same paper letter from Henry Martin to Mr. Browne [Cler. Parl.]. I conceive the request of this gentleman to be very reasonable and therefore enjoin you upon his taking up this commission to sign the fair one agreeing word by word with the original.

July 21. List of Committee of the Commons appointed to consider the certificate of the aldermen of London concerning the election of a locum tenens. C. J., II. 684. In extenso.

July 21. Letter from the Earl of Warwick, aboard the "James" in the Downs, to the Speaker of the House of Commons, in reply to letter of the Speaker of the 20th of July (see C. J., II. 680). The fleet is in general in good condition, but there are two or three old ships of the second rate that will not be so fitting to keep abroad in winter as others. I cannot give any advice as to the necessity of keeping the fleet out, that being better known to you who sit at the helm, but if you think fit to call in any, I hope you will take care that they be

not sent out again against us that stay abroad in service. My vice admiral has written to Captain Pett at Chatham for two cables for the "Guardland" and the "Antelope," which if he send not must be provided; and some of the ships will be speedily out of victuals. We have received 500l. for the stock of the ships and the discharge of sick men. I have written to Captain Walker in command of a ship about Guernsey and Jersey to take it to Milford Haven for the guard of that port. I yesterday received information that there are three Turks men-of-war come into the west, each of 30 or 40 pieces of ordnance. I hope some of our ships may light on them. This letter was read in the House of Commons, but is not set out in the Journals. C. J., II. 688.

July 21. Letter from Justice Reeve at Warwick to Lord North. Details the circumstances of the indictment preferred by Captain Robert Lee at the Warwick assizes against Lord Brooke for executing the militia, and opposing the Commission of Array. Prays his Lordship to make the matter known to both Houses of Parliament. See L. J., V. 256.

July 22. Petition of John Despagne, minister, and James Des Camps. In February 1640-1, an order was made by their Lordships, that Stephen Curzol, minister to the poor strangers inhabiting the Isle of Axholme and Hatfield Chase, should repay 30l. which he had, in combination with Dr. Farmery, chancellor of the diocese of Lincoln, wrung from the poor refugees. Curzol has never paid the money, and vexes the poor strangers with suits of law, having now two depending in the King's Bench and one in the Marshalsea. Petitioners pray that these suits may be stayed.

Annexed:—
1. Copy of order referred to in petition. 17 Feb. 1640-1. L. J., IV. 165. In extenso.

July 22. Order referring preceding petition to Justice Crawley. L. J., V. 230.

[July 22.] Petition of Francis de Neuillo to H. C.; petitioner, who was formerly a Capuchin preacher and superior in several monasteries of that order, having been converted to the Protestant religion, has come to this country for refuge. Having given up all his means of living, and being in great distress, prays some assistance from the House. C. J., II. 686.

July 23. Petition of William Gregory, late undersheriff of the county of Leicester. Prays that an early day may be appointed for the trial of his cause. L. J., V. 231.

July 23. Petition of Solomon Smithe, Marshal of the High Court of Admiralty. By a warrant dated 30th May last, under the hand and seal of the Earl of Northumberland, then Lord High Admiral, all the magazine conveyed from Hull was committed to the safe custody of petitioner. An order has since come forth from the Parliament for disposing of the said magazine. Petitioner prays that an order may be directed to him for his discharge thereof, and also for satisfaction for the money disbursed by him for the security of the same. L. J., V. 231.

July 23. Order in compliance with preceding petition. L. J., V. 231.

July 23. Order for the indemnity of the Earl of Stamford and others. L. J., V. 232. In extenso.

July 23. Order for payment of 4,000l. to Maurice Thompson. L. J., V. 233. In extenso.

July 23. Draft order for drawing men out of Ulster and Leinster to go into Munster. L. J., V. 234.

July 23. The King's answer to the petition of Parliament, with amendments in the King's handwriting. L. J., V. 235. In extenso.

July 23. Petition of Joane Brady, the relict of Garratt Brady, gent. Has greatly suffered in the general calamity of the distressed Protestants in Ireland, having lost all her estate. Prays for relief. A certificate, numerously signed, is added to the petition confirming petitioner's statements. See L. J., V. 238.

July 23. Affidavit of Francis Beard, under keeper, that he has seen Richard Barnard and others hunting deer in Windsor Forest.

July 23. Affidavit of Thomas Lyde that he has seen Bartholomew Luffe and others hunting deer in Windsor Forest.

July 23. Petition of Nicholas Higginson, Master of Arts. After being despoiled of the whole of his estate at Bealtirbirt, in the county of Cavan, by the rebels, was, with his wife and seven children, stript and turned naked out of doors, and compelled to travel with one of his children on his back to Dublin, almost 60 miles distant. Prays for relief.

July 23. Petition of George Charleton. Was de-

House of
Lords.
———
Calendar.
1642.

spoiled by the rebels in Ireland of an estate of 500l. per annum, barbarously handled, and cast into prison. During his imprisonment in the city of Wexford, he was in company with certain friars, and understanding their damnable plots he upon his enlargement discovered four ships full of provisions passing from Wexford into France for return of ammunition for the rebels, thereby afterwards taken by Captain Beatly; he has also discovered and impeached twelve rebels. Is now friendless and moneyless, and prays for relief. A certificate is added to the petition, signed Theo. [Lord] Docwra and Henry Jones, as to the truth of petitioner's statements, and that he is a fit recipient for the bounty of the House. Endorsed 5l.

July 23. Two copies of declaration of the Commons that the city of Bristol is a distinct county of itself, and ought not to have been mentioned in the Act for raising money for the defence of the kingdom, as in the county of Somerset. C. J., II. 688. *In extenso.*

July 25. Order in the cause between Sir Thomas Cary and the Bishop of Ardagh. L. J., V. 238. *In extenso.*

July 25. Petition of Sir George Garrett and Sir George Clarke, sheriffs of the city of London. Pray that an order may be made indemnifying them for bringing the King's writs and proclamations to this House, and leaving them there and not proclaiming them. L. J., V. 238.

July 26. Order for the Judge of Assize for the county of Hereford to see who will avow the paper, intituled "A Declaration or Resolution of the county of Hereford." L. J., V. 242. *In extenso.*

July 26. Order for the preservation of the magazines of the counties by force, if attempted to be taken away. L. J., V. 242. *In extenso.*

July 26. Copy of the reply of the Lords and Commons to the King's answer to their petition. L. J., V. 242. *In extenso.*

July 26. Order for 20,000l. to be paid to Mr. Loftus for the affairs of Ireland. L. J., V. 243. *In extenso.*

July 26. Order for the indemnity of the volunteers of King's Lynn. L. J., V. 243. *in extenso.*

July 26. Order for the Lord Lieutenant of Ireland to grant a commission to the Earl of Thomond, for a troop of horse and a company of foot. L. J., V. 243. *In extenso.*

July 26. Order for the indemnity of persons serving the Parliament. C. J., II. 693. *In extenso.*

July 28. Petition of Sir John Conyers, Lieutenant of the Tower. Prays that the Lord Mayor may be ordered to pay petitioner fees for his diet, &c. L. J., V. 244. *In extenso.*

July 28. Copy of letter from the Lords and Commons to the Lords Justices in Ireland, to send forces for the relief of Lord Esmond, in Duncannon Fort. L. J., V. 245. *In extenso.*

July 28. Order for the payment of monies due to Sir John Conyers and others. L. J., V. 245. *In extenso.*

July 28. Order concerning the raising of forces in Suffolk. L. J., V. 245. *In extenso.*

July 28. Narrative of Randall Laurence, the messenger, sent to attach Sir Lewis Dyves. L. J., V. 246. *In extenso.*

Annexed :—

1. Statement of Sir Thomas Alston, High Sheriff of Bedfordshire. In compliance with an order received from the Parliament, has made diligent search in Sir Lewis Dyves' house, and finds neither ammunition, arms, nor great saddles. 30 July 1642.

2. Certificate of Sir Thomas Alston, High Sheriff, and Thomas Rolt, one of the justices of Bedfordshire. On the 27th of July, after Sir Lewis Dyves had ridden away, and the riot was past, fourteen persons were produced, but there was no proof that any of them were actors in the riot, except Edward Stevenson, Thomas Cashe, and John Albonie. These were bound over in good security to appear at the next assizes, because it was thought that Sir Samuel Luke, and his servant Bennett, who were wounded in the riot, were in peril of their lives. 30 July 1642.

3. Information of Thomas Bedells, William Stevens, and others, concerning the riot. Taken before Sir Richard Conquest and William Rolt, Esq., two of the justices of Bedfordshire. 27 July 1642.

July 28. Petition of many of the parishioners of the parish of St. Mary Magdalene, Canterbury. Mr. John Marston, rector of the parish, although he hath been heretofore somewhat scandalous in regard of a suspected crime, for which he was imprisoned by order of the High Commission for the space of a quarter of a year, hath since his release so well demeaned himself, and hath been so diligent and painful in prayers, administering the sacrament, and preaching, that petitioners pray that they may still enjoy the benefit of his constant preaching, notwithstanding a petition recently presented against him by some few of the parish. See L. J., V. 245.

July 28. Affidavit of Robert Dickinson and Edmund Goodwin, of words spoken by Lieutenant Bodley, concerning the safety of London. L. J., V. 249. *In extenso.*

July 28. List of persons who have visited the Lord Mayor in the Tower since the 20th instant.

July 28. Letter from the Committee for the defence of the kingdom, to the Committee for the Irish adventurers. The distresses of the kingdom are so pressing and the disbursements have been so great that greater sums are now necessary for the defence of the kingdom than the Lords and Commons can for the present raise. The Committee for the defence of the kingdom desires therefore that the Committee for the Irish adventurers will advance one hundred thousand pounds by way of loan, upon the public faith, to be repaid in so short a time that it shall not be diverted from the purpose for which it was intended, or any way frustrate the acts already made on behalf of that adventure. C. J., II. 698.

July 28. Account of Edward Husband for printing done for the House of Commons, and request for early payment. See C. J., II. 698.

July 28. Order concerning the raising of forces in Dorset. C. J., II. 694. *In extenso.*

July 29. Message from the Commons for a joint committee upon Commissions of Array. C. J., II. 695. *In extenso.*

July 29. Certificate of Roger Lord Cork. The bearers, Andrew Hayes, clerk, late vicar of Tipperary, and Alexander Young, clerk, late minister of Salloghcutt, in the county of Tipperary, have with their wives and children been robbed and despoiled by the rebels of all they possessed, having with much difficulty escaped with their lives, it is therefore fit that they be permitted to embark from hence and pass into England.

July 30. Draft order for the Earl of Pembroke to be Lieutenant for the counties of Monmouth, Brecon, and Glamorgan. L. J., V. 248.

July 30. Affidavits of Thomas Burgis and James Rowley, of scandalous words spoken by Captain Slingsby and Captain Wake, against the Earl of Warwick. L. J., V. 249. *In extenso.*

July 30. Application of the French ambassador to the Parliament for leave to transport white wool for the use of the French king. L. J., V. 249.

July 30. Certificate of Sir Michael Eames, that George Payler, paymaster of the garrison of Berwick, hath often procured money on his own credit, whereby he hath given good satisfaction to the soldiers, who were otherwise likely to mutiny; and that he hath frequently, at his own cost, made journeys to London to solicit the Parliament for money to pay the soldiers. See C. J., II. 697.

[July.] Petition of William Poe, a distressed prisoner, in the King's Bench. Prays relief against an unjust sentence in the Star Chamber obtained at the suit of Sir Edward Bullock, who, notwithstanding the abolition of that court, by combination with the warden of the Fleet, prevented petitioner's discharge, and on his procuring a writ of habeas corpus committed him to the Fleet on an action for 200l. under the judgment of the Star Chamber. Petitioner has lost all his estate and some of his dearest friends by the rebellion in Ireland, where he has served as a commander, is ready for any further service, and prays for relief and enlargement.

Annexed :—

1. Certificate in support of preceding. 2 May 1642.

[July.] Account of monies paid by Sir David Watkins to the treasurers for his adventure for lands in Ireland.

Aug. 1. Petition of Thomas Jenyns, Esq., that Sir Filibert Vernatti, arrested under a writ ne exeat regno at petitioner's suit, may be ordered to give sufficient security for the demands in question before he obtains his discharge. L. J., V. 250.

Annexed :—

1. Writ ne exeat regno for arrest of Vernatti. 18 June 1642.

2. Copy of an order in the cause. 20 July 1642. L. J., V. 222.

3. Copy of Vernatti's petition praying that he may

be discharged upon giving good security. (Undated.)

4. Copy of certificate of Sir William Middleton and others, that they are willing to become sureties for Vernatti. 19 July 1642.

5. Statement by Jenyns of his objections to the proposed sureties.

Aug. 1. Order for the Committee for the Irish adventurers to lend 100,000*l.* to the Committee for the defence of the kingdom. L. J., V. 250.

Aug. 1. Order for the payment of 15,000*l.* to Mr. Loftus for a month's pay for the Scottish army in Ireland. L. J., V. 250.

Aug. 1. Order for the issue of 20,000*l.* proposition money, upon the order from the Committee for the safety of the kingdom. L. J., V. 251.

Aug. 1. Order for William Bartlett and Edward Anthony to receive the money and plate come in upon the propositions within the city of Exeter. L. J., V. 251. *In extenso.*

Aug. 1. Affidavit of Thomas Symonds of words spoken by Edward Teringham against the Parliament. L. J., V. 251. *In extenso.*

Aug. 1. Two copies of letter from the Scots Commissioners concerning the treaty. L. J., V. 262. *In extenso.*

Aug. 1. Letter from William March at Arundel House to the Lord Mowbray and Maltravers. The writer, who appears to have been an agent for the Earl of Arundel, gives a long and detailed account of moneys received and expended by him on behalf of the Earl, who was at that time abroad.

Aug. 2. Draft order appointing the Earl of Peterborough Lord Lieutenant of Northamptonshire. C. J., II. 700. *In extenso.* On the same paper,

Draft order for the Deputy Lieutenants and other officers of the county to act by virtue of their several commissions until the Earl of Peterborough shall have granted his deputations. C. J., II. 701. *In extenso.*

Aug. 2. Petition of Captain Robert Slingsby and Captain Baldwin Wake. Their Lordships were pleased to order that petitioners should be set at liberty upon bail. They have attended several days with their bail, but by reason of great affairs could not present them to their Lordships. Pray that their bail may be forthwith accepted. L. J., V. 256.

Aug. 3. Draft order for the indemnity of those who assisted in apprehending Sir Lewis Dyves. *See* L. J., V. 268.

Aug. 3. Agreement entered into by William Hickson, master of the ship "Mary," of Scarborough, to transport ten horses and a calash belonging to Prince Rupert from Rotterdam to some harbour between Harwich and Newcastle.

Aug. 4. Draft order for the indemnity of the Dorsetshire volunteers. L. J., V. 262. *In extenso.*

Aug. 5. Petition of Richard Brewton. Upon hearing petitioner's cause against Sir John Lenthall, their Lordships ordered the transcript of the record to be returned into the King's Bench, in order that petitioner might take out execution. Sir John Lenthall has since procured himself to be sworn of the Privy Chamber of His Majesty, and made over his estate in trust purposely to defeat petitioner of his remedy in law. Prays that this illegal proceeding and contempt may be taken into their Lordships' serious consideration. L. J., V. 263.

Aug. 5. Petition of the Right Hon. Basil Lord Viscount Fielding and the Lady Elizabeth his wife, the Right Hon. Oliver Earl of Bullingbrook, committee of the Lady Dorothy and Lady Ann Bourchier, daughters and co-heirs of the Right Hon. Edward, late Earl of Bath, deceased, His Majesty's wards. They complain that William Pagett, steward to the late Earl of Bath, refuses to give account of certain great sums of money which were raised as portions for the Earl's daughters. Pray that Pagett may be called upon to answer, petitioners being unable to proceed against him in law, because he stands upon his privilege as servant to Henry now Earl of Bath.

Aug. 5. Draft orders for Sir Ralph Hopton and others to be sent for as delinquents. L. J., V. 264. *In extenso.*

Aug. 5. Letter from Sir Richard Onslow to Denzill Hollis, Esq., or in his absence to John Hampden, Esq., concerning the arrest of Justice Malett. L. J., V. 264.

Aug. 5. Order for the release of John Gaskell and others, imprisoned for opposing the Commission of Array in the county of Chester. L. J., V. 267. *In extenso.*

Aug. 5. Letter from the Earl of Portland to the Lords in the High House of Parliament assembled. Knowing the clearness and uprightness of my own

5.

heart, I cannot so far forsake myself as by a voluntary quitting that right and privilege of Parliament which is due to me, make the world believe I am guilty of a crime which can never lawfully be fixed upon me. I do therefore, with all humility, pray and demand that which in right and justice belongs to me, which is my seat and vote in Parliament. From Sir J. Garrett's house, Sheriff. *See* L. J., V. 262, &c.

Aug. 6. Petition of Sir Faithful Fortescue. Petitioner is, by letters patent under the Great Seal, constable of Knockfergus [Carrickfergus] Castle, in Ireland, during life. Since Parliament has been pleased (for advancing the service of that kingdom) to dispose of the place to the Scots, petitioner prays that an order may be made for payment of what was due to himself and the warders up to the time the castle was rendered to the Scots; he also prays that some compensation may be given to him for the loss of his freehold of the castle, he being now destitute, having lost the whole of his estate by the late rebellion. L. J., V. 268.

Aug. 6. Petition of Scipio Le Squier, servant to His Majesty, Vice-Chamberlain of the receipt of Exchequer. Prays that Matthew Francis and others may be called upon to answer for their illegal proceedings, by which petitioner has been ejected from his house in Long Acre. L. J., V. 268. *See also* L. J., V. 303, where the case is stated at length.

Annexed :—

1. Affidavit of petitioner, detailing the circumstances of his ejectment. 22 July 1642.

2. Petition of Matthew Francis, praying for a copy of Le Squier's petition, and that a day may be fixed for him to answer the charge.

3. Another petition of Matthew Francis, praying that the business may be heard and determined by their Lordships, or dismissed to be heard at law. 10 Aug. 1642.

Aug. 6. Petition of Sir Filibert Vernatti. Was arrested upon a writ *ne exeat regno* at the suit of Thomas Jenyns. Prays for his discharge upon reasonable security. L. J., V. 268.

Aug. 6. Articles of the treaty concerning the reducing of the kingdom of Ireland to the obedience of the King's Majesty and Crown of England, agreed upon between the Commissioners for Scotland, authorised by His Majesty, and the Parliament of that kingdom, and the Commissioners for England authorised by His Majesty, and the Parliament of that kingdom at Westminster, the 6th day of August 1642. The Scotch at their own charge to levy and transport 10,000 men into the parts of Ireland lying nearest to Scotland. The English to provide arms for these men. Two English ships to be sent to attend on the Scotch forces in Ireland, and to preserve their communications with Scotland. Ten troops of horse to be sent by the English to serve with the Scotch foot under the Scotch commanders, and 1,200*l.* to be paid by the English for raising one hundred horse in Scotland. The officers of the Scotch army to have the same pay and allowances as the English. Carrinkfergus and Coleraine to be placed in the hands of the Scotch till the end of the war, their army to be then disbanded by regiments at a time, and to receive pay till then. The said towns to be stored with provisions and ammunition for the use of the Scotch forces. 2,000*l.* English money per annum to be at the disposal of the general of the army, to be disbursed upon fortifications, intelligences, &c., and 2,500*l.* to be disbursed upon account for providing artillery, horses, &c. The inhabitants of Ulster to obey orders from the Scottish commanders for providing food, forage, &c. The 10,000 Scotch to go as an army into Ulster, with power to their commanders to prosecute the war, as they shall think best for the Crown of England, to make terms with places and persons, provided no terms be made for toleration of popery or concerning the lands of rebels; the Scotch commanders to be answerable for their deportment to His Majesty and Parliament; but if it shall be found advantageous for the Scotch army to join with that of the King's Lieutenant in Ireland, in that case the Scotch commander shall receive instructions only from the King's Lieutenant or his deputy, and himself alone give orders to his own men, the armies to have the right and left hand, van and rear, charge and retreat, successively, without any mixing of the two armies whatever; no Scottish officer to be commanded by one of his own quality; and if the commanders of two troops sent from either army be of the same quality, they shall command the party by turns. The Scotch to be entertained by the English from the 20th of June

F

last for three months. To receive their discharge from the King and Parliament of England upon a month's notice. After expiry of the three months the liability of the English to pay the Scotch troops to cease upon their giving a month's notice to that effect.

These articles were under discussion for many months. A proviso and amendments were agreed to on the 6th August by the Lords, and a conference appears to have been had on the same subject on the 23rd Sept., but there is no mention in the Journals of the formal ratification of these articles. *See* L. J., VI. 268, 371.

Aug. 6. List of delinquents to be sent for from Shropshire. L. J., V. 269. *In extenso.*

Aug. 6. Order for 200*l.* to be paid to Lord Loftus, late Lord Chancellor of Ireland, in consideration of the great services he has performed in Ireland, and of the condition he is brought unto now in his great old age by reason of the rebellion. L. J., V. 270. *In extenso.*

Aug. 6. Petition of John Marston, praying for a mitigation of the severe sentence passed upon him for the words spoken by him against the Parliament. *See* L. J., V. 244.

Annexed :—

1. Statement of the charge against him.

Aug. 8. Affidavit of Edmond Syler and Jonathan Lawe, of words spoken by Stephen Jackson against the Parliament. L. J., V. 271.

Aug. 8. Petition of the Dukes of Vendosme, D'Espernon, and Soubize, the Marquis of Vieuville, and the Lord of Valiquerville, praying an order from their Lordships for leave to continue their abode in or about the city of London, with the same liberty and safety which they have hitherto peaceably enjoyed; or, if they desire it, to depart out of the kingdom without any other conduct or declaration. L. J., V. 272. *In extenso.*

Aug. 8. Order in accordance with prayer of preceding petition. L. J., V. 272. *In extenso.*

Aug. 8. Petition of the captain and other officers of the band of Volunteers of the Hundred of Rochford, Essex, the minister and people of the town of Raleigh, with other well affected persons in the said hundred, to H. C. Complain that the Volunteers of the hundred who have completely armed themselves, and chosen a captain to instruct them in the use of the arms for the defence of the country, have been shamefully abused and assaulted by William Tilford and others. Pray that the offenders, who are common enemies of religion, and who are continually slandering and reviling 'the Parliament, may be severely punished, to the terror of others. C. J., II. 712.

Aug. 9. Draft order for William Bartlett and Edward Anthony, receivers for the county of Devon, to pay 5,000*l.* to Sir George Chudleigh. L. J., V. 274. *In extenso.*

Aug. 9. Copy of letter from Sir Edward Nicholas to Sir John Sackville about contributions for the King. L. J., V. 295. *In extenso.*

Aug. 10. Petition of [Edmund Butler and others] six Irish gentlemen, now miserable prisoners in Newgate, for themselves and their servants; about eight months ago were arrested at Salcombe, Devonshire, on their way from France to Ireland, bereaved of all their goods, and sent prisoners to Newgate, where they have ever since remained in the greatest want, and though an order has been made for their trunks to be restored to them, they have not got them. They have now an opportunity of serving the King of Portugal, and pray for enlargement or competent relief. L. J., V. 280.

Aug. 10. Draft resolutions concerning Sir Richard Gurney, Lord Mayor of London. L. J., V. 280. *In extenso.*

Annexed :—

1. Precedents concerning the election of the Lord Mayor of London. (Two papers.)

Aug. 10. Order for Henry Herbert, Esq., a member of the House of Commons, to repair to Monmouth, and publish the declaration concerning the illegality of the Commission of Array. L. J., V. 280. *In extenso.*

Aug. 10. Affidavit of John Gosse, that the annexed papers remaining with the Clerk of the Parliaments are true copies of the several records concerning Henry Stewart and others, fetched out of Ireland by command of the House. *See* L. J., IV. 393.

Annexed :—

1. Copy of the warrant for bringing Henry Stewart and others to Dublin. 13 Aug. 1639.
2. Copy of the censure given against Stewart and others in the High Court of Castle Chamber, in Ireland. 7 Sept. 1639.
3. Copy of the votes of the Board against Stewart

and others, the Lord Deputy being present. 7 Sept. 1639.

4. Copy of the estreats upon the lands of Stewart and others.

Aug. 10. Petition of James Lord Awdeley and Earl of Castlehaven. In July last, by His Majesty's licence, petitioner departed into the kingdom of Ireland to dispose and order his estate there. During the time of this unhappy rebellion he has daily offered his services to the State, as the Earls of Ormond and Roscommon and other Lords of the Privy Council will certify. Divers of his servants have been slain, and the whole of his estate taken from him by the rebels, nevertheless he now stands indicted there of a supposed treason, exhibited by the malice of William Collins and Daniel Ennis, who are themselves indicted as rebels, and who offered to take off the prosecution for so inconsiderable a sum as 3*l.* This petitioner, knowing himself to be innocent of the least thought of treason, with great indignation utterly refused, and immediately repaired to Dublin, and tendered himself to the Lords Justices and Council, who have ever since restrained him of his liberty. Prays that, being a peer of England, he may be ordered to be transmitted to England, to be tried by their Lordships according to law.

Aug. 11. Order for the issue of writs of habeas corpus for the production of John Bastwicke, Robert Ludlow, and Lieutenant Rawlins, confined at York for performing the orders of the two Houses of Parliament. L. J., V. 283. *In extenso.*

Annexed :—

1. Petition of Susanna Bastwick, wife of John Bastwick, Dr. in Physic. On the 22nd of July last petitioner's husband with two other gentlemen engaged on the service of Parliament were violently arrested whilst riding peaceably on the highway by some of the King's cavaliers, who could show no warrant but their cocked pistols. They were first imprisoned at Leicester, and then carried on three lame jades, their own horses having been taken from them, to York, where they are now in prison, and threatened with indictment. Petitioner prays that measures may be taken to free her husband from imprisonment, that he may be sent up to Parliament, the honour and authority of which is concerned in the matter, with the warrant under which he was arrested. *See* L. J., V. 283.

Aug. 11. Draft of the judgment pronounced against the Lord Mayor. L. J., V. 284. *In extenso.*

Aug. 11. Draft order of the Commons for a message to be sent to the Lords to acquaint them with the great store of arms and ammunition at Knolle House. C. J., II. 714.

Aug. 13. Engrossment of " An Act for the better pay-" ment of several sums of money therein specified, by " and out of the estate of Sir Thomas Dawes, knight, " and John Dawes, gentleman, two of the sons of " Sir Abraham Dawes, knight, deceased." Brought from H. C. this day. L. J., V. 286. Committed 563, but not read a third time.

Aug. 13. Message from the Commons to impeach the Marquess of Hertford, the Earl of Northampton, and Henry Hastings, Esq. L. J., V. 286.

Aug. 13. Draft order against putting into execution the Commission of Array for Oxfordshire. L. J., V. 287. *In extenso.*

Annexed :—

1. Letter from the Warden and Corporation of Henley-on-Thames to Lord Say and Seale, Lord Lieutenant of the County, enclosing copy of circular letter received by them from the Commissioners of Array for Oxfordshire. 12 August 1642. L. J., V. 286. *In extenso.*
2. Copy of circular letter referred to in preceding. 10th August 1642. L. J., V. 286. *In extenso.*

Aug. 13. Report of Doctor Aylett and Doctor Heath upon the Gentleman Usher's Bill for extraordinary expenses. L. J., V. 287. *In extenso.*

Annexed :—

1. The Gentleman Usher's account. L. J., V. 287. *In extenso.*

Aug. 13. Letter from Sir Walter Erle at Dorchester to William Lenthall, Esq., Speaker of the House of Commons. The writer's fears and dangers are much increased since the coming of the Marquess [of Hertford] out of Somersetshire to Sherborne. Their numbers multiply daily and they fortify themselves at Sherborne, victualling the castle, and building huts for the soldiers; their horse are supposed to be betwixt 400 and 500, too great a strength for the writer to encounter. Will do his best to secure Dorchester and Weymouth, being in respect of their magazines of ordnance and powder (most considerable, but the places are not of strength, and he knows not of any help that is near at hand. Unless some course be taken for drawing forces out of other counties the public will receive more prejudice than is yet conceived, and this county will be in a worse condition than any in the kingdom, if the port towns of Weymouth and Poole be seized and fortified, and this and the neighbouring county come to be made a seat of war. Humbly requests that the money, paid in by the inhabitants of Dorchester for the supply of horse and arms, may be re-delivered to them, as the charges they have been put to for providing for the defence of the town, have been greatly increased, and on its safety depends the safety of the whole county. *See* C. J., II. 720.

Aug. 15. Petition of Henry Cowes and others, servants of Lord Cottington, having the charge of his Lordship's house at Hanworth. Complain that divers persons lately attempted to pull down the pales of Hanworth Park, and came with swords and guns in a riotous manner, and endeavoured to ransack and pillage the house under colour of a pretended power to search for arms, &c., by virtue of a warrant surreptitiously gotten, as petitioner's conceive, as it was directed to none there present. Pray that an order may speedily be given for apprehending the delinquents, and securing his Lordship's house and goods against any further attack. L. J., V. 289.
Annexed :—
  1. List of the rioters.
  2. Copy of the order for searching for arms. 4 July 1642. C. J., II. 649. *In extenso.*
Aug. 15. An inventory of the arms in the armoury at Knolle, belonging to the Right Hon. Edward Earl of Dorset. Signed by the Earl. L. J., V. 289.
Aug. 15. Letter from the Earl of Mulgrave to the Earl of Holland. One Copley, an old servant of mine, has, notwithstanding a protection given by myself, been arrested, and is detained contrary to our privilege. I pray your Lordship to move the House that he be set at liberty and freed to follow my occasions. L. J., V. 289.
Aug. 15. Order referring the petition of Richard Harding to Mr. Baron Trevor. L. J., V. 289.
Annexed :—
  1. Report of Baron Trevor. There are 15 actions for debt and trespass in the Court of Marshalsea, and six in the King's Bench now pending against Harding.
  2. List of the actions.
Aug. 15. Draft warrant to the officers of customs, searchers of ships, and others, to allow Mary Lovett to embark for Flanders with her infant son, her maidservant, and her goods. *See* L. J., V. 301.
Aug. 15. Copy of the general instructions to county Committees. C. J., II. 717. *In extenso.*
Aug. 16. Petition of the county of Devon, from their late general sessions to the Lords and Commons. L. J., V. 295. *In extenso.*
Aug. 16. Petition of the county of Devon, from their late general sessions to the King. L. J., V. 295. *In extenso.*
Aug. 16. Petition of Urbanus Vigors, a minister from Ireland to the Earl of Manchester. Petitioner, by reason of his long attendance and his great losses by the wars in Ireland, is in such sad condition that he is like to starve with his wife and children. Prays his Lordship that a comfortable answer may be returned to the petition presented by him to the House. *See* L. J., V. 296.
Aug. 16. Order for suppressing the Commissions of Array, and for apprehending the abettors of them. L. J., V. 297. *In extenso.*
Aug. 16. Copy of preceding.
Aug. 16. Draft of an order for the Lord General to prevent riots among the soldiers. L. J., V. 300. *In extenso.*
Aug. 16. Draft of an order for the lords lieutenant, deputy lieutenants, and justices of the peace to suppress riots. L. J., V. 300. *In extenso.*
Aug. 17. Draft order for the same instructions to be sent into Warwickshire that are sent into Somersetshire. L. J., V. 298.
Aug. 18. Petition of Colonel John Butler, praying for his discharge upon his giving security that he will not go into Ireland during the rebellion there. L. J., V. 301.
Aug. 18. Another petition of Colonel Butler praying that William Le Stunt, Esq., and Joseph Brandon,

Esq., may be accepted as his sureties, and that their Lordships will allow him some means to bear his charges out of this kingdom, and grant him a free pass for himself and three servants to Dover, and an order for the mayor and magistrates there to assist him with a passage to Flanders or France.
Annexed :—
  1. List of his debts. *See* L. J., V. 306.
Aug. 18. List of the insignia belonging to the City seized by the gentleman usher in the late Lord Mayor's house. L. J., V. 303. *In extenso.*
Aug. 18. Order for the Commissioners for Irish affairs to meet. L. J., V. 303. *In extenso.*
Aug. 18. Affidavit of Humanitas Mayo that the Constable of Staines treated their Lordships' warrant for the apprehension of the rioters at Hanworth in a scornful manner, and underhand gave the rioters notice of the warrant, and in consequence none of the delinquents were found. L. J., V. 303. *In extenso.*
Aug. 18. Report of Lord Chief Justice Brampton, upon the cause between Squire and Francis. L. J., V. 303. *In extenso.*
Aug. 19. Two draft orders in the cause of Massey against Rolfe. L. J., V. 305.
Aug. 19. Remonstrance of the lieutenant, bailiffs, jurats, ministers, and constables assembled in State and Common Council of the Island of Jersey, on behalf of Sir Philip Carteret, Lieutenant Governor and Bailiff of the island. They disavow all the charges made against Sir P. Carteret, which are calumnious, and made by those who, for their own interest, desire to trouble the good and quiet of the State. He has procured the passing of many good laws for the government of the island, administered good justice indifferently, kept the poor from oppression, protected the ministers of God's word, and preserved the merchants in their liberty of trade, not only in His Majesty's dominions but in foreign countries, where his reputation has procured them many favours. His return to the island will be to the exceeding content of all except those who envy him. (French.) L. J., V. 305.
Annexed :—
  1. Translation of preceding.
Aug. 19. Order for watches to be kept in Cambridge, Suffolk, and Norfolk. L. J., V. 306. *In extenso.*
Aug. 19. Copy of the Lord General's protection for Mrs. Nott of Chesewick, against her house being plundered.
Aug. 19. Examination of George Browne and Emery Hughes, concerning the assault committed by Peter Lyon upon Cecil Cave at Greenwich. *See* L. J., V. 301.
Aug. 19. Small paper endorsed "Mr. Pime's Noate."
" To send me the proclamation for raising the Kinge's " Standard."
Aug. 19. Petition of William Stamp, clerk, Vicar of Stepney, to the Commons. Was committed as a delinquent by order of the House, prays to be discharged upon good bail. C. J., II. 728.
Aug. 19. Notes of various votes of both Houses concerning the Earl of Essex, passed on this and previous days.
Aug. 20. Petition of Richard March, Keeper of His Majesty's stores, to Robert Earl of Essex, praying his Lordship to take into his consideration the annexed petition. L. J., V. 308. *In extenso.*
Annexed :—
  1. Petition of Captain Francis Conningsby, Richard March, and Edward Sherburne, officers of His Majesty's ordnance, to the House of Lords, praying for their discharge, having been committed by their Lordships for refusing to issue some munition in their custody. L. J., V. 308. *In extenso.*
Aug. 20. Order for transporting 15,000l. to Carrickfergus for the use of the Scottish army there. C. J., II. 721. *In extenso.*
Aug. 20. Amended draft of preceding. L. J., V. 310.
Aug. 20. Petition of Stephen Jackson, praying for his discharge. *See* L. J., V. 271.
Annexed :—
  1. Copy of order for his committal. 8 August 1642.
Aug. 22. Order for the Committee for Cornwall to use all diligence to apprehend the Earl of Bath and others. L. J., V. 315. *In extenso.*
Aug. 22. Draft order for payment of 5,000l. to Mr. Frost for provisions for Ireland. L. J., V. 316. *In extenso.*
Aug. 22. Order for payment of 1,000l. to Mr. Halsteed,

factor of Mr. Quarles, for arms provided for Ireland. L. J., V. 317. *In extenso.*

Aug. 22. Affidavit of Richard Allman, of the service of their Lordships' order of the 29th of July upon the plaintiff in the writ of error, Eales *v.* Covell. *See* L. J., V. 246.

Aug. 23. Draft of pass granted to Colonel Butler, to go to France or Flanders. L. J., V. 317.

Aug. 23. Draft order for Sir John Lucas and Mr. Newcomen, to be sent for as delinquents. L. J., V. 318.

Aug. 23. Petition of Sir Thomas Malet, Knight, one of the justices of His Majesty's Court of King's Bench, praying for his enlargement, and if their Lordships be not pleased to grant this, then that his wife may be allowed to remain with him during his imprisonment. *See* L. J., V. 337.

Aug. 24. Order for securing the town of Great Yarmouth. L. J., V. 319. *In extenso.*

Aug. 24. Petition of Michell Lesne, Sieur de Rabinet, of the town of Dinan, in France. Petitioners' ship, the " St. Nicholas," James Vallée, master, laden with wheat belonging to Mathurin Guerin, merchant, from St. Malo for Chester, was, in the beginning of July last, taken at sea by Captain Waters, commanding one of His Majesty's ships of war, carried into Plymouth and delivered to the Vice-Admiral. No gunpowder or ammunition was found in her, as was pretended, but petitioner has been unable to obtain leave from the Vice-Admiral either to carry away the ship, or to sell the wheat before it was utterly spoilt. Petitioner being a natural born subject of the King of France, this detention of his ship is a breach of the peace and union between the two Crowns, and he therefore prays that the ship may be forthwith returned, and satisfaction made to him for the damages he has sustained.

Annexed :—

1. Translation of the letters of charter between James Vallée, the master of the ship, and Mathurin Guerin, merchant, with reference to the voyage and cargo of the ship. 9 July 1642.

2. Copy of the application made by James Vallée and Mathurin Guerin to the Vice-Admiral, either to allow them to carry away the ship or to sell the wheat, allowing the money to remain in the hands of some merchants of Plymouth until the matter is settled. 26 July 1642.

3. Translation of the certificate of René Lesquier S' de la Menardays, Lieutenant-General of the Admiralty of France, in the Court of St. Malo, and seneschal of that place, that leave was given for the departure of the ship from St. Malo, after the officer and overseer of the court had visited her, and reported that he found in her no merchandise prohibited by His Majesty's ordinances. 6 August 1642.

4. Translation of depositions taken before the " Notaries note-keepers of the King, established " at St. Malo," as to the building, ownership, and cargo of the " St. Nicholas." 9 August 1642.

Aug. 25. Petition of Edward Sanderford. Was committed to the Fleet on Monday on a charge of having been hired to kill the Earl of Essex. Prays for his discharge. L. J., V. 321.

Annexed :—

1. Similar petition of same to the Earl of Essex.

2. Examination of Edward Sanderford, tailor, taken before Lord Chief Justice Brampston. Denies that he was set on by any man to kill the Earl of Essex, or that it was ever in his thought to do so. 27 August 1642. *See* L. J., V. 334.

Aug. 25. Message from the King at Nottingham to both Houses of Parliament, proposing a treaty for composing differences. (Signed by the King.) L. J., V. 327. *In extenso.*

Aug. 25. Copy of declaration of the Marquess of Hertford and the other Commissioners for Somerset to the people of the county. You have been summoned to hear such things as the Commissioners think necessary to be publicly known, that you may not be deceived by the malicious suggestions and deceitful pretences of those men who disturb the peace of the kingdom, and endeavour to bring in great changes in the Church and State against the King's consent and just authority. For the better effecting their wicked designs, they have cast all manner of slanders upon those men who they know are ready at all hazards to oppose them in their mutinous and rebellious enterprises. They give out that the Commissioners are papists or popishly affected, whereas it is well known that they have lived and are resolved to die, as their fathers have done in the practice

of the Church of England, while these men are known to despise the Common Prayer Book, and to favour Brownists, Anabaptists, and other disturbers of all order and government. They also give out that the Commissioners have power to take what they please of any man's estate, which is as foul an untruth as that of their being papists, since the commission was only to review the arms of the subjects, to see them muster, and to take care that no person of ability should be without arms ; this commission they are resolved to put in practice until it be better liked and understood. The quarrel which these men have with the commission is, that they would gladly have found all men unarmed but their own faction, for the more easy effecting of their wicked purposes, which manifest themselves in their levying armies against the King to the terror of all good subjects. The Commissioners therefore pray and require your assistance against such traitorous and rebellious practices. *See* L. J., V. 332.

[Aug. 25.] Copy of another declaration of the Marquess of Hertford and the other Commissioners for the county of Somerset. Whereas many false and scandalous imputations have been laid upon us for executing His Majesty's just commands, we do hereby declare and protest that we shall never be brought to execute anything that shall tend to the violation of the liberty or property of the subject, or to the hinderance of the true religion established by law, and we defy the authors of all such scandals and imputations, until it appears by any particular, that we have done anything in contradiction of this our solemn protestation. And whereas there have lately been assembled at Shepton Mallet great numbers of armed men, which the authors of these false reports would throw upon us, we think fit to declare the true passages, that all the world may know upon whose charge the whole fault may come. On Saturday evening the Lord Marquis and the rest of the Commissioners were informed that some persons of the best quality were come into Shepton Mallett under colour of eating venison, and that tickets of an unusual style, without any name subscribed upon them, were carried about inviting great numbers both of horse and foot to meet there. Although we were commanded hither for no other purpose than preserving the peace of the county, and it appeared to us that such meeting in arms in a time of peace could be for no good intent, we were so tender of giving any colour of raising forces on our side, that we did not so much as summon the soldiers, contenting ourselves with our own servants, which to most of us were very few, till we could see further what their intentions were. On Sunday afternoon a petition signed by the greatest part of the inhabitants of Shepton Mallett was brought to the Lord Marquess desiring his protection, as they were informed that a great assembly of armed men was appointed there for Monday, which put them in great fright, because they heard that Mr. William Strode and George Malliard had made great and unusual preparation of arms and ammunition in their houses in the town, and divers low persons had given out that such and such houses should be fired, and that the streets should run with blood. His Lordship seeing that it was now a business not to be neglected if he would answer the trust reposed in him by His Majesty, and that his own security as well as that of the petitioners might be concerned, answered that he would take care to provide for their safety, and there being in the county two troops of horse levied by the Earl of Bedford for His Majesty's service, the Lord Marquess held it necessary to make use of them, and thereupon caused them to draw to this town of Wells for the protection of it and the country adjacent, not intending to use them except in defence of himself and the gentlemen assembled there. On Monday morning his Lordship sent Sir Ralph Hopton with some justices of the peace and gentlemen with their attendants only, unarmed, into the town of Shepton Mallett, to see what people were there. Those gentlemen had been there but a short time conferring with the inhabitants and re-examining their petition, when Mr. William Strode came with his company armed with swords and pistols, and forbad the people to obey any such unlawful directions as Sir R. Hopton was giving them, whereas indeed he gave them none at all. After a little while, Sir R. Hopton, well knowing that there are informations against Strode for treasonable words and actions, arrested him on suspicion of high treason, and commanded him to the Constable George Malliard, who suffered him to escape. This done, there entered into the town great numbers of horse and foot who disarmed, as we are informed, all the honest inhabitants. Sir R. Hopton retreated out of

the town to avoid any accident that might possibly
have gone to blood, but which was prevented by his
and his company's good temper. This being the true
state of the passages of that day, we are confident no
just or understanding person can any way blame what
was done by his Lordship or any of us, or excuse this
riotous and tumultuous assembly so contrary to law and
His Majesty's commands. Endorsed. The declaration
set out by the Lord Marquess and other Commissioners
at Wells. The paper is undated and much mutilated.

Aug. 26. Draft order giving the Earl of Arundel
licence to transport eight black Dutch horses and one
white spotted horse beyond the seas, and six servants
to attend them in their passage. L. J., V. 321.

Aug. 26. Petition of Bartholomew de Mountague, a
stranger born. Complains that his house in Covent
Garden was broken into by Alsop Crosse, a messenger,
and his goods taken away on the grounds that he was
a Roman Catholic. Prays that his goods may be returned and that he may be granted a pass to return into
France, his native country. L. J., V. 322.

Annexed :—
1. Similar petition. (Undated.)
2. Affidavit of Humfrey Brock, in the matter. 24
August 1642.
3. Affidavit of Peter Lynn. 24 August 1642.
4. Affidavit of Randall Bickerton. 25 August 1642.
5. Affidavit of Bartholomew de Mountague.

Aug. 26. Draft order against the printing of parliamentary proceedings without authority. L. J., V.
322. In extenso.

Aug. 26. Ordinance prohibiting the importation of
currants. L. J., V. 322. In extenso.

Aug. 26. Draft ordinance for raising money in London. L. J., V. 323. In extenso.

Aug. 26. Draft order against plundering houses. L.
J., V. 327. In extenso.

Aug. 27. Charge against Gyles Thorne, minister of
St. Mary's church, Bedford, for speaking blasphemous
words, with list of witnesses to prove the charge. L. J.,
V. 326.

Annexed :—
1. Extracts from Thorne's sermons.

Aug. 27. Message from the Commons concerning the
answer to be sent to the King's message. L. J., V.
326. In extenso.

Aug. 27. Copy of the answer of the Lords and
Commons to the King's message proposing a treaty to
compose differences. L. J., V. 328. In extenso.

Aug. 27. Draft order to the officers of the dockyard
at Chatham to issue stores for the fleet under the Earl
of Warwick. L. J., V. 328. In extenso.

Aug. 28. Warrant by the Committee for the defence
of the kingdom to the keeper of the Gatehouse, to keep
in safe custody Captain William Legge, lately apprehended or levying war against the parliament. L. J.,
V. 395. In extenso.

Annexed :—
1. Petition of Captain William Legge, prisoner in
the Gatehouse ; prays to be allowed to have a servant of his own to attend upon him during his
confinement and that he may be visited by his
friends. (Undated.)

Aug. 29. Petition of Isabella Massey, praying that
certain lands may not be disposed of until her suit
against William Rolfe is determined by the Lord Keeper.
L. J., V. 331.

Annexed :—
1. Another petition to the same effect.

Aug. 29. Petition of Elizabeth, Countess Rivers,
Dowager. Complains that she has been despoiled of all
her goods to the value of 50,000l. Her two houses, the
one at St. Osithes, in Essex, the other at Melford, in
Suffolk, have been broken into by a rude multitude
raised for the most part in or about Colchester, who
threatened her life, carted away her goods, digged up
her corn, drove away her cattle, and destroyed her gardens, not leaving her so much as a change of apparel.
Prays that strict search may be made for the offenders
and her goods restored to her, and that she, her servants, and agents (who now go under peril of their lives)
may, by their Lordships' protection, repair to her houses
to assist in the search and to give information to the
justices. L. J., V. 331.

Aug. 29. Draft order for all mayors, justices of
the peace, and other officers, and especially Harbottle
Grimston, Esq., Recorder of Colchester, to assist Lady
Rivers and her servants in recovering her goods. L. J.,
V. 331.

Aug. 29. List of collectors appointed in the several
wards and parishes under the ordinance for raising
money and plate in London. L. J., V. 331.

Aug. 29. Certificate from Sir Richard Samwell and
another, that the order of the Lords of the 24th August,
directed to the sheriff of the county of Northampton
and themselves, has been received. See L. J., V. 319.

[Aug. 29.] Petition of distressed clergy of Ireland
resident in and about the city of London, to the Earl of
Holland. Upon a former motion made by his Lordship
it was ordered that petitioners should be recommended
unto the clergy of London, Westminster, and Southwark for the benefit of the collection at the next fast,
but (by what misfortune petitioners know not) the order
failed to be entered, so they cannot receive the benefit
thereby intended. Pray his Lordship to move the House
to give command for entering the order in regard
of the now approaching fast-day. See L. J., V. 331.

Aug. 30. Petition of justices of the peace and inhabitants of the town of Bedford. Pray for the removal of
Giles Thorne, parson of St. Mary's there, a turbulent
and profane person, who used to persecute in the High
Commission Court those who desired to abstain from
profanations, and now sets up divisions and factions in
the town. L. J., V. 332.

Annexed :—
1. Affidavit of James Elsbey that in a sermon at
the church of St. Mary's, Bedford, Mr. Giles
Thorne, the parson, spoke in favour of confession.
10 Sept. 1642.

Aug. 30. Order committing Gyles Thorne to the
Fleet. L. J., V. 332.

Aug. 30. Petition of Owen George, John Betton, and
Edward Davies. Dame Margaret Eyton, widow, died
at Shrewsbury on the 13th of this instant August,
having made her will, which was duly attested, and
leaving petitioners executors thereof. Two of petitioners on the day that she died sent up the will to the
third to be proved in London. Richard Betton, by
fraudulent practices, got the will from the post, and
then by force, with Richard Owen and about 100 persons, entered and took possession of deceased's dwelling
house, turned her servants out of doors, took away her
cattle, and reaped her corn. Richard Betton afterwards
came to London, and made oath before Dr. Aylett that
deceased died intestate, and that he and Richard Betton,
junior, were her nearest of kin, and thereby obtained
letters of administration to be granted to them. Pray
that the said letters may be revoked, and that Richard
Betton and Richard Owen may be sent for to answer
for their fraudulent proceedings. L. J., V. 332.

Annexed :—
1. Affidavit of John Betton as to the truth of the
statements in the petition. 24 Aug. 1642.

Aug. 30. Draft order for the ordnance and ammunition to be removed from Camber Castle to Rye. L. J.,
V. 333. In extenso.

Aug. 30. Letter from Dr. Thomas Paske, at Canterbury, to the Earl of Holland. We have found much
trouble from the troopers sent among us. Colonel
Sandes arriving here with his troops on Friday
night, caused a strict watch, and sentinels to be set
upon the church and upon our several houses, to the
great affrightment of all the inhabitants. This done,
Serjeant-Major Cockin came to me, and in the name
of the Parliament demanded to see the arms of the
church and the store of powder of the county, which
I showed him, and he then possessed himself of the
keys, and kept them in his own custody. The next
morning we were not permitted to enter the church
for the performance of divine service, but about eight
o'clock Sir Michael Livesey and Captain Player, attended by many soldiers, came to our officers and
demanded the keys of the church to be delivered to one
of their company. Then they departed, and the soldiers
entering the church giant-like began a fight with God
himself ; overthrew the communion table, tore the
velvet cloth from before it, defaced the goodly screen
or tabernacle work, violated the monuments of the dead,
spoiled the organs, broke down the ancient rails and
seats, with the brazen eagle that did support the Bible,
forced open the cupboards of the singing men, rent
some of their surplices, gowns, and Bibles, and carried
away others ; mangled all our service books, bestrewing
the whole pavement with the leaves. A miserable
spectacle to every good eye. But as if this were too
little to satisfy the fury of some indiscreet zealots, (for
many did abhor what was done already) they further
exercised their malice upon the arras hangings in the
choir (representing the whole story of our Saviour),

and finding a statue of Christ in the frontispiece of the Southgate, they discharged at least forty shots against it, triumphing much when they did hit it in the head or face. Nor had their fury been thus stopped had not the colonel and some others come to the rescue. They then departed for Dover, from whence we expect them this day, and are afraid that upon their return they will plunder our houses, unless steps be taken to prevent the same, as they have already vilified our persons, and offered extreme indignities to one of our brethren. I am confident that the Houses of Parliament being rightly informed herein, will provide against the like abuses and impieties in other places. *See* L. J., V. 346.

Aug. 30. Petition of Frederick de Bousy and Elisha Robins, citizens and merchants of London. In October last, petitioners shipped several quantities of ribbons and silk hose in a ship belonging to Robert Williams, an Englishman, bound for Rotterdam. The ship was taken on the voyage by a frigate of Ostend, carried into Dunkirk, and the goods condemned as good prize. Pray their Lordships to treat with the Spanish ambassador, or to appoint Sir Balthazar Gerbier to treat with him, for the restitution of petitioners' goods.

Annexed :—

1. Affidavit of John Lee and others that the goods were the property of De Bousy and Robins, freemen of the city of London.

Aug. List of officers and soldiers enlisted during the month of August 1642, under the command and in the regiment of the Earl of Stamford.

Aug. Petition of Wm. Turner, clerk and sexton of Brenchley, Kent, to H. C. ; hearing that a warrant of the House had been issued against him, he immediately gave himself into the custody of the sergeant, prays that he may be made an example of the clemency of the House, not of its justice. *See* C. J., II. 709.

[Aug.] Petition of Elizabeth Lucas, widow. Complains that a multitude of people came into her house, and carried away her plate, jewels, linen, and other goods. Prays that she and her servants and agents may have power to enter and search the houses of those persons by whom her goods are known or suspected to be detained, and that her case may be specially recommended to Harbottle Grimston, Esq., Recorder of Colchester.

Sept. 1. Draft order for the treasurers for the subscriptions of plate and money, to issue money to the treasurers of the army. L. J., V. 334. *In extenso.*

Sept. 1. Draft order for Captain Vernon to be Deputy Treasurer at War to Sir Gilbert Gerard. L. J., V. 334. *In extenso.*

Sept. 1. Letter from Dr. Thomas Paske to Henry Earl of Holland : was bold to tell his Lordship of the outrages committed by some of the troopers in the house of God, and so holds it right to inform his Lordship of an apology since made by Sir Michael Livesey, who, coming with his troopers to the town on Tuesday night, sent for the writer, and in the presence of the mayor and others said that he was commanded by the committee to demand the keys of the church only for the purpose of removing the arms and powder there, and gave direction to the Captain to behave civilly ; Sir Michael expressed himself as overwhelmed with sorrow for what had happened, and the writer is inclined to believe him, on account of his courteous usage that night, and care to prevent further mischief, and wishes the others had made the same excuses, but Captain Baynes and some of his company seemed to justify themselves ; doubts not Parliament will secure for the future the peaceable enjoyment of the house of God. *See* L. J., V. 346, &c.

Sept. 1. Petition of Colonel John Butler : by their Lordships' late order, petitioner was banished to foreign parts during the rebellion in Ireland (*see* L. J., V. 317) where all his property is, prays the House, in consideration of the evidences of loyalty that he has given, to protect his estates in Tipperary.

Sept. 1. Petition of Fenton Parsons ; petitioner being retained as counsel for nine of the Privy Councillors of Ireland, defendants in a cause at the suit of Henry Stewart, attended on several occasions for the hearing of the cause before a Committee and particularly on Tuesday last, when Stewart told him that he did not think that the cause would be heard that day, and afterwards tried to get the cause heard without giving petitioner notice ; prays that the cause may be heard by counsel at the bar.

Annexed :—

1. Affidavit of Fenton Parsons in support of preceding.

Sept. 2. Information of Robert Bumpus and John Ayerson of scandalous words spoken by Edward Sanderford against the Earl of Essex and others. L. J., V. 334. *In extenso.*

Sept. 2. Copy of order for James Wheeler and others, to appear and answer for not re-delivering to Mr. Peter Civell the goods they had taken from him. L. J., V. 335.

Annexed :—

1. Statement of Felix Carter, constable of Uxbridge, that he had shown their Lordships' order of the 22nd of August to Thomas Battye and Thomas Pitt, and that they refused to give up the goods of Peter Civell. 25 August 1642.
2. Statement of John Nelham, constable of Ruislip, that James Wheeler refuses to give up Civell's goods. 25 August 1642.
3. Statement of John Jennings, headborough of Pinner, that Charles Shippie and Edward Neeles refuse to give up Civell's goods. 27 August 1642.

Sept. 2. Order for securing the safety of the town of Oxford. L. J., V. 336. *In extenso.*

Sept. 2. Draft order for the banishment of the Capuchin Friars. C. J., II. 749. *In extenso.*

[Sept. 2.] Petition of Lewis Phillipps, under-sheriff for the county of Huntingdon, and of Henry Burnby, bailiff of the hundred of Toseland, in the same county ; have been prisoners in the Fleet for the last fifteen weeks by their Lordships' order, are heartily sorry to have offended, and pray to be released or bailed. *See* L. J., V. 155, 335.

Annexed :—

1. Similar petition of Lewis Phillipps. (Undated.)
2. Petition of Phillips and Burnby to the Earl of Manchester. Pray his Lordship to use his influence for their enlargement. (Undated.)
3. Petition of Henry Burnby. Is not in any way guilty of the crime for which he was committed. Prays to be discharged upon bail. (Undated.)

Sept. 3. Order for the rents of Lord St. John's lands in Essex and Bedfordshire to be reserved in the tenants' hands until the cause between his Lordship and George Benyon be decided. L. J., V. 338. *In extenso.*

Annexed :—

1. Motion for preceding order.

Sept. 3. Message from the Commons for the appointment of Sir Gregory Norton and others, as receivers for Midhurst and Chichester. L. J., V. 338. *In extenso.*

Sept. 3. Order giving leave to Sir Robert Dishington to transport two horses into France. L. J., V. 338.

Sept. 3. Petition of John Cooth, parson, and James Strode, clothier, of Shepton Mallet, to H. C. Having seen an order that they were to be sent for as delinquents, voluntarily submit themselves and pray to be discharged upon bail. C. J., II. 750.

Sept. 3. Petition of Sir John Conyers, Lieutenant of the Tower : Mr. Hume, petitioner's nephew, is captain of a foot company in the service of the United Provinces ; prays for leave to raise forty voluntary soldiers to send to his nephew to strengthen his company.

Sept. [5.] A true relation of the several passages acted by Sir John Seaton, Knight, and Edwyn Sandis, Colonels, together with some of the Committee whose names are hereunto subscribed, according to instructions agreed upon by the Committee of the Lords and Commons for the safety of the kingdom to be observed within the county of Kent. On Sunday, Aug. 14, they apprehended Sir John Sackvill coming to Sevenoaks church, then went to Knowle House, whence they brought away five load of arms belonging to the Earl of Dorset. On Saturday the 20th they placed a guard on Rochester Bridge, and afterwards took Upnor Castle by surprise whilst the soldiers were at bowls, and placed a guard there ; as they were returning they heard that Sergeant-major Douglas had captured Cobham Hall and arms and horses there, whilst Lord Roper had been stopped at Rochester Bridge and sent prisoner to Upnor Castle ; on Saturday they were well entertained at Rochester, and the same evening went to Chatham Dock, which was surrendered to them by Captain Pett, when he saw their warrant ; on Monday, the 26th August, they went to Gillingham, and put a guard on board the "Sovereign" ; on the 27th they went to the house of Sir Peter Ricoth (Rycaut), of Aylesford, a known rendezvous for malignants, took him and sent him to Upnor Castle, and seized arms and plate, some concealed in the roof of the house ; the same day they went to Allington Hall, Lady Wootton's, having information of horse and arms there, but found none ; and the same evening forced Sir William Butler's house at

Teston, after but slight opposition from a few servants who behaved insolently, Sir William not being there, some arms and money were found and seized; that night they were well received at Maidstone; the next day they went to the houses of Sir Edward Deering and Sir Robert Darrell, but did not find Sir Edward as they had expected, and only a small quantity of arms; thence they went to Hatfield to the Earl of Thanet's, where they seized one load of arms, and passed that night at Ashford, where they were joyfully received; the next day they went to Canterbury, where they were received by the mayor and sheriffs with acclamation, they took two loads of arms and six barrels of powder from the dean and prebendaries, and arrested Mr. Browne, a papist, of great estate in Berkshire in an alehouse, and sent him to Dover Castle, and took some plate from another papist, Mr. West; the next day they went to Dover where were many suspected persons, who however made a contribution for the King and Parliament to prove their fidelity, whilst Thomas Bargrave, the Dean's son, and others were arrested; by request of the Lord Admiral they sent to Deal Castle, which surrendered after a short parley; Walmer, Sandown, and Dover Castle, having already surrendered to him; the next day they went to Feversham, and were met with much affection by the mayor and other inhabitants, they searched the houses of Lord Roper and Mr. Pettit, papists, and took a quantity of plate; they were well received at Lydd, and the next day at New Romney and Tenterden; the next day they went to the houses of Sir Robert Philmer (Filmer) and others, but could neither find them nor anything of value: and so after examining the garrison at Rochester they came to Gravesend, and hearing that the Dean of Canterbury with a party had privately passed towards Rochester, they sent after him and brought him back, and sent him and Lord Roper by barge to his Excellency, and on the 3rd of September they marched into London. After the signatures follow some notes of informations against the Dean of Canterbury. See L. J., V. 339.

Sept. 6. Petition of Anne Viscountess Baltinglasse; her husband is so utterly ruined by the rebellion in Ireland, that he has no maintenance left for himself and his family; prays their Lordships to grant her some present support. L. J., V. 341.

Sept. 6. Petition of Symon Middleton, for relief against John Battie for unjust proceedings in the administration of the estate of Robert Gray, deceased. L. J., V. 341.

Sept. 6. Petition of the Earl of Portland: their Lordships have ordered that petitioner's wife and children should remove from the Isle of Wight after two days' warning, but it is impossible that they should be safe anywhere on the mainland, for petitioner's house near Acton has been broken open and robbed, his goods and trunks in London ransacked, his mother in Essex turned out of doors, the bed whereon she lay taken from her, and the poor people threatened who offered to receive her; prays that if his wife must remove out of the castle (Carisbrook) she may remain in the island until she can get a passage to France, and that a pass may be granted to her for herself, some of her children, and fourteen persons besides, with such goods and household stuff as she shall think fit, a small proportion of plate, and 300l. in money. L. J., V. 341.

Sept. 6. Order for the trained bands of Cambridgeshire and the Isle of Ely to prevent riots. L. J., V. 341. In extenso.

Sept. 6. Draft answer of both Houses to the King's message delivered on the 5th instant. L. J., V. 342. In extenso.

Sept. 7. Petition of Thomas Fulwar, Dr. of Divinity and Bishop of Ardfert, in Ireland, having been despoiled of his whole estate by the rebellion, prays to be recommended to the Commissioners appointed to distribute the money collected the last fast-day for the relief of the distressed clergy in Ireland. L. J., V. 342.

Sept. 7. Petition of Bartholomew Mountague: was a servant to King James, and is now a servant to the King and Queen; prays for a pass for himself, his niece, and three servants to France. L. J., V. 343.

Annexed:—

1. Blank pass in accordance with preceding.

Sept. 7. Letter from Sir Nicholas Slanning at Lostwithiel to the House of Lords; has taken notice of their Lordships' order that he should be sent for as a delinquent, but as he is a member of Parliament, and has taken the protestation, he submits that he cannot appear before their Lordships without the leave of the House of Commons. L. J., V. 364. In extenso.

Sept. 7. Commission from the King appointing William Courtenay, sergeant-major of the regiment of foot under the command of Sir John Beaumont, and captain over one company in the regiment.

Sept. 8. Draft order to punish breach of contract in soldiers who receive entertainment to serve the Parliament. L. J., V. 343. In extenso.

Sept. 8. Two drafts of order for the Lord General to restrain and punish disorders amongst the soldiers. L. J., V. 343. In extenso.

Sept. 8. Copy of resolutions respecting the inland post office, that the sequestration of the office to Burlamachi is illegal, and that he give an account of the profits of the office. L. J., V. 343. In extenso.

Annexed:—

1. Report concerning the office granted 22nd June 1637 to Thomas Witherings, sequestered 29th July 1640, for alleged misdemeanours in opening letters, not giving advices in due time, taking greater rates than usual, transporting prohibited commodities, not suffering the passage boat to be searched, not able to hold correspondence for want of language, breach of correspondence for want of paying foreign posts, none of which were proved; Witherings afterwards assigned his interest in the office to the Earl of Warwick.

2. Motion to be made upon preceding.

Sept. 8. Draft order for payment of 3,375l. to the receiver general of the county of Gloucester for timber, &c., by him to be paid to the Earl of Salisbury and Mr. Edward Tyringham. L. J., V. 344. In extenso.

Annexed:—

1. Petition of children and creditors of Mr. Tyringham to Edward Earl of Manchester for reference of their petition to the House of Commons.

Sept. 9. Request of John Yate, that he may have liberty to go abroad for his health, with his wife and son, and some three or four servants. L. J., V. 344.

Sept. 9. Petition of Captain Francis Coningesby, Richard March, and Edward Sherburn, officers of His Majesty's ordnance; petitioners were committed by order of the 17th August, for not issuing, upon a warrant from his Excellency (the Lord General), some part of the ammunition in the Tower of London entrusted to them by His Majesty's warrant; petitioners acted from no illfeeling towards Parliament, and pray that the conflict of command may be considered, and, now that the store has been disposed of, that they may be set at liberty and pardoned. L. J., V. 345.

Annexed:—

1. Copy of order of 17th August. L. J., V. 299. In extenso.

2-5. Two similar petitions, with two copies of order of 17th August annexed.

Sept. 9. Petition of the parishioners of the parish of All Hallows, Bread Street, in London: the rector, Mr. Lawson, is near his dissolution, and has for some years past been unable to officiate, during which time petitioners have at great charge provided Mr. Seaman to do the duty: they pray that when the place falls vacant, their Lordships would recommend the Archbishop of Canterbury, in whose care petitioners cannot confide, to appoint Mr. Seaman. L. J., V. 345.

Sept. 9. Draft order for finding out and regaining the goods of the Countess of Rivers, taken from her houses in Essex and Suffolk, and for encouraging her tenants to pay their rents. L. J., V. 331, 345.

Annexed:—

1. Printed copy of preceding.

2. Draft of amendments to same.

3. Petition of Elizabeth Countess Rivers, complaining that the preceding order has not been carried out, and that she and her children are consequently in want of subsistence. (Undated.)

Sept. 9. Letter from Peter Egerton, at Shaw, to Alexander Rigby, at his chamber in Gray's Inn: desires him, if possible, to obtain a pass for Robert Arderne, a Cheshire man, to go into France: Lord Strange is very active in the country summoning all before him, and disarming those who come not, trying to induce men to come in by giving out that a Parliament army is coming towards them, which has done great spoil to the King's subjects; should there be occasion to raise men in Cheshire and Lancashire, and the House should make use of him, he doubts not to do them good service.

Sept. 10. Petition of the inhabitants of Leighton, in the county of Bedford: the parsonage of Leighton, worth above 600l. per annum, is impropriate in the hands of the Dean and Canons of Windsor, and by them leased to Sir Thomas Leigh, one of the Commissioners of Array

in the county of Warwick; the vicarage, worth about
50l. per annum, is in the gift of a prebendary of Lincoln,
elected by the impropriators; the late vicar, Christopher
Slater, was a promoter of superstitious innovations and of
scandalous life, so that petitioners were obliged to maintain a lecturer, Samuel Fisher, for their better instruction in godliness, whom they pray may now be appointed
vicar. L. J., V. 345.

Sept. 10. Petition of Arthur Magneiss (or Magenness);
petitioner was on his way to Ireland, when he heard of
the outbreak of the rebellion there, and consequently
returned to West Chester, where, though a loyal subject,
he was suspected by the Mayor, and sent up to London,
and by their Lordships' order committed to the Tower,
where he has lain ten months; he fears that all his fortune, which is in Flanders, will be utterly lost, and
prays for enlargement, on the undertaking of the
Spanish Ambassador that he shall immediately go to
Flanders, and stay there during any rebellion in Ireland.
L. J., V. 346.

Sept. 10. Order for the Committee for the defence of
the kingdom to issue out monies in the absence of the
Lord General. L. J., V. 346.

Sept. 10. Draft of preceding.

Sept. 10. Draft order appointing treasurers and commissaries for Suffolk. L. J., V. 346.

Sept. 10. Draft ordinance for raising 2,000 foot for
Ireland. L. J., V. 347. In extenso.

Sept. 10. Copy of a letter from Lord Inchiquin, at
Cork, to [the Lords Justices of Ireland]; finding that if
some check were not given to the rebels the county of
Limerick would become wholly theirs, he determined
to attack them, and accordingly having noticed that
their forces were besieging the Castle of Liscarroll, he
started from Cork, sending word to other forces to join
him, and coming upon the rebels by forced marches
found them in a very strong position, the Castle of
Liscarrol having surrendered the night before; notwithstanding the difficulties of the ground, after some
slight firing of artillery the rebels were completely
routed, but were so nimble in flight that not above 500
are known to have been killed, but considerable stores
of arms, &c., were captured with the Castle, but
the writer was unable to advance, for his men were
without provisions, and the ruin of himself and his
men is only delayed, unless their Lordships can
send them a supply of men, money, victual, and munition, for the rebels are only annoyed by their late defeat and will soon rally again, so that without supplies
of all kind it will be impossible for the writer to maintain himself through the winter. Marmaduke Shafto
has lately come from Lord Dungarvan as commissary
over twenty draught horses, the writer requests that a
commission may be made out for him, and also that the
question of the command in those parts may be settled,
for the King's service suffers by a disjointed command;
the writer again earnestly entreats that assistance may
be sent to him, and in conclusion desires them to let
him know how he may advance Richard Gethney, who
has overture of a right nobleman's service, and to consider this letter as written to each of them individually.

Sept. 13. Information respecting the residence of
one Cheekley, ordered to be sent for as a delinquent.
L. J., V. 351.

Sept. 13. Petition of Thomas, Earl of Berkshire, that
he may either be heard, or have leave to be at his own
house upon bail. L. J., V. 351.

Sept. 13. Petition of the Earl of Carlisle, to be either
heard or bailed. L. J., V. 351. In extenso.

Sept. 13. Petition of Bartholmew Home, to be heard
or bailed. L. J., V. 352. In extenso.

Sept. 13. A note of the instructions for the Committee
to be sent into Ireland. See C. J., II. 764.

Sept. 14. The impeachment of James Lord Strange,
son and heir apparent of Wm. Earl of Derby, by
the Commons assembled in Parliament, in the name of
themselves and all the Commons of England, of high
treason. L. J., V. 354. In extenso.

Annexed:—

1. Deposition of Sir Thomas Stanley, of Bickerstaffe, concerning the proceedings of Lord Strange
in executing the Commission of Array in the
county of Lancaster. 5 August 1642.

2. Similar deposition of John Holcroft, Esq.
5 August 1642.

3. Deposition of Thomas Birch, Esq., in the same
matter. 5 August 1642.

Sept. 14. Certificate of the Mayor of Canterbury, that
William Edgforth, who is an inhabitant in the parish of
Christ Church, Canterbury, and a man of honest and

civil life, and no ways addicted to popery, had his house
broken into at an unreasonable hour of the night on
the 16th of August last, and his arms as one of the
trained bands taken away from him by some of Captain
Browne's company.

Sept. 15. Petition of William Le Ceur and others,
the creditors of Anthony Hooper, merchant, and of the
said Anthony Hooper: pray for an extension of the
time limited by the Commission for the examination of
witnesses in the cause, and for further powers to enforce
their attendance before the referees. L. J., V. 354.

Annexed:—

1. Copy of certificate from the referees, that owing
to the intricacy of the accounts and the imprisonment of Hooper, they have been unable to complete the case.

Sept. 15. Draft ordinance for settling Commissioners
for the navy. L. J., V. 355. In extenso.

Sept. 15. Draft order for the appointment of Mr.
Thomas Smith as secretary of the navy. L. J., V.
357. In extenso.

Sept. 16. Affidavit of Thomas Wright and others,
that Captain Davis, a pensioner in the Charter House,
tried to interrupt the sergeant who was calling upon
the people in Smithfield after beat of drum to serve
under the Earl of Essex, and said that it were no matter
if all were hanged that would so serve. L. J., V. 357.

Sept. 16. Draft answer of Parliament to the King's
last message, for conciliating differences. L. J., V,
358. In extenso.

Sept. 16. Draft order for the apprehension of Lord
Strange. L. J., V. 358. In extenso.

Sept. 17. Impeachment of Wm. Lord Marquess of
Hertford and others, by the House of Commons, for
summoning His Majesty's subjects together at Sherborne, in the county of Dorset, in August last, and
inciting them to take up arms; and for publishing a
paper containing malicious scandals against Parliament,
and actually levying war against the King, Parliament,
and kingdom. L. J., V. 360.

Sept. 17. Impeachment of John Weld, Esq., high
sheriff of the county of Salop, by the House of Commons, for proclaiming the Commission of Array in the
county, for inducing the grand jury in the name of the
county to sign a seditious declaration, &c. L. J., V.
360.

Annexed:—

1. Copy of declaration (mentioned in preceding),
expressing the loyalty of the subscribers to the
King.

2. Copy of resolutions concluded at Much Wenlock,
16 Aug. 1642, by the high sheriff and the rest of
the Commissioners of Array, for their mutual
protection.

Sept. 17. Petition of Bartholomew Mountague, Frenchman; Mr. Vayse, a haberdasher of small ware, living at
Paul's chain, will not deliver up petitioner's goods pursuant to their Lordships' order. L. J., V. 360.

Annexed:—

1. Affidavit in support of preceding.

Sept. 17. Certificate, numerously signed, delivered in
by Dr. Paske in support of his letter to the Earl of
Holland about the riot committed at Canterbury by the
soldiers; stating that Colonel Sands came to Canterbury on the evening of the 26th of August, and caused
a strict watch to be set upon the church and precincts;
and about two o'clock that night Captain Cockyn came to
Dr. Paske, and desired to see the arms of the church
and store of powder of the county, and took the keys
away then, and the arms and powder next morning; that
next morning, Saturday, no one was permitted to enter
the church for the performance of divine service at
six o'clock as usual, but about eight o'clock Sir Michael
Livesey and other officers went with many soldiers to
the vergers, who gave the keys to Captain Bayns, and
when Sir Michael was gone Captain Bayns with his
soldiers went into the church, when the following outrages were committed, the communion table was thrown
down the steps and turned legs upwards, the velvet cloth
was torn, and the gold fringe carried away, the screen
much defaced, the monument of Archbishop Chicheley
much violated, the keys and bellows of the organ cut
and spoiled, the ancient rails and seats, and the brazen
eagle supporting the Bible broken in pieces, the cupboards of the choirmen broken open, and their gowns,
surplices, and books, some torn and some taken away,
the famous arras hangings in the choir (representing
the whole story of our Saviour) were stabbed, ript, cut,
and slashed in many places, especially where the soldiers
observed any figure of Christ, whilst at another ancient

statue of Christ in the " frontispiece " of the Southgate, leading to the city, the troopers discharged their muskets, and there was much joy when they hit it either in the head or face; and Captain Bayns upon his return to Canterbury, on the 30th of August, seemed to justify these proceedings. L. J., V. 361.

Sept. 17. Letter from John Prowde, at Shrewsbury, to Humfry Mackworth, Esq., in London : I received your letter by Mr. Walsh, the post came not long after, but the Mayor sent to stop him at the gates and examined the letters in the Town Hall before they were delivered, and I doubt not would have opened any that he thought suspicious : we sent Mr. Walsh to Stafford to enquire after His Majesty, who heard there that the gentry and trained bands attended him at Uttoxeter on Thursday last, he was supposed to be then going to Newcastle, thence, perhaps, to Chester, no doubt he has had many invitations from Sir James Palmer and others in these parts; Sir Henry Jones has promised to bring much aid from Wales, but is not likely to do it; Mr. Barber, Mr. Charlton, and others have drawn towards Bristol, Mr. Charlton is thought to be there. Mr. Barber was detained at Bridgnorth by the Sheriff; Sir James Palmer has taken some lodgings here in case the King should come ; part of Lord Falkland's carriage is come with a direction that it should be placed near the King's lodging ; Lord Northampton was at Bridgnorth yesterday, and the latest news is that the King is expected to set up his standard here.

[Sept. 19.] Petition of the Earl of Portland : by long restraint in a very close and noisome house, petitioner is brought into a very ill state of health and fortune; prays that he may be restored to so much liberty as may preserve him and his family from ruin. L. J., V. 362.

Sept. 19. Letter from Sir Peter Courtney to Mr. Fish ; sends a copy of the King's direction to him to repair to Cornwall, and not to depart thence without leave (dated June 29th, 1642), from which will be seen what danger he would run by disobeying the King's command, but as soon as he has the King's leave he will with all speed appear before the House of Peers, when he doubts not his innocence will prove him a faithful subject. L. J., V. 364. *In extenso.*

Sept. 19. Two printed copies of the ordinance for the bringing in of plate, money, and horses (L. J., V. 121. *In extenso*), and of the instructions concerning the same, to be sent to the committees in the several counties. The instructions were ordered by the Commons to be printed this day. C. J., II. 773. *In extenso.*

Sept. 20. Petition of Dame Mary Carre, wife of Sir Robert Carre ; in February last their Lordships ordered that until petitioner's cause could be heard she should be protected from the violence of her husband ; who, having formerly conveyed certain property to the Earl of Northumberland and others in trust for petitioner and her children, afterwards forbade the tenants to pay their rents to the trustees, in consequence of which petitioner was obliged to bring an action against one of the tenants in the name of the trustees, and after much delay obtained a verdict, Sir Robert now threatens to bring a writ of error in the case of each several rent in order to delay the matter as far as possible, whilst petitioner is in great distress for want of the money ; she prays for a settlement of the matter by their Lordships, as she cannot obtain relief elsewhere in consequence of the absence of the Lord Keeper and obstruction of the Great Seal. L. J., V. 364.

Sept. 20. Petition of William Beale, Edward Martin, and Richard Sterne, Doctors in Divinity and Masters of Colleges in Cambridge; petitioners who were committed to the Tower by their Lordships' order of the 1st of September, are thereby forced to neglect their private affairs and public duties, whilst the fees and charges are greater than their estates can bear ; they pray for enlargement upon bond. L. J., V. 364.

Sept. 20. Petition of Owen George, John Betton, and Edward Davies, gent.; Richard Owen and Richard Betton were by order of 30th August last sent for as delinquents, Owen was attached at Shrewsbury by an officer of the House on the 7th instant, but Richard Gibbons, Mayor of Shrewsbury, with others, to the number of about 200 rescued him, and refused to obey their Lordships' order, saying that Owen was a Commissioner of Array, and must attend the Commission the next morning at Bridgnorth ; while the officer was informed that Betton the other delinquent was gone to the King at Nottingham ; pray that the rescuers may be sent for as delinquents and that Thomas Hunt, captain of the militia in Shrewsbury and his company may assist the officer to attach them. L. J., V. 364.

Annexed :—

1. Affidavit of Richard Cupman, deputy to the Gentleman Usher of the House of Lords, in support of preceding. 14 Sept. 1642.

Sept. 20. Draft instructions for the Committee to be sent into Ireland. L. J., V. 365. *In extenso.*

Sept. 21. Draft letter from the Speaker of the House of Lords to Secretary Nicholas, directing him to recommend to the King the preceding instructions, and the persons appointed by the Commons to carry them out. L. J., V. 365. *In extenso.*

Sept. 21. Instructions for Sir Thomas Pelham and others, Committees of both Houses of Parliament, for the raising money, plate, and horse for the defence of the King and kingdom in the county of Sussex. L. J., V. 365. *See* C. J., II. 773, where the instructions are given *in extenso*, but without any names.

Sept. 21. Petition of Richard Betton of London, merchant; upon a petition of Owen George, John Betton, and others, alleging a riot against petitioner and others, an order was made for their attachment, but only petitioner has been taken, who is a merchant in London and a factor for others in the country, so that if he be not soon enlarged, not only himself but others are likely to be utterly undone ; prays that the charge against him may be referred to the Lord Chief Justice, and meantime that he may be enlarged on bail. L. J., V. 366.

Sept. 21. Order giving power to the committee for taking account of the contributions to send for witnesses, records, &c. L. J., V. 366. *In extenso.*

Sept. 21. Draft of preceding.

Sept. 21. Draft order for the Lord Mayor and Sheriffs of London to be added to the committee for the militia there in the place of Sir John Gayre and Sir Jacob Garrett. L. J., V. 366. *In extenso.*

Sept. 21. Copy of declaration of the Commissioners of the National Assembly of the Kirk of Scotland, met at Edinburgh, thanking providence for inclining the English Parliament to accept the motion of the late assembly for union in religion and uniformity in kirk government, a work of great difficulty, and likely to meet with opposition from the locusts of the bottomless pit and the policy of worldly men, but for the accomplishment of which they trust in God and contribute their prayers and endeavours ; from prelacy, a tree God never planted, and the root of numberless evils in the people and ministers, the people of Scotland have mercifully been delivered, but it has taken deeper root in England, and they rejoice to think that it will be cut down, the stump even pulled up, and the ordinance of God planted in its place; episcopacy removed, the work of reformation will go on rapidly, for this end therefore not only the general assembly but the whole kirk and kingdom will unite their prayers. *See* L. J., V. 411.

Sept. 21. Petition of George Cantrell and Rebecca his wife, relict and executrix of Richard Butler, deceased, in the behalf of the orphans of the said Butler ; in 1636 Butler obtained judgment for 200l. against Charles Carey, but got no benefit thereby for Carey obtained privilege under the Earl of Dover; petitioners having now taken Carey in execution upon the judgment, he has produced a protection from the Earl of Nottingham, and has obtained an order from their Lordships for his discharge to the ruin of the orphans; pray that the order may be recalled, for Carey is no menial servant to the Earl, while the Lord Mayor presses to have the debt brought into the Chamber of London, and threatens to sue petitioners for the same for the benefit of the orphans.

Sept. 22. Petition of Sir Henry Bruce, praying for a protection for his safety, or a pass to transport himself, wife, children, family, and goods beyond seas. L. J., V. 367.

Sept. 23. Petition of Sir George Clerke, one of the sheriffs of the city of London, desiring to know how he is to dispose, on his going out of office, of Sir Robert Berkeley, now in his custody. L. J., V. 370. *In extenso.*

Sept. 23. Answer to the petition of Lucy Lady Hastings against Francis Poulton concerning the manor and rectory of Purton [Pirton], Herts, which were sold in 1633 by Sir Archibald Douglas for 1,500l. to Francis Poulton for 60 years, if Sir Archibald and his lady should so long live; with 700l. of the purchase money Sir Archibald bought himself an annuity of 100l. of Sir Humphrey Stiles, 360l. was paid to Benyon who held a mortgage of the premises, 200l. to Buck a silkman, who had a judgment against Sir Archibald, and the rest went in payment of debts. L. J., V. 370.

5.

G

Annexed:—
1. Affidavit of James Kenricke in support of preceding.
2. Declaration by Sir Archibald Douglas entirely disavowing the suit set on foot against Poulton by Lucy Lady Hastings on behalf of herself and Lady Eleanor Douglas.

Sept. 23. Petition of Dame Elizabeth Slingsby, widow: prays that Sir Faithful Fortescue, from whom she can get no answer to a Bill in Chancery respecting the settlement made on the marriage of his son with her daughter, on pretence of his service for the public, may not be allowed to depart until he has made answer, the matters being within his own privity, and not requiring above two or three hours' time. L. J., V. 371.

Sept 23. Draft order for soldiers to march to the rendezvous. L. J., V. 371. In extenso.

Sept. 23. Amendments in the Scots treaty for sending men to Ulster, and agreement respecting the same. L. J., V. 371. In extenso.

Sept. 23. Petition of Thomas Pitt and others; some soldiers, under command of Colonel Hollis, before the order of restraint, plundered the house of Mr. Civel, a papist, and openly sold the goods in the market, some of which petitioners ignorantly bought, in some cases at Civel's request for fear the soldiers should burn them; Civel afterwards procured an order from their Lordships for petitioners to appear and answer for their conduct, they appeared but could not be heard from press of business, and by Lord Mandeville's wish they departed till further notice, but were again summoned and committed for contempt of the former order; pray for discharge without payment of fees, and that Civel may be ordered on receiving again his goods, to reimburse them what they paid for them. L. J., V. 372.

Sept. 23. Draft order for the order respecting the Capuchin friars at Denmark House to be sent to Mr. Stricland, and notes of other proceedings. L. J., V. 372.

Sept. 23. Letter from the Lords Justices of Ireland at Dublin Castle to the Lord Speaker. They enclose a copy of their letter of the 24th of June last concerning the complaint of Henry Stewart and others after which they had hoped for a stay of all proceedings thereon; but they understand that the letter has not been read, while Mr. Stewart earnestly solicits further proceedings, they desire his Lordship to procure that their letter should be read, and that consideration may be had of the position and present circumstances of the accused, who are zealously engaged in the preservation of Ireland and ought not to be recompensed with dishonour.
Annexed:—
1. Petition of Sir Wm. Parsons one of the Lords Justices of Ireland, Sir Richard Bolton, Lord Chancellor, Sir Adam Loftus, Vice Treasurer, Sir Gerrard Lowther, Chief Justice of the Common Pleas, Sir George Radcliffe, and Sir Robert Meredith, Privy Councillors; petitioners despoiled by the rebellion, which they are daily toiling to suppress, are now threatened by their Lordships with imprisonment unless they pay 1,900l. damages to Henry Stewart and James Gray for a supposed crime in which they were most innocent, as they would have proved had their counsel been heard. Pray to be heard in favour of a rehearing of the cause. See L. J., V. 345.
2. Petition of Henry Stuart; is exhausted in estate by his long attendance, and unable to pay his creditors; will do so proportionably out of the first money he shall receive under the ordinance of both Houses; prays for protection for a time. See L. J., V. 345.

Sept. 24. Petition of Sir George Garrett, one of the sheriffs of the city of London, desiring to know how to dispose, when he goes out of office, of the Earl of Portland, now in his custody. L. J., V. 372. In extenso.

Sept. 24. Petition of Archibald Armestrong. John Scott, Dean of York, agreed to repay a debt of 200l. and interest to petitioner by half-yearly payments of 50l., to be made by Henry Earl of Danby out of the rectory of Pickering, but when petitioner had only received 50l., Dr. Laud Archbishop of Canterbury, under pretence of relieving the Dean of his creditors, interfered at the Council Board to prevent any further payment; prays that the Earl of Danby may be ordered to make the half-yearly payments until the debt be satisfied. L. J., V. 372.

[Sept. 26.] Petition of certain distressed ministers lately come from Ireland, deprived of their spiritual and temporal livings by the rebels; pray to be relieved out

of the collections made the next fast-day, as they can obtain no relief out of the collection made pursuant to their Lordships' former order. L. J., V. 373.
Annexed:—
1. Copy of order of 30th of August referred to in preceding. L. J., V. 333. In extenso.

Sept. *26. Two drafts of order for payment of 450l. to Captains Church and Beresford. L. J., V. 373. In extenso.

Sept. 27. Draft order for payment of 100l. to Sir Pierce Crosby in regard of his great losses in Ireland and his great deserts. L. J., V. 374. In extenso.

Sept. 27. Draft instructions for the committees at Lincoln. L. J., V. 374. In extenso.

Sept. 27. Petition of distressed ministers of Ireland, praying for further relief out of contributions to be made in London, Westminster, Southwark, and the suburbs thereof.
Annexed:—
1. Similar petition undated.

Sept. 27. Affidavit of Thomas Prittey and William Lynch, that Hercules Trew and others killed a doe in the Moat Park, Windsor. See L. J., V. 459.

Sept. 29. Two drafts of order for raising 1,000 dragoons with some troops of horse to be sent into Lancashire. L. J., V. 376. In extenso.

Sept. 29. Draft order for payment of 3l. per diem to the committees to be sent to Ireland. L. J., V. 377. In extenso.

Sept. 29. Copy of the declaration of the Secret Council of Scotland to Parliament, congratulating themselves on the prospect of unity in religion and uniformity in church government in the two kingdoms. Read in the House 11 Oct. See L. J., V. 393.

Sept. 29. Copy of the declaration of the Scotch Commissioners of the peace, to Parliament; are anxious to do all in their power to compose the distractions in England, and for this end have sent some of their number to use their endeavours with His Majesty and the Parliament, and desire a safe conduct for them. Read in H. L. 11 Oct. See L. J., V. 394.

Sept. 30. Petition of Sir Edmond Reve, one of His Majesty's Justices of the Court of Common Pleas; has been visited with a long and dangerous sickness and prays that his attendance may be dispensed with until his health is better. L. J., V. 377.

Sept. 30. Petition of Richard Le Grand, a French merchant and protestant. Crispin Desormeaux, a French merchant, has detained from petitioner about 400l. and goods to the value of 230l., and has arrested him for a pretended debt of 500l.; prays that the whole matter may be referred to the Lord Chief Justice of the King's Bench to examine and report thereon to the House, that petitioner may have relief. L. J., V. 377.
Annexed:—
1. Certificate of Sir John Brampston. The whole matter turns on the question whether the debt of 500l. alleged by Desormeaux to be due to him from Le Grand be true or not, and it was to save his goods from seizure till this point were decided that Le Grand went to prison 3 Oct 1642. L. J., V. 382. In extenso.
2. Further statement in the cause.
3. Petition of Richard Le Grand. Petitioner has laid in prison for eleven months at the suit of Desormeaux. Prays an order for his discharge upon common bail, and that his goods may be delivered to him.
4. Petition of Crispin Desormeaux. Prays that Le Grand's petition may be rejected as the statements contained in it are utterly false.
5. Petition of Le Grand, to Henry Earl of Holland. Prays that the word discharge may be substituted for the word security in the order made by their Lordship for petitioner's benefit.

Sept. 30. Names of deer stealers in Somersham Park. L. J., V. 377.

Sept. 30. Petition of Sir Thomas Dawes. In 1641, the Commons having voted the farmers of the customs delinquents for contracting with His Majesty for the farms before they were granted by bill, some of them offered 192,000l. by way of composition, which was accepted, and 31,495l. 11s. 8d. was apportioned upon the estate of Sir Abraham Dawes, petitioner's father, long since deceased, and now a Bill has been sent up from the Commons against the whole estate of petitioner and his father, and the question before their Lordships is, whether children are to be utterly undone for an error of their father not accused in his lifetime; petitioner was besides left engaged for his father's debts to the amount of 60,000l., and has been violently prosecuted by his creditors ever since the proceedings of the House of Commons in the matter, so that he dare not go out of his house for fear of arrest to the great damage of his estate and business. Prays their Lordships to grant him the same protection, whilst the Bill is before the House, that was given by the Commons in an order of the 11th of April last, that he may be able to instruct his counsel. L. J., V. 377.

Annexed :—
1. Copy of order of the Commons mentioned in preceding. C. J., II. 521. *In extenso.*
2. Another petition of Sir Thomas Dawes to the same effect.

Sept. 30. Petition of Sir Thomas Crymes and others, creditors of Sir Thomas Dawes. The Bill for the better payment of Sir Thomas Dawes' debts to His Majesty and others, has been five weeks before their Lordships, but only once read on account of press of business, whilst Sir Thomas is receiving the profits of his lands worth 2,000 per annum. Petitioners pray that the Bill may be read as soon as possible, and that the rents due at Michaelmas may be sequestrated towards satisfaction of the claims upon the estate, and that meantime no extents may issue against Dawes' estate. L. J., V. 377.

Annexed :—
1. Petition of Edward Russell, Esquire. Prays that Sir Thomas Dawes' Bill may not be allowed to pass until he has paid or secured to petitioner 1,000l., advanced by him to the late Sir Abraham Dawes.

Sept. 30. Draft order referring the two preceding petitions to the consideration of the Lord Chief Justice of the King's Bench. L. J., V. 377.

Annexed :—
1. Certificate of the Lord Chief Justice. The facts of the case are as stated by the petitioners, the extents desired to be stayed by the creditors are extents at the King's suit for the debt due by Sir Thomas Dawes. 4 Oct. 1642.

Sept. 30. Instructions for the Committee to be sent into Worcestershire. L. J., V. 377. *In extenso.*

Sept. 30. Request of Anne Roberts, wife of one of His Majesty's musicians, for a pass for herself, with her children, servants, and baggage into France, her native country.

[Sept.] Petition of Peter Smart, one of the prebendaries of Durham. Petitioner, during eighteen months that he has prosecuted his suit against Dr. Cosens and others upon the impeachment of the House of Commons, has spent above 1,200l., and has himself become heavily indebted and many of his friends beside, while Dr. Cosens and the others, though under recognizance to appear, have without leave gone down into the country, leaving only a solicitor to follow their business, and are embroiling the kingdom and endeavouring to raise both men and money (as they pretend) for the King, but really that whilst the public troubles increase they may escape their particular deserved punishments; while petitioner is excluded by them from his prebend, and reduced to extreme poverty, and they scoff at justice and rail upon the Parliament. Prays that a speedy day may be appointed for the conclusion of the cause, and that in case Dr. Cosens and the others do not appear he may have the benefit of their recognizances for his support and payment of his debts.

Oct. 1. Petition of William Arundell, Esq. In his former petition, petitioner showed that Lord Baltimore had influenced the late Lord Arundell, petitioner's father, in his last sickness, to charge certain lands and manors in a way he would never have done when in health. It was then directed that the Lord Keeper should proceed in the matter so far as the deeds were concerned, but that the criminal part should be reserved for their Lordship's hearing, but Lord Baltimore is endeavouring to get the manors sold in order to defeat their Lordships' intentions. Petitioner prays that stay may be made in these proceedings. L. J., V. 379.

Annexed :—
1. Copy of preceding.
2. Copy of order for Lord Baltimore to answer. L. J., V. 379.
3. Petition and answer of Cecil Lord Baltimore. Mr. Arundell's cause has been three times tried in the Court of Chancery, and on each occasion a decree has been pronounced in petitioner's favour. Prays that he may be freed from any further scandal and clamour, and that the execution of the final decree may proceed according to the rules and course of justice.

Oct. 1. Draft order of both houses for the magazine of arms at Droitwich to be kept by the bailiffs and officers of the town. L. J., V. 379. *In extenso.*

Oct. 1. Draft order respecting the 300l. collected for coat and conduct money, in Worcestershire. L. J., V. 379. *In extenso.*

Oct. 1. Draft order for payment of 2l. per diem to Captain William Tucker, assistant to the Committee going to Ireland. L. J., V. 379. *In extenso.*

Oct. 1. Draft order concerning the winter guard of shipping for England and Ireland, with list of the ships. L. J., V. 379. *In extenso.* (Two papers.)

Annexed :—
1. List of ships, headed " Guard for Ireland."

Oct. 1. Petition of Frederick Gibb, clerk, minister of Boxstead, in the county of Suffolk. Was sent for as a delinquent, and is now in the custody of the serjeant at arms, for reading the King's proclamation, concerning levies, in Boxstead Church. Prays pardon for his offence, which he committed in ignorance, never having heard of any order of the Parliament against publishing the proclamation. C. J., II. 789.

Oct. 3. Order in the cause between Le Grand, and Desormeaux, for the goods of the former to be restored to him. L. J., V. 380. *In extenso.*

Oct. 3. Names of persons to receive passes to travel. L. J., V. 380. *In extenso.*

Oct. 3. Petition of Francis Nicholls, of Westminster, poulterer. About twelve months since he took a piece of ground near Farnham, in Surrey, from Captain Coldham, captain of the trained bands there, and spent above 500l. in turning it into a warren and stocking it with conies, but now there are a multitude of disorderly people, who have of late destroyed all the deer in the Marquis of Hertford's park, and are destroying the deer in two parks of the Bishop of Winchester, at Farnham, and threaten when they have done there to destroy petitioner's warren, of which he is in hourly fear, and prays their Lordships to make a speedy order to protect him from ruin. L. J., V. 380.

Oct. 3. Petition of John Morris, servant in ordinary to the Prince, His Highness. Complains of arrest in August last, at the suit of Winkfield Molesworth, who said the case was now altered, and that the King's and Prince's servants had not now the same privileges, prays for release. L. J., V. 381. *In extenso.*

Annexed :—
1. Similar petition of same, undated.

Oct. 3. Order on preceding petition for discharge of Morris, and for Molesworth and the serjeants to be sent for as delinquents. L. J., V. 381.

Oct. 3. Draft order for issuing ammunition for Ireland. L. J., V. 381. *In extenso.*

Oct. 3. Draft order for the sheriffs of London and Middlesex to send one company of the trained bands to attend upon Parliament. L. J., V. 381. *In extenso.*

Oct. 3. Draft order for Captain Thomas Badnege to be a captain under Lord Kerry, in the room of Captain Thomas Watts. L. J., V. 381. *In extenso.*

Oct. 3. Petition of Adam Viscount Loftus, of Ely, in the kingdom of Ireland, against Sir George Wentworth, for not making repayment to petitioner pursuant to order of their Lordships. L. J., V. 381. *In extenso.*

Annexed :—
1. Affidavit of John Loftus in support of preceding. 20 Sept. 1642.

Oct. 3. Order providing security for those who should advance horses and arms for the thousand dragoons for Lancashire. L. J., V. 382. *In extenso.*

Oct. 3. Draft of preceding.

Oct. 4. Examination of William White, of the parish of " St. Pulcher's," London ; he wrought as a printer in the house of Gregory Dexter, and lately by his command printed a book called " King James's Judgment of a " King and of a Tyrant," but does not know who was the author of the book or how the copies were distributed. Examination of Abigail, wife of Gregory Dexter ; after her husband went away the book was printed in her house and by her order ; she knows who was the author but refuses to name him. L. J., V. 385.

Oct. 4. Two drafts of the orders appointing Mr. Hotham and the other committees in Yorkshire commissioners for receiving, money, horses, and plate, &c. L. J., V. 386. *In extenso.*

Oct. 4. Petition of Symon Norton, prisoner in the Fleet, to the Committee for the safety of the kingdom ; petitioner, as a sworn servant to His Majesty, was commanded to attend in person at Stoneley [Stoneleigh], in the county of Warwick, and after his departure thence upon his own affairs into Leicestershire, was apprehended and brought up prisoner to the Fleet, where he has remained fourteen weeks : since his departure into Leicestershire, his house near Coventry has been plundered, a barn burnt, timber trees cut down, and a manor house and barns entirely demolished; petitioner who rents much land in that neighbourhood, and employs many poor people, prays that he may be enlarged on bail, as if he should not receive his rents he will be unable to maintain himself and family, or pay his labourers their wages. C. J., II. 792.

Oct. 5. Message from the Commons, with an order for the Earl of Northumberland to be Lord Lieutenant of the county of Surrey, and for James Maine to be a Deputy Lieutenant for the county of Hertford. L. J., V. 386. *In extenso.*

Oct. 5. Two drafts of the instructions for Lord Willoughby of Parham, and the rest of the committees sent into Yorkshire. L. J., V. 387.

Oct. 5. Petition of Archibald Lord Archbishop of Cassell, in the kingdom of Ireland; has lost his worldly estate worth 9,000*l.* sterling, and what is worse, is put from his calling in preaching the Gospel; prays that unless he may have employment in some part of England, a pass may be granted for himself, his wife and family into Holland till peace be established in Ireland. L. J., V. 387.

Oct. 5. Petition of Thomas Hyde, Keeper of the great park at Farnham, in the county of Surrey. Andrew Wisdome and others, to the number of 100, on Sunday the 25th of September last, and on the last fast-day, and since, have riotously killed with dogs and guns, and carried away 200 deer at least out of the great park, and pulled down the pales and killed divers cattle, whilst others have been lost in consequence; they threatened to kill petitioner, who told them it were more fitting they should be at church according to the order of Parliament, saying they cared not what Parliament did or said; petitioner prays that they may be apprehended and brought before the House.

Oct. 5. Affidavit of Thomas Hyde in support of preceding. L. J., V. 387.

Oct. 5. Petition of Robert Earl of Warwick; the letter office of England was created by letters patent in June 1637, and granted to Thomas Witherings for life, whose estate is now vested in petitioner; in July 1640, the office was sequestered by the King's privy seal into the hands of Philip Burlamachi, who was directed by proclamation to execute the office; about the beginning of this Parliament a petition for relief was presented to the House of Commons, who, after hearing both sides, voted that the sequestration was illegal, that Burlamachi should account for the profits since the sequestration, and that the proclamation in pursuance of the sequestration was void, in all which their Lordships concurred; Burlamachi has not obeyed these votes duly served on him, and petitioner prays that he may be restored to possession of the office and Burlamachi punished for his disobedience. L. J., V. 387.

Oct. 5. Draft order for payment to Sir Thomas Barrington of the remainder of the 4,000*l.* appointed to be spent out of the contributions of the county of Essex, on arms, &c. for the county. L. J., V. 387. *In extenso.*

Oct. 5. Draft order for the Mayor of Colchester, to take charge of the arms and ammunition of the Countess of Rivers, at St. Osith, Essex. L. J., V. 388. *In extenso.*

Oct. 5. Certificate of the Lord Chief Justice in the case of Richard Betton against Owen George and others, relating to proceedings respecting the will of Dame Margaret Eyton.

Oct. 6. Petition of Scipio Le Squyre, Vice-Chamberlain of the Exchequer; prays to be restored, pursuant to the Lord Chief Justice's report, to a house in Long Acre, from which he was ousted by Sergeant Francis. L. J., V. 388.

Oct. 6. Petition of Sir Alexander Gordon; petitioner having been a servant to His Majesty for many years, and to King James before, was promised by the King a warrant for a certain sum of money for maintenance, but he fell into so severe a sickness from which he is not yet entirely recovered, that he could not get the warrant signed, meantime the rebels have seized all his estate in Ireland, and forced his wife and children to fly for safety to some remote place; prays for a pass to go to the King to get the warrant signed, and then to Ireland to seek his wife and children, and transport them to Scotland or elsewhere. L. J., V. 388.

Oct. 6. Draft declaration directing the Lords Justices of Ireland and others to assist the committee sent thither. L. J., V. 388. *In extenso.*

Oct. 6. Draft order for the defence of the town of Manchester. L. J., V. 388. *In extenso.*

Oct. 6. Draft order for 8,980*l.* 5*s.* to be paid to the several persons who have supplied corn, victual, clothing, and other necessaries for the services of Ireland. L. J., V. 389. *In extenso.*

Oct. 6. Affidavit of Richard Le Grand, that John Beverlette refuses to re-deliver to him his goods pursuant to their Lordships' order. *See* L. J., V. 397, &c.

Oct. 6. Information of Samuel Crossman and others, that William Price, of Bradfield St. Clare, in the county of Suffolk, called the members of both Houses base rascals, &c.

Oct. 7. Petition of Owen George, John Betton, and Edward Davies; that their cause against Richard Betton, senr., and Richard Betton, junr., concerning the administration of Lady Eyton's estate, may not be heard until all the parties and witnesses can appear. L. J., V. 389.

Oct. 7. Draft order for the Earl of Leicester, Lord Lieutenant of Ireland, to bring into the House his instructions lately received from the King. L. J., V. 389. *In extenso.*

Oct. 7. Draft order for payment of money due to Captain Dawson (or Davison) and others. L. J., V. 389. *In extenso.*

Oct. 7. Draft order for Oliver Pleddall, to have the Lieutenant's place of the troop of horse under Captain St. John, in Ireland. L. J., V. 389. *In extenso.*

Oct. 7. Petition of Dame Barbara Villiers, stating that for more than 20 years she has enjoyed a house in the Dean's Yard, Westminster, and that long before her time and since there was only a lodge at the gate for a porter for letting people in and out, that under colour of a lodge a great structure has been built with several sheds upon the waste ground and against the wall of her house without her consent, depriving her not only of the air and prospect, but of all privacy in her best rooms; and now higher stories and chimneys are being built, which will be still greater annoyance to her; she is unwilling that her landlord, Mr. Littcott, now employed in the service of Parliament, should suffer in his absence, and prays on his behalf and her own for stay of the buildings and for further consideration of the case. L. J., V. 390.

Oct. 7. Petition of George Wall, clerk, chaplain to the Earl of Essex ; the patronage of the church of Newington Butts, Surrey, has for almost 100 years been enjoyed by the Bishops of Worcester by virtue of an exchange with the Crown, but on the church becoming void about eight years ago, the Archbishop of Canterbury collated Thomas Stevens to the church, whereupon a *quare impedit* was brought against the Archbishop and Stevens by Mr. Bludworth, the grantee of the Bishop of Worcester, and upon a trial at the Common Pleas, a verdict was given in his favour, but Stevens having brought a writ of error merely for delay, Mr. Bludworth overruled by the Archbishop, waived the Bishop's presentation and accepted the living upon the Archbishop's collation ; the Bishop of Worcester, not knowing anything of this, granted the next presentation of the living to Nicholas Wall, petitioner's brother, in trust to present petitioner, then domestic chaplain to the Bishop, since which grant, the living having become void, the Archbishop has collated Mr. Meggs, parson of St. Margaret Pattens, London ; petitioner's cause was formerly referred by their Lordships to the common law, but having brought a *quare impedit*, he finds that he cannot make a declaration, and therefore cannot have any remedy in law, in consequence of the said collation of Mr. Bludworth by collusion ; prays that a trial may be directed to be had of the Bishop of Worcester's right to present, independently of this collusive collation. L. J., V. 390.

Oct. 7. Instructions for the Earl of Essex to deliver the petition of both Houses to the King with all speed. L. J., V. 390. *In extenso.*

Oct. 7. Draft order for an allowance to be made to Mr. Hawkins, Mr. Chambers, and Mr. Willis, attending the Commissioners for Ireland. L. J., V. 390. *In extenso.*

Oct. 7. Draft order for seizing horses and arms of ill-affected persons in Northamptonshire. L. J., V. 390. *In extenso.*

Oct. 7. Draft order for Captain Ashley, of the "Employment," to take the committees for Ireland to Dublin, and to bring the Earl of Antrim from Carrickfergus. L. J., V. 391. *In extenso.*

Oct. 7. Draft order that the persons appointed to take subscriptions of money, plate, &c., within London and Westminster, may also receive the said money, plate, &c. L. J., V. 391. *In extenso.*

Oct. 7. Draft order for payment of the regiments of foot and horse in Ulster. L. J., V. 391. *In extenso.*

Oct. 7. Draft order for sending ammunition to Ireland. L. J., V. 391. *In extenso.*
Annexed:—
1. Draft preamble to preceding, recapitulating the previous orders on the subject. Endorsed, " Not " to be entered."
Oct. 7. Petition of Wm. Gage; prays for a pass into France for himself, his wife, children, and servants. L. J., V. 391.
Annexed:—
1. Note that Mr. Gage lives at a house called Bentley, in Sussex, and has about 800*l.* per annum; he is generally beloved, and never suspected of doing or intending anything against the King or State; it is true he is a recusant, and until things are quieter he desires to go into France and have his estate paid him in England.
Oct. 7. Draft order for Lord Conway to send 1,000 men and a troop of horse to the relief of Munster, for providing clothing, &c. L. J., V. 392.
Oct. 7. Two drafts of the instructions to be sent to Mr. Walter Strickland, agent for the Parliament, with the States General of the United Provinces. L. J., V. 392. *In extenso.*
Oct. 7. Draft order for Mr. Wm. Pennoyer, to take up carts to carry match and powder to Bristol. L. J., V. 392. *In extenso.*
Oct. 7. Draft order giving the Committee for the safety and defence of the kingdom power to administer oaths. L. J., V. 392. *In extenso.*
Oct. 8. Request from the Earl of Portland for a pass for one of his servants into France to his lady with a trunk of apparel. L. J., V. 392.
Oct. 10. Two orders for Mr. Ashton (Ashurst) and others to be added to the committee for the raising of a thousand dragoniers. L. J., V. 393. *In extenso.*
Oct. 10. Two orders approving of Alderman Wollaston and others as treasurers for the same purpose, and for appointment of Captain Struce as Sergeant-major. L. J., V. 393. *In extenso.*
Oct. 10. Two orders for the appointment of a committee of the subscribers for the same purpose. L. J., V. 393. *In extenso.*
Oct. 11. Petition of Wingfield Molsworth, citizen and grocer of London. Petitioner was committed by their Lordships on the ground that he had arrested John Morris, embroiderer to the Prince, contrary to privilege; petitioner who acted in ignorance, is heartily sorry for his offence, and having withdrawn his action, prays to be released on bail, as he has nothing but his trade to maintain himself, his wife, and children. L. J., V. 394.
Oct. 11. Certificate of Sir Richard Stonnes, sheriff of the county of Huntingdon, and others; having received their Lordships' order for the apprehension of the delinquents (who killed the deer in Somersham Park), they sent to the house at Old Hurst, where the delinquents were supposed to be, but the officers were refused admittance. The offenders are desperate men and cannot be apprehended without raising the power of the county, for which there is no authority under the order of the House, and therefore further directions are desired in the matter. L. J., V. 394.
Oct. 11. Draft order for Captain Tucker to be admitted as assistant to the committee sent to Ireland. L. J., V. 395. *In extenso.*
Oct. 11. Petition of Daniell Farvack and Isaac Le Gay, of London, merchants; tobacco formerly belonging to Anthony Hooper, but adjudged to petitioners by order of their Lordships, has been seized in Guernsey by John Basley, who, in the absence of petitioners has obtained a sentence there in his favour, from which they have appealed. Pray that the case may be referred to the referees engaged in deciding between Anthony Hooper and his creditors. L. J., V. 395. *In extenso.*
Annexed:—
1. Copy of summons made upon the appeal in the Isle of Guernsey. 9 Sept. 1642.
Oct. 11. Order for the Earl of Warwick to repair to Parliament, and for Captain Batten to be Vice-Admiral in his absence. L. J., V. 396. *In extenso.*
Oct. 11. Draft of preceding.
Oct. 11. Draft order appointing Christopher White, Keeper of the Gatehouse. L. J., V. 396. *In extenso.*
Oct. 11. Draft order to prevent the conveyance of arms, &c. from Bristol to the Marquess of Hertford, in Wales. L. J., V. 396. *In extenso.*
Oct. 11. Draft order for Captain Venn to dispose of arms, &c. L. J., V. 396. *In extenso.*
Oct. 11. Order directing the sheriffs of Yorkshire to

assist the Committees in execution of the militia there. L. J., V. 396. *In extenso.*
Oct. 11. Draft of preceding.
Oct. 11. Informations against Captain Kettleby, captain of one of His Majesty's ships for the defence of the coasts of Ireland, who deserted that service. C. J., II. 803.
i. Copy of the King's warrant to Captain Kettleby, Admiral of the fleet on the Irish coast, to come to Newcastle. 23 June 1642.
ii. Copy of the King's warrant to the captain of any ship to receive the Duke of Richmond and Lennox on board and convey him abroad. 17 Sept. 1642.
iii. Examination of the master and officers of the " Swallow." That the morning after the storm, which happened on Michaelmas day, the captain called them all into the cabin, and tried to persuade them to agree to alter the ship's course and steer for Holland, but they said that they were under promise to repair to the Downs, the boatswain adding that there were fifty men on board who would cut the halliards rather than consent to such a step; upon which the captain turned them out of the cabin as if they had been traitors.
Oct. 12. Application from Mr. George Howard and others for leave to travel. L. J., V. 397.
Oct. 12. Letter from George Darell to his dear tutor, Mr. Acred. Desires his good services with his Lordship (the Earl of Mulgrave) that he would procure his release from prison, for the sergeant when he saw the writer's protection said, that if the debt were but ten groats he would not release him for any lord in England. L. J., V. 397.
Annexed:—
1. Letter from the Earl of Mulgrave to the person that arrested his servant George Darell. Will question him for this affront to the privileges of Parliament, unless upon sight of this letter his servant be released. (Undated.)
Oct. 12. Petition of Giles Thorne, clerk. Petitioner has been seven weeks committed on account of objection taken to some passages in his sermons; the case has been partly heard, and he prays that a speedy day may be appointed for the further hearing, or that he may be bailed. L. J., V. 397.
Annexed:—
1. Another petition of Thorne to be bailed. 14 Feb. 1642-3.
Oct. 12. Draft order directing the mayor, &c. of Exeter to fortify and defend the town and castle. L. J., V. 398. *In extenso.*
Oct. 12. Order for indemnity of the Yarmouth men for seizing a ship from Rotterdam with men and arms for Newcastle. L. J., V. 398. *In extenso.*
Oct. 12. Draft of preceding.
Oct. 12. Draft order for continuing forces in the county of Dorset. L. J., V. 398. *In extenso.*
Oct. 12. Draft order for payment of 300*l.* for the fortification of the castle and town of Exeter. L. J., V. 399. *In extenso.*
Oct. 12. Draft order for payment of 68*l.* 8*s.* to Sergeant Major Warren. L. J., V. 399. *In extenso.*
Oct. 13. Petition of Crispin Desormeaux, merchant in Paris, in France, by Giles Vanbrugg his procurator. Richard Le Grand, a pretended merchant, but formerly a Jesuit, has presented a false petition to their Lordships, which was referred to the Lord Chief Justice, and certain goods, now in the hands of John Beverlett, were ordered upon reading his report to be delivered up to Le Grand: these goods form part of goods out of which Le Grand has cozened many merchants in Paris, and should go in satisfaction of claims upon him. Petitioner prays to be heard before the goods are surrendered by Beverlett. *See* L. J., V. 399.
Oct. 13. Petition of Matthew Francis. The 10th instant was appointed for hearing the cause between petitioner and Scipio Le Squire, and whilst attending with their counsel and witnesses they agreed to refer all the matters in dispute to their counsel for decision; but afterwards Squire went back from his agreement. Petitioner prays for an order confirming the agreement.
Annexed:—
1. Affidavit of Francis in support of preceding.
Oct. 14. Petition of Sarah Berry. Petitioner after enduring great brutality from her husband, who attempted her life and then defamed her honour and turned her out of doors, was obliged at length to proceed against him in the Spiritual Court for separation and maintenance; the case depended there for a year but she could not bring her husband to answer, and that

court has now no power to compel him. Prays that her case may be referred to a committee of their Lordships. L. J., V. 399.

Oct. 14. Message from the Commons, with a note for the appointment of a select committee to take care of the affairs of Ireland. L. J., V. 400. *In extenso.*

Oct. 14. Draft order for payment of 100*l.* to Viscountess Baltinglasse. L. J., V. 400. *In extenso.*

Oct. 14. Draft order for payment of 10,316*l.* 13*s.* 4*d.* to the Treasurer at Wars for 6,000 muskets, &c. for the Scottish army in Ireland. L. J., V. 400. *In extenso.*

Oct. 14. Draft order for courts of guard, and posts, bars, and chains to be set up near Westminster. L. J., V. 400. *In extenso.*

Oct. 15. Order that the officers of the Court of Wards shall not henceforth pass the annual pensions arising out of that Court to the Duke of Richmond and others. L. J., V. 401. *In extenso.*

Oct. 15. Draft of preceding.

Oct. 15. Draft order for Giles Greene to be a commissioner for the customs. L. J., V. 401. *In extenso.*

Oct. 15. Order for erecting courts of guard in the suburbs, &c. L. J., V. 401. *In extenso.*

Oct. 15. Draft of preceding.

Oct. 15. Message from the Commons, with resolutions for securing those who do not contribute to the charge of the Commonwealth, &c. L. J., V. 402. *In extenso.*

Oct. 15. Draft declaration for putting the counties near the city of London in a posture of defence. L. J., V. 402. *In extenso.*

Oct. 15. Certificate of inhabitants of the county of Middlesex to the Lords and Commons, that Leonard Leonards of East Smithfield, is a man of quality and approved trust, and fit to be appointed captain to command and train the inhabitants of St. Katharine's and East Smithfield as a foot company, they humbly desire that their election may be confirmed by Parliament.

Oct. 17. Draft of the answer given by the House of Lords to Alderman Pennington, when presented for their approbation. L. J., V. 404. *In extenso.*

Annexed :—
1. Another draft with instructions respecting his taking the usual oaths before the Barons of the Exchequer.

Oct. 17. Draft order for payment of 40,000*l.* to the Scots Commissioners towards the brotherly assistance. L. J., V. 405. *In extenso.*

Oct. 17. Draft order for disarming Edward Lawrance and others in Dorsetshire. L. J., V. 405. *In extenso.*

Oct. 17. Draft order for payment of 2,000*l.* to Sir John Bamfield and Mr. Waddon for defence of Devon and Cornwall. L. J., V. 405. *In extenso.*

Oct. 17. Petition of Thomas Lord Coventry, he submits himself to the House, and is sorry to have offended in replying to their Lordships' summons, but he had also received His Majesty's summons to attend him at York. L. J., V. 405. *In extenso.*

Oct. 19. Petition of John Escott ; petitioner has undergone part of their Lordships' sentence, having stood in the pillory in Cheapside and at Westminster; he has lain in Newgate, where the sickness has been very hot for more than nine months ,by which his health is impaired, and his estate consumed by excessive fees. Prays to have liberty on bail in London and within six miles round. L. J., V. 406.

Oct. 19. Petition of Thomas Graves and William Shawe, in behalf of themselves and others, tenants of Sir Robert Carre, of lands, settled for the payment of 400*l.* per annum for his children's use ; by order of their Lordships of the 20th September, made upon a complaint of Lady Carre, petitioners were directed to pay their rents into the hands of the Earl of Northumberland and others, feoffees in trust for the use of the children ; Sir Robert affirms that the 400*l.* has always been duly paid for the use of the children, and directs the tenants to pay the rents to him ; they fearing to incur the penalties contained in their leases, pray to be discharged from obedience to their Lordships' order. L. J., V. 406.

Annexed :—
1. Petition of Richard King, Esq. As a neighbour of Sir Robert Carre and his lady upon some differences between them, he allowed his name amongst others to be used as lessee for years to the Earl of Northumberland and others under a rent of 600*l.* per annum for the lady's use, but never occupied a foot of the lands or received a penny of the rents, but has permitted them to be disposed of as before by Sir Robert Carre's direction. Petitioner is involved in a suit at law about them, and prays to be discharged from

obedience to their Lordships' order of the 20th of September.

2. Copy of order mentioned in preceding. L. J., V. 364.

[Oct. 19.] Petition of Richard Le Grand. Petitioner has been eleven months in prison at the suit of one Desormeaux and his goods attached; and by order of the 3rd of October it was ordered that the goods should be delivered up as having been unjustly attached (L. J., V. 382) ; and by an order of the 13th of October that John Beverlett should be attached for not delivering up the said goods (L. J., V. 399), and that petitioner should accept a declaration from Desormeaux before his discharge, but no declaration has been put in. Petitioner prays that he may be enlarged on bail and have his goods restored. *See* L. J., V. 406, &c.

Annexed :—
1. Complaint of (Richard Le Grand).
2. Copy of further order in confirmation of former orders. L. J., V. 406.

Oct. 19. Petition of the parishioners of Ryersh [Ryarsh], in the county of Kent. Petitioners have for more than a year past been without any resident minister, though Mr. Wm. Walton, the undoubted patron, has presented Mr. Sybbalds, Bachelor of Divinity, of Aberdeen, of whom they approve, but he is kept away in consequence of Mr. Trott, vicar of Starsfield, having raised a pretended claim to the living. Petitioners pray that Mr. Sybbalds' presentation may be confirmed. L. J., V. 406.

Oct. 19. Draft order for Mr. Trott to answer.

Oct. 19. Draft of the propositions for the raising of some of the trained bands of the several counties for the defence of London. L. J., V. 407. *In extenso.*

Oct. 19. Draft order appointing the Earl of Northumberland and others, Commissioners of the Navy. L. J., V. 407. *In extenso.*

Oct. 19. Draft order respecting their power. L. J., V. 407. *In extenso.*

Oct. 19. Draft order for payment of 300*l.* for relief of the poor protestants in Ireland. L. J., V. 407. *In extenso.*

Oct. 19. Draft order for ten ships to guard the Irish coasts. L. J., V. 408. *In extenso.*

Oct. 19. Petition of Sir Edward Henden, one of the Barons of the Court of Exchequer, for leave of absence on account of his health. L. J., V. 408. *In extenso.*

Oct. 19. Draft propositions for raising money, &c., in Devonshire. L. J., V. 408. *In extenso.*

Oct. 19. Draft ordinance for the sending out ships with letters of marque for relief of Ireland. L. J., V. 409. *In extenso.*

Oct. 19. Draft order in confirmation of the order of 31st May last, excusing the two ministers of the Island of Guernsey, nominated by Act of Parliament, from attendance at the assembly of Divines. *See* L. J., V. 94.

Oct. 19. Letter from the Lords Justices of Ireland to the Speaker of the House of Lords, recapitulating the arguments contained in their former letters for the dismissal of the complaint of Henry Stewart and John Gray against Sir John Parsons and other members of the Irish Council Board, especially as Stewart and Gray never paid the fine complained of, or any fees whilst in prison. L. J., V. 488. *In extenso.*

Annexed :—
1. A brief of the manner of the proceedings in Stewart's business against the Privy Council of Ireland in the Lords House of Parliament.
2. Petition of Sir Robert Meredyth. Was commanded by order from their Lordships to appear on the 1st July 1642 to answer the complaint of Henry Stewart and others, but as so few of the Council were at that time resident, he could not obtain leave to attend, and besides had been robbed of all his horses and goods by the rebels. Prays that the former directions in the cause may be suspended until he has been heard in his defence. (Undated.)

Oct. 20. Draft ordinance for making Philip Earl of Pembroke and Montgomery chief commander in the West. This ordinance was sent up from the Commons this day, and the Lords added the names of certain counties, and then referred the ordinance or commission to the Committee for the safety of the kingdom, after which it appears to have been dropped. It is noted " Not passed." L. J., V. 410.

Annexed :—
1. Names of counties added by the Lords.

Oct. 20. Draft answers of the Lords and Commons. L. J., V. 410, 411. *In extenso.*

i. To the Lords of the Privy Council of Scotland.

ii. To the Commissioners of the National Assembly of Scotland.

iii. To the Commissioners in Scotland for the preservation of the peace betwixt the two nations.

Oct. 20. Heads of the conference concerning an association for the defence of the kingdom. L. J., V. 412.

Oct. 20. Draft order appointing Mr. Henry Bulstrode, colonel of the trained bands and volunteers of three hundreds in the Chilterns, in the county of Bucks. L. J., V. 413. *In extenso.*

Oct. 21. Draft order for repayment of money disbursed by the Mayor of Plymouth. L. J., V. 414. *In extenso.*

Oct. 21. Draft order for securing the town of Exeter. L. J., V. 414. *In extenso.*

Oct. 21. Draft order to pay 1,040*l.* to James Sanderson for oatmeal sent for the relief of Londonderry. L. J., V. 414. *In extenso.*

Oct. 21. Draft order to pay 12*l.* to Tobias Norris, for clothing poor English in Dublin. L. J., V. 415. *In extenso.*

Oct. 21. Draft order for troops raised by the town of Bandonbridge to be taken into the pay of the State. L. J., V. 415. *In extenso.*

Oct. 21. Order appointing a day for hearing some cause not mentioned.

Oct. 22. Message from the Commons, with resolution for the appointment of the Earl of Warwick as captain-general of the forces to be raised in the parts about London. L. J., V. 415. *In extenso.*

Oct. 22. Draft of the Earl of Warwick's commission. L. J., V. 416. *In extenso.*

Oct. 22. Draft order for the Marshal of the Admiralty to make stay of ships for defence of the city of London. L. J., V. 417. *In extenso.*

Oct. 22. Draft order for the deputy lieutenants of the counties of Devon and Cornwall to take up ships for the service of the counties. L. J., V. 417. *In extenso.*

Oct. 22. Draft (much amended) of the protestation and declaration of the Lords and Commons in Parliament to this kingdom and to the whole world. L. J., V. 417. *In extenso.*

Oct. 22. Draft order for repayment to the committee and deputy lieutenants of the county of Cornwall of all money disbursed by them. C. J., II. 818.

Oct. 24. Petition of Robert Walley and George Norman, prisoners in the Fleet. Petitioners stand committed by their Lordships' order of the 18th instant for arresting George Darrell, servant to the Earl of Mulgrave; they acknowledge their fault, and pray to be discharged without payment of fees. L. J., V. 419.

Annexed:—

1. Similar petition to the Earl of Mograve [Mulgrave]. Noted, "Forasmuch as concerns myself " (if the House be pleased) I am satisfied."

2. Copy of order of 18 Oct.

Oct. 24. Petition of the Earl of Portland. Has now lain almost three months in close houses in restraint, and is thereby greatly prejudiced in his estate, and likely to be ruined; is not guilty of any crime against their Lordships, and therefore prays to be restored to his liberty, and to his right and privilege in Parliament. L. J., V. 419.

Oct. 24. Draft order to indemnify the inhabitants of Barnstaple for fortifying their town. L. J., V. 419. *In extenso.*

Oct. 24. Draft order for the King's children to be removed into London. L. J., V. 419. *In extenso.*

Oct. 24. Draft order for shutting up shops in London. L. J., V. 420. *In extenso.*

Oct. 24. Draft order for restraining prisoners in the Tower. L. J., V. 420. *In extenso.*

Oct. 24. Draft order for search to be made for horses in St. James, Clerkenwell. L. J., V. 420. *In extenso.*

Oct. 24. Similar order for St. Andrew's, Holborn.

Oct. 24. Similar order for St. Martin's in the Fields, St. Mary Savoy, and St. Clement Danes.

Oct. 24. Similar order for St. Giles in the Fields.

Oct. 24. Two drafts of the ordinance for safe conduct of the Scotch Commissioners. L. J., V. 420. *In extenso.*

Annexed:—

1. Proviso excluding the Duke of Lennox and Earl of Roxborough from the safe conduct. L. J., V. 420. *In extenso.*

Oct. 24. Draft order for appointment of justices of the peace in Lancashire. L. J., V. 421. *In extenso.*

Oct. 24. Draft order for securing and disarming recusants in Lancashire. L. J., V. 421. *In extenso.*

Oct. 24. Draft ordinance for making provision for maimed soldiers. L. J., V. 421. *In extenso.*

Annexed:—

1. Printed copy of preceding.

Oct. 24. Draft order for payment of 100*l.* to the Archbishop of Tuam. L. J., V. 421. *In extenso.*

Oct. 24. Draft order for payment of 100*l.* to Sir Francis Hamilton. L. J., V. 421. *In extenso.*

Oct. 24. Draft order for payment of 50*l.* to Robert Bailey. L. J., V. 421. *In extenso.*

Oct. 24. Information against Roger Clarke and others for refusing to subscribe the propositions. *See* C. J., II. 820.

Oct. 25. Two drafts of the order for putting London into a posture of defence. L. J., V. 422. *In extenso.*

Oct. 25. Draft order for an allowance to be made for support of the King's younger children. L. J., V. 423. *In extenso.*

Oct. 25. Copy of the declaration of both Houses in answer to His Majesty's declaration, intituled "His " Majesty's declaration to all his loving subjects after " his late victory against the rebels on Sunday, Oct. 23, " 1642." Rushworth, II., iii. 41. *In extenso.* *See* L. J., V. 423, where it is said that "a large declaration, " being an answer to a former declaration of the King, " which lays a scandal upon the Parliament," was read and approved and ordered to be printed and published. The last sheet of this copy is wanting.

Oct. 26. Copy of the King's proclamation, offering pardon to those who would submit to him, except those whom he has proclaimed traitors. This proclamation was to have been sent by herald to the Earl of Essex, and to have been dispersed in his army, but was forgotten in the hurry preceding the battle of Edgehill, which took place on the 23rd. The proclamation is entered *in extenso.* L. J., V. 423.

Oct. [27]. Petition of William Lord Archbishop of Canterbury. Upon sight of their Lordships' order of the 24th instant (for restraining the prisoners in the Tower), he dismissed all his servants save two. Prays that beside his two servants, "who are to make his bed, " and do other things necessary for his age, going on " with threescore and ten years of a weary life, their " Lordships would favourably allow him a butler and " a cook, without which he knows not how to live, " being not placed in any house in the Tower, but in a " solitary room, destitute of all company and other " help."

Oct. 28. List of Committee for receiving the despatches from the Committees in the several counties, with their instructions. C. J., II. 825. *In extenso.*

Oct. 28. Letter from the Lords Justices of Ireland at Dublin Castle to Mr. Speaker. Since their letter of the 12th instant, they have been earnestly solicited to send supplies of all kinds to Connaught, most of the men sent thither having died of mere want, whilst the rest are ready to disband, and the writers can do nothing without supplies from England. They have similar requests from the garrisons in Leinster, especially for powder, of which their own store is very short, and they therefore must repeat their former requests for speedy supply. The regiments under Lord Conway, Sir William Stewart, and others, are all in great distress, and the writers unable to help them. The rebels have lately published a proclamation, of which a copy is enclosed (wanting); they also enclose a copy of an Act of Council for celebrating the 23rd of Oct. by a public thanksgiving; they are in great want of mills, as they have all been destroyed, either by the rebels or their own soldiers, and request that a hundred steel mills may be sent them, and further that the drugs for which they sent by their agents may be hastened over, and those persons punished who supplied bad drugs on a former occasion. By their letters of the 7th of June they requested that if they were not to have the command of the Scotch forces in Ulster, those forces might be moved from Carrickfergus to Londonderry and other places more convenient for the defence of the province; this they again earnestly repeat, fearing that if it be not done the rebels will fall upon and reduce Londonderry. In derogation of the Royal authority the rebels have established courts of judicature, elected knights of the shires, and assembled in a pretended Parliament at Kilkenny. In conclusion, the writers repeat their earnest request for supplies of men, money, arms, powder, match, and other provisions mentioned in their former despatches. *See* C. J., II. 832.

Enclosing:—

Three printed copies of an Act of Council of the Lords Justices of Ireland, enjoining that the 23rd of October should henceforth be observed in all churches throughout Ireland, in thankful remembrance of the discovery of the plot for the seizure of the castle and town of Dublin and massacre of all the British and Protestants there, discovered only a few hours before its intended execution.

Oct. 29. Letter from the gentlemen of the county of Devon at Exeter to the Committee for the safety of the kingdom : have come from Plymouth to confer with the Deputy Lieutenants of Devon about the raising of men and money to oppose the malignants in the writers' own county, who grow stronger and stronger every day. The gentlemen of Devon are willing, but want money and arms ; they have written to the gentlemen of Somerset, Wilts, &c., for assistance. If the Earl of Pembroke were to come, there would be a cheerful access to him ; meantime they desire that Colonel Bampfield, with his regiment, may be sent to Exeter. *See* L. J., V. 425.

[Oct.] Petition of Captain Robert Slingsbie and Captain Baldwin Wake : have already been seven weeks in prison, and have had no benefit of the order made on their former petition that they should be bailed. Pray for enlargement on bail or otherwise. *See* L. J., V. 385.

Nov. 1. Draft order of the Commons for sending 10,000*l.* into Munster, sent up to the Lords this day. Noted, "To be further considered of." L. J., V. 425.

Nov. 1. Draft order for sale of the materials of the castle of Sherbourne, Dorsetshire. L. J., V. 426. *In extenso.*

Nov. 1. Draft order for payment of the officers of the garrison of Manchester out of the delinquents' estates. L. J., V. 426. *In extenso.*

Nov. 1. Two drafts of order for repayment of such as shall furnish men or money to serve under the Earl of Warwick. L. J., V. 426. *In extenso.*

Nov. 1. Draft order recommending Colonel Vavasor to be captain of a troop of Horse at Bandon Bridge. L. J., V. 426. *In extenso.*

Nov. 1. Draft order for sending clothes, &c. to Galway. L. J., V. 426. *In extenso.*

Nov. 1. Draft order for contracting for provisions for Ireland. L. J., V. 426. *In extenso.*

Nov. 1. Draft order for recruiting the fort of Galway. L. J., V. 427. *In extenso.*

Nov. 1. Draft order for sending clothes and ammunition to Connaught. L. J., V. 427. *In extenso.*

Nov. 1. Draft order for sending an agent from Parliament into Flanders. L. J., V. 427. *In extenso.*

Nov. 1. Draft order for payment of 200*l.* to the Archbishop of Armagh. L. J., V. 427. *In extenso.*

Nov. 1. Draft order for the Committee for Suffolk to retain 4,000*l.* for the defence of that county. L. J., V. 427. *In extenso.*

Nov. 1. Draft order for fortifying the town and castle of Exeter. L. J., V. 427. *In extenso.*

Nov. 1. Draft order that the 100 dragoons, lately raised in Devonshire, shall be under the joint command of the deputy lieutenants of the county and of the city of Exeter, during their billeting there. L. J., V. 428. *In extenso.*

Nov. 1. Draft orders for securing disaffected persons in the county of Derby, and for appointment of deputy lieutenants of the county. L. J., V. 428. *In extenso.*

Nov. 1. Two drafts of the order for securing apprentices, that enlist as soldiers, against their masters. L. J., V. 428. *In extenso.*

Nov. 1. Petition of the Dean and Chapter of the cathedral church of St. Paul, in London. The Lord Mayor, alleging an order in that behalf from their Lordships, has shut up the doors of the church, and taken the keys into his custody, by which many well affected persons cannot enjoy the frequent use of prayer, and some cannot bury their deceased friends by their ancestors as they desire. Pray that the church may be again opened for these purposes.

Nov. 2. Affidavit of John Howard (and copy of same), that Thomas Michell refused to pay the rent due from him to Lambert Osbolston for the impropriation of Biggleswade, in the county of Bedford. L. J., V. 429.
Annexed :—

　1. Copy of order referred to in preceding. 7 July 1641. L. J., IV. 304. *In extenso.*

Nov. 2. Draft order for payment of 800*l.* a month for the maintenance of the King's younger children. L. J., V. 429. *In extenso.*

Nov. 2. Petition of paviers and others employed about the work of paving the old palace. Pray that 100*l.*, by way of impress, may be delivered into the hands of the officers of His Majesty's works, with directions for them to pay the same to petitioners proportionably as they shall think fit, and petitioners will then

expect no more money, nor trouble their Lordships again till the work is finished. *See* L. J., V. 424.

Nov. 2. Warrant of the Commons committing William Dancke to Newgate. C. J., II. 831.
Annexed :—

　1. Petition of William Dancke, of Dartford, to H. C. Has been committed to the noisome gaol of Newgate, but for what cause he is altogether ignorant. Prays for his discharge.

　2. Certificate of inhabitants of Dartford, that Dancke has for divers years been one of the sheriffs' bailiffs there, and that during that time he has been of good behaviour, and has carried himself, both in the execution of his office and otherwise, honestly, civilly, and free from scandal, and in a better manner than men in that profession have usually done. 3 Dec. 1642.

Nov. 3. Draft petition of both Houses of Parliament to the King for restoring peace, sent by the Earls of Northumberland and Pembroke. L. J., V. 431. *In extenso.*

Nov. 3. Certificate of Mr. Justice Foster, respecting the cause between Sarah Berry and her husband, that a suit was depending in the prerogative court between them, and witnesses have been examined on behalf of Sarah Berry, to prove the gross brutality of her husband, but that as yet no witnesses have been examined on behalf of the husband. *See* L. J., V. 399.
Annexed :—

　1. Petition of Sarah Berry, praying that the preceding certificate may be read by their Lordships, and relief granted to her.

Nov. 4. Petition of Rice Williams ; prays that certain plate, &c. belonging to the Archbishop of York, left with him as security for some engagements he is under for the Archbishop, now seized by order of the House, may be re-delivered to him. L. J., V. 432.

Nov. 4. Certificate of the Earl of Danby, concerning the cause between the Dean of York and Archibald Armstrong. L. J., V. 433. *In extenso.*

1642, Nov. 4
to
5 Aug. 1643.
} Book of orders.

Nov. 5. Draft protest (unsigned) against the resolution of the Lords, to send two members of their House with a petition to the King, whilst, in his last letter, His Majesty intimates that some of their members are traitors. *See* L. J., V. 433.

Nov. 6. Two copies of the order to authorise Sir Gilbert Gerrard to pay monies upon the warrants of the Earl of Warwick. L. J., V. 434. *In extenso.*

Nov. 6. Draft order for all officers and soldiers to repair to the Lord General's army. L. J., V. 435. *In extenso.*

Nov. 7. Draft order for Captain Hill to receive money for raising dragoons. L. J., V. 437. *In extenso.*

Nov. 7. Declaration of Parliament, calling for assistance from Scotland. Sent up from the Commons on the 2nd (L. J., V. 430. *In extenso*), and agreed to by the Lords this day. L. J., V. 437.

Nov. 7. Amended draft of preceding.

Nov. 7. Draft order, engaging the public faith for the repayment of money to be raised weekly by the citizens of London. L. J., V. 437. *In extenso.*

Nov. 7. Copy of warrant from the Earl of Essex, for the conveyance of Charles Price and other prisoners from shire to shire to Coventry, there to be kept until further order. *See* L. J., V. 448.

Nov. 8. Draft order for securing the navy and provisions at Chatham. L. J., V. 438. *In extenso.*

Nov. 8. Two copies of the order for fortifying Chichester. L. J., V. 438. *In extenso.*

Nov. 8. Draft order for the prisoners in the Tower to have no communication with each other. L. J., V. 438. *In extenso.*

Nov. 8. Draft order to the sheriffs of London, not to publish the King's proclamations. L. J., V.438. *In extenso.*

Nov. 8. Draft order for payment of 1,000*l.* to Sir William Lewis, governor of Portsmouth. L. J., V. 438. *In extenso.*

Nov. 8. Sixteen printed copies of a proclamation of His Majesty's grace, favour, and pardon to the inhabitants of his county of Kent. Rushworth, Part III., Vol. II., p. 54. *In extenso.*

Nov. 9. Copy of warrant from the Lord Mayor Pennington to Captain Thomas Chamberlain to assist John Randall and others, with the trained bands under his command, in execution of an order of the Committee for the safety of the kingdom of the 1st instant (relating to the Duke de Vendome). *See* L. J., V. 399.

Nov. 9. Affidavit of Robert Freeman, that Thomas Andrews, sheriff of London, and John Towes, alder-

man, refuse to deliver up a hamper of plate, and a trunk and hamper of hangings, belonging to the Archbishop of York, pursuant to their Lordships' order of the 4th instant, unless he would covenant that the same should be forthcoming. L. J., V. 439.
Annexed :—
    1. Order mentioned in preceding. L. J., V. 432.
    In extenso.

Nov. 9. Draft order for martial law to be exercised in the Lord General's army. L. J., V. 439. *In extenso.*

Nov. 9. Petition of William Lord Archbishop of Canterbury ; understanding that his house at Lambeth is taken for some public service, he prays that the library there, and his own study of books, may be placed in security, and that he may have leave to remove such other goods as he there hath to Croydon or elsewhere. L. J., V. 439. (Holograph.)

Nov. 9. Message from the Commons, with votes of that House for the sending of the petition to the King, &c. L. J., V. 439. *In extenso.*

Nov. 10. Draft order for securing the town of Watford. L. J., V. 442. *In extenso.*

Nov. 11. Petition of Sir Hardes Waller, a colonel in the army in Munster, and employed on service to the King and Parliament in England, has been twice arrested for a debt of 40l., for which he is surety, by one Bowes and others ; petitioner, who is now ousted from a large estate in Ireland, prays that he may be freed from arrest, or receive the arrears of pay due to him. Noted, Ordered to be referred to the common law. L. J., V. 441.

Nov. 11. Draft order for payment of 200l., for the service of the town of Maldon, Essex. L. J., V. 441. *In extenso.*

Nov. 11. Draft order for all soldiers under the Earl of Essex to repair to their colours. L. J., V. 442. *In extenso.*

Nov. 12. Draft letter from Parliament to Lord Falkland, acknowledging the receipt of His Majesty's answer respecting a cessation of arms, &c. L. J., V. 443. *In extenso.*

Nov. 13. Certificate of inhabitants of Gothurst [or Geythurst], Bucks, that Sir John Digby has been constantly resident with his mother either at Gothurst or in Rutlandshire, and has not been with the King as was imagined.

Nov. 14. Message from the Commons with resolutions respecting the drawing up of a declaration to set forth to the world the efforts of Parliament for peace, &c. L. J., V. 444. *In extenso.*

No. 14. Draft order for turning Winchester House, Southwark, into a prison. L. J., V. 445. *In extenso.*

Nov. 14. Draft order, pledging the public faith for the expenses of those who volunteer from Essex to supply the desertion of the mercenaries of that county. L. J., V. 445. *In extenso.*

Nov. 14. Draft order pledging the public faith to the citizens of London for their expenses in raising soldiers, &c. L. J., V. 445. *In extenso.*

Nov. 15. Message from the Commons, with resolutions respecting the raising of light horse, by the citizens of London, &c. L. J., V. 446. *In extenso.*

Nov. 15. Draft order for Mr. Justice Berkeley to sit in the Court of King's Bench, &c. L. J., V. 446. *In extenso.*

Nov. 15. Draft order for soldiers to repair to their colours. L. J., V. 446. *In extenso.*

Nov. 15. Draft order for Major Hurry to go into Kent with dragoons, &c. L. J., V. 446. *In extenso.*

Nov. 15. Draft order for Mr. Bard and others to be commissioners to value horses seized for the public service, with amendments. L. J., V. 447. *In extenso.*

Nov. 16. Petition of divers of His Majesty's late Commissioners for causes ecclesiastical (signed by Sir Nathaniel Brent) ; in Trinity term last they presented a petition praying that they might be protected from suits against them as commissioners, unless corruption or other misdemeanor was proved, this petition was by their Lordships' order referred to a Committee appointed to consider cases of like nature ; but the committee has not yet had time to consider it, in consequence of other business, while one Flower has declared against some of the petitioners in the Court of Common Pleas, and obtained a rule for them to answer the first court day of this term ; petitioners pray that all proceedings on Flower's suit may be stayed until the Committee have had time to consider the petition. L. J., V. 447.

Annexed :—
    1. Copy of former petition.
    2. Copy of order referring the petition to a committee. 15 June 1642. L. J., V. 135.
    3. Copy of order originally appointing the committee. 23 March 1641-2. L. J., IV. 664.

Nov. 16. Draft orders for the safety of the Tower of London. L. J., V. 447. *In extenso.*

Nov. 16. Draft order for Captain Charles Price and other officers to be kept prisoners at Gloucester. L. J., V. 448. *In extenso.*

Nov. 16. Draft order to borrow some of the proposition money for the county of Surrey for present maintenance of the soldiers. L. J., V. 448. *In extenso.*

Nov. 16. Draft order, for payment of 20l. to Mr. Michell, an Irish Minister. L. J., V. 448. *In extenso.*

Nov. 16. Draft order for payment of 300l. for fortification of the town and castle of Taunton. L. J., V. 448. *In extenso.*

Nov. 16. Affidavit of Mark Barnes that Richard King, of Ashby, in the county of Lincoln, and other tenants of the lands conveyed by Sir Robert Carr to feoffees in trust for maintenance of his wife and children, refuse to pay the rents to the said feoffees pursuant to their Lordships' order of the 20th of Sept. last, being forbidden by Sir Robert Carr's agents. L. J., V. 448.
Annexed :—
    1. Similar affidavit of Thomas Rayner.
    2. Similar affidavit of Daniel Sheldon.
    3. Copy of order indemnifying the tenants for paying their rents to the feoffees. 19 Oct. 1642. L. J., V. 406.
    4. Copy of order of 20 Sept. 1642, mentioned above. L. J., V. 364.
    5. Motion for King and others to be sent for as delinquents.

Nov. 16. Draft answer of Parliament to the King's last message concerning the treaty. L. J., V. 449. *In extenso.*

Nov. 16. Warrant or writ from the King to James Duke of Richmond and Lennox, warden of the Cinque Ports, to cause publication of a proclamation to be made.

Nov. 17. Order for a pass for trunks, &c. of the Archbishop of Armagh to Oxford. L. J., V. 449.

Nov. 17. Draft order to Edward Lord Newburgh to recall the Commission of oyer and terminer for Lancashire. L. J., V. 449. *In extenso.*

Nov. 17. Petition of the Earl of Portland ; by four months' imprisonment is reduced to the same condition as if he had been convicted of the greatest crimes, yet is not guilty of any towards their Lordships ; prays to be restored to liberty. Noted, Nothing done.

Nov. 18. Petition of Richard Vaghan and Josias Casewell, prisoners in the Fleet by their Lordships' order ; pray for discharge, the rather as they are employed in the service of Parliament. L. J., V. 450.

Nov. 18. Draft order for payment of the contribution money in Yorkshire to Sir John Hotham. L. J., V. 450. *In extenso.*

Nov. 18. Draft order for Mr. Pickering to deliver the declaration concerning the Scots coming to the assistance of Parliament to the Scotch Council of State. L. J., V. 451. *In extenso.*

Nov. 18. Draft order for opposing Mr. Ford in the county of Sussex. L. J., V. 451. *In extenso.*

Nov. 18. Draft order for the counties of York, Lincoln, &c., to associate together to subdue the papists and malignants there. L. J., V. 451. *In extenso.*

Nov. 21. The woeful complaint and humble petition of divers well affected to the King and Parliament in the evil affected county of Hereford, for relief from their miseries suffered at the hands of the Cavaliers, to Henry Earl of Stamford, Governor of the city of Hereford. L. J., V. 453. *In extenso.* Noted, "This petition was " delivered me from these poor persecuted protestants, " and I have made provision for them in the houses " of the cathedral men, who have for the most part " abandoned this place. (Signed) Stanford " [Stamford].

Nov. 22. Petition of Dame Barbara Villiers ; in contempt of their Lordships' order of the 7th of October last for her protection, Edward Bromfield and others have continued to build the house in the Dean's Yard, Westminster, depriving her of air, prospect, and privacy ; prays that the workmen may be apprehended and the building demolished. L. J., V. 453.
Annexed :—
    1. Copy of order mentioned in preceding. L. J., V. 390.

Nov. 23. Petition of Joseph Alexander ; petitioner rides horses, and fits them for service with great saddles for the use of Parliament; and therefore prays that his horses may be protected from seizure. L. J., V. 455.

Nov. 23. Petition of Bartholomew Home; praying that his case may be heard or that he may be set at liberty. L. J., V. 455.

Nov. 24. Resolutions of the Commons respecting the alteration in the petition to the King. Agreed to this day. L. J., V. 456. *In extenso.*

Nov. 23. Letter from the Justices of Kent at Maidstone to the Speaker of the House of Commons; on the 11th instant Sir Vivian Mullinex, one Brewer, and others, having been apprehended, the oath of allegiance was tendered to them as papists, and on their refusing to take it they were committed to gaol. Sir Vivian has been released by order of the House of Lords, influenced, as is stated in a packet lately discovered, by the active spirit of the Lady of Banbury; whilst the writers were at Maidstone an order came from the House of Lords to take away Brewer. The trained bands were much troubled that papists should find so much favour, and though the writers will not complain of the discouragement to themselves, yet they think it right to acquaint the House of Commons with these passages, which are likely to breed a general discontent. See L. J., V. 456.

Nov. 24. Petition of both Houses to the King that he would return to them with his Royal not his martial attendance. L. J., V. 457. *In extenso.*

Nov. 24. Draft order to prevent deserters coming from Ireland to England. L. J., V. 457. *In extenso.*

Nov. 24. Two drafts of the order to stay provisions going out of London. L. J., V. 457. *In extenso.*

Nov. 24. Draft order for a deserter to be sent to the Lord General. L. J., V. 457. *In extenso.*

Nov. 24. Draft order for maintaining the forces in the town of Manchester. L. J., V. 457. *In extenso.*

Nov. 24. Two draft orders for maintaining the forces in the north parts. L. J., V. 458. *In extenso.*

No. 24. Draft order for the Committee of Irish adventurers to keep 5,000l. to be issued as occasion shall require, and for 548l. 2s. to be paid to the surgeons, &c. in Ireland. L. J., V. 458. *In extenso.*

Nov. 24. Draft order for maintenance of the King's younger children. L. J., V. 458. *In extenso.*

Nov. 24. Notes of proceedings in the Commons on the 19th, and drafts of various orders made this day. L. J., V. 456.

Nov. 24. Petition of Thomas Jenyns and Humphrey Bradbourne; Sir Philibert Vernatti, for whom petitioners are sureties for a large amount, is protected from arrest by order of their Lordships during the continuance of the suit between him and John Latch, which has now lasted almost two years; petitioners against whom judgments have been taken out, pray that they and their estates may have the same protection as Vernatti. *See* L. J., V. 476.

Nov. 25. Petition of Thomas Ken, one of the clerks of the House, for a trunk containing records, &c. to be restored to him. L. J., V. 459. *In extenso.*

[Nov. 25.] Request from the Committee, appointed o receive the account of the profits of the letter office, or a further report from the justices to whom the case was referred.

Annexed:—

1. Copies of the orders of both Houses in the matter of the 8th of Sept. 1642. Read this day. *See* L. J., V. 459.

Nov. 25. Petition of Sir Thomas Malet, one of the justices of the Court of King's Bench; has been seventeen weeks prisoner in the Tower, in consequence of which his wife and children are in great distress, and his own health decayed; is sorry to have offended their Lordships and prays for liberty, or for a reasonable time to answer the charges against him.

Nov. 26. Draft order for the Mayor of Exeter not to publish the King's proclamation of the 9th instant. L. J., V. 460. *In extenso.*

Nov. 26. Draft order for relief of the inhabitants of Brentford. L. J., V. 460. *In extenso.*

Nov. 26. Draft order for the Committee sent into the city about the raising of money to call some of the citizens to their assistance. L. J., V. 460. *In extenso.*

Nov. 26. Draft ordinance for securing and fortifying the city of Exeter. L. J., V. 461. *In extenso.*

Nov. 26. Draft ordinance to compel the inhabitants of London, &c., who have not already done so, to contribute for the support of the army. L. J., V. 462. *In extenso.*

Nov. 26. Letter from Sir Edward Hungerford and others, at Bath, to Mr. Speaker Lenthall; they hear that it is the intention of the Western Cavaliers to march upon Bristol, and the well affected of the city have solicited as-

sistance, which the writers are ready to send, but the mayor and aldermen make a scruple of entertaining the county forces without some order from Parliament; the majority of the aldermen are suspected of being malignants, but of the commons of the city there are three good to one ill affected member, the writers therefore desire that an order from Parliament, authorising the Mayor and aldermen of Bristol to take a thousand soldiers from the counties of Somerset and Gloucester to preserve the city from the plundering Cavaliers, may be sent back by their messenger with all speed. The danger they fear is near, for some of the Cavaliers have lately showed themselves at Marlborough, and they wish that the Earl of Essex would put a stop to the roving and straggling of these plundering Cavaliers, for it would very much comfort and satisfy the affrighted countrymen. *See* L. J., V. 469.

Nov. 28. Copy of the King's answer to the last petition from both Houses. L. J., V. 463. *In extenso.*

Nov. 28. Affidavit of John Saunders, Deputy-Keeper under Sir Arthur Manwaringe, that Hercules Trew killed a stag in Old Windsor Wood. *See* L. J., V. 459.

Nov. 29. Message from the Commons with an order for appointment of Captain Burrell and others to be commissaries to enrol and value horses and arms. L. J., V. 465.

Nov. 29. An explanation of the ordinance concerning the assessing of such persons as have not subscribed in London, Westminster, &c. upon the propositions for raising money, plate, and horses. L. J., V. 466. *In extenso.*

Nov. 29. Draft ordinance for the better provision of victuals and other necessaries for the army, and for payment and satisfaction to be made for such provisions. L. J., V. 466. *In extenso.*

Nov. 29. Printed copy of an ordinance for the speedy setting forth of certain ships (in all points furnished for war) to prevent the bringing over of soldiers, money, ordnance, and other ammunition from beyond the sea to assist the King against the Parliament in England. L. J., V. 467. *In extenso.*

Nov. 29. Draft ordinance for raising money upon the security of the ordinance for the assessing of such persons as have not contributed according to their estates. L. J., V. 467. *In extenso.*

Nov. 29. Draft order that the receivers of the King's and Queen's revenue shall not issue any money without acquainting the Houses. L. J., V. 468. *In extenso.*

Nov. 29. Draft order for Mr. Bedwell to be captain of the volunteers of Ipswich. L. J., V. 468. *In extenso.*

Nov. 29. Draft order for payment of 400l. for the defence of Norwich. L. J., V. 468. *In extenso.*

Nov. 29. Draft order of indemnity to the city of Norwich for training volunteers. L. J., V. 468. *In extenso.*

Nov. 29. Draft order for defence of the county of Chester. L. J., V. 468. *In extenso.*

Nov. 29. An ordinance of both Houses of Parliament concerning John Pickering, Esq. L. J., V. 469. *In extenso.*

Nov. 29. Draft of preceding.

Nov. 29. The names of the Commissioners for the county of Bucks, for the execution of the orders concerning provision for the Parliament forces. L. J., V. 469. *In extenso.*

Nov. 29. Draft order for the security of Bristol. L. J., V. 469. *In extenso.*

Nov. 29. Draft order for the security of the town and county of Southampton. Noted, "Mr. Holles who carried up this order, moved the Lords that the like order (mutatis mutandis) might be made for Southampton, and that their clerk might have power to issue out an order to this purpose. It is a business of great consequence and haste, and therefore if you please to despatch it and sign it, the messenger stays only for it. H. Elsynge." *See* C. J., II. 869.

Nov. 29. Draft order pledging the public faith for repayment of contributions advanced for the defence of Sussex. L. J., V. 469. *In extenso.*

Nov. 29. Petition of Abigail Dexter, now prisoner in the King's Bench; in the absence of her husband, who is a printer, and who went as a dragoon in the late expedition to Oxford, she caused "King James' Judgment" of a King and of a tyrant" to be reprinted, conceiving by the title that it was a work of the late King James, and therefore not likely to give offence, for this she was committed to the King's Bench prison, where she has lain seven weeks; her offence, for which she desires pardon, was committed from imbecility and ignorance, and she prays that she may be released from imprisonment, that her family be not ruined and all her customers lost. *See* L. J., V. 385, &c.

Dec. 1. Petition of Henry Earl of Bath, a prisoner in the Tower by their Lordships' order; his house and goods have been assaulted, and his horses, which are for his wife's daily use, arrested and likely to be taken from her; prays for an order for the protection of his house and goods. L. J., V. 469.

Dec. 1. Petition of Frances wife of Thomas Leverson, Esq.; her husband who has gone to France, appointed that she should receive 200*l.* per annum to be paid her by Francis Blunt, who was to receive the rent of her husband's lands at Wolverhampton, but Blunt a notorious papist, taking advantage of these distracted times, converts the allowance to his own use; she prays that her case may be referred to one or more of the judges, that upon report to the House she may have relief. L. J., V. 469.

Dec. 1. Order referring the preceding case to Mr. Justice Crawley. L. J., V. 470.

Dec. 1. Affidavit of Richard Poole, that the order of the 25th of Nov. for giving possession of the Letter Office to the Earl of Warwick, is disobeyed by Burlamachi and others. L. J., V. 470. *In extenso.*

Dec. 1. Similar affidavit of Fulke Hughes. L. J., V. 470. *In extenso.*

Dec. 1. Copy of a commission for a captain of a company of foot or dragoons, with amendments. L. J., V. 470. *In extenso.*

Annexed:—
1. Draft of a commission for a captain of foot.
2. Same in the county of Nottingham.
3. Same in the city and county of Canterbury.
4. Draft of a colonel's commission.

Dec. 1. Copy of a declaration made by the Earl of Newcastle, governor of the town and county of Newcastle, and general of His Majesty's forces raised in the northern parts of this kingdom for the defence of the same, for his resolution of marching into Yorkshire, as also a just vindication of himself from that unjust aspiration laid upon him for entertaining some recusants in his forces. Rushworth, III. ii. 78. *In extenso.*

Dec. 3. A true relation of the abuses and affronts offered to the Right Honorable Lord Bernard, Duke of Espernoone. L. J., V. 472. *In extenso.*

Dec. 3. Draft order appointing a committee of citizens to seize gunpowder in London and within twenty miles thereof. L. J., V. 472. *In extenso.*

Dec. 3. Draft order that no gunpowder be exported but by authority of preceding committee. L. J., V. 472. *In extenso.*

Dec. 3. Draft order for an allowance to be made from the Bishop of Winchester's rents for the repair of Winchester House, now used as a prison. L. J., V. 472. *In extenso.*

Dec. 3. Order that the captains in Sussex discharged by the King shall execute their commissions notwithstanding. L. J., V. 473. *In extenso.*

Dec. 3. Draft of preceding.

Dec. 3. Draft order for disposal of the money ordered to be paid to Sir Anthony Irby for Yorkshire dragoons. L. J., V. 473. *In extenso.*

Dec. 3. Draft order pledging the public faith for repayment of money advanced for the relief of Chester. L. J., V. 473. *In extenso.*

Dec. 3. Draft order for disposal of the money contributed in Lancashire. L. J., V. 473. *In extenso.*

Dec. 3. Order for relief of maimed soldiers. L. J., V. 473. / *In extenso.*

Dec. 3. Draft of preceding.

Dec. 3. Petition of George Kirke, gentleman of His Majesty's robes; petitioner was by order of Parliament appointed to receive 1,000*l.* out of the coinage money in the Tower of London, but by another order that money is ordered to be paid to Mr. Cornelius Holland, for the expenses of the King's children, who remain in London; prays for an order to the warden of the Mint to pay the 1,000*l.* to petitioner, as it is for provision of His Majesty's apparel. L. J., V. 474.

Dec. 3. Petition of John Read, merchant, prisoner in the Fleet; petitioner is imprisoned for a debt of John Dingley, for which he was surety, at the suit of Thomas Gunton, as no proceedings can be had this term in Chancery, prays that his case may be referred to the Judges of the Common Pleas, and that he may be enlarged on reasonable bail. L. J., V. 474.

Dec. 5. Draft order reported by the Earl of Manchester against the ordinance for the association of the counties of Derby, Leicester, Nottingham, &c. L. J., V. 476.

Annexed:—
1. Draft order referred to in preceding. Noted, Not resolved of. This order was subsequently agreed to with some alterations. *See* L. J., V. 493.

Dec. 6. Petition of Thomas Jenyns, Esq., and Humphrey Bradborne; Sir Philibert Vernatti, for whom they are sureties, is by order of the Committee for Petitions protected from all arrests and judgments during the dependency of their cause before the House; pray that they may have the same protection.

Dec. 6. Copy of order for protection of Jenyns and Bradborne. L. J., V. 476.

Annexed:—
1. Copy of order for protection of Vernatti. 30 Jan. 1640-1.
2. Petition of Abraham Vernatti, another surety for Sir Philibert, praying for the same protection that has been granted to Jenyns and Bradborne. (Undated.)
3. Copy of Sir Philibert Vernatti's original petition against Latch.
4. Copy of petition of Jenyns and Bradborne above mentioned.

Dec. 6. Petition of George Mynne, Esq.; petitioner was about eight years ago illegally ejected from the Hanaper Office by sentence of the Star Chamber, and having of late brought an assize in the Court of King's Bench for recovery of the office from Sir Richard Younge the disseisor, he is stopped on the ground that Sir Richard is privileged as one of His Majesty's servants; petitioner who is aged, and has no other remedy, prays leave to continue his trial at law. L. J., V. 476.

Dec. 6. Order for Sir Richard Younge to answer the preceding petition. L. J., V. 476.

Dec. 6. Petition of Richard Tyto, citizen and salter of London; Robert Shering having obtained judgment against petitioner in an action of trespass, petitioner sued for a writ of error, on which the record, &c. was ordered to be brought into Parliament by Sir John Brampston; but he has since received a " writ of ease," and Sir Robert Heath, now Chief Justice, is with the King; prays that the record, &c. may be brought in by some other justice. *See* L. J., V. 612.

Dec. 7. Message from the Commons with resolutions of that House respecting the removal of the King's children to St. James', &c. L. J., V. 477.

Dec. 7. An explanation of the ordinance for the assessment of London and Westminster, &c. L. J., V. 477. *In extenso.*

Dec. 7. Draft order for protection of those who have been proclaimed traitors by the King. L. J., V. 478. *In extenso.*

Dec. 7. Order for providing 2,000 horses out of the counties of Essex, Suffolk, &c. L. J., V. 478. *In extenso.*

Dec. 7. Draft of preceding.

Dec. 7. Draft order for Lady Seymour and her daughter and Mr. Vincent Goddard, to be kept in safe custody at Marlborough. L. J., V. 481. *In extenso.*

Dec. 7. Affidavit of John Greenhill and others, that the Earls of Carlisle and Suffolk, with other gentlemen, came over Smithfield at one o'clock in the morning, and rode on though the sentinel called to them to stop; that at Holborn conduit they were stayed by the constable and his watch, towards whom they were so violent that he was obliged to send to the court of guard for aid. *See* L. J., V. 481.

Dec. 7. Warrant from the King to the county of Suffolk, directing the inhabitants to obey the commission given to Thomas Player.

Dec. 8. Petition of William, Lord Archbishop of Canterbury. Sir Charles Cæsar, Master of the Faculties, is dead, petitioner desires the leave of the House to appoint either Dr. Heath or Dr. Aylett to the post. L. J., V. 481. (Holograph.)

Dec. 8. Message from the Commons with the votes of that House for the appointment of the Speaker, Sir John Lenthall, as Master of the Rolls. L. J., V. 481. *In extenso.*

Dec. 8. Petition of Richard Branthwaite; has been a prisoner in the Tower for sixteen weeks to the decay of his health, and to the harm of his own estate and the estates of others entrusted to him; prays that he may have the liberty of London, and live in some lodgings near the Temple. L. J., V. 481.

Dec. 8. Draft order for supply of provisions for Ireland. L. J., V. 482. *In extenso.*

Dec. 8. Draft order for levying a thousand dragoons in Somersetshire, &c. L. J., V. 482. *In extenso.*

H 2

Dec. 8. Order for fitting out ships for defence of the narrow seas. L. J., V. 482. *In extenso.*

Dec. 8. Draft of preceding.

Dec. 8. Draft order for the assessment of the several counties for the support of the army. L. J., V. 482. *In extenso.*

Dec. 8. Draft resolution for the Earl of Lindsey to recommend the declaration of Parliament to the Scots. L. J., V. 483. *In extenso.*

Dec. 8. Draft order of the Commons for the relief of those plundered by ill-affected persons. This order is entered in the Journals for relief of Mr. Bayles, of Witham, Essex. C. J., II. 881. *In extenso.*

Dec. 9. Order upon report from the Committee appointed to take the accounts in the case between the Earl of Warwick and Philip Burlamachi, for appointment of an auditor, production of books, &c. L. J., V. 483.

Dec. 9. Resolution for putting twenty men into the Castle of Carisbrook. L. J., V. 483. *In extenso.*

Dec. 9. Message from the Commons with preceding.

Dec. 9. Petition of Sir James Mountgomery and others about succours for the army in Ireland. This petition and the annexed papers are given *in extenso.* L. J., V. 483-484.

Annexed :—
1. Copy of petition to the King on the same subject.
2. Copy of the King's answer.
3. Propositions of Sir James Mountgomery and others on the same subject.

Dec. 9. Draft of a letter to the Countess of Roxburgh to be signed by the Earl of Manchester, Speaker, informing her of the order of Parliament for the return of the King's children to St. James', and desiring her to attend upon them as formerly, and not to allow their removal without acquainting both Houses. *See* L. J., V. 477.

Dec. 9. Copy of a report made by the fellowship of merchant adventurers, with the names of the merchant strangers of the intercourse, who have all equally enjoyed the benefit of the intercourse between the kingdom of England and the House of Burgundy, which benefit, the merchant adventurers think it fit that they should still enjoy.

Dec. 10. Petition of the mayor, deputy lieutenants, and captains of the city of Exon, praying for speedy reinforcements of both men and horse for the protection of the city. C. J., II. 884.

Dec. 12. Draft declaration of both Houses of Parliament to be sent to the States General of the United Provinces. L. J., V. 486. *In extenso.*

Dec. 12. Draft order authorising Mr. Strickland to deliver the preceding declaration. L. J., V. 486. *In extenso.*

Dec. 12. Message from the Commons with an order for providing match, and an order for payment of 1,000*l.* a week to the Committee in London, till 20,000*l.* is paid to provide arms, &c. L. J., V. 486. *In extenso.*

Dec. 12. Copies of preceding orders.

Dec. 12. Draft order for transporting of corn, &c. into Ireland. L. J., V. 487. *In extenso.*

Dec. 12. Order for the bells of Exeter Cathedral to be melted for ordnance, &c. L. J., V. 487. *In extenso.*

Dec. 12. Draft of preceding.

Dec. 12. Petition of the agents for the distressed city of Londonderry, to the Commons. There are 6,059 persons in the city, whereof 5,123 are women and children, or sick, aged, or impotent. Only 2,000 are inhabitants of the city, and the rest have fled there for safety. "Spotted fever" has broken out, the winter is approaching, and the rebellion increases. They therefore pray that a collection may be made on some of the fast-days for their relief. Noted, "Ordered collections " to be made the next fast-day in all churches (except " Westminster) in and about London." C. J., II. 885.

Dec. 13. Petition of Lieutenant Colonel Reade, praying that the strictness of his imprisonment may be so far eased that he may have a servant to attend on him, and such clothes and other necessaries as he now stands in need of. *See* L. J., V. 487.

Dec. 13. Message from the Commons with resolution that Mr. Holles should be desired to command the forces in the western parts, &c. L. J., V. 488. *In extenso.*

Dec. 13. Letter from Philip Burlamachi to [Lord Grey of Warke]; has been warned to attend this day before his Lordship and other Lords, but is unable to attend on account of illness. Prays his Lordship to represent the same to the House, and express his readiness to attend as soon as he is able.

Dec. 14. Affidavit of Gregory Isham, that he served Job Alibond with the order of the House about the Letter office. L. J., V. 490. *In extenso.*

Dec. 14. Copy of letter from the Parliament to the Prince of Orange, authorising Mr. Walter Strickland to negotiate certain affairs with the States General. L. J., V. 490. *In extenso.*

Dec. 14. Order for the deputy lieutenants of Somersetshire to attach Sir Ralph Hopton and others for raising volunteers to serve against the Parliament. L. J., V. 490. *In extenso.*

Dec. 14. Draft of preceding.

Dec. 14. An ordinance made by the Lords and Commons in Parliament assembled, for the better and more speedy execution of the late ordinance of the 29th of November (for compelling those to contribute who have not already so done). L. J., V. 491. *In extenso.*

Dec. 14. Draft of preceding.

Dec. 15. Affidavit of John Pope, of Maidstone; that on Friday the 30th of September last he rode to the farm of Bewell, a tenant of the Earl of Salisbury, to see about repairs there, and the next day, Sir Wm. Brook, when out hawking came to Bewell's house, and finding him and his dame out and only two maids in the house, sent one of them to see for her mistress, and the other with a message to some passers by, to tell Bewell he wanted to speak to him. Sir William having thus got the maids out went into the house and locked the doors, and would not let Bewell in until he attorned tenant to him, upon which Sir Wm. gave him his bond that he would save him harmless. Upon the same paper is a direction that the Earl of Salisbury should have possession of the lands in question between him and Sir Wm. Brook until the matter should be determined at common law. L. J., V. 492.

Dec. 15. Petition of William Beale, Edward Martin, and Richard Sterne, Doctors in Divinity and Masters of Colleges, in Cambridge. Pray for release upon bond, as they have been fifteen weeks prisoners in the Tower at excessive charges, and to the neglect of their private affairs and public duties. L. J., V. 492.

Dec. 15. Draft order for the exemption of the members and assistants of both Houses from the assessment. L. J., V. 492. *In extenso.*

Dec. 15. Draft ordinance for the association of the counties of Leicester, Derby, &c., for their mutual protection. L. J., V. 493. *In extenso.*

Dec. 15. Affidavit of Richard Poole, that he served John Caston, postmaster in Barbican, and Job Alibond, with the order of the 2nd instant (for the postmasters to deliver the mails to the Earl of Warwick), but that no letters have been delivered. *See* L. J., V. 490, &c.

Dec. 15. Petition of Sir Edmond Wright, alderman of the city of London. Petitioner's house is too small to lodge the Earl of Portland, with the servants that daily attend on him, as well as petitioner's own family. Prays that the Earl may be removed to some more healthful and convenient place. Noted, with a certificate from the treasurers of money and plate, that Alderman Wright has brought in 500*l.* upon the propositions, and 100*l.* towards the loan of 30,000*l.*

Dec. 16. Resolutions of the Commons that the forces raised against the Parliament are for the rooting out of the protestant religion, &c. C. J., II. 891.

Dec. 16. Copy of letter from Colonel Nathaniel Fiennes and Colonel Arthur Goodwin to the Lord General. On Tuesday morning we marched towards Winchester, making the more haste as the enemy that morning cut off a company of dragooners and took their colours, we galloped after them and overtook some of them before they got into Winchester, others came out of the town to help them, but we beat them back, and surrounded the place with horse and dragoons, and forced an entrance into the town, but evening coming on were unable to take the castle, where the sheriff had summoned all the soldiers and many gentlemen to meet to assess the county for maintenance of the King's army. The next morning Lord Grandison came out and surrendered the castle upon certain conditions (which are enclosed), but we were unable to enforce the observance of the condition for the protection of the commanders and gentlemen from violence and pillaging, for the soldiers were in such a state of mutiny, that the officers and gentlemen were not only some of them stripped and pillaged, but put in fear of their lives, whilst some of the soldiers actually shot at their own officers who tried to prevent this violence, by which, and by the plundering and outrages committed in and about the town, the glory of the action was much eclipsed, while if the arms and horses taken had been more equally distributed, the advantage to the State would have been greater. We enclose a list of the officers and gentlemen taken. We recovered our colours, but the enemy burnt their own during a desperate resolution to make a sally in the night. We march this day [Dec. 14] for Portsmouth, where we shall wait for orders, money, and reinforcements. Our loss is only one captain of dragooneers and four or five men, and two or three hurt. Lord Grandison has behaved very fairly and hopes for better terms than those granted to men taken in the field, because in order to prevent more bloodshed he delivered up a place which had still some strength left. He and those taken with him hope that if not allowed to return to the King, they may have the same terms that were granted to those at Portsmouth, but we only promised to represent this to your Excellency. Noted, These are true copies. (Signed) Essex. *See* L. J., V. 494.

Dec. 17. Draft declaration of Parliament, that if any violence is offered to Catesby, Lilborne, and others, prisoners at Oxford, reprisals will be made by Parliament upon the prisoners in their hands. L. J.,; V. 497. *In extenso.*

Dec. 17. Draft order for payment of 57l. 15s., for malt delivered at Dublin. L. J., V. 497. *In extenso.*

Dec. 17. Two drafts of order for payment of 204l. to Mr. Crone for wheat. L. J., V. 498. *In extenso.*

Dec. 17. Draft order for payment of 120l. to John Jones for hire of a ship. L. J., V. 498. *In extenso.*

1642, Dec. 17. ⎫ Minute book of proceedings in the
to ⎬ House of Lords.
22 April 1643. ⎭

Dec. 19. Petition of inhabitants of the borough of Horsham, Sussex. The vicarage of Horsham having become void by the death of the late incumbent, the Archbishop of Canterbury is about to present it to one Mr. Conniers, a man unfit to undertake the cure of so great a number of souls. Pray that the vicarage may be conferred upon Mr. John Chatfield, an able and faithful minister who has been lecturer in the parish for six months. L. J., V. 498.

Dec. 19. Instructions for the deputy lieutenants of the county of Lancaster. L. J., V. 499.

Dec. 19. Petition of citizens and inhabitants of London, &c. praying for measures for the restoration of peace. L. J., V. 501. *In extenso.* This petition was referred to a committee, as objection was made to it by another petition from the city presented this day.

Dec. 19. Draft order for 750l. to be paid to Colonel Carne for the garrisons in the Isle of Wight. L. J., V. 501. *In extenso.*

Dec. 19. Draft order for the payment of 1,500l. to Maximilian Beard for wheat for Ireland. L. J., V. 501. *In extenso.*

Dec. 19. Draft order for the payment of 548l. 10s. to Richard Lock and Edmond Clymer, for fish for His Majesty's army. L. J., V. 501. *In extenso.*

Dec. 19. Draft order for the payment of 100l. to the Bishop of Raphoe for his relief and support. L. J., V. 501. *In extenso.*

Dec. 19. Draft order for the payment of 318l. 4s. to Mr. Wollaston for herrings for Ireland. L. J., V. 502. *In extenso.*

Dec. 19. Draft order for the payment of 5,000l. to Mr. Nicholas Loftus for incidental expenses. L. J., V. 502. *In extenso.*

Dec. 19. Draft order for payment of 1,500l. to the Earl of Leicester for his allowance of 10l. per diem. L. J., V. 502. *In extenso.*

Dec. 19. Affidavit of Robert Maurice that he served their Lordships' order upon Sir Richard Yonge. L. J., V. 509. *In extenso.*

Dec. 19. Letter from the Earl of Stamford at Bristol to the Speaker of the House of Lords concerning the taking of Bristol, and the increase of his army. L. J., V. 511. *In extenso.*

Dec. 20. Petition of Elizabeth, Countess of Carrick. Prays to be restored to the possession of certain manors and lands in the counties of Norfolk, Suffolk, and Essex, demised to her by her late husband Sir Thomas Southwell, to whom she was bestowed in marriage by Queen Elizabeth, being at the time maid of honour to Her Majesty, and illegally kept from her by Sir Richard Crane and Sir Thomas Mennes. Petitioner is very aged and her case is unrelievable both in law and equity, she having no capacity to sue ; her husband, John Earl of Carrick, having deserted her twenty years ago and remained in the remotest parts of Scotland ever since. L. J., V. 503.

Dec. 20. Draft order for the Lord General to appoint William Lord Grey of Warke, Commander-in-Chief of the forces raised in the counties of Norfolk, Suffolk,

Essex, Cambridge, Isle of Ely, Hertford, and county of the city of Norwich. L. J., V. 503.

Dec. 20. Application for a warrant for Joseph Wolfgang Rumler, His Majesty's apothecary, to send certain apothecary's stuffs to Oxford for the use of His Majesty. L. J., V. 503.

Dec. 20. Two applications from the Venetian Ambassador for a pass for himself, family, and goods. L. J., V. 503.

Dec. 20. Petition of Dame Elizabeth Gerrard, relict of Dutton Lord Gerrard, late of Gerrarde Bromley, in the county of Stafford, deceased. On Friday night last certain officers came, and broke into petitioner's stables in Long Acre, and took therefrom two coach horses without giving any reason for so doing. This petitioner conceives to be against the privilege of Parliament (she being a Baroness), and therefore prays an order for the delivery of the horses to her in whose custody soever they shall be found. L. J., V. 504.

Dec. 20. Draft of some amendments to the propositions for accommodating differences. *See* L. J., V. 504.

Dec. 20. Draft order for a watch to be set in Southwark. L. J., V. 505. *In extenso.*

Dec. 20. Draft order for raising dragoons in Cambridge. L. J., V. 505. *In extenso.*

Dec. 20. Draft order of indemnity of Sir George Chudley and others, who have been proclaimed traitors in the county of Devon. L. J., V. 506. *In extenso.*

Dec. 20. Instructions for the lords lieutenant, deputy lieutenants, and other officers and commanders in the counties of Norfolk, Suffolk, Essex, &c. L. J., V. 506. *In extenso.*

Dec. 20. Petition of inhabitants of the city and liberties of Westminster and the duchy of Lancaster; for a speedy accommodation between the King and Parliament, &c. L. J., V. 507. *In extenso.* (Parchment collection.)

Dec. 20. Copy of the protest of certain lords against one of the articles of the propositions to the King. L. J., V. 508. *In extenso.*

Dec. 20. Affidavit of Robert Briscoe and Gregory Isham concerning the seizure of the West Chester mail. L. J., V. 509. *In extenso.*

Dec. 20. Affidavit of Fulke Hughes on the same subject. L. J., V. 509. *In extenso.*
Annexed :—
1. Copy of preceding.
2. Further affidavit of Fulke Hughes. 3 Jan. 1642-3.

Dec. 20. Affidavit of Matthew Dexter on the same subject. L. J., V. 509. *In extenso.*

Dec. 20. Copy of preceding.

Dec. 21. Petition of Wilks Fitchett and William Shallaker, praying for an order for payment of the balance of their account for provisions supplied for the service of the House. L. J., V. 508. *In extenso.*

Dec. 21. Order upon preceding. L. J., V. 509.
Annexed :—
1. Letter from Sir Robert Pye to the House of Lords. The Commissioners of the Treasury signed an order last summer for payment of 300l. to petitioners, whereof they have only received 100l., the said order and divers others being void by reason of the alteration of the Commission of the Treasury, except the same are renewed by the now Commissioners. 3 Jan. 1642-3.

Dec. 21. Petition of Sir Richard Yonge, touching the office of clerk of the Hanaper. L. J., V. 509. *In extenso.*

Dec. 21. Petition of the churchwardens and inhabitants of St. Anne's and St. Agnes', within Aldersgate, London, to H. C. Petitioners having obtained leave of the House to elect a lecturer for their church, have chosen Mr. John Rawlinson, a godly, learned, and painful minister. Pray for an order confirming their election. C. J., II. 898.

Dec. 22. Fragment of a draft of the declaration of the two Houses of Parliament in answer to the King's declaration after the battle of Edgehill. *See* L. J., V. 510; C. J., II. 881.

Dec. 22. Petition of Thomas Tallcott, that his suit against Edmund Harrington may be referred for trial at the common law. L. J., V. 510.

Dec. 22. Petition of Thomas Michell. Was arrested at the suit of Lambert Osbaldston. Prays that a day may speedily be appointed for hearing the cause ; and that in the meantime he may be discharged upon bail, as he has the command of a company which he raised in Hertfordshire for the service of the Parliament. L. J., V. 510.

Dec. 22. Petition of divers knights, esquires, gentlemen, ministers, freeholders, and others, of the abler sort of men inhabiting the county of Bedfordshire and amounting to the number of 3,700, to the Lords and Commons. Pray that Parliament will lay hold on His Majesty's gracious promises and intimations, and by that means put an end to the present war. L. J., V. 511. *In extenso.*

Annexed :—

1. Copy of a petition of same to the King, praying His Majesty to lend a gracious ear to such propositions as the Parliament shall present.

Dec. 22. Petition of divers inhabitants (especially citizens of the city) of London, and the parishes within the liberties thereof, to the Lords and Commons. Pray the Parliament to use means for the procurement of a happy peace. Fifteen sheets, very numerously signed. L. J., V. 511. *In extenso.*

Dec. 22. Copy of preceding.

Dec. 22. Petition of Richard Roe. Has been arrested contrary to privilege, being a servant to the Marquess of Winchester. Prays for discharge. L. J., V. 512.

Dec. 22. Copy of preceding.

Dec. 22. Petition of the parishioners of the parish of St. Ethelborowe's, within Bishopsgate, to H. C. Petitioners formerly presented articles against John Clarke, their parson, for innovations, for preaching transubstantiation, and for his scandalous life, he is now sequestered for a malignant. They pray that Mr. Thomas Emerson may supply the cure in the room of Mr. Clarke. C. J., II. 899.

Dec. 23. Petition of Thomas Michell, praying for an early day for the hearing of his cause against Lambert Osbaldston. L. J., V. 512.

Dec. 23. Application by Lady Byron for a pass for herself, children, and servants to go to Oxford. L. J., V. 512.

Dec. 23. Petition of Dame Mary Carre, wife of Sir Robert Carre ; prays that Richard King may be sent for to answer his contempt, in not complying with an order of their Lordships to pay petitioner certain rents for her maintenance. L. J., V. 512.

Dec. 23. Petition of Edward Lord Newburgh, chancellor of His Majesty's Duchy of Lancaster, concerning the re-calling of a commission of oyer and terminer, &c. L. J., V. 513. *In extenso.*

Annexed :—

1. Order for the re-call of the commission, &c. 17 Nov. 1642. L. J., V. 449. *In extenso.*

Dec. 24. Petition of the Earl of Carlisle, to be restored to his seat in the House. L. J., V. 514. *In extenso.*

Dec. 24. Petition of Philip Burlamachi. Was apprehended by their Lordships' order for not bringing in the books of account concerning the Inland Letter Office. Prays for discharge. L. J., V. 514.

Annexed :—

1. Petition of same : the cause about the Inland Letter Office, in which Lord Stanhope, the postmaster, and the Earl of Warwick as assignee of Mr. Withering are concerned, is still depending in the House of Commons, and petitioner, by their Lordships' order of the 6th of October last, was ordered to show cause why the sequestration should not be discharged and to account for the profits ; but the hearing was prevented by weightier matters. Prays that he may be heard before any order is made.

2. Petition of John Castlon and Edward Hutchins, two of the postmasters for London, in behalf of themselves and all their fellows, the postmasters of England ; petitioners during the late occurrences between England and Scotland received not only packets but post warrants from both Houses to supply gentlemen travelling on their business with horses, which they have always tried to execute, though the adjacent towns have been unwilling to supply horses at the rate of hire which petitioners themselves received, and hackney men, who keep horses, refuse in the same way ; petitioners pray that an order may be made that all persons shall supply horses to them for the the service of Parliament on notice given, or that they may have the establishment of 4,000l. formerly paid for doing His Majesty's service.

3. Petition of same, that no order may be issued restraining them from receiving, carrying, and delivering all such letters as His Majesty's subjects shall freely bring unto them, by which labours they maintain themselves and discharge the King and State of 4,000l. a year,

which sum was formerly allowed for that service. (Undated.)

4. Printed copy of the humble remonstrance of the grievances of all his Majesty's posts of England, together with carriers, waggoners, and others, miserably sustained by the unlawful projects of Thomas Witherings, sometime mercer of London.

Dec. 24. Affidavit of Thomas Barlow that he served two orders upon Roger Haughton, postmaster of Waltham, requiring him to deliver the possession of the Inland Letter Office to the Earl Warwick.

Dec. 24. Petition of Robert Aldus to H. C. ; bought 400 quarters of barley in Suffolk, and laded a great part at Woodbridge in three small vessels, intending to transport the same to Holland and Flanders, but by order of the House the barley has been stayed and seized, prays for leave to transport the barley as proposed, or else to bring it to London for sale. C. J., II. 901.

Dec. 24. Petition of the mayor, aldermen, and commons of the city of London to the Lords and Commons. Pray that all good and fit means may be pursued for obtaining such a peace as may consist with the security of religion, the honour and safety of His Majesty, the perfecting the work of reformation both in Church and State, and the vindication of the power and privileges of Parliament.

Dec. 26. Petition of William, Lord Archbishop of Canterbury. Prays their Lordships' approbation of the appointment of Mr. William Blackston, to the vicarage of Horsham. L. J., V. 515.

Annexed :—

1. Certificate, numerously signed, that William Blackston, clerk, is of sober carriage, and sufficiently learned and conformable to the doctrine of the Church of England. 21 Dec. 1642.

Dec. 26. Copy of order for Sir John Curson and Bartholomew Hone, Esqs., prisoners in the Tower, to be released upon bail. L. J., V. 516.

Dec. 26. Petition of the Fellows of St. John's College, Queen's College, and Jesus College, in the University of Cambridge. Pray that Dr. Beale, Dr. Martin, and Dr. Sterne, the principals of the said Colleges, who are now imprisoned in the Tower, may be released. L. J., V. 516. *In extenso.*

Dec. 27. Petition of Richard Brantwaite. Was committed to the Tower about twenty weeks since ; prays to be released upon bail. L. J., V. 516.

Dec. 27. Petition of some of the members of the French church in London. Pray that Mr. Stephen Oursell may be appointed their pastor. L. J., V. 517. *In extenso.*

Dec. 27. Petition of the Earl of Portland. Prays to be released and restored to his rights as a Peer. L. J., V. 517. *In extenso.*

Dec. 27. List of the prisoners in the Tower on this day. Signed by Sir John Conyers. *See* L. J., V. 511.

Dec. 29. Petition of Philip Burlamachi. Prays that his accounts may be audited by one of His Majesty's auditors, and his liberty granted to him. *See* L. J., V. 519.

Dec. 29. Another petition of same to the like effect.

Dec. 29. Draft letter from the Speaker of the House of Lords to Sir Edward Hungerford, not to demand money from Lord Cottington, who, as a Peer of the Realm, will be assessed by the House for the service of the Parliament. L. J., V. 517. *In extenso.*

Annexed :—

1. Letter from Lord Cottington, at Founthill, to the Earl of Pembroke. Has long been afflicted with stone and gout, and unable to leave his chamber. Sir Edward Hungerford threatens to bring his troops into the writer's house, unless he contributes 1,000l. for the service of the Parliament. Prays that a letter may be written to Sir E. Hungerford, which the writer conceives will be sufficient for his relief. 24 Dec. 1642. L. J., V. 517.

Dec. 30. Petition of Giles Johnson, Thomas Marshall, and others, that a day may be appointed for hearing their cause against Tallcott. L. J., V. 518.

Dec. 30. Order for John Harvie, clerk, to be vicar of Chard. L. J., V. 518. *In extenso.*

Dec. 30. Application by Sir Balthazar Gerbier, master of the ceremonies to the King, for a pass for J. De Lisola, the Emperor's resident, with his servants, to depart and return. *See* L. J., V. 515.

Dec. 30. List of prisoners committed by warrants from the Lords and Commons, in the custody of Sir John Lenthall, Marshal of the King's Bench. *See* L. J., V. 511.

Annexed :—

Copies of the warrants for the committal of the following persons :—
1. Thomas Hungate. 17 Aug. 1642.
2. Sir Basil Brooke. 27 Aug. 1642.
3. Thomas Killigrew. 3 Sept. 1642.
4. Sir George Devereux and William Martin. 10 Sept. 1642.
5. Robert Masters. 19 Sept 1642.
6. Captain Henry Fotherby, Captain Robert Bowles, and Robert Rookes. 20 Sept. 1642.
7. Abygall Dexter. 4 Oct. 1642.
8. Abygall Dexter. 5 Oct. 1642.
9. Captain Sydney Atkins. 8 Oct. 1642.
10. Sir William Flemyng. 1 Nov. 1642.
11. Thomas Gascoyne, Brackenbury Butler, John Dutton, and Matthew Rodstone. 8 Nov. 1642.

Dec. 30. Schedule of the names of such prisoners as are and have been committed to the Fleet since the beginning of the Parliament, together with the causes of their commitments where they did appear, also the day of the discharge of so many as have been discharged. *See* L. J., V. 511.

Dec. 30. Certificate of Cuthbert Hacket, keeper of the Poultry Compter in London, of what prisoners were committed to his custody. *See* L. J., V. 511.

Dec. 30. Particular of all such prisoners as are now in custody, committed by the Honourable House of Parliament to the custody of the Keeper of Newgate since the 4th of March 1641-2. *See* L. J., V. 511.

Dec. 30. Note of all the names of the Command men that are now in custody in Wood Street Compter, London, by order from Parliament. *See* L. J., V. 511.

Dec. 31. Petition of David Mathew and William Lissett. The ship " St. George," of London, laden with Spanish wools from Bilboa for Amsterdam, was by tempestuous weather driven into Falmouth, where she is detained under pretence of His Majesty's commands. Petitioners being agents for those to whom the goods were consigned, pray that a pass may be granted to them to go to the King in order to obtain a free passage for the ship to her directed port. L. J., V. 519.

Dec. 31. Draft of the order for the association of the counties of Warwick and Stafford, and parts adjacent ; instructions for the Lords Lieutenant, Committees of Parliament, and other officers and commanders in the counties of Warwick and Stafford, and cities and counties of Coventry and Lichfield, and the form of association of the said counties. L. J., V. 520. *In extenso.*

Dec. 31. Copy of preceding.

Dec. 31. List of commitments by the Houses of Parliament to the New prison. *See* L. J., V. 511.

Dec. 31. List of commitments by the Houses of Parliament to New Bridewell. *See* L. J., V. 511.

Dec. 31. Letter from the deputy lieutenants of Middlesex to Sir John Conyers, lieutenant of the Tower. Are commanded by the Earl of Holland, lord lieutenant of the county, to publish an order of the House of Lords of the 23rd of December, against the firing of muskets in the streets. Sir John is therefore required to charge the inferior officers of his company to take especial care for the due observance of the order. On the same paper is a copy of the order referred to. L. J., V. 512.

Dec. 31. Letter from the Earl of Stamford, at Bristol, to the Speaker of the House of Lords. Thinks it would be very convenient for the better securing of the place, that two good ships should be sent into the Channel. Is confident he shall make good use of them. Is now a naked man, having left all his own people behind him. Prays some relief by the aid of his fellow peers. What he wants in ability he will repair by his diligence. Prays their Lordships not to believe any reports they hear until advertised by himself or his officers, as he finds the Jesuits prattle much in these parts. Intends to be at Exeter on Sunday next.

Dec. Petition of James Phillipps, Edward Hall, and John Arnold, three of His Majesty's footmen in ordinary, to the Committee for the safety of the kingdom. Petitioners who came to town upon their own particular business, have been absent from His Majesty about three weeks. Pray for a pass to return, as their time of waiting is drawing nigh.

Annexed :—
1. Copy of petitioners' protection, as servants of His Majesty.

[Dec.] Propositions for the association of the counties of Suffolk, Norfolk, Cambridge, Hertford, Middlesex, Kent, and Essex, and for the raising of dragoons for the preservation of the peace of the kingdom.

[Dec.] Book of Custom Causes for Rye, from Michaelmas till Christmas 1642.

[Dec.] Petition of Symon Curnook, of Chancery Lane. Edward Dewell died in Virginia in 1636, leaving petitioner executor of his will. Humfrey Dewell, brother of the deceased, although he had a copy of the will, took out letters of administration. Petitioner has, after five years' suit, obtained two sentences in the Prerogative and Delegates Courts confirming the will, and now the only means left to him to get his rights is to sue his adversary upon a bond entered into in the Prerogative Court of Canterbury. Petitioner has therefore petitioned the Archbishop to assign the bond over to him, but his Grace answered that he was interdicted by the High Court of Parliament, and could not do so. Prays that leave may be given to his Grace to assign the bond to petitioner.

Annexed :—
1. Copy of Curnock's petition to the Archbishop of Canterbury.
2. Copy of the sentence of the Prerogative Court. 27 Jan. 1640-1.
3. Copy of the sentence in the Court of Delegates. 2 Dec. 1642.
4. Copy of bond entered into by Humfrey Dewell in the Prerogative Court. 24 June 1637.

[Dec.] Petition of Thomas Eyres and William Rawbone, keepers of the new prison and house of correction, in the county of Middlesex. About a month since 46 persons were apprehended at or near Brockley, in the county of Northampton, sent to London as delinquents, and appointed to several prisons, and on Friday, the 16th of Sept. last, four of them were sent to the New prison, and six to the House of correction ; but when brought in their poverty was such that they had no money to buy food even, and petitioners, to keep them from famishing, have been obliged ever since to relieve them at their own charge, which they cannot continue, as they receive no allowance from the county for prisoners, and therefore pray that some allowance may be made to them.

Account of customs on the cargoes of two ships leaving Cardiff and the members thereof, from Michaelmas to Christmas 1642.

Petition of Captain Dick and Thomas Cunningham, to the Commons, that a goodly ship of 500 tons and 30 pieces of ordnance and a frigate of 14 pieces, tendered by them for the service of the State, may be employed against the rebels, and that some members of the House may be appointed to treat with petitioners on the subject. *See* C. J., II. 943.

Petition of Henry Slingesby. In 1641 petitioner went into France, leaving all his deeds and documents under lock and key in his mother's house. She in his absence broke open his cabinets, and possessed herself of his deeds, &c., which he would not have complained of out of regard for her, but that he is likely to lose a suit in Chancery for want of them. Prays that she may be called upon to deliver up the deeds, or show cause for keeping them.

Petition of John Puntæus. By grant from His Majesty before the late troubles in England petitioner practised as a physician in Scotland, having his wife and children all the while in England. Prays for liberty to follow his profession anywhere in England.

List of Peers absent at a call of the House.

Request from Richard Sherburne, of Stoniers, in the county of Lancaster, that he may have leave to go to the waters of Bourbon with his wife, daughter, and servants.

Petition of several poor workmen and labourers in His Majesty's works at Whitehall and elsewhere. Great sums of money are due to petitioners for wages, the greater part whereof hath been owing 24 months and upwards. Pray that some speedy course may be taken for their relief, otherwise they are likely to beg, starve, and perish.

Petition of the eight rulers of the watermen. Complain of the unruly conduct of certain of the watermen upon the river Thames, and pray that a warrant may be issued to petitioners for the apprehension and punishment of the offenders.

Petition of Abraham Pont, gent., to H. C. Petitioner, by a former petition, complained of the oppressions done to him and his family by the Bishop of Raphoe. Prays that a day may be appointed for hearing his complaint, and that the bishop may be called upon to answer.

Petition of Dame Anne Herris, widow, for leave to proceed at law against John Earl of Bridgewater for recovery of a debt, notwithstanding the Earl's privilege.

Petition of divers distressed copyholders of the manor of the augmentation of Kenilworth, in the county of Warwick. Petitioners, ever since the dissolution of the Abbey of Kenilworth, have continued copyholders for lives in the manor for moderate fines, the nearest of kin having always been the next takers upon the decease of the longest liver. The manor was granted, 21st James I., to Robert Lord Carye, Baron of Leppington [created Earl of Monmouth in 1626], and regranted by the now Queen Henrietta Maria and others entrusted for her revenue unto Henry Earl of Monmouth, who has altered and subverted the customs, and outed many of the ancient tenants, and granted the copyholds to his own servants and to such strangers as' will give most for them. Petitioners pray that an ordinance may pass for re-establishing the ancient customs and moderating the fines to a certain rate, and that such of the tenants as have been outed by the said Earl may be restored.

Petition of Edward Johnson, of the Inner Temple, Esquire. Prays that no order may be made upon the Earl of Leicester's petition touching certain lands called Astell Grove, parcel of the manor and castle of Kenilworth, until petitioner has been heard by his counsel.

Petition of Francis Lord Willoughby of Parham. Petitioner in due course of law sued forth a writ for the extending of certain lands of the manor of Skettingthorpe, in the county of Lincoln, acknowledged to him by one Stone, since deceased, for a debt of 500l. Sir Edward Herne, the High Sheriff of Lincolnshire, being now in actual war against the Parliament, petitioner cannot procure the extent to be executed, and therefore prays that the tenants of the lands may be ordered to pay him the rents thereof, until his just debt is fully satisfied.

Petition of parishioners of St. Andrew, Holborn, that Mr. Vere Harcourt, brother of the late Sir Symon Harcourt, may be appointed their lecturer, in the room of Dr. Gauden, about to be removed.

Petition of Anne Grenewell, widow. Petitioner's late husband, William Grenewell, bought a 24th part of the French Wine Farm, which had been taken of His late Majesty late King James. Prays that Sir Nicholas Salter, the surviving patentee, and Sir Henry Garway and others, executors of the late Sir William Garway, the other patentee, may be ordered to pay her certain monies due to her late husband out of the profits of the said patent. The matter has been in litigation in the Courts of Chancery and Exchequer for more than 20 years.

Petition of John Scoble and Mary Scoble, widow, complaining of great oppression at the hands of John Fortescue, of East Allington, in the county of Devon, the lord of the manor there, and praying for relief.

Petition of the executor and creditors of the late Samuel Smalley, for relief against Viscount Beaumont and Sir John Monson touching certain lands conveyed to the late Samuel Smalley by Thomas, late Viscount Beaumont.

Petition of Thomas Skelton, servant to Thomas Lord Wentworth, arrested at Yarmouth at the suit of Thomas Spooner and others, contrary to privilege. Prays for discharge.

Petition of Edmond Savile. Has been imprisoned for eighteen months in the Fleet for not paying an annuity of 10l. per annum to William Meering, in compliance with an order of the Court of Requests. Prays for relief.

Petition of John Stone and others, inhabitants of North-more (North Moor), Oxon, complaining of the oppressions and abuses of Gowyn Champneys, one of the Chancery clerks, and praying for inquiry. Petitioners refer to "articles annexed" for details of their grievances, but the articles are wanting.

Petition of John Stephens and others, parishioners of Bisly, Gloucestershire, that Mr. Britton may have liberty to officiate in the church there, and that some part of the profits of the vicarage may be sequestered for his payment, the present vicar, Daniel Leyford, having led a scandalous life, and being now in the King's Bench Prison for debt.

Another similar petition.

Petition of Edward Trussell, mercer, Thomas Tutt, mercer, Edward Griffith, and William Scarborowe. Petitioners supplied Lewis Boyle, Viscount Killamakun (Kinalmeaky), with silks and wares for his marriage, he promising to pay ready money for the same. He Low refuses to pay, and as petitioners can have no relief in the ordinary course of law, the Viscount being servant extraordinary to His Majesty, they pray their Lordships to direct him to give them timely satisfaction.

Petition of same, with others, that the Earl of Cork or his son, Viscount Kinalmeaky, may be directed speedily to pay to petitioners the sum due to them. The Earl promised, that if petitioners would not press for payment until after the Earl of Strafford's trial, he would then give them satisfaction, and that in the meantime his son should not leave England. The Earl now denies this promise, and the Viscount is gone to Ireland. [Lewis Viscount Boyle, of Kinalmeaky, was slain at the battle of Liscarroll in this year.]

Petition of Thomas Gould, that their Lordships will hear his cause against Richard Prigg, clerk, touching the conveyance of certain lands at Ilchester and Northover by petitioner to Parson Prigg, as security for a loan.

Petition of Benjamin Hare, senior, that Sir Charles Herbert, Knight, His Majesty's Surveyor-General, may be ordered to pay certain moneys due to him for surveying and subdividing divers grounds in the great level of the Fens undertaken by the late Earl of Bedford.

Petition of Sir Edward Sydenham. By an order of the 7th March 1641-2 (L. J., IV. 629) he was allowed the benefit of the general order of the 13th July 1641 (L. J., IV. 312), for securing all persons in the quiet enjoyment of their possessions. Prays that the affidavits of his witnesses may be admitted in evidence, or further time allowed him to produce them.

Petition of Gamaliel Carr and Edmond Brewer, clerks. Daniel Strutt and Richard Browne, his uncle, of Castle Hedingham, being at strife, it was referred by certain of His Majesty's justices to petitioners (two neighbour ministers) to settle peace between them. Strutt has since brought many vexatious suits at law against petitioners, who pray to be relieved from further trouble in the matter.

Annexed :—

1. Certificate of Sir Thomas Honywood and James Heron, Esq., to whom the matter was referred by the Lords Committee upon a former petition of Strutt.

Petition of Henry Starkey, Esq., complaining of certain proceedings in the Court of Wards and Exchequer touching the manors of Oulton and Low, in the county of Chester.

Petition of John Long, gent., prisoner in the King's Bench, to the Committee assembled for defence of the kingdom. Petitioner having come out of Wiltshire to serve the State, enlisted and received pay, but was carried away prisoner to the King's Bench, from whence he had absented himself for three-quarters of a year, not by breach of prison, but by Habeas Corpus. Complains of the cruelty of Sir John Lenthall, marshal of the prison, and prays for discharge.

Petition of Sir Michael Wharton to H. C., prays that Sir John Mounson's patent for the "meliorating and better- " ing of surrounded grounds " may be examined, and parties restored to their former possessions, until Sir John Mounson evict them by legal proceedings in some Court of Record, he having brought in much ground, which never was surrounded, without the owners' consent.

Petition of Richard Watts, gent., prisoner in the Fleet, for relief against John Rye, scrivener, of London, touching a mortgage of petitioner's estate at Culworth, in the county of Northampton.

Petition of Giles Wright, son and heir and administrator of William Wright, deceased, complaining of the unfair dealings of Sir Henry Spiller touching the purchase of the manor of Kingsey, in the county of Buckingham, and praying for inquiry.

Petition of Samuel Graunt. Purchased the tithes of Thorpe Mandeville, in the county of Northampton, but has since been compelled to relinquish his title to them by an order of the Council Table, obtained against him by Mr. Bridges, the vicar. Prays for redress.

Petition of Robert Lane, Esq., to Edward Earl of Manchester, praying relief from his noble and kind kinsman, as he is in very great distress.

Petition of Bridget Vaughan, wife of James Vaughan, gent., commander of the Lord Cromwell's troop in the North of Ireland, to the Lords and Commons Commissioners of the Irish business. Prays for relief, the rebels in Ireland having burned, destroyed, or taken away all her husband's estate, and he having received no pay for a long time.

Petition of Digory Baker and Elizabeth his wife to H. C. complaining of an unjust verdict at the common law, obtained against them by Richard Smith by bribery and other unlawful means. Noted, Let him name the party who was bribed, and produce his proofs thereof.

Petition of William Downe to the Earl of Pembroke and Montgomery. Having served for twenty-one years in the Low Countries, returned to England and was appointed lieutenant of a company of foot. Was ordered into Devonshire, but falling very sick obtained leave to stay in London, where he has been five months under the surgeon's hands. Is in great distress, and prays his Lordship's assistance in obtaining his arrears of pay, and fresh employment in the service.

Petition of Thomas Coode, "your Lordships' Servant," to Henry Earl of Holland, &c. Lieutenant Williams coming into the yard of Mrs. Bigg in St. Giles' by virtue of a commission directed to Captain Roger, violently took away a black nag which Mrs. Bigg had bought of petitioner for 4l., which was to have been deducted from a debt owing to her. Petitioner has always paid all duties laid on him by Parliament, and therefore prays his Lordship to give order for the nag to be restored.

Petition of Roger Bragg, gent., to the Earl of Essex; petitioner's son, being an apprentice, has without the consent of master or parents listed himself under the command of Captain Owen, and now lies embarked in a ship at Tilbury Hope, waiting the pleasure of Parliament. Prays that he may be discharged, being a very sickly boy, and inconsiderable every way for any service.

Petition of Elizabeth Leigh, late of Porter Downe [Portadown], in the county of Armagh, widow. At the death of her late husband she was possessed of a good estate in her own right, of all which she was utterly deprived by the cruel and merciless rebels. She and her fatherless children have neither house nor clothes to cover them, and are like to perish through want, unless some speedy relief be afforded. Prays license to make collections for her relief in such parishes in and about London and Westminster, as to their Lordships shall seem meet.

Petition of Nicholas Arnold, to the Commons. A verdict in law has lately been given against him: is desirous of lodging a writ of error, but the great seal is so far distant, that he cannot obtain it in time; prays that writs of error, being lawfully issued out by the cursitors, and fees duly paid, may be allowed, and writs of supersedeas thereupon.

Two drafts of order for Dugaard Clarke, to be instituted to the rectory of Bradford alias Bereford.

Petition of the poor inhabitants of the city of Westminster, to the Earl of Pembroke, Lord Chamberlain to His Majesty, and to the two Houses of Parliament: pray that Mr. Robert White, who has been subcurate of the parish of St. Margaret, Westminster, and has been very careful in visiting and relieving the poor, may not be displaced from his cure for the private ends of a few.

Petition of Lieutenant Colonel Audley Mervyn to the Lords and other Commissioners for Irish affairs: in Nov. 1641 Sir Ralph Gore was commissioned by the King to raise a regiment of 500 men to oppose the rebels in Ireland, in which petitioner served as lieutenant colonel; prays that now Sir Ralph Gore is dead, he may be appointed colonel, and commissioned to enlarge the regiment to 1,000 foot and 100 horse.

Petition of Dame Margery Young, wife to Sir Peter Young: King James granted her a pension of 200l. per annum, which King Charles confirmed, in consideration of the services of Sir Peter, who was tutor to King James, and seven times ambassador for the making up of the match between His late Majesty and Queen Ann; of this pension the arrears now amount to 850l., and 3,000l. besides are due from His Majesty to petitioner's two daughters, she has in consequence become so indebted that she is in fear of arrest; prays their Lordships to give order for the payment of the money due to her, or of some part of it, for relief of her distress.

Petition of John Sherman to the committee for the safety of the kingdom: petitioner has served under the States of Holland, and the King of Portugal for six years past, and gained much experience in martial discipline; hearing of the unhappy differences now in his native country, and desiring to spend his dearest blood for the defence and welfare of the King, Parliament, and kingdom, he is newly come over to present his services to the committee, and prays, in regard of his readiness and known abilities, and the charge he has been at in coming over, that some place of command may be conferred upon him.

Petition of John Miller, His Majesty's servant in ordinary as tailor to the Duke of Gloucester His Highness; has been arrested by Edward Trussell of London, mercer, contrary to privilege; prays for speedy enlargement.

5.

Petition of Thomas Edwards, sealer, at the Great Seal of England; has for twenty-four years carefully performed the painful and laborious duties of his place, having only 4d. per diem for his certain fee, and 20s. per annum for livery, while the casual fees anciently belonging to his place are for the most part kept from him, "particularly the great seal when it is repudiated, appears by ancient records in the Tower, to belong to the "spigurnell, or sealer, as his fee;" but petitioner could never enjoy this nor many other privileges; prays for an examination of his place, and that he may have such fees and privileges as shall be found due to him, and meet to maintain him and three or four servants, and particularly that he may enjoy the old Great Seal, if it appears to be his due.

Annexed:—

1. Extract from the records in the Tower respecting the Great Seal.

Petition of William Crowe, gentleman, on the behalf of his brother Sir Sackville Crowe, His Majesty's Ambassador resident with the grand Seigneur at Constantinople; Sir Sackville obtained by letters patent under the great seal a grant in reversion, expectant on a term of years, lately expired, of the manor of Langherne, in the county of Carmarthen; about seven years since, upon his marriage with the Earl of Rutland's sister, he settled the manor upon her and their issue, and about three years since left the country on His Majesty's service, having assigned the premises for payment of his debts, &c., but Wm. Smaleman, being in possession of the property under the term for years, assigned the residue of the term to Thomas Perrott, who, by connivance with Smaleman and Henry Vaughan, has got possession of the property, and claims it under a pretended entail from the late Sir John Perrott, while Vaughan, a powerful man in those parts, has been purposely made steward of the manor, and holds courts, and threatens to ruin the tenants if they would not attorn to Perrott, and has no fear of the law. Prays that the confederates may be called to answer before their Lordships, and Sir Sackville Crow's agents be put in possession of the property.

Petition of Sarah the wife of Peter Treble of Wapping, mariner: petitioner's husband, now at sea, obtained a judgment for twenty and odd pounds against one William Penington in an action for assault; Penington, hoping to force petitioner to compromise, brought a writ of error in the King's Bench, this too was defeated, but now he is trying to make out that he is protected by the Earl of Cleveland, when he is only a starchmaker, and follows his trade in Stepney; petitioner prays that Penington may not be released until he has satisfied her claim.

Petition of Elizabeth, Katherine, and Mary Troughton: their father and grandfather conveyed lands at Hanslope, Bucks, worth about 300l. per annum, to Robert Wickens, and others, upon trust for petitioners; their father died about fifteen years ago, having made Richard Lane his executor; Lane and Wickens working upon the necessity of petitioner's mother, and her second husband, induced her to pass the lands in question to Lane for a very small sum, and procured the confirmation of the decree in Chancery in the minority of petitioners, and to their utter ruin; pray that Lane and Wickens may be summoned to appear and to produce the deed of trust and a copy of the decree in Chancery, and that Lane may be ordered to accept the money be paid for the land, with interest, and to account for the mesne profits.

Petition of Edward Ewell; from affection to Parliament he not only lent money, but brought his plate worth 30l. to the Guildhall; has for three years and upwards held the office of clerk and registrar in the Castle of Dover, but though he is ready to expose his life and estate in the service of Parliament, he hears that an endeavour is being made by some to oust him from his office; prays to be heard before the place is given to any one else.

Petition of Mrs. Margaret Moore and her children; petitioner lived in good condition in Ireland until the late rebellion, by which she was altogether despoiled of her livelihood; two of her nephews were slain in the service of Parliament, and she has now a son in the service in Ireland; she has received no relief since she came to England; prays for consideration of her case.

Petition of creditors of John Cremer of Snettisham, in the county of Norfolk, to H. C., against Robert Styleman, one of the feoffees in trust of Cremer's estate, who has provided for his own interest to the neglect of the other creditors; pray for a hearing of the case before their Lordships.

I

Petition of William Street, one of His Majesty's littermen, and a prisoner in Newgate; was on Saturday last arrested in Westminster Hall contrary to privilege, at the suit of Peter Williams, a brewer, for a pretended debt for drink due from petitioner's wife before her marriage; prays for release as one of His Majesty's servants.

Similar petition of same.

Petition of Sir Selwin Parker, Knight, and Elizabeth Parker, an infant of the age of six years, for relief against certain proceedings in the Court of Chancery and Court of Requests, arising out of the settlement made on the marriage of Robert Bowers with Elizabeth Parker, Sir Selwin's sister, both now deceased.

Petition of parishioners of Sundridge, in the county of Kent; encouraged by their Lordships' pious intentions to settle able and faithful preachers in all parts of the kingdom, they pray that if Dr. Hall, now rector, should cease to be their minister, their Lordships would move the Archbishop of Canterbury to appoint Tobias Blosse.

Petition of the inhabitants of the parish of Sudbury St. Gregory, and of the chapel of Sudbury St. Peter's thereto annexed, in the county of Suffolk; thereanciently belonged, and were paid to the church and chapel, great and small portions of tithes and oblations, to the value of 80l. per annum at the least, from the impropriate rectory, though the owner was a papist, and though one minister officiated both cures, but of late two ministers, Mr. Smith and Mr. Harrison, have officiated; in 1634 Oliver Andrew, and John his brother deceased, both protestants, became owners of the impropriation, and have ever since withheld great part of the ministers' stipends, besides torturing Mr. Smith in the High Commission Court; they have also enhanced the great and small tithes, troubled the inhabitants in several courts, have taken church dues, and injured the free school and hospital for lazars, and all this has gone on for near nine years; pray their Lordships to assign a new day for hearing the cause and to give compensation to the oppressed.

Petition of Elizabeth Moore, widow, to Edward Earl of Manchester; seven years ago petitioner in the name of Patrick Winch exhibited a Bill in Chancery against one Carpenter for relief from an extent upon a house in Fleet Street; after four several hearings, Carpenter was ordered to deliver up the statute to be cancelled and to pay 25l. costs, but his Lordship and Mr. Speaker have ordered that Carpenter should be discharged on paying 20 nobles; prays that the 25l. costs may stand.

Petition of Thomas Sumner; has been prisoner in the King's Bench for 18 months, and on account of his inability to discharge the marshal's dues was turned over to the common gaol, where he has undergone much misery for want of necessaries; yet by the means of Thomas Winch he is assessed at 20l., and as this is threatened to be distrained from his tenants, they refuse to pay their rents; prays for mitigation of the sum levied upon him.

Petition of Nicholas Wylliot, a Frenchman, to the Earl of Manchester, Speaker to the House of Peers. Petitioner being a stranger, took entertainment at the beginning of this war with the King's army, and being commanded with others to perform the duty of fetching of prisoners, and resistance being made, there happened to be a man slain by one of the party. For which action petitioner has been laid up in Newgate, and is informed that he is to be removed suddenly for trial in the country, where the act was pretended to be done. Prays that he may be tried in the usual way by a jury of his own countrymen.

Petition of Hugh Rosse, late His Majesty's servant at Dunkirk, in Flanders; petitioner was for many years employed by His Majesty and the State for the release of English subjects, prisoners in Flanders, and in this service spent large sums of his own money, besides becoming indebted to others, by whom he is now threatened with arrest. Prays for protection until his business now depending before Parliament is settled.

Annexed:—

1. Copy of similar petition of same to the King. Noted with a reference to the House of Lords, dated 19 March 1640-1.

Petition of Brian Smith, coachman. Petitioner has for the last quarter of a year attended with his coach and horses upon Thomas Viscount Wentworth, and there is now due to him upwards of 34l. Lord Wentworth has secretly conveyed away his trunk and other goods and absented himself, and his horses having been stayed by their Lordships' order, petitioner has no

means of recovering his debt. Petitioner prays that his debt may be satisfied before the horses are discharged.

Petition of divers of the inhabitants of Pinner, in the county of Middlesex. The curate of Pinner, which is a chapel of ease to the mother church of Harrow, only receives 10l. a year from the vicar for his maintenance, and seldom preaches or procures any other to perform that duty for him. Petitioners pray that they may have liberty to make choice of a lecturer, whom they will maintain at their own charge. See C. J., II. 723.

Petition of John Gerrard, late postmaster at Brickhill, in the county of Bucks; petitioner and his ancestors have enjoyed the place of postmaster for nearly fifty years, and there is now owing unto him the wages 374l. Notwithstanding this about three years since, Mr. Thomas Witherings sold the place to another, not in any way to advance His Majesty's service, but in order that he might himself reap the profit in selling the place. Prays that he may be restored to his place, or that Witherings may be ordered to give him recompense for the loss of it.

Petition of inhabitants of Cransley, in the county of Northampton. The lords of the manor of Cransley hold the parsonage, vicarage tithes, and vicarage house, under a pretended composition to pay the vicar a yearly stipend of 8l. About four years since the late Sir Henry Robinson left a legacy for the repair of the vicarage house, which is now in ruins, but the executors have neglected to repair it. The manor of Cransley is held in five parts, and certain of the holders refuse to contribute their shares for the competent allowance of the vicarage. Petitioners being destitute of a minister, were constrained to hire one at their own charge, until Mr. Goodman, hoping for competent allowance, was inducted, but he not prevailing has removed himself, leaving the inhabitants without cure ever since. Pray that a certain competent allowance may be settled for ever out of the vicarage and parsonage.

Draft letter from [the Speaker of the House of Commons] to —— respecting the disarming and dispersing of papists.

1642-3.

Jan. 2. **Petition of the paviers** and others employed about the work of paving the Old Palace of Westminster. Pray that they may receive payment of what is due to them by their contracts as the work is now finished. L. J., V. 523.

Annexed:—

Three other petitions of same to the like effect. (Undated.)

Jan. 2. **Draft order** for the accounts of the Inland Post Office to be delivered to the Earl of Warwick. L. J., V. 523. *In extenso.*

Jan. 2. **Order** for raising forces in Hertfordshire and places adjacent, to drive the King's forces from Brill. L. J., V. 523. *In extenso.*

Jan. 2. **The Lords answer** to the apprentices of London, who came to deliver a petition to the House. L. J., V. 524. *In extenso.*

Jan. 3. **Copy of the answer** of Parliament to the application of the Scots Commissioners for the payment of the arrears due to the Scots in Ireland. L. J., V. 524. *In extenso.*

Jan. 3. **Copy of the answer** of Parliament to the Scots Commissioners concerning the 40,000l. of the brotherly assistance due to them at Midsummer last. L. J., V. 525. *In extenso.*

Annexed:—

1. Letter from the Scots Commissioners asking for payment of the 40,000l. 24 Dec. 1642. L. J., V. 524. *In extenso.*

Jan. 3. **Petition of divers apprentices** and other young men in and about the city of London to the Lords and Commons. In favour of peace. L. J., V. 525. *In extenso.*

Jan. 3. **Order appointing a day** for hearing the cause between the Lord Balmerino and Lord Chief Justice Heath. L. J., V. 525.

Jan. 3. **Letter from Lord Carnwath,** at Oxford, to the Earl of Holland. Prays his Lordship to procure a pass for himself and four servants to go to Scotland. See L. J., V. 542.

Jan. 4. **List of persons** to be sent for as delinquents for killing the Earl of Carlisle's deer. L. J., V. 526. *In extenso.*

Jan. 4. **Draft order** for sending over victuals to Ireland. L. J., V. 528. *In extenso.*

Jan. 4. **Draft order** for the trained bands of London and Westminster to repair to their colours upon summons. L. J., V. 528. *In extenso.*

House of
Lords.
—
Calendar.
1642-3.

Jan. 4. Draft order for an allowance to be paid to Mr. William Hawkins for his attendance on the committee for Irish affairs. L. J., V. 528. *In extenso.*

Jan. 4. Certificate of the justices, in the case of Le Grand and Desormeaux. Dated 1 Nov. 1642. Read and entered this day. L. J., V. 528. *In extenso.*

Annexed :—

1. Petition of John Beaverley, committed for obeying their Lordships' order in the cause between Le Grand and Desormeaux, by which he was directed to deliver to Le Grand certain pieces of cloth left in his hands in trust; petitioner was quite ready to give up the cloth on having security from Le Grand that he would bear him harmless ; prays that the certificate of the judges in the cause may be read, and that he may be discharged from imprisonment. *See* L. J., V. 526.
2. Affidavit in support of preceding. 15 Nov. 1642.

Jan. 4. Petition of inhabitants of Essex, in favour of peace. L. J., V. 529. *In extenso.*

Jan. 4. Declaration of the Commissioners of the General Assembly of the Kirk of Scotland from their meeting at Edinburgh to the Hon. Houses of the Parliament of England. Inform the Parliament that they have sent a petition to the King by Mr. Alexander Henderson, praying his Majesty to disband all papists out of his army, to call an Assembly of Divines for settling an unity of religion and church government in both kingdoms, and to use all good means for the conversion of the Queen's Majesty to the true reformed religion. Entreat the Parliament on their part, to disband all papists, if any there be in their army, as is alleged in divers declarations, to constantly prosecute their desire for unity in religion and kirk government, to deal with His Majesty for calling an Assembly of Divines, and to give their serious thoughts and endeavours to the Queen's conversion.

Jan. 5. Affidavits of Dame Elizabeth Gurney and others, that Mr. Bard and Mr. Browne have refused to return Lady Gurney's horses in compliance with the order of the 15th of Nov. 1642. L. J., V. 530.

Jan. 5. Order for using Lambeth House as a prison. L. J., V. 530. *In extenso.*

Jan. 5. Order for the payment of 900l. to Mr. Loftus, for the freight of provisions, and clothing to Ireland. L. J., V. 531. *In extenso.*

Jan. 5. Draft of preceding.

Jan. 5. Two draft orders for Lord Petre's house in Aldersgate, and the Bishop of London's house near St. Paul's, to be used as prisons. L. J., V. 531. *In extenso.*

Jan. 5. Draft order for Lord Fairfax to continue the same way of payment to his army as he hath done hitherto. L. J., V. 531. *In extenso.*

Jan. 5. Petition of Francis Sadler and of Tempest Miller, and others, creditors of the said Francis Sadler. Pray that Toby Bose and certain other creditors, may be sent for to answer for their illegal proceedings in surreptitiously taking out a commission of bankruptcy against Sadler, in order to wrest his estate from him at an undervalue, and defraud the other creditors of their just debts.

Jan. 6. Petition of divers citizens and inhabitants of the city of London. Pray that the consideration of their former petition, referred by their Lordships to a committee, may be speedily proceeded with, and that it may also be referred to the committee to consider of the outrageous violence and injuries offered to petitioners in the preparation and prosecution of their said former petition. L. J., V. 531.

Annexed :—

1. Copy of former petition referred to in preceding. 19 Dec. 1642. L. J., V. 501.
2. List of committee to whom the petition was referred. 19 Dec. 1642. L. J., V. 499.

Jan. 6. Petition of Sir John Conyers, Lieutenant of the Tower, concerning a house built by William Felgate, near the Tower. L. J., V. 532. *In extenso.*

Jan. 7. Declaration of both Houses touching the illegality of Commissions of Array. L. J., V. 533.

Jan. 7. Draft declaration of the Lords and Commons against the agreement for the neutrality of Cheshire. L. J., V. 535. *In extenso.*

Annexed :—

1. Copy of the " Agreement made the three and
   " twentieth day of December, at Bunbury, in the
   " county of Chester, for a pacification and settling
   " the peace of the said county, by us whose names
   " are subscribed, authorised thereunto by the
   " Lords and gentlemen nominated Commissioners
   " of Array and deputy lieutenants in the said
   " county."

House o
Lords.
—
Calendar.
1642-3.

Jan. 7. Petition of Robert Harrington, Robert Goodwyn, and George Thimilby, agents for the distressed city of Londonderry, to H. C. By an order of the 12th of December last, all the money collected on the then three next fast-days was to be disposed of for the relief of the inhabitants of Londonderry, but by a subsequent order the money collected on the first of the fast-days was disposed of for the relief of the plundered ministers, whereby petitioners' intention of sending victuals in a ship called the " Prosperous," bound for Londonderry, is defeated. Pray that the order of the 12th of December may be confirmed, and that the collections made on the next fast-day after the two limited by the order, may be added to the other money, and that all ministers may be commanded to publish the order, and the churchwardens to pay over the collections to petitioners. C. J., II. 918.

Jan. 7. List of the prisoners in Lambeth House. [Jan. 7.] Petition of Bernard Alsopp, printer, prisoner in the Fleet. Prays for his discharge, having been committed for printing scandalous pamphlets, which were received and done by his servants during his absence in the country. *See* L. J., V. 533.

Jan. 9. Petition of Francis Richards, of Presteyne [Presteign], in the county of Radnor. On the 27th of October last, the captain of a troop of horse under the command of the Earl of Stamford, seized Captain Charles Price, knight for the county. Petitioner went in a neighbourly way to visit Price, and was then, without any cause, taken by the captain of the troop, and afterwards with Captain Price conveyed to Coventry, where he hath remained ever since in durance. Prays for his discharge. L. J., V. 536.

Annexed :—

1. Certificate of the committee at Coventry to whom preceding petition was referred. Richards was committed under a warrant of Colonel Essex. This is all the information the committee can obtain, as his commitment was from Gloucester, and his habitation is Presteign, sixty miles off. 17 Jan. 1642-3.

Jan. 9. Draft order for the removal of the prisoners from Lincoln Castle. L. J., V. 536. *In extenso.*

Jan. 9. Instructions for Francis Lord Willoughby, Lord Lieutenant of the county of Lincoln, and the committees of Parliament for the subscriptions of money, plate, and horse for that county, and other officers and commanders in the said county of Lincoln and parts adjacent. L. J., V. 536. *In extenso.*

Jan. 9. Draft of the declaration and ordinance of Lords and Commons for the defence of the county of Lincoln. L. J., V. 538. *In extenso.*

Jan. 9. Draft order for the discharge of all the present collectors of customs. C. J., II. 919. *In extenso.*

Jan. 9. Petition of Sir Francis Dowse, Knight, now prisoner at Portsmouth, to H. C. Was required by the Sheriff of Hampshire, in his Majesty's name, to appear at Winchester concerning the raising of some contributions for the payment of Lord Grandison's horse, whilst they were in that county. He appeared there accordingly, and his coach, and four horses were taken from him, and he himself was carried away prisoner to Portsmouth. Prays for his discharge, as he has always submitted cheerfully to all payments, and obeyed all the orders of Parliament. C. J., II. 919.

Jan. 10. Order for Ely House to be used as a prison. L. J., V. 542. *In extenso.*

Jan. 10. Order for raising forces in the county of Wilts. L. J., V. 542. *In extenso.*

Jan. 10. Order for securing the 3,000l. lent by the inhabitants of Bristol. L. J., V. 543. *In extenso.*

Jan. 10. Order for 2,516l. 4s. to be paid for necessaries for Duncannon Fort. L. J., V. 543. *In extenso.*

Jan. 10. Instructions for the deputy lieutenants of the county of Devon. L. J., V. 544. *In extenso.*

Jan. 10. Draft of preceding.

Jan. 11. Copy of the petition of the inhabitants within the county of Hertford to the Lords and Commons. In favour of peace. L. J., V. 545. *In extenso.*

Jan. 11. Petition of the ministers and elders of the Dutch and French congregations within the city of London ; pray that some order may be settled for suppressing disorders in their church. L. J., V. 546. *In extenso.*

Jan. 12. Order for fortifying the town of Lynn. L. J., V. 547. *In extenso.*

Jan. 12. Copy of preceding.

Jan. 12. Order for fortifying the town of Ipswich. L. J., V. 547. *In extenso.*

Jan. 12. Copy of the request and desire of Don Alonso de Cardinas, Ambassador for His Catholic Majesty of

I 2

Spain, propounded unto the Right Hon. Houses of Parliament concerning the lading of the ship "St. Clara," that ran away from St. Domingo, and came to Southampton. L. J., V. 551. *In extenso.*

Jan. 13. Pass for Sir Thomas Aylesbury to go to Oxford to attend the King upon his place as one of the Masters of the Court of Requests. L. J., V. 552.

Jan. 14. Draft order for raising money in the associated counties of Northampton, Leicester, Derby, Rutland, Nottingham, Huntingdon, Bedford, and Bucks. L. J., V. 554. *In extenso.*

Jan. 14. Ordinance prohibiting ships from going to Newcastle for coals. L. J., V. 555. *In extenso.*

Jan. 14. Order for the payment of 130l. for drugs for Ireland. L. J., V. 555. *In extenso.*

Jan. 14. Order for the payment of 3,336l. 1s. for clothes for the soldiers in Ireland. L. J., V. 555. *In extenso.*

Jan. 14. Order for the payment of 4,000l. for clothes for the soldiers in Ireland. L. J., V. 556. *In extenso.*

Jan. 14. Copy of preceding.

Jan. 14. Another copy.

Jan. 14. Order for the payment of 550l. for shirts for the soldiers in Ireland. L. J., V. 556. *In extenso.*

Jan. 14. Order for the payment of 165l. for necessaries for the army at Cork. L. J., V. 556. *In extenso.*

Jan. 14. Order for the payment of 180l. for beef and salt for Ireland. L. J., V. 556. *In extenso.*

Jan. 14. Order for the payment of 36l. for beef for Ireland. L. J., V. 557. *In extenso.*

Jan. 14. Order for disarming all those in London and Westminster who refuse to contribute upon the propositions. L. J., V. 557. *In extenso.*

Jan. 14. Order for fortifying the town of Gloucester. L. J., V. 557. *In extenso.*

Jan. 14. Order for supplying the churches of St. Martin, and St. Paul, Covent Garden, with ministers. L. J., V. 557. *In extenso.*

Jan. 14. Copy of preceding.

Jan. 14. Resolution of the Commons that they do not decline or intend to invalid the ordinance for the militia, by the seventh proposition. C. J., II. 928. *In extenso.*

Jan. 16. Pass for Clement Kynnersley to go to Oxford. L. J., V. 558.

Jan. 16. Certificate of Doctor Aylett and Doctor Heath that, in compliance with their Lordships' order, they searched certain chests and trunks at the Custom House belonging to the Earl of Arundel and Surrey supposed to contain silver, but they found in them nothing but pictures, and other household stuff warrantable. L. J., V. 558. *In extenso.*

Jan. 17. Order for the payment of money to the deputy lieutenants of the city of Exeter. L. J., V. 560. *In extenso.*

Jan. 17. Order for assessing the inhabitants of the county of Devon to defray the expenses of the army there. L. J., V. 560. *In extenso.*

Jan. 17. Letter from Colonel Bulstrode and Thomas Tyrrill at Aylesbury to the Earl of Essex. The writers being sorry to see their countrymen, who were well affected, daily plundered by the Cavaliers, though they wanted strength to undertake the chief harbour of them, yet resolved on Sunday last to attack them upon one of their quarters. Thought to have found a troop at Lurgishall about a mile and a half from Brill, but they had gone the afternoon before. Heard that at Piddington a mile further on there was another troop, so marched on and took the whole, men, horses, and colours, within sight of Brill without loss or hurt to any of the writers' troop. Some, who were afterwards taken in the town, will not acknowledge themselves to be of that company, but they are as bad as the worst, especially one Chadwell, who had a commission about him for captain of a company of dragooners, and Nicholson who is known to have been in actual service. Have sent all the prisoners, in number forty-nine, with the colours, whose motto is supreme and remarkable. Pray to be excused for so often soliciting more strength, but the enemy grows upon them, and the neighbouring county of Northampton. The writers' troop will not be recruited by the horses taken, as they are for the most unserviceable and poor, and as for arms they had very few. Have here in custody a man of this county, who posted up in the market towns the proclamation wherein Colonel Hampden and Colonel Goodwin were excepted from pardon, will keep him until they know his Excellency's commands. To this letter Colonel Goodwin adds, "I "beseech your Excellency to consider of Lieutenant "Greene as one of the chief plunderers of the house of "your humble servant." This is no doubt one of the

letters read in the House on the 21st January. *See* L. J., V. 566.

Annexed :—

1. Statement in the same handwriting as preceding; Skipwith had a commission for a troop of horse which he threw away; he was to be assisted with the troop we took at Piddington, and by Chadwell to raise his troop by taking horses where he could find them. The little gentleman with the silver lace and buttons on his coat was to have been cornet to Skipwith. Zouch, servant to Mr. Gardiner, went in their company only to plunder. Chadwell took five horses the day before from an honest gentleman of Moreton, and plundered a good minister's house at Water Stratford the same Sabbath day and took away from the minister's wife 18l. or 20l. The same company drove away eight or ten oxen of Sir Richard Ingoldsby's the day before.

Jan. 17. Application from Lady Spencer for a pass to go to Oxford. *See* L. J., V. 557.

Jan. 17. Order for stopping all carriages, waggons, and other conveyances going to or from Oxford without leave of Parliament or of the Earl of Essex. C. J., II. 931. *In extenso.*

Jan. 18. Petition of Patrick Carr, a Scotch gentleman, prisoner in Newgate; prays for his discharge upon condition of his leaving the kingdom. L. J., V. 561. *In extenso.*

Jan. 18. Pass for Doctor Mason, one of the Masters of the Court of Requests, to go to Oxford to attend His Majesty. L. J., V. 562.

Jan. 18. Copy of the King's answer to the petition of Parliament concerning the adjournment of the term to Oxford. L. J., V. 562. *In extenso.*

Jan. 20. Petition of John Hawkins, prisoner in the Fleet; was committed for refusing to obey the order of the Parliament forbidding shooting; prays for his discharge. L. J., V. 562.

Annexed :—

1. Another petition of Hawkins. On the 20th of January petitioner was ordered by their Lordships to be discharged, but he is still detained because he is unable to pay certain fees required by Mr. Browne and the rest of the clerks. (Undated.)

Jan. 20. Petition of Walter Lord Bishop of Winchester. Complains of the destruction of wood in Waltham Chase, parcel of the Bishop's manor of Waltham, by certain of the inhabitants contrary to an order of the House of the 3rd December 1641. Prays that the offenders may be sent for to answer. L. J., V. 563.

Annexed :—

1. Affidavit of Alexander Bowsher, that the order of the 3rd of December was duly published in the market place and church at Waltham, and that the persons named in the petition continue to cut and carry away the underwood and timber.

2. Order for the attachment of William Woodman, and the other persons mentioned in the petition.

Jan. 20. Petition of Sir Thomas Dawes. Prays that he may have his liberty in order to instruct and advise with his counsel during the passage of his Bill through the House. L. J., V. 563.

Annexed :—

1. Petition of John Dawes the younger, son of Sir Abraham Dawes, deceased. Prays to be further heard against the passing of Sir Thomas Dawes' Bill. (Undated.)

2. Copy of preceding.

Jan. 20. Petition of divers of His Majesty's late Commissioners for causes ecclesiastical. Pray that a suit brought against them by one Flower in the Court of Common Pleas may be stayed, until their Lordships have decided whether any proceedings can be taken against them as Commissioners, except for corruption, or misdemeanour, other than the illegality of their commission. The petition is only signed by Sir Nathaniel Brent. L. J., V. 563.

Jan. 20. Petition of the master and wardens of the Company of Vintners. Pray their Lordships to settle moderate prices for retailing vintners to sell by, for the ensuing year. L. J., V. 563. *In extenso.*

Jan. 20. Order for the payment of 10,000l. to Sir Gilbert Gerrard. L. J., V. 564. *In extenso.*

Jan. 21. Petition of Anne Blake, wife of William Blake. Prays that her cause against William Rolfe may be heard. L. J., V. 565. *In extenso.*

Jan. 21. Request for an order concerning the French and Dutch churches in England. L. J., V. 566. *In extenso.*

Jan. 21. Copy of preceding.

Jan. 21. Petition of James Tooke, Esq., one of the auditors of His Majesty's Court of Wards and Liveries. Prays that a pass may be granted to him to go to Oxford to attend to his office. L. J., V. 566.

Jan. 21. Draft order against removing the courts of law to Oxford. L. J., V. 567. *In extenso.*

Jan. 21. Draft order for continuing the ordinance concerning the subsidy of tonnage and poundage. L. J., V. 567. *In extenso.*

Jan. 23. Petition of the members of the French congregation, concerning the election of a minister for their church. L. J., V. 568. *In extenso.*

Jan. 23. Title to the Act for the utter abolishing and taking away of all archbishops, bishops, their chancellors, and commissaries, deans, sub-deans, deans and chapters, archdeacons, canons, prebendaries, and all chaunters, chancellors, treasurers, sub-treasurers, succentors, and sacrists; and all vicars choral and choristers, old vicars and new vicars, of any cathedral or collegiate church, and all other their under officers out of the Church of England. Read 1ª, L. J., V. 569. The Bill passed through all stages in both Houses. The last entry in Lords' Journals being an order of the House, that the title of the Bill be sent as a proposition to the King with the Bill. L. J., V. 572.

Jan. 23. Draft of an ordinance appointing ministers to ask pardon of God for the national sins of the kingdom. *See* L. J., V. 569.

Jan. 24. Petition of Lewis Mareschall, a Frenchman, and now an inhabitant of London. Was committed to the Fleet for presenting an unfitting petition concerning the French congregation. Prays for his discharge, as his offence was committed through his ignorance of the privileges of Parliament. L. J., V. 570.

Jan. 24. Copy of order of the Commons respecting Sir Benjamin Ayloffe. C. J., II. 941. *In extenso.*

Jan. 26. Application for a pass for Francis Bernardi, agent to the ambassador of Spain, to go to Oxford. L. J., V. 570.

Jan. 26. Pass for Ambrose Scudamore to go into Herefordshire. L. J., V. 570.

Jan. 26. Three drafts of the order for certain monies belonging to Walter Mountague, and attached by the sheriff of London, to be deposited in the hands of the Earl of Manchester, until the cause in Chancery between Mountague and Oliver Scandrett be heard. L. J., V. 570.

Jan. 26. Order for the payment of 138l. 4s. 1d. to George Evans for wheat for Ireland. L. J., V. 572. *In extenso.*

Jan. 26. Order for payment of 500l. to Sir William Cole for the garrison of Enniskillen. L. J., V. 572. *In extenso.*

Jan. 26. Order for the payment of 1,163l. 14s. to Nicholas Nagle for provisions for Ireland. L. J., V. 573. *In extenso.*

Jan. 26. Order for Captain Bingsley to keep his company in Ireland. L. J., V. 573. *In extenso.*

Jan. 26. Order for the payment of 41l. 5s. to Captain Isaac Thornton for arrears of his personal entertainment in the late Northern expedition. L. J., V. 573. *In extenso.*

Jan. 26. Order for payment of 400l. to Maurice Thompson and William Pennoyer, for providing a ship to carry some troops of horse and some clothes into Ireland. L. J., V. 573. *In extenso.*

Jan. 26. Order for assessing the county of Lancaster for the relief of Manchester, &c. L. J., V. 573. *In extenso.*

Jan. 26. Copy of preceding.

Jan. 26. Order for a constant watch or guard to be kept in the city of Norwich. L. J., V. 574. *In extenso.*

Jan. 26. Petition of Henry Muggeridge and others, footmen to His Majesty in ordinary, John Horring, footman to the Prince His Highness, Patrick Jerrell, footman to the Duke of York, and James Moutoth, yeoman usher of the guard to the Prince His Highness. Pray that passes may be granted to them to go to Oxford to attend their places.

Jan. 26. Petition of Dame Katharine Bromley, late wife of Sir Thomas Bromley, of Holte Castle, in the county of Worcester. Prays that Henry Bromley, son and heir of the late Sir Thomas, may be ordered to give up to petitioner the possession of the manor of Wick, intended to be settled upon her as a jointure by her late husband, who died without signing the settlement.

Jan. 27. Order for the Earl of Holland to appoint captains to the companies of the trained bands belonging to the Tower. L. J., V. 574. *In extenso.*

Jan. 27. List of the Committee of the House of Commons appointed to go with the Lords to the King with the propositions. L. J., V. 575. *In extenso.*

Jan. 27. Order that the money raised in Somersetshire upon the propositions shall be used for the maintenance

of the forces raised in that county. L. J., V. 575. *In extenso.*

Jan. 27. Order for assessing malignants in the county of Somerset. L. J., V. 576. *In extenso.*

Jan. 27. Letter from Sir Rowland St. John, Sir Richard Samwell, Sir Gilbert Pickeringe, John Crewe, and Edward Harby, Esq., at Northampton, to the Committee for the defence of the kingdom, concerning the assessment of certain lords who have declared against the Parliament. *See* L. J., V. 583.

Jan. 28. Petition of Sir Charles Berkeley. Prays that on account of his impaired health he may be removed from the Tower to Mr. George Kirke's house, upon giving sufficient security, and under such restrictions as their Lordships think fit. L. J., V. 576.

Annexed:—
1. Copy of preceding.

Jan. 30. Petition of Henry Arney. Was on Saturday last arrested by Robert Mayne and Henry Browne at the suit of Thomas Hutchinson, notwithstanding they knew he was servant to the Earl of Portland. Prays for his discharge. L. J., V. 578.

Jan. 30. Petition of Sir Basill Brooke, and Sir John Wintour. Pray their Lordships to resume the hearing of their cause against George Mynn, and that in the meantime all proceedings in the Court of King's Bench may be stayed. L. J., V. 578.

Annexed:—
1. Copy of preceding.
2. Order of the Committee for petitions with reference to the hearing of the cause. 19 July, 1641.
3. Copy of preceding.
4. Petition of Sir John Wintour, that their Lordships would look into the whole cause from the beginning, which relates to a lease of His Majesty's ironworks, and a certain quantity of cordwood in the Forest of Dean, and that time may be given for the examination of witnesses. (Undated.)

Jan. 30. Message from the Commons for an order for public thanks to be given for the success of the Parliament forces in the North. L. J., V. 578. *In extenso.*

Jan. 30. Draft of the declaration concerning Lord Fairfax's success in the North. L. J., V. 579. *In extenso.*

Annexed:—
1. Lord Fairfax's letter from Selby giving an account of his proceedings in the North. 26 Jan. 1642-3. L. J., V. 759. *In extenso.*
2. Letter from the Earl of Newcastle, at Pomfret, to Colonel Gilford Slingsby. Returns him thanks for the services he has done, and would be glad to give him all the assistance he desires in prosecuting the present levies, but cannot furnish him with any more men at present, for the following reasons, the forces of the bishopric were levied upon condition to remain in the county, and they are appointed to guard the ammunition through the county, and if need be further, which the Earl hopes they will obey. Hears that neither Colonel Huddleston nor Colonel Clavering can march for that convoy, as was intended, and has therefore appointed Sir Robert Strickland and desires Slingsby to do so too, as the Earl hears there is a design to surprise and secure it. As regards the lady, Slingsby is to use his own discretion, as the Earl has not been used to take ladies 'prisoners. Desires Slingsby to keep any goods or arms taken from disaffected persons, the goods upon account for paying the soldiers, and the arms for arming the men, and though they be part of the arms of the trained bands, yet being taken as a prize they shall be accounted so. As regards the fortifying the castle, the Earl does not understand of what consequence it can be except as a place of residence for Slingsby whilst he is raising his regiment. 8 Jan. 1642-3. This letter is noted as follows :—'' Slingsby, to whom " this letter is directed, is since taken prisoner " by Sir Hugh Cholmley, and is that Slingsby " mentioned in my Lord Fairfax's letter, and " with whom this letter and the instructions and " Sir John Henderson's letter was found.''
3. Instructions taken with Colonel Slingsby. The county (York) to be universally disarmed of all private arms, both of horse and foot, and those not borne in service to be brought into a magazine at York. The trained bands that rose with Hotham to be compelled to rise again, and serve in their persons, or every man to send an able-bodied man to serve for him. Considering Her Majesty intends to commit her person into

the protection of this county, a magazine is to be made at York to enable an army to subsist there in case of extremity or necessary retreat. All the gentry of Yorkshire to be unanimously moved to resort thither with their families and moveables, as the contrary faction do daily to Hull, by which means the persons and estates of such as are not well affected will be secured, as such as refuse or decline it shall discover themselves, and every man's fortune and family being there engaged they will more actually move with a joint concurrence for the preservation of the place, which must be the retreat for the safety of the Queen's person, no other place being defensible and considerable to balance Hull. Those that decline this proposition are to understand that they must at their own peril undergo the plunder of the soldiers, if any fall out. The garrison in York shall be daily employed in making regular works upon the avenue and outworks, and encroachments upon the hills and other places commanding the town. No markets or fairs to be held in any place in the county except York. Some of the iron ordnance, sent over by the Queen, to be sent for at the charge of the county to place upon the avenues and fortifications.

This and the Earl of Newcastle's letter are no doubt two out of the three papers referred to in the postscript to Lord Fairfax's letter. *See* L. J., V. 580.

4. List of the persons to whom the Earl of Newcastle granted commissions to raise forces. L. J., V. 580. *In extenso.*

Jan. 30. Ordinance for raising a loan for maintaining the army in Ireland. L. J., V. 580. *In extenso.*

Jan. 30. Copy of the propositions from both Houses to the King for accommodating differences. L. J., V. 581. *In extenso.*

Annexed :—
1. Draft of part of preceding, with Commons' amendments. *See* L. J., V. 561, &c.
2. Another draft.
3. Fair copy of part of preceding.
4. Another draft with amendments.

Jan. 30. Petition of Henry Cowes and William Goddard, servants to the Right Hon. the Lord Cottington. On Friday last one Austin, a corporal to Captain Harvey, of Cheapside, came with divers armed soldiers to the Lord Cottington's house, at Hanworth, and without any warrant from the Parliament, as far as petitioners know, forcibly entered the house and took away all the arms and weapons they found in it. Pray that the arms may be restored, or that petitioners may have license to furnish themselves and their fellow servants with others, to defend themselves against vagabonds, thieves, and robbers, as the house stands remote from any neighbour, and destitute of assistance from others in times of danger.

Jan. 31. Order for seizing the arms of all papists in Norwich. L. J., V. 583. *In extenso.*

Jan. 31. Letter from the Rev. Richard Culmer, at Canterbury, to the Earl of Warwick. The benefice of Chartham near Canterbury is now void, and is in the gift of the Archbishop of Canterbury, who intends, the writer understands, to bestow it upon one of the tribe of Lambeth. If malignants are permitted to advance their own party, and thereby their own cause, they will do great hurt, especially where malignant priests are so numerous. If the prelate's tyrannous patronage can be stopped, the writer prays that he may be taken into consideration, as he has a good testimonial for his life and doctrine, and has been deprived of his living for not reading the book for Sabbath sports. Is now so much engaged in advancing the association that he cannot wait upon his Lordship. *See* L. J., V. 585.

Jan. 31. List of servants of the Earl of Pembroke and Montgomery who attended him to Oxford.

Jan. 31. Letter from Captain Anthony Willoughby, at His Majesty's fort, near Galway, to the Lords in Parliament. Beseeches their Lordships to take his letters expressing the wants and dangers of the garrison into their serious consideration, and with all possible speed to hasten some relief both of men and provisions, otherwise their condition is likely to be very desperate. If not timely supplied the place may soon be endangered. Lord Clanricard is utterly unable, though most willing in any way, to relieve them, and the strength and success of the enemy increase daily in these parts. A small vessel to ride constantly in the harbour would much advance the welfare of the place by fetching such commodities as might be got in the adjacent islands and creeks. *See* L. J., V. 426, 720.

Jan. Instructions given by the commissioners appointed by the King's Majesty and Parliament of this kingdom (Scotland), for conserving the articles of the treaty, to John Earl of Loudon, Lord High Chancellor of Scotland, &c. You shall with all earnestness intreat His Majesty and Parliament that episcopacy may be totally removed, and that there may be unity of religion and uniformity of kirk government in all His Majesty's dominions: to this effect you shall solicit His Majesty and the Parliament for a meeting of sound divines of both kingdoms, who may prepare matters for the consideration of His Majesty, and the Parliament. You shall entreat and earnestly labour that His Majesty and the Parliament may in the depth of their wisdom take such fair and compendious ways as may remove the causes of these troubles without the effusion of more blood, and that there may be a more peaceable and amicable decision than by the sword. You shall shew that it is earnestly desired, that the Houses of Parliament would resolve upon the fittest ways of removing all prejudices and mistakes, and leave no fair means untried which may induce His Majesty to return to His Parliament, and you shall show His Majesty that it is our humble desire that he will hearken to the invitation, that by a happy conjunction with them the great public affairs may be settled. You shall earnestly beg that all papists now in arms in England shall be speedily disarmed and disbanded, and especially those in the Earl of Newcastle's army, because the most part thereof have been levied and have their residence near our borders, which may do us greater prejudice than the garrisons at Berwick and Carlisle, which were expressly contrary to the last treaty. You shall show to His Majesty that although we are bound by our commissions, when any difference arises to the disturbance of the common peace, to labour, to remove, and compose it, the present distractions are a work beyond our power and greater than can be remedied by us, and may come to that height before the next triennial Parliament, that any remedy that can come thereby will prove too late, and you shall therefore beseech His Majesty to indict a new Parliament to as short a day as his subjects may be legally warned there. Concerning the time of moving this demand, if you find the offer of our services acceptable, and that the King and his Parliament are like to agree, you may forbear proposing it, but if not, you shall instantly desire that a Parliament be indicted. You shall be careful that the whole articles of the former treaty be observed. You shall adhere closely and positively to our desires for the removal of episcopacy and the unity of kirk government, but in regard to differences in matters civil you shall desire that the Parliament give all satisfaction to His Majesty, so far as may stand with their liberties and religion, and that His Majesty may give contentment to his Parliament in all things that may stand with his honour and just authority. You shall show our earnest desire for the Queen's speedy return to England. You shall represent to His Majesty, that the commissioners have taken special notice of the excepting of Sir Archibald Johnston, of Warriston, out of the safe conduct, and desire His Majesty to take into his royal consideration what prejudice it may produce in the opinion of his good subjects, if any who are trusted in the public affairs of this kingdom, authorized thereto by His Majesty and the Parliament, shall upon any private information be rendered incapable of that trust, and you shall humbly beseech His Majesty to remove this stop, since we have made choice of him, as one who hath given sufficient proof of his fidelity, and hath never to our knowledge done anything to the prejudice of His Majesty's royal person, honour, and authority. *See* Clarendon, Vol. III., 498. Rushworth, Vol. II., Part III., 398.

Jan. List of prisoners in the Gatehouse, committed by the Lords in Parliament, and by the committee for the safety of the kingdom.

Feb. 1. Petition of Thomas Jenyns, Esq. The auditing of the accounts between petitioner and Sir Philip Vernatti was referred by their Lordships to Sir Charles Harbourd, Auditor Phillips, Auditor Povey, and Auditor Gwynn. Sir Charles Harbourd having gone beyond the seas, and his return being very uncertain, petitioner prays that the other auditors may certify in his absence. L. J., V. 584.

Feb. 1. Petition of Samuel Peck, scrivener, Francis Coles, and Francis Leach, of London, stationers. Were committed by their Lordships for printing and publishing a book, intituled " A continuation of passages for " the last week." Are heartily sorry for their offence and pray for their discharge. *See* L. J., VI. 16.

Feb. 1. Copy of preceding.

Feb. 1. Petition of Miles Burkitt, one of the vicars of Pattishall, in the county of Northampton. Complains of the oppressions suffered by him at the hands of his brother, William Burkitt, who is now in actual rebellion amongst the Cavaliers. Prays their Lordships to grant him a hearing.

1642-3. Feb. 1
to   } Book of orders.
1 June 1643.

Feb. 2. Petition of George Mynne, Esq. Prays that his cause against Sir John Wintour and Sir Basil Brooke may be left to the ordinary course of the law. *See* L. J., V. 578.

Annexed :—
1. Copy of order of Committee for petitions in the cause. 19 July 1641.
2. List of the Committee for petitions. 6 Nov. 1640. L. J., IV. 84. *In extenso.*
3. Copy of petition of Sir Basil Brooke and Sir John Wintour. *See* 30 Jan. 1642-3.

Feb. 3. Order that all members of either House who have actually levied war, or contributed towards the forces raised against the Parliament, shall be disabled from sitting during this Parliament. L. J., V. 584. *In extenso.*

Feb. 3. Message from the Commons with preceding order.

Feb. 3. Order for the commitment of negligent assessors or collectors, &c. L. J., V. 584. *In extenso.*

Feb. 3. Order giving power to the Committee for the navy to add thirty ships to the fleet. L. J., V. 585. *In extenso.*

Feb. 3. Ordinance for impressing seamen for the fleet. L. J., V. 585. *In extenso.*

Feb. 3. Ordinance for vindicating Ferdinando Lord Fairfax and others employed in the service of the Parliament. L. J., V. 586. *In extenso.*

Feb. 3. Order for sequestering the living of Whepstead, in the county of Suffolk. L. J., V. 586. *In extenso.*

Feb. 3. Order for sequestering the living of Allhallows, Barking. L. J., V. 587. *In extenso.*

Feb. 3. Ordinance for raising forces and money in the county of Wilts. L. J., V. 587. *In extenso.*

Feb. 3. Order for the payment of 4,000l. to Lord Fairfax, for the present supply of the army under his command. L. J., V. 588. *In extenso.*

Feb. 4. Order for the payment of 1,000l. to Sir Christopher Wray, for the troop under his command in the army in the North. L. J., V. 589. *In extenso.*

Feb. 4. Copy of preceding.

Feb. 4. Order for adding Sir William Bolestrode and others to the Committee for associating the counties of Stafford and Warwick. L. J., V. 589. *In extenso.*

Feb. 4. Order for removing certain prisoners from London to Windsor Castle. L. J., V. 589. *In extenso.*

Annexed :—
1. List of prisoners sent to Windsor Castle, the 11th of January 1642-3. L. J., V. 590. *In extenso.*

Feb. 6. Petition of Sir John Wintour and Sir Basil Brooke, by way of reply to the answer of George Mynne. Pray that the cause may be determined according to their Lordships last order. L. J., V. 590.

Annexed :—
1. Copy of an order of the Exchequer Chamber in the cause. 13 Oct. 1638.

Feb. 6. Two copies of His Majesty's further answer to the propositions of both Houses. L. J., V. 591. *In extenso.*

Feb. 6. List of Committee appointed to assess the assistants of the House. L. J., V. 591. *In extenso.*

Feb. 6. Petition of the governor, assistants, and fellowship of merchant adventurers of England, to H. C. Pray that they may have one general and final order, by which they may, without interruption, receive such moneys as come in upon the Act for 400,000l., until the principal and interest of the 70,000l., furnished by them for the use of the Parliament is cleared off, as petitioners' creditors of whom they took up the money are daily pressing them for repayment. *See* C. J., II. 956.

Feb. 7. Copy of letter from the Parliament to the Lord Willoughby of Parham, Lord Lieutenant of Lincolnshire, desiring him to suppress the riots in Sutton Marsh. L. J., V. 592. *In extenso.*

Annexed :—
1. Copy of an application for an order for suppressing the riot.
2. Affidavit of John Reade, concerning a riot in Sutton Marsh. 1 Feb. 1642-3.

Feb. 7. Letter from the Earl of Stamford, at Plymouth, to the Speaker of the House of Lords. Has by former despatches informed their Lordships of the condition of these parts. Is now besieged very close; the enemy are so cunning that they invite men, women, and children to come out of Cornwall into Devon to carry away the plunder of this town, for they are impudent enough to report that they have taken some of the frets and works. When by these delusions they have brought the ablest men into Devon, they, having guarded all the passes, keep them on this side and force them to serve. All here are resolved, they (the Earl's party) have able and good officers, hearty and stout soldiers. The mayor of the town is as brave a man as ever breathed, and they want nothing but his purse, credit, or power can help them to. The assistants, the members of the House of Commons, the deputy lieutenants, and the rest of the Council of War, sleep not in security, but are assistants day and night to perform the parts of gallant and brave men, so the writer doubts not to defend the place against the malice of the enemy, who do nothing but plunder this poor country most barbarously. Expects supplies of men out of the north, and east of Devon, for although they have store of horse and men in this place, yet the country about is so naturally fortified with hedges and breastworks, and so full of lanes and straight ways, that if they send out any parties they give them over, for until more force come up behind them it is useless making sallies or sorties. Is confident their Lordships will not impute the late misfortunes to any default of the writer. Shall refer himself to those noble gentlemen who can best report his actions. L. J., V. 603.

Feb. 8. Petition of Captain Thomas Nettervill, prisoner in Wood Street Compter, London. By an order of their Lordships, he was allowed 2s. a day for his maintenance, which for a long time was duly paid to him by Mr. Willis, clerk of the Crown. For the last three months petitioner has received nothing, and Mr. Willis says that all the money delivered to him for the purpose is expended. Prays that either his liberty may be granted to him, or the allowance continued. L. J., V. 503.

Annexed :—
1. Another petition of same. Petitioner has not yet received any benefit from their Lordships' order, and has in his extreme necessity been compelled to borrow his bread of his fellow prisoners. Prays that some other way may be appointed for his relief. (Undated.)

Feb. 8. Ordinance for the Earl of Warwick to command the fleet. L. J., V. 593. *In extenso.*

Feb. 8. Order for the treasurers to give acquittances to persons advancing money in London. L. J. V., 593. *In extenso.*

Feb. 8. Order for assessing persons in London, according to the ordinance of the 29th of November. L. J., V. 594. *In extenso.*

Feb. 8. Order for sequestering the living of Bushey, Herts. L. J., V. 594.

Annexed :—
1. Copy of preceding.
2. Petition of George Seaton, Doctor of Divinity. Complains that the order for sequestering the living of Bushey was obtained by misinformation. Prays that he and his accusers may be brought face to face, and that then whosoever is found, to have misinformed the House may receive exemplary punishment.
3. Petition of Philip Edline, Bachelor in Divinity. Prays that the order sequestering the living of Bushey may be discharged, as petitioner was duly instituted to the living upon the resignation of Dr. Seaton.

Feb. 8. Draft of the General Confession of National Sin, to be used at the fast. L. J., V. 595. *In extenso.*

Feb. 9. Petition of William Blake. Prays that the examination of the petition of Anne Blake, his wife, may be referred to some of the judges. L. J., V. 596.

Feb. 9. Petition of John Pulford, His Majesty's servant. Was arrested by John Hodges contrary to privilege. Prays for his discharge. L. J., V. 596. *In extenso.*

Annexed :—
1. Affidavit of Pulford concerning his arrest.
2. Petition of John Hodges. Is committed to the custody of the gentleman usher upon the unjust complaint of John Pulford, who pretends himself to be one of the King's servants extraordinary. Prays to be discharged upon bail, as he is employed in several services for the Parliament. (Undated.)

3. Another petition of Pulford.' He denies having spoken the words with which he is charged by Hodges, and prays that no further suggestion made against him may be credited without a full hearing. (Undated.)

4. Affidavit of Richard Perie. Hodges overtook his master Pulford, and himself, as they were riding across Hounslow Heath, and wanted to race with his master, and abused his horses, though worth 20*l.* and 16*l.* respectively, and finally struck him with a cudgel, when deponent drew his sword, upon which Hodges made off. 16 June 1643.

Feb. 9. Resolution of the Commons, that neither the King's Bench nor any other court shall have any jurisdiction over persons committed to the Parliament. C. J., II. 960. *In extenso.* Noted, Not passed.

Feb. 11. Order for the payment of 2,000*l.* in bills of exchange drawn by the Committee at Dublin. L. J., V. 598. *In extenso.*

Feb. 11. Order for the payment of 352*l.* to William Fletcher, and George Margette for matches. L. J., V. 598. *In extenso.*

Feb. 11. Copy of preceding.

Feb. 11. Order for the payment of 34*l.* to John Burston for necessaries for the fort at Cork. L. J., V. 598. *In extenso.*

Feb. 11. Order for the payment of 700*l.* to John Vernum for swords. L. J., V. 598. *In extenso.*

Feb. 11. Order for the payment of 280*l.* to Captain Whitscotte for twenty butts of sack. L. J., V. 598. *In extenso.*

Feb. 11. Order for the payment of 250*l.* to Abraham Vanden Beinde for pistols. L. J., V. 599. *In extenso.*

Feb. 11. Order for the payment of 280*l.* to Captain Whitscotte for sack. L. J., V. 599. *In extenso.*

Feb. 11. Order for the payment of 625*l.* 9*s.* to William Osbourne for wheat, butter, &c. L. J., V. 599. *In extenso.*

Feb. 11. Order for the payment of 359*l.* 7*s.* to Edmond Hunt for caps. L. J., V. 599. *In extenso.*

Feb. 11. Order for the payment of 359*l.* 7*s.* to Henry Paman for caps. L. J., V. 599. *In extenso.*

Feb. 11. Order for the payment of 563*l.* 14*s.* 2*d.* to the Mayor of Bristol, for victualling recruits, and forwarding them to Ireland. L. J., V. 599. *In extenso.*

Feb. 11. Order for the payment of 501*l.* 10*s.* 5*d.* to William Pennoyer and Richard Parr, for necessaries for the town of Bandon Bridge, in Ireland. L. J., V. 600. *In extenso.*

Feb. 11. Order for the payment of 500*l.* to William Pennoyer, for rye and cheese. L. J., V. 600. *In extenso.*

Feb. 11. Order for the payment of 62*l.* 4*s.* 1*d.* to William Pennoyer and Richard Parr, for necessaries for Munster. L. J., V. 600. *In extenso.*

Feb. 11. Order for the payment of 313*l.* 14*s.* 8*d.* to William Pennoyer and Richard Parr, for victuals for the fort and town of Kinsale. L. J., V. 600. *In extenso.*

Feb. 11. Order for the payment of 900*l.* 4*s.* to Thomas Downes, for herrings. L. J., V. 601. *In extenso.*

Feb. 11. Ordinance for raising men and money in Hampshire. L. J., V. 601. *In extenso.*

Feb. 11. Draft of preceding.

Feb. 11. Ordinance appointing Sir William Waller, serjeant-major-general of the forces in Gloucestershire, and adjacent counties, &c. L. J., V. 602. *In extenso.*

Feb. 13. Order for all moneys subscribed by the inhabitants of Devon to be employed for the defence of the county. L. J., V. 604. *In extenso.*

Feb. 13. Ordinance for seizing the effects of persons in Nottinghamshire who have been in arms against the Parliament. L. J., V. 604. *In extenso.*

Feb. 13. Copy of preceding.

Feb. 14. Petition of Lucy Mitchell and others, whose husbands are captives in Algiers. Petitioners have waited for two years in expectation of an order for their relief, and have spent all the small means they had, and pawned the very clothes off their backs; so unless their Lordships' compassion is extended towards them, they are like to perish. There was money allowed for the redemption of all captives upon the book of rates which lies dead in the Custom House. Pray that a set proportion may be allowed amongst petitioners for their husbands' redemption. L. J., V. 605.

Feb. 14. Application for a protection for Francois de Lissola, resident for His Imperial Majesty. L. J., V. 605.

Feb. 14. Petition of Francis Wortley, Esq., one of the gentlemen of His Majesty's Privy Chamber. Was arrested at the suit of Richard Thorneton, contrary to privilege, detained one day, and afterwards compelled to put in bail before he obtained his liberty. Prays that his bail may be discharged, and that he may receive some recompense for the affront offered to him. L. J., V. 605.

Annexed :—
1. Petition of Richard Thorneton, one of the soldiers of the trained bands for the county of Middlesex, parcel of the militia settled by ordinance of Parliament. Complains of the indignities to which he has been subjected by Mr. Wortley, and prays that all proceedings against him may be stayed, until their Lordships have heard and examined the truth on all sides.

Feb. 14. Petition of Anne Blake, wife of William Blake. Prays their Lordships to suspend the order of the 9th of February till after the hearing of the cause. L. J., V. 605.

Annexed :—
1. Copy of order referred to. L. J., V. 596.

Feb. 14. Petition of Henry Hughes, physician in ordinary to the Prince Elector's Highness. Prays for a pass from London to the Cinque Ports, and from thence into Holland. L. J., V. 605.

Feb. 14. Petition of inhabitants of the parish of St. Cuthbert's, Bedford. Mr. Thorne, parson of St. Mary's, Bedford, some years since engrossed into his hands the rectory of St. Cuthbert over the head of the incumbent, who was then living, since which time he has taken the profits of both the benefices, but wilfully neglects the cure of petitioners' souls, having only kept one drunken curate to officiate in both churches. Pray that Mr. Thorne may be compelled to afford a sufficient maintenance out of the profits of the rectory to Mr. Houlden, a godly and painful minister. L. J., V. 605.

Annexed :—
1. Certificate signed by the churchwardens and other inhabitants of the parish, as to the truth of the allegations contained in preceding petition.

Feb. 14. Petition of William James [Jhannes] that his suit against Daniel Fairefax may be referred to the Delegates. L. J., V. 605.

Annexed :—
1. Order referring the cause to the ordinary proceedings of the Delegates. 15 Feb. 1642-3.

Feb. 14. Draft ordinance for raising 500 dragoons in the county of Surrey. C. J., II. 964. The House of Lords ordered this ordinance to be respited for a time, and the county to be heard upon it, and no further proceedings appear to have been taken. Noted, Not passed. *See* L. J., V. 606.

Feb. 14. Petition of Richard Heron, printer. Was committed to the Fleet for printing something which has given offence to their Lordships. Prays for his discharge, as it is his first offence. *See* L. J., V. 596.

Feb. 15. Pass for a child of Sir Charles Berkley to be conveyed in a horse littor from Bruton, in the county of Somerset, to Oxford, to be touched for the King's evil. L. J., V. 606.

Feb. 15. Order for the repayment of 4,000*l.* to Sir William Waller and others, advanced by them for furnishing the forces in the county of Gloucester. L. J., V. 606. *In extenso.*

Feb. 15. Petition of John Bradley touching the administration of the estate of the late John Farrington. L. J., V. 607. *In extenso.*

Feb. 16. Ordinance for raising forces and money in the county of Sussex. L. J., V. 608.

Feb. 16. Ordinance for associating Shropshire with Warwickshire and Staffordshire. L. J., V. 608.

Feb. 16. Ordinance for raising forces and money in the county of Chester. L. J., V. 608.

Feb. 17. Petition of Ashton Nuttall, Esquire. Prays that the writ of error brought into the House by Gisborough and others may be dismissed. L.J., V. 608.

Feb. 17. Petition of Wilks Fitchett and William Shalliker. Upon a former petition their Lordships gave order to Sir Robert Pye to pay petitioners 817*l.* for provisions for the service of the House. Sir Robert Pye certified that he could not pay the same, because the commission from His Majesty to the Lords for his treasury was vacated and others chosen. Their Lordships then ordered Sir Robert Pye to draw up an order to send to the other commissioners, which was done, and petitioner has attended Lord Newburgh with it, but he answered that the commissioners cannot sign the order because the Parliament have made stay of His Majesty's revenues. Pray that some order may be made by which they may receive the money. L. J., V. 608.

Annexed:—

1. Copy of petition referred to in preceding.

Feb. 17. Letter from the Mayor and others of Kingston-upon-Hull to the Lords and Commons. Sir John Hotham has intimated that unless Parliament will furnish him with a speedy supply for the payment of his soldiers he will desist any further engagement, and immediately impose the charge upon the poor inhabitants of the town, alleging that the soldiers must not starve, and that therefore the inhabitants must provide for them. The writers have by the command of the Parliament entertained a garrison of soldiers amongst them, not only for the safety of the town and country adjacent, but as they conceive for the safety of the whole kingdom, and as the benefit may redound to the whole nation, so the charge, if it be imposed upon a poor corporation, may seem insupportable. They therefore pray that Parliament may resolve upon some way to secure them from the heavy burden likely to be cast upon them, for it is not the custom of the Governor to be dilatory in such resolutions. See L. J., V. 612.

Feb. 18. Copy of letter from the Speaker of the House of Lords to Lord Campden, desiring him to contribute towards the charges of the Parliament forces, as others of his rank have already done. L. J., V. 609. In extenso.

Feb. 18. Draft resolutions concerning the disbanding of the armies, &c. L. J., V. 610.

Feb. 18. Alterations proposed by the House of Lords in the ordinance for weekly assessments. L. J., V. 610.

Feb. 18. Order for the repayment to Mr. Stephens and Mr. Hodges, members of the House of Commons, of 720l. advanced by them for furnishing arms for the forces in the county of Gloucester. L. J., V. 611. In extenso.

Feb. 18. Order for seizing the estates of malignants in the county of Lincoln. L. J., V. 611. In extenso.

Feb. 18. Letter from the committee for Northamptonshire to the Earl of Manchester, Speaker of the House of Lords, concerning the taking of Lord Vaux's timber from Harrowden. L. J., V. 617. In extenso.

Feb. 18. Petition of William Arundell, Esq. Prays that an early day may be appointed for hearing his cause against Lord Baltimore. See L. J., V. 379, &c.

Feb. 18. Petition of Robert Shering. Prays that Richard Tito may be ordered forthwith to bring up his writ of error out of the King's Bench. See L. J., V. 612.

Feb. 18. Pass for Mrs. Elizabeth Walter to travel to Barnsley, Gloucestershire, about her own private occasions.

Feb. 20. Petition of Dame Dorothy Leventhorpe, late wife of Sir Thomas Leventhorpe, Bart., and now wife of Thomas Holford, Esquire. Prays that Thomas Holford may be ordered to carry out the provisions of a post-nuptial agreement, entered into between him and the petitioner, touching an estate left to her by her late husband. L. J., V. 611.

Annexed:—

1. Copy of preceding, and upon the same paper copy of the agreement referred to. 5 March 1641-2.

Feb. 20. Petition of Margery Page, widow, late wife of William Page, one of the Barons of the Exchequer. Petitioner's husband died three months since, and about a week afterwards her coach horses were taken from her by colour of an order of Parliament, and about twenty men and horses, employed in the Parliament service, were billetted at her house at Harrow on the Hill. Petitioner inhabiting in London during this winter was assessed at 100l. for the 20th part of her estate, and although it was well known that she had not received one penny of her jointure since the death of her husband, yet on the 13th of this month divers unknown persons of mean condition, to the number of about thirty, armed with charged muskets and other weapons, upon pretence of levying the said 100l. upon petitioner's estate, in a most barbarous manner broke into her house, and carried thence the beds whereon she lay, hangings, brass, pewter, and other goods, even all that she had, besides the deeds and evidences of her estate. Prays relief in her great extremity, and that her deeds, goods, and chattels, may be restored to her. L. J., V. 611.

Feb. 20. Petition of Anne Pratt, wife of Francis Pratt, haberdasher. Petitioner's husband, who has been assessed for the 20th part of his estate, is in the country, and will not return for a fortnight. Prays

S.

that in the meantime his goods, which have been seized, may not be taken away. L. J., V. 612.

Feb. 20. Draft order appointing a Committee of Lords to meet the Committee of the Commons to consider of the way of proceeding in the treaty, &c. L. J., V. 612.

Feb. 20. Petition of the inhabitants of Lambeth. On Sunday last some soldiers belonging to Captain Andrewes' company came into the church, during prayers with their hats on, and taking tobacco, and derided the service; when they were reproached for it they brandished their swords, and after they were driven out of the church, they slew one of the parishioners, and sorely wounded another. Pray that steps may be taken for repressing and punishing such disorder. L. J., V. 612.

Annexed:—

1. Affidavit of Edward Harper and others concerning the riot.

2. Certificate of the parishioners of Lambeth that it was Hugh Cocks, one of Captain Andrewes' soldiers, that killed Thomas Coe, one of the parishioners, in the churchyard. See L. J., V. 614.

3. Certificate of Richard Kellett, of the parish of St. Margaret's, Westminster, chirurgeon, that Edward Jones, of Lambeth, waterman, is so dangerously wounded with a shot through his thigh that he is not likely to live till tomorrow night. 21 Feb. L. J., V. 615. In extenso.

Feb. 20. Petition of Thomas Shering. Prays that the writ of error in the cause between him and Richard Tito may be brought in, and that Tito may be ordered to assign errors. L. J., V. 612.

Annexed:—

1. Another petition of Shering, praying that Tito may be ordered speedily to assign errors. (Undated.)

Feb. 20. Draft of the requests of the Lord Mayor, aldermen, and common council of the City of London about the raising of 60,000l. L. J., V. 612. In extenso.

Feb. 20. Application for a pass for a waggon containing goods belonging to the Countess of Carnarvon to go from London to Oxford. See L. J., V. 613.

Feb. 20. Petition of John Earl of Rutland. Prays that an order may be issued restraining certain miners from working in the manors of Haddon and Harthill, until a cause now pending between them and petitioner in the court of the Duchy of Lancaster has been heard and determined. See L. J., V. 624.

Feb. 21. Pass for Robert Makyn, yeoman of His Majesty's chaundry, to carry wax lights and torches to Oxford for His Majesty's service. L. J., V. 613.

Feb. 21. Draft order in the cause, Hooper v. Jhannes. L. J., V. 613.

Annexed:—

1. Petition of Anthony Hooper, praying that the preceding order may be revoked. (Undated.)

Feb. 21. Pass for a servant of the Marchioness of Hertford to go to Oxford with household stuff and other necessaries for her Ladyship's use. L. J., V. 613.

Annexed:—

1. A note of what is wanting in my Lady's chamber.

Feb. 21. Draft ordinance for rating sea coals. L. J., V. 614. In extenso.

Feb. 21. Copy of preceding.

Feb. 21. Draft ordinance for staying the shipping in the Thames. L. J., V. 615. In extenso.

Feb. 21. Copy of the King's message concerning the cessation of arms. L. J., V. 615. In extenso.

Feb. 21. Message from the Commons for a Committee to be appointed to consult with the Lord-General concerning the cessation of arms. L. J., V. 615.

Feb. 21. Petition of the parishioners of Mary Magdalen's, Bermondsey, in the borough of Southwark. Pray that Mr. Thomas Mawle, a plundered minister lately come out of Shropshire, may be assigned as their curate, Mr. Kem, who was heretofore appointed curate of the parish, having absented himself for three months and upwards. L. J., V. 616.

Feb. 21. Ordinance for sequestering the living of St. Margaret's, Lothbury. L. J., V. 616. In extenso.

Annexed:—

1. Petition of Humfrey Tabor, parson of the parish of St. Margaret, Lothbury. Prays that the preceding ordinance may not be put in execution until he has been heard by counsel for his defence.

2. Copy of preceding.

3. Another petition of Tabor. Prays that such allowance may be made to him out of the profits

K

of the living as will keep him, his wife, and three children from perishing.

4. Copy of preceding.

5. Petition of Elizabeth, the wife of Humphrey Tabor; prays their Lordships to mitigate the severity of the sentence against her husband.

Feb. 21. Order for the payment of 260l. to William Purefoy, Esq., advanced by him for the defence of the city of Coventry. L. J., V. 616. *In extenso.*

Feb. 21. Ordinance for sequestering the profits of the living of St. Martin's, in the Vintry, London. L. J., V. 616. *In extenso.*

Feb. 21. Pass for two servants and three horses of the Earl of Lindsey, to go to Warwick and back. *See* L. J., V. 612.

Feb. 21. Draft order that all orders and ordinances made for the advancing and levying of monies and other necessaries for the army raised by the authority of Parliament shall be executed, notwithstanding any treaty or cessation of arms. Noted, respited. C. J., II. 974. *In extenso.*

Feb. 23. Order for Sir William Waller to execute martial law in his army. L. J., V. 617. *In extenso.*

Feb. 23. Copy of the King's answer concerning the putting off the general assizes and gaol delivery throughout the Kingdom. L. J., V. 618. *In extenso.*

Feb. 23. Order for the removal of Lord Macquire and other prisoners from the Tower to Ludgate. L. J., V. 618. *In extenso.*

Feb. 23. Ordinance for sequestering the profits of the living of St. Nicholas Olave, Bread Street. L. J., V. 618. *In extenso.*

Feb. 23. Ordinance for Nathaniel Fiennes, Esq., to raise a regiment of horse in the counties of Gloucester, Worcester, and Oxon, and to seize horses and arms belonging to delinquents. L. J., V. 618. *In extenso.*

Feb. 23. Petition to the Commons of Dr. Echlyn, physician in ordinary to the Queen's Majesty, and by command of both the King and Queen's Majesty appointed to attend their royal children at St. James'; petitioner is in great want, because a pension of 100l. granted him by the King has not been paid for a year and a half on account of the distracted state of the King's revenue; prays the House to order the payment of his arrears, and of his pension in future, in consideration of his attendance on the royal children. C. J., II. 975.

Feb. 23. Petition of Daniel Featley, D.D., rector of Lambeth. Prays that John Goad and others may be called upon to answer for the false and scandalous articles exhibited by them against petitioner to the Committee in the Exchequer Chamber for plundered ministers. Goad and the others, who are obstinate separatists, took part with the soldiers against the parishioners in the late riots in Lambeth church.

Feb. 24. Message from the Commons for reducing the number of the Committee for the safety of the Kingdom. Rejected by the Lords. L. J., V. 619.

Feb. 24. Pass for John Craven, Esquire, and four servants, to travel into France. L. J., V. 620.

Feb. 24. Application for a pass for two servants of the Countess of Monmouth to go to Kenilworth. L. J., V. 620.

Feb. 24. Application for a pass for Robert Winde and William Harrison, and two servants, to travel into France. L. J., V. 620.

Feb. 24. Application for a protection for Wilks Fitchett, and William Shallaker. L. J., V. 620.

Feb. 24. Order for 100 marks contribution money to be paid for the relief of the poor English who have come from Ireland into the Isle of Wight. L. J., V. 620. *In extenso.*

Feb. 24. Petition of Katharine Fowler, daughter of Secretary Fowler, once secretary to Queen Anne. Complains that she was arrested in a barbarous manner, and imprisoned in the Marshalsea at the suit of Daniel Calt. Prays that she may be turned over to the Fleet, or that such bail as she can procure may be accepted. L. J., V. 620. *In extenso.*

Feb. 25. Order for the payment of 1,218l. 14s. to the Scots Reformado officers. L. J., V. 622. *In extenso.*

Feb. 25. Copy of preceding.

Feb. 25. Order for 300l. contribution money to be paid for the service of the Lough in Ireland. L. J., V. 622. *In extenso.*

Feb. 25. Copy of letter from the Speaker of the House of Lords to the Committee for Northamptonshire, concerning the taking of the Lord Vaux's timber from Harrowden. *See* L. J., V. 617.

Feb. 25. The true and humble answer of George Baker and others to the petition of Captain John

Bradley. Are quite ready to give up all accounts, books, and letters that may tend to the quiet ending of all differences between them and Bradley, and pray that the matter may be referred for settlement to some indifferent, honest, and able men.

Annexed:—

1. Copy of petition of Captain John Bradley. L. J., V. 607. *In extenso.*

Feb. 27. Pass for Robert Martyn, Esquire, and two servants to travel into France. L. J., V. 622.

Feb. 27. Order for the payment of 30l. to Captain Thomas Cupper for beef for the garrison at Cork. L. J., V. 623. *In extenso.*

Feb. 27. Petition of Richard Branthwayte. Prays leave to go to his house in Oxfordshire. L. J., V. 623. *In extenso.*

Feb. 27. Order for the payment of 1,500l. for arrears due to the garrison at Portsmouth. L. J., V. 624. *In extenso.*

Feb. 28. Petition of Thomas Jenyns, Esquire. Prays for an enlargement of the last order made by their Lordships in the cause between petitioner and Sir Filibert Vernatti. L. J., V. 624.

Annexed:—

1. Copy of order in the cause, 29 March 1642. L. J., IV. 682.

2. Copy of order, 27 May 1642. L. J., V. 85.

3. Copy of order, 1 Feb. 1642-3. L. J., V. 584.

Feb. 28. Petition of Elizabeth Wiseman, wife of Thomas Wiseman. Complains that one Quarterman came to her house in Great St. Helen's, Bishopsgate Street, when her husband was absent and forcibly took away goods to the value of 150l., under pretence of the Ordinance for Assessment of the 20th part, and afterwards arrested petitioner. Prays for her discharge and for redress. L. J., V. 624.

Feb. 28. Application for a pass for two sons of Lord Coventry, with their governor and four servants, to go into France. L. J., V. 625.

Feb. 28. Application for a pass for Richard Deards to go with some goods to Hillingdon. L. J., V. 625.

Feb. 28. Draft order for the committal of John Grimston and others to Newgate, for killing deer in Waltham Forest. L. J., V. 625.

Annexed:—

1. Affidavits of John Cocks and others, under keepers, concerning the killing the deer in Waltham Forest, and Havering Park. 9 Feb. 1642-3.

Feb. 28. Petition of Thomas Crewe and Anne his wife. Pray that Roger Mallock, the father of petitioner Anne, may be called upon to answer for converting to his own use certain monies which by an agreement entered into between him and Alice Hele, were to have been employed in the purchase of land for the use of petitioners. L. J., V. 625.

Feb. 28. Pass for John Saladin, his wife, five children, and two servants, to travel to Geneva. L. J., V. 625.

Feb. 28. Amended draft of the propositions for a cessation of arms. L. J., V. 625. *In extenso.*

Feb. 28. Copy of preceding.

Feb. 28. Order for the payment of 500l. for Sir William Cole's regiment at Enniskillen. L. J., V. 626. *In extenso.*

Feb. 28. Order for the payment of 102l. 12s. to Mr. Laurence Loe, chirurgeon to the Lord General's person and train. L. J., V. 626. *In extenso.*

Feb. 28. Petition of the governor, assistants, and fellowship of Eastland merchants. Pray that a pass may be granted to two of their company, with their secretary and a servant, to go to the King, as they have speedy occasion to address themselves to His Majesty with a petition for His Royal Letter to the King of Denmark for the restitution of a ship lately seized in the Sound, upon pretence of short entries made by the master. L. J., V. 626.

Feb. 28. Reasons why the ordinance now remaining unpassed in the Lords' House, for the raising of some moneys by some Staffordshire and Warwickshire gentlemen for the defence of the counties of Stafford and Warwick, and the counties of the cities of Coventry and Lichfield, should be presently passed. 1. The papists and ill-affected there are in actual rebellion. 2. The officers are now in town and cannot get to their charge without money. 3. The cessation of arms is to begin on Saturday, and unless the ordinance is at once passed, will begin before the officers can get to their charge and so the counties will be lost. 4. The ordinance is only in pursuance of the ordinance of association of the said counties. 5. The like reasons for the counties of Salop and other counties. *See* L. J., V. 627.

Feb. 28. Draft ordinance for raising money in the counties of Warwick and Stafford. L. J., V. 627. *In extenso.*

Feb. 28. Ordinance for putting off the assizes. L. J., V. 628. *In extenso.*

Feb. Printed copy of all the ordinances and declarations of the Lords and Commons assembled in Parliament for the assessing of all such as have not contributed upon the propositions of both Houses of Parliament for raising of money, plate, horse, horsemen, and arms for the defence of the King, Kingdom, and Parliament, or have not contributed proportionably according to their estates. Also divers orders of the committee of Lords and Commons for advance of money, and other necessaries for the army; and for the better execution of the said ordinances and declarations.

March 1. Petition of the Hon. Robert Fane, Esq. Petitioner, who is a student in the Middle Temple, prays that a pass may be granted him to go to his sister's, the Lady Elizabeth Cope's house at Bruerne to collect his rents, of which he is disappointed by reason of the troubles in Oxfordshire. L. J., V. 628.

March 1. Request of Sir Edward Rodney, for liberty to visit his family in the Old Palace Yard, and to walk in the College gardens and cloisters for his health. L. J., V. 629.

March 1. Draft Report of the Committee to whom was referred the cause between Lady Leventhorpe and Thomas Holford. L. J., V. 629.

Annexed :—
 1. Affidavit of Edward Lyndsell that he was unable to find Mr. Holford, and therefore served the order for the hearing of the cause upon one of his servants.

March 1. Petition of divers of the inhabitants of Lewisham, in the county of Kent. Notwithstanding an order of the House of Commons of the 26th of February 1641-2, that Mr. John Bachiler should preach a weekly lecture in the parish church of Lewisham, he has been much molested and hindered by Mr. Abraham Calfe, the vicar, and some of the parishioners. Pray their Lordships to confirm the said order. L. J., V. 629.

March 1. Copy of preceding.

March 2. Two draft reports from the Committee for assessing Lords in Northamptonshire and Rutland. L. J., V. 629.

March 2. Draft resolutions of Lords and Commons upon the King's " Proclamation forbidding all his " loving subjects of the counties of Kent, Surrey, " Sussex, and Hampshire, to raise any forces without " His Majesty's consent, or to enter into any association " or protestation for the assistance of the rebellion " against His Majesty." L. J., V. 630. *In extenso.*

Annexed :—
 1. Printed copy of the Proclamation. 16 Feb. 1642-3. L. J., V. 630. *In extenso.*

March 2. Order for the repayment of 700*l.* to Mr. Stephens and others, advanced by them for the equipment of Sir William Waller's army. L. J., V. 631. *In extenso.*

March 3. Order for a trial of the coin in the pix in the Mint by a sufficient jury. L. J., V. 632. *In extenso.*

March 3. Petition of Aurelian Townsend. Is threatened with arrest by Isaac Tulley, silkman, from whom he ordered silk and silver fringes for Lord Kinalmeaky. Prays protection from arrest, being the King's servant, and no ways indebted to Tulley. L. J., V. 632.

March 3. Ordinance for raising money for the maintenance of the Parliament army. L. J., V. 632. *In extenso.*

March 3. Ordinance for the security of those advancing money towards the 60,000*l.* to be raised in London. L. J., V. 633. *In extenso.*

March 3. Order for the payment of 794*l.* to the Lord Say and Seale for the household expenses of the King's children at St. James'. L. J., V. 634. *In extenso.*

March 3. Order for all merchants to perfect their entries in the Custom house. L. J., V. 634. *In extenso.*

March 3. Order for the Spanish merchants concerning the ship " St. Clair." L. J., V. 634. *In extenso.*

March 3. Order for sequestering the living of St. Andrew's Wardropp, London. L. J., V. 634. *In extenso.*

March 3. Order for sequestering the living of St. Alban's, Wood Street, London. L. J., V. 634. *In extenso.*

March 3. Order for sequestering the living of St. Mary Magdalen, near Old Fish Street, London. L. J., V. 635. *In extenso.*

March 3. Order for sequestering the living of Basishaw, London. L. J., V. 635. *In extenso.*

March 3. Order for sequestering the living of Rayne, Essex. L. J., V. 635. *In extenso.*

March 4. Petition of Captain David Forrest, executor of the will of David Ramsey, Esq. Prays that Fabian Philips may be ordered to account for the profits of the office of Philizer for the city of London, and to surrender that office, to which he was only admitted in trust for the benefit of David Ramsey, to whom the office was granted by the King. L. J., V. 636.

March 4. Copy of the Speaker's letter to the Lord General, concerning the molesting and searching of the Duke of Vendosme on his journey to Oxford, notwithstanding an order for his free passage. L. J., V. 637. *In extenso.*

March 4. Order for the muster of the trained bands, and volunteers at Taunton. L. J., V. 637. *In extenso.*

March 4. Order to compel the soldiers at Taunton to do their duty, and for a watch to be set there. L. J., V. 637. *In extenso.*

March 4. Ordinance explaining certain things in the ordinance for the weekly assessment. L. J., V. 637. *In extenso.*

March 6. List of Committee appointed by the Lords to confer with the Commons about the King's answers. L. J., V. 639. *In extenso.*

March 6. Application for a pass for Mr. George Sanderson, one of the Count of Egmont's gentlemen, to go to Paris. L. J., V. 640.

Annexed :—
 1. Draft pass for —— to go beyond seas.

March 6. Order for the payment of 1,000*l.*, with consideration to the executors of the late Lord Brooke, which sum was formerly lent to the Parliament. L. J., V. 640. *In extenso.*

March 6. Order for Mr. Samuel Cordewell to carry saltpetre and other materials necessary for the making of gunpowder to his works near Guildford. L. J., V. 640. *In extenso.*

March 6. Order for raising money for the relief of maimed soldiers and their families. L. J., V. 640. *In extenso.*

March 7. Application for a pass for Lady Stafford to go to Oxford. L. J., V. 641.

March 7. Message from the Commons concerning a committee to consult with the Lord General about the cessation of arms. L. J., V. 641.

March 7. Order for entrenching and fortifying the city of London. L. J., V. 641. *In extenso.*

March 7. Petition of John Vanhaesdoncke; complains that the inhabitants of Holme and Thornham, Norfolk, have pulled down the fences of certain reclaimed lands in the salt marshes there, of which petitioner has hitherto had possession in recompense of his great charge and industry in draining the said lands. Prays for an order for settling him, his tenants, and servants, in quiet possession of the lands. *See* L. J., V. 101.

March 8. Resolution insisting upon the nomination of the Earl of Northumberland and the Viscount Say and Seale, as committees to be sent to His Majesty. L. J., V. 642. *In extenso.*

March 8. Applications for passes for Sir Henry St. George, Mrs. Gerrard, and others. L. J., V. 642.

March 8. Petition of Thomas Overman and John Hardwicke against John Doughty, with reference to proceedings in a writ of error. L. J., V. 642. *In extenso.*

March 8. Copy of proceeding.

Annexed :—
 1. Petition of John Doughty that the cause may be speedily heard.

March 8. Printed copy of the King's proclamation forbidding all assessing, collecting, and paying of the twentieth part, and of all weekly taxes, by colour of orders or ordinances, and all entering into protestations and associations against His Majesty.

March 8. Certificate from Sir Charles Morgan, colonel of a regiment of foot, under the Lords, Estates, and Governor of Bergen-op-Zoom, that the bearers, belonging to Captain Floyd's company of the writer's regiment, are going to England to obtain thirty recruits for the company, and therefore praying all persons to whom it may appertain to let the bearers pass without let or hindrance.

March 8. Copy of a warrant from Lord Rivers and others [Commissioners of Array], for the seizing and sequestering of the goods of all persons within the city or county of Chester, who have or shall aid or abet the rebellion. There is the following note on this paper :—

" We lost some 5 men and some 20 wounded ; they lost " many more ; this was in the town ; they shot out at " windows. From Jo : Wyn, Nantwich, March 15, " 1642-[3]."

March 9. Application for a pass for Lady Isabella Thynne to go to Oxford. L. J., V. 642.

March 9. Application for a pass for two officers of the Wardrobe to go to Oxford. L. J., V. 642.

March 9. Pass for Valentine Wanley to go to Holland. L. J., V. 642.

March 9. Pass for John Daintrey and Joseph Atkinson, servants to His Majesty, to go to Oxford with gloves and other necessaries for His Majesty's use. L. J., V. 643.

March 9. Message from the Commons with votes respecting the marching of the Lord General, &c. L. J., V. 643. *In extenso.*

March 10. Pass for Sir Theodore Mayherne to go into Holland with his wife, family, and goods, and for Lady Mayherne to send a trunk there without being searched. *See* L. J., V. 641, 645.

March 11. Petition of Henry Noel, Esq., second son of the Lord Viscount Campden, touching his imprisonment by direction of the Lord Grey. L. J., V. 645. *In extenso.*

March 11. Petition of Thomas Moyser, Esq. Prays for further time to assign errors in the writ of error depending between him and Ashton Nuttall and others. L. J., V. 645.

Annexed :—

1. Copy of order for petitioner to assign errors. 17 Feb. 1642-3.

2. Affidavit of Thomas Moyser that the county of York, where petitioner's house is, is now in such great trouble that he is unable to go or send thither for his writings, without great and manifest danger. He has already had a foot post stripped stark naked, who was going to York with a letter. 7 March 1642-3.

3. Another petition of Moyser to Edward Earl of Manchester ; prays his Lordship to procure him further time to assign errors, as he has had his house plundered, and his books and writings taken away, his children, but young, driven he knows not whither, and the little estate he hath is wholly in the enemy's hands.

March 13. Petition of Thomas Coningsbie, Esq., High Sheriff of the county of Hertford. Petitioner's wife and children coming to town on Friday last, in their coach, to see him, one Gregson took away two of his horses by power of some warrant, but contrary to the ordinance of the 23rd of January last. Prays that the horses may be released. L. J., V. 646.

Annexed :—

1. Petition of same ; was in January last committed by the Commons prisoner to London House, and in March following removed to the Tower, where he has ever since continued without any charge having been brought against him ; prays that he may be brought before their Lordships by Habeas Corpus, and his case determined. (Undated.)

March 13. Order for sequestering the living of St. Bennett's Shenhog [Shereho̅g], London. L. J., V. 646.

March 13. Order for sequestering the living of Kirke Burton, in the county of York. L. J., V. 646.

March 13. Order for sequestering the living of Cranbrook, Kent. L.J., V. 646.

March 13. Order for the payment of 500l. for the supply and relief of Duncannon Fort. L. J., V. 647. *In extenso.*

March 13. Order allowing a third part of all prizes taken by the King's ships to the officers and seamen, and of those taken by merchants, one third to the officers and seamen, and one third to the owners. L. J., V. 647. *In extenso.*

March 14. The humble petition and remonstrance of Henry Noel, Esq., second son of the Lord Viscount Campden. Details at great length the circumstances of the attack upon his house at Luffenham, in the county of Rutland, by the forces under Lord Grey. Petitioner estimates his losses at 3,000l. and prays their Lordships to be a means to the House of Commons, by whom he

has been committed, for his discharge or that he may be released upon bail. L. J., V. 641.

Annexed :—

1. Letter from William Atton, at Brooke, (Viscount Campden's house) to Thomas Noel, Esq. There are forces at Wickham which have seized upon all my Lord's and Mr. Henry Noel's stock there, and have entered their houses and grounds, and discharged the tenants from their rents, and are now selling all the wood upon the ground, but by what law the writer cannot imagine. Desires to know (by his Lady's command) whether any warrant has been given herein by the Houses of Parliament. Believes it is Mr. Norwood who has procured some others like himself to do my Lord, and Mr. Noel this great injury. 8 March 1642-3. *See* L. J., V. 650.

2. Petition of Henry Skipwith, Esq. ; petitioner coming as a friend and near kinsman to visit Mr. Henry Noel in the county of Rutland, was there taken with Mr. Noel by Lord Grey and sent prisoner to London ; petitioner was not serving there or elsewhere against Parliament, yet had his horses and clothes taken from him. Prays for examination of the case and that he may be set at liberty upon bail. (Undated.)

[March 14.] Copy of the letter sent from the Speaker to the Mayor and aldermen of Bristol, to thank them for their activity in the service of Parliament. L. J., V. 648.

March 14. Application for a pass for Francois de Lizola, the Emperor's agent, to go to Oxford. L. J., V. 648.

March 14. Draft order to seize the estates of delinquents concerned in the late conspiracy at Bristol. L. J., V. 648. *In extenso.*

March 15. Petition of Thomas Nettervill, Esq., prisoner in Wood Street Compter. Prays that he may be released upon bail, as unless some speedy order be granted for his relief he must perish of famine. L. J., V. 649.

March 15. Petition of Thomas Horth, merchant, and others, owners of the ship " Mayflower " of Yarmouth. The ship having set sail for the Straits was by contrary winds driven into Falmouth, and was there made stay of by Sir Nicholas Slanyng for His Majesty. Prays that a pass may be granted to them to go to Oxford to petition His Majesty for the discharge of the ship. L. J., V. 650.

March 15. Petition of Anne Heycock, widow. Complains that John Tunbridge, her neighbour, by an encroachment, has interfered with the completion of her house now in course of construction in St. Clement's parish. L. J., V. 650. *In extenso.*

Annexed :—

1. Copy of report of Lord Maltravers and Inigo Jones upon the encroachments.

March 15. Application from the French Ambassador that three days may be granted to him to deliver in, in writing, his reasons why the Capuchin Friars at Denmark House should not be sent away. *See* L. J., V. 676.

March 16. Petition of Edward Hudson, clerk. Prays to be recommended for the living of Chartham, Kent. L. J., V. 679. *In extenso.*

March 16. List of committee to whom preceding petition was referred. L. J., V. 650.

March 16. Petition of Ralph Freke. Prays that a pass may be granted to him for himself, his wife, a kinswoman, and servants to go into Wiltshire where his estate lies. L. J., V. 650.

March 16. Application of John Holland and Thomas Skynner to the Earl of Manchester, for a pass to go to Oxford about the business of the merchant adventurers. L. J., V. 650.

March 16. Draft order for protection of the house and goods of William Savill, servant to the Earl of Rutland. L. J., V. 651.

March 17. Information of Thomas Wells and others of seditious words spoken by Edmund Rayner, of Lambeth, against the King. L. J., V. 651.

March 17. Information of George Fuller and others, of blasphemous words spoken by Edmund Cheesman, waterman. L. J., V. 651.

March 17. Petition of John Kayes, minister of the Gospel and lecturer of St. Nicholas Acons, London. Prays to be recommended for the living of Sundridge, Kent. L. J., V. 652.

March 17. Application for a pass for Lord Stanhope and his family to go into France. L. J., V. 652.

March 17. Draft order for passes for Robert Buchanan and Thomas Edwards, yeomen of the wine cellar to His Majesty to go to Oxford. L. J., V. 652.

March 17. Petition of Sir Thomas Malet, one of the Justices of the Court of King's Bench. Has been a prisoner in the Tower by their Lordships' order for two and thirty weeks. Prays that he may have leave to go abroad with his keeper to endeavour to provide for the relief of his distressed family, and return to his prison every night. L. J., V. 652.

March 18. Order for a pass to be granted to William Hustler, sadler to Prince Charles, to go to Oxford with two saddles, with their furniture, for the Prince and the Duke of York. L. J., V. 653.
Annexed :—
1. Copy of the pass.
2. Petition of William Hustler. Has been arrested at the suit of Ingram and his wife, and remains a prisoner in the Poultry Counter, notwithstanding the pass which had been granted to him by their Lordships. Prays for his discharge, and that Ingram, his wife, and Osborn the Serjeant at Mace who arrested him, and who knew him to be His Highness' servant, may be sent for to answer.

March 20. Draft order for the protection of the house and goods of Mr. Dewhurst of Cheshunt Nunnery, in the county of Hertford. L. J., V. 655.

March 20. Petition of William Rosse, Her Majesty's servant. Prays that the money taken out of his trunks by the searchers at Gravesend, on pretence that it was to be transported beyond the seas, may be returned to him, as he was only taking it to Scotland, where he was advised by his physicians to go for his health's sake, being sick in body inclining to a consumption. L. J., V. 655.

March 20. Petition of John Reynolds, a clerk in the Chancery, and Robert Thornton, chafe wax to the Great Seal. Pray that passes may be granted to them to go to Oxford to attend to their places. L. J., V. 655.

March 20. Copy of preceding.

March 20. Order giving power to the Committee appointed to go to Oxford to send one of their number upon any urgent occasion to take further advice of the Parliament. L. J., V. 656. In extenso.

March 20. Order for the Committee at Oxford to inform His Majesty of the robbery of certain waggons belonging to the counties of Somerset, Wilts, Devon, and Gloucester, by parties of His Majesty's army issuing out of Reading, notwithstanding His Majesty's late proclamation. L. J., V. 656. In extenso.

March 20. Information of Robert Bookham and others of blasphemous words spoken by Martha Drewitt.

March 21. Petition of Thomas Squire and James Noel. Petitioners arrested John Baynes for a debt due to them, but Baynes, pretending himself a servant of the Lord Morley, obtained an order for his discharge. Pray that the order may be indicted as Baynes is a papist convict upon record, and no servant to Lord Morley, and is very able to pay petitioners' debt. L. J., V. 657.

March 21. Draft of the instructions for Edmond Prideaux and Anthony Nicol, Esqs., members of the House of Commons employed in the county of Devon. L. J., V. 657. In extenso.

March 21. Draft order for adding certain persons to the Committees for the several counties for a weekly assessment. L. J., V. 658. In extenso.

March 21. Letter from the Committee at Oxford to the Speaker of the House of Commons giving an account of the presentation of the articles for the cessation of arms to the King. C. J., III. 14. This is a duplicate of the letter from the Earl of Northumberland to the Speaker of the House of Lords. L. J., V. 659. In extenso.

March 21. Petition of divers poor prisoners in the Bridewell, in Oxford, who were taken at Marlborough, to H. C. Petitioners were made prisoners whilst endeavouring to defend the town of Marlborough, and were dragged in the most inhuman manner to the Castle at Oxford, where they have endured hard imprisonment for the space of ten weeks, having been kept without food, sometimes for three days together, and now only allowed bread and water. All which cruelty has been exercised upon them to compel them to take an oath whereby they must swear that the Earl of Essex and all his adherents are traitors, and the war now raised for the destruction of them and the Parliament most just and necessary. Two and thirty of the petitioners have now been thrust into a moist, nasty, and stinking dungeon, and all persons are forbidden on pain of death to come to them, or relieve them with food or linen, by means of which inhuman cruelties many of them have fallen desperately

sick and all the rest are like to do so, as they have been threatened by Captain William Smith, Provost Marshal General of His Majesty's army, to be secretly stifled, poisoned, and affamished to death. Pray that some course may be taken whereby their lives may be preserved. See C. J., III. 11.
Annexed :—
1. Several articles of the cruel and unjust dealings and proceedings of Captain William Smith, Provost Marshal General of His Majesty's army, against many poor prisoners in Oxford Castle, and now in Bridewell.
2. Draft of the order of the Commons that the preceding petition and articles be printed and published, and that an express be sent to the Lord General to desire His Majesty that a speedy course may be taken for their relief. C. J., III. 11. In extenso.

March 21. Petition of divers of the inhabitants of Badwinter in the county of Essex, to Sir Thomas Barrington and Sir Harbotle Grimston, Knights for the county. Complain of the conduct of their minister, Mr. Drake, who refuses to administer the sacrament to them unless they come to the rail in the chancel. He has also walled up the chancel door and set two images upon the screen, and wears crosses and letters upon his surplice when he preaches. See C. J., III. 11.

March 22. Order for the prevention of disorders in the town of Lynn. L. J., V. 659. In extenso.

March 22. Letter from the Committee at Oxford to the Speaker of the House of Commons, giving a further account of the presentation of the articles for the cessation of arms to the King. This is a duplicate of the letter from the Earl of Northumberland to the Speaker of the House of Lords. L. J., V. 661. In extenso.

March 23. Order for marking the arms and horses belonging to the Parliament. L. J., V. 662. In extenso.

March 23. Declaration for a good agreement between the English and Scotch commanders. L. J., V. 663. In extenso.

March 23. Order for the payment of arrears due to the garrison of Northampton. L. J., V. 663. In extenso.

March 23. Order for sequestering the living of All Saints, Hertford. L. J., V. 663. In extenso.

March 23. Order for sequestering the living of St. Clement's, next East Cheap, London. L. J., V. 663. In extenso.

March 23. Order for sequestering the living of St. Michael's, Cornhill. L. J., V. 664. In extenso.

March 23. Order for sequestering the living of St. Mary, Abchurch. L. J., V. 664. In extenso.
Annexed :—
1. Petition of Jone Stone, wife of Benjamin Stone, parson of Abchurch, and now prisoner at Plymouth, prays for an allowance for herself, husband, and children, out of the profits of the living. (Undated.)

March 23. Order for sequestering the living of the church of St. Thomas' Hospital, Southwark. L. J., V. 664. In extenso.

March 23. Order for sequestering the living of St. Giles in the Fields. L. J., V. 665. In extenso.

March 23. Order for sequestering the living of Upper Winchenden, Bucks. L. J., V. 665. In extenso.

March 23. Copy of preceding.

March 23. Order for sequestering the living of St. Margaret, New Fish Street, London. L. J., V. 665. In extenso.

March 23. Order for sequestering the living of Northall, Middlesex. L. J., V. 666. In extenso.

March 23. Order for sequestering the living of St. Leonard, Shoreditch. L. J., V. 666. In extenso.

March 23. Order for sequestering the living of Halifax. L. J., V. 666. In extenso.

March 23. Order for sequestering the living of St. Olave, Old Jewry. L. J., V. 667. In extenso.

March 23. Order for sequestering the living of Hemel Hempstead. L. J., V. 667. In extenso.

March 24. Petition of John Plummer and George Errington. Pray for their discharge from custody, having been committed by their Lordships for opening a letter directed to the Earl of Holland, which they took from a gentleman whilst they were on scout service at Clapham. L. J., V. 667.

March 24. Petition of William Ridges, Thomas Spaldinge, and others, citizens of London. John Baynes [or Barnes] having been arrested by petitioners for debts due to them, was by their Lordship's order released upon the information of the Lord Morley, that Baynes was his servant. Pray that Baynes who is a recusant and no

servant of the Lord Morley may be called upon to give
satisfaction to his creditors. L. J., V. 668.
Annexed :—
   1. Statement that Baynes was convicted in January
   1640–41.
   2. Affidavit of John Owen that Baynes is a recusant
   convict, a Sabbath breaker, and one that hath
   lately been with the Cavaliers at Oxford. 23
   March 1642–3.
   3. Affidavit of John Usmer that Baynes said that
   he would kill 40 Roundheads with his own
   hand. 6 April 1643.
March 24. Draft resolutions concerning the cessation
of arms. L. J., V. 668. *In extenso.*
March 24. Draft of the answer of Parliament to the
King's message concerning the cessation of arms.
L. J., V. 668. *In extenso.*
March 24. Draft of the instructions to the Committee
at Oxford concerning the cessation of arms. L. J., V.
669. *In extenso.*
March 24. Statement respecting the arrest of Francis
Chamberlayne, His Majesty's servant in ordinary.
L. J., V. 669.
March 24. Ordinance for raising money, &c. for the
defence of Exeter. L. J., V. 669. *In extenso.*
March 24. Order for sequestering the living of
Weston Zoyland, Somerset. L. J., V. 669. *In extenso.*

March 25. Pass for Mrs. Lewson and her servants to
go to Oxford. L. J., V. 671.
March 25. Order for the payment of 100*l.* to the
Bishop of Ardagh. L. J., V. 671. *In extenso.*
March 25. Order for the payment of 4,000*l.* to Andrew
Dick, Esq. L. J., V. 671. *In extenso.*
March 25. Ordinance for the Commissioners of the
Customs to repay themselves 20,000*l.*, advanced by
them for the pressing necessities of the navy. L. J.,
V. 672. *In extenso.*
March 25. Application from the Bishop of Ardagh to
be dismissed from the various suits brought against him
by Sir Thomas Cary. *See* L. J., V. 658.
March 25. Petition of William March, servant to
Thomas, Earl of Arundel and Surrey, having the charge
of his Lordship's estate in his honour's absence beyond
the seas. The Earl has been assessed at 1,000*l.* for the
twentieth part of his estate. Prays that the prosecution
of the assessment may be forborne until petitioner has
written to the Earl for instructions, as for these six
months he has only been able to collect 300*l.* of the
Earl's revenues.
March 26. Letter from the Earl of Northumberland
at Oxford to the Earl of Manchester, Speaker of the
House of Lords, concerning the treaty, &c. L. J.,
V. 677. *In extenso.*
Annexed :—
   1. Copy of preceding.
March 27. Reasons offered by the Lords and Commons
to His Majesty why they cannot agree to the alteration
and addition made by his Majesty to the articles concerning the cessation of arms. L. J., V. 673. *In extenso.*
March 27. Amended draft of preceding.
March 27. Petition of Isabella Massey, widow, concerning her suit against Rolfe. L. J., V. 674. *In
extenso.*
March 27. Copy of preceding.
March 27. List of killed and wounded, headed "at
Uxiter." No doubt a list of killed and wounded at the
battle of Hopton Heath, which is in the neighbourhood
of Uttoxeter, as the first name amongst the slain is that
of the Earl of Northampton.
March 28. Statement respecting the tenants of Sutton
Marsh. L. J., V. 675.
Annexed :—
   1. Copy of an order of the Committee of Lincoln
   respecting the tenants of Sutton Marsh. 8 Feb.
   1642–3.
March 28. Draft order for adding Sir William
Brewerton to the committee for Staffordshire. L. J.,
V. 675.
March 28. Copy of order in the cause between
Anthony Hooper and his creditors. L. J., V. 676.
Annexed :—
   1. Petition as well of William Le Cner and others,
   creditors of Anthony Hooper, merchant, as of the
   said Anthony Hooper. L. J., V. 677. *In extenso.*
   2. Report of the referees to whom the cause was
   referred. L. J., V. 678. *In extenso.*
   3. Another petition of Hooper and his creditors,
   praying for an extension of time for taking
   accounts in the case. (Undated.)
   4. Further report of the referees. (Undated.)
March 28. Application for a pass for the Duke De
Espernon. L. J., V. 676.

March 28. Petition of the prebendaries of Christ
Church, Canterbury, now resident there, for protection,
for themselves, and the Cathedral. L. J., V. 676. *In
extenso.*
Annexed :—
   1. Copy of an order referred to in preceding. *See*
   L. J., V. 360.
March 28. Petition of William Rosse, Her Majesty's
servant, respecting money belonging to him seized by
the searchers at Gravesend. L. J., V. 678. *In extenso.*
Annexed :—
   1. Copy of order that the money referred to shall
   be delivered to petitioner upon his putting in
   security in the Court of Exchequer. L. J., V.
   655. *In extenso.*
   2. Affidavit of William Rosse that the searchers
   refuse to deliver up the money, notwithstanding
   he has put in security as required, and shewn them
   the preceding order. L. J., V. 678.' *In extenso.*
March 28. Order for sequestering the living of Horsham, Sussex. L. J., V. 678. *In extenso.*
Annexed :—
   1. Copy of preceding.
March 28. Copy of letter from the Earl of Northumberland to the Earl of Manchester concerning the treaty.
L. J., V. 682. *In extenso.*
March 29. Letter from the Earl of Northumberland at
Oxford to the Earl of Manchester, concerning the treaty.
L. J., V. 682. *In extenso.*
March 29. Copy of preceding.
March 30. Petition of Frances Dickinson, wife of
Lyming Dickenson, Esq., complaining of the oppressions
suffered by herself and her husband at the hands of
Thomas Gratwick and others. L. J., V. 681. *In
extenso.*
Annexed :—
   1. Copy of order dismissing Gratwick's petition.
   5 July 1641.
March 30. Petition of John Gibbon, prisoner in the
Fleet, praying that he may have leave to go abroad to
attend to his suit before their Lordships. L. J., V. 681.
In extenso.
Annexed :—
   1. Copy of order of the Commons for petitioner to
   be kept close prisoner within the walls of the
   prison. C. J., III. 19.
March 30. Petition of John Boughton, servant to
Katherine Lady Stanhope, governess to the Princess
Mary in Holland, respecting the payment of her Ladyship's jointure. L. J., V. 682. *In extenso.*
March 31. Letter from the Committee at Oxford to the
Speaker of the House of Commons. His Majesty, with his
Council, has sat constantly forenoon and afternoon about
the cessation of arms. At present he has not come to a
full resolution, as many difficulties arose upon the third
article about the removal of quarters, which the writers
did not conceive themselves enabled to resolve. Hope
the business will speedily come to a conclusion, and that
the House will receive it on Monday. *See* C. J.,
III. 26.
March 31. Letter from the Earl of Northumberland
to the Earl of Manchester. Duplicate of preceding
letter from the Committee at Oxford. *See* L. J., V. 685.
[1643, March.] Letter from Isaac Pennington, Lord
Mayor, to the Speaker of the House of Commons. One
Cheshire, a seditious preacher, was apprehended last
night; there will be charge enough against him if the
Committee think fit to commit him ; the writer also apprehended Griffith, rector of St. Mary, Magdalen, near
Old Fish Street, London, and Tuke, vicar of St. Olave's,
Old Jewry, very desperate fellows, and committed them
to Newgate, and sent their accusations to the House, but
they are bailed out, and are more insolent than ever :
knows not what may happen if an example be not made
of some of them.
April 1. Petition of Sir Thomas Cary, praying that
his former petition, and the Bishop of Ardagh's answer
thereto, may be referred to the consideration of one or
two of the judges. L. J., V. 686.
April 1. Copy of preceding.
April 1. Petition of John Gibbon, prisoner in the
Fleet, for leave to go abroad with his keeper. L. J., V.
686. *In extenso.*
April 1. Order upon preceding. L. J., V. 684.
April 1. Petition of Henry Noel, second son of the
late Lord Viscount Campden. Complaining that the
Committee for the Parliament at Lincoln refuse to
obey their Lordships' order made upon petitioners former
petition. L. J., V. 686. *In extenso.*
Annexed :—
   1. Copy of order referred to in preceding. 15 March
   1642–3. L. J., V. 650.

2. Letter from Za. Dale to Mr. Henry Noel. Received the Lords' order on Sunday night last, and went the next morning to Wickham, but Captain Harrington was gone with his forces to Lincoln, and had taken with him all the steers (18), and had killed six sheep and felled some young ashes for firing; he also left orders that no goods should be taken out of the grounds, and had put 12 horses where the beasts were, and had discharged the tenants from paying any more rent, giving one a special charge to look to the horses, and took away the bailiff prisoner to Lincoln. The writer next day went to Spalding, and showed the order to Captain Harrington's father, who said his son had not done anything but what he had an order for from the Committee at Lincoln. Went thence to Lincoln where he was guarded with muskets and pikes to the Committee, and presented the order, which Lord Willoughby and the rest of the Committee slighted very much. Sir Edward Hartop and Captain Wayte are in Rockingham Castle, and it is reported that Lord Grey will live in Mr. Noel's house, and Captain Wayte in Lord Campden's.

April 1. Two printed copies of the declaration and ordinance of the Lords and Commons assembled in Parliament, for the seizing and sequestering of the estates, both real and personal, of certain kinds of notorious delinquents, to the use and for the maintaining of the army raised by the Parliament, and such other uses as shall be directed by both Houses of Parliament for the benefit of the Commonwealth. The declaration is given in Rushworth (Vol. III., Part II., p. 309), with the exception of the names of the sequestrators, which are given *in extenso* in the Parliamentary Register, Vol. XII., 227.

April 1. List of persons accountable for monies received for the war in defence of the kingdom of Ireland against the rebels.

April 1. Draft of letter from [   ] calling a meeting at Leatherhead of the Commissioners for the county of Surrey, concerning the levying of the contribution money.

April 2. Petition of Charles Masselle, a poor distressed Frenchman, administrator of Daniel Hugo. Petitioner having obtained a decree against Thomas Gleane in the Court of Requests, Gleane subsequently obtained a prohibition in the Court of Common Pleas, whereby petitioner is prevented from proceeding further with his decree. Prays that Gleane may be ordered to pay the amount awarded by the decree with costs and damages, as petitioner is unable to be relieved by law, most of his witnesses being since dead, and the remainder living at Sedan in France.

Annexed:—
1. A similar petition of same. (Undated.)

April 3. Draft resolutions concerning the treaty with the King. L. J., V. 687. *In extenso.*

April 3. Report from the Committee upon the Riot at Lambeth. C. J., III. 27.

April 3. Draft orders of the Commons upon preceding report. C. J., III. 27. *In extenso.*

April 4. Order for sequestering the living of Thorley, Hertford. L. J., V. 690. *In extenso.*

April 4. Order for the payment of 70l. to poor women, wives of persons in the Train of Artillery in Ireland. L. J., V. 690. *In extenso.*

Annexed:—
1. Petition of Jane Hilliard and ten other poor women, whose husbands are employed in the Train of Artillery in Ireland, praying their Lordships to agree to the order passed by the House of Commons for their relief.

April 4. Order for the payment of 40l. to Mr. Higginson for wheat for Ireland. L. J., V. 691. *In extenso.*

April 4. Order for the payment of 400l. to Sir John Clotworthy for his service in Ireland. L. J., V. 691. *In extenso.*

April 4. Order for the payment of 138l. to Sir Robert King for cows, wheat, and beer barley for Ireland. L. J., V. 691. *In extenso.*

April 4. Petition of Thomas Holford, Esq. Petitioner has only recently heard of the order obtained by his wife Dorothy (late wife of Sir Thomas Leventhorpe), whereby he is restrained from taking any benefit of his wife's estate, until he can procure some further order from their Lordships. It has been impossible for him to attend to make good his case, as he has been for a long time sick of a fever, and in great danger of death. He therefore prays that he may be restored to the benefit of his freeholds, and that a day may be appointed for the further hearing of the matter, his own estate in the counties of Chester, Salop, and Flint, being under the sword of the array men, his subsistence for the present depends merely upon that which has been taken from him by their Lordships' order. See L. J., V. 611.

Annexed:—
1. Copy of order appointing a meeting of the committee, to whom Lady Leventhorpe's petition was referred. 25 Feb. 1642-3.
2. Copy of the report of the committee. 1 March 1642-3. L. J., V. 629.
3. Certificate of Theodore Deodate, Doctor of Physic, that Thomas Holford has been sick of a fever since the 16th of Feb., and that he is unable to give his personal attendance without danger of his life. On the same paper is an affidavit of Holford that Dr. Deodate's certificate is true. 4 April 1643.

April 5. Petition of William Latham, woollen draper in ordinary to His Majesty. Was arrested on the 27th of March last, when providing cloth to send away for His Majesty's last Maunday, at the suit of Simon Perrott. Prays that Perrott and others may be sent for to answer. L. J., V. 692.

April 5. Petition of Benjamin Spencer, minister of St. Thomas' parish in Southwark. Was committed to the Fleet for contempt of their Lordships' order. Prays for his discharge, and that some maintenance may be allowed to him until he take some lawful course, either in the ministry or otherwise, whereby he may get bread for himself and family. L. J., V. 692.

April 5. Petition of Sir Thomas Cary, that his cause against the Bishop of Ardagh may be referred to one or two of the judges. L. J., V. 692.

April 5. Ordinance for supplying the navy with mariners. L. J., V. 693. *In extenso.*

April 5. Instructions by the Lords and Commons in Parliament to Robert Earl of Warwick, by them appointed to be general and commander-in-chief of the ships which now are, or hereafter shall be set forth to sea for the better enabling him to the performance of that service. L. J., V. 694. *In extenso.*

April 5. Order for the payment of 200l. to Robert Paule for the freight of the ship "Paul" to carry clothes, victuals, &c., from London to Donegal. L. J., V. 694. *In extenso.*

April 5. Order for the payment of 430l. to William Hill for herrings. L. J., V. 694. *In extenso.*

April 5. Order for the payment of 50l. to Abraham Vanden Beindo for 20 pairs of pistols. L. J., V. 694. *In extenso.*

April 5. Order for the payment of 600l. to Alderman Towse for beef. L. J., V. 694. *In extenso.*

April 6. Order for the payment of 150l. to Leonard Towers for clothing for the soldiers in Ireland. L. J., V. 696. *In extenso.*

April 6. Order for the payment of 70l. to Peter Dyment for herrings. L. J., V. 696. *In extenso.*

April 6. Order for the payment of 16l. 8s. to Peter Dyment for herrings. L. J., V. 696. *In extenso.*

April 6. Order for the payment of 150l. to William Hodder for beef. L. J., V. 696. *In extenso.*

April 6. Draft resolutions of the Commons concerning the instructions to be given to the committee at Oxford. C. J., III. 33. *In extenso.*

April 6. Draft order of the Commons for the searchers at Gravesend to pay to the treasurers at Guildhall 800l. out of the monies seized by them and claimed by William Rosse. See C. J., III. 109.

April 7. Petition of inhabitants of St. Leonard's, Foster Lane, London. Pray that Mr. James Nalton, a godly and able minister, who hath been twice plundered and in danger of his life, may be instituted to the living of St. Leonard's, Foster Lane, which is now vacant by the decease of the late pastor, Mr. Smith. L. J., V. 697.

April 7. Petition of Thomas Jenyns, Esq. Prays that some speedy time may be appointed for determining his cause against Sir Filibert Vernatti, and that he may have leave, notwithstanding their Lordships' order of the 30th of January 1640-1, to take his legal course by way of arrest to secure the person of Sir Filibert Vernatti. L. J., V. 697.

Annexed:—
1. Copy of order referred to in preceding.
2. Copy of another order in the cause. 29 March 1642. L. J., IV. 682. *In extenso.*

K 4

3. Copy of another order. 6 Aug. 1642. L. J., V.
268.

4. Copy of another order. 28 Feb. 1642–3. L. J.,
V. 624.

April 7, Further addition of instructions agreed upon
by the Lords and Commons for the Committees of both
Houses at Oxford. L. J., V. 698. *In extenso.*
Annexed :—
1. Draft of a portion of preceding.
April 7. Order for the payment of 132*l.* to Edward
Logge for herrings. L. J., V. 698. *In extenso.*
April 7. Order for the payment of 24*l.* 11*s.* 6*d.* to John
Butler for butter. L. J., V. 698. *In extenso.*
April 7. Order for the payment of 48*l.* to Thomas
Hooke for herrings. L. J., V. 699. *In extenso.*
April 7. Order for the payment of 54*l.* 18*s.* 9*d.* to
Margery Hassard for peas, butter, &c. L. J., V. 699.
In extenso.
April 7. Order for the payment of 214*l.* 13*s.* 7*d.* to
George Wood for clothes and other provisions sent into
Ireland. L. J., V. 699. *In extenso.*
April 7. Petition of the advancing creditors of Sir
Thomas Dawes. Pray that certain evidences of the lands
of Sir Thomas Dawes, deposited by an order of the House
of Commons in the custody of Mr. Woolwich, Counsellor-
at Law, and now required by the counsel of Sir Thomas
Dawes for the purpose of drawing a proviso to his Bill,
shall be returned into the custody of Mr. Woolwich
within fourteen days after the delivery thereof. *See*
L. J., V. 286, &c.
April 8. Papers sent by the Earl of Northumberland
from the Committee at Oxford to the Earl of Manchester, Speaker of the House of Lords. The letter
enclosing these papers is wanting, but is, with the papers,
which are as follows, printed. *In extenso.* L. J., V.
699–703.
1. Questions from the King concerning the first
proposition.
2. The King's answer concerning the magazines.
3. The answer of the Committees to the King concerning the first proposition.
4. The King's answer about disbanding the army.
5. The reply of the Committees.
6. The desire of the Committees for an explanation
about the disbanding.
7. The King's explanation.
8. The desire of the Committees for a further
explanation.
9. The answer of the Committees about the disbanding.
10. The King's further answer about the disbanding.
11. The King's answer concerning his return and
the conclusion of the treaty.
12. The answer of the Committees about the fleet.
13. The King's reply.
14. The desire of the Committees for an explanation.
15. The King's answer.
16. The answer of the Committees about the towns
and forts.
17. The King's reply.
18. Questions from the Committees about the King
appointing the Lord Warden of the Cinque Ports,
governors of towns, &c.
19. The King's answer.
20. Questions from the Committees concerning an
oath to be taken by all officers, &c.
21. The King's answer.
April 8. Additional instructions for the Committees
at Oxford. L. J., V. 704. *In extenso.*
April 10. Petition of Captain John Hardwicke. Has
obtained a writ of *certiorari* addressed to the Lord Chief
Justice of the King's Bench, by whom it is to be
broken open ; this cannot now be done because his
Lordship is at Oxford. Prays that a pass may be granted
to some person whom petitioner may appoint to go to
Oxford with the writ, and return again. *See* L. J., V.
705.
April 10. Order for the payment of 650*l.* to William
Wade and John Parrott for wheat. L. J., V. 705. *In
extenso.*
April 10. Order for the payment of 89*l.* 10*s.* to William
Smart for peas and oats. L. J., V. 705. *In extenso.*
April 10. Order for the payment of 122*l.* to William
Hodder for wheat and oats. L. J., V. 705. *In extenso.*
April 10. Order for the payment of 87*l.* 18*s.* 7*d.* to
Giles Dobins for biscuits. L. J., V. 705. *In extenso.*
April 10. Order for the payment of 60*l.* to William
Smart for beef. L. J., V. 706. *In extenso.*
April 10. Order for the payment of 60*l.* to Swithin
Walton for beef. L. J., V. 706. *In extenso.*

April 10. Order for the payment of 100*l.* to James
Dier for beef. L. J., V. 706. *In extenso.*
April 10. Order for the payment of 163*l.* 2*s.* 6*d.* to
Charles Walley for shoes. L. J., V. 706. *In extenso.*
April 10. Order for the payment of 46*l.* 18*s.* to Maurice
Thompson for Captain John Brookehaven for salt.
L. J., V. 706. *In extenso.*
April 10. Order for the payment of 20*l.* to Sir John
Browne for beef. L. J., V. 706. *In extenso.*
April 10. Order for the payment of 56*l.* 5*s.* to Peter
Maunsell for beef. L. J., V. 707. *In extenso.*
April 10. Order for the payment of 160*l.* to James
Butler for herrings. L. J., V. 707. *In extenso.*
April 10. Order for the payment of 1,800*l.* to Michael
Casteele for beef. L. J., V. 707. *In extenso.*
April 10. Order for the payment of 526*l.* to Patrick
Englishe for rye. L. J., V. 707. *In extenso.*
April 10. Order for the payment of 22*l.* 10*s.* to John
Marshall for beef. L. J., V. 707. *In extenso.*
April 10. Order for the payment of 15*l.* to Elias Fitz
for beef. L. J., V. 707. *In extenso.*
April 10. Order for the payment of 63*l.* to Robert
Warner for beef. L. J., V. 707. *In extenso.*
April 10. Order for the payment of 70*l.* to — Buck-
stone for herrings. L. J., V. 708. *In extenso.*
April 10. Order for the relief of the Isle of Wight.
L. J., V. 708. *In extenso.*
April 10. Draft Ordinance for associating the coun-
ties of Warwick, Stafford, Cheshire, and Shropshire.
L. J., V. 708. *In extenso.*
April 10. Order of the Commons concerning the
passing of persons between London and Oxford without
passes. C. J., III. 37. *In extenso.*
April 11. Pass for Henry Brockden, servant to Lord
Morley, to go to Oxford to serve an order upon Sir
George Strode. L. J., V. 710.
April 11. Message from the Lords to the Commons
desiring the Committee for the safety of the kingdom to
be appointed to consider the state of the army. L. J.,
V. 710.
April 11. Message from the Commons respecting the
ordinance for the weekly assessment, &c. L. J., V. 710.
April 11. Ordinance for securing the money raised in
Dorsetshire. L. J., V. 710. *In extenso.*
April 11. Ordinance for adding committees to the
sequestrators for the county of Devon. L. J., V. 711.
In extenso.
April 10. Copy of the King's message in answer to
the request of the committees about disbanding the
army. L. J., V. 711. *In extenso.*
April 11. Petition of Edward Hudson, clerk. By
their Lordship's order of the 23rd of October 1641, the
Archbishop of Canterbury was directed not to bestow
any of the ecclesiastical benefices, which are in his disposing, until the names of the persons nominated by him
were approved by the House. The Archbishop very much
defraudeth this order by allowing his benefices when
they fall void to lapse into the King's gift, and then
uses means for his Majesty to present the same man as
the Archbishop intended for it. Prays that an order
may be made for the Archbishop to institute petitioner
to the rectory of Chartham, Kent. L. J., V. 712.
Annexed :—
1. Copy of order of 23rd October 1641 referred to in
preceding. L. J., IV. 402. *In extenso.*
2. Copy of order recommending Hudson to the
Archbishop for the rectory of Chartham. 28
March 1643. L. J., V. 675.
3. Another petition of Hudson praying their Lordships to grant a further order to the Archbishop
to collate petitioner to the rectory of Chartham.
(Undated.)
April 11. Message from the Commons concerning the
Earl of Kinnoul, the Duke D'Espernon, &c. L. J., V.
712.
April 11. Ordinance to explain the ordinance for the
weekly assessment of London. L. J., V. 713. *In extenso.*
April 11. Order for sequestering the living of Cottingham, in the county of York. L. J., V. 714. *In extenso.*
April 11. Petition of John Harrisson. Petitioner and
his father having been despoiled of all their estate in
the province of Connaught by the rebels were forced to
fly with their families to the castle of Boyle, where they
remained fifteen months, and were driven with the last
convoy for Connaught to come to Dublin. Petitioner has
since come to England to endeavour to obtain the payment of monies owing to him by Sir George Radcliffe
and Sir Robert King, but they answer that they have
no money whereby to give him satisfaction. Petitioner
prays that they may be called upon to satisfy his

just debt, otherwise he and all his family are like to starve.

Annexed :—

1. Copy of preceding.

April 12. Message from the Commons, with resolution for the Committee of that House attending the King at Oxford, to return on Saturday next to give an account of the proceedings of the treaty. L. J., V. 714. *In extenso.*

April 12. Order for sequestering the living of Gilston, in the county of Hertford. L. J., V. 715. *In extenso.*

April 12. Ordinance indemnifying the Mayor of Plymouth for seizing corn, &c. in that port for the supply of the stores there. L. J., V. 715. *In extenso.*

April 12. Ordinance for assessing persons in Yarmouth for the defence of the town. L. J., V. 715. *In extenso.*

April 12. Ordinance for raising forces in and about London. L. J., V. 715. *In extenso.*

April 12. Letter from the Earl of Northumberland at Oxford to the Earl of Manchester, Speaker of the House of Peers *pro tempore,* concerning the presentation to the King of the instructions received from the Parliament. L. J., V. 716. *In extenso.*

April 13. Petition of William Lord Archbishop of Canterbury. Denies the statements contained in the petition of Edward Hudson with reference to the living of Chartham, Kent. Petitioner received a letter from his Majesty requiring him to give the benefice to another man, or else lapse it to His Majesty in order that he might bestow it. Prays their Lordships to remember the long restraint and affliction of their poor petitioner, and not press him more about this benefice, considering he hath already given answer to His Majesty according to his duty, that he will obey His Majesty's gracious letters. Holograph. *See* L. J., V. 717.

April 13. Order for sequestering the living of Sawbridgworth, in the county of Hertford. L. J., V. 717. *In extenso.*

April 13. Order for the payment of 500l. to Mr. Frost for corn. L. J., V. 718. *In extenso.*

April 13. Order for the payment of 66l. to Lieutenant-Colonel Gibbs, arrears due to him for his services in the late Northern Expedition. L. J., V. 718. *In extenso.*

April 13, Copy of the King's message concerning the disbanding of the armies and his coming to the Parliament. L. J., V. 718. *In extenso.*

April 14. Order for two horses belonging to Mr. Carye, stayed by the court of guard at Tyburn to be returned to him. L. J., V. 719.

April 14. Pass for Sir Mathow Lyster, one of the doctors of physic to His Majesty, to go to Oxford and return to London. L. J., V. 719.

April 14. Draft order for the protection of the lodge, household stuff, and goods of Mr. Young, in the Great Park of Windsor. L. J., V. 719.

April 14. Order for the payment of 200l. weekly for the garrison at Aylesbury. L. J., V. 719. *In extenso.*

April 14. Order for the relief of Galway Fort. L. J., V. 720. *In extenso.*

April 14. Order respecting the arrears upon the Bill for the relief of Ireland. L. J., V. 720. *In extenso.*

April 14. Petition of William Lord Archbishop of Canterbury, prisoner in the Tower. Prays that he may not be any further pressed in the business of Chartham Rectory, both in regard that he hath already given by order of the House as many benefices as are worth 500l. a year, passing by, to his great grief, his own chaplains, and also in regard that he is not able to give any other answer than that already expressed. Holograph.

April 15. Application for a pass for William Hinton and his wife, and George Jhons, his wife, family, and servants to go into France. L. J., VI. 1.

April 15. Petition of Dame Margaret Manners. Prays for a pass for herself and servants to go to Flanders for the benefit of her health. L. J., VI. 1.

April 15. Application for passes for Francois Bernardi, agent to the Ambassador of Spain, and for Signior Gioseppe de Silvas y Vera and Philip Vordi, his interpreter, to go to Oxford and return. L. J., VI. 1.

April 15. Affidavit of John Cooke concerning the detaining of Mr. Carye's horses. L. J., VI. 1.

April 15. Letter from the Earl of Northumberland, at Oxford, to the Earl of Manchester, Speaker of the House of Lords *pro tempore,* concerning the treaty, &c. L. J., VI. 1. *In extenso.*

Enclosed :—

1. Paper from the Committee concerning the magazines, and enlarging the time for the treaty.
2. The King's answer.
3. Paper from the Committee concerning the Cinque Ports.

4. The King's answer.
5. Paper from the Committee concerning the fleet.
6. The King's answer.
7. Paper from the Committee concerning the oaths of officers.
8. The King's answer.
9. Paper from the Committee concerning disbanding the armies.
10. Paper from the Committee concerning the King's return to the Parliament.
11. The King's answer.
12. Further paper concerning the King's return.
13. Desire of the Committee for a further answer concerning the Cinque Ports, &c.
14. Paper delivered to the King upon the instructions concerning the disbanding.

The whole of these papers are printed *in extenso.* L. J., VI. 5–7.

April 17. Application for a pass for Edward Phillips to go to Spa with his family and servants. L. J., VI. 7.

April 17. Statement as to the income of the minister of Saint Thomas's parish in Southwark. L. J., VI. 7.

Annexed :—

1. Petition of inhabitants of the parish of St. Thomas in Southwark that the whole of the profits of the living, which only amount to 50l. per annum, may be paid to their present minister Mr. Bisco, and a contribution be made in the parish for Mr. Spencer lately sequestered by order of Parliament.

April 17. Petition of Edward Corbett, Fellow of Merton College, Oxford, praying to be confirmed in the rectory of Chartham, Kent. L. J., VI. 8. *In extenso.*

April 17. Petition of the Lady Honora, Baroness of Kerry. Prays for an allowance for herself and family. L. J., VI. 8. *In extenso.*

April 17. Petition of His Majesty's tapestry workmen at Mortlake, in the county of Surrey. Pray leave to transport some of their manufactures to Holland free of duty. L. J., VI. 8. *In extenso.*

Annexed :—

1. Another petition of same. Pray that some means may be taken whereby they may receive payment of 3,937l. due to them by His Majesty, as they are in great distress, many of them being ready to starve for hunger. (Undated.)

April 17. Report from the committee of examinations upon the seizing of Mr. Carye's horses by Captain Player. C. J., III. 48. *In extenso.*

Annexed :—

1. Order of the Commons made upon preceding report. C. J., III. 48. *In extenso.*
2. Order of the committee of examinations that the horses taken from Mr. Carye shall continue in Captain Player's custody, as Mr. Carye is suspected to come from Oxford, and doth usually pass byeways to avoid the courts of guards and watches. 14 April 1643.
3. Affidavit of John Cooke that he served the order of the House of Lords upon Captain Player. 17 April 1643.

April 18. Resolution respecting the enlisting of volunteers in London under Sheriff Langham. L. J., VI. 9. *In extenso.*

April 18. Ordinance to prevent the judges repairing to Oxford to keep the next term. L. J., VI. 9. *In extenso.*

April 18. Order adding Adrian Parmentor and others to the Committee for Norwich. L. J., VI. 10. *In extenso.*

April 19. Draft of pass for Lady Delavall to go to Oxford and return. L. J., VI. 12.

April 19. Petition of Hugh Cox, a soldier under the command of Captain Matthew Andrewes. Was committed by their Lordships to White Lion Prison in Southwark upon a misinformation, and has lain in chains in great weakness for six weeks. The business having been fully examined by the House of Commons, petitioner has been acquitted of the charges made against him, and therefore prays an order for his release. L. J., VI. 12.

April 19. Letter from the Earl of Lanerick [Lanark], at Oxford, to the King. Has received from His Majesty two "blanks," whereof he will give account whensoever His Majesty is pleased to require it.

April 19. Copies of various papers presented to the King by the Scotch Commissioners at Oxford, with His Majesty's respective answers thereunto. The first paper is dated 23 Feb. 1642-3, and the last 19 April 1643. Rushworth, Vol. II., Part III., 399. *In extenso.*

April 20. Petition of David Mathew, agent for Sir Arthur Hopton, His Majesty's Ambassador now resident in Spain. Prays that a pass may be granted to him to go into Warwickshire, Norfolk, and Suffolk, with his wife and one servant, to collect some rents due to Sir Arthur Hopton, and to labour to make some provision for his own subsistence. L. J., VI. 12.

April 20. Order for the payment of 42l. 15s. to Captain Richard Dowse, arrears due to him for his personal entertainment in the late Northern Expedition. L. J., VI. 13. *In extenso.*

April 20. Order for the payment of 41l. 5s. to Captain Edmond Hippisley, arrears due to him for his personal entertainment in the late Northern Expedition. L. J., VI. 13. *In extenso.*

April 20. Order for raising a regiment of volunteers in the county of Hertford. L. J., VI. 13. *In extenso.*

April 20. Letter from Sir William Parsons, Sir Richard Bolton, Sir Adam Loftus, Sir Gerrard Lowther, and Sir Robert Meredith, certain of the Judges and Council in Ireland to [the Speaker of the House of Lords]. Complain of the injustice of the judgment passed against them by the Lords in Parliament, whereby they are condemned as criminous persons to pay damages to Henry Stewart and James Gray. Have nothing left but their bodies to satisfy this condemnation ; they are truly confident of their own innocence, and that if their Lordships were only rightly and fully informed, the writers would be able to give them most ample satisfaction. Seventeen of the Lords and Privy Council were present in the Castle Chamber, when the sentence was pronounced against Stewart and Gray, yet the damages are adjudged to be paid only by eight. Stewart and Gray have not been damnified, for His Majesty has been graciously pleased to remit their fines, which the writers conceive he would not have done, if he had thought that his Councillors and Judges would have been further troubled. The writers delivered their judgment according to their knowledge and consciences, and upon the merits of the cause, as they understood it, and upon the public hearing thereof in open Court, in the presence of the defendants who have never alleged any bribery, partiality, or corruption against them, without due proof whereof, decrees of Judges were in all times, and still are, reversed without punishment or penalty to the judges. They, therefore, humbly entreat that their petition may be read and their counsel heard. *See* L. J., V. 345, &c.

April 21. Writ of error, &c., in the cause Shering v. Tyte. L. J., VI. 13. (Parchment collection.)

April 22. Petition of Thomas Jenyns, Esq., concerning his cause against Sir Filibert Vernatti. L. J., VI. 14. *In extenso.*
Annexed :—
1. Copy of order in the cause referred to in preceding. 7 April 1643. L. J., V. 697.
2. Affidavit of John Carter and James Parsons, in the cause. 18 April 1643.

April 24. Petition of William Lord Archbishop of Canterbury, prisoner in the Tower. Was in good hope that his last answer touching the rectory of Chartham would have given satisfaction to their Lordships. His answer must still be the same, that he is engaged both in duty and promise to His Majesty. Prays that this may be an acceptable answer to their Lordships, and that he may not be further pressed in the matter. (Holograph.) L. J., VI. 15.

April 24. Petition of Samuel Peck, scrivener, Francis Coles, and Francis Leach, of London, stationers. Were committed by their Lordships on the 7th of January last for printing and publishing a pamphlet intituled "The continuation of the News." Pray for their discharge upon bail. L. J., VI. 16.
Annexed :—
1. Copy of preceding.

April 24. Certificate of Baron Trevor and Justices Reeve and Bacon concerning John Baynes, servant to Lord Morley. L. J., VI. 16. *In extenso.*
Annexed :—
1. List of matters for which Baynes is in the custody of the sheriffs of London.
2. Copy of indictment against Baynes for recusancy in not coming to church.
3. Copy of the outlawry of Baynes upon preceding indictment.
4. Affidavit of Ambrose Hopton that Baynes is a servant of Lord Morley. 17 April 1643.

5. Petition of John Baynes, praying for his discharge, having been arrested contrary to privilege.

6. Petition of Thomas Spaldinge and others, creditors of John Baynes, a goldsmith, now a prisoner in the compter. Pray that Baynes may not be discharged until he shall have paid petitioners' just debts, as unless he do so they will be unable to continue their weekly payments. Baynes, who is a desperate and dangerous fellow, hath lately been at Oxford with the cavaliers and reports that he will beat up a drum for the King, and deeply swears that he will himself kill forty Roundheads, and that for twenty shillings he will procure my Lord Morley's protection for any man.

April 24. Order for restoring Edmond Lynold to the rectory of Heyling, in the county of Lincoln. L. J., VI. 16. *In extenso.*

1643, April 24 } Minute book of proceedings in the
to   } House of Lords.
4 Dec. 1643.   }

April 25. Petition of Elizabeth Viscountess Dowager of Campden. Prays to be relieved from the weekly assessment. L. J., VI. 17. *In extenso.*

April 25. Petition of the cursitors of the Chancery. Pray that a pass may be granted to Edmond Gardner, their messenger, to go to Oxford and return as often as necessary, to carry the writs out of the Chancery to be sealed with the great seal. L. J., VI. 18.

April 25. Draft of the letter from both Houses to Lord Fairfax, thanking him for his services, &c. L. J., VI. 18. *In extenso.*

April 25. Order for collections to be made for the relief of the captives in Algiers. L. J., VI. 19. *In extenso.*

April 25. Order for securing the repayment of money advanced for the support of the army under Sir William Waller, and Sir Arthur Haselrigg. L. J., VI. 19. *In extenso.*

April 25. Copy of preceding.

April 25. List of Committee of the Commons appointed to consider how the King's revenue may be received and improved to the advantage of the kingdom. C. J., III. 59. *In extenso.*

April 27. Petition of Elizabeth Countess Rivers. Petitioner having been barbarously assaulted and despoiled of her goods, their Lordships made an order for her protection (L. J., V. 331), and to encourage her tenants to pay their rents ; this they still refuse to do, whereby petitioner's debts remain unpaid and her children are deprived of all maintenance. Prays for a further order to enforce the payment of her rents. L. J., VI. 19.
Annexed :—
1. Copy of preceding.

April 27. Order of the Commons for a pass to be granted to the messenger to the cursitors of the Chancery to carry some writs to Oxford, &c. C. J., III. 61. *In extenso.*

April 28. Judgment against Mr. Ingoldsby, sequestering his living of Walton, in the county of Hertford, and committing him to the Fleet for publishing a book full of malignant expressions and imputations upon the proceedings of Parliament, and for preaching "That " those that have taken the protestation and do fight " against the King were foresworn." L. J., VI. 20.

April 28. Draft of preceding.

April 28. Affidavit of Thomas Shemonds, keeper of one of the walks in the Great Park at Windsor, that John Moore and others coursed the deer in the Park with greyhounds. L. J., VI. 21. *In extenso.*

April 28. Draft order for quieting the Earl of Suffolk's possessions at Newport in the county of Essex. L. J., VI. 21. *In extenso.*
Annexed :—
1. Affidavits of John Parish and John Flaske that they heard John Webbe and others say that they would turn their cattle into Lord Suffolk's mead called Newport-pond, and not permit his Lordship to enjoy the same, and that they would take advantage of these times lest they have not the like again. 25 April 1643.

April 29. Order for sequestering the living of Shenfield in the county of Essex. L. J., VI. 21.

April 29. Petition of John Childersley, Doctor in Divinity. Cheerfully submits to the order for sequestering his living of Shenfield, Essex, but prays that the arrears of rents, and tithes to Lady-day last may be paid to him, that he may have leave to sell his hay, wood, and other goods without interruption, and that some reasonable annuity may be allowed him as he is eighty years of age. L. J., VI. 21.

April 29. Judgment against Richard Nicholson sequestering his living of Stapleford Tawney, in the county of Essex, and committing him to Newgate. L. J., VI. 21.

April 29. Judgment against Henry Downhall sequestering his living of St. Ives, in the county of Huntingdon. L. J., VI. 22.

April 29. Judgment against John Reynolds, sequestering his living of Houghton-cum-Witton, in the county of Huntingdon, because there is proof that he is with the King's army. L. J., VI. 22.

April 29. Affidavit of Christopher Trench and others concerning the arrest of John Wyeman, servant to the Earl of Holland. L. J. VI. 22. *In extenso.*

April 29. Petition of Sir Thomas Malet, Knight, one of the Justices of His Majesty's Court of King's Bench. Prays for further liberty. L. J., VI. 23. *In extenso.*

Annexed:—
1. Petition of same. Is very sorry to have offended their Lordships, and humbly prays that he may be discharged from further imprisonment. (Undated.)

April 29. Petition of Edmond Cheeseman. Was lately committed to Newgate by order of Parliament for pretended words of blasphemy. Prays that he may be speedily tried or enlarged upon bail. L. J., VI. 23.

April 29. Petition of Lyming Dickenson, Esq., concerning his cause against Thomas Gratwicke. L. J., VI. 23. *In extenso.*

Annexed:—
1. Copy of order in the cause. 5 July 1641.
2. Affidavit of Lyming Dickenson that he served the preceding order upon Thomas Also and John Palmer, and that they treated it with contempt. 28 April 1643.

April 29. Certificate of Doctor Zouche concerning the goods of Sir Peter Ricault. L. J., VI. 23. *In extenso.*

Annexed:—
1. Copy of the paper presented by the Resident of Portugal, and copies of various letters on the subject of Sir Peter Ricault's goods, submitted to Dr. Zouche.

April 29. Order for sequestering the estates of delinquents in the county of Devon. L. J., VI. 23. *In extenso.*

[1643, April 29.] Draft ordinance for raising money in the associated counties of Norfolk, Suffolk, &c., for payment of the forces under Lord Grey of Warke. *See* C. J., III. 65.

April. Petition of Barnard Alsopp and Thomas Fawcett, distressed prisoners in the Fleet. Were committed about fourteen weeks since (7 Jan. 1642-3) for printing a scandalous book, intituled "His Majesty's Propositions" to Sir John Hotham and the Inhabitants of Hull, &c." Pray that they may be discharged, as their offence was committed not wilfully but ignorantly, or that they may be allowed their liberty upon reasonable bail. *See* L. J., V. 214, &c.

April. Petition of James East and John Freeman. There is at present great need of money for the service of the State, towards which petitioners conceive that 200l. or 300l. a week may be raised by making farthings, which may be brought into the Treasury at Guildhall, and thence issued out to captains and officers, who are willing to accept thereof, for their own and their soldiers' pay. Petitioners who have by the authority of Parliament seized the houses, instruments, and tools now used in the farthing office, and are willing to undertake the business in such way as Parliament shall direct, pray that they may receive order for the further process thereof. *See* C. J., III. 48.

May 1. Application for a pass for the Earl of Sancourt (a French lord), and his eight servants to go beyond the seas. L. J., VI. 24.

May 1. List of witnesses produced to prove that Francis Wright, parson of Witham, is a drunkard, &c. L. J., VI. 24.

Annexed:—
1. Copy of order of the Commons, sequestering the profits of the living of Witham, and appointing Edmund Brewer as preacher there. 6 April 1643. C. J., III. 32.

May 1. Copy of ordinance instituting the governors of the forces in Londonderry. C. J., III. 65.

May 2. Draft ordinance sequestering the living of St. Thomas the Apostle, in London from Wm. Cooper, and appointing James Moore in his place. L. J., VI. 25.

May 2. List of witnesses to show that Cooper is ill affected to Parliament. L. J., VI. 25.

May 2. Petition of Thomas Some, Dr. in Divinity, and Vicar of Staines, praying that Matthew Hales may be assigned him for counsel. L. J., VI. 25.

Annexed:—
1. Order for the hearing of the case. 28 April, 1643.
2. Petition of parishioners of Staines; Dr. Some has been vicar for twenty-six years, a man of unblameable life, opposed to popery and popish innovations, living peaceably with his neighbours, and endeavouring to keep them in love and unity amongst themselves; petitioners understand that he is now questioned before their Lordships for bowing to the altar and preaching against Parliament, both which they are ready to testify on oath that he has never done, and they therefore pray that he may continue their minister, and that he may be set at liberty so that they may enjoy the comfort of his preaching and godly and religious conversation. (Undated.)

May 2. Draft ordinance for Colonel Cromwell to seize the corn, cattle, &c., of delinquents in Cambridgeshire. L. J., VI. 26. *In extenso.*

May 2. Draft order for Sir Walter Earle to have command in Dorsetshire for the ordering of the military affairs there. L. J., VI. 26. *In extenso.*

May 2. Draft order for the execution of martial discipline in the trained bands. L. J., VI. 26. *In extenso.*

May 2. Draft order for the indemnity of the Barnstaple men for fortifying their town. L. J., VI. 27. *In extenso.*

May 3. Petition of David Durie, David Mather, Scotchmen, Edward Basing, and Thomas Ruther, Englishmen, in the behalf of themselves and divers other Englishmen, masters of several ships now lying at Dunkirk; petitioners bought ships at Dunkirk which had been adjudged lawful prizes, but they are kept in there by the Dutch fleet; they complained to the Earl of Warwick who said he could do nothing without an order from the House; petitioners then went with Captain Barker, commander of one of the ships belonging to the English fleet on board the ship of Sir Martin Van Trompe, Admiral of the Dutch fleet to speak to him, who told them that if the English Parliament ordered the ships to be brought away, and the order were sent to him by the Earl of Warwick, he would let them pass with the least convoy. Petitioners pray for a speedy order for their relief. *See* L. J., VI. 29.

May 3. Draft order for the appointment of two persons in each county for the speedy gathering of the weekly assessments. L. J., VI. 29. *In extenso.*

May 3. Draft of instructions for the persons so appointed. L. J., VI. 29. *In extenso.*

May 3. Draft order for the removal of Lord Macquaire, Hugh MacMahowne, and Colonel Read from the Tower to Newgate. L. J., VI. 29. *In extenso.*

May 3. Draft order for the suppression of riots in Dorset and Somerset. L. J., VI. 30. *In extenso.*

May 4. Petition of the petty canons and clerks of His Majesty's chapel within the Castle of Windsor; petitioners for declining to bear arms, as many of them were ministers, and others unfit for that service, were turned out of their habitations by Colonel Venn, with their wives and children, and forbidden to take their household goods. Pray that they may be restored to their houses and former maintenance. L. J., VI. 30.

May 5. Petition of Jane Wemes, wife of Doctor Wemes; her husband was so affronted in his ministerial office, disturbed in his pulpit, and prosecuted with such malice, that he was obliged to leave his habitation. Petitioner prays for further time to find him out, that he may answer before their Lordships in person, and for protection for herself and her children. L. J., VI. 32.

May 4. Draft order for payment of 1,366l. 13s. 4d. to Captain Bartlett and the ship's company of the "Confidence." L. J., VI. 31. *In extenso.*

May 4. Draft order for the garrisons of Portsmouth, Hurst Castle, &c., to be paid out of the King's revenue. L. J., VI. 31. *In extenso.*

May 6. Petition of Thomas Some, Doctor in Divinity, and Vicar of Staines; has been ordered to bring in a true valuation of the vicarage; hears that most of the sheep in his parish are now destroyed and the hedges and fences of most of his glebe land pulled up; desires that he may have further time to send in his estimate. *See* L. J., VI. 33, 42.

May 6. Order for sequestering the living of Alden-ham, Herts, from Joseph Soame the present vicar. L. J., VI. 33.

May 6. Petition of Lady Anne Maynard, Dowager; for a pass for herself, her three daughters, her physician Dr. Colladon, her servants, &c., to France, for the benefit of the mineral waters. L. J., VI. 34.

Annexed :—

1. Certificate of Sir Theodore De Mayerne that Lady Maynard is in need of change of air.

May 6. Draft order concerning assessments. L. J., VI. 34. *In extenso.*

May 6. Draft order concerning monies to be advanced by the city of London, and for securing the repayment thereof. L. J., VI. 34. *In extenso.*

May 6. Draft order for Sir Robert Harley to be mint master. L. J., VI. 35. *In extenso.*

May 6. Draft order for the searchers of Gravesend to restore 120l. to Captain Robert Moore. L. J., VI. 35.

May 6. Petition of Wm. Barker, of London, merchant, to H. C.; petitioner is heavily engaged for his brother, now a prisoner in Windsor Castle, who is therefore unable to take any steps to raise money. Petitioner prays that his brother may be removed in custody from Windsor to London. C. J., III. 72.

May 8. Petition of John Squier, Vicar of Shoreditch; has been turned out of his vicarage and put to very heavy expense since the order of April last sequestering his living; but has not yet been heard on account of the weighty affairs before Parliament; prays for a hearing. L. J., VI. 35.

May 8. Pass for Mrs. Jermine from Oxford to London and thence into Suffolk. L. J., VI. 36.

May 8. Copy of the King's message about the Bill for reducing the Irish rebels. L. J., VI. 36. *In extenso.*

Annexed :—

1. Draft answer of Parliament to preceding; they consider it unfit to enter into any discussion as to the merits of the Bill, but in answer to the charges againstParliament they send an account of the money raised for the service of Ireland, and of the manner in which it has been employed, which shows that the expenditure largely exceeds the receipts, so that if money intended for Ireland has been appropriated to other purposes it has been more than repaid. This answer was settled in the Commons on the 25th of May after a debate and division and was sent up to the Lords the same day, and was by them referred to a Committee on the 5th of June, but does not appear to have been further proceeded with. C. J., III. 102, 103. *In extenso.* L. J., VI. 81.

2. The true state of the account of all monies borrowed and received by virtue of any Acts or ordinances of this Parliament for the relief and defence of the kingdom of Ireland until the 11th of May 1643, according to the particulars of the said account certified by the treasurer at wars, the treasurers of monies due upon subscriptions of adventurers, and for voluntary contributions, and the Chamberlain of London, examined with the vouchers, and remaining with the auditor. 25 May 1643.

3. Copy of preceding.

May 8. Copy of letter from Sergeant-major Rosse at York, to Sir Hugh Chomeley, Governor of Scarborough. Lord Aboyne was going from York before my coming thence. I pray you to take as much care of his Lordship's ammunition as of Lord Antrim's. I write this as I am to start for Scotland. *See* L. J., VI. 47.

May 9. Application for a pass for Lady Debora Gerbier, with her sons and daughters and servants, to go into France. L. J., VI. 37.

May 9. Order for sequestering the living of Loose, Kent. L. J., VI. 37.

May 9. Order for sequestering the living of Pedmarshe [Pebmarsh], in the county of Essex. L. J., VI. 37.

May 9. Petition of Adam de Cardoneel, a French merchant residing in London; a ship belonging to his brother, who lives in Normandy, has been seized between Bristol and the Downs by some who pretend authority from the King of England; prays for a pass to His Majesty to solicit the release of the ship. L. J., VI. 38.

May 9. Petition of Joseph de Silva; has been engaged in a suit in the Court of Admiralty for nearly two years, and last April went with a pass to Oxford to defend his cause, but for want of some acts of court and other writings was obliged to return to London; prays for another pass to Oxford. L. J., VI. 38.

May 9. The names of those trespassers who have been lately taken coursing and killing His Majesty's deer in Farming Woods in the forest of Rockingham, in the county of Northampton.

May 10. Application from the Committee for Lincolnshire that Sir Jervais Scroope, sequestrator with Sir John Jacob of the lands in Sutton Marsh, now the subject of litigation between Lord Philip Herbert and others and the Duke of Richmond, may be put out of the sequestration, as the Committee utterly dislike that Sir Jervais should have anything to do with the receipt of the rents. L. J., VI. 38.

Annexed :—

1. Copy of letter from the Speakers of both Houses to Lord Willoughby of Parham, Lord Lieutenant of Lincolnshire, to suppress all riots upon Sutton Marsh. 7 Feb. 1642-3. L. J., V. 592. *In extenso.*

2. Affidavit of John Wrenham that he served the order of the 10th of May for the sequestration of the rents of Sutton Marsh, by Sir John Jacob, upon Thomas Welby; and that he afterwards attended the Committee for the county of Lincoln, and acquainted Lord Willoughby of Parham and others of the Committee with the said order. 15 July 1643.

3. Affidavit of J. Peeters, farmer of part of Sutton Marsh; was arrested by Mr. Welby for refusing to pay him his rent (notwithstanding the order of the 10th of May last), and detained until he entered into a bond for 600l., which he was compelled to do, under threat of having his stock sold before his face. The crops of corn now growing upon the marsh land are worth 5,000l., and are daily threatened to be destroyed by sundry ill-affected persons thereabouts. 19 July 1643.

4. Application on behalf of Lord Philip Herbert and Lord Dacre and their ladies. That the sequestration granted by the Committee of Lincoln upon the rents of Sutton Marsh may be discharged; that the money levied by those sequestrators may be repaid to Sir John Jacob; that the bonds which the tenants have been constrained to enter into may be given up; that the Lords will join with the Commons in an order for petitioner's relief; and that the lands may be protected from rapine and destruction. (Undated.)

May 10. Petition of Samuel Vandamm, of London, dyer; claims part of 400l. settled by Zacharie Ruytinge on his marriage with Katherine Mochart, and prays that the case, which has been long in suit, may be referred to two judges for decision. L. J., VI. 38.

May 10. Petition of Richard Kinge; petitioner was named lessee of certain lands belonging to Sir Robert Carre, with his consent, by the trustees for the use of Lady Carre, and the rent of 600l. was always paid by Sir Robert, but now Sir Robert will not so pay the rent, and petitioner has by various orders of the House become charged therewith; petitioner prays that the tenants may be ordered to make payment to him that he may be able to satisfy the trustees. L. J., VI. 39.

Annexed :—

1. Order respecting the payment of the rents. 20 Sep. 1642.

2. Another order. 19 Oct. 1642.

May 10. Petition of Benjamin Spencer, clerk, late minister of St. Thomas parish in Southwark, sequestered, now prisoner in the Fleet; has been allowed 30l. out of his late living for his maintenance, but the charge of his imprisonment will eat out all that allowance; prays for enlargement that he may the better provide for the subsistence of himself, his wife, and seven children. L. J., VI. 39.

May 10. Petition of William Simpson, sergeant, prisoner in the Fleet; petitioner acknowledges the justness of his sentence, though he never used the words (against the Earl of Holland) imputed to him; prays for enlargement and for abatement of fees on account of his poverty. L. J., VI. 39.

May 10. Memorial respecting the apprehension of Trew, Wilson, and other incorrigible deer-stealers. L. J., VI. 39.

Annexed :—

1. Affidavit of Thomas Shemonds, keeper of one of the walks of the Great Park of Windsor, that he and his man took Richard Wilson in the act of shooting a deer there, and that Wilson and Hercules Trew were in the park on May-day with dogs in pursuit of deer. 4 May 1643.

May 10. Petition of William Wombwell and Roger Melley (doorkeepers); have constantly waited upon their Lordships, and discharged their duties with care, yet Wombwell is assessed weekly at 10s., Melley at 4s. 6d., from which assessment they pray to be exempted. L. J., VI. 39.

May 10. Draft order to redress the abuses in taking horses for supply of the army. L. J., VI. 39. *In extenso.*

May 10. Draft order for seizing the effects of Francis Mosley and Nicholas Mosley, his son, for opposing the Parliament. L. J., VI. 40. *In extenso.*

May 10. Draft order for Colonel Mauleverer to raise a troop of horse in the North. L. J., VI. 40. *In extenso.*

May 10. Draft order for the Commissioners named in the Bill of 400,000l. for Suffolk to be the Committee for raising money in that county. L. J., VI. 41. *In extenso.*

May 10. Draft order for the assessment of the Clink, the Bankside, and St. Mary Magdalen's, Bermondsey, as part of the borough of Southwark. L. J., VI., 41. *In extenso.*

May 10. Draft order for Arthur Squibb, the younger, to be clerk of the Pells in the absence of Sir Edward and Mr. Edward Wardour. L. J., VI. 41. *In extenso.*

May 10. Draft order for payment of 1,000l., with interest, to Samuel Gardiner, Mayor of Evesham, for monies lent and expended by him. L. J., VI. 41. *In extenso.*

May 10. Draft order for Sir Wm. Springate, and others to be added to the Committee for seizing and sequestering the estates of papists and delinquents in Kent. L. J., VI. 41. *In extenso.*

May 11. Petition of Anne Bickley, daughter of Humphrey Bell, of London, silkman, and wife of John Bickley, of the same city, draper; her husband was a man of fair estate and good trade when she married him, and had with her about 1,200l. portion, and further induced her father and friends to become surety for him; he afterwards became idle in his business, and began to consume his estate in vain courses, leaving petitioner and her children in great want; and now in order to avoid providing for them he gives out that he is heavily indebted, and has procured a commission of bankruptcy to be taken out against him; petitioner who can get no relief by suit without great expense of time and money, prays that some able merchants may be authorised to examine her husband's estate, and to make provision thereout for herself and her children. L. J., VI. 42.
Annexed :—
1. Names of those to whom petitioner implores her case may be referred.

May 11. Copy of order for the persons apprehended for committing riot, and cutting down woods about Mere, Shaftesbury, and Frome-Selwood, Dorsetshire, to be brought up by the gentleman usher or his deputy. L. J., VI. 42.
Annexed :—
1. Copy of order for protection of the lands of Lord Bruce parcel of Gillingham forest, Dorsetshire, now disafforested. 24 April 1643. L. J., VI. 15.

May 11. Petition of Dr. Some; he cannot make any true valuation of the vicarage of Staines on account of the destruction lately caused to flocks, hedges, &c. by the two armies, and the fear the inhabitants have of their return, but prays that indifferent persons may be appointed collectors of the tithes, &c. for the ensuing year with directions to pay two-thirds thereof to petitioner, and one third to the officiating curate. L. J., VI. 42.
Annexed :—
1. Copy of order for sequestration of the living of Staines. 11 April 1643. C. J., III. 40.

May 11. Draft order for sequestering the living of Fyfield, Essex, from Dr. Alexander Read, for publishing the Book of Sports, bowing to the Communion Table, &c. L. J., VI. 42.
Annexed :—
1. Names of sequestrators proposed by Dr. Read.

May 12. Petition of Joseph Hunscott; Wm. Ashton, by trade a draper, having erected a printing press in the parish of St. Giles in the Fields, an obscure place, an order was made by the House on the 21st of Oct. 1641 for its suppression; and Michael Baker, one of the gentleman usher's deputies, taking with him petitioner, Nicholas Bourne, and other stationers, in pursuance of the order, carried away the press and materials

and deposited them in Stationers' Hall; for this petitioner and the other stationers have been molested by Bourne in the King's Bench, and have notice of trial for Saturday next; petitioner prays for an order for preventing the trial and for bringing the case before the House. L. J., VI. 42.

May 12. Petition of William Jhanns, merchant, that his cause against Anthony Hooper may proceed in the Delegates Court, or otherwise be heard before their Lordships upon the proofs taken in the Admiralty Court. L. J., VI. 42.

May 12. Petition of Edward Corbett, Fellow of Merton College, in Oxford; upon the recommendation of the Earl of Essex the House required the Archbishop of Canterbury to institute petitioner to the rectory of Chartham, Kent, but the Archbishop refuses to obey this order, desiring not to be troubled any more in that business; petitioner prays that Sir Nathaniel Brent, vicar general, may be required to institute him, as has been lately done in the case of Mr. Nalton of St. Leonard's, Foster Lane. L. J., VI. 42.

May 12. Copy of the King's proclamation convening the estates of Scotland to meet on the 22d of June.

May 13. Petition of Ezekiel Johnson, clerk; petitioner was by order of their Lordships put into possession of the living of Paulerspury, and by another order the Archbishop of Canterbury was not to collate any person to any benefice without the approval of the House, in contempt of which order he collated Mr. Ingram to Paulerspury; Ingram was ordered to appear before the House, but instead repaired to Oxford in Feb. last and having obtained a writ under the Great Seal, de vi laicâ amovendâ, has by colour thereof turned petitioner out of his living, sold his corn, &c., and forbidden the parishioners to pay tithes to him; petitioner prays for protection and redress. L. J., VI. 44.
Annexed :—
1. Affidavit of Charles Seller and John Stockle of service of their Lordships' order of the 1st July 1642, on Peter Ingram. 7 July 1642.
2. Affidavit of John Stockle of service of the same order on Sir Nathaniel Brent, and Sackville Wade. 8 July 1642.

May 13. Resolutions of the Commons concerning the army; reported from a conference this day. L. J., VI. 44. *In extenso.*

May 13. Draft answer of Parliament to the papers of the Scottish Commissioners touching the payment of their army in Ireland. L. J., VI. 45. *In extenso.*

May 13. Draft order for bringing masts from Kinsale to England. L. J., VI. 46. *In extenso.*

May 13. Petition of Sir Thomas Cary; prays for an order to prevent any further delay in the cause now in Chancery in Ireland between petitioner and the Bishop of Ardagh, and also for license to go into Ireland, and on the way to go to Oxford to solicit from his Majesty a grant of the office lately fallen vacant by the death of the Lord Viscount Ely.
Annexed :—
1. Report of the judges in the case. 3 May 1643. *See L. J., V. 692.*

May 13. Petition of John Bishop of Ardagh; has been long vexed by complaints and suits both before the House and in Chancery in Ireland, at the instance of Sir Thomas Cary, about certain lands and tithes now in the hands of the rebels, and those of near kin to Lady Cary, who is a papist and whose brother Captain Foxe is a chief commander among the rebels; petitioner who refers to the report of the referees to show the injustice of Sir Thomas's claim, prays that the case may be dismissed with costs until the courts and course of justice are open in Ireland, and he able to procure the necessary writings and witnesses.

May 15. Portion of the draft of the declaration of the Lords and Commons concerning the negotiations for a treaty carried on at Oxford in the months of March and April of this year. This declaration was agreed to by the Lords this day and ordered to be published. L. J., VI. 46. It is given *in extenso* in Husband's Collection, page 91. The first fourteen pages of the draft are wanting.

May 15. Draft ordinance for raising money in the county of Devon; by ordinance of 17 Jan. 1642-3 certain persons were empowered to assess those who had not contributed at all, or not according to their ability to the support of the army, but many ill-affected persons so assessed have conveyed away their goods or remain in prison to avoid payment, therefore the ordinance gives power to the assessors to let the lands, &c. of any such person for any term till the assessment and all expenses be raised, and protects tenants paying their rents to the assessors from their landlords. This ordinance was sent up from the Commons on the 18th, and referred by the Lords to a Committee, but nothing farther appears to have been done. L. J., VI. 51.

May 16. Draft order for the protection of James, Earl of Carlisle against riotous persons, who have destroyed certain ancient locks, mills, &c. on the River Lea, in the parishes of Waltham-Holy-Cross, Essex, and Cheshunt, Herts. L. J., VI. 47.

May 16. Petition of Thomas Killegrew; was committed by the Earl of Essex to the King's Bench on the 30th of Sept. last, on suspicion of raising arms against the Parliament, since which time Robert Punter and Michael Anderson have brought actions against him, one for 100l., the other for 30l., and are now ready to charge him in execution; petitioner prays that they may be ordered to stay their prosecutions, as he is committed by order of the Lord General. L. J., VI. 47.

May 16. Draft order sequestering the living of Southweald, Essex, from Dr. Samuel Baker, a double beneficed man, who does not believe the Pope to be Antichrist, licenses popish books in favour of auricular confession, bows before the Communion table, &c. L. J., VI. 47.

May 16. Draft order for sequestering the living of St. Mary, Bermondsey, from Dr. Paske, who has two benefices with cure, besides the mastership of ClareHall, the Archdeaconry of London, a prebend at York, and a prebend at Canterbury, altogether not resident at St. Mary's, Bermondsey, and a teacher of heretical doctrines, and who has thereby forced the parishioners to maintain a minister at their own charge. L. J., VI. 47.
Annexed:—
 1. Informations against Dr. Paske with his answers thereto.

May 16. Petition of Thomas Alse and John Palmer; petitioners are poor husbandmen, who have been five times fetched up from their farms in Sussex by the malicious prosecution of Lyming Dickenson, and then dismissed without any charge being brought against them; they pray that Dickenson may be ordered to pay their charges, and be further punished for his malignant opposition to the successes of Parliament. L. J., VI. 48.
Annexed:—
 1. Affidavit of John Palmer of Beddingham, Sussex; that Lyming Dickenson, clerk of His Majesty's stables, assisted the Commissioners of Array in the county, jeered deponent for lending 5l. for the service of Parliament, and caused him to be higher rated to the parish in consequence, and always repined at any success of Parliament. 14 May.
 2. Affidavit of Thomas Gratwick of Lewes, that Dickenson acted as an intelligencer between Mr. Ford, the pretended high sheriff of the county, and the malignants at Chichester and Oxford. 15 May.

May 16. Order for hearing the matter of the sequestration of the living of Stisted, Essex. L. J., VI. 48.

May 16. Draft order for protection of Dr. Cheshire during his removal from the living of Heston, Middlesex, to that of Dauntsey, Wilts. L. J., VI. 48.

May 16. Motion for protection of certain lands of the Earl of Suffolk at Haddenham in the Isle of Ely. L. J., VI. 48.
Annexed:—
 1. Copy of a previous motion in the same matter. 10 March 1641-2. L. J., IV. 640.

May 16. Petition of Alexander Read, parson of Fyfield, Essex; Robert Ashwell and others, farmers of his tithes, have for nearly two years past detained the tithes from him, and having been made assessors for Parliament have assessed him for the tithes which they withheld, and have thereby reduced him to the greatest poverty; prays for payment of his tithes and redress in other things. L. J., VI. 48.

May 16. Letter from the Committee at Aylesbury to Colonel Hampden, or in his absence to Colonel Goodwin or Bulstrode Whitlock, about the ravages committed by the King's forces. L. J., VI. 52. In extenso.

May 17. Petition of Alexander Read, parson of Fyfield, Essex; if now turned out of his house, his wife and children must lie in the streets, as no other house can be hired at this time of year in Fyfield; prays that those who are so desirous for a new minister may find him a furnished chamber for which he is ready to pay,

and that indifferent persons may be appointed to apportion the profits of the living, which all come in in this half year, between petitioner and the minister who is to succeed him. L. J., VI. 49.

May 17. The Committee's report of His Majesty's answer to both their papers delivered unto him at Oxford, concerning the Commissioners for conservation of peace sent from Scotland. L. J., VI. 49. In extenso.

May 17. Instructions for Mr. Michael Welden, sent from both Houses of Parliament to the Lords of the Secret Council, and the Commissioners for peace in Scotland. L. J., VI. 49. In extenso.

May 17. Draft of the order authorizing Mr. Michael Welden to go to Scotland, and of the order for sending to the Secret Council a copy of the letter from divers Scotch Earls intercepted by Lord Fairfax. L. J., VI. 49. In extenso.

May 17. Certificate of Sir Nathaniel Brent in the case between Ezekiel Johnson and Peter Ingram concerning the living of Paulerspury, that Ingram's collation was unduly obtained. L. J., VI. 49. In extenso.

May 17. Petition of Thomas Talcott; praying for a hearing of the case between him, Giles Johnson, Marshal, and others. L. J., VI. 50.

May 17. Petition of John Doughty, defendant in a writ of error brought by Thomas Overman and John Hardwicke, soap-patentees; that the plaintiffs may have no benefit of certain records which have been improperly certified. L. J., VI. 50.
Annexed:—
 1. Copy of order in the cause. 8 March 1642-3. L. J., V. 642. In extenso.

May 17. Ordinance for sequestering the jurisdiction of the Archbishop of Canterbury. L. J., VI. 50. In extenso.

May 17. Copy of preceding.

May 17. Petition of Henry and Micah French; John French late minister of Stradishwell [Stradishall], and uncle of petitioners, often promised to leave his estate to them, but at his death his widow, now wife of Richard Sadler published a will giving the whole estate to herself and her kindred, this will petitioners suppose to be forged; pray that she may be ordered to produce it before their Lordships as proceedings in courts of justice are so sore closed by the distractions of these times, that petitioners cannot bring their cause to trial in the ordinary courts. Noted, Read, nothing concluded.

May 18. Copy of a declaration made at Oxford, May 8, by Dr. Merrick, judge of the Prerogative Court, cancelling all acts done after the 10th instant by any man, who was before that his substitute. L. J., VI. 52. In extenso.

May 18. Petition of Ashton Nuttall, defendant in a writ of error at the suit of Gisbrough and others; prays that Gisbrough may be non-suited for not assigning errors within the time appointed by order of the House. See L. J., VI. 51.
Annexed:—
 1. Copy of order for assignment of errors. 11 March 1642-3. L. J., V. 645.
 2. Another petition of Nuttall to the same effect. (Undated.)
 3. Affidavit of Wm. Livesey. 1 Aug. 1642.

May 18. Petition of Cornelius Lord Maguire, Colonel Read, and Hugh Macmahowne. About eleven months since they were brought over as prisoners from Dublin and committed to the Tower, where they were kept close prisoners, but provided with all things necessary by their Lordships' order, they have now been removed to the noisome prison of Newgate, and there kept close prisoners, where they are without maintenance, and without a penny to buy themselves food; pray for an allowance fit for their qualities and for permission for a servant to attend them. L. J., VI. 51.
Annexed:—
 1. Petition of Hugh Mac Mahowne, close prisoner in the Tower. Prays that he may be brought to a speedy trial. (Undated.)
 2. Copy of order for the removal of Lord Maguire and the other petitioners from the Tower to Newgate. 3 May 1643. L. J., VI. 29.

May 18. Draft of letter of credence for Mr. Michael Welden, messenger from Parliament to the Council of Scotland. L. J., VI. 52. In extenso.

May 18. Draft order for the protection of the estate of the Earl of St. Alban's and Clanricard, a papist, from sequestration. L. J., VI. 53. In extenso.

May 18. Draft order for adding Sir Edward Patricke and others to the committees for the weekly assessment for Kent. L. J., VI. 53. *In extenso.*

May 18. Draft order appointing Sir John Chapman and others, a Committee for sequestrating the estates of delinquents in Sussex. L. J., VI. 53. *In extenso.*

May 18. Draft order for adding Sir Wm. Goreing and others to the Committee for the weekly assessments, &c. in Sussex, L. J., VI. 53. *In extenso.*

May 18. Draft ordinance for raising money for payment of the forces raised out of Essex, Suffolk, &c. L. J., VI. 53. *In extenso.*

May 19. Petition of Hugh Henn, praying for a pass to go to Oxford to serve his place as a page of the bedchamber to His Majesty. L. J., VI. 53.

May 19. Application for a pass for William Adams to go to the Spa with his wife and children. L. J., VI. 54.

May 19. Affidavit of Thomas Holden, clerk, and others, that Oliver Moakes had scoffed at an order of their Lordships directing that Mr. Holden should receive 20l. from the parson of St. Cuthbert's, Bedford, for officiating there, and that Mr. Thorne the parson had refused to pay the same. L. J., VI. 54.

Annexed :—
1. Petition of the parish of St. Cuthbert's, that the churchwardens may from time to time take up so much of the tithes as will satisfy the 20l. to Mr. Holden.

May 20. Petition of Richard Baker, collier; has for many years supplied the House with charcoal, and consequently obtained on the 6th instant an order for the protection of his carts and team of horses, but in contempt of this, on Thursday last, when petitioner was bringing coals from Chislehurst, two of his best horses were seized by Colonel Malleverer and Henry Garry; prays that the horses may be restored to him, and that those who have disobeyed their Lordships' order may be called upon to answer for their contempt. L. J., VI. 54.

Annexed :—
1. Copy of order of the 6th instant referred to in preceding. L. J., VI. 34.

May 20. Petition of Robert Barrell, curate and stipendiary of the Church of Maidstone, in Kent; prays that Mr. Byerley, of Gray's Inn, and Mr. Glover, of Lincoln's Inn, may be assigned him as counsel for his defence against the charges brought against him by the House of Commons. L. J., VI. 54.

May 20. Petition of Edward Corbett, fellow of Merton College in Oxford, praying for a nomination to the living of Charthain, Kent. L. J., VI. 54. *In extenso.*

May 20. Votes of the Commons concerning the making of a new Great Seal, reported to the Lords this day. L. J., VI. 55. *In extenso.*

[May 20.] Names of the peers appointed Commissioners of England to treat with Commissioners of Scotland about the peace of both kingdoms. L. J., VI. 55.

May 20. Draft order to the wardens of the Goldsmith's Company to make trial of the money in the pix in the Mint. L. J., VI. 56. *In extenso.*

May 20. Draft order for a thousand of the trained bands of Devon to repair to Exeter for defence of the city. L. J., VI. 56. *In extenso.*

May 20. Paper from the Scots respecting the extremities of their army in Ireland, desiring that provision may be made by Parliament for their subsistence, or that if no longer required due notice for their recall may be given. L. J., VI. 59. *In extenso.*

May 22. Copy of the King's message desiring an answer to his last message concerning an accommodation of differences. L. J., VI. 57. *In extenso.*

May 22. Letter from the Earl of Essex, at Reading, to the Earl of Manchester, Speaker of the House of Peers, *pro tempore;* encloses a copy of the desire of the Committee for the associated counties of Essex, Hertford, &c., that provision may be made for the payment of the forces sent from those counties, which he desires may receive a speedy despatch. This desire had been anticipated by the order of the 18th instant. *Vide supra.*

[May 22.] Petition of William Catherins, clerk to Edward Pitt, Esq., one of the tellers of His Majesty's receipt of Exchequer, to H. C.; several parcels of plate were committed to petitioner's custody by Mr. Pitt and others, but by an order of the House this plate (being in one trunk, two hampers, and a little red leather box), has been carried to Guildhall, and kept there; petitioner prays that the plate may be re-delivered to him, that he may be able to discharge the trust of an honest man. *See C. J., III. 96.*

May 23. Warrant for committing to the Fleet Ludovic Weames, Dr. in Divinity, Rector of Lambourne, Essex. L. J., VI. 58.

Annexed :—
1. Draft order of the Commons for sequestration of the living of Lambourne. 22 April 1643. C. J., III. 56.
2. Petition of Jane Wemys, wife of Dr. Wemys; prays that she may not be thrust out of doors, but may have the benefit of the parsonage house and two small closes till Michaelmas next. (Undated.)

May 23. Note that the Earl of Mulgrave moves for the living of Cranborne [Cranbrook], Kent, on behalf of his chaplain, Robert Cassinhurst. L. J., VI. 59.

May 23. Petition of Christopher Newsted, B.D.; petitioner, in recompense for long service abroad with Sir Thomas Rowe, was presented by His Majesty to the living of Stisted, Essex, but the parishioners threaten him with personal violence if he should attempt to come into the church or officiate there; they have detained all his means from him, and by misinformation have obtained an order from the Commons for the sequestration of the living; prays that he may not be put out of his living without a hearing. L. J., VI. 59.

Annexed :—
1. Copy of order for sequestration of the living of Stisted, Essex, and appointment of Edward Sparrowhawk thereto. 18 April 1643. C. J., III. 49.

May 23. Draft order for sequestration of the living of St. Botolph's without Bishopsgate. L. J., VI. 59.

May 23. Petition of the dean, prebendaries, petty canons, and clerks, and other the members and ministers of His Majesty's free chapel within the Castle of Windsor; as it has not seemed fit to Parliament that petitioners should remain in their present dwellinghouses within the castle, they pray that they may have an order for the removal and protection of their goods, utensils, and household stuff. L. J., VI. 59.

May 23. Petition of Mary Underwood, widow; prays for redress against Robert, the son, Wm. Underwood, the nephew, and Toby Maydwell, the son-in-law of her late husband, who have interfered with her in the administration of his estate, and thereby not only deprived her of the portion to which she was entitled, but exhausted all her means in legal proceedings. L. J., VI. 59.

May 23. Letter from Lord Fairfax at Leeds to Wm. Lenthall, Speaker of the House of Commons, about the taking of Wakefield. L. J., VI. 66. *In extenso.*

Enclosing :—
1. Letter from Lord Goring to his son, with directions as to the prosecution of the war. 17 May 1643. L. J., VI. 67. *In extenso.*

May 24. Information of John Minsterley and others, that Henry Toomes, speaking of the Lords of Parliament, called them roundheaded rogues and traitors. L. J., VI. 60.

March 24. Petition of Thomas Moyser and others. On the 11th of March last, it was ordered that all proceedings on the writ of error between petitioners and Ashton Nuttall should cease until the first day of Easter term following. Since then petitioner Moyser has done all he could to obtain his evidences, but now hears that his houses, goods, and writings have been burnt; petitioners pray that all proceedings upon the writ of error may be stayed until the times are quiet. L. J., VI. 60.

Annexed :—
1. Affidavit of Thomas Moyser; has endeavoured in vain to send to Yorkshire to get his writings, but is now informed that two of his mansion-houses are plundered, his rents seized on or stopped, nine tenements, together with stables and barns, burnt down, and two libraries, with all his books and writings, taken away. 23 May.
2. Order of 11 March, 1642-3, mentioned in petition. L. J., V. 645.

May 24. Affidavit of Richard Axtell and another, that Joseph Soane, late vicar of Aldendam, Herts, had interrupted Mr. Gilpin, appointed preacher there by Parliament, in the performance of his duties, and raised a disturbance in the churchyard. L. J., VI. 60. *In extenso.*

Annexed :—
1. Further information on the same subject.

May 24. Draft order for Colonel Walter Long to receive the sums unpaid under the ordinance for raising money in Essex, Hertford, and Bedford. L. J., VI. 61. *In extenso.*

May 25. Petition of Edward Hudson, clerk; their Lordships made several orders for the Archbishop of Canterbury to collate petitioner to the rectory of Chartham, Kent, in compensation for losses sustained at the hands of the Archbishop, on account of petitioner's affection towards the Parliament, but afterwards their Lordships being desirous of bestowing the said living on Mr. Corbett, petitioner freely submitted thereto, whereby his wrongs remain unredressed; the Archdeacon of Canterbury, the first author of petitioner's oppressions, in not inducting him to the rectory of Eythorn, Kent, is still alive, and well able to make satisfaction to petitioner, who prays that the archdeacon and his inferior officers may be called upon to answer, and that petitioner may receive satisfaction. The first part of this petition, relating to Mr. Corbett, is omitted in the Journal, the rest is given *in extenso*. L. J., VI. 62.

Annexed:—
1. Articles against Dr. Kingsley, Archdeacon of Canterbury, which petitioner desires may be added to his petition. As parson of Ickham he preached the poisonous doctrine. 1. That the laity ought not to search the scriptures. 2. That it was a question whether the Church of England was a true church. 3. That the Parliament sit for nothing but to undo the kingdom.

May 25. Draft order that the Earl of Chesterfield, now a prisoner, shall not be released or exchanged till he make satisfaction to Edward Johnson for goods of his taken from Hughes, a carrier. L. J., VI. 63. *In extenso.*

May 25. Draft answer to the paper from the Scots concerning the maintenance of their army in Ireland. L. J., VI. 63. *In extenso.*

May 25. Another draft.

May 26. Draft order for raising money for the army of Sir William Waller. C. J., III. 103. *In extenso.*

May 26. Draft order for the association of the county of Huntingdon with the counties of Cambridge, Hertford, &c., instead of with Leicester, &c. L. J., VI. 63. *In extenso.*

May 26. Draft order of the Commons for disposing of Mr. May's money. C. J., III. 58. *In extenso.* Endorsed, Not agreed to. L. J., VI. 64.

May 26. Notes respecting a conference about the restraining of prisoners on parole, the examination of Lord Wilmot, &c. L. J., VI. 64.

Annexed:—
1. Another paper of notes of proceedings on various days.

May 26. Draft ordinance for 10,000l. yearly to be paid to the Lord General, the Earl of Essex, out of the estates of delinquents. L. J., VI. 64. *In extenso.*

May 26. Draft order of the Commons for the imprisonment and examination of Lord Wilmot. C. J., III. 104. *In extenso.*

May 27. Petition of Captain John Hardwick and Thomas Overman; pray that some further time may be appointed for arguing the writ of error between them and John Doughty. *See* L. J., VI. 66.

Annexed:—
1. Petition of Thomas Overman and other soapmakers of London; petitioners, who had been brought up in the trade of soap-making, were in 1633 prosecuted in Star Chamber by certain knights and gentlemen, then lately incorporated as the Soapers of Westminster, severely fined, and sentenced never to use their trade any more, a prohibition extended to their journeymen and apprentices; petitioners endured twenty months' imprisonment, and were for five years kept out of their trade; upon review of these things the Commons passed the annexed votes upon the subject, but in consequence of the importance of other affairs nothing further has been done; petitioners confess that, in consequence of their sufferings, when they saw that the Soapers of Westminster made no white soap, they accepted a patent for making it, and undertook to pay 8l. per ton to the King, which came to almost a penny a pound, and to support this payment petitioners were obliged to take steps to prevent any from practising the trade who had not served to it, this they have since learnt to have been unjustifiable, and humbly desire that their offence therein may be remitted; under colour of this many persons, who never served to the trade, but were chandlers, barbers, coopers, and the like, have brought actions against petitioners for interrupting them therein, and many of them have obtained verdicts for amounts which petitioners cannot satisfy; they pray that as they cannot yet obtain any compensation from the gentlemen soapers, and are willing to satisfy all just claims as far as they can, the matter may be taken into the consideration of the House, as no other court of equity is now open, and that proceedings at law may be stayed.

2. Copy of resolutions of the Commons upon the soap business. 17 Aug. 1641. C. J., II. 260. *In extenso.*

May 29. Application of the creditors of Sir Thos. Dawes for attendance of Sir Paul Pinder and others at the hearing of their case.

May 30. Petition of John Brisco and others, inhabitants of Aldenham, Herts; petitioners have been attached by order of the House, and remain in custody, to their great cost and prejudice, and cannot learn the charge against them, nor, on account of the great affairs of the kingdom, obtain a hearing or discharge; pray for a present hearing, or that they may be discharged upon bail. L. J., VI. 70.

May 30. Draft declaration of the Lords and Commons against the adjournment of the term to Oxford. L. J., VI. 70. *In extenso.*

May 30. Draft ordinance for the assessment of all such persons as have not contributed proportionably according to the ordinance of the 20th part, within the city of London and twenty miles compass. L. J., VI. 71. *In extenso.*

May 30. Printed copy of preceding.

May 30. Draft order for Sir Gilbert Gerrard, treasurer at wars, to repay to the Commissioners of Customs, all moneys advanced by them to Sir John Hotham and others, upon bills of exchange. L. J., VI. 71. *In extenso.*

May 30. Draft order for appointment of Commissioners to search for goods and merchandize prohibited by law. L. J., VI. 71. *In extenso.*

May 30. Draft declaration and ordinance for the better securing and settling of the peace of the county of Kent. L. J., VI. 72. *In extenso.*

[May.] Application by the Countess of Dorset for a pass for Mr. Belsam, Robert Bickerton, and Richard Fulger, to go to Oxford with a coach and four horses, they being willing to be searched before they go.

June 1. Petition of Dorothie Brograve, widow; complains that administration of the estate of her late brother, Thomas Leventhorpe, has been granted to persons only distantly of kin to him, by Dr. Merrick, Judge of the Prerogative Court, to the injury of petitioner, who cannot on account of the distractions of the times prosecute an appeal with effect, and therefore prays for redress from the House. L. J., VI. 75.

Annexed:—
1. Petition of Edward Leventhorpe that the case may be left to the law. (Undated.)

June 1. Draft ordinance appointing additional committees for raising money for the maintenance of the army. L. J., VI. 76. *In extenso.*

June 2. Draft order for sequestration of the living of Maidstone, Kent, from Robert Barrell, curate and stipendiary, to Thomas Smyth. L. J., VI. 77.

Annexed:—
1. Affidavit of Jane Ellis, widow, that Mr. Robert Barrell said he wished that God would put it into the heart of the King to set the City of London on fire, and burn up the Puritans; and affidavit of Winifred Aymes, widow, repeats Ellis' statement, and says that Barrell said Parliament sat for their own ends, and that she has seen him drunk.

June 2. Message from the Commons with an ordinance revoking the ordinance authorising Colonel Long to raise money in Essex, and also for appointment of additional sequestrators in the county. L. J., VI. 77, 78.

June 2. Information against Sir Arthur Jenney and others for arresting Captain Martin contrary to privilege. L. J., VI. 78.

June 2. Information against Mrs. Wibrow, that she refuses to give up the possession of the parsonage house of Pedmarsh [Pebmarsh], Essex, pursuant to the order of sequestration. L. J., VI. 78.

June 2. Petition of the inhabitants of the city of Coventry and county of Warwick, to the Lords and Commons, praying for the appointment of some man of

honour and moderation to command them, who are now
dismayed by the sad and dangerous condition of the
country, and are like sheep without a shepherd. L. J.,
VI. 78.

June 2. Petition of John Grimston, Richard Staynes,
and Thomas Graves, poor distressed prisoners in Newgate; petitioners were committed to Newgate in Feb.
last for the fact expressed in the annexed mittimus,
they are truly penitent, and so miserable is their condition that they cannot long continue in life unless the
enlargement for which they pray be granted. L. J.,
VI. 78.

Annexed:—
1. Copy of mittimus from Sir Henry Wollaston,
Keeper of Newgate, that the prisoners were
committed by order of the House for killing the
King's deer in Waltham forest. 28 Feb. 1642-3.

June 3. Statement of the case of Johnson and others,
plaintiffs in a cause against Robert Talcott. See L. J.,
VI. 79.

Annexed:—
1. Statement of the case on behalf of Talcott.
2. Petition of Giles Johnson, Thomas Marshall,
and others; the question in dispute between
petitioners and Robert Talcott relates to the title
to a house, &c., at Colchester, worth 2,000l.,
which Talcott got from those who had no right
in it for 235l.; the cause has been thirty times
appointed for hearing, when petitioners have
attended with counsel, but Talcott has, unknown
to them, obtained an order for them to show cause
why the case should not be dismissed to the
common law or equity; petitioners can make no
title at law, but conceive they can in equity, but
complain of an order in Chancery, which that
court will not redress, so that the petitioners can
have no relief but from the House, from an injustice which has continued forty years; they
pray that a speedy day may be appointed for
hearing the cause. 24 Dec. 1642.

June 3. Affidavit of Elizabeth Parker, wife of Henry
Parker, of Limehouse, chandler, that Edmund Beanstone
said that if he had 500l. worth of plate he would not
carry in one penny worth for the Parliament's use, for
they know that for what they have done they shall lose
their heads. L. J., VI. 80.

June 3. Draft order for repayment of 5,000l. to Sir
Thomas Middleton, advanced by him for raising forces
in Wales. L. J., VI. 80. In extenso.

June 3. Petition of John Feriby, clerk; petitioner
was indicted at the Oxford Assizes last summer, and
bound to appear to answer the indictment at Oxford,
but not daring so to do on account of the forces lying
there and the threatening speeches against him, he sued
out two writs of certiorari to remove the indictment to
the King's Bench, but Mr. Justice Heath refused
to allow the certiorari, and sent forth a special writ to
attach petitioner, and hath privately sent for a pro-
cedendo in the cause; prays for an order to prohibit these
proceedings. See L. J., VI. 70.

June 3. Notes of proceedings this day.
June 5. Notes respecting the amendments made by
the Lords in the order concerning gunpowder, to which
the Commons disagree. L. J., VI. 81.

Annexed:—
1. Amendments and proviso.
June 5. Draft ordinance for raising 100l. weekly for
maintenance of the guards at Southwark. L. J., VI.
81. In extenso.

June 5. Petition of Giles Johnson and others; their
cause after a partial hearing on Saturday last was dismissed; they pray that a further and fuller hearing may
be granted before any final order be entered against
them. Noted, Read, debated, and rejected. L. J.,
VI. 82.

June 5. Propositions to adventurers for the reduction
of Newcastle, that London may be supplied with coals
from thence. L. J., VI. 82. In extenso.

June 6. Amendments to the ordinance for calling an
assembly of divines. L. J., VI. 84. In extenso.

June 6. Petition of Anthony Weldon; has long
attended in hope of employment, but seeing that there
is no want of officers, he prays for a pass to go beyond
seas to seek his fortune there. L. J., VI. 84.

June 6. Petition of Thomas Fayrye, Arthur Turner,
and Richard Clarke, for themselves and others, wood-
mongers and carmen of London; upon a former petition

5.

their Lordships referred their complaints, by an order
dated 16 June 1641, to Mr. Alderman Garraway and
Sir Thomas Gardiner, then recorder, both since deceased,
and others; nothing, however, has been done, and petitioners pray that the matter may be referred to Mr.
Serjeant Pheasant, now recorder, Sir John Geere, and
others. L. J., VI. 84.

Annexed:—
1. Order of 16 June 1641.

June 7. Petition of Blanche Lady Arundell, widow;
about five weeks since Sir Edward Hungerford besieged
petitioner and her family in Wardour Castle and burnt
down all the outhouses, and though she yielded the
castle, presuming that she and her children would be
provided for according to their quality, yet all the
household goods and stuff were carried away and her
husband's estate held by Sir Edward Hungerford, so
that she was left without a bed to lie on, and without
means to buy herself a house or furniture; she was
carried by Sir Edward to Hatch and then to Shaftesbury,
where she was kept till Prince Maurice and the Marquess of Hertford came to Salisbury, whither she went
in hope of finding her husband, but only to hear of his
death, she is still there in her distress in a lodging provided for her through the charity of Lord Hertford,
while every man is afraid to provide her with necessaries or to let her a house; she prays that she may be
free to get herself a house and furniture in the city or
close of Salisbury, and that herself and her goods may
be protected from violence. L. J., VI. 85.

June 7. Letter from T. N., at Dublin, to Robert Reynolds and Robert Goodwin, or either of them; recent
occurrences reported are these; the Earl of Antrim coming from England to County Down, was by a stratagem
induced by the Scotch forces to land, and was by them
made prisoner and taken to Carrickfergus Castle, while
his man, a papist, who helped his master's escape when
he was prisoner before, was tried by court-martial and
hanged; what the Earl's errand was the Scotch best
know, who obtained a full confession from his man; it
is declared also in a letter from Montrose to Colonel
Crawford, and if Montrose's account be true it is one of
the worst plots yet discovered, but the publishing of
this letter by some man, has given great offence to the
Council, and therefore the writer forbears to say more
about it. Lord Taff's business is kept very quiet, but is
supposed to be about a cessation, but nothing is likely
to be agreed upon unless the rebels contribute in good
measure to the maintenance of the army, if so, to die
without a cessation, will be as good as living on their
findings; the reason is that the army cannot subsist
without help from England; Sir Michael Ernley is still
abroad with his party, but can only get flesh, and has
to be supplied with bread from Dublin; Brent, the
lawyer, is going to England, but fears the ships lying
here will trouble him, though he holds a pass from His
Majesty, so why should he fear; if only the army could
keep the field this summer and carry off or burn the
crops, as was done partially last summer, the rebels
must starve next winter; the writer fears that he must
formerly have given some men a wrong character, but
the reason is the change in men, which is common in
England and Ireland; the letter-bark was chased at sea
last week by a Parliament ship, and not knowing what
she was the packets were thrown into the sea, so that no
certain news has been received from England since the
2nd of May; an active, wise, and religious deputy is
much wanted in Ireland; it is said that there is great
want amongst those about Kilkenny, and division too,
and that they will put Preston from his place of general,
and, if so, that he and his countrymen will offer their
services to the State here, this is hardly credible, but
"we are wonderfully charitable, and ready to believe
"what we desire to have, till the rest of our throats
"that remain yet alive be cut;" friends in Dublin long
to hear whether their letters have been received.

June 8. Notes of proceedings on this and subsequent
days.

June 9. Draft order for sequestration of the living
of Stanford-Rivers from Dr. John Meredith, who has
two livings, has not taken the protestation nor contributed to the support of the army. L. J., VI. 86.

June 9. Petition of Justinian Povey, one of the
auditors of His Majesty's Court of Exchequer; he and
his clerk have attended in London for half a year to
take the accounts of the great subsidy, at a charge to
himself of 200l., the Act of Parliament forbidding him
to take any fee or reward, and has besides paid all con-

M

tributions laid upon him; having a house at Hounslow he would gladly be there this long vacation in peace and quietness, and therefore prays for an order to secure him in going and coming, and to license him, being aged, to keep a couple of horses for himself and his man, and a horse to send for provision for his family. L. J., VI. 86.

June 9. Draft of the Covenant taken by the Lords this day. L. J., VI. 86. *In extenso.*

June 9. Amended draft of the Covenant to be taken by the whole kingdom. L. J., VI. 87. *In extenso.*

June 10. Petition of Ralph Macro and Anne Franckton. Pray that the 30l. deposited by petitioner, Macro, with the warden of the Fleet, in compliance with their Lordships' order made upon petition of Anne Franckton, may be delivered to them, they having agreed between themselves concerning the disposal of it. L. J., VI. 88.
Annexed:—
1. Copy of order referred to in preceding. 5 Feb. 1640-1.
2. Request of Ann Franckton to Mr. Throckmorton to deliver the order to Macro to receive the money from the warden of the Fleet.

June 10. Notes of proceedings in the case between the Earls of Bedford and Portland, and the inhabitants of Whittlesey, &c. L. J., VI. 88.

June 10. Draft ordinance reciting that a number of armed men calling themselves the King's forces, under the command of the Earls of Cleveland and Carnarvon, invaded the county of Bucks and robbed and pillaged there, and in particular burnt the village of Swanbourne, and murdered a poor woman there, and seeming to take delight in the desolation they caused, set guards to prevent anyone from attempting to quench the flames; in consideration of which the ordinance requires the Committees of Parliament in Northamptonshire and Buckinghamshire, to permit the persons, whose houses have been burnt, to cut and carry away timber from the forest of Whittlewood, from Lord Carnarvon's woods, and from those of any delinquents in the county of Buckingham for the purpose of rebuilding their homes. This ordinance was sent up by the Commons to the Lords, and by them read and respited: L. J., VI. 88.

June 10. Letter from the Lords Justices of Ireland, at Dublin Castle, to the Speaker of the House of Commons; having tried all means for providing subsistence for the army have been forced to try another way, as will be seen by the enclosed Act of Council, but they have only Dublin to work upon, and deprecate the idea that it will remove the necessity of sending supplies from England, of which they are in extreme need; one thing they cannot omit, namely, that the Protestant party has in these straights been forward to contribute towards the preservation of the kingdom, while all the opposition is from the Popish party. Postscript.—None of the ships intended to guard the Irish coasts attend to the harbour here, and the passage between this and England, but ships are daily chased by pirates, even at the mouth of the harbour, while the ships intended to guard the coast so interfere with those that would bring provisions, that all men are discouraged from adventuring, and the army is ready to starve. Under this is a note, but crossed out, " They do not observe how the ships in the King's ser- " vice take away the victual sent by [Parl.]." Endorsed, " Letter from yᵉ Lo; Justices of yᵉ 10th of June, but " not a word of Mountrose letter." L. J., VI. 119.
Annexed:—
1. Copy of an Act of the Council of Ireland: after reciting the extreme necessities to which the army is reduced, occasioned by the failure of the Houses of Parliament, who undertook the charge of the war, the ruin already caused by the heavy burdens incurred, and the justification of extraordinary measures in such cases, they proceed to impose a rate upon such commodities as they shall appoint, to be paid to the treasurer at wars for relief and maintenance of the army for the six months next ensuing, unless it be otherwise supplied in the meantime. 6 June 1643.

June 12. Draft ordinance for the association of Denbigh, Montgomery, and other counties in Wales, and for appointment of Sir Thomas Middleton as serjeant-major-general of all the forces to be raised in those counties. L. J., VI. 90. *In extenso.*

June 12. Draft ordinance for the appointment of Basil Earl of Denbigh, commander-in-chief in the associated counties of Warwick, Worcester, &c. and Lord

Lieutenant of the county of Warwick, in the room of Robert, late Lord Brooke. L. J., VI. 92. *In extenso.*

June 12. Ordinance for the calling of an assembly of learned and godly divines, and others, to be consulted with by the Parliament for the settling of the government and liturgy of the Church of England, and for vindicating and clearing of the doctrine of the said church from false aspersions and interpretations. L. J., VI. 92. *In extenso,* with the exception of the proviso at the end giving to substitutes appointed to supply the places of members who should happen to die the same powers as those members, and also strictly limiting the assembly to the exercise of the powers, &c. contained in the ordinance. (Parchment collection.)
Annexed:—
1. Printed copy of preceding.
2. Draft summons for persons nominated to attend the assembly. L. J., VI. 90.

June 13. Petition of the merchant strangers of the Entercourse, that they may be freed from the tax of the 20th part, and from the weekly assessments. L. J., VI. 94. *In extenso.*
Annexed:—
1. Copy of order of the Commons for the exemption of the merchants of the Entercourse. 5 April 1642. C. J., II. 512.
2. Copy of an order continuing preceding. 5 Jan. 1642-3. C. J., II. 915.

June 13. Petition of the Earl of Bridgwater; complains that soldiers under Captain Washington and others entered his park and house at Ashridge on Saturday last, beat down the ceilings, hewed down doors, though open to them, searched his evidence rooms and studies, took away plate, arms, and household stuff, killed not only male deers, but does ready to fawn, and fawns that could hardly stand, and turned the game as much as possible over the country; he forbears to mention losses formerly sustained by the taking away of forty-four valuable horses, but prays for reparation for these and protection from future losses. L. J., VI. 94.

June 13. Petition of Joseph Sone, clerk, prisoner in the Fleet; is heartily sorry for having contemned the ordinance for sequestration of his living; he prays for release and for permission to live in his vicarage where he has many things that cannot be removed without great loss, and crops growing which cannot be sold until they are housed, while his wife, child, and aged mother are dependent upon him. L. J., VI. 94.
Annexed:—
1. Similar petition of same. (Undated.)
2. Another petition. (Undated.)

June 13. Petition of William Jhanns, merchant; in compliance with the prayer of a former petition their Lordships began the hearing of the cause between petitioner and Anthony Hooper and others, but were interrupted by greater affairs; prays for a further hearing, or that the case may be left to the Delegates to decide. L. J., VI. 95.
Annexed:—
1. Copy of petition mentioned in preceding.

June 14. Judgment in the cause between Latch and Vernatti. L. J., VI. 95.
Annexed:—
1. Duplicate of preceding.
2. Certificate of the auditors.
3. Submission of Sir Thomas Dawes to the judgment.
4. Notes of the judgment.

June 14. Two printed copies of the ordinance for the regulating of printing, and for suppressing the great late abuses and frequent disorders in printing many false, scandalous, seditious, libellous, and unlicensed pamphlets, to the great defamation of religion and government, also authorising the masters and wardens of the Company of Stationers to make diligent search, seize, and carry away all such books as they shall find printed or reprinted by any man having no lawful interest in them, being entered into the Hall book to any other man as his proper copies. L. J., VI. 96. *In extenso.*

June 14. Draft of preceding.
Annexed:—
1. Explanation of same; that acts done in pursuance thereof by one of the persons authorised to carry it into effect shall be as good and effectual as if all the persons so authorised had joined together.

June 17. Petition of Elizabeth Countess of Exeter on the behalf of her son, the now Earl of Exeter; by virtue of an agreement made between the late Earl, her husband, and Thomas Maidwell, clerk, and others, inhabitants and commoners of Easton, Northamptonshire, the late Earl for a year and upwards before his death enclosed and held in severalty all the woods called Easton woods, with the exception of 130 acres called Bulgate Sale, Bark Sale, and part of Rogue Sale, which were to be kept in common for the use of the commoners; but of late, since the Earl's decease, divers of the commoners have broken open the inclosures in a violent manner, with threats to those that would oppose them, giving out that there is no law; petitioner prays for an order to secure her in peaceable possession, till the title to the premises can be determined at common law. L. J., VI. 97.

Annexed:—

1. Affidavit of Thomas Tampon in support of preceding.

June 16. Information that certain disorderly persons have broken into the park, chase, and woods belonging to James Earl of Suffolk, in the manor and soke of Somersham, have broken his fences and killed his deer, and that therefore an order is desired to the committees in Cambridge and Huntingdon to enquire into and repress these insolences. L. J., VI. 97.

June 16. Petition of Christopher Newsted, clerk; being rector of Stisted, Essex, and being interrupted in his possession by the inhabitants, the House, on his complaints made the annexed order for his protection, but he cannot get it executed, and therefore prays for further relief. L. J., VI. 97.

Annexed:—

1. Order referred to in preceding. 23 May 1643. L. J., VI. 59.

2. Affidavit of Christopher Newsted, that having obtained their Lordships' order he repaired to Stisted and demanded possession of the parsonage house from Thomas French, one of the churchwardens then in possession, who said he would not give it up before Michaelmas; the next day, being Sunday, he called upon the constable to help him, who refused; deponent with two friends then went to the churchyard and demanded the keys of the church from the sexton, who refused to give them up or open the door; deponent and his friends then sat down in the porch, but some women came and stoned his friends out of the porch and out of the village, and afterwards came back with others, and reviled deponent and tore his coat off his back, and drove him away, the constable actually helping them.

3. Petition of Thomas French and Robert Wood, of Stisted, Essex, now in the messenger's hands by order of the House; petitioners formerly exhibited articles against Mr. Newstead for malignancy and superstition, and he, out of mere malice, untruly accused them of disobeying an order of the House, but has not appeared to make good his charges; pray to be discharged from further attendance and for reparation. (Undated.)

June 16. Petition of William Flower, citizen and grocer of London; for having in his possession one book entitled "News from Ipswich," petitioner was detained nine months in prison by a warrant of the High Commission Court under the hands of Sir John Lamb and Doctor Basil Wood; upon complaint to the House of Commons, the Committee for courts of justice voted the warrant illegal, and the House confirmed the decision, but afterwards, being unable to proceed further in the matter on account of the great affairs of State, petitioner obtained leave to proceed at common law for redress, he now prays that he may not be hindered by any order of their Lordships. L. J., VI. 97.

Annexed:—

1. Order of the Commons confirming the decision of the Committee for courts of justice, &c. C. J., II. 158.

2. Order for Flower to proceed at common law. C. J., III. 94.

3. Undated petition of same recapitulating preceding petition and orders, and stating that he is stopped from proceeding at law by order of the House made upon a petition of Sir Nathaniel Brent (member of the late High Commission Court), for stay of petitioner's action. See L. J., V. 447.

June 16. Draft declaration of loyalty to the King. Reported in the House of Lords, and ordered to be communicated to the Commons, by whom no notice appears to have been taken of it. L. J., VI. 97. In extenso.

June 16. Petition of Henry Burnaby, bailiff of the hundred of Toseland, to Edward Earl of Manchester; for publishing one of the King's proclamations, which he did as the sheriff's officer, and for unseemly speeches against Sir Samuel Luke, petitioner was by their Lordships committed to the Fleet on the 20th of August last, he has obtained Sir Samuel Luke's pardon, and prays the Earl to commiserate his distressed estate and move the House for his enlargement. L. J., VI. 98.

Annexed:—

1. Petition of same to Sir Samuel Luke, member of the House of Commons; in proclaiming the King's proclamation he acted at the instance of Lewis Phelips, under sheriff, and on his bended knees he craves Sir Samuel Luke's pardon for his unseemly words, and prays him, out of compassion for his long imprisonment, and the deplorable condition of his wife and children, who, in these miserable days, have scarcely bread to eat, to take some measure for his enlargement. Noted, "I do freely remit any offence whatsoever committed against myself, and shall freely forgive him, being very sorry he should suffer so long, if the honorable assembly had nothing else against him, but the particular injury to me. Your Honors, in all humility, Sam Luke."

June 16. Draft declaration of the Lords and Commons assembled in Parliament concerning the present lamentable and miserable condition of Ireland. L. J., VI. 98. In extenso.

June 16. Printed copy of preceding.

June 17. Message from the Commons with an alteration in the ordinance for an assembly of divines, about sending Commissioners to Scotland, &c. L. J., VI. 99.

June 17. Petition of Thomas Smith, James Pickering, and others, owners, and William Rand, master of the ship "Unitie," of London. Above four years since the ship was taken by the Duke de Espernon, the petitioners lately arrested him and accepted bail, but hearing that those who had become surety for him were intending to leave the country they obtained a ne exeat regno against them, now they hear that a messenger has been sent to Oxford to procure a supersedeas; petitioners pray that John Vincent and James Pickering, with two servants, may have a pass to Oxford, or where the court shall be, that they may be enabled to prevent the malice of their adversaries. L. J., VI. 100.

June 17. Petition of the inhabitants of Boughton-Malherbe, in the county of Kent; their parson Robert Barrell, a man of considerable estate, has not resided amongst them for twenty years, putting curates upon them unapt to teach and of corrupt doctrine; he has been very remiss in preaching at his own church of Maidstone; has declared that the King's commands, even if illegal, ought to be obeyed; has abused those who seek for a reformation; has bowed to the Communion table and refused to read the declarations of Parliament; his drunkenness and wicked wish, that the King would burn London and the Puritans, have already been proved; petitioners pray that they may be eased from the heavy burden that Mr. Barrell is upon them, and that the profits of the living may be sequestered and paid over to John Osbourne, an orthodox and painful minister. L. J., VI. 100.

Annexed:—

1. Affidavit of Samuel Skelton in support of preceding. 19 May 1643.

2. Affidavit of John Zachary, minister of God's words at Itchingham [Itchingfield], Sussex. 19 May 1643.

3. Certificate of John Sedley and others. 1 June 1643.

June 17. Petition of Sir Arthur Jenney, in the county of Suffolk; in order to pay the sums levied by Parliament petitioner tried to recover debts due to himself and caused Mr. George Martin to be arrested for refusing to pay, upon this Martin produced an old commission for his protection from Lord Warwick, and obtained an order from the House for the arrest of petitioner and two bailiffs on the score of privilege; prays for release, and for liberty to recover the debts due to him. L. J., VI. 100.

June 17. Draft petition to the King for an accommodation proposed by the Lords to the House of Commons. L. J., VI. 100. In extenso.

June 17. Petition of all the chief inhabitants of Barnes, in the county of Surrey; John Cutts, parson, has been long absent, and is with the King at Oxford, and the living sequestrated, and upon a petition to the committee for sequestrations Mr. Robert Dingley was

M 2

approved as their minister, they pray for his appointment. L. J., VI. 101.
Annexed :—
1. Petition of same to the Committee for sequestrations mentioned in preceding.
2. Petition of inhabitants of Barnes ; on the sequestration of the living the House was wrongly informed that the inhabitants were destitute of a preacher, though Mr. Thomas Rutton had supplied the place of Cutts, and on this misinformation another was appointed ; pray the House to concur with the Commons in appointing Mr. Rutton. (Undated.)

June 19. A list of gentlemen appointed to take care of the houses and persons infected with the sickness at Lambeth, where there are about ten houses infected, and no care yet taken to keep the houses closed, or to convey the sick to the pesthouses. L. J., VI. 101.

June 19. Petition of Thomas Some, D.D., vicar of Staines, in the county of Middlesex. On the 11th of May last an order was made by the House for the sequestration of the profits of the living, of which one-third was to be paid to Mr. Burgess, for serving the cure and the rest to petitioner, the opponents of petitioner to have time to except to the names of the sequestrators proposed by him, no exception has been taken, but some of the tithes have already been lost by the delay ; prays that three or four of the sequestrators may be authorised to receive and distribute the profits of the living, and that his children may live in the vicarage, as Mr. Burgess has provided himself with a house near the church. L. J., VI. 101.
Annexed :—
1. Petition of same ; the sequestrators are interrupted in their proceedings by Mr. Burgess ; petitioner prays for enforcement of their Lordships' previous order. (Undated.)
2. Affidavit of Thomas Allen that Burgess was served with the order. 8 July 1643.
3. Certificate of the sequestrators that they have been interrupted in the collection of the profits of the living by Burgess. (Undated.)
4. Copy of order of 11 May 1643. L. J., VI. 42.

June 19. Petition of Nicholas Street ; as patron of the church of Leckhampstead, Bucks, petitioner presented George Holmes thereunto, a man well affected to Parliament, and for about twenty years schoolmaster at Guildford, Surrey, who was instituted by the Bishop, and is now in possession ; but one Thomas Langton has since tried to obtain a superinstitution from the Bishop upon a presentation from Sir Edmund Pie ; Sir Edmund and Langton are both at Oxford, and petitioner, fearing some powerful means from thence to induce the Bishop to superinstitute Langton, prays for an order to stop any such proceeding. Noted, Read. Nothing done.

June 19. Certificate that Mr. William Barton, late vicar of Mayfield, a man of godly life and able and orthodox in his ministry, has been forced to desert his flock and family by the plundering Cavaliers in Staffordshire.

June 20. Petition of Henry Earl of Bath ; has for three-quarters of a year been prisoner, and during that time continued in one lodging, but has been much disquieted by one White, who has produced an order from the Commons to put him in possession of the lodgings, and to dispossess petitioner. Prays for answer to his former petition for leave to go to the Spa, or at least that he may remain in his present lodgings. L. J., VI. 102.

June 20. Draft order for repayment of 6,000l. advanced by the Earl of Denbigh, for raising forces in Warwick, &c. L. J., VI. 102. In extenso.

June 21. Heads of what was thought fit to be offered by the Lords at the conference with the Commons at the communicating to them the petition for peace to be presented to the King. L. J., VI. 103. In extenso.

June 21. Draft order for payment of 100l. for the use of Sir William Waller out of the money raised for the aqueduct. L. J., VI. 103. In extenso.

June 21. Draft ordinance that an acquittance, under the hands of any three of the committee for Shropshire, shall be sufficient authority for repayment to the persons who advance money there for the service of Parliament. L. J., VI. 103. In extenso.

June 21. Petition of Dr. William Kingsley, Archdeacon of Canterbury, James Lambe, and Henry Jenkin ; petitioners have been charged by Edward Hudson with injustice in not giving him induction to the rectory of Eythorn, Kent, the truth being that Hudson produced an instrument purporting to be a mandate from the Archbishop of Canterbury for his induction, against which Dr. Bargrave, incumbent of Eythorn for nearly twenty-seven years, lodged a caveat, and the case was in due course heard before Sir Nathaniel Brent, and no further application was made by Hudson to petitioners, who pray to be discharged from further attendance in the matter.
Annexed :—
1. Copy of Hudson's petition. Vide supra 25 May 1643. L. J., VI. 62.

June 21. Copy of an Act of the Commissioners of Scotland for conserving the articles of the treaty, for the apprehension of the Earls of Morton, Roxborough, Annandale, Kinnoul, Lanerick, and Carnwath, under the terms of the Act of Pacification of 1641, as incendiaries between the two kingdoms, pursuant to information brought by Mr. Welden from both Houses of Parliament. See L. J., VI. 137.

June 22. Petition of Charles Best. An order was made by their Lordships to prevent carts passing through the Old Palace, Westminster, where there was no ancient way, to the disturbance of the House. A chain and posts were set up, and petitioner appointed by the gentleman usher to keep the key, in which duty petitioner and his wife have been much molested by Robert Hopkins and others. Pray that these offenders may be called upon to answer for their contempt. L. J., VI. 104.

June 22. Petition of the Lord Mayor, aldermen, and common council of the city of London, to the Lords and Commons, praying that the ordinance for listing and fitting for service all horses within and about the city and twelve miles round may be speedily passed. C. J., III. 140.

[June 22.] Wincott v. [Kester and Chapman]. Statement of Wincott. See L. J., VI. 104.

June 23. Draft declaration and ordinance for stopping all intercourse of intelligence between the city of London and Oxford. This intercourse, contrary to the custom of war, has been the means of setting on foot the late plot, and of providing monies for the continuance of the war ; no person under pain of sequestration shall in future be allowed to pass, without the consent of both Houses of Parliament or of the Lord General. Noted, This ordinance being read and the Lords asked their opinions they generally dissented unto it. L. J., VI. 104.

June 23. Message from the Commons with propositions for a subscription by adventurers for the relief of Ireland, and resolutions thereon. L. J., VI. 105. In extenso.

June 24. Draft order for prayer to be made by all ministers in their churches on behalf of the assembly of divines. L. J., VI. 106. In extenso.

June 24. Petition of His Majesty's poor knights of Windsor. Henry VIII. gave by will to the church of Windsor, lands of good value to pay the poor knights 12d. a day, and James I., considering the smallness of this allowance, gave them an additional 12d. a day, to be paid out of the Exchequer. Their allowance from the Exchequer has now been unpaid for two years and three quarters, and the church lands being sequestered, their church allowance has been unpaid for two months. Pray that an order may be made for payment of their arrears and for continuance of their church allowance, and that they may quietly enjoy their poor dwellings and goods which are now used at the pleasure and to the profit of others. L. J., VI. 106.

June 24. Draft ordinance for raising forces for the defence of the Isle of Wight. L. J., VI. 106. In extenso.

June 24. Letter from Lord Forbes, at Westminster, to the Earl of Manchester. A cousin of mine is prisoner in Flanders, and the Spanish Ambassador has promised that if I can obtain the release of petitioner [Ultas] under promise to leave the country and never to return without license either to Britain or Ireland, he will obtain that of my cousin, I should thus release a friend and be rid of a foe. Endorsed, Christopher Ultas.
Annexed :—
1. Petition of Christopher Ultas, an Irishman, close prisoner in the Fleet. Was taken in August last in the north of Ireland by Lord Forbes' fleet, shipped to England, brought before their Lordships, and committed to prison, where he is likely to perish. Prays that he may be discharged, and have leave to quit the kingdom.

June 26. Petition of Rachel Countess of Bath ; her husband being a prisoner in the Tower, she has been permitted by order of Parliament to keep four coach horses, but lately some soldiers, who said they were under the command of Sir Arthur Haselrigg, came at midnight and tried to break into her house and take her horses away, though she herself showed the orders for their protection, and the same men came again, and when asked for their warrant showed their pistols and broke open her stable and took her four horses; two of which have been taken for the service of Parliament, but two have been seen at work in hackney coaches; prays that she may at least have these two last restored and protected for the future. L. J., VI. 107.

June 26. Draft order and judgment in the case between the Earls of Bedford and Portland and the inhabitants of Whittlesey, to secure the Earls and their tenants in present possession of certain fen lands at Whittlesey, with liberty to the defendants to try their title at law. L. J., VI. 107.

Annexed :—

1. Petition of William Earl of Bedford, Jerome Earl of Portland, lords of the manors of Whittlesey, in the Isle of Ely and county of Cambridge, and of divers the landowners and tenants within the said town; petitioners have for divers years past been in possession of certain proportions of marsh grounds by virtue of an agreement with the tenants, confirmed by consent in the Exchequer Chamber, since which time most of the tenants have sold their proportions to petitioners, who have laid out large sums of money upon the improvement of the lands so bought, which were before waste and valueless; but many of the persons who sold their proportions have, with their servants, molested petitioners in their possession, attempting to destroy the fences and enclosures; in consequence five several orders have been at different times made by the House for securing petitioners in peaceable possession, by which means the riots have been in some degree prevented for a time, and petitioners have continued their improvements, and sown their lands with cole, rape, flax, barley, oats, and other grain; but on the 15th of May Jeffery Boyce and others, of Whittlesey, and the adjoining villages, to the number of above 100, proceeded, in defiance of an appeal from one of the justices, to throw down the division dikes, demolish the houses, and cut and destroy the crops on petitioners' lands, and endeavoured to destroy the general banks and sluices by which the whole country is secured; this they continued, their numbers constantly increasing, until the 17th, when the Parliament troops under Sir John Palgrave, lying at Wisbech, were forced to march towards them, upon which they dispersed, but, as divers of them have given out, with the intention of returning as soon as the troops should be withdrawn; petitioners pray that Jeffery Boyce and others, the chief ringleaders, in these riots, may be called upon to answer for their conduct, and that petitioners may be further secured in their possessions until their Lordships or some other court of justice shall determine the contrary. 29 May 1643.

2. Petition of some of the poor inhabitants of the town of Whittlesey, in the Isle of Ely, in the name of themselves and many others; on the 22nd April 1641 an order was made on behalf of the Earls of Bedford and Portland, lords of the manors of Whittlesey, that they and all claiming under them should quietly hold possession of the manors and divisions of tenants until good cause shown to the contrary; to this order petitioners humbly submitted; but since this order Mr. George Glapthorne, and others, have already enclosed above a thousand acres of ground, which formerly lay open, and which petitioners have time out of mind enjoyed as common, and are proceeding to enclose more, to the great impoverishing of petitioners and others, who obtain their chief livelihood from these commons; petitioners pray that further enclosure may be prevented until the question of right has been heard and determined. 31 July 1641. L. J., IV. 336.

3. Copy of preceding.

4. Order in the case 22 April 1641. L. J., IV. 224.

5. Order of 9 June 1641. L. J., IV. 269.

6. Order of 2 Aug. 1641. L. J., IV. 336.

7. Order of 24 May 1642. L. J., V. 80.

8. Order of 29 May 1643.

9. Order of 10 June 1643. L. J., VI. 88.

10. Affidavit of John Newton, of Wittlesey, that the rioters destroyed the fences, houses, and crops on the lands of the Earls of Bedford and Portland, and threatened George Glapthorne, Esq., a justice of the peace, with a pitchfork, when he called upon them to obey the laws of the realm, saying that he was no justice, for he was against the King and all for the Parliament. 29 May 1643.

11. Interrogatories administered to witnesses and their depositions taken on behalf of the Earls of Bedford and Portland. 17 June 1643. (64 pp.)

June 26. Draft order for securing Thomas May in execution of the will, and in disposing of the estate of Elizabeth late Viscountess Campden. L. J., VI. 108. *In extenso.*

June 27. Petition of Ralph Martin to Henry Earl of Holland; petitioner having taken a shop in the Strand, became indebted 21*l.* to one Webb, for which he has paid 20*s.* a quarter interest; prays the Earl to commiserate him under this extortion, and that as he is his Lordship's servant he may have the benefit of privilege. L. J., VI. 111.

June 27. Information of John Morgan, that on Saturday, the 17th, Captain Washington and Captain Burre came with troopers to Ashridge, and demanded the keys of the granary from Thomas Williams, the steward, and took away eight horses, and sent for horses and carts to carry away the grain. L. J., VI. 111.

Annexed :—

1. Information of [Thomas Williams], that when Captain Washington came to Ashridge informant showed him the orders of the House, and that on reading them Captain Washington was very angry, saying that he was accused of plundering and stealing.

2. Information of same that Nathaniel Hole, quartermaster to Major Fountain, came with twenty soldiers, and cried pish at their Lordships' order, and offered to lay wagers that it was gained for 5*l.* of John Brown, and took away what little was left of the oats and peas in the granary, and two horses not fit for any service.

3. Further information of same.

June 27. Petition of John Doughty, defendant in a cause in which Thomas Overman and John Hardwick are plaintiffs, that the question of law (whether the plaintiffs ought to have diminution) may be referred to the judges, and that upon their certificate a short day may be appointed for deciding the cause. L. J., VI. 111.

June 28. Draft resolution of the Commons nominating Mr. Dury one of the assembly of divines in the place of Dr. Downing, deceased. C. J., III. 148. *In extenso.*

June 28. Order of the Convention of Estates of Scotland, that a copy of the examination of the Earl of Antrim, and of Nane Dick, and James Stewart, his servants, and of the letter written by the Earl of Nithsdale and Viscount Aboyne to the Earl of Antrim, should be delivered to Mr. Welden, that he may acquaint Parliament therewith.

Annexed :—

1. Copy of the examinations of Nane Dick, the Earl of Antrim, and Master Stewart, taken before a council of war, held at Carrickfergus on the 24th of May, and the 12th of June 1643 under the presidency of General Major Munro. Nane Dick was examined as an accessory to the escape of his master, the Earl of Antrim, from Carrickfergus, in which he confessed his share, he was then desired to unburden his conscience before death of anything he knew of the plot of the Earl of Antrim and others against the kingdom of Scotland or the Scotch army in Ireland; he confessed that several letters concerning these matters passed betwixt the Earl of Antrim, the Earl of Nithsdale, Montrose, Aboyne, and others, and that a bark with ammunition and furniture of war was to be sent to Lord Aboyne and his friends in the highlands and Isles of Scotland, and another bark similarly laden to be sent to Carlisle to the Earl of Nithsdale and his confederates; that the Earl of Antrim told deponent that the intention was to do all the mischief they could by arms to Scotland, to overthrow the Scottish army in Ireland, and to bring all the forces they could out of Ireland to assist the King and the Catholic army in England against the Parliament. After this confession Dick was

M 3

judged worthy of death, and to be hanged " ex-
emplarlie " to others in satisfaction to justice.

The Earl of Antrim being examined, said that his
intention had been to levy forces for His Majesty's
service in England, in conjunction with the Earls
of Montrose, Airlie, Nithsdale, Lord Aboyne,
and others; the ammunition, &c. to be sent to
Lord Aboyne was to be employed in raising a
regiment for the Earl of Antrim, while Aboyne
was to make his way through Scotland to join the
Newcastle army, the ammunition was stopped at
York, and it was only on the Earl's earnest
request for Her Majesty that it was allowed to
proceed. Montrose was only to join them in a
legal way, and would not join in raising the
regiments. The Earl of Antrim declares the
statement of Nane Dick (who was hanged) to be
false; being asked if he had any warrant to Owen
Machart and Sir Philomie (Phelim) at Charlemont, or they had any warrant for joining with
him, he denied that he knew of any, but said that
it was by his warrant that his brother was sent to
them; the Earl declares that he came into Ireland
with the Earl of Newcastle's pass and private
instructions for making peace, with a promise that
if he could draw them to easy conditions the Earl
of Newcastle would obtain for him the King's
warrant for proceeding therein; being asked why
he offered 5,000l. to the general major, he said it
was only on condition that the general major
would suffer him to return to England; the Earl
declares that he knew nothing either of Sergeant-
Major Ross or Colonel Blair; Captain James
Wallace and Major John Monro being sent to
question the Earl, heard him say that he had
warrant to levy forces in any part of the King's
dominions for the King's service, and that some of
the English regiments were expected to join the
Earl of Newcastle, namely, the English about
Dublin and those in Ulster.

Master Stewart, servitor to the Earl of Antrim,
examined on oath under pain of torturing, stated
that he only knew that the Earl of Antrim had a
pass from the Earls of Newcastle and Derby;
he further confirms the Earl of Antrim's statements, and lastly, being threatened with the torture and death, except he should declare and free
his conscience in the truth by whose warrant and
direction the Earl of Antrim and others did
undertake the employment, he declared that as
the ammunition and arms were furnished by the
Queen's Majesty's order and command, so he
doubted not but the Earl of Antrim's employment, and that of others, was directed by Her
Majesty, and others, as was generally thought
by all and by him.

June 28. Copy of ordinance of the Commissioners of
Scotland for conserving the articles of the treaty; have
received through Mr. Welden, a desire from Parliament
to be informed what interrupted the proceedings of the
Commissioners sent by them to the King at Oxford, and
what propositions they had to offer for the peace of both
kingdoms, they therefore ordain that copies of the
instructions given to their Commissioners of the propositions presented by them to His Majesty, and of
His Majesty's answers thereto should be communicated
to Parliament. On the same paper is a copy of Mr.
Welden's address to the Commissioners.

June 29. Petition of the Clotworthies of the kindred
of Robert Gray, Esq., who is deceased without wife or
issue; the cause between petitioners and John Battle
and Richard Hunt, concerning the administration of
the estate of Robert Gray, valued at 49,000l., has been
in part heard, but owing to other great affairs has not
been decided, while Battle and others are taking advantage of the distractions of the times to defeat petitioners
of their rights; they pray that the case may be referred
to some persons to mediate therein, if they can, or to
certify the state of the case after hearing the parties for
the decision of the House. L. J., VI. 114.

June 29. Petition of parishioners of Halstead, Kent,
that Mr. John Cottingham, their present curate, may
with the consent of Mr. Thomas Whitfield, their parson,
who is also Vicar of Farningham, and willing to resign
Halstead, be nominated rector thereof. L. J., VI. 114.

June 29. Petition of inhabitants of Cranbrook, Kent,
thank the House for having, by order of 13th March last,
appointed John Williamson to preach and officiate as
vicar there, and pray that he may be appointed as their
constant and settled minister.

Annexed:—
1. Copy of order of 13 March 1642-3. L. J., V.
646.

July 1. Examination of the Earl of Portland before
a Committee of the Lords concerning Waller's plot. On
the 21st of June was removed to Alderman Atkins' house,
where he was visited by Mr. Waller, who said that he
was sorry he had brought him into this condition. That
it was a good while before he had done it, but at last he
had considered how to save himself, and wished the Earl
to do so too, as his guilt had not been great, and that he
(Waller) had been rather passive than active in the
business, and therefore desired the Earl to acknowledge
it. The Earl answered that he knew nothing of the
business, and therefore could acknowledge nothing.
Waller then asked if he did not know that Lord Conway
had agreed to be general, and Sir Hugh Pollard lieutenant-general, and said that Lord Conway had told him,
that the Earl of Northumberland liked the business.
The Earl informed him he knew nothing of it. Waller
answered it was proved, and that the Earl would suffer
much by it if he would not confess it. The Earl
answered that if it were proved it would be unjustly
and by false witnesses, and if he lost his life by it, he
should do it very innocently, and therefore contentedly.
Waller answered it would not reach his life, but he
would suffer much misery and long imprisonment, to
which the Earl replied that he must submit to it.
Waller said the Earl might save his own, and his
(Waller's) life by laying it upon Lord Conway and the
Earl of Northumberland. This he said with water
standing in his eyes, but the Earl answered that he
would never save himself by telling a lie. Waller then
said that Lord Conway and the Earl of Northumberland
were strangers, while he (Waller) was his kinsman and
entreated him for God's sake to save him. This was
the substance of what passed, Waller's whole discourse
tending to persuade the Earl to save himself, and Waller
by laying the blame upon the Lord Conway and the
Earl of Northumberland. L. J., VI. 116.

July 1. Draft order for the sale of Sir Peter Richaut's
adventure with the East India Company, and for the
payment of the money so raised to Sir William Waller
for maintenance of his soldiers. C. J., III. 151.

July 3. Draft order for apprehending rioters in Dorsetshire. L. J., VI. 118. In extenso.

Annexed:—
1. Letter from Matthew Davis, a justice of the
peace for the county of Dorset to the House of
Lords, enclosing depositions of witnesses concerning the riots in the Forest of Gillingham, near
Shaftesbury. 10 June 1643.
2. Examinations of John Godwin, Richard Ridgley,
John Belman, the younger, Nicholas Bowne, and
Morgan Horder, referred to in preceding. 10 June
1643.

July 3. Notes of proceedings this day. L. J., VI.
117.

July 3. Draft order for alderman William Billars to
be added to the Committee for the county of Leicester.

July 4. Draft orders respecting the government of
the town of Hull. L. J., VI. 119. In extenso.

July 4. Petition of Sir George Garrett, alderman
of the city of London. Petitioner heretofore, by foreign
attachment according to the custom of London, attached
in the hands of Oliver Scandrett the sum of 485l., being
the money of Walter Mountague, who was indebted to
petitioner in a greater sum. Scandrett removed the
matter by certiorari into Chancery, and obtained an injunction the question is properly triable by
law, and is no matter of equity. Petitioner cannot by
reason of the ordinances of Parliament proceed at Oxford,
either to procure bail or to dissolve the injunction, and
therefore prays that the money may be deposited with
the Earl of Manchester until such time as he is able to
proceed in Chancery in the matter. See L. J., VI.
119.

Annexed:—
1. Copy of preceding.
2. Order of the Committee for obstructions in courts
of justice for Sir George Garrett to appear and
answer the complaint of Oliver Scandrett. 12
June 1643.

July 4. Draft letter from the House of Lords, to the
Lords Justices and Council of Ireland, respecting their
treaty with the rebels. L. J., VI. 119. In extenso.

July 4. Draft letter from both Houses, to the Marquess of Ormond and Lord Lisle, concerning the behaviour of their officers and soldiers. L. J., VI. 120.
In extenso.

July 5. Application for a pass for Lord Lumley to go to Spa for the benefit his health. L. J., VI. 121.
Annexed :—
1. Certificate of John Fryer, Doctor of Physic, as to Lord Lumley's state of health, and that he is likely to receive benefit from drinking the Spa waters. On the same paper is a similar certificate signed Robert Arke, Med. Professor.

July 5. Petition of Levinus Hopper, of London; John Bickley, having a suit before their Lordships against Anne Bickley his wife, and being desirous to prevent petitioner appearing as a witness for her, repaired to petitioner's house in Great St. Bartholomew's within the liberty of the Earl of Holland, accompanied by four soldiers, who affirmed themselves to be of Colonel Mainwaring's regiment, and pretending they had a warrant of their Lordships to arrest petitioner as a malignant, broke open his door and carried him forcibly forth into the liberty of the city where they delivered him to two officers of Wood Street Compter, who arrested him upon an action of 6,000l. at Bickley's suit entered in the Sheriff's Court of London, whereas in truth petitioner never was indebted to him one penny. Prays that some speedy course may be taken for his enlargement, and for the exemplary punishment of Bickley, Thomas Mills, attorney, the officers who arrested petitioner, and the four soldiers who presumed to countenance their wicked proceedings. L. J., VI. 121.

July 5. Petition of Christopher Roper, serjeant-major in the regiment of the Earl of Kildare in Ireland. Petitioner became bound for a debt of his brother, the Lord Viscount Baltinglass, to Nicholas Abdy for payment on a day now past. Petitioner, who has served as an officer in Ireland against the rebels since the breaking out of the rebellion, having lately come over by licence from the lieutenant-general, has been arrested by Abdy. Neither petitioner nor his brother are able to discharge the debt for want of the pay and entertainment due to them, amounting to 2,800l. Is desirous to return to his charge in Ireland, as he understands that a speedy march is designed against the rebels, and therefore prays for his enlargement, or that Abdy may be satisfied out of the arrears due to petitioner and his brother. L. J., VI. 121.

July 5. Draft order for the assembly of divines to take the ten first articles of the Church of England into their consideration, to vindicate them from all false doctrine and heresy. L. J., VI. 121. In extenso.

July 5. Another draft.

July 5. Message from the Commons concerning Mr. Stockdale's letter touching the ill successes of Lord Fairfax's forces, &c. C. J., III. 155. In extenso.

July 5. Proclamation by the Earl of Newcastle, at Bradford, to the Governor and Commander-in-Chief at Manchester, and to the rest of the soldiers and inhabitants of that town. Presumes they are ignorant of the great success of His Majesty's army under the Earl's command, and the great desire to avoid the effusion of Christian blood, which moves him, before he proceeds further, to offer His Majesty's grace and mercy to those who will lay down their arms, so unjustly taken up, and immediately return to their due allegiance. Is authorised to receive them into His Majesty's grace and favour, and is as willing to do so, as to reduce them to obedience if they shall refuse. Wonders, whilst they fight against the King and his authority, they should so boldly profess themselves for King and Parliament, and scandalise those with the title of Papists, who venture their lives for the defence of the true Protestant religion. Has no other object than to let them see their errors, for his condition is such that he has no need to court them. If his (the Earl's) nature is forced they may expect such favour only as is due to so high contemners of His Majesty's grace and favour, now offered.

July 5. Protestation to be taken by every member at his first entrance into the assembly of divines. L. J., VI. 124. In extenso.

July 6. Petition of Edward Hudson, clerk. Prays that his cause against the Archdeacon of Canterbury, James Lambe, his surrogate, and Henry Jenkins, his registrar, may be referred to certain lords for hearing, the multiplicity of affairs of State preventing petitioner's cause being heard by the House.
Annexed :—
1. Petition of William Kingsley, Archdeacon of Canterbury, James Lambe, and Henry Jenkin. Pray that a certain day may be appointed for hearing Hudson's cause, and that in the meantime they may have leave to return home to discharge their cures.

July 6. Petition of Christopher Newstead. According to their Lordships' order of the 23rd of May last, petitioner repaired to Stisted in Essex, and demanded of Thomas French, the churchwarden, and Robert Wood, the constable, the possession of the church. French and Wood refused to assist petitioner, but allowed him to be beaten and his coat torn off his back. For this contempt they are now in the custody of the messenger, where petitioner prays they may remain until some day is appointed to hear petitioner and his witnesses. See L. J., VI. 97.
Annexed :—
1. Affidavit of John Bentall that Mr. Newstead is very sick in consequence of the ill-usage he received at Stisted, and is unable to travel without danger of further impairing his health.

July 6. Warrant from the Committee at Haberdashers' Hall for Mr. James Maxwell, gentleman usher, to pay 1,000l. according to the ordinance for assessing the twentieth part. See L. J., VI. 124.

July 6. Draft order for the demolition of Hornby Castle. This order was not agreed to by the Lords. C. J., III. 158. In extenso.

July 8. Information of [   ] that Sir Henry Mildmay and others killed a buck in Waltham Forest on Thursday last. L. J., VI. 125.

July 8. List of persons to be added to the Committees for the Isle of Wight, county of Huntingdon, &c. L. J., VI. 125. In extenso.

July 8. Draft order giving authority to the assembly of divines to send for papers, &c. L. J., VI. 125. In extenso.

July 10. Order in the cause Chapman and others against Wincott and Beale. L. J., VI. 125.
Annexed :—
1. Petition of Thomas Robson and Henry Chapman, that their cause against Wincott and Beale may be referred to certain referees.

July 10. Message from the Commons respecting the examination of the Earl of Portland, &c. L. J., VI. 125. In extenso.

July 10. Draft order for adjourning the assizes. L. J., VI. 126. In extenso.

July 10. Order for the indemnity of the mayor of Hull and others for seizing the town of Hull, and the persons of Sir John Hotham, Sir Edward Rodes, and Captain Hotham. L. J., VI. 126. In extenso.

July 10. Order for securing the town of King's Lynn, &c. L. J., VI. 126. In extenso.

July 10. Petition of the master, wardens, and assistants of the Company of Brewers of the city of London. The House of Commons in the rate of excise, now on foot for the maintenance and payment of the army under the Earl of Essex, have assessed two shillings upon every barrel of strong beer, and twelve pence upon every barrel of smaller beer, a rate which will undo all those that use the trade of brewing, and all those who depend upon their employment. Pray that a Committee may be appointed to receive such reasons as petitioners can give concerning the rate. Noted, Not heard.

July 11. Draft order for the payment of 600l. to Mr. William Rosse. L. J., VI. 127. In extenso.

July 12. Application for the removal of Richard Butler, apprehended for riot at Gillingham Forest in the county of Dorset, from the new prison in Clerkenwell to Newgate. L. J., VI. 128.
Annexed :—
1. Application on behalf of the Earl of Elgin that a Committee may be appointed to examine Butler concerning the riot.

July 12. Draft order appointing a Committee to consider the ordinance for the excise. L. J., VI. 128.

July 12. Ordinance for the encouragement of adventurers to make new subscriptions for lands in Ireland. L. J., VI. 128.

July 12. Draft order for raising forces in Holland, in Lincolnshire. L. J., VI. 129. In extenso.

July 12. Draft order appointing William White, clerk of assize on the Oxford circuit. L. J., VI. 129. In extenso.

July 12. Draft order confirming Sir William Waller in the office of chief butler of the kingdom of England and Wales, &c. L. J., VI. 130. In extenso.

July 13. Application for a pass for the Venetian Ambassador's goods to be transported to Roan [?]. L. J., VI. 130.

July 13. Draft order sequestering the living of Thornhill in the county of York. L. J., VI. 131.

July 13. Petition of Margaret Countess of Thanet. Prays that a pass may be granted to her to go beyond

M 4

the seas with her five children, servants, &c., and that a competent maintenance may be settled upon her out of the estates of the Earl of Thanet. L. J., VI. 131.

Annexed :—

1. Copy of preceding.

July 13. Application for a pass for two daughters of the Earl of Newport to go to Fotheringhay in Northamptonshire. L. J., VI. 131.

July 14. Petition of Thomas Taylor. Prays that a pass may be granted to him to go by ship to Hull and thence to York, Hilton, &c. to secure certain debts due to him. L. J., VI. 132.

July 14. Affidavit of John Bets, under-keeper of Lamborne Walk, in the Forest of Waltham, concerning the cutting down of a wood in the forest by Clarke, Charles, and others. See L. J., VI. 132.

July 15. List of persons to be added to the committee for the county of Sussex. L. J., VI. 132. In extenso.

July 15. Petition of Beatrice Nott and Benjamin Harrison, merchant; complain that Molins, Fuller, and Punter, pretending they were commanders for the Parliament, on the 22d of June violently entered the house of the petitioner Harrison, and took away the goods of Mr. Nott, husband of Beatrice Nott, although he is not as yet voted a delinquent, and there is no just cause why he should be so reputed, he not being with the King, and never having contributed towards the maintenance of the King's army, and having gone to Oxford upon no other occasion than to secure his debts there from some persons of quality. Pray that Molins, Fuller, and Punter may be sent for to answer. L. J., VI. 132.

July 15. Affidavit of John Barton that he served their Lordships' order of the 4th of July upon Oliver Scandrett. L. J., VI. 133.

Annexed :—

1. Copy of order referred to in preceding. L. J., VI. 119.

July 17. Draft of proceedings this day concerning the sending of the Lord Grey of Warke into Scotland, &c. L. J., VI. 134. In extenso.

July 17. Draft order of the Commons appointing John Rushworth, cursitor for the counties of York and Westmoreland. C. J., III. 170. In extenso.

July 17. The answer of the Commissioners of the General Assembly of the Kirk of Scotland from their meeting at Edinburgh, the 17th of July 1643, to the Honble. Houses of the Parliament of England, expressing their approval of the appointment of the Assembly of Divines. See C. J., III. 192.

July 18. Petition of the Lady Elizabeth Countess Dowager of Lyndsey. Prays that Jerom Freer, her servant, arrested contrary to privilege, may be discharged, and that Daniel Lee who arrested him, and Robert Keniston, at whose suit he was arrested, may be punished for their contempt. L. J., VI. 134.

July 18. Petition of Sir George Radcliffe, prisoner in the Gatehouse. Prays that he may have leave to go abroad with his keeper for his health, and necessary occasions, whereby he may be enabled to look after the broken remnant of his estate, without which it is impossible for him either to live or to discharge his conscience towards his sureties and creditors. L. J., VI. 134.

July 18. Order upon preceding petition. L. J., VI. 134.

July 18. Draft ordinance for raising money for the defence of the county of Huntingdon. L. J., VI. 134. In extenso.

July 18. Petition of the Lord Mayor, aldermen, and commons of the city of London, in Common Council assembled, to the Lords and Commons. Pray that an ordinance may be granted, that all the forces raised and to be raised within the city, and all places adjacent, mentioned within the weekly bills of mortality, may be under the sole command of the committee for the militia of the city, under the direction of both Houses of Parliament, and that Isaac Pennington, the present Lord Mayor, and other citizens and freemen may be added to the committee. C. J., III. 171.

July 19. Application for a pass for carrying the bodies of Mr. Henry Noel and his child to Campden, in Gloucestershire. L. J., VI. 136.

July 19. Draft order appointing the preachers at St. Margaret's Church upon the fast-day. L. J., VI. 136.

July 19. Draft ordinance for raising money for the defence of the county of Northampton. L. J., VI. 137. In extenso.

July 19. Petition of divers ministers of Christ, in name of themselves and sundry others, to the Lords and Commons. Pray that a public and extraordinary day of humiliation may be appointed, &c. L. J., VI. 138. In extenso.

July 19. Draft order appointing Friday the 21st of July to be kept as a day of public and extraordinary humiliation. L. J., VI. 139. In extenso.

July 19. Draft letter from the Parliament, to the Earl of Leven, requesting his Lordship to take the command, if the Scots should send any army for the assistance of the Parliament. L. J., VI. 139. In extenso.

July 19. Draft letter from the Parliament, to the Lord Chancellor of Scotland informing him that ships are ordered to guard the North Coast. L. J., VI. 139. In extenso.

July 19. Draft ordinance appointing John Earl of Rutland and others, commissioners to go to Scotland to treat of divers matters concerning the safety and peace of both kingdoms. L. J., VI. 139. In extenso.

July 19. Draft declaration of both Houses to the general assembly of the Church of Scotland. L. J., VI. 140. In extenso.

July 19. Draft amendments to the instructions of both Houses to the commissioners to the kingdom of Scotland. L. J., VI. 140.

July 19. Draft declaration of both Houses to the Kingdom and States of Scotland. L. J., VI. 142. In extenso.

July 19. Petition of Dr. Thomas Peyton, Rector of Northcotes, Lincolnshire. Having been robbed of his estate by the rebels in Ireland was preferred by his friends in England to a benefice of small value in Lincolnshire. Petitioner has a brother in the Low Countries, who is willing to support him in part of the charge of his wife and four children. Prays that a pass may be granted to him to take his wife and children, and one maid servant to his brother, who is one of the captains of the garrison at Busse, that he may there settle all or some of his children, having already taken care for an able and efficient minister to officiate for him in his absence.

July 19. Draft ordinance for raising money for the recovery of the town of Newcastle. Brought up from the Commons this day, but not agreed to by the Lords. L. J., VI. 136.

July 20. Petition of Anne Van-Enden, widow. Prays that her cause against Belton and others, which is so short that it will not take above an hour, may be heard this morning. L. J., VI. 143.

Annexed :—

1. Another petition of same. Prays for a speedy and final hearing of her cause. (Undated.)

July 20. Draft declaration concerning a rising in Kent. L. J., VI. 143. In extenso.

July 20. Notes of proceedings this day. L. J., VI. 143.

July 20. Petition of Lord Grey, Baron of Warke, now a prisoner in the Tower. Is sorry to have incurred their Lordships' displeasure. Prays for his discharge. See. L. J., VI. 134, &c.

July 22. Petition of Bartholomew Baker. Has been arrested contrary to privilege, being a menial servant to Lord Craven, who is now in France, and whose affairs will be much prejudiced by petitioner's restraint. Prays for his discharge. L. J., VI. 144.

July 22. Application for an order against the removal of certain goods belonging to the Earl of Arundel, from the Palace at Norwich, which goods the committee for sequestrations in the county of Norwich have ordered to be seized on pretence that they belong to the Lord Mowbray. L. J., VI. 144.

July 22. Draft order for the Lord General to move with his army in such manner as he shall think best. L. J., VI. 145. In extenso.

July 22. Copy of preceding.

July 22. Draft ordinance appointing Lord Fairfax, Governor of Hull. L. J., VI. 145. In extenso.

July 22. Draft letter from the Parliament, to Sir Henry Vane the elder, and others, to suppress the rising in the county of Kent. L. J., VI. 146. In extenso.

July 24. Petition of Raleigh Sanderson. Upon the misinformation of Thomas Smith, Robert Preston, and Arthur Collins that petitioner was in actual service in the King's army, and so a delinquent, he was sent for by the committee of sequestrations to appear and defend himself. He accordingly appeared on the 9th of June last, and being then ordered to appear again on the

12th, was arrested in Westminster Hall for 6,000*l.* by the said informers, and has ever since remained in strict imprisonment. This being a high breach and indignity to the honour and justice of Parliament, he prays that he may be forthwith released agreeably to the usual privilege of all courts of justice, and that the informers may be punished. L. J., VI. 146.

Annexed:—
1. Copy of preceding.
2. Certificate of the sequestrators, that they ordered Raleigh Sanderson to appear before them. 29 June 1643.
3. Affidavit of William Sanderson and Richard Street concerning the arrest of Raleigh Sanderson. 30 June 1643.

July 24. Petition of Lord Viscount Conway, praying for a speedy trial. L. J., VI. 146. *In extenso.*

July 24. Draft order concerning the wardship of the sons of those killed in the service of the Parliament. C. J., III. 179. *In extenso.*

July 24. Letter from Colonel Richard Browne, at Tunbridge, to the Earl of Manchester, Speaker of the House of Lords, or William Lenthall, Esquire, Speaker of the House of Commons. It pleased God by the abundance of rain that fell (almost two days without intermission) to hinder us above a day's march. Having stayed all Saturday at Bromley, we marched on Sunday to the rebels' quarters at Sevenoaks, which they quitted to our hand. Whither being come after a long and untoward march we were fairly promised some assistance from the country, for which we waited until 10 o'clock on Monday, but none came. We then advanced towards Tunbridge, where we were certainly informed considerable forces of the enemy were quartered. We received by the way letters which the enemy forced Sir Thomas Walsingham to write for them pretending a desire to yield upon such conditions as were propounded. We returned answer that if they would submit to the orders of Parliament, which had been already proclaimed to them, every man should receive pardon. But coming after a tedious march, and indeed before we knew whereabouts we were, the enemy instead of treating as they proposed fired upon our van. We then drew our men into battalia, resolving to fight it out without hearkening to their conditions, when, after a most gallant charge by such gentlemen as voluntarily came to accompany us, we gained the broken bridge on this side the town, making it passable by long planks laid over it. We then drew our men into several divisions towards the town and charged them again. The Green Regiment of Auxiliaries, together with the red coats, behaved very resolutely and like men, whereby after three hours and a half very hot fight, with the loss of five or six men, none whereof were considerable, except one Proudlove, Ensign to Lieutenant-Colonel Rowe, a very gallant man, and thirty or forty wounded, which much grieved me for want of chirurgeons, there being but one with us, we entered the town by force. We found about twelve of their men dead in the town and believe there are many more in hop gardens and hedges as yet undiscovered, besides many wounded. We have taken almost two hundred prisoners, and released that noble gentleman Sir Thomas Walsingham, and divers others of our friends, and for the present utterly routed the rebels. Our two troops of horse pursued the chase upwards of six miles and did good execution. We have resolved to give solemn thanks to God tomorrow, being Tuesday, for this our victory against so great odds. It is the opinion of the deputy lieutenants that it is necessary to leave garrisons in this town and in Sevenoaks and divers other places, which being done we shall have nobody to march withal. I desire the House will speedily raise another regiment for this service, and I request the recommendation of the officers whom I will choose out of those gentlemen who have voluntarily done so gallant service. This letter was read in the House of Commons 25 July 1643. C. J., III. 181.

July 25. Petition of Fabian Phillips. Prays that his cause against Forrett touching the office of Philazer of London, Middlesex, Cambridge, and Huntingdon, may be referred to the Lord Chief Justice and the rest of the Judges of the Court of Common Pleas. L. J., VI. 147.

July 25. Affidavit of Fabian Phillips that many of his witnesses are now out of London.

July 25. Application for a pass for the French Ambassador and his retinue to go into France. L. J., VI. 147.

July 25. Petition of Christopher Tench, John Wyeman [Wainman], and Elizabeth his wife. Pray that Thomas Ellicott and others may be sent for to answer

for their unjust proceedings, whereby petitioners have been cast into prison. L. J., VI. 147.

Annexed:—
1. Petition of John Wainman, one of his honour's watermen, to Henry Earl of Holland. Complains that Thomas Ellicott has by a wile caused petitioner and his wife to be clapped up in Newgate, where they remain in great distress. Prays his Lordship to take some course for their relief. See L. J., VI. 116. On the same paper, order referring the matter to Mr. Baron Trevor and Sergeant Whitfield (1 July 1643), and their report thereupon. 19 July 1643.

July 25. Petition of John Wright, printer. Prays for his discharge having been committed by the House of Commons for printing the book for excise upon commodities, although he received the order for doing so from their Lordships under the clerk's hand. L. J., VI. 147.

July 25. Draft order for the indemnity of Sir David Watkins and Sergeant Henry Clarke, concerning the payment to the treasurers of Guildhall of certain monies part of the fine for the wardship of Robert Smith. L. J., VI. 148. *In extenso.*

July 25. Draft letter from both Houses to the States of Holland concerning supplies for Ireland. L. J., VI. 148. *In extenso.*

July 25. Copy of preceding.

July 25. Notes of proceedings this day. L. J., VI. 149.

July 27. Petition of John Bishop of Ardagh in Ireland. Prays that a pass may be granted to him to go into Holland with his wife, one man and one maid. L. J., VI. 150.

July 27. Petition of Isabella Smith, wife of Thomas Smith. Raleigh Sanderson was arrested on the 12th instant by petitioner and her trustees upon a bond of 6,000*l.*, and has since petitioned to be released, alleging that he was arrested when attending by order of the Committee for sequestrations, although he could show no order for his protection. Prays that he may not be discharged but left to proceedings at law. L. J., VI. 151.

July 27. Draft ordinance for raising forces for the defence of the county of Surrey. L. J., VI. 151.

Annexed:—
1. Another draft.

July 28. Articles exhibited against Symon Paige, Parson of Hemingford Abbots, in the county of Huntingdon, by the parishioners of the parish. L. J., VI. 152. *In extenso.*

Annexed:—
1. Copy of order directing Sir Robert Rich and Mr. Page, two of the Masters of the Chancery, and assistants of the House, to examine witnesses in the matter. 6 July 1643. L. J., VI. 123.
3. Depositions of the witnesses. 7 July 1643.
4. Petition of divers freeholders and inhabitants of Hemingford Abbots, to H. C. Pray for the removal of Mr. Paige and the settling of a conscionable minister in his place.
5. Articles presented by the tenants and inhabitants of Hemingford Abbotts against Robert Paige, lord of the manor and patron of the living, and Symon Paige, rector of the parish.
6. Agreement entered into by certain of the parishioners for sharing the expense incurred in prosecuting any suits against the said lord of the manor and parson in any court of justice for the recovery of their rights. 1 April 1641.
7. Certificate of certain of the inhabitants of the town of Hemingford Abbotts, that Mr. Paige has always faithfully discharged his ministerial duties, and that he is a sober, godly, and peaceable man, and unblameable in his life and conversation. 21 July 1643.

July 28. Petition of the Earl of Portland. Has been for seven weeks a prisoner at the desire of the House of Commons upon the unjust accusation of Mr. Waller. Prays for his discharge. L. J., VI. 153. *In extenso.*

July 28. Petition of the Lord Viscount Conway. Has been for seven weeks a prisoner by reason of Mr. Waller's accusation, of which he is no way guilty. Prays for his discharge. L. J., VI. 153. *In extenso.*

July 28. Draft of letter sent into several counties concerning the raising of horse. See L. J., VI. 151.

July 28. Copy of preceding.

July 29. Draft order for the Countess of Dorset, to be appointed governess over the King's children, now at St. James'. L. J., VI. 154. *In extenso.*

July 29. Copy of the vindication of the late oath and covenant from misinterpretations. L. J., VI. 154.

July 29. Petition of Sir John Seaton, Knight, prays to be heard before any order is made in the cause between Sir Filibert Vernatti and Mr. Jenyns. L. J., VI. 154.

July 29. Draft order for the Lord Mayor and sheriffs to have the custody of the Tower during the absence of the lieutenant L. J., VI. 154.

July 29. Order for the payment of 491l. to Christopher Dew for grey coats. L. J., VI. 155. In extenso.

July 29. Order for the payment of 428l. 10s. to John Pococke for coats, and 3l. 10s. for petty charges. L. J., VI. 155. In extenso.

July 29. Order for the payment of 312l. 10s. to Francis Rowland for beef. L. J., VI. 155. In extenso.

July 29. Order for the payment of 85l. to John Read and John Gilbert for cheese. L. J., VI. 155. In extenso.

July 29. Order for the payment of 563l. 2s. 6d. to Thomas Prince for cheese. L. J., VI. 155. In extenso.

July 29. Order for the payment of 88l. 10s. to Jacob Ablyn for herrings. L. J., VI. 156. In extenso.

July 29. Order for the payment of 240l. 15s. 2d., to Robert Lawson for provisions for Ireland. L. J., VI. 156. In extenso.

July 29. Order for the payment of 132l. 16s. 6d. to Nicholas Bagbier for provisions for Ireland. L. J., VI. 156. In extenso.

July 29. Order for the payment of 50l. 13s. 4d., to Thomas Fossan for peas. L. J., VI. 156. In extenso.

July 29. Order for the payment of 156l. to William Smart for wheat, butter, &c. L. J., VI. 156. In extenso.

July 29. Order for the payment of 220l. 17s. 6d. to Thomas Rodbord for butter. L. J., VI. 156. In extenso.

July 29. Order for the payment of 135l. 9s. 2d. to John Cooke and George Younge for fish. L. J., VI. 156. In extenso.

July 29. Order for the payment of 86l. 3s. 7d. to William Pennoyer. L. J., VI. 157. In extenso.

July 29. Order for the payment of 297l. 18s. to Sir John Hippesley for salmon. L. J., VI. 157. In extenso.

July 29. Order for the payment of 42l. to Maurice Thompson for gunpowder and shot. L. J., VI. 157. In extenso.

July 29. Order for the payment of 32l. to Sir John Hippesley for iron. L. J., VI. 157. In extenso.

July 29. Draft ordinance for raising money for the defence of the county of Huntingdon. L. J., VI. 157. In extenso.

July 29. Draft order for selling unserviceable stores belonging to the navy, with list of stores to be sold. L. J., VI. 157. In extenso.

July 29. Draft ordinance appointing Adam Laurence, Derrick Hoast, Maurice Thompson, and Nicholas Cursellis, to receive subscriptions in Holland, for the relief of Ireland. L. J., VI. 158. In extenso.

July 29. Draft ordinance for the defence of London. L. J., VI. 158. In extenso.

July 29. Notes of proceedings this day. L. J., VI. 154, &c.

July 29. Affidavit of Henry Simpson, collector appointed by the sequestrators of the living of St. Ives, that certain of the parishioners refuse to pay him the tithes, saying they have the King's proclamation to the contrary. See L. J., VI. 174.

July 31. Petition of Thomas Jenyns concerning his cause against Sir Filibert Vernatti. L. J., VI. 159. In extenso.

July 31. Lists of persons to be added to the committee of sequestrations for Northamptonshire and Cambridgeshire. L. J., VI. 160. In extenso.

July 31. Petition of Jeffery Boys and others, poor distressed prisoners in the Fleet. Petitioners were by their Lordships' order committed for a riot upon the lands of the Earls of Bedford and Portland at Whittlesey. They have now made submission to the said Earls who are content they shall be enlarged upon bail. In addition to the fees required by the warden of the Fleet, the sum of 265l. is demanded of them by the gentleman usher for messengers' fees, which sum far surmounts in value all their estates. Pray that the fees may be mitigated according to their abilities.

Annexed :—

1. Copy of order referred to in preceding. 29 May 1643.
2. Copy of another order. 26 June 1643. L. J., VI. 107.
3. Recognisance subsequently entered into by petitioners. 6 Sept. 1643.

Aug. 1. Order for the Bishop of London, Dr. Turner, and John Juxon, to pay money received for the impropriations of the livings of Presteign and Aylesbury to John White and Samuel Browne. L. J., VI. 162. In extenso.

Aug. 1. Order for the payment of 200l. to Sir Thomas Wharton for his pay as Lieutenant-Colonel of the regiment commanded by the Marquess of Ormonde. L. J., VI. 162. In extenso.

Aug. 1. Order for the payment of 250l. to Mr. Francis Rogers, Lieutenant in the troop of horse commanded by Sir Richard Greenvill. L. J., VI. 162. In extenso.

Aug. 1. Copy of letter from the Lord General to the Committee for the militia of London, desiring them to forbear to take or list horses belonging to the judges, assistants, and attendants of the House of Lords. See L. J., VI. 152.

Aug. 2. Petition of Thomas Moyser. Prays for further time to assign errors in the cause Nuttall against Gisborough and others. L. J., VI. 163.

Aug. 3. Application for a pass for Sir Thomas Merry, one of the clerks of the green cloth, to go to Oxford. L. J., VI. 163.

Aug. 3. Order for the payment of 50l. to John Ogle, part of the pay due to him as captain of a foot company. L. J., VI. 163. In extenso.

Aug. 4. Petition of Edward Leventhorp. On the 1st of June last, an order was made in his cause against Brograve, which order still remains in the clerk's hands ; prays that the order may be issued forth, and petitioner discharged from further attendance. See L. J., VI. 75.

Aug. 5. Propositions for peace agreed to by the Lords and submitted to the Commons this day. L. J., VI. 171. The question of agreeing to these propositions was debated for three days in the Commons, and on the 7th of August a division was taken upon the question whether to take these propositions into more particular consideration, when the numbers were, Yeas, 81 ; Noes, 79. The division being so near, and the House not being satisfied with the report of the tellers, again divided, when the numbers were, Yeas, 81 ; Noes, 88. The House then resolved not to concur with the Lords in the propositions. C. J., III. 197. This paper and the Commons' reasons for their non-concurrence are here printed in extenso, as they do not appear in the Journals, and extracts only are given in Clarendon, Vol. IV. 183, and Parliamentary Register, Vol. XII. 362.

Most gracious Sou'signe,

Wee yo' Loyall Subiects the Lords and Comons in Parliament doe, w'th bleeding hearts, behould the miserable desoluc'on of this distracted Kingdome, and the inevitable approaching Ruyne of it, by the Calamities of this intestine Warr, occasioned by the great misvnderstanding betweene yo' Ma'v and yo' faithfull People, whose only desire the preservac'on of their just Rights and Liberties, And of that w'ch is farr more deare vnto them, their Religion : And therefore we haue w'th much Joy and Comfort seene a Protestac'on said to be by yo' Ma'v made before yo' receiving of the blessed Sacrament. By w'th yo' Ma'v professes that you intend the Establishment of the true Reformed Protestant Religion, w'thout any Connivance of Popery, And likewise a declarac'on of yo' Ma's lately Published shewing great desires to a Composure of theise vnhappy differences w'ch doth vnspeakeably reviue the hearts of yo' Peoples and makes them with a more tender Sence reflect vpon the present distemps, and the fearfull expectac'on of certaine distrucc'on, besides the irreconc'able Losse of the Kingdome of Ireland by their longer Contynuance, likely to make this Land like that, a Feild of blood, and worse, the Seat of Warre, for all Neighbouring Nations and the very Marke, and Prize of all the turbulent Spiritts of Christendom, if not prevented by the speedy interposic'on of the wisedome and Piety of yo' Ma'v and yo' two Houses of Parliament. Theise misserable distempers and distracc'ons haue bin the principall occasions of our not returning all this while an Answer to yo' Ma's Message of the 12th of Aprill requiring the Restituc'on of your Revennew, Magazeenes, Shipps, and Forts. And that the Memb'rs of both Houses voted out for adhering vnto yo' Ma'v in theise destracc'ons, may be restored to the same Capacity of Sitting, and Voting in Parliam't as they had in January 1641. And that yo' Ma'v and both Houses might be secured from Tumultuous

Assemblies by adiourning the Parliament to some other Place : To this wee giue yo' our humble Answer.

1. That wee are ready to giue yo' Ma'y a iust Accompt of somuch of yo' Reuennew as hath come to our hands, a good part whereof hath bin imployed in the maintenance of your Ma'ts Children, according to the allowance established by yo' self : And will giue satisfacc'on for such other sumes as haue bin Jmployed by vs ; And leaue it all to yo' Ma'y for the time to come ; That wee are likewise ready to deliu' vnto yo' the Navy, Forts, & Magazeenes, in a Trust and Confidence that they shalbe disposed and Jmployed for the Defence & Security of your Royall Person, and of yo' People, according to our humble desier expressed in our third Proposic'on following.

2. For the readmittance of our Members such as haue bin put out meerly for Adhering vnto yo' Ma'y in theise distracc'ons, wee shall endeavour to giue yo' Ma'y all due satisfacc'on, hauing regard vnto the P'uiledges of Parleam', w'h wee are bound by our duty in general, and pticulerly by our Protestac'on of the fourth of May 1641 to maintaine and preserue.

3. For securing yo' Ma'y from all Tumultuous Assemblies w'h is conceived can only be by adjourning the Parliament to some other Place. Wee beseech you beleeue that the Saftie of your Royall Person is vnto Vs a precious and most desired thing. That wheresoever yo' Parliament is, the Assurance of yo' Saftie is there evidently in the highest degree of Strength and Perfecc'on. Nor can yo' Ma'y and yo' two Houses of Parliament be in any Place of yo' whole Kingdome more Secure from feare, then in the Place where it now Sitts, yo' Citties of London and Westm' hauing bin faith-full to yo' Royall Predecessors who haue sate before you on the Royall Throne, and are still ready to express Fidelity and Affecc'on vnto yo' Ma'y, in all yo' occasions : Of which they Them-selues haue giuen yo' Ma'y pticuler Assurance by their Petic'on presented vnto you. And wee are most ready to confirme in yo' Ma'y this beleife of them, by any engagem', in any way your Ma'y will please to propose vnto vs, agreeable to our Duty and Allegiance. And wee doe now most humbly address our selues vnto yo' Ma'y, beseeching you graciously to accept what wee haue heere Rep'-sented, and to add yo' endeavo'' for the ending of this destructive Warre, and raise vnto vs a ground of confidence, by taking away the causes of our distrusts, and graunting vnto vs theise our humble desires, w'h only can su't the evill that hangs on' our heads, and produce that blessed Peace wherein yo' Ma'y & yo' Kingdomes may be made most happy.

1. That all Armes and Forces lately raised w'h in this Kingdom may be forthwith Disbanded & y' in order to such a disbanding a present Cessation of Armes may be agreed vpon.

2. That Religion and Church Gou'nment (the foundac'on of all Temporal Blessings) may be be setled in such a way as your Parliament shall desire, by the Advise and Councell of an Assembly of graue & Learned Diuines, to be approued of by your Ma'y.

3. That the Navy, Forts, & Magazeenes, may be intrusted in such hands as will be faithfull both to your Ma'y and the Parliament : And the Militia setled by Bill, for the Defence, & Satisfaction both of your Ma'y, and the King-dome.

4. That according to yo' Ma'ts gracious promise in yo' Message of the 12'h of Aprill, the Lawes may be put in Execution against Papists, And such other means vsed for suppressing of Popery in this Kingdome as shall by both Houses offred vnto your Ma'y for that purpose.

5. That such Delinquents as were Questioned & proceeded against in Parliament vpon Complaynt in the House of Comons before the first of January 1641 may be left to a Legall Tryall and Judgment of the Parliament.

6. That yo' Ma'y will graunt yo' free genn'all Pardon for the Releife & Comfort of your good Subiects, And that there may be an Act of Aboli-tion for the burying of all that hath hapned in this vnnatturall Warr, in a perpetuall Obliuion.

If in theise humble desires of ours, any thing shall appeare dubious, or obscure, or that yo' Ma'y shall not remaine vnsatisfied in any of theise per-ticulers, Wee humbly pray that your Ma'y would be pleased to appoint some Persons authorised from you, to meete w'h a Comittee of Lords and Comons to Treate of theise matters w'h may put a present stopp to all further effusion of the crying blood of your Loyall sub'ts Reestablish mutuall Confidence, betweene your Ma'y and them ; And (through the blessing of God), lay a happy foundac'on of Honour, Greatness, and Contentment to yo' Ma'y and of Peace and Prosp'ity to this and yo' other King-domes.

[Endorsed] The Proposicons,
5'h August 1643.

Reasons why the house of Comons cannott concurre w'h the Lords in the matter of y' Report concerning the Proposicons.

The Comons haveing taken them into their serious considerac'on though they fully concurre w'h their Lo'ps in their desires of a safe & hono'ble peace yett they can-nott concurre w'h them in these Proposicons for y' reasons ensueing.

The first Reason. They conceyve such concurrence w'h the Lords would bee a violacon of the publique fayth of the kingdome which both houses have engaged for repayment of all sumes of money to such as have lent or contributed any money, plate, horses or Armes to the Parliament for their iust defence in re-spect that no provision is made for the same by those Proposicons.

The seconde Reas' Whereas wee have sent Comittees by authority of both houses vnto o' Brethren of Scotland for their assistance with in-struccons likewise agreed vpon by both houses for that purpose, Our Concurrence with the Lords in these Pro-posicons would alter those Instruccons & make them voyd in the most materiall parts of them. And soe debarre vs of their assistance.

For first whereas wee have assured them that no pacificacon or agreement for peace shalbee concluded by the houses of Parliament w'hout sufficient caucon & provision for the security peace & safety of that Kingdome, the Indempnitie of all Persons & estates concerning the assistance w'h shall bee given to this Parliam' & Kingdome, the suppression of the Popish and ill-affected p'tie amongst them, There is no provi-sion att all in these Proposicons for the Indempnitie of Scotland, nor any thing at all in them concerning that Kingdome.

2. Secondly whereas by the Instruccons they are promised that sufficient Lands of Papists, Prelates and other malignants who have adhered vnto them shall by direccon of both houses bee sett forth out of w'h re-compence shalbee made to them for their forbearance And in part of their satisfaccon for the Arreares of the brotherly assistance, By these Proposicons all Papists and Prelates & their Adherents are pardoned as well as any his Ma'ts good Subiects.

3. Thirdly whereas wee have promised them a Guard of ships dureing their contynuance here All the ships are by these Proposicons to bee putt into the Kings owne hands.

4. Whereas for the reformacon of all erro's & abuses in the publique wor''p of Allmighty God & Church disci-pline & Gou'ment in such manner as shalbee most agreeable to the word of God & most effectuall for pro-cureing 'a neerer vnion w'h other reformed Churches they have called an Assembly of learned & godly Divines & have invited the Church of Scotland to send some from themselves vnto this Assembly who have accordingly nominated and appoynted some for that purpose, By these Proposicons the present Assembly is to bee dissolved vnless his M'ts Consent bee had thereto, And another to bee appoynted of such Persons whome his Ma'y shall approove of, w'h in likelyhood will never give their advise for setling such reformacon in the Church as is desyred.

The third Reason. Their third reason is because the Forts, ships & Magazins are wholly to bee re-signed into his Ma'ts hands w'hout any assur-ance or satisfaccon to the houses concerning the Persons who are to comand them. Which as it will amount to an acknowledgement that the two houses had no iust cause given them for seizing vpon them at the first, soe will it hazard the exposeing them & the well affected Protes-tants throughout the whole Kingdome to the malice of Papists, Delinquents, and of those ill Councellors who have brought the Kingdome into these distraccons.

N 2

For though by their first Proposicons to his Ma^{ty}, the Armyes on both sides are to bee disbanded yet considering that the Militia of the Kingdome is not setled, that the Papists in Ireland are in Armes, have publiquely declared themselves agaynst the two houses of Parliament & their intencons of comeing into the Kingdome, That the designe of the Papists and popeish p^{ty} here is the same with theirs, By putting the Forts, Ports, & Navy wholly into the King's hands to bee disposed of without consent in Parliam^t, They may bee placed in their hands who have bin the Contrivers of these troubles, And soe the Sea and Ports opened to Irish Papists & Rebells, & shutt up against our freinds.

For which reasons they cannott concurre wth their Lor^p. *And are discouraged to send any Proposicons at this tyme in regard y^t his Ma^{ty} by his Proclamacon dated the 20th of June last att Oxford hath declared that the Acts of the Persons now remayning in both houses are no longer to bee looked vpon as Votes of the two houses of Parliament.*

For which reasons as wee could not concurr with their lps in the propositions as they were framed, so wee could not in this time of iminent & pressing danger divert our thoughts or o' time from those necessary provisions as are to be made for the safety of the Kingdoms to the framing new propositions we having so lately p'sented propositions to his M^{ty} & by his answer receyv'd no satisfaction that we can not, at least with any hope, p'sent others at this time, when wee have cause to doubt his late success will make his royall assent more difficult; but such is o' love & desyer of peace, & of freeing this kingdom from these miseryes vnder wth it groanes, that wee shall with much earnestnes embrace all oportunities of offering such propositions to his Ma^{ty} as may secure through God's blessing our Religion & liberty, as likewise his royall souvreinty & Honor in such manner as may produce a lasting condition of happiness & safety to himself and all his people.

Aug. 5. Petition of Thomas Holden, clerk. Complains that the churchwardens of St. Cuthbert's, Bedford, refuse to obey their Lordships' order to pay him 20l. a year out of the tithes of the parish. Pray that they may be called upon to answer. L. J., VI. 171.

Aug. 5. Petition of Giles Thorne; prays that the trust of the souls of the parishioners of St. Cuthbert's, Bedford, may be committed to a more skilful and better qualified pastor than Thomas Holden, whom he charges with being a drunkard, ridiculously ignorant, a very stranger to good learning, and in no way able to distinguish truth from error. L. J., VI. 171.

Aug. 5. Petition of Thomas Jenyns. Prays that Sir Thomas Dawes may be ordered to produce certain deeds. L. J., VI. 172.
Annexed :—
  1. Affidavit of John Shelley of the service of the order for the production of the deeds upon Mr. Wilson, solicitor to Sir Thomas Dawes. 5 Aug. 1643.
  2. Copy of another petition of Jenyns in the same matter.
Aug. 5. Notes of proceedings on this and subsequent days. L. J., VI. 172, &c.
Aug. 7. Petition of Thomas Jenyns; prays to be dismissed from further attendance in the matter of Sir John Seaton's petition.
Aug. 8. Draft order in the suit between Catherine Pettus and the widow of Thomas Bancroft. L. J., VI. 173. *In extenso.*

1643. Aug. 8. to 22 Feb. 1643-4. } Book of orders made by the House of Lords.

Aug. 9. Petition of Mary Gray, Symon Midleton, and Katherine his wife. The cause between petitioners and the Clotworthies with reference to the estate of the late Robert Gray was referred, by an order of their Lordships, to certain referees. By a mistake in the drawing of the order, petitioners, though parties, are enjoined to be examined as witnesses against themselves, which is contrary to the intent of the order. Pray to be relieved from being examined, that the reference may be enlarged, and additional referees appointed, as those already named, by reason of other business, do not attend. L. J., VI. 173.

Aug. 9. Petition of John Viscount Purbecke concerning a rentcharge due to him from Sir Edward Cooke. L. J., VI. 173. *In extenso.*

Aug. 9. Petition of Edmund Nicholson; complains of a riot committed upon his lands in Gedney Marsh, and prays that the deputy lieutenants and the other officers of the Parliament may, in the absence of the sheriff and justices of the county, execute the order of the 13th of July 1641, for quieting possessions in Sutton Marsh. L. J., VI. 174.
  1. Copy of warrant of Sir John Brooke and Edward Heron, Esq., justices of the peace for Lincolnshire, for the apprehension of Erasmus Parkin and others for a riot at Gedney Marsh. 21 Sept. 1642.
  2. Affidavit of William Browne of Sutton, that the rioters burnt down three houses and a barn belonging to Edmund Nicholson upon Gedney Marsh, and dangerously wounded Nicholson. 22 Oct. 1642.
  3. Affidavit of Edward Townley concerning the riot. 3 Aug. 1643.

Aug. 10. Draft order for the Earl of Manchester to be Serjeant-major General of the forces of the six associated counties, &c. L. J., VI. 174. *In extenso.*
Aug. 10. Petition of Richard Wynde, William Carew, and William Taylor, inhabitants of St. Ives; petitioners, who stand committed for disobeying the ordinance for sequestering the tithes of the parish of St. Ives, pray for their discharge in regard that some of them are employed for the public service. L. J., VI. 174.
Aug. 10. Order for Stephen Estwicke, Francis Pecke, and Captain Player, senior, to provide clothes, &c., for the Earl of Essex's army. L. J., VI. 175. *In extenso.*
Aug. 10. Order for the payment of 10,000l. to Stephen Estwicke for clothes, &c., for the army in Ireland. L. J., VI. 175. *In extenso.*
Aug. 10. Order for the payment of 10,000l. to Sir William Waller. L. J., VI. 175. *In extenso.*
Aug. 10. Printed copy of an ordinance concerning the names of the Committee for the associated counties of Norfolk, Suffolk, Essex, Cambridge, Hertford, and Huntingdon, together with the instructions for the said Committee. And three special orders. 1. For the divines of the assembly to go into their several counties to stir up the people to rise for their defence. 2. For the Earl of Manchester to be Serjeant-major-General of all forces of the associated counties. 3. For the associated counties to raise a body of 10,000 foot and dragoons. L. J., VI. 174-176. *In extenso.*

Aug. 11. Petition of Michael Oldisworth, William Wise, and Robert Girlinge. By an order of the 13th of June 1641, the sheriffs and justices of all counties were to settle the possession of all men as they were the first day of this Parliament. John Trafford, by misinformation that he was in possession of certain lands at Tydd St. Mary on the first day of the Parliament, and that he was dispossessed thereof, obtained their Lordships' order to put the said order of the 13th of July in execution by power of the militia, thereby to continue him in possession. Petitioners pray that they may have the benefit of the general order and that Trafford's order, so unduly obtained, may be discharged. L. J., VI. 177.
Annexed :—
  1. Affidavit of William Wise in support of petition. 29 July 1643.
Aug. 11. Petition of John Trafford. Complains that William Wise made a forcible entry upon petitioners marsh land at Tydd St. Mary notwithstanding their Lordships' order. Prays that some course may be taken with Wise for his contempt. L. J., VI. 177.
Aug. 11. Order referring the two preceding petitions to Justices Reeve and Bacon. L. J., VI. 177.
Annexed :—
  1. Report of Justice Trevor thereon.
  2. Affidavit of William Pierson in the matter.
  3. Affidavit of Thomas Hatton.
  4. Affidavit of Simon Wood.
  5. Affidavit of William Wise.
Aug. 11. Order for Sir John Conyers to deliver the custody of the Tower into the hands of Sir Robert Harley until Sir John Conyers leaves the kingdom, when it is to be handed over to the Lord Mayor and sheriffs, according to a former ordinance. L. J., VI. 178. *In extenso.*
Aug. 11. Petition of John Doughtie, defendant, in a writ of error, wherein Thomas Overman and John Hardwicke are plaintiffs. Prays that without further delay he may have the benefit of the judgment awarded to him by their Lordships on the 5th instant. *See* L. J., VI. 171.

* The words printed in italics are struck out in the original, and the subsequent paragraph is on a separate paper, and in a different hand.

Aug. 11. Judges' report in the cause between Isabella Smith and Raleigh Sanderson. L. J., VI. 184. *In extenso.*

Annexed :—

1. Copy of order referring the cause to Justices Reeve and Bacon. L. J., VI. 150.
2. Copy of petition of Raleigh Sanderson. *See* 24 July 1643.
3. Copy of petition of Isabella Smith. *See* 27 July 1643.
4. List of bonds entered into by Raleigh Sanderson.
5. Order of committee for examinations, for search to be made in the house of Mr. Streete for arms and ammunition belonging to Mr. Sanders[on], who is suspected to employ the same against the Parliament. 4 April 1643.
6. Another order of the committee, that the pair of pistols and cases seized at Mr. Streete's house, and belonging to Raleigh Sanderson, who is at Oxford and suspected to be in actual war against the Parliament, shall be continued in Mr. Wright's custody. 10 April 1643.
7. Another order of the committee for the committee for Surrey and Middlesex to seize the wharf of Raleigh Sanderson and Francis Hanford, near St. Saviour's Mill, in the county of Surrey, and Shadwell wharf, in the the county of Middlesex, with the boats, lighters, engines, and other things belonging to the ballast business. 1 May 1643.
8. Receipt signed Charles Gheste for two rapiers, a dagger, and a case of pistols, received of Thomas Wright. 15 May 1643.
9. Affidavit of Arthur Collins that he knew nothing of the proceedings upon the sequestration of the estate of Raleigh Sanderson when he arrested him. 1 August 1643.
10. Affidavit of Robert Preston that he was told by Sergeant Wilde and some others of the grand committee that he might safely cause Sanderson to be arrested, there being no order made for his appearance. 1 August 1643.
11. Affidavit of Thomas Smith that he knew nothing of the sequestration of Sanderson's estate, but being informed that he was in town gave order for his arrest upon a bond of 6,000*l.*, as he hoped he might lawfully do. 1 August 1643.
12. Affidavit of George Plukenett. Hearing that Sanderson was arrested he gave notice and paid the fees to the Sheriff of Middlesex to charge him with action of 100*l.* upon a bond, but deponent knew nothing of the sequestration of Sanderson's estate. 2 August 1643.
13. Affidavit of William Sanderson and Richard Streete, detailing the proceedings before the committee upon the sequestration of the estate of Raleigh Sanderson, and his subsequent arrest.
14. Certificate of the sequestrators for the county of Surrey, that they, being dissatisfied with the proofs brought by Preston against Raleigh Sanderson appointed William Sanderson to send for his brother, the said Raleigh Sanderson, to come to London.
15. Affidavit of William Massey, one of the bailiffs of the county of Middlesex, that on the 12th of June he arrested Raleigh Sanderson, in Westminster Hall upon a writ *quo minus* taken out by Robert Preston, and that Sanderson informed the sheriff that he was ordered to appear that day before the committee for sequestrations. 2 August 1643.
16. Affidavit of John Calcott, under sheriff of Middlesex, that Arthur Collins insisted upon charging Sanderson, after his arrest, with a Bill of Middlesex at the suit of Daniel Giles, notwithstanding deponent informed Collins that Sanderson was sent for to attend the committee for sequestrations. 2 August 1643.
17. Affidavit of Edward Webb, servant to Raleigh Sanderson, that Robert Preston showed deponent a warrant signed by two of the collectors for the sequestrations in the hundred of Ossulston, and by virtue of that warrant received certain monies of the benefit and the profits of the wharf and ballasting business of Raleigh Sanderson. 2 August 1643.
18. Affidavit of Raleigh Sanderson that he is not and has never been in any service or employment in His Majesty's army, nor received any pay or promise of pay for any such service, and that he has never lent money to His Majesty or assisted any of His Majesty's forces with horse, arms, or ammunition. 2 August 1643.
19. Order signed by Robert Preston for an account to be made of what ballast hath been delivered at the wharf at Shadwell between the 2nd and 9th of May. On the same paper affidavit of Edward Webb that the preceding order is in the handwriting of Preston, and copy of order of the collectors for the hundred of Ossulston, appointing Preston to manage Shadwell wharf until the committee for sequestrations do further order.

Aug. 12. Application of Mr. Sergeant Whitfield to be exempted from paying the weekly assessment, in consideration of his having had four horses taken from him for the service of the Parliament. L. J., VI. 178.

Aug. 12. Ordinance for raising dragoons in the county of Essex. L. J., VI. 178. *In extenso.*

Aug. 14. Draft order respecting leave of absence to Mr. Ashe to go with the Earl of Manchester into the associated counties. L. J., VI. 179. *In extenso.*

Aug. 14. Draft order for the protection of Mr. Justice Reeve's house, in Chancery Lane, and his chambers in Serjeant's Inn. L. J., VI. 179.

Aug. 14. Similar order for the protection of his houses at Norwich and Wacton, in the county of Norfolk. L. J., VI. 179.

Aug. 14. Draft order for the protection of Mr. Justice Bacon's rooms in the house of Edmund Muggins in Chancery Lane, and his chambers in Sergeant's Inn. L. J., VI. 179.

Aug. 14. Similar order for the protection of his house in Norwich. L. J., VI. 179.

Aug. 14. Petition of Thomas Jenyns. Sir Thomas Dawes refuses to obey the orders to deliver certain bonds to the clerk of the House. Prays that some course may be taken for the delivery of the bonds. L. J., VI. 179.

Annexed :—

1. Copy of order referring the cause to certain of the judges. 31 July 1643.
2. Copy of the order of the judges appointing a day for hearing the cause. 31 July 1643.
3. Copy of order for Sir Thomas Dawes to produce the bonds. 5 August 1643. L. J., VI. 172.
4. Affidavit of Isaac Thomas that he served the preceding order upon Sir Thomas Dawes. 11 August 1643.

Aug. 14. Petition of Captain John Bond. Was on the 8th of July last arrested at the suit of one Gauthorne, and is now a prisoner in the King's Bench. Prays for his discharge as he is a sworn servant to His Majesty and (by the approbation and good liking of the House of Commons) in present employment in His Majesty's service. L. J., VI. 179.

Aug. 14. List of persons to be sent for as delinquents for refusing to bring in their horses. L. J., VI. 180. *In extenso.*

Aug. 14. Order for the payment of 150*l.* to Captain Gowre for his pay as lieutenant of a troop of horse. L. J., VI. 180. *In extenso.*

Aug. 14. Order for the payment of 365*l.* 8*s.* to Richard Wriglesworth and Daniel Fairvax, for clothes, &c. for Sir William Balfour's troop. L. J., VI. 180. *In extenso.*

Aug. 14. Order for the payment of 600*l.* to Thomas Haselrig, for clothes, &c. for Colonel Audley Mervin's regiment of foot. L. J., VI. 180. *In extenso.*

Aug. 14. Order for the payment of 43*l.* to Colonel Mainwaring and Mr. Croxton for ensigns for Colonel Audley Mervin's regiment. L. J., VI. 180. *In extenso.*

Aug. 14. Draft order concerning the payment of 10,000*l.* to Sir William Waller, and 10,000*l.* to Stephen Estwicke. L. J., VI. 180. *In extenso.*

Aug. 15. Petition of Mildmay, Earl of Westmoreland. Has now been in confinement for 10 months, to the danger of his health for want of fresh country air which custom hath naturalized to him. Would not have troubled their Lordships amongst their most weighty affairs, were not the consequence of more concernment than his own life, but having a wife and a house full of small children his fears for them increase daily as the church bells tell him the sickness increases near his house. Whilst, what through taxation, sequestrations, and often plunderings he hath not wherewithal to procure them bread here, where without money 'tis not to be had. Prays the House so far to compassionate his distressed condition as to give leave that he may with his family retire to one of his houses in the country, where his honor shall be as dear to him as it hath hitherto been. L. J., VI. 181.

N 3

Aug. 16. Ordinance for seizing the estates of the rebels in Kent. L. J., VI. 182. *In extenso.*

Aug. 16. Ordinance for the speedy raising of 20,000 soldiers in the six associated counties. L. J., VI. 182. *In extenso.*

Aug. 17. Petition of Cornelius Burges, vicar of Watford; 36*l.* 14*s.* 6*d.* is due to him for tithes from the Lord Capel's sequestered estate in the parish of Watford. Prays that the persons employed in sequestering the estate may be ordered to pay petitioner the sum due to him, as he has no means to recover the same in a legal course. L. J., VI. 183.

Annexed :—
1. Statement of the sums due to Dr. Burges from Lord Capel. 12 August 1643.

Aug. 17. Petition of Francis Newton, Thomas Mayo, and James Waddesworth, messengers. Their Lordships on the 15th of November 1641 ordered that any man who should discover any popish priests or Jesuits, and procure them to be apprehended, should be rewarded by the Parliament. Petitioners have brought many dangerous popish priests and Jesuits to their trial, conviction, and condemnation during the present Parliament, but have at present received no benefit from their labours, although they have in the prosecutions expended large sums of money. Pray that some recompense may be made to them for their past labours, and some annual allowance for the future to encourage their diligence. L. J., VI. 183.

Annexed :—
1. Copy of order referred to in preceding. 15 November 1641.
2. The names of the priests indicted and attainted at the Sessions House in the Old Bailey since the 22nd of July 1640, prosecuted and proved by Francis Newton, James Waddesworth, and Thomas Mayo, messengers to the Honourable Houses of Parliament, at their proper costs and charges.

Aug. 17. Draft ordinance for the committee of the militia for the city of London to administer an oath or vow to all those appointed to bear arms under them. L. J., VI. 184. *In extenso.*

Aug. 18. Petition of Peter Chamberlen, one of His Majesty's physicians : became bound for payment of 107*l.* in trust for Sir Wm. Middleton, and tendered the money to the day, deducting 50*l.* due to petitioner for diet and lodging afforded to Sir Wm. and his family, whilst he let part of his house (of the rent of 60*l.*) to the Lords Commissioners of Scotland for 420*l.* per annum, but Sir Wm., incensed by petitioner's former endeavour to restrain his unnatural and cruel conduct towards his mother, Lady Eliz. Middleton, since deceased, caused petitioner to be arrested in Fleet Street, and carried him in view of the trained bands and multitudes of people first to the St. John's Head in Ludgate, and then to the Rose in the Poultry, contrary to privilege, though the sergeants were told that petitioner was the King's servant; desires the consideration of the House. L. J., VI. 186.

Aug. 18. Petition of William Wombwell. Prays that 50*l.* due to him from Arthur Fry may be paid to him out of Fry's goods before they are otherwise disposed of, his estate having been sequestered, being one of the plotters in the late horrid conspiracy against the city. L. J., VI. 186.

Aug. 18. Draft order for all soldiers of the Lord General's Army to repair to their colours, &c. L. J., VI. 186. *In extenso.*

Aug. 18. Copies of some of the papers exhibited by Sir William Boswell, the King's resident at the Hague, to the Estates General of the United Provinces. L. J., VI. 187. *In extenso.*

Aug. 18. Draft order for pressing 2,000 men to recruit the army of the Lord General. L. J., VI. 190. *In extenso.*

Aug. 18. Printed copy of a letter from Mr. Marshal and Mr. Nye, appointed assistants to the Commissioners of Scotland, to their brethren in England concerning the success of their affairs. *See* C. J., III. 220.

Aug. 19. Petition of Arthur Samwell, Henry Kearsley, and other creditors of Sir Thomas Dawes. Sir Thomas Dawes having failed to bring in certain evidences in compliance with their Lordships' orders, petitioners pray that an order may be granted for searching his houses, chambers, studies, and other places for the said deeds, and also for the apprehension of the said Sir Thomas. L. J., VI. 191.

Aug. 19. Petition of John Gibbon. Is a prisoner in the Fleet in execution at the suit of Michael Fawkes, who is now with the King's army. Has petitioned

their Lordships for a hearing, but cannot now expect to obtain it on account of their other great occasions. Prays that a writ of habeas corpus may be granted to him to go abroad from time to time until his cause can be heard. L. J., VI. 192.

Annexed :—
1. Another petition of same praying that his cause may be referred to some four of their Lordships.
2. Another petition that order be given to Mr. Baron Trevor to grant him a writ of habeas corpus.

Aug. 19. Petition of John Perkins; Sir Alexander Hope and John Langston, two of His Majesty's servants, have long been indebted to petitioner to the amount of 40*l.*, and petitioner has obtained leave from the Lord Chamberlain to proceed against them at law notwithstanding their privilege. Langston being a servant in the Tower of London, petitioner would not presume to take course against him without their Lordships' approbation, and therefore prays that the leave already granted by the Lord Chamberlain may be confirmed by the House. L. J., VI. 192.

Annexed :—
1. Petition of same, to the Earl of Pembroke and Montgomery, Lord Chamberlain. Prays leave to proceed against Hope and Langston. Noted by the Earl, Hope and Langston to shew cause why the request should not be granted. 27 November 1640.
2. Petition of same, to same. Has shewn his Lordship's order to Hope and Langston, but cannot get any satisfaction. Noted by the Earl, Petitioner to take the benefit of the law if Hope and Langston do not give him satisfaction before the end of the present session of Parliament. 20 December 1640.
3. Petition of same, to the Earl of Essex, Lord Chamberlain. Prays leave to proceed forthwith against Hope and Langston who, instead of paying him his just debt, utter much evil language against him. Noted by the Earl, Hope and Langston to shew cause why the request of petitioner should not be granted. 25 January 1641-2.
4. Petition of same, to same. Has shewn his Lordship's order to Hope and Langston, who can show no good cause why his former petition should not be granted. Noted by the Earl, Petitioner may proceed against them in the ordinary course of law if they do not give him satisfaction within one month. 17 March 1641-2.
5. Petition and answer of John Langston, gent., porter to the Tower of London. Became bound for Sir Alexander Hope, His Majesty's carver, to John Perkins, but is unable at present to discharge the debt. Has offered to assign his wages, but this Perkins refuses. Three years' wages of 40*l.* per annum are due to him from His Majesty, and the King's army being now in the counties of Worcester and Northamberland, where petitioner has property, he cannot get any rents. Prays that until times are better Perkins may not have leave to arrest or implead him. 28 August 1643.

Aug. 19. Order of the Committee for the safety of the kingdom for the apprehension of all persons killing the King's deer and cutting down timber in Hyde Park. Signed by the members of the Committee.

Aug. 19. Warrant to the keeper of Ely House to take into safe custody Dr. Boale and others.

Aug. 21. Complaint of the Lord Morley that the rents of his manors of Hornsey, Tatham, &c., in the county of Lancaster, to the value of 1,200*l.* per annum, which is all that, for the present, he has to live upon, have been detained from him for the last 10 months, having been sequestered or otherwise seized upon by the Parliament forces. L. J., VI. 193.

Aug. 21. Petition of Katharine Pettus. Prays that she may be restored to the quiet possession of her manor of Santon, in the county of Norfolk, in compliance with their Lordships' order of the 7th instant. L. J., VI. 193.

Annexed :—
1. Certificate of Richard Carter and William Smith, two of the Commissioners appointed for sequestering the estate of the late Thomas Bancroft, that they have on behalf of Katherine Pettus demanded the possession of the manor of Santon from John Bancroft and others, who have forcibly withheld the same and utterly refuse to deliver it up. 12 August 1643.

Aug. 21. Petition of Anne Bickley. Prays that an
order may be made on her behalf in accordance with
the certificate of Sir John Nulls and Mr. Baron Leeke,
to whom her former petition was referred. L. J.,
VI. 193.

Annexed:—

1. Copy of her former petition. *See* 11 May 1643.

2. Copy of order referring her petition to Sir John
Nulls and others. 11 May 1643. L. J., VI. 42.

3. Certificate of Sir John Nulls and Mr. Baron
Leeke. 10 August 1643.

Aug. 21. Letter from Stephen Spratt, to the Lord
Howard of Escrick. Accuses his Lordship of having
pawned his honour in saying that the trunks and goods
lately taken from the lady of Banbury belonged to his
Lordship. If the House of Commons will let the writer
have a fair trial he will make it appear to the contrary
upon oath by divers witnesses both men and women. For
writing this letter, Spratt was sent for as a delinquent
and committed to Newgate. L. J., VI. 193.

Aug. 21. Application for a pass for William Hawkins
to go to Iver, in the county of Bucks. L. J., VI. 193.

Aug. 22. Order for the assembly of divines to consider of the doctrine of certain of the thirty-nine articles.
L. J., VI. 194. *In extenso.*

Aug. 23. Petition of the sequestrators of the living
of Aldenham, Herts. Complain that Joseph Soane, the
late vicar, refuses to give up possession of the vicarage
house and glebe lands. Pray for a further order in the
matter. On the same paper, affidavit of Richard Axtelly
that the sequestrators have often demanded possession,
but that Dr. Soane refuses them. L. J., VI. 194.

Aug. 23. Information respecting the searching of
Lord Hunsdon's house at Hunsdon for arms, &c.
L. J., VI. 194.

Aug. 23. Depositions of witnesses in the cause
between Sir Walter Devereux et al. and Sir William
Withypoole.

Annexed:—

1. Copy of order referring the cause to Sir Edward
Leech and Dr. Aylett. 18 August 1643. L. J.,
VI. 186.

2. List of witnesses. 19 August 1643. L. J., VI. 192.

Aug. 24. Application for a pass for the Portuguese
Ambassador, his interpreter, and attendants. L. J.,
VI. 194.

Aug. 24. Petition of Rose Fuller, a very poor widow,
on behalf of herself and her poor child. Petitioner's
late husband, Robert Fuller, was employed as a
chirurgeon by the East India Company and died about
four years since, having made his will, leaving petitioner sole executrix. Prays that the Company may be
ordered to pay her 18l. the residue of the sum due from
them to her late husband. L. J., VI. 194.

Annexed:—

1. Statement of the sums already received by
petitioner from the Company.

2. Copy of order for the East India Company to
answer. L. J., VI. 195.

Aug. 24. Ordinance for the repayment of 50,000l.
advanced by the city of London, for the payment of the
army raised by the Parliament. L. J., VI. 195. *In
extenso.*

Aug. 24. Ordinance for raising a body of horse for
the preservation, peace, and safety of the kingdom.
L. J., VI. 195. *In extenso.*

Aug. 24. Ordinance for fortifying Lovingland [Lo-
thingland], Suffolk, and East and West Flegg, Norfolk,
for the security of Great Yarmouth. L. J., VI. 196.
In extenso.

Aug. 24. Order for the payment of 100l. to Sir James
Barry in consideration of the losses he has sustained.
L. J., VI. 196. *In extenso.*

Aug. 24. Copy of preceding.

Aug. 24. Schedule of money and plate subscribed by
some of the inhabitants of the county of Warwick
for the service of the King and Parliament, and
brought into the Castle of Warwick. L. J., VI. 196.
In extenso.

Aug. 25. Draft letter from the Speaker of the House
of Lords, to the Earl of Lincoln and the Lords Bruce,
Dacre, and North, calling upon them forthwith to give
their attendance on the House. L. J., VI. 198.

Aug. 25. Petition of Francis Lord Willoughby of
Parham. John late Earl of Peterborough, who was
indebted to petitioner in the sum of 300l., died intestate,
and the Countess Dowager refuses to take out letters of
administration, although she acknowledges petitioner's
debt and desires he should be satisfied. Petitioner is
unable to take out letters of administration, because the

seal of the Prerogative office is at Oxford, and petitioner
is at Lincoln in the service of the Parliament. Henry
Compton and others are endeavouring to possess themselves of the estate of the late Earl, whereby petitioner
is likely to lose his debt. Prays that an order may be
made for seizing and disposing of so much of the late
Earl's personal estate as may satisfy petitioner's just
debt with damages for his forbearance. L. J., VI. 198.

Aug. 26. Petition of Daniel Breton. Petitioner took
a house of the Countess of Manchester called the Three
Kings, in Fleet Street, with a "bowling bare" thereto
belonging, part whereof is claimed by Sir Robert Rich
who refused to sell it to petitioner, but has since sold it
to Paul Williams, a broker, who intends to erect a new
edifice upon it contrary to law and greatly to petitioner's prejudice. Prays for relief. L. J., VI. 198.

Annexed:—

1. Affidavit of Daniel Breton. That he served
their Lordships' order upon Paul Williams, who
in contempt thereof continues to dig up his
bowling green and has commenced the foundations of his new building. 1 September 1643.
L. J., VI. 201.

2. Another affidavit of Breton; Paul Williams
having absented himself, his wife has encouraged
the workmen to go on building upon the "bowling
" bare " in deponent's possession in spite of their
Lordships' orders. 4 September 1643.

3. Another affidavit of Breton, similar to preceding.
15 September 1643.

Aug. 26. Ordinance for disposing of the houses of
those who have gone away and who have not paid the
weekly assessment. L. J., VI. 198. *In extenso.*

Aug. 26. Petition of the merchant strangers and
others concerned in the importation of plate and bullion
into this kingdom. Pray leave to import plate and
bullion without molestation. L. J., VI. 199. *In
extenso.*

Aug. 26. Order upon preceding petition. L. J., VI.
199. *In extenso.*

Aug. 26. Order conferring upon Dominique Petit,
Peter Delicques, and Claudius Fancault the sole right
for seven years of using an engine invented by them,
for drawing up out of the seas and rivers all or part of
ships, their lading, and cannons which are overwhelmed
therein. L. J., VI. 199. *In extenso.*

Aug. 29. Certificate of Sir John Franklin and Sir
John Hippisley, that George Longe of St. James',
Clerkenwell, who was formerly returned as a defaulter,
hath since sent in an able and sufficient horse with all
things necessary for the same. L. J., VI. 201.

Aug. 31. Petition of Sir William Withipoll. During
petitioner's absence beyond the seas Leicester Devereux,
who married petitioner's sole daughter and heiress, without any colour of title forcibly entered his house at
Ipswich, and possessed himself of goods to the value of
3,000l., and all the writings and evidences concerning
petitioner's manors and lands of inheritance. Leicester
Devereux has now, with his father Sir Walter, petitioned
their Lordships for settlement of a pretended marriage
agreement, whereby he hopes to obtain a title to the
said lands, taking advantage against petitioner by
occasion of the loss of his writings. Prays that Sir
Walter and Leicester Devereux may be forced forthwith
to make restitution, and that petitioner may be protected
from such unnatural and unjust violence. L. J., VI. 201.

Aug. 29. Paper endorsed My Lord's [Denbigh]
letter from Wellingborough to the committee at
Coventry. I desire you to meet me this day with all
the horse and dragoons you can spare at Hill Morton,
10 or 12 miles on this side of Coventry, in respect I have
desired the Northampton forces to convoy me until I
meet you.

Annexed:—

1. Letter from Sir Edward Littleton, to the Earl of
Denbigh; is glad to hear of his safe arrival at
Coventry, but the ways are so obstructed that the
writer only travels to Stafford, hoping to settle
peace there, but expects little without his Lordship's assistance; has gained the ill-will of many
by leaning to the honester part, and desires the
Earl to send a few lines to the House lest he
should be prejudiced by false accusations, and also
to obtain leave for him to stay in the parts where
he now is, from whence he expects to be able to
send useful information. (Undated.)

Aug. 30. Letter from Sir Richard Samwell, John
Crewe, and Edward Harby, at Northampton, to the Earl
of Denbigh. We hope your Lordship received our
answer wherein we offered to attend you if you had

pleased to command us. The Lord General sent a letter this day for your forces to meet him to-morrow at Bicester, with a postscript that if the foot could not come timely, then the horse only to go. We have acquainted Major Fraser, who will march with the horse accordingly, but the journey is too long for the foot. At the desire of your secretary we have despatched to the committee for safety the letters you sent from Wellingborough to us and to the committee at Coventry. We will be careful of the carriages left in our custody.

Aug. Petition of the merchant strangers of the Intercourse. Pray that a proviso may be inserted in the ordinance of excise to free them from all payments expressed and mentioned in the said ordinance, it having been declared by several orders of both Houses that they are exempt from all public subsidies, taxes, excises, and loans, as the society of English merchant adventurers is beyond the sea.

Annexed:—

1. Copies of various orders referred to in preceding.
2. Copy of certificate of the Fellowship of the Merchants Adventurers that the twenty-three persons named are the merchants of the Intercourse, and are all subjects of the seventeen provinces of the Netherlands, or of countries under the obedience of the King of Spain or the States General of the United Provinces. 29 August 1643.

Aug. The remonstrance and petition of the Lord of Kerry. Details at great length the circumstances under which he raised and transported a regiment for the defence of Ireland against the rebels, and the great hardship he and the regiment have suffered for want of their pay, and prays that the 1,000l. in money and 5,000l. victuals ordered to be sent for the relief of Munster, now nineteen months ago, together with the arrears of pay, and clothes and arms for his regiment, may be speedily sent, and if this cannot suddenly be effected, he prays that himself, his wife, and seven children may be taken into charitable consideration, that having lost all for their religion they may not be exposed to the extremity of beggary, and that the case of his officers who have all this time depended upon petitioner's purse, who is now no longer able to give them or himself relief, may be taken into consideration.

Sept. 2. Petition of the adventurers for lands in Ireland; against the rumoured cessation with the rebels. L. J., VI. 202. *In extenso.*

Sept. 2. Application from the resident of the King of Portugal for a pass for fourteen Portuguese men and women to Lisbon.

Sept. 4. Draft ordinance for making Lord Inchiquin, captain general of all the forces in Munster. L. J., VI. 203.

Sept. 4. Message from the Commons, with resolutions, making alterations in the committees of several counties. L. J., VI. 203. *In extenso.*

Sept. 4. Another draft of one of preceding resolutions relating to Cambridge.

Sept. 4. Copy of information against Steven Spratt, for saying that the Lords could not arrest any common subject without leave of the Commons, &c. L. J., VI. 203. *In extenso.*

Sept. 4. Draft order for the appointment of additional sequestrators for Nottinghamshire, &c. L. J., VI. 204. *In extenso.*

Sept. 5. Petition of Katherine Pettus, widow : Jeremy Aylett and others are now in custody for having taken violent possession of the manor of Santon in Suffolk and Norfolk, which had been sequestrated until a legacy, for many years owing to petitioner out of the estate of Thomas Bancroft, should be paid; petitioner prays that Aylett and his accomplices may not be discharged until she has been heard in favour of her claim to possession of the manor, and for payment of her costs. L. J., VI. 204.

Sept. 5. Petition of John Bickley, prisoner in the Fleet; petitioner who was arrested in his own house merely at the instigation of his wife Anne, prays for time to show cause why his estate should not be sequestrated. L. J., VI. 204.

Annexed:—

1. Draft order on a petition of Anne Bickley. 11 May 1643. L. J., VI. 42.

Sept. 5. Draft order for payment of 5,000l. for supply of arms for the forces under the Earl of Manchester. L. J., VI. 204. *In extenso.*

Sept. 5. Copy of order of the Commons for protection of Mr. Steward from arrest.! C. J., III. 228. *In extenso.*

Sept. 6. Affidavit of Richard Poole, that Fulke Hughes, a servant to the Earl of Warwick, has been arrested contrary to privilege by Duell, a sergeant of the

Poultry Compter, by the procurement of one Howett. L. J., VI. 207.

Sept. 6. Petition of Tho. Howett, citizen and wine cooper of London : arrested Fulke Hughes for a debt of 85l. 10s. which had been owing for ten months, and that after a chargeable suit; but since his imprisonment Hughes has unduly procured a protection from the Earl of Warwick ; prays for a warrant to secure Hughes until he make satisfaction. L. J., VI. 207.

Sept. 6. Draft ordinance for a weekly assessment from the associated counties of Norfolk, Suffolk, &c. for support of the forces raised in those counties. L. J., VI. 207. *In extenso.*

Sept. 6. Draft ordinance for Sir William Waller to take some of the trained bands and horse in London for the defence of the city of London and counties adjacent, for the assistance of the lord general, and for the preservation and recovery of the western parts. L. J., VI. 207. *In extenso.*

Sept. 6. Draft ordinance for Colonel Owen Rowe to contract with gunmakers and others for a supply of arms, &c. to the value of 5,000l. L. J., VI. 207. *In extenso.*

Sept. 6. Draft ordinance for levying arrears of rates, &c. in Suffolk. L. J., VI. 207. *In extenso.*

Sept. 6. Petition of Jeremy Aylett for himself and four of his tenants. Petitioner is a Commissioner appointed by Parliament for raising men, money, and horse in Essex, he and his tenants are now in prison for contempt of an order of their Lordships, which they never saw till after their arrest, and which was unduly obtained by Mrs. Pettus by combination with one Carter and Smith, a bailiff, by colour of a sequestration obtained in Chancery against the lands of Thomas Bancroft, deceased.

Annexed:—

1. Affidavit of Aylett in support of preceding.

Sept. 6. Letter from (Colonels) H. Mackworth and Tho. Mytton to Basil Earl of Denbigh. Express the loss they feel in his absence, and their sense of his zeal for the public service ; wiping off this stain will only make his honor shine the brighter; they pray that his spirit which would not have been overcome in the field may not yield to subtle and clandestine practices, but that he will prosecute his course of devotion to his oppressed country.

Sept. 7. Draft ordinance for appointment of an auditor and treasurer of the monies raised in Lancashire and Cheshire. L J., VI. 208. *In extenso.*

Sept. 7. Draft order of the Commons for discharge of Mr. Jeremy Aylett and his tenants. C. J., III. 231.

Sept. 7. Letter from [　　.] from his quarters at Cleeve to his brother : I know not what may be reported in London but the truth of our proceedings is as follows : —last week the Lord General met four or five regiments at Bayard's Green in Oxfordshire with about 7,000 foot and 4,000 horse, also Colonel Mainwaring with his city regiment of red coats, and a Kentish regiment consisting of eight colours, so that in all we were about sixteen or eighteen thousand men, and ever since we have marched together, which has caused us to endure hard quarters and want of victual, a barn and fresh straw we account a princely lodging, but the Lord be thanked we are all well and lusty ; last Sunday night we quartered at a little village called Addlestrop in Gloucestershire, and on Monday morning Prince Robert (Rupert) came to Stow-on-the-Wold and faced us on a hill over which we were to march ; our regiment that day led the van, the poor townsmen fell to their prayers, but we with joyful hearts went out to meet the enemy, who supposing the city regiments only to be there began to compass us round, for the lord general with his army was about a mile behind, we set ourselves in battalion pretty close to them, and our officers with great valour rode up and fired in their faces and so bravely retreated again ; as soon as the general came in sight he fired some drakes at them, which so amazed the rogues that they began to retreat, and the general's horse and his own regiment of foot charged them, and fired four roaring pieces at them, upon which they rode away as if the Devil were in them and we followed: what execution was done we know not, but hope well ; all the trophies of our victory were a cavalier's finger, which lay on the ground where they first faced us, and some prisoners ; the next day we were appointed to quarter at Prestbury where the cavaliers lay within six or seven miles of Gloucester ; as soon as we appeared in sight of the town they drew out into a corn-field, and our forlorn hope descended upon them, and the lord general let fly four pieces of ordnance at them, which made their guilty hearts quake and the

earth tremble, they rode away again as fast as their
horses would carry them, but we stayed some time by
the way and sold their welsh hobbies for 10s. a piece,
and that night they raised the siege of Gloucester and
burnt their cabins, which at first sight we thought had
been some town, and whither they are now gone the
Devil knows, for I think God hath nothing to do with
them; we are now wheeling about as we think toward
Worcester, we care not much whither, if God be for us
who can be against us.

Sept. 8. Notes respecting Mr. Justice Berkeley's
trial concerning ship money. *See* L. J., VI. 209.

Sept. 8. Printed copy of an ordinance to prevent the
coming over of the Irish rebels, together with three
special orders, all of which are given *in extenso* in the
Journals. L. J., VI. 210, &c.

Sept. 9. List of persons to be added to the committee
for Bucks for the weekly assessment. L. J., VI. 211.
In extenso.

[Sept. 9.] Petition of the officers of Sir William Waller's
brigade, to H. C., have served long under Sir William
Waller, but received little, to the exhausting of their
own and draining of their friends' means; are unwilling
to desist from serving, yet unable to subsist in the service; almost disenabled in a just way to prosecute their
just cause, and by necessity oppressing the countries
where they quarter, are forced to violate those privileges
which they fight to maintain; they appeal to Sir William
Waller to attest their fidelity, and pray that some part
of their arrears may be paid and the residue secured
to them. *See* C. J., III. 236.

Sept. 10. Copy of a letter from the Earl of Essex,
Lord General, at Tewksbury, to the Speaker of H. C.,
with news of the raising of the siege of Gloucester.
L. J., VI. 218. *In extenso.*

Sept. 11. Petition of John Kayes, minister of the
gospel; prays that Sir Nathaniel Brent, the Archbishop
of Canterbury refusing, may be ordered to institute him
to the rectory of Sundridge, Kent, upon the resignation
of Dr. Hall. L. J., VI. 212. *In extenso.*

Sept. 11. Copy of letter from Colonel Edward Massey
at Gloucester, to the Speaker of the House of Commons;
by the mercy of providence, the care of Parliament, and
the speedy march of the general, the enemy has risen
from before the town; he resumes his old suit that they
may be sufficiently strengthened to resist future attacks,
and endure the winter service, and that arrears of pay
may be satisfied, further desires reinforcements of horse
and foot sufficient to enable them to beat the enemy from
their quarters about the town, for if not, now that Bristol
is in the enemy's hand, unless Gloucester and the
country about be kept in subjection with a strong hand,
he sees not how to secure them to Parliament; without
a supply of ammunition, pistols, and carbines he cannot undertake to make the place good any further,
though there is no man more willing and ready to spend
his life in the service of Parliament than himself; he
trusts to the Speaker's goodness to signify these desires
and procure a speedy answer. *See* L. J., VI. 218.
where mention is made of this letter.

Sept. 12. Judgment of the House upon Sir Robert
Berkeley, one of the justices of the Court of King's
Bench, for his opinion in the case of ship money, with
an account of the proceedings of the House on delivery
of the judgment by Lord Grey of Warke, Speaker, *pro
tempore.* L. J., VI. 214.
Annexed:—
  1. Articles of impeachment of Sir Robert Berkeley,
  Knight, one of the justices of the Court of King's
  Bench, by the Commons in this present Parliament
  assembled in their own name, and in the name of
  all the Commons of England in maintenance of
  their accusation, whereby he standeth charged
  with high treason, and other great misdemeanours.
  Berkeley was impeached by message from the
  Commons on the 12 of Feb. 1640-1 (L. J., IV.
  161), but judgment in his case was not delivered
  till this day. L. J., VI. 214. The articles are
  given *in extenso* in Rushworth I., iii. 318. (Parchment collection.)

Sept. 12. Notes of proceedings this day.

Sept. 13. Affidavit of Richard Axtell, that Joseph
Soame (Sone), vicar of Aldenham, Herts, will not deliver
up possession of the vicarage house and glebe lands to
John Gilpin, pursuant to their Lordships' orders, though
duly served therewith. L. J., VI. 215.

Sept. 13. Petition of John Perkins; had leave from
the Earl of Pembroke and Montgomery (late Lord
Chamberlain) and afterwards from the Earl of Essex,
Lord Chamberlain, to arrest Sir Alexander Hope, His
Majesty's carver, and John Langston, porter of the

Tower of London, for a debt of 40l. long due: prays for
leave to proceed at law against Langston. L. J., VI.
215.

Sept. 13. Order upon proceeding, that if Langston
cannot show cause to the contrary by Monday week
next, Perkins may take his course at law.
Annexed:—
  1. Affidavit of Godfrey Austinson that when Sir
  Alexander Hope and Langston executed a bond
  for the money due to Perkins, Langston said he
  must be the paymaster, for he owed Sir Alexander
  much more than the 40l.
  2. Affidavit of Robert Burrows that the Earl of
  Pembroke and Montgomery gave Perkins a
  reference against Langston.

Sept. 13. Draft order for repayment of money advanced by the inhabitants of Ipswich, &c. for the use of
the navy. L. J., VI. 215. *In extenso.*

Sept. 13. Draft order for payment of 600l. weekly out
of the weekly assessment of Bucks, Herts, and Beds for
maintenance of the garrison of Aylesbury. L. J., VI.
216. *In extenso.*

Sept. 14. Petition of John Trafford. Mr. Wm. Wise
has caused petitioner to attend the House several days,
expecting him to present a petition about land in St.
Mary Tydd Marsh, in Lincolnshire, now in possession
of petitioner; but Wise, seeing that petitioner was
ready to answer, has done nothing in the matter.
Prays that Wise may have no advantage against him
without giving due notice. L. J., VI. 216. *In extenso.*

Sept. 14. Draft order of the Commons, nominating
additional Committees for the county of Cambridge and
Isle of Ely. C. J., III. 240. *In extenso.*

Sept. 14. Rough draft of order of the Commons, touching security to be given to those who advance money for
the use of Sir William Waller. C. J., III. 240. *In
extenso.*

Sept. 15. Message from the Commons, with an order for
Mr. John Maynard to be a member of the assembly of
divines. L. J., VI. 216.

Sept. 15. Draft order for securing the apprentices of
Thames watermen enlisted to serve under Sir William
Waller from the consequences of breaking their engagements with their masters. L. J., VI. 217. *In
extenso.*

Sept. 15. Draft resolutions of the Commons for rewarding Colonel Massey for his services, &c. C. J., III.
241. *In extenso.*

Sept. 16. Order for Lord Maitland and others to be
admitted to the assembly of divines. L. J., VI. 218.
In extenso.

Sept. 16. Order for the assembly of divines to set
forth a declaration of the reasons that have induced
them to give their opinion that the covenant may be
taken in point of conscience. L. J., VI. 218. *In extenso.*

Sept. 18. Draft ordinance concerning the excise.
L. J., VI. 220. *In extenso.*

Sept. 18. Draft ordinance authorising the Commissioners for the Customs, &c. to repay themselves
30,000l. advanced by them for supply of the navy.
L. J., VI. 221. *In extenso.*

Sept. 18. Draft ordinance for the relief of the distressed clergy of Ireland. L. J., VI. 221. *In extenso.*

Sept. 19. Petition of Katherine Pettus, widow, late
wife and administratrix of William Pettus, deceased;
details the wrong done her by Thomas Bancroft, as
executor of her late father-in-law, William Pettus, and
prays that his widow and executrix, Margaret Bancroft,
Jeremy Aylett, and others, may be called upon to
answer. L. J., VI. 223.

Sept. 20. Petition of Philip Thomas. Petitioner, one
of His Majesty's servants in ordinary, and messenger
of the chamber, was employed to attend the Commissioners for charitable uses in the city of London, where
he was arrested by two sergeants, John Burdett and
John Duell, at the suit of William Tooley, for a pretended debt of 40l., alleged to have been due thirteen
years, and is now detained prisoner in the King's
Bench, contrary to privilege. Prays for enlargement,
and for reparation from those who arrested him. L. J.,
VI. 223.

Sept. 20. Order upon preceding, appointing a day for
hearing the case. L. J., VI. 223. *In extenso.*

Sept. 20. Draft ordinance for the assembly of divines
to consider of a form of church government in the place
of that by archbishops, bishops, &c., now taken away.
C. J., III. 246. *In extenso.* This ordinance was agreed
to in the Commons on the 18th, and was sent up to the
Lords on the 20th, and by them "respited for awhile."
L. J., VI. 223.

Sept. 20. Order that every one taking any charge in the armies raised by the Parliament shall first declare his approbation of the covenant. L. J., VI. 224. *In extenso.*

Sept. 20. Draft of preceding.

Sept. 20. Printed copy of an ordinance, wherein the county of Lincoln is added in the association of the six counties of Norfolk, Suffolk, Essex, Cambridge, Hertford, and Huntingdon, for the mutual defence each of other against the popish army in the North, under the command of the Marquess of Newcastle; also giving power to the Earl of Manchester to nominate governors over the parts of Holland and Marchland; and if any person harbour a soldier that is imprested to serve under him, he shall be fined; if he refuse to pay his fine, his goods shall be sequestered, and he imprisoned till the fine be satisfied. With the names of the committees appointed for the collection of money to pay the forces raised for the preservation of those seven counties. L. J., VI. 224. *In extenso.*

Sept. 20. Draft of preceding, omitting the proviso at the end respecting the harbouring of pressed men.

Sept. 20. Resolutions of the Commons, upon report from the Committee appointed to consider of the papers, propositions, and results sent from the Commissioners of both Houses now in Scotland touching the business of putting in a garrison of Scots into Berwick, the payment of the arrears to the Scots army in Ireland, and the aid desired of the Scots by both Houses, and their condescending unto it, and the manner of it, and the propositions of the Scots thereupon, and the state and result upon the whole matter. C. J., III. 248. *In extenso.*

Annexed :—

1. Draft of preceding.

2. Copy of "the result concerning Berwick." Seeing the importance of providing for the security of Berwick, according to the terms of the treaty and covenant between the two kingdoms, the Commissioners of the Parliament of England and the Committee of the convention of estates of Scotland offer the following propositions on the subject, viz. : —1. A Scottish garrison shall be placed in the town, consisting of 600 foot and 120 horse, the chief officers to be approved by the two Houses of the English Parliament, or their Commissioners, this garrison to be part, and paid as part, of the Scottish army, which the Scots have agreed to bring into England; but as it is intended that that army should not fall short of the stipulated number, exclusive of this garrison, the cost of which will be 1,500*l.* monthly, it is left to the English Parliament to consider whether it would not be just for them to make up the monthly allowance to 31,000*l.* instead of 30,000*l.* 2. That Scotland shall guarantee that when the peace of the two kingdoms has been settled, their garrison shall be withdrawn and the works dismantled, and that whilst the garrison is there the liberties and estates of the inhabitants shall be respected; provided that if the English Parliament shall not approve of these articles, that they shall withdraw their garrison now there, otherwise it will be understood by the kingdom of Scotland as a breach of the large treaty between the two kingdoms. 5 Sept. 1643.

3. Another copy.

4. Reasons and grounds why a garrison of the Scottish nation upon this occasion should be settled in Berwick. If the assistance to be given by the Scots is to be effectual, they must have the town as a magazine for victuals and ammunition. It is the only safe passage for the army, and must always be open to them. An English garrison there would be of no use except as a help or hindrance to the assistance sent from Scotland. If Scotland were to assist England in any auxiliary way, they could not make terms unless some towns of garrison were granted them; much more reason is there for them to desire Berwick, when they are content to go on in such a joint and brotherly way with their brethren of England for their assistance. As the garrison at Berwick is only useful to the Scots in relation to their assistance to England, so when peace shall be restored all things shall be put into their former condition. 5 Sept. 1643.

5. The answers of the Committees of both kingdoms of England and Scotland unto the queries sent them from the mayor and corporation of Berwick by two of their own number, Mr. Clarke and Mr. Pratt, upon occasion of the said towns declaring for the King and Parliament of England at the desire of the English Commissioners : —1. What they do is done by authority of the two Houses of the Parliament of England; 2, and with the consent of Scotland. 3. Though the mayor and corporation of Berwick have bound themselves to stand for the King and Parliament upon their own defence, they may safely admit the Scots under the authority of the two kingdoms, without prejudice to the articles of pacification. 4. The number of men for securing the town is now under consideration. 5. They are to be maintained out of the public purse. 6. When peace is restored, the fortifications are to be destroyed, and everything put in its former condition; and during the occupation the rights and liberties of the inhabitants and the politic government of the town are to be respected. 7. No private person is to be questioned for the bygone. Two other things were propounded by word of mouth :—1. That the mayor might keep the keys of the town, and give the word till the garrison was fully settled, but it was thought necessary that Henry Darley should keep the keys during this time, allowing the mayor the use of them from time to time. 2. Provision has been made to secure the town from assessments. 5 Sept. 1643.

Sept. 21. Draft ordinance for the due and orderly receiving and collecting of the King's, Queen's, and Prince's revenue, and the arrearages thereof to the use of the Parliament. L. J., VI. 227. *In extenso.*

Sept. 23. Draft ordinance "to supply the poor and " all other degrees and sorts of people with wood, pay- " ing for the same, as by this ordinance is appointed." Whereas there is great scarcity of fuel in and about London, in consequence of the town of Newcastle being now in the hands of the papal and malignant forces, which is likely to produce great misery amongst the poorer people during the winter; and whereas the common sort of people, urged by necessity, have destroyed and are destroying great store of timber trees, which, if not timely prevented, may prove of dangerous consequence; it is ordained—1. That the circuit for cutting fellable wood and underwood shall be within sixty miles of London, and that the Committee of Lords and Commons shall appoint officers for the purpose. 2. That these officers shall have power to enter and cut wood upon the lands of any archbishop, bishop, deans, and chapters, in their "politic" capacity, or of any papists or other delinquents, or in any of the Royal parks or chases; that the poorer sort of every parish shall be served first, and afterwards the other degrees and ranks of people; that the wood brought to London shall be distributed in every parish by the churchwardens or such other persons as the Committee shall nominate, and at such easy rates as the Committee shall appoint : provided that this ordinance is not intended to give power of entry upon any of the lands above mentioned, if any private person, not being a papist or delinquent, has a real interest therein, nor upon any woods belonging to the site of any mansion house, nor upon gardens, orchards, or walks. 3. That none except persons duly nominated shall cut wood under pain of fine and corporal punishment. 4. That the officers shall have power to compel persons to convey the wood in carts or lighters upon reasonable hire for use in London. 5. That out of the sale of the timber the officers shall be repaid for fences put up and for their own trouble. 6. That none shall engross the wood so cut. 7. That the cutting shall continue till Parliament recall their order. 8. That in case of resistance to the officers the justices and deputy lieutenants shall assist them with any forces at their command. 9. That the officers shall be protected for their conduct, provided that due care be taken that no woods are cut without lawful authority.

This ordinance was sent up from the Commons this day, read by the Lords, and referred to a Committee (L. J., VI. 230); was reported on the 28th with amendments, read and agreed to, and returned to the Commons (233); whence it was sent back with further amendments on the 2nd Oct., which were agreed to, and the ordinance ordered to be printed (241).

Sept. 23. Another draft. Endorsed, "A later ordi- " nance drawn and passed."

Sept. 23. Draft order authorising the assembly of divines to adjourn to the Jerusalem Chamber, in the College of Westminster, from Henry the Seventh's

Chapel, on account of the cold. L. J., VI. 231. *In extenso.*

Sept. 23. Draft order for Mr. Baron Trevor to sit as puisne judge, to take the proffers of the late sheriffs for the grant of the sheriffwick, &c. L. J., VI. 231. *In extenso.*

Sept. 23. Draft order for payment of 610l. 13s. 7d. to Mr. Henry Finch and Mr. Henry Osborne, for butter, shoes, swords, &c., transported to Londonderry. L. J., VI. 231. *In extenso.*

Sept. 23. Draft order for payment of 215l. 2s. 7d. to Mr. Henry Finch, for victual and ammunition transported to Londonderry. L. J., VI. 231. *In extenso.*

Sept. 23. Draft order for payment of 661l. 16s. 8d. to Mrs. Jennett Russell, for corn and butter transported to Londonderry. L. J., VI. 231. *In extenso.*

Sept. 23. Draft order for payment of 145l. 0s. 7d. to Mr. Henry Osborne, for butter and salmon transported to Londonderry. L. J., VI. 232. *In extenso.*

Sept. 23. Draft order for payment of 605l. 12s. 8d. to Mr. Henry Osborne for corn, beef, and other provisions transported to Londonderry. L. J., VI. 232. *In extenso.*

Sept. 23. Message from the Commons with votes of thanks, &c., to the Lord General, after the battle of Newbury. C. J., III. 252. *In extenso.*

Sept. 23. Message from the Commons with resolutions for sending a committee to the City Common Council to represent the necessity of sending supplies, &c. to the Lord General's army. C. J., III. 252. *In extenso.*

Sept. 23. Letter from the Earl of Manchester, at Lynn, to the Lords in Parliament. Has formerly given an account to the Committee for the safety of the kingdom, how the town of Lynn was rendered into his hands, and also sent a copy of the articles of surrender. Since Tuesday last when he came to the town, he has received a letter from Colonel Cromwell, whom he had sent into Lincolnshire, to say that Sir Thomas Fairfax was landed in that county, between Grimsby and Barton, and that the enemies forces were interposed between his and those of Sir Thomas Fairfax, upon which the Earl sent him all the horse and foot he could spare, having regard to the security of his own neighbourhood, and also a bark with provisions to Sir Thomas Fairfax. He will press the deputy lieutenants to send in their proportions of horse and foot, and then he hopes to be able to move to the assistance of other counties. Before his coming some of the well-affected in the town were imprisoned by the mayor and their goods seized; he is very anxious to relieve these men, who are of great honesty and integrity, but desires the directions of Parliament, which he will always be ready to carry out. The articles upon which Lynn was surrendered are given in Rushworth, III. ii., 283. *See* C. J.,¹ III. 247.

Sept. 25. Papers relating to the covenant, inserted in the Calendar on this day, because it was the day on which the covenant was taken by both Houses of Parliament:

1. The Covenant as originally sent up from Scotland; some slight alterations introducing mention of Ireland were made by the Commons, and the fifth article relating to the maintenance of the late treaty was omitted, otherwise this draft agrees with the Covenant given *in extenso*, L. J., V. 219.

2. Copy of preceding with order of the Commons of 26 Aug. 1643, referring it to the consideration of the assembly of divines. C. J., III. 220.

3. Copy of the report of the assembly of divines to the House of Commons upon preceding. C. J., III. 223. *In extenso.*

4. Copy of the amendments made by the Commons. *See* C. J., III. 224, 229, 230.

5. Copy of a declaration of the House of Commons to their brethren of Scotland, concerning the fifth article of the Covenant. The Commons are most desirous to unite the two nations more closely, and think the taking of the Covenant most conducive to this end, but they have suspended their votes upon the fifth article (relating to the maintenance of the articles of the late treaty) thinking that many people would be less ready to take the Covenant, because there are many thousands who either know not the articles or know them only in part, and besides the public faith of each kingdom is engaged for the performance of the matter of that article, which is not the case with regard to the other articles of the Covenant. *See* C. J., III. 231.

6. Copy of commission from the general assembly of the Kirk of Scotland, empowering Commis-

sioners to treat with the assembly of divines in England, or any Commissioners appointed by Parliament concerning uniformity in church government, and to deliver a declaration to the Parliament of England, a letter to the assembly of divines, the answer of the assembly to His Majesty's letter, and also the answer of the assembly to the letter sent from some well-affected brethren of the ministry in England. 19 Aug. 1643. L. J., VI. 211. *In extenso.*

7. Answer of the general assembly of the church of Scotland to the declaration of both Houses; express their satisfaction at the progress of church reformation in England, their desire for a closer union between the two kingdoms, for which end they have sent Commissioners to treat with the assembly of divines, and have agreed on a covenant to be taken by the well-affected of both kingdoms. 19 Aug. 1643. L. J., VI. 212. *In extenso.*

8. Copy of answer of the general assembly of the Church of Scotland to the letter of the assembly of divines. Their letter was received with mixed joy and sorrow, joy at the work of reformation, sorrow for their sad condition, remembering the former assistance given by their brethren of England, they desire to assist them now, and to promote a closer union between the two nations.

9. Copy of answer of the national assembly of the Church of Scotland to the King's most Excellent Majesty. The remembrance of the duty they owe to His Majesty for his royal favour towards their kirk and government can never by any length of time be deleted out of their minds, whilst the sense of their obligations to him are increased by their religious feelings, they have therefore in their proceedings, in answer to the propositions made to them by the Commissioners of the Parliament of His Majesty's kingdom of England, and some divines assisting them, fixed their thoughts on His Majesty's honour and happiness, with no less intention than if His Majesty had been himself present among them, and in like manner have sent some ministers and others to the assembly of divines now in England, as next to the honour of God and the good of religion, may most serve for His Majesty's preservation and the peace of the kingdoms, on which subject the Commissioners of the last assembly have already fully expressed themselves to His Majesty. They pray His Majesty to judge them by the nature and necessity of their vocation, and the word of God, and not by the reports of ungodly men; and that His Majesty's heart may be inclined to the counsellors of truth and peace, that an end may be put to the present unnatural war. 2 Aug. 1643.

10. Copy of answer of the general assembly of the Church of Scotland, to some well-affected brethren in England; expressing their sorrow for their troubles, but reminding them, that they are only suffering like the saints of old, they must expect no mercy from papists and prelatists, but must quit themselves like men and seek deliverance in the work of the Lord.

Sept. 25. Copy of a letter from Sir Henry Anderson, at Oxford, to Mr. Speaker. Has heard of the hard, if not unjust, proceedings of the Parliament towards him for nothing but for his peaceable intentions for which he has suffered from both sides. The King's party being in power where his estate lay, seized and committed him prisoner to York Castle for fourteen weeks, during which time his goods were taken away and nothing left for the support of his wife and children, and when released by Captain Hotham's means he was not suffered to return to his wife or home, but sent a contrary way; after which he came to the Parliament and with difficulty procured means for his wife to join her daughter Hotham at Hull, where some persons by authority of Parliament broke into her chamber and took away all the means left her, upon which, as a member of the Commons, he moved the House that his goods might be restored, which was granted, but this order has since been revoked, to his great surprise, by men who pretend either law or honesty. In coming to Oxford his intentions were to procure the liberty of a son who has been twenty-three or twenty-four weeks prisoner for his service to Parliament, who did not seem likely to relieve him, also to get a pardon for some near friends; he had no other intentions unless anything tending to the peace of the kingdom might fall in his way. Since he parted with the

Speaker he has been fourteen days a prisoner at Wallingford; has not seen the King, but has been examined, and
no fault imputed to him but the taking of the covenant;
has been stayed at Oxford longer than he expected, but
will promote nothing except what will tend to an end
of the present calamities, which might be much better
concluded by an agreement than by war. Prays the
Speaker to move the House to restore his money and
goods forthwith, otherwise he will be obliged to move
the King to let him have satisfaction out of the estates
of those who have unjustly taken his property, which
he doubts not would be granted even out of the estate
of Mr. Speaker himself; but there are Sir Matthew
Bointon, Sir Wm. Allinson, and others, of the Hull
Committee, who have estates near, which no ordinance
of Parliament could save; he thought right that the
House should be informed of this that they might give
him a remedy which otherwise he must seek in a higher,
yet an honest way. *See* C. J., III. 219.

Sept. 25. Copy of a letter from Sir Henry Anderson
to Mr. Hollis. The King's long stay at Gloucester, and
the bloody issue to both sides, have frustrated the
writer's poor intentions for peace. The sight of so many
brought to Oxford, some dead, some wounded, since the
battle, would make any true English heart bleed. Entreats Mr. Hollis to use his endeavours for peace, the
time being not unsuitable, for which end he sends some
propositions of his own, which he desires Mr. Hollis to
consider and to return an answer by the bearer, who is
sent specially with a letter to Mr. Speaker, desiring the
restoration of the writer's goods taken at Hull; he
thinks the King would agree to the conditions sent.
Every man is desirous of peace, but yet with several
ends, and themselves to be the agents, he is desirous
that Mr. Hollis should have a share in the thanks and
honour of so good a work, in which he would do well to
consult with Sir John Holland, Mr. Selden, Mr. Maynard, or others. He believes there will be another
means used to acquaint Sir Philip Stapleton, who is
well thought of at Oxford, nor is there any ill impression
against Hollis. Sir Henry desires him not delay in the
work to which the King is well inclined, so his honour
be respected. *See infra.* 30 Nov. 1643.

Sept. 26. Draft order for publishing the ordinance
concerning the sequestering of the King's, Queen's, and
Prince's revenue. L. J., VI. 232. *In extenso.*

Sept. 28. Draft order for making provision for the
maintenance of the minister of the chapelry of Holland,
in the parish of Wigan, Lancashire. L. J., VI. 234. *In
extenso.*

Sept. 29. Draft order for Mr. Robert Duncan and
others to be added to the Committee for sequestrations,
&c., for Ipswich. L. J., VI. 235. *In extenso.*

Sept. 29. News pamphlet headed " A continuation of
" certain speciall and remarkable passages informed to
" the Parliament, and otherwise, from divers parts of
" this kingdome, from Thursday the 21 of September
" till Fryday the 29 of September 1643. Number 54.
" Printed for Francis Coles and H. Leach, in the Old
" Baly." Licensed and entered into the register book of
the Company of Stationers according to order, giving
some account of the battle of Newbary, and of the return
of the Earl of Essex to London, of the proceedings of
the Earl of Manchester in Lincolnshire, &c.

Sept. 30. Message from the Commons, with an ordinance for sequestration of the lands of city companies that
have not yet paid the rates imposed upon them by the
Common Council for the public service, unless they shall
forthwith pay the same. L. J., VI. 236. *In extenso.*

[Sept.] Petition of Sir Edward Hales, a member of
the House, to H. C.; has been a prisoner in the Tower
above eleven weeks, on suspicion of being concerned in
the insurrection in Kent; understands that an order has
been made for the sequestration of his estate; prays for
a hearing before the execution of the same. The order
was made on the 28th Sept. 1643. C. J., III. 258.

Oct. 2. Notes of scandalous words spoken by Mr.
Walker against the Lord Say and Seale, &c. L. J., VI.
241.

Oct. 2. Draft ordinance for Christ's Hospital to be
free from all taxes and assessments. L. J., VI. 241. *In
extenso.*

Oct. 2. Draft ordinance for fortifying the Isle of
Wight. L. J., VI. 242. *In extenso.*

Oct. 5. Petition of John Wynyard; as keeper of the
Palace at Westminster has a little house under the
Prince's 'tiring rooms, which the groom porter made
use of during his residence; he is now gone to Oxford,
and petitioner prays that he may enjoy the house,
which is properly his right, and may have the keys
and chains in the palace, and the ordering and dis-

posing of them for the service of the state. L. J., VI.
243. Noted, Nothing ordered.

Oct. 5. Draft ordinance enabling Adam Lawrence and
others, committees in Holland, to pursue the business
concerning Ireland, severally as well as jointly. L. J.,
VI. 243. *In extenso.*

Oct. 5. Draft order for payment of 886l. 18s. for
Captain Upton's troop of horse in Ireland. L. J., VI.
244. *In extenso.*

Oct. 5. Draft order for payment of 886l. 18s. to
Colonel Arthur Hill, three months' pay for one troop
of horse in Ireland. L. J., VI. 244. *In extenso.*

Oct. 5. Draft order for payment of 1,721l. 14s. for
arrears to men lately employed in the train of artillery
in Ireland. L. J., VI. 244. *In extenso.*

Oct. 5. Draft order upon a petition of Oliver Bowles,
giving him leave to land forty-five small casks of currants from Holland upon payment of customs. C. J.,
III. 263. *In extenso.* Noted, Not yet passed the Lords.

Oct. 6. Notes of proceedings on this and subsequent
days. L. J., VI. 244.

Oct. 7. Petition of inhabitants of Leighton Beaudesert
[Buzzard], in the county of Bedford, containing with
the hamlets above a thousand communicants; pray that
the parishioners may be ordered to pay the accustomed
tithes to the now vicar Mr. Rathband, and that a further
addition may be made to the vicarage out of the parsonage impropriate, and out of the tithes of the rest of
the lands of Lord Leigh, all of which are now sequestered
to the use of the Parliament. L. J., VI. 245.

Oct. 7. Petition of the University of Cambridge, to the
Lords and Commons; some members of colleges before
the war broke out sent plate to His Majesty, being
bound to him as their founder or as his chaplains, and now
some persons pretending authority from Parliament are
sequestering their libraries, goods, and revenues; they
pray for compassion that they may not be forced to
leave the University. L. J., VI. 246. *In extenso.*

Oct. 7. Draft ordinance for repayment of 30,000l. out
of the income from the excise to the merchant adventurers. L. J., VI. 246. *In extenso.*

Oct. 7. Draft order for repayment of those who shall
advance 8,000l. for the present supply of the lord
general's army. L. J., VI. 246. *In extenso.*

Oct. 7. Affidavit of Philip Thomas; that he served
two sergeants, John Burdett and John Duell, who arrested him, contrary to privilege, with their Lordships'
order to appear, and that Leech, solicitor to Tooley, at
whose suit petitioner was arrested, spoke contemptuously
of the order. L. J., VI. 246.
Annexed :—
    1. Affidavit of same, that Scriven, an attorney, told
Burdett and Duell, they were base rogues if they
appeared upon their Lordship' order.
    2. Similar affidavit of Gilbert Thomas.

Oct. 7. Answer of Clement Walker; refuses to submit to the judgment of the House as against the liberty
of the subject. L. J., VI. 247. *In extenso.*
Annexed :—
    1. Notes of preceding.

Oct. 9. Draft ordinance touching the lands of Sir
William Brooke, Knight, of Cooling Castle, in the county
of Kent, deceased. L. J., VI. 248. *In extenso.*

Oct. 9. Draft ordinance authorizing the committee at
Northampton to levy money for the defence of the
county. L. J., VI. 249. *In extenso.*

Oct. 9. Draft ordinance concerning forces to be sent
by the committee of the militia of the city of London
for the recovering of Reading. L. J., VI. 249. *In
extenso.*

Oct. 9. Draft answer to the French Ambassador
(Prince d'Harcourt) declining to release Mr. Walter
Montagu, sent secretly to England with letters from
the Queen Regent of France. L. J., VI. 250. *In extenso.*

Oct. 9. Draft ordinance raising the prices of wines
in consequence of the new excise, &c. L. J., VI. 250.

Oct. 10. Petition of the governor, assistants and fellowship of Eastland merchants; complain of the excessive duties imposed on their commodities by the
King of Denmark, and that five of their ships have
been seized and detained in the Sound, one outward
bound with cloth and other English commodities, and
the other four returning with hemp, flax, potashes,
pitch, and other goods of those parts: petitioners fear
not only this present damage, but also the future loss of
their trade, and that Holland will then become the
magazine of all Eastland commodities to the great diminution of British shipping : they pray their Lordships
to consider of some means to procure the release of their
ships. L. J., VI. 251.

Oct. 10. Draft ordinance appointing Mr. John Tilsley, vicar of Dean Church, in the county of Lancaster. L. J., VI. 252. *In extenso.*

Oct. 10. Petition of John Hart, one of His Majesty's bargemen; complains of having been unjustly arrested for debt by Thomas Blacklyn, a sergeant, at the suit of Hugh Busbye, a woodmonger in London; prays that he may have privilege of Parliament.

Annexed:—

1. Certificate of Nowell Warner and others that Hart is a sworn servant of His Majesty.

Oct. 11. Petition of Mildmay, Earl of Westmorland; petitioner was committed to the Tower, and a charge of 2,000*l.* laid upon him; of this sum 1,300*l.* has been paid by regular instalments, and whilst payment was going on Babington, a captain under Lord Gray, has plundered him of goods to a great value, so that all petitioner's losses, with the charge of his imprisonment, amount to 3,304*l.* 6*s.* 4*d.*; notwithstanding this the committees in the counties of Kent, Cambridge, and Huntingdon, have sequestered his estates in those counties; he prays for present and future protection from such sequestrations. L. J., VI. 253.

Oct. 11. Draft order for repayment of 8,000*l.* to the Commissioners of excise. L. J., VI. 253. *In extenso.*

Oct. 11. Draft order for the Earl of Manchester, to levy all monies that have been assessed and not paid in Suffolk, Herts, Essex, &c. L. J., VI. 253. *In extenso.*

Oct. 11. Petition of William Spencer, to H. C.; has been nine months and upwards prisoner by order of the House, but after various examinations nothing prejudicial to the State has been found against him; prays to be set at liberty. C. J., III. 273.

Oct. 12. Petition of George Clipson, Richard Flowood, Thomas Pouter, and Richard Clarke, prisoners in the Fleet; petitioners were committed on the 6th instant for selling wood out of Enfield chase, they are very poor men with wives and families dependent on their labour; they are heartily sorry to have offended, promise never to do so again, and pray for speedy enlargement. L. J., VI. 254.

Oct. 12. Certificate of Mr. Recorder Glynn, that Francis Newton, Thomas Mayo, and James Wadesworth, messengers, have performed the services stated in their petition, as appears by the annexed certificates, and are deserving of reward. L. J., VI. 254. *In extenso.*

Annexed:—

1. Order referring the petition to the recorder. 17 Aug. 1643. L. J., VI. 183.

2. Certificate of the clerk of the peace for the county of Middlesex, that John Hammond and others have been convicted as popish priests, and Margaret Powell for harbouring such persons on the prosecution of Newton, Mayo, and Wadesworth. 17 Dec. 1642.

3. Certificate of Ralph Briscoe, clerk of Newgate, of the names of nine persons, convicted as Romish priests on the evidence of Newton, Mayo, and Wadesworth, of whom seven were executed at Tyburn.

4. Copy of letter from the committee of the Commons for examinations, to the Lord Mayor of the city of London, recommending Newton, Mayo, and Wadesworth for recompense for their services in having procured the conviction of more popish priests and Jesuits, than have been convicted by any other means. 10 April 1643.

Oct. 12. Petition of the owners and merchants of the ship "Clare," lately arrived from the West Indies, with a cargo of money, cochineal, hides, ginger, and other goods, to the value of 80,000*l.*, to H. C.: petitioners complain of various orders under which 30,000*l.* has been taken from the ship, while it is expected that more money will be taken and the ship sold; petitioners are willing to pay 20,000*l.* over and above the 30,000*l.*, if they may continue to enjoy the privileges of merchants, subjects of the King of Spain, without disturbance upon any national quarrel. C. J., III. 274.

Oct. 12. Letter from Francis Lord Dacre, at Hurstmonceux, to Lord Grey of Warke, Speaker of the House of Lords, *pro tempore*; was advised last Thursday to retire into the country, because the woman where he lodged was sick of a violent fever, judged to be pestilential, and therefore hopes to be excused for his sudden departure; has received the order of the House to attend on Sunday morning (to take the covenant), but prays leave to be absent till that day sennight, on account of the ways, the weather, and his own infirmity, and then if he may do it without danger of bringing

infection, will not fail to attend their Lordships. *See* L. J., VI. 255.

Oct. 12. The Earl of Elgin [Lord Bruce], at Knowlton, to Lord Grey of Warke, Speaker of the House of Peers, *pro tempore*; is desirous to obey their Lordships' commands, but is in physic, and therefore fears he cannot come by Sunday, but will come next week unless their Lordships will dispense with his attendance for the present. *See* L. J., VI. 255.

Oct. 16. Draft letter informing Peers of the day fixed for the taking of the covenant, with list of Peers absent at the taking of the same, and notes of proceedings on other days. *See* L. J., VI. 255, &c.

Oct. 16. Message from the Commons, with an order for adding Thomas Sanders to the committee for the county of Derby. L. J., VI. 256. *In extenso.*

Oct. 16. Message from the Commons with an order for Mr. Daniel Cawdrey, to be a member of the assembly of divines in the place of Dr. Harris. L. J., VI. 257. *In extenso.*

Oct. 16. Draft order for the committee of Lords and Commons to enforce the payment of arrears of money assessed for the great affairs of the kingdom, by distress and imprisonment. L. J., VI. 257. *In extenso.*

Oct. 16. Draft ordinance for the repayment of all such sums of money as are or shall be lent by any person or persons for the speedy bringing of our brethren of Scotland into this realm for our assistance in this present war. L. J., VI. 257. *In extenso.*

Oct. 16. Petition of Edward Lord Howard, praying to have the wardship of his brother-in-law, Lord Boteler, an idiot. L. J., VI. 259. *In extenso.*

Oct. 17. Message from the Commons, with an order for appointment of a committee to advise with the Lord General for the speedy advancing of the armies. L. J., VI. 260. *In extenso.*

Oct. 17. Petition of the Mayor and commonalty and citizens of the city of London, governors of Christ's Hospital, and Anne Hawes, widow; upon a former petition against Nicholas Hawes, an order was made that he should sue out his livery; this he has now done, and petitioners therefore pray that their former petition may be dismissed the House, that so they may be at liberty to proceed at law for their further relief. L. J., VI. 260. *In extenso.*

Oct. 17. Draft orders of the Commons for invalidating the Great Seal of England, and all acts done by and under it, since it was taken away from the Parliament. C. J., III. 278.

Oct. 18. Draft order that 1,500*l.* belonging to the governors of Sutton Hospital, now lying idle in an iron chest in the custody of John Clarke, and a further sum of 500*l.* in his hands also belonging to the hospital, should be employed for the service of the Commonwealth in the maintenance of the garrison of Gloucester, to be repaid upon the public faith of the kingdom. Noted, Committed and considered of, but nothing done there n. L. J., VI. 261. On the 30th the committee reported that there were not enough governors of the hospital in town to consent to the taking of the 2,000*l.*, and that the Hospital was in arrears and would be dissolved if the money were taken, upon which the matter was dropped. L. J., VI. 283.

Oct. 18. Petition of divers officers and soldiers of several regiments under the command of the Right Hon. Henry Earl of Stamford, General of the western forces; petitioners have faithfully served Parliament for fourteen months, and have for the last five months been on hard service in the city of Exeter, and have received no pay for that time, notwithstanding the promises of the deputy lieutenants of the town and county; they have endured a siege of four months, and when the city was rendered, refused the offers of the enemy who promised them payment of all their arrears and great preferment if they would take service with them: petitioners could not even obtain a loan from the citizens of Exeter to bring them up to London, and might have begged or starved by the way if it had not been for the assistance of the Earl of Stamford; pray for payment of their arrears to encourage them in their resolutions of sacrificing their dearest blood for their country. L. J., VI. 262.

Annexed:—

1. Petition of Lieutenant Colonel Freeman and others: petitioners after receiving many wounds were taken prisoners at the defeat at Stratton, where they lost money, horses, and apparel, and though very weak, were compelled to march on foot to Truro, and were there long kept close prisoners in a lamentable condition, till at last some by escape and some by exchange got to

O 3

Barnstaple, where they did good service, until they were obliged to depart on the treacherous surrender of the town by the inhabitants; they have served for six months without receiving any pay, are now extremely in want, and pray for speedy payment of their arrears.

2. Certificate from officers employed in the West of England, that when the unfortunate city of Exeter was besieged, the mayor and deputy lieutenants promised them and their soldiers payment of the arrears due to them, and upon some hot assaults of the enemy, a gratuity of 100l. per regiment, but that they were obliged to leave the town without receiving one penny.

Oct. 18. Draft order for the trained bands of Middlesex, &c., to march where the Lord General shall direct. L. J., VI. 262. *In extenso.*

Oct. 17. Baron Trevor's answer to the impeachment of the Commons concerning ship money. L. J., VI. 262. *In extenso.*

Oct. 18. Petition of Sir Thomas Trevor, one of the Barons of the Court of Exchequer, acknowledging his error of judgment in the case of ship money, and submitting himself to the favourable consideration of the House. L. J., VI. 262. *In extenso.*

Oct. 18. Copy of preceding.

Oct. 18. Petition of John Clayton, recorder of the borough of Leeds, to H. C.; petitioner having represented to the committee for sequestrations that through his services and those of his son, a captain under Lord Fairfax, he had lost all his estate in Yorkshire, and been imprisoned sixteen weeks in Pomfret Castle, and that he could discover a rent of 120l. near London, not yet sequestered, belonging to a Yorkshire gentleman in arms with the Earl of Newcastle, desired that half the rent should be given to the State, half to himself; this has been agreed to by the committee after deducting 20l. for public charges, and petitioner prays the House to confirm their recommendation. C. J., III. 279.

Oct. 19. Printed book containing a copy of a declaration of the Lords Justices in Ireland of the 19th of Sept. 1643, ratifying and publishing the articles for a cessation with the Irish, also a copy of the articles, and of an instrument touching the manner of payment of 30,800l. agreed to be paid to the King by the Irish Roman Catholics. The declaration and articles given *in extenso* in Rushworth, III. ii. 548. This "printed book" was delivered to the Lords at a conference on the 18th, and reported to the House this day. L. J., VI. 263.

Oct. 19. Draft order appointing a committee to join with a committee of the Commons to consider the preceding declaration and articles. L. J., VI. 263. *In extenso.*

Oct. 19. Demand of the Commons for judgment against Baron Trevor. L. J., VI. 264. *In extenso.*

Annexed:—

1. Articles of the House of Commons, in the name of themselves and of all the Commons of England, against Sir Thomas Trevor, Knight, one of the Barons of His Majesty's Court of Exchequer, impeaching him for his judgment given in the case of ship money. Trevor was impeached by message from the Commons on the 22nd of Dec. 1640 (L. J., IV. 114), but judgment was not delivered till this day. L. J., VI. 263. The articles are given *in extenso* in Rushworth. I. iiii. 339.

Oct. 19. Petition of inhabitants of the town of Harwich, to the Commons; have lately received Thomas Wood as lecturer and preacher of their town, who informed the House that he was an orthodox divine; yet he enveighs against the Church of England, refuses to bury, baptise, or marry, except after a fashion of his own; has never administered the sacrament, saying that the congregation ought not to receive it together, has confessed himself a separatist; he was never brought up in schools of learning, but was a mere mechanic; he rails against the magistrates of the town, and makes controversies between neighbours; he promised to go away altogether and never did so, and calls two Anabaptist preachers, a tailor and a sailor, children of God. C. J., III. 281.

Oct. 20. Petition of Sir Thomas Trevor, Knight, one of the Barons of His Majesty's Court of Exchequer; praying to be released from imprisonment. L. J., VI. 265. *In extenso.*

Oct. 20. Doughty v. Overman and Hardwick. Writ of error, &c. L. J., VI. 265. (Parchment collection.)

Oct. 20. Draft order appointing a Committee to join with the Committee of the assembly to meet and treat

with the divines of Scotland, concerning a form of church government, &c. L. J., VI. 265. *In extenso.*

Oct. 20. Copy of preceding.

Oct. 20. Draft order for adding Lincolnshire to the ordinance for raising of the twentieth part. L. J., VI. 265. *In extenso.*

Oct. 20. Petition of Clement Walker, one of the deputy lieutenants and committees for the county of Somerset; petitioner has been summoned by the Lord General to attend a council of war, to justify what he has published in print about the surrender of Bristol by Colonel Nathaniel Fiennes, but being a prisoner in the Tower by their Lordships' order, he is unable to prosecute the matter; prays that on giving security to render himself again, he may have liberty for the present, to prepare for the council of war, and till it is over, to lie in his own house near Westminster Hall, for the better seeking of witnesses and despatching of business (the days now growing short), and he desires this the more as he has lost all his estate in the Parliament service, and finds going with a keeper very chargeable. L. J., VI. 265.

Oct. 21. Petition of Arthur Needham; prays that after the goods in the Black Lodgings, in the Inner Temple, formerly the Lord Keeper Littleton's, intrusted to petitioner by Sergeant Littleton, have been inventoried, they may be left in petitioner's custody. L. J., VI. 265. *In extenso.*

Oct. 21. Draft order appointing Richard Shute to the Cocket Office in the place of Sir John Wolstenholme. L. J., VI. 266. *In extenso.*

Oct. 21. Draft order for payment of 50l. to Captain Skrimpshire. L. J., VI. 266. *In extenso.*

Oct. 21. Petition of parishioners of St. Alphage, Cripplegate; the presentation to their parsonage, now void by the death of Mr. Sedgwick, belongs to the Bishop of London, who has promised not to present any one without the approbation of Parliament, and the good liking of petitioners; they pray that the choice may be left to them, and that they may have. till the end of the quarter to exercise it, and that meantime the profits of the living may be paid to Mrs. Sedgwick, who is left a widow with five children, petitioners engaging that the place shall be properly filled mean time.

Annexed:—

1. Petition of Nehemiah Dodd, minister of God's word in the parish of St. Margaret's, Westminster; on the recommendation of the Speaker of the House of Commons and others, the Bishop of London conferred the parsonage of St. Alphage, Cripplegate, upon petitioner, who went to the parish with letters of recommendation, wishing to make address to the parishioners for their approbation, but not finding them at home, left his letter with Mrs. Lee, wife of one of them; the parishioners have returned no answer, but are petitioners to the House, that they may have the quarter in which to make a free election; prays the House to consider of what consequence this would be to the patron, and to give him leave to proceed legally upon the former recommendation. (Undated.)

2. Letter from Denzil Holles and others at the Commons House to [the parishioners of St. Alphage, Cripplegate], recommending Nehemiah Dodd for acceptance as their minister. 20 Oct. 1643.

Oct. 23. Further articles of impeachment by the Commons assembled in Parliament against William Laud, Archbishop of Canterbury, of high treason, and divers high crimes and misdemeanors. L. J., VI. 267. *In extenso.*

Oct. 23. Draft ordinance for the more speedy raising of the monies formerly imposed, and yet unpaid within the city of London and liberties thereof. L. J., VI. 269. *In extenso.*

Oct. 23. Draft ordinance for the further enlargement of a former ordinance made for the speedy raising of monies, and furnishing one or more magazine or magazines of arms and ammunition, and other necessary charges for and concerning the raising of horse and other military forces within the hamlets of the Tower, the city of Westminster, the borough of Southwark, and other parts of the counties of Middlesex and Surrey, within the forts and lines of communication and parishes adjacent, mentioned in the weekly bill of mortality. L. J., VI. 271. *In extenso.*

Annexed:—

1. Amendments to preceding. 7 Oct. 1643. *See* L. J., VI. 245.

Oct. 24. Petition of six poor almsmen of Eastham, in the county of Essex, founded by Giles Breame, Esq. In 1640 petitioners' cause was by their Lordships' order referred to Lord Chief Justice Brampston, who made his report thereon; the petition and report still remain in this Hon. House, but can receive no determination, their Lordships having ordered that they will hear no private business. Petitioners pray their Lordships either to give a final hearing to their grievances, or refer the matter to the committee of obstructions. This petition is written on the fly-leaf of a small pamphlet entitled, A Breviate or true relation of the unchristian like dealing of Sir Giles Allington, the Lady Kempe, the Lord Keeper Coventry, Mr. Coniers, of Waltham Stow, in the county of Essex, Councillor at Law, and Mr. Draper, son to the Lady Kempe, in keeping the poor almsmen of Eastham from their right. L. J., VI. 271.
Annexed:—
1. Copy of preceding petition and pamphlet.
2. Petition of the almsmen presented 22 Jan. 1640-1.
3. Printed copy of preceding, with statement of their case.
4. Copy of report of Lord Chief Justice Brampston. 2 August 1641. L. J., VI. 335. In extenso.
5. Printed copy of preceding.
6. Another copy.
7. Petition of the almsmen, praying that their cause may be heard, or referred to the committee of obstructions. This petition is also written on one of the pamphlets mentioned above.
8. Petition of Dame Sarah Kempe, widow. Prays that some convenient day may be appointed for hearing counsel for all sides on the whole matter.

Oct. 24. Petition of Edward White, steward and receiver of the rents of the Right Hon. the Lord Petre, His Majesty's ward, for and on the behalf of his Lordship: Lord Petre was by the Court of Wards committed to the custody of the late Earl of Northampton, who placed him with a Protestant tutor at Oxford, where he is now pursuing his studies, and has never given any assistance against Parliament, nor indeed could do so, being but about 15 or 16 years of age, whilst his estates lying mostly in Essex, have contributed to all payments required by Parliament; notwithstanding this the committee for sequestrations, have sequestered two-thirds of his estate, real and personal, as if he were a papist and delinquent, when he is neither, and intend speedily to sell his goods, cattle, and woods to the ruin of his estate: petitioner prays for justice and consideration. L. J., VI. 271.
Annexed:—
1. A memorial of what has been paid out of Lord Petre's estate, in Essex, towards the service of the King and Parliament, with a statement in support of the petition.

Oct. 24. Petition of William Lord Archbishop of Canterbury, that he may have counsel assigned to him, may have some money out of his estate, and all his books and papers, &c. L. J., VI. 271. In extenso. (Holograph.)

Oct. 24. Petition of the committee of the additional forces by sea for Ireland, to H. C.; praying that means may be taken to force those adventurers who have not yet paid their proportions to do so at once, for petitioners are daily followed and solicited by seamen and others to whom money is due, who complain that they and their families are likely to perish for want of it, and so threaten petitioners that, they are in danger of their lives, both at home and abroad. C. J., III. 287.
Annexed:—
1. A list of the adventurers who have not paid their subscriptions, with the sums due from them.

Oct. 24. Notes of proceedings this day, &c.

Oct. 26. List of persons appointed by the Commons as their committees to go into Scotland. See L. J., VI. 273.

Oct. 26. Petition of the Society and Company of Gunmakers of the city of London. Petitioners are likely to be ruined for want of money owing to them by the State for arms supplied, while great store of foreign arms are imported, many of which break and kill or wound those who use them. Petitioners pray that these foreign arms may be put to the same proof as English, and that petitioners' arrears may be paid them. L. J., VI. 273.

Oct. 26. Petition of Clement Walker, one of the deputy lieutenants and committees for the county of Somerset. Notwithstanding their Lordships' order the lieutenant of the Tower will not accept the bail offered by him unless a day certain is fixed in the bond, whilst he has been moved to another and a worse lodging in the Tower, on purpose, as he believes, to prevent his friends from coming to him. He prays that the terms

of their Lordships' order may be carried out, that he may be better able to prosecute his business against Nathaniel Fiennes for the surrender of Bristol. L. J., VI. 273.

Oct. 26. Application for a pass for Mrs. Mary Powell, wife of the schoolmaster of Paul's school, into Berkshire and back, with a manservant, maidservant, a coach and four horses, and a saddle horse. L. J., VI. 273.

Oct. 26. Petition of George Earl of Desmond. Petitioner, in order to pay the assessment for the army within London and 20 miles compass, caused a sufficient proportion of timber to be felled at Osterley Park, but the poor of Brentford and the neighbourhood, under colour of a late ordinance for the cutting of underwood, have carried away most of the timber so felled, and though petitioner has treated for the cutting and sale of more, none will buy unless they can be sure of carrying it away. He prays for an order for protection of his timber, and ten days further time to make payment. L. J., VI. 273. In extenso.
Annexed:—
1. Order of the Committee of Lords and Commons for advance of money and other necessaries for the army; that as Lord Desmond has promised, that if within ten days he cannot pay the assessment his woods shall be felled, no prosecution shall be had against him meantime. 9 Oct. 1643.

Oct. 26. Petition of Richard Butler, servant to Dr. Bennett, assistant in the House of Peers; Dr. Bennett is in Wiltshire and too unwell to attend the House. Petitioner prays that Bennett may be excused from attendance for the present. L. J., VI. 273.

Oct. 26. Draft ordinance for payment of 40,051l. 18s. 8d. to Mr. Turner and others for commodities sent to Ireland. L. J., VI. 272.

Oct. 27. Papers presented at a conference by Sir Henry Vane concerning the affairs of the armies in Ireland, and the affairs in Scotland. These papers were read in the House this day and are given in extenso. L. J., VI. 275-277.
1. Letter from the English Commissioners in Scotland to William Lenthall, Speaker of the House of Commons, to hasten the propositions and treaty between the two kingdoms, the sending of money for the Scotch army, &c. 15 Oct. 1643.
2. Paper from the committee of estates of the kingdom of Scotland against the cessation of arms with the Irish rebels, and desiring that one of the Commissioners should go to England about it. 11 Oct. 1643.
3. Answer of the English Commissioners that they have determined to send one of their number to England about the cessation. 11 Oct. 1643.
4. Paper from the committee of estates of Scotland, desiring that the Commissioner sent to England should use all diligence in explaining the dangerous state of affairs in Ireland, and the necessities of the Scotch, &c. 13 Oct. 1643.
5. Act of the Commissioners of the general assembly of the Church, directing that the solemn league and covenant, as approved by the Parliament of England, should be sworn and subscribed throughout Scotland. 11 Oct. 1643.
6. Act of the Commissioners of the Convention of Estates of Scotland, approving preceding act and directing that no person should hold any place or employment under Government, who has not taken the covenant. 12 Oct. 1643.
7. Copy of letter from the King to the Council of Scotland, utterly disallowing a proclamation made by them in his name. 6 Sept. 1643. On the same paper is—
8. Copy of letter from the King to the Council of Scotland against the Covenant. 14 Sept. 1643.

Oct. 27. Votes of both Houses concerning the affairs of Ireland and Scotland. L. J., VI. 277. In extenso.

Oct. 27. Copy of the complaint of the Earl of Stamford against Mr. Anthony Nicholls, M.P., employed by command of the Parliament as one of the committees and deputy lieutenants of the counties of Devon and Cornwall. The Earl accuses Nicholls of having marched off with the horse to Bodmin without any authority for so doing, and of having delayed there, and taken the officers to breakfast at his mother's house, when the Earl had sent for the horse, and was actually engaged with the enemy at Stratton, the defeat at which place was owing to this conduct of Nicholls and to the treachery of Major-General Chudleigh, whose order Nicholls produced for removing the horse. (Two papers.) L. J., VI., 278.

Oct. 27. Petition of Clement Walker, one of the deputy lieutenants and committees for the county of Somerset; the lieutenant of the Tower still refuses petitioner's bail, as yesterday's order was worded in the same way as the preceding order; petitioner therefore prays that he may be bound only to render himself at the bar of the House. L. J., VI. 278.

Oct. 27. Petition of Steven Spratt. Has been seven weeks close prisoner in Newgate in misery and want, for contempt of the House in refusing to answer their Lordships' question. He was ignorant that to refuse to answer was a contempt; is now heartily sorry and ready to answer any question. L. J., VI. 278.

Oct. 27. Draft ordinance for pressing 3,000 soldiers in Lancashire. L. J., VI. 279. In extenso.

Oct. 27. Two drafts of an ordinance for Isaac Pennington, Lord Mayor of London, to execute the office of Lieutenant of the Tower. L. J., VI. 279. In extenso.

Oct. 27. Notes of proceedings this day.

Oct. 28. Petition of William Lord Archbishop of Canterbury; that Mr. Hales may be assigned him as counsel, in addition to those already named. L. J., VI. 282. In Dell's handwriting, signed by the Archbishop.

Oct. 28. Answer of Isaac Pennington, Lord Mayor, and Lieutenant of the Tower, to the complaint of Clement Walker. Walker refuses to execute a bond to render himself again in such terms as counsel advise, but the writer submits to their Lordships' pleasure. L. J., VI. 282. In extenso.

Oct. 28. Petition of Henry, Bishop of Chichester, that the sequestration of his estates may be stayed. L. J., VI. 283. In extenso.
Annexed :—
1. Copy of order of the Commons for sequestration of the Bishop's estates. 27 June 1643.

Oct. 30. Petition of the Clotworthies of the kindred of Robert Gray, deceased; for relief against John Batty, Richard Hunt, and Mary Gray, in the administration of the estate of the late Robert Gray, amounting to about 50,000l. The referees have made their report and sent in the depositions of witnesses in the cause, and petitioners pray that a day may be appointed for the hearing, and that all proceedings elsewhere concerning the estate may be meantime stayed. See L. J., VI. 283.
Annexed :—
1. Report of the referees. 12 Sept. 1643. With interrogatories to witnesses in the cause, and their depositions in answer.
2. Statement of Sir Henry Martin respecting the estate of Robert Gray, deceased.
3. Petition of Ellin Gray, spinster, in the behalf of herself and her sisters and brothers. An earlier petition relating to the same matter. (Undated.)
4. Petition of Joyce Powell, alias Clotworthy and others, the kindred of the late Robert Gray. Also an earlier petition relating to the same matter. (Undated.)

Oct. 30. Remonstrance of Henry Earl of Stanford (Stamford) to the Lords in Parliament, concerning his condition in his employments in the late wars. Has been employed as General of the Western forces for eleven months, and during that time received nothing but five weeks' pay for one troop of horse, while his house and estates have been plundered. Prays for payment of arrears, and that some malignant's house that is ready furnished may be allotted to him for his family. L. J., VI. 284. In extenso.

Oct. 30. Draft order for Sir Peter Killegrew to attend the French Ambassador, Prince d'Harcourt, from Oxford to London. L. J., VI. 284. In extenso.

Oct. 31. Petition of William, Archbishop of Canterbury; praying that it may be declared which of the articles of impeachment against him are intended to be charges of crimes and misdemeanors only, and which of treason; and that he may have further time to put in his answer. L. J., VI. 285. In extenso.
Annexed :—
1. Copy of order for the Archbishop to answer, &c. 24 Oct. 1643. L. J., VI. 272.

Oct. 31. Petition of Thomas Jenyns. Prays that if Sir Thomas Dawes persists in his contempt in neglecting to deliver in certain bonds to the clerk of the Parliament, in compliance with their Lordships' orders, a decree may pass for the cancelling of the said bonds. L. J., VI. 284.
Annexed :—
1. Copy of order in the cause. 5 August 1643. L. J., VI. 172.

2. Copy of warrant for the attachment of Sir Thomas Dawes. 14 Aug. 1643. L. J., VI. 179.

Oct. 31. Answer and petition of John Limbry, Arnold Brames, and John Cradock, merchants, to a petition preferred before their Lordships by John Langham, alderman of London, and others. Petitioners have already defended three suits at law in which Langham and the others were nonsuited, and one suit is now by consent to be tried in the King's Bench; they therefore pray that the matter may be left to be decided at law. L. J., VI. 285.
Annexed :—
1. Order upon Langham's petition for the matter to be referred to merchants, unless Limbrey show cause to the contrary. 18 Oct. 1643. L. J., VI. 262.

Oct. 31. Votes of both Houses for Alderman Kenricke to be one of the committees to reside in the north, &c. L. J., VI. 286. In extenso.

Oct. 31. Draft order that of the 508l. taken at the guards last night, 20l. be paid to the guards, and the residue to the Lord General and Sir Gilbert Gerrard. L. J., VI. 286. In extenso.

Oct. 31. Draft order for John Selden, Esq., M.P., to be keeper of the records in the Tower in the place of Sir John Borough. L. J., VI. 286. In extenso.

Oct. 31. Draft ordinance for the relief and maintenance of sick and maimed soldiers, and of poor widows and children of soldiers slain in the service of the Parliament. L. J., VI. 286. In extenso.

Nov. 1. Application for a pass for Sarah Lewes, Mrs. Lee's maid, and Mrs. Bringhurst, to Oxford and back. L. J., VI. 287.

Nov. 1. Draft of additional instructions for John Earl of Rutland and others, Commissioners in Scotland. L. J., VI. 288. In extenso.

Nov. 1. Three drafts of the votes of both Houses against the cessation of arms with the Irish rebels. With some votes of Sept. 30 on the same subject. L. J., VI. 238, 289. In extenso.

Nov. 1. Articles concerning the assistance to be sent by the Scots to Parliament. L. J., VI. 289. In extenso.

Nov. 1. Draft of propositions agreed on between the Commissioners of both Houses now in Scotland and the committee of the convention of estates in Scotland. L. J., VI. 290. In extenso.

Nov. 2. Petition of Elizabeth Countess Dowager of Exeter on the behalf of her son, the Earl of Exeter; on the 16th of June last their Lordships ordered that petitioner should quietly enjoy all the woods called Easton Woods, according to an agreement made with the commoners of the manor of Easton, but Thomas Cumbrey and others disobey the order, saying that there is now no law; petitioner prays that Cumbrey and the others may be apprehended and punished for their contempt. L. J., VI. 291.
Annexed :—
1. Order of 16 June 1643. L. J., VI. 97.
2. Affidavit of Thomas Tampon, that on the 25th of June last their Lordships' order was read in Easton church after morning prayer, and as soon as it was read many of the inhabitants rose up and said they would obey no order, and that deponent has frequently found the cattle of Cumbrey and others in the young springs in Easton Woods, and that when he told them of the order of Parliament they said they cared not for it. 28 Sept. 1643.
3. Affidavit of John Rastell, that Wm. Dunch spoke contemptuously of their Lordships' order.

Nov. 2. Draft ordinance for the government of the plantations in the West Indies. L. J., VI. 291. In extenso.

Nov. 2. Copy of letter from the Speakers of both Houses of Parliament, to encourage the soldiers in Ulster. L. J., VI. 292. In extenso.

[Nov. 2.] Draft declaration of the Lords and Commons against the Articles of Cessation with the Irish rebels; in their declarations of the 19th and 25th of July and 30th of Sept., they have shown the wicked attempts to set up popery in Ireland, and now on the occasion of this cessation think right to express their sense of the heinousness of this attempt; to this end they publish the King's letter of the 11th of June 1643 to the Lords Justices, empowering Commissioners to treat with the papists of Ireland, and a copy of the Articles of Cessation, with some observations thereon, and the votes of the two Houses, that Parliament may be seen to be guiltless of leaving unrevenged the blood of so many thousand innocent British, both men, women, and children; from the Articles it will be seen that the deputies from the bloody rebels are called Commissioners from His Majesty's Roman Catholic subjects; what an insult this is to the English nation, to the surviving relatives of the murdered protestants; what an encouragement to the rebels throughout Ireland; the articles provide that these Roman Catholic subjects shall not be disturbed in any province except Ulster. Are the protestants to traffic with them for their own goods, or stand still and starve whilst murderers feed on the fruit of their labours? Whilst to make it still more evident that the destruction of all the protestants was determined on, the rebels being privy to the day fixed for the cessation took nearly twenty castles just before it commenced, and in the quarters assigned to the betrayed protestant armies there is not corn enough for ten days for the army of Leinster, and not one cow amongst many hundred soldiers, whilst the rebels have whole counties well stocked with corn and cattle for present and future use; while if the war had been prosecuted and the present harvest destroyed, as proposed by Lord Lisle and Sir Richard Greenfield, the rebels might have been destroyed, whereas now under the terms of the cessation they will be able to reap two harvests; if to this it be answered, that they are to pay 30,800l. in money and beeves, what is that to the lives of the murdered, or to the money of which they have robbed the protestants, what are 5,000 cows to those they have carried off, specially at the present increased price, and when they are to be paid at times when they will most of them prove useless; while lest any protestant should resist these articles in defence of their religion the Marquis actually agrees to assist the rebels in preventing their so doing. It is shown that the malignant party in Ireland is in combination with the malignants in England, for the Marquis of Ormonde in the name of His Majesty, and Lord Muskerry in the name of the rebels, admits free trade with all ships coming with a pass from His Majesty. What measure then might they expect who should come even with provisions from any other authority? When further, the Marquis undertakes not to molest any ship of the rebels bringing arms, ammunition, or merchandize to Ireland. How different was His Majesty's conduct when treating with his protestant subjects in England: then he would not proceed until all the forts, magazines, and ships were entrusted to him. Let it be remembered also how he formerly expressed compassion for the protestants in Ireland, and horror at the barbarous outrages of the rebels; is it imaginable that after all those expressions rebels and papists should be taken into a league offensive and defensive, that traitors and murderers should be set at liberty, while Lord Justice Parsons and others, who have vigorously resisted the rebellion, are imprisoned upon the accusation of men, such as Lord Wilmot, Lord Dillon, and others, who are mere Irish or degenerate English; is it consistent with the King's professions that provisions and money intended for the protestants in Ireland should be converted to his own use, that his assent should be refused to bills for their benefit, that in his letter of the 11th of June he should call the Irish odious rebels, but now Roman Catholic subjects, and promise to do to them as shall be just and honourable. Is this cessation just to the spoiled protestants or to the English adventurers? Is it honourable to the King or the English nation? Finally, that this black work of darkness might be all of a piece, after His Majesty had cut off all human help from the protestants in Ireland, lest God should be entreated to help them he made a proclamation at Oxford, on the 5th of October 1643, that the day set apart by petition of both Houses and consent of His Majesty for prayer to be made for the sufferers should be no longer observed, as if prayer had too long been offered on behalf of the distressed protestants, or that this cessation would give them remedy for the past and provision for the future.

There is nothing to show that this declaration was agreed to; it was probably drawn up by the joint committee appointed to consider of the cessation on the 19th October, when the printed book and declaration of the whole business was read. In the preceding letter, however, to the soldiers in Ulster, it is said that Parliament has sent a copy of the Articles of Cessation, "together with what sense the two Houses of Parliament hath of it." This may refer to the present paper. *See* L. J., VI. 263, 293, and *supra.* 19 Oct. 1643.

Annexed:—

1. Copy of the King's letter of 11 June 1643, mentioned in preceding.

Nov. 4. Draft ordinance for the association of the counties of Hampshire, Sussex, Surrey, and Kent. L. J., VI. 294. *In extenso.*

5.

Nov. 7. Petition of Francis Mundy and Anne his wife; petitioners obtained a judgment in the Common Pleas against Sir John Chapman, late sheriff of Surrey, for the escape of William Hall, who was in his custody in execution for 180l., Sir John brought a writ of error in the King's Bench, where, after long debate, the judgment of the Common Pleas was confirmed, and now he has brought another writ before their Lordships only for delay; petitioners pray that a short day may be given him to assign errors. L. J., VI. 298.

Nov.-7. Draft order for the vintners to pay the arrears of the excise due from them. L. J., VI. 298. *In extenso.*

Nov. 7. Two drafts of the ordinance for John Pym the elder to be lieutenant of the ordinance. L. J., VI. 298. *In extenso.*

Nov. 7. Notes of various proceedings this day.

Nov. 8. List of inhabitants of the hundred of Edmonton, desiring to be added to the committees for Hertfordshire. L. J., VI. 298.

Nov. 8. Draft order for payment of 1,048l. 15s. 2d. to Lyon Beecher for wheat, peas, and butter for Ireland. L. J., VI. 299. *In extenso.*

Nov. 8. Draft order for sequestering rents in London belonging to Thomas Rowe, porter of the Old Castle in the Isle of Jersey, and others. L. J., VI. 299. *In extenso.*

Nov. 8. Draft ordinance for Mr. Lenthall, Speaker of the House of Commons to be Master of the Rolls, and to have the custody of the house or hospital of the converts situate in Chancery Lane, being from ancient time annexed to the office as a habitation for the Master of the Rolls. L. J., VI. 299. *In extenso.*

Nov. 8. Application from George Kirke, gentleman of His Majesty's robes, for a pass for John Daintre, a groom in the office, to go to Oxford with four dozen of gloves, which are much wanted by His Majesty, and four yards of "taby," two ells and a quarter of taffety, to be a tennis suit, and two pairs of garters and roses, with silk buttons and other necessaries for making up the suit. Noted, "Exped." The Minute Book of this date shows that the pass was granted, though there is no mention of it in the Journal.

Annexed:—

1. Similar application for a pass for John Reeve to go to Oxford with 27 pair of silk hose, 3 silk waistcoats and 6 pair of laced boot-hose for the use of the King and Queen's Majesty. (Undated.)

Nov. 10. Application for a pass for Richard Worthinton, a Dutchman, servant to the Spanish ambassador, to go to Flanders. L. J., VI. 301.

Nov. 10. Draft ordinance declaring void all acts done under the Great Seal of England since the 22nd of May 1642, for putting the new Great Seal into use, and appointing commissioners for the purpose. L. J., VI. 301. *In extenso.*

Annexed:—

1. Paper of amendments. *See* L. J., VI. 288.

Nov. 10. Two printed copies of preceding ordinance.

Nov. 11. Application for a pass for Sir Dudley Carleton, clerk of His Majesty's Privy Council, to go to His Majesty and the council at Oxford to attend the duties of his place and to return. L. J., VI. 302.

Nov. 13. Desire of Steven Spratt, to some congregation not named, for their prayers that God would give him patience and move the hearts of the Lords to do him justice.

Annexed:—

1. Anonymous letter to Lord Howard: I wish your Lordship would release Mr. Spratt, for there is great heart-burning in the city about his imprisonment, for he has done the State much service; I say again and again if you love yourself then release him, I would have put my hand to this letter if I did not fear to be laid in the same place as he is. Farewell.

Spratt was in Newgate for writing a scandalous letter to Lord Howard of Escrick. *See* L. J., VI. 193, &c.

Nov. 13. Answer of Wm. Archbishop of Canterbury to the further articles of impeachment brought against him, pleading Not Guilty. L. J., VI. 303. *In extenso.*

Nov. 13. Draft order for repayment to the Commissioners of Excise of 23,000l. advanced by them for the Lord General's army. L. J., VI. 304. *In extenso.*

Nov. 13. Notes of proceedings this day about the trial of the Archbishop of Canterbury, &c.

Nov. 15. Petition of Lionel Earl of Middlesex, to be heard against the assessment of his estate. L. J., VI. 305. *In extenso.*

Nov. 15. Petition of John Parker, John Partridge, and Thomas Harper, stationers; that an action brought against them by Lawrence Norcott may be stayed, and that he may be ordered to take a press and letters from Stationers' Hall, about which there has been litigation for many years. L. J., VI. 305. *In extenso.*

Annexed :—

1. Answer and petition of Lawrence Norcott, that he may have leave to carry the matter to trial, which is fixed for this week, and if he gain a verdict he will stay execution till their Lordships' pleasure.

Nov. 15. Two copies of the answer of Parliament to the French Ambassador's paper ·for promoting peace between the King and Parliament. L. J., VI. 305. *In extenso.*

Annexed :—

1. Translation of the French ambassador's paper. The original is given *in extenso*, L. J., VI. 302. 11 Nov. 1643.

Nov. 15. Draft ordinance for raising money for defence of Plymouth, &c. L. J., VI. 305. *In extenso.*

Nov. 18. Petition of the six poor almsmen of Eastham. Their Lordships were pleased to appoint the 13th of this instant November for the hearing of petitioners' cause, but the whole of that day was taken up with the Archbishop of Canterbury's business. Petitioners therefore pray that another day certain may be appointed. L. J., VI. 306.

Annexed :—

1. Particulars of the form of order desired by petitioners. (Printed.)

Nov. 20. Petition of Alice Wright, widow of Captain Gerrard Wright. Prays that an extent sued out of Chancery by her late husband, who was killed at the siege of Reading, may be assigned to her for the relief of herself and three small children. L. J., VI. 307. *In extenso.*

Nov. 20. Draft ordinance for the preservation and keeping together for public use such books, evidences, records, and writings sequestered, taken by distress, or otherwise, as are fit to be so preserved. L. J., VI. 307. *In extenso.*

Nov. 20. Printed copy of preceding.

Nov. 21. Letter from the Earl of Warwick in the Downs, to the Committee for the safety of the kingdom. Recommends to their favourable consideration a petition of some sea captains. Their petition speaks their suit, and is no more than land commanders have obtained.

The petition referred to is no doubt that of the sea officers of the 30th instant, praying that they may have some additional pay for service on land. *See* L. J., VI. 317.

Nov. 22. Petition of the Clotworthies, of the kindred of Robert Gray, deceased. Their cause against Mary Gray, John Batty, Symon Middleton, and others, about the administration of the estate of the late Robert Gray was appointed to be heard on the 16th instant, on which day, however, their Lordships did not sit. They pray that an early day may be appointed for hearing, and that all monies in the hands of Batty and certain debtors to the estate may meantime be paid into court. L. J., VI. 308.

Annexed :—

1. Schedule of debtors to Robert Gray, deceased.

Nov. 22. Draft order upon preceding petition, appointing the cause to be heard on the 27th instant. L. J., VI. 308.

Nov. 22. Petition of Sir Thomas Dawes. Thomas Jenyns having charged petitioner with absenting himself, in order to avoid the execution of the orders of the House against him, their Lordships, on 31st Oct. last, ordered him to appear personally before them on the 20th instant, but petitioner dares not go abroad, for some of his creditors, though they have got all his lands, still threaten his person with arrest. He prays to be allowed to appear by counsel. L. J., VI. 309.

Annexed :—

1. Order of 31st Oct., mentioned in preceding. L. J., VI. 284.

Nov. 22. Draft order upon preceding petition, for Dawes to be heard by counsel on Saturday next. L. J., VI. 309.

Nov. 22. Petition of Andrew Booth. Pursuant to their Lordships' order of the 31st of October last, petitioner is ready to bring in the deeds in his possession mentioned in the schedule belonging to Sir Philibert

Vernatti, deceased. These deeds were, however, deposited with petitioner as security for a debt, and he prays that Mr. Jenyns may be ordered to pay him the debt before he delivers up the deeds.

Annexed :—

1. Copy of order of 31 Oct. 1643 in the cause between Jenyns and Dawes.
2. Schedule of deeds mentioned in petition.

Nov. 22. Declaration of Lords and Commons that they will receive nothing from any foreign ambassador unless directed to one or both Houses or their Speakers. L. J., VI. 308. *In extenso.*

Nov. 22. Answer of both Houses to the French ambassador with respect to the paper for promoting peace between the King and the Parliament. When the ambassador shall propose anything in the name of his master to both Houses of Parliament, they will do that which shall be fit, and will justify their proceedings to all the world ; and with regard to the searching of his couriers, they desire it may be excused, as it was done without their privity. L. J., VI. 309. *In extenso.*

Nov. 22. Draft order that no captain of the guard presume to search or uncivilly use any of the servants of the French ambassador. L. J., VI. 309. *In extenso.*

Nov. 22. Draft order discharging the estate of Sir Wm. Morley from sequestration,· upon payment of 1,000*l.* L. J., VI. 309. *In extenso.*

Nov. 22. Draft order for the employment of nineteen of His Majesty's ships, and three and twenty merchant ships, as a winter guard for the narrow seas. L. J., VI. 309. *In extenso.*

Nov. 22. Draft order for raising money for the defence of Southampton. L. J., VI. 309. *In extenso.*

Nov. 22. Additional instructions with those that formerly were given by the Lords and Commons in Parliament of England to Theodore Haak and Robert Lowther for Richard Jenkes, appointed to repair to the King of Denmark, and from thence to the Queen of Sweden and other Princes and states of the Baltic sea, &c. L. J., VI. 310. *In extenso.*

Nov. 25. Petition of Henry Earl of Holland, for leave to go to his own house. L. J., VI. 311. *In extenso.*

Nov. 25. Papers delivered at a conference on the 22nd, reported and entered *in extenso* this day. L. J., VI. 311.

1. Copy of a letter from the Privy Council of Scotland to the King at Oxford, defending their late conduct in taking the covenant, and issuing a proclamation in His Majesty's name for raising forces. 19 Oct. 1643.
2. Copy of letter from the King at Oxford to the Commissioners of peace for Scotland, disallowing the proclamation made in his name for levying troops, and forbidding them to assist the English Parliament. 26 Sept. 1643.
3. Copy of a paper wherein the Lords of the Privy Council of Scotland agree with the General Assembly and Convention of Estates in the covenant, &c. 18 Oct. 1643.

Nov. 25. Message from the Commons, with an order for paying 1,000*l.* to Sir Wm. Waller for the forces at Farnham, &c. L. J., VI. 313. *In extenso.*

Nov. 27. Further remonstrance and humble desire of Henry Earl of Stanford [Stamford], as touching his former and present condition, since his return from the West. Has been long a suitor on behalf of himself, his officers, and soldiers, who have served in the West. A Committee has been nominated in the Commons to examine his charge against Mr. Nicholls, an undoubted complotter with young Chudleigh at Stratton, where the Earl's army was betrayed. As many of his witnesses are appointed to serve in the West, the Earl desires that a message may be sent to the Commons to nominate a joint Committee to take their depositions before they go, and to pass an ordinance for the present relief of the soldiers. The Earl will esteem himself very unhappy if, on account of sinister information, he has not influence enough to obtain consideration and pay, for himself and his men, after he has maintained and recruited them at his own charge for so many months. *See* L. J., VI. 314.

Nov. 27. Petition of William Langhorne, merchant. About the 19th of August 1642 petitioner was committed to the custody of the Gentleman Usher of the Black Rod for an alleged contempt in not performing an order of the House of the 17 Dec. 1641 in a matter in variance between the Earl of Warwick and Francis Mazzola, of Genoa; nothing has been objected against petitioner all this time, and he therefore prays that he may be set at liberty, and he will be ready to appear upon notice. L. J., VI. 314.

Nov. 27. Copy of letter from the Committee at Coventry, to the Lord General about the Earl of Denbigh, who has questioned the Lord General's right to appoint Colonel Barker Governor of Coventry, has ordered some troops from Coventry to Shropshire, and done other things which are likely to make a mutiny. L. J., VI. 321. *In extenso.*

Nov. 27. Message from the Commons, with an order against the adjournment of the term to Oxford, &c. C. J., III. 320. *In extenso.*

Nov. 27. Petition of the Cursitors of the High Court of Chancery. Petitioners have, for the despatch of business between party and party, sent writs to Oxford and other places, where the Great Seal was, to be sealed, but now an ordinance has been passed declaring all acts done by the Great Seal after the publication of the ordinance to be void, and that all persons putting the same in use are public enemies; petitioners have divers writs ready for the seal, which must bear date before that ordinance, and therefore pray that they may have leave to send these writs to be sealed as formerly. C. J., III. 320.

Nov. 28. Message from the Commons with an order for sending the horses raised in Middlesex to the Lord General. L. J., VI. 315. *In extenso.*

Nov. 28. Draft of the oath to be taken by the Commissioners of the new Great Seal. L. J., VI. 315. *In extenso.*

Nov. 28. Draft order for payment of 2,000l. to Colonel John Ven, Governor of Windsor Castle, for the arrears of the garrison. L. J., VI. 316. *In extenso.*

Nov. 28. Draft order for payment of 20l. to Richard Hart for demurrage of a ship at Dublin. L. J., VI. 316. *In extenso.*

Nov. 28. Draft order for the Commissioners of Excise to repay themselves 2,000l. advanced by them for Sir William Waller. L. J., VI. 316. *In extenso.*

Nov. 28. Draft of additional articles to the ordinance of excise. L. J., VI. 316. *In extenso.*

Nov. 29. Articles of the treaty agreed upon betwixt the Commissioners of both Houses of the Parliament of England, having power and commission from the said honourable Houses, and the Commissioners of the convention of the estates of the kingdom of Scotland, authorised by the Committee of the said estates concerning the Solemn League and Covenant, and the assistance demanded in pursuance of the ends expressed in the same.

This document is the original treaty signed by the Commissioners on both sides, and is dated this day, though the terms had been agreed upon some time before, the Covenant having been taken by the English Parliament on the 25th of September, and a proclamation for raising troops in Scotland for the assistance of the English Parliament having been issued on the 18th of August. These articles are given *in extenso* L. J., VI. 364.

Annexed:—
1. Draft of preceding. 25 Aug. 1643.
2. Heads of same.
3. Amendments to same.
4. Differences betwixt the articles of treaty signed by the Commissioners of both Houses of Parliament of England, and the Commissioners of the estates of the kingdom of Scotland, concerning the covenant and assistance, as they were agreed on before by both Houses of Parliament.

Nov. 29. Articles of the treaty agreed upon betwixt the Commissioners of both Houses of the Parliament of England, having power and commission from the said honourable Houses, and the Commissioners of the convention of the estates of the kingdom of Scotland, authorised by the Committee of the said estates, concerning the settling of the town and garrison of Berwick.

This document is the original treaty signed at Edinburgh on the 29th of Nov., though the terms had been settled some time previously. It is given *in extenso.* L. J., VI. 365.

Nov. 30. Message from the Commons, with an ordinance for sending forces from Hertfordshire to Newport Pagnell. L. J., VI. 318. *In extenso.*

Nov. 30. Draft ordinance for the Commissioners of Excise to repay themselves 2,000l. advanced by them towards the 5,000l. for Sir Wm. Waller. L. J., VI. 318. *In extenso.*

Nov. 30. Letter from Sir Wm. Armyn, and the rest of the English Commissioners at Edinburgh, to Wm. Lenthall, Speaker of the House of Commons; are sensible of the difficulties which press upon Parliament, yet are desirous of calling the special attention

of the House to the affairs of Ireland, and of justifying the course they have themselves pursued with regard thereto. The commanders of the Scotch forces in Ireland finding that they got nothing but promises, and seeing their soldiers naked, and their meal almost spent, and fearing to be left destitute if the Scotch were engaged in operations in England, determined to send a deputation to Scotland to represent their case. The writers thinking, that the disbanding of the Scotch army in Ireland would be attended with the most dangerous consequences, felt themselves bound to do all in their power to prevent it until they received full instructions from Parliament, which they daily expect; whilst the readiness of the commanders in Ireland for the service, if only maintenance were provided for them, has induced the writers to agree to their propositions for money, meal, and clothes, and as Scotland cannot provide the money and clothes, they desire that any provision already made for Ireland may be speedily despatched to them.

This letter, with a letter from the Scotch commanders in Ulster and other papers on the subject of their wants, was read in the House of Commons on the 12 Dec. 1643. *See* C. J., III. 338.

[Nov. 30.] Two copies of a paper taken upon Sir Henry Anderson at Leicester, being pretended propositions for an accommodation between the King and Parliament. The principal terms of these propositions are that the armies should be disbanded, the papists disarmed and confined to their habitations, and the laws against them put in strict execution; no papists to be about the Queen except foreigners, and they to take oaths to be prescribed by Parliament; the government of the church to be settled by learned divines commissioned by the King; the forts, navy, militia, &c. to be put into the King's hands; the persons to be appointed to commands and the great officers of the kingdom for the first five years to be such as Parliament shall approve; the King to take an oath every session that he will exercise his power legally; Parliament to be adjourned to Feb.; a general pardon to be issued, and all ordinances of Parliament made without the King's consent to be reviewed by a committee, and all record of those deemed dangerous to be destroyed.

Sir Henry Anderson confesses that the latter part of these propositions was written by him.

These propositions should be sent to the Lord General; if he agrees to them, as the writer supposes he will, peace will be restored; if he refuse all men will join with the King in reducing the opposers to obedience, for the cause of the war will be removed; for Parliament said they took up arms for defence of the protestant religion, the privileges of Parliament, and the liberty of the subject, but if the fulfilment of the King's promises be secured, and a general pardon granted, except to those who have been notoriously active against His Majesty, their reasons are gone. The chief difficulties are first, the oath to maintain the Earl of Essex, but if he should follow the war when all the preceding propositions are granted, men might justly forsake him, and secondly, the oath of the covenant, but an answer may easily be given to that, as it was taken only to the maintaining of the true protestant religion, as the person taking it should conceive, and to the leaving the papists to the law.

This paper was presented to the House by the Lord General as scandalous and much to his dishonour, particulars of it having been divulged abroad, whilst the paper itself was kept secret, whereupon an ordinance was proposed that all scandalous papers should either be burnt or speedily examined. L. J., VI. 318.

Dec. 1. Humble message and petition of the Assembly of Divines; praying for the appointment of godly magistrates to repress the growth of intolerable abominations, recommending a paper from some students of the University of Oxford, and desiring that an amanuensis may be appointed to assist the scribes of the assembly. L. J., VI. 319. *In extenso.*

Annexed:—
1. Paper mentioned in preceding, desiring that a College may be established in London for the benefit of those driven from their studies at Oxford. L. J., VI. 319. *In extenso.*

Dec. 2. Draft order for securing to the Guinea Company repayment for a loan of gold dust. L. J., VI. 321. *In extenso.*

Dec. 2. Draft order for adding Richard Grevis and others to the Committee for Staffordshire. C. J., III. 326. *In extenso.*

Dec. 4. Message from the Commons, with reasons why they cannot agree with the Lords in appointing a Committee concerning the Prince de Harcourt. L. J., VI. 322. *In extenso.*

Annexed :—

1. Copy of a letter from Louis XIV. to the estates of Scotland; desiring to maintain the ancient friendship between the two kingdoms, he sends M. de Boisivon to assure them of his affection, and to make certain propositions in which he expects satisfaction out of regard for their own interests, which he will always have at heart so long as their aim is to obey the King, their master. 24 Sept. 1643. (French.) On the same paper is a copy of M. Boisivon's propositions, he desires that they should not under any pretext whatever enter England in arms without commission from the King, their master; that the Lords of the Council of Scotland shall take no account of the difference in religion of those who serve in France, or are enrolling or shall enrol for service there, and that since the churches of Scotland have decided the contrary in their assembly, the Council shall recall this decision; these are the chief propositions and affect the maintenance or rupture of the alliance between the kingdoms of France and Scotland. (French.)

2. Translation of the French King's letter and of M. de Boisivon's propositions. L. J., VI. 322, 323. *In extenso.*

3. Another translation of the propositions.

4. Answer of the Council of Scotland to the propositions made to them by the most Christian King; are desirous of maintaining the ancient alliance between Scotland and France, but can only answer, that the question of preserving peace is now in the hands of Commissioners, that the National Assembly of the church is independent of the Council; they trust that the King will be better advised in his nonage than to make these things a cause of rupture between him and his ancient allies. L. J., VI. 323. *In extenso.*

Dec. 4. Draft order for a conference respecting recruiting the army on account of the King's advance to Basing. L. J., VI. 323. *In extenso.*

Dec. 4. Notes of various proceedings this day.

Dec. 5. Draft ordinance for the Commissioners of Excise to repay themselves 1,000l. advanced by them towards the 5,000l. for Sir Wm. Waller. L. J., VI. 327. *In extenso.*

Dec. 5. Draft order for payment of 400l. for the necessitous members of the assembly of divines. L. J., VI. 327. *In extenso.*

Dec. 6. Certificate of the committee in Cambridgeshire; their reason for sequestrating the Earl of Suffolk's estate was, that they received information from Mr. Yoward, solicitor for sequestrations, that an ordinance had been passed to that effect. L. J., VI. 328. *In extenso.*

Annexed :—

1. Letter from Humphrey March (one of the committee) at Ely to the Earl of Suffolk, that they were instigated to sequestrate his Lordship's estate by Mr. Yoward, who gave them his grounds for it in a written book. 9 Nov. 1643.

Dec. 6. Affidavits concerning persons who stole wood from Enfield Chase, and resisted the officers who endeavoured to apprehend them. L. J., VI. 328. *In extenso.*

1. Affidavit of John Butchett. 17 Nov. 1643.

2. Affidavits of John Butcher and others. 1 Dec. 1643.

3. Affidavits of John White and others. 1 Dec. 1643.

Dec. 6. Draft ordinance for repayment of 1,000l. to Sir Robert Harley, advanced by him for supply of the army. C. J., III. 330. *In extenso.*

Dec. 6. Petition of Lady Foster, wife of Sir Robert Foster, Knight, one of His Majesty's justices of the Court of Common Pleas; petitioner from the time that her husband left her remained at his house at Egham with her five children and twelve servants, and not only paid all taxes and assessments, but many times entertained commanders and soldiers, sometimes twenty, sometimes thirty at a time at free quarters, while fourteen horses have been taken from her, and by authority from committees for sequestrations, her husband's tenants have been forbidden to pay their rents, and her household goods have been inventoried under threat that they would all be removed; so being unable to keep house in the country, and having no horses to take her to church, when the ways were no longer fair enough for her to go on foot, she came with her children to a

lodging in town; she had been there little more than a week before she was served with a ticket intimating that she was assessed under the ordinance' of the 20th part at 350l., and thereupon arrested and carried to Haberdashers' Hall, when the committee there granted her ten days further time, but she was not set at liberty until she had paid 3l. 12s. for fees demanded by the men who arrested her; petitioner urges that neither she, nor her husband, who is an assistant of the House, and went to Oxford with leave, and cannot return without it, ought to be assessed by the committee at Haberdashers' Hall, and that if, after all she has suffered, her husband's rents are stopped and her goods taken away, she will have nothing left to maintain herself and her children, and therefore prays for protection.

Dec. 7. Draft ordinance to make Robert Earl of Warwick, Lord High Admiral of England. L. J., VI. 330. *In extenso.*

Dec. 7. Message from the Commons with an order for Walter Long to be Registrar of the Chancery. L. J., VI. 330. *In extenso.*

Annexed :—

1. Petition of Dame Mary Jermyn, the widow and relict of Sir Thomas Jermyn, late one of the members of H. C.; His Majesty by letters patent in 1638 granted the reversion of the office of Registrar in Chancery to the two sons of Sir Thomas Jermyn, which he had by a former wife; Sir Thomas died about two years ago, but before his death gave the patent to petitioner, saying it was all he, had to leave her and her children, as his lands were settled upon his other children; but since the office has become void Mr. Long has executed it and taken the profits; petitioner prays that the office may be given to her nominee, Mr. Robert Goodwyn, M.P., as it is the only provision for herself and her children. (Undated.)

Dec. 7. Draft order for payment of 500l. to Captain Crawley for the defence of the islands of Guernsey and Jersey. L. J., VI. 330. *In extenso.*

Dec. 7. Draft order for adding Joseph Widdmerpoole and others to the Committee of sequestrations for the town and county of Nottingham. L. J., VI. 331. *In extenso.*

Dec. 7. Petition of Henry Boone and Edward Fleet, chirurgeons; petitioners have spent all their time and much money in attending upon wounded soldiers from the Lord General's army; and in consequence are unable to pay the assessment for the twentieth part, they pray that this assessment may be taken off, and that they may be exempted for the future. C. J., III. 330.

Dec. 7. Letter from the Commissioners from Parliament at Edinburgh, to Wm. Lenthall, Speaker of the House of Commons: they represent that it would be convenient if some pious and prudent ministers were sent down into the Northern parts to instruct the poor people, whose ignorance has been much abused by the popish and prelatical party, and that if sent whilst the armies are there they would mutually help one another, whilst power might be given to the Commissioners to sequester the livings of malignant ministers, and provision be thus made for the preachers so sent down.

Dec. 9. Message from the Commons with orders concerning the sequestration of the estate of the Earl of Carnarvon, &c. L. J., VI. 334. (Three papers.)

Dec. 9. Draft order for payment of 400l. to Sir John Meldrum for his present despatch to Lord Fairfax. L. J., VI. 334. *In extenso.*

Dec. 9. Draft order that the Committee appointed to sit at Gresham College may sit at any other place within the city. L. J., VI. 335. *In extenso.*

Dec. 9. Draft order for reparation to be made to the well affected persons of King's Lynn by the malignants who injured them. L. J., VI. 335. *In extenso.*

Dec. 11. Draft order for the Commissioners of the Great Seal to present to Parliament the names of officers attendant on the Great Seal for approval. L. J., VI. 336.

Dec. 11. Petition of Joseph Zin Zan, alias Alexander, that he may have the use of the stable and yard at Winchester House, and have leave to build a riding school there. L. J., VI. 336. *In extenso.*

Dec. 11. Draft order for payment of 1,200l. for the garrison of Aylesbury. L. J., VI. 337. *In extenso.*

Dec. 11. Draft order for the Committee for Bedfordshire to go down there, and for the Lord General to provide for their security. L. J., VI. 337. *In extenso.*

Dec. 11. Draft order for the Commissioners of Excise to repay themselves 1,000l. advanced for Sir William Waller. L. J., VI. 337. *In extenso.*

HOUSE OF LORDS.
Calendar.
1643.

Dec. 11. Draft ordinance for Sir Walter Erle to be appointed Lieutenant of the ordnance. C. J., III. 337. *In extenso.* Endorsed, Not passed.

Dec. 11. Draft order for sending forces from Hertfordshire to Newport Pagnell. C. J., III. 337. *In extenso.*

Dec. 12. Draft order for repayment of 50*l.* to Mr. William Strode. L. J., VI. 338. *In extenso.*

Dec. 12. Draft ordinance for appointment of a committee for regulating affairs in the Isle of Wight. L. J., VI. 338. *In extenso.*

Annexed :—

1. List of persons subsequently added to the Committee. (Undated.)

Dec. 12. Petition of Captain John Bladwell, to H. C.; prays that 350*l.*, residue of a sum of 550*l.*, due for a troop of horse purchased from him by the State, may be forthwith paid, as he has himself been arrested for debt, which he cannot discharge whilst this money is unpaid. C. J., III. 339.

Dec. 13. Petition of William Archbishop of Canterbury; has been called upon to answer at the Bar on Monday next to an impeachment of the Commons on the complaint of Mr. Smart, though the case was long since in part heard without petitioner being called upon to defend it; prays that he may have a copy of the charge so far as it concerns him, and that the same counsel may be assigned him, that have been assigned him for the other matters now depending before their Lordships against him. L. J., VI. 339. In Dell's handwriting, signed by the Archbishop.

Dec. 13. Draft ordinance respecting the payment of the garrison of Berwick C. J., III. 341. *In extenso.*

Dec. 16. Draft order for repayment of 1,000*l.* to Captain William Danvers, advanced by him for defence of the county of Leicester, &c. L. J., VI. 341. *In extenso.*

Dec. 16. Draft order for Dr. Burges to be lecturer at St. Paul's, London. L. J., VI. 341. *In extenso.*

Dec. 16. Petition of John Craven, one of the scouts belonging to the militia of London, to H. C.; petitioner having been stripped of all his estate by the cavaliers, and forced with his wife and children to come to London, has done faithful service to Parliament and is resolved therein to die; is in great necessity in consequence of his losses, and prays that 52*l.* due to him on bond by Nicholas Wolf, a prisoner for bearing arms against Parliament, may be paid out of Wolf's estate now under sequestration. C. J., III. 342.

Dec. 16. Petition of Dame Jane Cooke, late wife of Sir Robert Cooke, one of the members of the House, to H. C.; the estate of Sir Robert being on the supposed delinquency of his eldest son at the disposal of Parliament, was upon her petition assigned to her, discharged of taxes and rates, for the maintenance of herself and younger children, in consideration of the losses sustained by her husband in the service of Parliament, but now by misinformation, as she supposes, the estate has been made liable to rates and taxes; she prays that it may be again freed from these impositions, and that she may be reimbursed the sums expended by Sir Robert in the service of Parliament. C. J., III. 342.

Dec. 16. Petition of Richard Brigham; on the marriage of petitioner's daughter to Leonard Ward, a private agreement was made between petitioner and Ward, which petitioner is ready to perform when Ward shall perform his part; nevertheless Ward has caused petitioner to be arrested contrary to privilege, though the matter in dispute is altogether matter of equity; petitioner has no remedy, owing to the distraction of the times, and prays for an order for his discharge from arrest.

Annexed :—

1. Certificate of Robert Boys that Brigham was and is sworn coachmaker to His Majesty. 4 Dec. 1643.

Dec. 18. Message from the Commons with names of persons to be added to the committee of the ordinance of association of Sussex. L. J., VI. 342. *In extenso.*

Dec. 18. Draft order for the Lord Admiral to be desired to issue 50 barrels of powder to Sir William Waller out of the naval stores. L. J., VI. 342. *In extenso.*

Dec. 18. Assessment upon the houses and estates in possession of the peers, assistants, and attendants of the House of Lords within the several places hereunder mentioned for the raising of 14,000*l.* for one or more magazine or magazines of arms and ammunition, &c. according to an ordinance of the Lords and Commons in Parliament. *See* L. J., VI. 342. The places are, the city of Westminster, St. Martin's-in-the-fields, St. Giles'-in-the-field, Clerkenwell, the Duchy Liberty, within the parish of St. Clement Danes, and the Savoy, Westminster Liberty in the parish of St.

Clement Danes, Chancery Lane and Rolls Liberty, Old Street Division, High Holborn Liberty, Sepulchre's parish, Islington.

Dec. 18. Two copies of preceding.

Dec. 18. Draft order that this assessment should not be drawn into a precedent for the future.

Dec. 18. Draft ordinance for further supply of power to the committee for volunteers for the county of Herts. L. J., VI. 342. *In extenso.*

Dec. 18. Draft ordinance for the erecting and maintaining of a garrison at Newport Pagnell, in the county of Bucks. L. J., VI. 344. *In extenso.*

Dec. 18. Petition of George Baker, merchant, to H. C. A bill of exchange was charged upon petitioner by Roger Skinner, of Chymney, in the county of Devon, but before it reached him, he received advices not to pay it, but upon complaint to the Commons an order was made for his commitment till he should pay the bill; petitioner had already given order for payment at Barnstaple, which he believes has been made; he prays to be cleared from payment of the bill and from further molestation. C. J., III. 343.

Annexed :—

1. Copy of order of the Commons mentioned in preceding. 2 Nov. 1643.

Dec. 18. Message and petition of the assembly of divines, to the Commons. C. J., III. 344. This is a duplicate of that presented to the Lords, 1 Dec. *Vide supra.*

Dec. 18. Petition of Joane Burdett, the wife of Richard Burdett, carpenter, close prisoner in Newgate, to H. C.; in commiseration of petitioner's sad condition the House on the 13th instant ordered that alderman Pennington should take bail for her husband, but the keeper of Newgate refuses to set him free on that order, and a writ has been procured for taking away his goods; she prays for further consideration as her husband is sickly, and she and his friends are denied access to him. C. J., III. 344.

Dec. 19. Affidavit of Thomas Hunt, of Walton-upon-Thames, that John Wheeler, constable of Walton, has pressed two of deponent's servants, in spite of an order of the House for their protection, as they are daily employed carrying wood and coals for the use of the House. L. J., VI. 345. *In extenso.*

Dec. 20. Petition of the Clotworthies of the kindred of Robert Gray, deceased, without wife or issue; that a day may be appointed for hearing their cause against Mary Gray and others, concerning the administration of the estate of the late Robert Gray. Endorsed, "Cause dismissed." *See* L. J., VI. 346.

Dec. 20. Message from the Commons, with resolutions, approving the advice given by the committee of safety to the Lord General, recommending him to send a detachment to Sir Wm. Waller at Farnham, and communicating to the Lords various letters on the subject. L. J., VI. 346.

Annexed :—

1. Letter from the Earl of Essex, at St. Alban's, to Lord Grey of Warke, Speaker of the Lords' House *pro tempore*, acquainting the House with the correspondence between himself and the committee of safety. 18 Dec. 1643. L. J., VI. 347. *In extenso.*

2. Duplicate of preceding to Wm. Lenthall, Speaker of the Commons. *See* C. J., III. 346.

3. Copy of letter from the committee of safety to the Lord General, the Earl of Essex. 14 Dec. 1643. L. J., VI. 347. *In extenso.*

4. Another copy.

5. Copy of the Lord General's answer to the committee. 14 Dec. 1643. L. J., VI. 347. *In extenso.*

6. Another copy.

7. Copy of a letter from the Lord General to the committee about the payment of his forces. 17 Dec. 1643. L. J., VI. 347. *In extenso.*

8. Another copy.

9. Copy of letter from the committee, to the Lord General, advising him to move forthwith to Windsor or some other place near Sir William Waller. 17 Dec. 1643. L. J., VI. 348. *In extenso.*

10. Another copy.

Dec. 20. Draft letter from both Houses, to the Earl of Essex, desiring him to pursue the advice given him by the committee, and move towards Windsor. L. J., VI. 349. *In extenso.*

Dec. 20. Draft letter from both Houses, to the Earl of Manchester, to move up his forces for the defence of the counties left unprotected by the march of the Lord General. L. J., VI. 349. *In extenso.*

HOUSE OF LORDS.
Calendar.
1643.

Dec. 20. Draft letter from both Houses, to the committee of Hertfordshire, to move their forces to Newport Pagnell. L. J., VI. 349. *In extenso.*

Dec. 20. Draft order of the Commons appointing Sir H. Vane senior, and others, to meet with a committee of the Lords to prepare a letter to be sent to the Lord General..

Dec. 20. Draft ordinance to disable any person within the city of London and liberties thereof, to be of the Common Council or any office of trust within the said city, that shall not take the late solemn league and covenant. L. J., VI. 348. *In extenso.*

Dec. 22. Petition of Lady Elizabeth Hatton. Thomas Johnson, a carpenter, in Shoe Lane, has begun to erect a tenement in the field at the north-east corner of Hatton House Garden, upon a new foundation, which will not only be a great annoyance to petitioner, but is not a fitting place for an honest habitation, but rather to receive and harbour ill-disposed persons, and is intended for an alehouse; she prays that the building may be stayed and Johnson ordered to pluck down what he has already erected.

Dec. 23. Order upon preceding, for stay of the building till the House be further informed in the matter. L. J., VI. 350.

Dec. 22. Petition of divers poor victuallers, and others, inhabitants within the county of Middlesex; upon petition to the Commons petitioners obtained an order that an allowance should be made to them for billetting the soldiers of Sir Wm. Waller; most of petitioners are so poor, that without present relief, they and their families are like to perish, they therefore pray their Lordships to confirm the order for their relief. *See* L. J., VI. 350.

Annexed :—

1. Copy of order of the Commons mentioned in preceding. 5 Dec. 1643. C. J., III. 329.

Dec. 22. Votes of the Commons for providing clothes, meal, and money for the Scotch forces in Ireland. C. J., III. 350.

Annexed :—

1. Propositions agreed upon between the Commissioners of England, and the committee of the convention of estates of Scotland, that the accounts of the Scotch army in Ireland should be made up, and clothes, meal, and money provided for them, that before the 1st of February 50,000l. should be paid at Carrickfergus for their arrears, that there should be one commander of all the British forces in Ireland, that if their arrears are not paid the forces should be transported into England, and maintained as the other Scotch forces there; that a supply of arms should be sent to Carrickfergus, and provision made for their maintenance, as long as they remain in the service of Parliament. 28 Nov. 1643. Some of these propositions are noted in the margin as having been resolved on, and are embodied in the preceding paper.

Dec. 23. Petition of John Brett and other poor people, on behalf of the Earl of Warwick and themselves. Pray that William Langhorne, now in the custody of the gentleman usher for contempt, may not be discharged until he has paid the damages agreed upon between him and petitioners, and that the Earl of Warwick may be informed of his arrest before he is discharged. L. J., VI. 351.

Annexed :—

1. Copy of order in the cause between Langhorne and the Earl of Warwick. 17 Dec. 1641. L. J., IV. 479. *In extenso.*

2. Affidavit of John Rich, that he served a copy of preceding order upon Langhorne. 13 Jan. 1641-2.

Dec. 23. Petition of John Wheeler; was employed by the committee for the safety of the county of Surrey, to impress the servant of Thomas Hunt, and for obedience to the committee was through misinformation imprisoned by their Lordships' order, but upon his humble petition order has since been made for his enlargement. Is notwithstanding this still detained in custody for not paying fees to the amount of 14l. and upwards, a sum altogether impossible for so poor a man to discharge. Prays to be relieved from the fees. L. J., VI. 351.

Annexed :—

1. Another petition of same, praying for his discharge.

2. Letter from the committee for the county of Surrey to the House of Peers; the constable of Walton-on-Thames, acted by direction of the committee in pressing Mr. Hunt's man. Hunt was himself imprisoned about last Midsummer for

carrying letters to Oxford, and is still under bail for it, the committee therefore desires that the constable may be set at liberty without paying any fees.

Dec. 23. Information of Henry Brodnax and John Gwinne against Stephen Spratt, for speaking scandalous words against Lord Howard of Escrick and the Parliament. L. J., VI. 351.

Annexed :—

1. Receipt for 3l. 1s. by Spratt for his time and charges for seizing the trunks of Lady Diana Newport, now owned by Lord Howard. 17 Aug. 1643.

2. Letter from Spratt, in Newgate, to Lady Diana Newport. Believes that her Ladyship had a great hand in his imprisonment. If the writer had prosecuted her for saying she wished God's curse might light on the Parliament, as eagerly as her friend prosecuted him, questions not that she would have seen some alteration before this time. Is confident it lies in her Ladyship's power to release him if she please. 5 Sept. 1643.

3. Letter from Spratt, in Newgate, to Sir John Woollaston. Details his proceedings in seizing Lady Banbury's goods, and prays Sir John to do him the favour to write to his (Sir John's) brother to procure him liberty to go abroad with his keeper. 5 Sept. 1643.

Dec. 23. Letter from the Earl of Stanford [Stamford] to the Lords in Parliament. His necessities with his servants and troopers are now so extreme, after four months' languishing, that unless some immediate care be taken they must either plunder or starve. Were it not for the goodness and charity of his honourable mother-in-law, the Countess of Essex, his wife and eight children might perish. Has served the Parliament faithfully since August 1642, and has endured as much hunger and suffering as any, having been besieged for six months in Plymouth and Exeter. His accounts have been audited, but his entertainment as general is not yet ratified. Prays that his miserable condition may be discovered to the House of Commons, with his earnest desire that there might be allotted to him for his present succour the 20th part of the ensuing estates, the Earl of Arundel's, the Dowager Countess of Rutland's, Lord Newburgh's, and Baron Trevor's. *See* L. J., VI. 351.

Dec. 23. Petition of Edward Trelawney. The cause in error between petitioner and Thomas Babb has been long depending. He has now nothing left to maintain his wife and children, and beseeches that a day for hearing the cause may be appointed. L. J., VI. 352.

Dec. 23. Draft ordinance concerning the sequestration of the revenues of the King, Queen, and Prince. L. J., VI. 352. *In extenso.*

Dec. 23. Draft ordinance for the Committee of the militia of the city of London to send the white and yellow regiments and other forces to the assistance of Sir William Waller. L. J., VI. 352. *In extenso.*

Dec. 23. Draft ordinance for Thomas Twiss, M.A., to be admitted to the rectory of East Horsley, Surrey. L. J., VI. 352. *In extenso.*

Dec. 23. Draft ordinance for reducing the duty on tobacco. L. J., VI. 352. *In extenso.*

Annexed :—

1. Petition of the traders in tobacco inhabiting in the city of London and liberties, and other parts adjacent. They hear that it is intended to put an excise upon tobacco, and pray that before this be done they may be allowed to give reasons to show that it will not produce the result expected, and will be prejudicial to many thousands of persons. (Undated.) Endorsed, Not heard.

Dec. 23. Petition of the Clotworthies, of the kindred of Robert Gray, deceased, without wife or issue, praying that for preserving the estate of the late Robert Gray such debtors to the estate as are willing so to do may pay their debts into some safe hands, and not to any of the parties, till the cause be determined.

Dec. 23. Order in accordance with the prayer of preceding. L. J., VI. 353. *In extenso.*

Annexed :—

1. Petition of Simon Middleton and Katherine his wife, administrators of Robert Gray, intestate: that the cause between them and the Clotworthies may be referred to some of the assistants of the House to decide whether the Clotworthies have any title in law or equity, and that the preceding order may be discharged. (Undated.)

Dec. 23. Letter from the Earl of Essex, at St. Alban's, to Wm. Lenthall, Speaker of the House of Commons. Finds that the differences between the Earl of Denbigh and the Committee at Coventry turn upon ordinances, commissions, &c., all of which are at London, and therefore refers the matter to Parliament. L. J., VI. 354. *In extenso.*

Dec. 23. List of prisoners, arms, and colours, taken by Sir John Meldrum at Gainsborough. C. J., III. 351.

Dec. 25. Order for discharging all officers of courts of record, who have assisted the King against the Parliament. L. J., VI. 354. *In extenso.*

Dec. 26. Copy of the King's letter to the Lord Mayor and aldermen of London. His Majesty is willing to grant a safe conduct to those persons appointed to present a petition from the city. L. J., VI. 371. *In extenso.*

Dec. 27. Copy of letter from Lord Digby at Oxford to Sir Henry de Vic, concerning the proceedings of the King's forces, and enclosing copy of the King's proclamation for the Parliament to meet at Oxford upon the occasion of the invasion by the Scots. L. J., VI. 368. *In extenso.*

Annexed:—
1. Copy of preceding.
2. Printed copy of proclamation. 22 Dec. 1643. Rushworth, Vol. II., Part III. 559. *In extenso.*

Dec. 27. Letter from Lord Digby to Mr. Curtius, His Majesty's resident at Frankfort. Duplicate of preceding letter to Sir H. de Vic. L. J., VI. 367.

Dec. 30. Petition of Lieutenant-Colonel David Forrett, executor of David Ramsay, deceased. Prays that his cause against Fabian Phillips may be speedily heard. L J., VI. 355.

Annexed:—
1. Copy of order in the cause. 25 July 1643. L. J., VI. 147.

Dec. 30. Petition of Peter Smart. Prays that his son Ogle, who is imprisoned at Winchester House, may have liberty to go abroad with his keeper. L. J., VI. 355.

Dec. 30. Draft letter from both Houses, to the Lord General to advance his army towards Windsor. L. J., VI. 356. *In extenso.*

' Dec. 30. Petition of Lord Newburgh. Prays leave to represent to their Lordships his sufferings and the condition he is reduced to, by the miseries of these times, before any further charge is laid upon him. He has been compelled to sell his plate, has been deprived of the benefit of his office, and of so much of his estate as abates two thirds of his yearly revenue. Has now no personal estate, but some ordinary and necessary goods, which he is engaged by marriage contract to leave to his wife after his death. His debts are three times the value of his estate, and increase daily, as he is compelled to borrow at interest to defray the ordinary expenses of his family. Notwithstanding this he has ever since the beginning of this Parliament attended at very great charge as an assistant upon their Lordships' House. *See* L. J., VI. 311.

Dec. 30. Letter from the Earl of Essex at St. Albans, to the Speaker of the House of Lords *pro tempore,* respecting the return of the Earl of Bedford to the Parliament. (Holograph.) L. J., VI. 356. *In extenso.*

Dec. 30. Petition of the Levant Company. Pray for license to import currants from the dominions of the Grand Seignior. *See* L. J., VI. 404, where the petition is set out almost *in extenso.*

Annexed:—
1. Copy of order of the Commons respecting the importation of currants. 24 Oct. 1643. C. J. III. 284.

[1643.]

Petition of divers of the parishioners of the parish of Austyn's, London; the present fixed maintenance for the ministry of the parish is not competent to maintain an able minister; petitioners therefore pray that the rent of certain houses in the parish belonging to the dean and prebends of Windsor, amounting to about 10l. per annum, may be annexed to their minister's stipend.

Petition of Alexander Baynham; prays that the dispute between him and the master and owners of the ship "John and Thomas," respecting certain goods shipped by petitioner at Genoa, may be referred to merchants by commission under the Great Seal.

Petition of Richard Beringer, to the Earl of Manchester, praying his Lordship to move the House to appoint another day for the hearing of the cause in error between petitioner and Cooke.

Petition of John Berry, of London, merchant; complains of unjust proceedings at law by John Southwood, and prays that, as now no relief can be had in equity, the case may be heard before their Lordships.

Petition of inhabitants of Caddington, in the counties of Hertford and Bedford. The Dean and Chapter of St. Paul's were heretofore lords of the manor of the Berry of Caddington, and received all the revenues, while the profits of the vicarage of Caddington were barely 30l. a year. Petitioners have for some years past maintained the present incumbent, an able and industrious minister, out of their own purses, which charge is now so much the more heavy in respect of the free quartering of soldiers and continual payments for the public. Pray that the rents of the manor may be allotted to the vicarage, or that a competent maintenance may be allowed out of the revenues of the prelates, since by the last oath and covenant prelacy is extirpated.

Petition of the vicars choral, Sherborne clerks, lay vicars, and other inferior officers of the church of Chichester, to the Lords and Commons. Having been deprived of the means of subsistence by the ordinance of Parliament sequestering the revenues of cathedral churches, and being incapable of other employment, pray that they may receive from the sequestrators what they formerly received from the Dean and Chapter.

Petition of Vincent de la Barr. Prays that his suit against Richard Chambers, concerning a bill of exchange, may be taken into their Lordships' consideration, or referred to some discreet merchants for settlement.

Petition of John Despagne, a French minister. Was pastor of the French congregation in the Level of Axholme and Hatfield Chase, and served very painfully for two years, but was, for want of his promised allowance, necessitated to depart from thence, having only received during that time 25l. Prays their Lordships to order that 135l. justly due to him may be paid by such members of the congregation as petitioner shall make choice of, they abating so much from their rents to the participants of the Level.

Petition of the inhabitants of Droxford, to the Hon. Committee for the county of Southampton. Petitioners have suffered much and are greatly impoverished by the late troubles, but have been always ready to testify their affection to the Parliament by the payment of all taxes. Their parish church has fallen into such decay that petitioners cannot with any safety use it for divine service, and they are unable to raise money for the necessary repairs. Pray that 100l. may be granted to them for the purpose out of the Deans' and Chapters' lands.

Petition of the poorer sort of feltmakers. In consequence of the scarcity of foreign wool, petitioners are now compelled to pay half a crown, and the excise, for what they formerly bought for 16d. or 18d., and their necessities are so great that they are often times forced to sell hats to the haberdashers for a less sum than the wool cost. They therefore pray that the excise may be taken off hats and felt.

Petition of James Gray, to the Earl of Manchester. Prays leave to proceed at law against John Digbie for the recovery of a debt, notwithstanding the Earl has granted him a protection.

Petition of Susan Hadnett. About two years and a half since petitioner extended certain lands in Middlesex and Lincolnshire belonging to Dame Elizabeth Gorges for 360l. forfeited for non-payment of an annuity. Lady Gorges has since died, leaving the lands to the present Countess of Lincoln, after payment of her debts. By the neglect of the petitioner's attorney the extent was lately quashed in the Court of King's Bench, and petitioner has since re-extended the lands, and has possession by virtue of such re-extent. Is informed that the Earl of Lincoln is endeavouring to obtain punishment against her and the Sheriff of Lincoln for this re-extent, pretending the lands to belong to his now lady, and that the proceeding is therefore a breach of privilege. Petitioner prays that she may be heard before either she, or the Sheriff, is troubled concerning the business.

Petition of Edward Hudson, clerk; has been for seven years past illegally kept out of the living of Goodmanham, Yorkshire, properly in the gift of Katherine Carlisle and her executor, by proceedings in law and equity, at the suit of Richard Potter, who is now in possession; prays for redress.

Certificate of Lawrence Norcott touching proceedings in the Court of Requests in a cause between Ann Adlington and Jane Philpot.

Petition of Francis Sadler, Tempest Miller, and John Colkowne, and of Humphrey Galbraith, on the behalf of himself and Lord Folliot, Sir Robert King, Sir Robert Forth, Sir Maurice Eustace, and others, in Ireland, the

P 4

creditors of the said Francis Sadler; Sadler was a great dealer in large sums of money between England and Ireland, and at the time of the rebellion was and still is largely indebted to petitioners, but knowing the difficulty of raising money in such distracted times, they did not press him for payment; meantime Edward Topp, to whom Sadler owed 500l., combined with Toby Rose, Anthony Boyse, and Thomas Garner, secretly to take out a commission of bankruptcy against Sadler at York, though he always kept church and markets at Bristol, Taunton, and Bridgewater, and Topp and the others further evaded all petitioner's efforts to join in the commission; petitioners pray that, as from the distractions of the times they cannot have any remedy elsewhere, their Lordships would call Topp and the others before them, that they may receive the punishment they deserve, and the petitioners have equitable relief.

Duplicate of preceding.

Application for a pass for Don Antonio Sarmierito, of the Council of War and Treasury of the King of Spain, who wishes to go from Flanders to Spain, and, being sick, desires to come to England and pass by land from Dover to Falmouth with his train, carriages, and all necessaries fitting for a person of his quality.

Petition of the copyholders of the manor of Thoydon Bois, Essex, to the Earl of Manchester. The manor is within the perambulation of the forest of Waltham, and petitioners have by the custom of the manor liberty to take estovers in the woods for their necessary fuel. They complain of the waste made by Edward Eldrington, Esq., the lord of the manor, in the cutting down of great quantities of trees, whereby petitioners are deprived of their common of estovers, and His Majesty is disinherited of his free liberty which he ought to have, according to the forest laws, for his deer and venison. Pray his Lordship to move the House of Lords to take some course to stay this great waste.

Petition of the gentleman porter and the forty warders of the Tower of London, to H. C.; at Midsummer, 1643, arrears of pay at 14 pence per diem a piece were owing to them for three whole years and a quarter, within the times of Sir William Balfour and Sir John Conyers, late Lieutenants of the Tower; they have during these troublesome times been tried by extraordinary service, and pray for payment of their arrears.

Petition of William Ware, that his case against Thomas and John Mitchell respecting a mortgage of lands near Chippenham may be referred to any two of the judges.

PROTESTATIONS.

Certificates or returns of the names of those persons who have made the protestation pursuant to order of the House of Commons of the 30th of July 1641. These returns are dated for the most part February, or March 1641-2. For a further account of them, see Report, page 3.

NAMES OF PARISHES.

BERKS—ABINGDON DIVISION.

*Abingdon (division).	Harwell.
——— (parish).	Kingston Bagpinge.
Appleford.	Lyford.
Appleton.	Marcham.
Ashampstead.	Milton.
Aston Tirrold.	Moreton, North.
—— Upthorpe.	——— South.
Basildon.	Moulsford.
Besselsleigh.	Radley.
Cumnor and tithings.	Shippon.
Drayton.	Steventon.
Dudcott (Didcot).	Streatley.
Frilford.	Sunningwell.
Fyfield.	Sutton Courtney.
Garford.	Upton.
Grampold (Grandpont).	Wittenham, Little.
Hagbourne, East and West.	——— Long.
	Wytham.

BERKS—NEWBURY DIVISION.

Aldworth.	Chieveley (including Courage Snelsmore and Oare).
Beedon.	
Boxford.	Chilton.
Brightwaltham.	Compton.
Brimpton.	Enborn.
Chaddleworth.	Farnborough.
Challow, East.	Fawley.
——— West.	

Berks—Newbury Division—cont.

Frilsham.	*Newbury (division).
Greenham.	Peasemore.
Hampstead Marshall.	Shalbourne.
——— Norris.	Shaw cum Donnington.
Hungerford.	Shefford, Little.
Ilsley, East.	—— West.
—— West.	Speen Church.
Inkpen.	Speenhamland.
Kentbury.	Stanford Dingley.
Leckhampstead.	Wasing.
Letcombe Bassett.	Welford.
——— Regis.	Winterbourn Danvers.
Midgham.	Woodspeen and Bagnor.
Newbury (parish).	Yattendon.

BERKS—READING DIVISION.

Aldermaston.	Reading, St. Mary.
Beenham.	Shinfield.
Blewbury.	Sonning.
Bradfield.	Stratfield Mortimer.
Bucklesbury.	Sulham.
Burghfield.	Sulhampstead Abbots.
Cholsey.	——— Banister.
Englefield.	Thatcham.
Padworth.	Tedmarsh.
Pangbourne.	Tilehurst.
Purley.	Ufton.
Reading, St. Giles.	Woolhampton.
——— St. Lawrence.	

BUCKS—BUCKINGHAM HUNDRED.

Addington.	Padbury.
Adstock.	Preston Bissett.
Akeley.	Radclive cum Chackmore.
Barton.	
Beachampton.	Shalston.
Biddlesden.	Steeple Claydon.
Caversfield.	Stowe.
Chetwode.	Thornborough.
Edgcott.	Thornton.
Foxcott.	Tingewick.
Hillesden.	Turweston.
Leckhampstead.	Twyford.
Lillington Dayrell.	Water Stratford.
Marsh Gibbon.	Westbury.
Moreton.	

BUCKS—COTTESLOW HUNDRED.

Aston Abbots.	Linslade.
Cheddington.	Marsworth cum Hawridge.
Choulesbury.	
*Cotteslow (hundred).	Mentmore.
Cublington.	Pitstone cum Nettleden.
Drayton Beauchamp.	Slapton.
——— Parslow.	Soulbury.
Dunton.	Stewkley.
Edlesborough.	Swanbourne.
Grove.	Whaddon cum Nash.
Hardwick and Weedon.	Whitchurch.
Hoggeston.	Wing.
Horwood, Great.	Wingrave.
——— Little.	Winslow.
Ivinghoe.	

CAMBRIDGE.

Letter of Thomas Bainbrigg, D.D., deputy Vice-Chancellor of the University, Master of Christ's College, forwarding certificates from the undermentioned Colleges of those who have taken, or who have not taken the protestation. (Undated.)

These certificates are signed by Dr. Bainbrigg, who classes those who have not taken the protestation under four heads:—1, sickness; 2, nonage; 3, absence; 4, not coming or going away without subscribing or telling their names, so consequently refusing it.

Christ's.	St. John's.
Clare Hall.	St. Katherine's Hall.
Corpus Christi.	St. Peter's.
Emanuel.	Sidney Sussex.
Gonville and Caius.	Trinity.
Jesus.	Trinity Hall.
King's.	Persons having the privilege of Scholars.
Magdalen.	
Pembroke Hall.	Public officers.
Queen's.	

---

* Clergy, churchwardens, overseers, and constables of the several parishes.

* Clergy, churchwardens, overseers, and constables of the several parishes.

CHESTER—CHESTER (CITY).

†Chester. St. Michael.
 Holy Trinity. St. Olave.
 St. Bridget. St. Oswald.
 St. Martin. St. Peter.
 St. Mary on the Hill.

CORNWALL—EAST HUNDRED.

Botus Fleming. Rame.
Callington. [St.] Anthony [Jacob].
Calstock. St. Dominick.
Camelford. St. Germains (borough).
*East (hundred). St. Ive.
Egloskerry. St. John's.
Landrake. St. Mellion.
Landulph. St. Stephen's by Launceston.
Laneast.
Launceston. —— by Saltash.
Lawhitton. St. Thomas.
Lewanick. Sheviock.
Lezant. South-hill.
Linkinhorn. South Petherwin.
Maker. Stoke Climsland.
Menheniot. Tremayne.
Northill. Tresmeer.
Pillaton. Trewen.
Quethiock.

CORNWALL—KERRIER AND PENWITH HUNDREDS.

Return of clergy, churchwardens, overseers, and constables only throughout both hundreds.

CORNWALL—KERRIER HUNDRED.

Breock [Breage]. Mawnan.
Budock. Mullion.
Constantine. Mylor.
Cury. Penryn.
Germoe. Perran Arworthal.
Grade. Ruan Major.
Gunwalloe. —— Minor.
Gwennap. St. Anthony in Meneage.
Helston. St. Keverne.
Landewednack. St. Martin in Meneage.
Mabe. Sithney.
Manaccan. Stedians [St. Stithians].
Mawgan in Meneage. Wendron.

CORNWALL—PENWITH HUNDRED.

Buryan [St.]. Paul.
Camborne. Penzance.
Crowan. Perran Uthnoe.
Gulval. Phillack.
Gwinear. Redruth [St. Uny].
Gwithian. St. Erth.
Illogan. St. Hilary.
Lelant [St. Ewny]. St. Ives.
Levan [St.]. St. Just.
Ludgvan. Sancreed.
Madron. Sennen.
Marasion or Market Jew. Towednack.
Morvah. Zennor.

CORNWALL—LESNEWTH HUNDRED.

Advent. Otterham.
Altarnum [Alternon]. Poundstock.
Davidstow. St. Clether.
Forrabury. St. Genny.
Lanteglos. St. Juliot.
Lesnewth (parish). Tintagell.
* —— (hundred). Treneglos.
Michaelstow. Trevalga.
Minster. Warbstone.

CORNWALL—POWDER HUNDRED.

Cornelly. Lostwithiel.
Creed. Luscallian [Luxulion].
Cuby. Merther.
Fowey. Mevagissey.
Gerrans. Philleigh.
Gorran [St.]. * Powder (hundred).
Grampound. Probus.
Kea. Roche.
Kenwyn. Ruan-Lanihorne.
Ladock. St. Allen [Alune].
Lamorran. St. Anthony.
Lanlivery. St. Austell.

CORNWALL—POWDER HUNDRED—cont.

St. Blazey. St. Michael Carthayes.
St. Clements. —— Penkevil.
St. Dennis. St. Sampson.
St. Erme. St. Stephens.
St. Ewe [Eva]. Tywardreth [Trewardreth].
St. Feock.
St. Just. Veryan.
St. Mewan.

CORNWALL—PYDER HUNDRED.

Colan. St. Breock.
Crantock. St. Columb Major.
Cubert. —— Minor.
Lanhydrock. St. Enoder.
Lanivet. St. Ervan.
Newlyn. St. Evall.
Padstow. St. Issey.
Perranzabulos. St. Mawgan.
Petherick, Little. St. Merryn.
* Pyder (hundred). St. Wenn.
St. Agnes. Withiel.

CORNWALL—STRATTON HUNDRED.

Boyton. North Tamerton.
Bridgerule. Poughill.
Kilkhampton. * Stratton (hundred).
Launcells. —— (parish).
Marham Church. Week, St. Mary.
Moorwinstow. Whitstone.

CORNWALL—TRIGG HUNDRED.

Blisland. St. Endellion.
Bodmin. St. Kew.
Breward [St.]. St. Mabyn.
Egloshayle. St. Teath.
Helland. St. Tudy.
Mynfrey [St. Minver]. †Trigg (hundred).

CORNWALL—WEST HUNDRED.

Boconnoc. Morval.
Broadoak. Pelynt.
Cardinham. St. Cleer.
Duloe. St. Keyne.
East Looe borough, and St. Pinnock.
 St. Martin's parish. St. Veep.
Lanreath. St. Winnow.
Lansalloes. Talland and West Looe.
Lanteglos-juxta-Fowey. Warleggon.
Liskeard.

CUMBERLAND—ALLERDALE-ABOVE-DERWENT WARD.

†Allerdale (ward). Irton.
Arleodon. Lamplugh.
Bootle. Lorton.
Brigham. Loweswater.
Chapel Sucken. Millom.
Cleator. Moresby.
Cockermouth. Muncaster.
Corney. Ponsonby.
Dean. St. Bees and townships
Distington. therein.
Egremont. St. Bridget's Beckermet.
Embleton. Thwaits.
Ennerdale. Ulpha.
Eshdale, otherwise Eskdale. Waberthwaite.
 dale. Whicham.
Gosforth. Whitbeck.
Haile. Workington.
Harrington.

CUMBERLAND—ALLERDALE-BELOW-DERWENT WARD.

All Hallows. Crosthwaite, and townships therein.
Aspatria. ships therein.
Bassenthwaite. Dearham.
Bolton. Gilcrux.
Bridekirk. Holme Cultram.
Bromfield, and townships Ireby.
 therein. Isell, and townships.
Caldbeck. Plumbland.
Camerton. Torpenhow.
Canonbury Cross. Uldale.
 Westward.

CUMBERLAND—CUMBERLAND WARD.

Aikton. Carlisle (St. Cuthbert).
Beaumont. —— (St. Mary).
Bowness. †Cumberland (ward).
Burghby-Sands. Dalston.

---

* Clergy, churchwardens, overseers, and constables of the several parishes.
† "The Mayor with the rest of his brethren and the commonality of this city."

* Clergy, churchwardens, overseers, and constables only.
† Clergy, churchwardens, overseers, and constables of the several parishes.

HOUSE OF LORDS.
Proceedings.

Cumberland—Cumberland Ward—*cont.*

Grimsdale.	Sebergham.
Kirk Andrews.	Thursby.
Kirkbampton.	Warwick.
Kirkbridge [Kirkbride].	Wetheral.
Orton.	Wigton.

CUMBERLAND—ESKDALE WARD.

Arthuret.	Hayton.
Bewcastle.	Irthington.
Brampton.	Kirk Andrews.
Castle Carrock.	Kirk Linton.
Crosby Eden.	Lanercost.
Cumrew.	Scaleby.
Cumwhitton.	Stanwix.
Denton, Upper and Nether.	Stapleton.
Farlam.	Walton.

CUMBERLAND—LEATH WARD.

Addingham.	Langwathby.
Ainstable.	Lazonby.
Castle Sowerby.	Melmerby.
Croglin.	Newton [Rigny].
Dacre.	Ousby.
Graystock and townships.	Penrith.
Hesket.	Renwick.
Hutton-in-the-Forest.	Salkeld, Great.
Kirkland.	Skelton.
Kirk Oswald.	

DENBIGH.

Denbigh (borough).	Ruthin (borough).
Holte "	

DEVON — BAMPTON, HALBERTON, HAYBRIDGE, HEMYOCK, AND TIVERTON HUNDREDS.

Return by the justices of the peace of names of clergy, churchwardens, overseers, and constables of the several parishes.

DEVON—BAMPTON HUNDRED.

Bampton (parish), (Patton and Shillingford).	Hockworthy.
Burlescombe.	Holcombe Rogus.
Clayhanger.	Morebath.
	Uffculme.

DEVON—HALBERTON HUNDRED.

Halberton (parish and tithings).	Sampford Peverill.
	Willand.

DEVON—HAYBRIDGE HUNDRED.

Bickleigh.	Nether Exe.
Bradninch.	Payhembury.
Broadhembury.	Plymtree.
Cadbury.	Sheldon.
Cadleigh.	Silverton.
Cullompton.	Talaton.
Feniton.	Thorverton.
Kentisbeare.	

DEVON—HEMYOCK HUNDRED.

Awliscombe.	Culmstock.
Buckerell.	Dunkeswell.
Church Stanton.	Hemyock (parish).
Clayhidon.	

DEVON—TIVERTON HUNDRED.

Calverleigh.	Tiverton (parish).
Huntsham.	Uplowman.
Loxbear.	

DEVON—BLACK TORRINGTON, HARTLAND, SHEBBEAR, AND WINCKLEIGH HUNDREDS.

Return by the justices of the peace of clergy and parish officials only.

DEVON—BLACK TORRINGTON HUNDRED.

Abbots Bickington.	Honeychurch.
Ashbury.	Inwardleigh.
Ashwater.	Jacobstowe.
Beaworthy.	Luffincott.
Belstone.	Milton Damerell.
Black Torrington (parish).	Monk Okehampton.
Bradford.	Northlew.
Bradworthy.	Pancrasweek.
Bridgerule.	Petherwin, North.
Broadwood Kelly.	Pyworthy.
Clawton.	St. Giles in Heath.
Cookbury.	Sampford Courtney.
Exbourne.	Sutcombe.
Halwell.	Tetcott.
Hatherleigh.	Thornbury.
High Hampton.	Werrington.
Hollacombe.	West Putford.
Holsworthy.	

DEVON—SHEBBEAR HUNDRED.

Abbotsham.	Little Torrington.
Alwington.	Martin [Merton ?].
Beaford.	Meeth.
Bideford.	Monkleigh.
Buckland Brewer.	Newton St. Petrock.
—— Filleigh.	Northam.
Bulkworthy.	Parkham.
Frithelstock.	Peter's Marland.
Huish.	Petrockstow.
Iddesleigh.	Putford, East.
Lancross.	Shebbear (parish).
Langtree.	Sheepwash.
Littleham.	Wear Gifford.

DEVON—HARTLAND HUNDRED.

Clovelly.	Woolfardisworthy.
Hartland.	Yarnscombe.
Wellcombe.	

DEVON—BRAUNTON HUNDRED.

Ashford.	Filleigh.
Barnstaple.	Georgeham.
Berrynarbor.	Goodleigh.
Bratton Fleming.	Heanton Punchardon.
Braunton.	Ilfracombe.
Buckland, East.	Kentisbury.
—— West.	Marwood.
Combe Martin.	[Morthoe ?].
Down, East.	Pilton.
—— West.	Trentishoe.

DEVON—BUDLEIGH WEST, HUNDRED.

Cheriton Fitzpaine.	Stockleigh Pomeroy.
Poughill.	Upton Helions.
Shobrook.	Washfield.
Stockleigh English.	

DEVON—CLISTON HUNDRED.

Broadclist.	Butterleigh.

DEVON—COLYTON HUNDRED.

Colyton.

DEVON—CREDITON HUNDRED.

Bishop's Morehard.	Kennerleigh.
Colebrook.	Newton Cyres.
Crediton.	Sandford.

DEVON—COLERIDGE (NORTH DIVISION) HUNDRED.

Ashprington.	Dartmouth, St. Saviour's.
Blackawton.	Dittisham.
*Coleridge (North Div.), hundred.	Halwell.
	Harberton.
Cornworthy.	Stokefleming.
Dartmouth, St. Clement.	Totness.
—— St. Petrox.	

DEVON—COLERIDGE (SOUTH DIVISION) HUNDRED.

Buckland Tout Saints.	East Portlemouth.
Charleton.	Sherford.
Chivelstone.	Slapton.
*Coleridge (South Div.), hundred.	Southpool.
	Stokeingham.
Dodbrooke.	

DEVON—†STANBOROUGH (NORTH DIVISION) HUNDRED.

Brent, South.	Morleigh.
Dartington.	Rattery.
Diptford.	*Stanborough (North Div.), hundred.
Huish, North.	

DEVON—†STANBOROUGH (SOUTH DIVISION) HUNDRED.

Allington, East.	Malborough.
Alvington, West.	Milton, South.
Churchstow.	*Stanborough (South Div.), hundred.
Huish, South.	
Kingsbridge.	Thurleston.
Loddiswill.	Woodley.

DEVON—ERMINGTON AND PLYMPTON HUNDRED.

Return by the justices of the peace of clergy and parish officials only.

DEVON—ERMINGTON HUNDRED.

Aveton Gifford.	Holbeton.
Bigbury.	Modbury.
Cornwood.	Newton Ferrers.
Ermington.	Ringmore.
Harford.	Ugborough.

* Clergy, churchwardens, overseers, and constables of the several parishes.
† A few returns for places in this hundred were sent with Haytor and other hundreds, see below.

Devon—Plympton Hundred.

Plymstock.
Plympton, St. Mary.
—— St. Maurice.
Revelstoke.

Shaugh [Prior].
Wembury.
Yealampton.

Devon—*Exminster Hundred.

Dunchidcock.
Exminster, parish.
*—— hundred.
Ide.
Kenn.

Kenton.
Mamhead.
Powderham.
Shillingford [St. George].

Devon—Fremington Hundred.

Alverdiscott.
Fremington.
Great Torrington.
Harwood.
Huntshaw.
Instow.

Newton Tracy.
Roborough.
St. Giles.
Tawstock.
West Leigh.

Devon—Haytor, Teignbridge, and parts of Exminster, Wonford South, and Stanborough Hundreds.

Letter from the members of Parliament for Devon, enclosing the returns hereafter mentioned, from Newton Abbotts. 14 Mar. 1641-2.
Returns by the justices of the peace of clergy and parish officials only.

Devon—Haytor Hundred.

Abbots Kerswell.
Berry Pomeroy.
Brixham.
Broadhempston.
Buckland-in-the-Moor.
Churston Ferrers.
Cockington.
Coffinswell.
Denbury.
Haccombe.
Ipplepen.
King's Kerswell.
—— Wear.

Little Hempston.
Marldon.
Newton Abbot and Woolborough.
Paignton.
St. Mary Church.
Staverton.
Stoke Gabriel.
Torbrian.
Tor Moham.
Widecombe-in-the-Moor.
Woodland.

Devon—Teignbridge Hundred.

Bickington.
Bovey, North.
—— South [or Tracy].
Hennock.
Highweek.
Ideford.

Ilsington.
Kingsteignton.
Lustleigh.
Manaton.
Moreton Hampstead.
Teigngrace.

Devon—‡Exminster (part only) Hundred.

Ashcombe.
Ashton.
Bishopsteignton.
Chudleigh.
Dawlish.

Doddiscombsleigh.
Teignmouth, East.
—— West.
Trusham.

Devon—§Wonford (part only) Hundred.

Combeinteignhead.
Ogwell, East.
—— West.

Stokeinteignhead.
St. Nicholas.

Devon—‖Stanborough (part only) Hundred.

Buckfastleigh.
Dean Prior.

Holne.

Devon—§Wonford (part only) Hundred.

Alphington.
Bramford Speke.
Bridford.
Chagford.
Cheriton Bishop.
Christow.
Drewsteignton.
Dunsford.
Exeter, All Hallows, Goldsmith Street.
Exeter, All Hallows, on the Wales.
Exeter, St. David's.
—— St. Edmund's upon the Bridge.
Exeter, St. George.
—— St. John's [Bowe].
—— St. Kerrian.
—— St. Lawrence.

Exeter, St. Martin's.
—— St. Mary Arches.
—— St. Mary Major.
—— St. Mary Steps.
—— St. Olave.
—— St. Pancras.
—— St. Paul's.
—— St. Peter's [Cathedral].
Exeter, St. Petrox.
—— St. Sidwell's.
—— St. Stephens.
—— Trinity.
¶—— The whole of the parishes.
Gidleigh.
Heavitree.
Hittisleigh.
Holcombe Burnell.

Devon—Wonford (part only) Hundred—cont.

Huxham.
Pinhoe.
Poltimore.
Rewe.
St. Leonard.
St. Thomas-the-Apostle.
South Tawton.
Sowton.

Spreyton.
Stoke Canon.
Tedburn.
Throwleigh.
Topsham.
Upton Pine.
Whitstone.
*Wonford.

Devon—Lifton Hundred.

Bradstone.
Bratton Clovelly.
Bridestowe.
Broadwood-Widger.
Dunterton.
Germasweek.
Kelly.
Lamerton.
Lewtrenchard.
Lidford.

Lifton (parish).
Marystow.
Okehampton.
Sourton.
Stowford.
Sydenham Dameroll.
Tavy St. Mary.
Thrushelton.
Virginstow.

Devon—Roborough Hundred.

Beer Ferris.
Bickleigh.
Buckland Monachorum.
Egg Buckland.
Meavy.
Plymouth.
St. Peter Tavy.

Sampford Spincy.
Shittestor Shee pstor].
Stoke Damerell.
Tamerton Foliot.
Walkhampton.
Whitchurch.

Devon—Sherwill Hundred.

Arlington.
Brendon.
Challacombe Rawleigh.
Charles.
Countisbury.
Highbray.

Linton.
Loxhore.
Martinhoe.
Parracombe.
Sherwill (parish).
Stoke Rivers.

Devon—Tavistock Hundred.

Brent Tor.
Milton Abbots.

Tavistock (parish).

Devon—North Tawton, South Molton, and Witheridge Hundreds.

Letter from John Chichester to Richard Culme, High Sheriff of Devon, enclosing the returns for those hundreds.
†Returns by the justices of the peace for the above hundreds.

Devon—North Tawton Hundred.

Ashreigny.
Atherington.
Bondleigh.
Burrington.
Clanaborough.
Dolton.
Dowland.
Down St. Mary.
High Bickington [Bickerton].

Lapford with Chawleigh, Coleridge, Brushford, Wembworthy, and Eggesford.
Nymet, Broad.
—— Tracy.
Tawton, North (parish).
Winckleigh.
Zeal Monachorum.

Devon—South Molton Hundred.

Anstey, East.
—— West.
Bishops Tawton.
Chittlehampton.
Knowstone.
Landkey.
Molland.
Molton, North.

Molton, South (town and parish).
Nympton, St. George.
Satterleigh.
Swimbridge.
Twitchen.
Warkleigh.

Devon—Witheridge Hundred.

Bishops Nympton.
Cheldon.
Chulmleigh.
Creacombe.
Crays Morchant.
King's Nympton.
Marleight [Mariansleigh].
Meshaw.
Oakford.
Puddington.
Rackenford.

Romansleigh.
Rose Ash.
Stoodleigh.
Templeton.
Thelbridge.
Washford Pyne.
Witheridge (parish).
Woolfardisworthy.
Worlington, East and West.

Dorset—Blandford, North and South Division—Bindon Liberty.

Bindon (parish).

Wool.

* See also below.
† Clergy, churchwardens, overseers, and constables of the several parishes.
‡ See also above.
§ These appear to have been sent up apart, hence their separation.
‖ For the remainder of this hundred, see above.
¶ Clergy, churchwardens, overseers, and constables, with some others, of the several parishes.

* Clergy, churchwardens, overseers, and constables of the several parishes.
† Clergy and parish officers only.

DORSET — BLANDFORD, NORTH AND SOUTH DIVISIONS —
COOMB'S DITCH HUNDRED.

Anderson.
Blandford [Forum].
———— St. Mary.

Bloxworth.
Winterborne Clenstone.
———— Whitchurch.

DORSET — BLANDFORD, NORTH AND SOUTH DIVISIONS—
CORFE CASTLE HUNDRED.

Corfe Castle (parish).

DORSET — BLANDFORD, NORTH AND SOUTH DIVISIONS—
HASILOR HUNDRED.

Arne.
Church Knowle.
East Holme.

Kimmeridge.
Steeple.
Tyneham.

DORSET — BLANDFORD, NORTH AND SOUTH DIVISIONS—
HUNDREDSBARROW HUNDRED.

Aff Puddle.   Tarners Puddle.

DORSET — BLANDFORD, NORTH AND SOUTH DIVISIONS—
OWERMOIGNE LIBERTY.

Owermoigne.

DORSET — BLANDFORD, NORTH AND SOUTH DIVISIONS—
PIMPERNE HUNDRED.

Bryanstone.
Durweston.
Fifehead.
Hammoon.
Haselbury-Bryan.
Langton Long.
Pimperne (parish).

Steepleton.
Stourpain.
Tarrant Hinton.
———— Keynston.
———— Launceston.
Winterbourne Houghton.
———— Strickland.

DORSET — BLANDFORD, NORTH AND SOUTH DIVISIONS—
ROWBARROW HUNDRED.

Langton Matravers.
Studland.

Swanage.
Worth Matravers.

DORSET — BLANDFORD, NORTH AND SOUTH DIVISIONS—
RUSHMORE HUNDRED.

[Zelstone] Winterborne.

DORSET — BLANDFORD, NORTH AND SOUTH DIVISIONS—
WINFRITH HUNDRED.

Chaldon Herring.
Coombe Keymes.
East Lulworth.
East Stoke.
Moreton.

Poxwell.
Wareham.
Warmwell.
Winfrith (parish).
Woodsford.

DORSET—SHERBORNE, CERNE (SUB-DIVISION), AND STUR-
MINSTER DIVISIONS.

*Returns by the justices of the peace.

DORSET—SHERBORNE DIVISION—SHERBORNE HUNDRED.

Beer-Hackwood [Hack-
ett].
Bradford Abbas.
Castleton.
Caundle Bishop.
———— Marsh.
———— Purse.
Compton Nether.
———— Over.
Folke.

Haydon.
Holnest.
Longburton.
Lydlinch.
North Wootton.
Oborne.
Sherborne (town).
[Shinborne] Lillington.
Thornford.
Up-Cerne.

DORSET —SHERBORNE DIVISION—YETMINSTER HUNDRED.

Batcombe.
Chetnole.
Leigh.

Melbury Bubb.
———— Osmond.
Yetminster (parish).

DORSET—SHERBORNE DIVISION—HALSTOCK LIBERTY.

Halstock.

DORSET—SHERBORNE DIVISION—RYME INTRINSICA LIBERTY.

Ryme Intrinsica.

DORSET—CERNE SUB-DIVISION—BUCKLAND [NEWTON] HUN-
DRED.

Buckland [Newton] and
tithings.
Mappowder.

Plush.
Pulham.
Wootton Glanville.

DORSET—CERNE SUB-DIVISION—WHITEWAY HUNDRED.

Chesilborne.
Hilton.
Ibberton.
Melcombe Bingham.

Milton Abbas.
Stoke Wake.
Woolland.

DORSET—CERNE SUB-DIVISION—PIDDLETRENTHIDE LIBERTY.

Mintern Magna.   Piddletrenthide.

DORSET—CERNE SUB-DIVISION—ALTON PANCRAS LIBERTY.

Alton Pancras.

DORSET—CERNE SUB-DIVISION—CERNE, TOTCOMBE, AND
MODBURY HUNDREDS.

Cattistock.
Cerne Abbas.

Compton Abbas.
Godmanstone.

DORSET—CERNE SUB-DIVISION—SYDLING LIBERTY.

Sydling.

DORSET—STURMINSTER DIVISION—STURMINSTER NEWTON
CASTLE HUNDRED.

Hinton St. Mary.
Margaret Marsh.
Marnhull.

Okeford Fitzpaine.
Sturminster Newton Cas-
tle.

DORSET—STURMINSTER DIVISION—BROWNSHALL HUNDRED.

Stalbridge.
Stock Gayland.

Stourton Caundle.

DORSET—STURMINSTER DIVISION—REDLAND HUNDRED.

Buckhorn Weston.
Child Okeford.
East Stower.
Fifehead Magdalen.
Kington Magna.
Manston.

Silton.
Sutton Waldron.
Todbere.
Twerne Courtnay.
West Stower.

DORSET—STURMINSTER DIVISION—STOWER PROVOST LIBERTY.

Stower Provost.

DORSET—BRIDPORT DIVISION.

* Return for the whole division.

DORSET—BRIDPORT DIVISION—BEAMINSTER HUNDRED.

Beaminster (parish).
Bradpole.
Charlstock.
Cheddington.
Corscombe.
Mapperton.

Mostertone, with South
Perrot.
Netherbury.
Stoke Abbas.
Wambrook.

DORSET—BRIDPORT DIVISION—BROADWINSOR LIBERTY.

Broadwinsor.

DORSET—BRIDPORT DIVISION—POORSTOCK HUNDRED.

Poorstock.

DORSET—BRIDPORT DIVISION—FRAMPTON LIBERTY.

Bettiscombe.
Bincombe.
Burton [Bradstock].

Compton Vallence.
Frampton (parish).
[Winterbourne] Came.

DORSET—BRIDPORT DIVISION—LOTHERS AND BOTHENHAMP-
TON LIBERTY.

Loders.   Bothenhampton.

DORSET—BRIDPORT DIVISION—WHITCHURCH CANONICORUM
HUNDRED.

Burstock.
Charmouth.
Chideock.
Marshwood.
Pilsdon.

Stockland.
Symondsbury.
Whitchurch Canonicorum
(parish).
Wootton Fitzpaine.

DORSET—BRIDPORT DIVISION—GODDERTHORNE HUNDRED.

Allington.
Skipton George.

Walditch.

DORSET—BRIDPORT DIVISION—EGGERTON HUNDRED.

Askerswell.
Hooke.
Longbredy and Kingston.

Winterbourne Abbas.
Wroxall.

DORSET—SHASTON DIVISION—COGDEAN HUNDRED.

Canford Magna.
Charlton Marshal.
Corfe Mullen.
Hamworthy.

Kingston.
Lytchett Matravers.
———— Minster.
Sturminster Marshal.

DORSET — SHASTON DIVISION — MONCKTON-UP-WIMBORNE
HUNDRED.

Chettle.
Cranborne and tithings.

Tarrant Monckton.

DORSET—SHASTON DIVISION—LOOSEBARROW HUNDRED.

Almer.
Morden.

Spetisbury.

DORSET—SHASTON DIVISION—KNOWLTON HUNDRED.

Long Critchell.
Gussage All Saints.

Woodlands.

---

* Names of clergy, churchwardens, overseers, and constables of the
several parishes.

* Clergy, churchwardens, overseers, and constables of the several
parishes.

House of Lords.
—
Protestations.

DORSET—SHASTON DIVISION—GILLINGHAM LIBERTY,
Gillingham.
Motcombe.

DORSET—SHASTON DIVISION—BADBURY HUNDRED.

Chalbury.   Hinton Parva.
[Tarrant] Crawford.   Horton.
Critchill Moore.   Shapwick.
Gussage St. Michael.   Wimborne Minster and
Hinton Martell.   hamlets therein.

DORSET—SHASTON DIVISION—CRANBOURNE HUNDRED.

Ashmore.   Oakford.
Belchalwell.   Pentridge.
Cranbourne (parish).   Rushton Tarrant.
Edmondsham.   Tarrant Gunville.
Farnham.   Turnwood.
Hampreston.   West Parley.
Holwell.   Witchampton.

DORSET—SHASTON DIVISION—WIMBORNE ST. GILES HUN-
DRED.
Wimborne All Saints.   Wimborne St. Giles.

DORSET—SHASTON DIVISION—SIXPENNY HANDLEY HUNDRED.

Cann (or Shaston St. Iwerne Minster.
  Rumbold).   Melbury Abbas.
Compton Abbas.   Shaftesbury St. Peter and
Fontmell Magna.   Holy Trinity.
Handley.

DORSET—SHASTON DIVISION—ALCESTER LIBERTY.
St. James.

DORSET—DORCHESTER DIVISION.
* Return for the whole division.

DORSET — DORCHESTER DIVISION — CULLIFORD TREE
HUNDRED.

[Broadway.]   West Knighton.
[Buckla]nde Ripers.   West Stafford and Froome
Chickerell.   Billet.
Mel[combe Regis].   Weymouth.
Osmington.   Whitcombe.
Rodipole [Radipole]. [Winterbourne Monk-
Upway.   ton.]

DORSET—DORCHESTER DIVISION—SUTTON POYNTZ LIBERTY.
Preston and Sutton Poyntz Stockwood.
(2).

DORSET—DORCHESTER DIVISION.
Wyke Regis (liberty).

DORSET—DORCHESTER DIVISION.
Isle of Portland.

DORSET—DORCHESTER DIVISION—GEORGE HUNDRED.

Bradford and Muckleford. Stinsford.
Broadmayne.   Stratton and Grimston.
Charminster.   Winterbourne St. Martin.

DORSET—DORCHESTER DIVISION—PUDDLETON HUNDRED.

Athelhampstone, Burles- [Puddleton.]
  ton, and Dewlish (North Tincleton.
  Blandford Hundred). Tolpuddle.
[Milborne St. Andrew.]

DORSET—DORCHESTER DIVISION—TOLLERFORD HUNDRED.

Chelborough, West.   Maiden Newton.
Frome Vauchurch.   Toller Porcorum.
Three returns, the names of which cannot be identified.

DORSET—DORCHESTER DIVISION—UGSCOMBE HUNDRED.

Chilcombe.   [Puncknowle.]
Fleet.   Swyre.
Hawkchurch.   Winterbourne Steepleton.
Langton Herring.   Dallwood
[Little Bredy.]   Fordington } Fordington
[Litton Cheney.]   Hermitage } liberty.
Portisham.   Puddle Hinton (liberty).

DORSET—BERE REGIS HUNDRED.
Bere Regis.   Winterborne Kingston.

DURHAM—CHESTER WARD.

Boldon.   Lanchester.
Chester - le - Street and Medomsley.
  townships.   Monkwearmouth.
*Chester (ward).   Muggleswick.
Ebchester.   Ryton.
Edmondbyers.   St. Hilda (South Shields).
Esh.   Tanfield.
Gateside [Gateshead]. Washington.
Hunstanworth.   Whickham.
Jarrow.   Whitburn.
Lamesley.   Witton-Gilbert.

* Clergy, churchwardens, overseers, and constables of the several parishes.

DURHAM—DARLINGTON WARD.

Auckland St. Andrew and Hamsterley.
  townships.   Haughton.
Auckland St. Helena.   Heighington.
Aycliffe.   Merrington.
Barnard Castle.   Middleton-in-Teasdale.
Brancepeth.   Sadberge.
Cockfield.   Stanhope.
Coniscliffe.   Whitworth.
*Darlington (ward).   Whorlton.
————— (parish).   Winston.
Denton.   Witton-upon-Weer.
Gainford.   Wolsingham.

DURHAM—EASINGTON WARD.

Bishop Wearmouth.   Houghton-le-Spring.
Castle Eden.   Kelloe.
Croxdale.   Monk Hesleton.
Dalton-le-Dale.   Pittington.
Durham, North Bailey. St. Oswald.
————— South Bailey. Seaham.
————— St. Giles'.   Sherburn Hospital.
————— St. Margaret's. Sunderland.
————— St. Nicholas. Trimdon.
Easington.

DURHAM—STOCKTON WARD.

Billingham.   Hart.
Bishop's Middleham. Hartlepool.
Bishopton.   Hurworth.
Dinsdale.   Long Newton.
Egglescliffe.   Middleton, St. George.
Elton.   Norton.
Elwick [Hull].   Red Marshall.
Greatham.   Sedgefield.
Great Stainton.   Sockburn.
Grindon.   Stranton.

ESSEX—HINCKFORD HUNDRED.

Alphamstone.   Lamarsh.
Ashen.   Liston.
Ballingdon.   Maplestead Magna.
Belchamp Otton.   ————— Parva.
————— St. Paul. Middleton.
————— Walter. Ovington.
Birdbrook.   Panfield.
Bocking.   Pebmarsh.
Borley.   Pentlow.
Braintree.   Rayne.
Bulmer.   Ridgwell..
Bumpstead, Steeple. Shalford.
Felstead.   Stambourne.
Finchingfield.   Stebbing.
Foxearth.   Stisted.
Gestingthorpe.   Sturmere, and hamlets.
Gosfield.   Tilbury-juxta-Clare.
Halstead.   Twinstead.
Hedingham Castle.   Wetherfield.
Hedingham Sible.   Wickham St. Paul.
Henny Magna.   Yeldham Magna.
*Hinckford hundred. ————— Parva.

HANTS.
Southampton.

HERTFORD—CASHIO HUNDRED.

Certificate of the mayor and others of the borough
and liberty of St. Alban's.

St. Alban's, St. Michael's. Redbourn.
————— St. Peter. Sandridge.
————— St. Stephen's.

HUNTINGDON—HURSTINGSTONE HUNDRED.

Bluntisham cum Earith. Raveley Parva.
Broughton.   Ripton Abbots.
Bury.   Ripton King.
Colne.   St. Ives.
Hartford.   Somersham.
Holywell cum Needing- Stukeley Magna.
  worth.   ————— Parva.
Houghton cum Witton. Warboys.
Pidsey cum Fenton. Wistow.
†Ramsey.   Woodhurst and Oldhurst.
Raveley Magna cum Up-
  wood.

* Clergy, churchwardens, overseers, and constables of the several parishes.
† The following is an extract from this document:—
"O. Cromwell. } "Wheatethall Awdley Esq., being at London about
"H. Cromwell. } paying in the pole money when the protestation
           was taken, he came and took it before us at Ram-
           say, the 24th of February 1641[2]."

HUNTINGDON—LEIGHTONSTONE HUNDRED.

Alconbury cum Weston.
Barham.
Brampton.
Brington.
Buckworth.
Bythorn.
Catworth Magna.
Coppingford cum Upton.
Covington.
Easton.
Edlington.
Gidding Magna.
—— Parva.

Gidding, Steeple.
Graffham.
Hamerton.
Keyston.
Kimbolton.
Leighton.
Molesworth.
Oldweston.
Spaldwick.
Stow.
Swineshead.
Winnick.
Woolley.

HUNTINGDON—NORMANCROSS HUNDRED.

Copy of the Speaker's letter to the sheriff and justices
of peace of the county, urging them to take the
protestation, and to see that others do the like.

Alwalton.
Caldecote.
Chesterton.
Conington.
Denton.
Elton.
Farcett.
Fletton.
Folksworth.
Glatton.
Haddon.
Holme.
Morborn.
* Normancross hundred.
Orton Cherry alias Over-
ton Waterville.

Orton Long alias Overton
Longville, with Bottle-
bridge.
Sawtrey, St. Andrew and
St. Judith.
Sawtrey, All Saints.
Standground.
Stibbington.
Stilton.
Water Newton.
Woodstone.
Woodwalton.
Yaxley.

HUNTINGDON—TOSELAND HUNDRED.

Abbotsley.
Buckden.
Diddington.
Eynesbury.
Fen Stanton.
Godmanchester.
Gransden Magna.
Hail Weston.
Hilton.

Offord Darcey.
Paxton Parva.
St. Neots.
Southoe.
Staughton Magna.
Toseland (parish).
*Toseland (hundred).
Waresley.

KENT—ST. AUGUSTINE LATHE—BEWSBOROUGH HUNDRED.

Beausfield [Whitfield].
Buckland.
Dover.
Ewell.
Guston.
Langdon, West.

Lydden.
River.
St. Margaret at Cliffe and
West Cliffe.
Sibbertswold and Col-
dred.

KENT—ST. AUGUSTINE LATHE—BLEANGATE HUNDRED.

Chislett.
Hearne.
Hoath.
Reculver.

Stourmouth.
Sturry.
Swalecliffe.
Westbere.

KENT—ST. AUGUSTINE LATHE—BRIDGE AND PETHAM HUN-
DRED.

Bridge.
Hardres, Lower.
—— Upper.
Nackington.

Patrixbourne.
Petham.
Waltham.

KENT—ST. AUGUSTINE LATHE—CORNILO HUNDRED.

Norborne [Northbourne]. Ripple.

KENT—ST. AUGUSTINE LATHE—DOWNHAMFORD HUNDRED.

Adisham.
Ickham.
Littlebourn.

Staple.
Stodmarsh.
Wickhambreux.

KENT—ST. AUGUSTINE LATHE—EASTRY HUNDRED.

Barfreston.
Betshanger and Pilman-
stone.
Chillenden.
Denton.
Eastry.

Eythorn.
Ham and Betshanger.
Knowlton.
Waldershare.
Woodnesborough.
Word [Worth].

KENT—ST. AUGUSTINE LATHE—KINGHAMFORD HUNDRED.

Barham.
Bishopsbourne.

Kingston.

KENT—ST. AUGUSTINE LATHE—PRESTON HUNDRED.

Elmstone. Preston juxta Wingham.

KENT—ST. AUGUSTINE LATHE—RINGSLOW OR THANET
HUNDRED.

Birchington.
Minster.
St. John's [Margate].
St. Lawrence.

St. Nicholas at Wade.
St. Peter's, Broadstairs
and Reden Street.

KENT—ST. AUGUSTINE LATHE—WESTGATE HUNDRED.

Hackington alias St. Ste-
phen.
Harbledown.
Holy Cross, Westgate.
St. Dunstan's.
Thanington alias St. Ni-
cholas.

*Walloon Congregation in
and about Canterbury.
*Christ Church, Canter-
bury (precinct).
†Longport (borough).

KENT—ST. AUGUSTINE LATHE—WHITSTABLE HUNDRED.

Blean otherwise St. Cos-
mus and Damian.

‡Seasalter.
‡Whitstable.

KENT—ST. AUGUSTINE LATHE—WINGHAM HUNDRED.

Ash.
Goodnestone.
Nonington.

Wingham.
Womenswould.

KENT—SHEPWAY LATHE—ROMNEY MARSH LIBERTY.

New Romney.

KENT—SUTTON AT HONE LATHE.

Certificate of justices of peace.

KENT—SUTTON AT HONE LATHE—AXTON HUNDRED.

Sutton at Hone.

KENT—SUTTON AT HONE LATHE—CODSHEATH HUNDRED.

Brasted.
Chevening.
Halstead.
Leigh juxta Tunbridge.
Otford.

Seal and Kemsing.
Sevenoaks.
Shoreham.
Sundridge.

KENT—SUTTON AT HONE LATHE—SOMERDEN HUNDRED.

Chiddingstone.
Cowden.
Groombridge.

Heiver.
Penshurst.

KENT—SUTTON AT HONE LATHE—WESTERHAM HUNDRED.

Edenbridge. Westerham.

LANCASTER—AMOUNDERNESS HUNDRED.

Aston cum Hothersall.
Bispham with Layton and
[Black]pool.
Bleasdale, Fulwood, and
Myerscough.
Broughton.
Garstang, with the fol-
lowing townships, viz.:—
Barnacre.
Bilborough.
Catteral.
Claughton.
Wyersdale.
Goosnargh, Newsham,
and Whittingham.
Kirkham, and townships
therein, viz.—
Bryning cum Kella-
murgh.
Clifton cum Salwick.
Freckleton.
Greenalgh cum This-
tleton.
Larbrick cum Eccle-
ston.

Kirkham—cont.
Medler cum Wesham.
Newton cum Scales.
Ribby cum Wrea.
Singleton Magna cum
Parva.
Warton.
Westby cum Plump-
tons.
Weeton.
Wharles.
Lytham.
Pilling.
Poulton le Fylde, inclu-
ding—
Carlton.
Hardhorn cum Newton
and Marton.
Preston.
St. Michael on Wyre.
Stalmine.
Wood Plumpton.

LANCASTER—BLACKBURN HUNDRED.

Blackburn parish and
places therein, viz.:—
Balderston.
Billington.
Clayton le Dale.
Darwen, Lower.
—— Over.
Lipshire [Wilpshire]
cum Dinkley.
Little Harwood.
Livesey.
Mellor cum Eccleshill.

Blackburn—cont.
Osbaldeston.
Pleasington.
Risheton.
Salisbaerie [Salesbury].
Samlesbury.
Walton in the Dale and
Overdale.
Tock[h]oles.
Witton.
Yate with Pictoppbanke
[Pick-up-Bank].

---

* These returns appear to have been sent up with those for the hun-
dred of Westgate.
† Now extinct; originally part of St. Paul's, Canterbury.
‡ With letter of justices of peace to the constables.

* Clergy, churchwardens, overseers, and constables of the several
parishes.

Lancaster—Blackburn Hundred—*cont.*

List of certain of the Inhabitants of some of the above-named places who refuse to take the protestation :—

Chipping.
Ribchester, including Alston, Dilworth, and Dutton.

Whalley, parish and places therein, viz. :—

Accrington.
Altham.
Aighton Bailey.
Bacobb [Bacup].
Brascliffe [Briercliffe].
Burnley.
Chadgley [Chaigley].
Chatburn.
Church Kirk with Osbaldwistle.
Clayton supra Moras.
Clitheroe (borough).
Cliverger.
Colne Trawden, &c.
Downham.

Whalley—*cont.*

Dunkinhalgh [Dunnockshaw].
Extwistle.
Filley Close.
Goodshawe [Goldshaw].
Habergham Eaves.
Hapton.
Haslingden.
Heyhouses.
Ightonhill Park.
Mearley.
Mitton, Henthorne, and Colcotes.
New Church, Rossendale.
New Church in Pendle.
Pediham.
Pendle.
Pendleton.
Reade.
Reedley Hallows.
Simonstone.
Wiswell.
Worsthorn cum Hurstwood.
Worston.

Lancaster—Leyland Hundred,

Brindhill [Brindle].
Chorley.
Croston, with—
　Bretherton.
　Byspham.
　Hesketh cum Beconsfaild [Becconsall].
　Mawdesley.
　Rufford.
　Tarleton.
　Walton.
Eccleston, with—
　Heskin.
　Parbold.
　Wrightington.
Hoole.
Leyland, with—
　Clayton.
　Cuerden.
　Euxton.

Hoghton, Withnell, Whealton, and Heapey.
Whittle-in-le-Wood.
Penwortham, with—
　Farrington.
　Houghton [Hutton].
　Howick.
　Longton.
Standish, with—
　Adlington.
　Anderton.
　Coppull.
　Charnock Heath.
　———— Richard.
　Duxbury.
　Langtree.
　Shevington.
　Welch Whittle.
　Worthington.

Lancaster—Salford Hundred.

Ashton-under-Lyne.
*Bolton and Dean parishes.
Bolton, including Bolton, Great and Little; Brightnett [Breightmet]; Haigh [Haulgh]; Harwood; Lever, Little; Lever, Darcy; Lostock; Sharples; Tonge; Edgeworth; Entwistle; Quarlton; Longworth; Turton; Blackrode; Rivington; Anlesarghe [Anglezarke].
Deane, including Farmworth; Halliwell; Heaton; Horwich; Hulton, Little; Hulton, Middle; Hulton, Over; Kersley; Romworth [Rumworth]; Westhaughton.
*Bury and Radcliffe.
Bury, including Cowpe; Eatenfield [Edenfield]; Lench; Musbury; Newallhey; Shuttleworth.
Tottington, Lower.
Radcliffe.
Middleton, including—
　Ainsworth.
　Birtle, Bamford, and Ashworth.

Middleton—*cont.*

Hopwood.
Leaver, Great.
Pilsworth.
Thornham.
Rochdale, including—
　Butterworth.
　Castleton.
　Huddersfield.
　Spotland.
* Manchester.

Manchester, including—
　Ardwick.
　Birch.
　Blakeley [Blackley].
　Cheetham.
　Chollerton [Chorlton cum Hardy], Haghend, Mansleache, and Hardie.
　Chorlton Row.
　Crumsall [Crumpshall].
　Denton.
　Didsbury, Withington, Burnage, and Levenshulme.
　Eccles.
　Flixton.
　Gorton.
　Harpar Hay [Harpurhey].
　Haughton.
　Heaton Norris.

Lancaster—Salford Hundred—*cont.*

Manchester—*cont.*

Newton Heath, Droylsdon, Bradford, and Failsworth.
Openshaw.
Prestwick cum Oldham, including—
　Akerington [Alkrington ?].
Heaton - upon - Faughfield.
Oldham.

Prestwick-cum-Oldham—*cont.*
Tonge.
Outwood within Pilkington.
Unsworth within Pilkington.
Whitfield within Pilkington.
Reddish.
Stretford.
Salford and liberties.

Lancaster—West Derby Hundred.

Leigh, with—
　Astley.
　Atherton.
　Bedford.
　Pennington.
　Tyldesley cum Shackerley.
　Westleigh.
Liverpool.
Wigan.
Winwick, including—
　Arbury.
　Ashton.

Winwick—*cont.*
Croft.
Culcheth.
Goulborne.
Houghton.
Hulme.
Lowton cum Kenion.
Middleton.
Newton.
Southworth.

Lincoln—Holland, parts of—Elloe Wapentake.

Cowbit.
Croyland [Crowland].
Gedney.
———— Fen.
Holbeach.
Lutton in Sutton.
Moulton.
Spalding.

Sutton, St. James.
———— St. Edmund's.
———— St. Mary.
Tydd, St. Mary.
Weston.
Whaplode.
———— Drove.

Lincoln—Holland, parts of—Kirton Wapentake.

Algarkirk.
Bicker.
Brothertoft.
Donington.
Fosdyke.
Frampton.
Gosberkirk [Gosberton].

Kirton.
Quadring.
Sutterton.
Swineshead Hill.
Wigtoft.
Wyberton.

Lincoln—Holland, parts of—Skirbeck Hundred [Boston].

Butterwick.
Fishtoft.

Frieston.
Leake.
Wrangle.

Lincoln—Kesteven, parts of—Winnibriggs and Threo, Beltisloe, Ness and Aveland Wapentakes.

*Certificate of the justices of the peace.

Lincoln—Winnibriggs and Threo Wapentakes.

Allington [West].
Barrowby.
Hayther [Haydor].
Honington.
Humby, Great.
Sedgbrook.

Somerby.
Stroxton.
Syston.
Welby.
Wilsford.
Woolstrop [Woolsthorpe].

Lincoln—Beltisloe Wapentake.

Basingthorpe cum Westby.
Bitchfield.
Burton Coggles.
Bytham Castle cum Counthorpe.
Bytham, Little.
Careby.
Corby.
Gunby.
Holywell and Aunby.

Irnham Bulby and Hawthorpe.
Levington [Lavington].
Skilington.
Stainby.
Swa[y]field.
Swinstead.
Witham, North.
———— South.
———— on the Hill.

Lincoln—Ness Wapentake.

Barholme.
Baston.
Braceborough.
Carelbie [Carlby].
Deeping Market.
———— St. James's.
———— West.

Greatford.
Langtoft.
Stowe.
Thurlby.
Uffington.
Wilsthorpe.

HOUSE OF LORDS.

Protestations.

LINCOLN—KESTEVEN, PARTS OF—AVELAND WAPENTAKE.

Aslackby.
Billingborough.
Bourne Dyke and Cawthorpe.
Denbleby cum Willoughby.
Dowsby.
Dunsby.
Folkingham [Falkingham].
Haceby.
Hacconby cum Steinfield [Stanfield].

Horbling.
Kirkby Underwood.
Morton.
Newton.
Pickworth.
Rippingale.
Semperingham.
Spanby.
Swaton.
Threckingham.
Walcot.

LINCOLN—KESTEVEN, PARTS OF—LOVEDEN WAPENTAKE.

Hoagham.

LINCOLN—KESTEVEN, PARTS OF—LINCOLN LIBERTY.

Bracebridge.
Branston.
Canwick.
*Lincoln City—
 St. Benedict.
 St. Botolph.
 St. Margaret's within the Close.
 St. Mark's.
 St. Martin.
 St. Mary Magdalen.

Lincoln City—*cont.*
 St. Mary Wigford.
 St. Michael on the Hill.
 St. Nicholas Newport.
 St. Paul's.
 St. Peter at the Arches.
 St. Peter in Eastgate.
 St. Peter in the Gowts.
 St. Peter in the Gowts.
 St. Swithin.
Waddington.

LINCOLN—LINDSEY, PARTS OF—LAWRESS WAPENTAKE.

Aistropp cum Thorpe [Aisthorpe].
Barlings.
Brattleby.
Broxholme.
Burton-next-Lincoln.
Carlton, North.
 —— South.
Cherry Willingham.
Dunholme juxta Welton.
Faldingworth.
Fiskerton.

Frysthorpe [Friesthorpe].
Gre[e]twell.
Netham [Nettleham].
Reepham [Repham].
Saxelby.
Scampton.
Scothern.
Snarford.
Sudbrook and Holme.
Torksey cum Hardwick.
Welton juxta Lincoln.

LINCOLN—ASLACOE WAPENTAKE.

Bishop's Norton.
Blyborough.
Cammeringham.
Cannbye [Caenby].
Coates.
Cold Hanworth.
Fillingham.
Glentham.
Glentworth.
Hackthorn.

Harpswell.
Hemswell.
Ingham.
Normanby.
Owmby.
Saxby.
Snitterby.
Spridlington.
Willoughton.

LINCOLN — LINDSEY, PARTS OF — BRADLEY HAVERSTOE WAPENTAKE.

Ashby juxta Fenby.
Aylesby.
Barnoldby le Beck.
Beesby.
Bradley.
Brigsley.
Cabourne.
Clee cum Thorpes.
Coates, Great.
 —— Little.
 —— North.
Cuxwold.
Fulstow Marsh.
Grainsby.
Hatcliffe.
Hawerby cum Beesby.

Healing.
Holton.
Humberston.
Ir[e]by.
Laceby.
Newton Wold.
Randall [Ravendale], East.
Rothwell.
Scartho.
Swallow.
Swinhope.
Tetney.
Thoresby, North.
Waith.
Waltham.

LINCOLN—LINDSEY, PARTS OF—LOUTH SESSIONS.

*Certificate of justices of peace.

LINCOLN—LINDSEY, PARTS OF—LOUTH ESKE HUNDRED.

Alvingham.
Anthorpe.
Burwell cum Walmsgate.
Calstropp [Calcethorpe].
Carlton, Great.
 —— Little.
Castle Carlton.

Cockerington, North, or St. Mary.
Conisholme.
Elkington, North.
 —— South.
Farforth cum Maidenwell.

Lincoln—Lindsey, parts of—Louth Esk Hundred—*cont.*

Garnthorpe [Grainthorp].
Gayton on the Wold.
Grimoldby.
Hallington.
Hangham.
Keddington.
Kelstern.
Louth.
Manby.
Muckton.
North Reston.
Raithby cum Maltby.

Ruckland.
Saltfleetby (All Saints).
 —— (St. Clement).
 —— (St. Peter).
Skidbrook.
Somercoates, North.
 —— South.
Stewton.
Tathwell.
Welton juxta Louth.
Withcall.
Yarborough.

LINCOLN—LINDSEY, PARTS OF—LUDBOROUGH WAPENTAKE.

Covenham, St. Bartholomew.
Covenham, St. Mary.
Fotherby.

Ludborough.
Ormsby, North.
Utterby.
Wyham cum Cadeby.

LINCOLN—LINDSEY, PARTS OF—CALCEWORTH HUNDRED.

Aby.
Alford.
Anderby.
Calceby.
Claxby.
Gayton in the Marsh.
Hogsthorpe.

Mablethorpe.
Maltby in the Marsh.
Mumby.
Strubby cum Woodthorpe.
Theddlethorpe St. Helen.
Trustropp [Trusthorpe].

LINCOLN—LINDSEY, PARTS OF—HILL HUNDRED.

Ashby Puerorum.
Aswardby.
Bag Enderby.
Brinkhill.
Claxby Pluckacre.
Fulletby.
Greetham.
Hagworthingham.
Hameringham.
Harrington.

Langton.
Ormsby, South, cum Ketsby.
Oxcombe.
Salmonby.
Sausthorpe.
Scrafield.
Somersby.
Tetford.
Winceby.

LINCOLN—LINDSEY, PARTS OF—MANLEY WAPENTAKE.

*Certificate of the justices of the peace.

Althorpe.
Appleby.
Auckborrow [Auckborough] cum Walcot.
Belton.
Bottesford and hamlets.
Broughton.
Burton super Stather.
Butterwick, West.
Crowle and hamlets.
Epworth.
Flixborough.
Frodingham, including Bromley and Crosby.
Halton, West.
Haxey, including Eastlound, Craizelound, Westwoodside and Burnham.

Hibaldstow.
Luddington cum Garthorpe.
Manton.
Messingham.
Owston.
Redb[o]urne.
Risby.
Roxby.
Scawby cum Sturton.
Waddingham, St. Mary.
 —— St. Peter.
Whitton.
Wint[e]ringham.
Winterton.
Wroot.

LINCOLN—LINDSEY, PARTS OF—CORRINGHAM WAPENTAKE.

*Certificate of justices of peace.

Blyton.
Corringham (par.).
Gainsborough.
Gra[y]ingham.
Heapham.
Kirton.
Laughton.

Lea.
Northrope [Northorpe].
Pilham and Gylbie.
Scotter.
Scotton cum Ferry.
Springthorpe with Sturgate.

LINCOLN—LINDSEY, PARTS OF—WALSHCROFT WAPENTAKE.

Binbrook, St. Gabriel.
 —— St. Mary.
Claxby.
Croxby.
Kelsey, South, St. Mary.
 —— St. Nicholas.
Kingerby.
Kirkby cum Osgodby.
Linwood.
Newton juxta Toft.
Normanby on the Hill.

Rasen, East.
 —— Middle.
 —— West.
Stainton le Hole [le Vale].
Tevelby [Tealby].
Thoresway.
Thorganby.
Thornton-le-Moor.
Toft.
Usselby.
Walesby.
Willingham, North.

HOUSE OF LORDS.

Protestations.

LINCOLN—LINDSEY, PARTS OF—WELL WAPENTAKE.

*Certificate of the justices of peace.

Brampton.	Marton.
Gate Burton.	Newton next Trent.
Kettlethorpe with Laugh-terton and Fenton.	Stow, St. Mary's.
	Willingham juxta Stow.
Kna[i]th.	

LINCOLN—LINDSEY, PARTS OF—YARBOROUGH WAPENTAKE.

Barnetby [le Wold].	Horkstow.
Barrow [on Humber].	Immingham.
Barton on Humber, St. Mary.	Keelby.
	Killingholme.
Barton on Humber, St. Peter.	Kirmington.
	Limber Magna.
Bigby and members.	Melton Ross.
Bonby.	Nettleton.
Brocklesby.	North Kelsey.
Cadney cum Housham.	Riby.
Caistor.	Saxby.
Clixby.	Se[a]rby cum Owmby.
Croxton.	Somerby juxta Bigby.
East Halton.	Stallingborough.
Elsham.	Thornton Curtis.
Ferriby, South.	Ulceby.
Goxhill.	Wootton.
Gresby [Grasby].	Worletby [Worlaby].
Haborough.	Wrawby.
Holton le Moor.	[Place unnamed.]

MIDDLESEX—EDMONTON HUNDRED.

Edmonton.	South Mimms.
Enfield.	Tottenham.
Hadley.	

MIDDLESEX—ELTHORNE HUNDRED.

*Certificate of the justices of peace.

Brentford.	Harmondsworth.
Cowley.	Heese alias Hayes.
Cranford.	Hillingdon.
Drayton, West.	Iokenham.
Greenford Magna.	Northall [Northolt].
——— Parva.	Norwood.
Hanwell.	Ruislip.
Har[e]field.	Woxbridge [Uxbridge].
Harlington.	

MIDDLESEX—GORE AND PART OF OSSULSTON HUNDRED.

*Certificate of the justices of peace.

MIDDLESEX—GORE HUNDRED.

Edgware.	Pinner.
Harrow.	Stanmore Magna.
Hendon.	Whitchurch alias Stan-more Parva.
Kingsbury.	

MIDDLESEX—ISLEWORTH HUNDRED.

Heston.	Isleworth.
Hounslow.	Twickenham.

MIDDLESEX—OSSULSTON DIVISION.

Finchley.	St. Giles, Cripplegate.
Fryern Barnet.	St. Leonard's, Shoreditch.
Hampstead.	St. James, Clerkenwell.
Hornsey and Highgate.	St. Sepulchre.
Islington and Stoke New-ington.	Willesden.

*Certificate of justices of peace of the Tower Division of Ossulston Hundred.

Bromley, St. Leonard's.	Stepney and Hamlets.
Limehouse.	Stratford-le-Bow.

MIDDLESEX—SPELTHORNE HUNDRED.

Ashford.	Littleton.
Bedfont.	Shepperton.
Feltham.	Staines.
Hampton on Thames.	Stanwell.
Hanworth.	Sunbury.
Laleham.	Teddington.

NORTHUMBERLAND—MORPETH WARD.

Berwick-upon-Tweed.   Morpeth.

NOTTINGHAM—BASSETLAW WAPENTAKE.

*Certificate of justices of peace.

Applesthorp.	Blyth.
Askham.	Bolle [Bole].
Beckingham.	Boughton.
Bilsthorp.	Burton, West.

Nottingham—Bassetlaw Wapentake—cont.

Carlton in Lindrick.	Littleborough.
Clareborough.	Markham, East, cum West Drayton.
Cla[y]worth.	
Cuckney cum Membris.	Markham, West.
Drayton, East.	Mattersey.
Dunham and Darlton.	Misterton.
Eakring.	Mysson.
Eaton.	Ollerton.
Edwinston cum Membris.	Ordsall.
Egmanton.	Ragnall.
Elkesly.	Rampton.
Everton.	Retford, East.
Finningley cum Aukley.	Saundby.
Gamston.	Stokeham.
Grove.	Sturton cum Fenton.
Harworth.	Sutton super Lound.
Hayton [Haughton].	Treswell.
Headon cum Upton.	Tuxford.
Kirkton.	Walkeringham.
Laneham.	Warsop.
Laxton [Lexington] cum Moorhouse.	Welley [Wellow].
	Wheatley, North.
Leverton, North.	——— South.
——— South.	

NOTTINGHAM—BINGHAM WAPENTAKE.

Bingham.	Knolton.
Bridgford, East.	Langar, including Barn-ston.
Broughton [Sulney].	
Car Colston.	Orston.
Colston Basset.	Owthorp.
Cotgrave.	Radcliffe super Trent.
Cropwell Bishop.	Shelford cum Membris.
Elton.	Skerington [Scarrington].
Flintham.	Staunton.
Granby.	Thorroughton [Thoro-ton].
Hawkesworth.	
Hickling.	Tithby.
Holm Pierrepoint.	Tollerton.
Kneeton.	Whatton with Aslacton.

Letter from the high sheriff of the county to the knights of the shire respecting the taking of the Protestation and the payment of Poll Money.

NOTTINGHAM—BROXTOW HUNDRED.

*Certificate of the sheriff of the county.

Annexed :—

i. Certificate signed by the sheriff and thirteen justices of the peace, that they had again taken the protestation.

Adenborough [Atten-borough], including Toton, Chilwell, and Bramcote.	Lenton.
	Linby.
	Mansfield.
	——— Woodhouse.
An[ne]sley.	Nottingham (town).
Arnold.	Papplewick.
Basford.	Radford.
Beeston.	Selston.
Bulwell.	Skegby.
Cossal.	Stapleford.
Eastwood.	Sutton in Ashfield.
Greaslie.	Teversall.
Hucknall Torkard.	Trowell.
Kirkby in Ashfield.	Wollaton and Bilborough.

NOTTINGHAM—NEWARK HUNDRED.

*Certificate of justices of peace.

Balderton.	Kilvington.
Barnby.	Langford.
Clifton, North and South, including Harby and Spandford [Spalford].	Shelton.
	Sibthorp.
Collingham, North.	Staunton and Flaw-borough.
——— South.	Syerston.
Elston.	Thorney, with Bro[a]d-holme and Wig[ge]s-ley.
Farndon.	
Girton, Besthorpe, and South Scarle.	Thorp in the Clotts.
	Winthorp.
Hawton juxta Newark.	

Letter from two of the justices to the knights of the shire, enclosing the certificates of the taking of the Protestation, and a certificate respecting the collection of the Poll Money.

---

*Clergy, churchwardens, overseers, and constables of the several parishes.

5.

*Clergy, churchwardens, overseers, and constables of the several parishes.

R

NOTTINGHAM—RUSHCLIFFE HUNDRED.

* Certificate of the justices of the peace.

Barton.	Normanton upon Soar.
Bonny [Bunney] cum Bradmore.	Plumtree cum Normanton.
Bridgford, West, and hamlets.	Radcliffe upon Soar.
	Kempstone.
Clifton cum Glapton.	Ruddington.
Cortlingstock alias Costock.	Stanford [upon Soar].
	Stanton-on-the-Wolds.
Edwalton.	Sutton Bonnington.
Gotham.	Thrumpton.
Keyworth.	Widmerpool.
Kingston upon Soar.	Wilford.
Leake, East.	Willoughby.
—— West.	Wysall.

NOTTINGHAM—THURGARTON HUNDRED.

* Certificate of the justices of the peace.

Averham.	Kneesal.
Bleasby.	Lomly [Lambley].
Blidworth.	Lowdham.
Burton Joyce.	Marnham.
Calverton.	Morton.
Caunton.	Muskham, North, with Batley.
Colwick.	
Cromwell.	Muskham, South.
Edingley.	Normanton [upon Trent].
Ep[p]erston.	Norwell.
Farnesfield.	Oxton.
Fiskerton.	Rolleston.
Fledburgh.	Scrooby.
Gedling.	Snenton.
Gonal[d]ston.	Southwell.
Halam.	Stoke.
Halloughton.	Thurgarton.
Hockerton.	Upton.
Holme.	Weston.
Hoveringham.	Winkbourn.
Kelham.	Woodborough.
Kirtlington [Kirklington].	Place unnamed.

OXFORD—BAMPTON HUNDRED.

* Certificate of justices of peace.

Alvescot.	Cockthorpe [Cokethorpe], Hardwick, and Elford.
Asthall.	
Bampton and hamlets.	Ducklington.
Black Bo[u]rton.	Grafton and Rotcot [Radcutt].
Broadwell, with Filkins and Holwell.	
	Kelmascott.
Brize Norton, alias Norton Broyne.	Kencott.
	Stan[d]lake.
Broughton Poggs.	Westwell.
Burford and hamlets.	Witney and hamlets.
Clanfield.	

OXFORD—BANBURY HUNDRED.

Chorlebury [Charlbury], with Finstock and Fawler.	Shutford.
	Swalcliffe, Sibford, Gower, and Sibford [Ferris].
Cleydon.	Wardington, Williamscott, and Cotes [Coton].
Cropredy and Bourton.	
Mollington.	

OXFORD—BINFIELD HUNDRED.

Harpsden.	Rotherfield Peppard.
Henley [upon Thames].	Sonning.
Rotherfield Greys.	

OXFORD—BLOXHAM HUNDRED.

Alderbury [Adderbury], East.	Drayton.
	Hanwell.
Alderbury [Adderbury], West.	Horley.
	Hornton.
Alkerton.	Milcombe.
Bardford St. John.	Milton.
Bloxham.	Tadmarton.
Bodicott.	Wigginton.
Broughton and Newington.	[W]roxton and Balscot.

OXFORD—CHADLINGTON HUNDRED.

Ascot-under-Whichwood.	Chastleton and Brookend.
Bruern.	Chipping Norton.
Chadlington.	Churchill.

---

* Clergy, churchwardens, overseers, and constables of the several parishes.

Oxford—Chadlington Hundred—cont.

Cornwall.	Over Norton.
Enstone and hamlets.	Ramsden.
Fifield Merymouth.	Rollright Magna.
Fulbrook.	Salford.
Hook Norton.	Shipton [under Whichwood].
Kingham.	
Le[a]field.	Shorthampton, Chilson, and Pudlicott.
Lyncham.	
Milton.	Spelsbury.
Minster Lovell.	Swinbrook.
North Moor.	Tainton.

OXFORD—LANGTREE HUNDRED.

Goring.	Newnham Murren.
Ipsden.	North Stocke [Stoke].
Mongewell.	

OXFORD—WOOTTON HUNDRED.

Aston, North.	New[ing]ton, South.
Aston Steeple and Middle.	Rowsham.
	Sandford and Ledwell.
Barford, St. Michael.	Shipton-on-Charwell.
Barton Steeple alias Barton Magna.	Stansfield [Stonesfield].
	Stanton Harcourt, and Sutton.
Barton Westcott.	
Begbrook.	Tackley.
Cassington and Worton.	Tew Magna.
Coggs.	Woolvercott.
Deddington.	Wootton.
Duns Tew.	Worton, Nether.
Glimpton.	Worton, Over.
Heythrop.	Yarnton.
Kiddington.	List of persons in the county of Oxford who refused to take the protestation.
Kidlington.	
Leigh, North.	
Leigh, South.	
Long Combe.	

OXFORD.—OXFORD UNIVERSITY HUNDRED.

The first page of this return is as follows:—

The Protestation by the House of Comons commended to the Vniu'sitie of Oxford was vpon ye 18ᵗʰ Februarie 1641, taken with such Marginall Notes and Interp'tations as are vnderwritten by the Heads of Houses or their Deputies whose names are subscribed.

I, A. B., doe in the presence of Almightie God promise, vow, and protest ᴬ to maintaine and defend so farre as lawfulle I ᴮ may with my life, power, and estate, the true reformed Protestant Religion, exp'ssed in the Doctrine of the Church of England against all Poperie and Popish Innovations within this Realme contrarie to the same Doctrine and according to the dutie of my Allegiance his Maᵗⁱᵉˢ Royall person, hono', and estate, ᶜ as also the Power and Privileges of Parliament, The ᴰ lawfull ᴱ rights and Liberties of the subiect, ᶠ and every person that maketh this Protestation in whatsoever hee shall doe in the lawfull pursuance of ye same. And to my power and as farre as lawfullie I may, ᶠ I will oppose, and by all good waies and meanes indeavo' to bring to condigne punishment, all such as ᴳ shall, either by force, Practise, Counsells, Plotts, Conspiracies, or otherwise ˙do anie thing to the contrarie of anie thing in this p'sent Protestation contained. And further that I shall in all Just and hono'ble waies endeavo' to p'-

ᴬ So farre as warrantable I may, and with subordination to the Oaths of Supremacie and Allegiance.

ᴮ And shall bee called thervnto by lawfull Authoritie.

ᶜ Against whom I verilie believe no Subiect of this Kingdome may with safe conscience take vp Armes either offensive or defensive.

ᴰ And common.

ᴱ So farre as the said Privilegee, Rights, and Liberties shall bee made knowne and evidenced vnto Mee to bee such.

ᶠ And shall bee called thervnto by lawfull authority.

ᴳ His Maᵗⁱᵉˢ Subiects.

Oxford—Oxford University—*cont.*

serve y° Vnion and Peace betweene the three Kingdomes of
England, Scotland, and Ireland : And neither for hope,
feare, nor other respect, relinquish this Pmise, vow, and
Protestation.

D'. Tolson, Pro vice chancello' and Provost of
Oriell Col.
D'. Fell, Deane of Christ-Church.
D'. Pinke, Warden of New College.
D'. Mansell, Principall of Jesus College.
D'. Baily, P'sident of St. John's College.
D'. Sheldon, Warden of All Soule's College.
D'. Potter, Provost of Queene's College.
M'. Richardson, Vice-Principall of Brazen-
nose College.

The Protestation by the House of Cofftons commended
to the Vniv'sitie was vpon the same day taken according
to the printed Coppie without the above-mentioned notes
by such Heads of houses or their Deputies whose names
are vnderwritten, viz'. :

D'. Wilkinson, Principall of Magdalen hall.
D'. Hood, Rector of Lincolne College.
M'. Rogers, Principall of New Inne hall.
M'. Trimnell, Vicegerent of Bailioll College.
M'. Boles, Vicegerent of Pembrooke College.
M'. Corbett, Subwarden of Merton College.
M'. Chapman, Vice-Principall of Alban hall.
D'. Airey, Principall of Edmund hall.
M'. Proctor, Sub-Rector of Exeter College.

Jn prātiā mei Johis French Notarij pubci
et Registrarij vniversitatis Oxon.

Then follow lists of the members of the several colleges, distinguishing those who have taken the protestation, or who were absent or sick, viz. :—

Christ's Church College.   New Inn Hall.
Merton College.   St. John the Baptist's
Magdalen College.   College.
New College.   Exeter College.
Brazen-nose College.   Oriel College.
Queen's College.   All Souls' College.
University College,   Wadham College.
Corpus Christi College.   Jesus' College.
St. Edmund's Hall.   St. Mary's Hall.
Magdalen Hall.   Trinity College.
Pembroke College.   Lincoln College.
Gloucester Hall.   St. Alban's Hall.
Balliol College.   Hart Hall.

There are many special provisoes and reservations
attached to the return ; thus, under Magdalen College
Robert Barrell and Will. Hobbes take the protestation,
" so far forth as it is not contrary to the maintenance
" of the King's Royal Prerogative, the doctrine and
" discipline of the Church of England by law esta-
" blished since the Reformation, the present statutes of
" the University of Oxon, confirmed under the King's
" broad seal of England, to all which they have been
" formerly sworn."

Mr. Good, of New College, gives his own explanation
of the protestation, whilst the other members of the
college take it with the same reservations as their
warden, Dr. Pinke ; so the members of Queen's take it
with the same reservations as their provost, Dr. Potter.
Mr. Sharsell, of Gloucester Hall, gives a special interpretation, while Joseph Crowther, of St. John's, " being
" doubtful in some passages of proposing the protesta-
" tion, and not presuming to limit the sense of it, till he
" understands how the Honorable House will admit any
" to do so, doth humbly and thankfully accept the in-
" dulged license of deliberating." John, Bishop of
Worcester, Rector of Exeter and Vice-chancellor of the
University, takes the protestation without reserve. Dr.
Kettle takes the protestation with this addition :—" I,
" Ralph Kettell, President of Trinity College, Oxon,
" having been brought up about sixty and three years
" in this University, do protest sincerely this protesta-
" tion tendered unto us as consonant unto the oaths of
" Supremacy and allegiance which I have often taken,
" that subscription which I have often subscribed, and
" that dutiful prayer which this Parliament time is
" published for the holy safety of this Church & realm
" in England."

SALOP—STOTTESDEN HUNDRED.
Bridgnorth   [Eardington].

SALOP—WENLOCK LIBERTY.
* Certificate of the bailiffs.

Badger.   Eaton and hundreds.
Barrow.   Madeley.
Beckbury.   Monk Hopton.
Benthall.   Wenlock Magna.
Broseley.   ——— Little.
Ditton Priors.   Willey.

SOMERSET—ABDICK AND BULSTON HUNDREDS.

Ashill.   Drayton.
Beer Crocombe.   Fivehead.
Bicknell [Bickenhall].   Ilminster and tithings.
Broadway.   Isle Abbots.
Buckland St. Mary.   Isle Brewers.
Cricket Malherbe.   Puckington.
Curland.   Staple Fitzpaine.
Curry Malet.   Stokelinch Magdalen.
——— Rivel.   Swell.

SOMERSET—BEMSTONE HUNDRED.
Perry.

SOMERSET—CARHAMPTON HUNDRED.
* Certificate of the justices of peace.

Carhampton.   Oare.
Culbone or Kitnor.   Porlock.
Cutcombe.   Selworthy.
Dunster.   Stoke Pero.
Exford.   Timberscombe.
Luckham.   Treborough.
Luxborough.   Withicombe.
Minehead.   Wootton Courtenay.

SOMERSET—CREWKERNE HUNDRED.

Crewkerne.   Misterton.
Hinton St. George.   Seaborough.
Merriott.

SOMERSET—GLASTON TWELVE HIDES HUNDRED.

Baltonsborough.   Glastonbury (St. John'n).
Bradley, West.   Meare.
Glastonbury (St. Bene-   Pennard, West.
dict).

SOMERSET—KINGSBURY AND CREWKERNE HUNDRED.
* Certificate of justices of peace.

SOMERSET—KINGSBURY (EASTERN DIVISION) HUNDRED.
Combe St. Nicholas.   Kingsbury.
East Lambrook.   Winsham.
Huish.

SOMERSET—KINGSBURY (WESTERN DIVISION) HUNDRED.
* Certificate of the justices of peace.

Ash Priors.   Wellington.
Fitzhead.   West Buckland.
Ford.   Wiveliscombe.
Lydiard Episcopi and
tithings.

SOMERSET—MILVERTON HUNDRED.
* Certificate of the justices of peace.

Ashbrittle.   Rownington [Bunning-
Badealton [Bathealton].   ton].
Kittesford.   Sampford Arundel.
Langford Budville.   Stawley.
Milverton.   Thorn St. Margaret.

SOMERSET—NORTH CURRY HUNDRED.
* Certificate of justices of the peace.
North Curry.   Thorn Falcon.
Stoke St. Gregory, and   Thurlbear.
hamlets.   West Hatch.

SOMERSET—NORTH PETHERTON HUNDRED.
Bridgewater.

SOMERSET—SOUTH PETHERTON, ABDICK, AND BULSTON
HUNDREDS.
* Certificate of justices of peace.

SOMERSET—SOUTH PETHERTON HUNDRED.
Barrington.   Seavington Dinnington.
Chillington.   ——— Mary.
Cricket St. Thomas.   Shipton Beauchamp.
Cudworth.   South Petherton and
Dowlish Wake.   tithings.
Knowle [St. Giles].   Whit Staunton.
Lopen.

* Clergy, churchwardens, overseers, and constables of the several
parishes.

R 2

SOMERSET—TAUNTON DEAN HUNDRED.
* Certificate of justices of the peace.

Angersleigh.
Bagborough.
Bradford.
Cheddon [Fitzpaine].
Combe Florey.
Corfe.
Cothelstone.
Heathfield.
Hill Bishops or Bishops Hull.
Hillfarence.
Kingston juxta Taunton.
Lydiard St. Lawrence.
Ninehead.
Norton Fitzwarren.
Oake.
Orchard [Portman].
Otterford.
Pitmister [Pitminster].
Ryston [Ruishton].
Staplegrove.
Stoke St. Mary.
Taunton.
Trull.
Wilton.
With[i]ell [Florey].

SOMERSET—WELLS FORUM HUNDRED.

Binegar.
Dinder.
Evercreech.
Litton.
Priddy.
Wells, (St. Andrew, Cathedral).
Wells (St. Cuthbert).
Westbury.
Wookie [Wokey].
List of names.

SOMERSET—WHITSTONE HUNDRED.

Allhampton and Sutton.
Batcombe.
Crenmor [Cranmor's] West.
Croscombe.
Ditcheat.
Hornblotton.
Lamyatt.
Lottisham.
Pennard, East.
Pilton and tithings.
Pylle alias Pull.
Wootton.
Wraxhall.

SOMERSET—WILLITON FREEMANORS HUNDRED.
* Certificate of justices of peace.

Bicknoller.
Brompton Ralph.
——— Regis.
Brushford.
Chipstable.
Clatworthy.
Cro[w]combe.
Dodington.
Dulverton.
Elworthy.
Exton.
Halse.
Hawkridge.
Huish Champflower.
Kilton.
Kilve.
Lilstock.
Monksilver.
Nettlecombe.
Old Cleeve.
Quantoxhead, East.
——— West.
Raddington.
Sampford Brett.
Skilgate.
Stogumber.
Stowey Nether.
† ——— Over.
Upton.
[Watchet otherwise] St. Decumans.
Winsford.
Withypoole.
Woodverd [Woodford].

STAFFORD—OFFLOW (NORTH AND SOUTH DIVISIONS) HUNDRED.
* Certificate of justices of peace.

STAFFORD—OFFLOW (NORTH DIVISION) HUNDRED.

Alrewas, Fradley, Orgreave, and Edinghall.
Bart-under-Needwood.
Bromley Regis.
Burton-upon-Trent.
Clifton, Campvifle, Haunton, and Harleston.
Hamstall Ridware.
Hanbury, Woodend, Draycoat, Stubby Lane, Fauld, and Coton.
Lichfield (City).
——— St. Michael.
Maveeyn Ridware.
Newborough and Hoarcross.
Pipe Ridware.
Rolleston and Annesley.
Tatenhill, Callingwood, and Dunstall.
Thorpe [Constantine].
Tutbury.
Whittington.
Wichnor.
Yoxall.

STAFFORD—OFFLOW (SOUTH DIVISION) HUNDRED.

Aldridge.
Armitage and Handsacre.
Barr, Great.
Bromwich, West.
Darlaston.
Drayton Basset.
Elford.
Far[e]well.
Hannesworth [Handsworth].
Harborne.
Hints.
Longdon.
Norton [under Cannock] and [Little] Wyrley.
Pelsall.
Rushall.
Shenstone.
Tipton.
Wednesbury.
We[e]ford.
Wigginton.
Willenhall and Bentley.

* Clergy, churchwardens, overseers, and constables of the several parishes.
† In the hundred of Cannington, but this return appears to have been sent with papers of this hundred.

STAFFORD—PIREHILL (NORTH DIVISION) HUNDRED.
Newcastle-under-Lyne.

STAFFORD—PIREHILL (SOUTH DIVISION) HUNDRED.
Stow.

SURREY—REIGATE HUNDRED.

Betchworth.
Buckland.
Burstow.
Charlwood.
Chipstead.
Gatton.
Horley.
Leigh.
Merstham.
Nutfield.
Reigate.

SURREY—TANDRIDGE (FIRST DIVISION) HUNDRED.
* Certificate of justices of peace.

Bletchingley.
Crowhurst.
Horne.
Limpsfield.
Lingfield.
Oxted.
Tandridge.
Place unnamed.

SURREY—TANDRIDGE (SECOND DIVISION) HUNDRED.

[Caterham.]
Chelsham.
Farley.
Tatsfield.
Titsey.
Warlingham.
Woldingham.

SUSSEX—ARUNDEL RAPE.
Letter of the justices of peace to the knights and burgesses of the county, respecting their taking the protestation. 1641-2, Feb. 28.
Certificates of the justices of the taking of the protestation by Sir John Leedes.

SUSSEX—ARUNDEL RAPE—AVISFORD HUNDRED.

Barnham.
Binstead.
Climping.
Eastergate.
Felpham.
Forde.
Madehurst.
Middleton.
South Stoke.
Tortington.
Walberton.
Yapton.

SUSSEX—ARUNDEL RAPE—BURY HUNDRED.

Bignor cum Buddington.
Burton cum Coates.
Bury.
Coldwaltham.
Fittleworth.
Hardham.
Houghton.
Loxwood.
Wisborough Green.

SUSSEX—ARUNDEL RAPE—POLING HUNDRED.

Angmering.
Burgham alias Burpham.
Ferring and Kingston.
Goring.
Limister.
Little Hampton.
Poling.
Preston, East.
——— West.
Stoke, North.
Warning Camp.

SUSSEX—ARUNDEL RAPE—ROTHERBRIDGE HUNDRED.

Barlavington.
Downcton [Duncton].
Egdean.
Kirdford.
Lurgushall.
Chapel, North.
Petworth.
Stopham.
Sutton.
Tillington.
Woolavington.

SUSSEX—ARUNDEL RAPE—WEST EASWRITH HUNDRED.

Amberley.
Billinghurst.
Chiltington.
Parham.
Pulborough.
Rudgwick.
Slinfold.
Storrington.
Wiggenholt with Greatham.

SUSSEX—BRAMBER RAPE—BRIGHTFORD HUNDRED.

Broadwater.
Clapham.
Findon.
Launsing [Lancing].
Sompting.

SUSSEX—BRAMBER RAPE—BURBEACH HUNDRED.

Auburton [Edburton].
Ifield.
Seal.

SUSSEX—BRAMBER RAPE—EAST EASWRITH HUNDRED.

Horsham (borough).
——— (parish).
Hitchingfield [Itchingfield].
Bullington.
Thak[e]ham.
Warminghurst.

SUSSEX—BRAMBER RAPE—FISHERGATE HUNDRED.

Kinson Bonsye [Kingston by Sea?].
Shoreham, Old.
Southwick.

* Clergy, churchwardens, overseers, and constables of the several parishes.

SUSSEX—BRAMBER RAPE—GRINSTEAD, WEST, HUNDRED.
Ashington.   Grinstead, West.
Ashurst.   Shipley.

SUSSEX—BRAMBER RAPE—PATCHING HUNDRED.
Patching.

SUSSEX—BRAMBER RAPE—SINGLECROSS HUNDRED.
Nutburst.   Warnham.
Rusper.

SUSSEX—BRAMBER RAPE—STEYNING HUNDRED.
Buttolphs.   Washington.
Coomes [Coombs].   Wiston. .
Steyning.

SUSSEX—BRAMBER RAPE—TARRING HUNDRED.
Tarring.

SUSSEX—BRAMBER RAPE—TIPNOAK HUNDRED.
Albourn and Woodman-   Henfield.
cote.

SUSSEX—BRAMBER RAPE—WINDHAM AND EWHURST HUN-
DRED.
Cowfold.   Shermanbury.

SUSSEX—CHICHESTER RAPE.
*Certificate of justices of peace.

SUSSEX—CHICHESTER RAPE—ALDWICK HUNDRED.
Lavant, East.   Slindon.
Pagham.   Tangmere.

SUSSEX—CHICHESTER RAPE—BOSHAM HUNDRED.
Funtington.   Thorney, West.
Stoke, West.

SUSSEX—CHICHESTER RAPE—BOX AND STOCKBRIDGE HUN-
DRED.
Alinbourne   [Alding-   Chichester—cont.
bourne]..   St. Olave's.
Appledram.   St. Peter's the Great.
Boxgrove.   St. Peter's the Less.
Chichester—   Chichester, city.
  Cathedral Close.   Donnington.
  St. Bartholomew with-   Eartham.
    out the West Gate.   Fishbourne, New.
  St. Pancras without the Hunston.
    liberty of the City.   Merston.
  St. Pancras within the   Mundham, North.
    liberty of the City.   Oving.
  St. Andrew.   Rumbald's Wyke.
  All Saints within the   Upwaltham.
    city.   Westhampnett.
  St. Martin's.

SUSSEX—CHICHESTER RAPE—DUMPFORD HUNDRED.
Chithurst.   Trayford cum Didling.
Elstead.   Trotton.
Rogate.   Turwick.

SUSSEX—CHICHESTER RAPE—EASEBOURN HUNDRED.
Bepton.   Linchmere.
Cocking.   Lodsworth.
Eastbourn [Easebourn].   Midhurst.
Farnhurst.   Selham.
Graffham.   Stedham.
Heyshot.   Woolbeding.
Iping.   Place unnamed.

SUSSEX—CHICHESTER RAPE—MANHOOD HUNDRED.
Birdham.   Sidlesham.
Earnley.   Wittering, East.
Itchenor [West].   ———— West.
Selsey.

SUSSEX—CHICHESTER RAPE—WESTBOURN AND SINGLETON
HUNDREDS.
Binderton.   Mid Lavant.
Compton cum Upmarden,   Racton.
Dean, East.   Singleton.
—— West, Chilgrove,   Stoughton.
  and Stapleash.   Westbourn.
Marden, East.   Two returns of places not
—— North.   named.

WARWICK—COVENTRY CITY AND COUNTY.
Anstey.   Sowe. .
Coventry (City.)   Stivichall.
Exhall.   Stoke.
Foleshill.   Wyken.

WARWICK—KNIGHTLOW HUNDRED.
Arley.   Ryton super Dunsmore.
Harbury.   Stoneley.
Leamington, Hastings,   Wappenbury.
  and townships.   Weston under Weatherley.
Napton-on-the-Hill.   Wolfhamcote.
Offchurch.   Wolston.

WESTMORELAND—EAST WARD.
Appleby (St. Lawrence).   Marton [Long].
———— (St. Michael).   Milburn.
Asby. .   Musgrave.
Brough [Burgh] under   Newbiggin.
  Stainmore.   Ormeshead.
Crosby Garrett.   Orton.
Dufton.   Ravenstonedale.
Kirkby Stephen, and   Temple Sowerby.
  townships.   Warcop.
Kirkby Thore.

WESTMORELAND—WEST WARD.
Askham.   Lowther.
Bampton.   Martindale in Barton.
Barton.   Morland.
Bolton.   Patterdale.
Browham [Brougham].   Shap.
Cliburn.   Strickland, Little, and
Clifton.   Thrimby.
Crosby Ravensworth.

WILTS—SALISBURY DIVISION.
One certificate containing the returns of the undermentioned places :—

ALDERBURY HUNDRED.
Alderbury and Waddon.   Platford.
Dean, West, and Grin-   Porton and Gomelden.
  stead.   Winterbourne Dautsey.
Idmiston.   ———— Earls.
Laverstoke and Ford.   ———— Gunner
Pitton and Farley.   Winterslow.

AMESBURY HUNDRED.
Allington.   Figheldean.
Amesbury.   *Lurgeshall   [Ludgers-
Boscombe.   hall].
*Breymaston [Brigmers-   *Milston.
  ton].   Netten [Durnford].
Bulford.   New Town.
*Chouldrington [Cholder-   Newton Toney.
  ton].   Normington.
Durnford, Great.   Salterton.
———— Little.   Tidworth, North.
*Durrington.   *West Wallow.

WILTS—SALISBURY DIVISION—BRANCH AND DOLE HUNDRED.
Bemerton.   Rollestone.
Berwick St. James.   Sherrington.
Burthenstall   [Burden's South Newton and Wish-
  Ball].   ford Parva.
Chilhampton.   Shrewton.
Fisherton Anger.   Stapleford.
Foulstan [Fuggleston St.   Stowford [Stoford].
  Peter], and Quidhamp-   Tilshead.
  ton.   Ugford St. Giles.
Langford Parva.   Wilton.
———— Steeple.   Winterbourne Stoke.
Madington.   Wishford Magna.
Orcheston St. Mary.   Wyly.

CAWDEN AND CADWORTH HUNDRED.
Barford St. Martin.   Harnham, West.
Baverstock and Hurcott.   Homington.
Bramshaw.   Netherhampton.
Britford and East Harn-   Odstocke.
  ham.   Stratford St. Anthony.
Burcombe, South.   Sutton Mandefield.
Combe Bissett.   Whichbury.
Foffont [Fovant].

---

* Clergy, churchwardens, overseers, and constables of the several
parishes.

* Clergy, churchwardens, overseers, and constables only.

Wilts—Salisbury Division—*cont.*

CHALK HUNDRED.

Alvediston.
Berwick St. John.
Bower Chalk.
Broad Chalk.

Ebbesbourn.
Fifield [Bavant].
Semley.
Tollard Royal.

DOWNTON HUNDRED.

Bishopston.
Bodenham.
Downton.
Fallerston.

Flambston.
Nunton.
Standlinch.

ELSTUB AND EVERLEY HUNDREDS.

Collingbourn Ducis.
En[d]ford.
Everley.
Fittleton and Hackton [Hackleston].
Ham.

* Little Hinton.
Nether Avon.
Overton, East.
Patney.
* Stockton.

FRUSTFIELD HUNDRED.

.'* Langford.

* White (parish).

UNDERDITCH HUNDRED.

Heale.
Lake.
Milford.
Stratford Dean.

Stratford Coen.
Wilsford.
Woodford, Great and
Little.

WORCESTER—WORCESTER (CITY).

All Saints.
St. Alban.
St. Andrew.
St. Clement.
St. Helen.

St. Martin.
St. Nicholas.
St. Peter.
St. Swithin.

YORK—NORTH RIDING—ALLERTONSHIRE DIVISION.

† Certificate of justices of peace.
Certificate of same of persons who refuse to take the protestation.

Borkby.
Brompton, nigh North Allerton.
Hutton Bonville.
[Kirkby] Sigston.
Leake, Knayton, Landmoth, and Nether Silton.
North Allerton.

Osmotherley, West Harsley, Ellerbeck, and Thimbleby.
Otterington, North.
Sessy-cum-Heaton [Hutton].
Thornton-le-Street.
West Rouncton.

Names of those who refuse to take the protestation in the Division of North Allertonshire.

YORK—WEST RIDING—AGBRIGG WAPENTAKE.

† Certificate of justices of peace.
One return including the following places, viz. :—

Agkton [Ackton].
Almondbury.
Alstofts.
Alverthorpe.
Ardslaw [Ardsley], East.
Austonley.
Batley.
Bretton, West.
Carlton.
Cartworth.
Churwell.
Criggleston.

Crofton.
Crossland-cum-Netherton and Armitage.
Dewsbury.
Emley.
Farnley Tyas.
Flockton.
F[o]ulston.
Gildersome.
Golcar.
Hepworth.
Holme.

Honley.
Horbury.
Huddersfield.
Kirk Burton.
Kirk Heaton.
Lenthwaite.
Lepton.
Lindley.
Lofthouse.
Longwood.
Marsden.
Meltham - cum - Netherthong.
Methley.
Middleton.
Mirfield.
Normanton.
Ossett.
Oulton.
Overthwonge [Upper Thong].
Rothwell.
Rothwell Haigh.
Sandall.

Shelley.
Shepley.
Shitlington.
Skamanden [Scammonden].
Slaithwaite.
Snydall.
Soothill.
Stanley.
Thornes.
Thornhill.
Thorpe.
Thurstonland.
Wakefield.
Walton.
Warmfield.
Whitley-cum-Breistwell.
Whitwood.
'Woodall [Wooldale].
Woodchurch [Woodkirk].
alias Westardly [West Ardsley].
Wrigglesworth.

YORK—WEST RIDING—MORLEY AND PART OF AGBRIGG WAPENTAKE.

Return for the whole wapentake, in which the following places are named :—

Adwalton.
Allerton.
Barkisland.
Birkinshaw.
Birstall.
Boulling [Bowling].
Bradford.
Calverley.
Clayton.
[Cleck] Heaton.
Clifton.
Crosland.
Crostone [Cross Stone].
Drighlington.
Eccleshall.
Elland.
Erringden.
Gomersall, Little.
Gre[e]tland.
Halifax.
Haworth.
Heartshead.
Heaton.
Hecmondwike.
Heptonstall.
Horton.
Hunsworth.
Illin[g]worth.

Kemerseidge.
Kirklees.
Lightcliffe.
Liversedge, Little.
Luddenden.
Manningham.
Norland.
Oakenshaw.
Pudsey.
Quick-cum-Sudlaworth.
Rastrike - cum - Fekesby [Fixby].
Rishworth.
Scholes.
Shipley.
Sowerby.
Sowerby Brigg [Bridge].
Soyland.
Spen.
Stainland.
Stansfield.
Taley [?].
Thornton.
Wadsworth.
Warley.
Wibsey.
Wike.
Wilsden.

YORK—WEST RIDING—CLARO WAPENTAKE.

Summary of persons who have, and also of those who refuse to take the protestation throughout the wapentake.
*Kirkby Malzeard and Ripon.
Middlesmoor.

YORK—WEST RIDING—OSGOLDERCROSS WAPENTAKE.

East Hardwick.
Ferrybridge (part of).
Hardwick, Tanshelf (part of), Ferrybrigge (part of), and Carlton.
Monkhill.

Pontefract.
———— Micklegate.
———— North Gate.
Tanshall [Tanshelf] (part of).

---

* Clergy, churchwardens, overseers, and constables only.
† Clergy, churchwardens, overseers, and constables of the several parishes.

* Summary of persons taking and refusing to take the protestation.

MANUSCRIPTS OF HIS GRACE THE DUKE OF SUTHER-
LAND, AT TRENTHAM, CO. STAFFORD.

The manuscripts from which extracts are given below consist of ten volumes of original letters written in the 16th, 17th, and 18th centuries; and the Commission is much indebted to Lord Ronald Gower for drawing attention to them, and obtaining the Duke of Sutherland's ready and liberal consent to their being brought to London for examination.' They are full of interest; and it will be seen that I have drawn largely from them. A few repetitions of the same items of news will be found, although I have excluded many others. The letters of several persons writing at the same period of public transactions must necessarily have much in common.

The first volume contains some letters by Admiral Sir Richard Leveson. In 1599 and 1600 it seems that there was fear of a Spanish invasion. In 1601 he was before Kingsale in Ireland, and gives an account of the siege of the town, then garrisoned by Spaniards; and at the end of the year he tells of the defeat of Tyrone, although Kingsale was not yet taken. In 1605 he seems to have gone to Spain with the Embassy of the Earl of Nottingham. After these come Sir John Leveson's papers relating to Kent, for about 30 years: they deal chiefly with Subsidies and military matters. In 1589 Lord Cobham was ordered to raise 1,000 men in Kent to go into France to aid the French King: and Sir John Leveson tells how the men were aggrieved at the thought of a stranger being appointed to command them, and how "he himself felt the slight of not being made their officer. In 1590 there was an order to raise 200 more for foreign service: and in 1595 a report of an intended foreign descent on the coast brought down an order to raise 600 men to aid in repelling it.

Mr. Burn, in his *History of the Fleet Marriages*, says that there does not appear to have been any clandestine marriage at the Savoy Chapel until after the passing of the Marriage Act. But from two letters in 1596 it is clear that irregular marriages there were frequent in the reign of Elizabeth. Lord Cobham's grandson and ward was married to his cousin at the Savoy in apparently an irregular way, and the chaplain who celebrated the marriage was committed to the Gate House.

In 1600 the Queen seems to have found fault with the clothing for soldiers which the county had been accustomed to supply; so she appoints her own clothiers. In this year there were levies for Ireland, and in 1601 for the Low Countries; and in the latter year the ancient courts for some of the Cinque Ports were revived after long disuse, much to the discomfort of many poor persons who were summoned to attend and pay for petty bits of wreck which they had found. Sir Edmund Barrett (who was created Lord Newburgh by Charles I.) went into Spain with the Earl of Nottingham in 1605; a letter by him is curious as showing the then wealth of Spain and abundance of coin there.

In vol. 2, a letter of 1626 mentions the fees payable on creation of Knights of the Bath. The Civil War letters are interesting. Some discontent appears at the favours shown to the Scots. Members of Parliament took instructions from their constituents as to the course they were to take in the Parliament. A news letter from York in June 1642 tells all that was going on there. In the same month Sir Edward Littleton (a Parliamentarian) tells Sir R. Leveson of an order made by the House of Commons that all members are to attend by the 16th instant. Sir Richard neglected this intimation, and at the beginning of August he and three others were served with a peremptory order to attend. In September 1642 he and his fellow declined to raise troops in their county, as requested by the Commissioners of Array. In December of the same year is an account of the Earl of Stamford's retreat from Hereford, and of Hopton's failure to raise troops at Ledbury. The ineffectual attempts of Lord Strange (soon afterwards Earl of Derby) to take Manchester are well told in diary by some one in the town in the last week of September 1642. There is news of the King at Salop in the beginning of October; and on the 15th of that month the Earl of Essex wrote a letter of contrition to the King. In 1645 Sir Richard Leveson was a prisoner at Namptwich, and he was obliged to get license from Col. Croxton to go to Trentham and to get sureties for his return. In the following year he compounded with the Parliamentary Commissioners, and he seems to have paid largely. (There are many papers connected with this.) There are accounts of the battles of Edgehill and Hylton Heath. A letter of Sept. 16th 1658 is curious for its satirical remarks on the late Usurper, and his daughter, Lady Claypole. Copy of articles for the surrender of Chester dated

Feb. 1st 1645. A letter of 1649 gives a notice of and extracts from Grebner's Prophecies about England in MS., which he presented to Queen Elizabeth, and which Dr. Neville obtained from her and gave to the Library of Trinity College, Cambridge. There are a few letters during the Interregnum giving foreign news, and some filled with joy at the restoration of King Charles the Second.

Vol. 3. contains letters from Lord and Lady Newport and their sons Francis and Andrew. There is Court news during the Interregnum. A letter from Amiens shows how exiled Cavaliers quarrelled and fought among themselves; notices of the escape of General Lambert, and the landing, and reception in London of King Charles II., and Court news during his reign. The letters of Francis Newport during the civil war are full of news. It seems from a letter here that King Charles the 1st offered to go into Hull with only 30 attendants, whereas, from Rushworth's account, it would be inferred that he stood out for taking with him his whole troop of 300. The letters of Francis Newport in 1642, he being an M.P., are full of interest. His letters of 1660 give details of the King's restoration, the desires of the rebels to get safety, and speculations about the King's marriage, and Court and foreign news. The letters of Andrew Newport* are of the same character. In 1658 he gives an account of the trials of Dr. Hewett and Mr. Mordaunt; and at the beginning of 1660, of the behaviour of Monck and the proceedings in Parliament. The doings preceding, at, and following the Restoration are detailed: the punishment of regicides, behaviour of Col. Harrison at his trial and execution; a notice of the contest between the Marquis of Hertford and the Earl of Worcester for the title of Duke of Somerset; the conference between the Bishops and Presbyterian ministers concerning Church government; the Commons' vote that the bodies of Cromwell, Ireton, Bradshaw, and Pride should be taken to Tyburn, and that the hangman for the time being should bear Cromwell's arms; and the Duke of York's proving his marriage to have been in September 1660.

In the other volumes, the letters during the Civil War are of course noticeable. There is again mention of and extracts from Grebner's prophecies, certainly written in the 16th century, which were construed to predict the execution of Charles I., the succession of Cromwell, and the restoration of Charles II. The MS. is in Trinity College, Cambridge. Of Lord Marlborough's book of Dumb Prophecies, p. 182 of the Appendix, I have had no previous knowledge. In one of the volumes is a series of good letters by Sir William Dugdale. The Commonwealth letters tell much news during that period: the anxieties of Oliver; his interviews with sectaries when *thou'd* him; his ill-health; his frequent putting off giving a decided answer to those who asked him to be a King; at one time coming out *en déshabille* to reply to a Deputation (p. 163); the people's dissatisfaction at the increased taxation; his own restlessness about Monk's inclinations, and the attempt to assassinate his son Richard (p. 166) must doubtless have made him splenetic; but still he could drink plenteously at a feast (p. 166), and allow dancing at his daughter's wedding. The respect paid by sovereigns to Cromwell is notorious; but privateers are no respecters of persons, and we find here (p. 165) that they landed in Kent and carried off a knight, and kept him for ransom. There are again several rather full notices of the trials of Dr. Hewett, Mr. Mordaunt, and Sir Henry Slingsby. Soon after Oliver's death the officers of the army met to discuss their grievances. In April before the Restoration is a capital letter about an ineffectual attempt to surprise York; and one in January, of the defection of Lambert's army. For some months before the Restoration, and after that event, the letters are numerous. The writers expatiate on the universal joy of the King's return and the splendour of his reception, and the rather slow business of the Act of Indemnity. Then we get personal notices of the King, his planting trees in St. James's Park, his tennis playing, and his bathing at Battersea; how the game of *Hombre* came into fashion; and how Mrs. Cromwell (the Protector's widow) failed in her attempt to carry off large quantities of furniture. Hugh Peters is said to be the man who decapitated Charles I.; and the authorities found the man who fixed to the scaffold the staples intended to confine the King in case he resisted. We read of the favour which Charles II. was obliged to show to the Presbyterians, and his neglect of the Cavaliers;† the long doubts as to

---

* The *Memoirs of a Cavalier* by De Foe certainly do not chronicle the actions of this Andrew Newport.
† Mention is made of the witty proposal for an Act of Oblivion for the King's friends, and of indemnity for his enemies.

the marriage of Anne Hyde with the Duke of York. Prynne's self-assertion was shown even in church, where he refused to kneel when taking part in the communion service ; the parson with the bread passed on, and refused to give it ; but he with the wine, not noticing the refusal of his coadjutor, gave the wine. This would form a good case for a Casuist. Speaker Lenthal's son was said to have two wives, and also to have counterfeited the Great Seal ; and several letters speak of the dispute about the title of Duke of Somerset and Beaufort, claimed by the Marquis of Worcester under what seems to have been a forged patent.

Among the letters of the last century those of pp. 18 and 19 of vol. 7 doubtless refer to the meeting of Parliament on the 9th of October, and the plot in favour of the Pretender, which the King by the Chancellor communicated to the Commons. Those of Lord North show his view with regard to the (then) American colonies ; and the good sense of Lord Thurlow's remarks on education will be admitted ; and his two long undated letters (pp. 210 and 211) are valuable contributions.

The letters by Pitt and Lord Thanet are thus explained. Lord Thanet was in court at Maidstone when O'Connor, a member of the executive directory of United Irishmen, was tried for high treason ; after O'Connor was acquitted, a detainer was lodged against him, and Lord Thanet was accused of complicity in the attempt to facilitate his escape, and was committed to the Tower.

The spelling of words has been nearly always modernised.

Vol. I.

Letters to and from the Vice-Admiral Sir Richard Leveson, from 1598 to 1605.

1. 1598, April 24. At the Courte. Gilbert, Earl of Shrewsbury, to Sir Richard Luson (Leveson) Kt., Admiral of Her Majesty's ships in the Narrow Seas. He has received his (Leveson's) letter and answers it " in " as great haste as you wryte some tymes to my Lo. " Admyrall when the ankers are in weyinge." He says that for the matter mentioned by Leveson he will use the advice of his cousin, Mr. Vincent Corbet, and if necessary write again. (Seal, a Talbot passant surrounded with the motto of the Order of the Garter.)

2. n. d. Draft of a Petition to King James by W. Leveson, of London. In the time of the late sovereign deceased, certain parcels of cloves were delivered unto the petitioner by the Commissioners then appointed for the selling of the Carrack goods brought in by Sir Richard Leveson, which cloves were both unmerchantable in respect of their ill condition, and also over rated unto the petitioner in respect of their high and unreasonable prices. He prays that His Majesty will grant a Privy Seal for so much as appeareth by the report of the Commissioners to be unmerchantable, and he will make speedy payment of the residue. He also prays some allowance for the pains he took in the King's service at Plymouth and London, about the Carrack goods, whereby he saved the King 4,000l., and in that service spent 100l. of his own money.

20. n. d. Sir Richard Leveson to Lord Hume of Berwick, Chancellor of the Exchequer and Lord Treasurer of Berwick. (A corrected draft in Sir Richard's handwriting).—Recommending the bearer who was sent down to Sir Richard at Plymouth, and was employed in unloading and bestowing the goods of the Carrack from the 25th of June to the end of August, or thereabouts, during which time he continued upon his own charges. And after the bringing of the goods to Leadenhall in London his labour and diligence continued until the death of the Queen. He does not know that the bearer has received any recompense.

3. 1599, July 17. London.—Sir Richard Leveson to his cousin Sir John Leveson. " The report of some " suddayne allarum hasteth me down into Kent, but " my own particuler occasions command me to stay." —He will visit Sir John as he goes.

4. 1599, Aug. 2. The Downs—Sir Richard Leveson to his cousin Sir John Leveson at Hallin.—He has safely landed Sir John's brother Peter at Ostend. He daily receives letters with alarms of the Spaniards approach, but from the sea hears no such thing. His ship is so leaky that he spends 10 hours out of the 24 in pumping her. He is now plying to the westward as far as Dungeness. About Thursday next he means to return to the Downs to take his youths [his cousin Jack and his brother] aboard, whom he prays Sir John to send.

8. 1600, June 20. Plymouth.—The same to the same. —He says that it seems that Her Majesty's ships under his charge were hastily set forth ; he is full of wants, especially of men. How his victuals will hold out he

does not know, and can only inform himself by the report of a religious purser, to whose conscience he must commit himself and the fortunes of his journey. The year being half spent he is troubled and fears he shall come too late. His instructions shall be precisely followed to avoid exception . . . . . If the Lords purpose to enlarge his father, he wishes it to be deferred until his return, because the manner of his enlargement may much import him (Sir Richard) both in reputation and otherwise.

5. 1600, Jan. 12. Downs.—The same to the same.— He has received Sir Tho. Wal[singham's] letter, the contents whereof concerning Sir He[nry] P[almer] he will believe till he sees the contrary. . . . . . In expectation of the Spaniards he has kept the coast of France these ten days past, and has he thinks suffered more foul weather than any of the Queen's ships ever did in this place. Asks him to send the [letter] enclosed with speed to London.

6. 1600, Jan. 18, Downs.—Sir Richard Leveson to the Earl of Nottingham, Lord High Admiral. In his last letter he imparted to the Earl the state of the service. This letter is about his wife, a daughter of the Earl.

7. 1600, Jan. 30. Dover Road.—Sir Richard Leveson to Sir John Leveson.—Thanks him for a letter and allows well of his judgment in suppressing his (Sir Richard's) letter to the Lord Admiral.

9. 1601, Sept. 2, Downs.—The same to the same. Understands that Sir John is to encounter the French gallants at Canterbury, he sends enclosed the names of those that by men of the best quality. Confides as a secret that the King will not be drawn in open terms to break out with the King of Spain, but like a true Machiavel will awhile look on, expecting the event of both our ruins, and then like a greedy fox will take his prey. Only he is content to contribute in money for the relief of Ostend.

10. 1601, Oct. 29, Quinborow.—The same to the same. —He is yet unpaid by the Treasurer of the Navy for what is due to him for his service in the Narrow Seas, namely 20 shillings per diem from the 9th of December last, to the 25th or 26th of September ; only he acknowledges the receipt of 100l. from Mr. Cooke. He asks Sir John to apply for the balance.—He hopes Sir John will remember him to the lady, &c.—" You told me of " pearl, gold, stones, &c., I did then scarce believe it, " but now I am assured of it, namely 4 bags of pearl " whereof one is one hundredweight, 8 bags of pisto- " lettes, one box of diamonds, cum multis aliis."

11. 1601, Nov. 7, Downs.—The same to the same.— He says that his entertainment in the Narrow Seas must be continued from the 9th of December to the 25th of September. If his note be otherwise it is false, wherefore he prays Sir John to correct it.

12. 1601, Dec. 10, Kingsalle.—Sir Richard Leveson to his cousin Sir John Leveson.—As to the business by land ; the Lord Deputy is still before Kingsale, incamping upon the north side of the town. The Lord President's force stretching out to the north-west. The first approach was made upon the north side about 30 score from the town. The second about 14 score off, which within a few days made a breach assaultable 40 yards in breadth as I conjecture. The breach being made it was not thought fit by our Captain and Council of War to enter for divers reasons, whereof I am unable to judge, being out of my element. Now that design is altered, the cannon removed from that place to the north-west side ; a breach must be made and assaulted. In the interim I must tell you that when the first breach was made, the Spaniards sallied out in the night very proudly, being in number 800, gave upon our ordnance, and pusht for them in our trenches, but were beaten back, losing at least 200 of their best men. . . . . . The Lord Deputy is a gallant fellow, a man temperate in council and valiant in execution. But here is the truth of his case. Time hath been omitted, not through his default but by some other accident ; Tyron and O'Donell are come down, being 7,000 strong, and hourly expected to lodge upon the backs of our camps. Don John de Aquila is resolved, and although he want flesh to eat yet he wanteth no bread, nor any muniments of war ; if the Lord Deputy do give upon the town, he must subject himself to the danger of a strong and a powerful enemy behind him. This being so, each part must stand upon his guard expecting who shall famish first, and new supplies must be sent out of England. To conclude, unless the business be more royally undertaken, I am much afraid that here is a perpetual war grounded : sed hoc tibi ; yet I must needs say that the Queen is very royal, having on this day 18,000 men in pay upon her charge within this kingdom, besides her ships. Now, sir, to that which appertaineth to myself, you shall

understand that the second of December the Lord Deputy received knowledge that six Spanish ships with 2,000 soldiers were come in to Castle Haven, being distant from Kingsale 9 leagues or thereabouts, whereupon I addressed myself for that place, leaving Sir Amias Preston at Kingsale with the one half of my fleet: the 5th of December I set sail from Kingsale, for sooner the wind would not give me leave; the 6th of December I arrived at Castle Haven, where I was received with 8 pieces of great ordnance planted upon the shore and 500 small shot at the least, the place being very narrow. It was my purpose and direction to have boarded, to the end that every Spanish ship might serve as a bulwark for ours against the ordnance upon the shore, but the Spaniards having up their ships so near unto the shore as I could not come unto them did prevent me in that, so I came to an anchor with my ships; within four hours after my coming into the harbour I forced the Spaniards to quit all their ships and sunk one of them down directly. The Admiral with nine foot of water in hold cut his cable and drove upon the rocks, the Vice-Admiral with one other did likewise drive to the shore. The next day following I was constrained to ride there still, the wind being south-east, and to suffer the fury of their ordnance from the shore, which did much annoy me. The night following I caused all my ships to warp out before me, and so came off safely with all my fleet (I thank God for it). In this fight I lost but 13 men and had 30 men hurt or thereabouts, only three of my own servants hurt, all the rest well, &c.

14. 1601, Dec. 15, Kingsale Road. — The same to the same.—He sends inclosed a letter from Capt. Brett. The bearer will acquaint Sir John with all affairs there.

22. n.d.—George Brett to Sir R. Leveson.—As Sir Richard desires to know whether Sir John Leveson did at any time hasten the dispatch of the shipping at Rochester, He says that Sir John sent him (Brett) twice to Sir Henry Palmer to enquire their forwardness, whereof once he understood by Mr. Bucke that all the victuals were not yet shipped, nor could they be provided until Wednesday in the next week; the next he demanded the same of Sir Henry Palmer, &c., and received the same answer, that they were as desirous as Sir John to embark the soldiers, but because they were not yet fully victualled they thought it best to stop two or three days. This being on the Saturday when he (Brett) was there.

13. 1601, Dec. 27.—Sir Richard Leveson to Sir John Leveson.—These times are dangerous for men to write news, much more to write opinions . . . . It has pleased God to bless us at last with a very happy and most strange victory strange, I say, that, being encountered with a soldier and a great captain as all the world accounteth Tyrone to be, having in his troops 4,000 able fighting men, and the number of our soldiers not exceeding 800 foot and 400 horse, that the day was ours. In this defeat there were killed of the enemy 1,000 bodies, seven or eight ensigns (I mean colours) taken in the field, and at least 1,500 arms of the enemy brought home by our people. The truth of it is this, as I understand by relation from others: Tyrone lying within four or five miles of our camp, purposed in the morning, about an hour before daylight, to give upon the camp and to charge it in every quarter; but the night being more spent than he imagined, the day appeared before he approached, by means whereof our scouts discovered his army, and our troops drew out. The enemy marching away in three bodies, very soldierlike as the judicial beholders do report, our horse charged one of their squadrons in the vanguard; but the enemy's foot delivering a volley of shot, our horse made a wheel. In the interim our seconds of foot coming up, the enemy's foot made a halt, whereupon our horse, discovering some fear in the Irish, charged again, and immediately the enemy broke order, cast away their arms, betook themselves to their heels, and never struck one blow after. Thus much for the state of the present affairs. Now I will be bold to deliver my opinion. Though it has pleased God to bless us with extraordinary success, yet I do not think that the town of Kingsale will be easily taken. That Don John will be drawn to composition, I cannot imagine; first because he is reputed to be a great captain and a gallant fellow; secondly, the colour of their pretence is masked under the cloak of religion, and all men's eyes of Christendom are now bent upon this business; thirdly, the cause being undertaken by the King of Spain and his first action of moment, and being seconded by the Pope, cannot be left off but with much dishonour. If then the town be not taken in by composition of necessity, it must be gained by force. And to withstand our force, I dare assure you there are yet 1,500 Spaniards in the town able to fight, the walls are indifferent defen-

5.

sible, and within the walls there are many castles which will require a time of gaining. Having now made the case as strong against us as I can, I make no doubt, notwithstanding, but the town of Kingsale will be ours: but when the town shall be taken, I cannot think that the war is at an end; for you shall understand that the Spaniard hath fortified divers other places upon this coast, as Castle Haven, Baltimore, and Beer Haven, all which are now possessed and kept by the Spaniard, and therefore will require a second work; moreover here is a general received opinion amongst us, and the intelligence is no less, that the King of Spain is now preparing a great army to be sent for these parts.

15. 1602, July 18, Plymouth.—The same to the same.—He regrets that he has been deceived by some person whom he had trusted. But he loves him still, and will think that his error proceeded rather out of weakness than out of baseness . . . . Asks Sir John to lay espial about all places, at Court especially, about the great Councillor, and ascertain two things, namely his love to Sir Richard's person and his opinion of Sir Richard's wealth. Asks him to be polite to F. C., and sound him as to his knowledge of Sir Richard's wealth; cannot understand how he has got any information . . . . Out of his poverty he will find something for that honourable lady to whom Sir John and he are so much bound.—He desires to be commended to Sir Thomas Walsingham.

16. 1603, May 17. The same to the same.—The general report is that the King goeth shortly to Chatham; but Sir Richard doubts it, because the Lord Admiral says he knoweth no such thing.

18. 1605, April 24, Corunna.—The same to the same. —Sir John's son John* has passed the seas in good health, and so continues. Since their arrival at Corunna on the 15th instant, my Lord has stayed for horse and carriage for his train, which being great in number cannot be provided without much pain to this poor country. Our entertainment at Court is prepared, as I hear, with much state and ceremony, which maketh me suspect that our journey will be long and tedious.—He sends remembrances to Sir Thomas Walsingham and Wymarke. He has written to Sir Henry Palmer about finishing his lodging at Chatham.

19. [1605.] The last of April, from the Heyght of 43. —The same to the same.—He refers Sir John (for news) to Capt. King, who will wait upon him.—Mentions his camerado, Frank Coppinger.

17. 1605, July 22. The same to the same.—Besides the anguish of his leg, he has laid 24 hours in fear of an ague.

21. n. y., 14 March, afternoon.—The same to the same.—He is glad he has not writ to my Lord, and hopes the answer to his last letter may succeed to Sir John's content.—Since Sir John's boy departed he has written to Jackson that, if he were an agent to Sir Amias, he (Sir Richard) wished him to prosecute the matter. He will suppress the letter to Jackson if Sir John wishes it.

Letters and Papers of Sir John Leveson relating to the County of Kent: 1582—1614.

23. 1581, Dec. 15, Rushbroke.—Robert Jermyn to Lord Cobham. — He sends an acquittance for 15l. which Lord Cobham had told him to send for half yearly.—Gives a good account of the progress in learning and good nature of his cousin Lord Cobham's ward.

24. 1587, June 8, Greenwich.—Copy Council Letter (signed by the Lord Chancellor Hatton, Lord Burghley, C. Howard, Francis Knollys, James Croft, Francis Walsingham, and J. Wolley) to [the Lord Lieutenant of the County of Kent], regarding a levy of men for the service and defence of the United Provinces of the Low Countries under the charge of the Earl of Leicester, the Queen's Lieutenant-General in those parts. The counties are not at present to be charged further than with ten shillings for every soldier towards the provision of a sword and dagger and for conduct-money, being careful at present to case them of all such other charges (as armour and coat money) as has been heretofore accustomed. None of those which were heretofore trained are to be employed in this service. When the deputy-lieutenants have made choice of the number appointed, Lord . . . . or his deputies are to have a view made of them before such captains as the Earl shall send down, so that he may have the liking or refusing of the persons: the men are then to be taken to the seaside, and be thence transported according to the directions

* He had on January 4, 1604, obtained a license to travel for four years. See Calendar of State Papers.

S

which the captain shall receive from the Earl. (From the indorsement it seems that 300 men were to be levied in Kent.)

26. 1588, June 18, Greenwich.—Copy of the Queen's letter to Lord Cobham, Lord Warden of the Cinque Ports, and Lieutenant of the County of Kent, or in his absence to the Deputy Lieutenants.—Thanks for obedience to her former orders to prepare resistance to foreign invasion.—Tells him (as the foreign army is already put to sea) to summon the best sort of gentry within his lieutenancy, and bid them have a larger proportion of furniture for horsemen and footmen, especially horsemen, and certify the result to the Privy Council.

25. 1588, Dec. 16, Warwick Lane.—Thomas Fanshawe to Lord Burghley, Lord High Treasurer.—Sends enclosed the names of those who were assessed at 6l. on land by the year, or at 8l. in goods, to the subsidy in the four hundreds in Kent, which Lord Cobham had written were omitted, namely, Maydeston and Eyborne, Sommerden and Goddesheathe. Lord Cobham had required to have the whole book of the last subsidy written out; but as he thinks his lordship cannot want all, he has only had his (Fanshawe's) own hundred copied.

27. 1588, Dec. 16. From the Court.—Lord Burghley to Lord Cobham.—He sends the book of the subsidy which Fanshawe had made out, and also Fanshawe's letter.

28. [1589], Sept. 22, Ospringe. — John Cobham to Lord Cobham.—Mr. Clifford, the young captain, says he will have the fear of the band, and not such as Sir Thomas Sondes and John Cobham shall appoint.—He assures Cobham that Clifford shall have none out of the hundred of Melton (?) and Tenham but such as have been trained in the band. Clifford has said that some of the better are ready to ride out of the country. As yet Clifford has shewn no commission, and (the writer is told) he will not. He desires Burghley's opinion.

30. 1589, Sept. 8, Westminster. — Council letter (signed by Burghley, C. Howard, and Francis Walsingham) to Lord Cobham.—Her Majesty being about to send forces into France to the aid of the French King, under the charge, it is hoped, of the Lord Admiral, to be landed at Dieppe, and the same to be of the chiefest of the trained bands of those counties nearest the sea coast, Kent is set down for 1,000 men armed and weaponed; and Lord Cobham is required to get them ready under the command of the chief gentlemen of the shire who for their own fitness for service and estimations and credit with the soldiers he shall think fit to be their captains and leaders.

29. 1589, Sept. 13. About mid-day, Shornhill.—(Sir) John Leveson to Lord Cobham.—He has received Lord Cobham's letter telling him Her Majesty's pleasure that the 1,000 trained to be levied in that shire should be led only by men of skill and experience in martial service. He is much grieved that he (not having been so exercised) is not to lead the soldiers, who are in a state of discontent at the thought of having a strange captain. He remonstrates, and says that Captain Raines has promised to accompany him, with whom he did not contract for the burdening of Her Majesty, but for his own instruction.—He tells how the men who have returned from the Low Countries and Portugal are loud in their complaints against their ill treatment by the captains, some having scarce clothes to cover them, others are half starved for want of meat, and all are penniless. His neighbours look for the like entertainment at the hands of like captains, and show bad feeling. If the order is to be carried out, he begs that he may not be made the hand to deliver over the men to any other captain, or be hereafter employed, as hitherto he hath been, for a sporting and unserviceable leader.

31. 1590, March 24, Greenwich.—Council letter (signed by Lord Chancellor Hatton, Burghley, C. Howard, Hunsdon, Buckehurst, T. Heneage, J. Wolley, and J. Fortescue) to Lord Cobham, Warden of the Cinque Ports and Lord Lieutenant of the County of Kent.—They refer to a former letter directing 200 men to be raised to serve the Queen beyond sea. They, with their officers and leaders, are to be forthwith assembled, fully furnished with armour and weapons, and apparelled with ordinary coats. Of these, 150 are to be at the Port of Sandwich on the 7th of April, and 50 at Gravesend at the same time, where there is shipping provided for them and other bands out of other counties; whence they shall be transported to Flushing in Zealand. The Queen allows four shillings for every coat; to every soldier a halfpenny per mile for conduct-money, or at Lord Cobham's option eightpence per day . . . . . He is to cause an indenture to be made between him and the captain, containing the furniture of the armour,

weapon, and apparelling of every soldier, and to send a copy to the Council; the cause being that the armour, &c. may be preserved, and on their return be restored to the country. " For such bands as are to be sent into " the Low Countries, besides their deduction of ten in " every hundred by the name of dead paies, you shall " also deduct out of the said number of every hundred " the officers, as the captain, lieutenant, ensign, ser- " jeant, chirurgeon, and dromme, because they are to " be accounted in the Low Countries as parcel of the " bands."

32. 1594, Oct. 22, St. Stephens.—Jo. Manwood to his brother [in-law] Sir John Leveson.—In answer to a letter he says, " Upon further consideration I thinke my " Lord of Dover or Mr. Archdeacon were fit to be on, " if any be elsewhere of that cauling, and for the " country Mr. Lieutenant and Mr. Edward Boys, which, " for their abiding in the country, experience and meet " places of dwelling, are fit."

34. 1595, July 31, The Court.—W. (Lord) Cobham to Sir John Leveson.—He sends a copy of Council letter, directing the forces of the shire to be put in readiness against any attempt by the enemy along the sea-coast, so that he may impart it to such as he shall think fit for the execution thereof.

41. 1595, Aug. 25, London.—W. (Lord) Cobham to Sir John Leveson, his deputy lieutenant. He received that morning the Queen's letter of mandate to cause 600 able and trained men within the county of Kent to be put in readiness and furnished with such armour and weapons as that the fourth part of them may be musketeers.—He encloses a copy, and prays Sir John to put it in execution.

37. 1596, May 29, Holywell. [Dr.] W. Lewyn to Lord Cobham. Expresses his grief at the disordered and inconsiderate marriage of his Lordship's grandchild and ward. Says that by the Canon law the children of brother and sister cannot marry; but by the Statute law of this realm all marriages made in the face of the Church are made good and lawful which are not contrary and repugnant to the law of God, as being not within the Levitical degrees, or otherwise forbidden by God's word. So that he takes this marriage indissoluble in regard of the Statute, in case the manner of solemnization were not contrary to the Statute; but the parties married, and the minister that married them in the night, and without consent of his Lordship, who was governor of one of them, and the persons that were present at the marriage, were all punishable by law, and that in very severe manner. He advises Lord Cobham, having possession of his ward, to examine him closely as to the circumstances of making and solemnizing the marriage, to see what strength the form of such marriage has, and how it may either be lawfully undone or necessarily stand and continue. " The Earl of Bath, " that now is, made an untimely marriage by night " with the daughter of Sir Thomas Cornwallys, which " was undone, and the Earl since married to another, to " the daughter (as I think) of the late Earl of Bedford." Says he will look at the Statute and deliver his opinion further. (See 33 post.)

39. 1596, June 7, Sheppie.—John Ayscough to Sir John Leveson.—Says that his neighbour Robert Allen has requested him to certify Sir John what arms and furniture he finds for the defence of that island, which is one corslet and two muskets furnished with able men to use the same, as appears by the muster roll made at the last musters taken by Mr. Thomas Gay . . . . . . He (Allen) is charged, the writer is informed, with two light horse, and so likewise is the writer's neighbour, William Haward, of Harty. He thinks those two horses should be converted into other furniture for foot to be employed in that island for the defence thereof against Her Majesty's enemies . . . . Mr. Lindsey, a gentleman of great ability and occupying in that country, findeth neither armour nor weapon, one bad caliver badly furnished excepted ; and the neighbours murmur that they shall be deeply charged, and he go so free; he suggests that Lord Cobham should summon him to shew cause why he should not more plentifully furnish this country with men and armour.

35. 1596, June 13, Tunstall. William Crowmer to Sir John Leveson.—He had hoped to have heard that Mr. Collier had accounted before Sir John or some other, so that it might appear what arms were taken for the last voyage toward Callis (Cadiz), and what had been restored again . . . ., and what money Mr. Michael Sondes had for that purpose received of Sir Thomas Clifford or Sir John Leveson, and what had been paid out of that to any of the soldiers, and what Mr. Collier had disbursed of the 7l. 10s. which he

received of Crowmer. Tells what he hears has been done to those who restored arms and to soldiers. Says he himself wants 41l. 19s. 6d., which he hopes may be soon restored to him; and asks Sir John to say what he thinks fit to be done for the renewing of the band of light-horsemen in those parts again.

33. 1596, June 14, The Savoy.—W. Moune (Master of the Savoy) to Lord Cobham (at Court).—He says he has been to the Archbishop of Canterbury and conferred with him concerning Mr. Bigge, the chaplain of the Savoy, who had given offence to Lord Cobham. On Friday last, after dinner, Mr. Bigge was called before his Grace, in the presence of Dr. Cosin, Dr. Lewin, Dr. Bancroft, and the writer, at Lambeth, and confessed his abuse. He said he thought he might well do it, as his fellow chaplains, Mr. Horwode and Mr. Lyllye, had married without licence as many or more than he had. The Archbishop committed Bigge to the Gatehouse in part punishment until Lord Cobham'n pleasure was known; meaning, it is supposed, at his next appearance by deprivation to displace him . . . . The writer says that he has examined John Field, a carpenter, who has been a special compounder of his mischief; he affirms that one Powell, servant to Mr. Ambrose Coppinger, and Dugdale his fellow servant, are sufficient (being well examined) to clear the substance and most of the circumstances of this unhappy marriage . . . The Archbishop has taken good order by commission that no such disorderly marriages shall be offensively in the Savoy performed.

36. 1596, June 21, Wrotham.—John Rychers to Sir John Leveson.—(After business matters) He encloses a list of those who refuse to pay the money assessed for the repair of arms within the hundred of Wrotham (16d. in the pound for land and 12d. for goods).—He recommends three persons for sharp example, and gives particulars of them.—(The list enclosed is of seven persons; one William Webb is said to be " a paritor " (apparitor), and lives by the sins of the people.")

40. 1596, Sept. 24, Wrotham. — Geo. Byng to Sir John Leveson.—Asking a fortnight's respite to accompt for some " common money" for which he had been made liable by another person.

38. 1596, Nov. 7, The Court at Richmond.—W. (Lord Cobham to Sir Thomas Wilforde and Sir John Levison, Knights, Thomas Fane and Thomas Walsingham, Esquires, his deputy lieutenants.—Alludes to his having not many days since sent to them a copy of a Council letter of the 31st of October last. about what was to be done in the county to withstand any attempt of the enemy; and alludes to his deputies' reply that they had given orders for the speedy performance of the contents of that Council letter. He incloses a copy of Council letter of the 6th November instant, directing further proceedings in the county, and directs them to take order for the performance of the contents thereof.

42. 1600, June 26, Greenwich. Council letter (signed by Tho. Egerton, C.S., T. Buckhurst, Notingham, G. Hunsdon, Ro. North, W. Knollys, Ro. Cecyll, and J. Fortescu), to Lord Cobham, Lieutenant of the County of Kent.—They refer to the Queen's letter of the 25th instant, stating her reasons for asking a levy in Kent of 50 foot for service in Ireland. Reprobate the choice of lewd and dissolute persons who run away before they embark or after they get to Ireland, and direct him to choose carefully, and to see that the arms be good and serviceable, and that in the said number of 50 there be 12 pikes armed with corselets, pauldrons. and good murryons ; 6 bills with long stems armed as the pikes, 6 muskets with good murryons and rests, 6 bastard muskets with good murryons, and 20 calyvers likewise with good murryons; and that care be had to furnish them with good swords and daggers (the swords to be of turkie blades and close hilts), of which there hath been very ill choice made heretofore . . . . Hitherto the apparel had been provided by the county; but now (for reasons given) the Queen adds 8s. at least per man to the allowance of the county, and orders some chosen men to provide apparel for the whole levy ; and, for the apparelling, Lord Cobham is to send to the Mayor of Chester so much as may suffice for the 50 men, at the rate of 40s. per man. For conduct-money each man is to have 8d. and their conductor 4s. per diem, for so many days as may suffice for their conduct to the port of Chester, where there are to be by the 25th of July, &c., &c. (2 pp.)

43. 1600, Feb. 24, Court. Henry (Lord) Cobham to Sir John Leveson.—Asks that, after the men are brought to Deptford and Greenwich, Sir John will repair to the Court to receive further directions. Sir (Thomas) Walsingham must remain behind with the 400 men. Sir —— Sonds is presently to repair unto the ships, and

to bring on 200 men with them far their safeguard. Hopes early to-morrow to see them.

47. 1601, July 19, Court at Greenwich.—Council letter (signed by Tho. Egerton, C. S., T. Buckhurst, Notingham, E. Worcester, Ro. Cecyll, J. Fortescu, and another), to Lord Cobham.—For provision of shipping and victuals to be made at Sandwich for 300 men, to be levied in Kent and sent to the Low Countries ; and for victualling and lodging of them there if they shall stay any time for their embarking, at the rate of 8d. a man by the day. (The indorsement says that this force was for the relief of Ostend.)

44. 1601, Dec. 18, Canterbury. Richard Culmer to Sir Henry Brook, Lord Cobham, Lord Warden of the Cinque Ports, and K.G., at the Blackfriars, London.— Tells who has the records of the courts of the manor of St. Austin's and the manor of Minster in Thanet; and offers, as he knows the customs thereof, to hold the courts for Lord Cobham. Says that he encloses a copy of Sir Thomas Fane's letter to Sir Edward Wotton about the wreck on the Hoope. The letter itself remains with Thomas Paramor of Canterbury, Sir Edward Wotton's droytgatherer.

46. 1601, March 6, Blackfriars. Henry (Lord) Cobham to Dr. Newman, at Canterbury.—After mentioning that there had not been for many years any court holden for the Admiralty of the Cinque Ports two ancient towns and their members under his charge and government, he appoints Dr. Newman to hold such courts, and determine all causes belonging and incident to the office of Admiral of the said Cinque Ports two ancient towns, and their members.

45. 1601, March 9, Dover Castle. (Sir) Thomas Fane to Lord Cobham.—He has received by post Lord Cobham's letter of the 6th, concerning the keeping of his Admiralty courts by Dr. Newman. After search, he cannot find a precedent of any Admiralty court being kept by any other than the Lord Warden's lieutenant, nor yet of any Admiralty court kept in the late Lord Cobham's time, except one by Mr. Oripse, one by Mr. Barry, and one begun by him (Fane), but kept only at Hethe and Romney in respect of divers wrecks, at the complaint and petition of certain merchants. To remedy this state of things, he has prepared a form of commission (in Lord C's. name) for Dr. Newman, and one other mandamus directed to the mayor and bailiffs of the ports, who otherwise would hardly be aiding to Dr. Newman as is requisite. Both drafts he encloses for alteration and correction.

48. 1602, July 22, Dover Castle. Mark Packnam t Lord Cobham.—Tells how he went to Canterbury and conferred with Dr. Newman about appointing a time for the next Admiralty court, and for taking depositions of witnesses concerning the Hope, because it is fit they should be examined before the court is opened. The Dr. says he must keep court at Canterbury next week, but has appointed to be at Dover on Monday sennight, being the 2nd of August.

51. 1601, July 27, at the general meeting at Romney. The Mayors, Jurats, and Commons of the Cinque Ports two ancient towns of Rye and Winchelsey, to Lord Cobham.—According to the ancient use and yearly custom of the Cinque Ports and two ancient towns of Rye and Winchelsey, they assembled that day at Romney. They have paid Lord Cobham's servant, Thomas Nowell, 10l. in full discharge of his claims for service in a suit concerning the general incorporation. Mr. Verrall, of Sandwich (also recommended to their notice by Lord Cobham), claims 24l. or 25l. for services in a suit touching the Cinque Ports two ancient towns. They asked for a bill of items, which he seemed unwilling to give; therefore they postpone his claim to their general meeting next year. (Indorsed "The " Assembly at the Brotherhood to my Lord.")

50. 1602, July 31, Dover Castle. Mark Packnam to Lord Cobham.—Acknowledges Lord C's. letter of the 24th. Has kept a copy of the book (sent to Lord C.) of the repairs done in Dover Castle in 1589. Dr. Newman had appointed to be here on Tuesday next to receive depositions concerning the Hope. John Bussher, of Margate, one of the principal witnesses, cannot be there on Tuesday, because he must be at Feversham fair to pay and receive money, but he will attend on Wednesday. Divers poor men are summoned to the Admiralty court on the 17th of August to pay small sums with which they are charged for goods which they have taken up and found;—they desire that they may pay the amounts to Lord Cobham's droytgatherer, instead of attending the court and paying there. The fishermen of Rye and Hastings have appointed to be at the Admiralty court for the controversies between them. (Enclosed is a slip of paper sent by Packnam, containing an extract

from the customs relating to the fine for taking flotsam, jetsam, or lagan, without satisfying the Lord Warden and Admiral his moiety. The penalty was that the finder should lose his own part, and to make fine to the value of all the goods, at the discretion of the Admiral.)

49. 1602, Aug. 13, Dover Castle. The same to the same.—On Tuesday last Dr. Newman was there, and took depositions of John Busaher and others, concerning wreck happening on the Hope and other places in Thanet. For other places in Thanet where other men claim wreck, they could not depose. Sends enclosed copies of the depositions. They privately examined John Underdowne, of Byrchington, who, they were informed, could depose well for Lord Cobham, and found that he answered wholly on Mr. Wotton's part, therefore they would not swear him and take his deposition.

52. 1603. A plott drawne by Tho. Dunn, the carpenter for Dover harbour, for certen works now in hand. —(A plan about 14 inches square.)

53. 1603, July 7. Dover Castle.—(Sir) Tho. Fane to Lord Cobham.—The works of Dover Haven are in good forwardness ; but if the harbour moneys promised by the Lord Treasurer out of the Exchequer this term be not paid unto Sir Thomas Fludd, treasurer for the harbour, the moneys already bestowed will prove to very little purpose. He says that the works are much admired.

54. 1605, May 24, Valladolid. (Sir) E. Barrett * to Sir John Leveson.—Since his coming into Spain (whereof he has intelligence in many letters to Sir John) he received at Seville 1,000 ducats (every ducat being 5s. 6d. there in value), for the repayment whereof he sent bills into Italy to Mr. Young, from thence to be sent to Mr. Slaneye ; those 1,000 ducats being spent, with accommodating of himself with clothes at Seville, he was forced to take order with Mr. Nevinson for some more money, because the residue of his thousand ducats was only sufficient to discharge him between Seville and Valladolid, where the last penny of it left him at his arrival . . . . . The exchange of money between Seville and London was 8 in 100. "This countrie is so " full of money that they esteem less of 5s. than we do " in England of 6d. ; and after this rate all things are " valued here ; . . . . my lodging here will cost " me 23 ducats a month, and I have only 3 chambers " for my money. I hear by some gentlemen that are " already arrived that my brother cometh along with " Sir Richard . . . . ., and next winter, if it be your " will, I shall be ready to carry him into Italy . . . . " My lord Admiral is expected here within these two " days, and I am to go and meet him ; there was never " Prince nor Embassador entertained with half the " respect nor magnificence as this shall be."

55. 1609, Dec. 13, Halling.—Sir J. Leveson to Mr. Jervis Hall at Wolverhampton.—He has perused at Halling all his papers and old deeds, whereof he has an extraordinary great many, of lands that belonged to Lilshul Abbey, and other lands gone from the Levesons. (Land business.)

56. 1613, Dec. 4. Henry Hobart (Lord Chief Justice) to Sir John Leveson.

57. 1613, Dec. 5, Mereworth Castle. (Sir) Thomas Fane to Sir John Leveson at Blackfriars.

58. 1613, Dec. 10, Eyton. Fra. Newport to Sir John Levoson.

59. [1613]. Dec. 11, Wolverhampton. Walter Leveson to Sir John Leveson.

60. n. d., Dudley Diggs to Sir J. Levison. (These five letters are of condolence with Sir John on the loss of his son.)

61. 1614, Sept. 17, Whitehall. Copy Council letter (signed by G. Cant (Abbott, Archbishop of Canterbury), T. Ellesmere, C., T. Suffolk, R. Somerset, Pembroke, E. Worcester, Ralph Winwood, Jul. Cæsar, and Tho. Lake) to the Sheriff and Justices of the Peace in the County of Kent.—Refer to their late letter to them asking a contribution for the supply of Ireland, for the provision of the cautionary towns in Holland and Zealand, and for the furnishing of the navy. The importance of these things is improved by the troubles in neighbouring countries. The Marquis Spinola has collected a large army (which he sometimes pretends to have done under the charge of the Archduke, sometimes under the name of the King of Spain, sometimes under the command of the Emperor, whereby we may conclude they all three have combined together), and has carried all the towns in the countries of Juliers and Cleves, situate upon the tract of the Rhine, whereby the Elector of Brandenburgh is deprived of towns long by him peaceably en-

joyed, whose right his Majesty is bound to defend by virtue of treaties between him and the Princes of the Union in Germany, and the person and states of the Elector Palatine and his princess, the King's only daughter, are endangered.—To prevent the danger to this kingdom which these forces threaten, his Majesty commands a general muster throughout the realm, and that all recusants be disarmed . . . . The sheriffs, &c. are told to employ their best endeavours for the speedy return of the contribution.

62. 1614, Oct. 3. Walter Story to Sir John Leveson.

65. 1614, Nov. 20. Same to the same. (Business letters by a bailiff.)

63. 1614, Dec. 3, Lilleshull. Frances Cumberford and Richard Moulton to Sir John Leveson.

64. 1614, Nov. 20. The same to the same.

65. 1614, Nov. 20. Newport.—Walter Story to the same.—These three last are by servants or agents on business matters.)

66. n. y., Jan. 18, Lilleshull Lody.—Richard Moulton to Sir John Leveson.—Upon the 24th the joiner will come to the Lody to make a portal for the bed-chamber. Moulton asks if he shall finish that work in Sir Robert Harley's chamber with old wainscot before Sir John comes down or not. Has no money but what cometh by selling corn ; cannot sell the corn above 2s. 6d. or 2s. 8d. the measure.

67. A note of lands.

Vol. II.

Fol. 1-6. One letter from Frances Duddeley, and six letters by Katherine Duddeley to Sir Richard Leveson. (These ladies were daughters of Sir Robert Dudley, called Duke of Northumberland and Alice his wife, who was created Duchess Dudley by Charles the First.) The letters are not dated, but were written before the marriage of Katherine to Sir Richard Leveson).—In one of the letters by Katherine she says that she sent him a ring only to shew the bigness, for otherwise it is most unworthy his acceptance. It seems to have been written shortly before the marriage, in reply to some enquiries by Sir Richard ; for in a postscript she says, " I am very " ignorant what belongs to these ceremonies, but I " think men give no garters nor ribbons, but gloves " and points ; but I am not sure what the fashions " now are."

Fols. 7-10. Four letters by Katherine to her husband, Sir Richard Leveson, dated respectively 8 May 1658, May 4, April 21 (or 27), and May Day. The last three are without the year. The writer seems to have been in London attending to some law business. In the letter of the 4th of May she says, " Lady Dorset was " here on May Day, and most of her children, and would " have had me to Hide Park with them, but I could " not go."

Fols. 11 and 12. Two letters from Edward 4th Earl of Dorset to Sir Richard Leveson.

Fols. 13-17. Ten letters by Richard 5th Earl of Dorset to Sir Richard Leveson. The first is in 1651, while only Richard Buckhurst; the latest is dated in 1659. They are on private matters.

Fols. 18-22. Nine letters from Frances Countess of Dorset to Sir Richard Leveson. This lady was eldest daughter of Lionel Cranfield, Earl of Middlesex. The earliest is dated 1655, and the last in 1658. In 1656, she and her husband wrote to Sir Richard to ask him to be godfather to the child then expected, who was afterwards Charles 6th Earl of Dorset; but it seems that Sir Richard and his wife were not able to attend.

Fol. 23. 1623, March 29, Whitehall.—Charles Stanhope to the Mayors, Sheriffs, Bailiffs, &c.—Order for supply of six able horses and a guide for Richard Lucem (Leveson), Esquire, who was going to Shrewsbury, and thence to Holyhead and back, about His Majesty's special affairs.

Fol. 24. 1626, April 10, Whitehall. (The Earl of) Pembroke to Sir Richard Lewson, one of the Knights of the Bath made at His Majesty's coronation.—The King says that he intends not the bill of fees rated and signed by the Earl Marshall and Lord Pembroke should conclude any other of his servants that have patents for fees not mentioned in that schedule ; and that the gentlemen ushers of the King's Privy Chamber, his gentlemen ushers, daily waiters, and serjeants-at-arms having by their several patents, granted by his father (King James) and himself, 5l. to each company apportioned them upon all manner of Knighthood, Sir Richard is, in consideration of his late Knighthood of the Bath, to pay the said fees, amounting in all to 15l., for their use to the bearer Thomas Bartholomew, one of the grooms of His Majesty's chamber appointed for the purpose.

---

* A pencil note says that Sir E. Barrett was son of Dame Christian Leveson, daughter of Sir Walter Mildmay, married first to Sir —— Barrett. Sir E. Barrett was created Lord Newburgh by Charles I.

Fol. 25. 16 . ., June 15, Longford. (The Earl of) Shrewsbury to Sir Richard Lewson.—Thanks for past favours, and asks for further aid.

Fol. 26. 1631, Dec. 10, London. John Marsham to Sir Richard Leveson.—Asks for payment of some money. (Seal of arms.)

Fol. 27. 1633, Sept. 24, Forest Hill.—Jo. Normansell to Sir Richard Leveson.—Asks Sir Richard to be careful on whom he confers the parsonage of Kinnersley; Fouke Crompton having said that he had the next presentation, and would not dispose of it without Sir Richard's advice.—Asks Sir Richard and his lady to write to the Bishop of Lichfield, to induce him to give to Normansell a prebend there (then void) formerly possessed by N.'s uncle Baily.

Fol. 28. 1637, Feb. 19, Dutchie House.— Edward Viscount] Newburgh to the postmasters at the several towns upon the road from London to West Chester.—Order to provide Sir Richard Leveson with four posthorses and a guide from stage to stage to West Chester, for himself and his companions, paying the usual rate.

Fol. 29. 1639, Feb. 26. Dutchie House. E. Newburgh to His Majesty's steward of the manor of Newcastle, co. Stafford, or his under-steward or deputy there. —Order to take the true quantity and number of acres of two pieces of land called the Lymes within the manor of Newcastle-under-Lyne, for the better preserving the rights of His Majesty's fee farmer (Mr. Saml. Terrick).

Fol. 30. 1641, May 20, Newcastle. — Edward Mainwaringe to Sir Richard Leveson.—Acknowledges receipt of Sir R.'s two letters of the 10th and 11th, and the printed paper enclosed. Upon Tuesday following, being their court day at Newcastle, he caused an Assembly of the whole borough, and found all ready to make the Protestation. Whereupon the mayor, the minister, the aldermen, the schoolmaster, capital burgesses, and common burgesses, in all above 100, did publicly and solemnly pronounce it. He observed no want of sincerity.

Fol. 31. 1641, Sept. 1.—Thomas Crompton to Sir Richard Leveson.—Last night he received a letter from Lord Cromwell, dated 29 August, by which he finds the Scots are certainly gone, and that divers of the better sort are preferred to great titles; among the rest General Lesley is made an Earl. Our army is not yet disbanded for want of money; we want 150,000l. ; but he hopes when the poll money comes, which cannot be long, that want will be supplied. Lord C. tells him that Parliament will certainly be prorogued that day sennight, being the 8th of that month, until the 20th of November next.

Fol. 32. 1642, April 28. Copy of a letter (1¾ pages of small and close writing) to the knights of some shire, by their constituents, regarding the course to be adopted in Parliament; in reply to answer by the knights to the constituents' letter of the 5th. (It takes the King's side.)

Fol. 33. 1642, June 17, York. News letter (3 folio pages).—Arrived there on Wednesday evening, and found the King, Prince, and Duke of York well and cheerful ; the Court full of Lords, many of the House of Commons and a multitude of other brave gentlemen.— York and the Northern parts loyal, a few inconsiderable men excepted. At present the King's guard of foot is 1,000, and of horse 200. No likelihood of levying a war against the Parliament. Does not hear of any intention to increase those numbers except upon extreme necessity. The King's going to Lincoln is yet uncertain. Lord Willoughby of Parham has done as much as may be in that county in performance of that ordinance of both Houses concerning the militia. . . The truth thereof is not much unlike the business of Buckinghamshire and Leicestershire. One at Sir William Pelham's table in that county said that they had a gallant appearance at Lincoln, where there were only 15 of the trained band met, instead of some hundreds I think, and this being complained of to Lord Willoughby for a jeere, the captain was committed, and is now upon bail. The Mayor of Lincoln has delivered the key of the county magazine (which was in the city) to Lord Willoughby, and refused to publish His Majesty's proclamation. The King thereupon sent for him, but Lord Willoughby, who keeps a court of guard at Lincoln, as we hear, sent up the messenger to the Parliament, with 12 horse and pistols for his guard. It seems the Mayor of Leicester and divers gentlemen of the county opposed Lord Stamford's proceedings at Leicester. The King sent the Mayor a letter of thanks, and desires to know the rest of the gentlemen's names, that he may do the like to them. On Wednesday last the Earl of Manchester went hence to Newcastle to be governor there . . . . I hear of no danger yet from the Scots. . . . Tuesday last arrived the Earl of Bristol and Lord Paget, the latter having submitted to the King, and acknowledged the error of meddling with the militia of Buckinghamshire; and he and

all the rest here did on Wednesday last subscribe certain articles, viz., to defend the King in his just rights, &c. . . . The King and Lords sate in Council on Wednesday afternoon. Certain propositions are to be sent up to both Houses; . . . with them the King will tender a full pardon to all except 12, viz., the six members formerly charged by him with treason, and Alderman Pennington, Mr. Venn, Sir Thomas Ludlow, Sir Peter Wentworth, Sir John Hotham, and Mr. Martin. Lord Fairfax, one of the committee here from the Commons, fell from his horse and broke two of his ribs last week. On Monday last a great stir here by some soldiers about the arrest of one of their fellows. It seems the Alderman at whose house the committee from both Houses lie, had some hand therein ; the soldiers pulled down the posts at his door and broke his windows.—Mentions the King's answer to the second Remonstrance, and that unparalleled piece his answer to the third Remonstrance.—Commissions of array are in hand to go down to the several counties ; the Commissioners in Warwickshire are the Earl of Northampton, Lord Dunsmore, &c., except such as Mr. Coombes and Mr. Purefoy, and others of that strain. Mr. George Sandon brought me yesterday to the Earl of Bristol, who told me that his nephew Lord Robert Digby died in Ireland last week. . . . This evening the messenger that was carried away from Lincoln towards London came to the Court, and the Mayor of Lincoln ; for whom they came to Grantham they better considered of the business, and so went no further. This evening came the Archbishop of York, and the Committee took leave of the King, and are to go to London speedily, all saving Lord Fairfax, who is hurt.

Fol. 34.—1642, June 6. (Sir) Edward Littleton to Sir Richard Leveson.—Tells him that an order has been made and printed that all members of the House of Commons who shall be absent on the 16th instant shall pay 100l. towards the war of Ireland. News that on Friday last was a great appearance at York : a petition of accommodation being to be presented, the Lord Savell (Savile) tore it in pieces; we have voted him and Lord Linsey incendiaries and enemies to the State ; we sent down a messenger, which the malignant party have imprisoned. Sir, we have those affronts offered which never Parliament had, which is no small trouble to all honest men. The King declares, and we declare . . . . We are in preparation of defence. We have sent down divers of the House to see the militia put in execution. The King makes Lord Lieutenants and Deputies and his Commissions to be sent into all counties. The Scotch stand very right, and I could wish the English did so.

Fol. 35.—1642, Aug. 6. Order by the House of Commons that Sir Richard Leveson, Mr. Frances Newport, Sir Richard Lee, Sir Robert Howard, members of the House, be forthwith summoned by the Serjeant-at-Arms, his deputy or deputies, to make repair to the said House . . . to do their service there. Signed by Henry Elsinge, Clerk of the Parliament. (Indorsed, Delivered by the messenger, 20 Aug. 1642, at Stafford.)

Fol. 36.—1642, Aug. 16, Beaudesert.—Will. Pagett to Sir Richard Leveson, Kt. Has received a commission from the King under the Great Seal of England for raising 1,200 foot for the defence of His Majesty's person, the two Houses of Parliament, the Protestant religion, the laws of the land, the liberty of the subject, and the privilege of Parliament ; has " sent this gentleman one of my officers to beat up my drummes in " your parts and about Newport." Asks Sir Richard's assistance.

n. d. The same to Sir R. Leveson, Baronett. Asks Sir Richard to meet him at Stafford on Saturday next, the 20th of August instant, upon special service for His Majesty.

Fol. 37.—1642, Sept. 2, Whitchurch. Letter by the Shropshire Commissioners of Array to the High Sheriff of the County of Stafford, recommending to him and the Commissioners of Array and the gentry of his county the result of their consultations at musters, the like whereof is sent to the other counties.—If acceptable, they desire to receive notice at Whitchurch on Thursday next, where some of them will weekly meet on that day to treat of their common security. Signed by (Earl) Rivers, Robert Killmorey, R. Cholmondeley, Tho. Savage, Tho. Aston, Tho. Cotton, John Weld, Ri. Lee, Tho. Hanmer, Paul Harris. (A copy of the Resolutions, dated 2 April 1642, is at fol. 41.)

1642, Sept. 5, Stone. Copy answer, addressed to the Sheriff by R. Leveson, Tho. Crompton, George Digby, Rafe Snoyde.—They decline "without supreme autho- " rity or greater motives of more demonstrable dangers " to raise the armes of their county."

S 3

Fol. 38. 1642, Sept. 3, Whitchurch. A letter to Sir R. Leveson, similar to the last but one above, signed by John Wild, Sheriff, Ri. Lee, Tho. Hanmer, Paul Harris, Thom. Eyton, Richard Sneyd, Richard Lloyd, Franc. Ottley, Francis Thorns, Gerard Eyton.

1642, Dec. 13. Hu. Elliott to Sir Richard Leveson. One from the parts of Worsteare (Worcester) and Hereford tells him that on Sunday morning the Earl of Stamford went away from Hereford, both bag and baggage, and left not anything in the town either of his or any others, for that it is said he plundered them incevorall (in several ?), and set three houses afire to keep them in action that they might not pursue him. On Monday, news came to Worcester that their carriages could not pass, but that they were all in a dirty lane in the way towards Gloucester . . . The Hereford people sent 700 horse after them, with what success not yet known. On Friday last Sir Hopton, who had promised the Earl of Stamford that he had 1000 dragoniers at four days' warning to be ready for his service, came into Ledbury and brought with him his colours and his drum, and there in a commanding manner called all the countrymen in order to bring in their dragonnes. The first man answered him that he had received His Majesty's book to the contrary, and that he durst not, lest he should be held a traitor. The others did answer alike, so that he went out of Ledbury, and his colours and drum were taken from him. It is said that Hopton has since come to Worcester and turned to the King's part. There is great store of horsemen in Bridgnorth, said to be the Earl of Chesterfield's servants, and likewise he himself, who has been lately plundered, and his lady much abused.

Fol. 41.—1642, Sept. 17, Court at Uttoxator. "Charles " R." to Sir R. Leveson. Being informed that Sir Richard has in his custody four brass field-pieces and 40 now pike-staves, the King directs them to be brought to his magazine at Shrewsbury.

Fol. 41.—1642. Sept. 2. Copy of the seven Resolutions at Whitchurch of the Commissioners of Array.

Fol. 42.—1642, Sept. 25 and six following days. (Diary by some one in the town of Manchester attacked by the Earl of Derby.)—Sunday the 25th the Lord Strange (now since the Earl of Derby) came accompanied with Lord Molineux, Sir Gilbert Houghton, Sir Gilbert Gerrard (lately made colonel by His Majesty), Sir John Girlington, High Sheriff of Lancashire, Sir Thomas Midleton, Sir Alexander Radcliffe, Sir Thomas Barton, Sir Cecil Trafford, Sir John Talbott, and most of the gentry of the county, with all or great part of the trained and freehold bands in the county, and many Welchmen, in all 3,000 strong, with 5 troops of horse, troop under the command of his lordship, under Lord Molyneux, another under Captain Windebank, all dragooners, another under Capt. Barton, second son to the Earl of Lindsey, and another under the command of Capt. St. John, who was after slain; in the afternoon they, in two bodies, marched within musket-shot of the town, when some bullets were exchanged, no great harm done on either side, only a young boy slain on the town's side; both sides continued shooting from their centuries (sentries ?) all that night. On Monday morning my lord sent for a parley, which was that the town would deliver up their arms and receive into the town a troop of horse, &c., &c. The town refused to billet any soldiers without consent of Parliament, or to deliver up their arms, which were their own, to be employed against the Great Council of the Kingdom, which they are bound to maintain in discharge of their late Protestation. His lordship's messenger threatened that the town should hear from him by the voice of cannon; the town said they expected no favour. About 2 p.m. his cannon began to play, and the town answered for about 7 hours. A barn at the end of the town and 8 houses were burned, but his lordship durst not approach the chains of the town. He lost in that attack above 120 men, as appears by the graves found in the fields about the town, and 5 men more were found in the sands of the river, and it is supposed that more were cast into the river, amongst whom was Mr. Mountain, a colonel of horse, and Capt. Skirton, a lieutenant, with others of note. The town lost only 3 men. Of about 100 cannon's iron bullets none did harm except to houses, altho' they were 8 and 9 pounds in weight.—On Tuesday Lord Strange made another attack without success. Seven troopers, with their horses, were taken by the town, and one quartermaster shot, with the loss of two townsmen.—On Wednesday Lord Strange sent for another parley, and offered that if the town would give him 50 muskets he would take bag and baggage and

begone. The town said they would not give him so much as a rusty dagger. Contrary to the truce, which was to have lasted the night, Lord Strange brought up some ordnance and planted them in Salford; he afterwards removed them (though with the loss of two men) or he would have gone home without them. One of the two slain was Capt. Standish, a gentleman of ancient family in Lancashire, who was to have married Mr. Archbould's kinswoman that married Sir John Harpur, of Cork.—On Thursday, about 10 o'clock, 100 musketeers, 50 pikes, and 50 halberds went out of the town to relieve a house near the town which Lord Strange's horse had taken. They were set upon by a troop of horse and about 100 musketeers; after an hour's fight most of the horse were driven into the river, and Capt. Snell and two more were drowned; the captain had two rings on his hand worth 80l. The town lost 5 men and had 8 more mortally wounded. On Lord Strange's side 13 were slain and two horsemen, well affected, taken prisoners.—On Friday Lord Strange's forces were so scattered that they durst not approach within pistol shot of the town.—On Saturday afternoon Lord Strange sent to the town for delivery of the prisoners, which were 85, in exchange for 16 whom he had taken, and this was done; and then he went away, with the loss of 220 men, as is conceived.

Fol. 43.—1642, Oct. 9, Salop. Ric. Weston to Sir Richard Leveson.—Finds that the Lords are possessed with a very ill opinion of the High Sheriff of Yorkshire, for they are certain he first invited Hotham to sally out of Hull, and are informed that he and Hotham were the first breakers of the capitulation, which has occasioned much trouble in the North; he is put from his office of sheriff, and Sir Richard Hutton succeeds him: his two brethren here in the army committed and cashiered from their several places. The troop in which he (Weston) is listed is commanded to march to-morrow. There is a rumour that the Earl of Derby has gotten the arms from Manchester, and will be here on Tuesday. The King intends to remove hence on Wednesday; his forces are great and increase daily. It is conjectured he will be above 25,000 strong before three days' march. The trained foot of this county he leaves behind to guard the town and county, and will leave in the town a garrison as great as they will require, and ammunition and ordnance.

Fol. 44. 1642, Oct. 25, Warwick Castle. (Copy.) Robert (Earl of) Essex to the King.—Begins, Most high and mighty illustrious Lord, the glimmering light of my life by which I now live, the law of my own conscience, hath taken from me, &c. (He asks the King's pardon for his rebellious acts.)

Fol. 45. 1643, June 13, Shrewsbury.—Arthur Capell to Sir R. Leveson. A printed paper, directing him to send four horses, men, and horse-arms, for the King's service, to Shrewsbury, by Monday the 19th of June, to the Red Lion, there to be received and listed. A MS. addition says that only two horse are expected, to make up those formerly sent, four in all.

Fol. 47. 1644, July 4, Evesham. The King's message to the Lords and Commons.

1644, Sept. 8, Tavistock. The King's message to the Lords and Commons.

(Both these are printed in the "Reliquiæ Carolinæ," and elsewhere.)

Fol. 46. 1644, Jan. 11. Copy of Propositions made at a meeting of the lords and gentlemen of the associated counties of Worcester, Salop, Hereford, and Stafford.—Twelve propositions, the first being that His Majesty would be pleased to declare Prince Charles his Highness, to be general of these associated forces.

Fol. 48. 1645, Nov. 20. Engagement to Col. Croxton (signed by Sir Richard Leveson) that, inasmuch as Col. Croxton has allowed him to go to Trentham for health and business, he will return to Namptwich and render himself a prisoner as before within 28 days after date.—Signed by Ri. Lee, Edw. Kinaston, Roger Whittacer, John Doodie, and Richard Atkins, as sureties for the performance by Sir Richard of his parole.

On the other half of the sheet of paper, Whittacer, Doodie, and Atkins sign an undertaking to pay to Marshal Travers all sums that Sir Richard stands engaged for, for the fees or diet of prisoners lately released from Namptwich, if Sir Richard do work his enlargement, be summoned to London, or do not return according to his engagement.

Fol. 49. 1645, Dec. 20. Engagement signed by Sir Richard Leveson, that as Sir William Brereton has allowed him to stay at Trentham for 14 days more, he will return to Namptwich and render himself a prisoner within 14 days after date.—Lee, Kinaston, Whittacers, and Doodie sign as sureties.

Fol. 50. 1645, Nov. 3, Nov. 12, Nov. 20, and Dec. 12.
—Four passes, signed by (Col.) Thomas Croxton, for 1.
Henry Smith, servant to Sir Richard; 2. Mr. Robson
and Robert Grimes, servants of Sir Richard; 3. Sir
Richard, with men and horses; 4. Mrs. Jane Brerewood,
going from Namptwich to Peover.

Fol. 51. 1645, Dec. 16, Namptwich. Matth. Graners
to Sir Richard Leveson.—Sends enlargement of parole
for 14 days.

1645, Dec. 20, Namptwich. (Col.) Thomas Croxton to
all commanders, officers, &c. Gives notice that Sir
Richard Leveson has had his parole enlarged by Sir
William Brereton for 14 days.

Fol. 52. (1646.) Foom of a warrant for pardon, under
the Great Seal to, and restitution of lands of, Sir R.
Leveson, he having been admitted to a fine of . . . l., for
deserting to the Parliament and adhering to the enemies
thereof.

Fol. 53. Rentall of the estate of Sir R. Leveson in the
co. of Salop, delivered to the Committees [at Goldsmiths'
Hall] upon oath.

Fol. 54. 1646, Feb. 27. Copy order by the Commissioners for compounding with Delinquents, that Sir
R. Leveson having paid and secured the fine imposed
upon him for his delinquency, the trunks, cabinets,
hampers, boxes, and bags of writings, papers, court rolls,
books, and evidences belonging to him and deposited in
Mr. Edward Jones's and Mr. Froude's houses in Shrewsbury, should be re-delivered to him. Signed by T.
Lincoln, Manchester, Mulgrave, Antho. Irby, Hen.
Darley, D. Watkins, John Ashe, Robert Jenner.

Fol. 55. 1646, March 9. Pass signed by Wm. Lenthall, Speaker, for Sir R. Leveson and six servants
(named), with his coach and horses, to go from London
to Trentham in Staffordshire, or Linsell in Shropshire,
and back.—Addressed to all courts of guard, officers, and
others whom it concerneth.

Fol. 51. Copy (2 pp.) of the Engagement and declaration of the grand jury, freeholders, and other inhabitants
of the county of Essex, in pursuance of their late petition presented to both Houses of Parliament the 4th of
May 1648. (It is in favour of the King.)

Fol. 62. 1648, March 29. A letter signed " Jero-
" boham," addressed to Mr. Tho. Langley, Esq. . . . . . .
For news, three counties of Wales are risen for his
Majesty, as also 2,000 of Major Langhorne's soldiers are
gone to Col. Poyer; they have relieved him, and taken all
their ordnance and ammunition; slain many. Among the
rest, Col. Fleminge is missing. They have taken Tinbey
(Tenby) castle, as also a ship that lay before Pembroke
Castle, by name the Expedition, with all the men and
arms. An express last night, thus : the Parliament of
Scotland have sent them [the Westminster men] their
last resolution, and that in three votes, 1. They will
maintain the King; 2. They will draw their kingdom
into a posture of defence, and that with an army; 3.
That they will send 12 of their Lords and Commons to
treat with the like number of ours here, and they shall
debate their business concerning both kingdoms, and
will send 12 hostages hither, and the Parliament must
send the like number thither. They also demand Manchester, Say, Wharton, with one or two lords more, with
Martin and Vane, and many more of that faction, and
that their Parliament is to end the 29th of this March.
. . . . . Last night we drank the King's health, in
abundant manner, being his coronation-day, and much
celebrated it with ringing of bells and bonefires more
than ordinary. . . . . The Parliament would fain draw
the City in again, but the tome fooles begin to be wiser;
they proffer them the militia in their own hands, as they
had it formerly, and the Tower also, and they will now
release their aldermen and much more; but two words
must go to a bargain.

Fol. 59. 1648, July 20, The Ligure before Colchester.
—Protection for the house at Trentham of Sir R. Leveson, and his person, family, horses, cattle, sheep, and
other goods. Signed by T. Fairfax, sealed with his
crest, and addressed to all officers and soldiers under his
command.

Fol. 60. 1648, Oct. 18. Pass for Sir R. Leveson to go
from Staffordshire to London about his composition, and
to return. Signed by T. Fairfax, and sealed with his
seal of arms (16 quarters), and addressed to all officers
and soldiers under his command.

Fol. 61. 1644, Jan. 10, Queen Street. Permission for
Sir Richard Leveson (he having made his composition
with the Parliament) to reside in town with his servants,
&c., and to go to Trentham and return. Signature of
T. Fairfax, and his crest.

Fol. 56. 1648, Jan. 12. Licence (by virtue of the
powers given by the order of the House of Commons of
the 5th of January instant), signed by Fran. Allein, for

Sir R. Leveson to reside in London, or within 12 miles
thereof, for 28 days, about the business of his composition.

Fol. 57. 1648, Feb. 2. Protection for Lady Leveson's
horses in Trentham Park, co. Stafford, and Linsell Park,
co. Salop. Signed by T. Fairfax, and sealed with his
coat of 16 quarters.

Fol. 63. 1649, May 12. Copy order of the House of
Commons (signed by Henry Scobell, Clerk of the
Parliament), that the cases of the delinquents standing
for consideration that day, touching the mitigation of
their fines, and also the cases of William Bassett, of
Claverton, co. Somerset, and Sir Richard Leveson,
should be taken into consideration that day sevenight.

Fol. 64. 1650, Jan. 15. Receipt (partly printed and
partly written), by Richard Waring and Michael Herring, treasurers of the moneys to be paid into Goldsmiths' Hall, to Sir Richard Leveson, for 1,923l. in full
of his 6,000l. (over and above 3,846l. allowed for rectories
by him settled towards maintenance of the ministers,
and for interest due on the latter moiety, 136l. 13s. 6d.),
imposed on him by the Parliament of England as a fine
for his delinquency to the Commonwealth.

Fol. 65. One page (probably written by Sir Richard
Leveson while a prisoner at Namptwich), stating his
desire to put in bail before Sir W. Brereton, " or the
" Governor of this garrison, as I did for my return when
" I went lately to Trentham," for his appearance at
Goldsmiths' Hall, rather than be taken to Shrewsbury
for that purpose.

Fol. 66. A poem "On Oxford Mayors Election."
Begins,—

It was when good Autumnus sheds the leaves,
That Mace from Mayor, as boughs from trees bereaves.
(60 lines. 17th century.)

Fol. 67.—A true relation of the battle of Edge Hill.
1 p. (Stated at the end to have been commanded by His
Majesty to be written, and to be sent to the Commissioners of Array in Cheshire.)

Fol. 68. 16—, Oct. 30, Oxford. An unsigned letter to
Mr. Bushill, giving a short notice of the battle [of
Edgehill] . . . . This morning news was that Essex,
Brooke, and their forces are marched to Northampton,
and it is thought to meet with Sir John Hotham, to lay
down arms by reason they be but 7,000 foot, most of
their horse being cut off. (1 p.)

Fol. 69. (1643, March 19.) Long news letter of three
pages, giving an account of the battle of Hopton Heath,
near Stafford, where the King's army defeated the rebels.
The writer is very severe in his remarks on the rebels,
for refusing to give up the body of the Earl of Northampton, except on the terms of receiving back their
eight drakes and ammunition, and prisoners taken by
the royalists.

Fol. 70. [1658], Sept. 16. News letter (2 pp.). "My
" servant Moses is dead," was Mr. Hugh Peters' text on
Sunday last. . . . . . Although Lord Lockhart of Dunkirk has often moved that Gravelin (being a maritime
town) should, according to the articles, be surrendered
by the French to the English, the French will give no
ear unto it; and, which is worse, news letters come
every day, informing of the lamentable mortality
amongst the English; and yet there are more of the old
soldiers, 20 out of every company, that are ordered by
the Council to be still transmitted into Flanders; be-
like to make a rare experiment if death or the grave
can be surfeited or not. It was spoken all about London
that the Lord Berkstead, Governor of the Tower, is
dead; but it is not so. As his tailor was taking his
measure to make him a mourning suit for His Highness,
he was corrupted by a dead palsy, a shrewd disease, and
which I believe that, although a long time it may keep
him company, yet none but the resurrection can cure.
I am informed that the Lady Claypoole, a great lover of
plays and piety, did on her death-bed beseech His Highness to take away the High Court of Justice, and spake
words which, leaving a deep impression on his heart,
did accompany him to the very close. We have printed
and published a libell representing that if theer must be
a protector over this nation, to govern as a single magistrate, it would doe better in the person of the King of
Scotland then of any other, which would reduce all
things into its lawfull and primitive channell, and be
the happy mother of peace and union in the nations.
This is highly resented, and much adoe their is to find
out the printer and the publisher of the said libell. I
am also credibly informed that many officers of the army
have put forth a remonstrance, desiring that the nation
may be governed by a parliament, according to their
institution, after their dissolution of Kingshippe; but
this bites as shrewd as the other, and the Long Parliament have showed to all posterity what may be expected

from such men of God (as the pulpits then flattered them), and from such worthyes of our Israel. I made mention in my last of an effigies of wax made to represent his late Highness. The charge of the wayters is great, &c. It is therefore not to continue above 14 days at the farthest. In the meantimes black velvet is bought all London over to hang in Whitehall and Somerset House; and because men cannot mourn enough for the death of His Highnes, the stones and walls are taught to do it. It is not amiss to conclude that the Swedes have bin stoutly repulsed from Copenhagen, and there is such a mortality in the army, by reason of theyr luxury, and not burying the garbidges of the beasts which they have brought in to feed them, that they are ready of themselves to rayse the seige, having bin five times notably repulsed by the Danes.

Fol. 71. A news letter of 1 page. *Begins*, Cardinal Mazarin is at last come to Paris, being met by the King himself and received in his own coach. He arrived there the 4th of February, new style, in the afternoon, &c. (French news.)

Fol. 72. 1645, Feb. 1. Copy of articles between the commissioners appointed on behalf of Lord Byron, Field Marshal General of North Wales and Governor of Chester, of the one part, and the commissioners on behalf of Sir William Brewerton [Brereton], Baronet, Commander-in-Chief of all the force in Cheshire, and at the Leager before Chester, on the other part, for the surrender of the city of Chester and the fort thereof. 18 articles. (2¼ pp.)

Fol. 73. [1625.] Copy (4 pp.) of the speech of the Speaker of House of Commons to the King, on the occasion of his being chosen Speaker.

Fol. 74. [1642 ?]. Copy of a Declaration or the Resolutions of the county of Hereford . . . . They resolve to maintain, 1. Protestant religion; 2. The King's just power; 3. The laws of the land; 4. The liberty of the subject. (This declaration is in favour of the King.) 2½ pp.

Fol. 75. 1657, Aug. 25, and 1658, Oct. 24. Two friendly short letters from C. Derby (Charlotte de la Tremouille Countess of Derby, the defender of Lathom House against the rebels) to Sir Richard Leveson.

Fol. 76.—1649, April 16, London. . . . to . . . 'Tis true the peace is concluded in France between the Queen and the Parliament of Paris; he (the writer) has seen letters from Paris saying that the Cardinal was not banished as it was demanded; he thinks that the Cardinal will revenge himself on the Italians. Those of Rouen and elsewhere bless themselves for their peace, and speak as if after a general one is made (as they are about it) all the neighbours Princes under the young King's banners will make a conquest of their land. The same letter advises a friend of mine to depart hence betime; to this purpose it shall not be amisse to send you a kind of prophesie that runs thus:—Grebnerius was in England with Queen Elizabeth, and presented her with a fair MS. in Latin, describing therein the whole future history of Europe, here and there limning in water colours some principal passages for turnes in the world of after ages. Dr. R Nevill, then Dean of the Closet, very intimate with the Queen, got this book of her, and bestowed it on the library of Trinity College, Cambridge, where it hath lain public to the eyes of all beholders over since. About five years since it was much defaced. In these predictions he described the troubles of Russia, and mentions the election of the Swedish King, Sigismund, King of Polonia, by which he should loose his inheritance; that of the Swedish usurper's race there should be one, Gustavus Adolphus by name, who should take a hint from the distractions in Germany to enter that empire with a small army, and really (really) into a mighty force, and fight many battels prosperously, but at the last pitched field he should perish. Then about that time should reign another Northern king, nomine Carolus, "qui " ducet uxorem Mariam papisticam ex qua evadet " regum omnium infelicissimus; tum populus ipsius " ditionis eliget alium regem comitem qui durabit " in imperio tres annos aut circiter, et postea idem " populus sibi eliget alium regem equitem, non ejus- " dem familiæ nec honoris, qui detrudet sub pedibus " suis omnia aliquando longiore tempore, et post " hunc nullum. Paulo post apparebit quidem Carolus " a Carolo descendens ab immensa classe in littus " ditionis patris sui, et cum auxiliis Suedicis, Dani- " cis, Hollandicis, Francicis, et Hispanicis prosternabit " adversarios suos et administrabit imperium suum " felicissime et erit Carolo magno major."[*]

Fol. 77.—1654, May 20, Rouen.—L. to Mr. John Langley at Trentham.— . . . . Our merchants are

joyful of the long-desired peace between England and Holland; they expect in brief to hear of the like between France and England. The King of the Scots is to have from the King of France 20,000 pistoles, and to go to Chambery to his aunt in Savoy, with the promise of an annual pension (if Mazarin will spare it) out of the King's coffer, who is profuse beyond measure in his plays and like shows, according to the Italian mode, to busy the King about toys and fooleries while he governs all the kingdom at will . . . . Though once he could call in derision and reproach all them that were for the Prince of Condé, Cromwells, out of *ratione di stato*, they are now good friends, as it appears by their great intelligence.—A report that Amsterdam will not henceforth acknowledge the young Prince of Orange their governor, as free to choose when and whom they please. The 1st of May last was the day the Queen of Sweden had set down to surrender her crown to her cousin Charles, Prince Palatine . . . . The King of France is to go to Rheims to be anointed with their miraculous oil and to be crowned.

1654, June 7. Jo. le Quesne to Sir Richard Leveson. —Notwithstanding Mazarin's subtle suggestion to the contrary, the King of France would go to Rheims to be crowned. The government of the province of Alsace being promised to M. de Harcourt, if he would surrender the town of Brisach into the king's hands, [he] did condescend to it; he, upon confidence of the agreement, went out of the town with some of his friends, came in again, went to the captain's house; being arrested, found a letter from Mazarin among his papers to take some good opportunity to lay hold on M. de Harcourt. The new politicians promise, and give order to break promise, all with one breath. The treaty between Sweden and England reported to be concluded but not signed.

Fol. 78.—1656, April 8, London. Jean le Quesne to Sir R. Leveson.—Mentions the successes of the King of Sweden against the King of Poland, and the anger of the Pope thereat. The Pope wants to effect a general peace, particularly a peace between France and Spain. To this purpose he has proclaimed a Jubileo, with plenary indulgence and general pardon, extending even to cases reserved to himself, to them that shall visit so many churches, &c., &c., and pray for rooting out the new heretics sprung up in the Catholic Church (he meaneth those that uphold Jean Sanius (Jansen's) opinions). . . . . The King of France is to answer the Pope's solicitations, who greatly taxes him for joining with the enemies of his Church in a peace and confederacy with Cromwell and with the King of Sweden. His Ambassador at Rome presented the Pope a letter from the King of France, and another " from " Mazarin showing a great zeal for a general peace, " nevertheless with this proviso, that it might be after " this summer." The Pope stormed, and said he saw the Court of France was not inclined to peace, and denounced Mazarin's ambition, and alluded to Mazarin having prevented a peace between France and Spain at the meeting at Munster, when he (the Pope) was then Nuncio from Rome. " Lately 500 persons have left the " town of Avignon to become Protestants, who have " dispersed themselves in several towns in France."

Fol. 80.—1660, June 21, London. Charles Talbot to Sir Richard Leveson.—Says that since he came from Dover, waiting upon the King to London, he had given Sir Richard an account of the landing. The House of Commons did on Tuesday last, after excepting seven from the Pardon for life, and finishing " the twentie for " estate," grant the King for his life Tonnage and Poundage and proceed upon Poll money, and are restoring the King's and Queen's lands, and have voted 20,000l. to her out of the taxes. There are six Commissioners for the Treasury and Navy, that is, the General, the Earl of Southampton, Marquis of Ormond, two Secretaries of State, and one more; and the King is making lords and deputy lieutenants for every county. . . . . As yet we ride 200 gentlemen of quality and officers as a guard to the King's person, and guard him by turn day and night (with the General's life guard) in the court on foot. . . . Mentions his (Talbot's) brother Langly. Says that the King has made his (Talbot's) brother Sir Gill. (Sir Giles Talbot) Master of the Jewel House, and knighted his (Charles Talbot's) son Jack, who is also sworn of the Privy Chamber in ordinary. The General has given him a troop of horse in the army; his second son is to have a troop at Dunkirk, and his youngest son is equerry to the Duke of Gloucester.

Fol. 81.—1660, May 29, London. Charles Talbot to Sir R. Leveson.—The King landed at Dover on the 25th, and this day arrived at London. Says he was one of the first that kissed the King's hand at his landing, and doubts not to be to him (as to his grandfather and father) a servant during life. On Saturday last, the King, at Canterbury, knighted Monck, and Winchilsey with Mordant for leading him up. After the Dukes of York and Gloucester leading Monck up to the King (Sir Ed. Walker leading them up), he made him Knight of the Garter, the King putting the George about his neck, and the Duke of York the Garter upon his leg, and the cloak with the Star was delivered him by the Herald, after reading of a parchment which declared that (for his princely blood and signal services he had done him) he did declare and make him one of the Honourable Order of the Garter, which emperors had desired, and that he should be farther considered.

1660, Nov. 24, London. Charles Talbot to Sir Richard Leveson.—Says he has spoken to Lord Brook about Sir Richard's commission for a troop, which shortly will be ready.—Says that the Parliament is to be dissolved the 20th of next month.

Fol. 82. 1660, April 26, London. Samuel Terricke to Sir Richard Leveson. This day the House has appointed a committee touching elections) and returned hearty thanks to the General for his great service done towards a settlement, and appointed this day fortnight for this place for a day of thanksgiving for God's mercies towards these distracted nations. It said there is a letter come to town from the King, to be presented to the Lords' House to be communicated to the House of Commons. The Protestant ministers of Rochelle and other places in France have given a large character of the King's constancy to the Protestant religion.

Fol. 83. 1660, May 3, London. Samuel Terricke to Lady Katherine Leveson.—His letter of the 1st of May told of the King's letters and declarations. . . . The 50,000l. is ordered to be forthwith paid to His Majesty, and 10,000l. the City presents him. A committee is appointed to take off all records of the Journal in the House of Commons since 1646 that are to the prejudice of the King. . . . In consideration of the Court of Wards, the House has allowed the King 100,000l. yearly. . . .

Fol. 84. 1660, Nov. 17, London.—Samuel Terricke to Sir Richard Leveson. A Bill is preparing for settling 80l. yearly upon every minister forth of the Dean and Chapter's estate, which is agreed upon between His Majesty and the clergy; six months' tax at 70,000l. a month passed last Wednesday for paying of the navy and remainder of the army; two regiments of horse and seven of foot yet to be disbanded. Poll money comes short of what is expected; a renew will be had thereof. The ambassadors of Holland have presented His Majesty with a rich bed, thought worth 10,000l., and 50,000l. in rarest pictures the world affords; there is a speech for a match with the King of Portugal's sister.—Notices some of the Parliament's votes of the 16th.—Mr. Calamy will be Bishop of Coventry and Lichfield. Serjeant Hales is Lord Chief Baron.

Fol. 85. 1660, Nov. 22, London. Samuel Terricke to Sir Richard Leveson. Mentions yesterday's votes in the House.

1660, Dec. 8, London. The same to Mr. John Langly at Trentham.

Fol. 86. 1660, Dec. 8, London. The same to Sir Richard Leveson.—No Bishop yet assigned for Lichfield and Coventry. Calamy that was intended is made Provost of Eton and Dean of some other place.

Fol. 87. 1660 May 1, Inner Temple. Sam. Baldwyn to Sir Richard Leveson. As soon as the House of Commons met this morning a letter was delivered by Sir Jo. Greenvill (a Gent. of the King's bedchamber) to the Speaker, with a declaration inclosed. 'Twill come out in print speedily. (Baldwyn mentions the King's offers, and the speakers in, and proceedings of, the House after the reading of the letter.) . . . . This place is transported with joy; the bells ring and bone fires are expected in every street.

Fol. 89. 1661, May 30. Rob. Milward to Sir R. Leveson.—Many are desirous to restore the impropriations to the right owners, but as yet it is not a fit time, though there is a Bill drawn.—Mentions the Bill to repeal the Act against Bishops and restore them to their votes in the House of Lords; and a vote that day for a Bill for a voluntary contribution for the present relief of his Majesty's necessities. "'Tis thought the Presby-
" terians, who were most forward for it, will give freely.
" I think there is not much expected from the Cavaliers ;
" some worthy persons of that party are not pleased
" with this vote."

Fol. 90. 16..., May 25. Rob. Leveson to Mr. John Langley at Trentham. Cannot wait on Sir Richard on Monday, but before Saturday will wait on Langley at

5.

Trentham.—Here is no news, the Parliament not sitting this day. The King and the Duke of York are gone by water down the [river], where the Duke treats the King.

Fol. 54. 1646, Oct. 1, Goldsmiths' Hall. At the Committee for compounding with delinquents. Order that Sir R. Leveson shall pay 9,876l. as a fine for delinquency. But if he settle the rectories of Trentham being of the value of 90l. per annum, Barlaston being of the value of 50l. per annum, Sheriff Hales being of the value of 60l. per annum, Lilleshull being of the value of 80l. per annum, Treshall and Seisdon being of the value of 20l. per annum, upon the several ministers and their successors for ever, then the fine will be 6,000l., half to be paid in hand, the remainder in three months. Signed Jo. Leech.

Vol. III.

Fol. 2. 1642, Sept. 16, High Ercall.—Sir Richard Newport to his brother (in law) Sir Richard Leveson.—By what you write of Lord Strange, that he is to join with the King at Chester, it may be conjectured that his lordship comes not to this county before the King; yet it is not certain but he may (he having an intention when I last writ unto you to have sent for me to him if he had then come) send to the sheriff 51, who are to be commanded by him to have me to subscribe to certain protestations, conclusions, and agreements which the Commissioners of Array have subscribed unto, and send about to others to get their hands unto, so that if it please you to accomplish my desire in my former letter (a copy whereof I send), &c.

In the former letter (a copy of which is with the above) Newport asks Sir R. Leveson to use his interest with Lord Strange that he (Newport) may not be made to engage himself to either side, so that he may use his influence to compose differences between them, as he had done on a former occasion.

Fol. 3. 1652, Nov. 20. Rachell Newport to her brother Sir R. Leveson. . . . . Lady Alice Egerton was married last week to the Earl of Carborough, she being his third wife, and he having divers children. Sir Robert Harley married his eldest daughter this week to the late Lord Derby's brother's son Mr. Stanley; the portion 1,500l., jointure 300l., maintenance 40s., settled 500l. The Marquis Dorchester is presently to marry with the Lady Derby's second daughter; he asks no portion but what she will give her when she is able, but takes her for love. . . . . The Earl of Worcester is taken and committed to the Tower. . . 30 or 40 of the Dutch fishing boats were taken by us; they were all sent home with a charge not to come and fish in our seas any more.

1657, Nov. 14. The same to the same. Little news, only the great wedding at Court on Wednesday last, and continues yet ; the Lord Falconbridge with the Lady Mary will be next, all things being concluded. Lady Middlesex is still in the west, and I hope will there continue ; her lord is wonderful brave in town, and I hope will think no more of her.

Fol. 4. 1658, July 13. The same to the same.—A fresh report of the death of the King of France. His Highness has made Lord Pembroke and his lady friends, and I hear Lord Middlesex will endeavour the same, now he has sold all her plate, most of the household stuff, and all Lord Bath's library : all goes in play and rioting. My daughter Bromley has a son come from Virginia; he has been there almost four years, and there is no profit to be had there, trading is so poor.

Fol. 5. 1658, July 20. The same to the same. . . On Friday and Saturday last came out of the Tower Lord Cleveland, Mr. John Russell, Sir William Compton, Sir Richard Willis, Col. Covert, and some others. The Duchess and Duke of Richmond are safe arrived in France from their creditors; great store of her servants are turned off, and her estate put into friends' hands to pay debts, which are very great. The Dutch ships are westward again, and they to return the East India ships of ours. Lord Dorchester's daughter was married to Lord Rosse on Thursday last, 10,000l. being paid down, and more promised after death.—Sir William Whitmore's match is made up with Merchant Harvey's daughter, 10,000l. being the portion. The King of France is alive and dead every 24 hours. . . . We are sending great store of men into Flanders.

1658, July 27. The same to the same. Lord Shrewsbury, your neighbour, is in motion to two sisters, Mr. Brudnell's daughters by two wives, the elder living with her grandfather, the Lord Bru[denell], being unhandsome and crooked, the younger tolerable; it is thought he will not have the elder. Yesterday, the 26th, my son Newport went out of town (for Trentham). It is

T

reported that Gravelines is besieged; great want of
rain, and the town very empty.

Fol. 6. 1658, Aug. 3, London. The same to the
same. . . His Highness, with his family, is settled at
Hampton Court; Lady Claypole being still very ill, and
the physicians much fearing her. There is a hot report
now of a coronation which shall be shortly, but it is
not believed until it is seen done. On Thursday last
Lord Bridgman's daughter was married to Sir Thomas
Slingsby, whose father was lately beheaded. There
being a very great wedding kept upon Saturday last,
I was invited, being one of the bride's kindred and
friends, and to which unkindness I went; since I kept
no coach of my own, six miles out of town going and
coming was a great journey. The town is extreme
empty, and the flux begins again in the town to be very
hot to [   ]; very hot and dry weather. Lord Falconbridge and his lady came out of the North last week, he
being presented at York with a pair of silver flagons and
60l. in gold; the like was done to my Lord Richard
at Bristol. My cousin Dodington, that married Lady
Temple's daughter, has bought the Remembrancer's
office in the Exchequer, which office formerly the Fan-
shaws had.

1658, Oct. 5. The same to the same.—Lady Manchester died this day sennight of a wheezing and
shortness of breath, her lungs growing fast to her sides;
. . . though her lord and she have been accounted
great Precisioners, she would have none but a Cavalier
minister to absolve her at her death, and desired her
lord to give him 10l. for a legacy. Lord Harry speedily
coming out of Ireland; he is lately made Lord Lieutenant of Ireland, and has power to make a deputy.
Judge Windham and Judge Weelis, their judges' places
are taken from them, because in their last circuit the
country places complained of their ministers that they
would not administer sacrament to them. Lord Bristol
is very sick in Flanders, and his lady gone over to him.

Fol. 7. 1658, Oct. 12. The same to the same. . . .
The news now is of our new Lord General, the Lord
Fleetwood; the army petitioning to His Highness for
it, and he refusing it modestly; but they resolved to
have him or Desborough; now they say he must not
be called Lord General, but must have the whole power
of the soldiers and militia in his hands, and nobody else
have anything to do with them. Alderman Allen and
his wife were both buried together last week; a mighty
funeral, and he died a very rich man; how it was gotten
God knows. The Lord Harry is not to come to England; he must look to keep that he hath in Ireland, for
there is no more to be got here.

1658, Oct. 26. The same to the same. . . . Col.
Pride is lately dead. The soldiers are not yet contented, but they say will petition for a Parliament. His
Highness's effigies has lain in state to be seen, and
his funeral will be the 9th of next month. A world of
sickness in all countries round about London. London
is now held the wholesomest place. . . . There is
a great death of coach-horses almost in every place,
and it is come into our fields. P.S. My Lord of
Shrewsbury's match with Mrs. Brudenell is off, and is
made up to Sir John Yates his daughter.

Fol. 8. 1658, Dec. 14. The same to the same.—Lady
Dorset has been to Dover to send her two eldest sons
into France. . . Mr. Pierpoint went yesterday to Sir
John Evelyn's, to the marriage of his eldest son, which
is to be on Thursday. Sir Richard Temple and his
sisters are gone out of town. We had a great wedding
at my Lady Whitmeare's, her daughter marrying with
a merchant's son. It is thought the Opera will speedily
go down; the godly party are so much discontented
with it. Writs are out for a new Parliament, but
nobody knows whether they will sit or no, the Levelling
party is so much discontented.

Fol. 4. 1658, Jan. 4. The same to the same.—Much
sickness in the town, especially feavers, agues, and the
small-pox. . . A report that Lord Devonshire's son,
Lord Cavendish, going out of France into Italy by sea
was taken by the Turks; we hope it is not true, because
a friend of Andrew's who we thought to be with him,
we received a letter from him yesterday from Florence.
Lord Goring, son to my Lord Norwich, is married, or
shortly to be married, to a rich widow, Mrs. Baker, he
having no fortune of his own. Mr. William is come
from Guernsey, and quite released out of prison, but
his brother John who came with him is gone this day
to the Tower again.

Fol. 8. 1660, March 27. The same to the same.—
Yesterday came out a very strict proclamation against
all disturbers of the present government, and against
agitators, offering 10l. a man for any that shall be
brought in. It is reported that Okey is up in Bedford-

shire with three of the regiments; two of the three are
to be disbanded suddenly. Scott, they say, is one of
the authors of this business, who desire to set up
the Rump again. Several of the countries there are
rising, and many of the General's soldiers are gone out
against them; it is feared some of them are inclined
that way, especially the discontented officers; it is
reported he should have been murdered amongst them,
if God had not prevented it.

Fol. 9. 1660, April 21. The same to the same.—
Lambert was near being taken this week, being hid at
a house in Millbank at Westminster; the house was
beset with soldiers to take him; he had intelligence, and
then dressed himself in woman's clothes and a mask,
gave 10l. to a neighbour to break a wall to pass through
the house; a coach being ready, he was conveyed away
immediately. Desborough, Hough, and some others are
taken at Homeby (Holmby); they talk and vapour much,
but I hope it will come to nothing.

1660, April 28. The same to the same. I wrote to
you on Tuesday last of the great appearance in Hide
Park both of horse and foot, a great number of them
volunteers, many of them persons of quality. Monck
was not there, but stayed for the examination of Lambert, who told him he was invited to it by part of the
army, to which Monck told him he did believe it an
untruth; he and those that were taken prisoners with
him were that night sent prisoners to the Tower, and
are kept very close. On Wednesday the House sat, and
part of the Lords, divers of the Lords being kept out;
but yesterday so many went in that I hear 40 were in
the House. No Oxford Lords are admitted yet, but it
is believed all will [be] next week. They have sent for
Lords Oxford and Southampton, and the rest will follow.
On Wednesday the Upper House sent to the Lower to
desire a conference, which some few withstood, but it
was carried by the major part against them . . . . . Sir
Harbottle Grimston is made Speaker . . . . P.S. They
have agreed for Monday to be set apart for a fast.

1660, Mayday. The same to the same.—A joyful day;
a letter was read in the House from the King, wherein
he refers all to the Parliament concerning himself;
. . . also a declaration from him, wherein he is ready
to forgive all offenders that seek for pardon, &c. . . .
Luke Robinson stood up and recanted, and promises
what a faithful subject he will be to the King. He was
the first that spoke after the letter was read. Lambert
has attempted twice to make his escape since he was
taken. . . . York was like to be surprised by some
of his party. My Lord Brook hath his castle again, and
turned out the Governor and put in one of his own.

Fol. 11. 1660, May 26. The same to the same.—
The King came to Dover upon Friday, but lay at anchor
upon the Downs at least a day, waiting for the coming
of the General. As soon as he landed and the General
received him, he fell on his knees a good while, and
gave thanks to God, as was supposed; from thence he
went to Canterbury, and this night 'tis said he lies at
Cobham, &c. &c. . . . To-morrow night we intend to
bury her (Rachel Bromley, who died on the night of the
25th) in Great St. Bartholomew, in my grandfather
Mildmay's vault.

Fol. 11. 1661, April 30. The same to the same.—
Great preparations for the coronation to-morrow, and the
next day the making of six new Earls and six new
Barons. . . . . Our cousin Lady Bath hath got her
place of being Lady Bath again, it cost her 1,200l.; she
has made two Knights of the Bath, George Fane's son,
and Sir Chichester Raye's son; her lord is very angry
at her changing her title; he says it is an affront to
him. The Duchess, my sister's mother, has been ill of a
fever. Lord Lee continues weak and ill. . . . Lord
Bruncard's (Brouncker's) brother is either married or as
good to the Widow Germine; great jointure and great
personal estate. Glin is recovered of the fall he had
when he was riding with the King; they jeer him in
the town, and say he vomited up a great deal of Penruddock's blood, whom he condemned in the West. Last
night was the funeral of the young Duchess of Richmond,
who died in childbed.—Kellsey hath got a pass from
the King to go beyond sea; under that colour they did
take Fewson and Dakey with him, but they are brought
back again. Yesterday the King did drive a chariot in
Hide Park with two horses. A proclamation is coming
out forbidding all sorts of lace silver, bone lace, black
or white, but what is made in England to be worn.

Fol. 12. 16 . ., Sept. 27. Eli. Newport to (Sir R.
Leveson).

Fol. 13. 16 . ., Sept. 4, n. s., Amiens. R.N. to Andrew
(Newport).—' Foreign news.—'Tis strange to hear of the
dissensions amongst the exiled English, Scotch, and
Irish in Flanders. I met with a captain of Lord New-

burgh's regiment in Calais, who told me that he was
fled thence three days before from Newport, for having
killed Lord Newburgh in the streets; the occasion
given was that his Lordship struck at him with a
cudgel; but the fellow is a senseless officer, which makes
me hope his relation is false. The next day I saw a
relation of a quarrel under my Lord Taaffe's hand
between him and a Scotchman of my acquaintance, one
Sir William Keith; the dispute was only for three
royals and a half at tennis. Sir Wm. Keith was slain
upon the place; upon this great occasion also were
engaged four persons besides the principals. Upon
Taffe's side Dick Talbot fought and wounded Dick
Hopton in two places; and on Taffe's side again one
Davis fought with Sir William Fleming, but no hurt
done. . . . H. Wroth would be much pleased to hear
that I have within these four days past waited upon the
Cardinal, who is received in all towns like a king, with
his arms upon the gates, and the burghers, magistrates,
officers, and all people pay him the greatest honour
imaginable. I waited his march, because the convoy
was like an army, and those of Hesdin would otherwise
have taken me in my journey to Paris. From Abbeville I retired for convenience of quarters and took
another road, being recommended by an Irish Bishop
into the company of the Pope's Nuncio, who has entered
already upon discourse of religion, to whom I have the
confession of my faith as a good Englishman ought to
do, and betwixt French (of which he has no great proportion) and Latin (of which I have less) we make shift
to hold upon discourse without coming to argument.
This night I lodge and am invited to supper with
Marshal d'Aumont, who hath a design to buy an
English gelding of mine for which he shall pay sauce.
. . . I desire you will shew this at Eyton and
Arly (Arley), to both which families I am a very
real servant, &c. . . . You will think it strange to
hear that the Protector hath spies in the French Court
and army, of which I was advertised by one that is much
in those secret affairs, so that it is necessary to keep
a watch upon our mouths here, as it is fit to do in
England, for whatever the Cardinal hears passes immediately into England; never was any alliance performed
with so much present tenderness; the time of jealousies
draws near, for the Protector's age and infirmities give
some of the moderate men considerations of the insta-
bility of their confederacy.—P.S. I met at Boulogne
your boy Robin, very miserable, and spirited over in one
of Capt. Cobb's company in Col. Cooke's regiment
newly landed; the next news of him will be that he
will be hanged for running from his captain, which he
told Patrick was already in his thoughts.

1642, Nov. 29, Dutchie House. F. Newburgh to
Sir R. Leveson.—Hopes that the example of the
Staffordshire justices in providing guards for the safety
of the county will be followed in other places. Com-
plains of the pillaging round about, particularly in
Essex and Suffolk. The fatal encounter at Braynesford
has dispelled the hope of an accommodation between the
King and the Parliament. The King's army is about
Reading and Oxford. Alludes to the burdens which
will arise by the contributions for the support of the
armies on both sides, the daily messages between the
King and the Parliament, and says that to the last sent
by the Parliament inviting the King to return, the
King gave an answer which in the first part was very
sharp, but in the end invited them to send propositions.

Letters from Francis Newport, M.P. for Shrewsbury,
to his uncle Sir Richard Leveson, at Trentham. They
contain principally notes of passing events, and a few
extracts are given. They commence in the year 1639,
and are continued to 1661.

Fol. 14. 1639, Dec. 4, London. Francis Newport to
Sir R. Leveson.—Complimentary.—You heare our cause
hath gone well with us, I am certayne of noe other
news though the rumour goes of the Spaniards truce
with the French and the Turks with the Persian, and
lastly of ours with Scotland, as I presume Mr. Langly is
able to informe you, &c. P.S. I have heard since the
writing of my letter that the Palsgrave was kept close
prisoner, and us'd with little more respect than an
ordinary fellow in the prison.

Fol. 15. 1642, April 26, London.—The same to the
same.—The Kinge went on Saturday last to Hull well
attended, and would have enter'd into the Towne. Sir
Jo. Hotham denyed him; then he offerd to enter onely
with 30 men, as few as he could with his dignitye; that
Hotham denyed too, expostulatinge with the King upon
the walls a longe tyme. Upon this the Kinge went backe
to York, and sent a message to the Parliament consist-

inge of the relation of this passage, tellinge us that he
had proclamd Hotham a traytor, and desiringe justice
against him. Upon this the House of Peers began three
votes to us: first, that Hotham had done nothing but in
obedience to the Parliament; second, that the Kings
proclayminge him a traytor, beinge a member of the
House of Commons, was a breach of our privilidge;
third, that doinge it without due processe of law was a
breach of the liberty of the subject. These wee joynd
with them in, and have sent Sir J. Hotham 2,000l. more
to pay his garrison, and have sent two ships more to
fetch away the magazine thence. One party is much
depressed at this newse and the other as much set
higher. The Elector and the Duke of York were in
Hull when the Kinge came there, havinge bin there
ever since the night before, and Sir Jo. Hotham made
some scruple of lettinge them out.

Fol. 16. 1642, May 3, London. The same to the
same.—Two messages wee have lately received from
the Kinge, which I have sent you inclosed. Since that
wee have had a relation from Rushworth the clarke,
who was sent downe into Yorkshire, of some passages
there, which were shortly to this purpose; the Kinge
made two propositions to the Yorkshire gentlemen:
1st. That they would defend his person from all
violence; 2nd. That they would vindicate his honor in
the affront hee received at Hull. To the first they
answered they would by all means warrantable by the
law of the land. To the second they desired him to
aske the advice of his great Councell. Some of the rest
of the gentlemen not satisfied with this answer retired
within themselves to consider of an answer to make to
His Majesty, which what it is yet wee know not;
amonge those a obeife was Sir Fr. Wortely, who drew
his sword, sayinge I am for the Kinge; another sayinge
this must be ended by the sword. The House was
putting the question to accuse Sir Fr. Wortely of High
Treason, but that they considered it was onely affirmed
by one that but heard it from another. The House is
thinkinge of an accomodation, and to that ende hath
referr'd it to a committee to draw a petition to the
House to desire him to come nearer his parliament, and
to hearken to the advice of his great Councell, express-
inge withall our loyalty and affection to him, and with
this they will sende downe instructions by members of
our house, Sir Ph. Stappleton, Lord Farefeaux, Sir Hugh
Cholmely, and the other is to bee Hen. Cholmely already
there, to preserve the peace of that county in case any
insurrection or takinge up of arms should bee. We
hope this petition will doe much good, and tis all our
prayers. Hen. Vernon was turn'd out of the House to-
day, upon his election, very strangely, and but by three
voices. We have very good newse often out of Ireland
of great defeates wee give the rebells there.

Fol. 18. 1642, May 10, London. The same to the
same.—Much business hath not bin dispatched this
week in Parliament. The most considerable passages
were: 1. We have made a vote to desire the Lords to joyne
with us to bestow 500l. in a jewell to be sent to my
Lord of Ormond in Ireland as a mark of their favour,
and to move the Kinge to make him Knight of the
Garter, and this for the good service hee hath done
there upon the rebels, and for his loyalty which hee pre-
serves to this Crowne. The House's declaration upon
the proceedings at Hull I have sent you, and the King's
message to us upon it, which hath troubled us much,
insomuch that Sir H. Ludlow said in the House that he
that wryt it did not deserve to be King of England.
He was challenged for it by two or three in the House,
but it was interpreted in a mild sense as applyed onely
to the writer, not to the King, how justly I do not question; soe that he onely had a reprehension in his place
for it, but the House hath in this as upon former messages voted the contriver of it to bee enemy to King
and kingdom; and we are framing an answear to it;
upon this we are resolved upon naminge evill councellors,
it should have bin are this, but it is put of a week longer.
The Bill for excluding the four shires is passed the
Lords' House. O'Neal is escaped last weeks out of
the Power, it is not knowne how. The Kinge hath send
for my Lord Bankes and all his servants in ordinary to
him. This day was a general muster of the trained bands
of the city in Finsbury Feilds, being in all 8,000. Both
the Houses of Parliament adjourned this day, that as
many as would might go to grace their worke, it beinge
the first putting of their ordinance of Parliament in
execution; many great lords were there on horseback
and in tents, and many commoners besides, much gentry
besides, and the infinite shole of people. My Lord
Savile is gone to Yorke.

Fol. 17. 1642, May 17, London. The same to the
same.—We received a message from the Kinge last

week, which I have inclosed, with an answer of the Houses to two former messages and a letter from our committees at Yorke, which told us the Kinge commanded them to bringe this his answer themselves, which they in all humblnesse denying, as beinge commanded by the Parliament to reside there; the Kinge told them there that if they stayd there to hinder his service, hee would lay them by the heeles. Upon signification of this to the House, they made this declaration, which I have sent you, and the Lords joynd with them in it. We received letters yesterday from our Committees againe, that told us the King had summoned all the county of Yorke to appeare before him there last week, where hee made this speech to them, which I have enclosed. The greatest body of them made answeare, and did desire His Majesty to have recourse to his Parliament in a businesse of this high nature, and durst not presume to interpose between him and them. Some others consented to a guard, and they meete next Fryday at Yorke; 'tis a guard of horse. Wee are preparinge an ordinance of Parliament someway to hinder this meetinge. All these last passages at Yorke are ordered to bee printed together; and 'tis some ill fortune that they will not come out tyll to-morrow, soe that I cannot send them you tyll next week. Wee have voted a longe Remonstrance to the kingdome, which will suddainly come forth in print. The Lords have sent us downe a Bill that noe Lord to bee made hereafter shall have a voice in Parliament without the consent of both Houses. Wee have sent to the counties of Middlesex and Surrey and those nere London to have the ordinance for the militia put in execution. Judge Berckly's triall is on Saturday in the Lords' House. The Bill for the Synod of Divines is ingrossd in our House. The Kinge to-day sent a command to Sargent Major General Skippon to attend him suddainly at Yorke, upon which wee have made these votes. 1. That for the Kinge to command any free born subject to attend his person that has noe relation of particular service to him is against the liberty of the subject and the law of the land. 2. That his sendinge for Skippon to attend him is against the law of the land. 3. That sendinge for him, beinge imployed in the service of the Parliament without their consent, is a breach of their privilege. 4. That we continue our commands to Skippon to attend our service.—The King hath likewise sent to my Lord Keeper to command him to issue out wryts and proclamations for the removal of the next terme to Yorke. The Lords have voted it illegall, and have commanded the Lord Keeper to issue out noe wryts nor proclamations to that purpose, &c.

Fol. 19. 1642, May 24, London. The same to the same.—There hath not been much business dispatched this week in Parliament, which hath been imployed much in consideringe how to get more moneys (the 400,000l. being all out already if it were come in) ; we do not know how to get it, but have resolved whatever comes in shall be retributed out of the forfeit lands in Ireland, and so must be beholding to any one that will bringe it in upon those conditions; for imposing any more they dare not venture on for fear of discontenting the kingdome. That compact of news from Yorke which I promised you last weeke Mr. Langley brings you now with the large remonstrance newly come out, the King's last declaration, his proclamation and letter to the gentlemen of Yorkshire, the votes and petition of both Houses, and the articles against the recorder. Many other pamphletts (it may be) he may bringe you, but these I send you are all pertinent and necessary for your knowledge. The last news that came from York is that there came 200 horse on Fryday last for the King's guard, and that hee dismissed all but 50 of them, and has there Sir Robert Strickland's regiment of foote attendinge on him, and has summoned all the gentlemen and freeholders of Yorkshire to bee there next Fryday again. Wee take the greatest care wee can to see the militia in all countyes put in execution, and have this afternoon made a Committee of Lords and Commons to consider which is the best way to secure the Parliament and kingdome against any force that may be offered, and a committee of our House to consider how to get moneys for a stock for the Parliament to imploy upon occasion for their service; for which purpose it is proposed a declaration shall go forth to invite all well-minded people to bringe in their moneys, their names beinge concealed as longe as the Parliament thinks fit, and shall be repaid again when the Parliament is able for it. The last news is that my Lord Keeper is gone downe to York with or after the seal without the Parliament's leave, for 'tis thought the seal was sent for from him (Tom Elliott coming to him from the Kinge), and that he is gone after it, it may be to get it againe;

'tis uncertaine how, but the Lords have sent for him back again with all speed, and have ordered, in case of refusal, the power of the county to bring him back. News comes to us that O'Neal is taken in Norfolk. Judge Berckly's triall was to-day in the Lords' House, but not half perfected. Wee are in as many doubts of the issue of things here as you are there ; I hope God will give a happy end to them.—P.S. The King sent for all his great horses at the mues on Saturday last, which went away on Sunday morn, and 'tis reported the Kinge intends to goe to Lincoln.

Fol. 20. 1642, May 31, London. The same to the same.—Most of this last weekes occurrences I send you printed. But you may please to know further that the magazine is come from Hull, the captaines of the ships that brought it rewarded with money and thanks. This last message of the King's a Committee is appointed to draw a declaration in answeare to it, and another to forbid any to have a hand in sellinge of the jewells of the Crowne, because wee heare of such an intent. Those committees were sent downe formerly to Hull : Sir Ed. Ascough, Hacker, and the rest, came up and are sent down again with large instructions to assist and advise Sir Jo. Hotham, and to preserve the peace of the county by requiring the people not to obey any commission coming from His Majesty under the Great Seal or otherwise to levy men. Divors Lords are, since the Keeper, gone down to the King, viz., Salisbury, Clare, Bath, Barkshire, Peterborough, Northampton, with others; Savile, you know, is suspended the House this sessions for refusinge to come upon the Lords' summons. Sir Jo. Corbet hath instructions to go down to Chester to see the regiments there and companies ship'd away, to informe what backwardnesse hath been in them. My Lord of Bristow's speech I have sent you, the last declaration of both Houses, the King's message and proclamation that came yesterday, with the votes and orders of both Houses. The Lords pass'd on Saturday 14 propositions to bee made to the Kinge, which wee have agreed to in our House; they are framed and collected out of the former evills and remedyes which were voted at Grocers' Hall. It is referred to a Committee to draw some propositions on the King's behalf, as these are on this subjects, to offer to him; and those shall bee forthwith presented to him, with a humble petition to return to his Parliament. If the King grant these, they are in great hopes of accommodation, and I think will bee willing, after they have set the businesse of Ireland in a good way, to dissolve the Parliament; otherwise things must go on as they begin.

Fol. 22. 1655, March 6. Francis Newport to Mr. John Langlye at Trentham. Meeting with this enclosed,* I have sent it you to shew my freind, that he may see what scandalous things are hatched notwithstanding the great care and prudence shown by His Highness and the Council for the discovery of all disaffected spirits and the disappointment of their practices ; yet the author of this libellous paper is conceived to bee a person of more bitterness towards His Highness and the Government then any of that party who now bear the great loade of that crime; that is Mr. Harry Nevill, formerly one of the Councel, whom His Highness may do well to make an example to all that shall dare to speak such bold untruths. News here is but little, save that there is like to be great disorders in our fleet, which it's fear'd will much retard the present expedition. I beleeve you hear that Vice Admirall Lawson, a man of great influence upon the mariners in generall, hath layd down his commission, and some other captaines have followed his example, which is soe much taken to heart by the rest that General Desborough and Col. Kelsey are gone down in great haste to compose the disorders that are among the seamen, which wee hope they will effect. Yet in these perplexityes and troubles the magnanimity of His Highness cannot bee sufficiently set forth, who, hearing that the Dutch had sold 40 sail of ship, to the Spaniard, sent for their embassadors lately to him, and bad them tell their masters that he thought he had sufficientlye stop'd their mouthes lately, but now hee saw nothing would serv their turne but beating out their teeth ; and about three days since they coming to him again to excuse the business to him, hee told them that it was indifferent to him whether he fought with one or both of them, meaning the Dutch and Spaniard. It may be you have heard by this of the misfortune His Highness had the other day; his coach and six horses coming over the water in the ferry boat in Lambeth, the boat sunk and the coach and three of the horses were drown'd; unhappy people make idle observations upon it, and say my Lord of Canterbury's coach and horses were drown'd in the same place a little before he

* There is nothing now enclosed.

was sent to the Tower; but no doubt there is a speciall Providence that guards His Highness and uppholds his authority. The most news is that it is current upon the Exchange that the Spanish Fleet, nere 60 sayle, are gone for the West Indyes, where they are too likely to devour all those few that are left in Jamaica; we have 30 sayl of our best ships there; God send they escape the Spanish power, which is like to find them and their men but very ill provided to fight, &c.

Fol. 23. 1657, Nov. 5, London. Fra. Newport to his uncle Sir R. Leveson, at Trentham.—The greatest discourse of the towne for this term hath bin the issue betweene Mr. Colt and young Dutton for Mr. Dutton's estate of Sherborne, which was try'd yesterday in the Upper Bench and held the Court from 9 in the morn till 9 at night, much gentry beinge present of both sexes; but it went with Mr. Dutton. The Lord Viscount Falconbridge is to marry the Protector's second daughter. The Swedes we heare are beaten every where, though the bookes confess it not; the drums beat here for volunteers for France and Swedeland, but with little successe. At the last businesse before Mardike, which the bookes tell you of, wee heare the King of Scots' horse's bridle was shot out of his mouth, and the Marquis of Ormond's horse killd under him. Wee have sent over severall ships of materialls for fortification thither, as of lime, brick, pallizades, &c., with many hundreds of beefes, and intend to keepe it, though at the dearest rate, &c.

Fol. 24. 1657, Nov. 14, London. The same to the same.—The freshest newse here is that the Dutch have taken 11 ships of the Portugal Braseel fleet which they have long waited for, having for a good while block'd up Lisbon with their own, and have declared war against Portugal. It is believed we shall not long keep fair with that nation falling foul upon our allies (however they have provocation enough), and for further probability of that we have for certain brought in a Dutch East India ship to Plimouth, which is there stay'd. This growing difference will not perhaps make more for the King of Scots' interest then the desperate sickness of the Prince of Conde makes against it. The Swedes begin look up againe with a late victory they have had against the Danes, havinge taken Frederick Ode, a strong hold upon the sound, by storm, and put 1,000 men in it to the sword; wee have a story of their late Queene, who is now at Fontainebleau, that havinge intercepted a letter of an Italian marquesse her domestique sent for Italy, wherein hee raillyed his mistresse, and related some of her extravagancyes, shee sent for him, and havinge given him but an houres time for confession caus'd two or three of [her] laqueyes to run him through. The Lord Fairfax cannot yet obtaine of His Highnesse the liberty of his now son, the Duke of Buckingham, to reside within his dominions, hee telling him that it is not in his power to grant it, and 'tis beleeved it will be remitted to Parliament. Great feasting and jollity hath been at Court this weeke for the nuptialls, which is all the novelles and discourse of this place at present, &c.

Fol. 30. 1660, April 5, London. Francis Newport to his uncle Sir Richard Leveson, at Trentham.—The city was almost all of a blaze on Tuesday night with bonefires. The next week there go six Lords and 12 Commoners from the Houses with their answers to the King, which, I am told, are full of dutyfull and humble acknowledgments: the city send some of themselves likewise with their answer; the Lords appointed are Oxford, Warwick, Middlesex, Barkely, Brooke, and Hereford:—the Commoners are not yet named, they are chosen by ballotting, which is not yet perfected; the Houses send the King 50,000l. which the city have sent them upon the public fayth, and the city send him 10,000l. in gold. To-day I hear the city have voted in their Common Councill to send the Queen 5,000l., the Duke of Yorke and Glocester and the young princess 1,000l. apiece. All the young lords are admitted into the Lords House to those of 48 which sat first, and they have since sent for the lords that were at Oxford, as Hertford, Dorchester, Linsey, &c.; upon which some of those lords that were created since the Great Seal went from London, went to the General and told him their right to sit as well as any others, as Lexington, Bellasis, &c.; the General told them he would not obstruct their sitting and confessed their right; but the King hath signifyed his pleasure for theirs and the Oxford lords' forbearance for a while, lest it give occasion to question the election of the unqualifyed members in the Lower House; so that there is none of the King's party lords sit that I know as yet but Barkshire, who does it only to secure him from his creditors. There are great numbers of the gentry dayly going over to the King, and 'tis

believed there will [be] little less than a thousand go over with the Lords next week, and as many out of the city; 'tis thought they will find but bad quarters for so many at Breda. The Houses send the King five Bills to pass before his coming; first, a previous Bill to make this a Parliament, to make all the other Acts good; though I see not how that will hold water; for if they be not two lawful Houses already (which they are not), the King's assent to Bills passed by them cannot make them real Acts of Parliament, but that they will stand to the venture of, being all that can be done at present. The other Bills are, 1, for confirmation of sales, till the Parliament take further order, or make satisfaction to the purchasers; out of which Act are excepted the estates of my Lord Craven, Sir John Stowell, and Alderman Bunce: the Duke of Bucks endeavours to get his excepted, but 'tis questioned whether it will be. 2. An Act of generall pardon and oblivion. 3. For tender consciences. 4. For the soldiers' arrears. The officers have all subscribed their obedience to, and acquiescence in, the determinations of the Parliament. I spoke with a gentleman yesterday as he came just from the King, and came by the fleet, who have all declared for the King, set up his colours upon all the ships, and shot off above a thousand cannon in token of their joy, while he was there. The Bills before-mentioned other Lord and Commons are to go with a week after the other, who are to attend his Majesty over; whose coming nothing now in the eye of human reason can hinder, if God permit. It is said Sir Harry Mildmay, Scot, Needham the news wryter, and some others are run away. Luke Robinson was the first man in the House, after the King's letter and declaration were read, that declared his assent for his coming in, the confessed he had been of a contrary judgment, and divers others such as he are mighty Cavaliers now; who say, as the boggars did in the play to their King, Who is not glad that thou art chosen King now thou art King? Great preparations are making for the King's reception, and everybody makes themselves as fine as they can; 'tis said most of the nobility and gentry of the nation will go to Dover to meete him. The Lords sent a message on Thursday to the Commons to acquaint them that they had added Lord Manchester to the Commissioners of the Great Seal, and desired their concurrence; but 'twas not assented to, but to-day I hear 'tis carryed in the affirmative. 'Tis believed to have a tendency to the removal of the Lord Chancelor Hyde; what effect it will have when the King comes will be seen. I believe there will little occur more worth your notice till the King comes, which may peradventure bee about three weekes hence, if not sooner, &c.

Fol. 46. 1660, May 12, London—The same to same.— The Lords and Commons went yesterday towards his Majesty, and with the desire of the Houses to hasten his coming when he could. It is expected he will be here this next week, but what day is not yet known, neyther how he will come, whether through London, or privately by water for avoyding of danger to his person. There were two sea captains brought up in chaines last night (they call them Clarke and Sparke) who would have seduc'd some seamen and engag'd them to have fir'd the ship the King was to have come in. The Lords bring no Bills over with them to the King to pass, save onely that for making this a Parliament; they have voted the Duke of Yorke 5,000l. more. Lest you should not yet have been told the story of Sir Arthur Harley, I shall stuff this letter with it. He told the Generall not long ago that if the King came in he should be hang'd; the Generall told him he would secure him for 2d.; not many dayes since he sends the Generall a letter minding him of his promise, and encloses 2d. in it. The General gives his wife the letter to answer, who sends Sir Arthur the King's declaration, and bids him take hold of that. The citizens never had such trading in their lives, their shops are fuller of customers than commodities.

Fol. 46. 1660, May 15, London.—The same to the same.—All that is remarkable which the House of Commons hath done since I wryt to you last is, that in the Act of Oblivion they have agreed upon seven in number to be excepted for life and estate, but have not yet nam'd them; others there are who were of the King's judges also, but perhaps did not sign the warrant for his execution, who will be excepted only as to their estates. All the King's judges who are living are order'd to bee seized upon, but I believe they will catch but few of them; yet some are in hold already; our kinsman Sir Henry Mildmay is gone. There is extant a very fair journal of every day's proceedings, both preparatory and at the time, of the King's trial, and of every person that was present, which was ordered at that time to be kept among the Parliament rolls and in all the Courts of Westminster, for the honor of those that were actors in it, but it will hardly prove so. They intend, as I heare, to attaint the blood of those that are gone before their fellows, and have this day voted a confiscation of the estate of Bradshaw and Ireton. The old Speaker's son, Jack Lenthall (dubb'd by Oliver), speaking to the Act of Oblivion on Saturday, and intending to throw a bone of contention amongst them, told them he saw no difference between those that ever had drawn a sword against the King, and those that more immediately acted towards his death, and did believe none would be made; which gave the House so great distaste that he was immediately call'd to the bar upon his knees, where he enter'd his peccavi. The King is expected speedily, but the time we yet know not; he is come down to the Hague, and the fleet (order'd to attend his command) gone to Skivelin. 'Tis expected he comes now with the first wind; but whether that will bring him eyther to Dover, Margeat, and Harwich, as some suppose, is not known; so that those that would set forwards to meet him know not which way yet to go nor perhaps will not till they hear where he is landed. The Lords, &c. that were sent to him I cannot hear yet are gone from Dover; they took no order about their shipping before they went hence, and the fleet was gone before they came, only some three ships left behind; nayther doe they know (as 'tis believed) where to repair to his Majesty sooner than in England if the wind serve him which is now against him, &c. P.S. An Ostender has taken a ship wherein many of the Lords' fair clothes were.

Fol. 31. 1660, May 22, London. The same to the same.—The General received advertisement last night from Dr. Clerges (now knighted) that the King intended to embarque as yesterday, and that if possible hee would come to Dover; whereupon to-morrow morning the General goes towards that place, and all the company, which is like to bee very numerous. My Lord Northampton hath gathered a troop of gentlemen and others to that purpose, as likewise the Earl of Lytchfeild, the Duke of Buckingham, the Earl of Lyncoln, my Lord Mordant, and Randolph Egerton, besides Robinson and Browne of the City. Wee had had a troup of our freinds and countrymen, but that many of our countrymen came not to town 'till Sunday morning, and in this short time they could not get themselves ready. The road is like to be much pestred with multitudes of people. There hath been some dispute between the Lords and Commons about the privilege of their Houses; the Commons voted the persons and estates of the King's judges to be seized, and sent the vote up to the Lords for their concurrence. The Lords voted the same thing, but did not join with them, but expressed in their vote that upon the complaint of the Commons they did it; which the House of Commons resent as a breach of their priviledge, though it be thought their vote to that purpose be a greater encroaching upon the jurisdiction of the Lords, who have the sole power of judicature. This day they had a conference about it, and are to meet again this afternoon; but I shall not be able to tell you at this time what the issue of it will be. We have newse out of Ireland that the old rebels begin to stir there, and have put some of the English out of possession, but no question our conjunction here will soon reduce them if they proceed. There is much complaint among the Lords that they hear of many blanke patents granted by the King of late years for honors which have layen dormant a good while, and now are sold for small sums to persons unworthy of them, such as Sir Richard Minshaw and others, which, as they hear, amount to a great number, and will be to the dishonor and the pesteringe, if not to the destruction of the Lords House; the consideration of which hath made many of us forbeare to make claims to our right of entrance there, lest we should lead the way to all the rest, some of whom I believe we never heard of, nor the King neyther; and this 'till the King's wisedome shall direct some moderation in the business. To this end and some other there hath been a Bill brought into the House of Commons to make void all grants pass'd by eyther of the Great Seales since the first seal went from London in 1642, both of offices and honors; but there will be a proviso in it, that it shall not extend to certain persons within such a qualification, which I am assured by those that brought in the Bill will not touch those in my capacity: the Bill hath been twice read and committed. Divers have bin committed for treasonable words against the King. To-morrow we make for Rochester, &c.— P.S. Desborough is brought in to-night, and the boys hoot him along the streets, Phanatique, Phanatique. Mr. Henningham (Heveningham) has petitioned, and says hee was misled by Bradshaw, if that will serve his turn. You know Sir H. Mildmay is taken.

Fol. 32. 1660, May 29, London. The same to the same.—I cannot forbeare telling you the joyfull news of the King's safe arrival at Whitehall, whither he came this evening, attended with such bodies of horse of the gentry and nobillity as I beleeve London scarce ever saw. The citizens played their parts very well too, but the particulars I must leave to the News Book to informe you of, it being too late now to undertake that taske. Monk and Montagu were made Knights of the Garter at Canterburye, the Duke of Yorke doing the former the honor to tye his garter about his leg; the latter had his sent him to sea. I went to see Sir Harry Mildmay in Dover Castle, who denyes to have any share in the judgment of the King, and desires me to try for his pardon; he is or pretends to bee very ill of the stone.— The King met the two Houses to-night in the Banqneting House, where he told Mr. Speaker in short that ho should be ready to grant any thing that should be desired of him for confirmation of the laws and settlement of the true religion, &c. P.S. The Hollanders entertained the King at the Hague most magnificently, and presented him in money, plate, and a bed, to the value of 60,000l., and are very apprehensive of a breach with us, which is apparent by all their discourse, as they say that come from there.

Fol. 45. 1660, June 16. The same to the same.—Harvest draws on, and such ministers who enjoy your impropriations may be perhaps forward enough to persuade with their parishioners to pay them their composition-rents before hand, that is before harvest; to prevent which I thought it fit for me to advertise you that all your impropriations settled on the Church will certainly revert to you, and that you may do well to give notice to all that formerly paid you tithes not to pay any, or any composition money in lieu of them, to the incumbent ministers, and at harvest to receive them yourself, as I mean to do with mine. No trustee will sue you, and the incumbent cannot. The King is making lords lieutenants in all counties. The House of Commons is still upon the Act of Indemnity, and every day except some and acquit others who are brought upon the stage. The House of Lords, their chiefest businesses are receiving of several petitions preventing destruction and sale of woods in the King's forests and chaces, and asserting their own privileges in several causes. They have been troubled to-day with Purbeck Villiers, whom they sent for for treasonable words and blasphemous speeches; but he denied his honour, and claimed the privilege of a member of the House of Commons, so he remains in the custody of the black rod. The King is upon the water almost every night.

Fol. 32. 1660, June 26, London. The same to the same.—There is no course taken yet concerning impropriations passed away by compounders . . . . P.S. Andrew is one of the esquires of the body.

Fol. 33. 1660, Aug. 26, Eyton. The same to the same. —Says he has presented Sir Richard's name to the King for one of the deputy lieutenants for Shropshire.

Fol. 27. 1660, Jan. 26, London. From the same to the same.—Here is inclosed a letter from the Councell to my Lo. Brooke (the like being; sent to other Lord lieutenants). He being with his mistress in Dorsetshire, I have sent it to you to be communicated to the rest of the deputy lieutenants of that county; I opened it least you should make scruple of it. I think I gave you notice formerly of a regiment of horse designed here to be raised under the command of the Earl of Oxford, who will now speedily be marryed to my lady Anne Digby; as also a regiment of foot under the command of my brother Russell; the charge of these with the life guards hath begot a resolution of disbanding all the inland garrisons, and amongst the rest ours at Shrewsbury and Ludlow, even in this time which their letters as you see speak to be full of danger, which will speedily be done, and which therefore requires the more circumspection from the deputy lieutenants to provide for the common safety. I have sent to those nearest hand in Shropshire that the next time you come over to Lillshall they wait upon you there to confer of matters. My Lord Chancellor's eldest sonne was married this week to my Lord Capell's sister that now is. The fair princess at Portsmouth is fallen ill again of a looseness, and we hear somewhat dangerously; Dr. Bates is gone down to her; she hath many prayers here for her recovery. I suppose you know my lord of Bristol hath bought Wimbleton of the Crown, &c.

Fol. 28. 1660, Feb. 7, London. The same to the same.—The chiefest errand of this is to acquaint you of you have not heard it already) that Sir Fra. Lawley and Sir Richard Ottley are thought tuo two fittest persons to be knights of the shire for Shropshire, and desire your assistance for them. The writs will issue speedily. My Lord of Bristol is going over to-morrow upon private business of the King's, but whither is not known with us ; tis supposed to view some lady ; but whether to Portugal, Germany, or Sweden, we are left to guess. The King dined yesterday at Bedford House. The coronation holds certaine now the 23rd April ; we have received our letters for our attendance.—The Earl of Anglesey is dead of the small pox.—P.S. The King hath given command for a new gallowes at Tiburne, and the three supporters of that triangle are to be Cromwell, Bradshaw, and Ireton.

Fol. 29. 1660, March 23. From the same to the same. —You heard of the stop of my Lord of Bristoll's journey to Parma, and of the management of some part of that affair, as is conceived, without the Chancelor's privity (by the Spanish Embassador, Lord of Bristoll, and Lord Aubigny), which is thought to be the occasion of it ; when we have a Queene, Mr. Montague (Lord Montague of Northamptshire eldest sonne) is to be master of her horse, Earl of Chesterfield her chamberlain, Mr. Harvey her treasurer. 'Tis I suppose no news to you that the Dutchess of Yorke is with child. Most of the discourse here now is about the coronation ; tis not yet declard who shall'be High Constable that day, but most thinke my Lord of Ormond. Harry Howard (Norfolk) expects and is like to be Earl Marshall. Tis no news to you that Lord Valentia is to be Earl of Anglesea, and Lord Brudenell Earl of Cardigan. The City their choice of Parliament men does not at all please the Court ; four rigid presbiterians, Fowke, Jones, Love, and Tomson. The Florentine Embassador had audience on Thursday, &c.

Fol. 35. 1661, April 2, London. The same to the same.—All the accompt can be given from this place at present is that the Portugal match is conceived to stand fairest of any ; and yet 'tis arriv'd that the Dutch have taken Goar in the East Indyes from the Portugee, which should have been part of the portion ; if the Spaniard take their country from them too, we marry their whole nation and must keep them. The Duke of Parma's brother is here, but private, and hath taken his leave, as hath the Florentine this afternoon. My Lord Steward is made Duke of Ormond, and four new Knights of the Garter we are to have, the Duke of Ritchmond, my Lord High Chamberlain, Lord Chamberlain of the Household, and the Earle of Strafford (as some reward for his father's sufferings). Tis believed the City election will be questioned by the Committee of privileges, as soon as the Parliaments sits. *

Fol. 36. 1661, April 30. The same to the same. —The only thing that engageth men's thoughts and discourse is the King's marriage, concerning which the Council sat yesterday morn ; but all the clarks were commanded out, and all the councillore enjoyned secrecy by the King himself, both before and after council ; but tis generally believed tis concluded for Portugall. The Duke of Cambridge is very ill and much feared. You may perhaps receive some intelligence of the taking of Ludlow, Okey, and Hewsen ; but it is not so. The books will describe the solemnitye of the coronation to you better than my pen.

Fol. 37. 1661, May 4. The same to the same.—The business of the match stands as it did then, generally believed for Portugall, but nothing declar'd. My Lord of Bristoll is expected dayly. We hear of some insurrection in Sicily occasioned by the Gabells, and another (though now over) in Naples upon the King of Spain's inquisitors coming thither, which the people would not endure, not so long as 'till the Vice Roy might send into Spain to know the King's pleasure; upon which the inquisitors were enforced to take their journey to Rome. The Dutch fleet is gone into the East Indyes, where they are likely to dispossess the Portugee of all, which will make our match the less considerable. A great dispute like to be about the Bishops coming into the Lords House ; though there be scarce room now for the lay Lords, &c.

Fol. 37. 1661, May 7, London. The same to the same.—The Duke of Cambridge dyed on Sunday in the afternoon, and was buryed yesternight without any solemnity ; noe mourninge in the Court for him (you may take it which way you will). To-day all the City Militia (trained bands and auxiliaries) mustered in Hyde Parke, six regiments of each and a regiment of horse ; the King was there and threw his collection among the people ; gammons of bacon, neates' tongues, and sweetmeats, which much delighted them. My Lord of Bristol is expected here to-night ; some think the Portugall match is yet doubtfull, but the learned agree it concluded ; to-morrow 'twill be likely knowne, at least tis expected that my Lord Chancelor will tell us some-

what of it in his speech to both Houses. If any thing may be concluded from raillery, there is this ground for it, that Sir Harry Bennet being lately come out of Spaine (one that the King hath a great kindness for), where he was an agent for the King, and promoted what he could the Spanish designs for the King's match, wearing his beard after the Spanish mode, the King jestingly told him he would cut of his Spanish beard with a paire of Portugal scissors. The King and Lords ride to-morrow from Whitehall to Westminster Abbey in Parliament robes.

Fol. 38. 1661, May 28, London.—The same to the same.—There is nothing yet done concerninge the impropriations; but there is a Bill depending in the House of Commons for the restoring of them to us, which hath been once read ; another for restoringe Sir Jo. Packington to his land about Alesburye which was extorted from him in the same way ; whether these Bills will pass, no man I suppose can yet say, but it is no ill sign when they are not thrown out at the first reading. . . . . The last occurence here was the making my Lord Ashley (that is Sir Anthony Ashly Cooper) Chancellor of the Exchequer; and since that, my Lord of Peterborough, Governor of Tangier, that Port in the mouth of the Straits, and on the coast of Barbary, which the Portugee put into the King of England's hands, to which place when he goes he is to carry 2 or 3,000 men. This day the Quakers desired to be heard in the Lords House, and after four or five of them had talk'd one after another after their usual manner, they were commanded to withdraw, and so far were they from prevailing in their desires of toleration of them in their way, that the Lords have made a committee to consider of the best way either of converting or suppressing them. . . . P.S. No body yet designed to go to fetch the Queen ; the Duke of Ormond goes not, and to avoid charge 'tis believed no other person of quality, besides the Vice-Admiral Lord of Sandwich.

Letters from Andrew Newport to Sir Richard Leveson.

Fol. 40. 1647, Jan. 25, London. Andrew Newport to Sir R. Leveson, at Trentham.—He encloses a pamphlet, of what moment he knows not, otherwise than as its censure of the army is somewhat severe, and may assure us that their pretences for liberty and law are but the delusory means to hedge in their own interests. 'Tis said that Jenkins and Sir John Stowell shall come to tryal on Thursday next. The rumour of the Prince's being in Holland last week was not true ; letters of late come out of France and assure us of his being at St. Germins. The letter he sent to the Parliament is by them endeavour'd to be conceal'd, but I am told it will be privately printed ; if it be, you shall not fail of one of the copies.—P.S. The impeached Lords are discharged from the Black Rod and sit in the House again.

Fol. 41. 1647, Feb. 1, London. The same to the same. —Though the House of Lords discharg'd their seven members from the Black Rod, and gave them liberty to sit again in the House, yet the Commons could not brook it, but have impeached the Lord Willoughby of Parham of high treason, and are preparing a pill for the rest too; Sir John Maynard of their own House lyes under the same impeachment also. It is ordered (but I think only by the committee of safety, not by the House because it should be less publick), that if the King desire Mr. Ashburnham should come to him, he should have liberty to wait upon him, but no other. The King lately sent to the Duke of York, bidding him not too much resent his confinement, himself patiently suffering it. Many last week did and still do confidently report the Prince to be gone out of France, but I have a letter from Sir Ri. Browne (the King's agent) in Paris, that assures us he is still there. 'Tis in every man's mouth that the Scots will suddenly invade England; grounded upon the protestations of some of the commissioners themselves. There is a very strict search made almost every night for those of the King's party that, contrary to the ordinance, stay in town, and money given to many to discover those that talk against the present proceedings, which stipend some that have been of the King's party most treacherously receive. Arthur Trevor lately made a supper, and amongst others invited Generall Mitton, who discover'd some discourse of Arthur Trevor's to some in authority, and caused him [to be] imprison'd, in which condition he now is. General Langhorne, lately going to Sir Thomas Fair. to take his leave, was check'd by him as a dangerous man, and is now upon bait in town. Some castles were delivered to Langhorne in South Wales, upon condition that the gentlemen in them should not be proceeded against as delinquents; the articles it seems are broken; the dishonour of which Langhorne supposes to reflect upon him, and having moved for performance of articles, but not heard, 'twas feared he might countenance those gentlemen if they should make head.

Fol. 23. 1656, May 31. [The same] to the same.—The honour of your concern for my enlargement does more endear it, and I should be very glad to know how I might employ that liberty I have in your service; as it is yet, I cannot do it so much as in giving you the ordidary occurrences of the town; hearing no more of them myself than is brought to me in a visit, by which means I cannot promise you the truth of any of it. They say our fleet did lately attempt the landing of some men at Cuba, and were beaten off with much loss. Our merchants here have lost this week near 20 ships (to the Dunkirkers), besides a Dutchman of 40 guns that was their convoy: 'tis sayd there is at Dunkirk neer 70 men of war of all sorts, but their chief employment is stealing. The French have cut off 3 Lorraine regiments wholly as they were going to Quenois. There is a discourse of an intention to sell all decimations at ten years' purchase to the owners, and in case of refusal to have the 10th part sever'd and sold to any other purchaser. Great talk of a Parliament intended, and of an enlargement of the Major Generalls' commission, but in what particular I hear not. All the Major Generals have often sat close at White-hall; Worsley is very sick, and many think will not recover. Thus, sir, I have layd my bagatelles before you; you may please to pardon the little worth of them as coming from one that lives not on the Change, but the suburbs and shires, not out of his shop neither. P.S. Young Sir Charles Sedley is at this time very sick of a feaver and the meazells, of which Sir William dyed.

Fol. 42. 1657, Dec. 3, London. The same to the same.—The Spanish foot are all drawn down about Dunkirk, which makes those in Mardike expect an assault, but by the officers' letters thence they seem not at all to distrust either their courage or force to defend it: they are very well mann'd, and since the arrival of store of deal boards hence, with which they have 'made them huts, in good health, which they formerly wanted by being in great numbers and measure exposed to the weather. The report here represents the Swedes to be in no good condition. The Dutch Embassadour, as you have heard, is gone home, but I can assure you upon no quarrel as yet between the two States, merely upon an account of his own. Some prizes (16 or 17 ships) that the Dutch lately took from the Portugais were by foul weather in their way to Holland drove into an English port, upon which the Portugall agent here caus'd them to be arrested, but a merchant told me lately they were again released to the Dutch. Sir Hugh Cholmely is dead, &c.

1657, Dec. 8, London. The same to the same.—This week's intelligence begins with the taking up of several Romish priests, eight in number, of whom there was such particular notice given that in each House they were call'd for by their names. In one house the servant mayde offer'd the priest the protection of her bed, and her company in it, that they might pass for a married couple; but the poor man chose rather to hazard his liberty than the scandal, and was taken. His Highness hath made lately several officers of his House, Sir Gilbert Pickering Chamberlain, Col. Phillip Jones Mr. Controwler, Mr. Waterhouse Master of the Greencloth. And 'tis said generally that he hath made Whittlocke Baron of Henley. Jack Corbett our countryman hath married his son to a niece of Mrs. Harris's, one Mr. Cambell's daughter, and, as he says himself, the match will be, first and last, worth 15,000*l.*, &c.

Fol. 43. 1657, Dec. 12, London.—The same to the same.—Two days since I met with a list of the persons appointed to sit in the Upper House, which I have herein sent you, but I believe there are some names wanting, these not making up the number of seventy, and if I find it to be so I shall send you the list corrected. The news of the sad miscarriage of Sir Jo. Reynolds, Colonel White, and some others, is come to towne lately, who coming from Mardike for England, and for the greater expedition adventuring upon a small boat to transport them, were cast away upon the Goodwin Sands; their trunks were afterwards found upon the shore. P.S. Lord Bellasis was lately to wait upon Lady Shirley as a suitor.

Fol. 25. 1657, Dec. 19, London.—[The same] to the same.—There occurs little to acquaint you with but our great expectations from Mardike, where there are great preparations making both for the assault and defence, the French having sent several of their guards to assist in its defence, and the Boores in Flanders undertaken to raise 8,000 men for the reducing it, and the clergy of Bruges have advanced 400,000 florins for the service. Prince Rupert hath the command of 8,000 men under the King of Hungary, who, they say, will owe his Empirate to his sword, in which the Duke of Sax &c. will assist him; the ecclesiastical electors are all of the French faction. The Swede loses, and is said to be very low reduc'd within his own contributions; 600 men that went hence to his assistance are drove back hither by contrary winds. New plots are said to be discoursed, and new confinements talk'd of. God bless us from a share in them, &c. P.S. Mr. Palmer that married Lord Westmoreland's daughter is lately dead.

Fol. 43. 1657, Dec. 26, London.—The same to the same.—After stating that he was suspected, and found he should not be long at liberty, he says:—Two nights since all the gentlemen at the comb-makers' ordinary were seized and sent to St. James's, prisoners. Yesterday several of the congregations that met for the solemnizing the day of the nativity were beset with soldiers, and most of the young men, not being housekeepers, retained prisoners; and this day divers gentlemen more were fetched out of the Tenniscourt and sent to St. James' also; and the general discourse of the towne is concerning a plot, and the Scottish King's intention to attempt something from abroad, so that how long my present liberty will continue, or why I should believe the stars more propitious to me then the rest, I know not, nor very well how to dispose of myself if they do not do it to my hand.

Fol. 39. [1658] June 1, Tuesday.—[The same] to the same.—This day Dr. Huatt and Mr. Mordaunt were brought before the High Court of Justice; the former us'd many arguments against the jurisdiction of the Court from the Act itself by which they sit, which the Court over-ruled, and required him several times to plead, which he did not, and soe was ordered to be taken away. After him Mr. Mordaunt was brought to the bar, who urg'd the same arguments against the jurisdiction of the Court as the former, but would not be allow'd of any force more to him than to the other; at last he pleaded not guilty, and two brothers of Sussex (Mr. Stapelys) witnessed that Mr. Mordaunt encouraged them to serve Charles Stuart, who, he said, would suddenly invade England, and that Charles Stuart had writ him word so; but he sayd this to them apart. The examination and confession of another (who hath since made his escape) to the same purpose was read upon the oath of Mr. Scobell that it was so. It remains in the breasts of the Court what shall become of them; no sentence or acquittal hath yet pass'd, and the Court is adjourned to to-morrow. The French have perfected their line before Dunkirk, and are making their approaches; they have 35,000 men. The Spaniard lies within two leagues of them at Fernes with 14,000, &c.

Fol. 25. 1658, June 3. [The same] to the same.—My last gave you an account of the tryals of Dr. Huatt and Mr. Mordaunt. Yesterday they and Sir Henry Slingsby were called together to the bar: the Doctor and Sir Henry Slingsby were both sentenced to die (to be drawn, hang'd, and quartered); Mr. Mordaunt was pronounced not guilty. The Court spent almost the whole day in the Painted Chamber in consultation upon these three persons; Mr. Mordaunt was saved but by one voice (the President's). The Court is now adjourned till this day seavennight. There was news upon the Exchange to-day that the Emperour was chosen. The siege at Dunkirke continues; there was a great sally made out of the town lately, and they beat up some of the French guards, but the English had the honour to force them in again. Lord Falconbridge is expected here again on Saturday.

P.S. My Lady Huatt preferr'd a petition yesterday to the Court in the Painted Chamber that her husband might be permitted to plead, but when he came to the bar they would not allow him to speak a word.

Fol. 44. [16$\frac{59}{60}$], Jan 10. The same to the same.—We are, God be praised, now freed from some fears we lately laboured under, my Lord Fairfaxe having layd down his arms upon the return of the Northern Army to their obedience, and Monke hath written the House word that Fairfax did nothing in the late rising without his privity and consent, which hath removed the jealousy he lately lay under for that action. Yesterday Sir Harry Vane was turned out of the House for acting against the Parliament during the late interruption, and banish'd the town. Fleetwood, Whittlock, Galoway,

Sydenham, Warreston, and some others will suddenly have the same measure. The House yesterday voted a bill to be brought in for confiscation of the estates of those persons that were engag'd with Sir George Booth, and gave the Council of State power to remand what prisoners they please that were released by the Committee of safety; the oath of abjuration is like to be laid aside. The nine officers that were voted out of the army by the Parliament when they sate last are banish'd the town to the remotest dwellings they have, and the inferiour officers also lately cashiered. Col. Morley is Lieutenant of the Tower. Nudigate will be Chief Justice; Withrington, Fountaine, and Terrill Commissioners of the Seal. Monke is to march hither with what forces he conveniently can, and the Northern Army lately under Lambert to go into Scotland under Morgan.

Fol. 44. [164⁵⁄₉] Jan. 28.—The same to the same.—The stream of Westminster Hall at last runs one way, and the opinions, so various of late concerning General Monke, are now reconciled, for he hath so clearly manifested himself (by letter) a faithfull servant to the Parliament as it now sits, that no further doubt remains of him. This night he layes at St. Albans, and next week we expect him here. We hear, notwithstanding, of addresses preparing in several counties for restitution of the secluded members, but the Parliament hath sent young Sir Robert Pye to the Tower for bringing one of that nature from Berkshire, and this lot of his we hope will make the rest take heed what they do. A troop of horse and a company of foot last night broke open the house of a draper in Paul's Churchyard, and carried away 4,000l. to Whitehall, for which they would shew the draper (a common councilman) no order. To-day the man was attending at the Parliament door, but what satisfaction he hath I do not yet hear. There is a tax of 100,000l. per month coming out.

Fol. 44. [164⁵⁄₉] Jan. 31. The same to the same.—On Saturday the Lord Richardson, Sir Her. Townsend, and Sir Jo. Hubbard delivered the declaration of Norfolk for the re-admitting of the secluded members and against the paying taxes, their representatives not sitting; they were threatn'd the Tower but not sent thither, and yesterday they presented the same to General Monke at St. Albans, who gave them no very good reception. Buckinghamshire, Northamptonshire, and most other countyes are either doing the same or have done it already. Yet the Parliament thinks fit onely to fill their House by new elections; to-day they consider'd the qualifications for them, and have voted that no cavalier, no secluded member, nor any that sate in Richard's Parliament (except such as now sit) shall be admitted. Generall Monke will not be here before Friday; on Thursday his rendezvous is at Barnott. The soldiers now in town are marching out to give place to General Monke's men.

Fol. 44. 164⁵⁄₉, Feb. 5. The same to the same.—The House hath not agreed the qualifications for the new elect Parliament, though they come daily under consideration. On Thursday the foot here were in a great mutiny for want of pay, and being commanded out of town, would not stir out of Somerset House, though a regiment of General Monke's foot were drawn up before the gate, till they had received some pay, and then they marched away quietly, as all the rest of the army formerly here hath done into remote quarters, to give way to Monke's army. Monke came in yesterday with about 6,000 men, but this malignant place shewed no great content at his entrance.

Fol. 70. [1660], May 8th, London. The same to the same.—This day the King was proclaim'd at Westminster, Temple Bar, and the Old Exchange, both Houses of Parliament attending the ceremony from first to last; but next week 'tis believ'd he will land, and that both Houses will wait upon him at the sea side; for this day they voted he should be desired to come as soon as might be, and have appointed a committee to consider of the manner of his reception, and to gather his revenue. No bills will be offer'd him till his landing, because they will not have them look'd upon as conditions of his reception, and 'tis said both Houses will wait upon him at the sea side. All proceedings in courts of judicature are to be in the King's name from hence forward. I will not derogate from the merit of this by offering any more intelligence. God make us thankful for this.

Fol. 70. 1660, May 15th. The same to the same.—By the last account we have of the King, we hear he intended to be at the Hague last night, whence without any stay he would come for England. The English fleet

hath been at Skeveling, within two miles of the Hague, these two days, to attend His Majesty, and the General said to-day at dinner that he would take ship this day, and by God's blessing we do not doubt but to see him here on Saturday; to-morrow I think the company will go hence to wait upon him, I mean the gentry; the General 'tis said will meet him a days journey off with five regiments of horse. The whole transactions of the late King's trial and of the committees meeting at several times in order to it being drawn fair in a book, with intention to have them register'd in all the Courts of Record in Westminster, and in every county also, was lately amongst other papers taken from Scobell, and read in the House of Commons, by which they know precisely who were every time at the meeting of the Committee, who signed the warrant for execution, and who sate in the High Court at sentence. Yesterday the debate was how many should be excepted in the Bill of Indemnity, and agreed that of those which sate in judgment upon the King there should not die above the number of seven, of which they have not yet named any, but sent out warrants to apprehend all that sate. To-day Thurloe was impeach'd of high treason for something he did lately, and they sent to apprehend him, but I cannot yet tell whether they met with him or not.

Fol. 71. 1660, May 19th. The same to the same.—The contrary wind prevents the King's intention to bo suddenly here, otherwise by this time he had been here, and will be so as soon as that will permit. Mean time he is highly courted at the Hague, and presented by the Hollanders with great sums of money. One Moorland, a clerk under Thurloe, hath discover'd a great many intelligencers, for which the King lately knighted him. Sir R. Willis is in the van of them, and hath betrayed the King all along. An order is sent to all sheriffs to seize the estates, both real and personal, of all the King's judges. Sir Harry Mildmay was taken two days since at Rye, attempting to go beyond sea. The old lords are so troubled at the great company of new ones, some of mean quality and less fortune, that 'tis thought there will be an expedient found to exclude many of them. 'Tis said the Princess Royal will come over with the King. The Spaniards are much troubled the King is out of their quarters, intending, as is supposed, to have put some conditions upon him, but God be thanked, he comes over without any engagement to any foreign prince or state.

Fol. 76. [1660], May 29th. The same to the same.—I am but newly come from Court, though it be almost ten at night, after a dusty but very pleasant march in other respects. The King came to Whitehall to-night, where both Houses met him, to whom he gave most gracious answers as to the laws and religion. Monke is Master of the Horse also, Jeffry Palmer, Attorney, Sir Orlando Bridgeman Chief Justice of the Common Pleas. The greatest acclamations through the whol town that ever were seen.

(46b.) [1660], June 9.—The same to the same.—The King, by the advice of his Council, is settling the militia in all counties under Lords Lieutenants. The King having press'd the expediting of the Act of Indemnity, and the Houses haveing an intention to punish in some degree divers others besides those seven that were the late King's judges who are to dye, which would take up much time, they have resolv'd first to confiscate the estates of all that sate in the High Court of Justice upon the King, excepting 3 only, Hutchinson, Lassalls, and another; and they have excepted out of the Act 20 more not yet named, who are to be punish'd as shall be provided in another Act not yet made, by fines as is suppos'd, in which number I believe you will find Haslerigge, Vane, St. John, Glynne, Maynard, Ellis, and divers others that have been active since 48. The King went yesterday to Hampton Court early and return'd by 12 at noon; he had by the way a great fall off his horse, but God be thanked no hurt; in the afternoon the House waited upon him, to claim the benefits of his declaration for pardon, in the name of themselves and all the Commons of England, which prevents the taking out of particular pardons; but this still with exception to those persons that the House have excepted and shall except.

Fol. 74. [1660], June 12. The same to the same.—Since my last the House hath been employ'd wholly or principally upon naming those persons they intend shall not have the benefit of the Act of Indemnity, but of the 20 they except, there are but few named yet, the favour that some of them find in the House making the debates long. Yesterday the great debate was con-

5.

U

cerning the old Speaker, Lenthall, in whose favour the General spoke much ; but upon division of the House the opposers of Lenthall were the major part by 80 ; so he will receive no benefit by the Act. Sir Harry Vane was excepted likewise, and found but one (Noe) in the whole Howse to favour him. To-day they have excepted one Major-General Burton of Norfolke. Luke Robinson was expell'd the House yesterday. Sir Harry Mildmay is sent for from Dover. I think I told you in my last that the militia will be settled in the countyes under Lords Lieutenants. P.S. Thurloe hath been with the King privately, and with the Chancellor since. 'Tis said he will be (as he us'd to call it himselfe), Ingenious.

Fol. 74. 1660], June 16th.—The same to the same.— The weather is not so hot, but the debates in the House equal it in warmth ; several persons guilty enough to bring them within the exceptions finding friends enough to excuse them ; amongst which Serjeant Glyn yesterday found great favour, and was laid asyde after much dispute. One Blackwell, a rich man, the same day was excepted, and to-day Alderman Pack. Villiers, that married Sir John Danvers his daughter, was yesterday sent for by the Black Rod ; he is now a member of the Lower House ; but the Lords look upon him as Viscount Purbeck, and so take cognizance of him, to-day he was brought before the Lords, and by my Lord Monmouth was accused to have said in his hearing at my Lord's table, that it was a very commendable and just action to put the last King to death ; that if an executioner had been wanting, he would have been the person, &c. He desired to advise with counsel before he answer'd, and a copy of his charge. It was told him that as yet there was no more but an information and no charge ; but order is given to the Attorney and King's counsel to draw up a charge. In the mean time he is committed to the Black Rod. He was offer'd his seat as Viscount Purbeck when he came in, but he refus'd it, and said he had searched the Petty bag for a patent, and could find none.—My Lord Middlesex asked him (when he was withdrawn), whose son he was, because he renounc'd his peerage, he said he was son to the lady that married the Lord Purbeck; My brother is Lord Lieutenant of Shropshire. The King to night sups with the Lord Mayor; last night he supp'd with the Lord Chamberlain Manchester.

Fol. 47. 1660, June 20. The same to the same.—The King pressing the House of Commons continually to hasten the naming of the 20 persons they intended to except, yesterday the number was completed as you will find by the book. To-day the proclamation of pardon to all but those the Houses except was proclaimed by the Heraulds in several places. The House to-day gave the King tonnage and poundage, and a Parliament man now tells me that the Committee of Religion to-day voted that all ministers that were put out of their benefices merely for their affection to the King, and were not otherwise scandalous, should be restored to their respective cures. Bourdeaux the French Embassadour that was, had new credentials sent him to the King, but the King refus'd them, I suppose upon Bordeaux his own account, because he hath been so great an enemy to his Majesty. Lord Craven is made Governour of Shrewsbury by the Generall in whose disposal all garrisons are. Sir, I humbly beg the favour of your minding Mr. Doughty to send me the terrier he promis'd me for my Lord Suffolke, with whom the Duke of Yorke intends to hunt often next winter.

Fol. 47. 1660, June 26.—The same to the same.—According to your command I have attended Mr. Sneade. An address of the same nature with that you propos'd, hath been in discourse among your countrymen already, and this afternoon they meet again to resolve whether they shall proceed or not ; to-morrow I wait upon him again and by next post 'tis possible you may have the result. The Act of Idemnity I believe will be sent to the Lords from the Commons to-morrow for their concurrence ; 'tis variously discours'd whether the Lords will except more persons or not. Mr. Scott is taken in Flanders, and by this time is in Dunkirke ; he is turn'd a good subject already, if you'll beleive his letter sent hither to one he desir'd would be his friend. There are new discontents in the army, to remove which I know no better remedy then to persuade your neighbours to part freely with their money ; the presbyter is not well pleased neither, but I hope God that hath given us this beginning will perfect our happiness. There is a Dutch Embassadour coming over with very rich presents ; six sets of coach horses and six coaches very rich with them, two suits of hangings, each of 10,000l., a suit of gold plate, two of silver plate, and all the jewels of the Crown

that were pawn'd there. 'Tis believed by many that the tythes that were pass'd away in part of compositions at Goldsmyth's hall, will be restor'd ; many intend to petition for it when the time is proper ; and if you please to give me order and direction to have it, I will cause one put in for you ; in the mean time it may not be amisse to warn the tenants not to pay them where of late they have. Sir I am much obliged for your concern for me in the employment His Majesty hath put upon me ; but your information was too favourable ; the bed-chamber had 14 in it before the King came over, which number is six above the establishment, and the supernumeraryes 'tis said will be reduc'd ; I think there was scarce one place in the whole court void of any consideration when the King came ; besides that he was pleased to bestow upon me (as he tells me) as an earnest of his further favour, which is, Squire of the Body, a place of honour, but small advantage otherwise then by being certaine of haveing the King's ear once a day. The General's title is Duke d'Albemerle (a place in Normandy belonging to the Plantagenetta from whom he derives himself), Earl of Toddington or Torrington, Viscount Coldstream, and Baron of Potheridge (his house). Coldstream is the river in the north that lay between him and Lambert last year.

Fol. 48. 1660, June 30. The same to the same.—There was a motion made for a longer day for the King's judges to come in, and 'twas press'd with much earnestness by some, but it was rejected at last, and according to the Proclamation all of them that rendered not themselves within the 14 days therein limited are to forfeit life and estate. There was a form of thanksgiveing publish'd to be us'd on Thursay last, and in the front 'twas said, Publish'd by authority ; the Presbyterians in the House are scandalised at it, and have appointed a committee to examine the printer by what order he did it. Tho Presbyterians are very high upon the King's bestowing favours upon some of them by the General's recommendation. St. John (late Chief Justice) got a proviso brought into the House to-day in his own favour, but 'twas thrown out. I cannot yet give you an account of Mr. Sneade and the other gentlemen of your country ; Mr. Sneade went early out of the House this morning, so that I could not speak with him. Your picture is gone down by Mr. Slannier.

1660, July 5.—The same to the same.—I am just now returned from the great entertainment the City gave the King and both Houses at Guildhall, the King sat under a state at the upper end of the hall in the middle of the table, the Duke of York at the end on the right hand, and Duke of Gloucester on the left ; a degree lower (divided with a rail), were four tables, two on each side of the hall for the Lords, and a degree lower than that, six tables, three on each side for the Commons, the King's own music on one side of the hall in a little gallery, and opposite to them 24 viols and violins in another, and long galleries round the hall full of women ; after dinner there was some pastime by men habited like lawyers, soldiers, countrymen, &c., which took up the rest of the day. I should have told you first that the King went in his coach, his Pensioners going on foot before him, and querries by the coach side on foot also ; he had gone in an open chariot but that the rain prevented him, and this is the Landskippe of this days business. The Bill of Poll money is engrossing, and will suddenly be sent up to the Lords, that of Indemnity will not so soon be ready by reason of the multitude of provisoes that were brought in and not yet all debated. We have great complaints of the negligence of the young men of the Commons House who either by the Court or other entertainment of the town suffer themselves so to be called away from attending the House and committees that many votes are lost by that supineness. At length I have met with Mr. Sneade, but he had not the address about him, having put it into the hands of one of the King's servants who was so employed this day that I could not get a sight of it. P.S. Lord Culpeper is very sick and like to die.

Fol. 49. 1660. July 21. The same to the same.—Says he did not fail to perform his (Leveson's) commands concerning Lady Anne Holborne and communicated with Sir Richard Temple who would see them obeyed. —The business of the Lords this week hath been much upon hearing the complaints of those persons whose relations suffer'd by High Courts of Justice in Cromwell's time, and some by Commission of Oyer and Terminer, as those particularly of Mr. Penruddock's party in the West ; by such a Commission, Judge Windham condemn'd some, as which time he declar'd the taking up of arms against the supreme magistrate de facto, to be High Treason by the statute of 25 Edw. III. ; and being call'd before a Committee of

・i

Lords this week, did avow it still to be his opinion; he is since sent to the Tower; Lady Huett and Sir Henry Slingsbye's relations have petitions depending before the same Committee. Lord Swinton, a Scotchman, one of Montrose's Judges, was sent yesterday to the Gate-house.—The Lords upon reading the Bill of Indemnity have excepted out of the bill all that gave sentence upon the King; what concurrence that vote will find in the Lower House we shall in a short time see. The Lower House hath spent much of this week upon tonnage and poundage, and have received a report of what the Committee of Religion voted on Monday last, deferring that debate until Oct. 23rd, desiring the King in the mean time to call some Divines to consult about Church affairs, and that vote was confirmed in the House, but not without opposition. P.S. The Portugall Embassadour had audience yesterday in the presence.

Fol. 75. Aug. 2. The same to the same.—The House of Lords are still upon debate of the several heads of the Act of Indemnity; the moderate speech of the King's (which I sent you) stopp'd the career they intended so that they have satisfied themselves with the excepting of 5 more persons for life to be added to the 7 that the Howse of Commons left to the law; and in estate none shall be punish'd: these 5 are Lambert, Haslerigge, Sir H. Vane, Coll. Axtell, and Coll. Hacker; the 4 first of these were of the 20 that the House of Commons intended to punish in their estates: Hacker was the man to whom the warrant was directed to see the King executed. But the House of Lords have order'd also that if any of the remaining 16 shall hereafter presume to bear any office, civill, military, or ecclesiastical, that they shall receive no benefit by this Act of Indemnity; 'tis disputed whether the House of Commons will allow of the pardon of these 16 when the Act is return'd to them. The House of Commons hath voted Sir George Booth 10,000l. out of the Excise for the repair of his losses in the action of last summer; to-day the concurrence of the Lords was desired, but they thought fit first to consult the King about it, because the Excise money being his, they thought it became them not to dispose of it without his consent; to-morrow I believe 'twill be order'd in the Lords House by the King's allowance. A months pay is voted by both Houses to the army. Jack Bromely is made a cornett to a troop of horse. I believe Sir John Talbott is married this day; for the women that are of the council are gone out of town to the house where his mistress (Mrs. Slingsby) lives in great privacy.

Fol. 76. 1660, Aug. 7.—The same to the same.—The greatest debates of the Lower House are at present concerning the bill of sales, and they have agreed that none of the King's Judges, of any High Court of Justice, of Barebones Parliament, of the Committee of safety, of Cromwell's counsell, nor any decimator shall have their purchases confirm'd. They are now upon the Poll bill again and excise. Yesterday the Lords upon the motion of Generall Mountague pardon'd Sir Gilbert Pickering, and after him one Major Lyuter who had sate once upon the King. To dispatch the bill of Indemnity the sooner yesterday, they threw out all the private provisoes therein which were very many. There was liberty given to some Lords to bring in Bills for reparation of their losses, and accordingly one was brought for my Lord Newcastle, Duke of Buckingham and Bristol: after some debate, my Lord Bristoll was desired to propose the question, which he did in these words, Whether their Lordships did consent to the Bill in favour of my Lord Newcastle without exclusion of the other Lords; the Duke of Buckingham finding my Lord Newcastle named, and himself not, stepp'd from, his seat, and in some heat more than usual asked my Lord Bristol why he named my Lord Newcastle and not him, and pressing him in an extraordinary manner for his reason in so doeing, my Lord Bristol told him he thought my Lord Newcastle a man of more merit than him; the Duke sayd he believ'd him not, and return'd in some anger; of which passage the King having immediate notice, they were commanded not to stir out of their lodgings, and so it rests yet. To-day the Lords thought fit to except some persons from receiving benefit by the Act of Indemnity that sate upon the Lords Hamilton, Holland, Derby, and Capell, and agreed that 4 persons should be excepted, for each Lord one, and 'twas resolv'd that 4 Lords in the House nearest of kindred to those that suffer'd should each of them name one presently; Lord Derby named Col. Croxton, Lord Pagett named one John Blackwell (for Lord Holland), Lord Denbigh named one Wiburd for Hamilton, and Lord Capell named Mr. Edmund Wareing, our late sheriff; and the whole House immediately consented

to the excepting those 4 persons. Lord Lauderdale is made Secretary of Scotland, Glencarne Chancellour, and Crawford Lyndsey Treasurer.

Fol. 49. 1660, Aug. 11. The same to the same.—Since my last, the King hath received notice of a design manag'd by the fanatick party to gain Portsmouth, the Governour and his deputy being absent, some attempts were made to corrupt the under officers, amongst which they met a man not for their purpose, who discover'd it. The Bill of Indemnity hath pass'd the Lords House, with some alteration and was this day sent down to the Commons where 'tis believed there will be some new dispute concerning it. Lord Devonshire is Lord Lieutenant of Derbyshire. Lord Chesterfield 'tis thought shall marry my Lady Elizabeth Buttler, daughter to my Lord of Ormond. There is some discourse of adjourning the Parliament.

Fol. 50. 1660, Aug. 16. The same to the same. . . . When the Lords sent down the Act of Indemnity to the Commons with their amendments, the House of Commons nevertheless adhered to their former votes concerning those that should die; only joined with the Lords in excepting Hacker; and for clearing 16 of the 20 they had formerly resolved to punish by a future Act in estate, they joyned with the Lords also, and so sent up the Bill again. The Lords upon reading the Bill adhered to their votes also, which occasioned a conference to-day in which the Lords gave their reasons for adhering to their first vote. . . . The King hath given order to Sir Ed. Turner to acquaint the House of Commons that by that clause in his speech, "If there be any other of " such dangerous principles that the safety of the nation " cannot consist with their liberty, they should alfso be " punish'd," he meant Haslerigge, Vane, Lambert, and Axtell.—The young Duke of Richmond is dead in France, and the Lord Lichfield son to the Lord Aubigny that was killed at Edge Hill, is now Duke of Richmond.

1660, Aug. 18. The same to the same.—Our great bodyes move so slowly that 'twill be the next post at least before I shall give you their resolution concerning the Act of Indemnity; the House of Commons are not yet of a mind what they shall do with the Judges of the King; the proclamation of summons seeming by implication to pardon them if they rendered themselves; all they did to-day in it, was to desire another conference with the Lords concerning it, which 'tis supposed will be on Monday. The Excise is continued for three months, and the King came to the Lords House to-day to pass that Act, Lord Roberts being deputy of Ireland, had some scruple how the forces of that nation should be commanded; for as the King's Deputy he had some pretence to it, but the General being by his commission Captain-General of all the forces in the three kingdoms, that command could not well be taken out of his hands; to solve it, therefore the General is made Lieutenant of Ireland.

Fol. 51. 1660, Aug. 23. The same to the same.—Our great expectation of the Bill of Indemnity is not yet satisfied; yesterday the Lords had a Conference with the Commons in which the Chancellor represented the sense of the Lords for adhering to their former votes for taking away the lives of all the King's Judges; the Commoners appointed to manage the Conference made their objections, and were answer'd very well by the Chancellour, one by one; to-day report was made to the Commons of yesterday's conference, and much debate there was, but they agreed only to have another conference with the Lords to-morrow; many are inclin'd to a concurrence with the Lords, and as many think themselves obliged by the Proclamation and their former votes not to take away the lives of those that rendered themselves. Marquis Hertford and Earl of Worcester, both pretend to be Duke of Somerset; Hertford by restauration, the other by patent from the late King; yesterday a Committee of Lords sate upon it; Worcester produced his patent, but with all said the King gave it him, with some conditions which he acknowledg'd were not by him perform'd, and therefore referred himself to the King. I saw a Petition to-day to the King subscribed by most of the Lords for restoring the Earl of Arundell to be Duke of Norfolk. Earl of Newport is made Gentleman of the bedchamber, which many wonder at. 'Tis now doubtful whether Lord Roberts will goe into Ireland to act as deputy under the General. 'Tis now believed that Wareing and the other three that sate upon the Lords, and Lambert and the other three that were excepted by the Lords with him will not die; they will ('tis sayd) be left out of the Act of Indemnity; but the two Houses 'tis thought will petition the King for his mercy towards them; I hear the King should say he would take such a course with them that they should not be able to give any disturbance.

1660, Aug. 25. The same to the same.—Yesterday the Commons shew'd their reasons why they could not agree with the Lords in excepting those of the King's Judges that rendered themselves; and to-day the Lords offer'd this expedient, that all the King's Judges should be excepted from benefit by the bill, (in which case they are left to the law which will certainly condomn them); but that those that rendered themselves upon the Proclamation should not be executed by any Act of Parliament: upon report of this to the Commons, they agreed with the Lords, and now, if the Act can so soon be ingross'd, 'tis believed, it will be pass'd by the King on Tuesday next. Haslerigge shall forfeit estate only; Axtell both life and estate: Lambert and Sir H. Vane are excepted both for life and estate also, but the Houses will petition the King to pardon the lives of these two. Wareing and the other three that sate upon the Lords are pass'd by wholly. The King returned last night from Hatfeild.

Fol. 52. 1660, Sept. 1.   The same to the same.—Mentions the proposed adjournment of the House upon the next Saturday until November 6th.—No more private business will be attended to; they will intend principally to the ordering of the money for disbanding the army and satisfaction of the arrears of the Fleet. My Lord Southesk, a Scotchman, killed a countryman of his (one Carre) t'other day in a duel, for which he is in prison. One that dispersed seditious pamphlets was this day brought into White-Hall. The Princess Royal (they say at Court) will be here suddenly.

Fol. 52. 1660, Sept. 4.   The same to the same.—The Duke of Gloucester hath been very sick and 'tis thought he will have the small poxe; Lord Oxford hath them aod is dangerously ill. Lord St. Albans, Lord Crofts, and young Harry Jermyn are come over. Mons. de Rovigny is come to demand the Princess Henrietta for the Duke of Orleans, and 'tis believed the King will give his consent. Hugh Peters was taken in Kent Street on Sunday last. The Admiral Mortague is gone to fetch the Princess Royal, and 'tis thought she will be here towards the later end of the next week. I believe the Prince de Ligny is landed by this time, Embassadour from the King of Spain. Lord Hertford will carry the Dukedom of Somerset.

Fol. 53. 1660, Sept. 8th.   The same to the same.—The House of Commons, upon computation of the King's revenue, found it to be 900,000l. per annum, and ordered an addition of 300,000l. per annum more, but have not yet agreed whence that shall issue. There is a bill to be brought in for annexing Dunkirke to the Crown. A bill is agreed for making Marquis Hertford Duke of Somerset. The army is to disband as soon as money comes in by the Poll Bill to pay their arrears; if that money shall not be sufficient they have voted the King two months contribution of 70,000l. per month to help; the order of disbanding is to be by lot; only the Duke of Yorke's and Gloucester's regiments and the General's are to be disbanded last, except those that are in fortified garrisons. The patents for late honours are to be brought in to the Chancellor to be inroll'd. The House of Commons hath given the King one month's contribution of 700,000l. for his present supply. The Committee of the Common Council had voted a petition for renewing the Covenant, but it was thrown out at the Common Council. Lady Dutchess of Richmond (the elder) is come to town from France. The Parliament adjourns not till Tuesday next, it being not possible to finish some bills sooner. P.S. Be pleased I beseech you to mind Mr. Doughty of the tarriers he promised me. The King will have the benefit of them this winter.

Fol. 53. 1660, Sept. 13. The same to the same.—The King went to the Lords House and passed about 20 bills, after which he spoke very well to the Houses, and after him the Chancellor made a large speech to them also. . . . . The Houses adjourned till 6th of November, but first voted a present of 10,000l. to be made the Princess Royal at landing, and as much to be sent the Queen of Bohemia. One of the bills pass'd to-day was for restoring the Marquis of Hertford to the Dukedom of Somersett, of whom the King spoke so obligingly that it was judged the greater honour of the two. Dunkirk was voted by the House of Commons to be annexed to the Crown, but the Lords thought it unseasonable now that the Spanish Embassadour was just upon his entry, & so it stopp'd at present. The Lords voted the bringing in of late patents of honour to be inroll'd, but that found a stop at the Commons House, so that sleeps too. The Spanish Embassadour

(the Prince de Ligny) came in to-day. In the Bill for restoring ejected ministers and confirming those in possession that are in places of dead incumbents, the Lords have reserved to themselves their presentations, but the Commoners have parted with theirs, pro hac vice. . . . . . The Duke of Gloucester is pretty well, but my Lord Oxford is very ill. P.S. 10,000l. was lately given the Duke of York and 7,000l. to the Duke of Gloucester.

Fol. 54. 1660, Sept. 15. The same to the same.—I did never with less satisfaction give you any intelligence that I now do . . . . death of that most incomparable [Duke of Gloucester]; when I writ on Thursday . . . . . . appearance, and the judgment of all the physicians as they had ever seen anybody the tenth day in that disease, at 6 a clock that night; he was thus when the physicians left him. Immediately after they were gone he bled at the nose 3 or 4 ounces, and then slept about half an hour; when he waked he presently lost his senses, and about 9 that night died. Next day he was open'd, and his lungs were found as full of blood as they possibly could hold, besides two or three pints of blood that lay about them, and much blood in his head, which took away his senses. The physicians never gave him anything from first to last, so well he was in appearance to every one; his body is removed to Somersett Howse. The court is in deep mourning and will continue so for 6 weeks; after that in half-mourning till the coronation of the King, the 6th of February next. The King is the most afflicted man for the loss of his brother. . . . . P.S. The Princess Royal is expected almost hourly at Gravesend; the barges are gone to meet her, but we hear not yet of her landing. The King puts not his footman, &c. in black nor any other.

Fol. 54. 1660, Sept. 22, London. The same to the same. On Thursday last Dr. Juxton, late Bishop of London, was install'd Bishop of Canterbury in Henry the 7th Chappel at Westminster. The Duke of Gloucester was buried there last night; his body was removed by water from Somersett Howse to the Parliament stairs, where the Duke of York, all the nobility, and the King's servants met it.—He hopes the militia is in good forwardness, as the discontented party, he hears, are preparing new troubles, &c.

Fol. 55. 1660, Sept. 25. The same to the same.—He thanks for the complement of the terriers, and bogs thoy may be sent up as soon as he (Leveson) has a conveniency, for 'tis sayd the King intends for New Markett within a fortnight or 3 weeks.—The Princess Royal came to Whitehall to-night, but is seen by none to-night; she is unprovided of mourning, having not heard of her brother's death till she was on ship-board. The Lord Hatton, I hear, will be Lord Privy Seal. Lord Chesterfield is married to my Lord of Ormond's daughter.

Fol. 55. 1660, Sept. 29. The same to the same.—We hear of Princes abroad though nothing to be transmitted of our own. The nobles and great officers of Sweden all apply themselves now to Christina formerly Queen of Sweden, and the last Queen and young Prince they say will be put out of the country. Our greatest discourse now is concerning Coll. Warden whom you found lately acquitted by the Council upon the petition of Sir George Booth and other gentlemen of that county, but Coll. Vernon, that first accused him, hath since been with Scott in the Tower, who hath accused him of all the villanies imaginable, even to the endeavouring to put the King into their hands when he escaped after Worcester fight, the betraying of Mr. Cooke, for which he had 500l., and giving notice of all that pass'd in Sir George Booth's business; this being read yesterday at the Council under Scott's own hand, there was an order issued for the apprehending him, and I hear since he is taken. We hear the King goes to Portsmouth next week and the Princess Royal to Hampton Court that while. We expect daily the proclamation concerning religion; the presbiterian ministers, we hear, are very unreasonable. Dr. Reynolds (the King of their Israel) they say accepts of a Bishoprick. P.S. He again asks for the terriers.

Fol. 56. 1660, Oct. 6, London.—The same to the same.—Thanks for the arrival of the terriers.—Disbanding the regiments.—The Queen hath sent word she intends to be here suddenly, within less than a month she is expected, and the young Princess with her; ships go suddenly to fetch her. The Prince de Ligny went hence to-day towards Flanders. There are such great villanies discoursed of Coll. Warden that was in Sir George Booth's engagement (by Mr. Scott), that 'tis a great question betwixt him and Willis which is the greater knave. The King's judges are to be tried on Tuesday next at the Sessions House in the Old Bayly. By your servant on Monday I shall acquaint you with some passages that are not fit to be sent by the common conveyance.

Fol. 57. 1660, Oct. 8, London. — The same to the same.—In mine by the last I told you that by the return of your servant you should receive an account of some passages that were not fit for the publique conveyance, which in short is this. There hath for some years been an amour between the Duke of Yorke and Mrs. Hyde; of late she hath kept her chamber and 'tis said she is with child; several discourses there are concerning it; some say with great confidence there was a contract, and that by some dexterity it is taken out of her hands again; others say there was no contract at all; the King hath been in much trouble about it, and the Chancellor is so still; for the dilemma must necessarily be of ill consequence both ways, how it will end is not yet known, but you shall have an early notice, &c.

Fol. 58. 1660, Oct. 11, London.—The same to the same.—There is little of discourse or action now in town, but what concernes the trials of the King's judges; yesterday they were first call'd, their indictments were read, and all but Sir Hardres Waller and Charles Fleetwood pleaded not guilty; but with some difficulty as the Diurnall will tell you; the other two confessed the fact and their guilt. To-day your neighbour Harrison was the only man tryed; for excepting against 35 jurymen (a privilege allowed in cases of treason), noe other could be heard this day: with much assurance and glory he avowed the fact, and spake as much treason and blasphemy now as he had acted before; he said he had often pray'd with tears that God would direct him, and it was revealed to him to be a just action to put the King to death, who (he said) had made war against the Parliament, and was guilty of all the bloodshed in the war; when they endeavoured to prove his hand to the warrant for execution, he wish'd them not to lose time, and calling for the paper, said he believed it to be his hand; the jury concluded him guilty without going from the bar, and he was immediately senteno'd to be hang'd, drawn, and quartered; after this he went away smiling without any appearance of trouble. Last night the Duke of Buckingham and Mr. O'Neale fell out in the Princess her drawing room; the lie was given to Mr. O'Neale; but the King being near came in immediately, and so it stopp'd; what is since done I do not yet hear, but the passage being so publick, I believe will have no ill success.

Fol. 58. 1660, Oct. 13, London.—The same to the same.—There is nothing here worth your knowledge, but the tryall of the King's judges, and in particular of your neighbour Harrison, who was bang'd, drawn, and quarter'd to-day at Charing Cross; he trembled much when he first came upon the ladder, but excus'd it by the ill-usage he had in Newgate since his condemnation, and said he thank'd God he came with as much content to die there as he did to commit the act for which he suffer'd; he was going he said to sit at the right hand of Jesus to judge us all. Yesterday Scroope, Carew, Scott, Clement, and Jones were condemned; to-day Hugh Peters and Cooke, and they say Hewlett will be proved to be the man that cut off the King's head. The main argument of all of them is that an Act of Parliament warranted them (supposing that small remnant of the Commons† House to be one), which Scott said was as much a Parliament as this that is now in being, and that irregularities ought not to be condemn'd in that if allowed in this. P.S. My Lord Treasurer's daughter, the Lady Audry, that should have married my Lord Piercy, died yesterday morning.

Fol. 59. 1660, Oct. 20.—The same to the same.—Last night the French letters came which say the Queen intended to begin her journey this way, yesterday; the Duke of York intends to meet her at Calais, to which purpose he goes hence on Monday or Tuesday next, and they say the King will go the later end of next week to meet her in Kent; Count Soisson is landed extraordinary Embassadour from France. The Portuguis make offers of very great advantage to England for the King's assistance against the Spaniard, but what car the King gives to them is not yet known. Axtell and Hacker were hang'd yesterday at Tiburne; Mr. Heveningham was condemn'd yesterday; his life 'tis thought will be sav'd, but his estate we hear will be given to my Lord Dover, grandfather to Mr. Heveningham's wife, who is daughter to Lord Rochford . . . . . The Duke of Somerset is like to die.

Fol. 59. 1660, Oct. 23, London.—The same to the same.—Yesterday a conference was held before the King

at the Lord Chancellor's, betwixt the Bishops and Presbiterian ministers concerning Church government; the Presbiterians agreed to an Episcopall government, but they would not have the Bishops have any power but joyntly with the presbiters, and with their consent; at last they agreed that the Bishop should act with the advice and assistance of his prebends and six ministers of the dioces: the Presbiterians pleaded much for power of suspension from the Communion to be given to ministers, but that would not be granted, and they yielded at last that power only to the Bishop and his assistants (as above); some liberty is given them to forbear some ceremonies if they please. Some parts of the Common Prayer (which are particularly mentioned) they must use, other parts they have liberty in, and some others are to have some small alteration; they are agreed in all matters and very suddenly. A declaration of Church government will be set out. During this conference Mrs. Hyde fell in labour, and notice being given of it, the King sent for the Lady Ormond, Lady Sunderland, and Lady Corke; these with some Bishops, the Lord of Ormond, Manchester, and the Secretary were commanded to be present at the birth, and to ask her (as they did) whose child it was; she said the Duke of York's; they further ask'd her if she were married; she said she was (to the Duke); they ask'd her also if any other man had known her, and with many imprecations she said, none; thus the matter rests; 'tis said 'twill be brought into Parliament. The Duke goes to meet the Queen on Thursday; the Princesse on Friday; the King on Saturday. Count Soissons comes in to-morrow, his audience will be on Friday. P.S. Mrs. Hyde's her child is a boy.

Fol. 60. 1660, Oct. 30, London.—The same to the same.—On Sunday last there were five Bishops consecrated in Henry 7th Chappel, Dr. Sheldon for London, Dr. Hinchman for Salisbury, Dr. Morley for Worcester, Dr. Sandreson for Lincoln, and Dr. Griffiths for St. Asaph. To-day the King's declaration concerning the affairs of the church came out, which I have herein sent you. We hear not yet of the Queen's landing; the King went to meet her on Saturday, expecting her to land at Dover on Sunday night, to which purpose he intended to be there that night also. When they return we shall hear what will become of the business betwixt the Duke and the Chancellor's daughter; some call her Dutchess of York already; in the Chancellor's house altogether so.

Fol. 60. 1660, Nov. 6, London.—The same to the same.—The Parliament being now met again, there will be a plentiful subject to write upon: and I hope they will be exquisite courtiers, for they have this first day of their sitting complemented the young Princess Henrietta with 10,000l., and ordered the Council to wait upon the Queen with their congratulations for her return hither; yet tis doubtful how long she will stay, she having promis'd to return into France within six weeks. An account was given into the House to-day of the disbanding of about 20 regiments of foot and four or six of horse; withall that the poll money by computation would not amount to above 250,000l., by reason the Act was not duely observed in many places . . . . The Chancellor is made Baron of Hinden, and his patent was this day read in the House. The old Countess of Carlile died yesterday suddenly of an apoplexy. My Lord Bath (lately Sir John Greenville) is Groom of the stoole. The Duke d'Anjou will marry our very pretty Princess Henrietta.

Fol. 61. 1660, Nov. 13, London.—The same to the same.—Though the Queen hath been so long here, and 'twas believed her coming was principally upon occasion of the Duke's late adventure, yet we cannot yet hear what end that affair will have; though the marriage be in a manner confess'd, yet her discoursing it before he gave leave which ('tis sayd) she promis'd not to do, hath so enrag'd the Duke that his affection had not greater measures than now his hatred has. The great delay in paying in the poll money and the underrating in many places, hath left the nation almost as much in debt as when that Act came out. The debt upon computation amounting to 1,300,000l.; to satisfy which, the House hath partly concluded upon a years tax of 70,000l. per month, and to-morrow they say 'twill be so resolv'd. There hath been some discourse, but without ground, that some others of the King's judges were suddenly to suffer, and I take the occasion to tell you so, because possibly you may have heard that report from other hands. The Queen intends her return to France within these three weeks. I think I told you before of Sir Harbottle Grimston's being made Master of the Rolls, and that Maynard and Glyn are the King's sergeants. The French Embassadour goes back about two days hence. There was a bill brought into the House lately against alimony, by Mr. Ferrers, of Derbyshire, which received a great debate, and the House was divided upon it; but the favourers of the Bill carried the vote by 16, and to-morrow, I think, 'tis to be read againe; the women begin to make strong parties against the Bill, yet how it comes to pass I know not, many of the young men are ill courtiers.

Fol. 61. 1660, Nov. 20, London. The same to the same.—The great business of the Court concerning the Duke's marriage is yet in a mist, which they say will not be dispelled till the Queen is gone, and her day of remove is appointed to be Monday sevennight. We are all troubled to lose our very pretty Princess Henriette. She goes with her mother into France, where she will be married they say this winter, and some say the Queen will return hither at spring. Yesterday young Lenthall (the old Speaker's son) was put into the Tower for counterfeiting a Great Seal. There is a pamphlet which undertakes to prove the Long Parliament not yet dissolv'd. The author* is taken, his book to-day voted seditious, and an impeachment to be drawn against him. I have sent you a 20s. piece of new gold, which you will receive by the means of Mr. Jenkyns, my brother's servant. I sent it by a tenant of mine to him, not daring to adventure it by the post.

Fol. 62. 1660, Nov. 27th, London. The same to the same.—The House being to dissolve the 20th of next month, and the Queen's journey intended to begin on Monday next, the King consider'd that if the wind should not be fair when he had brought the Queen to Portsmouth, they might stay so long there that he could not be here again to dissolve the Parliament; therefore the journey is deferr'd, as 'tis believ'd till after Christmas, for that will not be a time for travel; besides that the weather will be too cold for her. To-day the House of Commons voted the other half of the excise of beer, and ale, coffee, and other outlandish drinks, to the King for his life; the first half being perpetuated to satisfy for the Court of Wards. There hath been a long debate in the House of Lords about vacating a Fine in the case betwixt Leveston and Powell; they have voted allready upon hearing the evidence that the Fine was gained by terror and force, yet they are very tender of vacating the greatest assurance the law can give, especially since the business comes unduly before them, that is, by petition, not by writ of error, and therefore they give intimation to the complainers that they should bring in a Bill, that the Fine may be vacated by the legislative power.

Fol. 62. 1660, Dec. 1, London. The same to the same.—The passage of most remark this week in Parliament was concerning the King's declaration touching ecclesiastical affairs, which the Presbiterian party would needs have turned into an Act; and a Bill was brought in to that purpose, but after a very long debate, and a division of the House, it was carried by about 26 voices in the negative, at which John is very angry. The Spaniard hath had two losses lately, one of his fleets going with 5,000 Neapolitans against Portugall, which was wholly cast away, and as some say here the Portugalls have beat some of his men and taken many : besides this there is a report (but not assured), that Mexico is revolted from him, and declare a free trade with all comers. The Duke d'Anjou sent a gentleman lately to the King to desire his leave to write to his sister (the young Princess), which is granted him. P.S. All the estates of the King's judges will be settled on the Duke of York.

Fol. 63. 1660, Dec. 6, London. The same to the same.—I should have told you 10 days since the ill success we then had in the Lords House with the Bill we brought in thither to restore us to our impropriations, which, by the means of my Lord Chancellor (to gratify some of all sorts of the clergy), was rejected ; but though I was loath to be the first intelligencer of so ill news, yet I must humbly advise you now to take as little notice of it as may be, that the country parsons may not be encouraged the more to oppose us in it, for we that are concern'd here do not think ourselves much the further of them notwithstanding this, and do resolve to keep possession till a better opportunity offer itself in our behalfs. A Bill is depending for augmenting the small vicarages out of the impropriations of Bishops, but it touchs not ours. The Bill for restoring the Duke of Norfolk is pass'd both Houses. The City are much troubled at the Commons refusing to make the King's

declaration for ecclesiastical matters a law. A great consecration of Bishops last Sunday at the Abbey, and their feast at Haberdashers' Hall on Tuesday. Our Bishop is not yet resolved on since Calamy refused it. The House of Commons voted yesterday the carcases of Cromwell, Ireton, Bradshaw, and Pride, to be forthwith taken up and drawn upon a hurdle to Tiburne, there hung in coffins a while, and then buried under the gallows. It is intended to be mov'd that the hangman *pro tempore* may for ever hereafter give Cromwell's arms ; but that, perhaps, being a wrong to others of the name better deserving, may not be granted. It is uncertain whether the Queen will go so soon after Christmas, as [was belie]ved ; the King thinks it may become the Duke of Anjou [to fetch] his mistress, our young fair princess, better than for her to go . . . . . Here was a general belief that Col. Ludlow was taken in Mich. Oldsworth's house in Westminster, but it proves not true. It is believed the Coronation will be put of till May, but there is no declaration of it. Perhaps the phancye of this inscription upon some new medals of English coin to be presented to the King for his approbation, may somewhat persuade the protraction of it till that time, namely *Natus, renatus, coronatus* 29 *Maij.* Plays at Court every week. Lady Anne Digby to be married to Lord of Oxford, the King makes the joynture. Lord Cranborne is dead.

Fol. 64. 1660, Dec. 8, London. The same to the same.—I received yours, in which told me you had received the piece I sent you ; I believe I shall send you another shortly, for the King likes not this, though in the next there will be no other difference but what arises from the manner of stamping ; that I sent you being done with a hammer, the other with a screw, which makes a very great difference, though the cut be the same.—Parliamentary news.—The Chancellor is to be made Duke, but I know not yet his title. My mother hath sent you a book and the King's picture, by one Charnocke or Jarnock.

Fol. 64. 1660, Dec. 11, London. The same to the same.—I can now assure you that which is not yet confess'd, and hath so long been the great dispute of the Court, I mean whether the Duke would own his wife. I dare now give you my word he will, and that she shall be acknowledged Duchess of York as soon as the Queen is gone, whose journey begins the 26th of this month. The Queen is grieved much at it, and thinks there was never more want of the Pope's power here than upon this occasion. The Princess Royal is in as great a trouble, and for this reason only is resolv'd to return into Holland. More Dukes we shall have at the Coronation, Lord Ormond and Northumberland ; that the Chancellor would be one too I told you before. On Saturday night last, one of the King's frigates lying at Woollage (Woolwich), with the portholes of the lowest tier of ordnance open, the seamen being asleep, rolling by the strength of the great wind, took in so much water at the portholes, that she sunk, and the men in her were drown'd at a low water ; she lies pretty bare, and they have got some of her guns out already, and hope to weigh her up too.

Fol. 65. 1660, Dec. 15, London. The same to the same.—Since my last there is a discovery of persons that are now put to act the same game that but last year was the fate of honester men, and several are apprehended, but none of any quality, for endeavouring to make an insurrection. Amongst the rest, one Major White (a mean fellow), was endeavouring to corrupt one of the under porters of Whitehall gate (they having been comrades under my Lord Fairfax), who discovered him to the General ; he confesses little as yet, but that he said he would pull the white star off the General's cloak. In his chamber there were found several confus'd lists of men, of which they can make little. We have a report here that the ship in which Argyle and Leard (Laird?) Swinton were sent towards Scotland, is cast away, and they in it, and 30,000l. also lost there, that was sent to disband some men in Scotland. Upon our stages we have women-actors, as beyond sea. We hear nothing yet of the Parliament's being prolong'd, though some say there are endeavours made to obstruct the settling the King's revenue, that it may prevent the dissolution.

? Fol. 65, 16$\frac{60}{61}$, Feb. 5, London. The same to the same.—These two or three days last past have afforded us a more than probable discourse of that which will be an infinite satisfaction to the whole nation, a treaty for the marriage of the King with the daughter of Portugall, to which purpose principally they say the Portugall Embassadour is now return'd, but hath not yet had his audience, and the conditions they offer are

---

* Thomas Philips.

DUKE OF SUTHERLAND.

very considerable in their consequences besydes the money: 'Tis said they will give the King a good harbour in the Straits, two towns in the Indyes, by which means we shall recover that very great trade now almost lost, besides this they will give a very considerable sum of money 1,700,000*l*. In Portugall, by some that come thence we hear they looke upon it there as already concluded in a manner: My Lord Bristol goes hence on Friday beyond sea as 'tis thought for Portugall, but 'tis given out for Flanders to see his daughter there. Most of the nobility attended the Lord Treasurer to-day to Westminster to the Checquer chamber to be sworn. I believe you will heare of writs for a new Parliament sent out immediately after the term. There was a quarrel lately betwixt the Duke of Buckingham and Admiral Montague as they went over with the Queen; the Admiral sent him a challenge next morning, but they were prevented fighting, the quarrel being publick; the Duke is much blamed, and the King very angry with him for it, besides, 'tis beleived it may hinder his being restored to the Bed-chamber and Council, both which favours the King intended him.

Fol. 66, 16$\frac{60}{61}$, Feb. 16. The same to the same. Since my last we have had so general a report of the King's being married some time since to a lady in Flanders, niece to the Prince de Ligny, that having writ you word of a treaty with Portugall, I was unwilling to let my next want what moral assurance there could be of the idleness of this last rumour: for besides that there wants an invitation both from the person and interest, I do assure you the King himself laughs at this as at many other wives the world hath given him. 'Tis resolv'd now that a new Parliament shall meet the 8th of May next, to which purpose writs will issue on Monday if they cannot be ready to-night. I am told privately that the Duke of York intends to prove his marriage before the Council on Tuesday next.

Fol. 76, [1660], Feb. 21, London.—The same to the same.—The only notice I have now to give you is that on the last Council day the Duke of York proved his marriage before the Council to have been in September last, my Lord of Ossory and the Dutchesse her woman being present, his own Chaplain Dr. Crowder performing the Minister's part; he proved allso a contract in November was twelvemonth.

Fol. 66, 16$\frac{60}{61}$, Feb. 26, London.—The same to the same.—If the late obligation for the observance of Lent strictly appear severe to you that possibly cannot undergo the penance of a fish diet, I hear you will be absolv'd in some measure from it by a new and more indulgent order; for upon debate in the Council lately, I am told it was resolv'd that 3 days of the week should be dispensed with, (viz.) Sundays, Tuesdays and Thursdays, which will be more convenient for you in that I think, you have no Bishop as yet settled in your diocesse. The writs for the Parliament I hear will be ready to-morrow night, I have an intention to stand for Burgess of Shrewsbury, which will occasion my coming into your parts, then I shall at leisure give you a more perfect account of our transactions than by letter I can. A gentleman of my Lord St. Albans came on Sunday night to Whitehall; by him we hear that our Princess is to be married in Lent on St. Joseph's day, the only Saint that admits of marriage during that term: the Cardinal he says was pretty well this day sevenight when he came away, but letters bearing date since that time represent him very ill again: by the discourses in France of his estate he is very rich and leaves most of his estate to the son of Mareschal de la Meilleray who married lately his niece.

Fol. 67. 16$\frac{60}{61}$, March 2, London. The same to the same.—The Dutch having prepared a new Fleet of 20 sail, as 'tis suppos'd against Portugal, the King in friendship to the Portugais hath sent to the Dutch to desire that he may be judge betwixt them; some go further and say the King hath sent to them to declare their intention for that fleet, and that he gave them time but till the return of the Post, that if it were against Portugal he would send as many ships after them; this I cannot assure, but of the first I am certain. Prince Maurice of Nassau is this night come to town extraordinary Embassadour from the Elector of Brandenburg. My Lady Elizabeth Darcy (daughter of the late Lord Chesterfield) died to-day. The writs for the Parliament I hear were finish'd yesterday; if so, I believe they will be sent abroad to-night. Sir Fred. Cornwallis is to be a Lord at the Coronation.

Fol. 67, 16$\frac{60}{61}$, March 5. London.—The same to the same.—Since my last we have certain notice of the death of Cardinal Mazarin, and that he left the King of France 80 millions of livres in ready money besides 20 millions that he acquitted the King of which were due to him: he left his niece her husband, threescore thousand pistoles a yeare besides, and other great legacies to severall other persons. He deputed (or recommended) three persons to the management of affairs there, Monsr. de Lions, Monsr. Tillet and Fouquet the superintendant of the Finances. Yesterday there was a kind of a contract betwixt my Lord of Ormond's second daughter and my Lord Cavendish (my Lord Devonshire's son), the King joyning their hands, and the friends and parents of each party present, they are not to marry this year and half, she being but yonng and little. The writs for the Parliament are now upon distribution. There is now a treaty of marriage (or proposals at least) betwixt the King and the Duke of Parma's daughter, but 'tis not public yet.

Fol. 34. 16$\frac{60}{61}$, March 12, London. [The same] to the same.—The scene of marriage is varied again; the treaty with the Duke of Parma being at an end, and they say that with Portugall renewed. The Catholike faction here, as freinds to the Spaniard, prevail'd with the King for instructions to treat in Italy, and the Spaniard offer'd to endow any ally of his as his own daughter; upon this my Lord Bristoll went over. The Chancellor was not made acquainted with this treaty when first sett on foot; but discoursing it afterwards, hath now prevail'd so far that it is stopp'd, and my Lord Bristol sent for back: the Chancellor hath possessed the Council upon this occasion with the practises of the Spanish faction here amongst our Catholikes, and 'tis believed the Catholike Lords will be in danger of losing their personal sitting in the Upper House upon it, and sit henceforward by Proxy only. The Spanish Embassadour finds himself aggrieved at this proceeding, and told the King he found his master's concerns were not respected; that he heard the Portugall Embassadour should say he had outwitted him, but believed it not till now, supposing he had treated with more advantage with the King himself, than the other could do by the Chancellor, and wish'd the King to consider how dangerous it was for him to give ear to the counsels of him (in this affair) that had married his daughter to the Duke next heir to the Crown: in the end that if the King pursued the interest of Portugal, his master would be obliged to make war upon him; to which the King very shortly replyed the King of Spain might do what he pleased in that; he valued it not. Thus stands the affair of the marriage at present, &c.

Fol. 68. 16$\frac{60}{61}$, March 19, London.—The same to the same.—I have nothing new to acquaint you with but what we hear from beyond sea, first of the marriage of the Princess which was intended to be yesterday or Sunday last; the King sends my Lord Crofts, the Duke, Mr. Jermyn, and Mr. Rawlyns to congratulate. We hear likewise that Mr. Mountague (Watt Mountague) is in disgrace in the Court of France, and banish'd the Court for endeavouring to continue the administration of affairs in the Queen mother of France, and her cabinet; the King saying he would now have no more Premier minister but look to his own concerns himself, and that he would sooner have done it, but that the Cardinal had deserved very well of him, by his great services: Cardinall de Rets was coming to Paris expecting to be employed also, but is commanded back again. I have herein sent you Argylo's plea before the Parliament in Scotland; he hath also petitioned the King for his mercy.

Fol. 68. 1661, March 26, London.—The same to the same.—Our chief discourses are concerning elections for the Parliament, amongst which the late ones of the city much surprize us, some being chosen there that could never before find credit amongst them, nor had now (as 'tis believed) but for their known and remarkable opposition to the Bishops. The same interest is prosecuted with great earnestness in many countries, what success they will have the books will tell you. Our Princess is not yet married, though word was sent from France, the wedding would be on Sunday sevenight; three days since a gentleman was sent over for the King's approbation in writing, which was before forgot. We have little talk now of the King's marriage, and 'tis very doubtful where 'twill fall.

Fol. 69. 1661, April 2, London.—The same to the same.—The King of late hath been pleased to send the Garter to four of the nobility, the Duke of Richmond, Lord Lindsey, Lord Strafford, and Lord Manchester; the instalment intended at Windsor had like to have bene deferr'd for want of blue velvet to make the robes, which occasioned a discourse here that it was put off, and it had been soe, but that one hath undertaken to dye blue enough out of other colour'd velvets. The discourse that is of the King's marriage inclines yet to the Portugais side, the chief difficulty in it is whether the conditions offer'd will ballance the consideration of a war with Spain and the Low Countries against one in Portugal, against the other in the Indyes. I must not omit to acquaint you with the late bloody battle fought upon this quarrell betwixt four cooks of tho two several factions in which one was kill'd and the rest very much wounded. The King's cook (a French man) was kill'd, the others belong'd to the Spanish Embassadour, my Lord Bedford, and Lord Ossory. Though the Citty intended an example to the rest of the nation in their election, by the returns that are just come we find men of another temper in most places. Mr. Pierpoint lost his election for Nottinghamshire to a private gentleman, though he had the conjunction of several Lords in that country. My Lord Fairfax lost his also in Yorkshire. My Lord Crofts married 'tother day (the Lady Heale) whose husband died about two months.

Fol. 69. 1661, May 11, London.—The same to the same.—The King will go to Worcester this summer in July and to all the places where he was conceal'd in those parts in his escape.—Yesterday the King went to the House again and sate there in his crown and robes; the occasion of it was to hear first the Speaker's desire to be excused from his employment, which the King would not allow of, and then the Speaker accepted of it in an eloquent speech. The Queen of Bohemia 'tis sayd by some will be here suddenly, but I hear by others I have more reason to credit, that there is a frigate sent to stop her. The picture of our intended Queen is at Whitehall; by that and the report of those that have seen her she is a lovely little woman. The House of Commons have voted they will give thanks to the King for communicating his intention of marriage, and promise to stand by him in it. P.S. The Duke of York is now Governor of Portsmouth. Coll. Rutherford (long in the French army) made Lieutenant General of our forces in Flanders.

Fol. 72. 1661, May 18, London.—The same to the same.—The business of the House of late hath been first the passing a bill for security of the King, in which they have forbidden all covenants, tumultuary petitions, factious preaching, charging the King with an intention to introduce Popery, &c. On Thursday morning their whole debate was concerning Sir Jo. Morley, one of their members for the North upon a petition to proceed at law against him for having betrayed the King's Councell abroad, for which he received money of Cromwell; great part of the House thinking it fit he should be immediately suspended the House and confin'd lest being conscious of the fact he should escape; but after several hours debate, the vote was only for liberty to the petitioner to prosecute. Lord Roberts is made Lord Privy Seal. Last night about 12 a clock the Queen of Bohemia came to town, and yet the notice of a frigate sent to stop her (of which I gave you notice formerly) was true; for notwithstanding she received that message, she came, which troubled the King a little, in regard the reception that was fit for her to have and him to give could not so suddenly be prepared, insomuch that last night she was forced to lodge at Drury-House (my Lord Craven's). Yesterday there was a motion made for the burning the Covenant by the hand of the hangman, and that dispute lasted 5 hours; the opposers of the motion attributed the restoration of the King to it, and some others that said they had taken it, undertook to say they had served the King as well with that as others that were openly professed of his party; this made the heat much greater; at last being put to the vote, it was carried in the affirmative by 125 voices, and to-day they send to the Lords for their concurrence.

Fol. 71. 1661, May 21, London.—The same to the same.—Notwithstanding the confidence of some men here that the King's match with Portugal would occasion a war with the Dutch, in respect of the great competition betwixt those two nations for the trade of the Indies, in which 'tis believed the King will assist the Portugais, yet we are made believe now, that the Dutch desire our friendship as much now as ever, and at this instant the King hath prepared 20 or 23 good men of war, and the Dutch above 30 to joine in an enterprise upon Argiers and Tunis, where the Turk does so abound in ships which rob all passengers, that they resolve to fire them all. To-day we hear Argyle was to be hang'd in Scotland, the very day he caus'd Montrose to die; yesterday the Lords concurr'd for the burning the Covenant by the hangman, and to-morrow is the day appointed for the execution. The Militia bill

was this day debated, and in the end referr'd to a committee, 'tis said the Lord Lieutenants will have power given them to raise a month's pay as occasion shall offer, and to march into the neighbour counties to join with their neighbours if it is requisite. To-day the King christen'd a new pleasure-ship and nam'd it (himself) La Katherine, the name of the Infanta of Portugal.

Fol. 72. 1661, May 25.—At ten a clock every morning the Howse of Commons debates the several paragraphs of the Militia bill, so that that is the greatest business yet upon their hands and will be so a long time, for they proceed very slowly, and yet we had need to be constantly in some posture of defence, for t'other day in the north one (whose name I cannot yet learn) that lived in Leeds in Yorkshire had got 3 or 400 men ready to attempt something, but was chased his country and last night was taken in Holborn and this morning brought to White-hall; 20 or 30 witnesses are come up against him, in few days we shall have a perfect accompt of the whole; we do not yet hear when the ships go for the Infanta of Portugall. But some of the conditions of the marriage are now upon performance, particularly the delivery of Tangier (a town of the Portugalls in the bottom of the streights) into the King's hands. Mr. Noel, my Lord Cambden's son is married to one of my Lord Treasurer's daughters; Lord Cambden hath settled 8,000l. per annum. Sir John Nicholas (son to the secretary) is married to a sister of Lord Northampton. There is a bill now in the Lords House for the making a brook in Worcestershire navigable betwixt Seaverne and Shirbrige, that the coals there may be brought cheaper to Worcester, Gloucester, and these Lower Countreys, which will absolutely destroy all the water-sale of coals out of Shropshire, the trade of Bridgnorth and in part of Shrewsbury; yet it will certainly pass the Lords House, whatever it does that of the Commons.

Fol. 73. 1661, May 30. London.—The same to the same.—There were so many members absent of both parties from St. Margarets on Sunday last, when they were appointed to receive the Communion, that neither party thought fit to take notice of it in the House next day. Mr. Prynne and some few others refus'd to take it kneeling. 'Twas moved next day that Dr. Gunneing might have the thanks of the House for his pains, and be desired to print his sermon; Secretary Maurice and Mr. Prynne oppos'd it; the former said it was a scandalous sermon, but the House order'd thanks, and in waggery some desired that those two opposers should be the persons order'd to carry them, but not so order'd. Yesterday, being the day of the King's birth and return hither, was observed with great solemnity in all churches. To-day the House of Commons order'd a bill to be brought in by the solicitor, to enable the King to send commissions for receiving the free and voluntary contribution of his subjects towards the supply of his occasions. And another Bill to be brought in by the same person to vacate the Act (made in the Long Parliament) that excluded the Bishops from the Lords House. Some officers of the late King's were lately upon a design of petitioning the Parliament for some consideration towards their arrears, but have thought fit to stop for the present; however, I have sent you a paper publish'd by them, which may be worth your reading. P.S. 'Tis believed Argyle is by this time dead, as an express says that came thence, and saw the scaffold up.

Vol. 4.

Letters from Stephen Charlton to Sir R. Leveson.

Fol. 1. 1631, July 30, London.—Sends by bearer a book lately sent from France containing a long letter from Monsieur to his brother the King of France.—Hears that the Queen mother will remain at Ghent.

Fol. 2. 1642, Oct. 25, London. . . . . News this day of a great battle between the King's army and the Earl of Essex. There is one that proffered to pawn his life that the Earl of Essex has taken the King and the Prince prisoners, and routed the King's army . . . and that Prince Robert (Rupert) is slain. . . . . It is certainly reported that they have had a very great battle and a bloody one 5 or 6 miles beyond Banbury. . . . . The main battle began on Sunday last about one o'clock p.m. and lasted until 6 at night; and then it was hard to say who should have the better. But on Monday morning Lord Brook's forces and Col. Hampden's and Col. Goodin came up with 800 or 700 fresh men and 10 or 12 pieces of cannon, and fell upon the flank of the King's army and wholly routed them, and this is the general report; and they say that the King's horse had a great advantage over the Earl of Essex, but his foot they say fought like devils; and besides they say that the country came in pel-mell to help the Earl of Essex. "And yet " for all this I was all this morning at the Parliament " House, and no man could tell me that there was any " certainty of this. I saw my Lord of Newberg there, " and Mr. Robert Legh likewise, and they know nothing " of a certainty." . . . Some think that the King got the better and that the Earl of Essex was slain; it was a bloody blattle, 4 thousand men slain on each side, and neither King nor Prince within 3 miles of the armies when they fought. . . . . The Parliament put into Windsor Castle above 14 or 1,500 men at the news they heard that the King was coming to London or Windsor, but now they have sent them back again. One told that he heard that once the King was in danger, and there was a great cry in the army of Save the King. Order by Parliament yesterday that Pauls shall be kept shut, and all trades shall shut up their shops for a small time, and all prisoners that are in Tower or Gatehouse shall be kept close prisoners. Some 300 or 400 Scots are come by sea hither and more will come shortly. . . . It is certain that the Queen will be in France very speedily. . . . . She is daily expected there

1642, May 25, London.—Sends in a sealed box two pair of pendents, one for Lady Newport, the other pair for Mrs. Stevenson, price 60l.; if she do not like them she may return them within 14 days. . . . . . The foreign news, that for certain the Spaniards have given the French a mighty overthrow in Artoyse about Chattelar, where they have killed above 6,000 on the place and derouted the whole army and taken all their baggage, munition and cannon. . . . The Spaniards have also given them another overthrow at Perpignan or thereabouts. The Cardinal de Richelieu is so sick that it is impossible for him to live. The Swedes have given the Emperur a great overthrow lately.

1642, June . . . Fears for the peace of the kingdom. Refers for news to inclosed papers. The Earl of Warwick is come from sea on purpose to exercise his place of Lieutenant for the Militia in Essex; and this day he is to muster up the trained bands of that county at Burntwood. Now this is done by the appointment of the Parliament, and the King hath appointed another lieutenant for the same county (whose name I cannot yet learn), but it seems they have both chosen the same day and the same place for the mustering their men. . . . Because of the order which I send you, I hope you will be here by the 16th of this month, or else you will be in danger to lose 100l. . . . The Parliament advance but little, because of these great distractions, only make all the shift that possible can be for money to supply Ireland. The drums beat daily for that service both by sea and land; there is a further store of shipping [   ] for these parts of a matter of 18 or 20 sail. . . . Lady Newport's pewter plate trenchers are under the hands of the graver. . . . The Parliament have voted the Lord Savile and the Lord Lindsey enemies of the Commonwealth. . . . Last week this city granted to lend the Parliament 100,000l. for the Irish business, to be paid out of the 400,000l. last granted to be levied by the Parliament, and now the companies of the city are very busy in ordering the levistion (levy) of the said 100,000l.

Fol. 5. 1642 [   ], London. . . The Parliament have lately received a letter from the Earl of Essex intimating that he had sent to Lord Dorset to intreat him to acquaint the King that he had a petition to deliver to him from the Parliament. The King answered that his cares should always be open to any petition that the Parliament should make unto him, provided they sent it by any except those whose names were mentioned in his Declaration as traitors. This message the Earl of Essex sent to the Parliament upon Saturday night last from Worcester, and desired them to send down some of the Parliament men that are well acquainted with the counties of Hereford and Salop, and to advise with him concerning the state of those two counties. Sir Robert Harley and Sir John Corbet are two of those that are gone down to him for that purpose. . . This message took up all the day yesterday in both Houses, upon which they passed some votes: 1st, That the restriction in the King's answer did not stand with the honour and privilege of Parliament, &c. . . . The Earl of Bedford is come to the Parliament to vindicate himself from some scandals raised upon him about the passages before Sherbourne, and as I am told he has cleared himself. The Earl of Bath is taken in the west country, and they are bringing him and Sir Hugh Pollard and three more of quality up hither. News for certain that in Yorkshire there is an agreement of peace made in Yorkshire between those that stood for the King and those that stood for

the Parliament, Lord Fairfax being the principal man for the Parliament, and the Earl of Cumberland for the King; it is thought the Parliament is not well pleased at the agreement. The cavaliers whom the Marquis of Hertford left behind him in the west country, as soon as he was gone, wheeled about and went into Cornwall, and are now in Famoth (Falmouth) and in a very strong castle there close by, that was in the custody of Sir James Bagge's son-in-law. The Earl of Leicester is come to town and great preparation is making for [Ire]land, but he hath been strongly opposed [by some of the Ho]use of Commons, whereof one Mr. Martin was [   ] though Mr. Pym hath carried him through the [   ]; the Earl of Bedford is appointed speedily to return to his charge unto the Earl of Essex, and it is thought that it will be he shall carry the petition to the King. One thing more in the King's Answer, viz., that he will have the petition brought by day and not by night, and that a trumpet shall sound when it is brought to him. Certain news that the Earl of Warwick has taken the two ships which revolted from him, viz., Capt. Ketleby, captain of the one, and Stradly of the other; but Stradling escaped ashore at Newcastle, the other submitted. News, confirmed by several letters from Manchester, that those of the town have slain about 300 of Lord Strange's forces. . . . The Earl of Northumberland is married to Lady Elizabeth Howard, and I sold him my necklace of pearl to present unto her; I am to have 650l. for it. . . . I am at Charing Cross about the business of my pearl, and also about the selling of my Barbary nag to Mr. Holles.

Fol. 6. 1642, Aug. 9, London. . . Colonel [Goring] hath declared himself for the [   ], to keep the town and castle of Portsmouth for the King, and refuses the Parliament to have any interest therein, although within these few days he wrote a letter to them that he would stand for the Parliament with the hazard of his life and fortunes, 'till he had gotten 5,000l. from them to make some fortifications about the town; and so soon as he had got the money he was absolutely for the King. . . . It is thought he has made sure of the Isle of Wight likewise for the King; . . . . but for all this we are in good hope of pacification before they come to blows; for all Hampshire and those parts are stark wild at Col. Goring and swear they will cut his throat or else lose their lives, as is reported; they will not obey the Commission of Array there or in Somersetshire where the Marquis of Hertford has been much baffled, and all his followers, consisting in most of the prime gentry of that shire, only the clothiers of the country and the freeholders, insomuch that he was forced to retreat into Wells. . . . In Warwickshire the Lord Brook has carried the militia clean against Lord Northampton. . . . There was a little scuffling between them, but no harm done; and it was about 5 or 6 pieces of ordnance which Lord Brooke bought here in town to send to Warwick Castle which the Earl of Northampton would have taken from him for the King; but Lord Brook was too hard for him as you may perceive by a printed paper here inclosed. . . . . . Serjt. Hide of the House of Commons was sent to the Tower last week. Judge Malloc, upon Friday last, was brought from Kingeon Size (Kingston Assizes?) by a troop of horse to the Parliament for causing some distraction at the Assizes in Essex and Kent amongst the people. Sir Kenelm Digby was on Saturday morning sent for by the Parliament and taken in his bed, for raising some horse privately in the city, and have found out 15 or 16 of his horses in several stables about the city. The county of Essex have sent up 500 horse to go along with the Earl of Essex and sends the city word that they have 500 more at their service. This day news from Somersetshire that the Marquis of Hertford is taken prisoner in Wells, and a number of the noblemen and gentlemen that did assist him in the Commission of Array. (The writer refers to inclosed papers.) And from the inclosed from the High Sheriff of Yorkshire you shall understand of the truth there. . . . . . . I have sent Doctor Hinton the six dozen of pewter plates.

Fol. 7. 1642, Aug. [   ], London. I have learned that the Marquis Hertford was not taken, but fled away from Wells in the night with all his company; or he would have been taken the next morning; for there were gathered the next morning about Wells above 40,000 men for that purpose; and the Earl of Pembroke and the Earl of Bedford are gone down into all those parts with commission from the Parliament to raise forces and trained bands, and to pursue the said Marquis and all with him as traitors to the King and Parliament. We hear the King is now at Leicester, and thence he goes to Warwick and West Chester, and many fear he will cross the seas (which God forbid if it be his will). The Isle of Wight stands firm for the King and Parliament, and Lord Pembroke is made Governor of it. Lord Spenser is gone from the Parliament to the King, and Sir Jacob Ashley is gone from his government of Plymouth to the King. News this night that Lord Northampton has taken 6 pieces of ordnance from Banbury with 800 troops, but it is thought he will not carry them far. The Earl of Warwick has taken a ship bound from Holland to Newcastle, laden with 300 barrels of gunpowder and other munition of war, sent by the Queen. All this I have learned for certain since writing my other letter.

Fol. 8. 1642 [   ]. After referring to inclosed papers, he says there has been a great deal of distraction in this city (London) yesterday concerning a petition, which some considerable men in the city have underwritten for peace. (Copy inclosed.) The petition was carried yesterday to the Common Council for their approbation and advice on it, and as they were at Guildhall for that purpose in a civil way without any weapons, comes a troop of horse and some companies of foot (not of the trained bands of the city), and beset the Guildhall in a warlike manner, and abused these petitioners in a most uncivil manner . . . The Common Council then being sitting in the Hall, some wiser than some, caused the doors to be shut, and then they took away the drawn swords from those soldiers that were within the Hall . . . Some were hurt, but no great harm was done. At length the Common Council sent for their petition, and after long debate would by no means consent thereto, but have chosen seven aldermen and 19 common council men to draw up [another in] the name of the common council, and [   ] for peace, to be sent both to the King. News this day, out of the West country, that six troops coming out of Plymouth, commanded by Capt. Tomson, Capt. Pim, and others, have fallen upon Sir Ralph Hopton and routed his army, and taken prisoner the high sheriff of the shire, Baronet Senior, and his eldest son, and 9 or 10 more of quality, and shipped them at Dartmouth for London. Sir Ralph Hopton was forced to pass over a brick wall, or else he had been taken. News from Cheshire that they are all up in arms, and have put the Earl of Derby to flight; the Earl of Newcastle is got into York. (The writer then mentions a report of the Lords and Commons having agreed on an accommodation, and what he has heard of their propositions). Those that were baffled yesterday at the Guildhall are resolved to deliver their petition to the Parliament, and show their grievances, how they were abused.

Fol. 9. 1642 [   ]. Distraction in Shropshire.—We hear that the Earl of Essex with the greatest part of his army is hastening from Worcester into that county, having reduced that town already, altho' it has cost the lives of above 16 or 17 of his men, and of above twice as many of the King's side, as the news reports, Col. Wilmot being slain in the conflict, and Prince Rupert and Sir John Byron, and the rest of the King's forces that were at Worcester are retired to Bridgnorth, where it is thought the Earl of Essex will not let them rest long.—Charlton thinks that the Shropshire gentry have brought ruin on themselves, and that the houses which the King's forces have spared will be ruined by the Earl of Essex.—There is great preparation of dragoniers to send into those parts, because the Parliament are resolved to have a flying army, to consist mostly of horsemen, to follow the King wheresoever he goes. A report that the Marquis of Hertford has lost five of the seven pieces of ordnance which he had, and almost all his ammunition and provisions, as he was going from Miniard to pass over the river into Wales somewhere about Bristol. The county rose up against him, besides the pursuit which the Earl of Bedford made, so that he escaped very narrowly himself; many of his soldiers he has left behind him at Miniard [at the] mercy of the country. The Earl of Bedford [   ] told me yesterday that the Marquis of Hertford is utterly undone. They told me also that some in the P[arliament had] private intelligence from my Lord of [   ] that some of the commanders and some of the army had a resolution to revolt as soon as they could have the opportunity, but are discovered. They told me likewise that they heard there was a falling out between Lord Paulet and the Marquis of Hertford. We heare that Prince Rupert behaves himself so rudely, whereby he doth himself a great deal of dishonour, and the King more disservice. Here is a

number of money and plate brought to the Guildhall daily. I bear that Sir Peter Ricquart is come off by lending the Parliament 1000l. The Parliament have cast out of the House of Commons a matter of 46 for several misdemeanors, but I did not see your name in the list . . . Out of Ireland we hear that there has been a famous victory by our side against the rebels at Munster, our side being but 2,300, and the rebels being 10 or 12,000, and commanded by Lord Musketh, and our forces being commanded by one of Lord Cork's sons, and one that married Lord Ormond's daughter; there were slain of the rebels 670, and three pieces of ordnance taken from them . . . Our side lost but five men, whereof Lord Cork's son was one; it will certainly be to-morrow. They say that the King of France hath 18 or 20,000 men in Picardy not far from Calais, upon what design is not known; but the Parliament take special notice of it, and have given order to the Earl of Warwick to have an eye on those parts. Report that the Queen is expected at Newcastle the first fair wind, and that she hath bred a combustion 'twixt the States in Holland. The Emperor hath lately received another defeat of at least 4 or 5,000 men.

Fol. 11. 1656, April 29, London. News from Germany and France that the King of Sweden is absolutely beaten, and in a very bad condition. News from France that the Pope has sent two cardinals into France with a bull of excommunication against Cardinal Mazarin as a chief of a general peace between the Kings of France and Spain; the excommunication to pass unless he use his best endeavours to conclude the peace; and the Pope has written to the Archbishop of Rouen to assist the two cardinals. When the cardinals came to Paris, and delivered their message, Mazarin asked them to have patience for two days; but the next day the King and Mazarin ordered that 12 or 15,000 men in arms should be ready, and caused the two cardinals to be sent to the Bastille, and have sent soldiers to seize the Archbishop of Rouen. A quarrel is likely between the clergy and Mazarin; for all the clergy in France, except the Sorbonists, are for the peace. This coming upon the difference between the King and the Parliament of Paris and the other Parliaments, regarding the alteration of the money, of which the Cardinal is the chief, if the Cardinal do not play his part effectually it will be his utter downfall. If the King of Sweden and this Cardinal fall, the two best pillars of our hopes here are gone. We can not hear yet whether the King of Portugal has agreed to the articles which his ambassador and our Protector concluded, nor whether our fleet be gone out of Lisbon Road.

Fol. 12. 1657, April 4, London. On Tuesday last the Speaker in the name of the whole House went to the Protector, and acquainted him with the vote of the House, and they humbly desired him to take upon him the kingly government. After much discourse he told the Speaker it was a very weighty business, and therefore required time to consider, and that he would seek God in the business, and in a few days give the House his answer. Since which time we hear that the chief commanders in the army have had several meetings, and have sought God in the business, and are generally against the proposition, and also several of the Protector's own council . . . . This morning I was told that yesternight the Protector gave in his answer to the House that he would not take on him the kingly government. Some say that he will have the city of London petition him to take it upon him. News from France about the embargo upon all the Dutch ships in the harbours and ports of France, and all Dutch merchants goods in France, because of the Dutch having taken two of the French ships in Toulon roads in revenge for the French having a little before taken two of their merchant ships in the Straits . . . . The searchers and officers of the Custom House have been in the Downs, and have seized upon 20,000 pounds [   ], which they found in two or three ships that were outward bound for the East Indies, which makes some of our Eastern merchants look blank upon the business and dare not own it. There is five ships come into the Downs from the fleet], and have left 20 of their ships upon the coast of Cales, but we cannot hear of anything they have done worth their la[bour].

Fol. 13. 1657, April 7, London. The House is much troubled that the Protector refuses to take upon himself the kingly government. I am told that yesterday they have voted again that the kingly government is the most needful (for) this nation. Thereupon the House was very much divided . . . They say that the [army?] will have a rendezvous within a few days upon [Black]heath about (it). Many think that the city must [petition and] then it will be done.—News from France about the seizure of the Dutch ships.—P.S. It is reported by a Parliament man that the House is resolved not to alter a tittle of what they have voted concerning the kingly government.

Fol. 14. 1657, April 11, London. After a short notice of the meeting on the Wednesday previous between the Protector and the whole House in the painted chamber, and his then desiring a further time to consider their proposition of kingly government, the writer says—In the mean time here is discovered a new plot amongst the faction of Sindercome as it is reported; it is discovered but two days ago. They have apprehended at least 30 persons, and some of them in arms ready to perfect the plot, and many other arms and ammunition taken amongst them, and they say a matter of 5,000l. or 6,000l. in gold taken about them. The Protector has been himself there two nights till two or three o'clock in the morning in examination of them; and some he has sent to the Tower, and some to Lambeth House, and some he keeps in Whitehall; but they say they are all very obstinate and resolute fellows, and will not put off their hats to the Protector, and thou him at every word that they speak to him. The report goes that there are at least 10 or 15,000 of this gang, and this has bred as great a distraction at Whitehall as the business of kingly government: and these fellows go by the name of Fifth Monarchy men. This noon at Exchange I was told that Major Harrison and Col. Okey and another Colonel are in this plot and are apprehended and sent to the Tower: seven of our frigates are now before Dunkirk, and four before Ostend to try if they can keep their ships from going out or coming in.

Fol. 15. 1657, April 14, London. Yesterday the Protector and the Parliament had a conference according to appointment. . . . . He gave them some objections in writing against his taking the kingly government: this was all that passed and so they parted; and immediately the House chose a Committee to answer his objections. This was told me by a Parliament man yesternight, who told me that his opinion was that the Protector would not accept the kingly government, but withal he told me that he found five for one of the contrary opinion. The certainty of the great plot is without contradiction, and the report goes that it would have been the bloodiest business that ever was invented if it had taken effect, throughout all the kingdom, but especially in London, Whitehall, and all the suburbs. They say that the Tower should have been blown up, &c. &c. I am told that, besides those I mentioned in my last, Sir Henry Vane is one, Col. Rich, Col. Lawson and several others. The Protector immediately sent forces into several counties that he suspects by his intelligences to have any hand in the business. . . . He has those that are in hold continually in examination, and they say he examines them himself.

Fol. 16. 1657, April 18, London.—There have been several applications this week made by the House to the Protector to shew him the necessity that he should take upon him the kingly government: and twice he has put them off because of his indisposition of health. . . . They have solicited him to shew to him their Committee's answer (to his objections), but it seems he is not yet in perfect health to afford them a conference: and yesterday was promised them a resolution from him; but I hear this day upon the Exchange that it is put off till Monday next at 10 in the morning. The general report goes that never man was troubled as he is at this instant. The House as I hear are resolved to make a King, either him or some other; but that is hard to believe, because I think they have no such care, or else they must be confident that he will take it upon him in the conclusion. As it is generally thought, he will only stand for the City to petition him to it.—News from Holland that there they have seized Frenchmens shipping and estates as well, as they have done the Dutch in France, &c.—News that the Emperor of Germany is lately dead. Our ships at sea have met with a Dutch ship coming from St. Domingo with hides, indigo and tobacco and cochineal, and some friars in her, and it is supposed that there is some silver in her; they have taken her and brought her into the Downs.

Fol. 17. 1657, April 21, London.—Since writing the last, as I went home to Putney I called at Westminster, and there met with a Parliament man a kinsman of my wife, who told me more exactly what had passed on Thursday 'twixt the Protector and the House. As thus: the House having been two days before to speak with him, but could not because of his indisposition of health,

but on Thursday he came out of his chamber half unready in his gown, and a black scarf about his neck; and made his apology for the loss of their former labour; and when he had done his speech, Serjt. Glin spake to him in answer to all the objections he gave them in writing to shew them how he was not capacitated to take the crown upon him: and when Glin had ended, the Master of the Rolls, Lenthall, spake very boldly and [   ] in answer to the said objections and urged Magna Carta, and the Petition of Right, and that a kingly government was a right due and most proper for the people of this nation. When he had ended his speech, then spake the Lord Broghall (Broghill) excellently well to the same purpose; and after him spoke Whitlocke shewing invincible reasons and arguments of necessity that the Protector should take upon him the kingly government. When he had ended his speech, the Protector applied himself unto the Lord Whitlock and told them all that he must confess they had all convinced him in all his objections, insomuch that for the present he knew not what to say to them, but desired them to come to him the next day; the meantime he would take a farther consideration of it, and then he would give them satisfaction, so the House went to him on Friday, but they lost their labour; for he was not well and could not be spoken with. So they returned to the House and adjourned to the Monday following, which was yesterday. So yesterday they went to him again, and as I hear he hath put them off till this day in the afternoon 3 of the clock, and hath given them some slight hope that he will take it upon him. The opinion of most men is, that he will take it upon him. Report that the Queen of England is dead in France, and that our English ships coming from Smyrna have had a great fight with four Spanish men-of-war in the Straits, and that one of them is burned and the other sunk.

Fol. 18. 1657, April 25, London.—The Protector has given to the House some proposals whereby he may be capacitated to take the crown upon him; what the proposals are I cannot certainly relate, only I hear that he requires the laws to be regulated and some of the 12 articles moderated, and that they must add 600,000l. more per annum to the 1,300,000l. which they have formerly allotted to him for maintenance; then he will maintain the war with Spain out of that revenue. . . . It is reported that these proposals have given the House so much work to do that it will take them up a month's time at least before they can do anything else if they continue sitting. . . . . It is certain that the major part of them are much discontented, and would fain begone into their country. Report that the Spaniard has besieged a town belonging to the King of Portugal on the borders of Portugal, and is there with 20,000 men, with intent to break into Portugal.

Fol. 19. 1657, May 5, London.—We are still expecting what will be the Protector's resolution. . . . He still puts the House off with farther delays to take better consideration, and to seek God in so weighty a business. . . . . Upon his ultimate result the House adjourned till this day, and what will be done this day will be the work of my next advice. The news of the Prince of Conti is thought to be but a fable, because letters from France make no mention of it, but report that the Dutch and French are like to go together by the ears, their Ambassadors being commanded home on both sides. It is said that the Dutch Ambassador spoke so boldly to the King of France at his audience that he told him that the Cardinal Mazarin would undo him and his kingdom; which caused that the Queen Mother would not give him audience at all, nor the Cardinal either; [when] he came to take his leave of them. One of our State frigates called the Constant Warwick, meeting with three Spanish men of war of Biscay, is reported lately to have taken one of them and sunk the other two; another of our frigates have taken a Dunkirk man-of-war and brought her into Plymouth.

Fol. 20. 1657, May 23, London.—We have reports from several foreign parts, and in the first place from the East Indies, that the Hollanders have taken from the Portugals, a town called Columbus, upon an island from whence the Portugall had all the cinnamon which brought a great revenue to the King of Portugal; and it is said that the Hollanders have taken all that island, and are like to take more from the Portugalls in those parts; if this news be confirmed, the Hollander will go near to make the King of Portugall but a poor King; for most of his revenues came from those parts and from the Brazils; and it is thought, with the aid of the King of Spain, the Hollander will be masters of that ere it be long, and then the King of Spain, with the assistance of the Hollander, will quietly have the kingdom

of Portugal again, having already got footing in it; we
shall in time hear more of this business, which will be
of great importance. From Holland we hear that there
is more likelihood of an accommodation 'twixt them and
France; we hear from France that the King of France
and the Queen his mother are upon their journey towards
Bollen to view the 6,000 men from hence in those parts,
and it it said the King will have 40 thousand more to
join with them, so that it is the general opinion of all
men that they will lay siege to Dunkirk and make the
seat of war there for this summer; from Hamburg they
write that the Swede hath given such an overthrow to the
Pole that he will hardly recover it; the Princes of Germany are all preparing to be in a posture of arms about the
election of a new Emperor; what will become of it no
man knows; it is a general jealousy here that we shall
fall out with the Hollanders before it be long; we hear
no news at all of any action our navy have done at sea.
As for Parliament and Whitehall news, it is thought that
the Parliament will be dissolved within a few days and a
new one chosen at Michaelmas next, or this adjourned till
then; and then they are to meet again and the excluded
members shall be called to sit amongst the rest, and then
being a full House they shall vote a kingly government,
and it will be accepted of by the Protector.—P.S. Here
is a notable book cast up and down the street in nature
of a libel, and directed unto the Protector; it is by
report one of the strangest books there hath yet come
forth; first an admonition to the Protector and then to
the soldiers, and chargeth them with all the misery of
these kingdoms as causers of them and threatens them
God's judgment infallibly to fall upon them for it.

Fol. 21. 1657, July 11, London.—There is news come
from Calais that the King of France his forces have
taken the town called Momadie; it is a little garrison
which the Spaniard had in Luxembourg upon the
frontiers of Champagne, and did much trouble the
French in those parts, and they say it will be of great
importance to the French now they have it, because they
will have Commenance to come to lay siege to a town or.
two not far off that place, which are of greater importance; it seems this garrison was surrendered to the
French upon composition; we do forbear to believe the
truth of it till next post. We hear that at Frankfort
this next month will be the great meeting for the election of the Emperor: some say it will be the Archduke
Leopoldo that will carry it, others say that the Duke of
Bavaria hath a great party for him amongst them; for that
purpose the King of France sends two Ambassadors to the
election, and they are two of the greatest men in France
except the princes of the blood. Some say the Swede will
be in a strait before long, for the Dane is resolved to fall
upon his country with above 40,000 men, and the Muscovite on another part of his country with above 200,000
men, and the Tartar comes with a very powerful [army]
to assist the Pole, so that it is the general opinion that
he will be much worsted this summer. It is confirmed
that the Venetian forces by sea have had a great victory
over the Turk, having taken, sunk, and destroyed above
30 of his men-of-war, besides other ships of carriage.
Nothing more from Portugal . . ., but some say
that there is a fleet of Hollanders that lie before the port
of Lisbon, and will not suffer any provisions to go in.
Lord Montagu is gone down to the Downs to take command of the fleet now there and at Port[smouth] ready
to go out, but no man can tell their design: some say
for Dunkirk, others for Portugal.

Fol. 22. 1657, June 23, London.—Since his last, news
is come by ship from Portugal contradicting the report
given in his last of the success of the Portugal against
the Spaniard before Olmanza, for it is certainly reported
that the Spaniard hath taken Olmanza and another frontier town not far off, &c., and that the Grand Chamberlain of Portugal is revolted to the King of Spain.
(This Grand Chamberlain is he that was Ambassador
here, and had his brother beheaded here for the riot
done in the new Exchange.) It is here generally feared
that the Spaniard will go near to be master of all Portugal unless they have speedy aid from England and
France; and therefore it is thought the Protector will
with all expedition despatch away for Portugal 2,000
men, seeing it concerns him much to do it.—Other
foreign news.—It is said that we have 50 or 60 sail of
men-of-war at Portsmouth and in the Downs ready to
go upon some design; Lord Montague goes general of
them.

Fol. 23. 1657, June 27, London. News from France that
the Prince of Condy attempted to surprise Calais, but
failed, and was forced to retreat after he had burned some
houses in the suburbs, and is returned back to the main
body of the Spanish army, which is in the upper part of

Flanders waiting upon the French army to see what they
will do, &c., &c. Nothing more concerning the Portugal
business. . . . [　　] was performed the ceremony
of giving the Protector his oath in Hall and making him
Protector Royal. I doubt not but you will have it all at
large in the next Monday's pamphlet; the meantime I
will only acquaint you with what I heard, that there
were [a pair] of scaffolds built upon each side of a great
canopy [　　] at the upper end of the Hall where the
Speaker sate, and on [one] side sate all the Parliament
men, and on the other side sate the [　], the Lord
Mayor and all the Aldermen, and they say the [Earl of]
Warwick carried the sword before the Protector, and
[then after he was] sworn, he was proclaimed Protector
Royal in the [　]. Some say that those Dutch ships
that were seen in the Downs, mentioned in my former
letters, are gone in behalf of the Spaniard and their
own interest to block up Lisbon . . . ., for they have
likewise war with the Portugal. If this be true, the
Portugal will be in a sad condition before long, and
then Blake's fleet will want a place of retreat upon all
occasions, which will be a business of great concernment
for the Protector's designs against the Spaniard.

Fol. 24. 1657, June 30, London. The pamphlet that
came out yesterday will shew all about the late ceremony at Westminster. It is said it will be proclaimed
before the Exchange. In the meantime the merchants,
and generally all trades in the city, are much troubled,
and storm highly at the proceedings of this titular
Parliament, I will not say they curse them to the pit
of hell, for by the Acts they have made they have raised
yet more and more the customs and excise of almost all
commodities, to the destruction of trade.

1657, July 4, London. You will hear more at large
in Thursday's pamphlet, concerning the great triumphing through this city upon Wednesday last, in proclaiming the Protector and chief magistrate over the
three kingdoms and the dominions thereunto belonging,
especially before the Exchange. The Lord Mayor, in
his crimson velvet gown, and all the aldermen in their
scarlet gowns, attended with all the officers of the city,
guarded with the Protector's life guard, and 500 of the
best horse in the army, and 30 or 40 trumpeters of the
army, and all the trumpeters and waytes of the city, with
such a noise as never was heard. All the world is discontented at the Acts the Parliament have made concerning import and excise, which is the most abominable
thing that ever was heard of.—After some reports of
foreign news, the writer says, there are two or three
more ships come to Portsmouth from Blake's fleet; the
Dunkirkers have lately taken one of our frigates.

Fol. 25. 1657, July 14, London.—Here is nothing at
home but crying of Acts up and down the town.
1657, July 18, London.—The Protector hath taken
Major Lambert's commission away from him, and has
transferred all his soldiers under the command of Col.
Fleetwood, which many conceive will breed ill blood,
and hope the old proverb may prove true, that when
thieves fall out true men may come to their goods.
They say that Sir Gilbert Pickering and Col. Sidenham
are put out of the Council of State, and more removals
are expected. They say that the Protector is sending
an ambassador for Muscovy, to mediate the differences
between the Emperor and the Swede, for we begin to
fear that the King of Sweden is not in a good condition.
. . . . . Montmedy holds out still against the French.
The report goes that the Spaniard hath killed a great
number of the French before that place.—In a P.S. he
says that the Excise and Customs are let to farm to
Martin Nowell, Alderman Dethick, and one Blake, his
son-in-law, Sheriff Teaine, Alderman Frederick, Mr.
Ford, and three or four more, and that they are to pay
900,000l. per annum.

Fol. 26. 1657, July 25, London. News is come to the
Protector from General Blake, that he hath taken
a Flemish ship, which was coming from the Canaries,
bound either for Amsterdam or for Cales. . . . . She
had aboard her above 200 Spanish commanders and
300,000 pieces of eight, besides store of cochineal and
other rich commodities. News likewise this week from
Amsterdam that two Dutch ships are lately arrived there
with the value of 300,000l. sterling in pieces of eight,
from the Canaries, which is for the King of Spain's accompt to pay Don John d'Austria's soldiers. There is besides in these ships to a great value in P[　] commodities, all which goods and plate were part of that which
was [taken] in the Canaries out of those ships which
Blake destroyed at the Canaries, before they were
destroyed, and so were the goods and plate in this ship
which Blake hath now taken.—Reports from Portugal
and Germany.—Two of the King of Denmark's ships

are very great, carrying 104 pieces of ordnance apiece.
. . . . A flying report that Lambert should be taken at
Gravesend, in a ship, intending to go privately beyond
the seas, but was brought back and is sent to the Tower:
some question the truth of it; . . . but it is certain
that there came this week from Dunkirk shallops, which
landed a party of musketeers upon the Isle of Tennet
(Thanet), and went to a knight's house not far off the
sea, and plundered his house, and took from him a
matter of [   ] or 1,500l. in money, and carried the
knight away with them, and would have taken his eldest
son and his wife also [if it had not] been that he
engaged upon his honour to cease 1,000l. to be sent to
them in Bruges within a certain time for his ransom.
Meantime they have taken the knight for security till
the money be paid. It is supposed that they were most
of them Englishmen.

1657, July 28, London.—A report, since the French
letters came yesterday, that the siege of Montmédy is
raised. Several merchant ships are lately arrived in the
Downs from Smyrna and Leghorn, and one or two from
the East Indies, and at least 10 or 12 from the Barbadoes, most of them from Barbadoes laden with coarse
sugars. Our fleet is not yet gone out of the Downs,
neither can we learn upon what design they are bound.
At home very little moving, but very busy about this
new farming of the Customs and Excise. . . . Some say
that two or three of them do begin to fall off, and are
afraid to hazard their fortunes in so casual a business;
as indeed they had but a sad example in the late farmers
in the late King's time, which were all men of vast
estate, and are now all utterly ruined, and under the
judgment of a statute of Bankrupts.

Fol. 27. 1657, Aug. 1. Says he has taken Sir
Richard's clock to Joanes the watch maker in the
Strand.—News that Blake's fleet is come upon our
coast; some of his ships are at Plymouth, some at
Portsmouth, and other places. They say that Montagu
is gone out of the Downs with his fleet of 30 sail of very
good ships; he hovers to and fro about Calais and Dunkirk. I was told yesterday by a notable intelligent
person that Montagu and his fleet are bound for the
Baltic, upon design to relieve the King of Sweden, and
be revenged on the King of Denmark for imbarging our
ships at Copenhagen about two or three years ago. The
King of Sweden is in a sad condition and can expect no
aid but from the Protector. The news from Flanders
is that Montmédy is relieved, but the news from Whitehall is that it is taken by the French. They say that
an ambassador from Portugal arrived in the west country, who is supposed comes for aid from hence. A report
that the Earl of Stamford and two of his men have
murdered a man upon the highway near [   ] park.
Some say that he and his two men are condemned to be
hanged at the Assizes in the country; and that he hath
obtained a reprieve for 15 days, and is coming to London to (try if) he can get his pardon, which is thought
will not be granted. Our undertakers for the Customs
and Excise are still at a stand, and can not yet resolve
whether it is best to go on or [not].

1657, Aug. 4, London. — Report from France that
Montmédy is surrendered to the King of France upon
very noble terms, the Governor being slain and dying
the next day after he was wounded. . . . The news
of Blake's coming upon our coast is not so certain (for
aught I can perceive) as was reported upon Saturday
last, but it is generally confirmed that Montagu is gone
with his fleet for the Sound, and so for the Baltic Sea to
the relief of the Swede . . . . he hath no friends to
stick to him at this time but the Protector and the King
of France. The King of France cannot, having both
his hands full; and for our ships, they are thought will
come too late, if they should get clear through the
Sound, where it is thought they will find opposition.—
He says the report of the Portugal Ambassador having
arrived is a fable . . . . It is this day reported
that the Protector and those that have been in hand
to farm the Customs and Excise have now absolutely
agreed upon particulars. News yesterday from Leghorn, that the Turk's Tripoli men-of-war have taken
an English ship bound from Leghorn to Skandaroon,
very richly laden for the account of the merchants of
[   ] city; she is esteemed to be worth at least 40 or
50,000l., her lading was fine cloth and tin and 80,000
pieces of eight.—P.S. I hear nothing farther of the Earl
of Stamford's business. The ship's name that is taken
is the Recovery of London, of 350 tons, and 28 pieces of
ordnance.

Fol. 28. 1657, Aug. 15, London.—The Portugal [Am-
bassador] is come to Greenwich, where he will stay till
order is taken for his reception and entrance into the

City in state, as accustomed. He says that the wine
merchants and vintners of London had made several
addresses to the Protector for a longer time for the
putting of their wines at the rate accustomed, but that
he refused, "So that henceforth we shall have [   ]
and white wine for 7d. the quart and Spanish wines
and [   ] for 18d. the quart. The old company of
the East India [   ] have been likewise soliciting the
Protector for a patent [for a] joint stock for that trade
as it hath been formerly, but they are put off from day
to day for his resolution, so that many are of opinion he
will not grant it."

1657, Aug. 22, London.—News that Montagu with 30
sail of our ships is before O   and waits for the
King of France in person to come down into those parts
with 30,000 horse and foot, and it is supposed their
design is to lay siege to Dunkirk by sea and land.—News
from Antwerp of Don John of Austria's doings.—News
from Germany that the Swede has utterly routed the
Dane.—The Portugal Ambassador has not yet made his
entry into the City. The undertakers for the Customs
and Excise have not yet agreed with the Protector.

Fol. 29. 1657, Sept. 12, London.—A report on the
Exchange of an express from the Downs with news that
the French have besieged Dunkirk by land, and that
Montagu has besieged it by sea with 28 English ships.
. . . . If Dunkirk be not well provided it will not be
able to hold out long.

1657, Sept. 19, London.—No news from Holland or
Flanders these 10 or 15 days. . . . . This day I was
told that the French have not laid siege to Dunkirk.
. . . . Here is Col. Reynolds, that went Commander
over the English that went over into France, and hath
brought over with him the Governor's son of Calais;
they are come to fetch some mortar pieces and ammunition, which is granted them and have shipped it away,
and they are gone post after it. There are three or
four post packets now stopt in Dunkirk, and they will
not let them pass, which makes a great disturbance in
trade here.

Fol. 31. 1657, Sept. 29, London. Three posts have
come together from Holland, Flanders, and Germany,
which were stopt in Dunkirk, which confirms the taking
of Mardike.—News of great defeat of the Swedes by
the Danes at sea.—Other news from Germany.—A report, held true, of De Reuter having taken 10 Turkish
men-of-war.—For domestic businesses at Whitehall, they
are so closely carried that we can not learn anything
that is done there; but what they will have published
you will find in the pamphlets. This day was chosen in
Guildhall Alderman Cheverton to be Lord Mayor for
this next year.

1657, Oct. 7, London.—Report of the French forces in
Flanders.—Reports of three of our merchant ships of
considerable value, one taken in the Straits by the
Turkish men-of-war, and the other two coming from
Guinea and the West Indies are taken by the Spaniard.
—P.S. A sad business befallen the son of Sir Thomas
Eyton, a very wild young man . . . . he was placed
with a woollen draper, but played so many wicked pranks
that his master at last turned him away; . . . . and
then he fell into company with as mad blades as himself,
and upon the highway on this side of St. Albans, they
robbed a coach and killed   Lieut. Col. ; and now
young Eyton is taken for one of them, and is in Newgate and like to suffer for it.

Fol. 30. 1657, Dec. 19, London. It is certainly confirmed that the two great commanders mentioned in his
last letter were cast away on the Goodwin Sands in a
great fog, and a kind of a storm, and the bottom of the
ship that they were in was see[n] upwards by one that
was very near her when she was cast away . . . One
of their trunks is come ashore, and some swords and
rich belts known to be theirs.—There hath been some
brushing of late at Mardike, [   ] that the Spaniard
hath taken a matter of 60 of our men.—Report that the
Dane hath lately got some advantage of the Swede
. . . . The Swede is much threatened by the Pole
and Muscovite and German forces, which undoubtedly
will fall upon him heavily this next summer, and then
he must of necessity fall, for he hath neither men nor
money nor friends to help him, but the Protector and
the French, who have enough to do themselves this
summer, as it is supposed . . . there are about seven
or eight Jesuit priests apprehended, and are put in
prison on pretext of a plot.

Fol. 42. 1657, Dec. 29, London. — We conceive by
some late actions that our great one at Whitehall hath
a world of fears and jealousies in his breast, for on
Christmas and the day following he hath caused at least
five or six persons to be apprehended and sent to several

X 3

places of security; and some of the persons of quality, whilst they were at sermons and receiving the communion in private houses, namely, Dr. Wyld, and the greatest part that heard him at a private house, where he doth ordinarily preach and administer the sacrament at certain times appointed, and so soon as he had performed his exercises both he and the greatest part of his auditors were seized by a troop of horse and carried to St. James's, and in the same manner was another that preached at Exeter House, and the most part of his auditors likewise, and some others in London as well as they. And the next they took several persons out of Tennis Courts, and carried them to prison. They say some are sent to Windsor and some are set at liberty. Most of the Papists are apprehended and secured through all parts of the kingdom.—News from France and Germany.—Here is great store of shipping lately come into the Downs from all parts, as six ships from the East Indies, and others from Mallaga with wines and fruit, others from the Canaries with wines, and some from Barbadoes, with sugar, indigo, and cotton, and likewise from Lisbon; in all, by report, 40 sail.

Fol. 32. 165⅞, Feb. 15, London. Reports about contests between the Danes and Swedes.—The rumour continues that we shall have another Parliament very speedily, and that the writs are under hand; yet have I not so much faith as to believe it. The Governor of Dover Castle is put out, and another put in his place. What I wrote you in my last concerning his own regiment is certain in the main, but not all his regiment, but the greatest part of them. The Protector made a great feast in the Cockpit for all his chief commanders within two or three days after he broke up the Parliament, where (as it is reported) he drank wine very plenteously with them. No news from France, but that at Mardik our Englishmen die there wonderfully of an unknown infectious disease; and many are sent over hither very sick, and not one that comes over of 20 recovers, (he says that those that visit them, even the surgeons themselves are infected.) We expect daily some strange thing or other to come forth concerning the promoting of the present government, and a power or order for raising money by Privy Seal or the like . . . One told me that the Protector had sent a Privy Seal to Prideaux, the Attorney-General, for 3,000*l*. . . . . It is certain that above a fortnight ago the Protector sent for the present Lord Mayor, to demand a certain sum of the city, who said they were so poor, that they were forced to go from door to door to beg contributions for the relief of their poor, which were more than ever; and many families that formerly had good handicraft trades, and lived very well, and now for want of work were ready to famish for want of bread; and this is too true a story. The Protector told him for all that, if he would not undertake to procure him money, he knew how to do it himself, and so parted.

Fol. 33. 165⅞, Feb. 23, London. The Protector's eldest son, Richard, had like to have been shot by one of his own soldiers, who gave fire at him with a musket, but it did not go off, so he escaped that danger; but his fath(er) continues still sick and keeps his bed; the last news I heard of him was that he had a very dangerous impostume in his back, and yesterday, sent for Boone one of his our city chirurgeons . . whom I speak with to-morrow.—News from Germany and France.—News came yesterday of the taking four or five English ships by the Dunkirkers, which are for the Spaniards, and lie upon the coast of Biscay, and in those harbours and upon the coast of Spain, and scout up and down about the mouth of the Straits, and meet with many of our ships.

165⅞, March 20, London.—The city are [putting them]selves into a posture of arms, according to the Protector's [letter to the] court of aldermen and common council, and . . . the trained bands were commanded to shew their arms yesterday, which was done.—A report of Monck writing to the Protector that he should look to himself in England, and he would look to himself in Scotland.—News from Germany.

Fol. 34. 165⅞, March 6, London.—Refers to the proclamation by the Protector and his Council, that all Papists delinquents and those who had borne arms for the late King should depart from London to their own habitations, and not to go from thence above 5 miles. . . . It is reported that the Protector cannot take his natural sleep at night, but cries out upon Monck, Monck, so that it seems there is something in Scotland troubles him. . . . It is certain that the grandees of these times were never more put to their shifts than at this time; they say we shall have Privy Seals come forth very shortly . . . there is a report that an order given for the army to be drawn up to this city and round about it, which if it be, it will be to draw some blood from those of this city that are troubled with a pleurisy. Here continues still the rumour of setting out a fleet and sending 30,000 men into foreign parts; which cannot be done as the case stands at present; for many men say (I cannot say how they will stand to it) that [they] will know how they part with their money hereafter; and this is the common talk among many in the city; but when half a dozen red coats shall come to them they will be as tame as asses.—News from Germany.—A rumour for a long time, and it still continues, that we are like to have another squabble with the Dutch.

Fol. 35. 165⅞, March 9, London.—Here [is news come] to Whitehall that there is peace made 'twixt the Swede [and the Dane], but I cannot think how it can be done so suddenly. . . . The news was told me by Jo. Bu[ ] this day, who had it from a friend of his who was at Whitehall this morning, where he said was great rejoicing at the news. (He gives the conditions of the peace).—News upon Saturday from our fleet that lie before Dunkirk, that 5 Dutch ships would have gone into Ostend, and it seems they were empty ships, and our ships being resolved to search them, &c., which they refused, thereupon they fell into fight and our ships took 3 of them, and forced the other two to run ashore; and now some say they are Dutch ships and will cause a breach 'twixt us and them; others say they were ships that the Spaniards had bought from the Dutch. Immediately on the news order was given to General Goodson (one of our sea generals) to haste to the Downs and go forth with 16 or 20 sail of our ships of war that are ready in the Downs, and to examine all Dutch ships that should pass to and fro in our Channel, and to fight them if the Spaniard or the King of Scots have any interest in them, for we are very jealous that the Dutch will furnish them with ships to transport soldiers for some part of the North of England. Col. Lawson, a sea commander is lately sent to the Tower, and went in under the Traitor's bridge, as I am told, but upon what account I cannot learn.

165⅞, March 13, London.—News of the peace between the Swede [and the Dane] is confirmed. It is the opinion that we shall speedily fall out with the Dutch. The Lord Mayor of this city, and some of the Aldermen and Common Council men were yesterday with the Protector at Whitehall by his [order], where he made a speech unto them, and told them that this nation and this city were in great danger, because he was upon good ground certainly informed that the [King of] Scots and the King of Spain were preparing great forces to come for England, and had hired ships of the Hollanders for that purpose to transport their men and that here were many thousands in this nation ready to receive them, and to join with them, and therefore he sent for them to acquaint them with these things, and to give them order to put the militia of the city into a speedy posture of war, that they may be ready at an hour's warning upon all occasions, and that for his part he assured them he would live and die with and [not] stir from the city.

Fol. 34. 1658, March 27, London.—The report that the peace was bad for the Dane is confirmed. News from France that the Governor of Hesden in Picardy, not far from Amiens and Montreuil, has surrendered it to the Prince of Condy, being discontented at some pretended wrongs received from the Cardinal, &c. &c. At home we hear that great fears and distraction is amongst them at [ ] and in the army likewise, as it is reported that the whole army should be drawn off [from] London, and that there should be a general rendezvous upon Hounslow Heath; but that is altered, and train [bands] here in the city were ordered to be set up and a [day] appointed for a general training in Moorfields; but we hear that business is likewise dasht, and now they beat drums, for, volunteers both in city and country as (fast) as they can drive; for Cromwell himself hath [said] that the King of Scots hath come forth of Flanders [with a fleet] of ships, and will land in some part of England or Scotland; if he be not landed already for that? On Tuesday night last, here was a kind of alarm in this city; about 9 o'clock that night the Protector sent [order] to the Lord Mayor and Aldermen and Common Council to set a double watch that night in the city, and that each Alderman in his ward with the constables and Common Council men should, in person, go and make search in every tavern, inn, and alehouse for cavaliers and malignants, and suspected persons, and seize upon horses; which was done accordingly; the like was done in the suburbs by the soldiers, and some horses were taken and carried away to the Tower and other places, but I hear their owners came the next day and they had their horses again. There are 4 or 5 of their own tribe committed lately to the Tower; amongst the rest Sir William Waler (Waller?) is one.

Fol. 36. 1658, May 8, London.—Says that the report in his last of Dr. Hewet's death is false, and he is confident they cannot prove anything against him It is commonly reported that the High Court of Justice will not go up, but if there be any trial for the prisoners upon the score of this new plot, it will be at the King's Bench bar. . . . P.S. Since writing of the premises the High Court of Justice was proclaimed before the Exchange at noon, to begin upon Wednesday next.

Fol. 37. 1658, May 11, London.—The High Court of Justice will begin to-morrow. The speech goes that one Slingsby will be the first that shall be tried, and the next will be Dr. Hewett. It is not known who shall be Judge of that Court; some think it will be Serjeant Glin, and their reason is, because his opinion only amongst all the Judges was for setting up the High Court of Justice for this business. They say for certain that Dr. Channell (who was the first discoverer of this pretended plot) is now run since he is come to London, and Capt. Staple hath his pardon for his infamous confession of that which some say he cannot justly prove.

Fol. 38. 1658, May 15, London.—Some of the High Court of Justice met on Wednesday afternoon and adjourned the court till Monday next. . . . A report that there has been a smart fight lately between [   ] and the Spaniards about Mardik or Ostend wherein [   ] hath been worsted, and that the Duke of York and Marquis of Ormond are slain in the battle . . . but few or none believe it true. . . . P.S. Robert Waring is dead since he came over from beyond sea with Sir William Whitmore.

Fol. 39. 1658, May 29, London.—On Thursday last the High Court of Justice sat, and three or four of the prisoners were brought from the Tower to Westminster, but the court adjourned till Wednesday; none of the prisoners were brought to the bar but were sent back to the Tower. The chief witness that accuses Dr. Hewet is run away. I cannot hear anything more about the trial of Sir Henry Slingsby; some say that Lord Falconbridge has begged his life.—Some French news.

Fol. 40. 1658. June 1, London.—News from France.

Fol. 39. 1658, June 1, late at night, London.—The High Court of Justice sat this day. Dr. Hewet and the Earl of Peterborough's brother were tried. The Doctor would not plead but denied their power. The other did the same for a long time, but at length pleaded Not guilty; they produced several witnesses against him. Both were sent back to the Tower.

Fol. 40. 1658, June 3, London. . . . Yesterday the High Court of Justice passed sentence on Dr. Hewet and Sir Henry Slingsby (to be hung, drawn, and quartered). The Earl of Peterborough's brother is cleared. (He refers to the pamphlet for more particular relations.) . . . Sam. Terrick and his son are both broke for 20,000l., whereof 17,000l. is money taken up at interest.

Fol. 41. 1658, July 13, London.—News from France of the bankruptcy (for 300,000 crowns) of a great Paris banker, which distracts our Exchange.—A great wedding upon Thursday next; the Lord Rosse doth marry the Marquis of Dorchester's daughter, and a tailor told me, that the Lord Rosse hath made him one suit will cost him 800l. sterling.

1658, July 20, London. I heard to-day that Cardinal Mazarin narrowly escaped. The Duke of Anjou (brother of the King of France) asked for an order for some money; the Cardinal made a short denial; the Duke pulled a pistol out of his pocket and discharged it at him, but one of the Cardinal's attendants stept between the Duke and the Cardinal and received the shot and was killed. This was told me by one that said he saw a letter from Dunkirk which gave the relation. A report that ours and the French forces intend to lay siege to Newport, and that General Morgan going to take a view of that town was slain with a cannon bullet from the town of Newport.

Fol. 43. 1660, April 21, London.—Since my last Tuesday's letter, here hath been a strong report that the King will be here speedily. Several letters have been lately seen from him to the Council of State and to General Monck, and here hath been the Lord of Ormond and hath returned back again. The Earl of Newcastle and the old Lord Goring are come over and

remain here still, and have been with the Council of State and with General Monck, and have had civil reception by them. A report that a person of quality has arrived in the Downs; some say the King, others a person to treat with the Parliament about the King's business. . . . Here was ordered a general training on Tuesday next of all the trained bands and auxiliaries in this city to be kept in Hyde Park. . . News that yesterday General Monck and the Council of State received intelligence that a great party of the fanaticks are rendezvouzed at or about Edgehill, and therefore General Monck is resolved to march to them with all his forces, &c. (Charlton says he does not believe it.) P.S. This day the Council have sent Titchburne and Ireton to the Tower.

1660, May 1, London.—On Saturday last were brought letters from the King (they say Sir Richard Grenville brought them), one to the Houses of Lords and Commons, one to General Monck, and one to the Lord Mayor and Aldermen and Common Council of the city of London. The first and second were read this morning in the presence of both Houses and voted satisfactory; then they voted Charles Stewart the Second the lawful heir apparent to the Crown of England, Scotland, and Ireland; thirdly, they voted the Government of these three nations to be in the King, Lords, and Commons; fourthly, they voted a committee of Lords and Commons to be sent speedily into Holland to acquaint the King with these votes and fetch him home; and lastly they voted 40 or 50,000l. for the charge of bringing the King to England. (He gives briefly the substance of the King's letters.) P.S. We hear that many of the fanatick party are daily taken in the North and West; among the rest Major-General Harrison.

Fol. 44. 1660, May 5, London.—The city have granted a loan of 100,000l. to the Parliament, viz., 50,000l. to bring the King home, and 50,000l. to pay the arrears of the Navy and General Monck's soldiers. . . . Lord Craven and Sir John Stowell (as I hear) are in a very good way to recover their estates. The King's arms are now beginning to be set up in all churches and in the sterns of all ships and in all the halls in the city, and all the other arms pulled down, and ordered that the King shall be prayed for in all churches. They have voted 500l. for a jewel for Sir John Grenville for bringing the King's letter and declaration. . . . In Dorsetshire there hath been lately another rising of the fanaticks, but they were quickly suppressed and their chief captain taken prisoner with 40 more.

Fol. 46. 1660, May 8, London. This day the King was proclaimed in the accustomed places throughout London and the suburbs. All the trained bands and auxiliaries guarded the streets. The heralds of arms the maces, and the sword naked, accompanied with all the noblemen of the Parliament, the two Speakers, and all officers and judges, the Lord Mayor in a purple velvet gown, all the aldermen in their scarlet robes, General Monck with a number of horsemen of his own troop assisted with the city troops and a great number of volunteer citizens on horseback, all riding with naked swords, flourishing them above their heads.—Cannon firing; bells ringing. . . . They are going to make bonfires.

1660, May 26, London.—The King landed at Dover yesterday about 3 p.m.; they say he lay at Canterbury yesternight, and this night he is to lie at Cobham and then rest himself, and on Tuesday come to London.—Preparations in London.—The Duke of York is to lie at St. James's and the Duke of Gloucester at Somerset House.—The King hath knighted all the commissioners that went over into Holland, as well those of the Parliament that were not knights before, as also those of the city. Alderman Langham and Alderman Adams are knights and baronets.

Fol. 45. 1660, May 29, London.—(A long letter about the King's reception.) Great concourse of people in all the towns through which he passed from Dover. At Blackheath not less than 120,000 people, men, women, and children.—All the horse came along with the King to this city. The King's life guard and Col. Monck's life guard always next the King's person; and a little before the King came to the City, the Lord Mayor and Aldermen met him and performed those obedient ceremonies due in such cases; and after that the Lord Mayor and General Monck rode bare-headed before the King all along the City, and the Duke of York on the right hand of the King, and the Duke of Gloucester on his left; there was not one musket or pistol shot off ever since the King came from Dover till he was in Whitehall; for there was a prohibition to the contrary

X 4

upon pain of death.—On the King's landing at Dover, Monck fell on his knees; the King laid both his hands on his head, and afterwards took him on his arm and kissed him, and some say he called him father. He called for an Order of the Garter which the Duke of York had ready and gave to the King who gave it to the General, and the Duke of York took, and would by all means put it about his leg; and after that the King knighted him Knight Banneret of England, which being done, the King and the General had about an hour's discourse in private. . . . This morning the King was upon Blackheath by 9 o'clock, and there he was on horseback and thence to London. Sir Thomas Gower being in town told me you should hear from him by the post.

Fol. 46. 1660, June 9, London.—That design which the Presbyterians had against Bishops is come to nothing. —(He refers Sir Richard to the common constant weekly pamphlet for the proceedings in Parliament.) Report that the lives of some of the traitors are to be begged by some of the Court followers who are to have great sums of money for their pains, according to the degrees of the persons and the fact. . . . But your countryman Harrison will die, whoever escapes, for he justifies himself in his action and glories in it. His Majesty's only recreation as yet is at Tennis by 5 o'clock in the morning for an hour or two. Yesterday morning he went to Hampton Court and Richmond, and came back to Whitehall to dinner, only three or four to attend him. Lord Leigh and Lord Newport sit in the House of Peers.

Fol. 47. 1660, June 16. London.—Yesterday, in the House of Peers, Lord Purbeck was accused of some treason which he has spoken of the King, and likewise of blasphemy; and the same day in the House of Commons Serjeant Glin and Whitlocke for their actions in Cromwell's time, and they say Glin is got clear with much ado, but Whitlocke is put off till another time.— The trial of the regicides takes up most of the time of both Houses.—The King and the Dukes of York and Gloucester dined this day at the Lord Mayor's by a private invitation of themselves. The King has propounded to Dr. Reynolds and Calamy for the Presbyterian party to choose 10 others to join with them, and to Dr. Gawden and Mr. Bale for the Episcopal side to take 10 likewise to their assistance and decide the business of Church Government, and the King to be the Moderator. This is the news of the day.—The King and the Duke of York come every evening as far as Battersea, Putney, and Barn Elms, to swim and bathe themselves; and take a great delight in it and swim excellent well.

Fol. 45. 1660, June 19, London. At noon, Exchange was received the King's pardon for all those of his subjects, except those which the Parliament will not pardon. . . . A report that the Houses will shortly adjourn for a certain time till the funerals of the late King be solemnized, which time is not yet certainly concluded upon, but his corpse is to be fetched back from Windsor very speedily. . . . When they have done with those that have been the late King's tryers, they will fall on those that condemned Dr. Hewet and divers others in the same kind. Yesterday, the City sent some of the Aldermen and Common Council to invite His Majesty, the Dukes of York and Gloucester, and some of the Lords to a feast on next Thursday fortnight. A present from the King of Spain of 16 horses, both coach-horses and saddle-horses.

Fol. 48. 1660, June 23, London.—Scott being taken at Gant in Flanders was sent over and brought prisoner to Westminster upon Thursday last. The two Houses have finished the Bill for Pardon yesterday, and delivered it up to be ingrossed. . . . Lord Newport I hear is made Lord Lieutenant for Shropshire, the Lord Craven, Governor of Shrewsbury, and Sir William Whitmore his deputy. Great preparations for the late King's funeral. New Commissioners chosen for the Custom House, viz., Sir Job Harly, Sir John Werssenholme (Wolstenholme?), Sir John Jacobs, Sir Nicholas Crisp, and some others to be added.—Many applications for places at Court. Whitehall is like a fair all day, and many discontented and jealous that others are preferred.

Fol. 49. 1660, June 26, London.—The Act of Oblivion and Pardon is not yet finished: yesterday, Lord Leigh told me it was not come up to the House of Lords. . . . The King doth urge them very much to finish it. They have voted 20,000l. to the Queen in order to her coming over. Somerset House is preparing for her. I have sent you some pamphlets; amongst them are two of Waller's poems; I had much ado to get that which is

bound upon leather, they have been so bought up of late that there is none now to be had under 5s. a piece. (A note of the charges says that Natures Secrets cost 1s., and Waller's poems, 1s. 10d.)

Fol. 50. 1660, Aug. 11, London.—I hear that yesterday the Bill of Indemnity was passed in the House of Lords. . . . A Parliament man told me that he believed if the House of Commons found any difficulty in it for them to give their consent, they would refer it wholly to the King. I hear that the House of Lords have excepted 4 more for life out of the Bill of Indemnity, which was Major Crochson (Croxton) that was governor of Chester Castle, and one Colonel Blackwell, and one Wybourne, of this city, a shopkeeper . . . . Some say that Fairfax's name is in question.

Fol. 51. 1660, Aug. 14, London. . . . . I am told that Major Waring has procured a pardon from the King. . . . Lord Newport intends to go for Shropshire next week, but his lady stays here . . . . P.S. I am told that my nephew Job is the most leading man in the House of Commons and all before him when he appears and speaks; he is now chosen chairman in a committee for religion. He is to be made a serjeant-at-law the next that are made, and to be Chief Justice of West Chester, or, as some say, judge of the Marches of Wales; he is the highest man in the House for the King's interest.

1660, Aug. 18, London. . . . Reports about the Bill of Indemnity. . . . Hazelrigg, Vane, and Scott, that the Lords had excepted for life, they have since condescended that they shall be only excepted for their estates. The falling out between the Duke of Buckingham and the Earl of Bristol has caused a severe order by the King and his Council against their duels. The Lord Digby is put out from being Chamberlain to the Queen. On Wednesday last some members of both Houses came to the city to borrow 100,000l., and offered the Poll money for security; the Court of Aldermen and Common Council referred the matter to a Committee, in which some Presbyterians in the Common Council would have a petition drawn to be presented to both Houses to relate some grievances, the chief being, as I am told, that the King had not performed his promise in settling religion and the Church Government, because, say they, they see the King's whole design is to set up the Bishops; but I believe their motion did not take. . . . News here that the fanatics are up in your parts, and have seized upon the town of Stafford, and some say they are up likewise in Scotland.—News from Italy that there is an insurrection in Rome, and that the Pope has fled to a place of strength not far from Rome, where his treasure is. . . . . The States of Holland have sent His Majesty a most stately pleasure boat to sail up and down the river, all gilt very richly within and without.

Fol. 52. 1660, Sept. 1, London.—The day after my last letter the King signed the Bill of Indemnity and the Bill for Poll Money, and a Bill for Judicial Proceedings. . . . They are about disbanding the old army, but I am told they will have a new army maintained of 6 or 8,000 men for some certain time.—We hear that the Spanish Ambassador is arrived at Dover, and that the French Ambassador is at Calais ready to embark, so that we shall have a great deal of gallantry here in the city very shortly. It is reported that Major Waring will come off both for life and estate, but that Lambert and Sir Henry Vane will suffer death. Col. Scrope and Ludlow and Carye and Axtall are already voted in Parliament to die, and some others, yet it is thought the King will pardon many.

1660, Sept. 8, London.—The Parliament have voted the King 1,200,000l. . . . The Duke of Gloucester has been dangerously ill of the small pox or some such disease; the doctors say it is a disease between the small pox and the measles; he is now past danger of death for this bout as the doctors say. The Earl of Oxford lies dangerously ill of the small pox, it is thought he will hardly recover. The King has lately sent a letter to the Lord Mayor that it is his pleasure to have all the old Aldermen that are living shall take their places again that were put out because they refused to act against his late Majesty during the late troubles, and all those put out that have acted against him. The Earl of Anteram attempted to make his escape out of the Tower, but was prevented. Col. Ludlow has made his escape out of the hands of the serjeant-at-arms, whereupon a proclamation is come forth upon pain of high treason for any man to harbour him that doth not discover him, and 300l. for any man that shall discover and apprehend him. . . General Montagu is gone to Holland to fetch over the Princess Royal. We hear that Lord German (Jermyn) is lately come from France, and brings word that the Queen Mother is not willing to come over, but will stay in France to avoid inconvenience, and it is said the Duke of Guise is to marry the Lady Henrietta Maria.

1660, Sept. 11, London. It is thought the Parliament will adjourn this day week. Great preparations for the return of the Princess Royal, who is arrived at Dover, and the Duke of York is gone to meet her either there or by the way, also the great Ambassador from Spain. The Prince de Ligne arrived at Gravesend upon Sunday last, and this night they say he lies at Greenwich, and to-morrow makes his entry into this city; he comes out of Flanders and brings 500 attendants, also nine score horses, some coach-horses, and some for the great saddle; some to present to the King, some to the Duke of York, and some to the Duke of Gloucester, with three rich coaches, one to each of them, with six horses apiece. He comes extraordinary Ambassador. News from Plymouth of another Ambassador from Spain come to be Lieger here. Yesterday evening was proclaimed before the Exchange peace and free trade with Spain. . . . Ludlow was nearly taken; they took his coat and the coats and cloaks of two or three that were with him.

Fol. 53. 1660, Sept. 22, London. The Ambassador that came by way of Plymouth, and comes to lie Lieger here, is arrived and has taken up his quarters at Crouné House, at South Lambeth. We hear that the Princess Royal comes not over till the spring. because of the death of her brother the Duke of Gloucester. The Prince de Ligne upon Thursday last gave His Majesty a visit, but none of his attendants were there in mourning; yet they say there are at least 40 tailors at work making mourning for him and his followers at his own charge.

Fol. 54. 1660, Sept. 25, London.—The King and Duke of York went by water last Sunday afternoon to Gravesend, to meet the Princess Royal, who landed at Margate, where the King and Duke of York met her; thence they came to Gravesend, and this afternoon they brought her by water to Whitehall privately; only the Tower saluted them as they passed by, and so did all the ships in the river, with all their great guns.—Some of the judges are sent for to try the traitors.—The Duke of Gloucester was buried privately in Westminster on Friday night. Speaker Lenthall's son, who was knighted by Cromwell, is charged to have two wives, and is liked to be hanged; for, as I hear, it will be manifestly proved against him.

1660, Nov. 6, London. (To Mr. John Langley.)

Fol. 53. 1660, Nov. 10, London.—The Parliament have voted a fast, and have voted the Princess Henrietta Maria 10,000l., as a gift. . . . The Houses have been at Whitehall with the King, to thank him for his last declaration. . . . They are about settling the business of the Court of Wards, and how to raise 100,000l. in lieu thereof, and also upon the means to pay the rest of the army's arrears and the navy, and to make provision for the maintenance of the army hereafter. The East India Company were yesterday with the King, for some assistance from him towards the maintenance of that trade: he promised that in due time he could give them all the assistance they could in reason require. . . . It is thought that he will send next year about 25 sail of men-of-war into the East Indies, to curb the Dutch in those parts. The Queen Mother, it is thought, will return to France very shortly. P. S. A Frenchman has lately come with two very fine rubies, both of a bigness and goodness, 30l. a piece; also a very rare Oriental amethyst, price 28l. I shall endeavour to get them as cheap as I can. They are not to be matched in England.

1660, Nov. 13, London.—It was expected yesterday that Titchbourne, Henry Martin, Owen Ro, and Lilbourne, should have been executed; but it seems the Lieutenant of the Tower, and a vintner of the Castle in Cornhill have procured of His Majesty to have the execution deferred for some time, only for Titchbourne's sake; for Titchbourne absolutely saved the vintner's life from the gallows, and likewise the Lieutenant of the Tower, as they say . . . . but on the other side, Lady Capel, Dr. Hewet's lady, and Love's widow, are importunate petitioners to the King for justice upon them, and I hear that the Queen Mother sent her secretary to the Houses to demand justice upon all those that had been the late King's judges. . . . I am told she is to return from France speedily, with the Princess Henrietta Maria, to accomplish the match between her and the Duke d'Anjou, which they say is absolutely concluded. The French Ambassador is speedily to return to France, having freighted ships to carry his goods. It is now the general vote about the town that the D. of Y. is really married to the lady that lies in of a son in ex-

ceeding great state, and all in the family give her no other title than the Duchess.

Fol. 56. 1660, Nov. 14, London.—A debate in the Commons on a matter between the Lieutenant of the Tower and a member of the House, one Sir Hugh Owen, who, making a visit to a kinsman in the Tower, previously to his going into the country, was on returning stopped by one of the wardens at the Tower Gate, who kept him prisoner until the Lieutenant came in, on suspicion that he had been visiting Sir Arthur Hazelrigg, for all that he told him that he was a Parliament man, and why he came, &c., &c. The Lieutenant came in between 1 and 2 in the morning, foully drunk, and gave the knight some uncivil language, and would not let him go out that night, but lodged him and his two sons in a chamber, and put a padlock upon the door, and in the morning, upon better consideration, let him go at liberty: and now Sir Hugh presents the Lieutenant in the House of Commons, and yesterday the business opened in the House by one of the members (a Councillor, as it seems), and hath made such a crime that it is thought the Lieutenant will at least lose his place, if not be imprisoned besides . . . . The Count de Soissons, the French Ambassador extraordinary, is returned to France. . . . The match is agreed upon between the King of France's brother and the Princess Henrietta Maria.

Fol. 57. 1660, Nov. 20, London.—Report that the Lieutenant of the Tower will, by means of friends in the House, the King, and the Duke of Albemarle, get off at a genteel rate. The House busy for the last four or five days about ordering the tax and disbanding the remainder of the army by sea and land, and making provision for the navy for the future. This done, they will fall to the prosecution of those guilty of the King's death, which the Queen Mother, as I hear, prosecutes vigorously, before she returns to France. . . . Sir Henry Vane and Lambert will be tried and suffer death, and some others. (He says he has offered 56l. for the rubies; that the owner has trusted them to him, and he is resolved not to part with them, so begs Sir Richard that order may be taken with Robin Shelton for payment of the money.)

Fol. 58. 1660, Nov. 24. The King has sent a letter to the House of Lords, to be communicated to the Commons, that he intends to dissolve Parliament the 22nd of next month. . . . . News from Spain of a great loss of shipping before the bar of Cales (Cadiz); five galleons of the King of Spain, bound from Cales to the West Indies, richly laden to the value of three or four millions; likewise five or six ships with 5,000 soldiers from Naples, and bound for Portugal against the King of Portugal, and all cast away in a storm, besides four or five English and Dutch ships, bound from Malaga, with fruit and wine from England. I have heard this morning that the Governor of Mexico is revolted from the King of Spain, and assumes that place for himself, and will entertain any trade with any nation: and they say he that is Governor of Peru is brother to the Governor of Mexico, and it is thought they will join together and keep those countries to themselves. . . . The business of the Chancellor's daughter is yet doubtful, whether owned or not owned, for aught I can hear, by the major part as yet. (He says he has agreed for the rubies within 20s., which he is resolved shall not defer the bargain; he and a friend of better judgment are confident that there are not the like to be had in England.

Fol. 59. 1660, Nov. 27, London.—Nothing of moment in the Houses; only the fellow that made the rings and the pulleys upon the scaffold, if the King should resist that, then those things should force him to it, he was taken upon Sunday last, and taken to Newgate and will be hanged as is reported before Sunday next. (He has received 56l. of Robert Shelton and delivered the rubies to him.)

166?, Jan. 2?, London.—The King is in very good health and goes to Hampton Court often, and back again the same day, but very private; most of his exercise is the tennis court in the morning when he doth not ride abroad; and when he doth ride abroad he is on horseback by break of day, and most commonly back again before noon. The Duke of York continues his course of physic which I am told makes him look very thin. The Queen Mother and the Princess are still at Portsmouth. . . . . A rumour that the Prince of Condé begins to stir up troubles in France and that the Cardinal should be killed. The Duc d'Anjou is at Rouen waiting for the Queen and Princess coming over. The Duchess of York is lodged at Whitehall till St. James's is fitted up for her Court; further, that the Chancellor will lay out 40,000l. upon St. James's House for that purpose.

DUKE OF SUTHERLAND.

Fol. 60. 166$\frac{0}{1}$, Feb. 12, London.—The King's coronation is settled for the 23rd of April next; and for that purpose the King has sent to the Lord Mayor, &c., to meet him at the Tower and wait upon him all along to Westminster. The Spanish Ambassador has been with His Majesty lately to demand Dunkirk and Jamaica for the King of Spain. His Majesty answered they had cost too many of his subjects' lives to be rendered upon those terms; and that was all that passed between them. The Ambassador said he must return to Spain to acquaint his master, for he had no more business but that in England; and so took leave of His Majesty. Concerning the match with Portugal. . . . I hear that the King of Portugal has sent him a blank to set down his demands, and it shall be condescended unto. And the Princess hath sent him word that, for religion, she will refer herself to His Majesty's discretions.

Fol. 61. 166$\frac{0}{1}$, Feb. 16, London.—We hear that Lord Digby is sent upon some design, but where, or upon what account is not yet known. Great opposition against the match with Portugal by the Spanish and the Dutch factions.—Reports as to other matches proposed.—The City has ordered 6,000*l.* to be expended for devices and pageants for the coronation day. . . . I hear that Lent will not be so strictly enjoined as mentioned in the proclamation, because there cannot be fish sufficient to serve half the city in time of Lent, and therefore it is reported only Wednesdays and Fridays will be enjoined strictly to be deemed for fish days.

166$\frac{0}{1}$, Feb. 19, London. It is not known where or on what design the Earl of Bristol is gone.—Several reports about it.—Upon a secret business which is somewhat dangerous to relate till the truth be known; the rumour of it is up and down the town, but very uncertain, neither do I believe it, and I hope it is not so that the King should be married before he came out of Flanders to a relation of the Prince de Ligne, and that the Earl of Bristol is gone thither upon that account. All at Court is peaceable and quiet since the King hath new modelled his life guard. I hear that he is going down to Portsmouth to see the mariners paid their arrears;—and then give some satisfaction to them of London and Chatham, for they say some of them are three years in arrear.—P.S. In Scotland they have given Argyle his charge of high treason.

Fol. 62. 166$\frac{0}{1}$, March 2, London.—I must beg your excuse for not writing by last Tuesday's post, because I was at Putney with my family *a Shroving**. . . . Prince Rupert (as I am informed) is the only favourite of the King's, insomuch that he has given him 30 or 40,000*l.* per annum out of his own revenues for his present maintenance, and is resolved to make him Lieut.-General of all Wales, and president of the Marches;—meantime he is preparing to go for Germany to the Emperor to take his leave of that Court and to resign his military charge there and so return to England. . . . . I am told that the King went into the Palatinate with an intent to have procured some money of the Palsgrave, which was refused; Prince Rupert being then there, seeing the unworthiness of his brother in that particular, made use of all the friends he had, and procured His Majesty a considerable sum of money, which was an act of much love and civility, which His Majesty was very sensible of then, and now he will requite him for it. . . . We can not yet hear what is become of the Earl of Bristol; his business is carried very private. . . . Sir Thomas Corbet told me that Lord Capel is made Earl of Essex.†

166$\frac{0}{1}$, March 9, London.—The Duke [ ] Ambassador, has had an audience; some suppose it is about a match between His Majesty and the late Prince of [ ]'s sister, for this Prince Morice van Nassau is [nearly] related to her, and it is thought that the State have an interest in this embassage as well as [ ] of Brandenburg. Some say the Earl of Bristol is gone direct for France to the Queen Mother about the match between the Princess Henrietta Maria and the Duke de Juin (d'Anjou?) the King of France's brother. . . . His Majesty's chiefest recreation is to go twice or thrice a week to Hampton Court to oversee his workmen there; and most part of the rest of his time is to oversee his workmen in St. James's Park, where they are making stately walks and planting of trees for shade.

Fol. 63. 166$\frac{0}{1}$, March 12, London.—I am informed that the Earl of Bristol was sent to the Prince of Parma's Court to take an exact view of his daughter, but the King's mind altered, and he despatched a post to command him back again.—Report of a proposition for the marriage of the King with a sister of the late Prince of Orange. . . . The writ for chosing of burgesses is this day come down to the City. Yesterday the King sent to the City to borrow 100,000*l.* to pay the mariners; . . . . . but to-day he sent word that there was no occasion as sufficient money had come in from the several counties to the value of 30 or 35,000*l.* P.S. My cousin Francis Charlton of Apley, hath had his leg cut off, about the gartering place.

166$\frac{0}{1}$. March 23, London.—Charlton says that the election in the City not being pleasing to the King, as many letters as possible of those that were written into the county to incite them to follow the example of London, were sent to the Court so that the King might see what was written. He thinks that the King intends to draw up some more forces about the City to strengthen his own guard, as also to reserve the militia in all counties; this being very needful, seeing the Presbyterians, Independants, and Anabaptists, are leagued together in the plottings; their pretence being, as they give out, to be only against the order of Bishops; the King they say they will obey in all things as well in Church as State, but none but the King supreme in the Church.

Fol. 64. 166$\frac{0}{1}$, April 2, London.—Report of the match with Portugal being concluded.—This day all the colonels, captains, and officers of the trained bands of this city went to Whitehall to assure the King of their loyalty to him and to the Protestant religion.—His Majesty has 12 ships fitted ready to go for the Straits against the Turks, and the Dutch have 25 sail more in readiness for the same design. . . . A rumour that the Duke of York is shortly to go to Portugal to fetch the Lady for England. The Spaniard is making great preparations for this summer against Portugal. Lord and Lady Leigh with Lady Tracy came to town on Saturday. . P.S. There are 62 Knights of the Bath to be made, and 14 or 16 Knights of the Garter.

1661, April 9, London.—The match with Portugal is thought to be concluded, notwithstanding the opposition of the Spanish and Dutch.—Reports of what the King of Spain has offered.

Fol. 65. 1661, May 7.—The Duke of Cambridge* (the Duke of York's son) died on Sunday night last. This day all the shops in town are shut up because of the general training on Hide Park, so that this day is made holiday, and to-morrow will be the like, for the King's going to the Parliament. . . . Prince Rupert about 15 days past went for Germany.

1661, May 11, London. . . . The House adjourned till yesterday afternoon at 2 o'clock, when the Speaker of the House of Commons was presented to the King in the House of Lords, where the Speaker made a large and learned speech. This day they sit again. . . . All diligence is using to dispatch ships to Portugal to fetch the Princess. There is also an embargo of all shipping both in the Downs and in this river till the King's ships be gone. P.S. The Spanish ambassador is preparing to return for Spain, and I hear that the Portugal Ambassador doth return for Portugal in our fleet to carry the good news of the agreement of the marriage.

Fol. 67. 1661, May 18, London.—The Queen of Bohemia is arrived at Gravesend and is expected at court daily, if she be not come thither already very privately. . . I hear that His Majesty hath sent an express into Spain to know whether he will own his ambassador's action concerning the seditious pamphlets which he dispersed up and down the city, and till that express be returned the Spanish Ambassador is not to stir from hence. . . The Parliament have voted it to be a Premunire to say that His Majesty is popishly affected. I am informed they have damned the Covenant, and it is to be burned by the hangman; and when it was voted so, Prin (Prynne) stood up and made a motion that the Engagement might be burnt with it; another stood up and told him that it must be the work of another day. I heard this morning that His Majesty had gone by water to fetch the Queen of Bohemia.—A rumour that there is like to be civil war in France now the Cardinal is dead.

Fol. 66. 1661, May 21, London. A likelihood of an agreement between the Dutch and Portugese.—A rumour these 2 days that the Spaniard has got a footing in Portugal, &c., &c., but there are contrary news from Lisbon. . . . The Queen of Bohemia is come to town and lodgeth at my Lord Craven's house in Drury Lane, as I am told. The Solemn League and Covenant is to be burned to-morrow by the common hangman. P.S. The ships are not yet gone for Portugal, but ready to be

* For the various popular diversions on Shrove Tuesday, *see* Brand's Popular Antiquities (ed. Ellis, 1849), vol. 1, p. 63.

† He was made Earl of Essex, 20 April 1661.

* The patent for this title seems not to have been valid. *See* Nicolas's Historic Peerage (ed. Courthope).

gone so soon as the Duke of Ormond and his attendance
shall be ready.

Fol. 67. 1661, May 25, London.—Proceedings in Parliament.—I do not hear that they intend to give His
Majesty a power to raise money in the intervals of
Parliaments, though I wrote you so in my last.—Expects
daily to hear of the departure of the fleet for Portugal.
—The Hollander and the Portugal have referred their
business to His Majesty as umpire. The Spanish Ambassador has been very quiet lately, and something
melancholy as they say. The Solemn League and Covenant was burned on Wednesday in three places, viz.,
in Palace Yard, in Cheapside, and before the Old
Exchange. We hear that Argyle was hanged the 22nd
of this month in Edinburgh by order from His Majesty,
because the same day of the month was Montrose put
to death in the same place, and the Scotch Covenant
likewise burnt the same day. . . P.S. I am told that
all those prisoners that are condemned and are now in
the Tower shall suffer death, except Heveningham,
whose life is begged by Lord Rochford and the Earl of
Dover, who are to have 1,000l. per annum of his lands
equally between them.

Fol. 68. 1661, May 28, London.—Since my last Saturday's letter the two Houses of Parliament have received
the Sacrament, according as it was ordered to be celebrated, upon Sabbath day last, which they did unanimously, excepting 3 or 4, whereof 2 were our citizen
burgesses, viz., Love and Tenison who absented themselves. And Prynne was there, but would take it
sitting, and the minister that gave the bread saw that
he would not kneel and refused to give it him, and he
that came after thought that the other had given him
the bread and gave him the wine sitting and took no
notice, by a mistake, so that Prynne received but the
wine (as I am told), so that what they will do with
them that were absent we cannot tell. There was one
of the House of Commons desired the Speaker to excuse
him because there was a difference between him and
his wife and hath been for many years . . . ; and it
seems there is the like difference between the Speaker
and his wife. Saturday and yesterday the two Houses
were upon the damning of the Acts of No Kingly Government and the Engagement and the Instruction and
another Act which I cannot hear; but the 3 others
were condemned to be burnt, which was performed this
day at noon before the Exchange by the hands of the
hangman. . . . It is thought all the prisoners in the
Tower will suffer death according to the sentence. We
are expecting the truth whether Argyle was executed
as reported. To-morrow is to be performed a solemnity
of thanksgiving for the King's coming into England
and restoration to the Crown. P.S. The Spanish Ambassador remains still here and is very quiet. . . Our
ships are still in the Downs. To fetch the Queen to
England some say the Duke of Ormond is to go, some
say the Duke of Albemarle, others say both. One told
me the Queen of Bohemia is come purposely to mediate
a peace between the King and the Hollanders, and also
between the King of Portugal and the Hollanders.

Letters by Sir Richard Temple, Lady Temple, and
others, 1654–1658.

Fol. 69. 1647. [Sir Richard Leveson] to Lady Christian Temple, at Stow, near Buckingham.—About the
fine imposed on him for delinquency.

Fol. 70. 1654, Jan. 19. Christian Temple to Sir
Richard Leveson.—About her son John (who did not
seem able to settle steadily to any business or profession).

Fol. 71. 1654, Feb. 19. The same to the same. About
the same matter.

Fol. 72. 1658, Dec. 28, Whitehall. Richard Temple
to his uncle (Sir R. Leveson).—A letter of 4 folio pages
nearly all about the imprudent behaviour of his brother
(John). . . For affairs here, I do very much fear a
good agreement between the Protector and Parliament
for that I perceive the popular party much fixed on
their former replies (?) and though now the bill has
been twice read in the House and twice committed to
a grand committee, and earnest endeavours of late used
for a change of some things, viz., that the Council
might be for life, and not expire with every triennial
Parliament and a new chosen, that the provision for
the maintenance of the 30,000 continued for my Lord's
life might not determine every Parliament, that a
negative to the alteration of the Instrument might be
given to him, that a Parliament might not be called
immediately upon the choice of every Protector + to
beget faction and raise disturbance, yet but little unless
that of the negative like to be granted; besides a pro-

vision for the rest of the 57,000 men till they may be
disbanded, and likewise seeing the preparations that
are made on the other side with the army gives me
great cause to suspect it, and our time expiring on
Monday next, after which the 20 days of deliberation
are only reserved, so that I fear they cannot pass the
Bill in time. Our fleet is all gone out, bound I suppose
for Hispaniola to surprise that and some rich islands
neighbouring, upon design to fall into the Indies; but
this is a great secret and I can but guess.

Fol. 73. 1655, April 4, Stowe. Richard Temple to
Sir Richard Leveson.—Announces the death of his
mother about 4 p.m. of the day before.

Fol. 74. 1655, May 24, London. The same to the
same.—About his brother John and his sister Christian.
—For news here, the commitment of Serjeant Maynard,
Twisden, and Windham to the Tower for pleading the
cause of one Coney, a merchant, who refuses to pay
tonnage and poundage, as having no foundation in law
but upon ordinance of my Lord Protector and his
Council.

Fol. 75. 1658, June 1. Richard Temple to Sir Richard
Leveson. I have spent this whole day in attending
upon the trial of Doctor Hewett and Mr. Mordant. The
Doctor made many exceptions to the jurisdiction of
the Court. . . . He desired to know their commission;
this was declared to him by the President to be an Act
of Parliament and a commission under the Great Seal.
Then he desired to hear it read, but that was refused;
to hear his judges called by name, but this was told him
had been already done; he insisted that by the words
of the Act, if all did not sit they were no lawful Judicature, and brought precedents that where none were said
to be of the Quorum all must sit, and that the clause in
the Act empowering them to hear and determine, did
refer to the whole number and not to the 17 or more;
and he made other exceptions, as the Parliament was
impeached in their liberty of sitting, and that 150 of
them were kept out by force, and that a House of Commons were not a Parliament; but that which he principally insisted on and desired [was] counsel to be assigned
him : which, being refused, he offered to submit the expo-
sition of the Act to His Highness' Council ; if they would
declare that the court was lawfully constituted according
to that Act, he would proceed ; and this being denied,
and the Court asserting their own authority, he being
not suffered to speak further to the last exceptions, he
declared he would [not] bring such a scandal upon himself as to yield up the liberty of an Englishman, against
his conscience ; and so, after many interlocutions, he
was recorded to be guilty by standing mute and refusing
to plead. After that Mr. Mordent was brought to the
bar, who did not dispute the authority of the Court, but
insisted upon it, that by that Act they ought to try him
by Jury, because the Act did not refer to any other
manner of proceeding, and that it was said they should
proceed therein as in case of Treasons ; this was ruled
against him by the Court : then he urged for counsel,
and that he ought not to be tried the same day he was
indicted, and for this he produced many precedents ; but
this, upon long debate, was over-ruled, and so he proceeded and pleaded Not guilty. Then the two Sta . .
lyes of Sussex were produced, and gave very slender evidence against him ; all was but discourses tending to a
design, but the main was he did acknowledge Charles
Stewart had writ to him to encourage and stir up his
freinds to assist him when he should land; and that
if the forces in Sussex were not strong enough, those in
Surrey were ready to join with them, but what forces
these were, or what they were to do, was very dubiously
delivered ; and it appeared that if anything was intended
it was but newly begun, and came not to any perfect
design, and there was but a single witness to any one
thing or time. Captain Mallory being escaped, he [   ]
himself, so as might [   ] the mercy of the court, and
yet made a reasonable good defence. . . . It is
feared he may be condemned, but hoped that the nicety
of the case may prevail for a pardon. A rumour that
the King of France is retreated to Paris for fear of
the Prince of Condé, and that Lord Falconbridge is fain
to follow him.

Fol. 76. 1658, July 13, London. Richard Temple to
[Sir R. Leveson]. Some consultation about summoning
a Parliament, but no resolution taken yet, because the
Protector is informed that the boroughs in the West are
engaged by the Commonwealth party, as they call it ;
. . . but I believe it will be called upon short notice
and unexpectedly. . . . I hear it is under consultation
to prescribe some rules for the discharge of those of the
royal party still under restraint. The Protector's family
is dispersed ; Lord Falconbridge into the North with

his lady ; and my Lord Richard into the West with his lady ; and all, as I suppose, to engage the gentlemen and others of the country to assist such in the election as they shall propose. Lady Claypole is so troubled with the sins of her youth called the griping of the guts, that my Lord watched with her himself all Saturday night, and it is thought she hath bespoken a place in another world. Affairs in Flanders are in a good condition. The French King well recovered by the Cardinal his nurse, who watched day and night with him, which hath more endeared him to the young King.—Other foreign news.

Fol. 77. 1658, Oct. 18, Stowe. R. Temple to Sir R. Leveson.—Gives intelligence from those who were eye-witnesses though not perfect ear-witnesses of a general meeting on Thursday of all the officers of the English army at the chapel at Whitehall, occasioned, as far as could be learned, by some murmur and discontent of many of the officers and soldiers which, as some say, they were about to express in a petition or rather re-monstrance concerning the prerogative that the late Protector had exercised over them by turning divers of them out and taking their commissions from them without assigning any cause and without being convicted of any offence before a Council of War, and particular instance was given in the case of my Lord Lambert and others ; to prevent which for the time to come they desired : 1st, that the Protector that now is should appoint Lord Fleetwood his general-in-chief ; so the present Protector not having been a soldier, and so a stranger to their persons and merits, might leave the government of the army wholly to him, whom they did conceive for the reasons alleged, would have a greater care of their interests and respect for their particulars ; and further that no officer might be cashiered or have his commission taken from him without being adjudged by a Council of War. . . . Col. Berry, your late go-vernor of Salop and the counties adjacent, made a speech and was seconded by Col. Goff, son-in-law to Commis-sary General Whalley, a notable engine of the late Pro-tector in the army, and some little was also said by Lord Fleetwood ; but my friend being at some distance could hear but a little now and then, and that was to this effect, hinting the dangers that might ensue to the army by any division, and casting a fair gloss upon the late Protector's proceeding in this kind, pretending that it was his tenderness of them that were laid aside that put him upon it to choose that way rather than bring them upon the stage for things which would have brought upon them a greater punishment ; and lastly, that if they had any occasion of offence, directing them to address them-selves to their chief officers and in particular to Lord Fleetwood, who would be all ready to endeavour to rectify anything amiss in the places they were set in as well as if they had the absolute determination thereof committed to them. I hear that for the present they seemed all well satisfied, and my friend heard them all give a general hemme after Goffe's speech in token of satisfaction ; so that the Devil is laid at present.

Fol. 78. 1658, Oct. 23, London. Richard Temple to (Sir R. Leveson).—The business (mentioned in the last letter) has been chiefly animated by Major-General Des-borrowe, who married the late Protector's sister ; what his aim is therein as to his own particular, unless it be to make use of Fleetwood's softly temper to be a stirrup to himself to get into the saddle at last, cannot be imagined ; but all do judge it a strange attempt in him to venture so great grandeur as he is already in, being third man in the Government, but to bring it once more upon the dye ; whether he hath some fear he shall bear the sway as formerly, or what it is, none can compre-hend. The first address was intended to have been by Petition, but afterwards by timely notice of it, it was stopped by the Protector, and all the officers sent for to a conference, when I hear they found a reply beyond expectation from the Protector, in which he did express much courage and resolution not to part with the generalship, and told them he intended not to make any alterations amongst them, till he was better acquainted both with their persons and merits, but by Lord Fleet-wood's advice. This answer did for the present pacify them ; but, as I hear, the Devil is revived again, and yesterday a fast was kept by the officers at St. James's. Lord Fleetwood carries fair with both parties, and I suppose all endeavours are used by the Protector to engage him, if that can be effected. It is thought with some sudden and sharp course this cloud may be blown over, otherwise we may justly fear a tempest. I find the army endeavour much the restoration of the officers that were turned out by the late Protector, as Col. Okey, &c. Col. Pride is conceived to be dead by this

time ; he was very near it this morning. Goff and Ingoldsby and Whalley are thought to stand firm to the Protector, though none but Ingoldsby appears publicly in opposition. My Lord Protector and his Council set mighty diligently to manage this business as it concerns them. All persons, both foreigners and others that have made any addresses to the Protector, speak very well of his deportment, and say it is much beyond expectation. . . . Sir George Askue is made admiral for the Swedes, and hath liberty to choose his officers here ; his merits have been much neglected here, but it seems taken notice of abroad.

Fol. 79, no date. John Temple to Sir R. Leveson.—Promising good behaviour :—Says he has more inclina-tion to a merchant than to divinity, law, physic or court.

Fol. 80. Savile to Sir R. Leveson. Business.

Letters from John Dodington to his uncle Sir R. Leveson.
The first four are on family matters.

Fol. 84. 1654, Feb. 1. Several scandalous pamphlets against the Protector have flown up and down ; and this day a report that upon the countries refusal to pay more taxes the soldier shall take free quarter. . . . An epidemical fear of new troubles possesseth all men.

Fol. 86. 1655, May 28, London.—Mr. Recorder Steele was yesterday made Chief Baron : one Graves of Lin-coln's Inn, a poor sneaking fellow, is to succeed him, as is believed. By next term you must expect a new Lord Keeper who is Attorney-General Prideaux ; a new Master of the Rolls who is Lord Commissioner Lisle ; and Glyn Lord Chief Justice in Rolls his place, whose quietus is signed. Thus the statists of the times have disposed of affairs, but whether things must be thus or no is past my prophetic skill. There is a new recruit going with our Indian forces.

Fol. 87. 1660, June 5, London.—On family matters. —He mentions that his father (who had then returned into his own country) had suffered misfortune in the late King's service.

Fol. 88. 1660, May 15. Frances Doddington to Sir R. Leveson.—Family matters.

Letters from William Smith to Sir R. Leveson.
Fol. 90. 1642, Oct. 9, Shrewsbury.—On Tuesday we are commanded to march, but which way I know not as yet for certain, unless towards London as all men guess. It is here said that the General Essex is already gone towards Oxford, whence he intends to pass down his ordnance by water to London, and to post himself and his army after them. P.S. Before I could seal this letter here came one of Prince Rupert's trumpeters to me to let me know of his going to-morrow to the Earl of Essex ; for I have Captain Wingate whom the Prince took at Worcester in my custody : therefore you may know the Earl of Essex is not gone.

Fol. 102. 1647,* April 31. (William Smith) to Sir Richard Leveson.—You cannot but have seen the army's declaration which caused the ordinance to be passed next day for making null and void all that was done in the absence of Speaker Lenthall, though re-jected at 3 or 4 several days debate before. Since the Scots have pressed an engagement upon the Houses for the sending of the old Propositions agreed on by both kingdoms, and sent to the King to Newcastle, which the Houses not being able to denie have con-sented to send them, which will be a means to spin out time and hold the business further off from a conclusion, 'tis hoped the King and the army may correspond so well that he shall send such an answer to them as, though not satisfactory and consenting to them (which can never be expected) yet agreable to the sense of the army, and if so, their mediation will be so sufficient as will easily make it satisfactory. Upon the passing of this vote for the old Propositions the House adjourned on Friday till to-morrow. The King is at Hampton Court ; the head-quarters of the army at Putney, but nothing is resolved on 'till they see the King's answer to the Propositions ; and even then they themselves either know not, or (I can assure you) will not be thought to know what to determine. The Ministry of Scotland excite them there with all earnestness and violence to come into England as one (one ?) man to settle their cove-nant ; and 'tis believed they will, at last. Chancellor Lowden and Lanericke, Duke Hamilton's brother, are on their way hither, Commissioners from Scotland ; their errand is not yet known. Argyle was absent from

* The writer has not given the year ; but this year is written by a contemporary hand above the address.

the Council at their sending, and made a public protestation afterwards against anything that conduced to
the making of a breach between the two kingdoms.
Baten, vice-admiral of the navy, is engaged to no party,
and to his friends vows privately that he will obey no
commands but the King's; he is provided for four months.
They are still upon the disquisition of the late business
in the City, and upon a report of the progress they have
made in it they have committed some citizens, I hear,
yet none of the House. 'Tis likely you have heard that
Sir Philip Stapleton, who went over with five more of
the impeached members, died of the plague at Calais,
almost as soon as he landed: the people of the house
where he died made the rest of the members pay them
80l., before they would let them come forth, for bringing the sickness into their house: it decreased here 80
last week.

Fol. 89. 1647, Feb. 29, London.—We hear from
Scotland that the Council of State are met, and that
upon their first sitting the Lord Chancellor Lowden
made them a short rehearsal of what had passed between their Commissioners and the Parliament of England: it was moved that the Commissioners should
have thanks given them; some opposition was made by
alleging they ought not to give them thanks till they
were fully informed of what was done. After a short
debate it was put to the Question and carried in the
affirmative that they should have thanks; four only
voting the negative. I desire not to be mistaken; this
passed in the Council of State, not in the Parliament
of Scotland which meets not till the 10th of March.
There is order given in Scotland that Mr. Marshall
shall not be permitted to preach in any church within
that kingdom. . . . 'Tis said the Scots demand the
King should be brought back to Holdenby and reside
there according to their agreement when they delivered
him to the Parliament. . . . A Scotchman of credit
said very lately that he did believe though Hamilton
and Argyle should be in as great a measure friends as
they are enemies, and both endeavour to hinder their
countrymen from coming into England, that they could
not prevail. Some letters of the Queen and Duke of
York going to the King were intercepted; but the
Parliament not being able to decypher them, sent order
to the Isle of Wight to have the King's cypher searched
for, which was so well performed that the King's
Cabinet was broke open before his face; but by great
chance the King had the cypher in his pocket, and with
scorn to their incivility, burnt it before their faces.

Fol. 91. 1647, Sept. 27.—The Parliament are upon a
new model of propositions; some few of the old ones
will be taken, and some of the army's proposals:
. . . . but if they continue masters of the army, I
look for little good by them; if not, I look their propositions should break their own necks; for there has
been mapping lately in the House between some of the
root and branch men and the officers of the army that
are members. Ireton, moving the army's proposals
might be considered there, and sent to the King, gave
occasion to one Scot (an insolent fellow and enemy to
the proposals as all of that spirit are) to let the House
know that there had been underhand treaties between
the officers of the army and the King, to which end
Ashburnham and Sir John Berkeley were continually
at the head-quarters, agents for the King, which he
desired might be examined; to which Cromwell by way
of reply took occasion to vindicate his own innocency
and to declare his readiness to obey the Parliament's
commands, but if the House should think fit to examine
that business, he desired it might be examined withal,
which members of the House had been at head-quarters
likewise endeavouring to debauch the army and seduce
them from their principles of this violent party, though
there are not a considerable number in the House, in
opposition to the rest, yet there are too many of them
of the body of the army which causes continual dispute
and jealousies between the general officers and adju-
tators (sic) which is the greatest hope we have the
officers of the army will come to an agreement with the
King, for fear their own factions and the odium they
contract from the kingdom by being necessitated through
them to keep up their army the longer, will at length
undo them; if they do not I do not see how the King and
the Parliament can ever agree; for in their new propositions they have absolutely voted down the Bishops and
the sale of their lands, which the King making a matter
of conscience I believe will never consent to; and then
they have absolutely agreed he shall have no negative
voice in the Militia after the expiration of the time they
propose to have it settled in them, which is in effect to
have it in them for ever. They have accused the Lord

Mayor and 4 Aldermen with two or three Common
Councilmen of high treason. The aldermen are Bunce,
Langham, Cullen, and Adams. Some aldermen have
shaken off their furs and say they will serve in that condition no more. I hear the City will lend no money
which will cause the army to take some violent cause
for raising it upon them. A rumour that Hamilton has
undertaken the sudden disbanding of the Scotch army.
. . . . No man living can tell what the issue of this
business will be; . . . . yet Ash. and Be. are
in good hopes which is all the comfort I can give you.
Lord Digby and O'Neal are arrived in France lately
with great danger. Digby has gone for St. Germains to
the Queen, where he saw Prince Rupert (who is well recovered of his shot in his head, and now in great esteem
there) and my Lord Gerard to fight with, if the Queen
do not salve matters. Some of our Presbyterian ministers are found to have been interested in exciting the
apprentices in the late business of the City and are sent
for; I hear Calamye, Burgesse and Care named.

Fol. 90. 1658, Oct. 9. W. Smith to Mr. John Langley.
All our courtiers are preparing for the greatest funeral
that has been seen in England. Yesterday His Highness presented all the officers of the army with complete
mournings; nevertheless there are many discontented
persons among the Marshalists whose often assemblings,
though as often forbidden, do hold their meetings, insomuch that the obsequies being over, it is believed some
discontents will break out. It is said the funeral will
be solemnized on the 5th day of November next. . . . .
Much honour is performed to the corpse which lies at
Somerset House.—Foreign news.—We hear of a great
ship burnt at Chatham, it is said to be that which was
called the Princess Royal, which now is called the
Resolution, which ship was a better ship of war than the
Sovereign Royal.

Fol. 92. 1658, Oct. 23. W. Smith to John Langley.
—His Highness's funeral is designed to be on the 9th
of November. . . . The Dutch hold a reasonable
handsome correspondence with His Highness, their
Ambassador being daily received in a very respective
manner at Whitehall.—The French are not so much
caressed there as formerly.

Fol. 94. 1660, June 23, Drury Lane. W. Smith to
John Langley). . . . The fire between the Presbytery and the Episcopacy is not yet extinguished; for
Jack the Levite labours to confound Aaron the jure
divino priest; but God holds the balance and will do
justice. As to the Publicans Office the Parliament have
out-acted their predecessors and given His Majesty the
Customs during life; tho' before they have been given
only from one Parliament to another. . . . The
Commissioners use all means they can devise to raise
money from such as have been sucking and gathering it
per or nefas for these years of rebellion; but the
Lord General is composed all of mercy and has highly
interposed in the Lower House for favour towards some
of the most rich and potent of the Rump, whereby many
great offenders have found more favour than ever they
did, or intended to show to those that are now more
justly their judges; but his Lordship is now removed
to the Lords' House. (The writer then mentions all his
titles and offices.) I know no man for coat armour to
exceed His Excellency; this day I saw in a table of his
Achievements 90 several coats of arms in his quarterings.
. . . Lord Jermyn, Earl of St. Alban's, is soon going
to France and is to return with the Queen. . . . The
King is every night feasted by one or other of the
Lords.

Fol. 95. 1660, Aug. 4. W. Smith to John Langley.—
. . . . The Lords have delivered 63 of the regicides
to justice without mercy, and so many of them as can
be apprehended are speedily to undergo the execution
thereof; this sacrifice is offered only to the Manes of
his murdered Majesty. The Houses at present are about
inquiry into the other bloody Courts which have bereaved
the virtuous and loyal nobility of their lives. . . . .
The French Queen is said to be with child, and yet Her
Majesty's magnificent entry into Paris is delayed because Cardinal Mazarin is indisposed of the gout. For
Ambassadors, we look for Don Lewis de Haro's brother
from Spain with 300 followers, Prince Rupert with a
great train from the Emperor, and the Duc d'Espernon
from France with no less state.

Fol. 96. 1660, Aug. 12, Drury Lane.—William Smith
to John Langley.—As yet, no public persons come from
foreign Princes. The two Houses of Parliament look
still upon each other as if they had been long strangers.
The Lords pursue justice, though with mercy beyond
merit. The Commons prefer mercy, even to the detriment of justice; so as between their long debates the

Act of Indemnity has not yet received the royal stamp. His Majesty is in continual action and merciful expressions, insomuch as he rejoiceth all men's hearts who beheld the cheerfulness of his countenance . . . He is of late much invited to christen his servants' children, and after many such works of piety he went on Saturday last to the Tower, and performed the same work for Mr. Lieutenant's son there, during which solemnity the prisoners were carried all into the Mint, though some of them, as I hear, hoped and cried to have been carried to His Majesty. The Scots Commissioners have received great content from the King and his Council, and are going home filled with joy; the great officers are also settled, to their own desires; the Earl of Glencairn is made Lord Chancellor, the Earl of Crawford is Lord Treasurer, the Earl of Lauderdale, Secretary, and the rest are changed. On Thursday last His Majesty went below Gravesend aboard an East India fleet, consisting of seven goodly ships, returned with rich lading, amongst which one ship and her lading fell to his own share; for, as I hear, the ship and her lading were the adventure of Richard Cromwell . . . The same night, returning, he had the divertisement of dancing on the ropes before him in the great hall at Whitehall. Notwithstanding Mr. Calamy has lately, as I hear, petitioned His Majesty against his two royal brothers for going to plays.

1660, Aug. 18, Drury Lane. William Smith to John Langley.—The account between the Houses of Parliament comes off with discord, and is not like to be other so long as the Presbyterians can foment the difference. In the beginning of this week a committee of Lords and Commons went into the City to borrow 100,000l. The citizens not only denied it but told them that the Commons House were obstructing justice upon the murderers of the King and their loyal brethren. The members returned in wrath, and next day passed the Bill for Poll money, which the City bears with great regret; so, in short, the Parliament and City are all disjointed. About Wednesday next we expect the Prince de Ligné, Ambassador Extraordinary from his Catholic Majesty, who comes attended with 12 noblemen, each having three coaches with six horses apiece, and the ambassador six coaches in like manner, together with 20 lackeys and 20 grooms, besides pages. Camden House in London, together with Goldsmiths' Hall near adjoining, are prepared for the said ambassador. The extraordinary ambassadors of Denmark and the State of Venice are come already. The Earl of St. Alban's returns hither next week from France, and with him comes the most disconsolate Duchess of Richmond, having buried in France her only young son the Duke, who has left to the Earl of Lichfield his title of Lenox, together with his whole revenue. P.S. The Bill of Indemnity is again returned from the Lords' House, who will not be pacified without a proportionable sacrifice to justice; the City being of the same mind; God reward them.

Fol. 97. 1660, Aug. 25. William Smith to John Langley.—This has been a week both of action and passion. Almost every day there have been conferences between the two Houses, and yet they have not always parted like brethren. . . . Yesterday they came so near to agreement, as it is now resolved that Axtell, who was lately brought out of Ireland, shall be hanged and quartered, Vane and Lambert shall be left to petition His Majesty for their lives, and Hazelrigg shall not die, but lose his whole estate; . . . there is yet one scruple put to a further debate, viz., whether those who rendered themselves upon His Majesty's late Proclamation shall not find favour thereby; and this day a Conference is to be about that business. His Majesty came last night to Whitehall from Hatfield, the Earl of Salisbury's house, where he has been highly treated ever since Wednesday morning . . . The Danish and Swedish Ambassadors are arrived, but the Spanish and French not yet. The Earl of St. Alban's has returned from France, but not yet come to town, though Sir Kenelm Digby, Her Majesty's Lord Chancellor, is come. The Queen is sickly and weak, and therefore not judged fit to come from the pure air of France to our muddy climate, till the spring.

1660, Sept. 8, Drury Lane. William Smith to John Langley.—The Duke of Gloucester is taken with the small-pox, but, God be thanked, they come out full and kindly, and it is thought the worst is past.—Debates in the House about continuing the whole or part of the Army.—. . . The Sea-general, Montagu, is gone with 10 or 12 ships to bring over the Princess Royal of Orange, the King's sister.—A Frenchman has come over on behalf of the Duke of Anjou, that he may marry

the Princess Henrietta, the King's youngest sister, now in France with the Queen . . . The Earl of Winchelsea is speedily going Ambassador to Constantinople, and Sir Thomas Bendish is coming home, who is like to have a sad entertainment in regard of Sir Henry Hyde's death and Sir Sackville Crow's base usage.

Fol. 90. 1660, Sept. 15. William Smith to John Langley.—Last night the royal corpse (the Duke of Gloucester) was privately interred at Westminster Abbey. His Majesty and the Duke of York are this day gone to Hampton Court for fresh air . . . . On Monday last the Spanish Ambassador came very splendid to his audience at Whitehall, where His Majesty received him in a posture of melancholy, equivalent to the Spanish glory; his next appearance at Court will be as deep in mourning.—In daily expectation of the Count of Soissons as ambassador extraordinary from France. The Hollanders seem to be much troubled at a new Act of Parliament, which prohibits the foreign importation of any goods, but such as are of the same country's growth with the shipping which brings them. The Parliament have pretended great advancement to His Majesty's revenue, but the issue proves of little concernment to the proposals; the profits intended being raised out of His Majesty's estate already settled.

Fol. 99. 1660, Michaelmas day. The Princess Royal of Orange came with the King and Duke of York to Whitehall on Wednesday;—her loyal reception;—nevertheless, a miscreant villain in Kent getting into a pulpit affronted God with thanks for the death of the Duke of Gloucester, adding blasphemous desires for the same upon the rest of the royal stock. The rascal, as I hear, was yesterday brought to Newgate . . . . It is said that Lambert is set at liberty, and hath his own inheritable estate restored to him at the request of Sir George Booth and Lord General Monck. A lioness in the Tower is delivered of three whelps, whereas it is said they use to have but one; this is received as a good omen.—The Count of Soissons is still expected; . the Prince de Ligni yet continues here.

1660, Oct. 12, Drury Lane. William Smith to John Langley.—The week has been spent in sessions and trials upon the Rebels. . . . Your countryman Harrison began and led the dance of that black Masque, . . . being this day between 10 and 12 to be hanged and quartered where Charing Cross stood. Five more received the same sentence yesterday, viz., Scot, Cook, Carew, Scrope, and Jones. This day Hugh Peters comes to his trial, being the man, as is by all reported, and as they say proved, to have given the fatal blow.—We expect Her Majesty 10 days hence, with her beautiful daughter Henrietta, but is not long to stay as is said. The traitors Whaley and Goffe are gotten into New England, but soon expected to be sent over. Sir Michael Livesey of Kent (another of the murderers), being gotten into the Low Countries, was met with by a gentleman whom he had formerly highly abused in Kent, who, demanding satisfaction of Sir Michael, the knight refused to come his name; whereupon the gentleman required him to draw, else he would run him through the body; Sir Michael did so, but was soon disarmed; whereat the people coming in and demanding the cause of their quarrel, the gentleman said, That was one of the murderers of the King: the Dutch boors, without further examination, cut Sir Michael in pieces, and trod his body into the dust. Harrison is now hanged and quartered, not vouchsafing any expression of repentance, but blasphemously said he should rise again within three days, and at the right hand of God be Judge of his Judges, and so died, not being half an hour at the place before he was executed. The Presbyterians would not yet be quiet if they durst stir, nor are they content, though they have the best offices in Court and City, while we poor Cavaliers are ready still to starve.

1660. 1660, Oct. 20. William Smith to John Langley.—Refers to Harrison's death on the previous Saturday at Charing Cross.—On Monday John Carew died in the same place and manner. On Tuesday despairing Hugh Peters and John Cook, the only penitent, were hanged and quartered in the same place. On Wednesday Thomas Scott, railing, and Gregory Clements, howling, because he said his sin could not be forgiven, died as and where the rest; and an hour after came John Jones, and made no bones either of his fact or fortune, and he with Adrian Scroope, who all along desired the prayers of the people, ended their lives by the same death in the same place; and now the stench of their burnt bowels had so putrified the air, as the inhabitants thereabouts petitioned His Majesty there might be no more executed in that place; therefore on Friday, Francis Hacker, without remorse, and Daniell Axtell,

DUKE OF
SUTHER-
LAND.

who dissolved himself into tears and prayers for the King and his own soul, were executed at Tyburn, where Hacker was only hanged, and his brother, Rowland Hacker, had his body entire, which he begged, and Axtell was quartered. The rest of the condemned rebels are returned to the Tower 'till His Majesty and the Parliament resolve what shall be done with them.

1660, Oct. 27, Drury Lane. William Smith to John Langley.—This week, the Term beginning, Sir Robert Forster is made Lord Chief Justice of the King's Bench, Sir Orlando Bridgeman is removed from Chief Baron to be Lord Chief Justice of the Common Pleas, and Judge Hales is expected to be made Lord Chief Baron. On Thursday the new Serjeants at law (in number 15), invited His Majesty to their sumptuous feast at the Middle Temple Hall; but the King, having much domestic business, went not. On Wednesday the Duke of York and his royal sister, the Princess of Orange, went towards Dover, to prepare (the one by sea and the other by land) for bringing and entertaining the Queen's party. On Friday the great French Ambassador had his audience at the Banquetting Hall. This morning His Majesty went by the first of daylight towards Dover to meet his royal mother, who is expected to be this night at Calais, together with Her Majesty's most beautiful daughter, the Princess Henrietta . . . . who is to be speedily married to the Duke of Anjou, the French King's only brother,—after which Her Majesty will return and settle in England . . . Trade begins to flourish.—The Presbyterians have lately made some disturbances, which are reasonably well pacified by Bishoprics and Deaneries, which are conferred on half a dozen of the most quarrelsome of them. . . . . I am truly comforted in beholding His Majesty, but have not yet been benefited by his coming.

Fol. 101. 1661, April 13, Drury Lane. William Smith to John Langley.—The chiefest affairs now in hand are His Majesty's coronation and marriage, the first of which draws near, the four stately standing Pageants being now almost finished. The first His Majesty shall encounter is in Leadenhall Street, and it presenteth Anarchy and the confusion which that government brings: the second is erected at the Royal Exchange, and it holds forth Presbytery, and with it the decay of Trade; the third, which is the most sumptuous, stands in Cheapside, relating the honours due to the Hierarchy, and showeth the restoration of Episcopacy. In this magnificent building, His Majesty is to be treated to a stately banquet, and to show the power which Episcopacy hath over Presbytery, just at His Majesty's departure will arise the form of the old Crosse, which anciently stood at the same place, at whose appearance Presbytery vanisheth. The last, which is also very glorious, stands in Fleet Street, and represents Monarchy, whereby the former disorders are brought into their first conformities:—and these are to be the works of Monday, the 22d of this instant April. On Monday next His Majesty intends to go towards Windsor, to accomplish the instalments of the Garter; 20 or more knights are to be installed, with the Duke of Richmond, the Duke of Ormond (created also Prince of Tipperary), the Earl of Lindsey, and the Earl of Manchester, are the last receivers of that order. There are also divers to be made Dukes, Marquises, Earls, Viscounts, Barons, and Knights of the Bath.—Speaking of the expected marriage, the writer says, We rest our hopes and expectations on Portugal, at which the Spaniard swells; nevertheless, it is said the Earl of Bristol has concluded a truce between Spain and Portugal . . . . I am informed that our gracious Queen Mary will be speedily here; but I doubt it, because her last welcome was so starvingly expressed by this unworthy city, who again have showed their teeth in the election of their Parliament men, but the general elections of England in other parts have given better testimony of their loyalty . . . . For the Coronation, the Lord Wharton's furnitures for his horse (as is said), will amount to 8,000l., the bit of his bridle being valued at 500l. The Duke of Buckingham has written to some friends (as they say), that notwithstanding the malice of the cards and dice, he has bestowed 30,000l. upon a suit to attend His Majesty at his coronation.

Fol. 103. 1661, May 25. William Smith to John Langley.—I have been little in town for these 2 months last past. The principal news is in relation to His Majesty, and that towards his marriage, which you have in print from his own mouth. The Lady Infanta Katharina is expected about 3 months hence; on the 18th of July, His Majesty intends to begin his progress, which is intended towards Plymouth, there to meet the Infanta. In the Parliament, the last public work was

the hangman's, to burn the holy Covenant, which he did on Wednesday last in London and Westminster. On Tuesday (as it is reported for certain) the great traitor Argyle paid the debt due to his many treasons and murders in the same manner which he inflicted on that matchless convert Montrose . . . . The Dutch being to receive great sums of money from Portugal upon the conclusion of peace, would also have the benefit of their men-of-war abroad for 8 months which being resisted by His Majesty, it is thought we shall rather engage in the Portugal's assistance. . . . . Some soldiers are lately sent over to Dunkirk, where, it is said, the Spanish forces have very lately seized upon all the horse of the garrison as they were grazing under the town.

Vol. V.

Letters by Wm. (afterwards Sir Wm.) Dugdale.

1642, Aug. 28, Nottingham.—W. Dugdale to Sir Richard Leveson at Trentham.—I was required by Mr. Secretary to cause these printed things to be safely conveyed to you, who desires that you will please to disperse them so soon as is possible, and to the best advantage of His Majesties service. The two letters do require a speedy and trusty delivery, and some account of them accordingly. Men and arms will be welcome hither, and therefore what furtherance of either you can make at this present will be most acceptable. There be two reasons why I inlarge not myself more to you in particular, the one is haste, the other you may guess at.

Fol. 2. 1648, Oct. 16. W. Dugdale to [Dr. Hinton?] I yesterday received yours, and by reason that next week the same party who left my last letter at your house is to pass that way again, I have sent you these inclosed in the meantime to look over, if you have not yet seen this book, I know you will think your labour well bestowed in reading it; by the other which I received by the last post you will see what is like to be the issue of the personable intreatye (for soe my neighbours call it). I am very glad to hear that the noble knight and my good friend Mr. J. Langley be in health. —Sends Mr. Dodsworth's service.—I met with an acquaintance in Paris this summer who hath been out of England now near 7 years; he resided in Rome two years, and hath made the best use of his travels that I ever yet knew any do; he came to Paris about Christmas last, and in his return by Florence was most nobly used by the Ladies father at Trentham, whom he magnifies for one of the most accomplished men in the world, and says that he yet speaks as good English as if he had never lived out of this kingdom. This gentleman showed me a pedigree printed in two large sheets of paper drawn by the Duke of Northumberland himself of his own family, and very finely devised upon a ragged staff (in regard of his relation to the old Earls of Warwick). The print was cut in copper at the Duke's own charge, and the copies he gives to friends, whereof this was one. . . . I thank you much for your friendly intentions towards my daughter, and should be very glad to dispose of her to wait on any lady whom you think to be principled with loyalty; &c. P.S.—My wife commends her best service to you and Mrs. Hinton.

Fol. 3. 1655, Jan. 26, London.—The same to (J. Langley?) . . . . 'If I come into the country at Easter, which I hope to do, I shall be so busied about my Index that I cannot stir an hour. . . . I think I told you by my last of the honour done to Col. Pride, by knighting him; since that, the like is done to your quondam acquaintance Col. Barksted, the Lieutenant of the Tower. The sheriffs are all now in print; Mr. Thomas Chetwin for Staffordshire. On Monday last there was an unhappy accident at St. James; three gentlemen who had been prisoners about four months, the one his name is Holder (as I heare) son to him that escaped when Sir Louis Divee got away; the other Tirrell; and the third Jackson or Johnson; attempting to make their escape, and being pursued into the park by a soldier, shot the soldier with a pistoll and broke his arme, and being since taken about Spring Garden, are laid in irons. But this is not all; for I hear that those that were out upon bail are now called in again. . I am told that Col. Harvey (who hath the Bishop of London's seat at Fulham) though he be out of the Tower, is not forgiven his cosenage of the State; for they say that all he hath is seized on for no less then 56 thousand pounds, which they lay to his charge as pocketed by him unjustifiably. The Dutch are gone out with a great fleet, if reports here be true, no less than 80 sail of men-of-war and 15,000 landsmen, in aid of Dantzick against the Swede. I hope the Ecclesiastical History is with you before this time.

DUKE OF
SUTHER-
LAND.

Fol. 4. 1655, Sept. 8, London.—W. Dugdale 'to John Langley at Trentham.—I hope that the Rationale, I told you of, will be very shortly with you; for it is delivered to your cousin at the Three Crowns to be conveyed by the carrier, who was to come from hence yesterday (as he said). Admiral Pen is come back from Jamaica with part of the Navy, but hath left General Venables dead there, and many more, as most men say. Some talk of recruits, and I cannot tell what; but others fear that we have lost so much by this voyage that there will be little encouragement to adventure again. It is said that three of the best ships were blown up or fired, and many men perished in the accident. They say that Pen is at Portsmouth. There is one Sturgeon, of the Protector's Lifeguard taken and imprisoned, as a framer or disperser of the libellous Queres, of which I could never get a sight as yet. The Protector hath been very ill the last week, but they say he is now recovered. His uncle Sir Oliver Cromwell is very lately dead, by an unhappy accident; for I hear that he was out in the rain, and after his return sitting by a good fire without any company in the room, by some weakness or swoon fell into the fire, and was so scorched that he died about two days after. We hear of great hurt by floods, especially Northward, by the overflowing of the Trent, which they say here hath gone over cornfields. Here is now some talk of the speedy enlargement of those that are in restraint; and that we shall have a new Militia settled in 7 or 8 parts of the nation, each having their charge of those Malignants within their limits; and 'tis said that this is to be borne out by the Royalists only. Great preparation is making in Germany by the Emperor as I heare, so formidable is the Swede grown by getting this footing in Poland at such an easy rate.

Fol. 5. 1655, Sept. 15, London.—The same to the same.—I hope the Rationale is come safe to your hands. For news, I am to tell you that General Venables is printed to be alive again, though sick; but they say that our men die exceedingly at Portsmouth and other places since their return, the loss by this sea voyage being aggravated every day more and more, so far as people dare spoute. And they say that the Spaniard is lately gone out with 23 stout ships, which we doubt may meet with those 13 that are left behind at Jamaica. Mr. Palmer and Sir John Packington are out of the Tower; but the enlargement of others moves slowly either out of that place or any else. 'Tis now said that we shall not permit the Swedes to raise any men here. On Friday last week Bidle the Socinian was tried for his life at Newgate sessions; who confidently justified himself, pleading the Instrument of Government for his warrant, which holds forth toleration unto all that do profess faith in God by Jesus Christ except those that are popish or prelatical; so that they have set him aside, not knowing how to touch him, to the great grief of the presbyters. Very busy they are in most counties as I hear to establish godly ministers in all places, there being strict scrutiny made into those that are the present incumbents, in so much as they have questioned Lambert Osbaston for impudence, ignorance, and debauchedness, and having proved that he pledged an health about six years ago, have outed him of a rich parsonage in Hertfordshire, where he was very well liked of for his good hospitality.'

Fol. 6. 1655, Sept. 22, London.—The same to the same.—I hear that the Tryers are very busy in many places [in putting] such men out of Church livings as are scandalous in any respect; of which sort they have lately met with Lambert Osbaston, who had a fat parsonage in Hertfordshire, and, charging him with impudence, ignorance, and debauchedness, have outed him. For the first of these faults they judge him at large; for the second they say he is ignorant in the things of God; and for the last they had proof that he drunk a health about six years since. But we have sad news to our merchants, whose traffic is with Spain; for the Catholic King is so much incensed against us for the business of Hispaniola and Jamaica, that he hath caused all those merchants' goods and books which are within his dominions to be seized on and the persons of the men secured. And if the report be true that I hear this day, General Venables and Admiral Pen with some other that were in this unsuccessful expedition were yesterday committed to the Tower. We are afraid that the Spaniard will destroy those that we left in Jamaica, which are not many, there being 13 ships with them; for they are gone out with a great navy and above ten thousand men aboard whereof many are gentlemen. I hear that the Kentishmen and many others do get their liberty upon bail. Yesterday the Lord Mayor was feasted at Whitehall, and made a knight to boot.

Fol. 7. 1655, Michaelmas Day.—The same to the same.—For news we have very little here, except the imprisonment of Col. Venables and Pen in the Tower for that miscarriage in Hispaniola: but I hear that the merchants have certain intelligence that the King of Spain's Plate fleet is come home safe; so that then Admiral Blague may put up his pipes for this year. For want of matter I here send you some notes of a sermon for which it is said the preacher is committed; but there be that say that in his later prayer he prayed God to forgive His Highness for those things, and that he is not in restraint.

Brief notes of a sermon preached before the L. Protector at Hampton Court (by the Minister of Hampton) about the midst of August last. The text Prov. cap. 29. v. 2.

1. The imeriall actings of a bad ruler, like Absolon, who got into the Throne by flatteries.

2. Being advanced into it, he advanced only his own relations.

3. He lays heavy taxes upon the people to debase their spirits and subject them to his designs.

4. He gives God thanks for victories, that the people may think his cause is righteous.

5. He gives a toleration to all sects; and countenanceth all but the true religion.

6. Jehu like, he pretends Reformation, when he intends to set up Calves at Bethell.

7. He persecutes all that are not of his faction, and are contrary to his present interest.

Hast thou killed and } Here he spoke of Ahab tak-
taken possession.   } ing Naboths vineyard, &c.
He said that when David cut off the lap of Saul's garment his heart smote him, and so made a parallel betwixt that and cutting off the late King's head: and how David was troubled for what he had done, though he was ordained to succeed Saul.

Mr. Gage, his text to our English in Hispaniola wherein he preached to them, after they were beaten. Joshua, cap. 7. ver. 7.

Fol. 8. 1655, Oct. 9.* The same to the same.—I am very glad to understand (as I do by yours of Sept. 29th) that my noble friend is in good health, being much obliged to him for his valuation of my work in the press; which you may be sure I speed forward all that may be, but doubt that before Lent it will not be perfected. Of those Monuments in Pauls and other places I shall confer with you at our meeting, which I hope will be shortly; for I hear not of any new restraint like to be upon the Cavaliers as yet. Some are got out within these few days, upon security given to act nothing prejudicial to the present Government: but others do stagger at the latitude those would have, and to the time, being desirous that their bonds might have some limit, their sureties conceiving it too dangerous to seal such bonds, where the condition is subject to the interpretation of those that are not their friends; for what they say is prejudicial must then expose them to the danger of the forfeiture. But I was told about two days since by a principal person that is in this restraint, that they are now resolved at Whitehall to limit the bonds to a twelvemonth, and that it shall be particularly exprest in the condition, what they mean by such prejudicial acting, &c. For other news, we hear the Palsgrave is dead, so that having left an only daughter, Prince Rupert is to succeed as Palatine; but whether it be true that he is dead, a short time will discover. Winslow (a Committee man of Haberdashers Hall) died in the return from Hispaniola. I hear he raved much of Haberdashers' Hall in his sickness. Birkinhead (brother to our Oxford Aulicus) who betrayed Col. Booth and Mr. Wenman about three years since, died likewise in that voyage. We talk high here of sending another Armada to conquer Hispaniola, notwithstanding this ill success. It seems our superiors are not pleased that so much of these matters should be communicated by the press; for they have restrained all the pamphlets but Politicus, which is to be viewed by the Secretary of State. On Wednesday last came in a Venetian Embassador hither in great pomp. From Amsterdam we hear that the Swede is totally routed, and the King fled with xij men. If this prove true, 'tis great news. Hugh Peters lays about him to some purpose, to restrain the Presbyterians from growing up; the pulpits in divers places do ring with his declamations against them: He calls it a *periwig religion* and now magnifies the old. You will receive by the

---

* This date is not by Dugdale's hand and the month and day are indistinct.

carrier, two little books, one a journal of our late expedition to Hispaniola, which may not abide the light here; the other a discourse [by] James Howell called Some sober inspections into the passages of the late Parliament, wherein, cogging up [the] Protector (for to him he dedicates it) with some superlative language for destroying that monster (as he calls it) [he] hath taken the boldness to speak more truth, barefaced, than any man that hath wrote since they sate; nor doth he [sp]are the Scot and Presbyterian. Read it through, I pray you, upon my recommendation, though in some things he do commit little mistakes, and in others doth blunder a little.

Fol. 9. 1657, Feb. 13, London.—The same to the same. —This is to tell you that my printer finished yesterday, but my last plate will not be done till Tuesday, yet do I hope that I shall have two books bound to send away by the carrier for you on Fryday next. Our news is so little here, now that the Parliament is broke up, that it is scarce worth relating. On this day sevenight His Highness made a long speech to all the officers of his army, setting forth the story of our times from 3º Caroli, and therein his own, and how that the authority he hath is a thing far from his own seeking : as also of his calling this Parliament, whereunto, being advised by his council, he yielded, though he professed it, in his own judgment, no way seasonable. Next of the necessity of his dissolving it, in order to the public safety, professing his zeal thereto, and intention to govern by the laws, except in case of urgent necessity, wherein he must be constrained to have recourse to extraordinary ways : but it seems his rhetoric did not charm them all, for I hear that 17 or 18 have either laid down their commissions, or that they are taken from them, and 'tis said that 6 of the officers of his regiment of horse are in restraint at a private house near Charing Cross. Here hath been an expectance of a Declaration from His Highness to satisfy the world for this his dissolving this Parliament; but as yet we see it not. And a great noise we have had of a Proclamation for banishing the Cavaliers and Papists 20 miles from this city ; but I hope it will prove no more than a rumour. So likewise of new Decimations and many other ways for raising vast sums of money, which perhaps arise more from people's fancies then any true ground. I was this day told by one that saw a letter out of Oxfordshire, that 35 gentlemen in that county are newly secured ; but all is quiet and calm here as yet, which God continue.

Fol. 10. 1657, Oct. 17, London.—The same to the same.—You shall receive that book of the Tower Records which you mention by the carrier this next week.— The Duke of Buckingham will have but a short enjoyment of his fair lady in England, I doubt, unless his and my Lord Fairfax his friends, who labour hard to get the sentence pronounced against him to be recalled can prevail : for a troop of horse is gone down into Yorkshire to seize upon him, and where ever he is taken, he is to be conveyed to Jersey, there to be confined to a sad restraint, as I hear. Other news from hence there is none, but that we have sent 4,000 suits of clothes, with store of provision and warlike habiliments to our men in Flanders. But the rumour here is, which I hope is not true, that those in Mardike are very sick, and, which is worse, that the rest at Burbroke (2 leagues thence) where they were designed to winter, are for the most part slaughtered by the Prince of Conde, who fell in upon them with a strong party. . . . He fears the Swede will lose Pomerania and perhaps more.

Fol. 11. 1657, Oct. 24, London. The same to the same.—I hope you have, ere this, received that book of Mr. Prynne's setting out, intituled " An Abstract of the Records in the Tower."—Of news we are very barren. The troop of horse which went into the North for the Duke of Buckingham were answered by my Lord Fairfax, upon his honour, that he was not there, so that it seems he is slipt aside for the present. I am certainly told that my Lord Fairfax is coming up to mediate for him, and to endeavour to redeem him from this confinement to the isle of Jersey ; what the issue thereof will be, we shall shortly see. The young lady is transcendently pensive at this sad news in reference to her husband, and so is her mother. They were married by one Mr. Vere Harcourt (Sir Simon Harcourt's brother), a great Presbyterian, who assured my Lady Fairfax that he saw God in the Duke's face. Our news from beyond sea is not much. It is confest on all hands that the Swede is sinking apace. Rumours we have had of some disaster befallen our English at Burburgh, two leagues from Mardike, but I hear it not certainly confirmed.

Fol. 12. 1657, Nov. 14, London.—The same to the same.—For news we hear that the Dutch have taken xj. Portugal ships with rich lading, and that our navy hath

stopt an East India ship belonging to those butter boxes about the Lands End, so that some say we and the Hozen mogens are like to fall out. This is all that I can tell you from abroad. But from hence here is more ; for on Wednesday last was my Lord Protector's daughter married to the Earl of Warwick's grandson ; Mr. Scobell, as a Justice of the peace, tyed the knot after a godly prayer made by one of His Highnesses divines; and on Thursday was the wedding feast kept at Whitehall, where they had 48 violins and 50 trumpets and much mirth with frolics, besides mixt dancing (a thing heretofore accounted profane) 'till 5 of the clock yesterday morning. Amongst the dancers there was the Earl of Newport, who danced with Her Highness. There was at this great solemnity the Countess of Devonshire (grandmother to the bridegroom), who presented the bride with 2,000l. worth of plate. And ere long the other daughter is to be married to my Lord Fauconbridge, as 'tis said. I hear that my Lady Fairfax and her daughter (the Duchess) have been several times at Whitehall of late to wait upon the great ladies there ; but alas now, all this is not regarded, for I am told that the females there do say, Proud tits ! are their stomachs now come down ? There is talk of many that are to be summoned by His Highness to sit in the other House ; but forasmuch as 'tis not yet certain who they will be, I forbear to name them.

Fol. 12. 1657, Nov. 21, London. The same to the same.—Your character of Mr. Prynne's book, which I sent you is very suitable to it, and of the same mind do I perceive are other men of understanding here ; yet I must tell you that the Title thereof makes it sell, and at a very high rate.—I have sent you a catalogue of the nobility baronets of King James his time and King Charles, with the knights of King Charles, and those made by His Highness, newly printed, which sells here at double the true worth of a book of that size . . . From beyond sea we hear that the Dane hath had a foul blow by the Swede at Frederick Rode ; but all this will not help the Swede I doubt, so powerful is the Pole, and now in Pomerania against him. Some say that Cardinal Mazarin is sick, and that Marshal Turenne moves for a peace with the Spaniard. It seems that the Dutch have taken a great prize from the Portugals, no less than xj ships, valued at two hundred thousand pounds, so that 'tis doubted that these butter boxes adhering closely to the Spaniard will be our enemies, which is the rather supposed because that their embassador is newly gone from hence.

Fol. 13. 1660, Aug. 7. From the Herald's Office.— The same to the same.—I received your kind letter yesterday. I am well pleased that you jump so right with me in your esteem of Tom Philpot's book,[*] with Kilburnes and Guillims late edition. I have caused Mr. Secretary Morice his book to be delivered to your nephew to be sent to you . . . . . The Act of Indemnity is almost dispatched with the Lords, who, in pursuance of the King's desires, have struck off all the provisoes of moment (as I hear), excepting that for the murtherers of his father, and for Haselrig, Vane, Lambert, Axtell, and Hacker. I believe it will be sent down again to the Commons very speedily. Yesterday there passed some hot and high words in the Lords House betwixt the Duke of Buckingham and Earl of Bristol, by reason the Earl of Bristol did set a higher value on the Marquis of Newcastle's actings and sufferings for the King than of the Duke's ; in so much as it amounted to a challenge as some say ; whereupon by appointment of His Majesty they are required to keep their houses as I hear.

Fol. 14. 1660, Aug. 25, London.—The same to the same.—I thank you for your kind intimation of those old writings concerning Wolverhampton, and shall endeavour to get the sight of them as soon as I well can. I will deliver that book written by Mr. Blunt,[†] concerning the King's escape from Worcester, some time the next week, to your nephew. I know not yet any thing to the contrary, but that I shall set out of London towards Warwickshire on Monday next come sevenight. Our great expectance here is when the two Houses will finish the Act of Indemnity ; several conferences they have had about it, and 'tis hoped that upon their meeting again this day upon the same occasion they will dispatch it. The Commons do much insist upon it, that those of the King's murtherers who came and rendered themselves upon the King's proclamation, shall not be touched as to their lives, in regard there may be no cause to say that they were betrayed by that proclamation, which implyeth that in case they did come in and

---

* Villare Cantianum : fol. Lond., 1650.
† Thomas Blount's Boscobel, printed in 1660.

render themselves within a certain time therein pre-fixed, they should have favour: for it expresseth that if they did not so do, they should have no pardon for life or estate. Haselrig, Vane, and Lambert are like to have their lives saved, the Houses having resolved to make it their request to the King, that they may not be put to death. There hath been some obstacle in the passing of that Bill for restoring the Marquis of Hert-ford to his great grandfather's honour, in regard that the Marquis of Worcester did exhibit a patent under the Great Seal, pretended to be granted to him by the late King, at Oxford, for creating [him] Duke of Somer-set and Beaufort; but this being in truth suspected to be forged, there appearing no vestige of it at the signet or privy seal, nor any other probable way, and my Lord of Hartford being prepared to make such objections against it, as might have tended much to the dishonour of my Lord of Worcester before a committee of Lords, about three days since the Marquis of Worcester was pleased to tell the Lords that he must confess that there were certain private considerations upon which that patent was granted to him by the late King, which he performing not on his part, he would not insist thereon, but render it to His Majesty to cancel if he so pleased. So that my Lord of Hartford's business being now like to go on smoothly, it hath encouraged the family of the Howards to attempt the like restitution of the Earl of Arundel to the Dukedom of Norfolk, which, considering how much the greatest part of the House of Peers incline thereto, will out of doubt be granted. So, pre-senting my best service to the noble knight and lady whose farther honour by reason of the King's declara-tion of her mother to be a duchess, I do heartily congratulate, &c.

Fol. 15. 1660, Aug. 30, London.—The same to——. As touching the King's declaration upon his father's grant of the title of Duchess to the old lady you men-tion, with place and precedency to her daughter, this is the account which I can give you thereof, viz., that Sir Edw. Walker did draw a petition for this now Duchess to the King, and, being assisted by Secretary Nicholas, moved His Majesty in it, but could not prevail; for he told me in private, that he feared that the King had no great opinion of the truth of the pretended grant from his father, which they showed under the Great Seal, but deemed it to be one of those counterfeits which the now Marquis of Worcester is shrewdly suspected to be guilty of (there being one for himself, which creates him Duke of Somerset and a Knight of the Garter, nay which gives him power to create any degree of honour, under an earl, now in question before the Parliament, of which you will heare more perhaps very shortly). But not[withstan]ding that Sir Edw. Walker and the secre-tary could not set the whole agoing, one Doctor B . . . (one of the King's physicians), and one Thomas Kille-grew (an old courtier), as I am credibly [in pri]vate informed, did the business not without a good reward you may be sure. Mr. William . . . . . told me it was 500l. (I do not mean the 500l. in gold which Shirington Talbot gave.) And . . . ., women are highly pleased. My Lady Anne sent for me lately by Sir Tho. Leigh, and ask[ed] questions touching her place, &c., not worth troubling you with the relation. I have bespoke a seal for your lady with the bear and ragged staff, not in silver, but in steel [which is] farr better, which will be ready by the middle of next week, but no coronet over it, that [is] not justifiable for her in this case, though the daughter of a duke, and one who hath precede[nce of] a countess, for so she is now to have. I hope you will keep this letter private, for it [is] not fit that any but yourself should be acquainted there-with, nor would I impart so much to [any] one but an entire friend, as I know you are to me. I have here inclosed some queres from my good friend Sir Edw. Walker, which I shall intreat you [to] answer when you well can, and to convey this letter to Mr. Deg, the lawyer of your parts, which is upon the same errand. —Yesterday the King came to the House and past five Bills; the first concerning judicial proceedings in law, the second for interest money at six in the hundred, the third for an annual thanksgiving on the 29th of May for His Majesty's birth and restoration on that day, the fourth an Act of indemnity and oblivion (which hath been so long upon the anvil), and the fifth for Pole money. I assure you the Speaker of the House of Commons made a most excellent speech to the King upon the presenting him with those bills, and the King the like to both Houses, which I presume you will see printed within a few days . . . . . I believe there will be a recess within these few days, if not a dissolu-tion of this Convention. And I presume you will very shortly see a notable declaration of His Majesty touch-

ing religion. His patience and lenity hath hitherto been much abused by some, but you will now find (this Act of Indemnity being past) that for the future he will be of another temper, whereof he hath given a fair item and caveat in this his excellent speech. Ludlow (one of his father's murtherers) is broke out of custody and fled, and a proclamation sent after him with offer of 500l. to whomsoever shall take him. P.S. If you can satisfy Sir Edward Walker in some of these his inclosed desires, it will much oblige us both. I have herewith sent you the Act of Indemnity newly printed this day.

Letters by Mr. John and Mr. William and Mr. Thomas Langley, 1642 to 1661.

1642, May 10, London.—John Langley to Sir R. Leveson.—The impunity with which the fractious zelots triumph daily is a visible mark of the distempered government; in any country but here some heads before this time had paid for their tongues; as upon Saturday in the Commons House debating of the King's message (which is supremely well penned and startled them ex-tremely) one Sir Harry Ludlowe said, " He that writ " that message was not fit to govern nor wear a crown ;" being for it by some required to the bar, 'twas shuffled over by voting it not to be the King's, though Secretary Faulkland presented it to the Parliament under the King's hand and seal; in the like debate of Marquis Hartford's letter to be discharged of the Prince, where-upon some suspected His Highness might be trans-ported beyond sea, Peard said it was no great matter, for there were more of the line; there is nothing yet established upon the King's message, only a committee is appointed to prepare an answer for it : concerning the ammunition at Hull, they voted yesterday that it belonged to the commonwealth, and therefore they might fetch it away, though a former order held them some dispute wherein they had ordered it not to be removed without the consent of the King by the advice of his Parliament ; but 'tis said they may alter their orders as well as inferior courts; yesterday was appointed for naming evil councillors, but 'tis put of until Thursday. Earl Bristowe made a handsome speech one Saturday for some accommodation to be proposed, and not to run thus desperately on rocks; it was received with good appro-bation for the time, but I hear not of anything concluded upon it; another proclamation is issued forth against Lord Digby to charge him with high treason if he come not in within 16 days. Sir Louis Dives is at the Hague, and summoned to appear upon a penalty; the Commons sent for Messrs. End. Porter and Ashburnham, but the King excused them, the one attending himself, the other the Prince; which the House rejecting, hath warned them to appear at a day upon a penalty; they have sent for Sir Fr. Wortley and some others, York-shire knights, who refuse to come to them; Lord Grandison had a troop or company in Ireland, which he held to some profit, where his lieutenant hath lately done some considerable service, in reward whereof the House hath voted the lord's command (himself being now with the King), unheard, to his lieutenant; this day the citizens are busy in training 10,000 soldiers in Finsbury. . . . . eing to the new militia, which made the Houses rise timely to-day, that they might go thither to see and countenance their new ordinance, intending to set this as an example for the whole kingdom to imitate. Earl Essex is gone in a new guilt coach full of Lords, &c. ; the King hath sent for all the servants of his house, for his standing wardrobe, for Chief Justice Bankes, and Lane, the Prince's attorney; these two are gone to York, for what purpose is not known, though Banks will strictly pursue the genius of the Houses; the King's message is come forth while I was writing, and is here inclosed. O'Neale's escape out of the Tower is more thought of because they would chose a lieutenant to confide in who should be so negligent, which he only excused by saying the prisoner had the freedom of the Tower by their own order.—P.S. The last Declaration here inclosed concerning the militia (as you will find) full of gall and wormwood, &c.

Fol. 17. 1645, May 7, J. L. [John Langley] to ——. St. Philip brought me St. Mark's letter for answer ; be-sides my very hearty thanks, I can but recommend this bearer to be our historian, who hath heard and seen all our sufferings, since the malignancy of these times allow us not to discover our honest thoughts : Solomon was not wise enough, nor Alexander valiant enough, to satisfy the opinion of these new undertakers, whose judgments reach no further than their eyes, nor affections so far, otherwise they had forborne thus impiously to violate the peace and justice of the most glorious kingdom in

Christendom and usurp a brutish power to make us the continual objects of persecution; ambiguis ars strepet ipsa malis; in this equipage of fury we still preserve a hope of meeting again in safety, &c.

Fol. 17. 1645, Oct. 21, Nantwiche. (Sir R. Leveson) to the Right Honble. my dearest sister the Lady Newport in Worcester.—Domestic.

Fol. 19. 1647, May 17, Westminster.—Langley to Sir Richard Leveson.—The Lady Temple sent for me and acquainted me that Haberdashers' Hall had set your fine there at 2,000*l*. whereupon immediately we negotiated with Lord Howard, who is chairman, Mr. Gourdon and Mr. Darley being also of that committee, and 'twas so handled that it is brought to 1,000*l*., according to which here is a ticket inclosed, purposely sent to discharge you from the like demands of the country committee; but then, upon a further private dispute it was resolved that when it comes again into debate it shall be reduced to 500*l*. and Lady Temple hopes that bringing 300*l*. in ready money it shall serve turn or at least satisfy for a while. (The remainder of the letter is on the same subject.)

Fol. 20. 1647, May 18, Westminster. The same to [the same].—After more about the subject of the fine he writes—For news, much expectation depends upon the resolutions of the army, which demands their whole arrears before they disband, knowing that after they shall be put off with words only; some other high propositions are mentioned, but the particulars are not yet known; there is a letter come from the King acquainting them with the substance of that letter which was delivered him in private from the Queen, the party being in prison, it imparting her desire of His Majesties applying himself unto the Parliament, saving his conscience and honour, and besides that His Majesty would consent to some of their propositions, namely, to settle the presbitery for three years, and then longer if the kingdom liked it; to confirm the acts of their Great Seal if they would not question things done by his, &c.; this letter is to be read this day, however, they are preparing new propositions to send again unto His Majesty. Sir Arthur was so well pleased with his . . . that he carried him in his coach from Brooke House to his own at Islington.

Fol. 21. 1647, May 25, Westminster. The same to the same.—At the end of the letter he writes: Here is a calm of news, the present work is disbanding the army, voting them only two months pay with security for the rest; ten are to come hither out of every regiment to receive their money and calculate the remainder; next Saturday they are to disband at Chelmsford; Monday at Safron Walden; Tuesday at Huntingdon; Wednesday at Bedford; Thursday at Oxford, &c.; the soldiers are to leave their arms in the church of each place. Mr. Fr. Newport had obtained a qualification of fine in the Commons House if Clive had not unluckily come in when it had been long in agitation and barred it so as with his accusation as it still stands without abatement. . .

Fol. 22. 1647, June 1, Westminster. The same to the same.—General Fairfax was sent to the army last week to prepare them for disbandment; to this purpose his regiment was to be drawn together this day at Chelmesford in Essex, whither Earl Warwick, Lord de la Ware, Sir Gerrard, Sir Potts, Mr. Grimeston, and another went yesterday to meet them with their two months pay, and then to disband; but last night and this morning's post bring news whence 'tis whispered they will not disband, but require high demands; the regiment which should have been this day at Chelmesford is marched towards Yarmouth; General Fairfax is removed from Safron Walden to St. Edmunds Bury, further from the Commissioners, who may return as wise as they went; Oxford hath 1,200 soldiers under an independent governor, who fortify the works, have 80 great guns and 100 barrels of powder; some dragoons of the like stamp are lately put into Newport Pannell; these carriages startle our wise men, so as they begin to repair the decayed works in some places; here yesternight a list was taken of coach horses here about fit for service, yet 'tis said the King is still at Holmeby; what success this new enterprise may produce is very uncertain, though most think it will conclude in a money matter; however, I am advised from a very good hand in common prudence to be sparing a while in discovery of any resolution to either side, both having joined so far to ruin us, as little is left but our prayers for peace to enjoy the remainder; the result of these things I may send by next post, &c.

Fol. 23. 1647, June 29, Westminster. The same to the same.—After the subject of the fine, he writes,—The general's head-quarters are at Uxbridge; the King at Hatfield, though voted by the Commons House to

Holmeby again, yet 'tis thought ere long he will be at Hampton Court: there is good correspondence between His Majesty and the army; so is there between them and the city; much artifice hath he used to raise another army, but 'twill not take effect; this makes the presbiterians rail extremely at the Londoners; the eleven members have withdrawn themselves, yet may return when they please, but the army desires first to settle the greater affairs of the kingdom before they undertake to charge them; 'tis in proposition to choose eleven Commissioners from the Parliament, city, and army, to treat of accommodations; divers soothing votes and messages have been lately interchanged, yet 'tis thought each parties engagements have made them irreconcileable, distrustful of one another, and both suspicious to the cavaliers all, who looke upon the King's usage. Mr. James Leveson is safe returned from Guinea, with a rich ship for the merchants and something for himself, &c.

Fol. 24. 1647, Sept. 28, Blackfriars, London.—W. Langley to John Langley at Sir R. Leveson's.—He returns thanks for a present of a book that Sir Richard gave him before he left town and also for a letter received on the 2nd instant—I have little news; and truly I think London (like an ill liver in the body which turns the best nourishment it receives into corruption) does nova impuriora reddere, the very substance of good truths being suspected, if it but come from hence. The Newcastle propositions have lost another journey to Hampton Court, the King rather asserting the proposals of the army, which hath put the Parliament to a second trouble, and to that end are now new vamping their propositions, and then if His Majesty assent not, &c. 'Twas this day told me by one of the members of the Houses that there is a design that the propositions shall be prepared as in relation to this kingdom only; how Scotland will relish it many doubt; however, they are certainly disbanding their army. The British forces in Ireland, upon reasons to themselves best known, have joined in association, and resolved to admit of no other commanders-in-chief more than what they have already or other superior as yet, but require supply of both men and money; these things have for present unhinged those going under command of Sir Hardres Waller, and hath begot new disputes, so that as yet nothing is in that particular done. But some here believe that Sir T. Fairfax will not readily weaken, or remove his main body, till he be assured of the coming in of the Cities contribution, whose remissness in that particular hath caused him courteously to offer to free them from that trouble, and come and collect it himself; and lest any obstacle appear which might retard or hinder the proceed thereof, the Lord Mayor (last Saturday being Sept. 25th) with 4 aldermen to attend him were sent to the Tower. More of the City Common Councell with some of their colonels are to follow. The division in the army increases between Cromwell's and the Agitators' factions; these suspect Cromwell and his faction, who, they conceive, labour to insinuate too much into the King's favour; his faction on the other side labouring to new mould the agitators, who they conceive take too much upon them, as in relation to the dispossessment of things and the government of the kingdom; however, I have been certainly informed that Cromwell spoke much on the King's behalf, when his answer to the propositions was controverted in the House. They voted thus: first, that the King's answer, was a dividing answer; as to divide the kingdom of England from that of Scotland, by offering to satisfy each kingdom severally; next, to divide the army from the Parliament, in throwing himself upon the army's proposals; with much business to the like purpose. But some keener spirits went higher, as to assert that the King's answer was a denial of signing the propositions; that the King's denial to sign the propositions was an obstruction to the peace of the kingdom, that he was the Achan in Israel, the Jonas in the ship, &c.—P.S. Sir Robert Harley is put from his place of the Mint, and this day already is, or to be, committed to the Tower.

Fol. 25. 1648, June 6, Westminster. John Langley to (Sir R. Leveson). On the subject of the fine and other family business matters.

Fol. 26. 1648, June 20, Westminster. The same to (the same).—Business. . . . I lately heard that Mr. A. N. [A. Newport], is a pretender in courtship unto a daughter of Sir Hen. Herbert, the other being married unto Sir Simon Ivoryes son: they two are his co-heirs; Sir Hen. will give between them all his lands, 800*l*. per annum, &c.

Fol. 27. 1648, June 27. The same (to the same).—Relating to various payments, and commissions executed.

Fol. 36. 1649, Oct. 27, Westminster. The same to (the same). After mentioning Lady Temple's business, he says, "I doubt my lady's business will require some "money speedily, for two clerks are now employed in "writing copies of many books lately found in the Star "Chamber office at Gray's Inn, which, after the rate of "12d. a sheet, may arise to above 100l. Lady Newport "is removed into St. James's. . . . . Riding in the "Strand upon Thursday, I met Mr. Andrew, who told "me all there were in good health."

Fol. 37. 1649, Oct. 30, Westminster.—The same to (the same). Lady Temple's business.—Saturdays and Mondays the House sits not. The King is thought to be still in Jersey: little speech of him, less of the Scots: the subscription to the new government is refused by none, all submitting to it without scruple, and so will to any else that comes, whilst it stands, which makes some of that kind think it not a sufficient engagement.

Fol. 38. 1649, Nov. 3, Westminster. The same to (the same). . . . . The motions in the House are chiefly about taking off the great taxes; to this purpose the revenue of the Crown lands is designed for payment of soldiers' arrears; two-thirds of Papists' lands for payment of the army. with such other propositions hereunto pertinent. The young King is said still to be in Jersey.

Fol. 39. 1649, Nov. 6. Westminster. The same to the same . . . . Here is little news stirring, all negociations being carried with much greater secrecy than ordinary; the House is still debating upon a way for taking off the taxes; two days last week were spent about it, and this day it comes on again in course to be handled; they say their army in Ireland prospers with fresh conquests, yet that very many die daily of the country disease, and that Col. Trevor hath lately beaten up some of their quarters with much execution. The young King is said to be removed from Jersey for Scotland, being the only place left him; and venture he must, wherever he is. The design of our jar with France is thought to be purposely to provoke the common people there unto a distaste and breach with their own king, which hath wrought so far as they of Bordeaux have seized a strong castle there, and outed Duke Epernoun, the old governor of Gascoigne, and have petitioned their King to take off the embargo of English manufactures, expecting then that our prohibition of their wines will then be recalled. P.S. Here is a fresh report that Montrose is landed with some considerable force in Scotland, and that his design is for England; and that thereupon Lambert is drawing his strength together to prepare against him.

Fol. 29. 1649, Jan. 30, Coventry.—The same to the same.—I hear at Lichfield that the young Lady of Weston is courted by the Earl of Londonderry, the Lord Talbot, and another from Sir Henry Willoughbyes; being more than before I heard named; so as 'tis doubted a younger brother will not be entertained.

Fol. 31. 1649, Feb. 9, Westminster.—The same to (the same).—After relating his doings with regard to the business of the fine, he says, "'Tis reported that the "King is in France, that his treaty with the Scots "begins at Breda, the 15th March, that Cromwell will "be here shortly, but his stay not long, that the "French have recalled their prohibition of English "manufactures, and that the States here will do the like "for French wines."

Fol. 32. 1649, Feb. 16, Westminster. The same (to the same). . . . . Sir John Davers is put from the Council of State; Gen. Fairfax is melancholy mad, troubled in mind three or four times a week, yet hath not taken the engagement; some say Cromwell will be shortly here; others say he cannot come away thence.

Fol. 35. 1649, Feb. 27, at sunset, Coventry. — The same to the same.—His (Langley's) horse having been shoed by a smith in London so straight, and pared so near the quick, that at St. Alban's he was obliged to remove, and mend the shoe of his near fore foot; he must go so gently with him that he cannot be at Trentham before Friday evening.

Fol. 40. 1655. May 17, London. The same to the same.— . . . . Here's a deep silence of news. The Protector consults close and daily with his army officers. 'Tis thought he will settle a legislative power in himself: that the Judges act not according to their instructions is ill taken. Grey brought his Habeas corpus, which the Governour of Windsor refused to obey; one Cones, a London merchant, was imprisoned for refusing to pay custom; he also brought his writ of Habeas corpus last Saturday, when pleading for himself the case of ship-money, Prideaux, Attorney-General, told him the law was changed; his further hearing was adjourned to next Saturday. Some report the peace with France

is concluded, being purposely deferred, either to bogle the Spaniard in the enterprise of our navy at the West Indies, or to make his grand ambassador partaker of the affront.

Fol. 41. 1655, May 19, London.—(The same to the same.)—A London merchant, one Cones, lately desired to pay customs, for which his goods were seized and himself imprisoned. Upon Saturday last he brought his writ of Habeas corpus returned into the usurper's bench, where Sergeant Mainard and Sergeant Twisden with Mr. Windham, being of his council, spoke their sense of the law in that case for their client; against whom Attorney-General Prideaux prosecuted. In this dispute same pickant (piquant) words were interchanged of what was and was not law; but at that time the further hearing thereof was adjourned unto this day. In the mean time while yesterday, about 10 o'clock, those three great lawyers were summoned at Westminster Hall, to appear immediately before the Protector. After long attendance they were admitted to him, who told them they were factious persons and traitors to the Commonwealth, &c., and committed them instantly to the Tower, in three several coaches, that they might not confer together, where they remain close prisoners; yet this day Cones was brought again to the Upper Bench, where he spoke for himself modestly and stoutly. He required his former counsell. Judge Rolles said if he could bring them thither they should be heard. Cones replied if his lordship would declare it for law that in his case he ought to pay custom, he would pay it willingly; but the Court took exception at the return of the writ, and therefore adjourned the matter again unto Wednesday next, and remanded him to prison; he had counsell there, but it was not then seasonable for them to interpose. This stormy surprise startles the gownemen extremely. The Lord of Cherbury died about a week past at his house in the country.

Fol. 43. 1655, Sept. 19, Trentham. (Copy.) Sir R. Leveson to Frances Countess of Dorset. A complimentary letter.

Fol. 44. 1656, April 28, Trentham. (Copy.) The same to the same.

Fol. 44. 1656, May 17, London.—J. Langley to (Sir R. Leveson.)—About the disposal of Trentham Tithes. . . . . Some say the business of calling a Parliament, decimation, and doubling the taxes are set aside; others doubt it.

Fol. 46. 1658, April 24, London, Covent Garden. The same to the same.—Mentions the arrival in London of my Lady to her lodging at Mr. Coppinger's, next above the George, in Bedford Street, Covent Garden.—There is report that a higher Court of Justice is in forming; that Mr. John Russell's, Sir Compton, Sir Henry Slingsby, Doctor Hewet, a minister, &c., are commonly suspected to be in danger. That some blank commissions have been found, which have occasioned these proceedings.

Fol. 47. 1658, April 27, London.—The same (to the same). . . . . Mr. Andrew Newport was here on Sunday evening, and presents you with his kindest salutes, yet is not very visible by daylight.—I see many troops of horses trumpeting to and fro, and companies of foot grumbling with their drums daily in the streets; some thinking the pretences (pretence is?) of fears to form the high Court of Justice, and securing the royal party in prisons is chiefly occasioned to draw the soldiers about the town, for doubling his guards and strengthening himself for reception of Kingship, when the seasonable time comes by Parliament or otherwise. Infinite other conjectures there are, whereof 'tis like some may hit. . . . P.S. Sir John Wollaston died upon Sunday night last.—Left almost all to his wife, did little good unto any else, &c.

Fol. 48. 1658, April 29, London. The same to (the same.)— . . . . This morning was the trial at the upper bench, upon indictment of the Italian for forgery; the proof was very direct against him; the hearing held from 9 until 1 o'clock; then the jury went out and the judges rose; but the opinions of all the Court was so clear, that no doubt but the verdict will be for us, yet cannot be known until to-morrow morning. The two ladies were not there present, being otherwise advised by counsell, nor durst the pretended Duke appear in Court, nor could anything be proved against Sir James Croft, so he is like to escape. . . . . The only discourse now is about erecting a high Court of Justice, Commissioner Lile to be president, and that some will speedily be questioned, though others say it will be like a pedagogue's rod, only held up to awe the boys; however, few like it.

Fol. 48. 1658, May 1. The same to (the same.) . . . .
The trial upon the information passing so clear for the
ladies, their next work is, that the Italian being found
guilty of the forgery, and he, having four days' respite
to speak in arrest of judgment, which we suspect not,
then are we to move for judgment upon the verdict, and
that the forged writing in the register book may be cancelled and obliterate, which we expect will be easily
granted; for it must be done by special order of the
court, upon our counsell's motion; and except this be
effectually accomplished, all that hitherto hath been
performed signifies little. The forming of a High Court
of Justice seems to be at a stand for the Commission,
extending to about 150 persons, amongst whom all the
judges are comprehended to better countenance the procedures thereof; but they much boggle at it, and refuse
to act by it, conceiving the last Parliament, being a
stain'd company, was not of sufficient power to authorise
them safely to undertake the execution thereof against
the express provision of our known laws and divers
Statutes to the same effect. Thursday and yesterday morning both the Chief Justices were in long dispute at Whitehall, concerning these particulars, which
hath given some stop to that career; yet their fears or
something worse still possess them, for every night the
soldiers search divers houses, and take thence many
into prisons.—Earl Warwick's hearse (who died about a
fortnight since), with many mourners and coaches,
passed through London towards Essex unto burial.
Fol. 49. 1658, May 4, London.—The same to (the
same.)—Domestic. He then writes at the end of the
letter that "The judges still boggle at the High Court
" of Justice, the Prot[ector] told Chief Justice Glin
" that lawyers are always full of quirks. He replied
" it could not be otherwise, when soldiers drew up the
" Act; yet many think they will do their work that
" way which by a jury they could never perform. 4,000
" men more are shipped for Mardike."
Fol. 51. 1558, May 8, London.—The same to (the
same.)—This morning, after serious dispute, judgment
was granted in the Upper Bench against the Italian,
upon the verdict of forgery; the next work is to attack
and lay him in prison, if he run not away before. 'Tis
reported that the French lately have been trepened
(trepanned) at Ostend, being by secret confederacy to be
admitted into the town, upon a sign of hanging up a
white flag, and shooting off a gun at an appointed time;
and when they were entered, 1,500 of them were presently cut off, &c.
Fol. 50. 1658, May 11, London.—The same to the same.
—To-morrow the Commissioners for the Court of Justice
are to meet, and then to resolve upon what form they will
proceed, which is thought will be after the arbitrary way
without jury; then satis est accusare. Four principally
are said to be fixed upon; Sir Slingsby, a Cavalier uncom-
pounded, Dr. Hewet, a minister of the Royal party, young
Mordant, a Presbyterian, and one Gifford, a Papist.
This Court is to continue until the next session of Parliament, which is thought still will be about September.
These rigid proceedings offend most men's thoughts.
The business of Ostend was very foul; on the French
side, Marshal D'Aumont being prisoner, and almost all
his men slain. Parson Waring, who attended Sir Willm.
Whitmore, died lately of a violent fever; he is much
lamented by all, especially of that family.
Fol. 51. 1659, Feb. 2. Tho. Langley to his uncle, Mr.
John Langley.—This day, the soldiers being to march
out of town, the horse are gone; but the foot are mu-
tinied, because they had not their pay, and have pos-
sest themselves of . . . . house, and 'tis said killed one
of their captains last night, and do cry for a free Parliament; and just now the apprentices cry, Arms, Arms,
for a free Parliament. Now what we shall have God
knows.
Fol. 51. 1659, Feb. 29, Trentham. (Copy, by Mr.
Langley, of a letter from Sir Richard Leveson to Sir
Thomas Gower, at Stitnam, in Yorkshire.) — Complimentary.
Fol. 54. 1660, April 21. Thos. Langley to Sir Richard
Leveson.—We are here all in a bustle at present, hasting
into arms : and General Monk's army marching into
the country, it is said towards Edgehill, where Lambert,
as some say, is with 7,000 Quakers and Anabaptists.
Fol. 55. 1660, May 1. Thos. Langley to Sir R. Leveson. . . . . This brings you the joyful tidings of our
King's coming home, with all the speed as so great a
reception will allow, there having been several votes
this day in Parliament about it; also they have voted
three Lords and 12 Commoners, to be sent to him to
Breda. The high resentment of the news in this city is
expressed by ringing of bells and making of bonefires.

Fol. 55. 1660, May 3. The same to (the same). It is
resolved by the Parliament, that four Lords and eight
Commoners, shall go to Breda to fetch home the King,
and by this city that two Aldermen and four Commons
shall go with them, and to carry His Majesty 10,000l.
from this city, as a testimony of their loyal submission to
his royal authority, he being proclaimed at Westminster
already, and expected to be proclaimed in this city to-
morrow. Further, the Parliament hath voted our late
King's death to be murder.
Fol. 56. 1660, May 5. The same to the same.—I must
correct my last as to the proclaiming of the King, which
hath not been yet done; and now this city have chosen
21 Commissioners to go to fetch the King at their own
charge, being some of the most eminent persons of the
City, which are to carry him a letter and 10,000l. This
city also lent the Parliament 50,000l. to send the King,
who likewise send six of their Lords and 12 of their
Commons with it, and their letters. This city lends the
Parliament 50,000l., to disband four or five regiments
of their soldiers, all which moneys is already near
raised. It is said the whole Parliament do intend to
meet the King some part of the way. There are six rich
coaches providing to fetch him in. The Hollanders have
presented him with 200,000 dollars, and two very rich
coaches. His entrance here it's thought will be about
the end of this month.
Fol. 57. 1660, May 26. Tho. Langley to (Sir R.
Leveson). This morning about 3 o'clock came advice
to the Lord Mayor that the King was come to Canterbury last night, and landing about Deal or the nearest
part to that place; and this night it's thought
will come to Cobham Hall, and on Monday near London, and so make his entrance through here on Tuesday which is the soonest expected ; the bells here have
rang all day since 4 o'clock, and order given for bonefires this evening; the Earl of Cleveland leads out to
meet his Majesty that day of his entrance here the
gentry of Buckinghamshire and Hartfordshire; also
the three regiments of horse that came out of Scotland
with General Monk are likewise to go out that day to
fetch in the King, all in their armour as they marched
out of Scotland ; the King hath conferred many
honours of (on ?) General Monk, as Duke of Somerset,
Earl of Essex, vice-Chancellor of Oxford, Warden of
the Cinque Ports, Knight of the Garter, one of his
Majesty's Privy Council, and General at sea and land,
and more is said ; his Majesty hath also knighted all our
City Commissioners and made Mr. Callamy and Dr.
Reynolds two of his chaplains.
Fol. 57. 1660, May 29. The same to (the same).—Our
joy and admiration hath been great here this day of the
coming safe home of our most gracious Sovereign to
his lodging at Whitehall, where he is safe arrived,
blessed be God.
Fol. 58. 1660, Oct. 13.—Tho. Langley to his uncle, Mr.
John Langley.—This day Harrison was executed at
Charing Cross, carrying it out confidently to the last ; yesterday was condemned five others, Scott, Jones, Scroop,
Clemence, and Carew ; this day were condemned Cooke
and Peters ; Cooke delivered himself lawyer-like to the
judges for two or three hours in several cases, which
were answered effectually by Sir Orlando Bridgeman
and Sir Heneage Finch, the King's Solicitor; it is said
on Monday Scott is to be executed in the Palace Yard
at Westminster, and that the King hath been pleased
to give his wife his estate ; Captain Smyth tells me
Cromwell's wife is married to a courtier, an elderly man,
but he did not know his name, but a favourite of the
Kings.
Fol. 53. 1660, Feb. 19. The same to the same.—
Fol. 59. n.d. J. Langley to Sir R. Leveson.—Business.
—The Lord Keeper salutes you with much respect.—
This morning I was at Bedford house to visit Mr. Newport, but he was not stirring, however, I learnt from
Lord Newburgh, Sir Ed. Littleton, Sir John Jenings,
Sargeant Evers, Mr. Palmer, and others that the house
is full and no likelihood yet of calling or danger to them
that are absent; your nephew is the bravest gallant
about the town, in himself, his lady, coach and footmen,
&c.
Fol. 58. 1661, April 9. Thomas Langley to Mr. John
Langley. . . . This day there is chose for Parliament men in Southwark, Sir Thomas Bludworth and
one Col. Moore, both right honest men ; the presbiters,
independents, anabaptists, and quakers joined together
in abundance, but could not carry it; some of them
brought swords, and when they saw they could not have
their wills, drew them and hurt some of Bludworth's
men, but are sent to prison for it; there's many lying
reports scattered by them in the city, but so long as

amounts to no more, shall be passed by; yet I may mention one upon the Exchange to-day, that the King had sold his three kingdoms to the Spaniard, and that the life guards were most papists, and that in the countries all the papists were listed, and that there would be a general massacre; but an account of this report was carried up to Court presently; this serves to show you the present temper of ugly spirits.

62. Draft in J. Langley's hand of a letter by (Sir R. L.) to Mr. Crakenthorpe.—C. seems to have applied for a presentation to or promise of the next turn to Black Notley, to which his late father seems to have been formerly presented by Sir R. L.'s father. Sir R. commends Crakenthorpe for his works and virtues, but excuses himself from making any agreement for the living, for which to contract until a vacancy is in some sort a profanation of holy things. On a vacancy, if C. is unprovided for, Sir R. will be mindful of him.

On the back is draft of a Latin letter in L.'s hand, perhaps to C.

61. n. d. (J. Langley to Sir R. L.) Gives reports about the siege of Colchester, the movements of the Scots, and a pretended design to poison the King. The Prince of Wales has left the Court of France and gone to Holland.

LETTERS BY MR. SAMUEL HINTON.

Fol. 63. 1641, May 2. S. H. (Samuel Hinton) to Sir Richard Leveson. . . . News we have by the post from London who returns so speedily that ere we have read our letters he is gone. So, the petition sent by the Earl of Stamford and the gallant answer,—the petition of the gentry at York and the answer declaring the behaviour of the Governor at Hull and his being proclaimed traitor by the King and rewarded by the Parliament with 2,000l. for his good service,—Sir Francis Wortley and six more of the petitioners sent for as delinquents,—is only confirmation of what you heard before. That there be 1,000 English slain in Ireland by the rebells, but with a greater loss (for so it must be or the paper will not sell), and that all will be gone if supplies go not in greater numbers and more speed, is confidently reported here; but you are nearer to Chester and can tell whether His Majesty will be there, and at the Lord Stranges, which is rumoured here. The names of the divines chosen to assist in this Lay Clergy Synodical Assembly to make a new face of religion are printed. We hear that on the 29th of April 200 Kentish gentlemen, well appointed, went to the Parliament and presented their former petition; the Parliament rose, demanded their weapons (swords and pistols) which were delivered, and promised answer as this day. The Earl of Stanford and seven more are gone down with Commission and money to levy men to keep Hull; these things portend dangers.

Fol. 63. 1642, May 16, Coventry.—The same to the same.—The King's answer to the Declaration about Hotham being read in the House, Mr. Prin did attend it with a gracious smiling, which was favour enough for the King. One of the members said if it were the King's own act he had forfeited his crown. Some called a bar, but more votes were for interpretation, and that was by this moderate gloss (never Canonist made worse) that it was not forfeited but forfeitable. Your Lord Lieutenant moved to have the malignant party named, and a staff set at their doors. How safe it is to conjoin with these potent super-monarchs I leave to your wisdom to judge. P.S. This day I am informed that divers parliament men leave the House and go to the Bath, and some say they will yield up Hotham to be tried and are fearful.

Fol. 64. 1649, April 19. S. H. (Samuel Hinton) to Mr. John Langley.—My humble services to my noble Lady and Sir R. and give them this following relation :—One Grebnerus, a German, presented Queen Elizabeth with a manuscript declaring what future events should happen in Europe. Dr. Nevill, Dean of Canterbury, and Master of Trinity College in Cambridge, procured the book of the Queen and gave it to the library of the College. Mr. Will. Clutterbooke, library keeper there, since Manchester's expelling all honest men out of the college, &c., hath upon conference, with other excluded fellows, and rubbing up their memories, given to his friends this ensuing piece of Prophecy of England. Rex septentrionalis nomine Carolus ducet uxorem papisticam Mariam, ex qua evadet regum omnium infelicissimus. Tunc populus ipsius ditionis eliget alium sibi regem comitem, qui durabit in imperio tres annos aut circiter. Et postea idem populus eliget alium regem equitem non ejusdem familiæ nec honoris, qui detrudet omnia sub pedibus suis aliquanto longiore tempore; et post hunc nullum. Paulo post apparebit quidam

.Carolus ex Carolo, descendens ab immensâ classe, in littus patriæ suæ cum auxiliariis Danicis, Swedicis, Hollandicis, Francicis, et Hispanicis; et prosternabit suos adversarios; et administrabit imperium suum perfælicissime, et erit Carolo Magno major. Quod faxit Deus! Thus far I follow a copy; may I add (and that upon the faith of a Christian) this book I saw above 20 years since in that library. It had an epistle dedicated to Henry of Burbon, then King of Navarr; in which he told him he should be King of France. I saw much of the business of the war in Germany and I well remember that there was foretold the fall of the Earl of Essex, and to my best remembrance in these words. Hoc anno peribit Regulus quidam in Anglia infelici morte, cujus filius, &c., shall be greater or more famous in arms than his father. Sir Tho. Leigh had Clutterbooke to read to him in Camb[ridge] under his tutor, and he met him last summer or the year before, in London, and they had speech hereof; told him much of this above, and promised then to recollect himself and give him a fuller accompt. This for the credit of the truth that there was such a book, which is performed : do you muster up your thoughts with your best and latest intelligence from the first action it mentions. Now if this find acceptance, let me know if you have heard of the Dumb Prophecy presented to the Earl of Marlborough; if not, I will give you a full account of it, and as good testimony for the truth of its stranger predictions (I mean if it did foretell and is not forgot since events too sad are happened) as I have done for the former.

Fol. 65. 1649, St. Mark's Eve.—S. H. (Samuel Hinton) to Mr. John Langley.—Since you will have it, I will speak for the Dumb Prophecy. The particulars made known to me are tragical, but I will give you my relation and my authority. At the trial of the Earl of Strafford, the Countess of Marlborough was with much ado persuaded to be at the hall one day. Some great crime he so finely wiped off and cleared himself that the auditors thought he would be quit; a lady asking the Countess her opinion she said she thought he would perish, and gave this reason, that in her husband's Dumb Prophecies (a book only filled with pictures, but not one word writ or printed in it) she saw the representation of such a court, and such a man at the bar, and his face in that picture so like the Earl of Strafford, that she feared he would be cut off, in regard that in that book in the next leaf there was he again pictured with his head on the block or cut off. This was related to Mr. W. Dugd. (Dugdale); he afterward casually at Oxford, when it was a garison, met with the Marquis Hartford's secretary and one Mr. Longe, High Sheriff then of Wiltshire, who was near allied to Marlborough, who did assure him that it was a true relation. Upon farther discourse, Mr. Dugd. asked where the book was. Long replied it was burnt, and that he gave his consent to the burning of it; and gave this strange reason to him (some years now since at Oxford), that amongst other things there was the picture of some such other court, and the King as at the bar, and on the other (next) leaf an hearse and the Crown pictured as set upon it, and this W. D. told me, upon his faith, was true; and the secretary heard it as well as himself. . . . Let me tell you my opinion, that both this and the former of Grebner appear to me two of the strangest things that I ever heard in my days; and let me not forget that Sir Tho. Leigh told me he had all of the King in this book from the Lord Marlborough himself. P.S. I have forgot whether I formerly told you that I saw part this prophecy of Grebner printed (but not fully as my relation) in the end of a book writ by Brightman * many years since.

Fol. 66. n.d. July 27. The same to the same.— . . . . The Mayor and Sheriff of Coventry refusing to proclaim the proclamation for the Commission of Array, the High Sheriff of Warwickshire doing the same, Sir Arthur Haselrig and Lord Gray coming with 500l. and Dr. Bastwick to book (boot?) to keep the magazine which the Earl of Stanford had taken away, it pleased His Majesty to visit Leicester as he had Newark and Lincoln (his speeches in all 3 places printed now); his train was four miles at Leicester of gentry, priests, and others ; his approach made Haselrig and Gray fly, but Bastwick is taken and in Leicester Gaol, and next Assizes to be tried for waging war against the King. Some 60 men, hired by Sir Arthur Haselrig, kept the magazine, but on Monday resigned it, and it is kept in several hundreds. The King commands Serjeant Whitnide to

---

* Thomas Brightman. Predictions and Prophecies, written 46 years since, concerning the Churches of Germanie, England, and Scotland. 1641. 4to.

give the major and sheriff of Coventry notice that they must attend him as on Sunday last. The poor spirited rascals were ready to die (at Leicester they report of our major, as some write, of Ben and the Colonel), but they sent to Warwick to the Lord Brook three messengers, and divers of our inhabitants fled to that sanctuary; at last the major procured a rabble to say he should not go, nor went not. Brook had about 1,000 men in his castle, but the King went away yesterday towards Beverly, and Brook discharged part of his army. But the King will shortly see our parts and undeceive us. His answer and propositions to the Parliament are in print, gracious, full of strong reason, and trim'd with the same neat quipps as formerly. To-morrow the Earl of Northampton, Sir Dunsmore, Sir Tho. Leigh, and the rest of the Commissioners of Array begin at Southam to train: on Friday at Stratford-upon-Avon, on Saturday at Coleshill, and there I intend to be. This is all true.

Fol. 67. 16—, Sept. 20. Sam. Hinton to Mr. Thomas Davies at his house near the Butchers-row, Lichfield.—I had rather the news that I was last Saturday committed by the Council of War in our city to the custody of our sheriff should be made known to my friends from myself than by relation of another. The cause of my imprisonment I know not; only one Mr. Phipps, a physician, and now an officer in the army here, objected (after I was ordered to be committed) that two or three years since I should speak some words before him and Sir Tho. Leigh at Layton Buzard against old Parliament men, and wish for young twigs that might be easily bound; that I should, at a tavern, tell him that I liked the Popish religion better than ours, that I had been at counsells and consultations against the ways of the Parliament, and that I was a malignant party. Truth is, if Sir Thomas could remember discourses of Mr. Phipps after a plentiful meal, and Sir Tho. then taking physic, he would call to mind that Mr. Phipps was full in discourse against Bishops and the Church government, &c. . . . Lastly, I was told I set my hand to a petition to the King; I denied it not, but said I thought no honest man would have refused it. This is all I know why [I] am a prisoner; and although I requested to be confined to my own house, offering oath and bond to be a true prisoner, in regard of my wife's long sickness &c., to the sheriff's house I was sent, and there remain. . . .

Fol. 68. 1660, May 13. S. H. (Samuel Hinton) to Mr. John Langley. . . . His Majesty is thought to be at Dover, and on Tuesday to enter London. Will. Dugdale rides all this day to be there to meet him. The Lord Leigh of Stonly goes up on Tuesday, as many persons of quality do from all places. General Monk is made Duke of Somerset. The King sent his wife a jewel, his picture in it. The House of Commons cary (carry) all bravely for Church and King, thwarted the Lords' bill who proposed to have the nominating of the King's servants. You will hear that some have endeavoured to disturb business. . . . .

Mr. Ayloffe's Letters.

Fol. 69. 1652, Dec. 1 (or 11 or 21 or 31).—G. Ayloffe to Mr. John Langley.—Since the [engagement with the Dutch wherein we lost three ships] 'tis said we have lost five or six merchant ships off Malligo and Barbadoes; the Dutch fleet continue still to hang about our coasts, indeed to the blocking up our harbours (for indeed the State have sent over to all ports that no shipping stir out), a disgrace that never happened before to this nation that hath in all times been masters of our seas; but we are providing a good fleet that will be suddenly ready to set out; and so, if the winds do not, we will drive them away. The Dutch have set out a Placat (they call it) in Holland, declaring all enemies to their state that send ammunition or materials for war or shipping into England. The Spanish Ambassador has been at the House to appeal from the Admiralty about those ships of the King of Spain's plate and bullion that were taken, but they were directed to go on in the Admiralty; however some fancy the dispute is only to colour the paying for our taking the French ships and hindering the relief of Dunkirk. The French agent having mended (as it seems he had power to do, the superscription of his letters, which was at first *A mes tres chere et bones Amies le gens du Parlement de Engleterre*, but now *Mes Amies, le Parlement de Republique d'Engleterre*) had audience this day, not in the House of Commons, but only by a Committee in the Lords old house, which he took exceptions at, but was answered that if his Master or an embassador came [they] could but give him reception

in the Parliament House; so that passed; and he made a great compliment of his master's desire of the good understandings that might be between the two nations, &c.; however, we take him but for a spy. They say my Lord Digby is sent by the King of Scots into Holland, and my Lord Wilmott sent to the Diet, in Germany; here's a report that my Lo. of Bristol is dead.

Fol. 70. 1655, July 14. The same to the same. . . . . The council joined with a committee of the officers ('tis said) are close upon consideration of the persons under restraint, and some say are framing some engagement or oath of abjuration; 'tis thought shortly something shall appear. The apprehension (if any were) of the great Swedish army must needs be removed by this Embassador's or Agent's coming from the King of Sweden (he is expected suddenly, and Dorset House taken for him) and something the more, for the person being one of our own nation, one Sir Geo. Fleetwood brother to the deputy of Ireland; he has been ever a soldier in the Swedish wars. They say the Judges of the northern circuit, Chief Barons Steele and Parker, carry a particular commission to try the gentlemen of Yorkshire secured upon that rising; it may go ill with some of them 'tis thought. Some say that General Blake's fleet are come upon the coast of Spain. . . . There was like to have grown a little breach between the late married couple, the Earl of Middlesex and his lady, but 'twas quickly peaced; it seems he does not well brook some of her servants, and perhaps begins to think the articles too much derogatory to the honour of a husband; his mother perhaps doing not all the best offices.

Fol. 70. 1657, Nov. 17. The same to the same. . . . The discourse of the town has been much filled up with the great marriage at Whitehall, which was solemnised there three or four days last week with music, dancing, and great feasting, and it now begins for two or three days at the Earl of Warwick's. The marriage of the other sister to Lord Falkenbridge they say is concluded. They are now busy about the other House, as they call it; the Judges all had a meeting lately with the commissioners of the great seal to consult about framing the writ of summons; the old form or style does not fit; they say now it must go *viri notabiles.* . . . I forgot to tell you that amongst other lesser presents to the bride, the Lady Devonshire gave some pieces of chamber plate all of gold with] one (they call) *the piece royal :* 'tis such as I have seen used for the waiter to carry a glass upon. The Lady Claypoole's was two sconces of 100l. apiece, they say; and somebody I heard presented a good quantity of Barbary wine.

Fol. 71. 1658, May 15. The same to the same. . . . . The day after you went, I hear 60 of the commissioners of the High Court met at the Painted Chamber, but they say did nothing but appoint to meet upon Monday next. The judges of the Upper Bench were all there, and the Barons of the Exchequer, but my Lord St. John is sick. I heard it spoken, by one that pretends to know it, that writs for a Parliament are in hand. Here has this day a news gone about that the Duke of York and Marquis of Ormond are killed. 'Tis in some letters to Whitehall, they say, but not upon the Exchange that I hear, and some late letters from France mention nothing of it. 'Tis supposed by some at some attempt upon Mardike; others the French army beat up Spanish quarters, in which the Duke and Ormond were; for it is certain the whole French army is come near Calais, and the King himself in Calais; for I was told the French Ambassador sent away this morning to Calais some bottles of Canary for the King of France's own drinking. . . . Some wonder why Ormond should be named with the Duke, he not meddling in arms; and then why there should be such negligence about his quarters. . . . Here appears a little face of strictness about town; all those that were formerly prisoners at St. James are summoned in, and all that are in town gone thither this evening, and I hear that some are taken about the town here into custody this day; and I hear some troops of horse have been marching the city to-day, and 'tis rumoured as if it were to search for Charles Stuart, but some conceive the care and vigilancy is in respect of the sitting of this High Court, for their better and more assured quiet proceeding.

Fol. 71. 1658, July 15.—The same to the same.—Alludes to the death of Sir Ben. Ayloffe's wife, and his own preparations for his approaching trial at Carlisle Assizes.—Our Ambassador in France, Lo. Lockhart came out two days since, 'tis thought upon some great and private affairs with his Highness; yesterday all the Council attended with him at Hampton Court where the Protector is; 1,000 horse are gone or going for Flanders and divers regiments of foot; so as if we and the French gain farther there, some will doubt we may fall out in the sharing of it. The Dutch and we are peaced again; we have restored their ships, and they engage to do the like for ours taken by them in the Indies; here has been a day or two since a fresh report of the French King's relapse; but he is well, or at least able to go to Paris. This day was the marriage of the Lord of Ross and Marquis Dorchester's daughter. The Duchess of Richmond is gone into France; given out she goes to visit her brother, when the truth is conceived she even little better than runs away for dubt, and because she can live no longer here.

Fol. 72. 1660, May 15. The same to the same.
.... The Act of Oblivion is the thing they are now vigorously upon; wherein their indulgence to except but seven persons (which 'tis said the General was the occasion of) is much wondered at; though the numbers be resolved, yet I do not hear that the persons are yet established, which perhaps may be kept secret till as many as can be found may be secured, and that 'tis thought has made many hide themselves, for there is they say a stop upon all po[st]s; but 'tis said there are about 20 secured here and fetching up; 'twas moved that the executioner might be enquired out, and the Speaker said that would be known in due time. Here are frequent reports of the King's sudden coming, indeed, that he has been landed at Dover; but perhaps that has been cast out to hinder the great concourse of people going over to the King, which 'tis said he could wish would somewhat abate. I was told that the messengers of both Houses were still at Dover; only Mr. Holles I heard got over in a packet boat upon Tuesday, by whom His Majesty's pleasure may be known touching the manner of his reception and the house he will come to. Whitehall is forwardest in preparation, though St. James and Somerset are under the same order. The King had sent for the Navy upon Friday last, which attend as 'tis said at Helvetsluce; and His Majesty took the Hague in his way, and perhaps is there still; a barque went down yesterday to Dover, and 'tis said the General will march to-morrow. ... This day 'twas moved to name the seven, to put the others out of terror, but took not; they have ordered bills of Attainder against the late Protector, Bradshaw, Ireton, and Pride, for confiscation of their estates; 'twas moved the Lo. Gray of Groby might ha' been another, but was not. One thought the seven too few; he would have had of all professions, some soldiers, lawyers, courtiers, clergy, but 'twas not seconded; 'tis said divers are run away, as Mildmay, Ludlow, Lo. Mounson, Lisle, and Martin; but they have a plentiful world of these delinquents, enough to hang, enough to confiscate, enough to banish, enough to imprison, and enough to run away. They have secured Thurlow (Thurloe); some think rather to squeeze some discovery out of him, than for anything capital. Cromwell's wife and her daughter Rich, are gone from their lodgings in the Charter House, nobody knows where; great store of packs of hangings and other goods are secured in Thames Street by guards of soldiers, which the report goes, were ordered to be conveyed away upon her account.

Fol. 74. 1660, May 29. Gui. Ayloffe to Sir Richard Leveson.—Writes to give an account in short of this blessed day of the King's most glorious entrance into the city of London and so to Whitehall, which was with as high expressions of joy and affections of his people as is imaginable, being as well brought in with very gallant company and troops of the citizens as of very splendid troops of the nobility and gentry; of the nobility, the Earls of Derby, Northampton, Cleveland, Litchfield, Lo. Mordant, Lord Maynard; Lo. Faulkland, Lo. Gerrard who had the command of the lifeguard of His Majesty, all which with the General's lifeguard and Army Regiments, by estimation could not be less than 8 or 10,000 horses; the two Houses attended in the Banquetting house; after His Majesty had a very little while reposed, he sent for the lords into him, and then immediately came in to the House of Commons in the Banquetting house. The Speaker made some speech, to which the King desired to be excused for making any long reply by reason of weariness, but told them they should not be more ready to propose anything to him for the good of his people in laws, liberties, and religion, than he would be to grant, &c.; so the Speaker and every member kissed his hands; He rid very plain in cloathes, so did both his brothers; he and they shewed great courtesy to all balconies and windows of ladies, and moved their hats often; Gen. Monk has a blue ribbon; what office of state, or other honour will be conferred, 'tis better the next may tell you; they name him of two, Master of the Horse and High Treasurer; and perhaps it may be neither; the

uncertainty for other officers and Bishops silences me. Some think Bishop Juxon is too weak of body to be Canterbury, and 'tis doubted whether the Bishop of Salisbury will accept it; then 'tis feared it may fall upon the Bishop of Ely, which is not much wished; and if to neither of these, then Dr. Sheldon may chance to be the man. My Lo. Newport and Mr. Andrew went both to attend the King.

Fol. 73. 1660, June 5. The same to the same. . . . 'Tis not to be imagined how many are dissatisfied; innumerable flocks of people hovering ·here to see how they may light upon places and preferments; the Court and royal party grudging at every favour to the presbyterian, and they on the other side thinking they have not enough, and all that is done to them, being wrought by the General, has begot much murmuring at him; 'tis thought too much that Lord Manchester should be Lord Chamberlain, and four or five others of the Privy Council, as Hollis, Anseley, Mr. William Pierpont, Sir An. Ashly Cooper, and Mr. Secretary Morris; and besides there is some little competition between Sir Gilb. Gerrard, and Lord Seymour for Chancellor of the Duchy, which I conceive there is no great question, but his lordship's interest must carry if he please; some talk as if Sir Ed. Sidenam has almost got in again, and that Reynolds is knighted, and the cancelled knight baronetship of Sir Harry Wright restored; and all this the General's doing; Sir John Whitlock [and] Thurlow has been with the King; Whitlock presented divers medals and manuscripts that were the late King's; Thurlow 'tis said, has turned over a leave in a black book, that makes some tremble; 'tis said two of the Duke of Buckingham's servants and it may be higher; Banfield is slunk away, and others perhaps we may hereafter hear of. They are towards finishing the Act of Oblivion; yesterday they settled it, for accounts of all public receipts to be from 42; this day they fell upon the seven to be excepted for life; two I hear are agreed, Harrison and Gregory Clement; for the other five I hear they would box for them, but 'twas said the King's party in the House would be very fain to have excepted all that voted the abjuration of the family of the Stuarts; and 'twas debated with some heat, 'till the General interposed and told 'em that he knew His Majesty's mind (and had come to declare it) was inclined to moderation and mercy, and so mollified the matter. The dispute for the High Chamberlainship between the Earl Oxon and Linsey, is referred to a committee of Lords. There was a petition hatching,—the city to have churches settled according to the covenant; but it was blown off and received no birth.

Fol. 75. 1660, Sept. 11. The same to the same.—Mentions the adjournment of Parliament and the probable bills to be brought in for disbanding the army and the supplies for the King; and then goes on to say that— The great Ambassador from the King of Spain will come in to-morrow; the Prince de Lingia, that has been much a friend to our King in Flanders, he comes in the greatest equipage that ever was. Camden house and two other houses are provided for him. The Duke of York is gone away with a good part of the fleet to settle his sister the Princess of Orange, who will very shortly be here; the Duke of Gloster is in a good condition for one that has the small-pox. . . . The King has bestowed 7,000l. a year upon the Duke of Albemarle out of his own lands, and (which I am not so much pleased withall) most of it out of the Duchy. The whole manor of Enfield, with the manors, houses, and parks of Theobalds and Cheshunt, Ashdowne forest, the Grogle Chace, and other lands in Sussex, the honour, manor, and all lands belonging to Bullingbrooke, Beskcott park, and divers other things to him and his heirs male, &c. The report was that Ludlow was taken since the proclamation, but it proves not true. The proclamation for the peace with Spain, &c. came out yesterday.

Fol. 78. [1660], Sept. 13.—The same to the same.— Giving a short account of the death of the Duke of Gloster. Parliament was adjourned that morning, and 20 Acts were passed. P.S. The Prince de Lignia came to town to day; . . . his 12 coaches and chaises came yesterday before him. They say we shall have one out of France in as great splendour, some say the Prince of Anjou.

Fol. 76. 1660, Nov. 6. The same to the same. The list of sheriffs is as true as I could write by a copy I could scarce read; they were prickt yesternight by the King at the council table, and then Glin and Maynard made the King's serjeants; Sir Harbottle Grimston is Master of the Rolls, and they say Hales will quickly be Chief Baron. The old La. of Carlisle is dead; well yesterday morning and died last night. The Lo. Chancellor

DUKE OF SUTHERLAND.

is made Baron of Hendon in Wilts; he refused a higher title of Earl which was offered; the business of his daughter will go very smooth and well for aught appears; the King shows great testimonies of favour; goes often to his house. The Lo. Treasurer has had an odd kind of sickness; . . . the death of his daughter wrought deep (they say) upon him. The Queen is in very good health, and very good humoured; this day the King went with her to see her house of Wimbleton; 'tis given out she will return over a month, and that her resolution was so when she came away out of France; limiting the number of her train and herself but to two or three trunks, and her servants to small proportions of luggage; but perhaps these arguments and the resolution may not be infallible; 'twill be a cold winter voyage to go back.—P.S. There came in a Dutch Ambassador to-day. The Parliament met; the House of Commons voted to give the King thanks for the Declaration, and would have it pass in an Act, though the King declare in it that 'tis against his judgment. 'Twas moved to have a review of the Act of Pole money; it falls so extreme short of expectation.

Fol. 76. 1661, April 2. The same to the same.—The Coronation and inquiry after elections is the greatest subject of discourse. That example of London has not corrupted all places, for 'tis said in most the choices are good. Vast gallantry against the Coronation is provided, but many of the Lords have got dispensations to be absent, that there will be less than a 100 'tis thought ride; four new Knights of the Garter will then go forth; the Duke of Richmond, Earl Linsey, Earl Manchester, Earl Straford. They reckon upon 76 (70?) knights of the Bath, but I wonder why knight barronets already should be of the number, as I hear of divers as Sir Tho. Trevor, and Sir Ducy and others. The match with Portugal keeps much life still, though perhaps 'twill never be; nor is the Spanish Embassador gone. The Lord Crofts has got the great widow Heale, after her six weeks mourning. The King presented him, and 'twas done instantly; and now she's shod round.

Fol. 77. 1661, May 7. The same to the same.— . . . The Earl of Bristol landed yesterday at Deal, and is expected in town to-night. Last night was buried the Duke of Cambridge, the Duke of York's son: there appears no outward mourning, and perhaps there is little inward. The City Militia appeared this day in Hyde Park before the King, both trained bands and auxiliarys. The King honoured them both in the gallantry of himself and the rest of the Court, and also in taking a special view of them round about, where there was as high acclamations whilst he was present as their volleys of shot could make when he was gone; for till sooner they began not to exercise. We hear yet of no product of the meetings and consultations that has been between the Episcopal and Presbyterian clergy. . . . The Lady Jane Seymour, the Duchess of Somerset's daughter, was this day married to the Lo. Dungarvan; 'twas very private. The Lo. Chancellor was not well yesterday, but perhaps 'twas but in order to his being better to-morrow; that is the better provided for declaration of the King's pleasure to the houses.

Fol. 79. n.y., May 3. Guicciardine Ayloffe to Sir Richard Leveson.[*]— . . . . This business of Hull and Yorkshire takes up all the time of the House, and all the discourse of the town, and therefore you can expect no variety. Yesterday morning, Rushworth, the clerk assistant in the House, came to town out of Yorkshire, (whither he had been sent with a warrant to summon up those first petitioners) and gave a full relation of the state of things there; truly you'll easily discern in what case the King is by that last petition of the Yorkshire gentlemen: the gentlemen of the county being assembled by the King's commands, and after the King had delivered his mind to them requiring their advice and assistance touching Hull, and commanding the sheriff not to execute any warrant from the Parliament, they desired time to give answer (which in effect was that petition) and to chose 8 as a Committee to draw it. Sir Fra. Wortley and the party with him being denied to join with that Committee of the country, Sir Fra. and some 20 more drew their swords and flourishing them about their heads, cryed out, they would be for the King, and so went a little in the town and there settled to be as another Committee for the country, but what they did is not yet known: here Rushworth came away before they had determined anything but this act of Sir Fra. the House were about, and 'tis likely will conclude treason, though they did suspend it for the present. The consequence of Rushworth's relation was

to settle a committee to be sent down, which are my Lo. Howard of the Lords House, and my Lo. Fairfax; Sir Phill. Stapilton, Sir Hugh and Sir Henry Chomley; their power you may imagine was for the militia, the sheriff, the post passages, and what may be imagined necessary and conducible to that service; but at last there grew a question whether they should go to the King from the Houses; or if not sent, whether, if His Majesty should send for them, what observance to his commands they should give; these questions the two Houses last night were divided about, but I hear this day they are agreed they shall attend the King with a petition, which was this day a drawing. A petition to the King now? there's . . . said that I know of this business. There came a packet this afternoon from the King whether . . . . more in it besides a commission to pass the bill of tunnage and poundage (which I hear my Lo. Keeper instantly (did?), I do not hear of. . . They are setting out a declaration to the kingdom wherein they use the phrase (God so deal with us, &c.): they say 'twill be high and sharp both touching Hull and the militia. You know they sent 2,000l. down by the last committee to Hull, my Lo. Stamford, Willouby, &c., and this day they have concluded of 2,000l. more to be sent thither. 'Tis much talked they will fall to naming the evil councillors within this day or two, which I'll believe when I hear; there's Collonels Vavazor and Feelding with the King at York, of whom they say they have a very ill council. They have this day in the Lords House cleared my Lo. Loftus, the old Chancellor of Ireland, of all the charges laid against him by this late Lo. Lieutenant. The Queen is gone a little short progress to be out from the Hague some ten days. She was on Friday at Rotterdam, thence to Utrich and so about to some other towns.

Fol. 80. n.d. G. Ayloffe to Mr. John Langley.— . . . This day the House fell upon the adding some more persons to be excepted for estate, to be liable to fine and mulkt as the House should determine, which were St. Johns, Keeble and one Burton that was one of those that had his hand in the sentencing above 20 to death in Norfolk; but they had so many friends that it could not be done: this day 'tis thought St. Johns will escape through the net, though lesser fishes are caught; they will go on with them to-morrow: the General interposes much in all, but very earnestly for the Speaker Lenthall. They say the States of Holland are sending Embassadors with a noble present of a cubbard of plate of gold. There is a Chancellor of the Duchy settled by the King, my Lo. Seymour, who was pleased to send to me, and I think I shall be in the same employment again in the Duchy business, which I am not more ambitions of, for any ends of my own than to serve my friends. And truly the stewardship of Newcastle has been much in my thoughts, how I might preserve it for Sir Richard if he please; and because my interest is yet nothing, being but a new creature there, I could wish some first hand might be found to move it first: a word from my Lo. of Dorset or such like I should carefully second; I am not yet acquainted with the temper of this lord; my late ever to be honoured lord I knew well how little he would look upon such a thing in the gratifying a friend, &c.

Fol. 81. n.y. Feb. 15. ( ) to John Langley.— This day came out the declaration of the House of Commons concerning the King, which was not sent on to the Lords at all.—Mr. Ashurst and Mr. Birch sent letters yesterday of their arrival at Edinburgh, and that the convention of Assembly was put off for two days, at which time 'tis talked here they will declare to send to the Prince some of their Lords, though the business be concluded already, and we expect to hear shortly the Prince to be in Holland, for it is conceived that the Scots will come in, though the Parliament hope otherwise, and 'tis thought those commanders that are gone and going are to negociate the taking them off if possible they can; but the King's party have confidence they will not, and upon their coming in under shelter of that army may spring up an army of English which shall have an English general and not at all subject to the Scots; the Parliament, 'tis thought, apprehend something in this way, and provide. The General wrote to the House to-day that 'tis necessary to have the isle of Jersey taken, and the Parliament go high in everything; all the packets that came out of Scotland were broken open, and I heard that by some in the city immediately a post express was dispatch't thither to give notice before it could come by the ordinary, though I scarce understand the drift, yet it shows some active minds in some. The Lord Willoby would not stand to it and venture himself, but is gone into Holland; Judge Jenkins was

* This letter and the next but one are clearly of the time of Charles I.

5.

A a

brought yesterday to the bar before the two Speakers to answer some Bill which he had refused ; and being asked, told thme they were no lawful Judges, because not made by the King, and had never taken the oath that Chancellors ought and sat there with a counterfeit seal ; and told them that Mr. Sollicitor at my Lo. Strafford's trial urged that to offer violence to the law was to use violence to the King, which was high treason, and cast them down a paper of his reasons why he would not answer, which you may imagine had law enough in it, and 'tis said will come out in print. The servants that were about the King are all put away, so as now there are but a few persons that attend of all sorts ; Maule and Murray are there still, that the Scots may have an account of their King.

Vol. VI.

Contains letters of Mr. Bernard Grenville to Sir W. L. Gower and letters of Lord Granville of Potheridge and the Countess of Rochester, Dr. King, Sir William Wyndham, John Chetwynd, Esq., and Cornelius Wood, Esq.

Fol. 4. 1684, June 10, London.—B. Grenville to W. Loveson Gower.—That this paper may be more acceptable, I have robbed the Earl of Sir Richard Bulst[rodes] intelligence received this moment, that it may divert you in your country retirements, and am to add that the Dutch letters bring that Sir Thomas Armestrong was seized and secured at Leyden in Holland by the King's minister Mr. Chudley, and was immediately put on board one of His Majesty's yaughts that was attending the transportation of the Prince's French players for England expected with the prisoner this night. The Duke of Albemarle having taken up his quarters in my solitary house in York buildings until he can better provide himself, affords me no more time to lengthen our domestic intelligence.

Fol. 4. 1684, June 21, London.—The same to the same.—He complains of the non-payment of money by the Treasury. In a P. S. he says that Sir Thomas Armestrong was executed yesterday at Tyburn, as the sentence passed upon him.

Fol. 5. 1684, July 22, London. The same (to the same). Business.

Fol. 5. 1684, July 29, London. The same (to the same).—Various are the discourses on this trial of skill of the Lord K. and P. S. in planting their relations in the Treasury, which gives a ras (race ?) for the present where the White Staff was designed.—The King's day for his removal to Winchester is fixed for the 26th of the next month, and the Duchess returns from Tunbridge on Saturday next, and the Duke of Ormond and his secretary Sir Ceryll for Ireland the beginning of the next week ; the Earl of Pembroke is married to the Attorney General's daughter and the uncle Sir Cerill is not far from it. The young Countess of Yarmouth died suddenly this morning.

Fol. 6. 1684, Aug. 27, Marre. The same to the same. —Speaks of his having reached this northern corner, where Providence has cast his lot, after many heats and storms with contentious Lords and vexatious adversaries. His wife proposes more satisfaction and advantages from the innocent wheel and country plough than from her Court attendances and expectations. "Within " three or four days we are going more northward in the " Bishopric and Cleveland, to settle our concerns there ; " our stay will not be long in a place, but when I fix " my day as to my approaches back to vile London, you " shall receive fresh assurances, &c."

Fol. 7. 1684, Nov. 12, Marre.—The same to the same. —I was this week repairing to my duty at Court, resolving to try my fortune by my dilligence this winter in Whitehall, my Lady Bathe having kindly lent me her lodgings there, and the Duke of Albemarle is resolved to content himself this winter with my house in York Buildings. I gave him possession at my coming out of London, upon his being hurried into a sale of his Danby purchase. Thus the cedars at Court are as liable to changes as we shrubs.

Fol. 1. 1684, Jan. 17, Whitehall.—The same to the same.— . . . . By your letter to my brother B., I find some of your corporation of Newcastle are designing this way to establish their concerns: if my appearance personally may be useful to them or any particular persons your friends I will attend my Lord Chief Justice or the Attorney-General.—P.S. 'Tis the discourse at Court that your Lord Lieutenant, the Earl of Shrewsbury, is treating with the Lord Chamberlain for his white staff, and the Lord Bruce has bought the Lord Lindsey's Bedchamber place. My Lord of Ormond will not stay to deliver the sword to his successor. My Lord of Arran is returned.

—Mr. Bridges had contracted for his Bedchamber place, but His Majesty has denied him positively his consent to sell. The Duke goes for Scotland the next month, and my nephew Lansdowne for Spain.

Fol. 1. 1684, Feb. 3, Whitehall, 10 at night.—The same to the same.—Sends the most acceptable good news of the King's hopeful recovery, which yesterday we were almost in despair of : His Majesty being seized in his chair and bedchamber with a surprising convulsion fit, which lasted three hours, and accompanied with other dangerous symptoms which usually follow those distempers. But the physicians, I praise God, have been so successful in their timely applications by bleeding, cupping, blistering, and all such seasonable remedies and courses, that they now this evening declare him in no danger, without return of new fatal accidents, which God grant we may never see, but that his sacred life may be yet preserved many many years amongst his subjects. P.S. The young Lady Ossory is dead in Ireland.—My Lord Allington died on Saturday last.

Fol. 2. 1684, Feb. 10, Whitehall.—The same to the same.—Speaks of the universal grief on the occasion of the King's death.—His present Majesty's speech at Council gives some allay and great satisfaction, and when the approaching Parliament comes I doubt not but Mr. Levison will give fresh proofs of his hereditary loyalty to this Prince ; and when you come to town I will wait on you to him whenever you command my service.— 'Tis said the Lord Dartmouth succeeds Master of the Horse, Admiral Herbert (Mr. Sidnoy's) place in the Robes, and Mr. Grahmes' Privy Purse. Of the new Queen's syde, the Lord Clifford, Lord Chamberlayne, and 'tis believed the Earl of Peterborow will be Groom of the Stole ; how the fates will dispose of we old Bedchamber men, relies entirely on His Majesty's gracious goodness and charity towards us ; and in that number none more unhappy than myself, after 25 years' services in prosperity, and some in gaols and the worst of times. P.S. The Queen Dowager, 'tis believed, will remove to Somerset House ; Mr. Speaker Seymour kissed the King's hand yesterday.

Fol. 3. 1684, March 12, Whitehall.—The same to the same.—P.S. My brother has received his doom (his key and office), bestowed on the Earl of Peterborow, His Majesty having graciously promised him the continuance of his pensions and salaries of 5,000l. a year, with a compensation for his place, and his six years' arrears. God grant I may see it. Otherwise my brother in his old age will be uneasy in his fortune after 40 years' services. Sir Richard Mason, that occasioned my troubling you, died this morning in his lodging at Whitehall. A fever rages that proves very mortal, and gives great apprehensions of a plague. . . . Queen Dowager removes her Court to Somerset House the week before Easter.

Fol. 2. 1684, March 24, Whitehall.—The same to the same.—Hopes he may be returned to serve in the Parliament, and prove his loyalty.—There are reports spread in the Court that reflect on you in promoting elections of such as are not principled to contribute the supporting His Majesty and Crown.—My Lord Brandon is one named you vigorously appear for : i have adventured (to contradict these scritch owles), and that you only seek your own peaceable and regular election at Newcastle, out of no other consideration but that you may have an opportunity to serve your prince and country, as becomes a dutiful subject, and whose ancestors have always bled for the Crown, and that the same blood runs in your veins, and resolutions of shaking off all those calamnies cast upon you. If you approve I will show your last letter to the King, and pray in your next mention how unjustly grounded are these new scandals spread of you.

1685, Sept. 29. The same to [   ]. Apologises for not paying some money, "not having received 500l. " out of the Hearth Money. 'Tis true my son George, ", being under some wants and ill accidents at Paris, I " did, by Mr. Gay's help and assistance, procure from " Alderman Duncombe that sum to disengage him."

Fol. 11. 1686, July 28, London. The same (to the same). On business.—In a postscript, " 'Tis said " that His Majesty has denied leave to the Earl of " Danby and the Lord Weymouth, travelling beyond " the seas. . . . . . I have a second letter of the 4th of " June, from Captain John, from Malta, confirming the " Ambassador's death, and his sailing back to Leg- " horn."

Fol. 12. 1686, July 30, Windsor. The same to the same.—The great ministers meet at Whitehall on Wednesday, upon their new commission, and the Bishop of Durham is summoned to attend, and be of the Quorum. My Lord of Carlingford is recommended by His Majesty to the Prince of Orange, to the same command my Lord of Ossory had in the States service (of the King's subjects). Mr. Cutts is in the number of the wounded at Buda, which, 'tis feared [is] not yet taken.

Fol. 12. 1686, Aug. 10, London.—The same to the same.—The camp is this day broke up, and my brother's regiment has quitted the field, with the same reputation and favourable declaration from His Majesty that they had gained at their entrance. Their quarters for some time is to be at Portsmouth, towards which place they began their march this day. . . . . Captain Killigrew is going again to sea, and to be in the Mediterranean. . . . The Bishop of London appeared; [he] has given [to] him 'till Monday next to give his answer.

Fol. 14. 1688, Aug. 23, St. James.—The same (to the same).—You have before this the intelligence of the Lord and Lady Bathes preparing suddenly bag and baggage for Stowe; a letter from His Majesty yesterday quickens the Lord's journey, being commanded further to repair to his government. A general council is summoned to meet at Windsor to-morrow, and a new Dutch Ambassador daily expected; and, notwithstanding the approach of winter, a war between Holland and France is much discoursed. The Bishop of Rochester has voluntarily resigned his ecclesiastical commission, and written a letter to the Archbishop his reasons, with another letter to the Lord Chancellor to the same effect, Judge Allibone died yesterday.—The Duke of Ormond treated most splendidly the University of Oxford this day at his house in St. James' Square. The procession began at Northumberland House; the doctors and scholars walking in their formalities in the street to their new Chancellor's.

1686, Aug. 24, London. The same to the same.—His Majesty being gone his western progress as far as Bridgewater and Bristowe, I have now my quietus from Stowe to begin mine northward, which I do to-morrow.

Fol. 14. n. d. A fragment of a letter from the same to the same. We have another prodigious rise at court; the Lord Keeper's brother, Sir Dudley North, and the Lord Weymouth's, Mr. Henry Thynne, this day declared Commissioners of the Treasury; none unfortunate and contemptible but those that entirely depend on our master. Sir George Downing is likewise dead, and the other sheriff of London, Sir Peter Rich, succeeds in the Custom-house. The Duchess of Ormond died this morning.

Fol. 15. n. d. Part of a letter from the same to the same.—I am this morning come from Windsor where I found the Lord Montague received graciously both by King and Queen, and creeping, as 'tis said, into favour at court. The camp breaks up within 15 days, and to-morrow is to be the great day, the Lord Arran treating their Majesties. My brother writes me he has received orders from my Lord Treasurer to call a convocation in Parliament of Tinners.—Most of the volunteers, Spanish as well as English, are killed before Buds. Named in the last letters—slain : Captain Rupert the Prince's son, Mr. Wiseman, Mr. Talbot, Mr. Moore, Mr. Smith, and Mr. Bellase wounded, with some others. My Lord George Saville is in the number of the wounded volunteers, and Will. Herbert received his [wound] on the first attack before Buda. 'Tis said Dr. Cartret [Cartwright] shall be Bishop of Oxford.

Fol. 16. n. d., Tuesday at 2.—The same to the same. —His Majesty has been at last moved in your concern, and declares he is very well satisfied with you since my Lord of Bath's last engagement, and you have his free leave to go into the country and return when you please. These are His Majesty's words, &c.

Fol. 17. Two letters from John Granville, probably the Hon. John Granville, afterwards Lord Granville of Potheridge.

1688, July 31st, aboard the Bonaventura, in the Downs. J. Granville to . We are a second time returned out of Sole Bay into the Downs, where we shall continue till the King gooth for Portsmouth, where he intends again to visit us this summer. Last night Jack Lusons commission came down to be Captain of the Mary; since my being here I have seen three or four ships disposed of, and the Lord knoweth when will be my turn.

Fol. 18 et seq. Letters from Jane Lady Hyde, afterwards Countess of Rochester, daughter to Sir William Leveson Gower, to her sister-in-law Cathcrine Lady Gower; also to Lord Granville, of Potteridge, her uncle, on the subject of Sir William Wyndham's marriage. 1707. Letters from Lord Granville. Letters from the Earl of Rochester, &c.

Fol. 45. 1704, Dec. 31, Turin. J. Chetwynd to Lord Gower.—The enclosed paper will give you an account of a sally made from Verrue the 26th instant, which suc-

ceeded so well that we do not know but Monsieur de Vendome may be obliged to quit the siege; if he does not quit it, I hope this will not be the last serenade we shall give him. Monsieur de Chertogne was very much esteemed amongst the enemies and was to be Governor of Verrue, into which place we brought him much sooner then the Duke of Vendome could do; this siege costs the enemies very dear, and will so ruin their infantry then we hope they will not be in a condition to do any more mischief this winter, and before spring I hope we shall receive our succours, else we shall go nigh to lose his R. H., or he lose his whole country, for when the enemies are masters of Verruc we have only Turin left and not half troops enough to guard it, and it is impossible for us to get any recruits. It is not yet certain whether Mr Hill will go to Venice; if he does I am to stay here.

Turin, the 30th Dec. 1704, s. n. The 26th inst., in the afternoon, R. H. ordered about 1,000 men from Crescentin to Verrue to make a sally from thence to ruin the enemies trenches and batteries, and drive 'em from their advanced posts: the troops which were to make this sally were divided into two bodies, who marched out of Verrue about 4 of the clock in the afternoon, and gained the enemies batteries, which were the farthest off of the place before they wore discovered, which gave such a general consternation in the trenches that our people met with no great opposition in the execution of their orders; we levelled their trenches, destroyed several of their mines and nailed up 4 mortars and 14 or 15 pieces of cannon, and set fire to their carriages and everything else that was combustible. Mons. de Chertoigne, Lieut.-General, who commanded in the trenches was wounded in two places and taken prisoner with 8 officers more. Mons. d'Immecour, Major General, was killed in the actian, and de Chertoigne is since dead of his wounds; we lost about 200 men, but its believed the enemies between 4 and 500 men. At the time that this attack was made by the foot, General Feltz, who commanded the horse at Chivas, had received orders to pass the Po, and make a false attack on that side upon the enemies camp, which order he executed so well that the whole French camp was in confusion, and we are assured that several of the officers had already sent away their equipages from the head-quarters; if this sally had been but half an hour sooner, it is certain that the Duke of Vendome would have fallen into our hands, for he was then in the trenches.

170⅚, Jan. 13, Turin.—The same to the same.—Mr. Hill, being obliged to go to Genoa about six weeks since, he thought it for the Queen's service to leave me here, and gave me directions to present my credentials to H. R. H., which I did in a day or two after he went, and I have been here ever since upon the foot of the Queen's minister, and as such I attend H. R. H., and I have had the honour to write to Mr. Secretary Hedges every post.—I am now on my departure, for Mr. Hill has sent me directions to be ready to go upon the first orders; however, if he bids me to stay till his successor arrives, I will stay ; so far am I from standing upon punctilios, especially in anything that may relate to the Queen's service, but I am so far from being desired to stay here by anybody except his R. H., that your Lord Treasurer or Mr. Secretary Hedges have not been pleased to take the least notice of me in any of their letters to Mr. Hill, tho' he was so kind as to recommend me very kindly to both of them.

Letters from Cornelius Wood, Esq.

Fol. 46. 1706, Oct. 9. From our camp at Grames.— Cornelius Wood to my Lord (Lord Gower). . . . As for that affair of Cardugen (in which, by accident, I was), I will truly relate to your Lordship the whole matter; we made a great forrage towards Lisle, to cover which there was 6,000 foot and 600 horse, the whole commanded by a major-general of foot, and Cardugen as brigadier had command of the horse, whose escort was advanced a great way before the gross of the foot; the foot went out at 12 o'clock at night, and the horse escort at 3 the next morning, and the foragers went out at 6 the same morning. I went out about 7 in the morning out of mere curiosity, having no concern at all with this whole detachment; I met there my Lord Roby, who was also there in curiosity; my Lord Roby came to see Cardugen; but they, telling us he was gone to reconnoitre with two esquadrons, my Lord was returning, but I persuaded him to go on to those two advanced esquadrons; when we came at them, we espied some people bearing towards us, which we found to be the

French.—I did then advise Cardugen to draw his two esquadrons back, and occupy the mouth of the defiles, whereby he might with safety retire to the gross of his escort, which advice he at first embraced, one esquadron marching while the other fac'd the enemy, and I myself, with 8 English dragoons, advanced towards the enemy to amuse them : but he had (which I knew not of) sent for two other esquadrons, to support those two before mentioned, and had ordered his dragoons to ⁂ and line the hedges. I then went up and told him, Cardugen—This will throw all into confusion ;— you are too near your enemy to dismount your dragoons ; instead of one dismounting ten will run away. He then told me, but with great civility, that he had the direction of that affair, and was to answer for it. 'Tis true, said I, I have nothing to do here ; I would only have given you my friendly advice and assistance. I then galloped out to the 8 English dragoons which was next the enemy, being resolved to take my fate with the hindermost. The French, seeing our people in confusion, pushed upon us and entered the defiles pell mell with us, and 4 of the English dragoons that was advanced with me was taken.—The French pushed through the defile, but farther durst not advance, seeing the gross of the escort stand in the plain before them. There was not a horse lost of the forangers that day, and but 8 men killed of ours and three of theirs. I stayed there 5 hours after this, till all the forangers and escort was come home. My Lord, I have told you all this to let you see I commanded not there that day ; for if I had I should not have advanced my horse through those defiles, or, if so great an oversight had been made, I think I could have brought them back without being ruffled ; but some men's eyes are so dazeld with the beams of their superiors' favours, that they cannot see to explicate themselves from a difficulty which their want of experience may have thrown them into. While the water runs smooth every one is a good officer ; but 'tis only men that has been long accustomed to dangers that can stem the tide of a very evil accident.————— We are now covering the siege of Aioth.

1709, July 23, n. s.   Camp before Turney.—The same to the same.—We once believed that peace would soon have brought us to our native country, but you see the scene is changed, and war rings through every quarter ; so since the united consultations of so many refined politicians can't bring this war to a happy conclusion, we are trying what men of our boisterous profession can do. We are now besieging Turney, for which service there was detached 60 battallions of foot and 60 esquadron of horse and dragoons, amongst which number is your humble servant : we hope to be masters of the town in two or three days, but the citadel will require some time longer to take ; we go by way of sap to get the castle, they having many mines, one of which we discovered last night ; our grand army which covers the siege lies not far from us, and Marshal Villers we hear is still at his old camp between Lintze and Beliare, &c.

1709, n. s., Sept. 14.   Camp before Monse.—The same to the same.—On Wednesday last we fought a great battle with the Frenchmen, and obtained a very memorable victory, beating them from behind the strongest entrenchments I ever saw ; this victory came not to us without some loss, many brave officers and soldiers being killed ; but the joy of victory is so grateful to the living, that it banishes the memory of the loss of such as perished in the pursuit of it. I was all along at the siege of Turney, both of the town and of the castle, and brought the horse from thence to the grand army but the day before the battle ; and the foot from Turney came up but an hour before the battle begun, making more than ten thousand men in all, which was a very good addition to our forces ; I doubt not but this good success will bring forth something for the good of the world in general, of the Confederate in particular, and peculiarly for that of our own country. We are now going to besiege Monse, and I hope it will not be long before it is in our hands.

Vol. VII.

Letters to John, Lord Gower and his son from Lord Hatton, the 2nd Duke of Bedford, the Duke of Hamilton, Lord Cheyne, the Duke of Marlborough, Atterbury, Bishop of Rochester, the Marquis of Granby, Lord Wm. Manners, Lord Downe, the Earl of Winchelsea, the Duke of Kingston, the Earl of Kinnoul, the Earl of Cardigan, Sarah, Duchess of Marlborough, the Earl of Essex, the Earl Bathurst, the Earl of Carlisle, Lord Bruce, Lord Brooke, the Earl of Anglesey, Lord Banbury, &c. 1700–1725. Also letters to Katherine, Lady Gower, &c. from the Countess Granville, Lord Carteret (her son),

Mrs. Elizabeth Granville, Lord Landsdowne, &c., K. Duchess of Rutland, L. Duchess of Rutland, the Countess of Mar, Lady M. W. Montagu, the Countess of Gainsborough, the Countess of Plymouth, the Countess of Exeter, &c., and Mrs. Bridget Noel.

Fol. 1. 1702, Nov. 25, Kirby.   Lord Hatton to [Sir John Leveson Gower, afterwards Lord Gower].—" That " the Queen has thought fit to take into her councils per- " sons of your worth and character is such a satisfaction " to the most loyal part of her subjects as obliges them " to take all opportunities of expressing it ; and Her " Majesty having been pleased to confer upon you the " office of Chancellor of the Duchy, I am apt to think " it will not be disagreeable to you that I lay before you " what concerns the stewardship of the Duchy lands in " this country, and inform you that the stewardship of " the manors of Irthestoe and Raunds as also of the " Hundred Court of Higham Ferrars in this county was " in the hands of my father in the reign of King Charles " the 1st, and in mine all the time since the restoration " of King Charles the 2nd, till my Lord Stamford put " me out of it to place there some men more agreeable to " his humour."—Asks to hold the place under Sir John's authority.

1703, May 15, Southampton House.—The Duke of Bedford to John Lord Gower.   Mentions the marriage of Lord Granville, and speaks of him in complimentary terms.

Fol. 2, n. d.   The same to the same.—On money matters.—He speaks of his buildings in Covent Garden as having put him extremely out of money.

1705, May 11, Streatham.—The same to the same. —Says that he charged his servants some time ago not to stir on either side during the elections, until they should have further orders.   Asks for the names of those who have stirred, and what they have done ; he himself is inclined to help those that Lord Gower approves, but the reason he has been doubtful is that if he opposed Sir John Wolstenholm it might possibly make a turn in the election in Bedfordshire, upon which he owns his own mind is extremely set, and that it would be a great vexation to him (the Duke) to lose it.

Fol. 3. 1705, April 22, Preston.—The Duke of Hamilton to Lord Gower.—The gentleman you recommend to this place is so deserving that we ought to return your lordship thanks for affording so worthy a person to serve for the town ; we must all be ashamed that he is so ill matched in a brother burgess, but the gentry in these parts are not very fond of London journeys, for if anybody of tolerable character had stood they had infallibly have carried it from the two candidates, Mr. Molyneux and Rigby.

Fol. 6. 1706, Jan. 2.   The Duke of Marlborough to Lord Gower.—I have been some time without making any answer to the honour of your Lordship's letter, because I really don't know how to make any answer that is like to be agreeable.   Your Lordship can not but be sensible that both my Lord Treasurer and myself have given sufficient proofs of our desire and inclination to serve you, and I believe I may answer for him and for myself that we were both very sorry when you and your friends thought fit to put it out of our power to continue doing so ; much more might be said upon this head, but I choose to make it as short as I can, being unwilling to enlarge ; however, I do assure you that whenever I can think I may succeed I shall move Her Majesty as you desire.

Fol. 4. 1714, Oct. 16.   Lord Cheyne to Lord Gower. —Relates that Lord Paget professes great honour and friendship for him (Gower), and intreats his interest for his (Paget's) son, who is a candidate for Staffordshire, and that he would be merciful to the young man at first setting out, and not exert his interest to the utmost. Paget and Ward are joined.

1714, Oct. 30.   Lord Downe to Lord Gower.—Hopes that Sir Arthur Kaye, as he having joined their interest, will have Lord Gower's interest at the next election for the county of York.

Fol. 33. 1714, Nov. 3.   Lord Lansdowne to Lord Gower.— . . . . . .   I shall mention nothing more but what relates to the honours of the family, which I think ought to be insisted upon to be restored. My Lady Carteret having the Cornish estate, should be created Countess of Bath, and as I am entitled by virtue of King Charles's warrant to assume the Earldom of Corbell, as the direct male descendant from Sir Bevile, I cannot think a patent would be refused me for it, if it was represented to the King, as an article that would give peace to the family.   I would not have you indifferent in either of these articles, nor look upon them as vanity ; you will find them of use.   It is likewise my opinion that the Granville name should go along with the estate.

Fol. 5. 1714, Nov. 9, Lisle Street.—Lord Cheyne to the Rev. Mr. Plaxton, at Lord Gower's, Trentham.—He is sorry that Mr. Phillipson does not comply with Lord Gower's desires—thinks him (Gower) happy in having Mr. Plaxton's aid in putting his affairs in order; wishes him success.—Says nothing is dear in town but horse meat. Chair hire is as cheap as ever and more commodious for both sexes.

Fol. 5. n. d. [1715, March 17.]—The same to the same. —Thanks for papers received.—Hopes the surveyor is at work, and maps all the lands, &c.—He was in hopes that some bargains had been made for lands out of lease or lives filled up.—He (Cheyne) can only assist Lord Gower but as a trustee, &c.—Our Parliament met to-day; the King came to the House of Lords, the Commons came up to the bar of the upper House, where the Lord Chancellor told them that the King willed they should return back to their House, choose a Speaker, and present him on Monday noon at 12 of the clock at the bar of the House of Lords. Most people expect that this session will be a long and a warm one. P.S. The Bishop of Salisbury died this morning.

Fol. 10. 1715, Oct. 27, London. Duke of Kingston * to Catherine, widow of the first Lord Gower.—What I say I have several times thought of, and what makes me no longer delay telling it is the report of Lord Gower's having been here, which tho' not true makes me afraid of some inconvenient consequence to him. Taking for granted he has too good an understanding to trust his abbey land with a Popish prince, makes me ask if you think it not proper he do something like what I shall mention, he having been of age after the Parliament was sitting, and not coming up to it; come to town and assure the King he is not in the interest of the Pretender, as other Tory lords have done, or at least write a letter to whom he thinks proper to go to the King from him with such assurance; this can be no prejudice to his interest with any body but a Jacobite. Who would set up a Popish King to be the head of a Protestant church? Good God, what madness! If I am thought the first mover of it, it may not be so well approved of, as coming from a Whig; but 'tis no more than Lord Anglesey has done in Ireland, declared himself no Jacobite, but, as to the Church, the same principles he was of.

Fol. 8. 1720, Jan. 11, Kelham. The Marquis of Granby to Lady Gower. Offers congratulations on the marriage of her daughter.

Fol. 12. 1720, Aug. 28, Blenheim. The Earl of Cardigan to Lord Gower.—Congratulates him upon the birth of a daughter who will want a fortune if the South Sea continues to fall; he is almost frighted out of his little senses not knowing the true occasion of its fall; asks Lord Gower's advice whether to stand it or sell out.— I am got to Ombre every day, and lose my money as fast as I do in the South Sea, &c.

Fol. 13. 1722, July 10, Hamby.—The same to the same.—Complains of his ill health; he intends for Burleigh on Friday, to keep Lord Exeter's birthday.—Is not fit to undertake such a thing, but is resolved not to lose an opportunity of paying respects to him for reasons he (Gower) may guess.

Fol. 13. 1722, Feb. 20, London.—The same to the same. —Cannot answer you as to the time of the Parliament's rising, nor can Will. Morley; but he bid me tell you he defers writing till he can. The Lords have expunged the reasons for the Election Bill.

Fol. 15. 1723, Feb. 3, Hamby.—The same to the same. —Begs him to acquaint Mr. Cecil that an election is fixed for the 12th inst., and if his health will permit him to take so long a journey it would be of very great service to us; besides it would make him so popular that if ever he had any thoughts of standing for this county it would make all the gentlemen zealous to serve him. Sir Nevile Hickman and I were to wait on the peer at Burleigh last Tuesday; we all dined at Stamford where most of the gentlemen of that side of the country met us; the peer and I paid the expenses of that day; Sir Novill scarce met with any denial; I hear the other side brag much, but I can't find where their interest lies. Get Litchfield to send Sir Charles Buck down; I fancy Sir Thom. Sebright would come along with him if your Lordship would propose it. Tom Conyers is come to town; he is a very fit person to stir in this affair and to speak to those gentlemen who have votes, &c.

Fol. 9. 1716, June 13. Lord Winchilsea to Lord Gower.—Asks him to let Mr. Crompton know that Mr.

* The Duke of Kingston was father of Lady Gower, Lady Mary Wortley, and the Countess of Mar.

Bedford is to be found at his house near the King's Bench prison in Southwark; was desired by a friend of Lord Gower to say this.

Fol. 6. 1718, Oct. 10, Bromley. Fr. Roffen (Atterbury) to Lord Gower. Requests him earnestly to be present at the opening of the session and to persuade his friends also.—Asks him to urge the same to Sir W. Wyndham in as strong terms as he has written, and he will answer for Wyndham's allowing the reasonableness of the request.

Fol. 7. 1718, [ ] 25, Kelham.—The Marquis of Granby to Lord Gower.—On his return from Yorkshire found his Lordship's letter wherein is mentioned the gentlemen's desire of having the plate either before or after the day on which it is now fixt; to which he agrees, for his whole design in subscribing was to assist in promoting Lord Gower's pleasure, and to encourage a diversion he is so fond of himself as riding.—Begins his campaign to-morrow, and is of opinion that he shall end it successfully, having, tho' of different nations, a very good body of troops, and the new levies having already given signal proofs of their being capable of performing wonders.

Fol. 17. 1721, April 27. S. (Duchess of) Marlborough to Lord Gower. (The signature and address only are in the Duchess's writing.) Encloses a written paper for the perusal of Lord Gower, which she asks him to return as it will save a good deal of writing.—She hopes that he will read it not only because it relates to the Duke of Marlborough, but because it concerns that justice and equity to which every subject has the same right.— She knows the person whose reputation is chiefly concerned on the contrary side, makes use of all his abilities and all the opportunities a large acquaintance with the nobility gives him, to make very deep impressions on his own side of the question.—She only states facts fairly and justly and leaves it to others judgment.—She thinks her paper is drawn up in a more plain and intelligible manner than the lawyers, who must keep to particular forms, will suffer the printed case to be, &c.

Fol. 17. 1721, Aug. 17, Newpark. The Earl of Essex to Lord Gower.—Congratulates him on the birth of a son (who was afterwards 1st Marquis of Stafford).

Fol. 18. 1722, Oct. 5. The Earl of Bathurst to Lord Gower. — I received yours when Lord Strafford, Sir William Wyndham, and William Shippen, were with me. I communicated the contents to them, and they were so angry with you that it took up a great deal of time and several bottles of wine to appease them; that at this time of day Lord Gower should send to know whether he should attend in Parliament could not have been believed if it had not been under his own hand.— It was unanimously agreed that I should send a messenger on purpose to you that you may have timely notice to be here personally on Tuesday next, and we don't doubt but you will prevail with Lord Cardigan to come up with you; we desire also that you will give notice to all members within the week to be here at the opening of the session. We are all ready to vote any man into the plot who shall fail to attend upon this occasion; we shall attribute it to guilt or to a remissness which is equal to it. Give no room, my dear Lord, for any reflections to be made upon a character hitherto so unblameable, but come away immediately, and I will burn your letter and be ready to throw my gauntlet down to any man who shall dare to assert that you ever thought of staying in the country a moment after the sessions began.

Fol. 3. 1722, Nov. 17, Pasley.—The Duke of Hamilton and Brandon to the 2nd Lord Gower.—Recommends his cousin the Marquis of Annandale to his (Gower's) protection, he having been defendant in some law suits with his mother-in-law wherein he prevailed; and he is now called before the House of Lords by two appeals.—The Duke hopes for Lord Gower's interest and patronage for him.

Fol. 19. n. d. Lord Bruce to Lord Gower.—Friday morning.—It will be very material and necessary for as many of our friends as can to be here at our next meeting; I will take care to give notice to Lord Anglesey and Stawel; there are besides absent without proxies the Duke of Northumberland, Lords Exeter, Denbigh, Berkshire, Abington, Plymouth, Poulet, Strafford, Hereford, Broke, Maynard, Byron, Lexington, Barnard, Conway, the Archbishop of York, the Bishops of Exeter, St. David's, and Bristol. If you and other friends will take care of getting them to town, it will do very well.

Fol. 11. 1732, Feb. 22, Dupplin.—The Earl of Kinnoull to Lord Gower.—Apology for troubling him upon such a subject as a case in the House of Lords, but poor

Lord Hyndford's case will be so sad a one, if Coll. Cheston (Charteris?) caries his cause against him, that I'm sure you'll easily excuse my concern for him when I tell you that he's my near relation, and that if he loses this cause his family will be entirely ruined;—the merits of the case I leave to Lady Hyndford, who will be glad of an opportunity to inform your Lordship of her case. I have writ to Bathurst; I pray talk with him &c.

Fol. 21. 1712, Oct. 7, London. A news letter.—News from Brussells, Vienna, and the Hague.—Edinburgh, the 30th Sept. Nothing of news here, but I'le oblige you with a fresh piece of Presbyterian cant which was poured out on Sunday last by Mr. Mackleven in the Talbooth Church; in his prayer after sermon, viz., O ! Lord, there are two great beasts in the world, the Great Turk and the Pope of Rome; destroy them both and bring down that great enemy of Christ's kirk, the Tyrant of France. Bless our Queen; but, Lord, take a course with some dangerous and evil counsellors that are about her.—Falmouth the 2nd. Yesterday came in the packet boat in 7 days from Lisbon, with several passongers and brought letters of the 4th n. s. which give an account that the Spanish army under the Marquis de Bay, consisting of 15,000 foot and 5,000 horse, was set down before Campo Mayors, in which place is a garrison of 4,000 men, and Brigadier Maste has thrown himself into the same. We have an account from Cambridge that, on the 3rd inst., the Rev. Mr. Philip Brooks, B.D., follow of St. John's College, a very learned and worthy member of that body was unanimously elected University library keeper in the room of. Mr. Laughton, deceased. My Lord Treasurer has been indisposed, but Dr. Radcliff has set his Lordship to rights again. The Queen (God be praised) is in very good health, notwithstanding the Whigs give out the contrary amongst their party all the kingdom over, and further to cheer them they tell them that the Electoral Prince of Hanover will be here against the sitting of the Parliament.

Fol. 26. 1714. Dec. 20, London. Lord Cartoret to Lord Gower.—Mentions that the King has created his mother Countess Granville and Viscountess Carteret, which is a title Lord Gower could not have taken, having two sirnames already;—by this means the title of Bath is open to him (Gower), and he (Carteret) does not doubt he may get it.

Fol. 34. 1717, May 18. The Earl of Oxford to (Lord Gower).—Several of his friends advise him not to run the hazard of a third year's imprisonment, but to offer his petition to the House of Peers. Asks Lord Gower to be present; he is very ambitious of having the Duke of Rutland to present his petition, whom he esteems highly, and asks if Lord Gower thinks it would be agreeable for him to do so.

Fol. 33. 17⅛, Feb. 6, Lord Lansdowne to Lord Gower. —A committee of Lords, being appointed to meet on Saturday next in the Prince's chamber, at the usual hours of ten or eleven, about a Bill in which Lord Weymouth is interested, and it being expected that my wife and myself should appear to declare our consents, I entreat your Lordship to be there, and shall take it as a great favour if you will acquaint the committee that we are neither of us in a condition to attend, but that we freely consent to the Bill. — Asks Lord Gower to subscribe towards repairing the school and the church at Launceston : most of the Cornish gentlemen have subscribed, and he (Lansdowne) is their Recorder.

Fol. 32. 1721, Aug. 10, London. —— to Lord Gower. —This day the King came to the House and made a speech, but I design to be in bed before it will be cried about. The substance was to thank the House of Commons for the supplies the last Sessions, and for enabling him to pay the debts of the Civil list; for taking care to restore credit, after the late calamitous times, when the enemies of the government were by pamphlets and reports endeavouring to inflame the nation; that they did well in punishing those that were guilty, and in taking compassion of those that were sufferers; that he had given an act of pardon to those that were unwarily drawn in to be in some measure partakers without knowing what they did. He desired them to discountenance profaneness and immorality, and to preserve the public peace in their respective counties. And then the Chancellor, by the King's order, prorogued the Parliament to the 19th of October next. Cannot say anything for certain about a dissolution, but a friend was told within these four days by a very considerable man of the Treasury that, within a little time after the prorogation, there would come a proclamation to dissolve the Parliament. These reports are not to be

depended on. Lord Essex has been very dangerously ill at Newpark.

Fol. 32. 1722, May 1, London. The same to the same.—If every gentleman in England had exerted his interest with the same spirit that you have done, this new Parliament had been more agreeable to the inclination of the people in general than I am afraid it will prove; however, by a modest computation, I believe there will be about a hundred and seventy Tories; the new members are about two hundred, and, tho' they go under the denomination of Whigs, it may be a question whether they will dip their hands in the dirty work their predecessors have left behind them. The death of my Lord Sunderland has very much disconcerted the measures of the Court, and put their affairs into some confusion. As soon as he was dead, the executors and the Duchess of Marlborough sealed up his scrutore, till his son returned from his travels. But the Lord President of the Council, Lord Privy Seal, and the two Secretaries of the State came and tore off the seals, seized what papers related to public affairs, and carried them away; which, as the world says, has put the Duchess into a very great passion, and she threatens them with a law-suit.—I cannot pretend to tell you who will succeed him. The Duke of Dorset has the best pretensions to be Groom of the Stole, because he is the first Lord of the Bedchamber; whether there is any other person that has the same title to be first Minister of State, time must show.—Mr. Walpole's horses feel the weight of a first minister, for they never stand still from morning till night. His experience in affairs at home will gain a considerable share of power, but not being much conversant in foreign business, and not being able to talk at Court with the same easiness as he does in the House of Commons, the whole power will scarce fall to his lot. Our news from abroad seems to threaten war from all parts of the world, and we are very sensible of it here. There are great men daily going abroad to foreign parts, and 'tis now said that the middle of this month is fixed for the King himself.—If I am rightly informed there has been some dispute amongst the Ministry whether they shall meet and chose a Speaker, or be prorogued from time to time till His Majesty returns. The project of inoculation takes most prodigiously, notwithstanding the death of my Lord Sunderland's son. The young princesses they say are out of danger.—Sir W. Wyndham is expected in town shortly.

Fol. 45. n. d. Lady Mary Wortley Montague to Lady Gower.

Fol. 46. n. d. Countess of Gainsborough to the same.

Fol. 47 and 48.—Letters from Mr. B. Noel to Lady Gower. Condolences; and an arrangement for Lord Gower's funeral.

Fol. 39. 1722, Oct. 16. The same to the same.—If ever Mr. Proby designs being a Parliament man, he should not become now, and give it up, having so much the start and advantage of Mr. Piggott, tho' Manchester is gone down, who sent a man in Old Bond Street, down to Mrs. Lyton's; but she told the man she was engaged, and would give her interest to nobody but Mr. Proby. To-day they are in the House of Commons like to sit late about the Habeas Corpus Bill, and they say never so full a House was scarce known as was in it yesterday. Above 500 members, and a vast many design of the Lords' side, to speak to-day to endeavour shortening the time. It can't be strong enough to throw it out. I hear all is concluded between Lord Burford and Miss Worden, who has 5,000l. when she marries, in prospect. Lord Exeter did not take his place on Saturday, as he desired, not finding Lord Gower soon enough that day, who he had a mind to go with him, but will do it to-day. The town is very full, and full of thought, and both sides either way of thinking.

Fol. 43. May 18, at night. The same to the same.— . . . . Dyer's letter says Lord Anglesey is to be one of the Secretaries of State, and Lord Nottingham said at Burleigh he had a private letter of the same. Had Lord Gower been alive, I should have had reason for the sake of one, to have not been much displeased; but as it is, I have nobody I very much value can be turned out, or very much respect, or have a concern for, that will, I believe, be put in, since the Duke of Leed's age I fear, will make him not be any more at the helm, and consequently he or his friends have little advantage by a change in the Ministry. The Duchess of Shrewsbury, I perceive, 'tis said, has found the art none else could do, as given out, of making the Queen laugh since the Prince's death, till she has; since her Lord's being Chamberlaine has done it.

Fols. 35 to 43. Many letters from the Duchess of Rutland to Lady Gower, and her son and grandson.

The following extract only seems to relate to public events:—

Fol. 38. 1722, Sept. 29. The Duchess of Rutland to Lady Gower. We are here every day told of one or other taken up by the messengers, and of several more to be so; but I hope there is no other ground for some mentioned, than only their being of a party that won't give in to the measures of some of the Ministry, who would carry everything, and have no opposers to their villany. . . . . For in all reigns we have heard of sum creatures whose pride and malice have had no bounds, and have made Kings, that would in theirselves been the best of princes, through their artifices been lost in a great measure the affections of their subjects; but I hope that is not the case now, under the happiness, liberty, and property and riches we enjoy, in a King so tender and careful of his people; for I am confident His Majesty is under concern, to have been obliged to send the Bishop to the Tower, and the two Lords went there last night, Orrery and North and Gray, through their own want of consideration and indiscretion, 'twas said. Last night the Lord Arran was in custody also, but in this affair, as in all others, there is a world of false reports, and nothing scarce to be depended upon, but what one sees. Lord Exeter delivered the Stamford address, and was so graciously received, he did not wait two minutes, but was carried in by Lord Orkney to the King's closet. Some are of a very odd opinion, and that is, that this Parliament as soon as meets will be dissolved, and a new one chose; but this sure is hot brained fancies and conjectures, especially as care is, and will, 'tis likely enough, be taken to secure them who may do mischief, and are rude enough to not think right everything some would have them come in to.

Vol. VIII.

Letters of Sir Thomas Gower to Sir Richard Leveson, Mr. Langley and Mr. William Leveson Gower, 1632-71.

From the Earl and Countess of Bathe to Sir T. Gower, 1670-71.

From Lady Jane Gower to Mr. Wm. Leveson Gower.

From Lady Katherine Leveson to Mr. William Gower.

From Lord Danby, Lord Lansdowne, &c., to Sir Wm. L. Gower, and other letters, 1670-89.

From Mr. Edward Gower to Sir Richard Leveson, 1658-61.

Fol. 2. 1642, July 22, Stitnam. Thomas Gower to his uncle, Sir Richard Leveson, at Trentham.—Sent last week a large relation of all passages here. This week produces nothing but what you will hear from London; the petition from both Houses to the King, and his tart reply. Here the forces (I call them not army) lie quartered about Hull, the nearest about a mile off. Cannon baskets are providing, and materials for entrenching, but I believe the town will not be attempted, for the forces here are not 8,000, and the town hath 1,000 and more, and this week there are drawn out of several ships, lately come up, 700 musketeers, and besides the natural strength of the town, there are now outworks made, and they still add to them night and day. If you will have my opinion, I believe Hull is but the pretext to draw forces together, and will not be attempted. The Providence is drawn aground, and all the ordnance taken out of her for land service. Five regiments of horse are raising for the King, besides two of dragoons.

Fol. 3. 1642, Aug. 5, York.—The same to the same. —Since my last the blocking of Hull is as I always believed, proving to no purpose, for Sir John Hotham's pinnaces commanded the river, and the ships from the Parliament the sea, the King drew off his forces upon Sunday last; but first Sir John Hotham had taken some boats, and in them divers gentlemen, as Captains Markham, Horner, Galton, Mr. Egerton, Mr. Faltonstall, Mr. Wright, and others; and the Wednesday night before the same, wherein the King expected an answer from the Parliament, Captain Lowinger and Captain Legarde sallied by night, and avoiding the highways, by passing the dykes upon portable bridges, they came three miles from Hull, and making a stand with 40 horse and some 200 foot, they fell into the town of Anlaby, wherein Lieutenant-Colonel Duncumbe and the Major Frankland lay with their companies, and letting alone the corps du guarde, took all the rest between sleeping and waking, beat up the quarter, surprised the sentinel (whom they slew), hurt some others, and carried 12 or 13 prisoners away. They also fired a barn wherein their ammunition lay (being half a barrel of powder), and frighted the regiment so abominably, that the next

day at noon the highways were filled with runaways, and in three companies they could not muster 15 men. Some others such rising spread the contagion, and most of the trained bands began to examine why they should fight with one another, and why they whom it least concerned should lie in the works, and the Cavaliers more interes[ted] lie at Beverley, and neither case their watches nor assist in danger. Upon this, some horse were quartered near Beverley, all the foot called thither, and the magazine and ordnance is bringing hither as fast as possible. I need not tell you of the Leicestershire Warwickshire affairs, nor of the results of our Yorkshire meeting this day, all which will . . . . only thus . . . . our me . . . . ath failed expe . . . . both sides . . . . we hear an answer . . . . and remonstrance to the Parliament . . . . not fully appear, only 'tis manifest that the . . . . undertakes to raise, arm, and pay 5,000 cuirassiers, for three months, for His Majesty's security. The other day 40 men came out of Hull, who were charged by eight horse, who slew one or two, took four, and drove the rest headlong into the town. Fresh men come in daily, so, as 'tis supposed, there are about 2,500 men in the town. More are expected, and I apprehend they will send in so many as may awe this country, thereby to divert its assistance to the King. Every day we talk of the King's remove southward, but I cannot see how he can advance without better provisions, for as yet he hath more men than arms. The forces yet apparent are 500 horse of Carnarvon's regiment, 500 Grandison's, 500 Biron's, the Prince's guards, 500; Wilmot is raising as many. I have a command to raise 1,000 dragoneirs, Col. Heron, 600, others 400. Six regiments of foot are raising, but unless Prince Robert lands, I see not how they will get arms for them. The Hull business, and ill-carriage of things, makes the King's affairs in worse repute than otherwise they would have been.

Fol. 4. 1642, Oct. 5, Pontefract. The same to the same.—This unfortunate country is still the scene of trouble; Mr. Hotham is issued out of Hull with 1,000 foot and 2 troops of horse (or rather two in one), and many of the country is joined to him, and they expect daily two regiments of foot and two troops of horse from the south; he will much trouble us, by being master of the water, whereby he can take and leave when he pleaseth; and this country being full of rivers, and he having possessed Cawood castle (the Bishop's house), within 7 miles of York, standing upon the river, we cannot force him, and he is safe, having his retreat by water, and can return at his pleasure, which will haggle out this country which hath no help from the King, but a great part of our gentry with him, little money or ammunition. Notwithstanding these difficulties, according to my duty, I am raising the county, and with part of the forces drawn together I am now within six miles of him; the Earl of Cumberland is providing at York; but a treaty of peace concluded, and since strangely deserted by the gentry of his part, hath much retarded our preparations, yet incensed the people against him and them. You will shortly hear what will be done; in the meantime I have a mighty burden upon my shoulders, being now to oppose orders of Parliament (for oath binds me to maintain the county in peace as far as I can, and repress the disturbers) and this without money or means, but the bare assistance of the people which I cannot make a foundation upon. My wife dares not come in Newcastle because the plague is there.

Fol. 5, 1652, July 31.—Thomas Gower to Mr. John Langley.—My nephew Dodington hath had notable success yesterday, all his claims allowed; . . . . the same day was fortunate to the Countess of Darby, but unfortunate to the Earl of Worcester, who is come in without conditions or pass, and will (as most say) certainly smart for it. The additional Act passed yesterday and some private ones; our news at sea comes from Holland (and no other ways) that Blake hath taken nine Dutch men-of-war, sunk two, burnt one, taken as many loaves as contained 2,000 men, whom he hath sent home without ransom. Yesternight a Newcastle merchant (who came post) affirmed that he saw both fleets within less than three leagues of each other, so as here is now great expectations of the event. In France, the King since the retreat of the Spaniard grows in reputation; Normandy is almost agreed, and Beaufort since his killing Nimours is come to him. The King of Scotland is going into the Low Countries; he hath made five privy councillors, my Lord Gerrard, Sir John Berkley, Crofts, Cooke, and . . . . to the wonder of all about him. Mrs. Pooley and some others of that sort are coming for England, and Prince Rupert every day expected in Holland. The soldiers petition do much trouble the consciences of divers members of

Parliament; and this day happening to read some heads of it, the name of the new representative did so trouble the stomach of a fat black Yorkshire gentleman, that though he be as tall a trencherman as any that is much higher than himself, yet the leg of a chicken was more than he could swallow; and indeed the business grows past jesting; they talk also of calling some members to account, but lest I be in the same predicament I will say no more.

Fol. 5. 1652, Dec. 21. The same to the same.—Since I writ last the French envoy hath mended his title and had audience this day; his message I leave to the Diurnalls and will only tell you such things as the Gazettes (I believe) meddle not with all. In France the Cardinal Mazzarin preparing for his entry into Paris was, it seems, resolved first to remove the Cardinal du Retz, being jealous both of his great abilities, power with the people, and the Pope's favour to him, who affects him particularly and also keeps up his reputation to make use of it to the maintenance of his authority in France, and for counterpoise to Cardinal Mazzarine (whom he extremely hates); this latter hath prevailed with the King upon pretence of a new combination to commit him close prisoner to Bois de Vincennes together with Madame Chevereuse and Monsieur Grammond; upon which the Bishop of Paris and divers other Bishops and Abbots went to the Parliament desiring redress or at least intercession to the King; their answer was, they knew nothing of the cause nor any more but only Le Roy le commande; then they addressed themselves to the Duke of Orleans, who seeing how much he suffered in the person of his chief instrument Du Retz, and sensible, that it tended to his depression, used all means he could: but nothing prevailing, the body of the clergy went in procession through the streets of Paris and carried the sacrament publicly, imploring divine assistance for preservation of the liberties of the Gallican Church. The Pope resents it so high that at Rome they say they will interdict the Realm of France. The Prince of Condé hath at last a total rout, he hardly escaping, and among others the Earl of Castlehaven, who had command under him, is slain. The Portugall is agreed with us, and hath given 50,000l. for the goods of the merchants in his hands. The Lubeckers were bringing hither much provision for support of the fleet, and the Dutch have taken it by the way. The Spaniard rants high, in so much that Sir W. A.* (a Yorkshire member) told me he was a skirvy saucy fellow, but 'tis believed we shall not be long friends with Spain. The Swede demands restitution for the Ginny ships taken by us, and that in rough terms. 'Tis feared we have had a sore blow in Ireland, and that Phelim O'Neale is master of the field in Ulster. The Dutch be in the Channel betwixt Dover and Calais with 120 ships, and another fleet making ready. P.S. I was this day for the verses, but cannot get them yet, Sir F. Cobb being gone 10 miles. P.S. 2. —The French envoy had audience at a Committee of eleven, of which four understood him; he gave very good words; among other expressions he told them princes were not to be regarded unless they were just, and since it had pleased God to make them a state, his Master wished them much joy of it.

Fol. 6. 1652, Dec. 28.—The same to the same.—Here is little worth writing, most of the time being spent in endeavouring to take away the esteem held of Christmas Day, to which end order was made that who ever would open shops on that day should be protected by the State; yet I heard of no more than two who did so, and one of them had better have given 50l., his wares were so dirtyed; and secondly that no sermons should be preached, which was observed (for aught I hear) save at Lincoln's Inn. I must beg excuse for saying the Prince of Condé was totally routed; though several letters from Newport, Ostend, and other places assured it, yet they say now his rear payed the shot, together with his baggage, that he hath saved the rest sore shattered. The breach between the Courts of Rome and France grows still wider, and on no slight occasions besides what I wrote last; for the Pope sent to summon Mazarine to Rome; the Nuncio who brought the Monitory was stayed at Marseilles and his papers taken from him. The envoy from France dined with a friend of mine to-day; 'tis a witty drunken fellow, a good scholar, and a roundhead Huguenot; his business (setting by the pretences) is really to get trade between Bordeaux and England, that they may vend their wines, without which they are beggared, and the King desires to do something for that

* I suppose Sir Wm. Allanson, M.P. for the city of York.

town's satisfaction which stands yet in tickle terms; and next he is to mediate betwixt us and the butter boxes, who I assure you desire peace, and France no less, for fear of the advantages Spain gets by this war both by trade and other ways.

Fol. 4. 1652, Jan. 15. The same to the same.—The soldiers have appointed a Committee of 15 to order and present their petition or remonstrance, call it what you will, some here think to fool them as formerly; they say if this bout they do no good, the next shall; but I dare not tell you what judgment is here made of that affair. In France the King and Cardinal carries very high, but I should not say the Cardinal, for 'tis here believed that he hath laid down his Cardinal's cap, sent it to Rome, nay farther that he shall be High Constable and marry Madame de Longueville; Cardinal de Retz, his opposite, is to be at liberty and go Ambassador into Spain, as one whose great parts will be useful out of France but troublesome in it. The Duke of Lorraine is come down against the Hollander and hath taken Gelders; the pretence because he demanded his money of the Dutch out of the bank at Amsterdam, which they were not able to pay and he takes for denial; but, re vera, the King of Spain puts him on that business under hand, by that means doing the Dutch as much mischief as he could do himself, casing his own territories of that army which else must lie upon them, and himself maintaining the peace, his subjects have not the least detriment. The Hollander hath raised 10,000 men to resist him, which, they being so vastly in debt added to the burden of their great fleet, lies heavy on them, and hastens the underhand treaty with us. The Duke of York and Lorraign are fallen out, the former debauching the most of three regiments of Irish which were in his army to serve the French. The Pope hath seized upon a great sum of money of Mazarin's, discovered in the bank at Rome, and his choler is still high against France; all this tends to the advantage of Spain, who gets strength and reputation every day. Heert, the Spanish Ambassador, is discontented at the carriage of most of the English ladies who were at his entertainment, and they as much at him for giving the chief place and respect to Col. H. Martin's mistress . . . . they are also much displeased at her for being finer and more bejewelled than any, but whatever the matter was, she tarried there all night, and to that belongs a tale also; yet 'tis no small argument of the greatness of the Hogen Mogen Heeren Staten of England, that the Ambassador of the great monarch of Spain should make such an entertainment for such a property belonging to one of the Parliament of England.

Fol. 6. n. y., May 18. The same to the same.—I was forced to make use of my brother Howard's favour, to get a pass from the Lords of the Council to come to London to wait upon Sir Rich. Temple's extravagant meeting and undue practises, and that was the cause that I took not Trentham in my way . . . . . . I will not rob the Diurnal of the news of this great plot which hath fever shaken this city; they talk of firing, burning, ruining; the cavalry completely armed beat the pavement two nights together; the foot guards were tripled, many very mean persons seized, yet I saw no disturbance in the suburbs, which it may be is the cause that the fear hath not extended to Hyde Park, where the young gallantry, male and female, are notwithstanding very jovial, and 'tis believed have dark designs, and really they say smock treason prevails much there; and though other be discovered it lies concealed till the attempt hath succeeded, though sometimes with as hot service as the French had at Ostend, who are now drawing a line about Dunkirk, the King and court being at Calais, whither my Lord Fawconberge and my Lord Howard go on Friday morn with complement and something to boot. The Duke of York is killed here with a long pistol which reached from Bapaulm to the Haye.

Fol. 7. 1653, Feb. 18. The same to the same.—Since wrote last here hath been a Plot discovered; the books will tell you the intent and persons discovered; some say it is real, others a Fanfara; but certainly it hath been managing three months last past, for one of the last counsell of state told me that they then knew of it, had one among them daily, but despised it as a ridiculous thing managed by prentices and inconsiderable persons. However, some wise men believe that a couple of coy ducks drew in the rest, then revealed all, were employed to that purpose that the execution of a few mean persons might deter wiser and more considerable people. Beveringe hath had audience, tells the council that he hath a plenipotentiary power, that three other embassadors are to be here next week, and if any accident retard their arrival, that he will sign the articles of peace, which assurance was here exceedingly relished and some great persons much pleased. But, this morn comes a gentleman from Ostend, who tells a lamentable story, viz., that Grave Maurice, bastard to Prince Maurice, Count William and Beverwarden, in behalf of the house of Nassau, have taken the field with 10,000 men, &c. &c. . . . . . but *sit fides penes authorem*, the news is not here liked, therefore not believed here. Here are new books, among which the Case of the new Commonwealth stated, and a Justification of the last Parliament are much cried up.

Fol. 7. 1653, Feb. 21. The same to the same.—The news I last wrote concerning Holland is believed, but worse and more rugged comes from Ireland; for Lieut.-General Ludlow (as is said) hath a great interest in the soldiery, and followed by Sir Hardres Waller, Sir Charles Coot and others, expresseth no good opinion of our government; and though the report be suppressed by all means, yet it increaseth, and the rather because the Lord Henry Cromwell went post away on Saturday at midnight. Last night eight were drawn out of every company and sent away by boats to the ships, which raiseth many conjectures whether for Holland, France, or Ireland. The plot makes much noise, but few believe any thing of it, yet certainly there was something in it. From Scotland, for truth, Kenmore and Glencarne are beaten by Coll. Morgan; he had 1,200, they 3,000; yet, though totally routed, the Scots were so nimble that all scaped save 140; two castles were taken in the Highlands, one of them quitted, and upon the gates a sheet of paper fixed, and in great letters written—*we had no orders to fighte*.

Fol. 8. 1657, March 22, Stitnam. The same to the same.—. . . . The last week two of my brothers and many others are carried prisoners to York, and I have notice given not to stir out of my own house, nor will they declare whether I shall follow my friends; only say that the respect to my brother-in-law is the reason they extend not the full rigour to me. My brother Wm. Gower was but newly returned out of France with my son, and wishes himself there again, having had no suspicion that keeping himself free from the company of those of whom they are jealous, that he should be made a prisoner.

Fol. 8. 1658, June 26. The same to (the same).—. . . . . . Here is little news. My brother Phil. Howard landed yesterday from Dunkirk, he tells us, &c. (of the warfare between the Spanish and French).—Our foot suffered much in the late fight, but did gallantly; Fenwick and I think all the officers of that regiment are slain; divers of the volunteers, and among the rest Drummond, once Major-General to Montrose. The French carried themselves basely, and being three times desired to charge, cried *Ouy, ouy, ça ça*, drew their swords, advanced a few paces, and they cried *Attendez un peu*, put up their swords, and would not stir; they still keep Mardike, and much disgust there is betwixt our men and they. General Lockhart, our embassador (call him whether you will), made a long speech to the inhabitants of Dunkirk, told them the Protector was a man of a vast comprehensive soul, sought the good of all his subjects, though he was not of their religion, yet he had good thoughts and good will for all that believed in God and to be saved by Christ Jesus; that 'tis true the Papists in England were pressed hard, but it was not with his will, but being sworn to the laws of England he could not do otherwise, but they not being under the penalty of that law he would protect them in their own profession, and they should enjoy it without affront or trouble. The King of Hungary is certainly chosen Emperor, and a parliament will be after Michaelmas.

Fol. 8a. 1659, Dec. 17, York. Thos. Gower to Sir Richard Leveson.— . . . . News from the north here is little; I hear General Monk lyes at Coldstream betwixt Kelso and Norham upon the border, and General Morgan at Cowbrain, eight miles from Carlisle. General Lambert is at Newcastle, where they still treat, and he had like to have surprised Berwick, as in the other side they missed Carlisle narrowly, so no advantages are sought during treaty. There hath been a great meeting of several gentlemen of quality at York, which some take umbrage at. And a great part of the news we heard when I was with you, concerning Sir H. Vane's coming northward, and the jealousies betwixt principal officers here and at London, were all Fanfaras . . . .

Fol. 8a. 1659, Jan. 5. Thos. Gower to Mr. John Langley.—The last post there was no writing because of the stirs in this country which were occasioned and begun thus. The burden, but more the insolency of the soldiers, gave just occasion to all to consider seri-

ously of the consequences if they should give General Monk, against whom they were marching, the least raffle, or confirm their soldiers, if they should apprehend themselves the stronger by Monk's refusal to fight, which, though most rational in him, yet might, in his own and the adverse soldier's opinion (who looks not into the inside of business) be interpreted fear or weakness, and work effects accordingly. It was thought fitting also to give the city of London encouragement that they might see such a considerable province as this county join in the same design and endeavour to vindicate themselves from slavery; these and several considerations, too long for a letter, prevailed above the caution of many who thought it almost a desperate attempt to appear against 60 troops of horse quartered among and close by us; and therefore a considerable number of gentlemen gave assurance to meet at several places fit to join at a general rendezvous, but were a little hastened before the day, because the several meetings, not private enough, and some false brother had given notice at Newcastle; whereupon Lilburne was sent back to York with speed; three troops of horse and two companies of foot brought in more then before, and more upon their march, had they not been prevented; a party of horse were sent to seize upon my Lord Fairfax, and the Duke of Buckingham, who were at Appleton six miles from York; but a friend from the city giving timely notice they got away St. Stephen's night, and by daybreak went through Selbye, but lost one another, the old general passing Armin and Castleton Ferry into Marshland, the Duke over Lanrik Ferry towards Hull, whither his father intended also, but for some reasons went not; in the meantime it was given out and believed at York that they were gone to Leeds, from thence to Manchester, and Lilburne grew confident the design was broken; 'till Thursday night all was quiet save some parties of soldiers moving about, and the Quakers assembling at their several meetings; Friday morn by day, there met at Malton Sir Francis Boynton, Coll. Bethell, Sir Hen. Cholmley and many others, to the number of 300 horse, well armed and mounted, among whom Mr. Wm. Gower with above forty horse, half gentlemen, all well mounted and armed, and within an hour came in Capt. Strangways, of Lilburne's regiment, with most of his troop; as soon as he was arrived he accepted against Mr. Gower, professing he loved the man but could not be in a design where cavaliers were parties; the rest of the gentlemen generally opposed Strangways earnestly, but Mr. Gower, to avoid being a cause of separation, and it may be the ruin of the whole business, left the command of the men to Mr. Tho. Vavasour, and marched along as a private gentleman. I forgot to tell you that when the Duke of Buckingham lost his father in the night, after two days' wandering, remembering a meeting was to be at Malten, came to Huten, within two miles, to an old friend's abode there, and was at the meeting, and the like exceptions by the same captain were made against him, though tho Lord Fairfax was his father; that night they quartered six or seven miles off, and I met Mr. Gower at Gilling, where more men came to him, and persuaded him to go still, this being foretold him by myself; they rendezvoused at sunrise at Harealey, where Smithson (major to Lilburne), and Capt. Th. Lilburne, formerly put out by his Collonel and this Parliment, having been fetched back by his old soldiers, came in with their troops, and advertisement that the Irish Brigade, having left Lambert, would join with them, and notice also that my Lord Fairfax would meet them at Knaresborough; thither, being near 20 miles, they marched in deep snow; at Birrough bridge, formerly Isurium, they were faced by Hacker's regiment of horse, were drawn on both sides to charge, and the Duke of Buckingham put himself, with his sword drawn, in the head of Mr. Gower's party to lead them, and the old soldiers gave the new party leave to be in the front, who were ready enough to engage, but Hacker's men were content to draw off, and marched away. At Knaresborough they met the Lord Fairfax, who had with him 150 horse, and Capt. Wilkinson's troop come away from Lambert; in the meantime Lilburne demanded the city magazine of the mayor of York, who was ready enough to deliver it, but the Common Council opposed unless he would declare for Parliament, which he refused, and they sent to invite my Lord Fairfax, who next morn advanced towards York; at Hessam Moor the Irish Brigade being 9 or 10 troops met him, and jointly declared for Parliament, some being against single person and House of Lords, others of another opinion, yet all agreed against Lambert; all united under the Lord Fairfax's command with loud shouts, and faced York, sending a trumpet to summon it; Lilburne manned the walls, caused patrols of horse

to ride the streets to keep in the inhabitants, and denyed
to admit them without Lambert's order : they without
provided to storm in confidence of their party within,
when as fourscore of the citizens notwithstanding the
horse, yet (? got) with their arms into the minster
and rung the bell, and a party of Lilburne's own men
seized a church beyond the bridge, and cried *Fairfax;*
their Collonel advanced first to persuade, after to threaten,
but was forced to gallop off, and least all should serve
him so sent out that he would be content to admit the
Irish forces, but none of those of the gentry, and particularly excepted against those who had been his own
officers ; indeed he expected men from Lambert who lay
at Rippon, seven miles from Knaresborough, when my
Lord Fairfax lay there, as near York as he within four
miles, and hoped to persuade the Irish, having new
changed party. So they marched in, and next day my
Lord Fairfax, and all the company, increased by 400 foot
of Coll. Morleys, who came in to the Lord Fairfax also.
In the meantime all Lambert's men save 200 forsook him;
to those he made a brave speech and they resolved to
live and die together ; but within an hour he stole away
with one man, and I hear came to Newpark to Coll.
Lilborne's, who met him with a very few others, and
since, Lambert is not heard of, and the Coll. is private
in York. Upon news of this disbanding all the countrymen went to their several homes, and the Irish marched
out of the town to other quarters ; posts are gone up
to London, as also the Duke of Buckingham, and
whether the country shall have thanks or no is a
question ; and whether or not, they have surely prevented the Quakers, who had doubtless a furious design,
their letters to several of their meetings to meet with
arms the 6th day of the first month being intercepted.
I am just now told that General Morgan with a great
body of horse is within a day's march, sent from
G[eneral] Monk after Lambert ; and thus you have
the relation of the sudden ruin of an army, accounted
at least 9,000 men, without a blow, and by a divided
party who could hardly hang together but against
them ; add farther, just in Lambert's vertical point
when he was advancing, and a small favourable encounter had perfected his design. . . .

Fol. 9. n. y. (probably 16⅔) Jan. 19. The same to
the same. You are not to look for anything of importance here ; all will be at London, where the scene
at present lies, now General Monk is gone thither. I
waited upon him at his departure ; he carried three
strong regiments of horse and four of foot; four are
left here, one of which lies at Beverley, there being as
yet no positive answer to be got from the Governor of
Hull, but that he will deliver it to those who bear the
image of Jesus Christ. Many wonder at General
Monk's order, which he hath left in Scotland, there
being no field army at all there, or other force, save
what is in the citadel of Leith, St. Johnston's, Aire,
and Inverness, and the castles of Edinburgh, Stirling,
Dunbarton, Dunother, and some other few strong piles
rather than castles. He hath confined Argyle and most
of the chief of the Remonstrators, and seems to put a confidence in Glencarn, Rothes, Ogilbye, Dairly, and others
of Montrose's party ; he hath licensed all noblemen to
have arms for themselves and four servants, and all
gentlemen for them and two servants ; he hath above
20 sects in every foot company, and the Scots offered
him to furnish him with 13,000 foot and 3,000 horse,
and to give what assurance he thought fit not to meddle
in his absence. These propositions refused, they offered
1,000 gentlemen on horseback, and every man an attendant armed ; and at last, because he wanted horse,
1,000 horses. He gaineth in all places by his civility,
but is so close that not anything can be guessed of his
intentions, only he puts out and puts in which officers he
pleaseth. . . . . . . My Lord Fairfax hath laid down
his arms, and with them an opportunity, in some men's
opinion, to make himself great, and the nation quiet by
a free Parliament ; it is most certain he might have
done what he list ; Lambert's army disbanded and
melted, only by the fame of his rising ; the Irish
Brigade sent an officer to let him know that most of
them had served under him, and now offered themselves
to be ordered by him, and venture their lives wheresoever he would employ them ; most of Lambert's men
had the same resolutions. General Monk made a halt
till he heard what his proceedings were, and we are
assured London had their eye principally upon him ;
and though all this and more was fully represented, yet
he chose rather to sit down contented with the thanks
of the House, than to make use of these great opportunities. Some ascribe it to dulness, others that an
order of Parliament hath more power upon him then

all reason ; some to farther design not yet ripe; some
to one thing some to another, &c. . .
Fol. 10. (16⅔) Jan. 19. The same to Sir Richard
Leveson.
Fol. 10. 1660, June 14. The same to Sir Richard
Leveson.—Yesterday I sent my son post into Yorkshire
to manage an election at Scarborough, where a new
burgess is to be chosen. . . . This day Mr. Edw.
Progers returned from France, and now at court they
talk of the Queen's return, and that in short time ; her
secretary, Sir John Winter, is gone to her, and there is
a committee for vesting her jointure, and some say the
Duke of York goeth for her. Bordeau, the late resident, is going, if not gone ; and either Espernon or
Harcourt comes embassador extraordinary shortly.
Those who gaped for preferment and offices in this
great change fail of their account ; for they were divided
between the old servitors abroad and the new cavaliers
at home long ago, and before either could hope for so
happy change ; and at present all gratifications and
favours are the Presbiters' portion ; if any of the King's
party get anything it is inconsiderable. I forgot to let
you know that I performed your commands to His
Majesty, who spoke kindly of you and seemed pleased to
hear of you. I write nothing of news from the House,
it being wholly employed about naming the twenty.
Whitlock 'scaped this day, and Coll. Axtell supplieth
his place ; there is great endeavour in some to make the
Earl of Salisbury one of the number, and he will hardly
escape unless his fellow lords protect him. . .
Fol. 9. 1660, June 30. The same to the same.—The
King dined yesterday at Copt Hall, to-day at Roehampton ; returned both days in terrible rain and
thunder, so as the fine feathers and gay clothes are come
back utterly spoiled, and the brave gallants look like
drowned rats, or as if they had been rolled in puddles,
and the gilded coaches are become like to others. The
Court grows regular, and the old orders come again into
use ; the Prince's chamber and gallery begin to be free,
which before were pestered with mean people. The
Presbiters begin to stir, and discover their opposition to
ceremonies, and their desire to keep out the old ejected
clergy, and 'tis believed as soon as the Act of Indemnity
is finished that you will hear of greater opposition
in that nature. In the meantime many of the King's
party show much folly in putting in provisoes against
particular persons in things of small value, and which
rather show passion than judgment; but I believe it
proceeds from discontent, which ariseth from their
opinion that the Presbiterians engross both profit and
favour; and truly they do what may be to keep power
to themselves and others from it. Here is a rumour to-
day that the Princess Henrietta is privately married
to the Duke of Anjou, wrought by the Cardinal to
prevent the bestowing of her in the House of Austria,
being extremely jealous lest the Emperor should have
her ; but I have been with my Uncle Winter, who is
newly returned from the Queen, and he knows nothing
of it. There is a proviso this day put in the Act to bar
all the King's judges of the benefit of indemnity who
came not and rendered themselves within fourteen days.
Fol. 11. 1660, July 7. The same to the same.—. . .
All the provisoes are this day dispatched, and 'tis believed that Monday the Bill of Indemnity will be
finished and sent up to the Lords, who will be very
severe if their own words may be believed, nor do they
reject any proviso though put in by a Commoner. One of
the most active among them told me just now that the
Earl of Salisbury and his fellows who dissolved the
House of Lords in compliance to the army will be excepted, and that they will not spare one High Court of
Justice man who hath condemned any of the peers, and
according to that rule very many will suffer. The army
grumble much at the new collonels and like not at all
that the Earl of Northampton, the Lords Falkland,
Hawley, Langdale, Daniell O'Neale should have regiments, and as little that the trained bands are settling
in the ancient way by Lords Lieutenants and Deputy
lieutenants ; but I believe when money comes in they
will be yet more pleased. I hear at Court of a Don
coming from Spain, forerunner to an embassador extraordinary, a count of high esteem and near akin to
the Privado ; and it is believed that peace will be shortly
concluded with that crown to the great joy of this
city.
Fol. 11. n. d. The same to the same. . . . . It
is true the misfortunes of these times have fallen heavier
upon me than almost any of my estate, being forced to
pay again what the King had received of me; which
being his own, I could not refuse him ; and also the
largest sheriffs account of England to pass when my

bailiffs and officers by advantage of the war made no accounts, and their sureties either dead or undone ; so all falls upon me and turns to prejudice ; yet I say not this to decline charge, but to let you know that, but for these inconveniences and great losses, I should rather have exceeded than fallen short of expectations. . . . I am glad to hear that divers whose fathers were compounders are chosen ; yet none in these parts venture at it, nor was it thought expedient among us ; finding a great jealousy and aptness in the two parties to unite again against the royalists, it was thought better to decline particular satisfactions in order to general advantages ; besides great care was taken that such were chosen who were very honest, yet free from exception.

Fol. 12. 1660, Aug. 14. The same to the same.
. . . . The Bill of Indemnity is returned from the House of Lords and will be speedily dispatched ; the Commons for the most adhere to what they sent up ; only agree with the Lords in excepting Coll. Hacker for life, and all the 20 for estate ; the rest of the King's Judges to be banished, and the four grandees to be perpetually imprisoned, but that is not yet concluded. They are displeased that the Lords except none of their own House for life, there being as guilty among them as any in all things, saving being judges of the King. The last week Ludlow went from the Serjeant-at-arms, left a letter directed to the Speaker, told him that he had withdrawn himself, not out of distaste of the House of Commons upon whose words he had rendered himself, but for that he saw blood was thirsted for by those who hardly ever had attempted to draw any in either sort, and that attempted to invade the liberties of the Commons of England of which he hoped they would be careful ; that when ever the House of Commons signified their pleasure and that they would maintain what they had promised upon notice left at a place he named, he would readily return to the place from whence he went. Eight Lords and more Commoners are gone into the city to advance the loan of 100,000l. upon security of the Pole bill ; but it is suspected though the cow have milk she will not give it down ; and the rather because Recorder Wilde made a long speech, showed four reasons why the city could not lend ; 1. Delay of the Bill of Indemnity. 2. No performance with those who had laid out money upon public sales. 3. Innovations in church government, 4. Sudden decay of trade, which indeed is strangely gone, the most practised in that kind not knowing the reason, and though six India ships are returned very rich. The Hampshire frigate was assaulted by eight Spanish men-of-war, all as great as herself, yet is come off clear, extremely torn, to the great honour of our nation. But, sir, the great news is, which till more public, I pray keep to yourself, on Sunday the General refused to give the Lord Roberts [Robartes] Commission to govern the army in Ireland, which discontents the Chamberlain and others, and 'tis believed he will not go as being only trusted with civil but no military power. The consequences are many and important. . . .

Fol. 12. 1660, Oct. 17. The same to Mr. John Langley.
. . . . The Parliament endeavours to put whatever the King offers or is about, into an Act that their power may the least go along with the King's, to which purpose the Declaration at Breda, and that concerning Church government are turning into Acts to oblige His Majesty to whatever he hath offered when circumstances of time, occasions, ceremonies, emergencies, and indeed necessity gave him reason to offer more than there was reason to expect ; what is done concerning Lord Lieutenants and the Militia, I shall refer to the next, every day giving more light, though by this little day enough is seen. . . .

Fol. 13. 1660, Oct. 31, *(King Street, Westminster.) The same to the same. . . . I have been little at home since I saw you, being too much employed in country affairs, which our old lords and masters have left in extreme disorder, and the raising of the old number of 12,000 foot and the former proportion of foot hath been no small labour, especially there being few of the old stock of people left who had formerly managed business, and few of the new who knew which was to go about it ; we have also three Lord Lieutenants, and formerly but one, which makes it more intricate ; and though 12 regiments of foot, only five troops of horse, which are free troops not being disposed into a regiment ; my son is captain of one of those. . . . The King went hence Saturday last, and can hardly return till Saturday next, some say on Monday ; the Queen coming

* The Powterers, next to the Swan Tavern.

to Canterbury on Tuesday last ; this town is very empty till the return, although there did not so many persons of quality attend the King as was expected. I believe you hear of the young Ladies delivery of a goodly boy, who believes as well by that merit as other reasons to be a Duchess, she is very sick of the measles. . . . The Queen and Princess Royal are, in show, extremely discontented and her great enemies, and indeed the whole affair is in a mist, and not fit for a letter no more than the several reports relating to the whole affair. . . .

Fol. 13. 1660, Nov. 6. From the blew Lyon over against Salisbury House. Thos. Gower to Sir Richard Leveson.—The Houses met this day, and all I hear they have done, besides ordinary formalities, is the gift of 10,000l. to the Princess ; there was some sharp expressions against multitude of French now in town, who eat the bread out of the mouths of the natives, there being as they say no less than 35,000 silk weavers come hither since '57. The children of Belial are not forgot, and the great conflux of the offspring of Babel who are not fit to mix or be conversant with the sons and daughters of Sion ; they were the very expressions of a godly zealous member, and the noise in the streets agreeing with this and some pulpit doctrine, hath given the French Ambassador occasion if not desire to be gone, and the Queen begins to talk of return ten days hence. But the great news, and second to none but the King's happy restoration is this morn from Denmark, where as their own words speak it, in gratitude to their King's heroic magnanimity and sufferings for the safety of the people and kingdom and his singular virtues active and passive, they have by universal consent changed his election into a successive title, and given him and his successors the same power and succession by descent in his line and after the same manner as the Kings of France and England have, so as he is to be as absolute monarch as any King in Christendom ; and now we talk of a match with his sister as a matter of consequence, and though but common discourse, yet great persons speak of it seriously. I saw this day the two English French Abbots, Daubigny the only brother alive of the last Duke of Richmond, and Montague the Earl of Manchester's, together with Sir Kellam Digby, the Queen's Chancellor. The lady in childbed recovers of the measles, and the child also, and her father was created Baron two days since ; and if court whispers can be believed shall be a Duke, and if that be so, his daughter may without murmur be a Duchess ; whether it be so or not, the noise and slightings of her in every man's mouth almost last week are now stilled ; the consequences I leave to you. . . . The court is now splendid, so many Princes and Princesses being together, and the town incredibly thronged, so as most new come wish themselves at home again. The Presbyterian makes his advantage of all, and for ought I can see intends to make the Parliament long lived by tediousness in settling the King's revenue. Every day gives new light as well as discourse. P.S. The Dutch Ambassador came into town this afternoon.

Fol. 14. 1660, Nov. 13. The same to Mr. John Langley.—At present there is little considerable ; the French Ambassador Extraordinary hath taken his leave, and I hear goeth away to-morrow ; as yet the opinion that the Queen follows him within a fortnight is upheld, and the rather because she is exceedingly bent upon the match of the Princess with the Duke of Anjou. The lady who pretends to be a Duchess is daily in more hopes to be so indeed ; the King was on Sunday afternoon a long time at her father's, and the coarse language which was so rife when she first lay in is not only laid aside, but also they excuse themselves all they can who let any fall. The courtiers also make visits, which cause people who know how observant they are of every motion or appearance of favour, to make judgment accordingly. A few days will show what may be imagined ; in the meantime it is good to suspend in so delicate a matter. An ambassador is come from Venice and another not far behind from Florence. The Parliament are in consideration of the Militia, which, being the great quarrel before, is hoped will be done to the satisfaction of all concerned.

Fol. 14. 1660, Nov. 20. The same to the same. . . . The House of Commons having been employed about the manner of raising 1,200,000l. which they have promised for a revenue for His Majesty, settling the militia, attainting the rest of the King's judges, raising 100,000l. in lieu of the Court of Wards, where the great question is whether by a Lond tax upon the Excise or assessment according to estate of every individual person ; and from thence arise new questions which spin out time and still demonstrate that old ways wore good ;

there are other debates arising upon the manner of settlement, because some of these courses can only raise it for a time, whereas the consideration for the Court of Wards is to be for ever. The Presbyterian party get strength and power; some of the principal receiving daily the several marks of favour. Maynard and Glyn knighted and made the King's serjeants, Broun, judge in the Common Pleas; I will make no descant of the men, you have known them all. Here is again strange superstitions from the great tide on Friday night last; though I be far from one of that number who much regard them, yet I will give you an account of it, in regard it is strange. At five in the even there was the lowest ebb that I ever saw, and whereas it should have flowed only till nine, and was a land tide as they call it, and should have kept within the banks, it flowed till one, and went quite over the mill banks, and boats rowed in Westminster; then whereas it should have ebbed eight hours it flowed again within four, and was still water next morn at the bridge at ten of the clock; and the observers add farther that there was no wind or other accident which might cause alteration of tides. The Queen sets forward for France the 2nd of December, and is so earnest for the match of the Princess Henrietta with the Duke of Anjou, that the cold weather cannot allay the heat of that desire, nor the Princesses indisposition by a great cold retard the journey.

Fol. 15. 1660, Nov. 24.   The same to the same. . . . . Since the King declared that he would dissolve the Parliament, some of the old presbyterians assembled and were drawing up reasons why the King should only adjourn and not dissolve, there being so much business on foot that it cannot in so short time be dispatched; it was resolved first to present it to the Lord Chancellor, by him to be represented to the King, but upon better consideration I heard, not an hour since, they have let it alone. They of late build much upon the Chancellor's favour, I hope without ground though not without appearance; that party carrying all places and profits. Lenthall the last Speaker's son was committed to the Tower, for counterfeiting the Great Seal; his answer is slight, that a friend in Italy very curious in all seals desired the King's, whereupon he got the impression with such clay as tobacco pipes are made of. The news of Mexico holds yet, and of the Turks progress in Transylvania, as also the Queen's journey upon Monday seven night. The Bill for settling the Trained bands by authority of Parliament goeth on shortly, for the Fr. (Presbyterian ?) finds himself outwitted and that it will strengthen the King's power instead of lessening it; but it is called on, and if the short time hinder not, will pass. The Bill for restoring the Duke of Norfolk was read in the House of Commons, and must be so again of Monday, but was opposed, particularly by Bamfield, Sir J. Northcote, Pim, and others.

Fol. 15. 1660, Nov. 29. . The same to the same. . . . . I am to find out something whereby I may be reimbursed the money which I lent to the King; for to have it in money as yet there is no possibility; and it is as hard a matter to find any manner of profit whereunto there are not already several pretenders as may be. I am told that Hanbury Park in Staffordshire is the King's, and not disposed, at least not so but that a great advantage may be got by it, and that it may be attempted without prejudice to any; I pray if it be within your knowledge let me understand of what nature or value it may be, or as near as can be guessed without a strict or open inquiry, for that may be dangerous; and if it seem to be near the value, to which I pretend, I will, God willing, send purposely about it. . . . Alludes to the proposed marriage of his son with a daughter of Coll. W. Eure, whose father Lord Eure was slain at Marston Moor ; her sister is marryed to Mr. Danby.— Yesterday the Bill was brought into the House to turn the King's Declaration concerning Church government and ceremonies into an Act; it induced the greatest dispute of any yet, and with much vehemency, but was thrown out, the House being divided, 158 being for the Bill, 180 for casting it out. The Presbiter strove as for life, and which you will wonder at, some of the old commonwealth party joined with the Cavaliers. P.S. The news of the revolt of Mexico holds still, and the Queen stays here three weeks.

Fol. 16. 1660, Dec. 11. The same to the same. His son has gone abroad with his (Tho. Gower's) brother Howard (the new Earl of Carlile,* having exchanged his former title upon the death of the late Count (Countess ?) and not yet returned. . . . The Parliament, or some of them, are yet in hope of six weeks' time to sit; yet I

* According to Nicolas, Howard was not made Earl of Carlisle until 30th April 1661.

heard the Sol. Gen. Finch speak of it, and he is a knowing person; however they spin out time, and of late do little, as if they would cut out work. But I can almost assure you that the lady, newly churched, shall be acknowledged a Duchess shortly, whatever is said to the contrary. I must recall what I caused my son to write concerning the taking of Ludlow; another was mistaken for him, and could not persuade them the contrary. The King holds the Dutch to very hard terms, demanding not only reparation for the old business of Amboina, but also for 300,000l. laid to their charge by the Spanish merchants and adventurers of Guinny. I will not trouble you with the sinking of a ship worth many thousands intended for the Gold Coast in the great storm last Saturday night, &c. P.S. I am told that yesternight the King, Prince Rupert and the Duchess of Albemarle christened the child of the Duchess at Worcester House.

Fol. 17. 1661, May 21. The same to the same. . . . The House of Commons are wholly intent upon the two Bills for the Militia and the King's safety; against some clauses in the latter the two Aldermen of London made several objections, little to their commendation. The House of Peers debated till two this afternoon, whether the bill to condemn the Earl of Strafford should be nulled or repealed; it was carried for the latter by five voices, but disputed with great heat on both sides. A rumour is spread this morn that the Spaniard hath taken Olivenza, and is in a capacity to march to Lisbon, if not hindered by want of carriages for victual, seeing he can hope for none by water. Seventeen great ships and three victuallers are now in the Downs, which are believed by some must bring home our Queen, but certainly must touch at Portugal, though I suspect they go farther. The Dutch are arming apace ; 23 great men-of-war ride now in the Texel, besides the fleet already abroad, and the Spaniard hath drained all his garrisons as on the French as German frontier to lodge them about Dunkirk. We have a new fleet making ready with all expedition, and volunteers raising, most say for Dunkirk, but some few that they are to garrison Tanger as soon as we receive it from the Portuguese.

Fol. 18. 1661, May 26. The same to the same.—This day I understand from a wise man that the Spaniard and Portuguese are in treaty both in Madrid and Lisbon, that many articles are agreed, and whatever issue will be, it breedeth jealousy ; and some state astrologers will persuade themselves that the great tameness of the Ambassador of Spain is only to amuse us and take away the suspicion of what countermines they are working; they say his speeches and his actions agree not; that having declared he would go away as soon as he was certain the match with Portugal was concluded, and he now pretends new instructions lately received, when it is certainly impossible that they could come out of Spain hither since the King's public declaration. Out of this bulrush they pick nuts indeed, some which I must leave to your imagination. The news holds that the Dutch have made peace with Portugal and leave their own West India Company to shift for themselves, and offer to make our King umpire of all differences. The fleet is now all in the Downs save four ships, and is expected they set sail for the Mediterranean within eight days, but still it holds that they touch not in Portugal as they go, whatever they do in their return. Three days hence will produce much news.

Fol. 19. 1669, Oct. 8. Thomas Gower to (his son) William Leveson Gower at Stitnam.—After writing about business he sends " his service to my Lady Jane; " I doubt not she hath ere this received her letter in " blank verse, but she is to expect another from Sir R. " Howard unless his muse be out of humour, because " my Lady Bathe won his money at l'hombre last night ; " but if my lady have a rime from her uncle Prideaux, " she will easily believe that the Burgesses in Parlia- " ment drink rather water then wine, if the poetry be " rightly considered ; but whether all prove rhythme or " verse, they are, together with myself, who will venture " no higher than prose, her very humble servants."

Fol. 20. 1670, April 26, Stitnam. Thos. Gower to the Earl of Bath at Whitehall. On family business.

Fol. 21. Two letters from Thomas Gower to his son, W. L. Gower. One is dated 1671, March 22. On business.

Fol. 22. 1672, Feb. 22. The same to the same.— Written "From my bed." Business.

n. d. The same to the same at Stitnam.—I doe not say, as Sir Henry Blount did, that I am glad to hear it was reported I was dead, but give God thanks that I am in good health. . . . . . Yesterday Sir Job Charlton and myself were to dine with my Lord Bath in order to your affairs, but the Danish Ambassador came thither, so we quit the field as likely to be too hot for men of business. Sir P. Munckton is sheriff, T. Fairfax under-sheriff, but he will not hear of W. Hayes as too much friend to Mr. Peebles. The Lords have rejected the Bill of Judicature; the House of Commons have voted a Bill against Conventicles, and been this day hard upon Sir G. Carteret, so I believe we shall shortly be despatched. . .

Fol. 25. n. y. Feb. 23, Stitnam.—The same to the same. . . Sir William Wentworth prosecutes his pretences, claims the performance of the promises and engagements made when he desisted the last time to give way to Sir W. Frankland. My Lord of Darby was then engaged for him, and 'tis believed, will not break his word; the burrough holders acknowledge the contract made with him at the last election, and in order to the next, he hath given them two treatments; for they were begun to solicit before Sir Thos. Ingram died, and should he surcease, there is another dangerous competitor who appeared the last time, Mr. Robt. Wharton, who is backed by the endeavours of most of the neighbouring gentlemen. Mr. Talbotts, Menhills, and Lockwood have votes, are his kinsmen, yet in regard of former promise, the Menhills are for Sir Wm. Wentworth, but after him for Wharton above any, and the others solicit and treat the burrough men in Wharton's behalf. Sir John Key and Sir Jeremy Smithson are pretenders, but to little purpose, though the latter say he will spend 1,000l. and hath promised bribes to particulars. I opened the enclosed from Sir W. Frankland, and whatever neutrality he pretends, he with Mr. Linfield were soliciting for Sir Wm. Wentworth. "The burrough holders take any man's " treat, and while they are treated with cups will say " much but perform little." Says that without Lord Darby's interest he, Gower, is not likely to get on.— Lord Darby has already given Cowgates to several upon condition they vote for Sir W. Wentworth, &c. &c.

Fol. 23, n. d. Thos. Gower to Mr. John Langley. (The corner of the letter where the date might have been is torn of.)—Since the game is likely to be played here, if it grow desperate, I shall, God willing, timely advertise Sir Richard Leveson, that he may provide for the safety of his stake, whatever becomes of his servants here. After His Majesty's arrival, we were in a calm, 'till the unfortunate voyage to Hull raised this horrid storm, which hath ever since dangerously tossed us, and the worse because we have fallen asunder among ourselves, though as yet, God be thanked, we have only made paper wars. All which hath passed, printed or written, you shall receive entire; in the meantime rest content with this short account. His Majesty summoned us this day; his propositions were that treason was so countenanced that he feared danger, and therefore desired our advice and concurrence for a guard; we have chosen a committee to frame an answer, who cannot agree upon it; some desiring to refer it to the Parliament, others to offer freely. The freeholders being not called with the gentry, have delivered a protestation that nothing done without their consents shall bind them. Three hours ago His Majesty hath declared that he is resolved to raise a regiment of foot of the trained bands for his guard; the horse he desires to consider of; which hath caused above 1,000 of the gentry and freeholders to join in a petition wholly to decline any guard, but I have yet stayed the delivery in hope of concurrence, and I see some hopes of drawing things to a better way, for this must if followed on, produce such a breach as will hardly be repaired, and if we can devise how to satisfy the King and not do contrary to the present state and swing of affairs, you will say 'tis not ill handled. I hope my next . . . . bring you better news, in the meantime know we desire to obey the King . . . but not to sunder them but for the present we think him too low . . . . have a bad game to play, all my aim is to discharge my oath, my duty . . . . peace of this country if possible.

Fol. 24. n. y. 30 June. The same to the same.— Here is little news which the Diurnals will not give you an account of; that of Turkey is hoped will prove only a false alarm; but it is but hoped, for there are no letters contradict it; only one from Marseilles saith that all the English are clapt up and their goods seized, and that is the best they yet look for. The French are before Landrecy, and the Archduke preparing to relieve it; to which purpose the Emperor hath sent 12,000 men. The Swedes great army gives ombrage to friend and foe, and look a squint upon Holland and Poland. The commitment continues still, but for aught I can yet learn our good friend hath no manner of prejudice upon him. C. Backhouse is yet here, and those gentlemen which were

said to be sent to the Barbadoes are not gone, and some of them in the Tower yet. I saw this day a manifesto of the Duke of Savoy justifying his act against the Valdenses, &c.

Fols. 26 and 27. 1670, Feb. 13, and 1671, March 26, Whitehall.—Two letters from the Earl of Bathe to Sir Thomas Gower on family matters.

Letters of Jane, Countess of Bathe, daughter to Sir Peter Wyche, wife of John Earl of Batho. Also letters of Lady Jane Leveson, wife to Sir William Leveson Gower; and letters of Sir W. L. Gower; and letters of Lady Katharine, widow of Sir Richard Leveson, K.B.

Fol. 30. 1690, Jan. 15, London. — Sir W. Leveson Gower to Mr. Linfield (evidently his son's tutor).— . . . . My Lord of Leicester seems to be the wisest man of his country, if not of the age he lives in; he is civil to all the men of wit or soul who visit him, without taking notice of what opinion or party they are of, and leaves the stage free to those who have a mind to be actors.

Fol. 31. 1672, July —, and Nov. 18, Trentham.—Lady Katharine Leveson to her nephew Mr. William Leveson, the last is directed to him at the Earl of Bathe's lodgings at Whitehall.

Fol. 32. 1672, Sept. 8, Whitehall.—A true copy of the Right Hon. the Earl of Arlington's letter to Madam Danby.—The burgeship of Malton in Yorkshire, being vacant by the death of Sir Thomas Gower, he asks her to favour Mr. Leveson Gower with her credit in the election.

Fol. 33. 1672, Sept. 29. Madam Danby* to Lord Arlington.—Her tenants at Malton are ready to comply with her desire for the election of her cousin Leveson to the burgesship of Malton. If His Majesty's commands together with her own inclination to serve her cousin had not prompted her to assist him, his (Arlington's) desires would have been sufficient.

Fol. 33. 1672, Sept. 21. Madam Danby* to W. Leveson Gower. Advising him how to proceed in the above matter.

Fol. 34. 1670. Nov. 12, York. Phil. Monckton to William Leveson Gower at Stitenham. The writ for the election of a burgess for Scarborough will be there upon Monday, the election being on Wednesday. Asks for Leveson's company on Tuesday; he will meet him at Seamore where he will meet Sir Thomas Slingesby and others.

At the back of the letter are four verses of five lines beginning That I Aurelia do adore, ending, To attend her leisure.

Fol. 35. 1671, Aug. 13. Ed. Gower to William Leveson Gower.

Fol. 36. 1672. Oct. 16. Tho. Fairfax to W. Leveson Gower.—The King being at New Market the business cannot be prosecuted till his return. (About getting a friend an office.)

Fol. 36. n. y., March 3. The same to the same.

Fol. 37. 167⅔, Feb. 11, Stitnam. Plaxton to W. Leveson Gower.—He has been to Malton to get their and their adversaries polls reviewed—he and his friends are confident of success. Mentions those who are willing to come to town and gives other particulars relating to affairs at Malton.

Fol. 38. 1688, May 5, London.—(Lord) Granville to Sir William Leveson.—As for the ceremonial part of our journey, the compliments which were made my Lord wherever he past, and the manner of his being received by the gentry of the two counties, without doubt you know . . . . . . he gave great satisfaction to the country, so by the answers he has brought he has likewise pleased the Court, His Majesty having declared himself well satisfied with what he has done. The answers of the Roman Catholics were all positive to the questions; the dissenters were divided; some were positive, others doubtful, desiring that the questions might be debated by a free parliament, and in case a reasonable expedient or equivalent could be found, they were ready to serve His Majesty in all things, which was also the unanimous answer of those of the Church of England. These answers being delivered with great submission and duty, the King has been pleased to take them in good part . . . . . . The town is as empty of news as the Court; we have had a new play called The Fall of Darius (written by Crown), by which the poet, though he could get no fame, yet had a most extraordinary third day by reason of the King's presence at it; the first day of its acting Mrs. Bower was taken so violently ill in the midst of her part that she was forced to be carried off, and instead of dying in jest was

* In both letters the writer signs herself "Danby."

in danger of doing it in earnest. Mrs. Cook is dead and Mrs. Boute . . is again come upon the stage, where she appears with great applause. We are promised this week another new play of Shadwell's, called the Alsatia Bully, which is very much commended by those who have had the private perusal of it. Besides plays the town is fruitful in scandal; I have enclosed you a sample of that which some commend.—Mentions the high esteem in which Lady Wyndham is held in Somersetshire.

At the back of the letter is a poem, called "The New Litany," very much worn in places, evidently being the enclosure to which he alludes.

Fol. 39. 1688, Aug. 25, London. A news letter directed to W. Leveson Gower, at Trentham.—(There is a note signed R. B., and dated Stone, Aug. 27, on the cover.—This last night about 12 a clock came an express that went for Chester, with orders speedily to march the regiment that is there to Hull.)

The Marquis de Abbeville, that had leave to come from Holland is dispatched thither again with all expedition. An extraordinary council was held last night at Windsor, where I am told the calling of a Parliament was resolved on. The Commissioners of the Navy are gone down to Chatham and Portsmouth to hasten the fitting out 10 men of war with all expedition; they will be three and four rate frigates, and those of five and six rates that are now out will be turned into fire ships. The preparations of the Hollanders alarm us very much, but His Majesty has commanded such care to be taken that we shall be in such a condition as not to fear any insult from them. (Gives news from Brussels, Vienna, and an account of the battle of Belgrade.)—Yesterday Sir John Iles, one of the aldermen of this city, kissed the King's hand in order to be Lord Mayor for the year ensuing. Mr. Timothy Hall, pursuant to His Majesty's congé d'élire, directed to the Dean and Chapter of Christ Church, was chosen Bishop of Oxford the last week, and a return made thereof, but there was no Mandamus to admit him a Doctor.

Fol. 40. 1688, Dec. 4, London.—A news letter to the same. A trumpeter having been sent to the Prince of Orange for passport for the Commissioners that are appointed to treat with him not being returned, they went from hence on Sunday, and lay that night at Windsor, yesterday at Reading, the head quarters of the King's army, where they will stay to expect the return of the trumpeter. There are but three Commissioners sent, viz., the Lords Hallifax, Nottingham, and Godolphin. The Lord Dartmouth having received a letter that His Majesty had resolved to call a free Parliament, he immediately called a council of war, who have sent an address of thanks to His Majesty, signed by himself and all the captains of the fleet that were present, the substance of which was that they did believe the only way to preserve his person and government to him was by a free Parliament. With this address the Lord Berkeley and Captain Layton were ordered to attend His Majesty, which yesterday they did, and my Lord Berkley read it to His Majesty. Yesterday we received an account that the Princess of Denmark lay on Wednesday last at the Earl of Northampton's, went thence for Leicester, and was expected at Nottingham last Saturday, where a house is taken for her; several Lords and gentlemen went thence to meet her, the bells were ringing and other demonstrations of joy were preparing against her coming, and during her stay there she will be entertained by the Earl of Devonshire. The Princes of Orange and Denmark stayed at the Earl of Bristol's till Friday last, and went thence to Bruton, the Earl Fitzharding's house, and designed for Bristol, which city was delivered to the Earl of Shrewsbury, who is made governor of it by the Prince of Orange; he with 200 horse and 500 foot entered the place the 1st instant, and at the Tolsey was met by the Mayor and Aldermen, to whom he delivered a letter from the Prince, in which he assured them that he was come for the defence of the Protestant religion, their liberties, and properties; and therefore having great confidence in their fidelity he had sent no more soldiers, being unwilling to burthen them; while this letter and the Prince's declaration were reading, the soldiers were quartered, the people generally receiving them very well. Newcastle, Hull, Barwick, and Carlisle still hold loyal to His Majesty notwithstanding all reports to the contrary. The rabble have burnt a Popish school and chapel in Lincoln, which endangered sundry houses. On the 29th past, Admiral Herbert, with about 200 sail came into Plymouth Roads, having sailed from Torbay the Wednesday before, where they left 20 sail. All the report of the French landing in the west rose only from a French man-of-war putting

into Falmouth, the one to ship a leak, and the other went off to sea without landing one man. The Earl of Bath summoned all the deputy-lieutenants, justices of the peace, and other gentlemen of the county to meet him at Saltash, in Cornwall, the 1st instant, which they did; to whom he read the Prince of Orange's Declaration, and then the greatest part of them signed an Association in defence of the Protestant religion.

Fol. 41. 1688, Oct. 20, London.—A news letter for the same.—Precepts being issued out by the Lord Mayor of this city requiring the common council men to meet at the Guildhall, yesterday the greatest part of those that were living came about four in the afternoon, and being sat, Deputy Langhorne (one of them) desired to hear the instruments read that restored their Charter; which being done, he observed there was a clause in them that ordered the choice of common council men to fill up the places of those that were dead; and observing to my Lord that a common council was a temporary office, and only chosen for a year, he believed their year being long since expired they could not proceed to act anything. My Lord Mayor then asked the question of (? if) what Deputy Langhorne said was the sense of them all; they unanimously declared it was; upon which his Lordship adjourned, and desired them to consider of it; assuring them that he would send lawful summons to every Wardmote according to the custom of the city. Yesterday Sir Humphrey Edwine and Sir Thomas Lane were chosen Aldermen at wardmote, and returned to the court of aldermen, who swore them in the afternoon. This day the Lord Cornbury's regiment of dragoons marched through this city into Surrey.—Spanish news. —200 hackney coaches are added to the 400.—My Lord Dartmouth is now in the Gun Fleet Road, and will sail to-morrow for the Downs, where a Council of war will be held for opposing the enemies' landing. The Bishops being well assured of His Majesty's gracious intentions and favour for the Church of England, are gone into their respective dioceses to dispose the mind of the people to the defence of their King and country.

Fol. 42. 1689, Sept. 18, Chester. A news letter directed to Leveson Gower at Trentham. (On the back is a short letter from George Mainwaring saying that he sends all the news, and in a P.S. this day the Commissary by order from the Duke is going with all the wagons to Hylake to be shipped.)—Yesterday came to this city Mr. Palmer, Chaplain to Sir Hen. Ingoldsby's regiment; he left Carrick-Fergus on Friday last, and says that the Irish left the garrison of Charlemont as soon as they perceived the English approach without striking a stroke, and retreated to the Newry; being followed by the Duke's forces, they set fire to the town which consumed all but four houses before the Duke's could reach the place, and then they fled to Dundalk, which they left without doing any harm, being closely pursued by our army which followed them till within 8 miles of Tradarth near the Lurgan Race, where the Duke is encamped waiting for the big cannon and baggage which were shipped off at Carrick-fergus a Fryday last, and were expected there a Saturday; and from thence the Duke sent a message to King James that he had numbers of the Irish in his power every where about him, and if he see any more such doing as burning of towns, and if any house in Dublin were burnt or any Protestant there hurt, he would not spare man, woman, or child; there was also a messenger sent from King James directed for Count Schombergh, who was told that they formerly knew such a one in France, but that their General was a Duke and Peer of England, and if any message came for him it would be received. The Duke of Berwick is in Tradarth, and it's supposed that there are about 20,000 Irish in the town, and entrenched about it, where, if the Duke find any difficulty to beat them, he will proceed to Dublin another way; that upon the Duke's message to King James, most of the Protestants that were in restraint are at large, and allowed more freedom then of late they had; this minister assures us Mr. Harbord, with the money that went lately from hence, arrived at Carrickfergus a little before the great storm, as also did the Lord Huit's regiment and the rest that went with them.

Letters of Mr. Edward Gower.

Fol. 43. 1658, June 29, London. Ed. Gower to Sir Richard Leveson. . . . As for news there is little or none; that at Court was that the Swede was fallen with his whole army into East Frisland, but since, this is contradicted. The Hollanders have been put to a great fright; for the States General issuing forth some bills for the levying of some moneys which they had occasion for, caused little less than a mutiny upon the people, who denied to pay any, but since the business is taken up. They say the King of Hungary is certainly elected Emperor. Mr. Terrick having led the way, there is since him, some say six, some eight French merchants broke. Mr. Terrick oweth in all but 16,000*l.*; he offereth his creditors 7*s.* 6*d.* at pound; this is all he will give.

Fol. 48. 1660, April 15, Stitnam. The same to the same. . . . The militia for this county is settled in three regiments of foot, 1,000 in each regiment, and three of horse, 400 in each regiment, all in the hands of very honest men. Most of our burgesses are chosen, and though all our endeavours were used to the contrary, yet Luke Robison is returned burgess for Scarborough, upon Vice-Admiral Lawson's account; but a very wise man saith we shall not have above three scabbed sheep in our flock.

Fol. 48. 1660, April 21, York. The same to the same. —Upon Thursday the 16th instant, there came into York 32 soldiers of Capt. Peverall's troop; Smithson's Collonel to the regiment, Lilburne formerly Coll.; these dispersed themselves by two and three together to the Inns, where they were observed to demand quarter either without billet or officer to quarter them, which say some was the cause why Coll. Bethell suspected them; hearing also they gave out some high words, he (as Governor of the town) sent out some to enquire of some of them from whence they were, who was their officer, what their business, with such like questions, but could receive no good answer from any of them; which was the cause that he and one Major Walters coming privately to their inns, found their horses bridled up to the rack, their saddles on; about 12 of the clock in the night they went up into their chambers, where they found them asleep upon their beds in their clothes, their boots on, with their swords drawn, their pistols loaden, and some of them cocked; as soon as they had seized on them, and had them under examination, they confessed they had a design upon the city, and there were 80 townsmen that were to have been ready upon the same confederacy, and also that the foot then in the town, which were four companies, had some of them promised to assist them. This gave no small alarm to the city, who the next day agreed with those foot soldiers to give them crowns a piece to march out of the town, which they did accordingly; the town hath ever since kept very strong guards, 80 foot of townsmen at every gate, and they have four troops of Bethell's horse in the town. The townsmen that were discovered were all Lambertonians and sectaries. Upon Thursday the 19th there came another troop of the same regiment to the gates, and would have had entrance, pretending their business was to quarter in the town; but the guards kept them out; on Friday two more of the same, but were likewise refused. There are 1,000 citizens who have listed themselves under my Lord Mayor, who are resolved to keep very strong guards till they can get their militia raised, which is not yet done by reason of some false brethren, but will be done very shortly. The soldiers are very high, but 'tis thought all is but wind. Coll. Salmon was seen in this country on Thursday last, and a party of horse was employed to snap him, but 'tis not yet done. Lambert we hear nothing of as yet.

Fol. 49. 1660, May 4. Stitnam. The same to the same—and one to Mr. John Langley of the same date. Complimentary.

Fol. 50. 1660, May 22. The same to Sir R. Leveson. —I make no doubt you have intelligence by this post that the King is landed, of which as yet there is no certainty; only I was informed by one that came this day to London and from him on Sunday that he intended to move on Monday, and that his goods and servants were embarked; to-morrow I march with the General to meet him, where will be an incredible show of nobility and gentry. . . . Your kinsman Sir Henry Mildmay was taken making his escape beyond seas. . . . . Desborough is brought into Whitehall, prisoner, and Hewson is taken.

Fol. 52. 1660, May 29, London.—The same to the same.—I take the boldness to present you with this happy news of His Majestie's safe arrival at Whitehall, where, as also upon the road, he was received with the greatest acclamations of joy that possibly could be, such as it is impossible for me to express; he landed upon Friday at Dover, and went that night to Canterbury, where he staid till Monday. The volunteers that rid in the General's life-guard, which were near 120, were allotted to be His Majesty's life-guard, which they performed, though they were every night upon duty, with a great deal of willingness: amongst the crowd

I was one, and do not certainly know but that I may be upon the guard this night. . . . I see my Lord General Monk created Knight of the Garter; there were made Knights Bachelors, Philip Howard Captain of the life-guard, Coll. Rositer, Massey, Alderman Robinson, &c.; these were all made at Canterbury.

Fol. 53, 1660, July 12. The same to the same.—The discourse of the town is of the petition from Somersetshire and Dorset for establishing of the Church in the same splendor and ceremonies that she was in in King James' and Queen Elizabeth's times; for the votes of the House, the weekly pamphlets will furnish you only thus much; of Luke Robinson, he is turned out of the House, where, before his exit, he made a recanting speech at the bar of very near half an hour long, all bathed in tears; he served for Scarborough, where my father is now engaging his friends to choose him Burgess.

Fol. 53, 1660, Aug. 2. The same to the same.—Yesterday the Lords excepted these four following out of the Bill of Indemnity, viz., Sir Arthur Haslerigge, Sir Henry Vane, Mr. Thomas Scott, and Coll. Axtell. The Bill for Pole-money was returned this day to the Commons from the Lords, with some amendments which the Commons have approved of, and it will be shortly passed. The Court is modelling itself as it was in the late King's time, that is, that persons are to come near the King's person as they are in quality: a Privy councillor into a lobby near the bedchamber, a lord's son into the antechamber, others (except public officers), though persons of quality, no nearer than the Presence chamber or gallery, persons that do effectually wait for business into the Privy chamber.

Fol. 54, 1660, Aug. 9, Westminster.—The same to the same.—Yesterday the Commons made an order that no Bishop, Dean, nor Chapter, Prebend, or other clergyman should let any leases without first acquainting a committee, by them appointed for that purpose, with it; the Lords have made an order that those purchasers who were either abjurers, rumpers, decimators, or major-generals, shall not have any the least consideration allowed them, but they must return their unjust got lands; upon several petitions to the Lords concerning having those left to the law who sate as Judges in the pretended High Courts of Justice they are graciously pleased to give unto the several petitioners leave to pick out of every several high court of those that sate as judges, one such as they themselves shall think fit to be excepted out of the Bill of Indemnity, and to be left over to the law, which will undoubtedly make them examples according to their deserts; amongst the number I can hear as yet of no more that are pitched upon, saving these four following:—My Lord Capell's friends have pitcht upon Major Edward Wareing, Shropshire Waring, Lord Derby, Major Croxton, Lord Holland, Capt. Blackwell, who, I hear, is already dead, Duke Hambleton, Capt. Stone. The Prince de Linnye is coming over to desire the Princess Henrietta Maria for the Emperor; but we have a report here that the French will not part with her, but intend her for le Duc d'Anjou; she is worth striving for, being esteemed, for beauty and parts, the Phœnix of this age.

Fol. 54. 1660, Aug. 11. The same to the same.—This day the Lords returned the Bill of Indemnity to the Commons with several amendments and exceptions, as, for example, to have all suffer in general that sat as judges upon the late King, one out of every High Court of justice that sat, and such like, which the Commons will not as yet at all consent to, and say those whom they have already excepted they will confirm, but none more; their reason is this, many that were the King's judges and others have rendered themselves prisoners upon their proclamation; their words being passed, they cannot recall it; if they do, it will look like a trepanne to promise them their lives upon surrendering themselves within such a time, which they laying hold of, appear; and after this they to go back with their promise and declaration. This makes a great noise, and it is thought the Act will not pass yet in haste.

Fol. 50. 1665, Aug. 14, Westminster.—The same to the same.—Sir Richard having recommended him to learn Italian, and having given him an Italian dictionary and some other books, he, to show him his advance, has enclosed a translation of some Italian verses which he has made in his leisure hours. 16 lines. The Italian is on one side, and the English opposite. *Begin,*

"Beauty doth Madam 'bove all wonder shew."
"Donna, Belta sopra ogni maraviglia."

Fol. 56. 1660, Aug. 26, Stitnam. The same to the same.—News this barren soil produceth none, only that Dean Marsh, Dean of York, carried things on in order to a settlement of the Church here very high ; the singing men and organs are preparing. Prayers, I mean Common Prayer, are settled in the Minster, as formerly, twice a day.

Fol. 58. 1660, Nov. 3rd. From the Blue Lion, an apothecary's shop over against Salisbury house, in the Strand. The same to the same.—The Queen came yesternight late by water to Whitehall ; with her the King, Princess Royal, Princess Henrietta Maria, Duke of York, Princess Rupert and Edward, a most brave and full Court, all lodged at Whitehall. This morn Prince Rupert, who had a patent from the late King to be Lord President of Wales and the Marches thereof, delivered it up to His Majesty, with this compliment, that he would hold nothing by any greater right than his favour. There must be no standing regiments of horse nor foot in England ; all are to be reduced to 40 companies of foot for garrison, of whom there must be no collonels, only captains ; all Governors of towns are to be reduced to the same model, though he have several companies. in the garrison, he is but captain and receives no more pay, nor any thing for being Governor. 'Tis said also, and by persons near business, that there must be, say some 6, others but 4, troops of horse in the nature of guards ; the King's to be commanded by the Lord Gerard ; the Duke of York's, whose officer is not yet declared ; Prince Rupert's commanded by Collonel Thomas Daniell ; the Duke of Albemarle's by Sir Phillip Howard ; the other two not fully resolved upon are to be commanded by the Dukes of Buckingham and Richmond ; none to be commanded by a person under the quality of a Duke. As concerning the Chancellor's daughter rumours are uncertain as yet ; no result of any thing, only 'tis observed the Duke never yet saw her since she was brought to bed, &c.

Fol. 58. 1660, Nov. 10. The same to the same.—Yesterday morn the House was taken up with a squabble betwixt Sir John Owen, a Parliament man, and Sir John Robison, Lieutenant of the Tower ; the business is too long to relate, only thus much I shall make bold to tell you ; Sir John Owen, coming into the Tower with his two sons, went to see a kinswoman of his, the warder's wife, that keeps Hasslerigge ; upon his return the warder at the gate stopped him, and though Sir John Owen told him who he was, he would not let him go ; there he kept till twelve o'clock at night, at which hour the Lieutenant coming in, after some words in passion interchanged, the Lieutenant put him into a room with his sons, and put a padlock upon the door ; the next morn let him go without saying anything to him ; this was brought into the House, as an abuse to a Parliament man, and caused many disputes ; at last it was referred to the Committee of privileges to consider of ; this, though not worth your patience in hearing, yet was thought worth the canvassing in the House. There is a new Bill a drawing up against Sir Henry Vane ; upon Monday next my Lord Chancellor must be created Duke, the title I know not. My Lord Howard and his lady are reconciled and together again. The Earl of Carlisle and his lady * are both dead, and my Lord Howard is to have the title and to be Earl of Carlisle. This day was a Bill brought into the House to provide against women that separate themselves from their husbands, and after claim alimony, and take up things upon their score.
• It was, after much debate whether it should be thrown out of the House or no, at last referred to a committee. All is well at Court ; the only talk there is of the match betwixt our Princess Henrietta Maria and the Duke of Anjou. This day the House of Peers went generally to kiss the Queen's hands in the Banquetting house.—P. S. In the afternoon yesterday the House of Commons went to give the King thanks for his Declaration concerning ecclesiastical affairs, and are about to draw a Bill according to the heads of the Declaration. 'Tis said Sir Hen. Martin, Tichburne, August: Garland, and Hewlet will all four be hanged.

Fol. 59, 1660, Nov. 15. The same to the same.—Yesterday the French Ambassador, le Duc de Soissons, after having had the King's consent to the marriage between the Princess Henriette Marie and the Duke d'Anjou, went away well pleased. The Dutch Ambassador hath had his audience, and hath presented the King very richly with a bed and some gold plate, with other rich moveables ; this day the Dutch Ambassador was to kiss the Queen's hand, with four or five coaches and at least 50 or 60 lacqueys, all in mourning. Monday come three weeks, 'tis thought the Queen and the Princess Henriette Marie return for France. This morn the King went to Hampton Court ; this day the Lord

Chancellor was attended and complimented by the Vice-Chancellor of Oxford, and by many of the Masters and Fellows of the College in their red hoods and square caps. The Parliament have brought in many Bills, as for highways, for settling the rates, for the trained bands, for provision against alimony for wives that do without good cause separate themselves from their husbands, as also a Bill of attainder and confiscation of the estates of those that were executed, of those that are condemned, and of Ireton, Cromwell, Hewson, &c. Lisle is for certain got into a French monastery ; but they have passed but one Bill which is for 70,000l. a month during six months to begin in January next. . .

Fol. 59, 1660, Nov. 17, London.—The same to the same. . . . . The Commons, or some of them, were very fierce in voting down the Lord Lieutenants, and consequently the deputies, but upon second thoughts laid it aside ; this happened upon a misdemeanor committed against a parson by the Earl of Derby, or some of his men, the particulars of which I cannot learn ; only thus much I hear, there was a letter of complaint read against him in the House. The news upon the Exchange is that the Great Turk hath given them a great blow in Transylvania, and advanceth so that they begin to be fearful of him in Germany.

Fol. 60, 1660, Nov. 20, London.—The same to the same. —This morning the Parliament brought in an impeachment against Mr. Phillips, who writ the scandalous pamphlet The old Parliament Revived ; and it is sent up to the House of Lords. Yesternight at the Fleece Tavern, being much company and very merry with kettledrums and trumpets, there happened this disorder or rather mischance :—The gentlemen were discoursing of the play which they then came from, by name the Unfortunate Lover ;* at the latter end of the play there was a duel upon the stage ; which they, discanting upon, drew their swords in jest to shew wherein they failed ; in their folly Sir Robert Gaskholl received a chance thrust in the hand, which, with the ebullition of blood, caused a pass, in which Sir Robert Gaskholl his heels flew up, and the Scotchman unfortunately followed home his thrust, and ran him, sitting in his chair, through the body ; within half an hour he died, and the Scotchman is taken. Yesternight the King, Queen, Princess, &c. supped at the Duke d'Albemarle's, where they had the Silent Woman† acted in the Cock-pit, where on Sunday he had a sermon. This morn the Countess of Carlile was fetched from Salisbury House in great state, where she lay in state to be buried in the country.

Fol. 66. n. d. [1660, Nov. 22?] The same to the same.—This day the King hath declared to both houses that this Parliament shall be dissolved the 20th of the next month, and that he will immediately call another. The Parliament have given 100,000l. for ever, to be raised out of the Excise in lieu of the Court of Wards. The Irish debates were ended last night in prejudice of the Irish expectations, the sale of lands confirmed to the adventurers, yet so that no grant for service in, or arrear transmitted out of England be admitted, but only for the benefit of such as have served in Ireland, and with some consideration of the ancient proprietors. This was done at the Council, and the Duke of Albemarle, if he continue in that mind, hath declared that he will go for Ireland. This day brought news that the Vice Roy of Mexico hath revolted from the King of Spain, and is followed by all that great empire. This Lord Mayor of London is troublesome to the clergy of the old stamp ; the Bishop sent to him that the church might be fitted decently, and he would provide ministers to preach there ; his answer was that he would make no provision for any of the singing men, and when he saw the names of those he intended for preachers, if he liked them, they should have admittance. In the mean time the city do not pay the 100,000l. they promised to lend. This day the House of Peers voted the restoring of the Duke of Norfolk ; 'tis observed many of the Parliament men are not pleased at this their so quick dissolution as they term it, not knowing whether they may be chosen again or no.

Fol. 60, 1660, Nov. 24. London. The same to the same.—Here was a rumour that some of the Parliament men were about to draw up a remonstrance to let the King know that there were several undeniable reasons for their longer session, and that it was impossible for them to quit their hands of so much business as they have undertaken in so short a time ; but of this I hear no certainty. [This] morn the message from the House of Lords was read, which was to desire the consent of the Commons to pass a bill for the restoring of the

---

* In the Calendar of State Papers is the draft of a letter to Margaret Countess of Carlisle, dated December 19, 1660.

* Sir William Davenant wrote the Unfortunate Lovers.
† By Ben Jonson.

Duke of Norfolk; the bill was read in the House and is appointed to be read again upon Tuesday next, and 'tis said it will pass without much opposition. Sir John Lenthall is sent to the Tower for counterfeiting the Great Seal of England. His excuse is upon his examination that he hath a friend in Italy that is very curious in seals and that it was for him that he took the print; but this will not save him, for it was answered he might have had an old seal from off some patent; he hath taken out his pardon under the Great Seal, and by this means he had the opportunity of doing it. . . . My cousin Doddington's office he never enjoyed since, as I am informed, Thurloe had his exit; but I am sure he never had it since the King came in; it is Sir Thomas Fanshaw [his] office, who hath had a patent for it above 20 years, neither had John Doddington any consideration for his money, nor ever received above 6 months profit. The Queen is still resolved for her journey on Monday come a sen'night with the Princess Henrietta and Prince Edward; the Princess Royal stays all winter.

Fol. 61, 1660, Dec. 4, London. The same to the same.—It is confidently reported that the Parliament hath forty days longer given them to sit; this though hotly talked is not at all credited. On Saturday night at midnight was Major-General Ludlow taken at one Michael Oldsworth his house, Secretary to the late Earl of Pembroke; Ludlow married this Oldsworth's sister; he got out of the house, but was taken endeavouring to make his escape. The Parliament of Scotland is to sit within 10 days, &c. P.S. The bill for the Duke of Norfolk's restoring is passed the Commons yesterday.

Fol. 57. 1660, Dec. 8. The same to the same.—News we have little, nothing of certain; many things contradict, as that of Ludlow's being taken and the German Duke's being here. My Lord of Argile and Judge Swinton, one of Cromwell's judges for Scotland, are both sent to Scotland, there to receive their condign rewards. We hear the Parliament of Scotland have voted down the League and Covenant, and some say they have voted it treasonable. The Parliament here must sit no longer then the 20th instant, much against their wills. They have finished the Bill of attainder and given the King their estates with this proviso in the Act, that he may lease them out but cannot sell them. I hear by the bye that most of them are begged of the King before he hath got them. I hear nothing of the Bill for the train band nor for alimony for women. P.S. I hear all the prisoners that stand condemned and are in the Tower are to suffer.

Fol. 61. 1660, Dec. 13, London. The same to the same.—We have here some rumours of a plot, which we hope is discovered, of which I can hear no particulars, only that one Major White is taken, who is said to have in his pocket a list of 6000 men that have listed themselves in Ireland in order to oppose the present power; this White was a major in Ireland all these wars, and hath been since this late happy return in Flanders, where as it is said, he once saved Scott from being taken; he is now fast in the Gate House, and warrants issued forth for the apprehending of several other persons. We hear from Ireland that there are six troop of horse there that have refused to disband. Scotland proves honest above expectation; the Parliament there vote down Presbytery and the Government. 'Tis said this plot is as general in England as Ireland; 'tis hoped now the worst is past, and that the danger is over. The House are resolved to sit forenoons and after during this session; there were several complaints brought this day into the House against Lords lieutenants and their deputies, and the Act for settling the trained band was this day read, but referred, not passed. The Coronation must be the beginning of February; the Lords are stinted in the number of their footmen; a Lord is to have 6, a Viscount 8, an Earl 10, a Marquis 12, a Duke 14, the Duke of York 16, the King 20; this is new but certain every one must be known by their distinction as they pass.

Fol. 62. 1660, Dec. 15, London. The same to the same.—The rumour of this late conspiracy is still hot in the town, though many are of an opinion it signifies nothing. Major White is taken and clapt up in the Gate House, and as I hear was this day to be examined; there is but one witness against him, who is a porter. I hear there are four more seized of and sent to the Tower, and that Lambert should have been tampering with some in the Tower to have endeavoured an escape; this is but news. The Queen began her Christmas here this day, and will for France upon the 25th instant; the Parliament will dissolve upon the 20th; the Bill for the trained band was read twice; what is done in it I cannot hear. The Bill for settling the half of the excise upon the King as hereditary is passed, as also the

Bill for 100,000l. a year in lieu of the Court of Wards. We hear from Yorkshire of very tempestuous winds, many houses and churches overthrown, and that Argyle is cast away going for Scotland, and with him Swinton. . . . Sir John Hotham hath lost all the roof of his house and his chimneys in this storm.

Fol. 62. 1660, Dec. 20, London. The same to the same.—The Parliament do not dissolve till Monday night, the Lords will not agree to the Bill for taking away the Court of Wards, which the Commons are troubled at, and say if the Court of Wards must not be taken away they will not give their consents to the passing the Bills for settling half of the excise upon the King and his successors. The plot is not yet known so well as that I can have any perfect relation of it at any hand more than that there should have been such and such things done as I mentioned in my last; neither day nor hour appointed for the effecting of it. All agree some mischief was intended by reason that the heads of the Phanaticks from all parts of England were flocked thither; for my part, if I may be so bold as to spend my judgment, I think something was intended, but that it was crushed in its embryo. The Princess Royal is this day fallen ill of the small-pox, which hath occasioned, as I hear, the Queen and Princess to put off their intended journey. . . The Princess Henrietta is this night removed to Newport House; to-morrow she goeth to St. James's for fear of the small-pox. The Duke of York takes very well to his Duchess, carryeth her to plays, and several persons of quality go to kiss her hand; she is as yet at Exeter House with the Chancellor. Col. Desborough was taken upon Wednesday morning; after he was examined he was sent to the Gate House. Major-General Massey hath 3,000l. given him by the Parliament, and Captain Titus 2,000l. Mrs. Jane Lane, though deserving much more than both, but 1,000l.; 'tis observed the Presbyterians are best rewarded. Vice-Admiral Lawson (now Sir John Lawson) had letters from the King, Duke of York, Princess Royal, Princes Rupert and Edward, and from the Duke of Albemarle to the House of Commons in his behalf, intimating the good service he had done the King in being instrumental in the last happy change; but these proved not successful, for they moved the business and gave him not so much as the thanks of the House, whereas he expected a large gratuity or badge of honour.

Fol. 44. 1660, Jan. 16. The same to the same.—For news, here is none but talk of the Phanaticks who have not done anything since my last. The Princess is recovered of the measles. The King of France is come to Roan (Rouen), the Duke d'Anjou to Havre de Grace to meet the Queen. I have here enclosed sent the Scotch diurnall, not that there is anything of extra-ordinary in it, but because it is new, and the first of this kind I have seen.

Fol. 63, 1660, Jan. 19. The same to the same.—Upon Monday at the Old Bailey were sixteen tried of these late disturbers; all were condemned, eight executed this day, whereof Veneur, who through a mistake I formerly writ you word was dead of his wounds, was one and their head; six are to be hanged to-morrow; two, who were penitents, are reprieved. I hear there came one of their cabal in his shirt to the Sessions House, and told them he was come naked and without arms to tell them he was one of those that were in arms, and that he had done execution upon the Lord's enemies, and desired he might suffer with his brethren; he was apprehended, but not that I can hear of indicted; they all pleaded undauntedly, Not guilty; they were hanged upon gibbets in several places of the city, drawn thither as traitors upon a sledge or hurdle, though indicted for murder. I cannot hear that those that are reprieved confess anything, or that they discover any more of their confederates. The King's guards, both horse and foot, are now settled; three troops of horse, the first His Majesty's, commanded by Lord Gerrard; the 2nd, the Duke of York's, commanded by Sir Charles Bartley; the 3rd, the Duke of Albemarle's commanded by Sir Phillip Howard, the same troop that was the General's life guard; each troop must consist of 140 men; they are to have 3s. per diem. The foot guards are to be, some say, 20; the least that are spoke of are 14 companies of foot commanded by Coll. John Russell, my Lord of Bedford's brother. The oldest captain, his name I have forgot, was formerly one [of] His Majesties major-generals; most of these companies are to be commanded by those that served the King in Flanders, these three only excepted, that I can hear of, viz. Coll. Wheeler, Coll. Tho. Daniell and Lieutenant Coll. Thomas Howard, my Lady's brother; the common soldiers too are to be those that served the King in Flanders, who are now at Dunkirk; there are 1,300 of them; I hear they are about to come over shortly. The Princess is safe recovered, and some say safe arrived with the Queen Mother in France.

Fol. 63. 16$\frac{59}{60}$, Jan. 24, London. The same to the same.—The news here is of the grand revolt in France; it is credibly reported the King of France came not to Roan (Rouen), where he now is, so much in compliment to our Queen as because he was jealous of some troubles in Paris occasioned by the manufacturers joining with the Prince de Condé, who hath declared the King a bastard and himself the lawful heir to the Crown; 'tis said this discontent was occasioned by the King's forbidding of all sorts of laces, bone or loom, to be worn. The guards are to be settled as I mentioned in my last; persons of very good quality carry colours in this guard, namely, Sir John Talbot and Sir Henry Joanes: there is besides the three troops before mentioned one regiment of horse called the Royal Regiment, commanded by the Earl of Oxford; the Earl of Darby his second brother, carrieth the colours; they are to have 3s. per diem as long as they attend in the city, 2s. 6d. when they live in the country. My father was told by Henry Howard of Arundell House, that these reports of France are but chimeras and not one word true; more, that he had this night a letter from Paris, and that it mentioned not anything of it. If I may spend my judgment, I believe the Queen's stay at Portsmouth may have occasioned this; the reason why she stays I cannot hear, but am assured at court that all is well.

Fol. 64. 16$\frac{59}{60}$, Jan. 26. The same to the same.—I mentioned nothing in my last of the disgarrisoning all the inland garrisons of England; and the reason was I had no assurances of it, which since I have, and particularly those of York, Shrewsbury, and Ludlow; these four following Lords were all with the King yesterday contesting for a troop in the Earl of Oxford's regiment. My Lords Mandevill, Windsor, Richard Butler, and Falkland; the King answered one of them that if he had a troop in this regiment he must not think to stay here to play at Hombre, the new game at cards now in fashion at court, but to lie and quarter abroad in the country, there to attend his service. The news of France is all false; the Princess hath been very ill again of a fever, but is now recovered, who with the Queen is yet at Portsmouth. This day the King went to Hampton Court, and its thought he will return this night. By Prince Rupert's means my cousin John Dodington hath got to be secretary to the President of Wales, my Lord the Earl of Carberry: Sir Richard Temple, as I am credibly informed, is in treaty with the Earl of St. Albans to have his half sister in marriage, &c.

Fol. 44. 1660, Feb. 14. The same to the same.—We have it credibly reported here that we shall have a Parliament by the 6th of May, but I was told it by one of the Council this day that they heard nothing of it at the Council table. We shall have the coronation undoubtedly on the 27th of April, and I hope we shall enjoy your company here at that time. This day the Portugal ambassador had his audience, and, as a courtier told me, the King modestly denied his request, 'which was in order to a match with our King.

Fol. 45. 1660, Feb. 16. The same to the same. . . . I hear at Court that Goffe and Whaley are taken in the Indies, how true is expected.

Fol. 45. 1660, Feb. 19. The same to the same.—We have it credibly reported here that there is like to be a breach betwixt us and the Spaniard; the occasion was this; the Spaniards were building a bridge over a channel from Bourbourg towards Dunkirk, which the Governor saw might be of inconvenience if finished, and for that cause made it be fired by some of his men, which the Spaniard took so ill that he refused to send into Dunkirk the taxes agreed on by both sides, which the Governor knowing the King's pleasure concerning it hath sent to demand, and if they refuse prepares to endeavour to make them pay. 'Tis here credibly reported amongst many, though secretly, that the King is married to the Prince de Lynnie his niece, though it is thought by men pretending to know something, there is no such person in nature; some say to the Governor of Bruges his daughter; both which are false, if himself and friends may be credited.

Fol. 46. 1660, Feb. 26, London.—The same to the same.—I hear 'tis resolved at the council table that for the conveniency of the commonalty all people are for this Lent permitted to eat flesh three days a week, fish being very scarce, and indeed not to be had. No more plays at Court after this night, and but three days the week at the play houses.

Fol. 46. 1660, March 2. The same to the same. This evening came attended through the city with twelve coaches, every coach six horses in it, an ambassador from Portugal; his quality, titles, business, if I can by

any means learn, you shall hear in my next. My father is preparing to go for Yorkshire, to be, if he can, chosen a Parliament man, burgess for Malton. I could wish with all my heart he had some assurances of it, for in this ensuing Parliament he will have two particular businesses of more than ordinary concernment.—P.S. The Coronation is certainly to be April 23rd 1661.

Fol. 47. 1660, March 5. The same to the same.—The ambassador I mentioned in my last is Count Maurice de Nassau, who is come in a compliment to the King to know what shall be done with the Prince d'Orange; when the old Prince d'Orange died he left for guardians to his son the Princess his wife, Count Maurice de Nassau, and the Duke of Brandenburg; when the Princess Royal died, she prevailed with the King to supply her place, which he accepted of; the Cardinal of France is certainly dead, and 'tis said the Cardinal de Rhets [Retz] is to be Ministre d'Estat; our young Princess is to be married to the Duke d'Anjou upon Saturday next, and 'tis said the Queen is returning for England. The Duke d'Albemarle is to be Lord High Constable of England during the ceremony at the Coronation; that ended, his staff is to be broken.

Fol. 47. 1660, March 7. The same to the same.— Here are very strong endeavours to be Parliament men, especially by the Presbyters; 'tis generally believed the Bishops will be admitted into the House of Lords. The King went to Banst[ead] Downs to a horse course.

Fol. 66. 1661, April 10, Stitnam.—The same to the same.—We have been at the election at Malton, where my father had the majority of voices; but Mr. Darbye, Lord of the town, returned himself in an indenture with Sir Tho. Heblethwaites, so that it must come before a Committee of privileges. I have an answer from London that the number for Knights of the Bath are completed, and that they are to be but 70, so that I was much too late.

Fol. 67. 1661, April 30, King Street, Westminster. The same to the same. Encloses some of the best Panegyrics that are extant; the press floweth with them, but never were there so many barren ones as now, though they have so good and copious a subject . . . All our expectations now are who shall be our Queen; and the King hath referred it to his Council, and saith he will be guided by them in it; I hear yesterday it was debated at the Council table, and resolved for the Portugal, who will change her religion, and with whom we must have eight millions, and that the Duke of Ormond and my Lord of Inchiquin are shortly to go to Portugal to manage that affair. This morn my Lord Duke of Buckingham told me nothing was resolved of at the Council table, but put off till Thursday, but he verily believes it will be the Portugal. They talk already of raising an army to go for Portugal; and there is a proclamation to re-call all English mariners from foreign Princes service, and that they shall have employment at home. Another proclamation from the council table to forbid gold and silver lace or Flanders dentelles, more than to wear what are already bought, and some time given to put off those they have.

Fol. 68. 1661, May 2, London.—The same to the same.—I here enclosed send a paper, which on my opinion is a very great motive to make me credit the common report vogued here with the match with Portugal; to that effect this night the Duke of Ormond goeth towards Gravesend in the King's barge, and so for Portugal, together with my Lord of Inchiquin; 'tis reported here we must (I mean the King) be moderators between Spain and Portugal, and so drive on a general peace; which if it happen, he shall have the just title of peacemaker. Here is come out a list of the Parliament men elected, which because in many things it is defective, I have not sent. It is credibly reported Dr. Bates is dead, how true I know not. Yesterday the King and nobility were all at Hide Park in more then an ordinary equipage.

Fol. 69. 1661, May 2, London.—The same to the same.—I failed the last post; the truth is I was at a play at court engaged with some ladies, and got not home till after two o'clock at night. The news in the House is, that the citizens that serve for London seem dissatisfied at this vote to oblige them to receive the Sacrament; they were told if they did not observe the vote they must be made to undergo its penalty; they replied they are freely chosen to serve in Parliament, and 'tis not a vote in Parliament can thrust them out. The news is that the Spaniard have taken Puerta Porta, one of the chiefest and strongest towns in Portugal; 'tis reported also that they have made an inroad into the country as far as Bragn; but the latter is stiffly contradicted. The Spanish Ambassador, who formerly had ranted that he had instructions from his master to be gone as soon as the King should declare he would match with Portugal, did this day, having audience, profess his instructions were altered, and that now he was to stay; it was thought at first to be but a rant, now it is concluded so, and he is laughed at by most for his pains.—Enclosed some papers.—I hear the Parliament sits not to-morrow, but is adjourned till Monday by reason of taking the Communion on Sunday. P.S. Argile is condemned, and is to be hanged, as this day. Montrose his trial I will send you, but it is too large for a letter.

Fol. 70. 1661, May 7. The same to the same.—Upon Sunday last about 3 a clock at noon the Duke of Cambridge departed this world, lamented much by his mother; he was buried by torchlight on Monday, accompanied by some of the household, none of quality that I could see; very few lights, not above 30, and those carried by the King's and Duke's footmen in their liveries; a canopy of black velvet carried over him, supported by four mourners, the Duke carried under it by six more; all in deep mourning. None goeth into mourning for him unless it be the Chancellor. This day was spent by the King and Court at Hide Park, in viewing the city Trained bands with the auxiliaries, all commanded by my Lord Mayor as General; one regiment of horse, not at all liked, commanded by Sir Nicholas Crisp, where my cousin, John Bromley, carried a colours. There was at the west end of the park erected a scaffold, wherein was a chair of state for the King, and another chair for the Duke of York, with several scaffolds round about, where were persons of quality. After the King was seated, there passed by him only one regiment of foot, and Sir Nicholas Crisp's regiment of horse; then my Lord Mayor's troop of horse, commanded by Sir Will. Muddiman, all citizens. For state before him was led a goodlike horse, with bridle, saddle, and furniture, after the Indian manner, and a tall swarthy complexioned man leading him clad also in a loose garment, cap, and boots or buskins after the same manner. From about six score of the King's scaffold was the foot drawn up six deep in length and an interval betwixt, where the King passed through; this line of foot reached on both sides from the King's chair of state to the park gate; every regiment had his tent set up in the rear; the King stayed there about an hour and half, after whose departure the opposited regiments fired against one another in the manner of skirmishes. Great preparations are making against the grand ceremony we must have to-morrow.

Fol. 71. 1661, May 11, London.—The same to the same.—I, here enclosed, send you the King's and Chancellor's speeches, and can send little of news with them, save only that the Speaker waited upon the King at the Lords' House yesterday about four in the afternoon, where, according to the custom, the Speaker very urgently pressed his insufficiency, and made the closure of his speech in these words, That his inabilities were such to perform so weighty an office that he wanted abilities to excuse himself enough, and then made a pause; to which the Chancellor answered that he was so well known to the King, that he must give over excusing himself, and cheerful accept of the employment; with all added that the King was sensible of his abilities, and that he had showed himself a good orator and an able man in endeavouring, in such language or terms as he did it, to disable himself. Then the Speaker replied, since it was His Majesty's command that he should receive it with all cheerfulness, he did, and humbly begged that whatever he did or said amiss might be looked upon as rather an error in judgment then anything of willingness. Then he addressed himself to the King, and told him he hoped he would take it in good part if he declared that he was astonished at the glory of his presence, as that the presence of his glory and lustre had almost cast him into an ecstacy, and that he could almost say with St. Paul that now he was wrapt up into the third heaven. After having spoken much and very well in praise of the King, something of his undoubted descent and right to these crowns, next in commendation of the Lords, and last of all of the Commons; he concluded humbly begging in the name of the Commons these four things or petitions:—1. Freedom from arrests for all members and their servants; 2nd. Freedom of speech; 3rdly. Freedom of access; 4thly. A benign construction of their actions: all which, the Chancellor told them, the King, being assured of their loyalty, did grant them; after which the House dissolved till this morn at eight of the clock, when they chose a Committee of privileges to consider of double elections, which the said Committee is now sitting about. I must here, with Mr. Speaker, beg the favour of a benign construction of what I have written, fearing

I have been too bold in undertaking to deliver the heads of a speech whereof I was not suffered to take any notes, but I will make use of Martial's words for my apology:

Da veniam subitis non displicuisse meretur
Conatur studiis qui placuisse tibi.

. . . . I hear of a petition of some of the poorer sort of the King's officers are about to present to both Houses. The Duke of Ormond goeth for Portugal, and I desire a word from you whether you would advise me to go or not; I can get to go with the Duke. P.S. It is reported the Earl of Chesterfield goeth as General of the Fleet, who lately married the Duke of Ormond's daughter. I forgot to let you know the Chancellor told us the King intends a progress this summer in Worcestershire, and will, about the latter end of July, adjourn the Parliament.

Fol. 72. 1661, May 16. Old Palace Yard, at Mr. Aldridge's over against the Sun and Shears.—From the same to the same.—Yesterday the House spent in examining the impeachment that was given in against Sir John Marley, and after all, at last, referred him to the Common law; and I hear Mr. Liddle, his accuser, will let it fall, and so it will come to nothing. This morn was spent in providing a bill for securing the King's sacred person. The Lords have made an order that no petition shall be received by them that is not signed by a Grand jury; this day the great dispute between the Earls of Oxford and Lindsey was before the Lords; what was done in it I cannot hear; it was whether hath the more right to be Lord High Chamberlain of England. The Queen of Bohemia is landed at Gravesend and expected into town to-morrow. This evening my father's business came before the Committee for elections, whether he or his adversary were returned by the proper officer; my father was returned by the bailiff of the burrough chosen by the burghers to manage the election; Mr. Danby, his antagonist, is returned by the bailiff of the manor, who hath made former returns, and upon the question it was resolved neither bailiff had the right of returning burgesses, but that the right was in the burghers, and, therefore, neither party is to sit till the merits of the cause be heard. None appeared more against my father in this business than Sir Richard Temple, though a stranger to the other party.

Fol. 73. 1661, May 18, London. The same to the same.—As for my journey to Portugal, I shall scarce attempt it, by reason that neither the Duke of Ormond nor the Earl of Chesterfield goeth; only my Lord of Sandwich with whom I have no acquaintance. 'Tis reported here, but falsely, that the Prince Orange should be dead, of the small-pox. The Parliament have voted the League and Covenant to be burnt by the hand of the hangman and to be taken down in all churches and other public places. The Queen of Bohemia was landed this morn at two of the clock at Somerset stairs. Some Bills are preparing for indemnity, the settlement of the Militia, &c.

Fol. 74. 1661, May 28. The same to the same.— . . . Puerta Porta is not taken; Coll. Rudderforth is appointed governor of Dunkirk, a Scotchman; the Earl of Peterborough is Governor of Tangers, & yet we have of the Portugall by agreement in the mouth of the Straights; he is to choose whom he pleaseth for a deputy governor, and to have 15 companies of foot out of Dunkirk. This day some Acts of the late Rump Parliament were burned by the hand of the hangman by virtue of an order of Parliament to that effect. The Bill for the Militia takes up almost all the time in the House, and I cannot hear they have made any considerable progress in it yet. The warrant for the execution of Argyle is signed by the King, and sent down. To-morrow is a great feast here and I believe throughout the kingdom.

Fol. 75. 1661, May 30. The same to the same.—Yesterday was spent in solemnizing the great anniversary, which was observed in all churches very punctually, and a book printed on purpose for that day and published by the King's command. Doctor King, bishop of Chichester preached before the King; the close of the day was spent in ringing of bells and bonefires. This morn the House of Commons voted in the Bishops, and the repealing of the Act that excludes them; 'tis thought the Lords will scarce pass it with so little difficulty; some do not stick to say they will oppose it there. This morn also the Commoners voted the King a Benevolence; which, if every man's affections must be measured by their abilities in giving, will fall heavy upon the poor Cavalier, whose good will to His Majesty hath already drained their purses too much to be able to come in competition with the gaining Presbyter or serving neuter; many are highly displeased at these Benevolences, alleging it to be unparliamentary; but we think no man ought to be so, since in the House it was declared every man is left to his own will and discretion. I have here enclosed sent a list of the Lords of the Upper House.

Vol. IX.

Letters by Edward Gower, S. Charlton, W. Smith, Robert Shelton, Thomas Langley, Andrew and Francis Newport, and John and Charles Talbot.

1660, June 9, London. Edward Gower to Sir Richard Leveson.—Yesterday morning by five of the clock the King went for Hampton Court and returned before dinner; after dinner he had a conference with the Commons in the Banquetting house, where they gave him thanks for the gracious favour he had conferred upon them in giving them an Act of Indemnity, which they would accept of, and came to claim it in the name of the Commons of England. The King told them that as soon as they had excepted such as they would except he would confirm it, and desired them to do it with all the expedition possible. Here enclosed is a list of those that are already excepted out of the Act of Oblivion; more some report are already excepted, but I cannot hear it for certain, and therefore shall omit till I hear more. A party of horse went forth the last night to have apprehended Hugh Peters; they found clothes and writings but missed of him. Here is a report at Court that the Marquis de Caracena hath apprehended Scot in Flanders, and will send him over shortly, how true I know not, 'tis suspected. The French Embassador is gone and Prince Harcourt is to come over Embassador. The Queen Mother is sent to, to come over, and she must have her jointure. The King's chapel is making ready for him; amongst other things there are 12 singing boys provided, and a pair of organs setting up where Noll's seat was. We had the last week a great talk of the City's petition to the House of Commons against Bishops, but it was crusht in the shell, for (as I hear by some Parliament men) it was spoken of in the House and much resented which was the cause (the citizens having timely notice of it), it never came to light. Places here are none to be had for those that have not money to lay out. I am fearful my father will scarce get a grant confirmed which he had from the late King, though he hath it under his own hand, for the herbage of New Park in the Forest of Gawtress, not worth above 25l. per annum.

The names of those that are already excepted out of the Act of Indemnity: Major-General Harrison, Coll. John Joanes, Mr. Seay, Tho. Scot, Corn. Holland, Lord Lisle, John Backstead, Lieutenant of the Tower; Mr. Phellps, clerk; Cooke, Solicitor-General; Serjeant Dandy, Mr. Broughton. Some say Sir Hen. Mildmay who is prisoner in Dover Castle; he petitioned the Parliament to remove him to the Tower, for he thinks he shall be eaten up with lice where he is.

1660, Aug. 4, London.—The same to the same.—. . . The only tug is betwixt Episcopacy and Presbytery; the young men (though the old men who are generally presbyterians are more cunning) are careful not to be outvoted in this point; and though the Presbyter would have the church settled in Parliament, the other party are resolved to put it off with delay, and by that means compass their design, which is to have it settled by a Synod, where things may be fairly canvassed, after the dissolution of this Parliament. The chief rumour of the town is, and it is reported so at Court too though not credited, that the presbyterians of Scotland should be troublesome there and in arms. It is also reported that the Queen should be landed, which was caused by the going off of the guns at the Tower and the ringing of the bells. The reason of that noise was this, Alderman Robinson governor of the Tower, now Sir John Robinson, hath this day a son christened in the Tower, to whom His Sacred Majesty was godfather; great doings there was, and great feasting and banquetting. I hear Lambert, Vane, Haslerigge, and the rest of the prisoners were sent on shipboard during the time of the King's being in the Tower; the reason why is that the old custom ever was when the King came into the Tower to have all the prisoners released; this is only a bare conjecture.

1660, Aug. 7, London.—The same to the same. . . . Yesterday the House of Commons was very severe against the Bishops, and made an order they should have no power to let leases not till they had taken some order in that affair; this day they made the same, concerning Deans, Chapters, and Prebends.' The King had made an order empowering my father and another gentleman to keep this summer's profits of the Deans and Chapters'

lands of Yorkshire in their hands till it were decided by due course of law whose they were to be; which being told in the House, it was moved that my father might be sent for and examined by what means he had procured this warrant (which he knew not of till it was brought to him); but upon second thoughts he was not sent for; but this day I hear some of the House have prevailed so far with the King, as to call in the warrant and others of the same nature, in other countries. Here is a complaint at Court that the young men absent themselves from the House, and by that means give the old men, who are most of them presbyterians, the advantage; nor pleasure nor profit ought to be thought of where business of such concern as this of church government and purchasers' estates are in debate. This morning there happened an unlucky dispute in the House of Lords betwixt the Duke of Buckingham and my Lord of Bristoll.—(Gives an account of it much the same as in previous letters).—I hear the Lords are resolved to take the life of one Commissioner of each High Court of Justice that sat. P.S. My Lord Duke of Buckingham hath the regiment granted to him which was last Major-General Gibbons his; it lies now in Kent.

1660, April 26, London.—A Jamais (S. Charlton) to (Sir Richard Leveson).—Both Houses of Lords and House of Commons sat yesterday according to their appointment; there were of the Lords 18 or 20 the first day, and to-day it is thought there will be half as many more, and in the House of Commons there were above 300; the Lords have chosen the Earl of Manchester their Speaker, and the House of Commons have chosen Sir Harbottle Grimston for their Speaker; it is thought this Parliament will not sit above 3 weeks or a month, before which time be expired it is really believed that the King will be here, and then he will call a real Parliament; this is the opinion of most men.

1660, April 28, London.—The same to the same.—There hath been no new matter, nor like to be, till Tuesday next, because both Houses have adjourned till then, and have ordered a fast to be kept by both Houses upon Monday next at St. Margaret's, Westminster, where Dr. Reynalds, Dr. Gaudin, and Mr. Callamy, perform the exercise for the whole day. Some say that upon Tuesday the grand business for the voting of the bringing in of the King will be resolved upon.

1660, May 10. The same (to the same).—The two Houses of Parliament have voted the Crown and Bishop's lands to be restored; also they have voted the King to be sent for with all expedition; and therefore they have ordered General Montague to make all possible haste for Flushing, and by him they have ordered 30 thousand pounds to be sent to pay the King's charges. A Parliament man told me all this yesterday night, and moreover he assured me that, if it pleased God to send him a safe passage, that the King would be at Dover by Tuesday or Wednesday next, and that the Parliament Commissioners and the City Commissioners are resolved to set forth from hence toward Dover upon Monday next, and General Monk with some of his own troop and many volunteers and the auxiliaries of this city are ready to march towards Dover to meet the King and to conduct him in London; the Parliament man told me likewise that General Monk is to be created Duke of Somerset so soon as the King comes over; the same party told me that the House of Lords send down to the House of Commons that they would give their consent that they might have the nomination of the King's servants of his household, but they refused their motion and were very much discontented at them for it, and returned them answer that they thought it all the reason in the world that it should be left to his own freedom; the Houses have voted the King a hundred thousand pounds per annum in lieu of the Court of Wards; this day all shops have been shut up in this city and suburbs, and so strictly observed for thanksgiving in all churches for our deliverance from the late tyranny and oppression. P.S. I am told that the Oxford Lords do sit in the House.

1660, May 15, London. The same to the same. In his last he gave a hint of some proceedings in both Houses against those that sat in judgment upon the late King's death.—I shall now assure you that they do now very vigorously prosecute them, in so much that they make them fly, and they know not whither to go for shelter; for the hand of God is powerfully and justly against those cruel murderers, and no man pities them; they have voted that the Serjeant-at-arms shall forthwith take them all into safe custody and secure them, and order taken that all the ports of England, Scotland, and Wales shall take notice and apprehend them. The Parliament hath an exact register of all the names of those that had any hand in the King's trial, and all the passages to a man, to a day, to an hour, and to a tittle, of what passed in that trial; and I am told that the Parliament is resolved not to let any one man that is alive that had a hand in that trial escape without condign punishment; they have resolved already that seven or eight of them shall suffer without mercy or pardon, and some of the rest shall forfeit their whole estates, and the rest shall be banished. All that have bought Deans and Chapters' lands, and Bishops' lands, must restore them again, some to the King, which the persons are not living that possessed them before these times, and those that are living shall enjoy their own, and those that have bought Debentures at a low value must pay the full value or be reimbursed of their money they paid for them. The benefit of these businesses will be ordered by the Parliament. They say Coll. Joyce hath hanged himself. We shall not know yet who the persons be that are designed to suffer in this business without mercy. Tichborne is thought will be one, and Scot another. There are seven of them in the House, and they have submitted to the mercy of the Parliament. This is all I can learn of the proceeding in both Houses. By this time we suppose the Commissioners are arrived in Zealand, and will not be 12 hours after they are landed before they will be with the King, and after they are with the King, it is thought they will not stay above a day, but will wait upon His Majesty for England, and, if the wind stand fair, he may be at Dover upon Saturday night or Sunday next.

1660, June 3, London. S. Charlton to (Sir Richard Leveson). He had heard from a Parliament man, and a near friend, that the Parliament had not finished the qualifications which are to be mentioned in the Act of Pardon; eleven of them they have gone through and finished. They were also upon settling a tax of a hundred thousand pounds for 12 months, which money being raised, would pay all the nation's debts, so that afterwards there will be no more taxes. His friend also told him that,—yesterday Prin fell upon Sir Anthony Ashley Cooper, for putting his hand to the instrument to settle the Protector, and that my nephew Job Charlton seconded Prin, and was very violent against Sir Anthony; how he will come off my friend could not tell me. . . . The King and the two Dukes dined upon Saturday last at Roehampton, at the Countess of Devonshire's, and General Monk with them, where they were gallantly treated, and after dinner the King and the two Dukes danced with the ladies above an hour, and danced rarely well, as one that saw them dance told me, who hath very good judgment. . . . Sir Thomas Leigh is come to London; Mr. Charles Leigh's brother-in-law, Mr. Brown, is knighted. We have such a number of new knights and knight baronets made every day, that they are too common; a man may have a patent for a knight baronet for 300l. or 400l.; if any man in your country has a mind to one at that rate, I can procure him one. P.S. The French Embassador, Mons. de Bordeaux, that hath lain so long here, is gone for France; he would fain have had audience of the King, but He would not grant it him, nor hear of him, so that he was defeated and went privately away. The Queen Mother will be here very speedily, and the Princess Royal of Orange.

1660, May 19, London. A Jamais to (Sir Richard Leveson). They have been ever since upon the business of the late King's Tryars . . . . . have so frighted them that they are all fled and gone. . . . but here is a rumour that some of them are taken here. . . . . A strict order that all their estates shall be immediately seized . . . . , their persons apprehended and secured wheresoever they may be found. I doubt not but Mr. Thomas Langley doth constantly send you the weekly pamphlets that come forth. . . . . Here are several pictures in black and white of the King and his brother and General Monk, which I intend to send you some. We cannot yet hear that the King is come from the Hague; only it is supposed that he is there, because the last news that came from Breda was by one that came from thence, and was in Breda upon Friday last was a sennight, and then the King was there, and did intend to set from thence towards the Hague upon Monday last; and as this person was coming over he met the ships that carried the commissioners half seas over, so that it is thought they are with the King at the Hague, and that they will make all the haste with conveniency that possible may be for their return; but for these three or four days we have had very blustering winds, which do continue still, so that it is thought the King will not venture to sea 'till the weather be better settled; here are great preparations making both in Kent and Essex and in Suffolk for his entertainment and reception, and a

number here in the city only wait for the news of his landing, and then they resolve to begin with all expedition; and some say the General will not stir 'till then, because they are uncertain whether he will land in Kent or in Essex. Both the Houses have begun to do something in order to the settlement of Religion and Church government; they have absolutely confisked to the King's use all the estate of Oliver Cromwell, deceased, and Pride's and Bradshaw's, and Ireton's that married Cromwell's daughter, and own nobody that are tenants to the King's lands, or dean and chapters' or delinquents' lands will pay one farthing of rent. Sir William Brearton at Croydon had caused a great deal of wood to be taken upon the Bishop's lands, but nobody dare buy it or carry it away. My Lord Leigh came to town two days ago; but neither he nor my Lord Newport will sit in the House till the King comes, &c.

1660, May 22, London.—The same to the same.—Gives an account of the preparations to meet the King at Dover, and of the intended escort to London and his reception there . . . . The wind being now very fair, we expect that he will be at Dover by to-morrow night. Here is such a general desire of his arrival, the like was never known. I heard yesterday for a certain that it was Hugh Peters that struck off the late King's head, and there is one that will take oath of it.

1660, June 30. W. Smith to Mr. John Langley.— Here are daily expected Embassadors from all Princes; none are yet come but a Dutch Embassador and an envoy from Brandenburg. . . . The Duke of Epernon is expected to be here next week from France as an extraordinary Embassador; and then the Lord Jermyn Earl of St. Alban is to go for France in the like condition, and is also to bring our gracious Queen and her most beautiful Princess Royal the Lady Henrietta, who now resides with Her Majesty. The Parliament have advanced and presented 20,000l. for Her Majesty's accommodation at present; and such of her lands as they have rescued from the rebels are again returned into Her Majesty's possession. The Parliament endeavour to raise estates for their Royal Highnesses the two Dukes out of the confiscations of such traitors as they daily convict; as yet none of the villains are brought to their arraignment, because the Courts of justice are not filled, nor are either of the Chief justices as yet appointed. His Majesty and his royal brothers are daily feasted; till yesterday they were usually entertained at supper; but then the Earl of Middlesex feasted them magnificently at his house at Copthall, after they had spent the morning in hunting with great content in Waltham forest. This day they are all gone to Roehampton near Putney to be princely entertained by the Countess Dowager of Devonshire, where it is hoped the same will savour of Aurum Potabile or rather Portabile. . . . We have now little said of our great General (whose titles he sets forth). General Mountagu is Earl of Portsmouth, Lord Admiral in present charge under the Duke, and Knight of the Garter. P.S. As yet men of my loyalty have only [our] mouths filled with laughter, and our heav[   ]. His Majesty, having not hitherto found enough in honours and offices to satisfy his enemies, expects his loyal friends will stay till he be more able; nevertheless some unhappy wit, amongst other queries scattered in a paper in the Privy Chamber made one whether it were not fit His Majesty should pass an Act of Indemnity for his enemies and of Oblivion for his friends.

1660, June 30, London.—The same to the same.— Last Thursday was a day set apart for thanksgiving for His Majesty's restoring to his lawful inheritance, which was performed very zealously in all churches here in the City and in all neighbour parishes in these parts. Yesterday I spake with my Lord Leigh, who told me that there was little or nothing done in the Lords' House; for it was motioned there that the House should adjourn 'till Tuesday next, but it was carried to the contrary; and the reason was because of the daily vast charge of 2,000l. a day for the army, and therefore it was necessary that they should not adjourn but rather use all labour and diligence to take burden off the nation; so that [it] is supposed that that business will be the chiefest employment of both the Houses 'till they have found out some remedy to take it off; the Presbyterians have been very busy and earnest to hinder the settlement of religion in the Episcopal government, and many Scots are come hither to assist that work; but they cannot prevail. Alderman Sir John Robinson is made Lieutenant of the Tower, and they say Major-General Massy shall be Major of the city militia. I was yesterday at Dorset House. . . . It seems the Chancellor Hyde hath his lodgings in that house, and in the hall he keeps the Seal such days in the afternoon according

Cc 3

as he doth appoint it. P.S. The King went yesterday to Copt-Hall to hunt the buck; the Lords invite the King very oft, and the two Dukes, and [He] is very freely merry with them, and he will not have them provide above ten or twelve dishes for him at most.

1660, July 7, London. The same to the same.—The Bill of Indemnity and qualifications therein to be inserted are not yet finished, which is all the business the House of Commons, upon the main, have been employed in this week past. Upon Thursday last the great entertainment of the King, the two Dukes of York and Gloucester, and all the Lords and Commons of Parliament was performed with as much sumptuousness as can be imagined, which cost the city as it is reported about 5,000l.; but the day was not so favourable as it could have been wished, which did wholly eclipse the glory of it; for it rained all the forenoon and most part of the afternoon, so that the King and all the nobles came in coaches, which otherwise were resolved to have passed through the city on horseback; which if it had performed after that manner, would have been a very glorious sight, for all the citizens were prepared in all their gallantry in as high a manner as when he first came into England.

1660, Aug. 4, London.—(The same to the same? The signature is torn off.) The only business that hath passed in the House of Lords since my last is that they have excepted four more for life then were excepted before, that is to say they have left them out of the Bill of Indemnity, to be tried by the law; and these four are Sir Arthur Haselrig, Sir Henry Vane, Major Lambert, and Collonel Hacker; they say there is one more or two, but I cannot tell their names for certain; but the report goes that Desborow is one of them. I hear that His Majesty hath given out warrants to take possession of all his lands in all counties, and immediately to take them out of the hands of all those that have bought them, during the Rebellion, and the like speedy course is taken for Deans and Chapters and Bishops' lands. I heard another say that those that have bought the King's lands do proffer the King two hundred thousand pounds and the fifth part of the true value of the yearly rent if His Majesty will pass the lands over to them by a fee farm, and they will pay him the fee farm rent besides; which His Majesty will not hearken to as I am told. The Bill of Indemnity cannot be yet passed in the Lords House. His Majesty is gone this morning to the Tower, to be godfather to a child of Sir John Robinson's, Lieutenant of the Tower. I hear Sir Thomas Midelton is made a viscount, Sir George Booth, a baron, and Mr. Perpoint, a baron; the Lord Robarts is to go deputy for Ireland.

1660, Aug. 7, London.—The same to the same.—The Bill of Indemnity is not yet past in the House of Lords, neither is it like to pass in haste; for I am told that the Lords have had several conferences with the House of Commons, but cannot agree upon several particulars which the Lords would have altered in their Bill; and likewise the Lords would have many more excepted in the Bill, which the House of Commons will not consent unto; and that the case stands at present 'twixt the two Houses, so that the House of Commons lets the Lords go on in their work, and the meantime the House of Commons are fallen [to] the business of the Church government; and the King lets them both alone, and he settles the Bishops both for Ireland and England, and his own chaplain for his household; but I hear that yesterday there was an untoward falling out betwixt the Duke of Buckingham and the Earl of Bristol, &c., &c.

. . . . As for Whitehall, it is every day in the morning as full that a man can scarce wedge in between them; a number of the clergymen and the rest petitioners for proferment and places about the court. Here are seven of our East India ships lately arrived in the Downs from several parts of those Indies that belong to the new joint stock; my Lord Leigh hath got leave of the House to go home for a month or such a matter for his health's sake, so that to-morrow he goes thence towards Stoneleigh; and from thence as I understand he intends to go to the Bath. This day I saw Mr. Goode here in London, who is newly come from Oxford, where this last act he proceded Doctor.

1660, July 9, London.—Robert Shelton to Mr. John Langley.—Since my coming hither it hath been my whole business to wait upon Mr. Andrew Newport and Mr. Sharington Talbot. I delivered Mr. Andrew Newport both letter and token, who orders me to call upon him a little before my coming down. Mr. Talbot orders me to come to him to-morrow morning by six of the clock, for he intends to present the gold to His Majesty before ten of the clock, for he is ordered by the King to come pt.

(post?) to-morrow to the Lord Digby's about some business of concernment, and from Cossll intends our master to visit at Trentham, and give him an account from His Majesty concerning the reception of the purse which I have bought and in readiness against morning; this day hath . . . . . play day for His Majesty, Dukes, General, and . . . . others accompanying them have been pr . . . . . feasted at Yeild Hall by the Lord Mayor . . . . . the Assizes are not yet known; there are no m[ore new] Judges yet added, only Judge Atkins in the Exchequer and made knight, &c. (Seal, a pelican in her piety with R. H. in right hand corner.)

1660, April 28, London. Samuel Torrick to Sir R. Leveson. Yesterday being Friday, the House adjourned till Tuesday next, and then at 8 o'clock in the morning it meets to take into consideration the grand business for a settlement; for till that be perfected nothing will be binding that we do. . . . . . It is whispered that the General hath a letter from the King to present to the House; if so, then shall have it Tuesday; he intends to cast himself wholly upon his Parliament.

1660, May 8, London. Samuel Torricke to Lady Katherine Leveson. Mentions the proclamation of the King in Palace Yard and other places, and the Houses' desire for the King's speedy return, and that the House has appointed a committee to consider of a yearly revenue for the King, with power to receive information &c., for the discovery of the Crown Jewels, &c.

1660, May 15, London. The same to the same.—Mentions that the Commissioners of both Houses with a letter signed at Sion House by 118 ministers Episcopal and Presbyterian had gone to meet the King at Breda, and that it is expected that the King will stay at Cobham House for some days on his landing.—Parliamentary news.—There is 10,000l. sent the Duke of York, and 5,000l. to the Duke of Gloucester; the King of Spain hath presented His Majesty 25,000l.; the Dutch, it is believed, will present him with a very considerable sum; there will be a discovery made of 20,000l. to a committee of Parliament; likewise there hath been seized goods to a great value which were concealed [by] Mrs. Elizabeth Cromwell, late wife to Oliver. . . . . . This day the House hath assigned 30,000l. for the putting of Whitehall, St. James, and Somerset House into order for the reception of the King. This day Secretary Thurlo is charged with high treason, and ordered to be taken into custody. P.S. Alderman Viner, a goldsmith, is ordered this day to provide a crown and sceptre with all speed.

1660, 3 July, London. Samuel Terricke to Sir Richard Leveson.—Mr. Ayliffe tells me that he hath acquainted you that my Lord Seamer, Chancellor of the Duchy, hath appointed you Lord Steward as formerly, which I know will be pleasing to the copyholders. Your name is inserted in the address to His Majesty.

Letters by Mr. Thomas Langley.

1660, April 26. Thomas Langley (to Sir Richard Leveson).—Yesterday in Parliament when the Lords s[ent] to the Commons to join with them in observing of [the] fast next Monday, Luke Robinson stood up and asked the Speaker who made them a House of Lords? and to that purpose, having done what he had to say, Henry Finch the Councillor spoke, and told the Speaker that they had heard a very good sermon that morning by Dr. Reynolds, who told them they were to be the physicians and healers of the nation, being sorry that the gentleman that spoke last should forget it so quickly in moving that question, (or to the same purpose), desiring the Speaker that it might be put to the vote whether there was a House of Lords or no, which was done, and the House generally formed it.

1660, May 8. The same to the same.—Account of the King's proclamation by the Lord Mayor, &c. (which he sends in print).

A letter of the same date to his uncle Mr. John Langley, giving a similar description.

1660, May 11. The same to Sir R. Leveson.—To-morrow the King is to be proclaimed in Southwark by our Lord Mayor, &c.

[1660] May 12. Thomas Langley to Sir Richard Leveson. The Commissioners are gone towards the King; those of the army that are appointed march about Tuesday or Wednesday next; there's a thousand apprentices and young gentlemen out of the city are to go all in white doublets with bloome colour scarfs about them to bring the King in, who go on foot. Whitehall is fitting up for His Majesty's reception. . . . The prisons here grow full of such as cannot rule their tongues, and many of the grand rebels are run away. The old beldam protecteris is also gone; being searched after, ten load of her rich goods were seized last night by the water side, in a costardmonger's house, supposed for to be shipped away.

1660, May 19. The same to the same.—There is a report that the King is gone to Amsterdam, invited by that place to receive their treatment, who its said will present His Majesty with 100,000l. and from thence will take the first wind to come for England, &c.—Five of the late King's judges, with Haselrig, Liles, Scott, Mildmay, and another taken near Dover.—Orders for the King's reception.

1660, May 22. The same to the same.—We expect to hear every hour of the King's landing. . . . General Monk, it's said, marches to-morrow with his lifeguard only; the rest of the army lies still, there being several volunteer troops of gentlemen and citizens very richly habited and bravely mounted led by several eminent persons, as Coll. Robinson, the troop of citizens all in buf cotes very richly laced, the Lord Mordant a troop of Spanish merchants, all in black velvet coats, the Lord Maynard a troop of Essex gentlemen, Squire Hales a troop of Kentish gentlemen, the Earl of Northampton another troop, and his brother Sir William Compton leads a troop called the Lady Monk's troop, and some others go to meet the King and march away to-morrow. Disborrow was brought prisoner to town this night out of Essex. To-morrow the Papists are to be banished from about the City.

1660, May 24. The same to the same.—The King came to anchor yesterday morning at 9 o'clock in Dover road; a letter being sent to the General Monk that His Majesty would not land till Monk came to him, which post met Monk at Greenwich as he was going, who so soon as he had read the letter drove away with all speed, saying he would not sleep till he came to His Majesty, which is conceived he is before this time, and that the King is not yet landed; for as soon as he lands, the great guns are so ordered and laid along the coasts in forts and ships which are to take the report one from another, till it come to the Tower of London, that we shall hear of it in three or four hours time, when the King lands; besides the life guards and several commanders of the army, there is gone first the Lord Maynard's troop, next the Earl of Northampton's troop, next went Coll. Robinson's troop, next the Spanish merchants, Mr. Fowler leading one of the divisions of it with their footboys in white doublets; last went the Duke of Buckingham with his troop; all these are volunteers in such high equipage not to be expressed. This day went two army regiments, the Lord Howard's, and the Lord Falkland's; the commanders and officers rich and brave. General Browne is preparing to be not inferior for garb to march out some ten miles that day the King comes through the city. P.S. Brown's troop are in silver doublets, and their swords hung in black scarfs.

1660, June 7. The same to the same.—There past in the House this morning to be exempted from pardon five more besides the seven in the book; Coll. Harrison scorns to ask pardon; he saith the Protector kept him in prison a great while, and now the King is come he will take away his life and ease him of that trouble.

1660, June 16. The same to the same.—You shall receive by the carrier the Act for Assessment, wherein your honour is a Commissioner for Staffordshire; there's some thirteen agreed on by the Parliament towards making up the 20 that are to be excepted, besides those that were the King's judges. Whitlock is got off with much ado; they are coming among our Aldermen again; the Earl of Salisbury shall be degraded it's said. The King and Dukes are all gone by now to the Lord Mayor's to a supper or banquet in their coaches, it being about 10 o'clock at night.

1661, May 16. Robert Milward to Sir Richard Leveson.—The Presbyterian is so inconsiderable in the House that the more prudent men of that party are silent. An Act passed the House this day, and ordered to be ingrossed, wherein the Covenant is condemned, as also the legislative power of the Lords and Commons without or against the King; and whosoever shall by word seek to maintain either incurs the penalty of a Premunire: it is ordered that the Committee of confirmation of public acts shall not ravel into the late acts of the court of wards, the judicial proceedings, His Majesty's revenues and the Act of Oblivion. I can assure you the last would never have received a full confirmation, however it may yet fall out, but in obedience to His Majesty's desires, who is not only the Sovereign but the favourite of the kingdom. As to the Act concerning Ministers, I believe we shall make bold to correct it. The Queen of Bohemia is landed, and daily expected here.

[1660], May 12, Saturday. Andrew Newport to Sir Richard Leveson. The commissioners of both Houses went hence yesterday towards the King, and 'tis believed they will meet him upon his way, so that we expect him here this day sevennight at farthest: much company will go hence on Monday and Tuesday to meet him at his landing. . . . To-day the House was upon the Act of Indemnity, and in discourse of what persons were concerned in putting the King to death; young Lenthall said that those persons which first raised arms against the King were equally guilty of the King's death with those that sate in judgment upon him; which so enraged the Presbyterians that he was ordered to withdraw, and it was much pressed he should be sent to the Tower and expelled the House; but at last he was only called to the bar upon his knees, where he recanted, and was restored to his place. Those members that were the King's judges and to-day in the House were required to speak for themselves. Coll. Ingolsby began, and confessed his fault with great penitence, and desired the mercy of the House, which he will undoubtedly have; after him four more did the like, Morley, Gourdon, &c., but what their lot will be is uncertain; several in the same qualification are run away; Sir H. Mildmay, Scott, &c. Commissioner Lisle hath put a petition into the hands of several members, but it will not be read in the House. There are two captains sent hither to-day from the fleet, and put in irons into the Tower, for designing to blow up the ship that the King should board; this makes it believed the King will come privately hither; besides that several desperate persons threaten him much when he comes, some of which are daily sent to prison. Mr. Pryn told the House to-day that he would discover 200,000l. sent hither to the factions party to enable them to keep out the King; and a Committee is appointed to consult about it; 'tis said that the Cardinal sent it and offered further assistance of money and men. The fleet is ordered to be at the King's command, and he is desired to make haste to the exercise of his regal power. P.S. Coll. Okay went to the King t'other day, and was on his knees to ask the King's pardon for being one of his father's judges, but the King referred him to the Parliament.

1660, Aug. 7, London. Fra. Newport to Sir Richard Leveson. The Act of Indemnity, I believe, will not now long stay with the Lords; this week I think will give a despatch to it, if the Commons will agree to those' alterations by them made, which is doubtful. This day the Lords agreed upon one of every Court of justice that sat upon their own members to be excepted out of the Act of Indemnity, and that the nearest relations of those Lords who suffered should name those single persons, and likewise, I should have told you, one of the Court martial to be excepted who sat upon the Earl of Derby. My Lord of Derby for that court named Croxton; Lord Paget for Lord of Holland, whose daughter he married, named one Blackwell, that is dead, and would name no other; Lord of Denbigh, for Duke Hamilton, who married his sister, named one Wibert; and my Lord Capell, for his father, named our countryman Waringe the late sheriff; and these four are as they now stand wholly excepted out of the Act. The Pole money bill stays for the Act of Oblivion, which the Commons will have go hand in hand with it; all private provisoes which have been offered to the Bill of Oblivion are agreed by the Lords to be laid aside, which otherwise would never have retarded the passing of the Bill. . . . We can have no answer yet from the House of Commons concerning our writings by which we passed away the impropriations; some of them say they have them not, and many of the Presbyterians labour hard to have them confirmed to the churches; but I hope we shall prevent them by a Bill first put in for the restoring of them to us; in the meantime we gather them de facto. Prince de Liague is expected Embassadour from Spain, but the King can get ne'er a House here to receive him. The last letters from France said the Cardinal continued ill. No Master of the Rolls is yet named here. 'Tis said the match is agreed on between Monsr. of France (the King's brother) and our young Princess Henrietta Maria, who is said to be one of the handsomest ladys in the world. No doubt my brother Andrew hath told you that as the Act of Indemnity now stands with the Lords, all that sentenced the King or signed his death are wholly excepted, and only four more wholly excepted, which are four of those twenty the House of Commons sent up to be excepted, but not as to life; and these four to-day named before; how far the House of Commons will agree with us in these votes we yet know not.

[1661], May 21. Robert Leveson to Sir Richard Leveson.—Yesterday there was a conference of both

Houses, and there was imparted to them letters from
Scotland importing that the Scots having made it appear
how much they rejoice in the happy restoration of His
Majesty to his most just and undoubted right, and
having by their actions given signal testimonies of their
faithful zeal and affection as well as obedience, they
now desire that His Majesty will trust them so far as to
trust them with their own country, and will please to
take out all the English garrisons, and only reserve
some small inconsiderable English force in some few
centre places which His Majesty shall think most fit.
The same day the King was at the House to put them
in mind that they should not offer to entrench upon
the Act of Indemnity; this day the Bill for the Militia
was passed in the House of Commons, intituled to be an
Act for the further securing and preserving the King's
person and these kingdoms. I suppose you have heard
already of the resolves for burning the Covenant; and
this day the Lords passed the same, and to-morrow it is
to be burned in the Palace Yard, Westminster, and over
against the New Exchange, Temple Bar, Fleet Conduit,
and Cheapside, and over against the Old Exchange, by
the hand of the common hangman.

n. y., April 26. John Talbot to Sir Richard Leveson.
—The Gazette only omits this, that yesterday four of
the nobility took their places in their House; Earls of
Middlesex, Dorset, Rivers, and Lord Peters; some of
the others which are under the notion of the young
nobility, that is such who are no otherwise incapable
of sitting but because they acted not heretofore with
the Lords, they have been desired to forbear for a few
days, but 'tis believed will shortly sit also : this day we
requited their kindness, for we sent Mr. Herbert to
acquaint them that the House had appointed this day
fortnight for a day of thanksgiving to be observed in
London and Middlesex, and this day month for the rest
of the nation, and desired their concurrence, which
they assented to; this morning was spent in the nominating a Committee of privileges, and this afternoon
they did sit to consider of double returns, which are
many, and report thereon to-morrow to the House ;
the bugbear of qualifications is not yet taken notice of,
and I do not find the temper of the House to be so
Rumpish.

1660, May 15th. Charles Talbot to Sir Richard Leveson. 'Tis believed that the King will be at Dover upon
Thursday night next, and that General Monk and we all
shall march out of Town that day to meet him' in as
much glory and gallantry as the time will permit, and
we hope his coronation day will be the 29th of this
month which is his birthday. The Houses sit close, and
are upon the question of the late King's murtherers ;
and some say not above seven of the Judges that are
living will be spared. Thurloe was this day impeacht
of high treason, and we hear apprehended ; who yesterday said that if he were hanged 'he had a black book
which should hang half of them that went for Cavaliers,
from which accusation you and I are free. Dick Willis
and his brother are condemned of treason. The murtherers of the King were so confident in their villainy
that they have left their names and seals in a book
covered with black velvet which now discovers them.
A ship is stopped that was carrying two hundred thousand pounds in money and goods over for the King's
service.

1660, July 2, London. The same to the same.—
Thanks Sir Richard for his letter and says that in the
latter part of it he desires Talbot to recommend him to
the King ; promises to do it, but urges him to do it
himself " knowing you are (as you have ever deserved
" to be) highly valued by the King, who does not forget
" such friends, and the addition which you intend to
" confirm it by, being so highly noble, will both imprint
" you in his memory for ever and be a great advantage
" to me although but your messenger." . . . . The
factious here hinder the justice which we expected upon
several wicked men condemned and of more daily taken ;
the settling of the King's revenue and the militias of
the counties, the Deputy lieutenants not being nominated ; nor do we know what will become of our guards ;
for one day 'tis reported we shall stand, and the next
that we shall not ; but if so all will not go well. P.S.
The King hath made choice of an army regiment of
horse to be his own, and great men will be officers in it,
and I hope good men soldiers. The two Dukes have
each a regiment also.

1660, Aug. 7, London. The same to the same.—
Although I find the King still gracious to me, yet other
people supplant me in all my designs, so that I have the
good fortune to serve my friends but cannot benefit
myself any way; therefore I intend not to stay long
here , , , , , . The Lords have this day voted that

four men which did judge the four Lords should die, of
which old Waring and Coll. Croxston are two ; and the
Act of Indemnity is past their House, and to be sent to
the Commons, who this day sent to them the Bill for
Pole-money, and they are hastening the Bill for Excise, after which 'tis thought the Parliament will be
adjourned or dissolved . . . . .

1707. An account of what bucks have been killed in
Lillieshall Park by Francis Salt, keeper of the said park.
Total 21.

1710, May 8. A copy of inventory and appraisement
of the goods, cattles, and chattells of John Lord Gower,
baron of Stitnam, taken at Lillieshall Lodge in the co.
of Salop upon the 23rd of Feb. 1709. (Total 70l. 19s. 6d.)
There are many letters from J. White, who was evidently a steward or bailiff, to Lady Gower.

1709, June 25th, Newcastle. Will. Burslem to Lord
Gower. In a postscript,—At the sealing up of this Mr.
Thos. Fenton brought me the inclosed poem made by
his brother Elijah who is schoolmaster at Seven Oak in
Kent ; it is intended to be printed, but not without your
Lordship's approbation, which is desired may be known ;
it will not be printed alone, but with other poems of the
like nature.

1710, Oct. 11. Trentham. Pa. Wood to Lady Gower
at Belvoir. The election for this county at a meeting of
the gentlemen on Wednesday last was settled, and Mr.
Paget and Mr. Ward agreed on for this time, and Mr.
Bagott the next ; Sir Bryan Br . . . ns interest was
taken little notice of, and what he had he offered to
Mr. Ward in hopes to have kept open the breach between Mr. Bagott and him, but is happily prevented by
their accommodation. Mr. Foley and Mr. Chetwind are
returned for Stafford Town ; but Mr. Hen. Vernon
petitions against the latter upon the right of the
electors, and hath a good colour for it.

A poem, intituled " Dr. Wilds Ghost on His Majesty's
declaration for liberty of conscience, April 4th 1687.
(84 lines)—

Begin, How liberty of conscience that a change
        Bilks the crape gown and mortifies L'Estrange.

Vol. X.

Letters by Lord North, Lord Thurlow, William Pitt,
and others.

Eleven Letters by Lord North to Earl Gower.

1771, June 13. Downing Street.—Has received a
summons to a Council at St. James's. If necessary, he
will be there, otherwise he will be glad to be excused.
" I am now, like Prince Volscius, with one boot on and
" the other off, and wait for your Lordship's decision."
" P.S. I have written by His Majesty's command to
" the Bishop of Lichfield and Coventry, to offer him the
" vacant bishoprick of Durham."*

(1771), Sept. 30. Sir Lawrence Dundas not having
received much benefit from the great doctor Le Fevre
is advised to pass the ensuing winter at Nice. He
presses for the dignity of a Privy Councillor before
going abroad. Lord North wishes that the request had
not been made, but the King consents if Lord Gower
has no objection.

1773, July 22, Bushey Park. In order to accommodate the holders of unlawfully diminished coin, to
forward the purposes of the Act passed in the last
session of Parliament, and to restore the gold coin of
these kingdoms if possible to its legal value without a
re-coinage, the Treasury has proposed to the Bank to
receive all unlawfully diminished gold money by weight
at 3l. 17s. 10½d. per oz., and have promised to recommend to Parliament to indemnify them for any loss
they may suffer by carrying this measure into execution.
The Treasury has directed the inclosed order † to be sent
to the receiver of the Public revenue. . . . . The
necessity of taking this step without delay has prevented
me from communicating it previously to His Majesty's
confidential servants, but I hope you will not disapprove
of it.

1773, Oct. 18, Bushey Park.—Sends a copy of an
extraordinary and rather captious letter which he
received last night. As it equally concerns the rest of
His Majesty's servants, he has desired a Cabinet to be
called on Thursday next to consider of the answer which
it may be proper to return.

1774, Sept. 30, Downing Street. His Majesty has
this day dissolved his Parliament, and I am no longer a
member of the House of Commons. I hope, however,
very soon again to be in that august assembly and to

* See the letter by Lord Uxbridge, p. 213, col. 2.
† Not with the letter.

meet all your Lordship's friends there. . . . . Has written to Mr. Whitworth who, he thinks, has been misrepresented to Earl Gower.

1774, Sept. 30, Downing Street. When I wrote to your Lordship yesterday I forgot the principal business I had to mention, viz., that the Lords of the Cabinet at London and in the neighbourhood have thought it right to make some alteration in the list of the 16 Peers and to remove those Lords who are not able to give due attendance in Parliament. In consequence, your Lordship's brother-in-law, Lord Dunmore, will be omitted, but another brother-in-law of your Lordship, Lord Galloway, will be put in his room. If Lord Dunmore should return to England to reside here he will certainly have a preferable claim upon a vacancy. Your Lordship will find one peer left in the list whose attendance in the House of Lords is not very constant, but we trust you will not complain of our partiality, though his name is continued there, and Lord Dunmore's omitted; I mean the Earl of Bute. I shall see Lord Mount-Stuart this morning, and ask him if his father chooses to continue. If he does, a Dowager first Lord of the Treasury has a claim to this distinction, and we do not now want a coup d'état to persuade the most ordinary newspaper politician that Lord B. is nothing more. . . . . Either Mr. Robinson or myself will be always upon the spot (Downing Street) during these bustles.

(1776, Nov. 20; so indorsed), Downing Street.—"Some "days I spoke with your Lordship at James's, I had "received His Majesty's directions to acquaint Lord "Buckingham with his intention of nominating him "to the Lieutenancy of Ireland, but I had not executed "his commands, having been stopped by a conversation "His Majesty had held with Lord Dartmouth. Lord "Buckingham was certainly not the first object of my "choice. But when he applied to me I told him that "if the persons whom I had recommended should not "succeed, I should be glad to see the Lieutenancy "conferred upon him." All his recommendations having failed, he was obliged by his engagement with Lord Buckingham to propose him. "His Majesty hesi-"tated for some time, but having no objection to the "person, and perceiving how I stood pledged, he gave "me authority to apprize Lord Buckingham of it which "he has since confirmed." But for these circumstances he would gladly have obeyed Earl Gower's commands in soliciting the Lieutenancy for Lord Carlisle.

1778, Feb. 10, Downing Street.—Compliments Lord Gower on the public-spirited offer which he had made, but says that there is no new arrangement on foot, nor could there be any arrangement with the interest of the King and public by which Lord Gower could be permitted to leave his present situation. All that had passed respecting a great man (which was very little) had been communicated to Mr. Rigby, and it did not amount to much. Most of the members of Parliament whom I have been able to sound prefer a declaration that the British Parliament will not tax America to the repeal of any Acts. The latter measure is equally mortifying, but the former more effectual to the purpose of inducing the Colonies to treat with this country. The possibility of levying taxes in America by the authority of Parliament is universally given up, and therefore they say that nothing material is lost; besides that, if an expectation of a contribution on the part of America is held out, and that business seriously recommended to the Commissioners, this measure is more consistent with my conciliatory proposition than the other. I wish to have your Lordship's opinion on that point, and for that purpose to see you here with the rest of the Cabinet at 11 o'clock to-morrow morning.

1778, May 8, Friday night, 10 o'clock, Downing Street.—A note of three lines, with a copy of the following letter—

1778, May 8. Lord North to Lord Sandwich. (Private.) I have shown your Lordship's letter, the letter which you received from Admiral Duff, and the list of the Spanish fleet, together with the inclosed extract of the advices from Paris, to Lord Weymouth, Lord Dartmouth, Lord Gower, and Lord George Germain. They are all of opinion that nothing contained in these papers will justify a change in the destination of Admiral Byron's fleet; they continue to think that every dispatch should be used to send the fleet off to North America, unless you should, before the departure, receive certain accounts that the Toulon fleet is arrived at Cadiz, and either continues there, or has sailed in a route which clearly indicates that its destination is towards a different quarter of the globe. I think it highly probable that you may already have received by the Proserpine such intelligence as must put out of doubt the proper line to

be followed. In the meanwhile the sentiments of all the Cabinet Ministers in town are unanimous for sending the fleet to North America as soon as it can sail. It may be the intention of Spain to assist Mr. D'Estaign with a squadron in his expedition to North America. In that case, it is to be wish'd that our fleet should be stronger, and this contrary wind, if it continues, will afford an opportunity of adding some ships to Mr. Byron's squadron. Although I am not one of those who think an invasion of these islands impracticable, nor am convinced that France and Spain will not attempt it, yet I think the enterprise so arduous that they will not for some time be able to carry such a project into execution. The danger of our army and fleet in North America appears to me more probable and more immediate. Besides, altho' I pay little credit to the sincerity of the Court of Spain, and believe that they harbour very hostile designs against us, I cannot conceive it possible that they would hold such a pacific language just at the very moment that they intend to unite in an attack upon our possessions in Europe. P.S. If you can contrive to send a ship load of prisoners to be exchanged in America, I should think it advisable to do it without delay.

1779, Oct. 17, Waldersh.—The King not having any prospect of forming an Administration upon the plan of a coalition with parts of the Opposition, which promises in His Majesty's opinion any good to himself or the public, has ordered me to resume my former plan, and I have accordingly written to Lord Carlisle according to what I mentioned to your Lordship last week, notwithstanding the little hopes your Lordship's conversation gave me . . . . . His acceptance of a place at this moment can give you no uneasiness, and will not appear to you inconsistent with the close connexion which subsists between you.

No date.—Informing Lord Gower (lest the King's message had not reached him) that the King intended to appoint Lord Bathurst President of the Council to-morrow.

Twenty-two letters by Lord Thurlow to Lord Gower.[*] The earliest are indorsed as 1779, Oct. 12 and 18, and Feb. 1780. These, and one without indorsement are seemingly political, but written in such obscure terms, that few, if any, but the addressee could understand them. That of Feb. 1780 relates some talk with Lord No. (North).

[1780, Feb. 7.] . . . . . Your objection is indisputable; first because it is a matter of feeling which is not directly a subject of dispute; and, secondly, because leaving your proxy with a Minister might have been thought liable to cut very close, if not to cross the idea on which you resigned . . . . . . But I don't suppose the same objection would have lain against giving it to the Duke, who seems to have stood all along in the same situation in which you are now placed.

1781, Sept. In this, after remarking upon the affectionate and intelligent nature of Leveson (Lord Gower's son), he says, "I suspect that the reason why promising "parts so often disappoint the expectations conceived of "them, is because they are not taught to command "their attention. It seems to be the habit of attention "which produces memory, reasoning and the other "powers which are comprised in the general word "understanding; and attention seems to be the effect "of curiosity; and that again is abundantly excited in "lively minds by all things around them, particularly "new objects; but the ideas must be simple or at least "distinct, and perfectly comprehensible; and in the "ordinary course of accident, elementary notions, such "as science is made up of, certainly do not stand the "fairest chance . . . . What I propose will appear "a strange substitute for a dry employment (i.e., the "exercise of learning mere words), but I fancy it will be "attended with other advantages which will make the "experiment a good one. It is Arithmetick, to be "followed up afterwards with Geometry, and at length "Algebra. All which I verily believe a boy might well "master before he goes to the University; and if not "before, not one in a thousand will master them after-"wards; and yet they are the indispensable foundation "of a great part of science, which is both useful and "ornamental; and for the rest, they form a kind of "practical logick, of ten times more use than the art "so called, which for the most part is rather a curious "refining upon language, attended, however, I admit "with no inconsiderable advantages . . . . At what-"ever time of life they are learnt, the rationale of them

_____

[*] Two undated; only two or three have his name signed; some have only T., and some have no signature. Lord Gower has on some indorsed dates, probably of the days when he received them.

" is so immense that the elements must at first be got
" merely by rote."

. In the following (undated) letter on the same subject,
Lord Thurlow says : " If they were compatible, I should
" prefer Arithmetic and Geometry to Languages. . . .
" Besides, I am afraid, that if these dry elements are
" not learned early, they will not have so good a chance
" for attention afterwards as Languages will."

1782, July 6, Saturday. . . . The measure and
degree of the present agitation remain uncertain, and .
still more the time and manner of its subsiding Lord
Rockingham's death opened the scene. You know the
lictors and their parts. Had he lived through another
session, the machinery (there is room to imagine at least)
would have broke down ; not so much by the incongruity
of, its essential parts and internal construction, as for
want of external bearing and sufficient effect upon the
object it should have acted upon. . . . Upon the
death of Lord Rockingham the principal pretender to the
succession was Charles Fox. If that had proceeded
smoothly, the place would have been occupied with more
energy ; but the measure might have met with some
degree of unfavourable acceptance to counterbalance
that. The last idea, or some other wishes of the party
prevented the pretension from taking that simple, form,
and the Duke of Portland's name was held forth, or some
other without naming him of a similar description. The
King cut this short by naming Lord Shelburne ; explaining that such was his original idea in the forming
the new Administration ; but that way was given to Lord
R. personally. The party professed to acquiesce for
some time ; and even Charles Fox seemed to think it
might be endured, if other arrangements, and particularly the new modelling of the Cabinet, were admitted.
This at least was the style of his conversation on the
Wednesday. But on the Thursday he turned short.
About 3 o'clock he told Rigby that he had brought the
Seal with him to Court. But after that he conversed
with Lord S. in the window, and acquainted him that
before he could resolve upon staying, he must ask them
one question, Was he to go to the Treasury ?—Yes.—
Then I must resign. But I wish to accommodate, and to
hold the Seal for so many days as may be thought necessary to a new arrangement. Lord S. told the King this ;
and Mr. F. went in immediately after and left the Seal.
This last conversation lasted about three minutes, the
King recommending it to him to reconsider it, and he
declining. Lord John came in only in respect to Lord
R. and he declined that or any other office. It was at
first understood amicably enough, and scarcely with positive refusal ; but that stiffens, and the report of to-day
(but I don't know this), is that Mr. Fox's resignation is
one of his reasons. It is confidently said by Charles Fox
and indeed expected, that the D. of Portland will also
resign, and C. told me he was going to meet him at
Wolbeck. Lord Keppel's situation seemed impossible
to be given up so abruptly in the first outset of his
campaign, and he had agreed accordingly to stay till
winter. Some few of the Board of Treasury, Lord
Althorp included, were expected to follow, and this seems
to close them. Mr. Pitt was to take a capital place,
either Chancellor of the Exchequer or Secretary of
State as the occasion might require ; and Lord Temple
or Lord Grantham were thought of for Foreign Secretary. You guess how that deliberation would be weighed.
But the thing seems to be going much further now ; for
I have just received a letter from Lee to resign the office
of Solicitor General (of which you will not talk because
I have not seen him, and I mean to try, tho' without
expectation of success, to persuade him to stay). In his
letter he refers not only to the death of one excellent
friend but to the succession of a great many others.
How far this goes I don't know. There was a meeting
this morning at Lord Fitzwilliam's, and I know that
Lord Temple and C. F. were to be there amongst others.
Till this term the D. of Richmond stood firm, and Conway, Camden, Grafton, &c. These last were not of that
meeting, and if they shrink it will not be in concert
with the former. . . . By Monday I shall hear
more and give you a better account. . . . . .

1782, Thursday, 12, Buxton.—Has learned on the road
that our fleet was to sail on last Friday : and of Sir Wm.
Pepperel's letter he only knows that if it be true it
flatters him (Thurlow) and supports the opinion he has
always entertained of things in that quarter. . . .
The absence of Lord Mansfield, who has been with the
Bishop of Worcester, made it necessary for me to stay the
prorogation of Parliament, which is, as you know, to the
10th of October : and Lord Shelburne talks of carrying
it over Christmas ; but this was upon an occasion when
the perfect order and œconomy of the Treasury was upon

the tapis, ... This is my second day at Buxton ;
after a battery and regular drinking of the water and a
very long ride, I have dined at a side table with Lord
Frederick Cavendish.

(n. d.) Having nothing else to do, I go to bed before
nine, I dine at a side table with Lord Hoode and his
ladies, amongst whom are three of the greatest beauties
of this place.

Another letter (evidently while at Buxton or shortly
after leaving), gives an account of an excursion.

n. d. Gives the hint last given to him that the Parliament is likely to be prorogued again. . . . The
coach is at the door, and I must go to meet a Committee
of East India Directors. (He mentions that summer is
coming on.)

Thursday.—I have staid so long at court that I have
not time to write. . . . The loss of the Island seems
to be nothing in comparison of the 700 men which are
taken. Nor am I very sorry for the 160,000l. belonging
to the former plunderers supposed to be captured there.
The Marquis de Bouillon make an attack with a less
number than those he besieged, and of that number
could land no more than 300, and then his boats having
steved by going to a wrong part of the island. If
treachery could have found a plausible reason for giving
up the other, the works were undermined, and the
soldiers had no ammunition ; 5 rounds instead of 60 ;
although the Commander had notice openly given him,
which he affected to slight the day before.

Friday morn.—I was sent for this morning to the
King, chiefly I think that I might not understand myself to have been so wrong as I thought. But His
Majesty thinks, and very justly, that your opinion is
better, or at least so good an addition that it ought not
to be omitted. He therefore sent me hither to desire
you would go to the Queen's House as soon as you can
make it convenient.

An undated letter is written after his return from
France, where he went in August.

(An undated letter of 8 pages.) . . . . I feel very
pressingly the want of that assistance which I had in
the beginning of the year, and without which I could
not have acted at all ; with this difference, that then I
was obliged to act, and now I can hold back. In the
Conversations I am now referring to, your name, as you
may easily imagine, did not fail to be mentioned in
terms which only you can give an answer ; but which you
cannot answer without a larger communication than can
easily be made in this manner. (But he says there is
nothing in it to bring Lord Gower up before the time
he had appointed.) The only business of which notice
has been given is the East Indian ; but no particulars of
that plan, which can be depended upon, have yet tran-
spired. That which is talked of is appointing. the
Directors by Parliament, and also nominating the
Council in the same manner ; by which measure the
modesty of the Ministers seems to mean to transfer
from themselves the credit of withdrawing Mr. Hastings, &c., and appointing Mr. Francis, General Smith,
and Mr. W. Burke in their places, only receiving to
themselves the patronage, in a shape for which the
King is to have no thanks, and over which he is to
retain no power. This is thought, I suppose, to be
their wish, and from thence inferred to be their purpose,
but it appears to me so unprincipled, irregular, and
rash, that I do not impute to them so much want of
common sense. The rumour, however, proceeds to
suppose that they have divided about it, and that Lord
Stormont still retains a contrary opinion, but that
Lord North has been reconciled to it by being allowed
to nominate his faithful friend Mr. Francis, who is
become so at the instigation of those more faithful
Counsellors under whose conduct he has taken that
creditable part for which the world is now admiring
him. To this last article his Lordship's late conduct
affords some countenance. When as Secretary for the
Home Department he allows the Secretary for the
Foreign not only to read the speech at the Cockpit but
to make the motion relative to the East Indies, which
is the proper business of his office. For the rest of their
publick politicks the same rumour says that they have
hazarded very lavish propositions to every Court of
Europe to procure that, or the appearance of that, for
want of which among other, a thousand other, causes
we suffered much abroad and the Ministers no less at
home. Russia for example is said to [have] the offer
of 15 ships of the line to be sent into the Mediterranean,
and after that an armed neutrality in imitation of that
foolish but mischievous vanity in the late war, is proposed with Spain. Supposing a perpetual enmity

between us and France to be the irrevocable doom of Heaven, and the false and peevish conduct to be not the accidental caprice of this hour, but the natural result of her situation; supposing on the other hand the disposition of Russia and Spain to be more steady to their actual interests than the form of Government in both, and additional circumstances in the last seem to promise; the first conception of the idea seems to be just, and to depend only on the discretion and reserve with which it may be conducted for its real value and merit. But it was observed that Mr. F. played the game of politicks as dashingly as he had done that of cards, and if the new adventure should turn out like the old one,————. As to their private or interior politicks the same rumour says they proceed in the very channel in which they set out, and consequently tend still to fret and imbitter more than to conciliate. This is perfectly astonishing, because a line of conduct seems to open, so obviously wise and so merely simple, that no objection can be made to it but the downright honesty of it—I mean the line of employing their power and opportunity which are manifestly in their hands, to arrange the Prince in the prudent, reputable, and agreeable part of duty to the father and kindness to his brother as the price of those gratifications which seem to engage his attention. But this line is not taken, and things remain accordingly in a situation painful to the Individual and mischievous to the Publick. On the other hand your experience in affairs does not want the assistance of what passed in the spring to form the reflections which that suggests and impresses deeply on me. The danger of relapsing into that situation must prevent any step being taken without having prepared an arrangement which promises, and that pretty confidently, a different upshot from the former. When those who acted in that scene present themselves to the view, it is impossible to forget either the events or the causes which appeared to produce them, and consequently to proceed without seeing to their being removed. This sensation probably has effect where any movement ought, I think, to begin; for I can't bring myself to like it as well, that it should begin elsewhere. The same sensation will produce a degree of reluctance in others to coalesce in a system which may possibly end so very contrary to their public opinions and genuine judgments. This end, however, seems to be the object of few, and they seem to be growing sensible both of their need of assistance and of the necessity of conforming in some degree to the publick and genuine sentiments of those whom they are looking to. Such communications as these have led to the Conversations I alluded to before respecting you, and I believe this outline (loose and shadowy as it appears) is almost as distinct a view as I know how to convey in this manner. . . .

(n. d., 8 pp.) . . . As to our Politicks, altho' there is affectation enough of consulting me, I don't feel myself at the bottom of them. Some little natural jealousy is irresistible, that when I speak of our bottom as much too narrow, it may be that I am weary of standing alone in a strange land. This is so true in fact, that I am not surprised it should be observed; nor that it should operate to the effect of creating suspicions. And yet I mistake things strangely if I am not right in my thoughts of the matter. Fox, who certainly turned out the last minister *proprio marte*, and must certainly have a certain following, carries out with him the immediate friends of Lord Rockingham, all the Cavendishes, Spencers, Keppel, Burke, &c., to the number of about 50 or 60, as Rigby computes it, in the House of Commons. Keppel professes to stay only in reference to his situation. Such an apology for staying seems, in my poor judgment, a fair extent of the reward due to the measure; and yet I have heard a bird in the air sing that he is to receive extraordinary compensation for so indispensable a piece of condescension. The Duke of Richmond seems to preserve his connections with his nephew, and remains to do God knows what; but he remains. The rest of the Cabinet is differently affected, but with what variety both of sentiment and energy you know us all enough to weigh. For the rest, the Government is sufficiently disabled and impotent by the loss of these opportunities to conciliate, without which I protest I don't see how the thing is to be done; and our acquisitions and substitutions are surely not all of the most promising sort. You will have heard of the list which kissed hands yesterday; *Lord Shelburne, William Pitt, young Elliot, Jackson K. Counsel, Thos. Townsend, Lord Grantham, Pratt, Awbrey, Sir Geo. Younge,

* The following names are in two columns. The 2nd column beginning with Lord Rockingham.

Lord Rockingham, Lord John Candish, Montague, Lord Althorpe, Lord Shelburne, Mr. Fox, Lord Duncannon (Admiralty), Jack Townsend, Tho. Townsend.—I don't know the news of this morning, but I understood this morning that Col. Barré was to replace Burke at the War Office, which I confess I wished for the Lord Advocate, who it seems is to succeed Barré as Treasurer of the Navy; but I have not heard upon whom his situation falls; I mean of Lord Advocate, for the Signet is to be given him for life, with a great sweep I suppose in Scotland. Unless there were some one to whom it might be desirable to give his place, I should think a little more ceremony in the profusion of the few things there is to be given might be advisable. The place of Solicitor General is talked of for Sir Pepper Arden. If this does not demonstrate too narrow a plan, perhaps you know how to explain it otherwise; for I hear you have had an express sent down to you, which must mean nothing or furnish you with the means of giving me a better notion than I yet possess of things. You will have heard from other hands that Fox undertook to explain to the world the ostensible reason for quitting; which he wished should be understood some great and essential ground of Politicks, and in particular some one on which the prospect of peace would mainly depend. In this he entered so fiercely on the abuse of Lord Shelburne, and was followed with so much acrimony by the rest of his friends, that he is said to have left an impression much to his disadvantage. It seems to have been confessed by them all that if his friends or the D. of Portland or of Richmond could have succeeded, there would have been no resignation. At the same time many people doubt whether the House in general entered more into his invective against his rival or the contempt of him and his motives. In the meantime Lord North seems to have fared better than usual: for his former enemies have prodigious advantage by comparison with his present successor. Yesterday Lord Shelburne took an opportunity of retorting; which Lord Derby took an opportunity of a strange sort to call for an explanation of to-day while we were waiting for His Majesty. Fox had writ to him in the morning to complain, and insisted that either he should retract an assertion which fell from him that Mr. Fox had never imparted to him any other reason for resigning than his, Lord S. taking the Treasury. Fox acknowledged this would have been a sufficient reason, but insisted that he had on the Sunday before declared in the Cabinet, that he would resign. It was true that he had so declared, but it was promised it should not be imparted to the King, and as F. said, for fear of hurting Lord Rockingham's health. Lord S. contended that he had many times made such peevish declarations before, and if he had meant that for peremptory it would not have consisted with any duty to the King to keep it a secret from him, whatever it might have been proper to do as to the rest of the world; and as it was admitted no other declaration had been made, he thought himself justified in the opinion he delivered of it.

n. d. Stratford-on-Avon.—He notices the richness and populousness of the country between Stafford and Stratford-on-Avon, and calls " The Stars " the worst house in Stafford, whence he posted to Wolverhampton, and finds fault with " The Swan " there. He wished, but could not go to see Warwick Castle, because of bad roads.

n. d. In the next letter (written a few days after) he tells how he went to Woodstock, and went to Blenheim, where he was much pleased with the Duke and Duchess of Marlborough and their daughters, the Ladies Elizabeth and Caroline. He got to Salthill the same night, and reached town only time enough to attend the Levée. . . . . Of public news I can give you no account, having seen no ministers; but I find that the account from Gibraltar is confirmed in all its parts. Baccelli has written to the D. of D. that the siege of G. is raised, that the fleet is arrived at Algesiras, but comparing circumstances, that is the combined fleet. There is also good news from the E. I. (East Indies?). I go to Oudland to-morrow.

n. d. There is no use in telling you, that we are under dreadful apprehension of a third party, unless I could bring together the thousand little circumstances which foment that apprehension, to which must be added comments upon defective or misrepresented stories, conjectures, &c., &c. To these must be added a number of false views, ill-conceived aims, unreasonable pretensions, causeless jealousies, and all that muddle which makes the intricacy of low and foolish Politicks. If I rate these things properly, and am right in laying them quite aside, Lord North, who is watched as the Leader of this

Phantom, a third Party, was it not in his power to go wrong, at least at the head of a Party, in anything essential to the present Government, and if he has it in his inclination, which I doubt, that will also cease when he discovers the extent of his power. If he really holds off, perhaps he has some particulars to arrange, which will probably bring him forward with less credit, and I think with less advantage, than if his line had the appearance of being quite his own. I know this *esquisse* is as indistinct as the rack of a cloud; but I shall let it go, because it would be a volume to give you the whole detail, if I could be sure of remembering it all. I am going to dine with Lord S. to-day, and shall try to give him your intimation. Anything from you will catch his attention, which is much upon the stretch to know how people feel at this time. He asked me the other day when you would come to town. I answered with much simplicity, that I had not heard you say a syllable about it. At the meeting of Parliament, to be sure? I said I really could not tell. But, as the conversation did not drop, I also told him, that Leveson had informed me he expected you about the end of the month. But I declined speculating upon it to him : with you I may speculate, and I rather suppose you will be at the meeting of Parliament at all events, if a Peace should be brought forward. The subject is of too much consequence to suffer you to be absent; and tho' that is either not very forward, or I don't know the channel well in which it is proceeding, yet I think one of the steps which has been taken towards it, I mean the abandonment of America (for so the progress to it must, I am afraid, be termed), must needs, I suppose, come before Parliament ; and that also seems to be a subject, which, all things considered, will make it impossible for you to stay away. For the rest, the terms proposed by France are more moderate than you would expect. I must go to dinner, and I shall leave this open till I return. It will be too late to run over the terms, and I shall be on thorns till I know you have received it. In Newfoundland, a fishery divided by coasts, each exclusive ; Dominique and St. Lucie in the West Indies ; Dunkirk in Europe ; the exchange of Senegal for Goree in Africa. Less reasonable pretensions in Indostan will make the subject of discussion, and I don't care to enter further into them in this channel. Spain throws out an unshaped idea, muddled by the ill-temper and incapacity of D'Arenda ; not'sing material, or more than some loose (and in the States popular) suggestions about the new Law of Nations, invented by that great luminary of law and politicks, the Empress of Russia, is heard of from Holland. . . . We are in anxious expectation of news from Gibraltar ; the latest accounts, and those not confirmed, going only to the 13th. But of those I shall say no more, because I enclose them.

Six letters by William Pitt.

1784, Sept. 5, Brighthelmstone.—He asks Lord Stafford if he would consent to take the office of Lord Privy Seal, so that Lord Camden might take the office of President then held by Lord Stafford. Lord Camden (he says) " has a great dislike to coming forward in a station " which has no sort of connection with the habits of the " Profession to which he has belonged." . . . "There " seems little difference between these two high offices " except that the Privy Seal has rather less confinement. " . . . . Notwithstanding the disturbances which " have prevailed in Dublin, the last accounts give a " more favourable prospect. Secret information has " been given of plots supposed to have been formed by " the discontented party. But there seems every reason " to think them greatly exaggerated. . . . In the mean-" time many of the counties have, I find, come to Resolu-" tions expressing a strong disapprobation of the extra-" vagance of the Aggregate Meeting, which will certainly " strengthen the hands of Government. The situation " of the Continent seems to call for a good deal of our " attention during this recess, and may, I trust, afford " an opening for gradually gaining some ground there." . . . . (With this is a copy of Lord Stafford's answer dated 8 Sept. 1784, in which he says that the motives which induced him to enter again into His Majesty's service were that he might contribute towards removing a set of Ministers, of whose principles he had the worst opinion, and in giving his little assistance to such of whose principles he had formed a contrary judgment, and who he thought were most likely to give ease to the King's mind and relief to this debilitated country. In short he had the most perfect confidence in the intentions and abilities of Mr. Pitt, and his (Stafford's) friend the Chancellor. He then expresses his willingness to do what Mr. Pitt asked, but says he should wish that the

change should be made on his own request, and that nothing should be done before he came to town early in November.)

1797, Aug. 25, Downing St.—He puts a Prebend in Rochester Cathedral at Lord Stafford's disposition in favour of Mr. Woodhouse ; and says that after having seen as much as he lately has done of Lord Granville, he (Woodhouse) has a strong claim in addition, if the tutor can be judged of from the pupil. (With this is a copy of Lord Stafford's answer of thanks.)

In the early part of July 1799 Lord Stafford prepared a letter to the King, soliciting His Majesty's clemency towards Lord Thanet. A copy of this (with these papers) he sent to Mr. Pitt on the 14th of July with a letter stating his intentions to intercede with the King.

1799, July 15, Tuesday. Hollwood.—Pitt, without discouraging Lord Stafford's intentions, says that he has strong doubts whether a disposition to lenity can be indulged consistently to what is due to the considerations so properly stated in Lord Stafford's letter, Public Justice and Example, and that the King cannot be advised to form any decision without reference to the Court by whom the sentence was past. With reference to Lord Stafford's wish to resign the Lieutenancy of Staffordshire, he takes it for granted that it would be agreeable to Lord Stafford that Lord Gower should succeed him. With this is a letter from Lord Thanet to Lord Stafford, dated from the Tower, Aug. 8, 1799, thanking Lord Stafford for having (as he had learned) before he left town made a representation to the King on his behalf. He says that he does not think it will be successful. " Having been deceived after all the intimations I had " received from so many quarters previous to the day " when judgment was given, and in particular from the " Chancellor, who in almost a direct message desired " that I would not emit going to court on the first fol-" lowing Wednesday, I never can entertain the smallest " hope of my confinement being either shortened or " even mitigated."

1800, June 18, Wednesday, Downing Street.—Is sorry to learn from Canning that Lord Granville does not wish to vacate his seat at present, and thus cannot accept a seat at the Admiralty. Pitt therefore proposes the seat for his friend W. Eliot and thinks that such an arrangement will be agreeable to Lord Stafford. (With this is a copy of Lord Stafford's answer of thanks.)

1764, July 26, London.—Lord Northington to [Lord Gower].

[1771, June,*] Monday morning. Lord Uxbridge to Lord Gower. I cannot resist sending you the enclosed, containing, as it does, sentiments that do the worthy bishop so much honour. I shall ever respect him for his plain dealing and sincerity upon this occasion, which, at your leisure, I wish you to tell him, that he may be saved the trouble of a letter from me, reserving myself 'till he gets to Canterbury. Bangor is a very good resting place, and I am told not unlikely to become vacant ; should it be the case, I should have a double interest in wishing him success.

1774, Oct. 8, Eccleshall.—B[rownlow] [Bishop of] Lich[field] and Cove[ntry] to [Lord Gower].—Hopes to hear that Lord Gower's friends have met with success at Newcastle.— Lord North has been at Banbury and is elected by this time without trouble ; he was robbed a day or two before on his road to Bushy, and his postillion wounded. — Mentions the peaceable election of Messrs. Meynell and Whitworth at Stafford.—Mr. Trevanion is likely to come in for Dover by a manœuvre of Mr. Fectors, who says he meant to *serve* Government by it.

1778, Feb. 16. Lord Bathurst to [Lord Gower].—He says that he has in a letter to Lord North desired His Majesty's permission to have his name struck out of the list of his Confidential servants.

1780, March 17, London. [The Duke of] Hamilton and Brandon to [Lord Gower].—Mentions his intention to bring before the House of Peers his claim to a seat in that House as Duke of Brandon, which he has delayed in hopes Lord Gower would have been in London.— Asks Lord Gower to devote a little time to the question, and move it in the House of Lords.

1785, Nov. 13, Blithfield. - Lord Bagot to Lord Gower.

1792, Oct. 9, London. Henry Dundas to Lord Stafford. I asked the King's permission to send to your Lordship for your perusal a paper respecting the debts of the Prince of Wales some time ago transmitted to His Majesty in a letter from Lord Thurlow, together with a

---

* See Lord North's letter of 18 June 1771, *ante* p. 208, col. 2.

copy of the answer which, by the King's command, I have this day sent in a letter from me to Lord Thurlow. I am just setting out for Scotland.

1792, Nov. 9, Hague.—Lord Auckland to Lord Grenville. Refers to Lord Elgin's account of affairs in Brabant and Flanders by dispatches of the 7th instant.—Alludes to the fatal misdirection and failure of the allied armies, the disgraces and losses in Savoy and on the Rhine; but more particularly to the successes of M. Dumourier's army in Brabant. He thinks it possible that Flanders and Brabant may fall into the hands of France, or of a revolted class of the inhabitants; and that the United Provinces may be attacked by France. If the Austrian armies are driven out of the Low Countries there will no apparent means of armed resistance on the Continent. He hopes for instructions of a nature to calm the anxiety often expressed to him by Ministers of the Republic. (Copy of extract, 4½ pp.)

1792, Nov. 13, Whitehall. Lord Grenville to Sir Morton Eden, K.B.—Alludes to the King having hitherto declined to make himself party to the enterprise of the courts of Vienna and Berlin for terminating the war. But now, the French successes in Flanders have brought forward the consideration of the common interests of Him and the King of Prussia; sends inclosed the declaration which the ambassador at the Hague is to deliver. Eden is to give a copy to the Prussian Ministers, and tell them that the King wishes for open and candid correspondence with the King of Prussia on the state of affairs; and that Mr. Straten will receive orders to make to the Austrian Ministers at Vienna a communication similar to the present. (Copy, 3 pp.)

Copy of the Declaration referred to in the last letter.—It assures the States General of the King's determination to execute the Stipulations of the Treaty of 1789.

1801, March 24, Palace Yard.—Henry Addington to [the Marquis of Stafford]. As Lord Gower has resigned the Lieutenancy of the county of Stafford, the King will not have any one appointed until it is known whether it will be agreeable to Ld. Stafford to resume it. He is authorized to say that no arrangement would be so acceptable to the King. (With this is a draft of Lord Stafford's reply (dated from Bath) declining the office by reason of age and infirmities.)

A folio volume written in the 17th century, containing copies of Royal and other letters, speeches, &c., of the 15th, 16th, and 17th centuries.

Some of the documents copied in this volume are known; but as some may be new or little known, I have ventured to give notes of all.

p. 1. 1564, Feb. 21, Dunkell. Henry Darnley to the Earl of Leicester. Begins—My especiall good Lord, your accustomed friendlyness during my continuance in the Court.—Assures the Earl of his gratitude and readiness to serve him.

2, 1600, King James to Dr. Hambleton. Begins Although I have never doubted.—Tells him to assure all Englishmen that when he (James) comes to the Crown he will not only maintain and continue the profession of the Gospel, but will not permit any other religion to be professed and avowed within the kingdom.

4. Henry, Earl of Richmond before he was King, to his friends here in England from beyond the seas, &c. Begins, Right trusty, worshipful, and honourable good friends and our allies, I greet you well. Being given to understand your good devoir and intent to advance me. . . . Says that when he is certified by them of their force and leaders he will be prepared to come over. Asks credence for the bearer.

6. A survey of the three great Kingdoms of Europe as the state of them was in King James's time. Begins. These three great kingdoms, France, England and Spain as they now stand are to be compared to the election of a King of Poland. (Seven reasons are given for the probability of France joining with England and Holland against Spain.)

9. Sixteen brief maxims under the head Temperance. 1st. Be humble in thy owne sight.—Twelve brief maxims under the head Domus. 1st. Seek thy wife for vertue only.

11. Hen. Beaufort, Bishop of Winton, his letter to the Duke of Bedford, Regent of France upon the falling out betwixt him and his nephew Humphrey Duke of Gloucester, Lord Protector, 4 Hen. VI.—A short letter asking the Duke to come over at once. "For by my " troth, if you tarry, we shall put this land in adventure " with a field, such a brother you have here; God make " him a good man." (Dated on Allhallow even.)

12. The Declaration of the Earls (Northumberland and Westmoreland), on the rising in the North.

14. The Earl of Leicester to Queen Elizabeth. Begins I received this morning the 17th of August two letters by my cozen Blount.—Says that if the Queen will continue the countenance of the war there (the Low Countries) she must also increase her charge there. Alludes to a report of a treaty of peace between the Queen and the Prince of Parma, and advises against it. In a P.S. he says that if the King of Spain's army is on the sea, the Queen must not spare any cost in the world or trust to any treaty. (The words "fifteen days ago " about the time of the loss of Sluys" fix the date to 17 Aug. 1587.)

24. 1593, Nov. 12. Queen Elizabeth to the French King Hen. IV. upon the changing his religion, translated out of French. Begins, Ah, what delours! oh, what griefs! (An English version is in Camden's History of Queen Elizabeth, fol. Lond. 1688, p. 475.)

26. 1563, April. Henry Earl of Huntington to the Earl of Leicester.—Alludes to the Queen having given his wife (at her last visit to the court) a privy nip, especially concerning himself.—Denies any such ambition as that of which the Queen seemingly suspects him, and which he attributes to the suggestions in a foolish book foolishly written. Asks Leicester's good offices with the Queen.

29. Queen Elizabeth to the Queen Dowager of Scotland.—Letter of credence for Sir W. Cecil and Dr. Wotton, whom she has sent to join certain of her Ministers in the North parts to meet Commissioners, sent by the French King to treat for a peace.

31. A note of Queen Mary of Scotland and her marriages.

33. 1587, January. Queen Elizabeth to Sir Amias Paulet on the death of his son in Paris.

36. 15 . ., Nov. 18, Knoll. Archbishop Cranmer to King Henry VIII.—Gives a translation into English from the Italian of a letter by " John Bianchett, a " Bononois born, sometime my servant, and now ser- " vant unto the Cardinal, which was late Bishop of " Worcester," relating the good entertainment at Rome by the Pope of Mr. Reginald Pole.

40. 1644, Sept. 11.—The Archbishop of Canterbury's Re-capitulation after his long hearing. — Begins, My hearing began March 12, 164⅘.

83. 1646, May 26. The City of London's desires in their Remonstrances,—thirteen items. 1st. That some strict and speedy course may be taken for the suppressing of all private and separate congregations.

86. A copy of the dittay or indictment of the Earl of Bothwell upon the murder of the Lord Darnley, King of Scotland.

88. 1567, March 17. Of Hownslowne.—A copy of a letter from the Earl of Lennox to the Queen of Scots about the murder of his son, &c.

91. 1567, April 5, Seyton.—A copy of the contract for marriage made between the Queen and Earl Bothwell.

A Memorandum at the end says that this Contract was made within 8 weeks after the murder of the King, who was slain on the 10th of February; and 7 days before the Earl was acquitted; and before any sentence for divorce or suit begun; for it was not till April 26th as appears by the records, &c.

96. Some remarkable passages collected out of the Queen's letters to Earl Bothwell found in the little trunk.

105. A copy of a letter of the late Earl of Arundel to the Queen's Majesty.—Begins, As the displensure of a prince (See Camden's History of Queen Elizabeth.)

136. 1584, Feb. 14, from the Tower.—A letter by Dr. Parry to the Queen. (See Camden.)

138. 1583, Sept. 12.—The heads of a conference between the King of Scots and Secretary Walsingham.

152. Note of such especial heads as by the King's Majesty of Scotland were delivered to Secretary Walsingham to be communicated to the Queen's Majesty. (See Calendar of State Papers relating to Scotland for this and the preceding items.)

154. An abstract touching the Queen's marriage, by Sir Thomas Smith. (This is an abstract of Nos. III. and IV. of the Appendix to Strype's Life of Sir Thomas Smith.)

166. Sir Walter Rawleigh to Sir Robert Carr. Begins, After many great losses. (Printed.)

170. Sir W. Rawleigh's letter to his wife the night before he expected execution. (Printed.)

175. [John Dudley] Duke of Northumberland's letter to the Earl of Arundel, Fitz-Alan.—Entreats (in abject terms) intercession for his life,

179. Lord Northumberland's letter to Sir Francis Vere.—Challenges him to fight. (This and the other letters and papers in the matter were printed by Peck.)

D d 3

181. The Countess of Nottingham's letter in answer to the King of Denmark's disgraces to her husband. (This was printed by Mr. Payne Collier in the Egerton Papers; for the Camden Society. It had been previously printed in the *Cabala*.)

183. A letter of Secretary Walsingham to the Chancellor of Scotland touching the death of the King's mother.

204. [Received 1583, May 8.] Queen Elizabeth to the Lord Treasurer Burghley. *Begins*, Sir Spirit, I doubt I doe nickname you. (Printed in Nares's Life of Burghley, vol. 3, p. 213.)

206. 1645, Jan. 15. His Majesty's (Charles I.) letter. (Printed.)

211. 1645. The Parliament's answer to His Majesty's 2 letters concerning his personal treaty with them, the one dated the 26th, the other the 29th of December last.

216. 1644, Jan. 29. His Majesty's letter to the two Houses of Parliament. (Printed.)

226. 1645, Sept. 4. Sir Thomas Fairfaxe, his letter to Prince Rupert when he summoned Bristol.

231. 1645, Aug. 25. Engagement, signed and sealed by Fairfax and Cromwell, for the safety of the persons and estates of the citizens of Bristol, if the city should surrender.

233. Further instructions to the citizens of Bristol that shall endeavour the delivering up of that city to the Parliament forces.

236. 1645, Oct. 14. Basingstoke. — Lieut.-General Cromwell to Mr. Speaker upon the taking of Basing House.

241. Lord Treasurer Burghley to Queen Elizabeth. *Begins*, I know not in what manner of words.—He laments the Queen's displeasure and offers to surrender all public employments. (*See* Nares's Life of Burghley, vol. 3, p. 212.)

247. Lord Treasurer Burghley to his son. A long letter, giving rules for conduct in life. *Begins*, Son Robert, the vertuous inclination of thy matchless mother. (Printed in the Appendix to Nares's Life of Burghley.)

259. 1572, Oct. 9. Sir Edward Dyer to Sir Christopher Hatton. (Printed in Nicolas's Life of Hatton.)

265. 1640, Aug. 28. Petition by the Earls of Bedford and Essex and eight other Lords, that the King would summon a Parliament.

271. 1578, July 2, Antwerp.—The substance of Her Majesty's Ambassadors negotiations with the Prince of Orange, and others deputed by the States of the Low Countries.

292. 1592, July 28, Antwerp. The substance of the Conference between the Lords and the Emperor's ambassador.

304. Instructions to A. B. to be sent to the Scottish Queen. (These are for Robert Beale and not for Walsingham as stated in the margin of the MS.. The Calendar of State Papers for Scotland gives the date as 4 May 1584.) Beale was to see if Mary would stand to her two offers made to Wade : 1. That she would get her son to deal favourably with Angus and Mar, and the rest of the English faction in Scotland. 2. That she would order the Bishops of Glasgow and Ross, her Ministers in France, to stay their practices against England.

312. Secretary Walsingham to the Regent of Scotland. (What seems to be an abstract of this letter is in the Calendar of State Papers relating to Scotland under the date of June 4, 1574 ; but the letter is said to be from Queen Elizabeth. The writer of the letter in the volume now under description could not have been the Queen ; she would not have written. " In the mean- " time I most humbly take my leave.")

313. The conditions whereupon the Queen of Scots will be content to resign her estate to her son.

315. 1564, Feb. 6, Edinburgh. Thomas Randolph to the Earl of Leicester.—The Queen of Scots is favourable to the proposition that she should marry Leicester.

322. 1575, March 13 (15th ?). Queen Elizabeth's speech in the Parliament House. (An eloquent speech. Its effect was that she declined to marry. It is not mentioned in Sir Simonds D'Ewes's Journal.)

331. Instructions for certain gentlemen sent abroad.

333. The effect of a speech from John Crook, Esq., Speaker of the Parliament, to Her Majesty, in the name of the Commons, the last of Nov. 1601, at Whitehall, in the Counsel Chamber.

337. The Queen's speech.—(This and the preceding item are, with considerable variations, in Sir Simonds D'Ewes's Journal.)

ALFRED J. HORWOOD.

THE MANUSCRIPTS OF THE MOST HONOURABLE THE
MARQUIS OF LANSDOWNE.

SHELBURNE MSS.—II.

(For the arrangement of these papers *see* p. 125 of 3 Rep.
of the Hist. MSS. Commissioners.)

COLONIAL AFFAIRS AND PEACE WITH AMERICA, 1766–1783.

Vols. 43—88.

The majority of the papers in the volumes comprised under this division are either copies of papers or
original letters written to or by Lord Shelburne during
the period of his official connection with American
affairs. Interspersed with these, *e.g.* in Vols. 45 and 46,
are papers relating to the foreign politics of Europe.

Several of the papers in this Report are printed in
Vol. 1 of my Life of Lord Shelburne. Others will appear in the succeeding volumes.

Vols. 43 and 44.

Two large folio volumes labelled Assiento papers.
They contain copies of papers, and many original letters
and documents relating to the Assiento affairs, from 1718–
48. Each volume has at the beginning a list of its
contents. The Assiento is the name by which histori-
cally the contract between the King of Spain and other
papers for furnishing the Spanish dominions in America
with negro slaves is known. It was transferred to England and vested in the South Sea Company, in 1713, by
the Treaty of Utrecht. The differences with regard to
it were one of the causes of the war with Spain in 1739,
and the fall of Sir Robert Walpole. The Treaty of Aix
la Chapelle continued it in the hands of the South Sea
Co. for four years, after which it reverted to Spain. As
all the papers in these two volumes relate to the same
subject, no detailed list has been given.

Vols. 45–46.

Two volumes bound in red morocco and labelled
"American Papers." The first volume contains copies
of queries to Governors, and their answers, with projects,
plans, representations, &c., from 1705 to 1724. The
second volume contains copies of several letters and
documents from 1686 to 1766. Both volumes are important for the early history of the American colonies.

Vol. 45.

Orders and instructions to the Captains General and
Governors in Chief in and over our colonies and islands
in America, and of the several laws relating to trade
and navigation.

Answers to the Board's queries relating to the state
of the Island of Jamaica. 21st Nov. 1741.

Jamaica.—Letters, queries, and answers. 21st Nov.
1741.

The form of making out a list of ships and vessels
outward bound from any port, &c.

Barbadoes.—Answers of his Excellency Henry Green-
ville, Esq., to the queries sent him from the Right
Honourable the Lord Commissioners for Trade and
Plantations. 7th Feb. 1748.

Bermuda.—The answers of Governor Popple and
Council to the Board's general queries. 2nd May 1749.

South Carolina.—The answer of Governor Jas. Glen to
the Board's general queries. Received 13th Sept. 1749.

Virginia.—The answer of Colonel Lee, Commander-
in-Chief of Virginia, to the Board's general queries
29th Sept. 1750.

New York.—The answer of Governor the Honourable
George Clinton to the Board's general queries. 23rd
May 1749.

New Jersey.—The answer of Governor Belcher to
the Board's general queries relating to the state of that
province. 21st April 1749.

Memorandum relating to the trade with the follow-
ing colonies, viz.:—Nova Scotia, New Hampshire,
Massachusetts, Rhode Island, Connecticut, New
York, New Jersey, Pensylvania, Maryland, Virginia,
North Carolina, South Carolina, Mississippi. Dated
8th Sept. 1721.

New Hampshire.—The answer of Governor J. Belcher
to the queries sent him from the Right Honourable the Lord Commissioners for Trade and Plantations. Dated, Portsmouth, New Hampshire, 4th April
1737.

Bahama Islands.—Answer of the Governor to the
general queries of the Board. 17th July 1745.

Leeward Islands. Answer of General Matthews to
the Board's general queries. Received 10th July 1746.

Massachusetts Bay.—Answer of the Governor to the
Board's general queries. Boston, 2nd March 1736–7.

North Carolina.—Governor Captain Burrington's representation of the present state and condition of that
colony. 1st Jan. 1732–3.

Maryland.—Governor Samuel Ogle's answer to the
Board's general queries. Annopolis, 16th Dec. 1749.

Connecticut.—Answer of Henry Willis, secretary to
the Governor, to the Board's general queries. Hartford,
9th Sept. 1730.

Answer of P. Gordon, Lieut.-Governor of Pensylvania,
and counties of Newcastle, Kent, and Sussex on the
Deleware river, to the Board's general queries. 15th
March 1730–1.

Rhode Island.—Answer of Governor J. Jencks to the
Board's general queries. 9th Nov. 1731.

Proposal for a scheme towards the better government
of the West Indies.

A copy of a representation to His Majesty, with a plan
of general concert and mutual defence, to be entered
into by His Majesty's colonies in North America.
Signed by Halifax, Jas. Grenville, Fran. Fane,
And. Stone, Jas. Oswald, Rich. Edgecumbe, and Thos.
Pelham, Lords Commissioners for Trade and Plantations.

Copy of a representation of the state of the colonies
in North America. Drawn up by the Commissioners at
the Congress of Albany, July, 1754.

Plan for a union of the northern colonies. Drawn up
by the Commissioners at the Congress of Albany. July
1754.

Copy of a letter from P Schuyler to the Lords Commissioners for Trade and Plantations. New York, 27th
April 1720.

Copy of a letter from P. Schuyler to the Board. New
York, 9th June 1720.

Copy of a letter from P. Schuyler to the Board. July
1720.

Journal of Laurence Claussen, the interpreter from
the Sinnokies country, to Octjagara, pursuant to the
instructions of Myndert Schuyler and Robert Livingson.
Albany, 22nd May 1720.

A letter from W. Burnet, Esq., Governor of New
York, to the Board. New York, 27th Aug. 1720.

A copy of a letter from Governor Burnet to the Board,
dated New York, 12th July 1721, together with a
memorial from John Durant, late chaplain to the Fort
of Cataracony. Dated New York 16th Oct. 1721.

Propositions made to the five nations of Indians by
W. Burnet, Esq., Governor of New York. Albany, 7th
Sept. 1721.

Answer of the five nations of Indians to W. Burnet,
Esq., Governor of New York. Albany, 9th Sept. 1721.

A letter from Governor Burnet to the Board, together
with a memorial from Archdeacon Kennedy, Adjutant
of the four companies of New York. New York, 2nd
Dec. 1721.

A letter from Governor Burnet to the Board. New
York, 21st Nov. 1722.

Propositions made to the aforesaid five nations of
Indians by Governor Burnet. Albany, 27th Aug. 1722.

Answer of the five nations of Indians to Governor
Burnet's propositions. Albany, 1st Sept. 1722.

Propositions made to the River Indians by Governor
Burnet. Albany, 31st Aug. 1722.

Answer of the River Indians to Governor Burnet.
Albany, 31st Aug. 1722.

Further propositions made to the five nations of
Indians by Governor Burnet. Albany, 13th Sept. 1722.

The second answer of the five nations of Indians to
Governor Burnet. Albany, 14th Sept. 1722.

Propositions made to the five nations of Indians by
His Excellency, Alexander Spotiswood, Governor of Virginia. Albany, 29th Aug. 1722.

Answer of the five nations of Indians to the Governor
of Virginia's propositions. Albany, 6th Sept. 1722.

Further propositions made to the five nations of
Indians by the Governor of Virginia. 10th Sept. 1722.

Further propositions of the Governor of Virginia to
the five nations of Indians. 11th Sept. 1722.

Further answer of the five nations of Indians to the
Governor of Virginia. 12th Sept. 1722.

Propositions made to the five nations of Indians by
Sir W. Keith, Governor of Pennsylvania. Albany, 7th
Sept. 1722.

Answer of the five nations of Indians to the propositions of Sir W. Keith, Bart. Albany, 10th Sept. 1722.

The four days' conference of the five nations of Indians,
with their reply, to the propositions made to them by
the Honourable John Wanfau, Lieut.-Governor in
Albany. Albany, 19th July 1701.

Notes taken at a meeting of the Commissioners for
Indian affairs in Albany. 29th May 1723.

Notes taken at a meeting of the Commissioners for
Indian affairs. Albany, 30th May 1723.

D d 4

Right margin: MARQUIS OF LANS- DOWNE.

Notes taken at a meeting of the Commissioners for Indian affairs. Albany, 31st May 1723.

A letter of W. Burnet, Governor of New York, to the Board. New York, 9th August 1724.

Notes taken at a private conference held by W. Burnet, Esq., with the Sachims of six nations, and their reply. Albany, 14th Sept. 1724.

Propositions made to the Sachims of the six nations by the Governor of New York. Albany, 15th Sept. 1724.

Answer of the Sachims of the six nations to the propositions of the Governor of New York. Albany, 17th Sept. 1724.

Further propositions made to the Sachims of the six nations by the Governor of New York. Albany, 19th Sept. 1724.

Answer of the Sachims of the six nations made to the Governor of New York. Albany, 20th Sept. 1724.

Propositions made to the Sachims of the Schaahkook Indians by the Governor of New York. Albany, 19th Sept. 1724.

Answer of the Indians to the Governor of New York. Albany, 19th Sept. 1724.

A proposition made by the Commissioners of the Province of Massachusets to the six nations of Indians. Albany, 16th Sept. 1724.

Answer of the six nations of Indians to the Commissioners of Massachusets. Albany, 18th Sept. 1724.

The affidavits of John Groesback, Jun., and Duke Schuyter on the state of the Indian trade.

Vol. 46.

An account of Foreign Linens imported and exported in 1713, 1714, 1715, 1735, 1736, 1737, 1738, 1739, 1740.

Observations on the trade with Germany, dated Ratisbon, $\frac{18}{28}$th April 1716.

Observations of the company of Merchant Adventurers in Hamburgh to the Lords Commissioners on the state of their trade.

Observations of the Levant Company on the state of their trade.

Observations of the Muscovy Company on the state of their trade.

Grant and other papers to the Duke of York of lands in New England, dated 20th Feb. 166$\frac{3}{4}$.

An account of the quantity of Spanish long cloth exported quarterly from England to all foreign ports in 1714.

Instructions to Colonel Thos. Dongan, Governor of New York, for observing the Acts of trade and navigation, dated Windsor, 20th June 1686.

Letter to Col. Dongan to publish the treaty of neutrality, dated Whitehall, 26th Dec. 1686.

The appointment of Thomas Dongan, Esq., to be Governor of New York. 1686, 20th May.

Instructions for Col. Dongan. Windsor, 29th May 1686.

Letter from the Committee to the Governor and Council of New York to return journals and accounts of all matters relating to the government. Whitehall, 3rd June 1686.

Letter to John Spragg, Esq., secretary of New York, to return to the committee quarterly accounts of all things done in his office. Whitehall, 10th June 1686.

Letter from Col. Dongan to the Lord President concerning a French invasion, &c. 8th Sept. 1687.

Letter from Col. Dongan to the Lord President on his apprehension from the French, &c. New York, 12th Sept. 1687.

Instructions for Capt. Palmer relating to the French invasion by Col. Dongan. 8th Sept. 1687.

Letter to the Governor of New York to protect the Indians. Whitehall, 10th Nov. 1687.

Correspondence of the Commissioners (the Sieur Barillon and the Sieur de Bonrepaux) appointed by the French King to treat as to the execution of the treaty of neutrality in America with Lord Middleton and Lord Godolphin.

Memorial of the French Commissioners touching the Iroquois.

Memorial of the English Commissioners touching the several matters and differences.

Letter to Colonel Dongan for preventing acts of hostility. Whitehall, 22nd Jan. 1687.

Instrument for preventing acts of hostility. Whitehall, $\frac{1}{11}$ December 1687.

Letter to Col. Dongan to report the boundaries of his government. Whitehall, 1st April 1688.

Letter of revocation for Col. Dongan. Whitehall, 22nd April 1688.

Letter from the Lieutenant Governor and others at New York on the state of the government. New York, 15th May 1689.

Letter from the King Will. III. to Captain Francis Nicholson, Lieutenant-Governor of New York. Whitehall, 30th July 1689.

Letter from the Council of New York to the Earl of Shrewsbury on the state of the government. New York, 10th June 1689.

Memoranda of the Board of Trade concerning New York, and recommending that a governor be sent thither. Whitehall, 31st Aug. 1689.

Memoranda. Two companies of foot to be sent to New York. 13th Sept. 1689.

Letter from the Earl of Shrewsbury to the Lords of the Committee for trade, &c., acquainting them with the appointment of Henry Slaughter, Esq., to the government of New York. Whitehall, 25th Sept. 1689.

Commission for Col. Slaughter to the Governor of New York.

Copy of a supplication exhibited to King Henry VI. by the inhabitants of the county Palatine of Chester, complaining of the demand of a subsidy voted by the Parliament at Westminster.

The King's letter to the county to discharge them of the subsidy.

List of civil officers employed in North America in Jan. 1766.

A state of paper money emitted in Virginia from 1755 to 1762.

Additional taxes laid on the Virginians to redeem and sink the paper money emitted in that colony for the aid of the war.

The Lords protest against the repeal of the Stamp Act. 11th March 1766.

Ships belonging to Liverpool employed in the African trade, and the number of slaves sold in the West Indies and America, from 1758 to 1764.

Observations on the cotton manufacture.

Vol. 47.

A small folio volume containing an examination of the Acts of Parliament relative to the trade and the government of the American colonies. The different constitutions of government in those colonies considered, with remarks formed into a Bill for amendment of the laws of this kingdom in relation to the government and trade of the said colonies. By James Abercromby, May 17th, 1752.

Vol. 48.

A folio volume labelled "Papers and Proposals " relative to North America, from 1764-1767." Most of these papers are copies. There are, however, several important original letters and papers by Jacob Blackwell, John Walker, P. Syman, George Croghan, John Harvey, James Grant, Charles Dalrymple, and Edward Montagu. This volume also contains the petition of Lord Egmont for a grant of part of the island of Dominica. Most of the undated papers belong to the year 1763.

Thoughts concerning America, by Mr. Hasenclever.

Observations on West Florida, by Jacob Blackwell, with three plans.

Plan proposed by General Phineas Lyman for settling Louisiana, and for erecting new colonies between West Florida and the Falls of St. Anthony.

A letter from Mr. John Walker on the importance of Florida, from its climate and possible produce.

Hints respecting the settlement of Florida.

Thoughts concerning Florida.

Propositions for settling the new Sugar Islands, roughly thrown together.

Thoughts concerning the colonies.

A letter from Sir William Johnston to Mr. Secretary Conway, containing his opinion of settling a colony at the Illinois.

Reasons for establishing a British colony at the Illinois, with some proposals for carrying the same into immediate execution.

A letter from Mr. P. Lyman to Lord Shelburne, concerning the navigation of the Mississippy.

A letter from G. Croghan to General Gage, on the best method of supplying Fort Chartres with provisions.

A letter to the Earl of Shelburne, January 16th, 1767, mentioning the discovery of some remarkable bones like those of elephants.

A letter from G. Croghan to Dr. Franklyn, January 27th, 1767, relating to the trade, &c. of the Illinois country.

A letter from G. Croghan to General Gage, containing an account of his negociation with the Illinois Indians, 16th January 1767.

Journal of an expedition along the Ohio and Mississippy, by Captain Harry Gordon, 1766.

Observations relating to North America, 1761.

A plan for settling a township in America, to consist of one hundred thousand acres, with an estimate of the expense, &c.

Thoughts concerning the sale of lands in the West India Islands, by John Harvey, 13th August 1763.

A short discourse on the present state of the colonies in America, with respect to the interest of Great Britain.

A sketch of a proposal for seals for Canada, East and West Florida; and the ceded islands.

Advantages arising from keeping up armed vessels on the lakes in North America, by Joshua Loring.

A list of His Majesty's vessels on the lakes in North America.

Commission to Joshua Loring, Esq., for building boats for the use of the army in N. America.

An estimate of the expense of one of His Majesty's vessels on the lakes, on their present footing.

An estimate of the freight that might be made in His Majesty's vessels on the lakes, by carrying the merchants' goods.

A draught of a Bill for an American custom house.

A letter from P. Lyman to the Earl of Shelburne, 31st August 1766, containing an account of the navigation of the Mississippi.

A description of the harbours upon the East Coast of Nova Scotia, from the Gut of Canso to the Harbour of Fourchu, showing the number of large ships each may contain. By Thomas Fryer, pilot.

A description of the several towns in the province of Nova Scotia, with the lands comprehended in and bordering upon the said towns, drawn up by order of the Hon. Jonathan Belcher, Esq., Lieutenant Governor and Commander-in-Chief of the said province.

Remarks relating to New France in 1754, addressed to Marshall Belleisle.

Remarks relating to New France in 1758, addressed to Marshall Belleisle.

The importance of settling Nova Scotia.

An estimate of the expense of settling 20,000 acres of land in East Florida, with 75 Greek families, each family one with another to consist of 1 man, 1 woman, and 2 children; also with 20 negroes to clear land the first year.

An estimate of the expense of settling 20,000 acres of land in East Florida, with foreign Protestants, as required by the grant within three years.

Hints relative to the settling of our acquisitions in America.

A list of the number of fighting men of different nations of Indians through which Dr. Franklyn passed, living at and near the several posts.

Uncleared lands.

Extract of a letter from Sir Jeffrey Amherst to the Earl of Egremont, dated New York, 30th November 1762, recommending Detroit as a proper seat for a new government.

A letter from Governor Grant to James Pownal, Esq., 20th July 1763, on the best method of settling the new colonies in America.

An account of the Island of Dominica.

A letter from C. Dalrymple to the Earl of Shelburne, dated Rouseau, in the island of Dominica, 12th September 1768, concerning the free ports (with ? a map of the Island of St. Domingo).

Lord Egmont's petition for a grant of part of the Island of Dominica.

An estimate of a sugar plantation of 300 acres.

An account of the quantity of raw sugar imported into England from Christmas 1756 to Christmas 1761, distinguishing the countries whence imported.

An account of the quantity of prime Muscavado brown sugar imported into England from Christmas 1756 to Christmas 1761, distinguishing each year.

Hints respecting the settlement of our American colonies.

Hints respecting the civil establishments in the American colonies.

Some thoughts on the settlement and government of our colonies in North America.

Hints relative to the division and government of the conquered and newly acquired countries in America.

General propositions about the form of government to be established in the new colonies by Governor Pownall.

5.

Some hints for the better settlement of the ceded islands.

Supplementary hints for the more speedy and effectual settlement of the ceded islands.

An account of the method of making pearl ashes.

An account of pig iron from America, to be imported.

A catalogue of such useful foreign plants as will thrive in the different climates of our American dominions.

Hints relating to the office of provost, marshal, &c. at Barbadoes, by Mr. Walker.

Remarks on the Caiques and Turks Islands.

An account of the importance of West Florida, by Jacob Blackwell.

A letter from Edward Montagu ? dated 6th May 1767, relating to the paper currency of North America.

A plan of the London merchants in favour of paper currency in North America.

Reasons for restricting the jurisdiction of the Courts of Admiralty in North America, by Mr. Cooper.

The opinion of the Attorney General, &c., concerning the jurisdiction of the Court of Vice-admiralty in North America, and the King's commission to the Earl of Northumberland for the purpose of establishing its jurisdiction.

Vol. 49.

This volume is marked "America," and contains miscellaneous papers from 1703-1767. These are mostly copies.

A List of Papers in the Plantation Office since the year 1664, relative to the Boundaries between the Provinces of New York and New Jersey.

"System of geography," under the title of America. Page 523 and 4 extracted.

Things to be considered of in North America.

Thoughts on the colonies by S. G.

State of the case relative to the lands reserved by the Creek Indians in Georgia, and of the claims and pretensions of the Bosomworths with respect thereto.

List of such Acts, passed in the Massachusetts Bay, as have been reported on between the year 1703 and the present time.

List of Acts of Parliament relating to the plantation trade.

List of such Acts passed in the colony of Virginia, as have been reported on by the Board of Trade between the year 1703 and the present time.

List of Acts passed in New York from 1703 to the present time, which have been reported on.

List of such Acts, passed in New Jersey, as have been reported on from the year 1702 to the present time.

List of such Acts, passed in New Hampshire, as have been reported on between the year 1753 and the present time.

The decision of the Privy Council in the case of John Colebrook.

Extracts from the votes of the Assembly of Pensylvania, Oct. 21st, 1741.

Observations on the revenue of South Carolina, by Mr. Tomson. (Original.)

A letter from the agent for South Carolina to Lord Shelburne, dated Inner Temple, 3rd June 1763, concerning the boundary of that province. (Original.)

A representation of facts relative to the conduct of Daniel Moore, Esq., Collector of His Majesty's customs at Charles Town, (printed) South Carolina, by the merchants of Charles Town.

Observations relating to the boundaries of Carolina.

Warrants granted by his Excellency Thos. Boone, Esq., Governor, &c. of South Carolina, for lands to the south of Alatamaha River to several petitioners, the 5th of April and 3rd of May 1763.

A letter from Governor Boone to the Earl of Egremont, dated Charles Town, 1st June 1763, relating to a treaty with the Indian nations, after the peace of 1763.

A report of the Board of Trade, relating to a plan of concert of the North American Provinces for the common defence, 1754.

A letter from Lord Egremont to the Lords of Trade, on the advantages to be derived from the peace of 1763, 5th May 1763.

A sketch of a report, with observations on the commission, and instructions for the Governor of Grenada.

A reference from Lord Egremont, approving the report of the Board of Trade of the 8th of June, with further suggestions as to the waste lands. 14 July 1763.

A report from the Lords of Trade concerning that part of North America which lies to the west of the

E e

old colonies, and which was acquired at the Peace in 1763. 5 Aug. 1763.

Mr. Pownal's sketch of a report concerning the cessions in Africa and America at the Peace of 1763.

The report of the Lords of Trade relating to the cessions at the Peace of 1763. June 8, 1763.

Various complaints from the West Indies and the North American colonies, from 1689 to 1757.

Extracts on the subject of a requisition of a compensation to the sufferers by the riots in America on occasion of the Stamp Act, 1766.

The representation of the General Assembly of New York to the King, concerning the administration of justice in that province, 11th Dec. 1762. Signed W. Nicoll, Speaker. An original.

The representation to the Governor of Virginia by the House of Burgesses, May 1763, concerning the paper currency.

Extract of a representation from the Board of Trade to His Majesty, dated 9th Feb. 1764, concerning the paper currency in America.

Copy of a letter to the Earl of Hertford concerning the regulations for the settlement of the conquered Sugar Islands, with two appendices, entitled—
1. On means to remedy, if not prevent, the illicit trade of North America.
2. On means to obviate the inconveniences to be dreaded from the sinking, all at once, the paper currency of the provinces. Written at Paris in the year 1765, by L. M.

Memorandum of some facts relative to the administration of colony affairs, from Mr. Pownal, 6th January 1766.

Resolutions at a meeting of the committee of the West India and North American merchants at the King's Head Tavern, 10th March 1766.

The petition of the merchants of the city of New York, in the colony of New York, in America, relating to the paper currency. 28 Nov. 1766.

A letter from W. Patterson to the Earl of Shelburne, on the preservation of his Majesty's timber in America.

Offer of a treaty for the sale of Lord Granville's district in North Carolina to the Crown. Signed by the second Lord Granville.

The humble representation of the council and assembly for the province of West Florida, stating what is wanted for the support and encouragement of the province. 22 Nov. 1766.

Papers relating to a proposal of Messrs. Baynton to supply Fort Chartres with provision.

Letters, &c. relating to the distribution of the troops in North America; one original from Wm. Ellis.

List of His Majesty's ships stationed, or to be stationed at Newfoundland, &c., in America. Printed.

Extract of a letter from Major-General Gage to the Secretary at War, dated New York, 22nd Feb. 1767, on the disposition of the troops.

A letter from General Gage to Lord Shelburne, 22nd Feb. 1767, accompanying the journal of Captain Gordon, Chief Engineer of North America, and descanting on the subjects to which it refers. There is a very useful map accompanying this letter.

General distribution of His Majesty's forces in North America, 22nd Feb. 1767.

Cantonment of the forces in North America.

A letter about reducing the duties on coffee and cocoa imported from the ceded islands, and afterwards exported, March 1767.

Abstract of acts and proceedings relating to the North American plantations, from 1660 to 1757.

Remarks on the present state of America from Mr. Morgann, April 1767.

Letters of Mr. Thos. Moffatt, relating to his claim of indemnity for his sufferings in the riots occasioned by the Stamp Act. (Original.)

A private letter from Governor Bernard to Mr. Pownal, 16th Dec. 1766, relating to the appointment of a separate agent for the House of Assembly, and other business. (Original.)

The Boston Gazette for 24th Nov. and 1st Dec. 1766.

Letters, &c. relating to Mr. Bowen's making sago and vermicelli, 1766.

Contents of Vol. 50, endorsed, "Miscellaneous Papers "and Estimates relative to Indian Trade."

Representation of the state of the Colonies in North America, 1754, and a plan for the union of the Colonies, &c., signed by Lord Halifax and the other Lords of Trade.

Lord Shelburne's remarks on the cessions made by France and Spain, and the commercial advantages that may be derived therefrom. (Original.)

Lord Barrington's plan relating to the out ports, Indian trade, &c., with remarks, 10th May 1766.

Remarks on Lord Barrington's plan No. 1.

Remarks on Lord Barrington's plan No. 2.

Some advantages for carrying on the Indian trade at the back of Virginia.

Proceedings of the Ohio Company about the settlement, &c. of the Ohio.

A letter from G. Croghan to Dr. Franklin, about the boundary of the six nations, dated Lancaster, 2nd Oct. 1767. (Original.)

A letter from J. Galloway to Dr. Franklin, dated Philada., 8th Oct. 1767, relating to the Indian boundaries. (Original.)

Two letters from S. Wharton, relating to the Indian boundaries. (Original.)

Reasons for establishing a British colony at the Illinois, with some proposals for carrying the same into immediate execution.

Observations of Sir Jeffery Amherst, relating to the Illinois settlements, Nov. 1767.

A letter from General Lyman to the Earl of Shelburne, relating to the settlement of the Mississipi.

A letter from the General Lyman to the Earl of Shelburne, dated Oct. 28th 1766, relating to the navigation of the Mississipi.

Plan proposed by General Lyman for setting Louisiana, and for erecting new colonies between West Florida and the falls of St. Anthony.

Considerations submitted to the Board of Trade relating to the superintendent of Indian affairs.

Minutes submitted to the Cabinet in the beginning of summer, 1767, relative to the system of Indian traffic.

The substance of what passed between Lord Shelburne and Mr. Dyson about the superintendants given to Lord Clare, Nov. 1767.

Notes by Lord Shelburne concerning the superintendants in America. (Original.)

A memorial of the Indian trade sent by Governor Carleton to the Board of Trade, 1767.

Some thoughts on Indian affairs.

A memorial of Indian affairs, dated Montreal, 20th Sept. 1766.

A short abstract of Col. Bradstreett's congress with the Indian deputies in Sept. 1764.

A letter from G. Croghan to Dr. Franklin, relating to the trade, &c. with the Illinois, dated New York, 27th Jan. 1767.

State of the King's rights and revenues at the Detroit, &c.

Various estimates for provisioning troops, &c. in North America.

Extract of a letter from Sir Jeffery Amherst to the Earl of Egremont, dated New York, 30th Nov. 1762, recommending a seat of Government at Detroit.

Extract of a letter from Major-General Gage to Mr. Secretary Conway, New York, 15th July 1766, relating to the trade with the Illinois.

Extract of a letter on American affairs, advising that the salaries of Crown officers may depend upon the Crown.

Estimate of officers' salaries, &c. in the southern department of Indian affairs annually.

Estimate of the amount of the Deputy Quartermaster-General's department in the district of New York for the year 1766.

List of the officers of the northern department of Indian affairs under the superintendancy of Sir William Johnson, Bart., with their respective salaries, and also those appointments intended by the plan for the better management of Indian affairs, &c.

Abstract of the contingent charges in North America for the year 1767, distinguishing such as are annual, together with charge for provisions for 1767.

Observations on the Indian trade by B. Frobisher, dated Quebec 10th Dec. 1766. (Original.)

Plan for the future management of Indian affairs proposed when Lord Hillsborough was at the head of the Board of Trade, with remarks.

This vol., 51, is endorsed, "Abstract of Letters from "the American Governors, &c. in 1766 and 1767."

Major-General Gage to Mr. Secretary Conway, New York, 28th March 1766, on the provision for the troops in the back settlements, &c.

Abstract of the despatches, received 27th Oct. 1766, by the New York packet from Governor Franklin, New Jersey, 8th and 11th Sept., and from Major-General Gage, 11th and 13th Sept., on the Indian affairs, and the disposition of the troops.

MARQUIS OF LANSDOWNE.

Abstract of despatches from Major-General Gage, 8th Oct. 1766, received 10th Nov., on the disposition of the troops, and Indian affairs, &c.

Major-General Gage to Lord Barrington, New York, 11th Oct. 1766, with several estimates.

Major-General Gage to Lord Barrington, New York, 28th Oct. 1766, with estimates.

Major-General Gage, New York, 11th Nov. 1766, on the quartering of troops, on Indian affairs, &c.

Abstract of a despatch from Major-General Gage, transmitted by Lord Barrington, with estimates. 9th Dec. 1766.

Major-General Gage, 23rd Dec. 1766, on the war with the creeks.

An account of the Mississippi and the forts, &c. on its banks, given by Lieut.-Colonel Maxwell as described by Major Chisholme. In Major-General Gage's despatch of the 23rd Dec. 1766.

State of the Island of Cape Breton. In Major-General Gage's despatch of the 23rd Dec. 1766.

Governor Johnstone to Colonel Tayler, Pansacola, 4th Oct. 1766, on the necessity of a war with the Creeks.

Major-General Gage, 10th Oct. 1766. on the hardships of the inhabitants about Detroit.

Major-General Gage, 17th January 1767, on the state of Pensacola and the Mississippi, &c.

Major-General Gage, 20th Feb. 1767, on the peaceable disposition of the Indians, on quartering some troops at Boston, and on his correspondence with General Pitken about quartering the German recruits.

Major-General Gage, 22nd Feb. 1767, on the Indian trade.

Major-General Gage, 3rd April 1767, on the quartering of the troops at New York.

Major-General Gage, 4th April 1767, on the reduction of expenses.

Major-General Gage, 5th April 1767, on the quitrents of North America.

Major-General Gage, 15th May 1767, on the Indian wars, the quartering of troops in Carolina, &c., and the behaviour of the Spaniards in the Mississippi.

Lord Barrington, 20th May 1767, on the quartering of the troops in Canada.

Abstract of despatches from Major-General Gage, dated 28th and 29th of April 1767, and received 5th June 1767, on the smuggling trade.

Abstract of a despatch from Major-General Gage, 27th May 1767, on the state of Pensacola, disposition of the Indians, &c.

Major-General Gage, 13th June 1767, on the Indian boundary, &c.

Major-General Gage, 20th Aug. 1767, on the misbehaviour of the traders.

Major-General Gage, 24th Aug. 1767, on the disposition of the troops arrive from Ireland, Indian trade, &c.

Major-General Gage, 31st Aug. 1767, on the Spanish Cartel and disposition of the troops, &c.

Major-General Gage, 10th Oct. 1767, on Indian affairs.

Major-General Gage, 19th Oct. 1767, on a Mutiny Bill in the Bermudas, encroaching upon the prerogative of the Crown.

Major-General Gage to Lord Barrington, 20th Oct. 1767, on the misbehaviour of Major Rogers.

Mr. John Stuart to the Lords of Trade, 23rd Sept. 1766, petitioning for a grant of land.

Mr. John Stuart to the Lords of Trade, 16th Nov. 1766, on the prospect of an Indian war.

Governor Johnstone to Mr. John Stuart, 30th Sept. 1766, on the disposition of the Creeks.

Mr. Charles Stuart to Mr. John Stuart, 1st Oct. 1766, on the murder by the Creeks.

Major-General Gage to John Stuart, Esq., 30th Aug. 1766, on Indian Wars.

Mr. Stuart, 1st April 1767, on the disposition of the Creeks.

Mr. Stuart, 1st April 1767, Indian affairs.

Mr. Stuart, 11th April 1767, Indian trade, &c.

Mr. Stuart, 11th April 1767, expenses of the treaties with the Indians, &c.

Mr. Stuart, 28th July 1767, Indian trade, &c.

Mr. Stuart, 22nd Aug. 1767, on the hostilities with the Creeks.

Mr. Stuart, 3rd Oct. 1767, on murders committed by the Creeks.

Extract from Sir William Johnson's letter to the Lords of Trade, 31st Jan. 1766, on the use to be made of the Illinois country.

Extract from Sir William Johnson's letter (to the Lords of Trade), 28th Feb. 1766, Indian boundary.

Extract from Sir William Johnson's letter to the Lords of Trade, 22nd March 1766, designs of the French.

Sir William Johnson to Mr. Sec. Conway, 28th June 1766, on the discontents of the Indians.

Sir William Johnson to Mr. Sec. Conway, 10th July 1766, on a proposal for erecting a colony at the Illinois.

Sir William Johnson to the Lords of Trade, 20th Aug. 1766, on a treaty with the Indians.

Sir William Johnson to the Lords of Trade, 8th Oct. 1766, on a plan for Indian affairs.

Sir William Johnson, 15th Jan. 1767, on the complaints of the Wappinger Indians.

Sir William Johnson to the Lords of Trade, 15th Jan. 1767, on a treaty with the Illinois.

Sir William Johnson, 1st April 1767, on the intended settlement on the Ohio.

Sir William Johnson, 30th May 1767, on the Indian boundary treaty.

Sir William Johnson, 30th May 1767, on a treaty with the six nations about a boundary.

Mr. Holland to Mr. Macklean, 31st July 1767; an account of expenses.

Sir William Johnson, superintendent of Indian affairs for the Northern District, 14th Aug. 1767, and another extract from a letter of his, without date, on the complaints of the Indians.

Abstracts of despatches from Commodore Palliser to the Lords of Trade, (dated 28th and 29th Aug.?) and 9th Sept. 1766, on complaints about the fees of the Customs House officers.

Abstracts of a despatch from Commodore Palliser to the Lords of Trade, 21st Oct. 1766, on the designs of the French with respect to the fishery, by means of the Nova Scotian Indians.

Major Farmer to (Lord Barrington), Secretary of War, 19th March 1766, complaining of hardships.

P. E. Irving, Esq., to the Lords of Trade, 7th Aug. and 20th Aug. 1766, on courts of judicature, &c.

Report of the Attorney-General of Quebec of the persons who refuse to pay duties to the Receiver-General. 19th Aug. 1766.

Lieut.-Governor Carleton to the Lords of Trade, 18th Oct. 1766, on Indian Trade and boundary.

Lieut.-Governor Carleton, 18th and 25th Oct. 1766, on the internal factions, Indian trade, &c.

Lieut.-Governor Carleton, 9th Nov. 1766, recommending Mr. Joncaire for his address and knowledge of the Indians.

Abstract of despatches from Lieut.-Governor Carleton, dated 17th, 21st, and 24th Nov. 1766, and received 24th Dec., on church affairs, revenue, fees of office, Abbé Joncaire, and Mr. Walker's affair.

Lieut.-Governor Carleton, 29th Nov. 1766, on Mr. Walker's affair.

Lieut.-Governor Carleton, 3rd Jan. 1767, on grants of lands.

Abstract of despatches from Lieut.-Governor Carleton, dated 14th Feb. and 4th and 5th March 1767, on the discovery of a mine, the state of the forts, Mr. Walker's affairs, &c.

Abstract of despatches from Lieut.-Governor Carleton, dated 15th and 28th March 1767, on Mr. Walker's affair and Indian trade.

Lieut.-Governor Carleton to the Lords of Trade, 28th March 1767, on Indian trade.

Abstract of a despatch from Lieut.-Governor Carleton, 15th April 1767, on the revenue, and notice of Mr. Hey's letter, dated 14th April 1767, about Mr. Walker's affair.

Lieut.-Governor Carleton, 14th May 1767, on the fees of office.

Abstract of despatches from Lieut.-Governor Carleton, dated 8th and 14th of July 1767, on Mr. Chabert's case, and on mines.

Abstract of despatches from Lieut.-Governor Carleton, 11th June and 29th Aug. 1767, on mines, &c.

Abstract of despatches 22nd, 24th, and 26th of Sept. 1767, recommending Mr. de Lery, &c.

Lieut.-Governor Carleton, 9th Oct. 1767, on Major Roger's conduct.

Lieut.-Governor Carleton, 30th Oct. 1767, on a Canadian bishop.

Mr. Francis Mackay, 30th Oct. 1767, on His Majesty's right to the timber of some estates.

Abstract of despatches from Mr. Green, of Nova Scotia, dated 14th June, 17th July, 8th, 22nd, and 24th Aug. 1766, and from Lieut.-Governor Francklin, dated 24th Aug., 3rd and 16th of Sept. 1766, all addressed to the Lords of Trade, on the general state of the country.

Lieut.-Governor Francklin, 10th Sept. 1766, on the sale of spirituous liquors.

MARQUIS OF LANSDOWNE.

Abstract of despatches from Lieut.-Governor Franklin, of Nova Scotia, to the Lords of Trade, dated 30th Sept. and 1st and 6th Oct. 1766, on coal mines, &c.

Abstract of despatches from Lieut.-Governor Francklin to the Lords of Trade, 13th and 30th of Sept. and 15th of Oct. 1766, relating to posts, Romish priests, and expenses on account of the Indians.

Abstract of despatches from Lieut.-Governor Francklin, dated 31st Oct., 19th, 21st, and 22nd Nov., and 1st of Dec. 1766, on the peaceable state of the colony, state of manufacturers, and debts of the province.

Lieut.-Governor Franklin to the Lords of Trade, 22nd Nov. 1766, on a survey of the coasts and the laws of debtors.

Governor Lord William Campbell, 5th Dec. 1766; complains of the extensive possessions of Lieut.-Governor Franklin.

Address of the Council and House of Assembly of the Province of Nova Scotia to His Majesty, on the state of their debts. In Lord William Campbell's letter to the Lords of Trade, 5th Dec. 1766.

Lord William Campbell, Governor of Nova Scotia, 27th February 1767, on the roads of country.

Lord William Campbell, Governor of Nova Scotia, 4th April 1767, on the expenses of the Government.

Lord William Campbell, Governor of Nova Scotia, 6th April 1767, with lists of vessels, &c.

Lord William Campbell, Governor of Nova Scotia, 20 and 21st of May 1767, on the ill-behaviour of the Spaniards, and on roads.

Abstract of despatches from Lord William Campbell, Governor of Nova Scotia, dated 24th, 25th, and 27th June 1767, inclosing account of fees, &c.

Lord William Campbell, Governor of Nova Scotia, 7th Sept. 1767, inclosing estimates for the support of Government, &c.

Abstract of despatches from Lieut.-Governor Francklin, dated 7th Sept., 10th and 24th Oct. 1767, on the conduct of the Acadians.

Estimate of the charge of maintaining and supporting the civil establishment of Nova Scotia for the year 1768.

Mr. Holland to Mr. Macleane, Gasper Bay, 31st July 1767, with the survey of the coasts, showing expenses incurred from 24th Dec. 1765 to 24th Dec. 1766.

Abstract of despaches from Governor Bernard to the Lords of Trade, dated 16th, 18th, 21st Aug. and 3rd and 4th Sept. 1766, on a disturbance about a boundary between New York and New England.

Abstract of a despatch from Governor Bernard, 1st Sept. 1766, wherein he acknowledges the receipt of the Duke of Richmond's letter of 23rd May.

Abstract of despatches from Governor Bernard, dated 4th, 10th, 12th, and 15th Oct. 1766. Disturbance on account of the customs and a petition from the judge of the Court of Admiralty, with an abstract from Mr. De Berd's despatch, 2nd Jan. 1767, relating to the depositions of the inhabitants of Boston respecting the behaviour of the Custom House officers, &c.

Governor Bernard to the Lords of Trade, 15th Oct. 1766, on the case of Mr. Auchmuty in the Court of Admiralty.

Governor Bernard, 10th Oct. 1766, &c., on the opposition to the Custom House officers, the boundary, &c.

Governor Bernard, 14th Nov. 1766, on the riots at Boston.

Governor Bernard to the Lords of Trade, 15th Nov. 1766, on manufactures in the province.

Lieut.-Governor Hutchinson, 15th Nov. 1766, on the compensation for damage done in the riots at Boston.

The House of Representatives of Massachusets Bay to the Earl of Shelburne, 4th Dec. 1766, expressing their concern that they should be represented to His Majesty as the cause of reviving disagreeable disputes, &c.

Governor Bernard, 6th Dec. 1766, on a compensation or damages in the riots.

Abstract of despatches from Governor Bernard, 22nd, 24th, and 30th Dec. 1766, rise of the disturbances in Boston; history of James Otis, Esq.

Governor Bernard, 4th Jan. 1767, on the addition to his salary.

Governor Bernard, 24th Jan., 7th, 14th, and 18th Feb. 1767, on the progress of the disturbances, provision for troops, &c.

Abstract of despatches from Governor Bernard, dated 21st and 28th Feb. and 2nd March 1767, on the Lieut.-Governor's seat in Council, riots at Falmouth, expenses of the government, &c.

(Governor Bernard's) observations on the account of the expenses of the government of Massachusets Bay.

Governor Bernard's additional observations (on the same subject (in his dispatch of 2nd March 1767).

Abstract of despatches from Governor Bernard, dated 23rd, 28th, 30th March, 13th April, and 4th and 9th May 1767, on the boundary, fees, revenue, and agents.

Governor Bernard, 30th May 1767, on the Lieut.-Governor's seat in the Council.

Governor Bernard, 6th June 1767, on his disputes with the Assembly.

Governor Bernard, 22nd June 1767, on the appointment of an agent.

Governor Bernard, 27th July 1767, on the faction losing ground.

Governor Bernard, 24th Aug. 1767, on the faction reviving.

Abstract of despatches from Governor Wentworth, dated 16th and 23rd June 1767, on preparing estimates.

A paper marked Rhode Island. No accounts received from it. Undated and without signature.

Governor Ward of Rhode Island, 25th June and 6th Nov. 1766, on the money due to the colony, &c.

Governor Ward of Rhode Island, 6th Nov. 1766, on the money due to the colony.

Governor Pitkin of Connecticut, 4th Aug. 1766, address of the Assembly on the repeal of the Stamp Act.

Deputy Governor Sharpe (of Maryland), 9th Dec. 1766, compensation voted by the Assembly to the persons who suffered loss by the mob.

Governor Gitkin (Pitkin), dated Hartford, 22nd Sept. 1766, acknowledges the gratitude of the people of Connecticut for Act of Parliament passed in favour of America.

Governor Pitkin, Harford, Connecticut, 4th Dec. 1766, on apprehensions of the resentment of the Indians.

Governor Pitkin to the Lords of Trade, Hartford, 5th Dec. 1766, an account of manufactures.

Governor Pitkin of Connecticut, 1st June 1767, on the expenses of government.

Abstract of despatches from Sir Henry Moore transmitted by the Board of Trade, dated New York, 12th and 18th Aug. 1766, disturbances by the Indians.

Sir Henry Moore, 11th Oct. 1766, on the boundary of the province, &c.

Sir Henry Moore, New York, 8th Nov. 1766, on the boundary of the province and grants of lands.

Abstract of despatches from Sir Henry Moore, 3rd, 4th, and 7th April 1767, on the Wappinger Indians, augmentation of the council.

Sir Henry Moore to the Lords of Trade, 4th April 1767, on the Canadian boundary.

Abstract of despatches from Sir Henry Moore, 20th, 25th, and 26th April 1767, on the fees of officers, intrusions on the Crown lands.

Abstract of despatches from Sir Henry Moore, 17th, 22nd, and 23rd May 1767, probate of wills, and a petition of some soldiers for land.

Abstract of despatches from Sir Henry Moore, 9th and 10th June 1767, petition of S. Robinson, New England boundary, and provision for the troops.

Abstract of despatches from Sir Henry Moore, 21st and 22nd Aug. 1767, on quartering of troops and Crown lands.

Abstract of despatches from Sir Henry Moore, 1st, 4th, and 5th, Oct. 1767 on the low state of the magistracy, quartering of troops.

Lieut.-Governor Colden of New York, 20th Oct. 1767, desires a compensation for his losses in the riots.

Abstract of dispatches from Sir H. Moore, Governor of New York, 24th Oct. 1767, on quartering troops.

Marquess of Granby to the Earl of Shelburne, 5th March 1767, with the list of the ordnance office.

Mr. Penn, Deputy Governor of Pensylvania, 21st Jan. 1767, on the murder of Indians.

Mr. Penn, Deputy Governor of Pensylvania, to the Lords of Trade, 21st Jan. 1767, on manufactures.

Mr. Penn one of the proprietors of Pensylvania, 11th April 1767, on the revenue of the province.

Abstract of dispatches from Governor Franklin (of New Jersey), dated 19th June 1766, 11th Sept., 18th Dec. (1766), 23rd Dec. 1767, and 21st Feb. 1767, on the quartering of troops, murder of Indians, quitrents, &c.

Governor Franklin of New Jersey, 18th Dec. 1766, on the murder of Indians.

Governor Franklin of New Jersey, 18th Dec. 1766, on the quartering of troops.

Governor Franklin of New Jersey, 21st Feb. 1767, on expenses of government.

Abstract of dispatches from Governor Franklin of New Jersey, dated 22nd Aug., 6th and 22nd Oct. 1767, on quartering troops, &c.

Abstract of a dispatch from Sir Henry Moore, Governor of New York, transmitted by the Lords of Trade, dated 15th Nov. 1766, on paper currency and firmness of the Assembly.

Extract from the journal of the General Assembly of New York, 9th Dec. 1766, with complaints against Captain Norwood for seizing a ship.

Sir Henry Moore, Governor of New York, to the Lords of Trade, 10th Dec. 1766, with complaints of the Assembly about restrictions on commerce.

Sir Henry Moore to the Earl of Shelburne, New York, 19th Dec. 1766, complaints against the Assembly.

The Board of Trade to the Earl of Shelburne, White-hall, 29th Jan. 1767 (New York petition).

Sir H. Moore, Governor of New York, to the Lords of Trade, 19th Dec. 1766, and transmitted by the Board of Trade 6th Feb. 1767, on the paper currency, &c.

The address of the General Assembly of New York to Sir H. Moore on the quartering of troops, dated 15th Dec. 1766.

Governor Moore's speech to the General Assembly on the quartering of troops, 17th Nov. 1766.

Abstract of dispatches from Sir Henry Moore, Go-vernor of New York, dated 19th and 22nd Dec. 1766, on the complaints of the Wappinger Indians and on quartering the troops.

Abstract of dispatches from the Lords of Trade, dated 10th, 12th, 14th. and 17th Jan. 1767, on cutting down pine trees and the state of manufactures.

Sir Henry Moore, 17th Feb. 1767, on the payment of bills in Paris, &c.

Abstract of dispatches from Sir Henry Moore, 20th, 21st, 22nd, 23rd, and 24th Feb. 1767, on quitrents, ex-penses of government, and New England boundary.

Vol. 52.

This Vol., 52, is endorsed, " Abstract of Letters from " yᵉ American & West India Govᵗ in 1766 & 1767."

From Deputy-Governor Sharpe, Anapolis, 27th June 1766, on the repeal of the Stamp Act.

From Deputy-Governor Sharpe, Anapolis, 9th Dec. 1766, on the state of manufactures.

From Deputy-Governor Sharpe, Anapolis, 9th Dec. 1766, on a compensation for riots.

From Deputy-Governor Sharpe, Anapolis, 23rd Dec. 1766, behaviour of the Indians.

From Deputy-Governor Sharpe, Anapolis, 20 Sept. 1767, on the receipt of the Act to grant certain duties in America, &c.

Lieut.-Governor Fauquier, of Virginia, 26th July 1766, &c., on illegal settlements, &c.

Lieut.-Governor Fauquier, of Virginia, Williams-burg, 1st Sept. 1766, petitioning in favour of Mr. Wormley, junr., for a comptrollership.

Lieut.-Governor Fauquier, of Virginia, Williamsburg, 12th Sept. 1766, on the repeal of Stamp Act.

Lieut.-Governor Fauquier, of Virginia, Williamsburg, 10th Nov. 1766, his speech and the address of the Assembly on the repeal of the Stamp Act.

Lieut.-Governor Fauquier, of Virginia, Williamsburg, 18th Nov. 1766, and on illegal settlers. Address on the repeal of the Stamp Act and state of manufactures.

Lieut.-Governor Fauquier, of Virginia Williamsburg, 22nd Nov. 1766, and in favour of Mr. Wythe to be Attorney-General.

Lieut.-Governor Fauquier, of Virginia, Williamsburg, 2nd Feb. 1767, on the Indian boundary.

Lieut.-Governor Fauquier, of Virginia, Williamsburg, 27th April 1767, and on discontents, expenses of Govern-ment and murder of Indians.

Lieut.-Governor Fauquier, of Virginia, Williamsburg, 4th June 1767, in favour of Mr. J. Page, for a seat in the Council.

Lieut.-Governor Fauquier, of Virginia, Williamsburg, 25th June 1767, inclosing various accounts.

Lieut.-Governor Fauquier, of Virginia, York, 30th July 1767, in favour of J. Page, &c., for the vacant places in the Council.

Governor Tryon, Brunswick, N. Carolina, 1st Aug. 1766, Act as to forts, &c., repeal of the Stamp Act.

Governor Tryon, Brunswick, N. Carolina, 2nd Aug. 1766, &c., on the repeal of the Stamp Act, the appoint-ment of a Solicitor-General, nomination of the trea-surer and clerks of the Pleas.

Governor Tryon, Brunswick, N. Carolina, 2nd Aug. 1766, on the repeal of the Stamp Act.

Governor Tryon, Brunswick, N. Carolina, 30th Dec. 1766, requesting the appointment of a Solicitor-General.

Governor Tryon, Brunswick, N. Carolina, 15th Nov. 1766, &c., on ship, timber, state of manufactures.

Governor Tryon, Brunswick, N. Carolina, 30th Jan. 1767, &c., on the state of manufactures.

Governor Tryon, Brunswick, N. Carolina, 31st Jan. 1767, on the nomination of a treasurer.

Governor Tryon, Brunswick, N. Carolina, 27th Feb. 1767, &c., on the appointment of a clerk of the Pleas.

Governor Tryon, Brunswick, N. Carolina, 7th March 1767, on the appointment of a treasurer.

Governor Tryon, Brunswick, N. Carolina, 28th March 1767, on the sale of the brigantine " Fox."

Governor Tryon, Brunswick, N., Carolina, 8th July 1767, on a boundary line.

Governor Tryon, Brunswick, N. Carolina, 14th July 1767, on the Cherokee boundary.

Governor Tryon, Brunswick, N. Carolina, 28th July 1767, on the Cherokee boundary.

Governor Tryon, Brunswick, N. Carolina, 29th June 1767, &c., on public accounts, account of taxables, Cherokee boundary, Land Office.

Lord Charles Greville Montague, South Carolina, 12th Aug. 1766, in favour of John Hume having an addition to his salary.

Lord Charles Greville Montague, South Carolina, 19th Sept. 1766, on the nomination to the offices.

Lord Charles Greville Montague, South Carolina, 8th Dec. 1766, on produce and manufactures.

Lord Charles Greville Montague, South Carolina, (no date), complaints of the Indians, various lists.

Lord Charles Greville Montague, Charles Town, 5th March 1767, disturbances among the Indians.

Lord Charles Greville Montague, Charles Town, 14th April 1767, Indian traders.

Lord Charles Greville Montague, South Carolina, 12th May 1767. Suspension of C. Skinner from the Office of C. Justice.

Lord Charles Greville Montague, South Carolina, 14th Aug. 1767, public funds, fees of office, quartering of troops.

Lord Charles Greville Montague, South Carolina, 5th Oct. 1767, &c., disturbance on account of the customs.

Governor Wright, Savannah, 23rd Aug. 1766, on the silk culture.

Governor Wright, Savannah, 28th Oct. 1766, on the repeal of the Stamp Act.

Governor Wright, Savannah, 18th Nov. 1766, on the number of inhabitants, produce, &c.

Governor Wright, Savannah, 29th Nov. 1766, dis-turbances from the Indians, state of the province.

A general state of the trade from Oct. 1765 to Oct. 1766.

Governor Wright, Savannah, 5th Jan. 1767, murder of Indians, temper of the province.

Governor Wright, Savannah, 6th April 1767, opposi-tion to the quartering of troops, paper currency, pro-vincial agent, tar Bill.

Governor Wright, Savannah, 15th May 1767, public moneys, &c.

Governor Wright, Savannah, 15th June 1767, the erection of a lazaretto, disposal of gunpowder, &c.

Governor Wright, Savannah, 23th July 1767, fees of officers.

Governor Wright, Savannah, 14th Aug. &c., quarrels with the Indians, defenceless state of the province.

Governor Wright, Savannah, 24th Oct. 1767, &c., quarrels with the Indians, provision for soldiers.

Governor Wright, Savannah, 17th Sept. 1767, &c., accommodation with Indian troops of the province.

Governor Grant, East Florida, 5th Aug. 1766, &c., on the encouragement to settlers, manufacturers, importa-tion of Greeks by Dr. Turnball.

Governor Grant, East Florida, 5th Aug. 1766, Bermu-dian settlers.

Governor Grant, East Florida, 21st Aug. 1766, and from Commodore Palliser, Newfoundland, 23rd Oct. 1766, war with the Greeks, repeal of the Stamp Act, peaceable state of the fishery.

Governor Grant, St. Augustine, 4th Nov. 1766, on the receipt of an Act of indemnification, &c.

Governor Grant, St. Augustine, 25th Nov. 1766, ac-count of manufacturers.

Governor Grant, St. Augustine, 27th Nov. 1766, dis-appointment of the Bermudan settlers.

Governor Grant, St. Augustine, 17th Jan. 1767, &c., damage to a fort by an hurricane, a bridge over St. Sebastian's creek, Dr. Turnbull's conduct.

Governor Grant, St. Augustine, 22nd Feb. 1767, peaceable state of the Indians.

Governor Grant, St. Augustine, 18th April 1767, &c. return of a draft for building a bridge, Indian affairs.

Governor Grant, St. Augustine, 27th June 1767, diffi-culty with Dennis Rolle's Grant.

Governor Grant, St. Augustine, 16th June 1767, general state of the province.

E e 3

MARQUIS
OF LANS-
DOWNE.

To the Lords of Trade, Whitehall, 9th April 1767, on the settling of Greeks in East Florida.

To the Lords of Trade, Whitehall, 28th April 1767, on the commitment of Mr. Douglas in Jamaica.

To the Lords of Trade, Whitehall, 28th April 1767, on the petition of the inhabitants of Louisbourg.

To the Lords of Trade, Whitehall, 28th April 1767, on the complaint of some Canadians on account of the boundaries of the province.

To the Lords of Trade, Whitehall, 11th May 1767, to lay before the House of Commons, the Journal of the House of Representatives of Massachusets Bay.

To the Lords of Trade, Whitehall, 15th May 1767, about papers to be laid before the House of Lords.

To the Lords of Trade, Whitehall, 15th May 1767, about papers to be laid before the House of Commons.

To the Lords of Trade, Whitehall, 21st May 1767, to lay before the House of Lords papers relating to Quebec.

To the Lords of the Treasury, Whitehall, 25th Nov. 1766, about expenses on account of some Indians who were in London.

To the Lords of the Admiralty, Whitehall, 28th April 1767, for an account of the Court of Admiralty in America.

To Governor O'Hara, Whitehall, 17th Oct. 1766, on the incroachment of the French on the River Gambia.

To Governor O'Hara, Whitehall, 6th June 1767, on the trade up the River Gambia.

To Governor * Major-General Gage and His Majesty's governors in America, &c., Whitehall, 9th Aug. 1766, acquainting them that they are to correspond with him as Secretary of State.

Circular to the Governors of North America and the West Indies, Whitehall, 9th Aug. 1766, with a copy of the revocation of an Order of Council of 11th March 1752, concerning the Board of Trade.

Circular to all the Governors on the continent of America, Whitehall, 13th Sept. 1766, on the murder of some Indians.

Circular to all the Governors on the continent of America, except Newfoundland, Whitehall, 11th Dec. 1766, to procure an estimate of the civil establishment.

Circular to all the Governors of North America, except Newfoundland, Whitehall, 13th Jan. 1767, to procure an account of the fees of officers.

Circular to the Governors of Senegambia, Nova Scotia, and Georgia, Whitehall, 11th April 1767, with the estimate of the civil establishment.

To Lieut.-Governor Carleton, Whitehall, 26th May 1767, relating to the assassination of Mr. Walker, and other matters.

To Lieut.-Governor Carleton, Whitehall, 20th June 1767, expressing approbation of his conduct and that of the Chief Justice of Quebec in the affair of Mr. Walker.

To Sir Henry Moore, Whitehall, 9th Aug. 1766, about the quartering of the troops.

To Sir Henry Moore, Whitehall, 11th Oct. 1766, on the seizure of the lands of some Indians.

Copy of Lord Shelburne's letter to Sir H. Moore for General Greene, Whitehall, 9th Nov. 1766, in favour of Mr. Hasenclever, on account of the manufacture of hemp, iron, and potash.

To Sir Henry Moore, Whitehall, 11th Dec. 1766, on the difference between New York and Massachusets Bay.

To Governor Sir Henry Moore, Whitehall, 20th Feb. 1767, on the provision for the troops.

To Sir Henry Moore, Whitehall, 14th March 1766, on the pay of some provincials who acted with the regulars.

To Sir Henry Moore, Whitehall, 11th April 1767, on the grant of lands in the west side of Connecticut river.

To Governor Franklin, Whitehall, 13th Sept. 1766, on his account of the decent behaviour of the province in the time of the Stamp Act.

To Lieut.-Governor Fauquier on the punishment of those concerned in the violation of the treaties with the Indians, Whitehall, 19th Feb. 1767.

To Lord Wm. Campbell, Whitehall, 19th Feb. 1767, on a proper conduct to the Indians and the improvement of the colony in general.

To Lord Wm. Campbell, Whitehall, 17th March 1767, in favour of Mr. George Spence and others who had a grant of St. John's Island.

To Lord Wm. Campbell, Whitehall, 26th May 1767, refusing the grant of the coal mines of Cape Breton, &c.

---

* Governor in original list of the contents of this volume.

To Lieut.-Governor Franklin, Whitehall, 20th June 1767, on his taking the government of Nova Scotia in the absence of Lord Wm. Campbell.

To Governor Bernard, Whitehall, 13th Sept. 1766, on some discontents which appeared after the affair of the Stamp Act.

To Governor Bernard, Whitehall, 11th Oct. 1766, recommending to his care four Indians who had been in London to complain of the injustice of the English.

To Governor Bernard, Whitehall, 11th Dec. 1766, on the difference with New York on account of boundaries.

To Lord Charles Montague, Whitehall, 25th Oct. 1766, on the quarrels with the Indians, occasioned by the traders, &c.

To Lord Charles Greville Montague, Governor of South Carolina, Whitehall, 3rd Feb. 1767, to grant Mr. Robt. Raper leave of absence.

To Lord Charles Greville Montague, Whitehall, 19th Feb. 1767, about making peace with the Greeks.

To James Grant, Governor of East Florida, Whitehall, 25th Oct. 1766, approving his conduct with respect to the Indians.

To James Grant, Governor of East Florida, Whitehall, 11th Dec. 1766, on the keys of Florida and the Indians.

To Governor Grant, Whitehall, 19th Feb. 1767, approving his conduct to the Indians.

(To Governors Browne and Grant) Governors of East and West Florida, Whitehall, 11th April 1767, inclosing estimates of the colonies.

To Governor Grant, Whitehall, 14th May 1767, encouraging the settlement of Greeks in the province.

To Governor Johnstone, Whitehall, 22nd Sept. 1766, giving him leave to come to England.

To Lieut.-Governor Browne, Whitehall, 22nd Sept. 1766, appointing him to supply the place of Governor Johnstone.

To Governor Johnstone, Whitehall, 19th Feb. 1767, recalling him from his government for engaging in a war with the Indians.

To Lieut.-Governor Browne, Whitehall, 19th Feb. 1767, appointing him to supply the place of Governor Johnstone, and to put an immediate stop to the Indian war.

To Lieut.-Governor Browne, Whitehall, 20th June 1767, acquainting him with the appointment of Capt. Elliot to succeed Governor Johnstone.

To Governor Wright, Whitehall, 22nd Sept. 1766, recommending a proper conduct with respect to the disturbances occasioned by the Stamp Act.

To Governor Wright, Whitehall, 19th Feb. 1767, to promote peace with the Indians.

To Governor Tryon, Whitehall, 19th Feb. 1767, to promote peace with the Indians.

To Governor Tryon, Whitehall, 20th June 1767, about the Indian boundary and other matters.

To Lieut.-Governor Penn, Whitehall, 26th May 1767, to bring to punishment the author of a murder committed at sea.

To Sir Wm. Johnson, Whitehall, 13th Sept. 1766, on the misconduct of the Indian traders.

To John Stuart, Esq., Whitehall, 13th Sept. 1766, to promote peace with the Indians.

To Sir Wm. Johnson, Whitehall, 11th Oct. 1766, on the complaints of the Indians.

To John Stuart, Esq., agent and superintendant for Indian affairs in the south district, Whitehall, 11th Dec. 1766, to promote peace with the Indians.

To Sir Wm. Johnson, Whitehall, 11th Dec. 1766, on the plan for regulating Indian affairs.

To Sir Wm. Johnson, Whitehall, 19th Feb. 1767, to promote peace with the Indians.

To John Stuart, Esq., superintendant of Indian affairs for the southern district, Whitehall, 19th Feb. 1767, to promote peace with the Indians.

To Sir Wm. Johnson, Whitehall, 20th June 1767, on the plan for the first settlement of Indian affairs.

To Major-General Burton, Whitehall, 9th August 1766, approving the behaviour of the Indians.

To Major-General Gage, Whitehall, 13th Sept. 1766, on quartering the troops at New York.

To Major-General Gage, Whitehall, 13th Sept. 1766, to pay the owners of a sloop that had been impressed for the service of the garrison at Quebec.

To Major-General Gage, Whitehall, 11th Oct. 1766, on the birth of a princess.

To Major-General Gage, Whitehall, 11th Dec. 1766, on the settlement of Indian affairs, the disposal of the troops and the reduction of the expenses.

MARQUIS
OF LANS-
DOWNE.

E e 4

To Major-General Gage, Whitehall, 19th Feb. 1767, to promote peace with the Indians.

To Mr. Verchild (President of the Council at St. Christopher), Whitehall, 11th Dec. 1766, to procure an estimate of the establishment.

To Mr. President Verchild, Whitehall, 20th June 1767, approving the behaviour of the inhabitants of the Leeward Islands.

To Governor Melville, Whitehall, 3rd Feb. 1767, on the suit of Mr. Riquebourg.

To Governor Melville, Whitehall, 19th Feb. 1767, granting him leave of absence for 12 months.

To Governor Bruere, Whitehall, 19th Feb. 1767, on the claims of the owners of vessels seized by the Spaniards.

To Governor Bruere, Whitehall, 20th June 1767, on the payment of his salary and other matters.

To Governor Shirley, Whitehall, 20th June 1767, on the payment of his salary.

To Mr. Symmer, Whitehall, 20th June 1767, on his plan for the settlement of the Caicos Islands.

Vol. 54.

This Vol. 54 is endorsed, "Drafts of letters to " American and W[t] India Governors, from June " 1767 to y[e] end of y[t] year."

Circulars to all the Governors in North America and the West Indies, 11th July 1767, for granting certain duties in America, &c., and a new seal for the Colony.

Lord Shelburne to General Gage, 14th Nov. 1767, on the establishment of new governments in the back settlements, &c.

Lord Shelburne to General Gage, 19th Dec. 1767, on the complaints against Major Rogers, &c.

Lord Shelburne to Sir William Johnson, 19th Dec. 1767, on the Indian boundary.

Mr. Macleane to Brigadier Carleton, 24th Oct. 1767, inclosing copies of former dispatches.

Lord Shelburne to Brigadier Carleton, 14th Nov. 1767, the case of Mr. Chabert. Conduct of Jesuits in Canada, &c.

Lord Shelburne to Governor Bernard, 17th Sept. 1767, on the appointment of the Lieut.-Governor to a seat in the council, the agency, &c.

Lord Shelburne to Governor Bernard, 8th Oct. 1767, on the appointment of H. Hatton, &c. to be Custom House officers.

Lord Shelburne to Governor Bernard, 14th Nov. 1767, on a printed paper reflecting on the Government.

Lord Shelburne to Sir H. Moore, 18th July 1767, transmitting the Act to suspend the Legislature of New York till they had assented to the Mutiny Act.

Lord Shelburne to Sir H. Moore, 14th Nov. 1767, approving of his conduct with respect to the Mutiny Act.

Lord Shelburne to Governor Franklin, 18th July 1767, requiring an entire acquiescence in the Mutiny Act.

Lord Shelburne to Lieut.-Governor Fauquier, 8th Oct. 1767, on the claim of the Ohio Company to certain lands.

Lord Shelburne to Lieut.-Governor Fauquier, 14th Nov. 1767, requiring him to compleat his boundary line.

Lord Shelburne to Governor Tryon, 14th Nov. 1767, recommending the completion of his boundary line.

Lord Shelburne to Lord Charles Montague, 8th Oct. 1767, disapproving his suspension of the Chief Justice.

Lord Shelburne to Governor Wright, 18th July 1767, requiring a compliance with the Mutiny Act.

Lord Shelburne to Governor Wright, 14th Nov. 1767, approving the methods he had taken to conciliate the Indians, and his erection of a lazaretto.

Lord Shelburne to Colonel Grant, 14th Nov. 1767, approving his treaty with the Indians and his method of opening a communication between some provinces.

Lord Shelburne to Lieut.-Governor Elliston, 11th July 1767, transmitting the Act to grant certain duties, &c., and a new seal.

Lord Shelburne to Governor Melvill, 8th Oct. 1767, requiring him to send intelligence of the state of the province.

Lord Shelburne to Governor Spry, 2nd Aug. 1767, acquainting him with his appointment to the Government of Barbadoes, and recommending Captain Williams.

Lord Shelburne to Governor Shirley, 14th Nov. 1767, with a pardon for P. Duseau, and acquainting him with the appointment of his son to the Government of the Bahama Islands.

Lord Shelburne to President Rous, 14th Nov. 1767, on the non-residence of several members of the council.

Lord Shelburne to Mr. Symmer, 8th Oct. 1767, checking his forwardness to settle a Civil Government in the Turks Islands.

Vols. 55, 56.

These Vols. are endorsed, " Answers to American " Circulars. In the years 1766 and 1767." There is an Index.

I.

Circular from the Lords of Trade to all the Governors on the continent of America, to procure an account of the manufactures, Whitehall, 1st Aug. 1766.

Governor Bernard to the Lords of Trade (Massachusets), 15th Nov. 1766. State of manufactures in the (Province of) Massachusets Bay.

Lieut.-Governor Fauquier to the Lords of Trade (Williamsburgh) 17th Dec. 1766, on manufactures in Virginia.

Governor Wright to the Lords of Trade, Savannah in Georgia, .18th Nov. 1766. State of manufactures in Georgia.

Governor Grant to the Lords of Trade, St. Augustine, 25th Nov. 1766, state of manufactures in East Florida.

Governor Pitkin to the Lords of Trade (Connecticut), 5th Dec. 1766, state of manufactures in Connecticut.

Governor Sharpe to the Lords of Trade, Annapolis, 9th Dec. 1766, state of manufactures in Maryland.

Address of the House of Delegates of the Province of Maryland to the Lieut.-Governor, 6th Dec. 1766, on the manufactures in the Province.

Governor Sir Henry Moore to the Lords of Trade, Fort George, New York, 12th Jan. 1767, state of manufactures in the Province of North York.

Deputy-Governor Penn to the Lords of Trade (Pensylvania), 21st Jan. 1767, state of manufactures in Pensylvania.

Lieut.-Governor Browne to the Lords of Trade (West Florida) 25th Jan. 1767, state of manufactures in West Florida.

Governor Tryon to the Lords of Trade, Brunswick, (North Carolina), 30th Jan. 1767, state of manufactures North Carolina.

Governor Tryon to the Lords of Trade, Brunswick, 2nd Feb. 1767, state of the saw-mills in the Province of North Carolina.

Lieut.-Governor Franklin, Halifax, Nova Scotia, 21st Nov. 1766, state of manufactures in Nova Scotia.

Circular to all the governors on the continent of America, Whitehall, 11th Dec. 1766, to procure an account of the civil establishment, and of the manner of imposing quitrents and granting lands.

Circular to all the governors on the continent of America, Whitehall, 13th Jan. 1767, to procure an account of the fees of offices.

Governor Sir Henry Moore to the Earl of Shelburne, Fort George, New York, 20th Feb. 1767; state of quitrents and grants of lands in New York.

Docquet of lands granted in New York from 31st Oct 1765 to 13th Feb. 1767.

Governor Franklin to the Earl of Shelburne (Burlington, New Jersey), 21st Feb. 1767 ; state of quitrents in New Jersey, and expenses of government.

Governor Bernard to the Earl of Shelburne, 2nd March 1767, on the expenses of government, &c. in Massachusets Bay.

An account of the mode of granting lands in the province of Massachusets Bay.

Governor Sir Henry Moore to the Earl of Shelburne, Fort George, New York, 21st Feb. 1767, on the expenses of the Government of New York.

* Observations on the account of the expenses of the Government of Massachusets Bay. Inclosed in letter of Feb. 20th.

Mr. Penn, one of the proprietors of Pennsylvania, (Spring Gardens), 11th April 1767, on the expenses of government.

Lord William Campbell to the Earl of Shelburne, Halifax, Nova Scotia, 4th April 1767, on the expenses of government in Nova Scotia.

Governor Franklin to the Earl of Shelburne, Burlington, New Jersey, 12th April 1767, on the fees of offices in New Jersey.

Sir Henry Moore to the Earl of Shelburne, Fort George, New York, 25th April 1767, on the fees of offices in the province of New York.

Governor Bernard to Lord Shelburne, Boston, 30th March 1767, on the fees of offices in Massachusets Bay.

---

* In the margin of p. 160 is the following note:—" For Governor " Bernard's observations, &c., vide 14 pages forward." (viz., p. 172).

Governor Wright to the Earl of Shelburne, Savannah in Georgia, 15th May 1767, on the expenses of government in Georgia.

Lieut.-Governor Fauquier, to the Earl of Shelburne, Williamsburg, 20th May 1767, on the fees of offices in Virginia.

*J Blair to the Governor, on the manner of imposing quitrents in Virginia.

An account of grants of lands in Virginia.

· An account of salaries and fees of office in Virginia.

Lieut.-Governor Carleton to the Earl of Shelburne, Quebec, 15th April 1767, expense of the Government in Canada.

Extract of a letter from Lieut.-Governor Carleton, Quebec, 14th May 1767, on the fees of offices in Canada.

Deputy Governor Sharpe to the Earl of Shelburne, Annapolis, 14th May 1767, on the expenses of government in Maryland, and grants of land.

Deputy Governor Sharpe to the Earl of Shelburne, 14th May 1767, inclosing an Act of Assembly made in 1717, regulating the collectors and naval officers' fees in the province of Maryland.

Extract from the Act of Assembly passed in Maryland, 26th Nov. 1763, on fees of offices.

Lieut.-Governor Fauquier to the Earl of Shelburne, Virginia, 25th June 1767, on the fees of the naval officers in Virginia.

Governor Grant to the Earl of Shelburne, St. Augustine, 16th July 1767, on the expenses of government, and grant of lands in East Florida.

II.

Governor Wright to Lord Shelburne, 20th July 1767, on the fees of officers in Georgia.

Lieut.-Governor Browne, 8th July 1767, to Lord Shelburne, on the grants of land and fees of offices in West Florida.

Lord Wm. Campbell to Lord Shelburne, 27th June 1767, on fees of office in Nova Scotia.

Conditions on which lands are granted in Nova Scotia.

Governor Pitkin† to Lord Shelburne, 1st June 1767, on the expense of government in Connecticut.

Governor Pitkin† to Lord Shelburne, 1st June 1767, on quitrents in Connecticut.

Lord Charles Greville Montague, to the Earl of Shelburne, 14th Aug. 1767, on the mode of granting lands in South Carolina.

List of fees taken in South Carolina.

Governor Grant to the Earl of Shelburne, 8th Aug. 1767, on the fees of office in East Florida.

Governor Tryon to the Earl of Shelburne, 21st July 1767, on the fees of office in North Carolina.

Governor Tryon to the Earl of Shelburne, 16th and 17th July 1767, on the mode of granting lands in North Carolina, &c.

An account of the ordinary and extraordinary expenses, both civil and military, of the government of North Carolina, which are defrayed by provincial funds of the said government.

An estimate of monies emitted and raised in North Carolina, from 1748 to 1766, both years inclusive, and to what purposes the same was raised, by what taxes sunk, replaced, &c.

Deputy Governor Penn to the Earl of Shelburne, 24th April 1767, on the expenses of government in Pennsylvania.

Deputy Governor Penn, to the Earl of Shelburne, 25th April 1767, on the fees of office in Pennsylvania.

Vol. 57.

This volume is endorsed "Accounts of American Ex-
" pense, both Military and Civil, and Proposals for
" better regulating the Indian Trade, with Observa-
" tions."

State of the King's rights and revenues at Detroit, and conditions on which lots were granted in the town and lands in the settlements in the time of the French.

Sales of lands in the Southern Caribbee islands (1765 and 1766).

Military establishment of America for the year 1765.

Governor Gage to the Secretary at War, New York, 11th Oct. 1766, inclosing estimates of the military expenses.

Estimate of expenses attending the Secretary's office in time of peace.

Estimate of the expense of fire, candles, &c., for the King's barracks in N. America, and of the expense of furnishing these and keeping the furniture in order, with explanatory remarks, and a detail of the expense.

Estimate of the expenses attending two troops of rangers in Georgia for the year 1766.

Estimate of the expenses of carrying on His Majesty's service in the department of the Commissary General, from 25th Dec. 1765 to 24th Dec. 1766.

Estimate of the expenses of the works at the forts in the district of New York for 1766.

Estimate of the expenses attending a regular post to and from New York to Albany for 1766.

An estimate of the naval department on the lakes for 1766.

Estimate of the naval stores necessary for the several vessels on the lakes for 1766.

Estimate of the expenses incurred in one year in South Carolina and Georgia, for transporting provisions from the places of deposit to the forts Augusta, Prince George, and Charlotte, and to three sergeants for issuing the provision there.

Estimate of the annual expense of the Deputy Quartermaster-General's department in the district of New York for the year 1766.

Estimate (for the year 1766) of the expenses of the Commissary Muster Master's office in North America, which according to the disposition of the troops, but as they now stand for 1766.

Estimate of ordinary contingencies in Nova Scotia for one year (1766).

Estimate of the yearly contingent expenses of the garrison of Louisbourg, Island battery and colliery.

Estimate (for the year 1766) of the annual expense attending the Commissary-General of stores and provisions department in Canada.

Estimate (for the year 1766) of the annual expenses of His Majesty's hospital in the garrison of Quebec.

Estimate (for the year 1766) of the annual expenses attending the Brigadier-General's department for the northern district.

Estimate (for the year 1766) of the expense attending the Assistant Deputy Quartermaster-General's department under the Brigadier-General commanding in the northern district.

Estimate for repairing the Church of St. Francis at St. Augustine for soldiers' barracks (1766).

Estimate for building five kitchens.

Estimate (for the year 1766) of the expenses necessary for the repair of the several yards and store houses for the ordnance service and batteries at Halifax, Nova Scotia.

Estimate (for the year 1766) of the expenses that will attend the repairs of Fort Cumberland, Fort Frederick, and Fort Edward in Halifax, Nova Scotia.

Governor Gage to the Secretary at War, New York, Oct. 28, 1766, inclosing other estimates.

Estimate (for the year 1766) of the annual expense of Fort Amherst in St. John's Island.

Estimate of the supposed expense for the year 1766 of the Quartermaster-General's department at Albany.

List of the officers of the northern department of Indian affairs under the superintendency of Sir William Johnson, Bart., with their salaries, and also those appointments intended by the plan for the better management of Indian affairs, &c.

Extract of a letter from Governor Gage to Lord Barrington, dated New York, 9th Nov. 1766, inclosing estimates of provisions, &c.

An estimate of the expense of provisions issued to His Majesty's troops and condemned and destroyed in one year in North America.

Abstract of the several estimates transmitted to the Secretary at War, New York, 11th Oct. 1766.

Estimate of officers' salaries and other contingencies (presents) in the southern,* department of Indian affairs annually. In General Gage's, 21st Dec. 1766.

Estimate of the expenses at the forts for the year 1767.

Estimate for inclosing the public building, and building two stone block houses, and some necessary repairs at Niagara, for the year 1767.

Estimate of the expense of works necessary to be carried on at Detroit for the year 1767. In General Gage's, 21 Dec. 1766.

An estimate of the expense of provisions issued to His Majesty's troops and others, and condemned and destroyed in one year, in West Florida. In General Gage's of 15th Jan. 1767.

Estimate of officers' salaries and other contingencies, annually, in the southern department of Indian affairs,

---

† In the margin J. Adair. The letter is signed John Blair.
† In previous volumes there is reason to think that Gilkin is written for Pitkin, and in Vol. 56, pp. 19, 38, 39, and 40, we find Pitkin.

* Northern in original list.

exclusive of general meetings and congresses. Inclosed in Mr. Stuart's letter to the Earl of Shelburne, 11th April 1767.

State of the expenses of government at Nova Scotia, and how the same is defrayed.

Particulars of that part of the expense of government at Nova Scotia for the year 1766, which was defrayed by a grant of Parliament.

Particulars of the expense of the government of Nova Scotia, which was defrayed out of the provincial funds.

The particular duties and taxes which constitute the provincial funds at Nova Scotia, and the duration of the laws by which such taxes are laid and duties imposed, together with the appropriation thereof, with an abstract of the state of the provincial funds in Nova Scotia. Transmitted by Lord William Campbell, 4th April 1767.

General distribution of His Majesty's forces in North America according to the disposition now made, and to be completed as soon as practicable, 29th March 1766.

Establishment of the (forts) forces, staff garrisons, &c. in North America, for the year 1767.

Abstract of the contingent charges in North America, distinguishing such as are annual and such as are not, together with the charge for provisions for 1767.

Mr. Macleane's account of the state of the preceding papers.

Expenses of America for one year.

Mr. Bradshaw to Lord Shelburne, Great George Street, 4th Sept. 1766, relating to the contingent expenses for America.

A summary of some expenses for Nova Scotia, &c.

Queries relating to some articles of American revenue with answers.

Account of His Majesty's duty of 4½ per cent., for 39 years from 1721 to 1760.

Account of money drawn for by Governor Melville for the service of the islands under his command.

Annual expenses of America.

Memorandum from Mr. Townshend of expenses on account of America, &c.

Annual expense of the civil establishment of America.

Plan of forts and garrisons proposed for the security of North America, and the establishment of commerce with the Indians, &c.

Lord Barrington's observations on the forts and Indian posts, with remarks by General Gage, dated 10th May 1766.

Plan for the future management of Indian affairs, with a list of the Indian tribes in the northern and southern districts of North America.

Remarks on the preceding plan by Dr. Franklin.

Remarks on the preceding plan by Mr. Jackson.

Remarks on the same plan (anonymous).

Circular to all the governors on the continent of America, except Newfoundland, Whitehall, 11th Dec. 1766, for the estimate of supporting the several establishments.

Lord Shelburne to Major-General Gage, Whitehall, 11th Dec. 1766, relative to Indian affairs, the quartering of troops, and on American revenue.

Lord Shelburne to Sir Wm. Johnson, Whitehall, 11th Dec. 1766, on the regulation of Indian affairs.

Lord Shelburne to John Stuart, Esq., Whitehall, 11th Dec. 1766, on Indian affairs.

Circular to all the governors on the continent of America, Whitehall, 13th Jan. 1767, for an account of the established fees for the grant of lands.

Lord Granby to Lord Shelburne, Knightsbridge, 5th March, 1767, inclosing an account of the state of the artillery.

The principal officers of the ordnance to the Marquis of Granby, inclosing an account of the artillery in England and New York. Office of Ordnance 30th Jan. 1767.

Vol. 58.

This volume is endorsed " Papers relative to the In-
" demnity Act passed in Massachusets Bay and
" to the American Mutiny Act, both under con-
" sideration of Parliament in the year 1767."

A minute about the right of the Lieut.-Governor of Massachusets Bay to sit in Council to put a negative upon such members of the Council as he disapproves of, and to appoint a provincial agent, with the Attorney-General's opinion upon those three points.

Abstract of American correspondence (from 1765 to 1767) laid before the Parliament, 12th March 1767.

A narrative of occurrences in the province of Massachusets Bay since the repeal of the Stamp Act.

Extract of a letter from the Hon. Daniel Dulany, Esq., of Maryland, to the Right Hon. Lord Baltimore on the repeal of the Stamp Act.

Extracts from the minutes of the House of Lords. relating to the repeal of the American Stamp Act.

Extracts from the votes of the House of Commons, relating to the repeal of the American Stamp Act.

The practice relating to quartering troops in Ireland and Scotland.

Mr. Pownal's opinion concerning the suspending clause in Acts of American Assemblies.

A proposal relating to the defraying the expenses of quartering the troops in New York conformable to Act of Parliament.

Abstract of Sir H. Moore's letters of the 10th of June and 21st of Aug. relating to the Act for quartering the troops in New York.

The copy of a minute relating to the Mutiny Act from Sir H. Moore's letters.

Extract from the Act of Parliament for rendering more effectual in America, "An Act for punishing " Mutiny and Desertion, and for the better payment of " the Army and their Quarters."

Extracts from the letters of General Gage and Sir Henry Moore, relating to the proceedings upon a requisition of a provision for quartering, &c. of the troops in America in pursuance of the Act of Parliament.

An account of the manner in which the several provinces in North America yielded to the Mutiny Act.

State of the case, relative to the Act for punishing mutiny, &c. in Bermuda, abstracted from Governor Bruere's and General Gage's letters.

Mr. Secretary Pitt to the Governors in North America, 30th Dec. 1757, respecting the raising of troops in the last war.

Penalties and forfeitures attending the breaches of the several acts of trade, recoverable only in the King's Courts, &c.

Extract from Governor Bernard's Commission.

An account of several acts of grace.

Original questions as to the King's prerogative of pardoning.

Queries concerning the Bill of Indemnity and Oblivion, with judges' opinions.

The form of an Order of Council for disallowing Plantation Acts.

Report of the Committee of Council on the Massachusets Act of compensation, &c.

Queries concerning the quartering of troops at New York.

Mr. Dunning's opinion concerning acts of grace.

Abstract of several acts of grace with queries relating thereto.

Copy of the 6th Article of the General Instructions to the Lieut.-Governor of Virginia in 1609.

The case of Virginia relating to its defence against the Indians.

Copy of an order to prepare a Bill for the pardon of the Governor and Assembly of Virginia for passing certain acts of Assembly at the threatening of N. Bacon, &c.

Copy of the order for new charters for the provinces of New England, 22nd Feb. 1688.

Reasons alledged in the scire facias for vacating the charters of the Massachusets Bay in New England, in the reign of Charles II.

An Act for reuniting to the Crown, the government of the several colonies and plantations in America.

A minute of the Council relating to the proprietary governments, 16th May 1689.

Mr. Usher's case, Receiver-General of New England, who levied taxes when the charter was abrogated, Dec. 1689.

Extract from the journal of the Committee for trade, and plantations at the Council Chamber, Whitehall, Friday, 8th July 1692, relating to the pardon of offences in the disorders at New York.

Address of the Lords Spiritual and Temporal in Parliament to his Majesty, about the state of the trade of this kingdom, with reference to the plantations in the West Indies, 18th March 1696.

Copy of an Order in Council (Whitehall), 31st Aug. 1699, declaring null and void an Act passed in Pennsylvania for preventing frauds and regulating abuses in trade.

The opinion of Sir Edward Northey, the Attorney-General, on the incapacity of Papists to purchase lands in the plantations, dated 21st June 1704.

Extract of an address of the House of Lords to Her Majesty, dated 12th March 1705, to repeal two Acts of the Carolina Assembly.

' Copy of a report of Sir Edward Northey, Attorney-General, relating to Papists in Maryland, dated 8th Oct. 1705.

A Commission to pardon some rebels in the Leeward Islands and to send others to be tried in England.

' A Bill for the better regulation of charter and proprietary governments in America, and for the encouragement of the trade of this kingdom and of Her Majesty's plantations, dated 20th June 1705-6.

' Report of the Solicitor-General to the Lords of Trade, advising the repeal of two laws of the Carolina Assembly, 17th May 1706.

An order for the repeal of two laws passed, in the Carolina Assembly, 10th June 1706.

Repeal of a Barbadoes Act, 9th June 1709.

Extract from an order of Her Majesty in Council, 24th Oct. 1709, to show the laws could not be repealed in part.

Preamble of an Act for granting a revenue to Her Majesty to arise within the province of New York, in America, for the support of that Government, 1711.

Orders of Council and other papers (six in all) relating to the settlement of a revenue for defraying the charges of a Government at New York, 1710.

An Order of Council abrogating an Act of a provincial Assembly, 1718.

Extracts from the journals of the House of Lords, relating to the state of manufacturers in the Colonies, 1733, &c.

Preamble of an Act passed in New Jersey, relating to riots and disturbances, 1745, &c.

Copy of the preamble of an Act passed in New Jersey, 16th Feb. 1747-8, to pardon persons guilty of riots in that province.

An Act to pardon the persons guilty of the insurrections, riots, and disorders raised and committed in New Jersey, 1748.

Report of the Attorney-General, 7th April 1756, on an Act passed in Pensylvania, relating to the quartering of the troops.

An Act to render more effectual in His Majesty's dominions in America, the Act for punishing mutiny and desertion, 1765.

A letter from Governor Colden to Mr. Secretary Conway, 24th June 1766, relating to the damage done by a riot.

Minutes from the American Mutiny Act.

Abstract of an Act to amend and render more effectual in his Majesty's Dominions in America, an Act intituled " An Act for punishing Mutiny and Desertion."

Order in Council directing the Board of Trade to consider the Colony Acts.

Extract from the minutes of Assembly of New York, 9th Dec. 1766, relating to a complaint against Captain Norwood.

A letter from Governor Colden to the Earl of Shelburne, 26th Dec. 1766, relating to losses sustained in the riots.

Extract from the votes of the House of Assembly of the province of New York, on the 9th day of Dec. 1766, relating to Governor Colden's losses in the riots.

A letter from Governor Bernard to the Earl of Shelburne, 24th Dec. 1766, relating to his opposition to Mr. Otis, &c.

Extracts from the journals of the House of Representatives of Massachusets Bay, 1761, &c., relating to the requisitions from the Crown.

Preamble of the Compensation Act, passed in New York, 19th Dec. 1766.

A letter from Mr. Dexter to Mr. Deberdt, dated Dedham, 6th Jan. 1767, relating to the dissatisfaction of the people at the conduct of Governor Bernard.

The reply of the House of Representatives to the message of Governor Bernard, 30th Jan. 1767, relating to his providing for the artillery companies.

An account of the Mutiny Act in America, 1767.

A representation from the Board of Trade on the Barrack Act of New York, 26th March 1767.

Report of the Board of Trade on the Act passed in Massachusets Bay, for compensation and indemnity, 13th April 1767.

Repeal of an Act of the Assembly of New York, relating to furnishing the barracks with firewood, &c., 13th April 1767.

A letter from Governor Grant (St. Augustine, 18th April 1767), relating to his draughts for the building of a bridge over St. Sebastian Creek.

A letter from Governor Grant (St. Augustine, 19th April 1767), relating to treaties with the Indians.

A letter from Governor Bernard to the Earl of Shelburne, 4th May 1767, relating to his altercations with the House of Assembly.

A repeal of an Act of Assembly of Massachusets Bay, relating to the pardon of offenders in the riots, 13th May 1767.

Dates of proceedings, &c. relative to the Act of Compensation, Indemnity, and Oblivion passed by the Governor, Assembly, and Council of Massachusets Bay, from the 6th Dec. 1766 till 15th May 1767.

An Act to restrain the Assembly of New York from passing any Act till they have made provisions for troops.

Part of the American Mutiny Bill.

Vol 59.

This volume is endorsed " Papers relative to the Church " in America."

The Bishop of London to the Board of Trade on the provision for the clergy in the colonies, &c., 1st March 1766.

Notes of the statutes, &c. extending to the colonies.

Heads of a plan for the establishment of ecclesiastical affairs in Quebec.

A letter from the Archbishop of York, dated Dartmouth Street, 10th April 1767, relating to the church in Canada. (An original.)

Resolutions of the House of Lords relating to the laws of the colonies, 5th April 1734.

Thoughts upon the ecclesiastical establishment in Canada by the Archbishop of York, 11th April 1764.

Heads of a plan for the establishment of ecclesiastical affairs in the province of Quebec, April 1767.

Thoughts upon the present state of the Church of England in America, June 1764.

Vol. 60.

This volume is endorsed " Correspondence relating to " the Indian Trade."

The commission of Queen Anne concerning the Mohican Indians, 1703.

A warrant to the Governor of Connecticut with respect to the Mohican Indians, 23rd March 1704.

An account of Sir William Johnson's letters, &c., relating to Indian affairs.

A letter of Mr. Capacin to Mr. Bpt. Campeau, dated du Coste Vincent, 7th June 1765.

Extract of Sir William Johnson's letter to the Lords of Trade, dated 31st Jan. 1766, on gaining the possession of the Illinois.

Extract of Sir William Johnson's letter to the Lords of Trade, dated 22nd March 1766, concerning the artifices of the French.

A letter from J. Stuart to J. Pownal concerning his transactions with the Indians, dated Charles Town, 24th Aug. 1765.

Extract of a letter from Mr. Alexander Cameron to Mr. Stuart, dated 10th May 1766, concerning the fixing of a boundary.

A talk from Ouonnastolah, Willinnawar, Ottassettee, Killagusta, Indians, &c., to the Hon. William Bull, Esq., Lieut.-Governor of South Carolina, at Toguah, 11th July 1765, concerning a boundary.

A letter from Governor Johnstone on the rupture between the Chactaws and Creeks, Pensacola, 19th May 1766.

Abstract of a letter from John McGillivray to Charles Stuart, Esq., Deputy Superintendent of Indian affairs, dated Mobile, 10th May 1766, on the war between the Chactaws and Creeks.

Copy of Governor Johnstone's letter, dated Pensacola, 3rd June 1766, on the apprehension of a war with the Creeks.

Extract of a letter from His Excellency Governor Wright, dated Savannah, 10th July 1766, to John Stuart, Esq., relating to the apprehended war with the Creeks.

The Wolf King's answer to a joint talk received from His Excellency James Wright, Governor of Georgia, and John Stuart, Esq., Superintendent of Indian affairs, dated at Mucolassee, 29th April 1766.

A letter from Sir William Johnson to Mr. Secretary Conway, 28th June 1766, on the apprehension of an Indian war.

A return of the Lower Creeks.

A letter from Governor Grant, dated St. Augustine, 1st Dec. 1764, on the Indian trade.

Extract of a letter from Major-General Gage to Mr. Secretary Conway, New York, 15th July 1766, on the clandestine trade between the French and the Indians.

Remarks relating to fixing a boundary with the six nations, with the list of the different nations or tribes of Indians in the northern district of North America.

On the method to prevent giving any alarm to the Indians by taking possession of Florida and Louisiana.

Lord Shelburne's observations upon a plan for the future management of Indian affairs.

Remarks on Lord Barrington's plan for the settlement of the conquered countries in America, private, to the Earl of Shelburne.

Captain Roche's remarks on the state of the forts, ports, and communications in North America, 7th Feb. 1767. (An original.)

Vol. 61.

This Vol. 61 is endorsed " Reports of Attorney and " Solicitor-General from 1689 to 1768." A very important collection.

Letter from J. Pownall, 11th June 1767, inclosing reports of the Attorneys and Solicitors-General on plantation business.

Letter from J. Pownall to the Earl of Shelburne, 20th Oct 1767, inclosing reports of the ·Attorney and Solicitor-General.

Reports of the Attorney and Solicitor-General, relative to warrants issued by Mr. Usher, Receiver-General of New England, for raising money in New England in 1686, dated 2nd Dec. 1689.

William Popple to the Attorney and Solicitor-General, Whitehall, Oct 1697, relative to the right to constitute ports in New Jersey.

Report of the Attorney and Solicitor-General to the Lords Commissioners of the Council for Trade, &c., relative to the right to constitute ports in New Jersey, dated 18th Oct 1697.

Report of the Attorney and Solicitor-General to His Majesty, concerning letters of denization granted by Governors in the plantations, 1699.

Report of the Attorney and Solicitor-General to the Lords Commissioners for Trade, &c., relative to the King's right to commission any of his governors to approve or disapprove proprietary or charter governors, 10th Jan. 1699.

Report of the Attorney and Solicitor·General to the Lords Commissioners of the Council of Trade, &c. on appeals from Massachusets Bay, 4 April 1699.

William Popple to Attorney and Solicitor-General, Whitehall, 4th April 1699, about a clause in a Commission, preparing for Colonel Codrington, relating to martial law in the plantations.

Report of the Attorney and Solicitor-General to the Lords Commissioners for Trade, &c., about a clause in Colonel Codrington's Commission, relating to martial law in the plantations, dated 7th April 1699, and in the margin, 7th and 12th April 1699.

Report of Sir Charles Hedges, Judge of the Admiralty (Court), to Mr. Popple, relative to appeals from the Vice-Admiralty Courts in the plantations, dated 21st Sept. 1699.

Report of the Attorney-General to the Lords Commissioners for Trade, &c., relative to appeals from the Vice-Admiralty Courts in the plantations, dated 28th Sept. 1699.

Observations by Mr. Northey on the Maryland Act, as it relates to a vestry, dated 16th Jan. 1700.

Report of the Attorney and Solicitor-General to His Majesty, relating to the qualification of Scotchmen to bear offices in the plantations, dated 11th May 1700.

Report of the Attorney and Solicitor-General to the Lords Commissioners for Trade, &c., on appeals from Connecticut, dated 15th May 1701.

Report of the Attorney-General, relative to actions brought by Messrs. Bayard and Hutchins against their judges and grand jury, dated 8th March 1702-3.

Report of the Attorney-General to the Lords Commissioners for Trade, &c., relative to the effect of an Act of Naturalization in the Colonies, dated 11th March 1702.

Report of the Attorney-General to the Lords Commissioners for Trade, &c., in regard to levying a duty of 4½ per cent. in the conquered part of St. Christopher's, dated 13th Jan. 1703.

Report of the Attorney-General on a clause in the charter of Massachusets Bay, relating to the erecting of courts, dated 21st March 1703-4.

Report of the Attorney and Solicitor-General to the Lords Commissioners for Trade, &c., on the case of a natural born subject of England, but residing in a Danish Island in the West Indies, trading with Queen's enemies, dated 22nd March 1703-4.

Report of the Attorney-General to the Lords Commissioners for Trade, &c., on an Act passed at Montserrat, 13th June 1702, for quieting men's estates, and for avoiding litigious lawsuits, &c., dated 4th May 1703.

Report of the Attorney-General on regulating of coin in the plantations, 31st May 1703.

Report of the Attorney and Solicitor-General to the Queen, on the governor of Massachusets Bay, commanding the Militia of Rhode Island, 1703.

Report of the Attorney-General to the Lords Commissioners for Trade, &c., on barring estates, 1704.

Report of the Attorney and Solicitor-General to the Lords Commissioners for Trade, &c., relating to members of the Assembly of Barbadoes absenting themselves, dated 1st Feb. 1704-5.

Report of the Attorney-General on a clause in the charter of the Massachusets Bay, relative to established courts, dated 21st April 1703-4.

Report of the Attorney-General to the Lords Commissioners for Trade, &c., on the renewal of Commissions for trying pirates in the plantations, dated 24th June 1704.

Report of the Attorney-General on the capacity of Papists to purchase lands in the plantations, 21st July 1704.

Report, additional, of the Attorney-General to Her Majesty, relating to the Members of the Assembly of Barbadoes absenting themselves, dated 28th March 1705.

Report of the Attorney-General to the Lords Commissioners for Trade, &c., on the erecting a Court of Chancery in Antigua by Act of Assembly, dated 13th June 1705.

Report of the Attorney-General to the Lords Commissioners for Trade, &c., respecting Jesuits and Papists in the plantations, dated 18th Oct. 1705.

Report of the Attorney-General to the Lords Commissioners for trade, &c., on the proclamation for settling the rates of foreign coin, dated 19th Oct. 1705.

Report of the Attorney and Solicitor-General to the Lords Commissioners for Trade, &c., relative to two unwarrantable Acts passed in Carolina, 17th May 1706.

Report of the Attorney and Solicitor-General to the Lords Commissioners for Trade, &c., relative to the proprietors of the Bahama Islands, having forfeited their charter, dated 17th May 1706.

Report of the Attorney-General to the Lords Commissioners for Trade, &c., relative to the Crown's right to appoint governors of proprietary colonies, 1707.

Report of the Attorney-General to the Lords Commissioners for Trade, &c. on letters of administration in the plantations, dated March 1707.

Report of the Attorney-General to the Lords Commissioners for trade, &c., on several Acts passed in the Massachusets for fining persons who had traded with the French, dated 24th March 1707.

Report of the Solicitor-General to the Lords Commissioners for Trade, &c., on several Acts of Virginia, &c., dated 20th Aug. 1707.

Report of the Solicitor-General to Mr. Popple, relative to the breach of an Act of Parliament in which no penalty is expressed, 1708.

Report of the Solicitor-General to the Lords Commissioners for Trade, &c., relative to a negro and her children disposed of by the Governor of Jamaica as an escheat, dated 2nd April 1708.

* Report of the Attorney-General on prize goods taken in America, dated 25th May 1708.

† William Popple, jun. to Mr. Solicitor-General ? (Attorney-General), Whitehall, 11th July 1708, relative to the governors of colonies right to appoint naval officers.

‡ Report of the Solicitor-General (Attorney-General ?) (to the Lords Commissioners for Trade, &c.,) relative to the governors of colonies right to appoint naval officers, dated 13th July 1708.

Report of the Solicitor-General to the Lords Commissioners for Trade, &c., on a petition for passes for four Spanish ships to come from the Spanish West Indies to Barbadoes to fetch negroes, dated 29th Oct. 1708, in answer to Wm. Popple's letter annexed, dated Whitehall, 26th Oct. 1708.

Report of the Solicitor-General relative to the impressing of men at New York, dated 17th Sept. 1709.

Copy of an Order in Council on a report of the Attorney and Solicitor-General relative to the disobedience of the Proprietary and Charter Governments to the Queen's proclamation for settling the rates of foreign silver coin, dated 22nd Jan. 1707.

---

* If the endorsement on the report is correct, Sir James Mountague was Attorney-General in May 1708, then the report, †dated 13th July 1708, p. 185, which, as well as the preceding is signed by him, is by the Attorney-General and not by the Solicitor-General as endorsed, and Mr. Popple's‡ letter of 11th July 1708, should have been addressed to Attorney-General instead of the Solicitor-General.

MARQUIS OF LANSDOWNE.

Report of the Attorney-General on an Act of Jamaica for quieting possessions, dated 27th Oct. 1709.

Report of the Attorney-General to the Lords Commissioners of Trade, &c., relating to ambergrease seized in Jamaica and the prosecution thereupon, dated 23rd Nov. 1709.

Report of the Solicitor-General to the Lords Commissioners for Trade, &c., relative to trees fit for masts in Massachusets Bay, dated 12th May 1710, to which is annexed, Wm. Popple's letter to him on the subject, dated Whitehall, 24th April 1710.

Report of Sir Charles Hedges and other civilians on complaints of the seizure of several vessels belonging to Bermuda by the Spaniards, dated Drs. Commons, 4th March 1713-4.

Report of the Attorney-General to the Lords Commissioners for Trade, &c., on an Act passed at St. Christopher's for settling possessions, dated 14th July 1713.

Report of the Attorney-General to the Lords Commissioners of Trade, &c., on the passing and transmitting temporary laws, dated 22nd July 1714.

Report of the Attorney-General to the Lords Commissioners of Trade, &c., relative to escheats in Jamaica, dated 6th August 1713.

Report of the Attorney-General on the abuses committed at Newfoundland contrary to Act of Parliament, dated 31st Jan. 1715, in answer to Wm. Popple's letter to him, which is annexed, dated Whitehall, 25th Jan. 1715-6.

Report of the Attorney-General, relative to proceedings in the courts of justice in cases where the Governor is concerned, dated 20th May 1715.

Report of the Attorney-General on the case of Mr. Tulon, who employed French servants in the fishery on the coast of Newfoundland, dated 28th Jan. 1716-7.

Report of the Attorney-General on the Governor of the Massachusets Bay, commanding the militia of Rhode Island, &c., dated 5th April 1716, in answer to Wm. Popple's letter, which is annexed.

Report of the Attorney-General to the Lords Commissioners for Trade, &c., relative to Acts of Parliament concerning wool in the plantations, and the penalty to be recovered thereupon, dated 22nd Nov. 1716.

Report of the Attorney-General to the Lords Commissioners for Trade, &c., on an accusation against Lord Archibald Hamilton, Governor of Jamaica, dated 24th Nov. 1716.

Report of the Attorney-General to the Lords Commissioners for Trade, &c., on an Act passed in New York for a general naturalization of foreign Protestants, dated 2nd Jan. 1717-8.

Report of the Solicitor-General to Mr. Popple, on a petition for land between Nova Scotia and the province of Main, dated 15th Feb. 1717-8.

Report of the Attorney-General to the Lords Commissioners for Trade, &c., on an Act passed at New York for the better settlement and assuring of lands, dated 12th March 1717-8.

Report of the Attorney and Solicitor-General to the Lords Commissioners of Trade, &c., relative to a proclamation promising pardon to pirates, dated 14th Nov. 1717.

Report of the Attorney-General on the surrender of several of the proprietors of the Bahama Islands, dated 10th Dec. 1717, in answer to Wm. Popple's letter to him, which is annexed, dated Whitehall, 10th Dec. 1717.

Report of the Attorney-General to the Lords Commissioners for Trade, &c., relative to appeals from decrees given in the plantations, dated 19th Dec. 1717.

Report of the Solicitor-General to the Lords Commissioners for trade, &c., on a trial for piracy by the Governor of the Massachusets Bay, dated 5th March 1718-9.

Report of the Solicitor-General on an Act of Carolina laying a duty on British commodities, dated 5th April 1718.

Report of Mr. West to Lords Commissioners for Trade, &c., on an Act of Montserrat for quieting possessions, dated 27th May 1718.

Report of the Solicitor-General prohibiting artificers from going out of the realm without licence, dated 12th Nov. 1718.

Report of Mr. West to the Lords Commissioners of Trade, &c., relative to Spanish ships trading with the British colonies, dated 29th Jan. 1719-20.

Report of the Solicitor-General to Mr. Popple, relative to Spanish ships trading with the British colonies, dated 4th Feb. 1719-20.

Report of Mr. West to the Lords Commissioners for Trade, &c., on the power of a Governor to prorogue the General Assembly under an adjournment, dated 27th May 1719.

Report of the Attorney-General to the Lords Commissioners for Trade, &c., relating to the negative voice reserved to the Governor of the Massachusets Bay by the charter, dated 27th Feb. 1720.

Report of Mr. West to the Lords Commissioners for Trade, &c., relative to a piracy, and the Admiralty jurisdiction in the plantations, dated 20th June 1720.

Report of the Attorney and Solicitor-General to the Lords Commissioners for Trade, &c., relative to a patent for the sole curing of sturgeon in America, and importing the same into this kingdom, dated 18th July 1720.

Report of the Attorney and Solicitor-General to the Lords Commissioners for Trade, &c., on the right to the Islands in the Delaware River, dated 5th Aug. 1721.

Report of the Attorney and Solicitor-General to the Lords Commissioners for Trade, &c., on the time when the three years for the Crown to approve or repeal Massachusets Acts is to commence, dated 2nd June 1722.

Report of the Attorney and Solicitor-General to the Lords Commissioners for Trade, &c., on two Acts passed in the Islands of Jamaica relative to His Majesty's revenue, dated 21st May 1723.

Report of the Attorney-General to the Lords Commissioners for Trade, &c., on the Crown's right of altering the constitution of the Assembly of New Jersey, dated 16th Sept. 1723.

Report of Mr. Richard West, counsel, to the Lords Commissioners for Trade, &c., on the question whether a governor can sit and vote as a member of the council in the plantations, dated 8th Jan. 1724-5.

Report of Mr. Richard West to the Lords Commissioners for Trade, &c., on the shipwrights' petition respecting the great number of ships built in America, dated 4th Dec. 1724.

Report of the Attorney and Solicitor-General on the case of a mate of a ship being killed by a shot from a fort in Barbadoes, dated 17th April 1725.

Copy of an Order in Council, including a report of the Attorney and Solicitor-General, on the encroachment upon the prerogative of the Crown by the House of Representatives of the Massachusets Bay, dated 1st June 1725.

Report of the Attorney and Solicitor-General of a trial of a person for the murder committed in Spanish Town, one of the Virgin Islands, dated 18th Dec. 1725.

Report of the Attorney and Solicitor-General to the Lords Commissioners for Trade, &c., on the King's right to the woods, dated 23rd Dec. 1726.

Report of the Attorney and Solicitor-General to the Lords Commissioners for Trade, &c., on two Acts of Montserrat relative to the courts of justice, &c., dated 28th July 1730.

Report of the Attorney and Solicitor-General to the Lords Commissioners for Trade, &c., on the validity of certain grants made by the Lords proprietors of Carolina, dated 28th July 1730.

Report of the Attorney and Solicitor-General to the Lords Commissioners for Trade, &c., on the power of the Colony of Connecticut to make laws affecting property, dated 1st Aug. 1730.

Report of Dr. Sayer on prosecuting an appeal from the Vice Admiralty Court in New England relative to cutting pine trees without licence, dated 6th Dec. 1730.

Report of the Attorney and Solicitor-General to the Lords Commissioners for Trade, &c., relative to the validity of Acts in Rhode Island, notwithstanding the Governors dissent, &c., dated 5th Aug. 1732.

Report of the Attorney and Solicitor-General to the Lords Commissioners for Trade, &c., on fines and recoveries in plantations, dated 15th Dec. 1730.

Report of Mr. F. Fane to the Lords Commissioners for Trade, &c., relative to the privileges of the Russian Company, dated 17th June 1734.

Report of the Attorney and Solicitor-General on the question whether a governor can sit and vote as a member of the Council in the Plantations, dated 15th Jan. 1735.

Report of the Attorney and Solicitor-General to the Lords Commissioners for Trade, &c., relating to the King's right to the woods in the county of York, dated 20th Jan. 1735.

Report of the Attorney-General to the Lords Commissioners for Trade, &c., on the scheme for erecting a land bank in Boston, in the Massachusets Bay, dated 10th Nov. 1735.

MARQUIS OF LANSDOWNE.

Report of the Attorney and Solicitor-General on the case of the blank patents in North Carolina, dated 11th February 1737.

Report of the Attorney and Solicitor-General to the Lords Commissioners for Trade, &c., on an Act passed in Georgia relating to trade with the Indians, dated 28th July 1737.

Report of the Attorney-General relative to Royal mines in Jamaica, dated 20th Dec. 1737.

Report of the Attorney and Solicitor-General respecting the power of the Crown to erect a Court of Exchequer in South Carolina, dated 12th June 1738.

Report of the Attorney-General to the Lords Commissioners for Trade, &c., on an Act passed in the Island of Bermuda in 1740 to prevent lawsuits, dated 4th Feb. 1743.

Report of the Attorney and Solicitor-General to the Lords Commissioners for Trade, &c., relative to the Assembly of Pensylvania being obliged to provide for the defense of the province against a foreign enemy, dated 19th Oct. 1744.

Report of the Attorney and Solicitor-General to the Lords Commissioners for Trade, &c. relative to the Assembly of New Hampshire's refusal to admit the representatives of new towns to sit and vote in the choice of a Speaker, dated 18th March 1747.

Report of the Attorney and Solicitor-General to the Lords Commissioners for Trade, &c., on the validity of an Act of North Carolina passed in 1715, and whether it be repealable by the Crown, dated 3rd Jan. 1747.

Report of the Attorney and Solicitor-General to the Lords Commissioners for Trade, &c. relative to the issuing writs for choosing representatives for a new Assembly without dissolving the old one, dated 18th June 1748.

Report of the Attorney-General relative to the power of taking cognizance of capital crimes in Newfoundland, dated 27th March 1750.

Report of the Attorney and Solicitor-General to the Lords Commissioners for Trade, &c. relative to the power of the King's Bench in Bermuda, and other matters in that Government, dated 13th April 1750.

Report of the Attorney and Solicitor-General to the Lords Commissioners for Trade, &c., on two Acts passed in North Carolina relative to the members of the Assembly, public offices, and courts of justices, dated 1st Dec. 1750.

Report of the Attorney-General to the Lords Commissioners for Trade, &c. relative to giving the Governor of Newfoundland power to execute criminals convicted of capital offences, dated 16th May 1751.

Report of the Attorney-General to the Lords Commissioners for Trade, &c., on an Act passed in Nevis relating to papists, dated 6th Aug. 1751.

Report of the Attorney and Solicitor-General to the Lords Commissioners for Trade, &c., on the proposal of the trustees of Georgia to surrender their trust to the Crown, dated 6th Feb. 1752.

Report of the Attorney and Solicitor-General to the Lords Commissioners for Trade, &c., on the properest method of administering the government of Georgia upon the surrender of the charter by the trustees, dated 25th Feb. 1752.

Report of the Attorney and Solicitor-General to the Lords Commissioners for Trade, &c., on the instructions relative to appeals, dated 7th April 1753.

Report of the Attorney and Solicitor-General to the Lords Commissioners for Trade, &c., on a petition of Lord Baltimore respecting his claim to a tract of land called Avalon, in Newfoundland, dated 5th April 1754.

Report of the Attorney and Solicitor-General to the Lords Commissioners for Trade, &c., relative to appeals from the Plantations to the King in Council, dated 17th July 1754.

Report of the Attorney and Solicitor-General to the Lords Commissioners for Trade, &c., whether the governor and council of Nova Scotia have power to enact laws, dated 29th April 1755.

Report of the Attorney and Solicitor-General to the Lords Commissioners for Trade, &c., on the qualification of a person to sit in the Assembly of Jamaica, who had been convicted in England of uttering treasonable expressions, dated 29th April 1755.

Report of the Attorney and Solicitor-General to the Lords Commissioners for Trade, &c., on writs for electing members of Assembly in Jamaica, dated 29th April 1755.

Report of the Attorney-General to the Lords Commissioners for Trade, &c., on an Act of Pensylvania extending the Mutiny Act to that province, dated 7th April 1756.

Report of the Attorney and Solicitor-General to the Lords Commissioners for Trade, &c., on martial law, dated 28th Jan. 1757.

Report of the Attorney and Solicitor-General to the Lords Commissioners for Trade, &c., relative to the crime of counterfeiting and uttering Spanish dollars and pistareens in the colonies, dated 18th May 1757.

Report of the Attorney and Solicitor-General to the Lords Commissioners for Trade, &c., on the case of the Deputy Postmaster-General of Jamaica being removed by the Lieut.-Governor of that island, dated Lincoln's Inn Fields, 3rd Dec. 1759.

Report of the Advocate and Attorney-General to the Lords Commissioners for Trade, &c., on several cases relating to the seizure of the effects of the French inhabitants, and the forfeiture, sale, and escheatage of lands in the island of Grenada, dated Lincoln's Inn, 25th Jan. 1764.

Report of the Attorney-General to the Lords Commissioners for Trade, &c., on the questions whether those subjects of the crowns of France and Spain who remain in the ceded countries in America are to be considered as aliens, dated Lincoln's Inn Fields, 27th June 1764.

Report of the Attorney and Solicitor-General to the Lords Commissioners for Trade, &c., relative to the disabilities, &c. of the Roman Catholics in the countries ceded to His Majesty, in America by the treaty of Paris, dated Lincoln's Inn, 10th June 1765.

Mr. Yorke's opinion relative to the grenades, &c., dated 12th June 1767.

The Attorney General's opinion relative to privileges claimed by the Lieut.-Governor of Massachusets Bay, dated 25th Aug. 1767.

The Attorney General's opinion on the seizure of the ship "Liberty" at Boston, in New England, by the officers of the Customs, 1768.

Report of the Advocate, Attorney and Solicitor-General to the Earl of Hillsborough, on the method by which the prisoners in custody at Philadelphia may be legally tried for murder committed on the high seas, dated 10th May 1768.

Report of the Attorney and Solicitor-General to the Lords of the Committee of Council for Plantation Affairs, relative to the acts and proceedings of the legislature of New York in their last session of Assembly, 24th July 1768.

Vol. 62.

This volume is endorsed, "To and from the Lords of "Trade and American Office."

A representation of the Board of Trade on the claim of the Dutch with respect to Cape Apollonia, in Africa. An original, dated 29th July 1767.

A representation of the African merchants concerning the claims of the Dutch to Cape Apollonia.

Certificate and evidence relating to the claim of the Dutch to Cape Apollonia, and representation from the Board of Trade upon Count Wildren's memorial, together with their Lordships' letter to the Earl of Shelburne, dated Whitehall, 29th July 1767.

A report of the Board of Trade to the King, relating to the claim of the Assembly of Jamaica to superintend the receipt and payment of the public money and other matters. Whitehall, 15th Oct. 1754.

A report of the Board of Trade to the House of Commons relative to the state of Jamaica. Whitehall, 22nd Feb. 1753.

Minutes of the proceedings of the Lords Commissioners for Trade and Plantations upon the order made by the Lords of the Committee of Council for Plantation Affairs on the 23rd of May 1767 relative to the Island of St. John.

The advice of the North American merchants to the Board of Trade about the Indian trade. London, 30th Oct. 1767.

From Lord Shelburne to the Board of Trade, Whitehall, 27th Oct. 1767, concerning the settlement of Turks Islands.

Report to the Lords of Trade concerning the sale of gunpowder in Georgia, dated Whitehall, 14th Nov. 1767.

A report to the Lords of Trade concerning the Court of Exchequer in North Carolina, dated Whitehall, 14th Nov. 1767.

Draft of a letter to the Lords of Trade, dated Whitehall, 14th Oct. 1767, with reference to the land between Quebec and New York.

Draft of a letter to the Lords of Trade, dated Whitehall, 14th Nov. 1767, relating to the case of John Kerr and deputy commissaries in North America.

The Earl of Shelburne to the Lords of Trade, dated Whitehall, 17th Dec. 1767, concerning the appointment of an agent for the House of Assembly, in Massachusets Bay.

A letter from Lord Hillsborough to the Earl of Shelburne, dated Whitehall, 13th April 1768, communicating papers relating to the detention of some negroes by the Spaniards in America.

Copy of Mr. Symmer's letter dated Turks Islands, 16th Dec. 1767; an account of the detention of some negroes by the Spaniards of Monti Christo (in Lord Hillsborough's of 13th April 1768).

Translation of a letter from Don Pedro Ziron to And. Symmer, Esq., dated Montpxto, 13th Oct. 1767, on the delivery of the negroes. In Mr. Symmer's of the 16th of Dec. 1767.

Translation of a letter from Don Pedro Ziron to A. Symmer, Esq., dated Montpxto, 27th Oct. 1767, respecting the delivery of negroes. In Mr. Symmer's of the 16th Dec. 1767.

Lord Hillsborough to Lord Shelburne, Whitehall, 18th July 1768, communicating some papers relating to the government of Grenada.

Considerations and propositions respecting the island of Grenada, 18th July 1768.

Lord Hillsborough to Lord Shelburne, Whitehall, 19th July 1768, concerning the insurrection in Boston in New England. An original.

Vol. 63.

This volume is labelled "Occurrences in the Province " of Massachusets Bay, since the Repeal of the Stamp " Act." It contains a narrative of the above-named events without the name of the author being given.

Vol. 64.

Volume 64, endorsed "Papers and Memorials relative " to the Government of Canada and Quebec," contains copies of various documents and several letters, original letters, and papers from A. Mabane and P. Irving to General Murray on the state of Canada, 1753–67.

Patent to the Earl of Cholmondeley to be surveyor and auditor-general of all the revenues of the Crown in America. 20th November.—25 Geo. II.

Report of the Government of Quebec and dependencies thereof by J. Murray, to the Earl of Egremont, dated 5th June 1762, with a list of the papers referred to in the report.

1. King's arrest of the 15th March 1732, directing the settling of the lands granted already within a certain time limited, on pain of forfeiture.

2. Tariff of duties on imports and exports (dated 17th March 1761).

3. List of the officers employed at Quebec in the year 1758 for the collection of the King's revenues, with their several yearly salaries.

4. Ordinance on the rate of exchange. Quebec, Oct. 1758.

5. Extract of a letter to Governor Murray, giving some account of the Indian trade in the upper country, dated Albany, 10th August 1761.

6. Number of souls in the Government of Quebec, 1761.

7. Quantity of furs exported in 1754, with the Quebec prices of the several species.

8. Quantity of furs exported in 1755, with the Quebec prices of the several species.

9. Imports and exports in 1754.

Seven plans for fortifications for Quebec.

Project for building a citadel at Quebec.

Return of the posts or lands granted by Governor Murray in the Government of Quebec and Dependencies thereof to the 22nd July 1763 inclusive.

A proclamation for settling the Government of Quebec, the 17th day of Oct. 1763.

Attorney and Solicitor-Generals' report on the Government of Quebec, 6th Aug. 1764.

Copy of Governor Murray's letters to the Lords of Trade relating to the outrage offered to Mr. Walker, dated Quebec, 2nd March and 24th June 1765.

John Frazer to the Earl of Shelburne, 1st April 1767, relating to the affair of Mr. Walker.

Journal of the proceedings at Montreal during the assizes, 28th Feb. 1767.

Messrs. Streetwall and Crafton to Lord Shelburne, 3rd Oct. 1766, about the affair of Mr. Walker.

Case of Mr. Walker, with the opinion of Mr. Jackson, 27th Jan. 1766.

An Order of Council requiring the King's officers in Quebec to send an account of whatever they think defective in the judicature of the province, dated St. James's, 28th day of August 1767.

Report of the Attorney and Solicitor-General to the Lords of the Committee of Council for Plantation affairs, relative to the Civil Government of the province of Quebec, endorsed "Instructions to the Governor of " Quebec relative to Juries," dated 14th April 1766.

Additional instructions to Governor Murray relative to juries. Approved in Council the 17th Feb. 1766.

Notes relating to the revenue of Canada, dated 14th June 1765.

Abstract of a letter from Mr. Collins, deputy surveyor-general of Quebec, to the Lords of Trade, dated 22nd July 1766, relative to the King's wharfs, &c., at Quebec.

Advertisement of the receiver-general at Quebec in confirmation of an exclusive right of Thomas Dunn, &c., to the Indian trade, 9th August 1766.

P. Irving to Governor Murray, Aug. 23rd 1766, on the then state of Canada.

P. Irving to Governor Murray, 24th Oct. 1766, remonstrating against an innovation in the council, &c.

A. Mabane to Governor Murray, dated Quebec, 26th Aug. 1766, on the state of affairs in Canada.

Governor Murray to Lord Shelburne, 30th Aug. 1766, on the state of Canada.

Report of the Board of Trade on the Acts of the Governor and Council of Quebec, relating to the establishment of courts of judicature and other civil constitutions, 2nd Sept. 1765, to which is annexed the following papers, viz.:—1. Names of persons appointed to be of the council upon the 13th Aug. 1764. 2. Copy of an ordinance for regulating and establishing the courts of judicature, justices of the peace, &c. in this province (Quebec), passed 17th Sept. 1764. 3. Copy of an ordinance for ratifying the decrees of Quebec, Montreal, and Trois Rivieres, passed 20th Sept. 1764. 4. Report of the Attorney and Solicitor-General that the Roman Catholics in Canada are not subject to the penalties which those in England are under.

Extract from a report of the Board of Trade, 2nd Sept. 1765, against the exclusion of Roman Catholics from courts of justice in Canada.

Copy of a letter from Quebec, 30th Sept., received 4th Nov. 1766, of the insolence of the Catholics on the indulgence granted to them, and the complaints of the Protestants, and other matters.

Governor Carleton to the Board of Trade, Quebec, 18th Oct. 1766, on the monopoly of the Indian trade, &c.

Remonstrance to the Governor of Quebec about a nomination to the Council.

Dr. Mabane to the General, dated Quebec, 21st Oct. 1766, on the affair of the Council, &c.

Notes of letters, &c. relating to Canada, from 1763 to 1767.

Draft of resolutions (of* the House of Lords) relating to Canada (1767).

Notes of proceedings relative to Canada.

Notes on the affairs of Quebec.

Lord Shelburne to the Board of Trade on the appointment of an assembly, and other things necessary to the settlement of Canada (dated 17th May 1767).

Notes relating to the oaths proper to be proposed to the French inhabitants of Canada.

Dates of certain proceedings relating to Canada, from Oct. 1763 to April 1766.

Various notes and hints relating to Canada.

Lord Egremont to the Board of Trade, dated Whitehall, 5th May 1763, on the settlement of North America after the peace.

Lord Egremont to the Board of Trade, dated Whitehall, 14th July 1763, on settling the government of Canada, East and West Florida.

An account of the state of Canada from its conquest to May 1766.

On the subject of religion with respect to Canada, 31st May 1763.

List of the French officers of justice in Canada when it was in the possession of France.

List of the inhabitants of Canada who want employment in his Majesty's service, with the number of families and men able to bear arms.

List of papers relative to Quebec received from the Council Office, 16th May 1767.

Abstract of Quebec papers continued since Lord Shelburne came into office, 7th July 1766.

Agreement between the Duke of Richmond and Count Guerchy.

* Inserted because found in the original list of documents in this volume.

An account of a conference with the Count de Guerchy about the paper money of Canada.

Observations on the Canada paper money, 28th Oct. 1766.

Observations on the Canada paper money, 28th Oct. 1766.

Answers to objections relating to the paper money of Canada.

Observations of the British Commissary for Canada paper, submitted to the Earl of Shelburne, London, 20th Sept. 1766.

An historical account of the paper money of Canada.

Vol. 65.

This Volume 65, endorsed "Newfoundland Papers" contains copies of papers on Newfoundland, and some original papers and letters by Sir Hugh Palleser, and others, from 1763–67.

A letter from the Earl of Egremont to the Board of Trade, dated Whitehall, 8th March 1763, recommending to their consideration the articles of the peace relating to the Newfoundland fishery.

Copy of the representation from the Board of Trade to the King relating to the Newfoundland fishery, dated Whitehall, 15th March 1763.

Instructions to Captain Graves, Commander at Newfoundland, after the peace in 1763.

Copy of additional instructions to Captain Graves, Commodore at Newfoundland, and to the commanding officers of all His Majesties ships in America.

A letter from Lord Egremont to the Board of Trade, dated Whitehall, 17th March 1763, directing them to prepare a draft of instructions for the Governor of Newfoundland.

A letter from the Board of Trade to the Earl of Egremont, dated Whitehall, 18th March 1763, promising to comply with the preceding requisition.

A representation from the Board of Trade to the King's most Excellent Majesty, with a draft of instructions for Newfoundland, 21st March 1763.

Copy of a representation from the Board of Trade to the King's most Excellent Majesty, with a copy of instructions for Governor Graves of Newfoundland, 29th March 1763.

A letter from H. Pallisser to Lord Shelburne, 10th Dec. 1766, with an account of the French and English fisheries for 1766, to which is annexed a plan of York or Chateaux Bay on the coast of Labrador, and a plan of the Block House at Pitts Harbour, Labrador.

Mr. Palisser's answer to the complaints of the French, relating to Newfoundland in the year 1766.

John Lemesurier to Lord Viscount Howe, dated Guernsey, 22nd Jan. 1767, relating to the English on the coast of Newfoundland, carrying their oil and cod fish to the islands of Saint Peter and Miquilon.

A letter from Mr. Pallisser to L. Macklane, Esq., Secretary of States. Office, Whitehall, dated London, 18th Feb. 1767, enclosing,—

(1.) A letter from Mr. Palliser to Mr. De Berts in answer to complaints from the Assembly of New England, London, 18th Feb. 1767.

(2.) Memorandum of the substance of what passed at a conference between Mr. Pallisser and the French Ambassador on the 4th March 1767 and 31st March 1767.

(3.) Memorandum by Mr. Pallisser, concerning the oppression of the Newfoundland fishermen by their employers.

Regulations to prevent quarrels between the English and French fishermen about taking of bait.

A letter from J. Cawthorne to the Earl of Shelburne, dated Gwyns Buildings, Islington, 23rd March 1767, inclosing a plan for settling Newfoundland to the southward.

An account of what fortifications are necessary to defend the Newfoundland fishery.

About the fortifications, &c., Newfoundland, with particulars, relative to St. John's in Newfoundland, addressed to the Earl of Shelburne.

A letter from H. Pallisser, Governor of Newfoundland to M. Francois d'Angeac, Governor of St. Pierre, &c., dated Great St. Laurence Harbour, 22nd June 1767, relating to the dispute between the subjects of the two Crowns, expressing his satisfaction at their termination.

A letter from D'Angeac, Governor of St. Pierre, to the Governor of Newfoundland, in answer to the preceding, dated à St. Pierre de Terre neuve, 25th June 1767.

A letter from the Governor of Newfoundland to the Commander of the French ship of war, 10th July 1767, complaining of his arrival as an evasion of the treaty of peace in 1763.

An answer to the preceding by the French Commander, insisting upon his right to protest the French subjects, dated Enrade de St. Pierre de Terre neuve, 20th Aug. 1767.

A declaration of Hugh Pallisser, Governor of Newfoundland, relating to a memorial from the ship Adventurers at Labrador, respecting the fishery on the coast of Labrador, Pitts Harbour, Labrador, 10th Aug. 1767.

A memorial from the ship Adventurers at Labradore to Governor Pallisser, praying to be protected in their rights and privileges, Aug. 1767.

Governor Pallisser's order for sending home from Newfoundland men that are useless in the country after the fishing season is over, 2nd June 1767.

A general account of the French fisheries at Newfoundland, at St. Pierre's, and Miquelon, in the Gulph of St. Lawrence, and on the banks, 1767.

Governor Pallisser's report to the Earl of Shelburne, relating to the French fishery in the year 1767. Dated London, 15th Dec. 1767.

A particular account of ships and men employed in the Newfoundland fishery, from 1764 to 1767 (by H. Pallisser).

Governor Pallisser's report of occurrences, &c., respecting the state of the British fishery, dated London, 15th Dec. 1767.

Governor Pallisser's scheme with regard to the fishery.

A general scheme of the fishery and inhabitants of Newfoundland for the year 1767.

Vols. 66 and 67.

These two volumes, labelled American affairs, contain a very important collection of papers from 1765 to 1783, relating chiefly to the details of American politics. They fall under four heads :—

(1.) Copies of documents.
(2.) Newspapers.
(3.) Original notes by Lord Shelburne.
(4.) Private letters, mostly originals.

Contents of Volume 66, endorsed "American Affairs, " Vol. I."

Memorial of the merchants trading to Canada and other colonies in North America to the Earl of Egremont.

Copy of an ordinance made by the Governor and Council of Quebec on the 17th Sept. 1764, for regulating and establishing courts of judicature in the province of Quebec.

Report of the Lords Commissioners for Trade and Plantations, together with heads of a plan for the establishment of ecclesiastical affairs in the province of Quebec, dated Whitehall, 30th May 1766, sent to the Lords Committee of His Majesty's Privy Council for Plantation Affairs.

Representation of the Board of Trade to His Majesty, proposing that an assembly should be called in Quebec and the Governor ordered to return to this kingdom to give an account of the state of the province, 2nd Sept. 1765.

Report of the Attorney and Solicitor-General to the Lords of Committee of Council for Plantation Affairs, relative to the civil government of the province of Quebec, 14th April 1766.

Copy of draught of instructions to James Murray, Captain-General and Governor of Quebec.

Substance du Discours qui a ete fait a . . . . . . par les Principaux Chefs de Canada pour être communiqué a la Cour de France. In Lord Rochford's Secret and Confidential of 14th April 1768.

M. Morgann to Lord . . . . . Quebec, 30th Aug. 1769, relating to reports on religion, revenue, &c. &c.

H. Caldwell to Lord . . . ., Caldwell Place, near Quebec, 9th Jan. 1775, on the situation and prospects of the province of Quebec and the benefit of that country to Great Britain, with remarks on the merchants, Roman Catholic clergy and the Protestant Religion in that province.

Major H. Caldwell to Lord . . . ., Quebec, May 1775, relating to shutting the courts of justice, the state of the country, and the proceedings of Arnold, Allen, and others.

Francis Maseres to Lord Shelburne, Inner Temple, 9th Aug. 1775, inclosing copy of a letter dated Quebec,

22nd June 1775, in which the writer complains of an Act of Parliament (the Quebec Bill) by which he is deprived of the rights of an Englishman, the Roman Catholic religion is supported, and the Protestants and their religion neglected in the province (of Quebec). Gives an account of a riot, and the doings of the provincials at Ticonderoga, &c.

Francis Maseres to the Earl of Shelburne, dated Inner Temple, 24th Aug. 1775, relating to the position and doings of the provincials after they took Crown Point and Ticonderoga, and the refusal of the Canadians to act offensively against the Americans, &c.

Thoughts for conducting the war from the side of Canada, addressed by Lieut.-General J. Burgoyne to Lord George Germain, and dated Hertford Street, 28th Feb. 1777.

General Sir William Howe to Sir Guy Carleton, New York, 5th April 1777, relating to operations to be taken against the rebels in America.

Lord George Germain to Sir Guy Carleton, dated 26th March 1777, relating to the operations to be taken against the rebels in America.

Memorandums and observations relative to the service in Canada, submitted to Lord George Germain by J. Burgoyne.

Copy of a letter from Sir Thomas Mills to Lord George Germain, dated London, 19th March, and one from Lord George Germain to Governor Haldimand, dated Whitehall, 21st March 1781, relative to the Lieut.-Governor Cramahes being ordered home to answer for the expenditure of money in the province of Quebec.

Lord Barrington and the Right Hon. H. F. Carteret, Postmaster-General to the Right Hon. William Ellis, dated General Post Office, 27th Feb. 1782, relative to appointing Mr. Finlay (their Deputy in Canada) to be superintendent of the post roads between Quebec and Montreal, to which is annexed a memorial from Hugh Finlay, dated London, 20th Feb. 1782.

Henry Hamilton to Lord . . . . ., dated London, 9th April 1782, relate to his case from 1775, when he was appointed Lieut.-Governor and Superintendent at Detroit.

Anonymous letter to the Earl of Shelburne, endorsed Quebec, 18th April 1782, about the establishment of a General Assembly at Quebec; the Popish Act, &c.

Substance du Discours qui a ete fait à . . . . par les principaux Chefs de Canada pour être Communiqué à la Cour de France. In Lord Rochford's Secret and Confidential, of 14th April 1768.

Letter from Peter Livius, Chief Justice of the Province of Quebec, dated London, 19th March 1782, relative to the secret cause of the usage he received in Canada, and his removal from the chief justiceship of Quebec.

Memorial of Peter Livius, Chief Justice of the Province of Quebec to the Lords Commissioners of H. M. Treasury, dated London, 15th March 1782.

Copy of a letter from the Earl of Dartmouth to General Carleton, Governor of the Province of Quebec, dated Whitehall, 23rd May 1775, relating to Mr. Livius' appointment to the judgeship of the Common Pleas in Montreal, and his desire to have a seat at the Council Board, &c.

Recollection by the writer (Peter Livius, Chief Justice of Quebec) of his argument in the case of Brooke, Watson, and other assignees of L. Carignan, a bankrupt, against Richd. Dobie, 30th April 1778.

Mr. Livius, Chief Justice of Quebec, on the reasons for his instituting a suit against Sir Guy Carleton, London, 20th May 1782.

Memorandum relating to Mr. Livius' action against Sir Guy Carleton, and his desire to have a grant of the seigneurie, fief, &c. of Saint Maurice, &c., dated 12th June 1782.

Lewis Guerry to Lord . . . . . ., dated Duke Street, Westminster, 5th June 1782, asking renewal of his leave of absence from Quebec.

Warrant signed by the Earl of Dartmouth for Guy Carleton, Esq., Captain General and Governor in Chief of the Province of Quebec, to collate Lewis Guerry, clerk to a church and parish in the Province of Quebec, dated Court of St. James, 7th April 1775.

Baron de Kutzleben to Lord . . . . . ., dated Sackville Street, 21st June 1782, about the baggage expected at Portsmouth for Hessians, in Canada.

Estimate of the expenses of the province of Canada for six years and four months, ending in Oct. 1782.

An account of the quantity of such goods as have been imported from Canada and Nova Scotia, and are entitled to bounty for five years from 1776 to 1770, and for five

5.

years from 1776 to 1780 inclusive, distinguishing each year.

Copy of a paper of Observations "sur le dernier "Memoire remis par My Lord George Lennox à M. le "Duc de Choiseul, le 17 Avril dernier," relative to Newfoundland, delivered by Count Guerchy, the 8th May 1766. (Copy sent to Commodore Palliser, 29th May 1766.)

Copy of a letter signed Richmond, &c., to Lord George Lennox, dated Whitehall, 3rd June 1766, relating to disputes about fishing on the coasts of St. Pierre, Maquelon, and Belle Isle, &c.

Commodore Palliser's observations of the island of Belle Isle, Newfoundland.

R. Edwards to Lord . . . . ., Hollis Street, Cavendish Square, 26th March 1782, relating to the fortifications and defence of Newfoundland, with a list of the Newfoundland squadron, and the number of troops in that island in 1781.

Lieut.-Colonel Pringle's memoranda from the plan of a general defence for the island and fishery of Newfoundland, laid before Governor Shuldham, in 1772, and Governor Montague in 1778.

Lieut.-Colonel Pringle's proposal with General Conway's observations thereon.

Remarks on Lieut.-Colonel Pringle's memorial to Lord Shelburne.

Proposed establishment of the Newfoundland Corps, 15th April 1782.

Instructions to Commissioners sent to visit the Massachusetts soon after the Restoration.

Extract from a letter from Governor Bernard to the Earl of Shelburne, dated Boston, 21st Jan. 1768, relating to the proceedings of the House of Representatives of the Province, &c.

Extracts from Mr. Otis' "Rights of the British Colonies."

Extracts from the "Farmer's Letters."

Extract of a letter from the Earl of Dartmouth to Governor Gage, dated Whitehall, 3rd June 1774, about upholding the authority of the kingdom over its colonies, and a Bill for quartering troops.

List of Councillors. In Governor Gage's of the 27th Aug. 1774.

Extract of a letter from Hampshire County, 10th Aug. 1774. In Governor Gage's of the the 27th Aug. 1774.

Copy of a letter from Governor Gage to the Earl of Dartmouth, dated Salem, 27th Aug. 1774, relating to Acts of Parliament for regulating the government of Massachusetts Bay, the appointment of a council, removal of sheriffs, impeachment of the Chief Justice, and agitated state of the country, &c.

Copy of minute of council held at Boston, the 31st of Aug. 1774. In Governor Gage's of the 2nd Sept. 1774.

Extract of a letter from the Hon. Governor Gage to the Earl of Dartmouth, dated Boston, 2nd Sept. 1744, relating to disturbances in several provinces in America, and the state of the country, &c.

Extract of a letter from the Hon. Governor Gage to the Earl of Dartmouth, dated Boston 3rd Oct. 1774, about the manner in which the cause of Massachusetts Bay is espoused by the American colonies, the proceedings of Congress, and the proposed meeting of the provincial Congress at Concord.

Extract of a letter from the Hon. Governor Gage to the Earl of Dartmouth, dated Boston, 17th Oct. 1774, despairs of any overtures for a reconciliation being accepted by the people of America unless recommended by the continental Congress.

Extract of a letter from the Hon. Governor Gage to the Earl of Dartmouth, dated Boston, 30th Oct. and 2nd Nov. 1774, relating to the proceedings of the Provincial Congress and the Continental Congress at Philadelphia, and the state of the continent, &c.

Extract of a letter from the Hon. Governor Gage to the Earl of Dartmouth, dated Boston, 15th Nov. 1774, relating to resolves of the Continental Congress being received by the people, and the encouragement shown to it by the rest of the New England provinces, &c.

Memorials of the English and French Commissaries concerning the limits of Nova Scotia.

Memorials of Commissioners concerning limits of Nova Scotia, printed 1755. (Endorsed Mr. Pitt's notes.)

Francis Legge to the (Earl of Shelburne), dated Pinner, Middlesex, 17th July 1782, relative to his memorial to him enclosed.

Memorial of Francis Legge, late Governor of Nova Scotia, to the Earl of Shelburne, dated Pinner, Middlesex, July 1782.

G g

Memorial of Francis Legge, late Governor of Nova Scotia, to the Earl of Shelburne, dated Pinner, 4th Sept. 1782.

Extract from letters, &c., relating to the complaints against Governor Legge of Nova Scotia, 1776.

A letter from Mr. Finucane to Lord . . . ., relative to the rights of the Crown in Nova Scotia, 20th Jan. 1782.

Remarks concerning the territorial rights of the Crown in the province of Nova Scotia, and the lands adjoining (in Mr. Finucane's of 20th June 1782).

John Calef to the Earl of Shelburne, dated Davis', Russell Court, Covent Garden, 11th April 1782, intends going to Penobscot by the first conveyance to resume the charge of his district there.

General P. Wadsworth's proclamation, dated Thomastown, 18th April 1780, to which is annexed a resolve of the General Assembly of Massachusett's Bay.

The state of the inhabitants of the District of Penobscot, March 1782.

John Calef to Lord George Germain, dated Crown, Russell Court, Covent Garden, 10th Dec. 1780, with copy of a paper about America, delivered to him Dec. 12th 1780, a letter dated Russell Court, March 2nd 1781, and a memorandum dated March 1782, endorsed Penobscot Papers.

Capt. H. Mowat to Lord G. Germain, dated Albany, Majabigwaduce, 9th May 1780, relating to Mr. Calef, and the state of America.

Memorial and petition of John Calef, Esq., agent for the inhabitants of the territory of Penobscot, to the King, &c. 12th July 1780.

Resolves of the House of Commons, 31st March 1766.

Certificate of Col. Goldthwaite, in behalf of John Calef, Esq., dated London, 16th Oct. 1781.

Certificate of Capt. MacDonald, in behalf of John Calef, Esq., dated London, 20th Feb. 1782.

John Nutting to the Earl of Shelburne, dated London, 22nd April 1782, relating to the advantage of establishing a post at Penobscot.

Certificates of General Thomas Gage, and Thomas Flucker, Secretary of the Province of Massachusetts bay, in favour of John Calif, Esq., dated, Portland Place, 26th Feb. 1782, with an extract of a letter for Governor Hutchinson to the Earl of Dartmouth, dated Boston, 30th Dec. 1772, respecting Mr. Calef.

Mr. Goldthwaite's account of the eastern part of the province of Massachusett's bay, with some remarks thereon.

A list of the number of inhabitants settled on lands eastward of the river Sagadahock to the river St. Croix, in Massachusett's bay, taken Oct. 1772.

An account of the annual exports of the country lying between the river St. Croix and Kennebeck, from the year 1772 to 1775 inclusive, with the prices sold for.

Proposal for making a new province in America to be called New Ireland, with an estimate of the civil establishment for that province, approved of by the King the 11th Aug. 1780.

An opinion relative to the King's right to grant certain lands petitioned for lying between Nova Scotia and the province of Main, dated 18th Dec. 1717.

Mr. Isaac Ogden to Chief Justice Smith, relating to an action between the Vermonteers and Albanians. Received 23rd March 1782.

Extract of a letter from Mr. Edward Lutwych to Mr. Leonard, dated New York, 18th March 1782, relating to a disagreement between Congress and Vermont, &c.

Mr. Wm. Smith to Major-General Tryon, New York, 23rd March 1782, about the war with Vermont.

Major-General Tryon to the Earl of Shelburne, dated Upper Grosvenor Street, 28th April 1782, relative to Mr. Smith's despatch from New York.

A ninth list of prizes, part whereof hath been condemned in the Court of Vice-Admiralty for the province of New York to His Majesty's use, dated New York, 6th May 1782.

Governor Wm. Tryon to the Earl of Shelburne, dated Somerley, Suffolk, 15th July 1782, relating to Mr. W. Smith, whose letter he transmits to him.

Governor Wm. Tryon to the Earl of Shelburne, dated July 1782, relating to General Skinner, whose letter he encloses.

Return of provisions in store for the troops under Sir Henry Clinton.

Mr. Skene to the Earl of Shelburne, dated Chelsea, 26th Sept. 1782, enclosing letters from Mr. Chief Justice Smith and Mr. Cuyler.

Chief Justice Smith to Governor Skene, dated New York, 10th Aug. 1782, relating to the means which

should have been taken to secure the tranquillity of the Empire, &c.

Remarks relative to North America, and the state of the forts, &c. in the King's possession, 1782.

Demand of artificers wanted from England for service of the Royal Artillery in North America, dated New York, 7th Dec. 1781. In Lord Townshend's letter of the 12th March.

State of the brigade of Royal Artillery in North America, under the command of Lieut.-Colonel William Martin, dated New York, 3rd Jan. 1782.

Disposition of ordnance at New York, also the number of pieces of ordnance in America, and proportion of officers and men of the Royal Regiment of Artillery, Jan. 1782.

(Lord) Amherst and others to Lord Viscount Townshend, dated Office of Ordnance, 23rd Feb. 1782, relative to ordnance, &c.

A demand of ordnance, stores, &c. wanted from England for the field and garrison service in North America, dated Ordnance Office, New York, 6th Dec. 1781. In Lord Townshend's letter of the 12th March.

Draft of a letter to the Duke of Richmond, dated Whitehall, 1782, relating to ordnance and stores to be sent to New York.

Lord Viscount Townshend to the Hon. Welbore Ellis, dated Office of Ordnance, 12th March 1782, enclosing report on the demand for stores for New York.

W. H. Drayton to Lord . . . ., dated Charles Town, South Carolina, 1st Sept. 1774, relative to the late five Acts of Parliament, relating to America, the light in which they are considered by the Americans, and the consequence to be apprehended in attempts to defeat their operation.

Henry Lawrens to Wm. Manning, relating to the treatment of the Americans by the English Government, the commencement of hostilities by the King's troops between Concord and Boston, and the readiness of the people to support the "common cause," &c., dated Charles Town, 22nd May 1775.

Letter from . . . . . to Wm. Manning, Esq., dated Charles Town, South Carolina, 27th Feb. 1776. About the warlike preparations of the people of Charles Town, who are ready to put the torch to their town in preference to submitting to their enemy, and the feeling of the Americans towards Great Britain produced by the speech and answers at the opening of Parliament, &c.

A. Turnbull to the Earl of Shelburne, dated Charles Town, 1st Aug. 1781, relating to the state of the province of South Carolina, &c.

Reasons for restoring the entire province of South Carolina to the King's peace, compared with those for confining its limits to the posts established by Lord Rawdon, dated 24th Oct. 1761 ? (1781).

Question proposed to be put to the judges relative to the case of the American Colonel Hayne, executed at Charles Town in 178 . . ?

Mr. Thomas Taylor to the Rev. John Wesley, dated Savannah, 28th Feb. 1782, relating to the proceedings of the rebels and the murder of Col. Grierson, &c.

Sir James Wright to . . . . . ., dated Sept. 1782, giving a concise view of the situation of the province of Georgia for three years past.

Messrs. Greenwood and Higginson to the Earl of Shelburne, dated London, 19th Oct. 1782, relating to the claim of the late John Gordon on account of lands purchased in 1763 of Spanish subjects in East Florida.

Memorial of Wm. Greenwood and Wm. Higginson to the Earl of Shelburne, dated London, 17th Oct. 1782, relative to a claim to land purchased by John Gordon in East Florida, of Spanish subjects in 1763.

State of the Plantations in the village of Rolle, on St. John's River, East Florida, 1783.

Dr. Andrew Turnbull to the Earl of Shelburne, St. Augustine, 14th March 1780, relating to his treatment by Governor Tonyn. Endorsed 178(2) ?

Dr. And. Turnbull to Lord George Germain, St. Augustine, 16th March 1780 ; complains of Governor Tonyn's tyrannical proceedings against him and others. Encloses papers relating to a suit in Chancery against him by Lady Mary Duncan, with an opinion respecting the "Ne exeat Regno vel Provincia, served upon him in that suit by order of the governor.

Dr. Turnbull to the Earl of Shelburne, St. Augustine, 25th March 1780 ; asserts that through Lord George Germain neglecting to attend to his complaints, Governor Tonyn has been encouraged to proceed further in his ill-treatment of him ; complains of Governor Tonyn stopping civil suits against a man of the Council ; his proceedings in the trial of his own coachman for murder, suspending Chief Justice Drayton, and appointing an unfit man in his place, &c. Endorsed 1782.

Dr. Andrew Turnbull to the Earl of Shelburne, Charlestown, 23rd May 1782, congratulations on the change of ministers and wishes of success.

Dr. Andrew Turnbull to the Earl of Shelburne, Charlestown, 21st June 1782, solicits employment until he can get a subsistence by his profession. Gives an account of his family, &c.

Dr. Andrew Turnbull to the Earl of Shelburne, Charlestown, 24th June 1782. Apologises for writing an importunate letter to him (on the 21st instant).

Dr. Andrew Turnbull to the Earl of Shelburne, Charlestown, 3rd July 1782; complains of Governor Tonyn's treatment of him, and being apprehensive of his attempting to hurt him with his Lordship, therefore troubles him with the memorial enclosed.

Memorial of Dr. Andrew Turnbull to the Earl of Shelburne, dated Charlestown, 3rd July 1782, with a P.S. dated 7th July.

Memorial of Andrew Turnbull to the Lords Commissioners, for Trade, &c., dated 19th Sept. 1776. In his memorial of the 3rd July 1782.

Memorial of Andrew Turnbull to the Lords Commissioners for Trade, &c., dated London, 5th Dec. 1776. In his memorial of the 3rd July 1782.

Andrew Turnbull to Patrick Tonyn, Governor of East Florida, dated St. Augustine, 9th Aug. 1778, relating to his intention of acting in his offices of secretary and clerk under his government. In Dr. Turnbull's of the 3rd July 1782.

Patrick Tonyn to Andrew Turnbull, dated St. Augustine, 11th Aug. ? 78. Refuses to let him act as secretary of the province (of East Florida), and clerk of the Council. In Dr. Turnbull's of the 3rd July 1782.

Andrew Turnbull to Lord George Germain, dated Charlestown, 13th June 1781, complaining of Governor Tonyn. In Dr. Turnbull's of the 3rd July 1782.

Dr. Andrew Turnbull to the Earl of Shelburne, dated Charlestown, 7th July 1782, relating to his complaints against Governor Tonyn, and the joy of the inhabitants of East Florida about the orders for dissolving the civil government, &c. being countermanded.

Andrew Turnbull to the Earl of Shelburne, Charlestown, 31st July, relating to his imprisonment in East Florida, and Governor Tonyn's treatment of him and others.

Dr. Andrew Turnbull to the Earl of Shelburne, Charlestown, 6th Dec. 1782. Thanks for recommending him to Sir Guy Carleton, whose aid he will not ask for himself, but will solicit him to give his eldest son an appointment in the Commissary Department. Complains of Governor Tonyn.

J. Bruce to Lord . . . . . ., 22nd Aug. 1782, respecting West Florida.

Charges incurred in East and West Florida in three years, between 1st of Jan. 1779 and the 1st of Jan. 1782, exclusive of the military establishment.

Memorial of the merchants of London, formerly trading to West Florida and others, setting forth the importance of the English possessing that country, which might serve as an asylum for American loyalists, dated London, 31st Oct. 1782.

Vol. 67.

E. Wright, Wm. Franklin, and other American governors to the Earl of Shelburne, 2, Fludyer Street, 12th Feb. 1783, relating to the petition from the agents of the American loyalists.

Abstract of a letter from Dr. Franklin to Lord Dartmouth, dated 21st Aug. 1773, relating to the friendly feeling of the people of the province of Massachusetts towards Great Britain, &c.

Abstract of the declaration of the Congress, setting forth the causes and necessity of their taking up arms, dated 6th July 1775.

A paper containing different opinions on the subject of America.

Mr. Dunning's remarks on the rebellion in America, Feb. 1775.

Notes by Lord Shelburne relative to America during 1780–81, &c.

Notes relating to the Prohibitory Act, and other American subjects.

Richard Henry Lee to his brother (Arthur Lee), Williamsburg, 19th May 1769. The dissolution of the assembly here was immediately followed by an association against the importation of goods. Only friendly measures can secure the obedience of America to Great Britain.

Arthur Lee to Lord Shelburne. Bristol, Wells, 3rd July 1769, relating to scholarships for the Colleges in America, and his Lordship being entitled to a grant of land in Pensylvania, encloses a letter from his brother.

Proceedings at a meeting of deputies appointed by the several counties of Maryland, at Annapolis, from the 8th to the 12th of Dec. 1774. Extracted from the Maryland Gazette, received from Robt. Eden, Esq., Deputy-Governor of the said province, 17th Feb. 1775.

Letter to Lord Shelburne, dated Skeensborough, 15th July 1777, relating to the affair at Habberdon, and the improbability of the colonies being subdued. A copy.

Resolutions and motions in Congress respecting fishing at Nova Scotia, &c., 22nd March 1778.

A paper containing the proceedings of Congress (on 19th and 23rd June 1779) respecting fishing on the banks of Newfoundland, &c.; endorsed "Release from "bond of secrecy respecting fishery, &c. 19th June "1779."

Robert Hodgson to Lord Shelburne, Mount Row, 1st July 1779, relating to his memorial now at the Board of Trade, and of his being about to be called upon to use his knowledge of the middle part of America, &c.

Plan for securing the future dependence of the provinces on the continent of America. The date is about 1764.

The American account current, with its vouchers, stated by an American, 1781.

John William to the Earl of Shelburne, Harley Street, 20th Jan. 1781, relating to the imprisonment of Mr. Jarvis, son of the President of Antigua, the state of commerce, and indications of the amity of Holland, &c. towards America.

Letter from Sir H. Crosby to General . . . . . ., endorsed New York, 28th July 1781, relating to the proceedings of Lord Cornwallis, the number of troops under some of the British generals in America, and the number of French troops, &c. which Washington has at his call.

Sir H. C(rosby) to . . . . 20th Aug. 1781. Complains of the intimations thrown out by the minister in his letter of March, printed by the rebels, and of the language held in Parliament, that he was at New York with the Governor's army.

H. Clinton to . . . . . . London at Sea, 19th Oct. 1781. (Admiral) De Grasse entered the Chesapeake with 27 sail of the line, from the West Indies, on 29th of Aug., and Admiral Graves, being joined by Sir S. Hood, with 14 sail, had a brush with De Grasse, in which he suffered a good deal. Washington has moved southward to meet the French troops, &c. which De Grasse brought with him.

Sir H. C(rosby) to G. G., Dec. 1781. Complains of Lord Cornwallis's letter of the 20th Oct., from which it may be supposed that he is to blame for the post his Lordship took at York Town. Mentions the arrival of General Washington's troops at Williamsburgh, and the capitulation (of Lord Cornwallis and his army), and the probable cause of their misfortunes.

Sir H. C(rosby) to C. J. N. York, 7th Dec. 1781. Attributes the cause of their late misfortune (the surrender of Lord Cornwallis and his army) to the want of promised naval superiority under Sir G. Rodney, and gives Lord Cornwallis's statements respecting some insinuations in his letter of the 20th Oct.

Copy of a letter from General Arnold to Lord George Germain, dated London, 3rd Feb. 1782. Enclosing considerations on the American war, and plan for prosecuting it.

Original letter from General Arnold to Lord George Germain.

Propositions for the employment of His Majesty's forces now in North America, submitted to the consideration of His Majesty's confidential servants, by Lord George Germain.

James Anderson to the Earl of Shelburne, dated Monkshill, near Aberdeen, 28th May 1782. Relating to the emigration from Scotland and Ireland to America, having caused great alarm before the American war, and the desire of the American colonies for independence, with proposals how that may be secured to them.

Samuel Estwick to the Earl of Shelburne, dated Lower Berkley Street, Portman Square, 13th June 1782, notes on the West India Patent Offices.

List of the officers of the colonies residing in Great Britain, not dated.

Duty and situation of officers in the colonies, not dated.

John Maffett to Lord Shelburne, dated Castle and Falcon, Aldergate Street, 15th July 1782, relating to American matters.

Baron de Knoblauch to the Earl of Shelburne, dated New York, 17th Jan. 1783. Gives an account of himself, and is known to Sir Joseph Yorke.

List of civil and naval officers in the West Indies and American colonies, with an account of their salaries, &c.

The Boston Evening Post and General Advertiser, 4th May 1782.

Copy of the report of a committee of American merchants, dated New York, Coffee House, 16th Aug. 1782. Enclosed in their letter of 26th Aug.

The committee of American merchants to Lord Shelburne, dated 26th Aug. 1782, relative to the evacuation of His Majesty's garrisons in America.

Objections to the mode of sending out annual presents to the American Indians, received 9th Nov. (1782), from Mr. Wm. V(aughan).

Wm. Vaughan to Lord Shelburne, dated Mincing Lane, 9th Nov. 1782, transmits a paper relative to presents to Indians.

A list of materials for shipbuilding in West Florida, 10th Dec. 1782.

Memorandum of the American rank of General Haldimand and Sir Guy Carlet .

John Blackburn to Thomas Orde, Esq., dated Scots Yard, 28th June 1782, respecting the payment of *salary* to the *Chief Justice* of New York.

Declaration of the Board of Directors of Associated Loyalists, dated New York, 28th Dec. 1780, in Mr. Leonard's of 30th March 1782.

Copy of a letter from Moses Brown, one of the members of the meeting for suffering in New England, to a friend in Philadelphia, dated Providence, 2nd first month 1776.

Copy of what the Meeting of Friends, held at Providence, New England, 21st of the 11th month 1775, prepared to present to Generals Howe and Washington.

Copy of a letter from Mr. S. S. Blower to Sir Wm. Pepperrell, Bart., dated New York, 23rd March 1782. Conduct of the Loyalists since Lord Cornwallis's surrender.

Mr. George Leonard to the Earl of Shelburne, dated Pimlico, 30th March 1782, in behalf of the American Loyalists. Is ready to give information.

Mr. Frederick Smyth, late Chief Justice of New Jersey, to the Earl of Shelburne, dated New York, 12th Aug, 1782, offers his services in the absence of Governor Franklin. Represents his services and sufferings.

List of American sufferers who now receive annual allowances from the Treasury, dated 3rd June 1782.

List of Americans applying for allowances, whose cases have not yet been considered, dated 3rd June 1782.

The Earl of Dunmore to the Right Hon. Thos. Townshend, dated London, 24th Aug. 1782, proposition to dispose of the Provincials and Loyalists, to settle them in the Mississippi, and if it be meant to carry on the war against the Americans, to put the loyalists with regulars under separate leaders, is ready to support this idea in person.

Remarks upon the Minute of the Board of Treasury, referred to Mr. Hartley for his consideration.

Letter signed (unknown) to the Earl of Shelburne, dated Oct. 1782, about the present enquiry into the claims of American Loyalists.

Mr. Motteux to (the Earl of Shelburne), dated Walbrock, 22nd Jan. 1783, encloses an anonymous letter sent to Charles Town, 11th Dec. 1782, relative to rendering useful the American Loyalists.

Draft report of John Wilmot and Daniel Parker Coke, Esq., to the Lords Commissioners of Her Majesty's Treasury, relating to the cases of all the American sufferers already deriving assistance from the public, and of those who are claiming the same.

Report of John Wilmot and Daniel Parker Coke, Esq., to the Lords Commissioners of His Majesty's Treasury, dated Whitehall, 29th Jan. 1783, on the cases of all the American sufferers already deriving assistance from Government, in which are three schedules, viz. : 1. List of American sufferers according to their rank, &c. 2. Persons of the 2nd class in Schedule 1, more particularly recommended to the patronage of Government. 3. List of the American sufferers, with the allowance to each, also an account of the general state of the American sufferers, to which is annexed Messrs. Wilmot and Coke's letter to George Rose, Esq., dated Whitehall, 29th Jan. 1783, requesting him to transmit their report to their Lordships.

Sir James Wright, Bart., Wm. Franklin, Esq., and other (American) Governors, to the Earl of Shelburne, dated Fludyer Street, Westminster, 6th Feb. 1783, asking to see his Lordship about the American Loyalists.

Petition intended to be presented to Parliament by the late American governors in behalf of the American Loyalists, praying for an adequate compensation for their losses, and (if necessary) to be heard by counsel, in support of their claim, dated 8th Feb. 1783.

(E. Gower) to Captain Jervis, Rio Janeiro, 19th April 1782. Gives an account of Rio Janeiro, Isle of Trinidad, the best latitude for crossing the Line, and an account of the devastation in Peru by Tupar Amaric.

Translation of five letters, dated Santa Fee, Caracas, and San Carlos, 1781, relative to the insurrection in the Santa Fé, in Spanish America, with a note of the capitulation of the rebels at Santa Fé.

Precis of several intercepted dispatches from the Government of the province of Venezuela, in South America, to the Minister of the American Department at Madrid, dated 1781.

Precis of Spanish letters intercepted on their way from Caracas, in South America, to Old Spain, dated 1781.

Intelligence enclosed in a letter from John Stables, Esq., dated Rio de Janeiro, 3rd June 1782, received by him from Capt. McDonall, of H.M. ship "Africa," who speaks Portuguese, and commanded three years on that coast.

Vols. 68–69.

These vols. contain copies and duplicates of despatches and some original letters from General Conway and Maurice Morgann. The latter are very interesting.

Extract of a letter from Lord George Germain to Earl Cornwallis, dated Whitehall, 9th Nov. 1780. Sends His Majesty's thanks for his Lordship's victory over the rebels near Camden. Approves of his determination to punish those traitors who had repeated the violation of their oaths of allegiance, broken their parole, and taken arms against the King. His civil regulations in South Carolina are approved of, and it being the King's desire to convince the people of America that no abridgment of their former liberties is intended, he is, therefore, to throw the conduct of civil matters into their former channels, as far as he shall judge expedient. Understanding that Congress evades an exchange of the Convention troops with the garrison of Charlestown, suggests ways of getting rid of the prisoners of war, for the purpose of saving the public the expense of maintaining them.

General Clinton to General Grey, dated New York, 3rd July 1779. Complains of the reinforcements due in May not having arrived there, and of his having no camp equipage to enable him to continue his move. Was lucky in his first attempt to seize Varpland and Stoney. S. W. Howe's army at Brandywine amounts to 13,000 men, Mr. W[ashington] can meet him (Genl. Clinton) with 14,000 men besides militia. The eastern provinces are starving. Has not heard from Europe for three months, and has no money. Would not see another campaign so neglected for all the world.

Extract of a letter from Lord George Germain to Sir Henry Clinton, dated Whitehall, 3rd Jan. 1781. Gives his reasons for regretting that Col. Ferguson's misfortune compelled Lord Cornwallis to require Gen. Leslie to quit the Chesapeak and proceed to Cape Fear river. Fears the second abandonment of Portsmouth, after taking possession of it, will be productive of the worst effects to the King's service. Thinks the French will send part of their force into the Chesapeak when they hear that they (the English) have abandoned it. The King desires him to send a detachment from New York on an expedition to the Chesapeak. British recruits are embarking at Gravesend for Charlestown.

Extract of a letter from Lord George Germain to Sir Henry Clinton, dated Whitehall, 17th Feb. 1781. Approves of his orders for establishing a permanent post at Elizabeth river. Trusts that the troops he is preparing for embarkation are to be employed in reducing Maryland and Pennsylvania to the King's obedience, while Lord Cornwallis and Brigadier-General Arnold subdues Virginia, for such is the low condition of the authority and finances of the Congress, and the weakness of Washington's army, that little opposition is to be expected from that quarter. Accounts from France of M. de Ternay having sailed from Rhode Island on the 25th Dec.

Abstract of a letter from Lord George Germain to Sir Henry Clinton, dated Whitehall, 7th March 1781. As the revolt of the Pennsylvania line and Jersey brigade will affect Washington's present force, and prevent its being reunited by new levies, thinks Sir Henry will avail himself of that General's weakness by sending a considerable force to the head of the Chesapeak. The effect of General Arnold's successful enterprise up James river. The American levies in the King's service are more than the whole of the enlisted troops in the service of the Congress. Measures to be adopted for enlisting American prisoners for the service in the West Indies. The westerly winds for the last two months have prevented the Warwick and Solebay, with their convoy, getting further than Plymouth.

Extract of a letter from Lord George Germain to Sir Henry Clinton, dated Whitehall, 4th April 1781. Lord Cornwallis, after gaining two advantages over the rebels, passed beyond Salem, in North Carolina. The King approves of the behaviour of Brigadier-General Arnold and others mentioned. Has received private news of the inhabitants soliciting arms, to use in conjunction with the King's forces. He has a favourable opportunity of assisting them, as Washington's army is in a low condition. It is said that 26 sail of the line, under Count de Grasse, and seven transports, with 7 to 12,000 land forces, sailed from France on the 22nd of last month. Six of these ships are to go to the East Indies, and the rest to the West Indies. The fleet under Admiral Darby was waiting off Cape Clear on the 25th of last month. The associated refugees are sensible of Sir Henry's kind attention to them, for whom he is to find rations.

Extract of a letter from Lord George Germain to Sir Henry Clinton, dated Whitehall, 2nd May 1781. Vice-Admiral Arbuthnot overtook the French fleet before they entered the Chesapeak, and defeated the French Admiral's project of carrying his squadron and a detachment of French troops to attack Gen. Arnold in concert with the rebel forces. Major-General Phillips arrived in James river with reinforcements, and it is hoped that Lord Cornwallis will affect a junction with him. Informs him, by command of the King, that the recovery of the southern provinces, and the prosecution of the war from north to south, is to be considered the principal object for the employment of all troops under his command.

Extract of a letter from Lord George Germain to Earl Cornwallis, dated Whitehall, 4th June 1781. The French fleet, defeated from Rhode Island, by Admiral Arbuthnot. Lord Cornwallis's victory at Guildford. Instructions for carrying on the war.

Copy of a letter from Lord George Germain to Sir Henry Clinton. Whitehall, 6th June 1781. Is pleased that Lord Cornwallis sees the importance of pushing the war on the side of Virginia. Hopes that the troops from Ireland will arrive in time to join his Lordship, or form another army under Lord Rawdon, to drive the enemy out of the upper country, while Lord Cornwallis and Gen. Phillips are employed in reducing the lower parts.

Extract of a letter from Lord George Germain to Sir Henry Clinton, dated Whitehall, 4th July 1780. Measures to be taken for obtaining the submission of the inhabitants of Charlestown, &c. Trusts he will find an opportunity of prosecuting his plan of operations in the Chesapeake, from the success of which, added to the reduction of Carolina, he expects the recovery of the whole of the southern provinces in the course of this campaign. The Hessian and Anspach are about to embark.

Extract of a letter from Lord George Germain to Sir Henry Clinton, dated Whitehall, 7th July 1781. The King approves of his pushing the war southward, with all the force he can spare from New York. Three regiments, 3,000 British recruits and 2,000 Germans, have been sent home. The French fleet will proceed to North America, and Sir Geo. Rodney will follow them, to prevent their interrupting him in his operations, and the better to effect this, Admiral Digby will reinforce Rodney with three ships of the line.

Extract of a letter from Lord George Germain to Sir Henry Clinton, dated Whitehall, 17th July 1781, relating to the causes which have increased the prospect of bringing the southern colonies to obedience.

Substance of several conversations had with Major-General Phillips on the subject of operations in the Chesapeake before his embarkation on his expedition thither, 26th April 1781. Signed by H. Clinton.

Sir Henry Clinton to (Major-Gen.) Phillips, New York, 30th April 1781, about the proceedings of Lord Cornwallis and others, and the southern army.

Sir Henry Clinton to the Earl Cornwallis, dated New York, 11th June 1781. Wishes that he could send his Lordship a second army. Proposes that Philadelphia should be attacked.

(Lord Cornwallis) to Lord George Germain, Wilmington, 24th April 1781, relative to his marching into Virginia, and his junction with Major-General Phillips. Encloses copy of his letter to Major-General Phillips.

Lord Cornwallis to Major-Gen. Phillips, Wilmington, 24th April 1781. The damages likely to ensue to his Lordship's army and LordjRawdon from Greene marching into South Carolina. Proposes to form a junction with Phillips' army.

Lord Cornwallis to Sir Henry Clinton, Wilmington, 23rd April 1781. Being apprehensive of Greene marching towards Camden, he has determined to march to-morrow. His (Clinton's) army is in want of everything but shoes.

Letter to Sir Henry Clinton, dated Bird's Plantation, North of James River, 26th May 1781. Proposes to dislodge La Fayette from Richmond. His opinions as to the manner in which the war should be conducted. Gives particulars about the southern army, &c.

Extract of a letter from Sir Henry Clinton to the Hon. Lieut.-General Leslie, dated 20th Dec. 1781. Force of the King's troops in southern provinces of the the latter end of 1781. Project of General Greene's attack of Savannah, whether best to attack it or abandon the place.

State of His Majesty's forces serving in North America and the West Indies, according to the last returns to Dec. 1781.

Lord George Germain to Sir Henry Clinton, dated Whitehall, 6th Feb. 1782. Informs him that he is permitted to quit his command in North America, and is to resign the command of the King's forces to Major-General Robertson.

Lord George Germain to Major-General Robertson, Whitehall, 6th Feb. 1782. Instructions to him on his being appointed Commander-in-Chief of all the King's forces in North America.

Right Hon. W. Ellis. to Sir Henry Clinton, Whitehall, 12th Feb. 1782. About his being appointed Secretary of State.

Sir Henry Clinton to Lord George Germain, dated New York, 18th March 1782, relative to the civil officers of government of the province of South Carolina. The police of Charlestown. Mr. Irving, Mr. Camden, &c., encloses several letters respecting these matters.

Extracts of a letter from Lieut.-General Leslie to Sir Henry Clinton, dated Camp near Charlestown, 18th Feb. 1782, relating to the demands of the Loyalists.

Extract of a letter from Sir Henry Clinton to Lieut.-General Leslie, dated 20th Dec. 1178, relating to the augmentation of the salaries of the police of Charlestown, and the payment of salaries of the civil officers of the province of South Carolina.

Copy of a letter from the Board (of Police at Charlestown), signed by Lieut.-Governor Bull, to . . . . . . Charlestown, 18th Feb. 1762, relating to the police of Charlestown.

Thomas Irving, Receiver-General of South Carolina, to Lieut.-General Leslie, dated Charlestown, 4th Dec. 1781. About paying the salaries of the civil officers (of South Carolina), &c.

Thomas Irving, Receiver-General of South Carolina, to Lieut.-General Leslie, Charlestown, 4th Dec. 1781. Asks to be re-established in his office of Receiver-General in place of Mr. Cruden.

Thomas Irving to Lieut.-General Leslie, dated Charlestown, 31st Jan. 1782. About the Board of Police at Charlestown, and the support of civil officers there, &c., &c.

Lieut.-General Leslie to Sir Henry Clinton. Camp near Charlestown, 2nd Feb. 1782. About the officers of Mr. Irvine (Irving) and Mr. Cruden.

Extract of a letter from the Lieut.-General Leslie to Sir Henry Clinton, dated Camp near Charlestown, 2nd Feb. 1782, relative to the Board of Police at Charlestown.

A list of the civil officers of South Carolina who received allowances on account of the loss of emoluments of their respective employments during the suspension of the King's authority in the province of South Carolina. Dated Charlestown, 5th Dec. 1781.

Copy of Lord Cornwallis's commission to John Cruden, Esq., appointing him commissioner for the management, &c., of the seized estates of the rebels (in South Carolina). Dated Waxham, South Carolina, 16th Dec. 1780.

Sir Henry Clinton to Lord George Germain, dated New York, 22nd March 1782, relative to the revival of the civil government (iu the province of New York), &c., &c.

Lieut.-General James Robertson to Sir Henry Clinton, dated New York, 21st March 1782. Gives his opinion relative to the revival of the civil government in the province of New York, and encloses the opinion of the council there upon that subject.

Lieut.-General James Robertson to Sir Henry Clinton, dated New York, 22nd Mar. 1782. About the inhabitants of the counties of Duchess and Ulster, and their message to him, and the claims on government for the rent of houses, &c.

Sir Henry Clinton to Lord George Germain, dated New York, 23rd Mar. 1782. Encloses a copy of the decree of the Court of Admiralty respecting the prises made in the Chesapeake in April 1781.

Sir Henry Clinton to Lord George Germain, dated New York, 24th March 1782, relating to provision being made for the widows of provincial officers.

Sir Henry Clinton to Lord George Germain, dated New York, 24th March 1782. Desires that Lieut.-Governor Graham may be appointed deputy superintendent of Indian affairs in the western division of the southern district in the place of the late Mr. Cameron. Encloses copy of a letter of recommendation in his behalf from Sir James Wright, dated Savannah, in Georgia, 2nd Jan. 1782, and one from the Council of the province of Georgia, dated Savannah, in Georgia, 31st Dec. 1781.

Sir Henry Clinton to Lord George Germain, dated New York, 12th April 1782, relating to sending troops to raise the seige of Brimstone Hill, or to succour Jamaica, &c.

Archibald Campbell, Lieut.-Governor of Jamaica, to Lieut.-General Sir Henry Clinton, Jamaica, 8th March 1782. Being informed that Jamaica will be attacked by the French and others he therefore solicits his aid.

Sir Peter Parker to Rear Admiral Digby, Sandwich, Port Royal Harbour, Jamaica, 7th March 1782. Preparations for the defence of Jamaica. Asks him to send reinforcements thither. Encloses intelligence, dated 27th Feb. 1782, respecting the preparations of the French and Spanish for attacking Jamaica.

Intelligence from Charlestown, 30th March 1782, respecting the capture of a Spanish transport, and the fleet bound from Havannah to Cape Francois being dispersed in a storm.

Sir Guy Carleton to the Earl of Shelburne, dated New York, 12th May 1782. It being improbable that sufficient transports can be procured this year for the removal of the troops from New York, they are therefore likely to stand or fall there.

List of transports serving in North America, dated New York, 10th May 1782.

Sir Guy Carleton to the Earl of Shelburne, dated New York, 14th June 1782. Recommends Captain Coote.

Sir Guy Carleton to General Conway, dated New York, 16th Aug. 1782. Asks for leave to return home.

General Conway to the Earl of Shelburne, Little Warwick Street, 18th Oct. 1782. On Sir Guy Carleton's conduct, &c.

Copy of a letter from Evan Nepeau, Esq., to Alexander Adair, Esq., dated 30th June 1782, relative to Sir Guy Carleton being appointed to command the 84th Regiment of Foot.

Sir Guy Carleton to the Earl of Shelburne, dated New York, 8th and 9th Oct. 1782, relative to the exchange of Lord Cornwallis.

Substance of a conversation between General Knox and Mr. Elliot at Tauppan, on 26th Sept. (1782), respecting Lord Cornwallis's exchange.

Abstract of the state of the army under the command of General Sir Guy Carleton, dated New York, 1st Dec. 1782.

Sir Guy Carleton to the Earl of Shelburne, dated New York, 16th Dec. 1782, about proposals for peace with America, the demand of the French Minister at Philadelphia that Rhode Island should be held in pawn for the money lent by France. Opinion respecting what government is suitable for America.

List of transports, army victuallers, storeships, &c. at New York, dated 16th Jan. 1783.

List of ships expected at New York, dated New York, 16th Jan. 1783.

Distribution of troops in America and the West Indies, dated 18th Jan. 1783.

Copy of a letter to the President of Congress, dated Office of Finance, 29th July 1782, relating to monetary affairs of the American Government.

Copy of a letter to the President of Congress, dated Office of Finance, 30th July 1782. Encloses estimates for the service of the year 1783.

Sir Guy Carleton to the Right Hon. Thomas Townshend, dated New York, 19th Jan. 1783. Transmits letters, &c. to him.

Abstract of the state of the army under the command of General Sir Guy Carleton, dated New York, 10th Jan. 1783.

Sir Guy Carleton to Governor Parr, dated New York, 22nd Dec. 1782. Solicits for the Loyalists a grant of the lands adjoining Rosway harbour.

Extract of a letter from Admiral Hugh Pigot to Mr. Stephens, dated "Formidable," New York, 9th Oct. 1782. Gives his opinion respecting the small vessels commissioned in the King's service at New York and the West Indies.

Rear-Admiral Digby to the Earl of Shelburne, dated "Prince George" off New York, 11th Oct. 1782. Complains of tobacco being brought clandestinely to New York. Points out the disadvantages arising from sending (American) prisoners to them (the English). Proceedings of the leaders of the rebellion.

Extract of a letter from Rear-Admiral Digby to Mr. Secretary Townshend, dated 25th Oct. 1782, relating to naval affairs in America and the West Indies.

Rear-Admiral Digby to Mr. Secretary Townshend, dated New York, 15th Dec. 1782. Hopes that the trade of privateers will be knocked up this winter. Fears that the convoy at Philadelphia will escape. The defence of New York must depend upon Admiral Pigot next spring.

Rear-Admiral Digby to Mr. Secretary Townshend, dated New York, 19th Nov. 1782, about the Loyalists, &c.

Maurice Morgann to Lord Shelburne, dated New York, 10th May 1782, about the state of America.

Maurice Morgann to Lord Shelburne, dated New York, 12th June 1782. Reasons on the present state of America, the temper of the people, and the prospect which now offers of peace.

M. Morgann to Lord Shelburne, dated New York, 17th June 1782, desires to leave America.

M. Morgann to Lord Shelburne, dated New York, 17th Aug. 1782, relating to the effect produced by the publication there of the proposal of independence.

M. Morgann to the Earl of Shelburne, dated New York, 11th Sept. 1782. The publication of the offer made by Mr. Grenville at Paris had produced a stillness among the mass of the people in America. Encloses a paper by order of Sir Guy Carleton.

A paper headed "Mr. Williams about 10th Aug.," relating to the committee of the General Assembly of Massachusets, and the feeling of the people of Hampshire, &c. towards their leaders and Great Britain. In Mr. Morgann's of 11th Sept. 1782.

M. Morgann to the Earl of Shelburne, dated New York, 4th Oct. 1782, about the state of the provinces, the proceedings of the American leaders to enlarge their power, &c.

Copy of information from the county of Albany, dated 29th Sept. 1782, relating to the desire of the people for peace, and the feeling towards the French and American armies.

M. Morgann to Lord Shelburne, dated New York, 4th Oct. 1782, about himself and his situation.

M. Morgann to Lord Shelburne, dated New York, 9th Oct. 1782, relating to the mode of paying the provincial corps (in America).

Maurice Morgann to Lord Shelburne, dated New York, 11th Oct. 1782. Encloses for the Earl of Shelburne a printed extract from a newspaper, dated Philadelphia, 5th Oct. (1782), containing the resolution of Congress not to treat for a separate peace.

M. Morgann to Lord Shelburne, dated New York, 29th Oct. 1782. Thanks his Lordship for the pension granted him by the Treasury. Gives his opinion as to the fate of the American provinces as soon as the external compressions of England are taken off them. Complains of Mr. Edmund Burke, &c., who may be very anxious "to represent himself as the friend and "champion of the people, but is really only the trum-" peter of a particular connection."

M. Morgann to Lord Shelburne, dated New York, 16th Dec. 1782. Gives an account of the state of the country. Desires to return home.

Vol. 69.

M. Morgann to Lord . . . . ., dated New York, 16th Jan. 1783. Encloses copy of a report (to Sir Guy Carleton) and papers relative to American money.

Report of Messrs. William Smith, M. Morgann, and others (to Sir Guy Carleton), dated New York, 30th Dec. 1782, relative to compelling the money contractors' agents to draw Bills of Exchange for the use of the military chest below par, to which is annexed, Sir Guy Carleton's commission of 1st Dec. 1782, appointing them to enquire into that matter; minutes of their proceedings therein, Harley and Drummond's account, and an account of cash deposited with Messrs. Gordon, Biddulph, and Gordon, and by them appropriated to the public. In Mr. Morgann's of 16th January 1783.

Considerations on the nature of American money on the issuing the dollar by authority at 4s. 8d. sterling, for the pay and subsistence of the army on the nature of the contract for the remitting of money for the use of the military chest, and of the rate of exchange between New York and London, the causes of its falling, and the probable means of prevention.

Considerations on the compelling the army to receive its pay in dollars valued at 4s. 8d. sterling. In Mr. M. Morgann's of 16th Jan. 1783.

Mr. M. Morgann to . . . ., dated New York, 19th Jan. 1783. Encloses provincial newspapers for Lord Shelburne.

Remarkable contents of American newspapers from 11th Dec. 1782 to 11th Jan. 1783. In Mr. Morgann's of the 19th Jan. 1783.

Brook Watson, Commissary General, to Richard Burke, Esq., dated New York, 17th Aug. 1782. Gives an account of the state of his department, from 14th June to the present time.

Brook Watson to the Marquis of Rockingham, dated New York, 18th Aug. 1782. Has spared no pains to reduce the contingent expense of the army. Thinks that 15,000 men might have been added to it without additional expense. This letter is marked private.

Brook Watson to the Earl of Shelburne, dated New York, 12th Sept. 1782. Encloses duplicate of his private letter of the 18th Aug. to the Marquis of Rockingham, whose death compels him to solicit the Earl's attention to it.

Joshua Upham to General Carleton, dated New York, 12th Nov. 1782. States that the common people of America desire to be at peace with Great Britain, and gives the terms for peace which they are willing to accept.

A note to the Earl of Shelburne, dated New York, 26th July 1782, enclosing an extract of a letter from a gentleman of New York, dated New York,15th June 1782, relating to the intended messages of peace from Great Britain being accepted by America; the feeling of the Americans towards their leaders; Washington's position, and his expectation of help from France, the arrival of 30 odd vessels at Cape Hatteras; the feeling towards Rochambeau's army, and the doings of Rodney and Hood.

Extract of instructions from the Minister of Finance of the United States of America and the Secretary of the Board of War, dated Philadelphia, 11th July 1782, containing propositions to be made to the German prisoners of war at Reading, to which is annexed Captain Bowen's address at Reading on the 30th July 1782, in which he laid those propositions before the prisoners there.

Walter Patterson to Lord Shelburne (duplicate), dated Island Saint John, 22nd June 1782. Congratulates him on being appointed Secretary of State.

Major General J. Patterson to the Earl of Shelburne, Halifax, 29th Oct. 1782, relating to Nova Scotia and measures taken for the protection of its inhabitants.

A sketch of the province of Nova Scotia, and chiefly of such parts as are settled. In Major-General Patterson's of 29th Oct. 1782.

Governor Parr to General Grey, Halifax, Nova Scotia, 23rd Oct. 1782, mentions his arrival at Halifax in Oct., and describes his home there; his quietness disturbed by providing for families from New York who have come to settle in Nova Scotia. Complains of the fortifications at Halifax which cost 180,000l.

Governor Parr to Lord Shelburne, Halifax, Nova Scotia, 14th Nov. 1782, relating to the German recruits, and the benefit it would be to the service where he is if he were restored to his rank in the army.

Governor Parr to the Earl of Shelburne, Halifax, Nova Scotia, 29th Nov. 1782. The people of this province appear to be much attached to Government, except in that part, called Cobiquid at the head of the basin of Minas, where dissenters from the North of Ireland are settled; 300 refugees have arrived at Annapolis from New York and more are expected.

Report of the state of the fortifications at St. John's, Newfoundland, 1782. Signed Robert Pringle.

General scheme of the Newfoundland fishery for the year 1782. Signed by Vice-Admiral John Campbell, Governor, 28th Oct. 1782.

Captain Twiss, commanding engineer in Canada, to the Earl of Shelburne, dated Quebec, 24th Oct., but endorsed 21st Oct. 1782. Thinks no European power could long support Canada by force against America independent.

Thomas Carleton to Lord Shelburne, Quebec, 16th Sept. 1782. Presents Captain Twiss to his Lordship. Intends going to England if he does not find anything going on at New York. (In Captain Twiss' letter of 21st Oct. 1782.)

General abstract of expenses incurred in Canada under the instruction of the Controller of Works between 1st July 1776 and 30th June 1778. In Captain Twiss' letter of 21st Oct. 1782.

Abstracts of expenses incurred under the commanding engineer in Canada, between 1st July 1778 and 31st Dec. 1781. In Captain Twiss' letter of 21st Oct. 1782.

Lieut.-General Leslie to General Sir Guy Carleton, Charlestown, 18th Nov. 1782. His intentions of assisting the Loyalists in returning the enemy; their negroes have proved abortive by the behaviour of Mr. Matthew, the rebel governor, and General Green. The Loyalists going to the East Florida and Jamaica will, he apprehends, complain to Sir Guy about their allowance of provisions.

The embarkation return of His Majesty's troops under the command of Lieut.-General Alexander Leslie from Charlestown, 30th Oct. 1782.

List of transports appointed to receive the garrison of Charlestown.

List of ships gone to Halifax under convoy of His Majesty's ships "Perseverance" and "Ceres."

List of ships left at St. Augustine to be sent to New York in the spring.

List of ships bound to St. Lucie under convoy of His Majesty's ship "Hornet."

List of ships bound to Jamaica under the direction of Lieut. Curling, &c.

List of ships to England under the direction of Lieut. Arnold, and under convoy of His Majesty's ship "Adamant."

Abstract of the list of transports appointed to receive the garrison of Charlestown, 19th Nov. 1782.

Vol. 70.

A folio volume bound in red morocco and labelled "Correspondence with Mr. Oswald, the Commissioner at "Paris." It contains copies of despatches from 21st May 1782 to 20th Jan. 1783. A very important collection. A full list is appended.

Correspondence with Mr. Oswald, the Commissioner at Paris.

Lord Shelburne to Benjamin Franklin, dated 21st May 1782.
Lord Shelburne to Richard Oswald, dated 21st May 1782.
Lord Shelburne to Benjamin Franklin, dated 21st May 1782.
Richard Oswald to Lord Shelburne, dated 13th May 1782.
Lord Shelburne to Richard Oswald, dated 21st May 1782.
Lord Shelburne to Benjamin Franklin, dated 25th May 1782.
Richard Oswald to Lord Shelburne, dated 9th June 1782.
Lord Shelburne to Richard Oswald, dated 30th June 1782.
Richard Oswald to Lord Shelburne, dated 8th July 1782.
Benjamin Franklin to Richard Oswald, dated 27th June 1782.
Richard Oswald to Lord Shelburne, dated 8th July 1782.
Richard Oswald to Lord Shelburne, dated 10th July 1782.
Richard Oswald to Lord Shelburne, dated 11th July 1782.
Richard Oswald to Lord Shelburne, dated 11th July 1782.
Benjamin Franklin to Richard Oswald, dated 12th July 1782.
Benjamin Franklin to Lord Shelburne, dated 12th July 1782.

Extract from the Maryland Gazette, 16th May 1782. Signed W. Harwood, clerk, and J. Maccubbin, clerk.

Richard Oswald to Lord Shelburne, dated 12th July 1782.

Lord Shelburne to Richard Oswald, dated 13th July 1782.

Richard Oswald to Lord Shelburne, dated 16th July 1782.

Thomas Townshend to Richard Oswald, dated 19th July 1782.

Thomas Townshend to Richard Oswald, dated 26th July 1782.

Richard Oswald to Thomas Townshend, dated 31st July 1782.

Thomas Townshend to Richard Oswald, dated 3rd Aug. 1782.

Richard Oswald's commission from the King, signed Thomas Townshend, dated 25th July 1782.

Richard Oswald's order and instructions, signed George R., dated 31st July 1782.

Thomas Townshend to Richard Oswald, dated 10th Aug. 1782.

Richard Oswald to Thomas Townshend, dated 5th Aug. 1782.

Richard Oswald to Thomas Townshend, dated 6th Aug. 1782.

Richard Oswald to Thomas Townshend, dated 17th Aug. 1782.

Minutes of conversation with the American Commissioners to Thomas Townshend, dated 7th Aug. 1782. Signed Richard Oswald.

Conversation with Doctor Franklin, &c., to Thomas Townshend, dated 13th Aug. 1782. Signed Richard Oswald.

Observations to Thomas Townshend, dated 15th Aug. 1782. Signed Richard Oswald.

Draft proposed by Mr. Jay, 10th Aug. 1782. George the Third to Richard Oswald.

Richard Oswald to Thomas Townshend, dated 18th Aug. 1782.

Richard Oswald to Thomas Townshend, dated 21st Aug. 1782.

Richard Oswald to Thomas Townshend, dated 27th Aug. 1712. Copied 1783.

Thomas Townshend to Richard Oswald, dated 1st Sept. 1782.

Richard Oswald to Thomas Townshend, dated 10th Sept. 1782.

Richard Oswald to Benjamin Franklin, dated 5th Sept. 1782, with copy of extract, dated 1st Sept. 1782, and draft answer to Lord Howe and General Clinton's letters, enclosed.

Extract of a letter in answer to the letters and papers from the Earl of Carlisle, &c., dated 17th June 1778.

Extract from the proceedings of Congress, dated 18th July 1778.

Benjamin Franklin to Richard Oswald, dated 8th Sept. 1782.

Note of Richard Oswald to Lord Shelburne, dated 10th Sept. 1782.

Sketch of a letter proposed by Mr. Jay to be made in His Majesty's commission, for treating with the Commissioners of the Colonies, dated 10th Sept. 1782.

Richard Oswald to Thomas Townshend, dated 11th Sept. 1782.

Minutes regarding the intended treaty with the Commissioners of the Colonies, and what is required of me by His Majesty's instructions on that head, dated 29th Aug. 1782.

Richard Oswald to Thomas Townshend, dated 19th Sept. 1782.

Thomas Townshend to Richard Oswald, dated 20th Sept. 1782.

Thomas Townshend to Richard Oswald, dated 24th Sept. 1782.

Commission from George R. to Richard Oswald, dated 19th Sept. 1782. Signed Thomas Townshend.

Resolutions by the United States in Congress assembled, dated 12th Aug. 1782, with letter of Sir Guy Carleton and Admiral Digby, dated 2nd Aug. 1782.

Richard Oswald to Thomas Townshend, dated 2nd Oct. 1782, with copy of the commission of the United States of America to Benjamin Franklin and others, dated 15th June 1781. Signed Sam. Huntingdon, enclosed.

Discharge from parole of Captain Fage, dated 1st Oct. 1782. Signed B. Franklin.

Richard Oswald to Thomas Townshend, dated 3rd Oct. 1782.

Richard Oswald to Thomas Townshend, dated 5th Oct. 1782.

Richard Oswald to Thomas Townshend, dated 7th Oct. 1782, with articles of a final treaty proposed between Great Britain and the Thirteen States of America, signed Richard Oswald, dated 8th Oct. 1782, enclosed.

Richard Oswald to Thomas Townshend, dated 8th Oct. 1782.

Thomas Townshend to Richard Oswald, dated 11th Oct. 1782.

Richard Oswald to Thomas Townshend, dated 11th Oct. 1782, with minutes of sundry articles recommended in my instructions not included in the treaty, dated 17th Oct. 1782, signed Richard Oswald, enclosed.

Thomas Townshend to Richard Oswald, dated 23rd Oct. 1782.

Thomas Townshend to Benjamin Franklin, dated 23rd Oct. 1782.

Richard Oswald to Thomas Townshend, dated 23rd Oct. 1782.

Thomas Townshend to Richard Oswald, dated 26th Oct. 1782.

Lord Shelburne to Thomas Townshend, dated 26th Oct. 1782.

Lord Shelburne to Richard Oswald, dated 23rd Oct. 1782.

Thomas Townshend to Richard Oswald, dated 28th Oct. 1782.

Richard Oswald to Thomas Townshend, dated 29th Oct. 1782.

Thomas Townshend to Sir Guy Carleton, dated 23rd Oct. 1782.

Certificate of Richard Oswald, dated 29th Oct. 1782.

H. Strachey to Thomas Townshend, dated 29th Oct. 1782.

Richard Oswald to Thomas Townshend, dated 5th Nov. 1782.

Benjamin Franklin to Thomas Townshend, dated 4th Nov. 1782.

Richard Oswald to Thomas Townshend, dated 6th and 7th Nov. 1782.

Extract from the Pensylvania packet of the 5th Oct. 1782. Signed Blair, Mr. Clenachan, chairman.

Extract from the Pensylvania packet of the 5th Oct. 182. Signed Charles Thompson, secretary.

Richard Oswald to Benjamin Franklin, John Jay, and John Adams, dated 4th Nov. 1782.

John Adams, Benjamin Franklin, and John Jay to H. Stachey, dated 6th Nov. 1782.

John Adams, Benjamin Franklin, and John Jay to Richard Oswald, dated 7th Nov. 1782.

H. Strachey to Thomas Townshend, dated 8th Nov. 1782, with articles agreed upon by and between Richard Oswald on the one part, and Benjamin Franklin, John Jay, and John Adams on the other part, enclosed.

Richard Oswald to Benjamin Franklin, John Jay, and John Adams, dated 4th Nov. 1782.

H. Strachey to the American Commissioners, dated 5th Nov. 1782.

H. Strachey to Thomas Townshend, dated 8th Nov. 1782.

Richard Oswald to H. Strachey, dated 8th Nov. 1782.

Richard Oswald to Thomas Townshend, dated 15th Nov. 1782.

Richard Oswald to H. Strachey, dated 15th Nov. 1782, with letter to Benjamin Vaughan to H. Strachey, dated 14th Nov. 1782, enclosed.

Evan Nepean to H. Strachey, dated 27th Nov. 1782.

J. Barry to Thomas Townshend, dated 27th Nov. 1782.

H. Strachey to Thomas Townshend, dated 29th Nov. 1782, with articles enclosed.

H. Strachey to Thomas Townshend, dated 29th Nov. 1782.

H. Strachey to Evan Nepean, dated 29th Nov. 1782.

Alleyne Fitzherbert to Thomas Townshend, dated 30th Nov. 1782.

Richard Oswald to Thomas Townshend, dated 30th Nov. 1782, with articles agreed upon by and between Richard Oswald on the one part, and John Adams, Benjamin Franklin, John Jay, and Henry Laurens, on the other part, signed and sealed, enclosed.

Richard Oswald to Thomas Townshend, dated 30th Nov. 1782.

Richard Oswald to Thomas Townshend, dated 4th Dec. 1782.

Richard Oswald to H. Strachey, dated 4th Dec. 1782.

Evan Nepean to Richard Oswald, dated 11th Dec. 1782.

Richard Oswald to Evan Nepean, dated 18th Dec. 1782.

Evan Nepean to Richard Oswald, dated 21st Dec. 1782.

Richard Oswald to H. Strachey, dated 16th Dec. 1782.

Thomas Townshend to Richard Oswald, dated 8th Jan. 1783.

Richard Oswald to Thomas Townshend, dated 20th Jan. 1783.

Vol. 71.

This Vol. 71 is endorsed, "Peace 1783. Correspon- "dence. Provisional and Preliminary Articles, No. 1."

1782.

Richard Oswald, Commissioner for treating of a peace with certain colonies in North America. Draft of his orders and instructions, dated St. James', 31st July.

Richard Oswald, memoranda of general instructions to, in conversation, 28th April.

Richard Oswald, further memoranda of instructions to. (No date).

Lord Shelburne to Richard Oswald.

Richard Oswald to Lord Shelburne, 11th June.

Dr. B. Franklin to Richard Oswald, 11th June.

Copy of Dr. B. Franklin's discharge of Lord Cornwallis' parole, dated Prasy, 9th June.

Richard Oswald to Lord Shelburne, 12th June.

Richard Oswald to Lord Shelburne, 12th June.

Lord Shelburne to Richard Oswald, 27th July.

Richard Oswald to Lord Shelburne, 5th Aug.

Richard Oswald to Lord Shelburne, 6th Aug.

Richard Oswald to Lord Shelburne, 18th Aug.

Richard Oswald to Lord Shelburne, 11th Sept.

Mr. Jay to Richard Oswald, 10th Sept.

David Hartley to Dr. B. Franklin, 26th July.

Richard Oswald to Lord Shelburne, 19th Sept.

Henry Laurens to Richard Oswald, 10th Sept.

Henry Laurens to Richard Oswald, 12th Sept.

Henry Laurens to Mr. Day.

Lord Shelburne to Richard Oswald, 3rd Sept.

Lord Shelburne to Richard Oswald, 23rd Sept.

Richard Oswald to Lord Shelburne, 3rd Oct.

Richard Oswald to Mr. Townshend, 3rd Oct.

Copy of the articles of the treaty proposed to be concluded between Great Britain and the United States of America. Signed R. Oswald, and dated Paris, 8th Oct.

Richard Oswald to Lord Shelburne, 11th Oct.

Lord Shelburne to Richard Oswald, 21st Oct.

Richard Oswald to Lord Shelburne, 24th Oct.

Richard Oswald to Lord Shelburne, 29th Oct.

Henry Strachey to Hon. Thomas Townshend, 29th Oct.

Richard Oswald to Lord Shelburne, 5th Nov.

Lord Shelburne to Richard Oswald, 23rd Nov.

Richard Oswald to Lord Shelburne, 30th Nov.

Richard Oswald to Lord Shelburne, 4th Dec.

Richard Oswald to Lord Shelburne, 26th Dec.

Minutes relative to the freedom of neutral navigation, Paris, 15th Dec.

Richard Oswald to Lord Shelburne, 29th Dec.

Richard Oswald to Lord Shelburne, 29th Dec.

Lord Shelburne to Richard Oswald, 31st Dec.

1783.

Richard Oswald to Lord Shelburne, 5th Jan.

Richard Oswald to Lord Shelburne, 8th Jan.

Richard Oswald to Lord Shelburne, 8th and 9th Jan.

Dr. B. Franklin to Richard Oswald, 14th Jan.

Richard Oswald to Lord Shelburne, 23rd Jan.

1782.

Lord Shelburne to Mr. Grenville, 5th July.

Lord Shelburne to Mr. Grenville, 13th July.

Alleyne Fitzherbert to Lord Shelburne, 31st July.

Alleyne Fitzherbert to Lord Shelburne, 17th Aug.

Alleyne Fitzherbert to Lord Shelburne, 3rd Oct.

Alleyne Fitzherbert to Lord Grantham, 7th Oct.

French memorial, viz., Le Roi pour repondre à la Notte de la Cour de Londres remise per Mons. Fitzherbert, le 4 Août dernier, proposes les Articles suivants pour servir de base à la future pacification entre sa Majesté et le Roi de la Grande Bretagne. Art. 1. Peche de Terre Neuve. Art. 2. Afrique et Traite des Negres. Art. 3. Indes Orientales. Art. 4. Indes Occidentales Antilles. Art. 5. Dunkerque. Art. 6. Commerce. Dated Versailles, 6th Oct. 1782. Signed De Vergennes.

Spanish memorial (written in French) containing the terms of peace proposed by the Court of Madrid, dated Paris, 6th Oct. 1782. Signed Le Comte d'Aranda.

Lord Shelburne to Alleyne Fitzherbert, 21st Oct.

Alleyne Fitzherbert to Lord Shelburne, 23rd Oct.

Alleyne Fitzherbert to Lord Shelburne, 5th Nov.

Alleyne Fitzherbert to Lord Shelburne, 4th Dec.

Alleyne Fitzherbert to Lord Shelburne, 4th Dec.

Alleyne Fitzherbert to Lord Shelburne, 17th Dec.

Alleyne Fitzherbert to Lord Shelburne, 18th Dec.

Alleyne Fitzherbert to Lord Shelburne, 24th Dec.

Alleyne Fitzherbert, precis of his letter of the 24th Dec.

Lord Shelburne to Alleyne Fitzherbert, 20th Dec.

Alleyne Fitzherbert to Lord Shelburne, 26th Dec.

(24th Decr. 1782) Rapport fait au Roi dans son Committé de la Lettre de Rayneval du 20th Dec., et de ce qui avoit été exposé le 23 par Mr. Fitzherbert de l'ordre de sa Cour, dans une conference avec le Comte de Vergennes, touchant la Dominique, Versailles. 26th Dec. 1782. Signed De Vergennes. In Mr. Fitzherbert's, Dec. 26th 1782.

1783.

Alleyne Fitzherbert to Lord Shelburne, 5th Jan.

Alleyne Fitzherbert to Lord Shelburne, 5th Jan.

Lord Shelburne to Alleyne Fitzherbert, 9th Jan.

Alleyne Fitzherbert to Lord Shelburne, 15th Jan.

Alleyne Fitzherbert to Lord Shelburne, 19th Jan.

Alleyne Fitzherbert to Lord Shelburne, 25th Jan.

Alleyne Fitzherbert to Lord Shelburne, 3rd Feb.

Alleyne Fitzherbert to Lord Grantham, 9th Feb.

Alleyne Fitzherbert to Lord Grantham, 8th March.

1782.

Comte de Grasse to Lord Shelburne, 10th Aug.

Comte de Grasse to Lord Shelburne, 18th Aug.

Lord Shelburne to Comte de Grasse, 3rd Sept.

Comte de Grasse to Lord Shelburne, 21st Sept.

Comte de Grasse to Lord Shelburne, 25th Dec.

1783.

Lord Shelburne to Comte de Grasse, 28th Jan.

Comte de Grasse to Lord Shelburne, 21st Jan.

1782.

Comte de Vergennes to Lord Shelburne, 6th Sept.

Préliminaires. Projét de Préliminaires remis par le Comte de Grasse, comme le resultat de ses conversations avec Mi lord Shelburne, dated 17 Août 1782. (In my Lord's handwriting).

Préliminaires. Remarques à faire sur une Notte confidentielle, sur les Moyens d'achominer les preliminaires de la Paix, Sept, 1782.

Lord Shelburne to Comte de Vergennes, Sept.

Comte de Vergennes to Lord Shelburne, 15th Nov.

Lord Shelburne to Comte de Vergennes, 23rd Nov.

Lord Shelburne to Comte de Vergennes, 23rd Nov.

Comte de Vergennes to Lord Shelburne, 25th Nov.

Comte de Vergennes to Lord Shelburne, 28th Nov.

1783.

Comte de Vergennes to Lord Shelburne, 20th Jan.

Lord Shelburne to Comte de Vergennes, 24th Jan.

1782.

M. de Rayneval to Lord Shelburne, 10th Sept.

M. de Rayneval to Lord Shelburne, 28th Sept.

Lord Shelburne to M. de Rayneval, 21st Oct.

Lord Shelburne to M. de Rayneval, 13th Nov.

M. de Rayneval to Lord Shelburne, 1st Dec.

M. de Rayneval to Lord Shelburne, 4th Dec.

M. de Rayneval to Lord Shelburne, 4th Dec.

M. de Rayneval to Lord Shelburne, 17th Dec.

M. de Rayneval, Résumé des Observationes faites par, Dec.

Comte de Vengennes to M. de Rayneval, Dec.

1783.

M. de Rayneval to Lord Shelburne, 6th Jan.

M. de Rayneval to Lord Shelburne, 20th Jan.

M. de Rayneval to Lord Shelburne, 14th Fêb.

M. de Rayneval to Lord Shelburne, 20th March.

1782.

Comte d'Aranda to Lord Shelburne, 17th Dec.

Lord Shelburne to Mons. le Comte d'Aranda. (No date).

Comte d'Aranda's offers in treating for a peace, Oct.

1783.

Messrs. de Berkenroode and de Brantsen to Lord Shelburne, 20th Jan.

Lord Shelburne to Messrs. de Berkenroode and de Brantsen, 1st Feb.

1782.

Treaty, provisional, between Great Britain and North America, dated at Paris, 30th Nov. 1782. Signed Richard

Oswald, John Adams, B. Franklin, John Jay, Henry Laurens. Attested, Caleb Whiteford, Secretary to the British Commission, W. T. Franklin, Secretary to the American Commission,

1783.

Preliminaries. Articles. préliminaires de Paix, entre sa Majesté Britannique, et le Rois très Chrétien, signés à Versailles, le 20 Janvier 1783, Alleyne Fitzherbert, Gravier de Vergennes. (Printed.)

Preliminaries. Articles préliminaires de Paix, entre sa Majesté Britannique, et le Roi d'Espagne signés à Versailles, le 20 Janvier 1783. Alleyne Fitzherbert le Comte D'Aranda. (Printed.)

Vol. 72.

Contents of Vol. 72 endorsed "Peace 1783. Papers of "Negociation. Informations and Opinions, No. 2."

The Duke of Grafton to the Earl of Shelburne. Euston, 14th Nov. 1781.

America. Persons of note with the people of, viz. :— Dr. Franklin, Messrs. Adams, Laurens, the two brothers Livingston, Morris, of Philadelphia, Izard, and Moses Gill of Boston. From Mr. Jackson to (the Earl of Shelburne.

America. Memoranda from Mr. Digges, relative to treating for peace with, 30th March 1782. Account of what passed between Mr. Digges and Mr. Adams.

A transcript of the foregoing.

Lord Shelburne. Memoranda relative to truce or peace with America, Commissioners in Europe to treat thereof.

Maryland. Unanimous resolution of, respecting independence. 16th May 1782.

Peace. Propositions and reasoning concerning, submitted to Lord George Germaine, 25th July 1781. Endorsed 1782.

Paper headed "Peace, Breviate concerning." 7th Feb. 1782.

Dr. Franklin to D. Hartley, Esq., Passy, 5th April 1782. Relating to making peace, and the manner in which the English conducted the war in America.

Dr. Franklin to D. Hartley, Esq., Passy, 13th April 1782. Lord North's propositions to the French ministers for them to abandon America, and their answer thereto.

Dr. Franklin to D. Hartley, Esq., Passy, 14th April 1782. If the new ministry are disposed to enter into a general peace, Mr. Laurens is ready to receive their propositions relative to time, place, &c.

Dr. Franklin to D. Hartley, Esq., Passy, 16th Feb. 1782. Relating to making peace between Great Britain, America, &c.

Dr. Benj. Franklin to Henry Laurens, Esq., Passy, 12th April 1782. Congratulates him on his enlargement. Hopes the terms exacted by the late ministry, will now be relaxed when they are informed he is one of the commissioners for a peace. Encloses a copy of the Commission, the purport of which he may communicate to the ministers.

Preliminaries, five articles of, May 1782.

Mr. Thomas Walpole to Lord Shelburne, Paris, 18th June 1782. A letter from his Lordship to Mr. Oswald.

Le Comte de Vergennes. Proposition touching the Newfoundland fishery.

Newfoundland fishery. Memoranda thereon, in Lord Shelburne's handwriting.

Newfoundland fishery. Particulars as to St. Peter's Isle, on the coast of Newfoundland; also of Langley island, and Mequilon. To fortify those islands would avail little against a naval power of little importance to our free navigation, their being in the hands of the French, March 1783.

Peace, articles thereon, touching Newfoundland, Africa and Negro trade, East Indies, West Indies, Dunkirk, and Honduras, with observations.

Honduras. The English establishments in the bay of, to be abandoned, proposed article thereon between England and Spain.

Logwood merchants, their representation to Lord Shelburne, relative to the 4th article of the preliminaries with Spain, 31st Jan. 1783.

British merchants trading to Spain, their memorial to Lord Grantham, Secretary of State, 22nd Jan. 1783.

Preliminaries of the Dutch negotiation, from 4th March to 29th Oct. 1782.

Cabinet, the sense of, touching preliminaries with America, 15th Nov. 1782. Approved by Mr. Townsend and Mr. Pitt.

Lord Shelburne's notes relative to the negotiation, 22nd Nov. (in his own handwriting).

Minutes relative to the situation of England in the present war. 48 pages, folio Paris, 26th June 1782 and 1st July, at the end.

Objections and queries, relative to the future peace and safety of Great Britain, Paris, 3rd July 1782.

Supplement to the preceding papers, Paris, 5th July 1782.

Monaghan to . . . . (no date). Considerations on the war with Holland. Artifices of the French. Stipulations in the treaty of 1674 might be amended by a new treaty of commerce. Sketch of Mr. Wentworth's character.

Mr. George Harris to Lord Shelburne, 27th May 1780, on the treaty with Holland in 1674.

On a general treaty and Congress, Brussels, 1st Nov. 1782, endorsed "The Earl of Shelburne will not "offend his great political talents by condescending to "glance his eyes over the crude thoughts of an indi- "vidual who was long expected, but now reveres the "superior powers of his Lordship. His Majesty's speech "from the throne on Thursday last will perpetuate the "name of the Earl of Shelburne."

Anonymous letters, two, in the same handwriting; the first to Lord Shelburne, against the independence of America; the second to Col. Isaac Barre, with a plan of operations to be pursued towards America and the West Indies. (No date.)

America, conduct towards, which should have been held at the time Parliament deprecated the continuance of the war. (No date.)

French and Spanish perfidy, copies of letters from Dr. Franklin, Deane, and. Lee, Count de Vergennes, Count Florida Blanca, &c., in 1777 and 1778, to show the same.

America, hints drawn up in 1780, when a reconciliation with, was talked of.

Law of nations, memorial for the improvement of, at the present Congress at Paris for establishing a general peace, 8th Jan. 1783.

Naval establishment in time of peace, memorial on the necessity of keeping up a respectable one, 8th Jan. 1783.

Dr. Franklin to Mr. Wm. Hodgson, merchant in Coleman Street, Passy, 31st Oct. 1781. Four letters relating to advances to be made to various American prisoners in England, and similar subjects.

American prisoners in Mill prison, Forton, prison and Kinsale (10th April 1782, total 1050), memoranda concerning the exchange of.

W. L. to . . . . Brussels, 2nd April 1782. Thoughts on the present prospect of peace. Allusion to the possible influence of Lord Bute. A separate peace with America not to be expected. America has got independence, and now only wants peace; her connexion with France must grow stronger while the war continues, which the French ministry is aware of. A mad prince here, the Prince de Ligne, always protests against the King of France being crowned King of Navarre, which, he says, is his kingdom.

Henry Laurens, Esq., to Benj. Vaughan, jun., Esq., Exeter, 2nd April 1782. Lord Shelburne's intimation of his desire to see him; will bring him to town as fast as his health will permit.

Benj. Vaughan, Esq., to Lord Shelburne, 4th April 1782. Enclosing Mr. Laurens letter from Exeter.

Benj. Vaughan, Esq., to Lord Shelburne, 24th April 1782.

Mr. Laurens and Lord Cornwallis. Conversation between them, relative to their exchange, 29th April 1782, in the presence of Moses Young, Secretary, of the latter.

Note on the tax levied in Pennsylvania during the last war.

Mr. J. Simpson to Lord Shelburne, Leicester Street, 27th April 1782. His sentiments and reasoning as to the latitude it may be advisable to give to persons appointed to treat of peace with America. 12 pages folio.

Anonymous to Lord Shelburne (no date) with the sketch of a Bill.

Act to enable His Majesty to conclude a peace or truce with certain colonies in North America, 15th June 1782. (Printed.)

America, ideas relative to peace with, 1783.

Anonymous, subscribing himself a true Briton to Lord Shelburne, July 1782, against American independence, this letter though directed to Lord Shelburne is really addressed to Mr. Pitt.

Mackenzie (Mr. Kenneth) to Lord Shelburne, Charlotte Street, near Portland Chapel, 12th July 1782, with an extract of a letter from New York, relative to the temper of the American rulers, and the affection of the people towards the mother country.

Tilghman (Mr. James) to Lady Juliana .... Penn, Chester Town, Maryland, 14th Aug. 1782. Relative to proprietary estates, and particularly that of Will. Penn.

Tilghman (Mr. James) to the same, Chester Town, 14th Aug. 1782. A duplicate of the former. A copy transmitted to Mr. Oswald at Paris, 26th Oct. following.

Connolly (John, Lieut.-Col.) to Lord Shelburne, Charlotte Street, Portland Chapel, Sept. 1782. Containing much information respecting the revolted and loyal colonies of North America.

Anonymous to Lord Shelburne, 22nd Feb. 1782, respecting the East Indies, and the French settlements there. Hints from a knowledge of that country, acquired by upwards of 20 years.

Mr. Fras. Baring, to Lord Shelburne, 27th Sept. 1782. Two points material to the existence of our power in India, viz. :—1. That the Cape of Good Hope shall not be in the hands of the French. 2. That no foreign (European) power shall establish themselves in Bengal and Orissa, so as to prevent us from taking their forts, &c. at pleasure, with remarks.

Mr. Fras. Baring to the same, 2nd Oct. 1782. Enclosing remarks relative to Chandernagore. A slight illness has prevented his completing some remarks on the Honduras trade.

East India company, extract of a note from the Secret Committee of the, to Lord Grantham, 23rd Oct. 1782, relative to the forming of proposals to be offered in case of a treaty for peace.

East India Company, Lord Grantham's answer to the foregoing, Whitehall, 24th Oct. 1782.

East India Company, the Court of Directors of; their observations on the 14th and 16th articles transmitted by Lord Grantham, 29th Jan. 1783.

East India Company, Secret Committee of, to Lord Grantham, 4th Feb. 1783.

East India Company, Lord Grantham to the Secret Committee of, 3rd Feb. 1783. (Private and most secret.)

India, sketch of the orders to be sent to, in consequence of the preliminary articles agreed on, between the Crowns of Great Britain and France, 4th Feb. 1783.

India affairs. List of captured French and Dutch settlements, 1782.

A postscript belonging to a letter at p. 385.

St. Bartholomew and St. Martin, observations on the islands of, 4th Dec. 1782. Received from Sir Charles Middleton.

Anonymous subscribing himself "Impartial observer " to Lord Shelburne," Salisbury, 25th Nov. 1782. Containing hints relative to the importance of several West India islands.

Mr. Jo. Hog to . . . Exeter, 8th Feb. 1783, on the Newfoundland fishery, the great injury thereto by such an extravagant grant to the French.

Anonymous to Lord Shelburne, March 1783. The importance of fixing the English and Spanish boundaries on the Mosquito shore, sometimes called the Spanish main.

Campeachy trade long lost to this country. Groves of logwood trees upon its banks, &c.

Mr. Fr. Baring to Lord Shelburne, 26th Sept. 1782, on the importations of logwood and mahogany from the bay of Honduras.

Mr. Fr. Baring on the bay of Campeachy.

Mr. Fr. Baring's remarks on the article of logwood, 3rd Dec. 1872.

——— to Lord Shelburne, 18th Sept. 1782. Importance of the gum trade from Africa, Senegal the grave for Europeans. The benefits derived from its trade cannot compensate for the numbers that perish. Goree of still less value than Senegal. Senegal when in the hands of France did not produce one fourth of the gum that has been imported by the English. No place on the coast of Africa can be ceded to France of so little importance to England as Senegal and Goree. Besides this there are various particulars relative to the principal articles of the African trade (slaves, gum, ivory) and the settlements where they are to be had.

Mr. F. Baring to Lord Shelburne, 24th Sept. 1782, on the African trade, Cape of Good Hope, &c.

Mr. F. Baring to Lord Shelburne, 18th Oct. 1782. Madagascar. On object of the greatest national concern, the slaves from thence the hardiest, best, well-disposed, and cheapest.

Mr. F. Baring's remarks on the fourth article of the proposed treaty.

Mr. James Simpson, Attorney-General of South Carolina, to Lord Shelburne, 15th Jan. 1783; Review

of American affairs, and opinion of the future commotions which may be looked for.

Lieut.-Colonel John Conolly to Lord Shelburne, 1st Feb. 1783. On the Canadian boundaries. Proposes an amendment of the treaty which he considers as too partial to the Americans on the score of trade with the Illinois and other Indians.

Mr. Peter Thoppison to Lord Shelburne, Feb. 1783. On the Canada boundaries. Some few interested men without just cause complain thereof. Canada at present costs government 1,000,000l. per annum, Bounties and drawbacks should be taken off in lieu of new taxes and the navy debt funded.

Massachusets bay. Query.—What claim has the province of, to the province of Main, or the country between Nova Scotia and New Hampshire. Answer.—The old charter of Massachusetts bay being forfeited was vacated, and a new charter granted, An. 3 William and Mary, in which were united with it, the colony of New Plymouth, the province of Main, the territory of Sagadahoe and Nova Scotia.

Canada' merchants to Lord Shelburne, New York, Coffee House, 6th Feb. 1783, on the Canada boundaries and the loss which this country and Quebec is likely to sustain by the line of partition settled by Art. 2 of the provisional treaty with America, which cuts off almost the whole of the fur trade.

Representation of the Canada merchants enclosed to Lord Shelburne, 31st Jan. 1783. Their objections to the intended new boundaries of the province of Quebec. N.B. Mr. Thoppison's letter (No. 80), appears to have been written in consequence of the foregoing letter and representation of the Canada merchants, S.P.

Quebec merchants, regulations proposed by the, to secure and withdraw their property dispersed throughout that part of the province now about to be ceded to the United States of America, Feb. 1783.

Mr. Geo. Dempster's memorandum to Lord Shelburne, respecting debts due in America to the merchants of Glasgow, 22nd April 1782.

J. Pownall, Esq., to Lord Shelburne, 30th Jan. 1783, relative to the future regulation of the commercial intercourse of Great Britain with the United States of America.

J. Pownall to Lord Shelburne, 2nd Feb. 1783. Review of the Statutes necessary to be revised in consequence of the provisional treaty with America.

J. Pownall, Esq., to Lord Shelburne. 7th Feb. 1783. Proposed commercial regulations with America.

Draft of an Act to enable his Majesty to conclude a definitive treaty of commerce, and in the meantime to make temporary regulations for mutual convenience of Great Britain and America. In Mr. Pownall's of 17th Feb. 1783.

Sir Roger Curtis to Mr. Nepean. Thectis, Portland road, 2nd Feb. 1783, review of the peace of which he thinks very highly.

Sir John Jervis' arguments for the peace deduced from the state of the navy, in reply to "the political " necessity of pulling down the naval power of our " enemies before we make the peace, 1783."

Memoranda for Mr. Townshend's immediate consideration.

Vol. 73.

A folio volume bound in red morocco and labelled Jamaica. It contains an account of the constitution of Jamaica, 1678–1680, and copies of 38 appendices relating to the same subject.

Contents of volume 74, endorsed "West India Miscel- " laneous Papers."

A miscellaneous collection (1724–64), of which the most important papers are,—

(1.) Considerations which may tend to promote the settlement of our new colonies in the West Indies, &c.

Some general heads submitted concerning the most eligible plan of government for the new acquired islands of Dominique, St. Vincent, Grenada (with the Grenadittees), and Tobago, by Governor Melville.

Objects to be attended to in granting lands in the newly-acquired islands.

Branches of the Jamaica revenue appropriated to the use of the island by Act of Parliament, passed in the year 1728.

Extract of P. Yorke and C. Weary, Attorney and Solicitor-Generals' report to the Board of Trade, dated 18th May 1724, concerning taxes in Jamaica.

(2.) Papers relating to the Mosquito shore.

Vol. 75.

A folio volume labelled "South Seas." It contains an account of discoveries and copies of reports and despatches relative to the West Indies and the South Seas down to 1768. The most interesting papers are,—

(1.) Mr. Sutton's Abstract of Transactions relating to the West Indies, from Queen Elizabeth's time to the Treaty of Utrecht.

An account of the discoverers, &c. of America.

Abstract of Pope Alexander IVth's Bull.

Extracts from the treaties between the Kings of England and Spain, of 1529 and 1542.

Copy of the 9th and 10th Articles of Peace between Philip III. of Spain and King James I., 1604.

Articles extracted from treaties of peace between England and Spain, concluded in the years 1604 and 1630.

Abstract of Sir Richard Fanshawe's letters from Spain, 1664, 1665, and 1666.

Abstract of Lord Sandwich and Sir William Godolphin's correspondence with Lord Arlington, from 1664 to 1671.

Extracts of treaties between England and Spain, 1670, 1713.

Sir William Godolphin to Lord Arlington. Madrid, 13th July 1670, with the articles of the treaty concluded July 1670.

Sir William Godolphin to the King, Madrid, 29th July 1670. On sending the preceding treaty.

Commission of Council for Plantations, 30th July 1670.

Letters to and from the plenipotentiaries at Utrecht in the Paper Office, relating to the Spanish West Indies, 1712.

Utrecht correspondence 1713, relating to the Spanish West Indies.

Articles proposed by Lord Lexington, respecting the West Indies, 1670.

An account of discoveries, &c. in America and West Indies.

Sir Richard Fanshaw's negociations with Spain, relating to the West Indies.

Abstract of Sir Richard Fanshaw's correspondence with Spain. Madrid, 1664 and 1665.

Discoveries in America (from 1492 to 1670).

Treaty between Charles II. of England and Charles II. of Spain, relating to America.

Letters from Lord Sandwich to Lord Arlington, relating to the treaties with Spain, deciphered, 1666.

Letter from Lord Sandwich to Lord Arlington. Madrid, 23rd Feb. 1666. Difficulties in settling the treaty.

Letter from Lord Sandwich to Lord Arlington. Madrid, 11th May 1667.

From same to same, 23rd Dec. 1667.

Sir William Godolphin to Lord Arlington. Madrid, 10th May 1672. On the cutting of logwood.

Propositions by Lord Lexington to the Court of Spain, 21st Oct. 1712. With the answers.

(2.) Mr. Keene's correspondence with successive Secretaries of State, relating to various questions of minor importance connected with the West Indies, 1729 to 1732.

(3.) Extracts from the King of Spain's grant of a 10-years assiento for a company to trade between Cadiz and the Phillippine Islands.

Mr. de la Paz to Messrs. Keene and Vandermeer, Seville, 4th Sep. 1732, relating to the Phillippines.

Sir James Grey's letters to the Earl of Shelburne. Madrid, 4th and 18th Feb., 11th April 1768, about the Phillippines.

A paper given to Count Weymouth by Count Welderen, relating to the Spaniards going to India by the Cape of Good Hope.

(4.) Mr. Keene's negociations about Falkland's Isles, 1749.

Duke of Bedford to Mr. Keene. Whitehall, 26th Oct. 1749. On the commerce of the two nations (France and Spain).

Copy of a paragraph in Lord G. Lenox's letter to Lord Shelburne. Compeigne, 17th Sept. 1766, relating to the Falkland Isles.

Discourse held to the Spanish Ambassador in Sept. 1766, relating to the Falkland Isles.

Extracts translated from Grotius's Mare Liberum.

Situation of Falkland Isles.

Historical notes, relating to the Falkland Isles.

Extracts from navigators and other authors, relating to Falkland Islands, 1593 to 1712, &c.

Extracts from the Earl of Rochford's correspondence relative to the Manilla ransom and Falkland Islands.

Sir Charles Saunders to the Earl of Shelburne, 8th Nov. 1766, enclosing a list of the vessels which had been sent to Falkland Islands. (Original.)

An account of Captain Macbride's voyage to Falkland Islands. Port Egmont, 6th April 1766.

Abstract of a letter from Captain Macbride, of the "Jason," dated Downs, 21st March 1767, containing an account of transactions at Falkland Islands.

(5.) A table of the latitudes observed and longitudes west from London, both by account and observation of the places the "Dolphin" was at and saw in her late voyage in 1766, 1767, 1768.

Captain Wallis to Lord Egmont. London, 19th May 1768, with an account of his voyage in the "Dolphin."

An account of the names, latitudes, longitudes, and variations of the compass, of lands discovered, on board His Majesty's ship the "Dolphin," in 1767.

Chart of the Straits of Magellan, &c.

Contents of Vol. 76, endorsed, "On the Limits of the "Spanish and Portuguese Settlements in South "America." 1701-1765.

Précis dans lequel on demontre, la portion de païs appartenant au Portugal dès l'extremité du sud du Brasil jusqu'à la Rivière de la Plata, et la Garantie de la Grande Bretagne, &c.

Article 5, du Traité signé entre le Portugal et l'Espagne, le 18e Juin 1701, ou l'Espagne renonce aux Droits qu'elle puisse avoir sur la Colonie de Sᵗ. Sacrement.

Treaty signed at Lisbonne, 16th May 1703, renouncing all claims to the possession of Portugal.

Tractatus Fœderis Defensivi inter Lusitanos, Anglos and Batavos adversus Hispanorum et Gallorum Incursiones, initi Ullissipone, die 16ᵉ May 1703.

Article 5, of the treaty of peace concluded at Utrecht, 6th Feb. 1715, between Portugal and Spain, relinquishing all conquests made in the war.

Article 6, of the treaty of peace concluded at Utrecht, relinquishing all right to St. Sacrement, &c.

Article 20, of the treaty of alliance between England and Spain concluded at Utrecht, the 13th July 1713. England's guaranty to the peace.

Article 22, of the treaty of peace between Portugal and Spain, Utrecht, 6th Feb. 1715, when they accept the guaranty of England.

Treaty between Spain and Portugal, signed the 12th Feb. 1761, annulling all former treaties.

Memorial presented by order of the Court of Portugal to Lord Egremont, upon the negociation of the peace, and to which no answer was made. Complaining of want of confidence, and of a due regard to the honour and interests of Portugal.

Deduction on l'on demontre les Termes, and l'Intelligence de la Paix, signée à Paris le 10ᵉ Fevrier 1763, entre le Portugal and l'Espagne.

Memorial given by the Portuguese Ambassador to the Marquis de Grimaldi, at Madrid, the 6th Jan. 1765, complaining of infractions of the Peace in Brazil.

An answer to the above, the 6th Feb. 1765.

Accounts of military preparations of the Spaniards against Brazil.

Copy of a letter from the Comte Da Cunha, Viceroy of Brazil, to Mr. De Mendoza, Secretary of State, dated Rio de Janeiro, the 8th March 1765, requiring succours against the invasion of the Spaniards.

A treaty between Spain and Portugal to settle the limits of Brazil. Madrid, 13th Jan. 1750.

Vol. 77.

A folio volume labelled description of the Islands of St. John, Cape Breton, Magdalen, Grenada, St. Vincent, and Dominica. The description is dated 1767, and is preceded by a letter to Lord Shelburne.

Contents of Vol. 78, endorsed, "West India Information. Jamaica; Barbadoes; General Mathew; Grenada; Tobago, and St. Vincents'; Africa."

An account of the quantity of pigments, cotton, rum, dy(e)ing and other woods, drugs of all kinds, imported from His Majesty's sugar colonies in America, from yᵉ year 1757 to yᵉ year 1764, and likewise the quantities of the said commodities exported from England, distinguishing each year.

An account of the total quantities of imports from North America to the British West India Islands, for the years 1771, 1772, and 1773.

An account of the imports to the British sugar colonies from North America for three years last past, distinguishing each year, viz., 1771, 1772, and 1773.

An account of the importation of sugar and rum into the port of London, with the number of ships, from 30th March 1762 to 1776, distinguishing each year and island.

Précis of a letter from Lieut.-Governor Campbell, Jamaica. Persons recommended for engineers. Loss by the fire at Kingston amounts to 400,000l. News concerning Spanish ships, troops, &c.

Précis of a letter from Governor Cunningham, Barbadoes, relating to the defence of Barbadoes, Hood's ships, and a proposal for a grant of money to be applied to fortifications.

Précis of a letter from Governor Brown, Bermuda. Has restored the officers of the Crown who were suspended by the Lieut.-Governor. Thinks the spirit of privateering will draw the resentment of the enemy. Wants supplies from England.

Précis of a letter from Governor Maxwell, Bahama. Suspects Mr. Symmers' integrity, though he approves of his estimate. Desires to return to Europe.

Letter from Mr. Izard, dated 12th September 1778, relating to the Floridas and Fishery.

Mode of communication recommended to be kept up for the better security of the West India Islands, with which is the form of the letter that Mr. Manning and Mr. Baillie are prepared to write, dated London, 22nd April 1782.

Memorial. To consult General Conway on the subject of the enclosed papers, viz. :—Supplies for the West Indies, &c., state of the fleet there, stores, provisions, and troops for Newfoundland. The paper relating to the state of the fleet in the West Indies is dated 15th March 1782, and endorsed, "From Admiral " Kepple, 29th March 1782," as is also the paper about stores, &c. for Newfoundland.

Letter to the Lords ——, dated 30th May 1782, relating to the defenceless state of Barbadoes, St. Lucia, and Antigua, in the absence of Sir Geo. Rodney, exposed to the French troops.

Mr. Charles Payne Brotherson, Captain Commander of Saint Martin's Island, to the Right Hon. Lord Wycombe, dated St. Martin's, 31st July 1782.

Proposals to the Marquiss De Bouillée, Captain General and Commander-in-Chief of His Most Christian Majesty's forces in the West Indies, relative to the French part of the Island of St. Martin's. Signed Charles Payne Brotherson. And the Marquiss De Bouillée's answer thereto. In Mr. Brotherson's of 31st July 1782.

Governor Valentine Morris to the Earl of Shelburne, London, 28th Nov. 1782. The Island of Becquia and others should be held as appendages to St. Vincent and not to Grenada.

Governor Valentine Morris to the Earl of Shelburne, 10th Feb. 1783. Proposed stipulations with the French respecting the Caribbs. Hopes to be restored to his government of St. Vincent's.

Governor Valentine Morris to the Earl of Shelburne, 14th Feb. 1783. Objects of immediate resource for increase of the West India revenues.

A list of the officers of the Customs at the several Islands mentioned, restored on the peace, Feb. 1783.

Arguments for protecting the West India Islands, Feb. 1782.

List of exports from the Island of Jamaica to Great Britain and Ireland for the year 1775.

List of exports from the Island of Jamaica to North America for the year 1775.

Samuel Jones to Lord ——, Kingston, Jamaica, 10th Sep. 1779. Mentions Dr. Irvine, inventor of making salt water fresh; the engagement off Grenada, &c. As soon as the news arrived at Kingston of a French fleet of 120 sail having gone to Cape François, the Governor proclaimed martial law. Describes the preparations for defending Kingston and other places in Jamaica against an attack by the forces under D'Estaign, who declared " that so far from leaving the King of England " a sugar island, he did not intend to leave him British " sugar enough to sweeten his tea for breakfast by " Christmas." Mentions the movements of D'Estaign's fleet, &c.

Lord Geo. Germaine to Stephen Fuller, Esq., agent for Jamaica, Whitehall, 14th Oct. 1779. Relating to troops for service for Jamaica.

General Dalling to Vice-Admiral Sir Peter Parker, Port Antonio, 21st Dec. 1781.

Governor John Dalling to Lord Geo. Germaine, Port Anthonio, Jamaica, 21st Dec. 1781.

Governor John Dalling to Mr. Robinson, Secretary to the Treasury, Navy Office, 23rd March 1782.

General John Dalling to Lord Shelburne, Arlington Street, 29th March 1782. Has some papers to show his Lordship.

Stephen Fuller, agent for Jamaica, to the Earl of Shelburne, Upper Harley Street, 29th March 1782. Fearing that Jamaica will be attacked by 25,000 or 30,000 men, entreats his Lordship to send some veterans from North America. Encloses an extract of a letter, dated Bruxelles, 27th Feb. 1782, containing intelligence respecting the sailing of the Brest fleet on the 11th Feb., and its destination, the number of ships De Grasse has at Martinico (Martinique), and that Monteil is in the windward passage with five French and seven Spanish ships of the line, and that Jamaica is to be attacked by 25,000 men.

Stephen Fuller to Lord Shelburne, Upper Harley Street, 2nd April 1782. Gives an account of the state of Jamaica, and the requisites for that island to sustain the enemy's attack.

Stephen Fuller to the Earl of Shelburne, Upper Harley Street, 8th April 1782. The report that the planters are perfectly easy respecting Jamaica since the arrival of the last packet is not true.

Mr. Grigson to Lord Shelburne, 15th April 1782. Great scarcity of provisions at Jamaica, the worst to be feared on that account.

Stephen Fuller to the Earl of Shelburne, Upper Harley Street, 26th April 1782. Sends copy of a letter from the committee of correspondence at Jamaica, dated Spanish Town, Jamaica, 4th March 1782. Asks for reinforcements.

Mr. Fuller to Lord Shelburne, Upper Harley Street, 28th May 1782. Sends papers relating to Jamaica, from 1772 to 1781.

John Price to the Rev. Mr. Jervis, Penzance, 27th April 1782.

R. Lewing to John Price, Esq., Spanish Town, Jamaica, 6th March 1782, about the state of Jamaica, and the attack meditated against that island. An enclosure.

Robert Hodgson to Lord Geo. Germain, Kingston, Jamaica, 27th April 1782. The British white people on the Spanish main, particularly at Black River on the Mosquito shore and Rattan, have been swept away by the Spaniards, which he thinks is a good riddance, many of them being adverse to the interests of the Crown. Expects soon to be put once more on his legs there, &c.

Mr. Fuller to the Earl of Shelburne, 20, Upper Harley Street, 14th May 1782. Sends the postcript of a letter he received from Jamaica, dated 17th March 1782, in which it is stated that 16 sail of the line arrived at Cape St. Domingo from Martinico (Martinique) for immediate attack of Jamaica.

Governor Archd. Campbell to the Earl of Shelburne, Jamaica, 20th Sept. 1782.

Duplicate of the above letter.

Governor Archd. Campbell to the Earl of Shelburne, Jamaica, 4th Nov. 1782.

Mr. Robert Butcher, Naval Officer of Barbadoes, to the Earl of Shelburne, Walthamstow, 22nd April 1782. About the employ of naval officer and deputy naval officer at Barbadoes.

Mr. John Adlam to Robert Butcher, Esq., Barbadoes, Nov. 1780.

John Adlam to Robert Butcher, Esq., Barbadoes, 14th July 1781.

Robert Butcher to John Adlams, Walthamstow, 6th Oct. 1781.

Samuel Eatwick to the Earl of Radnor, 30th April 1782. Governor Cunningham, of Barbadoes, to be recalled directly. Proposes dropping the idea of impeachment, as Mr. Estwick means to pursue him at law.

John Gay Alleyne, Speaker of the House of Assembly of Barbadoes, to the Earl of Shelburne, Barbadoes, 6th July 1782. Transmits to his Lordship the vote of the House of Assembly of Barbadoes on the re-call of Governor Cunningham.

Joshua Steele to the Earl of Shelburne, Barbadoes, 24th July 1782. Encloses an extract of the statutes relative to fees.

Memorial respecting collecting 4½ per cent. duty at Barbadoes, the restoration of Mr. Weekes to the judgeship of the Court of Admiralty at Barbadoes, and obtaining instruction from His Majesty to consent to the passing of an Act of the Island (of Barbadoes), for prevention in future of the abuses committed by the late governor there, in exacting fees from the people without the consent of the legislature.

Extracts from the statutes of Barbadoes relating to the exaction of extraordinary fees. Enclosed in Mr. Steele's, of the 24th July 1782.

John Adlam, Deputy Naval Officer (of Barbadoes), to the Lords Commissioners of His Majesty's Treasury, Barbadoes, 15th May 1782. Encloses a list of vessels entered inwards and cleared outwards at the Naval Office at Bridge Town, Barbadoes, between 11th Feb. and 10th May 1782.

Proceedings of an hospital board held by order of Baigadier General Christie, Commander-in-Chief of His Majesty's forces in the Leeward Islands. Dated General Hospital, St. Lucia, 16th Sept. 1781, and signed by John Stewart. To these proceedings is attached a paper relating to them.

State of His Majesty's troops at the Islands of St. Lucia and Antigua, under the command of General Edward Mathew, Commander-in-Chief, dated 1st April 1782.

State of His Majesty's forces in the Leeward Islands, commanded by General Mathew, by the latest returns received the 4th June 1782.

Edward Mathew, Commander-in-Chief, to the Collector and Comptroller of His Majesty's Customs at Saint Lucia, Morne Fortune, 9th April 1782, relating to the port and trade of St. Lucia. In General Mathew's of 26th April 1782.

Major-General Edward Mathew to the Right Hon. Welbore Ellis, St. Lucia, 22nd April 1782, on account of the labour attending the supplies for this garrison.

Major-General Edward Mathew to the Right Hon. Welbore Ellis, St. Lucia, 26th April 1782, transmits the following paper.

Queries put by Admiral Rodney and General Mathew to the Attorney-General of Barbadoes, with the Attorney-General's answer, dated Barbadoes, 25th March 1782.

Governor Thomas Shirley to General Mathew, Antigua,19th Dec. 1782. His proceedings upon receiving information of the Marquis de Bouillé being at Guadeloupe with 4,000 men and seven vessels, and intended to attack Antigua. Encloses a copy of the resolution the council entered into upon receiving the above information.

General Edward Mathew to Governor Shirley, Barbadoes, 29th Dec. 1782. His proceedings with regard to the defence of the island, upon receiving the intelligence he communicated to General Prescott, &c.

Extract of a letter from Major-General O'Hara to General Mathew, dated St. Lucia, 30th Dec. 1782, relating to the embarkation of troops on board Admiral Pigott's ships there (for Jamaica).

State of His Majesty's troops at Barbadoes, St. Lucia, and Antigua, dated Barbadoes, 6th Jan. 1783. Signed Edward Mathew.

Major-General Edward Mathew to the Right Hon. Thos. Townshend, Headquarters, Barbadoes, 7th Jan. 1783, relating to the embarkation of troops at St. Lucia for Jamaica, &c., &c.

Extract of the review made at Fort Royal, Grenada, showing the number of officers, soldiers, &c. there on 25th June 1780, dated 1st July 1780.

A printed letter from the British planters and merchants in the land of Grenada to the proprietors of estates and others in the said island, residing in Great Britain, dated Grenada, 15th Nov. 1779, relating to what has passed in Grenada since it was captured.

List of names, at the bottom of which is written " Many of the most considerable Manchester, and " Lancaster familys."

Private information of the present state of the Island of Grenada, and its dependencies,' and of its value to the crown of Great Britain, submitted to the consideration of His Majesty's ministers by the British proprietors.

A paper relating to the state of the Island of Grenada, and its dependencies, and of its value, &c. to Great Britain, submitted to the consideration of His Majesty's ministers by the British merchants.

Geo. Johnstone to Lord Shelburne, Kensington Gore, 11th April 1782, suggests that his Lordship should see Captain Pasley, who is able to give a just account of the Island of Trinidad.

A French account of the taking of Tobago, dated 1781.

The memorial of Edmund Lincoln to the Earl of Shelburne.

Copy from the minutes of the Assembly of Tabago, dated 14th and 29th April and 6th May 1780.

Thos. Fairholme, Speaker of the Assembly of Tobago, to the Hon. Edmund Lincoln, Tobago, 13th May 1780.

Walter Robertson, K. F. Mackenzie, and others, commissioners, appointed to value estates in Tobago, to Governor Geo. Ferguson, Tobago, 7th July 1781.

Memorial of Lieut.-Governor Ferguson to Lord Geo. Germain, dated London, 6th Dec. 1781.

Governor Ferguson to the Right Hon. Welbore Ellis, Jermyn Street, 11th March 1782.

W. Tod, Alex. Willcock, and others, to the Earl of Shelburne, London, 29th Oct. 1782.

Memorial to the Earl of Shelburne from the committee of Tobago Island.

Governor Geo. Ferguson to the field officers commanding Tobago, artillery and battalion of militia, and others, Tobago, 9th June 1781.

Governor Geo. Ferguson to the Right Hon. Welbore Ellis, Jermyn Street, 11th June 1782.

The memorial of the proprietors and others interested in the Island of Tobago to the Earl of Shelburne. The above papers all relate to the defence of the island against the French.

Valentine Morris to the Earl of Shelburne, Antigua, 29th March 1780. Thanks his Lordship for his remarks in the House of Lords relative to his conduct when Governor of St. Vincent. Remarks concerning the loss of that island, the Carib sedition, &c.

Eleven papers relating to the charges against Governor Morris, and the proceedings relating to his case before the Hon. Henry Sharpe, President of His Majesty's Council and Chief Justice of the Court of Common Pleas for the Island of St. Vincent, in 1778.

T. Poplett, Lieutenant of the African corps, to the Lords Commissioners of the Treasury, Goree, 10th July 1782.

T. Poplett, Lieutenant of the African corps, to the Earl of Shelburne, Goree, 10th July 1782. Complains of Commandant Wall.

Contents of Vol. 79 ; endorsed "West Indies Lord
" Rodney ; Mosquito and Honduras ; Demerary,
" Bermuda ; Merchants' Petitions ; Sugar Refiners."

Letter from Admiral Sir George Rodney, dated St. Lucia, 6th March 1782. British fleet. Hopes of engaging the enemy.

Letter, dated on board of the "Formidable," at sea, 28th April 1782, containing an account of the action between the fleets of Great Britain and France on the 9th and 12th of April 1782. Received from Sir Charles Douglas, first captain to Lord Rodney.

Letter from Lord Shelburne to Admiral Lord Rodney, R.B., dated Whitehall, 30th May 1782. Informs him of His Majesty's approbation of his conduct in the victory obtained by the fleet under his command, his being made a peer, and that the thanks of both Houses of Parliament will shortly be sent him.

Letter from Lord Shelburne to Rear-Admiral Lord Hood, dated Whitehall, 30th May 1782. Informs him of His Majesty's satisfaction with his conduct in the victory over the French fleet commanded by the Count de Grasse, and of his being made a baron of Ireland.

Extract of a letter from Lord Rodney, at Jamaica, of 5th May, giving an account of the capture of the "Jason" and " Caton," &c., and of the condition of the two fleets since their last engagement, dated Admiralty, 16th June 1782.

Letter from Mr. Hodgson to the Earl of Shelburne, dated 6th June 1781. " With propositions relative to " South America."

Copy of a memorial from Rt. Hodgson, Esq., late His Majesty's Superintendent, Agent and Commander-in-Chief on the Mosquito shore, to the Right Hon. Lord George Germain, relating to charges laid against him by Mr. White, in two memorials to the Board of Trade, dated 11th Nov. 1773 and 4th June 1775.

Letter from Rt. Hodgson to the Earl of Shelburne, dated Jamaica 15th May 1782, relating to the island of St. Lucia, the people of Black river, Rattan, and Sir George Rodney's prisoners.

Letter from Wm. Dalrymple to the Earl of Shelburne, dated Wigmore Street, 24th May 1782, relating to the Mosquito Indians, and an expedition to the bay of Honduras.

Letter from James Ferrall, James McAulay, and others, to General Wm. Dalrymple, dated at the quarters of Honduras Fuzileers in St. Fernando De Omva, 27th Oct. 1779. They acknowledge that it is through him they are now in possession of St. Fernando De Omva, and express their gratitude for his civility to them while under his command, and wish him a pleasant passage to England.

Letter from Richard Hoars, James Ferrall, and others to Wm. Dalrymple, Esq., dated Rattan, 12th March

1781. They approve of his plan for an expedition to the Bay of Honduras, and promise nothing shall be wanting on their part to give it effect.

Extract of a letter from Major Laurie, Superintendent of the Mosquito shore Indians, to Major Dalrymple, dated Black River, 22nd March 1781. Hopes that Dalrymple will command the expedition from hence.

Information respecting the old General Isaac, the young King, and Admiral Richards, who are chiefs of the Indians on the Mosquito shore.

Observations and information relative to plan for an expedition to the Bay of Honduras, laid down by Major Dalrymple.

Letter from Robert White to the Earl of Shelburne, dated Mount Grove, Hampstead, Middlesex, 23rd May 1782, refers to papers delivered at the office to Mr. Nepean the 15th inst., relative to the Mosquito shore and Rattan Island.

Letter from R. White to the Earl of Shelburne, dated Mount Grove, Hampstead, 23rd May 1782. Encloses a paper, received from Mr. Dyer, to whom it was addressed, containing intelligence respecting the Mosquito shore and Rattan Island, in a letter from a gentleman in Jamaica, concerned in the settlement at Rattan, to his correspondent at London, dated Kingston, Jamaica, 17th March 1782.

Letter from the Court of Demerara to Lieut.-Colonel Kingston, dated Demerara, 14th Oct. 1781. The oath of allegiance presented by Commodore Edward Thompson, having caused much uneasiness, they ask Governor Kingston to give them an explanation, signifying that they shall not bear arms against the seven united provinces, for reasons mentioned.

Letter from Robt. Kingston to the Director-General and Court of Essequibo, dated Demerara, 14th Oct. 1781. Asks upon what grounds the attempt was made to set the Colony of Demerara against the appointment of an English governor, and what foundation the Court of Essequebo had for asserting that the governor would bring a train of people that would put the colonies of Demerara (Essequebo and Berbice) to an annual expense of 25,000l., when the governor had found that the whole expense for the colony establishment for the two rivers did not usually amount to 7,000l. per annum.

Declaration of Robert Kingston to the Hon. the Council and the inhabitants at large of Demerara, Essequebo, and Berbice, with all their dependencies, relating to the articles of capitulation granted to by His Majesty's Commander-in-Chief to Demerara, Essequebo, and Berbice, and the advantages likely to arise therefrom to the inhabitants of these colonies.

Letter from R. Kingston to the Right Hon. Lord George Germain, dated Demerara, 16th Jan. 1782. Respecting the State of Demerara.

Letter from R. Kingston to the Comte K. Saint, Commander-in-Chief of His Majesty's forces. Has executed the articles of capitulation proposed by him for himself and the inhabitants and merchants at Demerara.

Letter from R. Kingston to . . ., Esq., Member of Council, dated on board the "Oronoque," Demerara, 30th Jan. 1782.

Letter from P. Van Schuylenburch and others to R. Kingston, Esq., dated 30th Jan. 1782. The surrender of the colony of Demerara demanded.

Letter from R. Kingston to the French Commander-in-Chief of His Majesty's forces, dated River Demerara, on board the "Oronoque," 31st Jan. 1782. Encloses proposals on behalf of the inhabitants of Demerara.

Letter from R. Kingston and Wm. Tahourdin to the Commander-in-Chief of His Majesty's forces, dated 1st Feb. 1782. Encloses their proposals for the capitulation of Demerara.

Letter from M. le Comte de R. Saint to Mr. Kingston, Governor-General of Demerara, Berbice, and Essequebo, relating to the capitulation of Demerara, dated 1st Feb. 1782.

Letter from R. Kingston and others to Comte R. Saint, dated on board the "Oronoque," in the River Demerara, 1st day of Feb. 1782, relating to the capitulation of Demerara.

Preliminary articles of capitulation of Demerara and Essequebo, between Comte R. Saint, Commander-in-Chief of His Most Christian Majesty's forces employed in this expedition, and Robert Kingston, Esq., Lieut.-Governor of Demerara, Essequebo, and Berbice, and Captain William Tahourdin, Commander of His Britannic Majesty's squadron.

Proposals of capitulation from R. Kingston, Esq., Lieut.-Governor of Demerara, and Captain William Tahourdin, Commander of His Britannic Majesty's ships and vessels, to the Commander-in-Chief of His Most Christian Majesty's forces both by sea and land, employed on this expedition, relating to Demerara &c., &c., 3rd Feb. 1782.

A list of English and French forces at Demerara, 3rd Feb. 1782.

Letter from R. Kingston, to the Right Hon. Lord George Germain, His Majesty's principal Secretary of State, dated Demerara, 8th Feb. 1782, relating to the measures taken by himself and others to defend Demerara against the French and the capitulation of that colony.

Letter from R. Kingston to the Right Hon. Lord George Germain to His Majesty's principal Secretary of State, dated Demerara, 9th Feb. 1782, relating to Demerara and Berbice.

Memorial of Lieut.-Governor Kingston, late Lieut.-Governor of Demerara, has expended more than 800l. in supporting the honour of his istuation. Prays relief. Dated 26th Oct. 1781.

Produce for taxes delivered for Demerara, Essequebo, and Berbice, 26th Oct. 1781.

Letter from Robert Traill to the Right Hon. Lord North, &c., &c., dated Custom House, Bermuda, 7th April 1782. Intended attack of those Islands, their importance from situation as to commerce.

Letter from Robert Traill to Right Hon. Lord Shelburne, dated Custom House, Bermuda, 19th Sept. 1782. Points the advantageous position of the island of Bermuda for commerce, and their use to Great Britain in time of war. From the 5th of Jan. last 93 prizes have been brought into their port by the privateers of this island.

Letter from R. Triall to the Right Hon. the Lords Commissioners of His Majesty's Treasury, dated Custom House, Bermuda, Jan. 30th 1783, relating to the depredations made about these islands, (of Bermuda,) upon the vessels that are cast upon them.

Letter from Robert Traill, Collector to the Right the Lords Commissioners of His Majesty's Treasury, Customs House, Bermuda, 17th Feb. 1783.

Letter from R. Traill, Collector to the Right Hon. Lord Shelburne, &c. &c., dated Custom House, Bermuda, 10th Feb. 1738. Believes that these islands (of Bermuda) must, from their situation, &c., prove the most valuable possessions His Majesty holds in this quarter of the globe.

Letter from Mr. Geo. Bruere to the Earl of Shelburne, dated Fotheringay, 1st April 1782, state of Bermuda isles, requisites for their defence.

Address and Petition of the Assembly of Jamaica to the King, 20th July 1781.

Copy of the Petition of the West India planters and merchants to the King, on the subject of the general seizure of private property, found in the Dutch islands of Saint Eustatius and Saint Martin, dated 6th April 1781.

Petition to the King from the West India planters and merchants, 2nd Jan. 1781.

Minute of the West India planters and merchants, 20th March 1782.

Minute of a general meeting of the West India merchants, 26th March 1782, Messrs. Long and Neave to wait on Ministry, with petition of West India planters and merchants, and their application to the late Ministry for protection of the West India islands.

Resolution of a general meeting of the planters and merchants of St. Christopher's and Nevis. London, 17th April 1782.

Account of British plantation. Sugar refined or consumed raw in England in the following years, from 1731 to 1780. N.B.—The capture of the outward bound West India fleet, in summer 1780, has occasioned a considerable part of the crop of that year to be delayed till 1781.

Observations from a gentleman in town to his friends in the country, relative to the sugar colonies, proving their importance to England, and explaining the tendency of the request made by the refiners to manufacture foreign sugar, and to put it on a footing with the British.

Letter from Nath. Farman to the Earl of Shelburne, dated Distaff Lane, 17th April 1782, relative to the sugar trade.

Copy of a memorial presented to the Lords of the Treasury by a committee of the sugar refiners of London, dated 13th April 1782, relating to the sugar trade.

Reasons in favour of a Bill to permit prize sugars to be entered for home consumption, under a moderate duty, humbly submitted to the consideration of the members of both Houses of Parliament.

A paper containing remarks against the importation of foreign sugar.

Facts relating to the sugar trade, with a refutation of the assertions made in a paper called " Reasons against " the application for lowering the duties on foreign " prize sugar." Humbly submitted to the consideration of both Houses of Parliament.

State of the prices of raw sugar for seven years, and proof of the decline of the consumption, dated May 1781.

" Reasons against a Bill to permit sugars, the pro- " ceeds of the British islands in the West Indies, to be " warehoused in this kingdom, under certain restric- " tions."

The report of the Honourable the Board of Trade and Plantations to the Right Hon. the Lords of the Trea- sury, on the matter of certain memorials from the sugar refiners of London, to which are prefixed copies of the said Memorials' Report, dated Whitehall, 31st of March 1871. Printed in the year 1781.

Letter from Richard Neave to the Earl of Shelburne, dated May 1782. The chairman of the committee of West India merchants and planters.

Petition of the sugar planters and merchants, in- tended for Parliament, in opposition to the application of the sugar refiners. In Mr. Neaves' of the May 1782.

Vol. 80.

This volume is labelled " Minutes of African Affairs." Copies of papers relating to the British settlements on the coast of Africa.

Vol. 81.

This volume contains copies of papers and despatches and some original letters, one of them from Henry Fox relative to Senegal affairs, from 1756 to 1768.

Vol. 82.

This volume is endorsed " Papers relating to Minorca."

An account of the Government of Minorca, with proposals for the improvement of it. By the Lieut.- Governor.

Copy of the report of Mr. Attorney and Mr. Solicitor- General on the memorial of Lord Carpenter, Governor, and Colonel Kane, Lieut.-Governor of Minorca, about erecting a court of appeals in that island, &c., 17th Aug. 1731.

Mr. Hope to Mr. Conway, containing a plan for making Minorca useful to England, 30th July 1765.

Hints of some things that might contribute to im- prove His Majesty's island of Minorca.

Mr. Townshend to Sir Richard Littleton. Mahon, 20th Aug. 1765. Disposition of the Barbary Powers, and various schemes of internal improvement.

Lieut.-Governor Johnston. Mahon, 21st Dec. 1765. On the pretended privileges of the islanders.

Governor Johnston to Lord Rockingham. Mahon, 17th Dec. 1765. On the building of barracks.

Plan for establishing a chamber of health in Minorca, submitted to the consideration of the Right Hon. Mr. Conway, &c., by Governor Johnston.

Report of the commissioners on the complaint of the Universities in Minorca, against Governor Johnston. Mahon, 20th Dec. 1765.

Minutes of some regulations proper to be made for the better government of the island of Minorca, in its different branches, the administration of justice, the augmentation of the royal revenue, and the improve- ment of the estates of the individuals of it, submitted to the Right Hon. the Earl of Shelburne, and others of His Majesty's Ministers. By Governor Johnston.

Petition of Governor Johnston to His Majesty in Council, on the elections of magistrates in Minorca.

Governor Johnston to the magistrates of Minorca, on the admission of persons to ecclesiastical seminaries.

Extract of a petition from the magistrates of Minorca to Lieut.-Governor Johnston, for confirmation of their privileges.

Governor Johnston's answer to the preceding pe- tition.

Petition from the Jurats of Minorca to the Duke of Argyle, and the Duke's answer in behalf of their civil and religious liberties, 1712.

Copy of the 5th article of Lord Tyrawley's instruc- tions of 8th Oct. 1753 concerning religious privileges.

Letter of Governor Johnston and the confirmation of the rights and privileges of the island of Minorca by this present king, 1765.

Order of Lieut.-Governor Johnston, 27th Oct. 1763, against the treaty of peace.

The constitution of the Island of Minorca, by their agent.

A brief account of the Government and State of the Island of Minorca.

Mémoire instructif sur l'Isle de Minorque, et Moyens proposés pour son amélioration, par J. Segui et Sanxo, ce 11e Oct. 1766.

Mémoire sur l'amélioration de l'Isle de Minorque, et augmentations des productions, par J. Segui, Fiscal de Minorque.

Lettres patentes du Roi, en forme d'edits, pour l'ad- ministrations de la justice dans l'Isle de Minorque, données a Versailles au mois de Mai, 1757.

The King of France's appointment of a criminal assessor.

The British merchants in Minorca to Mr. Borrowes, with their petitions, May 1764.

Sir Richard Littleton to Lord Halifax, May 1764, with the petitions of the merchants.

The petition of the British merchants residing in the island of Minorca, against the residence of French merchants in the island, 1764.

Complaint of the British merchants in Minorca to Lord Halifax. Mahon, 29th April 1765.

Complaints of the British merchants in Minorca, transmitted by Mr. Hope, 29th April 1765.

The Earl of Hallifax to Colonel Townshend at Mi- norca, 31st May 1765, to allow Mr. Segui a recompence for giving passes.

Colonel Townshend to Lord Hallifax, Mahon, 14th April 1765, relating to Mr. Segui.

In favour of Mr. Segui's memorial, St. Philip's, 8th April 1765.

The humble representation of Dr. John Segui and Sauxo, His Majesty's Advocate-Fiscal in the Island of Minorca, to the Right Hon. the Earl of Shelburne, one of His Majesty's Principal Secretaries of State.

Dr. Segui's petitions to the King.

Reasons for making Mahon, in the island of Minorca, a free port.

Theodore Alexiano in behalf of himself and the other Greek residing in Minorca, 20th Nov. 1766.

Sir B. Keene to the Marquis de la Paz, on the com- plaint of the clergy against the Governor of Minorca. Seville, 6th March 1732.

The Attorney-General to the magistrates of Minorca, 29th Dec. 1765, relating to an alarm on the subject of religion.

Governor Johnston's Declaration, Mahon, 14th Jan. 1766, repealing an order relating to taxation.

Messrs. Pons and Syndick, agents for Minorca, to Mr. Sutton, complaining of Governor Johnston, 24th March 1768.

Further instructions to prove the inefficacy of the Orders in Council issued in Aug. 1753. By Messrs Pons and Syndick, agents for Minorca, 1768.

Questions on the Ecclesiastical Jurisdiction, relating to the Priest of St. Philip's being put under arrest for theft, by order of Governor Johnston, 1767.

Memorial of Messrs. Pons and Syndick, agents for Minorca, as delivered to the Council Office, 7th April 1768.

Petition of John Pons and Andrew Syndick, and representatives of the Civil and Ecclesiastical States of Minorca to the King.

Letters annexed to the Syndick of Minorca's Memo- rial, 7th April 1768.

Memorandums relating to Governor Johnston's disputes with the inhabitants of Minorca, 13th Oct. 1763.

Earl of Shelburne to Governor Johnston, 28th Aug. 1767, requiring a state of the case relating to the quartering of soldiers.

Abstract of a letter from the deputies of Minorca, 28th June 1767, on the quartering of troops.

Short state of the complaint of quartering at Alayor.

Memorandum relating to the barracks of Minorca, Office of Ordnance, 7th April 1767.

Governor Johnson to the Earl of Shelburne, Mahon, 20th April 1767, claiming a share of the Stanque duty.

Account of the Stanque duty of Minorca for the year 1766.

Account of Anchorage duty of Minorca, for the year 1766.

Particulars of the Stanque duty at Minorca.

A paper relating to the Stanque duty at Minorca.

Queries relating of Minorca.

Mr. Pons's memorial to the King in Council, com- plaining of Governor Johnston, 13th July 1768.

Minorca. Complaints before the Committee.

Minorca. Papers before the Secretary of State.

Points relating to Minorca that seem to require dispatch.

Governor Johnston to the Earl of Shelburne, justifying himself against Mr. Pons. Mahon, 9th Nov. 1768.

Proceedings of council relating to the complaints of the inhabitants of Minorca against their Governor, Anstruther, &c., from March 1748 to 1753.

Vol. 83.

This Vol. is endorsed, "Gibraltar Importance, 1782. "Minorca. Instructions to Governors in 1753 and "1763.

Elliot's (General) letters, abstract of, from No. 9 to No. 19 (the year not mentioned but apparently of 1782).

Elliot's (General) letter to Lord Hillsborough, Gibraltar, 10th March 1782. (Extract.)

Debbieg (Colonel Hugh) to Lord Shelburne, 13th June 1782, containing general remarks upon general Elliott's letters, papers, plans, &c., from 6th March to 7th May 1782.

Dickenson (Edward, the late receiver-general and cashier of Gibraltar.) Account of the executors of, from 1st July 1781 to 30th June 1782.

Gibraltar. Supplies for, 13th June 1782.

Gibraltar. Expenses incurred for the garrison of, in 1780, 1781, and 1782. Extract from the treasury books, viz., in 1780, 212,950l.; 1781, 339,976l.; 1782, 262,156l.

Gibraltar. Paoli, General, to Lord Shelburne, 15th May 1782. On the means of supplying Gibraltar. Advises sending four or five old India ships on that service, with the fleet going out, to shew them at Cape Finisterre, and proceed on; their formidable look would deceive and be their security. (Endorsed, Copied for the King.)

Jervis (Sir John, K.B.) to Lord Shelburne. Fondrogaut at sea, 16th July 1782. Proposal for a sudden and unexpected relief of Gibraltar.

Jervis (Sir John) to Lord Shelburne, Portsmouth, 19th Aug. 1782. Proposes the sending a small squadron immediately to the relief of Gibraltar, which may otherwise be lost. As these and several captains senior to himself, it may be improper for him to command the detachment. Shall be glad to go in a subordinate character.

Jervis (Sir John) to Lord Shelburne, Fondrogant at sea, 22nd Oct. 1782. Six 64 gun ships, sufficient to supply Gibraltar with provisions during winter. Too great a risk to send the whole fleet into a strait not wide enough to navigate half the number in, with an enemy of superior force.

Jervis (Sir John) ———, Britannia, 29th Oct. 1782. Peas, oatmeal, and gunpowder the only real wants at Gibraltar. Some account of Captain Curtis and of Colonel Lowther.

Jervis (Sir John) to Lord Shelburne, Exeter, 4th Dec. 1782. Anecdote of Sir Edward Hawke in 1756.

Cooke (Mr. Nathl.) to Lord Shelburne, 26th Aug. 1782. Thoughts on the state of Gibraltar.

Towry (Lieut. Geo.) to Lord Shelburne, 14th Dec. 1782. On the non-importance of Gibraltar.

Motteux (Mr. John) to Lord Shelburne. Wallbrook, 16th Dec. 1782, with some remarks on the English trade in the Mediterranean. On Gibraltar, &c.

Motteux (Mr. John) to Lord Shelburne. The said remarks. The trade to and from the Mediterranean, in time of peace, almost wholly carried on by English ships. Enters into the several articles of the trade.

Gibraltar. Considerations for and against the possession of, from Mr. Garbett, Dec. 1782.

Brimstone is the principal ingredient used in making oil of vitriol, the best from Talamona in Italy. In time of war, difficult to be procured.

Gibraltar. The importance of, with regard to commerce and merchant ships in time of peace. From Mr. Baring, 28th Dec. 1782.

Gibraltar and Minorca. Memorial respecting. From Mr. Sinclair of Park Street, Westminster, 1782.

Ferguson (Dr. Adam) to the Duke of Montagu. Edinburgh, 15th Nov. 1782. A gentleman in whose ingenuity the Dr. has much confidence, says he knows of a method of attack against which Gibraltar is not provided, and by which it might be taken. He also knows of means to keep vessels afloat, when in danger of sinking at sea, and which would be effectual to raise the "Royal George" now sunk at Spithead.

Hind, John, and Thomas Field to Lord Shelburne. London, 10th Dec. 1782. In behalf of themselves and other inhabitants of Gibraltar who have suffered in

their property, houses, cargoes, &c. during the blockade and bombardment.

Cowper (Henry), George Boyd, and Eliz. Terry. Their petition to Lord Shelburne, in behalf of themselves and other inhabitants and sufferers during the siege of Gibraltar. Praying that in case a rumoured exchange of that garrison should take place, they may be compensated for the loss of their landed property, houses, &c. London, 9th Dec. 1782.

Fuller, (Mr. Stephen) to Lord Shelburne, 22nd Jan. 1783, with a copy of a memorial this day presented to the Secretary of State, begging his Lordship's support.

Gibraltar. Memorial to the King of Stephen Fuller and Rose Fuller of London, merchants, and of Stephen Robinson and John Bowman, of London, navy agents, appointed attorneys and agents by Governor Elliott, and other principal officers, to receive the head money, bounty money, &c. arising from the defeat and destruction of the ten Spanish battering ships on 13th Sep., and the "Saint Miguel," ship of war of 72 guns.

Instructions to Governors.

Instructions for Sir Richard Lyttleton, K.B., Lieut.-General and Governor of Minorca, 22nd April 1763.

Instructions for James Lord Tyrawly, Governor of Minorca, 8th Oct. 1753.

Minorca. Order in Council, approving some new regulations for the island of, 28th May 1752.

Minorca. Don Bernardo Olives, of the island of, his humble petition to the King, in behalf of the University of Cindadela or General University; and of the Universities of Alayer, Macadal, and Ferrarias in said island.

Minorca. Report of the Committee of the Council, upon the affairs of, Kensington, 11th Aug. 1753.

Minorca. Original Latin of English translation of the 11th article of the treaty of Utrecht, respecting the island of.

Pringle (Colonel Henry) to Colonel Barré, Barcelona, 1st May 1782. His journey to, arrival at, and stay at Minorca during the siege. Left in Spain as a hostage.

Minorca. John Martin Baker, many years English resident in the island of. His petition to Lord Shelburne, praying compensation for his losses, his brewery, houses, stores, &c.

Minorca. James Niven and Arthur Gibbons, to Lord Shelburne. Beg to be admitted to his Lordship, and to have his opinion of their memorial of 22nd Feb. Answer. Under present circumstances can give no answer to their memorial.

Minorca. James Niven and Arthur Gibbons. Their memorial to Lord Shelburne in behalf of themselves and others, setting forth their great losses, and praying compensation, 18th Feb. 1783. Their property, as well their own, ———, as in trust, seized by the Spaniards after taking possession of the island.

Vol. 84.

This volume, or rather parcel, contains—

(1.) Papers relating to Eustatius. Among them are several original letters from Sir J. Jervis, Benjamin Vaughan, Lord Stanhope, Lord Sydney, Maurice Morgann, Jennings, J. Jekyll, Robert Sidney, J. Gouverneur, Evan Nepean, John Smith, and drafts of letters by Lord Shelburne.

(2.) Copies of official correspondence relative to the coast of Africa, 1767-1768, with an original letter from Joseph Debat, Lieutenant-Governor of Senegal, of 13th Aug. 1767.

(3.) Constitution of Minorca and alterations proposed, and official correspondence with the Governor of Gibraltar and Minorca. All copies except a private letter from Lieut.-General John Stone to Lord Shelburne, 6th July 1768.

Vol. 85.

This volume contains papers relating to American affairs in 1766 to 1769. These papers are very important. Most of them relate to the American Mutiny Act, and the question of the amnesty granted by the Assembly of Massachusetts to the rioters.

1766.

Governor Pownall on laying out townships in Nova Scotia, New York, Virginia, and South Carolina. At the end there are some notes in Lord Shelburne's writing.

Extract of a Journal from Monday, 7th Oct. to Monday, 14th Oct. 1650. (The original was printed.) Relating to the Prohibitory Act on the trade between the American colonies and West India Islands, and the consequent disturbances in the former.

A paper endorsed " Copy of a sheet from one of Capt. " Hodgson's Books called Rough Material. Wrote " when there was expectation of a Spanish war."

A paper endorsed " Some thoughts on the importation " of sugar from the Mosquito shore, by Capt. Hodgson. General distribution of His Majesty's forces in North America. New York, 10th Oct.

1767.

A table of such English and British statutes as are expressly or virtually extended to His Majesty's colonies in America, alphabetically arranged under general heads, to the fourth year of the reign of His Majesty King George the Third.

A letter to Lord Shelburne on American Commerce. Anonymous.

A paper in French on the military advantages of Fort Johnson. Signed by Capt. Follet, commander of the fort.

A paper endorsed on the Government of Canada.

Two papers relating—
  1. On the American trade, 1767.
  2. On the Indian boundary and trade.

Three papers relating—
  1. To the Massachusetts Amnesty Act, 1767.
  2. To Mr. C. Townshend's proposed taxes.
  3. To the American Mutiny Act.

A paper endorsed " Minutes of the American Business," and in pencil, Duke of Grafton to-morrow, Col. Barré, and Sutton.

A paper endorsed " Minutes for the New York Mail."

A paper endorsed " New York." It contains abstracts of Sir Henry Moore's letters, 1766 and 1767.

A paper endorsed " Reasons for not diminishing " American expense," 30th March.

Extract of a letter from Lord Shelburne to Lord William Campbell, Governor of Nova Scotia, 19th Feb. On the subject of road making.

A paper endorsed " Georgia." It contains abstracts of Governor Wright's letter.

Mr. Melville to Lord Shelburne, April 14th, on the affairs of Grenada.

Draft of a letter from Lord Shelburne to Governor Bernard May, giving him leave of absence.

Abstract of despatches from Mr. Symmers, agent for His Majesty at Turks Islands, 15th May.

A paper endorsed " Grenada," containing an abstract of Governor Melville's despatches.

Draft of a letter to Sir Henry Moore, June.

Draft of a letter to Lieut.-Governor Hutchinson, June.

Minutes of letters by American Governors to be answered by the West India and New York packets, 10th June.

Draft of a letter to Major-General Gage.

Copy of letter of recall to Governor Moore, June.

Copy of letter to Cadwallader Colden, appointing him to be the *locum tenens* of the Governor.

A paper endorsed " Report concerning the Appoint- " ment of County Sheriffs in South Carolina, in lieu of " a Provost Marshal," 22nd July, addressed to the Board of Trade.

A paper endorsed, " Minutes of American Business " for the West India Mail," 18th Aug.

Copy of the proceedings at a council held on the 28th Aug. relating to the Canadian judicature.

Draft of a letter from Lord Shelburne to Governor Bernard, Oct.

Draft of a letter from Lord Shelburne to Governor Bernard, 14th Nov.

1768.

Mr. Hewitt, from Dominica, to Lord Shelburne. Unimportant. 9th April.

Paper endorsed, " Extract of a Letter from Governor " Wentworth to the Earl of Shelburne." New hampshire, 25th March. With an enclosure.

Draft of circular by Lord Hillsborough to all the Governors on the continent of North America, except Massachusetts Bay, East Florida, and Quebec, 21st April.

Draft of a despatch from Lord Hillsborough to Governor Bernard, 22nd April.

Mr. Bradshaw, of the Treasury, to Mr. Phelps, of the Department of Secretary of State, enclosing a copy of the memorial of the Commissioners of the Customs in America, dated 12th Feb. 1768, for the information of Lord Hillsborough.

Copy of a letter from Lieut.-Governor Franklin, of Nova Scotia, 16th June, to Lord Hillsborough.

Copy of a letter from Lieut.-Governor Franklin to the Lord Hillsborough, 11th July.

Copy of a letter of 16th July, from Governor Bernard to Lord Hillsborough.

Copy of the draft reply of Lord Hillsborough of the 30th July.

Copy of the minutes of the proceedings of a council of Massachusetts, 29th July.

Copy of a letter of Governor Hodgson to Lord Hillsborough, relating to the Mosquito shore, 3rd Sept. Also a detail of some circumstances concerning it and the late superintendent (the said Capt. Hodgson) to 22nd July 1778.

Copy of a letter from Lord Hillsborough to Governor Bernard, 14th Sept.

1769.

Three unimportant letters relating to West India affairs.

Vol. 86.

This volume is labelled Miscellaneous American Papers, Newfoundland.

It contains :—
  (1.) Copy of a memorial of Captain Hugh Debberg to H.M. minister on a survey of Newfoundland, 1764. Additional proposal, 1st Jan. 1787.
  (2.) A report by Captain Debberg on the fortifications of St. John in Newfoundland, 8th Jan. 1766.
  (3.) An account of the harbours in Newfoundland, by Captain Debberg, 19th Feb. 1767.
  (4.) Original letters and copies of several papers relating to the Newfoundland fisheries.
  (5.) Considerations on the rights and interests of adventurers in the Labrador fisheries, and an original letter from G. Cartwright.
  (6.) Project for the navigation of the St. Lawrence river, July 1782.
  (7.) Extracts of letters from British Governors in Africa, America, the West Indies, &c., 1766.
  (8.) An account of the Mosquito shore. A plan for receiving settlements there and promoting a trade to the Pacific by the lake of Nicaragua. Two memorials on the subject by Captain Speer, 1760. An account of the flag of truce to carry despatches to San Fernando, detained by the Spaniards, from 4th April to 4th Sept. 1763.
  (9.) A memoir of the Canary Islands, by George Chalmers, 1762.

Vol. 87.

This volume contains papers chiefly relating to American affairs during 1782, 1783, and 1784.

1782.

State of the case of Mr. Thomas McKnight of the province of North Carolina. An American Loyalist who suffered great losses in consequence of the war, dated 26th March.

1st April. A letter signed C. W. J. Rejoices at Lord Shelburne's accession to the ministry, and tenders advice.

5th April. Samuel Peters to Lord Shelburne ; considers himself capable of being useful among the people of Connecticut in restoring the King's Government, and encloses copies of letters written to Mr. Ellis and Sir Guy Carleton with a similar object.

5th April. Mr. James Burrow to Lord Shelburne, advises treating with General Washington rather than with Commissaries of Congress.

Four letters from Mr. Trafford to Lord Shelburne, March and April 1782, enclosing a scheme relative to America.

6th April. Mr. D. Braham states his case and appeals for protection.

7th April. Mr. Lidderdale, late Consul of Carthagena, encloses a plan of peace for America.

6th May. The Hon. Hobart sends a proposed sketch by Messrs. Mauropas, in 1779, for an accommodation between the powers of war.

14th May. Governor Cunningham of Barbadoes solicits protection.

Three letters from Mr. Joshua Street, dated 1st and 16th June from Barbadoes, relative to the sugar trade, and Governor Cunningham's resignation.

6th June. Mr. James Drummond to Lord Shelburne; contains intelligence about the French and Spanish dominions in the West Indies.

10th June. Mr. John Pattson appeals to Lord Shelburne ; was collector of Customs at Philadelphia ; has had great offers from the American Government, being connected with important persons in that country.

11th June. Mr. Crawford, M.P. for Dumbarton, encloses memorial of the Glasgow merchants interested in North American trade before 1766, praying attention to their debts from North America, before that date.

12th June. Mr. Thomas Boon; his lands in South Carolina have been confiscated by the Assembly of that province, asks for compensation.

19th June. Mr. Drummond. Information about the French Windward Islands.

24th June. Mr. Peter Taylor. About his confiscated estates in South Carolina.

24th June. Mr. Keane. Two regiments come to Barbadoes from Charlestown. Reported that General Mathews had taken Monserat.

28th June. Mr. Landi offers to make some discoveries relative to Spanish America.

June. Mr. George Saxby formerly member of Council in South Carolina reduced by confiscation of his estates in South Carolina, and prays for relief.

8th July. Sir George Saville. His reasons for preferring to make a recognition of American Independence a preliminary to the treaty of peace and not part of the treaty itself.

10th July. Mr. John Wilmot congratulates Lord Shelburne on the complete triumph in point of argument of Mr. Pitt and General Conway gained in the House of Commons on the previous night over Lord John Cavendish and Mr. Fox.

24th July. Mr. W. Wrixon; contains an account of an interesting conversation between Mr. Samuel Adams and the writer, relative to a projected division in the American colonies after the establishment of their Independence and the conquest of the remaining English colonies.

27th July. Mr. Breen; his quitting the kingdom.

27th July. Mr. Cells. Importance of Island of Curacoa to Great Britain.

3rd Aug. Mr. Butcher. Dispute concerning his employ of naval officers at Barbadoes.

8th Aug. Mr. Charles Hamilton encloses thoughts on the means of pacification of America.

9th and 13th Aug. Mr. Hake sends plan of the pacification of America.

14th Aug. Mr. Neilson can procure authentic intelligence of Dr. Franklin by a member of Congress now at Paris. Endorsed. "An impostor."

26th Aug. Mr. Bridging sends extracts of a letter from the Low Countries recommending that American Independence should be unconditionally recognised.

1st Sept. Draft of Richard Oswald at Paris. The same subject.

6th Sept. Lady Charleville, Sir J. Coghell's ideas respecting New York against evacuating it.

26th Sept. Mr. John Breen renews his application to be employed.

27th Sept. Observations about Jamaica.

29th Sept. Mr. Wilmot about his and Mr. Cook's joint enquiry into the cases of the suffering American Loyalists.

29th Sept. Mr. Redmund Burke requests the King's pardon for having held an American appointment with the American army.

5th Oct. Mr. Watson. Proposal for a commercial intercourse between England and America through Amsterdam.

15th Oct. Lord George Gordon wishes to know if it true that American Independence is to be unconditionally recognised.

17th Oct. Mr. Andrew Allen's conversation with Mr. Silas Deen at Spa.

23rd Oct. Mr. Caldwell wishes to be appointed Receiver-General of Quebec.

27th Oct. Lord Dumore sends a letter from Mr. Smith at New York.

20th Nov. Lord Dunmore thinks the salaries or pensions to American sufferers should be continued them, till the commissioners have determined upon their claims.

26th Nov. Mr. John Marsh. Provisions are being shipped from Cork under neutral flags for the French navy.

1st Dec. Mr. Drummond sends information about the West India Islands.

8th Dec. Mr. Watson on American commerce.

11th Dec. The Earl of Bristol transmits the address of the city of Londonderry to Lord Shelburne. Knows a gentleman who would undertake to bribe the leaders Congress and General Washington.

12th Dec. Mr. Barclay proposes settling the American Loyalists on the waste lands of England.

12th Dec. Captain Durnford can give information about West Florida.

31st Dec. 1783. A letter signed J. P., not addressed to Lord Shelburne, protests against the delays in the negotiating the peace with America.

(Undated.) A paper on American Independence, sent to Lord Shelburne, no signature, urging a re-union of America with England.

A letter neither signed nor dated, endorsed Considerations on America.

Part of a French letter on peace with America.

A letter signed C. W. J., enclosing newspaper extracts in reference to American affairs and the peace.

Fragment of a letter on West Indian affairs.

Consideration on American money and the rate of exchange.

Memorial of the merchants, &c. interested in the trade to North America before 1766.

Mrs. Wooldridge's memorial to the Treasury.

Mr. Williams' offer of service in connexion with American affairs.

Notes of a conversation between Mr. Oswald and Dr. Franklin.

1783.

A variety of papers containing arguments for the peace 1783, they are apparently the notes of a speech.

1st Jan. Copy of a letter from Monsr. De Vergennes. The present position of France. On the back are some verses.

6th to 10th Jan. Copies of extracts of letters from Monsr. de Vergennes, relating to European politicks generally.

6th Jan. Mr. Motteux to Lord Shelburne, with an extract of Franklin from Paris.

10th Jan. Mr. Allen to Lord Shelburne, enclosing a letter from Silas Deane.

16th Jan. Several papers relating to Barbadoes. Unimportant.

21st Jan. Lord Keppel to Lieut.-General Sir Charles Gray on the appointment of the latter to succeed Sir Guy Carleton in America.

24th Jan. Mr. M. G. Lloyd congratulates Lord Shelburne on his success as minister.

26th Jan. Mr. Hutton about Dr. Franklin's coming to England on his way home from America. Congratulations on the peace.

27th Jan. Congratulations on the peace.

2nd Feb. Extract of a letter from Sir Roger Curtis to Mr. Evan Nepean, on the peace which he considers very favourable.

4th Feb. Rev. Bennetaller to Lord Shelburne, relative to the stoppage of his allowance at the Treasury, as an American sufferer.

14th Feb. Mr. M. Parker's congratulations on the peace.

15th Feb. The merchants of Glasgow through Mr. James Richie to the Lord Advocate, thanking the administration for the attention given to their concerns in the negotiations for peace.

16th Feb. Mr. Allen to Lord Shelburne about his pension as an American sufferer.

26th Feb. Sir John Rouse to Lord Shelburne. The Counties of Suffolk, Cambridge, and Kent will present addresses in favour of the peace.

26th Feb. Mr. Lytton to Lord Shelburne, recommends a dissolution of Parliament.

28th Feb. Mr. Lettsom to Lord Shelburne. Congratulations on the peace.

March. Several letters and other papers relating to the address of the corporation of Ipswich, approving of the peace.

Copies of the 4th article of the peace preliminaries and the 6th article of the definitive treaty.

18th March. Some notes relating to naval operations in the Indian Ocean, and other Indian subjects.

March. An extract from Captain Cook's Journal, relating to the small importance of the French possessing St. Pierre and Miquelon, compared with our free navigation in those parts.

April. Mr. Keane to Lord Shelburne, from Barbadoes. Popularity of the peace at the West Indies.

6th April. Governor Campbell, of Jamaica, to Lord Shelburne French and Spanish preparations.

6th April. Governor Steel, from Barbadoes, to Lord Shelburne. Affairs of the island.

2nd May. Mr. Steel to Lord Shelburne, enclosing several papers relative to the affairs of Barbadoes.

24th June. Governor Parry to Lord Shelburne. West India affairs.

27th and 30th Aug. Copies of extracts of two letters from Mr. Lovell and Mr. Oliver, on the West Indian trade. Mistakes committed in the definitive treaty of peace.

25th Sept. Printed copy of letter addressed by Mr. Samuel Eastwick, agent to the Speaker of the House of Assembly at Barbadoes.

5th Oct. Copy of letter of Sir Guy Carleton to Lord North. Prospects of Nova Scotia.

Copy of a.memorial of William Deane Poyntz, late Deputy Paymaster-General of his Majesty's forces at New York, to the Right Hon. the Lord's Commissioners of his Majesty's Treasury.

30th Dec. Governor Shirley to Lord Shelburne. Unimportant.

Paper endorsed, Proposal for Taxes. It contains a variety of propositions with reference to taxes and currency between England and America, but is unimportant.

Observations respecting Porta Rica, West Florida, and Trinidad, from Mr. B. Vaughan.

Notes on the English possessions on the West Coast of Africa, with reference to the peace, 1783.

1784.

Some memoranda about the American Loyalists, enclosing a copy of the letter of Benjn. Franklin to Richd. Oswald, dated Paris, 26th Nov. 1782.

Peltries exported from Quebec, with the duties.

Paper headed. Some hints given to Lord Penhryn to be made use of if necessary by Mr. Pitt. Feb. 7th, they relate to the trade between America and the West Indies.

Copy of correspondence between General Arnold and various ministers relative to his position and pay, from the 8th Aug. 1783 to 2nd March 1784.

Governor Parry, from Barbadoes, to Lord Shelburne. Information about the island.

12th Nov. Lieut.-Governor Hamilton, from Quebec, to Lord Sydney. Affairs of the province. Encloses four letters on the same subject.

A memorandum on the right of England under the 7th article of the treaty of peace, to withdraw certain negroes from the States.

Vol. 88.

This volume contains five different sets of papers.
1. Miscellaneous papers chiefly American, from 1770 to 1780.
2. Miscellaneous chiefly American, from 1785 to 1793.
3. Letters from Dr. Turnbull.
4. Letters from Governor Parr.
5. Miscellaneous.

1.

Joseph Warren to Lord Shelburne, Boston, 1770. The events of the 5th of March.

Extracts of letters to Lord Dartmouth from Governor Hutchinson, Governor Tryon, and others, from 15th Nov. 1773 to 3rd Jan. 1774. They relate to the duty upon tea.

Mr. Deane to Lord Shelburne, 17th Oct. 1776. The action at Long Island and General Washington's reply to Sir William Howe's proposal of a negociation for peace. Lord Shelburne's reply to the above letter written in Paris.

Extract of a letter from an American gentleman. Philadelphia, 7th June 1776. Impossibility of reconciliation between the two countries.

Sir William Howe to Lord George Germaine. New York, 29th Dec. 1776. The royal proclamation limiting the time within which His Majesty's general pardon should be granted.

Sir William Howe to Lord George Germaine, on the same subject, 30th Nov. 1776.

Lord Howe to Lord George Germaine, 20th Sept. 1776. Interview with the Commissioners of Congress, Dr. Franklin, Mr. John Adams, and Mr. Rutledge. Their refusal to treat except on the basis of independence. Encloses copy of Royal proclamation issued in consequence.

A detail of the operations of the American and English armies during their campaign in the autumn, 1777.

Mémoire present par Mons. M. Le Chev. Yorke, 21st Feb. 1777. Sir Joseph Yorke in his paper complains of the imperfect observation of its neutrality by the French Court in the American war.

Copy of two letters from Williamsburg, Virginia, sent by way of Spain to a foreign gentleman, and trans-

lated into English. The first is signed T. J., and the second, C. Bellin.

Copy of a petition of the West India planters and merchants, presented 16th Dec. 1778. Distress in the Sugar islands.

Fragment on the inefficient manner in which the war has been conducted on the part of England ; there is an allusion to Burgoyne's defeat.

Several papers endorsed "Rough Drafts of a Petition " on American Affairs." The petition was apparently drawn up by Dr. Price and annotated by Lord Shelburne.

Two letters from Mr. Parry to Lord Shelburne, 13th April, and 1st Aug. 1788.

Reply to the address of the Assembly of the Island of St. Vincent by Governor Morris, 2nd Jan. 1799.

Address of several leading inhabitants of the Island of St. Vincent to the Governor.

Short, clear, and comprehensive view of the British Empire, from the first hostilities in North America in 1775 to 1780.

Governor Morris to Lord Weymouth, 29th March 1780. Capture of the Island of St. Vincent. Defence of his own conduct.

Copy of part of a letter relating to West Indian affairs and military and naval operations.

Paper relating to the defence of Newfoundland.

Mr. Samuel Jones to Lord Weymouth, relating to Spanish America.

2.

Feb., State of the trades with Indian countries.

Mr. William Smith to Lord Lansdowne, April 1785. On the effects of the American Independence upon England, the English colonies, and the United States.

1st Jan. 1785. The American Loyalists; relations of the United States.

1st May 1785. Congratulations on step in the peerage. The American Loyalists. Population of the province.

27th June 1785. Unjust attack made upon him by Mr. Wentworth, an imaginary relation of the late Lord Rockingham.

31st July 1785. Progress of the province.

Letters from Governor Parr to Lord Lansdowne, 28th Sept. 1785. The American whale fishery.

Extract from a letter dated St. John's, 9th May 1785, relating to the Canadian Trade.

Copy of a letter dated Quebec, 6th Aug. 1786. On the trade that may be carried between Canada and the West India Islands.

Mr. Hoard to Lord Lansdowne, Dominica, 27th Sept. 1786. Affairs of the island.

Anonymous letter. Philadelphia, 27th Oct. 1786. American affairs generally.

Governor Parr to Lord Lansdowne, 7th Aug. 1786. Religious sectaries.

Governor Parr to Lord Lansdowne, 15th May 1786. Affairs of Nova Scotia.

Extract of a letter from Boston, 1st Jan. 1788. Trade of the United States.

Return of the effectives of His Majesty's forces serving in the West India Islands, 11th Dec. 1787.

Governor Parr to Lord Lansdowne, Barbadoes, 14th June. Commercial treaty of 1783.

Desirability of complete free trade. Affairs of the continent. Opinion of Mr. Burt.

Mr. Bingham to Lord Lansdowne, Philadelphia, 4th March 1787. Effects of independence on the United States. Their constitution. Necessity of substituting a fedral for a confederate system.

Mr. Hamilton to Lord Lansdowne, St. George's, Bermuda, 16th Aug. 1789. Affairs of the island.

Mr. Bingham to Lord Lansdowne, 22nd Oct. 1791. Lord Wycombe's projected journey to the United States. Reported commercial treaty between the United States and Great Britain. Joins Lord Lansdowne in regreting the defection of the Marquis De'Bouillé from the revolutionary cause in France.

Abstract of a declaration made by the King of Spain, Dec. 1793, relative to the policy to be pursued towards France.

Some unsigned notes on the prosecutions for treason in Canada, dated Temple, 13th Nov. 1792. Qv.

Mr. John Adams to Dr. Priestly, 27th Feb. 1793. Discusses the question of emigration to the United States. Regrets the injury done to the cause of Republicanism by the excesses of the French.

Mr. Keen to Lord Lansdowne, St. Vincent, 4th Aug. 1793. West Indian affairs.

Mr. Joshua Steel to Lord Lansdowne, Barbadoes, 18th Oct. 1793. American and West Indian affairs.

3.

Dr. Turnbull's letters.

London, 1st Sept. 1766. Enclosing a "Narrative" which proposes encouraging the emigration of Greek colonists into Florida.

Port Mahoon, 10th July 1767. Difficulties thrown in the way of Italian emigration to America by the local authorities at Leghorn.

London, 1st May 1767. Appointment as secretary and clerk of the Council for the province of East Florida.

Leghorn, 15th June 1767. On Minorca.

Gibraltar, 4th April 1768. Colonists for Florida.

27th Feb. 1768, 4th April 1768, and 3rd May 1768. Emigration to Florida.

Minorca, 28th Feb. 1768. His sending some antique marbles found in Turkey.

Smyrnea, East Florida, 24th Sept. 1769. Emigration into colony. The antiques sent from Turkey.

Smyrnea, East Florida, 24th Sept. 1774. His opinion on American taxation. Progress of the colony.

Smyrnea, East Florida, 20th Dec. 1774. Lord Granville's estate in North Carolina.

American taxation, an appeal to arms will probably take place.

New York, 9th Nov. 1777. Military operations. Improbability of the end of the war being favourable to Great Britain.

New York, 10th Dec. 1777. The East Florida settlement broken up by the machinations of Governor Tonyn.

St. Augustin, 16th Dec. 1777. The same subject.

St. Augustin, 23rd Dec. 1777. The same subject, enclosing memorial to Lord George Germaine.

Extract from a letter from Mr. Holmes, a merchant in Pensacola, to Dr. Turnbull in St. Augustin, 18th Feb. 1780. Danger apprehended from the Spaniards.

St. Augustin, 14th March 1780. Outrageous conduct of Governor Tonyn.

St. Augustin, 25th March 1780. The same subject, and enclosing copies of the memorial he has addressed to Lord George Germaine, and of the legal proceedings in which he has become involved in connexion with the affair of Smyrnea.

Charlestown, 13th May 1783. Congratulates Lord Shelburne on having concluded a peace, and expresses his conviction that posterity will justify it notwithstanding its present unpopularity.

4.

Preston, 22nd July 1778. Danger of a number of Scotchmen in the army. Discontent in Scotland. Objects to the Highland dress.

Seven letters of Aug. and Sept. 1779, written from London at the time of the expected invasion after the action off Ushant.

19th April 1782. Unimportant.

Four letters of 19th May 1782, 9th and 25th July, and 25th Oct. 1783. From Halifax, Nova Scotia, giving some account of the province.

Nine letters of 24th Jan., 22nd March, 22nd April, 1st May, 16th June, 26th July, 13th and 17th Aug., and 16th Oct. 1784, relating to the same subject.

Halifax, 9th Oct 1789. The same subject.

5

Two unimportant letters relating to South America and Tristan d'Acunha.

Vol. 34.

A folio volume, labelled "Foreign Courts. Letters, "1782-3. Information." It contains sets of papers.

(1.) Copies of despatches to and from English ministers at foreign courts.

(2.) Original letters from abroad addressed to Lord Shelburne.

(3.) A great mass of statistical information as to foreign countries, especially Russia.

One or two papers of an earlier date have got mixed with those in this volume. None of these are of much importance.

The contents of this volume are printed in Division II., and not in Division I., to which they would seem more naturally to belong, for the reasons given at p. 140 of the Appendix to the Third Report of the Commissioners.

1. Keith, Sir Robert Murray. Extract of a letter from, to the Right Hon. Ch. J. Fox, dated Vienna, 4th May 1782.

Prince Kaunitz's remark on the English mode of negociating at Paris. "I am told," said he (somewhat deridingly), "there is again a flock of English at Paris. "Is it possible that your ministry can hope to reap any "advantage from such a mode of negociating with the "French Court."

2. Trevor, the Hon. Jo., to Mr. Secretary Fox, dated Ratisbon, 16th April 1782. Account of a conversation with a son of M. de Brentano, one of the Elector Palatine's ministers at the Diet, Aide-de-camp to the Comte de Rochambeau. He very incautiously mentioned when, where, and with whom the latter was to embark on his return to America (the Duc de Lauzun, the Marquis de la Fayette, the Marquis de Laval, and the Baron de Viomenil). He says that the French have but a bad opinion of their affairs in that country, they consider the present Congress as much degenerated from that which governed America two years ago. Congress not very fond of the French. Public virtue on the decline in that country. Cabal and intrigue prevail in their public elections. The French consider them as a steady persevering people, without activity, virtue, or spirit of union to preserve an independence; that they have neither the vices nor the virtues of the English; some of their greatest admirers at a distance are disappointed in their national character upon a nearer view, and surprised at the long exertions they have made in support of their union and independence. Nothing was clearer than that the people might be conquered by well disciplined European troops, but that the country was unconquerable. The paper money (now worth little), amounted to between 200 and 300 millions of livres. France rather doubtful but that America may return to the mother country, and prefer some honourable and easy connection with Great Britain, short of independence, to a dangerous and precarious independence of its own.

3. Sir James Harris to Mr. Fox, dated Petersburg, 24th May/4th June 1782 (extract). Has not received any ministerial answer from the Vice-Chancellor, but believes that the Empress is pleased with his letter, and that he shall receive in his first conference with Count Osterman strong assurances of her friendship. She dreads nothing so much as being drawn into a war.

4. Lord Shelburne to Sir James Harris, at Petersburg, 27th July 1782. (Extract.) On the Russian mediation.

5. Sir James Harris to Lord Grantham, dated Petersburgh, 9/20th Dec. 1782. Report of what passed between him and the Russian minister, Count Goertz, on the subject of a triple alliance between Russia, Sweden, and France, to form which were the first instructions of the latter.

6. Sir James Harris to Lord Grantham, dated Petersburg, 20/31 Jan. 1783 (secret and confidential). Conversation with Prince Potemkin on the neutral flag. He speaks very unguardedly of the Empress. "Here," said he, "we never look backwards or forward, and are "governed solely by the impulse of the hour. A good "and faithful subject can never know how to regulate "his conduct. If I was sure of being approved when "I did good, or being blamed when I did wrong, I "should know on what I was to depend, but these dis- "cerning qualities are wanting, and if the passions are "flattered, the judgment is never consulted."

7. Sir Jo. Stepney to Lord Grantham, dated Berlin, 22nd Oct. 1782. Account of his first audience, and of the long conversation he held with his Prussian Majesty on the general politics of Europe, the British possessions in the East Indies, the American war, the state of Gibraltar, &c. The letter continues, "His appearance was in "all respects exceedingly good, considering his years "and known infirmities."

8. Sir Jo. Stepney to Lord Grantham. Berlin, 8th Feb. 1783. (Extract.) Anecdote of Prince Henry of Prussia.

9. Sir Thomas Wroughton to Fox. Stockholm, 3rd May 1782 (in cypher). Account of the French subsidy of 3,000,000 livres to Sweden, for naval uses, in four quarterly payments. The King has represented the services he has rendered to France, by being the first promoter of the armed neutrality, procuring her naval stores, carrying on her commerce under neutral flags, &c. Has laid a plan before the French ministry for building three line of battle ships a year. The King's partiality to the French is well known; of late the ridiculous distinctions he has shown to some

I i 3

French travellers has given offence. The French Charged'Affaires is treated with peculiar favour.

10. Extract of a letter from Mr. Eden, dated 22nd June 1782. Russian frigates arrived from Cadiz, bring advice of the combined fleet consisting of 36 sail of the line. The attack of Gibraltar has been laid aside till September preparatory to which boats are building, eight to carry 20 guns each, and to be covered over in the manner of *casemates*. The constructions enormous and unweildy, such is the report of the Russian officers, which is scarcely credible.

11. Mr. Eden to Lord Grantham. Copenhagen, 26th Oct. 1782. (Extract.) Containing curious particulars relative to the Danish trade companies. Paper currency. The Danish West Indian colonies, &c. Letters from the Isle of France contain an account of the defeat of General Munro by Hyder Ally. The foregoing French intelligence sent from Mr. Hanbury at Hamburgh to Mr. Fox. Rec. 29th April 1782.

12. Sir William Hamilton to Fox. Caserta, 30th April 1782. (Extract.) Great preparations making at Cadiz, Algesiras, and in the Camp of St. Roche for a more than ever vigorous attack of Gibraltar.

11. Sir William Hamilton to Fox. Caserta, 7th May 1782. (Extract.) Project for a general attack upon Gibraltar by sea and land. The French to act in concert with the Spaniards. This plan cannot be ripe for execution before the middle of July.

13. Lord Mountstuart to Lord Hillsborough. Turin, 13th April 1782. (Extract.) The Spaniards determined to press the seige of Gibraltar. Spanish navy in bad condition.

14. John Collet, Consul at Genoa, to Fox. Genoa, 22nd June 1782. The Spanish floating batteries against Gibraltar : the attack is said to be deferred until August ; the combined fleet, five French and 25 Spanish ships of the line, sailed from Cadiz the 4th inst.

15. Sir Robert Ainslie to ————. Constantinople, 1st May 1782. (Extract.) Inclosing an extract of a letter from Bussora which follows.

16. William Digges La Touche, Esq., to Sir Robert Ainslie. Bassora, 17th March 1782. Military operations in India.

17. William Digges La Touche, Esq., to Sir Robert Ainslie. Bussora, 14th May 1782. (Extract.) Trincomalee taken by storm by Sir Edward Hughes, 8th Jan. Callicut surrendered to Major Abingdon, 13th Feb., after their grand magazines had been blown up. The former is in the principal bay of the island of Ceylon, the latter on the Malabar coast belonging to Hyder Ally ; the conquest of great importance ; the Governor and Council may be supplied from it with timber which there is much want of. The principal horde of Arabs of Bussora has since been pretty quiet. From Shiraz it is said that Ally Morul Cawn has put to death Acbar Cawn, his prime minister, and several of the principal Cawns for a conspiracy against him, &c.

18. The Hon. Edward Hay, Envoy Extraordinary at Lisbon, to the Duke of Richmond. Lisbon, 12th July 1766. (Extract.) Inclosing a decree of the King of Portugal, whereby shares in the several trading companies established in Portugal shall be deemed chattels personal to circulate in trade, and to answer all the purposes of ready cash. Mr. Hay's remarks thereon ; judged to be very prejudicial to foreign trade.

An English translation of the foresaid decree. 21st June 1766.

19. Robert Walpole to Fox. Lisbon, 24th April 1782. (Extract.) Great preparations making for an attack on Gibraltar by land and sea.

20. Robert Walpole to Lord Grantham. Lisbon, 23rd Nov. 1782. ! Inclosing duplicates of the despatches sent by the Antelope "packet" which was taken by the French on her way from Lisbon to Falmouth. Several British subjects who had abandoned their royal allegiance to the King of Spain and retired into Portugal, have been given up to the Spanish Government. The Portugese lending their ships to Spain and covering Spanish effects returning from America, &c.; is evidently assisting the enemies of Great Britain.

21. Robert Walpole to Lord Grantham. Lisbon, 23rd Nov. 1782. Orders from Madrid for preparing 24 ships of the line at Cadiz to sail with 14 French ships and 14,000 to 16,000 troops, and eight more French ships expected from Brest to go against Jamaica and the rest of the British settlements in America. Camp at St. Roc, there remain there from 15,000 to 20,000 men. Count D'Estaign is arrived at Madrid. It is said he is to command the expedition preparing at Cadiz.

22. Robert Walpole to Lord Grantham. Lisbon, 5th Oct. 1782. Success of the garrison of Gibraltar in de-

stroying the Spanish floating batteries, in which was killed, 390; wounded, 641; drowned, 80; taken prisoners, 397. Spanish ships in bad condition, and indifferently manned ; their crews, it is said, discouraged by our late successful fire on the floating batteries. At Cadiz there are only 2,000 men in garrison ; the walls on the side of the bay with the ramparts have 42 pieces of artillery with some 12-inch mortars ; the land gate is dismantled ; the Castle of Sebastian has 18 pieces of 24. The King is resolved to continue the siege by sea and land. Approves of the Duc de Crillon's conduct.

23. Sir John Hort to Lord Shelburne. Lisbon, 10th Sept. 1776. Some account of Count Shulenberg, Count de la Lippe, and other German officers in the Portuguese service. Present policy respecting the wines of Portugal, prejudicial to the trade thereof. Their Brazil settlements well provided and in a good state of defence. The Portuguese have an utter hatred to the Spaniards, full as strong as at the Revolution in 1640 ; their present army of 18,000 effective troops may do something provided nine out of ten of the officers are foreigners, not else. Sir John's opinion touching the revolted colonies in America which he had communicated to Lord Rochfort. An Italian improvisatore has directed the people of Lisbon for some months, and is on the point of departing for London. Intends giving him a letter to Sir Sampson Gordon.

24. Sir John Hort to Lord Shelburne. Lisbon, 19th Sept. 1777. The military in Portugal not liable to prosecutions for debt. Sir John not at that time upon speaking terms with Mr. Walpole. Political state of Portugal. Sir John's opinion of the state of affairs in America somewhat different from that of his Lordship and Colonel Barré.

25. Sir John Hort to Lord Shelburne. Lisbon, 11th Jan. 1780. Inclosing a letter from Captain Blanket at the Cape of Good Hope, which had been kept up a fortnight by Mr. Walpole ; it came in a Portuguese Indian ship. The Queen of Portugal given over by her physicians.

26. Sir John Hort to Lord Shelburne. Lisbon, 18th Sept. 1780. Count Nesselrod, the new Russian minister, speaks with extraordinary respect of his Lordship. Has invited the Court of Lisbon to join in the League of the armed neutrality, which has been refused. The Russian fleet.

27. Sir Jo. Hort to Lord Shelburne. Lisbon, 22nd Feb. 1782. Affairs at Gibraltar. Account by Capt. Blankett. Affairs at Gibraltar, second letter.

28. Sir Jo. Hort to Lord Shelburne. Lisbon, 19th Aug. 1781. M. de Crillon, 27th July, was then on his passage from Carthagena to Minorca with nearly 50 transports, containing 10,000 Spanish troops, escorted by four ships of the line and two frigates. The combined fleet at their departure from Cadiz consisted of no less than 54 of the line. They carried with them a large store of fascines and 300,000 sacks for sand bags. The Plate fleet of 20 sail arrived safe at Cadiz the 28th ultimo. Report of a rebellion in Persia. The new Ynca's manifesto thereon.

29. W. Grenville, Esq. Lettre a Mr. Mitchell, St. James, 31 d'Aout, 1762 (Traduction) et lettre separée au même de la même date. Mémoire pour servir à reponse aux remarques contenues dans la lettre a Mons. Mitchell, en date de 18 de Sept. 1762. Replique au mémoire remis par Mons. le Comte Finkenstein, au Sieur Mitchell, Ministre Plenipotentiaire du Roy de la Grande Bretagne, auprès le Roy de Prusse, dans une lettre dattée a Berlin 1 Oct. 1762.

30. Sir Jo. Hort to Lord Shelburne. Lisbon, 15th March 1782. Specifying the restrictions on British trade. The King of Morocco has declared his late treaty with Spain at an end, and the English restored to all privileges. Surrender of Morocco.

31. Sir Jo. Hort to Mr. Fox, Lisbon, 25th April, 1782. (Extract.) The new Book of Rates, very inimical to the British trade, from the extraordinary high duties. Of woollens alone among 52 British articles four only are kept within the stipulated bounds of 23 per cent. More than three fourths are from 30 to 50, and even above 70 per cent. Some relaxations, however, towards Irish importations.

32. Mr. Jos. Green to Sam. Corbett, Esq. Birmingham, 3 Aug. 1782. Respecting a petition of his brothers, which Sir John Hort has forwarded to the Queen of Portugal.

33. Mr. William Green to his brother Joseph at Birmingham. Lisbon, 21st Aug. 1782. On the hardships the hardware manufacturers are like to suffer by the new book of rates, with a copy of the new duties on sundry articles.

34. Sir Jo. Hort to Lord Shelburne. Lisbon, 25th April 1782. Is not very clear about giving his Lordship joy on his promotion; considers it at a "fearful period." Bad state of the Portuguese military, officered by valets de chambre and men cashiered 20 years ago by Count la Lippe for crimes or incapacity. Great preparations at Cadiz for a general attack upon Gibraltar.

35. Sir Jo. Hort to Lord Shelburne. Lisbon, 6th June 1782. Hardships of the British commerce, Taxgatherers, lawyers, and priests consume full three fourths of the substance of Portugal. The Brazilians discontented, and in the very capital whisper their right to free trade. Remonstrances against the new book of rates, and tumults threatened on its first coming into operation on the 14th inst. Gibraltar formidably attacked by land and sea; the garrison ready to receive them. Provisions there unsound but abundant. Mr. de Pombal protested when dying, "That of his King and country he had "no pardon to ask for any of his counsels, alluding "it was thought to the great executions of the nobility, "whose families, all but the Aveiro branch, after 24 "years have had an acquittal." Sir John is desirous of returning home.

36. Sir John Hort to Lord Shelburne. Lisbon, 23rd June 1782. Various intelligence. The book of rates was opened on the day appointed with general acquiescence. The King of Portugal, "though he hates a heretic "worse than the devil," betrayed an extraordinary gladness on the late victory at Dominica.

37. Sir Jo. Hort to Lord Shelburne. Lisbon, 1st Aug. 1782. Mr. Edmund Burke is delivered after suffering hard usage in the Castle of Santi Petri, near Cadiz, from misinterpreting the signal. Portugal is said to have acceded to the Neutral Alliance, and the acknowledgement of American Independency, both arising from apprehension and the impotent state of their army and navy. By advices from Buenos Ayres, through Rio de Janiero, the rebellion continues in Peru. 50,000 Spaniards are said to have been slain in and out of battle, including the miners; the engines destroyed and the mines filled up.

38. Sir John Hort to Lord Shelburne. Lisbon, 22nd Aug. 1782. Count St. Vincente, the only tolerable man in this country for the first naval place, is just made second.

Inclosing a Lisbon Almanack, or Court Calendar, the first ever composed here; the effect of the new Academy of Sciences, and some Rodney Ribbons, a present to Lady Shelburne. The fashion was led by Mrs. Walpole, the handsomest Englishwoman in Lisbon.

39. Sir John Hort to Lord Shelburne. Lisbon, 10th Nov. 1782. State of the combined fleet. The garrison of Gibraltar in perfect health and spirits. The enemies carcases had not displaced one stone. The asserted breach was an absolute lie.

40. Sir John Hort to Lord Shelburne. Lisbon, 23rd Nov. 1782. On some misrepresentations respecting the British and Irish trade; the Spaniards misreport the state of the combined and British fleets in the engagement. 20th Oct. 1782. Encloses a list of the combined fleets.

41. Sir John Hort to Lord Shelburne. Lisbon, 19th Jan. 1783. Further particulars of the Siege of Gibraltar. D'Estaing is to carry 19,000 troops with him in his intended expedition against Jamaica.

42. Sir John Hort to Lord Shelburne. Lisbon, 25th Jan. 1783. Advices is received of the embarkation of the troops at Cadiz.

43. Sir John Hort to Lord Shelburne. Lisbon, 9th Feb. 1783. On the accession of the Court of Portugal to the Neutral Alliance. Siege of Gibraltar.

44. Sir John Hort to Lord Shelburne. Lisbon, 2nd March 1783. Congratulations on the conclusions of the preliminaries. The Portuguese forward in their compliance to the North Americans. Mr. Howard has visited every prison and hospital at Lisbon, and approves their management. Proceeds in a few days for Spain. Encloses a decree of the Court of Portugal, 15th Feb. 1783, for re-admitting North American ships. (Printed.)

45. Alexander Graham, British Consul at Fayal, to ————. 12th July 1782. (Extract.) Affairs in South America.

46. Letter to Monsieur Semolin, dated St. James's, 4th May 1782. On the Russian mediation for a separate peace with Holland.

47. Mr. Secretary Fox to Mr. de Semolin. St. James's, 28th June 1782. On the Russian mediation.

48. ———— to Count de Luni. St. James's, 9th May 1782. About refusal of the Russian mediation.

49. ———— to Count de Luni. St. James's, 6th May 1782. On the Russian and Prussian alliance.

Here follow a great number of statistical papers respecting the trade, &c. of Russia and other countries, of which a letter of Captain Blankett, 25th Dec. 1774, is the most interesting.

Corsica. A paper from General Paoli, describing of what advantage that Island would be to Great Britain. May 1782, grounding thereon the proposal of an offer to give up Gibraltar and Minorca to Spain in return for the sovereignty of Corsica.

Vol. 35.

The reasons for printing the contents of a portion of this volume in Division II. and not in Division I., to which it would naturally belong, have been stated at page 140 of the Appendix to the Third Report of the Commissioners.

16. A la Venerie, 8 Juin 1782.—Sardaigne (le Roi de) au Marq. de Cordon. Signed de Hauteville. Influence of Lord Rodney's victory over De Grasse. France will not treat separately from her allies. Conduct of Holland.

17. De Mirabel (le Comte) au Marq. de Cordon (Extrait.) No date. Negociations and conduct of Lord Rockingham's ministry.

25. 24 May 1782.—M. Simolin (M.) a Mr. Marcoff, on Mr. Fox's speech in Parliament about Mr. Grenville's mission. In Lord Shelburne's handwriting.

26. Londres, le 26 Novem. 1782.—The same, au Comte d'Osterman (decypherrd). Arrival of M. de Rainoval from Paris. His interview with Lord Shelburne. Cordiality of the latter, who is anxious for peace, but it must be recollected that the war party in England is still strong. Rumours as to the conditions proposed. Exchange of Gibraltar for Porto Rico.

31. Londr., 23 Avril 1782.—De Lusi (le Comte) (au Roi de Prusse. Mr. Fox offers Carte Blanche to the K. of Prussia, as Mediator for Peace, and mentions the terms he, Mr. Fox, would be ready to subscribe to. Projects for a Northern Alliance.

32. Londr., 26 Avril 1782.—The same subjects.

33. Londr., 11th Juin 1782.—(Extrait.) The same subject.

34. Potsdam, le 17 Juin 1782.—Prusse (le Roi de) au Comte de Lusci. Reply to the preceding letters.

35. Potsdam, 27 Juin 1782.— The peace and the projected Northern Alliance.

36. Breslau, 26 Aout 1782.—The same subjects.

*36. Berlin, 3 Sept. 1782.—(Extrait.) The same subjects.

37. No date. The same, au meme (Extrait). He is assured that Spain has offered Minorca, Oran, and Masalquivir in exchange for Gibraltar, and he thinks England would be a gainer by the bargain, on account of the expense of maintaining Gibraltar, &c.

38. Potsdam, 27 Jan. 1783.—The same, au meme. Probability of England preserving a strict neutrality for at least ten years to come.

39. Montbrillant, 11 Juin 1768. Extract from a letter addressed to the same, au Baron Diede de Furstenstein (Extrait), marked under Baron Bernstorff's cover on a separate sheet, but not in his handwriting. Journey of the Prince Royal of Prussia to Hanover.

43. Passy, 31st March 1782.—Franklin (Dr. Benj.) to David Hartley, Esq. Congratulates him on the change in the disposition of the English towards America, hopes the change of the ministry will be attended with salutary effects; he is but one of five in the Commission (Messrs. Adams, Jay, Laurens, and Jefferson, and all the others), and has no knowledge of their sentiments; in case of the death or absence of any, the remainder have power to act.

44. Passy, 31st March 1782.—The same to Mr. Wm. Hodgson, Merchant, Coleman Street. Has just heard there are 200 American Prisoners in Ireland destitute, and dying in numbers. Kindness to captives on both sides may promote a reconciliation; he has no correspondent in Ireland, and wishes to be put in a way to sending them some relief; does he think the new Ministry better disposed than the last? if so, would wish him to lay before the former propositions for the exchange of prisoners slighted by the latter; he wishes to finish this devilish contest as soon as possible.

46. Londr., 12 April 1782.—Bourdieu (Mons'. James,) à Mr. Vander Oudermonlen (Extrait-interceptée). Relates to the negociations for peace with Holland.

47. Londr., 12 Avril 1782.—The same to Mons. Pache, l'ainé (Extrait intercepte). A commercial intrigue suggested as the first step towards a negociation for a general peace.

48. *Ostende*, 17 *Mai* 1782.—Larcher (Mons. G.) a Valentine Thurne, at Mr. *Mawley* (or Mawby), No. 3, *Southampton Row*. A letter of caution. Relates apparently to the secret negociations for peace with Holland.

49. *Londres*, 28 *Mai* 1782.—Bourdieu (Mons). Extracts of two of his letters to Mons. *de la Sonde*. The same subject.

50. *Paris*, 6 *Juin* 1782.—Pache *l'aîné* lettre a Mr. J. Bourdieu. Prospects of peace. Naval operations.

51. *Paris*, 6th *June* 1782.—Alexander (Mr. W.) to Wm. Adam, Esq., *Adelphi*.

52. *Paris*, 17th *June* 1782.—J. N. to Mr, Philip Wray (*viâ Hennesy and Co., at Ostend*). On the French politics of the time, and chiefly adverting to the expected peace. " On Sunday evening Mr. Grenville received his new " powers, which are now extended so as to include " America, to the exclusion of Mr. Oswald, who is how- " ever, it seems, ordered to remain here. . . . If " peace should not ? be made a separate distinct treaty " between England and America will probably be " thought expedient."

53. *St. James's*, 7th *Aug.* 1782.—Fraser (Mr.) to Lord Shelburne. Inclosing a copy of a letter from *Paris*, written in *white ink*.

54. *Paris*, 21st *July* 1782.—Chalmers (Mr. G.) to Mr. Philip Wray. · French politics of the day. This is the letter mentioned in the preceding number, enclosed in Mr. *Fraser's* to Lord *Shelburne*, 7th Aug.

55. *Nantes*, 10th Aug. 1782.—Laurens (Henry, Esq.) to James Bourdieu, Esq. (written partly in *Cypher*). He has been extremely ill; is about to return to *America*, as soon as he can provide proper means.

On various points in the negociations for peace, especially the terms to be given to the American loyalists, the whole tone of the letter is very defiant of the English ideas on these subjects, and seems to have aroused the indignation of the maker of the index to this volume, who indulges in some severe observations.

57. *Londres*, 23 *Aout*. 1782.—French spy, *name un-known*, a *Mademois' Ez*, under cover, a *Mademois' de Frances, Rue basse de Rampart, Paris*, dated *Londres*, 23 *Aout* 1782. Fox is in Ireland, Grantham is on the continent, Flood is in Paris. The latter is come to watch the negociations for peace with a view to their effects on Ireland.

58. *Bruxelles*, 11 *Octor*. 1782.—Tort (Mons'.) a Mess". *Bourdieu* and *Cholet*. Ambiguous conduct of M. de Vergennes en Mons. Tort threatens to " mordre comme " un chien enragé."

59. *Paris*, 28 *Nov.* 1782.—Pache l'aîné, M'. a Mons'. *Bourdieu*. Negociations for peace. Preparations for the continuance of war. French finance.

60. *Londres*, 10 *Jánv*. 1783.—Bourdieu, Chollet, and Bourdieu, au Marq. de Castries. M. Pitôt has been captured on his way from Ireland, and has had to throw his despatches into the sea.

61. *Victory, St. Hellens*, 31 *May* 1778. — Blankett (Capt. J.) to Ld. Shelb.

62. *Versailles*, 4 Sept. 1781.—De Vergennes (le Comte) a Chev' de la Luzerne. Copy (decyphered). Attitude to be observed by France with regard to the American Congress, in the stability of which M. de Vergennes does not seem to have any great confidence. This letter has Lord Shelburne's pencil marks in the margin.

63. *Versails.*, 22 Oct. 1780.—The same subject.

64. *Sept. and Oct.* 1780.—His opinion of certain leading characters among the *Americans*, to wit, *Franklin, Silas Deane, Adams, Izard*, and *Arthur Lee*. Extracted from the previous letters.

65. *Versailles*, 9 Janv. 1781.—Letter on *Chiffres*. au *Chevr. de la Luzerne*. This dispatch was taken in *America*, and sent from thence to be decyphered. It relates to military and naval operations. An original.

66. *Newport*, 27th May 1781.—De Rochambeau (le Comte) au Chev' de la Luzerne a *Philadelphie* (decy-phered). The same subject.

67. *Philadelphie*, 10 *Fevrier* 1782.—De la Luzerne (le Chev') a . On French commerce with America. Original.

68. 21 Janv. 1782.—Baudoin (Mr. J.), Negociant a Boston, Traduction d'un *Mémoire* adressé a M'. de la Luzerne. The same subjects. Original.

69. *Boston*, 21 Jan. 1782.—The same. The substance of the above in *English*.

70. *Philadelphie*, 27 *Fevrier* 1782.—De la 'Luzerne (le Chevr.) au *Comte* de Vergennes, *decyphered*.) Exchange of prisoners. Prospects of the war.

71. *Fevrier*, 1782.—Harrison (Mr. Gouverneur de *Virginie*) au Chev' de la Luzerne, Fevrier 1782, sur

l'Envoy des *Armes* dans la *Riviere James* (*Traduction, decyphered*).

72. *Philadelphie*, 28 *Fovr*. 1782.—De la Luzerne. (*le Chevr.*) au *Comte de* Vergennes (*decyphered*). Differences with the State of Vermont.

73. *Philadepph.*, 1 Mars 1782.—De la Luzerne (*le Chevr.*) au *Comte* de Vergennes.

74. *Fevrier*, 1782.—The same. Etat du *Change* des *Especes* contre les Traites et le Papier Monnoye a *Philadelphia* pendant le Mois de Fevrier 1782 (Inclus dans sa Lettre du 1 Mars).

75. *Philadelphie*, 9 *Mars* 1782.—De Marbois (Mr.) au Comte de Vergennes. (*On the Finances decyphered*.)

76. *Philadelph.*, 13 *Mars* 1782.—The same au meme. Feeling in Carolina towards France and England re-spectively. Question of the fisheries.

77. Rutlege (Mr. Jean, Gouverneur de la Caroline Meridionale Discour de, a l'Assemblée generale de cet Etat. (*Traduction.*)

78. *Philadelph.* 15 *Mars* 1782.—De la Luzerne (le Chev') a Mr. le Baron de Grimm. (The same was sent to the *French Ambassr. at Madrid*.) Capture of York Town. American commerce and finance.

79. *Philadelph.*, 21 Mars 1782.—De Marbois (Mr.) au Comte de Vergennes. A very interesting paper, giving an account of the composition and character of the American Congress.

80. 7 Fevrier 1782.—Gazette de Philadelphie, Ex-trait de la, 7 Fevrier 1782. Mr. Silas Deane a traitor. Gazette de Philadelphie, undated. The same subject.

DIVISION IV.

Vol. 161.

A folio volume labelled "Minutes of Cabinet, Falk- " land Island. Instructions for Lord Bristol, Sir J. " Gray and Mr. Lyttleton. Foreign miscellany." The minutes of the Cabinet are in Lord Shelburne's hand-writing. All the other papers are copies, 1766, 1768.

Vols. 162, 163, 164.

Three folio volumes labelled Treasury Minutes. The first volume includes July and August 1782. The second, October, November and December 1782. The third, January, February and March 1783. All the papers in these volumes are copies.

Vol. 165.

This volume is marked "Minutes of motions on various Parliamentary subjects."

Le Chevalier de Pinto, 2 June 1780, a card touching Lord Shelburne's intended motion respecting northern affairs.

Le Comte de Verscheffer, 11th April 1787. Questions préliminaires au sujet d'une neutralité armée.

Mr. Dunning's notes on the subject of the note in 1780.

Mr. Dunning on the American war. · No date given.

Notes on Extraordinaries, Private contracts, &c.

Number of men voted, exclusive of augmentations, for 1776 to 1781.

Commissioners of accounts. Memorandum from their report. West India garrisons.

Clause of an address to His Majesty on the want of foresight, ability, and integrity in his ministers.

Notes of an address to His Majesty on the war with America.

References to Parliamentary register; remembrances, etc. in 1775, 1776, 1778.

Various notes on the conduct of the ministry chiefly in 1780, respecting the war with America, by Lord Shelburne.

Remarks on the commissioners proposals to the Americans.

On the dangerous condition of national affairs.

On American independence.

Remarks on the treaty between France and Spain.

Extract of a letter from J. Berney Petit, relating to a county meeting, 1780.

Commission of accounts to consist of nine members of the House of Commons.

Additional words proposed in 1762 to voting the German troops.

Parliamentary reform, the necessity of, in 1783.

Mr. W. Tollomache's letter to the County Palatine of Chester, 29th April 1780.

The address of the city of London for the reform of Parliament.

MARQUIS
OF LANS-
DOWNE.

General meeting on œconomical reform, equalising the representation and shortening the duration of Parliaments.

Notes of Lord Shelburne on the bill for embanking the Thames.

" The province of a statesman heretofore far less complicated than at present." A paper on this subject.

Observations on officers of high rank in the army having been lately dismissed without the judgment of a court martial.

Regency. Notes of a speech on the Regency Bill of 1765.

Mr. Dunning to Lord Shelburne, touching a misconception of the Duke of Richmond, and the dismemberment of America. 20th Jan. 1782.

Lord Suffolk to Lord Shelburne acquainting him that the Opposition is gathering all its strength for Monday, 2nd May 1769.

Lord Shelburne to Count Sarsfield, about misrepresentation in the newspapers as to what passed in the House of Lords, 21st May 1775.

Lord John Cavendish to Lord Shelburne, 1780. Proposed motion in the Houses of Lords and Commons.

Mr. Bayley, 18th April 1780, to Lord Shelburne on the state of affairs.

Vol. 166.

This volume contains papers of 1782 and 1783, and others of an earlier date.

Draft of Mr. Burke's bills for economical reform, 1782.

Copy of the first six reports of the commissioners of accounts, 1782.

Persons examined twice or oftener by the commissioners of accounts, 1782.

A paper containing some short notes on the projected economical reform, 1782.

Inspection into certain offices in the Exchequer with remarks proposed therein by the committee of accounts, 1782.

Abstract of the first report of the commissioners of accounts, 1782.

Abstract of the second report.
Abstract of the third report.
Abstract of the fourth report.
Abstract of the fifth report.
Abstract of the sixth report.

W. Moleson, Secretary to the Commissioners of Public Accounts, to Ld. Shelburne. Has prepared lists of the persons who have sums of public money unaccounted for. 14 Feb. 1783.

Miscellaneous extracts from the Lords Journals. Heads for an address, remonstrance, and petition of the City of London. (The date is probably 1780.)

Motions intended to be made by Lord Rockingham. 1782, November.

Notes made on the day of Lord C(hatham's) speech, undated and relating to private affairs.

Observations on Lord Shelburne's speech as quoted in the London Courant. 2nd June 1780.

Mr. John Berens to Lord Shelburne. Foreign politics. 8th Jan. 1781.

Dr. Frampton's remarks on Mr. Gilbert's Poor Bill. Oct. 1781.

Mr. H. Allnutt on the same subject. 23rd May 1782.

An account of the income and expenses of the Turkey company, 1781.

An account of the sums granted to the Turkey company by Parliament.

Mr. Richardson on the reform of the customs to Ld. Shelburne, 30 July 1782, with enclosures on the same subject, viz :

(1.) Proposed oath against fraudulent practices within the Customs.
(2.) Proposed income tax.
(3.) Copy of motions to be proposed to the House of Commons. This last paper is endorsed, " Three " motions intended to have been proposed in " the House of Commons if a change of Minis- " ters had not taken place."

Notes on the importation of barley.

Plan for an independent Parliament by Mr. Harvey. 1st Aug. 1782.

A plan of Parliamentary reform by Mr. George Edwards. 11th Oct. 1782.

Further thoughts on Parliamentary reform. The King's answer to the Quakers in 1760, 1761, 1763.

Mr. Mayor on the price of paper as affected by the duties. 18th Nov. 1782.

5.

Proposals as to payment of Ministers abroad. 9th Feb. 1782.

A hint relative to the speaker. 18th July 1782.

List of Peers written to for hearing the speech, and at Shelburne House. 4th Dec. 1782.

Forms of notes for certain occasions to Peers.

Address moved in the Peers as it stood. 17 Feb. 1783.

List of Scotch members for and against the address. 17th Feb. 1783.

Draft of the King's answer to the address of the Commons condemning the peace, and the amended answer. 24th March 1783.

Heads of the bill for the better regulation and government of the British settlements in India, and for the security and preservation thereof, by Frances Russell, Esq.

Bill for the better payment of the land tax, and notes on the same.

Notes on Lord Mahon's bill for preventing bribery at elections.

Vol. 167.

A folio volume in red morocco, labelled Rights of Burroughs. Mr. W. Masterman's Compendium of the Rights and Privileges or mode of election of members to serve in Parliament, drawn alphabetically in tabular form, with an abstract of the gradual alterations in the Representation.

Vol. 168.

Political papers from 1763-1797. A very miscellaneous but interesting collection.

1763.

Papers and precedents relating to Wilkes, containing amongst others, three opinions of Serjeant Glynn (?).

1764.

Another opinion on the case of Wilkes.
Opinion of Mr. Dunning on the Bill of Rights.
Two opinions of Mr. Dunning on private affairs.

1765.

Letter relating to a petition from Clare College, Cambridge, presented to the House of Lords by Lord Shelburne.

Two letters relating to questions arising out of the Treaty of 1763, one is by the Chevalier D'Eon.

1766-7. Two papers entitled Symptoms of War at Different Courts of Europe in 1766-7.

22nd December 1766. Letter from the Committee of Oporto Merchants.

Abstract of the Tripoli Ambassador's letter to the Earl of Shelburne and of two other papers.

A paper on Colonial Commerce.

18th Sept. 1767. Mr. Weston to Mr. Sutton.

Copy of an answer of the Royal Court of Jersey to the petition of Doleance, of Mr. Peter Phade Gruchy on behalf of Mr. Nicholas Fist.

16th Sept. 1767. Mr. Attorney-General's Report on the petition of the Warmly Company for the grant of a charter of incorporation, and on several petitions against the same.

17th Sept. 1767. Mr. Rivers to Mr. Sutton on respiting criminals.

Notes by Lord Shelburne on the Bank Charter.

List of His Majesty's ministers, &c., in the Southern department.

Foreign ministers in the Southern department.

Notes on events during 1767.

9th May 1768. List of correspondence in the Paper Office about Corsica.

1768.

Notes upon smuggling.

30th May. Lord Barrington to Lord Shelburne, inclosing precedents of orders given by the Secretary of State for the troops to support the civil magistrates.

1769.

17th Oct. King of Poland to Lord Shelburne recommending a friend.

1770.

18th March. Mr. Serjeant Glynn's opinion on the proposed remonstrance.

Notes on Lord Shelburne's journey abroad in 1771.

1778.

A letter of Lord Shelburne to Count Sarsfield.

MARQUIS
OF LANS-
DOWNE.

1780.

Papers relating to the county meetings.
Extracts from several French letters relating to the affairs of Holland.
Papers relating to the armed neutrality.
Motions, 15th Dec. 1779 and 8th Feb. 1780.

1785.

Extract of a letter of the 12th July. M. de V. à M. de R.
Three letters from the Prince of Anhalt Dessau.
Letter from Frederick the Great, sent through the Prince of Dessau.
Draft of Lord Shelburne's answer.
29th Nov. Mr. Palmer of the Treasury to Lord Lansdowne on his appointment.
Notes upon private art collections and an academy by Lord Lansdowne.

1790.

Paper headed reasons in favour of the permanency of the French Revolution.

1791.

Notes on the Priestly riots at Birmingham.

1782.

26th March. Mr. Mackintosh remarks on the present state of affairs.
Paper entitled Army and Fleet contains precedents.
Correspondence relating to French prisoners of war.
Secret intelligence received from abroad, several papers.
17th April. Intelligence received from Lord Viscount Keppel.
24th April. Intelligence of ships fitting out and repairing in English ports for France and Holland.
18th Dec. Mr. Pitt to Lord Shelburne. Minutes of the cabinet held in May 1782.
22nd April. Minutes as to the reform of the Civil Service.
Copies of the standing orders transmitted by the Lord High Treasurer Rochester, in the year 1685, to the several public accountants to be by them observed as standing instructions in conformity to the rules established by him to prevent delays in accounting, &c.
Rules established by the Lord High Treasurer and the Lords of the Treasury for the government of the auditors of the imprest to prevent delays in accounting which are greatly prejudicial not only to His Majesty but many times also to the accountants themselves.
Observations of the auditor on the rules established by the Lord High Treasurer, &c., and proposals for further regulations respecting such accounts as have been created since the first establishment of those rules.
Notes relating to the King's speech in opening Parliament in 1782 and 1783.
Paper relating to the expenses which have attended the coinage.
Schedule of papers delivered over by the executors of William Lowndes, Esq., late Secretary of the Treasury.
Paper relating to victualling the army in America in 1782.
Report concerning the repository of papers in the Treasury, viewed 12th and 13th Sept. 1782, by James Matthews, Librarian to the Earl of Shelburne.
15th July. Burgesses, &c., of Lyme Regis, request my Lord to defer consideration of petition for a new charter, for a few days, and until a counter petition of the freeholders and inhabitants can be prepared against it.
Warrant to authorise the Earl of Shelburne to countersign commissions.
Epiniceum on Lord Rodney's victory.
Elegy on the death of the Marquis of Rockingham.
27th March. Minute of Lord Shelburne being sworn Secretary of State.
26th March. Mr. Bell to Lord Shelburne.
Notes on the militia before Charles I.
Outlines for a general commutation Act, proposed by William Richardson, Esq., to the Marquis of Lansdowne, when First Lord of His Majesty's Treasury.
Three private letters, unimportant.

1783.

12th Jan. Sends copy of a letter to Wm. Sheridan, Esq., being a report on "The Defence of the Earl of

"Shelburne," and intended (if approved by his Lordship) for publication from Ignotus.
Bribery Bill, 1788.
25th March. Mr. Rose sends Treasury Reform Minute as it now stands, and the former one, with the alterations made in it. Treasury minute wanting.
A computation of the expense to government of victualling 70,000 men for 1783.
26th Feb. Draft of the answer to the address of the City of London by Lord Ashburton.

1784.

Correspondence between Lord Shelburne and Lieut.-Gen. Cunningham, of Barbadoes, relating to the supersession of the latter.
Abstract of a report of the commissioners for reorganising the Civil Service.

1786.

Extract of a letter from M. Dumont to M. le Comte de Mirabeau.

1787.

27th Jan. Copy of a letter of Ld. Lansdowne on the poor laws.
Notes on the repeal of the Test Act.

1789.

Copy of a French letter on Dutch affairs, anonymous.
Papers on the Westminster election of 1789.
6th June. Draft of a letter apparently by Ld. Lansdowne to the King.

1792.

28th Aug. Extracts of letters about Poland.

1794.

Paper in French entitled Reflexions sur l'alliance de la Russie avec l'Autriche, ou avec la Prusse, l'Angleterre, par M. le Comte de Hertzberg.
Index of parliamentary papers, 1790 to 1800.
Extrait d'un mémoire du Comte Francois de Carletti, relatif à la conduite du Lord Hervey, ministre de la Maj : Britanique auprès du grand Duc de Toscane.
Notes on the Bank Charter, &c.

1795.

1st Feb. M. de Talleyrand to Lord Lansdowne, with an account of America.

1797.

Paper entitled Ld. Granville's explanation of Lord Auckland's assertion.
Papers relating to the trial of Lord Edward Fitzgerald.
A bundle of papers marked miscellaneous, mostly unimportant.

V.

On General and Private Correspondence.

The letters which are of any public interest will be printed in my life of Lord Shelburne, one volume of which has already appeared. It is therefore unnecessary to give any extended notice of them here.

DIVISION VI.

ANCIENT MANUSCRIPTS.

For the probable origin of this collection, which is of a very miscellaneous character, see page 126 of the Appendix to the Third Report of the Commissioners.

No. 169.—A fol. vol., in blue Turkey, labelled Sea Dominions. Lecture on Navigation. Pepys Index. It contains copies of miscellaneous papers relative to navigation, and of an Index to the Pepys MSS. There is an index.

No. 170.—A fol. vol. in vellum, containing a paper entitled Anne R. An establishment, with incidents for housekeeping. Also wages and board wages to the officers and servants of our house, chamber, and stables, with the expense of the chappells, and provisions for horses. Also, allowances, stipends, and pensions to old and supernumerary servants and widowers, to commence the first day of July 1702.

No. 171.—A fol. vol., in red morocco, being an account of the revenues of the Crown for one year, ending at Michaelmas, quinto Edwardi sexto, with the establishment of His Majesty's household, and civil government, with the salaries then allowed. Also, remonstrances for increasing His Majesty's revenue.

It is a fine MSS., and in excellent preservation. There is a modern index to its contents. It seems an office book.

No. 172.—A fol. vol., bound in vellum, and containing a MS., entitled The generall state of receipts and issues of the publick Revenues between the Feast of St. Michael, 1693, and the Feast of St. Michael, 1694. It has a modern index to its contents.

No. 173.—A fol. vol., in vellum, labelled *A General Index of Crown Lands*. It contains an alphabetical account of the land revenues belonging to the Crown, as they appeared by the Parliament surveys and books of entry in the Surveyor-General's office since the year 1650.

It is a very choice MS. Its contents are divided into ten columns, viz. :—

1. County.
2. Names and situations of the estates.
3. To whom granted.
4. For what term.
5. Yearly rents.
6. Improvements.
7. Dates.
8. In what surveys and entries to be found.
9. Fines.
10. Occasional remarks and references.

No. 174.—A fol. vol., in vellum, labelled *Exchequer Officers and Fees*. Its title as it stands in the MS. is, A book of all y⁰ severall officers of y⁰ Court of Exchequer, together with the names of the present officers in whose gift and honꝛ admitted. With a briefe collection of y⁰ chief heads of what every officer usually doth by virtue of his office, according to the state of y⁰ Excheqꝛ, anno Dini 1692. It has a modern index.

No. 175.—A fol. vol., in vellum, containing Revenues, &c., of the islands of Guernsey, Alderney, Sarke, Arne, and Gethow. It is an authentic copy, with the greenwax seal appendant. Every page is signed by the examining jurats, with a certificate in French, subscribed, Eleazar le Marchant, Bailiffe; Law. Fiott, and Samuel Bonamy, Jurats. 16 August 1755.

No. 176.—A fol. vol., in vellum, containing "The " accompts for the year ending the 29 September " 1692, of receipts by loans and repayments in satis-" faction thereof. Incomes and issues of the Exchequer, " Customs House, Excise Office, Post Office." A fine MS.; the title is richly illuminated. There is a modern index.

No. 177.—A fol. vol., containing Names of Popish recusants, convicts, and Papists, who have registered their estates, together with most of their titles, additions, and places of abode, or the parishes or townships where their lands lie, and the names of the tenants in possession, and an abstract or total of each person's estate, as the same have been returned by the clerks of the peace for the several counties to the commissioners, trustees, &c. for the forfeited estates. Total of the estates in the several counties, 386,746l. 4s. 10¾d. These returns were made on the project of Jo. Cosins that Papists should pay two thirds of their income.

No. 178.—A fol. vol., containing "A schedule of all " the entry books, surveys, papers, writings, and muni-" ments belonging to the office of Surveyer-Generall " of His Majesty's lands, revenues, and now lying in " the hands of Daniel Pulteney, Esq., as administrator " of the personall estates and effects of John Pulteney, " Esq., deceased, late Surveyer-Generall." An original MS., dated 1726, and signed Charles Gibbons, G. Cartwright. There is a modern index to it.

No. 179.—A fol. pamphlet, being an authentic copy of " An establishment or list containing all payments to " be made for civil list affaires, from the 25th day of " March 1709," in the 8th year of our reign for the kingdom of Ireland. It has a modern index.

No. 180.—A fol. pamphlet, containing "An account " (no name nor date), of an expedition against Cartha-" gena, in South America." (Admiral Vernon.) Copies of letters on the state of Ireland, in 1756, in case of a French invasion. Copies of two letters of Count de Schaumbourg Lippe in 1757. An account of Gibraltar in 1751.

No. 181.—A fol. vol., in vellum, containing "A copie " of His Majesty's Grant, anno 1671, to the Receivers-" Generall and Farmers of the Duty on proceedings at " Law." A fine MS. of the time.

No. 182.—A MS. fol. in vellum, having no generall title. It is divided into two parts, with heads in Latin, though written in English.

A. (1.) *Pars Prima.*—De Jure Maris et Brachionum ejusdem. (2.) *Pars Secunda.*—De Portibus Maris. (3.) Appendix concerning the five ports, their names, privileges, and charges.

B. A MS. fol., marked "on the Customs," with other papers on the same subject.

This MS., though written in a different hand from A., I believe to be a continuation of it. It begins "Pars " Tertia," and in cap. I. the author says, " Having in a " former part, as preparatory to this, gone through the " examination or history of the Ports, I now descend to " the history or narrative of the King's Customs."

No. 183.—A fol. vol. labelled *Revenues Opinions*. It contains references from the Treasury Board to the Attorneys and Solicitors-General on various points relative to the revenues, from 1673 to 1707.

No. 184.—A fol. vol. labelled *Court of Admiralty*. It contains (1) Admiralli Angliæ ab anno 1307 ad annum 1670. (2) An account of patents, records, &c. to 1703, and some other papers. A curious MS.

No. 185.—A fol. vol. labelled *Invasiones Tempore Elizab.* It contains extracts of papers referring to the invasion in 1588, and to various incidents subsequent to that period.

No. 186.—A fol. MSS. pamphlet being a schedule of the ancient surveys or rentals before the Rebellion. The surveys made in the time of the Rebellion and the surveys since the Restoration, &c., 1713.

An original MS., signed by S. Elphinstone and W. Munday.

No. 187.—A quarto vol. labelled *Paper Office Catalogue*. It is a catalogue of the treatise and other instruments, books, and papers in His Majesty's Paper Office. It contains also an index to the papers and MS. of Sir Leoline Jenkins.

No. 188 and 189.—Two 4to vols. labelled *Extracts out of the Secretary of State's Books*, from 1661 to 1725. They also contain a few extracts for the year 1757.

No. 190.—A 4to vol. in red morocco, labelled *Council Book of Henry VIII., &c.* It contains copies (1) of the Council Book of Henry VIII. in 1540 and 1541; (2) Of a book of the King's power of pardoning, by the Earl of Nottingham, Lord Chancellor; (3) Of some doubts on Poining's Acts in Ireland; (4) Of the King's warrants for beheading the Earl of Strafford, 1641.

No. 191.—A fol. pamphlet, being A brief collection concerning the manors of the Duchy of Cornwall, which are commonly called "Assessionable or Ancient Dutchy," from 7 Edw. III. to 44 Elizb. With a table wherein are set down the present rents, compared with those which were answered in the 7th year of King Edw. III. and all the casual profits, &c. compared.

A very neat MS. No date nor any name of the author.

No. 192.—A thin fol. vol. containing " A rental of " His Majesty's land revenues within the several coun-" ties of North Wales, with the annual tithes." It has no date.

No. 193.—A 4to vol., in calf, containing copies of the manner of the most happy return into England of our gracious Sovereign Lord King Charles II., and his proceeding through London upon Tuesday, the 29th of May 1660. The preparation for His Majesty's coronation, &c. at Westminster, the 23rd of April 1661.

The proceeding to the coronation of King Charles on Thursday, the 2nd of February 1625.

It is a copy attested by St. George Clarenceux in 1694.

No. 194.—A quarto vol., in parchment, labelled *A Discourse of the Parliament*. It contains "A discourse of the High Courte of Parlyament and of the aucthoritie of the same, collected out of the common Lawes of this lande, and other good aucthors." It has no date nor name of the author.

No. 195.—A small 4to vol. containing schedules of fees and lists of officers; viz., a schedule of the usual fees taken at the Treasury by the secretary for himself and clerks, 24th April 1695.

Charges of the establishment, anno 1702, 297,549l. 1. 6d.

Fees for payment of money in the receipts of the Exchequer taken by the two deputy chamberlains called the Bally Court.

Schedule of the fees payable to the auditor imprests.

List of officers of the Custom called the Patent Officers, with their salaries, &c. List of officers of the excise collections, collectors, supervisions, &c., with their salaries, &c.

No. 196.—A small 4to vol. in blue Turkey, containing particulars and date of the receipts and issues of the public revenues, taxes, and loans, during the reign of His late Majesty King William, from Ladyday 1688 to Michelmas 1710. An interesting volume.

No. 197.—A small 4to vol. containing *Elementa Jurisprudentia*. Are studies possibly by Lord Shelburne, when young.

No. 198.—A small 4to, in vellum, labelled *Victualling Contract*, 1677. The parties are,—Our Sovereign Lord the King, of the one part, and Richard Brett, Samuel Vincent, and J. Parsons, of London, on the other. Dated 19th Dec. 1677. By writ of privy seal signed Piggott.

No. 199.—A small 4to vol. labelled *Court of Admiralty*. It is a collection of several matters concerning the power and rights of the Lord High Admiral, and the jurisdiction of the Court of Admiralty.

No. 200.—An 8vo volume containing a catalogue of Mr. Secretary Pepys's library.

Vol. 201.

This set of volumes of a miscellaneous set of papers.

A. Account of ways and means and supplies from 1715–1760. They are perhaps contained in Sir Charles Whitworth's work.

B. A pocket-book, in vellum, lettered Various accounts from 1754 to 1760. Bounties from 1744. Civil list from 1728. It seems to be in the hand of James West, who was many years Secretary to the Treasury.

C. A short history of the Custome House Affairs of North Brittaine since the Union, to the 5th of May, 1709.

D. List of incidental allowances to the officers in the Port of London and the Outports. Ladyday, 1748.

E. An abstract of the Civil List Act, 1782.

F. The Civil Establishment of Ireland on the 28th Jan. 1773.

G. The military establishment of Ireland as it stood the 1st Dec. 1772, including military pensions, half pay, barracks, etc.

H. A pocket-book, in vellum, labelled "Treasury," containing—"the Method of Business at the Treasury " on coining Money." "Distribution of business among " the several clerks." "Contents of Treasury books " and index."

I. A pocket-book, in vellum, containing Various public accounts, 1750–1759, with accounts of the Sinking Fund, 1722–1759. It seems like B., in the hand of James West.

K. A pocket-book, in vellum, containing Various public accounts, 1749–1751. In Jas. West's handwriting.

L. A small volume in morocco with silver clasps, containing a list of His Majesty's Royal Navy, 1st Aug. 1768.

Four vols. of Ryder's British Merlin, for 1767–1768, 1776, 1771, with some notes in pencil by Lord Shelburne.

I cannot conclude this Report without again expressing my sense of the courtesy and kindness experienced by me from the officials of the Public Record Office, and acknowledging the great assistance I have received from them.

EDMOND FITZMAURICE.

THE MANUSCRIPTS OF THE MOST HONOURABLE THE
MARQUIS OF SALISBURY.

1588.

Jan. 4. Th. Symes to [E. of Essex?].
Jan. 8. "876°" (Earl Bothwell) to [Arch. Douglas?].
Jan. 16. Thos. Lake to same.
Jan. 18. Sir F. Walsingham to same.
Jan. 19. Aldn. Billingsley to Ld. Burghley.
Jan. 19. Ric. Douglas to Arch. Douglas.
Jan. 20. Sir F. Walsingham to same.
Jan. 23. Jo. Marshall to same.
Jan. 26. Ric. Douglas to same.
[1588?] Jan. 28. R. Aston to Tho. Fowler.
Jan. 29. Sir Jo. Selby to Arch. Douglas.
Jan. —. Articles proposed in the Assembly of Nanci.
Jan. —. King of Scots to the State.
Feb. 2. Don Guillaum' de St. Clement to the Duke of
Parma.
Feb. 5. Causes of the great charges of Sir John
Norreys and Sir Francis Drake "about this journey."
Feb. 6. Agreement between W. Anderson and Arch.
Douglas touching perfection of a medicine called Uni-
versal.
Feb. 18. Ric. Douglas to Arch. Douglas.
Feb. 20. Lands offered to be assured to the Queen by
Lord Norris for a loan.
Feb. 21. W. Fowler to Arch. Douglas.
Feb. 21. Tho. Holdfort to same.
Feb. 24. Sir J. Morgan to same.
Feb. 26. Earl Bothwell to Musgrave, Capt. of Bean-
castle (this ought to be after 1593).
Feb. 26. Ld. J. Hamilton to Arch. Douglas.
Feb. 27. The Queen to Sir Thos. Shirley.
Feb. 28. Ric. Douglas to Arch. Douglas.
Feb. —. State of the lands of Lord Norris.
Feb. —. Names of the Lords Lieutenants in England
and Wales.
Mar. 1. Sir Jo. Peyton to Sec. Walsingham.
Mar. 1. Mayor of Lynn to same.
Mar. 1. P. Carvyll to Arch. Douglas.
Mar. 1. J. P. Tourner to same.
Mar. 3. Sieur de Tremblecourt to Count Charles,
Palatine of the Rhine.
Mar. 4. G. de Prouvency to Signor d'Allen.
Mar. 4. James Douglas to John Douglas.
Mar. 4. List of twenty barons who enjoy their baro-
nies in right of their wives.
Mar. 6. Sir F. Walsingham to Arch. Douglas.
Mar. 9. Ld. Sinclair to same.
Mar. 12. Ric. Douglas to same (2).
Mar. 15. John Montgomery to John Montgomery.
Mar. 16. The Queen to King of Scots.
Mar. 16. King of Scots to Arch. Douglas.
Mar. 18. Same to the Queen.
Mar. 19. Sir James Melville to Arch. Douglas.
Mar. 19. W. Douglas to same.
Mar. 20. John Smith to same.
Mar. 20. Lord J. Hamilton to same.
Mar. 20. R. Abercrombie (Burgess of Edinborough) to
same.
Mar. 24. Ric. Douglas to same.
Mar. 28. Same to same.
Mar. 30. Sir C. Stafford to the Queen.
April 4. Ric. Douglas to Arch. Douglas.
April 7. Charlotte de la Marck (afterwards wife of
Turenne) to the Duke Casimir.
April 11. Ld. Burghley to Mr. Wooley.
April 13. Ld. Zouch to Hy. Middlemore.
April 17. Nich. Evrington to Arch. Douglas.
April 26. Ric. Douglas to same.
April 27. Same to same.
April 27. James Melvill to same.
April 28. Ric. Douglas to same.
April 30. W. Douglas to same.
April 30. Privy Council to Ld. Burghley.
April —. Remembrances for Mr. Bodley touching the
matters of musters.
May 17. Ric. Douglas to Arch. Douglas.
May 20. P. Denais to Sec. Walsingham.
May 23. Ric. Tenys to Ld. Burghley.
May 26. Ric. Douglas to Arch. Douglas.
June 3. Sir F. Walsingham to same.
June 7. —— to ——.
June 8. Sam. Borthwick to Arch. Douglas.
June 10. Master of Gray to Ed. Johnston.
June 16. Instructions for Mr. Robert Cary sent into
Scotland.
June 18. W. Selby to Arch. Douglas.
[1588?]. June 20. James Colville to same.
June 22. Sir F. Walsingham to same.

June 27. The Queen to Ld. Burghley.
June 28. R. Beale to same.
June 28. Advertisements from Paris.
June 29. The Queen to Ld. Burghley.
June —. Ric. Douglas to Arch. Douglas.
June —. —— to the (K. of Scots).
July 4. The Queen to Ld. Burghley.
July 5. The English Commissioners to Dr. Dale.
July 7. E. of Derby to the Privy Council.
July 8. Sir Ja. Crofts to Ld. Burghley (Murdin).
July 8. E. of Derby to same.
July 8. The Queen to same.
July 8. The Queen to same.
July 9. Earl Bothwell to Arch. Douglas.
July 10. Ric. Douglas to same.
July 11. Sec. Herbert to same.
July 13. Nich. Evrington to same.
July 15. Hotman? to same.
July 16. The Queen to Ld. Burghley.
July 18. W. Selby to Arch. Douglas.
July 18. Th. Smith to Henry Killegrew.
July 18. Sec. Herbert to Arch. Douglas.
July 19. Ric. Douglas to same.
July 21. Jo. Brown to same.
July 22. Sec. Walsingham to same.
July 23. R. Carvyl to same.
July 27. Sec. Walsingham to same (Murdin).
July 28. The Queen to Ld. Burghley.
July 28. Sultan Murad the 2nd to the Queen.
July 31. W. Douglas to Arch. Douglas (of Whit-
tingham).
Aug. 1. Ric. Douglas to Arch. Douglas.
Aug. 3. The Queen to Ld. Burghley.
Aug. 3. John Robinson to same.
Aug. 4. King of Scots to the Queen.
Aug. 5. Ric. Douglas to Arch. Douglas.
Aug. 11. Tho. Fowler to same.
Aug. 11. Examination of two mariners of North Hol-
land, in Spanish Fleet.
Aug. 12. Charlotte de la Marck to E. of Leicester.
Aug. 13. Six Senators of Denmark to the Queen.
Aug. 14. Ric. Douglas to Arch. Douglas.
Aug. 14. Confession of Gilbert Gifford, prisoner in
Paris.
Aug. 22. Inventory of munitions in Limerick Castle.
Aug. 24. The Queen to Ld. Burghley.
Aug. 27. Robt. Bowes to Arch. Douglas.
Aug. 29. Sessions at Cork. Attainted lands of late E.
of Desmond in Waterford.
Aug. 30. Sam. Cockburn to Arch. Douglas.
Sept. 7. Ja. Colville to same (of Schiennes).
Sept. 7. King of Scots to same.
Sept. 8. Barges on the river Lee.
Sept. 8. Ordnance in custody of John Fagan, clerk of
munitions in Cork.
Sept. 8. Certificate of the arbitrators between the
Bishop of Hereford and Silvan Scorie for dilapidations.
Sept. 9. R. Douglas to Arch. Douglas.
Sept. 11. —— to Ld. Cobham.
Sept. 11. R. Douglas to Arch. Douglas (Lodge).
Sept. 11. W. Raven to Ld. Burghley.
Sept. 12. G. Beverley to Ld. Deputy of Ireland.
Sept. 16. R. Douglas to Arch. Douglas (Lodge).
Sept. 20. W. Raven to Ld. Burghley.
Sept. 25. Mr. Ortell to Arch. Douglas.
Sept. 28. Anth. Bacon to Lord Burghley.
Sept. 29. Privy Seals for payments, from 1571.
Oct. 5. J. P. Tourner to Arch. Douglas.
Oct. 5. The Queen to Ld. Scroope.
Oct. 8. Same to King of Scots.
Oct. 8. Anth. Bacon to Ld. Burghley.
Oct. 11. Money due to officers and soldiers serving in
Low Countries for two years ending
Oct. 14. Ld. Audelay to Ld. Burghley.
Oct. 17. Master of Gray to Arch. Douglas.
Oct. 22. Papers referring to Spanish pistoles taken
by Sir Francis Drake.
Oct. 23. Thos. Hodgson to Ld. Buckhurst.
Oct. 25. Thos. Arundel to Ld. Burghley.
Oct. 29. T. Fowler to Arch. Douglas.
Oct. 30. A. Durham to same.
Oct. —. J. Grenway to the Council.
Nov. 1. C. S. to Arch. Douglas.
Nov. 2. Calthorpe, Lord Mayor, to Ld. Burghley.
Nov. 2. Alderman Thos. Skinner to Arch. Douglas.
Nov. 4. Dr. Hammon to Ld. Burghley.
Nov. 5. Thos. Brune to same.
Nov. 6. Gilbert Fawle (?) to Arch. Douglas.
Nov. 6. Case of the Portreve of Mollingar and Theo-
bald Dillon.
Nov. 9. John Proband to Arch. Douglas.

Nov. 14. W. Cornwalleys to Ld. Burghley.
Nov. 20. Countess of Leicester to same.
Nov. 22. Ric. Douglas to Arch. Douglas.
Nov. 22. Same to Purie Ogilvey (Murdin).
Nov. 24. John Maye to Thos. Fowler.
Nov. 25. Thos. Fowler to Arch. Douglas.
Nov. 25. Sir John Selby to same.
Nov. 29. "876" to same.
Dec. 1. The Queen to King of Scots.
Dec. 1. The Queen to Ld. Burghley.
Dec. 3. Thos. Miller to Arch. Douglas.
Dec. 5. Sir John Selby to Arch. Douglas.
Dec. 9. J. P. Tourner to Arch. Douglas.
Dec. 16. "876" to same.
Dec. 20. Ric. Stonley to Ld. Burghley.
Dec. 20. Robt. Petre to same.
Dec. 20. Sir A. Cornwalleys to same.
Dec. 31. Sir Thos. Cornwalleys to Ld. Burghley.
Dec. 31. Sir W. Stewart to Arch. Douglas.
Dec —. James Douglas to John Douglas.
Dec. —. Privy Council to Sir Jo. Morgan.
—— R. Grahame to Arch. Douglas.
—— Ric. Douglas to the same.
—— Mr. Harris to Ld. Burghley.
—— R. Cooburne to James Sincler.
—— John Colville to Arch. Douglas.
—— J. P. Tourner to same.
—— Governor of St. Michael's Mount to the Privy
Council.
—— Auditor Peyton to the same.
—— De Nassau (?) to Arch. Douglas.
—— Sir Jo. Selby to Arch. Douglas.
1588. Extraordinary payments in the Low Countries.
1588. Rates of pay for the officers and crew of a
Flemish ship of war in the English service.
1588. Instructions to Don Martin de Pashilla, captain-
general of the gallies of Spain, as regards the discipline
of the men while at sea.
1588. Names and number of ships that serve against
the Spanish fleets.
1588. Offences and sentence of Gilbert Sherington.
1588. Collection of accidents, chiefly foreign affairs,
from 1578.
1588. Answers to queries respecting ores.
1588. Treaty between Elizabeth and Phillip II.
1588. Answer to Ambassadors of Scotland.
1588. Oration by G. Gifford to Cardinal of Seville.
1588. Declaration of K. of France (Hen. III.) to the
Queen Mother against peace with the Leaguers.
1588. Ships of Spain for invasion of England (orig.
draft).
1588. Genealogy of the Siteilts of Haultereinnos in
Eves, Hereford, in two branches. Sir W. Cecil, Ld.
Burghley, and Wm. Siteilt of Haultereinnes.
(1588.) Mem. of Salt-matter at Burwaje.
(1588.) Answer to queries respecting ores.
(1588.) Brief discourse on League (Fr.).
(1588.) Discourse touching Duke of Guise, his taking
arms, &c.
1588. Scripturarum et Patrum Testimonia ad defensionem Religionis Ecclesiæ Anglicanæ.
Doctor Hammon to Lo. Burghley on offices of Bishop
and Presbyter in New Testament.
(1588.) Risposta data dalla Reina d'Inghilterra all'
Ambass. del Re di Polonia et di Suecia.
1588. Questions to and replies of James Digges,
Muster Master of the Low Countries.
1588. Certificates for the pay of two lancers under
the Earl of Leicester.

1589.

Jan. 1. Lup La Tras to Tho. Wilks (Spanish).
Jan. 2. Rafe Lane to Ld. Burghley.
Jan. 12. E. Bothwell to Arch. Douglas.
Jan. 13. "Y" to Sec. Walsingham.
Jan. 15. Apostiles to doubts set down by James
Digges, as to the Low Country Musters.
Jan. 27. Sec. Walsingham to Arch. Douglas.
Jan. 28. Sir Thos. Smith to Ld. Burghley.
Jan. —. Defects in the treaty with the Low Countries.
Feb. 4. The Queen to Ld. Burghley (2).
Feb. 4. Same to same.
Feb. 4. Sec. Walsingham to Th. Wilks.
Feb. 4. Privy Council to Ld. Burghley.
Feb. 5. Same to Ld. Burghley.
Feb. 9. Sec. Walsingham to Arch. Douglas.
Feb. 10. J. Hudson to same.
Feb. 17. Countess of Leicester to Ld. Burghley.
Feb. 17. J. Constable to Arch. Douglas.
Feb. 20. Countess of Leicester to Ld. Burghley.
Feb. 22. Privy Council to same.

Feb. 25. The Queen to King of Scots.
Feb. 28. W. Douglas to Arch. Douglas.
Mar. 1. Master of Sprot to Arch. Douglas.
Mar. 1. Justices of Norfolk to Privy Council.
Mar. 1. Inventory by Dav. Dod and Wm. Normanby,
of household stuff of Ld. Cobham, in Blackfriars,
London.
Mar. 2. J. Hamilton to Arch. Douglas (of Coverton).
Mar. 4. Ld. Willoughby to Privy Council.
Mar. 7. Ric. Douglas to Arch. Douglas (of Coverton).
Mar. 13. G. Grahame to same.
Mar. 13. E. Johnstone to same.
Mar. 13. W. Billingsley to Ld. Burghley.
Mar. 13. C. S. (an officer of rank in the Scotch guard
of France) to Arch. Douglas.
Mar. 16. Humfry Fryers to same.
Mar. 16. Countess of Leicester to Ld. Burghley.
Mar. 17. Sir Jo. Fortescue to Auditor of the Ex-
chequer.
Mar. 19. Sir E. Denny to Sir F. Walsingham.
Mar. 20. "Y" to Sir F. Walsingham.
Mar. 20. H. Billingsley to Ld. Burghley.
Mar. 20. Roger Aston to Arch. Douglas.
Mar. 22. Ric. Douglas to same.
Mar. 23. Chancellor Hatton to Ld. Burghley.
Mar. 29. Geo. Comerford to Ld. Deputy of Ireland.
April 1. R. Grahame to Arch. Douglas.
April 3. —— to Ed. Isham.
April 5. —— to Sec. Walsingham.
April 6. "876-" (Earl Bothwell) to Arch. Douglas.
April 6. —— to Arch. Douglas.
April 9. Ric. Douglas to same.
April 9. Alex. Bonus to Sir F. Walsingham.
April 10. T. Fowler to Arch. Douglas.
April 11. R. Carvyl to same.
April 11. Contents of letters written to the Queen from
foreign parts.
April 11. "876" to Arch. Douglas.
April 11. Sir Jo. Wogan to Sec. Walsingham.
April 12. Same to Sir Julius Cæsar.
April 13. Chancellor Maitland to Arch. Douglas.
April 13. Sir. Jo. Wogan to same.
April 13. Archbp. of Canterbury to Ld. Buckhurst.
April 21. Ja. Somers to Arch. Douglas.
April 22. King of Scots to Arch. Douglas.
April 23. C. S. to same.
April 26. The Queen to Ld. Burghley.
April 27. Occurrents out of Scotland.
May 1. Protest of Clement Dray of London, prisoner
for debt.
May 2. The Queen to Ld. Burghley.
May 2. Same to the King of Scots.
May 3. Sir R. Constable to Sec. Walsingham.
May 3. Sir James Melvile to Arch. Douglas.
May 5. T. Fowler to same.
May 6. —— of Galbardes to same.
May 10. Ld. Deputy and Council of Ireland to the
Commissioners.
May 10. Commission to certain of Council as Com-
missioners for pacification in Conaught.
May 10. Sir W. Herbert to Ld. Burghley.
May 16. Chr. Perkins to Sir F. Walsingham.
May 19. Geo. Beverley to Arch. Douglas.
May 19. The Queen to King of Scots.
May 20. King of Navarre to Ld. Burghley.
May 20. Master of Gray to the Queen.
May 22. Dr. Hammon to Sir F. Knollis.
May 23. Chanc. Maitland to Arch. Douglas.
May 24. Sir F. Knollys to Ld. Burghley.
May 26. Privy Council to Ld. Burghley.
May 27. Sir Jo. Norris to Capt. George.
May 27. Les Defences et Procedures touchant l'em-
prisonnement et la ransom de Monr. l'Evesque de
Rosse.
June 7. Ph. Howard to Ld. Burghley (E. of Arundel).
June 7. Anne Countess Arundel to same.
June 18. Ld. Burghley to Arch. Douglas.
June 25. J. Fowler to same.
June 27. J. Johnston to same.
June 27. James Innes to Geo. Car.
June 27. Master of Gray to Ld. Burghley.
June 27. Bp. of Ross's testimonial of character for
Jas. Gispatrick.
June —. Instructions to Geo. Earl Marshal, Ld. Keith
and Altories, lieut. in the North, and Ld. Dingwall, &c.,
ambassadors for marriage of (James) with Princess of
Denmark.
July 2. Obligation of Hen. Ld. Cobham to his brother
for 200l.
July 6. Privy Council to Ld. Burghley.
July 8. J. Dervinz to Herr Brokis.

July 11. The Queen to Ld. Burghley.
July 13. Privy Council to same.
July 20. Sir F. Walsingham to Arch. Douglas.
July 22. Customer of Sandwich to Ld. Burghley.
July 24. Privy Council to same.
July 29. Hotman to Arch. Douglas.
July 31. Ric. Douglas to same.
[1589.] Aug. 1. J. Colville to Arch. Douglas.
Aug. 6. Advertisements from St. Malories.
Aug. 12. Ric. Douglas to Arch. Douglas.
Aug. 16. Sir Jul. Cæsar to Sec. Walsingham.
Aug. 16. The Queen to Ld. Burghley.
Aug. 16. Ric. Douglas to Arch. Douglas.
Aug. 20. R. Sydney to Lord Burghley.
Aug. 23. Ric. Douglas to Arch. Douglas.
Aug. 29. Ld. North to Ld. Burghley.
Aug. 31. Capt. Ed. Garett to Capt. Ed. Waynman.
Sept. 1. W. Cockburn to Arch. Douglas.
Sept. 8. Ld. Burghley to same.
Sept. 10. Ja. Colville (of Schiennes) to same.
Sept. 11. Sir H. Nevil to Ld. Burghley.
Sept. 17. Ric. Tomson to Sir F. Walsingham.
Sept. 25. Debts due to H.M. payable in Exchequer, and others payable by customers, collectors of subsidies, and fifteenths.
Sept. 26. Philip Howard to Lord Burghley (Earl of Arundel).
Sept. 28. Sir Thos. Arundel to same.
Sept. 29. Money paid on Privy Seals from Exchequer Feb. 8, &c.
Sept. —. Charges of Capt. Yorke about a pinnace of Odyner in France.
Oct. 7. T. Fowler to Ld. Burghley (Murdin).
Oct. 13. Geo. French to Arch. Douglas.
Oct. 17. Certain Captains to the Privy Council.
Oct. 18. R. Lang to Arch. Douglas.
Oct. 20. Th. Fowler to Ld. Burghley.
Oct. 20. Same to Arch. Douglas.
Oct. 24. Jo. Colville to Ld. Burghley.
Oct. 25. Duc de Bouillon to M. de la Fontaine.
Oct. —, Queen Elizabeth to the Q. of Navarre.
Nov. 1. Ld. Burgh to Ld. Burghley.
Nov. 2. (Ric. Douglas) to (Arch. Douglas).
Nov. 2. (Same) to Monsr. Constable.
Nov. 8. T. Fowler to Ld. Burghley.
Nov. 9. H. Billingsley to same.
Nov. 13. Privy Council to the Auditor of Bedford.
Nov. 13. W. Selby to Arch. Douglas.
Nov. 23. Journies of Pet. Værhalius in Sweden, &c., commencing 1 Sept.
Nov. 24. Accounts of Sir W. Pelham, lieut. of ordnance.
Nov. 30. H. Billingsley to Ld. Burghley.
Nov. 30. Issues of a Privy Seal for 8,000l. for forces in Ireland.
Dec. 7. T. Fowler to Arch. Douglas.
Dec. 8. "M" to "F" (Walsingham).
Dec. 9. R. Douglas to Arch. Douglas.
Dec. 12. Geo. Leicester to Mr. Daniel (Bergen op Zoom.)
Dec. 12. R. Carlisle to Arch. Douglas.
Dec. 12. Florence Macarthy to Ld. Burghley.
Dec. 13. H. Billingsley to Ld. Burghley.
Dec. 13. Chr. Sclander to Arch. Douglas.
Dec. 18. H. Billingsley to Ld. Burghley.
Dec. 19. Adam Wachendorf to Sir F. Walsingham.
Dec. 20. [Ric. Douglas] to [Arch. Douglas].
Dec. 24. The Queen to Ld. Burghley.
—— W. Hunter to Arch. Douglas.
—— Ld. Cranston to same.
—— Magistrates of Edinburgh to same.
—— E. of Essex to Sieur de la Noue.
—— Same to Vice Chamberlain (Murdin).
—— Countess of Leicester to E. of Essex.
—— Account of Receiver of the Court.
[1589.] The Queen to K. of Navarre (3).
1589. E. of Arundel to the Queen.
1589. Privy Council to Lieuts. of Shires.
1589. Paul Wentworth to the Queen.
[1589.] [Arch. Douglas] to [Ld. Burghley?].
1589. Orders for the more speedy arming and furnishing of the Herts soldiers by Ld. Burghley.
1589. Relation of such things as Wm. Pyttes had intelligence of, being prisoner in the Groynes.
(1589?) Instructions to the Earl of Leicester (by Arch. Douglas).
(1589?) Instructions to Sir F. Walsingham (by Arch. Douglas).
1589. Entertainment per diem of the Lord General, &c. in Low Countries.

1589. View of yearly values, deductions, &c. of manors, lands, &c. in sundry counties, escheated by attainder of Philip late Earl of Arundel.
1589. Mem. as to Bond for 315l. granted by Sir F. Walsingham to Arch. Douglas, and of 500l. owing by Douglas to Walsingham.
(1589.) General syllogisms and points of a most imperious and virulent book.
(1589.) Considerations touching the peace of France by M. Bucenval.
(1589.) Declaration des justes causes qui ont constraint le Roy de Navarre de recourir aux armes.
(1589.) Cost of cutting, &c. two diamonds for the Queen.

1590.

Jan. 7. The Queen to Lieutenants of Counties.
Jan. 7. H. Billingsley to Ld. Burghley.
Jan. 9. Tho. Morgan to Captn. Bradford.
Jan. 20. Fran. de Civille to Sir F. Walsingham.
Feb. 5. Ric. Douglas to Arch. Douglas.
Feb. 5. H. Billingsley to Ld. Burghley.
Feb. 9. Ric. Douglas to Arch. Douglas.
Feb. 12. Same to same.
Feb. 12. Declaration of account of Arth. Atye, Receiver of Fines 24, Jan.
Feb. 13. Skinners of London to the Queen.
[Feb. 13.] Same to Ld. Burghley.
Feb. 17. License to Fran. Le Forte to transport goods from the East through England to France.
Feb. 26. Ric. Douglas to Arch. Douglas.
Feb. 27. Dr. W. Aubrey and Sir J. Cæsar to Ld. Burghley.
Feb. 27. Exchequer accounts.
Feb. —. Prohibitio formata de Statuto Articuli Cleri.
Feb. —. E. of Essex to bailiffs, &c. of Leinster.
Mar. 1. Justice Clerk to Arch. Douglas.
Mar. 4. Thos. Wyat to Sir F. Walsingham.
Mar. 6. Vincent Skinner to Ld. Burghley.
Mar. 7. E. Grimeston to same.
Mar. 7. Vincent Skinner to Lo. Burghley.
Mar. 9. Ric. Douglas to Arch. Douglas.
Mar. 16. T. Douglas to same.
Mar. 23. Syndic & Council of Geneva to Ld. Burghley.
Mar. 23. Same to the Queen.
Mar. 23. Genealogia Dominorum de Lacy. Pedigrees of Lancashire and other families.
April 1. Burninus, Dux Stetin, &c. to the Queen.
April 3. R. Bruce to Arch. Douglas.
April 3. Ric. Douglas to same.
April 5. —— to Sec. Walsingham.
April 9. Ric. Douglas to Arch. Douglas.
April 10. Receipt for money for soldiers provided by co. Cambridge.
April 12. Sir J. Conway to Sir F. Walsingham.
April 12. Undertaking of Jacques de Barlaer to furnish intelligence from the Low Countries.
April 17. Robt. Carvyl to Arch. Douglas.
April 17. The Queen to King of Scots.
April 18. Lord Setoun to Arch. Douglas.
April 22. C. S. to same.
[1589?] April 28. Henry the Fourth to E. of Essex.
April 29. H. Billingsley to Ld. Burghley.
May 8. M. de Buzenval to Lagny.
May 14. Sir R. Sidney to Ld. Burghley (Murdin).
May 15. John Douglas to Arch. Douglas.
May 19. Sir Jo. Fortescue and Sir Jo. Wolley to same.
May 20. Th. Holdfort to same.
May 26. The Queen to Sir Tho. Heneage.
May —. Proceedings touching the imprisonment of the Bp. of Ross.
June 3. Earl of Emden to the Queen.
June 3. Countess of Emden to same.
June 5. Henry IV. to French Ambassador in England.
June 5. Lords Willoughby and Burgh and others to the Queen.
June 9. Henry IV. to the French Ambassador in England.
June 11. W. Dundas to Arch. Douglas (Lodge).
June 13. J. Gibson to same.
June 13. M. de Beauvoir, French ambassador, to Lord Burghley.
June 15. Sir F. Gorges to E. of Essex.
June 16. E. of Essex to Sir Thos. Heneage.
June 17. The Queen to Ld. Burghley.
June 23. Jo. Woodward (priest) to Ld. Seton.
June 24. Bp. of Ross to King of Scots.
June 24. Bp. of Ross to Duke of Lennox.
June 24. Same to E. of Huntly.
June 24. Same to Countess of Huntly.

June 24. Same to Lord Seton.
June 25. Same to Tho. Ogilvie.
June 25. Same to Lord Pryor of Pluscardin.
June 25. Same to Mrs. Helen Lesly.
June 26. Same to George Car.
June 26. Same to David Clephane.
June 26. Same to Andrew Lisle.
June 26. Same to W. Leslie.
June 26. Same to Richard Irving.
June 27. Bp. of Ross's testimonial of character for
James Gispatrick.
June 27. Bp. of Ross to Tho. Ogilvie.
June 27. Thos. Leslie to Alex. Leslie.
June 29. The Queen to Ld. Burghley.
1590. June 29. Thomas Leslie to Jeane Keythe.
[June.] Mr. Udall's submission.
July 1. Sir Jo. Wolley to E. of Bath.
July 12. Sir Thos. Heneage to Sir R. Cecil.
July 12. The Queen to Mr. Wilkes and Mr. Bodley.
July 20. Summons to Archibald Douglas to appear
before the Court of Sessions, Edinburgh.
July 22. Andrew Martinho to Ld. Burghley.
July 22. List of English & Irish in the service of the
Prince of Parma.
July 27. Sir F. Allen to E. of Essex.
July 28. Privy Council to Ld. Burghley.
July —. Les troupes commandées pour le voiage de
France (Parma's).
(July) Matters concluded in the Edinburgh con-
vention.
July 16. Grant to Lo. Hen. Seymour of 300l. annuity.
Aug. 19. Sir R. Melvil to Arch. Douglas.
Aug. 20. Geo. Blincoe to same.
Aug. 24. E. of Huntingdon to Sec. (Walsingham).
Aug. 25. Sir J. Cæsar to Arch. Douglas.
Aug. 26. Sir Jo. Stanhope to same.
Sept. 5. Joachim Fredericus (eldest son of Mary of
Brandenburg) to King of Scots.
Sept. 6. The Queen to the States (2) (Murdin).
Sept. 6. Same to divers towns of the Low Countries.
Sept. 7. H. Billingsley to Ld. Burghley.
Sept. 7. The Queen to Sir R. Sydney.
Sept. 7. Same to Sir F. Vere.
Sept. 9. Same to Sir Thos. Bodley.
Sept. 10. Same to Ld. Mayor of London.
Sept. 12. Same to Ld. Burghley.
Sept. 12. Linen washed for Sir John Perrot, from the
2d May.
Sept. 13. John Greenwood and Henry Barrow to Ld.
Burghley.
Sept. 17. Ric. Douglas to Arch. Douglas.
Sept. 18. John Greenwood and Henry Barrow to Ld.
Burghley.
Sept. 18. Bp. of Ross to Arch. Douglas.
[1590?] 19. Henry IV. to E. of Essex.
Sept. 22. Sir Jo. Wogan to Ld. Burghley.
Sept. 22. The Queen to ——.
Sept. 22. Same to the Receiver.
Sept. 22. Same to Lord Scroope.
Sept. 23. Mr. Freake's certificate of sale moneys in
Ireland.
Sept. 29. Cæsar Walpcott to Mr. Dewhurst.
Sept. 29. Carlyle to Arch. Douglas.
Sept. —. Same to Sir Jo. Lucy and others.
Oct. 2. E. of Essex to Bailif, &c. of Leominster.
Oct. 6. —— to Sec. Walsingham.
Oct. 6. The Queen to Lieutenants of Counties.
Oct. 9. Ld. Hunsdon to Sir Thos. Heneage.
Oct. 11. The Council to Sir W. Fitzwilliam (2).
Oct. 15. Francis Merbury to Ld. Burghley.
Oct. 24. (Sir) W. Stewart to Arch. Douglas.
Oct. 24. E. of Essex to Sir H. Unton.
Nov. 3. Causes moving the Catholic league of France
to join with the King of Spain.
Nov. 7. Parsons, the Jesuit, to Dr. Barret.
Nov. 8. Robt. Naunton to Mr. Reynolds.
Nov. 10. Ld. Burghley to Arch. Douglas.
Nov. 12. Caius Coll., Cambridge, to E. of Essex.
Nov. 14. Estimate of probable payments from the
Exchequer.
Nov. 19. Sir Th. Bodley to Arch. Douglas.
Nov. 20. The Queen to Ld. Burghley.
Nov. 21. Same to same.
Nov. 21. Otwell Smith to Ld. Burghley.
Dec. 2. Lesly, Bp. of Ross, to Arch. Douglas.
Dec. 4. Sir F. Walsingham to same.
Dec. 18. Michael Moody to Sir Thos. Heneage.
Dec. 21. Hotman to Arch. Douglas.
Dec. — The Queen to Sir E. Norris.
(1590?) Declaration of John Gatacre.
—— E. of Essex to Sir H. Unton.

—— Sir W. Ralegh to Sir R. Cecil.
—— Sir T. Vavasour to same.
1590. The Queen to the Ld. Admiral and others.
1590. Captain Baker to the Queen.
1590. Sir Tho. Bodley to [? Lord Burghley].
1590. Earl Bothwell to Arch. Douglas.
1590. M. Leman to Privy Council.
1590. Geo. Thorisby to Sir R. Cecil.
1590. Privy Council to Ld. Deputy of Ireland.
1590. The Queen to Lo. Sheffield.
1590. Fran. Hastings to Duke Broke.
(1590.) Extracts of letters written from Calais.
1590. Account of the battle of Ivry, by a Leaguer.
1590. Matters to be seen into of the Lady Lennox's
lands.
1590. Agreement between France and England for
the sending of 6,000 men into Brittany.
1590. Of the offices of the moral law.
1590. Points to be considered in the articles for
acknowledging the laws ecclesiastical, &c.
(1590.) Captain Borthwick's discourse on the marriage
of James, &c.
1590. Treasury of the Chamber payment.
1590. List of Mayors for Coventry, with chronology
of events, from 1347.
1590. Copie du Serment fait aux Etats Unies par la
Royne d'Angleterre et le Prince Maurice.
1590. Report of Dr. Cæsar and Mr. Waad.
1590. A short progress for Her Majesty.
(1590.) Answers of Geo. Collymore to articles of ship
"Christopher" of Kirkaldy by Ambassador of Scotland.
1590. Diet and ransom of Spanish prisoners, by Edw.
Burnham.

1591.

Jan. 6. Th. Moffet to E. of Essex.
Jan. 7. The Queen to Ld. Burghley.
Jan. 8. Maurice Kiffin to E. of Essex.
Jan. 22. J. Moubray to Arch. Douglas. Duc de
Bouillon to Mr. Edmonds.
Jan. 24. (——) to Mr. Hayes.
Feb. 1. The Queen to Ld. Burghley.
Feb. 8. Instructions for Musters, &c. from Privy
Council to Lo. Deputy of Ireland.
Feb. 13. J. Garts to Lord Burghley.
Feb. 19. Customers of London to same.
Feb. 22. J. Harpur (priest) to N. Williamson.
Feb. —. W. Cornwalleys to Sir R. Cecil.
[Feb. —]. [Hen. de la Tour F] to ——.
Mar. 1. The Queen to Ld. Burghley.
Mar. 2. E. of Southampton to E. of Essex.
Mar. 10. Sigr. Filiarzi to Lo. Burghley.
Mar. 16. The Queen to same.
Mar. 29. [Ld. Burghley] to [Ld. Mayor of London].
Mar. 27. Dr. Aubrey and Sir J. Cæsar to the Privy
Council.
Mar. —. Ricardus Baro Arembeginus, legato Scotorum
regis, Lundini.
Mar. —. Dormant Privy Seals and others for pay-
ments out of Exchequer. From Easter 1590.
April 5. R. Carmarden to Ld. Burghley.
April 6. The Queen to same.
April 13. R. Parsons (Jesuit) to Juan Jicilio, y Juan
Fixerio, Clerigos Yngleses on Lisboa.
April 14. The Queen to Casimir, Count Palatine of
the Rhine.
April 20. R. Norton to Juan des Ambras.
April 24. R. Carmarden to Lord Burghley.
April 30. Jacques Barbaer to Sir Jo. Conway.
April 30. The Queen to Lord Burghley.
April —. The Queen to same.
April —. Charge of town of Chesthunt.
April —. Information to be obtained by Jacques
Barbaer in Low Countries.
May 6. Ld. Burghley to Arch. Douglas.
May 10. Jas. Boylo to Sir Jo. Conway.
May 14. Customers of London to Ld. Burghley.
May 15. King of France to E. of Essex.
May 16. Ric. Douglas to Arch. Douglas.
May 17. Queen to Ld. Burghley.
May 18. Ric. Douglas to Arch. Douglas.
May 21. King of France to E. of Essex.
May 28. Gilbert, E. of Shrewsbury, to Lord Burghley.
May —. Order for 500 men for Britanny, in L.
Burleigh's hand.
May —. Defects in answer of Th. Cartwright and
others.
June 2. Sir R. Cecil to Lord Burghley.
June 8. E. of Essex to Sir H. Unton.
June 11. W. Fowler to Arch. Douglas.
June 13. Sir Den. Rowghane (priest) to the Queen.
June 13. King of France to same.

June 15. The Queen's allowance and the Lo. Mayor's demand for conduct money.
June 18. King of France to E. of Essex.
June 20. Same to the Queen.'
June 23. Mayor and Corporation of Bristol to the Privy Council.
June 26. Mayor and Corporation of Southampton to same.
June 28. Magistrates of Bridgewater to Ld. Burghley.
June 28. Mayor, &c. of Lynn to the Council.
June 28. McGrahan Roman Catholic Abp. of Armagh to ——.
June 28. Gamon McGabren to Capt. Oliviera.
June 28. Magistrates of Barnstable to Ld. Burghley.
June 28. Mayor of Padstow to same.
June 28. Paul Lombard to Th. White, Louvain.
June 30. Magistrates of Hull to Ld. Burghley.
June 30. The Mayor, &c. of Newcastle to Privy Council.
July 2. Bailiffs of Yarmouth to Privy Council.
July 5. Hen. Nisbet to Jo. Nisbet.
July 11. The English commander to Ld. Burghley.
July 16. Lo. Burghley to Arch. Douglas.
July 19. R. Carmarden to Ld. Burghley.
July 26. M. Morgan to the E. of Essex.
July 26. T. Morgan to same.
July 28. E. of Bath to W. Peter and A. Worth.
July 29. Ric. Douglas to Arch. Douglas.
July 30. Ld. Willoughby to E. of Essex.
July 31. John Harper to Wilson.
July —. Confession of John Lewys (relating to the succession).
Aug. 1. Anonymous to Father Will. Holte.
Aug. 3. Sir H. Unton to Earl of Essex.
Aug. 7. Sir Thos. Sherley to same.
Aug. 7. Anth. Pembrugge to same.
Aug. 12. Sir Thos. Heneage to Sir Jo. Fortescue.
Aug. 14. E. of Essex to Treasurer of Wars.
Aug. 15. King of France to the Queen.
Aug. 17. Ric. Douglas to Arch. Douglas.
Aug. 19. King of France to E. of Essex.
Aug. 22. M. de Montmorency to same.
Aug. 26. John Hamilton (of Everton) to Arch. Douglas.
Aug. 30. King of France to E. of Essex.
Aug. —. Edw. Prime to same.
Aug. —. Marq. of Guasto to same.
[   ] Same to —— Raulet.
Sept. 6. Sir Rog. Williams to E. of Essex.
Sept. 6. —— Mony to same.
Sept. 7. Sir R. Williams to same.
Sept. 9. [Marq. Guasto] to same.
Sept. 10. R. Downhale to same.
Sept. 10. Sir R. Williams to same.
Sept. 14. King of France to same.
Sept. 15. [Maq. Guasto] to same.
Sept. 16. A Secretary of the E. of Essex to Lady Essex.
Sept. 16. H. Kyllegrew to E. of Essex.
Sept. 17. King of France to same.
Sept. 18. Sir H. Lee to Sir Thos. Heneage.
Sept. 19. —— to E. of Essex.
Sept. 22. H. Killegrew to same.
Sept. 22. Sir Thos. Shirley to Sir R. Cecil.
Sept. 24. Sir R. Williams to E. of Essex.
Sept. 24. Wm. Wylie to Mr. Ashby.
Sept. 26. Sir A. Ashley to E. of Essex.
Sept. 27. Marshal Biron to same.
Oct. 1. Marq. of Guasto to same.
Oct. 3. De la Fontaine to same.
Oct. 4. R. Brackenbury to same.
Oct. 4. The Queen to same (Murdin).
Oct. 5. Sir Chr. Hatton to same (do.).
Oct. 7. M. M(oody) to same.
Oct. 9. Sir E. Grimston to same.
Oct. 12. Ld. Burghley to Sir Thos. Heneage.
Oct. 13. Henri de Bourbon (Prince de Conde) to E. of Essex.
Oct. 14. T. (Moody) to —— (2).
Oct. 14. F. de Rihon to Mr. Reynolds.
Oct. 14. T. Smith to Mr. Reynolds.
Oct. 15. Sir Thos. Leighton to E. of Essex.
Oct. 17. The Queen to the Ld. Chancellor.
Oct. 20. Sir R. Williams to E. of Essex.
Oct. 20. King of France to same.
Oct. 20. Jo. Lindsay to Arch. Douglas.
Oct. 22. Ld. Burghley to E. of Essex (Murdin).
Oct. 23. Ric. Douglas to Arch. Douglas.
Oct. 24. The Queen to Merchant Adventurers, &c.
Oct. 24. W. Forske to Mr. Reynolds.
Oct. 25. M. Kyffen to E. of Essex.
Oct. 26. W. Foulkes to Anthony ——.

Oct. 27. Sir H. Unton to E. of Essex.
Oct. 29. Privy Council to Mayor of Padstow.
Oct. 29. H. Killegrew to E. of Essex.
Oct. 30. Marshal de Biron to same.
Oct. 30. Same to same.
Oct. 31. H. Killegrew to same.
Oct. —. R. Fouller to Arch. Douglas.
Nov. 1. R. Carmarden and Thos. Middleton to Lord Burghley.
Nov. 1. De la Noue (?) to E. of Essex.
Nov. 1. Ld. Cobham to Th. Wilks.
Nov. 2. King of France to E. of Essex.
Nov. 2. H. Killegrew to same.
Nov. 3. Sir Tho. Acton to same.
Nov. 5. Judgment of Matt. Carew and Keeng Pawle of property of Thos. Fowler.
Nov. 8. Instructions for Austin Halfdone sent to Spain.
Nov. 10. Hughe Allington to Barnard Dewhurst.
Nov. 10. De la Noue (?) to E. of Essex.
Nov. 11. R. Wright to Mr. Reynolds.
Nov. 14. Montmorency to E. of Essex.
Nov. 15. King of Scots to Lord Burghley.
Nov. 23. Sir Jo. Conway to J. de Barlner.
Nov. 27. E. of Essex to Privy Council.
Nov. 27. S. Pettingarre to —— Reynolds.
Nov. —. Estate of co. Devon for horses for Queen's service. Signed R. Champernown.
Dec. 2. W. Foulkes to —— Reynolds.
[Dec. 4.] Particulars of ships and goods, salt, &c. from Scotch traders.
Dec. 9. Thos. Smith to Sir R. Cecil (Murdin).
Dec. 10. Sir W. Russell to E. of Essex.
Dec. 11. Thos. Smith to Dr. White.
Dec. 13. Jo. and Lau. Beresford to the Queen.
Dec. 14. The Queen to Ld. Burghley.
Dec. 16. W. Foulkes to —— Reynolds.
Dec. 16. The Queen to Ld. Burghley.
Dec. 18. Grant of lease to Kath. Hooper, daughter of John Frankwell, gentleman usher, Greenwich. Signed by the Queen.
Dec. 20. E. of Northumberland to Lord Burghley.
Dec. 21. Lo. Cobham to Thos. Milles.
Dec. 23. E. of Essex to Sir R. Cecil.
Dec. 23. Jo. Gerdos to Ld. Burghley.
Dec. 24. The Queen to the E. of Essex.
Dec. 26. Privy Council to Ld. Burghley.
Dec. 26. The Queen to same.
Dec. 29. Grant of lease to Matt. Petley, yeoman of the chamber, Richmond. Signed by the Queen.
Dec. —. Mem. by Lo. Burghley of the state of the Conclave upon the death of Pope Innocent IX.
Dec. —. Roger de Bellegarde to E. of Essex.
Dec. —. Sir M. Arundel, R. Frake, &c., to Ld. Hunsdon.
Dec. —. Gaspar Dias (an attendant to the late Antonio) to (E. of Essex ?).
Dec. —. Countess of Essex to same.
Dec. —. Ric. Lee to same.
Dec. —. E. of Essex to the Gov. of Dieppe.
Dec. —. L. St. (anonymous) to [E. of Essex].
Dec. —. Sir Rog. Williams to Ld. Burghley.
Dec. —. Sir T. Baskerville to E. of Essex (2).
Dec. —. Ministers of the Reformed Church at Dieppe to E. of Essex.
Dec. —. Philippe de Mornay to same.
Dec. —. Sir E. Stafford to same.
Dec. —. Mayor, &c. of Weymouth to Privy Council.
Dec. —. Royal visits to Lo. Burghley at Theobalds, from 1572.
Dec. —. Divisions of forces for Devon into three parts.
Dec. —. Officers of Queen's army in France, under E. of Essex.
Dec. —. Jo. Heath to Rob. Whyte.
——. Mems., requisition for forces, etc.
1591. Discorso a la Sacra Catolica Real Magistad.
1591. Political state of Spain, &c., by Antonio Perez.
—— Explanatory memor. of Italian correspondence.
1591. Parishes in Hayeton Coleridge, Devon, for Sir Jo. Gilbert's and Mr. Carye's private bands.
1591. Grant of manor of Battersea to Eliz. Rydon and Johan Hollcroft. Signed by the Queen.
[1591.] Grant to Barth. Fawkyner, Alb. Holland, and Avery Butcher.
[1591.] Mem. of a cavalry skirmish.
[1591.] Grant to Thos. Gerrard of a company of 150 men, by death of Capt. Rainsford.
[1591.] Information concerning John Wilson [seminary priest].

5.

[1591.] —— to ——, waggons and horses for army,
and draft of same.
[1591.] —— to —— of a page and money upon a
treaty of marriage.
[1591.] —— to —— of Lieut. Floyd's return into
England.
[1591.] Payment to Sir Rog. Williams, Capt. Gorge,
Capt. Cumberland, and Capt. Ranesford.
[1591.] Questions for one out of Ireland having been
in Spain.

1592.

Jan. 6. Privy Council to Sir W. Raleigh.
Jan. 14. Apostles to consideration of checks re-
spited by Ja. Digges.
Jan. 15. Middleton, Bp. of St. David's, to the Queen.
Jan. 16. Ed. Palmer to Ld. Burghley.
Jan. 17. Sir W. Malorye to E. of Essex.
Jan. 18. The Queen to Ld. Burghley.
Jan. 22. W. Waad to Sir R. Cecil.
Feb. 7. Advertisements from Spain to Lo. Cobham.
Feb. 8. Edm. Palmer to Lo. Burghley.
Feb. 9. Ric. Douglas to Arch. Douglas.
Feb. 10. Edm. Palmer to Lo. Burghley.
Feb. 12. Account of Arth. Atie, Receiver General of
Fines, &c.
Feb. 16. M. de Soldaigne to Mr. Reynolds.
Mar. 1. Ja. Morrice to Ld. Burghley.
Mar. 1. Committee to confer with House of Lords.
Mar. 4. Sir M. Arundel to Sir R. Cecil.
Mar. 4. Geo. Henderson and 13 others to Arch. Doug-
las.
Mar. 8. Anonymous to Privy Council.
Mar. 8. Committees for relief of maimed soldiers and
mariners.
Mar. 10. Francois Curio (?) to Monr. de Dauveny.
Mar. 14. Ordnance for St. Mary Isle, Scilly. F.
Godolphin.
Mar. 19. John Brown to Arch. Douglas.
Mar. 20. Chaderton, Bp. of Chester, to Arch. Doug-
las.
Mar. 20. Memorial of Ric. Cary to the Queen, of sub-
sidies and loss by number of manors, &c. vested in one
person.
Mar. 26. J. Douglas to Arch. Douglas.
Mar. —. Horses for Queen's tenants to find for service
on borders.
April 6. The Queen to the states of Holland.
April 7. The Queen to Ld. Burghley (2).
April 10. Prince of Parma to the K. of Spain.
April 12. Sir H. Unton to Ld. Burghley.
April 15. The Queen to Ld. Burghley.
April 17. (Sir) Jo. Wedrington to Ld. Hunsdon.
April 24. The Queen to Ld. Burghley.
April 24. Inhabitants of Brecknock to —— Consent
for collection to Bp. of St. David's.
April 24. Sums due to officers, &c. for service in Low
Countries for two years ending 11 Oct. 1588, perfected
by Sir T. Sherlic.
April 25. Funeral of Lady Mildred Burghley,
Mourners, &c.
April 26. Sir Thos. Markham to E. of Essex.
[April or May?] A Secretary of Essex's to ——.
April —. Memoranda as to the French King.
May 3. Testament of Sir John Perrot.
May 7. The Queen to Ld. Burghley.
May 10. The Queen to P. Osborn.
May 18. The Queen to Ld. Burghley.
May 18. Anonymous to M. du Even Guymale.
May 20. Patent of Hatfield to Sir John and William
Fortescue.
May 22. Fran. Torman (?) to Arch. Douglas.
May 23. Sir R. Cecil to Sir Thos. Heneage.
May 24. Sir Ro. Southwell to Sir R. Cecil.
May 25. Privy Council to Sir W. Raleigh.
May 26. The Queen to Sir Geo. Carew.
May 27. Privy Council to H. de Montmorency.
May 29. Lord Admiral to ——.
May 30. P. de Sadare to Jaques le Gourante, Londres.
May —. Advertisements from Spain to Ld. Cobham.
June 1. P. de Sadare to Jaques le Gourante, Londres.
June 1. M. Decigarondo to Guil. Tute.
June 2. Vincent Erbs to Sr. Fr. Aprimal.
June 4. Fr. Torman (?) to Arch. Douglas.
June 5. Sir H. Lee to R. Lee (his brother).
June 6. Sir T. Morgan to Lord Burghley.
June 13. King of Scots to Sir R. Cecil.
June 16. H. Anderson to E. of Huntingdon.
June 16. Mayor, &c. of Portsmouth to Ld. Burghley.
June 19. Justice Young to same.
June 19. Will of Sir Rog. Williams.

June 22. Reponse pour le Capitaine Philippe de
l'Espine . . . chansons jettes hors de Stenbeeck.
June 22. The Queen to Ld. Burghley.
June 25. Grant of lands to Jane, wife of Malivery
Kattelyne, Whitehall, signed by Fr. Walsingham.
June 29. Jo. Heath to Ro. White.
June 29. Lady D. Porrot to Dowager Lady Russell.
June 31. Warrant for munitions for Ireland.
[   ] Remains of munitions in account of Sir Geo.
Carewe, late master of ordnance in Ireland.
July 2. Opinion of Meich to adventurers of articles,
by M. Caron, agent for United Provinces.
July 3. Warrant to discharge first fruits of the late
Bp. of Exon.
July 4. Transportation of 20 bands of footmen out of
Low Countries into Brittany.
July 11. Aldermen Billingsley and Carmarden to Ld.
Burghley.
July 12. Messrs. Cave and Dawse to same.
July 16. Sir Anth. Sherley to E. of Essex.
July 18. The Queen to Ld. Deputy of Ireland.
July 23. Same to Ld. Burghley.
July 23. Grant to Ro. Wingefield, nephew of the Lord
High Treasurer, of site of the disparked park of Torpell,
Greenwich, signed by the Queen.
July 26. The Queen to E. of Tyrone.
July 26. Sir R. Palmer and Burrough to Ld.
Burghley.
July 27. The Queen to same.
July 27. Fran. Ormand (?) to Dav. Garve.
July 28. Warrant to Lo. Deputy, &c., to receive
instructions from Sir J. Fenton.
July 30. The Lord Admiral to Ld Burghley.
July 31. The Queen to Lord Deputy of Ireland.
July 31. Ch. Chester to Sir R. Cecil.
July —. Sir W. Ralegh to Sir R. Cecil.
July —. Same to same.
Aug. 3. The Queen to the Ld. Deputy.
Aug. 10. Grant of lease to Sir Hen. Wodderington,
marshal of Berwick. Signed by the Queen at Nonsuch.
Aug. 10. Grant to Edw. Darcy, groom of the presence
chamber, of manors of Ebbesham, Sutton Callesden,
and the rectory and church of Ebbesham. Signed by
the Queen at Nonsuch.
Aug. 13. E. of Bath to the Privy Council.
Aug. 20. Warrant for E. of Essex for 300l. per annum
out of Royal parks now disparked.
Aug. 21. The Queen to Sir T. Bodley.
Aug. 21. Powder, &c. for castle of Jersey, from 21 Apr.
Aug. 26. The Queen to Ld. Deputy of Ireland.
Sept. 4. The Queen to Ld. Burghley.
Sept. 15. Instructions for Sir R. Cecil and Thos. Mid-
dleton as commissioners of prize causes.
Sept. 16. The Queen to Sir R. Cecil.
Sept. 21. Same to King of Scots.
Sept. 26. D. Anderson to Arch. Douglas.
Sept. 26. Sir Jo. Gilbert to Privy Council.
Sept. 27. Orders set down by commissioners at
Dartmouth.
Sept. 28. King of Scots to Roger Aston.
Sept. 30. Same to Arch. Douglas.
Sept. —. Lading of the " Carrack."
[.] Mr. Carye's answer to Sir John Gilbert's
allegations of trained bands in Haytor and Colridge,
Devon.
Oct. 1. J. Cisbett to Arch. Douglas.
Oct. 17. Sir Thos. Heneage to Ld. Burghley.
Oct. 20. The Queen to same.
Oct. 23. Privy Council to same.
Oct. 24. Dr. Parkins to same.
Oct. 30. The Queen to Ld. Burghley, Sir R. Cecil,
Sir J. Fortescue, and Sir W. Killegrew.
Oct. 30. Same to Ld. Burghley.
Oct. —. Instructions touching recusants in Lanca-
shire, with lists of the same.
Nov. 3. Jo. Pound to Sir R. Cecil.
Nov. 14. Thos. Middleton to same.
Nov. 15. Thos. D'Argues to same.
Nov. 17. Ld. Burghley to Arch. Douglas.
Nov. 21. Mr. Justice Young to Sir R. Cecil.
Nov. 22. Same to same.
Nov. 22. Bill exhibited to L. Treasurer by Mr. Wardour,
with answer.
Nov. 24. Mr. Justice Young to Sir R. Cecil.
Nov. 24. Ld. Elphingston to Archd. Douglas.
Nov. 24. Resolution of the States for reformation of
limits.
Nov. 26. The Queen to King of Scots.
Nov. 27. Justice Younge to Sir R. Cecil.
Nov. 28. Same to same.

[Nov. —.] John Anwick's defence of the Bp. of St. David's.

Nov. —. " Reponce que moy Thomas D'Argues faitz aux VII. articles interrogatoires que me fait Mons. Yonge, Juge.

Nov. 29. The Queen to the Lord Deputy.
Nov. 29. Justice Young to Sir R. Cecil.
Dec. 5. The Queen to Ld. Burghley.
Dec. 6. Sir J. Gilbert to Sir R. Cecil.
Dec. 7. Ld. Burghley to same.
Dec. 9. Justice Young to same.
Dec. 9. Thos. D'Argues to Mr. Justice Young.
Dec. 12. Wm. Bereblock to Sir R. Cecil.
Dec. 20. —— to Arch. Douglas.
Dec. 22. Thos. Horton to Sir R. Cecil.
Dec. 22. Lord Elphinstone to Arch. Douglas.
Dec. —. The Queen to Lord Deputy of Ireland.
Dec. —. Same to same.
Dec. —. The wounded officers to the court of Parliament.
Dec. —. The Queen to the King of Scots.
Dec. —. Anonymous to the Queen.
Dec. —. Hen. Bourcher to the E. of Essex.
Dec. —. Petition of certain Spaniards to Essex for an audience.
Dec. —. Sir Ant. Sherley to same.
Dec. —. Charges in recovering goods of the " Golden Lion " and " Red Lion," wrecked on the Goodwins.
——, Bryan Annesley and F. Harvie to the Queen.
——, E. of Essex to Sir H. Unton.
——, Marquis d'Havre to Countess de Berghé.
——, F. de Mendoza to — Gifford.
——, Appointment by L. Burghley of Rob. Woodrington of London as weigher in the Customs.
—— Beer for Galway in Ireland.
—— Commission concerning encroachments.
—— Fines upon ale-house keepers, &c.
—— Names of recusants throughout England and Wales.
—— Spanish writing found at Exon by Wm. Blackstone of London, goldsmith.
—— Of the Great Carrack "Madre de Dios" captured by Sir W. Raleigh.
—— Scotch King's instructions to Spain. (Spanish invasion of England).
—— Mem. upon Act touching denizens.
——, Grant to Ant. Wary, of the manor of Aston and Purye, Northampton.
—— John Stanley's adventures in Spain and Portugal.
—— Case of Sir F. Englefield.
—— Names of pensioners to K. of Spain, by Rob. Russell.
—— Articles against purveyors.
—— Names of seminary priests in Yorkshire.
——. Reformation sought to be made in matter of Recusancy.
——, Grant of a lease to John Newton of Aghrim.
——, For Her Majesty, to Mr. Kelgray. Inventory of cloths, &c. in the trunk.

1593.

Jan. 3. —— to R. Gray.
Jan. 7. The Lord Admiral to Sir John Gilbert.
Jan. 8. Capt. Rob. Duncombe to Lord Burghley.
Jan. 8. E. of Derby to Ld. Burghley.
Jan. 8. Same to Sir R. Cecil.
Jan. 8. Purie Ogilvy to Arch. Douglas.
Jan. 17. G. B. Castiglione to De Beauvois.
Jan. 18. B. Beard to Sir R. Cecil.
Jan. 18. Examination of Griffith Jones at Dover.
Jan. 20. Lord Buckhurst to Sir R. Cecil.
Jan. 22. E. of Derby to same.'
an. 23. The Queen to Ld. Burghley.
Jan. 23. A. Ashley to Sir R. Cecil.
Jan. 23. Certificate of allowances to controllers of the checks and musters and of works at Berwick.
Jan. 23. Extent and yearly value of manors, &c. of the late Arth. Ld. Grey of Wilton, now of Thomas his son.
Jan. 25. Privy Council to Lord Burghley.
Jan. 25. Sir Thos. Sherley to Sir R. Cecil.
Jan. 28. Magistrates of Chester to Ld. Burghley.
Jan. 29. Jo. Crane to same.
Jan. 30. The Queen to same.
Jan. 31. Aldermen Billingsley and Carmarden to same.
Jan. —. Certificate for Ecclesiastical Bill agreed on in Convocation.
Feb. 1. Justices of Norfolk to Privy Council.

Feb. 1. Account of cordage received by Chr. Baker of agents for the Muscovy Company, signed by Sir J. Hawkins, B. Gonson, and Chr. Blake.
Feb. 2. Articles against Edw. Rogers, by John Harrington.
Feb. 5. Jo. Standish to his father.
Feb. 5. Sir Fr. Drake to the Privy Council.
Feb. 6. Declaration of John Danyel touching Tower, city and ships to be burned.
Feb. 8. W. Jemmett to Ld. Cobham.
Feb. 10. Sir F. Drake to Sir R. Cecil.
Feb. 11. Sir Thos. Pratt to Ld. Burghley.
Feb. 12. E. of Pembroke to the Queen.
Feb. 13. Ant. Atkinson to Sir R. Cecil.
Feb. 14. J. Cecil to same.
Feb. 15. E. of Huntingdon to same.
Feb. 17. H. Longe to Mr. Shute.
Feb. 21. Request of Ant. Powlet in behalf of the Isles.
Feb. 21. H. Leighe to Sir R. Cecil.
Feb. 25. Sir W. Ralegh to same.
Feb. 26. E. of Essex to same.
Feb. 26. Lady Ralegh to same.
(.) Depositions before Sir T. Norreys; vice-president of Munster. (Mention of John FitzEdmonds of Clare.)
Mar. 1. E. of Essex to Sir R. Cecil.
Mar. 1. Mr. Windebank to same.
Mar. 3. Sir H. Norris to same.
Mar. 3. Jo. Crane to same.
Mar. 4. Sir W. Ralegh to same.
Mar. 4. Ld. Cobham to same.
Mar. 4. E. of Essex to same.
Mar. 6. Request of Philip de Carteret, Seigneur of St. Omer, of the Isle of Sark, for ordnance.
Mar. 7. W. Waade to Sir R. Cecil.
Mar. 7. Sir H. Palavicino to same.
Mar. 8. Ld. North to same.
Mar. (10). Inhabitants of Jersey to the Queen.
Mar. (10). The Queen to Ld. Burghley.
Mar. 13. Ld. Burghley to Arch. Douglas.
Mar. 14. Promise of 400l. by deputies of Jersey towards new fortifications.
Mar. 15. Ld. Lumley to Sir R. Cecil.
Mar. 16. Ld. Burgh to same.
Mar. 16. Ld. Cobham to same.
Mar. 16. N. Hilliard to same.
Mar. 17. Sir H. Saville to same.
Mar. 18. Sir Thos. Morgan to same.
Mar. 19. Proceedings against Emanuel Lewis and Stephan Ferrerade Gamma, conspirators with De Lopes.
Mar. 20. Sir E. Brooke to Sir R. Cecil.
Mar. 20. S. Cooke to same.
Mar. 24. Order for fortification in St. Hiliers, Jersey.
Mar. 25. Sir N. Clifford to Sir R. Cecil.
Mar. 29. Ric. Carmarden to Ld. Burghley.
Mar. 30. Jo. Budden to Sir R. Cecil.
Mar. —. King of Scots to Lord Burgh.
—— Scotch king's answers to propositions of Q. Eliz., by the Ld. Burgh.
April 5. Articles for jurors of Cumberland and Westmorland upon decay of houses, castles, &c. since the 10th year of the present reign. Newcastle, with verdict, signed Huntingdon.
April 7. Sir J. Cæsar to Sir R. Cecil.
April 9. Articles and verdict for bishopric of Durham. See April 5.
April 9. Articles and verdict for bishopric of Northumberland.
April 10. Certificate of debts due to the Queen for customs, imposts, subsidies, 15ths and 10ths.
April 10. R. Carmarden to Ld. Burghley.
April 11. W. Cecil to Sir R. Cecil.
April 14. Privy Council to Lord Burghley.
April 15. —— to R. Parsons (the Jesuit).
April 16. Sir H. Lee to Sir R. Cecil.
April 18. R. Carmarden to Ld. Burghley.
April 22. Examination of Ric. Ireland.
April 22. The Queen to Mr. Barton.
April 22. Sir R. Cecil to Ed. Winter.
April 23. Mayor of Dover to Ld. Cobham.
April 26. Ld. Cobham to Sir R. Cecil.
April 28. E. Dyer to same.
April 28. R. Carmarden to Ld. Burghley.
April 28. Neville de Latymer to Sir R. Cecil.
April 28. W. Cecil to same.
May 3. Aldermen Billingsley, Carmarden, &c. to Ld. Burghley.
May 4. Sir R. Barklay to Sir R. Cecil.
May 4. The Dean, &c. of Trinity Coll., Cambridge, to same.

MARQUIS
OF SALIS-
BURY.

May 5. The Queen to Ld. Burghley.
May 6. Examination of H. Baily respecting Dr. Crothe out of Spain into Ireland.
May 8. E. of Essex to Sir R. Cecil.
May 10. H. Owen to John Owen.
May 10. Chateau-Martin to Lord Burghley.
May 10. Sir W. Ralegh to Sir R. Cecil.
May 11. Sir Tho. Stanhope to same.
May 12. Sir R. Sydney to same.
May 12. Chateau Martin to Lord Burghley.
May 12. W. Cecil to Sir R. Cecil.
May 13. Ed. Winter to same.
May 14. Remembrance to Privy Council for Guernsey.
May 15. Weekly payments to the Queen's forces in Low Countries for two months ending
May 15. Sir G. Carew to Mr. Beadwell.
May 16. Same to Lord Burghley?
May 17. Causes between Alderman Watts and Sir M. Morgan.
May 20. Suits of officers of the port of Boston, with answers for Corporation.
May 20. Sir Thos. Fane to Lord Cobham.
May 20. Justice Shuttleworth to Sir R. Cecil.
May 21. Ld. Hunsdon, Sir R. Cecil, and Sir Jo. Wolley to the Ld. Keeper, Ld. Treasurer, &c.
May 21. Lord Burghley to Sir R. Cecil.
May 22. G. Fenner to Privy Council.
May 22. Lord Burghley to Sir R. Cecil.
May 22. Jo. Stanhope to same.
May 23. Lord Cobham to same.
May 26. G. B. Giustiniani to same.
May 26. Ld. Burghley to same.
May 26. H. Noel to same.
May 26. Mr. Gilpin to E. of Essex.
May 26. H. Maynard to Sir R. Cecil.
May 27. Dr. Chr. Parkins to Lord Burghley.
May 28. Chateau-Martin to same.
May 29. E. of Essex to Sir R. Cecil.
May —. The Lord Admiral to same.
June 2. Chateau-Martin to Lord Burghley.
June 3. Same to same.
June 4. A. Hode to Ld. Dacre.
June 11. E. Harvardo to G. Holt.
June 11. W. C. to Sir W. Stanley.
June 12. P. Worthington to Jo. Petit.
June 12. Chateau-Martin to Ld. Burghley.
June 13. Dr. Jacomel to M. de Beauvois.
June 14. The Queen to Ld. Burghley.
June 15. Sir W. Ralegh to same.
June 15. Manuel Dundrada to same (2).
June 20. Ant. Standen to Ant. Bacon.
June 23. E. of Cumberland to Ld. Burghley.
June 29. Ant. Rolston to —.
June 30. Mayor of Chester to Lord Burghley.
July 3. Manuel Dandrada to same.
July 10. Sir Jo. Fortescue to Arch. Douglas.
July 11. W. Goldsmith to Sir R. Cecil.
July 13. Sir Ant. Powlet to Ld. Burghley.
July 16. Same to same.
July 16. The Council to Ld. Burghley.
July 18. Sir Ric. Bingham to Sir R. Cecil.
July 18. Sir H. Cocke to same.
July 19. Sir Thos. Leighton to same.
July 20. Minute of Council against Sir H. Barkeley for refusing to permit the felling of timber in Norwood Park.
July 23. P. de la Haye to — Percival.
July 23. Privy Council to L. Burghley.
July 26. Sir Ant. Sherley to Sir R. Cecil.
July 28. Chateau-Martin to Lord Burghley.
July 30. Privy Council to same.
July 31. Ld. Burghley to Sir Jo. Fortescue.
July —. H. Noel to Sir R. Cecil.
July —. The Queen to King of France (2).
July —. The Queen to King of Scots.
Aug. 1. Sir Jo. Fortescue to Archd. Douglas.
Aug. 2. Ld. Cobham to Sir R. Cecil.
Aug. 2. Sir Jo. Fortescue to Arch. Douglas.
Aug. 2. Ro. Manners to Sir R. Cecil.
Aug. 2. Sir G. Carey to same.
Aug. 3. H. Noel to same.
Aug. 5. Sir W. Knollys to same.
Aug. 5. Sir Thos. Heneage to same.
Aug. 5. Ant. Bacon to E. of Essex.
Aug. 6. A. Standen to Sir R. Cecil.
Aug. 6. R. Taillor to same.
Aug. 7. T. Drury to Sir R. Cecil.
Aug. 7. Sir H. Cocke to same.
Aug. 8. Mayor of Canterbury to same.
Aug. 8. Sir H. Palavicino to same.
Aug. 9. Justice Younge to same.

Aug. 9. Geo. Margitts to same.
Aug. 10. The Queen to Ld. Burghley.
Aug. 10. Thos. Spencer to Steph. White.
Aug. 10. Jo. Stylman to Sir R. Cecil.
Aug. 10. Sir Jo. Norris to Sir Am. Powlet.
Aug. 10. Sir Thos. Blount to Sir R. Cecil.
Aug. 10. Manuel Dundreda to Lord Burghley.
Aug. 10. E. of Essex to Sir H. Unton.
Aug. 11. Sir C. Carroule to Sir R. Cecil.
Aug. 12. Sir F. Greville to same.
Aug. 12. Sir J. Norris to Sir A. Pawlet.
Aug. 13. The Queen to Ld. Burghley.
Aug. 13. Note for W. Maxwell of things to be bought in England for Jersey.
Aug. 13. Ld. Cobham to Sir. R. Cecil (2).
Aug. 14. Chateau-Martin to Lord Burghley.
Aug. 14. Ch. Collarth to Sir R. Cecil.
Aug. 14. Jo. Stylman to same.
Aug. 15. Sir W. Ralegh to same.
Aug. 15. Manuel Dundreda to Lord Burghley.
Aug. 15. W. Morant to Sir R. Cecil.
Aug. 16. H. Maynard to same.
Aug. 17. T. Myddleton to same.
Aug. 18. Mr. Godfrey to same.
Aug. 19. Sir Am. Powlet to same.
Aug. 19. Sir H. Palavicino to same.
Aug. 20. Paul Yne to same.
Aug. 22. Sir. H. Unton to same.
Aug. 23. The Queen to King of Scots.
Aug. 24. Lord Lumley to Sir R. Cecil.
Aug. 25. Advertisements from Spain.
Aug. 27. Sir W. Ralegh to Sir R. Cecil.
Aug. 27. Geo. Margitts to same.
Aug. 27. Bennet Shawe to Sir Am. Powlet.
Aug. 27. D. Aubrey to Sir R. Cecil.
Aug. 29. Sir J. Fortescue to Arch. Douglas.
Aug. 30. Sir A. Powlet to Ld. Burghley.
Aug. —. Sir H. Cocke to Sir R. Cecil.
Aug. —. Thos. Drury to same.
Sept. 4. Thos. North to same.
Sept. 5. Lord Willoughby to same.
Sept. 6. Privy Council to Sir R. Bingham.
Sept. 9. Sir A. Cooke to Sir R. Cecil.
Sept. 10. G. B. Giustiniani to same.
Sept. 10. M. Brandaye to M. Hickes.
Sept. 13. Chateau-Martin to Lord Burghley.
Sept. 15. Sir Am. Powlet to Sir R. Cecil.
Sept. 16. Arth. Gorges to same.
Sept. 18. Ric. Sutton to same.
Sept. 18. Sir W. Fitzwilliam to same.
Sept. 18. Mr. Edmondes to [Lord. Burghley?].
Sept. 19. King of Scots to the Queen.
Sept. 19. Sir Ant. Cooke to Sir R. Cecil.
Sept. 19. Jo. Stylman to same.
Sept. 20. Thos. Middleton to same.
Sept. 20. The Queen to King of France.
Sept. 20. Same to French King's sister.
Sept. 20. Lord Windsor to H. Brooke.
Sept. 21. Ld. Strange to Sir R. Cecil.
Sept. 23. Margery Lady Norreys to same.
Sept. 23. The Queen to the French King's sister.
Sept. 25. Charles de Sturry? to Lord Cobham.
Sept. 25. Mr. Peter's office by patent and oath.
Sept. 25. Weekly imprest for 600 footmen, &c. in bands for Guernsey and Jersey for eight weeks.
Sept. 25. Ar. Gorges to Sir R. Cecil.
Sept. 26. Ld. Strange to same.
Sept. 28. Chateau-Martin to L. Burghley.
Sept. 29. Custom upon silk brought into London for one year.
Sept. 29. Stone pots and heath brush brought into port of London, March 1592 to
Sept. 29. Provision and wages in fortifying Castle Cornet, Guernsey, 9 April to
Sept. 29. Tin shipped from outports, from Mich. 1592.
Sept. 30. Dr. Mount to Sir R. Cecil.
Sept. 30. B. Beard to same.
Sept. —. Ann, Lady Wentworth to Sir R. Cecil.
Oct. 2. Ric. Hesketh (who attempted to seduce the E. of Derby to assume the title of King) to his wife.
Oct. 2. Same to Thos. Hesketh.
Oct. 3. The Queen to Lord Burghley.
Oct. 3. Sir Jo. Fortescue to Arch. Douglas.
Oct. 3. Thos. Middleton to Sir R. Cecil.
Oct. 5. Privy Council to Steward and Bailiff of Westminster.
Oct. 7. The Queen to King of Scots.
Oct. 7. The Queen to King of France.
Oct. 8. Sir W. Ralegh to Sir R. Cecil.
Oct. 8. Geo. Margitts to same.
Oct. —. W. Paterson to — Margitts (2).

Oct. 8. Ld. Burghley to Lord Mayor of London.
Oct. 8. Geo. Margitts to Sir R. Cecil.
Oct. 9. Ant. Ashley to same.
Oct. 10. Sir W. Fitzwilliam to same,
Oct. 10. Interrogatories to Ant. Tyrrel, before
Justice Young.
Oct. 11. Earl of Essex to Sir R. Cecil.
Oct. 13. Sheriffs of London to same,
Oct. 14. Ant. Standen to same.
Oct. 15. Ric. Hesketh to Ld. Cobham and the same.
Oct. 16. Sheriff Houghton to Sir R. Cecil.
Oct. 17. Sheriff Bayning to same.
Oct. 18. H. Finch to same.
Oct. 20. E. of Derby to same.
Oct. 20. Justice Young to same.
Oct. 20. Chateau-Martin to Lord Burghley.
Oct. 21. Sir E. Hoby to Sir R. Cecil.
Oct. 22. Provost, &c. of Eton to the Queen.
Oct. 23. Ant. Shirley to Sir R. Cecil.
Oct. 24. Lord Burgh to same.
Oct. 25. Th. Digges to same.
Oct. 25. W. Becher to Sir Thos. Shirley.
Oct. 25. Vincent Skinner to Sir R. Cecil.
Oct. 25. Bp. of Coventry and Lichfield to Sir Thos.
Stanhope.
Oct. 26. Vincent Skinner to Sir R. Cecil.,
Oct. 26. Sheriff Bayning to Ld. Buckhurst and the
same.
Oct. 27. Vincent Skinner to Sir R. Cecil.
Oct. 27. Ric. Holland to Ld. Cobham and the same.
Oct. 27. Ant. Astley to Sir R. Cecil.
Oct. 29. Sir Jo. Savage to Ld. Cobham and the same.
Oct. 29. H. Brooke to Sir R. Cecil.
Oct. 31. Ld. Burgh to same.
Oct. 31. Bp. of Coventry and Lichfield to Dean of
Coventry.
Nov. 2. Sir Thos. Shirley to Sir R. Cecil.
Nov. 2. Mr. Townshend to same.
Nov. 2. Sir H. Norreys to Sir R. Cecil.
Nov. 3. Ld. Crumwell to same.
Nov. 3. Sir Jo. Fortescue to same.
Nov. 4. R. Hesketh to Wm. Waad.
Nov. 4. Sir B. Cecil to Warden of the Fleet
Nov. 5. Chateau-Martin to Lord Burghley.
Nov. 5. Ric. Hesketh to Wm. Waad.
Nov. 6. E. of Essex to Lord Cobham
Nov. 8. Sir B. Cecil to Mr. Sheriff Bothe (2).
Nov. 8. E. of Derby to Sir R. Cecil.
Nov. 8. Sir M. Blount to same.
Nov. 9. Same to same.
Nov. 9. Matters concerning Mr. Thornbower, Wis-
beach, Lo. Bp. of Cumberland, Lady Arabella, Jos.
Sir Hen. and Sir Rob. Constabells, &c.
Nov. 10. Sir Jo. Fortescue to Sir R. Cecil.
Nov. 10. E. of Derby to same.
Nov. 10. Sir Thos. Shirley to same.
Nov. 11. Ld. Cobham to same.
Nov. 11. Jos. Newton to — Beard.
Nov. 11. Sir R. Cecil to the Sheriffs of London.
Nov. 11. James Parry to Mrs. Shelley.
Nov. 12. Jo. Stylman to Sir R. Cecil.
Nov. 12. The Queen to King of France.
Nov. 12. Lord Cobham to Sir R. Cecil.
Nov. 13. Jo. Budden to same.
Nov. 13. Sir Jo. Danvers to same.
Nov. 14. Sir Fr. Danvers to same.
Nov. 16. Sir M. Blount to same.
Nov. 17. Chateau-Martin to Lord Burghley.
Nov. 19. Nic. Francois to Lord Cobham.
Nov. 20. Dr. Parkins to Sir R. Cecil.
Nov. 20. Sir Jo. Puckering to Lord Burghley.
Nov. 20. Italian books delivered by Thos. Barnes to
Edm. Brus, sent to Sir Chas. Danvers.
Nov. 21. Jo. Budden to Ld. Burghley.
Nov. 21. Ld. Cobham to same.
Nov. 21. Justice Younge to Sir R. Cecil.
Nov. 21. Jo. Penruddock to same.
Nov. 22. Dr. Chr. Perkins to same.
Nov. 23. E. of Shrewsbury to same.
Nov. 23. Sir M. Blount to same.
Nov. 23. Jo. Budden to same.
Nov. 24. The Queen to King of France.
Nov. 24. Words used by Ed. Pemberton, prisoner in
the Marshalsea.
Nov. 25. Lord Cobham to Lord Burghley.
Nov. 26. Dr. Chr. Perkins to Sir R. Cecil.
Nov. 26. Ld. Keeper Egerton to same.
Nov. 27. Sir Thos. Heneage to same.
Nov. 27. Jo. Budden to same.
Nov. 28. W. Waad to same.
Nov. 29. Sir Thos. Heneage to same.

Nov. —. Sir Jo. Stanhope to same.
Nov. —. Sir R. Cecil to Sheriff of London.
Nov. —. Countess of Derby to same.
Nov. —. Sir Jo. Puckering to same.
Nov. —. Ld. Stafford to Sir R. Cecil.
Nov. —. Ann Lady Wentworth to same.
Nov. —. E. of Derby to same.
Nov. —. Advertisements from Calais.
Dec. 2. Sir M. Blount to Sir R. Cecil.
Dec. 4. Chateau-Martin to Lord Burghley.
Dec. 5. Ant. Tyrrel to Sir R. Cecil.
Dec. 6. B. Beard to same.
Dec. 6. Chateau-Martin to Ld. Burghley.
Dec. 8. B. Beard to Sir R. Cecil.
Dec. 8. King of Scots to the Queen.
Dec. 8. Thos. Stephenson to Hesketh.
Dec. 8. Same to Mr. Leigh (2).
Dec. 9. Mrs. J. Shelley to Mr. Beard.
Dec. 12. B. Beard to Sir R. Cecil (2).
Dec. 13. Same to same.
Dec. 13. The Queen to Sir Ch. Blount.
Dec. 13. Sir Ch. Danvers to Lord Hunsdon and Lord
Cobham.
Dec. 15. E. of Derby to Sir R. Cecil.
Dec. 16. E. Phytton to same.
Dec. 16. Sir Ch. Blount to same.
Dec. 18. Rog. Loppes to Harman (Winchester).
Dec. 18. Chateau-Martin to Ld. Burghley.
Dec. 20. Ben. Beard to Sir R. Cecil.
Dec. 20. Sir Thos. Stanhope to same.
Dec. 20. Sir Ch. Blount to same,
Dec. 21. Sir G. Carew to same.
Dec. 21. Sir T. Leighton to Lord Burghley.
Dec. 21. Sir G. Carew to Sir R. Cecil.
Dec. 21. E. of Huntingdon to same.
Dec. 21. A. Ashley to same.
Dec. 21. The Queen to Lord Burghley.
Dec. 21. John Stylman to Sir R. Cecil.
Dec. 23. E. of Huntingdon to same.
Dec. 23. Thos. Middleton to same.
Dec. 26. Sir Ch. Blount to same.
Dec. 26. Lord Zouche to same.
Dec. 26. Sir E. Hoby to same.
Dec. 26. Sir Hor. Palavicino to same.
Dec. 27. Ann White to same.
Dec. 27. Tho. Bellote to same.
Dec. 27. Attorney General to same.
Dec. 27. Bp. of Worcester to same.
Dec. 28. Sir Ch. Danvers to same.
Dec. 28. Sir H. Palavicino to same.
Dec. 30. Same to same.
Dec. 31. Sir C. Danvers to same.
Dec. 31. Justice Young to same.
Dec. 31. Privy Council to Lord Burghley.
Dec. 31. The Queen to same.
—— E. of Northumberland to Privy Council.
—— The Brush Makers to Sir R. Cecil.
—— B. Walton to same.
—— Mr. Faucon to Hesketh.
—— Chr. Carlisle to the Queen.
—— H. Melvil to the E. of Essex.
—— Company of Pewterers to the Queen.
—— R. Drake to same.
—— H. Bennet and S. Thompson to Sir R. Cecil
and Lord Burghley.
—— Dowager Lady Russell to Sir R. Cecil.
—— W. Grosvenor to the Queen.
—— The Queen to [Duc de Bouillon ?].
—— The Queen to the King of Scots.
—— Catherine of Navarre to the Queen (2).
—— Calvacati to the Queen.
—— Le Chevalier Guichardin to the E. of Essex.
—— Capt. Malbie to E. of Essex.
—— The Queen to Ld. Burghley.
—— Advertisements from St. Malo of the Spanish
army at Bluet.
1593. Gentlemen fit to be Treasurer at War.
1593. First Bill against Recusants.
1593. De Antiquitate Burgi Yernemouth in Comitatu
Norfolciæ.
1593. Church plate found in a ship at Erith.
1593. Matters concerning Skydmore, Garret, Apleby,
Typpin, Paget, &c.
—— Plot of late Mr. Peter's lodgings in St. Stephen's,
Westminster.
—— Abuses by purveyors of corn by color of licenses.
—— Goods saved upon coast of Kent.
—— Export of pipe staves out of Ireland.
—— Remembrance of Paul Juy (Jue, &c. or Jovius,
Italian engineer) for assistance in fortifications of
Jersey.

—— Charge of works in Jersey.
—— Official report by E. of Huntingdon of harms done in the East and Middle Marches, from 26 Eliz.
—— Notes of a sermon on Adversity.
—— Report of case between Sir Edw. Hobie and Brasenose Coll., Oxford.

1594.

Jan. 1. Sir W. Ralegh to Sir R. Cecil.
Jan. 1. Sir H. Danvers to E. of Essex.
Jan. 3. Ja. Grahame to Douglas.
Jan. 3. "42" to M. de Colville, à Londres.
Jan. 4. Confession of Thos. Hall respecting Grace Maurice.
Jan. 4. Dr. W. Day (Dean of Windsor) to Sir R. Cecil.
Jan. 5. Thos. Webbe to Rog. Manners.
Jan. 6. Ld. Burghley to Sir R. Cecil.
Jan. 6. F—— M—— to Eliz. Holt.
Jan. 6. Bap. Guistiniani to Sir R. Cecil.
Jan. 7. J. Cardenagh to same.
Jan. 7. The Queen to Ld. Deputy of Ireland.
Jan. 7. E. of Huntingdon to Ld. Burghley.
Jan. 7. J. Guicciardini to E. of Essex.
Jan. 9. Examination of John Philips and wife Judith, alias Doll Pope, and Geo. Burnell, touching the cozening of the Widow Maacall.
Jan. 10. Thos. Fleming to Sir R. Cecil.
Jan. 11. E. of Cumberland to same.
Jan. 13. Certificate of issue of Privy Seal for 8,000l.
Jan. 14. Dr. Day, Dean of Windsor, to Sir R. Cecil.
Jan. 14. N. Jeffe to same.
Jan. 17. Dr. Chr. Parkins to same.
Jan. 17. Mayor of Northampton to the Privy Council.
Jan. 17. Thos. Lyly to Sir R. Cecil.
Jan. 17. Francesco Florio to same.
Jan. 1?. —— Topclyffe to same.
Jan. 20. Viscount Byndon to same.
Jan. 20. Sir H. Unton to same.
Jan. 22. Sir F. Greville to same.
Jan. 23. The Contractors to Ald. Billingsly.
Jan. 24. Anth. Bacon to E. of Essex.
Jan. 25. Sir Edm. Vuedall to Ld. Burghley.
Jan. 25. Hutton, Bp. of Durham, to Sir R. Cecil and Sir J. Wolley.
Jan. 25. King of Scots to the Queen.
Jan. 25. R. Wingfield to Sir R. Cecil.
Jan. 25. Alderman Billingsley to Ld. Burghley.
Jan. 25. R. Wingfield to Sir R. Cecil.
Jan. 27. Note concerning French ship at Lisbon.
Jan. 28. "4" (Moody) to F. Morse.
Jan. —. Practises of devises by Hillarye Dakins, seminary priest, with evidence of witnesses against him.
Jan. —. Examination of John Jennens, and John Winfray of Portsmouth.
Jan. —. Arthur Throckmorton to Sir R. Cecil.
Jan. —. Privy Council to Bp. of Durham.
Feb. 1. H. Maynard to Sir R. Cecil.
Feb. 1. Sir H. Palavicino to same.
Feb. 1. W. Carmarden to Ld. Burghley.
Feb. 2. Jo. Stylman to Sir R. Cecil.
Feb. 3. Sir Th. Cecil to same.
Feb. 3. Francesco Florio to same.
Feb. 3. Sir Post. Hoby to same.
Feb. 4. Grant to Bp. of Winchester of the Keepership of Waltham Park.
Feb. 5. Sir Thos. Bodley to the E. of Essex.
Feb. 5. R. Kisbey to Sir R. Cecil.
Feb. 5. Sir Thos. Bodley to Ld. Burghley.
Feb. 7. Sir E. Norris to the E. of Essex.
Feb. 7. W. Nichols to R. Halling (London).
Feb. 8. Geo. Boleyn to Sir R. Cecil and Sir John Wolley.
Feb. 8. Sir M. Stanhope to Sir Thos. Heneage.
Feb. 8. Neville Latymer to Sir R. Cecil.
Feb. 9. The Queen to the Grand Seignor.
Feb. 9. Ed. Vnedale to E. of Essex.
Feb. 10. Attorney Gen. Coke to J. Stanhope.
Feb. 10. H. Fitz(herbert ?) to N. Longford.
Feb. 10. Th. Honiman to Sir R. Cecil.
Feb. 11. Fletcher, Bp. of London, to same.
Feb. 11. R. Topelyffe to same.
Feb. 11. Sir F. Vere to E. of Essex.
Feb. 11. J. Guicciardini to same.
Feb. 12. Ld. C. Mountjoy to Sir R. Cecil.
Feb. 12. Ld. Keeper Puckering to same.
Feb. 13. Sir Jo. Fortescue to same.
Feb. 14. Sir Th. Bodley to E. of Essex.
Feb. 16. Hutton, Bp. of Durham, to Sir R. Cecil.
Feb. 16. Chaderton, Bp. of Chester, to same.
Feb. 17. Geo. Margitts to same.

Feb. 17. Chateau-Martin to Lord Burghley.
Feb. 18. J. Guicciardini to E. of Essex.
Feb. 18. Ld. Mayor of London to Sir R. Cecil.
Feb. 19. Dr. W. Whitaker to same.
Feb. 19. Nich. Fitzherbert to G. Smith, Civita-Vecchia.
Feb. 20. Ld. Mayor and Aldermen to Sir R. Cecil.
Feb. 20. G. Smith to Mr. Beestone.
Feb. 20. W. Warrington to Widow Warrington, Wimborne Minster.
Feb. 21. Ld. Zouche to Sir R. Cecil.
Feb. 21. M. Scott to same.
Feb. 21. Sir H. Palavicino to same.
Feb. 21. W. Waad to E. of Essex.
Feb. 21. Capt. A. Proston to Sir R. Cecil.
Feb. 22. E. of Huntingdon to same.
Feb. 22. Th. Bodley to the E. of Essex.
Feb. 22. Same to Lord Burghley.
Feb. 23. Sir E. Norris to the E. of Essex.
Feb. 23. Lord Chancellor and Sir R. Cecil to E. of Pembroke.
Feb. 24. Ld. Hunsdon and Sir R. Cecil to same.
Feb. 24. Dowager Lady Russell to Sir R. Cecil.
Feb. 26. Earl Bothwell to Capt. Musgrave, of Beaucastle.
Feb. 26. Th. Bodley to the E. of Essex.
Feb. 28. Arth. Gregory to Sir R. Cecil.
Feb. 28. W. Waad to E. of Essex.
Feb. 28. Anonymous to [Earl of Essex ?].
Feb. 28. Wm. Lee to Sir R. Cecil.
Feb. —. E. of Essex to same.
Mar. 1. Wickham, Bp. of Winton, to same.
Mar. 1. Ant. Mildmay to same.
Mar. 1. Jo. Stanhope to same.
Mar. 2. Th. Bodley to E. of Essex.
Mar. 3. Sir Ch. Danvers to Sir R. Cecil.
Mar. 3. W. Carmarden to Ld. Burghley.
Mar. 4. Chateau-Martin to same.
Mar. 4. Mr. Bodley to same.
Mar. 4. Same to the E. of Essex.
Mar. 4. Sir E. Denny to Sir R. Cecil.
Mar. 5. Capt. Ashenden to same.
Mar. 5. Sir N. Clifford to same.
Mar. 6. Capt. Lambert to [E. of Essex ?].
Mar. 7. E. of Sussex to Sir R. Cecil.
Mar. 8. Sir H. Killegrew to Ld. Burghley.
Mar. 8. E. of Huntingdon to same.
Mar. 8. The Queen to same.
Mar. 8. Speeches by Humfrey Bonner, late Mayor of Nottingham, concerning the E. of Shrewsbury.
Mar. 9. Sir W. Cornwalleys to Sir R. Cecil.
Mar. 9. Books received from my Lo. of Canterbury.
Mar. 10. E. of Huntingdon to Ld. Burghley.
Mar. 10. Lord Burghley to the Sheriffs of Warwick.
Mar. 10. Beauvoir la Noue to Earl of Essex.
Mar. 12. Jo. Gilbert to ——.
Mar. 13. Ld. Hunsdon to Sir R. Cecil.
Mar. 14. Geo. Gilpin to E. of Essex.
Mar. 14. Examination of James and Edm. Williamson.
Mar. 14. Whitgift, Abp. of Cant., to Ld. Burghley.
Mar. 14. Thos. Bodley to E. of Essex.
Mar. 14. Thos. Bodley to Lord Burghley.
Mar. 14. N. Williamson to E. of Essex and Sir R. Cecil.
Mar. 14. Sir R. Martin and Wm. Waad to Sir R. Cecil.
Mar. 14. Wm. Waad to same.
Mar. 14. N. Williamson to same.
Mar. 15. Ld. Cobham to Sir R. Cecil.
Mar. 15. Aldermen Billingsley and Carmarden to Ld. Burghley.
Mar. 16. Thos. Williamson to Ed. Williamson.
Mar. 17. Sir F. Vere to E. of Essex.
Mar. 18. Thos. Bodley to E. of Essex.
Mar. 18. Same to Ld. Burghley.
Mar. 18. G. Gilpin to E. of Essex.
Mar. 19. Wm. Waad to Sir R. Cecil.
Mar. 19. Ed. Williamson to Wm. Waad.
Mar. 20. The Queen to Ld. Burghley.
Mar. 20. Wm. Waad to Sir R. Cecil.
Mar. 20. E. of Oxford to Ld. Burghley.
Mar. 20. Dr. Jul. Cæsar to the Ld. Admiral.
Mar. 21. N. Williamson to Sir R. Cecil.
Mar. 21. Ot. Smyth to E. of Essex.
Mar. 23. Florence Macarthy to Sir R. Cecil.
Mar. 23. W. Fleetwood to same.
Mar. 23. E. of Oxford to Ld. Burghley.
Mar. 24. Sir Jo. Wolley to Sir R. Cecil.
Mar. 24. Same to same.
Mar. 24. Sir John Gilbert to same.
Mar. 24. Sir R. Cecil to Sir Thos. Egerton.

Mar. 24. King of Scots to W. Bowes, treasurer of Berwick.
Mar. 25. Ferrara's Will.
Mar. 25. Chateau-Martin to L. Burghley.
Mar. 26. Sir R. Cecil to ——.
Mar. 30. Examination of Simon Knowles, of Spanish practices as to England.
Mar. 31. E. of Huntingdon to Sir R. Cecil.
Mar. 31. Matters disclosed by R. Barwàys, priest.
Mar. 31. Ed. More to Sir R. Cecil.
Mar. —. Sir N. Clifford to same.
Mar. —. Concerning bakers and license for starch.
Mar. —. Countess of Cumberland to Sir R. Cecil.
April 1. Capt. Duffield to same.
April 1. Sir Ant. Shirley to same.
April 2. Sir H. Palavicino to same.
April 2. E. of Derby to same.
April 2. P. Maurice Nassau to the Queen.
April 2. Information by Knowles of news from the Netherlands.
April 4. Jo. Harmar to Sir R. Cecil.
April 6. Geo. Goring to same.
April 6. T. Jeffreys to same.
April 7. Mayor of Boston to Ld. Burghley.
April 7. Chateau-Martin to same.
April 7. Lord Hunsdon to one of the Gentlemen Ushers.
April 7. Sir G. Carew to Sir R. Cecil.
April 7. Sir E. Vuedale to same.
April 7. Ld. Hunsdon to same.
April 8. T. Jeffreys to same.
April 8. Messengers for levy of 1,500 men for Ireland.
April 8. Sir G. Carew to Sir R. Cecil.
April 8. E. of Essex to Sir H. Unton.
April 10. Sir Jo. Gilbert to Sir R. Cecil.
April 10. Caldwell, Bp. of Sarum, to Hon. Brooke.
April 11. E. of Derby to Sir R. Cecil.
April 13. King of Scots to the Queen.
April 13. Geo. Goringe to Sir R. Cecil.
April 14. Dr. W. Aubrey to same.
April 14. Sir W. Ralegh to same.
April 14. Lord Hunsdon to same.
April 14. Same to Ld. Burghley.
April 15. Jo. Crane to Sir R. Cecil.
April 16. Att. Gen. Coke to same.
April 17. Sir H. Palavicino to same.
April 18. Sir E. Vuedale to same.
April 18. Ld. Buckhurst and Sir Jo. Fortescue to same.
April 18. Sir M. Blount to same.
April 20. Sir H. Palavicino to same.
April 21. Nàn Countess Warwick to same.
April 21. Privy Council to Ld. Burghley.
April 21. Geo. Goringe to Sir R. Cecil.
April 22. Ld. Keeper Egerton to Sir Thos. Heneage.
April 23. Don Juan d'Aquila to M. Rodriguez.
April 24. Sir Jo. Stanhope to Sir R. Cecil.
April 25. Sir M. Blount to same.
April 26. Ld. Keeper Puckering and Ld. Buckhurst to same.
April 26. Geo. Goring to same.
April 27. Geo. Hull to same.
April 28. Sir Geo. Carey to same.
April 28. Jo. Colville to H. Lok.
April —. Mem. endorsed, Sir Robt. Sydney, concerning reinforcement of a troop of horse.
—— Sir N. Clifford to Sir Thos. Heneage.
May 2. Ld. Mayor of London, to the Privy Council.
May 2. Ld. Keeper and Ld. Buckhurst to Sir R. Cecil.
May 2. E. of Shrewsbury to same.
May 2. Th. Wilbraham to same,
May 3. Sir N. Clifford to same.
May 3. Sir Th. Cecil to Sir R. Cecil.
May 3. Jo. Colville to H. Lok.
May 3. E. of Essex to Sir R. Cecil.
May 4. Ant. Gregory to Sir R. Cecil.
May 5. E. of Essex to same.
May 5. Sir N. Clifford to same.
May 5. Franc. Antonio to Jor. Franciotti.
May 6. Sir N. Clifford to Sir R. Cecil.
May 7. W. Cade to same.
May 7. E. of Shrewsbury to same.
May 8. W. Medelay to same.
May 9. Dr. Ric. Webster to same.
May 9. Countess of Derby to same.
May 10. Jo. Colville to H. Lok.
May 10. Sir Th. Cecil to Sir R. Cecil.
May 12. Geo. Goringe to same.
May 12. Sir Th. Fane to same.

May 12. The Queen to the Master and Receiver of the Court of Wards.
May 13. Sir H. Lee to Sir R. Cecil.
May 13. W. Hickman to same.
May 13. Ld. Cobham to same.
May 14. H. Lok to same.
May 14. Ld. Burgh to same.
May 16. Walt. Hickman to same.
May 16. Rog. Manners to same.
May 16. E. of Huntingdon to same.
May 17. Bailiffs of Yarmouth to same.
May 18. Sir Th. Egerton to same.
May 18. Sir Ch. Blount to same.
May 18. Examination of Ric. White, &c. before Justice Young.
May 19. Sir Jo. Danvers to Sir R. Cecil.
May 19. And. White to same.
May 20. Th. Windebank to same.
May 22. M. Greensmith to same.
May 23. Antonio Perez to same.
May 23. Sir R. Cecil to Ant. Perez.
May 23. Same to Fr. Bacon ?
May 25. R. Brus to E. of Essex.
May 25. G. Gilpin to same.
May 25. M. B. Combes to Sir R. Cecil.
May 25. Sir Ch. Blount to same.
May 26. E. of Cumberland to same.
May 27. Alderman Martin to same.
May 27. Ld. Burghley to same.
May 29. The Queen to Lord Burghley.
May 30. Wm. Waade to Sir R. Cecil.
[May —.] Intelligence from Scotland.
June 1. W. Anderson to Archd. Douglas.
June 1. Chateau-Martin to Lord Burghley.
June 2. Examination of W. Turner, merchant of Colchester.
June 4. Examination of Wm. (?) Smythe, of Colchester, seaman.
June 5. King of Scots to the Queen.
June 5. Order from Court of Wards or Duchy Court.
June 6. Sir H. Palavicino to Sir R. Cecil.
June 8. Giov. B. Caresana to the Queen.
June 8. Ric. Douglas to Arch. Douglas.
June 9. R. Carvyl to same.
June 10. Chateau-Martin to Lord Burghley.
June 11. Barth. Gilburd to Sir R. Cecil.
June 13. Anth. Atkinson to same.
June 16. M. de Lancy to E. of Essex.
June 17. Sir Th. Leighton to the Privy Council.
June 18. Chateau-Martin to Lord Burghley.
June 18. M. de St. Luc to E. of Essex.
June 20. Chateau-Martin to Lord Burghley.
June 21. Sir W. Ralegh to the Ld. Admiral.
June 23. The Queen to Ld. Burghley.
June 24. Ld. Buckhurst to Sir R. Cecil.
June 24. Capt. Jo. Houghton to same.
June 25. W. Selby to Arch. Douglas.
June 29. John Bristowe (Moody) to — Robyn.
June 29. Ld. Cobham to Sir R. Cecil.
June 29. Justice Townsend to same.
June 30. Ld. Scroope to same.
June 30. Sir G. Carew to same.
June —. Misdemeanour of Th. Douche against Marg. his mother.
July 2. Sir H. Palavicino to Sir R. Cecil.
July 4. Hutton, Bp. of Durham, to same.
July 4. The Queen to the admiral and commanders of Her ships.
July 5. R. Brus to (E. of Essex).
July 6. Same to same.
July 7. W. Waite to Sir R. Cecil.
July 8. Alderman Billingsley to Ld. Burghley.
July 8. Sir Th. Shirley to Sir R. Cecil.
July 9. Th. Edmonds to (E. of Essex).
July 9. Sir Timothy (Hesketh, name erased) to Sir R. Cecil.
July 13. Lady Bacon (the mother of Sir F.) to the same.
July 13. Sir Ant. Powlet to Sir R. Cecil.
July 13. Dr. Webster to same.
July 13. Mayor of Southampton, to same.
July 13. Chateau-Martin to Lord Burghley.
July 15. Countess of Cumberland to Sir R. Cecil.
July 15. Memoranda for Brest.
July 15. Ric. Scribel to Th. Myddleton.
July 15. Ant. Powlet to Ld. Burghley.
July 16. The Queen to the same.
July 16. Sir H. Palavicino to Sir R. Cecil.
July 17. R. Carmarden to same.
July 17. Sir Th. Shirley to same.
July 17. Jo. Byrd to same.

MARQUIS
OF SALIS-
BURY.

July 17. Ld. Cobham to same.
July 20. Sir Jo. Gilbert to same.
July 20. Sir W. Ralegh to same.
July 21. Capt. M. Dawtrie to same.
July 21. Sir H. Palavicino to same.
July 22. E. of Lincoln to Ld. Burghley.
July 24. Sir Geo. Carew and A. Gorges to Sir R.
Cecil.
July 25. Th. D'Arques to same.
July 26. Ld. Cobham to same.
July 27. Mayor of Ipewich, to Ld. Burghley.
July 28. Maitland Ld. Thirlstane (Chanc. of Scot-
land) to same.
July 28. Privy Council to same.
July 28. Sir Th. Throckmorton to Sir R. Cecil.
July 28. R. Douglas to Arch. Douglas.
July 30. C. Hussie to Sir R. Cecil.
July 31. Th. D'Arques to same.
July 31. The Queen to Sir Jo. Norris.
July —. Th. Robinson to R. Carmarden.
July —. Officers of Southampton to Ld. Burghley.
July —. Mem. of Conveyances by Edw. VI., of lands
of Bishopric of Winchester, annulled by 6 Mary, now re-
enacted.
July —. Names of seminary priests in England, and
with whom resident.
Aug. 2. Sir H. Lee to Sir R. Cecil.
Aug. 3. Spanish Deputy to D. Juan Idiaquez.
Aug. 3. F. Spinola to Sr. Est. d'Yuarra.
Aug. 3. Dr. Parkins to Sir R. Cecil.
Aug. 4. E. of Lincoln to Ld. Burghley.
Aug. 5. Sir W. Cornwalleys to Sir R. Cecil.
Aug. 6. Sir Th. Heneage to same.
Aug. 6. H. Brooke to same.
Aug. 6. The Queen to Ld. Burghley.
Aug. 6. Same to E. of Bath.
Aug. 12. Th. d'Arquez to Sir R. Cecil.
Aug. 12. R. Carmarden to same.
Aug. 13. "4" (Moody) to Th. More.
Aug. 14. Confession of Steph. White to avoid the
torture, and his proceedings with John Moody.
Aug. 15. Conference of Adrian Delange and Steph.
White.
Aug. 16. Mayor of Plymouth, to Sir R. Cecil.
Aug. 16. Examination of Nich. Flute, of Dartmouth.
Aug. 17. P. Corsini to Sir R. Cecil.
Aug. 17. The Comte de St. Paul to the Queen.
Aug. 20. Jo. Colville to Sir R. Cecil.
Aug. 20. Dr. Ch. Perkins to same.
Aug. 20. Ld. Mountjoy to same.
Aug. 20. (30th.) Joanes Aveden (?) to L. Buy Vile
lascada.
Aug. 25. Sir W. Ralegh to (Sir R. Cecil ?).
Aug. 25. Geo. Margitts to same.
Aug. 25. Sir Th. Cecil to same.
Aug. 25. Arth. Gregory to same.
Aug. 26. R. Topolyffe to Ld. Burghley.
Aug. 26. The Queen to same.
Aug. 28. Lord Sheffield to Sir R. Cecil.
Aug. 29. Ro. Manners to same (2).
Aug. 29. John Stafford to same.
Aug. 29. Cheverny to E. of Essex.
Aug. 30. The Queen to M. of Winchester.
Aug. 31. Examination of Gilb. Smyth, of Exon,
merchant.
Aug. —. Sir Chas. Danvers to Sir R. Cecil.
Aug. —. H. Lok to same.
Aug. —. Ch. Carty to same.
Aug. —. W. Hamone to same.
Aug. —. The Widow of Dr. Lopez to the Queen.
Sept. 1. Mayor of Exeter to Sir R. Cecil.
Sept. 1. Wm. Brocas to same.
Sept. 1. Sir Geo. Carey to same.
Sept. 2. Th. Townson to same.
Sept. 2. Sir H. Palavicino to same.
Sept. 2. Th. d'Arques to same.
Sept. 3. L. Lewkenor to same.
Sept. 4. E. of Shrewsbury to Sir R. Cecil.
Sept. 5. Capt. W. Lane to same.
Sept. 6. Capt. Dawtrey to same.
Sept. 6. Wm. Brocas to same.
Sept. 6. Le Duc de Mayne to Rog. d'Espaigne.
Sept. 7. Same to Card. de Joyeuse.
Sept. 7. Sir Ro. Williams to Sir W. Cecil.
Sept. 7. Mayor of Exeter to same.
Sept. 7. E. English to H. Maynard.
Sept. 9. Geo. Margitts to Sir R. Cecil.
Sept. 10. Sir W. Ralegh to same.
Sept. —. Jo. Colville to K. of Scotland.
Sept. 12. Same to E. Bothwell.
Sept. 12. Sir H. Palavicino to Sir R. Cecil (2).

Sept. 13. Dr. R. Webster to same.
Sept. 13. Ed. Prynne to same.
Sept. 13. Dr. Jo. Cowell to H. Brooke.
Sept. 17. Th. D'Arques to Sir R. Cecil.
Sept. 17. —— to ——.
Sept. 18. Aldermen Billingsley and Carmarden to Ld.
Burghley.
Sept. 18. R. Perceval to Sir R. Cecil.
Sept. 18. R. Carmarden to Ld. Burghley.
Sept. 19. Aldermen Lee and Bennet to Sir R. Cecil.
Sept. 19. Geo. Margitts to same.
Sept. 19. Dr. Th. Ridley to same.
Sept. 19. (Moody) under the name of Bristow to Th.
More.
Sept. 21. Ld. Lumley to Sir R. Cecil.
Sept. 21. Th. D'Arques to same.
Sept. 22. Th. North to Ld. Burghley.
Sept. 22. Ch. Carty to Sir R. Cecil.
Sept. 23. Interrogatories for Ralph Sheldon.
Sept. 24. R. Carmarden to Sir R. Cecil.
Sept. 25. E. of Cumberland to same.
Sept. 26. Th. Edmonds to E. of Essex.
Sept. 26. [English Ambassador ?] to [Lord Burghley ?]
Sept. 27. M. Hickes to Sir R. Cecil.
Sept. 27. Dr. Jul. Cæsar to same.
Sept. 28. Ri. Skevington to same.
Sept. 28. H. Brouncker to same.
Sept. 28. M. Hickes to same.
Sept. 28. Capt. E. Waymann to same.
Sept. 29. Duc de Montpensier to E. of Essex.
Oct. 1. Hen. Brooke to Sir R. Cecil.
Oct. 3. Ld. Lumley to same.
Oct. 3. Sir Jo. Wolley to same.
Oct. 5. Sir H. Palavicino to same.
Oct. 6. Wm. Waad to Ld. Burghley.
Oct. 8. Sir Jo. Fortescue to Sir R. Cecil.
Oct. 8. Ld. Burgh to E. of Essex.
Oct. 9. F. Derrick to H. Wickham.
Oct. 10. Sir Geo. Carew to Sir R. Cecil.
Oct. 10. Moody to Th. Harrington.
Oct. 11. Sir W. Cornwalleys to Sir R. Cecil.
Oct. 11. Jo. Colville to same.
Oct. 11. Earl of Essex to same.
Oct. 12. Arth. Gregory to same.
Oct. 12. Payments by Sir Th. Shirley, treasurer at
war, of forces in Low Countries extraordinary, from 1 Feb.
1586.
Oct. 14. Jo. Colville to Sir R. Cecil.
Oct. 14. Dr. Day, Dean of Windsor, to same.
Oct. 16. Dr. T. Ridley to same.
Oct. 16. Att. Gen. Coke to same.
Oct. 16. T. Windebank to same.
Oct. 17. Jo. Bristow (Moody) to "A. Versamen."
Oct. 17. (Antonio) King of Portugal to Earl of Essex.
Oct. 18. Ric. Douglas to Arch. Douglas.
Oct. 19. Sir H. Palavicino to Sir R. Cecil.
Oct. 20. Howland, Bp. of Peterboro', to same.
Oct. 20. Lucy Lady St. John to Sir R. Cecil.
Oct. 20. Sir R. Cecil to M. Richardat.
Oct. 22. Jo. Colville to Sir R. Cecil.
Oct. 22. Same to H. Lok.
Oct. 26. — Edgecumbe to directors of the mines.
Oct. 27. Sir A. Pawlet to Sir R. Cecil.
Oct. 31. Sir R. Cecil to M. Caron.
Oct. —. The Queen to M. Richardat.
Oct. —. Privy Council to same.
Oct. —. Merchants of the[E. Country to Ld. Burghley.
Oct. —. Warrant of E. of Essex as patentee of sweet
wines to the Livonians.
Nov. 2. Sir Jo. Fortescue to Sir R. Cecil.
Nov. 3. King of Scots to R. Bowes.
Nov. 4. Whitgift, Abp. of Cant., to Sir R. Cecil.
Nov. 7. R. Beale and Sir H. Killegrew to Roger
Saunders.
Nov. 8. Maynard to Sir R. Cecil.
Nov. 8. Ed. Suliarde to same.
Nov. 8. Sir H. Palavicino to Sir R. Cecil.
Nov. 11. E. of Derby to Ld. Burghley.
Nov. 13. Th. Edmonds to E. of Essex.
Nov. 13. The Queen to French King's sister.
Nov. 13. Vincent de Vinconzo to —.
Nov. 13. Questions by John Bassadona to Vincenzo,
with answers.
Nov. 17. Stan. Passy to Topclyffe.
Nov. 21. Rog. Manners to Sir R. Cecil.
Nov. 23. M. de Sancy to the E. of Essex.
Nov. 26. Weekly payments to forces in Low Countries
for two months.
Nov. 26. Legacies for godly uses by John Freiston of
Altosts, York, to Univ. Coll., Oxford, Emanuel Coll.,

Camb., almshouse at Pontefract, free school at Norman-
ton, free school at Wakefield, &c.
Nov. 27. F. Greville to Sir R. Cecil.
Nov. 27. N. Geffs to same.
Nov. 30. Justice Young to the Queen.
Nov. —. E. of Essex to Sir R. Cecil.
Nov. —. Sir R. Cecil to M. Caron.
Nov. —. Jas. Douglas to Wm. Douglas.
Dec. 2, Sir H. Palavicino to Sir R. Cecil.
Dec. 2. —— to P. Halling.
Dec. 3. Sir W. Waller to Sir R. Cecil.
Dec. 4. Th. Horniman to same.
Dec. 6. W. Lee to same.
Dec. 6. Sir W. Cornwalleys to same.
Dec. 6. Whitgift, Abp. of Canterbury, to same.
Dec. 7. N. Longford to same.
Dec. 7. H. Lok to same.
Dec. 7. Fletcher, Bp. of Worcester, to same.
Dec. 8. Same to same.
Dec. 9. Declaration of Th. Brookes of diamond
pawned to Giles Simpson.
Dec. 10. Sir R. Cecil to Bp. of Lincoln.
Dec. 11, Hutton, Bp. of Durham, to Sir R. Cecil.
Dec. 13. R. Wrothe to same.
Dec. 14. Chaderton, Bp. of Lincoln, to same.
Dec. 15. Examinations of Alice and W. Hamor and
Bart. Gilbert respecting diamonds Dec. 13.
Dec. 15. Ald. Martyn to Sir R. Cecil.
Dec. 18. Sir H. Palavicino to same.
Dec. 19. Ld. Keeper Puckering to same.
Dec. 19. Ri. Carmarden to same.
Dec. 20. Sir W. Cornwalleys to same.
Dec. 20. Ernest (Archduke, Gov. of Low Conntries)
to King of Spain.
Dec. 20. —— to Douglas of Sprot.
Dec. 21. Les Etats de Provinces Unies to Comte
d'Essex.
Dec. 21. Fletcher, Bp. of Worcester, to Sir R. Cecil.
Dec. 21. Sir W. Ralegh to same.
Dec. 22. T. Edmonds to E. of Essex.
Dec. 23. R. Willughby to Dr. Hawkins.
Dec. 23. H. Maynard to Sir R. Cecil.
Dec. 24. Chaderton, Bp. of Lincoln, to same.
Dec. 24. Ld. Keeper Puckering to same.
Dec. 25. R. Carmarden to Ld. Burghley.
Dec. 26. Dr. Th. Ridley to Sir R. Cecil.
Dec. 26. Sir W. Ralegh to same.
Dec. 27. Maurice of Nassau to E. of Essex.
Dec. 27. King of Portugal to Queen Elizabeth.
Dec. 28. B. Clere, searcher at Ipswich, to Ld. Burghley.
Dec. 29. Hutton, Bp. of Durham, to Sir R. Cecil.
Dec. —. Sir R. Cecil to Ld. Buckhurst and Sir Jo.
Fortescue.
Dec. —. Officers of Southampton to Lord Burghley.
Dec. —. Privy Council to Bp. of Durham.
Dec. —. Sir W. Ralegh to Sir R. Cecil.
Dec. —. Carew Reynell to same.
Dec. —. Dr. Th. Ridley to same.
Dec. —. Hen. Bunre (?) to the Queen.
Dec. —. Leases in Bishopric of Winchester which
previous Bishops have usually granted to Her Majesty.
Dec. —, Jo. Burrell to Lord Burghley or E. of Essex.
Dec. —, Sir H. Danvers to E. of Essex.
1594. Treasons and attainder of Pat. Collin or
Cullen, Ri. Hesketh, and Wm. Purrye.
1594. Names of United Provinces which de jure ought
to discharge half the general debt.
1594. Accusations against K. of Spain's ministers
touching English fugitives, Ibarra, Sir W. Stanley,
Father Holt, Garrett, Moody, &c.
1594. Act for surety of the Queen's person.
1594. Note out of the Civil Law to maintain the
Queen's demands notwithstanding extract sent to
Mr. Bodley.
—— Capt. Hayes to Ld. Burghley.
—— John James to — Clifton.
—— Gr. Markham to Mr. Reynolds.
—— The Queen to King of Scots (E. of Essex's).
—— Declaration of John Bernardus de Carcsano.
Narrative of his life.
—— Custom on gold and silver, thread and lace.
—— Calculations of Sir R. Cecil upon copper
mines.
—— Interrogatories for Ciprian Gabriel.
—— Engrossing of tin in Cornwall.
—— Fines of E. of Oxford.
—— Conveyances by Geo. E. of Shrewsbury to his
son Hen. Talbot.
—— Essex described by John Norden, with pen
and ink map coloured.
—— Mem. of war between Spain and France.

—— Mem. of Sir R. Cecil of harbouring priests by
M. Tasborough.
—— Memoriæ Nativitatum et aliarum rerum
gestarum. From 1521.
1594. Relief of Hen. Leigh, keeper of Rockliff Castle
on the Borders.
1594. Commodities and revenues of the manor of
Farnham.
1594. Claim for a lease granted by Th. Goodricke,
Bp. of Ely, to his brother John, temp. Hen. VIII.
1594. Memoranda on wars between France and Spain.
1594. Discours de la prise du Marquis d'Aremberg,
par. Mon. le Mareschal de Biron.
(1594.) Instructions to Rob. Bowes, ambassador in
Scotland, upon a writing to the K. of Scots' secretary,
by Lo. Zouche (Papistical Lords).
(1594.) Answer to Earl Bothwell (Pap. Lords).
(1594.) Advertisements touching Scottish Roman
Catholics.
(1594.) Instructions of Scotch King to D. of Lennox,
ambassador in France.
(1594.) Words spoken by one Sutcliff against Lord
Burghley and [Sir R. Cecil].
(1594.) Paper upon the succession.
(1594.) Description of John Gerrard.
(1594.) Grant to Hen. Broucard of customs in Ireland.
(1594.) Army account in French for 2½ years.
(1594.) [Arch. Douglas's] reckonings.
(1594.) (An officer of the Treasury) to [Lord Burgh-
ley], of Lady Fortescue.
(1594.) Sir Ro. Sydney to Lo. Burghley.
(1594.) Authoritas Sacræ Scripturæ, for reformation of
errors in the Church. On Papal supremacy and the
temporal power.
(1594.) Misdemeanors of Hillarie Dakyns.
(1594.) Account of Dr. Rog. Lopez's treason.
1594. Don Hurtado de Mendoza to the Queen.
1594. Lawrence Smith to Countess of Warwick.
1594. Gilbert E. of Shrewsbury to Sir R. Cecil.
1594. Privy Council to Lord Willoughby.
1594. Contractors for pepper to the Queen.
1594. E. of Essex to M. Viedame.
1594. Same to Sir H. Unton.

1595.

Jan. 1. E. of Shrewsbury to Sir R. Cecil.
Jan. 1. Sir Ed. Norris to E. of Essex.
Jan. 3. Sir G. Peckham to Sir R. Cecil.
Jan. 3. Co. of York to same.
Jan. 4. E. of Derby to same.
Jan. 4. Sir John Fortescue to Barnard Dewhurst.
Jan. 4. Sir Th. Bodley to Ld. Burghley.
Jan. 5. Bapt. Giustiniani to Sir R. Cecil.
Jan. 5. Sir Ed. Norris to E. of Essex.
Jan. 7. The Queen to Ld. Mayor, London.
Jan. 7. Claude de la Tremouille to [E. of Essex ?].
Jan. 8. R. Douglas to Arch. Douglas.
Jan. 9. Auditor Hill to Sir R. Cecil.
Jan. 10. Jane Carvell to Arch. Douglas.
Jan. 10. Sir H. Palavicino to Sir R. Cecil.
Jan. 11. Jo. Lee to same.
Jan. 12. Ger. Lowther to Jo. Stanhope.
Jan. 14. Lady Varenne to E. of Essex.
Jan. 15. F. Mascoll to Sir R. Cecil.
Jan. 15. Otwell Smith to E. of Essex.
Jan. 15. Sir Ph. Boteler to Sir R. Cecil.
Jan. 16. Ja. Dillon to same.
Jan. 16. E. of Cumberland to same.
Jan. 16. Geo. Goring to same.
Jan. 17. Sir H. Unton to E. of Essex.
Jan. 17. Same to Lord Burghley.
Jan. 17. Same to the Queen.
Jan. 18. Privy Council to Collectors of Subsidies.
Jan. 18. Ph. Honnyman to Sir R. Cecil.
Jan. 18. Sir W. Ralegh to Sir R. Cecil.
Jan. 18. H. Houger to same.
Jan. 19. Sir H. Lee to same.
Jan. 19. Same to same.
Jan. 20. Th. Mascoll to same.
Jan. 20. Sir H. Palavicino to Sir J. Fortescue,
Jan. 21. Sir Jo. Forster to Bp. of Durham.
Jan. 21. Capt. R. Moryson to E. of Essex.
Jan. 21. The Queen to King of France.
Jan. 21. Same to Queen of France.
Jan. 21. Lord Burghley to Arch. Douglas.
Jan. 22. R. Staper and E. Holmden to Sir R. Cecil.
Jan. 23. Mathews, Bp. of Durham, to Ld. Burghley.
Jan. 23. Geo. Goring to Sir R. Cecil.
Jan. 23. — Cope to same.
Jan. 24. Sir Jo. Foster to Ld. Burghley.

5

Jan. 24. Duc de Bouillon to Comte d'Essex.
Jan. 25. Jo. Ferne to Sir. R. Cecil.
Jan. 25. Geo. Gilpin to E. of Essex.
Jan. 25. Sir Th. Bodley to Ld. Burghley.
Jan. 25. Th. Mascoll to Sir R. Cecil.
Jan. 25. Sheriff of Somerset to same.
Jan. 25. Duc de Montpensier to E. of Essex.
Jan. 25. Sir H. Palavicino to Sir R. Cecil.
Jan. 25. M. de Montmartin to E. of Essex.
Jan. 26. Th. Honnyman to Sir R. Cecil.
Jan. 26. Sir Jo. Rooper to same.
Jan. 27. Jo. Ferne to same.
Jan. 27. Bapt. Giustiniani to same.
Jan. 27. Dowager Lady Russell to same.
Jan. 27. Sir H. Unton to Lord Burghley.
Jan. 28. Th. Lake to Sir R. Cecil.
Jan. 28. H. Brooke to same.
Jan. 28. The Queen to Q. of Scots.
Jan. 28. Th. Lake to Sir R. Cecil.
Jan. 28. Jo. Stanhope to same.
Jan. 28. Same to same.
Jan. 29. Fulke Greville to Lord Burghley.
Jan. 30. Jo. Rolsterne to Arch. Douglas.
Jan. 30. Mathews, Bp. of Durham, to Ld. Burghley.
Jan. 30. Sir Th. Bodley to same.
Jan. 30. Sir E. Dymoke to Sir R. Cecil.
Jan. 31. Geo. Gilpin to E. of Essex.
Jan. 31. Sir Th. Wilks to Sir R. Cecil.
Jan. —. Duc de Montpensier to E. of Essex.
Jan. —. M. de Beauvoir to same.
Feb. 1. Th. Arundel to Sir R. Cecil.
Feb. 1. Sir Th. Shirley to same.
Feb. 2. Sir R. Crofts to same.
Feb. 2. Jo. Car. Marquis of Baden to the Queen.
Feb. 3. Sir H. Unton to Lord Burghley.
Feb. 3. Same to the Queen.
Feb. 3. Vaughan, Bp. of Bangor, to Sir R. Cecil.
Feb. 4. The Queen to Lord Burghley.
Feb. 4. Sir H. Unton to the E. of Essex.
Feb. 4. Sir Ed. Norreys to same.
Feb. 5. Advertisements from Rome.
Feb. 5. Sir R. Wynter to Ld. Admiral and Sir R. Cecil.
Feb. 5. Jo. Vere to same.
Feb. 6. Sir Wm. Russell (Lord Deputy of Ireland) to Lord Burleigh.
Feb. 7. Ld. Cobham to Sir R. Cecil.
Feb. 8. Sir Th. Leighton to Privy Council.
Feb. 9. Ed. More to Sir R. Cecil.
Feb. 9. Sir R. Berkley to same.
Feb. 9. Speech of W. Lucke, goldsmith, at the Mitre in Cheapside, with examination.
Feb. 9. Beauvoir la Noue to E. of Essex.
Feb. 9. Mr. Bodley to Lord Burghley.
Feb. 10. Geo. Gilpin to E. of Essex.
Feb. 10. M. Sancy to M. Bussenville.
Feb. 10. Commission for a Provost Martial.
Feb. 10. Geo. Crytton (Jesuit) to Rev. P. Jacobo Tyrio.
Feb. 10. Same to Aquaviva.
Feb. 10. The Queen to Sir Th. Wilson.
Feb. 11. Maurice of Nassau to E. of Essex.
Feb. 12. Advertisements from Venice.
Feb. 13. Sir H. Unton to E. of Essex (2).
Feb. 13. Pat. Cuming to Arch. Douglas.
Feb. 14. H. Maynard to Sir R. Cecil.
Feb. 14. Sir A. Cope to same.
Feb. 14. Instructions of Sec. King to Wm. Stewart, amb. to States General.
Feb. 14. M. de Mony to E. of Essex.
Feb. 15. Purefey and Ferne to Ld. Burghley.
Feb. 15. Sir Th. Leighton to Privy Council.
Feb. 16. The Mayor, &c. of Hull to Sir. R. Cecil.
Feb. 17. E. of Essex to same.
Feb. 17. R. Bowes to Ld. Burghley.
Feb. 17. Sir Th. Wilks to Sir R. Cecil.
Feb. 17. Mem. of stores, rigging, &c. to authorities at Portsmouth for salvage.
Feb. 17. H. Noel to Sir R. Cecil.
Feb. 18. Sir H. Unton to Lord Burghley.
Feb. 19. Sir H. Danvers to E. of Essex.
Feb. 19. Advertisements from Vienna.
Feb. 20. Mathews, Bp. of Durham, to Ld. Burghley.
Feb. 20. Day, Bp. of Winchester, to Sir R. Cecil.
Feb. 21. Sir Ed. Coke to same.
Feb. 22. Ant. Atkinson to same.
Feb. 22. Sir F. Vere to E. of Essex.
Feb. 23. Sir E. Stanley to Sir R. Cecil.
Feb. 23. Advertisements from Antwerp.
Feb. 24. Ld. Burgh to Sir R. Cecil.
Feb. 24. Jo. Harmar to — Beeston.
Feb. 25. Th. Ferrers to Sir R. Cecil.

Feb. 25. Attorney General (Coke) to same.
Feb. 25. Sir F. Vere to E. of Essex.
Feb. 26. M. de Sancy to same.
Feb. 26. Lord Burghley to Arch. Douglas.
Feb. 27. Arch. Douglas to Ld. Burghley.
Feb. 27. Sir H. Unton to E. of Essex.
Feb. 28. The Queen to Ld. Burghley.
Feb. 28. Mathews, Bp. of Durham, to same.
Feb. 28. Bailiff of Colchester to Sir R. Cecil.
Feb. 28. Geo. Gilpin to E. of Essex.
Feb. 28. Lady Riche to Sir R. Cecil.
Feb. 28. Gar. Gwifo to Ld. Burghley.
Feb. — Concerning Vice-Chancellorship of Duchy of Lancaster.
Mar. 1. W. Medeley to Sir R. Cecil.
Mar. 1. Duc de Bouillon to Comte d'Essex.
Mar. 1. Sir F. Willughby to Sir R. Cecil.
Mar. 2. Aymar de Chastes (Gov. of Dieppe) to E. of Essex.
Mar. 2. Duc de Bouillon to Comte d'Essex.
Mar. 3. Th. Arundel to Sir R. Cecil.
Mar. 3. Lord Burghley to Arch. Douglas.
Mar. 3. Capt. Hen. Dooray to E. of Essex.
Mar. 4. Privy Council to Ld. Burghley.
Mar. 4. Sir H. Unton to E. of Essex.
Mar. 4. Same to Lord Burghley.
Mar. 6. A. Atye to Sir R. Cecil.
Mar. 6. Attestation of those who apprehended W. Kindmont on the Borders.
Mar. 7. Ld. Admiral to Sir R. Cecil.
Mar. 7. Sir E. Norris to E. of Essex.
Mar. 7. Sir E. Wilton to same.
Mar. 7. Sir F. Vere to same.
Mar. 8. E. of Essex to Sir R. Cecil.
Mar. 8. Issue of Privy Seal for money for 1,000 footmen for Ireland.
Mar. 8. Caldwell, Bp. of Salisbury, to Sir R. Cecil.
Mar. 8. Sir R. Cecil to Ld. Willughby d'Eresby.
Mar. 9. Th. Ferrers to Ld. Burghley.
Mar. 9. Sir F. Vere to E. of Essex.
Mar. 9. Bp. and Justices of Durham to Ld. Burghley.
Mar. 10. Dr. Chr. Parkins to Sir R. Cecil.
Mar. 10. Hutton, Abp. of York, and the Council to Ld. Burghley.
Mar. 10. Same to same.
Mar. 12. T. Smith to Sir R. Cecil.
Mar. 12. Sir W. Hatton to same.
Mar. 12. Sir H. Cooke to same.
Mar. 12. Sir Foulke Greville to same.
Mar. 12. Sir R. Barkley to same.
Mar. 13. Sir R. Martyn to same.
Mar. 14. E. of Oxford to Ld. Burghley.
Mar. 15. R. Cole to same.
Mar. 15. Governor of Bayonne to E. of Essex.
Mar. 15. Th. Ferrers to Ld. Burghley.
Mar. 16. Sir Jo. Gilbert to Sir R. Cecil.
Mar. 16. Sir E. Norris to E. of Essex.
Mar. 16. Countess of Bedford to Sir R. Cecil.
Mar. 16. W. Moys to H. Maynard.
Mar. 17. Th. Windebank to Sir R. Cecil.
Mar. 17. Same to same.
Mar. 17. Ld. Admiral to same.
Mar. 17. Sir H. Unton to Lord Burghley.
Mar. 17. Same to E. of Essex.
Mar. 17. Wm. May to H. Maynard.
Mar. 17. Sir. H. Unton and W. Edmonds to E. of Essex.
Mar. 18. Warden, &c. of New Coll., Oxon, to Sir R. Cecil.
Mar. 18. Sir A. Powlet to his brother.
Mar. 20. Lady Ralegh to Sir R. Cecil.
Mar. 20. Sir H. Unton to Lord Burghley.
Mar. 20. Hutton, Abp. of York, to same.
Mar. 20. Capt. M. Bradgate to Sir R. Cecil.
Mar. 20. Th. Arundel to same.
Mar. 20. E. of Derby to same.
Mar. 21. Abp. and Council of York to Ld. Burghley.
Mar. 21. W. Paule to E. of Essex.
Mar. 21. Sir T. Bodley to Ld. Burghley.
Mar. 21. H. Morgan to Sir R. Cecil.
Mar. 23. Th. Ferrers to Ld. Burghley.
Mar. 24. Sir T. Bodley to same.
Mar. 24. Sir Ed. Norris to E. of Essex.
Mar. 25. Sir Ant. Powlet to Sir R. Cecil.
Mar. 25. W. Halliday to same.
Mar. 25. E. of Oxford to Ld. Burghley.
Mar. 25. M. de Montmartin to E. of Essex.
Mar. 25. Sir Th. Shirley to Sir R. Cecil.
Mar. 26. — Champernoun to same.
Mar. 27. Beauvoir la Noue to the E. of Essex.
Mar. 28. Sir F. Vere to same.
Mar. 28. Same to same.

Mar. 28. E. of Oxford to Ld. Burghley.
Mar. 28. E. of Huntingdon to Sir R. Cecil.
Mar. 28. E. of Oxford to — Hickes.
Mar. 31. Sir F. Zouche to Sir R. Cecil.
Mar. —. Drafts of commissions by E. of Essex as commander of forces assisting France.
April 1. Sir Art. Gorges to Sir R. Cecil.
April 1. Geo. Gilpin to E. of Essex.
April 1. E. of Oxford to Ld. Burghley.
April 2. Benedict Harvey to ——.
April 3. Goodman, Dean of Westminster, to the Queen.
April 3. Issue of Privy Seal of money for forces returned from Brittany.
April 4. Sir Th. Cecil to Sir R. Cecil.
April 4. Maurice of Nassau to E. of Essex.
April 5. The Queen to Ld. Burghley.
April 6. Nich. Bomer to E. of Essex.
April 6. Paper endd. Nich. Williamson. (Morton and Berwick mentioned.)
April 7. H. Lok to Sir R. Cecil.
April 7. Lady Ralegh to same.
April 8. Jo. Sparhawk to same.
April 8. Sir Foulke Greville to same.
April 9. E. of Oxford to Ld. Burghley.
April 12. Ld. Anderson to Sir R. Cecil.
April 12. Duc de Bouillon to Comte d'Essex.
April 13. Sir Th. Bodley to Sir R. Cecil.
April 13. Same to Ld. Burghley.
April 13. E. of Oxford to same.
April 15. Sir E. Norris to E. of Essex.
April 15. Fletcher, Bp. of London, to Sir R. Cecil.
April 15. Sir H. Palmer to Ld. Admiral.
April 16. W. Wayte to Sir R. Cecil.
April 16. Ld. Admiral to same.
April 16. The Queen to Ld. Burghley.
April 16. Hutton, Abp. of York, to Sir R. Cecil.
April 17. Same to same.
April 17. Ld. Buckhurst to Ld. Burghley.
April 17. E. of Oxford to same.
April 17. R. Carmarden to same.
April 17. Sir Ant. Shirley to Sir R. Cecil.
April 17. Ri. Pownal to Ld. Buckhurst.
April 18. Ld. Burghley to — Francis.
April 19. Mathews, Bp. of Durham, to Sir R. Cecil.
April 20. King of France to the E. of Essex.
April 21. Jo. Stanhope to Sir R. Cecil.
April 21. Confession of Edw. Codrington, taken in Flushing.
April 21. Ld. Willughby to Sir W. Knollis.
April 23. R. Capcots (Deputy of the Mercht. Adventurers) to same.
April 23. Sir Th. Bodley to Ld. Burghley.
April 24. E. of Oxford to Sir R. Cecil.
April 24. G. Lowther to Sir Th. Heneage.
April 25. G. Gilpin to E. of Essex.
April 24. Sir F. Vere to E. of Essex.
April 25. Ber. de Caresana to the Council of the Queen of England.
April 26. Same to same.
April 26. Countess of Hertford to Sir R. Cecil.
April 26. Examination of Sam. Whaiton and Th. Richardson, signed by them and Sir Wm. Waade, as Clk. of the Council.
April 26. Note of proceedings concerning evidences at Belvoir since the death of Edw. E. of Rutland.
April 28. Rog. Ld. North to Sir R. Cecil.
April 28. Sir G. Carew to Lord Buryhley.
April 28. Sir H. Saville to Sir R. Cecil.
April 28. Ld, Admiral to Sir R. Cecil.
April 28. Ric. Willughby to Dr. Hawkins.
April 29. Ja. Yetswent to Sir R. Cecil.
April 29. John Clapham to same.
April 30. Ld. Hunsdon to same.
April 30. Sir E. Hoby to same.
April 30. Sir R. Cecil to John White.
April 30. Ld. Buckhurst to Ld. Burghley.
April —. Ld. Admiral to Sir R. Cecil.
April —. Advertisements from France.
April —. Pat. Moyle to Ld. Burghley.
April —. W. Jones to Sir R. Cecil.
May 1. Th. Dawet to Ld. Burghley.
May 2. Beauvoir la Noue to E. of Essex.
May 3. Sir Ed. Norris to same.
May 3. Geo. Gilpin to same.
May 3. Sir H. Palavicino to Sir R. Cecil.
May 3. Ld. Cobham to Ld. Burghley.
May 4. Sir Foulke Greville to Sir R. Cecil.
May 6. Bar. Dewhurst to same.
May 7. R. Carmarden to Ld. Burghley.

May 7. Ld. Buckhurst to Sir R. Cecil.
May 7. —— Edgecombe to same.
May 8. Jo. Colvill to ——.
May 8. Jo. Lee to Sir R. Cecil.
May 9. Ro. Walmsley to Ant. Kemp.
May 9. Sir H. Palavicino to Sir R. Cecil.
May 9. M. de Sancy to E. of Essex.
May 9. E. of Huntingdon to Sir R. Cecil.
May 10. Th. Fane to same.
May 11. Patent of starch, Mr. Ellis's interest in, through Mr. Young.
May 12. Dr. Alex. Nowell to Sir R. Cecil.
May 12. H. Maynard to same.
May 13. Maurice of Nassau to E. of Essex.
May 13. Jehan de Oldenbarnevelte to same.
May 13. Declaration of Sam. Whaiton.
May 14. The Queen to Ld. Burghley.
May 14. Pat. Robinson to Arch. Douglas.
May 14. Geo. Goring to Sir R. Cecil.
May 14. Sir E. Hoby to same.
May 14. Ed. More to same.
May 14. — Edgecombe to same.
May 17. R. Bellot to same.
May 17. Sir H. Gray to same.
May 17. Sir Th. Shirley to same.
May 17. Sir H. Palavicino to same.
May 17. Information concerning Rob. Sweet.
May 17. Declaration of Th. Richardson.
May 18. Sir Th. Shirley to Sir R. Cecil.
May 19. Sir R. Cecil to Att. Gen. Coke.
May 19. Countess of Shrewsbury to Sir R. Cecil.
May 20. Whitgift, Abp. of Cant., to same.
May 20. Lady Jane Townsend to R. Stanhope.
May 20. Gr. Markham to Sir R. Cecil.
May 20. M. of Winchester to same.
May 21. Tho. Pergan to same.
May 23. Ld. Keeper Puckering to same.
May 23. Sir Ed. Hoby to same.
May 23. Lady Lumley to — Stanhope.
May 23. Ri. Broughton to E. of Essex.
May 26. Jo. Stanhope to Sir R. Cecil.
May 26. R. Hayes to same.
May 26. Sir M. Morgan to same.
May 27. Lady M. Nevylle to same.
May 27. Examination of Whaiton.
May 28. Sir Hor. Palavicino to Sir R. Cecil.
May 28. Same to same.
May 29. W. Fleetwoode to same.
May 29. Lady Mary Norris to same.
May 29. R. Carmarden to same.
May 29. Examination of Jas. Holt.
May 29. Chateau-Martin to Lo. Burghley.
May 30. Sir Ch. Danvers to Sir R. Cecil.
May 30. Sir Jul. Cæsar to same.
May 31. King of Scots to the Queen.
May 31. Sir H. Palavicino to Sir R. Cecil.
May —. Ed. Linton to Sir R. Cecil.
May —. Note touching writings and goods of N. Williamson at Wilno.
June 1. Ernest D. of Brunswick to the Queen.
June 1. Examination of Geo. Herbert at Middleburgh and intelligence by Mr. Daniel, now prisoner in the Tower.
June 2. Th. West to Sir R. Cecil.
June 2. Beauvoir la Noue to E. of Essex.
June 2. —— to ——.
June 3. Ld. Lumley to Sir R. Cecil.
June 4. Th. Arundel to same.
June 5. Sir Ar. Gorges to same.
June 6. Sir H. Palavicino to Sir R. Cecil.
June 7. Sir Geo. Carew to same.
June 7. Same to same.
June 7. Sir E. Hoby to same.
June 7. Lady Riche to same.
June 8. E. of Huntingdon to same.
June 8. Sir F. Gorges to E. of Essex.
June 9. Sir Th. Bodley to Sir R. Cecil.
June 9. Nicholas de Menze to same.
June 11. N. Bellamy to same.
June 11. R. Wrothes to same.
June 11. R. Dudley, afterwards titular E. of Northumberland, to same.
June 12. M. Topclyffe to same.
June 12. Lady Riche to same.
June 13. E. of Cumberland to same.
June 13. Sir T. Egerton and B. Coke to same.
June 13. Speeches, &c. of Th. Williamson by Th, Pearsall.
June 14. G. Gilpin to E. of Essex.
June 14. Charles de Bourbon to King of France.

June 14. Examination of Dav. Lawe (a priest), relating to E. of Shrewsbury and his servant Th. Williamson.
June 15. Capt. W. Morgan to Sir R. Cecil.
June 16. Jo. Harpur to same.
June 16. Sir Jo. Fortescue to Arch. Douglas.
June 17. Hutton, Abp. of York, to Sir H. Cecil.
June 17. Sir H. Palavicino to same.
June 19. Ld. Mayor to H. Maynard.
June 20. Disorders in London, from the 6th to the 16th.
June 21. Ld. Lumley to Sir R. Cecil.
June 21. E. of Lincoln to same.
June 21. W. Wayte to same.
June 21. La Fontaine to E. of Essex.
June 22. Chaderton, Bp. of Lincoln, to Sir R. Cecil.
June 23. Ed. More to same.
June 23. Geo. Gilpin to E. of Essex.
June 23. Sir H. Palavicino to Sir R. Cecil.
June 23. Att.-Gen. Coke to same.
June 24. Advertisements from Rome.
June 25. Sir F. Vere to E. of Essex.
June 25. Hugh Bethel to Arch. Douglas.
June 26. Sir H. Unton to Sir R. Cecil.
June 28. Demandes de M. le Duc de Mayenne et la reponse du Roy.
June 28. Sir Ed. Norreys to E. of Essex.
June 28. R. Grey to Sir R. Cecil.
June 28. Jo. Harpur to same.
June 29. Ric. Topclyffe to same.
June 29. Mathews, Bp. of Durham, to same.
June 30. E. of Cumberland to Sir R. Cecil.
June 30. Keeper of the Gatehouse to same.
June 30. The Queen to Ld. Burghley.
June 30. Sir H. Palavicino to Sir R. Cecil.
June 30. Advertisements from Venice.
July 1. Advertisements from Rome.
July 1. Ric. Osberne to Sir R. Cecil.
July 2. Sir H. Winston to same.
July 2. Ric. Kelly to same.
July 6. Mayors, &c. of Newcastle to Privy Council.
July 6. Agreement between Ric. Broughton, trustee of Walter late E. of Essex, and the present Earl, for payment of accounts.
July 6. Certificate of Geof. Storie's service in Ireland.
July 7. Jo. Scudamore (priest) to Mr. Fitz-Herbert.
July 7. The Parishioners of St. Owestrie and St. Martin's, Salop, to Lord Burghley.
July 7. King of France to his sister.
July 7. Advertisements from Venice.
July 8. The Queen to Ld. Burghley.
July 8. Sir Th. Heneage to Sir R. Cecil.
July 8. Ld. Keeper Puckering to same.
July 8. Sir Ed. Norris to Earl of Essex.
July 8. Geo. Gilpin to same.
July 8. Ld. Burgh to same.
July 8. Advertisements from Rome.
July 8. Ld. Keeper Puckering to Sir R. Cecil.
July 8. King of Scots to the Queen.
July 9. Sir Th. Cecil to Sir R. Cecil.
July 9. Sir Edm. Anderson to same.
July 10. Sir Fran. Godolphin to same.
July 10. Adrian Nicolai to M. de Caron.
July 10. Acknowledgment of Book of Proofs from Sir Th. Heneage by Ld. Burghley, against Edw. Seymour, E. of Hertford, and Lady Cath., daughter of the late D. of Suffolk, attainted on charge of matrimony. (To be kept in Exchequer.)
July 11. Sir Th. Bodley to Ld. Burghley.
July 11. Jo. Harper to same.
July 11. Noel de Caron to Sir R. Cecil.
July 11. Ric. Percival to same.
July 12. Sir Th. Heneage to same.
July 12. Geo. Goring to same.
July 13. Ld. Cobham to same.
July 14. Att. Gen. Coke to same.
July 14. Advertisements from Venice.
July 14. Jean Nidan to M. Noel de Caron.
July 14. E. of Essex to Sir H. Unton.
July 16. Capt. Ferd. Gorges to E. of Essex.
July 17. E. of Essex to Sir R. Cecil.
July 17. Dr. T. Bilson to same.
July 18. Ch. Justice Popham to same.
July 19. Geo. Gilpin to E. of Essex.
July 19. Sir H. Cocke to Sir R. Cecil.
July 20. Ld. Burgh to E. of Essex.
July 20. Ottwell Smith to Sir R. Cecil.
July 20. Jo. Harpur to same.
July 20. Sir F. Vere to same.
July 21. Ld. Burgh to E. of Essex.
July 22. Sir F. Vere to same.
July 22. Duc de Bouillon to Comte d'Essex.

July 22. E. of Essex to Keeper of Norwood Park.
July 22. Ld. Admiral to E. of Essex.
July 22. Capt. Ant. Kemes to same.
July 22. E. of Derby to Sir R. Cecil.
July 24. Ottwell Smith to E. of Essex.
July 25. Lady Balegh to Sir R. Cecil.
July 25. Sir Th. Heneage to same.
July 26. Capt. N. Clifford to E. of Essex.
July 27. Privy Council to Ld. Burghley.
July 27. Morgan, Bp. of Landaff, to Sir R. Cecil.
July 28. Sir H. Cocke to same.
July 28. Ottwell Smith to E. of Essex.
July 28. Ed. More to same.
July 28. Sir Th. Dennis to same.
July 28. Arth. Gorges to Sir R. Cecil.
July 29. Countess of Southampton to same.
July 29. Ld. Mayor, &c. of London to same.
July 29. Jo. Harpur to same.
July 29. Sir F. Drake and Sir J. Hawkins to E. of Essex.
July 30. Privy Council to Ld. Burghley.
July 31. Sir T. Heneage to Sir R. Cecil.
July 31. Haberdashers Company to the Privy Council.
July 31. W. Lane to Sir R. Cecil.
July —, Lady P. Riche to same.
July —, W. Cecil to same.
July —, Estimate for repair of St. Martin's church, Salop.
Aug. 1. The Queen to "The Generals."
Aug. 1. Sir E. Norris to E. of Essex.
Aug. 1. E. Wiseman to same.
Aug. 1. E. Wilton to same.
Aug. 2. Ld. Burgh to same.
Aug. 2. Ottwell Smith to same.
Aug. 2. Duc de Bouillon to Comte d'Essex.
Aug. 2. Countess of Southampton to Sir R. Cecil.
Aug. 3. Lady Mildred Read to same.
Aug. 3. Ld. Mountjoy to same.
Aug. 3. Sir Post. Hoby to same.
Aug. 3. N. Williamson to same (3).
Aug. 4. Same to same.
Aug. 4. Ld. Euro to same.
Aug. 5. Ld. Burgh to E. of Essex.
Aug. 5. Jo. Harpur to Sir R. Cecil.
Aug. 5. Sir Thos. Gerrard to same.
Aug. 6. N. Williamson to same.
Aug. 6. Sir F. Vere to E. of Essex.
Aug. 6. Of suspected persons to arrive in England.
Aug. 7. Information of Joan Aylinge, of Fittleworth.
Aug. 7. Duc de Nevers to the Queen.
Aug. 7. W. Webbe to Sir R. Cecil.
Aug. 7. Sir H. Palavicino to same.
Aug. 8. Lord Mountjoy to same.
Aug. 8. Ld. Admiral to same.
Aug. 8. Capt. Ed. Wylton to E. of Essex.
Aug. 8. E. Wiseman to same.
Aug. 8. Sir R. Sydney to same.
Aug. 8. Justices of Sussex to Ld. Buckhurst.
Aug. 9. Co. of Southampton to Sir R. Cecil.
Aug. 9. The Queen to Ld. Burghley.
Aug. 9. Ld. Buckhurst to Sir R. Cecil.
Aug. 9. Ld. Mountjoy to same.
Aug. 9. Jo. Harpur to same.
Aug. 10. Sir Th. Leighton to Sir Geo. Carey.
Aug. 10. Privy Council to Ld. Burghley.
Aug. 11. Ld. Buckhurst to Sir R. Cecil (2).
Aug. 11. Capt. E. Wylton to E. of Essex.
Aug. 11. List of English at Rome.
Aug. 12. Lo. Burgh to E. of Essex.
Aug. 12. Sir E. Denny to Sir R. Cecil.
Aug. 12. Governor of Dieppe to E. of Essex.
Aug. 12. Ottwell Smith to same.
Aug. 12. Sir Jo. Gilbert to Sir R. Cecil.
Aug. 12. E. Wiseman to E. of Essex.
Aug. 12. Advertisements from Rome.
Aug. 13. Sir F. Drake and Jo. Hawkins to E. of Essex.
Aug. 13. Sir Th. Baskerville to same.
Aug. 13. Sir Th. Gorges to same.
Aug. 13. Demands to be made to the Generals by Baskerville.
Aug. 14. N. Williamson to Attorney General.
Aug. 14. Lo. Burgh to E. of Essex.
Aug. 14. Th. Trelloy to Sir R. Cecil.
Aug. 14. Governor of Dieppe to E. of Essex.
Aug. 15. E. of Cumberland to Sir R. Cecil.
Aug. 15. Sir T. Bodley to States General.
Aug. 15. Mem. of ruinous state of Chichester and necessity to fortify.
Aug. 16. Sir F. Drake and Jo. Hawkins to the Queen.
Aug. 16. The Queen to Sir F. Drake and Jo. Hawkins.
Aug. 16. Sir F. Vere to E. of Essex.

Aug. 16. Comte de St. Paul to same.
Aug. 16. Mat. Twens (?) to Sir R. Cecil.
Aug. 17. Sir R. Sidney to E. of Essex.
Aug. 17. Governor of Dieppe to same.
Aug. 17. M. de Salignac to same.
Aug. 17. King of France to same.
Aug. 17. Geo. Gilpin to same.
Aug. 17. Sir T. Bodley to Ld. Burghley.
Aug. 18. Nic. Williamson to Attorney General.
Aug. 18. Sir F. Drake, Jo. Hawkins, T. Gorges, and T. Baskerville to Sir R. Cecil.
Aug. 18. Advertisements from Venice.
Aug. 18. Sheriffs of London to Privy Council.
Aug. 19. Ottwell Smith to E. of Essex.
Aug. 19. Advertisements from Rome.
Aug. 19. Sir Th. Cecil to Sir R. Cecil.
Aug. 20. H. Lok to same.
Aug. 21. —— to ——.
Aug. 21. Duc de Bouillon to Comte d'Essex (2).
Aug. 22. Sir R. Cecil to N. Williamson.
Aug. 22. Tho. [Ld.] Burgh to E. of Essex.
Aug. 22. Nic. Williamson to Attorney General.
Aug. 22. Same to Sir R. Cecil (2).
Aug. 22. Mr. Halliday to same.
Aug. 22. Gov. of Dieppe to E. of Essex.
Aug. 22. Sir F. Vere to same.
Aug. 22. H. Brooke to Sir R. Cecil.
Aug. 22. Dr. Chr. Parkins to same.
Aug. 22. Lo. Chandos to same.
Aug. 22. Sir R. Sydney to E. of Essex.
Aug. 23. Ld. Cobham to Sir R. Cecil.
Aug. 23. M. de Sourdean to E. of Essex.
Aug. 23. Sir R. Martyn to Sir R. Cecil.
Aug. 24. Sir F. Vere to E. of Essex.
Aug. 24. Gov. of Dieppe to same.
Aug. 24. Sir R. Sydney to same.
Aug. 25. Wm. Waad to Sir R. Cecil.
Aug. 25. Mr. Champernoun to same.
Aug. 25. Sir Th. Heneage to same.
Aug. 25. Antonio (ex-King of Portugal) to E. of Essex.
Aug. 25. Examinations of Edm. Moore and his wife touching Rog. Waltham.
Aug. 25. Account of letters delivered by Casey to Mr. John Stanhope, Wm. Waad, &c.
Aug. 25. Advertisements from Venice.
Aug. 27. Rob. Herbert to Wm. Waad.
Aug. 27. Sir Th. Bodley to Lo. Burghley.
Aug. 27. Geo. Gilpin to E. of Essex.
Aug. 27. Wm. Wade to Sir R. Cecil.
Aug. 27. Mr. Halliday to same.
Aug. 28. Geo. Carey to same.
Aug. 29. M. de St. Luc to E. of Essex.
Aug. 30. —— to ——.
Aug. 30. Gov. of Dieppe to E. of Essex.
Aug. 31. Sir Jo. Hart and Alderman Halliday to Sir R. Cecil.
Aug. 31. Sir F. Vavasour to same.
Aug. —. Of patent for starch, Ellis and Sir John Pakington.
Aug. —. Capt. N. Clifford to E. of Essex.
Aug. —. Persons of credit in Spain.
Aug. —. N. Williamson to Sir R. Cecil.
Sept. 1. Alderman Holliday to same.
Sept. 1. Capt. Chilcot to same.
Sept. 1. Merchant adventurers to same.
Sept. 1. Gov. of Dieppe to same.
Sept. 1. Examination of John Colbron touching Rog. Waltham.
Sept. 2. Sir Th. Heneage to Sir R. Cecil.
Sept. 2. M. du Perron to the King of France.
Sept. 3. H. Maynard to Sir R. Cecil.
Sept. 3. —— to ——.
Sept. 3. Sir F. Vere to E. of Essex.
Sept. 3. Sir Th. Shirley to Sir Th. Heneage.
Sept. 4. E. of Derby to H. Scarebreck, W. Lucas, and W. Radcliffe.
Sept. 4. Same to Sir Th. Gerrard.
Sept. 5. Capt. E. Wylton to E. of Essex.
Sept. 5. Capt. of Rochelle to same.
Sept. 6. Geo. Gilpin to same.
Sept. 6. Sir Th. Egerton to same.
Sept. 6. Mr. Denssell to ——.
Sept. 6. R. Carmarden to Sir R. Cecil.
Sept. 6. Lo. Cobham to same.
Sept. 6. E. of Rutland to same.
Sept. 6. Sir H. Palavicino to same.
Sept. 6. Same to Lord North.
Sept. 6. E. of Rutland to Sir R. Cecil.
Sept. 7. Th. Treffey to same.
Sept. 7. Sir Th. Wilford to same.

Sept. 8. Lady Norreys to same.
Sept. 8. Jo. Owen to same.
Sept. 8. Ad. Clar. Equitem R. Cecilium, By Jo. Owen.
Sept. 9. Sir Th. Heneage to Sir R. Cecil.
Sept. 9. Dr. Chr. Parkins to same.
Sept. 9. Th. Myddleton to same.
Sept. 9. Jo. Stanhope to same.
Sept. 9. Whitgift, Abp. of Cant., to same.
Sept. 10. W. Cordell to same.
Sept. 10. Sir Ro. Williams to E. of Essex.
Sept. 10. Sir Jo. Fortescue to Sir R. Cecil.
Sept. 11. N. Williamson to same.
Sept. 11. Sir R. Sydney to E. of Essex.
Sept. 11. Sir T. Bodley to Ld. Burghley.
Sept. 14. Ed. Wiseman to E. of Essex.
Sept. 14. Capt. Ed. Wylton to same.
Sept. 14. Sir F. Vere to same.
Sept. 14. Mr. Ashley to Sir R. Cecil.
Sept. 14. Ld. Burgh to E. of Essex.
Sept. 14. R. Carmarden to the Queen.
Sept. 14. Sir Geo. Carew to Sir R. Cecil (2).
Sept. 15. —— to E. of Essex.
Sept. 15. Th. Adams to Sir R. Cecil.
Sept. 15. Th. Myddleton to same.
Sept. 15. De la Fontaine to E. of Essex.
Sept. 16. Geo. Gilpin to same.
Sept. 16. Ld. R. North to Sir R. Cecil.
Sept. 16. E. of Rutland to same.
Sept. 16. W. Sanderson to same.
Sept. 17. Mayor, &c, of Exeter to same.
Sept. 17. Ld. Burghley to same.
Sept. 17. Ld. Keeper Puckering to same.
Sept. 18. Sir Geo. Saville to same.
Sept. 18. Sir Ed. Norris to E. of Essex.
Sept. 18. M. de Saldaignes to Ottwell Smith.
Sept. 19. Sir R. Sydney to E. of Essex.
Sept. 19. R. Carmarden to Sir R. Cecil.
Sept. 20. G. Gilpin to E. of Essex.
Sept. 20. Lo. Burgh to same.
Sept. 23. R. Carmarden to Sir R. Cecil.
Sept. 23. Mr. Stallenge to same.
Sept. 24. Ld. Burghley to Sir T. Bodley.
Sept. 25. Sir T. Bodley to Ld. Burghley.
Sept. 25. Duc de Bouillon to Comte d'Essex.
Sept. 26. Mr. Beeston to Sir R. Cecil.
Sept. 27. Sir R. Sydney to E. of Essex.
Sept. 29. Sir Th. Shirley to Sir R. Cecil.
Sept. 29. Fletcher, Bp. of London, to same.
Sept. 29. E. of Rutland to same.
Sept. 29. Customs of different ports for one year.
Sept. —. Licenses upon export of beer.
Sept. —. Sir E. Leigh to Sir R. Cecil.
Sept. —. Lady Ralegh to same.
Oct. 1. Capt. Crosse to same.
Oct. 1. De la Fontaine to E. of Essex.
Oct. 1. M. de Mouy ? to [same ?].
Oct. 2. Capt. E. Wylton to same.
Oct. 2. Lady Norreys to Sir R. Cecil.
Oct. 2. Amoassador Rogers to same.
Oct. 2. W. Borough to Ld. Burghley.
Oct. 2. Lady Dorcas Martyn to Sir R. Cecil.
Oct. 2. Ld. Burghley to Dep. Gov. of Stoad.
Oct. 3. Ambassador Rogers to Sir R. Cecil.
Oct. 4. Extracts from divers French letters.
Oct. 5. King of France to E. of Essex (2).
Oct. 5. Dr. T. Ridley to Sir R. Cecil.
Oct. 5. Description of Panama by Batista Antonellas (in Spanish).
Oct. 6. Hen. Dyrickson to Peter Van. Lever.
Oct. 6. Mr. Goring to Sir R. Cecil.
Oct. 6. H. Constable to E. of Essex.
Oct. 7. Sir F. Vere to same.
Oct. 7. Rogier de Bellegarde to same.
Oct. 8. Ld. Burgh to same.
Oct. 8. Sir R. Sidney to Le Grave.
Oct. 8. Sir Ant. Pawlet to Sir R. Cecil.
Oct. 8. Capt. John Brooke's receipt for 130 men out of Kent.
Oct. 9. Ld. Cobham to H. Brooke.
Oct. 10. Ld. Dudley to Sir R. Cecil.
Oct. 11. Mr. Ashley to same.
Oct. 11. Mr. Skymer to same.
Oct. 12. Sir W. Corke to same.
Oct. 12. Sir R. Sydney to E. of Essex.
Oct. 12. Florence Macarthy to Sir R. Cecil.
Oct. 12. Sir R. Cecil to Sir Jo. Norreys.
Oct. 12. Jo. Ferne to Sir R. Cecil.
Oct. 12. M. de Lomenie to E. of Essex.
Oct. 13. E. of Essex to Sir Jo. Norreys.
Oct. 13. Th. [Ld.] Burgh to E. of Essex.

Oct. 13. Sir Jo. Foster to Ld. Burghley.
Oct. 13. Sir H. Palavicino to Sir R. Cecil.
Oct. 13. James Douglas to Arch. Douglas.
Oct. 13. Sir R. Sydney to Ld. Burghley.
Oct. 14. M. Guicciardini to E. of Essex.
Oct. 16. Sir R. Sydney to same.
Oct. 16. Ld. R. North to Sir R. Cecil.
Oct. 16. Capt. E. Wylton to E. of Essex.
Oct. 17. W. Stallenge to Sir R. Cecil.
Oct. 17. Sir Th. Cecil to same.
Oct. 18. Sir Ri. Fynes to same.
Oct. 18. Justices of Devon to Sir W. Ralegh.
Oct. 18. E. Ashley to Sir R. Cecil.
Oct. 18. Geo. Gilpin to E. of Essex.
Oct. 19. R. Percival to Sir R. Cecil.
Oct. 19. Sir T. Bodley to Ld. Burghley.
Oct. 19. Lord Hunsdon to Sir. R. Cecil.
Oct. 19. Sir Tho. Cecil to same.
Oct. 19. Starch. Information of Ric. Cranmer against
F. Pope, of Salisbury.
Oct. 20. Justices of Man to E. of Derby.
Oct. 20. E. of Oxford to Sir R. Cecil (2).
Oct. 20. Cause between John Phillips and Hen.
Curwen of incumbency of Archdeaconry of Man, decided
by Sir T. Gerrard.
Oct. 21. P. Proby to Sir. R. Cecil.
Oct. 22. Sir T. Bodley to Ld. Burghley.
Oct. 22. B. Fitzjames (Le Glave) to (E. of Essex?).
Oct. 22. O. Smith to E. of Essex.
Oct. 23. Sir Jo. Foster to E. of Huntingdon.
Oct. 23. Franc. of Bourbon, to the E. of Essex.
Oct. 25. Lo. Cobham to Sir R. Cecil.
Oct. 27. Florence Macarthy to same.
Oct. 27. Mayor of Chester to E. of Derby.
Oct. 28. Ottwell Smith to E. of Essex.
Oct. 28. W. Stallenge to Sir R. Cecil.
Oct. 28. Corporation of Colchester to same.
Oct. 29. Sir P. Hoby to same.
Oct. 29. M. de Lomenie to E. of Essex.
Oct. 31. Arth. Gorges to Sir R. Cecil.
Oct. 31. Dr. T. Bilson to same.
Oct. 31. M. de Lomenie to E. of Essex.
Oct. 31. De la Fontaine to same.
Oct. —. List of 18 places void in her Majesty's and
others gift.
Nov. 1. R. Champernoun to Sir R. Cecil.
Nov. 1. Coldwell, Bp. of Sarum, to same.
Nov. 1. Frater Jacobus Carolus to E. of Essex.
Nov. 2. Tho. [Ld.] Burgh to same.
Nov. 3. Capt. W. Constable to same.
Nov. 4. Dr. Ri. Vaughan to Dr. Webster.
Nov. 4. Magistrates of Hull to Sir R. Cecil.
Nov. 5. P. de la Haye to same.
Nov. 5. Wm. Waad to same.
Nov. 6. Sir R. Sydney to E. of Essex (2).
Nov. 6. H. Deryckson to P. Van Lore.
Nov. 7. W. Stallenge to Sir R. Cecil.
Nov. 8. Rog. Houghton to same.
Nov. 8. And. King to same.
Nov. 8. Lease from Wm. E. of Derby to Sir Walt.
Raleigh, of Hasilbertree.
Nov. 8. Beauvoir la Noue to E. of Essex.
Nov. 8. Ottwell Smith to same.
Nov. 8. Lands to the Crown by attainder of Leonard
Dacre and the E. of Arundel.
Nov. 9. Capt. E. Wylton to E. of Essex.
Nov. 9. Sir R. Sydney to same.
Nov. 9. P. Fitzjames (Le Grave) to Sir R. Sydney.
Nov. 10. Sir F. Vere to E. of Essex.
Nov. 10. Florence Macarthy to Sir R. Cecil.
Nov. 10. John Dowland to same.
Nov. 11. M. Guicciardini to E. of Essex.
Nov. 11. Sir Jo. Foster to Ld. Burghley.
Nov. 11. Sir W. Ralegh to Sir R. Cecil.
Nov. 12. Coldwell, Bp. of Sarum, to same.
Nov. 12. Frater Jacobus Carolus ad Reginam.
Nov. 12. Sir R. Sydney to E. of Essex.
Nov. 12. Same to Ld. Burghley.
Nov. 13. Same to E. of Essex.
Nov. 13. Sir W. Ralegh to Sir R. Cecil.
Nov. 16. Ld. Burghley to Mr. Ferrers.
Nov. 18. Lord St. John to Dr. Tyndall (Master of
Queen's Coll., Camb.)
Nov. 18. Sir Jo. Winter to Sir R. Cecil.
Nov. 19. Sir H. Palavicino to the Queen.
Nov. 20. M. Cardinal to Sir R. Cecil.
Nov. 20. F. Chenye to same.
Nov. 20. An English priest to his cousin.
Nov. 22. Sir F. Greville to Sir R. Cecil.
Nov. 22. Sir Ch. Danvers to E. of Essex.
Nov. 22. Gov. of Dieppe to same.

Nov. 22. Sir Ch. Danvers to Sir R. Cecil.
Nov. 23. Co. of Kent to same.
Nov. 23. Capt. Durham to E. of Essex.
Nov. 24. Whitgift, Abp. of Cant., to Cambridge Uni-
versity.
Nov. 24. Geo. Gilpin to E. of Essex.
Nov. 24. Ant. Ersfield to same.
Nov. 25. Sir W. Ralegh to Privy Council.
Nov. 26. Justice Walmsley to Sir R. Cecil.
Nov. 26. Privy Council to F. Ferrers.
Nov. 26. Answer of Sir Jo. Foster to articles by Sir
W. Bowes and others, commissioners.
Nov. 27. W. Stallenge to Sir R. Cecil.
Nov. 27. Sir T. Bodley to same.
Nov. 27. Lords Cobham and Buckhurst to same.
Nov. 27. Fletcher, Bp. of London, to same.
Nov. 27. Sir R. Sydney to E. of Essex.
Nov. 27. Enormities of Mr. Darcy's patent for mak-
ing, &c. of leather, with letter from Mayor of London.
Nov. 28. H. Dyrickson to Van. Lore.
Nov. 28. N. Williamson to Sir R. Cecil.
Nov. 28. E. Christovad to E. of Essex.
Nov. 29. The Queen to Privy Council.
Nov. 30. Sir W. Ralegh to the Lord Admiral.
Nov. 30. Account of A. Paulett for St. Heliers.
Nov. —. Sir E. Wynter to Sir R. Cecil.
Nov. —. Sir W. Ralegh to same.
Nov. —. Sir M. Arundel to same.
Nov. —. De la Fontaine to E. of Essex.
Nov. —. Articles of inquiry for state of Middle
Marches.
Nov. —. Dower of the Viscountess Bindon.
Dec. 1. Jo. Daniel to the Queen.
Dec. 2. Same to Sir R. Cecil.
Dec. 2. Attorney General Coke to same.
Dec. 3. The Queen to Ld. Burghley.
Dec. 3. Sir N. Parker to R. Cecil.
Dec. 3. De Lomeine to same.
Dec. 4. E. of Huntingdon to Sir R. Cecil.
Dec. 4. Capt. Durham to E. of Essex.
Dec. 5. Th. Smith to Sir R. Cecil.
Dec. 5. E. of Essex to same.
Dec. 5. Levant merchants to same.
Dec. 6. Sir F. Vere to E. of Essex.
Dec. 6. Sir R. Molyneux to Sir R. Cecil.
Dec. 7. Chief Baron Periam to same.
Dec. 7. Sir E. Hoby to same.
Dec. 7. H. Constable to E. of Essex.
Dec. 8. Sir Th. Wilkes to Sir R. Cecil.
Dec. 8. Henri de Bourbon to E. of Essex.
Dec. 8. H. Crofts to Sir R. Cecil.
Dec. 9. Sam. Wharton to same.
Dec. 9. Mayor of Plymouth to same.
Dec. 9. Confession of Th. Wharton at Plymouth.
Dec. 9. Declaration of magistrates of the Brill to the
Queen of England (in Dutch).
Dec. 10. W. Cope to Sir R. Cecil.
Dec. 10. Geo. Gilpin to E. of Essex.
Dec. 10. Wm. Wade to Sir R. Cecil.
Dec. 10. Jo. Gylls to T. Myddleton.
Dec. 10. E. Dyer to Sir R. Cecil.
Dec. 10. Ld. Cobham to same.
Dec. 11. Jo. Ferne to Sir R. Cecil.
Dec. 11. Maurice Berkley to Ld. Burghley.
Dec. 11. M. Noel de Caron to Sir R. Cecil.
Dec. 11. E. Dyer to same.
Dec. 12. Lady Hawkins to same.
Dec. 12. Rob. Lo. Sempill to E. of Essex.
Dec. 12. Jo. Ferne to Sir R. Cecil.
Dec. 12. Sir E. Stafford to same.
Dec. 12. Lady Hawkins to same.
Dec. 12. Sir R. Sydney to E. of Essex.
Dec. 13. Jo. Danyel to Sir R. Cecil.
Dec. 13. Lo. Cobham to Mayor of Sandwich.
Dec. 13. Whitgift, Abp. of Cant., to Sir R. Cecil (2).
Dec. 13. Sir W. Cornwalleys to same.
Dec. 13. Lo. Ro. Northe to same.
Dec. 14. Sir Hor. Palavicino to same.
Dec. 15. Rog. Manners to same.
Dec. 15. R. Carmarden to same.
Dec. 15. An English Romanist to his cousin.
Dec. 17. W. Williams to E. of Essex.
Dec. 18. The Queen to the Abp. and Council at York.
Dec. 18. Sir Ed. Norris to E. of Essex.
Dec. 18. Sir P. Boteler to Sir R. Cecil.
Dec. 19. Levant Merchants to same.
Dec. 20. Capt. Morysine to same.
Dec. 20. M. Kyffins to same.
Dec. 20. Capt. Waynman to same.
Dec. 20. Examination of John Gough of Dublin.

Dec. 21. Charges of Mayor, &c. of King's Lynn, for setting forth ship "Expedition."
Dec. 21. E. of Cumberland to Sir R. Cecil.
Dec. 21. Jo. Ferne to same.
Dec. 21. Sir R. Berkley to same.
Dec. 21. Jo. Daniel to same (2).
Dec. 21. Hutton, Abp. of York, to Ld. Burghley.
Dec. 21. Abp. and Council at York to same.
Dec. 22. Same to same.
Dec. 23. Montmorency, Constable of France, to E. of Essex.
Dec. 24. Whitgift, Abp. of Cant., to the Lord Keeper and Lord Buckhurst.
Dec. 24. Sir R. Cecil to same.
Dec. 25. Jo. Ferne to Sir R. Cecil (2).
Dec. 25. Sir R. Sydney to E. of Essex.
Dec. 25. Sir Hor. Palavicino to Sir R. Cecil.
Dec. 27. Sir E. Dymok to same.
Dec. 28. King of France to Duc de Montpensier.
Dec. 28. Same to M. Dessetiees.
Dec. 28. Same to E. of Essex.
Dec. 29. H. Maynard to Sir R. Cecil.
Dec. 30. Examination of Jane Baxter, &c. at York, for coining.
Dec. 30. M. Guicciardini to E. of Essex.
Dec. 31. Mr. Gilpin to same.
Dec. 31. H. Noel to Sir R. Cecil.
—— King of Scots to the Queen (2).
—— The Queen to King of Scots. (Copy.)
—— E. of Essex to the Queen.
—— The Queen to the Lord Treasurer.
—— H. Gorneld to Sir R. Cecil.
—— H. Lok to same.
—— Jo. Merrick to ——.
—— E. of Northumberland to E. of Essex.
—— M. de Tremouille to same.
—— The Count St. Pol to same.
—— M. Beauvoir la Noue to same (3).
—— M. Campagne to same.
—— Baptiste Castillion to ——.
—— M. de la Fontaine to the Queen.
—— Same to E. of Essex (5).
—— M. de Mouy to same.
—— Mr. Wetenhall to Arch. Douglas.
—— Jo. Rawlins to Edw. Reynolds, sec. to E. of Essex.
—— Account by Th. Bilson, of Treasure of College of Winchester, from 1581.
—— Advertisements of state of Spain.
—— Advertisements from France.
—— Sir W. Paddy to Sir R. Cecil.
—— P. Proby to same.
—— Jo. Smith to ——.
—— Capt. R. Turner to E. of Essex.
—— Capt. Walker to Sir R. Cecil.
—— Justices and Commissioners of Peace for England and Wales, from 1592.
—— Principal men in divers shires.
—— Answer of Sir Ed. Codrington to E. of Lincoln.
—— Mortgage ordered by Ld. Buckhurst to be granted by Hen. Mogges to Hen. Reynolds.
—— List of Muster Masters in every county.
—— Request of Sir Th. Shirley to be discharged of payments for army in Low Countries.
—— Mem. as to ships' provisions, &c., Rochelle.
—— Upon making glass in Ireland, by Geo. Longe.
—— Instructions for Capt. Clifford to take charge of ships, &c. to blockade the Spanish in French ports.
—— Note from Mr. Mylls of movements of Italians.
—— Mem. as to the K. of Spain's authorising Dr. Rog. Lopes's conspiracy, with account and publication of same.
—— Outrages by the Scots in E. Marshes since death of Sir Jo. Selbye.
—— State of Heralds and Pursuivants.
—— Note touching John Killegrew.
—— Interrogatories for Nich. Williamson.
—— Memorial of E. of Shrewsbury's causes.
—— Mems. by Sir R. Cecil. Of Cardinal Salviati, &c.
—— Recusants certified out of counties, from 1582.
—— Remembrance for the E. of Essex in behalf of the E. of Huntingdon.
—— Note of corn due from farmers yearly on Cobham estate.
—— Woods sold for this year on the same.

1596.

Jan. 1. J. Tourner to Arch. Douglas.
Jan. 1. Sir F. Vere to E. of Essex.
Jan. 1. Jo. Daniel to Sir R. Cecil.
Jan. 2. M. Guicciardini to E. of Essex.

Jan. 2. Sir Gr. Markham to Lo. Chamberlain.
Jan. 3. The Queen to Mr. Bodley.
Jan. 3. Sir Hor. Palavicino to Sir R. Cecil.
Jan. 3. Officers of Ipswich to Ld. Burghley.
Jan. 3. Sir F. Vane to Privy Council.
Jan. 4. Sir E. Uvedale to E. of Essex.
Jan. 4. Vidame de Chartres to same.
Jan. 4. The Queen to King of Scots.
Jan. 5. Sir Hor. Palavicino to Sir R. Cecil.
Jan. 5. Mr. Barber to ——.
Jan. 5. Sir A. Ashley to Sir R. Cecil.
Jan. 6. Capt. Legat to same.
Jan. 6. Sir Hor. Palavicino to same.
Jan. 6. Sir F. Gorges, &c. to same (3).
Jan. 6. Sir Gr. Markham to same.
Jan. 6. Jo. Daniel to same.
Jan. 6. François d'Orleans to E. of Essex.
Jan. 7. Sir Hor. Palavicino to Sir R. Cecil.
Jan. 7. M. Guicciardini to E. of Essex (2).
Jan. 7. Sir F. Vere to same.
Jan. 8. Sir F. Chaloner to same.
Jan. 8. E. of Essex to Scottish Clergy.
Jan. 8. Sir Hor. Palavicino to Sir R. Cecil.
Jan. 8. King of France to E. of Essex.
Jan. 9. Mr. Cherry to Sir R. Cecil.
Jan. 9. Sir R. Sydney to E. of Essex (2).
Jan. 9. W. Stallenge to Sir R. Cecil.
Jan. 10. Sir H. Vere to E. of Essex.
Jan. 10. Capt. Bosville to Sir R. Cecil.
Jan. 10. E. of Lincoln to same.
Jan. 11. Sir R. Sydney to E. of Essex.
Jan. 11. Lady Willughby to Sir R. Cecil.
Jan. 11. Jo. Norburie to same.
Jan. 11. E. of Oxford to same.
Jan. 12. Sir Gr. Markham to same.
Jan. 12. Lady Stoweton to Lady Cecil.
Jan. 13. M. de Saldaigne to Ottwell Smith.
Jan. 13. G. Gilpin to E. of Essex.
Jan. 13. W. Stallenge to Sir R. Cecil.
Jan. 13. The Queen to Lord Burghley.
Jan. 14. Sir H. Palavicino to Sir R. Cecil.
Jan. 15. Sir Gr. Markham to same.
Jan. 15. State of chest as found by auditors Neale, Sutton, &c.
Jan. 15. Sir H. Palavicino to Sir R. Cecil.
Jan. 16. Art. Gregory to same.
Jan. 16. Sir Geo. Peckham to same.
Jan. 16. Sir G. Markham to same.
Jan. 16. Sir E. Norris to E. of Essex.
Jan. 17. Sir F. Vere to same.
Jan. 17. Tho. [Lord] Burgh to same (2).
Jan. 17. G. Gilpin to same.
Jan. 20. E. Stanhope to Sir R. Cecil.
Jan. 20. A. Loftus, Lord Chancellor of Ireland, same.
Jan. 20. Capt. E. Wylton to E. of Essex.
Jan. 20. Sir R. Sydney to same.
Jan. 21. Same to same (2).
Jan. 21. Sir F. Vere to same.
Jan. 22. King of Spain to E. of Tyrone.
Jan. 22. Examination of Geo. Rosett, a Frenchman of St. Malo.
Jan. 22. King of France to the Queen.
Jan. 22. Wm. Waad to Sir R. Cecil.
Jan. 22. Ld. Dunsanin to same.
Jan. 22. French Privy Council to Sir H. Unton.
Jan. 23. W. Udall to Ric. Wharton.
Jan. 23. Sir W. Cockes to Sir R. Cecil.
Jan. 23. Sir H. Corke to same.
Jan. 24. Sir W. Raleigh to same.
Jan. 24. Sir M. Arundel to same.
Jan. 24. Sir R. Sydney to E. of Essex.
Jan. 24. Sir T. Chaloner to same.
Jan. 25. W. Lille to same.
Jan. 25. Lord Admiral to Sir R. Cecil.
Jan. 25. Sir E. Hoby to same.
Jan. 26. R. Barton to E. of Essex.
Jan. 26. Sir Jo. Aldrych to same.
Jan. 27. E. Stanhope to Sir R. Cecil.
Jan. 27. Dean and Chapter of Westminster to same.
Jan. 27. Jo. Daniel to E. of Essex.
Jan. 27. G. Gilpin to same.
Jan. 28. Sir R. Sydney to same.
Jan. 29. Sir T. Baskerville to Sir R. Cecil.
Jan. 29. Sir H. Vere to E. of Essex.
Jan. 30. Account by Capt. Docra of defeat of Spaniards at Turnhout.
Jan. 30. Capt. Jo. Barkley to E. of Essex.
Jan. 30. M. de Mony to same.
Jan. 30. Capt. H. Docra to same.

Jan. 30. R. Carmarden to Sir R. Cecil.
Jan. 30. M. P. de Regomontes to E. of Essex.
Jan. 30. T. Gurlyn to Sir R. Cecil.
Jan. 31. Sir A. Cookes to same.
Jan. 31. Duc de Bouillon to Comte d'Essex.
Jan. —. Same to same.
Jan. —. E. of Derby to Sir R. Cecil.
Jan. —. King of France to the Queen.
Jan. —. The Queen to King of France.
Jan. —. Ecclesiastical Bill in the Commons House.
Jan. —. Attorney General to Sir R. Cecil.
Jan. —. M. de la Fontaine to E. of Essex.
Jan. —. M. Legrand to same.
Feb. 1. Mayor of Limerick to the Queen.
Feb. 1. Sir F. Gorges to Privy Council.
Feb. 1. Sir R. Sydney to E. of Essex.
Feb. 1. Lady Cobham to Sir R. Cecil.
Feb. 2. M. Noel de Caron to E. of Essex.
Feb. 2. Sir W. Ralegh to Sir R. Cecil.
Feb. 3. E. Stanhope to same.
Feb. 3. Jo. Daniel to same.
Feb. 3. Sir R. Sydney to E. of Essex.
Feb. 3. Lord Burgh to Sir R. Cecil.
Feb. 4. Sir E. Norris to E. of Essex.
Feb. 4. Ant. Percy to same.
Feb. 5. Sir H. Palavicino to Sir R. Cecil.
Feb. 6. E. of Essex to same.
Feb. 6. Sir F. Gorges to same.
Feb. 7. Sir H. Lee to same.
Feb. 7. Sir F. Gorges to same.
Feb. 8. Ld. Dunsany to same.
Feb. 10. Ld. Admiral to same.
Feb. 10. M. de Sancy to E. of Essex.
Feb. 10. R. Carmarden to Sir R. Cecil.
Feb. 11. Duke of Florence to the Queen.
Feb. 12. G. Gilpin to E. of Essex.
Feb. 13. F. Cherrye to Sir R. Cecil.
Feb. 13. Sir F. Gorges to same.
Feb. 14. Jo. Ferne to same.
Feb. 14. Munitions remaining at Dieppe shipped for
London.
Feb. 14. M. Desiguieres to E. of Essex.
Feb. 14. Sir R. Sydney to same.
Feb. 14. Sir H. Palavicino to Sir R. Cecil.
Feb. 16. Ott. Smith to same.
Feb. 16. Sir A. Mildmay to E. of Essex.
Feb. 16. Duc de Bouillon to same.
Feb. 17. E. of Thomond to Sir R. Cecil.
Feb. 17. Sir R. Sydney to same.
Feb. 17. W. Lille to E. of Essex.
[.] Essex to the Council of Sir Ra. Crosse,
Alfarez, and the Admiral of Holland.
—— Examination of a Spaniard taken at Dover.
Feb. 18. R. Mason to Mr. Smith.
Feb. 18. G. Gilpin to E. of Essex.
Feb. 18. Lo. Admiral to Ld. Burghley.
Feb. 18. Commissioners at Portsmouth to Sir R. Cecil.
Feb. 19. Mr. Brouncker to same.
Feb. 20. Sir T. Arundel to same.
Feb. 20. Sir E. Norris to E. of Essex.
Feb. 20. R. Carmarden to Ld. Burghley.
Feb. 20. Sir F. Vere to E. of Essex.
Feb. 21. The Queen to Ld. Burghley.
Feb. 21. Dr. Chr. Parkins to Sir R. Cecil.
Feb. 21. Capt. M. Bredgate to same.
Feb. 21. Sir T. Baskerville to Privy Council.
Feb. 23. Ld. Eure to Ld. Burghley.
Feb. 23. W. Stallenge to Sir R. Cecil.
Feb. 24. Sir A. Savage to same.
Feb. 24. W. Stallenge to same.
Feb. 25. Sir W. Woodham to E. of Essex.
Feb. 25. Instructions for Capt. Mat. Bredgate for
voyage to Barbary.
Feb. 26. Sir R. Cecil to Ld. Burghley.
Feb. 26. The Queen to same.
Feb. 27. M. Verdiani to ——.
Feb. 27. Sir R. Sydney to E. of Essex.
Feb. 28. Sir F. Vere to same.
Feb. 28. Ant. Kemis to same.
Feb. 28. G. Gilpin to same.
Feb. 29. Capt. Swaine to Sir R. Cecil.
Feb. 29. T. Philipps to same.
Feb. —. Sir W. Cornwallis to same.
Feb. —. Sir R. Sydney to E. of Essex.
Mar. 1. H. Dodds to Sir R. Cecil.
Mar. 1. Sir R. Fenys to same.
Mar. 1. W. Stallenge to same.
Mar. 1. Sir T. Baskerville to Privy Council.
Mar. 1. Chief Justice Popham to Sir R. Cecil.
Mar. 1. P. Corsini to same.
Mar. 2. Ld. Eure to Ld. Burghley.

Mar. 2. Capt. Wenman to Sir R. Cecil.
Mar. 2. Searcher of Sandwich to Ld. Burghley.
Mar. 2. Ottwell Smith to Sir R. Cecil.
Mar. 2. Venetian Ambassador to Sir H. Unton.
Mar. 2. Capt. E. Wylton to E. of Essex.
Mar. 3. Ld. Eure to Ld. Burghley.
Mar. 3. Sir Jo. Fortescue to Sir R. Cecil.
Mar. 3. N. Williamson to same.
Mar. 3. W. Stallenge to same.
Mar. 3. Rog. Aston to same.
Mar. 3. E. of Bath to same.
Mar. 3. Sir T. Arundel to same.
Mar. 4. E. Molyneux to same.
Mar. 4. Zach. Lok to same.
Mar. 4. Demands of Sir T. Fludd touching the office
of Treasurer of Low Countries.
Mar. 4. Mayor of Southampton to Sir R. Cecil.
Mar. 4. G. Brooke to same.
Mar. 4. Ordnance devised by Emery Molineux.
Mar. 5. Examination of Wm. Thomson as to threats
of Talbot and White (priests) to kill Burghley.
Mar. 5. Bailiffs of Worcester to Sir R. Cecil.
Mar. 6. Th. Philips to same.
Mar. 6. L. Lowther to Arch. Douglas.
Mar. 6. Marquis of Tarento to E. of Essex.
Mar. 6. W. Lille to same.
Mar. 6. Lo. Admiral to Sir R. Cecil.
Mar. 6. Sir A. Mildmay to E. of Essex.
Mar. 7. W. Lille to same.
Mar. 7. Sir T. Chaloner to same.
Mar. 7. La Fontaine to Sir R. Cecil.
Mar. 8. D. of Holstein's agent to same.
Mar. 8. Sir T. Shirley to Ld. Burghley.
Mar. 8. M. de Tarento to E. of Essex.
Mar. 9. E. of Rutland to Sir R. Cecil.
Mar. 9. W. Stallenge to same.
Mar. 9. W. Lille to E. of Essex.
Mar. 10. Ott. Smith to same.
Mar. 11. House of Ormond or Ossory, by John
Daniel.
Mar. 11. Jo. Ferne to Sir R. Cecil.
Mar. 11. Jo. Daniel to same.
Mar. 11. Arthur Alye to Mr. Downall.
Mar. 11. Duke of Tuscany to E. of Essex.
Mar. 12. Sir R. Sydney to same (2).
Mar. 12. Sir T. Chaloner to Ant. Bacon.
Mar. 14. Ld. Keeper Egerton to Sir R. Cecil.
Mar. 15. W. Berchen to Ld. Burghley.
Mar. 15. Dr. Chr. Parkins to Sir R. Cecil.
Mar. 15. Sir Jo. Foster to same.
Mar. 15. Sir R. Sydney to E. of Essex.
Mar. 16. Governor of Brest to same.
Mar. 16. Sr. Bassadona to Ld. Burghley.
Mar. 16. E. of Essex to Sir J. Condy.
Mar. 17. Sir R. Sydney to E. of Essex.
Mar. 17. Ld. Cobham to Sir R. Cecil.
Mar. 17. Countess of Huntingdon to same.
Mar. 17. Ar. Gregory to same.
Mar. 18. Sir F. Godolphin to Sir R. Cecil (2).
Mar. 18. Ed. Maxey to same.
Mar. 18. Capt. E. Wylton to E. of Essex.
Mar. 18. Th. Palliser (a priest) to Wm. Waade.
Mar. 19. Sir Jo. Fortescue to Sir R. Cecil.
Mar. 19. Sir E. Norris to E. of Essex.
Mar. 19. Governor of Bayonne to same.
Mar. 20. Sir R. Sydney to same.
Mar. 20. Sir E. Norris to same.
Mar. 20. Sir W. Cocke to Sir R. Cecil.
Mar. 21. F. la Forte to same.
Mar. 21. Mayor of Plymouth to same.
Mar. 21. Capt. Bredgate to same.
Mar. 22. M. Guicciardini to E. of Essex (2).
Mar. 22. Capt. Fr. Rinshaw to same.
Mar. 23. Sir H. Palavicino to Sir R. Cecil.
Mar. 23. Sir Jo. Aldrich to E. of Essex.
Mar. 23. M. Drake to Sir R. Cecil.
Mar. 23. Arth. Gregory to same.
Mar. 24. May, Bp. of Carlisle, to same.
Mar. 24. M. Cole to same.
Mar. 25. M. Becher to Ld. Burghley.
Mar. 25. Whitgift, Abp. of Cant., to Sir R. Cecil.
Mar. 26. Mr. Solicitor Fleming to same.
Mar. 26. Sir Th. Shirley to Ld. Burghley.
Mar. 26. Diets of the Abp. and Council at York, from
1 Jan.
Mar. 26. Sir F. Vere to E. of Essex.
Mar. 27. E. of Essex to Sir R. Cecil.
Mar. 28. T. Phelips to same.
Mar. 28. Sir F. Gorges to same.
Mar. 29. Sir H. Palavicino to same.
Mar. 29. H. Brooke to same.

Mar. 29. Ld. Mountjoy to Ld. Burghley, E. of Essex, &c.
Mar. 29. W. Stallenge to Sir R. Cecil.
Mar. 29. M. Ferrers to same.
Mar. 30. Sir F. Vere to E. of Essex.
Mar. 30. Sir H. Palavicino to Sir R. Cecil.
Mar. 30. Hutton, Abp. of York, to Lord Burghley.
Mar. 30. R. Godfrey to T. Bell.
Mar. 30. Same to M. Hudson, agent for the K. of Scots.
Mar. 30. Dr. Parkins to Sir R. Cecil.
Mar. 31. Fr. Edmunds to Arch. Douglas.
Mar. 31. Commissioners at York to Ld. Burghley.
Mar. 31. Lord Admiral to Sir R. Cecil.
Mar. 31. Geo. Gilpin to E. of Essex.
Mar. —. Lord Admiral to same.
Mar. —. E. of Cumberland to same.
Mar. —. —— to M. de Mandreville, Comte de Dampiere in Cypher.
Mar. —. Noel de Caron to Sir R. Cecil.
Mar. —. Quotations out of divers books of law touching ordinaries.
Mar. —. Advertisements from Geneva, Nantes, &c.
April 1. Sir F. Vere to E. of Essex.
April 1. Charges about the bark "Raven," for New-castle.
April 1. Alderman Billingsley to Ld. Burghley.
April 2. Ld. Sheffield to Sir R. Cecil.
April 2. Ex Governor of Calais to Lord Admiral.
April 2. Allegations maintaining the Bp. of Sarum to have the keeping of all Rolls and Records of any Court holden in Sarum since the statutes of 27 Hen. VIII. and 3rd Edward VI. unto this time.
April 3. Sir H. Palmer to Lord Admiral.
April 3. R. Gray to Sir R. Cecil.
April 3. Earl Bothwell to E. of Essex.
April 3. Sir E. Norris to same.
April 4. Fletcher, Bp. of London, to Sir R. Cecil.
April 4. Lord Admiral to same.
April 5. Fletcher, Bp. of London, to same.
April 6. H. Maynard to same.
April 6. Officers of Ipswich to Ld. Burghley.
April 6. Fr. Rizzio to Sir R. Cecil (2).
April 7. Deputy Lieutenants of Dorset to E. of Essex.
April 7. Governor of Dieppe to same.
April 7. John Van Olden Barnevelt to same.
April 7. Charges of the ship "Elizabeth Jonas," of Hull, for the Queen's service.
April 8. Orders by justices for relief of the poor in Cornwall in this time of great dearth.
April 8. Fellows of Eton. Coll. to Sir R. Cecil.
April 8. The Queen to Ld. Burghley.
April 9. Examination of Enoch Machin.
April 9. Bp. of St. David's offensive sermon against the Queen. His petition for pardon upon imprisonment, and letter to Sir R. Cecil.
April 9. Sir H. Palmer to Lord Admiral.
April 9. Sir Th. Leighton to Sir R. Cecil.
April 9. Sir F. Carew to same.
April 9. Rudd, Bp. of St. David's, to Privy Council.
April 9. Same to Sir R. Cecil.
April 9. Sir F. Vere to E. of Essex.
April 9. Geo. Blunt to Bp. of Durham.
April 10. Ld. Burghley to Sir R. Cecil.
April 10. Sir Th. Shirley to Ld. Burghley.
April 11. E. of Essex to Sir R. Cecil.
April 11. Hatonval (?) to the Governor of Calais.
April 13. T. Ferrers to Ld. Burghley.
April 13. Same to the Queen.
April 13. Countess of Warwick to Sir R. Cecil.
April 13. Lord Admiral to same.
April 15. Ld. Compton to same.
April 15. Earl of Cumberland to same.
April 16. Sir T. Arundel to same.
April 16. Sir Geo. Carew to same.
April 16. Dr. Tucker to same.
April 16. Lo. Admiral to same.
April 16. Comte de St. Pôl to E. of Essex.
April 18. —— to ——.
April 18. Joos de Moor to Heer Palmer.
April 18. E. Standen to Sir R. Cecil.
April 19. Purefey and Ferne to Ld. Burghley.
April 20. Lord H. Norris to Sir R. Cecil.
April 20. Sam. Cockburn to Arch. Douglas.
April 20. Sir T. Gerrard to Sir R. Cecil.
April 20. Justice Shuttleworth to same.
April 21. Ric. Douglas to Arch. Douglas.
April 21. Examination of Th. Arundel before Essex, &c.
April 21. Sir F. Gorges to Sir R. Cecil.
April 22. Capt. Troughton to same.
April 22. Ld. Dudley (?) to same.

April 22. R. Godfrey to T. Bel (?).
April 22. Bat. Giustiniani to Sir R. Cecil.
April 22. Coldwell, Bp. of Sarum, to same.
April 22. Sir W. Courtney, T. Denny, &c. to Privy Council.
April 24. Day, Bp. of Winton, to Sir R. Cecil.
April 25. Sir W. Courtney to same.
April 26. Sir T. Arundel to same.
April 26. E. of Essex to same (2).
April 26. J. Drue to Arch. Douglas.
April 26. Survey of Harbottel Castle. etc. by Ant. Felton, specifying repairs done by Sir John Foster, late warden of the Middle Marches.
April 27. Foulke Greville to Sir R. Cecil.
April 27. Sir Jo. Gilbert to same.
April 27. Sir H. Palavicino to same.
April 27. Jo. Spilman to same.
April 27. E. of Essex to same.
April 27. Rob. Goullam (?) to Sir T. Leighton.
April 28. Ld. Morley to Sir R. Cecil.
April 28. Mr. Ashley to same.
April 28. Whitgift, Abp. of Cant., to same.
April 28. Mr. Michel to same.
April 29. Sir T. Leighton to same.
April 29. Sir Geo. Carey to same.
April 29. Lady Riche to same.
April 29. R. Godfrey to T. Bell.
April 29. Duc de Bouillon to Comte d'Essex (2).
April 29. Effect of patent to Th. Carew and Th. Gage for keeping of Hurst Castle.
April —. Sir C. Danvers to E. of Essex.
April —. Sir M. Arundel to Sir R. Cecil.
April —. Charges of ship "Elizabeth," of Hampton.
April —. Ditto of the Indeavour (of Toppinham set forth by Mayor of Exeter under E. of Essex.
May 1. Obligation of the Duc de Bouillon and M. de Sancy for defence of Boulogne-sur-Mer, &c.
May 1. E. of Essex to Ld. Burghley (3).
May 2. Jo. Daniel to Sir R. Cecil.
May 3. Dr. T. Bilson to same.
May 3. Sir W. Ralegh to same (4).
May 3. Matthew, Bp. of Durham, to Ld. Burghley.
May 3. E. of Essex to Sir W. Ralegh.
May 4. R. Bridges to Sir R. Cecil.
May 4. B. Guicciardini to E. of Essex (2).
May 4. Sir W. Ralegh to Sir R. Cecil.
May 4. E. of Essex and Lord Admiral to same.
May 5. G. B. Giustiniani to same.
May 6. Sir W. Ralegh to same.
May 6. Ld. Eure to Ld. Burghley.
May 6. Lord Keeper Egerton to Sir R. Cecil.
May 6. E. of Essex to the Queen.
May 6. Same to Sir R. Cecil.
May 8. Same to same.
May 8. Sir T. Baskerville to same.
May 8. Sir T. Baskerville to Ld. Burghley.
May 8. Examination of W. Whitehead, of Munck-wearmouth, Durham, before the Bishop, regarding Matt. Goodman.
May 10. Dr. T. Bilson to Sir R. Cecil.
May 11. R. Carmarden to Ld. Burghley.
May 11. The Queen to same.
May 12. E. of Essex to Sir R. Cecil (2).
May 12. G. B. Giustiniani to same.
May 12. Fr. Bunny to Bp. of Durham.
May 13. G. B. Guistiniani to Sir R. Cecil.
May 13. Sir W. Ralegh to same.
May 13. Sir H. Palavicino to same.
May 13. Examination of H. Parkinson by Bp. of Durham.
May 14. E. of Essex to Sir R. Cecil.
May 14. Matthews, Bp. of Durham, to same.
May 15. A. Ashley to same.
May 15. Sir T. Fane to same.
May 15. Sir J. Cæsar to same.
May 15. E. Hayes to same.
May 16. Dr. T. Bilson to same.
May 16. Sir T. Arundel to same.
May 16. Dr. T. Bilson to same.
May 16. Fellows of Winchester to same.
May 16. A. Ashley to same.
May 16. Lo. Deputy of Ireland (Sir W. Russell) to the Queen.
May 17. Sir T. Knollys to Sir R. Cecil.
May 17. M. Stanhope to Jo. Stanhope.
May 17. E. of Derby to Sir R. Cecil.
May 17. Mr. Staple and Mr. Cordell to same.
May 17. Lo. Mayor to same.
May 17. Mr. Halliday to same.
May 18. Generals of the Expedition (Lord Admiral, Ld. T. Howard, Sir Geo. Carew, and Sir F. Vere) to same.

May 18. Sir F. Vere to same.
May 18. Sir F. Gorges to same.
May 18. E. of Essex to same,
May 19. Same to same.
May 19. Dr. T. Bilson to same.
May 20, Mr. Maynard to same.
May 20. French Bonds with my Lord (Burghley).
May 21. Ld. Mountjoy to Sir R. Cecil.
May 22. Sir E. Wotton to same..
May 22. Th. Edmonds to same.
May 23. The Queen to same.
May 23. Ld. H. Howard to same.
May 24. A. Ashley to same.
May 24. Ld. Buckhurst to same.
May 24. Ld. Zouch to same.
May 24. Sir E. Stanley to same.
May 24. E. of Essex to same.
May 25. Sir R. Cecil to Sir T. Leighton.
May 26. Sir R. Barkley to Sir R. Cecil.
May 26. Sir W. Ralegh to same.
May 26. Ld. Buckhurst to same.
May 26. A. Felton to Ld. Burghley.
May 27. Ld. Burghley to Sir R. Cecil.
May 27. Ld. Buckhurst to same.
May 27. Sir T. Wilford to Ld. Cobham.
May 27. Sir W. Courtney to Sir R. Cecil.
May 27. R. Leigh to Abp. of Cant.
May 28. Dr. Chr. Parkins to Sir R. Cecil.
May 28. Lo. Lumley to same.
May 28. Abp. of York and Council of the North to
Ld. Burghley.
May 29. Alderman of Hull to Abp. of York.
May 29. H. Cuffe to Mr. Downhall.
May 29. Sir G. Carew to Sir R. Cecil.
May 29. Sir W. Ralegh to same.
May 29. H. Wotton to same.
May 30. E. of Essex to same.
May 30. Capt. Crosse to same.
May 31. Th. Webbe to same.
May 31. A. Ashley to same.
May 31. Sir G. Carew to same.
May 31. Sir E. Hoby to same.
May 31. Jo. Bomel to ——.
May 31. Council of the North to Ld. Burghley.
May 31. Abp. of York to same.
May —. E. of Essex to same.
May —. Sir T. Knollys to Sir R. Cecil.
May —. Sendam (?) to E. of Essex.
May —. Lady H. Howard to Sir R. Cecil.
May —. E. of Essex to same.
May —. Declaration of English merchts. at Bordeaux
to Chas. Soldayne, councillor of the Fr. King, upon
griefs at Ragan.
June 1. Sir A. Knivet to Sir R. Cecil.
June 2. J. Lancelot to same.
June 2. Proposition by Pennet, canon of Notre Dame
in Rouen, to Parliament against Protestants.
June 3. Sir F. Gorges to Sir R. Cecil.
June 4. Wm. Waad to same.
June 5. Sir W. Fitzwilliam to same.
June 5. G. B. Giustiniani to same.
June 5. Sir F. Gorges to same.
June 6. Wm. Waad to same..
June 7. Dudley Narton to same.
June 7. S. Cockburn to Arch. Douglas.
June 7. Ld. R. North to Sir R. Cecil (2).
June 7. Privy Council to Ld. Burghley.
June 7. Council of the North to same.
June 8. T. Farrers to Sir R. Cecil.
June 8. The Queen to Ld. Burghley.
June 8. Jo. Lee to Sir R. Cecil.
June 8. Sir Jo. Fortescue to same (2).
June 9. Lady F. Kildare to same.
June 9. Sir E. Stanley to same.
June 11. G. B. Giustiniani to same.
June 12. Fletcher, Bp. of London, to same.
June 13. E. of Essex to Privy Council.
June 14. T. Myddleton to Sir R. Cecil.
June 15. The Dowager Lady Russell to same.
June 15. Mr. Staples (Gov. of Levant Co.) to same.
June 15. The Queen to Ld. Burghley.
June 18. Bilson, Bp. of Winchester, to Sir R. Cecil.
June 18. Sir Jo. Fortescue to same.
June 19. Sir R. Barkley to same.
June 19. G. Beeston to same.
June 19. Bills for wardships.
June 20. Sir J. Fester to Ld. Burghley.
June 20. Petition of Rog. Felhame, of Waddingworth,
Linc., of wrongs by E. of Lincoln.
June 23. Dr. Bennet to Sir R. Cecil.
June 23. Lo. Dunsanny to same.

June 24. The Queen to K. of Scots.
June 24. Report of Jos. Meric of Exeter, of a dan-
gerous person he met near Ashburton.
June 25. License to do services in Scotland of Ld.
Eure to John Armstrong (for faults committed).
June 25. Bp. of Winchester to Sir R. Cecil.
June 25. Lady K. Howard to same.
June 26. E. of Lincoln to same.
June 26. Certificate of Arth. Hevenyngham and Jo.
Peyton of state of coast of Norfolk against invasion,
musters, &c., with description of Flegge and Hoving-
land,
June 27. Attorney General Coke to Sir R. Cecil.
June 27. Sir E. Hoby to same.
June 28. Sir Ch. Danvers to same.
June 29. Sir J. Fortescue to same.
June 29. Apparel out of ship " Mary and John."
June 30. N. Saunders to Sir R. Cecil.
June 30. C. H. (Ld. C. Howard) to Span. Admiral.
June 30. Sir G. Carew to Sir R. Cecil.
June 30. Russell, Ld. Dep. of Ireland, to the Queen.
June 30. E. of Essex to ——.
June 30. Rog. Wilbraham to Sir R. Cecil.
June —. E. of Essex to same.
June —. Foggs Newton to same.
June —. Fellows of Winton Coll. to same.
June —. Capt. T. Lovell to Ld. Burghley.
June —. H. Lok to Sir R. Cecil.
June —. Capt. Tho. Lovell to Ld. Burghley.
June —. Foggs Newton to Sir R. Cecil.
June —. Reasons for Rog. E. of Rutland, a ward,
against petition of Isabel Countess of Rutland.
[.] Debt to the Queen of the orphans of the Bp.
of London, their house at Chelsea.
July 1. Special things inwards, Customs, London,
from 1st of June.
July 1. R. Beale to Sir R. Cecil.
July 1. E. of Lincoln to same.
July 1. Ld. Mountjoy to same.
July 1. Sir T. Arundel to same.
July 1. Sir R. Fiennes to Ld. Burghley.
July 1. E. of Essex to Sir R. Cecil.
July 1. Jas. Anderton to same.
July 2. Ernest Duke of Brunswick to Ld. Burghley.
July 3. Capt. Billington to Sir R. Cecil.
July 4. Th. Smith to same.
July 5. G. Gilpin to E. of Essex.
July 5. Capt. N. Saunders to Privy Council.
July —. Petition of John Reynolds, agent for Phillips-
town, Ireland, to Sir B. Cecil. Of the O Connors.
July 6. Mr. Jones to Sir R. Cecil.
July 6. Lord St. John to same.
July 6. Abstract of French letters to M. Fontaine.
July 7. Officers of Ipswich to Ld. Burghley.
July 7. Sir G. Carew to Sir R. Cecil.
July 7. Commissioners at York to same.
July 7. Dr. E. Fletcher to same.
July 7. Proceedings of counsel in the north against
Bi. Atkinson of Ripon.
July 8. Sir H. Cocke to Ld. Burghley.
July 8. The Queen to same.
July 8. Advertisements from Madrid.
July 9. Ld. R. North to Sir R. Cecil.
July 9. Jo. Procter to same.
July 9. Lewis, Dean of Gloster, to same.
July 9. Mr. Honneman to same.
July 9. H. Maynard to same.
July 9. Sir G. Carew to same.
July 9. Bilson, Bp. of Worcester, to same.
July 9. G. B. Giustiniani to same.
July 10. Commissioners at York to Privy Council.
July 10. Same to Sir R. Cecil.
July 10. Same to Ld. Burghley.
July 10. E. of Lincoln to Sir R. Cecil.
July 10. Dr. W. Tucker to same.
July 10. Jo. Cooke to same.
July 10. Sir F. Gorges to same.——
July 10. R. P[arsons?] to ——,
July 10. Lady M. Hoby to Sir R. Cecil.
July 11. R. Sackville to same.
July 11. E. of Lincoln to same.
July 11. M. T. Herriot to same.
July 12. Ld. R. North to same.
July 12. G. Gilpin to same.
July 13. Mayor of Plymouth, to same.
July 13. N. Saunders to same.
July 13. Sir E. Stanley to same.
July 13. Sir A. Mildmay to same.
July 14. Sir Jo. Carey to same.
July 14. Garret de Malines to same.

MARQUIS OF SALIS- BURY.

July 14. E. of Ormond to the Queen.
July 14. Dr. Ch. Parkins to Sir R. Cecil.
July 15. Lo. Mayor, London, to same.
July 15. Lord St. John to same.
July 16. Th. Edmonds to same.
July 16. Lady Hawkins to the Queen.
July 17. Watson, Bp. of Chichester, to Sir R. Cecil.
July 17. Bilson, Bp. of Worcester, to same.
July 17. Recusants in Worcester diocese.
July 18. The Setting forth the ships "Costeley" and "James" from Ipswich.
July 18. Sir A. Powlet to Sir R. Cecil.
July 18. Lady E. Danvers to same.
July 18. Sir G. Carew to same.
July 19. Ld. Cobham to same.
July 19. Noel de Caron to same.
July 19. Sir R. Fenys to same.
July 20. E. of Pembroke to same.
July 20. W. Stallenge to same.
July 20. Ld. H. Howard to same.
July 20. Officers of Yarmouth to same.
July 20. Mayor, &c. of King's Lynn, to same.
July 21. Officers of Ordnance to same.
July 21. G. Gilpin to E. of Essex.
July 21. Sir W. Courtenay and Sir T. Dennys to Sir R. Cecil.
July 21. Ld. Mountjoy to same.
July 21. Customer of Lynne to same.
July 21. Jo., Earl of Cassalis to Scottish Amb.
July 21. Officers of Bridgwater to Sir R. Cecil.
July 22. Mr. Udall to same.
July 22. Customers of Hull to Ld. Burghley.
July 22. Wm. Purveyes to Sir R. Cecil.
July 22. Sir F. Gorges to same.
July 22. Mayor of Bristol to same.
July 23. Ld. Cobham to same.
July 23. Council of the North to same.
July 23. G. Goringe to same.
July 23. Sir A. Capel to same.
July 23. Dr. W. Tucker to same.
July 23. N. Saunders to same.
July 23. Lady Hawkins to same.
July 23. Confession of Miles Dawson, priest.
(.) Funeral of Hen., Ld. Hunsdon, late Lord Chamberlain.
July 24. Earl of Leicester and officers of Newcastle to Ld. Burghley.
July 24. Arrest de la Cour de Parlement de Paris en faveur de Madame la Princesse de Condé.
July 24. Bilson, Bp. of Worcester, to Sir R. Cecil.
July 24. E. of Essex to same.
July 25. Sir D. Drury to Sir R. Cecil.
July 25. Aldermen of Newcastle to same.
July 25. The Queen to Ld. Burghley.
July 25. E. of Essex to Sir R. Cecil.
July 25. Customer of Poole to same.
July 25. Ld. Cobham to same.
July 26. Earl of Cumberland to same.
July 26. Sir T. Cecil to same.
July 26. Sir E. Carey to same.
July 26. Officers of Southampton to same.
July 26. Magistrates of Southampton to same.
July 26. Sir W. Knollys to same.
July 27. Sir E. Stanley to same.
July 27. A. T. Salusbury to same.
July 27. E. of Lincoln to same.
July 27. Officers of Plymouth to same.
July 27. Sir Jo. Norrys to the Queen.
July 28. Sir Jo. Knevet to Sir R. Cecil.
July 28. Sir A. Ashley to Sir G. Mervase and Mr. Cuffe.
July 28. Sir P. Hoby to Sir R. Cecil.
July 28. Sir E. Hoby to same.
July 28. J. Panulja [?] to the Queen.
July 29. Ld. E. Crumwell to Sir R. Cecil.
July 29. H. Lok to same.
July 29. W. Cecil to same.
July 29. C. Reynell to same.
July 29. H. Knowles to same.
July 29. Sir R. Fenys to same.
July 30. Mrs. M. Arundel to same.
July 30. Sir R. Carey to same.
July 30. Russell, Lord Deputy of Ireland, to same.
July 30. Wronges done by Ld. Cromwell.
July 31. Ric. Douglas to Arch. Douglas.
July 31. Capt. Lovell to Sir R. Cecil.
July 31. Day, Bp. of Winchester, to Ld. Buckhurst.
July 31. Sir G. Frenchard and Sir R. Horsey to Sir R. Cecil.
July 31. M. Noel de Caron to E. of Essex.
July —. (Sir) T. Arundel to Sir R. Cecil.

July —. Sir E. Carey to same.
July —. Mrs. M. Carey to same.
July —. W. Cecil to same.
July —. Lady Marg. Hoby to same.
July —. T. Edmonds to the Queen.
July —. Ld. Hunsdon to Sir R. Cecil (2).
July —. Lady Ralegh to same.
July —. Lady Riche to same.
July —. Jo. Sanderson to same.
July —. The Queen to K. of Scots.
July —. Bonds of States for Palavicino's debt.
July —. Charges for 12 ships, 2 pinnaces, and 1,200 men by city of London under Essex and Lo. High Admiral.
Aug. 1. Names of seminaries and Jesuits in London prisons.
Aug. 1. Dowager Lady Russell to Sir R. Cecil.
Aug. 1. Officers of Gloster to same.
Aug. 1. Ar. Gregory to same.
Aug. 1. E. of Essex and Ld. H. Howard to the Queen.
Aug. 1. E. of Essex to Sir R. Cecil.
Aug. 2. John Carey to same.
Aug. 2. Sir R. Carey to same.
Aug. 2. M. de la Fontaine to the E. of Essex.
Aug. 2. E. Darcy to Sir R. Cecil.
Aug. 2. Sir E. Dymock to same.
Aug. 2. Mr. Bellot to same.
Aug. 2. W. Stallenge to same.
Aug. 2. Sir R. Sydney to E. of Essex.
Aug. 2. Wm. Cecil, of Alterennes, to Ld. Burghley and Sir R. Cecil.
Aug. 3. E. Stanhope to Sir R. Cecil.
Aug. 3. Countess of Essex to same.
Aug. 3. Lord Audley to same.
Aug. 3. Geo. Gilpin to E. of Essex.
Aug. 4. R. Drake to Sir R. Cecil.
Aug. 4. N. Noel de Carron to same.
Aug. 4. Bailiffs of Yarmouth to same.
Aug. 6. Sir Thomas Fane to Lord Cobham.
Aug. 7. Extracts from Hulst.
Aug. 7. Mayor and Aldermen of Newcastle to Bp. of Durham.
Aug. 7. Lady Hunsdon to Sir R. Cecil.
Aug. 7. Ro. Moore to same.
Aug. 7. Sir Fred. Gorges to same.
Aug. 7. Same to same.
Aug. 7. The Mayor, &c. of Exeter to same.
Aug. 7. R. Douglas to Arch. Douglas.
Aug. 8. Sir Ferd. Gorges to Sir R. Cecil.
Aug. 8. Wm. Killegrew to same.
Aug. 9. Sir Geo. Carew to same.
Aug. 9. Sir F. Gor and W. Stallenge to Sir R. Cecil.
Aug. 9. Wm. Killegrew to same.
Aug. 9. Same to same.
Aug. 10. Sir A. Ashley to same.
Aug. 10. Mr. Pillart to E. of Essex.
Aug. 10. Sir Geo. Trenchard and Sir R. Horsey to Sir R. Cecil.
Aug. 11. W. Stallenge to same.
Aug. 11. Privy Council to the Lord Admiral.
Aug. 11. [?] M. Villeroy.
Aug. 11. Sir Post. Hoby to Sir R. Cecil.
Aug. 12. Wm. Stallenge to same.
Aug. 12. Capt. Crosse to same.
Aug. 12. Sir A. Ashley to same.
Aug. 12. Bailiffs of Ipswich to same.
Aug. 13. Sir W. Ralegh to same.
Aug. 13. Sir C. Cecil to Mr. Killegrew.
Aug. 13. Sir Ferd. Gorges to Sir R. Cecil.
Aug. 13. Lord Lumley to same.
Aug. 13. Mr. Myddleton to same.
Aug. 14. Mr. Killegrew to same.
Aug. 14. Philip the Second (of Spain) to O'Rourke.
Aug. 14. Mr. Stileman to Sir R. Cecil.
Aug. 14. Ant. Aston to Mr. Fowler.
Aug. 15. Sir F. Vere to Sir R. Cecil.
Aug. 15. Wm. Stallenge to same.
Aug. 15. P. Tourner [Earl of Essex].
Aug. 16. Council of the North to Sir R. Cecil.
Aug. 16. Dr. Matthews, Bp. of Durham, to same.
Aug. 17. Jo. Carey to same.
Aug. 17. King of Scots to the Queen.
Aug. 18. Andr. Martingho to Sir R. Cecil.
Aug. 18. Roger Walton to same.
Aug. 18. Sir Th. Fane to same.
Aug. 19. Sir R. Carey to same.
Aug. 19. Jo. Carey to same.
Aug. 20. Wm. Killegrew to same.
Aug. 20. Geo. Gilpin to E. of Essex.
Aug. 20. Sir H. Palavicino to same.
Aug. 22. Wm. Stallenge to Sir R. Cecil.

MARQU OF SAL BURY.

Aug. 22. Dr. G. Goodman to same.
Aug. 23. Dr. R. Webster to same.
Aug. 23. Sir Ant. Ashley to same.
Aug. 23. Same to same.
Aug. 23. Geo. Gilpin to E. of Essex.
Aug. 23. Sir E. Norris to same.
Aug. 24. Wm. Stallenge to Sir R. Cecil.
Aug. 24. Sir Ed. Hoby to same.
Aug. 24. Freightage of a ship of Middleboro' to the Canaries.
Aug. 25. R. Beale to Sir R. Cecil.
Aug. 25. Sir Ar. Savage to Privy Council.
Aug. 25. Sir E. Norris to E. of Essex.
Aug. 25. Inquisition taken at Portsmouth of ships, &c. from fleet employed at Calais.
Aug. 26. Roger Walton to Sir R. Cecil.
Aug. 27. The Queen to Lord Burghley.
Aug. 27. Report of Dav. Collman, mariner of Lubeck, being come from Port Real.
Aug. 28. Sir A. Ashley to Sir R. Cecil.
Aug. 28. Lord Deputy Russell to the Queen.
Aug. 28. Philip Corsini to Sir R. Cecil.
Aug. 28. Sir R. Cecil to Sir Th. West.
Aug. 28. The States General to E. of Essex.
Aug. 28. Same to same.
Aug. 29. Sir R. Sydney to same.
Aug. 29. Sir R. Bulkeley to the Queen.
Aug. 29. Sir Th. West and Mr. Cotton to Privy Council.
Aug. 30. Th. Drake to Sir R. Cecil.
Aug. 30. Sir Ant. Ashley to same.
Aug. 30. Sir Ed. Hoby to same.
Aug. 30. The Mayor, &c. of Hull to same.
Aug. 31. Sir Wm. Fitzwilliam to same.
Aug. 31. Sir Thomas West to same.
Aug. 31. Governor of Dieppe to E. of Essex.
Aug. 31. Goods found at Weneson? Southampton, in custody of Sir Oliv. Lambert.
Aug. —. Duc de Bouillon to E. of Essex.
Aug. —. Sir F. Greville to Sir R. Cecil.
Aug. —. E. Reynolds to same.
Aug. —. Duc de Montpensier to E. of Essex.
Aug. —. Count Hohenlo to same.
Aug. —. Lord Sheffield to Sir R. Cecil.
Aug. —. Dr. E. Grant to same.
Aug. —. Th. Arundel to same.
[.] Ships arrived in Plymouth of E. of Essex's squadron, the Lo. Admiral, and of Sir Walt. Raleigh.
[.] Statement of Fr. Chambers touching pearls and gold on board the " Golden Dragon," of London.
Sept. 1. Her. Croft to Sir R. Cecil.
Sept. 1. Sir E. Vuedall to same.
Sept. 1. Jehan Van Oldenbarneveldt to E. of Essex.
Sept. 1. Count Hohenlo to same.
Sept. 2. Capt. Dalton to Sir R. Cecil.
Sept. 2. Geo. Goringe to same.
Sept. 2. Sir Ferd. Gorges to same.
Sept. 2. Sir R. Sydney to E. of Essex.
Sept. 2. Lady M. Stanhope to Sir R. Cecil.
Sept. 3. Jo. Sanderson to same.
Sept. 3. Sir A. Ashley to same.
Sept. 3. Jo. Stileman to same.
Sept. 3. Countess of Kent to same.
Sept. 3. Geo. Gilpin to the E. of Essex.
Sept. 4. Sir R. Cecil to Sir O. Lambert.
Sept. 4. R. Carmarden to Sir R. Cecil.
Sept. 4. Justice French to same.
Sept. 4. Goods seized by divers officers of customs in port towns.
Sept. 5. Jo. Bland to Sir R. Cecil.
Sept. 5. Capt. Norton to Lord Burghley.
Sept. 5. Maurice de Nassau to the Queen.
Sept. 6. E. of Oxford to Sir R. Cecil.
Sept. 6. Mayor of Southampton to same.
Sept. 6. Restalrig to Arch. Douglas.
Sept. 7. R. Topclyffe to Sir R. Cecil.
Sept. 7. W. Waad to same.
Sept. 7. Scottish Ambassador to the King of Scots.
Sept. 8. E. of Shrewsbury to Sir R. Cecil.
Sept. 8. Ar. Gorges to same.
Sept. 8. Sir Ferd. Gorges to same.
Sept. 8. Wm. Stallenge to same.
Sept. 9. Sir Jo. Levison to the Lord Chamberlain.
Sept. 10. Privy Council to Lord Burghley.
Sept. 10. Sir Ferd. Gorges to Sir R. Cecil.
Sept. 10. Officers of the Port of Lyme Regis to Lord Burghley.
Sept. 10. Ant. Atkinson to E. of Essex.
Sept. 10. Capt. Bosseville to Sir R. Cecil.
Sept. 11. M. de Villeroy to Duc de Bouillon.
Sept. 11. Wm. Stallenge to Sir R. Cecil.

Sept. 12. M. de Busanville to E. of Essex.
Sept. 12. Sir R. Sydney to same.
Sept. 12. Intelligence from Spain, dated the Escurial.
Sept. 13. Robt. Vernon to E. of Essex.
Sept. 13. M. de la Fontaine to same.
Sept. 13. Governor and Company of Turkey Merchants to Sir R. Cecil.
Sept. 14. Sir A. Ashley to same.
Sept. 14. R. Carmarden to same.
Sept. 14. Sir E. Norris to E. of Essex.
Sept. 15. The Queen to Lord Burghley.
Sept. 15. Philip Corsino to Sir R. Cecil.
Sept. 15. The Queen to Lord Burghley.
Sept. 15. Countess of Shrewsbury to Sir R. Cecil.
Sept. 15. Bennet, Dean of Windsor, to same.
Sept. 16. R. Beale to same.
Sept. 16. [Sir R. Cecil ?] to Wm. Stallenge and Mr. Honyman.
Sept. 17. Ar. Gregory to Sir R. Cecil.
Sept. 17. Bilson, Bp. of Worcester, to same.
Sept. 17. E. of Oxford to same.
Sept. 17. R. Beale to same.
Sept. 17. Don Emanuel to same.
Sept. 17. Report of money, plate, jewels, and goods taken at Cales [Cadis], in Spaigne, brought to light by Commissioners, 2 Aug. to 17 Sept. 1596.
Sept. 18. Lord Mountjoy to Sir R. Cecil.
Sept. 18. Sir A. Ashley to same.
Sept. 18. Mr. Browne to same.
Sept. 18. Sir R. Sydney to E. of Essex.
Sept. 18. Duc de Bouillon to same.
Sept. 19. Th. Windebank to Sir R. Cecil.
Sept. 19. M. de Dinenwowd to E. of Essex.
Sept. 20. Lady M. Hawkins to Sir R. Cecil.
Sept. 20. E. of Bath to same.
Sept. 20. Lord Hunsdon to same.
Sept. 21. Lord Burghley to same.
Sept. 22. Th. Mun to E. Hickman.
Sept. 22. M. Hickes to Sir R. Cecil.
Sept. 22. Wm. Stallenge to same.
Sept. 22. Geo. Gilpin to E. of Essex.
Sept. 23. R. Kingsmill to Sir R. Cecil.
Sept. 23. Maurice de Nassau to the Queen.
Sept. 23. M Rean to E. of Essex.
Sept. 23. Anonymous to ——.
Sept. 24. Sir R. Sydney to E. of Essex.
Sept. 24. Jo. Danyell to Sir R. Cecil.
Sept. 25. E. of Cumberland to same.
Sept. 25. Sir A. Ashley to same.
Sept. 26. Mary Windebank to same.
Sept. 26. Lady M. Hawkins to same.
Sept. 26. Lord Willoughby, Sir E. Dymoke, and Sir G. St. Pôl to Ld. Burghley.
Sept. 26. Sir Ant. Mildmay to Sir R. Cecil.
Sept. 26. R. White to same.
Sept. 26. Sir Ant. Ashley to same.
Sept. 27. Lord Keeper Egerton to same.
Sept. 27. Sir H. Knivet to same.
Sept. 28. Sir E. Hoby to same.
Sept. 28. Anonymous to ——.
Sept. 29. M. Rean to E. of Essex.
Sept. 29. Sir Ferd. Gorges to Sir R. Cecil (2).
Sept. 29. Dr. Th. Ridley to same.
Sept. 29. Payments to Sir T. Shirley for pay of officers and 2,000 men.
Sept. 29. Impost upon sweet wines, at various ports.
Sept. 29. Estimate for payments by Treasury of chamber and household expenses.
Sept. 29. Account of Hen. Glanvile, Steward of Household, to Wm. Lord Cobham, Lord Warden of Cinque Ports, and Lord Chamberlain, for one year.
Sept. 30. Sir A. Ashley to Sir R. Cecil.
Sept. 30. P. Furtado to W. Waad.
Sept. —. The Queen to King of France.
Sept. —. A. Gorges to Sir R. Cecil.
Sept. —. The Queen to King of France (2).
Sept. —. Mr. Lichat to E. of Essex.
Sept. —. Ar. Gregory to Sir R. Cecil.
Sept. —. Louis of Nassau to E. of Essex.
Oct. 1. Mayor and Aldermen of Lincoln to Lord Cobham and Sir R. Cecil.
Oct. 1. Th. Chester to E. of Essex.
Oct. 1. Mathews, Bp. of Durham, to Sir R. Cecil.
Oct. 2. Sir H. Norreys to E. of Essex.
Oct. 2. Wm. Waad to Sir R. Cecil.
Oct. 2. Duc de Bouillon to E. of Essex.
Oct. 3. [Sir T. Edmondes ?] to ——.
Oct. 3. Lord Rich to E. of Essex (2).
Oct. 3. Whitgift, Archbp. of Canterbury, to Sir R. Cecil.
Oct. 3. Sir H. Newton to same.

Oct. 3. Virginio Orsino to Ant. Percy.
Oct. 3. E. of Shrewsbury to E. of Essex.
Oct. 3. Names of soldiers delivered to Capt. Arth. Chichester at Hertford by dep. lieut. of the said county under Lord Burghley.
Oct. 4. Sir R. Sydney to E. of Essex.
Oct. 4. Geo. Gilpin to same.
Oct. 4. Th. Fowler to Sir R. Cecil.
Oct. 5. Ant. Alye to Mr. Downhall.
Oct. 5. Second examination of Miles Dawson, priest.
Oct. 6. Sir Ferd. Gorges to Sir R. Cecil.
Oct. 6. M. de la Fontaine to E. of Essex.
Oct. 6. The Queen to the Lord Mayor of London.
Oct. 6. Drs. Herbert, Stanhope, and Swaile, to Privy Council.
Oct. 6. Examination of John Berrington, a Roman Catholic.
Oct. 7. The Mayor of Southampton to Sir R. Cecil.
Oct. 7. Sir Ant. Ashley to same.
Oct. 7. Same to same.
Oct. 8. Jo. Danyell to same.
Oct. 8. Ro. Poly to Lord Cobham.
Oct. 9. E. of Lincoln to Sir R. Cecil.
Oct. 9. Sir R. Hopper to H. Maynard.
Oct. 9. Lord Buckhurst to Sir R. Cecil.
Oct. 9. Names of soldiers prest in London for Picardy.
Oct. 10. Lord Mayor of London to Lord Burghley.
Oct. 11. Jo. Michell to Sir R. Cecil.
Oct. 11. M. Noel de Caron to same.
Oct. 12. M. Skinner to same.
Oct. 12. Messrs. Waad, Vaughan, and Stevyngton to same.
Oct. 12. W. Willaston to E. of Essex.
Oct. 13. E. of Shrewsbury to same.
Oct. 13. Lord Rich to same.
Oct. 13. Dr. Parkins to Sir R. Cecil.
Oct. 13. Council of the North to same.
Oct. 14. Sir Ant. Mildmay to E. of Essex.
Oct. 15. Countess of Shrewsbury to Sir R. Cecil.
Oct. 15. R. Mylner to Mr. Willies.
Oct. 15. Capt. Bredgate to the Lord Admiral.
Oct. 15. [Sir R. Sydney] to ——.
Oct. 15. Sir Post. Hoby to Sir R. Cecil.
Oct. 15. P. Proby to same.
Oct. 16. Don O'Connor Sligo to same.
Oct. 16. Sir R. Sydney to E. of Essex.
Oct. 16. E. of Shrewsbury to same.
Oct. 17. Sir John Stanhope to Sir R. Cecil.
Oct. 17. Mr. Perceval to same.
Oct. 17. Sir R. Sydney to Lord Burghley.
Oct. 18. Lord E. Seymour to Sir R. Cecil.
Oct. 18. P. Proby to same.
Oct. 18. Geo. Gilpin to E. of Essex.
Oct. 20. Sir H. Bagnell to Sir R. Cecil.
Oct. 20. Sir R. Sydney to E. of Essex.
Oct. 21. The Mayor, &c. of Newcastle to Sir R. Cecil.
Oct. 21. Rich. Laing to [Arch. Douglas ?].
Oct. 22. Sir R. Sydney to Sir R. Cecil.
Oct. 22. Wm. Willaston to E. of Essex.
Oct. 22. Sir R. Sydney to same.
Oct. 22. The Deputies of the States of Holland to same.
Oct. 22. Mr. Maynard to Sir R. Cecil.
Oct. 23. Jo. Roper to same.
Oct. 23. Sir H. Danvers to E. of Essex.
Oct. 23. Sir Ch. Danvers to same.
Oct. 23. The Customer at Milford to Lord Burghley.
Oct. 23. Sir H. Palavicino to Sir R. Cecil.
Oct. 23. Sir Jo. Smith to same.
Oct. 23. Advertisements from Genoa, Milan, &c.
Oct. 24. Sir Ant. Pawlet to Sir R. Cecil.
Oct. 24. Don Emanuel to E. of Essex.
Oct. 24. Sir R. Sydney to same.
Oct. 25. Wm. Cecil of Alterennes to Sir R. Cecil.
Oct. 25. Sir W. Knollys to same.
Oct. 25. J. Guicciardini to E. of Essex.
Oct. 25. The Constable of France to same.
Oct. 26. Report of search in Raby Castle by Sir W. Bower, &c.
Oct. 26. Sir Geo. Carew to Sir R. Cecil.
Oct. 26. Garrett de Malynes to same.
Oct. 26. Sir R. Sydney to E. of Essex.
Oct. 26. King of Scots to R. Bower.
Oct. 26. Lord H. Seymour to Sir R. Cecil.
Oct. 27. M. de Guiennes to E. of Essex.
Oct. 27. Sir F. Gorges, the Mayor of Plymouth, &c., to Sir R. Cecil.
Oct. 27. Wm. Stallenge to same.
Oct. 27. Wm. Lilley to the E. of Essex.
Oct. 27. Sir F. Gorges to Sir R. Cecil.

Oct. 27. Wm. Borough to same.
Oct. 28. Lord Sheffield to same.
Oct. 29. Advertisements from Genoa.
Oct. 30. Wemyss of Logie to the E. of Essex.
Oct. 30. Mathias Holmes to same.
Oct. 30. Justice Popham to Mr. Bacon, Mr. Carey, and Mr. Ashley.
Oct. 30. Jas. Anderton to Sir R. Cecil.
Oct. 30. Sir R. Bingham to same.
Oct. 31. The Queen to Lord Burghley.
Oct. 31. Wm. Camden (the historian) to Sir R. Cecil.
Oct. 31. Sir Tho. Wilkes to same.
Oct. 31. Th. Smith to same.
Oct. 31. Baldi (Colonel of the Swiss) to E. of Essex.
Oct. —. Duc de Montpensier to same.
Oct. —. Sir R. Sydney to same.
Oct. —. Same to Lady Riche.
Oct. —. M. Stanhope to Sir R. Cecil.
Oct. —. Money paid to Sir Jo. Stanhope for provision of light horse out of sundry dioceses.
Nov. 1. Geo. Gilpin to E. of Essex.
Nov. 1. Earl of Northumberland to Sir R. Cecil.
Nov. 1. Advertisements from Turin.
Nov. 2. Ditto.
Nov. 2. The Queen to Lord Burghley.
Nov. 2. Sir F. Gorges to Sir R. Cecil.
Nov. 2. Ed. Cecil to same.
Nov. 2. Noel de Caron to same.
Nov. 2. Sir Geo. Carew to same.
Nov. 3. Sir Th. Shirley to same.
Nov. 3. Wm. Stallenge to same.
Nov. 3. Earl of Essex to same.
Nov. 3. Sir F. Gorges, the May. of Plymouth, &c., to same.
Nov. 3. Sir R. Sydney to E. of Essex.
Nov. 3. Same to same.
Nov. 3. Sir H. Norreys to same.
Nov. 4. Jo. Danyell to Sir R. Cecil.
Nov. 4. M. de Rean to E. of Essex.
Nov. 5. Justices of Cornwall to Privy Council.
Nov. 6. Capt. Crofts to Sir R. Cecil.
Nov. 6. Wm. Stallenge to same.
Nov. 6. M. P. de Regemonte to E. of Essex.
Nov. 6. —— "Suo Amico in Inghilterra."
Nov. 7. Rich. Carew to Privy Council.
Nov. 8. Occurrences between Turkish and Christian armies.
Nov. 9. M. de Rean to E. of Essex.
Nov. 9. Schedule for imprest and entertainment for officers of bands to be levied in Wilts and Southampton, for Isle of Wight.
Nov. 10. Bailiffs of Yarmouth to Sir R. Cecil.
Nov. 10. R. Bowes to same.
Nov. 10. Sir H. Palavicino to same.
Nov. 10. Jo. Gyles to E. of Essex.
Nov. 11. Nouvelles de la part des Comptoirs d'Amsterdam, being news from France, Germany, Italy, &c.'
Nov. 12. Jo. Beverley to Lord Burghley.
Nov. 13. H. Brooke to Sir R. Cecil.
Nov. 13. Capt. J. Brooke to same.
Nov. 13. Mat. Holmes (Chaplain to the Merchants at Middleburgh) to [E. of Essex ?].
Nov. 13. M. Holmes to Lady Walsingham.
Nov. 14. Wm. Waltham (Mayor of Weymouth) to Privy Council.
Nov. 14. Powder delivered into the Ordnance, with cost.
Nov. 16. Sir A. Pawlet to Sir R. Cecil.
Nov. 16. Same to same.
Nov. 16. Sir F. Gorges to same.
Nov. 16. Wm. Stallenge to same.
Nov. 16. The Mayor of Plymouth to same.
Nov. 16. Deputies of the States to the E. of Essex.
Nov. 18. A. Gorges to Sir R. Cecil.
Nov. 18. Warrant to Dr. Th. Neville of Trinity Coll., Cambridge, to let parsonage lands.
Nov. 19. Sir H. Palavicino to Sir R. Cecil.
Nov. 19. Jehan de Dunenuoir (Dutch Admiral) to E. of Essex.
Nov. 19. Th. Nichols to P. Halynes ?
Nov. 20. Sir G. Markham to Sir R. Cecil.
Nov. 23. Lord Hunsdon to same.
Nov. 23. Officers of the Port of Ipswich to same.
Nov. 23. Lord Hunsdon to same.
Nov. 23. Wm. Lilley to E. of Essex.
Nov. 24. Jo. Gyles to same.
Nov. 25. The Queen to Lord Burghley.
Nov. 26. Lady M. Willoughby to Sir R. Cecil.
Nov. 26. Th. Nicols to P. Halyne.
Nov. 27. E. of Essex to Sir R. Cecil.

Nov. 27. Countess of Bedford to same.
Nov. 27. Wm. Stallenge to same.
Nov. 27. Capt. Ed. Morgan to E. of Essex.
Nov. 28. Th. Fane to Sir R. Cecil.
Nov. 29. The Queen to Lord Burghley.
Nov. 29. Sir E. Stafford to Sir R. Cecil.
Nov. 30. Same to same.
Nov. 30. Lord H. Howard to same.
Nov. 30. R. Vernon to E. of Essex.
Nov. —. Customs of special commodities, London, for the month.
Nov. —. E. of Essex to Sir R. Cecil.
Nov. —. Sir R. Sydney to E. of Essex.
Nov. —. Sir W. Cornwallis to Sir R. Cecil.
Dec. 1. Lord Mountjoye to same.
Dec. 1. Sir R. Sydney to Lord Burghley.
Dec. 1. Sir A. Ashley to Sir R. Cecil.
Dec. 1. Arth. Warwicke to Mr. Percivall.
Dec. 2. Aldermen Billingsley and Saltonstall to Lord Burghley.
Dec. 2. Sir R. Sydney to E. of Essex.
Dec. 2. Same to same.
Dec. 2. Le Sieur de Rean to same.
Dec. 2. Geo. Gilpin to same.
Dec. 2. Officers of the Port of Ipswich to Sir R. Cecil.
Dec. 2. The Dean and Chapter of Westminster to same.
Dec. 3. Noel de Caron to E. of Essex.
Dec. 4. Sir F. Gorges to Sir R. Cecil.
Dec. 4. Lord Buckhurst to same.
Dec. 5. H. Sadler to same.
Dec. 5. The Queen to Lord Burghley.
Dec. 5. Lord Hunsdon to Sir R. Cecil.
Dec. 5. Sir R. Sydney to E. of Essex.
Dec. 5. Examination of Th. Addequot before Dr. Cæsar, &c.
Dec. 6. Lord Buckhurst to Sir R. Cecil.
Dec. 6. Dr. Cæsar, &c. to same.
Dec. 7. Sir E. Norreys to E. of Essex.
Dec. 7. Pierre de Moucheron to Sir R. Cecil.
Dec. 8. Jiacomo Marenco to E. of Essex.
Dec. 8. Sir E. Stafford to Sir R. Cecil.
Dec. 9. Lord Buckhurst to same.
Dec. 9. Lord R. North to same.
Dec. 9. Dr. E. Lilley to same.
Dec. 9. Th. Phillips to E. of Essex.
Dec. 9. Fr. Cherrie (for the Muscovy Merchants) to the Queen.
Dec. 9. Advices for M. Le Fort, containing particulars of the loss of the Spanish fleet.
Dec. 10. Lord Cobham to E. of Essex.
Dec. 10. Same to Sir R. Cecil.
Dec. 10. Sir A. Cope to same.
Dec. 10. Wm. Stallenge to same.
Dec. 10. Th. Phillips to E. of Essex.
Dec. 10. Sir F. Gorges to Sir R. Cecil.
Dec. 10. Examination and confession of Jo. Wemys, of Lojie, at Campvere.
Dec. 11. Duc de Bouillon to E. of Essex.
Dec. 11. Th. Phillips to same.
Dec. 11. Alvares to Jer. Ybanes.
Dec. 12. Sir R. Sydney to E. of Essex.
Dec. 12. P. de Ragemonte to same.
Dec. 13. Sir Jo. Aldrich to same.
Dec. 13. Capt. E. Wylton to same.
Dec. 13. Wm. Lilley to same.
Dec. 13. Certificate concerning the foot bands serving in Picardy.
Dec. 14. Capt. Chichester to E. of Essex.
Dec. 15. Sir E. Stafford to the Lord Admiral.
Dec. 15. P. Del-Calille to ——.
Dec. 15. Sir H. Palavicino to Sir R. Cecil.
Dec. 15. Dr. Julius Cæsar to same.
Dec. 15. Sir Grif. Markham to same.
Dec. 15. Lady D. Willoughby to same.
Dec. 16. Sir E. Stafford to same.
Dec. 17. H. Maynard to same.
Dec. 18. The Queen to Lord Burghley.
Dec. 18. Th. Fane to Sir R. Cecil.
Dec. 18. R. Carmarden to Lord Burghley.
Dec. 20. R. Castlefield to same.
Dec. 20. Lieutenant-Governor of Bayonne to E. of Essex.
Dec. 20. Sir G. Markham to Sir R. Cecil.
Dec. 20. Jacomo Marenco to E. of Essex.
Dec. 20. Mst. Holmes to same.
Dec. 21. M. de Rean to same.
Dec. 21. M. Guicciardini to same.
Dec. 21. Sir E. Norreys to same.
Dec. 21. F. Basques to Jer. Ybanes.
Dec. 21. E. of Cumberland to Sir R. Cecil.

Dec. 21. P. del Catilla to E. of Essex.
Dec. 22. Sir R. Sydney to same.
Dec. 22. Money lent to Arch. Douglas by Sebastian Harvie.
Dec. 22. Remembrances recommended by Mr. Arth. Bacon, with remarks by E. of Essex.
Dec. 23. Sir G. Markham to Sir R. Cecil.
Dec. 23. Immanuel Martinez to ——.
Dec. 24. The Lord Mayor, &c. of London to Privy Council.
Dec. 24. The Customer of Weymouth to Sir R. Cecil.
Dec. 26. Alonzo Nunes de Herrard to E. of Essex.
Dec. 26. Noel de Caron to Sir R. Cecil.
Dec. 27. Sir R. Sydney to E. of Essex.
Dec. 28. Sir E. Vuedale to Sir R. Cecil.
Dec. 29. Jo. Danyel to same.
Dec. 29. R. Douglas to Arch. Douglas.
Dec. 29. Capt. Dantry to Sir R. Cecil.
Dec. 30. Sir A. Mildmay to the Queen.
Dec. 31. Messrs. Burroughs, Carmarden, and Middleton to Lord Burghley.
Dec. —. Sir F. Grevyll to Sir R. Cecil.
Dec. —. M. Stanhope to same.
Dec. —. H. Hughes to same.
Dec. —. Mr. Wymarke to same.
Dec. —. List of forces in Ireland, and where disposed.
[1596.] King of Scots to the Queen (7 letters).
[1596.] The Queen to the King of Scots.
[1596.] Catharine of Navarre to E. of Essex.
[1596.] —— to ——.
[1596.] S. Shinkrodes (?) to T. Arundel.
[1596.] Jo. Barvitius to same.
[1596.] Th. Arundel to the Signor de Tilly.
[1596.] The same to E. of Essex.
[1596.] The Queen to the Emperor.
[1596.] Sir M. Arundel to Mr. Budden (Feodary of Dorset).
[1596.] Dr. Bennet to the Queen.
[1596.] Capt. Buck to Sir R. Cecil.
[1596.] The Lord Admiral to E. of Essex (3).
[1596.] The Spanish pledges to same.
[1596.] Sir R. Carey to Sir R. Cecil.
[1596.] Lord Chief Justice Coke to Lord Burghley.
[1596.] Sir H. Croft to E. of Essex.
[1596.] C. to E. Bothwell ?
[1596.] E. of Essex to Sir H. Unton.
[1596.] W. Downhall to E. Reynolds.
[1596.] Lord Dunsany to Sir Jo. Stanhope (2).
[1596.] The Queen to E. of Essex ?
[1596.] Lord Ra. Eure to Sir R. Cecil.
[1596.] Le Roy et M. de Villeroy to French Privy Council ?
[1596.] Sir R. Jermyn to E. of Essex.
[1596.] Th. Keylwey to Lord Buckhurst.
[1596.] Lady Riche to Sir R. Cecil.
[1596.] Sir R. Sydney to E. of Essex.
1596. Jo. Taylor to Lord Burghley.
1596. Mr. Traheron to Mr. Waad.
1596. Capt. Troughton to the Queen.
1596. Sr. de Lenglie to the King [of France ?].
1596. [Colville ?] to [E. of Essex].
1596. Sir Charles Danvers to E. of Essex.
1596. Sr. de Rean to Sir R. Cecil.
1596. [La Fontaine] to [the Queen].
1596. The Inhabitants of Harwich to Privy Council.
1596. The same to Sir R. Cecil.
1596. Hen. Lok to the Queen.
1596. Sir G. Merrick [?].
1596. Virginio Orsino to the King of France.
1596. Ant. Perey to Mr. Naunton.
1596. [?] to Ant. Perey.
1596. [Sir H. Palavicino ?] to [Sir R. Cecil ?]
1596. Cases already adjudged for Her Majesty.
1596. Orders taken with certain prisoners and examinations.
1596. Examination of Pedro Ramus of Moores in Galizia, touching the loss of the Spanish fleet.
1596. Notes of Privy Council orders.
1596. Spanish advertisements of the riches in Cadis.
1596. Things especially considerable in the taking of the town of Cadis, by Sir R. Cecil.
1596. Names of the pledges delivered by the town of Cadiz.
1596. Reason for the disappearance of treasure, in charge of Mr. Topclyffe, taken at the capture of Cadis.
1596. Matter in difference between Plymouth and Sir Ferd. Gorges.
1596. Fines paid by Aldermen and Commons of London of late years from bearing of offices.
1596. Commissioners for West Riding of Yorkshire.

1596. Cadiz Expedition, draughts of warrants under hands of Generals for service of Cadiz.
1596. Memoranda of E. of Essex of ships and land force.
1596. Proportion of men and servants for the E. of Essex for a five months' voyage.
1596. Preparations for the voyage to Cadiz, with names of captains and men out of various counties.
1596. Note of shipping with tonnage.
1596. Strength of horsemen and footmen in the Middle Marches.
1596. Pay of officers of the field and men in Picardy for six months.
1596. Captains for Ireland, with 1,000 men.
1596. Reasons why Mr. Champernowne cannot be a Colonel, or raise a third regiment in the south division.
1596. Reasons for displacing Mr. Gibbes of his captainship.
1596. Leaders of horse fit to be employed.
1596. Names of captains that served at Cadiz.
1596. Schedule of men to be levied of the captains, &c.
1596. Note of armour found wanting by the City intended for Cadiz.
1596. Note of armour left when soldiers were set forth out of the county of Middlesex.
1596. Note of armour for succour of Cadiz.
1596. Misdemeanors by Cuthbert Armourer and his sons, &c.
1596. Exceptions against the subscription that is to be intruded upon ministers in Scotland.
1596. Case of Wm. Carew and Edm. Fortescue, of lands sold.
1596. Life of Horne (Bishop of Winchester?).
1596. Geof. Fenton's petition as secretary and surveyor in Ireland.
1596. Latin verses by Lady Russell to Sir R. Cecil.
1596. Customs for velvets, satin, taffeta, cambric, lawn, sewing silk, &c., London.
1596. Reasons to induce the Queen to continue the Dean of Bristol (Dr. Watson) in the rectory of Cheynham by commendam.
1596. Respecting the grant of a lease of the rectory of Godmanchester by the Dean and Chapter of Westminster. The immunities of St. Martin's-le-Grand desired by the Crown.
1596. Dr. Tucker and dispensation of the statutes of Winchester College.
1596. Days of assignment to Cofferer of Household, 1583 to 1596.
1596. Demands of Sir Thomas Leighton for Guernsey.
1596. Mem. of a suit to the Queen for keeping county books.
1596. Revenues of Guernsey.
1596. Rules and regulations of a proposed association of Roman Catholic priests.
1596. On the captainship of Norham, its value, &c.
1596. Charges for setting forth the ship "Grace of God," of Yarmouth.
1596. Charges for one ship by the town of Plymouth.
1596. Quello ha proposito un Gentilhomo, &c.
1596. Advertisements from Venice touching Ant. Shirley.
1596. Sonnet to E. of Essex, &c., Lo. General of Eng. Army.
1596. Notes out of Spanish letters from Havana in June and July last, taken by an English man of war from a small pinnace.
1596. Examination and proofs against Robt. Talboys, Esq., for offence at Bristleton Hill, 10th of August, when horsemen were appointed to attend the Lord Warden of the Middle Marches, &c.
[1596.] Scotch advertisements for Wm. Waade.
[1596.] Orders for discipline of trained bands in City of London in 1588 now revived, about 1596.
—— State of possessions and liberties of St. Albans, &c.
—— Prescription of Dr. Smyth and Dr. Langton.
—— Memorial to Sir Th. Egerton with lists of justices for New Sarum.
—— Bill of Wheler of things melted for Felton.
—— Ecclesiastical matters out of Fitzherbert's Abridgment.
—— Writing of Cecil respecting agreement between the E. of Derby and Countess Dowager.

1597.

Jan. 1. Virginio Orsino to E. of Essex.
Jan. 1. Wm. Stallenge to Sir R. Cecil.

Jan. 1. Books out of Calendar of Sec. Walsingham's writings.
Jan. 4. Lady Bargh to Sir R. Cecil.
Jan. 4. The Queen to the King of Scots.
Jan. 5. Sir E. Wynter to Sir R. Cecil.
Jan. 6. Sir H. Palavicino to same.
Jan. 7. Lord Dunsany to same.
Jan. 7. Mr. Gerald to Privy Council.
Jan. 7. Sir Th. Wilkes to Sir R. Cecil.
Jan. 7. B. Carmarden to H. Maynard.
Jan. 7. Capt. Crosse to Sir R. Cecil.
Jan. 7. Carew Ralegh to same.
Jan. 8. Maurice de Nassau to Lord Burghley.
Jan. 9. Mr. Borough to Privy Council.
Jan. 9. Dr. Webster to Sir R. Cecil.
Jan. 9. Sir H. Palavicino to same.
Jan. 9. Countess of Bedford to same.
Jan. 10. Earl of Cumberland to same.
Jan. 10. Sir R. Sydney to E. of Essex.
Jan. 10. Louis Comte de Nassau to same.
Jan. 10. R. Carmarden and Mr. Wright to Lord Burghley.
Jan. 11. Geo. Carey to Sir R. Cecil.
Jan. 11. Geo. Gilpin to E. of Essex.
Jan. 11. Cyprian Gabriel to same.
Jan. 12. Dr. Bilson, Bp. of Winchester, to Sir R. Cecil.
Jan. 13. Sir Ed. Coke to same.
Jan. 14. Sir Jo. Cutts to same.
Jan. 14. Sir Ro. Crosse to same.
Jan. 14. Ro. Smythe to the Lord Admiral.
Jan. 14. The Lord Admiral to Sir R. Cecil.
Jan. 15. Sir Ro. Crosse to same.
Jan. 15. Sir H. Palavicino to same.
Jan. 15. Jo. Danyel to same.
Jan. 16. Sir Walter Ralegh to Lord Burghley.
Jan. 17. Sir A. Ashley to Lord Cobham.
Jan. 17. Memoranda of bands in West Country, their pay, &c., by W. Meredith.
Jan. 18. Jo. Philips to Sir R. Cecil.
Jan. 19. M. de Moucheron to E. of Essex..
Jan. 20. S. Cocks to Sir R. Cecil.
Jan. 20. Capt. Bosseville to same.
Jan. 21. Sir R. Sydney to E. of Essex.
Jan. 22. The Queen to Lord Burghley.
Jan. 22. Beauvoir de la Noue to E. of Essex.
Jan. 22. Th. Fane to Sir R. Cecil.
Jan. 22. Sir R. Crosse to same.
Jan. 23. W. Lilley to E. of Essex.
Jan. 23. Earl of Shrewsbury to Sir R. Cecil.
Jan. 23. Capt. E. Scott to Mr. Reynolds.
Jan. 23. P. Proby to Sir R. Cecil.
Jan. 23. W. Selby to Lord Burghley.
Jan. 24. Sir H. Palavicino to Sir R. Cecil.
Jan. 25. Sir R. Sydney to E. of Essex.
Jan. 25. Sir R. Cecil to Arch. Douglas.
Jan. 25. T. Fane to Sir R. Cecil.
Jan. 25. Philippo Corsini to same.
Jan. 27. Sir Mat. Morgan to E. of Essex.
Jan. 28. Countess of Bedford to Sir R. Cecil.
Jan. 28. The Queen to Lord Burghley.
Jan. 28. Serjeant Hele to Sir R. Cecil.
Jan. 29. Sir R. Sydney to E. of Essex.
Jan. 29. Same to same.
Jan. 29. Maurice of Nassau to same.
Jan. 29. Th. Fane to Sir R. Cecil.
Jan. 29. Capt. Crosse to same.
Jan. 30. Same to same.
Jan. 31. Louis of Nassau to E. of Essex.
Jan. 31. Wm. Lilley to same.
Jan. —. Catherine of Navarre to same.
Jan. —. Her. Crofts to Sir R. Cecil.
Jan. —. Th. Arundel to same.
Jan. —. The Dowager Lady Russell to same.
Jan. —. Capt. Shute to same.
Jan. —. Earl of Cumberland to same.
Jan. —. Lady Bedford to same.
Jan. —. Memoranda of manufacturers against import of playing cards.
Feb. 1. — to the Queen.
Feb. 4. The Queen to Lord Burghley.
Feb. 4. Th. Fane to Sir R. Cecil.
Feb. 4. Ro. Savage to [Sir R. Cecil?].
Feb. 5. Capt. Hum. Parker to E. of Essex.
Feb. 5. M. de Sancy to same.
Feb. 6. Peyton (Lieutenant of the Tower) to Sir R. Cecil.
Feb. 6. M. St. Luc to M. de Basqueville.
Feb. 6. Geo. Brooke to Sir R. Cecil.
Feb. 6. Hun. Besse to W. Wollaston.

Feb. 8. Whitgift, Arch. Bp. of Canterbury, to Sir R. Cecil.
Feb. 9. R. Carmarden to Lord Burghley.
Feb. 10. Commission for Guernsey.
Feb. 11. E. of Essex to Sir R. Cecil.
Feb. 12. Same to same.
Feb. 13. Sir Jo. Danvers to Sir C. Danvers.
Feb. 15. Lord Burghley to Sir R. Cecil.
Feb. 16. Capt. Gode to E. of Essex.
Feb. 12 & 16. Memoranda touching the treaty between the Queen of England, King of Spain, and the States.
Feb. 12 & 16. Extracts of letters from Spanish Commissioners at Verviers to Cardinal Albert.
Feb. 17. R. Carmarden to Lord Burghley.
Feb. 17. Sir R. Sydney to E. of Essex.
Feb. 17. Sir E. Conway to same.
Feb. 17. Sir R. Sydney to same.
Feb. 17. Examinations of Antonio Memey, a Portuguese, concerning the Spanish preparations from Brittany and Biscay.
Feb. 18. Sir E. Conway to E. of Essex.
Feb. 18. Submission of Brian Orwack (O'Rourke ?), the chief of his name.
Feb. 18. Submission of Shane McManus Oge O'Donnel, of Tyrconnel, for himself and others, at the Abbey of Boyle.
Feb. 19. —— to Geo. Heldiver.
Feb. 20. Sir A. Sydney to E. of Essex.
Feb. 20. R. Carmarden to Lord Burghley.
Feb. 21. The Queen to same.
Feb. 23. Geo. Gilpin to E. of Essex.
Feb. 25. The Queen to Lord Burghley.
Feb. 26. Sir Alex. Radcliff to E. of Essex.
Feb. 26. Anth. Bacon to Sir R. Cecil.
Feb. 26. Sir R. Drew to same.
Feb. 26. M. Le Grand to E. of Essex.
Feb. 26. Earl of Shrewsbury to Sir R. Cecil.
Mar. 2. Emperor of Russia to the Governor of Evan Gorod.
Mar. 2. Examination of Helen Fortescue and her two daughters, for harbouring a priest.
Mar. 3. Adam Loftus, Archbp. of Dublin, to Sir R. Cecil.
Mar. 4. Ed. Gray to Lord Burghley.
Mar. 6. The States General to the E. of Essex.
Mar. 7. Jo. Colville to same.
Mar. 8. Duke of Florence to same.
Mar. 9. Passport of the Adalantado of Spain to two Englishmen.
Mar. 10. H. Constable to the E. of Essex.
Mar. 10. Philip Count of Hohenloe to E. of Essex.
Mar. 10. Maurice of Nassau to same.
Mar. 12. Points and articles of Sec. of Merchant Adventurers to the States General, for leave of residence in the United Provinces, with answers.
Mar. 13. P. de la Haye to Lord Burghley.
Mar. 13. Sir H. Palavicino to Sir R. Cecil.
Mar. 14. M. Guicciardini to E. of Essex.
Mar. 14. H. Cuffe to Hen. Saville.
Mar. 18. Sir R. Ker to Sir R. Carey.
Mar. 20. Jean, Count of Nassau to E. of Essex.
Mar. 20. Jo. Udall to same.
Mar. 20. Survey or muster of forces for Portsdown division of Hampshire.
Mar. 22. M. Guicciardini to E. of Essex.
Mar. 22. Sir A. Barkley to Sir R. Cecil.
Mar. 23. Tho. Laple to E. of Essex.
Mar. 23. Commissioners for the Peace to Privy Council.
Mar. 24. E. Seymour to Sir R. Cecil.
Mar. 24. Dudley Norton to same.
Mar. 26. Wm. Lilly to E. of Essex.
Mar. 26. Sir T. Shirley to Sir R. Cecil.
Mar. 27. Sir Ed. Norreys to E. of Essex.
Mar. 27. Lord Sheffield to Sir R. Cecil.
Mar. 28. Sir R. Sydney to Earl of Essex.
Mar. 29. Sir T. Shirley to E. of Essex.
Mar. 29. The Mayor of Plymouth to same.
Mar. 29. Dean Nowell to same.
Mar. 30. Jacomo Marenco to E. of Essex.
Mar. 30. Tho. Throckmorton to Sir R. Cecil.
Mar. 30. Countess of Bedford to same.
Mar. 30. Watson, Bp. of Chichester, to same.
Mar. 31. Governor of Dieppe to E. of Essex.
Mar. —. Capt. Wynn to same.
Mar. —. Jacomo Marenco to the Queen.
Mar. —. The Company of Pewterers to same.
Mar. —. Don Juan de Ribas, Governor of Calais, to ——.
Mar. —. Wm. Udall to Bishop of Lymerick (2).

April 1. Sir R. Sydney to E. of Essex.
April 2. M. Stanhope to Sir R. Cecil.
April 2. Jean Castel to E. of Essex.
April 2. M. de Bellegrande to same.
April 3. The Mayor of Plymouth to Sir R. Cecil.
April 3. P. de Regiomonte to E. of Essex.
April 3. King of France to same.
April 4. John Earl of Cassilis to Sir R. Cecil.
April 4. Louis of Nassau to E. of Essex.
April 4. Sir Th. Shirley to Sir R. Cecil.
April 4. Sir Jo. Aldrich to E. of Essex.
April 4. Marshal de Biron to same.
April 5. Arth. Gorges to Sir R. Cecil.
April 6. Capt. Horde to same.
April 6. Sir A. Mildmay to E. of Essex.
April 7. H. Lok to Sir R. Cecil.
April 7. Jo. Danyel to same.
April 7. Sir A. Mildmay to E. of Essex.
April 7. Watson, Bp. of Chichester, to Sir R. Cecil.
April 7. Whitgift, bp. of Canterbury, to same.
April 8. Sir M. Molyns to same.
April 8. Lord Mountjoye to same.
April 8. R. Carmarden to same.
April 8. The Queen to Lord Burghley.
April 9. Mr. Darrell to Sir R. Cecil.
April 9. Capt. Dawtry to same.
April 9. Lord Mayor of London to same.
April 10. The States Deputies to Privy Council.
April 10. Wm. Lilley to E. of Essex.
April 10. Capt. Wylton to same.
April 10. T. Philips to Arch. Douglas.
April 10. Sir R. Cecil to Duke of Holstein.
April 10. The Queen to the King of France.
April 10. Justin de Nassau to E. of Essex.
April 11. Wal. Travers and Jas. Killertone to Sir R. Cecil.
April 11. Lord Mountjoye to same.
April 11. Sir Ed. Norris to E. of Essex.
April 11. Sir Jo. Smith to Sir R. Cecil.
April 11. M. Fonquerelles to E. of Essex.
April 12. Sir R. Sydney to same.
April 12. The Mayor and Jurats of Dover to Sir R. Cecil.
April 13. W. Lilley to E. of Essex.
April 14. Sir R. Sydney to same.
April 14. Confession of John Storm, suborned by the Cardinals to murder Sir Edw. Norreys.
April 15. M. Van Heile to Sir R. Cecil.
April 15. Juan de Aguia y Vergari to the Queen.
April 15. Arch. Douglas to Sir R. Cecil.
April 15. Capt. Maye to same.
April 15. Sir A. Shirley to same.
April 16. Sir Ed. Wylton to E. of Essex.
April 18. Baron Ewens and Serjeant Drewe to same.
April 18. Th. Fane to Sir R. Cecil.
April 18. R. Swifte to same.
April 18. Jo. St. Leger to same.
April 18. Dr. Goodman, Dean of Westminster, to same.
April 18. Sir F. Vere to E. of Essex.
April 20. Rich. Davies, Bp. of St. David's to Sir R. Cecil.
April 20. Jo. Danyel to same.
April 20. Ar. Gorges to same.
April 21. Memoranda of men and pay in the garrisons at Jersey, Guernsey, and the Isle of Wight.
April 21. A description of the state of England connected with the charge against Th. Arundel.
April 22. Geo. Gilpin to E. of Essex.
April 22. Ed. Kirkeham to Sir R. Cecil.
April 22. Capt. E. Wylton to E. of Essex.
April 22. The Queen to Lord Burghley.
April 22. Mr. Champernowne to Privy Council.
April 22. Geo. Chamberlayne to E. of Essex.
April 22. M. Montmartin to same.
April 22. Dr. Goodman, Dean of Westminster, to Sir R. Cecil.
April 23. Sir Geo. Saville to same.
April 24. Sir E. Fytton to same.
April 24. Sir W. Ralegh to Lord Burghley.
April 24. Th. Fane to Sir R. Cecil.
April 24. Sir Fr. Vere to E. of Essex.
April 24. W. Lilley to same.
April 26. Lord H. Norreys to Sir R. Cecil.
April 26. Lord Burgh to same.
April 27. Sir R. Sydney to E. of Essex.
April 27. Mr. Beecher to Lord Burghley.
April 28. Wm. Stallenge to Sir R. Cecil.
April 28. E. of Essex and the noblemen with him to Sir R. Cecil.
April 29. The Queen to Lord Burghley.

April 29. Sir R. Sydney to E. of Essex.
April 29. Same to same.
April 29. The Deputies of the States to E. of Essex,
Lord Admiral, and Lord Buckhurst.
April 29. Sir R. Sydney to E. of Essex.
April 30. Sir Th. Shirley to Sir R. Cecil.
April 30. W. Cecil to same.
April —. Ed. Darcy to same.
May 2. M. de Sancy to E. of Essex.
May 2. Th. Windebanke to Sir R. Cecil.
May 2. Sir. Jo. Aldrich to E. of Essex.
May 2. Dr. Goodman, Dean of Westminster, to Sir R.
Cecil.
May 2. Sir A. Ashley to same.
May 2. Sir Anth. Mildmay to same.
May 2. Capt. Chichester to E. of Essex.
May 2. W. Lilley to same.
May 3. Mr. Solicitor Fleming to Sir R. Cecil.
May 3. H. Cavendishe to same.
May 3. Th. Myddleton to Mr. Wilkes.
May 4. Sir A. Pawlet to Sir R. Cecil.
May 4. Sir E. Hoby to same.
May 4. Capt. H. Power to E. of Essex.
May 4. Sir Ed. Norreys to same.
May 4. Lord Burgh to Sir R. Cecil.
May 4. Countess of Desmond to same.
May 5. Sir F. Carew to same.
May 6. Sir Humph. Parnell to same.
May 6. King of France to the Queen.
May 7. Ro. Baer to Sir R. Cecil.
May 7. E. of Essex to same.
May 7. Sir H. Drewett to same.
May 7. Sir F. Vere to E. of Essex.
May 8. Mr. Cherry (for the Muscovy Merchants) to
Sir R. Cecil.
May 9. Sir R. Sydney to E. of Essex.
May 9. T. Arundel to Sir R. Cecil.
May 9. Sir G. Fenton to same.
May 9. R. Beale to same.
May 10. Geo. Chamberlayne to same.
May 10. Lord Burghley to same.
May 11. Sir F. Carew to same.
May 11. E. of Essex to Lord Burghley.
May 12. Sir H. Drewit to Sir R. Cecil.
May 12. Lord H. Cobham to same.
May 12. Sir G. Carew to same.
May 12. Sir R. Sydney to E. of Essex.
May 12. Same to same.
May 13. Lord Burghley to Sir R. Cecil.
May 13. Same to same.
May 16. Sir R. Sydney to E. of Essex.
May 16. The Doge of Venice to the Queen.
May 16. Sir Jo. Foster to Sir R. Cecil.
May 17. Sir H. Drewit to same.
May 17. Quarles to Mr. Babington and Mr. Bromley.
May 17. Ant. Rolston to E. of Essex and Sir R.
Cecil.
May 18. Lady Ann Cobham to Sir R. Cecil.
May 18. Wm. Waad to same.
May 19. Same to same.
May 19. Fitting, victualling, and paying four ships.
May 19. Wm. Lilley to E. of Essex.
May 19. Sir Fr. Vere to same.
May 19. Sir F. Gorges to Sir R. Cecil.
May 20. W. Medeley to same.
May 20. The Queen to Lord Burghley.
May 21. Sir N. Parker to Sir R. Cecil.
May 22. Sir R. Sydney to E. of Essex.
May 22. Capt. L. Kemys to Sir R. Cecil.
May 22. Geo. Gilpin to E. of Essex.
May 23. Jacomo Marenco to same.
May 23. Jo. Danyel to Sir R. Cecil.
May 23. Attorney General Coke to same.
May 23. Sir Ant. Mildmay to E. of Essex.
May 23. Sir H. Danvers to Sir R. Cecil.
May 24. Sir R. Sydney to E. of Essex.
May 24. Same to same.
May 24. E. of Essex to Sir R. Cecil.
May 25. Sir Fr. Vere to E. of Essex.
May 25. Countess of Desmond to Sir R. Cecil.
May 25. Hen. Masterson to E. of Essex.
May 25. A. Champernowne to Sir R. Cecil.
May 25. Capt. Moryson to E. of Essex.
May 26. Sir Hor. Palavicino to Sir R. Cecil.
May 26. Geo. Gilpin to E. of Essex.
May 26. T. Mildmay and J. Petrie to Lord Burghley.
May 26. R. Carmarden, Mr. Middleton, &c., to same.
May 27. Lord H. Cobham to Sir R. Cecil.
May 27. F. Grevillo to same.
May 27. Sir R. Sydney to E. of Essex.
May 28. Bilson, Bp. of Winchester, to Sir R. Cecil.
5.

May 28. Capt. J. Throckmorton to E. of Essex.
May 28. Gervase Babington, Bp. of Exeter, to Sir
R. Cecil.
May 28. Geo. Gilpin to E. of Essex.
May 28. Sir Jo. Aldrich to same.
May 28. Jo. Danyel to Sir R. Cecil.
May 28. Attorney General Coke to Lord Burghley.
May 28. M. Guicciardini to E. of Essex.
May 28. Tho. Bellot to Sir R. Cecil.
May 29. Same to same.
May 29. Capt. Brett to E. of Essex.
May 29. Sir E. Norreys to same.
May 29. Bilson, Bp. of Winchester, to Sir R. Cecil.
May 29. Bill of Exchange for Spanish Paymaster
General in Low Countries.
May 30. Sir R. Sydney to E. of Essex.
May 30. Duc de Bouillon to same.
May 30. Sir Fr. Vere to same.
May 30. Jo. Browne to Sir R. Cecil.
May 30. Lord Sheffield to same.
May 30. Th. Palliser (priest) to Wm. Waad.
May 30. Wm. Waad to Sir R. Cecil.
May 30. Sir Hor. Palavicino to same.
May 31. English prisoners in Spain to the Queen.
May 31. Sir R. Sydney to E. of Essex.
May 31. Louis of Nassau to same.
May 31. Capt. Dowcra to same.
May 31. Sir W. Bowes to Lord Scroope.
May 31. The Sheriff of Devonshire to Sir R. Cecil.
May 31. Vincent Skinner to Lord Burghley.
May 31. Acknowledgment of Th. Lake of an obligation
for debt due by Duke Brooke of Temple Court, Soms.
May —. Tho. Arundel to Sir R. Cecil.
May —. Privy Council to "One of the messengers of
" Her Majesty's Chambers."
May —. Mem. by Sir R. Cecil on pay, &c. to troops in
France.
May —, Pledges required by the Marches of England
of the Marches of Scotland and Liddesdale.
June 1. Sir R. Sydney to E. of Essex.
June 1. Sir Hor. Palavicino to Sir R. Cecil.
June 1. M. de Sancy to E. of Essex.
June 1. Things propounded to the Senate of Lubeck
as to the chief of the Hanse Society by Count of Bar-
liamonite, Geo. Westendorffe, and Jo. Newark, Spanish
Ambassadors.
June 2. Sir R. Carey to Sir R. Cecil.
June 2. Mrs. E. Hampden (the mother of Jo. Hamp-
den) to same.
June 2. E. of Essex, the Lord Admiral, and Sir R.
Cecil to Sir M. Arundel.
June 2. Lord Scroope to Sir R. Cecil.
June 2. E. Stanhope to same.
June 3. H. Maynard to same.
June 3. M. de Mouy to E. of Essex.
June 3. Sir B. Barkeley to Sir R. Cecil.
June 3. Th. Fane to same.
June 3. English prisoners in Spain to same.
June 4. Capt. Ar. Chichester to E. of Essex.
June 4. Sir M. Mollyns to Sir R. Cecil.
June 4. Mr. Edgecumbe (ancestor of E. Mount Edge-
cumbe) to same.
June 4. H. Fadys to same.
June 4. Jas. Perott to same.
June 4. Jacomo Marenco to E. of Essex.
June 4. H. Lok to Sir R. Cecil.
June 4. Sir R. Carey to same.
June 4. Florence Macarthy to same.
June 5. Sir Fr. Vere to E. of Essex.
June 5. W. Lilley to same.
June 5. Ar. Gregory to Sir R. Cecil.
June 5. R. Carmarden to Sir W. Ralegh.
June 5. Wm. Stallenge to Sir R. Cecil.
June 5. R. Bowes and Sir W. Bowes to same.
June 5. Sir Jo. Aldryoh to E. of Essex.
June 6. Jo. Danyel to Sir R. Cecil.
June 6. Sir R. Sydney to E. of Essex.
June 6. Sir W. Fitzwilliam to Sir R. Cecil.
June 6. Sir E. Denny to same.
June 6. Sir Rich. Verney to same.
June 6. Th. Fane to same.
June 6. Capt. Jo. Barkeley to E. of Essex.
June 7. Robert and Sir W. Bowes to Lord Burghley.
June 7. Sir R. Sydney to E. of Essex.
June 7. Same to same.
June 7. Maurice of Nassau to same.
June 7. Countess of Desmond to Sir R. Cecil.
June 7. E. of Shrewsbury to same.
June 7. E. of Kent to the Privy Council.
June 7. Th. Bodley to E. of Essex.
June 7. Geo. Gilpin to same.

June 7. Names of 100 soldiers, with arms, &c., delivered to Capt. Th. Allen for the county of Bedford by Henry, E. of Kent, Lo. Lieutenant.
June 8. Sir R. Sydney to E. of Essex.
June 8. Sir R. Barkeley to Sir R. Cecil.
June 8. Chr. Keynell to E. of Essex.
June 8. Sir H. Palavicino to Sir R. Cecil.
June 8. Same to same.
June 9. Earl of Essex to Sir R. Cecil.
June 9. Sir Ed. Coke to same.
June 10. R. Topclyffe to same.
June 10. Wm. Cecil to same.
June 10. Soldiers with armour delivered to Capt. Dacres for co. Herts.
June 11. King of France to E. of Essex.
June 11. Robert Bowes to Sir R. Cecil.
June 11. Duc de Bouillon to E. of Essex.
June 11. Time of a journey between London and Madrid.
June 12. Sir R. Carey to Sir R. Cecil.
June 12. Th. Bellot to same.
June 12. Sir Ant. Ashley to same.
June 12. Wm. Stallenge to same.
June 12. Jo. Carey to same.
June 13. Sir R. Bingham to same.
June 13. Sir R. Martyn to same
June 13. Mr. R. and Sir W. Bowes to same.
June 13. Wm. Waad to Sir R. Cecil.
June 13. Mr. R. and Sir W. Bowes to Lord Eure.
June 13. E. of Essex to Sir R. Cecil.
June 14. Th. Fanshawe to same.
June 14. Nic. Degles to same.
June 14. H. Cuffe to H. Saville.
June 14. M. Guicciardini to E. of Essex.
June 14. Lord Scroope to the Privy Council.
June 14. Hen. Lok to Sir R. Cecil.
June 15. Capt. Ed. Wylton to E. of Essex.
June 15. R. Marshall to Sir R. Cecil
June 15. Sir Gef. Fenton's man to same.
June 15. Th. Arundel to same.
June 15. Sir R. Martyn to same.
June 15. Capt. Arthur Chichester to same.
June 15. E. of Essex to same.
June 15. W. Cook to same.
June 16. Wm. Stallenge to same.
June 16. Lord H. Cobham to same.
June 17. Sir W. Bowes to Lord Eure.
June 17. Wm. Waad to Sir Jo. Stanhope.
June 18. E. of Essex to Sir R. Cecil.
June 18. E. of Cumberland to same.
June 18. Countess of Kent to same.
June 20. Sir T. Wilkes to same.
June 20. Sir R. Barkeley to same.
June 20. Sir A. Standon to same.
June 20. Fred. Moore to same.
June 20. Wm. Waad to same.
June 21. Wm. Stallenge to same.
June 21. Sir H. Palavicino to same.
June 22. Sir H. Knyvet to same.
June 22. Sir Jo. Hollis to the Lord Keeper.
June 22. Mr. Houghton to Sir R. Cecil.
June 22. Lady Hungerford to same.
June 22. Lord Scroope to same.
June 22. E. of Essex to same.
June 22. Same to same.
June 22. Wm. Waad to same.
June 23. Sir A. Shirley to same.
June 23. H. Maynard to same.
June 23. Roger Manners to same.
June 23. Sir M. Arundel to same.
June 23. E. of Essex to same.
June 24. The Dowager Lady Russell to same.
June 24. Mr. Budden to same.
June 24. Countess of Kent to same.
June 24. Sir W. Bowes to same.
June 24. E. of Essex to same.
June 25. Sir W. Russell to same.
June 25. Earl of Essex to same.
June 25. Sir J. Hollis or Holohis to Lord Burghley.
June 25. Sir W. Russell to Privy Council.
June 25. Joseph Mayne to Sir R. Cecil.
June 25. Indenture by Sir Geo. Horne and Geo. Younge, Scotch Commissioners in Border causes, delivered to Sir W. Bowes.
June 26. Sir W. Bowes to Sir R. Cecil.
June 26. Earl of Essex to same.
June 27. Lord Eure to same.
June 27. Sir R. Cecil to Sir M. Arundel.
June 27. W. Stallenge to Sir R. Cecil.
June 27. Capt. May to same.
June 28. Sir W. Brereton to the Privy Council.

June 28. Wm. Waad to Sir R. Cecil.
June 28. Mrs. E. Hampden to same.
June 28. Whitgift, Abp. of Canterbury, to same.
June 28. E. of Essex to same.
June 29. Andrew Bushey to same.
June 29. Mr. Vavasour to same.
June 29. Dean and Chapter of Westminster to same.
June 29. Lord Scroope to same.
June 29. Sir Hor. Palavicino to same.
June 29. Proclamation for apparel, and additions of certain particularities.
June 30. Sir T. Fane (gov. of Dover Castle) to Sir R. Cecil.
June 30. Sir T. Wilkes to same.
June 30. Dr. W. Cooke to same.
June 30. And. Norton to same.
June —. The Dowager Lady Russell to same.
June —. R. Beard to same.
June —. Sir E. Fitzgerald to same.
June —. Sir T. Arundel to same.
June —. Countess of Desmond to same.
June —. Lord Th. Howard to same.
June —. Foulke Grevyll to Mr. Knolles.
July 1. Lord Dunsanny to Sir R. Cecil.
July 1. Th. Windebank to same.
July 2. The Queen (Privy Seal) to Lord Burghley.
July 2. Sir T. Fane to Sir R. Cecil.
July 3. T. Harriot to the same.
July 3. Lord Burghley to same.
July 3. Sir R. Barkley to same.
July 4. Edw. Conway to same.
July 4. Sir T. Fane to same.
July 4. T. Coverte to the Lord Admiral.
July 4. The Queen to Lord Burghley.
July 4. R. Bowes to Sir R. Cecil.
July 4. Dr, Duport to same.
July 4. Sir H. Winston to same.
July 5. Same to Lord Burghley.
July 5. Countess of Kent to Sir R. Cecil.
July 5. Geo. Cranmer to same.
July 6. Lord Admiral to same.
July 6. Justice Owen to same.
July 6. Florence Macarthy to same.
July 6. Sir J. Carey to same.
July 6. The Commanders of the Fleet to same.
July 7. Bilson, Bp. of Winchester, to same.
July 7. Sir F. Carew to same.
July 7. H. Maynard to same.
July 8. Sir J. Ley to same.
July 8. R. Busse to same.
July 9. M. Hicks to same.
July 9. Justice Owen to same.
July 10. Examination of John Steele at Sibthorp before W. Sutton, Ed. Stanhope, and Ri. Whalley, Justices of Notts. Counterfeit begging license.
July 11. Sir W. Cornwalleys to Sir R. Cecil.
July 11. W. Sanderson to same.
July 11. Dowager Lady Russell to same.
July 11. Mey, Bp. of Carlisle, to same.
July 11. Lord Keeper, Lords North and Buckhurst to same.
July 12. Th. Smith to same.
July 12. Jo. Daniel to same.
July 12. The bailiffs of Colchester to same.
July 12. Mr. Atkinson to same.
July 12. The Attorney and Solicitor General to same.
July 13. Bilson, Bp. of Winchester, to same.
July 13. Earl of Rutland to same.
July 13. Mr. Sandys to same.
July 13. Lord Buckhurst to same.
July 14. Capt. Dawtry to same.
July 14. F. Compton to same.
July 15. Peter Wentworth to same.
July 15. R. Manners to same.
July 15. Lord Barry to same.
July 16. M. Eliano Calvo to same.
July 17. Louis, of Nassau, to E. of Essex.
July 17. Mr. Crompton to Sir R. Cecil.
July 17. Sir T. Leighton to same.
July 18. Sir T. Shirley to same.
July 19. Project of an advice at war in the journey of the Lord Deputy to Lough Foyle, directed to the Lo. Chancellor and Council of Ireland and sent by Sir Ralph Lane.
July 20. Sir T. Leighton to Sir R. Cecil.
July 20. Same to same.
July 21. Sir H. Norreys to Privy Council.
July 21. Bennet, Dean of Windsor, to Sir R. Cecil.
July 22. Lord Keeper Egerton to same.
July 22. Christ. Anthonius and the Dutch congregation at Sandwich to [Sir R. Cecil ?]

July 23. Sir R. Sydney to Sir R. Cecil.
July 23. Sir R. Fenys to same.
July 23. Same to Sir Jo. Stanhope.
July 23. Sir Hen. Ley to Sir R. Cecil.
July 23. Jas. White to same.
July 24. Bilson, Bp. of Winchester, to same.
July 24. W. Borough to same.
July 25. Dr. Knight (Sir R's. chaplain) to same.
July 25. Tho. Edmonds to same.
July 25. The Queen's oration to the Polish ambassador at Greenwich.
July 26. T. North to E. of Essex.
July 26. Sir Hor. Palavicino to Sir R. Cecil.
July 27. Sir Julius Cæsar to Lord Burghley.
July 27. Mr. Hext to Sir R. Cecil.
July 27. R. Beale to same.
July 27. Sir J. Stanhope to same.
July 28. Jo. Styleman to same.
July 28. E. of Northumberland to same.
July 28. Ordnance, &c., in charge of Sir F. Gorges for defence of the fort at Plymouth, 1 Jan. 1596 to
July 29. Sol. Fleming to Sir R. Cecil.
July 29. Babington, Bp. of Exeter, to same.
July 29. P. Wentworth to same.
July 29. Points of the Scotch King's letter compared with overtures for quiet of the Borders.
July 30. Jo. Young, Bp. of Rochester, to Sir R. Cecil.
July 30. Lord Eure to Lord Burghley.
July 30. Sir H. Palavicino to Sir R. Cecil.
July 31. Countess of Arundel to same.
July 31. Jo. Young, Bp. of Rochester, to same.
July —. Friár John (Aguirre y Vergara) to same.
July —. Lord Dunsany to same.
July —. Sir E. Fitzgerald to same (2).
July —. The Lord Admiral to same.
July —. Lord Th. Howard to same.
July —. Mrs. Cath. Malby to same.
July —. Dowager Lady Russell to same.
July —. E. of Rutland to same.
July —. E. Wymarke to same.
Aug. 1. Noel de Caron to same.
Aug. 1. W. Medely to same.
Aug. 1. E. Gorges to same.
Aug. 1. The Emperor Rudolph to his subjects.
Aug. 1. Proclamation of the Emperor Rudolph touching Merchant Adventurers.
Aug. 2. Bailiffs of Colchester to Sir R. Cecil.
Aug. 2. T. Bellot to same.
Aug. 2. Instructions for Sir R. Cross for transporting the Lyon and other merchant ships with victuals for the fleet under the Earl of Essex.
Aug. 3. H. Croft to Sir R. Cecil.
Aug. 3. E. Reynolds to same.
Aug. 3. Mr. Edgecumbe to same.
Aug. 3. Sir Ed. Coke to same.
Aug. 4. The Dean of Windsor to same.
Aug. 4. The Mayor, &c. of Sarum to same.
Aug. 4. J. Aguirre y Vergara to same.
Aug. 5. T. Alabaster to same.
Aug. 5. D. Hilles to Arch. Douglas.
Aug. 5. E. of Essex to Sir R. Cecil.
Aug. 5. Sir M. Morgan to same.
Aug. 6. Sir R. Cecil to Mr. Darrell.
Aug. 6. The Privy Council to E. of Essex.
Aug. 6. E. of Shrewsbury to Sir R. Cecil.
Aug. 6. Sir R. Cecil to Sir John Cutts.
Aug. 6. E. of Essex to Sir R. Cecil.
Aug. 6. Dr. Dupont to same.
Aug. 6. Wm. Borough to same.
Aug. 8. Sir Hor. Palavicino to same.
Aug. 9. Mr. Darrell to same.
Aug. 9. Sir H. Harrington to Mr. Waad.
Aug. 9. E. Miller to Sir R. Cecil.
Aug. 9. Sir John Packington to same.
Aug. 9. Countess of Derby to same.
Aug. 9. H. Lok to same.
Aug. 10. E. of Essex to the Privy Council.
Aug. 10. Sir Jo. Cutts to Sir R. Cecil.
Aug. 11. Sir H. Palmer to same.
Aug. 11. Mr. Topclyffe to same.
Aug. 11. Sir E. Fytton to same.
Aug. 11. Lord Dunsany to same.
Aug. 11. Sir Geo. Carew to same.
Aug. 11. E. of Essex to same.
Aug. 11. Same to same.
Aug. 11. The General and Council of the Expedition to the Privy Council.
Aug. 11. R. Carmarden to Lord Burghley.
Aug. 11. Lord Th. Howard to Sir R. Cecil.
Aug. 12. Ar. Gorges to same.

Aug. 12. Mr. Bradgate to same.
Aug. 12. E. of Essex to same.
Aug. 12. T. Fane to same.
Aug. 13. Lord Burghley, the Lord Admiral, and Sir R. Cecil to E. of Essex.
Aug. 13. Sir R. Weston to Sir R. Cecil.
Aug. 13. E. of Essex to same (3).
Aug. 13. Vaughan, Bishop of Chester, to same.
Aug. 13. Lord Mayor of London to same.
Aug. 13. E. of Essex to Mr. Reynolds.
Aug. 13. Philippo Corsini to Sir R. Cecil.
Aug. 14. E. of Essex to the Privy Council.
Aug. 14. Same to Sir R. Cecil.
Aug. 15. Mr. Edgecumbe to same.
Aug. 15. Mr. Solicitor General Fleming to same.
Aug. 15. Lord Buckhurst to same.
Aug. 15. Sir H. Palavicino to same.
Aug. 16. Earl of Pembroke to same.
Aug. 17. Mr. Darrell to same.
Aug. 17. Countess of Desmond to same.
Aug. 17. T. Bellot to same.
Aug. 17. Sir R. Martin to same.
Aug. 17. Sir Jo. Gilbert to same.
Aug. 17. Provisions found on board Spanish ships lately taken.
Aug. 18. Sir J. Gilbert to Sir R. Cecil.
Aug. 18. Ant. Mildmay to same.
Aug. 18. Sir T. Gerrard to same.
Aug. 18. H. Powlet to same.
Aug. 19. Lord Burghley to same.
Aug. 19. Wm. Stallenge to same.
Aug. 20. Lord Keeper Egerton to same.
Aug. 20. King of France to the Deputies of the Reformed Church.
Aug. 20. Whitgift, Abp. of Canterbury, to Sir R. Cecil.
Aug. 21. W. Lilley to E. of Essex.
Aug. 21. Sir R. Cecil (to Lord Deputy of Ireland?)
Aug. 21. Earl and Countess of Derby to Sir R. Cecil.
Aug. 23. Wm. Stallenge to same.
Aug. 24. Sir T. Shirley to same.
Aug. 24. The Auditors to same.
Aug. 24. Francis Dacres to Lord Burghley.
Aug. 24. Earl of Shrewsbury to Sir R. Cecil.
Aug. 26. Dr. Duport to same.
Aug. 26. Wm. Stallenge to same.
Aug. 27. Earl of Lincoln to same.
Aug. 27. Earl of Shrewsbury to same.
Aug. 27. The Commissioners, Th. Wilkes, &c. to Lo. Keeper of G. Seal, Lo. Treas., Lo. Buckhurst, and Sir John Fortescue, Chanc. of Exchequer.
Aug. 28. Earl of Essex to R. Knollys.
Aug. 28. F. Greville to Sir R. Cecil.
Aug. 29. R. Graham to Arch. Douglas.
Aug. 28. Lord Admiral, Lord Chamberlain, and Sir Robt. Cecil to Mr. Skinner and Sir Ferd. Gorges.
Aug. 30. Lord Lumley to Sir R. Cecil.
Aug. 30. F. Greville to same.
Aug. 30. Lord Admiral to same.
Aug. 30. R. Coningsby to same.
Aug. 31. Noel de Caron to same.
Aug. 31. Dr. Stanhope to same.
Aug. 31. Bancroft, Bp. of London, to same.
Aug. 31. Lord General and Council of the expedition to Privy Council.
Aug. 31. Sir Geo. Carew to Sir R. Cecil.
Aug. 31. Lord Mountjoy to same.
Aug. —. W. Bruester to same.
Aug. —. Sir E. Fytton to same.
Aug. —. Same to Sir R. Cecil.
Aug. —. Sir G. Gifford to the Queen.
Aug. —. Lord Grey to same.
Aug. —. Lord Herbert to same.
Aug. —. Lord Th. Howard to the Queen.
Aug. —. The Privy Council to E. of Lincoln.
Aug. —. Countess of Pembroke to Sir R. Cecil.
Sept. 1. Mayor of Dartmouth to same.
Sept. 2. Bp. of London, Dr. Stanhope and Dr. L. Andrews to same.
Sept. 4. Lady Denny to same.
Sept. 4. Geo. Leslie to Mr. Brown.
Sept. 4. R. Maynard to Sir R. Cecil.
Sept. 4. Lady Desmond to same.
Sept. 5. Lady Cobham to same.
Sept. 6. The Cardinal Albert to M. de Billy (Commissioner at Lisle).
Sept. 6. Sir Jo. Gilbert to the Lord Admiral.
Sept. 8. Sir Walter Ralegh to Sir R. Cecil.
Sept. 8. R. Butler to same.
Sept. 8. The States General to the Queen.
Sept. 8. Sir T. Fane to Sir R. Cecil.

Sept. 9. Sir W. Cornwallis to same.
Sept. 9. Wm. Stallenge to same.
Sept. 9. Foulke Grevyll to same.
Sept. 10. The Dean and Chapter of Exeter to same.
Sept. 10. Sir Geo. Carew to same.
Sept. 11. Hutton, Abp. of York, to same.
Sept. 10. Le Prince d'Espagne, aux Prélats, Nobles, &c., du Pays Bas.
Sept. 12. Sir R. Fenys to Sir R. Cecil.
Sept. 12. Sir W. Clerke to same.
Sept. 13. Sir Geo. Carew to same.
Sept. 13. Wm. Stallenge to same.
Sept. 14. Sir T. Shirley to same.
Sept. 14. Bailiffs of East Grinstead to same.
Sept. 14. Sir Cha. Percy to E. of Essex.
Sept. 15. Lord Hunsdon to Sir R. Cecil.
Sept. 15. T. Dagley to same.
Sept. 16. E. of Essex to same.
Sept. 16. Sir A. Mildmay to same.
Sept. 16. Lord Keeper Egerton to same.
Sept. 16. A. Ashley to Sir Ralph Horsey.
Sept. 18. Duc de Bouillon to the Queen.
Sept. 19. Wm. Stallenge to Sir R. Cecil.
Sept. 19. Sir R. Wrothesley to same.
Sept. 19. F. d'Azevedo to Wm. Stallenge.
Sept. 20. Sir Th. Bodley to E. Smyth.
Sept. 21. Gef. Storie to Sir R. Cecil.
Sept. 21. Examination of John Dewrance of Enfield, touching the head of a dead man found in the Chace said to be that of "Feagh Mackheugh", (an Irish traitor).
Sept. 22. R. Skevington to Lord Admiral and Sir R. Cecil.
Sept. 22. R. Percival to same.
Sept. 23. Whitgift, Abp. of Canterbury, to same.
Sept. 23. F. Dacre to E. of Essex.
Sept. 23. Wm. Stallenge to Sir R. Cecil.
Sept. 24. A. Gorges to same.
Sept. 24. Lady Riche to same.
Sept. 24. R. Lytton to same.
Sept. 25. H. Apsley to same.
Sept. 25. Sir H. Palavicino to same.
Sept. 25. Sir Jo. Gilbert to same.
Sept. 25. Same to the Lord Admiral (2).
Sept. 25. Sir W. Clerk to Sir Robert Cecil.
Sept. 25. Sir Jo. Gilbert to same.
Sept. 25. Sir H. Palavicino to same.
Sept. 25. Wm. Stallenge to same.
Sept. 25. F. Dacre to Elinor Dacre (his daughter).
Sept. 25. Lady Montague to Lord Buckhurst.
Sept. 26. Dr. Chr. Parkins to Sir R. Cecil.
Sept. 27. Same to same.
Sept. 26. Sir Jo. Gilbert to same.
Sept. 26. Lord Burghley to same.
Sept. 26. Lord Buckhurst to Lord Burghley.
Sept. 27. Sir H. Lee to Sir R. Cecil.
Sept. 27. Sir F. Gorges to same.
Sept. 27. Sir T. Leighton to same.
Sept. 28. Hutton, Abp. of York, to Sir R. Cecil.
Sept. 28. R. Beale to same.
Sept. 29. Countess of Pembroke to same.
Sept. 29. Mathews, Bp. of Durham, to same.
Sept. 29. Bancroft, Bp. of London, to same.
Sept. 29. H. Lok to same.
Sept. 30. Dr. Jegon to Lady K. Howard.
Sept. —. Countess of Essex to Sir R. Cecil.
Sept. —. Lady Ralegh to same.
Oct. 2. Sir A. Mildmay to same.
Oct. 2. Dean of Westminster to same.
Oct. 2. Mr. Huet to same.
Oct. 3. Manner and form of election of a Knight of the Shire made at the castle of York, with various papers upon the election of Sir John Saville.
Oct. 4. Bailiffs of Colchester to Sir R. Cecil.
Oct. 4. Mr. Trefyll to Mr. Bevill.
Oct. 5. Justices of Yorkshire to Sir J. Stanhope.
Oct. 5. Abp. and Council at York to Privy Council.
Oct. 5. Sir P. Hoby to Sir R. Cecil.
Oct. 5. Sir J. Peyton to same.
Oct. 6. Mr. Gaul to same.
Oct. 6. W. Poyntz to same.
Oct. 6. A. Ashley to Sir Ralph Horsey.
Oct. 7. G. Carey to Sir R. Cecil.
Oct. 7. W. Stallenge to same.
Oct. 8. Mayor of Plymouth to same.
Oct. 8. Dean and Chapter of Exeter to same.
Oct. 8. Lord Burghley to same.
Oct. 9. Mr. Cuffe to same?
Oct. 9. Mr. Stapell to same.
Oct. 10. Amy Cottel to Lady Ralegh.

Oct. 10. M. de Neufeville and M. de Villeroy to M. de la Fontaine.
Oct. 10. Lord Admiral to Sir R. Cecil.
Oct. 10. Lord Keeper Egerton to same.
Oct. 10. W. Kirkham to same.
Oct. 11. Sir E. Vuedale to same.
Oct. 11. Privy Council to Council at York.
Oct. 11. Mr. Roe to Lord Admiral.
Oct. 11. Sir F. Gorges to Sir R. Cecil.
Oct. 12. Lord Riche to same.
Oct. 12. Sir Tho. Lucy to same.
Oct. 12. Lord Cobham to same.
Oct. 12. Countess of Arundel to same.
Oct. 12. R. Carmarden to same.
Oct. 13. Sir W. Ralegh to same.
Oct. 14. Mr. Purveye to same.
Oct. 14. Sir E. Fytton to same.
Oct. 14. Sir E. Hoby to same.
Oct. 15. Chaderton, Bp. of Lincoln, to same.
Oct. 15. M. Villeroy to M. de la Fontaine.
Oct. 15. Bailiffs of Stockbridge to Sir R. Cecil.
Oct. 15. V. Skinner to same.
Oct. 15. Sir Ed. Coke to same.
Oct. 15. Concerning three colts of the breed of Coole and Castlepark sent to the E. of Essex.
Oct. 15. Presses, &c. needful for the safe custody of Records under the Banqueting House, Whitehall.
Oct. 16. H. Maynard to Sir R. Cecil.
Oct. 16. Lord Norreys to same.
Oct. 16. The Queen to E. of Essex.
Oct. 17. Sir T. Wilkes to Sir R. Cecil.
Oct. 17. Lord Norreys to same.
Oct. 17. Lord Cobham to same.
Oct. 17. Hutton, Abp. of York, to same.
Oct. 18. Sir E. Hoby to same.
Oct. 18. Lord Keeper Egerton to same.
Oct. 19. Th. Windebank to same.
Oct. 19. E. of Essex to Privy Council.
Oct. 19. Statement of Sir H. Palavicino of alum purchased for Her Majesty in 1578.
Oct. 20. Sir F. Gorges to Sir R. Cecil.
Oct. 20. Capt. R. Hawkins to E. of Essex.
Oct. 2L. E. of Essex to Sir T. Jermyn.
Oct. 22. Sir T. Leighton to Sir R. Cecil.
Oct. 22. The Dowager Lady Russell to same.
Oct. 23. Sir F. Gorges to same.
Oct. 23. E. Stanhope to same.
Oct. 24. Countess of Essex to same.
Oct. 25. Lord Mountjoy to same.
Oct. 25. Sir M. Stanhope to Mr. Petsenall.
Oct. 26. R. Smith to Sir R. Cecil.
Oct. 27. E. of Essex to same.
Oct. 27. Mr. Bellot to same.
Oct. 27. E. of Essex to Privy Council.
Oct. 28. Privy Council to the Ports.
Oct. 28. Sir E. Hoby to Sir R. Cecil.
Oct. 28. Mr. Powlett to same.
Oct. 28. Privy Council to E. of Essex.
Oct. 28. Payments for victualling the fleet from 5 November 1596 to ——.
Oct. 29. Lord Th. Howard, Lord Mountjoy, and Sir W. Ralegh to E. of Essex.
Oct. 29. Lord Hunsdon to Sir R. Cecil.
Oct. 29. Mathews, Bp. of Durham, to Lord Burghley.
Oct. 29. Dr. R. Parkins to Sir R. Cecil.
Oct. 29. Capt. Somers to E. of Essex.
Oct. 29. Sir N. Parker to same.
Oct. 29. Lord T. Howard to Sir R. Cecil.
Oct. 29. Sir W. Ralegh to same.
Oct. 29. Sir Jo. Gilbert to same.
Oct. 29. Lord Cobham to E. of Essex.
Oct. —. Mrs. Arundel to Sir R. Cecil.
Oct. —. E. of Essex to same.
Oct. —. Sir E. Hoby to same.
Oct. —. Sir G. Merrick to same.
Oct. —. Lord Burghley to the Justices of the Peace.
Oct. —. Sir W. Ralegh to Sir R. Cecil.
Oct. —. The Council at York to same.
Oct. —. Ed. Reynolds to same.
Oct. —. Things to be ordered from Portsmouth.
Oct. —. Relacio del viaje del Adelanaido (Spanish expedition to Ireland).
Nov. 1. Lord Cobham to Sir R. Cecil.
Nov. 1. Lady Wharton to same.
Nov. 1. Sir F. Vere to E. of Essex.
Nov. 1. Lord T. Howard to same.
Nov. 1. Lords Howard and Mountjoy, Sirs W. Ralegh and F. Gorges, to same.
Nov. 1. Sir T. Blount to same.

Nov. 2. Sir T. Blount and Mr. Pawlet to Privy Council.
Nov. 3. Sir C. Percy to E. of Essex.
Nov. 3. Sir H. Palavicino to Sir R. Cecil.
Nov. 3. Sir Ar. Capel to same.
Nov. 3. Sir Geo. Carew to same.
Nov. 3. Sir S. Bagnall to same.
Nov. 3. Sir F. Godolphin to Sir W. Ralegh.
Nov. 3. Wm. Hunt to Sir R. Cecil.
Nov. 4. Lord Hunsdon to same.
Nov. 4. Sir R. Barkley to same.
Nov. 4. Sir C. Moryson to same.
Nov. 4. Lady Joyce Carew to same.
Nov. 4. Sir A. Pawlet to same.
Nov. 4. Lord Hunsdon to same.
Nov. 5. Lord Mountjoy to same.
Nov. 5. Countess of Bedford to same.
Nov. 5. Sir Geo. Carew to same.
Nov. 5. Lord H. Cobham to same.
Nov. 6. Geo. Carey to same.
Nov. 6. Geo. Carey and Wm. Stallenge to same.
Nov. 6. Lords Howard and Mountjoy, Sir W. Ralegh, and Sir F. Vere to Privy Council.
Nov. 6. Sir E. Norreys to E. of Essex.
Nov. 6. Sir F. Gorges to same.
Nov. 7. R. Carmarden to Sir R. Cecil.
Nov. 7. Jo. Manners to E. of Rutland.
Nov. 7. Geo. Chamberlayne to Ferd. Rogel (Madrid).
Nov. 7. Same to Sig. F. Buquer.
Nov. 7. Same to Father Cresswell (Madrid).
Nov. 8. Advertisements out of Spain touching the Spanish fleet.
Nov. 9. Lord H. Cobham to Sir R. Cecil.
Nov. 9. Sir R. Sydney to E. of Essex.
Nov. 9. Lord Dunsany to Sir R. Cecil.
Nov. 10. Lord Grey to same.
Nov. 10. Wm. Lilley to E. of Essex.
Nov. 10. E. of Essex to Sir R. Cecil.
Nov. 10. Names of the Committees on Monopolies, &c.
Nov. 11. Wm. Lilley to E. of Essex.
Nov. 11. Duc de Bouillon to same.
Nov. 12. States General to the Queen.
Nov. 12. Same to the Privy Council.
Nov. 12. Sir T. Fane to Sir R. Cecil.
Nov. 12. E. of Essex to same.
Nov. 13. Geo. Gilpin to E. of Essex.
Nov. 13. T. Cave to Sir R. Cecil.
Nov. 13. Mr. Ward to Mr. Willys.
Nov. 14. Geo. Carey to Privy Council.
Nov. 14. Serjeant Yelverton to Sir R. Cecil.
Nov. 14. R. Carmarden to same.
Nov. 14. Earl of Rutland to same.
Nov. 15. John Danyel to same.
Nov. 15. Names of the Committees on Subsidies, &c.
Nov. 17. The Muscovy Company to Sir R. Cecil.
Nov. 18. Sir Th. Shirley to same.
Nov. 18. Justices of Merionethshire to same.
Nov. 18. Capt. Lyon to [Mr. Gilpin?]
Nov. 19. R. Carmarden to Sir R. Cecil.
Nov. 19. Mr. Cooke to same.
Nov. 19. Examination of Francis Godoy, a Spanish Captain.
Nov. 21. Sir John Holles to Sir R. Cecil.
Nov. 21. Jo. Hare to same.
Nov. 22. The Queen to Lord Burghley.
Nov. 22. R. Wheeler to Sir R. Cecil.
Nov. 22. Capt. Crosse to same.
Nov. 23. Ant. Bacon to same.
Nov. 23. Sam. Fox to same.
Nov. 23. Examination of Jos. Constable at York.
Nov. 24. Hanibal Vyvian to Sir R. Cecil.
Nov. 24. Sir Th. Bodley to same.
Nov. 24. Ch. Topclyffe to same.
Nov. 24. Sir R. Sydney to E. of Essex.
Nov. 24. The Council of the North to Lord Burghley.
Nov. 24. Examination of Chr. Simpson at York Castle.
Nov. 25. Capt. J. Price to Sir R. Cecil.
Nov. 26. Examination of Th. Hayley.
Nov. 27. Paul Toebast (?) to same.
Nov. 28. Sir R. Sydney to E. of Essex.
Nov. 28. R. Vernon to same.
Nov. 28. Duc de Bouillon to same.
Nov. 29. H. Alington to Sir R. Cecil.
Nov. 29. Sir R. Molyneux to same.
Nov. 29. Justice Beaumont to same.
Nov. 29. Capt. Baynard to same.
Nov. —. Lady Cheke to same.
Nov. —. Lord Grey to same.
Nov. —. Countess of Southampton to same.

Nov. —. Th. Strafford to Mr. Waad.
Dec. 1. Sir E. Stafford to Lord Burghley.
Dec. 1. Mr. Rante to R. Bowes.
Dec. 1. Examination of Mich. Pearson.
Dec. 2. Sir H. Lee to Sir R. Cecil.
Dec. 2. Examination of Chr. Simpson and others upon an escape of prisoners from York Castle, 24 Nov. to 2 Dec. 1597.
Dec. 3. Mr. Beverley to Sir R. Cecil.
Dec. 3. King of Spain to the Chief Treasurer.
Dec. 6. Sir A. Ashley to Sir R. Cecil.
Dec. 7. F. Cherry to same.
Dec. 7. Sir W. Clerke to same.
Dec. 7. Sir H. Killegrew and Mr. Beale.
Dec. 7. Council at York to Lord Burghley.
Dec. 7. "Philophonus Flimon" to the Queen.
Dec. 7. Council of the North to Lord Burghley.
Dec. 8. Sig. Marenco to E. of Essex.
Dec. 8. Jo. Danyel to Sir R. Cecil.
Dec. 9. Sir A. Ashley to same.
Dec. 9. Roger Manners to same.
Dec. 9. Ferd. Genibeli to same.
Dec. 9. Sir E. Fytton to same.
Dec. 10. Sir W. Lane to same.
Dec. 10. Sig. Antonio Perez to E. of Essex (2).
Dec. 10. Francisco Gusto [Perez ?].
Dec. 10. Jacomo Marenco to E. of Essex.
Dec. 12. Conseil d'Etat to King of Spain.
Dec. 12. Capt. Crosse to Sir R. Cecil
Dec. 14. Sir Post. Hoby to same.
Dec. 14. E. Stanhope to same.
Dec. 14. Dr. Parkins to same.
Dec. 14. R. Marshall to same.
Dec. 17. The Queen to Lord Burghley.
Dec. 18. Borehart Bruckman to Sir R. Cecil.
Dec. 18. Earl of Huntingdon to same.
Dec. 18. R. Carmarden to Lord Burghley.
Dec. 19. H. Lok to Sir R. Cecil.
Dec. 20. W. Lilley to E. of Essex.
Dec. 20. Philip de Nassau to King of Spain.
Dec. 22. V. Skinner to Lady Russell.
Dec. 22. Lord H. Cobham to Sir R. Cecil.
Dec. 22. R. Topclyffe to same.
Dec. 22. E. of Essex to same.
Dec. 22. M. St. Le Sieur to same.
Dec. 23. Sir A. Astley to same.
Dec. 23. Lord Burghley to Mr. Necton.
Dec. 24. Dr. Crompton to Sir R. Cecil.
Dec. 24. King of Scots to the Queen.
Dec. 25. The Wardens and Fellows of All Souls, Oxford, to Sir R. Cecil.
Dec. 26. J. Hudson to the same.
Dec. 26. Philip Corsini to Lord Burghley.
Dec. 26. Sir F. Gorges to Sir R. Cecil.
Dec. 26. Privilege of Henry IV. to "Fabry et sept Fils" for device in husbandry.
Dec. 28. Julius Cæsar to the Lord Admiral.
Dec. 28. Bayliffs of Colchester to Sir R. Cecil.
Dec. 30. Sir T. Shirley to the same.
Dec. —. [Sir Ed. Norris] to [E. of Essex].
Dec. —. The same to the Queen.
Dec. —. Th. Arundel to Sir R. Cecil.
Dec. —. Lord Scroope to same.
Dec. —. James Antony to same.
Dec. —. Note of Bills passed in Parliament.
1597. Her. Crofts to Sir R. Cecil.
1597. The Merchant Adventurers to Privy Council.
1597. Pinners and Needlers of London to Sir R. Cecil.
1597. H. Lindley and Mr. Reynolds to Sir R. Cecil and the Queen.
1597. Sir R. Sydney to E. of Essex.
1597. The Children of Fletcher, Bp. of London, to the Queen.
1597. The Privy Council to Sheriffs of Counties (2).
1597. [Jo. Udall] to Sir Ed. Dyer.
1597. [Lord Willoughby] to [E. of Essex].
1597. E. Gray to Sir R. Cecil.
1597. Lord T. Howard to same.
1597. Lord Hunsden to the Queen.
1597. Clement Medeley to Sir R. Cecil.
1597. H. Malbie to E. of Essex.
1597. Pierre Beauvoir to Sir R. Cecil.
1597. Lord Mountjoy to same.
1597. [Th. Arundel] to [E. of Essex].
1597. Mr. Neile to Sir R. Cecil.
1597. Sir H. Nevill to same.
1; 97. E. of Northumberland to E. of Essex.
1597. [The Parliament] to the Queen (2).
1597. The Queen to the [E. of Essex].
1597. Capt. Wylton (?) to same.

1597. Sir W. Ralegh to Sir R. Cecil.
1597. The same to E. of Essex.
1597. Lady Russell to Sir R. Cecil.
1597. E. of Rutland to same.
1597. Lord Sheffield to same.
1597. Lady Southwell to same.
1597. Countess of Southampton to same.
1597. W. Stafford to the Queen.
1597. Same to Serjeant Fowles.
1597. Mr. Thornborough to the Queen.
1597. Roger Walton to E. of Essex.
[1597]. Duc de Bouillon to the Queen.
[1597]. Duc de Biron to the E. of Essex.
1597. Lord R. North to same.
1597. Petition on increase of popery in Salop.
1597. Names of Sheriffs, and those forborne.
1597. Reasons for the suit of the town of Yarmouth for continuance of liberties against molestation of Lowestoffe.
1597. Charges by Edith Richer and three sisters against Sir Jo. Saville and Hugh Hare.
1597. Claim of Ric. Champernown to have the south military division of Devon to be newly divided, with answers of Lord Ed. Seymour.
1597. Bref discours d'une cruaute plus que barbare executée en la ville de Tonnerre en Bourgayne, contre le corps mort de feu M. Isaac de Laune, Docteur en Medicine, et ce pour le faict de la Religion.
1597. Bills passed in the Lower House.
1597. "Avisos," offer by writer for liberty of services to England, &c.
1597. Bishoprics void to be supplied.
1597. Accusations against students and merchants of the obedient parts of Ireland preferred to the Council of Spain by Hen. O'Neale son of the E. of Tyrone.
1597. Minute concerning the Bill against Accountants.
1597. A Bill touching the Statute of Recognizances.
1597. Objections against the Bill for the increase of people.
1597. Memoranda for "A legation of this nature," (preparations for Sir R. Cecil's journey into France) with a list of gentlemen proposing to go.
1597. Preparations against the Spanish designs upon England.
1597. Mem. from Sir R. Cecil to Lord Burghley on Irish and Scottish despatches.
1597. Notes for the Parliament.
1597. Remembrances of Sir W. Bowes on arrest.
1597. Commission for taking accounts of Sir G. Carew, Master of Ordnance, in the two voyages southwards.
1597. Powder for furnishing ships in this last voyage.
1597. Remembrances touching the Army, &c.
1597. List of captains in several counties.
[1597.] Reasons of State for the Bills of Buildings and of Tillage.
[1597.] Description of the Island of Jerceira with a discourse on its loss, from Baptista Serarje to Capitano Secresto.
1597. Articuli de Sacramento Matrimonii per theologos disputandi.
1597. Mr. Udall's confession of opinion touching points of ecclesiastical government.
1597. Speech in the House of Commons on Bill against Inclosures.
1597. Considerations pour lesquelles les convoies licetes, et autres imposts nouveaux et extraordinaires, ne devroyent estre exigez des Marchants Adventuriers par les Estatz Generaux des Provinces Unies; with reasons of the convoy, &c.
1597. Wares and merchandize of the Low Countries.
[1597.] [Commission] for E. of Essex reciting his gallantry in France, &c.
1597. Response donnée par trois Conseilleurs de sa Majesté à la proposition des Deputés, de Messieurs les Estats Gneraux du Pays Bas.
1597. Accounts between Giles de Vischer and Ludolph Euglested concerning ordnance.

A MANUSCRIPT BELONGING TO THE MARQUIS OF RIPON.

Small thick folio, parchment, double columns, very early in the 14th century (and seemingly by an English hand).—Incipit Lilium Medicine oditus a magistro B. de Gordonio.—It is in seven parts. The exordium begins:—
" Interrogatus a quodam Socrates; and ends Inchoatus
" est liber iste cum auxilio magni dei in preclaro studio
" montispessulani post annum 20ᵐ lecture nostre anno
" domini 130? mense Julii."

At the end of the 24th and last chapter of the 7th part is the following colophon:—"Expletus est liber
" benedictus deus in secla: bene possum igitur dicere
" Hoc opus exegi quod nec Jovis ira nec ignes nec ferrum
" nec edax poterit abolere vetustas."
At the end of the 3rd part are two pages of receipts.
At the end of the 4th part are three columns headed:
" Ars ad aquam vite faciendam;" at the end of which
" Ista sunt rescripta de simplici aqua vite at de compo-
" sita et de perfectissima ad exemplar originalis extracta
" ex diversorum dictis philosophorum medice artis que
" F. scripsit episcopus Ginuensis Romanole juxta Bono-
" niam."
After the end (given above) of the 7th part is a heading (cut by the binder). Incipit liber brevis et . . . . super regimine acutarum egritudinum traditus a magistro Bernardo de Gordonio.—Begins: regimen acutarum egritudinum consistit. Ends: (on the 5th page) diutissime in ore tenendo. Hæc omnia facta sunt post lecturam continuam xi. annorum, &c. Then comes
" Ingenia curacionis morborum quantum est de presenti
" sunt decem (5 pp.)" Ends: " Facta fuit hec ordinatio in
" preclaro studio montis pessulani anno domini, 1299,
" mense Junii die mercurii post festam beati marcal'.
" Et quia aliqui ex sociis volunt scire quid est dandum,
" intelligendum est quod longa sunt tempora valde
" quod nos abbreviavimus regimenta acutorum, et
" venit ad manus multorum; postea compilavimus
" opus totum de crisi et criticis diebus breviter et cum
" integritate sicut solitis. Explicit tabula ingeniorum;
" benedictus deus salvator mundi, amen."—A fifteenth century hand here has added the words Explicit lilium.
After a blank leaf is a short tract of nearly two leaves beginning " De causis in quibus flebotomia debet
" suspendi."—Then 18 leaves containing " Thesaurus
" pauperum " beginning " In nomine sancte et individue
" Trinitatis." The author says he wishes it to be so called, and gives certain cautions to the users of the remedies and receipts.
On a fly-leaf facing the first page is the following inscription showing that the volume was once the property of Fountains Abbey. " Liber sancte Marie de
" fontibus ex dono domini Willelmi Pecke vicarii
" Collegii Ripon, liberatus domino Marmaduco Abbati
" per manus fratris Thome Rydde monachi ejusdem
" anno domini mᵉ quingentesimo xvi (1516)." An owner's name above this has been erased. There is an erasure on the fly-leaf at the end.
Thomas Dempster claims Bernard de Gordèn as a Scotchman; and in Dr. Mackenzie's Lives and Characters of the most eminent writers of the Scots nation (fol. Edinb. 1708) is a short account of Bernard de Gordon and his various writings. The Lilium Medicine was printed several times in the 15th century, and was also printed in the 16th century. It was translated into French and Spanish, and both of these versions were printed in the 15th century.

ALFRED J. HORWOOD.

THE MANUSCRIPTS OF THE RIGHT HONOURABLE LORD HATHERTON, AT TEDDESLEY, CO. STAFFORD.

These are not numerous, but they present points of interest. It is usually stated by historians and antiquaries that Richard I. was the earliest of our Kings who used the plural form (Nos) in charters and patents. The original charter by King Henry II., noticed below, shews that Madox had warrant for his statement that Henry the 2nd in the latter part of his reign wrote in the plural number. (See Madox's Epistolary Dissertation concerning the most ancient great roll of the Exchequer.)
A deed of settlement by Justice Littleton, author of the celebrated work on Tenures, temp. Edward IV. shows the large landed property then possessed by him.
There are autograph signatures (to letters) of Edward IV., Henry VIII., and of two of his wives, viz., Anne and Katherine (Parr), and of Queen Mary and Edward VI.; letters by Lord Stafford (on the eve of his trial), Churchill (afterwards Duke of Marlborough), Swift, Addison, and Washington. A translation of one of Juvenal's satires by Geo. Stepney has an interesting note by Alexander Pope, showing his appreciation of Dryden's poetical excellence and of his generosity.

12th century. Latin charter on vellum. King Henry (the 2nd), addressing all in whose bailydoms Henry del Broc holds lands, grants to Henry del Broc the forestary and all lands and all tenements which Brunus held, with the daughter of the said Brunus, hereditarily as fully as ever any of his ancestors in the time of Henry his (the King's) grandfather held; and acquits him from county, hundred, and all other suits. Witness, Ranulf de Glanville at Westminster. (N.B.—The King uses the plural form *Nos.*) Part of the Great Seal remains.[*]

28 Edw. I. Copy made in the last century of the boundaries of Teddesley Hay and Galey Hay, taken from the record. (In French.) It follows nearly the perambulation next mentioned.

26 Edw. I. (Copy made about the middle of the 16th century.) Perambulation of Cannock by the view of Malcolm de Harle, John of Crokesley, Sir W. de Stafford, Ralph Basset, and many others. Begins with the bounds according to a charter of Edward I., which commences at Faresley, in the Water of Thame. (About two feet long and one foot broad.)

6 Edward I., Sept. 10, Westminster. Grant by the King to Hugh le Blunt in fee of a fair at Penkridge, on the 28th and 29th of September, and three following days. The witnesses are R. Bishop of London, J. Bishop of Chichester, J. Bishop of Norwich, Gilbert de Clare, Earl of Gloucester and Hertford, Aymer de Valence, Earl of Pembroke, John de Warren, Earl of Surrey, Hugh de Despenser, W. le Latymer, and Edw. de Mauley, steward of the household. The great seal in green wax remains.

20 Hen. VI. Richard, Archbishop of Dublin, the canons, proctors, prebendaries, and chaplains of the King's Chapel of St. Michael the Archangel, of Penkridge, make a lease to Thomas Moore, of Moore Mill Pool.

36 Hen. VIII. Richard Hopkis, the elder, Mayor of Walsall, and Thomas Yardley, and Richard Dyngley, Masters of the Guild of St. John the Baptist, of Walsall, demise a pasture in Bradeley, called St. John's ground. Seal of the guild: oval, about three inches by two inches; the Virgin under a canopy.

Some 15th century deeds show that one Adam Pynson had three sons, William (described as late of Sareden, co. Stafford), Nicholas, and Richard, and that Richard had two sons, William and John.

22 Edw. IV., April 27, Greenwich. To the keeper of our Hay, called Teddesley Hay. The King is informed that the game, by excessive hunting and otherwise, is greatly diminished.—He, intending by God's grace to take pleasure, orders the keeper to suffer none to hunt, shoot, or course; but to keep the game.—If any person break these commands he is to certify, that the King may provide punishment.—The King's autograph E. R. is at the top. (Seal is gone.)

12 Edw. IV., March 18th. Feoffment by Thomas Littelton, one of the justices of the Common Bench to Roger Wille, clerk, one of the canons of the Cathedral Church of Lichfield, W. Cambeforde, one of the prothonotaries of the said bench, Humphrey Salway, Esq., Thomas Waldife, gent., John Campian of Worcester, mercer, W. Wyghts of Frankeley, and Robert Chilelton of Pollesworthe, of his manors of Specheley, co. Worcester, and all lands, &c. which he has in Specheley, Cuddeley, Bradicote, Whiteladiaston, Collesdone, Upton super Snoddesbury, Crowle, and in the vill of Worcester and the suburbs thereof, in Stone, near Kidderminster, and in Moreley, within the desmesne of Kyngesnorton, in the said county of Worcester; and a moiety of the manor of Boysterley, co. Worcester; also all lands, rents, &c. in Lichfield, co. Stafford, a messuage in Breredon, in the said county, which he lately bought to him and his heirs, and all lands, &c. in Halisowen, co. Salop;—to hold to them and their heirs and assigns.—Warranty.—He appoints Robert Oxclif, John Byshull, John Wyllys, John Pale, and John Meryng, attorneys to deliver seisin.—Also he demises to the trustees his manor of Areley, co. Stafford, for seven years, without rent and without impeachment of waste.—The premises and all the contents were for the performance of his last will.—Signature *Thomas Littelton.* (The seal is gone.)

A letter undated by George Washington to General Lincoln (said to be indorsed by Lincoln, as June 16th, 1779): " Sir, Major Campbell advises by letter just " received that the enemy are advancing towards Ven-

" becter's bridge; I wish you to send out fresh parties " immediately, and to make the earliest report. If this " report is confirmed by your scouts, you will order " your tents to be struck, and put into the waggons, " and have every thing in readiness to move.
" I am, Sir, your most h^ble servant,
" G. Washington."

A printed folio page. Oxford, 14 Feb. 19 (Car. I.), 1643. " Charles R." at the head, and signed at the foot by Ed. Littleton, C. S. and Samp.   addressed to Edward James, gentleman, co. Stafford, boro' Kynnaston.—Subjects of England and Wales are bound to resist and suppress our subjects of Scotland who have entered or shall hereafter enter this kingdom.—Instead of personal service they may lend 20l., or the value in plate; toucht plate at 5s., untoucht plate at 4s. 4d. per oz.; and pay or deliver it within seven days to the high sheriff of the county, who is to pay the same at Corpus Christi College, Oxford, to the Earl of Bath, Lord Seymour, Mr. John Ashburnham, and Mr. John Fettiplace, or any of them, treasurers for receiving and using thereof by the said members (of both houses).

1647, Feb. 24th. " Fer (2nd Lord) Fairfax." Certificate that Col. Christopher Copley did in Feb. 1642 raise a troop of horse, as appears by the certificate of commissioners of musters, and was mustered in his (Fairfax's) presence on the 22nd of February aforesaid, and from that time was in actual service as captain of the said troop till the 6th of August 1643, upon which day Fairfax appointed him major of his regiment of horse by commission under his hand, and from that time he continued in actual service as major of that regiment till the 1st of April 1644, when by virtue of a commission from Fairfax he raised a regiment of horse, and was in actual service as colonel thereof till the 25th of June 1645; all which time he behaved diligently and faithfully.

16—, Aug. 5th, Clifton. The Earl of Holland to the Earl of Essex.—" The King hath altered nothing of his intention for the jornies of his progress; purposing to be at Sidbury upon the 11th of August; his remove is from Lesseiter thether, where I do not conceive it is so fitte for your lordship to attend him as in your own shire; your lordship can best advise your selfe in what manner, but in my opinion I would shunne any extreme either of to many or to bee to privat; your near friends it is proper should accompany you, for whom I will undertake they shall not want that usual respect given to gentlemen upon the like occasion; this I will not only promise, but all the expressions of respect and love that can possibly be given you by your lordships most humble and faithful servant, Hollande." (1½ pp.)

Copy of the above letter.

n. y. Aug. 25th, Windsor.   " Charles R." (at foot) to my Lord Bronker. " The Dutches of Cleaveland has satisfied me it is both for her advantage and those in the reversion that Nonsuch should be suddenly disparked, to avoid all sutes and contests between her and the Lord Berkeley, and that she intends to let it out at a rent which is to be reserved to her Grace for her life, and after to the Duke of Southampton and others in the reversion. Therefore I do agree and think it reasonable you, according to the power given, shall make a lease thereof for what number of years she shall require, not exceeding one and twenty years."

1665, Nov. 4th, Oxford.   " James " (at foot), countersigned by W. Coventrye (wafer seal at the beginning). James, Duke of York and Albany, Earl of Ulster, Lord High Admiral of England and Ireland, Constable of Dover Castle, Lord Warden of the Cinque Ports, and Governor of Portsmouth, to Richard Gibson, gentleman, of Yarmouth.—Appoints him surveyor of the victualling of His Majesty's navy in the port of Yarmouth;—he is from time to time to send accounts, &c. to Samuel Pepys, Esq., Surveyor General of the victualling affairs, and follow the instructions of the Duke, the principal officers and commissioners of His Majesty's navy, or the said Samuel Pepys:—yearly salary of . . . . hundred pounds quarterly.

(1678) July 12th, London. (General) J. Churchill to Dr. Charles Litelton.—Excuses for not writing, being in the country from whence he could " write no nuses, but now we are again very furious upon the warre, so that I hope it will not be long before I have orders to come over. At my arrival here Mr. Beavoir told me of the Duke having removed your neveu from the major's company, which had I been in town I would have hindered, knowing that you had rather that he should have continued in a garrison company.—My brothers ensigne has been very sike (sick), but now he is pretty well again so that he shall come by the first opportunity. My Lord Treasurer has promised to give money to release the Virginian men; as soon as it is done the Duke intends to send you the company of grenadiers and thirty men, that is to recruit that company that was Mideltons.—If there be ought in what I can be serviceable to you herein, I beg you will command me, I being with all respect your faithful umble servant, J. Churchill.

My service to my Lord Midelton and the rest of my friends.

1694, Aug. 28th, Oates.   J. Locke to [Mr. Clarke?].

" Dear Sir, I am glad to hear of your safe arrival in town, and when you are a little setled in your gears there I hope to receive from you now and then a litle account how the world wags. My long stay in town the last time made so lasting an impression on my lungs, that I have scarce yet got it off, tho' I find a very sensible advantage since I came hither; so that unless my own business or any service I can doe you call me to town, I shall not be very forward to come thither yet a while; I return my thanks to Madam for her kind remembrance, and shall be very glad of her recovery and health, wether from the Bath waters drank at Bath or at home, as from anything else. My service to her, my wife, and the rest of the young folks. I conclude you will now stay in town. I desire to know, intending to trouble you with a letter of attorney to receive my salary in the Excise. My service to all my friends that come in your way; particularly remember me kindly to J. F. if he be in town.

P.S.—Sir Francis, my lady, and all here give their service to you and Mrs. Clarke. I hope you found Master well."

1702, May 14th, Versailles. · (A print filled up with MS.) Pass signed by Louis (and Colbert) for Sir Philippe Anglois going to England by Calais. (A wafer seal.)

1705, Oct. 31st. (Prince) "George," Lord High Admiral, &c. to Captain Richard Canning, Commander of H. M. ship Worcester.—Order to receive on board Anthony Oldfield, gentleman, formerly a volunteer in the "Ranelagh," and to bear him as a volunteer during the time he shall serve on board. (A printed form filled up.)

1726, Nov. 23rd, Dublin. Jonathan Swift to Mrs. Greenvil, at her house in Abby Court, Chester.— " Madam, I have had a letter by me above six weeks, expecting every day to have sent it with the picture by a gentlewoman who was to go for England, but hath now put off her journey. This was the reason of your not hearing from me sooner. I have at last heard of a Chester owner, one Mr. Whittle, who hath undertaken to deliver it to you. It is the best of the several cuts that have been drawn for me, and is made up as well as our workmen here can do it. I hope Mr. Greenvil and you are in health, as well as your girl, if you have not spoiled her with fondness. When you see Mrs. Keach (or Kench) pray give her my thanks for the friendly care she took of my goods which came all safe."

23 pp., 4to. The eighth satire of Juvenal; headed, " This is in Mr. Stepney's hand." After the argument the poem begins—

What signifies high birth ? What reall good
To trace from long descent our ancient blood?
To have our monumental grandsires known
By counterfeits of canvas or of stone?
Ends—
Nor ere confess your honours ancient source
Was some poor shepherd boy or something worse.

At the end of the poem is the following note, which, as well as the note at the head, are said by the indorser to be in the handwriting of Mr. Pope. " Who com- " pares the original of Mr. Stepney with that printed " in Dryden's Juvenal, will see the vast advantage it " received from passing under his hands. I question " not the same would appear of the other translations " there, if the originals were extant to make the same " comparison. This was what that great man did for ". almost all his acquaintance."

32 Hen. VIII., Feb. 6th, Hampton Court. "Henry R." to the Bishop of Exeter and the Dean and Chapter there.—Whereas the King's servant, Thomas Winter, Archdeacon of Cornwall, has leased to the King's ser- vant, William Bodye, his archdeaconry for three years to three years, for 32 years yet to come or thereabouts, and W. Bodye spent much money in getting the lease and since, and will lose if Winter die,—the King asks

them to confirm Winter's grant under their seal, i.e., the Episcopal and Chapter seal.

36 Henry VIII., March 6th, Greenwich. "Kateryn the Quene, K. P.," to the Bishop of Exeter, the Dean or his deputy, and the Chapter there.—Is desirous to prefer. John Throgmorton to some honest promotion.—Asks them to give him the next advowson of any one prebend that shall chance to be void in their church of Exeter.

[155-] March 24th, Palace of Westminster. "Marye the quene" to the Dean or Canons of the Cathedral Church of Exeter.—Asks them to pay the money they owe her (here inclosed) to her servant, John Aylworth, Esq., one of her general Receivers.

n. y. March 26th. "Anne the quene" to our trustie and well beloved the Dean and Canons resident of my lordes Cathedral Church of Exetir, and to every of theym.—As their tithes in the parish of Hevitre are on lease to the Abbess of Polslowe, for a term which will soon expire, which ferm is like within brief time to be void add in their order, by reason that the same abbey shall be dissolved ;—asks them to grant a lease to John Sowdon, junior, for 60 years to begin at the expiring of the other lease, at the same yearly rent as the Abbess pays.

2 Edw. VI., Feb. 10th, Palace of Westminster. " Edward " (countersigned by E. Somerset) to the Dean and Chapter of Exeter.—The Bishop of Exeter passed a grant under his seal to Sir W. Paget, Kt. of our 'Order and Comptroller of our household, which we send unto you herewith—Prays them to confirm it and send it by bearer (At the foot Pro edibus epi. in London).

3 Edw. VI., Dec. 1st, Westminster. " Edward " to the Dean and Chapter of Exeter.—By advice of his Council, he has sent letters to John Bishop of Exeter, requiring him to grant to Sir Andrew Dudley, Kt., one of the chief gentlemen of the Privie Chamber, and one of the four Knights appointed to attend upon his person, and to his heirs and assigns, the manor of Pawton, co. Cornwall, the manors of Bishops Teynton, Radways, and Weste Teyneyemouthe, with the parsonages of Bishops Teynton and Radway, and the advowsons of the vicarage of Bishops Teynton and Radway, co. Devon ;—which grant ought to be confirmed by them. He requests them to confirm it. Signed by—

J. Warwick.	W. Saint John.	J. Russell,
Thomas Ely.	William Paget.	T. Cheyne.
H. Dorsett.	T. Darcy.	R. Sadleyr.
J. Wyngfeld.	Edward North.	W. Northt.
W. Herbert.		

1704, Sept. 13th, Magdalen College, Oxford. H. Sacheverell to Mr. Edward Wilson, at his house in Cannock, near Lichfield.—He has been with the gentle- men of Christ Church College, who say they have received his (Wilson's) pedigree, and think it clearly made out, but they ask for a disproof of the pretensions of the others.—Is sorry Mr. Noel's son is not qualified for the place, for he would be put in on the account only of a collateral relation to his (Wilson's) lady's family, who are the regular lineal descendants from Frost, in deficiency at present of his (Wilson's) &c., &c. Desires his service to Wilson's good lady, Brother Perry and Wilson's sister, with the writer's old friend, Mr. Gataire and honest Major Ryves, &c.

Another folio contains the following letters :—

1696, Aug. 1st. From Sir W. Booth's house in James Street, Westminster.—Edward Littleton to the Honble. W. Blathwayt, Esq., principal secretary to His Britannic Majesty in Flanders (1 p.). Strongly advising a march into France ;—might march to Paris if he please, the country being so fine ;—and there can be no opposition. —The country abounds with provisions in this time of harvest, and the people would pay great contributions to ransom their goods and horses. " But you might " justly sacrifice some places to the flames, in revenge " for Spires, Worms and Heidelberg."

1696, Aug. 3rd. The same to the same.—He again urges the advance with 20,000 or 30,000 horse and dra- goons; proposes a line of march, as the opinion of him- self and his friends.

1701, Aug. 9th. The same to the same.—"Your candid acceptances of my letters during the last war hath given me encouragement to presume now further upon you. It seems not advisable that we should engage in the war (if we can help it), unless Italy and Germany do vigorously engage likewise. The Italians are hindered by their timorous, over cautious, and selfish htmour; the Germans by their divisions and discontents.—Among the divisions are religion and the great Electorate. In the business of religion the Protestants must not recede an inch from the treaty of Westphalia. The great electorate was created by the Emperor in opposition to both religions."—Littleton advises that the heir apparent to the English throne should renounce it; (the Electorate) with the Emperor's consent.

1711, May 19th, Southwark. H. S[acheverell] to ———— (Indorsed as by Dr. Sacheverell, but it is quite in a different hand from the other letter, and looks more like a copy.) He is sorry that Mrs. James has married without the consent of her mother . . . " Was there no one but that miscreant in the country to join their hands " (abuses him well). From the first part of the letter it seems that Sacheverell would have married her if her father had complied with his (Sacheverell's) endeavours.

1715, July 20, St. James. Copy council letter to Henry Earl of Uxbridge, Lord Lieutenant of Scotland, sent to Sir Edward Littleton, Bart.—They hear that the Pretender is preparing to invade.—Refer to the Act of 13 & 14 Car. II. Direct him to seize the arms of papists and nonjurors. Signed by Nottingham, Dorset, Devonshire, Orrery, Manchester, Hay, and Sunderland.

1715, Sept. 16th.—Copy Council letter to the same; sent to Sir Edward Littleton.—Rebellion in Scotland. —The Castle of Edinburgh attempted to be surprised. —The intended invasion of England by the person who during the life of the late King James II. pretended to be Prince of Wales, and since his decease has taken upon himself the style and title of James III., King of England, and James VIII., King of Scotland, being bred up in the Popish superstitions, &c. Tell him to cause the whole of the militia within his lieutenancy, horse and foot, to be in readiness to meet upon the first orders, and give directions to the proper officers of the Militia to seize, with the assistance of a constable, the persons and arms of Papists, Nonjurors, or other persons he has reason to suspect to be disaffected to His Majesty, &c. Signed by Somerset, Manchester, Nottingham, Sunderland, Grafton, W. Boscawen, Bolton, Marlborough, and others.

The meeting of the deputy lieutenants was to be at 10 o'clock on Monday, the 26th instant, at the Rose and Crown, Stafford.

Account of money found at Pileton in 1741 and 1749, when the last Sir Edward Littleton pulled the house down.—It was found behind a casement. In 1741 nearly 10,000l., in 1749 upwards of 5,700l., making in all 15,749l. 4s. 3d. (in 25 packets), consisting of single Johns, Moidores, half Moidors, guineas, double Johns, Sceptres, and Broads.

1792. To Moreton Walhouse, Esq., High Sheriff of the co. of Stafford. Petition by gentlemen, clergy, and freeholders of the county of Stafford, for meeting to petition the House of Commons to abolish the African slave trade. Twenty-six signatures, amongst them are Walter Bagot, W. B. Gresley, Edward Sneyd, W. Wolseley, and J. Sneyd.

1808, Aug. 21st, Keswick. Robert Southey to Sir Edward Littleton, Bart. Thanks him for notes on Plot [Plot's History of Staffordshire], and for a book on some North American language. He has ordered a copy of his work on Spanish history to be sent to Teddesley.—He alludes to extracts from a poem six or seven hundred years old, translated by Frere, whom he lauds.

A folio of the 16th century. The visitation of Staffordshire, arms in trick and pedigrees, 4 + 95 leaves; and copies of seals from charters at the end.

At the top of one page is Ro. Glo. Som. (Robert Glover, Somerset Herald).

At 75b. Names of those who were disclaimed as gentlemen.

p. 77. Copy of Somerset's letter, Aug. 1583. About those bearing the title of esquire or gentleman, who have no right. (1 p.)

p. 77b. Copy of Somerset's letter to John Berwick, bailiff of the hundred of Cudleston. To warn esquires and gentlemen to appear before Somerset, marshal and deputy to Norroy, at Stafford, on   day to bring arms and crests, &c.

p. 78. Form of summons to a man who refused to bring his arms, &c. He was to come before the Earl Marshal.

33 Hen. VIII. (Copy.)* Grant by the Bishop of Lichfield and Coventry to Littleton of the Ridership of Cannock Chase, with the appurtenances (except the fee of 60s. and 8d.) in tail. Instead of that, which was a fee, the bishop grants an annuity of 60s. and 8d., with

power of distress over Langton and Beaudesert. (The annuity is still paid.) The grant was confirmed by the dean and chapter, and inrolled in the bishop's register, 34 Henry VIII.

A folio volume.

1679, May 10th, From the Tower. (Lord) Stafford to Mr. Henry Vernon.—"I desire you will doe mee the favor as to come to towne with all the hast that you can to be heer at my tryall, I having an order from the House of Peers to that effect; and you will very much oblige me to come."

1679, May 24th. George Vernon to H. Vernon (his brother) at Wolverhampton.—About Henry Vernon's coming up as a witness in Stafford's tryal.—Notices the bad state of things; betraying the navy, firing houses, and bribing members of Parliament.

1679, May 10th. Copy order of the House of Lords for Henry Vernon to attend to give evidence on the 13th of May. (In a letter by Ralph Lawson to Henry Vernon.)

On the cover of a letter.—"The respective postmasters on the road to Wolverhampton are required to forward this letter with all possible diligence as they will answer the contrary, it being for His Majesty's special service, Whitehall, 12th Jan. $\frac{78}{75}$, 9 at night, hast, hast, post hast. "Monmouth."—Received in Barbycan past 10 at night, Dorothy Askew.— Then come notes of its having been received at 12 at night.—At St. Albans, past 10 in the morning.—At Dunstable at about 5.—At Brickhill at 8.—At Daventry past 1.—At Coleshill at 8."

A paper folio found among the writings of Richard Persehouse, Esq., of Reynolds Hall, near Walsall; (his ancestor, Richard Persehouse, temp. Car. I., was a magistrate then, and also in the reign of Charles II.)

1642, Oct. 16th. "Lindsey." A protection for Richard Persehouse, who is dutiful to the King.

Copy of His Majesty's protestation against popery; dated July 25th, 1643, before taking the sacrament from the hands of the Archbishop of Armagh.

1645, June 24th. Assessment made on that date for a contribution to His Majesty's garrisons for one month's pay. (1½ pp.)

1645, Nov. 7. A levie made for two weeks pay to His Majesty's garrison at the Close at Lichfield. (3 pp.)

(1646, May.) A letter unsigned and undated. About the surrender of Dudley, the writer being there.

1647, Jan. 15th. John Persehouse to his father Richard Persehouse. — Family matters. — The Scots begin to raunt so high, for we believe they want more money. The House of Lords have not as yet given their doom on the rial [royal] prisoner. Next Monday the House of Lords are to satisfy the Upper House what they intend concerning Monarchy, Peership, and the establishment of religion;—whether in deposing the King they intend utterly to subvert monarchy or not. It is reported the Scotch have much courted the Prince to command their army . . . . . This I am confident, the Scots endeavour to bring a general odium upon the Parliament in their papers, and Parliament is not slow in the remuneration.

1647, April 10th, Wednesbury. John Carter, high constable. Sends a copy of the warrant (below), and tells the addressee to send it on to the other constables whom it doth concern.

1646, March 24th. The warrant is signed by Edward Brougham, Richard Flyer, Mich. Biddulfe, and Thomas Snead.—To the constables, churchwardens, and head boro' of Walsall, boroughs of Rushall and Goscott, Cunnoll, Norton, and Wynsley.—Telling them (by virtue of several ordinances of Parliament and commissions to them and others) forthwith to inquire what money, plate, horses, arms, ammunition, household stuff, goods, rents, profits, &c. have been received, taken, collected, raised, &c. by virtue or colour of any Act or Ordinance of the present Parliament, or upon any pretence for the public service ;—from whom and to whom paid, &c.; and who since Michaelmas 1640 have been employed as fitting constables or otherwise in collecting, &c.—They are to leave notice in writing at every dwelling house :—Penalty on any refusing to make return. Make up accounts in a book and send it by the 1st of June to Mr. Sherwyns, Walsall, at the Three Swans.

1647, May 31st. Copy by Richard Persehouse of his letter to Capt. Tuthill.—Refers to the warrant.—He says Capt. Tuthill is not ignorant of the losses he (Persehouse) has sustained by his party.—Before making the return he would confer with him.

---

* The original document was lent to the Marquis of Anglesey in 1828 for his inspection, at his request, by the late Lord Hatherton. It was never returned, and it appears, from correspondence on the subject, to have been by some means mislaid.

1648. Nine receipts in 1648 of sums of money for monthly payments for Fairfax's army. The sums vary from 3 shillings to 19s. 6d.

Parodies of the Ten Commandments, Belief, and Lord's Prayer. The first commandment.—Thou shall have no other gods but us the Lords and Commons, &c.

The Belief.—I believe in Cromwell, the father of all schism, sedition, heresy, and rebellion; and in his only son Ireton, &c., &c.

The Lord's Prayer.—Begins, Our fathers which think your Houses of Parliament to be heaven.

1649, June 6th, Goldsmiths' Hall.—Commission for compounding with delinquents.—John Peircehouse, of Reynold's Hall, co. Stafford, gentleman, petitioned to compound and pay what was imposed;—he paid.—Order to all committees, &c. not to sequester or molest him in person or property.—Signed by Wm. Monson, Peter Wentworth, John Dove, William Allanson ?, Ed. Ashe, John Oldfield.

1649, June 16th. Receipt for 7l. 6s. for the payment of what is imposed.

Particulars of his (John Peircehouse's) estate. Freehold for his life, the remainder to his first, second, third, and other sons in tail; remainder to the right heirs of his grandfather.—A messuage and land in Walsall, worth 5l. per annum before the wars; and a horse worth six pounds.

1649, April 16th, Chigwell, John Peircehouse to his father Richard Peircehouse.—About the business of compounding. (2 pp.)

1649. Four receipts for horses for the army from Humphrey Piercehouse.

1649, Sept. 23rd, Cokenhatch. Edward Chester to his brother Richard Piercehouse.

1650, Jan. 25th. Letters of Administration granted by the Keeper of the Liberties of England to John Piercehouse of the effects of his father Richard Piercehouse.—Latin.—Signed by Mich. Oldisworth and Henry Parker.

Copy petition to Oliver Cromwell by Har. Bagott, Rich. Leveson, Rand. Egerton, George Digby, Thos. Lane, J. Persehouse, Thos. Leigh, T. Warde.—They acknowledge the benefit of the general pardon;—disclaim the acts of some rash persons;—they ask to be freed from payments and penalties now demanded by new Instructions, and engage to be obedient and faithful to him and the then present government.

Particulars of the estate of John Piercehouse.—4 items, 165l. 10s. per annum.

1650, March 21st. B. Lechmere.—Opinion on a case that an estate acquired after composition is not liable to sequestration for former delinquencies.

1651, June 25th. Copy order by the commissioners for compounding. To certify why J. Persehouse's estate was sequestered.

1651, Jan. Certificate.—The commissioners find that he (J. Persehouse) had purchased the estate from his father; and so did not press the sequestration.

Draft petition by J. Persehouse.

1651, April 9th, Stafford. Copy of the committee's letter at Stafford; to the same effect.

1651, April 22nd. The Commissioners for compounding write to the committee at Stafford that a suspension is not a discharge, and that J. Persehouse must produce his deeds.

Draft petition by J. Persehouse.

Opinion by F. Parson on a case.

1657, March 12th. License (signed by Gil. Pickering) for J. Persehouse to travel from his house to Stafford, and to remain to the end of the Assizes where he has a tryal.

1658, April 24th. J. Persehouse says that when he was 17, he was betrayed into the war raised by the late King against the Parliament, and continued two years as a private person, not bearing command;—he then turned to the Commonwealth, and when Charles Stuart, the pretended King of Scotland, invaded, he offered Fairfax to raise a regiment to oppose, and gave security for 10,000l. for the faithfulness of himself and it. Fairfax said he had no order, but would remember Persehouse's readiness;—his person and offer were presented to Fairfax by Col. Alex. Popham, and Col. Algernon Sydney, then Governor of Dover, and Dr. Ernely, formerly Judge Advocate of Ireland;—he vows and protests fidelity to Oliver Cromwell. Signed John Persehous. (A canting letter.)

1660, July 11th. Her. Bagot to (John Pershouse). —He has received his letter.—The confidences of those people were grounded on an incouragement they had of corrupting the army; the power they had in the House by over voting, but the absent members are returned

and now they submit; the present debates being concerning religion, the plot being discovered I dare not venture the relation of it, as from good hands it is said a vast sum of money is sent from Mazarin. The Earls of Argyle and Antrim are both taken prisoners. Sir Henry Vane, Sir Arthur Haselrig, and very many others are seized on this account. One of the army regiments of horse did present an address to the King. The commidoonarie (?) officers were immediately discarded, and very honourable persons supply their commands.— Lord Northampton commands a regiment of army foot. Lord Falconburgh has surrendered his regiment to the King. Yesterday I was in the court when Capt. Bacons was forced to quit his employment, and it is believed this day will be a prisoner. The Act of Oblivion is past the House of Commons, and no reliefe for our past actions of ware : you would suddenly see a nue fase in relation to government, had the King but money to pay off the army. I am now fixed at the court . . .
. . . . . If any of your insolent neighbours speak against His Majesty or His Majesty's government, a severe legal course will be taken against them. If any one should refuse justice on this account, send me speedy notice, and a severe course will be taken against them. This is the King's command.

n. d. The same to the same.—Acknowledges Pershouse's letter of the 4th of August ; he did not answer it by the next post, as he (Bagot) wanted to tell him that the Act of Indemnity had past the House of Lords, and is to be an Act of Oblivion. The judges who sat on the King are to be excepted, and four more for this four lords which were murdered, your neighbour, Sheriff Haring[ton], Col. Croxton, of Chester, and one Henningham.—He mentions the House of Common's vote that ejected ministers should retake their benefices without legal prosecution.—Animosity in the House of Lords between Buckingham and the Earl of Bristol is reconciled.—Prince Rupert will be here very suddenly, and so will the Princes Royal.

1660, Dec. 4, Brookehouse.   Fr. Parker to John Pershouse.—On musters.

Same date. Warwick. Robert Charnocke to John Pershouse.—On the same subject.

1660, Dec. 4th, Whitehall. E. Vernon to John Pershouse. — Mentions the intended confiscation of estates of rebels in or since 1642, and the intended exhumation of Cromwell, Ireton, Pride, and Bradshaw.

An address to John Pershouse, as Justice of Peace for the co. of Stafford. Walter Grosvenor, Thomas Congreave, and others certify that Elizabeth Byrch, who had accused Thomas Smith of ill words against the King, was a woman of ill fame, and made like charges against persons under the usurper.

Draft of John Pershouse's answer.—The father and the daughter are bound to prosecute ; he never saw the mother, he was obliged to commit; but he will join with another in her bail.

1661, May 4th. John Pershouse to Lord Brooke.— Account of the Lichfield election.—Col. Lane and Sir Theophilus Biddle were elected.—Sir Harry Vernon and . . . Diot lost.

1641. April 13th. The Earl of Strafford's speech at the conclusion of his defence. Begins—My Lords there remains another treason. Ends—Te domine confitemur.

n. d. R. Fox to R. Parkshouse (Pershouse). About his delinquency.

Other papers ; and papers in an action of trespass, Leigh v. Stamford, for breaking into Rushall.

A letter by John Pershouse to R. Pershouse.—Army doings.

Debate on a bill to attaint Sir J. Fenwick in the House of Lords.—Division list, Dec. 23rd, 1696. The Bill was passed by 68 to 61.

A protestation by 48 peers.

Mercurius Pragmaticus, &c., from Jan. 25th to Feb. 1st, 1647. (7 leaves.) Begins—

Three kingdoms brought to a fine passe
Whilst that our saviours rule,
This countrie is become an asse
The city but a mule.

(4 verses, 1 p.) The rest in prose.

A thick and large folio.—Collections for the history of the Littleton family by Mr. Fernyhough, from 1235 downwards. — Arms, pedigrees, biographical notes, extracts from deeds and records, original drawings and engravings, &c.

1694, March 3rd. H. (General) Gough to Sir E. Littleton, at Pilluston.—Mentions the perplexity about how to raise taxes.—Mentions loss by clipping of money and sending sailors abroad.—State of the streets between

Whitehall and Westminster;—indecencies and villany committed on women by the rabble and multitudes who flock about Whitehall to see the Queen lie in state.—Ladies in the crowd have all their clothes cut off behind; some have their coats pinned up to their backs, and exposed, and not able to help themselves; others abused by two or three at a time whilst they are defending their heads, and their modes are taken away frequently.—Children are trod upon and pressed to death.

I beg to return my best thanks to Lord Hatherton for his hospitality at Teddesley.

ALFRED J. HORWOOD.

SIR E.
LECHMERE,
BART.

THE MANUSCRIPTS OF SIR EDMUND LECHMERE BART., OF RHYDD COURT, UPTON-ON-SEVERN, WORCESTERSHIRE.

Perhaps the most valuable item in this collection is a Taxation roll of the time of Edward the First for the county of Worcester, giving the names of the landholders (clerical and lay) and the sums at which they were assessed. I conclude the tax to have been on landholders because the same person is often found taxed in several places. There are some early deeds of great interest. One is very remarkable for having the seal pendent by its label from the centre of the document. Early deeds by Ralph de Mortimer* and the Earl of Mellent; a writ by King Henry II., and a deed by Osbert Fitz-Hugh about the bounds of Cornwood; many deeds relating to Worcester Priory, one of them stating the termination of a dispute about land by battle; another showing that the Convent gave aid to their landlord on the occasion of the marriage of his eldest daughter (but they got a lease of land for it); the original deeds terminating the sharp dispute between Gilbert de Clare, Earl of Gloucester and Hertford, and Joan his countess, on the one part, and the Bishop of Worcester on the other part, about the foss which the Earl had made on top of the Malvern Hills; a curious award by the Earl of Warwick in the early part of the reign of Henry V. of the penance to be done and amends to be paid by Nicholas Burdet for (seemingly) an assault on one Thomas Compton in Worcester Cathedral. The foundation deed of a Chantry in the reign of Edward II. (recited in an Inspeximus) gives a long list of things which each chaplain was to leave for his successor.

There is a Chronicle of England, the same as that printed by Caxton.

Among the later MSS. is a volume containing notices by Sir Nicolas Lechmere (a Baron of the Exchequer temp. Car. II.) of his ancestors, and of himself and family, and of events, public and private, from the year 1651. In this volume is an original letter by John Thurloe, written a few days after the Protector's death, expressing confidence in the stability of Richard's succession; and an original letter by Oliver. Also a contemporary copy of a letter by Bishop Bonner to the Privy Council asking their aid against the Archbishop of Canterbury and others.

A volume of parchment leaves about 13 inches square; only 18 leaves are filled. It contains entries of pedigree matters, and notices of events by Sir Nicholas Lechmere, Kt.

Thomas Lechmere, the great great grandfather of Nicholas, married Eleanour daughter of Humphrey Frere, of Blanket.—Eleanour first married one Leth, and was afterwards married to Thomas Lechmere; she was born at Blanketts on the 22nd of April 1474. The grandfather of Nicholas was Edmund Lechmere, and his father, who died in 1650, was the only son of the above, and was Edmund Lechmere of the Middle Temple; he was born in 1577, married first —Blacknall, who died without issue; secondly (in 1610), Margaret daughter of Sir Nicolas Overbury, and sister of Sir Thomas Overbury who was poisoned in the Tower. Sir Nicholas Lechmere was the third son, and was born the end of 1613, and married 1642 Penelope daughter of Sir Edwin Sandys, of Northborne, co. Kent, by Katherine daughter of Sir Richard Bulkeley. His (Nicholas Lechmere's) great grandfather was Richard Lechmere, who married Margery, one of the daughters and co-heirs of Thomas Rooke, of Ripple, a lawyer; he died in 1563; they were married in 1542.

1651, Aug. 22, Tuesday. The King with a numerous army, most Scots, some English, by long uninterrupted

* It has been suggested, with show of probability, that Mortimer (de Mortuo mari) is the Latin form for Lechmere.

SIR E.
LECHMERE
BART.

marches from Sterling to Worcester sodainly possessed himself of the city of Worcester, and in a few days fortified it beyond imagination. At the same time the Scots broke down Upton Bridge, Beawdley Bridge, Powick and Branceford Bridges.

Aug. 25. Massie, Major-General to the King, with about 130 Scottish horse, quartered in my house at Hanley; he treated my people civilly, but threatened extirpation to me and my posterity because I was joined to the army of the Parliament.

Aug. 27. 150 Scots horse quartered at my house at Hanley.

Aug. 28. The Parliament army under command of Lord General Cromwell advanced before Worcester, and at the same time Major-General Lambert gained Upton Bridge from the Scots, in which enterprize Massie was wounded and some few of the enemy slain.

Aug. 29. The Parliament army drew close to the city of Worcester.

1651, Sept. 3. Total overthrow to the Scottish army by God's blessing on the army of the Parliament of England, commanded by Lord General Cromwell; the battle began on the west side of the city (in those very fields where my brother-in-law, Col. Edwin Sandys, the 23rd of Sept. 1642, fought with Prince Rupert and received the wounds whereof afterwards (1st Dec. 1642) he died); but was ended (and was sharpest) on the east side. The morning the battle was fought General Cromwell made a bridge over the Severn (a little above Teme mouth), and another bridge close by over the river of Teme, whereby there passed over his army from side to side as he saw occasion. The battle began about 1 o'clock and lasted 'till night; I was present at it; in pursuit of the victory the city of Worcester was taken by storm, and all the wealth in it became booty to the soldiers. (24 lines are erased.)

(At the foot.) Add hereunto while I was embroiled in these turmoils, my wife, Saturday, Aug. 23rd 1651, was delivered of a son named Sandys. She was at Lord Paget's house, Dean's Yard, Westminster.

(On the verso of this leaf.) 1648, July 4. I was, by the inhabitants of Beaudley, nullo contradicente, chosen burgess to the Parliament then sitting in the place of Sir Henry Herbert, Knight, high sheriff of this county, and on the 10th of the same month admitted to the House of Commons. This Parliament continued to of April 1653.

fo. 5. 1654, July 12. I was chosen one of the knights for the county of Worcester for Parliament to be held at Westminster 3rd of September following.

(6 verso.) 1656, Aug. 20. He was chosen knight of the shire co. Worcester for the Parliament to be held the 17th September following.

1656, Jan. 28. Note of purchases of land from Lord Coventry and his brothers.

1657, Aug. 26. This year 1657, many died in this parish of Hanley; at least 40, but of no pestilential or infectious disease.

Printed paper, 9½ lines.—At the top is written, "Nicholas Lechmere, Esq., Attorney of the Duchy, in "your morning gown and hood." You are desired to attend the funeral of the most serene and most renowned OLIVER, late Lord Protector, from Somerset House, on Tuesday, the 23rd of November instant, at eight of the clock in the morning at the farthest, and to bring with you this ticket; and that by Friday next you send to the Herald's Office, near Pauls, the names of your servants that are to attend, in mourning, without which they are not to be admitted; and also to take notice that no coaches are to pass on that day in the streets between Somerset House and Westminster. Seal of arms, a lion rampant. In the corner, "Recept. 18th Nov. 1658, N. "Lechmere."

fo. 8. 1658, Friday, Sept. 3. About 4 o'clock in the afternoon at Whitehall died Oliver Cromwell, Lord Protector of England, Scotland, and Ireland, having, according to the humble petition and advice of the last preceding Parliament, declared his eldest son, the Lord Richard Cromwell, his successor, who was the next day solemnly proclaimed in London and Westminster, and throughout England the week following. Shortly after he was proclaimed in Dunkirk, then in the possession of the English (won by his father, together with Mardike, from the Spaniard in 1658) . . . In December following write issued for summoning a Parliament for the 27th of January.—The 19th of January was the day of election for this county; myself and Thomas Foley were chosen knights of the shire. The election was very costly. The expenses at several inns in Worcester (taken up by Mr. Foley and myself for the entertainment of our friends) amounting to 614l., which we paid to a penny. All this was occasioned by our competition with Mr. John Talbott, of Salwarp, and Mr. John Nanfan, of Birds Norton, joining against Mr. Foley and myself. Geo. Coventry, Esq., eldest son to Lord Coventry, then high sheriff.

Parliament was dissolved the   day of 1659, and shortly afterward the old Long Parliament, which had been interrupted the 19th of April 1653, and discontinued to the 7th of May 1659, then re-assembled; and shortly after was Richard the Lord Protector laid aside, his brother Henry, Lord Lieutenant of Ireland, commanded home, and both retiring to a private life, the Parliament restored the Government in the way of a republic, as it was before their interruption.

This summer was an (here is a word erased) insurrection made by Sir George Booth and Sir Thomas Middleton in Lancashire and Cheshire.

8b. Notices of himself and a copy of verses sent to him by Wm. Ligon, Esq.; 14 lines, beginning—Sir, though your serious thoughts frequent the barr; end— Our love and friendship's lasting monument. This accompanied a poem composed by himself (Ligon), much savouring of a devout, holy mind; the title was The Triumphs of Sion, or the Victory of Grace in Sufferings.

fo. 9. 1659, March 16. The Long Parliament (first assembled by writ of King Charles I., Nov. 3, 1640) after many wonderful changes by them made upon Church and State, and many unprecedented alterations and impressions made upon themselves as (from their first consistence of King, Lords, and Commons), acting by the power of the Lords and Commons, without and against the King, and after by the power of the Commons only (or rather a small part of the Commons), without and against the King and Lords, and after many interruptions of that remaining part of the Commons, the first by Oliver Cromwell, from the 9th of April 1653 to the 7th of May 1657, and the other by Col. John Lambert and other officers of the army, from   day of   to   day of   1659, the Long Parliament, the said 16th of March 1659, by act of its own, dissolved itself. But before its dissolution an Act was made by them for assembling another Parliament on the 25th April 1660, which assembled accordingly. Note, the Commons were summoned by writ made under the then Great Seal, under the style of the Keepers of the Libertys (a name invented by the Long Parliament after they had declared themselves a Republic), and no writs at all issued for summoning of the peers, but they assembled gratis, and acted as a House of Peers.—A note of the accession and landing of Charles II. after the dissolution of the Long Parliament, " of which I was an unhappy member. I applied myself " to His Majesty, [9b] then at Bruxelles, for his pardon, " which he at Breda, 4th April 1660, granted. I shortly " after received it under the Great Seal. The chief " instrument in procuring it was Viscount Mordaunt, " by the mediation of Thos. Beverley, now Sir Thomas " Beverley."

Note of the Coronation, April 22nd 1661.
fo. 12. 1665. This year there was great mortality in London.

12 b. Fire of London.

fn. 13. 1668, March 1. Entered upon readings at the Middle Temple, relating to that branch of 33 Hen. VIII. c. 39, which subjects estates tail to the King's debts by judgment, recognizance, &c.

13 b. 1669, Jan. 3, died George Duke of Albemarle.
1669, Dec. ., Sir Henry Sandys, of Northbarn, Kent, was a birding, the gun went off unexpectedly and shot him dead.—Other notices of the family of Sandys.

fo. 16. 1689, April 25. I received His Majesty's writ to take the degree of serjeant-at-law.—May 1. I appeared in Chancery and took the oath.—On Wednesday, May 8th, I received my patent to be Baron of the Exchequer— took the oath.—On May 24th received the King's writ to attend in the House of Peers, and attended: the King came in state, and assented to three Bills; the first, Indulgence to dissenting Protestants; second, reversing the attainder of Lady Lisle, beheaded by Jeffrey in the West; the third, for selling some houses in Piccadilly formerly belonging to Mr. H. Coventry. (The writ mentioned above is in the volume.) The last entry in the volume is the 26th of Nov. 1703, mentioning a dreadful storm of wind.

On the last leaf is the entry of the death of Sir Nicholas Lechmere, on the 30th of April 1701, 88 years of age.

In the volume are two letters by R. Ligon, about his book which he sent to Sir N. Lechmere and some family letters; also the following letters:—

1658, July 20, Hampton Court. Jo. Thurloe to N. Lechmere, Esq., Attorney of the Duchy, about office business.

1658, Sept. 9, Whitehall.—The same to the same.—I find by yours of the 6th instant, that you have heard of the great breach the Lord hath been pleased to make upon us at Whitehall by taking away His Highness, as also of the succession of his sonne in the Government; so that I need not trouble you with the particulars of that, save only to assure you that his new Highness hath the blessings of a very easie and peaceable entrance upon the government. All parties centringe in him as one deserving it of himselfe, as also being the eldest sonne of the bravest man that ever this nation bred. The army will be and are entirely his; those that were most doubted threw themselves most forward in his establishment. You are very right about the proclamations, and according that which you mention was emitted upon Saturday nighte; it could not be done before, in respect His Highness, before he entered upon his government, was to take the oath in the Petition and Advice, and he was to be proclaymed before he tooke his oath. The last night we had the newes of a great defeate given by the French to the Spanyard near Ypres, where the French killed and tooke neare 4,000 horse and foot; a party commanded by Prince de Ligne, who was to relieve Ypres, a place streightened by the French. This was done upon Friday, the same day His Highness died, it being alsoe the 3rd of September.

I am your affectionate cosen and most humble servant, Jo. Thurloe.

A vellum roll, Latin, 14th century, in three pieces (many membranes), between 30 and 40 feet long, and 5 inches wide.—The beginning is absent. It contains, apparently, short heads of discourses for Sundays (with a text at the head of each). Also on Saints' days; and Narraciones.—Those for Sundays have several heads (short).—Those for Saints and Apostles are longer.

1549. Oct. 26, Marshalsea. Contemporary copy of a letter by E. London (Bonner) to Lord Chancellor Ryche and others of the Privy Council (2½ pp.).—He has complained and prayed redress against my Lord of Canterbury, Lord of Rochester, Dr. Smith, and Dr. Maye; yet, because Dr. Smith, being a minister to the Duke of Somerset, and they both his deadly enemies, have laboured his ruin, staying his remedies and suits, having help of the two others, he asks them (the Lords) again to be allowed to sue for honest and lawful liberty to prosecute his appellation and supplication to the King, and according to law to make suit for redress of injuries by the said persons.—As an argument, he says the collection of the King's subsidy in his (Bonner's) diocese is stayed.

1562, May 2, 4th Eliz. Edmonde Boner, clerk general. Release of actions to Richard Lechmere, of Hamley, co. Warwick.—Seal, E. B., with Ita est, Edmondus Boner clicus antedictus, by Bonner's hand.

1641, June 30. George (Bishop of) Hereford certifies that Roger Lechmere, of Fownhope, gentleman, having been formerly indicted and convicted a recusant, has oppeared before two justices of the peace, and submitted himself to the State and Church of England. He has taken the oath of allegiance and supremacy, and has protested by certificate that he would for the future conform. And he has received a certificate that Lechmere had for more than a year conformed and frequented the parish church of Fownhope, and taken the Sacrament.

1654, March 24, Whitehall. "Oliver P." to Sir John Walsh, Serjeant-at-Law, and the rest of the justices of the peace for the county of Worcester, or any of them, to be communicated to the rest, or, in his absence, to Nicholas Lechmere, Esq. (Wafer seal of arms, six quarters, the arms of Cromwell in the first quarter.)

"Gentlemen,—We doubt not but you have heard before this tyme of the hand of God goeing along with us in defeating the late rebellions insurrection. And we hope that through His blessing upon our labours an effectual course will be taken for the totall disappointment of the whole designe. Yet, knowing the restlesness of the common enemy to involve this nation in new calamityes, we conceive ourselfe, and all others who are intrusted with preserving the peace of the nation, obliged to endeavour in their places to prevent and defeat the enemye's intentions. And therefore, as a meanes specially conducing to that end, we doe earnestly recommend to take orders that diligent watches (such as the law hath appointed) be duely kept for taking a strict account of all strangers in your country, which wil not only be a meanes to suppresse all loose and idle persons, but may probably cause some of those who come from abroad to kindle

SIR E.
LECHMERE,
BART.

fires here to be apprehended and seized upon; especially if care be taken to secure all those who cannot give a good account of their busines; and may also break all dangerous meetings and assemblings together. Herein we doe require and shall expect your effectual endeavours; knowing that if what by law ought to be don were done with diligence in this respect, the contrivance of such dangerous designes as these would be frustrated in the birth, or kept from growing to maturity. I rest your very affectionate friend, Oliver P."

1655, July 17. Parchment under the Great Seal.—License by Oliver Cromwell to Nicholas Lechmere, of the Middle Temple, Esq., to practise within the bar of the several courts at Westminster.

1658, Oct. 23. License by Richard Lord Protector to Nicholas Lechmere, as above.

A small book of about 24 leaves, containing list of causes in the various terms during the years 1666, 7, 8, $\frac{9}{10}$, at Gloucester, Hereford, Salop, Stafford, Worcester, Oxford, &c., being apparently those causes in which he pleaded.

1658, Dec. 16. Appointment by Richard Lord Protector of Nicholas Lechmere to be Attorney-General of the Duchy of Lancaster. Under the Great Seal of the County Palatine, and the seal of the Duchy of Lancaster.

A rather small folio volume, vellum, 15th century. Chronicle of England (the same as printed by Caxton). On the first leaf verso, And whaöe Dioclician her fador herde of þese þingis he was wondre wroth.

Cap. 244. Hen. V. And after þe deeþe of King Henry þe IIII. reigned King Hari þe Vᵗ his son.

Cap. 245. Of þe geting of Rome . . . . he helde his parliament. Ends on the eighth line, Strengthen hym in his ritt and þann anone he . . . . (Of the first leaf of the work only a fragment remains, and p. 3 is rubbed and illegible.)

A large fine red Great Seal of King Stephen. The legend is Stephanus Dei Gratia Rex Anglorum. The King is seated on a broad chair, sword in right hand, a ball, cross, and dove in the other; on the reverse, Stephanus Dei Gratia Dux Normanorum; a man on horseback with shield and sword; the action of the horse is good, but the legs are thin; the horse's neck is well curved.—A charter must once have been there with it; a slip of paper says Roger Bishop of Salisbury died 1140, who was one of the witnesses; so that the date of the charter must be 1135–1140.

12th century. William, son of Wido of Offeni, releases to the prior and monks of Worcester his part of Huneltone, which Hunel Isnardus his grandfather and Emma his wife bequeathed to them. Witnesses, Gilbert Bishop of Hereford, Walter the Archdeacon of Salop, Master Geoffrey de Clifford, Master Godfrey nephew (nepos) of the prior, W. de Beauchamp, Richard la blaca, Osbert le brun, Siward de linderigga, Thomas . . . . . . and Thomas his son, Simon Albus, Thos. do Chichely. Alan de Bradewud.—A fine round seal about 2½ inches. A man on horseback with a shield and sword. Sigillum Willelmi filii Widonis.

n.d. Ego Rad. de Mortuo mari concedo terram meam de Wrabenhalle que est in estimacione unius virge liberam ab omni servitio seculari excepto Geldo si contigerit ad victum et dñiü monachorum sicuti Tustinus eam donat cum filio suo Girardo. Hoc quia de me feodeo est concedo pro anima mea et uxor mearum et dominorum et filiorum et parentum meorum hoc mea* propria manu confirmo + assensu filiorum et hominum meorum ut sit firmum et stabile in perpetuum. Ego vero Tustinus licencia domini mei confirmo mea + manu. Testes sunt Bern' Oxpac, Gislebertus, Johannes, filii, Ebrardus de Doutone, Roger Walterus Radulfus, Balduinus Rogerus. Seal of white wax (nearly a hemisphere), with device of a lion and part of the legend, [Sigill]um [Rad]ulfi . . . M . . . . .

12th century. G. Comes Mell. Willelmo de bello Campo filio suo sat. I direct you to quit claim to the Prior and monks of the Church of St. Mary of Worcester the forestage of Tibritune and all places. of that forest, so that henceforth you claim no forest rights pertaining to that vill; for you know that for the soul of me and my countess, and Rodbert my son, and of my father and mother, I concede and pardon to the Prior and Monks the King's gild which to me belongs, and all customs and services and forest rights which were formerly the King's and then mine in the said vill. As to the land which they held in service of me (one carucate), which is of the Bishop's fee, I cannot

intermeddle pro itinere meo. But whatever my brother the Earl of Leicester and you do on my part, I grant to the Prior and monks. For know that there are no monks in my domains whom I love so much, nor in whose prayers I so much confide; and if God grant I return from the Pilgrimage safe and sound, I will well shew it to them. So I ask you, as my dear son, that them and all of them for the love of me you will maintain. Witnesses, Wm. the Chaplain, Ralph de Auro Monte, Hugh son of Galer and Gervase bailiff of Mellent. (Seal is gone.)

12th century. A deed by Osbert filius Hugonis. The long dispute between me and the monks of Worcester about the bounds of Cornewda by counsel of my knights and neighbours and lawful men is thus ended. That they may hold what we have marked out by foss through the midst of the whole wood between me and them. Witnesses, Hugh de Sai my brother, Roger de Solers, Robert de Sturmi, W. de W . . . . . W. Carbonel, Eustace d'estas', Philip de Wornell, Symon Blunde, Andrew Ethelin de Lawe, David his brother, John de Wdesetune, Ralph his son, Horn son of Ketelbi, and others. Seal, round, 3 inches. A man on horseback in armour, with sword and shield. Legend . . . berti filii Hugonis.

Hen. II.—H. King of England and Duke of Normandy and Aquitaine and Earl of Anjou, to the Bailiffs of Worcestresir and Salopesire, greeting. I command you that without delay you cause the monks of Worcester to have their common which they ought to have in the wood of Cornewnde, of which Osbert son of Hugh deforces them. If not let my Sheriffs of Worcester and Salop do it, so that I hear no more clamour for want of right. Witness, G. Archbishop of Canterbury, at Evesam. Part of the Great Seal, the King seated; reverse, a man on a horse.

10 John. Gloucester, before the King, &c. Fine between Ranû Prior of Worcester, and Hugh de Cinctetone, of half a hide in Cinctetone, to the Prior and Convent of Worcester.

14 Hen. III. Worcester, morrow of Trinity. Fine between Christiana de Kankletone and the Prior of Worcester, of the fourth of a virgate and nine acres in Kankleton, to the Prior and Church of Worcester.

29 Hen. III. Octaves of the Purification. Fine between the Prior of Worcester by attorney, and Ralph Gundi and Grecia his wife, of half a virgate in Tetindone, to the Prior and Church of Worcester.

30 Hen. III. Westminster, three weeks of Easter. Fine between Richard Prior of Worcester, by Geoffrey de Croppethorne his attorney, and Nicholas de Yardel and Christiana his wife, of half a virgate in Tedingtono, to the Prior and Church of Worcester.

33 Hen. son of John.—Agreement between William de Bracy and Richard Prior of Worcester. He releases to the Prior, &c. a pasture in Tybertone, and gives them liberty to enclose a field called Purnewdc, in the same vill. They may have a way (of 8 feet) through his wood of Warmedone, from the manor of Tybertone to the King's highway which goes to Worcester; they are to make a hoc to protect the corn. For this the Prior gives a messuage and croft in Trottcswolle and 10 marks of silver. Witnesses, Sir W. de Beauchamp, Sir W. de Sautemareys, Simon de Robeford, Walter Fitz Warin, Adam de Crumbe, Master W. de Foywyke, Thos. de Stokes, and others. Seal of arms, a fess, two stars in chief. Sigillum Willelmi de Braci.

13th century. Odo de Michegros to all, &c. The plea which was in the Court of the Prior of Worcester by precept of the King, about one hide of land with the appurtenances in Elfsiston, between me plaintiff, as attorney for Eleanor my wife, and Godfrey of Elfsiston tenant, thus was terminated per finem duelli in the court, by Peter de Wicke my champion, and Richard de Dunie (or Dunic), champion for Godfrey ; namely, that Godfrey and his heirs should. make to me and my heirs by Alianor homage for the land, and I and my heirs to the Prior of Worcester. When the prior and convent ought to receive their rent, we or our heirs will send to the house of Godfrey or his heirs and will receive from them the rent, and immediately before we leave the house will repay it to them as our stewards, to be paid by them in our behalf to the Prior and convent. They also quitclaim per finem dicti duelli to the Prior and convent all right in five virgates of land and a mill in the parish of Un'b'o and all claim whatever. Witnesses, Adam de Duderhulle, Sheriff of Worcester, Walter le Poher, Sheriff of Warwick and Leicester, ... Philip de Muttone, ... and others. Round seal, a bird, wings spread. Sigillum Odonis Michegros.

SIR E.
LECHMERE
BART.

---

* The label on which the seal is, is suspended from the vellum at this point.

13th century. W. de Beauchamp of Elmeley gives to God and St. Mary, and the Prior and Convent of Worcester, all that *solum* with the appurtenances in Bredone of which there was an agreement between him and them in the King's Court, before the Justices Itinerant in Worcestershire, namely, Roger de Thurkelby, Gilbert de Preston, Symon de Wakdone, and John de Cobham, in 33 Hen. III., saving to him and his son common of herbage in the said soil, and to take stone in the quarries there. The grantees to have the services of the land of Clement Porkil and his heirs, &c. Witnesses, Lord Richard Muscegros of Wullafeshall, Robert de, Penedok, John le Poer, and another. Round seal of arms, a fess; at top of the shield a crescent, and on each side a star. *Sigill. Willi. de Bea . . . . mp.*

13th century. Geoffrey de Abedetock, Lord of Hyndeloph, to the Prior and Convent of Worcester; he gives a right of way in a road from Worcester to Coderugge, in frank almoign. Witnesses, Robert Vicar of St. Johns, Nicholas le Bodel, &c., &c. Seal of arms broken : two lions passant; a star at the top and on each side of the shield.

13th century. Petrus de Saltumarisco gives to William de Saltumarisco, his brother, all his land in Dunehamstede. Witnesses, Lord Walter de Beauchamp, Lord Henry Luvot, Sheriff of Worcester, Lord Robert Folet, Eudo de Beauchamp, W. de Chadintone, Osbert de Abbetot, Hugh le Poiher, Rad. Haket, and five others (named), and others. Seal, a shield with fess. *Sig . . . . Petri de Saulmareis.*

13th century. Peter de Saltumarisco gives to William de Saltumarisco, his brother, all his land in Dunehamstede. Witnesses, Lord Henry Lovet, Sheriff of Worcester, Hugh le Power. (This deed is by a different scribe, and I do not think that the seal is from the same mould as the last. The order of words in the charter differs.)

n.d. (Earlier than the last.) W. de Saltemareis to all. I have received from . . . . . the Prior and the Convent of the Church of Worcester, *grauam* which is between the wood of Heddeclover and Sedwelleliche (Sedwellsiche ?), and *grauam* which is on the other part of the meadow, which is between Duewda and Linches *grua*; to hold in fee, paying to the Church of Worcester yearly 5s.—Among the witnesses is Roger Dod.—Seal round, nearly 2 inches, broken at the foot. Man on horseback, with sword and shield, *Sigill. Wil . . . mareis.*

n.d. Agreement between the Prior and Convent of Worcester on the one part, and Richard de Witfeld on the other part. Richard grants to farm to them all his land of Tymberdene, with the men and other appurtenances, *ad usum Elemosinarie sue*, except two men, namely, Reginald Cok and W. Huctred. To hold from Michaelmas 1243, for fifty years, paying 1 lb. of cummin to Richard and his heirs yearly by the hand of the Elemosinary of Worcester. The men of the said vill in common (*Comunit'*) shall acquit the said lord of royal and foreign service. For this, on his urgent occasion, namely, the marriage of his oldest daughter, they gave to Richard 36 marks of silver. Witnesses, Master W. de Poywike, Sheriff of Worcester, Lord Peter de Wyke, Lord Hugh de Pirie, Thos. de Stoke, Symon the Clerk, Robert of St. Godwale, Peter Colle, Richard the Clerk, W. Wareford, Luke de Novalanda, Drago de Piritone, J. de Nottcolive, W. de Papancker, Simon Clerk of Borbure, and others. A round seal, a fleur-de-lis. *Sigillum Ric. fil. Ric. Dafleia.*

n.d. Wm. le Poer, Kt., son of Roger le Poer, to all. Whereas Richard de Wichefeld leased to the Prior and Convent of Worcester all land which he held of William in Tymberdone, with the men and their services, except the services of Reginald Coc and W. Huttred, from Michaelmas 1243, for 50 years : He (William) confirms it, and will not distrein for the default of Richard; consideration. 60s. Witnesses, Sir Richard de Boudon their officer, Master W. de Powyk, W. de Bowelle, Sheriff of Worcester, Walter de la Dene the bailiff of the Bishop, &c. Seal of arms of William le Poer.

13 Ed. I. Oct. Trin. A Fine in which Thomas de Woyland was plaintiff, and the Prior of Worcester deforciant, of the advowson of the Church of Great Sobbiry; to the Prior of the Church of St. Mary. As the consideration, they receive him to the benefit of all prayers in the church.

19 Ed. I. Tewkesbury. Saturday before the Feast of St. Dunstan. Godfrey Bishop of Worcester, Gilbert de Clare Earl of Gloucester and Hertford, and Johanna Countess of the same counties, to all faithful in Christ. —Recites a dispute between Godfrey Bishop of Worcester on the one part, and the said Earl and Countess on the other part, about a foss made by the Earl and

Countess on the top of Malvern Hill on the land of the Bishop, to the nuisance of the said Bishop and Church of Worcester; by the intervention of friends, particularly Robert, Bishop of Bath and Wells, it is appeased; namely, that the Earl and Countess hereby grant to Godfrey and his successors two fat bucks on the vigil of the Assumption of the Virgin, and two fat does on the vigil of the Nativity of the Lord, out of their forest and chase of Malvern, yearly at his manor of Kemeseye; on failure, other two bucks and does within the octaves of the said terms, and doubled for every octave; on failure, they submit themselves to the King or the bailiff of any other whom the Bishop shall name, who may distrein them (the grantors). And they will give to the Prior and Chaplain of St. Mary, Worcester, when the see is vacant, or to their attorney asking for them, at the Castle of Hanlegh, the above bucks, &c. Godfrey with the assent of the Prior and Chapter of Worcester allows the foss to continue, and gives to the Earl and Countess in fee all their lands and messuages outside the foss and contiguous thereto towards Hereford. Seals of both the parties, and the seal of the Bishop of Bath and Wells, in whose presence the deed was made. The first seal is oval green wax, a Bishop with crozier, and hand blessing, about 3 inches high; the legend is gone. The second and third seals, of the Chapter and the Earl, are gone. The fourth seal is a small round one, a shield with three lions passant, no legend, but a scroll; on the right side of the shield is a lion courant, on the left a castle. The fifth seal is gone.

19 Ed. I. Saturday before the Feast of St. Dunstan, Tewkesbury. Another deed by the same parties relating to the squabble about the foss. The seals are, first, that of the Bishop of Worcester; second, the Chapter of Worcester (the secretum is a gem, a woman beside a short column, on which is a cupid, and the legend, *Habundans Cautela non nocet*); the third is a large one of the Earl on a horse in chain armour, with sword and shield charged with three chevrons; the horse's trappings are charged with the same (well cut); the heads of the horse and man and the feet of the horse are gone; on the obverse is a large shield of the arms; the fourth is that of the Countess, a small seal, three lions; the fifth, Bath and Wells, head gone. (The second seal is engraved in the new edition of Dugdale's Monasticon, but the legend is wrongly given thus, *Abundans cautela nocet*).

19 Ed. I. March 10, Ichyntone.—The King writes to Malcolm de Harlec, Escheator this side of the Trent, to find by a jury if damage will arise if he license Robert Blanket to give one message and one virgate in Tymberdene to the Prior and Convent of Worcester in augmontation of the alms of their house, &c., &c.; and to make a return.—Inquisition of lands, &c., of Robert Blanket, in Tymberdene, at Worcester, taken Tuesday after the feast of St. Clement, before the sub-escheator, 20 Ed. I., by the oaths of 12 named, who say he may do it without damage to the King. It is of the fee of Roger le Poer, and owes suit of court every three weeks, and is worth 20s. per annum.

End of the 21st year of Ed. I. 6th of the Ides of November, Hathenhale.—William le Poer, Knight, Lord of Hatenhale, confirms to the Lord Prior and the Convent of Worcester, for the use of the almoner, all donations, by Osbert Blanket of, &c., in Tyberdene, and he releases to them all services. Witnesses, Lord Robert de Bracy, Henry le Walleys, and two other knights, Osbert Blanket, and one other.—Seal of arms, a fess, and two stars in chief.

34 Ed. I. Monday, on the Feast of St. John the Evangelist, Worcester.—John Lovet, of Elmeleghe, Knight, releases to the Prior and Convent of the Church of St. Mary of Worcester, and their successors, his right for life in 20d. in rent, which he receives from them out of a croft which they had from Reginald le Leche, of Worcester, which croft John Comyn, of Worcester, holds *extra Losemere de Wygorn.* Witnesses, Richard le Mercer, William Colle, William Roculf, Richard le Belleytere, Richard de Evesham, Henry de Uptone, Ad. le Pirie, and others. (Seal gone.)

7 Edw. II. Feb. 16, Castle of Hanleye, Feast of the Purification. Gilbert de Clare, Earl of Gloucester and Hertford, gives to Sir Roger Tyrel, Robert the son of Robert le Grava de Hanleye "our naif," with all his sequel and lands and chattels. Seal, three chevronels.

16 Ed. II. Monday after the Feast of Mary Magdalene, in the Priory of Worcester.—John de Holeway quitclaims to the Prior of the Church of St. Mary of Worcester and the convent, his right in the lands, &c. which he had in Coutertone, within the manor of Overbury.

Witnesses, Nicholas Russell, Sheriff of Worcester, and four named, and others.

Inspeximus, by Thomas Bishop of Worcester, of a charter by John Salemon of Stretforde, clerk, saying that Edward II. gave license to give land in Rippel to two chaplains in the Church of Rippel, and he with the consent of Walter de Bedewynde, Rector of the Church of Rippel, Worcester diocese, gave it to God and St. Mary, and to Philip David, of Ewininge, chaplain, to say masses for him and his father John and mother Lettice, and Alice, Avice, Christian, and Jone his sisters, and all, &c., and for Thomas de Cobham, Bishop of Worcester, and his ancestors, &c., and John de Sapi and Sibil his wife, &c., and Lord Walter de Beauchamp and Alice his wife, and Walter, William, and Giles their sons, and Petronilla their daughter, and Simon de Crombe, &c. The chaplain was to be presented by him while living, and then Philip and his successors were to leave to their successors the following things (if they be): "melius plaustrum vel carectam, unam carucam cum pertinentiis, " unam herciam, unam archam, unum tonellum, unam " cunam, unam cudum, unam tinam, unam ollam eneam, " unam patinam, unum urceolum, unam craticulam, " unam mensam, unam formam cum trestellis, unam map- " pam, unum toellum, unum lavatorium, unam pelvim, " unam scalam, unam tentorium, unum saccum, unum " bussellum ad mensurandum bladum, unam corballum ; " videlicet de quo libet eorum melius vas quod habe- " bitur tempore vacacionis dicte Cantarie." Witnesses, William de Beauchamp, John de Sapi, Symon (?) de Crombe, Knights, &c., 1320, 14 Ed. II.—Then follows the King's charter of license to amortize, dated at Hertfordbrigge, in Northumberland, 14th of August, 13th year of Ed. II.—The Bishop then ratifies the foundation of the chantry. Dated at Bredone, Wednesday after the Feast of St. Bartholomew in the year above. (The gift was of a messuage and 48 acres of land, 12 of meadow, 3 of pasture, and 3s. of rent in Rippel.)

4 Ed. III. July 5, Wodestok. Edward the King gives license to the Prior and Convent of Worcester that they the church of Overbury, with the chapels of Wephe-bourne, Tedyntone, and Borghe annexed to the said church, in Worcester diocese, and of their patronage, may appropriate and hold for their own use, notwithstanding the Statute of Mortmain. By writ of privy seal. Great Seal of England, nearly perfect, in green wax. The King seated under a canopy with sceptre and ball, a fleur-de-lis on each side. On the other side, the King on a horse, with sword and shield ; the sword is fastened with a chain : lions on the trappings of the horse.

8 Edw. III. In a deed of this date Adam de Fecken-ham, bailiff of Worcester, is named.

1347, June 9, Worcester.—Indenture made in the presence of Wolstan, Bishop of Worcester, between Hugh le Despenser, Lord of Glamorgan and Morg', patron of the Monastery of St. Mary of Tewkesbury, of one part, and John by divine permission Abbat of the same monastery and the convent of the same place of the other part. Whereas Hugh gave them in frank almoign three acres of land in Lantrisant in Meskyn in Morgan, in the field of the said Hugh called Crokbobruan, of the land called Tyrmoyl, with the advowson of the church of the vill of Lantrisan ; and Hugh caused the said church at his own expense to be legally and canonically appropriated, and gave them possession : Hugh with their consent and that of the Bishop orders that from the Nativity every year while Hugh lives, and on the anniversaries of his death, a certain expenditure of money and certain religious services should be performed. As a penalty for non-observance Hugh and his heirs may distrein on the manor of Forthampton : in their default the Bishop may distrein ; on his default the Prior and Chapter of Worcester may distrein. Four seals : 1st, seal of Despenser ; 2nd, seal of the Bishop of Worcester ; 3rd gone ; 4th round.

5 Ric. II. John Russel, Lord of Strengesham, Knight, and Agnes his wife, declare that whereas Joan relict of Laurence de Hanleys in her widowhood gave to Sir John Haddon, chaplain, and two other clerks, in fee five solidates of rent in the manor of Bradecote ; they have attorned. Seal of John Russel ; a chevron between three cross crosslets fichées. The other seal, the front of a church with two steeples ; legend Mons Syon.

7 Ric. II. Feb. 19, Westminster. Letters patent under the Great Seal. License to the Prior and Convent of St. Mary of Worcester to acquire lands to the value of 10 marks per annum of lands holden of the King in capite.

16 Ric II. Memorandum (indorsed on the above) that on the 3rd of Sept. they had got lands of 100s. per annum in part satisfaction.

1389, Chapter House of the Monastery of Lesser Malvern.—Richard Prior of the Monastery or Priory of Lesser Malvern, of the Order of Benedictines, Worcester diocese, considering the loss which, by reason of the appropriation of the parish church of Whatekole lately given to us and our monastery by Henry Bishop of Worcester, will arise to the Prior and Chapter of the Cathedral Church of Worcester whenever the see is vacant, they grant to the said Prior and Chapter of the Cathedral Church of Worcester and their successors, and the said Cathedral Church, a yearly amount of 3s. 4d. Oval seal, 3 inches high. An ecclesiastic in robes, with staff and book ; legend broken, ... illum Sci Egid . . . atis nove m . . . . . .

2 Hen V. June 6, Warwyck (French). Richard Beauchamp, Earl of Warwick, to all.—John Fordham, Prior of the Church of our Lord of Worcester, and Thomas Burdet of Arewe, co. Warwick, Kt., in November, 1 Hen. V., for him and Nicholas his son, were bound in 500 marks sterling, i.e. the Prior and Avery Trussel, Kt., and the said Thomas to W. Beauchamp of Powyk, Kt., to be paid at certain times, to abide the award of Thomas Wallewayne and John Barton or other persons in their place to be named on the part of the Prior, their men and servants, and Richard Whillyngton and Thos Harewell or other persons in their places on the part of Thos. Burdet and Nicholas and their men and servants ; and if the award was not made by a certain time, then to stand to our ordinance and arbitration. The parties with counsel appeared at Tewkesbury on Tuesday in Easter week last past. The award was that the Prior and Thomas shall be friends ; Nicholas as soon as he comes to England out of Ireland for fear of the execution of a process of law against him, shall, before he goes to his father's inn, go to Worcester, and there in the Cathedral Church of Worcester, at the image of our Lady before the high altar, shall offer a taper of wax of 5 lbs. between his hands in honour of God and our Lady on some Sunday or feast day at the hour of mass, for the offence and trespass to the said church by him done ; and that taper in form of penance, and not with an assembly of people, shall offer ; and from the said image shall go to the Chapter House, and in the said house of the Prior and his co-monks ask pardon for the offence done to God, the church, the Prior and co-monks. Thomas Burdet to be bound to us in 300 marks, so that Thomas or Nicholas do no damage or corporal injury to the Prior or his co-monks or servants. The Prior and his men, indicted in the co. of Warwick, and Thomas and Nicholas, indicted in co. Worcester, are to procure respectively their deliverances according to law without disturbance. Thomas and Nicholas are to pay to Thomas Compton of Shipston 100s. for damage done to him by Nicholas.—A large seal (rather broken) of the Earl ; four quarters, two bears supporters, helmet, and (the crest is broken) ; first and fourth chequy a chevron charged with . . . ; second and third a fess between six cross crosslets.

1474, Oct. 12, Evesham Chapter House. Richard Abbat of the Monastery of St. Mary the Virgin, and Egwin Bishop and Confessor of Evesham, of the Order of St. Benedict, Worcester diocese, ad Romanam Ecclesiam nullo medio pertinentis, and the convent of the same place, to all, &c. Considering the damage, by the appropriation, annexation, and consolidation of the Monastery of Alm-cestria, alias Rutherford, Worcester diocese, to us and our monastery, lately made by John Bishop of Worcester, done to the Prior of the Cathedral Church of St. Mary's Worcester, during vacancy ; we give an annuity of 6s. 8d. to the prior and chapter, with power of distress on Almcestre.

1 Ed. VI. March 4. A roll of vellum about 2 feet in length. Hundred of Pershore, co. Worcester. A direction to Richard Lechmar, of Hanley Castle, gentleman, high collector of the said hundred, to gather the sums below mentioned for the second payment of the subsidy granted in 37 Hen. VIII. It gives the names of the petty collectors and the sums to be received from each. Total, 224l. 7s. 9d. Signed by Geo. Wylloughbie, Will. Cokesay, Rich. Sheldone, the King's three Commissioners.

A Taxation roll for Worcestershire of the time of Edward the First.—There are 17 membranes sewn together so as to make a long roll, and to the last are fastened eight other membranes pendent like the Plea Rolls. There is no heading to indicate in what year or for what purpose the taxation was made. From the traces of thread holes at the top of the first membrane it is probable that the heading has been lost. The writing is very good ; the entries are in two columns. The city of Worcester comes first on the list of places. As the entire roll is being copied for the purpose of publication by an Archæological Society, my extracts here are short.

Wygorn. *Warda Sancti Clementis.*

De Waltero de Clynclade. 8d.
Twelve names; summa 17s. 4d.
Eight of the names and sums are struck through with the pen.

Omnium Sanctorum, 64 names, summa 10l. 14s. 6d.
Warda Sancti Nicholai, 25 names, summa 4l. 6s. 8d.
Warda Sancti Martini, 44 names, summa 13l. 10s. 10d.
Warda Sancti Petri, 39 names, summa 43s. 4d.
Alia Warda, 78 names, summa 38l. 11s.
Warda Sancti Andree, 52 names, summa 14l. 19s. 4d.
Summa totalis Civitatis Wygorn, 82l. 11s. 6d.
And by another hand, Summa totalis 87l. 3s., et sic excedit 4l. 11s. 6d.
(From each ward several of the names and their assessments are struck out, one of them in St. Peter's Ward being Henricus Imaginator.)

Taxatio dimidii Com. de Wych, quero in capite rotuli.

Forfelde, 10 names and one struck out, summa 61s. 10d.
Broctone, 25 names, summa 104s. 8d.
Swyneforde, 40 names, summa 8l. 0s. 20d.
Villata de Wych, 85 names, summa 27l. 13s. 2d.
Duddeleye, 41 names, summa 6l. 7s. 4d.
Kydermunstre, 58 names, summa 9l. 5s. 4d.
Cradeleye, 23 names, summa 4l. 7s. 10d.
Pelemore, 24 names, summa 108s. 4d.
Haggeleye, 27 names, summa 6l. 9s. 8d.
Beine Bruyn, 16 names, summa 62s. 2d.
Beine Simonis, 12 names, summa 49s.
Muttone Walter, 13 names, summa 47s. 4d.
Muttone, 16 names, summa 60s. 4d.
Mancrin do Bremesgrave et Nortone, 256 names, summa 60l. 13s. 4d.
Sequitur hundr de Dodintre inferius in curtis rotulis.
Summa totius hundredi dimidii Com., 328l. 8s. 6d.

Then follow the names of the various villa in the hundreds of Dodintre, Oswaldeslowe, and Blakehurste; below the name of each vill are the names of the landholders and the sum at which each was taxed.—The sum of the whole hundred of Dodcistre was 146l. 5s. 8d.; of the hundred of Oswaldeslowe, 496l. 3s. 4d.; and of the hundred of Blakehurste, 162l. 14s. 8d.

I must be permitted to express my sincere thanks to Sir Edmund Lechmere for his hospitality at Rhydd Court.

ALFRED J. HORWOOD.

THE MANUSCRIPTS OF SIR JOHN MARYON WILSON, BART., OF CHARLTON HOUSE, KENT.

A volume of 167 leaves of thick parchment, about 5½ inches high and 4½ inches wide. The writing seems to be of the 14th century; the abbreviations are numerous. It contains the Code of Icelandic Laws, known as *Jonsbok,* given by King Magnus (in substitution for the code known as *Jernsida*) in 1280. This code was printed in small 8vo. at Holm in 1578. On comparison, this MS. and the printed text are found to agree substantially, but the spelling and order of the words vary, and the order of some of the chapters is different, and in a few instances the MS. contains more or less than the print.

In the *Landzleigum* the wording of the MS. differs much. The appendix of the MS. contains some documents not in the appendix to the print. A few of the leaves seem palimpsest, and there are traces of scroll ornaments in the margins of some of the leaves, which seem not to have been originally intended for the Code of Laws. The initial capital letters are coloured variously, lake, yellow, green, and vermilion, and some are gilt. At 35b is a very large F, beautifully interlaced with conventional foliage. In the initial P at the commencement of the *Thiofa Balk* is a rude drawing of a man hanging from gallows.

On the first flyleaf are,—the name *Magnus Bjirnsson* (in writing about 150 or 200 years old), and a later autograph of *Olafur Thorlaksson;* another illegible; and *Magnus Thorleifson me possidet.* At fo. 49 some writing has been erased, but the date, 1622, is just visible. On the last leaf of the volume there is the name of *Magnus Thorlaksson.*

The text of the Code occupies all but the last 26 leaves. After the Code come 9 leaves of appendix, and

---

15 leaves of index, and 2 leaves containing seemingly computations of the values of money.
The MS. has *Bat* where the print has *Path;* and *lier* where the print has *leggr.*

1559, Nov. 29. Ferrara. A diploma granting to Thomas Wilson the degree of Doctor of Laws.

Inventory of the goods and chattels of Thomas Wilson, secretary to Queen Elizabeth (about 20 feet long and 5 or 6 inches wide).

1640. The like of John Wilson; one roll of vellum and one of paper.

1596. Folio, 7 written leaves. An English Quid for a Spanish Quo; or a most royally renowned resolution. Expedition and most memorable exployte performed by God's assistance and Her Majesty's loyal navy and army at Cadiz, on the coast of Spayne, in the year of Christ our Savyour 1596. Exceript per me R. Ro.—It contains a list of the sea and land regiments, English and Hollanders, noblemen, knights, gentlemen, and captains, English and stranger volunteers, &c. &c. A short account of the departure for and arrival at Cadiz. —A copy of the Queen's prayer.—A copy of the Lord Admiral Howard's letter to Lord Hunsdon, giving an account of the affair at Cadiz, dated from on board the "Ark," July 8, 1596.—A short notice of the subsequent doings of the fleet, and its return to England.—At the end, " In gratiam gratorum gratiis, A. C. 1598, May 29 : " inscript. per me Ricard. Robinson." (This MS. was printed not quite correctly in the periodical paper called *Long ago* for November 1873. The Admiral's letter is printed nearly at length in Birch's Memoirs of the reign of Queen Elizabeth, vol. 2, p. 52.)

1627, Oct. 6. A sheet of vellum, with the seal attached of Gustavus Adolphus, King of Sweden. It recites that King Charles had determined to admit Gustavus into the Order of the Garter, and had therefore sent Sir James Spens, of Wormeston, Peter Young, Esq., gentleman of the bedchamber, and Henry St. George, herald at arms, to make the investiture. The King Gustavus Adolphus certifies that all was done properly, and that he will observe the rules of the order. (Latin.)

4to., Latin paper, 17th century. Paradigmata quædam et loci communes ex novem primis libris partis secundæ moralium Plutarchi collecta.—By Edward Burton.—Dedication to Doctor Langton, President of Magdalen College.—About 22 leaves, followed by some sermons in English.

4to., Latin, paper, 17th century. Metaphysics from Aristotle.—A treatise on the eye.—De Astronomiâ : extract from John de Sacrobosco. (This Edward Burton was son and heir of Sir Edward Burton, Kt., of Eastbourne, in Sussex, and the last heir male of that ancient family. He was of Magdalen College, Oxford, and Doctor of Divinity, and one of the chaplains in ordinary to King Charles I. He was rector of Broadwater, in Sussex, where he died 9th Aug. 1661. Mary, the daughter of Judith, his first wife, by her first husband, Francis Haddon, of London and of Kent, grandnephew of Walter Haddon, Esq., LL.D., master of the Court of Requests to Queen Elizabeth, and her ambassador, was wife of Sir William Wilson, of Eastbourne, Baronet.)

In a roll of several papers are the following :—

1520, Oct. 10. Copy presentment of the Customs of Ashdowne, co. Sussex. (About 5½ feet by 7 inches.)

1607. Presentment of abuses in Ashdown forest. *Inter alia,* the Earl of Dorset is presented for taking a piece of land.

1656. John Earl of Thanet and Lady Margaret his wife, eldest daughter of one of the co-heirs of Richard, late Earl of Dorset, are seised in fee of the manors of Bolbrook, Bassets, St. Ties, and Churtnces in Hartfield, co. Sussex. They claim wood for firing.

1625, Nov. 2. Hampton Court. Printed form of Privy Seal, addressed to John Wilson, of Sheffield, in Sussex, for a loan of 10l. to the King Charles I. Sir Henry Tompson was to receive it, and at the foot is his receipt to Mr. Wilson. Large seal of red wax at the back.

1631. John Tye spoke insulting words of John Wilson, Esq., of Eastbourne. The Earl Marshal compelled Tye to make an apology, and engage to behave well. There are also a letter by the Earl, deposition about Tye's speech, and Tye's undertaking, &c.

1704, Nov. 1. Warrant signed *George* (Prince of Denmark), appointing Edward Jocelyn to be chaplain of the Prince's own regiment of marines, commanded by the Right Honourable Richard Viscount Shannon.

Among a number of old deeds is one of the time of Henry VI., which mentions William Say, valet of the

buttery of the King. In one of the time of Henry VIII.
is mentioned "Robert Hogen, magister pro ore domini
"regis in coquinâ suâ." A deed of 30 Elizabeth is a
conveyance from Thomas Hog, of Buxtedd, co. Sussex,
to James Burgess, of a house in Buxted, which bears
the indorsement, "In this house lived ralp Hog, who
"at the then furnace at Buxted cast the first cannon
"that was cast in England."

There are two volumes containing copies of letters in
the 17th and 18th centuries by members of the Wilson
family and others; and copies of the letters and papers
above noted about John Tye's slanders (the originals,
except those about John Tye, I did not see); and personal notices of some of the Wilsons. There are interesting letters from Francis Wilson, who took military
service with the Dutch, and afterwards with the Swedes,
temp. Car. I.; and a little later curious accounts of the
way in which William Wilson (afterwards made a
baronet) defeated a search by Cromwell's soldiers for
compromising papers, and of the kidnapping and sale
as a slave of his son Thomas; an account by Sir Thomas
Spencer Wilson of the battle of Minden, at which he was
present, and other letters. Everything of interest in
these volumes has been printed under the editorship of
Mr. W. R. Blencowe, in the 10th and 11th volumes of
the Sussex Archæological Collections.

Sir T. Spencer Wilson's daughter Jane married the
Right Hon. Spencer Perceval, who was shot by Belling-
ham. The assassin was hung. At Charlton House is
a copy of the account of a dream by a gentleman in
Devonshire (several days before the event) three times
in one night, in which he seemed to see the act of
assassination and the place of it. On going to London
after the news came down he recognised from inspection the place, the murderer, and his victim, and the
dresses worn by them at the time.

Alfred J. Horwood.

A MANUSCRIPT BELONGING TO SIR JOHN LAWSON,
BART., OF BROUGH HALL, YORKSHIRE.

The York Ritual or Manual mentioned in the last
Report was afterwards found, and was sent to London by
Sir John Lawson.

It is in small folio, written on vellum in the 14th
century. It has 176 leaves including the fly-leaf at the
end. It commences with a calendar, one page for each
month; then comes a table to find Easter from 1403
occupying four pages. (The calendar and table are by a
later hand than is the text of the volume.) The text
follows. From the calendar I extract the notice of English
persons. Such parts of the text as are in English, I
have thought it desirable to copy, as specimens of 14th
century English.

Jan. 7. Deposition of St. Edward, king and confessor.
March 2. St. Chad.
March 20. St. Cuthbert.
April 24. Translation of St. Wilfred, archbishop of
York.
May 19. St. Dunstan.
June 8. St. Wilfred, Archbishop of York.
July 2. St. Swithun.
July 7. Translation of St. Thomas (erased).
Aug. 5. St. Oswald, king and martyr.
Aug. 23. St. Hilda.
Aug. 31. St. Aydan, bishop and confessor.
Sept. 1. St. Giles, abbat.
Sept. 4. Translation of St. Cuthbert.
Sept. 5. St. Bertin, abbat.
Oct. 2. St. Thomas of Hereford.
Oct. 12. St. Wilfrid, archbishop of York.
Oct. 13. Translation of St. Edward the king.
Oct. 15. St. Wulfran, bishop and confessor.
Nov. 6. St. Leonard, abbat and confessor.
Nov. 7. St. Willibrod, bishop and confessor.
Nov. 21. St. Edmund, king and martyr.
Dec. 29. St. Thomas (erased).

At the foot of each page of the calendar are "Festa
"colenda" (two or three special feasts named).

The text of the volume commences on the 9th leaf. It
is written with very black ink in a large, firm, Gothic
hand (21 lines in a page). The large initial letters are
ornamented, blue and red; the smaller capitals are
alternately red and blue.

Fol. 9. The seven penitential psalms.
17b. The Litany ends.
18. Various prayers.
19. Deus, Deus meus, respice in me.

5.

24a-44. Officium defunctorum (agrees pretty well
with the Roman ritual).
45, &c., are occupied with rubrics regarding the ceremony; benediction of salt and water; mixture of salt
and water.
48. Ordo ad catechuminum faciendum (baptism, with
variations for infants and adults).
60. A rubric for parish priests to teach often their
parishioners the form of baptism, and it is given in
English; "I cristen þe in þe nayme of þe fadyr and
"þe sone and of þe haly gayste."
61. A long rubric for Matrimony.
62. "Here I take þe N. to my wedded wyfe, to hald
"and to have at bed and at borde for fayrer for layther,
"for betta for wers, in sekenes and in hele till ded us
"depart,* and þair to I plyght þe my trowth."

The form for the woman is the same, with the necessary difference "to my wedded housband," and better is
written instead of betta.
62b. Wyth þis ryng I wedde þe and wyth þis gold
& sylvere I honoure þe and wyth my gyftys I dow
þe.
65-67. Prefaces with music for Trinity, Holy Spirit,
Corpus Christi, Holy Cross, and Commemoration of
the Blessed Mary.
67b. Coloured picture of Christ on the Cross between
the Virgin and St. John standing below.
68. Prayer for all. (The Pope is erased.)
70. Sacrament to the husband and wife.
72b. Benediction of couch.
73a. Thurification (secundum morem antiquum) of the
thorus and thalamus.
73. Order of visiting and anointing the sick.
80. Ordo in agenda mortuorum cum anima in agonia
fuerit, &c.
89b. Procession for the dead.
93. Absolution over the body in the sepulchre.
96. Benediction of bread on Sundays.
Benedictio pere et baculi (of a pilgrim).
97b. Benediction of Cross, and of those going to
Jerusalem.
98. Benediction of the shield and staff of a man going
to fight a duel.*
99. Benediction of new fruits, butter, cheese, &c.
100. Benediction of all food and drink, a new house,
&c.
101. Absolution on bull of indulgence (the part where
the Pope is mentioned is erased).
101b. Sententia excommunicationis.†
At the bygynnyng god and haly kirk corses all thais
that the frunches of halykirk brekes or disturbes and all
that es ogayn the pes of the ryght of tho state of halykirk, or the therto assentes with dede or counsail, and
all tha that halykirk prives of right or makes of halykirk layfe that es halud or sanctified. Also all thais
that wytandly or wilfully tendis falsly and gifes noght
to god and to halykirk the tend parte of the tenth pene
of ilk awynning lefully won in marchandys or with any
other craft, withdrauand anly the expenses and the
costage that nedfully behoves to be made about the
thyng that the winnyng es gatyn of, noght tendyng the
wynning of amarchandys with los of another. And also
all thais that of the fruyt of the erthe or of bestalle or of
ilk athyng that now es in the ƺore, gyfes noght the
tyndes haly with owten any withdrawing of the costage.
Also all thais that for ilwill of the person or the parispreste or the clerk or of any other minister of halykirk
wighaldes tyndynges, rentes, offerandes, mortuaries, or
oght that falles to be gyfen to god or to halykirk. Also
all tha that the fredom of halykirk lettes, brekes, or disturbes, that es to say, If a man fle to the kirk or to kirk
ƺord, wha so hym lettes or owt drawes or thor to procours or assentes. Also all tha that dos sacrilege, that
es, for to tak haly thyng ont [of] haly place or unhaly
thyng out of haly place, or halud thyng out of unhalud
place, that es for to say, If chales or westment ware
borne in to a howse in the towne for to kepe for the
mare surte. Also all tha that letters purchesis in any
lordes court that the proces of right may noght be de-
tinued (? detmned, i.e., determined) ne jugged. Also alle
that the pes of the land disturbes. Also all thais that
blod drawes of any man or woman in violense or in any
other felony in kirk or kirk ƺerd whar for the kirk or
the kirk ƺerd es enterditet or suspend or polut. Also
all tha that er agayne the kynges ryght. Also all that

Q q

---

* In the margin is a 15th century interpolation "If holy kirke it
" wille ordayn."
† This was for a litigant's champion in battle to decide a Writ of
Right.
‡ Words in italics have been re-written in the MS. For convenience
in printing, the letters th have been substituted for the Anglo-saxon þ.

there were sustens agayne the kynges pes wrangiusly.
Also all robours and revors bot it be tham selfe defend-
and. Also al tha that er ogayn the gret charter of the
kyng the whilk es confermid of the court of rome.
Also al tha that fals wytnes bers or procours tham
wityng, namly, in cause of matrimon in what court
so it be or out of courte. Also al tha that fals
witnes bringis forth rigth to deserit of land or of
rent, tenement, or any other catel, and al fals advocates that for mede puttes forth fals excepcions or
querils whar for right matrimon es fordon. Also all
tha that for mede or fovor or for any other encheson
maliciusly outher man or woman bringis out of thar
gode fame in to wiked, or gars thaim los ther wareldly
gode or honours, or puttes wrangiusly to thar purgacion.
Of the whilk there was no fame befor. Also al tha that
lettes malyciusly or disturbes the right presentacion of
a kirk whilk the verra patron suld presente or tharto
procours with word or dede or with fals enquest. Also
al tha that mede takes to disturb pes, thar love suld be,
or contak or strif mayntens with word or dede and till
that thai have yolden agayn the mede to thaim of wham
thai it tok, thai may noght be assoled. Also alle tha that
enteres houses, maners, or graunges of persons or vicars
or any other man of halykirk ogayne thar will : or agayn
thar attornes wil, and any maner of gode, movabil or
unmovabil, away bers with strenthe or wrangiusly away
drawes or wastes, on the whilk cursyng thai may noght
be assoled, to thoi have made a seth to thaim that the
wrang es don to. Also alle tha that any manor of godes
with violens bers out of halykirk or of houses of religion
the whilk es thar inleved be cause of warantyse or so-
cour or to kepe, and tha that thar to assentes or procours. Also alle wiches and al that on thaim leves.
Also alle tha that lais hand on preste or clerk in malis,
bot it be thaim self defendant. Also all women that
there generacions or childer distrues under with drinkes
or with ony other craft. Also alle tha thai thare childer
wranguisly fadirs thaim wittyng or thare childer wites
on any man maliciusly. And alle tha that wikkedly
slaes thair childer or leves thaim in feld or in toune or
at kirk dores or in gatechadiis, or in any straunge place,
and fleis fra thaim, when the childer er of unpower.
Also al tha that fals mony makes or thar to assentes.
Also all tha that gode mony clippes thaim to avantage.
Also alle tha that . . . . . the popes bulles or
countirfotes the kynges seile. Also al tha that byes or
selles with fals mesours or fals weghtes that es to say
bies with ane and selles with another. Also al tha that
falses the kynges standerd thaim wyting. Also al thais
that maliciusly disturbs man or woman wedded or un-
weddit to make thair testament lanfully and thai that
lettes the edecucion of the testament laufully made.
Also alle tha that forsuers thaim of the halidom willing
or wittyng for niede or for hatredin or for to gar any
man los his werldly gode or his honour. Also al tha
that brinnes kirkes or houses of any mans in land of
pes. Also al robers and revors oponly or privily be day
or be night that any man gode steles for whilk godes
men whor worthi to sofer dede. Also al tha that with
haldes any mans godes that has bene askid opunly in
halykirk thaim selven wittyng. Also al feloners and
thair mayntenors. Also al conspiratours or fals suerers
in assises or in any other courte. Also al tha that any
fals playntes putes forthe ogan the fraunches of hali-
kirk or of the king or of the rewme. Also al that of-
ferynges that er offerd in haly kirk or in kirk3erd, in
chapel, or in oratory, or in any stede with in the province of York, that es with halden or put away in any
other place ogaun the person wille, or his parispreste of
the parische that it es offerd in, bot if thai be priva-.
leged. Also al tha that thair gudes gifes in drofie
of dede in fraude of halykirk, or for to forbar thair
dettes, and al tha that swilk giftes takes and thairto
counsailis or helpes. Also alle tha that lettes prelates or
ordiners of halykirk for to hald consistori cession or
chapetir, or to enquere of synne, or of excesse that nede
be for hele of saule. Also al crotikes that trowes noght
in no sacrament of the auter the whilk es godes awen
body in flesche and blode in forme of brede and other
sacrementes that touches hole of sanle. Also al userers,
as if a man len his catel to another to take avantage be
covenaud, for loving of his catel, for if thair uere any
swilk in a cyte, tho gite suld be ontirdite that no sacrament suld be don thair in, to thai wer puttid oute of tho
cyte. Thies er the poyntes of the gret cursing that our
haly fadirs papes erchebishops and bishops has ordaned
and thai awght for to be pupplis at the lest thrice in the
3ere in ilk a parischekirk, that es to say, the first sonanday of lentyn, or the secund, and also som sonanday
affir the maudelaines, or els be for, als it may best fal,

and also sum sonanday in the advent be for the yole ; and
thus halykirk uses thurgh cristendum.—Siquis exco-
municat excommunicacionem in scriptis proferat et
causam excommunicacionis ex presse conscribat propter quam excommunicacio proferet; exemplum .vero
scripture hujusmodi teneatur excommunicato tradere
infra mensem si fuerit requisitus; super quam requi-
sicionem fieri volumus puplicum instrumentum vel
litteras testimoniales confici, sigillo autentico consig-
natas. Quando quisque solempniter excommunicat
sic dicat, et autoritate dei patris omnipotentis et filii et
spiritus sancti et sanctorum apostolorum canonum et
nostri ministerii excommunicamus et anathematiz-
mus atque liminibus sancte dei matris et ecclesie
sequestramus illos qui hec mala fecerunt vel consen-
serunt vel terras sancti petri depopulati sunt ut non
haberent partem cum deo nec cum sanctis ejus, et
nisi respuerint ad satisfaccionem venerint sic extin-
guatur lucerna eorum in secula seculorum, Amen.

105. Pro precibus dominicalibuz. Deprecemur deum
patrem omnipotentem pro pace et stabilitate sancte
matris ecclesie, 3e sal mak your prayers specially
till our lord god almighti and til his blissyd moder
mary, and till alle the haly court of heven, for the
state and the stabilnes of al halykirk, for the pape
of rome and al his cardinals and for the archebischop of
York, and for al erchebischops and bischops, and for al
men and women of religion and for the person of this
kirke that has your saules to kepe, and for alle the
prestes and clerks that has served or serves in this kirk
or in any other. And for al prelates and ordiners and
al that halykirk reules and governs that god len thaim
grace so forto reuel thes popil and swilk ensaumpil for
to tak or scheu thaim, and thaim for to do thare after,
that it may be loving unto god and salvacion of thaire
saules. Also 3e sal pray specially for the g0de state of
this reume, for the kyng and the quene and for al tho
peris and the lordes of this lande, that god send love
and charite thaim omang ; and gif thaim grace so for
to reule it and govern it in pes, that it be loving to god
and the comons un to profit. Also 3e sal pray specially
for tham that lely and trwly payes thare tendes and
thaire offerandes til god and halykirk, and for al that
other dos that god thaim amende. Also 3e sal pray
specialy for thaim that this kirk first biggid and edefied,
and al that it up haldes and for al that thar in findes
boke or chales, vestment, lyght, or towell, or any other
anourment, whare with godes scrvys es sustend ; and
for thaim that halybred gaf to this kirk to day and for
thaim that first began and langest haldes on. And for
al land tilland, and for al seo farand, and for the wedir,
and for the fruyt that es on erthe, that the erthe may
bring forthe his fruyt cristenmen to profit ; and for al
pilgrymes and palmers and for al that any gode gates
has gane or sal ga. And for thaim that brigges and
stretes makes and amendes, that god giit us parte of
thare gode dedes and thaim of oures. Al so 3e sal pray
for alle our parischyns whar so thai be on land or on
water, that god save thaim fra al missaunters, and for
alle wymen that er with chield in this parische or in any
other that god delyver thaim with joy and gife tho child
cristendom, and thaim purificacion, and for al that er sek
and sary that god al mighthi conforth thaim and tham
that er un (in?) gode lyfe that god hald thaim there in.
For tham that er in dette or in dedly synne or in prison
that god bring tham out thare of ; for tham and for us
and for al cristen folke for charite says a pater noster
and a ave. Priest, Deus miseriatur nostri, etc. Gloria
patri, &c., &c. . . . . Deus a quo sancta desideria. Al
so 3e sal pray specialy til oure lady sanyt mary that
sche bocum oure avoket and [th]at sche pray for hus
specialy till hir dere son. And also 3e sal pray specialy
for the breders and the sisters of saynt petir minster of
York, and of sant Jon of beverlay, and of saynt Wil-
fryde of rypon, and for al that 3e er halden un to and
for al that god wald 3e prayed for. Says a pater noster
and Ave. a Ave regina colorum. In tempore paschali.
a Regina celi letare. Versio. Post partum virginis.
Oratio. Famulorum tuorum. Also 3e sal pray specialy
for oure fader saules and oure moder saules and for oure
god fader saules and oure god moder saules and for oure
brether saules and oure sisters saules and for our eldir
saules, and for al tho saules of whame the bodis es berid
in this kirk or in this kirke 3erde. And for al saules
that in purgatori godis mercy abydes and for al cristen
saules of whame we have had any god of, says specialy a
pater noster and ave.

107. De sancto spiritu missa : officium.

109b. In veneracionem sancte crucis.

110b. De sancta Maria in Adventu.

112. Officium de Dominica, ab Oct. Epiph. usque ad Purificationem.

113b. Do. in tempore Paschale.

114b. Rubric. Hoc modo dicetur Missa de dña usque ad fest. S. Trinitatis (but with certain variations for other periods).

115b. Missa de festo Corporis Christi.

117. Missa de Angelis.

118. Missa pro familiaribus.

121. De Cruce tempore Paschale.
De omnibus sanctis tempore Paschale.

121b. De omnibus sanctis in Adventu.

122. Pro serenitate aeris; pro infirmo vel infirmâ.

123. Pro vivis et mortuis.

124b. Missa pro defunctis. Pro sacerdote, oratio. Pro corpore presenti.

127. Pro confratribus.

127b. Pro episcopo defuncto. Pro famulo.

128. Pro benefactoribus. Pro patre et matre. Pro omnibus defunctis.

129–138b. Music. The genealogies, &c. Purification of Mary. Benediction of fire, &c.

139. Benediction of wax candles.

Several rubrics on the following leaves.

141. Benediction of palm and other leaves.

142b. Rubric. On the Sabbath of Easter, fire is to be gotten from beryl or flint, &c., &c. Other rubrics and forms.

145. Rubric for double féasts, &c. For the Purification.

Music and rubrics to the end of the volume.

169. St. Wilelm archbishop (cancelled).

The last rubric is for Feria Quinta in die cene post nonam.

The volume has the names of Christopher Lodge (as owner), and John Lodge in writing about 200 years old.

ALFRED J. HORWOOD.

THE MANUSCRIPTS OF SIR HENRY MILDMAY, BART., OF DOGMERSFIELD PARK, CO. HANTS.

These are very few; there are, however, two of great interest although indifferent degrees. One is the original order by Oliver Cromwell for the arms and flag to be used in the Navy in substitution for those used under the King. The other is part of the original manuscript by Abraham Tucker of his work called The Light of Nature pursued. This work was published by him (under the pseudonym of Edward Search), in 7 vols., 8vo., 1768–78; reprinted in 1805. The late William Hazlitt executed an able abridgment of the work, and it was published in one volume in 1807.

34 Hen. VIII., July 23rd. Grant to Thomas Mildmay and Avice, his wife, of the manor of Mulsham, in Essex, late the property of the monastery of St. Peter of Westminster.

1 Mary, Oct. 3d. The Queen's general pardon to Thomas Mildmay, one of the auditors of the Court of Augmentation and Revenue of the Crown, alias T. Mildmay, Esq. Auditor of our Duchy of Cornwall, alias T. Mildmay, Esq. Sealed with the great seal of Edward VI.

1573, June 25th. (Wa. Mildmay to . . . .) Roger Iveson, one of the Queen's messengers, prays the allowance for service by him done at the command of the Right Hon. Sir Walter Mildmay, Kt., one of the Queen's Privy Council, and Chancellor of the Exchequer. There are several items. At the foot is the warrant for payment, thus—Allow for this bill to 6s. 8d. Wa. Mildmay.

1 Jac. I., March 3d. General pardon to Sir George Harvey, Lieutenant of the Tower of London.

2 Jac. I., March 28th. General pardon to Sir Gawin Harvey, of Markes, in the parish of Hornechurch, co. Essex.

1 Car. I., Feb. 10th. General pardon to Sir Henry Mildmay.

1648, Feb. 23rd., Derby House. "O. Cromwell". Prœses pro tempore to . . . . Gentlemen, there has been a report made to the Council by Sir Henry Mildmay of your desire to be informed what is to be borne on the flags of those ships that are in the service of the State, and what to be borne on the stern in lieu of the arms formerly there engraven. The council resolve they shall bear the red cross only on a white flag quite through the flag, upon the stern the red cross in one escutcheon and the harp in the other, being the arms of England and Ireland; both escutcheons joined according to the pattern herewith sent. The flags to be provided with all expedition for the ships for the summer guard, &c. Signed (by Oliver Cromwell as above) in the name and by the order of the Council of State, appointed by the authority of Parliament.

1652. May 18th. Committee for the Public Revenue sitting at Westminster. By virtue of an ordinance of both Houses of Parliament, 21st of Sept. 1643, and order of the Trustees for the maintenance of Ministers of the 31st of March 1652, these are to require you out of money in hand of the profits of first fruits and tenths payable to the commonwealth since 8th June 1649, to pay to Mr. Robert Asby, minister of Stratford, co. Suffolk, 20l. for half a year due 25th of March last, for the yearly sum of 40l. granted to him by order of the Committee for the reformation of the University, of the 13th of June 1651. Signed by H. Vane, Hen. Mildmay, and three others.

The following letters from King William III to the Earl of Galway are copies in writing of the last century. I made abstracts of all, but find that all except one are given in "Letters of William III. and Louis XIV., and of their ministers, &c. 1697 to 1700," edited by Paul Grimblot, 2 vols. 8vo. London, 1848.

1697, Oct. 19th.
1697, Nov. 26th.
1698, July 16th.
1698, Jan. 27th.
1699, June 1st.
1699, Aug. 14th.
1700, May 11th.
1700, July 2nd.
1700, Aug. 15th.

1698, Oct. $\frac{7}{17}$. Au Genr. The king acknowledges the Earl of Galway's letter of the 10th September. He has not been able to send orders with regard to the assembly of Parliament in Ireland; being so far off he (the King) cannot well give orders. Refers the Earl of Galway to the Lord Justices in England. He knows that many in England do not wish the session of the Irish Parliament to turn out well. He fears that the hatred against the chancellor Methuen will be a great obstacle. All he can say is, provide for the subsistence of the troops in Ireland. It is of consequence that there be a good session in Ireland.

1803, July 23d. Hartford Bridge. Original memorandum for an association for the defence of the country (by raising a corps of cavalry). Signed by H. St. John Mildmay and 52 others.

Pedigree of the Mildmays, of Moulsham Hall, Essex, and also of the St. Johns, of Farley. 4to. London, printed 1803.

Four volumes, folio, blue morocco. A manuscript copy of the Light of Nature by Abraham Tucker. The first 24 chapters, ending in the second volume, are by the author's hand. The rest of the volumes are copied.

ALFRED J. HORWOOD.

THE MANUSCRIPTS OF SIR ALEXANDER MALET, BART., AT QUEENSBERRY PLACE, KENSINGTON.

These are very interesting, and some of them are of great historical value. They range over two centuries and a half, beginning with the reign of Henry VIII. Being arranged in nearly chronological order, reference to them is comparatively easy, and research is further facilitated by tables of contents, which Sir Alexander Malet has prefixed to the volumes in which the papers are bound up.

One of the papers is of the reign of Henry VI., and is the beginning of a petition by the Commons to the King against the Duke of Suffolk.* There are early copies of letters from Sir Thomas Boleyn, while the King's agent in the Low Countries in 1509 and 1510 ; and from Sir Thomas Spinelly, at Brussels, to the King in 1513 and 1514, and original letters from the King to James V. of Scotland and to the Earl of Arran ; a letter by Sir John Cheke, while a prisoner in the Tower of London in 1556 ; and a copy of Queen Mary's will. The Scotch papers in the time of Mary Queen of Scots are of special interest. In 1559 are the original instructions by the Duke of Chatelherault and others of the Council, given to Lethington on the occasion of his embassy to Queen Elizabeth ; an original letter in 1567 to Lord Gray from the confederated Lords Morton, Mar, and four others (and signed by them), for deliverance of their Queen, the preservation of the Prince, &c. ; a copy of the Declaration of the Earl of Morton in 1568 regarding the finding of the silver box and the letters and sonnets therein ; in 1561 a long letter from James Stuart to Mary Queen of Scots, giving remonstrance and advice ; letters from Maitland to his Queen ; letters by Cecil and the Earl of Leicester ; copies of letters by Elizabeth to Mary and to James ; and a holograph letter to the Earl of Leicester by King James, written between the trial and the execution of his mother, which seems to show that he was rather indifferent to her fate. There are several letters by important persons on religion during the reign of Elizabeth.

Out of their proper place are two long and important letters by Lord Wharton to the Earl of Hertford, telling in detail the writer's ravages in Scotland towards the close of the reign of Henry VIII.

An original petition to the King by Arabella Seymour is strongly worded. There is also a letter by her.

There are letters by Grindal Archbishop of York and Abbot. Archbishop of Canterbury, John Selden (and several to him), Sir Simonds Dewes, Gerard Langbaine, Charles I., Lord Keeper Coventry, and Secretary Windebank ; papers by Archbishop Laud about his right to visit the University of Cambridge ; and letters to Whitelocke in Sweden. Some papers here show that Oliver Cromwell intended to found a new college at Oxford ; and that Lord Ashley (first Earl of Shaftesbury) projected writing a history of England. In 1653 Whitelocke seems to have had the custody of the *Codex Alexandrinus*, and to have been authorised by the Council of State to lend it to Brian Walton and others, who signed an undertaking to keep it safe and return it. Walton afterwards asks for a grant from the Treasury towards the expense of printing the celebrated Polyglot Bible. There are letters by Charles II., James II., Algernon Sidney, Gilbert Burnet ; several letters to Henry Coventry (Secretary of State, temp. Charles II.), and by his brother Sir William Coventry, on naval affairs ; many interesting letters to the Earl and Duke of Lauderdale, who advocates stern measures with the Scotch Covenanters.

Letters by Lord Clarendon ; a series of letters by Sir Thomas Higgons, our agent at Venice in 1675 and later years ; and some by the Duke of Ormonde ; several letters from Cardinals at Rome to Charles II. giving birthday congratulations ; a letter by the Duke of Monmouth ; a curious letter by Bushworth to the Honorable Thomas Thynne, M.P., accounting for certain suppressions in the *Historical Collections* ; letters from the Earl of Orrery to Sir J. Malet, in 1678, giving Irish news ; papers about Oates' plot ; letters from Louis XIV. to the Duke of York ; and by the Duke of Tyrconnel (in 1688) to James II. ; and an account of the seizure of the latter at Faversham. There are also letters by Atterbury, Bishop Ken, and David Garrick.

The parentage of the Old Pretender was for a long time the subject of discussion : a volume in this collection

* A long petition or complaint against the Duke (wanting the beginning is printed at p. 879 of the Appendix to the Third Report.

is wholly occupied by papers (printed and manuscript) about it.

The salient points of Sir Alexander Malet's MSS. are indicated above ; brief notes of nearly every document are given below.

VOL. I.

Folio, vellum, 12th century. Ten leaves in double columns, containing 23 letters,—1. Anselm to Pope Urban. 2 and 3. Letters by Pope Pascal. 4. Pope Pascal to Anselm. 5. Pope Pascal to King Henry. 6 and 7. Anselm to Pope Pascal. 8 and 9. Pope Pascal to Anselm. 10. Pope Pascal to Henry King of England. 11. Pope Pascal to Osberne, Bishop, and the Church of Exeter. 12. Pope John to Anselm, elect of Canterbury. 13. Pope Benedict to Anselm. 14. Anselm to Pope Pascal. 15. Pope Pascal to Anselm. 16, 17, and 18. Pope Pascal to King Henry. 19. Pope Pascal to Matilda Queen of England. 20. Pope Pascal to the Bishop of York. 21, 22, and 23. Pope Pascal to Anselm. The MS. ends on the first column of the last leaf. In the margins of the leaves are references to Anselm's works in the edition of Paris 1675, where most of the letters are printed, but Nos. 1, 5, 10, 11, 12, 16, 17 and 18 are not marked as there printed.

Folio, paper, 13 pp. Cotemporary copy of articles for the marriage of Henry VIII. with Catherine of Aragon. It contains the letter of Ferdinand and Isabella, King and Queen of Castile, &c., *beginning*, In omnibus hujus seculi negotiis. At p. 4 is King Henry's letter.—Following these, in a page and a half by a later hand, is a copy of the definitive sentence by Pope Clement for the validity of the marriage of Henry VIII. with Catherine, and against his marriage with Anne Boleyn. Dated at Rome in 1534.

Secret instructions containing certain points and articles wherein it is the King's pleasure that his ambassadors shall diligently enquire and ascertain his Highness and the Emperour. (To move the Emperor to invade the French King on the frontiers of Guyenne, as it is more at length touched in the open instructions.) 3 pp., 17th century.

Folio. paper, 17th century, 17 pp. Copies of letters by Sir Thomas Boleyn, agent in the Low Countries, to the King, touching all the affairs with the Emperor Charles. 1510.
1. Pleaseth your Grace to understand that we have not as yet declared to the Emperor, &c., &c. (because the Emperor had written to despatch the French ambassador). Dated, Brussels, 4th June. (2 pp.)
2. Pleaseth your most sovereign Grace to understand that the 16th day of the present month I wrote my last letter. (He says that in his last he told of Thomas Spinelly's coming and delivering the King's letters of the 10th of the month.) Dated Brussels, 19th June. (6 pp.)
3. Pleaseth your Grace to call to your remembrance that the 19th of this present month we wrote our last. Dated, Brussels, 22 June. (2½ pp.)
4. Another dated Brussels, 27 June 1510. (Nearly 6 pp.)
5. Beginning of another, referring to his letter of the 27th :—*ends*, As yesterday, which was the 28th day, my lady sent word that shee thought is it right meet that one of us should go.
1513, July 19, Brussels. Sir Thomas Spinelly to the King. Refers to his letter of the 17th. (3½ pp. Copy, 17th century.)
1514, Aug. 2, Brussels. Copy of joint letter by Wingfield and Spinelly to the King. (2 pp.)
1514, July 21, Brussels. The same to the same. (1½ pp.)
1514, Aug. 1, Brussels. T. Spinelly to the King. (2 pp.)
Copy letter by the King to . . . . Refers to the addressee's letter dated Mechlin the 19th instant (Nov.), he having late come to the presence of the Duchess of Savoy. (1½ pp.)
n. d. Copy of a letter to the King's Commissioners in Flanders. They refer to their letter from Bruges of the 9th instant :—a business with the Prince of Castile about an *intercose* of 1506. (5½ pp., ends imperfectly.)
Copy of another letter regarding an armed assistance to the Emperor by Henry VIII. (8 pp.)
(1528) Oct. 1. "Henry R" to James V. of Scotland. An original letter to dissuade him from pursuing the Earl of Angus, or coming on or near the Borders. Wafer seal, and superscription.
15th century. Beginning of a petition by the Commons to the King against the Duke of Suffolk. Begins,

Shewyth & pytuously compleynith; *onds*, and many dyverse.*

(1543) 35 Henry VII., Oct. 27, Ampthill. "Henry R." to the Earl of Arran.—A scolding letter for his conduct in not contradicting the Cardinal who, in the presence of the King's ambassador, affirmed that the King's covenants passed with Scotland 'were passed by private authority. The King says that "the Cardinal powdored his speech with lies."

Copy (by Dr. Harbin) of Ann Bullen's letter to the King, found among Cromwell's papers; now in the Ashmolean Museum. *Begins*, Your Grace's displeasure and my imprisonment. Datod, 6 May 1536.

Answer made by the King's Highness unto certain articles given by way of Informacion on the behalve of his derest brother and nephew the King of Scots unto his familiar servitor Patrick Sentclare, and by him shewed and declared unto the King's grace as followeth. —Signed at the end by the King. (10 pp. Border Matters, &c.)

33 Hen. VIII. Copy of the letter by the King to the University of Oxford, asking them to send, by the bearer his chaplain, Edward Leighton under their seal, the articles of the condemnation of Wyclif by the University, and the confirmation thereof by the Council of Constance.

1534. Copy of the second letter by the King to the University of Oxford about the decision of the questions touching the Primacy. Dated, 18 May. And copy of proceedings in 1534. Dated, 27 June 1534. (2 pp.)

Copy of lotter by Henry VIII. to Stafford Duke of Buckingham, to bind his servants to good behaviour in the Marches of Wales. Dated at Woodstock, 6 June. (This is an official copy. The letter was seen and allowed by Burghley; and on the 10th May 36 Elizabeth, Edward Stafford prayed that it might be enrolled in Chancery, and it was so enrolled. (3½ pp.)

(1547, Aug. 30.) Stephen Winton (Gardiner) to Mr. Mason, a visitor in his diocese; against homilies "of only faythe."

1547, May 6. The Earl of Arran to Pope Paul the Third, and a letter in French to the King of Scots:—about absolution to those concerned in the murder of the Cardinal of St. Andrews. (Both are cotemporary copies.)

License by Philip and Mary (with signature of "Mary the quene") to Robert Shepardo, of Romford, co. Essex, one of the yeomen of her chamber, to sell wine. Countersigned by "Nicholas Ebor. Canc."

Copy of a similar licence by Queen Elizabeth.

1556, July 15, Tower.—John Cheke to the Queen. A letter asserting his faithfulness, and that he had declared his mind to the Dean of St. Paul's.

Copy of Queen Mary's Will, from the original in Mr. Hale's hands at Alderley in Gloucestershire. (20 pp. and a codicil of 5 pp.) The witnesses to the will are H. Bedingfeld, John Throgmorton, Thomas Wharton, R. Wilbraham. The witnesses to the codicil are Edmund Peckham, Thomas Weudye, John Wallis, Barnard Hampton. The will begins with saying that she thinks she is with child.

1559, May 20. Copy of Instructions by Queen Elizabeth to the Earl of Pembroke, Lieutenant of the counties of Wilts and Somerset.

1559, Nov. 10, Sterling. Instructions given by the Duke of Chatelherault and utheris of the conseil to the young lard of Lethyngton, secretary of the realm presently direct to the quenes majeste of England to be declayrit to hir majeste or hir mayst honorable council. —Signed by Hamilton, W. Argyll, and 8 others.—Indorsed by Cecil.

1567, June 12, Edinburgh. A letter to Lord Gray from the Confederated Lords;—for deliverance of the Queen from her thraldom, and that the Prince may be preserved and the murderers of his father may be tried. They pray him to come to Edinburgh with his honest friends and servants.—Signed by Morton, Mar, Sympil, Hume, Sanquhar and another.

1568, Dec. 29, Thursday. Copy of the declaration made and presented by the Earl of Morton to the Commissioners sitting at Westminster.—1568, Dec. 29th. The trew Declaration and Report of me James Earl of Morton how a certain silver box overgilt conteyning dyvers missive writings, sonetts, contracts, and obligations for marriage between the Queen Mother to our sovéran lord and James some tyme Erll Bothwell was found and usit.—He says that George Dalgleish was taken to the Tolbooth, and threatened with torture. In

fear, he calls for [the Earl's] cousin Mr. Robert Douglas; who coming, he went forth to the potterraw, and from under the seit of the bed took forth a silver box which he had brought from the castle the day before. The Earl opened it on the 21st of June, and he and others examined the contents, letters, sonnets, &c., and kept them unchanged.

1567. Copy of a letter *endorsed*, Copy of a letter given to Secretary Cecil. *Begins*, On the 19th June I dynt at Edinburgh, the Lord of Ledynton, secrotario was with me. (1½ pp.)

1573, last of July. Original deposition taken in the presence of Allan, Lord Cathcart, Sir John Bellenden, of Ancherville, Kt. Justice Clark, Master James Halyburton, provost of Dundee, and George Douglas of Parkhead, captain of the Castell of Edinburgh.—Doposition by Alexander Lord Hume concerning the Regent Murray conspiring the death of the King. Signed by those present and by Hume. (1 p.)

1573, Aug. 3, Holyrood House. Deposition to the same effect made by W. Kirkaldy in the presence of Lord Boyd, Sir John Bellenden, and Master James Lowson.

1560, Feb. 11, Paris. F. Bedford to Lord Robert V. M. of the Queen's Majesty.—Good beginning of religion there.—Juan Manriques, the King of Spain's ambassador has bedn there.—The young Queen of Scotts should before my coming be removed to Reymes; but now is that journey differred; yet shall she afterwards thither, and so to Jumpeville, there to abide. M. Dampville or M. Vielleville shall, it is thought, come shortly into England to congratulate the new King. So doth this Duchess of Ferrara send over one of her chief gentlemen to visit the Queen's Majesty, who is ready to depart hence.

1560, May 30, Barwick. Thomas (Duke of) Norfolk to the Duke of Chatelherauld and the rest of the Lords of the Congregation in Scotland.—About relief to the Scots from France; he says he hears from Court of the recent arrival of one M. de Randon, with a Commission from the French King to the Bishop of Valence, La Brosse, Doysell and himself or two of them, so as the besieged persons need not be called out of the town to treat with others to be appointed by the Queen. (1½ pp.)

1560, May 22, Amboise. Nicholas Throckmortou to Lord R. Dudley; (much in cypher decyphered).—Mr. Portunary has lately advertised me, &c. . . . . Recommends F. as good for fortifications and engineering. (Not important.)

1560, July 20. Edwin Wigorn (Sandys, Bishop of Worcester) to Lord R. Dudley, excusing himself, by reason of a synod at Lambeth, to execute a deed of lease of a parsonage or some such thing.

1570, Jan. 3, Paris. Henry Norris to the Earl of Leicester.—Religious.—Many people pleased at the report of Leicester concerning them. (1½ large p.)

1570, Jan. 19. Ed. London (Grindall, Bishop of London) to the Earl of Leicester. Asking him to intercede with the Queen for him and not to believe his enemy. (1 p.)

1571, May 20, Cork. Sir John Perrot to the Earl of Leicester. Refers to his own letter of the 26th of April, wherein *inter alia* he spoke of his determination to set forward against the rebel James Fitzmaurice.—Gives an account of his doings. (3 close large sides.)

1571, July 30, London. Christopher Goodman to the Earl of Leicester.—Thanks him for his intervention with the Archbishop of Canterbury.—He was imprisoned and stayed from preaching.

1571, July 16, Edm. Ebor. (Grindall, Archbishop of York), to the Earl of Leicester. State of religion as he found it during his visitation. In a P.S. he says he hears that Leicester's old schoolmaster Willoughby is asking the Queen for an office in his church belonging to his gift.

1571, July 20, Halden. Sir H. Sydney to Lord Leicester (unimportant).

1571, July 28, Putney. John Hales to the Earl of Leicester.—A long letter of thanks for favours.—For the two young men Robert and William Bele he asks Leicester to place Robert where Her Majesty at Leicester's suit determined :—for William he asks that he may be made a canon in Oxford. (4 pp. and 5 lines.)

1571, Aug. 2, London. Acerbo Vellutelli to the Earl of Leicester. Letter in Italian. Sends a person for a letter of favour to Dr. Ghibius, and one from the Admiral.—Ship business.

1572, March 4th, Fulham. Ed. London to the Earl of Leicester.—Hears that Gerald the Portingale has complained at the Court as if he had been ill used :—abuses him and intimates that he ought to have been killed. He has had mass in his house Sunday and Friday for

* It is the beginning of the Petition which is printed in the Rolls of Parliament; vol. 5, p. 177.

Q q 3

SIR A. MALET, BART.

12 months; there resort there twenty at least of Her Majesty's subjects.—Asks him to tell the Queen that the idolater may be punished.

1572, March 21, Chester. William (Bishop of) Chester to the Earl of Leicester.—According to his (Leicester's) letters he has installed Goodman the preacher Archdeacon of Richmond. On Palm Sunday one of his chaplains W. Wright, M.A., of Cambridge, coming from his sermon, was put in the stocks and pelted by the women with rotten eggs, and ill used. (2½ pp.)

1572, April 20th, Cork. Sir J. Perrot to the Earl of Leicester. Irish affairs:—and his own doings. (6 pp.)

1572, Oct. 8th, Paris. Sir Francis Walsingham to the Earl of Leicester.—Acknowledges Leicester's letter of the 22nd of September. Recommends a Captain Sasetti for service in Ireland;—he has offered him service;—mentions another;—is sorry that union with Scotland is not already made.—Recommends the union. (1¾ pp.)

1572, Nov. 8, Salcy forest. John Wake to the Earl of Leicester.

(1572); Jan. 12th. Edmund Roffen (Freke, Bishop of Rochester) to the Earl of Leicester.

1575, April 8th. F. Knollys to the Earl of Essex, Her Majesty's Governor of Ulster.—As there were difficulties since Captain Malbie's coming hither, he says he offered Her Majesty to go himself to Ireland (about the Earl's service in the plantation), but she delays; he did that to hope to get the Queen to send money. She said Essex had no grave man with him. (3 lines are blotted out.)

VOL. II.

1561, June 10, Edinburgh. James Steuart to the Quene's Grace:—dissuading her from interfering in religious matters. (5 pp.) In the fifth page he says: Take stinte Madam; judge this with yourself that thair is na man that knoweth perfectly the present estate of your realm, and desireth with true affection the advancement of your grace's service that ever will advise your grace to meddle with matters of religion at this time. If it shall please your grace to credit me and follow my foresaid advice proceeding from an unfeyned heart that truly willeth your grace's advancement, then fear not that your grace shall have a perfect obedience in despite of any will press the contrair, whateir they be (God willing), and thereupon I will bestow my own life most willingly.

1562, March 9th, Westminster. (Copy.) W. Maitland to the Queen. *Begins:* Your Majesty may please to understand that upon the 4th day of this month I wrote to your Majesty some beginning of a conversation that passed between the Spanish Ambassador and me. Yesterday I dined at his house; the French Ambassador was there. (After dinner the French Ambassador went to Court, and the other and he talked.) *At the end:* I received yesternight last a packet of letters for your Majesty dated at St. Andrews the last of Feby., and shewing a discourse of Chattelard's matter, the execution whereof being so wysely and orderly done cannot but redound to your Majesty's high honour. It is so long since the matter was brought to my ears, I believe Mr. Randolph writ either to the Queen or to Mr. Secretary, but always it was very humbly reported and almost . . . in the same manner as the discourse bears; this only differed, that was that when at the first your Majesty was so angry that you would needs have him slain or ever he passed out of the place, and commanded Colemanye to do it out of hand, but that my lord of Murray said it was more convenient to execute him by justice. (5½ pp.)

1562, June 10th, Greenwich. W. Maitland to the Queen, touching the meeting of the two Queens.—Thinks the time will be appointed for Mary to be at York on the 24th Aug. or thereabout.—Warning is given to all officers to make provisions.—Safe conduct will be given for 1,000, but they will be glad if she (Mary) will make the number less.—Speaks strongly of Elizabeth's affection for Mary.—Tells Mary to write as if she were in love, and because she has not experience in such matters she is to consult some of her ladys;—she is sure to have good counsell of the Lord of Mar, who has been long acquainted with love matters. (3½ pp.)

1567, Aug. 20, Windsor. W. Cecill to (Randolph). It begins, with *Sir*, but on the second page the writer says, *My Lord*.—The letter is full of religious expressions and hatred of Antichrist. On p. 2 he says, The reiteration of the purpose intended by the Guises in marriage of your Queen to the French King to disturb the realm, and consequently to stir mortal war betwixt the two kingdoms can never be tolerable to this realm. On p. 3 he says he will never consent to it. *Ends*, Yours in god, and in the concord of this Ile inseperable, W. C. (*Indorsed:* Cecils letter to Randolph, touching the Queens marriage in Spane.) (Holograph, 3 pp.)

SIR A. MALET, BART.

1568, July 15th. From the Court at Havering. W. Cecill to (Your Grace) L. S.—Has received letters to him, and imparted hers to the Lords of the Council, saying that Sir John Southworth has been before her and cannot be persuaded to conformity; therefore he is to remain where he is. P.S. (autograph) About a complaint by the Spanish Ambassador that there was a collection here by ecclesiastics to relieve Count Ludovic, whom the ambassador terms a rebel. (½ p.)

1570, June 18, Oatlands. W. Cecill to the Earl of Leicester (holograph). On the importunity of the French King, Her Majesty will hear what offer the Queen of Scots has to make; she has license to send into Scotland for some of her part to come hither. (1 p.)

The mind and opinion of Rodolph Gualter, of Zurich, concerning the meaning of surplises and priests cappes. *Begins:* It troubles me not a little. (1½ pp.)

1571, Feb. 11th, Isle of Ely. R. Cox, Bishop of Ely, to Rodolph Gualter. About ceremonies; in Latin. (1½ pp.)

1566, Dec. 16, Receipt of 144*l*. 4*s*. 4½*d*. from the Earl of Leicester for half a year's rent of the Archbishop's Manor of Southwell, co. Notts. Signed by Tho. Ebor.

1566, kal. Junii, from my house at Croydon. Letter from *Tuus bonus amicus* (Matthew Parker Archbishop of Canterbury?) to Haddon in Latin.—Lamenting the audacity of some who opposed authority. (1 p.)

1567, July 15th, Richmond. Council letter, signed by Pembroke, R. Leycester, E. Clynton, W. Howard, W. Cecill, and another, to the Archbishop of York, President of the Council in the North.—Recommending Mr. Pever's cause.

Cotemporary copy of the engagement made at Stirling condemning the carrying off Queen Mary and the carrying her to Dunbar; and to set her at liberty and defend her.

Answer to the Instructions of our Most Noble Sovereign and her dearest spouse the Duke of Orkney, committed to the credit of my Lord Boyd, communicate to the Earl of Morton the 28th of May 1567, at the free school. *Begins:* In so far as it may anywise appear to their Graces that some suspicion may be collected against me for convening in Stirling upon the 1st of May, &c. (1 p.)

1561, July 13th, Edinburgh. James, Regent, to Mr. John Wood, attending at Court in England. (2 pp. and 3½ lines of cypher at end.)—Acknowledges letters, and has written others which Wood is to present to the Queen.

1569, May 16. The Earl of Leicester to the Regent Murray.—Touching your causes, John Wood is able at length to make report.—Thinks that Lethington is the best man he (Murray) can send over. Lord Boyd has moved the Queen to ask Murray for his liberty;—presses for it, as he thinks Boyd is reasonable. (Holograph, 1½ pp.)

1570. Chamæleon; by George Buchanan against the Lord of Lethington, Secretary of Scotland in 1570,* followed by,

An invective against the family of Hamilton by G. B. 1570. *Begins:* It may seem to your Lordships that I meddling with high matters. (14 pp. folio.)

1573, Dec. 2, Hanworth. E. Hertford to . Is coming home and intends to be at Wallop Hall Friday next. (14 lines; the direction is torn off.)

1573, Nov. 28th, Blackfriars. H. Knolles to Sir J. Thynne at Longleat. . . . The Queen came suddenly from Greenwich because of the death of the Mother of the Maids; she went to Leycester House in London, and remained there all the next day; she is now at Somerset House.—A postscript contains foreign news. (1½ pp.)

1574, Sept. 18, Paris. E. Seymour to his brother the Earl of Hertford. (½ p.)

1576, Sept. 6, Middelbourg. Instructions in French (signed by Guill. de Nassau) of what Mons. Bartley is to say to the Queen of England from the Prince of Orange; he is first to kiss hands. (3 pp.)

1577. Customs presented on the 17th of March, of the Manor of Amesbury, &c.

1582, Sept. 29. A remembrance of that we have declared to, &c. Sir George Carey, Kt., Ambassador for our dearest sister the Queen of England at Stirling

* Printed, London. 8vo. 1710.

on the 29th Sept. 1582. Signed at the end, "James R."—Is pleased with his letter and has given some grace to the Earl of Angus.—Asks that Archibald Douglas, one of the murderers of his father, may be given up.

1582, March 18th, Richmond. Sir Francis Walsingham to the Archbishop of Canterbury.—On the alteration of the Calendar.

1583, March 29, Richmond, From the same to the same.—On the same subject.

Reasons against the alteration of the Calendar. (1 leaf.)

1578, March 20, Argentorati. Joan Sturmius to Edm. Grindal Archbishop of Canterbury.

1583, April 4th. Copy of a letter by E. Archbishop of Canterbury, and the Bishops of London, Sarum, and Rochester.—They could not agree to the alteration in the Calendar without consulting other churches.

1585, July 15th, Tutbury. Nau to Sir Francis Walsingham.—Asks him to give dispatch in his mistresses affairs. (In French, ⅓ p.)

1584, Sept. 4th. Enterprises found on a Scottish Jesuit taken on the seas, for the invasion of the realm. (7½ pp.)

Latin speech to the Pope. (2 pp.)

1584, Feb., Somerset House. Copy of a letter by Queen Elizabeth to Queen Mary.—About the Association, and Nau's conclusion on what the Master of Gray said that James had not agreed to the Association. (1½ pp.)

Copy of Queen Elizabeth's letter to James. Begins: When I consider right, dear brother, that all the chaos whereof the world was made. (She promises on the faith of a King.)

Copy of another letter by Queen Elizabeth to James.—The gentleman, who for your allowance, &c. (sends one to lay open her grievances.)—Trusts that coming may blot all out of her memories book.

Brief of the Bill in the Star Chamber put in against To. Cartwright and eight others. Quarto in two columns, Bill and Answer.—All about religion and discipline. (8 leaves.)

1585, Nov. 4th, Lambeth. Jo. Cantuar. (Whitgift, Archbishop of Canterbury) to the Earl of Hertford.—Contains a good many Latin quotations from St. Ambrose. It is to reconcile Hertford with the writer and some others. (1 p. and 4 lines.)

1585, Jan. 23rd, Greenwich. "Elizabeth" to the Archbishop of Canterbury. To levy money to help to find lances (1,000 promised) to assist the Low Countries against Spain.

1585, April 12th, Lanfey. Robert (Earl of) Essex to the Countess of Leicester.—An apology for a supposed offence.

Mr. Knell, chaplain, to Walter Earl of Essex, his letter to Sir H. Sydney, of the manner of the Earl's sickness and the causes of suspicion of poison. (This is a later indorsement.) . . . . . The copie of the letter written touching his opinion of the cause of the death of the late Right Honble the Earl of Essex. Begins As concerning the cause of the death of the said Earl of Essex; being commanded by the R^t Honble Sir Henry Sidney, Kt., Lord Deputy of France, for diverse reports to put in writing what I know." (3 pp.) Then follow, in Latin, particulars of lands and tenements of Walter Marshal in Ireland between the heirs of the said Walter and Ancelin. 1 Hen. III. 3rd May 1217. (6 pp.)

1584, Feb. 15th, Holyrood House. Copy of letter by James to Queen Mary, in French.—On her complaints of his Ambassador, which he thinks may be placed under these heads:—1. That he has not treated jointly on James' affairs with hers. 2. That he has not worked for her liberty. 3. That he denied that the Association passed.—The first is an impossible thing. Secondly, he appeals to her whether he must not first get himself steady. Thirdly, he admits it. But he will always acknowledge her for Queen Mother during her life. (1 p.)

1586, Dec. 4, Holyrood House. Holograph letter, signed at the end "James R.," to the Earl of Leicester.—Is glad that Leicester was out of England when his mother was condemned.—Cannot deny that her cause was to be hated by all good christians and lovers of this isle, but affirms that the proceeding was slanderous to all princes in Europe and dishonourable to Elizabeth.—Asks him to cause the rest of the trajedie to be unperfected until the arrival of his Ambassador which will be in as few days as possible.—If his offers be not found reasonable, then Elizabeth may do as she pleases. (3 pp.)

1571, Jan. 16. The whole discourse of the Duke of Norfolk's arraignment. Begins: First the oyer was made as followeth, &c., &c. Names of the judges: Then was Robert Catlye Chief Justice of England, &c. Ends, was buried in the chappel of the Tower by Mr. Deane of Paules. (5 folio leaves closely written.) Then follows the examination of Mary Queen of Scots, living at the castle of Fotheringay, by the Lords of Her Majesty's Honourable Privy Council and other Commissioners appointed for that purpose, for the hearing of the same, 1586. Begins: Upon Wednesday the 12th of October 1586 the Lords Commission for the hearing of the Scotch Queen came. Ends: The blood and clothes with the blocks and whatsoever was bloody were burned in the fire made in the chimney in the hall hard by the Scaffold. (15 pp.) The letters between Mary and Babington are introduced.

1588, July 25th. Council letter signed by Hatton, Canc., Burghley, and five others to the Archbishop of Canterbury.—To order parsons to get people to pray against the Spaniards.

1589, Nov. 12th, Edinburgh. R. Naunton to D. Copcoat, Master of Corpus Christi College, Cambridge. (Religious chiefly.)

1589, Sept. 21st, Oatlands. Council letter, signed by Hatton Canc., Burghley, C. Howard, Huntingdon, and others, to the Archbishop of Canterbury.—For money for the levies to aid the French King.

1593, March 13, Greenwich. Council letter to the same and signed by the same.—The Queen has allowed, on the request of Lady Anne Catesby that her husband, Sir William Catesby may go to the Bath:—let him go:—he is to return fifteen days after warning.

1590. March 18, the Fleet. Thomas Cartwright to Mr. D. Bancroft, one of Her Majesty's Commissioners.—Complains that the time is bad for study and the place worse, and he wants books. 1½ pp. close writing.)

1590, March, Ely. Copy of my letter to Mr. Cartwright.

1592, Sept. 24th. Court at Oxford. W. Burghley to the Archbishop of Canterbury.—About recusants: he mentions one Ruckwood in Suffolk. (Burghley in a P.S. gives a list of eight, at Banbury.)

1590, Sept. 7th, Heidelburg. Fr. Junius to "Reverende præsul." Latin. (½ p. folio.)

1592, 6 kal. Jul. Lipsius to Abr. Ortelius. Latin. (1 p.)

1592, Dec. 23. John (Bishop of) London to the Lords of Her Majesty's Privy Council.—About the Bishop of London for the time being having the allowing of preachers to come to Paul's Cross. (1 p.)

1592, Dec. 26. Council Letter to the Archbishop of Canterbury.—Refers to the Bishop of London's letter complaining of the disobedience of those who are summoned to preach, and telling him to have care of it, and, if necessary, apply to them.

Letter by John Knox to Queen Elizabeth. Begins: As your graces displeasure against me unjustly conceived. (Written on half the page; and on the opposite column are remarks by or for the Queen.) (4 pp.)

1596, Jan. 12th, Littlecote. J. Popham to Sir J. Martin and others.—Against abuses of corne-masters, maltsters, ingrossers of corn and toplers. (1½ pp.)

1595 or 96. Considerations to move His Majesty of Scotland to give ears to the offers of those princes who can and will help him. 1. That His Majesty considereth that his honour requireth no less than to show himself grateful to His Holiness, whom the writer assureth to have meant and intended nothing else but His Majesty's advancement and repose from the tyranny of the ministers and the Queen of England, &c. The last consideration (24th) is, That His Majesty get what he can from Spain. (3 pp. folio.)

1600, April 9, My lodging near the Savoy. Safe conduct for the Earl of Gowry, who had come from foreign parts, and his going home. Signed by T. Buchurst and Ro. Cecyll.

Certain hellish verses devised by the Atheist and traitor Rawley, as yet is said (nearly 60 lines). Begin, "When first this circle round this building fair,
   Some God took out of this confused masse—
What God, I do not know nor greatly care—
   Then every one his own director was."

1605, last of June, Whitehall. Council letter to the Earl of Hertford.—About Musters.

1608, Sept. 19, Hampton Court. Copy of a council letter to the Archbishop of Canterbury (about Musters), and a letter by R. Cant. to the Bishop of London, enclosing it.

1608. Sept. 4. R. Cant. to (the Bishop of London). About supplies to the Queen.

Sir A. Malet, Bart.

15-. Sir Thomas Wharton to the Earl of Hertford. Account of his doings by way of exploits in Scotland, from the 22nd of Oct. to the 8th of Nov., dated from Carlisle. (8 pp.)

From the same to the same.—On the same subject. (Nearly 4 pp.)

1600. Council letter to the Earl of Hertford.—About composition for his lands. His title was suspected to be defective.

n. d. A. S. (Arabella Stuart) to her good Cousin.—Sends thanks to the Queen and commiserates her own case. (1 p.) It looks like a copy.

Original petition to the King by Arabella Seymaure. She asks for her liberty.—Consider what a miserable state I had been if I had taken any other course than I did; for my own conscience witnesses before God that I was then the wife of him that now I am; I could never have matched with any other man, but to have lived all the days of my life as a harlot, which your Majesty would have abhored in any, especially in one who hath the honour (how otherwise unfortunate soever) to have any drop of your Majesty's blood in them.

n. d. Arabella Seymour to ———. To ask the Earl of Northampton to interfere with the King for her relief. (1 p.)

1605, May 3, Brussels. The Earl of Hertford to the King. — Account of the grand reception he met on his passage to the Archduke on His Majesty's service. (1 p.)

1611, Jan. 25th, Lambeth. G. Cant. to the King.—About Sir John Yorke, and Gerard the Jesuit. (2 pp.)

1554. Considerations why lands of Abbeys and other religious houses taken by King Henry VIII. and aliened to divers may be held by dispensation. (1½ pp. Latin.) (The original of this is in the King's Paper Office at Whitehall, April 16th, 1616. G. Cant.)

1615, Feb. 17, Paris. De Mayerne to the King. (French.) Concerning his conversation with De Thou about Mary Queen of Scots. De Thou will write as well of the Queen as times permit. De Thou wants the King to order Sir N. (R.?) Cotton to continue his memoirs to the end of Queen Elizabeth, so that he (De Thou) may benefit in his history. (1¾ pp. large.)

1615, last of Nov. Sir Ed. Coke (at Serjeant's Inn), to the King.—About Sir Thomas Mounson's business at the Guildhall. (2 pp.)

1615. Another letter from the same.—Similar business.

1618, Feb. 20. Henry Yelverton to the King.—A curious letter about the examination of Sara Swarton, who was threatened with the lash, but confessed, having asked it might be *sub sigillo*; but she confessed the Lady Ross to be the only naile that has thus scratched the Lady Exeter.

Copy of the Lords' advice to the King how to suppress the growth of recusants. (3½ pp. folio.)

Interrogatories and answers of the Earl of Bristol. Twenty interrogatories.—(7 leaves.)

1624, Sept. 18. Copy of Cardinal Richelieu's letter to the King.—About concessions to Catholiques. (1 p.)

Vol. III.

1627. Æræ Dionysianæ, Prid. Kal. Dec. Pontanæ.—A short Latin letter by Ja. Armachanus (Archbishop of Armagh) to Selden, written on the back of a Scheme of Chronology since the Patriarchs.

Catalogue in Mr. Harbin's hand, of letters by several hands to John Selden, in a folio volume in the possession of Matthew Hale, Esq., of Alderley, co. Gloster (220 letters of the 17th century).

163¾, Jan. 30th, London. (Lord) Conway and Kilulta to J. Selden.—Is sorry the plague has kept him in the country.—A friendly letter. (1 p.)

1644, July, London. — Abra. Hayne to J. Selden. (Latin, 1½ pp.)

1646, Sept. 23, Queen's College, Oxford. Gerard Langbaine to the same.—The reasons you have given why, without eminent prejudice to ourselves, the General's letters could not hitherto be published, do thus far satisfy. But he objected again that the longer they are kept the more they may decoct of their virtue.—Note on the Monastery of West Sherburn, co. Hants, its endowments, and some tithes thereof belonging to Queen's College, Oxford. (2½ pp.)

Copy of the foundation charter of Sherburn (temp. Hen. I.), by Henry de Port. (1 p.)

1646, Sept. 28th and Oct. 27th. Two letters from Gerard Langbaine to J. Selden, from Queen's College, Oxford.

1646, Nov. 19th. From the same to the same. (Selden was in Whitefriars).

1652, Feb. 8th. The same to the same.

1656, Sept. 15. Gerard Langbaine to Wm. Burton. On his *Græcæ linguæ Historia*.

1648, Oct. 23, Oxford. (Dr.) Edward Reynolds, Vice-Chancellor, to J. Selden.—To get him to make interest in the Parliament that King James's benefits to the Law Professors and Lady Margaret's Lecturer might be considered.

164⅔, Postridie kal. Feb. Simonds Dewes to J. Selden. (Latin.) Speaks of his German, Latin, and English Lexicons. — Acknowledges Selden's gift of Anglo-Saxon fragments of the laws of Edgar and Canute. —Sends a gold coin of Tiberius.—L.S.

A letter in Greek from W. Jackson to J. Selden.

1619, Feb. 3, London. Draft in Selden's writing of a letter by him to Edward Herbert, Minister to the Christian King. (Latin.)

Draft of a grant by the Vice-Chancellor, Master, and Scholars of the University of Oxford, of the office of Chancellor, granted in Convocation.

1653, March 2, Whitefriars. Draft of a letter to his Excellency the Lord Whitelocke, Lord Ambassador, from the State of England, &c., to His Majesty of Sweden.—Complimentary.

Prid. idus Aprilis. The Vice-Chancellor and Scholars of Cambridge to J. Selden. (Latin.) Thank him for his gift of Oriental books.

1629, July 6th, Durham House. Thomas Coventry, C. S., to Mr. Justice Jones and Mr. Justice Whitelocke. —The King takes notice of the smallness of his revenue, yearly answered by the forfeitures of Popish recusants. —They are to inform themselves of the estates of all able convicted recusants, and take notes of the manors, &c. (1 p.)

(1625, April 17th.) Extrait des Actes du Synode provincial de l'isle de France, Picardie, Champagne, et Beausse tenu a Charenton le 17 April 1625, et autres jours. Signed by Durat, Moderateur, &c. (A protest by the reformed churches against disturbers of the peace).

1626. Copy of Reponse du Conseil du Roy sur les plaintes et demandes de ceux de la religion. (9 pp. in 2 columns.)

1628, Nov. 23. (Indorsed the 24th.) Bref du Pape Urban VIII. sur la prise de la Rochelle. (1½ p.)

1629, March 12th. Copy of a letter from the General Assembly at Nismes, written to the King of Great Britain. (2½ pp.)

1629, March 12th, Nismes. Copy of a letter by Henry de Rohan to the King of Great Britain.—About the loss of Rochelle, &c.

Copy of Apology of M. le Duc de Rohan, on the late troubles of France by reason of religion. (11 pp. in French.)

165½, Feb. A brief information of the present condition of the religion in France, and of the way to provide for their redressment in the present juncture. (English, 3 pp.)

1634, Jan. 23. Francis Windebank, at Westminster, to (A. Hopton).—A letter of advice to be cautious not to bind the King to inconvenience.

1634, Jan. 24th. "Charles R." and Francis Windebank to Arthur Hopton. — About a commission to Spain.

1643, Oct. 23. "Charles R." and Nicholas to the University of Oxford.—The Earl of Pembroke and Montgomery being in rebellion, the King tells them to choose another Chancellor.—They choose the Earl of Hertford. —Signed, John French, Register.

1634, Oct. 16, Westminster. Francis Windebank to Arthur Hopton. Nearly all in cypher, not decyphered. (9 pp.)

Another letter, the same to the same, of 8 pp.

Articles by which may be settled the arming of a fleet of 20 ships by His Majesty, with the assistance of the King of Spain. (Indorsed as An agreement between the two kings and sent to Davis.) (5 pp.)

Exceptions (in Spanish) taken by the Resident to the articles, and sent in Spanish. (Indorsed as penned by His Majesty's order and sent by Davis.) The first complaint is that he is not styled Catholic Majesty. (3 pp.)

Five pages in cypher.

1634, Oct. 16th st. vet. Francis Windebank to (Arthur Hopton in Spain.) (7 pp.)

1634, Oct. 17th. st. vet. From the same to the same. (1 p.)

1634, Oct. 17th st. vet. Ditto. Nearly all in cypher. (2 pp.)

Articles for maritime alliance (in Spanish). (4½ pp.)

Copy of the English articles above. *Indorsed*, Copy of articles given by me, 21 March, 1635, s. n. to Conde Olivares.

Proposals from the Honourable Council of State for their better carrying on their affairs in Spain and the coasts thereof, for the advance of the trade of the nation, and the great hindrance to all others. There are eight items. (2½ pp.)

To the Council of State.—Remonstrance of the London merchants trading to the Canaries. (1½ pp.)

Copy of a letter to the King of Spain (in English), against injuries to merchants trading to Malaga. (1 p.)

A Citation for the Universities for a Visitation. (It is so headed.) *Indorsed*, The Cardinal's Citation at Cambridge. Dr. Pearne being Vice-Chancellor. (Latin, 1 p.)

1485, 3 kal. Dec. Copy of Pope Eugenius's Bull of Exemption for King's College, Cambridge. (2 pp.)

That the Archbishop of Canterbury ought to visit both the Universities metropolitically. (7 pp.) Written in a neat hand, and endorsed by the same hand, " Concerning my visitation of the two Universities, " Oxford and Cambridge."

The public disorders as touching Church causes in Emmanuel College, Cambridge, in 1603.

Concerning disorders in the University. *Indorsed*, Received 23rd Sept. 1636. Certain disorders in Cambridge, to be considered in my Visitation. (3 pp.)

Reasons sent by the Vice-Chancellor and heads of the University of Cambridge why Cambridge is exempt from Metropolitical Visitation. (3½ pp.)

1635, last of December. Copy of my letter to Dr. Smyth, Vice-Chancellor of Cambridge, in answer to the reasons.

1635, Dec. 19th. To the Archbishop.—Letter signed by Dr. Smyth, Vice-Chancellor, and Samuel Ward, S. Collins, Thos. Parke, Thos. Bainbrigg, Thos. Comber, B. Lang, Ralph Brownrigge, Thos. Bachcroft, W. Sandcroft, Jo. Cosen, Richard Lowe, Thos. Eden. (Sending the reasons as above.)

1635, Dec. 20th. Henry Smyth, pro Canc. to the Archbishop ; to accompany the other.

Vol. IV.

16⅓, May ⅓⅓, Paris. A letter to Edward Hide, at the Middle Temple.—Apology for leaving London in a hurry ; the writer had a sick mind.

1671, Feb. 2nd. *Indorsed by Bulstrode Whitelocke*, My letter to Lord Ashley.—About his intention of writing a history of England.

1644, March. John Ridley to B. Whitelocke.—On church government. (3 pp.)

1652, March 1st. B. Gerbier to the Lord General and the Lord Whitelock.—Sends a paper of his general confession to lay up with other papers in a book.

A summary relation of Sir B. Gerbier's proceedings since this Parliament assembly and his final ends thereby. *Begins,*—

1. In 1642, he discovered to Parliament how Lord Cottington and others had betrayed the nation ; who were the Pope's pensioners, and other foreign princes. (5 pp., signed 1 March 1652.)

1653, Jan. 7th, Whitehall. Sir Ch. Wolseley to Lord Embassador Whitelock in Sweden.—Tells him how the English Government is now conducted, and speaks of Cromwell and how he is liked.

1654, March 28th, London. Sir Jo. Holland to Lord Ambassador Whitelocke.—Gives an account of his interview with Oliver, who thinks well of Whitelocke. (1½ pp.)

1656, April 15, Cassel. John Davy to Lord Commissioner Whitelocke at London.—Understands from Mr. Hartlib that the State doth intend to employ Whitelocke in an universal embassy towards all Protestants in Germany. (He discourses thereon). (2 pp.)

1656, July ⅓⅓, Chanlny. W. Swyft to Lord (Whitelocke.)—Foreign news.

1636, May 13th, Canterbury. W. Somner to ——, About proof of prerogative Wills at Canterbury. (1 p.)

1656, Nov. 19, London. W. Somner to W. Burton, at Kingston-upon-Thames.—Sends a pamphlet for perusal, written 15 years ago. It might admit of enlargement by reason of a treatise by Malbranuq, who, writing to De Morinis, pitches on Sandgate for the situation of the port.

1639, March 24th, 14th year. " Charles R." to Sir John Bancks, Attorney-General, and Sir Edward Littleton, Solicitor-General.—To prepare a grant of 40,000l.

5.

a year to the Queen for 60 years, if she so long live, to be charged on certain customs.

" Charles R." Instructions to the Earl of Northumberland, Lord High Admiral, and General of such forces as shall be raised in all places on this side of the Trent, or in our dominions of Wales. 5 points. No seal or countersign. (½ p.)

1642, last of July, York. " Charles R." to Justice Sir Thomas Mallet, Judge of Assises, co. Surrey.—Tells him to go home and await a despatch. (1 p.)

1645, Aug. 25th, Huntington. Copy letter of Charles I. to Secretary Nicholas.—He has received his of the 13th, and four printed Oxford papers concerning his published letters.—States his resolve that whatever happens to him he will not give up the Church to the government of Papists, Presbyterians, or Independants, or lessen the Crown of that ecclesiastical and military power which his predecessors left him. (1 p.)

His Majesty's paper of the 2nd of October, delivered to the divines attending the Commissioners, and being the sense why he cannot absolutely consent to the proposition concerning the Church, which, with their answer and His Majesty's reply, are, although here inserted, extrajudicial and no part of the Treaty. *Begins,*—

" I conceive that Episcopal Government."—p. 2. The names of the divines.—We do fully agree without hesitation.—p. 9. His Majesty's reply to the answer of the Commissioners and Divines to his Majesty's paper of the 2nd of Oct., delivered on the 6th of Oct. 1648. (Ends on p. 17.)

A Proposition concerning the Militia, dated from Newport, Oct. 9th, answered by His Majesty. (7 pp.) *Begins,*—That the Lords and Commons in Parliament, &c., shall during the space of 20 years. . .

Other propositions and answers.

1648, Oct. 21, Newport. The King's Answer, " His " Majesty conceives that his former answer." (4 pp.)*

Copy of Warrant for execution of the King.

1633, July 6th. Receipt of money from James Moriverer by Wentworth.

1636, May 26th, Lambeth House. Warrant signed by W. Cant. for the confirmation of the digest of the statutes for the University of Oxford. (½ p.)

Approbation of the proof of the Polyglot Bible, and recommending it; signed by J. Armachanus (Archbishop of Armagh), and J. Selden. (A large space is left between these two names ; and others were to have signed.)

1637, Aug. 2nd, Romisford. Henry Ball to Sir Thomas Thynne, at his house in Cannon Row, Westminster.—Account of the proceedings at Cirencester for raising the Ship Money.

1640, Postr. nonas, Oct., St. Grog, Amsterdam. Ger. Joa. Vossius to the Archbishop of Canterbury (W. Laud), in Latin. (1 p.)

1642, April 18th, York. Lord Hertford to Dear Lamb (his wife).

Letters by Brian Duppa, Bishop of Sarum, to the Marquis of Hertford.

Dr. Thomas Smyth's papers concerning the Marquis of Hertford's conference with Oliver Cromwell.—About Cromwell's pressing Lord Hertford to come to him ;— he at last came ; Cromwell said he was weary of it ; and asked advice. Hertford told him to call back Charles II. Cromwell said No ; he (Charles) would never forgive.—They parted, but Hertford never had any prejudice.

Copy of the covenant taken by the Lords on the 15th Oct. 1643 (in Harbin's hand) from the original on vellum, in the hands of Lady Lansdown, Dec. 29th 1718.

1643, Aug. 2. Pass by Lenthall, Speaker, for Bartholomew Hall and wife and servants to go to Wimborne, co. Dorset.

1645, June 12th, 14th, 16th. Examination of Lord Savil taken before the committee of the Lords (10 pages with alterations).

Petition of Lord Savill to the House of Commons.

1645, June 26th. The information of Denzil Hollis, Esq., taken before the Committee of the Lords and Commons.

1646, Feb. 18th. John Parker to —— Burton.—About Church government.

1651, Oct. 26th., Louver, Paris. " James" (Duke of York ?) (and seal) to John Harbin, English merchant at Morlaix.—Thanks for 500l.

* The above have been printed.

1651, Oct. 28th, Louver, Paris. Edward Wolley to
Harbyn.—Complimentary on the gift. (Wolley wrote
the Duke's letter, I think.)

1646, June 24th. Printed pass by T. Fairfax for the
Earl of Dorset, Lord Chamberlain to the King and his
household.

1647, Putney. Opinion by a Committee of Officers
touching the Articles of Oxford.

1650, Jan. 14, Hagh. Copy of a letter by Walter
Strickland to the Speaker to the Lord Commissioner
Whitelocke). Mentions the States having prohibited
Defensio regia pro Carolo primo, supposed to be by Sal-
masius who has incurred their displeasure; and 500
guelders fine on the printers and publishers.

Imperfect draft of a project of Oliver Cromwell for
creating a new college at Oxford. (4 pp.)

A paper on the scarcity of corn and bullion.

Easy way to raise money for the use of the Commonwealth of England.

1652, July 14th. Certified copy of warrant by the
Council of State to Christopher Mayo to raise 3,000
foot in Ireland, out of such natives as have been in
active arms against the Parliament, and transmit them
for service of the King of Spain to Bilboa, and St.
Sebastian and other parts in Spain equally distant from
England.

Jo. Fitzjames, Jo. Griffith, his actions with regard to
Dunkirk; the anger of the government; and that Whitelocke (and two others named), disavowed his having any
instructions but to demand prisoners.—Says he did his
best for the State. (2 pp.)

4¼ pp. more, unsigned, relating to the same subject.

1652, March 12th, Dunkirk. Dastrades to ——
About Dunkirk. (1 pp.)

The benefits to be made of the place. What may be
in mine added to the place. (2¼ pp.)

1657, Private articles between the King of France,
and Lord Oliver, Protector of England. Dated from
Paris, 10th May n.s. 1657.—26 articles. (8¼ pp.)

1657, April 20th. The true relation of the destroying
the Spanish ships at the cite of Teneriffe, the 20th of
April 1657, from the first intelligence we had of them as
we lay before Cales. (7 pp.)

165—, James Howell to the Council of State. Proposes
a new Treatise on the Sovereignty of the Seas, *apropos* of
the late clash with Holland;—if he is employed he will
not only give Selden's reasons and authorities but
others:—it should be published in French as well as in
English.

A Memorial on the state of the Roman Empire.—
England is to protect Protestant interests and to
cultivate good understanding between and with Continental Protestant States. (3 pp. neat and close.)

A deduction of things relating to the Sound in the
years 1658 and 1659, with some reflections thereupon by
Sir Philip Medows. (19 pp. 4to.) He says that after the
peace concluded at Roschild in Feb. 1657, he was remanded out of Denmark by order from England, and
sent to the King of Sweden.

The Petition of the French church in Somerset
Chapel. To the supreme authority of this nation the
Parliament of the Commonwealth of England.—They
first worshipped at Durham House, and then by favour
of the Council of State, and permission of the Committee for regulating the late King's houses, in the
Chapel where formerly the Capucins had their exercises
by Somerset House. They pray that it may be given
to them absolutely. The petition is subscribed in the
name of the whole congregation by Jespaigne, Minister
of the Gospel, Oardoing, Oheret, P. de Chair, Hilaire,
Cresse, John le bon, Pierre Haller, Pierre Lanwell,
Jehan Lallamayn.

1651, March 23, R. Boyle to John Mallet, Esq., at
Poynington, Somersetshire. (2 pp.)

1651, Jan. 22, Youghall. The same to the same.—
The Torys have of late been very destructively active,
particularly to the prejudice of divers of my tenants.
(2 pp.)

1658, April 17, Oxford. The same to the same.
(2 pp. of note paper.)

1653, Feb. 4, Whitehall (received 2nd of March).
Jo. Thurloe to —— Whitelocke in London. (2¼ pp. partly
in cypher.)

1653, Feb. 10 (received 2nd of March). The same to
the same. (1¼ pp.)

1653, Feb. 16 (received 15th of March). (2½ pp.)

1653, Feb. 24 (received 23rd of March). (2½ pp.)

1653, Aug. 15. Whereas Lord Commissioner Whitelocke is desired by the Council of State to deliver to
them a MS. of the Greek Septuagint commonly called
Tecless Septuagint, containing 4 volumes, they promise

to keep it safe and return it.—Signed by Wm. Fuller,
Brune Ryves, Sa. Baker, Brian Walton, and Rich.
Drake.

16—, Elsinore, Nov. 13. Algernon Sydney to my Lord
[Whitlocke]. Since his (Sydney's) of the 25th of Sept.
he has received no letter from England except from
persons so far away from news that they did not know
of the liberty granted us by the Parliament and Council
to return home.—Foreign politics.—P.S. Hears that
Monk is marching into England; hopes Whitlocke has
ordered matters so as to keep the army united. (1 p.)

A fragment (of 1½ pages) partly in cypher apparently
about the landing of Charles II.

VOL. V.

1654, Sept. 25, Court at Aix. Instructions signed by
" Charles R." for Henry, Earl of Rochester, who was on
a mission to the elector of Brandenburgh, signed C.R.
at the end. (2½ pp.)

1652, Dec. 25, Paris.—Present instructions for the
Earl of Rochester, my ambassador in Germany.—
" Charles R." at the head and C. R. at the end. (Holo-
graph, 1 p.) To raise men.

1653, Nov. 13, Chantilly.—Holograph letter by King
Charles to the Earl of Rochester.—Acknowledges
Rochester's letter of the 30th, which has revived him.
(1 p.)

16—, July 30, Spa.—Copy of a letter by the same to
the same.—As he is setting his family in order, tells him
to deliver to the bearer Fox 6,000 gilders out of his
(Charles's) German money.

Latin address by Henry, Lord Wilmot, Earl of
Rochester, to the Emperor to move him to incite the
Dutch, and to persuade the Pope to stir up the English,
Scotch, and Irish Romanists, in King Charles's favour.
(66 pp.)

Brian Walton to the Council of State.—A Polyglot
can be printed at about one-fifth of the cost of the Paris
Bible.—As the foreign former editions have been
printed at the public cost, he asks an advance from the
Treasury.

1660, July 14. Certificate of respectability and loyalty
of Theophilus Sacheverell by Gr. Peachey, John Dymocke, and five others.

1662, Oct. 14, Cockpitt. The Duke of Albemarle to
the Duchess of Somerset.—As Lord Lieutenant he is to
inform himself of the value of peers' estates ;—asks for
a return by her.

n.d. Gilbert Burnet to Henry Coventry.—Sends a
petition enclosed, and asks Coventry to present it to the
King and show it to H.R.H.

1664, March 15, Navy Office. S. Pepys to Mr.
Coventry.

1664, Jan. 8, Navy Office. The same to the same.
Both letters are on naval and official affairs.

1664, Nov. 25, Whitehall. Thomas Clifford to the
Hon. Mr. Coventry.—Notice of the King's speech and
proceedings in the House of Commons on that day, and
expressing regard for the safety of the person of H.R.H.
in the war. (7 pp.)

1669, Aug. 11, st. n., Brussels. Sir W. Temple to
——. Sends news enclosed (which is not there). It
is thought the French will try to take Cambray, because
Cambray, being within their quarters, it is dangerous,
and last week 500 of their horse went 12 leagues into
France, and plundered a little town called Rippemonde,
&c.—Just alludes to an encounter with the Dutch in the
Thames. (2 pp.)

16—, Aug. 19, Plymouth. (The Earl of) Bathe to
Secretary Coventry.—Says that the King has given the
living of Calstocke in the Duchy of Cornwall to Mr.
Trelawny, son of Sir Jonathan Trelawny.

n. d. Lisburn to the King.—Offering his services.—
Says he has served in the Duke of Monmouth's regiment
abroad.

16—. John (Bishop of Galloway) to the Earl of
Lauderdale.—The Archbishop of Glasgow is dead : suggests himself for the see.

1667, March 5, Broomhill. The same to the same.—In
favour of Lord Viscount Kenmore, who had suffered for
the King.

1665, June 29, Brechin. Da. Brechinen (Bishop of
Brechin) to the Earl of Lauderdale, Secretary for the
kingdom of Scotland.

1667, July 18, Edinburgh. The same to the same.

1665, March 3,   do.   do.   do.

1665, Jan. 28,   do.   do.   do.

1661, May 9 and Dec. 16.   do.   do.

1661, Dec. 13. Do. About his intended resignation.

1661, Nov. 13. Do. On the same subject, he speaks as
if he had left.

16—, R. Leighton (Bishop of Dunblane) to the Earl of Lauderdale.

Reasons for the town of Edinburgh for reducing and declaring void and null the pretended election of Sir Andrew Ramsay to be Provost.

Copy of the Protestation by Robert Eliot, deacon of the Wrights, that they did not acknowledge Sir Andrew Ramsay to be Provost.

1679, March 24, Justice Court of Edinburgh. Certificate regarding the proceedings against Wm. Veatch *alias* Johnson a prisoner in the Tolboth; he is to be proceeded against according to law. (Signed by Ro. Martin.)

1666, April 10 and March 31, Antwerp.

1666, April 13, s. n. Hague.

1666, April $\frac{13}{23}$ s. n. Antwerp and other places to $\frac{May\ 30,}{June\ 9,}$ at Antwerp. Upwards of 30 pp. of copies of news letters, and letters of advice from foreign parts between the above dates about the Dutch fleet, &c.

1664, April 24. Considerations in order to a Dutch war (so indorsed).

1. Paper of 4½ pp. by Coventry to Lord ———. About the money necessary for a Dutch war.

2. 2½ pp. in columns. Considerations in relation to the Dutch.

Copy delivered to His Royal Highness, April 24th 1664, *begins*, Whether any directions shall be given to Sir J. Lawson for his behaviour towards the Dutch fleet in the Streight.

1664, May 5th. Copy of a memorial for H.R.H. About war with Algiers. (½ p.)

1664, June 25th. The affairs of Tangier having necessitated Sir John Lawson to quit his station before Argiers without making peace, &c. :—with a note by Sir W. Coventry and the original draft for this paper by Sir W. Coventry. (*Indorsed*, Considerations about the war with Argiers, with some regard to the war likely to be with the Dutch.)

Original letters by Sir Wm. Coventry to Lord Falmouth. (After Lord Falmouth's death these letters were returned by Mr. Bridgeman.)

1665, April 1st. *Endorsed*, Justifying myself about the liberty of the seamen in the matter of prizes :—Concerning a conference with the Lord Chancellor and Lord Arlington, and shows I was against the Dutch war. (3 pp.)

1665, April 1st, Royal Charles.—Desiring particular instructions from the King or his Royal Highness. (3½ pp.)

Reasons against sending commanders to sea who have not used the sea. (5 pp.)

A paper about the Dutch wars showed once to Lord Falmouth and to no one else. (6 pp.)

1665, May 5th. Copy of a letter to Lord Arlington, but not entered in my book. Against taking off embargo and liberty of privateers, for hiring or building new ships,—for pressing the Dutch in every shape to bring them to a battle. (2¼ pp.)

1665, May 19th, Royal Charles.—About rectifying a list of ships, justifying myself in the matter of the two captains, &c.

1665, Oct. 3rd, Oxford. Sir William Coventry to Wm. Penn.—About getting ready more ships to make a show.

Copy of a paper left with the Duke of Albemarle when His Royal Highness went to sea and left the care of the navy to him. (7 pp.)

1666, Oct. $\frac{4}{14}$. Copy of a letter by the King, countersigned by Arlington, to (the States) acknowledging their letter of the 16th ult. by a trumpet, who has since delivered the body of Sir W. Berkbley into the hands of his friends.—Thanks them.—Replies to their proposals for peace. (13 pp.)

List of ships at the Nore on the 12th of May 1666, with additions by Coventry. (1 p.)

1666, May 21st. List of His Majesty's fleet in their several squadrons and divisions.—Red, white, and blue, with names of the Admirals (a large sheet).

1666, May 21st, Royal Charles. The Duke of Albemarle to Sir W. Coventry.—Expresses great assurance of Sir W. Penn's care and diligence.

1666, May 21st, Royal Charles. Prince Rupert and the Duke of Albemarle to His Royal Highness—Victuals and money desired.—Sir J. Norris to be sent down and Sir W. Penn to hasten ships in the river.

1666, May 26th. The Duke of Albemarle to Sir W. Coventry.—Desiring directions whether he should fight with less than 70 sail.

1666, May 27th. The same to the same.—Declaring his unwillingness to retreat from the Dutch though he has but little force, 54 ships.

1666, May 28th. Copy of a letter by Sir W. Coventry to the Duke of Albemarle.—Stopping of the post. Additional ships for Prince Rupert to meet him at Torbay.

1666, May 28th. Copy of the Duke of York's letter to the Duke of Albemarle (and Coventry's draft of it). Leaving it to Albemarle to fight or not.

1666, May 29th. List of ships that went with Prince Rupert and are in the Downs. (1 p.)

1666, May 29th (indorsed May 30th). Division of His Majesty's ships under the Duke of Albemarle. (1 p.)

1666, May 30th. The Duke of Albemarle to Sir W. Coventry.—Sends the enclosed letter from one of our scouts. (The following is, I suppose, the enclosure.)

1666, May 30th. Tho. Ewen, H.M. Ship, Kent. News of Flemish fleet.

1666, May 30th. The Duke of Albemarle to His Royal Highness.—Says he will go next morning to the Swin between the gun fleet and the Middle ground, and intimates they judge fit to remain there till they have 70 ships.

1666, May 30th, Royal Charles in the Downs. The Duke of Albemarle to Sir W. Coventry.—About costs of arms and stores.

1666, May 31st. Sir W. Coventry to the Duke of Albemarle.—His Royal Highness approves anchoring in the Swin.

1666, May 31st. Copy of a letter by H.B.H. to the Duke of Albemarle.—News of the Dutch fleet, and commanding the recall of Prince Rupert.

1666, May 31st. Sir W. Coventry to the Duke of Albemarle.—Gives notice that the Dutch fleet were but 72 sail, and hints at Prince Rupert's recall.

1666, June 5th, Harwich about 8 at night. Silas Taylor to Sir W. Coventry. (*Indorsed*, Hast, hast, post hast.) Defeat of the Dutch yesterday. Narrative of the engagement. (2 pp. large.)

Plan of the fleets as they were drawn up to fight. (2 pp.)

Draft in Sir W. Coventry's hand of relation of the battle. (10½ pp.)

List of officers changed since the fight in June 1666. (1½ pp.)

List of ships. (1 p.)

1666, June 28th, Royal Charles at the Buoy in the Nore. Prince Rupert and the Duke of Albemarle to (Sir W. Coventry).—Sir W. Penn's case to be represented to His Majesty.

1666, July 9th. The same to His Royal Highness.—That Sir Robert Holmes and Sir Jermy Smith with men from the fleet be sent up to bring down ships ;—and asks Sir W. Penn's care to assist.

1666, July 27th. Prince Rupert to His Royal Highness (signature R.).—Refers to the bearer Sir Thomas Clifford for the relation of what passed ;—hopes he will be satisfied with their endeavour; admits some errors not of courage but of conduct.

1666, July 25th. Narrative of the engagement of the fleets. (3 pp.)

1666, July 28th. 3 leagues off Orford. (Copy.) Came last night from our fleet which has beaten the Hollanders into these parts.—Our fleet intend to lye 12 leagues off the Texel.—Encloses account of the wants of the fleet. (It is inclosed and is 1 p.)

Copy of the Duke of Albemarle's narrative of the miscarriages of the war particularly concerning the division of the fleet in 1666. Sent to the House of Commons. (9 pp.)

Copy of Prince Rupert's narrative of the same. (5 pp.)

Nearly 8 pp. of Coventry's notes for answers to Prince Rupert and the Duke of Albemarle's narratives.

VOL. VI.

1666, July 7th. The Emperor Leopold to James, Duke of York.—Recommends his envoy Baron d'Isola. (Latin, signed and sealed.)

1660, May 23rd, Breda. Edward Hyde to the Earl of Winchilsea.—Complimentary. (1 p.)

1667, May 7th. Extract from a letter by Lord St. Albans (in France) to ———. Partly in cypher decyphered.—The French Court are anxious of the arrival of our Ambassador at Breda, and promise to do all they can to get the island for England; if not, a reasonable recompense. (1½ pp.)

May 17th, Clarendon House. Clarendon to Lord Ambassador Coventry at Breda. Mostly in cypher

Sir A. Malet, Bart.

Sir A. Malet, Bart.

deciphered.—Directions for his replies to certain matters, principally about Pouleson (which the Dutch were resolved not to give up).

1667, May 27th, Clarendon House. The same to My Lords.—On the same matters. (Nearly all cypher decyphered.)

1667, May 31st. The same to My Lord. (Cypher decyphered.) (2 pp.)

1667, June 7th. The same to the same. (Cypher decyphered.) (3½ pp.)

1667, June 14th. The same to My Lords. (Cypher decyphered.) (3½ pp.)

1667, June 21st. The same to My Lord. (1½ pp.)

1667, July 1st.* The same to the same. (Cypher decyphered.) (1 p.)

1667, Aug. 2nd. The same to My Lords. (Cypher decyphered.) (3½ pp.)

1668, March 24th. List of His Majesty's ships abroad and fitting out to sea.

(166$\frac{7}{8}$), Feb. 18th, Aleppo. Robert Frampton to your Excellency (the Earl of Winchelsea, Ambassador Extraordinary to the Grand Signor).

1668, Aug. 19th, Aleppo. The same to the same.—Waited on Lord Maidstono at Hyland, who in three days sets out for Damascus and is going to Jerusalem.

Jan. 23rd, Oates. J. Locke to Ed. Clarke, Esq.—Thanks the College for their kind remembrance of him, &c. (1 p. note paper.)

1669, Jan. 24th. J. B. to his sister Mrs. Margaret Beavis at the Earl of Northumberland's at Blois. (2½ pp.)

166$\frac{8}{9}$, Feb. 22. (Copy.) "C. R." Instructions for Ralph Montagu, Esq., master of the horse to the Queen, going to France as ordinary ambassador.—There are 13 heads. (9 pp.)

n. d. Copy of warrant to seize and imprison R. Montagu, because he came to England without license, and while in France held secret correspondence with the Pope's nuncio.

Copy of reasons to induce the Duchess of York to embrace the Roman Catholic religion, as it was written by her own hand. *Begins*, Being from youth brought up in the Protestant religion. (3 pp.)

Notes and extracts concerning the Poor by Sir W. Coventry (4 pp.); and 7 pp. of a clerk's writing on the same subject, dated 1670, Dec. 3rd.

Remembrances concerning the funeral of Sir J. Stowell, K.B. (They went from Hamme, co. Somerset to Cotherston in the same county, on horse; there is a list of the attendants.)

1672, Oct. 1st, Paris. The Earl of Sunderland to Secretary Coventry.—It is more difficult than he thought to get the exemption which the King designs for M. de la Zuleistein. (2 pp.)

1672, Oct. 15th, Edinburgh. Sir George Mackenzie to the Duke of Lauderdale (His Majesty's Commissioner). It contains much about Sir Andrew Ramsay's election, and the town not wishing to justle with him. (2 pp.)

Two letters by Geo. Mackenzie, Ja. Foulis and Murray to the Duke of Lauderdale.—About town business.

About 25 letters to Lauderdale the King's Commissioner in Scotland, wholly relating to Scotch affairs. Most of them appear to be written by James Foulis, some by George Mackenzie, some by both, and Murray. One is about Convention; another refers seemingly to the murder of the Archbishop of St. Andrews, and says that all the prisoners will be put to the torture.—In another are mentioned interviews with the King, the Duke of York, Monmouth and Secretary Williamson.

In another letter dated 28th of May 1678,—The King has so engaged himself with us now that we may expect any thing of him.—One mentions the condemnation of Rebels and forfeiture of estates, and in another he (Mackenzie who was Lord Advocate) says, I have this day served the King heir to the Duke of Lenox.

George Mackenzie to the Duke of Lenox.—The inquest brought in a verdict after a whole night; they found all 29 guilty of high treason.—The point debated was, whether when one witness saw a rebel in one place and another in another place their depositions could be joined, since the witnesses were not *contestes*. He was forced to argue;—never had a harder task. The *preparation* is of great use to the Crown.

George Mackenzie to the Duke.—The Chancellor and I waited all this day at Leith examining witnesses, and certainly Hackston of Rathalrick was he who struck the postilion and turned the coach; but is not taken. One Stick is taken who is said to have given the first stroak. Camron's brother is taken who certainly wounded the town-major and probably was at this murder. A merchant woman who gave them brandy and ale at the house where the murder was committed, is in prison. It seems that Irish dernie, who is now killed, did command the party. He was killed by Achmutie who was the Duchesses page. Many who are suspect are taken, but no clear probation against them; but we will put them all to the torture. Remember the King that King Alexander the 2nd killed 4,000 for the death of one Bishop of Caithness, and gelded them: and what law had he for that?

1678, last of April. George Mackenzie to the Duke of Lauderdale.—Says he came to London on Monday and kissed hands;—talked with the King and the Duke of Monmouth. (3 pp.)

1678, May 7, 23, and 25. Letters from the same to the same.

16$\frac{78}{79}$, Feb. 10. The same to the same.

16$\frac{78}{79}$, Feb. 19. The same to the same.—I have forfeited yesterday six of the most considerable of the rebels Machiesmore, Crecklie, Kellock, Earlstown the elder, and the younger Culvernam, with sound of trumpet and tearing of their arms.

1679, April 8. The same to the same.—Asks him to tell the King at the request of a meeting that the 6th Act of the third Parliament of James V. is the best security against field meetings. (3 pp.)

Three letters with no date to His Majesty's High Commissioner (the Duke of Lauderdale) from G. Mackenzie.

n. d. From the same. Was with the Duke, who entreated me to tell you that you nor we should not mistake his admitting those people to kiss his hand, for he did it merely to get them to go about in the Convention, and to tell them that opposing the King would not do their business. This Claverhouse tells me he told them when they came to him, and he told them also that this Convention was an infallible test of their duty; it is my humble opinion that your Grace should give them fair weather and smooth things till the Convention be over, &c. (2 pp.)

Another letter of 3 pp. with no year but the date of July 6.

n. y. March 5, Edinburgh. The same to the Earl of Lauderdale.—At Lauderdale's parting from Edinburgh yesterday there was such a crowd that Mackenzie failed to take his leave, &c. (1½ pp.)

1679, Jan. 15. Lord Arlington's defence before the House of Commons. (5½ pp.)

1673, Aug. 16, Whitehall, Jo. Cooke to [Secretary Coventry].—The Lord Chancellor drinks the waters every morning.—No particular account yet of the late engagement at sea between the Prince and De Ruyter on the Monday preceeding.

Letters from Lord Arlington.—they are generally in cypher, three figures to one letter; the first is dated from the Hague in 1674, Nov. 24, s. v.

1674, Nov. 24, s. v., Hague. Lord Arlington to the King.—Gives an account of his conversation with the Prince of Orange who wished to be taken into favour. (6 pp.)

1674, Nov. 27. Since writing the letter, the Prince came into my chamber (nearly 2 pp. of cypher partly decyphered).

Sir Thomas Higgons' speech in Parliament about the the Duke of York's marriage to the Princess of Modena. (Autograph, 2½ pp.)

1674, May 18, Paris. Thomas Higgons to———. (1½ pp.)

1674, Sept. $\frac{1}{4}$, Venice. From the same.—Chiefly about the mode of his reception in the college, which was at first thought insulting. (3 pp.)

1674, Oct. 2. Copy of a memorial in Italian, presented in the college, about some custom levied.

A second copy of the memorial.

1675, Jan. 14. Reply to the above, and another dated on the 13th of Sept. (in all 9 pp.)

1674, Nov. 16, Venice. T. Higgons to Secretary Coventry.—Suggests that a few frigates should be sent to the Mediterannean for defence against the Tripolines. (2½ pp.)

1674, Dec. 21 and 28, Venice. Two letters from the same to the same, the first is of 2 pp. and the second of 3 pp.—News.

1675, Jan. 4. Xmas Day, 1674. The same to the same. (3½ pp.)

1675, Jan. 18.	The same to the same.		(2 pp.)
1675, Jan. 25.	Do.	Do.	(1 p.)
1675, Feb. 1.	Do.	Do.	(1 p.)
1675, Feb. 8.	Do.	Do.	(3 pp.)
1675, Feb. 15.	Do.	Do.	(2½ pp.)

Sir A. Malet, Bart.

1675, April 12. The same to the same. (2½ pp.)
1675, April 19. Do. Do. (2 pp.)
1676, Oct. 16. Do. Do. (2 pp.)
1676, Oct. 30. Do. Do. At the King's solicitation Mr. Patrick was delivered from the galleys where he had been eight years. (1 p.)

1676, Dec. 4. The same to the same. (1½ pp.)

1676. Xmas Day, s. n. Lord Winchelsea arrived here with his lady and family. (1 p.)

16$\frac{76}{77}$, Jan. 15. Signor Brusoni, now historiographer of the house of Savoy, wrote the general history of Italy from 1625 to the present year, wherein are several things thought prejudicial to the interests of the house of Savoy;—he wrote this before he was in the service of Madame Royale and sold the copy to some printer at Venice. Now he wished to correct it, and print it in some other form; but the printer having bought and got license to print, Brusoni knows not how to hinder it. San Tomaso, chief minister to the Duke of Savoy and also to Madame Royale, wrote to Higgons to assist Ct. Matthioli, who was coming from Turin to Venice about it. Count Matthioli having business of his own at Milan, stays so long by the way, that before he gets to Venice, the book is printed, and on the stalls;—so it is too late for Higgons to suppress the publication. Matthioli wanted Higgons to let him seize the books by violence under cover of the English Envoy's authority.—Higgons refused. (1½ pp.)

16$\frac{76}{77}$, Jan. 22. Lord Winchelsea notwithstanding the cold, embarked this day in the English ship "William" for Zante; thence he says he will go to Patras, thence to Smyrna, and so to Constantinople. (2 pp.)
16$\frac{76}{77}$, Feb. 19. The same to the same.
16$\frac{76}{77}$, March 5 and 12. Do. Do.
1677, April 9. Do. Do.
Epitaph on Sir Hugh Wyndham. (8 lines.)

Vol. VII.

1674, March 13th. Minster Lovell.—Henry Coventry to (his brother) Sir John Coventry.—A draft letter of 3½ pp., in which he tries to persuade his brother to marry.

Copy of Dr. Burnett's deposition relating to the Duke of Lauderdale (found among the papers of Sir John Malet of St. Audrey, Co. Somerset, then M.P., and was written with his own hand).

1675, April 23rd. Gives an account of his conversation with the Duke of Lauderdale on the first Saturday in September, 1673. It was about Scotland, particularly about suspending penal laws in matters ecclesiastical. He said the people in Scotland that were at such a distance could not imagine what to make of the King's speech and declaration; the Duke said *Hinc illæ lachrymæ*, and that all had forsaken the King but he and Lord Clifford.

Copy Petition against the Duke of Lauderdale by the Commons to remove him from all employment and from the King's Council, referring to the Duke's saying that the King's edicts were equal to laws and ought to be observed. (2 pp.)

Copy by Sir John Malet of the King's answer. (1 p.)

Copy of (Lauderdale's) speech on the opening of Parliament. *Begins*, the last time I had the honour to serve the King in this place. (He told them of the King's grounds for war against the State. He wants peace; the Swedes proposed Dunkirk as a place of treaty; the enemy refused.—The King accepted Cologne proposed by the enemy.—Another reason for keeping this session is to punish field Conventicles).

1675, Aug. 30th. T. Howard, of Richmond and Carlisle, to . . . . . (concerning Lord Cavendish). Against severity to Catholics; about the talk of Lord Cavendish and another in St. James's Park about the French retreat over the Rhine.—On the 3rd page is the following note:—In obedience to the order of the House writ to T. H., asked if he owned the papers: He declined to answer.

Copy (7 pp.) of my letter to the Earl of Essex, Lord-Lieutenant of Ireland, upon the subject of his reiterated proclamation for banishment of all the Popish prelates and all regular priests too; permitting the secular priests to remain at home unmolested, viz., according to and in performance of the address made for that purpose to His Majesty by the House of Commons in 1674.—This letter shows that all the stress of the said proclamations and address fell on the few loyal remonstrant regulars, which I believe the said House of Commons could not intend, but rather would have desired His Majesty to protect such men were their case known to them. The letter is signed P. W. (*i.e.*, Peter Walsh.)

Letters from the Duke of Ormond to Secretary Coventry.

1674, Aug. 12th. Acknowledges his kindness to Sir S. Lane.—Supposes it too early to think of the meeting of the Parliament: it may be hard to saw how long it will sit. (1 p.)

1674, Nov. 11th. Speaks well of the farmers of the Irish revenue. The bearer is employed by them. (1 p.)

1676, April 7th. Thanks for Coventry's interfering with the King for Ormonde's son, John, for the Government held by the last Earl of Donegal. (1 p.)

1678, Nov. 5th. Concerning the ecclesiastical promotions and disposal of the primacy.—Declares the apprehension the Protestants have of the Papists, and the bad state of the forts. (3 pp.)

1677. Giving an account of the state he found Ireland in at his first arrival. (7 pp.)

167$\frac{4}{5}$, Feb. 12th. The Scotch bishops to Lauderdale, against toleration; signed by St. Andrews; Alexander, Edinburgh; Jo. Gallovidian; Ro. Brechinen.

n. d. R. B. (Rd. Baxter), to the Earl of Lauderdale; docketed (a canting letter to the Lord Lieutenant). (1¾ p.)

1672, Aug. 14th, Whitehall. "Charles R" and seal (countersigned by Henry Coventry) to John Shelley, Esq., at Thackham, Co. Sussex.—An order to give certain large coins or medals lately found in Sussex to Elias Ashmole.

1678, Nov. 30th. "Charles R" to the Sheriffs of London and Middlesex.—Was lately informed that the head and quarters of Wm. Staley, executed for high treason, which he gave leave to be privately interred, were buried with funeral pomp; and it was ordered in Council that they should be disinterred and set up in public quarters.—Mistake in the information.—Stop execution of the said order until further pleasure.

167$\frac{8}{9}$, Feb. 28th, Whitehall.—Letter of "C. R." (the signature at the foot) to the Duke of York to go beyond sea (bad spelling). At the end, "for my dearest friend "the Ducke of Yorck." (¼ p.)

1676, June 2nd. Ch. duc Dudley, &c., to the King, (French). Although born out of England considers himself a subject.—Cardinal Norfolk will assure the King of his submission. (A short letter.)

1676, Nov. 12th, Zutliew. "Jean R." (Sobieski) to the King.—Concerning the death of Mr. Christmas, H.M. Trumpeter. (French 2 pp.)

1675, Nov. 30th, Roma (Italian). Cardinal Rospigliosi to the King. Assurance of his desire to serve him, and hopes the solemnities at Christmas will be pleasing to him.

1676, April 11th. The same to the same.—Acknowledges the King's letter of the 9th of March in last year.—Speaks of his great desire to serve him.

1677, Nov. 27th. The same to the same.—Alludes to *il vicino natal santissimo.*

1678, Nov. 26th. The same to the same.—On the same subject.

1675, Dec. 11th, Rome. Cardinal Barberino to the King.—Sends good wishes for the new year.

1676, Dec. 8th. The same to the same.

1677, Nov. 27th. The same to the same.

1676, March 31st. Cardinal Altieri to the King.—Acknowledges the King's letter praising the Cardinal of Norfolk.

1677, Dec. 6th. Rome.—Flavio Duke of Bracciano to the King.—Christmas congratulations.

1688, Sept. 28th. Munich. Josephus Clemens, Elector, to the King (Latin). Announces that by his election, &c. he has obtained the Archbishopric of Cologne, and also Papal confirmation of it.

167$\frac{7}{8}$ March (Ostend). The Duke of Monmouth to the King.—Mentions his arrival at Ostend with Lord Howard's five companys, four of the Duke's, and a hundred of the guards.—The Spaniards here are miserable creatures, only 400 of them, and that is all the garrison in Ostend except what Monmouth brought.—Asks for more men. (2½ pp.)

1678, Aug. 17th. Louis (XIV.) and Arnauld to the King.—Tells him of the signature of peace between him and Spain on the 10th of August.

12th March. Princesse de Chastillon to King Charles. Asks for a passport to travel. (5 pp., 4to.)

The same to the Queen. (9 pp.)

1674, Nov. 10th. Cypher between the King and the Lord Chamberlain. Indorsed, "For His Majesty." (One large sheet, and a little sheet.)

1677, Sept. 6th. Jo. Rushworth to the Hon. Thomas Thynne, M.P., at Drayton.— Thanks for letter.— Mr. Secretary has delivered him all the papers, and excepted to nothing but some passages on the beginning of Parliament, 3rd of Nov., 1640—words spoken by Lord Digby, Faulkland, Culpeper, Hide, &c.; some reflecting upon Bishops, Judges, projects, &c. He knows the passages were spoken, but he objects to sanction the publication. So Rushworth agreed to break off before that point. The secretary is to have a copy to see whether the copy that goes through the press differs from the copy with him. All quiet at Whitehall.—Saw at Bartholomew fair the Duke of Buckingham, Madame Mazarin, and other ladies. The Duke and the Lord Treasurer are far from being friends.—Merchants on the Exchange are calling in their concerns in the Spanish dominions, fearing a sudden rupture. P.S. Muddiman is in custody for writing so confidently that the Spaniard intends war against us, and yet the merchants will not credit the contrary.

1677, Sept. 22nd. London. The same to the same. Containing town news and news from an Edinburgh news letter.

1677, Dec. 6. Canterbury. Jo. Tillden to Secretary Coventry. — About Coventry's application for Mr. Ivory for the living of Exning. The Chapter have given it to Mr. Balk, Fellow of Queen's College, Cambridge, his (Ivory's,) superior in learning and standing.

1688, Oct. 23rd. The same to Lady Coventry.

1678, Nov. 1st. The Duke of Buckingham, Lords Winchester and Halifax, and H. London (Bishop) to Secretary Coventry.—It being referred to them to take examinations concerning the murder of Sir Edmund Bury Godfrey, they want all the evidence; they tell him to send to the Marquis of Winchester's house in Lincoln's Inn Fields the examination of Charles Atkins, which Sir Philip Howard delivered to Coventry, and the examinations of John Child and Mr. C. Atkins, and the body of Samuel Atkins then in their custody.

Copy of Coventry's narrative. *Begins*, Since the reiterated address from the Houses of Parliament, the unexpected successes of the French alarmed the King, and he sent to his ministers to inform him of the condition of the Confederates. (3½ pp.)

1678, Oct. 7th. Henry Coventry to the King. About Oates, Coleman, and Rumball. (2 pp.)

1675, Nov. Copy of Lord Shaftesbury's speech in Parliament. *Begins*, Our all is at stake and therefore you must give me leave to speak freely before we part with it. (9 pp.) It is on the subject of Appeals.

Lord Shaftesbury to ―――― (of Carlisle). *Begins*, I very much approve of what Lord Mordant and you told me you were about:—says he can't come up to town as he intended, for he hears it reported that an office with a strange name is prepared for him.—He will come when the addressee sends for him. (1 p.)

1677. Copy of (Hydes?) Speech to the King of Poland.—The King has agreed with the King of France to assist in establishing the King of Poland.

1701. That part of Dr. Smith's letter to Mr. Bennet, the bookseller, which relates to the paper published against the Earl of Rochester. (The True Patriot Vindicated.) He tells which speech it was that he Latinised, and that there was nothing about religion in it.

The Earl of Orrery's letters (from Castle Martyr) to Sir J. Mallet, M.P., as follow :—

1678, Jan. 1st and 14th, March 7th and 21st, June 24th and 28th, July 16th, Oct. 22nd, Nov. 26th, Dec 3rd, 6th, 10th, 20th, and 27th. (It seems that Sir John Mallet sent news; and the Earl of Orrery tells him a little Irish news; these letters are generally of one page.) In the letter dated 3rd of Dec., he says very few of the Romish Titular and regular clergy had gone out of the Kingdom, notwithstanding the late Proclamation requiring them to do so; and very few firearms have been brought in.

In the letter of the 20th of Dec., he says, the 12th instant a damned plot was detected at Dublin for murdering the Lord Lieutenant ; a young Englishman, one John Jephson, was to have committed the villany at the instigation of four Irish Roman Ecclesiastics, of whom two are taken; one is in France and the other not known where.

Copies of some depositions in Irish Plots in 1678.

Copy of an unsigned letter on the Plot. (3 pp.)

There are other letters from the Earl of Orrery to Sir J. Mallet in 1679, March 28th, April 4th, 8th, 28th, 29th, May 2nd, 6th, 13th, and 23rd.

1678, Aug., Arington near Hungerford.—W. Jones to ――――. His opinion concerning words spoken by Mr. Malet, which he thinks are criminal. (1 p.)

1678, April. Copy of a letter by the State of Genoa to their agent touching the murder of the Duke of Somerset. *Begins, Magnifico nostro Agente.* (2 pp.)[*]

1677, Sept. 19th. Unsigned newsletter to Thomas Thynne, M.P. (8 pp.)

1677, Oct. 18th, London. Ditto. (3 pp.)

1677, Oct; 24th, London. Ditto. (3 pp.)

1677, Dec. 4th, London. Ditto. (1 p.)

1677, Oct. 23rd, Whitehall. ―――― to his brother Thomas Thynne.—Yesterday the King declared his resolution of giving Lady Mary to the Prince of Orange ; the Duke being called in declared, his desire and consent. (1 p.)

1678, Jan. 1st, The Hague. (*Indorsed* Mr. Hyde to Secretary Williamson.) About the treaty of peace and the wording of it. (16½ pp.)

1679, Jan. 4th, Vienne. Guillaume de Schrotters (or Schrolders) to the King.—Sends a powder to counteract fever.

1679, Oct. 20th. (*Endorsed*, This paper was presented to the King by the Duke of York.)—That about May or June last Col. Fitzherbert delivered to the Pope's internuncio at Brussels a letter and paper signed by four Roman Catholic bishops, two of whom were Plunket, Archbishop of Armagh, and Tyrrel, Bishop of Clogher, recommending Fitzherbert to be the only person fit to be entrusted general of an army for establishing the Roman Catholic religion in Ireland, under the French sovereignty, &c. (¾ p., 4to.)

Extracts touching Charles II.'s Restoration.

16 ―, April 24th, Windsor.—The Earl of Sunderland to ――――. About Sir Gilbert Gerrard.—To ask him on oath, when he comes again, if he knows anything of a black box much talked of, or of a paper on such a box, or anything that relates to Dr. Cousens, bishop of Durham, having married the King to the Duke of Monmouth's mother.

1680, April 24th. Sir Gilbert Gerrard being asked by Secretary Coventry whether &c.—Says he knows nothing of the box, nor had he any such box intrusted to him, nor papers relating to any such matter. Asks to be excused from taking the oath. Will wait on the King.— Deposition taken in the presence of Henry Coventry and H. Thynne.

1683, May 3rd. Newsletter to Lady Weymouth.

Vol. VIII.

(1665), June 22nd. St. Germains. Louis XIV. to the Duke of York.—In reply to his letter of the 15th, giving an account of a victory over the Dutch. Alludes to the Duke being covered with the brains of the Comte de Falmout (the Earl of Falmouth).

1682, March 19th. St. Germains en Laye.—The same to the same. Is glad he (the Duke) is going to see the King at Newmarket, and thinks the Duke's firmness is necessary to confirm the King in his resolution to accept the means which he (Louis) offers for peace. —Credence for Barillon.

1685, March 8th. Louis XIV. to the King.— On the death of Charles II. Lord Churchill had been sent to tell him.

Parallel of the penal laws of France against the Protestants with the penal laws of England against those of the Roman religion. (10 leaves.) And a discourse on the foregoing Parallel. (7 leaves.) Both papers are in French.

An expedient for a limited Toleration. (1 p.)

Some considerations concerning the obstructions that have hitherto hindered the reduction of the Universities to the Catholick religion. (7½ pp.)

Address to the King with reference to the Proclamation following.

Copy of King James the 2nd's [proposed?] Proclamation for daily serving of morning and evening prayer in all churches and chapels, &c. (2 pp.)

Comments upon the above proclamation.—Revenue to arise from dispensations from it.

Considerations relating to an Apostolic Vicar.

Observations on our Saviour's prayer in the garden. (2 pp.)

A Memorial of the Dean and Chapter of the English secular clergy to his most sacred Majesty James II., 1685. (Against the admission of a Vicar Apostolick.— Prays first that the bishop to be sent have not only leave to exercise the power of an ordinary, but that in his Breve he be declared a true and proper ordinary of

---

[*] This was Duke Francis. In a former report I inadvertently remarked upon Duke William as the person assassinated. Duke William died in 1671 ; his successor Duke John died in 1675; and Duke Francis in 1678.

SIR
A. MALET,
BART.
___

the Catholics in England, and that be first expressed in the Patent.)

2ndly. That the appointment be declared to be temporary.

De Chevigne, pere de l'oratoire, to King James. M. de Canaples will explain the writer's sentiments on the King's accession. Congratulations, &c. (1 p.)

168$, Feb. 5th, Dublin Castle. The Earl of Clarendon to the King.—In favour of Lord Clanricard. Praises the appearance of the King's guards.

1685, Dec. 13th, Stowe. The Earl of Bath to King James II.—Is sorry he was absent last session: he asks for arrears of pension.—Asks that he may stay there till after Christmas.—The town of Plymouth is now as loyal and dutiful as the garrison.

1685, Aug. 29th, Dublin. (Tirconnel to King James). The nomination of Lord Clarendon as Governor of that country terrifies the Catholics. (2 pp.)

1688, March 14th, The Hague. Marquis of Albeville to the King.—Has sent by last post to Lord Middleton, a list of all the officers gone over in the yeacht; he now sends a list of those that go over with Col. Walling or with Major Killicue.—There went over in the yacht one Capt. Connock (whom he leads), formerly a Capt. of Dragoons in England.—In the time of the Plot he became a Roman Catholic and lost his employment.

1688, March 17th. Duke of Tirconnel to James II. —About the pay of the army, and calling a Parliament here (? Ireland).—Is sorry that the King intends the reducement of 10 men in each company. Hopes be will put as many Catholic officers into the three new regiments as he can . . . Regimental and army business.

1688, March 19th. The Hague. [Marquis of] Albeville to the King. (5 pp.)

1688, April 2nd. The Hague. The same to the same. (7 pp.) He refers to his long dispatch to Lord Middleton as necessary to be read by the King.—It is now publicly avowed by the States that the only thing that unites them with the Prince of Orange is their belief that if the Catholic Religion should be settled in England, this state must fall with the Protestant religion in Christendom, and that 'must ensue if the test and penal laws be taken away.—Says that the Prince makes Her Royal Highness believe that the King will not keep his engagement for succession in the true line, and the Jesuits will prevail with the King to act against his present assurance.—Is sorry to say that the Prince and Her Royal Highness are sponsors to Burnet's child.

1688, March 28th. Tirconnel to the King.—Sending a scheme of two Bills for giving as little disturbance to Protestants as possible, and to restrain Catholics no more than what seems absolutely necessary to render them considerable or capable to serve the King.

n. d. Dr. P. Walsh to the King.—Asks for an interview to tell the King that the French King would have given support to raise troubles. (1½ p.)

1687, Aug. 14th. Windsor. "James R." (and Sunderland) to H. F. Thynne, keeper of the library at St. James.—Whereas he thinks fit to allow his chaplains the Benedictine Monks at St. James', the use of such books out of our library there as they shall desire; he tells Thynne to deliver them, taking a receipt of Father Thomas Howard for re-delivery.

1688, Aug. 13th. (Copy.)—"James R." to the Warden, &c. of All Souls, Oxford.—Recommending John Cartwright, M.A., of Trinity College, Cambridge, to the vicarage of Barking, Essex, resigned by Thomas Bishop of Chester, which he held in Commendam.

1688, Aug. 27. Copy of the Earl of Sunderland's letter.—They have not complied.—The bishop is to hold still in Commendam.

Letter to the Earl of Sunderland in reply by L. W. Finch, Warden, and the Fellows of All Souls, Oxford. They say they were not disobedient, but the thing was extraordinary :—They took advice and find that the surrender should have been enrolled in Chancery : then they would consider it.

1688, Sept. 6th. All Souls.—L. W. Finch to (the Earl of Sunderland). On the same subject.

1688, Dec. 10th. Copy of James the II.'s letter to Lord Feversham.

1688, Dec. 12th. James II. to the Earl of Winchelsea. Telling him he had been seized by some of the town : he would not make himself known.—Asks him to come. (Copied from the original lately in the possession of Henry, Earl of Winchelsea, the 9th Jan. 172¾ by J. Creyk.)

1688, Dec. 12th. Account of what happened to King James upon his being taken at Faversham, by way of diary, from the 11th to 15th of Dec. (10 pp.)

An imperfect account of the taking of King James and bringing him to Faversham, and what befel him there, Dec. 1688, written by Capt. Southouse, at the time Major of the town, or Amis, who commanded the boats. (8 pp.)

168$, Jan. 17th, London. J. F. to my Lord.—Comments on Lord . . . remarks on Varillas' history.— Relations between France and Genoa.—Her Majesty has almost made an end of Maimbourg's treatise about the progress and grandeur of the Bishop of Rome ; in a few weeks it will come abroad ; only two copies are in the kingdom, one for the King and one for the translator.—Character of a Trimmer.—From Scotland there are further proofs of the last plot.

1667, May 9. Louis XIV. to the States. Sending a copy of the letter to the Queen of Spain about the rights of Louis's Queen and son.

1688, Sept. 6th. Copy of Louis XIV's letter to the Cardinal d'Estrée.

1688. Copy of the Emperor of Morocco's letter to the English Parliament. (For peace and trade.) (1½ pp.)

1688, Dec. 12th. Sir W. Portman to Mr. Blewet at Woodhouse.—Have dispatched into the west and north-west parts of the county to get loans for the Prince. Asks Blewet to help the protestant cause.— Names some who have, and what they sent.

1691, May 9th, London. The Duke of Ormond to Baldwin Mallet.—Appointing him Deputy-Lieutenant.

1691, Jan. 23rd. Sir Samuel Morland to Lord Weymouth (written by him when blind by help of a ruler).—Asks Lord Weymouth to get him put among the exceptions in relation to pensions.—The doctor gives him hopes of restoring his sight as soon as the warm weather comes.

Certain observations on the Government ; with several reflections by three several hands.

1. By George, late Marquis of Halifax.
2. By Mr. Charles Mountague.
3. By John Lord Somers.

1st. That a prince who falleth out with laws breaketh with his best friends. (33 heads.)

2nd. A supplement by Mr. Charles Mountague. (14 heads in all.)

3rd. By Lord Somers. (44 heads. 17 pp., 4to, in all.)

1694, Oct. 24th. T. (White) Bishop of Peterborough to Dr. Frampton Bishop of Gloucester.—Complimentary.

1720, Dec. 24th. Bromley.—T. Roffen (Atterbury) to Dr. Harbin, and six other letters of no importance. —In another he says, "When you see Mr. Bedford." In another "Mr. Bedford was with me yesterday."*

1709 and 1710. Three letters from Is. Walton to Dr. Harbin. (He and Atterbury talk about the articles of 1571.)

1691 June 7. Thomas (Ken) Bishop of Bath and Wells. Draft of a petition by the clergy of the diocese of . . . . on behalf of the Archbishop and Bishops under censure.

Jan. 22nd. Winchester. Two other letters and the same to Dr. Harbin.

Copy of the inscription for his tomb by Bishop Ken. G. Smalridge to Dr. Harbin.

1712, Oct. 10th. The Hague. Robert Hales to ——. (On note paper.)

1713, May 19th. The Hague. From the same. Both are about his tours, gardening, and books.

1723, Dec. 20th. Geo. Bishop of Bath and Wells to Dr. Harbin.

1725, Nov. 9th. Rome. Copy of the Chevalier's letter to his wife. Begins : Your behaviour to me, the threats I have received. . . . On fo. 5, a copy of the Chevalier's memoir. Fo. 9, copy of Lord Inverness's letter to a friend from Rome, Nov. 17th, 1725.— Ends on fo. 11. (On his wife's retiring to a convent.)

Memorial from the Chevalier.—About the clergy abhorring his restoration. (2 pp.)

A folio of 16 pages (copy) by an adherent of the Chevalier, about his cause.

168$, Feb. 19th. Copy of Sir R. Sawyer's letter to Dr. Cook, of Jesus College, Chancellor of Ely. About King James's abdication. (1½ pp.)

Copy (by Harbin) of the Duke of Wharton's letter, dated from Madrid, June 17th, n. s. 1726, to his sister Lady Jane Holt.—After and à propos of his attainder. (5½ pp.)

SIR
A. MALE
BART.
___

___

* It will be recollected that Hilkiah Bedford was fined and imprisoned, as the (supposed) author of The Hereditary right of the Crown of England asserted, fol. 1713.

Rr 4

1761, Oct. 17th. Piccadilly. Lord Egremont to Mr. Malet, on his being appointed Secretary of State.

1762, Aug. 24th. Hampton. David Garrick to Warton. Acknowledges his observations on the Fairy Queen of Spenser.

A BOUND VOLUME.

(Temp. Car. 2.) Considerations about the true way of suppressing popery in this Kingdom. (43 folio pp.) *begins:* Amongst the ignorant Vulgar instructed by malicious men.

The Illustrious Sclaves. Nov. the 2nd, A.D. 1672.

An abridgement of the Historie of the illustrious Sarra (*Sclaves* it should be). The faire Sarra, a Moore's daughter by adoption to Barberousse a pyrate and King of Tunis, &c. (1 p.) (These are the contents.) The history *begins:* It was when the sable clouds had covered the skies, &c.—The Moor hears complaints; fights and rescues Sarra. (28 folio pp.)

Essay concerning the decay of rents and the remedy, written by Sir W. Coventrye, about 1670. (5 folio pp.) *begins:* That rents decay every landlord feels.

Some of the consequences that are like to follow upon the lessening of interest to 4 per cent. (by Mr. Locke, directed by Lord Ashley). (8 large folio pp.) *Begins:* It will be a gain to the merchants.

Some important and urgent reasons for the immediate reformation of cloathing. (8 reasons in 1 p.)

170¾, March 1st. Dublin, W. Percival to ——. About leaving out Sir G. Rooke from the Address of the Convocation of Ireland. (5½ close folios.) (The address was to congratulate on the success of the last campaign.)

Ex bibliotheca Cotton, Vitell. B. 12. S. Gardiner to Cardinal Wolsey, dated from Greenwich. Vitellius, B. 13. Vitellius, B. 9, B. 10, B. 11. (54 pp. in all, by Harbin; Henry VIII.'s business.) Vitellius, B. 12, 1 p., 4to. (These are extracts by Dr. Harbin from the Cotton MSS. in the British Museum.)

Seven pages of extracts from a manuscript on paper in the Imperial Library at Vienna, bought by Busbequius at Constantinople, and written out by John Price at Vienna in 1637. Greek words beginning with the letter A. And similar extracts from a MS. supposed to be by Tzetzes. (The extracts are signed by G. Harbin 1695.)

Other extracts from a Greek MS. by George Gemistius, &c.

Copy of a letter to Bishop Fowler, Sept. 4th, 1703. Account of what Mr. Bedford, minister of the Temple parish, told the writer of a friend of his who conversed with spirits (about 13 years ago). It is a narrative about Thomas Perks, a man about 20, who lived with his father at Mangerfield, co. Gloster. (8¾ pp.) (Nonsensical proceedings.)

Various readings in MSS. of Epistle of St. John, c. 5. v. 7. (Harl. MSS.)

Ambassadors confined or ordered to depart. 1523–1635. (8 instances are given.)

1731, Nov. 27th. Letter (or copy). J. T. to ——. Sending verses supposed to be written by Mr. Swift.

The place of the damned.

Begin: All folk who pretend to religion or grace,
Allow there's a hell, but dispute of the place.

Eight Latin verses, hexameter and pentameter, written under Cromwell's picture presented to the Queen of Sweden, by Andrew Marvell. *Begin:* Bellipotens virgo septem regina Trionum.

Epigrams and other poetry.

1703, 11th $\frac{M}{3}$ (3rd month?) Copy of a letter by W. Penn to the Lords Commissioners for Trade and Plantations; signifying his willingness to resign the government of Pensylvania to the Crown.

1703, May 12th. Whitehall. (Copy.) W. Popple to W. Penn.—Asks him to lay before the Lords his proposals.

1703, May 18th. (Copy.) W. Penn says he thinks he has said enough.

1703, May 21st. Robert Cecill, Ph. Meadows, W. Blathwayte, John Pollexfen, and Mat. Prior, to the Earl of Nottingham—They send copies of the letters, and say they cannot get on without the Queen's directions.

1703, May 22nd. W. Popple to W. Penn.—Says that he has sent copies of the letters to the Earl of Nottingham.

Notes about Charles I. chiefly from books.

A printed folio sheet, about the collection of Civil War tracts, near 30,000, from 1640 to the Restoration, and 100 manuscript pieces.—They were shifted about for safety under Cromwell.—A pretended bargain was made with Oxford for the sale of them, and 1,000*l.* deposit paid.

Copies of Sir J. Hotham's letters from the originals. Begins, p. 1–7, 1642, from Nalson's Collections.

Comédie du Prince d'Orange sur la leveé du Liege d'Oudenarde, et ce que sest passé en la bataille de Senef. —Personages; Le Prince d'Orange et Moulerey Sargans, Fabrice fou du prince, aussi sargant. (14½ pp., 4to.)

Case and copies of opinion of Fr. Pemberton and H. Finch about the legality of the King's mandate to Cambridge to admit Alban Frances, a Benedictine, to be M.A. without oath, and dispensing with all statutes, &c. They say it was against the Statute of Elizabeth. 4 & 5 Eliz.

A volume of papers and prints about the birth of the Pretender, as follows:—

1715, Oct. 18th. Bat. (Bar?) le Duc. Copy of a letter in French by J. R. to the Etats Generaux. (1 p.)

April 7th, N. S. Nat. Spinks to Dr. Harbin.

170¾, March 23rd. The same to the same. Mrs. Pearce, widow of Mr. Pearce, the King's surgeon, says she never heard the Prince had an issue.—Her husband attended him at Richmond in sickness day and night, and went with him to Windsor, after which he was no more sick.—Does not believe Mr. Page's story, unless it be one Pearce, of Drury Lane.

April 9th. The same to the same.—Spinks seems to believe in Page's story, and notes discrepancies in Mrs. Pearce's story.

170¾, Jan. 31st. R. J. (Jenkins) to Lord Weymouth. Telling Page's story, viz., that he made an issue in the arm of a child said to be the Queen's; in four days he went, and saw no issue, though the child was still said to be the Queen's.

Extracts from Sir George Mackenzie's MSS. (6½ pp., quarto.)

Account of the birth of the pretended Prince of Wales, as it is believed by the Lord Bishop of Worcester. *Begins*, The Countess of Clarendon said the Queen increased. (6 pp. folio.)

1688. Form of prayer for the 17th of June instant for the delivery of the Queen and the birth of the young prince. (4 leaves, 4to.)

A hue and cry after Daniel Foe and his Coventry beast, with a letter from that worthy horse courser to a friend of Mr. Mayo, in Coventry, that lent it him. London: Printed and sold by the booksellers of London and Westminster, 1711; price one penny. Foe was accused of having stolen a horse that he hired at Coventry.—In his letter he says he will give full satisfaction. He then defends the birth of the Pretender. (2 leaves, quarto.)

De Ventre, inspiciendo, or remarks on Mr. Ashton's answerer in a letter to a Friend. 2 copies together.

A full answer to the Deposition, &c., with map of St. James's Palace, and the Court there, describing the place wherein it is supposed the true mother was delivered, with the particular doors and passages through which the child was conveyed to the Queen's bed chamber. London: Printed for Simon Bruges, 1689. With title and one leaf of apology, and 21 pages (of two columns) of text, and plates.

Confession of Judith Wilkes, the Queen's midwife, with full account of her running away by night and going into France. (1 leaf.)

Collection of addresses from Societies and Corporations to King James concerning the conception and birth of a Prince. (16 pp.)

1688, Oct. 22nd. Part of the proceedings of the General Council about the birth of the Prince and the statements of various persons. (2 leaves.)

Memorial from the English Protestants for their Highnesses the Prince and Princess of Orange, addressed to Monsieur Benting at the Hague. (28 pp.)

A BUNDLE.

Notes of the Impeachment of Lord Clarendon. (3 pp.)

Copy of Clarendon's letter to the Lords. *Begins:* I cannnot express the insupportable trouble. (5¼ pp., fol.)

167¾, Jan. 28th. Notes in the House of Commons. (1 p.)

Brief of Bill for annexing Tangier to the Imperial Crown of this realm. (½ p.)

1678, Nov. 1. Proceedings in the Houses; and notes of the execution of prisoners in the Plot.

SIR A. MALET, BART.

Resolution of the Judges of England upon deliberation upon all the several questions touching Popish recusants. 17 questions and answers. (2½ pp.)

Draft of petition to the King to get rid of Lauderdale.

1675, March 31st. Whitehall.— Copy of Council order to take into custody James Bedford, a Nonconformist preacher, lately apprehended for holding a conventicle, and asserting that the King did not intend laws to be enforced. Addressed to the Keeper or Deputy Keeper of the Gatehouse.

1673, Nov. 2. H. Stubbe to Sir J. Mallet. Complaining of his arrest by an order written by Bridgeman, and signed by Arlington; no cause being expressed. (1½ pp.)

1675, Nov. 12th. At a Committee, to whom the matter of the Narrative concerning M. de Luzancy, and also to enquire what priests and Jesuits have of late been committed or released, are referred, Sir J. Malet being in the chair,—Sir John Havil, Recorder of London, was ordered to attend with all warrants, &c., in the matters.

1675, Nov. 9. Order that Mr. Coleman attend.—Other papers about it.

(The narrative was written by Luzancy, and translated into English by Lewis Champian.)

Memoire pour servir de réponse à un écrit que le pere St. Germain Jesuite a mis entre les mains de Sn Majesté pour justifier la violence qu'el a faite au Sr Luzancy. (10 leaves.)

Luzancy's case in English.—(The way he was entrapped by Jesuits and their persecution of him.) (6 pp.)

Printed proclamation for the apprehension of St. Germain and his complices in the late violence offered to M. Luzancy, alias Chastelet. (Luzancy was converted from Rome to the Protestant religion.)

I must be allowed to acknowledge my obligations to Sir Alexander Malet, who most kindly in every way facilitated my labours for the Commission.

ALFRED J. HORWOOD.

THE MANUSCRIPTS OF SIR GERALD FITZGERALD, BART., OF THURNHAM HALL, LANCASHIRE.

SIR G. FITZ-GERALD. BART.

After the report on the MSS. at Thurnham Hall (see p. 246 of the Appendix to the 3rd Report of the Commission), Sir Gerald sent for examination the following:—

Pedigree of the House of Desmond, from Morice Fitz-Gerald son to Gerald of Windsor and Nesta daughter of Rhesus, Prince of Wales, who went to Ireland 16 Henry II., down to James Fitzjohn, 14th Earl who married Joan, daughter of Viscount Roche. Honora, one of the daughters of the daughter of the 14th Earl " married Mc Oarthy More, by whom she had issue " Ellen, wife to Florence McCarthy now prisoner in " England." This account of the family occupies 3½ pp., foolscap size, closely written. The writing is of the early part of the reign of King James I.

1686 (Nov.) 4th.* Thomas Nugent to Sir John Fitzgerald, Bart. Tells of Sir John's poor friend Edmund Fitzgerald, being persuaded to meet an antagonist in order to a reference, and that on the word of a gentleman and Christian no further trouble should be offered him, both of which he forfeited by taking poor Ned and sending him to gaol at Cork. Edmund sent word to Nugent, who wrote to the mayor that Edmund was one of Sir John's soldiers and consequently not to be arrested without Sir John's leave, or orders from higher powers ; in which he finds that they have taken Edmund into their own custody, and that he was to be kept at the Guard Chamber until Sir John's pleasure was known. Nugent says that the pass makes Edmund Sir John's soldier, and thinks that Sir John should write to Capt. Colgrave to say that he does not wish to cover any to defraud his neighbour, but that until they address him or the higher power he will not expose the King's soldier or friend. "You were extremely want- " ing at Cork, last night being Gunpowder Treason. " Capt. Colgrave discoursed nie three days ago about " what he should order that night. I told him he " should act as he thought convenient, but that if he " had a mind to imitate the King he should use noe " ceremony ; for I living this time twelvemonth in " London, the King ordered that bone-fires nor noe " other ceremony should be used ; notwithstanding " which he drew out the regiment and made them fire

* This should be (perhaps it is) 5th, because of the reference in the letter to Gunpowder Treason.

5.

" a volley of commemoration to their former principles ; " this is what we get by such commanders in chief ; " if more falls in their way, we shall not be forgot ; " let us give our friends thanks."

SIR G. FITZ-GERALD. BART.

1689, Dublin. John Callaghan to Sir John Fitzgerald, Bart., at his house in Limerick.—Sir John will find by the letters he (Callaghan) lately wrote to him that the prospect of having a company elsewhere was not his motive for quitting his employ under Sir John, but his indisposition (which yet was so much that he could do nothing with his right hand, but writing by the help of a table to support it). Thanks Sir John for continuing him in his ensign's place. 'Tis true he might have a company raised in September last, but Sir John having then sent for a commission for him in Lieut. Lavallen's place, and he (C.) finding Sir John willing to advance him further and there being a talk of their marching to the north, he was ashamed to move for a discharge ; but now seeing he cannot draw his sword he is forced to receive the discharge. Sir John says he (C.) may continue until he is provided with a captain's place, which he doubts not to have next campaign if he be able to manage it ; but if he do not recover the use of his hand by the end of the month or the beginning of February, he will resign. Thanks Sir John for his kindness ; so does Col. Dennis Callaghan. . . 'Tis said His Majesty goes towards Cork, Kingsale as some say, on Thursday, and as others say on Monday next. The major was here for money, and went away on Sunday, and Capt. Fitzmaurice along with him ; he said if he did not come himself he would write to Callaghan about consulting Councillor Butler in order to get the regiment removed to Munster, after the taking of Kenagh. Some of Sir John's officers at Dublin, but Capt. Roche and Capt. Creagh. Sir John's brother was still there ; he had expected to go to Scotland, but now he did not know where to go.

ALFRED J. HORWOOD.

THE MANUSCRIPTS OF LEWIS MAJENDIE, ESQUIRE, M.P., OF HEDINGHAM CASTLE, CO. ESSEX.

L. MAJEN-DIE, ESQ.

These are few. The most important is a long Bede Roll of the end of the 12th century, shewing that 120 churches acceded to the entreaty of the Abbess of the Convent of Hedingham to pray for the Soul of her predecessor Lucy the Countess of Oxford. The various styles of writing make this a most valuable document for palæographical purposes, as well as for the notices of churches then existing.

The topography of the Manor of Castle Hedingham at the latter end of the 16th century is amply shewn by a volume of descriptions and plans compiled for Lord Burghley who was the then owner.

There are many letters, from 1753 to 1763, from the Archbishop of Canterbury and others to the Revd. John James Majendie, D.D., relating to relief from England to Hungarian, French, and other foreign Protestants I. Notes of them are given below.

A parchment roll, about 20 feet long and seven inches wide. This was sent to various religious houses in England by Agnes the humble servant (minister) of the Church of the Holy Cross and St. Mary of Henigeham, so that they might testify to their offering prayers for the soul of Lucy Countess of Oxford (wife of Aubrey de Vere, 3rd Earl of Oxford), foundress of the priory of Heningham, Co. Essex. The letter by Agnes to the religious houses is in Gothic characters. About four-fifths of the certificates by the religious houses are in corrupted Lombardic or Norman characters: some are in modern Gothic and some few in Lombardic small letters. There are three well executed drawings occupying the whole width of the roll. The first represents Christ on the Cross between Mary and John, and to the right hand are the Virgin seated with the infant Jesus. The second represents two Angels drawing up a lady in her shroud to heaven. The third represents the sprinkling and thurification of the lady in her coffin ; monks and nuns are in attendance. At the top of each drawing are some Latin verses. The churches which certified their compliance with the request are as follows :—

Christ and Sts. Botulph, Julian, and Denis of Colchester; St. John the Baptist of Stoke, St. Mary of Colum, St. Mary Wicsnie, Sts. Peter, Paul, and Mary of Osyth, John the Baptist of Colchester, Sts. Peter and Paul of Hockel, St. Mary of Coggeshall, St. John the Apostle and Evangelist of Lega, St. Mary of Dunmawe, St. Mary of Hatfeld, Sts. Mary and Martin of

S 2

Mendon, St. Mary of Perchewell, St. Mary and St. Laurence the Martyr of Blakemere, St. Mary and the Holy Cross of Suldham, St. Mary and St. Ethelburga of Barking, St. Mary of Snape, St. Mary of Strafford, St. Leonard of Stratford, the Holy Trinity of London, St. Mary of Southwark, St. Saviour of Bermondsey, St. Bartholomew of London, St. Peter of Westminster, St. John of Haliwell, St. John the Baptist of Latton, St. Mary of Tyleley, St. Mary of Cippell, St. Paul of Newenham, St. Mary of Ixewich, St. Peter of Dunstaple, St. Mary of Lelford, St. Sepulchre of Teford, St. Mary of Derham, St. Katherine of Blakeborge, St. Mary Magdalen of Plantuney, St. Mary and All Saints of Welfacre, St. Mary of Castle Acre, St Mary of Rudham, St. Mary of Walsingham, St. Mary of Wardone, St. Mary and All Saints of Wambun (Wamborough?), St. Mary of Chik (Chickney?), St. Andrew of Bromholm, St. Mary and St. Augustine of Hikeling, St. Benet of Hulme, St. Faith of Horssam, St. Mary of Karrowe, St. Trinity of Norwich, St. Cross of Bungay, St. Michael of Romburg, St. Peter of Wangeford, St. Mary of Blibro, St. Mary of Sibecun, St. Mary of Leeston, St. Mary of Buttel, St. Mary of Campesse, St. Knut of Ipswich, Sts. Peter and Paul of Ipswich, St. Mary at Merit, St. Leonard of Brisete (?), St. Thomas the Martyr of Liesne, St. Andrew of Rochester, St. Mary Malling, St. Mary of Boxle, Sts. Mary and Nicholas of Leeds, St. Saviour of Kaversham, St. Mary Magdalen of Davintune, Christ Church Canterbury, St. Sepulchre of Canterbury, St. Gregory of Canterbury, St. Augustine of Canterbury, St. Martin of Dover, St. John the Evangelist of Hortone, St. Mary of Robertsbridge, St. Martin of Battle, St. Pancras of Lennes (the names of many men and women are at the foot of this), Sts. Mary and Blaise of Bongrave, Sts. Peter and Grimbald of Hyde, Sts. Mary and Edburga of Winchester, Sts. Peter and Paul and St. Swithin of Winchester, Sts. Mary and Ethelfleda of Rumsey, Sts. Mary and Edith of Wilton, St. Mary of Shirborne, Sts. Peter and Paul of Montacute, St. Peter the Apostle of Muchelney, St. Mary of Glastonbury, St. Augustine of Bristol, St. Mary of Keynesham, Sts. Peter and Paul of Bath, St. Mary Magdalen of Ferley, St. Mary of Bradenestoke, St. Mary and St. Aldelm præsul of Malmesbury, St. Peter of Gloucester, St. Oswald of Gloucester, St. Mary of Llanthony near Gloucester, St. Mary of Tewkesbury, Sts. Mary and Egwine of Eversham, Sts. Mary and John of Godstow, St. Mary of Oseney, St. Frideswide of Oxford, St. Mary of Abingdon, St. Mary of Reding, St. Mary of Hurley, St. Mary of Missenden, St. James of Waled, St. Mary Magdalen of Yeland, St. Thomas the Martyr of Cruceroys, St. Mary of Woburne, St. Mary of Elverstone, St. John Baptist and John the Evangelist of Caudewell, St. Neot, Sts. Andrew and Giles of Barnewell, St. Radegund of Cambridge, the Friars Minor of Cambridge, St. Peter and St. Ethelreda Queen and Virgin of the Church of Ely.

The form of entry for each Church is "Titulus ecclesie" (the name of the church) followed by a short prayer for the Lady.

In some cases the entry was perhaps made by one of the persons bearing the roll; but many are evidently made by the authorities at the different churches : and this roll is a most interesting and important document to shew the various styles of writing in the last decade of the 12th century. It is noticed in Morant's History of Essex and in Astle's History of Writing. A descendant of Mr. Astle presented it to Mr. Majendie.

22 Hen. VIII. Rental of Poris*. A roll about three feet long. Total annual rent, 27l. 6s. 11d.

3 Edw. VI. Rental, as well free as copy, of Hedingham. A roll about three feet long. Total annual rent, 35l. 10s. 11d.

1592. A' folio volume. Extent of the Honour and Manor of Castle Hedingham, &c., parcel of the possessions of Lord Burghley and late of E. de Vere, Earl of Oxford, &c. 222 leaves including an index. The plans are very neatly drawn and they and the descriptions of the houses and lands are very numerous and precise. The volume was compiled by Israel Amyce.

A folio volume, paper, 17th century. La discipline Ecclesiastique des Eglises réformées de France. — Mémoire de tous les Synodes nationaux (from that of Paris 1559 to that of Alençon 1637.)—Titles of the Chapters of " La Discipline Ecclesiastique" (fourteen in number; 1. Des Ministres et Pasteurs; 14. Des Reglements, et Advertissement pour les particuliers).

1644. Rental of the Manors of Hedingham upland, Hedingham Nunnery, Prayers and Grays (about three

---

The name of Poris is in the margin. The contents of the roll seem to relate to the manor of Prayers or Preiers in Essex.

---

feet long). The names of tenants are placed alphabetically. The rental was 36l. 5s. 9d.

Folio, 16 leaves. Antiquities of Hedingham ad Castrum, and Sible Hedingham, and Colne Earles. It contains an account (5 pp.) of Sir John Hawkwood, born at Sible Hedingham.

A folio volume containing letters inlaid. 1753 and 4. Letters from Thomas (Herring) Archbishop of Canterbury to John James Majendie, on the subject of an application by Hungarians for aid. In the third letter he tells Mr. Majendie to thank Mr. Rimius for his letters, and particularly for the curious detail of his interview with Cossart, in which he thinks that Rimius conducted himself like a man of spirit.—In the fourth letter (Sept. 22, 1754) he acknowledges the receipt of the Hungarian representation of their case :—he will read it, and if necessary alter and submit the alterations to Majendie and others. Will answer Mr. Professor's letter and that of the President of Zurich. Would like to acquaint Mr. Professor that he approves and would encourage the publication of the letters which he mentions :—that he could get assistance from the Bench of Bishops, but they are all in the country and nothing can be attempted until they return. Nothing effectual can be done for the Hungarians until winter, and even then he fears nothing can be done but some present assistance. Asks Majendie to tell Mr. Kolmar that the reason why he does not answer the two letters is not from neglect or want of regard to the President and College of Zurich and Mr. Professor, but that he is disabled by the season of the year, which keeps London empty. Asks Majendie to return some letters to Mr. Duplan :—thinks his answer to Mr. Pomaret's letter very good. Is concerned at the appearance of the severe spirit in Languedoc, and particularly for the hard fate of Lafage :—he had the detail of that cursed execution some days ago, and thought it of moment enough to put it in the hands of the Ministry.

1754, Nov. 22. Says he is in earnest in desiring to assist the University of Debritzen in its present difficulties. Suggests that Mr. Wiespresni shall go round with a petition to all the Bishops.

1754, Dec. 22. Says that Mr. Rimius does well to go on with his work, and having shewn the dirty nonsense of the Moravian enthusiasm, it will of consequence be demonstrable from facts that they have imposed on the Legislature, and that their principal assumes a power dangerous to the State. Is much concerned about the poor Hungarians ;—hears that an annual subscription will not go down ; doubts if they can hope for much aid at present. The Bench are pressed upon these applications from abroad, and many others at home, beyond their abilities.

1755, Jan. 8. Is despondent about aid to the Hungarians.

1755, May 4. Sends the Bishops subscriptions and his own. Thinks they should be placed in the Funds.

1755, Nov. 17. Thinks so well of the men and the sad case of Debritzen that if they return to England he will do anything for them he can.

1755, Nov. 30. Will set about getting aid for honest Rimius.

1755, Dec. 17. Ask Majendie to wait on the Bishop of London and Dr. Nichols at the Temple. Has 40 guineas for Rimius.

1756, Feb. 15 and March 2. In the last he gives a form certifying that the bearer, Mr. Stephen Weazpresmi of the University of Debritzen in Hungary, produced to him and the rest of the Bishops satisfactory credentials of his character; and being convinced of the low and compassionate state of that Protestant University they contribute to the relief of the Students there.

1756, June 7. Is glad that the poor people of Debritzen have had some success at Cambridge. Hopes they will have the same at Oxford. Is sorry that Rimius is disappointed : says that he did the best he could for him.

1758, April 17, Exeter. G. Exon [George Lavington, bishop of Exeter] to Majendie.—Says that Majendie's and Mr. Planta's letters came safe :—will take care to recommend him to his Grace of Canterbury. If there is a catalogue of the late Mr. Rimius's book he would like to have one.

1758, July 17. G. Exon to Majendie.—Is glad of Planta's success. His Grace of Canterbury told him (the writer) that the Lord Keeper and the Speaker had agreed to appoint Planta to be an Assistant. Mr. Planta says that Moravianism is dissipated at London. The writer, however, fancies that the Count abroad is renewing his attempts, and perhaps composing what he calls his great work to keep up or recover the spirits of his party.

1758, Sept. Copy of letter by Thomas [Secker] Archbishop of Canterbury to the Gentlemen of the Committee at Geneva for the relief of the distressed.

1758, Sept. 20. Thomas [Secker] Archbishop of Canterbury to Majendie, asking him to revise and translate the above.

1759. A letter about French Protestants.

1759, April 15. The Bishop of Winchester [Benjamin Hoadly] to Majendie, about the presentation to a living in Guernsey entrusted to him and Majendie by Lord Delawarr.

Two others by him and one by the Bishop of Exeter about a bounty to French Protestants, and one by the Archbishop about an application by German Protestants.

1761, April 24. Copy of a Message from the Protestants in France by M. Gibert. (3 pp.)

"Mr. Majendie and Mr. Muyssan, two French clergy-
"men, brought to me M. Gibert, a French Protestant
"Minister officiating in France, with credentials from
"several of his brethren and the Act of a Synod in the
"Upper Cevennes in 1758, all expressing that they
"would leave the country if they could not be relieved
"from the hardships which they now suffer on account
"of their religion."—The writer gives an account of his communication of the matter to the Duke of Newcastle, Pitt, and Lord Bute: they agreed that application to France might retard a peace and expose us to applications on behalf of Papists. If they left their country they should be received well in England, Ireland, or America. The King was visited, and he said he should like to help them, but could not interfere then without hurt to them; but that they should be well received if they came over.—Above 1,700l. was given by the King for French ministers: this was now more than sufficient; part might be applied to the ministers who came over. (This seems to be a Memorandum of some one who had an interview with the King.)

1761, Sept. 29. Thomas Secker, Archbishop of Canterbury, to Majendie. Hesitates to deliver Du Plan's letter to the King because he cannot affirm all contained in it. Du Plan says that in 1695 the Commons voted 15,000l. a year to the French refugees, and this is in M.'s book, Les Plaintes, &c. But the 7 & 8 W. 3. cap. 30. § 31, only authorised raising any sum not exceeding 15,000l., and that but for once. The writer thinks that the 15,000l. a year given afterwards was the voluntary bounty of the Crown. (3 pp.)

1761, March 13, &c. The same to the same. (3 letters.)

1762, March 1. Lord Ligonier to the Archbishop.—Acknowledges his letter about La Riviere and Causse; will recommend them to Parslow (the Governor of Gibraltar?), and thinks that the Archbishop's recommendation will get them an additional douceur.

1763, Jan. 7. Lord Egremont to the Archbishop.—Handed the Archbishop's letter to the King, who says that the same assurances which were given to Mr. Gibert should be repeated in the manner proposed.

Other long letters by him on the subject; and account of the King's opinions.

1763, Nov. 3. The Archbishop to Majendie. He has a Greek letter from one who signs himself Nectarius Protosyncellus to the Patriarch of Antioch; saying that he was a presbyter in the Greek and Russian Church at Amsterdam until he was convinced that they worshipped bones and wood like Idolaters.—Makes enquiries about him.

Two more letters about Nectarius.

Nov. 22. Poor Nectarius is in despair and thinks of returning to Amsterdam. "Give him 5 or 10 guineas "for me."

Other letters by the Archbishop (who seems to have been very charitable).

1767, March 4.—Mr. Sharpe, Clerk of the Council, says that the first step for the poor Vaudois is to have a Petition to the King in Council, signed by some one on their behalf.

1767, Sept. 5. Has received 206l. 5s. for half a year's pension to the Vaudois, due Oct. 10, 1766. Of this 134l. 1s. 3d. belongs to those in Piedmont.—He saw the Queen on Thursday, and sent her two dozen of figs the same morning.

Letter by the Archbishop about the Vaudois.

Statement of or by the Community of Bobby or Bobbio, a valley of Luzern, sufferers from the overflow of Pellice.

Copy Petition to the King in Council by the Vaudois, a Protestant Canton in the valley of Piedmont (inhabiting the valleys of Luserne, Perouse, and St. Martin), telling of their sufferings from persecution by Papists, from storms and floods; and asking aid by a Brief for Charitable Collections throughout England and Wales.

Particulars (in. French) of the Expenses of a Pastor in the Valleys, who had six children, a servant, and a horse.

1771. Copy of a Memorial to Majendie by Samuel Chaufepié concerning the application to be made of the interest on the sum collected for Piedmont.

Copies of two Letters by Majendie to the Commissaries of the Churches.

1763. Printed memoir about them. (7 pp.)

Letters in 1763 (2), 1768 (1), 1769 (3), 1770 (1), by J. Samuel Chaletain at Amsterdam about the Church.

Long letter by the Archbishop to Mr. Majendie about a paper by Majendie on the management of the Brief.

A few other papers on the subject.

I beg to acknowledge, with thanks, the hospitality of Mr. Majendie at Hedingham Castle.

ALFRED J. HORWOOD.

THE MANUSCRIPTS OF THE REV. H. T. ELLACOMBE, OF CLYST ST. GEORGE, DEVONSHIRE.

These comprise a great number of letters (chiefly of the 17th century) of the family of Newton of Barr's Court, co. Gloucester; but very few of them contain matter of public interest. A notice of Barr's Court and of the masters of that place was contributed by Mr. Ellacombe to the 4th volume of the Herald and Genealogist (1868).

There are some original Court Rolls and Hundred Rolls for the manors of Bitton, Oldelonde, &c., in the co. of Gloucester. An account of the manor of Bitton (by Mr. Ellacombe) is in the above-mentioned volume of the Herald and Genealogist.

A small collection of early Bristol deeds seemed worthy of the details which I have given below. The volume containing abstracts of Bristol wills is interesting.

There are a great number of papers relating to Kingswood Chase, and the trespasses, enclosures, and encroachments there in the 17th century.

Among the letters are—one by Charles II. regarding State Papers embezzled by the regicide Bradshaw; two giving news and reports shortly before and just after the flight of King James II.; and some of the time of Charles II. give notices of the Rye House Plot and the conspirators. Papers here show how Francis Creswicke, of Hannams Court, was thrown into prison on suspicion of communicating with Monmouth's officers when his army was at Keynsham, and how he got released.

A grant by the Abbess of Lacock 7 Hen. VIII. should be noticed.

The only papers and letters of general interest are the following:

Temp. James I. One page. Argument against giving parliamentary confirmation of grants of crown lands (to Scotchmen); and that even if such confirmation be granted, there should be a confirmation of leases therein made by the late Queen either for money, consideration or for good service.

1 p. 4to. The oath of a burgess (of the city of Bristol). This is printed in black letter. At the foot is a written certificate by Thomas Pott the Chamberlain sealed with his seal of office, that Fraunces Creswicke was, on the 19th December 1608, admitted into the liberties of the city; Mr. John Butcher, Mayor, and Thomas Moore and William Yonge, Shreves.

1646, Dec. 15. A printed form of license, by the Committee at Goldsmiths' Hall for compounding with Delinquents, to Henry Creswick, whose composition was not perfected, to continue within the cities of London and Westminster or elsewhere within the lines of communication or within 20 miles distant from the said lines, for attending his said composition. Signed by John Ashe, Robert Jenner, Antho. Irby, and four others.

1661, Aug. 8, London. Ossory to the Mayor of Bristol on his absence to Mr. Thomas Longton. He received lately advice of a writ directed to the coroners of Bristol at the suit of John Knight, and backed by Robert Yeamans. Asks him to inquire about it and let him (Ossory) know the result and he will do what he can according to the mayor's directions. In a P.S. he offers to write to Knight and doubts not he shall easily take him of (off).

1665, Aug. 23, Hynam near Gloucester. George Lane to . . . . acknowledges the addressees' joint letter of 22 Aug. and sends inclosed the Lord Lieutenant's letter to the Lord Chancellor on their concern, with a flying seal, so that when they have perused, they may seal and deliver it.

1670, Feb. 22, Whitehall. Copy of order in Council (the King, the Duke of York, Prince Rupert and 12 others present) on the petition of the Earl of Rochester, Sir John Newton, Bart., Thomas Chester, John Meredith and William Player, Esqs., lords of the several manors adjoining the chase of Kingswood, co. Gloucester, on behalf of themselves and their tenants and other freeholders, commoners within the chase, complaining that Sir Baynham Throckmorton, Kt. and Bart., instead of getting a patent for the rangership, had obtained from the King a lease for 60 years (contrary to all former example) of all the King's rights and oppressed the commoners and cottagers. Ordered that a copy of the petition be delivered to Sir Baynham Throckmorton, who is to return an answer in writing to the Board on the 1st of March, and the petitioners and he were then to attend and bring with them counsel learned if they pleased.

1681, Feb. 14, London. G. Newton to his father Sir John Newton at Barras Court near Bristol . . . . On Sunday last there happened a sad accident to Esqre. Thynn who lately marry'd the Lady Ogle, as he was riding in his coach through the Pall Mall; three or four foreigners came up and one of them fired a blunderbuss and killed Thynn. He says the cause of the assassination was conjectured to be in respect of an outlandish Count, who they say had received some affront from Esqre. Thynn; the Count was formerly a pretender to the Lady Ogle.

1682, July, Bristol. Richard Towgood, Dean of Bristol, and Samuel Crossman, treasurer, to Sir John Newton at Barr's Court. They ask his assistance towards erecting "a great fair organ and other ornaments" in the cathedral.

16 . . Oct. 16. P. (Peter Mew, Bishop of) Bath and Wells to Sir John Newton at Harptry.—Is sorry he cannot comply with the proposition of Lord Grandison (with regard to a patent affecting the Forest (of Kingswood?). He will maintain the ancient custom.

1688, April 16. Will. Sacheverell to his father-in-law Sir John Newton at Barr's Court.—Understanding that Sir John is to have his trial on the 16th of May, he will be in London on the 10th. (Seal of arms, 6 quarters.)

1691, March 3. Jane Sacheverell to her brother (Sir John Newton) . . . . Has not written to her brother Stringer to meet him. As for Will. Sacheverell going to Cambridge, they will discuss of that when the addressee comes.

1688, Sept. 9, Longleat. Visct. Weymouth to Sir Jno. Newton.—Not hearing that Sir John intends to stand for Knight of the Shire, he asks Sir John's support for his (the writer's) brother Thynne.

1688, Nov. 8. V.R. to Sir John Newton. Since the first account they had of the Prince of Orange's landing several expresses have come, but the matter kept very private; . . . 'tis believed the King will not go into the field until the apprehension of another landing in the north be over . . . . Much fears that Bristol will be aimed at, and that near Sir John will be the seat of war. Most people hereabouts bury their plate and secure themselves as well as they can, tho' he fancies they have least reason to fear. Lord Peterborough's regiment marched to-day, and on Saturday or Sunday a train of artillery will go out. Report of the bishops being desired to sign an abhorrence of the Prince of Orange; they have all refused to do it, upon the account the King would not let them see the declaration, wherein they were told they as spiritual lords were mentioned.

1688, Dec. 13 (London?). Last night we were all alarmed about 1 o'clock. Nothing was heard in our street, but To arms, to arms, telling us that the Irish, &c. were committing all manner of outrages, as murder, &c. . . . it was a false alarm . . . . The King left us on Tuesday last at 3 in the morning, and my Lord Chancellor went away about the same time; but the Lord Chancellor was taken yesterday at Wapping in a little ale house and was brought up to town and committed to the Tower; they have also taken 35,000 guynies besides a great deal of silver which he had sent on board a collier, that was to have transported him beyond sea. To-day, news that the King is stopped near Feversham: he was in a little hoy and with him

Sir Edward Hales and two priests. The King will be in town to-morrow. It is said that as soon as the news was brought that the King was stopped, the Lords here in town sent a petition to him to return back to Whitehall. The Prince's vanguards are at Brenford, and will be in town to-morrow, and the Prince is at Staynes, and is expected on Saturday.

1692, March 30. Certificate signed and sealed by Robert Fisher, Nicholas Beck, and Thomas Ireland, three of the commissioners for executing the Act of Parliament for raising money by a poll for carrying on the war against France, that Sir John Newton of Barr's Court is liable for a horse and horseman with arms for his lands in the county of Lincoln.—On the same paper, 1692 May 4, Certificate by the same persons that John Newton of Calverthorpe is liable for a horse, horseman and arms for his lands in the county of Lincoln. Both were for the militia.

16 . . Badminton, Friday night. (The Marquis of) Worcester to Sir John Newton at Barrows court. Finding by consultation with some of the deputy lieutenants that alarm is taken already by the disaffected, especially towards Oxfordshire, where they have searched already,—he thinks it best that they should all search at the same time, and asks Sir John to send his horse and friends and servants to Winterborne on Tuesday to accompany Mr. Burnell in the search. Asks him to send by the bearer two of the orders they signed and keep the other till he meets with Mr. Chester.

The Costs and Charges of our journey to London on the Lord Chamberlain's warrant (1 p.): from Saturday, 9 July 1692, until the following Saturday, 18l. 13s. 5d. They came with a messenger; and had to procure bail and justify them. The taverns mentioned are the Raven and Three Tuns, the Cheshire Cheese, the King's Head, and the One Bell. They went by boat from Blackfriars to the City; on the Thursday they had to wait all day at the King's Head with the bail (being four) for Lord Justice Treby's return to his chamber; and they paid the messenger there for not confining them at all, 3l. 5s. One item in the bill names "Mr. Till Adams, and self."—The indorsement on the paper is "Wm. Prewetts account of cost of going to London before the Lord Chamberlain."

1695, Feb. 29, Pensoford. J. Langton and Cir. Lyde to Sir Jno. Newton.—John Weekes, an Ensign in Sir Bev. Green's (Grenville's) regiment, with two serjeants, being taken up on suspicion against the government, were brought to them at Penseford. Weekes informs them that he is well known to Captain Newton, having a grandfather living near Barr's Court, to whom he has written the inclosed letter. They ask Sir John to return by the bearer a testimonial of the Ensign's reputation.

1696, July 16, Bristol. William Cox to Sir John Newton . . . . Dyer in his letter, now as well as last post gives an account, that there is peace concluded between the French King and the Duke of Savoy . . . . one of the reasons assigned was, that the Spaniard owed him 2,000,000l. of money, and the Duke of Savoy was to give the Duke of Burgundy the county of Nice, as a portion with his daughter. At the same time King William has published an order in the camp, that no person presume to talk of a peace on pain of a common soldier being hanged and an officer cashiered. But it is all the discourse at the Hague, and that it is proclaimed at France.

M. Cr. to Rochford (so indorsed).—Copy of a letter interceding for her husband's liberty; she having six children, who would have starved if Mr. Scrope had not given assistance. If her husband be at liberty he will doubtless put her in a position to perfect the agreement made with the addressee. She has begged Mr. Poley and Mr. Scrope to intercede.

1708, Jan. 19, Louth. Gervase Scroop to (his uncle) Sir John Newton.—Having made public profession of the Protestant religion, he asks Sir John to effect his reconciliation with his father; and to try to get him a post in the army; or in the fleet that is expected to go to sea next summer, under Lord Pembroke the High Admiral.

1704, Jan. 22, Gibraltar from on board the Siren (?), gally. John Euer to Mrs. Bridget Hort, at Temple Street, Bristol.—They intend to sail that night for Levorna (Leghorn ?) . . . That day they parted company with Sir Clondesley Shovel and 125 sail of ships more bound up the Straits. They met with a hard storm the 2d of January, in which they lost their maintopmast and sprung the head of their mainmast, but the storm abated and they have their mast rigged again.

1711, July 25, Bishopsthorp. Jo[hn Sharp, Archbishop of] York to Sir John Newton, at his house in
Soho Square, London.—All he can tell of Mr. Claring-
horn is that he was educated in the Popish religion and
took holy orders in that Church; that afterwards
having great scruples in his mind about that religion,
he applied himself to the writer; and upon further
reading and consideration being satisfied of the errors
thereof, he, by the writer's order, made a public renunciation of it, and was received into the Protestant communion. About a year after (viz. in 1701) the writer
bestowed the living of Conisborough on him. The
writer has not seen him for some years, but hears that
he behaves himself as he ought, is acceptable to his
parish and is a popular preacher, so that Sir John need
not scruple to give him the living Sir John mentions,
worth 60l. per annum.

1711, Aug. 3. W[illiam Wake, Bishop of] Lincoln, to
the Rev. Mr. Archdeacon Rogers;—telling him that he
may let Sir Jo. Newton know that until Mr. Stokes is
well enough to come to him (the Bishop) for institution,
he will, upon the archdeacon's account, take no advantage of any lapse that may occur to him. The writer
says that he wrote a long letter to the archdeacon by
the last post about the affair of Dadlington.

Copy of an address to a jury summoned to meet by
virtue of an Act of Parliament of the 12th of Queen
Anne, for making the river Avon, in the counties of
Somerset and Gloucester, navigable from the city of
Bath to Hannam's Mills. (The jury were impanelled
to give compensation to persons whose lands were taken
or affected by the works.)

1719, March 21, Berkeley Castle.—H. Berkeley to
Francis Creswick, Esq., at Hanham.—Having been, at
the Assizes, nominated for candidate at the ensuing
election, he asks the vote and interest of Creswick.

A packet of letters from Thomas Oldfield (a solicitor)
dated from Bristol and London (1682-1700) addressed
to Sir John Newton, chiefly relating to a suit about
Kingswood.

1683, June 23, London. He says that there is a plot
discovered of a design that was laid to kill the King
and Duke as they came from Newmarket, wherein Mr.
West, Mr. Nelthropp, and Mr. Wade, barristers of the
Temple, Col. Romsey, Capt. Walcot, Goodenough and
his brother, with divers others, are reported to be
concerned, and it's certain all he has named are fled;
but Mr. West last night rendered himself and was this
day examined before the King and Council at Hampton
Court, and hath discovered the design and the confederates, amongst which there were four of the King's
and Duke's guards.

1683, July 5. It is generally believed the conspirators
will be tried next week and found guilty, for Col.
Romsey it is said has made a great discovery.

1684, June 12, London. Sir Thomas Armstrong was
brought yesterday in the evening before the Council at
Whitehall, but refused to answer those questions he
was examined to, as I am told; and it is likely to be
true, for he returned back to Newgate in a very short
time.

1688, Dec. 22. It is said the King is still at Rochester,
and the Prince's guards with him, but whether he is
under a confinement by them is not certain, as I can
hear, but I am told he has liberty to go where he
pleases. There was a great Council at St. James's
where the Prince is, Wednesday last, and another Thursday. The Princess of Denmark and Prince came to
Whitehall Wednesday with the Bishop of London. The
Chancellor has petitioned the Prince, acknowledging
his crimes to be as numerous as his enemies, begging
pardon and promising to discover secrets relating to the
succession. It is said Sir Robert Atkyns the elder will
be a great man in Westminster Hall. One letter I am
told mentions that the King is gone to Calais, but the
rest say he is at Rochester.

1687, Feb. 4. This day, our late Mayor, Mr. Lane, the
sheriffs, with several aldermen and common councilmen,
(in all about 28) were by the King's command displaced,
and Mr. Day nominated Mayor, and Sanders, a haberdasher, and Hine, a grocer, sheriffs, and divers new
aldermen and common councilmen appointed. Alderman Lawford, Alderman Crabb, Alderman Creswick,
Sir Richard Crump, and Sir Wm. Hayman, continue
aldermen. Sir William Meyrick, Mr. Yate, Mr. Blackwell, and six more of the former common council are
left in. Mr. Wade is our town clerk.

1688, Oct. 13, Bristol. The letters say that the
Bishop of Winchester has order from His Majesty to
restore Dr. Hough and the rest of the fellows of Magdalen College, and that the Dutch fleet was at sea, but
driven in again by contrary winds.

1688, Nov. 30, Bristol. By a letter yesterday received, I was informed that the city of London refused
to quarter soldiers, and it is said the bridges at Staines,
Kingston, Windsor, and Maidenhead are to be broken
down and stands to be raised. The Princess of Denmark. with the ladies Churchill and Berkeley, went
privately away Sunday night, but it is not said whether
the Duke of Newcastle, Earl of Derby, and Lord Fairfax
have seized York and put out Sir John Reresby, the
governor. The Earls of Devonshire, Derby, Rutland,
Exeter, Chesterfield, Lords Delamere, Lumley, Cholmley, Latimer, and 6 or 7 more, are reported to be about
Northampton with 7,000 men. Sir Edward Hales is out
of the Tower and Skelton put in, who took the oaths
Tuesday last, and that day was a great council, the king
(who came to town the day before) and all the Bishops
and Lords in and about London being present and many
preliminaries to a Parliament were debated, in which
they were to deliver their opinions the day following,
as to a regulation of the Council, cessation of arms, and
discharging of Catholic officers, most of which it is
supposed would be agreed to; and no papists were at
that council. It is said Sir Jonathan Guyse and Col.
Trelawne with some regiments of the prince's will be
here this day or to-morrow. . . One come from Gloucester says that Lord Lovelace was carried off thence
by five bold fellows, Wednesday last.

A great number of original depositions in the suit
(Newton v. Creswicke) about Kingswood Chase, and a
great number in the matter of a riot there. And a
number of papers relating to the Chase and the claims
of commoners. And a 12mo. volume (temp. Car. II.), containing a copy of a charter by Charles II., and numerous
copies of, or extracts from records (from very early times)
relating to the Chase.

A portfolio contains a large number of letters to and
by Sir John Newton, Bart., and to his son. A few are
by Col. John Seymour to Sir John Newton. All except
those by Col. Seymour are on purely domestic or
business matters.

1695, April 9. Jo. Seymour to Sir John Newton,
Bart., at Barr's Court (franked by Edw. Norreys). . . .
Most of our foot in Flanders are already encamped, on
the enemies endeavouring to strengthen and enlarge
their lines, and it is believed some action must ensue
upon it.

1695, Feb. 22, London. The same to the same.—
Sorry my honest comrade, Gervais, will be called away
so soon; it being the King's positive order for all
officers to go with the next convoy, and it will be ready
for the 6th of March. . . . I am not yet assured of my
stay this summer in England, but our great ones tell me
I shall. Your old acquaintance, Ned Rowse, is made
governor of Upnor Castle, near Chatham, and C. Wortley, one of Gervas br. (brother ?), captains has his company in the guards.

1691, Feb. 25, London. The same to the same.—The
news of the town is a little strange, to have so horrid
a thing carried on at the court of France, seconded by
Englishmen. The Duke of Wirtemberg is at Ostend
with 26 battalions, ready to embark if the French dare
to land any men on the coast, with ships ready to transport them; and it is not to be doubted but Admiral
Russell with 38 good men-of-war will be about Bulloigne
Bay (the place it is said their men are to embark at)
by to-morrow, which will put a stop to this bloody
armada.

1693, March 3. The same to the same.—Every hour
brings in some of the conspirators, and I believe most
of them will be tried this week. There are 17 French
merchant ships taken by the Guernsey privateers, laden
with brandy and wines, and we are in hourly expectation of some good news from Mr. Russell. It is credibly
believed that 80 transport ships are passed towards
Scotland with 8 men-of-war, and the Scotch noblemen
are posted away thither, in case their assistance be
wanted.

1694, Feb. 20. The same to the same.—Our friend,
Mr. Blaithwayte, went hence this morning and intends
to be at Dirham [on] Monday :—my cousin, Berkeley,
has this morning lost his dear wife . . . Lord Portland has the Garter, being elected into the order last
night.

1697, April 20. The same to the same . . . . Lord
Sunderland is made Lord Chamberlain; Sir H. Hobart
and Col. Wharton, Commissioners of the Admiralty;
and Mr. Pelham, Lord of the Treasury. There will be
other changes, which are not yet public.

1697, Oct. 12, London. . Jo. Seymour to Sir John Newton, Bart., at his house Barrecourt, near Bristol.—Sir, This morne we had a mail from Holland, which brought order for the disbanding five regiments of foot, three of horse, and two of dragoons, forthwith; these were last raised here about three years since; the peace is proclaimed in Holland, and my Lord Portland is hourly expected, who will bring directions to have it proclaimed here likewise. The King will be here in three weeks. God send him a good passage to his joyful subjects; we have a very ill account from poor Nevill and his squadrons, himself being dead, with a great many officers more, and 1,500 seamen of sickness and ill provisions. I wish the ships and surviving few were returned.

Several bundles of letters, to and from Sir John Newton and other members of the family, and letters on business. Out of these I could only collect the following slightly interesting passages.

1689, Nov. 9. G. N(ewton) to Sir John Newton. A letter giving parliamentary proceedings from the 4th instant.

1710, July 21. (Dr.) John Radcliffe to (Sir John Newton). A letter prescribing medicine for Lady (Newton).

A bundle of papers and letters of the Creswicke family.

1668. Inventory of the goods and chattels of Sir Henry Creswicke, late of the city of Bristol, merchant.—In the great parlour were (inter alia) one organ and virginals, and twelve pictures, valued at 6l. 2s. 6d. In the two long galleries were 51 pictures, valued at 2l. 10s. (these surely must have been prints). One of the rooms was called the Melancholy Chamber. The valuation of the goods at his houses in Bristol and Hanham amounted to 313l. 14s. 4d. He had besides plate of the weight of 754 oz.

Copy of will of Arthur Hathway, of Bitton, victualler, 1679.

A parcel of miscellaneous papers containing inter alia,—the names of the innholders and alehouse keepers in Easton, March 16, 1674. They were in number 44, and about three-fourths are marked as "not fit."

Names of the justices of the peace for the county of Gloucester (temp. James II.), 3 pp. folio.

Printed oath of a burgess of Bristol, 1703.

Certificate (printed) that Henry Creswick took the oath against the Pretender, 1723.

A folio unbound of 69 written pages, containing, according to an endorsement on the cover, "Abstracts of "wills, places of burial, names of streets, &c., from "1381." The first page begins with the words "Coll. "out of the Great Book of Wills." The first will abstracted is that of John Wodrow, 6 Ric. II. At p. 13, is a short note of the will of William Rowley, 1479, stating that he gave several charities, particularly to the parish church of the Blessed Virgin at Dam, in Flanders, where he was buried, and to the nuns of St. Agnes, of the order of St. Austin, in that town, and to two places in Spain. (The reference is to p. 210.) At p. 7, the will of Simon Canynges is noticed (the reference is to p. 120). At p. 23, is an extract from the will of William Cannings, 1474, who had been five times mayor, and was the builder of St. Mary, Redcliffe. The latest will is of 13 Eliz. On the 55th page begin "other collections out of the Book of Wills and Enrol-"ments of Deeds not before extracted by me." All the extracts relate to Bristol and Bristol people. The writing seems to be about 200 years old.

A parcel of early deeds (Latin).

John Huse, Lord of Charlecumbe, grants to Nicholas de Lyuns and his heirs, two marks of annual rent out of the four marks of annual rent which William de Paris pays out of land in Bristol, lying in Wynchestrete, between land of the said Nicholas and land of Walter de Tylli; he reserves by way of rent a pair of white gloves or one penny at the option of Nicholas. Power of distress. The consideration for the grant was 20 marks of silver. The witnesses were William Clerk, then mayor of Bristol, William de Beaumont, and Robert de Kilmein, bailiffs of Bristol; Thomas Long, William son of Nicholas, Walter de Paris, Amand Clerk, Robert de Leghe, Gibert de Merlberge, Elias Aky, Martin Bat, John Clerk.—Seal 1½ inches in diameter, shield of arms (seemingly three bars ermine), with inscription Sigillum Johannis Huse.

A rather later grant by the same John Huse (here written Hose) to the same Nicholas de Lyuns (here called de Leonibus), of (the other) two marks of annual rent which William de Paris paid out of the aforesaid

land. He reserves a similar rent. The consideration was 20 marks sterling. The witnesses were the same as above (Kilmein being here written Kilmeynan), with the omission of John Clerk. Seal as before.

A.D. 1284, Michaelmas. Thomas de Lyons demises to Thomas de Westone, his heirs and assigns, a house in Bristol opposite the Pillory at the north end of Wynche-street, for 600 years from Michaelmas then instant; the lessee is to keep the house in repair and perform all services and secular demands to the chief lord of the fee. Witnesses, Thomas de Hamedene, mayor of Bristol. (No other witness is named, and the label although prepared for a seal does not seem to have borne one. The conclusion is that the deed was not executed.

A.D. 1286, Nativity of St. John Baptist. Thomas de Lyons demises to Thomas de Westone and Boysia his wife, and their heirs and assigns, two shops which Stephen Painter now holds, near the entrance to the mansion of the said T. de Lyons in Wynchestrete, in Bristol, thenceforth for 30 years. The lessor to keep the shops in repair, and the expenses of repairs paid by the lessees by reason of the default of the lessor he is to repay; and in default of his so doing the lessees may hold over beyond the term until they are indemnified. Witnesses, Richarde de Manegodesfelde, mayor of Bristol, William de la Marine, who together with the said Thomas de Westone was bailiff of Bristol, John de Wycombe, Walter Young (Yuvene), tanner, Ralph Wyneman, Geoffry Stots, William Dale, Roger Carpenter, tanner, John Boydin, clerk, and others. Seal of green wax. Device, a lion grappling with, I think, a dragon or serpent, of very beautiful execution. The legend, S. Thome de Lihouns.

Thomas de Lyons grants to Thomas de Weston, and his heirs and assigns, his house cum Cocke, which is beyond the gate and the land behind the house, which house is called Piscina, and is in Bristol, on the old wall behind the house late of his father, Nicholas de Lyons, in Wynchestret, between the messuage late of his sister, Alice de Lyons, and land of John de Pedertone (other abuttals and the measurements are given). He grants a way through a certain gate, and a duplicate key. Rent, ½d. Consideration, a sum of money not specified. Witnesses, Everard le Franceys, Mayor of Bristol, William de Marina and John Clerk, bailiffs of Bristol, Richard de Manegodesfeld, Thomas of St. Albans, John . of Kerdyf (Cardiff), Henry of Berewycke, Walter le Franceys, Richard le Ropere, Ralph Wyneman, John de la Leygrave, John de Wycombe, Roger the Fisher, John Boydin, clerk, and many others. Seal the same as the last.

Thomas de Lyons grants to Thomas de Westone, his heirs and assigns, a messuage in Wynchestret, in Bristol, nearly opposite the pillory at the north end of the said street, between land late of William de Parys and land of Master Robert Zeuare. Rent, to Thomas de Lyons his heirs and assigns, one silver penny, and to the King, 4½d. for landgavel, and to Sir Adam de Buctone, Kt., one silver halfpenny.. Witnesses and seal (broken) the same as to the last.

Thomas de Lyons grants to Thomas de Westone, his heirs and assigns, a cellar (with right of entry and exit), in Bristol, behind the grantor's messuage in Wynche-stret. Rent, one silver penny. Witnesses, Richard de Manegodesfelde, mayor of Bristol, William de la Marine, who with the said Thomas de Westone was bailiff of Bristol, Geoffry Suel and Henry Horncastel, seneschals of Bristol, Richard Draper the younger, Thomas of St. Albans, Henry le Waleys, Matthew le Packare, John Boydin, clerk, and others. Seal as the last.

17 Edw. I., Wednesday on the morrow of the feast of St. Thomas the Apostle, Bristol.—Matilda relict of Thomas de Lyuns, late burgess of Bristol, releases to Thomas Nas, burgess of Bristol, and his heirs and assigns, all her right by way of freebench or otherwise in the tenement in Wynchestret, Bristol, in which the said Thomas de Lyuns lived and died, being between the tenement of the said Walter Nas and the tenement in which Walter called the Yunge lived. Witnesses, Richard le Draper, Mayor of Bristol, Geoffry Agodeshalf and Simon de Boritone, prepositi of Bristol, Richard de Manegodesfelde, Walter Francoys, Adam Welischote, Ralph Wyneman, Stephen Painter, Matthew le Pakkere. John de Wycumbe, Henry Kam, Giles clerk, and others.

Thomas de Westone grants to his son John, and his heirs and assigns, the house in Wynchestret, Bristol, nearly opposite the pillory. Rent to the grantor a rose, and to Thomas de Lyons a penny of silver, rent of assize, and to the King 4½d. for landgavel, and to Sir Adam

Rev. H. T.
Ellacombe.

de Butler ½d. of silver. Witnesses the same as to the last but two, omitting Richard le Ropere and John de Wycombe.

Lucy Gray, relict of Walter de Kerdyf, grants to Thomas de Westone and Roysia, his wife, and their heirs and assigns, all her land and buildings in Bristol, in Wynchestrete, opposite the Jewry, between land late of William de Bruges and land late of John Gileberd, They were to hold of the grantor, but to pay the rents and services due to the chief lord. Witnesses, the Mayor, bailiff, and seneschals, as in the last but two, Ralph Wyneman, John de la Leygrave, Thomas de Lyons, John de Wycombe, Adam de Wylisole, John le Mareschal, John Barry, John Boydin, clerk, and many others.

Roger le Heyr de Bartone grants to Ralph Leuelance and William, his brother, and the heirs of William, three capons of annual rent wont to be received of Walter Hasting, of Wolleward, for four acres of land which he held of him in Farnberuhe. Rent, nominal. Consideration, 5s. of silver. Witnesses, Thomas Lord of Little Wollewarde, William le Wayte of Bartone, Robert Oliver, Adam de Wolleward, Peter Oliver, and others.

Temp. Henry III. William the son of Walter of Budestone, grants to Reginald Cook and Edith his wife, and their heirs, all the land which he has or may have in the manor of West Kingeham, of the inheritance of Cecily his wife, middle daughter of Martin le May; with power to devise, sell, and assign, as well in sickness as in health; rent ½d. If he or they fail in warranty, they (the grantees) shall have exchange out of his best land in Budestone, and to the value of buildings according to the valuation of lawful men of the neighbourhood. Consideration, 10 marks sterling. Witnesses, Sir Richard de Ripariis, Adam Yue, Walter Dru, William Plusbel, William Gernon, Stephen Clerk, Henry Hereberd of Budestone, William de Aswell of Budestone, Herbert, of the church of the said vill, and others.

8 Edw. II., Wednesday before feast of Nativity of St. John the Baptist, Bartone.—Thomas le heyr. of Bartone Hentmersh, grants to John son of Walter le Kynth, of Tatlesthrope, and his heirs and assigns, all his piece of arable land, over against and next Blakethurne. Witnesses, Robert le Mareschal, Simon le Wayte, John le Wayte, Robert at Garden, Walter at Barre, Robert son of Ivo, Roger le Eyr, and many others.

12 Edw. II., Sunday in the feast of the Nativity of St. John the Baptist, Bristol.—John de Westone, son and heir of Thomas de Westone, formerly burgess of Bristol, demises to Richard de Bourtone, and Agnes his wife, their heirs and assigns, his cellar, with the appurtenances at Wynchestrete, in Bristol, lying in breadth behind the tenement formerly of Thomas de Lyons, and the curtilage, late of Agnes Dale; and extending in length from the tenement now held by John le Leche to the land which was of the said Thomas de Lyons, for the term of six years from the date; rent, 2s. of silver. Consideration in hand, a sum of money not specified. Witnesses, Richard Tylloy, Mayor of Bristol, Ralph le Wyte Irmangere, Richard de Faynes, bailiff of Bristol, Symon Forstal, Thomas le Fourbour, John le Leche, Richard le Mareschal, Richard le Cartere, and many others. Sealed by lessor and lessee; but the seals are gone.

18 Edw. II., Feast of St. Leonard the abbat, Bristol.—John de Westone, son and heir of Thomas de Westone, late burgess of Bristol, demises to Richard de Bourtone, burgess. of Bristol, and Agnes his wife, for their lives and the life of the survivor, the cellar above described; rent, and other consideration as in the last charter. Witnesses, Rog. [or Reg.] Tortle, Mayor of Bristol, John de Romeneye and Walter de Prentiz, bailiffs of Bristol, Simon Forstal, Thomas le Forbor, John le Leche, Richard le Mareschal, Richard le Cartere, William Gylomyn, clerk.

28 Edw. III., Tuesday, in the feast of the Annunciation of the B. V. M., Portesheved.—Richard le Carpenter, burgess of Bristol, and Elena his wife, grant to John Mareys the elder, co-burgess of the said town, and son of the late Thomas Mareys, of Salt Marsh, and his heirs and assigns, all the lands which they then had in the manor of Portesheved, and which Ralph de Webbe, of Bristol, late husband of the said Elena, acquired from John son of John Richard of Portesheved. to them the said Ralph and Elena, and the heirs and assigns of the said Elena by charter. Witnesses, William Capel, William Kempe, John Spescy, Richard le Rene, Richard Peche, and others.

12 Hen. VII., Sept. 12. Exemplification under the seal of the town of Bristol, of seven documents exhibited by John Bagot, late merchant of Bristol. The first is the will of Walter Stodeley, merchant of Bristol, dated in 1390, opened in 1390. The documents are fully set out. The seal is nearly perfect, 4 inches in diameter, and well engraved on both sides.

7 Hen. VIII. Feb. 11, Lacok Chapter House. Johanna, abbess of Lacok, and the convent of the same place, demise to John Tayloure, and Julia his wife, and William their son, a tenement and curtilage, &c., in the parish of Button, for the lives and life of the lessees and the longest liver, at rent of 13s. Oval seal, red wax, not quite perfect, nearly 3 inches by 2 inches. Virgin and child seated under a canopy, and underneath a single figure standing under a canopy.

1533, July 17. Prerogative probate of this date of the will, undated, and codicil 3rd of April 1533, of Thomas Yonge, of Bristowe, grocer. Red wax seal, not quite perfect, representing the murder of Becket.

2 Hen. V. Christine Frome, late wife of Thomas Frome, and Thomas Frome, her son and heir, convey to John Cokkes, son of James Cokkes, a tenement in Wynchestreet; and because their seals are unknown to many they get the mayor (John Droys) to append his seal of office. All the seals remain.

22 Hen. VI., April 3. A deed by David Brenan, rector of the church of St. Maria de Foro, is authenticated in the same way; and a conveyance to him also.

In the reign of Henry VIII. . . . Weston of Oldland seals with the arms of three fleurs-de-lis, and a mullet for difference.

1660, Jan. 8. Copy of council letter signed by Edward Hyde, C., Albemarle, and 10 others, addressed to the Marquis of Ormonde, Lord Lieut. of the co. of Somerset—authorizing him and his deputies to disarm persons of all principles or who have since the Act of Indemnity shown disaffection to the King or Government, and to administer to them the oaths of supremacy and allegiance and take security for their good behaviour and proceed against recusants.

PAPERS CONNECTED WITH MONMOUTH'S REBELLION.

(Notes.) Francis Creswicke stands indicted for talking with the rebels at Kynesham.—At the two following assizes he petitioned to be tried, but his prosecutors, Sir John Newton, &c., pretended not ready. The 3rd assizes Mr. Attorney-General gave him a certiorari and at the same assizes it was allowed and he then indicted a tenant of Sir John Newton for suborning 2 witnesses against him, which bill the grand jury then found. At the hearing before the King and Council the Duke of Beaufort declared to his Majesty that he did believe that Creswicke did not talk with the rebels with any ill intent, for that he gave his grace the best intelligence that he had in the west of England. To pray a Noli prosequi to free him from the malice of his prosecutors.

Petition to the King, of Francis Creswicke of Hannams Court in the co. of Gloucester now a prisoner in the castle of Gloucester.—In this he charges Sir John Newton with malice on account of a suit at law about Kingswood Chase, and prays that he may be heard before the King and Council, and that Sir John Newton may be ordered to attend.

Petition by Francis Creswicke to Sir William Gregory, one of the barons of the exchequer and judge of the assize for the county of Worcester.—After mentioning the device by which his tryal had been delayed and noticing the malice of Sir John Newton and Mr. Player, two of the most violent opposers of his Majesty's right of chace in Kingswood,—he asks that the Judge will take bail for his appearance at the next assizes held for the county.

Another petition (at the back of the last) asks the Judge to allow him to remain in Gloucester jail till he can have his habeas corpus to appear at the King's Bench.

Petition to the King by Dame Elizabeth Davies, relict of Sir Thomas Davies, deceased, Lord Mayor of London in 1676 and 1677—asking that her brother-in-law Francis Creswicke may be bailed, and that his wife and relations may have access to him.—And another by her asking that Creswicke may be heard before the King and Council, and that Sir John Newton might be ordered to attend; or that he might be discharged or bailed.

Another petition by Creswicke to the King. Creswicke being then removed by habeas corpus to the King's Bench Bar.—Alludes to the malice of his neighbours by reason of his having got a decree in the

S s 4

matter of Kingswood Chase: and that they charged
him with having had discourse with the rebels at
Keynsham. Says that his house being half a mile from
Keynsham, he went there to get intelligence for the
Duke of Beaufort, but did not go near Lord Grey.—
Asks that the attorney may be allowed to consent to his
(Creswicke) being bailed, and that he and Lord Grey
may be confronted.

1 James II., Aug. 31. Original deposition by James
Phipps of Bitton, cole-miner, sworn before J. Lowforde.
—Says that on Thursday 25 June last about 2 p.m. he
was at a mead called Sydenham in the parish of Bitton
near Keynsham, looking on the rebels there, viz., the
late Duke of Monmouth and his army: he saw a
trooper ride out of the said army towards Francis Creswicke, who was then walking in the path in the said
mead, and alight, go up to Creswicke, and soon afterwards return. He saw William Hawkins, of Bitton,
and the said Creswicke immediately come and stand by
the wall there for the space of one hour about 60 yards
from the place where the Duke of Monmouth was.
When the rebels cried Horse and away, Creswicke and
Hawkins were standing with the deponent. Says that
Creswicke did not deliver any papers or speak to the
Duke of Monmouth or Lord Grey. Says that there were
near a hundred people looking at the rebels, and that
Hawkins is a person of ill fame.

Draft affidavit by F. Cr. (Creswicke) that Sir Ric.
Hart, of Hannam, is the son of a decimator, who deci-
mated the deponent's father in the late usurper's times,
and lately married a sister of Sir Wm. Jones, formerly
Attorney-General to his late Majesty, and that Lady
Hart declared, as the deponent is credibly informed,
when the Duke of Monmouth and rebels were at Keynsham, that if the Duke had come a little further into
Gloucester she would have given him some hundreds of
cheeses, she keeping then a dairy on a farm called
Filgrove, near that place. That soon after the last
sessions of Parliament held at Oxford, Sir Richard Hart,
a member thereof, declared that he was for the Bill of
Exclusion, and after that made his brags ('tis reported)
that he had opposed the delivering in the charter of
Bristol to his late Majesty.

Copy of Sir T. Bridges's affidavit.—That on the 25th
of June last when the rebels were at Keynsham, Creswicke came and (deponent's house being taken up for
Mormouth's quarters) asked him to go and stay at
Hannam. As they were going they met an old man
whom the deponent sent to a place called Syddenham
mead, to get intelligence that the deponent might send
to the Duke of Beaufort. Creswicke thought the old
man not capable, and offered to go himself, if deponent
would go to Hannam alone. In about two hours Creswicke returned and gave deponent some account of
what he had seen and learned there in the camp as he
pretended. They both then went on to Hannam and
lodged there that night. Next morning Creswicke
came early to deponent and asked him to write to the
Duke of Beaufort that the rebels were gone from Keynsham towards Bath or Warminster, as he, Creswicke,
was informed, and the deponent did so, and sent the
letter the same morning by his own servant from Creswicke's house.

A few short memoranda of what Thomas Harrison,
Thomas Rose, and Anne Siswek had deposed (or could
depose) about Sir R. Hart's sayings.

(Indorsed.) William Hawkins and John Isles, their
testimony as T. Rosse gave me.—28 June 1685. " Wil-
" liam Hakens made othe be fore the gostes apase
" (Justice of Peace).—He says that he saw the squire
" (Creswicke) in Sydenham give 2 papers to Lord
" Grey, one about a foot long, and the other about a
" foot and a half long, and that Lord Grey gave them
" to a man that was by him with a star on the left
" breast," &c.

1685, July 8. Thornbury. Copy (by Creswicke) of
letter to the Duke of Beaufort.—He says what Bridges
says in the deposition above :—" The contents of Sir
" Thomas's advice I know not : what I observed was
" that Monmouth's army consisted of above 1,000 horse
" and about 8,000 foot, 8 field pieces with some Drakes,
" and 30 ploughs, whereof 4 was teemes of good horses
" and the rest oxen : his men some well armed, others
" indifferent, and some not at all, only having an old
" sword or a sticke in their hand ; however, I observed
" many musketts and other ammunition in their car-
" riages. Gray, Ferguson, Wade, Tyler, and Specke
" were there at Keynsham."—Defends himself against
Sir John Newton's accusations.

(Indorsed.) Copy of the Kalendar, my affidavit,
D. of Beaufort's Mittimus, and Sir W. Atkyns Mittimus.

John Stone to be hang'd, drawn, and quartered.
Elizabeth Lumbart to be hang'd, but after re-
    prieved.
John Asplin to be transported.
Christopher Tilly remain as before.
George Martin, burnt in the hand and acquitted.
William Randle, the like.
Robert Peere, ⎫
Thomas Stephens, ⎬ To find bail for appearance
Hanna Gale, ⎭   the next, and acquitted.
Peter Rivers to find bail for his appearance the
    next sessions of the peace for the county, and
    acquitted.
Philip Cambridge, to be sent into Somersetshire
    to be tried for high treason.
Francis Creswicke, ⎫ Accused for high treason,
Geo. Saunders,   ⎬ to remain in Goale.
Tho. Skyn, to find bail before one of the justices
    of this county, to appear the next.

Copy of an affidavit by Creswick, regarding Sir Jno.
Newton purposely keeping away a witness so as to delay
Creswick's trial.

1685, July 1. Duke of Beaufort to Col. John Jefferyes.
—Order to send two troopers to assist the constable in
taking Francis Creswicke and Geo. Saunders to Gloucester Gaol. (Copy.)

1685, July 1. Rob. Atkyns to the keeper of ye castle
of Gloucester.—Order to receive the bodies of Creswicke
and Saunders. (Copy.)

1685, Nov. 30. Affidavit by Thomas Attwood of the
Inner Temple, Gent., sworn before F. Wythens, that on
28th instant Creswicke attended on Lord Grey and
asked him whether he had any conference with, or received any paper from Creswicke on the 25th of June,
at or near Keynsham, and the Lord Grey declared the
negative, nor did he ever see Creswicke before to his
knowledge.

1686, Jan. 13. Whitehall. Sunderland to the
Attorney-General.—Directs him to enter a Noli Prosequi
on the record of the indictment against Creswicke.
(Copy.)

1686, Jan. 17. R. Sawyer to Sir Samuel Astey, Kt.,
His Majesty's coroner and attorney in the court of K. B.
—Says that an indictment was preferred at the assises
at Gloucester on March 3, 2 James II., against Creswicke
for holding correspondence with the late rebels in the
west ; and that by virtue of the King's sign manual,
dated 13 January 168⅚, he authorises Astey to enter a
Noli Prosequi. (Copy.)

1686, Feb. 23. Stapleton. Tho. Stubbs to Capt.
Seamer (Seymour?).—A challenge to fight. Seymour
was to meet Stubbs at the sign of the White Hart at
Hungerford, between Marlborough and Newbury.

With the papers relating to Creswicke is a copy (3½
close folio pp.) of a paper indorsed Creswicke's Case,
made by Mr. Ellacombe in 1823 from the original then
in possession of a Creswicke. It gives a full account
of the going to, and return from, Sydenham mead,
above mentioned, and of what took place between him
and Sir Thomas Bridges.

166⅘, March 8. Whitehall.—" Charles R. " to the
mayor of the city of Bristol. After stating that George
Bishop then inhabiting within the city of Bristol,
had therefore had the custody of the papers and
writings of John Bradshaw, who (the better to carry on
his execrable designes) took divers papers and writings
out of the office of the King's Library at Whitehall,
which could not yet be recovered,—The King directs
him to call up and examine Bishop, and take measures
for the recovery of the papers and writings, and to
make a catalogue of any such found, and with a copy
thereof together with the proceedings, to give a full
account to Thomas Raymond, clerk and keeper of the
papers and records of State.—Countersigned by Edward
Nicholas. Wafer seal at the top.

1730, Aug. Bitton.—Berkeley Seymour to . . . .
In default of a satisfactory answer by the bearer about
repayment of money, which he alleges that the addressee and Mr. Creswicke and the other scrub managers
of Hannam took from his tenants,—" I will demand
" justice of you this afternoon at your door with my
" sword. If your neighbour, Mr. Justice Creswicke,
" has a mind to divert himself that way, my cousin
" Bowles, who is come from Bristol on purpose, has
" a sword at his servis ; and if the tall learned divine,
" Dr. Creswicke, the present worthy dean of Bristoll,
" has any inclination to be of the party, the habit of a

" dragoon which he generally wears will be proper for
" the occasion: a young fellow of Kings Collegde
" under Master of Arts, shall throw more Greek &
" Latin in his teeth then he will be able to digest in
" twelve months."

(A note by Mr. Ellacombe says that the Bitton
Seymours originated from a bastard brother of Lady
Jane, and that the last of these Seymours was hanged at
Gloucester for murdering his brother Berkeley, in Jan.
1742, and was brought home and buried under the communion table, Seymour at that time being the lay
impropriator of the great tithes.)

Folio, 17 century, 25 pp.—Copy of the allotments on
the partition (27 Jan. 21 Eliz.) of the estates of Robert
Braine, Esq., deceased, between Dame Eme the wife of
Sir Charles Somersett, Kt., and Anne the wife of
George Winter, Esq., sisters and co-heirs of the said
Robert Braine.

The manor place or mansion house of St. James in
the city of Bristol was actually divided into eastern and
western portions between the ladies. The property
was nearly all in Gloucestershire; a little was in the co.
of Monmouth. The items are very many. The manor
of Staunton in Gloucestershire was divided. Of the
manor house there, it is said that nothing but some
broken old walls remained.

Manor of Oldelonde, co. Gloucester.

The following are original rolls, with modern transcripts:—

18 Ed. III. Rental of the tenants of Simon Bassett.
18 Ed. III. Court roll.
25, 28, and 29. Court rolls.
37 Ed. III. Rental of 2 parts of the manor and of
the 3rd part.
Edward III. Court rolls for years 40, 42 (curia
legalis), 44 (2), 45, 47, 48, 50 (2).
Richard II. Years 1 (2), 3 (2), 4 (2). 6, 8, 9, 17 (1s
Court Domini Johannis Deveros), 17, 20. and 21. And
three or four rolls where the year of the King cannot be
ascertained.
Oldelande and Bytton. Rental. 13 Hen. VII.
Bytton, Hannam, and Oldelande. Court baron of
Lady Katherine Newton. 44 Eliz.
Badgeworth. View of frankpledge, with court baron
of Lady Katherine Newton. 44 Elis., 1 Jac. I.,
2 Jac. I.
Weere Burgus. View of frankpledge and court baron
of Lady Katherine Newton. 1 Jac. I., and 2 Jac. I.
Bitton Hundred Rolls. 5 Ric. II., 8 Ric. II., 9 Ric. II.,
16 Ric. II. (and III., where the year of the King cannot be ascertained), and 1 Hen. IV. (2). The heading
is *Hundredum legale,* except in the roll of 5 Ric. II.,
where the word *regale* is used. At each court four
knights were chosen, and took an oath. The knights
at the court of 5 Ric. II. were Roger Marmyon, William
Brown, Robert Kyntone, and Henry Freeman.

Manor of Bitton, co. Gloucester.

Views of frankpledge in the years 1719, 1722, 1724,
1725, 1729, 1737, 1738, 1739, 1746, and 1747. These
are on foolscap paper, and contain the names of the
suitors and jurors, returns by the tything-man of the
names of the inhabitants summoned to appear, and
presentments by the jury (with original signatures).
Down to and including the year 1729 the lord of the
manor was Sir John Newton, Bart.; in 1737, 1738, and
1739 the lord was Sir Michael Newton, Bart.; and in
1746 and 1747 Susan Archer, widow, was lady of the
manor.
A large number of copies of Records from early times
relating to the parish and manor of Bitton.

Three extracts from a Register of Lacock Abbey, in
the possession of Mr. Talbot, regarding its possessions
within the parish of Bitton.
Letters, 1665 and 20 years following, by and to Sir
John Newton and other members of the family, relating
to Barr's Court and the possession of it.
Oldland, Hannam, &c., co. Gloucester.—Many depositions on oath before Richard Hart, or Henry Creswick, or Thomas Long (and in many cases before
Richard Hart and Henry Creswick), Justices of the
Peace, concerning assaults and other offences, in the
years 1729, 1730, 1732, 1735, 1736, 1738, 1739, and
1740. The greater number are in the year 1738.

5.

Four packets of papers, indorsed Lewton MSS. In
these I find—
Returns by the assessors of rates made on the following places in Gloucestershire, viz., Bitton, Oldlands,
Hanham.
Bitton. 1677, Aid to build ships of war (2); 1691,
169½, Aid; 169¾, 1698, 1705, 1717, Land tax; 1708, aid;
1724, Poor rate.
Hanham. 1695, Aid to the King; 1698 and 1699,
disbanding the army and providing for the navy; 1703,
money for the Queen and for war with France; 1704,
Aid to the Queen by Land tax; 1705, the same; 1709,
the same.
West Hanham. 1662.
Oldlands. 169½, aid; 1691, Aid; 1695, Assessment of
real estate to the 4s. in the £; 1703, Aid by a land tax;
1704, for the land tax; 1705, the same; 1707, the same;
1708, the same; 1712, the same; 1715, Aid; 1717, Aid;
1720, Aid by Land tax; 1736, the same.

ALFRED J. HORWOOD.

THE MANUSCRIPTS OF WALTER CHARLES STRICK-
LAND, ESQ., OF SIZERGH CASTLE, WESTMORELAND.

For more than 600 years, by evidences in the
Castle, and from remoter times, the Stricklands have
been seated at Sizergh, and Mr. Strickland has, preserved in three large volumes, a very curious and
perhaps complete series of the deeds relating to the
property, commencing in the 12th century. Nearly
100 years ago Mr. Thomas West (the author of The
Antiquities of Furness) made accurate abstracts of
them, and these are in a single volume.

Among the early deeds are two relating to the Priory
of Watter, and a grant to the Abbot and Convent of
Bruer; and portion of a roll cartulary of the Abbey of
Cokersand, and a grant to the Priory and Convent
of Kertmell.

A deed of 8 Richard II. by John de Wyndesore has
a note by Mr. West that one Wyndesore was engaged
with Alice Perrers, and was privately married to her
before the King's death. (But it was William de
Wyndesore who married her, and Lowth, in his Life of
Wykeham has shown that he did not marry her until
after Edward III. was dead.)

In the 27 Hen. VI. are seen the terms in which
Walter Strickland served as a military retainer to the
Earl of Salisbury.

In the 15th century are two papal dispensations for
marriage.

In the 39th Elizabeth is a list of the tenants on
the Strickland estate, with the rents, fines, services, &c.
And a list (temp. Hen. VIII.) of the servants and
tenants able to bear arms, bowmen and billmen, horsed
and unhorsed, and all harnessed : 280 in all.

There are a few civil war documents, and among
them a letter asking Colonel Strickland to furnish fowl
for King Charles's table at York.

There are large bailiff's accounts of the manors of
Margaret Countess of Richmond (mother of King
Henry VII.).

A folio volume. Abstract of the ancient writings
belonging to Thomas Strickland, of Sizergh, Esq.,
made by Thomas West (author of The Antiquities of
Furness), 1778. This volume consists of 188 pp. and
an index.

No. 1, temp. Richard I. In this deed Sizergh is
spelt Sigaritberge. W. de Lancaster grants lands to
Gervaise de Ainecuria (Deincourt). One of the witnesses
is Roger Dapifer.

No. 2. Gilbert son of Roger Fitzrenfrid, Baron of
Kendal, grants to Gervaise de Ainecuria and his heirs
that they shall be free of Noutgeld for all lands in
Westmoreland and Kendal, which Noutgeld Gervaise
paid for lands held by military service.

No. 6. A witness to this is John de Bellocampo,
sheriff of Appleby (temp. John).

By another deed Sir Walter de Stirkeland grants to
the church of St. Mary of York, and the Prior and
monks of Wederhill, four acres of land in Great Stirkeland. Among the witnesses are Walter, Dean of
Westmoreland, and Michael, Vicar of Moreland.

A witness to another is Thomas son of John, Sheriff
of Westmeringland (Westmoreland) and Cumberland.

No. 9. Peter de Brus to William de Strickland and
Elisabeth his wife. Release and exemption from service at the Baron's Court;—from the *pultura* of the
land-serjeant, both in man and horse; and from the
witneema ; in respect of all their lands in Hakethorp
. . . . and Sizergh.

No. 14. In this is named William de Daker, Sheriff of Westmoreland.

No. 15. Ralph de Ayncurt to John Gernet. Ralph obliges himself to find a mill and miller in Hencaster to grind John's corn multure-free when the hopper is empty, unless the corn of Adam Gernet or his heirs be in the mill. John Gernet and his heirs are to furnish the miller with reasonable entertainment while the corn is grinding.

No. 21, temp. Ed. I. W. de Stirkeland grants Crosscrake Chapel to the Priory and Convent of Kertmell. They were empowered to choose a chaplain and provide for him out of the revenues of the chapel, to celebrate divine service and pray for the souls of the founder and his successors, and to be exempted from receiving lepers and other infirm persons.

No. 23 (temp. Ed. I.). Lease from Sir W. de Sterkeland to Sir Richard de Preston and Anabel his wife, of land in Great Sterkeland for 12 years; rent 54s., and they were to grind the corn growing upon the said land at his mill, at the rate of the 13th dish. (Sir William held the land of Margaret de Ros.)

1642, Oct. 20th. H. (Earl of) Cumberland to Sir Robert Strickland, Kt. and Col.—Order to raise the regiment of which he, Strickland, is colonel, and lead it to York, where he is to receive further orders, to defend the country against marauders on horse and foot, who are neither authorised by His Majesty nor by the Earl.

16—, March 17th. Robert Strickland to his son Sir Robert Strickland, M.P. 'Tis sad news to hear the Lords and you should go contrary. God grant good; I fear it. 'Tis reported the King's a wise young man. In the name of God let him play Rex to God's glory, his own preservation, and the kingdom's good. (Sir R. Strickland was M.P. 1661.)

1666, Oct. 28, Ripon. Robert Strickland to Lady Curwen at Wakinton.—On business.

There are a few family letters on business.

16—. List of Her Majesty's [Catherine of Braganza?] servants and their wages. (Sir Thomas Orby and Sir Rd. Minshull are mentioned.)

1663, April 8th. Francis Nevile to Sir Thomas Strickland, M.P. He hears that they are about to banish all Jesuits and priests; that may, probably, hinder the growth of popery.' But surely if you could so educate priests that they would by their sound doctrine, good lives, and conversation become good examples to the people, that would [work] such a cure as would prevent all fears of relapse. But this will hardly be done so long as you suffer pluralities, by which it appears that some of our priests abound, others as good as those wholly want, which is as ill as banishment. For the excuse, if you could prevent the extortions and oppressions of the collectors, that revenue would never be lessened, altho' out of the matter a larger, surer, and more certain revenue may be raised to the Crown with far less chance and much less charge. —If you would take care to purge all electors of . . . . . . governors or trustees for charitable uses, governors of money in lands or stocks, &c., all or most of them being now [such] as neither affected our last government (?) either of Church or State, nor this, it would much redound to the peace of this kingdom. I commend these things to your consideration.

16—. Jane Strickland to her husband, Sir Thomas Strickland. Domestic.

1671, Nov. 16th. Jo. Kaye to his uncle.

1673, Dec. 1st. Jo. Hudleston to Madame Harper.

16—. Draft of a letter by Thomas Strickland to Lord Ar(lington?).—I cannot but acquaint your Lordship how the alterations made and making at Court are resented here by all those whom I ever esteemed the most passionate lovers of His Majesty's person, and the most faithful subjects to the Crown, every man being full of threats and the like discourses. Anglesey outed, Littleton and Osborne in his place, the Duke of Ormond out, Lord Orrery and Sir Robert Howard in his place, the standing forces to be disbanded, Henry Nevill and St. John daily expected. Whether all this be true or not I know not, but it fills many men with fear and wonder, and at least this conclusion is made by all that it will teach others to complain, and the complaining part will easily make an orator, if that be the way to gain favor and preferment. And if I mistake not in my measures, these alterations will not agree with the sense of the kingdom, if the people's sense be represented in their epitome, the House of Commons, but it's said the Parliament shall never meet. Yet if that were, I fear the King's occasions

would occasion the calling of another, and I am confident many of the same would appear again, and I hope the same temper, I pray God not a worse.—He does not think these alterations have his (Lordship's) concurrence.

1748, April 16th, Whitehall. A pass for Thomas Strickland, Mary and Henrietta Strickland, and James and Thomas Brown, and two servants, to pass from Dover to Calais on board the James sloop; and to return. Signed by the Duke of Bedford.

The following deeds amongst others are in a small black box.

(n. d. Hen. III.) John de Fischer gave to God and St. Mary and the convent of the House of Watter, in free alms, a bovate of land which he had of the gift of John, son of Ankelin of Lokintun, for the souls of his father, mother, and self. Witnesses : Richard, chaplain of Watter, Reginald and Terri, chaplains of Killingwic, Stephen the deacon, Walter the deacon, Alan the clerk, Oyartin, clerk of Killingwic, &c.

15 Edw. L., Hockday. Emma, widow of Roger le Devencys of Myddelton lease to the abbat and convent of Bruer, one acre of meadow with the appurtenances in the Emede of Middleton, for five years.

15 Ed. I. Richard son and heir of Roger de Deveneys of Myddelton grants a similar lease. Dated at Bruer.

A deed poll. Robert Talun, son of Robert Talin, with the assent of his heirs makes the cellarer of the House of Watter his steward to do foreign service to the superior lord of the barony, which was of W. Fossard, de feudo dimidii militis, videlicet de quinque carucatis terræ cum pertinentiis in territorio de Killingwic, whereof tho canons and brethren of the House of Wattre had his gift. (Therefore here 10 ploughlands made a knight's fee.)

1460. Brother Robert, prior of the order of Mary the Mother of God of Mount Carmel, to [blank]. Gives participation in the benefit of all 'masses, prayers, fastings, vigils, &c. as well in life as in death.

1291, Prid. Id. Aprilis 19, Ed. I. W. Michel gives to God and St. Mary, and the abbat and convent of Bruer, all that he had from Westharpetre, by way of exchange for his land in Westaipton. Witnesses, Sir Roger de Nodras and Sir John Galafre.

1333, St. Peter ad Vincula. Warton-in-Kendal. A deed by Robertus filius Roberti filii Radulphi de Pontefracto de Warton in Kendal.

1334, June 29th, York. Richard —— to John the chaplain of ——. Gives the sum of six marks to say divers services in the church of —— for the souls of his three wives, Beatrice, Agnes, and Dionisia. Witnesses : Henry de Belton, mayor of York, Richard de Laycestre, W. de Grafton, W. le Sporier, bailiffs of the city (and others named). Seal of the grantors and the large seal of York. The secretum of Henry de Belton is a shield charged with a hand between two stars. The crest looks like a cross.

8 Ric. II., Dec. 20th, London. Letter of Attorney from John de Wyndesore to Sir Walter Strickland.—Appoints him guardian of his estates in Westmoreland and Lancashire. (About this time one Wyndesore was engaged with Alice Perrers, and was privately married to her before the King's death. See Ayliffe's Calendar under the article Irish Records.)

27 Hen. VI., Sept. 1st. Indenture of release from the Earl of Salisbury (Richard Nevill, 8th Earl), to Walter, son and heir of Sir Thomas Strickland.—Walter engages to serve the Earl against all men except the King.—The Earl is to give Walter yearly 10 marks in time of peace, and in war the same wages as men of his rank are accustomed to have; Walter to be well horsed and armed and arrayed;—he is always to be ready to wait on the Earl at home and abroad, and to be accountable to the Earl for one third of the profits made in war.—When any captain or man of rank is taken, the Earl is to have him, paying a reasonable reward for him. (Walter Strickland slew the traitor Henry Talbot, and thereby gained the reward of 1,000 marks, which he released to the King, 18 Hen. VI., for which the King made him Master of his harriers and Keeper of Calgarth Park.)

1458, July 22nd. A dispensation from Vincent Clement, the Pope's Nuncio, for W. Redman to marry Margaret Strickland, being within the fourth degree.

16 Ed. IV. A dispensation for Thomas Middleton to marry Johanna Strickland, widow. It is directed to the Archbishop of York or his Vicar-General, and is dated from Rome, Nov. 9th, by Pope Sixtus IV.

5 Hen. VII. 6 kal. April (27th March). Dispensation from the Roman Penitentiary for Walter Strickland to marry Elizabeth Salkeld, being within the fourth

degree of consanguinity, under seal of office, 7th of Pope Innocent VIII.

(About 38 Hen. VIII.) A book of Walter Strickland, Esq., containing the names of all domestic servants and tenants able to bear arms, with their habliments of war,—

Bowmen, horsed and harnessed -	- 59
Bilmen, horsed and harnessed -	- 74
Bowmen, without horse, harnessed	- 71
Bilmen, without horse, harnessed	- 76
	280

At this period Walter Strickland was Deputy Steward of Kendal.

39 Eliz. A book containing the names of all the tenants of Thomas Strickland, Esq., in the manors, &c., of Sizergh, &c., with their rents and services, reliefs and heriots. The fines were arbitrary; in the same hamlet some tenants pay nine or ten years' rent at the charge of the tenant. The *gersuma* sums were oppressive.

14 Car. 1, 1638, Sept. 18th. Commission from "Wentworth," Lord President of the Council in the North, to Robert Strickland, Esq., to command a regiment of 900 trained band soldiers in the North Riding of Yorkshire.

1640, April 6th. "Northumberland" to Col. Robert Strickland. Orders to march his regiment at Newcastle-upon-Tyne.

1640, April 4th. Copy order by the King to the Vice-President of the North to call together all the colonels of the county of York, or lieutenant-colonels or mayors, to give orders for marching six regiments of train bands to Newcastle; to have two weeks' pay in advance. The colonels are to be excused attendance in Parliament, and the Vice-President is not to move out of his presidency, though chosen a member. The regiment is to be relieved when the King's troops come up.

1640, July 17th. Copy of the King's commission to the Earl of Strafford to raise and array all men capable of bearing arms and of serving in the war. He is to appoint a deputy and put martial war in force. (This copy is signed by Strafford.)

1640, Aug. 10th. Commission signed by "Strafford" appointing Robert Strickland Deputy-Lieutenant in the North Riding of Yorkshire.

n. d. A letter from Sir Edward Osborne to Colonel Strickland, acquainting him with the King's arrival at York, and requesting him to favour him with some fowl for the King's table. Desires him to wait on the King, who intended to speak with all the commanding officers of the North. (Sir Edward Osborne was Vice-President of the King's Council for the North, and Lieutenant-General of the forces raised in that part of the country. —He was father to Sir Thomas Osborne, the first Duke of Leeds.)

1640. Copy petition to the King from the Lords and gentlemen of the county of York, to be excused from raising two months' pay in the county for the support of the train bands, and offering one months' pay. It seems that the King promised, as an encouragement to the expedition against the Scots, that the heirs of all who died in it should be free from wardship. The petition is signed by the leading men of the republican party; amongst them are Philip Wharton, Fairfax, Bellasis, Falconbridge, and John Hotham.

Copy of the King's answer.—Council letter of the 17th August 1640.—Reproaches for passing by the Lord Lieutenant, whom they are desired to consider as their sovereign, and to apply to him before troubling the King.—The King charges them with a false return of the charge of last year's service, which they stated at 100,000l.—Says that the billotting of soldiers is the ancient right of the Crown, and that he cannot divest himself of it; and that he cannot march armies without it, provided that provisions be paid for according to Petition of Right. He promises that the army shall be duly paid, and shall require no more than free lodging and the debt contracted to be paid by the captain of the company, provided it did not exceed 6d. per day.

Copy of the petition of the Scotch army after the affair of Newborne-upon-Tyne, desiring leave to approach the King's person. They call themselves Commissioners of the late Parliament.

Copy petition for the redress of grievances, signed by eleven lords. On the resolve of the King to meet the nobles at York on the 24th of the month.

1640. last of Aug. Warrant from the Lord President at York for raising a supply of 26s. 8d. for each soldier. Signed by Edward Osborne.

1640, Aug. 25th, York. "Charles R." (and seal) to Col. Robert Strickland, to draw together the train bands under his command, and such others as he can, and to be at the rendezvous at North Allerton on the 29th.

1640, Aug. 25th. Order signed by Holland, Goring, and another, to all mayors, &c., &c., to furnish Col. Robert Strickland with ten carts for the use of his regiment marching to the Border.

1640, Sept. 3. Warrant under the hand of (the Lord President) Edward Osborne, to the King's messenger, to apprehend all to be named by Col. Strickland, who refused to join the regiment commanded by Col. Robert Strickland, to oppose the Scots who had got to Newcastle.

1640, Sept. 7th. Copy of Strafford's orders to the chief constable to tell the deputy lieutenants, justices of the peace, and other gentlemen, to attend the deputy lieutenant at York on the 11th of September, the day appointed by the King to be there.

1641, July 3. A sheet of vellum, signed by "Essex." The Earl of Essex and Ewe, Viscount Hereford and Bourchier, Lord Ferrars of Chartley, Lord Bourchier and Lovayne, Lord Lieutenant of the county of York, appoints Robert Strickland, Esq., to be a deputy lieutenant. Attached is a copy (signed by Essex) of the King's letters patent appointing the Earl to be lieutenant of the county.

1641, July 3rd. Commission from the Earl of Essex to Robert Strickland to command 800 train bands in the North Riding of York.

1642, May 14. York. "Charles R." and seal.—Commission to Thomas Strickland, Esq., to command a company of 114 train-band soldiers.

1643, March 25th. W. (Earl of) Newcastle appoints Walter Strickland to command a company in a regiment of foot under the command of Col. Robert Strickland, to be raised by beat of drum in the north of England.

1643, June 2nd. A captain's commission from the Earl of Newcastle to Sir Robert Strickland to command a troop of horse called the North Riding troop, to be raised by sound of trumpet.

1644, July 15, York. A safe conduct for Sir Robert Strickland, of Thornton bridge, and his family, to return from York, with a protection for his house and estate. Signed by the three generals for the Scotch and English army at York, viz., Leven, Fairfax, and Manchester. (The battle of Marston Moor was fought on the 3rd of July. Prince Rupert was beaten.)

1646, April 9th. "Leven" with his seal.—To the Lords and Commons for sequestrations.—Having taken into consideration the articles made upon the surrender of the city of York, and particularly the 11th article, namely, that all citizens, gentlemen, &c., should when they pleased remove with their families and goods, &c. yet, understanding that Sir R. Strickland, notwithstanding that he is within the benefit of the articles, has his estate sequestered. Tells them that if Sir R. Strickland hath acted nothing against the Parliament since the rendering of York, he might in justice possess his estate free from sequestration.

166—. A certificate signed by Castleton, Fra. Wortley, T. Fane, Henry Cholmeley, and about 20 others, including William Fairfax, that Sir Thomas Strickland would be a proper person to have the farm of the Excise of beer and ale.

1672, May 25th. The King grants to Sir Thomas Strickland a lease for 21 years of duties on foreign salt, imported into England from beyond seas.—The rent was 1,000l.

(1673.) A draft letter by Sir Thomas Strickland to a fellow M.P., thanking him for excusing his absence in Parliament. He says he would not "swear negatives "to speculative matters of divinity." He protests his loyalty.

1682, July 18th. A regrant of the lease of duties on foreign salt, &c., to Sir Roger Strickland, on his succeeding Sir Thomas Strickland. Rent 2l.

1685, Oct. 31st. Renewal of the lease by James II.

1745, Nov. 10th. Copy of Prince Charles' (Regent) letter to the Mayor of Carlisle. Seeing that the Mayor intends to resist the Prince, puts before him (the Mayor) the dreadful consequences of a town being taken by assault.

7 to 8 Hen. VII., Michaelmas to Michaelmas.—A roll of 12 skins written on the dorse also.—Accounts of all the Ministers of manors of Margaret, Countess of Richmond, mother of the present King. (This roll relates to Kendal.)

The moneys were paid to Sir Reginald Bray the receiver. On the 10th skin the total owed was

700l. 12s. 10d. 11th skin, the account of W. Walter Chaplain, deputy of Sir Reginald Bray. In the margin " Dominium de Kendal, officium receptoris." This is a summary. Total 339l. 10s. 2d. 12th skin, sum of all allowances and livings 324l. 17s. 11½d. He owes 14l. 12s. 1d., out of which there were allowances.

Roll 7 Hen. VII. (paper), 16 leaves, about 1½ foot long. Kendall Castrum.—Accounts of shepherds, stock-keepers, &c.

Paper rolls ; 12 sheets. Accounts of Thomas Warren, bailiff, and various others, 5 Edw. 6, &c., beginning with Nateland.

There are about 70 or 80 paper rolls of bailiffs accounts for Nateland, &c. ; and relating to the property of the Nevills before their intermarriage with the Stricklands.

1569. Roll of vellum, about 10 feet in length and 5 inches in width. Inventory of the goods and chattels of Walter Strickland, Esq., appraised April 1569 upon the book oaths of (three persons named). The totals are, —at Sizergh, 660l. 11s. ; May 1569, at Hanaby, 358l. 13s. ; Thornton bridge, May 1569, 118l. 19s. 1d. Grand total, 1,138l. 3s. 8d. In the Lord's chamber was a throned bed. Under the head of plate, cups and spoons of a kind called wherteren (sometimes querteren) are valued at 5s. 6d. per oz. Two lyverraye potts of 86 oz. are valued at 6s. 3d. per oz. The value of the plate was about 130l.—There were mattrass, thrawen bed, cover-let, counterpoynte, bolstar, sheets, blankets, pillows.—Numerous horses and other cattle.

With ready money the whole personal estate was 1,364l. 11s. 3d. The debts were 331l. 12s., leaving 1,032l. 19s. 3d., from which was to be deducted 200l. owing for the wardship of Isabel Place, leaving a net balance of 832l. 19s.

A roll of vellum of the 16th century, about 6 feet long by 4 inches wide, containing boons and services to Sir Thomas Strickland, payable by his tenants in Nat-land, Stainton, Sigiswick, Hincaster. The greatest number of hens payable by one person was 6 ; none did more than one days harrowing or four days shear-ing. The total number of hens payable was 34 dozen and 9, besides 14 capons.

32 Henry VIII., June 11. Copy grant of the site of Halton Priory to Thomas Culpeper in fee.

A folio volume. Convencions of servants wages by Mr. Robert Colynson, prior, anno Domini 1531. Names of some servants and wages and particulars. 23 written leaves.

Fol. 2–4. Copies of 16th century documents and letters relating to the priory of Hawtempryce, co. York.

Fol. 6. Redditus resolutus of all the lands and tene-ments of the monastery of Hawtempryce.

Willesby, A.D. 1532 ; rents payable at Pentecost. Cottingham rents payable at Pentecost and Martinmas, St. Peter ad Vincula, and the Purification. Haulaghlye and Wolferton. Rentals for Hessill. Rentals for 1533, 1534, 1535 and 1536.

At the end, Copia vera per me Wm. Goundsell, 1613.

A folio of about 36 leaves, 1571, being a book of pay-ments and receipts paid and received by Alyce Stryk-land, widow, from the 1st of August, anno 14 Eliz.—Receipts for rents, fines, and corne. Payments for servants wages at different times.—Also in 1572 and several following years.—This volume is covered with a leaf of the book of Ecclesiastes of the 12th century.

A folio. A note of all such money as Nicholas Wright of Thornton Brigge hath received to the use of his right worshipful master, Sir Thomas Boynton, Kt. since the 7th of January in the 25th year of Elizabeth.

33 Hen. VIII., Feb. 13th. Henry Bekwith to Lancelot Alford. Some of the King's tenements and jetties, parcel of His Majesties exchanged lands about Hull want repair ;—if not attended to will cause damage to the inhabitants and double cost to the King.—Deliver to Wm. Graves, collector of the rents, such timber as is felled within the King's woods.

c. 1300. A roll of about 4½ feet long in two mem-branes. (A skin or skins is wanting at the top.)—A cartulary of Cokersand Abbey.—Abstract of about 35 documents ; three on the dorse are in a later band.—The names of the donors are Gilbert le Noble, Orm son of Adam de Kellet, Robert de Hotonrice, William de Newbigging, William son of William de Newbigging, Robert de Hoton, Adam de Hotonruc, and Alice his wife, Adam de Lupton. Roger de Barton, Adam dean of Lancaster, Ralph de Beckley, Henry son of Henry de Redman, William son of Gilbert the clerk, William son of Roger de Burton, Roger de Yeland, Henry son of Norman de Redeman, Orm son of Thovo, Gilbert son of Patrick de Curwen. Thomas de Betham, and Thomas son of Gospatric.—The lands given were in Frebank, Newbiggin, Hotone, Lupton, Writhtintone, Burton, Hildreston, Yeland, Benetham, &c.

14th century. The last skin of a roll of vellum, con-taining six documents.

1. John son of Sir John de Eynell, Lord of Egman-ton, gives notice to all his tenants and reseants in Cun-dale and Thornton or Swale, that he granted all services to Alexander de Ledes. Dated at Pontefract, Tuesday after Trinity, 17 Ed. II.

2. Copy of the deed of grant of the two manors of Cundale, &c., dated from Cundale, Wednesday before the Nativity of John the Baptist, 17 Ed. II.

3. Copy of a deed of grant by John de Eynell to Alexander de Ledes and Elizabeth his wife, of the watermill of Faldington on Swale ; dated Tuesday before the Feast of St. John of Beverley, Archbishop, 14 Ed. II.

4. Copy of a deed of grant by John de Eynell to Margaret his daughter of his vill of Leteby, &c. Satur-day after the Feast of St. Swithin, 14 Ed. II.

5. Copy of a deed of grant by John de Eynell to Alexander de Ledes, and Elizabeth his wife, of the parke of Leteby. Saturday, after the Feast of St. Gregory, Pope, 15 Ed. II.

6. Copy of a deed of release by John de Eynell of A. de Ledes from a bond of 200 marks, which he gave in security to refeoff John de Eynell for life of the park of Leteby. Sunday after Michaelmas, 18 Ed. II.

My best thanks are given to Mr. Strickland for his hospitality at Sizergh Castle.

ALFRED J. HORWOOD.

THE MANUSCRIPTS OF REGINALD CHOLMONDELEY, ESQ., OF CONDOVER HALL, SHROPSHIRE.

R. CHOL-
MONDELEY,
ESQ.

The greater part of this collection consists of documents, letters, and papers written or possessed by John Smyth, of Nibley, co. Gloucester, steward of Lord Berkeley, and M.P. for Midhurst, co. Sussex, in 1620. Another portion consists of collections in the 18th century, by William Cowper, of Chester, for the history and antiquities of Chester, and of the Isle of Man. There is a well filled volume of notes made by Mr. Smyth while he sat in Parliament, but they do not seem to contribute any information beyond what is already known. There is a fine early copy (on a roll of parchment) of the poem called *The Stacions of Rome*, giving an account of the various churches and shrines at Rome, of the reliques there, and indulgences consequent on visits to them.

The Abbey of Kingswood, in the co. of Wilts, was founded in 1139, by William de Berkeley. Dugdale (in the Monasticon) gives an account of the foundation of the house, extracted from a Register of the Abbey, then (A.D. 1651) in the possession of John Smyth, of Nibley. This Register does not appear to be at Condover Hall; but from among Mr. Smyth's papers and deeds I collected several early rolls, and upwards of 50 early charters of and relating to the Abbey, and not noticed by Dugdale. Short notices of these are given below.

In the beginning of the reign of King Charles II. the Court of the Marches of Wales claimed jurisdiction in Gloucestershire, and their claim was resisted: it was very likely to support the resistance that Mr. Smyth obtained the folio volume which contains copies of the case and arguments, temp. Car. I., where the jurisdiction of the Marches Court over the four shires of Gloucester, Worcester, Hereford, and Salop was debated at length.

Three folio volumes contain the names and personal descriptions of nearly all the able-bodied men in Gloucestershire in 1608.

The collections for Cheshire history and the Municipal history of Chester are considerable. Among them is a copy of Archdeacon Roger's Breviary for the city of Chester, (Mr. Wilbraham's copy has been described in a previous Report); Cowper's Life of St. Werburgh; Bostock's poem on the Earls of Chester; Flower and Glover's Visitation of Cheshire in 1580, with additions in 1609; an account of the doings in and about Chester during the Civil War, and Malbon's account of Nampluych, 1642-55.

For Lancashire there is an account of the Earl and Countess of Derby, and of the siege of Lathom House. There are also collections for the Isle of Man, and copies of prayers and meditations and letters by the Earl of Derby before his execution, and a copy *signed by the Countess* of the articles for the surrender by her of Castle Rushen and Peel Castle.

The papers and printed books about Virginia and the Somer Islands (temp. Jac. I.) are valuable.

Numerous letters and papers in 1641 and 1642 tell of the affairs of Chester during the war, and the transport of troops thence to Ireland; and one in Feb. 1641-2 shows Algernon Sidney as Captain of a company of foot.

In 1597 the Earl of Essex asks the bailiffs, burgesses, &c., of Shrewsbury to be allowed to nominate their burgesses for the Parliament about to be summoned.

The rules for the domestic service of Sir Thomas and Lady Berkeley at the end of the reign of Elizabeth are so curious that they are given in full below, as also the agreement in 1609 between Sir Thomas and Mr. Smyth, regarding the service and expenditure in the household. In the same portfolio with these is a copy of a secret Article to the Treaty of 1729 between Spain and England, whereby the King of England absolutely gives up Gibraltar. It purports to have been executed in due form. Another portfolio contains a series of letters and papers in 1642 about Berkeley Castle and the siege and surrender thereof, including the original articles for the surrender, signed by Col. Forbes for the Parliament, and by John Smyth for Lord Berkeley. In 1673 is a letter from the Earl of Castlehaven, at Brussels, to the Duke of Ormonde, complaining of his uncomfortable state and expressing a desire to quit his appointment. The Duke of Ormonde had an anxious time while his grandson, the young Earl of Derby, was in ward to him, as the letters in 1673-5 from the Earl and his governor (in France) show.

The school of Wootton Edge was in the time of James I. the subject of law proceedings, and here are some papers connected with it. There are several

original papers and opinions by foreign Doctors, taken in 1634 or 1635 on the question (for fiscal purposes) whether tobacco was a victual.

R. CHOL-
MONDELEY,
ESQ.

The letters are several hundreds in number. From these I have selected some of interest for notice below, including a letter from Edward VI. to the Mayor, &c. of Chester about some matter not disclosed; a letter by Queen Mary to the same persons, dated only six days after the death of Edward VI., against the Duke of Northumberland and Lady Jane and her husband; a long letter by Queen Elizabeth about the coin; a letter on vellum, signed by James I., to the Emperor of Japan; and three letters by Charles I., of which one is to tell the Mayor of Chester to endeavour to seize Hollis, Hampden, Pym, Hazelrigg, and Strode, accused of high treason and fled; and a letter by Charles II., in 1684, asking contributions for Chelsea Hospital, in which he had already spent much money. Many letters are and by the Duke of Ormonde, and a few by the Duke of Albemarle. It appears by a letter from Arlington to the Duke of Ormonde that James II. at the beginning of his reign ordered the revival of an ancient service or allowance called *All Night*, which was to be served up in the Prince's Chamber. In 1689 a *quondam* Cook at Oxford is recommended by the Bishop of Winchester and the Duke of Ormond to the Vice-Chancellor of the University, as a fit person to keep a billiard table in Oxford. A number of letters chiefly in 1642 and 1643 show the state of Gloucestershire during the Civil War, and a long letter dated from Youghal in August 1642, gives an account of the fighting in Ireland. A letter in 1706, by Mr. Loup, tells of the battle of Ramillies, and gives the contents of two letters, by Capt. Butler, detailing the siege and taking of Barcelona; and in another he gives the contents of a letter by Butler, detailing the taking of Carthagena.

Among a few letters to Mr. Cowper by literary men is an original by Alexander Pope. It is slightly imperfect, but is accompanied by a copy made from the original when perfect. A letter in 1755, by David Hume, acknowledges a correction in his History of England made by Mr. Cowper. There are two letters signed by Sir John Fielding when he was blind; and a letter from Mr. Hinton, telling of the burial of Dryden on the previous Monday at the expense of the Kit-Cat Club; and another saying that Kennet and Tanner were to furnish Dr. Wake with materials for an answer to Atterbury's attack on Wake's book (on Convocation).

There are numerous papers of assessments for Berkeley, North Nibley, and other places in Gloucestershire in the 17th century to rates and royal aids.

A roll of vellum nearly 14½ feet by 12½ inches wide. It is composed of five membranes, but one had more; there is a hiatus between A.D. 520 and A.D. 800. It contains universal history from Adam downwards; but after the first membrane Roman and British history are the special subjects. The chronicle ends (about two thirds down the back of the roll) with the marriage of Henry VI. of England, and a head of Edward IV. of England, in whose reign this copy was probably written. The composition is nearly all in double columns, between which the succession of patriarchs, emperors, and kings, is given in shape of a pedigree, their names, and sometimes crowns, and sometimes fancy portraits, being placed within circles; the so-called portraits are well drawn and the two types of face which serve for all our kings have great character. There is a coloured drawing representing the temptation in Paradise. Twining round the stem of a tree is a human form with a serpent's body from the waist downwards offering an apple; immediately in front under the tree Eve offers one to Adam. Another drawing is of Noe taking juice of the grape from a vine tree. The text *begins, Tempora summa lineamque descendentem ab exordio mundi cum successoribus quorumdam regnorum et regum ad eruditionem futurorum duximus annotare, ut ex brevibus lector devotus plura colligere possit.* Under the year 206 from King David, the compiler places the reign of King Leir in Britain, and gives briefly the story of his three daughters. Under A.D. 444 he gives the letter of the Britons to Aetius. Under A.D. 503 he says that Aurelius Ambrosius was succeeded by his brother Uter, who, according to the History of the Britons, *si fas est credere*, by the aid of Merlin brought from Ireland the *corea gigantum*, which is now on Salisbury plain and called Stonehengis. The accessions and a few of the chief events in the reigns of English sovereigns are given; the last entry is the marriage of Henry VI. in the 23rd year of his reign.'

T t 3

A roll of vellum 15 feet 3 inches long by 4 inches in breadth (14th century). It contains the English poem called the Stations of the Cross, in writing of about the end of the 14th century. The first 7½ inches of the roll are occupied with two paintings in colours; the lower one represents Christ crucified (between the two thieves) and V. Mary and St. John standing in either side of his cross. In different parts are seen the lance, reed and sponge, and ladder. Two embattled niches supported by three columns make a framework to the figures, the figure of Christ obscures the centre column. The picture above represents four persons, apparently two male and two female, with a diapered wall for background and arches over head; both paintings are much rubbed. Preceding the poem are the following sentences in Latin.* Quicumque intuebitur hec arma domini nostri Jhesu Christi de peccatis suis confessus et contritus habet tres annos indulgentie ex concessione sancti Petri primi. Item triginta . . . . . fices dederunt quilibet . . . . . dit centum dies indulgencie. Item centum viginti . . . . . pontifices quilibet illorum de . . . . . ginta dies indulgencie.

The poem begins—
He yat wil his soule leche
list to me i wil him teche.

This edition of the poem is somewhat like that printed in 1866 at p. 113 of vol. 15 of the publications of the Early English Text Society; but there are many variations.

Quarto, vellum, 14th century, Latin. A Homily.—Augustinus de Spiritu et animâ.—Liber Pastoralis Curæ. (St. Gregory to John Bishop of Ravenna).—Isidorus de summo bono.—Augustinus ad Comitem. (There is a note by an early hand saying, that the writer does not think that this work is by the Great Augustine). It begins, O mi frater, si cupias scire.—Liber Magistri Hugonis de instructione Noviciorum. Begins, Non preter solitum facere quosdam judicabo.—St. Augustine de similitudinibus.—The following note of ownership occurs, "Rowland Oseley owith this book."

Quarto, vellum, 14th century, Latin, 278 leaves. This is a collection of numerous alchymical, astrological, and medical treatises. The first begins, Magnifico principi et illustrissimo domino A. primogenito Regis Jerusalem et Sicilie Dei Gracia, Duci Calabrie ac in regno Sicilie vicario generali, A frater de ordine p'cl' capellanus ejus, &c. Cum prima causa est summa . . . . . hic autem liber de Essenciis intitulatur. It contains two principal books; 1st, of real essences; 2nd, de intentionalibus. The first contains nine treatises (1. of the essence of the Creator, 9. of the being and essence of Accidentals).

Compositiones divinorum ignium. Suus suo Amiens amico Anselmus Ferario pro amore, &c.

A treatise compiled from a Latin translation of an Arabic work by Albubery Acazy, son of Sacharia, a philosopher of Damascus.

Dixit Messazlat ore dicta Hermetis. Ends, explicet Liber Hermetis de quatuor parlitres.

Incipiunt figure septem planetarum.

(40b.) Liber de triginta verbis (Alchimical).

(44.) Incipit liber A, B, C dictus.

(46b.) Incipit Epistola Avicennæ Abyucene de Alkymiâ; et est bonus liber.

(54.) Tractatus Magistri Ric. Fornivale de Alk.— Begins, Dixit Arthurus expositor hujus operis, Accipe arsenicum. Ends, Dixit Arthurus, qui est Ric. de Fornivale, ne vilipendatur ista operatio quis nunquam nisi nunc exnit filia principis ita nuda, &c.

(61.) Tractatus Alberti de plantacionibus arborum et conservacione vini. Begins, Modus incisionis arborum multiplex est, sed magis usitatus et magis communis est ut evellas ipsum urtulum a sua matre sub uno nodo ad longitudinem duorum unguium diviso. Ends, qui residet in fundo vasis ut putrescant.

(72.) Philosophia dividitur in tres partes, viz., &c.

(129.) Liber de spiritu occultate Alkymiæ. Begins, Dixit Mereheris ad fledum, Serva quod dicam tibi et scribe. Sume ex lapide ubique reperto qui vocatur robio et nascitur in duobus montibus. Ends, est philosophice (phice) preferenda.

(156.) Septem sunt corpora, Saturnus, Jupiter, &c. Ends, Explicit tractatus Richi.

(159.) Quidam accepit unam unciam et dimidiam unciam de Kibvit et dimidium lune et dimidiam salis armoniaci. Ends, vermilionem fixum.

(169.) Incipit exposicio bona super librum O venerande pater. (Alchymy).

(172b.) Incipit liber Arythmetice. Begins, Quantitatum anima (aª) centuria que magnitudo dicitur. Ends, Consonancie musicales. Ista sufficiant pro summa hujus libri.

(191.) Summa de Kirbit oleo coctum. Ends, ut invenies quod cupis de tribuente de fratre Osberto.

(193b.) Incipit liber vocatur A, B, C. Begins, Habeatur de lunata eris li. 6 vel plus.

(196.) Proprietas et opera animalium et piscium et avium ven . . . . . extracta de libro Alberti quem composuit de moribus et naturis animalium, per Shlinzin de Sandhz, &c. Begins, Sicut dicit philosophus. The 1st Chapter is De vermibus. The last is De vermibus.

(215.) Cum ego Rogerius rogatus a pluribus sapientibus, do separatione ignis ab oleo, &c. &c. Redigamus corpora ad suam originem. Ends, Explicuit Mziusm et Orhmsin, &c., &c.

(216.) Cum tibi promisi mittere duos cedulas subsequentes, unam ut dixi mitto et hoc de mixtione, &c. Ends, Expluit Mzhat, &c. (ut supra).

(218b.) Cum de ponderibus utilis sit distinctio. Ends, Et si aliqua dicta sit penes te ligata rescribas et solvam ligamenta cum auxilio unius dei in trinitate et trinitatis in unitate. Vale. Explicit Verdhsm . . . . . ad patrem hlgznûc de ozrht alk.

(230.) Incipit in nomine domini brevis exposicio summe totius libri universalis operis et majoris tû hermetê patrem.

(230b.) Iste liber qui dicitur de Salibus. Enarratio Archillar. (At the beginning he says that before he made the translation he was rich and afterwards was poor, because he lost all in opere alkumiœ;—he prayed; he was told to go into the desert;—he went where Alexander went. Ends, explicit liber de corporibus et spiritibus (by Archileus the philosopher).

(244b.) Incipit liber de secretis naturæ secundum diversos auctores, et dicitur liber Dioscoridis de finicis ligaturis, et sunt hic plura bona. Begins, Nemo cquius inter stolidos reputare debet.

(255.) O Moriene, primum querere libet. Conversation between Morienus and King Kahalid.

(265.) Sinonomia Alkumye, per A., per B., &c.—And another, imperfect tract; 278 is the last leaf.

From a number of deeds three have been selected on account of their age, and a fourth because its contents are interesting.

Henry, son of Herbert, to all his friends and men. He gives to William de Aubenes, for his service, in fee (feodotale) and hereditarily, and to his heirs, the land of Bochude, free from all service, and the land of la blaque welle, and at Caen, denrû quandam, near the mill of Gaimar. The witnesses are Henry, the lord's son, and Richard and John, clerks, Thomas de franco vallo, and Alexander, his brother. This charter was made at Caen in the house of Henry, the son of Herbert, on the last of the kalends of July, witness Duranne, the clerk who made it, and witness also, William de Terra Wasta, and John, son of Roger, and many others. (12th century. The seal is gone.)

Maurice, Lord of Berkeleye, gives to John Taber, in fee, for his homage and service, all that land which Eaditha, relict of Roger Roke, sometime held of him, with a messuage in the vill of Newport, viz., &c., &c.; and land in Reham between a meadow of the Abbat of St. Augustine of Bristol, and a meadow of Ralph Dole. Rent 30d. quarterly. Gersuma 20s. Witnesses, Sir (dominus) Maurice de Salso Marisco, Sir Roger de Lokintun, Robert de Hales, then seneschal, Andrew de Brokeslane, John de Egintun, Nicholas de Crauleye, Thomas Mathias, Adam Flambard, Robert Herde, Hugo, son of Juel, and many others. (13th century. Seal gone.)

Isabel de Longchamp, daughter of Henry de Mineriis, grants to the church of St. Oswald and the canons there all her land in Culkerton, which came to her hereditarily; for the souls of her and her ancestors, to be holden in frankalmoign. She also grants other lands specified. Witnesses, Ralph Musard, John (?) de Eyton, Peter de Eggeswere, and others named.

1528, Aug. 18. Thomas [Wolsey] Cardinal, Priest of the title of St. Cecily, Archbishop of York, Primate of England, and Chancellor, and Legate de latere of the Apostolic See, to Richard Bromeley, monk of the monastery of Vale Crucis of the [Cistercian] Order, in the diocese of St. Asaph, a priest having professed a regular

---

* The red paint is rubbed off in several places. In other respects the roll is in fine condition.

life.—Absolves him from the guilt, if any, of apostacy incurred by him by the not wearing his habit, and from all ecclesiastical penalties hitherto incurred, and from all excesses (except those reserved to the Holy See) hitherto by him committed, and gives him permission (because of his weakness of body) to use linen next his skin, and long leggings (*caligia*) of a decent colour, also . . . . under his hood during divine service as well in the choir as in the cloister, and to talk in a low voice in the dormitory and elsewhere, and in his chamber, after . . . . to eat and drink moderately, and on a journey to choose a fit confessor secular or regular, and to hear confessions from those who should come to confess to him, and to absolve them from all excesses not reserved to the Holy See, and to be elected abbot of any monastery of the said order, or take any other claustral dignity which he can conscientiously assume . . . Dated from his house near Westminster. Oval seal of red wax (about 5 inches by 3 inches) in case. Figures of Sts. Peter and Paul in niches under a Roman pediment. Underneath is the coat of arms of Wolsey surmounted by a Cardinal's hat. The legend is "Sigillum Thome Archiep. Eb]or, Legati dc latere, ad dispensationes;" portions of the inscription and coat of arms are lost. At the foot (left corner) is the name of John Hughes and (right corner) the name of Claibun the Datary. The document states Bromeley to be the son of a monk by an unmarried woman. (Latin.)

THE ABBEY OF KINGSWOOD, CO. WILTS [GLOUCESTER].

A.D. 1240. A skin of vellum, 2 feet 1 inch long, by 5½ inches in breadth. Reragia W. Cellerarii de Kingeswode ad festum S. Petri ad vincula, anno gracie M.CC.XL. xii. ixsol. 1d.—Recepta a suprascripto termino et deinceps usque ad festum Sancti Andree, viiili.—Summa totalis xixl. ixsol. 1d.—The accounts on the front of the skin are in 2 columns, under the heading, "Expense de " suprascriptis reragiis et receptis." Numerous items of payments occupy nearly the whole of the column, but a surplus of 3l. 10s. 10d. was in hand. Then, from the feast of St. Andrew to the feast of the Purification, the cellarer received 7l., and thence to the feast of St. Peter ad Vincula 1241, he received 17l. : total, with the arrears, 27l. 10s. 10d. The second column of the front, and the single column of the back of the skin, contain other expenses ; and the sum total of expenses on both sides of the skin amount to 24l. 1s. 5½d., up to the feast of St. Peter ad Vincula, 1241, and the Reragia were 3l. 9s. 5d. (together 27l. 10s. 10½d.), against 27l. 10s. 10d., for which the cellarer was accountable.

A.D. 1242. A skin of vellum 14 inches long, by 5 inches in breadth.—Reragia Bursariorum Domus de Kingeswode, anno gracie M.CC.XLiᵒ. ad festum S. Petri ad Vincula de omnibus receptis domus. viᵐ xx. li. et xvli. vs. ob. tota lana et lok simul computatis et xx. libr de arreragiis lane anni xlii. The receipts to the feast of St. Andrew (for flock, rents, sale of sheep, &c., &c.) were 166l. 10s. 6d., including the arrears. The expenses from the feast of St. Peter, 1241, to the same feast day of St. Andrew, were 153l. 14s. 9d. The receipts from the feast of St. Andrew to that of St. Peter, A.D. 1242, were 290l. 7s. 3½d. with the arrears, and the expenses for the same term were 115l. 10s. 2½d.—The arrears (or surplus) were 174l. 16s. 11d. In the latter expenses are payments to the cellarer, the sub-cellarer, the shepherd, 10 marks to the use of the church, 18l. 0s. 0½d. for building a new inn (hospitium).

A.D. 1255. A skin of vellum 18 inches long, by about 7 inches in breadth. Stipendia domus de Kingeswode, anno gracie Mᵒ.ccᵒ.lvᵒ. (Two columns in front, and one on the back.) The payments are to ploughmen, drivers, and others at various estates of the Abbey ; the sum total of all the payments " tam in stipendiis quam " in messionibus " for the whole year was 77l. 9s. 11½d. The left hand column contains the Stipendia de Hokedaye.

The back of the skin contains payments for the same estates for the year 1256. The sum total is not given.

A piece of vellum 9½ inches by 7½ inches, being the lower portion of an account (for about this time) of the expenditure of the Abbey. One item is 8d. for the expenses of the Abbot going to Tintern. The vellum is of the same width as that last described, and the accounts are written by the same hand, and although it is clean and in good preservation, it may be assumed to be part of the second membrane of the account next described.

A.D. 1262-3. A piece of vellum 20 inches long by 7½ inches in breadth. An old English capital E. is at the head. It has lost, from damp, much of the left and

some of the right column. It is written on both sides, and contains receipts for the year 1262-3.

A.D. 1288. A piece of vellum 10 inches long by 5 inches in breadth. Computus of brother William de Cumb. for the granges of Cherthull, Baggestone, Hull, Aldrinton, A.D. 1288. (Written on both sides.)

A.D. 1311. A piece of parchment 14 inches long by 5 inches in breadth. Account of the cellarer of Baggeston (sale of stock : the murrain is mentioned. It seems to be only the 1st membrane of the account.)

A.D. 1316. A piece of parchment 8½ inches long by (on an average) 4½ broad. Computus of the Cellarer from the feast of St. Lawrence, 1316, to the feast of St. Michael in the same year. Sum of receipts 28l. 18s. 11d., and of expenses 31l. 7s. 1d. Below are other expenses amounting to 33s. 2d.

14th century. A piece of parchment 10 inches long by 3½ inches in breadth. The computus of brother Walter for the grange of Egge.

14th century. A slip of parchment, 10 inches long by 3½ inches in breadth, containing a series (in Latin) of questions to an inquest, and answers by them regarding the tenure of certain lands by and under the Abbey.

15th century. Two membranes sewn together, each about 9 inches long by 5 broad. The first entry is " Johannes Scoche dedit l. vaccam operi ecclesie pressli " viii. s." Then come (on both sides of the first skin) names with sums of money opposite. It may be inferred that this is a list of donors to the church.

24 Hen. VI. A piece of vellum 13 inches long by 4½ inches in breadth. Rental of the Abbey of Kingeswood. (Torn at the bottom ; it is evidently only the beginning.)

Robert de Berkelai, for the souls of his father and mother, and for the health of his own soul, confirms to God and the church of St. Mary, of Kingeswode, and the monks there serving God, the gift to them by Gilbert de Tudenham of seven acres of land in the fields of Niwentone, of his fee, to be holden in frankalmoigne. Witnesses, Roger de Berkelai, his uncle, Juliana, his wife, Oliver de Berkelai, Eustache de Camme, Thomas, his seneschal, William de Hesele, Thomas, parson of Niwintune, Thomas de Loventi, William de Seai, and many others. Circular seal nearly 3 inches in diameter. Man on horseback, sword in hand, on left arm a shield charged with a bend sinister ; legend broken. Secretum 1½ inches broad ; man on horseback ; legend, Sigillum Roberti de Berkelai.

Robert de Berkelai, for the health of his soul and the souls of his two wives, Juliana and Lucy, and of his father and mother, and of all his ancestors and successors, gives to God and the church of St. Mary of Kingeswode, and the monks, &c. in frankalmoign, one virgate of land in his manor of Wottune, at Sumheie, with the messuage and all appurtenances, viz., that virgate which Liulph Durant held, and all the land which Richard de Bisseford held with a messuage and mill, and all issues (*sequelis*), which the said mill used to have. Witnesses, Roger de Berkelai, Henry, his son, Philip and Oliver, brothers of the said Roger, Jordan le Ware, John de Craulega, Simon de Olapenne, William de lahessler, Alexander the chaplain, Hugh de Bradelega, William his brother, Maurice, son of Nigel, John de Eginton, Adam de Grava, William de Hagelega, Robert Disse, Richard lesbut, Robert, son of Master Alured, Hugh Pistor, Henry the clerk of Bradelega, Nicholas de King ; and many others. (Seal gone.)

1230. 14 kal. Aprilis. William, by the grace of God, Prior of St. Oswald of Gloucester, and the Convent, with the assent of Walter, Archbishop of York, primate of England, in consideration of 100l. sterling, sell and quit claim to the monks of St. Mary, of Kingeswode, all lands and possessions which the vendors had in Culkertone. Sealed by the archbishop and the vendors. Witnesses, William de Putot, sheriff of Gloucester, Peter de Eggesworth, and five others named.

1232. Purification of the B. V. M. Roger, son and heir of Adam of Cherletone, confirms to K.* all gifts by his father Adam and Henry de Ribbesford, in Cherleton. Witnesses, Bartholomew la banc, Oliver de Berkeley, Geoffrey de Chausi, William de Rodmerton, Laurence de Lasceles, Nicholas, son of Henry of Culcreton, Walter de Uptune, Roger de Duttune, Philip de Tettebury, William son of Elyas, Geoffry Custance, Roger Barelli, Walter Bernard and others.

1239. Feast of St. Philip and St. James the Apostles. William Mannsel grants to K. for 20 years his lands in Culcretune, with the vileins, &c., in consideration of 40 marks paid by the monks. Witnesses, Oliver de

---

* The letter K. indicates the Abbey of Kingswood.

Berkeley, Robert de Rocheford, Robert, Dean of Kene-
pole, W. de Mineriis, Bartholomew la banc, Roger de
Duttune, Walter de Uptune, Philip de Reteburi, John
le New, Richard Colin, of Culcretun, Hen. Bernard,
Geoffry Custance, Nigel de Ollurthe . ., Walter Tysen,
Roger Calfhage.

1243. Feast of St. Martin. John del Egge grants
to K. all land which Gilbert, his father, held, and
which descended to him (John), at le Egge, in the manor
of Sunundeshale, in exchange for the land which the
monks had at Rocwde, in the parish of Bisleye. Witnesses, Peter de Eggewoth, Oliver de Berkelai, William
de Troham, Richard de Abbenessi, Robert de Mulecot,
Henry de Strode, Roger Petipas, and others.

Nones of July ( ), year of Pope Gregory IX.
(1227-1241), Otto Cardinal, deacon of St. Nicolas in
prison, legate of the Apostolic See, to all, &c. He has
seen letters of Pope Honorius in this form, Honorius to
the Cardinal Archbishop of Canterbury and the Archbishop of York, and the suffragans, &c. of the provinces
of Canterbury and York : Whereas the abbats of the
Cistercian Order, in the time of the General Council
under Pope J., decreed that thenceforth the brethren of
the Order, lest by occasion of their privileges, churches
should be oppressed and pay tithes of property which
they should cultivate by themselves or at their expense to
the churches to which they were formerly paid, and that
Pope J. wished to extend the rule to other Orders ; and
that disputes had arisen. Honorius says that abbats
and brethren of that Order should be free from tithes
as well of possessions had before the General Council,
as of newly tilled land (novalibus), whether acquired
before or after the General Council, which with their
own hands or at their own expense they cultivate ; also
of gardens, &c., &c. Dated at the Lateran, 7 kal. July,
the 6th of his Pontificate.—The transcript was made at
the prayer of the abbat, &c., of Kingeswode.

1280. Feast of St. Mark the Evangelist. Agreement
between the abbat &c. of K. and brother Adam, prior of
the Hospital of St. Bartholomew of Gloucester. The
former give to the latter five acres of land in Acche-
cumbe over against Olepenno (the parcels are minutely
described.)

William Bretun gives to God and the Abbey of K.
one cottelda of land in Osleworth, with the appurtenances
which Alice Roke sold to him for five marks. Rent to
Alice and her heirs of one white glove at Easter or one
penny, and to the chief lord 1 lb. of cummin. Witnesses,
Geoffrey de Chausi, Oliver de Berkeley, Bartholomew
labanc, Nicholas Ruffus, John le New, Nigel de Osleworth, Henry de linez, Walter clerk of Hillesloge,
William de Bradelege, and others.

Roger de Niwentune gives to the Abbey of K. land
of Bollacok, between Ywolege and Egge, near le Ros,
in the manor of Niwentune. Witnesses, Sir (Dominus)
Geoffrey de Chausi, Henry de Linez, Peter de Ywelge,
Walter de Neylesworth, Hugh de Ryllocote, Robert de
Uptune, and others.

Roger de Niwentun, son of Philip de Berkele, gives
to K. an acre of land in Niwentun (the boundaries are
stated).

Agreement between the Abbat of K. and Luke de
Chirintune. The abbat, &c. gives to Luke land and a
messuage in Chirintune, formerly of Walter de Brac-
kele, which he gave to the monks of Bethlesdene, and
which the monks of Bethlesdene sold to the monks of
K. Rent 6s. sterling. The abbat asks Luke not to
sell or pledge it without the consent of the monks of K.
Witnesses, Bartholomew labanc, Roger de Duchtune,
Thomas de Rodeburwe, William de Rodmertune, Henry
Hardewine, Nicholas de Leppesete, Geoffrey Custance,
and others.

Adam de Cherletune gives to K. one virgate of land
in Cherletune, portions lying in Garstone, Carnete-
crundle, Sepestalle, Hareburne, Hadenhulle, Cleihulle,
Wensierd, Olledene, Froggaputtesforlong, Westlang-
forlong, Brodesierd, Buledone, &c.; viz., half which,
&c., and half which, &c.: the two half-virgates of land
ita per campos jacent divise. Witnesses, William Came-
rarius, Geoffrey de Chausi, Roger de Almundestre,
William Scai, Adam his son, Robert de Dudim, Henry
de Culcretun, John of Tetbiri, William Butevilain,
Adam Barete, Alured Barete, Nicholas de Kingeswode.

(In this charter the acreage of the numerous portions
is given, and all together amount to 32 acres.)

Alured Barete gives to K. two acres in Culcretune.
Witnesses, Henry de Culcretune, William Scai of Tre-
sham, Adam his son, Henry son of Bernard, Nicholas
de Kingeswode, Geoffrey son of Custance, Adam de
Culcretun, William Butevilain.

Roger Barette gives to K. a messuage super fontem,
with a curtilage and the appurtenances in Culcretune.
Witnesses, Bartholomew labanc, William de Rodmertun, Nicholas de Culcretun, ... William de la
Planke, Roger de Calfhage.

Agreement between Roger Baret and K. It states
that in 1243 Roger Barette, on Michaelmas day, gave to
K. one acre in the fields in Culcretun, viz., &c., for
10 years, until they should have received 5 croppos from
one acre and 5 from the other, "exceptis inhokis si forte
contigerint fieri in eadem villa :" that the prior took
the first crop from the two acres in the autumn of 1244,
and would take the last crop in the autumn of 1253,
besides crops de inhokis quotiens contigerint. For this
they gave Roger 6s. After the term the lands are to
revert to Roger. Witnesses, Walter de Rodmerton,
Lawrence de Lasceles, Robert Passelewe, G. Custance,
Nicholas de Culcretune, Walter, Henry Bernard.

Agreement between Thomas the Abbat and the Con-
vent of K. and Adam son of Henry of Chirintun. They
grant to Adam the land which the said Henry held of
K. in Chirintun, and an additional croft which they
had of Walter de Burton and land in Smalecumbe.
Rent 8s. Witnesses, William de Rodmertune, Robert
Passelewe, Ralph Hereward, Lawrence de Laceles,
William de Westrop, Hugh son of Nigel, Henry, parson
of Rodmerton, Henry de Culcretun, Roger Barete,
Geoffrey son of Constance, and others.

The following five deeds are tied together :—

Henry Bernard, of Culcreton, releases to K. (his
lords) all his right in certain land upon Littledune, near
the way leading to Rodmertun, at the north part of
Culcretun, so that the monks for ever may cultivate,
plough, and reap; together with the field of Littledun,
in which the aforesaid land lies; notwithstanding any
common right of him and his heirs; saving, however, to
them common pasture of the said land after harvest
(messem), with the beasts of the monks. Witnesses,
Roger de Ducktune, Walter de Uptune, Henry the
serjeant (serviente), Com. Ric. de Tetebur: Master
Robert de Segrei, . . . Robert de Passelewe, Lawrence de Lasceles, and others.

Walter son of Henry Bernard releases to K. the same
lands as last above, in the same woods. Same witnesses.

Geoffry Custance, of Culcretune, releases to K. the
same land in the same woods. Same witnesses.

William Mansel releases to K. the same lands.
Among the witnesses, Henrico serviente Comit. Ric.
de Totuburi.

Elizabeth, who was the wife of William de Gam-
mages, releases to K. the same lands.

The following nine deeds are tied together :—

Alice Toky, in her widowhood, releases to William
Bretton in fee, for a gersuma of 5 marks of silver, a
cotella of land in Oslewurthe, to be holden of her. Rent,
a pair of gloves or 1d. Witnesses, Geoffrey de Chausi,
Oliver de Berkeley, Richard Burgens: Walter the
writer, William de Sumery, Robert le New, Nigel de
Osele, Roger Petipas.

Alice Toki, of Gloucester, says that while a widow
she gave to K. one cotelda of land in Oslewrthe, paying
to the chief lord of Oslewrthe what she did, viz., one
pound cimini at Bristol fair, and regal service. Witnesses, Geoffrey de Chausi, Oliver de Berkeley, Richard
Burgeis, Walter le escriven, Walter Tisun, and other
witnesses, as in the preceding.

Henry de Belesby grants to K. a tenement in Oslewrthe, and all right in the vill which he has or may
have from William de Rocheford, brother of Thomas de
Rocheford. Rent, a pair of gloves, price 1d., or a silver
halfpenny. Witnesses, Lords John le Brun, Richard de
Cromhale, William le Maunsel, and John de Wanton,
Knights; Henry le Lyncz, Peter de Ewelege, Robert
le Ductun, Richard de Wockeseye, Walter de Neylesworth.

Robert de Rochefort confirms to K. the donation by
John Culling of all lands, &c. which he had in Osleworth, they finding all necessaries, and a burning lamp
day and night in the church of St. Nicholas of Osle-
wrth, as John Culling was wont. Witnesses, Oliver
de Berkeley, &c.

Richard le Oure, son and heir of Gillard de Oure,
confirms to K. the lands in Oslewrthe, which came
from his mother. Witnesses, John de Lokynton, rector
of the said vill, and others. (This deed is imperfect.)

William de Rocheford, brother and heir of Thomas
de Rocheford, gives to Henry de Belesby, for his
homage and service, the tenements in Oslewrthe, &c.,
and what may come to him after the death of his

R. Chol-
mondeley,
Esq.

brother, Thomas de Rochefort. Witnesses, R. le Bret,
. . . John de Kellecote, Hugh de Kellecote . . .

Master Henry de Bolesby gives to K. the woods of
Oslewrthe, which he had from William de Rocheford.
Witnesses, Sir (*Dominus*) John le Brun and Sir Richard
de Cromhall, Kts. ; Ric. le Breth . . .

Robert de Rocheford gives to K. his wood called the
Frith. Witnesses, Oliver de Berkeley and others.

Bernard de St. Waleric (for the sake of God and his
soul and the souls of Henry the King and Eleanor his
Queen and all their successors, and the souls of his
mother M. and his wife A, and their successors) gives
to K. and the monks, &c., who for a little time dwelt
at Tetteburi, 40 acres of land in Myreford, near the
lands which the monks had of the gift of King Henry
and Roger of Berkeley, founder of the abbey ; to found
and rebuild their church, with the whole abbey, if they
will. And he confirms all that they had when they
dwelt at Tetteburi and Horemaredoune. Witnesses,
Simon, Bishop of Worcester, the Abbot of Malmsbury,
the Abbot of Tyntern, Roger son of Roger of Berkeley,
Aanore, wife of the grantor, Kenaud de Syrecamp,
. . Walter de Albamara, ... Hugo Machars,
Osmund the chaplain, Arnulph the clerk.

Robert de Rocheford gives to K. such liberty in Osel-
worthe, of him and his heirs, as, if they are impleaded
and liable to be amerced, they shall be free from the
amercement ; none of their sheep or beasts shall be
impounded, unless found in his covert or fenced grounds.
If they trespass they shall be summoned according to
law to make satisfaction in his court, or to hold their
own court, and there satisfy the complainants, if their
court shall be first adjudged to them ; and then if they
do not, they shall be compelled by their beasts and not
by their sheep. Witnesses, Oliver de Berkeley . . . . .
Roger Petiplas, Colin de Colkerton, Walter Tylun,
Robert le Stabler, and others.

Henry de Robbeford grants to K. a virgate of land
in Cherletune, and two messuages, which Mabel and
Muriel formerly held, and 6 acres of meadow in Ned-
dreswolleslade, and pasture for 200 sheep, and other
lands, which came to him by descent from his brother
Tristram ; and for which his lord Adam de Oherlton,
after the death of Tristram, received his homage and
relief, and gave seisin. Witnesses, Bartholomew Iabanc,
Oliver de Berkeley, Laurence de lasceles, Adam de
Cherletuna, Nicholas, the son of Henry of Culcretun,
Walter de Uptune, Roger de Ductune. G. Custance,
Roger Baret, . . , and others.

Roger de Newintun grants to K., Bollecote, lying
between Ywelege in Egge, near le Ros, in the manor of
Newintun. Witnesses, Geoffrey de Chausi, Henry de
Linez, Peter de Ywleg, Walter de Neylesworth, Hugh
de Kylliock, Robert de Upton, and others. (There is a
duplicate of this deed).

Nicholas de Newintun, son of Roger de Newintun,
confirms to K. all the gifts by his father, of Bollecote.
Witnesses, Milo de Langehoe, Bartholomew de Olepenne, Robert de Stone, Robert de Bradestane, Ralph
de Camme, John de Olepenne, and others.

Henry de Culcretun confirms to K. the donation by
William Butevilain, of 16 acres of land in Culcretun, of
Henry de Culcretun's fee, viz., &c. Witnesses, W.
Chamberlan, William de Bodenham, William Parson,
of Tetebiri, Adam de Cherletun, Robert de Ducton . . .
Henry, the son of Bernard, Alured Baret, Robert
Muschet, Nicholas de Kingeswode.

Maurice de Berkeley, son and heir of Sir (*domini*)
Thomas de Berkeley, releases to K. a rent of 10*d*. out
of lands at La Egge, in his manor of Symundeshale,
which they had by gift from Thomas de Berkeley, uncle
of the said Sir Thomas his father ; and a rent of 3 capons
out of land in Pokhampton in the manor Hynetun, given
by Sir (*dominus*) Robert de Berkeley, brother of Sir
Thomas, grandfather of Thomas, his father. And he
grants that if they move their water conduit from his
park of Hairemare, he will do certain works. Witnesses,
. . . . Thomas de Berkeley, son of Sir Thomas de
Berkeley, and others.

John del Egge grants to K. the land which Gilbert
his father held and came to him hereditarily, situate at
le Egge in the manor of Symundshale (see *ante*, 1243).

Nigil de Kyngescote grants to K. (for the souls of
himself and Petronilla, his wife, and Walter de Wottone), one acre in the field of Newentone, abutting on
the road from Cullicote to Kingeswode.

Ralph Mercator, of Sowire, grants to K. the burgage,
with the appurtenances in the burg of Sowire, near the
bridge, against the house late of Ralph de Rupe. Witnesses, John de Actune, W. de Fromptone, Adam Pistor,
and others (named).

5₄

Jordan de Budeford confirms to K. the gift of his
father, Geoffrey de Buddeford, which was *in hæc verba,*
viz. : Geoffrey grants to K one load (*unam carratam*) of
hay from his meadow of Avekesbury ; so that when
Geoffrey or his heirs cut hay, the monks may come to
fill one wagon with the best, and carry it off. Witnesses,
Sir (*dominus*) de Maunsel, Sir John de Wautone, Sir
Robert de Veel, knights ; Elias de Cumbe, Yvo de
Cumbe, Thomas le Archer, Richard de Colewiche, and
others.

R. Chol
mondele
Esq.

Henry Passelewe, of Rodmerton, gives to K. 3½ acres
of arable land in the field of Culcretun (described
in pieces). Witnesses, John de Hanekyntone, Elias
Bokerel, Roger de Blez, James Folioth, John Neel,
Roger de Couwesmere, and others.

William le Engleys, of Chiggelewe, son and heir of
Simon le Engleis, gives to K. four acres of land in
Culkerton, which W. Butevilain the elder gave to the
said Simon, with Alice William's mother. (13th century, much damaged).

Brother W., called Abbat of Kingeswode and the
convent, make known to all that they have granted to
the Lady Warebrugge, of Bristol, their friend and
intimate, that they will every day celebrate one mass
for her soul specially, and the souls of Vitalis her
husband and Elias her son, and the souls of her other
children and of all the faithful dead, at their old abbey,
in the chapel of St. John the Baptist, by their secular
chaplain, to whom they will supply all necessary food
and raiment, or by one of their monks, if they have not
a secular chaplain ; and if not, then by the said chaplain, or a monk, in their abbey.

5 Edw., Oct. 11, London. Edward, King of England,
Lord of Ireland, and Duke of Aquitaine, to all, &c.
License to Adam de Smetheleye to grant a messuage
and virgate of land in Culkertun to the abbat and convent of Kingeswod and that they may take it to them
and there successors for ever, notwithstanding the
Statute ; saving to the chief lords, &c.

1317. Wednesday next after the feast of Pope Gregory,
in the chapter at Kingeswode.—Richard, Abbat of Kingeswode, of the Cistercian Order, and the convent, re-
collecting the favours of Sir John de Berkeley, son of
Sir Thomas de Berkeley, Lord of Berkeley, and Lady
Hawyse, wife of the said John ; they grant that two
masses shall be said by two monks for the souls of
them and of their father and mother and ancestors,
in the chapel of the Virgin Mary at the gate of the
Abbey for ever ; except one day in every month at the
election of the abbat and convent, when the masses are
to be said in the parish church of Wottone. Special
directions for the mass. Their obits are to be in the
Martyrology. On the vigil of the Anmunciation seven
monks are to say Placebo and Dirige, &c. Sealed with
the convent seal and with the seal of Thomas de Berkeley on the part of the executors of John de Berkeley.
Seal of arms of Thomas de Berkeley.

13 Edw. II. Feast of St. Faith the Virgin. Agreement
between Richard, abbat of the church of St. Mary of
Kingswode and the convent, and Hugh Lanfoul.
They give to Hugh and the wife whom he shall first
marry after the execution of that agreement for their
lives a toft in the vill of Culkerton and 24 cases of land
in the fields of Culkerton. Rent 6*s*. 8*d*.

24 Edw. III. Feast of St. Martin the bishop. Agreement between the abbat and convent of K. and Richard
Ardarne and Matilda his wife. They grant to Richard
and his wife a tenement and 1½ virgates of land in
Culkerton. Witnesses Richerus de Cherleton, Henry
le Warner, William Macherling, William Contance,
Henry Passelewe and others. (The acreage of the
numerous pieces is given, and the total is 73 acres.)

14th century. A son cher bienveillannt Dann Henri
de Hortone par la grace de Deu Abbe de Kyngeswode,
Marie de Breus saluz et honur. En droit de la mus-
traunce Sire qe vus nus feistes par vostre lettre, qe
nostre baillif de Tetteburi ne vus suffre pas pestre la
pasture en Suthebay cum vus soletz fere solom le purport del Escrit fest cyrographe entre mon seygnur qe
deus asoille et vus ; Sachez, Sire, qe nus avoms de ceo
arene le Baillif, et il nus ad dist qo il ne vus ad pas vie
a pestre la diste pasture de vos boefs en la manere cum
les autres francs homes communers la pesent de cuis,
et ceo veut le escrit, et vus en autre manere ne devez
voler de la fere pestre ne autre estat aver en la diste
pasture, ne vus serra suffert ; Kar nus savoms bien
meyment qe les autres communers ne deivent entrer fors
ove nos boefs. A deu, Sire, qe vus garde toz Jurs.

20 Hen. VI. Feast of St. Thomas, the Apostle. In
the chapter's house.—John Wodeland, Abbat of Kingeswood, co. Wilts, of the Cistercian Order, Worcester

diocese, and the convent, give to Thomas Wodeward, the office of warden of the woods of Kingswood and Effulespen within the demesne or manor of Osulworth, co. Gloucester, and also the office of supervisor of all their other woods and underwoods in the counties of Wilts and Gloucester, to be exercised by him, or his sufficient deputy, for life. His fee was to be 40s. and three yards of coloured cloth, and meat and drink sufficient for him or his deputy whenever he came to the monastery. The abbat, &c. are to fence. Power of distress in the manor of Osulworth. Under the common seal (gone). Witnesses, Nicholas Alderlegh, Nicholas Daunt, Thomas Forde, John Badcok, John Taylour, tanner, Robert Forde Towkere, Richard Eyrermanger, &c.

Folio, paper, 17th century. 240 pp.

1. The state of the cause concerning the President and Councell established in the Marches of Wales.—There were anciently eight counties in Wales . . . .

p. 3. Reasons against the Court out of books and statutes.

p. 4. Reasons to abolish the Court of Marches.

p. 15. (In the margin is the name *Trotman*.) May it please your Lordship, concerning this business and the exercise of jurisdiction by the president and council of Wales . . . .

p. 35 and 36. (Bacon's argument ?) It standeth admitted that this pretended jurisdiction . . . .

p. 37. Councell and Marches of Wales.—For the government of Wales and the Marches thereof. . . .

p. 45. Anno Domini 1641. Arguments proving the jurisdiction used by the President and Council in the Marches of Wales over the counties of Gloucester, Worcester, Hereford, and Salop, to be illegal and injurious, and a mere encroachment beyond their appointed limits.—Touching the illegality. . . .

p. 49. Records.

p. 50. Upon Mr. Attorney's arguments these points arise and are examinable.—Whether without the aid of an Act of Parliament. . . .

p. 66. Reports, in French, of arguments in Parliament 17 Car. I.

p. 74. The effect of the first argument of the King's Sol.-General, Sir Francis Bacon, in maintaining of the council of the Marches over the four shires.

p. 82. The effect of what was spoken by Mr. Serjeant Hutton.

p. 86. The reply of the King's solicitor.

p. 97. The third and last argument of the King's solicitor in reply to Serjeant Harris.

p. 120. The petition of the Commons.

p. 122. The King's answer.

p. 125. That the Counties of Gloucester, Hereford, Salop, and Wigorn were never parcel of Wales or the Marches thereof.—The King's writ doth not run within Wales . . . .

p. 133. Some papers concerning the Marches of Wales and the illegality and grievance of that jurisdiction over the counties of Gloucester, Worcester, Hereford, and Salop.

p. 134. Motives and grievances, urging the inhabitants of the four counties to be exempted from the jurisdiction.

p. 139. The reasons and motives and argument to maintain the Bill for the exemption, &c.

p. 144. An Act for the exempting, &c.

p. 148. The state of the cause, &c.

p. 157. A treatise on the jurisdiction. *Begins*—This dispute hath fallen into two questions.

p. 230. There remaineth yet a second part of the enquiry . . . *ends*—than a journey to Ludlow.

In this volume are the following letter and papers; the first being probably the cause of Mr. Smyth obtaining the volume.

1661, March 14. Ludlow Castle.

"Carbery" (Lord President of the Marches) to the High Sheriff and Justices of the Peace of the county of Gloucester.—He notices the bad state of the roads in that county, and calls upon them to put in force the statutes relating thereto.

1662, March 25. Draft of a declaration by the Justices of the peace, alluding to Lord Carbery's letter, and denying that the co. of Gloucester was within the Marches of Wales or within the power or jurisdiction of his Lordship's Commission. It has the autograph signatures of 21 Justices of the Peace.

Copy of a presentment by the Grrand Jury to Lord . . . . that processes were issued out of the Court of Marches of Wales against some inhabitants of the county of Gloucester, for matters arising within that

county; and that the Lord President had sent the letter noticed above and praying him to present the matter to the King, that redress might be had.

Form of a Bill in the Court of Marches.

Small 4to, paper, 206 pp., end of 17th century.—Fair copies of letters between Ant. Pagi and Wm. Lloyd, Bishop of St. Asaph, on Roman Consular Chronology. These end on p. 123. The remainder of the volume contains copies of letters on the same subject between Father Noris and the Bishop, with the interpolation at pp. 145-156 of a letter by Henry Dodwell (at Cookham) to the Bishop. All the letters except Dodwell's are in Latin, and are dated in the years 1686 and 1687.

Small 4to., paper, 42 leaves. c. 1600.—Collection of all the offices of England, with the fees and allowances belonging unto them in the King's gift. (This is similar to that described at p. 404 of the Appendix to the Fourth Report.) At fo. 36. The valuation of the several livings of all the Bishopricks of England, with the tenths that every of them payeth to his Majesty yearly. At 37b. The valuation of the several livings of the Deanerys with their tenths *ut ante*. At 38b. The Nobility of England according to their degrees, with a list of Barons created by King James. At 41b. The descent of Queen Elizabeth. At 42b. The number of parish churches in England (the number in each county).

Small 4to, paper, 72 leaves.—Journal of a tour abroad in the years 1682 and 1683. The first leaf is absent. The journal opens imperfectly with a description of Canterbury Cathedral (April 1682). The writer thence went to Dover and crossed over to Calais, where he "saw Count Coningsmark, talked of much in England "for being an accessory in the murther of Mr. Thin." He travelled through France and went into Switzerland; the last place mentioned is Fribourg. On a leaf at the end of the volume is the name of George Smith (the writer of the journal), and there are bills of exchange drawn by him on his uncle, James Smith, of the Red Lion, in Fenchurch Street. Probably there was a second volume of the journal, as one of the bills of exchange shows him to have been at Rome in Feb. 1684. In 1683 and 1684 are several bills of exchange drawn by Richard Blackmore on James Smith, dated respectively from Nismes, Montpelier, Geneva, Venice, Strasbourg, Rotterdam, and Rome.

Small 4to, paper, 17th century, 123 leaves.—A Breviary or Collections of the most anchant Cittie of Chester, reduced into these chapters following, by the Reverend Mr. Ro. Rogers, Bachelor in Divinity, Archdeacon of Chester, and one of the prebends (*sic*) of the Cathedral Church in Chester; written anew by his sonne, D. R., a well wisher to that anchant Cittie. (See p. 416 of Appendix to the Fourth Report.) The 10th (and last) chapter is headed " Certain commendable deeds done for " the wealth and estimation of the Citti of Chester by " certain that have bene maiores of Chester, by some " others that have bene borne there, and other good men " dwellinge there." The 2nd page of this ends, " is not " so trulye imployed as it ought; thus farr Da-Rogers, " &c." Then follow statements of various gifts by mayors and inhabitants of plate and money. The volume ends imperfectly in the statement of the 15th, viz., Mr. Hugh Ollwy's gifts.

Quarto, paper.—A summary of the Life of St. Werburgh (by Wm. Cowper).

Summary of the Life of St. Werburgh, &c., &c., by a citizen of Chester, William Cowper, Esq.]. 4to. Chester, 1749. pp. 31. This copy is interleaved and has large additions by Mr. Cowper.

Quarto, paper, 18th Century, 58 pp.—Historical Verses, composed by Richard Bostock of Tattenhale, in Cheshire, Gent., who was buried in that Parish Church, 21 April 1663.

Begin, " When Saxon Harold Godwin's Son
        " Who had been King without all right" . . .
The poem has 53 verses of eight lines each, and ends on the 18th page. The remaining pages and the margins of the poem are occupied with Mr. Cowper's Annotations and elucidations of it, and of the history of the Earls of Chester.

Folio, paper, 18th century, 25 leaves. Copies of Summons to Parliament down to and including 13 Ed. II., taken from the Close Rolls.

Folio, paper, 16th and 17th centuries.—1. Visitation of Cheshire, taken by William Flower, alias Norroy King of Arms, and with hvm Robert Glover, Somerset Herald, his Marshall, A.D. 1580. (97 leaves.) The arms are well tricked, and there are copies of deeds and their seals which evidence the pedigrees and arms.—There are some additions supposed to be made by William Smith, of Old Haugh, Rouge Dragon, Pursuivant at

Arms, in 1609. Leaves 74–80 are nearly blank. The leaves 90–96 have arms only, " taken out of a Book in " the office, written temp. Hen. V.—2. Paper of a larger size. Visitation for Cheshire temp. Elizabeth by Somerset Herald. Leaves 31b–39 and 55–62 are in a different hand. After 64 the leaves are blank except 4 pp. of Arms, copied out of Churches and Houses in Yorkshire, 1584.

Folio, paper. Copy of a MS. written about 1591, concerning the destruction of religious Houses in England. *Begins*, Forasmuch as the religious Houses. Colleges, Charities, Churches, Chapels, Hospitals, and all other Houses for the maintenance of the poor were in building and founding by the space of 1,000 years. *Ends* (p. 94), Therefore, I would wish all good people to take example . . . . than the Common weal or God's service. To whom be all praise.—pp. 95–100. Some further account of the Dissolution of Religious Houses in England, at and before the Reformation. (This is in Cowper's hand.)—At p. 104, is a copy of a long letter by Sir S. Digges to Mr. Digby of Sandon, who lent him Sampson Erdeswicke's MS. view of Staffordshire. The volume ends at p. 114.

Three volumes folio in vellum covers. 1. Names and surnames of all the able and sufficient men in body fit for His Majesty's service in the wars in the divisions of Kistesgate, co. Gloucester, wherein are contained the hundreds of Kistesgate, Deerhurst, Cleeve, Tyboldstone, Chottenham, Tewxbury, Westminster and Slaughton; with their ages, personable statures and armours; viewed by the Right Honble Lord Berkeley, Lord Lieut. of the said county by direction from His Majesty in the month of Aug. 1608. 6 James I. (331 pp.) 2. A like account within the division of the seven hundreds within the co. of Gloucester, wherein are contained the hundreds of Cirencester, Crowthorne, and Minty, Rapsgate, Brightwelsbarowe, Bradley, Longtree, Bisley and Whitstone. 1608 (214 pp.) 3. A like account for the division of Berkeley, co. Gloucester, wherein are contained the hundreds of Berkeley, Grombaldsark, Swyneshead, Langley, Pucklechurch, Henbury, Thornbury and Barton near Bristol. 1608. (318 pp.) The three volumes are all compiled on the same plan.

Folio, 1760; 44 leaves interleaved; by Dr. Cowper. Collections for Broxton Hundred. Such as are extracts from Daniel King's Itinerary (published in Vale Royal of England, 1656) are in inverted commas. More than 200 arms are blazoned. At the end is an index of names.

Folio, unbound.—A digression concerning the deport of the Earl of Derby and his lady in the late troubles, with some remembrances of the things done in the two sieges of Lathom House. 35 pp.—*Begins*, Amongst the Nobles that appeared unto His Majesty at York when the seditious and insolent routs of the Londoners drave him from Whitehall, James, Earl of Derby, was one of the first. *Ends*, and she died at Knowsley House with that Christian temper and piety with which she had lived.—In another hand are 7 lines, extracted from Dugdale, showing who the Countess was.

In the margin of the following tract of 25 leaves is this note "Malbon's account of Nampwyche, Co. Cest. from 1642 to 1655." The tract is headed "A brief and " true relacion of all such passages and things as hap- " pened and were done in and about Namptwich, in the " county of Chester, and in other places of the same " county, together with some of the things in other " counties . . . . . by some of the commanding " officers and soldiers of the said town of Namptwich, " after the same was made a garrison for King and " Parliament, since the 10th of August 1642, so truly " as the writer hereof could come by the knowledge of " the same, viz.—Upon or about the 11th day of August " 1642. Sir William Brereton and the Deputy Lieu- " tenants for the said county of Chester." *Ends*, (after the surrender of Beaumaris in 1648), " there were not " above 20 on the Parliament side slain and wounded; " but of the other parties a great number.—per me " Thomam Malbon, 1651."—After this the last 1½ pp. contain notices for the years 1651, 2, 3 and 5.—There is the autograph, " Thomas Malbon owith this booke " 1651."

Folio, paper, 17th century.—fo. 1. Oaths of the Mayor, Recorder, and Sheriffs of Chester.—A collection of the Mayors who have governed the city of Chester. *Begins*, Before the nomination of the said Mayor it is requisite.—This is followed by extracts from Speed.

Fo. 6. Divers collections by the worthy and grave citizen William Aldersey, the elder.

Fo. 8b.—Abridgment of my Collections gathered by Robert Rogers, Archdeacon of Chester, divided into 7

chapters. (There only 4 here). Then come some blank leaves. Then names of Mayors, from 24 Hen. III. There are columns for the years and the 12 months; the names of the Mayors are put in their proper places, and there are some notes of events. The original hand ends with 19 Charles I. Thence the tables are continued to 1701.—Then come notes of proceedings at Assembly. And Notes of charitable gifts (several pages).

Folio, paper, 17th century, about 100 leaves.—Chester Foundation. *Begins*, Two Colleges of Llegions in Cronicle wee read, on in South Wales in the time of Claudian. (4 pp. of early history.) A description of the county. *Begins*, The county Palatine of Chester is one of the shires.—There is a long description of the Cathedral. —Description of several hundreds.—Account of the Earls of Chester.—Copy of the Charter of 21 Hen. VII. —Deaths of the plague between June 1647 and April 1648 :—particulars ; total number of deaths 2,099.

Quarto, paper, 18th century. Copy of a letter by James, Earl of Derby, in answer to Commissary General Ireton's summons to deliver up the Isle of Man. Dated Castle-town. 12th July 1649.—The private Devotion of the Right Honble. that glorious Martyr the Earl of Derby, composed by his Lordship on several occasions in the Isle of Man. 1650. (About 70 leaves). The first is dated August 1st. 1650.—Copy of his letter to his wife soon after he was taken prisoner.—His plea (6 leaves).—His last letter to Lady Mary, Mr. Edw. and Mr. William (1 leaf).—Relation of Mr. Humphrey Baggarley, touching my Lord's death and some passages before it :—and his speech (10 leaves).—A poem of 5 pp. on the Earl by S. R.

Collectanea Devana. 2 vols. folio. (These are from various authors ; a list of them is on p. 1.)

Vol. 1. 330 pp. Collections for the city of Chester down to 1757. The Earls of Chester down to 1648. Part 2 begins at p. 123. It consists of fragments and lists and notes of Mayors, Sheriffs, &c.

Vol. 2. Pages 1 to 49 are occupied with the Sheriffs down to 1755, and additions down to 1802. A new paging (1 to 41) contains A collection of certain passages and occurrences in the Civil War begun A.D. 1642, concerning Chester and other places mostly within the distance of a day's journey from that city. *Begins*, Several of our English writers. It *ends* with a letter (6 pp.), dated Pulford, 17 March 1642, signed by Thomas Aston (the contents certified by 10 other signatures) about the conduct of Aston in the affair of Middlewich. It is addressed to Earl Rivers and Viscounts Cholmondely and Kilmurrey, and others.

Quarto, paper, 18th century. Villare Com. Cestri. 342 pp., besides tables at the end. It is headed, " Dr. " Williamson's Collections from Holme's MSS., with " some additions and annotations." The names of places are in alphabetical order, one name to each page. The last date is 1701, when the book was compiled. (It is said to be " out of the library of Dr. Wil- " liam Cowper, of Chester.")

Folio, paper, 18th century. Statuta Ecclesiæ Cathedralis Cestr. 54 pp. and 1 p. of index to the Statutes. The Latin text is on one page, and an English translation on the opposite page. Book-plate of [Dr.] E[dward] Harwood, M.A.

A square folio, written A.D. 1764. 38 pp. An account of the siege of the city of Chester, 1645. *Begins*, 1642. The war between the King and the Parliament, being now begun, it was thought necessary to fortify Chester. *Ends*, with an account of the demolitions during the siege, " to the full sum of 200,000l." At the end of the volume (loose) are some letters and papers. Letter from the Rev. Dr. T. Gower at Chelmsford to E. Harwood, and letters from Thomas Falconer, of Chester, and others on Chester matters. This volume also has the book-plate of E. Harwood.

A folio volume, bound, with the arms of Cholmondeley on the sides. It is lettered on the back " Dr. " Williamson's Collection of Cheshire Evidences." MSS. by William Cowper, of Clutton, ludimagister. There is a reference from Dr. Gower's Sketch of materials for a new and completed History of Cheshire. 4to., London, 1800. This volume is described at fo. 90; it was lent to Gower by the Rev. William Stones, of Chester, whose father was a historical collector.

A thin folio volume of 54 pp., contains official extracts (signed by J. Cayley, Keeper of Records) from Ministers' accounts, 32 Hen. VIII., for Vale Royal Abbey, preceded by extracts from Tanner's Notitia Monastica. There are a few loose papers in the cover.

Folio, 212 leaves, preceded by a copious Index of names. Extracts from *Inquisitiones post mortem*, for Cheshire, from 1 Hen. VIII. to 12 James I.

U u 2

Folio, unbound, 62 pp. The antiquity of the most ancient and famous city of Chester, collected by the learned and experienced authors of great antiquity, being here born and laboured much in this work in their times. And first of the names of the city of Chester 1. Neomagus, (11 names in all). *Ends*, with a chapter on the Antiquity of the Gabell Rent.

A paper-covered folio, wrongly labelled A Visitation of Cheshire, by Glover (formerly belonging to E. Harwood, of Chester). It contains Notices of the Antiquities of Chester :—Foundation of the Abbey of Vale Royal :—Abstracts of the Chronicles of the Earls of Chester :—Extracts from Domesday, and the Red Book of the Exchequer :—Account of St. Werburgh. (Down to this point the contents are in Latin.)—Abstracts of charters in Latin and English, with arms neatly tricked in the margins :—Pedigrees from Inquisitions and charters : —Gentlemen of Cheshire knighted by the Earl of Hertford at Leith.—Names of persons disclaimed by Richard St. George, Norroy, 1613. (1¼ pp. in 2 columns.) —Index of names.

A quarto volume of about 80 leaves.—History of Chester and lists of the Mayors and Sheriffs. It begins temp. Edward III., A.D. 1335. "King Edward, by the "charter before mentioned, dated at Pomfret, granted "to his son the Black Prince."

A quarto volume contains Brief Notes of the Antiquity of the famous city of Chester. (31 leaves.) It deals with the Bishops, Earls, Mayors, and Sheriffs.

A quarto volume of 87 leaves contains some Collections relating to the Ecclesiastical Affairs of Chester. *Begins*, "So many authors." The last date is 1492, at p. 87. It deals with Bishops, Prebendaries, Deans, Archdeacons. (This is numbered 13 of Cowper's Collections.)

A quarto volume of 68 leaves, seems to be a continuation of the last volume. The last 18 leaves contain an Account of the Abbey of St. Werburgh. (This volume is numbered 11 of Cowper's Collections.)

A quarto volume contains Account of the Mayors and Sheriffs of Chester. (This is numbered 7 of Cowper's Collections.)

A quarto volume of 89 pp. contains Collections concerning the City of Chester. *Antiquam exquirite matrem. Begins*, Chester the Metropolis. It ends with the death of Charles II. (This is No. 12 of Cowper's Collections.)

Another quarto of only 6 leaves contains an account of the Streets of Chester. (No. 10 of Cowper's Collections.)

Folio, unbound. The proper Qualifications of a good Governor in the management and conduct of a young Nobleman or gentleman in his travels through forrain countryes.—*Vita beata in virtute posita.*—Written in the year 1693 by T. M. The Introduction *begins*, The Almighty Lord of the whole universe.

A quarto volume contains a List of Gentlemen who appeared at Chester in the Grosvenor interest at the election of Geo. Johnson to be Mayor in 1732. And the following, apparently by W. Cowper :—

Poetical translation, Book 1, of Silius Italicus.

Some Memoirs of the first Duke of Ormonde, by the Earl of Longford. (28 pp. of note paper.)

Historical Catalogue of the Bishops of the Isle of Man.

Some Collections from others, and observations of my own, being a small sketch of the Isle of Man, wrote during the few days which I staid in that Island, July 1729. *Begins*, Dear Sir, when I took leave of you. (81 pp., small quarto.)

An Essay. The Conflagration, partly extracted from Dr. Burnet's Theory of the Earth. (English poetry, 43 pp.) This volume has the book-plate (of arms) of W. Cowper, of Colne, Esq. 1728.

Another quarto with a like book-plate. On the fly leaf is the Note, "Nov. 9, 1701. Dr. Humphreys, Bishop of "Bangor, gave me this book. R. D. The former part of Alfred's History was not thought worth copying, because Bishop Lloyd judged it but a transcript of Jeffrey, as appears by his letter annexed."

Copy of part of Alured of Beverley ; beginning, Finito regno Britonum, Britanniæ regnum ad Anglos est translatum.

Bishop Lloyd's letter to Thomas Price of Llanvyllen, concerning Jeffery of Monmouth's history. (12¼ pp. 4to.)

Selden's answer to Sir John Sempill, transcribed out of a MS. in the Ashmolean Library, No. 830. T. 6. (25 pp., 4to. About Tithes.)

A Latin play with the title "Sanctus Tewdricus sive "Pastor bonus, Rex et Martyr," in 9 scenes, composed

respectively by Richard Simons, William Parry, Richard Smith, Frances Simons, Daniel Gifford, Henry Chamberling, Charles Peeters, Thomas Beveridge, and Nicholas Tempest. The personages are St. Tewdricus, Maurice, King of the Silures, and Arthur his brother, and Malcolm and Ulfadus, *Mauricio et Arthuro chari proceres*. At the end is a song with music, by Beveridge. The title page was written by Henry Matthew Chamberling.

About 35 leaves of copies of letters, in 1744 and 1745, on naval and military affairs. (Many and perhaps all are from newspapers.)

A tract of 96 pp. (pp. 1 and 2 are absent) by Hend. Toren, giving an account of transactions during his stay in the Island (of Man). It relates to a quarrel between Thomas Wilson, Bishop of Sodor and Man, and Alexander Horne, Governor of the Island. It seems to be about a slander on a Mrs. Hendricks, wife of an innkeeper of the Island, and other cases which led to quarrels between the Bishop and the Governor.

Folio, paper, 18th century.

Latin poem on the death of Thomas Hesketh, of Rufford, by W. C[owper], with translation into English on the opposite pages (ends pp. 15 and 16).

On the relict sitting by the bust of her husband, drawn by H. Winstanley.

Inscription, in English, on Hesketh, who died in 1735, in his 37th year.

Copy of inscription in the east cloister of Westminster to Daniel Pulteney, supposed to be by Viscount B.

Other inscriptions: one to Susanna Walker, third daughter of John Walker, of Honger Hill, who died 4 Nov. 1736, æt. 18.

English translation of Addison's Latin poem on the Resurrection, painted over the Altar of Maudlin, Oxford.

Epitaph on the Rev. Mr. Cowper (John Cowper), A.M., of Brazen-nose.

Latin translation of Pope's Dying Christian to the Soul.

On the death of the Queen.

Under a picture of Alexander Pope, died 1744, æt. 57.

On the death of Thomas Lister, ob. 1745, M.P. for Clitheroe.

(All the above are on 4to. paper in the volume above noted, containing a Digression concerning deport of the Earl of Derby, &c. &c.)

A small quarto, 19th century, contains copies by the late Thomas Heber, of inscriptions in Hodnet and other places, and drawings by him of places and arms.

VIRGINIA AND THE SOMER ISLANDS.

1616, July 14, Somer Islands.—Bryan Cave to Mr. Thorpe, one of the Adventurers for the Sommer Islands. Understanding that Thorpe was discouraged about his share and held back from supplying money until he heard the truth, Cave encourages him, and doubts not that if he supplies plants and other necessaries, his commodities shall be greater. Their great enemies are the rats, which threaten the subversion of the plantation. The Governor, whose industry he praises, has given orders that the inhabitants shall work their confusion by poison and traps.

In the margin is a short note by Daniel Tucker to Thorpe, saying that not having leisure, he has got Cave to write ; recommends Thorpe to send supplies to his land and provisions for two or three men, and says that to that effect he has written to the Countess of Bedford.

A folio volume of 2 pages of table, and 155 pp. of text, The table is as follows :—

The Patent of the Bermuda or Somer Islands, anno 13 Jacobi R. ; fol. 1.

The Patent of Virginia, anno 7 Jacobi ; fo. 37.

Another Patent for Virginia, 9 Jacobi ; fo. 25.

The Indenture to Sir William Throckmorton and others for plantation in Virginia ; p. 53.

The Commission given to Captayne Woodleefe ; fo. 61.

Mutual Covenants, between Sir William Throckmorton, Richard Berkeley, George Thorpe, John Smyth, and John Woodlefe ; fo. 64.

Remembrances given to Capt. Woodleefe, at his departure for Virginia ; fo. 71.

The list of men sent with Mr. Woodlefe, for Virginia ; fo. 73.

The Certificate of the Mayor of Bristol ; fo. 76.

The letter of Sir William Throckmorton and others, sent to the Governor of Virginia at the ship's departure ; fo. 77.

The letter of Sir Edwin Sandys, sent to the said Governor with the said ship ; fo. 78.

The particular charges in furnishing out the ships; from fo. 79 to fo. 94.

The Charter party with Mr. Williams of Bristol for the hire of his shipp; fo. 94.

The Certificate of Sir George Yardley of the arrival of our ship in Virginia; fo. 97.

The particular charges in a supply sent into Virginia in March 1619, in the ship from London wherein Mr. Thorpe went; fo. 98.

The Indenture of Assignment of Sir William Throgmorton's 4th part to Mr. William Tracy; fo. 100.

The Orders and Ordinances for governing the Virginian Court and the land in Virginia; from fo. 103 to 122.

A Commission for Mr. Tracy from the Treasurer and Company to ship himself for Virginia; 123.

A revocation of the Commission and authority conferred heretofore on Mr. Woodleefe; fo. 124.

A Commission to Mr. Thorpe and Mr. Tracy to govern our people in Virginia; fo. 125.

The quadrupartite Articles of Agreement, between Mr. Berkeley, Mr. Thorpe, Mr. Tracy, and Mr. Smyth; fo. 127.

A general letter sent by Mr. Berkeley and Mr. Smyth to Mr. Thorpe, of Virginia affairs, which Mr. Tracy carried; fo. 129.

The Agreement with Richard Smyth and others, undertakers, to the halfes in Virginia; fo. 132.

The Agreement with Mr. Pawlet to goe preacher, physician, and surgeon; fo. 133.

The Charter party with Mr. Ewens for the ship wherein Mr. Tracy went in Virginia; fo. 134.

The Certificate of the Mayor of Bristoll; fo. 137.

The list of men sent in Virginia; Sept. 1620, fo. 138.

The accompt of monies paid since the 16th of Sept. 1619, touching the last year's voyage; fo. 140.

The accompt for hire of the first ship to Mr. Williams and the wages of Toby Felgate, pilot; fo. 142.

The accompt of the charge in furnishing and setting out the supply in Sept. 1620; from fo. 142 to fo. 150. (The following are not in the Table.)

The accompt of monies laid out since Mr. Tracie's departure, 18 September 1620, untill Michaelmas 1621; fo. 151.

The accompt of the charge of the 4 servants sent into Virginia in the ship called " The Furtherance," in the month of May, 1622, 20 Jac., with Mr. Sampson, master thereof; fo. 153.

The accompt of the charge of a small supply sent over into Virginia in April 1623, anno 21 Jac., in the shipp called the " Bonny," belonging to Mr. Barbor, upon advertizement of our servants great necessity; fo. 155.

Ferdinando Yate's account of his voyage to Virginia in 1619. (11 pp., 4to.) It is preceded by an address (in 2 pp.) to George Thorpe, of Wanswell, Esq., and John Smith, of Nibly, Esq. The 16 day of September anno domini, 1619, he set sail in Kingrod in a bark of Bristol called the Margaret.—They made land on the 28 Nov. and landed at Keeketan in a good harbour on the 30 of Nov. The writer tells of nothing but the weather and the damages to the ship.

1620, June 1. " Copy of my (John Smith's) letter to Mr. Berkeley about our accompts for the Virginia ship then returned." (2 pp.)

1620, July. Mr. Russell's project touching artificiall wyne in Virginia. (1 p.) It was to be made from a vegetable which grew there; it could be made cheaply, easily, would keep well, and would not intoxicate. Russell asked that upon consideration of it here to the Company he might have 1,000l., besides the benefit in Virginia of serving the colony. At the foot, Smyth has written that it was agreed, with some little variation, with Mr. Russell, the acmunist and chimist; and that Sir John Brooke, 2 April 1621, told him that of his own knowledge the wine was made of sassappras boyled in water; he had of the drink.

1620, Sept. 20. Copy of the Account which Smyth sent Mr. Thorpe into Virginia. (½ p.)

1620, Dec. 19. Southampton Hund. George Thorpe to John Smith, at North Nibley. Is busy examining witnesses concerning Captain Argoll. Will write more by the next [ship], against which time he hopes Captain Woodleefe's tobacco will be ready. Says that the country is very healthy, and that they have found a way to make a good drink from Indian corn, which he prefers to good English beer. Recommends Smyth to send over his second son.

1620, March 24. A note for Mr. Felgate to receive his freight by March 24, 1620, Signed by " Geo. Thorpe." (1 p.)

1621, Dec. Receipt signed by Nicholas Farrar of 6l. 13s. 4d. from Mr. John Smyth, upon his subscription in the Roll for the trade for furs, and another for 10l. upon his subscription in the Roll for the building of pinnaces, boats, and dwelling-houses, for the use of the planters in Virginia. For each he was to receive his rateable share of profits according to his adventure.

1623, March 7; 1624, June 28, Dec. 20, Jan. 3, Feb. 8, and March 7. (3 pp.) Copies of Orders made at Courts for the Company, regarding the debts of Capt. Thorpe, in Virginia.

1634, April 10. Inventory of the goods and estate of Capt. George Thorpe, deceased, appraised by three persons (named). They are valued at pounds of tobacco; total, 1,323½ lbs. (3 pp.)

1634, Aug. 14. Bristol. William Thorpe, son and heir of George Thorpe, to Mr. Taylor, asking him when he arrived in Virginia to enquire when George Thorpe died, what goods and lands he had, who was their Governor, whether an inventory was taken, and what lands he had in Berkeley Town. (1 p.)*

An engraved map of Virginia, about 18 inches broad and 14 inches deep, said at the foot to be " Discovered and Discribed by Captayn John Smith. Graven by William Hole." In the left hand top corner is an engraving, below which it is said that " Powhatan held this state and fashion when Capt. Smith was delivered to him prisoner." Powhatan is on a raised seat, with an attendant on each side of him; on the floor is a smoaking wood fire between two double rows of seated natives. On the right side of the map is a well engraved figure of a native armed with a bow and a club.

A large broadside, headed " By the Treasuror, Councell and Company " for Virginia," addressed to the Governour of Virginia and the Councell of Estate there residing. It is dated the 17th of May 1620, and contains directions and rules for the management of, and works in the colony. At the head are engravings representing both sides of the seal of the Company; one side representing the King in his robes, with crown, sceptre, and ball, and the legend, " Sigillum regis Magne Britannie, " Francie, et Hibernie;" and the other side containing the royal arms, with the legend, " pro concilio suo Virginia."

A tract in 4to, called " Virginia's God be thanked." The title is wanting. (Lowndes states that it is by Patrick Copland, and was published in 1622.) Sheet A is of four leaves (the 4th blank), containing a dedicatory letter to Sir Thomas Smith, Governor of the East India Company, dated 24th April 1620; two letters to Capt. Martin, Pring, Governor of the Sea Mayor of the E. I. Company in India, dated respectively the 22nd January 1619 and 20th May 1620 (all dated from the Royal James), and repetitions in Latin of the same letters. The text follows on 36 pages, top 1 and 3 of the text are absent; p. 3 is on the first leaf of signature B. The lower half of the back margins of the tract are destroyed by damp.

A Declaration of the State of the Colonie and Affaires in Virginia, with the names of the Adventurers and summes adventured in that Action.—By his Majesties Counsell for Virginia, 22 Junii 1620. (Portrait of the king and legend as in the Broadside above.) London. Printed by T. S., 1620. The Declaration ends on p. 11. Then follows 16 pp. (1-16). A note of the Shipping, men, and provisions sent to Virginia by the Treasuror and Company in the yeere 1619. Then on 50 pp. (1-50), the names of the Adventurers, with their several sums adventured paid to Sir Thomas Smith, k'., late Treasuror of the Company for Virginia. The names are in alphabetical order, and comprise peers of the realm and other noblemen and gentlemen and City Companies. Then on a pp. (1-4). Names of Adventurers, with the sums paid by Order to Sir Baptist Hicks, k'; and The names of the Adventurers, with the sums paid to Sir Edwin Sandys, k', Treasuror of the Company from the 28th of April 1619 to the 27th June 1620. Then come on 29 pp. (1-30), Orders and Constitutions, partly collected out of his Majesties Letters Patents, and partly ordained upon mature deliberation by the Treasuror, Council, and Companie of Virginia, for the better governing of the actions and affairs of the said Company here in England residing. Anno 1619 and 1620.

A second edition of the above (printed by Thomas Snedham, 1620), on 92 consecutively numbered pages, besides the leaf containing the title. This is followed by an order of Council given in the Great and General Quarter Court held 13th Nov. 1620, pp. 93-97.

Bound up with the last is the following 4to tract, " Observations to be " followed for the making of fit rooms to keep silkwormes in; as also " for the best manner of planting of Mulbery trees to feed them. Published by authority for the benefit of the Noble Plantation in Virginia. At London. Imprinted by Felix Kyngston, 1620. (21 pp, including title.) Then comes (pp. 25-28). A valuation of the Commodities growing and to be had in Virginia, rated as they are there worth.

Folio, 4 pp. A note of the shipping, men, and provisions sent and provided for Virginia by the Right Honorable Henry Earl of Southampton and the Company, and other private Adventurers, in the years 1621, &c.; at p. 2. Other occurrents of note; p. 3. Gifts; p. 4. Patents granted this yeere.

Another edition of the above, with impressions of the Seal of the Company at the head; and this clause at the end, " Whosoever trans " ports himselfe or any other at his own charge unto Virginia, shall for " each person so transported before Midsummer 1625, have to him and " his heirs for ever fifty acres of land upon a first, and 50 acres upon a " second division."

A plaine and true relation of the goodnes of God towards the Sommer Islands, written by way of exhortation, &c. &c., by Lewis Hughes, minister of God's word. At London. Printed by Edward Allde, dwelling neere Christ's Church, 1621. (4to, 24 leaves, including title.) The exhortation ends on the 11th leaf. The remainder of the tract is coupled with questions and answers concerning keeping holy the Sabbath day, Publique exercises of religion and the Lord's Supper; Grace before and after meat; and prayers for the morning and evening.

Orders and Constitutions partly collected out of his Majesties Letters Patents, and partly by authority and in vertue of the said Letters Patents; ordained upon mature deliberation by the Governour and Company of the City of London for the Plantation of the Summer Islands; for the better governing of the actions and affairs of the said Company and Plantation, 6 Febr. 1622. At London, imprinted by Felix Kyngston, 1622. 4to, 43 numbered pages, besides the leaf containing the title. On the reverse of the title page is an engraving of a lion rampant in face, holding in front a shield charged with a ship in a storm. The motto is, " Quo fata ferunt."

A Declaration how the monies, viz., 70l. 5s. 6d., were disposed, which was gathered (by Mr. Patrick Copland, preacher in the Royal James) at the Cape of Good Hope (towards the building of a free schoole in Virginia) of the gentlemen and mariners in the said ship; a list of whose names are under specified, &c. 4to, 7 pp. imprinted at London by F. K. 1622.

R. CHOL-
ONDELEY,
Esq.

CHESTER.

1 Henry VIII. The award between John Abbot, of the monastery of St. Werburg, and the Mayor and Citizens of the city of Chester, made anno 1 H. VIII.—This is an epitome in 19 items of the award. Following in another hand is a copy of Henry VIIth charter to the city of Chester. (16th century. 3 pp.)

1 Henry VIII., Aug. 7. A full copy of the award, made by Charles Boothe, Sir William Uvedale, and George Bromley, three of the King's Commissioners, and Anthony Fitzherbert, Serjeant at Law, and William Rudall, the Queen's Attorney. (It is about St. Werburg's fair and other liberties. 8 pp.) 16th century.

Memorandum that the 9th day of January, 31 Hen. VIII., Raffe Wryne, then being Recorder of this citie, was made clarke of the Pentice of the same citie, and the 5th daye of October, 32 Henry VIII., the particular fees following were ordered to be paid unto him. And the same have ever since been challenged and received by the recorders of this citie successively as incident to the office of recorder. And the clarke of the Pentice, who by himself and his servants executed all the buisnes, had notwithstanding noe part thereof.—This is followed by lists of fees on 4 pages. (16th century.)

Memoranda or notes referring to the privileges of the Mayor and Citizens of Chester, and the encroachments of the Dean and Chapter, And notes of passages in two of the Dean's sermons, in which he attacked the Mayor. (1½ pp. 16th century.)

1569, May 14, from the Court. R. (Earl of) Leycester to Sir Hugh Cholmondeley, V. P. of Wales; Sir John Throckmorton, Justice of Chester; William Gerrard and Richard Pates, Esqrs.;—requesting them to repaire to the city of Chester for trial whether the same were decayed or not, and the cause of such decay. (Contemporary copy.)

1602, May 26. Court at Greenwich. Copy of Council Letter to the Mayor of Chester, and the rest of the Commissioners, for viewing of the souldiers at that port;—about the raising and keeping together soldiers and their embarkation from Liverpool [to Ireland].

1607, April 7. Attested cotemporary copy of award in a dispute between the Mayor and Citizens of Chester on the one part; and Peter Sharpe, B.D., and Roger Ravenscroft, M.A., prebendaries of the Cathedral Church of Chester, on behalf of the Dean and Chapter of the other part.—The Mayor and Citizens were to be at liberty to pass and repass through the great west door of the church at the time of any funeral or attendance upon any corpse to be buried in the said church; and as often as the Mayor repaired to the church to hear divine service or sermon, or upon any just occasion, he was to be at liberty to have the sword of the city borne before him, with the point upwards.

(n. d., temp. James I.). Draft of a Petition to the King by the Mayor, Aldermen, and Citizens of Chester. The King had, by letters dated 22 Nov. last, delivered to them the 15 of January instant, recommended Hugh Mainwaring an utter barrister of Lincoln's Inn, to the place of Recorder. The late Recorder died on the 6th of January, 20 miles away from Chester, and they only knew of his death on the 15th January. Inasmuch as Hugh Mainwaring is young and inexperienced, and some of their own aldermen and citizens are of great judgment and well practised in the laws, and some (sic) of them a bencher in the Inner Temple, they pray to have their free election to the office.

1612, November. Money received [by the Mayor] of several persons for the several causes upon their names appearing. (1 p.)

1612, November. Another paper similar.

1609. The aldermen and stewards of every society and company draw yourselves to your said several companies, according to ancient custome. And soe to appeare every man with your said several companies, every man as you are called upon paine that shall fall therein.—The aldermen and stewards of 26 different companies are named in the list underwritten. On the back of the page is a copy of the Mayor's "proclamation on the "Roody upon St. George's Day, A.D. 1609. All "persons assembled to see the ancient race are to keep

"the peace and be of good behaviour; horses, other "than those in the race, are to keep off the course."

Articles to be performed for certain orders touching the running of a race for two bells and likewise for a cup, to be run for at the ringe upon St. George his day, being the 23rd day of April, as followeth.—Six rules for the furnishing of the bells and cup, the award thereof to winners, payments for entries, the mode of payment of expenses, the keeping of and security for the cup, &c. (1½ pp.)

Dr. Cowper's remarks on the Eastgate of Chester taken down. 1766. 3 pp.

Remarks on the criminal jurisdiction of Cheshire barons. (1½ p.)

R. CHOL-
MONDELEY,
Esq.

ISLE OF MAN.

1651, Oct. 31. Copy of Articles between Sir Thomas Armstrong and Mr. Samuel Rutter, on behalf of the Countess of Derby of the one part, and Col. Thomas Birch, Lieut.-Col. William Michell, Commissioners appointed by the Hon. Col. Robert Duckinfield, Commander-in-chief, on the other part, touching the surrendering of Castle Rushen and Peele Castle.—This is a copy attested as true by Chr. Musgrave and Bernard Hatton. Below their names is the following "This a true copy of the "Articles of which I approve and have already sur- "rendered Castle Rushen. C. Derby." (The signature is that of the Countess.)

1733, Jan. 23. Bishops Court. The (Bishop of) Sodor and Man to Dr. Cowper. A letter of two and a half pages, with which he sent some collections for the history of the Isle of Man.

A fragment, pp. 82–195 note paper size, of a History and Chronicle of the Kings of Man (by Dr. Cowper.)

1734, Nov. 19, Manchester. Robert Thyer to William Cowper, Esq., at the Isle of Man, 3 pp., about the history of the Isle of Man.

1751; Dec. 24. A.B. to William Cowper, Esq. The letter is preceded by a Latin inscription for a portrait of Dean Swift in the Bodleian Library placed by John Barber, Alderman and Mayor of London. The letter begins "Good Sir, As some addition to your Dean Swift, " and with which I take my leave of Sir T. Bodley's " gallery, I send you this" . . . The writer says he is going to the metropolis on Friday.—On the other side of the page is a Latin inscription under the portrait of Alexander Pope (on a level with the Dean's).

GLOUCESTERSHIRE.

List of Sheriffs from Hen. 2 to 1638. 7 pp.
Copy of speech of Mr. Gregory to the Duke of Ormonde when he visited Gloucester.

SHREWSBURY.

1589, Oct. 28, Lincoln's Inn. Thomas Owen to the Bailiffs of Shrewsbury.—Mr. Fenes having obtained the office of Alnager of Shrewsbury, by grant from Her Majesty, Owen's opinion is that the bailiffs cannot hold the same office by law from Her Majesty's said patentee, and advises them to correspond with Mr. Fenes. As to the coming election of members of Parliament, he tells them that they are under no obligation to choose one resident within their town.

1586, Aug. 23, Condover. The same to the same. Is informed that they have given him a yearly fee of five marks; he gives it back again with thanks, being content with his former fee of 20s.

39 Eliz. Aug. 23. Edward Screven, Sheriff of Salop, to the Bailiffs of Shrewsbury; with a copy of the writ directing the choosing a member of Parliament.

1597, Aug. 27. Copy of Council letter on the same subject.

1597, Aug. 13. Plymouth. "Essex" (Robert Devereux) to the Bailiffs, Burgesses, and Commonalty of the town of Shrewsbury.—Being at Plymouth expecting a good wind, he hears that Her Majesty is resolved to call a Parliament. Asks that they will grant him the nominating of their burgesses, nothing doubting he shall be returned from the present expedition for her Majesty's service in time convenient for the nomination. Asks them to send an answer to the Court to his Secretary Edward Reynoldes.

1597, Aug. 27, London. Thomas Owen to the bailiffs of Shrewsbury. Asks that they will choose his son Roger Owen to be one of these burgesses for the Parliament to be holden the 24th of October.

1650, Aug. 21, Shrewsbury. Thomas Hayes, Chas. Denyon, Richard Llewellen and Ow. George to . . .

A single page in folio, containing a copy of a proclamation by His Majesty's Councell for Virginia, giving license to any in Virginia, and all who shall from time to time go there in person, to return to England without any other restraint than to ask leave of the Governor. A large broadside. The inconveniencies that have happened to some persons which have transported themselves from England to Virginia without provisions necessary to sustaine themselves, hath greatly hindered the progresse of that noble plantation. For prevention of the like disorders, &c. (It gives a list of necessaries for families or single persons with the prices.)

. . Lament the desolation of them by plague and pestilence, 156 having died in two months; there are among them near 3,000 cast upon common charity. Ask the addressees to have a day of humiliation in their city to implore God on behalf of Shrewsbury, and also to give them some assistance for their poor.

PROCLAMATIONS AND BROADSIDES.

1599. For better observance of Fish days, suppressing of unnecessary number of alehouses, and punishing rogues, &c. (In 3 sheets.)

1611. For arresting the Lady Arbella and William Seymour escaped from the Tower.

Reasons why the contribution of 1d. per ton of every ship that goeth forward and backward on the North coast of England, towards the maintenance of the lighthouses at Winterton, should not be any grievance, etc. (In 3 sheets.)

20 James I. Copy of patent to Benedict Webbe to make oil from rape seed.

1625. For Coronation of Charles I. (In 2 sheets.)

Petition of the barbers and chirurgions of London that in any Act confirming the King's grant to the physicians of London, the petitioners' rights may be saved.

1630. Regulations for those coming to be touched for the King's Evil.

1640. Petition of 15,000 porters, against the Papists in England and the rebels in Ireland.

1640. Proclamation for a general Fast on the 8th of July.

1644, April 8, Oxford. Proclamation against swearing and cursing, and for better observing prayer and preaching in the King's army, city of Oxford, and other parts.

1659, July 29. Proclamation for a solemn fast on 21 August.

1659. Dec. 14. For summoning a Parliament to meet on 24 January next.

1660, April 17. Declaration and address of the gentry of the county of Essex (addressed to Monck).

1678. Jan. 24. For a Parliament to meet on 6th of March next.

1688, Nov. 6. Proclamation by King James II. against the Prince of Orange.

1688. Dec. 17. Declaration of the Lord Lieutenant, &c., of the county palatine of Chester, city of Chester and county of the same, in favour of the Prince of Orange.

1689. The case of Richard and Ann Ashfield, (two of the younger children of Sir Richard Ashfield Bart., and Mary Lady Ashfield his first wife, who was one of the daughters and coheirs of Sir Richard Rogers) respondents, to the appeal of Dorcas Lady Ashfield, second wife of Sir Richard Ashfield, to reverse a decree in Chancery.

1689. Proclamation by King William and Queen Mary for appointing Commissioner for putting in execution the Act for raising money by a poll and otherwise towards the reducing of Ireland.

5 Edward 6, July 7, Greenwich. "Edward" to the Mayor and Sheriffs of the county of Chester.—He sends her writ, with certain other things devised by him, with the advice of his counsel for the better order of that county. He orders them not to break up the seal of the writ until the morning of the 9th instant, and to do it within the county mentioned in the libel of the writ; they or their under-sheriff are to take testimony at the day to see them break it up; they are then to follow the terms of the writ circumspectly, and not to disclose the tenor of it or of the cedule annexed until the time of publication, except to the under sheriff or other minister who shall execute the writ, whom they are to swear to follow the tenor thereof.—Signed by E. Somerset, R. Ryche, Canc., J. Warwick, Willm. Paget, T. Dorset, W. Herbert, John . . . . (The signature of the King seems effected by means of a stamp.)

1 Mary, July 12, Keninghall. "Marye the quene" to the Mayor and inhabitants of West Chester.—She states that on the death of her brother she caused herself to be proclaimed Queen in Norfolk, Suffolk, and elsewhere; that it has come to her knowledge' that John Dudley, calling himself Duke of Northumberland, with a few complices, has proclaimed " one Lady Jane " daughter to the Duke of Suffolk, for quene of our said " realm, which he hath married to one Gulforde his " soone, whom he entendeth to make King," and that he intends to lead a force against her. She commands them to raise as great a force as they can and repair to her at Keninghall or elsewhere in the county of Nor-

folk . . . . Wherefore [ryght] trustie and well-beloved ay ye true Inglysshemenne faile ye not, &c. (The word [ryght] has been struck through with a pen, and the words in italics have been inserted by a different hand in a space left between the words ye and fail. Indorsed "Received on the 22° and proclaimed the " same day."

3 & 4 Phil. and Mary, June 26, Palace of Westminster. "Philipp and Marye the Quene" to the Mayor and Aldermen of the city of Chester.—They are sending Sir Henry Sydney with convoy of treasure and munition to Ireland. After noticing a proclamation of the war and license by another proclamation to all their subjects " to go to the seas and take their vauntage upon the " enemye," and not doubting that they (the Mayor and Aldermen) have furnished such ships as they were able for keeping the seas quiet and annoying the enemy;—Require them to see Sir H. Sydney and the treasure and munition safely conveyed over the seas.

2 Eliz. Oct. 12, Hampton Court. "Elizabeth R." to the . . . . . brethren . . . .—Since the proclamation for the decry of base testons, inconvenience arose from the inability of some persons to distinguish one from the other, and the marks first added to the basest testons are worn out; she has therefore appointed persons to be at certain places to inform the people and stamp the said testons, and directs to appoint a justice of the peace, and another to use for stamping the testons the two stamping irons and a round plate of steel, which she sends, one of the irons bearing the print of a greyhound and the other a portcullis. She gives particular directions for the use of them. She trusts within a month to send down a quantity of fine money. (2½ pp., torn and damaged).

1590, May 1, Court.—W. (Lord) Burghley to Sir Henry Winston at Standish.—The late Earl of Warwick has left certain lands in Gloucestershire to his widow for payment of his debts. She is anxious to use Winston's friendship in her causes there. Burghley is overseer of the Earl's will, and he asks Winston's lawful assistance to Lady Warwick's tenants and affairs for the redress of any disorder or indirect dealing offered them by any others, as far forth as he being in the commission of the peace may give. The Lady will be willing to requite him with any office there belonging to her or with any other good turn. (Endorsed, "The Lo. Burghley's " letter to Sir Henry Winston about entering into the " Countes of Warr. Business against the Lo. Berkley.")

1593, July 9. Court at Otelandes.—W. (Lord) Burghley to Mr. John Fetter, Mayor of Chester.—Acknowledges the receipt of a letter from the Mayor to the Lords of the Privy Council dated the 1st instant, whereby it appears that according to their direction, this Mayor had, with the help of the Vice-Admiral, made provision for the transport of 600 soldiers to Ireland; prays him to cause the same shipping to be staid until further direction. With the Mayor of Chester's letter, he (Burghley) has received the letter from the Mayor of Liverpool, who has provided shipping for the like number. The present letter is to be sent to him in answer thereof. (An indorsement signed by Burghley, directs that this letter shall be sent over directed to the Lord Deputy by the first passenger.)

9 James I., Jan. 10, Westminster. "James R." to the Emperor of Japan, &c.—Has written several times but has received no reply; this he attributes to the distance; he renews his offers of friendship, as he is confident that his people will behave well, so he doubts not they will be protected by the Emperor. (A short letter beautifully written on vellum, about 18 inches by 15. Three sides have a beautifully ornamented gilt border, and the many capital letters and some words of the letter are gilt. The address on the outside is also ornamented and gilt.)

Copy (5½ foolscap pages) in English of the King of Morocco's letter to the King of England.—He has had success in the Conquest of Sullie, and hopes for the like success in war against Tunis and Algiers; and asks if the King of England will assist him with such forces by sea as shall be answerable to those he provides by land.

James I. M . . . . 3, Westminster. "James R." to the Mayor and Justices of the city and county of Chester. (The letter has been torn and the right half is gone. It is indorsed "A letter of King James the 1st " against Alehouses.")

n.y. Aug. 7, Chiselhurst. William Camden, Clarenceux, to Sir Michael Stanhope, Kt.—Right Worshipfull Sir, I cannott warrant all that is sett down in your note for the Lord Berckley, allthough for the most part true. It maye be sufficient when you have not particulated all

the titles of the Earle of Sussex to add no more than this
and Elizabeth married to George L. Berkley, lineally descended from the Mowbraies- Dukes of Norfolk. I know
that the Lords Berkley have used the said titles as well
as the Howards Dukes of Norfolk, but not without some
repining, and in my opinion may be very well spared
in this your epitaph.
1636, March 16. Receipt signed by Francis (Earl of)
Bedford for 30l. paid by Mr. Smith, officer and receiver
of Lord Berkeley, for the use of the poor of Chenies, by
virtue of a grant made to them by Ann, Countess of
Warwick, deceased, at Lady Day, 1637.
1640, March 23. Roger Kirkbie to Sir Gilbert Hoghton,
Bart., and the rest of the Commissioners appointed for
the assessment of 4 subsidies within the county Palatine
of Lancaster.—He says that, that day in the Parliament
House, Sir Robers Pye gave him a certificate directed
to him and his fellows, appointed by the House of Commons to be the receivers of the four subsidies granted
by the last Act. Sir Gilbert has some doubts by reason
of some mistakes in the Bill. Kirkbie says that they
have passed a Bill amending the mistakes and it has
gone up to the Lords. He thinks Hoghton may go on
with the business, although the Act has not yet come
to his hands. (Copy.)
1641, Feb. 8. William Brereton to Mr. Cooper,
Mayor of Chester.—This day he read to the House
Cooper's letter and the warrant enclosed, and moved
that if they thought fit to discharge Sir George Hambleton, his warrant might be restored, which was not
assented unto, but they determined he should be
brought up by Habeas Corpus. It would have been
sent by that post, but for the mistake of one who should
have delivered it to Brereton.
1641, Feb. 24. "George Monck," Lt.-Col. to the
right honourable the Earl of Leicester, Lord Lieutenant
of Ireland and General of His Majesty's forces for this
present expedition, certifies that Thomas Printon, master
of the Grace of Chester, has brought to Dublin 16 horses
of the officers of his excellency's regiment.
1642, May 20. William Lenthall, Speaker [of the
House of Commons], to Sir George Booth, Sir Richard
Wilbraham, Sir Thomas Delves, Sir Richard Grosvenor,
Thomas Stanley, Richard Brereton, Harry Bunbury,
John Greive, and the rest of the justices of the peace of
the County Palatine of Chester, and to the Mayor of
Chester, and to Charles Walley and William Edwards,
Aldermen of Chester.—Notices complaints received
from persons in the county and city of Chester that
they have suffered much from soldiers billetted on
them without their consents, and who had committed
outrages, and had departed without making satisfaction either for themselves or their horses. He then
gives the particulars of the orders of the House of
Commons on the subject of troops passing through the
county on their way to Ireland.
1642, Sept. 18, Court at Stafford.—"Charles R." to
the Mayor of Chester.—Announces his visit to Chester
on Friday next, and bids him have the Train Band
ready, and provision for him and his retinue.
17 Car. I., Jan. 4, Whitehall.—"Charles R." to the
Mayor of the town and port of Westchester, the Searchers, Comptrollers of the passage, and all other his
officers there whom it may concern.—Whereas Mr.
Denzill Holles, Sir Arthur Hazelrigg, Mr. John Pim,
Mr. John Hampden, Mr. William Strode, having been
by the Attorney-General accused of High Treason and
of high misdemeanours, have fled, and they will probably
endeavour to escape into foreign parts; he tells the
addressees to use diligence to arrest and keep them in
custody till (having advertised the Privy Council) further orders.
18 Car. I., Sept. 26, Court at Chester.—"Charles R."
to Thomas Couper, Mayor of Chester, James Earl of
Derby and John Earl Rivers, Robert Vire Cholmondeley, Robert Brerewood, Recorder, William Gamul,
Charles Walley, and Thomas Thropp, Aldermen of
Chester.—Tells them, with the assistance of the Sheriffs
and others, to search the several houses of Sir William
Brereton, Bart., William Edwards, Alderman, and
Thomas Aldersey, Alderman, the Red Lyon and the
Golden Lyon, situate in the said City, and to seize and
take for the use of the King all arms and ammunition
found there which they shall suspect to be intended to
be used against the King.
1644, June 19. (The Earl of) Derby to all His Majesty's loving subjects whom it may concern.—Protection for William Farrington, of Werden, Esq., and his
wife (and his goods, chattel, or cattle), who had been
taken prisoners by the enemy, and released by the
garrison at Lathom.

1648, Aug. 1, Gray's Inn.—Jo. Bradshawe to Mr.
Robert Wright, Mayor of Chester.—Has received a
letter from Wright and three other Aldermen. They
know why Chester was omitted the last time, and if the
like or other sad impediment do not happen, they may
be sure he will not alter from the usual place of holding
the grand Sessions. He promises attention to the welfare of them and their city conditionally on their constant compliance with the directions of Parliament.
1650, Sept. 19, Council of State at Whitehall. Jo.
Bradshawe, President, to the Mayor of Chester.—Sends
10 Acts of Parliament for a Thanksgiving, &c., and tells
him to cause them seasonably to be distributed into all
the parishes of his jurisdiction, so that none may pretend ignorance thereof, of which a strict account will
be required. (Wafer seal of the Council of State.)
1662, May 27, Cockpit.—Albemarle to Thomas Earl
of Ossory.—Recommends the bearer, Thomas Monck,
for an Ensign's place in one of the Companies in Ireland.
1662, Sept. 30, Whitehall.—(Prince) Rupert to Lord
. . . Recommends a business of the bearer, Sir
William Carr (long a servant in the Prince's family).
n. d. (Sir) Matthew Hale to Mr. Smith.—Opinion as
to the liabilities of the county at large to the repairs of
Ower Bridge, near Gloucester. (2 pp.)
16 Car. II., July 5, Office of Arms in the City of
London.—William Dugdale, Norroy King of Armes to
the Town Clerk of the City of Chester.—A printed
form signed by Dugdale, and having his large wafer
seal of office, whereby he denounces certain persons,
whose names are annexed, as having usurped Arms,
Cognizances and Crests, and the style of Esquire or
Gentleman, and directing that they shall not be addressed as esquires or gentlemen until they shall justify
the same by the law of Arms. (The names of 38 persons in Chester, and their places of abode, are given.)
15 Car. II., Dec. 10. The King's warrant under the
seal of the Council of the Marches of Wales to apprehend James Bridgeman, and attach him as a rebel to
answer to such contempt as shall be objected to him by
Thomas Dewzell and Margaret his wife.
1681, Nov. 6, Albemarle House.—(The Duke of) Albemarle to (Duke of Ormonde).—Sends a petition, on
which the King declares in his favour. Hopes to find
favour from him (Ormonde), like as he gratified Albemarle's father on former occasions.
n.d. M. (Duchess of) Ormonde to the Duke of Ormonde.—She expected to have seen him last night,
because his coach went to Wicomb the day before, and
everybody has been at London; the Duke of Grafton,
Lord Clarendon, Lord Churchill, and in short everybody but him. Sir John Mead wrote to him the last
post from Ireland, and said there was great need of
making a sheriff, for the prison had been broken twice
since last Assizes. She says she has made Mr. Gascoine
send him a blank Warrant, which he will please to sign
and fill up, if there be no hopes of his coming soon,
which she hopes he will do.
1684, Nov. 4, Whitehall. "Charles R." to the [Arch-
bishop of Canterbury].—Seeing that many who served
his Royal Father and then followed him (Charles II.)
abroad are reduced to poverty, and that in his guards
and garrisons others may become unfit for service, he
has resolved to found and erect at Chelsea a perpetual
hospital, in which more than 400 aged or otherwise disabled soldiers might then (and so successively the like
number for ever) be lodged and supplied with necessary
supports of life. He has already expended great sums
of money on the fabrick. But as his particular bounty
is not sufficient, he calls on other of estate and quality,
particularly the Clergy, and asks [the Archbishop] to
send circular letters to all the Bishops of his province,
inviting them to get subscriptions from the Clergy.
1684, June 14, Convent of St. Saviour at Jerusalem.
Latin Certificate by Brother Petrus Antonius Grassus,
&c. &c., and keeper of Mount Sion and the Holy Sepulchre, that John Just, an Englishman and a Londoner,
had been to Jerusalem and visited a number of Holy
Places (specified). Oval wafer seal of the Guardian of
the Convent of Mount Sion. On it are represented a
large assembly and a man seated having his feet washed
by another (probably Christ washing the disciples' feet),
and above them a number of beatified saints surmounted
by the Holy Ghost.
1685, June 30. Arlington to the Duke of Ormonde,
Lord Steward, and to the Treasurer and Controller and
rest of the officers of the Board of Greencloth.—His
Majesty, having commanded that the ancient service

and allowance of All Night,* heretofore served up in the King's Presence Chamber, should now be again revived and served as formerly, he (Arlington) desires the Duke will give order that the same be served up as formerly.

1686, July 12, Windsor. "James R." to the Duke of Ormonde, Lord Steward of the Household.—Order to admit the bearer, Sir Winston Churchill, into the place of Second Clerk of the Greencloth in Ordinary, vacant by death of Sir William Boreman.

1688, Sept. 24, Dublin.—William (Bishop of) Kildare to the Duke of Ormonde.—Congratulations on the Duke's accession to the honours and patrimony of his great ancestors. Commends the care and industry of Dr. Hinton, the Master of the School at Kilkenny.

1689, April 9, Chester. Charles Thompson to Henry Gascoigne, at his Grace the Duke of Ormonde's, in St. James' Square.—People arrived yesterday who left Dublin on Saturday, and say that King James had set up his Standard on the Castle of Dublin, whose motto is Now or Never. Now and Ever; he was to march on Monday last to Carrickfergus and thence immediately to Scotland, where they say are many thousands to join his force. . . . . There were some highland lairds with King James in Dublin to receive his commands whether they should come to Ireland or not; he thanked them and ordered them to stay in Scotland where were many thousands more; they said they had 5,000 men in their neighbourhood ready; King James told them he was going to the North in order to go to Scotland, where he would be in a few days.—Movements of the Duke of Berwick and Lord Tyrconnel.—Poor Londonderry and Coleraine it is feared cannot hold out long, having no relief; the ships and men designed thither were in this port yesterday; there are some frigates that came from France left in Ireland, and, it is said, are to bombard Derry. King James is to be in Captain Hercules Davis's house in Carrickfergus. . . . The Queen is to lye in in Ireland, who they say is big with child. All things in Ireland are governed by the French Ambassador, as if Ireland were the French King's, and King James under him. . . . . This morning is discovered that the well in the Castle of Chester is poisoned. . . . . Sends a list of those who came with King James into Ireland. (This list is inclosed, giving the names of 45 persons, French, English, and Irish. Among them are Col. Kenan, Simon Lutrell, and Marshal Boufflers with 500 officers, and 1,500 English, Scotch, and Irish, all coming from Brest with all speed.

1689, January 30, Westminster. P[eter Mew, Bishop of] Winchester, to the Duke of Ormond.—Recommends the bearer, Alexander Denton, as a person fit to continue the employment for which he petitions.—Enclosed is an unsigned letter by the Duke of Ormonde to the Vice-Chancellor of Oxford, saying that Alexander Denton, a Cook at Oxford, had brought to him his own petition and the Bishop of Winchester's letter, and recommending him as having (as he is informed) kept a civil orderly House, and requesting that he might have leave to keep up his Billiard Table as long as the V. C. might judge it reasonable, according to his good behaviour in the management of it without prejudice to any of the members of the University.

1609, Feb. 26, Whitehall. Copy of Council letter (to the Sheriff and Justices of the Co. of Gloucester), complaining of the incorrectness of the returns made by the Sheriffs of the counties, of the lists of freeholders, and commanding them to send true and perfect certificates; and also directing the Sheriff every half year to send up a true calendar of all such returns of panels as well concerning trials as inquisitions as he had made of the two terms and assises next precedent; and also requiring him not to omit returning for Jurors such as have procured writs de non ponendis in assisis, except they be manifestly from age or impotency within the meaning thereof.

1613, Aug. 24, Stoke. (Sir) Edw. Coke to Lord Berkeley. Is glad to hear of his Lordship's return to his castle of Berkeley, and that he is so free from harm where there was so eminent danger. "But it hath " pleased God to preserve us to see the comfort and " fruit of this so much applauded and happely begunne " marriage . . . . Diverse judges and others are " with a large commission to doe justice and punish " oppressions, &c. sent over into Ireland; my brother " that was joined with me in circuite as one of them

" that is gone; my Lord Russell and Sir Thomas " Dennys are lately dead. Sir Patrick Murrey has " married Sir Francis Vere's widowe. The Prince " yesterday went from his hunting in and about " Windsor to Richmond, blessed be God, in greate " prosperitie and good health." Thanks him for remembering Sir William Throckmorton's matter, and promises to do his utmost to proceed in it.

1618, Oct. 24, Oldburio. Henry Townshend to John Smith, in London. Says he was commissioned to appear at Wickwar to inquire for concealed lands. The Commissioners were Sir John Poyntz, Sir John Stafford, Sir Richard Hill, and an old gentleman whose name he did not know. How he (Townshend) was left out he does not know; but the Jury found the land for the King. Some friends of his that served in the Jury told him that Smith had made sure word before hand, or else they should have no verdict. Smith's adversary, Clookhay, pleaded very hard to have them found 36 tenements with land for charitable uses, but could not prevail.

1660, Feb. 9, London. Baynham Throkmorton to John Smith, at Nibley.—Understands that Sir Thomas Overbury has lately, at Gloucester, declared that he will not stand to be Knight of the Shire, and that the Ld. Lieutenant will be one, and Mr. John How makes himself sure of the other. The cost deters the writer from standing, but he dislikes the thought of How coming in, because he thinks himself above all men. Asks Smith to use his endeavours with others to have two persons selected without going to the poll. Asks that any reply may be directed to him at the Crown below Charing Cross, over against Stanhop (Stanhope) House.

1625, Oct. 24, Clowerwall. Sir William Throkmorton to John Smith. He is in trouble about his son, Baynham, who has gone off, and he fears that he is with his enemy, Sir Richard Catchmaye, and intends to go abroad. Asks Smith to endeavour to get some deeds (which he needs executed by himself) executed by his Son. (There are several other later letters by Sir W. Throkmorton, and one in 1606 by John Throkmorton, on business matters.)

1633, June 6. Robert Poyntz and two others to John Smith, at North Nibley. By virtue of their Commission under the Great Seal, they ask for a contribution towards re-edifying St. Paul's Church, in London. (An indorsement by Smith says that he sent 20s.)

1630, March 9, Whitehall. (Copy of) Council letter to 19 Gentlemen of the County of Gloucester (John Smith of North Nibly is one), directing them to appear at Whitehall and compound for not attending at the King's Coronation.

1638, Feb. 18. R. Berkeley and Mau. Berkeley (Deputy Lieutenants) to John Smith, directing him to furnish for the trained force of the Co. of Gloucester a man, horse, arms, and furniture, as understated; they charging him with a Cuirassier instead of a Light Horse as formerly.

1639, Feb. 18. Barbican. G. Berkeley to John Smith, Steward of his lands in Gloucester. At the instance of the Lord Chamberlain, he asks Smith to vote for and get support for Sir Ralph Dutton, to be one of the Knights of the Parliament for Gloucester.

1641. Copy of form of a warrant, dated at Chorley, to the high Constable of . . ., Co. Lancaster, to collect a Benevolence for the relief of the distressed subjects of Ireland.

1641, Dec. 15, Cirencester. Letter to . . . signed by Ro. Poyntz, Mau. Berkeley, Ry. Berkeley, Thomas Chester, Thomas Veel, John Smythe, and four others, soliciting subscription to a Petition, and directing that the paper be sent to Sir William Mosten, at Cirencester, on the 11th of January, when they have appointed the next meeting.

1641, Feb. 7. Francis Creswicke (Sheriff of the County of Gloucester) to John Smith, of North Nibley. In obedience to a letter from the Speaker and a letter from the Knights of the County he appoints a public meeting at Cirencester, at Mr. Portlock's, to take and publish the protestation and petition therewith sent.

Petition and remonstrance of the knights, gentry, freeholders, and inhabitants of the county of Gloucester whose names are subscribed, with several Schedules thereunto annexed (the schedules are not there).

It is a petition in favour of Episcopacy.

(1642.) Petition to the King by divers of the true Protestant religion in the County Palatine of Lancaster.

1642. Saturday, Alveston. Tho. Veel to (John Smith). Incloses a letter, which he says he received that morning; the gentleman that brought it told him that Lord . . . received letters on Thursday last that the King would be as that or the last night at Warwick with

* This Service is several times mentioned in the Ordinances and Regulations for the Royal Household, printed by the Society of Antiquaries, &c., Lond. 1790, pp. 58, 79, 157, 321, 365.

R. CHOL-
MONDELEY,
Esq.

considerable power, and he conceived he would come amongst them.

1642, June 8, Euxton. Hugh Anderton to William Farrington, Esq., at Werden.—Has received by the bearer a letter from Captain Somner for money behind to him and his company for pay. Complaints of this kind are common; but he has no money in his hands, as appears by his account delivered·yesterday evening to Sir William Gerrard and the General Major. . . . . Is surprised that in their hundred, out of so much money taxed, there should not be sufficient to maintain 30 men at half pay. Begs Farrington, if he have any of the money, to let Capt. Somner have 20l. or 30l. upon account, that he may keep his men together.

1642, Aug. 11, Sudeley. Chandos to Captain Veale. Notifies a public meeting at the Ram at Cirencester on Monday next, to consider the course to be taken in the distracted state of the kingdom.

1642, Aug. 29. John Thomas (High Constable) to the Petty Court or Tithingmen of North Nibley. The Parliament has appointed Visct. Say and Sele to be Lord Lieutenant of the County of Gloucester, and he has appointed Sir Robert Cooke, John Fettiplace, Edward Stephens, Nathan Stephens, Thomas Morgan, and others, to be Deputy Lieutenants. He directs them (by virtue of a warrant to him) to summon all captains, &c. of trained bands in the tithing, &c.; and also 6, 8, or 10 to supply defects in the train bands to appear at the Riding, near Sodbury, on the 1st of Sept. next; and the captains are to bring in their master rolls.

1642, Sept. 26. Na. Stephens and Tho. Hodges to John Smyth.—They met on Thursday last at Gloster (being the day appointed at the 1st meeting of the gentlemen, it being agreed they should meet once a fortnight). Very few were there: hopes that Smyth and others will come on Thursday next, to advise what is best for the good of the country in these times of extremity and danger.

1642, Oct. 3. Jo. Seymour. John Codrington, and Edw. Stephens, to John Smith.—The gentlemen in other parts have subscribed according to the propositions set forth by the Parliament, and have taken the subscriptions of others, what money, plate, horse, and arms they will lend or furnish to the Parliament. In pursuance of a warrant 300 are summoned to meet on Saturday, and other 400 on Monday. Smith is on Friday to send in to the Ridings at Chipping Sudbury such horse of service as he is taxed at, there to be trained and exercised.

1642, Oct. 19. Ro. Cooke, Na. Stephens, and Edw. Stephens, to John Smith.—Intreating him to meet them and the rest of the gentlemen at Gloucester at the Boothall on Monday the 14th (sic.) of the present month to consider what is best to be done for the common safety of themselves and the County.

1642, Nov. 25, Chipping Sudbury. Jo. Seymour and Edw. Stephens to John Smith and Anthony Kingscote, or either of them. Dangers are near approaching; therefore they think good to call in the Dragooners that they subscribed that they may have them in readiness for the safety of the county. They ask Smith and Kingscote to cause the Dragooners subscribed before them in the hundred of Berkeley to appear on Saturday at Chipping Sudbury with horses, armour, and a month's pay.

1643, Aug. 15, Barkley. (The King's Commissioners), to the high Constables of the hundred of Berkeley. (Copy.) The King's army under the command of Prince Rupert has entered the County of Gloucester and subdued Bristol and other places, and the King intends to settle garrisons in the said City and other places. He has fixed 6,000l. per month as the proportion of the County of Gloucester for maintenance of the garrisons; on payment of which the county shall rest secure from prejudice; the payments are to begin on 8th of August 1643. The High Constables are to assemble the inhabitants of the hundred and exhort them to pay the sums underwritten, which sums when collected are to be paid to Thomas Walter of St. Nicholas parish in Bristol, merchant, within 10 days after the date of the letter.—Annexed is a list of 22 ville in Berkeley Hundred, with sums of money opposite each, amounting in all to 4971. 5s.

1642, Aug. 10, Youghal . . Henry Rugge to John Smith. . . . Will give, though briefly, yet true intelligence of those occurrences which have happened in these parts since the beginning of the late universal insurrection of the Irish Papists in this kingdom. The province of Munster is the most southernly quarter in Ireland, lying opposite to Devonshire and Cornwall, under the government of a President with the Council of the Province.

This part remained 2 months quiet after all the rest had revolted, and we conceived good hopes of its continuance till about 12 days before Christmas, when certain rebels out of Leinster came in and disturbed our hoped security. The Lord President was not idle all this while, but having secured Cork (the most remarkable place of his Province) the best he could, in the extreme want of men, money, [and] ammunition, with 3 troops of horse and 50 musketeers (a bold attempt) he fell upon that enemy which has foraged in the counties of Waterford and Tipperary, and within a few days destroyed about 600 of the rebels without the loss of one man; and having visited the cities of Waterford and Casshel, with the townes of Clonemell and Cacrig, &c., he returned to his house at Donneraile, Dec. 28. But ere the holidays were half spent, Richard Butler, brother to the Earl of Ormond, Purcell Baron Loghnash, Philip O'Dwyer, great men in Tipperary, revolted; the city of Casshel, townes of Clonmell, Fodder, Carrig &c. did the like; and suddenly the Lords of Dumboine and Cahir, with that whole county, turned rebels; the Lords of Brettus and of Castlooonell did the like in the county of Limerick in Kerry McFinan, with the rest of the Irishry there rebelled; so did O'Sydnam in the west of the county of Cork; Waterford revolted, city, and whole county, save a few places which lie on the river of Youghal. Thus, on a sudden, all things were become desperate; robbing, stripping, murthering of the English Protestants in every quarter; we who by God's great mercy escaped with our lives, fly some to Cork, some to Youghall, some to Bandon; others betake them to castles in the country. The Lord President draws all the force he could make into the field in January; expecting the approaching of the enemy, he encamped near Kildarerrey, in the County of Corke; the rebels approach, but are afraid to come down into the plains, fearing our horse; the rebels were 14,000, we about 700 foot and 300 horse. The enemy dares not fight; ours much desire it, being weary of their bad winter quarter in the open fields. About the second week in February the Lord President made an honourable retreat to Cork from the great army of the rebels, not having lost a man, and then not being able to doe any more provideth only for defence. The Erle of Corke is at Youghall to guard it with the Viscount of Dungarvan, the Erle of Barrimore at Castle Leghan, the Lord Braughall, at Lismore, the Lord Kinallmely at Bandon, the president with the Lord Inchiquin at Corke; the Lord of Rovy is sent into England; and so stood the present condition of the English in Munster untill Shrovetide; the Irish revolting in every quarter. Shrovemunday, Sir Charles Valvasor, with 1,000 foote landeth at Youghall; on the next weeke the Lord President brings such forces as he could spare out of Corke, and they both march to Dungarvan; they take the towne and receive the castle on composition; while they ly at the seige of Dungarvan, the Lord of Muskry revolteth, drawes 4,000 men within 3 miles of Corke, the president by hard marches getts to Corke in 2 dayes; about the 23rd of Aprill the Lord of Inchiquin and Sir Charles issue out of Corke with two troopes of horse and 300 musketters; they assault Muskry, rout his army, take . . . tent and wagon, kill Captain McFinan, the stoutest of all those rebells, with 400 others, the rest fly; Muskry himselfe goeth to Limericke, wher the others of his faction meet him. The President overgrowth weake of body, and yet on the coming over of the two last regiments he removes into the field; they take many castles from the enemies; the enemy about June draws towards our forces, on St. Peter's days they fight, God gives us the victory, a handfull of our men routs the rebels' army; we there tooke from them five ensigns; the same weeke the president dieth. The next weeke the Lord Braughall went to releive Sir Richard Osborne nere Dungarvan, and in his returne, having with him a troope of horse and 300 foot, was encountred by 800 rebels neere Cappoquin, but by God's blessing he slew almost 300 of them with the losse of one man onely. Verely God hath done great thinges for us, but we are defective to ourselves, our new soldiours are half dead, and yet ther hath not bene 20 slaine in all the skirmishes against the enemy. Things are not right with us, the soldiers want pay, our army is made weake, not by the power of an adversary, but by ourselves.

1643, Nov. 4(?). Berkeley Castle. George Maxwell to Mr. Smith of Nibley.—The reason for not waiting upon him that day was that he heard the enemy was abroad and had been at Beerston (Beeston?) Castle.

1643. Nov. 17. Berkeley Castle. The same to the same.—Has written to Sir Francis Haly concerning the state of the castle. Has suffered as much as he can with his credit and has trusted to their very fair promises, but he thinks they only want to gain time. When the King raised the seige of Gloucester he sent Maxwell four pieces, but he could not then get them into the castle and he cannot now have one of them. The King gave him an order at Gloucester for 320 men to be in garrison in Berkeley Castle, of which 320 men, the Prince's Company was to be 200; now they have taken away the Prince's company. Complains that he has neither victuals nor money. Hears that Sir Francis Haly has ordered that he shall have no entertainment for his soldiers. Lord Hapton's company there is duly paid and has victuals besides. His own men are for the most part run away. He cannot withstand the enemy if he thinks the intention is to put an affront on him. Says (in confidence) that he has sent his lieutenant to the Prince, with his commission.

1643, January 3, Bristol. John Smyth to Sir Edward Hyde (a signed Draft).—He acknowledges Hyde's letter to him, and one enclosed to Lord Berkeley, of whose fidelity and allegiance to the King Hyde may rest assured, but his long illness and failure of almost all his revenue may defer that assistance in person or purse or both that might justly be expected. He (Smyth) will send a message rather than the King's letter, which in the condition he (Smyth) is in is almost impossible. Lord Berkeley may be heard of at his house in Great St. Bartholemew's; the Earl of Clare and Lord Conway are his chief friends.

1634, Feb. 22, Whitehall. Copy of Lord Deputy Wentworth's propositions for the kingdom of Ireland read and approved at the Council Board the 17th of Feb. 1631, and of the King's orders thereon. There are nine propositions. 1st. That his Majesty may declare his express pleasure that no Irish suit by way of reward be moved of any of his servants or others before the ordinary revenue there become able to sustain the necessary charge of the Crown, and the debts thereof be fully cleared. (3½ pp.)*

16. .. Dec. 6, Cirencester. Letter signed by Ro. Cooke, Na. Stephens, John Fettiplace, John Stephens, and John Georges, addressed to John Smith at Nibley, saying that it was agreed that 300 Dragooners should lie in garrison at Cirencester; that none of the dragooners of his parts or hundred had come for the guard thereof; and desiring him to issue warrants to summon them to come in to garrison for the safety of the town, and to appoint the officers of every parish to bring in the moneys that are for the payment of the dragooners to three persons (named), who had been appointed receivers thereof.

16. .. Dec. 9, Cirencester. John Georges to John Smyth at Nibley. In reply to Smyth's letter he says that if the horses which Smyth mentions are sent with an allowance of 2s. per diem, if Capt. Peyler cannot find riders for them he (Georges) will do it there; and all that come are to be under the command of Lieut.-Col. Carr and his officers, till there may be a fit number to distribute into several companies, and then fit captains will be placed over them. Attributes the mutinous language of the people to the dilatoriness of those who have been specially employed and relied on by the Parliament, the Lord General, and the Lord Lieutenant.

1642, Oct. 21. Warington. (Copy.) At a meeting at Warington, by the Earl of Derby the Earl Rivers and divers other Lords, Knights, and gentlemen of the counties of Lancaster and Chester, whose names are subscribed, it is concluded and agreed upon as follows :— Twelve heads, for calling out the trained bands and freehold bands and horse of the two countries for the defense thereof; for fixing places of rendezvous; for payment of the troops (every soldier to have 12d. the day, out of which the captains and officers to have 4d. the day for their pay and the provision of powder, bullet and match); to bring about an association with the counties of Salop, Flint, Denbigh, Cumberland, and Westmoreland. Signed by the Earl of Derby and 23 others, among whom are R. Cholmondeley, Tho. Cholmondeley and John Davinport.

1666, Oct. 2, Gloucester. Wm. (Bishop of) Gloucester to Her Majesty's Justices of the Peace now met at Gloucester to keep the quarter sessions. A long letter with Biblical and classical quotations, urging them in strong terms to put in force the Acts against Conventicles.

1661, Jan. 23. Copy return of the Constable of Wotton under Edge unto his Majesty's commission at their sitting, of those who have subscribed and paid and those who have subscribed and not paid. (27 persons are in the former category and 26 in the latter.)

1672, Dec. 23. Copy of the King's license, countersigned by Arlington, for a room or rooms in the house of Mary Tovy, of the parish of Vly in Gloucestershire, to be a place for the use of such as do not conform to the Church of England, who are of the persuasion commonly called Presbyterian, in order to their public worship and devotion.

1696, Aug. 20. Council order under seal and signed by Wm. Bridgeman, directing George Smith, Esq., J. P. for Gloucestershire, to send to the Council Board all such informations upon oath and examinations as had been taken relating to Captain William Wintour and the other persons proposed by Smith to be named in a proclamation. (Smith had written to Mr. Newton, Warden of the mint, about several persons accused of clipping and counterfeiting the current coin of the kingdom.)

1708, April 29, Drumlanrig. Philip Davies to George Smyth, Esq., at North Nibley . . . . . The only true news is that they have 15 of their nobility in the Castle of Edinburgh, and that very day part of them were ordered for London, a second part on Saturday, the other part on Tuesday. Wishes them a safe deliverance, but does not expect to see them all back in Scotland. He mentions a preacher on the mountains who caused great disturbance, having congregations of 700, 800, or 1,000, and was at the point of writing four or five sheets of paper against the Union; but an order of council was issued against him last week and proclaimed him a rebel at the Cross of Edinburgh; hears that three parties of horse are after him, and that he has 18,000 men with him in the mountains; the paper he wrote was in the nature of a roll; thinks it was near five yards long; he brought 100 or 150 men in arms, horse, and foot, and nailed [it] to a cross in a place called Jankers belonging to the Duke, about six miles from Drumlanrig; he (Davies) saw the taking of it; this was done in December. Davies does not like the Scotch houses; the only windows are those to let out the smoke; the fire is made in the middle of the house, and they sit round it and talk, but cannot see each other for the smoke.—He finds fault with the bread, the beer, and the women of the country. He seems to have recently left England, and at the time of his letter to be employed as agent to the Duke of

A short account of the methods used by the Irish for the importing of their wool and woollen yarn from the southern coasts of that kingdom into France. (1 p.)

Petition to the King   by Robert Gower and Edward Harle; setting out the abuses in the supply of drugs for the army and navy, and suggesting the appointment of one or more apothecaries general, from whom all surgeons are to procure their medicines, the price to be paid by the Treasury and deducted from each surgeon's stated allowance; and praying that the petitioners, on sufficient testimony of their ability, may be established in that Imploy.

1660, March the (   ), St. Johnes. Lord Berkeley to Mr. Edward Smith, at Nibley.—Intends to be at the next meeting of the Committee at Gloster, for settling the Militia. Lord Bruce is returned from Bedfordshire Commander-in-chief of all the forces there :—He (Berkeley) will take it kind if his countrymen give him leave to command a regiment of horse, without having any superior commander over him in the country.

1664, Sept. 15, London. Sir Edward Fust to John Smyth, at Gloucester . . . . . Prince Rupert is preparing with 22 good ships for Guine, and another fleet preparing to follow, which makes some think there may be [an] engagement on our seas before. There is a daily pressing of men for sea. Col. Massey goes with the Prince with 1,000 foot, as 'tis reported. Some say the King of France medinates, but not yet that I hear of publiquely. The packet boat, by accident or design, is stopped, as by the news book; if no good account, the D. of York will send his Mercuries to Sir G. Dowings for intelligence. The King and Council sit close, and a great hum in the town about the Dutch affair.

1665, March 17, Southw[arke]. Edward Smyth to (his father) John Smyth, at Nibley. A long letter; from which it appears that Edward Smyth and Sir Thomas Clarges were contending candidates for a seat in Parliament. On Tuesday the bailiff at 10l. charge, divided the Artillery Ground, at Horsey, (Horsley) Down, intending to make the election there the day following. This was the same night countermanded by a letter from the Lord General. The next morning two companies of foot were sent over; one took possession of the hall where the writ was to be read, and the other the artillery ground. Sir Thomas Clarges by riding about got together about 2,000 men from Newington, Lambeth, Westminster, &c., of which only 500 were thought to be able to poll. The crowd was so great that Smyth and his friends could hardly get up; but they numbered a little over 1,530, so that when the other party were garbled of all their unpollable men, Smyth must carry it by great odds. Lord Craven, Sir P. Howard, and others of the Court were there. The Lord Mayor who came to read the writ was forced to stand in the street in the crowd. The writ was read; Smith demanded a poll; the Lord Mayor appointed St. George's Fields; Smyth insisted that Horsey Downe was the fit place. The Lord Mayor went to the Council, and got an order to adjourn to St. George's Fields. On Wednesday they went there; Sir Thomas Clarges and he have a parley; Smyth perceives that his supporters do not come up so strong as formerly; the end of it is that he agrees to give up to Sir Thomas: and they both went together to the place appointed to take the poll; he made a speech to the people recommending Sir Thomas, and persuaded his friends to vote for him, which was done; Sir Thomas and he naming 20 of each other's parties to seal the indentures.

1666, June 9, Badminton. Lord Herbert to John Smith, of Nibley. Notices the backwardness of many in payment of the weekly tax lately assessed, and of the arrears of the three months tax theretofore rated. In order to prevent the necessity of proceeding with rigour, he asks Smith to explain to the people their duty and the necessity of paying. In pursuance of the King's orders, Smith is to have it ordered at the present sessions that Beacons be provided in the usual and convenient places of the county, and that they be duly watched whereby notice may be given of any approaching danger.

1666, Oct. 4, Fort Bellaagh. Thomas Smyth to Mr. Edward Smyth at the Bridge House, near the bridge foot in Southwark, London . . . . . Thanks for making Col. Cooke his friend. Says that his garrison is the remotest in this kingdom, 120 miles from Dublin, 32 miles from any post office, a mile from any market town. He is governor of the fort, where he lives, praised be Jove, in great plenty. The place stands in the middle of a bog, 10 miles every way; without it as much wood, and beyond it mountains. Wishes he had the convenience of a painter, for he believes the whole world does not afford the like landscape.

1666, Dec. 14. Sir Edward Fust to John Smyth at Nibley.—Directions to tender the oaths of supremacy and allegiance to Popish recusants, or those suspected to be so; the names of those who refuse to take the oaths to be sent to Fust.

1662. Copy of certificate by Thomas Smyth, that one William Vizer, served Charles I. as an officer under his (Smyth's) command, and died in service, leaving a wife and six small children; and of an order by Sir Gabriel Lowe and John Smyth, Esq., Justices of the Peace, co. Gloucester, that the widow should have 4l. per annum from the Treasurer of the county in pursuance of the Act of Parliament authorizing them.

1666, Jan. 12, Gloucester. William (Bishop of) Gloucester to John Smith, Esq. Alludes to Smith's declaration at Todbury (Sodbury ?) that excommunicate persons are liable to the penalty of the Statute for their absence from the Liturgy, notwithstanding they are excluded by the church censure. It is so powerful a way to reduce many refractory persons that he (the Bishop) will endeavour that it shall have its effect. He likes it better than the Significavit, which is chargeable and troublesome.

1669, April 26, Gloucester. Henry Ockold, Mayor, to John Smith.—Assures him that a person named had not been arrested, and that the serjeants are and have been commanded to forbear to make any arrests in the time of the Assizes or Sessions, so that that no just occasion should be given for the removal of the Assizes or Sessions.

1678, Feb. 6. Copy of the King's answer to the address of the House of Commons. (About the proposed treaty offensive and defensive with Holland against France.) This is followed by a copy of the Commons address on Feb. 1.

1694. April 2, London. William Stephens to George Smyth at Alderman Man's house.—Is glad that Symth is so well employed; doubts not that what he has written is very honest and useful and necessary at this time . . . . He never knew any time when the Church was more caressed by the Court than now, so that if Smyth is anything but sweet upon the Church, his book will not be licensed, nor will Sir Robert

Atkins like his dedication. He says that his own sermon gave great offence to the church because he did not speak honourably enough of Conquest and Passive Obedience, and for want of a sufficient quantity of railing upon the Dissenters; and he believed it would not have passed the licenser's approbation and therefore was printed only by virtue of the order of the Lord Mayor and Court of Aldermen.

1706, March 25, Council Chamber, Kensington. (Copy.) Council letter to Charles Earl of Berkeley, Custos Rotulorum of yᵉ co. of Gloucester, but in his absence to the Justices of the Peace. Urging the exercise of the "Act for the encouragement and increase of "Seamen and for the better and speedier manning Her "Majesty's fleet," by finding out and impresting such seamen and able-bodied landsmen and prisoners for debt as are intended by the Act.—It was with a view to a fleet against the common enemy (France).

1706, June 4. William Loup to George Smith.—He doubts not Smith has heard of their noble champion's second glorious victory (Ramillies). He gave them a Jeroboam stroke, and the Danes did not forget how their poor natives were sacrificed at Calcinedo (Calcinato) in Italy; so that when their generals bid them halt, they drove on, Jehu like, giving no quarter, and cutting the enemy all to pieces for several miles; but our brave English boys who, with their horse quickly routed their (the French) right wing, were more merciful and granted quarter to the regiment Du Roy, who laid down at their horses' feet their arms and begged for their lives. Is loud in praise of Marlborough, says that last Friday he received two letters from his dear friend Capt. Butler, the first dated 30th of April by which he gave the following melancholy account;—On the 27th April they anchored in the bay of Barcelona with five sail of ships of battle, Monsieur Tholouse having timely notice of their coming, and they being becalmed, gallies towing them, they escaped very narrowly, but to their great surprise they found that Fort Mountjoy was not only taken but demolished 15 days before their arrival, and the Lord Donegall killed when the enemy entered, and most of the English and Dutch. The enemy having intrenched themselves close to the foot of the town bastions fired from six several batteries, and several bombs at the same time fell into the town, and had been taken in two days if our fleet had not come so happily to their relief; the inhabitants were tired with extraordinary dutys, and many killed, and poor King Charles had got into a boat to save himself, but went ashore immediately after we had landed our forces, we being about 10,000 strong; afterwards, by night, several deserters came over to us telling us that the Duke of Anjou looked very sorrowful altho' it is computed he had about 15,000 men, yet in all likelihood has besieged himself not being able to look round him without seeing a sad passage of ruin, being surrounded with 40,000 Mucquelletts; the only deliverance they expect is by taking the town, having not above four days' provision. The Mucqueletts are resolved to revenge the cruelty the French treated them withall when they came hither; and if they enter the wall they certainly [will] be cut in pieces, we having raised inward works and are all resolutely bent to defend it sword in hand, and our brave King also. As matters stand to-day all things promise to our success, for they cannot get any advantage, all which must have an end in a short time.

The 2nd letter.—May 1st. At 3' this morning the enemy went off in great confusion leaving behind them 27 mortars, 140 brass canon, 40,000 cannon balls, 5,000 barrels of powder, with shell of all sorts to a great number, pickaxes, spades, about 10,000, with great store of other warlike necessaries, sacks of meal for 12,000 men for 8 months, and great quantities of other provision, and 3 large hospitals of sick and wounded, being it is thought about 5,000. They are pursued by the Macqueletts, from which we expect a miserable account of such an army going off in mutiny and disorder; they went away offering no attack to the . . . ne. Although governed by the Duke of Anjou, Marshal de Thosse and Count Noilles, being attacked all the way by the Macqueletts, and, as we believe, making towards Provence. Count do Thessie at his going away wrote in short to Lord Peterborough that the glory of the day was his; that the French fleet was gone, and the English gained the victory; but prayed his Lordship to use humanity and kindness to preserve the sick and wounded. Accordingly he ordered a guard for their security; but the Macqueletts had destroyed some of them before they came . . . . I expect the whole monarchy is, or will be in a short time, devoted to King Charles. We are all in good condition and hope this will not be the last stroke we shall give them this summer. This account I took at the King's Palace, being the very same he had himself. The letter is dated from "The "Dorsetshire, Barcelona." Loup adds that when the army marched off the sun was totally eclipsed in those parts.

1706, July 27, Whitehall. Jos. Tily to John Smyth . . . . Here is more life than ever in the business of Lorraine; therefore pray think of it; for upon a peace, the barriers of Europe will come first into consideration . . . Sends an inclosure [not with the letter] concerning the sending of wool from Ireland to France; against which pernicious practice the writer inveighs, and recommends Smith to get such of his neighbours as are clothiers, to join with the Backwell Hall in an address for the purpose of stopping the practice. He says that there is a post come that afternoon, and it is said that the French in a Council of War had agreed to raise the siege of Turin; the forces designed for the descent are all shipped, and only wait for a wind to carry them to France.

1706, Sept. 3, Lambeth. William Loup to George Smyth.—Has received two letters from Capt. Butler, the first dated June 28th brought by Lord Chalemont (Charlemont) and another to the Archbishop, giving an account of the taking of Carthagena on the 13th of the same instant, without the loss of one man, and Le Conde de St. Cruise came to our fleet in two galleys, equipped and manned with 1,000 men and 48,000 dollars, which he had on board to pay off the garrison of Oran, on the Barbary Coast belonging to Spain; and I have formerly been there; it [has] a strong garrison, but the Conde, a great grandee of Murcia, suspecting him to be in King Charles III.'s interest, designed to imprison him; but he was too cunning for them. The Miqueletts have destroyed 3,000 of Count Tessi's army since the raising of the siege of Barcelona. They likewise expect Sir Clowsley (Sir Clondesley Shovel) daily and hourly to join, them which is a mystery to us at home.—In his second letter he gives us an account that Brigadier Gorge came from Valencia with about 500 foot and 300 horse, and there was drawn from the fleet 500 seamen and 800 marines; with these forces they lay before the suburbs of Alicant five days, taking and retaking some small outworks, whilst 8 men of war laid to batter the City, suburbs, and 3 fortifications under Sir George Bings, which reduced the place to a bad condition, and made several breaches through the walls; and Sir J. Leake, my intimate acquaintance and good friend, ordered all the boats to be manned with 500 seamen, and armed with the rest of the marines entered with sword in hand into the city through the breaches. An Irishman, General Mahoney, stood the last man to oppose but was forced to fly, with those people he could get, up a mountain into a castle; but they hope in a little time to have him and his castle. Sir, The wind proving contrary and being late in the year, it was hazardous for our capital ship to go to sea, so that all our first rates and second rates, except two or three, are returned home, but the whole fleet continues still at Torbay and Sir Clowsley and my Lord Rivers are aboard of the "Association"; no person knows where they are to go. but they have alarmed all the seaports of France, and all from 16 to 60 are to bear arms. It is my opinion that they will cross over the Bay to Bayonne or Caronna (Corunna) to hinder the communication between France and Spain, and to intercept Anjou. Our great General has taken Manin, which Mons. Vauban calls the flower of his garden, and the mighty Vendosme, who came from Italy, durst not venture a battle for so important a fortress.—We expect to be masters of Dundermund in a short time, and our army lays before Manin till the breaches are repaired. Prince Eugene goes on successfully, and it is thought will join the Duke of Savoy; if so, the siege of Turin must be raised. We are sending a great fleet of men-of-war to the West Indies, to look after the Spanish Flota. Lewis le Grand was never so perplexed and put to his trumps as now . . . . He gives a list of ships under Sir George Byng, which commanded the city and suburbs and castles of Alicant, July 29, 1706. (8 ships carrying 586 guns).

CHESTER IN THE CIVIL WAR.

1641, Nov. 4, York House. A. (Earl of) Northumberland (Lord High Admiral) to the Mayor of Chester.—The Lords have had information that divers officers of Flanders and others are going towards Bristol, Chester, Holyhead, and other places, with intention to take ship for Ireland to join the rebels there.—The Mayor is directed to stop the port of Chester and the members

thereof, and not to suffer any to pass over sea unless they can show they are not of the number of these Flanders commanders or soldiers.

1641, Nov. 23, Chester. Thomas Cowper, Mayor, and Thomas Mottershead, to the Lord High Admiral.—In pursuance of his order of the 15th of Nov. they send to him the body of Arthur Progers: and complain of the expense of conveying him and other delinquents.

1641, Jan. 14, Carnarvon. Jo. Griffith, Vice Admiral of North Wales, to the Mayor of Chester.—In obedience to the Lord High Admiral's orders, Griffith had stayed Col. Butler, who was about to take ship at Holyhead. Butler went to stay with Dr. Griffiths, Judge of the Admiralty, and then went to Beaumaris, where he pretended to make a journey to Carnarvon to see Jo. Griffiths, but, instead, went to Chester. Whyte the Mayor of Beaumaris sent word, and the Mayor of Chester attached him (Butler) and wrote to Jo. Griffiths to know the reasons for his detainer: in answer to that letter Jo. Griffiths wrote the present letter.

1641, Jan. 15. Copy of letter by the Mayor of Chester, and some of his brethren, to the Lord High Admiral. —Mr. Thomas Nettervill (son to Lord Viscount Nettervill of Ireland), being at Chester and declaring himself bound for Ireland, they, understanding that Viscount Nettervill and his son Luke are out in the rebellion in Ireland, and thinking that Thomas who had been a soldier in the Low Countries might be a dangerous person, had arrested him: and as he could not give security not to go to Ireland without license from the State of England, they detain him until they know the Lord Admiral's pleasure.

1641, Jan. 17, Beaumaris. Henry White to Thomas Cowper (Cowper), Mayor of Chester. On the same subject.

1641, Jan. 19, West Chester. List taken from the Muster Rolls of four troops, viz., Viscount Lisle's, Sir Rd. Grenville's, Capt. Vaughan's, and Capt. Marrow's. 1 p. signed by Dudley Wyatt, Commissary of the Musters.

Same date. Another list of the same, with the sums of money to be paid on their account added.

Same date. Receipt for 1,000l. from the Mayor of Chester, in part payment of one month's entertainment for four troops of Horse, consisting of 300 besides officers. Signed by Ri. Grenville, Dan. Treswell, Will. Vaughan, and John Marow.

1641, Jan. 23. Receipt to the same for 100l. for Sir Richard Grenville. Signed by Francis Hope.

1641, Jan. 22, Chester. Copy of letter by the Mayor and two others to the Earl of Leicester, Lt.-Genl. of Ireland, at Leicester House.—They acknowledge his letter of the 14th, and the two Bills of Exchange accepted by Mr. Pinder, one of which has been paid, and they have paid the amount to Sir R. Grenville, &c. (see the receipt above). Hope to receive the other 1,000l. the beginning of next week, and then will pay the remainder of the month's entertainment. At the pressing request of Lt.-Col. Monk they have let him have for the Earl's regiment of foot then in Chester 100l. They have assisted Sir R. Grenville in providing ships to transport troops to Ireland. Say that the Citizens suffer, provisions being scarce and dear by reason of the troops quartered there, and the influx of 700 English fled out of Ireland then resident in the city, besides many hundred of distressed Irish that daily resort to the same. Ask that if any more troops are to be embarked they may be billetted in the country and in the town of Leverpoole.

1641, Jan. 22, Chester. Copy of letter by the same to Sir Robert Harley, K.B., about receipt and payment of money as in the letter last above.

1641, Jan. 22. Copy of letter from [the Mayor of Chester] to the Lord High Admiral.—Acknowledges his letter about bringing up Mr. Nettervill to the Lords in Parliament. In accordance with the contents of a letter from the Mayor of Beaumaris he has arrested Col. Butler, an Irishman, as reported of great experience in military affairs, and he is in the custody of one of the Sheriffs. As the Sheriff is much busied about the troops (there being four troops of horse and the Lord Lieutenant-General of Ireland's own regiment of foot then in the City) the writer begs that Nettervill and any others that may be stayed, may be delivered by the Sheriff of the City to the High Sheriff of the County Palatine of Chester, and so be passed from County to County up to London. Complains much of the expense to the City.

1641, Feb. 1. Copy (signed by H. Elsynge) of the Order by the House of Commons that Sir. W. Brereton should write to the Mayor of Chester to send the examinations of suspected persons staid at Chester.

1641, Feb. 2.—Receipt by Capt. John Boys for 132l. 6s. from the Mayor and two Aldermen of Chester.

1641, Feb. 8, Covent Garden. Tho. Smithe to the Mayor of Chester.—As the Citizens feel aggrieved by the intention of their apprentices to go for Ireland as soldiers, he puts the Mayor in mind that by Statute four Justices may compel an apprentice to serve his time. He and Franc. Gamull attended the Lord Lieutenant yesterday, who promised them that it should not be so (i.e. that apprentices should not be taken). (1 p.)

1641, Feb. 19. Copy of Order of this date of the House of Commons referred to in the next letter.

1641, Feb. 21, Covent Garden. Tho. Smithe to the Mayor of Chester.—Incloses copy of order of House of Commons, so that now having an order of either house the Mayor and the Sheriff may (notwithstanding any habeas corpus) convey prisoners who may be stayed at Chester from Sheriff to Sheriff. Will obtain an Order that no soldiers shall have arms delivered until they are ready to be shipped. "Those members of our House that "have the Protestation are not put to take it again."
. . . Thinks the Mayor may, like his predecessors, use his discretion in conniving at slaughtering and eating of flesh when fish and white meat is scarce, especially at this time, considering the great confluence of soldiers and others to Chester.

1641, Feb. 4 and 9, and 10, and 16, and 18, Puddington; Feb. 18 (no place); Feb. 20, New Key.—Seven letters of these dates by Sir Richard Grenville to the Mayor of Chester, about supplies to men and ships being transported to Ireland. And an account (signed by Grenville) of 100l. received by him from the Mayor to pay for provisions for four horse troops to be transported from Chester to Dublin.

1641, Feb. 22, Yorkhouse. A. (Earl of) Northumberland (Lord High Admiral) to the Mayor of Chester. —The Mayor having given a pass to one Connell, servant to the Recorder of Dublin, notwithstanding the Mayor knew he was a Papist, the Earl warns him to be cautious how he gives passes to Papists, as an ill construction may be made thereof.

1641, Feb. 24. Certificate signed by Will. Cope, that Thomas Prenton, Master of the Grace, of Dublin, had safely landed in the haven of Dublin the Company of Capt. William Cope, in number 100 soldiers and 10 officers, with 10 soldiers belonging to Capt. Sidney.

1641, Feb. 26. Copy of letter by Thomas Cowper, Mayor of Chester, to the Earl of Northumberland, explaining the circumstances under which he granted the pass to the servant of Mr. John Bysse, the Recorder of Dublin.

1641, Feb. 28, Dublin Castle. Council letter to the Mayor of Chester, requesting that as coals are scarce at Dublin, he will order all ships coming from Chester to bring some coals, which shall be paid for at once. Signed by W. Parsons, Jo. Borlase, La. Dublin, Ad. Loftus, J. Temple, and four others.

1641, March 2. Receipt signed by Edward Dymocke, Lieutenant to Capt. Biddulph (by order of Parliament and direction of Sir W. Brereton, M.P.), for 60l. 4s. 8d., paid by the Mayor and Aldermen of Chester, for pay due to Dymocke and others.—Attached is a copy of the order of the House of Commons dated 16 Feb. 1641.

1641, March 7. Receipt signed by Richard Williamson, for himself and partner, Brian Mercer, owners of the Anne, of Leverpoole, for 12l., paid by the Mayor and Aldermen of Chester, for transportation from Liverpool to Dublin of 20 horses, part of Capt. Vaughan's troop. Attached is a certificate signed by Sir Richard Grenville, that the "Anne" had brought the horses with men and arms to Dublin, on the 21st of February.

1641, March 7. Similar receipt and certificate for 12l. 12s. for 120 horse of Lord Lile's troop. The vessel was the Edward, William Johnson, owner.

1641, March 8. Similar receipt for 12l. for Captn. Shirley Snellings company, consisting of 110 soldiers and 10 officers. The vessel was the James, of Larges, in Scotland, David Boyle, owner.

1641, March 8. Similar receipt and certificate for 11l. 8s., for 19 horses of Capt. Treswell's troop. The vessel was the Swan, of Liverpool, Richard Harrison, owner.

1641, March 8. Similar receipt and certificate for 9l. 12s., for 16 horses of Sir Richard Grenville's troop. The vessel was the Mary, of Liverpool, William Rimmer, master and owner.

1641, March 8. Similar receipt and certificate for 21l. 4s., for 200 soldiers and 12 officers, being his Excellency's company under the command of Capt. Guy Moldsworth. The vessel was the Grace of God, of Battan Wyme. Robert Cooke, owner.

1641, March 8. Similar receipt and certificate for 15l. 12s., for 26 horses of Capt. Marrow's troop. The vessel was the Mary Flower (May Flower in Grenville's certificate), of Helbree, William Wright, owner.

1641, March 8. Similar receipt and certificate for 14l. 8s., for 24 horses of Capt. Vaughan's troop. The vessel was the Katherine, of Fornby, Thomas Gilberson, owner.

1641, March 11. Similar receipt and certificate for 18l., for 30 horses of Capt. Marrow's troop. The vessel was the Hopewell, of Liverpool, Thomas Andowe, owner.

1641, March 17. Similar receipt and certificate for 21l. 12s., for 36 horses of Capt. Vaughan's troop. The vessel was the Fortune, of Leighton, John Houghe, master.

1641, March 8. (Indorsed, Copy of a letter sent to my Lord Lieutenant, 12 March 1641). The writer (the Mayor) defends himself from the charge of inhospitality to the soldiers at Chester.

1641, March 11. Information of Thomas Knowles and William Bromfield, prisoners in the Northgate of the City of Chester, about Lieut. Cole coming to the prison with some of his company and forcibly liberating two soldiers there. On the same sheet of paper is a deposition, dated 10 March 1641, of Rose Johnson, wife of Edward Johnson, of Chester, Chapman, about two soldiers coming at night to their house and their violent behaviour, they coming as they said to search for a rogue that had killed a man.

n. d. A paper (¾ p.) signed by Lieut. Lawrence Cole, and witnessed; confessing fault in and expressing his regret for having of his own authority set at liberty two soldiers who were imprisoned. He had returned the prisoners to the same place till satisfaction might be made.

1641, March 12. Chester. Draft or copy of certificate, or intended certificate (by the Mayor), that one Pagett had not, as was reported, nor had any other deposed before him that the Earl of Clanrickard had turned rebel. Made at Dr. Donellan's request.

1641, March 15. Thomas Smithe and F. Gamul to the Mayor and Recorder of Chester.—Acknowledge their letters, and will have an eye to anything that shall be offered in the House touching the proceedings of Mr. Edwards; think he would better end the matter at home than bring the matter before Parliament. Sir William Brereton seems desirous that the matter may be composed in a fitting way.—On the outside F. Gamul has written, "Since the enclosure the Attorney-Gene-" ral is acquitted."

1641, March 16. Receipt signed by Thomas Crosse, of Chester, for the use of Thomas Prenton, master of the grace of Chester, for 21l. 12s., from the Mayor and Aldermen of Chester, for transporting from Chester to Dublin 16 horses of the officers of his Excellency's regiment, and 100 soldiers and 10 officers under the command of Capt. William Cope, and 10 soldiers belonging to Capt. Sydney.

1642, March 26. Copy of a letter to Thomas Cowper, Mayor of Chester, to Sir Thomas Smithe and Mr. Francis Gamul. Refers to an order of the House of Commons made 9 Sept. 1641, for removing scandalous pictures from churches; he says that he believes the order has been observed in all churches in Chester, except the cathedral, where he is informed there are several scandalous pictures. Mr. Bispham, the sub-dean, to whom he sent a message on the subject, said that he could not move without the dean and the rest of his brethren. Incloses the sub-dean's letter, and asks that it, and if necessary the writer's letter, may be laid before the House.

1642, April 12. Covent Garden. Thomas Smithe to the Mayor of Chester.—Acquainted Mr. Pim with the examinations, and divers others of the House; they are delivered to the Chairman of the Committee for Informations. Tells him to advise with the Recorder and indict Mr. Codford for his words; but there is no evidence against Mr. Bruen, but that scandalous minister's, who, he (the mayor) knows, denies what three or four have deposed . . . so advises him to inflict such a punishment on Mr. Codford as may rid him out of Chester.

(1642, April.) A statement of and signed by John Mason, a Lieutenant in Captain Sidney's troop, of the movements of his troop while waiting for embarkation to Ireland, and the reasons (for want of shipping) of the delay. (1½ pp.)

1642, June 20. Copy of a letter to the Sheriffs of Chester, signed by Will. (Earl of) Derby, Thomas Cowper, Maior (Earl) Rivers, R. Cholmondeley, William Gamull, and Cha. Walley.—By virtue of H. M. Commission directed to them, they tell the sheriffs to warn the train bands and inhabitants of the city, able to bear arms, to appear before them on the morrow at Pentice, in the Rood dee.

1642, Aug. 14, York. "Charles R." to Thomas Cowper, Mayor of Chester.—Being informed that some goods of the Duchess of Buckingham are arrived out of Ireland and landed at Neston, not far from Chester, he requires the Mayor, for greater security of the goods, to take them into his own house or other place in the city where they may be secure. (Large wafer seal of the Royal Arms.)

(1642), Aug. 31, Rock Savage. (The Earl of) Rivers to the Mayor of Chester.—Tells him that he hears that some horse are come into Chester under the name of Lord Leicester's men, but they say troopers to lie here upon the country; likewise that there is many horse come to the Northwich in the same manner. Gives him timely notice, so that he may take the best way for the peace of the city.

1642, Sept. 27. Memorandum signed by Thomas Cowper, Maior, and William Ince, Alderman and one of the Treasurers of the city of Chester, that they did deliver unto Geo. Bennett, of the said city, merchant, the office of keeper of the Common Hall, by delivering to him a waight in name of possession of the said office.

16 ., Aug. 23, Whitchurch. Tho. Hanmer to the Mayor of Chester.—Understands that the Mayor has committed one Loghlyn Ameloone for some words that he had spoken, and is informed that he was fair in drink at that time and is sorry. He was entertained a week since by the writer's brother, Capt. Hanmer, for the King's service, and is in pay. Asks that he may be released.

1641, Oct. 30. Deposition at Chester by Thomas Cremer, of Gray's Inn, in the county of Middlesex, gentleman, before Thomas Cowper, the Mayor, and other Justices; that on Tuesday last he met one Magenes, brother to Lord Magenes, who said he was going to Ireland (being lately come from Spain), to see Lord Macquere, and that he hoped that ere long the Irish would drive the Scots out of Ireland, and that he had returned 800 or 900 out of London into Ireland, to raise forces for the King of Spain; and that there was another in his company who called himself Readman, who drank a health to the confusion of the Protestants in Ireland. That Magenes said that since the business was discovered he would go to London with Cremer if Cremer would lend him some money. Signed by Tho. Cremer and by Thomas Cowper, mayor, and others, one is Randle Holme.

1641, Oct. 30. Examination at Chester of Arthur Magneis or Magenes, who said he came from London to Neston, in Woorall, where he had been about six days, intending to go to Ireland, but determined to return to London and then go to Flanders, when he heard of the rebellion in Ireland. He feared to go to Ireland because he, as a cozen german of Lord Mackquere, might be suspected. He was to go to raise a company for the King of Spain, in Flanders; had neither a commission nor money, but was promised by his Colonel, Owen O'Neale, a patent of a Captain's place if he brought over a company. Denies that he returned money to Ireland, but says that there was 800l. returned by one Captain Con O'Neale now in Ireland, which he had from the Spanish Ambassador in London; denies that he was sent for to Ireland; denies saying that he hoped to see the Scots driven out of Ireland; admits he heard it reported that the Scots demanded leave of the King to conquer Ireland; says he has been a soldier for three years in Flanders, but without office or pay. Signed by Arthur Magneiss and by the Mayor and three other Justices.

1641, Nov. 1 (at the foot of the above). On further examination he says he has been a student some 3 years in Doway, in Flanders; has not entered into orders; will take the oath of allegiance, but not the oath of supremacy, that being against his conscience in some things. Signed by Arthur Magneiss, and by the Mayor and other Justices.

1641, Nov. . Copy of a letter by the Mayor and Justices to the Lords of the Council, enclosing copies of the information by Cremer and the examination of Magneiss. On searching Magenes they found nothing, but on his footboy they found a false beard, near the colour of his master's hair, which was something reddish. While this was doing, Magenes took out a letter and burned the name and part of the postscript thereof, and tore the remainder, which shows that he meant to go to Ireland, notwithstanding he said he intended to return to London. The man Redmond, an Irishman

whom Cremer mentioned, is out of their jurisdiction. They have bound Cremer to appear before the Lords.

1641, Nov. 2, London. (Sir) Henry Bruce to his nephew Lieut.-Col. John . . . ad. .—Bruce had not long before landed [from Ireland], and he wrote from Chester. . . . . Expects the King's coming.—Supposes his nephew has heard of the Marquis of Argyle's retreat from the King and Parliament. The King is very violent against them; they would gladly be back again, but the King will have their cause examined in open Parliament. . . . . The Marquis hath written two (tow) letters to Mr. Murrey to make his peace with His Majesty; but Bruce thinks it will not do; so much doth appear, he will never be courted any more. Hears of some stir in Ireland; " some report it " is Magyre, and that sort of the old rebels; there is " not the less damage, for he is but a drunken fellow of " no importance, and it will not much harm you that I " think. I pray you send me the true relation of every-" thing of that business, and let not Arthur stay."

1641, Nov. 5. Copy order by the Lords in Parliament that Arthur Magennis and Redmond Comyn (then under restraint at Chester) should be brought before them :— and below,

1641, Nov. 10. Copy Order of the Lords that Magennis and Comyn were to be brought apart one from the other, and not be allowed to have commerce together; and that such suspicious persons as were in their company were to be pursued with Hue and Cry, and when apprehended, be sent up to the Parliament.

1641, Nov. 6. Three several depositions before the Mayor of Chester, by and respectively signed Thomas Whitstone of Tredagh, Matthew Spell of Tredagh, and John Johnson, sometime servant to Thomas Westropp, of St. Martin's in the Fields, Esquire.—The effect is that that day they were in company with one Prodgers (servant to Col. Sir Henry Bruce), who told them he was going to Ireland for news. Whitstone told Progers that such letters as he had brought from Ireland for the Lord Primate (whose servant Whitstone was) were searched in Chester. Prodgers said he had 2 letters, and rather than any should peruse them he would burn them. Progers told Spell that his letters should not be opened, because he was employed by Col. Bruce on the King's behalf unto Col. Reade, living in Tredagh and a great Papist. Progers told Johnson that he was going to Dublin to receive hundreds of money for his master's use. Spell and Johnson said that Progers said that England and Scotland had been together by the ears, and that then Ireland was in rebellion, and that they kept the King in Scotland, and he thought that the Prince would be crowned very shortly.

1641, Nov. 7. Examination of Arthur Progers, servant to Sir Henry Bruce, Kt., Gentleman of the Privy Chamber to the King. — Upon Tuesday last he left London and reached Chester on Thursday. Says he is to go to Dublin and thence to Tredagh to receive 600l. or 700l. from one Lieut.-Col. Read for his master's use, as appears by his master's letter to Read. Denies saying that he had 2 letters which he would rather burn than have opened; denies having any other letter than the one delivered to the Mayor, except one which he delivered to Mr. Alderman Walley from his master. Admits saying that the King had sent for his winter clothes to Scotland, and for English beer, and that the Parliamont had sent for the army from Oatland to London. He will take the oath of allegiance, but says the oath of supremacy is not for one of his religion. At the end are 2 short supplemental examinations of Progers, the last being on Nov. 8. All are signed by Arthur Proger and by the Mayor and several other Justices.

Provisions to be imbarked for 4 horse troops from Chester to Dublin for 360 men for 4 days' provision. horse and man. (1 p.)

For 28 days' pay for the 4 troops of horse now at Chester as underwritten, being the 3rd of January. Lord Leslie's troop, 123 horses and 100 men and 10 officers; Sir Richard Grenville's troop being 103 horse and 80 soldiers and 6 officers; Capt. Vaughan's troop being 83 horses, 60 troopers, and 6 officers; and Capt. Marrow's troop being 83 horses, 60 troopers, and 6 officers; and wagons for each troop. Total, 1,405l. 18s.) 1 p.

A fair copy of the last. The several amounts have been three times added up; after two failures the total is made 1,406l. 0s. 8d.

1641, Jan. 29. Copy of letter by the Mayor of Chester to the Lord High Admiral.—Will observe his Lordship's directions contained in his letter of the 25th, with the order inclosed therein As to his Lordship's directions concerning the stay of Flemish Commanders and others suspected of fomenting the present rebellion in Ireland, the Mayor says, that yesterday being the 28th, he was informed that Sir George Hamilton was in the City expecting a passage to Ireland. As he was a papist and might be suspected the Mayor sent for him. Sir George was willing to take the oath of allegiance but refused to take the oath of supremacy. On the Mayor saying that he could not suffer him to pass to Ireland until his Lordship was certified thereof, Sir George produced the King's warrant for his passage to Ireland, dated Windsor, Jan. 19th. But the Mayor stays him in the hands of a private man of good quality until directions from his Lordship, whom he prays to acquaint the King or the Lords in Parliament with the matter.

1641, Feb. 2. Receipt by Tho. Parramore, Captain of a company of his Excellency's regiment of foot, consisting of 100 men besides officers, from the Mayor and Aldermen of Chester of 132l. 6s. in full of one month's pay.

1641, Feb. 2. Receipt by Hercules Hannay, for the use and by the appointment of Algernon Sidney, Captain of a company of his Excellency's regiment of foot, consisting of 100 men besides officers, for 132l. 6s. in full of one month's pay.

1641, Feb. 19, Chester. Copy of a letter by the Mayor of Chester. Mr. William Gamull and Mr. Walley to the Lord Lieutenant.—They wrote to him on the 20th of January, telling him how far they had proceeded on his further directions. They understand he has received it from his Secretary Battier's letter of the 21st, wherein he intimates to them 3,000l. sent by Mr. Loftis, which they have received; and with that and the remainder of the first 2,000l. they have paid both the regiments of horse and foot, together with the 400 firelocks, and all their officers, for one month's entertainment, and have paid for the provision put aboard for transportation of both the said regiments of horse and foot into Ireland. They have engaged themselves to the owners of the ships for their freight, which they suppose will amount to as much as the remainder. Tempestuous weather has done much hurt to the shipping and spoiled much provision: &c.

1641, Feb. 19. Copy of letter by the Mayor of Chester to Sir Thomas Smythe and Mr. Thomas Gane; requesting them to get the House of Commons to say whether they mean the Protestation to be tendered to such as had already taken it; and to move the House that inasmuch as they had no provision of herrings or other fish to furnish the City for that Lent season, the House would grant him power to appoint 6 butchers out of the City, or otherwise out of the County, to slaughter and kill victual towards the maintenance of the citizens and others that might in that season be billetted in the City.

1641, Feb. 21, Chester. Certificate by Dudley Wyatt, Commissary, that Thomas Cooper the mayor and Mr. Gamul and Mr. Walley had paid to 8 troopers of Viscount Lisle's troop and to 6 of Sir R. Grenvile's troop one week's pay, amounting to 9l. 16s., and 28s. for hay and oats. (Attached is a paper containing the names of the 14 troopers, signed by Dudley Wyatt.)

1641, March 2, Dublin Castle. Council letter to the Mayor of Chester, telling him that John Clearke, owner of the barque the Gift of God, of Calburne, in Scotland, had received 16l. 4s. for the freight of 27 horses, 27 horsemen, and their boys from Chester to Dublin.—Signed by W. Parsons, Jo. Borlase, Ad. Loftus, J. Temple, and four others.

1641, March 19. Copy of letter by the Mayor of Chester to Sir W. Brereton.—Mr. Edwards, one of the aldermen, had complained to Sir W. B. of the Mayor's proceedings against him. The Mayor acknowledges Sir W. B.'s letter of the 15th, and justifies his own proceedings. (The letter was sent to Sir Thos. Smith and Mr. Francis Ganell, to be delivered to Sir W. B.)

1641, March 24, Chester. Copy of letter by the Mayor of Chester to Sir Thomas Smyth and Mr. Francis Gamull, sending a list of all such as have taken the Protestation within the city (of Chester), none to their knowledge having refused.

1642, March 25, Dublin. Thomas Sandford to the Mayor of Chester.—Certificate that the bearer John Davice (Davies), owner of the barque Gift of God, of Culberne, in Scotland, had landed at Dublin 105 soldiers and 3 officers, and that he had also brought with him 2 men of the company of Capt. Dimock.

1641, May 2. Receipt by John Davies for 10l. 16s. for the transport of the above men, under the command of Capt. Thomas Sandford.

1642, April 1, Chester. Copy of the Mayor's letter to the Justices of the Peace at or near Stone, or. Staf-

ford.—Encloses copy of a letter dated 26 March to him from the Irish Council for the apprehension of two suspected persons who had taken away certain of the King's moneys. Asks them to search for those persons, and obey the orders of the Irish Council.

1642, April 2. Examination of Robert Lanan, late of Hollowaydrath, near Dublin, Shoemaker, taken before Thomas Crompton, Esq., J.P. for the co. of Stafford.—Lanan says he knew one Patrick when in Dublin, but did not know until lately that his surname was Carvan (Garvan?), or that he was servant to Mr. Peter Beaghan, one of the Remembrancers of His Majesty's Court of Exchequer; denies that he had any part with Patrick in robbing Beaghan, or any part of the money supposed to be taken out of Beaghan's chest, &c.—Signed by Thomas Crompton.

1642, April 2. Stone.—Warrant under the hand and seal of arms of Thomas Crompton to all mayors, bailiffs, constables, and other King's officers in the direct from Stone to Chester.—Patrick Garvan and Robert Lanan are charged by the Council of Ireland with having robbed Peter Beaghan of 70l. 19s. 6d. In accordance with the Mayor of Chester's letter, he has arrested Lanan, and now desires the addressees to pass him on from constable to constable direct to Chester, so that he may be brought before the Mayor there.

1642, April 2, Stone. Copy of Crompton's letter to the Mayor of Chester, on the occasion of sending Lanan.

1642, April 6. Copy of the Mayor of Chester's letter to the Lords Justices of Ireland, telling them of Lenon's (Lanan?) being apprehended, and that he was in the Northgate, and that the other (Garvan) should likewise be committed to the Northgate.

1642, April 15. Declaration by Dudley Wyatt, Commissary of the Army, before the Mayor of Chester and John Moore, Esq. (signed by all three), that the money ordered to pay the troops at Chester arrived not until Monday was sennight; that he then signed their books, and they were paid one month's pay; that soon after they marched to the seaside; all except one troop are gone, and the rest are imbarking.

1642, June 11. Copy of letter by the Lords Justices and Council of Ireland to (the Mayor of Chester).—They have employed and do require and authorize the bearers, Capt. Henry Smith, Lieut. John Bernard, and Lieut. Arnold Cosby, to convey to London as prisoners the traitors Lord Macguire and Hugh MacMahowne, and also Lieut.-Col. John Read, and deliver them to such person as the Lord Lieutenant of Ireland shall appoint. And they require all Mayors &c. to furnish horses a strong guard and all necessary assistance.

1642, June 26, Dublin Castle. License to William Fitzwilliams, Esq., son of Thomas Vice-count (Viscount) Fitzwilliams, of Merion, to go to France. Signed at the head by W. Parsons and Jo. Borlase, and at foot by Ormond Oserye, Cha. Lambart, Ad. Loftus, Roscommon, J. Temple, Tho. Rotham, Ja. Ware, Rob. Meredith.—Below is a certificate by David Lloyd that William Fitzwilliams took the oath of allegiance before the Mayor and Robert Brerewood, Serjeant at law, Recorder of the City of Chester, on the 15 of Aug. 1642.

1642, July 2. H. Rigby to the Mayor of Chester.—Advising him to look well after a prisoner in the Northgate charged with having stolen a mare, because he had "an art to dissolve anie boltes laid on him."

1642, July 7. The accounts of Thomas Cowper, Mayor, William Gamull and Charles Walley, Aldermen of the City of Chester, for 2,000l. charged by Sir Job Harrie and Sir John Nicolls upon Mr. Peter Pinder, Collector of H.M. Custom House at Chester, and ordered by his Excellency the Lord Lieutenant of Ireland for the payment of one month's pay for 4 troops of horse mustered at Chester, according to a list of pay, received from his aforesaid Excellency, as also for the transportation into Ireland. (4 pp.)

n.d. Copy Petition to the Right Honourable Court of Parliament of the nobility, knights, gentry, and freeholders of the County Palatine of Chester, whose names are subscribed. (The names are not copied. The Petition is in favour of Episcopal Government in the Church.)

n.d. Copy of a Petition intended to have been presented to His Majesty for the fortification of Chester.

Two papers about negligence of ships engaged to transport troops to Ireland.

1648, Feb. 23, Goldsmith's Hall. The Committee for compounding with delinquents to the Committee and Sequestrators for the county of Chester.—Robert Tatton, of Wilbenshaw, county Chester, has submitted to a fine, and paid and secured the same according to order. They are to forbear all further proceedings in the sequestration of the estate of the said R. Tatton, compounded for according to the particular annexed. If further estate is discovered, the same is to be sequestered until compounded for.—Directions concerning his estate. —Signed by John Ashe, Ed. Ashe, Richard Vennar, and four others.—The particulars of Tatton's estate are on the following leaf.

Aguste 1601. Orderes set downe by my lady to be observed by the gentle men in every respecte, the which dirrecones shall remayne in the gentleman usheres hands to thende that none of them shall for theyr excuse, plead ignorannce uppon the breach of theyr appointed orderes by for geatinge any of them but to cute of that inconvenience I do here appointe that every one of the gentellemen may at any time resorte to the gentle man usher and such as can rede may here see from time to time what those orderes bee where by they may be the better instructed of theyr dutyes and orders appointed to be observed by them.

Dirrecones for the gentelmen.

The gentellman usher to see my gentlemen in housholde to live in descente order to be diligent and reverent in theyr services to my lo: and me and to obay all othere good orders sette downe by me in the yomens booke with out any brech or contempte of any of them where by both you shall greatly contente my lo: and me with your obedience and wele behavyour and tractablenes and besides be an ocasione to procuer the meaner sorte of my servaunts in cawlinge to amend theyr faultes by your good examples; and though I do referr yon for the moste of them to those ordres all redie sett downe for brevetye yet I thought it not good to passe over with out derectinge some orders unto you as the chiefeste to be observed.

To come every morninge to see the dininge chamberes in good order.

The gentleman usher to come every morninge in to the dyninge chamber and with drawinge chamber in the winter season at viii of the clocke and in summer at vii of the clocke. If straingers bo there then at more earlyer howres and to see that the yomen of those chambers do kepe fyers there in the winter and order well and dresse uppe every thinge in those chamberes accordinge to my former dirrecones sete downe. And if you find any lacke in them to see those faltes presently amended whereby this place shalbe kept orderly to the contentemente of my lo: and me, and besides shall be in decent order at all times for the enterteinenge of straingers; likewise in the summer time to see the chimneys trimed with grene bowes and the windowes with herbes and swete flowers and the chambers strowed with greene rushes.

To atende at service tyme.

The gentleman usher all the service dayes appoynted to cume upp dalye with the residewe of my gentlemen to here the service aside, before my lo: and me, and to cume upp som what before the yomen; and after service he and reste of the gentlemen to remaine in the dyninge chamber and not to go downe with the yomen, which is moste disorderly; for as the hall is a fytte place for the yomen so is the dyninge chamber most conveniente for the gentlemen to make theyr moste abode in.

For wearinge theyr livery Cotes for a time.

Further when any straingeres be here, though but one in number, if thaye be of that calinge that they do come into the dyninge chamber, then my pleasure is that the gentleman usher and all the reste of gentlemen shall presently put on theyr livery cotes for the firste nighte and all the nexte day folowinge, unlesse it be sunday or holiday, then to put on theyr clokes but the nexte day that it is a working day to were theyr livery cotes then after howe longe so ever any straingeres do tarye, unlese newe straingeres do come before the olde be gone, then agayne to were theyr livery cotes the firste and the nexte day after theyr cominge, and all the time after they may with my likinge were theyr clokes, so the former appointed times be observed; and from hensforth neither my gentleman usher nor the reste of my gentlemen to depard either with theier winter liveryes or theyr sumer liveryes till newe cotes be geven them; and I do further appoynt that neither my gentlemen usher nor anye other of my gentlemen shall, at anye time when my lo: or I ride abrode durenge the time of our benge in jorneye, were anye other upper garment either cloke or other wiesse, but only his livery cote; and when theire liveries be firste given, though no

straingers be here, yet to were them two dayes together unlesse it happen to be one holy day or sunday, at what time they do weare theyr livery cotes to keape them on all day with out usenge to were any other garment for that time.

Not to cume into the dininge chamber with cotes or cloke.

Further my pleasure is that neither my gentleman usher nor any other of my gentlemen shall come into the dyninge chambers nor sitt at play with my lo: and me in his girken or doublett, but either in his livery cote or in his cloke; and I do licence from hensfoorte the gentleman usher and the residewe of my gentlemen thoughe no strainger be here to come in to the dyninge chamber at any time whene my lord and I am at play there at any kinde of game.

To atende in the greate chamber.

And when straingeres be here, then my pleasure is that they both after dynner and supper and at all other times, bothe the gentlemen usher and the reste of my gentlemen, shall kepe moste in the dyninge chamber to make showe of themselves both for the honor of my lo: and me and to be redie to do such other service as shall be comanded then.

My lo: walkinge abrode.

Further when I shall walk any way out of the parke, as into the fyldes, as more or any of my out warde groundes, then would I have the gentleman usher and the reste of my gentlemen be in a redynes to wayte uppon me.

In the parke.

Further when I do walke in the parke then I do licence the gentlemen either to walke, bowle, shoote, or use aney other pastime or a . . . . where I walke in this order If do wake in the hye walke then they may be in the lower walke; if I do walke in the lower walke then they may be in the uper walke. I do not set downe this as an expresse comandment that I woulld have them be there only; I do licence them to be there or to be absente as they shall thinke good.

Licence to com in to the garden.

And at any time when I am in the great garden my selfe, I do for the time of my beinge there, as well when no straingers be here as when aney be here, licence the gentleman usher and the reste of my gentlemen to com into the garden and there either to bowle or remayne there as longe time or as shorte as they will, or to com in or not to com in they are disposed; for I do not sette this downe as an expresse comandmente I woulld have them to be there at such times as I walke there, but rather do geve them leave with out my mislike to come in wher they will durenge the time of myne abode there or to be absente as they shall thinke good.

Diligent atten- dance diner at dynner and supper.

And duringe the time my lo: and I am at dynner and supper and do sitte a brode, my pleasure is that the gentleman usher and the reste of my gentlemen shall with due reverence and grete diligence wholly geve theyr attendance to wayte uppon us, and non for those times to go to reste themselves in other places or to be absente, but to wayte diligently and not to go to any bye places to eate mete in corneres, nor to take or geve away aney mete but by the gentlemen usher's soffrance and licence, but to geve good attendance till they go all together to take our revercion, and therein All to behave themselves cively like gentlemen without makenge aney grete noise or usinge aney other unseviell orders, to use no playinge fence nor disorderly pastimes in the hall, which causeth great disorder and geves cause of offence by the grete noise that comes by that meanes.

Not to broke dayes having leave to go foorth.

At what time that either the gentleman usher or any other of my gentlemen craves leave either to see their frendes or to dispatch erneste busines, none of them in any wise but uppone grete occasion and apparaunte cause to breake the day appointed of theyr returne, and besides not to go unles they do obtaine leave of myselfe.

For grete play.

Further my pleasure is that neither the gentlemane usher nor none of the reste of my gentlemen shall use grete play neither at dice, tables, nor cardes; for excese of gameninge ympoverisheth your estate and causeth maney disorderes and contencions to be amongest felloves; but in stede of this games to exercise yourselves in all manner of sctivity, as bowlinge, and chieflye exercise of your longe bowe where in I take grete delighte.

Interteininge of straingers.

The gentlemen usher to see all straingers well entertayned for my lo: honor and myne: every man accordinge to his callenge likinge and estimacion that is to be made of him; to see those that are of creadite to be dulye served with livery; none to have aney in my house under the degree of an esquier of an hundreth pounds a yere of inheritance at the leaste; your ofice benge gentlman usher is not neither yet any other of my gentlemen to be at the servinge of any liveryes under the degree of a baron; gentlemenes liveries to be served only with yomen, unlesse it be a knighte a knightes sonne and heire or a gentleman of five hundred marke landes of inheritance.

An eries sonne or barones sonne. then one gentleman to go with his livery and to place the bredde drinke and plate uppon the cubborde in his chamber.

Enterteinments in strayingers Chambers. The gentleman usher to geve good enterteinmente to all gentlemen; to see them wante nothinge in theyer Chambers; to see them have theyer brekfast in due time or aney thinge else that they lack or theyer servantes that is fitte to offer to straingers for theyer better enterteinmente; and when aney gentleman of callinge comes to the house, he and the reste of my gentlemen to be ready to bringe them into the dyninge chamber; and when they go a way, the gentleman usher and the reste of my gentlemen to bringe them to theyer horses.

Endevor of good orderes. And as for observinge of all other good orders, with the eschewinge of any breach to the contrarye, my pleasure is that the gentleman usher and the resedue of my gentlemen should endevour then selves to the uttermoste they may to live orderly, the which good orders thoughe they be at large sett downe in the yomens orders in the end of the booke, yet I thincke good to make a breffe rehersall of them here.

To keepe private the offices. My pleasure is that non of my gentlevate the offices. men, onley the gentleman usher excepted, shall cume into aney of the offices, as Buttry, pantrye, celer, breuhouse, backhouse, kichin, squallary, larders, neither yet into the landrye or dey house, nor in those too laste rehersed not the gentleman usher to come into them; neither yet he nor aney of the reste of my gentlemen to use any carowsinge in any house to make one an other drunke, or to presse any strainger to carowse; to frequente no alehouse; note to use private swearinge nor aney other unhoneste kind of life, but to behave them selves orderly and sively like gentlemen.

Quarelinge. No gentleman to falle oute or quarrel one with an other, but to live lovingly to geather, without fighinge or contencion.

For beinge not a nightes out. Neither the gentleman usher nor none of the reste of my waitinge gentlemen to ly out anightes, but to come into theyer owne lodginges appointed for them by nine of the clocke at night.

Tendinge at the dresser. The gentlemen to come at the firste call of the usher to the dresser, and there to use them selves decently with out loud noice or any rude behavyor.

Houres for drinckinge. The gentleman usher and the reste of my gentlemen to keepe due houres for drinckinge, for the morninge at viij of the clocke, at night at eight of the clocke, and to come to drinckinge two and two to gether.

Orderly ridinge a brode. When my lo: and I do ride abrode, the gentleman usher to see the gentlemen ride afore two and two to gether orderly without usinge aney undecentnes as in loude speach or rude sportes one with an other.

Moderate speach in the hall. My pleasure is that when the usher of the hall, heringe grete noise at dinner or supper time, shall bydde make lese noise, no gentleman to seme to scoffe or reste at him, but orderly to use modrate speach for the better example of others.

Further my pleasure is that both to contribute my lo: and me to make more services the more acceptable to us who doth so greatly mislike those disorders, and allso to geve good maners to your fellowes of mener *For the due observinge of my la: direcions.* callinge, that even as you all tender my favour, the gentleman usher and all the reste of my gentlemen to frame your selves to the obeyenge of these reasonable orders sette downe by my lord and me, and with all dewtyc to endevour youre selves to obay and observe them with out aney breach of any of them so nere as you can possibell, and all you my waytinge gentlemen to be obedyent to my gentleman usher to do what you shall be commanded by him toucheinge the decent and good ordringe of your selves and doinge diligentle and dutifull servis to my lo: and me; and by cause you shall well knowe all this orders are sett downe by my selfe, hopinge you will the more willingly with obedyence frame your selves and service according to this direcions, I have in the ende set to my hande and therefore do expecte these orders shall be the. . . . . .

In the margin of the last page is written "found at "Cranford, June 1635." And at the top of the same page an old hand has written "Lo: Berkleys orders."

Articles agreed upon between, Sr Thomas Barkley, knight, and the lady Elizabeth, his wife, and John Smyth gent. the xvith day of December 1609, Annoque Septimo Regis Jacobi, touching the expences and governement of his houshold at the lodge in Neweparke in the county of Gloucester.

1. Imprimis, it is agreed that the said family shall not exceed the number of xviij. persons over and besides the said Sr Thomas Barkely and his lady and their children.

2. Item, the said Sr Thomas Barkely promiseth hereby to delyver every yeare to the said John Smyth towards the charges of the said house the some of cocxli, by two equall payments, to be made within one month after the severall feasts of the Anuncyacon of our lady and of St Michaell tharchangel, save that 65l.,[*] of the first payment is nowe to be delyvered to the said John Smyth, which at this present remayneth in the hands of the Right honorable the lord Barkley, beinge the money of the said Sr Thomas.

3. Item, the said lady Elizabeth and John Smyth hereby undertake to mayntayne and keepe the said family in that estate, degree, and callinge, that standeth with the reputation of a knight and his lady, beinge both of them descended of honourable parents, with all manor of necessaryes for houskeepinge in bread, beere, wine, Acates, fire, wood, hay, litter and oates.

4. Item, the said Sr Thomas promiseth not to keepe in his Stable at any one tyme tegeather above the number of foure horses, geldinges, and mares.

5. Item, the said Sir Thomas promiseth in the word of a true gent. that after one or two admonitions and noe amendment hee will not keepe in his said family any drunkard, swearer, incontinent, or any other disorderly person, but will give credit to the informacon of the said John Smyth touchinge the same.

6. Item, it is agreed that the said lady and John Smyth shall not be charged with reparacions of the said house or stable, nor with fyndinge any lynnens, brasse, pewter, implements or furniture of houshold, but that the same is to be at the charges of the said Sr Thomas or the said Lo. Barkeley.

7. Item, it is agreed that this agreement shall stand duringe the lyfe of the said Lord Berkely, unles the said Sr Thomas shall give three monthes warnynge for the dissolution of his family.

8. Item, it is agreed that the said lady and John Smyth shall keepe all the yeare longe six cople of hounds for the said Sr Thomas Delight and recreation with the hunsman.

Signed by T. Barkley, Eliza Berkley, and John Smythe.

Carmina Henrici Vaux primo geniti Domini Willelmi Harrowdon in Passione[m] Jesu Christi. (3½ pp. folio), *Begin,* Supplicium domini referens cædemque nefandum.

End, Sanctoramque greges resonantes dulciter himnos Henricus Vaux anno ætatis suæ 13°.

An Apologie of the Earl of Essex, &c. &c., dedicated to Mr. Anthony Bacon, 1598. *Begins,* He that eyther thinketh he hath. . avcd.

An account of money paid for the Earl of Northumberland while he was a prisoner in the Tower for supposed complicity in the Powder plot. (4 pp. and part of a 5th, and part of a 6th; the last is signed by the Earl); the sum total is 621.0s. 2d. Sir William Wade's man is mentioned. The rewards to servants and messengers are many. He had to pay for mending the windows of his chamber; he bought a gridiron, a shovel and tongs; he gave half-crown to the man who brought the lions for him to see; he frequently lost money at play; he bought shuttlecocks; he purchased bacon, wine, many pounds of almonds; and 2 lb. of tobacco for 3l. 10s.; he gave 10s. to a blind harper, and 5s. to Tom fool. When the Earl of Essex was married, Lady Suffolk's gentleman usher brought Northumberland a pair of gloves and had 2l. as his reward. On the occasion of being taken to the Star Chamber he paid 1s. for a pen and an inkhörn; one of the warders of the Tower accompanied him and had 1l. as his reward (this was on the 27th of June). The year is not mentioned and the number of days over which the account extends is not stated.

Sir Walter Ranleigh his Apologie for his last action at Guyana. *Begins,* Because I know not whether I shall live . . .

Sir Walter Rawleighes speech at his death.

Chancellor Bacon's letter to the Lords of the Upper House, May 1621. *Begins,* It may please your Lord-

[*] 85l. substituted for 83l.

R. CHOL-
MONDELEY,
ESQ.

ship, I shall humbly crave at your Lordships hands a benigne interpretation.

Temp. James I. The manner of the progression of the Masque. (6½ pp.);—

Thomas Basset, the Lancashire Bagpipe, and John Seywell, the Shalme, riding abreast together, and two men to lead their horses and two torch bearers. *Fancy*, riding single, *Opinion and Confidence*, riding together, and a pair of torch bearers to each. *The Jews harp, the Tongs*, and *the Byad*, with three men to lead their horses, and two torch bearers. Projectors, viz. the jooky, the countryman, the lamp-man, the case, the Carrot man, the seaman, John Morton the Byad, each with two torch bearers. The Magpie, the Crow, the Jay, and the Kite riding in a quadrangle with the Owl in the middle; these have five men to lead their horses and four torch bearers. Three satyrs have four torch bearers. Two dotterells have two men to lead their horses and two torch bearers, and a single dotterell has a horse leader and two torch bearers. The Myne Mill, a Fantastique and the Dancer have each two torch bearers, and the dancer has a horse leader. Seven pair of trumpeters, each pair having two torch bearers. One hundred gentlemen riding two and two together, each gentleman having two of his own men torch bearers and a groom. The marshal and his 40 men. The first chariot for Musicke, Sir Henry Fane's coachman is charioteer; it carries eight persons and has three flambeaux bearers on the right and three on the left. The second chariot for Musicke, the Earl of Northumberland's coachman is charioteer; of this chariot are the Genies, Ampbilucke, Irene (Mr. John Lanier), Eunomia, Diche, and five Constellacions (the fourth is Mr. Henry Lawes); it has three flambeaux bearers on the right and three on the left; two pair of gentlemen riding together and two torch bearers for each pair; a chariot of orange and silver with four masques in it, with two horse leaders, and four flambeaux bearers on the right and four on the left; two pair of gentlemen riding together, and two torch bearers for each pair; a chariot of blue and silver with four masks in it, with two horse leaders, and four torchbearers on the right and four on the left; two pair of gentlemen riding together, and two torchbearers for each pair; a chariot of crimson and silver with four masks in it, two horse leaders, and four flambeaux bearers on the right and four on the left; two pair of gentlemen riding together, with two torch bearers for each pair; a chariot of white and silver with four masks in it, two horse leaders and four flambeaux bearers on the right and four on the left. The two Marshals of London and a guard of 200 halberdiers.

1616, April 26. His Majesties debts and destined how to be paid.—Debts uppon the Ordinary att the Annunciation 1616. There are 30 items amounting to 385,518*l.* Among them are Lady Elizabeth's transportation, 2,000*l.*; naval fight, 693*l.*—Then follow debts uppon the Extraordinary. There are 23 items amounting to 59,858*l.* Among them are, Lady Elizabeth for jewels given at her departure 2,000*l.*; [Sir Hugh] Middelton for waterworks, 2,069*l.*; present to Spayn, 442*l.*; Pott, for dogges, 275*l.*; Queen's creditors, 20,000*l.*; Gosson, for a cheyne of diamonds, 200*l.*; late Prince [Henry] funeral, 5,633*l.*; Mr. Herriott at Michaelmas last, 1615, 10,000*l.*, for this the King pays interest. Then follows, ready money borrowed (from 12 persons named), amounting to 25,000*l.* besides interest. Sum of all the debts, 470,426*l.* Then follow other debts to be considered of, there are 7 items amounting to 151,200*l.*—Making a grand total of 620,676*l.*

With the above are lists of pensions decreased and pensions increased between Michaelmas 1613 and Michaelmas 1614; the former amounting to 6,516*l.* 16*s.* 8*d.*, and the latter to 3,686*l.* 10*s.* Among the former are Isaac Casaubon, 300*l.* Among the latter are Isaac Cusanbon's wife and his son, 300*l.*—Lists of fees decreased and fees increased between the same dates; the former amounting to 1,063*l.* 13*s.*, and the latter to 2,412*l.* 9*s.* 3*d.*

Folio, seven leaves (13 written pages), A.D. 1620, endorsed, *My Collection of Monopoly Patents.* There are particulars of 96, all in the reign of James I. One dated 30 Oct., 13 James I., is to Roger Wood and Thomas Symcott for 30 years of the sole imprinting of all briefs and other things upon one side, except Proclamations and other things granted by Patent. Another is for the making and selling a back skreen for the ease of the back. Another is to Don Diego de Sarmiento de Acunas, Earl of Gondomar, and his heirs, to carry out of England yearly six horses, six hawks, and 12 dogs without any taxation or imposition. Another is for making a stone to imitate marble.

Folio, 3½ pp. Copy of the Lord Chancellor's opinion on Authority in excommunicating of bishops and translating of prelates according to the laws of Holy Church.

1633, An abstract of His Majesty's patent for the fishing of Great Britain and Ireland. With a list of such as have already subscribed and a copy of their agreements. This is followed by a memorandum (unsigned) by a brother of Sir Thomas Bowe (one of the subscribers) of what Sir Thomas wrote in June last.

Articles about the Prince's marriage with the Infanta. (Latin, 6 pp.) 25 articles, of which the first is that the marriage is to be carried through by dispensation from the Pope, to be obtained by the Catholic King.

Quarto, (14 pp.) The danger wherein the kingdom now standeth and the remedie, by Sir Rob. Cotton, followed by a copy of the King's speech. 17 March 1627 to the Parliament.

1640. Sept. 24. The King's speech to the Lords at York.

1640, Sept. 4. Copy of petition to the King by the Lords of the late Parliament and others of his Majesty's loyal subjects of the kingdom of Scotland. *Begins*, That whereas after many sufferings.—And answer by the King on the 5th Sept. On the back of this paper is a long pencil memorandum in short-hand, and another ink memorandum partly in short-hand.

1640, Sept. 1 to Sept. 8. Diurnal occurrences of proceedings in Parliament.

Quarto, 13 pp., 17th century. Expositions upon the Statute of 43 Elizabeth (as to the power of Justices of the peace).

Copy of the Act of Attainder of Thomas Earl of Strafford, and a catalogue of the Earl of Strafford's friends which voted against the Bill of his Attainder in the House of Commons, April 22, 1641.

Burnet's character, by Mr. Lesly, who perfectly knew him. (1 p., folio.) *Begins*, He was zealous for the truth, but in telling it always turned it into a lye. He was bent to do good but fated to mistake evil for it.

1729. (Found in one of Mr. Hornby's book's on sale, Dec. 11, 1739.) The Secret Article between the Kings of Spain and Great Britain. (2½ pp.) Dated 23 Nov. 1729. —His Britanick Majesty gives up Gibraltar and Port Mahon to the King of Spain and renounces them for himself and his successors.—It is said to be done at Seville in the closet of his Catholick Majesty, and to be signed by the Marquis de la Pas and Don Joseph Patinho on the part of the King of Spain, and by William Stanhope and Benjamin Keene on the part of his Britannick Majesty.

1630, April 30. William Russell, Jo. Wostenholme, and Kenelme Digby to (the Lords of the Council). Copy of a long letter (4 very closely written pages of foolscap size) in reply to the Lord's letter of 24 of March last, about the complaints and examination sent to the writers by the Lords, against Mr. Hilliard and Mr. Stevens, saltpetermen, and their deputies and servants.

1631. Complaint of Thomas Bond, Esq., against Thos. Hilliard, the Peterman (2 pp. close, copy).

1631, April 16, Whitehall. Copy of warrant (signed by Lord Dorchester), to the Attorney General to draw a new commission for the Petermen.

(In the letter of 1630. and the complaint of Thos. Bond, the oppressions, abuses, and flagrant misdeeds of the Saltpetermen are fully detailed.)

1640, Nov. 3. Copy of the King's speech.

1644, March 12. Oxford. Copy of the King's Commission to the Earl of Glamorgan to make further concessions to the Irish Roman Catholics.—This is set out in,

1645, Sept. 3. (Copy.) Agreement between the Earl of Glamorgan for the King and Viscount Mountgarret, Lord President of the Supreme Council of the Confederated Catholics.

Folio, 3 pages. (Indorsed, Mr. Towne Clerk, his Coppie of . . .) 1637. October 17th.

Edward Overman. The collector of

Michael Davys. Keeper cleane of the markett. in Newgate markett, Collector of Toll there, setting out of the stalles in Leadenhall and upper Laborer or keeper of the greene.

John tilling. Weigher of meate at Leadenhall and setting out of the Stalles there, and weigher of meate at Bishopsgate.

Nicholas Barrie. Clarke of the Court of Requests and Beadle of the same.

Richard Falconer. Clarke of the Cittie works, keeper of the reparacion stuffs, and Porter of the Bridghouse.

John Bedell. Weigher of meale at Newgate markett.

R. CHOL-
MONDELEY,
ESQ.

. 24th October 1637.

John Bromfeild, London, Esq., sonne of John Bromfeild of the Inner Temple, Common Serjeaunt and Judge
of the Sherives Courts.

William Bromfeild, sonne of the said John, Town clark
and Stewardshipp of Southarke.

Thomas Bromfeild, sonne of Tho. Bromfeild, of Odemer
in the county of Sussex, Esq., Attornie in the Maiors
Cortt, and clarke of the Assayers.

John Smyth, of the Middle Temple, London Esq., Common Pleader.

Edward Smyth, sonne of the said John, Secondary.

John Bromfeild, soone of Robert of St. Savior's in
Southarke, Esq., Comon cryer.

Edward Bromfeild, sonne of the said Robert, Keeper
of Ludgate.

Edward Bromfeild, sonne of John Bromfeild of Odyner
aforesaid. Keeper of the compters.

William Bromfield, sonne of the said John Bromfeild,
Bailiff of Southarke.

Henry Bromfeild, sonne of the said John Bromfeild,
Clarke of the Bridgehouse.

William Keeling, sonne of William Keeling of Hertford in the county of Hertford, gent., Attornie in the
Sherives Court.

Edward Keeling, sonne of Edward Keeling of Mitcham,
in the Countie of Surrey, gent., Clarke of the Chamber
and clarke of the compters.

William Wall, Keeper of the wood and coales for
the poore and keeper of the   Leadenhall.

Daniel Overman, sonne of Daniell Overman, Fishmonger, common 'outcroyer.

Tho. Eppindale sonne of John Eppindale of Barton in
Staffordsheire, Esq., Oterbailiff.

Henry (Francis is written above) Jackson sonne of
Henry Jackson, Clarke of the compters.

William Greene, sonne of William Greene of Westminster, gent., Common hunt.

Daniel Dorsett, keeper of the sessions house in the
old Baly and upper laborer of the Bridghouse.

William Vernon, sonne of Walter Vernon, Esq., Pro-
thonotarie and clarke of the Court of Requests.

John Lynche, sonne of John Lynche, of Grove, in the
county of Kent, gent.

James Newman, sonne of James Newman, keeper of
the Guildhall.

Beaconfeild Forrentake, keeper of Morefeilds and
drawer of water at Dowgate.

(1688) Dec. 17 . . . Dongan to Col. Fitzpatrick,
Park Place, St. James' Street. He was going for Ireland, disguised as was necessary, otherwise he should
be stopped both by parties of the Prince and their own.
He left London the night the King did, and came
through to Wales near Denbigh, when the country unfortunately was up'for fear of a party of the King's army,
which they said was making their way to Ireland. He
was recognised by Sir Richard Middleton and sent to
Chester Castle. He desires Fitzpatrick to solicit a
passe to go to Ireland, or to be sent on to London decently out of hand.

BERKELEY CASTLE.

1642, Sept. 23. A paper expressing the desire of
Lord Berkeley's tenants of the county of Gloucester,
that they may have his leave to man and guard Berkeley Castle and the parks there, for his Lordships use
and benefit, and their own safety, against all violence
that should be offered; they promising to obey the commands of him or his deputy. Mr. William Thorpe, Mr.
Thomas Smythe, and four others are named, each of
whom was to have the command of six others then chosen
and agreed upon, and those six were to take their directions from one of the first named persons.—Regulations
for absence of any.—In case any on watch are distressed,
then on ringing of the Castle bell, the country have
promised to come to the defence.—Signed by John
Smyth and eight others. (1 p.) On the other leaf of the
sheet are the names of the six, and of the six others who
are to be under each.

1642, Feb. 11, at 6 o'clock in the night. Articles for
surrender of Berkeley Castle by John Smyth, Esq., to
Lieut.-Col. Arthur Forbes, in the name of the King and
Parliament.—All goods belonging to Lord Berkeley
were to remain there without pillage. The arms to
remain for the use of Lord Berkeley and the county.
Goods of any person in the Castle who has assisted the
King and Parliament, to be on enquiry delivered to him.
Will. Wright, the usual servant of Lord Berkeley, to
remain to look after the goods of Lord Berkeley. All
soldiers and gentlemen in the Castle may march out

without harm. "All which the said Lieut.-Col. Forbes
" doth promise on his part faithfully to perform, as he is a
" souldier and a gentleman." Signed by Ar. Forbes and
John Smyth. (1 p.)

1642, Feb. 11. Fair copy of the above as altered, also
signed by Forbes and Smyth.

1646, Aug. 26. Thomas Morgan to Capt. Mathews.
Tells him to issue warrants to the chief constable of the
hundred of Berkeley to summon a sufficient number of
men to meet at Berkeley, to demolish the works about
the Castle, the gates, and some part of the walls, that an
enemy may not on a sudden take any advantage thereby;
according to the ordinance of Parliament. (Copy.)

1646, Sept. 9. Order of the Committee by ordinance
of Parliament for Gloucester, Hereford, &c. to Capt.
Richard Mathews and Capt. James Bailey.—As by
order from Parliament, the garrison of Berkeley Castle
is to be taken off, and the works about the Castle to be
slighted and demolished, they are required to summon
sufficient men within six miles of the Castle, to repair
thereto with spades pickaxes, &c. to work in demolishing the works and walls in part about the castle. The
guns, amunition, and drawbridge are to be taken to
Gloucester. Signed by Sil. Wood, Jo. Fettiplace, Jo.
Seymour, and six others. (Copy.)

1646, Sept. 17. John Smyth to Sir John Seymour.
Says that report has cast him under the censure of Sir
John and the Committee at Tetbury for opposing the
slighting of Berkeley Castle; a thing contrary to truth;
he refers them to Mr. Richard Stephens and Mr.
Fowler: "with this request, not to suffer for decency,
" a peere to see that damage in his castle under pre-
" tence of servis, the like not don to any other, no not a
" delinquent, which is wholly contrary to the members
" of parliament of this county's undertaking with my
" Lord Berkeley." (Draft by John Smyth.)

Draft or epitome (in Smyth's writing) of a warrant (by
virtue of an order of an order of Parliament) to Col.
Berrowe to make search for goods taken from, and to
cease from further spoil of the castle, and to bring back
the goods, and to enforce obedience to the order.

1646, Oct. 22. Joseph Hatch to Col. Berrow, at
Berkeley . . . . For discovery of the goods of Lord
Berkeley. He never to his best remembrance had or
hath or knows where is any of the said goods; for they
were all left (for his part) with Major White, and what
he did with them he (Hatch) does not know.

n.d. Deposition of John Hathorne (or Fathorne).—
That being by order from Col. Berrow summoned to
appear before him at Berkeley this 23d of October, concerning the goods of Lord Berkeley sold out of the
Castle and conveyed away, says it was done before he
came there or had any command there; but after he
came the gentry came, by virtue of the order of the
Committee for Gloucester, to slight the castle, and committed abuses, and he, being summoned at Gloucester
for the soldiers pay, was not able to preserve the said
castle, &c.

1646, Oct. 23, Berkeley. Letter by Robert Stevenson
to Major William White, Capt. George Raimand, Capt.
Joseph Hacke, Capt. Robert Stevenson, Capt. William
Brotherton, Capt. John Davies, Capt. Henry Pegler,
L. Godfrey Elles, L. Gey. Sillcokes, and Chap. (sic)
John Holford.—As for my part at the taking of Berkeley
Castle where I commanded in chief, Col. Ransbrowe
and Col. Morgan having given to the soldiers the free
bowte of what was in the Castle, I had a share in bringe
of the goods to satisfie the soldiers 5s. a pece, which
goods was the Ennemies. As for the defacing of the
Castle or any of my Lord's household rooms, I left all
safe as I found them with Major White, who commanded
when I was commanded to Monmouth by my Colonel,
Thomas Morgan, &c.

Notes of names of a number of captains, colonels, and
other persons, of whom certain specified enquiries
are to be made regarding the goods taken from the
Castle. (1 p.)

1646, Oct. 23. Answer of John Halford, clerk, minister unto the forces of Gloucester employed at the taking
in of Berkeley Castle, in humble obedience unto the
order of the Right Honourable the House of Lords, concerning the materials of my Lord Berkeley's Castle.
On the 24th Sept. 1645, the churchyard adjoining to the
Castle and the chief strength of the said Castle was
desperately stormed by forces under Col. Ramsborough
and Col. Morgan. Col. Ramsborough, to incourage
his men, had procured them the free plunder of the
Castle. When Sir Charles Lucas was forced on the
26th of September to surrender the Castle, Col. Ham-
borough was much perplexed how to satisfy the soldiers,
because before the storming and at the instant of it,

he had received several orders from Sir Thomas Fairfax to march towards the West, and he thought that the plundering and the consequences would delay his march, and feared that his soldiers and the Gloucester forces might quarrel about the division of the plunder. The men were at last induced to accept 5s. each in lieu of plunder. Thereupon, Halford returned to Mr. Margett's house in Berkeley, and in lieu of 545l. deposited to satisfy his brigade and Col. Morgan's soldiers, he sealed and delivered a bill of sale of all the moveables in the Castle to Major William White, Capt. Robert Stephenson, Capt. George Raimond, and Capt. Joseph Hatch, who took in others, viz., Capt. William Brotherton, Capt. Jo. Davis, Capt. Henry Pegler, Lieut. Godfry Ellis, Lieut. Guy Silcox, and Halford, as sharers with them in the sale of the said moveables, to make unto them satisfaction for several sums of money which they had laid down to make up the sum aforesaid. Halford took some old goods which he believes to belong to Lord Berkeley, towards repayment of a great part of the sum (20l.) lent by him, and of which he is ready to give an account. Denies that the Castle was defaced by any of the gentlemen above named, or that anything mentioned in the order of the House of Peers was embezzled or taken away by any of them.—At the foot is a declaration testifying the truth of Halford's declaration, and signed by Henry Pegler, John Davis (his mark), and Godfrey Ellis. (3 pp.)

1646, Oct. 23. Deposition by Henry Knowles, brazier, of Gloucester, that for any part he bought of Lieut. Ellis, a citizen of Gloucester, bought in the open market of Gloucester brass of him, that came to 5l., where the Lieut. had it he cannot tell.

1646, Oct. 24. Draft (by Smyth) of a letter saying that in obedience to their Lordships' order of the 2d of October instant, the writer had been to Berkeley Castle and found that the spoil and destruction mentioned in Lord Berkeley's petition was true in a high measure.— Further particulars.—The evidence house broken open and near 700 material pieces of evidence taken thence, some hundreds more cast into the dirt and wet, many of the ancient charters torn and their seals broken for benefit of the silk strings to which the seals were fastened, and the rest being many thousands confusedly cast together for gain of the bags and boxes wherein they were placed, in contempt of their Lordships' order for their preservation.

———

1673, June 30, Bruxelles. The Earl of Castlehaven to the Duke of Ormond. (Enclosed is a news letter in French, dated Liege, 28 June 1673, giving news from the seat of war and of the King of France's doings.) He says all accounts agree with the letter, only the King's loss was in the Sunday attack more than the letter says, when Sir Larie Johns was killed . . . . . Thinks that Maestricht will soon be the King's, for when the outworks are gone the body of the place is of no strength, &c., &c.

1673, July 4, Bruxelles. The same to the same. Acknowledges the Duke's letter of the 19th, Maestricht being over, we here know not where the King will pitch next. 6,000 of his men are towards Breda, yet we fear here as those in Holland. For the Duke of York, I never was much in his favour, nor ever understood his ways; but I suspected no good issue, knowing some of his counsellors. What his meaning is in this last action of quitting, the world will make many judgments, but I can think of none to his advantage, or to the end that people say he would be at: the wiser sort of my religion in England never liked the declaration nor the carrying it on, and so I believe may as little approve this action of the Duke and my Lord Treasurer. I hear that you are advanced from the gallery to the cabinet . . . . . I am an unlucky man; for many years I have been persecuted for having been of your party, and now I am as bad here for justifying the King in many things untruly said of him, and by it I have made myself so uneasy with this governor that I am thinking to quit this service for his sake only; my judgment being still, as ever you knew it, for a good understanding between England and Spain, and in the interest of the King to maintain this country in the Spaniards hands, which will necessarily fall shortly to the French, if the King have not a care in time. I have all the reason in world to quit, for no gentleman hath ever been so unworthily used as I have been by this proud ignorant governor, who really is by his folly likely to be the loss of this country in having given so much reason of offense to the two Kings. You would do me a favour truly to let me know the King's and your own sense on this matter, that if I quit, I may write to Spain for my discharge; for I being a general must have it from the Queen.

A packet of letters relating to the Earl of Derby while abroad in 1673, 1674, and 1675. The Earl was a minor under the guardianship of his grandfather, the Duke of Ormonde, and a gentleman named James Forbes was, by appointment from the Duke, in attendance on the Earl as his governor. Forbes from time to time wrote to the Duke. His first letter is dated Paris, 2 Sept. 1673, in which, after giving foreign news, he hints at the great expenditure of money by the Earl, as do also his letters of the 9th and 20th of Sept. In a letter of the 11th of Oct. he alludes to Madame de Brinvilliers and her poisonings. The Duchess of Ormonde was also in correspondence with Mr. Forbes; for on the same 11th of October he wrote to her a letter, in which he states how he impressed on the Earl the necessity of not consorting with his own countrymen if he was to learn the French language; and mentions a quarrel which the Earl had had with a servant. On the 18th October Forbes wrote to the Duke that he had taken the Earl to see the French King at Versailles, where he had just returned. They saw the King in his caleche, with a mistress on each side of him; he seemed much altered and very chagrined and out of humour. He says that Lord Derby begins to ply his exercises and language more than he did at first. Forbes' letter of the 22nd Oct. to the Duke is filled with foreign news. The Earl took offence at Forbes's remonstrances against his course of life; for on the 25th October Matthew Portley, servant to the Earl, wrote from Paris to Mr. Knollys, that in consequence of Forbes not countenancing the Earl's companions, they had plotted against his life, and that though he had escaped death for the present, he was dangerously wounded in three places by one Merret, who with his boy had assaulted Forbes. He adds that Merret and his boy were in prison; that the Earl would not allow him (Portley) money to carry him home, and threatened him with death if he went near Forbes. The Earl got Forbes committed to prison, and on the 13th of Nov. Bi. Mulys wrote a long letter to the Duke on the matter, and the differences between the Earl and Forbes, and sends a copy (inclosed) of the Interrogatories to and Answers of Forbes made and taken by Claude Lefebure conseiller du Roy, bailly, juge ordinaire civil et criminel du baillage de St. Germain des Pres pour messieurs les Religieux prieurs et convent de Labbaye du dict lieu. On the 12th of November the Earl wrote to the Duke, complaining violently of Forbes's rude behaviour, and saying he could bear him no longer; and on the 18th of November wrote another letter, saying he had been obliged to tell him to quit the room. On the same day Forbes wrote to the Duke his account of the affair. He says that a person named Merret, son of a physician in London, had made the Earl's acquaintance, and had led him into dissolute behaviour.—It seems that the Earl's fondness for Merret had induced strong remonstrance from Forbes, and hence the quarrel with the Earl and the assault by Merret. Many letters passed between the Duke and Forbes and the Earl, and the Dowager Countess of Derby wrote to the Duke, expressing her regret for her son's treatment of Mr. Forbes. Mr. Mulys writes long letters to the Duke. Forbes was discharged at once, the judge evidently perceiving the absurdity of the accusations brought against him by the Earl. Merret was condemned to nine years banishment, charges, damages, and a fine to the poor. The Earl was very indignant, and after more than one application succeeded in getting the King's order for his release. On the 18th of December the Duke writes that he has recalled Mulys. Afterwards Mr. Stanley and Captain (afterwards Major) Thomas Fairfax were in attendance on the Earl, and there are letters from Fairfax to the Duke in August 1674, dated from Lyons, to Sir Nicholas Armorer in September from Lyons, to the Earl of Arran in January 167¾ dated from Rome, and to the Duke in February of the same year and June the following year dated from Paris. A copy of the Duke's letter to the Earl and of one to Major Fairfax, both dated in June 1675, seem to intimate that the Earl would come to England in the following year.

Printed case of the Earl of Derby, as it did appear before the Lords, for the manors of Hawardin, Hope and Mould, in the co. of Flint, purchased by Sir John Trevour, Col. Twisleton, Capt. Ellis, and Serjt. Glinne. Copy of protest of several Lords against the Bill for restoring the manors to the Earl.

1662. Copy of part of a speech or letter by the King, saying that he did not pass the Bill, but that it was not from want of affection to that noble family. He doubted not to make a better end for the Earl than he would attain if the Bill had passed.

A packet of letters and papers relating to the Earl of Derby's possessions under the guardianship of the Duke of Ormonde, 1673–5. These include letters from Henry, (Bridgman) Bishop of Soder and Man, Sir Peter Brooke, Robert Ropert, the Earl of Derby, the Duke of Ormonde, Henry Nowell (Governor of the Isle of Man), William Bankes, and the Bishop of Chester.—These are about the Isle of Man and the Estate at Knowsley. Some are addressed to Henry Gascoigne, the Duke's Secretary.

THE EARL OF STRAFFORD'S LETTERS.

1673, May 28, Wentworth Woodhouse.—The Earl of Strafford to the Duke of Ormonde.—Is glad to hear from the Duke that his treaty with the Earl of Derby is brought to a satisfactory conclusion. Hopes to hear of the marriage soon. Asks him to persuade his (Strafford's) nephew Derby to go to France before September.

1673, Aug. 25. Copy of Ormonde's letter to the Earl of Arlington.—About Lord Strafford's pecuniary difficulties. Suggests that Arlington should get Strafford's pension paid.

Part of a letter by Strafford to the Duke of Ormonde, saying that Mr. Verigny waited at Lord Derby's table, and saying that it was customary abroad for gentlemen to sit at table, and bespeaking his interest for Verigny.

1673, Sept. 6, Wentworth Woodhouse. The Earl of Strafford to the Duke of Ormonde.—About Lady Athol's Portion. Thanks for favour to Verigny.

1673, Sept. 20. The same to the same. Recommends Mr. Chantrell (not a year and a half these seven years out of the Earl's House), a Westminster Scholar and B.A. of Cambridge, and asks that the Duke will speak well of him to the Bishop of Man (Sir Orlando Bridgeman's brother).

There are seven more letters from the Earl to the Duke, and two from his Countess to the Duchess, and three letters by the Duke in reply in the years 1673 and 1674. They relate chiefly to the Earl's difficulties, and the behaviour of the Earl of Derby. The last letter is from the Earl of Strafford, asking the Duke's aid for Mr. James Greenhalgh to have the next good living in the Earl of Derby's disposal.

1688, Dec. 19, Chester Castle. The Earl of Derby to the Duke of Ormonde.—Sends inclosed the desire of the gentlemen who were officers in that garrison to have laid down their arms on sight of the King's letter to Lord Feversham. . . . He continues their restraint, being all Roman Catholics, until he receives directions. Their case is hard; he does not hear of any in their circumstances being detained. Has written to Lord Churchill much to the same purpose. Asks favour for Sir Edward Byron, who has just come in.

1688, Dec. 19, Chester Castle. Earl of Derby to the Duke of Ormonde.—Asks the Duke that the Prince of Orange may have a true account of what he has done. Mr. Egerton and Captain Oldfield have gone up for his (the Earl's) sake, to inform about the state of the county. Condoles with the Duke on his late loss.

1688, Dec. 27, Dublin. Charles Thompson to Mr. Henry Gascoigne, Secretary to the Duke of Ormonde :—On the news from England that the Duke, his Lord and Master, was coming with an army for Ireland. His and his friend's disappointment, they having made preparations to pay their duty to the Duke.

168⁴⁄₉, Feb. 7, Thursday. Extract from the Commons Journal, containing form of oath of fidelity to King William and Queen Mary.

A portfolio containing seventeenth century copies of Records, extracts from old deeds, law cases, and pedigrees. With them are 10 folio leaves of Readings, one in Furnivall's Inn, eight of the leaves are occupied with a reading by Lowe (the reader), Aug. 2, 1812, on the Statute of Simony, 31 Eliz. c. 6. These readings are in Law French. There are also copies of the following wills :—

1624, Dec. 31. Will of Sir Roger Newinson, of Eastry, in the county of Kent; and a codicil dated 9th March 1624 (1625), and another codicil dated 6th July 1625. (5½ brief sides.)

1632, Sept. 22. Will of Thomas Warren, of Barton-on-the-Heath, in the county of Warwick, gent. (1 p.)

1646, Feb. 11. Will of William Hopton, the elder, of the parish of Berkeley and county of Gloucester. (1½ brief sides closely written.) Although said to be only a copy, it is signed by William Hopton, and his seal (a

branch of hops issuing from a tun, being a rebus on his name), is at the top of the first page.

1680, January 24. Will of Moore Fortune, of North Nibley, in the county of Gloucester, clerk.

A packet of papers in the matter of a suit regarding the School at Wootton under Edge, founded by the Countess of Warwick. There are a few paper Court Rolls, temp. Henry IV. and Queen Mary, and various petitions and papers in the suit temp. James I.
Church Rates and Poor Rates of Nibley.
A small packet of papers of the years 1601, 1602, 1603, 1614, 1619, 1629, 1630, 1631, 1636, and 1660.

15 Car. 1. Copy agreement between the churchwardens of Nibley and Henry Neale, of Somerford Cames, county Wilts, bell founder, for making five bells for Nibley Church ; musical bells as deep in note as those of Slimbridge or Dursley, or half a note deeper ; two to be new cast, and the other three in Nibley steeple to be chipped out, so that all five be brought to be musical.

1639. Rate for the new bells and frames for the old, and a screen in the chancel and other church work. (4 pp.)

1642. Names of payers to the poor in the parish of Slimbridge. (3 pp.)

A packet of Informations and Depositions taken before John Smith, as Justice of the Peace, temp. Charles II. The J. P. business papers range from 1618 to 1663.

Printed copy of the Letters Patent (22 James I.) to Benedict Webb, for making oil from rape seed ; copy of a Bill in Chancery by Webb against Richard Warner and others in 1626 ; and letters by Webb and other papers in the matter, and a paper (brief size, closely written) by Webb containing " A narration of " my " employments sithence I came to discretion."

TOBACCO.

1635, Feb. 19, Whitehall. John Coke (secretary), to Mr. Gerbier. (Copy). That tobacco is no victual, hath appeared by the declaration made by Divines, civilians, and physicians on that side, and now his Majesty for his own satisfaction hath required the opinion of our best learned here in the sea laws, who have under their hands confidently averred that to judge tobacco victual is consonant to no law by which treaties of princes ought to be expounded. It must therefore be concluded that the admiralties of Dunkirk and Bruxelles have pronounced against law. . . . . . Gerbier is to declare to the Infanta and his Council of State, that if His Majesty now shall give leave to reprisal the fault is not his, but the injustice is on their side . . .

With this are,—A long opinion by the College of Louvain, under their seal, and under the hands of the President and four other members ;
A short opinion under the hands of six Brussels physicians, agreeing with their brethren of Louvain ;
Long separate opinions of two Paris physicians, an opinion by the King of France's physician in ordinary ;
An opinion of four physicians of Douay, and separate opinions by two Jesuits at Brussels ;—that tobacco is not an aliment.
And lastly, an opinion signed by Matthew Kellison, S.T. doctor and president of the English College at Douay, and Ed. Stratford, S.T., doctor and professor, and William Hyde, S.T., professor ; that, although they considered that a priest could not celebrate after taking tobacco, yet they did not dissent from the doctors and professors of medicine, who said that there was no aliment taken in the smoke.
The opinions are in Latin.

A packet of papers about Hearth money in the county of Gloucester, temp. Charles II., including a printed proclamation in 1666, and an original council letter in 1671.

LETTERS FROM LITERATI TO MR. COWPER.

Pope's Elegy to an unfortunate lady was translated into Latin hexameters by Mr. Cowper. He sent a copy to Pope, who acknowledged it by the following letter. The ends of the first seven lines of the original letter are lost, but a copy of the entire letter made about the beginning of this century, supplies the missing words.

173⁴⁄₉, Feb. 5, Twitenham, in Middlesex. Sir, some accident [and above all] the sickness of a very deserving parent h[ave prevented] till now my acknowledgement of the receipt [of your obliging] Letter and Verses. Pray think I am one wh[o would nei]ther be insensible to a civil, or neglectful [to an ingeni]ous man. I shall use you with the justi[ce and the free]dom, which is due to both: and at the sa[me time that] I congratulate you upon the Revival of your Taste for the Ancient Authors, exhort you not to cultivate them negligently, but by frequent Imitations of them. No Pleasures so well suit with Exercise as those of the Imagination, which can be pursued even in the Field, and when your Dogs are at fault, can fill up the Intervall; none better suit with a Country Life than those of Poetry. Your choice indeed of my writings is what I cannot approve as the best, but if mine lead you [to better] they will have some merit, and I shall thank [you for thin]king so. When you write better (as you cer[tainly will if] you proceed) you will find Authors among y* [Moderns more] worthy of your pains; but in the mean[time (to giv]e you, Sir, a proof that what you have done [pleases me)], I sh⁴ not be sorry if you tryed y' hand upon [Eloisa to Abe]lard, since it has more of that Descriptive and (if I may so say) Enthusiastic Spirit, wh^ch is the Character of the Ancient Poets, and will give you more occasions of imitating them. I am sensible (Sir) of your Partiality to me, and desire you to thinke me

Your most obd' humble servant,
A. POPE.

(A copy of the Latin translation of the Elegy is with this letter).

1745, Dec. 7, Coventry. (General) Will. Douglas to Dr. William Cooper (Cowper) at Chester.—After compliments in allusion to his stay with the Doctor at Chester, he praises Cowper's Elegy on his friend Heskett, but hints its too great length; praises unreservedly Cowper's Epitaf (sic) on his own tenant, but thinks his version of Moliere's epitaf (sic) rather falls short of his other translations. "I am afraid Bendish made you "exceed in the Bottle, and damp'd your Poetical fire. "I suppose your Ladies are now easy, and no more ap- "prehension of a visit from the bare a——d hero's of "the North; they wander about so, that I'm afraid we "shall have a wild goose chace with them."

174½, Feb. 1, London. The same to the same.—He acknowledges receipt of Cowper's second attempt on Moliere's epitaph, and his fine version of part of Pope's Messiah.—He has made a fair and just representation to the Prince and the Duke of the good disposition his [Cowper's] city [Chester] was in.—Alludes in complimentary terms to Cowper's friend, Sir Robert; says he has "stood by him at Court when the King took the "greatest notice of him, and talked very graciously "and familiarly to him, your city mostly the subject." Thinks his second attempt on the Epitaph is better than the first; acknowledges the difficulties mentioned, particularly from the jeu de mots, which cannot easily be turned from one language to another. Says that he (Douglas) gave it knowing it would be a sort of trial. Thinks his version of the Messiah excels, if possible, the original in nobleness and sublimity of the phrase and expression.

1749, Dec. 10, Dublin. (Earl of) Orrery to William Cowper, Esq., at Chester.—Thanks for the exact account sent of Lord C.'s unfortunate affair. . . . "Lucas has "withdrawn his person, and has left his spirit among "us. He does his business like Belzeebub, who walks "no more to and fro upon the earth, but sends his "influence from the regions of Hell. He is in your "neighbourhood at Liverpool." . . . "We have two "new actors just come upon the stage that are like to "make considerable figures. The name of one is "Diggs, the son of Col. Diggs, and nephew of Lord "Delaware. The other is an Hibernian, his name is "Mossup, the son of a clergyman. They promise "wonders or Garricksisms."

1752, Dec. 2, and 1754, Jan. 2, Marston House. The same to the same.

1755, Oct. 2, Edinburgh. David Hume to Dr. Cowper.—Sir, I acknowledge myself to be very much oblig'd to you for the Information which you have had the Goodness to convey to me. The Proofs, which you give me, convince me of my Mistake, when I asserted that the King was at Shrewsbury when he received Intelligence of the Action at Powick Bridge near Worcester. The King had marchd along with the Army from Nottingham to Shrewsbury, where the Army then lay: No Historian had mentioned his leaving the Army to go to Chester. This had led me into the Mistake, which I shall take care to correct by the first opportunity.

I am likewise sensible of the other Mistakes, which you take notice of. I doubt not but many more wou'd occur to you in reading my History, and those more material; I always esteem myself much oblig'd to any one, that inform me of my Errors; and so far am not

unworthy of the Favor you have conferr'd on me. Farther Favors of the same kind shall always be gratefully acknowleg'd.

I am, Sir,
Your most obedient and most humble Servant,
DAVID HUME.

1761, July 16, London. Sir Eardley Wilmot to Dr. Cowper, at Overlegh, near Chester.—Says that he has examined the poem which Cowper sent, and thinks there is as much merit in the performance as the nature of the subject would admit. (An indorsement says that the poem was Il penseroso.)

1745, Feb. 4, March 8, and 1746, March 26, Woodston, near Peterborough. Robert Smyth (rector of Woodston) to (Dr. Cowper). Three letters about a proposed list by himself of the sheriffs of all the counties in England and Wales, and about pedigree matters.

1749, Feb. 14, York. F. Drake to Dr. Cowper. Archæological.

1750, July 13, Glodeth. Thomas Mostyn to Dr. Cowper.—Will lend him the Annals of the Abbey of Chester as soon as he gets to Mostyn. Recommends a work in progress, entitled "Originals," by the Rev. Mr. Holloway, Parson of Middleton Stoney, in Oxfordshire.

1752, Nov. 17, Salop. G. Edwards to Dr. Cowper. Sends copies of two Latin inscriptions lately found at Wroxeter, once a Roman station by the name of Uriconium; both fair and legible; one 6 feet high and 2 feet broad; the other about 2½ square.

1756, Feb. 27. Codicote. G. North (F.A.S.) to Dr. Cowper, at Bath.—Thanks for specimens of coins found in digging in the foundations of a Priory and sent by Mr. Wood. . . . Has received from Lord Willoughby news that the King of Naples has discovered the ruins of the city of Pompeii. The letter of Camillo Paderni just received from Naples by the Royal Society is being translated.

1757, Dec. 15, Chester. Letter from Dr. William Cowper to [Godolphin Edwards], asking for loan of any Collections he may have relating to Chester and the neighbourhood in the Civil War, commencing 1642.—(A note on the back says that no MS. belonging to Godolphin Edwards, of Shrewsbury, was to be found in the study of the late Dr. Cowper; though in Oct. 1769 Mr. Edwards, by Mr. Latham, said he lent one pursuant to the within request.)

1766, Jan. 11, Chancery Lane. William Norris to Dr. Cowper.—Sends a list of the names and dates of elections of members of the Society of Antiquaries preceding Dr. Cowper. Mentions the Society having presented a copy of their works to the King, who had made inquiries what they were doing.

1765, June 8, London. William Norris to Dr. W. Cowper. Thanks for "your very elegant poetical "Epistle to your nephew."

1767, Sept. 15, British Museum. W. Maty to the Rev. W. Norris, consenting to let Dr. Cowper have a facsimile of Hugh Lupus's sword.

(1767, letter end of Sept.) Dr. William Smith, Dean of Chester, to Dr. Cowper.—Suggesting and giving (in reply) a form of inscription for an image of a little Bacchus, digged up at Chester.

1767, Oct. 4, Trevellyn. Thomas Boydell to Dr. Cowper.—His brother has given up engraving, but will get engraved for Dr. Cowper a drawing of the East Gate of Chester.

1767, May 5, Bow Street, and May 23, London. Sir John Fielding to William Cowper, Esq., at Overlegh.—About Mr. Pleasant, charged with forgery, who had been taken, and the parties injured refused to pay the twenty guineas offered for their capture. Advising a good watch to be kept at Parkgate, which was a favourite post for felons to escape to Ireland. (Both signed by Sir John Fielding when blind.)

(1742) March 10, Bond Street. Copy of a letter by Thomas Hervey to Sir William Bunbury.—A challenge to give him satisfaction (by duel), and do justice to the child of Lady Hanmer. (1½ pp. foolscap. It was printed in 1742.)

Three letters from Edward Hinton, at Westminster, to his cousin, the Rev. John Cooper, at Chester. In one, dated May 14 (no year), he mentions the case at Westminster of David Jones, a student of Christ Church, Oxford, who had been expelled from the University by the Vice-Chancellor. Jones obtained his discharge from the Castle by reason of an informality in the V.-C.'s warrant, but Treby, C. J., would not hear Jones when he wanted to apply for a Mandamus to make the V.-C. take off the expulsion, and another to make the Dean and Chapter of Christ Church continue him a student there. He says that Dryden was buried by the

Bishop of Rochester at the Abbey on Monday; that the
Kit Cat Club were at the charge of his funeral, which
was not great, and that Mr. Montague had engaged
to build him a fine monument. Dr. Garth made a Latin
speech, and threw away some words and a great deal of
false Latin in praise of the poet.

In another, dated June 6 (no year), he says that there
is going to be a 2nd edition of the book against Dr.
Wake, with some additions and alterations. The author
of this book is certainly Mr. Atterbury. The Dr. is
preparing an answer to it, and Kennet and Tanner are
to furnish him with materials.

LORD GEORGE SACKVILLE.

1760, March 18, 20, 21, 25, 26, 29, and April 3.—
Seven letters from Thomas Cowper, junior, to William
Cowper, Esq., giving accounts of the proceedings and
evidence in the Court Martial on Lord George Sackville. In the letter of April 3 (when Lord George ended
his defence) he much praises the eloquent speech of
the defendant.

A portfolio of papers, two of which relate to the
Assessment of John Smyth to ship money, and the others
relate to his composition for delinquency, 1643–1655.—
Also copies of Assessments to Poll monies.

ASSESSMENTS TO POLL MONEY AND AIDS.

1650, North Nibley. A Rate for the collecting of the
Poll money granted by Act of Parliament assessed by
us whose names are subscribed, 24th of Sept. 1660.—
Seven columns of names with the amount rated on
each.

1666. Return of an Assessment for Ashleworth. Some
letters and papers regarding Assessments in the years
1661, 1664, &c.

1673, May. Berkeley Hundred and Thornbury Hundred.—Eleven returns of Assessments in various parishes,
according to the Act of Parliament for supply of His
Majesty's extraordinary occasions. The names of those
assessed and the charge on each are given.

1689. Seven returns of a rate and Assessments made
pursuant to Acts of Parliament for granting a present
aid, For supply of their Majesty's necessary occasions,
For reducing Ireland, and For defence of the realm.

Remembrances, 1609, 1639, one in 1662, and some undated. Riot at Slimbridge in 1609; for visits to and
law business at London. One in Novr. 1636 is indorsed,
" When I intended to have sent Wm. Archer to London
" when the plague raged, but went not till 1 Feb.
" after,"

Receipts and expenses.

A 4to book containing receipts and expenses, 1601–
1618.

A number of separate sheets of the like, 1602–1640;
and a few undated.

A duodecimo-sized volume containing 141 leaves, on
which John Smyth, of Nibley, M.P. for Midhurst, has
written his notes of proceedings in the House of Commons, from 30 Jan. 1620 to 19th Dec. 1621.

An unbound quire of 16 leaves (12° size), containing
" Apte & fit similes taken out of learned men's Ser-
" mons in Oxford, 1590, begun the 22nd of April." Of
these only 17 pp. are written.

A PORTFOLIO OF FAMILY (SMYTH) LETTERS OF THE
16TH AND 17TH CENTURIES.

The only letters of general interest are those from
Wm. Smyth to his father John Smyth at North Nibley.
Three of them are dated from Verasheroone, the 24th of
Dec. 1658, the 29th of December 1659, and the 12th of
January 1660.

In the first, the writer says that the country agrees
with him very well, " it being at present not much
" hotter than with you in the midst of summer; but
" we are in the autumn, and therefore must expect it
" hotter. I have given the Company an account of
" our voyage to Acheene . . . we lost our voyage; the
" cause was the Dutch have wars with the Queen of
" Acheene, as well as with many others her neighbour-
" ing kings, which they stick not to do, provided they
" can see but a profit to be made; wherefore they are
" generally hated. I have sent to my master an account
" of our voyage from our first setting sail from the
" Downs until my arriving in this place . . . there you
" may see how God went along with us; for one of the
" 3 ships which accompanied us after our departure
" from him was carried away, but the men saved; the
" ship's name was the Persia Merchant. I am placed
" in the healthiest place in all India or the coast of
" Cormondell. It is an inland town, some 40 English
" miles from the Metropolitan port and factory, which

" is called Metchlupatam. This country is level for
" 100 miles and more, not one hill to be seen : abun-
" dance of wild fowl; the chiefest of our diet all the
" year long is wild ducks and such like. Mr. Acourt,
" our chief, and Mr. Seymour, our second, do very well
" agree, which is the life of our trade . . . Had I a
" good cloth coat with a large silver lace, which is all
" the wear here and the badge of an Englishman; and
" on the contrary, without it and others answerable to
" it, not esteemed nor regarded. The chiefest thing
" needful is a good hat . . . I suppose you have
" heard of the death of Sir Henry Skipworth, who died
" about a year and a half since, as I am informed, of
" grief, he having, as is said, lost his estate by a vessel
" which was cast away : he died about some 7 miles
" from hence, at one Mr. Winter's house, an Englishman
" . . . this country is a very cheap place of residence
" were it not for the state & multiplicity of servants,
" we strangers are constrained to keep; all men being
" respected according to his train and habit. We have at
" present belonging to our Factory near 70 persons, to
" whom we covenant to pay between 4s. and 5s. sterling
" per month each, they finding themselves all provisions
" and necessaries : these servants are allowed when
" they travel, or are sent abroad on our business, 2d. per
" diem, which is the rate we give to all day labourers
" and porters we usually employ to carry burdens 50,
" 60, or 100 miles outright, which is the usual convey-
" ance we make use of for all sorts of goods . . . All
" sorts of provisions are extreme cheap; the usual
" rates of beast is from 5s. to 8s. (he says they can
" rarely get them because the people believe that their
" souls go into Calves, Cows, &c.) ; goats and sheep in
" great plenty from 6d. to 10d. apiece ; hens, 2d.

In the second letter he says that he has written twice
since leaving England, the last time by the ship
" William and Thomas," which, as the Dutch say, foun-
dered in the sea near the Cape of Good Hope. He
says, I find not India to answer to mine and other men's
expectations . . . . It is as difficult a thing to get
a livelihood as in any other country, especially if a man
have but a small beginning . . . . The last night
I received news that I was in mention to go for Acheene
in commission with one Mr. Ralph Conyngsby, a very
accomplished gentleman, and formerly a student in one
of the Inns of Court.

In the 3rd letter it appears that he started for Acheene,
but they were driven down to Bay Bengalla, where their
ship was cast away and their goods much damaged.
In the month of June last Mr. Roger Seymour, second
of Verasheroone, was drowned while attempting to pass
a river on horseback.

A few years ago, a copy of the Vulgaria Terentii,
printed evidently by Roode and Hunte at Oxford, in the
15th century, was sold in London by public auction for
a large sum. It was a quarto of 4 quires ; the signatures
n, o, p, and q, showed that it was part only of a larger
volume. In a box of MSS. at Condover Hall I found a
volume in its first binding of oaken boards containing
quires f to q of the entire volume. The treatise which
precedes the Vulgaria Terentii, is Compendium totius
grammaticae ex Laurentia Valla Servio et Perotto. (It was
composed by John Anwykyll, who was Master of Magdalen College, Oxford, about 1482 or 3, and he
composed it at Archbishop Warham's request. For this
information I am indebted to Mr. Henry Bradshaw, of
King's College, Cambridge.)

I can not close this report without expressing my obligations to Mr. Cholmondeley, not only for his warm hospitality at Condover Hall, but also for his allowing me
to bring the Kingswood Charters and many of his other
papers to London, so that I might examine them fully.

ALFRED J. HORWOOD.

THE MANUSCRIPTS OF STANHOPE GROVE, ESQ., COM-
MANDER, R.N., OF TAYNTON, NEAR GLOUCESTER.

Mr. Grove was pleased to send to London the documents noted below ; and he mentioned in his letter to
the Secretary that his ancestor, Col. Pury (named in the
documents), held high command in Gloucestershire in
Cromwell's army: and that the Colonel was the son of
the then Member of Parliament for Gloucester, who
defended the city against the King, and that he subsequently held a commission in the army of Charles the 2nd.
He adds that the histories of Gloucestershire tell of the
part undertaken by both father and son in that critical
period.

Monck kept up to the last his apparent devotion to
the authorities of the Commonwealth : and the letters

by him before the Restoration, noted below, give no indication of any leaning to the Royal cause.

1648, Oct. 16, St. Albans.—T. Fayrefaxe to all officers and soldiers under his command.—Mr. Edward Barker has bought of Mr. Benedict Hall several quantities of wood lying in the counties of Gloucester and Monmouth, a great part of which has been taken away by soldiers under pretence of tythe. They are to permit Mr. Barker or his agents to carry it away, and are to oppose all tumults about it. (Copy.)

1655, Dec. 18, Sarum. John Disbrowe to Thomas Pury, junior, Esq., at Gloucester.—The Lord Protector and the Councell having issued Orders and Instructions for securing the peace of the Commonwealth whereby Pury and others were appointed to execute the same in the County of the City of Gloucester, the writer in obedience to the Protector's command gives Pury notice to be present at Gloucester on the 26th, at which time and place the writer purposes, through the blessing of God, to give his attendance and communicate the said Orders and Instructions. (Seal of arms.)

1659, July 20, Councell of State att Whitehall. Appointment of Thomas Pury the younger, Esquire, to be Captain of a Company of Foot, consisting of 100 soldiers besides officers, of such well affected persons as should voluntarily list themselves under him in the City of Gloucester, for the present defence and security of the said City and the Commonwealth against any the Enemies thereof, &c. Signed in the name and by order of the Councell of State appointed by authority of Parliament, H. Jhonston, præsident. '(Written on a sheet of vellum; with wafer seal of the Councell of State.)

1660, March 27. "George Monck," Captain General and Commander-in-Chief of all the Forces in England, Scotland, and Ireland, to Colonel Thomas Pury, Lieut.-Col. Thomas Ffrench, Major William Neast, or the officer in Chief present with the said regiment of foot now and for the time being.—A Commission to them or either of them to call a Court Martial consisting of the Commission Officers of the said regiment, as often as need shall require, and there to hear, examine, and determine all offences and misdemeanours committed by officers or soldiers of the regiment against the Laws and Ordinances of War, and to bring them to trial and inflict punishment. The Commission is not to extend to the trial of any officer in Commission or to the inflicting any punishment to the taking away of life or member without notice to an order from Monck. (At the top are the arms of Monck in red wax)

1660, March 29, St. James's. George Monck to the officer or officers that command the Forces in Herefordshire. Understanding there have been disorders lately committed in Herefordshire, and divers affronts offered by the Cavaliers to the well affected party there, he desires them to assist Major Harley in keeping the peace of the country.

1660, April 1. Jo. Butler, Quartermaster General to Col. Pury. "Collonell Pury is to have Monmouth, "Uske, and Abegeveny for Quarters for 3 Companies "of his regiment till further order."

1660, April 11, St. James's. George Monck to Col. Pury or the officer in chief with his regiment at Hereford.—Lord Lambert having escaped out of the Tower last night, Monck tells Pury to be very careful of his duty and not suffer any officers to be away from their charges, and to have an eye that no agitators come among his soldiers to withdraw them from their duty. Pury is to secure any such and send them to the Martial Generals at the Mewes: if any officer or soldier apprehend Lord Lambert he shall have 100l. "I would "have you take care that there be still heere a "Comission officer of your regiment. I desire you "alsoe to take."

1660, April 19, Hereford. T. Scudamore, Edward Harley, Ro. J. Lepel, Tho. Blayney, and Ro. Hurley to Col. Pury. Being informed of attempts on foot to disturb the peace and safety of the nation, and in particular of that City and County, they desire him draw into the City the Company of Foot of his regiment then quartered at Rosse. As the matter is too pressing to wait for the previous order of the General, they will endeavour to obtain his Excellency's approbation. (The endorsement states that the writers were Commanders of the Militia of Hereford.)

1660, April 20, St. James's. George Monck to Major Robert Harley.—Requires him to preserve the peace of the counties of Hereford, Worcester, and Gloucester, and the parts thereabouts. The officers commanding

Col. Sir Arthur Hesilrige's, Col. Alured's, Col. Purye's regiments, or of the troops and companies belonging to them in these shires or the parts thereabouts which were not commanded by the Lord Howard were to observe such orders as they should receive from Harley. (Stated to be under his hand and seal: but there is no seal.) Below is an autograph note by Robert Harley to Col. Pury, desiring him to execute the contents of the above order and substituting him thereunto.

1660, April 21, Whitehall. The Conncell of State to the Governor of Hereford.—After noticing that there were distempers and animosities in those parts, they tell him to keep strict guard and to suffer no suspicious persons to pass near his command, nor soldiers without order from the Lord General or their Colonel or other Commander-in-Chief. He is to continue at his charge and not remove upon any private occasions of his own without special leave. If necessary to preserve the peace, he is to call to his assistance the army and militia forces near. They have written to the same tenor to the Governors of Shrewsbury, Cardiff, Chepstow, Worcester, and Gloucester, that they might be mutually helpful. He is to apprehend and secure all stragglers and other suspected persons.—Signed in the name and by order of the Councell of State appointed by authority of Parliament. "Arthur Annesley, President." Wafer seal of the Council of State.

1660, April 23. George Monck to Col. Thomas Pury. Refers to the annexed Information against some soldiers of Captain O'Keshott's troop in Col. Alured's regiment. Authorizes Pury from time to time, within six weeks, to call a Court Martial and try to punish the three soldiers. He is also to try any other soldiers who have said or done anything tending to mutiny or sedition, &c. No punishment to extend to life or member without first acquainting Monck therewith, and the grounds and reasons of the judgment. Authorizes him to administer an oath to witnesses. At the top is Monck's seal of arms in red wax.

(Annexed) Information against John Thrift, Peter Curtis, and Thomas Osburne, troopers in Capt. O'Keshott's troop in Col. Alured's regiment.—Thrift had said, at the White Hart at Tewkesbury, that Monck was a rogue, and that they (meaning Lambert and his party) should have a day for it, and that Smyth the bayly of Tewkabury would have a troop ready for them. —Curtis had said at the sign of the Dog in Tewkesbury, that Monck was a fellow of no principle, and that no good was ever to be expected from him.—Osburne had spoken, at the White Hart, revilingly and dishonourably of Monck, and said that Monck was a Monky face.— Certified by Thomas Margetts, Advocate, to be a true copy of the original remaining with him.

1660, June 11, 12 Car. II. Commission (on vellum) for Thomas Pury the younger to be Colonel of a regiment of foot and Captain of a company of foot in the same regiment. Signed by George Monck. Wafer seal, Monck's shield of four quarters at the top.

1660, Oct. 11, Cockpitt. "Albemarle" to Lord Herbert or the Commander-in-Chief with his regiment at Hereford.—Col. Birch is authorised by the Commissioners appointed for disbanding the Army to take care of the disbanding of Lord Herbert's regiment. Lord H. is to observe Birch's directions on the matter. The King having given a week's pay to the non-commissioned officers and soldiers in each regiment; if Lord H. take up the money in the country and charge it by Bills of Exchange upon Mr. William Clarke, at 15 days sight, it will be answered. (Sealed with the shield of arms of Monck, surrounded by the Garter and its motto, and surmounted by a ducal Crown.)

1660, Oct. 22. The Commissioners for disbanding the army to Col. Thomas Pury, or, in his absence, to the officer in chief of the Lord Herbert's regiment at Hereford or elsewhere.—Order that Lord Herbert's regiment of foot should be disbanded and paid off their arrears on or before the 29th of October instant; the officers and soldiers are to obey the directions in the matter given by persons authorised. The chief officer now at the head of the regiment is to take notice of the order and publish it to the companies.—Signed by Albemarle, Wm. Prynne and Rob. Scawen.

1660, Oct. 27, Cockpitt.—Albemarle to the Officer in chief of the Lord Herbert's regiment. Tells him that Col. Birch is one of the Commissioners for disbanding the army has been appointed for the disbanding Lord Herbert's regiment, and desires the chief officer to draw the regiment together and assist Col. Birch.

ALFRED J. HORWOOD.

The MANUSCRIPTS of EVELYN PHILIP SHIRLEY, Esq.,
of Ettington Hall, co. Warwick.

This is a miscellaneous collection consisting of more
than 150 volumes, and short notices of such of them as
seemed within the scope of the Commission are here
given. These are,—an account of the unfortunate attempt of Robert Devereux Earl of Essex, to raise the
Londoners on his behalf; notes of furniture supplied to
him when in the Tower; inventories of his plate, linen,
&c., both before and after his death; and a very singular
account in Latin, (in form of a dialogue) of his pedigree.
Treatises relating to the contentions between Queen
Elizabeth and Mary Queen of Scots, (some of which have
been printed). Copies of letters by Dr. Laurence Humphry (16th century) on the subject of ecclesiastical
vestments; of verses composed by Queen Elizabeth; of
letters by Roger Marbecke. Original correspondence
of James Stanhope (afterwards Earl Stanhope) with Lord
Treasurer Godolphin during the war with Spain, 1705–8.
Common-place book and original compositions by Philip
second Earl of Chesterfield, and of Philip Dormer third
Earl of Chesterfield; among them are the original MSS.
of the celebrated *Characters*, the greater number of
which were for the first time printed by the present Earl
Stanhope. An account of a great fire at Peasmore co.
Berks in 1736; a curious letter in 1754 showing the
large sums spent in contests for seats in the House of
Commons, and the venality of the Whig electors of the
place in question. A Journal by the Honourable Lewis
Shirley in 1700–1702 of his voyage to and from China,
contains much information. A 17th century
volume contains numerous poems by members of the
University of Oxford.

The heraldic and genealogical volumes are many.
Among them is a very beautiful volume presented to
Queen Elizabeth in 1572; three Leicestershire Visitations
(one of the 16th century, and two in 1619), and a visitation for Oxfordshire of the 17th century. The rarity
and value of *Halstead's Genealogies* is well known to
literary men; vol. 56 of Mr. Shirley's collection contains portions of the original MS. There is Sir Fulwar
Skipwith's diary in the middle of the 17th century.
There are copies of Commodore Barnett's letter-book
and papers, 1743–6; lists of the king's officers in the
American colonies in 1764; a register of official letters in
the affairs of the Army, Navy, and Ordnance, 1701–1718,
a short journal of a journey to the Peak in Derbyshire
in 1650, ending (in Johnsonian phraseology) with dissatisfaction with Chatsworth gardens. There are three
tracts on Transubstantiation by Bishop Morley, the last
of which has not been printed. Richard Symond's diary
of the doings of the royal army during the civil war
has been printed by the Camden Society; Mr. Shirley
has his Common-place book, an entry in which intimates
that he made collections for the county of Essex. Three
small note books of a member of the House of Commons
give notes of proceedings and debates in 1679 and 1680.
A 4to. volume of the 17th century contains copies of
interesting official documents, and of statutes of the
University of Oxford. A 12th century manuscript (of
foreign execution) on the office of the Mass seems of an
unusual character. Forms of legal pleading on various
writs are given in a volume written in the 14th century.
The volume containing copies of Oxford documents
gives two notices of a man who did good service to literature and to the University—the industrious printer
Joseph Barnes; during his lifetime he was fain to keep
a tavern in order to support himself and his family; but
he died in very reduced circumstances. The acquaintance of Barnes with Starkey the emblem-painter is
perhaps a new fact.

No. 6. A quarto MS. on vellum of 16 folios in the author's
own handwriting, with his signature, intituled " Pronos-
" tique historial de la felicité de l'an mil cinq cens et
" douze " by *Jehan le Maire* (Brotagne), Queen of Louis XII. It is
apparently the presentation copy. On the first leaf under
a golden star* having in three concentric circles in the
centre the word Bona repeated, are these lines,—

Annus esto bonus Anne bone Magne
Duodenus plenus bonus semper annus
Magnus prosper annus condigne regine
Anne Magne, bone annus sit benignus.

(This volume is not printed, and there is no MS. in
the Bibliothèque Imperiale. It is probably unique.—
Note by the late John Holmes of the British Museum.)

No. 7. In this volume (loose) are the following notes
and letters.—Such nowes as came to the Bishop of Bangor

from London. (The Bishop was Henry Rowlands, elected
in 1598, he died on the 6th of July 1616. Sir Robert
Williams Bart. from whom this paper came, was descended from a brother of the Bishop.) Sunday Feb. 8th.
The Earl was sent for to the Council but would not
come . . . The Lord Keeper and others came to
talk with and examine him; he would not answer. He
and his friends (about 300) went all to Essex House
with their swords and rapiers, not drawn, but with their
poynts up, they go to Ludgate, &c.; the Londoners
showed themselves favourable to the traytors or too
timorous, every one seeking only the defence of his own
house. My lord of Sussex, coming upon Sunday at
night when all was done, was nevertheless (because he
came upon Essex's letters) committed. Heyden, Baynam,
and others likewise are committed.

Copy of the Earl of Essex's letter to the Lords of the
Council on his departure from Plymouth. *Begins*,
Having taken order for all things that belong to our
land forces. (4 pp.)

1600, Feb. 11th. Warrant by (the Earl of) Notingham
and Ro. Cecyll to Sir Henry Bronker and Mr. Michael
Stanhope.—Essex being now a prisoner in the Tower is
unfurnished of these things here-under written.

Deliver to the bearer Geo. Partridge servant to
Mr. Lieutenant :—A table for himself and another for
the outward chamber, a carpet for his table, a foot carpet
for the floor, two cushions, a pair of silver candlesticks,
a chamber pot, a fire shovel and tongs, a pair of bellows,
a pan to burn rosewater, bedding for Mr. Warbert and
his man; A silver salt and a spoon, two silver pots for
wine.

Receipt for the above by Partridge, and for two hangings more.

23rd Feb. Court.—The Earl of Notingham to his
brother Mychael Stanhope. There is some cause to
youse (use) the late Earl's Collar and Garter this day at
the Tower, therefore I pray you send the Collar and
Garter unto me, and after they be used I will see them
safely kept and be answerable for them.

1597, Michaelmas. Inventory of all such implements
and household stuff as remaineth in several places at
Wansted taken at Michaelmas 1597. (6 folios.)

A note of the stuff sent from Wansted to Essex house
by Sir Gillies Mereoke command on the 29th of September. The same on the 20th of Sept., ditto Feb. 2nd 1598,
ditto March 8th, and March 15th 1598, ditto May 28th.
A page for each note. There are nine other leaves of
similar things.

Note of wardrobe stuff remaining in Essex House on
the 28th of March 1599 in the custody of Randall Shard
for the time of my Lord's being in Ireland. (5 leaves.)

An inventory of all the aparell, &c. in my charge at
Bishops Gate and at the court this 10th of March 1600.
(4 leaves.)

1600, July 21st. Note of such linen as remaineth
in the custody of Robert Pitchford 21st of July 1600.
(1 p.)

1600, Aug. List of plate. (½ p.)

1633, July. Sylver vessels delivered to E. Home.

1600, July 23rd. Inventory of plate as belongeth to
the Right Hon. the Earl of Essex, Marshal of England,
(2½ pp.); and inventory of linen at Essex House, Aug. 24th
1600, (1½ pp.) A brief inventory of all the wardrobe stuff
remaining in Essex House set down on the 8th of Aug.
1600. (3 leaves.)

Inventory of goods and chattels of the late Earl of
Essex by reason of his attainder and conviction &c.,
valued by virtue of a commission directed to Michael
Stanhope, Esq. and others, 28th of March, 43 Eliz.
1602. (7 pp.)

Francis Bacon's counterfeit letter to the Earl of Essex.
(4½ pp. quarto). *Begins*, Her Majesty proceeding thus
by gradation." The Earl of Essex to Bacon. *Begins*, Mr.
Bacon I thank you for your kind letter. (1½ pp.) At the
foot " My book, Jo. Manwood."

1600, March 17th, Whitehall. Letter signed by Lord
Buckhurst, the Earl of Notingham, Ro. Cecyll, and
J. Fortescue, to Mr. Michael Stanhope.—Lady Walsing-
ham informs us that she has divers parcels of stuff in
Essex House which she offers to swear belong to her.—
They tell Stanhope to deliver to her what she affirmeth.

1600, March 11th. List of goods, and the oath of Mat.
Carew to that effect.

Note of such stuff as came from Walsingham House
to Essex House. (1½ pp.)

Charges of diet at Essex House for Sir H. Bronkard
and two others, and their servants. (1½ pp.)

1600, Feb. 6th. William Cholmley (clerk to the Earl
of Essex) to the Earl the Lord Admiral, praying for payment of 210l. 19s. 0½d. and 10l. for the weekly expense

---

* Over the star, in a scroll, are the words *Non mudern*.

of dyett of the Earl from 11th of January 1600 to the 6th February 1600; and for Sunday February 8th and Monday, 10£.

1600, March 13th, Sackville.—T. Buckhurst to Michael Stanhope.—The Queen has granted to Mr. Brown, clerk of the Green cloth, in respect of a debt of 333£. due to him by Sir C. Blunt, late condemned for treason, all such goods as were remaining in Essex House of the said C. Blunt. After choice by Her Majesty's servants and note taken of the jewels they shall choose, the residue to be delivered to Mr. Brown.

1596, April 23rd. Inventory taken of goods of the Countess of Leicester and Sir C. Blount in Essex House. (5 folios.)

A letter about Sir C. Blount's goods.

1600, Feb. 21st. Council order signed by Egerton, C. S., T. Buckhurst, Notingham and Ro. Cecyll. Order to deliver certain goods for the use of Sir Gylly Merrick (as below).

A great number of receipts in 1599 and 1600 of sums of money paid by Sir Gilly Meyrick to various persons. —Thomas Lee (who was executed for high treason), Mr. Woodhouse, Ellis Jones, William Bigman, P. Edmondes, Peter Wyn, Laurence Lyndley, Alphonse Lanier, Capt. P. Edmonde, Capt. William Norreys, Rafe Constable, Thomas Dillon, Thomas Bager, Ellys Jhones, Ralph Rokeby, Richard Pye, Thomas Sutton, Henry Cuffe (June 22nd 1600), and Fra. Canc.

Execution of Sir Gilly Meyrick and Mr. Cuffe at Tyburn on the 8th of March 1600.

No. 6. Folio volume.

1600. Apology of Robert Earl of Essex and the considerations and reasons of peace and war.

The Lord Keeper's letter to him, and his answer.

An apology, &c. written to Mr. A. Bacon in 1600. *Begins*, He that either thinketh, &c. (This copy is said to differ from the printed one.)

21 b. A treatise touching the right, title, and interest as well of the most excellent Princess Mary, as of the most noble King James, her Grace's son to the succession of the crown of England by John Lislewe (Leslie) Bishop of Ross. 1586.*

A declaration of the table following, &c. (10 lines). *Begins*, Certain it is and assuredly tried and known to all men.

25 b. A further proof of the said title of succession with a resolution of the objections of the adversaries. *Begins*, We say then and affirm. *Ends*, my pen in my hand trembleth to write thereof.

Fol. 48. An exhortation to the English and Scotch nations that after so long warres they would now at last agree and joyne together in one true league of fast freindship and amatic. *Begins*, If we will remember the manyfold hurts and ould calamities. *Ends*, 53 b. Let us all continually pray to Almighty God the supreme Governor and ruler of the whole world. Amen.

No. 9. Folio volume, 16th century. (This MS. was formerly in the library of the late Mr. Pitts of Kingston, (Dorsetshire.)

6 kal. Nov., Lisbon. Copy of a Latin letter by Osorius Bishop of Lisbon to Roger Ascham.— He say that Thomas Wilson has sent greeting in Ascham's name, and that Ascham was suffering from fever. He came to Lisbon expecting that as soon as some business was done he should return to his diocese, but business presses on him. Letters will reach him at Algarve. Wilson will give Ascham a book in which he (Osorius) praises Walter Haddon.†

Reasons to move the Queen's Majesty's conscience to proceed with severitie in the case of the Queen of Scots. *Begins*, The word of God which is the only director of conscience and a certain rule for all estates.

3 b. An argument that the Queen's Majesty ought to have in conscience a great care of her own person. *Begins*, Every prince being the minister of God and a public person. *Ends*, This poisonous serpent that ceaseth not continually to thrust the sting of his venomous working into Her Majesty's safetie and possession of her crown.

4 b. A letter of Dr. Laurence Humfry concerning surplices unto the Bishop. *Begins*, Your lordship's letters directed to us by our Vice-Chancellor complaining that since old mass attires be so straightly commanded, the mass itself is shortly looked for. A sword is now put into the hand of those that under Queen Mary have drawn it for Popery.—Asks him to speak to the Queen, the Chancellor and Secretary that the proceedings may sleep. (1½ pp.)

5. Idem Episcopis Angliæ eadem de Materia. *Begins*, Et novam et singularem videri potest. (1½ pp.),

6. Idem ad reginam Angliæ de re vestiariu cadem. *Begins*, Si quoties peccant homines sua fulmina mittat Jupiter, exiguo tempore inermis erit.

Liceat enim mihi, Serenissime Regina, hoc carmine, affari majestatem tuam.

6 b. Alia ejusdem ad Reginam. *Begins*, Vere et ex animo tibi Elizabetha Regina. (1½ pp.)

7. A sermon made at St. Peter's-in-the-East by Mr. Rainoldes, A.D. 1576. The text was from Eph. c. 5 " Be ye therefore followers of God." The sermon *begins*, The prophet Esaie lamenting the miserable state of the children of God.

12. 1576, Feb. 8th. Dr. Matthews writing to Lord Leicester, having given occasion of offence in a sermon at Paul's Cross concerning succession (from Gal. 6). " We have by one," &c. *Begins*, Discoursing upon this text, I came at length.

13 b. Dr. Mathue his prayer usual in the pulpit.

Mr. Wentford's (Wentworth's) speech in Parliament for which he was afterwards committed to the Tower. *Begins*, Mr. Speaker, I have found written in a little volume these words in effect, " Sweet in deed is the " name of liberty."* (8½ pp.)

18. Supplicatio Polonorum ad Regem Gallie olim Poldnorum regem designatum. (Nearly 4 pp.)

20. 1570. M. Matthei oratio habita in adventum nobilissimi Leicestrensis Comitis in Cimeterio S. Marie, nonis Septembris. *Begins*, Quis deus adjunxit nostris sua nomina votis ? Sic olim poeta cecinit, &c.

21 b. Verses made by the Queen's Majesty.† (8 verses.)

> *Begins*, The doubt of future foes
> Exiles my future joy,
> And wit me warns to shun such snares
> As threatens mine annoy.
> *Ends*, My rusti sworde thro' reste
> Shal firste his edge employ
> To pul (poll) their tops who seke such
> things
> Or gape for future joy.
>
> Vivat Regina.

22. M. Rogeri Marbecci Epistolæ. (Latin.)

1564, Nov. 21st. To the Queen.

1564, Nov. 19th. To the Earl of Leicester.—To the same.—To Thomas Thornton.—To the Earl of Leicester. —To the Archbishops of York and Canterbury.—To the Earl of Leicester.—To the Bishop of Salisbury.—To John Dolabert (4 letters).—To Henry Blage.—To W. Clerke.—To Clerk and Morison, his disciples.—To Cardinal Pole.

28. To Lord E. Rosse.

29. Master Barnard, Canon of Christ Church.—To the Bishop of London in praise of eloquence (long).— Oration of Marbec at vespers (in vesperiis).—Oration of Nicholas Balguy of Magdalen College, Oxford, on the coming of the Bishop of Winchester as visitor. (2 pp.)

Periculosum est in rebus arcanis principum et regnorum nimis velle sapere, &c. Thomas Smith. (English.) *Begins*, In so great a matter which we have in hand which concerneth the whole realm. *Ends*, And for the love of his country to give place to truth quietly. (14 pp.)

Orationes duæ magistri Joannis Rainoldes exempla consilia injuriæ malorum facienda esse bonis. *Begins*, Epaminondam illum celeberrimum. (9 pp.)

Oratio secunda in Joannis Rainoldes de Maleficiis. *Begins*, Etsi vestros sensus. (10½ pp.)

A dialogue of the marriage of Queen Elizabeth compiled by Sir Thomas Smith. *Begins*, As I was walking in my garden. *Ends*, jesting one another at their new names. (Printed in Strype's Life of Sir Thomas Smith.)

The manner of the Earl of Essex's departure out of this life, who died the 21st day of September, and was buried the 27th of November 1576. *Begins*, Walter the noble Earl of Essex and Earl Marshall of Ireland :—with the six verses (of four lines each) which he sang the night before his death (by Francis Hindemersh). (6½ pp.)

1575, 6 Id. Julii. Petition in Latin to Queen Elizabeth of the Provost and Students of Christ Church, Oxford, founded by Hen. VIII., for the advancement of William James to a deanery.

---

* Lowndes says that this was printed in 1584.
† Printed at p. 455 of the collection of Ascham's letters, 8vo. Lond. 1703.

* See Sir Simonds D'Ewes Complete Journal, &c., p. 236, &c.
† Printed (with some variations) in Puttenham's " Arte of English Poesie," and in Nare's Life of Lord Burghley, vol. ii., p. 365.

1575, 16 Id. Julii. Latin letter to the Earl of Leicester by the Academy of Oxford.

To Burghley of the same date.

Exhortation of the Gauls besieged in Rochelle to Queen Elizabeth that she would defend her party. *Begins,* Haud dubie Regina iis qui nova deposcunt beneficia. (10 leaves imperfect at end.)

Two leaves of English.

Nos. 12 and 13. Quarto common-place books, and extracts, by Philip, second Earl of Chesterfield.

Octavo common-place book, &c. by the same in 1670.

No. 14. Folio. Correspondence of James Stanhope, afterwards Earl Stanhope, with Lord Treasurer Godolphin.

1705. Sept. 30th, Windsor. Sir Charles Hedges to [the Earl of Godolphin]. Sends three letters by Mr. Methuen, which came by Lisbon mail this morning. Sends extract of the one to Hedges.

1706, June 15th. Extract of a letter to Mr. Secretary Hedges from Barcelona. Lord Galway writes the allies will have an army of 17,000 foot and 5,000 horse, and the Spaniards will not be above 8,000 of the former and between five and six thousand of the latter. He designs to besiege Badaios or to march into Andalusia, but he finds great difficulties with the Portuguese. Brigadier Shrimpton makes great complaints of the naked condition of Gibraltar and want of all things necessary for repairing fortifications. . . . . When the fleet returns the Earl of Peterboro' has instructions to leave the place in as good a condition as he can. Her Majesty has given out her commands relating to the Lord Keeper and the Earl of Abington.

1706, Aug. 11th. n.s. Camp of Gundalajam. General Stanhope to Lord Treasurer Godolphin.—A descent by Sir Cloudesley Shovel and his fleet on Galicia would be of use. Laments the bad state of affairs. Unless they can win a battle, nothing but wintering a strong squadron in the Mediterranean can save this army from ruin. The Portuguese have not a shilling.—If we had money we could raise a considerable number of troops in Aragon, Valencia, and Catalonia, which provinces are as firm as possible in our interest.—Spain is divided into parties, as it was formerly, into the Crowns of Castile and Aragon. All the latter we are possessed of. —The division he laments.

1706. Aug. 25th. Camp at Chinchon. (8 pp.)—Oct. 6th and 24th from Valencia. The same to the same.

1706, Oct. 24th, Valencia. The same to Secretary Hedges, with copies of other letters.

1706, Oct. 29th, Valencia. The same to the Lord Treasurer.

1706, Nov. 8th and 24th, Valencia, and Dec. 14th. The same to the same.

1706, Dec. 14th and 25th, Valencia. The same to Secretary Hedges.

1706, Dec. 26th, Valencia. The same to [Lord Treasurer.]

1706, Oct. 24th, Valencia. Duplicate copy of the same date as above.

1707, Nov. 7th. Duplicate letter.

1708, June 22nd. Extract of letter from the Lord Treasurer to Mr. Stanhope.

1708. Aug. 24th, Barcelona. General Stanhope to [Sir John Leake].—Congratulations on success at Sardinia.

n.d. Ordem de Battalha do exercito chamado dos duas oroas mandado pelo Senhor Duque de Anjou.

(These letters are mostly written by James Stanhope, afterwards Earl Stanhope during the military operations in Spain in 1706, and were formerly in the possession of my grandfather Arthur Stanhope; they appear to have been lent to the great Earl of Chesterfield. See indorsement on the letter of Aug. 24th, 1708.)

No. 15. Original " Characters, &c." by Philip Dormer Stanhope, Earl of Chesterfield. (This shows that Walpole was misinformed, when he said that the Earl burnt the originals before he died. Letters, vol. iv. p. 73.)

Seventeen characters, *George I.,* the Mistresses of George I. and II., George II., *Queen Caroline,* Lord Townsend, Popo, Arbuthnot, Bolingbroke. *Pulteney, afterwards Earl of Bath, Sir Robert Walpole,* Lord Grenville. Mr. Pelham, Richard, Earl of Scarborough, Lord Hardwick, Duke of Newcastle, Duke of Bedford, *Henry Fox, Mr. Pitt.* (Those in italics were first published in 12mo. in 1777. Lord Mahon (now Earl Stanhope) printed the remainder.

Some thoughts upon the Clergy.

A dialogue between Villiers, Duke of Buckingham, and Sir J. Cutler.

A dialogue between Horace and Dr. Bentley.

My thoughts for the education of my godson Philip Stanhope.

My thoughts concerning the future education of my godson Philip Stanhope, who is, and in my opinion deservedly, the object of my tenderest care and wishes. (All autograph.)

No. 16. Quarto. Fragments by Philip Dormer, Earl of Chesterfield. (Autograph.)

1. On the administration of the Earl of Bute, written in 1763 (p. 1 to p. 18). *Ends* with a character. " He had honour, honesty and good intentions. He was too proud to be respectable or respected. Too cold and silent to be amiable, too cunning to have great ability, and his inexperience made him too precipitately undertake what it disabled him from executing."

2. Anecdote how the excise scheme came to be so unexpectedly dropped, written in 1761. (19–21.)

3. Fragments. (Inter alia.) An anecdote concerning the marriage of the French King Louis XV. with the daughter of Stanislaus Seczinsk, King of Poland (22–26). The chambermaid of Madame de Prie, the Duke of Bourbon's mistress, suggested to her mistress the daughter of Stanislaus as wife for the King.

4. Essay on the duty and utility and the means of pleasing; a fragment. Anecdotes, aphorisms, &c., (27–32). *Begins,* The desire of being pleased is universal.

5. Advice to the late Earl of Chesterfield (33–46). *Begins,* My dear boy. *Ends,* with a recommendation not to be in debt, and a quotation from Voltaire thereon.

6. The same with considerable additions and alterations (47–64). *Ends,* with P.S. I am sure I need not recommend Dr. Dodd to your care and friendship. You are sensible, I know, of the great obligations you have to him, and whenever you have either interest or power. I charge you to exert them with zeal to serve him.

7. " Some thoughts on the duty, the utility and the " means of pleasing," addressed to the late Earl of Chesterfield (64–85). Begins as before.

8. Anecdotes, &c. (86–89).

No. 19. A thick folio. Executorship account under the will of Thomas Fermor of Somerton, county Oxford, Esq., dated 15th of June 1580.—George Shirley was one of the executors. (See Archæological Journal, vol viii.)

No. 24. A quarto containing 47 letters by the Rev. Ralph Shirley, and one by his son John Shirley, 1714–54, to Wm. Archer, Esq., of Cooper Sale, near Epping, mostly dated from Wickham, the parsonage house of Welford, county Berks, of which place Mr. Shirley was rector. He died in Dec. 1760 æt. 50. according to the Gentleman's Magazine, but by some mistake, as he was born in the 17th century. (Ralph Shirley was of Baliol College, and was M.A. in 1707.)

1726, Jan. 26th, Ralph, Shirley to William Archer. Account of bell-ringing on his (Archer's) wife's delivery of a daughter. The bells were first rung by female, and then by male ringers. The women got in first and rung much, only letting in one man who got the keys of the church for them, and so enabled them to keep the men out ; when tired out, they let the male ringers come.

1729, Sept. 2nd, Wickham. The same to the same. Soho Square. Mentions the illness of Mr. Packer who is not likely to recover. In event of a vacancy Mr. Bertie thought there would be four candidates, yourself, Mr. Winchcombe Packer, Mr. Vansittart and Mr. Aston. He (Shirley) thought that Vansittart would not stand, and that Aston might be prevailed on to desist, having but a poor chance, and that it lay between him (Archer) and Packer.

It appears that on the 27th July 1736 a great fire broke out at Peasemore, county Berks ; it broke out through a high wind, did much damage, 1575l. 6s. 4d. at a moderate computation. Here is a copy of a letter by two justices of the peace, giving leave to the poor cottagers' agent or agents, for six months, to ask charity for them from house to house within the county, but not a license to the sufferers, they being so many.

1754, June 11th, Peasemore. Ralph Shirley to ——. Mr. Strode, lately chosen, is dying. Mr. Gore told Lord Craven that you were pitched on to succeed him and support the interest. It is my duty to let you know that the electors, principally of the Court side, have been remarkably venal. At the close of the last Parliament but one, Mr. D—— d who sat in the House but six weeks, upon an appeal spent, some say, 13,000l., others 11,000l., the least 9,000l. His canvass this time cost (Lord Craven hears) 3,000l., and what his appeal will come to (for he is resolved to petition) who can say ? His appeal is not against Mr. Strode, but Lord Fane.

The electors on the Tory side (Mr. Strode's) are comparatively upright.

No. 28. Folio. A book of dialling with drawings by Edward Shirley, formerly schoolmaster in H.M. Navy, afterwards purser of a ship, by interest of Admiral Vernon. He died on a voyage to the East Indies, in the fleet under the command of Commodore Barnet. (13 leaves, the last three are drawings of dials.) Many other drawings of dials, for different latitudes, and of different shapes. (20 pp. and 3 leaves.)

No. 32. Folio. Temp. Car. I. A book of prescriptions. Copied from one written by Sir Samuel Sandys, of Ombersley, co. Worcester. (541 pp. + Index.) p. 362. Recipes by Sir Walter Raleigh. p. 460. Recipes by Sir Jo. Finett.

No. 34. Folio. A book of prescriptions by Richard Beete in 1691. Names of people and the prescriptions for them. In it are some prescriptions by Hans Sloane and Richard Mead. On the cover are stamped, on one side *Joanna Henryson*, and on the other side *Musica Medicina Mentis.*

No. 38. Journal of the Honourable Lewis Shirley (fifth son of Robert Lord Ferrers of Chartley, afterwards Earl Ferrers 1st Viscount Tamworth, born 1685, died on a voyage to China 1710).

Journal of a voyage taken by me (God permitting) from London to Emois in China on board the ship Neptune, Capt. Lesley Commander, in 1700.

Began, Thursday, December 5th, 1700. Left Billingsgate, Deal, Canterbury (which he describes). Dec. sailed out of the Downs. On Tuesday, 28th January, saw Teneriffe; June 3rd Palma (he gives description of it); Sunday, 15th June, 1701, Batavia (described).

July 24th journal at Amois (17 leaves).

View of the trade of China taken from the port of Emor, in the province of Tokieu, anno 1701. (73 pp.)

At the other end of the volume is a journal of a voyage from Emoy towards England, in the ship Neptune Capt. Lesley, Feb. 6th, 170¼; ends at fol. 46.

Tuesday, 15th Sept. 1702, Wednesday and part of Thursday at Dover. He kept a log. There are some drawings, and good observations.

No. 37. 1684-7. Lord Ferrers' household book.

No. 39. 4to. Miscellany, poems, and translations, 1697; by R. (Shirley) eldest son of the first Earl Ferrers. (70 leaves.)

Among them is Prospect of Staunton by the Honourable W. Shirley, imitated and enlarged in English by the Honourable R. Shirley.

No. 40. 12mo. Temp. Car. II. Poems, &c. (8 being on the delivery of Sir Robert Shirley's lady).

Latin oration on the death of the learned John Blagrave, A.M. and Fellow of St. John's Oxford, ob. March 11th, 1655, by Samuel Christopher, A.M. of St. John's.

Speech (Latin) by Dr. Wyat of St. John's for the grade of Master.

News from Newcastle, or New Castle Colopita. *Begins,*
England a perfect world and Indies too,
Correct your maps, Newcastle is Peru.
(4 pp.) by Thos. Winnard.

Upon the late inundation of the river Trent, by Thos. Winnard, A.B. St. John's. The scene Muscham and Holme two opposite villages on the river side near Newark. *Begins,*
When heirs and widows hoarding fresh supplies,
Bottle up tears wrung from St. Swithin's eyes.
(4 pp.)

On Sir Robert Shirley's lady delivered of a son on the Sabbath day.

On the Thanksgiving day. *Begins,*
Enjoy the angry powers do fret away
The scene of your high crimes and judgement day.
(2¼ pp.)

Lines on the City's present to the General. (8 lines.)
To the Lieutenant-General. (10 lines.)
A short grace after a long dinner. *Begins,*
We thank thee, Oxford, thou hast given us grace,
And made us Doctors of thy learned race,
We thank thee, London, ... each citizen,
For you have made us more great gifted men.
Ab auctore ignoto sed suspecte. T.W.

Divers English and Latin verses. Elegiacal, Panegyrical, Satirical, Genethliacal, Epithalamial, &c.
On Thomas Paynter of John's A.B. death. *Begins,*
Ab authore ignota sed suspecto. Joh. Shaxton.

The pious memory of Dr. Speed. *Begins,*
Here lies a multitude let none infer.
By Richard Painter, A.M. of John's,
On a Doctor of medicine (Dr. Speed) in Latin.
By William Walwin of John's,
A song on Prince Charles his birth. *Begins,*
Welfare the muse while in well chim'd verse.
(1¼ pp.)

An owl of Athens, or, a relation of the entrie of the Earl of Pembroke as chancellor into Oxford, April 11th 1649. *Begins,*
Nay Blackwater now look to't you must away.
(2¼ pp.)
On the Nativity of Christ. *Begins,*
Be dumb unhallowed oracles and more. (½ p.)
By Jo. Blagrave.
On the death of Dr. Clayton. By Will. Taylor, A.B. John's. (½ p.)
Trajedy of Mr. Christopher Love, beheaded on Tower Hill, Aug. 22nd 1651. *Begins,*
New from a slaughtered monarch here I come.
There are five short acts. (3¼ pp.)

A brief expression of the delight apprehended by the author at the seeing of the solemn triumph of the gentlemen of the Inns of Court riding with a masque presented before his Majesty, Feb. 3rd 1633. *Begins,*
Now did Heavens charioteer the days great star,
I'th' western ocean leave his weary car. (1 p.)
Upon the freckles of a ladies forehead.
By Samuel Filer, of All Souls.

Other poems, among them—
On the death of Mr. John Bragg.
On Kent's insurrection. *Begins,*
Bravely resolved, brave hearts, I see some good.
By Dr. Taylor of John's.
Latin verses :—
On the Passion.
On the Resurrection.
On the Ascension.
On the 3rd of September.
On the 5th of November.

The 5th Ode of the first book of Horace, a little changed, to an Oxford girl.
English verses.
On a study. *Begins,*
Studies are orbs, books stars, and scholars are
The proper intelligences of each sphere.
On woman's speeches. (4 lines.)
On the 5th of November.
On Night.
On the sale of College lands.
On a perpetual glutton.
On one who bestowed a gratuity of 20l. on St. John's Library.
Upon spring, &c. (All by T.E.)
On the defeat of King Charles at Worcester.
On the general cold.
At the other end of the volume are—
Oratio Jo. Blagrave habita in publicis comitiis cum esset senior comitiarum. Oxon. 1653.
Oratio D. Syms collectoris, jun. in quadrages. Anno 1654.

No. 43. A folio of 39 leaves, and seven leaves of table of pedigrees in Latin.
41. Eliz. Dec. 25th. To Robert Devereux, &c., &c., quidam antiquariolus anonimus S. P. D. 1599.
A prose account in dialogue of the pedigree of the Earl. Interlocutors, *Momus, Dadleor, Tervinor.*

No. 44. A folio of 132 pages containing 502 coats of arms. Book of the nobilitie given to the Queen's Majesty 1572. It begins with William Duke of Normandy, and at page 130 the last entry is William Cecill, Knight, Baron of Burley. There are perhaps in a different hand appendices and seven coats of arms, the first being Reginald Grey Earl of Kent, and Lord Grey of Ruthin, next heir male to Reginald Grey, Earl of Kent, nominated in January 1571. The seventh coat of arms is that of Peregrine Bertie, Lord Willoughby of Evesby, in the right of Lady Catherine his mother, Duchess of Suffolk, daughter and sole heir of William Lord Willoughby of Evesby, admitted to that dignity in November 1580.
On smaller paper are 10½ pages by the same hand as that of the appendices. Errors and oversights escaped in the books of the nobility given to the Queen's Majesty anno 1572.
The arms are very beautiful, and the colours and gilding and even the silver are quite fresh.

No. 45. Folio. Arms and pedigrees of the ancient nobility of Britain, with proper blazons from the Conquest to 1572, and then continued to 1606. (211 leaves. There are three coats of arms in a page.) Note.—" MS. given " me in 1798 by the Revd. John Lockman, Canon of " Windsor, *Leicester.*" It was probably compiled by Robert Cooke, Clarencieux, and is supposed to be the original of No. 1440 art. 23 of the Harleian Collection. (It is perhaps a transcript from it, Wanley supposed it to be different.)

No. 46. Quarto. Temp. Henry VIII. on vellum of 20 leaves. Arms of the Knights of the Garter. There are 52 coats of arms, the last is the Earl of Southampton in 1545.

No. 47. A folio. Names and blazon of arms of families of different counties, in the autograph, by Samuel Todde, at the latter end of the reign of Queen Elizabeth. (100 leaves with alphabetical index of nine leaves in two columns, no tricks.) :

No. 50. A folio, of which 27 leaves are filled. Arms of peers. There are nine in a page.

No. 51. Quarto. Leicestershire visitation in 1619. It contains the arms of the City of Leicester and private arms. (100 pp.) In pencil are the arms of London and those of the companies and guilds, four in a page.

No. 52. A large folio. Temp. Car. II. Arms of peers with supporters and mottoes.

No. 55. Quarto. Collection of several things concerning the law and practice of arms, and Holmes of Chester his boldness. I desire the reader to consider these collections seriously.— (In another hand.) My clarke was mistaken in the collections, for he mist low coats of arms, and three or four crests, the explancing the reader which is a Armeris will discover that fault, for it cannot well be mended in the book without defacing it.—Heraldry and anecdotes to p. 63. At p. 64, a description of the happy coronation of her serene Majesty Queen Anne, which was celebrated 23rd of April 1702. Then three pages of various coats of arms blazoned. At p. 95. Forms of proceedings at the coronation of William III. and Queen Mary, May 11th, 1689. Engraved heads and engravings of procession and printed coats of arms.

No. 56. A large folio. MS. pedigrees and proofs of Halsteds Genalogies. It contains all the pedigrees of the Mordant family, and the descents of the following houses who are merged in the Mordants. Alno or De Alneto, Broo, Latimer, Drayton, Manduit, Greene, and Vere. The following are wanting: the first part of Fitzaleur's and that of Howard Duke of Norfolk. The work was printed in 1681, it was drawn up by the second Earl of Peterborough, who died in 1697, and Mr. Rows his chaplain. Only 24 were printed. (43 leaves, engravings and original drawings.)

No. 71. 12mo. Diary of Sir Fulwar Skipwith, Bart. of Newbold Hall, great-great-grandfather to Sir Thomas George Skipwith, the last baronet, who married Selina eldest daughter of the Honble. George Shirley by whom he had no issue. Sir Fulwar Skipwith was born at Shacklewell in Middlesex on the 12th of September, 1628. In 1645 he went abroad by sea. On the 10th of Aug. 1645 cast anchor at Grand Canaries and fought with two Parliament ships and beat them. The last entry is in 1667. Came to London with wife, daughters, and servants. (23 written leaves).

No. 74. 12mo. A prescription book (like No. 34).

No. 76. Folio written by Philip Earl of Chesterfield, about cookery, medicine, and chemical receipts.

No. 77. Lists of pictures at various places. *Quere* by Horace Walpole. (35 pp.)

No. 80. Folio. 17th century. The Earl of Anglesey's discourses upon two long conferences had between the Houses, upon the bill for an additional imposition on several foreign commodities, &c. This same sets forth the jurisdiction of the Lords and power of the Commons in granting money, &c. The aforesaid conference was entered at large in the Commons Journals, 20th and 22nd of April 1671. *Begins,* The Commons having shown great earnestness. (127 pp., about 30 lines on a page.)

No. 81. Copy of the establishment of the yearly charge of the salaries to the officers and servants of Her Majesty's house, to commence on the 1st of July 1761. (About 12 leaves.)

No. 82. 1761. Establishment of the ordinary wages and allowances for Queen Charlotte. (8 leaves.)

No. 83. Quarto. List of the governors and other officers in His Majesty's colonies in America in 1704. Gives the office, the officers, and how appointed, and if for life or pleasure, the value, out of what fund paid. Observations. This volume came from the Stanhopes.

Lovel Stanhope was Under Secretary of State. (About 24 leaves.)

No. 84. Folio. Copies of Commodore Barrett's letter book and naval papers in 1743 to 1746. Copies of orders, &c. Begins with, 25 April 1744, a letter by Barrett to several captains desiring them to get stores and provisions for ships ordered on a particular service. (Between 80 or 90 leaves.)

No. 85. Folio. 1775-6. The journal of Alexander Thistlethwayte, Esqre. Begins November, at Genoa, ends at leaving Paris on the 14th March, 1776. He visited Pisa, Leghorn, Florence, was at Rome on the 24th of Dec. 1774, at Naples 17th of April 1775, at Portici May 1st, 1775, went to Pompeii and Paestuni, he did not admire the Temples, went back to Rome, and left it on the 22nd of May and visited Narni, Terni, Foligno, Loretto, Ancona, Pesaro, Imola, Bologna, Modena, Parma, Mantua, Verona, Vicenza, Padua, Venice, where he saw a great many paintings, the only thing worth notice at Venice was the arsenal ; he returned by Padua, Verona, Trent, Bozen, Satzburg, Vienna, Munich, Angsburg, Ulm, Schaffhausen, where the falls were 120 feet, Berne, Neuchatel, Lausaune, Secheron near Geneva, Lyons, Paris.

No. 86. A thin folio containing verses. It belonged to the third Earl of Chesterfield.

On the death of A. Pope, Esqre. *Begins,*
   Arise ye glittering stars of wit
   For, lo, the son of verse is sett.
Imitation of Horace, &c., and translation.

Stella's birthday, 9 years old. (30 lines.) *Begins,*
   Stella's so womanish and wise
   She cheats the most discerning eyes.
Ends, Thus far from mortals may be giv'n
   The rest the wisest leave to Heav'n.

Horace B. ii. Ode 14. (14 verses.) *Begins,*
   Perhaps nine days or scarce so much
   Your form survives and may be more
   Then Orrery, alas ! is such
   As Orrery who went before.

Stella's birthday, 10 years old. *Begins,*
   Whether my landlord or his dame.
Stella's birthday, at 12 years old, when she died.

No. 87. Folio. A register of official letters on the Navy, Ordinance, and Army in four columns, viz. date, to whom, for what, sums issued.
Navy, 29th of December 1701 to March 12th 1701 (45 pp.)
Army, from 22nd of December 1701 to 12th of March 1701. (80 leaves.)
Ordinance, from 20th January 1701 to 12th of March 1701. (6½ pp.)

No. 93.—Large Quarto, 56 leaves of vellum ; in French double (columns ; 15th century. Le livre du Roy Modus. *Begins* after a fragment) *Laprentis* demande comme leu doit lessier courre au cerf quant il est trouve. *Modus* respont &c. The last chapter is headed (in red) Ci devise coment on doit affetier esprevier et coment ils doivent estre mis en arroy. There are many coloured drawings in the book.

No. 97. 12mo., 1690. Iter boreale, or a journey into the Peakes. *Begins,* Alti consentur septem miracula pecci Ædes mous barathrum binas fons antraque bina. .
Staunton.—Dedication by B. Deioux to Lord Ferrers. (He seems in 1690 to have been tutor in the family of Robert first Earl Ferrers.) Dedication, preface, and work, 127 pages. Contents, The Peak, Pools Hole, Buxton Wells, Tydes Wells, Elden Hole, Peaks Arse, Chatsworth. *Begins,* Having turned our backs to the sweet place, we afterwards returned to   the full point of our small circle. *Ends,* (Chatsworth gardens) they having nothing extraordinary but their situation, nothing wonderful but their cost, and nothing unusual but their solitariness.

No. 107. Quarto vellum. Temp. Eliz. Arms of the Knights of the Garter done apparently for Henry IV. of France, his arms being the first in the book, two shields France and Navarre. There are 15 or 16 arms well executed.

No. 108. A catalogue of all the Earls of Pembroke that have been sithence the Conquest in order as they succeeded with the ysaues of diverse of them together with thyre proper coate armor and a briefe remembrance writen touching some matters of the eche of the saide Erles &c. &c. by Geo. Owen. Dedicated to the Right Honorable the Earl of Pembroke (written after 1621). Presentation copy to the Earl of Pembroke. (Vellum cover with arms on the sides.) (36 leaves.)

No. 110. 12mo. square in a case. Herefordshire Arms; one coat on each leaf; at the first the arms of the twelve tribes &c. down to about fo. 48.

No. 111. 12mo. Vellum, early in the 14th century. Statutes and 98 leaves of forms of pleading on various writs. (On the cover are the arms of Wymbousshe in the 16th century; quarterly sable and argent, a crescent in centre point impaled with, &c.

No. 114. Small quarto containing several hundred coats of arms, including all the English nobility and many of the gentry of the 15th century, with 19 large escutcheons of kings and emperors. About the end Edw. IV. Many Norfolk arms; nine in a page. On the fly-leaf is written Samuel Waker his book, 1676. The first coat of arms is the Spelman coat armor, the second, Chamberlin. There are some others which are more modern than the original. (About 70 leaves.)

No. 119. Folio c. 1600. (Thomas Wyndham) bought from the Lauderdale Collection of MSS., Feb. 4th, 1691. List of nobility in various reigns. Arms coloured and descriptions of the persons.

No. 120. Folio.—Arms of a Visitation of the county of Leicester, taken by Sampson Lenard, alias Bluemantle, and Augustin Vincent, poursuivants-at-arms, A.D. 1619. (49 pp., + index.) Four shields on a page.

Arms &c. taken at a Visitation of the county of Oxford. 17th century. (2 pp. of Index and 22 pp. of Arms, pp. 23–30, are in a modern hand.) One of Edmondson's MSS. afterwards Dr. Meyricks.

No. 122. A volume formerly belonging to Sir George Naylor, Garter, from Charles Joseph Harford, Esqre. of Stapleton Bristol.

Statutes of the Garter in English on vellum. (30 leaves.) The Royal Arms on the binding, and the initials E. R.

No. 123. A 12mo. volume. Description of both the Universities of Cambridge and Oxford, with their arms and the arms of every college of both of them, with the first founders and principal benefactors to those Universities; drawn out of divers authors by A. Lewis, sometime student in Cambridge, as followeth. 326 pp. followed by mottoes of the peers, and some notes. The arms are coloured. A few pages are blank.

No. 124. A quarto volume written by Bishop Morley.

1. To his Excellency James Duke of Ormonde from his most humble and affectionate friend, George Worcester. Our doctrine concerning the Sacraments, especially the Eucharist or Lord's Supper.

Begins, The word Sacramentum or Sacrament is not in the Scriptures. *Ends,* (p. 62) and send him away abundantly satisfyed and refreshed by it.

(This treatise does not appear to have been printed.)

2. The argument drawn from the evidence and certainty of sense against the doctrine of Transubstantiation, &c. (21 pp.)

3. A vindication of this argument (drawn from sense against Transubstantiation) from a pretended answer to it by the author of a pamphlet called A treatise of the nature of the Catholick Faith and Heresy. Cap. 2., pp. 54, 55, 56. (28 pp.)

(The 2nd and 3rd items were printed in 1683.)

No. 127. Folio. 17th century. Arms and pedigrees of Essex families. (51 leaves + Index.) These descents following were taken in the last Visitation for the county of Essex by George Owen, alias York Herald, and Henry Lilly, Rouge. Rose, anno 1634.

No. 128. 12mo. Archbishop Laud's speech when beheaded. MS. of the period. (17 leaves, and a Latin translation.)

No. 131. Volume, paper, of the 16th century. (42 leaves, some blank.) The arms and names of knights, esquires, and gentlemen within the county of Leicester living in 1564, set out as it was performed by Robert Cook then Chester Herald; and index. The first name is Sir Thomas Neville, and the last is Everard of Shenton. " The original that this was copied forth of was done " on Velom in colours, in the hands of Henry Ferrars, " of Baddesley Clinton, co. Warwick, 1593."

No. 135. Folio. Commonplace book of Richard Symonds native of Black Notley, co. Essex, for which county he made collections in three volumes now in the Heralds College ; he was author of other MS. volumes preserved in the Harleian Library and other collections in the British Museum. His diary of the doings of the royal army during the civil wars printed by the Camden Society in 1859. Symonds was born in 1617. At p. 235 " my collection out of Smyth's lives of the Berkeleys, " p. 142," *Ends* 557 with an epitaph on Alexander Symonds in Latin. At the beginning is a list of books and records cited, 103 in all. Two columns, small writing, but all the pages are not filled ; at the end are two epitaphs dated in 1691. At p. 335, " my collections for

---

" Essex 1. 366." At p. 407 account of an earthquake at Withham, co. Suffolk, on Sept. 8th 1692 (558 pp.)

No. 137. Oblong folio, end of the 16th century. Pedigrees of Cheshire families, by J. Boothe, with arms, and sometimes illegitimate issue. There are some additions in 1613, and some even as late as 1655.

No. 138. Quarto, paper. Arms of all the gentlemen in Kent, temp. James I. Arms of Grey, Earl of Kent, at the foot of the title. (34 leaves. Nine coats of arms on each page arranged alphabotically. All the pages are not full. Arms and names only.

Three small volumes like narrow pocket books.

A pencil note says :—" They were found amongst the papers of the family of Viscount Ashbrook which were " in the possession of an attorney at Shipston-on-Stour, " and given by him to a boy, from whom I bought " them. They must have come to the attorney from " the Dowager Lady Ashbrook. Seem to be note books " of Thomas Flower,* of , who died in 1700, " and was father of the first Lord Castle Durrow." The dates of the notes are 1679, '80, &c. They do not seem to contain any new information.

Quarto. Copies (c. 1650) of Oxford and Cambridge documents.

1578, June 19th. Certificate of dispensation for non-residence to three beneficed persons. Addressed to Sir C. Wray, Chief Justice of England, and the others of the Queen's Bench, by the Vice-Chancellor. (Dudley, Earl of Leicester, was Chancellor.)

1578, Feb. 18th. Testimonial letter for a traveller, namely, Johannes Huldridius A. Gachnanus Tigurinus, who had staid eight months at Oxford ; by Dr. Martin Culpeper, V.C.

1576, July 6th. Lord Burghley, Chancellor, and the masters and scholars of the University to all. Testimony to the learning in Hebrew and Aramaic of " Philippum Burgannum Bignonnen : Britogallum."

License to eat flesh given by Daniel Barnard, Vice-Chancellor, to John Bale and Frances, his wife, residing at the University.

1520, January 15th. John Stokesley, Vice-President of Maudlin, to his fellows. On the 15th August 1520 they assembled to elect a president, and intend to proceed with it on the 30th. Summons them to appear before him on the day, and proceed with the election. Sealed with the seal of the Archdeacon of Oxford, because his own may not be known ; and D. Higden, LL.D., official of the archdeacon, has put his seal.

21 Eliz. Dr. Martin Culpeper, Vice-Chancellor, gives license (on the recommendation of Oliver Wythington, Med. Doc., Thomas Knowles, of Brasenose, A.M., and Stephen Rowsham, curate of the parish church of St. Mary, in the city of Oxford,) for John Dutton, of Cheshire, Esqre. (who is staying in the University), to eat flesh.

Oliver Withington, Dr. of Physic, Deputie of Martin Culpeper, the Vice-Chancellor, gives license to G.L., of the parish of St. Peter, in le baylye in Oxford, to kill and dress flesh and sell to persons who are sick and authorised to eat it in Lent.

To William Bishop of Lichfield and Coventry, John Underhill, Professor of Theology, sends greeting. Certificate that David Jenkyns, of Brasenose, had studied six years in Oxford, and was respectable.

27 Eliz., July 19th. John Wythens, D.D., Professor of Theology, late of Brasenose, now of Jesus, Griffin Lloyd, LL.D., Principal of Jesus, and Peter Manewe, Surgeon, of the University, came before Edmund Lillie, Professor of Theology, as Commissary of the Earl of Leicester, then Chancellor, and Justice of the Peace of Oxford and Berks, in a matter wherein one party is a privileged person. J. Wythens gives recognizance for 40l., the other two for 20l. each, to keep the peace towards Richard Aldworth.

Letter by Edmund Lillie to all, &c., giving notice of the above, and to forbear to arrest J. Wythens.

3rd Feb. Edmund Lillie's certificate that William Wright, clerk, student in Broadgates, has diligently studied a whole year.

A similar certificate for William Dier, who had studied for 10 years, with intervals, in Brasenose.

1590. Dec. 6th. Nicholas Bonde, D.D., the Vice-Chancellor, to Thomas Ynte, gentleman, collector of the subsidies, within the co. of Oxford, and his deputies. Certificate that Henry Jackson, maniple of All Souls, is taxed to subsidys, &c., according to the Quarter ; therefore he is not to be taxed otherwise.

---

* [I do not find that Thomas Flower was M.P

34 Eliz., Jan. 21st. William James D.D., and Vice-Chancellor to the High Sheriff, &c., &c., of the co. of Berks. The Chancellor, &c. have the view of the assize of weights. &c. Some of you have distrained a cow of William Noakes, cook of Magdalen Hall, because he brought not his bushel before H.M. Clerk of the Markets to Abington, co. Berks. Tells them to deliver up the cow, and not molest Noakes who is a privileged person.

W. James, D.D., Vice-Chancellor of Lord Buckhurst, to Thomas W———. License to teach the elements of grammar and Latin, and the art of writing, within the precincts of the University of Oxford.

Nicholas Bond, Professor of Theology, and Vice-Chancellor of Lord Buckhurst, certifies that Joseph Barnes, printer and bookseller, and Sampson Starkey, " pictor artis statuarie sive emblematum peritissimus" have long resided there respectably, and asks that they, going to Holland, and then returning to England and Oxford, may be assisted.

Certificate by Nicholas Bond, Vice-Chancellor of Sir C. Hatton, that Richard Hughes of Gloucester Hall, had studied for more than six years in the University, and had taken the degree of Bachelor of Arts.

1580, Dec. 6th. Martin Culpeper, M.D., warden of St. Mary's. Winton, in Oxford, and the scholars give to James Pollexfen, alias Polson, LL.B. the office of clerk and auditor of the accounts of all bailiffs.

(Fol. 20 b.) 1574, Jan. 21, 17th Eliz. Magdalen College, Oxford. Authentication by Lawrence Humphrey, Vice-Chancellor. attested by Robert Ponde, Gerbrand Harton, Conrad Miller, Richard Joyner, Nicholas Todde, and Nicholas Bodde, Notaries Public, of a notarial certificate by Thomas Collins, notary public, witnessed by Robert Ponde, LL.B., and official of the Archdeacon of Berks, John Bodinger, B.L., notary public, Nicholas Todde, and Richard Joyner—that on that day at the residence of Walter Bayly, M.D., Public Professor of Medicine, there appeared personally before Thomas Collins, notary public, and the witnesses named below, the said Walter Bayly and Anna his wife and appointed her father, Hermann Evans, then of Cologne, and Leonard Cruder, of Wassenberch, of Cologne, their joint and several proctors in a lawsuit wherein the said Walter Bayly and Anna his wife were plaintiffs, and Charles Awirdt (one of their relatives) was defendant, for the purpose of undoing a sale to the said Charles Awirdt of certain of their patrimonial goods at in the Duchy of Juliers and neighbouring places, made by the said Hermann Evans for less than half their real value.

1550, Oct. 10. Grant by the Warden and Fellows of Christ's Church, Oxford, to three persons (not named) of the next presentation to the parish church of Shipton, for the purpose of presenting thereto a fit person on the next avoidance.

26 Eliz., Feb. 12. Westminster. The Queen's warrant (issued by Wray, C.J.) to the Mayor and Bailiffs of Oxford, and the V.C. of the University, and the keeper of her prison of Bocardo there, to bring up the bodies of John Parrat, gentleman, Leonard Williams, gentleman, and Henry Aunsell (in their custody) before William Ayloffe, one of her justices, on the 27th of Feb. at Oxford.

Following the above is the answer of Thomas Thorneton, V. C. of the University.—He says that the three named in the writ were arrested within the precincts of the University at the suit before the V. C. of certain privileged persons, the Dean and Chapter of Oxford Cathedral, in a cause of Trespass sine damni injuria data ; and that the three refused and still refuse to give bail to appear and stand to a trial; therefore they were imprisoned. He pleads the Royal Charters which gave the University authorities cognizance of all pleas except those touching freeholds) within the Oxford and the suburbs, and the four hundreds adjoining, &c.

1590, Feb. 28. William James, Vice Chancellor (of Sir C. Hatton) licenses Cromwell Lee, Esq., to eat flesh during that Lent.

Commission by Edward Archbishop of York to . . . to visit Queen's College, Oxford.

Another form for a College not named.

Testimonial by the Master and Warden and Fellows of Clare Hall, Cambridge, to Edmund Bishop of Norwich, stating the fitness of Thomas Bond for orders.

1574, Feb. 24. Testimonial by Edward Hawford, Master of Christ's College, Cambridge, and some of the fellows, to Edmund Bishop of Peterborough, of the learning and good conduct of Michael G. one of his fellows.

Testimonial by . . to . . (for orders) in favour of W. T., Bachelor of Arts and Student at Clare Hall, Cambridge.

Form of appointment by E. Hownd, B.D., Master or Warden of Katherine Hall, Cambridge, and the fellows, of certain persons (not named) to be their proctors in suits affecting their College.

1579, July 28. Court at Greenwich. Sir C. Hatton to the Vice Chancellor and other his assistants.—Finding that R. B., a poor scholar, had been expelled from Caius College by the Master and some of the fellows thereof, he asks that as R. B. had been admitted a fellow on the Queen's letter of recommendation, the V. C. would examine the matter, and restore him to his place.

23 Eliz., Oct. 27. Certificate by Andrew Perne, V. C. of Cambridge, to the Queen and her Council, &c., &c. that Francis Bertie was a perpetual fellow of King's College, Cambridge, and a scholar and Bachelor of Arts, and therefore entitled to the privileges of the University.

14 Eliz., May 19. The Queen to the V. C., Regents, and Non-regents of the University of Cambridge.—Inasmuch as William'Falke, B.D., is required to attend upon the Earl of Lincoln the High Admiral of England, she requests that he may be admitted to the degree of D.D. notwithstanding his absence for the short time, which otherwise would be required from him.

1642, April 28. Testimonial by Gilbert Sheldon, the Master, and the fellows of All Souls College, Oxford, that John Wainewright, M.A., and fellow of the College had resided seven years, very learned and perfectly orthodox, and fit for any employment in Church or State.

Blank form of appointment of Proctors for an Appeal. Another blank form in the same matters ; with a reference to p. 210 (evidently of the book containing the original form.)

Such fees as have been and are usually payable in the Chancellor's Court of the University of Oxford; sub manu Registrarii Rogeri Jones, viz.—(the items occupy 4 pages, among them are—

Pro generali privilegio, præter sigillum, 8s. ;—rarissimè.

Pro licentiâ ad mactandum carnes, 4s. } obs.(obso-
Pro licentiâ ad edendum carnes, 2s. 6d. } lete ?)

Pro præcepto custodi { Carceris } 12d.
                     { Bocardo }

Pro certificatorio afferentium pisces marinas et alia victualia aliunde empta ; præter sigillum, 3s. 4d.

Pro certificatorio pauperi scholaris peregrini, 12d. —Obs.

Fees for excommunication and absolution.

1644. Jan. 30. The President and Scholars of Corpus Christi College, Oxford, appoint John Hillersden, B.D., and James Hyde, M.A., of Magdalen College, their general proctors. (2½ pp.)

1624. July 29. William, Earl of Pembroke, High Chamberlain of the King's Household, and Chancellor of the University of Oxford, to all, &c. After reciting that Joseph Barnes in his lifetime not only kept a printing office, but also, by license to him and to his wife Barbara, built and kept a tavern in Oxford; and that he died, leaving his wife and children almost reduced to poverty ; specially his wife Barbara and his daughter Anne ;—He, the Chancellor, gives and confirms to the said Barbara and Anne, and the survivor, license to carry on in Oxford in the house so built by Joseph Barnes in the parish of St. Mary the Virgin, and elsewhere, in the University, the business of selling all kinds of wine by all lawful measures.

Latin Statute prescribing the books and time of study before the degree of Bachelor of Arts, and fines for non-attendance on Lectures. (3 pp.)[*]

A decree that the following course of study was to be followed, and the following writers to be explained. In Grammar, either Linacro or Virgil or Horace, or some portion of Cicero's Epistles. In Rhetoric, either the Præceptiones or Orations of Cicero, or the books of Aristotle on Rhetoric. In Dialectics, either the Institutes of Porphirius or Aristotle on Dialectics. Boethius or Gemma Frisius in Arithmetica. In Music, Boetius. In Geometry, Euclid: Orontius on the Sphere, or John de Sacrobosco, in Astronomy: Aristotle on Physics or his work on the Heaven and the World, or his work of Meteors, or his work De Parvis Naturalibus, or concerning the Soul in Natural Philosophy. In Moral Philosophy, Aristotle on Ethics, or his work on Politics, or Plato on

* These do not appear in the Munimenta Academica. Ed., Anstey. (Rolls Series.)

a Republic. In Metaphysics, Aristotle on Metaphysics. Let the above be explained in the Schools.—A student must be four years in the University before he can be a Bachelor of Arts ; of this period he is to devote two terms to Grammar, four to Rhetoric, five to Dialectics, three to Arithmetic, two to Music. Then for three years more he is to master other things, devoting two terms to Geometry, two to Astronomy, three to Natural Philosophy, Moral Philosophy, two to Metaphysics. Then he may go for the degree of M.A. (The reference to Linacre shows that this regulation must be temp. Hen. VIII. or later ; therefore it does not appear in the Munimenta Academica, edited by Mr. Anstey for the Rolls Series in 1868.)

(Fo. 27–34.) Nova Academiæ Oxon. Statuta.

1. Pro Scholaribus. *Begins*, Vetera Statuta observabunt.

17. Statuta de vestitu et ornatu corporis &c.

(Fo. 34 b.–44.) Statuta de modo litigandi ex Libro Senioris Procuratoris descripta, ex. fol. 70. *Begin*, Cum advocatorum. (Some are printed in the Munimenta Academica.) At fo. 42 b. are extracts from the Senior Proctors book, fol. 103 of Statutes published 13 March 1515. Warham Archbishop of Canterbury being the Chancellor and John Cottiford and William Fossey being Proctors.

(Fo. 44 b.–50.) Other statutes extracted from the Senior Proctor's book ; some against carrying weapons, &c., &c., A.D. 1313, and one in 1482 about those who are privileged to carry them.

(Fo. 49 b.–50 b.) An Act of Convocation, 22 Feb. 1592, about Appeals.

(Fo. 52–55.) Decrees of the Convocation for the better observation of the publiq exercises and avoyding of some disorders in the Universitie, 1576, October.

(Fo. 55 b.–57.) Decrees and orders made by authority of the Convocation, holden 23 and 27 June 1576, for reformation of excesse and some disorders in apparel.

(Fo. 58–60.) Latin preface or epilogue for a compilation of the statutes of the University ; briefly noticing what had been done in the times of Hen.8., Edw. 6, and Queen Mary and lastly of the Earl of Pembroke and the Archbishop of Canterbury under the patronage of King Charles.

(Fo. 63–75.) 14 Hen. VIII., April 1. Charter of the King to the University of Oxford, granted at the instance of Wolsey.

(Fo. 75–82.) 1575, May 12. Orders made by the Lords of the council, &c. for the composing of the controversies between the University and City of Oxford, &c.

(Fo. 83–86.) 1 Mary, 2 May. Charter by Queen Mary granting to the University the rectories of Southperwin, co. Cornwall, Olnescroft, co. Leicester, and Holme Cultram, co. Cumberland, and the chapel of Newton Arloche.

86 b.–93. 7 Eliz., 27 January. Inspeximus and confirmation of various charters to the University of Oxford.

The Proctor's Book cited in the above volume is that called B. by Mr. Anstey in "Munimenta Academica," edited by him in 1868 for the Rolls Series, and several of the items are printed by Mr. Anstey.

(Several quires are absent from the volume.)

In a folio. The rental from 1657 to 1665 of the Shirley property. Expenses of building the church of Stanton Harold, the only church in England built temp. Oliver Cromwell, for which Sir R. Shirley, father of the

first Lord Ferrers, was fined 1,000l. " Since he is so " fond of building churches," quoth Cromwell, " and so " rich, he shall build me a ship."

A volume of original letters laid down.

1602. Aug. 16th. George Ryves, Vice-Chancellor of Oxford, to George Shirley, thanking him for a present of 40l. to the new library lately erected by the worthy Mr. Thomas Bodley, with a copy of the list of books purchased from the register of benefactors.

1699. April 27th. Thomas Lord Weymouth to Lord Ferrers, enclosing agreement made by his agent, Mr. Dobbs, with a proposed tenant for those lands which my Lord is willing to give up to Lord Ferrers.

1695 and 1706. Two letters from the same to the same.

12th century. 8vo. vellum (71 leaves). De Officio Missæ.

Oratio Sacerdotum (5 leaves).
De Sancta Maria. (A prayer to her.)
Alia. (A longer prayer.)
Oracio penitentialis.
De offerenda (long).
De oblatione (short).
De silentio post offerenda (long).
De secreta.
De Te igitur.
Qui pridie quam pateretur usque in mei memoriam.
Materia (long disquisition on it).
Intentio.
Utilitas.
Unde et memores domine usque calicem salutis perpetuo, &c.
Norma recte credendi.
Ratio Sancti Augustini de Anima.
In libro Officiorum.
Ex ordine Romanorum.
A gustinus in libro de verbis Domini.
A gustinus ad Paulinum.
Augustinus in epistola ad Felicem.

DEEDS.

34 Ed. III.   Pardon to Sir Thomas Shirley for the death of John Waryn of Lockesley ; Ita tamen quod stet recto.

34 Ed. III. Two receipts by Milicent, the widow of John Waryn, for 20l., in two sums, paid by Shirley for the death of John Waryn.

20 Ric. II., Dec. 6th.   Seal, circular, two inches. Sigillum Willelmi de Bellocampo. A fess gules, between six cross crosslets or, a crescent for difference.

21 Ric. II. A bond by the King to the Abbat of Pershore in 20 marks lent. (Part of the Great Seal in white wax.)

20 Hen. VI.   W. de Ferrars, Lord of Groby.   Seal, circular, two inches.   A shield charged with seven mascels voided.

20 Hen. VI.   John Bishop of Bath, John Viscount Beaumont, William Lord Lovel, Richard Lord Grey of Wilton, and John Durward, Esqre.   Large seals of Bath, Beaumont, and Lovel.   Power of attorney to give seisin of the manors of Heath and Fekenho, in the counties of Oxford and Warwick.

To Mr. Shirley I must express my thanks for his kind hospitality at Ettington Hall.

ALFRED J. HORWOOD.

THE MANUSCRIPTS OF JOHN RICHARD PINE COFFIN,
ESQ., AT PORTLEDGE, NORTH DEVON.

(Second Report.)

Since the date of writing my first Report upon the ancient deeds and muniments preserved at Portledge, a further search has been made, by Mr. Pine Coffin's direction, which has resulted in the finding of a vast number of old documents and letters, of various descriptions. With his sanction, a selection from them, to the extent of some hundreds, has been made by me; the whole of which have been since subjected to examination, with the following results:—

The earliest among the ancient rolls is a Computus, or Account (in Latin), of John Walter, Provost, or Reeve, of the manor of Monkelegh, (near Great Torrington, in the county of Devon) for the 37th year of King Edward III. (A.D. 1363). The account consists of three long skins of parchment, sewed together; rendered illegible, at the beginning, by damp. A few items are here extracted from it, as indicating ancient names of localities, or illustrating the state of agriculture in those days.

The Receipts come under the heads of "Rents of "assize" (assessed rents), "Ferm of the mill and the "fishery," the mill being that of "Frisenam," and the fishery being "in the water called Torryg:" "Sales of "Wheat;" "Sales of Stores;" "Sales of labour (ope-"rum):" "Issues of the Manor;" "Perquisites of Court;" "Sales over and above the account." 29s. are received for "one bull and 3 cows, sold, witness, David Carswylle:" 12d. for "one mutton sold, arising from the heriot of "William Church ende;" 12d. for 4 geese, and 22½d. for 15 hens. Under "Issues of the Manor," the milk of 10 cows fetches 15s. for the year. Pastures, or feeding-grounds, are let in various localities in the manor, called "Python," or "Pychon," "Ridmore," "the "Merch near Loxford," and "Lobbethorn;" and a rent of 2s. is received for "the Sand-Way."

The Account then goes on to expenditure, under the heads of "Costs of buildings and dove-house;" "Neces-"sary costs, and Fold expenses;" "Hoeing and reaping;" "Grinding of grain;" "Autumn expenses;" "Out-"door payments;" "Livery (in kind) and stipends to "reapers, with wages;" "Moneys paid (to the lord)."—A woman "hired to pull out the straw for (covering) the "hall of the grange" receives 2d. Thomas Kens receives 8s. "for making the pigeon-house, by the job." One peck of oatmeal costs 3d., one peck of salt 2d. A charge of 2s. is entered for reaping the field called "Wylhay." Walter de Stephynstone receives 40s. for his fee, as steward of Mounkelegh and Mountolme; with various items on holding each of the Lord's Courts. The shep-herd receives 3s. for 36 weeks, his "livery" in wheat being entered on the other side, but effaced by damp: repair of his house is elsewhere mentioned. Payment to the lord is made "through the hands" of various persons, among them, "Dan (Dompnus) Denis;" an ecclesiastic, elsewhere called "Frater," or "Brother," Denis. This Denis receives also, for himself, 10s. 7d. "by tally," with 2 geese. William Penros is named as the preceding Reeve.

On the obverse of the roll, the beginning of which is illegible, particulars are entered as to the then stock upon the farm, and its increase, or receipts, in kind: 3 salmon are received "as rent," and "one pound of "pepper, proceeding from the rent of Peatecumbe;" a payment in kind which originated by deed in the time of Edward I., and is still received yearly by Mr. Pine Coffin, as representing the then grantor of the land. Two bushels of apples represent the whole of the garden produce in store. John Walter was evidently not looked upon as a trusty reeve, for many of his items in the latter list are crossed out by the "lord and auditors," and he is surcharged in respect of them. Thus whereas he makes out that there are 10 of the last year's geese on the farm, and but 6 of the produce, the later number is scored out, and 20 is substituted. His "petition for "favour" as "the late reeve," is attached to the roll; in which, among other things, he says that he has been surcharged for 17 geese (as having been sold by him) 5s. 8d.; but that there was "default of produce" to the amount of 14, and that a fox ran away with the three others. An interlineation states that he was allowed a reduction upon this item, to the extent of 3s. 4d.

The next Computus, in date, is that of Richard atte Hole, Reeve of Monkelegh in 43, 44 Edward III. (A.D. 1369, 70). 12 pence is entered as received for clay dug at Clampitte; places called "Cloynsysyre" and "Ridde" are also mentioned. For "one pair of thick "gloves" the charge is 3d., and for one "gesse" (a ringed

strap for the legs) for falcons 3d. 3 stone of cheese, costing 2s. 3d., and butter costing 22d., are bought for the labourers working in autumn : luxuries that are not to be found in those days, in connexion with that class, in other parts of England. They do not seem, however, on this occasion to have had any ale or cider given them. Bread for 18 "customary tenants," who carried the lord's hay, cost 16d., and one stone of cheese for them 8d. Mowing the meadow called "Medpark" cost 19d.; men being paid 2d. for tossing and getting in the hay. A portion of this Computus, which is also in a mutilated state, is illegible.

Computus of Simon Atte Warde, Reeve, or Provost, of Monkeleigh, 17 and 18 Richard II. (A.D. 1393, 4); partly illegible from damp. Loxdoune, Playstrete, Lorwex, Bordmourmede, and Okewell More, are places mentioned. A stack of wheat is sold, in gross, by the lord to John Stewlake, for 22s. 4d. The lord also sold, in gross, to Ralph Daubon, 43 sheep, 3 "hoggesters," and 39 lambs, for 60s. A reeder was paid 3s. 7d. for working at the grange 9 days, covering the hall, kitchen, and cowhouse (if that is the meaning of "baiers.") Gloves bought for the bailiff, the reeve, and servant, of the lord, cost 6d.: the latter, Martin Southleigh, by name, had 10s. yearly for his wages. When the lord visited the place, about the Feast of St. Peter (29th June), 23d. was spent for ale. "Paid a man for his expenses for carrying "4 salmon to Mountags 7d." The Monastery of Mente-oute, in Somerset, is meant. Sir Walter atte Zoo [Yeo] is pardoned 6d. for his rent of assize. As to the geese on the farm, 4 were given to a monk of Barstapul by the lord : one was consumed by John Glovere, when engaged on the business of the lord ; another by John, the lord's servant, just before Michaelmas; and 4 when the lord was there; at which time also 3 hens were eaten.

Another of these rolls contains proceedings of the "Law Court of the Manor of Parkeham," in the county of Devon, in the 20th and 21st years of Edward IV. (A.D. 1481-2). Its contents are of but little interest: John Drew is to be distrained to make his part of a foss on the south side of the vill of Brodeaysshe ; a foal of black colour has been found astray at Southerdowne ; Alice, the wife of John Bolyn, surrenders, to the use of Thomas Seller the younger, a tenement called "Olde Mille," the lord's fee thereon being one cow, valued at 3s. 10d. The Decenniers (or Jury) also present that Baldwin Vaggescombe, John Beare, John Nicholle, and Robert Mattecote, have severally broken the assize, by making, each of them, one brewing of ale; for which they are severally fined 4 pence. John Fortescu, Richard Robyne, John atte Combe, John Borisdone, and John Gyffard, are severally fined for neglecting to appear, as owing suit of court, the first four 3d. each, and Gyffard one penny. Thomas Bagilhole and Robert Mattecote are sworn into office as Ale-tasters. John Dure makes plaint against John Drewe that he has committed a trespass, by stopping up the way at Venyate. John Deare "puts himself upon inquisition "against John Mussell, in a plea of debt, for that he "detains one yard and a half of woollen cloth, of "red colour, to the value of 15d., delivered to him "at Parkeham for safe keeping for the said com-"plainant." A similar plaint is also made as to de-tainer of 2 pounds of white wool, delivered at Brude-aysshe to the same John Mussell.—These entries seem to indicate that woollen cloth was then made in this place.—Plaint is also made against Richard Holecombe, that he stopped up the way at Langelonde. In addition to the preceding, there are several other ancient Ac-count rolls, more or less defaced by damp.

The three following deeds, found among Mr. Pine Coffin's papers, deserve notice, as containing names of ancestors of John Gay, the poet, (whose family after-wards removed to Barnstaple) and of Risdon, the histo-rian of Devon. Both of these families were connected with the manor of Goldsworthy, in the parish of Park-ham, in North Devon.

Indented copy, on parchment, of an Inquisition (in Latin) taken at Great Torrington, in the county of Devon, on the 15th of November in the 22nd year of King Henry VII. (A.D. 1506), before Richard Garlond, the King's Escheator, on the oath of John Holbeme (or Holbeine) and eleven other jurors; who find that John Gaye, late of Gulworthy, was seised of the manor of Gulworthy at the time of his death, and of lands in Kyngysforde, in the parish of Kentysbere, and in Neuland and Columptonc, and elsewhere.

A parchment deed, or copy of court roll, in good condition, bearing date the 21st of April, in the 8th year of Elizabeth (A.D. 1566). It states (in Latin) that Philip Risdon, William Risdon, and John Risdon, in presence of certain tenants of the manor of Goldworthie, (in North Devon) had, out of court, surrendered into the hands of the lord a tenement situate in Stoke, within the said manor, to the use of Thomas Vyvyn, alias Fayne, Thomasin, his wife, and, Philippa, their daughter, upon payment to the said Philip Risdon of 46 *li.* Whereupon, the said Thomas, Thomasin, and Philippa, had appeared in court, and had received the said tenement from Thomas Gaye, Esquire, lord of the said manor of Goldworthy, and Alice, his wife, for the term of their lives and the life of the longest liver of them; they paying yearly 8s. 9½d. to the said lord and his wife, their heirs, and the assigns of the said lord, together with two days' ploughing, and two days' reaping, yearly, in autumn. There are two small seals attached, and the words are written at the foot (evidently with great difficulty),—"By me, Thomas Gay." Another signature, probably intended for that of Alice Gay, is only an unintelligible scrawl.

A long parchment indenture, in English, dated the 29th of August, in the 21st year of Elizabeth (A.D. 1579), made between Giles Risdon, of Parkcham, in the county of Devon, and William Risdon, his son, executors of the last will and testament of Antony Risdon, deceased, another son of the said Giles, and John Coffyn, of Portledge, Esquire. A term of 60 years had been granted by Alice Gay, widow of John Gay, in the 16th year of the same reign, in the capital messuage and barton of Gouldworthy, otherwise West Gouldworthy, in the county of Devon, to Philip Risdon, another son of the said Giles; which Philip assigned the said term to Antony, whose executors now assign to the said John Coffyn, for the unexpired part of the said term of years. There are two wax seals attached; one of them, apparently, representing a figure standing before a tree, has somewhat the appearance of being the impression of an ancient gem.

The Letters in the possession of Mr. Pine Coffin, belonging to the latter half of the seventeenth century, are very numerous; being, nearly all of them, addressed to his ancestor, Richard Coffin, of Portledge (who was High Sheriff of Devon in 1685,) or to members or connexions of his family; his second wife being a daughter of Edmund Prideaux, of Padstow, in Cornwall. These letters, with a few miscellaneous papers, are exactly six hundred in number: and the following is some account of a number which have been selected for notice, commencing with sixteen of a miscellaneous nature, arranged in chronological order.—

" Honoured Sir. Since my last, the face of things " heer outwardly is much changed, and our hopes at " present for such men as might bee truly serviceable, " are very small: a resolution (as they give out) is " taken up by the chief ones heer to make choice of " no one but he that is actually a burgesse. And ac- " cordingly, to render him capable by that rule, and in " order to his election (as is conceived) Mr. Nic: Denys " was yesterday made a burgesse; and another of this " towne (as the rumor goes) is pitch't on also. So that " your friends that desired to serve you (and in you the " publique interest) are at a stand, and know not how " to proceed. However, we shall observe how things are " carryed, and if an oportunity present, it shall be taken " hold of, and improved by, Sir, Your very reall friend " and servant, J. Hanmer. Barstaple, 23th March 1659." Addressed. " To the Worshipfull his much honoured " friend Richard Coffin, Esquire, at his house at Port- " ledge, these present." Written in a beautifully neat and legible hand. This is probably the nearest approach that Mr. Richard Coffin ever made towards obtaining a seat in Parliament.

A Letter from Edmund Prideaux, of Padstow, in Cornwall, (father of Humphrey Prideaux, Dean of Norwich,) to his daughter, Mrs. Ann Coffin, dated October 27th 1678. The Romish plot, denounced by Dr. Tongue and Titus Oates, is here alluded to.—" The con- " spiracie against the life of the King appeares everie " daye worse and worse, exceeding the Gunpowder " Treason, and I feare the danger is not yet over, in " regard Sir Edmond Godfrey, a justice of peace, who " had been active against them, was found dead, being " baselie murdered by them, not far from his house. " I beseeech God to prepare us, everie daye, for the " worst of times." In reference to family matters, he says,—" Will Pendarves and his wife [the writer's " daughter] returned hither from Werington, where " it seemes their entertainment was greater and more " noble than ever your husband and you, or your mother " and myself, at anie time, met with there." There are eight other letters in the collection, written by Edmund Prideaux the elder, who died in 1683. They

are very legible, and written in a beautiful hand. Werington, near Launceston, was the seat of Sir William Morice.

A Letter from Edmund Prideaux to his sister, Mrs. Ann Coffin, dated London, 2nd May 1685, the year of the Shrievalty of her husband, Richard Coffin. The following is an extract, in reference to the coach which she had lately set up.—" Your coachman is a silly fellow, to " tell you that your coach is too high to bring to Port- " ledge; for I had it made one purpose for your roads, " and 'tis noe higher then the other coaches that are " made for the gentlemen of Devon; for he that made " it, doth worke for most of the gentry of Devon. It " seemes the coachman is afraid of spoyling his face in " our busshie lanes, for his head will be at least two " foote higher then the toppe of the coache. If you " doe resolve to make it lower, you will only spend " your money to spoyle the coach."

A Letter, with a list of books inclosed, thus labelled, in Richard Coffin's hand:—" Mr. Dight's letter, wherein " he gives mee an account of the bookes bought for " mee at the auction of Dr. Heinsius, in Holland; but " not dated, but received about the beginning of June " 1683."

A copy of a Letter sent by the Mayor of Taunton to the Mayor of Exeter, such copy being sent to Richard Coffin, as the then High Sheriff of the county of Devon: —" Sir. By the inclosed copies of 2 letters intercepted " in these partes, you may perceave an intencion of an " insurrection forthwith in the west, and this day an " examination of a miller and wife was taken upon oath " before Mr. Justice Tymewell, that aboute 80 horsemen, " supposed armed, did passe, about one of the clocke " this morninge, a byway near this towne of Taunton, " and soe into a part of the west of England. Wee have " apprehended and secured five suspicious persons in " our towne; and now tis fair time many persons " pretending busines to the fair, flock to Exeter, tis " desired and not doubted but that your Worship will " make strict scrutiny in Exeter, and keepe watch and " ward, and send to the remaining deputy lieutenants " to get up your militia of your county; other militia " are up. Bee pleased to examine the letters that come " this post. Excuse haste From your servant Ber. " Smith, Maior of Taunton. If your Worship thinke " fitt to disarme all persons that come into your gates, " and persons already lodged in the innes; for tis " supposed the beginning wil bee at the fair. Taunton " June the 1, 85. To the Right Worshipful the Mayor " of Exeter, or, in his absence, to his representative, " These. This is a true copy." This commotion, it deserves to be remarked, took place nearly a fortnight before the Duke of Monmouth's landing at Lyme Regis, in Dorset.

A Letter, written to Mr. Richard Coffin, by Sir George Chudleigh, dated " Ashton, the 12th of September " 1685," in a very firm and legible hand:—" Honored " Sir. I am very sorry the infirmitys of my old age " will not permit mee to attend you with my personall " service at this solemnity, and to congratulate the " honor and happines of your place and authority at " this tyme. But to supply the defects of my old age, " and to testify the true and sincere affection I beare " unto your person and famaly, which hath beene of " ancient acquaintance and alliance, I have ordered " this bearer to present you with the venison of the " best bucke my parke affords at this tyme, which " humbly craves your acceptance, as a testimony of " that affectionate and ready service I owe you, and to " assure you that were my abillityes answereable to my " desires, no friend in the world should be more ready " to obey your commandes then Sir Your most humble " servant and affectionate kinsman George Chudleigh."

A short Letter, written by Sir William Morice, of Werington, to Mr. Richard Coffin, Sheriff of Devon, in 1685:—" Sir. I was in hope you would have saved the " expense of another assizes, but since it falls out other- " wise, my men shall not fail to wait upon you at Cre- " diton at the time appointed. My daughters and my " sister went this day to Dunsland . . . but Sir John " Carew is not with them . . . Your affectionate kins- " man and servant Will. Morice." He was son of the Secretary of State, of the same name. Richard Coffin's wife's brother-in-law, Mr. Bickford, lived at Dunsland.

A Letter to Richard Coffin, written by John Prince, author of the " *Worthies of Devon* " (publ. 1701).— " Hon^d Sir. According to my promise, and your many- " fold obligations on me, I have sent you Mr. Hooker's " Chorography and History of the Province of Devon " (as he calls it). I should desire it may be carefully " preserv'd, and, as soon as conveniently you may, re-

"turn'd. There ar many things of good note in it,
"which with other collections I have made, and
"farther intended to have procured, I had some-
"tymes the vanity to have thoughts of printing for the
"good of our country. But I am glad, Sir, that that
"undertakeing is like to be the province of one soe
"excellently qualefyed, both with learning, judgment,
"manuscripts, leisure, and estate, as yourselfe, which
"I hope you fully purpose and intend. . . . It is all
"att present from him who is, kind Sir, your most
"obliged and affectionate friend and servant John
"Prince. Berry Pomray Mar. 20th 1686."

A Letter from John Blake, Mayor of Barnstaple, to
Richard Coffin, dated 14 February 1686(7), and beginning :—"Honored Sir. Accordinge to your charitable
"intention, I have taken advise for distribution of the
"five pounds amongst the poore Protestants that fled
"hither from France, that by reason of the markett
"day being the Frayday, and the Saterday being
"throng with businesse of the towne, I could only
"acquaint Mr. Mosee, the minister, and Mr. Barber,
"an honest merchant, that also is to give you a list of
"the persons, and of what is given to them."

The following is an extract from a Letter of Edmund
Prideaux, brother of Humphrey, to his sister, Mrs. Ann
Coffin, dated "London 12 September 1688." After
stating that he had married, six weeks since, a widow,
who "had a good fortune both in land and money," he
continues,—"The news you had in the country about
"the distruction of Smyrna by an earthquake and
"fier is too true, for I have the misfortune to feele it
"severely, having a good estate there devoured by the
"fire, that hath laid the whole citty in ashes, after it
"was levealed to the ground by the earthquake."
The writer was a Turkey merchant, and lived at Crosby
Square, in the City.

A Letter of news, written to Richard Coffin by Mr.
Henry Brayley, from "Bydeford, Tewsday 16th 88"—
endorsed as meaning "16th Ocotober 1688." The invasion by the Prince of Orange being anticipated,—"I
"heer that all women and children are put out of the
"Tower, as being uslis; . . . and som hav bin with
"the King, desiring he will introst the Tower with
"Protestantes, but no anserr ; and that such a on cam
"from Holand by way of France, and tels the King
"the Prince of Oring went abord the fleet the 3 in-
"atent with 16 or 17 thousand gentelmen, as volun-
"teers with him . . . I heer also that our letter today
"spoke of som 16 or 17 seymen prest at London, and
"sent down the river by barg with a file of mosco-
"teeres ; bot the seymen threw the moscoteers over
"bord, and so got away."

A Letter from Edmund Prideaux to Mrs. Ann Coffin,
dated London 2nd July 1689 : in it is this passage.—
"Sir John Berry, by his Majesty's comand, is this day
"gone for Plymouth, where hee will bee the begining
"of the next weeke ; his business, as I understande,
"is to see if (there) bee any place there to make docks
"for accomedating our men of warr, in case they
"should want reparation when they put into the port.
". . . I doubt whether hee have time to visit his friends
"in the north of Devon."

A Letter written by John Coffin, to his father, Mr.
Richard Coffin, when at school, under a Mr. Rainer, at
some place not named ; in the beginning of the year
1695, immediately after the death of Queen Mary :—
"When orders was given that every one should go into
"mourning for the Queen, some Jacobite hung Tyburne
"in mourning, with a paper fastened to it, with this
"inscription on it,—' I mourn, because you dyed not
"' here.' The Jacobites in Bristol caused the bells to
"bo rung out, and went dansing through the streets,
"with musick playing,—' The King shall enjoy his own
"' again.' Almost every one here hath put himself
"and his fimily in moorning. Most of the gentle-
"mens' sons in our school aro in moarning, excepting
"myself. If you intend that wee should go in moarn-
"ing, (which is very fit we should), I desire you would
"send me word by tomorrow or next duy at farthest,
"that it may be rred by Munday." John Coffin afterwards was a member of Wadham College, Oxford, succeeded his father in the estate at Portledge in 1699, and
died in 1703, leaving a widow, but no issue. He was
succeeded by his younger brother, Richard, a Spanish
merchant, in London.

A Letter from John Prideaux, at London, dated the
18th of September 1698, to his aunt, Mrs. Ann Coffin :
the following is an extract :—"As to the condition of our
"trade, (it) is mostly to Barbary, at Tetuan, and the
"adjacent places thereabouts. We furnish the people
"mostly with cloth, exported from England, about 6

"shillings a yard ; we most commonly send mixt
"cloths, that is, of severall dyes and colours, and also,
"several species of cloths. . . . What we have ex-
"ported from Barbary, is cheifly wax, dates, ouchancal,
"estridge [ostrich] feathers, and hides ; but the greatest
"thing we trade in is wax ; and that and most of things
"I mention, we send to Cadix from Barbary. At Cadix
"we have a correspondent that sells those commodities
"there, and make[s] us return home in wine or bills of
"exchange. . . . As for my couzen, I doubt not but
"that in little time my master would qualifie him for
"a merchant, but I cant promise as to other matters.
"He is a man of a very penetrating witt, very ingenious,
"proper not only to commence butt to carry on and
"accomplish any enterprise with success. He was
"a slave in Sally [Sallee] ; but being so very under-
"standing above the rest of the captives, was sent to
"King Charles from the King of the Moors with let-
"ters, as an ambassador, to treat about the redemp-
"tion of captives. Had not such a thing happnd,
"he would be a slave to this day." Though the
writer complains of his want of education, this letter is
very neatly written, and the spelling is superior to that
mostly seen at that day. This John Prideaux was probably a son of John Prideaux, a brother of Dr. Prideaux and Mrs. Ann Coffin. In some portions of Dr.
Prideaux's Correspondence a John Prideaux, a nephew,
is alluded to, as having come to ruin ; and John Prideaux,
the brother, in one of these letters, is mentioned in
strongly disparaging terms.

A Letter from John Coffin to his mother, Mrs. Ann
Coffin, dated at Versailles, November 30, 1699. He had
recently left Oxford, and was now on his travels. The
following is an extract.—"If the danger of traveling in
"these parts is the only objection you have to make
"against my journey the next spring, I finde noe
"obsticle at all, for a traveller may with more safety
"pass thro' France then England, robberys not being
"soe frequent, and the people as obligeing. And as to
"their religion, as it is not much observ'd, soe is little
"or never talkd of in company, except by some bigoted
"priests, who make it their business to exclaim against
"all other opinions, except their owne. Such sort of
"people I take care to avoide, or if by chance I hit
"into their company, I have no reason to declare my
"religion, when it will doe me nor noe body els any
"service, but only contrary, cause broils and cavels
"between us."

A Letter from John Coffin to his mother, dated from
Genoa, 18th May 1701, giving an interesting account
of that place. The following are some extracts :—"I
"now am at Genua the Superb, as they call it, and
"indeed it deserves that title ; for in all my travells I
"never saw any one towne soe full of pallaces, soe-
"magnificent and stately : but the pride of the people
"is intollerable ; the nobles are distinguishd into two
"classes, the antient and modern, and those of the
"antient rank are soe haughty, as they will not visit
"nor converse with those of the second, nor marry into
"their family, tho' they are tenn times as rich. The
"Doge is almost a perpetual prisoner ; never goes out
"of his pallace without leave of the Senate. The Italians
"are very grave ; the nobility, both men and women,
"weare black flowerd silck, and this habit distinguishes
"'em from the citizens, who generally goe in coloured
"cloaths. . . . Perhaps you have heard of the warlike
"Amazons of this city in the time of the Holy Wars,
"when the greatest parte of the ladys of quality went
"to engage themselves in that war ; they story is here
"still very memorable, and their armour is now re-
"polished in the arcenall."

Two Latin speeches which were spoken at Bideford,
(in the Grammar School, probably,) on St. George's Day
1685, in honour of the Coronation of King James. The
writing is very distinct, and the copy, not improbably,
was handed to Richard Coffin, as being present as High
Sheriff of Devon, on this occasion. The two speeches
are not merely complimentary, but adulatory to ful-
someness, in a remarkable degree.

A very long paper, occupying from 6 to 7 sides of
foolscap, closely written, in a beautiful hand, and
headed,—"Reasons humbly offerd to the Duke of Albe-
"marle, against his going Governor of Jamaica." The
whole "revenue of the Government" is but 2500 li.
yearly. It is spoken of as "such a pittiful one (com-
"mission) as has noe other competitor for it but Sir
"Th. O.;" and it continues, — "Besides, doe you not
"thinke the same people will use you as they did when
"you were in the west and at Whitehall? They will
"have continuall spyes upon you, and misinterpretb
"every thing you do." Christopher Monk, Duke of

J. R. PINE
COFFIN,
Esq.

Albemarle, to whom this long Expostulation is addressed, accepted the governorship of Jamaica, in spite of this remonstrance, in 1687, and died in that island in 1688. Hans Sloane accompanied him, as his physician. Towards the close of this ably written paper, the author of which is not named, the following passage occurs :—
" That you may know that this is not mine alone, but
" the generall voice of the whole towne, read but all
" the lampoons with which the town hath swarmed of
" late ; which, though otherwise not much to be re-
." garded, yet when so very universall, they shew at
" least the sense of the times ; for the voice of every
" body is called the voice of God [Vox populi, vox Dei],
" and thus one of them speaks :—
" Let a disbanded peere, kicked out of Court,
" And made some upstart statesmans common sport,
" Sneake like a dog, and beg he may be sent
" With a great character to banishment.
" Since he is pleased to be made such a tool
" What's that to me :—
There are 5 or 6 more lines to the same purpose."
Not improbably, Richard Coffin was the author of this Expostulation.

In addition to the preceding there are 41 miscellaneous letters and papers, not here noticed, eight of them written by Edmund Prideaux to his daughter, Mrs. Ann Coffin, and one by her mother, Bridget Prideaux : one also the writing of Bridget (Bokenham), the wife of Dr. Prideaux. There are also 21 letters, in addition to those above quoted, from Edmund Prideaux to his sister, Anne Coffin.

Mr. Thomas Northmore, of St. Thomas's, Exeter, was Assistant Deputy Sheriff to Mr. Richard Coffin, in his year of office as Sheriff, in 1685 ; a year made memorable by Monmouth's abortive attempt to deliver this country from the rule of James the Second. The following is a selection of extracts from nine of the letters written by Mr. Northmore during this period, there being 26 in all preserved.—

8 June 1685. . . "[The] Duke of Albemarle, with
" Major Walker, came hither y[esterday] ; the Duke's
" regiment are ordered to bee raised, (as I heare) : the
" occasion of his comeing is not certenly declared. Its
" thought it is on the supposition of an insurrection or
".rebellion here in the west, by reason of a ship which
" the Tiger, one of his Majesty's frigates, lately took at
" sea, and brought into Plymouth, loaden with drums
" and ammunition. I waited on his Grace as soon as
" hee came, and gave him your service : hee was glad
" to hear of your recovery, and dranke your health."—
The Duke of Albemarle, it is said, shewed neither aptitude nor courage on this occasion : and hence, not improbably, his wish to escape further censure by accepting the governorship of Jamaica, as already mentioned.

15 June 1685.—" This morneinge the Mayor and
" Dean of Exon received a letter from his Grace the
" Duke of Albemarle [Lord Lieutenant of the county
" of Devon], whereby they are ordered to send to mee
" to give you notice to bee here at Exeter with the
" Posse Comitatus ; which letter I saw. But the Mayor
" and Deane, who are both Deputy Lieutenants of our
" county, thought it not adviseable for you to raise
" the Posse till you come att Exeter ; where you are
" desired to hasten, only the Mayor and Deane advise
" you to come with about 200 horsemen, as well armed
" and provided as they may be, of the most able and
" loyall men. To which end, you may require the
" gentlemen of the best quallity neare you and other
" substantiall men, by vertue of your writt of assistance
" to joyne with you and come up att Exeter, in order
" to the suppressinge of the present rebellion. They
" also did advise that you send to Sir Jonathan Wreys
" howse, where its said are fower or five good suites of
" armour : you may desire two or three of them. There
" is noe doubt of a ready complyance in all the loyall
" gentry and comonalty in this emergency to serve
" theire Kinge and country . . . Wee had this morninge
" an accompt from Honyton that the Duke of Monmouth
" with about 1000 men, about 8 or 9 of the clocke last
" night, were at Bridporte, about 6 or 7 miles from
" Lyme, where they mett with about 600 of the militia
" of Dorsetshire, whoe engaged them ; there were about
" 10 killed of each side (as its said) and the Duke of
" Monmouth wounded ; and that the Duke of Monmouth
" and his party retreated, and the militia followed them,
" and tooke some of theire guns, which were left in the
" flight."

22 June 1685. . . " Monmouth is removed from Taunton toward Bridgwater, and some of the King's army

" are now in Taunton. Its said Monmouth hath about
" 10000 with him, rabble and all."

4 July 1685. . . . " Its thought that the enemyes
" army is againe in or about Taunton. My Lord
" Churchill and my Lord Feversham, with the King's
" forces, are in pursute of them, but its supposed they
" are att some distance. There was a reporte yesterday
" that a scoute of the enemyes horse was then att
" Taunton, and some few others in and about Cullompton. Its conjectured theire designe may bee to
" march off to some of your northern ports. . . . I
" question not but you have already sett good and
" strict watches att all the ports and creakes in your
" parts, as Appledore, Barnestaple, Biddeford, Combe
" Martyn, Ilfracombe, Clovelly, and other adjacent
" places."

8 July 1685. . . " The Duke of Albemarle charged
" mee . . . to advise you to send out scouts in your
" northerne partes to apprehend such as are scattered
" there ; some were examined here yesterday who confess that about 200 of them [Monmouth's troops] went
" toward Ilfracombe, and dispersed, some one way some
" another, neere that place, and one of the witnesses
" saith hee, with Ferguson and about 30 others, went
" off in a boate at sea at Ilfracombe, but were driven
" backe, seeing the King's shipping making toward
" them."

10 August 1685—Postscript—" Sir Arthur Northcote
" giveth you his service : hee is now with mee, and
" would have lent his coach, if occasion, and company."
St. Thomas. 1 October 1685. (Letter mutilated).
" I ridd to Wells purposely to save you what I could of
" the extraordinary charge of whipping and executinge
" the prisoners, wherein I gott some mitigation. However, the charge will bee very greate. The quarters
" of the rebells are to bee sent to the severall townes
" hereunder written . . . The Under sheriff is this day
" gonne to Coliton to execute those two prisoners that
" were to bee executed there, and on Saturday [a] Crediton man is to bee executed there : it had been donne
" formerly, had wee knowne how to dispose of his
" quarters, and there was noe day assigned [either] in
" the Kellender or in the warrant for his execution ; all
" the other executions will be done with all speed. I
" hope you will [have] ceased the great trouble and
" charge of it ; brick cannot bee made without straw,
" pains and care shall not be wanting on my part. . . .
" Places where quarters and heads of rebells are to bee
" sent, are, Honiton, Axeminster, Coliton, Ottery, Crediton, Biddeford, Barnestaple, Torrington, Tiverton,
" Plymouth, Dartmouth, and Tottnes."

St. Thomas (Exeter). 12 October 1685. . . " I was driven
" to ride to Wells, and there to tarry all the Assizes, for
" a mitigation of the whipping, and about disposeing of
" the quarters of the rebells : I acquainted my Lord,
" (then Cheife Justice, now Lord Chancellor) that wee
" have many markett townes in our county, soe by
" Charter, that scarce retaine at this day the name of
" marketts, in some of which very few, in others not
" any, did resort to buy and sell, but as in other little
" villages where no marketts ever were. To which
" my Lord [Jefferies] answeared that the whipping
" should be onely in the greater and more generall
" marketts ; and for the quarters of the rebells, they
" are ordered to bee sett up at Honyton, Axminster,
" Coliton, Ottery, Crediton, Biddeford, Barnestaple,
" Torrington, Tiverton, Plymouth, Dartmouth, Tottnes.
" On Saturday next, at Axminster, is the last execution
" to bee done, and one more then at Honyton, unles
" reprieved, endeavours being makeing per expresse,
" who is not yet retorned. Three were executed at
" Honyton Saturday last. Quarters are already sett up
" at Colliton, Honyton, Ottery, Crediton ; others are
" brought hither to bee sent as above. The quarters are
" already boyled and tarred ; warrabts are to bee sent to
" the Mayors, to sett them up. I saved you considerably
" by my journey to Wells, and endeavour to save you
" what expences I can ; however, it is exceedinge
" chargeable and troublesome ; another such yeeres
" trouble will I not undertake for 500 li. . . . There
" were about 400 condemned at Taunton ; and 700 at
" Wells. Its thought about 100 are and wilbee executed ; the rest transported, unles perhaps a few may
" be pardoned. You fared better than the Sheriffe
" there,"—who would have to pay the expenses of the whippings and executions.

26 October 1685. . . " Wee are about to send quarters
" of rebells, and those to bee whipt, at Torrington,
" Barnestaple, and Biddeford, and soe about to Plymouth."

J. R. Pine
Coffin
Esq.

From 1683 to within a year or two of the death of Mr. Richard Coffin (in 1699), Dr. Humphrey Prideaux, Prebendary, and afterwards Dean, of Norwich, kept up a correspondence with his "Honoured brother," who had that relation towards him as having married Ann, his sister, who was the Doctor's senior by about 8 years. Some of these letters are rendered more or less illegible by damp, others, no doubt, have perished: the following are selections from eleven out of the twelve which have survived. The leading subject is endorsed on each, in Mr. Richard Coffin's hand.—

Oxford, February 16, 1684(5). . . "A Parliament will " shortly be called, which will give you an occasion of " another jorney to Exeter, and the opportunity of " befriending the Protestant religion, which I hope you " will make use of, as far as rightly you may; soe that " men of such temper be sent of your country, as will " neither exasperate the King by denying him reason- " able things, or on the other hand be too faint to " grant what may prejudice our religion. But come " what will, we must submit to what God will have " come to passe, who often makes tryal of us by afflic- " tions, and proves us by adversity. His Church is not " to be triumphant here; but if we look backward into " the historye of it, we shall ever find it strugling under " difficultys and persecutions, and always best thriving " under them."

Oxford, June 10, 1685. . . "The Scotch rebellion is " like to continue the Parliament longer then at first " designed. It seems it is a bad businesse; Argile " haveing shown himself herein a man of design as " well as resolution, for his plot is very deeply layd, " and cunningly contrivd. I wish it doth not create " us furthor disturbance then we at present imagin. " Trenchard hath escaped from the King's messengers " sent to apprehend him; and it is imagined gon into " Ireland, with designe from thence to passe over into " Scotland to him that heads his party. As his flying " discovers his guilt, soe the manner of it, I doubt, will " be the undoeing of his father-in-law, Mr. Speake, " who, in a very riotous and rebellious manner, got men " together, and beat of those that came to sease his son- " in-law, and thereby gave him an opportunity to make " his escape."

Saham [Norfolk], October 31, 1692. . . "Wadham Col- " lege hath the best reputation, but there is a yong man " chosen Warden there [whom] I do not know. At " Edmund Hall there is one Dr. Mills, a man of very " eminent work, [who] is Principall; whom I think " the considerablest man of that University, and whom " of all others I would soonest trust with any friend of " mine. But if you incline to send your grandson to " Cambridge, that is nigh me, and perchance I can " better serve you there then at Oxford, and I can have " continuall advice how matters there goe with him; " as I must confesse I think the Cambridge method of " education preferable to that of Oxford, though as to " the discipline, it is too loose for this age in both of " them . . . I am well acquainted ther with severall " of the Masters of Colledges, but by what I hear, I " best like of Sidney Colledge, and Doctor Johnson, the " Master, I am well acquainted with." Edward Pine, the orphan son of Richard Coffin's eldest daughter, Bridget, is here alluded to : he ultimately became a Fellow-commoner of the College of Sidney Sussex, Cambridge.

Saham. 8 October 1694. . . "I am now again re- " moving to Norwich, being driven hence by the un- " healthiness of the place, and indeed we had left it " above a month since, but I first, and after, my [wife, " were] taken with the sicknesse of the place, which is " the ague : however, the next week we intend [to bid " a] totall farewell to this place, for I have resigned " the liveing, in which I have acted [on my owne] " judgement, contrary to that of many others, who would " have dissuaded mo [from it] : but I could not persuade " myselfe to take the wages of a minister where I " intended never [more] to do the work, and therefor " would not for any gain charge my conscience with " this matter. I hope none of my friends will blame " me on this account; for there are many other things " to be valued besides money . . . . were it the treasury " of Crœsus, I could have noe content in it, when held " with injustice. And since to me nothing seems more " unjust, then that the maintenance appointed to the " support of God's worship should goe to such as never " attend it; and on this account I have on many " occasions, especially where I am Archdeacon, dis- " couraged non-residence, to the utmost of my power, " I am resolved I will never practice it myselfe, and " therefore I have sent to the patrons to present another

" minister to the liveing; and the person they have " agreed upon (for the patronage belongs to New Col- " ledge in Oxford) is nephew to Oliver Cromwel], being " son to one of his sisters."

May 22, 1695. . . "I should be glad to know how you " designe your younger son, and which way you think " he may be properest provided for. Often a younger " brother's profession proves more beneficiall then the " elder brother's estate; but then it must be chosen " soe as will best suit his genius, for every one is not " fit for every thing."—"Non omnia possumus omnes " was probably in his mind when he wrote the last sentence. Richard, the younger son, afterwards became a Spanish merchant in London.

August 16, 1695. . : "[As to] Bishop Williams, my " Lord [Lord Spenser] is but a yong man, and speakes " his censures by other mens judgements [than] his " owne. Had Laud been halfe as honest a man, we had " not been in that wretched state we [now are]. One " man hath layd the foundation of all the mischiefe " that hath since followed, and the other [has been] " bronded because he was his opponent. One act at " last is a remaineing blot upon [him, his] goeing over " to the Parliament; but for that he hath his apology. " But Clevelond Satyr . . . long abroad to make it " heard. To give the man his due, he was the gal- " lantest personage, [whether we] looke on him either " as gentleman, statesman, or divine, and I wish he " had a better historian [for] his life; for that booke " is stuffed with too many impertinences and needlesse " digressions. However, in it you have many things " of the secrets of those times, which you will not find " [elsewhere]." . . Hacket's Memorial etc. in reference to Lord Keeper and Archbishop Williams, is probably the book alluded to. Williams was a gross pluralist, and a man of, at least, questionable character ; facts which make Dr. Prideaux's admiration of him the more remarkable. This letter has been partly destroyed by damp.

Norwich, October 11, 1695. . . "I confess neither of " the University are in that condition I could wish. " I like Oxford most [qy. "least"], perchance the " reason is, that I know it best. Those that have now " the government of Colleges in that University [are " most] of them, such as I could scarce committ a dog " to their charge. I hope Cambridge may not be soe " [bad]: however I would reather desire my cosin [for " "nephew"] to be placed ther, that being nigh me, " I [may have] the opportunity of doeing him the " better service . . . [The] genius of the age is run " into libertinisme, and this is gon through all bodys " and orders of men in the kingdom, and the Uni- " versitys have drunk too deep of it."

Norwich, February 7, 1695(6). . . "I have made the " best inquiry I can, concerning Oxford, and upon the " whole I find it the opinion of all those I consult with, " that Wadham College is the best place for you to put " your son at, it beeing the best governed College in " the University, and stockd with the best Fellows. " Mr. Whiting they speak well of, but prefer Mr. Doyly " as the fittest person for a tutor in that College, but " he having been spoken to, declines undertaking it. " My opinion is, to commit him to the Warden, and " to leave it to him to provide a tutor for him, who " best knows his Fellows; and that will engage him to " be the more carefull of him." Mr. Doyly is again mentioned, in the Report upon the Archives of Wadham College, Oxford, included in the present Report.

Norwich, February 19, 1695(6). . . "In this place I " am so far out of the way of hearing anything from " Oxford, that I am myselfe very much a stranger to " that place, haveing noe opportunity of beeing in- " formed anything concerning it, all of these parts " goeing to Cambridge. I hope at Wadham College " your son will find all those advantages in his edu- " cation which you can wish. The greatest regard is " to be had to the company which he keeps, and in that " College the Fellows being a very good sett of men, " I hope he will have all manner of advantage by his " converse with them . . . . My sister in her last men- " tioned Exeter College. Whoever advised you there, " was noe friend : that is worse then Christ Church, " for at the latter there is something of ingenuity and " gentele carriage in the genius of the place, but in the " other, I never knew anything all the while I was at " Oxford but drinking and duncery." Prideaux himself had been a Student of Christ Church, of whom he here speaks with but very faint praise: his father, Edmund, had been a member, first of Sidney Sussex College, Cambridge, and, after that, of Exeter College,

Oxford, under Dr. John Prideaux, as Rector, afterwards Bishop of Worcester.

Norwich, March 29, 1697... "I have ordered a booke " to be left with my brother in London for you, which " I have desired him to convey to you with the first " opportunity. It is just now come out of the presse, " a Defence of Christianity against the Deists, a sect " who now very much prevaile. Its purport sets forth " what an imposture is, in the life of Mahomet . . . " proves that Christianity cannot be such ; those who " run away with those impious notions being mostly " the young gentlemen of this age, clever enough not " to read any thing that will much work their heads. " I thought it the best way to come at them by an " History, which sort of bookes they are willing enough " to read."

Norwich, May 12, 1697.—"I hope er this you have " received the book which I ordered to be sent you : " I wish you may find it worth your acceptance. I am " sorry the wickednesse of the present age makes us " soe much need such bookes. I had much rather there " were no occasion for them, but since there is, I was " willing to put to my hand in greatest measure I can, " for the support of that holy religion which we pro- " fesse." His *Life of Mahomet*, which he published this year, is the book alluded to.

Dr. Prideaux also kept up a constant correspondence with his sister, Mrs. Ann Coffin, from the year 1673, probably down to 1705, the year of her death. Some of these letters are much injured by damp; and many, no doubt, have perished. Extracts are here given from 27 out of the 66 which still survive.

November 1673. . . . "The new Dutchesse of York " will be at London next week, where she is accom- " panyed by her mother. She bringeth with her a " portion of 400000 crowns, being about an hundred " thousand pounds of our mony : which is payed by " two of her unkles, which are Cardinalls, and the King " of France, who was the cheefe matchmaker, and made " such haste to make it up, that without especting any " ratification from England, he concluded the busi- " nesse soe that she was upon her journey before they " heard any thing of the businesse at Whitehall ; to " their great astonishment, and, I suppose, indignation, " but that they dare not show it, for fear of their " disobliging their master, the King of France, who " ruleth here as he pleaseth, and hath reather imposed " a wife on the Duke, then procured for him. She " is young, not above 15, hunch-backd, and ugly, and " the daughter of a poor beggerly prince, whose re- " venues doe not exceed ten thousand pounds a year of " English mony, and hath nothing else to make him " considerable, but that he is absolute over Modena " and Rheggio, 2 petty villages in Italy."

Norwich May 9, 1674. . . . "As for my brother's pur- " chasing, you have no reason to expect that, till he " gives over tradeing ; for altho at present he hath " had misfortunes, yet, if it please God to give peace, " he is a bad merchant, that cannot make six times as " much of his money by trade as he can by land. Al- " tho' merchandise be not my trade, yet I chuse reather " to keep my estate in money than in land, for I can " make twice as much of it this way, considering what " taxes are upon land, and what advantages there are of " making money upon the publick funds."

Oxford, November 10, 1674. . . . "The Earl of Mid- " dleton is dead, and that family extinct, the estate, " worth 3000l. a year, was settled by will on the Lord " Buchurst, his nephew, who hath thereon declared " himself marryd to the Countesse of Faumouth, an " infamous relict of the Lord Clifford's. The King being " lately at Newmarket, admitted severall Cambridge " men to preach before him, beeing sollicited thereto " by their Chancelour, the Duke of Monmouth ; but " beeing very much offended by their long periwigs, " which some of them wore, and at the readeing of their " sermon, which all the Cambridge men are guilty of, " esteeming it affected to doe otherwise, hath sent an " expresse command to the governours of the University " to take care for the future that none of their devines " either ware periwigs or read their sermons. We like- " wise expect the same orders here, although our Uni- " versity is not soe guilty of either of those faults as to " need such commands for a reformation . . . . . The " Dutchesse of Yorke expecteth speedyly to ly in, her " mother will suddenly be here, her daughters lyeing " beeing the pretense of her comeing; although I sup- " pose her cheife end is to receive more presents, haveing " speed soe well the last journey as to have got more " here and in France then the revenues of Modena are " worth in 2 years. But it is the fate of those that

"marry beggerly princes allways to have beggers at " their heels."

Oxford, August 8, 1676. . . . "At Ford, I found the " old attorney's lady, who was very kind unto me . . . " My aunt was very inquisitive after (the) Bake family ; " she lamented much the death of my grandmother, " but as for Sir Walter, I find that all in that family " have a very ill opinion of him." Sir Walter Moyle, of Bake, in Cornwall, a kinsman of the family, is meant. The "old attorney" was Edmund Prideaux, Attorney-General under the Commonwealth, and connected with the introduction of the Post Office into this country.

Oxford, March 29, 1683. . . . "As for old Josias' death " I am not much concerned ; I suppose those that are " nearer related to him are glad of it, especially the " young Josias. But as for my Lady Moyle, I am very " much troubled at her losse [*i.e.*, loss of her] ; she was " the cheife support of the family : and I fear Sir " Walter will sufficiently want [miss] her, especially " in respect of the children she hath left behind her. " As to my liveing . . . the name of it is Blaydon, 5 " miles distant from Oxford. The town of Woodstock " is in my parish . . . my chief parishioner is his Ma- " jesty, who hath in my parish a mannor house, formerly " much resorted to by his predecessors, especially " King James; but the house being almost totally " ruined in the late wars, the King hath not been at " it above twice since his return; but were the house " rebuilt, I believe he might be here as often as King " James, who seldom fail'd to spend some part of the " summer at it. My other parishioners are the Earle " of Litchfield and his Countesse, one of the Dutchesse " of Cleveland's daughters by his Majesty ; the old " Countesse of Rochester and her two grandaughters, " daughters to her son the late Earle of Rochester; a " Baronett, and severall other gentlemen of good note. " The situation of the place is the most pleasant and " healthy that I know anywhere in England."

Oxford, April 20, 1685. . . . "I am at present a " mourner for the death of one of the best friends I " had in this place, Dr. Marshall, Rector of Lincoln " College, a person of as eminent worth, both for good- " ness and piety, as well as learneing, as any that he " hath left behind him ; and his losse was the greater " to me, because of a more than ordinary kindnesse he " designed me, had it pleased God be had lived till next " Michaelmas, that I might have capacitated myself " for it, by takeing the degree of Doctor in Divinity ; " for then he would have resigned unto me his Deanery " of Glocester, which would have placed me in an " honourable station, altho as to profits it be one of " the least that bears that name, the value of it not " exceeding 250l. a year."

Norwich, February 1, 1688 (9). "I perceive by yours " you are soe much in love with your Mons'. Jeureu " [Jurieu] that I believe if my brother were dead, you " would make him your second husband. Since I per- " ceive you so dote upon this man, I shall be sure to " say noe more of him that may offend you. You wrot " to me to know my judgement of his booke and the " man, and you are angry with me when I give it you, " tho it be noe other than what is after the judgement " of the best and learnedest of his own countrymen, " Mons'. Allix and others, whom I am acquainted with, " and who know the man better then I doe. His books, " when I read it, appeared to me a perfect romance, as " contained the inventions of a phancyfull brain, with- " out ground or reason. It hath been a practice for " this last age or two for to apply the prophecys of the " Revelations to the actions of the time : thus Bright- " man expounded them all of Scotland, and others of " the affairs of Germany, in the time of Gustavus, and " now Mons' Jieuren is driven out of France, all must be " expounded of that country, to make way for his return " home again ; and I think it the weakest performance of " any that hath been attempted this way. And for the " good deliverance which you imagin we have obtained " by the Prince of Orange comeing hither, I wish it " may prove soe; but I must tell you I have other " notions of that matter. I should be glad to be de- " ceived in my apprehensions, but as things now goe, " I can see nothing but a long series of confusion like " to come upon this land, which neither we or our " children may ever live to see an end of. . . . For " these two years I have been expecting continually to " be turned out of all, and therefore I have my mind " the better prepared for to bear it, when it comes " from another hand, as I expect er long it will ; oaths " and tests being like to be put upon us, which I can " never take ; and this I doubt not will voyd churches " enough for all your beloved phanatiques to come in

" upon their own terms, and then I hope you will be
" satisfyed."

Norwich, February 11, 1688 (9). . . . " The news from
" London concerning the settling of the Crown, I sup-
" pose y)u have heard of. What may be the consequence
" of it time must show. For my part I must confesse
" I expect noe good ; the next thing will be to require
" us to take a new devised oath of allegiance to the
" new King and Queen, which many thousands among
" us thinke we cannot take with a good conscience,
" considering the oath already taken to the late King ;
" the consequence of which will be, the turning out
" of us all. What the oath is, I doe not yet know ; but
" I hear the Bishops cannot get over it, but will rather,
" all of them, quit their bishopricks then take it ; if soe
" they and the Church must goe down together, and
" then your friends, the present Dissenters, may have
" their will and once more act as they did in the late
" times, which nothing but French dragooning can
" parallell."

Saham, June 27, 1692. " Dear Sister. I have received
" your letter, but perceive you have very wrong notions
" of matters, concerning which I shall enter into noe
" dispute with you. God knows the world is bad
" enough with us, and the Dissenters, who are so much
" in your favour, have helped forward to make it soe,
" as much as any party of men in the nation ; and
" now we have a King and Queen ready to sett forward
" a reformation, and Bishops who labour hard to effect
" it, yet nothing can be don, because that party in
" Parliament who are for the Dissenters, obstruct all
" offers made this way ; because unlosse they can bo
" uppermost, they will consent to nothing, but are
" desirous reather to make things worse, that soe they
" may the better compasse their own designs upon us.
" Severall very good Acts were offered by the Bishops
" last Sessions, but none could be past ; especially
" one for takeing away plurality of benefices with cure
" of souls. The reason urged against it was, that it
" being the privilege of the Lords to qualify ministers .
" for pluralitys, to take this way would be to devest
" them of their peerage ; but the true reason was, the
" party disaffected to the Church of England would
" not foregoe so plausible a theme of declaimeing
" against it ; and I have the most reason to know it,
" because I was the person employed by some of the
" Bishops to draw the bill. However, they will offer
" at it again next session ; but I foresee it will be to
" noe purpose. . . . For this I am sure, 'there never
" was a Parliament ever sate in England, which is
" more averse to the doeing of anything for religion
" and the service of God, then that which is now in
" beeing. . . . As to the Universitys, although at pre-
" sent some of the Colleges have fallen into the hands
" of ill men, as to the government of them, yet still
" there are very good men in both, where young men
" may be instructed in virtue and learneing, as well as
" in religion. Exeter College is totally spoyld, and
" soo is Christ Church, and for that reason, when lately
" chosen Canon of Christ Church, and Professor of the
" Oriental languages, in Dr. Pocock's place, I refused
" to goe."

Saham, August 21, 1692. . . . " As for your foolish
" neighbour, that will put force upon her son, that you
" mention, she will certainly ruin him to all ends
" and purposes, and by her method of education breed
" him up only to be a plague unto her all her life after.
" She hath no right to chuse a religion for her son ;
" every one is to looke after his owne soul, and must
" have the greatest right to chuse for its salvation,
" because he hath the greatest interest therein ; only
" it becomes parents, as long as their children have
" not judgment for themselfs, to guide them by their
" [example], as well as they can, and to give them the
" best education they are able ; I say this is the rule,
" did all people act sincerely, but wickednesse and
" faction is in the bottom of most of the divisions and
" dissentions about religion that are now among us ;
" but soe it hath been from the begining, and ever
" will be, and nothing is more foolish than the expecta-
" tion of that reformation which some would have ;
" for it is not consisteing with our lapsed condition,
" and therefore never can be had in this life. . . . The
" Act of Toleration hath added this mischeife, that
" since the liberty granted by it, a great part of the
" nation worship God noe way at all, but are degene-
" rated into perfect atheisme ; and although the Act
" doth not directly give them this liberty, yet it is soe
" ordered that now such a liberty is given to others,
" it cannot be avoyded but every one takes to doe what
" he pleases in matters of religion ; it being too difficult

" a matter to distinguish between those absentees from
" church that goe to conventicles, and those that doe
" not, that every one now is free to do what he pleaseth ;
" and soe it will be till there be a regulation of this
" Act ; which I believe will never be obtained from an
" atheisticall gentry in Parliament, who seem to aim
" at nothing so much as a totall libertinisme in manner
" as woll as religion. I foresee the event of this will
" be, the Church will be again torn in pieces, and the
" end thereof will be either the ruin of the Protestant
" religion or the ruine of Christianity among us ; for
" whenever the present establishment is overthrown,
" Popery must come in its stead, or nothing."

December 10, 1692. . . . " I am exceeding sorry that
" the Bishop's behaviour is so bad ; it is a great in-
" felicity that such a man is put into such a station.
" When I were last in London, it was talked with much
" hopes among the other Bishops that he was in a dying
" condition ; but I suppose they took this only by way
" of conjecture from his disorderly living ; it would
" be a great blessing to the Church were we rid of
" him, and one or two more of King James's Bishops,
" for the rest are indeed very worthy and good men,
" and I hope God will show mercy unto his Church by
" their ministry. . . . I expect a sweeping calamity,
" that will take us from one end of the land to the
" other, and I pray God protect my stars . . . In your
" next, give me some particulars of the Bishop's mis-
" carriages ; and whether he will never be removed
" higher." . Sir Jonathan Trelawny, Bishop of Exeter,
was promoted to the See of Winchester in 1707, and
died in 1721. In this letter, the roads between Norwich
and Cambridge are said to be impassable for carriages.

Norwich, November 8, 1693. . . . " The whole world
" is grown corrupt ; this nation is like to rue it for
" ages to come, that King Charles the 2nd ever reigned
" in this land ; his example hath soe corrupted all
" orders of mon among us, that there is scarce any
" religion, honour, or common integrity, left in the
" land, and God is gooing, I fear, to punish us in tho
" severest manner for it. At the same time the French
" sett soe hard upon us abroad, the party at home is
" labouring as hard for our ruin ; nothing will satisfy
" them but the pulleing down both of the Church and
" Monarchy. The Dissenters are now their tools to
" effect this, and if ever they carry the day, perchance
" they may faro under such men as bad as we ; for they
" are most, if not all, most profligate atheist[s], that
" are the head managers of this designe, who have
" already made shipwrack of their honour, their con-
" scienco, and their estates, and would now repair
" themselves upon the ruin of the publick interest of
" the kingdom. These men may make way for the
" King of Franco to swallow both us and them ; but
" for their designs, they will never take in this land,
" when they come to be publickly owned, however at
" present they may gull many under this cloake of the
" publick good, to which in reality they are the greatest
" enemys. . . . . . . These men have framed a councill
" for carrying on of their designes. God only knows,
" as to my selfe, perchance they may speedily give me
" reason enough to visit my friends in the West." Extracted from a very long letter, on the political aspects
of the times.

Saham, February 11, 1693 (4). . . " I have now 2 sons
" and a daughter ; the latter, I tell her I will send to
" her Aunt Honour, for she is exactly of her spirit and
" humour. She makes sport for the whole house, and
" will govern all, wherever she comes. She is, I thank
" God, a very sprightly, witty, child, and very healthy ;
" which hath encouraged me to venture 200 li. on her
" head in the Million Fund ; which will bring her 28 li.
" per annum ; and will be a reserve to keep her from
" starving, whatever misfortunes she may meet with
" in the world."

Date about March 1695.—" The Queen was buryed
" while I was at London, but I had not curiosity to
" incommode myself by ten hours setteing in a gallery
" to see that ceremony. While there, I met my
" old friend and relation Mrs. Bury ; the Bishop of
" Exeter haveing at last driven her husband out of the
" College, he hath settled himself in London. I can-
" not justify him for the hooke he wrot, but as to
" that which was the merits of his cause, I think he
" hath the hardest measure possible, hee being expeld
" the Colledge for expelling a Fellow, father of 2 bas-
" tards in one year. I have had a great deal of discourse
" with Wat Moyle, and hope that those storys which goe
" of him in the country may not be true. I have once
" more put him into the hands of the Bishop of Salisbury,
" who promised me to take pains with him in removing

J. R. PINE
COFFIN,
Esq.

" his prejudices, if there be any such rooted in him."
It would seem that Dr. Bury was removed from the
Rectorship of Exeter College by Dr. Trelawny, Bishop
of Exeter, the Visitor. Walter Moyle, thus committed
to the care of Gilbert Burnet, Bishop of Salisbury, was
a kinsman of Dr. Prideaux and one of the wits and
free livers of the day.

August 13, 1695. . . "The great divisions and parleys
" we fell into immediately on King James' departure
" made me always fear it would come to this, and this
" made me resolve to retire into the country, and
" avoyd all overtures of higher advancing myself in
" the Church; and indeed I have with greater industry
" avoyded in this particular then other men have
" sought; for the lowest stations are safest in trouble-
" som times; and, God helpe us, we are like to find
" troublesome ones enough."

Norwich, December 8, 1695. . . "My brother hath
" wrot to me about your son, and I should be glad to
" doe you all the service I am able. Cambridge being
" nigh me, I can there doe you the best service, and
" therefore I advised my brother to place him there;
" and I must confesse I have the better opinion of
" Cambridge, although perchance it be only that I doe
" not know it so well as Oxford, which to my great
" griefe, I know to be bad enough."

Norwich, August 11, 1697. . . "I hope my brother
" hath received the book I sent him. I published it
" to meet with an impiety that very much prevails
" in our day. It seems we have wrangled soe long
" about religion, that too many of us begin to be
" weary of it, and, instead of reforming, would now
" cast it all of at once. I hope my designe may not be
" without some good effect; two whole impressions
" of the booke haveing been already sold of." His
" Life of Mahomet " is the work alluded to.

April 20, 1698. . . " As to the books you inquire after,
" if you had Geddie's ' History of the Church of Ethiopia,'
" and his ' History of the Church of Malabar,' they
" would please you. As to the Jesuits in China, all the
" progresse they have made there is, to get the Chinese
" to worship Jesus Christ, the Virgin Mary, and
" St. Peter, among the rest of their heathen Gods."
This letter is much mutilated.

June 30, 1698. (Speaking of John Coffin, then on
a visit to him from Oxford.) . . "He hath a mind to see
" Ports[mouth on] his return, [and hath] a phancy to
" passe over into the Isle of Wight. [But] this I
" disswade him from, because he can see nothing worth
" the hazard of passing the sea to it; and he has
" [agreed] to let it alone."

February 1, 1698 (9). . . (In reference to Walter
Moyle) " He is a young, inconsiderate, rash fellow, that
" out of a pragmaticall humour, and an opinion of his
" own understanding, hath too much delighted to talke
" against the common received opinions of others; and
" as far as I can learn, all this talke of him hath pro-
" ceeded from this free pragmaticall way of talking,
" when formerly in the country. As to his religion,
" I believe as yet he hath some, and as the world now
" goes, few gentlemen really have, and I believe a
" libertine humour is in the bottom of it. When age
" makes him more serious, I hope he may become
" another kind of man. He hath hitherto acted in
" every particular a most indiscreet part. The Court
" would have preferd him, and the circumstances of his
" family putt him in need enough of it; but instead of
" behaveing himself soe, last Parliament, as to recom-
" mend himself to the favour intended for him, he
" joyned with the King's most bitter enemys, opposed
" his interest in everything, and hath affronted his
" person in a libell which he is supposed to have had
" an hand in, to that degree that he will never be
" pardoned it, or can expect to signify anything
" further then his estate can make him."

Norwich, May 8, 1699. . . "As to the Greeks at
" Oxford, I understand not that project, or doe I think
" it hath any encourager, but only Dr. Woodroff, a
" man of a magotty brain, and a singular method of
" conduct from all mankind besides. I have lett him
" know my judgment about it, that this matter can
" come to nothing, and you need not fear that they
" will be corrupted by us to the love of Liturgys; for
" nothing is more fixed among them then their own
" Liturgys, and they doe indeed what you think we doe,
" idolize their Common Prayer Books, for some of them
" they derive from the Apostles themselfs. As for foreign
" Christians, you would doe well first toe understand
" the Church you are of, before you sette soe far abroad.
" I think never any church was better established than
" ours, or more unreasonably opposed, and the tole-

" ration which is now allowed them that doe oppose it,
" makes only way for the driving of Christianity out of
" the land, for the only sect that grows upon it are
" the Quakers, who are noe Christians; all sects besides
" begin to dwindle to nothing; I am sure they doe so,
" where I am concerned."

Norwich, June 9, 1699. . . " Since you are for your
" son's goeing into France, I have wrot to London to
" procure him to goe over thither in the retinue,
" and under the protection, of the Earle of Manchester
" [Charles Montagu], who is goeing Ambassador to
" Paris. As to the persecution, that will not reach
" him, and I am much rather for his goeing into
" France than Holland. The French are the most
" polite people in Europe, and there most may be
" learnt by one that would profit by travell, but I advise
" by noe means that he goe either into Italy or Spain.
" . . . As to the liberty of conscience which you mag-
" nify; it is the mother of confusion, and hath made a
" greater step towards driving Christianity out of this
" realme then any that hath been made since it came
" into it; for it tolerates men that are noe Christians,
" I mean the Quakers. I am not, neither ever was I,
" for prosecuting any with penall laws, merely upon
" the account of religion; but such an unlimited tolera-
" tion as this is, will soon extinguish all religion among
" us, since it is now claimed by a vast number of
" people to be of noe religion at all. One piece of news
" you tell me, which looks very strange to me, and that
" is, that you were bred a Presbyterian; if you were
" bred soe, you were bred alone by yourselfe, out of our
" knowledge and observation, for none of us else were
" bred soe, and I am sure my father never intended
" any such breedoing for you. These men have broke
" the peace of the Church without any just reason for
" it, and have thereby overwhelmed us with endless
" confusion and distractions, and now are at an end
" themselfes; the Independent party have swallowed
" them up, and brought them to nothing. As to the
" Greek project, it is only the maggot of one private
" man; it can come to nothing, nor signify anything,
" and soe I told the projector, when he advised with me
" about it some years since. But he is a man of a
" singular way by himselfe, without judgement, pru-
" dence, or conduct."

Norwich, August 19, 1699. . . "As to Wat Moyle,
" I wish him well marryed, and I am sorry his ill
" character still sticks to him, but am glad people
" with you have such a regard to religion as their
" aversion to him on this account doth expresse. I
" did indeed wish a wife for him to Sir Walter in this
" country; but at the same time I told him it would
" be inconvenient for him to come soe far for a wife,
" and I was not certain that shee would goo soe far for
" an husband, and I should be content to hear noe
" more of it. She hath indeed 7000 li., and I could
" safely make the match, if she would be content to
" goe so far." Walter Moyle, his kinsman, has been
before mentioned. Moyle's literary works were published at London, in 1726; and in them are several
letters to him from Dr. Prideaux, in reference to his
" Old and New Testament connected."

Norwich, November 6, 1700. . . "Dear Sister. As
" soon as my son got well, my daughter fell downe of
" the same distemper, and, I thank God, got very well
" through it without any danger, and now she is well,
" my wife is fain down. I took all the care I could, to
" preserve her from the contagion, by removeing her
" from me; but what God willeth noe care of man can
" prevent. I am in the utmost concern for her, because
" I fear I must loose her; and her losse will be very
" great to me, especially if it should please God that I
" should dy too before my children are bred up. For
" in a strange country, where I leave no relations of my
" own to depend upon, whom shall I have to take care
" of them! This will make the calamity the greater,
" if God please to make it my lot." Shortly after the
date of this letter, he had the misfortune to lose his
wife.

Norwich, May 26, 1701. . . "My children, I thank
" God, are very well, and I am taking all due care to
" give them as good an education as I can, but I much
" want their dear Mother to help me in this matter. I
" am mightily pressed to marry again, with abundance
" of offers, and very valuable ones; but considering all
" circumstances, I shall think of makeing noe more
" changes till I make my great change of this life, as
" I hope, for a better, and I have some reason to appre-
" hend that I am at noe great distance from it. Had it
" been convenient for me to take another wife, I should
" soon have determined my choice upon a gentlewoman,

J. R. PINE
COFFIN,
Esq.

" whom I have long known to be a very good and
" discreet woman, although not very beautyfull. Her
" father was Knight of the Bath at the Coronation of
" King Charles the 2nd, and of the antientest and most
" honourable family in this countrey. At his death he
" left an estate of about 1000 *li.* a year, which this
" gentlewoman, with three other sisters, on the death
" of their elder brother, doth now inherit. . . She is
" passed 40, and was never yet married." Dr. Prideaux,
notwithstanding his apprehensions of failing health
(being then probably threatened with the complaint of
the stone) survived till the year 1724, when he died, in
his 77th year.

Norwich, September 15, 1701. . . "As to the Greek
" Patriarch you enquire after, I suppose he is one that
" wants bread at home, and is come hither to beg it.
" There is noe account made of him, or is there any
" notice taken of him. Such sort of people we have
" often come over. As to their religion, it is made up
" with a multitude of rites, and they reguard little
" else in it, beeing very ignorant and superstitious, and
" ready, in the giving of their judgements, to declare
" either for the Papists or the Protestants, according as
" it will best tend to their interests."

Without date. . . "Here men will be always sinners,
" and as long as clergymen are men, they will be soe
" too, for they have the same infirmitys with other men,
" the same corrupt affections and depraved desires;
" and act always under the same, and oftener under
" much greivouser, temptations then other men, and
" therefore you must not think it strange that they
" also fall like other men. Therefore pray be not any
" more distressed at this, for as long as this world shall
" last, there will be evill men among clergymen as well
" as other orders of men, and perchance as many : and
" as the present circumstances are, it is the great mercy
" of God if there are not more clergymen wicked then
" otherwise. For livings being trusted for the most
" part in the disposall of the gentry, and they having
" gotten a trick of selling, it hence comes to passe, when
" a patron hath a liveing void, he goes about seeking
" one that will be perjured for it; whereby it comes to
" pass that the worst men that are bred in the Uni-
" versitys get all the livings, and they that best deserve
" them, and whose labours would be most usefull to the
" publiok, are condemned to their College chambers all
" days of their lifes, and the publick totally loose the
" benefit of their learning and piety ; and this is what
" the Church of England cannot help."

Among the Portledge papers there is a long series of
letters written by Mr. Richard Lapthorne, of London,
to Mr. Richard Coffin, between the years 1683 and
1697 ; if there were originally any others of an earlier
or a later year, they have now disappeared. Mr. Lapthorne, from what he says in one of his letters, appears
to have been a native of Plymouth or its vicinity ; but,
from the peculiarity of the name, it seems not improbable that he was a member of the Lapthorne family
who were residing at Hartland, in North Devon, (in the
close vicinity of Portledge), in the earlier half of the
17th century. His residence was in Hatton Garden,
but what his calling or profession was, does not appear ;
most probably, he was an attorney, or in some other
way connected with the law. He speaks in one of his
letters of a son of his being elected a scholar at " Eaton,"
and as, in later years, proceeding to Pembroke College,
Oxford. Mr. Lapthorne may be fairly said to have been
Richard Coffin's " London agent," receiving from him,
as he states in several of his letters, a certain sum
yearly for his services. His main duty seems to have
been to purchase books, at auctions or elsewhere, for
the fine library which Mr. Coffin was then forming at
Portledge ; and many particulars are to be found in
these letters, relative to the then prices of books. Another of his duties was, to write, at least weekly, to
Mr. Coffin a letter of news, enclosing that week's
printed Gazette, the " chatt " in fact, as Mr. Lapthorne
habitually styles it, of the day ; he invaribly signing
himself " Your faithfull servant, Richard Lapthorne."
The larger portion of his political intelligence was in
general to be found, no doubt, in the current Gazette;
but many other notices are given in addition therein,
in reference to the passing occurrences of the day.
Mr. Richard Coffin was evidently an extensive grower
of hops ; and Mr. Lapthorne each year keeps him well
posted up as to the prices then current in the markets
for hops, both old and new. As in the case of the letters
previously mentioned, many of Mr. Lapthorne's letters
are much defaced, if not almost wholly illegible, from
damp ; while others of them have entirely perished, no
doubt, from the same cause. Those which have sur-

vived are no less than 409 in number ; like the rest of
these papers, they have all been submitted to a careful
and thorough examination, and the following is a series
of extracts from 139 of the letters in question :—

7 June 1687. . . . "Doctor Tillotson, the Dean of
" Canterbury, had an apploplectick or epilectic [*sic*] fit
" seized on him Friday sevenight last, falling from his
" chair as he sate by the fire at his house at Edmington ;
" but by bleeding and purging is pretty well recovered.
" Some think that it proceeded from greefe at the late
" death of his only daughter."
(The Letter much mutilated from damp, and not dated,
but, from an endorsement in the hand of Mr. Richard
Coffin, "supposed" by him to belong to December 1687).
Speaking of an auction that had recently taken place.—
" There was amongst them and I wonder [you] tooke
" no notice of them, a greater rarity, [and one] which
" was much prized ; viz, 4 manuscripts of the works of
" Wickcliffe, bought by the Earle of Kent [Antony
" Grey] at 21 *li.* od money. I could have almost wished
" I had bought them myselfe at that price, but I veryly
" beliefe my Lord would have bought them, [if he had]
" given 50 *li.* for them." It would be interesting to
know what works of Wyclif are here referred to.

21 Jany. 1687(8). "It^s reported there is a house in
" Lincoln's Inn Fields fitting up for the Capuchine
" Fryers. It seems there is some idle brayne hath
" made a lampoone relating to the late Thanksgiving,
" and a strict enquiry is made after the author, who, if
" hee bee discovered, will, according to his deserts, bee
" severely punisht." The Thanksgiving was published,
on the disclosure, by proclamation, of the pregnancy of
the Queen, Mary of Modena ; Thomas Sprat, Bishop of
Rochester, and Nathaniel Crewe, Bishop of Durham,
being, in part the composers. The well-known lines,
beginning " Tom, Dick, and Nat, in council sat," are,
not improbably, the lampoon alluded to.

28 Jany. 1687 (8). . . . "This weeke I carried my
" little boyes to see a Swetzer, 38 years of age, and but
" 2 feet and 7 inches in stature, and had a manlike
" countenance, and voyce as thick almost. Along
" (therewith) bee sung, danced, and discoursed. My
" younger son is not 7 till May next ; and is accompted
" very litele of his age, and this Switzer, measuring
" with him, came but a little above his waste. The
" wonders of God are seen as well *in minimis* as *maxi-
" mis,* as Pliny observes of Nature, in forming the
" flie."

17 March 1687 (8). . . . "I was told by a Frenchman
" that I know very well, that the Dauphin presented to
" the King, his father, a list of all the Protestants that
" were departed the kingdom since the beginning of
" the persecution, with a designe to mollify him ; but
" hee gave him this answer :— ' Son, when you come to
" ' raigne, take your own course ; but I am resolved to
" ' finish what I have begun ;' and threw him back the
" paper."

29 April 1688. . . "One Mr. Rous, a Midlesex gent of
" reasonable quallity, comly personage about 62 yeares
" of age, who lodged next dore to us, was with some
" company and taking a pipe of tobacco, and very
" merry, and in seeming good health, his pipe dropt
" out of his mouth, and hee instantly dyed, without
" speaking a word. Its said this Mr. Rouse was of the
" Lord Russell's Jury."

5 May 1688. . . . "Sir Charles Pym, dying at a
" taverne in Old Fish Street, in London, an unhappy
" quarrell ariss betwixt him and a stranger in another
" roome in the house ; who by chance going out to-
" gether from the house into the street, he drew, and
" Sir Charles was run through, and dyed presently."

12 May 1688. . . . "The King [James II.] hath bin
" this weeke to Chatham to view the shipping, and was
" wanting 3 days. In the interim the Queene receiving
" a letter of the sicknes of her brother, the Duke of
" Modena, fell very ill upon it ; insomuch that the King
" was sent for, and came presently away, without his
" guard ; but the Queene is now well againe."

25 May 1688. . . . "It seemes Sir John Norborow
" [Narborough] hath not bin successfull in his fishing
" for more of the Spaniards plate ; having gotten but
" one tun and a halfe, which comes to 12,000 *li.,* and is
" brought hither, but will not quitt [? requite] uss."

25 July 1688. . . . "On Tuesday next, at night, will
" bee a great entertaynement of fireworks on the
" Thames, to congratulate Her Majesties [Mary of
" Modena] coming abroad, after the birth of the Prince.
" I heard an Italian say, who is and hath bin imployed
" about these fireworks, that it will cost his Majesty five
" and twenty thousand pounds, according to the cal-

J. R. PINE COFFIN, Esq.

" culation of their works, and that 300 men have bin
" imployed near 4 months about them."
21 July 1688. . . . "Tuesday night last was per-
" formed the great entertaynment by fireworks on the
" Thames, about 11 of the clock. I heare but of one
" that was killed; there were, as I am informed, above
" 100,000 spectators. It lightned exceedingly all the
" while. . . . . The Lord Chancellor Jefferys son was
" this week married to the late Earl of Pembroke's
" daughter, by the Dutches of Portsmouth's sister. . . .
" The French fleet lying before Argeire [Algier] and
" throwing in many boombes, they sent word to the
" Admirall that if hee desisted not, they would send him
" in a canon the French Cons ull; but hee persisting,
" they made good their prom ise, (I suppose his head
" only). And the French, by way of revenge, having
" 30 Argerene slaves aboard, cutt them in peeces, and
" layd their quarters on planks, and by the waves
" floated them towards the towne."
28 July 1688.— . . . "Judge Rotheram is gon Ox-
" ford Circuit, and tooke one Mr. Burgess, an Non-
" conformist minister, with him as his Chaplin. This
" Burgess is a man of extraordinary ripe parts, and
" before the Circuit hee was wished by the Judges to
" penn a short tract for instruction and admonition to
" such criminalls as should be condemned, in order to
" their preparation for death, to bee distributed by him
" as there should be occasion." There were several
Puritan preachers of the name of Burgess; the one here
mentioned was probably Daniel Burgess, whose chapel
was burnt in the Sacheverel Riots, 1710.
31 August 1688. . . . "The great preparations of the
" Dutch, and equipage they are at present . . hath
" much amazed their neighbours. We heare his Ma-
" jesty is in much forwarded in his navall preparations,
" and so intent upon that affaire, that the carpenters
" work Sundays, seamen are pressed at the Downs
" that are come home from voyages, and the drums
" beat up for volunteers towards the waterside and about
" Tower Hill. Judge Allibone lies in state." Allibone
was one of the Judges who supported the King in the
trial of the seven Bishops.
15 Septr. 1688. . . . "There hath bin great noys
" about a captain tossing the Mayor of Scarborough in
" a blanket, who hath bin at Windsor to make his com-
" plaint, and is now at London."
6 October 1688. . . . "Notwithstanding this con-
" cussion of affaires, its to bee wondered that the
" people are no more affected with the danger; their
" countenances making but little shew of the dark ap-
" prehensions they should have of this expedition."
The intended expedition of the Prince of Orange is
alluded to; and the above passage was written probably
in a spirit of covert irony; as both Lapthorne and his
correspondent evidently sympathized with the Whig
party.
13 October 1688. . . . "I doe not perceive the people
" here to bee under any great consternation, notwith-
" standing the impendent menace of an invasion."
27 October 1688. . . . "On Sunday last, two Irish
" soldiers, passing the street by St. Michael's church
" in Corn[h]ill, and some roguish boys abusing them,
" the soldiers being strangers, run into the church for
" protection, and cried out 'Mercy, mercy.' But the
" people, being frighted, mistooke it for 'Massacre,
" 'massacre,' and so the whole congregation was put
" into disorder, and some harm received by it."
10 November 1688. . . . "This day the King's
" artillery set out towards the West. As for other news,
" you cannot now expect, because of the King's last
" proclamation, only perticular occurrences. Wee may
" mention two citizens of London are lately dead,
" vastly rich, viz. Alderman Jefferys, the Tobacconist,
" or Smoaker, who left an estate behind him of three
" hundred thousand pounds, but nether wife nor child :
" the other was Alderman Lucy, who died very rich,
" and left only one daughter. There is a passage very
" remarkable relating to this discourse; viz. that those
" two gents were intimate frends and associats in their
" life tyme. The first, Jefferies, lay a considerable
" tyme sick, and some two or three days before his
" death, as hee lay in his bed, had this expression :—' I
" ' wonder,' quoth hee, ' that never a one of my servants
" ' is at leasure to take in a funerall ticket for mee to goe
" ' to Alderman Lucy[s] buryall.' Now Lucy being then
" in good health, they thought it was only a delirious
" whim : but Lucy (tho then well) fell sick and dyed
" within 2 or 3 days after."
11 December 1688. . . "All the goodes at Whitehall
" are removeing as fast as they can bee carried out;

" and the mobile are at their old work, of pulling down
" Mass houses, and making bonefires of the matterials;
" and what mischeafe they will doe of this kind this
" night, God knows."
15 December 1688. . . . "Wee heare the King is at
" Rochester, and wilbe at White ball tomorrow; and
" the Prince of Orange is at Windsor. The Lord
" Mayor [Sir John Chapman], when the Lord Chan-
" cellor was taken and brought before him, fell into a
" strange epileptick fitt, and scarce yet recovered."
29 December 1688. . . . "Some in towne who came
" from Calix [Calais], say they saw there the Bishop
" of Exeter, and Lord Cheife Justice Herbert, with
" some others who lately left London. The Lord Chan-
" cellor [Jefferies] is close confind at one Mr. Bulls, a
" warders, but allowed pen, inke, and paper, which hee
" hath much used. The Tower church was very full on
" Sunday, in expectation to see him, but he came not
" out. . . . On Sabbath day last, the Bishop of St.
" Asaph preacht before the Prince; after which, his
" Highness received the Sacrament from the Bishop of
" London, with an exemplary devotion." This letter is
of great length, carefully written, in an almost feigned
hand, and without signature; probably, the times considered, by way of precaution.
9 March 1688 (9). . . . "The King and Queene being
" proclaimed at Bongay, a market towne in Suffolke,
" on Thursday, ult. Febr., being market day; at which
" solemnity great joy being expressd, on the next
" morning, being Fryday, a fire broke out, and con-
" sumed all the towne, out [except] one house. And its
" said that immediately before the fire a gun was heard
" to goe off, and then the fire broke out at 4 different
" quarters of the towne at once. It seemes the towne
" was of some bignes, for they say there were 2 churches
" in it." The Topographical Dictionaries say that this fire
occurred in 1688 : the right date, no doubt, is here given.
Not one house only, but one small street, was saved.
13 August 1689. . . . "But, Sir, I should deale un-
" kindly with you, upon so short a notice, to goe off
" and not recomend another to serve you in my roome;
" and therefore (if you shall thinke fitt) doe propose
" unto you one Mr. Bagford, of whom I have had much
" experience, and thinke him very fitt to bee employed
" by you. Hee was a tradesman, but his genius has run
" much in collecting books, and of late yeares has bin
" assisting to auctions, and hath bin imployed by
" Mr. Powle, Master of the Rolls and Speaker of Parlia-
" ment, to collect books for him. Hee is a man that
" will expect no great matters from you; what you
" allow me, I know will content him. I have proposed
" it to him (if you shall think fitt), and he thankfully
" imbraceth it." Mr. Lapthorne was at this time con-
templating the acceptance of some appointment, which
would have rendered it impossible for him to continue
to act as agent and book-collector for Mr. Richard Coffin.
The present extract deserves attention, as containing a
very early notice of the once famous John Bagford, the
typographical antiquary, who died, an inmate of the
Charter-house, at Islington, in 1716, aged 65. The Bagford Collection now forms an item in the Library of the
British Museum.
28 October 1689. . . . "I just now come from Mr.
" Oliver Cromwell, son to the Protector Richard, and
" grandson to Oliver. Wee met about common affairs;
" viz. debtor and creditor, wherein I chanced to bee
" concerned, and are to meet againe on Munday."
22 November 1689. . . . "This day, we heare, was
" committed to the custody of the Serjeant-at-arms, Sir
" Richard Haddock, Sir John Parsons, Alderman Sturt,
" and Fenn, Victuallers of the navy, for their mis-
" carriages therein; it being affirmed, that in the
" bottoms generally of the casks of beere were found
" gutts, and a sediment like coprice etc. Wednesday
" night, some rude and frantick fellow cutt off from the
" King's picture (hanging in Guildhall) the hand,
" scepter, and crowne, and the Lord Mayor and Court
" of Aldermen, have issued out their order for 500 li.
" reward for a discovery."
20 December 1689. . . . "On Wednesday night, being
" the anniversary of the King's coming into London,
" was celebrated with a representation in effigie, by a
" procession through the Citty, with 1000 lights to
" Temple Bar, of the capitall ministers and officers that
" governed in the late King, James, tyme. Also, a
" triple galloes was carried before them, and sate up
" within Temple Bar, which was the period of their
" perambulation; and after some cerimonies and dis-
" courses, the criminalls in effigie were huug up, about
" 11 or 12 altogether, and by it a monstrous bonefire.

J. R. PITT
COFFIN,
Esq.

" But tae triple tree chanced to crack and fall; and
" then gallows and criminalls, with stocks, pillorys,
" whipping postes, etc., were all thrown into the flames."
8 March 1689 (90). . . . " Its reported that Lady
" Ogleby is taken at Chester, in man's apparrell, going
" with letters to King James. I was informed that the
" minister of Crooked Lane in London, silenced by the
" late Act, pulled another out of the pulpit, the last
" Lordes Day, that was appointed to preach, which
" caused much disturbance in the church."

28 March 1690. . . " Wee heare from Ireland, that
" there are discontentes amongst the Irish about the
" measures of governing. Terconell truckles under
" the King of France, but Colonel Searsfeld refuses so
" to doe, and each have partys dependant on them. . .
" The Irish used some of our soldiers very barbarously,
" strangling them in their quarters, and burying them
" in the church with their cloathes on, for conceale-
" ment; for which there is now an inquisition, and its
" hoped they will have their reward."

26 April 1690. . . " On Satturday last, being Easter
" Eve, about 7 at night, 2 powder-mills, with a vast
" quantity of powder, was blown up at Hackney, and
" about some seaven persons killed, all French, one of
" them a minister. It shaked . . . houses, some at
" least 3 or 4 miles distant."

3 May 1690. . . " Yesterday were brought to town
" from Malden, a maritime towne in Essex, 7 ruffians
" going over to France, to carry out some intregues
" for King James; and being at sea, were frighted
" back into Malden by one of our men of war; on sight
" of whom, they drew [threw] a great many papers
" overboard, but some others are found about them,
" that discover their designe."

24 May 1690. . . " There was lately a poor woman,
" a laborer's wife, neer us, delivered of 4 children at a
" birth, 3 lived to be baptised, named Faith, Hope, and
" Charity; which being presented to the view of the
" Queene, she gave the parentes tenn guinnees."

8 June 1690. . . " This being our Sessions week,
" one Crowne, that was indicted last Sessions for
" bringing seditious papers and commissions from King
" James, some of them found in a key; it was then put
" off to be tryed this Sessions, and yesterday he received
" a faire tryall, and the Jury were all for finding him
" guilty, but one man; who indeed is a man of good
" quallity and understanding, and freind to the present
" government; but was not cleerly convinced as to this
" poynt : so that the Jury were together all night, and
" for ought I know till now, it being 4 post meridien.
" I wish wee had had some such in our late King's
" Juryes, when the state bloodhounds were pursuing
" their prey."

14 June 1690. . " Crone that was tryed, is condemned,
" and sentenced to be executed on Wednesday next.
" Yesterday was the generall execution-day, and one
" criminall hanged at Newgate, for killing his keeper.
" 7 others were carryed in carts to Tyburne, but a re-
" preeve came, and brought them all back alive. Mr.
" Ferguson is bayled, and Gadbury, the astrologer, seized
" for dispersing King James's Declarations; and what
" is remarkable, its sayd Mr. Partridge, in his last yeares
" Almanack, hath prognosticated his fate this yeare."

21 June 1690. . . " 3 of the 7 malefactors, brought
" from the gallows that day sevennight were yesterday
" carried thither againe and executed; its sayd, for
" great rudeness and insolent carriage in the prison
" since the repreeve."

28 June 1690. . " Its sayd Crone, that was repreived,
" hath made greate discoveries, but would doe nothing
" till he understood Gadbury, the astrologer, who is
" also in custody, had broken the ice."

16 August 1690. . " On the Lord's Day, Dr. Burnett,
" Bishop of Salisbury, preached at Winsor Church in the
" afternoone, where I was present, in the crowd of a
" numerous auditory; and it so happened as the Bishop
" was in his sermon, a pillar of one of the gallerys, by
" reason of the press, sunck, and the gallery cracked;
" which caused greivous skreeks, and crying out that
" all the church was falling down, which put the people
" into great consternation and horrible confusion, but
" no great hurt don."

29 August 1690. . . " I suppose you have heard of
" a great contest lately in Oxford, about the censuring
" of a booke said to bee written some tyme since by
" Dr. Bury, Rector of Exon [College], as being repug-
" nant to the Church hierarchy, etc.; and that they
" doomed it to bee burnt by the hangman, and have
" suspended the Doctor as to his place. Hee is now in
" London, and its supposed hee will by way of appeale

" make a vigourous defense for himselfe. The booke is
" titled 'The Naked Gospell.' " The case of Dr. Bury
has been previously mentioned.

13 September 1690. . " Yesterday, being execution
" day, 6 men were executed, and of them the two most
" notorious, criminalls for robbery, who behaved them-
" selves insolently when tryed, in the presence of the
" Judges, as they were in their march to the gallows,
" called for wyne, and drank King James his health,
" and sleighted the Ordinary's exhortations at the place
" of execution, and bid him and the people goe home
" and give obedience, and send for King James, or else
" they were reprobates. By this you may perceive of
" what race some of his advocates are."

20 September 1690. . . " Wednesday last was the day
" for our monthly Fast; and the people generally did shut
" up their shops, intending to goe to church; but the
" church dores were shut, the clergy having determined
" the fast to bee at an end; but it was strictly kept by
" all the Nonconformists at their meetings."

18 October 1690. . " On Sunday morning broke out
" a fire near the timber windmill on the Bankside in
" Southwork; which consumed 8 houses and much
" timber . . . There hath bin a discourse of earth-
" quake in many places . . . and its sayd that severall
" partes of this towne have bin sensible of these shakings,
" as in Quen Street and in the Inner Temple etc."

25 October 1690. . . " There was a day or two since
" a notorious highwayman taken in Southwark, called
" 'the Goulden Farmer.' When discovered, hee went
" through the streets with his pistolls in his handes, on
" foot, and a great while the people looked on, but
" afrayd to touch him; till at last, some butchers
" ventured, with some others, and yet hee killed one,
" and hath dangerously wounded severall others."

1 Nov'. 1690. . . " There was lately a difference in a
" coffee house neer Grays Inn, betwixt the Lord Wemm
" (Lord Jefferies son) and another gent, and both
" wounded; but its said, Lord Wems' black bitt a
" peece of the other gentleman's face of, upon which
" the gentleman thrust his sword in his back, and some
" say [he] is dead."

22 Nov' 1690. . . " Severall women of late have bin taken
" violently away, being fortunes; as a coachmaker's
" widdow in Long Acre, worth ten thousand pounds, by
" a Frenchman; also, one Madam Wharton, a young
" lady, worth 1500ll. per annum, by one Mr. Camfeild,
" a son, or nearly related, to the Earle of Arguile; but
" the women are both retrived." As will be seen in
another passage, it was Sir John Johnston, who abducted
Mrs. Wharton.

13 December 1690. . . " A poor widdow woman, not
" far from us, on Munday last, hanged hirselfe. It seems
" she had, in her husband's life time, lived in a pretty
" plentifull condition; but being now reduced to poverty,
" its conjectured was the basis of this temptation. Shee
" had severall children, and 2 lived with her, a boy of 9
" and a girle of 11, yeares old. The girle could say but
" litle, only thus; that the day the fact was don, there
" was a strange man in black with her mother, and had
" discourse with her, but she knew not what it was.
" But when hee went away, shee heard her mother say to
" him,—'But what then wil become of my poor children?'
" To whom hee replyed, 'Take you no care of them, they
" ' wilbe provided for '; and that his voyce was hoarse.
" This relation' I had from a respectable citizen, who,
" being constable, was present, and heard the examina-
" tion. Its a wicked age, and what this black man was,
" God knows." If only from the disclosures in these
letters, we must agree that it was a wicked age; and
the suggestion in the last two lines savours of the superstition of the age as well.

18 Dec'. 1690. . . " The Spanish Flota is safely arrived
" at Cales [Cadiz], with vast treasure from the Indies,
" thirty thousand millions [!!] of mony; narrowly
" escaping the French men of war, which lay ready to
" swallow them up. Captain Phipps hath entred and
" taken considerable of the French territories in the
" islands of the Canada, in the West Indies . . There
" were 22 condemned to dye this Sessions, and 4 re-
" markable : the Goulden Farmer, a notorious robber,
" who killed 2 men, to bee executed in Fleet Street,
" and hanged in chayns on Bagshot Heath, Sir —
" Johnston, for stealing Mrs. Wharton, to bee executed
" at Queen Street end in Holborne etc." Mr. Lapthorne's geographical knowledge seems to have been
at fault, in this instance, as to the " islands of the
" Canada, in the West Indies."

26 December 1690.—" Sir John Johnston, that was
" confederate in the stealing Mrs. Wharton, on Tuesday

J. R. PITT
COFFIN,
Esq.

J. R. PINE
COFFIN,
Esq.

" morning last was carried in a large mourning coach
" to Tyburne, the herse following the coach, to receive
" the corps after execution. Hee made a strenuous
" speech at the gallows; such it seemes, that proved so
" insinuating to the foolish mob, as to draw teares from
" their eyes, insomuch as, I was told by some, that a
" little prompting would almost have prevayled with
" them for a rescue; which seems credible, in regard
" they afterwards offered violence to Mrs. Wharton's
" lodgings, by breaking the windows, etc. But the
" next night, about 7 of the clock, hee was carryed
" from Fleet Street in a herse, attended by 30 coaches,
" to St. Giles, to be interred, and its sayd the Earl of
" Arguiles immediately followed the herse."

9 January 1691. . . "A young gentlewoman was taken
" in the night by the watch at Charing Cross, and put
" into the Round House, and before morning hanged
" herselfe with her garter . . . One that came, in
" St. Clement's Parish, to a baker's to lodge, by the
" name of Captaine Wickham, a gent of a good estate in
" Oxfordshire, made his will, and gave 1500 li. to the
" baker and his wife, and gave severall other legacies
" to . . . but a stranger to the baker; and within a fort-
" night after hee came, dyed; and upon inquisition, the
" deceased proves to bee a cheat, Captain Wickham
" being alive."

7 February 1690 (1). . . "The Lord Danby having
" supped in the City, and riding home late at night
" in a hackney coach, in the Strand, there being a
" scuffle betwixt his coachman and page and some
" foot passengers pretending to be press-masters, my
" Lord, coming out of his coach, drew his sword, and
" the constable and Mr. Watche coming into the fray,
" the Lord Danby was knockt down, and was after very
" ill. This business was lately under examination,
" but what is don in it, I yet know not."

14 February 1690 (1). . . "On Saturday last were
" seized at the Castle Taverne, in Paternoster Rowe, a
" collection of pictures and relicts, and rare peices of
" antiquity, belonging to the Lord Melford, who is with
" King James in France; they are appraysed to the
" value of some thousand pounds."

28 February 1690 (1). . "There is much chat of late
" about a demoniack, or gentlewoman possessed, in Duke
" Street, neer Covent Garden. There have bin a Colledge
" of Theologists to make their observations on her; and
" in order to consult about a way to restore her, (viz.)
" Dr. Hornick and others. There will a voyce sometymes
" blasphemously speake within her, when her lips and
" teeth are shut, and this very audible; and sometymes,
" sitting in her chayre, she will visibly bee lifted up,
" togeather with her chayre, a great distance from the
" ground, no one touching the same, that can be per-
" ceived. I heard this morning that Major Blackmore,
" once a great man in the West, and who hath bin for
" some tyme governor of St. Helena, is brought hither
" prisoner for some offence comitted there in the
" executing his government. Its sayd Sir Cloudsly
" Shovell is maryed to the Lady Norborough."

7 March 1690 (1). . "Many persons have been taken
" up, as suspected, at clubbs; amongst others, Sir
" Roger L'Estrange, which is out on bayle . . . I heard
" Captaine Roope, the governour of Dartmouth, read a
" letter from a justice of the peace in our cuntry, that
" examined the English prisoners that came over in a
" ship to Dartmouth lately from St. Mallows; who de-
" clared upon oath the miserable condition the French
" were in in those parts by reason of the extremity of
" the warrs. Their grounds lay waste, and the grapes
" rotted on the vines, because the inhabitantes would
" not bee at the charges and paines of pressing them;
" the cuntry very sickly, and could not hold out much
" longer." The cultivation of the grape for wine, about
St. Malo's, could hardly have been a matter of the
importance here represented.

14 March 1690 (1). . . "From Ireland, wee have this
" remarkable in its kind; that 3 of our soldiers deserters
" going off, were met with 4 deserters coming from
" King James to our army; who brought our deserters
" back, and since (they) are executed. The deserters
" that came from the Irish, say that there is a great
" difference arisen in the army, betwixt King James'
" men and the French, about some mony that Terconell
" had to pay the army, which hee claymed as his own,
" and so deteyned."

22 March 1690 (1). . . "There is much pressing for
" seamen; but wee heare of a fleet of 400 collyers coming
" into the river; which will, we hope, lessen the price
" of coales, that have bin excessive deare all this
" winter."

4 April 1691. . "Wee have had severall strange
" relations of its (Mons) being relcived, but the first
" proved a trick . . . occasioned by one in the habit of
" a millitary man, riding, as it were, post through the
" Citty and about 6 at night, and when before the Old
" Exchange, as posting by, cryed out, Mons was releived,
" and King William in it. But this, as its supposed,
" was a contrivance of some betters, that had wagers
" about it, in order to some surprize to retrive their
" bettes." Mons was surrendered to the French on
the 7th of April. This story reminds us of a charge
made of conspiracy of a similar nature about 120 years
later.

11 April 1691. . "Thursday night last, a terrible fire
" broake out at Whitehall in the stone gallery, and hath
" consumed a great part of that pallace. It began,
" its sayd, in the Duchess of Portsmouth's lodgings,
" now preparing for the Duke of Glocester, occasioned
" by a mayd's burning off of a single candle from the
" pound, insted of cutting it with a knife; and so,
" going hastely away before the flame extinguished,
" caused the eruption of this great conflagration . . .
" I hear the Duke of Glocester's lodgings are burnt
" down, as also the Lord Devonshire's, the Lord Over-
" kirk's, and a great part of the Earl of Monmouth's."

18 April 1691. . . "On Thursday last, one Mr. Brabant,
" once an officer in the Custom House, and put out
" lately, as hee sayd, by Sir John Lowther, one of the
" Comissioners of the Treasury, and a Privy Councellor,
" came to Sir John Lowther, and reproved him for
" what hee had don, and held a pistoll to him, and told
" him, if hee would not fight with him, hee would shoot
" him. Upon which, Sir John went with him to Hide
" Park, and they fought; and its sayd Sir John hath
" received two wounds, but not mortall, but Brabant is
" fled."

25 April 1691. . . "This week was our Sessions,
" where were convicted some cittizens for giving great
" sums, to have greater repayed, if Dublin were in the
" possession of King William and Queen Mary at a
" certaine time; and fined 200l. each, and to be im-
" prisoned till paid." Their disloyalty consisted, in fact,
in betting against the probability of Dublin being out
of King James's possession at a certain future date.

16 May 1691. . "This week was sentenced at the
" King's Bench bar a parson of Buckinghamshire (being
" convicted at the Assizes in the cuntry, for drinking
" King James's health, and confusion to King William
" and Queen Mary; hee had taken, notwithstanding, the
" oaths of Aleageance and Supreamacy,) to pay 100 marks,
" and [be] caryed before all the Courtes in Westminster
" Hall with a labell on his hat of his offence, and the like
" to bee don at 3 Assizes in the cuntry. Hee sayd, by
" way of excuse, hee was drunk (a sweet apology for a
" devine). . . Its sayd, Dr. Beveridge, elect for Bath
" and Wells, refused to take it, and so is put out of
" being the King's Chaplyn." He became Bishop of
St. Asaph in 1704.

31 May 1691. . . "There was tryed this weeke an
" experiment of a new engine for diving for wreck;
" the inventor exposing himselfe in person on the first
" essay. Tis invented, in order to fetch up Spanish
" bullion and coyns, that was cast away in Scotland in
" the Spanish invasion (1588), the guns and some gould
" haveing already bin taken up. The figure which
" incloses the diver, is in the shape of a bell, and an
" expedient to convey with it barrells of ayre for the
" diver's better subsistance in the deepe."

6 June 1691. . . . "It is much admired here that
" Monseur St. Ruth is sent over from France to bee
" Generall there, who hath bin so monstrous a perse-
" cutor, that even the Papistes themselves cry out
" against him; and its thought his coming thither will
" cause a difference betwixt the French and the Irish;
" tho' its sayd hee hath shewed some kind of lenity
" towards the Protestants, since his arrivall there."

13 June 1691. . "I am informed Spelmans Coun-
" cells (Concilia), both partes, are printing in one
" volume; the 2d part is very scarce, and of a pro-
" digious price, by reason it was burnt in the Fire of
" London."

21 June 1691. . . "They say there is an express that
" our King hath sent a challenge to the King of France
" to fight him, and that if he do not come out into the
" feild with his army for that purpose, hee will breake
" on upon him with his."

4 July 1691. . . "There is just now a fray betwixt
" the Whitefriar's men, called ' Alsatians,' and the gen-
" tlemen of the Temple; the Templers shutting up the
" back gates against them, they have broken them open,

J. R. PINE
COFFIN,
Esq.

3 B 3

J.R. PINN
COFFIN.
Esq.

" and some part of the wall. The Sherriffes are gon to
" quiet them. . . . Since the above written, I under-
" stand that the Sherriffe, with his posse, hath van-
" quished the White Fryers Raparees; but with the loss
" of one of his officers, who was killed, and sevorall
" men wounded. But the pest are fled from their
" quarters, and about 70 of them sent to the severall
" prisons within the gates."
11 July 1691. . . "Major Diamond, that brought
" news of the taking of Athlone to the Queene, was
" since murdered by three Irish Papists, as hee was
" talking with a gent in the Strand, in the midle of the
" day. One of them was presently seized, who dis-
" covered the other two."
18 July 1691. . . "It is sayd that the Lord Dartmouth
" was taken into custody for having some of King James
" his plate, and a tryall hath bin against the Lord Cas-
" tlemaine for keeping some plate which hee sayd hee
" had when he went his embassage unto Rome, and
" that, since, King James gave it him; but it appearing
" at the tryall that it was after the abdication, the Jury
" found 3,000 li. and odd money for the King."
25 July 1691. . . "Here hath bin lately acted a very
" sad tragedy by a young gent of Grayes Inn, viz., one
" Mr. Bird, who was a student there, and lived in his
" father's chambers. His father was bred an attorny
" in the North cuntry, and called lately to the bar in
" his old age. Hee had gotten a great estate, but many
" children; was very fond of this his eldest, and took
" much care to breed him up, so that he might be
" eminent in his calling, and so marry him so as to
" have a portion that might contribute to the advance-
" ment of the younger children. The young man came
" not long since from the University of Oxford; where
" it seems, unknown to his father, hee marryed with
" the butler's daughter of the Colledge. She came
" lately to town, big with child, lodged neer Hyde Park.
" This match being discovered to the father, made him
" outragious in anger towards his son . . . which took
" so much impression, as is supposed, on the son, that
" on Fryday was sevennight, in the evening, hee wrote
" a letter to her, to meet him in some feild neare Hyde
" Park; wher being mett, she was murdered by having
" her throat cutt by him; his letter to invite her there
" being found in her pocket, and nothing taken from
" her, nether rings, cloathes, nor mony, her husband
" was fourthwith apprehended, who had newly changed
" his cloathes, but his handes cut and bloody." From
other letters we find that he was finally hanged at
Tyburn, and his body buried in the church of St.
Andrew's Holborn.
15 August 1691. . . "Last Sunday night, a young
" gent of the Cursitors Office, about 10 o'clock, going
" through Grayes Inn Lane, passing by two inhabitantes
" there, one a shoemaker, having a pipe in his mouth,
" without any provocation, broke his pipe with his
" gauntlet frenge glove; and the man only saying it
" was not faire, hee drew his sword, and run him
" through the body, and killed him; for which hee was
" by Mr. Buck, a Justice in Hatton Garden, sent to
" Newgate." From other letters we learn that, being
sentenced to death, he was taken to Tyburn in a coach,
and hanged; and that his body was buried in the church
of St. Andrew's Holborn.
22 August 1691. . . "This morning two granadere
" soldiers were shot to death in Hyde Park, according
" to martiall sentence, for mutynny against their officer,
" a leiftenant."
29 August 1691. . . "Wee are informed that Sir Jo.
" Knight, the Mayor of Bristol, and others, should send
" a message to Exeter to the Judges at the Assizes, to
" let them know that if they came to Bristoll that
" season, they could not be enterteyned at the charges
" of the citty; and that the Judges returned answer
" that, as to theyr enterteynment, they would not dis-
" pute it, but were resolved, according to course, to
" come there, and doe justice."
13 Sept. 1691. . . "Mr. Axe, Sir William Portman's
" servant, whom I knew well, lately dyed, and by his
" will hath given 1,000 li. to incourage some mathe-
" maticall students to finde out the true Longitude, for
" the benefit of navigators."
17 October 1691. . . "Its sayd that when the bone-
" fires and ringing of the bells was, for the surrender
" of Lymericke (the next day being the late King
" James' birthday); after the clock stroke twelve, which
" was the beginning of the other day, a fresh bonefire
" was made in some part of the town, and the bells
" rung out afresh, according to a secret reservation

J.R. Pinn
COFFIN.
Esq.

" under the umbrage of the other celebration, which
" was taken notice of."
7 November 1691. . . "Wee have gotten a new way
" of expressing our solemnity; viz., instead of bonefires,
" illuminations; that is, all the windows towards the
" streets, and bell conics, fitted with candles burning,
" which makes the night like day :"—In reference to
the Gunpowder Plot, and the Anniversary of King
William's landing, 5th of November.
20 Dec. 1691. . . "It is sayd that General Ginkle
" is to bee made Duke of Buckingham." De Reede
Ginkle received only the Earldom of Athlone, in the
Peerage of Ireland. In the same letter, mention is
made of a Mr. Richard Opie, once of Plymouth, but
afterwards of Basingstoke, being found drowned near
London Bridge.
30 January 1691(2). . . "One parson Smith, Reader,
" or Lecturer, of Chelsy, was yesterday comitted (by
" the Lord Cheif Justice Holt) being accused for being
" concerned in many robberyes, and assisting high-
" waymen."
6 February 1691(2). . . "On Thursday there was a
" tryall in Westminster Hall touching a wager about
" Lymericke being in King William's possession by
" the 3d of October; whereas there was but a part in
" possession. But there being present at Westminster
" the Lord Athlone, Lord Cutts, and General Talmash,
" et al. [and others] who gave evidence that tho part
" were then only delivered in possession, yet they
" might, according to the articles, have had all, but for
" some reasons which they alledged in Court, they
" thought fit not to take possession of all till some days
" after; and so the verdict was given against the
" Jacobite party, there being many wagers for many
" thousand pounds, depending on the same basis."
21 February 1691(2). . . "Altho the thaw begun a
" week since, yet on Thursday there were some that
" passed over the Thames without a boat. The last
" Lord's Day there was an Italian sermon preached in
" the afternoone at Guildhall Chappell, and I heare it
" is to bee continued weekely there as a Lecture, to
" gratifie some of our London merchants. Dr. Wood-
" ruffe read at the same time the service of the Church
" of England in the Italian language. . . . On Saturday
" night last, or rather, Sunday morning, one Mr. Lawes,
" the schoolmaster of Maydston in Kent, being at an
" inn and drinking with Serjeant Wyatt's son, upon
" some quarrell, Lawes killed Wyatt, and fled for it.
" Its sayd that his Majesty, understanding that the
" Countesse of Marlborough continued with the Princess
" of Denmark at the Cockpit, signified his dislike of it';
" upon which, the Princess, not liking the message,
" not only dismissed the Countess, but also hath ac-
" quitted the lodgings herselfe, and is gone to Syon
" House. On Thursday, at 10 in the night, a gent was
" killed with his own sword by two watermen in St.
" Paul's Churchyard; the watermen fled, and are not
" taken."
5 March 1691(2). . . "There was a duell fought lately,
" as we heard, by the Lord Berclay and Collonel Green-
" vill, about Madam Temple, one of the Mayds of Honor;
" but no great hurt don, saving, its sayd, the last re-
" ceived a slight wound. There dyed one morning the
" last weeke, as hee was making himselfe ready in the
" morning, one Mr. Panceford, aged twixt 60 and 70."
9 April 1692. . . "Murders have been committed
" almost every day this weeke last past. On Thursday
" last, one Captain Baker was killed at Whitehall; and
" a day or two before, an officer of the army or navy
" killed the Bedlo of St. Clementes in the midle of the
" afternoone; for which hee is in Newgate. Also, one
" Mr. Thornecroft, a Cursitor, killed Mr. Cansdall at
" Hide Park in a duell, and one Mr. Cooke, of the Six
" Clerks office, I suppose, is now on his tryall for killing
" a man a while since in the Strand. Harrison, that
" hath layne some tyme in Newgate, accused for mur-
" dering Dr. Clench, hath bin tryed, and found guilty
" of the murder, and, amongst other remarkable cir-
" cumstances, one was the evidence of a semestress who
" possitively proved that bee bought the hanchircheif of
" her, which was found about the Doctor's neck." Dr.
Clench, a physician, on pretext of being summoned
to attend a patient, was strangled in his coach.
16 April 1692. . . "Yesterday was executed Harrison,
" in Holborne, for the murder of Doctor Clench. He
" was convicted by a multitude of concurring circum-
" stances, tho' he denyed the fact at last. His tryall
" and execution will come out, 6d. a part, which you
" shall have."

23 April 1692. . . "Its sayd that some gentlemen
" from France landed lately at Rumney Marsh ; three
" were taken, two made their escape, but one is in
" custody. Its also sayd they have some treasonable
" papers in the ship ; its sayd likewise that the last
" night a sham declaration from King James was posted
" up in this towne."

30 April 1692. . . This day were installed the call of
" new Serjeants, and Sir J. Treby made Lord Chief
" Justice of the Common Pleas. The formality of
" walking was dispensed with, by reason of the ex-
" ceeding wet weather ; they being carried in coaches.
" The motto of their rings is, ' Lex domi, arma Jovis.'
" Mr. Row, who should have bin one, lyes a dying ; hee
" is our countryman. Mr. Smyth, of the Midle Temple,
" refusing it, Mr. Bonithan, a Comissioner, had that
" vacancy."

7 May 1692. . . "The busines about the French their
" discent on us is so confusedly talked of, that I know
" not how to methodize it for a relation ; but that they
" designed it, as also that they were incouraged to it
" by some Bedleme Protestantes as well as Papistes
" here, I doe not doubt ; but our fleet being out, and
" we awake, its supposed they are prevented this tyme.
" Its sayd wee are encamping about Portsmouth ; a
" 100 carriages past through the City this day towards
" that place." A few days after this, the French fleet
was destroyed in the battle off Cape La Hogue.

14 May 1692. . . "On Munday, a malitia for Middle-
" sex appeared in arms before the Queenes Majesty in
" Hide Park ; and the day following the malitia for
" London did the like, the Lord Mayor in a millitary
" habit on horseback, being their leader, which her
" Majesty took very kindly. The last night was a great
" search for horses in and about the towne ; and an
" imbargo, by order of Councell, for the stopp of all
" horses whatsoever till further order ; and its sayd the
" Counsell will not sit till Munday ; so that, thes being
" Whitsaun Eve, many gallantes are hendred from
" travelling to Epsom and other places of pleasure ; as
" well as many others from journeying about their
" lawfull occasions. There was a search made for Sir
" John Fenwick (on the proclamation) the last night,
" who narrowly escaped out of his bedchamber ; they
" seized his breeches, etc. Yesterday there having
" been a hearing in Chancery before the Lords Com-
" missioners of the Great Seale, of a cause between the
" Earle of Clare and the Earle of Thanet ; after which,
" the two Lords casually meeting in Lincoln's Inn
" Feilds, had a rancounter, both being wounded, but
" not mortally."

21 May 1692. . . "Since my last, the Lord Lucas,
" Lieutenant of the Tower, seized the Lord Midleton,
" late Secretary to King James, and another lord, and
" one Sir — Forrester, in a widdow woman's house at
" Wapping ; who are committed to the Tower, and she
" to Newgate. Mr. Raytter, that maryed the Lady
" Chichester, was seized and committed to Newgate,
" but is out on bayle." The letter then gives news of
the recent victory, on the 19th of May, off Cape La
Hogue.

2 July 1692. . . "There was lately apprehended one
" Cole, a plumber, and committed to Newgate, upon
" suspicion to be one of the murderers of Dr. Clench.
" Hee was accused by the widdow of one Miller, who
" lately dyed in Cole's house, and supposed hee was
" poysoned by Cole ; and Miller told his wife, a little
" before his death, that Cole and himself were the two
" persons that murdered him."

18 August 1692, . . "Our pacquet boat from Holland
" is blown up, 100 persons in it, 60 perisht, and 40
" floating on the water, their lives were saved by an
" Ostender."

3 September 1692. . . "I saw Captaine Salisbury
" that brought the expresse of a party of our army
" being gon towards France. Hee was in the paquet
" boat that was blown up, and was thrown 3 fathom
" under water ; but as hee got up, his head struck
" against a plank, and plunged him down againe as
" deepe as before ; but getting up againe, hee took hold
" of the plank, and so was saved by the help of the
" Ostender, that they thought to bee their enemy ; hee
" told mee hee saw the man executed that was tryed
" for designing to kill King William."

10 September 1692. . . "I tremble almost to relate
" it—That on Thursday last, about 2 in the afternoone,
" there happened a generall earthquake, or shaking of
" the earth, throughout all London City and suburbs,
" and about 20 miles as some say, others less, others
" more, in the circumferong counties. I must confesse

" I, nor no one of my family, perceived the shaking,
" tho most of my neighbours did, and even ran out of
" their houses . . . only I had this symtome, which,
" upon discourse, most others had ; viz., a giddines in
" my head at the time : the stroak, or shock, lasted not
" above a minute, or, as many say, but an halfe minute.
" . . . What controvercy God intends further with us,
" is only known to Himselfe. P.S. The superstructure
" of the buildings not only shaked, but the ground itself ;
" and those that were in vaults and cellers affected with
" the shock, as well as those in chambers. Even those
" which sate on the benches on the Royall Exchange
" were shaken, as they sate."

17 September 1692. . . "I perceive by your letter
" you felt not the earthquake in your parts. It was
" felt in the King's camp, also at Amsterdam and
" Ostend, and in most places within 60 miles, and
" further, about London."

24 September 1692. . . "I was last night with Mr.
" Petit, that assisted Dr. Burnet in searching the Par-
" liament Rolls, when he wrote the Reformation, and hath
" now Mr. Pryn's place of Record Keeper of the Records
" in the Tower ; and, hee tells me Sir Robert Cotton hath
" for some tyme given him the free use of his Manu-
" script Library, where hee hath bin for some tyme very
" busy." William Petyt's Collection of MSS. is now in
the Inner Temple Library, and has formed the subject
of notice in a previous Report of this Commission.

15 October 1692. . . "I had a short view of Sir R.
" Cotton's Library. It is scituated adjoyning to the
" House of Commons at Westminster, of a great highth,
" and part of that old fabrick, but very narrow, as I
" remember, not full 6 feet in breadth, and not above
" 26 in length ; the books placed on each side, of a
" tollerable highth, so that a man of an indifferent
" stature may reach the highest. Over the books are
" the Roman Emperors, I mean, their heads, in brass
" statues, which serve for standards in the Catalogue, to
" direct to find any particular book, viz., under such an
" Emperor's head, such an number. . . . I had not time
" to look into the books ; some relicts I took notice of,
" besides the books ; viz., I saw there Sir H. Spelman's
" and Buchanons pictures, well don ; also, Ben John-
" son's and Sir R. Cotton's, and in the staires was
" Wicliff's. I had in my hand the sword of Hugo Lupus,
" Earle of Chester, that came in with the Conquest. I
" saw Pope Eugeneus his Bull to the King of England ;
" the originall in a faire Greek character in parchment,
" anno 1500 [?] and od yeares. Instead of wax seales,
" were the Cardinalls' heads in metall, that subscribed
" it. I also saw Dr. Dee's instruments of conjuration,
" in cakes of bees wax almost petrified, with the images,
" lines, and figures, on it."

29 October 1692. . . "The last night, a young gent,
" one Mr. Chester, heire to a good estate, went in alone
" to supp at the Fountaine Taverne in Covent Garden,
" upon a dozen of larks ; and sending the boy for a
" tart to close his supper, when the drawer returned,
" (he) found him dead, having shott himself with a
" pistoll. A gent of my acquaintance saw him dead
" this morning."

2 December 1692. . . "This day sevennight, in the
" night, certain ruffians broke into the house of Mr.
" Johnson, the Lady Russell's Chaplain, who in King
" James' tyme, underwent almost the same punish-
" ment with Dr. Oates ; and assarscinated [? assaulted]
" him in his bed, (and) wounded him ; but the people
" of the house crying out, the watch prevented
" murder."

11 December 1692. . . "This week hath bin boystrous
" and tempestuous for the most part ; and hath had its
" sutable effect on mens minds, for there have bin 3 or
" 4 duells fought here, within 3 or 4 days, viz.—The
" Lord of Banbury fought with his brother in law,
" Captain Lawson, and killed him, and is now on his tryall
" at the Old Bayly. Also, one Young, a young clerk,
" fought with another clerk, one Graham, of Clifford's
" Inn, the later was killed ; and yesterday the Lord
" Mohun fought with a player, and killed him. . . . I
" am told that 15 smiths were seized at once in Kent
" Street in Surry, working on instruments to breake
" houses, and clipping and coyning of mony ;"—Montfort the player, was, in reality, murdered, in cold blood,
by Lord Mohun.

28 January 1692 (3). . . "I have bin at the cane shop,
" and made an essay for a cane ; I wish you had men-
" tioned the length, for canes being exceeding deare,
" the shorter will come much cheaper ; so that I have
" resisted the buying one till Mr. Fyne's return, because
" I would have his advice thereon. . . Yesterday being

" our execution day, many highwaymen were executed
" at Tiburn; and Whitney, the ringleader, was caryed
" in a cart with them, but had his repreive at the
" gallows, and brought back on horseback, behind one
" of the Sheriffs' officers."
4 Feb'. 1692 (3). . . "The grand highwayman, Whit-
" ney, notwithstanding his repreive, was executed at
" Cow Crosse, neer Smithfield, Wednesday last."
11 Feb'. 1692 (3). . . " Wee have a strange distemper,
" that of late years raigns much amongst us, which was
" rare amongst our ancestors; but some are of opinion
" that it was more frequent then, but not so much taken
" notice of; it is a diabetes. Some languish away in it
" sooner than others. Some have had it upon them 2
" or 3 yeares. I met with one that told me hee had had
" it 2 yeares, and thought it would end his dayes. The
" Lord Brooke died of it, in 6 weekes sickness."
18 February 1692 (3). . . Mr. Young, the parson, that
" hath bin formerly convicted for forgeries, and stood
" in the pillory, according to sentence, stood 3 times
" during this week in the pillory for forging writings,
" and endeavouring to bring the Bishop of Rochester
" [Thomas . Sprat] and others, in a plott against the
" government."
25 February 1692 (2). . . " Yesterday morning was
" taken upp a man in ecclesiastical vestmentes out of
" the Thames, dead, being wounded in severall partes of
" his body. Some say its the schoolmaster of Camber-
" well."
14 May 1693. . . . . "One Captain Winter was
" condemned the last Sessions for killing a man in a
" ryott, 12 months since, in White Fryers, and having
" gotten a repreive for some dayes in order to a pardon,
" the Lord Mayor and Aldermen have bin at Whitehall
" to desire the Queen that he may be executed, and,
" the busines being debated in Councell, its sayd hee
" wilbe executed neer the place where the fact was
" comitted."
27 May 1693. . . "I have bin in great consultation
" with myselfe, what periwigg to send, since you did
" not give particular order about the size. I have
" been veiwing the shoppes, both in London by the Old
" Exchange, and in the Strand, and find that short
" perriwiggs, which they call ' bobbs,' are generally
" worne this summer, and especially by young gentle-
" men; so that I could not meet with one large peri-
" wigg of faire haire ready made, fitt for your son's
" wearing, and therefore send the short one, which is
" very fashionable, and I beleive will become him; it
" must bee combed out before it bee worne, it cost
" 22s. . . . Against the winter, if you give directions, I
" will see that a larger and more generous one shalbe
" made."
10 June 1693. . . "A woman of the play-house, being
" heard to sing a beastly lampoon on the Queene, an
" officer was sent to seize her, and in her lodgings were
" found severall of the libells, and one of her own
" handwriting. She was offred a pardon if she would
" discover the author, which refusing, she was tryed,
" and sentenced to be exposed on the pillory at 3
" severall places."
18 June 1693. . . "Yesterday was executed Anderton,
" the printer, at Tyburne, with 6 other criminalls: and
" Mrs. Lettice, the player, stood upon the pillory in the
" Strand, for singing and publishing a beastly lampoone
" against the government."
22 December 1693. . . " Wednesday last, being ex-
" ecution day, was a sad instance:—2 young gent' (the
" sons of Colonel Broame, a gent of quallity of Kent,
" their father dead,) were caried in a coach to Tyburne,
" and there executed, for killing an alehouse-keeper in
" Fleet Street. Here is of late a great discourse touch-
" ing a kind of miracle that cured a lame French girle,
" about 13 years old, the case thus.—The girle, when
" about halfe a yeare old, dropt out of her father's arms,
" and put her thigh and one toe out of joynt, which
" could never bee replaced. On a Lord's Day in No-
" vember, as she was in a deformed posture hobling
" long the streets, the boys mockt her; at which,
" being disgusted, when she returned home, acquainted
" her mistress therewith, who advised her to bear it
" patiently, for it could not be holpen. Presently after,
" the girle, looking into the New Testament, and read-
" ing the place where our Saviour performed such
" cures, sayd she,—' Its a wonder those Jews would
" ' not all beleive our Saviour, and come and bee
" ' healed; if hee were now on the earth, I would goo to
" ' him, and make noe doubt hee would heale mee, as
" ' he did some in those days.' Upon which, at the
" very instant her bones snapt, which was heard by the

" people in the roome, and from that time her dislocated
" limbs are set, and she perfectly well. The Bishop of
" Salisbury, and many persons of quallity, have been to
" see her. I spoke with a surgeon, who was sent by
" Doctor Ridgely, an eminent doctor of 80 yeares old,
" to see her, and the surgeon gives this account according
" to the relation, and believes it."
13 January 1693 (4). . . "Satturday night-last was a
" great entertaynment made for the Prince of Baden
" at Kensington, where was dancing and gaming, and
" a great supper; and banquets of sweetmeats all com-
" mon to such as were admitted in to bee spectators :
" and I was informed by one that was present, that hee
" supposed there could not be less than one thousand
" persons: but it was 5 of the clock in the morning
" before some of them could get home."
17 February 1693 (4). . . "The Commons have fallen
" upon many excellent pointes lately, whereof one is,
" that there bee a middle punishment for highway men,
" betwixt hanging and squitting, viz., exposed to la-
" bour; and that workhouses bee set up for that pur-
" pose, and also for imploying beggars and poor people."
The first germs of systems which have since been
adopted.
10 March 1693 (4). . . " Yesterday was convened before
" the House of Commons a parson of Essex, for saying
" that Sir — Marsham, one of the Knights of that shire,
" was a pentioner; for which hee was ordered to be
" taken into custody, and so remayns."
31 March 1694. . . " I suppose the news of the dread-
" full storme at Gibleator [Gibraltar], mentioned in the
" Gazet, cam to you before these. One Sir — Boveree,
" an eminent merchant of London, had 20,000li. in the
" fleet, and, its sayd, 3 sons; and hee being ill before,
" the news hastened his death."
6 April 1694. . . " Wee have news from Shrewsbury,
" of a horrid murder there committed on the body of
" one Captain Brown, who hath an estate there, and
" not long since lived at Sea-Hoe, in London. The
" murder was committed by 3, one of them his servant,
" for the love of 20 li. Its sayd an apparition made
" some signs of this murder to some of his freinds."
The above mode of spelling the then recently-named
locality of " Soho," deserves notice.
14 April 1694. An account is given of the death, in
that week, of Mr. Wilson (generally known in those
days as " Bean Wilson") in a duel, fought in Blooms-
bury Square, " with one Mr. Laas [Law], a Scotchman."
According to Mrs. Manly, in the New Atlantis, Wilson was
supported on a scale of magnificence, for some years, by
one of the mistresses of Charles II. His apparent
opulence, as compared with his prior poverty, with the
mystery as to the source from which it was derived, is
here also alluded to. Law escaped from Newgate, after
being found guilty of murder, eventually to start in
France the Mississippi Scheme, the explosion of which
convulsed that country. Some biographies state that
Law was born in 1681; but it is evident from this letter
that an earlier date must be assigned for his birth.
29 April 1694. . . "A gent., on Thursday last, that
" came lately out of the country, told a friend of his,
" my acquaintance, and in my hearing, this passage;
" viz., that the last Lord's Day, on his journy to London,
" hee being at a gentleman's house in Bucks, went with
" him to his parish church, where hee heard a very
" good sermon on these words—' Wherefore walk cir-
" ' cumspectly, etc.' and that in the sermon hee gave
" them caution to take care of being deluded, etc. That
" this gent, discoursing at dinner about the sermon,
" his friend told him the occasion of the sermon was
" remarkable; for that another minister of the Church
" of England, not far from the place, reputed always
" to bee a sober man, had lately pretended to visions,
" and declared that it was revealed to him, that at Whit-
" sunday our Saviour would personally appeare on the
" earth, which would cause a strange change, etc. But
" there is this very odd circumstance; hee advised the
" people to provide for a Judaicall sacrifice of oxen,
" sheep, etc., and sayd this, as a precept, was also re-
" vealed to him. Now this is contrary to Scripture;
" and this gent sayth that 6 or 7 families of this minis-
" ter's congregation, that preached this sermon, were
" gon with their goodes and treasure to this prophet's
" place of residence. I have made inquiry, and others
" doe affirme that they have heard of this enthusiast."
2 June 1694. . . " Here is a report that the Bishop
" of Hereford [Dr. Gilbert Ironside] was present and
" caused to be rased and obliterated an inscription
" which was on the tombe of Collonel Birch, some

" while since dead; which. is like to cause great ani-
" mosity."

30 June 1694. ., " One Mr. Cary, that was partner
" with Sir Thomas Cooke, and one Mr. Guy, a book-
" seller, were chosen Sheriffs, but upon their refusall
" and desire to fyne, there is to bee speedily another
" election." The future Founder of Guy's Hospital is
here meant.

7 July 1694. . . . . . (mutilated) " of the Society of
" the Middle Temple against the Benchers, and some
" indecent actions committed; as throwing down the
" Benchers' tables and looking the Hall doore, and
" keeping them. out of commons. This hath been re-
" presented to the Lord Chief Justice Holt, and yester-
" day both sides were convened before his Lordship at
" Serjeant's Inn; where, on hearing the matter, his
" Lordship, like a man of courage, sharply reprimanded
" the young gent[s], and told them hee would take
" care that they should bee severely prosecuted and
" punished."

4 August 1694. . " One thing may be remarkable to
" hint, viz., of a feald near Meadston in Kent not
" tilled these 3 or 4 yeares, which beares this year, with-
" out plouwing or sowing, a faire crop of wheat, and
" Mr. Freke that came lately from Tunbridge, in my
" hearing sayd, hee saw a crop from one root which
" boro 58 stalks, I mean, cares; and that it hangs up as
" a *monument* there."

27 October 1694. . . . " 42 people in the beginning
" of the night, in Acton rode, near Tiburne, were stript
" by robbers on the highway, and turned into a common
" feild . . . Lord Clancarty has made his escape out of
" the Tower, being a prisoner of war there."

10 Nov'. 1694. . . " There is an estate of between 2
" and 3,000 li. per annum fallen lately, besides a great
" personal estate, to the widow and relict of Major
" General Ludlow, who dyed in Switzerland; and there
" being one Mr. Thomas, a young man of about 30
" yeares of age, a leiftenant in the King's army, who
" pretended clayme to some part of the estate, she
" hath lately marryed him, shee being 62 yeares of
" age." Major General Ludlow died at the age of 91.

11 January 1694 (5). . . " Sixteen children, about
" the time of the late thaw, being upon the Thames,
" near Stanes, the ice breaking, were all drowned;
" and four of them were one man's children."

18 January 1694 (5). . " Its also reported there are 3
" goldsmiths of note, one of Lumbard Street, that are
" in Newgate, upon the account of clipping [the coin].
" . . . Two remarkable passages happed not many
" dayes before the Queen's death; an eagle shot by
" Mr. Hart, son to Sir Percivall Hart, in Kent, on
" Christmas Day last; and an old lyon refusing meat
" and dying, alike before the Queene. Both I have
" from good handes."

26 January 1694 (5) . . . " The Parliament, as I am
" informed, were yesterday upon laying a taxe upon
" all christenings, weddings, and buryalls."

6 February 1694(5). . . . " The Lord Admirall Russell,
" at Christmas last, at his cuntry appartments at Cales
" [Cadiz] made an extraordinary feast; 750 dishes, the
" first course an ox, roasted whole; 12 hogsheads of
" punch in a fountaine, in which was a little boy that
" was in a boat swimming on the punch sea, and
" delivered it to the companie. The Admirall had 800
" men to wait on him: this was very amazing to the
" Spaniards."

23 February 1694 (5). . . " This day sevennight, Mr.
" Guy, Secretary to the Lords Commissioners of the
" Treasury, (a man deemed to be worth at least an
" 100,000l., and a member of Parliament), was com-
" mitted to the Tower for being faulty in his office,
" where he still continues." It deserves notice, that
Thomas Guy, the bookseller, already mentioned, who
afterwards (1721) founded Guy's Hospital, entered Parliament this year, as member for Tamworth, but at a
later date.

9 March 1694 (5). . . . " At Hartford, one Mr. Hynton
" (the son of a woollen draper in Paul's Churchyard), a
" young man of about [2]2 or 23 yeares old [was con-
" demned] for robbing on the highway. Hee hath bin
" formerly tried for other roberies, and transported;
" but being so notorious and audacious, according to
" speciall order of the judge, hee was executed the
" same day sentence passed, for feare of an escape.
" At Winchester was condemned an Alderman's son, of
" that towne, as I take it, for robbing on the highway;
" and also one Captain Clark, (late governor of Cows
" in the Isle of Wight) for either clipping or coyning."

5.

15 June 1695. . . " On Munday night last, being the
" anniversary of the. Nativity of the Prince of Wales,
" some lewd heroes assembled at the Dog Tavern in
" Drury Lane, and there caused a bonefire to bee made,
" and had a drumme and other military musick, and
" drunk, and inforced others that passed by to drink,
" the Prince of Wales health. But the mob soone got
" about them, and broke the vintner's windows, and
" would have don more damage, had not mony been
" given to them to prevent it. One of them is taken,
" and severall others of the ringleaders discovered."

29 September 1695. . . " One Saunders' Chamber was
" broken open in the Inner Temple; where they found
" 50 li. of money clipt, and the clippings, and all the
" engins and instruments for doing it: but hee, not
" being within, hath fled for it, and since, its sayd, one
" Berry (a gentleman's son of good quallity) of the
" Temple, is taken into custody for the like crime, and,
" its sayd, Saunders is a Somersetshire gentleman's
" son."

7 December 1695. . . " Mr. Johnson, the minister
" that was so lamentably scourged, when Doctor Oates
" underwent his sentence, (or much about the tyme),
" hath obteyned the King's grant, as I am credibly
" informed, for 1000 li. in ready mony to pay his debts,
" and 300 li. per annum, during his and his son's life."

28 December 1695. . . " Mr. Litlebury, the famous
" bookseller, dyed on Christmas Day, of a cancer in his
" mouth, at the 74th yeare of his age . . . Wee have
" news here that a parson neer Exeter is in prison there
" for clipping and coyning; it is a sad case, if it bee so,
" that a minister of the Church dare commit such a
" fact."

15 February 1695 (6). " I have placed my son in
" Pemebrook Colledge, the Society being under the care
" of the Bishop of Bristol, Dr. Hall, who is Master, and
" constantly resident. . The house, tho it bee but a
" litle one, yet is reputed to be one of the best for
" sobriety and order."

28 February 1695 (6). " The Earle of Castlemayne
" hath surrendered himself, and Goodman, the player,
" is in Newgate; who is his Dutchess' favorite. Mr.
" Porter, in the proclamation, being in custody, they
" say hath made a large discovery of the whole plott."

7 March 1695 (6). . " I was told this morning that Sir
" Roger L'Estrange is dead in Newgate; also, that tho
" Lord Cutts seized a Frenchman in an inn in Smith-
" field, who had a muster roll of the English and
" others, engaged and in pay here to carry on this con-
" spiracy."

2 May 1696. . " On Tuesday last, the Venetian Em-
" bassadors made their entrance. Their garbe was
" black gowns, laced; the representation was very
" stately, both at the entrance and the audience, which
" was last night. I heare Prender[gast, who] first
" discovered the plott, hath his pardon, 3000 li. in
" money, and 500 li. per annum."

16 May 1696. . " The graziers will not bring their
" catle to towne, by reason of the scarcity of good
" mony. The goldsmiths faulter much in bringing
" fourth their best mony, and would still put the peo-
" ple off with clipt. Severall of them have been lately
" arrested, though men reputed very wealthy. Guineas
" are scarce, but wee hope a litle tyme will make great
" alteration for the best."

11 July 1696. . " There was lately one seized neare
" the Isle of Shipay in Kent, a man in a beggers habit,
" that had for some tyme gon about a begging; but
" one night at the house were hee lodged, bespoke a
" joynt of mutton for supper, and talking somewhat
" more portly than beggers use to doe, the people of
" the house discovering it to the neighbors the next
" day, after he went out, persued him and tooke him,
" and, upon examination and search, found he had
" quilted about him 500 guynees. So hee is now in
" Maydston Goale, upon suspition to bee the Lord
" Mountgomery, in the procl[amation]."

12 Sept'. 1696. . . . " A great many clippers and
" coyners are apprehended, and mills seized for coyning;
" and a proclamation is issued against one Captaine
" Wintour, a gent of about 800 li. a yeare, in Glocester-
" shire; and severall other his accomplices, charged
" with the same crimes."

17 October 1696. . . " My neighbour, Dr. Williams,
" is made Bishop of Chichester, and yesterday the
" drums, hoeboys, and musick, saluted him."

24 October 1696. . " Yesterday, ten malefactors were
" executed at Tiburn, some for clipping and coyning;
" one for carrying news into France, formerly a

3 C

" stationer in Chancery Lane, his name Pike : hee was
" quartered : and the Frenchman that killed his father
" in law, who hath bin for some tyme repreived ; and,
" as I this day am informed, hee was carried in a
" coach to St. Giles Church, some tyme before the
" rest : where was a sermon preached to him."

31 October 1696. . . . " Wee have abundance of rotten
" sheepe here, and never more plenty of mutton. I
" was told this morning that sheepe were sold in Smyth-
" feild the last Fryday (some) for 1s. 6d. a sheepe."

30 January 1696 (7). After given an account of Sir
John Fenwick's execution on Tower Hill. . . " Hee sayd
" nothing to the spectators, scarce looking on them,
" but delivered his speech to the Sheriffes, which is since
" printed, and here inclosed. Hee behaved himselfe
" well composed enough, as far as I can understand,
" that did not see him."

6 February 1696 (7). . . " I have lost a very old
" acquaintance since my last letter, viz., Mr. Slingsby
" Bethell, once Sherriffe of London, who dyed Thursday
" last, being 84 yeares of age. Hee was a man of great
" knowledge and understanding, and had bin a great
" travailler. I sate a good while with him the weeke
" before his death, and (he) discoursed with mee very
" hartily, and brought mee to the dore." Slingsby
Bethell was noted for his independence and for his
frugality ; the last quality closely approaching to mean-
ness. This is referred to by Dryden in his *Absalom and
Achitophel*,—" Cool was his kitchen, though his brains
" were hot."

20 Feb*. 1696 (7). . . " There hath bin some discovery
made lately by an astrologer of some treasure hid by

" the Jesuites in the Savoy, and many have bin yester-
" day and this day set on work to digg, and a guard
" attending them ; but its thought will signify nothing."

27 February 1696 (7). . . " Since my last, one Mr.
" Dekins, who marryed Sir — Bucknall the great
" brewer's widdow, fought in Hyde Park a duell with
" his son-in-law, Mr. Bucknall, and killed him ; Dekins
" is in custody."

7 August 1697. . . . " Here goes a comecall relation
" of a strange match between Lady Kingston, a
" widdow to the Lord Kingston, an Irish lord, and
" a leiftenant of the King's foot ; that she, having a
" mynd to marry him, sent him a challenge to meet at
" a tyme and place to fight, not naming the challenger,
" and hee coming there, tho' she was unknowne to him,
" and looking about for the challenger, at last saw a
" lady in a mask, who told him she was the person hee
" looked for, and then told him the occasion, and after
" some discourse carried him off in her ca[rriage], and
" in a very few bowers marryed him ; and its sayd,
" hath 1500 li. per annum estate, and worth 10,000 li. in
" money . . . . There [was] about a weeke since a
" great hubbub in the Temple, [from] an attempt to
" arrest Mr. Burlace [Borlase] of Cornwall, a gent of
" the house, resisting the officers, and tooke him from
" them ; many were wounded in it, and some of them
" have since had a conference with my Lord Chief
" Justice Holt about it ; and the Templars justify their
" defence, having [as] they say, antient preveledges for
" so doing."

HENRY THOMAS RILEY.

THE MANUSCRIPTS OF THE REVEREND EDMUND
FIELD, M.A., LANCING COLLEGE, CO. SUSSEX.

It would gratify many an owner of an old county hall
to be able to exhibit, for the illustration of his familiar
story, such a collection of documents as the records
which have come to the hands of the Reverend Edmund
Field, of Lancing College, through his connection with
the extinct family of Barker of Lyndon, in the county
of Rutland. The writings are in fact the collection
of a county family, that emerged from the ranks of
prosperous, gentle yeomanry in the earlier years of the
17th century, and after attaining the fullness of its
dignity and influence under the later Stuarts died out in
the present reign. The fittest resting place for these
memorials would be the old muniment-room of the
stately house which Sir Abel Barker built towards the
end of his life in his native county; but they are not
misplaced in a scholar's studious chamber to which the
sea breeze comes over a fine sweep of Sussex downs.
Comprising the patent of Sir Abel Barker's baronetcy
(conferred in the 17th year of Charles the Second);
the Pardon under the Great Seal which the Rutland
squire obtained from the Crown for his reluctant compliance with the revolutionary government, to which
he had yielded from prudential motives; a dozen or
more of such commissions as accumulate quickly in
families whose chiefs are required to fill offices of
dignity in their counties: and some 150 deeds (the
earliest being of the time of Edward II.), at this
time useful only to the local annalist, tracing upwards
the history of small patches of land; Mr. Field's collection contains also Sir Abel Barker's Private Letter
Book, the large number of letters (covering more than
150 years) set forth in the present report under the
title of the Barker Correspondence, and the Papers
relating to Taxation and Public Affairs in Rutland and
the adjoining counties in the 17th century.

(a.) *Private Letter Book of Abel Barker, afterwards
Sir Abel Barker, Bart., 1642 to 1665.*

Containing 308 copies of letters, written to 80 persons whose names are given in full, and several persons
whose names are only indicated by initial letters; this
manuscript book is from the first to the last line in the
handwriting of Sir Abel Barker, of Hambleton, co.
Rutland, who was high sheriff for Rutland in the
year 1646, and was created a baronet, September 9,
1665. Sir Abel died in 1679, leaving a son by his first
wife, Anne, daughter of Sir Thomas Burton, Baronet,
of Stockerson, co. Leicester, and two daughters by his
second wife, Mary, daughter of Alexander Noel, Esq.,
of Whitwell, co. Rutland, and niece to Sir Jeffrey
Palmer, Charles the Second's attorney-general. With
the exception of 15 letters, the originals of the epistles
transcribed into the Letter Book were all written by
their transcriber for the maintenance of intercourse
with his friends, or the furtherance of his numerous
affairs of business. The collection of papers exhibits
the career from early manhood to mature age of an
equally active and courteous man who, whilst managing
his own estate with vigilance, and farming lands which
he held as the tenant of neighbouring proprietors,
bestirred himself in the public business of his county,
and found leisure for social diversions. Whilst some
of the letters show their writer to have been a discreet
and clever man of business in his own interests, it is
seen from others that he was often required to act as
the adviser of acquaintances who prized his judgment
and yielded to his influence. Abounding with minute
facts for the topographer, the letters afford many agreeable illustrations of the general state of manners and
domestic life of our ancestors in the 17th century. That
Sir Abel possessed scholastic attainments, unusual in
country gentlemen of his period, appears from the
facility with which he could pen a letter in Latin to
his brother Thomas on private matters. The evidence
is no less conclusive that he was considerate for the
feelings and welfare of his dependents and less prosperous kinsmen. Of the 15 epistles, that did not come
in the first instance from the transcriber's pen, one is a
note from Sir Abel's sister Mary to her London dress-
maker, and two are letters from his mother to Sir
Thomas Burton, making overtures for her son's marriage with Sir Thomas's eldest daughter; whilst 10
were written by the last mentioned lady during the
brief period, between her engagement to Mr. Barker
and her death, which followed quickly on the birth of
her only offspring, the second baronet. These 13 letters
from three ladies, who may be regarded as fair examples

of the homely and gentle womankind of our 17th
century, are a welcome addition to a kind of literature
that has strong attractions for the historical explorer,
and is much less plentiful than he could desire. In
cataloguing the papers of this interesting collection,
I shall mention them in the order in which they
appear in the Letter Book, where they are entered
with an occasional disorder of dates, which indicates
that they were not entered into the book immediately
after the writing of the originals, and also that the
transcriptions of the Letter Book were, at least in many
cases, made from copies. The variations of the colour
of the inks, successively used in the Letter Book, afford
additional evidence that the transcriber was accustomed
to enter the letters in "batches," from time to time,
when a considerable interval had elapsed since the composition of the earlier papers of the latest accumulation
of copies. Moreover, in forming his judgment of the
oldness of the transcripts, the peruser of the Letter
Book should not fail to observe that it is written
throughout in precisely the same style of penmanship.

1. Abel Barker to the Worshipfull Thomas Wayte,
Esq., at his house in St. Jones in Middlesex. Respecting the extent of the Lordship of Tugby, co. Leicester,
being part of Mr. Wayte's estate.—Hambleton, March 7,
1641. Mr. Wayte was one of Abel Barker's landlords.

2. Abel Barker to the Right Worshipfull Sir Kenelme
Digby, Kt. at his lodgings in St. Martin's Lane. Enquiring where Sir Kenelme would like to receive his
next Lady Day's rent; whether in town or country;
and if in town, at what place. The letter begins with
"Noble sir," and ends with "I shall remain your
obsequious tenant and humble servant." Hambleton
in Roteland, March 9, 1642. Sir Kenelme Digby was
another of the writer's landlords.

3. Abel Barker to Thomas Wayte, Esq. Concerning
the assessment, in respect of "the 4 great subsidyes,"
on Mr. Wayte's land in Keytharpe and Goadby, of
which the writer is tenant. "I desire," says the
writer, "you will please to take some order for payment thereof, because it would be prejudiciall to me
if my cattle should be driven at this tyme of the
years." The writer describes himself "your affectionate friend and ready servant." Hambleton, May
3, 1642.

4. Abel Barker to his loueing brother Walter Good-
man. Excuses himself for not meeting W. G. at
Mr. Palmer's, as he has business at Lincoln Assizes.
Hambleton, July 23, 1642.

5. Abel Barker to his much respected friend Thomas
Leve, Esq. Asking for the loan of Mr. Leve's "legier
booke of all the conveyances of Sir German Poole's
land in Lincolnshire." The writer alludes to his
lawsuit with a person named Winell. Hambleton,
August 9, 1642.

6. Abel Barker to his good neighbour William
Andrew, now staying "at one Mr. Webster's in the
Bell Yard in the Strande." Entreating him to move
Sir Robert Py to accede to the writer's wishes re-
specting certain land on which he wishes to build a
house. "I have," he says, "greate occasions for
building, and I would not overslip this summer."
No date.

7. Abel Barker to the Right Worshipful Sir Kenelme
Digby. Asking for a renewal of his term in the Wood-
field, which he holds, as his father formerly held it,
under Sir Kenelme. The writer regrets he has been
referred, on the subject of his letter, to Sir Kenelme's
cousin, James Digby. Signs himself "your faithfull
tenant and humble servant." Hambleton, June 20,
1642.

8. Abel Barker to his loving friend Clement Dorman
at Tugby.—Excusing himself for remissness in not
calling on Mr. Dorman's lady sooner, as he has since
his journey to Lincolnshire been occupied "with the
welcome company of" his "kind landlords." The
writer will see her ladyship within two days, when he
hopes to "take the grounds of her." Hambleton,
August 14, 1642.

9. Abel Barker to his loving friend and most faithfull and obsequious kinsman, Thomas Collin. Regretting
that his sister "will not allowe the matter" or admit of
Mr. Collin's "dedication." The writer soothes his
kinsman's feeling by remarking, "a reason is not
always found in love." Hambleton, August 11,
1642.

10. Abel Barker to his loueing friend Mr. William
Gladwine. Concerning 530 todds of wool of the value
of 530l. sold by the writer to W. G. Hambleton, September 10, 1642.

3 C 2

11. Abel Barker to his worthy friends John and Francis Wayte in St. Jones. Applying for the payment of 10l., for which he sends a receipt; and stating that Mr. Gladwine has been instructed to pay the rent due to them from the writer. Hambleton, October 3, 1642.

12. Abel Barker to the same. Acknowledging the receipt of the 10l. The writer speaks of his recent negociations with Sir Kenelme Digby, and informs his correspondents that their tenants at Tugby are dissatisfied with Browne, the collector of their rents, who hath insulted over them heretofore. October 31, 1642.

13. Abel Barker to his loveing friend Mr. Thomas Sergyant. An urgent application for money. Hambleton. October 31, 1642.

14. Abel Barker to his loveing friend John Favill. Respecting 100l. which the writer has ordered to be paid to his correspondent, and 240 trees which he has bought. " I doe now perceive," the writer adds, " the " bargaine wilbe harder unlesse my landlords please to " amend itt, for beside that the place is worse seated " then I imagined for the sale of wood, the distractions " of this tyme are a cause that neither this nor any " other commodity in our countrey will give any money. " Itt will not be amisse therefore (if they so please) to " stay the cutting of the hedgerowes one yeare longer, " vntill these troubles be a little over for they will not " now give any money." Hambleton, January 11, 1642.

15. Abel Barker to John and Francis Waite. Announcing his recent interview " with Mr. Burton the " feodary, who sayth that soone as the tymes are more " quiet, he will send the tenants;" and informing his correspondents that they must prove that Tugby is held in soccage, Mr. Burton being confident that " itt " is held of the Abbey of Croxton in capite." No date.

16. Abel Barker to Francis Wayte. Sending a bond, due from a very sufficient man in payment of his rent ; and speaking much of the hardness of the times:— " But truly, sir, the distractions are so great in " generall and more particular in these partes wherein " we live, yt what money I had within me is all dis- " bursed by reason I dare not keepe any by me, ex- " pecting dayly when my house should be plundered, " myselfe carryed away (as most of our gentry already " are), and my goods bee exposed to the fury of the " mercilesse troopers : and from this also doth arise as " great an infelicity that hereby our commerce is " detayned so that we cannot for any commodity we " haue raise a considerable somme of money : and, if " these tymes continue, landlords with vs must expect " lottle or no rent, or if any very slowly, neither do I " for my owne part expect to receive the one halfe of " my rents due unto me." The writer begs his land-lord to pay taxes in respect to which he is threatened with a seizure of his stock. No date.

17. Abel Barker to Robert Edmund. Reproaching him in severe but stately terms with his repeated breaches of faith, and enjoining him to keep his word on Friday next. March 15, 1642.

18. Abel Barker to his uncle, Ephraim Wright. A fervid letter in which the nephew, upbraids the uncle for " seizing upon 25l. of my money, and converting " the same to your owne vse." After enumerating his several pecuniary services to his uncle, which give the delinquent's dishonesty a colour of signal ingratitude, the writer says, " That the tymes are ill for money, tis " true, therefore the more vnreasonable that you who " pay no rentes shonld detaine my money who pay so " many." He signs himself, however, " Your loueing " nephewe." Hambleton, March 30, 1643.

19. Abel Barker to Mr. Gyles Harys at London. A long and fervid letter in which the writer complains of his landlord's (i.e., Sir Edward Harington's) unfairness ; and Mr. Harys is instructed to press upon Sir Edward the writer's title to compensation for " haning beene " compelled to pay 160l. purposely for his sequestrod " rents." Offering to refer his claim to the arbitration of Mr. Harys and Mr. Collin, the writer concludes, " but if he bee not pleased to doe this he must excuse " me withdraweing from that landlord for whom I " haue suffered so much." Hambleton, December 24, 1644.

20. Abel Barker to Sir Edward Harington, Kt. and Baronet, at his house in Seething Lane, London. On the same subject as the preceding letter. After alluding to the occasion when he was " carryed prisoner " to Beluoir castle," and compelled to pay the same rent once and againe, and affirming that he has paid Sir Edward "more rents since these late distractions " than all his other tenants in these parts," he concludes

with " it is impossible for me any longer to continue " tenant to your grounds unlesse some remedy be " speedily applied." Hambleton, January 15, 1644.

21. Abel Barker to Mr. Harys. Another letter on the same matter of difference between the writer and Sir Edward Harington. Hambleton, Feb. 10, 1644.

22. Abel Barker to Mr. Gyles Harys at London. Respecting proposals about rent for the ensuing year for Sir Edward Harington's land. Mr. Harys is requested to urge Sir Edward to pay the monthly taxes due on the 20th of March, respecting which the writer has " beene much troubled by the troopers," and also another month's taxes, due on the 18th instant. Hambleton, April 28, 1646. Mr. Gyles Harys appears to have been Sir Edward's steward.

23. Abel Barker to Andrew Collin. About money claimed from Mr. Collin by his chapman, and money " paid in " to Sir Arthur Haselrig by John Canham for the writer's brother Goodman. West Smithfield, October 4, 1645.

24. Abel Barker to John Musson. Directing John Musson (the writer's farm-bailiff, and agent) to press a debtor, named Neuil, for money ; and to go to Uppingham for his master's mare. The writer wants news about his wethers ; has received 20l. of P. Woodcocke ; sends love to his mother and sister. West Smithfield, October 6, 1645.

25. Abel Barker to John Musson. Containing instructions with respect to his sheep, and expressing much sorrow at his brother Goodman's mishap, which, it is feared, is irrecoverable. Sends condolences to his sister Goodman, and wishes his mother or sister to go and comfort her. West Smithfield, October 11, 1645.

26. Abel Barker " fratri suo plurimum dilecto," J. Barker. Concerning the writer's recent interview with Sir Edward Harington, with whom he is at issue on questions of rent and taxes. John Barker is requested to speak with Mr. Harys on the points of difference, and furnish testimony against Sir Edward's proposals. West Smithfield, October 13, 1645. John Barker died in 1648 (Vide Wright's " History of Rutland "):

27. Abel Barker to his brother, Andrew Collin. Announcing his receipt of money due to his correspondent on bond from Mr. Robert Canham, and expressing his great sorrow at his brother Goodman's death. Together with other matters, the writer mentions the steps he has taken to secure for his sister Goodman the ward-ship of her son. In conclusion he says, " I desire you " wilbe pleased that I may speedily heare from you " the condition of our countrey, and when you conceive " I pay with safety come doune, for I desire to doe my " best with you in my sister's behalf." West Smith-field, October 17, 1645.

28. The same to the same. Announcing steps taken to secure to the widow Goodman the administration of her husband's estate, and to ascertain what money belonging to it is in Mr. Collin's hands. West Smith-field, October 20, 1645.

29. Abel Barker to John Musson. Containing orders about the flock ; and desiring the steward to press George Larrat for immediate payment of 40l. West Smithfield, October 20, 1646.

30. The same to the same. About the writer's flock and business. John Musson is ordered to buy wheat, " and have it brined after the Lincolnshire fashion " to avoyd blasting." West Smithfield, October 27, 1645.

31. Abel Barker to his brother Andrew Collin. About the receipt and payment of certain money, and his sister Godman's letters of administration. West Smithfield, October 30, 1645.

32. Abel Barker to John Musson. Dealing with matters of his business in Lincolnshire, especially the flock, and mentioning his sister Goodman's affairs. West Smithfield, November 3, 1645.

33. Abel Barker " matri suæ charissimæ, Eliz. " Barker." Declaring his deep grief for his sister Good-man's affliction, and setting forth what he has done in her affairs. West Smithfield, November 3, 1645.

34. Abel Barker to Robert Mackworth. Announcing that he is appointed to pay Robert Mackworth 10l., which the latter may receive at any time of P. Woodcocke at " the Adam and Eve over against " Smithfielde pens." Robert Mackworth's mother would not consent to give a larger amount, but is ready to buy and furnish a chamber for her son. Ham-bleton, January 1, 1645.

35. Anne Barker (i.e., Abel's first wife) " to the much honoured lady the Lady Frances Burton. These pre-sents with my humble duty. Madame, I had wayted

upon you before this to have given you thanks for your many fauors to me, had not Mr. Barker's extraordinary occasions, and my owne sicknesse prevented me. But now that your ladyshipp is neare cominge into the countrey (which I am glad to heare), I hope you wilbe pleased to doe me the honor to see Hambleton, whither you and all your good company shall be very welcome to Mr. Barker and me; & in y⁰ meane tyme that you wilbe pleased to accept the presentacion of our most humble duty to yourselfe & my father, & our best loue to my sister Jane, wishing her as happy a bride as, your dutifull and obedient daughter till death. A. Barker." Hambleton, June 26, 1647.

36. Anne Barker "to Mr. Augustine Crofts at the Nageshead in the Old Bailey near the pumpe there. Mr. Crofts, I thanke you for all your fauors, and I would desire you to buy me twelue elnes of a deepe watchet sarconett for a bed, and a sleight fringe for it of the same colour not aboue sixe yards and a q' lunge, and a small fringe for the topp of the bed. I pray you buy me fiue dozen of small silke buttons and a sett of prynts suetable to this inclosed patterne and send them downe. And I desire you would doe so much as goe into Lumbard Street to one Mr. Whyte a drugster, and buy me an ounce of his best parmacity and sexe graynes of beaten boazar. Mr. Barker will returne you the money by the first opportunity: he sent you the last by Mr. Woodcocke. I hope you haue received it before this. I pray you remember my loue to my brother Caluerly if he be in toune. I should be glad to know how he doth and how his business goes forwarde, & thus with my loue to your selfe and your wife I rest, your truely loueing friende." Hambleton, June 26, 1647.

37. Anne Barker to Mr. Augustine Crofts. "Mr. Crofts. My best loue remembered vnto you, with "many thanks for your paynes in buying my things, "all which I haue received by Sewell the carrier. I "haue sent here enclosed a bill of exchange for your "money. Mr. Woodcocke, who is to pay it, wilbe in "towne before you can receive this letter. . . ." Hambleton, July 14. 1647.

38. Mary Barker (Abel's sister) to John Swinfield, in Drury Lane. "I haue sent you herewithy all three "elnes of black tabba, which I desire you would match "with as much of the same bredth and goodnesse as "will make me a goune, & make it vp for me. You "needs not make it so wyde as you made my tafaty "gowne by a neale. You may lay vpon it such lace "and in such manner as is the newest fashion. I pray "you buy me as much tabba of the same bredth either "grasse greene or willowe greene as will make me a "petticote & stomacher, and make it vp with as much "gold and siluer bone lace of about 2s. 6d. y⁰ yard as "will go once about, and twice vp before. I would "haue you likewise buy me a winter sergo gowne of "some pretty greenish color, and very good serge, & "lay it with a pretty bone lace of gold and siluer as is "most in fashion. I pray make me also according a "riding coate & hood of scarlet serge, neately trimmed, "& let your wife buy me a plaine borgett of cuffs of "the neatest fashion, & a loue hood and a double "curle hood of the largest sorte, and a doz. paire of "bandstrings of seuerall sortes. Pray let her buy "me 3 or 4 yards of bone lace of seuerall sorts, a "yarde of a sorte, of about 5s. a yde. and 4 or 5 "elnes of rybon of seuerall sorts, some silk & silver, "and some tafaty. My brother hath appointed Edw. "Scotney to pay you 10l., whom you shall finde at "Adam & Eue in Smithfelde; the residue so soone "as I shall know what it comes to shalbe speedily sent "you by your loving freind, M. Barker." Hambleton, Septembris 10, 1648.

39. "Ex epistola respons, T. Burton mil. & bar. "filiæ primogen' dat' apud Lond. mense Febr. 1645. "What you acquaint me with, if you like, I knowe "nothing to y⁰ contrary but you have my consent. I "am very willing to giue you all content you haue euer "deserued well from me & I will expresse my loue to "you."

40. Elizabeth Barker (Abel's mother) to Sir Thomas Burton, Kt. and Baronet. Worthy sir. The distance of place denying opportunity of personall conference makes me presume vpon so small acquaintance to make these lines messengers of my desires vnto you: which are y' you will be pleased to graunt vnto my sonne that he may with your consent & approbacion prosecute that affection which he beares to your daughter, Mrs. Anne Burton. Sir, if vpon enquiry made of him & his estate you shall vouchsafe to gratifie me with a lyne or two in answere hereof, I shalbe ready to give

you suche further satisfaction therein as you shall desire from your humble seruant, Elis. Barker. No date.

41. Sir Thomas Burton to Mrs. Elizabeth Barker at Hambleton. Declaring approval of her overtures, but referring her son's suit to the wishes and judgment of his daughter, of whom he speaks proudly. "I thinke," he concludes, "you knew me in my youth, & I will "be glad to renue that acquaintance when it please "God I may come with safety into the countrey. In "the interim I leaue your desires to my daughter's "will." London, Feb. 1645.

42. Elizabeth Barker to Sir Thomas Burton, Kt. and Bart., &c. Worthy sir, I haue hitherto deferred my answere to your letters, in respect you was pleased therein to referre me to your daughter's pleasure. But because I could not expect satisfaction from her in that which more properly concerns yourselfe, I haue presumed once more to addresse myselfe vnto you. Sir, I suppose by this tyme you haue informed your selfe of my sonne & his estate, & (if you esteeme him worthy) I hope I shall not scome offensive in desireing what your pleasure is to give in porcion with your daughter, & what you wilbe pleased to require in joynture for her. The good character your selfe haue afforded her in your letters hath preuailed with me to aske no more then 1500li., & will I hope preuaile with you to granto no lesse. Sir, I shall heere be sparenge in repeatinge my sonnes deserts in that I am his mother desirringe rather you should know them from others, yet I haue had such experience of his obedience toward me in matters of lesse consequence that I doe not doubt of his obseruance in this. That former acquaintance which you are pleased to remember, I humbly thank you for, & shall accompt it my happinesse if I may become known vnto you in a nearer relacion; in the interim my request is these lines may present my owne & my sonnes seruice to your selfe & your lady from her that desires to rest, your most affectionate friend to serue you." Hambleton, April 2, 1646.

43. Abel Barker to Mrs. Anne Burton, at London. Mrs. Anne, though the distance of place denyes vs. our accustomed communication, yet the intercourse of letters may, if you be so pleased, supply that defect; wherein that you may not iudge me oblivious of our forepassed amity, I haue presumed to breake the ice, in confidence that you will not disdaine to wade after, & impart the present condicion of our affaires: for change alter the minde of, yours you know howe & howe. Hambleton, June 25, 1646. (Shortly before the writer's marriage with the lady.)

44. Mistresse Anne Barker "to the much honoured "lady the Lady Frances Burton this present with my "humble seruice. Madame, I am sorry that I cannot for "the present wayte vpon you to giue you thanks for your "many favours and bounty to me, but after Michaelmas "I hope Mr. Barker will giue me leaue to come myselfe "to present my humble duty to you, in the meane tyme "you shall neuer be forgotten in the prayers of your dutifull "& obedient daughter till death." Stockerson, August 15, 1646.

45. Mistresse Anne Barker to her noble Cousin Henry Heron, esq., Cosen, I am sorry I could not see you at my weddings for truely I wrote for you, although I did not know the day certaine. I chose rather to haue had you lost your labour then to haue wanted your sweete company; but now my suite is that you would be pleased to come to Hambleton & solemnize my weddings there. Pray doe me the fauour to present my humble duty to my Lord Cobham & my Lady & my seruice to your sisters when you see them. I hope you wilbe pleased to honour with your presence in truth your humble seruant & kinswoman. Mr. Barker presents his seruice to you. No date.

46. Mistresse Anne Barker to her "deare sister Mrs. "Jane Burton, Swete Sister, I thanke you for your "paines in buying my things, but I rather wished "you had danced with me in the dyneing roome then "about the strectes, who infinitely wanted your com-"pany. I would intreate you to buy bone lace & "satten for a gowne & kirtle, and a laced handker-"chief & cuffs made & starched, & a loue hoode, & "I pray good sister doe me the favour to buy for my "father & my lady my Lord Cobham & my lady "& your selfe & my cosen H. Heron & Walter "Caluerly the best fashioned gloues you can gett. "I pray doe you present my fathers & my mothers "& W. Caluerlyes, and get Wat to present the rest "together with Mr. Barkers seruice & my owne. "Mr. Barker's man will giue you money for the gloues. "Mr. Barker presents his seruice to you, wishing you

" in the like condicion with my selfe & in the meane
" bath caused me to subscribe myselfe your assured
" loueinge sister."

47. Mrs. Anne Burton to Sir Thomas Burton, Kt. and
Baronet, at his house in the upper part of Holborne
neare the Elme tree. Alluding to the miscarriage of
letters; and observing that she sends him what he
wants by the Uppingham carrier, whereas "but for
" the soldiers" she "had sent it by John Musson,"
she adds, "The foulnesse of the way & illness of the
" weather (though I thinke they was neuer worse)
" should not haue kept Mr. Barker & me from wayt-
" ing vpon you & my lady before this tyme had we
" not lined in dayly apprehensions of the troopers
" whom we haue already quarteringe with vs almost
" these three weekes." Hambleton, December 23, 1646.

48. Abel Barker to his worthy friend Mr. William
Sherman at Leicester. Announcing courteously that
his sister cannot satisfy Mr. Sherman's desires, as
"she hath disposed of her thoughts some other way,"
Hambleton, December 24, 1647.

49. Mistress Anne Barker to Mrs. Jane Burton.
Deare Sister, I hope father hath received his leoparde
safe which I sent by Uppingham carrier the last weeke.
I haue made bold to sonde my lady a countrey cake to
chuse kinge and queene with. You shall finde the
pea & the beane where two little stickes bee. Sister,
I giue you many thankes for your many favours &
paines for me, & so hopeing my father and my lady
bee in good health, and wishing you all a merry new
yeare, I rest, your assured loueing sister.
P.S. Sister, Mr. Barker presents his most humble
duty to my father & my lady, & his loue to your
selfe. Hambleton, December 31, 1646.

50. Mistress Anne Barker to Mrs. Matilda Booth at
Okeham. Excusing herself for not having waited on
Mrs. Booth,—remissness for which the bad weather must
be held accountable; and enquiring for the character
of a maid servant. Hambleton, December 17, 1646.

51. Mistress Anne Barker to her sister Jane. Deare
Sister, I desire you would dop me the fauour to giue
the bearer hereof John Musson my little gilded trunke
& my furre boxe, & if you can finde the cloth that
went about the cake, sow it about the trunke. I thank
you for your care of them. I shall now haue vse for
them in the country. I pray remember my husbands
& my most humble duty to my lady (my father, I
thanke God, is very well) & our loue to your selfe
& your seruant when you see him, wishing you all
the joy & happinesse that could be expressed in a
husband. I shall be glad to know if it be no prejudice
to you, when your wedding is, though I can doe no other
seruice if it be in London but to send you a bride cake.
I pray you send my loue to Mr. Cokayne & the 2
Nans & to all others that aske how I doe. I hope
I shall see my lady & you in the countrey this summer
and have the happinesse to enioy your company at
Hambleton, where you shalbe very welcome to your
assured lo. sister. Hambleton, Aprill 10, 1647.

52. Abel Barker to his honoured father Sir Thomas
Burton, Knight and Baronet. Declaring himself ready
to serve one of Sir Thomas's friends; entreating to
be tenant of any of his father-in-law's lands that
become vacant at Fresby or Stockerson; and enquiring
as to a high sheriff's obligations to make presents to
judges on circuit, and to give fees to their servants.
Hambleton, January 20, 1646.

53. Abel Barker to his worthy brother, Henry
Caluerly Esqr. Thanking him cordially for a
brotherly service. Hambleton, Jan. 20, 1646.

54. Abel Barker to Andrew Burton, Esq. Binding
himself to become the tenant of Mr. Burton's grounds
in Gunthorp, and signing himself "Your kinsman
"most affectionate to serue you." Hambleton, Jan. 20,
1646.

55. Abel Barker to his kinsman John Musson. Directing him to seek Laurence Staie, at the Crosse Keyes,
St. John Street and at the Charterhouse, in order that
a conveyance of certain land may be effected, and to
execute other commissions. "It wilbe," says the writer,
" requisite you sende me worde so soone as it is knowne
" when our assizes are, what judges ride this circuit, and
" what company we must expect from London, that we
" may prouide accordingly. You must buy two fether-
" bed tickes and bolsters, and halfe a dozen yards of
" jacke chaynes, & halfe a dozen paire whyte gloves,
" and if there be any thinge else necessary that you can
" thinke on, which wee have forgotten, you may buy
" it for your very loueing kinsman." Hambleton,
Jan. 26, 1646.

56. Abel Barker to Mr. Peter Sergyant at Melton
Mowbray. About some negotiations for the purchase
of land. Hambleton, February 15, 1646.

57. Abel Barker to Mr. Richard Louth in his chamber
in Clement's Inne. About the writer's arrangements
for entertaining the judges and his need of copies of
the Parliamentary Ordinance for a day of humiliation. "I desire," writes the sheriff of Rutland, "you
" would wayte vpon Sergyant Clarke & certifie him,
" that in respect the judges haue alwayes for about
" these 20 yeares lodged at Mr. Olineres, & I was
" ignorant of his desires to the contrary, I had pro-
" uided that house for them before the receipt of your
" letter, & layd therin in beere & other prouisions
" there which wilbe inconuenient to remoue, & there-
" fore if they please to accept of that for this tyme only,
" I will doe my best indeavour to prouide them one to
" their own contentment against the next, although I
" knowe not in such a poore towne where to haue a
" more conuenient vnlesse they wilbe pleased to lodge
" in an inne." Hambleton, February 17, 1646.

58. Abel Barker to his friend Mr. Thomas Fleminge
at Fotheringhay Park. Enquiring if he can enter into
possession of certain land next Lady Day. Hambleton,
February 26, 1646.

59. Abel Barker to his friend Mr. Augustine Crofts
at the Nag's Head in the Old Bailey neare the pumpe.
Bogging him to call on Mr. Peter Woodcocke, at the
Adam and Eve, near Smithfield Pens, for certain money
in payment of Mrs. Barker's purchases, &c. Hambleton,
February 25, 1646.

60. Abel Barker to his much honoured father Sir
Thomas Burton. Mentioning the provisions made by
the writer for the entertainment of the judges, and
asking to become tenant of certain of Sir Thomas's
lands. "As for Sergyant Clerke," says the writer,
" I appointed my undersheriffe to wayte vpon him.
" I hope I shall give them both content: I haue pro-
" uided the house they have vsually lodged in with fuel
" & such like materialls, & haue layd in beere & ale
" of myne owne. I intende to present them with a
" fatt sheepe & a calfe & some such like present."
Hambleton, March 4, 1646.

61. Abel Barker to his much honoured friend Sir
Thomas Hartopp, Knight, at Leicester. Sending a
declaration concerning one Samuel Oates, a weaver,
" who preacheth constantly in this country," for the
consideration of the judges, who may see fit to issue a
warrant for his arrest and conveyance to the assizes at
Okeham. Hambleton, March 19, 1646.

62. Abel Barker to Sir Edward Harington, Kt. and
Baronet, at his house in Seethinge Lane, London.
Promising to send his Lady Day's rent by messenger
to Sir Edward, as soon as the Assizes shall be over.
Hambleton, April 1647.

63. Abel Barker to his friend John Reene of Chesterton in Cambridgeshire. Asking where one Mistress
Newman dwells, how she lives, "what her name is,"
and where she can be spoken with. Hambleton, April
27, 1647.

64. Abel Barker to Sir Thomas Burton, Kt. and Bart.
at Holborne. About several matters of business. Hambleton, June 15, 1647.

65. Abel Barker to the Commissioners for compound
ing with delinquents. Acknowledging the receipt of
the Commissioners' letters, and announcing that proclamation, in accordance with their instructions, has
been made in full market at Okeham and Uppingham,
" the two onely market townes of this county of Rut-
" land." Hambleton, July 24, 1647.

66. Abel Barker to John Musson at the Adam and
Eve, in Smithfield. About payments of money and other
affairs of business. Hambleton, August 14, 1647.

67. Abel Barker to his friend Mr. Peter Woodcocke at
the Adam and Eve in Smithfield. Ordering him to receive
of Mr. Johnson the sum of 100l. due on an enclosed bond,
and to lodge the money with Mr. Lakin. Vppingham,
September 8, 1647.

68. The same to the same at the same address.
Instructing Mr. Woodcocke to pay the writer's
Michaelmas rent and tithe (16l. 18s.) to Sir Edward
Harington. Hambleton, September 22, 1647.

69. Abel Barker to Sir Richard Wingfield at Tiken-
cote. Offering apologies for not having written sooner,
and announcing that his sister, on hearing Sir Richard's
proposition in behalf of a friend, finds herself "al-
" together unwillinge to entertain that motion."
Hambleton, November 27, 1647.

70. Abel Barker to Sir Thomas Burton Kt. and Bart.
at Holborne. Announcing that, though Mrs. Barker's

time of labour is near at hand, it has not yet arrived. Hambleton, December 1647.

71. Abel Barker to Sir Thomas Burton, Kt. and Bart. at Holborne. Announcing that Mrs. Barker has given birth to a son after a "short (if not too short) conflict," The young mother is "very hearty ;" Mrs. Kneeland, the midwife, reports well of her patient ; and the writer begs his father-in-law to be one of "the witnesses to "the baptisme" of his grandson. Hambleton, December 26, 1647.

72. Abel Barker to Mr. Lion Falkener at Vppingham. Regretting that he cannot be present at a commission on Monday next, by reason of "the sad accident which "hath befallen me." The writer describes himself "your sorrowful friend." Hambleton, January 14, 1647.

73. Abel Barker to the same at Vppingham. Respecting the business to be transacted by the commission, when the writer cannot be present. Hambleton, January 15, 1647.

74. The same to the same at Vppingham. Consenting to sit on the commission against a person named Tayler, at Leicester, on Thursday. Hambleton, January 1647.

75. Abel Barker to his honoured brother Henry Caluerly, Esq. at Caluerly. Announcing in pathetic language the birth of his son and the death of his wife; and begging for a continuance of his correspondent's affection "though it hath pleased God to take to his "mercy the first occasioner thereof." Hambleton, January 17, 1647.

76. Abel Barker to his euer honoured father Sir Thomas Burton Kt. & Bart. Giving particulars respecting his wife's death; and entreating Sir Thomas to cherish love for his godson and grandson. Mrs. Barker's death is attributed secondarily to "her "owne feares and the too much haste of a hard-hearted "midwife." Hambleton, January 26, 1647.

77. Abel Barker to his uncle Mr. John Farbecke at Ketton. Beginning "Good Unkle, I have herewith "(sent you fiue yards of Spanish cloth, which I desire "you would be pleased to make into a suite and cloake, "and weare it as a sad remembrance of her who was a "great louer of you and me." The writer hopes that he may see his uncle in a day or two, and sends love to his aunt and cousins. Hambleton, January 31, 1647.

78. Abel Barker to Mr. Richard Munne, rector of Stockerson. Inviting Mr. Munne, the rector of Mrs. Barker's native parish, to attend at the delivery of her funeral sermon. "I desire therefore that I may haue "your company at Hambleton on Tuesday next to heare "a sermon and dine with me, and that you would doe "me the fauour to invite in my name your neighbours "of Stockerson to come with you. Onely because some "of them perhapps are not prouided of horses for such a "jorney, I desire you would giue to so many of the "poorer familyes as to you shall seem conuenient five "shillings a peece and invite all the rest." Hambleton, February 5th, 1647.

79. Abel Barker to Mr. Andrew Butler, rector of Hallaton. Inviting him and Mrs. Butler, in regard for their intimacy with the writer's "deceased wife," to "meets the rest of her friends at Hambleton vpon "Tuesday next to heare a sermon and dine with their "sad but assured friend." Hambleton, February 5th, 1647.

80. Abel Barker to Mrs. Thomasyn Collin at Easton. Informing her that the funeral meeting at Hambleton has been postponed to next Wednesday, and asking her to bring "little Euerard Goodman along with her." Hambleton, Feb. 5, 1647.

81. Abel Barker to his "euer honoured brother Henry "Caluerly, Esq. at Caluerly." Thanking Mr. Caluerly for expressing affection the writer's orphan infant, and for recommending a "gouernesse to initiate him in "vertue," but observing that the boy's tender age makes it desirable that he should be left for a time in the custody of the nurse chosen by his mother. Hambleton, February 18, 1647.

82. Abel Barker to Mr. Lion Falkener at Burton, in Lincolnshire. Enclosing a warrant for Mr. Falkener's signature, and begging him to oblige Sir Thomas Barker by attending promptly to certain business. Hambleton, March 8, 1647.

83. Abel Barker to his much esteemed brother Mr. Hugh Watts at Leicester. Begging him to search the register of the town of Houghton on the Hill for the proof of the age of Thomas Heyricke, son of John Heyricke, who was born about the year 1619. Vppingham, March 25, 1648.

84. Abel Barker to his "loueing brother" Mr. Andrew Collin at Easton. Concerning 60l. which Mr.

Collin deposited for his correspondent with Mr. Lakin, and which the writer has lent to William Andrew of Hambleton. Hambleton, May 15, 1648.

85. The same to the same at Easton. Instructing him to enquire at the Six Clerks Office what progress is being made in a certain business, and to "bring "downe with" him "three latitats." Hambleton, June 3, 1648.

Though this letter and the preceding epistle are directed to Easton, their contents show that they were written to Mr. Collin at London.

86. Abel Barker to his "loueing sister" Mrs. Elizabeth Goodman at Blaston. Expostulating with her earnestly and at great length on her purpose to intermarry with her deceased husband's brother, of the half blood. After setting forth the sin and social obloquy attending uncanonical marriages, the writer implores Mrs. Goodman not "to impinge herself vpon such a "rocke, which besides other discommodityes will at "once make shipracke of her conscience by the lawe "of God and her estate and posterity by the law of "man." Hambleton, May 30, 1648.

87. Abel Barker to Mr. John Wright, at the Six Clerks Office in Chancery Lane. Instructing him what to do in certain proceedings of law. Hambleton, June 7, 1648.

88. Abel Barker to Mr. Augustine Crofts, at the Nagg's Head in the Old Bayly. Begging him to buy for the writer, and send to Hambleton by the Haringworth carrier, a "blacke mourning suite . . . the "doublet of sattin and the hose of good Spanish cloth." Hambleton, June 28, 1648.

89. Abel Barker to the Honourable the Lady Abigail Sherrard at Stapleford. Avowing himself bound by his respect for her to do any service in his power for her tenants in Whissondine; but regretting that he can not accomplish her wishes concerning the levies for Sir Thomas Fairfax and Ireland. Hambleton, July 1, 1648.

90. Abel Barker to his "very loueing friend" Mr. Peter Sergyant at Malton. Sending a copy of Mr. Smithby's bill against them in Chancery, for Mr. Sergyant and his mother to peruse and then return to him. Hambleton, July 31, 1648.

91. Abel Barker to the same at Melton. Sending another copy of the same bill, and requesting to know by the bearer thereof what Mr. Sergyant and his mother intend to answer to it. Hambleton, August 10, 1648.

92. Abel Barker to his "honoured brother," Henry Caluerly, Esq., at Caluerly. A letter of affectionate assurances and courtesies. Hambleton, September 20, 1648.

93. Abel Barker to Mr. Henry Johnson and John Buston at Coggshall, Essex. Announcing that 150 todds of wool are on the road to them, and that 200 other todds will follow as soon as possible. The writer begs them to pay 500l. at the Adam and Eve in Smithfield on Friday, Nov. 10 next; and to lend him another 500l., or procure a loan of that sum from "any of their "neighbours hauing occasion to vse any money in the "writer's country." Hambleton, October 10, 1648.

94. Abel Barker to the same at the same place. Advising them that he has sent them another 75 tods of wool, to be followed by another 50 tods, making in all 200 todds to be paid for at the rate of 29s. per todd ; and requesting urgently that the money may be paid punctually on Nov. 10, the writer having unusual need for money. Hambleton, October 24, 1648.

95. Abel Barker to Mr. William Haries at Keldon, Essex. Requesting payment of 8l. 10s. at the Adam and Eve, Smithfield, on the 9th of November next. Hambleton, October 24, 1648.

96. Abel Barker to Mr. Johnson and John Buston at Cogshall. Announcing that he has sent off the last 50 tods of his wool, containing 376 fleeces, and also 12½ tods of his brother's wool, containing 97 fleeces. Hambleton, October 30, 1648.

97. Abel Barker to his "much esteemed" brother Henry Caluerly, Esq., at London. Regretting the failure of his endeavours to raise money for him. In talking with moneyed men he finds "them vnwilling to "discourse they have any, much lesse to part with "it these perilous tymes." Hambleton, October 30, 1648.

98. Abel Barker to his "euer honoured father" Sir Thomas Burton. Announcing that he takes the tythes of a close and meadow for six years at 34s. rent. Hambleton, November 30, 1648.

99. Abel Barker to his uncle Samuel Barker, Esq. About the examinations of persons suspected of having

stolen some of the writer's wool. Hembleton, April 9,
1649.

100. Abel Barker to Mr. Robert Gilbert at Melton
Mowbray. Enquiring whether he can have assurance
for the speedy payment of money due to him from
William Trigge, or must enforce the bond next term by
legal process. Hambleton, April 28, 1649.

101. Abel Barker to the "much honoured" Sir
Edward Harington, Kt. and Baronet. Apologising for
a delay in the payment of his rent, and making arrangements for the money. The writer also complains of the
excessive taxes laid on his county, and speaks of the
cost of the troopers quartered on him, in respect of Sir
Edward's land. "Sir," he says, "I beleeve Mr. Harys
" hath giuen you notice of 3 troopes of horse of Col.
" Lilburne's regiment which are come to quarter in
" this county. You haue foure for Gunthorps whom
" we quartered at Mr. Meakins at three shillings a
" peece per diem, which was as cheape as we could get
" them in respect of the dearnesse of these tymes. , I
" haue since so farre preuailed with their captaine who
" quarters at my house that he hath eased you for the
" present and remoued them all to another place. I
" know not how longe we shall continue that, but my
" indeauour shall not be wantinge therein. They haue
" already cost 5l. 6s. 6d." Hambleton, May 5, 1649.
The writer, for the first time in the letter book, signs
himself "your affectionate kinsman" to Sir Edward, as
well as his humble servant.

102. Abel Barker to Col. Thomas Wayte at London.
Begging him to use influence to procure for the bearer,
a poor kinsman of the writer, a vicarage in Leicestershire. Hambleton, May 10, 1649.

103. Abel Barker to Sir Edward Harington at London.
Expressing great annoyance that his rent to Sir Edward
should be again over-due, through Peter Woodcocke's
remissness. "Col. Lilburne's troopes," he adds, "are
" still quartered in this county, & intende to continue.
" The captaine vpon receipt of your orders for their
" removall into Worcestershyre, sent up to London to
" his Col. to know his pleasure, by whom he hath re-
" ceived orders from Maior-Generall Lambert that he
" shall not remoue without farther orders from him out
" of the country. We haue received of the troops who
" quartered vpon Gunthorp aboue 40l. so that your
" charge will not be more then 3l., whereas if I had
" not taken that opportunity of the captaine's quarter-
" ing at my house for their remouall, they would haue
" cost you 10l. before this." Hambleton, May 18,
1649.

104. Abel Barker to Sir Edward Harington at London.
About rent and taxes. The writer regrets that his kinsman is offended with him, and attributes Sir Edward's
displeasure to malicious report. Hambleton, May 30,
1649.

105. Abel Barker to Mr. William Gladwine at Cogshall in Essex. About wool and payments of money.
Hambleton, Aug. 1, 1649.

106. Abel Barker to Mr. Augustine Crofts at the
Naggs Head in Old Bayly. Requesting him to buy
and send down by the Haringworth a "good handsome
" coat" for the writer's son who "is about a yeare and
" a halfe olde, and hath newly begun to goe." Hambleton, August 11, 1649.

107. Abel Barker to his very loueing brother Mr.
Hugh Watts at Leicester. A letter of affectionate
assurances and courtesies. Hambleton, August 18, 1649.

108. Abel Barker to his "loueing brother" Henry
Caluerly, Esq., at Stanford. Regretting that he missed
seeing him at Stanford, and giving a good account of
his correspondent's little nephew. Hambleton, September 10, 1649.

109. Abel Barker to Mrs. Anne Stace at ———
Asking for the title-deeds of a little close which Mr.
Stace intended to exchange with the hospital at Stanford.
Hambleton, September 17, 1649.

110. Abel Barker to his "much honoured father Sir
" Thomas Burton at Stoekerson." Inviting him to dine
at Hambleton. Hambleton, September 18, 1649.

111. Abel Barker to a lady, (whose name does not
appear). Announcing that as soon as bodily indisposition shall permit him to make the journey, he will
come over to Gothurst, and pay his respects to her ladyship. Hambleton, October 10, 1649.

112. Abel Barker to Sir Edward Harington at London
About the rent and taxes of Gunthorp, and misunder-
standings between the landlord and tenant. Hambleton, November 17, 1649.

113. Abel Barker to the "much honoured the Lady
" M. D." Promising to wait on her ladyship at G. as
soon as possible. Vppingham, December 11, 1649.

114. Abel Barker to his much esteemed friend B. N.'
Esq. Regretting that severe cold prevented him from
keeping an appointment to meet B. N. at E., according
to the order of B. N. about L. E. Hambleton, December 28, 1649.

115. Abel Barker to his "much respected" brother
E. G. Inviting him and his sons to dine at Hambleton
on the morrow. Hambleton, February 1, 1649.

116. Abel Barker to Sir Edward Harington at London.
A long letter about rents and taxes, and the disagree-
ments of the landlord and tenant. The writer proposes
that his difference with Sir Edward shall be settled by
arbitration. Hambleton, January 18, 1649.

117. Abel Barker to Mr. Peter Woodcocke at the
Adam and Eve in Smithfield. Instructing him to pay
rent to Sir Edward Harington, and to transact other
affairs of money. Hambleton, March 16, 1649.

118. Abel Barker to Sir Edward Harington at London.
About rent and taxes. Hambleton, March 20, 1649.

119. Abel Barker to Mr. J. K. Regretting his inability to meet him on the morrow, as he is about to
start on a journey. Hambleton, March 26, 1650.

120. Abel Barker to his brother, Mr. Thomas Burton.
Regretting that he cannot satisfy Mr. Burton's desires at a "time when money is most wantinge with
men of the writer's profession." Hambleton, March 8,
1650.

121. Abel Barker to the "much honoured Lady,
M.D." Regretting that he "cannot consent to her
" motion," with respect to a third person. Hambleton,
April 30, 1650.

122. Abel Barker to his loueing friend Mr. Richard
Wilson at Castlebytham. Thanking him for his care
and pains in their common cause ; promising to consult
Mr. Skipwith's son and Mr. Archer ; and expressing
confidence that Mr. Laurence Stace might by diligent
search find a certain decree. Hambleton, May 19, 1650.

123. Abel Barker to Mr. Dr. Hurst at Barraby.
Announcing that his brother and sister Collins main-
tain the resolution already announced to the doctor by
Mr. Chesseldine. Hambleton, June 20, 1650.

124. Abel Barker to Mr. Edward Browne, at Allhallows in Stanforde. Announcing that, out of respect
for his correspondent, he has furnished the bearer with
" shift and apparell" ; and advising that Mr. Browne
should appoint one Huddlestone, a baker, to receive
the disorderly person's money. Hambleton, July 10
1650.

125. Abel Barker to Mr. John Lambe at his house in
St. Martins. Advising him to pay to Huddleston, the
baker, what he allows to the "neer-do-weel," mentioned in letter 124, who "hath lately sold his clothes,
" pawned his gowne, and for want of shift is growne
" noysome to his companions." Vppingham, July 10,
1650.

126. Abel Barker to his "euer honoured father,"
Sir Thomas Burton. Advising Sir Thomas to effect
the amendment of a commission in which he is insufficiently described as "knight," whereas he is both
knight and baronet. Hambleton, August 11, 1650.

127. Abel Barker to Mr. Peter Woodcocke, jun., at
Caldecot. Instructing him to pay rent for Gunthorpe
to Sir Edward Harington "who, if he be remoued from
" Seathinge Lane, is at my Lord Thanet's house in
" Aldersgate Street." Hambleton, September 24,
1650.

128. Abel Barker to Mr. J. K. Regretting that he
cannot at present fulfill J.K.'s desires. Vppingham,
September 25, 1650.

129. Abel Barker to Sir Edward Harington at his
house in Aldergate Street. Announcing that Mr.
Peter Woodcocke has been instructed to pay the rent
for Gunthorpe. Hambleton, September 23, 1650.

130. Abel Barker to Mr. Thomas Skipwith at Grantham. Asking for a paper book left with Mr. Ellis ;
and also the draught of a plea, in order that Mr. Palmer
may peruse it. The attorney is also instructed to
execute a commission. Hambleton, September 28,
1650.

131. Abel Barker to Mr. Thomas Skipwith at Grant
ham. Instructing the solicitor about the plea, and the
suit of which it is a feature. Hambleton, October 4,
1650.

132. Abel Barker to his "good brother," Mr. Thomas
Barker at Hambleton. Announcing the steps taken in
respect to the suit ; and instructing Thomas Barker on
matters of money. Smithfield, November 20, 1650.

133. Abel Barker to Mr. Richard Coxe at his Chamber
in the Temple, in the Paper Buildings. About the law
suit. Hambleton, December 7, 1650.

134. The same to the same at the same address. On the same business. Hambleton, January 4, 1650.

135. Abel Barker to Mr. Thomas Skipwith at Grantham. About the law-suit. No date.

136. Abel Barker to Mr. Peter Woodcocke at the Adam and Eve in Smithfield. Desiring him to pay rent for Gunthorpe to Sir Edward Harington, and to receive moneys from certain persons. Hambleton, March 15, 1650.

137. Abel Barker to Sir Edward Harington at his house in Aldersgate Street. About rent and taxes. Hambleton, March 19, 1650.

138. Abel Barker to his "loueing cosin" John Wright at Mr. Cator's house in Coleman Street. Declining in friendly terms to comply with a request. Hambleton, June 7, 1651.

139. Abel Barker to Mr. Edmund Wright at London. Declining to lend money, having "more than ordinarily "engaged himselfe in a purchase from which he has "not hitherto recouered; and being at present involved "in some law-suits which occasion a further expense of "money." Hambleton, June 7, 1651.

140. Abel Barker to Mr. Arthure Coldwell at Oundle. Declining to pay for medicines charged for by the druggist; the writer regarding the demand as unreasonable, as he paid the doctor for his services, and never ordered any drugs of Mr. Coldwell. Hambleton, June 18, 1651.

141. Abel Barker to Sir Edward Harington at his house in Aldersgate Street. About rent and taxes. Hambleton, October 4, 1651.

142. Abel Barker to Mr. Peter Woodcocke at the Adam and Eue in Smithfield. Directing him to pay rent to Sir Edward Harington, and to call on Mr. Grayes, in Nicholas Lane, for 14l. due from Mr. Buston on a bond. Hambleton, October 4, 1651.

143. Abel Barker to Mr. Robert Flatman at his deske in the Six Clerkes Office. About proceedings in a law-uit. Hambleton, October 18, 1651.

144. Abel Barker to Edward Skipwith, Esq., at Grantham. About proceedings in a law-suit. Hambleton, Oct. 20, 1651.

145. Abel Barker to his much respected brother Euerard Goodman, Esq. Thanking him for the refusal of certain grounds, about which the writer will see Mr. Goodman. Hambleton, October 23, 1651

146. Abel Barker to Mr. Thomas Barker at Hambleton. Announcing that much progress has not been made in a certain business, to which the writer alludes with studious caution: London, December 11, 1651.

147. The same to the same at Hambleton. A Latin letter giving the particulars of some land, which the brothers are about to purchase. London, December 13, 1651.

148. The same to the same at Hambleton. On the same subject. The latter half of the letter in Latin. London, December 18, 1651.

149. Abel Barker to Mr. Merrifield at his chamber in Clement's Inne. Respecting a law-suit in which the writer's brother John (who has died, leaving Abel his executor) was concerned. Hambleton, January 9, 1651.

150. Abel Barker to Mr. Lyon Falkner at Vppingham. About the business of letter 149. Hambleton, Jan. 19, 1651.

151. Abel Barker to John Musson. Directing him to get certain paper books from Sir Thomas Hartopp, and learn therefrom the particulars of a manor and lordship about which the writer has been misinformed. No date.

152. Abel Barker to Mr. Thomas Barker at Hambleton. Announcing that he sends a hat and clothes for his brother, and a "butt & suite" for John Musson. Thomas Barker is instructed on certain affairs of money, and asked to give John Musson some orders about sowing oats and peas. London, Feb. 20, 1651.

153. Abel Barker to his "much respected brother Mr. Andrew Collin. Announcing that search has ascertained that a certain "Commission of Bankrupts issued "out on Jan. 29, 1651." No date.

154. Abel Barker to Mr. Peter Woodcocke at Adam and Eue in Smithfield. Requesting him to procure money for the payment of rent. Vppingham, March 17, 1651.

155. The same to the same at the same place. Desiring him to pay rent to Sir Edward Harington. Hambleton, March 24, 1651.

156. Abel Barker to Sir Edward Harington, Kt. and Baronet, in Aldersgate Street. About rent, taxes, and other business. Hambleton, March 24, 1651.

157. The same to the same. About rent and taxes. The writer would gladly hold Gunthorpe for another at a reasonable rent, but declines to give what Sir Edward asks for the land. April 2, 1652.

158. Abel Barker to Sir James Harington, at his lodgings in Whitehall. Aannouncing his decision not to remain tenant of certain lands on the terms proposed by Sir James. Hambleton, April 3, 1652.

159. Abel Barker to Mr. George Merifield at his chamber in Clement's Inne. Requesting him to renew a "scire facias," and to send it down by the Haringworth carrier, who lodges at the Bell in Smithfield. Hambleton, April 3, 1652.

160. Abel Barker to John Musson at Hambleton. Announcing that he has taken more land of Sir Edward Harington, and giving particulars of the hearing of the writer's suit in Chancery, which has resulted to his advantage. Strand, May 11, 1652.

161. Abel Barker to Mr. Thomas Barker at Hambleton. Asking for information about his flock and business in Rutland, and announcing a triumph in the law-suit. June 24, 1652.

162. Abel Barker to Mr. Thomas Barker at Hambleton. Repeating the enquiries of letter 161, as he fears that letter has miscarried. "I desire," the writer adds, "you would send me a measure of my son's capp, and "of the length and circumference of his coate, that I "may prouide for him here." Strand, June 30, 1652.

163. Abel Barker to Mr. Thomas Barker at Hambleton. Announcing the satisfactory conclusion of the suit in Chancery. Strand, July 25, 1652.

164. Abel Barker to Sir Edward Harington, Knt. and Baronet, in Aldersgate Street. About rent and taxes. Hambleton, August 21, 1652.

165. Abel Barker to Sir James Harington, Knt., at Whitehall. Announcing that his rent will be punctually paid, and repeating that he cannot enlarge his term of certain lands at the rent required by Sir James. Hambleton, August 31, 1652.

: 166. Abel Barker to Mr. Peter Woodcocke at the Adam and Eue in Smithfield. Desiring him to pay the rent for Gunthorpe. Hambleton, September 25, 1652.

167. Abel Barker to Mr. Woodcocke at Caldecott. Desiring him to pay 106l. 5s. 6d. to Sir Roger Smith, at his lodgings in St. Jones, and to attend to other affairs of money. Hambleton, October 14, 1652.

168. Abel Barker to Sir James Harington, Kt. and Baronet, at Whitehall. About rent, and proposals for a new term of his tenancy under his landlord. December 24, 1652.

169. Abel Barker to Sir James Harington, Knt. and Baronet, at Whitehall. Expostulating with Sir James on an order given to John Winprey to sell all the trees on Gunthorpe, and begging that the order may be limited to such trees as are worth 10l. apiece. Hambleton, February 1, 1652.

170. The same to the same. About rent, &c. The writer hopes that his new lease has been sealed. Hambleton, March 12, 1652.

171. The same to the same. Entreating that two leases may be engrossed, in accordance with agreement and enclosed particulars. Hambleton, March 28, 1653.

172. Abel Barker to Mr. Peter Woodcocke at Caldecott. Instructing him to wait on Sir James Harington, see the new leases duly sealed and executed, surrender an old lease, and pay Sir James certain moneys. Hambleton, April 5, 1653.

173. Abel Barker to Sir James Harington, Knt. and Baronet, at Whitehall. On the business of letter 172. Hambleton, April 8, 1653.

174. The same to the same. Announcing that the leases have been sealed and returned. Hambleton, April 30, 1653.

175. Abel Barker to Samuel Barker at Grays Inn. Giving particulars concerning the lordship and manor of S——, about which Samuel Barker requires information for a friend. Hambleton, May 7, 1653.

176. The same to the same. Giving further particulars about the same manor. Hambleton, May 9, 1653.

177. The same to the same. On the same subject. Hambleton. May 16, 1653.

178. Abel Barker to J. K. Regretting his inability to answer a question in the absence of a certain "Act," but promising to get sight of the act in London, and then reply. Hambleton, May 16, 1653.

179. Abel Barker to T. W. "We are all quiet here "for 7 of your F. returned on Wednesday last, H., F., J., "A., & the V. being left behind: they are very reserued, "neither could I discouer any thing of their successe "untill I understood the same by E. S., and your lotters, "They are something eleuated with the speedy accep-

"·tance of their P., & hope that the rest will bring
" them acceptable newes vpon their returne, which will
" yet be before the wet wether, because (as the V. writes
" unto his ducke), the gent who dd. their P., & whom
" they most depend upon, is at present out of towne.
" Nothing else at present more than my respects."
Hambleton, May 16, 1653. This is the first of several
mysteriously worded letters that relate to an opposition
to the enclosure of lands in Lincolnshire, and the doings
of the opponents who, at least on one occasion, were
guilty of riot and other disorderly violence in breaking
down fences, &c. V. is the vicar of the place, who
appears to have been the leader of the opponents, his
wife being styled his "ducke."

180. The same to the same. On the same subject.
Hambleton, May 19, 1653.

181. The same to the same. On the same subject.
Hambleton, May 23, 1693.

182. The same to the same. On the same subject.
Hambleton, May 28, 1653.

183. The same to the same. On the same subject.
Hambleton, June 25, 1653.

184. The same to the same. On the same subject.
Hambleton, August 19, 1653.

185. Abel Barker to Mrs. Joanna Hippisley at Whissondine. Regretting that he cannot send her a certain
book. Hambleton, September 19, 1653.

186. Abel Barker to Euerard Goodman, Esq., at
Blaston. Announcing that John Musson's appointment
with Sir Thomas Burton prevents him for meeting Mr.
Goodman on the morrow. Hambleton, September 22,
1653.

187. Abel Barker to Sir James Harington. Asking
where he shall send rent to Sir James, now that the
latter has left Whitehall. Hambleton, September 23,
1653.

188. Abel Barker to C. T. W., at L. Containing particulars of the opposition to the Lincolnshire enclosures. Hambleton, Oct. 18, 1653.

189. The same to the same. On the same subject.
Hambleton, October 22 1653.

190. The same to the same. On the same subject.
October 25, 1653.

191. Abel Barker to Mr. Broune at Tolesthorpe. Enclosing a synopsis of the rates assessed for many years
in Rutland. Hambleton, December 18, 1653.

192. Abel Barker to E. T. W. at O. Announcing his
departure for London. Hambleton, February 9, 1653.

193. Abel Barker to K. D. at S. Promising to wait
upon him. Hambleton, Jan. 27, 1653.

194. Abel Barker to Mrs. E. P. in the Strand. Declining to act immediately on her suggestion. Hambleton,
February 25, 1653.

195. Abel Barker to C. T. W. at O. Announcing that
he has seen a certain petition against· him, and giving
its substance. London, February 18, 1653.

196. Abel Barker to Mr. John Borden at his house in
Burbolt Court. Fleet Street. Acknowledging the safe
arrival of the riding suite and hood, wherewith the
writer's kinswoman is well pleased. Hambleton, March
11, 1653.

197. Abel Barker to Sir James Harington in Aldersgate
Street. About rent and taxes. Hambleton, Mar. 11, 1653.

198. Abel Barker to Mr. P. Woodcocke at the Adam
and Eue in Smithfield. Instructing him to pay rent to
Sir James Harington.

199. Abel Barker to Mr. John Borden in Burbolt
Court. Acknowledging the arrival of a parcel, and desiring Mr. Borden to apply for payment to Mr. Woodcocke. Hambleton, April 3, 1654.

200. Abel Barker to C. T. W. at O. About the opponents to the Lincolnshire enclosures. January 27, 1653.

201. The same to the same. On the same subject,
March 26, 1654.

202. The same to the same. Promising to attend a
meeting. Hambleton, April 25, 1654.

203. Abel Barker to Sir James Harington in Aldersgate Street. Announcing that he has been served with
a writ for taxes on Gunthorpe, due from Sir James.
Hambleton, May 20, 1654.

204. Abel Barker to Mr. Peter Woodcocke, at the
Adam and Eue. Announcing that he will be in London
on Tuesday, when he will take 100l. from Mr. Woodcocke. Hambleton, May 27, 1654.

205. Abel Barker to Christopher Broune at Tolesthorpe.
Appointing to meet him on Tuesday at Sir Thomas
Hartopp's house at Normanton. Hambleton, June 12,
1654.

206. Abel Barker to his loueing kinsman John Blane
in Wbrooke. "My cousin tells me you are acquainted
" with a wincoop who sells good wine. I desire you

" would doe me the fauor to buy me 3 doz. of bottles;
" one doz. of· sacke, another of claret, & the third of
" white wine. I would haue the bottles all pints and of
" glasse, which you may buy of any glassman." Hambleton, July, 2, 1654.

207. Abel Barker to Sir James Harington in Aldersgate Street. Concerning leases of lands in Gunthorp.
Hambleton, July 8, 1654.

208. Abel Barker to the same. About rents and taxes.
Hambleton, Sept. 29, 1654.

209. Abel Barker to Mr. Woodcocke. Desiring to pay
rent to Sir James Harington. Hambleton, September
29, 1654.

210. Abel Barker to Col. Thomas Wayte at Orton.
About the assessment of taxes in Hambleton. Hambleton, August 14, 1654.

211. Abel Barker to Sir James Harington. Stating the
result of his endeavour to induce Sir James's tenants to
surrender their leases. August 18, 1654.

212. The same to the same. About rents which the
writer has received for Sir James Harington. Hambleton, Nov. 18, 1654.

213. Abel Barker to Mr. Woodcocke at the Adam and
Eve. Desiring him to pay certain moneys to Sir James
Harington. November 18, 1654.

214. Abel Barker to his kinswoman Mrs. Ursula Bland,
at the 3 Sugar Loaves in Walbrooke. Asking his cousin
Bland to "buy 2 rundletts of wine of 4 gallons apeece,
" one of sack, and thothers of claret5," and send them
down by the Haringworth carrier. Hambleton, December 3, 1654.

215. Abel Barker to Mr. Edmund Wright, at Mr.
Petticotte's in the Strand. "Pray doe me the favour to
" buy me a booke called Pembrooke's Arcadia lately re-
" printed with the life of Sir Phillip Sidney the author."
Hambleton, December 6, 1654.

216. Abel Barker to the Lady Frances Burton, at
Stockerson. Thanking her for many kindnesses and
much good advice, and saying "but I cannot find in
" myselfe any inclinacion to alter (as yet) my present
" condition." Hambleton, Dec. 22, 1654.

217. Abel Barker to Edmund Wright, in the Strand.
Sending him an order for 3l., 41 shillings of which are
to be paid to "cosen Bland," and the rest enjoyed by
Edmund Wright. Hambleton, Jan. 7, 1654.

218. Abel Barker to Sir Thomas Hartopp, at Norman
ton. Sending a calculation of the value of 2,000l., payable
six years hence. Hambleton, Jan. 24, 1654.

219. Abel Barker to Mr. Peter Woodcocke. Desiring
him to receive money due on an enclosed bond, and to
pay rent to Sir James Harington. Hambleton, March
13, 1654.

220. Abel Barker to Sir James Harington. About
rent and taxes. March 25, 1655.

221. Abel Barker to Mr. Thomas Barker, at Hambleton. Inviting his brother to come to town and announcing that he has sent his horse back by Peter Woodcocke.
John Musson is to put the animal to grass. Strand, May
17, 1655.

222. Abel Barker to Mr. Edmund Wright at London.
Acknowledging with thanks kindness shown to his boy,
repaying 47s. 6d. spent on the lad, and giving the writer
several small commissions to execute. "Get my cosen
" Bland," he says, "to buy me 11½ yards more of the
" same chequered stuff he made my coats of." Hambleton, June 24, 1655.

223. Abel Barker to Sir James Harington. About
rents and taxes. Hambleton, July 8, 1655.

224. Abel Barker to Geffrey Palmer, Esq. (subsequently
Attorney General to Charles the Second). Acknowledging kindnesses, and announcing that he has fixed his
affections on Mr. Palmer's neice. "I held it," he says,
" my duty to intimate so much vnto you, as the author
" of that happiness I propose to myself therein, and to
" desire your permission for my prosecution thereof."
Hambleton, July 24, 1655.

225. Abel Barker to Mr. Edmund Wright at London.
Enclosing a note for delivery to Mr. A. N., and enquiring
if Mr. Wright intends to come into Rutland during
next vacation. Hambleton, July 22, 1655.

226. Abel Barker to Mrs. Anne Primott, at London.
Declining to visit London at present. Hambleton, July
24, 1655.

227. Abel Barker to Mr. Edmund Wright. Avowing
that he would not have his petition detain Mr. Wright
in London, and wishes to defer the matter. Hambleton,
July 29, 1655.

228. Abel Barker to Geffrey Palmer, Esq. Thanking
Mr. Palmer for great kindnesses, and for his influence
with Mr. Noell (the father of the young lady referred to
in letter 224), and begging him to draw the marriage

settlements from documents enclosed. "I haue," he adds, "sent you also my former wine's joynture, as I "promised your brother at the beginning, that you may "see I haue not desired more of him, than was formerly "granted me by another." Hambleton, August 23, 1655.

229. Abel Barker to Mr. John Buston, at Coggshall. About wool and payment for it. Hambleton, August 23, 1655.

230. Abel Barker to Sir James Harington. About rents and taxes. Hambleton, August 23, 1655.

231. Abel Barker to Sir Thomas Hartopp, at Normanton. Expressing his readiness to serve Sir Thomas' friend, Francis Laurence. Hambleton, August 26, 1655.

232. Abel Barker to Alexander Noell, Esq. Announcing that the "writings" have arrived from Mr. Palmer, and that he will wait on Mr. Noell in the morning. Hambleton, September 2, 1655.

233. The same to the same. "I haue perused the act "and doe not perceive the cause of your feare to be an "essentiall but circumstantiall part, nor neede you "make the same appeare. I haue beene with the justice "who hath allowed the certificate and wilbe ready to- "morrow at two of the clocke." Hambleton, September 5, 1655. At which date the Marriage Act of the Parliament of 1653 requiring marriage to be performed in a magistrate's presence, and declaring no form of matrimony but the civil one to be valid, was still in force.

234. Abel Barker to Mr. John Bland at London. "I "desire you would make me a blake mourneing suite, "doublet and hose, but not a cloake, and send them "downe by this returne of Haringworth carrier. I "would haue the hose trimmed with fancyes, not points, "& the doublet collar not so wide as the last you made "me. Pray send me a little coate of blacke frissado, "a paire of Cordovans gloves, & cipresse hatband." Hambleton, September 23, 1655.

235. Abel Barker to Sir James Harington. About rates and taxes. No date.

236. Abel Barker to Mr. John Buston, at Coggshall. About payments. Hambleton, October 13, 1655.

237. Abel Barker to his cousin Walcott, at Stockerston. Asking to be informed when the executors come next time to Stockerston, and observing that 900l. are due to him from them. Hambleton, October 14, 1655.

238. Abel Barker to Sir James Harington. About rents and taxes. Hambleton, October 21, 1655.

239. The same to the same. About taxes. Hambleton, November 9, 1655.

240. Abel Barker to Geffrey Palmer, Esq. Sending copy of a bond respecting which Mr. Palmer has engaged to give an award; and speaking of cattle and other stock which the writer has inspected in his correspondent's interest. Hambleton, Nov. 9, 1655.

241. Abel Barker to Mr. Edmund Wright. Acknowledging the arrival of 2 rundlets of wine, costing 16l. 17s. Hambleton, Nov. 11, 1655.

242. The same to the same. Acknowledging his receipt of a petition and answer, and giving instructions about the business, to which they relate. No date.

243. Abel Barker to Geffrey Palmer, Esq. Giving particulars of a valuation of farm-stock made for Mr. Palmer. Hambleton, November 24, 1655.

244. Abel Barker to Sir James Harington. Enquiring if Sir James still wishes to sell certain land. November 24, 1655.

245. Abel Barker to Mr. Edmund Wright. Sending him an order for 20l., and instructions about several matters of business. Hambleton, December 15, 1655.

246. Abel Barker to Sir James Harington. Repeating the enquiry of letter 244. Hambleton, October 15, 1655.

247. Abel Barker to Mr. William Ducy at Islington. About taxes for Gunthorpe. Hambleton, December 19, 1655.

248. Abel Barker to Mr. Woodcocke. Instructing him to pay to Mr. William Ducie the Michaelmas rents of his tenants at Gunthorpes. Hambleton, January 9, 1655.

249. Abel Barker to his uncle, Ephraim Wright, at Okeham. Announcing that his mother declines to accede to Mr. Wright's demands for money, and returning him an insolent letter. Hambleton, January 19, 1655.

250. Abel Barker to Mr. Edmund Wright at London. Thanking him for judicious action in an affair of business. Hambleton, Jan. 19, 1655.

251. The same to the same. Announcing that the late Sir Thomas Burton's will has been proved in London; and begging Mr. Wright to send him a copy of it. Hambleton, February 24, 1655.

252. The same to the same. Acknowledging the arrival of the copy of the will, and draught of a license. Hambleton, March 2, 1655.

253. Abel Barker to Mr. Peter Woodcocke. Desiring him to receive 200l. due on enclosed bonds, and to pay his rent for land at Gunthorpe to Mr. Ducie. Hambleton, March 17, 1655.

254. Abel Barker to Geffrey Palmer, Esq. Giving particulars of certain lands he has viewed for Mr. Palmer. Hambleton, March 22, 1655.

255. Abel Barker to Mr. Edmund Wright at London. Approving Mr. Wright's action in the matter of the license. Hambleton, March 26, 1655.

256. The same to the same. Requesting him to order cousin Bland to send down 2½ doz. of wine, a doz. of sacke, a doz. of claret, 4 bottles white and 2 Rhenish, "the bottles glasse, most quarts, the rest pints." Hambleton, May 25, 1656.

257. The same to the same. Announcing that Mr. Woodcocke has been ordered to pay cousin Bland 5l. 12s., viz., 3l. 8s. for a boy's suit, and 44s. for the wine. Hambleton, July 5, 1656.

258. Abel Barker to Mr. Woodcocke at Smithfield. Ordering him to pay the 5l. 12s. to Mr. Bland of the 3 Sugar Loaves in Walbrook, and 7s. 4s. to Mr. Hart, "a taylor at the Catt and Fiddle over against "St. Dunstan's Church." Hambleton, July 5, 1656.

259. Abel Barker to his brother Watts at Leicester. Asking for payment of some of the money due to him from Sir Thomas Burton. Hambleton, July 26, 1656.

260. Abel Barker to Mr. William Ducie at Islington. About the rents which he takes for Mr. Ducie at Gunthorp. Hambleton, August 6, 1656.

261. Abel Barker to Mr. Christopher Broune. Thanking Mr. Broune for certain intelligence, and expressing disdain for William Jephson's untrue statements. Hambleton, August 16, 1656.

262. Abel Baker to G. P. at L. (i.e., Geffrey Palmer). Enclosing a copy of Sir Thomas Burton's will, and requesting him to "draw a bill in Chancery." Hambleton, October 13, 1656.

263. Abel Barker to Mr. Edmund Wright. Instructing him in a matter of business. Hambleton, October 13, 1656.

264. The same to the same. Instructing him as to proceedings against Sir Thomas Burton's executors. Hambleton, October 22, 1656.

265. Abel Barker to Geffrey Palmer, Esq., at London. About the same proceedings in Chancery. Hambleton, Oct. 22, 1656.

266. Abel Barker to F. H., at Westminster. About a negociation with a person (not named), who seems disposed to act reasonably in a matter of business. Hambleton, Oct. 22, 1656.

267. Abel Barker to his brother-in-law, Sir Thomas Burton. Congratulating him on his recent marriage, and expressing desire for an amicable arrangement to the Chancery suit, in which Sir Thomas is required to be a defendant. Hambleton, November 12, 1656.

268. Abel Barker to F. H., at W. Stating what he has done to induce Col. Waite to abate something of the too high sum he asks for his Rutland estate. No date.

269. Abel Barker to William E., Esq. About another suit in Chancery to which the writer is a party. Hambleton, January 20, 1656.

270. Abel Barker to Mr. William Ducie, at his house in Islington. About the rents and taxes of Mr. Ducie's estate in Rutland. Hambleton, January 10, 1656.

271. The same to the same. On matters relating to the same estate. Hambleton, June 30, 1658.

272. Abel Barker to Mr. Dobson at his house in Blackefryers. Ordering clothes of Mr. Dobson (a tailor), and complaining that the last clothes sent to Hambleton were packed so badly that they arrived "all in wrinkles." Hambleton, June 30, 1658.

273. Abel Barker to Mr. John Buston at Coggshall. About wool and payment for it. Hambleton, August 9, 1658.

274. Abel Barker to Hugh Ducie, Esq. at Islington. Explaining why he was unable, when last in London, to see his correspondent. Hambleton, August 24, 1658.

275. Abel Barker to Mr. Peter Woodcocke. Requesting him to pay rent to Mr. Hugh Ducie for Gunthorpe. Hambleton, October 18, 1658.

276. Abel Barker to Mr. Woodcocke. Requesting him to pay the rent for Gunthorpe. Hambleton, April 30, 1659.

277. Abel Barker to Mr. George Pretyman at London. About an executorship. Hambleton, May 18, 1659.

278. Abel Barker to John Pretyman, Esq., at Loddington. Making an appointment to see him. Hambleton, May 31, 1659.

279. Abel Barker to Philip Sherard, Esq., at London. Showing what injustice was done to Northamptonshire, Rutland, Lincolnshire, and Derbyshire, by the parliamentary arrangements of 1647 or 1648, for the raising of taxes ; and urging that action should be taken for relieving those counties of their excessive burdens. Hambleton, July 28, 1660.

280. Abel Barker to Mr. John Buston at Coggeshall. About wool and payments for it. Hambleton, August 4, 1660.

281. Abel Barker to William Cutler, Esq., at Rutland House. Announcing that Dr. Sterne has been made Dean of Lincoln, and advising Mr. Cutler to take prompt measures for renewing a lease of lands from the Dean and Chapter. Hambleton, Aug. 5, 1660.

282. Abel Barker to T. H., at L. Giving intelligence of measures taken with a view to an election in the county. Hambleton, December 23, 1660.

283. Abel Barker to Alexander Noel, Esq. About certain business of the county of Rutland, in respect to which the writer has been charged with "subtle designs." Hambleton, March 13, 1660.

284. Abel Barker to Captain Sherard. Repudiating indignantly the charge of mala fides and subtle design, and demanding the name of his culminator. Hambleton, March 16, 1660.

285. The same to the same. Repeating the demand of the previous letter. Hambleton, March 17, 1660.

286. Abel Barker to Alexander Noell, Esq. About the intrigues for the election, which appear to have agitated the county of Rutland greatly, and caused much ill-feeling. March 26, 1661.

287. Abel Barker to (name, probably John Buston, omitted). About wool and payments for it. Hambleton, July 28, 1661.

288. Abel Barker to Mr. Wray, a scrivener between the two Temple Gates. Enquiring if Mr. Audley still wishes to sell certain land. Hambleton, August 12, 1661.

289. Abel Barker to Sir Hugh Ducie at Islington. About rent, and the writer's hope to procure the passing of an important Act of Parliament. Hambleton, August 17, 1661.

290. Abel Barker to Sir Geffrey Palmer, Kt. and Baronet, at London. Giving full and minute particulars, at great length, respecting Colonel Hutchinson's estate, the lordship of Losby, which Sir Geffrey thinks of buying. Hambleton, September 16, 1661.

291. The same to the same. About a subscription for a voluntary present from the loyal gentry and clergy of the county to the King, which will probably amount to 1,000l. Hambleton, September 22, 1661.

292. Abel Barker to Sir Thomas Meres at Brooke. Announcing that he has heard from the Earl of Lindsey. Hambleton, October 1661.

293. Abel Barker to Mrs. Jane Parker at Carleton. Regretting that a member of his family has offended his correspondent, and promising to visit the lady. Hambleton, October 9, 1661.

294. Abel Barker to Mr. Thomas Templer at London. Explaining why he cannot lend money on the terms desired by Mr. Templer. Vppingham, October 16, 1661.

295. Abel Barker to (name omitted). About affairs of money. Hambleton, October 26, 1661.

296. Abel Barker to Sir Geffrey Palmer at London. Giving particulars of another estate, valued at 17,000l. which Sir Geffrey thinks of buying. Hambleton, January 5, 1661.

297. The same to the same. On the same subject. Hambleton, January 7, 1661.

298. Abel Barker to Mr. William Goodman. Requesting speedy payment of 300 and more pounds, long due to the writer. Hambleton, January 13, 1661.

299. Abel Barker to Sir Geffrey Palmer at London. Announcing Mr. Noel's acceptance of Sir Geffrey's proposal in a bargain. Hambleton, March 15, 1661.

300. Abel Barker to Valentine Sanders, Esq., at London. Announcing that Mr. Noel has come to Sir Geoffrey's terms. Hambleton, March 15, 1661.

301. The same to the same. On the same business. March 28, 1662.

302. Abel Barker to Euers Armyne, Esq., at Ketton. Respecting a lease of two pits, with a disputed title. Hambleton, April 2, 1662.

303. Abel Barker to Mr. Thomas Hayes at Melton. About a payment of money. Hambleton, April 10, 1663.

304. Abel Barker to Robert Markland, at the Rose in Smithfield. Instructing him to pay the writer's rent for Gunthorp. Hambleton, July 11, 1663.

305. Abel Barker to Sir William Ducie at the Lord Seymour's house in St. Martin's Lane. Informing him of the instructions, about rent, given to Mr. Markland. Hambleton, July 11, 1663.

306. Abel Barker to Mr. Peter Woodcocke at London. About rent to be paid "into the proper hands of "William Ducie, an infant," Sir William Ducie's nephew. Hambleton, September 22, 1664.

307. Abel Barker to Sir Geffrey Palmer at London. Giving precise reasons for declining to become surety for Mr. Samuel Hofbech, at Sir Geffrey's request. Hambleton, September 22, 1664.

308. Abel Barker to Mr. Thomas Barker, at the Rose in Smithfield. Requesting him to pay the rent for Gunthorp into the hands of William Ducie, Esq., an infant. Hambleton, May 6, 1665.

(b.) The Barker Correspondence : — Including the Whiston Papers and other Documents illustrative of Social Life in the 17th and 18th centuries.

1. Letter from Elizabeth Barker, (widow of Baldwin Barker, yeoman, who died in 1603) to her son Abel, the father of Sir Abel Barker. Demanding a separate residence, and money due to her by reason of her late husband's will. It begins, "Deare Sonne, harp not so much upon my death, I desired your life much before "I had you." 1604.

2. Letter from Samuel Barker, son of the abovementioned Elizabeth, to his brother Abel at Hambleton. Requesting that certain money be not paid to Samon, who has complained to the justices of peace for Rutland at Quarter Session. January 27, 1610, Staple Inne, London.

3. Letter from Abraham Wright to Mr. Barker at Hambleton. Begging Mr. Barker to accept a present of quinces for marmalade. No date.

4. Letter from William Wright to Abel Barker, Esq., at Hambleton. Begging for the loan of 300l. so that the writer and his brother may establish themselves in business. No date.

5. Release from George Cooke of Seaton, co. Rutland, to Abel Barker, in respect to the estate of the late Bawldwyne Barker. November 10, 1603.

6. Release from Fawstine Sculthorpe, gentleman, to Abel Barker of Hambleton, in respect to Baldwyne Barker's estate, and all other matters from the beginning of the world. May 24, 1607.

7. Letter from Thomas Fleetwood to Abel Barker, at Hambleton. Asking for three "lodes of heay,"to be repaid by six loads of hay at a convenient season, or bought at a reasonable price. April 3, 1630.

8. Letter from Edward Hunt, Esq., to Lord——. Offering to sell to his lordship an estate, including the manor of Lyndon, and yielding an annual revenue of 744l. 6s. 8d. February 27, 1633.

9. Letter from Robert Corbett to Abel Barker at Hambleton. About a claim for money. The Kinges Benches, July 10, 1634.

10. Letter from Sir Philip Digbye to his tenant, Abel Barker at Hambleton. Requesting Mr. Barker to pay 200l. to Mr. Edward Bead. Gothurst, October 31, 1634.

11. Francis Saunders to his kinsman Abel Barker, at Hambleton. About taxes, rent due to Mr. Digby, and other small matters of business. Lyndon, October 18, 1637.

12. Copy of the will, with codicils, of Abel Barker of Hambleton, father of Sir Abel. 1637.

13. Letter from Thomas Barker to his brother Abel, at "Mr. Vaughan's, a barber at the netherend of Chancery "Lane, near Sergeant's Inn." Announcing his purpose to be in town during this term, when he hopes to put an end to a troublesome suit. Medborne, February 7, 1637.

15. Receipt of Mary Barker (Sir Abel's sister), for 1,250l. paid to her by her brother Abel, in full settlement of her claims on her father's estate, and also on the estate of her brother John. September 26, 1645.

16. Letter from Sir Thomas Burton, Knight and Baronet, to his daughter Anne, wife of Abel Barker. Dated "from my house in the upper parte of Holborne, "neare the Elme Tree." December 9, 1646.

17. Letter from the same to the same. No date.

18. Letter from the same to Abel Barker, beginning "Sonne Barker." No date.

19. Letter from (Pastor) Laurence Hungerford to Abel Barker, High Sheriff. Announcing the writer's departure from his home, and making arrangements

for the performance of duties during his absence. March 10, 1646.

20. Letter from William Neale to Abel Barker. Begging for the loan of 20s.; "taxes indangering" the writer's "living." Dec. 11, 1646.

21. Letter from Jeremiah Ipshley to Abel Barker at Hambleton. Begging Mr. Barker to settle for his "quarterings," and to arrange about taxes with the townsmen of Edgington. Dec. 11, 1646.

22. Letter from Tho. Farbecke to his louing cosen Mrs. Anne Barker at Hambleton. Reminding her pleasantly of her old wish to be a High Sheriff's wife, and mother of a High Sheriff's heir, and hoping that the second part of the wish may be fulfilled as agreeably as the first. December 28, 1646.

23. Letter from Henrie Calverly to his "good brother" Abel Barker. Condoling with Mr. Barker on the untimely death of his wife. January 17, 1647.

24. List of the bailiffs and servants who attended High Sheriff Barker at the Okeham assizes, April 1647, together with details of the High Sheriff's supper and dinner at the Bell Inn, and of his presents of good cheer to the judges. These items of the Sheriff's official expenditure amounted to 50l.

25. Letter from Richard Lowth to High Sheriff Barker. Announcing the judicial arrangements for next assizes in Rutland. "When I came through Hatfield "on Tuesday last, the King was there, and on Thurs- "day he removed to Windsor Castle." London, July 5, 1647.

26. Letter from Robert Horsman to the High Sheriff. About the seditious action of a "dangerous schismatick" preacher, namely, Samuel Oates. Stretton, October 6, 1647.

27. Letter from the same to the same. Announcing the writer's satisfaction at delivering the same disturber of the church into the High Sheriff's hands. Stretton, October 8, 1647.

28. Copy (in Abel Barker's handwriting) of a judge's charge to a grand jury. The judge is not named, nor is the place mentioned where the charge was delivered. Dated July 12, 1648.

29. Letter from Abel Barker to his sister Goodman. Exhorting her not to make an uncanonical marriage. The writer copied this epistle into his letter book. May 30, 1648.

30. Letter from Katharine Walcott of Uppingham to her "very louing friend" Abel Barker at Hambleton. Entreating him to use his influence with a captain, quartered in his house, to relieve her of a soldier billeted upon. She writes "I am burdened with a "souldier to whose maintenance I am weekly to pay "halfe-a-crowne, with farre passeth my ability,beeing "a widow woman and hauing a great houshold to man- "taine, and but a littel liuing." May, 1649.

31. The original of a letter, about rent, taxes, and agreements, from Abel Barker to Sir Edward Haring- ton, which was copied into the letter book. Hambleton, January 18, 1649.

32. Letter from Sir Edward Harington to Abel Barker, at Hambleton. Begging for prompt payment of rent, as the writer has urgent occasions for money. Aldersgate Street, September 19, 1650.

33. Receipt of Henry Greene the elder of "Wyken "in the county of the city of Counterry," Esq., and Henry Greene of Roleston, co. Leicester, for 1,250l. paid by Abel Barker as the marriage portion of his sister, Mary, wife of Henry Greene. November 18, 1650.

34. Letter from Samuel Barker to his nephew Abel Barker at Hambleton. Asking for particulars (as to extent, quality of soil, and annual value) of Mr. St. John's manor of Sapcots. Gray's Inne, May 5, 1653.

35. Letter from Sir James Harington to his "dear "cousin Barker" at Hambleton. Respecting a new lease and the landlord's arrangements for settling the contract. Whitehall, May 12, 1653.

36. Letter from John Morgan, tailor, to Abel Barker at Hambleton. Announcing that the writer has sent his customer "a cloth sute of very goode clothe a "fashonable culler tremd with fancies according to "the fashion." London, October 6, 1653.

37. Letter from Anne Dixon to her "much respected "friend" Abel Barker at Hambleton. Begging him and his brother Thomas to join with other friends in arranging amicably a difference that has arisen between her and her son. "Some friends are to haue the heare- "ing of it," she says, "and I have maid choyce of you "for oue." Edmonthorpe, 1653.

38. Letter from Edmund Wright to Abel Barker at Hambleton. Announcing that "Generall Blake hath

"sett vp his standard in the streights, & men are "pressed & drawne out for the expedicion," and that the writer's brother Abel sends his remembrances to old friends in Rutland, from the Torrington frigate, and asks for their prayers and good wishes, "the trouble "and dangers of the sea being more then by land." London, Thursday.

39. Letter from Edmund Wright to his euer honoured kinsman Abel Barker at Hambleton. Announcing on the authority of rumour, "that Count Wm. Nassau "hath beseiged Amsterdam, and the fleet is designed "for Holland, and . . . is suddenly to set forth." London, December 7, 1654.

40. Letter from Edmund Wright to his "euer honoured "kinsman" Abel Barker at Hambleton. Announcing that the fleet with the writer's brother Abel and other friends on board has left Portsmouth, but whither it is bound is not yet known. "Cousen Bland," says the writer, "presents her service to you, and desires me to "let you know that her husband and Abel with her "on shipboard had you in remembrance with the rest "of our friends with you in a glass of wine." A post- script adds that the navy is thought to have sailed for "High Spaniola." January 4, 1654.

41. Letter from Rebekah Parsett alias Partesoyle to her "much respected friend" Abel Barker at Ham- bleton. Declining with a rather frigid civility an offer of marriage made to her by Abel Barker. "I cannot," the writer says after several expressions of courtesy, "thinke of committing my selfe and estayt into the "hands of any man vpon the terms you desier, more "espeshally your condision considered, as you have a "sonn. I doe acknowledge my selfe much ingaged to "you for the good thoughts you haue of me though "it be altogether without deserts." July 30, 1655. The letter book shows that six days before the date of this refusal Abel Barker was making overtures through Mr. Geoffrey Palmer for the hand of Miss Mary Noell.

42. Letter from Alexander Noell to Abel Barker, shortly before his daughter's marriage with the latter. —Sir. This is to certifie you that the mony for my daughter's portion will be readie by 7 o'clock in the morning, & I desire you will either com or send to reseaue & tell the mony early in the morning. If Mr. Musson bee not come with the writings, it is no matter betweene you & myselfe at present. We may seale them sum other time, but I much desire you should haue the mony. You must send bag to put the money in. Sir, in haste I rest y' true friend and seruant, Alex. Noel. No date.

43. Certificate (parchment) of the civil marriage of Abel Barker of Hambleton with Mary Noell, daughter of Alexander Noell of Whitwell, co. Rutland, on Sep- tember 6, 1655, in the presence of Euers Armyne, justice of the peace, and in accordance with requirements of the Marriage Act of the Parliament of 1653.

44. Letter from Edmund Wright to Abel Barker at Hambleton. About the progress of certain affairs in which the writer appears to be acting as Mr. Barker's attorney. March 13, 1656.

45. Letter from Mary Barker to her husband Abel Barker, at Mr. Brassington's in Clement's Churchyard. "Deart heart, I heare you goot safe and well to Lond, "and by this time are ready to retorne to her who "mournes for youre deare company. I trust to God "you will stay no longer then needes you must, &c., &c. "Your faithfull loueing wife, Mary Barker." In a postscript she adds, "Remember to by me som sherry "of amber: Pres you by me a lased pinner and quioufe "of the new fashiou for myselfe, and I would haue a "satten mantell for my child to crisen it in. Lette "it be ether blew or read satten, which you can best "got, and lased with a brod siluer lase and lined with "sarsinet." Hambleton, May 10, 1656.

46. Letter from C. Browne to Abel Barker at Ham- bleton. Reporting divers rumours that may be prejudicial to Mr. Barker's interest at a coming election, and also hurtful to his honour. Tolethorp, August 16, 1656.

47. Edward Greene to his loving brother Mr. Richard Triste, jun'. at Maydeford. Announcing the fortunate celebration of the writer's marriage, and sounding the praises of his bride in terms of fantastic extravagance. March 2, 1657.

48. Letter from Abel Barker to his brother Thomas at Medburne. Announcing the death of "unkle Barker "yesterday at 3 o'clocke in the morning," and the arrangements for his burial on the "morrow at one in "the afternoon." Hambleton, August 15, 1658.

49. Letter from Nathaniel Barker, John Barker, and Bridget Barker to Abel Barker, at the Rose in Smith-

field. In which Abel is thanked for his efforts to arrange a family difference, and is entreated to let the matter stand over till Uppingham Fair. North Luffenham, January 25, 1659.

50. Letter from Lord Campden to Abel Barker at Hambleton. Asking Mr. Barker to induce the magistrates of his county to "order an allowance to Will. " Colby, his lordship's muster-master." Lord Campdon has written to Sir Richard Wingfield on the same business. April 9, 1660.

51. Declaration of loyalty to Charles the Second, signed by fifty inhabitants of Rutland, 1660.

52. Declaration of the same kind, made and signed by William Shield, 1660.

53. Letter from Mary Barker to her husband Abel, " at the Dogg and Ball in Fleetestreete near the New " Pageant." A letter of dismal gossip about the ailments of their children and grevious sickness of their neighbours. Small-pox is raging at Hambleton, and the writer is in a panic for the safety of her babes who are down with whooping-cough. "I am in a sad con- " distion," she writes, "for my pore children who are " all so trobled with the chinconfe that I am afread it " will kill them. There is many dy out in this town, " and many abrode that we heare of. I am faine to " have a candell stand by me to goo in too them when " the fett comes." Hambleton, May 26, 1661.

54. Letter from the same to the same, at the same address. Another dismal note; Mrs. Barker, sen'. is weakly and lives within a yard of the small-pox, which is also in the house of Mary Barker's nearest neighbour. The children are still " all sadly trobeled with the chin- " cofe. Moll is much the worst. They haue such fits " that it stopes theare wind, and puts me to such frits " and feares, that I am not my selfe." Hambleton, June 2, 1661.

55. Letter from the same to the same, " att the Rose " in Smithfeeled near the penns." Giving Mr. Barker some gossip about his neighbours. The children are better, but the small-pox is still in the village. Hambleton, June 30, 1661.

56. Letter from the same to the same, " at the Flower " de Luce & Crowne, ouer aganest St. Clement's " Church dore in the Strande." Beginning like all the other letters of the series with " My Dearest Heart," and mentioning the several wants of the children who are getting over " the chincoafe." "I desire a paper " of losenges for them," says Mrs. Barker, " and a pare " of stokings for somer, and a pare of shows for them " both, sum perfumes for the champers, and one pare " of long white holland glufs for my selfe . . . " Bell is as ragedy as a beger boy. I prae you let him " haue a sute."

57. Letter from Richard Verney to Abel Barker. Soliciting Mr. Barker to get a small allowance for an old and disabled soldier, who fought for the late king. July 17, 1661.

58. Letter from Mary Barker to her husband, at " Sir " Geffrey Palmer's Old Chamber in the Temple Church- " yard." Expressing the writer's longing to see her " dearest heart" once again. No date.

59. Letter from Sir Geoffrey Palmer to Abel Barker, Esq., at Hambleton. Announcing that Mr. Awdeley is willing to sell Lyndon to Mr. Barker. October 16, 1661.

60. A note from Abraham Wright to———. Begging the receiver of the letter to accept a present of grapes. October 22, 1661.

61. Letter from Alexander Noel to Abel Barker. Begging Mr. Barker to give 3l. to his brother-in-law Andrew Noel, who is in London, treating with Colonel Trevers for the purchase of land in Armagh. January 19, 1661.

62. Letter from H. Ducie, Esq., to Abel Barker, Esq., at Hambleton. Thanking Mr. Barker for instructions respecting the duties of a sheriff, and mentioning the terms on which the writer has assisted one of their common friends. December 4, 1661.

63. Accounts of the personal estate (amounting to 10,315l.) of the late John Barker, Abel's brother. Jan. 22, 1662.

64. Receipt for 400l. (four years' rent) from Abel Barker, signed by his mother. January 16, 1662.

65. Accounts between Abel Barker and his brother Thomas, on the purchase of an estate. June 1, 1662.

66. Further accounts between the same persons. March 2, 1662.

67. Letter from Henry Kempe, Esq., to Abel Barker at Hambleton. Reporting an interview the writer has had with Mr. Fisher, guardian of Sir Hugh Ducie's heir, William Temple. March 29, 1666.

68. Proposals for settlements on the marriage of Henry Noel, Esq., with Elizabeth, daughter of Sir William Wale, Knt. August 14, 1669.

69. Letter from William Greenhaugh, and Jane his wife, to Sir Abel Barker, Knt. and Baronet, at Hambleton. Entreating Sir Abel to get ecclesiastical preferment for William Greenhaugh, who is a clerk, and has married one of Sir Abel's kinswomen. February 10, 1669.

70. The last will and codicil of Sir Abel Barker, dated in the year 1670.

71. Letter from William Greenhaugh, and Jane his wife, to Sir Abel Barker, who has presented Mr. Greenhaugh to the living of Lyndon. Rettendon, Essex, December 5, 1670.

72. Letter from Lady Barker at Hambleton to her husband, Sir Abel, " at Mr. Pawlins, a shoomaker in " the Strand, betweene the Maypole and St. Clement's " Church, London." Announcing her sore need of a fit mourning costume, wherein to render fit respect to the corpse of her uncle. " I would not if I could anoyd it " meat the body of my unkell, by reson I haue nothing " hansom to goo in, at such a time." May 16, 1670.

73. Letter from the same to the same, at the same address. Giving particular directions for her new mourning costume. " Let the goune," she writes, " be a plane " black sattine, with a peake, and a pare of sad colered " glufs, and a twisted role for my head, lased with " blake satten, and one lase with a wealt abote the hem, " and a pare of sleves to it, which is the fashon for " morning this sommer. My Lady Mackworth toulde " me so. The Ladys at Wisindine are so; and Mrs. " Mackit tould me the like last Sonday, who cam on " purpose to let me know the gentill man, her son was " a prentis with, deed worke to the young duchis of " Albemarle, and tow other duchis, and that he is a " very fashonabel tayler." Hambleton, May 17, 1670. The name of the dead uncle is not given in these letters, but probably he was Sir Jeffrey Palmer, who died in the last-named year.

74. Letter from the same to the same, at London. Giving the gossip of the Hambleton neighbourhood. " I had," says Lady Barker, " a grate dale of compnay " all the 3 halladays, which hath drunke us dry." Mr. Mathi's child has been christened, and a matron of Hambleton has broken her leg in playing at ball. Hambleton, June 1, 1672.

75 Letter from Walter Kirkham, Esq., to Sir Abel Barker. Making overtures for the marriage of Sir Abel's son and heir with one of Mr. Kirkham's kinswomen. " She is left," says the letter, " by her father, " Sir Walter Walker, three thousand pounds; she is " a handsom lady, and well bread." May 20, 1674.

76. Letter from Lady Barker to Sir Abel, " at Mrs. " Slaughter's, a stationers ouer against Sergyant's " Inne in Chancery Lane." Assuring the writer's " Dear Heart" that their son Thomas looks after the farme and business. Hambleton, November 25, 1675.

77. Two lists, in Sir Abel's handwriting, of things bought, or to be bought in London.

78. Small 12° MS. volume, containing, in 283 pages of singularly small and accurate penmanship, Sir Abel Barker's private accounts from the year 1665 to the Michaelmas of 1677. Furnishing evidence that Sir Abel carried on his business of a large sheep farmer in his later years, this volume contains much precise information as to the expenses and profits of farming in the 17th century. It gives also the particulars of the baronet's domestic expenditure, whilst he and his wife and children maintained friendly relations with the first families of their county. From the " Accomput ux. " M. Barkor," it appears that Lady Barker's allowance for housekeeping was 200l. per annum, and that she spent no more than 50l. per annum in dressing herself and three daughters. The page of the record, headed " Remembrances," gives the full list of the writer's children, two of whom died in infancy. The account book gives also the particulars of John Musson's will and estate.

79. MS. newsletter from London. May 6, 1678.
80. Do.   do.   May 8, 1679.

81. Inventory of the chattels in Sir Abel Barker's house at Lindon, at the time of death, dated Sept. 30, 1679. Shortly before his death, Sir Abel moved from Hambledon into the house which he built on his estate at Lyndon.

82. Inventory of his plate.

83. Letter from James Armeston, Esq., to Christopher Dighton, Esq., Elm Court, Temple. Requesting Mr. Dighton to buy a sword for the writer. Hinckley, October 31, 1687.

Rev. E. Field, M.A.

84. Letter from Andrew Noel, Esq., to his nephew, Christopher Dighton. Requesting him to buy a present of sturgeon for Lord Ganesborough; and mentioning a false report that many "thousands of Roman Catholics "were up in arms about Northampton," by which news the country has been greatly alarmed. December 15, 1688.

85. Letter from Andrew Noel, Esq., the younger, to Christopher Dighton. Announcing that Lady Northampton has obtained for him the place of a gentleman usher to the King; and enquiring if he would do well to accept the office. Exton, March 1, 168$\frac{8}{9}$.

86. Letter from A. Noel, Esq., senior, to Christopher Dighton. On the same subject. Exton, March 4, 1689.

87. Letter from Andrew Noel, Esq., the younger, to Christopher Dighton, Esq. Announcing the death of Lord Ganesborough, and ordering new mourning to be worn in token of respect for that nobleman. Exton, April 2, 1689.

87a. Letter from Andrew Noel, Esq., the younger, to Mr. Hingle, "at the Honble John Noel's lodgings, near "the Hand and Periwig in the Pell Mell." Ordering clothes for the writer to wear on Lord Burleigh's birthday, and perhaps at the wedding of his (the writer's) brother. April 24, 1695.

88. Letter from Colonel Parsons to his brother-in-law, Sir Thomas Barker. Describing minutely the pomp with which the writer's wife (Sir Thomas's sister) was buried at St. Margaret's Church, Westminster. December 25, 1697.

89. Letter from Thomas Clerke, Esq., to Christopher Dighton, Esq. Advising what steps should be taken for Mr. Noel's advantage in respect to his interests in Ireland. Dublin, March 19, 169½.

90. Letter from Richard Allin to the Revd. William Whiston at Lowestoft in Suffolk. In reply to Mr. Whiston's criticisms of the writer's opinions on certain questions of biblical chronology and theology. Whitchurch, November 29, 1699.

91. Letter from George Antrobus to the Revd. William Whiston. On the marriage of the writer's daughter with Mr. Whiston. Tamworth, June 12, 1699.

92. Letter from Richard Allin to the Reverend William Whiston. On questions of chronology. Sydney College, March 19, 1700.

93. Letter from Marm. Alford to the Reverend Dr. Richard Bentley, Master of Trinity College, Cambridge. Announcing that Dr. Bentley's "Patent was passed the "Broad Seal, and perfected," and enclosing the "particulars of the Fees and Expences in passing the "Patent." Whitehall, June 26, 1707.

94. Letter from Richard Allin to the Revd. Mr. Whiston, at Tamworth, in Staffordshire. On questions of biblical chronology. Sydney College, August 29, 1707.

95. Inventory of the chattels in Sir Thomas Barker's house, at Lyndon, at the time of his death. Dated March 7, 1708.

96. Circular (dated May 1706) announcing the revival of a social club, called "The Honourable Order of "Little Bedlam," and giving the list of the members of the association, together with the names they bore at the meetings of the society. "Whereas," runs this singular record, "the Right Hon. John Earle of Exeter, "lately deceased, did in the year 1684 constitute a "Society, called the Honble Order of Little Bedlam at "Burghley:" And whereas no chapter or assembly of the members had been held since his decease. These are to give notice, That the Right Hon. John (now) Earle of Exeter, intending to renew & continue the said hon. society, did upon the 18th day of May 1705 call a chapter to be held in Little Bedlam by some members of the society who were near at hand, and as Great Master of the Order did take upon himself the title of Lyon. At which chapter were elected and admitted in this honble society:—

	Titles.
The Right Honble Baptist Earle of Gainsburrough	Greyhound.
The Honble William Cecill	Panther.
Sir Thomas Mackworth	Badger.
The Honble Charles Cecill	Bull.
Charles Tryon, Esq.	Otter.

At which chapter it was ordered, amongst other things, that the former rules shall stand good, and that the register shall give notice hereof to all such members as were formerly of the society, and were not present at this chapter, to know whether they are pleased to continue in the society, under the Right Honble the Lyon, Great Master of the Order. Which intention to continue in this honble order, you are desired to give notice to the register, Daniel Clark, at Burghley, before the 15th day of May 1706. Otherwise your picture will be taken downe, and the master will proceed to a new election to fill up your place, that the society may be kept full.

The List.	Titles.
The Right Honble John Earle of Exeter, Great Master	Lyon.
His Grace William Duke of Devonshire	Leopard.
The Right Honble Earle of Denbigh	Tyger.
The Right Honble Earle of Gainsburrough	Greyhound.
The Right Honble Lord Lexington	Lamb.
The Right Honble Lord How	Hare.
Anthony Palmer, Esq.	Eliphant.
The Honble John Noel	Wildhorse.
George Choke, Esq.	Wolphe.
The Honble Charles Bertie	Stagg.
Sir Thomas Barker	Ramm.
The Honble James Griffin	Wildboar.
The Honble John Verney	—
Henry Nevil, Esq.	Fox.
Thomas Hatcher, Esq.	Bear.
Samuel Tryon, Esq.	Tarrier.
Signr Antonio Verrio	Porcupine.
Sir Godfrey Kneller	Unicorne.
Sir James Robbinson	Buck.
Richard Sherrard, Esq.	Mule.
Timothy Lanoy, Esq.	Antelope.
George Leafield, Esq.	Guiney Pig.
Greg. Hascard, De. of Winsor	Cock.
The Honble William Cecill	Panther.
Sir Thomas Mackworth	Badgier.
The Honble Charles Cecill	Bull.
Charles Tryon, Esq.	Otter.

Note.—All peers are placed at the first, and then the others as they were admitted. Daniel Clark, Register.

97. Letter from William Whiston (the mathematician and theological disputant) to Robert Nelson, Esq., in Ormond Street, near Gray's Inn, London. Replying combatively to an epistle in which Nelson (the author of "Festivals and Fasts of the Church of England") urged Mr. Whiston to recant opinions set forth in his "Sermons and Essays." "I run no hazzard," writes Whiston, "as to another world, because I keep close to "the Faith and practice which was once delivered to "the Saints, without suffering any synod or humane "authority to turn me at all out of the way: whereas "you venture the most sacred concerns to believe and "practice as the countrey & church wherein you were "educated happened to instruct you, and seem to "think it a piece of impiety to do otherwise." Cambridge, July 31, 1710.

98. The MS. volume in which William Whiston kept the minutes of the proceedings of "The Society for "promoting Primitive Christianity."

99. Letter from William Whiston to the Society for Promoting Christian Knowledge. Explaining why the writer has become an infrequent attendant at the meetings of the society. Union Court, December 1710.

100. Letter from William Whiston "To the Right "Rev. my Lords the Bishops and the Lord Bishop of "Lincolns in Deans Court, Westminster." Entreating for "a fair and publick examination of his MS. papers "before any censure be past upon him." The writer says, "I still offer to suppress my books in case that "a tenth part of the original evidence, which I have "to produce on my side, can be alleg'd for the opposite "doctrines." March 17, 17$\frac{19}{20}$.

101. Letter from Roger Cotes to William Whiston. Respecting one of Mr. Whiston's scientific proposals. Cambridge, December 2, 1714.

102. Letter from William Whiston to Samuel Barker, Esq., at Lyndon near Okeham, Rutland. Alluding to one of his projects for discovering the longitude, and accepting Mr. Barker's proposal for marriage with his daughter, who is however regarded by her father as too young at present for wedlock. London, January 27, 171$\frac{4}{5}$. William Whiston's daughter became in due course the wife of Samuel Barker, a member of Abel Barker's family.

103. Copy of the letter in which Samuel Barker made his offer of marriage to Miss Whiston. Lyndon, January 171$\frac{4}{5}$.

REV. B.
FIELD, M.A.

104. Letter from Richard Allin to William Whiston. On Mr. Whiston's observations of the eclipse. Sydney College, April 24, 1715.

105. Letter from John Jackson to William Whiston. Extolling the disputant's Primitive Christianity. Repington, October 31, 1716.

106. Letter from the same to the same. On questions of theology. April 17, 1717.

107. Letter from William Whiston to Samuel Barker, Esq., at Lyndon. Announcing the return of his wife and children from the country. November 9, 1717.

108. Letter from William Whiston, junr., to his sister Mrs. Samuel Barker, at Lyndon. Giving the news of the town, and its talk about quarrels and dissensions in the Royal Family. December 26, 1717.

109. Letter from William Whiston, junr. (son of the mathematician) to his sister, Mrs. Barker, junr., of Lyndon. In which the writer says, "My mother having "sent you an account of Dr. proceedings "in order to exclude my father from St. Andrew's "Church, I need not trouble you with it over again. "Only I shall let you know that he is not obliged to "stand in the isles on Sundays, as he did lately; for "the lawyers of Staples Inn have ordered their butler, "who opens their pews, to let him into one of their "pews, which is in the middle isle." London, February 11, 171⅞.

110. Letter from the same to the same. Alluding to the agitation caused by "the Peerage Bill." London. April 15, 1719.

111. Letter from Mrs. Samuel Barker to her husband in London. Imploring him to return to her, and rejoicing at the failure of the design of certain persons to prosecute him for heresy. July 24, 1721.

112. Letter from the Reverend John Jackson to William Whiston. On theological questions. November 4, 1721.

113. Prospectus (and list of subscribers) for raising a fund to enable William Whiston to continue his observations for discovering the longitude at sea. 1721.

114. A letter from William Whiston, senr., to "His "Grace the Lord Archbishop of Canterbury, at his Palace "at Lambeth." Recalling past courtesies and kindness from the primate to the writer, who regrets his Grace's change of sentiment on certain matters, and speaks at considerable length of incidents arising out of the religious controversies occasioned by his writings. Cross Street, Hatton Garden, May 18, 1721.

115. A letter from William Whiston, senr., to the Right Honourable the Lord Trevor, Lord Privy Seal, at Peckham, Surrey. Soliciting Lord Trevor's patronage for the writer's sons, who have been ordained at Cambridge under Dr. Laughton of Clare Hall, so that they are "qualified for several posts of life." Great Russel Street, over against Montague House, March 8, 172⅘.

116. A letter from William Whiston, senr., to his nephew Mr. William Whiston, at Luton, Bedfordshire. Expostulating affectionately, but in terms of strong reprobation, with the young man on his vanity, extravagance, and dissolute habits. It appears that the nephew had formerly been in Sir Isaac Newton's service, and that on leaving it he entered on a course of self indulgence and profligacy. London, September 14, 1725.

117. Petition of William Whiston to the Commissioners appointed by Act of Parliament for the discovery of the longitude at sea. 1730.

118 and 119. Letters from William Whiston, junr., of the Inner Temple, to his brother George. Announcing the arrangements for his marriage with Miss Plaistow. Aug. 1734.

120. Letter from the same to the same. March 2, 1734/5.

121. From the same to the same. 1734.

122. William Whiston, senr., to his son, Mr. George Whiston, at Samuel Barker's, Esq., at Lyndon, Rutland. Announcing that the Master of the Rolls is highly pleased with George Whiston's reports of his pupil, Mr. Jekyl. The writer proposes that his son should come up to town to see the Master of the Rolls, and consult Dr. Crowe, the physician. London, March 29, 1735.

123. A letter from the same to the same, at the same address. In which George Whiston is affectionately and urgently entreated to take steps for the benefit of his health, which is suffering greatly from excessive application to study. "Dr. Crowe," the father writes, "thinks that if you could abide cold bathing, which "might be come into at home gradually, it would go a "great way in your cure. He has also a great opinion "of Islington waters for your case." London, April 21, 1736.

REV. B.
FIELD, M.A.

124. Letter from William Whiston, junr., to his brother George. Giving the particulars of Queen Caroline's death. November 22, 1737.

125. Letter from the same to the same. Containing the particulars of the will of Sir Joseph Jekyll, Knt., Master of the Rolls, who left William Whiston, the elder, an annuity for life of 20l. Sept. 30, 1738.

126. Letter from the same to the same. On the same subject. October 7, 1738.

127. Letter from the same to the same. Enclosing prescriptions for George Whiston from Dr. Wilmot, who recommends his patient to drink the Stenfield waters, which are similar to the Scarborough waters. June 9, 1739.

128. Letter from the same to the same. Commending the speech made by Mr. Speaker on presenting the Supply Bills. June 16, 1739.

129. The elder William Whiston's receipt for 12l. 10s., one quarter's payment of the pension granted him by the King's warrant, dated March 22, 1737. The receipt bears date April 1740.

130. Letter from William Whiston, junr., to his brother George. Containing the political news of the week. April 19, 1740.

131. Letter from William Whiston, senr., to his son at Lyndon. Announcing that Mr. Edwards wishes to place his nephew, Mr. Salmon, as a pupil with George Whiston on such terms as the tutor had for teaching Mr. Jekyl. May 17, 1740.

132. Letter from Mr. Chetwoode to William Whiston, junr. Condoling with him on his ill health; and urging him ,with equal affectionateness and firmness, to resist his disposition to melancholy. August 28, 1740.

133. The memorial of William Whiston, clerk, sometime professor of mathematicks in the University of Cambridge, to the Rt. Hon. the Commissioners for exercising the office of the Lord High Admiral of Great Britain. June 20, 1740.

134. Letter from the Rev. John Jackson to Mr. George Whiston. On questions of biblical theology. March 19, 1742.

135. Letter from the same to the Rev. William Whiston at Lyndon. On questions of Jewish history. Mar. 19, 1742.

136. Letter from T. Fraser to the Rev. William Whiston. On questions relating to oriental languages. May 8, 1742.

137. Letter from the Rev. John Jackson to the Rev. William Whiston. On questions of biblical history. Oct.16, 1742.

138. Letter from the same to the same. On questions of biblical history. Nov. 13, 1742.

139. Letter from the Rev. John Jackson to Mr. George Whiston. For the most part on points of ancient history. Feb. 18, 1743.

140. Letter from the same to the same. On questions of ancient history. April 16, 1743.

141. Letter from William Whiston, senr., to the Earl of Westmoreland, Hanover Square, London. Asking for 50l. to enable the writer to bring out his projected edition of "the Four Gospels; according to the Greek "part of the MS. of Beza." Lyndon, May 23, 1744. Lord Westmoreland having taken no notice of this application, the writer sent him another copy of the letter, with an additional postscript.

142. Letter from the Privy Council to the Deputy Lieutenants of Rutland. Announcing the landing of the Young Pretender in the north-west of Scotland, and requiring them to disarm all "papists, non-jurors, "and all other persons that shall be judged dangerous "to the peace of the kingdom," within the said county. May 10, 1745.

143. Brief note:—"By express that arrived at 1 o'clock "this afternoon come into Derby 2 quartermasters and "demanded billets for 12,000 men, and we expect them "there to-morrow. That is all the information at "present as to the situation of our army." Leicester, December, 4 o'clock, in the evening. No signature or direction to this note.

144. Letter signed J. Wyche, and beginning with "My Lord." Announcing that "the Chevalier's ad- "vanced guard marched yesterday to Mansfield, and "the body to Alfreton," and that the rebel army, numbering only 4,600 men that can fight, is sure to be surrounded and destroyed. Stamford, December 6, 5 o'clock, afternoon.

145. Unsigned note, announcing on the authority of Lord Gainsborough's messenger, who has just returned from Nottingham, that the rebels have left Derby and

marched again for Ashbourn. December 6, 1745, ½ after 7 at night.

146. Letter from the Reverend John Jackson to Mr. Samuel Barker, of Lyndon. Describing a sharp encounter between the rebels and some country people; and giving particulars of the entry of the Royal army into Lancaster. December 31, 1745.

147. Unsigned letter, giving the latest news of the rebel army. Thursday, 8 o'clock, night.

148. Letter from J. Whiston in London, to his sister Mrs. Barker, of Lyndon. Reporting the panic in London. "Many are in great fears about them, and a camp will " be certainly formed on Monday on Finchley Common " of about 5,000 regular troops and 2 regiments of our " trained bands. I haue just heard that the Duke is " got between these plunderers and us." December 7, 1745.

149. Letter from the Rev. William Whiston to the Archbishop of Canterbury. Reflecting strongly on the remissness of the Church of England in neglecting to offer up prayers to God for the abatement and removal of "the long and sore murrain or plague now destroy- " ing the horned cattle;" and begging that search may be made at Lambeth for an "admirable collect of " thanksgiving and prayer on occasion of the Great " Storm of November 27, 1703." Lyndon, January 13, 174½.

149. Copy of the Archbishop's reply to the last-men- tioned letter, together with a copy of the form of prayer asked for by Mr. Whiston. "What you hint," the Primate observes, "about the Form of Prayer, your age, and " learning and experience give you a right to say, but it " becomes those who have less of all those to be a little " more reserved." Kennington, January 28, 1747.

150. Letter from the Rev. William Whiston to the Lord Chancellor, in Ormond Street. Soliciting his lord- ship's influence in behalf of the writer's son George, who is seeking under the government a place "that may be " easy and advantageous to him, and that without " burdening with what his weak nerves will not at " present bear." The writer alludes to the death of his son, William. London, February 6, 174¾.

151. Letter from the Rev. William Whiston to Samuel Barker, Esq., at Lyndon. Announcing that the writer's autobiography is ready for subscribers. London, August 31, 1748.

152. Letter to George Whiston from his old pupil, Mr. Jekyll. Inviting the latter to stay with the writer for four or five months, in order that they may resume their studies. Nov. 15, 1751.

153. Letter to the same from the same. Regretting that George Whiston cannot accept the flattering and affectionately worded invitation. Dalkington, December 10, 1751.

154. Letter from Thomas White (brother of Gilbert White of Selborne) to the Rev. William Whiston. "Reverend Sir, from the various performances that you " have favoured the world with (the nature, as well as " the number of them), and from the memoirs you haue " given us of your own life, I can plainly discern that " Nature designed you to be silent in your generation. " This I thought good to let you know, before you leave " a world, that, in fact, you have been of so little true " service in. I am, sir, your plain speaker, but your " real friend, Th. White." This curious piece of inci- vility to an aged and virtuous man is dated January 1, 1752, the year of William Whiston's death.

155. Letter from George Whiston to Speaker Onslow. Regretting that "severe miseries" forbid him to under- take at once the office of a librarian in the British Museum, and begging earnestly that he may for a brief while be allowed to discharge the duties of the place by deputy. February 12, 1756.

156. Letter from the Rev. J. White (a brother of Gilbert White) to Thomas Barker, Esq., at Lyndon, Giving measurements of rainfall at Gibraltar, and speaking of the death of the writer's sister at Selborne. Gibraltar, May 22, 1771.

157. Papers, containing a collection of facts, made by Mr. Samuel Barker, William Whiston, junr., and others, with a view to a new edition of Wright's History of Rutland.

158. A curious collection of tradesmen's bills, bear- ing dates from the year 1647 to 1760. The earlier bills, especially those from tailors of the seventeenth century, are interesting, and might be studied with ad- vantage by writers on the costumes and fashions of that period. One of the more noteworthy of these accounts is an undertaker's bill for the funeral of Madam Leigh (Christopher Dighton's sister) in London, in the year 1697. The lady, though not necessitous, was far from

5.

wealthy, and the interment cost 38l. 5s. 4d. Sending the account to Sir Thomas Barker, Mr. Dighton asks the baronet if he will "contribute anything" towards its pay- ment.

In addition to the letters, noticed in this list, the Barker Correspondence comprises several letters of sympathy or compliment, addressed to William Whiston, the elder, by his friends in England and in foreign parts. There are also letters, that passed between the younger members of the mathematician's family; letters of no considerable interest, on matters of history and science, addressed in the eighteenth century to Samuel Barker and Thomas Barker of Lyndon; and a number of letters by Gilbert White, grand-uncle to Mr. Field, who could not show them to me on the occasion of my visit to Lancing, as he had unfortu- nately lent them to a friend at a distance. All that is of public interest in these last-named letters will appear in the edition of "The Natural History of Selborne," now in course of preparation by Professor Bell, F.R.S.

(c.) *Papers relating to Taxation and Public Affairs in Rutland and adjoining counties in the 17th century.*

(1.) Indenture (parchment roll) made July 4, 22 James I., between the Commissioners of co. Rutland for collecting the first of three entire subsidies granted to the King by Parliament, of the one part, and John Butler of Okeham, co. Rutland, the High Collector, appointed by the said commissioners, of the other part. Names and titles of the Commissioners:—Edward Lord Nool, Sir Edward Harington, Knt. and Bart., Sir Thomas Mackworth, Bart., Sir William Bulstrode, Sir Gui Palmes, Sir Henry Myn, Knt., Richard Halford and Abraham Johnson, Esqs. The roll gives the complete assessment of county, under the headings of the several hundreds and parishes, with the amount assessed on each person. Those who refused or failed to pay the amounts charged upon them are marked "recusant."

(2.) May 13, 1625. Writ addressed by William Bull- strode and Guie Palmes to the Chief Constables of the Hundred of Martinsley (in compliance with letters from the Lord Lieutenant of Rutland and the directions of the Privy Council), requiring the said Chief Constables to appear before them at Okeham on the next Monday at 7 a.m., and to give notice to every petty constable of the hundred to appear at the same place and time, bringing with them 2, 4, or 6 men (according to requi- sition laid on each parish) not of the trained bands, ready to march forth to Plymouth and serve the King beyond seas. The petty constables are required to collect under-written moneys from their respective parishes for the coats, conduct money, and other charges of the recruits. Any petty constable, failing to bring the men required of him, will be himself impressed to serve the King as a soldier.

(3.) February 15, 1626. Writ from Justices of the Peace (signed Ed. Harington and William Bulstrode) to the Chief Constables of the Hundred of Martinsley: "These are in his Maᵗⁱᵉˢ name to will & require you, that " you make your warrants to all the pettye constables " within your hundred, that they and ev'ry of them " give warneinge to all taverne keepers, inholders, ale- " housekeepers, cooks and butchers to appear before " vs at Uppingham vpon Tuesday next, being the xxth " day of this instant monthe of February, by eight of " the clocke in the morninge there to enter into recog- " nizance with suertyes, that they and eu'y of them will " not kill, sell, dresse nor utter any fleashe dureinge " this tyme of Lent, accordinge to his Matics. proclama- " tion, which wee haue receaved for such purpose."

(4.) Indenture (parchment roll) made August 14, 4 Charles I., between the commissioners for collecting the two first of five subsidies, in co. Rutland, of the one part, and John Butler, of Okeham, Gent., of the other part. Commissioners, Sir Edward Harington, Knt. and Bart., Sir Henry Mackworth, Bart., Sir William Bulstrode, Sir Guye Palmes, and Sir Henry Mynn, Knights, and Thomas Lovitt, Esq. The roll displays the complete assessment of the county, with the names of the taxpayers, and the amounts charged upon them, arranged under the names of their parishes and hundreds.

(5.) Similar indenture, of the same date, with list of assessments for the county of Northampton.

(6.) January 27, 1629. Warrant from Justices of the Peace (signed Henry Mackworth, Guie Palmer, Francis Bokenham, Thomas Lovet), to the High Constables of Martinsley Hundred, Rutland, requiring them to raise in the several parishes of the hundred certain underwritten sums of money for providing two hundred fat wethers for the King's household, in accordance with a composition long since made by the county with the officers of the said household, "by reason of which " agreement noe takinge is made of the goods of anye " his Maties subjectes w^{th}in the said countie." The money on collection to be paid to the High Collector, Mr. John Butler of Okeham.

(7.) February 1, 1629. Warrant addressed to the constables of Hambleton by William Chisseldyne, requiring them to collect 2l. 14s. 5d. in the town of Hambleton, and 53s. 1½d. in Little Hambleton, and pay the money to John Butler of Okeham, gentleman, for the provision of His Majesty's household.

(8.) November 24, 1633. Warrant to the constables of Coltemore to collect in their town and parish certain underwritten sums of money, and pay them at or before the 10th of January, to Abel Barker of Hambleton, gentleman, for the provision of the Royal household.

(9.) November the 26, 1634. Warrant (signed Richard Campion) to the constables of Tigh, requiring them to collect money, and pay it to Abel Barker of Hambleton, for the provision of the Royal household.

(10.) April the 7, 1634. Order (signed William Marston) to the owners and occupiers of Reathorp, requiring them to pay certain moneys for the provision of the King's household.

(11.) February 11, 1631. Warrant (similar to that of Feb. 15, 1626) to the High Constables of Martinsley Hundred, for ensuring general abstinence from flesh in Lent. Signed by Hen. Mackworth and Fran. Bodenham.

(12.) January 31, 1632. Writ from Lord Keeper Coventrye and Attorney General William Noye to the Nathanael Gulston (who obtained the rectory of Lyndon from some patron, other than the Crown), requiring him to exhibit sufficient title to the living, the advowson of which is claimed for his Majesty the King.

(13.) July 12, 1633. Order signed by Sir Henry Mackworth, to the High Constables of Martinsley Hundred. "For as much as we have lately reseaued a " commission under his M^{ties} Broad Seale of England " for the assumaning this county to bestow their " benevolences towards the reparation of the decayed " church of St. Paul's in London, theise are therefore " to require you forthwith to send your warrants to " all the petty constables in your hundred to cause " all the landed men and all other sufficient men in " their towne to come before us at Okeham at the " signe of the Crowne the xxth of this month by eight " a clock in the morning."

(14.) February 17, 1633. Warrant to the High Constables of the hundred of Martinsley, for binding all inn-keepers and victuallers to observe the orders against dressing flesh in Lent. Signed by Lord Campden and Sir Henry Mackworth.

(15.) July 10, 1633. High Sheriff's Writ to the Chief Constables of the hundred of Martinsley, to provide horses, &c. for the King's use. "Whereas appointment " is given by the Lords of his Maties most hon^{ble} priuie " counsell to me Anthony Colly, Knight, shirenie of " this countye, to prouide horses to attend his Maties " returne from Scotland: Theise are therfore in his " Maties name straightly to charge & comande you " that presently vpon the receipt herof you take order " to prouide twentie of the best sufficient able horses " with good sufficient sadels & bridells, & able men " for guides for to carie the horses to Post Witham, " to be redie to attend his Maties vppon Fryday morning " betwixt 7 & 8 of the clock, which shall be the sixth " day of this present month."

(16.) March 1, 1632. Warrant to the High Constables, of the Hundred of Norton, co. Northampton, to collect underwritten moneys "for the service of the great and " smale provisions" of the King's household.

(17.) January 14, 1634. Warrant (signed, Jeremy Vinall) to the Constables of Ryall cum Belmsthorpe to collect certain moneys and pay them to Abel Barker of Hambleton, at Okeham, on or before next February 11.

(18.) February 1, 1635. Indenture between John Barker, of Hambleton, co. Rutland, gentleman, of the one part, and Richard Jacobb, of the city of Westminster, butcher, of the other part; whereby the said Richard Jacobb, in consideration of two separate sums of money,—the first of 95l., and the second of 90l.,— binds himself to provide, by certain stated times, two lots of sheep, a hundred sheep in each lot, for the provision of the Royal Household, taking the King's price for each of the said sheep, i.e., 6s. upon every sheep of the first lot, and 7d. for every sheep of the second lot.

(19.) September 10, 1635. Warrant to the Chief Constables of Hundreds, co. Rutland, to take steps for assessing and raising a contribution towards the sum of 1,000l., to be raised in the county for maintaining one ship of war of 100 tons.

(20.) September 30, 1635. Warrant to the Chief Constables of the Hundred of Martinsley, to raise in their hundred certain underwritten sums of money "for " the getting forth & maintaineinge of one shipp of " warre for the parte defence of the kingdome."

(21.) October 28, 1635. Letter of extraordinary assessment of ship-money, addressed to William Fynne of Hambleton, by Frank Bodenham, Sheriff of Rutland " Willm. Fin.—By virtue of his Maties writt directed " to me for the assessing & leavying of one thousand " pounds upon this countie of Rutl. for prouideing of " one ship of warre for the defence of the kingdome, I " doe assesse you for yor extraordinary ability, the sum " of 20s. besides the moneys which you pay vpon the " assessm^t of your neighbours, & I intreate you to " pay itt to this bearer, or bring it to me before " Munday next, when I goe to London, least you force " me to distraine or returne yor name to the Lords & " you be a president herafter: soe I rest yor Lo. frend, " Fran. Bodenham, Vic. I pray you refuse me not for " I intend to fauor you."

(22.) June 16, 1636. Letter addressed by Sir Edward Harington to the Commissioners of Taxes and chief taxpayers of Rutland, urging them to hold meetings and take steps for a more equal assessment of the county. A postscript, by Lord Campden, enjoins the taxpayers to give one another good notice of the meetings, called for this purpose.

(23.) October 6, 1636. Circular warrant to all the High Constables of Rutland (signed, Ed. Harington, Guie Palmes, and Jo. Osborne), to summon certain underwritten gentlemen of the county to a meeting at Okeham, for the purpose of agreeing on a general assessment "to pay his Maties provision."

(24.) January 27, 1636. High Sheriff Sir Edward Harington's warrant to the High Constable of Martinsley Hundred, to enquire into complaints against the constables of Uppingham, and to settle the discontents of that town by needful alterations of the assessment for ship-money. "Whereas," runs Sir Edward's letter, " I am informed of much partiality used by the Con- " stables and Churchwardens of Uppingham in there " assessments of the inhabitants there for the raisinge " of the somme imposed by me vppon the saide towne " for the furneashinge of one shipp of warr for his " May^{ties} service : These are to will and require you in " his Majestie's name, all business sett apart, to repaire " to Uppingham aforesaid vppon Monday next, and to " caull the saide constables and churchwardens before " you, and after the hearinge of the just complaintes of " all sutch as shanll seeme greeued with the inequality " of the said taxation, to settle all things in a just and " equall way, so neare as yow can, that no man may " be oppressed according to his Majesties roiall " intendment."

(25.) July 7, 1637. High Sheriff Sir Edward Harington's warrant, to the Chief Constables of East Hundred, to distrain and sell sufficient goods or corn, belonging to Samuell Waterfall of Belmethorpe, to cover the 20s. of ship-money he has neglected to pay in. contempt of his Majesty and the law.

(26.) Nov. 9, 1638. Letter of "advice and instruc- " tions," addressed by the Privy Council to the High Sheriff of Rutland, in respect to his Majesty's writ, directed to the Sheriff of the said co., and also to the sheriffs of cos. Lincoln and Leicester, and to mayors and other head officers of all corporate towns within the same cos., requiring them to raise between them 4,900l., for providing, furnishing, and manning a ship for the defence of the country ; the county of Rutland being charged with 350l. of that sum. The letter directs that "noe persons bee assessed to the same " vnlesse they bee knowne to haue estates in money or " goods, or other means to liue, over and above what " they get by their daily labor." Sixteen signatures to this letter. Among them are the autographs of Archbishop Laud, Bishop Juxon, Lord Keeper Coventry, the Earls of Manchester, Lindsay, Arundell and Surrey, and Pembroke, and Sir Harry Vane.

(27.) July 25, 1639. Treasury receipt (bearing signatures of Sir William Russell and Henry Vane, treasurers of the King's navy) for the 350l. ship-money, levied in Rutland in compliance with the King's writ of Nov. 5, 1638.

(28.) December 14, 1644. Military requisition (signed, Will. Fowler) on the occupiers of the land in Gunthorp

for " one quarter of otes " to be sent on Monday next to
" the Garison in Bourligh."

(29.) January 20, 1644. Acknowledgment (signed,
Robert Horsman) that 25 quarters of oats, and five
horses, belonging to Mr. Barker of Hambleton, were
taken to Rockingham Castle "for the service of the
" King and Parliament," by virtue of a warrant from
Lord Grey of Grooby.

(30.) July 24, 1644. Official receipt for 10l. " propo-
" sicion money," assessed upon Abel Barker, and
distrained for " after the tenne dayes specified in the
" Ordinaunce."

(31.) August 25, 1644. Official receipt for two quarters
of oats, taken upon a warrant from Mr. Barker of
Hambleton.

(32.) "November 12, 1644. Recd. then of Mr. Abel
" Barker upon a warrant from the committee· sixe
" quarters of oates. I say recd. for· the vse of this
" garrison of Burley. Jarvice Goodwin."

(33.) Memorandum, in Abel Barker's handwriting, of
money and goods (to the sum of 208l. 10s.), " lent vpon
" the publicke faithe," i.e., taken from him with promise
of payment.

(34.) August 25, 1644. Another military requisition
for oats addressed to Abel Barker. " Theise are to
" require you vpon sight hereof, you send to Burleigh
" Garrison two quarters of oates for the publicke vse,
" and you shall receive satisfaction for them." Signed,
Jo. Osborne.

(35.) December 4, 1644. Receipt for five quarters of
oats taken from Abel Barke or the garrison of Burleigh. Signed, " The marke + of Thomas Betts."

(36.) " A note," in Abel Barker's handwriting, " of
" all the otes & peese deliuered in to Burly by a
" warrant from the Committee, of the 12th of Decem-
" ber "; the requisitions amounting to the sum of
19l. 0s. 9d.

(37.) Another bill " From Abel Barker of Hamble-
" ton ":—

Taken by Edward More 3 horses and by
Leiuetenant Burry 2 horses, and carryed to
Rockingham and imployed there for the
seruice of the state as by a certificate
under the hand of Colonel Horsman appeares, which 5 horses were worth

Carryed by warrant to the sayd castle 25 qrs.
of oats as by certificate of the sayd Colonel
may appeare, wth oats were worth -

Taken by Captain Wollaston . and Captain
Butler's troopes vpon their seruice for the
Cõmittee of this county from his barnes
in Gunthorpe, 10 quarters of oates and 16
sacks, worth -

Sent in to Burley vpon seuerall warrants
from Mr. Osborne and others of the Cõmittee vpon promise of payment 84 qrs. of
oats at 47^{ll}, as by seuerall receipts for the
same will appeare, for which there is still
due vnto him -

Sent to Burly vpon warrant from the Cõmittee one horse worth -

Sent in to Burley vpon the Cõmittees warrant
2 bedds worth -

	£	s.	d.
(5 horses)	40	00	0
(25 qrs oats)	12	10	0
(10 qrs & 16 sacks)	06	00	0
(84 qrs oats)	32	10	0
(one horse)	08	0	0
(2 bedds)	06	00	0."

(38.) Duplicate of the above bill. And a separate
acknowledgment (signed, Michael Catesbye and James
Tiptaste, collectours) of oats and provisions, valued at
32l. 10s.

(39.) 1645. List of the several sums assessed on the
parishes of the five hundreds of Rutland for the
monthly tax.

(40.) May 13th, 1645. Warrant (signed, Jo. Osborne
and Jo. Hatcher) to the Constables, Occupiers, or
Tenants of Gunthorp. " By vertue of an ordinance of
" ye Lords & Cõmons assembled in Parliament for
" maintayneing of forces for ye defence of ye kingdom
" & for y^t we desire ye ease of y^t country of billeting
" & . free q^u of souldiers & to y^t satisfieing for oates &
" prouision formerly brought into this garrison & in re-
" gard we finde ye country very forward to leauy collect
" & carry in great summes of money to the enemy at
" Belvoir and Wynorton, these are therefore straightly
" to charge & cõm̄ nd you forthwith, vpon the sight
" hereof, to assesse &̃ collect within your constabulary
" the summe of fower pounds and eighteene shillinges
" imposed vpon your say towne for one moneth's tax
" for ye purposes aforesaid, and y^t you bring & pay the
" same at this garrison to Jo. Cole, gent., treasurer of
" ye county att or before the six and twentieth day of
" this instant Maye."

(41.) Aug. 20. 1646. The appeal of Nathanael Goulston,
Rector of Lyndon, to the Lord of the manor of Lyndon,

praying him to pay the arrears of rent due to his
petitioner, in accordance with an arrangement (set forth
in the paper), securing to the incumbent of the said
parish an annual rent instead of tithes.

(42.) December 5, 1646. Acknowledgment of quarters.
" Hambleton. Will. Ranse, cornett to Major Tomlinson
" in the Regimt. of Sr Rob. Pye, knight., qr. himselfe
" one man and three horse with Mr. Barker from the
" eighth of December till the 26th of the same in the
" yeare abbone sayd: also Will. Pettye, Corporall,
" vnder the same command, as longe. Wittnesseth
" this cornett's one hand. W. Ranse."

(43.) September 24, 1646. Schedule of the several
" townes and tythes " of Rutland, taken at North
Luffenham.

(44.) Copy (in Abel Barker's handwriting) of an order
by General Ireton to the army in Rutland. " For
" Capt. Brage or any other officer of the Army in
" Rutlande :—All the horse of Sr Robert Pyes & Col.
" Graues his regm^t are forthwith vpon notice hereof
" to departe out of the county of Rutland & repaire
" into the North to their colo^u ; except it be such
" officers serv^m as were left wth their horses, troopers
" vnmounted, or whose horses are lame or sicke, or
" men sicke themselues, and those left to looke to
" such : and if any shall not depart vpon notice hereof
" except as before, they may & ought to be apprehended
" by the next justice of the peace or person in authority,
" and sent in safe custody to the Marshall Generall at
" the head quarters to be punished by a connooll of
" warre, &c." Signed, H. Ireton. A supplementary
note (signed, W. Stane) to Capt. Brage, is attached to
the order.

(45.) March 3, 1646. Letter (signed, Fr. Thorpe) from
the Parliamentary committee (appointed to examine the
petition to the House of Commons from the Clothiers of
the old and new· draperies of divers counties) to the
sheriff of Rutland. Requiring him to give notice in
his county that the petition will be heard in the Exchequer Chamber, Westminster, on the second Wednesday of next Easter term, at 2 o'clock.

(46.) October 6, 1647. Warrant (signed, Robt. Horsman) to the constables of Stretton, for the arrest of
Samuel Oates on a charge of " gathering togeather of
" vnlawfull and disorderly· assemblies."

(47.) Schedule (in Abel Barker's handwriting) of the
lands, revenues, &c. of the " Manor of Foderinghay and
" the Colledge in the county of Northampton." The
survey, giving the particulars of this schedule, was made
in the year 1604.

(48.) February 17, 1650. Cos. Warwick and Leicester.
A brief declaration of the state of the accompte of
William Greene, Esq., receiver of the revenues of the
late King Charles in the said countyes, by vertue of
letters patent, dated 1642.

(49.) September 4, 1651. Warrant (signed, William
Fowler) to the constables of Gunthorpe to collect money
" towards ye reliefe of the maymed. souldiers &
" maryners and for ye reliefe of poore prisoners of y^e
" Upper Bench and Martialsey."

(50.) February 13, 1655. Summons (from the Commissioners for removing obstructions in sale of ye honors
of the late·King and Queen and Prince) to John Trist
to appear before the said Commissioners at Worcester
House, in the Strand, to answer for his conduct in preventing Samuel Chidley, purchaser of the Ladyfields,
co. Northampton, from felling and taking away the
timber of the said lands.

(51.) June 22, 1658. Warrant (signed, William Fowler)
to the assessor of Gunthorpe to levy and gather taxes.

(52.) October 1, 1660. Letter of instructions (issued
by the King's order, and signed, Edw. Nicholas,)· to
Baptist Viscount Campden, Lord Lieutenant of Rutland,
with respect to the ordering and drilling of the trained
bands of the county.

(53.) May 8, 1660. Magistrate's order to Abel Barker,
Esq., treasurer of the county, to pay the sum of 20s. to
Thomas Crampe, carpenter of Okeham, who is stricken
" with the uncleane disease of leprosy."

(54.) September 18, 1660. Schedules of the taxes of
Rutland, with the names of payers and amounts of their
respective assessments.

(55.) October 1, 1660. Certificate of Commissioners of
Taxes for the Isle of Ely, certifying that John Swaine,
of Leuerington, has paid his taxes for his estate in
Rutland as well as in the Isle of Ely.

(56.) October 26, 1660. Certificate of Commissioners
of Taxes for Middlesex that Hugh Ducie, Esq., has paid
an assessment of 10l. for his " degree at Islington."

(57.) October 12, 1660. Certificate of Commissioners of
Taxes for Westminster that " Sir Kelham Digby, Knt.,"

of the parish of St. Martin's, has paid an assessment of
20l. towards disbanding and paying off the forces.

(58.) January 12, 1660. Schedule of assessments of the
several parishes of Rutland to the tax for "disband-
" ing the remainder of the army and navy."

(59.) 1661. List of the sums raised in the several
parishes of Rutland, and of the amounts subscribed by
the principal contributors towards a present to King
Charles the Second.

(60.) April 25, 1661. Letter from Charles Crichton to
Abel Barker, Esq., reporting that Sir Richard Wingfield advises that a magistrates' warrant should be sent
to the constables of Uppingham to keep strict night
watch and to "suppress Anabaptisticall meetings."

(61.) July 17, 1663. Schedule of a rate set upon the
co. of Rutland.

(62.) March, 1663. Warrant to the chief constables of
Rutland to levy taxes.

(63.) September 19, 1663. Assessors' bill for Normanton in respect of two subsidies.

(64.) 1663. Schedule of assessments in North Luffenham in respect of two subsidies.

(65.) September 14, 1663. The same for the parish of
Exton.

(66.) September 19, 1663. The same for the parish of
Liddington.

(67.) October 1663. Warrant to the chief constables of
the Hundred of Alstoe to collect taxes.

(68.) March 11, 1664. Schedule of assessments and
valuations of the parishes of Rutland.

(69.) March 11, 1664. Schedule of the first quarterly
payments of the Royal aid in co. Rutland.

(70.) February, 1665. Schedule of assessments of the
parish of Hambleton.

(71.) March 30, 1665. Circular for the suppression of
sedition, addressed by Lord Clarendon to the magistrates
for the co. of Rutland, and signed by him.

(72.) Dec. 8, 1665. Schedule of the new valuation of
the county of Rutland.

(73.) February 1, 1666. Magistrate's warrant (with
several signatures) to the chief constables of the Hundred of Oakham Soake, to collect taxes.

(74.) February 6th, 1666. Letter from Lords of the
Treasury to "His Majesty's Commissioners for the
" money to be raysed by a poll within the county of
" Rutland," enjoining them to exercise their powers
vigorously, and to return the names of defaulters to the
Exchequer.

(75.) September 13, 1667. Letter from the Privy
Council (signed by Sheldon, Archbishop of Canterbury,
Lord Keeper Bridgeman, the Duke of Albemarle, the
lords Arlington and Ashley, and others) to the justices
of the peace for the county of Rutland, for the suppression of Popery ; enjoining the magistrates to enforce
the law, in accordance with His Majesty's proclamation,
against all persons making, or striving to make, converts
to the Roman Catholic faith.

(76.) 1667. Letter from Lords of the Treasury to
" the Commissioners for the Royal Ayd in the county
" of Rutland," urging them to collect arrears of taxes,
and to use all their powers for that end.

(77.) June 27, 1667. Letter from Lords of the Treasury (signed by Albemarle, Ashley, and Clifford) to
Justices of the Peace for the county of Rutland, urging
them to take measures for the more efficient and complete collection of the duty on fire hearths ; many
complaints having been made to their lordships of the
tumultuous and unlawful resistance which the farmers
and collectors of the tax encounter from disaffected
persons.

(78.) September, 1667. Warrant from the Lords of
the Treasury (signed by the Duke of Albemarle and
others) that taxes, to the amount 3l. 5s. 6d., shall
be forthwith recovered from Charles Dale, Esq., who
has refused to pay them. In case the money is not
obtained from Mr. Dale's estate, it will be levied against
the county of Rutland.

(79.) September 11, 1668. Memorandum (signed by
seven Commissioners for taxes of the county of Rutland), than no further alterations of the allotments of
taxation in the county shall be made except at a full
and general meeting of the Commissioners. It is
noticed in the memorandum, that some recent alterations in the apportionment of taxes have been made by
a minority of the Commissioners.

(80.) July 7, 1668. Letter (signed, Will. Doyley),
addressed, at the command of the Lords of the Treasury, to the Commissioners of Taxes in Rutlandshire ;
ordering them to call in arrears, and act stringently
against defaulters, with view to a clearing of accounts.

(81.) June 12, 1671. Schedule of "the yearly valua-
" con of the Lordshipp of Normanton," supplied to
Commissioners of Taxes.

(82.) June 10, 1671. Schedule of assessments of
Belton, co. Rutland.

(83.) June 10, 1871. Schedule of assessments of
Hambleton.

(84.) June 12, 1671. Schedule of assessments of the
parish of Teigh.

(85.) June 10, 1671. Schedule of assessments of the
parish of Greetham.

(86.) June 10, 161. Schedule of assessments of the
parish of Edgelton.

(87.) April 23, 1673. Schedule of assessments for the
whole of Rutland.

(88.) May 10, 1677. Schedule of assessments for the
whole county.

(89.) May 29, 1677. Schedule of assessments for the
parish of Aston.

(90.) 1678. Schedule of assessments of a poll tax for
Lyndon.

(91.) July 10, 1678. The same for the whole co. of
Rutland.

(92.) June 22, 1681. Letter from Lord Aylesbury,
Earl Marshal, to Sir Thomas Barker, Bart., High
Sheriff of Rutland, announcing that "Francis Burg-
" hill, Esq., and Gregory King, Rougedragon Officers
" of Armes," are about "to visitt the county of Rut-
" land and to register the arms, pedigrees, marriages,
" and issue of the nobility and gentry ;" and entreating the sheriff to assist the heralds in the performance
of their duties.

(93.) September 1, 1694. Warrant to "the collector
" of Lyndon" to assess and collect taxes.

(94.) October 28, 1715. Letter from J. Watts to Samuel Barker of Lyndon. Announcing that if Mr. Barker
will supply the Militia horse, which he and "his
Grace" are required to find, the Duke will contribute
half the charge. A bill for the horse and accoutrements
(amounting to 6l. 13s. 9d.) is attached to the letter.

(95.) A curious collection of 93 receipts for rents,
tythes, and taxes ; the earliest of the acknowledgments
bearing date April 16, 1595, and the latest bearing date
1789. Several of the older receipts are in Latin, and
acknowledge payment of rent from the tenant of lands
called "Ladyfeeld parcell manerii de Greensnorton,"
co. Northampton, pertaining to the Crown. The receipts
of the Commonwealth period are noteworthy.

It would be well for students of our Commonwealth
history, and all readers who take especial interest in
the affairs of Stuart England, if one of our archæological societies would undertake to publish Mr. Field's
17th century papers, and engage him to edit them.

JOHN CORDY JEAFFRESON.

THE MANUSCRIPTS OF A. C. RANYARD, ESQ., OF
LINCOLN'S INN, BARRISTER-AT-LAW.

Among the manuscripts which Mr. Ranyard sent for
examination are the following :—

A quarto volume of parchment, 68 leaves, writing of
the end of the 12th century. It contains, 1st, A short
account in Latin of the doings of the Crusaders in the
Holy Land, A.D. 1095-1099. It is the first of the works
printed by Bongars in the Gesta Dei per Francos (fol. Hano-
viæ, 1611) and occupies there 29 folio pages. The MS.
varies slightly from the print, and in some parts contains
a little more. Some of the names of persons are given
more correctly than in the print. Some leaves of the
MS. are absent, notably the last three of this tract, containing the last four lines of p. 28, and the whole of
p. 29 of the print.—The second tract in the volume is
seemingly an edition of so much of Paul the Deacon's
Historia Miscella as contains Eutropius's Roman History.
But it is much abbreviated, and differs (in the additions)
from Paul's History as printed in the Augustæ Historiæ
Scriptores. Some leaves of the MS. are absent and it
ends imperfectly at section 14 of Book 10 of Paul's
work, and at section 10 of Book 8 of Valpy's edition of
Eutropius.

At the top of the first page of the MS. a 13th century
hand has written Lib. S. Marie de Kenill., and below is
the autograph T. Marowe (16th century).

Folio, vellum, end of 14th century.—Boethius de Con-
solatione Philosophiæ, beautifully written by an Italian
hand. At the end of the work the scribe has added the
letter of Theophrastus, which Jerome sent to his friend
Jovinian to dissuade him from matrimony.

The volume came from the Pinelli collection.

Folio, 25 leaves, 17th century.—Letters between Sir Kenelm Digby and Lord George Digby about traditions, &c. Copyed out of one lent by . . . . 1646, &c. The volume has the book plate of Jeremiah Miller, D.D. (The contents were printed 12° Lond. 1651.)

Folio, 9 pp., 17th century.—Part of the Duke of Buckingham's relation of proceedings when the Prince was in Spain.—(This contains in brief the substance, with some slight additions and variations, of pp. 224–232 of vol. 3 of the Lords Journals.)

Fol., 50 pp., 17th century.—A list of what ships and goods have been condemned in the Admiralty Court since the beginning of the War (from 1 Feb. 1664 to 26 Sept. 1667). The first entry is "The Bergan of " Alogmark & goods in the same not claymed." The last is "The Charity of Amsterdam Course, Johnson, " Mr, and goods not claymed."

Folio, paper, 342 pp., 17th century.—Latin explanations of words in the first 12 and part of the 13th books of the Iliad of Homer.

The Greek words are in red ink.—Half of the first page is occupied with an introduction, which *begins* " Priusquam ad explicationem verborum incedit Eusta-' " thius nonnulla quasi preludii loco premittit," and *ends* " Homerus hic atque illic prout bonum arbitretur " quæ novem annis precedentibus Troie facta sunt " miro cum artificio intertexit. Sed hæc hactenus." The text *begins* Μηνιν est accusat. cas. nominis μηνις, μηνιος; and *ends* with the word χρυσοβορος . . . . . . aureum solum habens. The first four books occupy 182 pp.

Folio, paper, 88 leaves and 74½ leaves. 16th century. This is a beautifully written Greek manuscript, in Eastern binding. It contains two works, the first is astronomical, and the second is a comment on Aristotle's treatise on generation and corruption.

On the first flyleaf is the following sentence by a 16th century hand towards determining the authorship of the first and perhaps the second treatise :—και τοδε προς τοις αλλοις δημητριου Ισαυρου . . . Ισαυρου, το περι ουρανου· και το περι γενεσεως και φθορας.

The first treatise is headed υπομνημα συνοπτικον και ζητημα εις την περι ουρανου πραγματειαν. It *begins* [Ε]! ουτις νενλυσ εις ποδων μεγιστηρθε; and *ends* νοουμενης τε και το . . . τ* There are many diagrams in the work.

The second treatise is headed υπομνηματα και ζητηματα εις τους αριστοτελους περι γενεσεως και φθορας βιβλιον κ. τ. λ. It *begins*, Ανωρις ου μηφα τοις εξηγηται.

Quarto, paper, 15th century, 33 leaves. A treatise called *Computus cyrometralis* in 2 books. It consists of a number of hexameter verses (many of them made up of words of no real meaning, but as a *memoria technica*) accompanied by an extensive commentary and several diagrams. It is an astronomical work composed chiefly with a view to assist ecclesiastics in determining the feast days and proper services of their churches. At the end is the colophon in red ink, with " Et sic est finis " computi cyrometralis sub anno 1432°." (M. Libri had a copy of this work, N° 1095 of the sale catalogue of his MSS. in 1859, but unfortunately he has not described the contents.)

Folio, paper, 18th century. A vellum bound volume of large sized paper, of which between 80 and 90 leaves are filled. It is labelled *Precedents, Money Matters.* The treatise or collection is headed " A state of the " matter with relation to the amending of Money Bills " brought up from the House of Commons to the " Lords." *Begins*, There does not appear in their Lordships' Journals anything remarkable touching that matter till the Restoration, when the Lords from that time to the year 1695 frequently amended money Bills of all kinds.—At the 52nd page a different handwriting begins, and the precedents are taken from 1702 to 1733, where the volume ends. It seems to collect all the cases from 1660 where the Lords made amendments.

Serjeant Davis, his Charge to the Jurors of the Grand Inquest for the mainteyning and contynuing the publique peace by the execution of justice. (50 pp. foolscap size.) *Begins:* You my masters that are sworne. *Ends:* The publique service we have in hand. (17th century.)

1736, June 20. Certificate (on parchment) that at a general ordination in the Cathedral of Gloucester, Martin, Bishop of Gloucester, admitted George Whitefield, of Pembroke College, Oxford, to the order of Deacon. Signed *M. Glocestr.* Seal gone.

1741. Sept 11. Certificate of the Rev. Mr George Whitefield being that day made a burgess and gildbrother of Glasgow, and that he gave his oath of fealty. Extracted out of the Gild book by Jo. M'Gilchrist, Dep: Clerk. On the back are painted the arms of Glasgow.

ALFRED J. HORWOOD.

The labour of examining Miss Conway Griffith's manuscripts has been considerable, but far from fruitless. Comprising some two thousand separate documents, the collection is very miscellaneous. It is also notably deficient in arrangement. Indeed, save that Miss Conway Griffith, who takes an antiquary's interest in her literary possessions, had gathered into separate folios a few of the more attractive writings, no attempt had been made to classify her documents, or to reduce their mass by withdrawing worthless material, when they were entrusted to me for inspection. In consideration of its heterogeneousness and general neglect, the collection may be described as one of those undigested accumulations of domestic and official manuscripts, which grow steadily in families whose chiefs, from superstitious tenderness for the writings of their forefathers, or from indisposition for the labour of bringing them into order, allow their moth-eaten records to rest undisturbed, , whilst covering them from time to time with comparatively recent bundles of receipted bills, obsolete indentures, cancelled bonds, and old letters.

Such an accumulation necessarily contains a considerable proportion of uninteresting parchments and papers. Comprising bonds for the payment of small sums of money from obscure individuals, drafts of bills and answers in trivial law suits, attorney's letters about insignificant affairs of strictly private business, friendly notes yielding no single illustration of character or manners, pecuniary memoranda that can have scarcely been intelligible to the writers twelve months after they were made, tradesmen's bills affording no new information respecting the details of commerce, shreds of unsigned papers covered with numerals which may be presumed to have some reference to items of personal expenditure, and imperfect records of the receipt of cottagers' rents, which at the present would not afford so much as a note for the local annalist or parochial antiquary ; the majority of the Carreglwyd manuscripts lie far outside the fields of historical research. The proportion of these papers is the larger because, whilst some are in duplicate and even in triplicate, others of them have been multiplied four times by the copyist's industry.

In dealing with a multifarious collection, so largely loaded with literary refuse, I have exercised my discretion in dividing the valuable material from the material of no value. Of the several items of the latter element of the collection, no mention is made in my lists. It is well, however, to observe that, whilst declining to swell my catalogues with entries which could not be serviceable to any inquirer, I have made my comprehensive schedules of selected papers with full consideration for the needs of topographers, antiquaries, and social illustrators, as well as of labourers in higher departments of history.

Commencing with a few parchments and papers of the fourteenth century, the oldest of the Carreglwyd documents are comparatively modern. The important writings of the collection are, without exception, of dates subsequent to Henry the Eighth's time. Some of the letters and indentures, penned in the reign of Elizabeth and the three earliest of her Stuart successors, are of considerable interest. Attention may be claimed for the leases which show that, from the time of Elizabeth down to the later decades of the seventeenth century, it was usual for the tenants of farms in Anglesey to pay their rent in the three separate forms of money, presents, and service, and that in cases where a tenant was exempt from the two last-named kinds of obligation, his lease generally stated expressly that the money, which he had agreed to pay as rent, covered the dues commonly rendered to landlords in labour and gifts. The presents thus exacted by landlords and rendered by their tenants, were for the most part articles of agricultural produce. Sometimes, however, they were offerings of another kind. For instance, so late as Charles the Second's time, Hugh ap William held a small farm. the Tythin Clay, in the county of Anglesey, of Mr. Owen Holland at a yearly rent " of 6l. 0s. 0d. in money, two " capons, and *a hundred red herrings* in presents, and six " days of mason's work in service." It would be interesting to ascertain whether this practice, on the part of landlords, of inserting in their leases special stipulations for the payment of presents at principal feasts of the year, first became general in Anglesey in consequence of a growing disinclination, on the part of tenants to render dues which had been purely spontaneous before custom made them unavoidable obligations. The Carreglwyd leases are not of sufficient oldness to show whether the practice prevailed in Anglesey before the middle of the sixteenth century, when the farmers of various parts of England exhibited decided reluctance to pay the customary tributes, which they had come to regard as extortionate exactions rather than as items of their landlord's just and proper rent.

Another class of instruments, contributing in no small degree to the general value of Miss Conway Griffith's writings, consists of settlements of property drawn in anticipation of marriages celebrated amongst her ancestors of the seventeenth century. The marriage settlement, dated Feb. 13, 1642, which settled on the bride of Mr. Owen Holland, of Berow, co. Anglesey, and her issue, certain "seates, sittings, kneelings " and buryinge places" in Llanerhangel Eskeiviogo in the same county, may be esteemed nothing more than a curiosity of the conveyancer's art, produced for the gratification of a proprietor who had, at considerable cost and after much vexatious opposition, established his right to and property in the seats and burying-places. Regarding it as an illustration of life and manners, the reader will not fail to assign a greater value to the indenture in which a gentleman of Denbighshire, in the reign of James the First, whilst settling a landed estate on his son in tail male on the eve of his marriage with a gentleman's daughter, stipulated that during his life the young man should " worke " and labour " for him " as a labourer," and that the bride should during the same time " labour and work " for him as domestic servant.

But though the writings which illustrate the social condition of Anglesey and other northern parts of the Principality, are of considerable interest, even higher value may be assigned to those of the Carreglwyd documents which relate to the public affairs of North Wales during the Civil War and the Commonwealth. For many of these writings, as well as for the majority of her official and domestic papers having reference to the public affairs of England in the seventeenth century, Miss Conway Griffith is indebted to her ancestor John Griffith, Esq., a lawyer of Gray's Inn, who acted throughout several years as private secretary to James the First's Lord Privy Seal, Henry Earl of Northampton, the second son of the earl and poet, Surrey. In discharging the various important duties of this office, Mr. John Griffith gained his patron's confidence so completely that, having first appointed him a trustee of a deed for the execution of benevolent undertakings at Greenwich, co. Kent, Rising, co. Norfolk, and Clunn, co. Salop, the Earl made him one of the executors of his last will. Of the several noteworthy papers, which coming into Mr. John Griffith's hands during his residence in the Earl of Northampton's household, remained in them after that nobleman's death, one of the most interesting is Robert Fletcher's " Briefe and true " discours of the King's majesties cart-takers," particular mention of which will be found in my list of English writings. Surviving the Commonwealth, and persevering in official habits formed in the service of his first patron, Mr. John Griffith continued to the last to watch public events attentively, and to maintain relations with men of political affairs. Most of his papers are endorsed in his own handwriting; and though the majority of them consists of copies of papers well known to students of history, they comprise a minority of more or less noteworthy documents which, like Fletcher's " Cart-takers," have never been given to the world. The Carreglwyd collection contains also some writings from the hand of John Griffith's near kinsman, Dr. Griffith the Bishop of St. Asaph, and a large number of private or official documents drawn by Dr. William Griffith, the chancellor of the dioceses of St. Asaph and Bangor, and a notable advocate of Doctor's Commons, in the seventeenth century.

It should be observed that before she sent her manuscripts to the Record Office for examination, Miss Conway Griffith, acting on my suggestions, branded every parchment and paper of the collection with this stamp, " Carreglwyd papers, Anglesey, N.W." At the same time, she had the forethought to number every document and separate scrap of writing. Her labour in thus numbering all the manuscripts of the miscellaneous and unarranged collection has enabled me to produce lists which, whilst exhibiting the nature of the valuable part of the documents, may also serve as indexes to the inquirer who wishes to extract any of the registered writings from the mass of valueless material, in which they are put away. The same number, which precedes an entry in the catalogues, will be found in the manuscript to which the entry refers.

1. English Writings, i.e. Documents illustrative of social life and public affairs of England; and more particularly of England in the seventeenth century.

(No. 698.) Copy of Perkin Warbeck's proclamation beginning, " Whereas were in our in our tender age " escaped by godes might out of the tower of London " and were secretly conveyed ouer the sea into diuers " countries, " &c.; published on his entrance into England, with the "ayde and supportacion of the kinge of " Scottes."

(No. 786.) 1 Elizabeth. "Copy of the petition of " Gregory Fynes, esq., brother and heir of Thomas " Fynes, esq., who was son and heir to Sir Thomas " Fynes, knt., late Lord Dacres of the Sowthe (attainted " of felony temp. Hen. VIII.) ; praying her Highness " the Queen that he may be restored in blood."

(No. 792.) 20th November 1579. Copy of the "Com- " missio serenissimæ dominæ Reginæ Elizabethæ pro " matrimonio tractando inter ipsam dominam Reginam " et Franciscum Valois illustrissimum Andegaviæ du- " cem." Also copy of " Articuli contractus matrimonii " inter serenissimam Angliæ reginam Elizabetham et " Franciscum Valoys illustrissimum ducem celebrandi " anno 1581."

(No. 710.) 24 October 1584. The certificate of Ambrose Potter, " portreve of Gravsend," under " the towne " scale of Gravsend," that Roger Bolker and Robert Selbye, pencioners in Gravessend bulworke, and Rychard Warde and William Banokes, pencioners in Mylton bulworke, " are in full lyffe, desyryng youre " honour of youre certificathe vnto the quenes maies- " ties Receyvor of Kent, acordyng to my lorde Trea- " surer warrant, which the said receyvor hathe for " the payment thereof."

(No. 905.) 1590. Paper endorsed " Gentlemens Pro- " testations att-Ely." Containing a copy of orders from lords of the council (i.e. Lord Chancellor, Lord Treasurer and Lord Chamberlain) to the officer having charge of the Catholic gentlemen imprisoned in Ely Palace, for the considerate and better treatment of the said prisoners. From this document (dated from the court at Otlandes, 26 August 1590) it appears that the imprisoned gentlemen had complained of the needless hardships of their condition. Although they perceive " by the re- " porte of those gentlemen, to whome " it was committed " to examyne the griefes of the recusants vnder your " charge that the occasion of theire complaint was not " altogether so great " as the sufferers represented, the lords of the council admit that the complaints were not groundless, and add, " Therefore you shall accordinge " as the said gentlemen tooke order haue care that they " maie haue sweete and holsome water both for the " dressing of ther meate and other necessarye vses, " and permitt theym to inioye the libertye of the " gardens and orchardes and the leades to walke in. " And for the better preservacion of ther healthe you " shall not onelye suffer them to take the aire of a mile " or two in your companye, but the company of suche " other trustie parsons as you may be assured of, so they " may be in safety." Then follow copies of declarations of loyalty and allegiance to the Queen, embodying protestations of the readiness of the declarants to imperil their lives and estates in the defence of her person from the attacks of her enemies, and of her realm against the pope and every potentate whatsoever. (1.) The protestation of Sir Alexander Colepepper, Knt., made on 23 October in her majesty's 30th year. (2.) The protestation of Sir John Arrandell, Knt. Date not given. (3.) The protestation of Sir Thomas Fitzsharbert, alias Fytsharbott, Knt., who describes himself as " a brused old bodye within seaven yeares " of Torescore, prysoner at Elye." No date. (4.) The protestation of Willyam Catesby, made at Elie, in the year 1588. (5.) The protestation of John Talbott of Grafton, made 28 October 1588. (6.) The protestation of Sir Thomas Tresame alias Tressam, Knt., dated 22 October 1588 and endorsed "The humble " protestation of my allegiaunce to her Majestie exhi- " bitted by mee vnto Mr. Doctor Prone, deane of Elie, " and Mr. Doctor Legg vice chauncelour of Cambridge " authorized to receive the same of me Sir Tho. Tres- " sam, knt., prisoner in the Pallace of Elye." (7.) The protestation of William Trewhitt, alias Triwhitt, dated 23 October 1588. (8.) The protestation of John Leeds, dated 24 October 1588. (9.) The protestation of Edward Rockwood. No date. (10.) The protestation of Edward Sulyard, of Suffolk, Esq., dated 23 October 1588. (11.) The protestation of George Cotton, of Warhlington, co. Southampton. No date. (12.) The protestation of Richard Owen, dated at Elye, 23 October 1588. (13.) The protestation of

Thomas Wilford. No date. (14.) The protestation of Gylbert Melles. No date. (15.) The protestation of Michael Hare, dated 24 October 1588.

(No. 806.) List of the "Captens casired by the Erle "of Essex in Ireland." Giving the names of thirty-nine captains.

(No. 794.) A survey and sketch of Romney Marsh on a single sheet of paper, with an estimate of the small population of the level, and remarks on the indefensible nature of the district in case of a foreign invasion. The entire population of level (28 miles in compass) is computed at 590 men. "The danger," the draughtsman observes, "in landinge of the enemye is greate for they " may lande where they will (takinge their tyme and pro-". vision agreeable) from the west part of Bromehill unto " Heth which is some xii miles longe, and beinge landed " they may not only boorne and destroie Romeney, but " also in one houre may cutt vpp and make gutters crosse " Romeneymarshe walle, and the walles about Wallan-" mershe and Bromehill to lett in the sea and drowne the " saide marshes, containing as aforesaid 43000 acres."— No date.

(No. 755.) Causes of the decay of the Harborough *alias* Rye Haven. No date.

(No. 793.) "A survey of the state value and nomber of certaine Woodes lyinge in the East Riding in the countie of Yorke; i.e., Ricall Parke and Dighton Springe (held by the lord Kneuet by lease from the late queen), Wignum Groundes and Wignum Spring (held by Leonard Harbert, by lease from the same queen), Wheldrake Parke, Dorell Hagg, and Baygarth Woode (held by Sir Henry Vaughan, knt., by lease from the same queen)." No date.

(No. 985.) Fragmenta Regalia Or Observacioens on the late Queene Elizabeth, her tymes and Favourites. Written by Sir Robert Naunton, Knt., Master of the Court of Wards and Liveries. A carefully executed copy of Sir Robert Naunton's sketch of Elizabeth and her times; made probably by an amanuensis in the service of the Earl of Northampton, several of the copies of papers, endorsed by Mr. John Griffith, being in the same handwriting.

(No. A. 825.) Paper entitled "Her Highenes ordy-" nary corses vsually taken in her house, and in all " townes and villages neare the court." A set of directions to " the clarke of the checks," " the quenes porters," and the marshal of the royal household ; for excluding unauthorized visitors from the Queen's (Elizabeth's)? court, and for relieving its neighbourhood of vagabonds and other suspicious characters. No date.

(No. A. 45.) The congratulatory address of an orator, addressing James the First in a highly euphuistic style, and " in the names of these grave magistrates," the king's " most faithfull shervyes of London and Middle-" sex," and giving His Majesty a loyal and hearty welcome to the city of London. The references to Queen Elizabeth indicate that the speech was delivered soon after James's accession to her throne. No date.

(No. B. 51.) 12 March 1604. Patent, under the great seal, of a grant from the crown to Richard Prytherch of the Inner Temple, London, Esq., and Tobias Mathews, their heirs and assigns, for ever, of the manor of Penryn, co. Carmarthen, and of the Little Forest of Brecon, *alias* the little forest of Brecknock in the lordship of Brecon ; with lands and tenements in Carmthaar, co. Anglesey ; and also of lands and tenements in Westminster, viz. :— (1.) a piece of waste ground, near the stone wall, which surrounds the old palace of Westminster, and between the Parliament " stayres" and the " slnce" running down from the college of Westminster to the Thames ; (2.) a piece of waste ground, opposite the aforesaid piece, and between the Parliament stairs and another sluice, running down from the Parliament-house to the river ; (3.) another piece of waste ground, recently laid out in gardens, between the said wall and the way leading from the inner " chort" of the said palace to the slaughter-house ; (4.) another piece of waste ground, recently laid out in gardens, between the said wall on the east, and the way leading to the slaughter-house on the west ; (5.) another piece of waste ground, likewise laid out in gardens, between the said wall on the west, and the said way to the slaughter-house on the east ; (6.) a tenement called the "Blackhowse," lying near and within the palace called " Whitehall" ; (7.) a tenement lying within the aforesaid " chort" of the palace of Westminster ; (8.) a small area, opposite the east part of the said tenement, and enclosed with walls, late in the occupation of Charles Hanmer, deceased ; (9.) a piece of waste ground, lately used for three separate gardens, with the building upon it, called the " water-woorke," for conveying water from the river to divers houses and places in Westminster ;

(10.) all the tenements on the said piece of ground ; (11.) the stable or " le coachehowse," on the east of the same piece, with the entrance thereto ; (12.) a piece of ground, granted for a " garden by letters patent of Queen Elizabeth, and since that concession used as a way to the " wood warff " ; (13.) a piece of open ground, used by tolerance as a footway to the messuages lately in the tenure of John Dore and John Bennett ; (14.) the tenement or " gardinhouse " lately built in a garden, lately held by Hugh Brown ; (15.) another garden-house lately built on ground lately held by William Lancaster ; (16.) a little garden-house, on ground lately in the occupation of Thomas Hamlett ; (17.) another small garden-house, lately built on ground held by William Carter ; (18.) the little " shed " or garden-house in a garden lately held by Francis Morris ; (19.) another shed, in a garden lately in the tenure of John Bennet ; (20.) another " shed," in a garden lately held by Robert Brigges ; (21.) a shed or garden-house, in a garden lately held by Ralph Foster ; (22.) and also a piece of open ground, taken out of the river near to the stairs on the north, and to the wood-wharff on the south, which was appointed for the convenience and use of " le water-worke."—The local historian, dealing with the topography of Old Westminster, should examine the minute and carefully precise descriptions of the purlieus of the palace, contained in this charter.

(No. 764.) 29 Aug. 1605. Oratio Serenissimi Regis Jacobi habita in ecclesia Sanctæ Mariæ, 29° mensis Augusti 1605.

(No. 699.) Reasons given by the University of Cambridge why the said university is exempt from Episcopall and Archiepiscopall jurisdiction. No date.

(No. 696.) — 1605. A list of the officers and servants appointed to attend Charles Earl of Nottingham on his journey into Spayne ; together with a list of the lords, knights, and gentlemen of ranck which go with his lordship on this jorney. The officers and servants numbering 144 ; and the lords, knights, and gentlemen, making a retinue of 40 persons.

(No. 701.) — 1605. A list of " my lord of Hartford " his company to the Archduke," viz., The Lords Cromwell, Saye and St. John of Bletao, Sirs Edward Hobby, John Hollis, John Seymour, Henry Goodyer, John Hungerford, John Brooke, Giles Wroughton, Sir Edward Gorges, Sir Hughe Smithe, John Rodney, Francis Popham, Jaspar Moore, John Earnley, Thomas Thynne, Knts. ; Mr. Portman, and Sir John Stanhop's son, of Nottinghamshire.

(No. 634.) 15 October 1605. A briefe and true discours of the kings majesties carttakers, or rather a description of them and their offices ; bothe for the removes of the kings most honorable household, &c. from Standing House ; as in the progress tymes with the nobilitie, &c. Intituled to the most honorable and woorthy of Titles, for honor, learning, wisdom, and judgement, as also for the tender and most regardfull care and love to countrie, Henry earle of Northampton, &c. By Robert Fletcher, yeoman-purveyor of carriages for the removes onely of his majesties most honourable houshold ; wherein he hath servid 30 yeares and more with great troble, losses, and skandall.

Written by the James the First's yeoman-cart-taker (who had served Queen Elizabeth in the same capacity) for the information of the Lord Privy Seal, when the conduct of the royal cart-takers, as on the occasion of the King's progresses to Farnham, Basing, Salisbury, and Wilton, and their still worse conduct on the return journeys from Winchester to Wilton, and from Wilton to Hampton Court, had provoked a general entry against the grievances of wainage and the corrupt practices of the officers, empowered to impress horses and vehicles for the King's service on his journeys ; this tract gives a singularly vivid picture of the dishonesty of individuals, and of the abuses of a system. Affording a great deal of minute information respecting a department of the public service that was a fruitful source of popular discontent, it abounds with illustrations of character and manners that should be considered by historians of Elizabethan England. The staff of the King's regular cart-takers consisted of four officers, viz., the yeoman cart-taker and his three grooms, who during " every progress time " or midsommer quarter," were assisted by two " aids " or " extraordinary cart-takers," sworn into the cart-takers, office for the season, and empowered by " the grenecloth," to seize carts and animals, like the permanent officers. In the previous reign Robert Fletcher had replied to murmurs against the excesses of his subordinates by reducing the number of carts, impressed for a royal progress, from 600 to 400 ; and though an adverse official influence defeated his endeavours to limit the baggage-train to so small a number, he assures the Earl of Northampton with proper management, 400 carts ought to be enough for the requirements of the court on a journey: At the same time the writer " propounded a limitacion of myles, and " within the compas of twelve myles procurid that " cartes should serve to the full at all generall removes " at the rate of xs. a cart, and iid. a myle, the quenes " price, which xs. a removo was paid by those dwelling " without the list of xii. myles, and this held as the best " compos and most easy composicion that ever was " ordained, vntill her late majestie deceased." The extraordinary number of carts impressed for the progress of the King and his court from Wilton to Hampton is accounted for by the unusual number of His Majesty's retinue, by the badness of the roads "in the " deep of winter," and also by the fact that "the " Scotish people knowing no facion but their own ladid " there cartes with half lodes of stuff, and overloadid " the same with people. There was some tymes 16 and " more great bodies of men and women vpon one cart." Robert Fletcher speaks in strong terms of the outrageous dishonesty of grooms, still serving under him, as well as of grooms who sold their places and retired from the service, which they had disgraced, shortly after Queen Elizabeth's death. Having described the condition of his own department, the writer speaks with similar frankness and minuteness of detail of another service of royal cart-takers, styled "the cart-takers of London," during the last four years or otherwise called the " yeomen purveyors of carriages for his majesties " buttry, &c. and spicerye," consisting of chief and subordinate officers, authorised to impress carts and animals for conveying provision to the King's palaces in the neighbourhood of London. This service is said to have originated in the obligation of the city to provide means for carrying provision to "his highnes howses," not more than "25 myles from the citie"; and an interesting sketch is given of the growth, suppression, and revival of the department, which is represented as surpassing even the writer's own department in corruption and fraudulent usage. "These are the cart- " takers," Robert Fletcher says, " of whom preachers " in their pulpitts do proclaime, as namely Mr. Dean " of Pauls in a sermon before the late Quene, vpon " Ashwensday, 1585, and Mr. D. Neale before all the " lords in the chapell at Whitehall, when her late " majesties corps lay there not interrid. These are " those cart-takers, whoe doe daily and owerly take " carts in London, whether there be cause or noe cause; " and whoe are said to take money owerly and con- " tinewally. And these do sōm tymēs straie vpon an " ignorant poor carter, who having laiden his cart, for " Norwich Yermouth or places of like distans from " London. He is taken by one of thies cart-takers, " commaunded to unload, and to load a Tunn of drinck " and convey the same to the courts &c. There he " sheweth a commission—Brode seale &c. The poor man " drawith his purs and payeth v li., iiii li., v markes, &c., " to be freed of this cart-taker and his broade seal. A " nakid sworde were even as lawful." The concluding part of the tract, of twenty closely written folio sheets, relates to the insolence and extortionate practices of other purveyors, viz., the King's purveyors of sea-fish, his purveyors of wine, and his purveyors of oats, hay, and straw for the royal stables.—This official paper should be published. Students of social history would like to have it on their shelves.

(A. 154.) Copy of a petition to James the First for more effective measures against the agents of the Roman Catholic Church. The recital alludes to the gunpowder plot as a recent event.

(A. 797.) 2 May 1607. Copy of part of the warrant to the Keeper of Wardrobe, to furnish the Earl of Salisburie and the Lord Viscount Bindon, and either of them, with xviii. yards of "velvett crimsin for their " liveries for the order of the garter viz. for roabe, " kirtle with hoods and tippetts at xxxiiis. the yard," and "xii. yards di. of white Taffata to line the same " roabes at xvs. the yard."—The same paper exhibits the copy of a similar warrant for the Duke de Hulst, dated at Greenwich, 22 April, 3 Jac. I. The endorsement of the note states that the robes of the Earl and Viscount were to be worn "at the installation of the " garter."

(No. 785.) 24 March 1608. Copy of circular letter from the Privy Council, respecting the best means of levying an aid for making the King's eldest son, Prince Henry, a knight. It recommends composition, as a better process than inquisition, in that it is less troublesome to individuals, and requires no production of

evidence, capable of prejudicing its producers on future occasions, under certain contingencies. Signatures:— Rich. Cant., Tho. Elesmere, Chaunc, R. Salusbury, H. Northampton, Notingham, T. Suffolke, E. Worster, E. Wotton, L. Zouche, J. Stanope, Jul. Cæsar, Tho. Parrye.

(No. 293.) Copy of instruccions gyven to his majesties commissioners for the Leavying of ayde to make the most highe and noble Prince Henry his majesties eldest sonne knight. No date.

(No. A. 795.) 24 April 1610. Indenture of agreement between Henry Earl of Northampton, of the one part, and John Foyle, gentleman, of the other part; whereby the said earl grants to Mr. John Foyle, the next presentation to the rectory or parsonage of Cottistocke, co. Dorset, in case the present incumbent, John Mayo, clerk die within the next four years.

(No. A. 779.) Sept. 1610. A Declaracion of the quarrel between my Lord of Walden and Sir Edward Herberte. Signed by J. Peyton (who accompanied Lord Walden to the ground appointed for a duel between his Lordship and Sir Edward Herbert, in consequence of a challenge sent by the latter to his antagonist, who had struck him a blow), this lengthy narrative was drawn in Lord Walden's interest, to preserve his honour from any injurious misrepresentation of the affair. Sir Edward Heberte's challenge was dated 11 Sept. 1610 at Disseldorpe. The adversaries failed to meet one another in the appointed wood, though each is credited by the narrator with an honest purpose of fighting.

(No. 735.) Copy of instructions for the most Reverend Father in God, George Lord Archbishop of Canterbury, concerning certain orders to be observed and put in execution by the severall bishops in his province. Endorsement of the paper in the handwriting of Mr. John Griffith. No date.

(No. 796.) The liste of my lordes (i.e. Lord Northampton's) seruantes appointed to waite and attend my Lorde to Windsor. Giving the names of eleven "howshold seruaunts," and twenty-nine "receyvours." No date.

(No. 808.) 3rd November 1612. Copy of the articles of the contract of marriage between the Palgrave and the Princess Elizabeth, daughter of James the First.

(No. A. 809.) 24 February 1613. Copy of "The " Inscription upon the first stone laid with my lords" (i.e. Earl of Southampton's) "his owne handes of the " hospitall at Grenewich, devoutly kneeling vpon his " knees in fervent prayer to the holy Trinetie to blesse. " and prosper the foundacion." In the hand-writing of John Griffith.

(No. A. 790.) 1 Mar. 1614. Letter from the bishop of Chichester to the bishop of Lincoln, respecting the recent difference at Cambridge between the vice-chancellor and senior regent. "The blaze of this ignis " fatuus," says the writer, "hath flashed as farr as the " court at New Markett."

(No. A. 847.) 2 March 1613. Letter from the Bishop of Lincoln to Mr. John Griffith. Excusing himself for calling so seldom to inquire after the Earl of Northampton, and charging Mr. Griffith to assure the Lord Privy Seal of the writer's respect and care for him.

(No. B. 22.) 14 June 1614. The last will (in the testator's own hand-writing) of Henry, Earl of Northampton, baron of Marnehill, Lord Privy Seal, Lord Warden of the Cinque Ports, Knight of the Garter, Chancellor of the University of Cambridge, and one of the Privy Council. Avowing his gratitude to God for " deliveringe " him" in many and sondry tymes, from the most " subtile and entrappinge combinaciouns and practizes " of his enemies," the testator says " I do a trewe con- " stant servaunt of his, and a member of the catholike and " apostolike church, sayenge, with St. Jerome. In qua " fide puer natus fui, in eadem senex morior." After directing his executors to inter him in the chapel of Dover castle, and declaring his loyal affection for the king, he continues, " I most humbly beseech his excellent " majestie to accept, as a pore remembraunce of me his " faithfull servaunt, a cupp of gold of one hundred " pounds value, with one hundred Jacobino peces of " twenty-two shillings a-pece therin, on which cup " my desire is there shold be this inscripcion ' Detur " Dignissimo." To the most noble and hopefull Prince " Charles I give my best George. To my most dere " and entirely beloved nephewe, the earlo of Suffolke, " I give my jewell of the three stones, on of them " beinge that Ruby, which his excellent majestie sent " me owt of Scotland as his first token." He bequeaths to the same earl " a cross of diamondes given me by " my lady, my mother"; and his second George to the earl of Somerset. Other legacies:—2,000l. to his nephew, the Lord William, (it being in " some equity " that the testator should remember this nephew, in " respect of Clann intended by his father vnto him, " and now come to my hands"; a "suite of new " dressed hanginges," formerly in the possession of Lord Barckley, "to the nowe L. Barkeley, my warde"; an annuity for life of 20l. out of the lease-lands at Grenewich bought of the Earl of Salisbury's executors, to Jhon Southerwood; an annuity, for life, of 40l., out of the same lands to Jeames Symondes; 20l. to the poor of the parish of St. Martin's in the Fields, co. Middle-sex; a piece of plate of the value of 20l. to Lord Worcester; twenty nobles to each of the gentlemen, and five marks to each of the yeomen, being menial servants then attendant on the testator in Northampton House, (the said legacies being given to "bye them blackes"), with the use of their several lodgings in Northampton House, and their allowances till Michaelmas next; and furthermore the following special legacies to certain of his servants,—200l. to Edward Willys; remission of a debt of 100l. and restoration of a patent to Thomas Jermy; 100l. a-piece to Francis Wyndham, Jhon Heydon, Giles Savage, Hughe Chomeley; 50l. apiece to William Holler, Robert Lewyes, Jhon Wynn, Thomas Culpeper, Jhon Hickes, Henry Mildmay, Edward Gent, Andrewe Juill, Christopher Harris, and Arthur Lenney; 100l. to John Taggard and his wiffe; 40l. apiece to Panckroosse Fathers, William Foxe, Samuel Fisshe, Richard Larder, Peter Webster, and Thomas Scott; 20l. apiece to Ferdinand Kelley and Jhon Holmes the taylor; 10l. apiece to William Sowland and William Bland; 5l. apiece to William Yomans and Jeames Foster; 40 shillings to Will the boy; 500 marks to each of the testator's executors, besides their expenses in executing the will; 20l. to the chapel of Dover Castle; 20l. to the poor of Dover; and 10l. to Thomas Willies. The executors appointed by the will are the testator's servants, John Griffith, William Burge, and Robert Cole, gentlemen, who are required to render a yearly account of their proceedings in respect of the testators will, at Northampton House, to the Earls of Suffolk and Worcester, and Lord William Howard, who are appointed overseers of the testament. Directions are given for the founding and incorporation of the testator's hospitals at Risinge and Greenwich, and for the completion and endowment of his hospital at Clonn. "I will," the testator says of the two first-named of these charities, "myne heir for ever shall haue " the aominacioun, placinge and displacinge of the pore " of the hospitall of Risinge; and the Company of " Mercers in London, of the pore in the hospitall at " Greenwich, yet so as they chose xii. out of Grenowich, " and thother eight out of Shotesham in Norfolk, where " I was born." It is also mentioned in the will that the testator has leased, for 10 years, to his executors, all his "jewelles, goodes and other thinges in that lease " expressed," in trust for the payment of his debts and legacies, and for the performance of "other things men-" tioned in the same lease." The will was proved 18 June 1614.

(No. A. 830.) 8 July 1614. Sets of Latin verses by Serjeant Hoskyns. 1. On his committal to prison on the above-named day. 2. After his liberation, 8 July 1615. 3. De seipso, 1634. Also, on paper No. A. 828, two sets of Latin verses, endorsed by Mr. John Griffith thus, " 6 June, 1630. A coppie of verses made by Dr. " Sharpo and Serjeant Hoskins upon the appearance " of a starr that day in the sermon tyme at Paules " Crosse (the kinges majestie beinge present) of the " birth of a Prince."

(No. 791.) 17 November 1614. Copy of a letter from John Griffith, at Graye's Inn, to Lord Norreys, about the dress to be provided for the late Lord Northampton's almsmen, after the fashion of the "almesmens gounes " at Thame," and other matters connected with the earl's charitable bequests. The writer undertakes to enjoin Lord Northampton's almsmen to pray for Lord Norreys, and adds, in excuse for tho shortness of his letter, "my recesse from all attendance in Court dis-" ables me to geve your lordship any advertisementes of " newes."

(No. 778.) 16 June 1614. Copy of Sir John Brooke's acknowledgement of 1viii. vs. iiiid. received from Sir Robert Brett, Knt., by the appointment of the High Treasurer of England, being part of the money received by the said Sir Robert of the executors of the late Earl of Northampton, "for the repayre of Deale Castle."

(No. 897.) 16 July 1614. Copy of "a Schedule In-" dented of all such evidences and writinges concerning " the manor of Clunne and Bishops Castle, in the " countie of Salop, late the inheritance of the right " honourable Henry late earle of Northampton, de-

" ceased: delivered by John Griffith, esq., the sixteenth " day of July, 1614 to the right honourable Thomas " earle of Suffolk, Lord High Treasurer of England."

(No. 752.) 12 of August 1614. Letter from the earle Clan Ricard, at Sommer-hill, to Mr. John Griffith (or Griffin, as the name is spelt by the earl), entreating Mr. Griffith to "delever the mony allotted for Ferdorogh " OKelly nowe vnto hym befor yo' departur from " London into the country," as urgent affairs require O'Kelly's speedy return to Ireland. From John Griffith's endorsement of this paper it appears that "the " money" was the legacy bequeathed to Mr. O'Kelly by Lord Northampton.

(No. A. 789.) 5 Feb. 1615. Lord Chancellor Ellesmere's letter to James the First, praying, in consideration of his infirmities, to be discharged of his great place. "Most gracious Soueragne," he begins, "I find through " my great age accompanied with many greefs and " infirmities my sense and conceits is become dull and " heauy and memorie decayed, my judgment weake, my " hearing imperfect, my voice and speech fayling and " faltering, and in all the powers and faculties of my " mind and body great debillities." The plaintive petition ends, "I am unable to sustaine the burthen of " this greate seruise, for I am come to St. Paul's desier, " Cupio dissolui et esse cum Christo." Endorsed by Mr. John Griffith.

(No. 889.) 24 September 1616. An abstract of the accounts between Mr. John Griffith, Henry Howard, and Lord Arundel, in respect of the late Earl of Northampton's charities.

(No. 930.) 27 Sept. 1616. A note of the moneys to be received, the debts and legacies to be paid, and the works and other things yet to be performed, by Mr. John Griffith, as executor of the late Earl of Northampton.

(No. 801.) 21 March 1617. A coppie of Sir Walter Rawlegh's lettre to the Kings Secretarie of England. Written from the island of St. Christopher at the above-given date, and beginning with, "Sir, as I haue not " hitherto given you any accompt of our proceedinges " and passage towardes the Indies: so haue I no other " subject to write of since our arivall ther of the greatest " and sharpest misfortunes that haue euer befallen any " man."

(No. 777.) April 1617. Copy (in the handwriting of John Griffith) of a letter of petition from the Earl of Arundell, in Scotland, to Sir Francis Bacon, Lord Keeper of the Great Seal of England, praying from the Lord Keeper a decree that the writer may enter into possession of the lands which his uncle of Northampton leased to his executors for 10 years in trust "to be a " suplye to his personall estate towardes the perform-" ance of his will and other charitable workes by him " intended; the rents and profittes wherof haue been " since receyued and imployd by Mr. John Griffith to " the use accordinge to the late Lord Chancellor's orders " and decrees." The earl represents that he has suffered in this business from delays occasioned by the late Lord Chancellor's sickness and the negligence of his lawyers. He also solicits from the Lord Keeper a speedy hearing of a "cause dependinge befor you be-" tween me and one Parkes." At the close of this private letter the earl describes himself as the Lord Keeper's "affectionate true frend."

(No. A. 787.) 19 March 1620. Copy of Lord Bacon's letter to the House of Peers, of that date. Endorsed by John Griffith, "My lord St. Albans letter to the lords " of the parliament."

(No. 824.) Two sets of verses made by the Kinge his majestie (i.e. James. I.) when he was at Burley Howse, intertayned by the Marquis of Buckingham.

(1.) The heavens that wept perpetually before,
Since we came hither, showe theyr smyling cheore;
This goodly howse it smiles and all this store
Of huge provisions smyles vpon vs here.
The Buckes and stagges in full they seeme to smyle,
God sende a smiling boye within a while.

(2.) A Vow or Wishe for the felicitye and fertility of the owners of this howse.

If ever in the Aprill of my dayes
I sat vpon Parnassus forked hill,
And there inflam'd with sacred fiery still
By pen proclam'd our greate Apollo's prayse,
Graunt glistering Phœbus with thy golden rayes
My earnest suite, which to present theo here
Behold my * * of this blessed couple dere,
Whose vertues pure no tounge can duly blaze,

Thou, by whose heate the trees in fruit abound,
Blesse them with frute delitious, sweete and faire
That may succeede theym in theyr vertues rare ;
Firm plant theym in theyr naytive soyle and ground.
Thou Jovo, that art the only god indeede,
My prayer heare : sweete Jesus intercede.

(No. A. 818.) Copy of Lord Bacon's humble submission to the House of Lords. Signed, Francis Saint Albon, Canc.

(No. 695.) Jan. 1621. A true copy (with a translation into English) of the Latin oration addressed by Lord George Offolinski (chamberlain of and ambassador from the King's Maiestic of Poland) to James the First at Whitehall, on Sunday, 11 March 1620.

(No. 754.) 1 May 1621. Copy of the Latin entry on the close roll of the circumstances under which the Great Seal passed from Francis, Viscount St. Alban, to Lord Keeper Williams.

(No. 772.) 4th of May 1621. Copy of the acknowledgment, by the commissioners for raising the first payment of the second of two entire subsidies granted to the King by Parliament, that Simon Thelwall of St. Andrewes, in the Wardrobe, London, has paid his contribution to the said tax.

(No. 785.) 7 June 1621. Copy of a note, stating for the information of Mr. John Griffith where the writer has left in safety the great part of the pulpit cloth, the communion-table cloth, and other articles, including the "evidences for the hospitall and thother two hospitalles." The copyist's endorsement certifies that the letter was written by Mr. Swale, who was probably relinquishing some subordinate office having relation to the late Earl of Northampton's trusts for charitable uses.

(No. A. 804 and 805.) 12 August 1622. Letter from the Archbishop of Canterbury (George Abbot) to the Bishop of London, for the correction of the extravagances of unsound preachers ; embodying a copy of the King's letter to the primate on the same subject ; and enclosing the schedule of orders for the restraint of the same preachers and the encouragement of catechismal exercises on Sunday afternoons. The third of the said orders directing, "That noe Preacher of what title " soever under the degree of a bishop, or deane at the " least, doe henceforth presume to preach in any popular " auditory the deepe pointes of Predestination, Election, " Reprobation, and of the Universality, efficacy, resist- " ability or errosistability of God's grace &c." Endorsed by Mr. John Griffith.—See also, No. 80. A copy of the foregoing (circular) letter from the primate to the bishops of his province, with a copy of the afore-named orders.

(No. 687.) 1622. Petition of Hugh Barker, D.C.L., commissary and chancellor of the Bishop of Oxford, by letters patent under the episcopal seal, (granted 19 July, 17 James I., and subsequently confirmed by the dean and chapter of Christ Church in Oxford) to the Bishop of Lincoln, Lord Keeper of the Great Seal ; praying for an injunction to restrain the said Bishop of Oxford and one Humphrey Jones from combining to deprive the petitioner of the powers and emoluments of his said office ; and praying further that the said Bishop of Oxford may be required to appear before the Lord Keeper in the Court of Chancery, to answer to the allegations of the petition.

(No. A. 887.) 4 Sept. 1622. Letter from the Archbishop of Canterbury to the Bishop of London ; for the staying of unsound and dangerous preaching. Endorsed by Mr. John Griffith, as the primate's "second letter" on the subject, to the bishop.

(No. 714.) 5 Sept. 1622. Copy of a letter (signed John Lincoln, C.S.) from Lord Keeper Williams to the Custos Rotulorum and justices of the peace of Berkshire, ordering them to put in force the laws, for suppressing vagrancy, &c., against the "whole troupe of rogues, beggors, " Ægiptians, and idle persons," who infest their county to the injury of the King's poor subjects, and "the deepe " aspersion " of the present government. Requiring them, furthermore, "to correct the extortionate prices " charged, in their county, for hay and oats at inns and " hosteries, for flesh at shambles, and bread in bakers' " shops," by "apporcioninge such reasonable rates on " all theis particulars as in equitie and conscience shall " be found fittinge."

(No. A. 798.) 17 Jan. 1623. Letter (signed Isabell Stafford) from Lady Stafford to her much respected friend Mr. John Griffith, begging him, as the executor of the late Earl of Northampton, to deliver to her cosen, Thomas Forster, or to the writer's brother, "tho cove- " nants which Lord Stafford entered vnto," and deposited with the Earl of Northampton, "when he " acknowledged the statute of his land ;" the lady

having especial need of them "for settlinge of my " daughter's joynture while my lord Stafford is livinge, " which before my sons death was left raw and vnper- " fect." She adds, "If we now neglect it, perhaps " hereafter my lord will not be in so good a mynd."— Endorsed by Mr. John Griffith.

(No. 713.) 15 March 1623. A coppie of Dr. Turner. his proposalles at a committee that day in parliament. Comprising six articles of enquiry against the Duke of Buckingham.

(No. A. 815.) 20 April 1623. Copy of Gregory the Fifteenth's letter to the Prince of Wales.

(No. 789.) 17 June 1623. An inventory of John Griffith's "heddinges and other implements of house- " hold " in his lodging at Greenwich.

(No. 788.) 9 October 1623. "A note of my disburse- ". mentes of 6l. 5s., that I receyued for one yeare and a " quarter ended at Michaelmas last of the annuityes of " 5li. payable to the hospitall at Rysinge out of the " Marsh land purchased at Greenwich with the stock of " my lords hospitalles." For the hand-writing of John Griffith who, at the foot of the bill, makes note of the expenses of a journey to Rising, "Besydes my charge in " travell from London to Rysinge, wherin spent " 8l. 9s. 6d."

(No. 787.) Nov. 1623. "A note of my disbursements " of 7li. that I receyued for one yeare ended at Michael- " mas last of the annuities payable for keepinge of my " lords tombe, and of the Earl and Countes of Surrey " their tombe out of the marsh land purchased at " Greenwich." In the hand-writing of John Griffith (secretary and executor of the late Earl of Northampton), whose signature is attached to the account, which contains three entries of moneys spent on the Earl of Surrey's, tomb in "the church of Framingham," i.e. Framlingham, co. Suffolk. At the foot of the account, a "Mem. that these annuityes are hereafter as they be " receyued to be payd to the warden of the hospitall at " Grenwich, and he is according to statute to pay them " severally in one entyre payment yearlie at Allhaloutyd " in such sort as therein is provided for the mayntenance " of the sayd tombes.—John Griffiths."

(No. C. 103.) Copy of the articles of an agreement for marriage between Charles, Prince of Wales, and the Infanta ; i.e. "Articuli m'r'onalis conventus " habiti inter Seren^m. Wallie Principem et Seren^am " Infant et conuues eorund' coñissarios."—Endorsed by John Griffith, secretary to Henry Earl of Northampton.

(No. 685.) A coppie of a letter from the Spanish ambassadour to the kinges Majestie ; with the heading " Legatus Regis Catholici apud Anglos Jacobo Regi. The letter in which the 'Ambassador spoke indignantly of the Duke of Buckingham's demeanour in Spain :— " An Dux Buckinghamius contra auctoritatem et rever- " entiam Serenissimo Principi multa non fecerit ? Si " stante et præsente Principe non solitus fuerit sedere, " modo indecenti, pedes alteri sedi innixus ? &c." Endorsed by Mr. John Griffith.

(No. 707.) Paper, endorsed "Some Parliamentary " Newes." On the latest particulars respecting Prince Charles's adventures in Spain, and the explanations given to Parliament by the Prince and the Duke of Buckingham with regard to their action in that country. " The Spanish ambassador," says the letter-writer, " demaunds Buckingham's head, in justice to his master. . . . The king referrs all to his Parliament, who haue " honourable acquitted the Duke." No date.

(No. 759.) 23 April 1624. His Majestie's answere to a petition, deliuered him by the Houses of Parliament.

(No. 899.) 26 Nov. 1624. Memorandum that James the First (by letters patent under the Great Seal, 3 Sepf. in the first year of his reign, directed to the Lord Treasurer of England), put an impost of ten shillings on every hundredweight of white starch imported into his realm, and of five shillings on every hundredweight of starch made by the company of starch-makers within his realm, and that, on 21 March in the said first year of his reign, his said Majesty leased the same impost for twelve years, from the next Feast of the Annunciation, to Henry Earl of Northampton, at a yearly rent of one-fourth of the profits thereof : and further that (on a surrender of the aforesaid lease), his said Majesty, on 28 November, in the sixth year of his reign, granted to the same earl another lease of the same impost on white starch for twelve years, at a yearly rent of 333l. 6s. 8d. The paper is endorsed by John Griffiths, thus, " 28° November, 1624. " A coppie of the note that I delyuered that day to Sir " Jo. Ingram of the Generall Grauntes to my Lord of " the imposition vpon starch."

(No. 691.) 15 January 1625. Warrant from Sir Richard Blount, Knight, Sheriff of Oxfordshire, to bailiff of the hundreds of Banbury and Bloxham (in accordance with the King's writ, certifying his determination to be crowned, and directed to the said sheriff,), to make proclamation in his bailiwick, that all men therein, having xl*i*. per ann. in lands or rent, in their own hands or to their use in the hands of feoffees, and having had the same lands or rent for the space of the three years, are to take upon themselves the order of knighthood. The bailiff aforesaid to make a return to this precept, " at the " signe of the kinges heade at Oxon at or before " Wednesday the 25 of this instant Januarye."

(No. 748.) The coppie of Mr. Francis Phillip his petition to his majestie for his brothers inlargement out of the Tower.—No date.

(No. 700.) An answeare to the relation of the lord Ambassador of Spaine, towchinge his law suites in the Admiralty.—No date.

(No. 742.) A list of sums levied on Lordes and Ladyes for " their severall subsidyes for the first payment " graunted the last parliament." Endorsed by Mr. John Griffith. This paper affords data for estimating the wealth of the peerage and its several members in the earlier half of the seventeenth century.—No date.

(No. A. 793.) 24 April 1625. Order (dated at Whitehall, and signed " Arundelle Surrey "), and addressed to Sir Bevys Thelwall, Knt. His Majesties will is that he is pleased that the nobility of this kingdome shall attend the funerall of our late soverayne king James, as mourners, soe that it be intimated to euery man that shall send for blacks, that non vpon paine of his highe displeasure keepe the blacks, which will not or cannott really mourne, and doe honor to the funerall, as well in the proceeding as at the ceremonies in the church. And as euery one is to haue notice given of this commandement at the wardrobe, see noe doubt all will obey it, and not take their blacks, when they know their occasions will not permit them to attend the service.—On the other side of the sheet is a " List of such Lords and Ladies as " are to attend his Majestie to Dover for the reception of " the Queene appointed by himselfe ;" the 11 of May being the day appointed for the meeting at Dover. The paper is endorsed by Mr. John Griffith.

(No. A. 682.) 15 May 1625. A coppie of a letter from the earle of Oxford to his lady, written at Gertrugdenberg.—I have to lett you see by gevinge you this testimony vnder my hand, that I am well, least reportes might erre. Yesternight oure Generall drewe out 6,000, intendinge to endeavour the reliefe of Breda by breakinge vp th enemyes quarter at Tersydo, where we arrived at breake of dayo : the English havinge the vauntguard vnder the commaund of the Lord Generall Vere and my selfe. Our nation lost noe honour, but many brave gent their lyves : amonge which number my lord Ambs. nowe maryed neece her husband, Sir Tho: Wynd' kylled with a great shott, Capt. John Cromwell dangerously hurt, Capt. Tubb I beleive will not escape, Capt. Terrott shot through the body close vnder the left papp, but I hope he will liue, my ensigne Thomas Stanhope, kylled vpon the place, and diuerse other officers and gent of good quality hurt and kylled ; we fought as long as our munition lasted, and beate thenemye out of 3 houses. But the Dutch faylinge to (word eaten away by moth) and our ponder and shott being spent, wee were forced to retyre. In which retreat we lost most of those named. I returned not without a shott on my left arme : but so favourable a one, as drewe no bloude, nor hinders me to relate this tragedye. I am not willinge to bee a messenger of ill newes, otherwise I would haue written to my lord Ambassador.

(No. 776.) 4 August 1625. A copy of " his ma- " jesties speach in Christs Church hall in Oxford, to " the lords and commons there assembled, the 4th of " August, 1625 ;" beginning with " My lords and you " the commons, We all remember that from your de- " sires and advice my father nowe with God brake of " those two treaties with Spaine." Endorsed by John Griffith.

(No. 689.) August 1625. The coppie of the petition of the Lords and Commons assembled in parliament to the Kinge: and his Majesties answeares. Endorsement in the handwriting of Mr. John Griffith.

(No. 706.) 12 August 1626. The coppie of a protestation of the House of Commons of their loyaltie and readines to suply his Majestie in a parliamentary way. Endorsed by Mr. John Griffith.

(No. A. 159.) August 1625. A paper, headed " Reasons " conceaved by the parliament adjourned from West- " minster to Oxford the 27th of July, and there begun " the first of August and broken off the xii. of August

" 1625." Arguments for granting the King liberal supplies. Endorsed by Mr. John Griffiths.

(No. A. 148.) 3 Nov. 1625. Copy of the " Articles " sett down by the lords and others of his majestie " most honourable priuie counsell accordinge to the " tenor of the commission graunted by his majesty, " bearing date the second of November, 1625, for such " marchauntes and owners who haue or shall haue leave " from my Lord Admirall or his lieutenant to repayre " to the seas against the subiectes of the King of " Spayne, by vertue of the aforesaid commission." Endorsed by Mr. John Griffith.

(No. 688.) 17 Nov. 1625. Coppie of his majesties order to the Lord Admirall to giue present order to the officers of all the portes of England, to keep them straightly, that no English children be transported to the seminaryes beyond the seas. Endorsement in the handwriting of John Griffiths.

(No. 712.) 24 Nov. 1625. A list of the Privy Seales for Oxfordshire. The paper gives the particular sum required of each recipient of one of the said writs. Endorsement in the handwriting of Mr. John Griffith.

(No. 709.) The Duke of Buckingham's speech to the Commons on the requirements of the navy, and his measures for keeping an adequate force at sea. Alluding to his public service and private embarrassments, the speaker says, " My journey into Spayne was " all of my owne charge. I had not one penny of my " master. To France I confesse my charge was borne. " But that of the Low countries was my owne charge " without any thing from the king. I am accused to " be the cause of the losse of the narrowe seas, and " of the damage there sustayned." Deriding the suggestion that the fleet was sent out last summer at the instigation of private resentment ; the Duke speaks of the King of Spain's manifest attempts for an invasion, which compelled the King of England to send out a fleet. Admitted that, in discharging the duties of his office, he has made mistakes, the Duke palliates his errors by declaring them no offspring of ignorance, corruption, injustice, or oppression. No date.

(No. 686.) The coppie of one of the Kinges speeches to the Lords and Commons assembled in parliament. Condemning the shameful disorder of some of his subjects in resorting to the houses of foreign ambassadors, and in contriving " that their children should be so bred " here as if they were brought up cyther at Madrid or " in Rome." Endorsed by Mr. John Griffith.

(No. 811.) 7 Feb. 1626. Letter from Lewes, Bishop of Bangor (whilst in London for Charles the First's coronation), to his father-in-law, Sir Sackvill Trevor, Knt. at Place Newydd. Containing particulars of his gracious treatment by the King and the Duke of Buckingham, and other great personages ; and of the success of his suit with the King and Duke on behalf of his correspondent. After stating that, on the night of the last Monday in January, he " allayted at the red lion in " Grayes Inne lane where the plague has not been all " the Infection tyme," the writer says, " On Tuesday, " the next day, I wayted on the king at dinner. After " I had kyssed his hand and receaved as gracious a " welcome as ever I had in my life, I moued his ma- " jestie in your behalf with no litell ernestnes. Tyme " will not suffer me to write the summe of the wordes, " but the effect of his majestie aunswer was this, that " by his troth he would do for you, and that you weare " a very honest and able man." Further on he says, " I thancke god I never had so much favor in my lif " from his majestie, as I had synce I cam vp last. I " was one of the Busshops who held the cloth over his " head whilst his majestie was annointed, and after his " annointing he graciously kissed me and some 5 bus- " shops that weare at the annointing, as the ceremony " is, and when his majestie sate vpon his throne, on a " high scaffold with a crowne on his head, we did our " homage to him and then wee kissed hym. I thank " god I am now growen againe in extraordinary favor " with the Duke of Buckingham." The writer of this long and interesting epistle observes, " My Lord of " Rutland at the very coronation holding the sworde " asked me very hartilie how his cosen Anne did, and " whether she was come vp to London, and whether " she had a boy or a girle and very chearfully glad to " heare of her." Dated from the writer's lodging in Mr. Frost's house, in Westminster Cloyster.

(No. A. 48.) 26 March 1626. The coppie of his majesties letter to the Speaker of the Commons house of parliament, given at Westminster, 26 March, 1 Car. A.D. 1626. Endorsed by Mr. John Griffith.

(No. 690.) March 1626. The coppie of his Majesties answeare to the petition by the house of Commons con-

3 F 2

cernininge religion, delivered by the Lord Keeper. Endorsed by Mr. John Griffith.

(No. 738.) 4 April 1626. A coppie of his Majesties speech and the Lord Keepers to the Lordes and the House of Commons, sent to me that daye. This endorsement is in the handwriting of Mr. John Griffith. The papers set forth, 1. An abstract of the king's address to the Lords and Commons; 2. The Lord Keeper's speech; 3. The King's additional and concluding remarks to the Commons.

(No. A. 145.) 6 April 1626. Copy of the humble remonstrance of the Commons, now assembled in Parliament, to the King's most Excellent Majesty. Endorsed by Mr. John Griffith.

(No. 740.) 8 April 1626. An abstract of Sir William Walter's speech that day at a committee in the Lower House of Parliament. This endorsement of the paper is in the handwriting of Mr. John Griffith. The paper itself is headed "Sʳ William Walter his speech in the " Lower House of Parliament," and begins with these words, " On Munday afternoone Sir William Walter " proposed that the cause of all the greivances was that " all the Kings Counsell ride upon one Horseback, and " therefor that the Parliament was to advise his Ma- " jestie, as Jethro did Moses, to take vnto him assistants, " with theyr qualities. Exod. 18. 21." The qualities which the speaker desired to see in the King's advisers are then set forth in eight separate articles.

(No. 768.) 1 May 1626. Articles of the Earle of Bristoll, whereby he chargeth the Duke of Buckingham the first of May 1626. Endorsed, in the handwriting of the body of the paper, " The Earle of Bristolls Articles " against the D. of Buckingham."

(No. A. 775.) 6 June 1626. Copies of Charles the First's complimentary letter to the University of Cambridge, on the election of the Duke of Buckingham to be chancellor of the University; and of the Duke's letter in acknowledgment of the distinction conferred on him by the professors of learning, whose good opinion he prizes highly, notwithstanding his want of scholarship. " Yet I cannot," the Duke says, " attribute this honour " to any desert of mine, but to the sacred memory you " beare to my dead Mʳ the king of schollers, who loved " you and honoured you oft with his presence, and to " my gratious Mʳ uow livinge, who inheriteth with his " blessed father's vertues the affeccions which he bore " to your University."

(No. 898.) 19 Aug. 1626. Paper of memoranda endorsed by John Griffith, " Remembrances of sundry businesses " whereof I may have use vpon many occasions." The first of these memoranda is that, on 11 May, 1625, he had carried to Lord Arundell the copies of the statutes of the hospitals of Clunn and Rysinge, together with certain books, and a list of " the names and ages of the poore " men and women in both houses beinge xxvi who make " between theym two thousand eight and twenty." Another memorandum is that he must caution " Sir " Robert Howard hereafter not to be so forward in dis- " posinge his vncles charitie contrary to his will and " institution to pleasure either freind or seruant."

(No. A. 41.) 26 Jan. 1627. Letter from Hugh Owen at Worcesthowse to his worthy cousin John Griffith, Esq. at Bloxham, near Banburie. After giving his correspondent the latest gossip of the town about the blockade of Rochell, " by sixty men of warre frenche and " spanishe," and about " a huge great navie a-preparing " n spain," the writer adds, " Your noble frend, and our " best shelter and succour (I meane my Lord Privic Seale) " is sicklie, but whither of the gowt his owne diseaso or " otherwise we can not discerne. He kept his bedd this " 3 weeks or more, see weake in bodie that he hath taken " nothing but a little broth and gelic, till Thursday " last that he called for beefe and brewes, but could not " eate it, and yesterday he desired a dishe of "buttered " eggs, and did but tast it, yet he speaks better within " these 2 or 3 dayes than he did before, makes his bar- " gains himself and calls for his accomptes of vs; which " puts us in great hope of his recoueryo. Thus with my " deerest love to yourself, to Mr. Griffith, and your good " brother, his bedfellow, my cousen Richard Hughes, " I rest, &c." Endorsed by Mr. John Griffith.

(No. 761.) 17 March 1627. The Lord Keeper's speech in Parliament on March 17, 1627, beginning with " My " lords and you the knights and burgesses of the house " of Commons. If I had bene delighted in long speak- " inge, yet the example and commaunds of his Majestie " were more than enough to restraine the superfluitie of " that humor. But there is yett more for that excellent " compacted speech, which we haue heard from his " Majestie, beginning with a reason, that this is a time " for action and not for speech."

(No. 790.) 30 of April 1627. A paper entitled " The " effect (i.e. purport) of the speech delivered by the " Lord Primate before the Lord Deputy and the great " assembly at his Majesties Castle of Dublyn the last day " of Aprill, 1627."

(No. 270.) A list of the names of the persons slayne and taken prisoners in yᵉ Isle of Ree.

(No. A. 313.) A relation of the armyes landing in the isle of Retz. A lucid and graphic account of the naval and military operations by an eye-witness.

(No. 803.) 2 March 1628. Coppies of Sir John Elliottes and Mr. Seldenes speeches at the breakinge up of the parliament.—The endorsement of the paper in John Griffith's handwriting.

(No. 747.) 6 of May 1628. The Lord Keeper his speech that day to the House of Commons.

(No. 783.) 30th of January 1629. A coppie of his majesties and the Commissioners Orders in the cause between the Deane and Canons of Christchurch and the students of that house. Being a minute of the proceedings at Whitehall on 30 Jan. 1629, when the king was " gratiously pleased to heare the complaintes of the " studientes against the Deane and Canons of Christ " Church in Oxen, with their learned counsell on both " sides about the gouernment of the house, and the al- " lowances of the revenues belonginge to the same for the " maintenance of the studientes, whoe pretended to haue " bene of late much abridged of thejre allowances by " the said Deane and Canons." Failing to prove their case to the satisfaction of " his majestie and the lords to " whom the hearinge of this business was committed," the students were censured for " theire impertinente com- " plaintes," and were " enioyned by his majestie to re- " turne backe to theire studies and submitte themselves " to the Deane and Cannons."

(No. 894.) 9 Feb. 1629. Letter from Richard Hughes to Mr. John Griffith. About the late Lord Northampton's charities, and the action of the Mercer's Company, Lord Arundell, and Lord Suffolke in respect to them.

(No. 775.) 17th of March 1629. Copy of the articles proferred by Mr. More to the Lords Commissioners against the warden of New Colledge about the choise of the proctor. The articles charged the warden of New College, with exercising unfair influence in the election of a proctor, to the prejudice of Mr. More and the advantage of Mr. Stringer, candidates for the office. Endorsed by John Griffith.

(No. 942.) 17 April 1629. The last will of Richard Williams, " auncient-bearer vnder Captaine Thomas Powell" and nephew of Mr. John Griffith; containing numerous legacies of minutely described articles of wearing apparell. It would be serviceable to a writer on costume in Charles the First's England. It appears from one of the legacies that the auncient-bearer's monthly pay was iii li. v s.

(No. 410.) Packet of sixteen papers, receipts for rent of a set of chambers in Doctors Commons. The earliest of these acknowledgements runs thus :—" Rec'd. this xxᵗʰ " of October 1629 of Mr. Dr. Griffith for one halfe " yeares rent of certaine Chambers situate in the Dcors. " Com'ons London late in the possession of Dr. Wood- " house deceased due to Mr. Fellowes and Schollers of " Trinity Hall in Cambridge at the feast of St. Michael " the Archaungell past the sum of—xs. George Cole " Recr." The series of receipts shows that the advocate continued to be tenant of the same chambers at the same rent, till Lady Day 1641.

(No. A. 845.) 28 May 1630. Copy of a letter from the Bishop of London (Laud) to " his vice-chauncellor and " the heades of houses " of Oxford University. Urging the careful observance of " formalities which are in a " sort the outward and visible face of the university." Endorsed by Mr. John Griffith.

(No. A. 859.) 7 July 1630. A coppie of a decree in Chauncery in a matter between the bishop of Durham and Sir Harry Martyn. Endorsed by Mr. John Griffith.

(No. 925.) 23 Jan. 1631. A codicil to the last will of John Griffith, Esq. of Bloxham, co. Oxford, formerly secretary to the late Earl of Northampton, Keeper of the Privy Seal to James the First. It revokes two conditional legacies of 100l. to each of his nephews George Griffith and John Griffith, clerks, as they have each obtained an ecclesiastical benefice worth more than 40l. a year; and divides the money, thus recalled, amongst three of the testator's neices.

(No. 858.) 23 May 1631. Memorandum of the settlement made by Sir Henry Marten, Knt., (Dean of the Arches), of certain " differences in poynt of jurisdiction " that have fallen out betweene the Lord Bishop of " Bangor and his Chauncellor." Signed Lewes Bangor.

**Miss C.
Griffith.**

(No. A. 802.) The names of those that are appointed to preach in Lent, anno Dom. 1633. Dr. Hackett's name appears in this list.

(No. 739.) 13 Dec. 1633. Paper endorsed "His " Majesties Order for Civilians to bee Masters of Re- " quest and Masters of Chancery," being a copy of the memorandum entered on the Council Book, at White- hall, on the above-named day, of the King's order that to encourage "the breedinge up of able and sufficient " professors of the Civill and Cannon Lawes .. all " places that shall become vacant of Masters of Requests " to his Maiesty, and likewise eight of the ealeven " places of the Maisters of the Chauncery shall be " supplied with men of those professions of the Civill " and Cannon Lawes." The paper gives the names of the members present at the meeting of the council.

(No. 809.) 7 March 1634. Note (signed E. Nicholas) addressed to Sir Henry Martin, Judge of the Admiralty, requesting the judge to certify the Commissioners of the Admiralty whether there be on the record of the Admiralty any article to this effect :—" That noe maner " of persons otherwise then such as doe continually " through the yeare occupy fishing, and doe solely im- " ploy themselfes and servants to the same, or naviga- " cion, and noe other trade, or have ben bounde " apprentise to shippemasters and fishermen shall " occupie or vse any maner of fishinge crafte." The judge is further requested to state "whether he conceave " yt fitt that the same shold be putt in execusioun by " vice Admiralles."

(No. 779.) List of the preachers that are appointed for Lent, 1634.

(No. A. 796.) 11 Dec. 1637. Warrant, dated at White- hall, and signed Fran. Windebank, to all mayors, sheriffs, post-masters and others. To furnish two good and able posthorses, as occasion may require, to Dr. William Griffith, one of the masters in Chancery, who is repair- ing to St. Asaph on the King's service.

(No. A. 801.) List of the Lent preachers at court for 1635–1636.

(No. 743.) 1 May 1638. The list of the servants entertained by the Prince. The roll of the servitors in the prince's household (beginning with the Earle of Newcastle, sole gentleman of the prince's bedchamber and master of his horse, and closing with the names of the yeomen of the robes, Mr. Thelwall and Mr. Sun- comb) mentions only the principal retainers, who as gentle serving men, were rated above the "many others " below stayres."

(No. 765.) 16 Dec. 1638. Copy of order in council for completing and increasing the number of horse in every county; directing "that euerye person haueinge " lande of inheritance of the cleare yearlye value of " two, or three hundred pounds per annum within the " countye, or other estate equivalent therevnto should " be chargeable with an horse, viz., two hundred pounds " per annum, with a light horse, and three hundred " pounds per annum with a launce, at the discretion of " the Lord Lieutenant of the countye."

(No. A. 799.) List of Lent preachers for 1638 and 1639.

(No. A. 832.) Copy of "the humble petition of John " the most unfortunate Bishopp of Lincolne" to the King. Imploring pity of the King's "grace and good- " nesse," which are "the liveliest representation here " on earth of those attributes of God above," and further time for the preparation of his defence against ten distinct charges; "unless," the petition ends, "your " Majestie be grationalie pleased to take such other " satisfaction from your petitioner, as to change his im- " prisonment in the Tower dureing pleasure to a per- " petuall imprisonment of all faculties of his soule and " bodie to doe your majesties commaunds."

(No. 87.) Oct. 1639. Latin letter, beginning with " Raro alias pertinaciori studio versa falsis rumor per- " miscuit: jam comperta, aut pro compertis apud pru- " dentes habita, sic fere narrantur." Giving an account of Van Tromp's victories over the Spanish fleets off the Downs, on the tenth inst., and two following days. The writer ends with these words, " Hunc exitum " habuit classis Hispanica, capta, exusta, depressa, " sparsa." No date, signature, or direction to the epistle.

(No. 731.) —— 1640. A list of the King's and Princes chaplaines in ordinary, as they were in 1640.

(No. A. 751.) —— 1640. Report of proceedings in the House of Commons, when John Earl of Bristol appeared within the bar of the House, to reply to a charge of "delivering a message to his Maty from " Sir Richard Temple, tending to the dishonour of his " house, and breach of priviledge in particular as to

" Sir Richard Temple," together with a full report of the earl's speech in exculpation of Sir Richard Temple, and in explanation of his recent conversation with the King.

(No. 745.) The Duke of Lenox his Speech at the Councell Table diswading the King's Majestie from wageingo warre with the Scotts. No date.

(No. A. 827.) A poem in defence of the new adorning of Christ Church in Oxford, made by Mr. West, a student of the Colledge thereunto pertaining. No date.

(No. A. 820.) 20 Sept. 1642. Copy of Charles the First's warrant to the Chancellor, to make letters patent under the Great Seal, granting the place and office of one of the King's "learned counsel extraordinary" to Sir Wil- liam Ryves, Knight, formerly the King's Attorney- General for Ireland, "and nowe one of the judges of" the King's "court of cheife place theire," who," haueinge " lost all his fortunes in that kingdome," is about to re- turn to practice at the bar. In connexion with Sir Wil- liam Ryve's commission of K. C., may be noticed No, A. 819, the indenture, 3 Jan. 1643, by which he conveyed to his son, Sir John Ryves, all his lands and tenements, including the town of Corran, in the county of Cather- logh.

(No. A. 794.) 6 May 1641. Writ for the strict stopping of all the ports of England, in obedience to the order of the Lords spiritual and temporal to that effect; and also, in compliance with same order, for the arrest of Henry Percie and Henry Jermin, Esqs., Sir John Suckling, William Davenant, and Captain Billingsley, and their " safe conduct into the howse." Dated from Yorke Howse. Signed, Northumberland.

(No. A. 822.) 1641. Verses on Lord Strafford's Fall, entitled "My Lord Lieutenant of Ireland his Farewell." A poem of nine stanzas.

1.

Goe emptie ioyes
With all your noyse,
And leaue me here alone,
In sweet sad silence to bemoane
Your vaine and fleet delight :
Whose danger none can see aright,
Whilst your false splendor dims his sight.

2.

Goe and insnare
With your trimme ware
Some other easie wight ;
And cheat him with your flattering spight :
Raine on his head a shower
Of honour, favour, wealth and power,
Then snatch it from him in an houre.

3.

Fill his bigge minde
With gallant wind
Of insolent applause ;
Let him not feare ill-curbing lawes,
Nor King nor people's frowne,
But dreame on something like a crowne,
And climeing toward it tumble downe.

* * * * *

9.

Now tis too late
To imitate
Those lights whose pallidnesse
Argues not inward guiltinesse ;
Their course one way is bent,
The reason is, theres no dissent
In Heaven's high court of Parliament.

(No. A. 831.) 12 May 1644. A copy of "The Speech " of Thomas earle of Strafford, intended to bee spoken " on the scaffold the day hee was beheaded (12 May " 1641); but being interrupted hee delivered it to his " brother, Sr George Wentworth : from whose originall " coppy vnder the earl's owne hand, this is word for " word transcribed."

(No. 736.) Nov. 1641. The Service against the Rebells at Lisnegarvy in Nov. 1641, wherein Sir Arthur Tyring- ham commanded. A narrative of the circumstances under which the garrison of Lisnegarvy, co. Antrim, under the command of Sir Arthur Tyringham (with 500 foot, Lord Conway's troop of horse, and part of Lord Grandison's troop, and some three or four score men upon "small nagges with some shott amongst,") repulsed the rebels under Sir Phelim O'Neale and Sir Con Magenis, and drove them back from Lisnegarvy, on the occasion of their assault upon that town, on Sunday

**Miss C.
Griffith.**

Nov. 28. The account gives a vivid picture of the affair, and the subsequent attitude of the two forces. The writer estimates the strength of the rebels before the attack at 4,000, and their loss at 300 men, left dead in the streets and backsides of the town, and many wounded.

(No. 47.) Two sets of satirical verses. 1. A copy of one of the several attacks which Sir John Suckling brought upon himself by his famous gift of a troop of horse to Charles the First, *beginning*—

I tell thee, Jack, th' aat given the king
So rare a present, &c.

And *ending*—

Since under Mars thou wert not borne
To Venus glide and thinke no scorne
Let it be my aduise,
Leaue warre and thankful be to fate
Recouered hath thy lost estate
By carding and by dice.

Sir John Suckling's Answere, *beginning*—

I'le tell thee, Fool, who ere thou be
That made a fine sing-song of mee,
Thou art a very sott
Thy very lines doe thee betray,
Thy barren witt makes all men say
'Twas some rebellious Scott.

(No. 732.) Oct. 1642. A Declaracion of the Battaile late fought between Keynton and Edghill by his Majesties Army, and that of the Rebells. Together with other successes of his Majesties army happening since.

(No. 45.) Verses against the Presbytery and Parliament, *beginning*—

The wisest king did wonder when he spied
The nobles march on foote, the vassalls ride;
His Maⁱᵉ may wonder now to see
Some that would needs be kings as well as he,
A sad presage of danger to the land
When Lower striue to gett thuppor hand,
When prince and peares to peasants must obey
When laymen must their teachers teach the way.

(No. 46.) Copy of a royalist poem ("as with great ap-"plause it was presented to the king in his most just "arms to suppresse the rebellious practises in the king-"dome of Scotland,") *beginning*—

But you who whiles you would to heaven aspire
See heaven torment and sett the world on fire
Bould sonnes of tumult, that so long assay
To rule the sunne vntill you loose the day
What rage enflames you that see deepe yee wound
Your nations honor and profane her ground.

(No. 741.) 12 June 1643. The Names of those Parliament Men and Diuines, which make up the Assembly at Westminster for the Reformation of the Church of England in Doctrine and Discipline, convoaked and entitled by ordinance, 12 Junii, 1643.

(No. 718.) Satirical verses on the Westminster Assembly of Divines, entitled "The New Assembly."

(No. 760.) 30 Sept. 1644. Charles the First's proclamation, "declaringe his majestyes resolution for settinge "a speedy peace by a good accommodation, and invita-"tion to all his majestyes lovinge subjects to ioyne "together for assistance therin." This proclamation was printed by the King's printers, Robert Barker and John Hill, at Bristol, 1644.

(No. 766.) Proposicions offered to the consideracion of the Honorable Houses of Parliament. Nine satirical proposals for the amendment of usages observed at "the "tyme of good tidinges which the kings men commonly "call Christmas." The ninth and last of these proposals urges that, having sequestrated for the public use the revenues of the bishops, cathedrals, and many lay-landlords, the Parliament would do well "to sequester "all new yeares guiftes, as capons, turkys, hens, geese, "and such things as will live, for the use of the king "and parliament."

(No. 737.) Paper having on the one side a copy of "The Officers and Souldiers of Sᵗ Jhoᵒ Fairfax his "Army Their demands" (no date), and on the other side a memorandum of "A petition exhibited (21 April, "1647, being Wednesday in Easter Weeke) to his "Majestie by an Officer in the name of the army," praying the King to commit himself to the army, "who "would restore him to his former honor," with His Majesty's reply to the petitioner.

(No. C. 258.) 25 September 1660. Letter from Dr. William Griffith (Chancellor of St. Asaph and Bangor), Doctors Commons, London, to his cousin John Griffith, Esq., of Carreglwyd. After touching on an affair of business, the writer says, "The news that is, is new and joy-"full: just now I am retired to my chamber from seeing "the noble Princes, the Princes Royall of Orreng, landing

"att White Hall with his Maiety and the Duke of York, "which went to meet her to Graues end. Att her pass-"ing the tower there was aboue a hundred ordinances "shott. All thinges are well and quiet here. The army "is every day disbanding."

(No. A. 713.) Temp. Car. II. Curious letter to Mr. John Rowlandes, written by Edward Lloyd, one of the grooms of the Privy Chamber to Charles II., giving directions for the suitable interment in Westminster Abbey of Mr. Moris Wynn, also a groom of the same chamber, "For "though," says the writer, "he often sayd he desired a "private decent funeral and no rings vnlesse to his "brethren, yet for the respⁱᵉᵗ I had for him, and that "he may be interred according as he lived with creditt, "I desire it may be handsomely carry'd on, that I hope "those who were his friends att Whitehall, and our "countreymen in town who were acquainted with him "may be invited to the funeral, and hauo rings, of such "value as are usually given on the like occasion, only "our brethren the gromes ought to have 20s. rings or "thereabouts, and my Lord of Rochester." The writer has no doubt that "the Lord of Rochester will give leave "that he may be interred in the Abby as his desire was," and gives directions for bringing together a proper train of coaches for the procession. "I think," he says, "it is "gloves that is usually given to coachmen."

(No. 951 to No. 972.) Twenty-one neatly written paper of pedigrees, and extracts from records and muniments of various kinds, illustrative of the family of Talbot.

(No. A. 80.) 3 Oct. 1688, Badminton. "Having had "the King's grace by his gracious letter under his Privy "Signett and Signe Manuall to giue deputations to as "many of those gentlemen whose commissions I had by "his order called in, as I should judge ready & fitt to "serue him againe in that employment. Looking upon "you to bee one of that number, I send you this, to lett "you know yow are restored, and desire you will act by "the commission you formerly had, (the supersedeas to "which I hereby supersede), and which I doubt not you "will make use of for his Majesties service. And so "bidding you heartily fare well I remain.—Your Loving "Friend—Beaufort."—To John Griffith esq., Anglesey.

(No. A. 814.) A list of "The names of the persons that "voted for a Standing Armie." No date.

(No. A. 152.) Copy of "The Answere" of Newcastle-on-Tyne, "to the suppositions wherevpon the intended "act is grounded." No date.

(No. 729.) 3 Jan. 1705. Letter from Mr. Hugh Wynne, at London, to William Griffith, Esq., at Carreglwyd. Gossip about Saccheverell's last Sunday's sermon before the University of Oxford, and the questionable character of the Rev. Mr. D'Assigny who has established himself as a schoolmaster at Conway. "The Lord Keeper," the writer observes, "hath (to his great honour) refused all "presents usually made to Lord Keepers upon New "Year's Day, and will advise with the Archbishop about "the disposall of all Church Preferments in his gift."

(No. B. 128.) 28 Aug. 1706. Certificate on illuminated vellum, and under the public seal of the Bermuda *alias* Somer Islands, and with the signatures of the Lieutenant Governor [Benjamin Bennett, Esq.,] and the gentlemen of the Council and General Assembly of the said islands, attached thereto) that the Reverend and Worthy Thomas Holland, clk, sometime rector of the town and parish of St. George's, has during his residence in the said islands won the sincere respect of their inhabitants, who testify their sense of his merit by this document on the eve of his departure for England.

(No. 906.) 23 Sept. 1706. Letter commendatory, under the public seal of "the island of Bermuda in America," given by His Excellency Benjamin Bennett, Esq., to the Reverend Thomas Holland, on the departure of that gentleman with his wife and family from the said colony; to be exhibited by the bearer to any enemy into whose hands the vessel, in which the clergyman is about to return to Europe, may chance to fall. The letter declares that Governor Bennett has distinguished himself by humanity to prisoners, subjects of the king of France, brought into his island.

(No. A. 812.) A.D. 1753. Paper with this heading, "Copy of what Dr. Cameron intended to have de-"livered to the Scherif of Middlesex at the place of "execution and which he left in the hands of his wife "for the purpose writ by himself on different slips of "paper."

(No. 264.) 16 June 1786. Letter from John Berry, glasier, at Hornham near Salisbury, to John Lloyd, Esq., Conduit Street, Hanover Square, London.—"Sir, "This day I have sent you a Box full of old Staind and "Painted Glass as you desired me to due wich I hope it "will sute your Purpose it his the best that I can get at

" Present. But I expet to Beatt to Peccais a great deale
" verey sune as it his of now use to we and we Due it for the
" lead if you want Eney more of tae same sorts you may
" have what thear his, if it will Pay for Taking out, as it his
" a Deal of Trublo to what Beating it to Peceais his you
" will send me a line as sune as Posobl for we are gosin to
" move oro glasing shop to a Nother Plase and thin we to
" savo a greatt Doalo moro of the liko sort wich I ham
" your most Om^ble Servnt John Berry."—This letter is
endorsed "Berry ye Glazier about beating the fine
" painted Glass Window at Sarum to piéces to save the
" Load !!!"

II.

2. Welsh writings, i.e., documents illustrative of
social life and public affairs in North Wales (and more
especially in the county of Anglesey in the seventeenth
century).

(No. A. 194.) 1347-8. Extract from the account of
Richard earle of Arundell, sheriff of co. Caernarvon, of
all the issues of his bailiwick from Michaelmas of the
20th to Michaelmas of the 21st year of Edward III.

No. 810.) A.D. 1353. The Extent of commote of
Menay, co. Anglesey, by John de Delues, Lieutenant of
the Earl of Arundel, Justice of North Wales, and steward
of the said commote.

(No. B. 19.) 6 July 1454. Conveyance of lands and
tenements in a certain Wolo, called Wele Hoell, in
the township of Skoviok, in the comote of Menay, co.
Anglesey, in consideration of a sum of money, from
Hoell ap Jeunr ap Dauid, freeholder of the King's township of Skoviok, to Ithell ap Hoell &c. the freeholder of
the King's township of Berw Issa, of the same comote
and county.

(No. 107.) The vigil of Saint Thomas, St. Judea, 1455.
Receipt for xiii li., paid at Beaumaris by Syr Jones ap
Morys, rector of the church of St. Hilary, co. Anglesey,
to David ap Madoch ap David ap Hoelle and Res ap
Madoch ap David ap Hoelle; the said sum having been
due to the recipients thereof for lands and tenements,
" de Trefgo and Gllenhounok " in the hundred of Tal-
lebolion, co. Anglesey.

(No. C. 89.) ——— 1503. Rentale comot. de Menay
factum anno regni Henrici Septimi decimo octavo.

10th Dec. ——— 11. Hen. (.) Writ to John Griffith,
Esq., late sheriff of co. Anglesey, directing him to
deliver all writs, records, &c., pertaining to the shrievalty
and in his keeping, to John Owen of Presadfed, of the
same co., his successor in the said office.

(No. B. 120.) 20 Feb. 1522. Release and quitclaim by
John Owen, chaplain, son and heir of Owin ap Ethell, of
Merrowe, co. Anglesey, in Northwales, for himself and
his heirs for ever, to Edward Holand, esq., his heirs
and assigns, in respect of all those messuages, houses,
lands, meadows, &c., in Berrow yssa, Berrow Ucha,
Tree Byrthe, Tree Varthyn, Bodlow, Tree Yvan, Ras-
colyn, and elsewhere, in co. Anglesey and Caernarvon
which the said Owen Holand now holds and occupies, and
which descended to the said John Owen by the death
of his said father, or of his brother Hugh Owen.

(No. A. 198.) 18 Hen. VII. A rental of the King's
bands in the hundred of Menay. Imperfect.

(No. B. 265.) 22 Dec. 1537. Release and quit-claim
(in consideration of fifty marks sterling paid to him by
Griffith Richard, esq., and Ethelreda his wife, late the
wife of Owen Holand deceased, and Edward Holland,
son and heir of the said Owen, in accordance with a
decree of John Pakyngton, esq., the king's justice of
North Wales, in addition to eighty pounds paid to him
by the said Owen Holland in his life), executed by John
Owen, clerk, son and heir of Owen ap Ethel, late of
Berowe, co. Anglesey, in favour of the said Griffith
Richard, and Ethelreda his wife, and Edward Holond,
and the heirs and assigns of the said Edward, in respect
to all the said John's title and right to the houses, lands,
&c., &c., in Berrowyssa, Berowe Ucha, Tree Byerth,
Tree Varthen, Tree Ivan, Porthamell, Gwydryn and
Llangeven, and elsewhere in cos. Anglesey, Caernarvon,
and Merioneth, lately belonging to the said Owen ap
Etholl, or the aforesaid John Owen, or either of them.

(No. A. 768.) 28 Hen. VIII. The bill of costes in
Wales. A°. H. VIII. xxix°. At the Feest of Saincte
Kenelme the King, the yere of oure souerayne abouesayd. A bill of costs (in a suit the nature of which
does not appear); affording some testimony as to
legal and official fees in Wales, temp. Hen. VIII.
For instance:—It' pro feod marescall' et proclaim cur',
vd.; It' pro fœdiis quatuor s'uient ad legem, xiii s. iiii d.;
It' pra fœdiis duorᶜ attorn' iiis. iiiid. It' pro feodo
Justic' s'edm' vsū prē vd. At the foot of the sheet
appears the signature of John Pakyngton.. Other

chargos written in English, with the same signature,
appear on the back side of the sheet: for instance,—It'
for the knowlogyng of a Fyne before the Justes vis. viiid.;
It' for his clerkes fees iis.; It' for tho knowlegyng of a
release to be inrolled vis. viiid.

(No. 69.) 26 of July, 1560. Lease to farm, in consideration of a certain sum of money, paid before the
sealing of the lease, by William Hampton, of the county
of Anglesey, gentleman, and Elyn Graff', his wife, to
John ap Jennr of the same county, of " too tenementes'
" of landes with all their appurtenances commonly
".called Tethyn, &c., &c.," for eight years from next
feast of All Saints, at a yearly rent of "xs. of lefall
" money of England at the feastes of thapostell Phelippe
" and Jacobbe, and all Seyntos, by too equall porciounes,
" wyth too gese as presentes at christmas, and too
" capons at Ester, and one day of reapinge in harvest
" time, or iiid. in money yerely duringo the scyd
" terme."

(No. B. 287.) 1 of July 1565. Lease to farm, for 25
years, of the township of Eskiviock, with lands and
tenements there, and also in Heredrevayke, in the
hundred of Mency, co. Anglesey, to Sir Nicholas
Bagnall, Knt.; with liberty to dig and sell coal.

(No. B. 115.) 8th of Oct., 11 Eliz. Exemplification of
proceedings in the suit of William ap David ap Rees
alias Conwey v. Griffin ap Hughe ap Res, heard and
decided in the court of great session of the county of
Anglesey, held at Beaumaris (Bellum Mariscum), before
Reginald Corbett, justice of the said court, in the fifth
year of Queen Elizabeth; whereby the said plaintiff recovered from the said defendant possession of five messuages, one hundred acres of arable land, forty acres of
meadow, and forty acres of pasture with their appurtenances in Carnethor, Trevadock, Dyronwy, and Bod-
nowlwyn.

(No. A. 540.) 23 May 1572. Schedule of the several
houses and lands held by Robert Power, by virtue of
letters patent of the above date, in the township of Aber-
law, in the hundred of Talabolion, co. Anglesey, parcel
of the principality of North Wales.

(No. B. 204.) 20 of Sept. 1583. Indenture of lease
for fifteen years, granted (in consideration of thirty-one
pounds, thirteen shillings and fourpence, " paid in the
name of a fyne,") by Hugh Lewes (attorney of Sir
Nicholas Bagenalle of the Nowry, Knt., Hor Majesty's
farmer of her township of Eskivioge) of the tenement
of lands, &c., called Tuthin-bulche-gwyne in the said
township, at a yearly rent of vs. iiid. payable in equal
portions at Michaelmas and the feast of Sts. Philip and
James, and also of " six capones or sixpence in money
" price of euery one of the same capones," payable in
equal portions at the feasts of Christmas and Easter,
" with one dayes worke in plowinge, one day rapinge,
" and one daye mowinge yerly during the said terme,
" or els xiid. for plowinge vid. for repping and vid. for
" carringe, or els to carry so many peckes of coales as he
" hath bene accustomed to do from the said townshippe
" to the sea syd yerly during the said term."

6th of April 1586. Writ to the sheriff, co. Anglesey,
directing him to make a return of the rents, pertaining to
the crown, in the hundred of Mensi. With the duplicate
of his return attached to the said writ.

(No. C. 200.) 20 July 1587. Lease to farm (in consideration of fyve shillinges paid before the sealing of
the lease) by Owen Holland, of Berw Issaph, co. Anglesey,
Esq., and Elizabeth, his wife, to John ap Jenner ap Gruf
and his assigns, for eighteen years from Michaelmas
next to come, of the house and tenement, known by the
name of y Kay helig and kay yr geilwad, with all the
lands, &c., pertaining thereto, at a yearly rent of vis. viiid.
(paid in equal portions at the " feastes of thannunciacioun
" of oure ladie the virgyn and Saincte Michaell the Arch-
" angell "), and of " foure good capons yerelye, that is to
" saye tow at either of the saide tow feastes, together
" with the rente, in the name of presentes, and one dayes
" worke in harrowinge and one dayes worke in reapinge
" and one dayes worke in careingo of corne in tho
" harvest yerely, duringe tho seide terme, in the name
" of seruice."

(No. B. 106.) 9 March 1588. Writ to the sheriff
of Anglesey requiring him to make inquisition by the
sworn evidence of honest and discreet men, as to a
certain right of way leading from a tenement in tho
occupation of Thomas Bulkeley, Esq. in the township of
Berrowe, to a highway. The return of the sheriff's
inquisition is attached to this writ.

(No. A. 998.) 18th of March 1593. Lease to farm, by
Owen Holland, of Berw Issaphe, co. Anglesey, Esq., to
Richard Gruff, of Kefn y Vyrwen in the same county, and
Eleanor his wife, for the whole term of the said Eleanors'

life, of a certain tenoment and lands in Kefn y Vyrwen aforesaid, at a yearly rent " of the somme of thryttye " and three shillings and fourepence of currant money " of England at the feastes of Phillippe and Jacobe " thappostells and All Saintes by equal porciouns, for " all maner of rentes presentes and services, due vnto the " said Owen Holland or his heires and assiynes out of " the same."
(No. B. 303.) Aug. (   ), 1596. Indenture of agreement between Owen Holland, of Berrowe, co. Anglesey, Esq. of the one part, and Griffith Bagnall, second son of Sir Henry Bagnall, Knt., of the other part ; whereby the said Owen transfers to the said Griffith, all his lease to farm for thirty years of crown lands in Eskiviock, in the hundred of Meney, co. Anglesey, with the right to raise and sell coals therein, during the said term ; in consideration of the sum of 150l. to be paid to the said Owen by Sir Henry Bagnall, Knt., and of the said Sir Henry's undertaking to assure the fee simple of the residue of the township of Eskiviock to the said Owen and his heirs. The agreement reserves to Owen Holland a moiety of the coals, coal mines, and waste grounds affected thereby. The recitals of the instrument are interesting, viz. :—I. Lease to farm for forty years, granted by Hen. VIII., in the 23rd year of his reign to William Sackvil, one of the grooms of the King's chamber, of the township of Eskiviok, and of all lands and tenements, &c. there pertaining to the crown, with licence to take and sell coals therein, at a yearly rent of vii li. viii s. viii d. to be paid into the King's exchequer at Carnarvon ; the said farm and lands to be held and enjoyed by the grantee as fully and completely as they were held and enjoyed by " Llwelyn ap Rees ap Tudder ap Llwelyn, a native of the towneshippe " aforesaid.—II. Lease to farm of the premises, 1 July 7 Eliz., from the crown to Sir Nicholas Bagnall, knight, with liberty to dig and soll coals, for twenty-five years from, the Michaelmas of 1571, or from any earlier time at which Sir Nicholas's interest therein should terminate, at the yearly rent of vii li. viii s. viii d. to be paid into the receipt of the exchequer at Westminster, or to other authorised receivers. III. Lease to farm of the premises, 16 Dec. 18 Eliz., from the crown to Henry Harvy, Esq., one of Her Majesty's "gentlemen penciouners," for thirty years from Michaelmas, 1595, at the same rent, with " licenso " to take and sell the sea-coales within the towneshippe " aforesaid." IV. The deed, 20 Feb., 18 Eliz., whereby the said Henry Harvye conveyed his interest in the premises to Owen Holland aforesaid.
(No. B. 79.) 10 August 1596. Indenture of agreement between Sir Henry Bagnall, Knt., of the one part, and Owen Holland, Esq., of Berowe, co. Anglesey, of the other part, for the definition of interests and rights, affected by, but insufficiently considered in, a previous agreement, whereby on 8 August 38 Eliz., the said Owen Holland " granted and assigned to Griffith Bagnall " second son of Sir Henry Bagnall, diuerse landes and " tenementes with thappurtenances within the towne- " shippe of Eskyviogo in the countie of Anglesey, " amounting to about the value of moytie or an half of " the said towneshippe of Eskyvioge for the tearme of " thirtie years."
(No. B. 293.) 8 Aug. 1596. Indenture of an assignment by Sir Henry Bagnall, Knt. to Owen Holland, of Berrowe, co. Anglesey, Esq., and his heirs, of an assignment of a moiety of the township of Eskyviog, with right to raise and sell coal there, held by the said Sir Henry Bagnall, his heirs and assigns, in fee farm for ever under grants from the crown. The deed recites the already mentioned grants to Sir William Sackevile, Sir Nicholas Bagnall, and Henry Harvey.
(No. B. 297.) Last day of February 1598. Indenture of a lease for twenty-one years, granted by Owen Hollande of Berowe, co. Anglesey, to Hugh ap Robert ap John of Roskolin, in the same county, of a tenement of lands with houses and buildings thereon in the said parish, in consideration of five marks to be paid to the said Owen or his assigns at or before next Michaelmas ; at a yearly rent of five shillings, to be paid in equal portions at every feast of Philip and James, and every Michaelmas, and also of "four sufficient capons" to be delivered at every feast of Christmas.
(No. 612.) Paper roll (much moth-eaten). Tallabollion, Anno Domini 1602. August yᵉ first. A true copie of the muster booke of Thomas Glynne, Esquire, Captaine of the trayned souldiours of the Comot of Tallabollion, in the countey of Anglesey, as well of the olde as of the newe cessoment, With certaine marginall notes signifinge all kinds of defects, as by rules shall be expressed in the end of the booke. Entries on the outer leave of this roll give the number of the musters in the

years 1599, 1600, 1601, 1602, 1603, "In anno, 1599, " there was 5 trayninge musters not vpon the Sundayes."
(No. 190.) 30 July, 1605. A True Coppie of a Rentrowle of his Maᵗⁱᵉ cheofe Rents within the jurisdiction of the Late Abbote of the late dissolved monasterie of St. Marie at Conwey, within the seuerall Townshipps of Vilheldress, Cornwy Lys, Treveibion, Madlog, and Leunzmynyth, co. Anglesey.
(No. B. 309.) 4th of Feb. 1607. Special pardon, (in consideration of xls. paid to the King's farm,) by virtue of letters patent of Elizabeth the late queen, to Owen Holland, of the alienation, without license from the said queen, whereby the said Owen, 8 Aug. 38 Eliz., acquired from Henry Bagnall, Knt., the half of the township of Skeyviocke, which is held in capite of the crown. With further grant to the said Owen and his heirs for ever of the said half of the said township, to be held by the ancient and usual services.—The great seal, attached to this charter, is perfect.
(No. 753.) 12 Feb. 1608. Copy of the commission, under the great seal, to John Herbert, Knt., authorising and requiring him to survey and value the timber, trees and small wood, living or dead, on the King"s lands in co. Carnarvon ; and to return the particulars of the survey and estimate to the barons of the Exchequer at or before the octaves of Michaelmas next to come.
(No. C. 111.) 10 June 1608. Indenture of agreement between Catherine Moyle of Llanvaythly, co. Anglesey, "gentlewoman widow and late wife of John Winne " Owen of Llanvaythly aforesaid, gentleman," of the one part, and John Griffith, of London, Esq., " secre- " tarie to the right honorable the Earle of North- " ampton," of the other part ; whereby the said Catherine Moyle conveys to the said John Griffith, certain arable lands and waste in the town of Clegroke, alias Cleyrog, of the commotte of Tallabollion. co. Anglesey, being part of the principality of North Wales, to have and hold the same for three score years from Michaelmas 1621, under and in accordance with the letters patent whereby Queen Elizabeth, on 2 March in the 40th year of her reign, granted the premises, for the said term, to Nicholas Morgan and Thomas Horne, pages of her chamber. The instrument concludes with the mark (for signature) of Catherine Moyle.
(No. 90.) 13 June 1608. Appointment (made by Sir John Herbert, knight, one of the King's secretaries and Privy Council, by virtue of a special commission directed to him under the seal of the Court of Exchequer, and dated 15 February last past) of Sir John Wynne, Knt., Sir Wiliam Glynne, Knt., John Bodvel, Esq., William Glynne, Esq., Robert Gruffyth, gent., and Hugh Owen, gent., to survey and value the King's timber, trees and coppices, in the county of Caernarvon, as well all " trees which are tymber, as other great trees " which are no tymber, and also all dead and decayed " trees and all singular his majestics coppices," in his " forests cheses parkes and landes, as well in his majesty " owne handes and possessions as in the possession " of his farmers and tenants in the said county; with instructions to certify to the said Sir John Herbert, Knt., the survey, number, marks, and valuation of the said timber, trees, &c. at or before 1 October, next to come, so that the same may be certified into the Court of Exchequer in accordance with the requirements of the aforesaid commission.
(No. 750.) The humble petition of Robert Griffith, gentleman, to Robert earle of Salisbury, lord-highe Treasurer of England. Praying for payment for work done by the petitioner, during the previous summer, at the order of Mr. Secretary Herbert, in surveying and valuing His Majesty's woods in Merioneth and Carnarvon. No date.
(No. B. 275.) Three writs stitched together. 1. Commission (10 Nov. 6 Jac. I.) for Thomas Holland, Esq., to be high-sheriff of Anglesey, during pleasure. 2. Mandate (10 Nov. 6 Jac. I.) to the King's lieges in Anglesey to aid and assist the said Thomas Holland, Esq., in all matters pertaining to his shrievalty of the said county. 3. Writ to Thomas Holland, Esq. (10 Nov. 7 Jac. I.) on the appointment, during pleasure, of his successor in the said office of sheriff of Anglesey, directing him to deliver to William Owen, Esq., the newly appointed sheriff, all rolls, writs, and memoranda pertaining to the office.
(No. 436.) 1610. The petition of John Roberts, of co. Anglesey, to the King's Chief Justices of the Great Sessions of Anglesey, charging Henry Lloyd, Esq., with the abduction of his wife, and with a design to marry his (the said Lloyd's) daughter to the petitioner's son and heir. Also the answer of Henry Lloyd, who tra-

verses all the petitioner's assertions with direct counter-statements.

(No. B. 140.) 6 July 1611. Fine levied in the court of Great Session, co. Anglesey, at Beaumaris, before Richard Barker, Esq., the King's Justice of the said court, between Robert Holland, plaintiff, and William Hampton, deforciant, in respect of a messuage, a cottage, and a garden, with appurtenances, in Beaumaris: whereby the said William, the deforciant, acknowledges the right of the said messuage, &c., to be in the said William, the plaintiff, and executes release and quitclaim in respect to his title thereto.

(No. C. 254.) 10 Sept. 1611. Lease to farm, for twenty-one years, (in consideration of vii li. vi s. viii d. paid before the sealing of the indenture) by Lewis Gruffith ap Llein of Tre Ednyved, co. Anglesey, yeoman, and Richard Lewis Gruffith of Caernether, son of the said Lewis, to Robert Gruffith of Nantwych, in the same county, of a messuage and tenement of lands in Caernether, at an annual rent of sixpence to be paid at every feast of All Saints in the said term, "for and in the " name of all maner of Rentes, presentes, dueties, and " services."

(No. B. 277.) 20 Aug. 1612. Indenture of agreement between Gruffith ap Rees ap David ap Rees of Soughtyn, co. Flint, gentleman, of the first part, Edward ap William ap Howel of Gwesany, in the same county, gentleman, of the second part, and Gruffith ap Edward ap William, of Gwesany aforesaid, gentleman and son and heir apparent of the said Edward; whereby (in consideration of a marriage to be had and solemnized between Gruffith ap Edward ap William, and Jane verch Gruffith, daughter of the afore-named Gruffith ap Rees, and also in consideration of "marriadge money herein-after " expressed") the said Edward ap William ap Howel conveys to Gruffith ap Edward ap William the tenement whereon the said Edward ap William ap Howel now dwelleth in Gwesany, co. Flint, in trust for the said Edward ap William for life, and then to the use of the said Gruffith ap Edward, for life, with remainder in tail to the issue of the said Gruffith ap Edward and Jane. After providing for numerous contingencies, the indenture sets forth the following stipulations and concessions:—"And the said Edward ap William for him and " his, &c., &c., doth counaunte and graunte to and " with the said Gruffith ap Edward and his, &c., &c., " that he the said Edward shall during his natural life " fynd, myntaine and keepe the said Gruffith ap Edward, " Jane his wief and such children as the sayd Gruffith " ap Edward and Jane shall lawfully beget between " them during the said terme with meat drinke howse-" roome fire candle beddinge washeinge wringing " apparelle and all othere necessaries befitting their " degrees and callinge (exoepte apparell only of the said " Jane daring the said term which the said Edward is " not to fynd), and the said Gruffith in consideracion " of the maintenaunce and fynding of hym and of hys " said wief and children duringe the saide terme is to " worke and labour as a labourer vnto the said Edward, " for him and at his commaundemente, and also the " said Jane to labour and worke when she is theire vnto " lawfully required by the said Edward or his wief " duringe the said terme."

(Note A. 173.) Last day of February 1614. Warrant to Thomas Holland, Esq., captain of the trained band of the hundred of Tindaethwy, co. Anglesey, to train his company and complete its efficiency.

(No. 920.) Letter from Richard Boulton to his friend, Thomas Holland, Esq., captaine of the trayned band within the hundred of Tindaethwy, Begging the captain to excuse the bearer, Daniel Morris, at the next muster day for failing to appear with the "calis complete " furnisht," to which he has been cessed, and with which he will, on the writer's guarantee, be provided by the muster-day after the next muster. No date.

(No. A. 197.) 21 June 1614. Copy of a decree in Chancery in the cause between Sir Edward Herbert, Knt., and others, plaintiffs, and Peter Gruff, Esq., defendant; touching the title to the manor of Penrhyn, and other manors and lands in North Wales. Decree for the plaintiffs.

(9th of March 1614.) Copy of the King's licence, given under his signet at Westminster, to the Bishop of Bangor, exempting him from attendance at the Parliament summoned for the fifth day of April, in consideration of the prelate's age and infirmity of body, which make it impossible for him to travel without danger to his health: on condition that the bishop sends his proxy in convenient time to some competent person, who may speak and vote for him in the said Parliament.

(No. 603.) October 1614. Tallabollion. Muster booke of the trained bands of the said hundred. Neatly written; and almost perfect.

(No. 642.) Paper Roll (much injured by moth) of 17 long slips, entitled, Tallabollion: The Muster Booke of ye same hundred made vpp in October, 1614. The book opens with the list of officers, viz. Hugh Owen, cheftaine; Hugh Bulkeley, lieutenant; John Griffith, auncient; John ap Hugh, Rowland Owen and Richard Griffith, serjeants; Robert Jonas, drommer. The record gives the names, degree, and various arms of every soldier of the force, the entire strength of which was 237 men, i.e., 8 officers, 88 "armemen" (10 gentlemen targetiers, 22 men furnished with corselets and pikes, 52 men with "unarmed pikes," 5 billmen), and 141 shottmen (59 musquetiers, 82 caliverers or small shottmon).

(No. 10.) 16 April 1615. Grant from James the First, for himself and his heirs, to John Griffith, his heirs and assigns, in perpetuity, of the fishery and liberty of fishing in Aber Alow alias Aberalaw, in and through the river and water called Anon Alow and Aberalaw, in the hundred of Tallabollion, co. Anglesea; subject to a yearly rent from the grantee, his heirs, and assigns to the crown of two shillings and four pence.

(No. 11.) 11 July 1616. Collections out of diuerse Recordes in the courte of augmentation concerning Caernether and Aberalaw, and other thinges in Anglisey. The notes of this collection relate to matters temp. Hen. V., VI., and VIII.

(No. 14.) 11 August 1616. A collection of the estate of those fiue welleys and hamlett of land in Aberallaw purchased of his matie. by John Griffith.

(No. 621.) Tallabolion, 25 Sept. 1616. A True Enrowlment of the Trained Band of Souldionros of the said hundred of Tallabolion, now vnder the Leadinge of Hugh Owen. Paper roll, much injured by moth.

(No. C. 322.) 18 Feb. 1617. Schedule of annuell rentes of Rice Robertes late deceased; with a schedule of debts due to the executors of the same Rice Robertes, whose rent-roll did not exceed xiiili. vs.

(No. C. 332.) 3 August 1618. Memorandum of the articles of "housholdstuffe implementes and vttisen-" siles," belonging to Hugh ap Robert, Owen ap Robert, and their sisters, "sould at Bodwine for the " somme of thirteene shillinges and fourpence;" with a schedule of other goods and live-stock sold at the house in Fretmell. This schedule mentions—

Two ould fetherbeddes, a blankett and a peece of a blankett, for xxxvs.

A coult, for xliiis. viiid.

Another coult, for iiiili. iiis. viiid.

A nagg, for xxxvis.

(No. A. 182.) 3 August 1619. Warrant from deputy-lieutenants co. Anglesey to the High Constables of the hundred of Tyndaethwy, to cause the petty constables of a certain parishes in the said hundred to apprehend certain underwritten persons, guilty of default in respect to cessment for arms for the service of the trained band, or guilty of absenting themselves unlawfully from the musters of the company; with further orders to put the delinquents of the first-named kind in prison until the arms charged upon them shall be furnished, and to keep the delinquents of second sort in gaol for ten days.

(No. A. 81.) Three discoloured and much worn sheets of paper, containing some of the articles of accusation against the bishop of Bangor, who is charged with celebrating the marriage of persons within the prohibited degrees; with extorting money from persons in his jurisdiction; with uttering "slanderous and " intollerable speaches" against men of station and honour; with "stopping burials and casting out seates " from the church of Bangor;" with "suffering the " cathedral church to fall into decay;" with being a " common striker of men and women;" with extorting exorbitant fees for letters of orders; with giving exemptions from his majesty's military service to "such " persons as are neither his menial servants nor have " any relation vnto him;" and with uttering "wicked " execrations." One of the accusations is that "in his " last convocation in 1624, in mense Novembris he did " extenuat theuctority of the judges of assize, calling " them justices or petty judges, and also calling the " gentry of the country generally his vyllaynes, more " particularly Sir William Williams, Barronett, by name, " and . . also he called the Dean of Bangor sturdy knave " at his chapter." Another article charges him with a violent assault on "the dean's wief of Bangor whom he " thumped in the brest, being great with chyld, inso-" much that she was in daunger of her lif, and like to

" myscarry," and also on Mrs. Hallowes, " whom he
" likewyse did beate." It does not appear by whom,
or for whose information these articles were drawn.
No date.

(No. A. 178.) 4 May 1621. Warrant (signed by deputy-
lieutenants, co. Anglesey) to Thomas Holland, Esq.,
captain of the trained band of Tindaithwy ; to muster
and train his company.

(No. A. 181.) 1 Aug. 1621. Warrant to Thomas
Holland, Esq., captain of the trained band of the
comote of Tindaithwye, to return to the undersigned
deputy-lieutenants, " an exacte liste and roule of the
" names of all the persons charged with armes, and also
" what armes euerie of them stand charged with, with
" theire seuerall defects, and the names of all the per-
" sons," trained in the band, and also of persons
insufficiently charged, or not at all charged, in the
comote, with armes.

(No. 795.) 29 Oct. 1621. An Iventorie of the goodes,
catelles and chatelles of Rowland Owen ap Hugh ap
Jenr, gentleman, deceased.

(No. B. 280.) 6 Nov. 1622, Jac. I. Commission for
Thomas Holland, Esq., to be sheriff of co. Anglesey,
during pleasure. A portion of the great seal remains
attached to this parchment.

(No. 884.) Manual of directions for the Christian to
observe in preparing himself for taking the sacrament
of the Lord's table ; with notes on matters pertaining
to religious discipline and practices. " In some
" churches," says the writer, " they have lanterns
" which they lett downe, that the people may light
" their candles, and afterwards they take or hoyse it vp
" againe. See Christ was lett downe as a lanterne to
" our feete and as a light to our steps, but now is
" ascended on high." No date.

(No. 628.) List of articles (24 in number), " to be
" inquired of for the hospitall and schoole of Ruthin,"
by the Commissioner appointed by the Lord Bishop of
Bangor to visit the said hospital and school. Together
with the answers to the said articles. No date.

(No. 799.) Jane Stoddart's account of moneys spent
for and at her masters funeral. Containing these items,
—To three strange men that tooke speciall paines in
bringing home the corps, 7s. 6d. ; For the children to
offer 11s. 6d. ; To two poore people that received the
almes ouer the corps, 2s. No date.

(No. A. 180.) 22 Nov. 1624. Warrant (signed by
Richard Bulkley, William Owen, and William Griffith,
deputy lieutenants, co. Anglesey) to Sir Thomas Holland,
Knt., captain of the trained foot-band, in the comote of
Tyndaethwy ; to muster and train his foot-band at some
convenient place within the comote, on the 3rd day of
next December, and to observe accompanying orders
for maintaining the efficiency of the company.

(No. A. 174.) 19 July 1625. A muster roll of the
trained bandemen of the hundred of Tindaethy.

(No. 610.) 17 Aug. 1625. Letter addressed by Richard
Bulkely, William Gryfflyth and Rowland Whyte to Sir
Thomas Holland, knighte, captain of the trained bands
of foot in the hundred of Tindaithwy, reflecting on
the defective equipment and discipline of the said force,
and requiring him in the king's name to take measures
for raising it to proper efficiency.

(No. A. 519.) 27 Nov. 1627. A note of some writeings
concernge my owne estate. The catalogue (in the handwriting of John Griffith, Lord Northampton's secretary)
opens with mention of " My Letters Patentes of Caerne-
" ther dat. 12 Martii, A°, 11 Jacobi, with the assign-
" ment from Mr Protherek and Mr Tobie Mathew."

(No. 879.) 17 Feb. 1628. A schedule endorsed by Mr.
John Griffith, " A brief note taken out of the letters
" patentes of the kinges majesties landes in Anglesey
" lately purchased by the Londoners."

(No. C. 302.) 13th of May 1629. The last will of Arthur
Williams, of Llanbadrick, co. Anglesey. A good specimen of the several wills of the same period in the
Carreglwd collection. The testator bequeaths " towards
" the reparacioun of the cathedral church of Bangor,
" xiid." " towards the reparacioun of the church of
" Llanbadricke, vs.," " to be deuided betweene the poore
" of the parish of Llanbadricke yerely during the term
" of a hundred and one yeares now next ensuing the
" sum of vis. viii.," out of the issues of certain
messuages ; to his " nephew Arthur ap Richard Williams
" one feather [bedd with the furniture and appurtenances
" thereto belonging," and to his niece Anne Williams
" one feather bedd with the furniture and appurte-
" naunces thereto belonging."

(No. C. 314.) 12th of Oct. The accountes of Thomas
Holland, esquier, one of the executours of the last will of
Mr. Daniel Bulkeley, of all such of the late debtes of the

said Daniel (appearinge in his debte bookes) as came to
the bandes of the said Thomas.

(No. 16.) 4 Aug. 1630.) A note of ye sevyrall demises
of ye fishing of ye ryuer of Alow, since the sixt yeare of
Henry ye eight. 1. Grant, during pleasure, from Hen.
VIII. in the sixth yeare of his reign, to John ap Rees
ap Howell, at the yearly rent of iiiid. 2. Grant, during
pleasure, by Hen. VIII., in the sixth year of his reign,
to John Trolam, at a yearly rent of iis. 3. Grant, for a
term of years, by the same king, in the fifteenth year of
his reign, to the said John Trolam, at a yearly rent of
iis. iiiid. 4. Grant, by lease, by Queen Elizabeth, in the
fourth year of her reign, to John Moyle, at the same
rent ; which lease continued till the fishery was granted
to John Griffith.

(No. 58.) Rough draft of John Griffith's petition in
the Court of the Exchequer, praying Henry Viscount
Maundevile, the Lord High Treasurer, Sir Fulke Grevile,
Knight, Chancellor of the Exchequer, Sir Lawrence
Tanfield Knight, the Lord Chief Baron, and the other
barons of the said court, to grant a writ of subpœna, to
be directed to John Lewis, Esq., David ap Owen, and
William ap Robert (who have invaded the orator's
fishery of Aberalaw); commanding them to appear in the
Court of Exchequer, to discover what grant or conveyance of right they, or any of them, have in the said
fishery, and to abide by their lordships' decision on the
matter in dispute.

(No. 723.) 5 Sept. 1630. Letter from the minister
and churchwardens of Amwegh to Dr. William Griffith,
chancelor of Bangor ; rendering an account of the manner in which they have distributed (in accordance with
the chancellor's direction), amongst the deserving poor
of the parish, the sum of fifty shillings, " being a com-
" mutation of a penance enjoyned by ' the chancellor '
" upon Richard Parrey, gent., of the said parish, for for-
" nication by him committed."

(No. 680.) Oct. 1631. Written order, for " Hugh ap
" Robert of Rythin, joiner, to make and set up in the
" Cathedrall Church of St. Asaph before Christmas next
" the particulars following :—1. A pulpit of wainscot of
" 4 ft. in height and breadth, with a desk on three sides
" and a botom of boards, upon four foot in height. 2.
" A seate in length 8 foote, in breadth 4 foot, wains-
" cotted behind in height 8 foote, before 4 foote, with a
" wainscott couering ouer all, supported with 2 fair
" turnd pillars, a chair in the middle of the seate and
" a faire deske before. 3. Seates about the church, 26
" yards, all with turn'd frames. 4. Of wainscott 12
" yards to bee sett behind the seates that shall be aboue
" the stepps that goe to the Communion Table ; and
" also behind the Communion board. The wainscott
" hee is to make for 2s. the yarde, and the rest for 20
" nobles, whereof he hath receaued 5 Oct. 1631, before-
" hand, 3 li." Underwritten is Hugh ap Robert's receipt
for " 3 li. more, 24 Dec. 1631."

(No. A. 770.) 14 Feb. 1634. Letter from Tho : Williams, a lawyer of Lincolnes Inne to his client, Sir
Thomas Holland, of Berowe, co. Anglesey, about matters
of legal business. " I will," says the writer, " meete
" you att Bridgenorth where the sizes are nowe kept the
" sixteenth of March, & my Lord Chiefe Baron rides
" that circuite nowe with Mr. Justice Jones . . . for
" counsell you have Mr. Sergeant Heath, Mr. Platt, Mr.
" Charles Johnes."

(No. 611.) 3 March 1634. Letter from Garter King-
at-Arms :—I understand that you doe challenge vnto
yoʳ selfe and give for yoʳ armes the coate of Holland Duke
of Exeter, wᶜʰ I suppose you would not doe but vpon
good ground, yet because I am ignorant, by what title
you assume the same, I desire you betwixt this and the
next terme to send me yoʳ claimo and dissent, that I
may accordingly be resolued, whether they doe of right
appertaine vnto you or not, of wᶜʰ I request you not to
faile for auoyding of yoʳ further trouble and charge.
Soe I rest your Louinge friend John Borough Garter
Principall King at Armes. From the office of Armes
next Doctors Commons in London 3 March 1634.

(No. C. 67.) 31 May 1634. Bill of Complaint in the
court of the council for the Marches of Wales, by
Thomas Williams, clk., against Sir Thomas Holland of
Berowe, and Hugh Williams, William Thomas, William
ap Evan ap Moris, of Eskiviog, Lewis Thomas of Caerwen, William Probert, of Caerwen, who have interrupted
the plaintiff in the exercise of his right of common of
pasture, and common of turbary in townships of Eskiviog and Tregarneth, co. Anglesey.

(No. C. 61.) Copy of the answer of the defendants to
the above bill of complaint. No date.

(No. C. 64.) 27 of June 1635. Letter of congratulation by a writer (whose name has been removed from

the moth-eaten sheet of paper), to Sir Thomas Holland of Berrowe, beginning with these words, "Dear Sir " Thomas, I am heartily glade to heare y⁰ your adver-" saries haue fayled there pourpose of troblinge you " nboute your vndowted coate of armes."
(No. C. 308.) 9th of March 1634. A true and perfecte Inventory of all such goodes, catells, chattells, and credit of Rees ap Mathewe, late of Llangeinwen, co. Anglesey, and in the diocese of Bangor, deceased, intestate, as remayne as yett unadministered by Elizabeth Griffith, his late wief and his administratrix.
(No. B. 292.) 25 November 1635. Certificate on illuminated vellum, under the signature and seal of John Borough, Knt., Garter Principall King of Armes, that Sir Thomas Holland of Berrow co. Anglesey (whose right to bear for his arms Azure a Lion Rampant Gardant between five flowers de Lice Argent, has been challenged on the ground that the said arms belong properly to the family of Holland sometime Duke of Exceter) has demonstrated his descent from Hockin alias Roger Holland, who lived temp. Edw. III., and has furthermore demonstrated that the said arms have been borne by divers gentlemen, his kinsmen, being descendants of the said Hockkin : In regard for which demonstrations, and also for the unquestionable gentility of Sir Thomas Holland (who, besides being dignified with knighthood, is a justice of the Peace and Deputy Lieutenant of his county), it is further certified that the said Principal King at Arms has declared the said Sir Thomas Holland and his heirs entitled to bear the said arms.
(No. 836.) 8 June 1636. Letter, signed by the Archbishop, authorising the son of the late Bishop of Bangor to receive from the clergy of that diocese, a tenth granted by way of benevolence to the said bishop towards his expenses in repairing the church of Bangor ; the money to be spent in carrying out the late bishop's intentions respecting the cathedral.
(No. A. 319.) 30 Aug. 1636. An elegie vpon the much lamented death of the vertuous gentlewoman, Mrs. Margaret Lewis, who deceased the 30th of August 1636. Composed by her poorest servaunt, who unfeignedly laments her death. The following lines of the poem show what district of the island of Anglesey was supposed to be most familiar with the lady's virtues :—

Mourne, Llyvon mourne, for thou alasse hast lost
Thy hopeful mistress, neyther canst thou boast
Of any thing but griefe, since she is gone
Who was thy dearest, and thy onely one.

(No. 583.) 10 Sept. 1636. An accompt of all my Receipts and Disbursements for or to y⁰ vse of my Brother M' D' Willm. Griffith Chancellor of St Asaph and Bangor from . . . St. Peter's tide, viz. 29 June 1636, to the day aforesaid. Together with my charge at y⁰ beginning of this accompte.
The Account of Disbursementes "Towards his building " at Carreg-lwyd" contains the following items, illustrative of the remuneration of several kinds of labour in Anglesey, in Charles the First's time.

To Owen John Elmor the joiner for his worke for 49 dayes and a halfe at 12d. p. diem - - - - 002 09 06
To Hugh ap . . . the carpenter and his boy for theire worke, viz. y⁰ one for 58 dayes, and the other for 59 at 12d. & 7d. p. diem - - - - 004 12 05
To Parrie ap John ap William the mason for his 51 dayes worke at 18 p. diem - 003 16 06
To three other masons for their worke viz. one for 53 dayes, the other for 54 dayes, & the third for 45 dayes, at 14d. p. diem apiece - - - - 008 13 04
To James Foukes the mason for 54 dayes worke - - - - 001 07 00
To Owen ap Evan and his sonne for their worke, viz. the one for 17 & the other 14 dayes at 6d. & 2d. p. diem a-piece ; And for 32 dayes dim. a piece at 12d. & 8d. p. diem besides 12d. they had for Bearage for their first weekes work woh. was bestowed - - - - 003 17 04
To Rees ap Howell for 66 dayes worke in burning of lyme at 10d. p. diem - 002 15 00
To 15 Labourers for their seuerall worke at 6d. p. diem. a piece, saving 4 woh. were 5d. per diem - - - 015 15 00
(No. C. 186.) Hilary Term, 1636. Copy of Sir Thomas Holland's affidavit in the Court of Exchequer, respecting the course of the river Kefney, co. Anglesey, and injury done to him by Richard Bulkley, of Bewmares, and Thomas Cheadle his undertenant, who have stayed and

diuerted the said river by means of a stagne, placed across and athwart the stream, contrary to the engagement made by them seven years since, when the complainant first had recourse to the Court of Exchequer for protection in this matter. This dispute had its origin thirty years before, when Sir Richard Bulkeley, Knight, grandfather of the aforenamed Richard Bulkeley, constructed a " stagne " in the river, and was indicted for so doing in the Great Sessions for Anglesey by the deponent. Several of the legal papers of the collection have reference to this cause of quarrel, and litigation arising therefrom.
(No. B. 306.) 26 Nov. 1636. Inspeximus of proceedings in a suit, PRYTHERG v. HOLLAND, in the court of the council of the Marches of Wales, whereby the plaintiff, Richard Prythergh of Mevirian, co. Anglesey, Esq., sought to establish his right to a certain way, in Treviriwth, leading from his ancient dwelling-house and estate over the lands of Sir Thomas Holland, Knight, of Berrowe, in the same county, with the depositions of several witnesses in the suit ; and also with the decision of the council of the said Marches, which was in the plaintiff's behalf,—leave, however, being granted to the defendant to have the case tried and decided by Nisi Prius, within the county of Salop, within the space of two years, after which time, should he neglect to avail himself of the privilege thus accorded to him, he must, abide by the aforesaid judgment of the court of the Marches of Wales.
(No. 44.) 8 Nov. 1636. General synod of all the clergy of the diocese of Bangor held and celebrated by Edmund, by the divine providence, bishop of Bangor, on abovenamed day. The list contains the names of all the clergy present, with their respective offices, preferments and cures.
(No. 812.) 15th of December 1636. Writ from the council in the marches of North Wales, to underwritten officers within the principality and marches, for the apprehension of Katherine Lloyd and Robert ap William ap William, who are to be brought as "rebbells " before the said council.
(No. A. 987.) 3 July 1637. The humble petition of Edward Moris of Llansilin to the archbishop of Canterbury, praying that he may be dismissed out of the court of High Commission, where he " is questioned for set-" tinge up a seate in the chancell of the said parish " church, which was formerly pulled down by the " churchwardens of the said parish by order of Dr. Wil-" liam Griffith, the chancellor of the lord Bushoppe of " St. Assaphon." The petitioner urges in justification of his action in thus replacing the pew, that Dr. Griffith had ordered the churchwardens to restore it, when he had ascertained that " the seat was in no way prejudiciall " eyther to the standing of the communion table alter-" wayes or to any other part of the said chancell." The petition is referred by the primate to Dr. Gruffith for proper examination and treatment.
(No. C. 168.) 28 Sept. 1639. Return of an inquisition held on a writ of " diem clausit extremum," at Beaumaris co. Anglesey, respecting the estates of Arthur Bagenall, deceased.
(No. 773.) 20 Feb. 1640. Letter (obscurely worded on some affair of business) from John bishop of St. Asaph (Joh: Asaphen) to his " right worshipfull and his very " loving cosen Dr. Griffith chauncellor of St. Asaph and " Bangor."
(No. C. 44.) 9 Feb. 1641. Fourty-four sheets of a mutilated copy of the petition, presented to the Rt. Hon. William viscount Say and Seale, one of his Majesty's Privy Council, and Master of the Court of Wards and Liveries, in behalf of Nicholas Bagenalle, a minor, son of Arthur Bagenall, deceased, who was elder son of Sir Henry Bagenall, "knt. and marshall of the kingdome of " Ireland." Only the opening pages are preserved of this petition, which is a strong exparte statement of the intercourse between Sir Henry Bagnall and the Hollands of Berow, in which Sir Henry (who lived habitually in Ireland, and was imperfectly acquainted with his interests in Eskiviock and other parts of North Wales) is represented to have been outwitted and over-reached in various bargains by the Hollands who, as resident proprietors keenly alive to their interests, were still persisting in a course prejudicial to the said minor. Having set forth several more substantial injuries done to the estate of the minor, the petitioners urge, "And the said " Sir Thomas Holland hath erected seates or pues in the " chauncell of Eskeiviog church, the same places where " he see erected the saide seates beinge, and all or most " parte of the saide chancell belonginge to the saide " Nicholas Bagenall and his ancestors as well as in re-" gard of his and theire ranke and quallity as in the

" right of the saide seucrall messuages, tenements, and
" greate estates here and they time out of memory hadd
" and haue in the said parishe." It is further alleged
that " of late, takinge advantage of the minority of the
" said Nicholas Bagenall, Sir Thomas Holland of Be-
" rowe had, on some partial information "unduly
" procured from the archbishop of Canterbury without
" any suite. and the see of Bangor beinge then full,
" within which the saide parish is, a faculty or license
" to breake downe the chauncell wall of the North side
" of the saide churche, and there to erect a chappel for
" him the saide Sir Thomas Holland and his heires to
" the disinherison of his majesty's warde, whoe hath
" right on the seate and sittinge-place adjoyninge and
" annexed to the saide wall, so licensed to bee broken
" down, notwithstandinge the Bishopp of the diocese
" refused to grant any such license."
(No. B. 307.) 13 Feb. 1642. Indenture (covering four
large and closely written skins) of settlement of property
(belonginge to Sir Thomas Holland, Knt., of Berow, in
the parish of Trevarthyn, co. Anglesey, and his nephew
Owen Holland of the same places), made between the
said Sir Thomas and Owen of the first path, and Piers
Lloyd of Llygwy, co. Anglesey, Esq., John Gruffith the
elder of Llyu'n, co. Carnarvon, Esq., Owen Woode of
Llangwyfen, co. Anglesey, Esq., Robert Wynne of Voylas,
co. Denbigh, Esq., Hugh Wynne of Llannuda, co. Carnarvon, Esq., and Robert Wynne of Holyhead, co. Anglesey, of the second part : Whereby, in consideration of a
marriage agreed upon between the said Owen Lloyd and
Jane daughter of the said Piers Lloyd, and of the sum of
1,300l. to be paid to them by the said Piers Lloyd, as a
marriage portion for his daughter, the said Sir Thomas
and Owen convey to the persons of the second party, in
trust for the purposes of the agreement, the manor-house
and demesne of Berow aforesaid, with messuages, lands,
tenements, &c. in the towns, fields, and hamlets of
Bedfordd, Keneglwys, Rhoscolyn, Caerdgogo, Mathe-
warne, Wyan, Pentraeth, Nanlynrva, Bodlen, Klynocho,
Vechan, Llanvaes, Bewmares, Swydryn, and elsewhere,
together with all their "seates sittinge kneelinge and
" buryinge places easementes commodities and advan-
" tages in the parish of Llanorhangel Eskieviogo in the
" said county of Anglesey and all that chapel to the
" said church pertaininge and lately built by Sir Thomas
" Holland and all the seates sittinge kneelinge and
" buryinge places in the south side of the chancel of the
" said church, and all other seates sittinge kneelinge
" and buryinge places &c. in the said church or any
" other of the premises &c. &c. used or enjoyed by the
" said Sir Thomas Holland or any of his auncestores."
(No. B. 296.) 18th of Feb. 1642. Indenture of agreement (between William Griffith of Carnethour, co.
Anglesey, Doctors of Law, and Chancellor of the
diocese of St. Asaph, of the first part, Robert Owen,
son and heir apparent of John, Lord Bishop of St.
Asaph, and Francis Owen of London, gentleman, of
the second part, and the said bishop of the third),
whereby " in consideration of a marriage hereto-
" fore had and solemnized between him the said
" William Griffith and Mary his now wife daughter
" of the said lord bishoppe of St. Asaph, and of the mar-
" riage portion of the said Mary," the said William
Griffith conveys to the said Robert and Francis his man-
sion-house at Carnethour, with other estate of land in
for the benefit of his said wife and their issue.
(No. 945.) 15 Aug. 1642. Letter from Hughe Johnes
and William Thomas to Mr. Doctor Griffith at his house
in Carnethor, co Anglesea, respecting the death and last
will of his uncle Hugh Owen.
(No. A. 172.) 1642. Copy of the decree (pronounced
by Sir John Lambe, Doctor of Laws, and Judge of the
Arches Court of Canterbury) dismissing, with costs, the
petition of Sir Arthur Torringham, Knt., now deceased,
and his wife lady Terringham for the revocation of the
faculty conceded to Sir Thomas Holland to build a
chapel on the north side of the chancel of the church of
Eskiviogo.
(No. A. 193.) 3 July 1643. Copy of the articles proferred, in the Great Sessions of the county of Anglesey,
against Arthur Michael, Roger Phillips, Symon Donall,
William ap Jenur and others, who are accused of riotous
conduct in the parish church of Eskiviog.
(No. A. 783.) 5 Oct. 1643. Writ to the high sheriff
and others of the county of Anglesey, for the suppression
of riotous meetings near the parish church of Eskiviog,
and the apprehension of persons concerned in the disorderly assemblies.
(No. A. 773.) 1 Dec. 1643. Last will of William
Griffith, D.C.L. of Caernether, co. Anglesey. After
making a general bequest of his household stuff to his

wife, should there be no necessity to sell it or any part
of it for the payment of his debts, the testator adds, " To
" this bequest of Household stuff my meaning is that my
" wife should have the vse of all during her life, but the
" propertie of all standards together withall Bedsteeds,
" Tables and Liuery Cubbord I giue and bequeath to
" my heyre." He appoints for executors his " well be-
" loved Brethren George Griffith of Llanymynech in the
" county of Salop, Dr. of Divinity, John Griffith of
" Llanvaithlo in the county of Anglesey, cleark and Mr.
" of Arts, and Hugh Griffith of Caernetherr aforesaid,
" gent."
(No. A. 55.) Letter from the commissioners of array
for the county of Anglesey to a right honourable person
(whose name does not appear), praying him to prevail
on the king to follow the example of his royal predecessors and " exempte this island from any presse of
" men, att his time." This entreaty is provoked by the
king's writ, lately directed to the said commissioners,
requiring them to "presse and raise twoe hundred and
" fifty alle " (? able) " men in this county for his ma-
" jesty's service." The petitioners ground their petition
on the burdens they and their fellow-islanders bear, and
the difficulties they encounter for the safe custody of an
island, which is exposed to the attacks of Irish rebels
and the parliamentary forces. " First we are," they
say, " an island situat betweene Ireland and Lancashire,
" lyinge open and subject to invasion on all partes,
" beinge dayly robbed on our coaste by the rebbells of
" Ireland and parliamentary shipps, which are many in
" number att this time in Liuerpoolo, and threaten
" dayly to invade and possesse themselves of this Island,
" being of the greatest consequence of any other place
" in these partes vnto them."—No date.
(No. A. 786.) 21 Sept. 1645. Captain Hugh Griffith's
memorandum of money received by him of the cessment
made for the providing of new armes insteed of those
sent to Denbighshire and repayment of the advance
money then paid to the souldiers.
(No. 235.) 14 April 1644. Muster-roll of the Trayned
Band of Tallybolion.
(No. 219.) 21 Feb. 1645. List of the soldiers selected
from the Trained Band of the hundred of Talabolion,
to serve in the force of "sixteene able and sufficient
" fire-men of the trayned men and auxiliaries of each
" comott," of the county of Anglesea, appointed to
guard the "river of Menai."
(No. A. 833.) 21 Feb. 1645. Letter from John bishop
of St. Asaph (signed John Asaphen) respecting the disturbances in and near Conway. The town is in a ferment; but the writer does not think it needful at
present that his son, and his correspondent's son, should
" forsake the school " there.
(No. A. 838.) 8 April 1645. Memorandum of the bequests made (the day before her death) by Mrs. Griffith,
wife of William Griffith, doctor of laws, to her nearest
kindred and servants. The legacies to her children are
expressive of maternal tenderness. The lady's gifts to
her servants are, also, characteristic :—" To Jane Stod-
" dard my painefull and carefull maid I giue 5 li. and
" the rest of my better sort of wearinge apparell. Some
" of my more ordinarie cloaths I desire should be giuen
" to my other maydes that haue taken paines with me.
" And to Elin Pugh, my children's nurse, I giue first
" the frize gown I now weare. To Mary Draycott,
" poor wench, 5 li. besides her share of some of my
" cloathes."
(No. 232.) 12 Dec. 1645. Captain Hugh Griffith's
accompt of Powder, Match, and Bulletts bought and
received for the use of the Trained Soldiers of the
Hundred of Tallybolion.
(No. 613.) Not dated. Draught of 9 resolutions to be
adopted by the gentlemen of Anglesey, respecting the
taxation of the island for the maintenance of the forces
of the Parliament. 1. That the state was att no charge
for the reduction of Anglesey, whereupon it may justly
be desired that they contribute not for the reduction
& payinge of the soldiery in other counties. 2. That
they of Anglesey have maintained the parliament forces
quartered in their countie, & payd them duly, without
the helpe and assistance of any other countie euer since
their submission, though it were to the charge of a fift
part of their yearly meanes generally. 3. That the
gentlemen who mett at Denbigh had no commission
from the countie to encrease the charge, that layes
heavy upon them, nor to consent to pay any proportion
of the 1200 li. mencioned, or to any greater proportion
of troopers. 5. That they are ready to make paym' of
the assessm' of their share of the 60,000 li. as is required,
however disproportionably soever, till the hon'ble houses
relieve them. 6. That if there be any arrears, due to

the commaunders & soldiers, they may be payd out of their assessments of the 60,000 li. 8. To have the garrison as much decreast as may be. The Island being of the nature of a garrison in itselfe, able to defend itselfe ag⁸ᵗ any ordinary invasion.

(No. 77.) Copy of the humble petition of the Gentry Commons and Inhabitants of the Iland of Anglesey in Northwales, To the right honourable the Lords and Commons of England assembled in Parliament at Westminster.—Sheweth, that euer since the warre began we haue made much preparation for a defensive posture to preserue the inoffensiue Iland from incursion of the Irish Rebells and other insolencies incident to warre, without any thought or ingagement to oppose the honourable parliament, which we haue esteemed to be the onely meanes to preserue the churches peace and the subjects right. Neuertheles the king's partie appearinge amongst vs (and no particular invitation or protection from the parliament), we were necessitated to some complyance with them, yet with such caution and distance that we permitted not the Lord Byron, who was made gouernor of this Island by his Majestie, nor none of his forces, nor any els to rest themselues nor possess any strong hold at all amongste vs, being resolued vpon the firste opportunitie to render our obedience to the kinge and Parliament, which after a solemn summons from Maior Generall Mytton, your honours most faithfull agent and chiefe commander in these partes, wee did seriously in seuerall publique meetinges debate and willingly and readily submitt vnto him as may appeare by subscriptions vnder our hands to his commissioners imployed in that service. However since some particular distractions happened touchinge the surrender of Beaumaris Castle, which wee were no way off but laboured and endeavoured to compose a reconciliation as the Commissioners can testifie. In tender consideration and in regard of our vnanimous constant resolution to remaine firme for Kinge and Parliament against all opposers. Wee most humbly pray your honours dispensacion of delinquencies for the Island according to Maior Generall Mitton's mediation, and we shall ever pray for a blessinge vpon your honours vnwearied labours which shall be recorded to all posteritie. No date or signatures.

(No. A. 784.) May 1646. Copies of letters that passed between General Thomas Mytton, and the Lord Bulkeley, and other gentlemen of Anglesey. 1. General Mytton's demand (dated Carnarvon, 7 May 1646) that the gentlemen of the island comply with the Parliament and surrender their garrisons to him for the service of the King and Parliament. 2. The reply of Lord Bulkeley and the said gentlemen to General Mytton's letter (dated Bewmares, 12 May 1646); urging that they have raised a force only to preserve peace and testify their obedience to the King, and requesting that they may send a gentleman (protected by the General's "pass") to His Majesty. Signed by thirty-five gentlemen, including three of the family and name of Griffith. 3. General Mytton's letter (dated Carnarvon, 13 of May) enclosing a copy of an order which precludes him from allowing them to send one of their number to the King. 4. The copy of the said order, "Whereas you intimate you have "given a Passe to Sir William Byron and two servants to "goe to the King, we desire that henceforth there may "be noe passes granted to any of the enemy, vpon what "pretence soever, we conceauing that it may proue "prejudiciall to the state. Signed in the name, and "by the warrant of the committee of both kingdomes "by your lovinge friends, P : Wharton, Charles Artkin." "Addressed to Colonell Mytton, and dated Darby House, "24 April, 1646."

(No. 749.) May and June 1646. Copies of four letters that passed between General Mytton and the gentlemen of Anglesey. 1. Letter from the general requiring, amongst other things, that "Beaumaris Castle, "and all other forts and garrisons in the said island be "delivered into his hands." Dated, 26 May, 1646, at Denbigh, II. Reply to General Mytton from Lord Bulkeley and ten other gentlemen of the island, declaring their "readiness to comply with the Parlia-"ment." Dated 30 May, at Beaumares. III. The letter to General Mytton, whereby the said gentlemen of Anglesey submit themselves to the King and Parliament ; only renewing a former prayer for leave to send one or more gentlemen to speak for them at Westminster. Signed: Bulkeley, Rich: Prythergh, Wm. Griffith, John Bodwell, H. Owen, O. Woods, Row: Bulkeley, Ow: Holland, Hen: Owen, Ri: Owen Theodor, Wm. Bold. Dated, 2 June 1646, at Llangefin. IV. General Mytton's answer to these two letters frm the gentlemen of Anglesey. Consenting that the said gentlemen

may send a deputation to the Parliament at Westminster, and promising to use his influence with the Parliament in their behalf ; but insisting that they immediately surrender Beaumaris Castle, or be prepared for a siege of the said castle, to cover the costs of which their estates shall be confiscated.

(No. A. 568.) 13th of May 1646. Letter from General Thomas Mitton to lord Bulkeley and the rest of the gentlemen and inhabitants of the island of Anglesey. Gentlemen, I received yours verie late last night in answere whereto I thought fitt to send this bearer with theis lines, and to deale plainely with you. I feare by your answere and acciouns in receiving those that come vnto you out of the towne of Carnarvon and releuinge of them you will bring miserie vpon your selves, it being no lesse then open hostilitie against the parliment, the great counsell of the land, which I must endevour as much as in me lyeth by all meanes to provente, it being also repugnant to that parte of your answere whereby you conceaue your selfes by your demeanour to giue no just cause of offence, As for your desire to haue a passe fur a gent To goe to the king, were it for your good and in my power, I should withall readilie grant it. But giue me leaue to acquaint you that the disafeccioun of the king to the kingdomes and churches cause by reason of the euill counsellors that were and are about him hath brought vpon vs all theis miseries, and therefore for you to send vnto him will tender you enemies to the State. But I conceaue that parte of your answere was deuised by some of those foreuamed counsellours, that are by God's greate power beaten out of all the rest of the kingdome into your Island undone all places by the way wherein they came, which I desire you seriously and with all speede to consider.—That it lioth not in my power to grant you such a passe, I haue sent you the enclosed, which I desire you to send me by bearer, noe way doubting but it will satisfie you therein.—Gentlemen, I haue been somewhat tedious. but it proceeds from my desire to saue shedding of blood and the ruine of your countrie, which you will surely bringe vpon yourselves, if you persist in your way, I being commanded by the Parliament to endeavour the reducing of all such places and persons into their obedience in those partes that stand out against them, and I beleevo you cannott be ignorant of the power God hath put into their hand, by blessing theiro vnwearied pious endeavours for this his cause. Carnarvon, 13th of May 1646.

(No. 782.) 4 January. Letter from tho committee of the Lords and Commons for the army, to the Commissioners for raysinge the monthly assessment for the army in the counties of Northwales. Accompanying the Parliamentary order of 24 Dec. for disbanding the forces under Major-General Mitton's command, with the exception of certain companies specially mentioned in the letter.

(No. C. 97.) —— 1646 and 1647. A Noate showing how much corne hath beene threshed (i. e. at Berow) this yeare 1646. Beginning the tenth day of October, 1646. Similar note for the year 1647.

(No. 762.) 25 Jan. 1647. Instructions (signed at Denbigh by E. Vaughan, Gym : Shellwall, Jo : Jones) to Mr. Hugh Courtney. The first of the instructions runs thus :—"Inprimis, you are with all possible speed to "repaire to London and make your addresse to the "Committee of the Army for the supply of disbanding "money for North Wales. And likewise to his Excel-"lency and the Speaker of the House of Commons, for "the same end. You are likewise to repaire to the "Gentlemen that serue for North Wales for theyr assis-"tance in this negotiation."

(No. C. 320. 1647. Single sheet of a deposition made in writing by Owen Holland, as defendant in a suit arising out of Sir Thomas Holland's purchase of Sir Henry Bagnall's interest in the crown lands of Eskeviiog, from which it appears that Sir Henry Bagnall died shortly before the month of January, 19 Jac. I., and that Sir Thomas Holland had died at some date subsequent to the day of October 1643, when he made and declared his last will and testament.

(No. 614.) 2 Feb. 1647. (Much moth-eaten.) Certain Heads of Proposalls to be offered to the Gentlemen of Northwales for yᵉ speedie effecting yᵉ worke of Disbanding. By the Members of Parliament appointed to attend the said service at Ruthen. On the other side of the sheet appears (dated 3 Feb.) the proposals of the Commissioners, appointed to assess 60,000li. on the counties of North Wales, for raising "by way of volun-"tary advance from particular persous in each county" the sum of 6,220li. and 1,200li., by which sums the fund raised by the assessment falls short of the required

Miss C.
GRIFFITH.

60,000*li.* The proportions of the 6,200*li.* assigned to the several counties are as follows :—Denbighshire 1,492*li.*, Montgomeryshire 1,492*li.*, Carnarvonshire 998*li.*, Anglesey 746*li.*, Flintshire 746*li.* Merionethshire 746*li.*

(No. A. 40.) 8 Jan. 1648. Appointment (by Magdalen Tyringham, sister of Gruffith Bagenall, Esq., deceased) of William Bold and Henry Wynne, Esqrs. co. Anglesey, and cousins of the said Magdalen, Mr. Thomas Williams, his brother Mr. Lewis Thomas, and Mr. John Gybbard to enter upon the moiety of the township of Eskeivioge, and take the rents, &c. formerly pertaining to Gruffith Bagenallo for life.

(No. 668.) Writ of summons to the right worshipfull Hugh Williams, D.D. to appear before the right worshipfull Sir John Lambe, Knt., doctour of Law and Judge of the Arches Court of Canterbury, or his deputy, "in the parish church of St. Bowe London," on the eighth day after service, &c. to "answere to certaine "articles concerninge your supine neglecte in serveinge "of the cure of soules of the parishe of Llanddynam."

(No. 788.) Letter addressed by William Lenthall, Speaker, to Mr. Thelwall, Mr. Edward Vaughan and Collonel Jones, members of the House of Commons; and ordered "to bee communicated to the committees "for raiseing the monethely assessments in the seuerall "counties of North Wales." No date.

(No. A. 785.) 27 June 1653. Warrant to levy an assessment of 223*l.* 7*s.* 4*d.* in the hundred of Menay "towards the maintenance of the armies and navies of "the commonwealth."

(No. A. 648.) 15 Oct. 1656. The petition of John Trevor of Trevor, co. Denbigh, to the Hon. Lord Bradshaw, chiefe Justice of Chester, Flint, Denbigh, &c. Praying for the appointment of a day for the hearing of the petitioner's cause to be tried before his lordship, at "this present greate Sessions in the county of Den-"bigh." With underwritten appointment of a day, signed—Jo Bradshawe : Tho : Fell.

23 April 1656. Bill in Chancery, of Richard Stacy, shoemaker in the parish of Saint Martins in the Fields, against Owen Holland and Arthur Bulkeley of the county of Anglesey; in which the plaintiff asserts his title to certain lands, &c. in the township of Cardegoge and elsewhere in co. Anglesey, formerly belonging to his maternal grandfather, Arthur Williams late of Llanbadrig, co. Anglesey, gentleman, and alleges that he is fraudulently excluded from his said inheritance by the aforenamed Owen Holland, Arthur Bulkeley, and others.

(No. B. 117.) 7 October 1656. Tallabollion co. Anglesey. A True and Perfect Rentrowle of the Chiefe Rent (in Welch, Cyllid) of the Commotto of Tallabolion aforesayd for one whole yeare made at Llanvairynbornwy in the sayd commotte the seaventh day of October, in the grace of our Lord God 1656.

(No. C. 174.)—1663. Copy of interrogatories ministred for the examinacions of witnesses on the parte and behaulfe of Thomas Holland, esq. plaintiff against Robert, Lord Bulkeley, viscount Cassells in Ireland, defendant.

(No. C. 177.) — 1663. Bill of Complaint to the Hon. Timothy Littleton, Sarjeant att Lawe, and Thomas Jones esq., his majesty's justices of the Great Sessions cos. Anglesey, Carnarvon and Merioneth, by Thomas Holland of Berrw, an infant aged seventeen years (prosecuting by his mother, Jane Holland, a widow) alleging that wrong has been done him, in respect to the boundary of his estate in Eskiviog and adjoining parishes by Robert Lord Viscount Bulkeley of Barnhill in the same county, grandson of Sir Richard Bulkeley the elder of Bewmares, knt., deceased.—The bill recites the deeds by which the complainant's greatgrandfather, Owen Holland, acquired the property in Eskiviog; and sets forth with sufficient clearness the several stages of the long enduring controversy between the two neighbouring families, respecting the bounds of their estates.

(No. C. 173.) 23 Sept. 1663. Copy of bill filed on the above-named day in the same suit; with the defendant's answer.

(No. C. 176.) 3 Oct. 1663. The Answeare of Robert Lord Buckley viscount Cassiles in Ireland Defendant to the Bill of Complaint of Thomas Holland, esq., an Infant, by Jane Holland, widowe, his mother and guardian, complainant, filed on abovenamed day.

(No. B. 80.) 7 September 1663. Commission of John Griffith, gent. (by the appointment of Sir Richard Vaughan, earl of Carbery, Lord President of Wales and marches thereof) to be "cornet to Captaine Thomas "Bulkeley his troope in the militia of horse raised, or "to be raised, within the county of Anglesey, in North-"wales, in the regiment of which the right honorable

"Edward lord Herbert of Cherbury is colonel," under Lord Carbery's command.

(No. C. 8.) 28th of Jan. 1663. Part of the memorandum of an agreement, whereby George Griffith, D.D., bishop of St. Asaph, and brother of the late William Griffith, doctor of laws, consents to accept, in annual instalments of one hundred pounds ten shillings and sixpence, payment from his nephew John (son and heir of the said William, deceased) of the sum of 603*l.* 3*s.* 1*d.*, which he (the said bishop) has provided at divers times for the use and benefit of the said nephew during his minority; and whereby the said bishop engages to take up a sum of 200*l.*, on which the John Griffith stands indebted to Edward Cotton of the town of Salop: Provided that the nephew gives his uncle sufficient security in land for the payment of the said sums.

(No. A. 525.) Sept. 1664. Last will of Jane Griffith *alias* Wood, "the now wife of John Griffith of Caernether co. Anglesey.

(No. B. 224.) 17th of July 1666. Commission of John Griffith of Carreg Loyd, to be a deputy-lieutenant for co. Anglesey, by the appointment of the Earl of Carbery, Lord President of Wales and the Marches.

(No. C. 236.) 9 July 1668. "A Perfecte rentrolle of "Mr. Owen Holland's late lands as they were sett in his "time, and how they are now sett," from which it appears that most of the tenants on Mr. Holland's estate paid their rentes in money, presents, and service. For instance, Evan ap Roberts held his tenement at the yearly rent, in money, of 7*l.* 10*s.*, in presents, of foure geese, two capons, and, in service, of two days harrowing, two days' reaping, two day's of carrying corn. In like manner Hugh ap William John, held Tythin Clay at a yearly rent of 6*l.* in money, of two capons and a hundred red herrings in presents, and of six days of mason's work, in service.

(No. 798.) 28 Sept. 1668. Warrant from John Griffith of Caernether (his majesty's fee-farmer of the township of Caerdegog, co. Anglesey), to his bailiffs Rees Jones and Owen ap Richard Dauid of Llanvaithley, to collect the King's "chiefe rents" and pay them into the Exchequer, or to his Majesty's receiver-general for North Wales.

(No. 800.) 28 Nov. 1668. Treasury warrant (bearing the signatures of Albemarle, Ashley and Clifford) to the commissioners of assessments co. Anglesey, for the immediate levying of the eleven months tax, "lest any "trouble or doubt should arise amongst the commis-"sioners of the county of Anglesey whether the same "can be assessed after the first of February next."

(No. 517.) 16 May 1678. Warrant signed by deputy-lieutenants of the isle of Anglesey for levying money by rate, wherewith to provide ammunition for the forces of the island, and afford encouragement to the inferior officers of the said forces.

(No. 518.) 18 Jan. 1678. Warrant for the same purpose, for money to be levied in the hundred of Tallabollion.

(No. 519.) No date. A returne of the comott. of Tallabolion, according to the contents of the deputy-lieutenants warrants, giving the number of the arms formerly charged upon the hundred.

(No. 237.) No. date. A list indented of the trained bande of the Comott of Tallabolion in the countie of Anglesey, and the names of the captain and officers of the bande.

(No. C. 203.) Anglizey: Com. Talabolion. A List of the Trained Band of the said Commote with the names of the officers of the said band. No date.

(No. 218.) Talabolion : Account of the Powder to be delivered to the Trained souldiers of the said hundred. No date.

(No. 217.) Two papers, tattered and defaced; part of a muster roll of a trained band in the county of Anglesey. No date.

(No. 236.) Muster Books of all the inhabitantes of the hundred of Llyvon with the armes cessed upon them accordinge to the last general muster houlden at Beumares, before Sir Richard Bulkeley, Sir Sackeville Trevor, knightes, Richard Bulkeley, Esq., and William Griffith, Esq., deputy-lieutenants of the said county of Anglesey. No date.

(No. 633.) Paper Roll (frayed and moth-eaten). The Muster Roll of the Trained Bands of the Hundred of Livon. No date.

(No. 221.) No date. List of "The names of the most "frequent Defaulters at Musters within the hundred of "Llyvon, co. Anglesey."

(No. 222.) Paper much defaced, with date torn away. List of horse soldiers to be raised, within a comote of the island of Anglesey, to serve "in a moving body

" under the command of Capt. John Owen." It is ordered that " these horses are to be serviceable w'hall, " w'th able riders, and w'th swords pistolls or Carbiners, " and to haue for their mantynaunce seaven shillings is a " weeks allowaunce by the owners, to be repaide by the " hundred." With names of the persons on whom the horses (31) are levied.

(No. A. 791.) An agreement of seven articles, made by certain of the gentlemen of Anglesey, for lessening the burdens laid on the high sheriffs of the county. 1 That no sheriff (elected from the subscribers to the compact) shall have more than twelve livery-men attending on him at Great Sessions or elsewhere. 2. That the liverymen shall wear buff coats with buff belts, and bear javelins (instead of halberts) to be bought by the subscribers, and kept for the use of the sheriff's attendants. 3. That no sheriff shall lend the said coats, &c. to any person, or allow them to be abused or torn. 4. That the charge at the sheriff's ordinary shall not exceed eighteen pence for himself and friends, or eight pence for his men. 5. That the subscribers to the agreement shall pay their own scores at the sheriff's table. 6. That in case any sheriff (being a subscriber to the compact) is fined by the judges on a slight or frivolous account, his fellow-subscribers shall combine to procure the remission of the fine, or pay it in equal shares levied amongst themselves and friends. 7. That the articles of the compact may be amended by a majority of the subscribers. The preamble to this curious agreement states that, notwithstanding an Act of Parliament of the 13th year of the present reign for diminishing their charges, the sheriffs of the co. have been put to " insupportable " expenses by dietinge the judges, defrayinge the charge " of their lodgings, servants, and horses and other ex-" travagant and vaine glorious expenses."— No date. The reference to the statute 13 & 14 Car. 2. c. 21 proves however that the agreement was made in the time of Charles the Second.

(Nos. 280 to 300, and Nos. 351 to 394.) Two packets of schedules of assessments of taxes in parishes of Anglesey (for the most part of the hundred of Talabolion); and of receipts for rents, paid in respect of lands held by John, William, or Elizabeth Griffith, of the Principality of Wales or of the crown. The schedules of assessments are of the years A.D. 1663, '67, '74, '83, '84, '88, '92, '93, '97, '98, '99, 1700, 1706, 1709. The receipts for rents were given in the years 1694, '97, 1709, '24, '34, '38, '43. The local historian, dealing with the hundred of Talabolion, would do well to look at these papers.

(No. C. 271.) 1696. Eleven papers: being list of assessments of the king's taxes in different places of the hundred of Talabolion.

(No. C. 199.) 4 Nov. 1596. Letter from Edward Lhwyd (at Oxford) to the honoured Howel Vaughan, Esq., at Aberffrydlon, Montgomeryshire (Salop post, Montgomery bag). Begging for the loan of four manuscripts from Mr. Vaughan's library, and announcing that " Mr. W'm Wyn has just finish'd Cradog of Lhan Garvan's " History with Dr. Powel's notes &c., and will put it in " the Presse before Christmasse. He has put it into " modern English and has a very large preface to it, " wherein he maintains Geofrey of Monmouth's History " (the ridiculous fables therein excepted) with very " plausible arguments as they seem to me, and good " judgment and ingenuity. I was telling him that your " grandfather had writ some Notes upon the Triades." The writer with the enthusiasm of a special student declares, " I can think of nothing more necessary than " the perusing our ancientest Welsh MSS."

(Nos. A. 443 to A. 519.) Notice to pay rents, delivered to John Griffith and William Griffith, of the island of Anglesey, to be paid and receipts for rents duly paid by them, to the use of the king and parliament, the commonwealth, or the king (temp. Car. I., Commonwealth, Car. II., Jac. II., and William and Mary), in respect of farms of crown lands, &c.

(No. B. 168.) 10 Aug. 1703. Commission of William Griffyth to be a deputy-lieutenant of co. Anglesey, by appointment of Hugh Viscount Cholmondeley, lord-lieutenant of the cos. of North Wales, and of the county-palatine of Chester.

(No. C. 306.) 15 July 1708. Tallabolion : Schedule of assessments in the hundred by virtue of an Act of Parliament for granting an aid to Her Majesty by a Land Tax, to be raised for the year 1708.

(No. B. 52.) 10 Nov. 1740. Acknowledgment (engrossed on vellum) by the Rev. Henry Williams, rector of Llanfaethly, that, though he has watered his cattle, levant and conchant on his glebe and other lands, during his residence at Llanfaethly, at the brook or rivulet

running by Carreglwyd, he has done so not of his own right, but at the permission of William Griffith and Griffith, Esqs., of Carreglwyd.

From the diversity of the spelling of names of persons and places, the reader has of course inferred that in each entry names are spelt as they appear in the writing to which the entry refers.

JOHN CORDY JEAFFRESON.

THE MANUSCRIPTS OF ROBERT WALTER PRIDEAUX, ESQ., OF DARTMOUTH.

The following 34 documents are selected from about sixty in the possession of Robert Walter Prideaux, Esqre., of Dartmouth; who very courteously placed them before me for my inspection, when visiting Dartmouth, and lent me them for further examination, and notice in the present Report.—

A small parchment deed, in Latin, dated " at Dorte-" mue, on Wednesday [die Mercurie] the morrow of " St. Lucy the Virgin,". 18th Edward I. ; whereby Hervey Makeglad grants to his son, John, a tenement in Cliftone of Dertemue, which he had of the gift of John Aubin, situate between the tenement of Juliana Boys and that which William de Ho and John Webbs hold : at a yearly rent of 7 pence. Witnesses, Gilbert de Fawy, Ralph Reynot, Robert de Pole, William Hemmeng, William de Pruce [of Prussia], Ralph Makeglad, " and " others." The seal, in green wax, slightly broken, represents a galley, with one mast, and a star on either side of it.

A parchment deed, in Latin, with an oblong seal in green wax, a flower, with legend; whereby Isobel, relict of Thomas Wodegrene, grants to William Brento and Joan, his wife, her right and claim in a tenement in Hyesthardenasse, which the said Thomas and Isobel bought of Sir Peter de Fisacre, it being near the tenement of Roger Solaz; for a yearly payment of 6 pence to the said Sir Peter, at Christmas, and 2 shillings for relief, when falling due; they having paid to the said Isobel 27 shillings sterling beforehand. Witnesses, Gilbert de Fawy, William Joye, William Hemyng, Yllary Crok, Richard the Baker, Henry Peryce, Richard Kalewa, " and many others." Without date given, but temp. Edward I.

A small parchment deed, in Latin, whereby Elias, son and heir of Thomas Wodegrene and of Isobel, his wife, quit-claims his right in a tenement which William Brente and Joan, his wife, bought of his mother, Isobel, for 5 shillings to him paid. Witnesses, Gilbert de Fawy, William Joye, William Hemmyng, Henry Peryes, Edward Salcok, " and others." Without date, but temp. Edward I. Only a fragment of the seal, in green wax, is left.

A small parchment deed poll, in Latin, wherein Sir Peter de Fissacre states that he has inspected a deed of William Brente, from Isobel, relict of Thomas Wodegrene, stating that she had granted to the said William and his heirs, all her right to the tenement in Hardenasse which the said Thomas and Isobel bought of Sir Peter de Fissacre, near the tenement of Roger Solaz, the said William, his heirs, and assigns, rendering yearly, at our Lord's Nativity, 6 pence to the said Sir Peter de Fissacre ; the said William Brente having given to the said Isobel 27 shillings sterling beforehand. Witnesses, Gilbert de Fawy, Gilbert de Pole, William Joye, William Hemminge, Hillary Croc, Richard tho Baker, Henry Bissop, Richard Cowla, " and others :"— which deed he thereby confirms and ratifies. Witnesses, William Gora, William de Cumbe, Nicholas Adam, Henry de Colapitte, William Man, " and others." The deed belongs to the earlier part of the reign of Edward I. On the seal, in green wax, somewhat broken, a shield with a chevron may be traced, also for legend, " Petri " . . . ssaker."

A small parchment deed, the seal broken, in green wax, with fleur-de-lis and a legend; whereby Roger Tubbe grants to Henry Miller, for his homage and service, a messuage and garden in Hardinasse, at the nearest corner of the land of Sir Martin de Fissacre; between the way which leads from Hardinasse to Fluteshaued and the cliff [falesiam], to hold to him, his heirs and assigns, religious houses excepted ; for a yearly rent of one pair of white gloves, at Easter, and to Sir Martin de Fissacre, his heirs, or assigns, 12d. yearly, in four payments: 4 shillings being paid beforehand. Witnesses, John Clobard, Martin du Bois, William Albin, Edward Burd, Bartholomew de Fawy, Elias de Hamme, " and " many others." Temp. Edward I.

A Latin deed, on parchment, whereby John Sangere, of Hardinasse, grants to Stephen de Portelemuthe, and Joan, sister of the said John, a moiety of his messuage in Hardinasse, between the tenement of John de Coletone and that of Roger Swengelot, and near the high road leading to the chapel of St. Clair; to hold to them and the heirs of their bodies, at a yearly rent of 12 pence to Richard de Woleston, his heirs, and assigns. Witnesses, Richard Pody, Geoffrey Ode, Gilbert Salcoke, John Bregeman, Odo Jay, William Person, "and " many others." Dated 3rd Edward III. The seal is lost.

A small parchment deed, in Latin, the small seal, in red wax, mutilated, with a fanciful device; whereby John, son and heir of Martin Fakes, grants to John Marchaunt of Dertemuth, his freehold curtilage in Southtoundertemuthe, extending from the road leading from Dertemuth to Stokoflemyng, on the west, towards the harbour [portus] on the east, and near the curtilages of Richard Gordoun and William atte Wylle; for a yearly rent of one penny to the chief lords of the fee. Witnesses, Richard Gordoun, William Smale, William Polymond,—Heromyte, John de Launceton, "and others." Dated at Southtoundertemuthe, on Friday the Feast of St. Germanus the Bishop, 13th Edward III.

A Latin deed, on parchment, finely written, whereby Joan, daughter of William Verst, "in my pure " virginity," grants to Joan, daughter of John de Hamele, and Alice, her daughter, a piece of land out of her curtilage at Hardinasfeorde, between the curtilage of John le Man and the land of Roger Dauwa, and near the road from Hardinasfeorde to the church of St. Clement at Tunstall; at a yearly rent of 4 pence to the chief lords of the fee. Witnesses, William Bacon, John Gordon, William Hemmyng, Gilbert de Pole, Walter Gordon, John Sangere, John Selman, "and many " others." Dated at Hardinasse, in the 14th year of Edward III. The seal, in brown wax, has a fine impression, a child kneeling before a figure seated, apparently in the act of benediction; with the legend, " S. Thome " de Coletone :" perhaps the former seal of Thomas, a priest of Colyton.

A small parchment deed, in Latin, the seal lost, whereby Joan Keadelond, widow, grants to William Alayn her messuage in Hardenasse, near the tenements late of Thomas Wodegrene and of Roger Solax; also, her curtilage "in the Cumbe," between the curtilage formerly belonging to the pillory " in the Cumbe," the curtilage of Richard Modberd, and the curtilage, with piece of land adjoining, in Monkenestrete. Witnesses, Thomas Borberel, Nicholas Peris, Stephen Borne, John Henery, Richard Veysi, "and others." Dated at Hardenasse, the Friday after our Lord's Epiphany, 26th Edward III.

A parchment deed, in Latin, whereby Simon Gardiner, and Dionisia, his wife, grant to Richard William and Letice, his wife, all their part of a tenement, and 2½ feet without the wall thereof, which they had of the gift and fooffment of Roger Beamund; such tenement being situate in Hardinasse, near to the mill-dam and the tenement of John Raleghe and Dionisia, his wife; for a yearly rent of 2 pence sterling. Witnesses, William Ayschedene, Mayor, John Mathu, John Clerk, John Whetene, William Henry, "and others." Dated in the 32nd year of Edward III. Of the two seals, in red wax, fragments only are left. One, representing an anchor, would seem to have been of great antiquity.

A parchment deed, in Latin, whereby John Coggere, of Kyngiswere, grants to John Ralegh and Dionisia, his wife, a piece of ground at the Roptacle [? Rope-walk], situate between the ground of Walter de Cornesende and that of John Seygger, and between the curtilage of the men of Hardenasse, on the south, and the way from Hardenasfeorde to the church of Tounstalle, on the north; at a yearly rent of one penny to the chief lords of the fee. Witnesses, John Clerke, Mayor of Dertemuthe, William Assheldene, John Whetene, William Henre, "and many others." Dated on Sunday after the Feast of St. Peter's Chains, 36th Edward III. The seal, in red wax, has, on a shield, a fanciful cross.

A parchment deed, in Latin, the seal lost, whereby Alice, daughter of Martin de Estone, grants to Richard Stokehaye a moiety of a messuage and of a curtilage, between the messuage and curtilage of Joan, widow of Martin de Estone, and the tenement of John le Maan, and the curtilage of Joan, daughter of William Vere, and the way from Hardinasfeorde to Thounstalle; to hold to the said Richard, and to the heirs of the bodies of the said Richard and Alice, lawfully begotten. Witnesses, William Asseldene, John Clerk, William Henry,

John Wetone, Roger Pole, Walter Gordone, John Mathou, "and others." Dated at Clyftone Derthemouthe, in the 38th year of Edward III.

A parchment deed, in Latin, whereby John Paytefyn grants to Alice, daughter of Richard Stokehaye, his curtilage in Hardinasse, near the curtilage of Agnes, widow of Adam le Hopfre, and the king's highway, leading from the Fluteshencde towards the church of St. Clement of Tounstalle; to hold of the Lord Abbot and Convent of Torre, the said Alice paying to them one penny of silver, in equal portions, at the 4 principal terms of the year. Witnesses, William Henry, John Clerke, Roger Pole, Walter Gordon, John Matheu, John Weton, William Asseldene, and others. Dated in the 38th year of Edward III. The seal is lost, and the writing so faint as to be hardly legible.

A parchment deed, in Latin, whereby to John Raleghe and Dionisia, his wife, grant to John Edward and Isabel, his wife, a moiety of a piece of ground in Hardinasse, walled in, with 2½ feet without the wall, between the lands of John Hawele and John Clerk; at a yearly rent of one penny, in equal parts, at the four principal terms of the year. Witnesses, John Hawele, William Hyllay, Peter Cok, William Bovy, John Totyng, "and " others." Dated in the 48th year of Edward III. The small seal, in green wax, a fine impression, represents the sun, the moon, a star, waves, and a fanciful key, the legend, " SEEL FORIS IVANOS ;" a seal significant of travel, and befitting a Raleghe. It had once belonged probably to a foreigner.

A parchment deed, in Latin, whereby Nicholas Lange, tailor, and Roger Piers, Chaplain, grant to Henry Cooke and Isabel, his wife, the tenement in Cliftone Dertemuthe Hardenasse, with 3 gardens adjoining, which they had of the gift of the said Isabel, situate in Newportstret, in Hardenasse, between the tenements of Isabel Rowele, Robert Rendel, and John Loperige, on the east, and the tenements of Richard Prallynge and William Bovy, on the west, the mill-dam, on the south, and the tenement of Henry Canele on the north. Witnesses, John Bakere, William Bovy, John Loperige, William Aleyn, "and others." Dated in the 48th year of Edward III. Two small seals are attached, of green wax, with fanciful devices.

A parchment deed, in Latin, whereby Roger Wythenow and Alice, his wife, and John Leyman and Margery, his wife, grant to Hugh de Westone and Alice, his wife, a tenement and a moiety of a garden adjoining, at Hardenasse, between the tenements of Peter Paris and John Sampson. Witnesses, John Hauleye, Mayor of Dertemouthe, John Clerke, Thomas Assheldene, William Henry, William Knolle, "and others." Dated in the 49th year of Edward III. Of the four seals, only a small fragment of that of Roger now remains.

A parchment deed, in Latin, whereby William Aleyn, and Joan, his wife, grant to John Sodbiry and Alice, his wife, a messuage in Hardenasse, "within the liberty " of the vill of Clifton Dertemuthe and Hardenasse" and between the tenement of Nicholas Pipore and that of John Piers and John Skynnere, and the tenement of Richard Modberd, on the south, and the sea, on the east. Witnesses, John Hawlegh, Luke Bacon, Bailiff of the vill, William Harry, Gilbert Fawy, "and others." Dated in the 50th year of Edward III. There are two seals, in red wax, one of which, with the legend . . . . . " Sobir " . . . . bears the impression of a cross, of fanciful design.

A small parchment deed, in Latin, whereby Joan, widow of John Dartour, of Dertemuthe, quit-claims to Hugh Westone and John Westone, all kinds of actions, real and personal, from the beginning of the world. Sealed with her own seal, and that of the office of Mayor. Witnesses, John Prestecote, John Kentecombe, Richard Henry, "and many others." Dated in the 51st year of Edward III. The small seal, of Joan, representing an ape's head, in red wax, is slightly broken; that of the Mayoralty, in green wax, is in fragments.

A parchment deed, in Latin, whereby John Leyman and Margery, his wife, grant to Hugh de Westone and Alice, his wife, his moiety of a garden in Hardenasse, the other moiety having been lately granted to them by the same grantor, by fine levied in the Court of Clyftone Dertmouth Hardenasse; such garden being between the tenements of Peter Parys and John Sampson. Witnesses, Richard Henry, Mayor of Dertemouthe, John Hauleye, Thomas Assheldene, William Henry, William Knolle, "and others." Dated in the 3rd year of Richard II. The seals, in red wax, are tolerably perfect; that of Margery round, with a fanciful cross and the letters M. I. (not L.), and that of John Leyman, a shield, bearing, apparently, a lion rampant. A contemporary endorsement states that a fine was duly levied thereon, in the Court of Dertemouthe.

An official extract, or copy, in Latin, from the Court rolls of Dertemouth, Monday after the Nativity of St. John the Baptist, 3rd of Richard II. ; being an acknowledgment by John Leyman and Margery, his wife, that the 2 several moieties of a garden, in Hardenasse, are the right of Hugh de Westone and Alice, his wife, as being the gift, by deeds and feoffments, of the said John and Margery ; John Berrye, Seneschal of the liberty of the vill aforesaid, setting his seal of office thereto. The large seal, in brown wax, appended thereto, is in fine condition. It has for legend, " Pro officio Senescalli de " Dertemuth Clift'. H." The steward's horn is represented laid transversely upon the arms of Guido de Brienne, the lord of the Liberty ; the horn bearing reference probably to the original meaning (as supposed by some) of the word " Seneseallus," one who calls the flock together ; represented also by the word " Sty- " ward," or " Steward."

A parchment deed, in Latin, whereby William Hicke, and Blissa [elsewhere Blissota], his wife, grant to Robert Justis and Alice, his wife, a piece of land within the liberty of the vill of Cliftone Dertemuthe Hardinasse, at Hardinasse, near the Chapel of St. Clair, between the tenements of John Olyvere and Adam Bers ; they rendering yearly 4 pence to the chief lords of the fee. Witnesses, John Haule, Richard, Henri, Nicholas Miltone, Richard Clocke, Adam Bers, " and " others." Dated in the 3rd year of Richard the Second. The seals, in green wax, are still attached, but the impressions are very indistinct.

A parchment indenture, in Latin, whereby William Ferreris, son of John de Ferreris, of Churchetoune, grants to Thomas Hoygge and Amy, his wife, for term of their lives, a messuage and two gardens in Hardinasse ; the messuage being between the tenements of William Bovy and Martin Ferreris ; remainder to William Hoygge, their son ; at a yearly rent of 8 pence, payable at Michaelmas and " le Hokke " [Hocktide]. Witnesses, William Bovy, Richard Scoys, John Loperygge, John Gefferey, William Kent, " and " others." Dated at Hardenasse, in the 11th year of Richard II. The seal is lost.

A parchment deed, in Latin, with two seals in red wax, the impressions nearly effaced; whereby Richard Stochay and Alice, his wife, grant to Hugh Weston and Alice, his wife, a tenement near the tenement late of John Tosere, and the way leading from the chapel of St. Clair towards Hardenasworth. Witnesses, John Haule, Mayor of Dertemouthe, Richard Harry, William Harry; Walter Worthi, Edward Justyse, " and others." Dated in the 12th year of Richard II.

A parchment deed, in Latin, with a small red seal, representing a star, formed by intersecting triangles ; whereby Margery, relict of John Leyman, releases and quit-claims to Hugh Westone and Alice, his wife, her right in a tenement and garden in Hardenasse, bought of her late husband and herself (as above stated, under the third year of this reign). Witnesses, John Hawele, Mayor of Dertemouthe, Thomas Aysscheldone, Richard Harry, Walter Worthi, Edward Justyse, " and others." Dated 12th Richard II. The seal of the Mayor, which, it is stated, was originally appended, is lost.

A large parchment deed, in Latin, whereby Richard Stokhay and Alice, his wife, of Brodehomstone, grant to John Bodele and Rose, his wife, one message with curtilage adjoining, in Cliftone Dertemuthe Hardenasse, between the messuages of Joan, widow of Martin of Estone, and of John le Mean, and between the curtilage of Joan, daughter of William Veere, and the way from Hardenasseforde to Tounstalle, south and north ; at a yearly rent of 4 pence sterling to the chief lord of the fee. Witnesses, John Hauleigh, Mayor, Walter Worthi, Bailiff, Thomas Asshendene, Hugh Westone, Walter Russell, " and many others." Dated in the 12th year of Richard II. There are two seals, in red wax, one of which is the seal before used by John Ralegh, but not from the same matrix ; the other having a very similar fanciful device.

A parchment deed, in Latin, whereby John Raleghe, of Hardinasse, grants to Hugh Westone and Alice, his wife, a piece of land at Ropetacle, between the land of Walter de Tounesende and that formerly of Nicholas Clerck, and the curtilage of the men of Hardinasse, on the south, and the way from Hardinasforde to the church of Tounstalle, on the north; at a yearly rent of one penny to the chief lords of the fee. Witnesses, John Combe, John Pers, Gervase Cottebi, John Dau, John

Nicol, " and others." Dated at Hardinasse, in the 13th year of Richard II. The impression of the seal, in green wax, is like that given under the 48th of Edward III., and from the same matrix.

A parchment indenture, in Latin, with a small seal, in red wax, with a fanciful device, stars, and apparently, a beacon; whereby John Raleghe, of Dertemouth, grants to Hugh Weston and Alice, his wife, his tenement in Hardinasse, near the tenement of John Polkysfen, and the highway leading from Hardinasforde to the church of St. Clement of Tounstall on the north, and the tenement of Stephen Modberd and the palissaded place [palatium] of Edward Justyse, on the east ; for a yearly rent of 10s., for the life of the grantor. Witnesses, Edward Justyse, Henry Dele, Stephen Modberd, John Polkysfen, Walter Bayle, " and others." Dated on Thursday after the Feast of St. Matthias the Apostle, 13th Richard II.

A parchment deed, in Latin, whereby William Brege tone grants to William Croft and Soromunda, his wife, all his messuages at Hardonasse in the manor of Nortone, which he lately had of the gift of the said William. Witnesses, William Clerke the younger, Mayor of Dertemouthe, Walter Worthy, Gervase Cottesbury, Nicholas Hake, Richard Harry, " and many " others." Dated at Hardenasse, the first year of Henry IV. The seal, in red wax, has a diminutive impress of a cross, of fanciful design.

A parchment deed, in Latin, whereby Peter Coke, of Hardenesse, and Margery, his wife, grant to Blissota Hicke a rent of 4 pence to be received from their piece of ground in Hardenesse, near the Chapel of St. Clair and the place of William Scherefeld ; with power of distress. Witnesses, John Persone [? the Parson], John Sampsone, Henry Dele. Dated at Hardenesse, in the 2nd year of Henry IV. Of the two seals, in red wax, one represents a fanciful cross, the other, apparently, the Virgin and Child.

A parchment deed, in Latin, with a fragment of a fine seal, in green wax; whereby Blissota Hycke, relict of William, grants to Peter Coke, of Hardenesse, and Margery, a piece of land in Hardenesse, in the manor of Nortone, near the Chapel of St. Clair, and the land of William Scherefilde. Witnesses, John Hauley, Mayor of Dertemuthe, William Knolle, Gervase Cottebury, Edward Justice, John Knolle the younger, " and others." " Given at the Burgage of Nortone," the Tuesday after Easter, 2nd Henry IV.

A large parchment deed, in Latin, whereby John atte Wode and Elinora, his wife, grant to William Brokedone, and Isabel, his wife, a tenement in Clyftone Dertemowthe called " the Wellehowse," between the tenement of William Clerke, on the south, and the tenement of the aforesaid William Brokedone, on the north, and between the garden of William Rowe, on the west, and the lane near the churchyard, on the east ; rendering to the chief lords of the fee the services due and accustomed. Witnesses, Thomas Asschendene, Mayor of the vill of Dertemowthe, Henry Goldsmyth, Bailiff, William Rowe, John Amery, John Boune, John Brether, Clerk, " and many others." Dated the 8th year of Henry VI. This William Brokedone, it may be observed, was not improbably an ancestor of Brokedon, the painter of Alpine Scenery, whose picture of the raising of the Widow's Son, is over the altar in the church at Dartmouth.

A parchment deed, in Latin, whereby John Combe and John Bodrugen grant to Juliana, late the wife of John Cok, the tenement in Cliftone Dertemouth Hardenesse, between the tenement late of John Cok, and the highway leading towards Hardenesseford, on the north, and the deep sea, on the south ; to hold for her life, with remainder to William Weryn and Cecily, his wife ; who, after the death of the said Juliana, are to keep the Anniversary of the said John Cok and Juliana his wife, and of Peter Cok and Margery, his wife, in the church of St. Clement, at Tonstalle, on the Friday next before Palm Sunday in each year ; they to pay in the said church for the priests, the poor, and other necessaries in keeping such Anniversary, the sum of 3s. 4d. Witnesses, John Hawley, Esquire, William Clerk, John More, Hugh Yon, " and many others." Dated in the 14th year of Henry VI. There are two small red seals with fanciful devices, attached.

A parchment deed, in Latin, with a small seal, r of fanciful form, in red wax ; whereby Julia the wife of John Cok, of Hardenesse, grants Combe, John Westone, Richard Sendelle, Joh Richard Rake, William Foterell, Nichola

5.

Walter Stertyng, Walter Mono, John Barry, and John
Knyght atte Wyke, a messuage in Hardenesse, between
the vacant place of John Treboso and the highway near
the chapel of St. Clair, and near to the house of the
heirs of John Foughell; to hold the same of the chief
lords of the fee. Witnesses, John Coplestone, Esquire,
Robert Stephyne, Mayor of the vill of Dertemouth,
John Brusshforde, Richard Carswelle, Richard Tucker,
" and others." Dated in the 24th year of Henry VI.
This was a conveyance to feoffees, no doubt, secretly
to religious uses, in evasion of the Statute of Mortmain: Juliana's name in connexion with the church
of St. Clement at Tunstall (of which the Church of St.
Saviour, in Dartmouth, was only a Chapel), being
mentioned elsewhere. In a hand of about the time of
Elizabeth it is indorsed,—" Julian Coke's graunt to the
feoffees."

A parchment deed, in Latin, whereby Ammia [?Amy]
Veere, daughter of Richard Veere and Alice, his wife,
grants to her mother Alice, her tenement, with garden
and palisaded place [palatio] adjoining, situate in Clyftone Dertemouthe Hardenasse, between the tenements of
Richard Tucker and John Brussheforde, on the east and
west, and between " the salt sea," on the south, and the
way which leads from Hardenysworthe towards the
chapel of St. Clair, on the north, for her life; paying
yearly to the said Ammia and her heirs one red rose on
the Feast of the Nativity of St. John the Baptist; the
said Alice, at her own costs, keeping the same in repair.
Witnesses, Robert Welyngtone, Richard Carswylle,
John Brussheforde, Robert Stephyn, Richard Lambyll,
" and many others." Dated in the 26th year of Henry
VI., at Clyftone Dertemouthe Hardenasse.   The seal is
lost.

HENRY THOMAS RILEY.

THE MANUSCRIPTS OF CANTERBURY CATHEDRAL.

Public Record Office,
DEAR SIR,   March 26, 1874.
PURSUANT to your instructions I inspected the
Archives of Canterbury Cathedral on March 24, in the
company of Canon Robertson and Mr. Sheppard.

The Archives are preserved in cupboards and drawers
in the muniment room, and were to a certain extent
arranged and catalogued by Mr. Cyprian Bunce, in the
beginning of the present century.   He divided the documents into three classes, Cartæ Antiquæ, Libri Registrales,
and Rolls.

Of the Cartæ Antiquæ there are nearly 5,000, ranging
from the Conquest to the Reformation, of which a large
number are of the 11th and 12th centuries.   They are
arranged in drawers, alphabetically, according to the
subjects to which they refer, and though they principally
relate to the estates of the church, each drawer contains
a number of miscellaneous papers, which refer to other
matters, such as litigations between the Cathedral and
other religious foundations, royal privileges, the wine
granted to the Cathedral by Louis VII., etc.

For instance, the box marked D. contains documents
relating to Deepham, Dacoomb, Dover, &c., including
a grant of land by Stephen—" Taxatio Ecclesiæ, 1226,"
—and many papers concerning a dispute between the
Cathedral and the priory of Dover, concerning the
authority of the former, and a brief from Pope Alexander IV. on the subject.   In this box there are 11 documents of the 12th century, 69 of the 13th, 17 of the 14th,
and 8 of the 15th centuries.

Another box contains the submissions of the bishops
of the province of Canterbury to the Archbishops
(Langton and others); in some cases the original submissions are stitched together, in others they are
entered on a roll.   There are also many documents concerning the dispute between Canterbury and York as
to the carrying the Cross, and concerning the quarrel
between Christ Church and St. Augustine's, and the
detection of forgeries executed by the brethren of the
latter house.

In addition to the book of Saxon charters which
Kemble used, there are about ten loose charters, of
which some are probably unedited.

There are some very curious documents in this class,
including a grant of land by Suuithulf, Bishop of
Rochester, A.D. 888;[*] the will of Athelstan Atheling,
1015,[†] and a confirmation by William I. of an English
charter, in which the signatures seem to be autographs.

The Libri Registrales are 28 in number, and are
marked with letters   Most of them contain copies of
leases, &c., but the following are curious.

D. Containing copies of wills from 1500, and lists of
    ordinations held in the cathedral.

G. Copies of bulls from 1060, and of charters, of which
    the earliest is granted by Canute.

H. A treatise on " Husbondrye " in English, and other
    miscellaneous matters.

O. Copies of charters from A.D. 615, regulations for
    the cellarer, &c.

The Rolls consist principally of bailiffs' accounts,
from the 12th century.

Many of the documents which do not refer to estates
had been mislaid, and have been only recently recovered.
These have been very carefully examined by Mr. Sheppard, and he is now engaged in mounting them in books.
Three folio scrap books are already filled.   They commence in the reign of Henry III., and include household accounts, one or two ballads, letters, and other
materials for the history of the Cathedral.

There is another volume called " the Christ Church
Letter Book," which contains royal and other letters,
one of the 14th century, but most of them late in the
15th century.   Many of these are letters from the monks
in London to the prior.   There are also the accounts of
the prior's visits to London.

Another volume in the library contains State papers
of the time of Elizabeth, some being originals, and others
contemporary copies.

I was also shown a copy of the indenture between
Henry VII., the Abbot of Westminster, and the Prior of
Christ Church, for the saying of masses for the King's
family.   The binding is blue velvet, ornamented with gilt
portcullises and roses, and the first page is illuminated.

The mortuary roll of John Hotham, Bishop of Ely,
contains an illuminated portrait in the capital letter.

Another roll of 6 membranes is a copy of the ordinances imposed upon Edward II. by the Earl of Lancaster in 1315, with full details.   Another roll contains
documents of the reign of Henry III., viz. the letter of
the French King about the Barons' war; the letters of
the barons and of Henry III. consenting to refer the
matter to the French King; Urban IV.'s protest against
the provisions of Oxford; his commission to a legate to
absolve the King from his oath to observe the provisions; the letter of the barons to the King; and Prince
Edward's defiance of the barons, dated a day or two
before the battle of Lewes.

Mr. Sheppard has also arranged and mounted the finest
specimens of seals.   There is a fragment of a seal of
William I.; several of the Plantagenets and later Kings,
and archiepiscopal seals from Anselm, giving several
representations of the martyrdom of St. Thomas, some
of which are of great beauty.   There are also many fine
specimens of the seals of other religious houses, and of
private persons.

Mr. Sheppard has devoted much time and infinite
trouble to the arranging and preservation of the
Archives, and, as Canon Robertson tells me, gratuitously, entirely out of love for the work.

As I only spent one day in looking through the
Archives of the Cathedral, this account of them is but a
general one, but I hope sufficient to show you the interesting character of the collection.

I am,
Yours faithfully,
Sir T. D. Hardy, D.C.L.,   CHAS. TRICE MARTIN.
&c., &c., &c.

DEAN AND
CHAPTER
OF CANTER-
BURY.

REPORT OF AN EXAMINATION OF THE HISTORICAL
MSS. BELONGING TO THE DEAN AND CHAPTER
OF CANTERBURY.

The documents in this collection, many of which deal
with subjects of great political interest, have been used
by writers of history from very early times, and hence
it happens that a large number of the most important
of them have found their way into chronicles, and
thence into text-books. This circumstance, whilst it
adds to their value, as being the sources from whence
much information concerning the Church and kingdom
of England has been drawn, takes from them the
freshness which belongs to a newly-discovered hoard.

That the collection has been well kept together, from
the time when the documents first began to accumulate
in the early Middle Ages, is proved by the number of
MSS. of pre-Norman date which Mr. Kemble found in
it at the time when he compiled the Codex Diplomaticus; but the Canterbury MSS. in the Cottonian
collection, and the occasional appearance in a London
auction room of a parchment which once belonged to the
convent of Christ Church, show that these muniments
have not entirely escaped spoliation.

The whole collection is divided into two distinct
parts.

I. *The Registers*, of which it is proposed to give an
account in a later part of this report.

II. *The Chartæ Antiquæ*, detached MSS. about 5,000
in number, ranging in date from the eighth century to
the sixteenth. A very large proportion of these, certainly 4,000 out of the 5,000, may be described as title-
deeds, interesting, as preserving the ancient names of
persons and places, of fields, boundaries, and woods,
but not having sufficient historical value to entitle them
to detailed notice in this report.

The MSS. which remain after the separation of the
title-deeds treat of a great variety of subjects, but all
have more or less reference to the religion and politics
of bygone days, and are therefore valuable to the
antiquary and historian.

These Chartæ Antiquæ have been examined and endorsed at least three times, so that at the present day
many of them have three descriptive titles, which in a
few cases are discordant with each other.

Those which are dated before the reign of Henry II.
bear on the back a short clear description, written in a
strong thick character, with ink which still retains much
of its blackness. This is the work of an anonymous 12th
century librarian.

During the priorate of Henry of Eastry, who died in
1331, the MSS. were again looked over, a title being
endorsed upon those which had none, and in many cases,
a date or some additional explanation being appended
to the work of the 12th century editor.

The ink of this endorser, who wrote in a clumsy hand,
with a full pen, has faded to a reddish brown iron mould.

The third and last complete examination of the
Chartæ was made in 1806 by Mr. Cyprian Bunce, who
then compiled the Great Catalogue which is still in use.

At that time the muniments seem to have been regarded only as law papers, valuable in proportion as they
related to the title by which the cathedral body held their
estates, and hence it occurred that many MSS. of considerable antiquarian value were thrown aside, stowed
away in chests and hampers, and omitted from the catalogue. These rejected documents have now again been
brought into daylight, and arranged in four volumes,
three of which are known as "Scrap Books A. B. and
C." (" S. B." of the references in this report), and one
especially interesting volume labelled "Ch. Ch. Letters."

All those deeds which retain their ancient seals have
lately, by direction of the Dean and Chapter, been
separated from the bundles in which the MSS. have
hitherto been tied, and (each seal having been mounted
on card, or bound in a brass rim, as occasion required)
they are now placed in two large cabinets, where they
fill more than 20 spacious drawers.

Those MSS. which have no seals, having been cleaned
and smoothed, now occupy the drawers of another
cabinet. They are kept in portfolios, each of which
corresponds, as to its contents, with a division of the
Great Catalogue.

In the "Index of Subjects" the Chartæ Antiquæ are
arranged under the following heads:—

Abbeys foreign.

C. 1283, circ. 1193. R. Abbot of Pontigny recommends his proctor Brother Hugo to Geoffrey Prior of
Christ Church.

"Copiosa vestre benignitatis horrea, et promptuaria
vestre promptitudinis largiflua, nunquam nobis et
nostris desideriis clausa vel abscondita, sed indesinenter
reserata fuerunt in multorum ubertate favorum et
habundantia multiplicum gratiarum, et idcirco vestre
discretioni gratias quas possumus referimus, licet non
quantas debemus," &c.

M. 376, 1311. A copy, under the seal, now lost, of the
Commissary of Canterbury, of letters of attorney constituting two proctors for the abbey of Pontigny,
"presentibus litteris per duos annos tantummodo
"duraturis."

Alien Abbeys and Ecclesiastics holding English
Benefices.

M. 371, c. 1374. A list of ecclesiastical benefices in
Kent held by foreigners. This parchment is not dated,
but the mention of William Cardinal Archdeacon of
Canterbury indicates some year not long before 1374,
the date of his death.

"Dns. Willms. sacro-sancte Romane ecclesie Cardinalis, alienigena, optinet Archidiaconatum Cantuarie, et
not residet in eodem, cujus verus valor . . . . . . so
extendit ad vii. c. florenos. Et Dns. Arnaldus Savage
miles, et Johannes Barter Rector ecclesiæ de Westwell
. . . procuratores, ut dicitur, dicti Dni. Cardinalis . . .
occupant et tenent per se et suos fructus . . . . dicti
archidiaconatus, et eos occuparunt per duos annos
ultimo preteritos excepta quarta parte unius anni.

"Abbas et Conventus Monasterii de Lollay [Lonlay,
in the province of Tours] alienigene optinent ecclesiam
de Folkstan . . . . . cujus valor . . . . se extendit
ad xxxiii. marcas.

Frater Petrus Prior de Horton et confratres sui . . . .
optinent ecclesiam de Brabourne, ... que valet
xlv. marcas, ... et occuparunt . . . per quinque
annos et amplius.

"Abbas Sci. Bertini et conventus ejusdem, alienigeno,
optinent ecclesiam de Chilham cum capella de Molessh.
. . . que valet per annum xl. lib. et eciam ecclesiam de
Thrulegh . . . . que valet xxxv. lib. quarum fructus et
proventus autumpnales ultimi anni preteriti occuparunt,
auctoritate Dni. Regis Frat. Egidius de Ardenburgh
monachus dicti monasterii alienigena vocatur Prior de
Thrulegh et residet in eadem . . . . &c.

"Abbas et Conventus de Insula Dei, [L'Isle-Dieu, in
Normandy] alienigene, habent ecclesiam de Upchurcho
. . . . que valet per annum xxxv. marcas . . . . &c.

"Abbas et Conventus Monasterii de Pontiniaco,
alienigene, habent . . . . ecclesiam Sci. Nicholai de
Romenal cum capellis suis, que valent . . . . xv. marcas.
Et fructus . . . . de tribus . . . . annis occuparvit
Johannes Frauncoys . . . . tanquam fermarius Dni.
Regis, ... sed a festo Omnium Sanctorum Rob.
Bregge jam vicarius ecclesie de Romenal, ex concessione
Dni. Regis, ut dicitur, occupavit . . . . et occupat.

"Abbatissa et Conventus Monasterii de Gynes, alienigene, habent . . . . ecclesiam de Nywentun juxta Hethe
. . . que valet per annum . . . . xx. marcas, ... ac
eciam ecclesiam de Promhell, ... ac eciam ecclesiam
de Grenseto . . . . &c.

"Magister Hugo Pegm. alienigena, optinet redditus
ecclesie de Maydenstane . . . . que valet per annum
octies viginti marcas . . . . &c."

R. 51, 1060. Inspeximus of a charter of Edward the
Confessor, by which he gave to the church of St. Mary
of Rouen "villam quamdam nomine Ottregiam," in
England. Probably Ottery St. Mary, Co. Devon.

R. 56. Exemplification of a charter of Henry II. by
which he confers upon the church of St. Mary at Rouen
one half of the manor of Killum [Kilham, near Hull?]
to be appropriated to the table of the canons there.
The charter is especially addressed to the King's
subjects in "Eboraciscyra."

I. 229, I. 250, and R. 53. Certificates referring to the
foregoing charter, attested by Richard Bishop of Evreux, and R. Abbot of St. Audoen. Two of these are
dated 1227 and 1236.

R. 52. Inspeximus by the Abbots of Bec, Jumièges,
and St. Audoen (or Ouen, at Rouen)of a charter of
Henry II., granting to the Dean and Chapter of St.
Mary, Rouen, a weekly market, and a fair lasting two
days, at their manor of Killum.

C. 1264. Inspeximus by the same abbots of a charter
of Henry II., conferring the manor of Clare upon the
church of St. Mary, Rouen. Inspeximus dated 1227.

R. 54. Inspeximus of the same charter, and of its
confirmation by Richard I.

B. 391, 1220. A certificate of the Abbot of Faversham
and others, reporting the result of an inquiry which,

3 H 2

by the Pope's command, they had made concerning
matters in dispute between the monastery of St. Bertin
and Margaret de Loveland. Margaret had built a
chapel on her own land at Loveland, to the prejudice of
the church of Throwley, and the monastery, as patrons
of the church, applied to the Pope (Honorius III.) for
redress. The Abbot of Faversham and two others were
delegated to be judges in the cause; they called the
parties before them and effected a compromise; the
chapel was licensed, and the monastery obtained the
patronage.

B. 392, circ. 1200. An entire skin of parchment
covered by exemplifications, in different hands, of eight
deeds referring to the English possessions of St. Bertin's
abbey.

1. The first gift of the church of Chilham. This was
witnessed by Silvester, Abbot of Saint Augustine's, and
it contains a clause which provides for the maintenance
of two priests, who were to live in the house belonging
to the monastery, to receive all their sustenance and
"victualia, tam equis quam hominibus" from the stores
of the patron, except their straw (palea), which they
were to furnish for themselves.

Henry de Chastell, Archdeacon of Canterbury, and
his vice-archdeacon are witnesses to this inspeximus.

2. Confirmation by Hamo de Truiloe of his father's
donation of the church of Throwley to the abbey of
St. Bertin. As a consideration for this confirmation the
abbey is to receive De Truiloe into society, (as a con-
frater), to write his name in the Martyrologium which
is annually recited in the chapter-house, and to admit
him to all the benefits of their masses, alms, vigils,
fasts, and prayers.

Clarembald the first Abbot of Faversham, Bartholomew de Badelsmere, and Peter his son, are among the
witnesses.

3. Hugo de Dover's gift of the church of Chilham to
St. Bertin's. In this copy the donor is named Hugo de
Chilleham filius Fulherti de Dofra.

4. Confirmation, by Adrian IV., of the churches of
Chilham and Throwley to the abbey of St. Bertin's.

7. Warren, son of Simon le Pick of Dover, conveys
to the abbey of St. Bertin two acres of woodland, at an
annual rent of tenpence, the consideration being a
money payment of twenty-nine shillings.

8. John, son of Ralph de la Dane, conveys an acre of
woodland to the abbey.

At the end of the membrane is a crowded paragraph
containing a list of these instruments, together with
many others.

L. 383, circ. 1130. A formal recognition by Alexander
Bishop of Lincoln of the title of the abbey of Bec to
certain possessions in England. The churches of Wedon
and Winecomb, with their lands and tithes, are mentioned, but the donors of these are not named. The
other endowments, which all lie in the neighbourhood
of Wallingford, are said to be presented by Milo Crispin
and Matilda de Walingeford his wife.

B. 397. A confirmation by Henry III. of all the gifts
and endowments, both in Normandy and England, conferred by his grandfather and others upon the abbey of
Bec.

B. 371, 1190. A bull of Clement III. confirming to
the abbey of Bec all the English endowments which
they owned at the date. "Clemens. . . . . Quociens
" postulatur a nobis quod religioni et honestati con-
" venire dinoscitur . . . . . Ea propter, dilecti in Dno.
" filii, vestris justis postulationibus grato concurrentes
" assensu, Ecclesiam de Glinde . . . . . vobis et per
" vos ecclesie vestre auctoritate apostolica confirmamus,
" et presentis scripti patrocinio communimus."

The leaden bulla is still attached by a silken cord.

B. 397, 1227. A confirmation by Henry III. (Manu
Radulfi Except. Epi. Cancellarii) of a charter of his
grandfather.

The original charter of Henry II. had approved of
endowments conferred upon the abbey of Bec by Matilda the Empress and thirty-two other benefactors. The
donors, whose gifts lay both in England and Normandy,
came from all classes of society, the Earl of Essex being,
after the royal family, the first of a series of benefactors
which descended to Wil. fil. Radl. Ostiarii, who contributed an annual sixteen shillings in tithes.

The great seal which corroborates this deed is impressed on green wax, and is the finest specimen in this
collection.

S. 333. Archbishop Winchelsey confirms to the church
of St. Phillibert a pension, first granted by Abp. Langton, issuing from the church of Saltwood. This pension
is dealt with in the next deed.

S. 384, 1297. A commission addressed by Boniface
VIII. to the Dean and Precentor of London, appointing them judges to decide a cause in which the Abbot
of Bec claims a pension from the church of Saltwood.
The suit had been before several officials who had delayed their decision, and therefore the Pope sent this
commission, requiring the delegates to conclude the
matter within three months.

The bulla secured "filo cannabino" remains affixed
to this instrument.

G. 187, 1202. Abp. Hubert sends a mandate to W.
Gernon, reciting a letter of Innocent III. "Innocen-
" cius Episcopus, &c. . . . . . Ex siquidem dilecti filii
" Magistri Johannis de Columpna qui suo probitatis
" obtentu, intuitu quoque consanguineorum suorum
" quos sincera in Dno. diligimus caritate, carus est
" nobis admodum et acceptus, fuit propositum coram
" nobis quod W. de Brueira, cum quibusdam fautoribus
" suis, ecclesiam suam de Gatesden per violentiam oc-
" cupans, fructus ejus quos invenit ibidem contra justi-
" ciam asportavit, et ei restituere contradicit. Quo-
" circa fraternitati tue per apostolica scripta manda-
" mus." &c.

P. 53, 1236. John of Ferentino gives general notice
that Gregory IX. has conferred upon Gregory of Anagni the "provision" in Ch. Ch. Canterbury which the
Cursor of Innocent III. formerly held, and that the
proctor of the monastery has compounded by paying
" decem marcas bonorum, novorum, et legalium ster-
" lingorum," in consideration of which payment the
Pope has surrendered all claim to the "provision."

Endorsed in 14th century, "Composicio inter Grego-
" rium et procuratorem capituli, de quietancia unius
" provisionis quam petebat, pro x. marcis. Tempore
" Gregorii Papæ IX."

S.B. a. 11, 1270. Theodosius de Camilla, non-resident
rector of Wingham, has allowed the ornaments of the
church to go to decay, and the Prior of Ch. Ch., with
the consent of the proctor of the alien rector, has seized
coin and other chattels found on the premises to furnish
money with which to replace the ornaments, and also to
pay a fifteenth to the King.

W. 187, 1281. A citation from the Dean of St. Audoen, addressed to the prior and convent of Canterbury,
requiring them to appear at St. Audoen to answer in
a suit in which Theodosius de Camilla is plaintiff.
Theodosius is described as "capellanus Dni Pape et
" Rector Ecclesie de Winham " (Wingham).

S. 411, 1333. The proctor of an alien patron consents
to an exchange of benefices. The proctor describes himself as "humilis et devotus clericus Bernardus Vinen-
" tis, venerabilis et discreti viri Dni. Vitalis de Testa,
" Canonici in ecclesia de Sarum, et collegiate ecclosie de
" Wingham Cantuariensis, et Rectoris ecclesiarum de
" Schorham Roffensis, et de Henneye Sarum diocesium,
" ac patroni ecclesie de Halstede dicte Roffensis diocesis
" . . . . procurator."

S.B. a 33, 1349. A mandate requiring an inquisition
to be held to inquire into the status of the church of
Lynsted. The preamble states that a new vicar has
been presented by Raymond Pellegrini, the proctor of
Peter Cardinal of Sta. Maria Nuova, Archdeacon of
Canterbury, and therefore patron of Lynsted. [This
Petrus (Rogerius) was nephew of Clement VI., and
afterwards himself Pope, with title Gregory XI.]

S. B. c. 80. and c. 149, 1374. Inquisitions to assess
dilapidations at Lymne, Teynham, and Hackington.
William Judicis, Archdeacon of Canterbury and Rector
of Lymne, Hackington, and Teynham, was a nephew
of Clement VI., and a cardinal of the Roman Church.
When he died, in 1374, his successor in the archdeaconry, Henry Wakefeld, caused these inquisitions
to be made; the first of these parchments being
the returns sent in by the assessors, and the second
the schedules containing details of the dilapidations.
Ornaments, roofs, windows, books, vestments, enclosures, and parsonages were all in a state of ruin
and decay, partly caused by neglect, and due, in some
cases, to the portable materials having been sold by the
late incumbent. The total sum, which the assessors
considered to be necessary for restoring the property of
the archdeaconry to a lawful condition, amounted to
666l. 16s. 8d. in the money of the time.

Aqueduct.

In the 12th century Prior Wibert caused a copious
supply of spring water, brought by leaden pipes from a
hill about a mile away, to be conducted into all the
offices of his monastery. There are among the Chart.
Antiq. nine documents which refer to this subject, seven

DEAN AND CHAPTER OF CANTERBURY.

of the nine being agreements between the prior and the owners through whose land the pipes were carried. The contracts provide that, in consideration of a small annual payment, the prior shall have free access to the pipes when they require repairs or alterations. The canons of St. Gregory, through whose orchard the pipes passed, were allowed to attach a branch for supplying their house.

W. 224. " Theobaldus dei gratia . . . . toti Hali-" moto de Sco. Martino . . . . Sciatis nos dedisse " . . . . dilectis. filiis nostris priori . . . . paulo-" plus quam unam acram paludis . . . . in valli " apud Horsfalde ubi fontes erumpunt et defluunt usque " ad stagna eorum, ut melius et liberius possint fontes " suos curare, et stagna sua emendare, et utilius custo-" dire." &c.

W. 232. Two extracts, one in French, the other in Latin, in Somner's writing, " concerning the conduits " at Christ Church."

These are taken, 1. From a MS. in " Sir Simond " Dewes his library ; and 2. " From a martyrologium in " the library of the Earl of Arundell." The extracts, which are quite uninteresting, have translations annexed.

For details of the distribution of this spring-water, see an article by Professor Willis in the " Archæologia " Cantiana," vol. vii.

Appointments to Offices.

These are MSS. which show the procedure in the conferring of monastic and other offices.

C. 179. Abp. Richard appoints a " custos curiæ mon-" asterii."

S. B. a. 183, 1300. The Abp. requires the prior to admit a person whom he has appointed " senescallus " aulæ prioratûs."

S. B. a. 183, 1304. The Abp. requires the prior to invest his " senescallus aulæ hospicii" with the office of " custos magnæ portæ curiæ prioratûs."

C. 233, 1397. The convent confirm the Abp's. appointment of a " senescallus aulæ."

A. 200, 1478. The Abp. appoints, and the prior confirms, a new bedell.

A. 19, 1529. The Abp. appoints an appraiser to serve him in the city of London.

S. B. a. 118, 1533. The Abp. appoints a " custos " manerii" for Lambeth. The salary is threepence a day, with perquisites.

S. B. c. 89, 1534. The prior appoints two woodreeves, who are to hold office for life. This is rather a lease granted for a consideration, than an appointment to an office.

A. 22, 1536. The Abp. appoints to the office of Penitentiary of Ch. Ch. one monk, selected from three presented to him by the chapter.

Archbishops, Elections of, and Transactions incident upon Vacancies of the See.

A. 30, 1125. A slip of parchment, addressed by Honorius II. to Wm. of Corboil, Abp. of Canterbury, entitled " Ne bona ecclesiæ dissipentur, defuncto Archiepi-" scopo." The writer confirms to the church all the possessions which belong to it, and prohibits that " detest-" able custom" by which, at the death of an archbishop, the goods of the monks are devastated. This spoiling of the church is prohibited by a very strong penal clause. If any person, lay or clerical, having been once, twice, and thrice warned, shall retain ecclesiastical goods unlawfully obtained, " potestatis et honoris sui dignitate " carere, reamque se divino judicio existere de perpetua " iniquitate cognoscat, et a sanctissimo corpore ac san-" guine Dei ac Domini Redemptoris nostri Jhu. Christi " aliena fiat, atque in extremo examine, districtæ ultioni " subjaceat."

A. 187, 1206. A peremptory letter from Innocent III. to King John, requiring him to consent to the promotion of Reginald, the sub-prior, to the archbishopric of Canterbury. This letter, the tone of which is very characteristic, hardly supports the account of the Pope's wishes on the subject of this election as it is recorded by Paris :—

" Si regiæ petitiones libenter admittimus, et eas, " quantum honestas patitur, efficaciter promovemus, " indignum existeret si nostras preces et monita recusares " admittere ; præsertim cum nostri propositi non existat to " aliquando interpellare pro aliquo quod te non decent " exaudire . . . . Licet enim tuam volimus magnificen-" tiam honorare, ne in hiis exaudire propensius quæ tuæ " sint benoplacita voluntati, quia tamen deferre deo magis " quam hominibus nos oportet, nullius precibus vel amore " declinabimus in dextram vel sinistram, sed via regiâ

procedentes, quantum nobis Dominus dignabitur inspirare, quicquid postulaverit ordo juris investigare curabimus, et non habentes respectum ad hominem, sed ad Deum, ipso duce, studebimus adimplere."

S. 369, 1233. Congé d'élire under the great seal of Henry III. The King, addressing the prior and convent, says that he has received two monks, who report the bereaved state of the church, and therefore he grants to the chapter permission to proceed to the election of an archbishop, with this caution, " Rogantes " quatenus, prout pro oculos habentes, talem vobis et eis " eligere curetis in pastorem, qui deo devotus et " ecclesiæ vestræ regimini idoneus, et nobis, et regno " nostro utilis esse dinoscatur."

A. 188, 1272. A public instrument reciting Apostolic letters received from Pope Gregory X. The letters are addressed to Abp. Kilwardby, the elect of Canterbury ; they relate the exceptional circumstances of his election, and request him to provide money out of his official revenues to compensate Adam Chillenden, who, after election as archbishop by the convent, had gone to Rome and there, at the Pope's suggestion, resigned his office.

S. 372, 1278. A deed marking a stage in the long-continued dispute between the suffragan bishops of the southern province, and the priors of Christ Church who claimed archiepiscopal authority during the vacancy of the see of Canterbury.

The endorsement gives the sense of the instrument : " Composicio inter nos et Episcopos suffraganeos ecclesiæ " nostræ de jurisdictione nostra, sede vacante, in diocesi " et provincia Cantuariæ, et de creatione officialis Capi-" tuli Cantuariensis, et aliis sub signis vii. suffraganeo-" rum."

Six of the seals remain.

S. 410, 1293. The official of the prior and convent canonically coerces some misdemeanants. That is, the prior and convent exercise, and delegate, the spiritual authority of the archbishopric, sede vacante.

A. 189, 1294. Abp. Winchelsey gives notice to the Chapter of Christ Church that certain rectors and vicars excommunicated by them during the vacancy of the see, have desired a hearing, and that he has given them a day. The prior is informed that he can appear at the same time if he consider it necessary to do so.

S. B. a. 49, 1313. Congé d'élire granted by Edward II. after the death of Abp. Winchelsey.

A. 195, 1313. The instrument by which the monks of Christ Church depute three of their number to select seven others to form a committee for choosing an archbishop :—" Vobis plenam et specialem concedimus poten-" tatem, usque ad consumpcionem finalem candelæ in " lucerna coram vobis reposito duraturam, ut vos, vice " vestra et nostra, eligatis et eligere valentis septem per-" sonas idoneas alias a vobis de commonachis et confra-" tribus nostris . . . . quæ septem personæ, aut quatuor " de ipsis, plenam habeant potestatem, usque ad præsentis " diei noctis tenebras duraturam, ... ecclesiæ nostræ " vacanti de pastore idoneo providere."

S. 392, 1328. An instrument in all respects similar to the last.

A. 196, 1333. Letters of attorney appointing two monks to be proctors of the convent, for the purpose of announcing to the Pope that the chapter had chosen John (Stratford) Bp. of Winton to be their archbishop.

A. 411, 1333. A patron presenting a clerk to a benefice requests the prior and convent, sede vacante, to institute him.

S. B. a. 47, 1333. Abp. Mepham being dead, the prior and convent ask permission from the King to proceed to the election of a successor.

S. 416, 1374. The see of Canterbury being vacant, the clergy of the deanery of Sandwich appoint a proctor who shall in their behalf profess canonical obedience to the prior and convent of Ch: Ch., the spiritual head of the diocese.

A. 192, 1374. In 1368 Abp. Simon Langham resigned his office and went into exile, having forfeited the King's favour by accepting the dignity of cardinal. Six years after, coming to England in the character of nuncio and Bishop of Præneste, he was again chosen by the convent to fill the see of Canterbury. This instrument is the formal record, under the hand of a notary, of the cardinal's re-election. The King, greatly incensed, refused to assent to the choice of the monks, and perhaps it is from this cause that the present parchment has been violently torn, not out, into three pieces.

S. 419, 1375. The Prior of Ch. Ch., sede vacante, is authorised by the Pope's nuncio, who is also the " col-" lector" in England, to absolve the rector of a parish who has been excommunicated for delaying his payments.

DEAN AND CHAPTER OF CANTERBURY.

A. 199, 1443. Draft on paper of the Notarial Act of the election of Abp. John Stafford.

X. 15, 1443. "Solutiones expensarum facto per
" Johannem Priorem Ecclesie Xpi. Cant., sede vacante,
" circa diversas causas vacationem contingentes," &c.
"Fratri Will° Plympton, ordinis predicatorum, predi-
" canti in vulgari in die parasceues . . . . appari-
" tori commissarii misso ad Otteford pro Episcopo
" Roffensi . . . . pro sacro crismate conficiendo, ac
" ordines generales Sabbato sancto celebrandos.
"Magistro Rogero fratri predicatori pro sermone
" dicendo in visitacione.
" Rob° Byen equitanti ad citandas diversas personas
" ecclesiasticas.
" Expense Dni. Prioris equitantis London . . . . . ad
" informandum Dominum Regem de die electionis.
" Cuidam servienti Dni. Archepi. defuncti adducenti
" iij equos pro usu futuri Archiepi.
" Expens. Dni. Prioris equitantis in visitacionem apud
" Fevyrsham. Dat. Johanni Wodnysburgh pro appro-
" batione testamenti Willelmi Twaites.
" Priori equitanti usque Ledys in visitacione sua
" ibidem.
" Vicario de Assheford collectori procurationum de-
" canatus de Cherryng pro expensis suis.
" In regardo Apparitoris sui."

S. 417, 1374. The Rector of Hollingbourne certifies the Prior of Ch. Ch., sede vacante, that, in obedience to his mandate, he has imposed public penance on a culprit.

S. B. c. 119, 1485. Draft memorandum, in the writing of Prior W. Selling, reporting the death of Abp. Bourgchier, and the election, installation, and enthroni-sation of Abp. Cardinal Morton.

A second paragraph announces that during the vacancy of the see W. de Waynflete, Bishop of Winton, had died, leaving that diocese vacant, and that the prior had performed all episcopal functions at Winchester, excepting only the conferring of orders, the consecra-tion of churches and altars, and the granting of indulgences, these being functions inherent in episcopal orders.

S. 399, 1486. Prior W. Sellyng, for himself and his convent, sede vacante, gives this licence to. Thomas Goldstone, authorising him to preach "latino vel vul-" gari, clero et populo," in all lawful places in the province of Canterbury.

The Scrap Books contain a large number of presenta-tions to benefices bearing date 1349. These came into the hands of the prior in consequence of the frequent vacancies of the see at that time, there having been four Abps. within thirteen months. To the great pestilence or " Black death," which is known to have caused at least one vacancy of the see of Canterbury, may be attributed the number of these presentations. To the confusion which sprang from the same cause we may refer another group of documents in these books. These are letters of attorney by which all the clergy in each Kentish deanery commissioned a proctor to act for them collectively in ecclesiastical suits.

Archdeacon of Canterbury.

C. 15. A small neatly-written parchment addressed by Abp. Theobald to the convent of Ch. Ch.

The writer acknowledges that the monks have a right to exclude from their chapter-house not only his own chaplains, but even the Archdeacon of Canterbury. If the chapter require the advice of the archdeacon, he is bound to come at their summons without delay; in the chapter-house he shall sit on the footstool of the Arch-bishop's seat, but he shall not intrude his vote, or en-deavour to control the proceedings of the chapter.

Also the Abp. writes that, although the convent have at their own expense roofed a house of his with lead, this shall not be construed into a precedent " cum non Con-" ventus Archiepiscopis, sed Archiepiscopi Conventui, " et edificia construere, et bona alia multa conferre, ut " boni patres amore ducti filiorum, a priscis temporibus " consueverint."

A. 43, Dec. 1227. " Carta S. Arepi. de revocatione ec-" clesiarum exemptarum tempore Baldwini et Huberti. " Et de revocatione dignitatis Archidiaconatus."

In this deed the Abp., after reciting the diminution of dignity and jurisdiction which the Archdeacons of Canterbury had suffered through the injustice of his predecessors, who had wished to exalt their new founda-tions at Hackington and Lambeth at the expense of Canterbury, restores to the actual archdeacon (his own brother Simon) the authority which belonged to the office in ancient times. This authority consisted " tam in " correctione morum, quam in ecclesiarum visitatione."

H. 99, 1227. In order to render the income of the Archdeacon commensurate with his dignity, Abp. Lang-ton gives the churches of Teynham and Hackington to be attached " tanquam de corpore Archidiaconatus."

H. 101, 1227. Simon Langton, Archdeacon of Canter-bury, guarantees that the convent of Ch. Ch. shall not in any way suffer from the appropriation of the churches of Teynham and Hackington to the arch-deaconry.

A. 43 to 47, and A. 101 to 106, are documents marking the various stages of a long dispute between Rd. de Fer-ring, the Archdeacon of Canterbury, and the Prior of Ch. Ch., concerning jurisdiction, sede vacante. Many of these are statements under the hand of a notary, and were intended to be sent to Rome to be used as evi-dence in the appeal which one of the parties made to the Holy See; others relate to steps taken at home.

M. 255, 1293. Henry Prior of Ch. Ch. appoints two of his officers " ad monendum canonice Magistrum Ri-" cardum de Feringes, qui se dicit Archidiaconum de " Cantuar, ac eciam per suspensionis et excommunica-" tionis sententias, et alias censuras ecclesiasticas, si ne-" cesse fuerit, compellendum et cohercendum eundem, " ne . . . . . impediat seu impedire presumat; necnon " ceteros quoscunque, cujuscunque dignitatis preemi-" nencie aut status seu condicionis existant, qui jura " et libertates ecclesie nostre Cantuariensis violaverint, " molestaverint, seu perturbaverint . . . . sentenciis " ac censuris prenominatis cohercendos, karissimo dno. " nostro Dno. Edwardo, dei gratia Rege Anglie, et ejus " liberis duntaxat exceptis, vobis conjunctim et divisim " committimus vices nostras."

A. 45, 1298. Is the last document in the cause. The Archdeacon of Bedford, and a canon of Lichfield were appointed to arbitrate by Nicholas III., and by Boniface VIII., and, after receiving many affidavits and examin-ing witnesses on both sides, they drew up this report. This is not a judgment deciding the suit, but rather a certificate authenticating the affidavits which were sent to Rome at the same time. The delegates seem to have been but lukewarm in the matter, for they write : " Im-" pedimenti tamen supervenientis fatalitas seu eventus, " videlicet regni et incolarum Anglie communis pertur-" bacio, rerum discrimina, et adversorum negociorum " personas nostras tangentium occupatio, finem nulla-" tenus perducere permittebant."

S. B. a. 142. Not dated. The rector of Ashford, hear-ing that R. de Clyve, the commissary of the prior and convent, has threatened mischief to all who adhere to the side of the archdeacon, fearing that he may be included in the denunciation, appeals to Rome.

Autograph Signatures.

Royal signs-manual and signatures of persons known to history are found in the Chart. Ant., but they are not numerous.

A. 2 exhibits the crosses of William I. and his Queen, followed by the undoubted autograph signatures of Lanfranc, Hubert the Legate, Walkelin Bp. of Win-ton, Wulstan of Worcester, Remigius of Dorchester, and the mark of (H)erfastus of Thetford. (See under " Primary.")

Some leases are signed by Elizabeth ; her minister the Earl of Leicester gives a receipt for money ; and Cecil Earl of Salisbury signs a document emanating from the Court of Wards and Liveries.

Ecclesiastical dignitaries are represented by an auto-graph " Fiat" of Innocent VIII., and by the signatures of Hubert, Sudbury, and Warham, Abps. of Canterbury, Galfridus, Prior from 1191 to 1206, John Abbot of Abingdon, the Abbot of Battle in 1534, Prior Gold-stone, Prior Sellyng, and some other officers of Christ Church.

The volume of " Ch. Ch. Letters " contains examples of the signs-manual of Henry VI., Edward IV., Henry VII. and of Elizabeth his Queen. The parchment H. 112 bears the symbol, possibly copied, of Innocent II., and the signatures, apparently in autograph, of eight car-dinals.

Articuli and gravamina Cleri.

" C. 254.,c. 1213. G. fil. Petri Comes Essex Justiciarius, " E. Comes Bolonie, R. Comes Cestrie, W. Comes " Warrene, W. Marescallus Comes Pembrochie, W. " Comes Arundel, W. Comes de Ferrariis, Will. Bra-" wer, Rob. de Ros, Gillebs filius R. ejusdem, Rogerus " de Mortuo Mari, et Petrus filius Herberti, salutem " et debitam reverenciam. Sciatis quod bona fide " studebimus quod Dns. Noster Johannes Rex Anglie " pactum et securitatem vobis et aliis, tam clericis quam

" laicis, negotium quod inter ecclesiam Anglicanam
" et ipsum Regem versatum est contingentes, firmiter
" observabit . . . ." &c.

This is the original guarantee given to the church by
twelve of the great barons, thirteen days before John's
submission to the legate at Dover.

Eleven of the seals, more or less damaged, are still
pendent from the parchment. The " pactum et securitas "
alluded to were given by John at the same time, and
tne whole history is to be found in Wendover (ed Coxe,
vol. iii. 248).

O. 138. Endorsed " Concilium provinciale Oxoniense,"
then in a later hand, " Temp..Dni. S[tephani Langton]
Cantuar Archiepi. " Anno dni. MCCXV." This is
a contemporary copy, on three membranes, of the
proceedings of the Council of Oxford. The endorser,
misled by a reference to the Lateran Council, antedated
the MS. by six years.

The canons here propounded are printed in Spelman's
and in Wilkins's Concilia.

M. 260, 1299. " Articuli liberati Dno. Edwardo Regi
" ex parte prelatorum et cleri Anglie, in parliamento
" suo Londonie in quadragesima A.D. MCC nona-
" gesimo nono, tempore R. [Winchelsey] Cant. Ar-
" chiepi. Et postea in parliamento Lyncolnie in Octa-
" bis Sci Illarii, A.D. MCCC. iidem articuli liberati
" fuerunt Dno. Regi in presencia prelatorum et pro-
" cerum tocius regni."

This is a contemporary copy of thirty-four articles in
which the clergy complain of grievances and oppressions.
Twenty-eight of the articles deal with violations of
sanctuary, imprisonment of clerks by secular judges,
presentations of vicars by laymen, &c.; whilst the last
six are concerned with lighter matters, such as the seizure
of horses for the use of the King, and the confiscation of
the goods of alien religious foundations. The substance
of this document, with other gravamina, is given by
Wilkins (ii. 316 seqq.) under the date of 1309.

M. 289, 1294. A general protection granted to the
clergy by Edw. I., after they had yielded to him a
subsidy amounting to a half of their income. This
instrument is addressed " Capitaneis marinariorum, et
" eisdem marinariis, vicecomitibus et omnibus Ballivis."
The preamble runs: " Cum prelati et totus clerus de
" regno nostro medictatem beneficiorum et bonorum
" suorum . . . . liberaliter concesserint et grat-
" anter; Nos eorundem prelatorum et cleri quieti et
" tranquillitati ex hac causa libencius providere
" volentes, suscepimus in protectionem et defensionem
" nostram specialem . . . ." &c.

A mutilated seal is attached to the writ, and the word
" Cantuar" written in the lower margin implies that the
document was a " circular " of which a copy was sent to
all the parties concerned. Wilkins (ii. 200) printed it
from the Worcester Register.

C. 255. An undated document, endorsed " Articuli
" corrigendi in isto sacro concilio in diocesi Cantuar."

K. 11; 1310-11. A contemporary copy of the ordinances drawn up by the Barons' committee for the regulation of the King's household, and of the kingdom in
general. Many of these provisions touch the privileges
of the clergy, but as they are well known to historians
it is not necessary to enumerate them here.

Abbey of St. Augustine.

The Abbots of St. Augustine's, dependent, "nullo
" medio," upon the Roman Church, claimed exemption
from episcopal jurisdiction; on the other hand, the Archbishops of Canterbury, and, sede vacante, the Priors
of Christ Church, demanded submission from the monastery, which was situated in their diocese; from these
incompatible claims arose numerous law-suits and appeals to Rome, various stages of which are related in
the documents forming this group.

A. 49 and A. 51, circa. 1151. Endorsed, " Professio
" Silvestri Abbatis Sci. Augustini Cant. facta Theo-
" baldo Archiepiscopo ad preceptum Adriani Pâpæ."
This instrument in duplicate, fortified by the seals of the
Bishops of London, Evreux, Bath, Norwich, Chichester,
Hereford, and Lincoln, relates how Silvester the Abbot
professed canonical obedience to the Archbishop of Can-
terbury in the presence of the subscribers.

This MS. is valuable inasmuch as that it contradicts the
historians who assert that Silvester received benediction
without making his profession. The abbot is said to
have yielded on the production of the record of a precedent which was inspected by the attesting bishops.

C. 117, 1099. This is the precedent which convinced
Abbot Silvester:—

" Ego Hugo, ecclesie Sanctorum Petri et Pauli, at beati
Augustini Anglorum primi Archiepiscopi, electus Abbas,

promitto Sancte Dorobernensi ecclesie et tibi reverende
Pater Anselme, ejusdem ecclesie Archiepiscope, tuisque
successoribus canonicam per omnia obodientiam."

A. 48. Writ from William II. to the Abbot of St.
Augustine's:—

" W. Rex Anglie, Abbati Sci. Augustini salutem.
Defendo ne alium ordinem, neque consuetudinem, in
ecclesia Sci. Angustini ponas, quam habuisti tempore
Lanfranci Archiepiscopi; et illum honorem quem tempore Lanfranci Archiopiscopi, et subjectionem erga
matrem ecclesiam Cantuarie, habuisti, illum eundem oi
modo obediendo impendo, tu et monachi tui, tam in cam-
panis sonandis, quam in aliis consuctudinibus. Et vide
ne indo amplius audiam clamorem. T. Eudone Dapifero."

A. 209. Alexander III. to the elect of St. Augustine's.
This appears to be addressed to Abbot Clarembald, the
intruder, in 1163. The Pope writes: " Quia tua bene-
" dictio ultra 'quam decuit sep. noscitur dilata fuisse, et
" inconveniens prorsus existit ut religioso conventui
" presse debens, et officio ac nomine magistri carere;
" per apostolica tibi scripta precipiendo mandamus,
" quatenus a venerabili fratre nostro T[homa] Archie-
" piscopo, ... opportunitate suscepta, benedictionis
" munus accipias, et eidem omnem reverentiam . . . ."
&c.

A. 50 to A. 60 are papers in suits and appeals in
which Christ Church and St. Augustine's were alternately
plaintiffs and defendants, A. 53, A. 54, and A. 55 being
compromises and agreements which failed to bring
peace. The dates extend from the middle of the
thirteenth century to the early years of the fourteenth.

A. 193. In a letter to the prior, Archbishop Winchelsey forbids him to communicate consecrated oil or
chrism to St. Augustine's Abbey, which he says would
be to assist his adversaries.

A. 62. Endorsed, " Qualiter Augustinenses venerunt
" ad falsa privilegia sua."
This MS., of which A. 61 is a duplicate, tells an extraordinary tale of forgery, executed by Guerno, a monk of
St. Medard's, at Soissons, in order to support the pretensions of St. Augustine's monastery. The original
letter was addressed by Hugh, Abp. of Ronen, to Adrian
IV.; and it is accompanied by a certificate from Giles,
Bishop of Evreux, addressed to Alexander III., the
successor of Adrian. These letters are printed by Wharton in the preface to vol. ii. of his " Anglia Sacra,"
where, however, the first letter, as well as the certificate, is attributed to the Bishop of Evreux.

Archbishop Becket's Kinsmen.

M. 372, 1168. Pope Alexander III., in the lifetime of
Archbishop Becket, writes to beg that the Archbishop
Elect of Sens will assign to Gillebert, the nephew
" venerabilis fratris nostri T[home] Cantuariensis Ar-
" chiepiscopi," a pension which his kinsman Geoffrey
has previously received.

H. 89. Prior Alan confers upon John, the nephew of
St. Thomas by his sister Agnes, a vicarage in the
church of Halstow.

H. 90. Abp. Baldwin confirms the last gift.

L. 4. Prior Alan confers upon John, nephew of St.
Thomas by his sister Rohesia, a vicarage in the church
of St. Mary Bothage, in the city of London.

C. 165, 1221. A long roll of payments made by the
treasurers of Christ Church, Cant. Among the items
are some which refer to this subject:—

" Pro sotularibus Willelmi clerici et Andree nepotum
Sci. Thome reparandis contra natale xiid.

" Pro sotularibus Willelmi consanguinei Sci. Thome
reparandis vid. eidem Willelmo xiid.

" Pro lineis pannis Thome consanguinei Sci. Thome
xvid. pro sotularibus ejusdem vid. ob.

" Pro sotularibus Andree consanguinei Sci. Thome
contra pascham xxd.

" Pro sotularibus Andree consanguinei Sci. Thome
reparandis vid.

" Pro pannis laneis Rogeri consanguinei Sci. Thome
venientis de Terra Sancta vilx. ixd. ob.

" Pro pannis lineis ejusdem xviiid.

" Pro sotularibus ejusdem xxxd.

" Pro habitu monachico filii. H. de Cobeham et Willelmi consanguinei Sci. Thome lvs."

No especial favour appears to have been shown to
these nephews; in this account they take their place,
not with the more dignified brethren, but rather with
the " conversi," some of whom received gifts of clothing
at the same time as the archbishop's kinsmen.

It is to be noticed that it is only in this group of
papers that the Chart. Ant. present the archbishop as a
creature of flesh and blood; in all other instances where
the name occurs he is alluded to as a supernatural per-

sonage. It seems probable that the name has been weeded out from these archives for political reasons.

Bishops, Election and Consecration of.

C. 109, 1215. A charter of John, given at the instance of the Abp. of Canterbury, and the Bps. of London, Ely, Hereford. Bath, and Lincoln, granting freedom in the election of bishops. This instrument is dated from the New Temple, in London, on the 21st November, and is therefore distinct from a similar charter given at Dover.

Cauciones.—The documents grouped under this head consist chiefly of guarantees given by bishops consecrated, or about to be consecrated, elsewhere than in the church of Canterbury, that such consecrations shall not be used as precedents to the injury of the metropolitical church. With these guarantees, or as they are called in the endorsements "cauciones," are mixed a few letters of excuse from bishops who, having been summoned to take a part in consecrations, were unable to be present. Urgent affairs or weak health are usually alleged as the impediments, but two Welsh bishops were detained within their own frontiers "propter "guerram."

C. 120. A roll of 8 membranes written in the early part of the 15th century. This MS. sets forth the authorities upon which the prior and convent relied for supporting their claim to have the consecrations of all bishops of the southern province performed in their church.

The authorities are quoted in the following order:—

1. Carta Sci. Thome Martyris.

This is a transcript of the charter, and of its confirmation by Gregory IX., certified by the Prior of St. Gregory and the Dean of Canterbury.

The Abp., who apparently foresaw what would be the end of his opposition to the will of the King's party, writes that the church of Canterbury through its connexion with himself has incurred much odium, and from the same cause has suffered loss and damage, "quod tota " fere novit Latinitas"; also, rather than the church should be further injured, "quodlibet tormentum, sed " et mille mortis genera, si tot occurrent, libencius ex-"cipiemus. . . . Nos itaque, licet parati simus pro " pace et indempnitate capud et corpus persecutoribus " exponere, et ne pereat vel ne quid modicum perdat, " perire . . . . ipsam ecclesiam sub Dei protectione " et nostra ponimus." After giving the chapter authority to employ ecclesiastical censures against invaders of their rights, he adds: "Prohibemus ne Episcopi suffra-" ganei alibi consecrentur quam in ecclesia Cant. cui " tenentur ex professione et debita subjectione, nisi de " communi consensu tocius Capituli Monachorum Cant. " Nec crisma vel oleum per Cantuariensem provinciam " dividendum aliunde quam ab ecclesia Cantuariensi " aliquo tempore percipiatur."

This charter, which runs to a great length, is not dated.

2. Confirmation of the foregoing charter by Gregory IX. Dat. Lateran xii. kal. Febr. Pontificatus nostri anno primo.

3. "Protestatio Edmundi Arepi. Cant. de jure Capi-" tuli in consecrationibus Electorum." The spirit of the protestation is contained in the words, "Cum per " libertatem Cant., ecclesie suffraganei sine assensu " Capituli Cantuar. alibi quam in ecclesia Cant. nulla-" tenus debeant consecrari.",

4. Confirmation of the same by Gregory IX.

5. De eadem materia. Innocent IV. assures the prior that all suffragans whom he or his successors may consecrate shall still be bound to profess obedience to the church of Canterbury.

6. A cautionary letter from Gregory IX., promising that the consecration of Robert (Grosseteste) Bp. of Lincoln shall not be prejudicial to the church of Canterbury.

7. A letter from Alexander IV. to Abp. Boniface. He writes that R(oger) Elect Abbot of St. Augustine's has, after great labours, arrived at the Curia, and that he complains that Boniface has refused to give him the benediction in his own monastery. The Pope, having conferred benediction on the abbot elect, sends this letter giving information of the fact, and promising that through his act no damage shall accrue to Christ Church.

From this point to the end, the roll is occupied by copies of about 50 cauciones, the originals of which are in the Chart. Antiq.

C. 125, 1245. A letter from Abp. Boniface, dated from Lyons; he says that he is hindered on his journey to England, and he requires the Bp. of London to consecrate R. Elect of Exeter at Reading.

C. 143, 1327. Notarial act drawn up so that, if necessary, it may be used as evidence of the due observance of all proper formalities in the election of M. de Englefield Bp. of Bangor.

R. 47. "Transcriptum privilegii Alexandri Papæ de " subjectione Roffensis Ecclesie." This is a copy of an apostolic letter sent by Alexander III. to Prior Alan of Canterbury, confirming to him and his successors the supremacy which they have heretofore held over the church of Rochester.

C. 129, S.B. b. 231, X.2. These documents contain the story of Walter Scamel, Bp. of Sarum : how he was consecrated by Abp. John Peckham, extra Cant., the permission of the prior not having been obtained; how the prior appealed to Rome, and to his immediate patron the archbishop, sending at the same time a denunciatory letter to the bishop; all concluding with a general forgiveness and ratification of peace.

S. B. c. 125, 1327. A large part of the Bull of provision by which John XXII. supplied Bp. Grandison to the see of Exeter.

Brus, Robert &c.

S. 270, 1291. A contemporary copy in French of the two clauses of the treaty of Norham, made between Edward I. and the Scots. By the first clause, dated on the Tuesday after Ascension, the claimants, "Florenz " Counte de Hollaunde, Robert de Brus Seingnur de Val " Dununt (Annandale), Johan Baillol Seingnur de " Ga(llo)weye, Johan Comyn Seingnur de Badenough, " Patrick de Dunbar, Counte de la Marche, Johan de " Vescy pur son pore, Nichol de Soulis, e Willame de " Ros," agree to submit themselves to the arbitration of the King of England.

By the second clause, executed on the next day, they consent that Edward shall, under certain restrictions, occupy the strongholds of Scotland, pendente lite.

This document was sent by the King to the convent of Canterbury in order that an authentic record of the facts might be preserved. "Mittimus vobis sub sigillo " scaccarii nostri presentibus appenso transcripta quar-" undam litterarum que in Thesauraria resident." Endorsed, "Rex precipit quod ista transcripta ponan-" tur in cronicis." Published in fac-simile in "National "MSS. of Scotland," vol. ii.

M. 378, 14 Sept. 1318. This MS., which occupies more than a whole skin of parchment, contains a notice addressed by the Cardinals Gaucelinus and Luke, the Papal legates, to all religious persons and corporations in England and Scotland, requiring them to denounce "Robertum de Brus, non Regem, duntaxat regni guber-" natorem Scocie," and with extinguished tapers and tolling bells to pronounce sentence of excommunication against him and his adherents "ter et amplius in quali-" bet missa sollempni, semel post epistolam, secundo " post Evangelium, et tercio post communionem." This. notice is endorsed, "Processus Cardinalium " contra Robertum de Brus et Scotos."

Bulls, Original.

H. 112. A Bull of Innocent II. affecting the church of Hereford. The autograph signatures attached to this Bull are remarkable.

B. 371. Clement III. The leaden bulla "filo serico " is still attached.

S. 334. Boniface VIII. The leaden seal is in this case attached by a hempen string, "filum cannabinum."

S. B. c. 125. A Bull of provision by which John XXII. appoints a bishop to Exeter.

Canterbury, Christ Church sequestered.

C. 1,274, 1284. A parchment document, considerably decayed and greatly discoloured, which contains the history of the seizure of the priory of Christ Church by the King's escheator, with the appeal to the King, and its consequences. A prior having resigned, the King's escheator took possession of the revenues of the house, alleging that " priorata vacante " they belonged to the Crown.

" Memorandum quod anno MCCLXXXIIII. regni vero " Regis E. filii Regis H. XIII° Dns. Thomas Ringe-" mer qui tunc fuit Prior . . . . resignavit, et " habitum nigrum exuens habitum Cisterciense induit " apud Bellum-locum [Beaulieu]. Hoc audito Magr. " H. de Bray tunc Escaetor Dni. Regis citra l'rentam, " statim totam prioratum cepit in manum Dni. Regis, " dicens custodiam prioratus ad ipsum Regem perti-" nere, prioratu vacante ; quod nunquam prius oculus " vidit, nec auris audivit."

After the seizure the sub-prior hastened to the King in Norfolk, who, deferring the consideration of the matter until after he had met his council and parliament, ultimately acknowledged that his predecessors had never claimed the custody of the monastery, and withdrew the sequestration.

After a lapse of 13 years, driven to fury by the Bull "Clericis Laicos," fortified by which Abp. Winchelsey and his clergy refused to contribute to the King's wars, Edward I. again took possession of the monastery, and by sealing up the granaries and stores brought the monks to the borders of starvation.

On Ash Wednesday, being Feb. 27, 1297, John Dymoke, the King's officer specially appointed for the purpose, came, accompanied by the sheriff of Kent and others, into the court of the priory, and affixing seals upon the doors, took formal possession of the premises. The monks made no opposition, but secretly, fearing to do so openly, they introduced a notary, who drew up a precise statement of all the acts of oppression of which he was a witness, attesting the truth of his narrative by affixing his notarial mark.

X. 6, is the narrative thus drawn up and corroborated.

He says that he found Dymoke in possession, and calling himself the King's servant; the doors were all sealed with green wax, having an impression "quasi "leonis rapacis"; and to the monks he found Dymoke "alimenta vite necessaria, esculenta, et poculenta, "quibus ipso die vesci debebant, penitus denegantem."

C. 169, 1297. On the 6th of March following Dymoke's entry, the Granetarius requested the notary to visit the monastery once more, in order that he might testify that the granary was sealed up, and that the corn had spoiled from "heating." He says, "Ascendi in quod- "dam solarium ad caput granarii, et per quandam "fenestram inspiciens, vidi et inspexi dictum bladum "ad centum summas frumenti videlicet estimatum .. ". . eo quod erat ita calidum in palpando quod in eo "bene calefieri frigida posset manus, et fumus . . . . "exibat ab eo," &c. Here the story ends, as far as it is told by the Chart. Ant.

Schola Cantuariensis.

The schoolmaster at the beginning of the 14th century, working in a high-handed manner, attempted to use the thunders of the church for punishing little culprits who, in modern times, would be corrected by the cane.

X. 4. S. B. b. 19 and 20. Are four documents, three of which are notices to offenders, the fourth being a solemn investigation undertaken by the [rural] Dean of Canterbury in order to ascertain if the master was entitled to the power he claimed.

In the first case, the summons begins, "Acta in scolis "Cant. die Junii," &c.; it then goes on to charge against John Medi that "violentas manus injecisse Stephano "Borstede scolari meo," appointing next Saturday for settling the dispute. Violent laying on of hands is still often settled on a Saturday afternoon.

In the next case, Thomas Birkwood has offended in that "in Walterum clericum vice-monitorem meum ". . . . . manus injecisti temere violentas . . . . . "in sententiam excommunicacionis majoris in hujus- "modi, injectores manuum latam, ipso facto incidendo."

Again, he writes solemnly to the Dean, informing him that he has excommunicated "Ricardum de Aula propter "suas multiplicatas et manifestas contumaciones," and he requests that the clergy of the deanery may be required to publish the sentences in their churches "inter "sollempnia."

Once more, he announces to Roger Lymburner that he has already summoned him once, and that, as he did not appear, he now summons him for the second and last time, after which, if he be still contumacious, the usual penalty will follow.

The last document is one of a very formal and official character.

John Everard, the schoolmaster, propounds before the Commissary of Canterbury a document written by Abp. Peckham in 1291. This instrument really does confer upon the schoolmaster the powers which he claims, and the commissary is constrained to require the Dean to publish the sentences when requested to do so by the master.

From which it appears that the Dean had hitherto dealt tenderly with Richard de Aula.

C. 1,267, 1569. An agreement, under the seal of Corpus Christi College, Cambridge, by which the master and fellows consent to prefer the scholars of Canterbury to their foundation.

5.

S. B. b. 174. An eighteenth century master, whose name has been cut off, resigns his office into the hands of the dean and chapter.

Canterbury City.

C. 1,226. The monks of Canterbury had provided timber to assist in fortifying the city; fearing that this act might be used as a precedent, they obtain this guarantee from Hubert de Burgh, the justiciary, who certifies that the wood was provided out of goodwill, and not from any service or duty which the monks owed to the city.

C. 49. A certificate, having the same tenour, given by the (Dowager) Queen of Henry II. The motive cause which prompts her to conciliate the monks is, in her own words, "Audito quod karissimus filius noster Rex "Anglie . . . . detentus est ab Imperatore Romano, "venimus ad memoriam beati et gloriosi martyris . . ". . . ut liberationem Dni. Regis filii nostri pos- "semus, ejus intervenientibus meritis et precibus, "optinere."

C. 79, 1294. Part of a court-roll of the city of Canterbury.

C. 1,228, 1227. A certificate given by Rob. de Ely, citizen of London.

He relates that the King, having required the city of Canterbury to furnish a certain number of men-at-arms "pro guerra sua Scocie," the bailiffs called upon the convent to contribute their proportion. The convent, asserting that they were exempt from all secular service, refused their contribution, whereupon the mayor and commonalty assembled for the purpose of contriving a plan for coercing the prior and convent by the powers of the law. It happened that W. de Ely was present at the meeting, and out of love for the church, not being pressed or even asked, (he speaks in his own person) "predictos Ballivos et Burgenses instanter rogavi "quod ab omnibus dampnis et gravaminibus dictis "Priori et Conventui comminatis et inferendis penitus "desisterent et cessarent, et quia dicti Ballivi et Bur- "genses hujusmodi petitione mei gratanter annuerunt, "Ego . . . . predictos Ball. et Burg. de propriis "bonis meis competenter respexi," &c. An endorsement shows that the compliment which W. de E. paid to the bailiffs amounted to 10l. money of the time.

C. 1,230, 1428. A bond given by the bailiffs of Canterbury to the prior and convent, as a surety that they will abide by the award of two arbitrators to whom, by common consent, they had referred a dispute. The arbitrators were John Martin, Justice of the King's Bench, a Kentish man living at Graveney, (where a fine brass memorial of him still exists in the church), and Geoffrey Lowther. This bond marks a stage in the chronic dispute which embittered the relations of the prior and convent with the city of Canterbury.

It appears that the citizens seized some fish which the maniciple of the convent had purchased at the seaside, alleging that this act amounted to the offence of forestalling, and that their rights were thereby infringed. The matter was submitted to the decision of the arbitrators, with what result does not appear.

C. 1,231, 1432. Exemplification, under the seal of the bailiffs of Canterbury, of the record in a suit of novel disseisin, frissce forcei, in which the prior and convent were the plaintiffs, and Nicholas Barbour defendant. The cause of action was the withdrawal of a rent of 3s. 6d. issuing from a messuage and two shops in Canterbury.

C. 875, 1443. Lease from the citizens to the convent of a piece of land within the city wall, at Queningate, for a term of 13 years, at a rent of 6s. 8d. The land here dealt with is that which the convent obtained in fee simple fifty years later. See C. 1,233 below.

C. 1,233, 1492. A deed of composition made between the prior and convent of Christchurch on the one part, and the mayor and commonalty of the city of Canterbury on the other. The preamble states that discords have long existed between the parties, arising from points of contested privileges and jurisdiction, but that, by the advice of the "counsell and frendys of "eyther of the said parties, they at length have come to a final concord. The deed, on two whole skins of parchment, sets forth the concessions which each party agrees to make in order to purchase a lasting peace. The most important clause is one by which the city resigns to the convent all claim to that part of the city wall, including the bastion towers, which runs between Burgate and Northgate, together with the waste land, and the lane within and adjoining to the wall.

By this concession the city was relieved of the burthen of keeping the wall in repair, that expense

3 I

being taken off their hands by the convent who, on their part, obtained a great advantage in being able to use the newly acquired wall as one of the boundaries of their precincts.

At the time of this composition there was little fear that the city would be called upon to face a siege, and hence a clause which allowed the monks to pierce the fortification with a new postern, and to construct a bridge over the "dyke of the seid cite," was not as imprudent as it would have been in earlier and more turbulent times.

C. 1,154, 1492. The gift and grant from the city to the monastery of the above-mentioned wall and towers, being the corollary to the deed of composition.

C. 1,332 and 1,335, 1500. Record of a trial in which W. atte Wode, the Mayor of Canterbury, and several of his fellow citizens, were indicted for riot with assault, the prosecutor being the Prior of Ch. Ch. The story, which is told in six paper rolls and two parchments reads as follows :—The mayor, to try a right, went outside the Westgate, and being, according to his view, still in the city, he arrested some of the prior's servants, against the peace, &c. He was indicted, he pleaded, the prior rejoined, and at last a jury gave a verdict which was adverse to the mayor.

The prior's "complaynte" relates that the mayor with others to the number of two hundred, arrayed in manner of war, assembled on the 16 of July and issued from the city into a meadow called "the Rosiers," in the county of Kent, and not within the jurisdiction of the city. In the meadow they cut down certain trees called "welowes," and they stopped a dyke which had been made for the "avoiding" of the water in the time of flood. One Thomas Megge, assisted by others, "assauted on "Damp. Thomas Ikham, monke of the seid prior, being " late afore sore sike and walking in the felde for his " recreation, and then and there put him in grete " juberdie of his lyf." Also they "assauted on, bete, " and yll intreted" divers servants of the prior, carrying them into the city, when they took from them certain goods, such as a woode-knyff, a cap containing five shillings and two pence, two swords, a bow and shafts, and a byll, after which they imprisoned them for three days. Meeting Sir Thomas Jure, one of the priests of the almonry, with a "sparhawk" upon his fist, they " assaunted on " him and took away his hawk. The language of the citizens requires that great allowance should be made for changes in manners and customs, for, besides crying "Kylle the horesons," and "Stonde " horeson and yeld thy knyff," they taunted Dan Thomas the sick monk, seizing him by the "grabatum" and saying "Yeld the, horeson monke, comest thou her " to be a captayn this daye?"

On the day after the Westgate riot the mayor violently removed the fishmarket from Burgate Street, where it was conveniently near to the priory gate, to another street, to the great hurt and damage of the convent.

Again, when the "catour" of the church went to the new fishmarket and bought a "halybutte," the citizens took it from him as he was carrying it from the market to the priory gate, "contrarie to all ryght and good " conscience."

The prior, unable to purchase fish in the Canterbury market, sent his manciple to the seaside, where he bought a seme of fish; but this also was seized, as it came into the town, by the riotous citizens, "disapoyntyng in the " same the brethren of the place of ther deners." In addition to these breaches of the peace, the mayor and his fellows committed offences against the laws by trespassing, by building bridges and diverting watercourses, to the damage of the prior.

They also omitted various courteous ancient customs; thus "while hit hathe ben used of a laudable custom of " the mair and other citizens, that at the feste of Crist- " mas have assembled theym selfe in the church at the "tombe of Archibyshopp Sudbury, ther seying divers " orysons and prayours for the sowle of the same " Byshopp, for the greate actes he hath don to the seide " cite, the same maior and citizens, for the greate " malice and grugge as they owed to the seid prior' " and convent, at the fest of Cristmas last paast ab- " sented theym selfe from the seid church, and with- " drew there prayours from thense, and kept there " prayours and orysons under the prisonhous called " Westgate of the seid cite." Lastly, they abstained from joining the nobleman who brought the King's offering to St. Thomas at his feast at Christmas-tide, a thing before unknown. The mayor's reply contains no denial of the facts, but he recriminates, charging the prior with various offences, the taking away of the mace from the

city serjeant being one, and the befouling of the city ditch with sewage another.

The verdict gives detail of the riot, with the accompanying foul language, much more full than even the prior's complaynte. Altogether the jury collected from the evidence and handed down to us a lively picture of the manner in which angry people acted and scolded in early Tudor times.

S. B. b. 186. A memorandum made at the time of the mayor's riot.

"Thes byn the namys of my Lordys [the Prior's] " servauntes that hadde theyr wepnys takyn from " them." The "servauntes" were supposed to be peaceful haymakers, and invalids strolling for their health, and therefore it is odd to find that they were deprived of three swords, a bowe with schaffts, a bowe, a dagger, a bylle, a payer of briganders, and a payer of splints.

C. 1,236, 1501. A petition to the King from the Prior of Cant. This MS., written upon parchment, refers to a later development of the dispute last noticed. The mayor disregarded the verdict, and was summoned to the Star Chamber, where, for want of leisure, the affair was passed over, much to the discontent of the prior, who here begs the King to again summon his adversary " to appere afore your Highnesse or your councell, at a " tyme and place at your plesure to be lymyted, to " annswere to the premisses for the love of God and in " the waye of charite."

M. 256. Three narrow strips of parchment sewn end to end, forming a roll of about 5 feet long, and containing a list of the Mayors of Canterbury, from the first in 1448 to the 106th in the 3rd Philip and Mary.

The earlier entries consist only of the date of the year and the name of the mayor, but scraps of history are interspersed in the latter half of the MS. Thus, under the year 1544, we find :—

"XCIIII. (he being 94th mayor) Johannes Freman. This yere was the towne of Bolon wictoriously won and conquered by Kyng Henry the eight, the xiii day of Septembre.

"1554. Thys yere was the rysing of S. Thomas Wyat. Thys yere Quene Mary was married unto Philipe Prince of Spayne a fore Seint Jamis day at Winchester.

"1555. This day Carnale Pole came from Rome, and was receyved at Calyse by my Lord Clynton . . . . and so came to Cantourbury the xxi day of Novemb. at v of the cloke at afternone.

"Itm. the same yere the xii day of Julii was brent iiii heretykes.

"Itm. the xxi day of August was brent vi heretykes."

In the same yere the mayor and sheriff met the King, going to the continent, and carried him to Christ Church, where he was received by the college. The sheriff carried a white rod before the King, and was proud of it.

"The v day of September was brent v herytykes.

"My lorde Cardynall Pole . . . . . came thorow Cantourbury, and so went on to Calyce, and sat yn a generall councoll . . . . to conclude a peace betwixte the Emperour and the French Kyng, and so retornyd . . . . . into Englond and came to Cantourbury upone Corpus Xpi. day, . . . and went yn processyon with the College after the Sacrament, bareheadyd, and causyd Mast. Mayre of the citie with all the Aldermen to go . . . . next him, save only II lordys, in scarlett, and so on the Sonday after, the Sacrament was borne yn generall processyon, and Mast. Mayre with all the Aldermen went nexte my Lorde in scarlett, and my Lorde Cardynall canayd vi of hys owne gentylmenservants to carry vi torchys of waxe, of his owne proper costys and chargys."

"1556. The xxx day of Januarii, An° Phil. et Marie 2° & 3°, was brent one man and four women, then beyng Shryffe of Kent Sir Thomas Kempe, and Shryffe of Cantourbury John Semarke."

C. 1237. "Collection of evidences upon my Lo. Arch- " bishop Abbot his Quo warranto against the city of " Canterbury."

The perennial quarrel between the City and the Church, which in the 17th century had inherited the privileges ("tot et tanta et talia") of the dissolved monastery, was not ended by the dissolution.

The Archbishop and the college took the place of the prior and convent in the unextinguished feud.

This document, containing 18 sheets of brief-paper, is filled with precedents favourable to the Abp's. case. The writer has noted in the margin the authorities from whose works his arguments are derived. He refers to Bæda, Lambarde, Camden, Codex MS. Roffens, Domes-

day, Antiquitates Ecclesiæ Brittanicæ, Historia Ead-
meri, W. Malmesbury, and to many of the MSS. in this
collection, quoting, not the originals, but copies in
several quaintly named registers; among these occur
the following:—1. " Liber compositionum." 2. " Liber
privilegiorum." 3. " Liber niger, incipiens Barthon."
4. " Liber C." 5. " Liber Winchelsey." 6. " Hasp-
" Book." 7. " The knopped book." 8. " Liber ruber."
In the portfolio with these papers is a copy, in Somner's
writing, of the composition C. 1233.

Catalogues, Ancient, of the Chartæ Antiquæ.

C. 250. A paper book of 36 duodecimo pages, apparently written in the 17th century, containing items
selected from some register. The titles of some of the
Cart. Ant. are to be found in this list, but the majority
are at present unknown to the collection.

C. 232. A paper book in which Somner has copied a
14th century catalogue of the Cart. Ant.
The title of the original from which Somner copied
was, " Archivum Ecclesie Christi Cantuariensis, sive
" descriptio, atque supervisio, omnium chartarum et
" munimentorum, quæ in vasis tam Borealibus quam
" Australibus Armarii Chartophylacis Facta per Joh.
" de Glocesteria et Joh. de Eastria, A.D. MCCCLXX.—
" Custodes."
On the verso of the last leaf is written: " The original
" of this catalogue is preserved in the Chapter House at
" Westminster, in the county bags in the chief clerk's
" office. Title Kent. W. Illingworth, 10 Dec. 1806."
A. 17. " Extracts e registro privilegiorum sedis
" Archiepiscopalis Cantuariensis." A sheet of paper
containing 20 extracts, by a hand of the 17th century,
all relating to presentations to the church of St. Michael
in the Poultry.
A. 40. " Libertates Sci. Thome," a 15th century copy
of an inspeximus of 1252. Four charters are recited,
three of which, Will. I., Hen. I., and Hen. II., are still
in this collection.
C. 204. A roll upon which a 13th century hand has
made copies of early charters given by Edward the Confessor and his successors up to Richard I. Among these
are three from the Archbishops Anselm, Theobald, and
Thomas.
S. B. a. 149. A decayed sheet of paper, written in
double column and on both sides, by a 14th century
hand. It is not impossible that this is the original
draft from which was copied the catalogue mentioned
under C. 232 as being among the public records.

Chantries.

C. 145, 1363. A confirmation, under the seal of Abp.
Islip, of the foundation of a chantry in Christ Church
Canterbury, by Edward the Black Prince.
The foundation deed distinctly declares that the ordination of this chantry was the price exacted by the Pope
before the Prince could obtain permission to marry his
cousin Joan, to whom he was related within the prohibited degrees.
The deed contains the usual provisions for appointing
and removing the priests of the chantry, and the manor
of Vauxhall is assigned to the prior and convent, to
furnish the funds for supporting them.
F. 49 to F. 53. Are deeds relating to the manor of
Vauxhall, which came into the possession of the monastery by gift from the Black Prince.
The original foundation deed of this chantry was catalogued in 1806, but a pencil note now appended to the
entry declares that it was " missing temp. Dr. Russell."
W. 214, 1443. Foundation deed of a chantry, endowed by Joan Brenchley, widow, and to be established
in the chapel of our Lady in the parish church of
Bixley. In addition to this foundation she desires her
executors to sell her lands in Kent, and to bestow the
money so obtained in pious uses, such as " in chirches,
" fowle wayes, poor men and women, and other good
" deeds of charity."
B. 357. The feoffees of Joan Brenchley carry out her
wishes and found the chantry. This deed recites all the
steps in the process of the foundation, the King's licence
in mortmain, the bishop's consent, the endowment,
which gives the incumbent priest power to distrain for
arrears, &c. This complete establishment of the chantry
is dated 1458.
B. 356, 1458. Deed of foundation of a chantry in
Canterbury Cathedral Church, to be called Brenchley's
chantry. The priest is, on all Sundays and festivals, to
observe the canonical hours, with mass, and Placebo and
Dirige, at the altar of St. John the Baptist. At foot
is a confirmation by Abp. Stafford.

C. 151. The feoffees grant the patronage of Brenchley's chantry to Abp. Stafford and his successors.
C. 152. The feoffees assign a house in the parish of St.
Alphege as a residence for the priest of Brenchley's
chantry, at the same time charging certain named lands
in Kent with the payment of a stipend of 10l.
C. 252. Bourgchier's chantry in Ch. Ch. A copy on
paper, probably the draft, of a deed by which Henry VII.
was made patron of, and partaker in the benefits of
Bourgchier's chantry at the altar of St. Stephen in the
north transept of the Cathedral Church of Canterbury.
The document tells how Abp. Bourchier had endowed a
chantry, but having neglected to obtain the King's
licence to suspend the statute of mortmain, his bequest
became void, and only by the King's special grace was
the endowment given to the convent, who in gratitude
constituted the King patron and co-founder.
1482. One part of a trepartite indenture by which the
prior and convent of Llanthony juxta Gloucester bind
themselves, in consideration of favours received, to perform pious offices for Cardinal Bourgchier, his father,
and Anne Countess of Stafford, his mother. The other
two parts of the indenture were left in the hands of the
Cardinal and the Prior of Llanthony.
C. 154, 1529. The foundation deed of Warham's
chantry, which assigns, with the King's licence, lands in
Chislet for the maintenance of one or perhaps two
priests who shall say daily mass for the soul of the Abp.
The prior and convent, the trustees, agree to pay annually, through New Coll. in Oxford, a sum of sixty
shillings to three scholars of the college " vulgariter
" appellati Canterbury College."
On the founder's anniversary shall be said the mass
which is usually said on the death of an Abp., and on
the next day a mass of requiem, for which the prior, if
present, shall receive 6s. 8d., and the sub-prior 3s. 4d.
To every other official of the monastery is assigned a
fee, large or small, in proportion to his dignity; the
ringers are not forgotten, and even the candles are
provided for. This MS. bears the autograph signature
of the founder.
C. 147, 1339. Foundation deed of Buckyngham's
chantry in Ch. Ch. Cant. The executors of John Buckyngham, Bishop of Lincoln, stating that the deceased
had, to their knowledge, intended to found a chantry
in his lifetime, assign lands, and make regulations for
the maintenance of two priests, who shall for ever perform divine offices for the soul of the founder. The
priests were to be housed in a building specially erected
for them in the monastery of Ch. Ch.; they were to
have new clothing once a year, and a suit of the same
livery to wear when they walked into the town.
C. 146. Abp. Arundel's confirmation of the foundation.
C. 149, 1423. W. Daventre, alias W. Richee, was a
priest in Buckingham's chantry, and he was informed
that by an ambiguity in the deed of foundation he could
claim, as one of his predecessors had done before him, a
stipend of 20 pounds instead of one of 20 marks which
was usually considered to be the value of his office.
Disdaining to take advantage of the quibble he acquits
the prior of any liability beyond the 20 marks.
C. 150, 1433. John Forest, Dean of Wells and formerly Canon of Lincoln, the only surviving executor of
the will of Bishop Buckingham, uses the right reserved
to the executors, and explains and supplements the
foundation deed of the chantry.
The previous deed shows that the provisions of the
founder's deed were not clear enough to banish litigation;
and hence this amendment.
C. 148. Deed of foundation of a chantry of two priests
in Arundel's oratory in the nave of Ch. Ch., and of
one priest in the church of Maidstone, all three to be
endowed from the goods of Abp. Arundel the founder,
for whose soul, together with those of Abp. Courtenay,
Prior Chillenden, W. Topclive, and Elizabeth his wife,
the three priests were bound to say the usual masses,
collects, and psalms; the priests were required by the
deed to take part in all the solemn processions which
were formed in the church, on which occasions they
were to be dressed in the vestments provided at the
founder's expense.
S. 413. Copy of a deed by which R. de Bourne, executor of Rob. Vintier, founds a chantry in the chapel of
the nunnery of St. Sepulchre, Canterbury. The establishment is to consist of one priest, whose duty will be
to perform a daily mass with mention of the name of
Robert Vintier the testator. The executor gives as the
reason why such an obscure position has been chosen
for the chantry, that the nuns of the house were too
poor to secure the regular services of a priest, and that

by means of this chantry they would have daily service whilst the founder's soul would still enjoy the benefits arising from the masses.

S. 380, 1380. A notarial instrument providing for the singing of a daily mass, at the altar of the Holy Ghost in the church of the Cistercian Convent of Stratford, for the benefit of the soul of Thomas Hatfield, Bp. of Durham. This deed differs in two points from the ordinary foundation deeds of chantries; first, the penalties for omission of the daily duty are very severe, accumulating rapidly with the duration of the neglect; secondly, the causes by which the rites may be legitimately suspended are minutely stated, "Utpote per communem pesti-
" lenciam in provincia Cantuariensi, et precipue in locis
" vicinis dicte domui nostre, aut discrimina guerrarum,
" vel invasionem hostium, vel per subitam combus-
" tionem domus nostre supradicte, aut tantam aquarum
" inundacionem, ita notoriam et notabilem, quod per
" aliquod hujusmodi impedimentum seu infortunia
" prenominata, quod absit, adeo bona dicte domus
" consumpta fuerint, ut ad necessaria omnia ordinaria,
" et sine quibus debita religio in dicta domo nostra non
" potuerit observari, sufficere non potuerint."
C. 144, deed 1321, inspeximus 1325. Inspeximus by Edw. II. of a deed by which Prior Henry endows a chantry of six priests in the almonry of Christ Church. No new funds were provided for these priests, but certain "liberaciones," which hitherto had been other-wise bestowed, were diverted to them. Two "libera-
" ciones Lanfranci" were to be given at once to two of the priests, and other four were to be assigned to them as they fell vacant. Each "liberacio" entitled the holder to "unam panem monachalem, et unam lagenam et
" dimidium cerevisiæ monachalis, vel unum denarium
" et obulum de Thesauraria nostra pro cerevisia, si con-
" tingat Conventum vinum bibere in communi;" beside which there was a payment of 20l. annually; but it is not clear whether this was an additional endowment for the chantry priest, or whether it was an integral part of the "liberacio." "Sacerdotes pares sint et socii
" in camera et in mensa, et nullus ipsorum super alium
" extollatur."
M. 221, 1369. Royal licence granted to the exor. of R. Vyneter of Maidstone, empowering him to establish a chantry for two priests at Maidstone, endowing it with lands, mills, &c. to the amount of 20l. a year.
N. 17, 1316. "Ordinacio cujusdam Cantarie quatuor
" Sacerdotum in Norwic. facta per Dm. Johannem
" ejusdem loci Episcopum A° D° MCCCXVI."
This is a deed of confirmation executed by the Prior of Ch. Ch., who was remotely concerned in the founda-tion. This instrument gives a good example of the method by which religious houses became rectors, a vicar undertaking the charge of the parish, a stipulated, small proportion of the profits of the church being assigned for his sustenance. This collection furnishes great numbers of instances of churches so appropriated.
A. 219, 1333. A notary's narrative of the resignation of the chantry priest who served the altar of St. Mary at Tarring, the inquisition consequent upon the vacancy of the benefice, and the acknowledgment of the patron's right to present.
E. 159, 1392. The Prior of Ch. Ch., as mesne lord, gives licence to the corporation of priests in Elys' chantry in St. Peter's. Sandwich to accept, and to certain donors to give, real property to the chantry. The payment of five shillings and a halfpenny upon each vacancy, being the custom of the manor of Sand-wich, is to be continued.
M. 340, 1427. A draft presentation to the vicarage of St. Michael Royal, in the city of London.
The patrons were the prior and convent of Ch. Ch., and the presentee was at the time filling the office of master of the college founded in the same church for Richard Whityngton of happy memory.
At the foot is written a memorandum, " Et le roy,
" comande qe nul feire nie marchi soit tenuz deinz
" seyntuaries par lonour de seynt esglise."
C. 1,304, 1483. Three parchments which relate to the resignation of one chaplain and the presentation of another to serve the altar in the chantry of Buckley, in the parish church of Charing.
M. 27, 1347. Licence in mortmain from Edw. III., empowering the Prior of Ch. Ch. to purchase lands of the annual value of 20l. for the endowment of the chantry of St. Thomas "juxta portam prioratus."
A. 15, 1361. The will of Abp. Islip, who bequeaths to the convent some rich vestments, valuable pieces of plate, and 'lastly a thousand ewes, the number of which is never to be diminished, but the offspring and the wool are to become the property of the prior and con-

vent. He arranges for an annual inspection of the flock with a view to the maintenance of the health and number of the ewes. In return for the latter bequest he requires that after daily mass the following prayer shall be recited, " Deus qui inter apostolicos sacerdotes
" famulos tuos dominos Simonem et Johannem ac
" ceteros Archiepiscopos hujus ecclesie Pontificali et
" Archiepiscopali dignitate censeri fecisti, presta quod,
" ut quorum vicem ad horam gerebant in terris, eorum
" perpetuo consorcio letentur in celis."
Placebo and Dirige are also required to be sung upon certain stated occasions, a gratuity being assigned to the officiating priest.
W. 48a. Among the Chartæ Antiquæ is preserved the volume which contains the original agreement made between Henry VII. and the prior and convent of Canterbury, providing for the saying of perpetual masses for the founder and his kin.
The book, which, beside fly-leaves, contains 34 pages of parchment, is finely bound in boards of oak, covered with blue velvet, and fastened by two clasps of cast brass. Each corner of the lids is decorated with a brazen portcullis, and in the centre of each is a Tudor rose of the same material.
The volume measures 12 inches by 9, and the upper edge of the boards is cut into an undulating form to correspond with the "indenture" which they enclose.
The text is written in the centre of the pages, with a broad clear margin, this margin in the title-page being occupied by a band of coarse illumination, in which roses, grapes, and nondescript flowers are repre-sented on a ground of reddish-yellow.
The central space of the large initial letter is parted per pale, argent and vert, and upon this field are depicted the royal arms supported by a dragon and a white greyhound, the portcullis again appearing among the decorations. Three thick, plaited silken strings connect the document with the seals of, 1st, the King, 2, the Mayor of London, 3, the Abbot and convent of St. Peter, Westminster, each of these being enclosed in a box of turned brass.
The substance of the agreement is as follows :—
" This indenture quatrepartite made between the moost
" Cristen Kyng Henry the Seventh by the grace of God,
" &c., the twenty day of November, the twenty yere of
" his mooste noble reigne, on the oone partie; John
" Islipp, Abbott of the Monastery of Seynt Peter of
" Westminster, of the secunde partie; and Thomas,
" Prioure of the Metropolitan Church of Crist of Canter-
" bury, and the convent of the same place, of the III°
" partie; and the maire and commonalty of the citie
" of London of the fourth partie; witnesseth."
The deed goes on to say that the founder has settled upon the abbot an estate of the annual value of six pounds thirteen shillings and fourpence, the profits of which are to be paid to the Prior of Ch. Ch. in order to meet the expenses of the King's anniversary, which is to be observed in the church of Canterbury for ever.
The persons who are named for commemoration in the anniversary services are the King himself, " Elizabeth
" late Quene of Englond his wife," " theire children and
" issue," " the right excelent prynce Edmonde late Erle
" of Rychemond fader to our seid soveraigne lord the
" King," and " after her decease, the right excellent
" prynces Margarete Countesse of Rychemond and
" Derbey moder unto our . . . . lord the King."
The remainder of the book is occupied by the details of the annual celebrations, including the formulæ of the various collects which were to be recited on behalf of the several persons above mentioned. In the case of the King and the Duchess of Richmond, who were living at the time of the execution of this deed, one form of collect, a petition for worldly prosperity, was to be used, the person commemorated still surviving; whilst another, being a prayer for the soul of the deceased, was substi-tuted after the death of the person.
This covenant brings into strong contrast the two dis-tinct kinds of prayer which were offered for the living and for the dead.

Cloth Livery

C. 186, 1472. A contract made between the Prior of Ch. Ch. and a London alderman, by which the latter agrees to sell 16 pieces of livery cloth, described as " moustered villers," every cloth when wet to contain 24 yards in length and 7½ quarters in breadth. Two pieces are to be fit for gentlemen's livery, nine for yeomeh's, and 5 for grooms'. All the cloth is to be clear of " rowe,
" stour, cokell, vagite, grete bole or any other defaute,"
and the price is to be 39l. 14s.

C. 347, 1475. A similar contract made with John Hamsmyth of New Salusbury, "Raymaker." In this case the gentlemen's cloth is to cost 35s. the piece, the yeomen's 32s. 8d., and the grooms' 30s.

Each piece is to contain 24 yards of assize, and the breadth is to be one yard within the "lysts." Every yard is to have "eight rayes suyngly and no mo."

C. 241, 1480. A similar contract.

C. 244, 1499. Bill of John Marten of Hadley, who has sold 18 pieces of cloth of the three usual qualities, and of a "plaine blewe colour," and also several other "pieces" "de le Ray," called. also "syngule ray "clothes."

S. B. a. 91. A Cranbrook clothier contracts to supply russet cloths; gentlemen's at 3l., yeomen's at 4 marks; and grooms' at 7 nobles for each piece.

S. B. b. 6, S. B. c. 147, S. B. b. 125, S. B. c. 103, S. B. c. 147, are all contracts or bills relating to cloth of the prior's livery. In one case the colour chosen is "a "sad tawney."

The chamberlain's accounts in the Scrap Books afford much information as to the quantities and prices of black Benedictine cloth, and all other articles of monastic apparel.

Charters, Royal.

These are to be found in the Chart. Antiq. in considerable numbers, and of all dates from the eighth century to the time of Elizabeth. Many of the earlier examples have been printed in the Codex Diplomaticus, and in the references given below each charter so copied is distinguished by Kemble's number in Roman numerals:—

Ethelbald of Mercia, A.D. 742, M. 363, LXXXVIII.
Offa of Mercia, A.D. 788, M. 340, CLIII.
Offa of Mercia, A.D. 790, C. 69, CLIX.
Coenulf of Mercia, A.D. 812, C. 1278, CXCIX.
A fac-simile of this has been published by the Palæographical Society.
Ecgberht of Wessex, A.D. 830, C. 1279, CCXXIV.
Berchtnulf of Mercia, A.D. 840, C. 1280, CCXLIII.
A fac-simile of this has been published by the Palæographical Society.
Ethelbearht of Wessex and Kent, A.D. 863, M. 14, CCLXXXVIII.
Ælfred of Wessex, A.D. 898, F. 150, CCCXXIV.
Æthelstan, A.D. 937, E. 206, CCCLXIX.
Æthelstan, A.D. 937, T. 37, CCCLXX., a faulty contemporary copy of the last.
Eadred, A.D. 949, R. 14, CCCCXXV.
This is the celebrated charter written by Abp. Dunstan's own hand. A duplicate is in the Cottonian Collection.
Ethelred II., A.D. 972, B. 1, DCCIV.
This is written in the vernacular.
Ethelred II., A.D. 1006, C. 194, DCCXV.
Cnut, A.D. 1023, S. 261, DCCXXXVII.
Cnut, A.D. 1023, S. 260.
A translation of the previous charter in the vernacular.
Eadward, A.D. 1049, C. 1,281, DCCLXXXVII.
Eadward, R. 51, DCCCX.
Eadward, C. 3.
William I., A. 1, A. 2, C. 45.
William II., C. 6.
Henry I., C. 7, C. 9.
Stephen, C. 11, C 12, C. 13.
Henry II., C. 8, C. 10, C. 16, C. 17, C. 18, C. 20, C. 21, C. 22, C. 23, C. 24, C. 25, C. 26, C. 32, C. 40, C. 52, C. 74, C. 75, C. 197, C. 749, F. 9.
Richard I., C. 28, C. 76.
John, C. 30, C. 31, C. 109, C. 199, F. 11, I. 228.
Henry III., C. 33, C. 78, C. 1,075.
Edward I., C. 41, C. 86, C. 142, C. 1,266, C. 1,218.
Edward II., C. 54, C. 81, C. 82, C. 83, C. 144, C. 387, C. 818, D. 96.
Edward III., A. 164, C. 42, C. 84, C. 87, C. 88, C. 89, C. 103, C. 104, C. 1,217, C. 1,219, E. 177, E. 178.
Richard II., C. 44, C. 95, C. 388, C. 1,220.
Henry IV., C. 58.
Henry V., C. 96, C. 1,246, C. 133.
Henry VI., C. 62, C. 97, C. 98, C. 101.
Edward IV., C. 65, C. 99.
Henry VII., C. 100, C. 1,221.
Henry VIII., W. 183.
Mary Tudor, C. 190 (with Philip), C. 871, C. 1,271, C. 1,272.
Elizabeth, C. 273, C. 1,060.

A few of these charters are gifts of land, but nearly all of the later examples are grants of privileges, and exemptions from burthens, given by the several Kings to the monastory of Ch. Ch., one King after another confirming the charters of his predecessors. The charters of Henry II. stand apart from the others, being both

more numerous and more varied in character, owing to the King's desire to allay the odium which attached to him in consequence of the murder of Archbishop Thomas.

C. 21. Appears to be the actual grant extorted from him by the importunity of Prior Benedict of Canterbury, assisted by an ominous vision. The story is told in the Winchester MS. of the miracles of St. Thomas, written by William of Canterbury. The charter which is there recited agrees word for word with the present MS., but with this variation, there the date is Wallingford, here Marleberge. (See vol. i. of Materials for the Hist. of Abp. Becket in Chron. and Mem. of Great Britain.)

The charters of Edward the Confessor and William I. are in English; those of their immediate successors, up to Henry II., are in Latin, with an English translation subjoined; and after Henry II. Latin alone is used.

The right of free warren, so greatly prized as a means of procuring sport and dainty food, was first granted by Henry III., and frequently confirmed by his successors.

Exemptions from the operation of the statute of mortmain, either general, or limited to estates of a certain annual value, exist here in large numbers, and may be found under the names of the various manors to which the exemptions apply. It is to be noticed that the Kings were jealous of the acquisition of real property by religious foundations long before the passing of Edward's great statute, and that we have examples of permissions to deal in land asked for by, and granted to, the convent, dated at the beginning of the 12th century. For example, A. 63 and A. 64 are two charters of Henry I. which give permission to the monks of Ch. Ch. to exchange some land with the monks of St. Augustine's.

The charter of Cnut (S. 261) is remarkable for the character of the gift. "Ego Cnut . . . . basileus, "propriis manibus meis, capitis mei auream coronam "pono super altare Xpi. in Dorobornia ad opus ejusdem "ecclesie, quâ concedo eidem ecclesie, ad victum mona- "chorum, portum de Sandwico."

Discipline, Monastic and Ecclesiastical.

C. 163. A regulation of Abp. Theobald providing for the punishment of repenting deserters from the cloister. He allows that they may be again received, but he orders that they shall be placed in the lowest rank, there to remain for life, passed over by all the newly-admitted brethren, "ut degradationis sue intuitu era- "bescant, et humilientur." This MS. is fortified by the seals of the Abp. and of the Chapter.

P. 60, 1174-79. Alexander III. writes to Abp. Richard, "Cum sis monasticam religionem professus, "et religionis habitum geras, expedit tamen honestati "tue, viros honestos et idoneos, consimilis religionis, "circa te retinere. Inde est quod . . . . mandamus "quatenus aliquem monachorum ecclesie tue idoneum "et honestum circa te teneas, cique sigillum tuum "portandum committas, quia si aliena persona idem "sigillum deferrit, tibi, et ecclesie tue multa exindo "possint incommoda provenire."

S. B. c. 130, 12th cent. A small portion of the evidence in a suit, R. de Melksham v. M. fitz H. de Winton.

The witnesses testify that in the reign of Stephen one Theodbaud, a priest, veiled Eva the mother of Henry, and that Bp. Joscelin gave her the benediction, after which the convent of Wilton sent and took her away, that she remained at Wilton for a year, but "nescio "quomodo illa abstracta fuit."

S. B. a. 14, 13th cent. A scrap of parchment sent from the archdeacon to his Sompnour.
"Citentur infrascripti ad diem Mercurii proximum "post festum Sti. Petri."
After this title there follow a number of names of Canterbury residents, male and female, in several instances bracketted in couples. After each name is written the offence for which the archdeacon intends to proceed against the culprit. Most of the offenders are to be cited for immorality, but in a few cases executors are called upon to answer charges connected with their office.

S. B. b. 31, 13th cent. An archdeacon's memoranda of offences, and deficiencies in the churches of Herne, St. Nicholas, and All Saints. Books are deficient, chancels out of repair, executors are remiss, and Agnes Curteys is a standing temptation to sin. One parishioner has been allowed to die intestate.

C. 1,295. Prior Henry of Eastry warns all good people to give no credit to R. de Baners, a monk who for the third time has forsaken the cloister.

M. 368, circ. 1300. A monastic prosecutor's bill of indictment against H. de Cretinge and R. Blundell, monks of Ch. Ch., who appear to have been much employed at the outlying manors of the monastery, there acquiring what their prosecutor calls "secular" manners.

The language is so hyperbolical that it is not improbable that the shocking depravity laid to the charge of the delinquents is as much overstated as the style is inflated. The first paragraph will serve as a specimen :—" Si ista dies ita longa esset sicut dies orit " magni judicii, non posset gesta istorum duorum fra- " trum, scilicet H. et. R., secundum majus et minus in " qualitate et quantitate, recipere delictorum .... " loca sequencia, si possent oris et lingue uti beneficio, " clamarent et dicent, Heu ! iste venit a seculo ut pejora " faceret in claustro," &c.

C. 1294, C. 1296. S. B. c. 146. These MSS. contain as much as is known about a bitter quarrel which arose about the year 1320, between Henry [of Eastry] the prior and benefactor of Ch. Ch. and a faction of the monks of his own chapter.

S. B. c. 146. Appears to be the earliest of these records. It contains copies of several letters written by two of the malcontents, R. de Thaneto "in curia Romana " degens," and R. de Alendon, who remained in his convent at Canterbury. The MS. occupies a parchment about 24 inches by 12, which is so injured by damp that only a small part is legible.

These letters seem to have been collected in their present shape to be used in the interest of the prior as evidence against the writers.

The Roman correspondent writes to Alindone "fratri " suo adoptivo in Xpo. dilectissimo." He appears to be badly in want of evidence to support his accusation against the prior, and he continually begs his friend to send him all the proofs he can collect, " et omnes " articulos que (sic) nostis contra priorem, tam de " visitacione quam post, ... seu per ipsum com- " missos, seu per complices suos."

He hints that he is backed by a cardinal, whom he describes as "Dominus meus," and also " per quosdam " alios Cardinales." Some idea may be formed of the offences which he objected against his prior from the fragments of a schedule of grievances which is written on the back of the document.

"M⁴ quod prior sine conventus consensu .... fraudu- " lenter . . . , &c.

" Itᵐ W. de Ledeburi et J. de Winchel . . . . com- plicibus dixit . . . . &c.

" Itᵐ M⁴ quod frater Alanus de Cruce furavit . . . . &c.

" Itᵐ Idem Alanus furavit de R. de . . . . cereos in nocte quando R. Archiep. . . . . " &c.

The writer incidentally mentions that the Pope (John XXII.), who "minus facit pro Cardinalibus et per ipsos," had prepared many measures against ecclesiastical persons, and especially against monks, and that he only awaited the arrival of Robert of Sicily to put these measures in force, intending to proceed, backed by Robert's troops, "manu armata."

C. 1294a. Is the prior's copy of the articuli which R. de Alindon objected against him. In what is supposed to be the prior's own writing is an endorsement, " Arti- " culi famosi quos R. de Alindon scripsit dno W. et " R. de Thaneto."

C. 1294a. A letter, dated 18th Feb., from Abp. Walter Reynold to the prior, referring to some monks whom he had sentenced to sequestration from their fellows, apparently in consequence of their complicity in the rebellion of Alendon and Thanet. The writer says that he shall soon come to Canterbury to complete the visitation which he has left unfinished. He enjoins upon the prior still to keep sequestered those monks upon whom he had imposed that penalty in the chapter-house during his visitation, but he wishes them to be supplied with "congrua necessaria." like the other brethren. "Verumtamen octo fratres quibus erat indic- " tum jejunium panis et aque sextis feriis, sicut ad " rogatum vestrum eis concessimus, pane et vino, seu " cerevisia et potagio, illis diebus refici toleramus. ". Ad fratrem J. de Maldon, racione status quem optinuit " in ecclesia nostra, respectum habemus, volumus quod " in persona sua, quatenus potueritis salva religionis " honestate, temperetis rigorem, ita quod septa monas- " terii non exeat quousque duxerimus ordinandum."

C. 1294c. A letter from Abp. Walter to the prior. It explains that the King has written to the Abp., requiring him to compel the prior to release some of his monks (amongst whose names that of R. de Alendon appears) whom he had committed "carcerali custodie."

The Abp. plainly states that he writes this order unwillingly, being irresistibly urged by the King, who in his turn is also an unwilling agent, being compelled to interfere by the pressure put upon him by certain intercessors, whom he describes as "quidam Burgenses " de Sandwyco, et alii quidam milites et scutiferi de " dicto domino Rege speciales." This letter is endorsed by the prior, " Istam litteram recepimus primo die Junii " per manus Gilberti (appre)ciatoris de Westmonas- " terio, vesperis decantatis, pro deliberatione J. de " Valoyns, Th. de Sandwyco, et R. de Aledon a cus- " todia carcerali, in presencia fratrum Thome Stoyl, " Dyonisii, et Willelmi de Estrya monachorum."

In one of R. de Thanet's letters this Thomas Stoyle is said to be " radix multorum malorum."

C. 1296, circ. 1275. The record of an earlier mutiny of the monks of Ch. Ch.

This MS. contains the several accusations which R. Pikenot and W. de Tong, the representatives of the discontented monks, intend to charge against their prior, Thomas Ringmer.

They assert that he is guilty of perjury, theft, sacrilege, falsehood, dilapidation, and transgressions of the canons and monastic rule; that, although often excommunicated, he intrudes himself into the services of the church ; that he has oppressed and imprisoned thirteen monks who appealed to Rome against him ; that he has appropriated the goods of the church to the value of a thousand marks; and that he has given away 520 large oaks, fifty-six pounds twelve shillings in money, and jewels to the value of more than 46 pounds.

Further they say that he has encumbered the church with a debt of 4,000 marks, and applied the money " in " proprios non usus sed abusus." Assisted by a layman he has violated the shrine of St. Thomas, carrying off gold and precious stones of great value.

This prior, disgusted with the flock over whom he was called to rule, left his convent, and laying aside the Benedictine habit assumed the white robe of the Cistercians, the symbol of a stricter discipline. It was after his resignation that the King sequestrated the goods of the convent (see " Ch. Ch. sequestrated").

S. B. c. 8a. Robert and Alexander Poncyn, Prior Ryngmer's proctors, appoint Philip de Pomonte to be their substitute, for promoting the suit of the prior at Rome.

S. B. b. 205. Prior Ringmer sends twenty shillings and a " monile aureum " as a refresher to Philip de Pomonte, his proctor at the Roman Curia.

P. 21. "Capitulum celebratum in Ecclesia Omnium Sanc- " torum in Palenta [the Pallant] de Cicestria, die Jovis " proximo post festum conversionis Sci. Pauli, A.D. " MCCCXXXIII., per Johannem Pic clericum, com- " missarium in decanatu de Pagham, sede Cantuar. " vacante, specialiter deputatum."

Twenty-eight delinquents were summoned to appear before this chapter, of whom twenty-four were charged with immorality ; two persons were accused of breach of a promise to pay money to a rector and a vicar ; the remaining two cases were connected with the probate of wills.

C. 1,301, 1388. The Prior of Ely gives to Bro. Peter permission to change his convent. Peter wishes to leave Ely, " cujus situm, propter aeris intemperiem, " pretendit sue complexioni hactenus fuisse, et adhuc " esse, valde contrarium et nocivum," and he thinks he shall do better at Canterbury " prout per aliquantulam " moram, quam illic nuper traxerat, asserit se fuisse " personaliter expertum."

S. B. b. 193. A scrap of paper upon which some monastic censor has made notes of the delinquencies of his fellow monks :—

" Dns. T. Goldstone sepius est in curia, absque licencia, et raro vel nunquam in completoriis, in claustro, et quando est allocutus dedignat presidentes suos.

" Dns. Jacobus Harteye pejus servat claustrum, sed melius completoria. Pater reverende, scrutatores vestri nichil faciunt in officiis suis, scrutando observancias ecclesie ; intantum quod dns. N. Harste dixit pupplice, coram Magistro Priore, in loco quo erat proclamatus, hec verba 'Ego faciam clamores,' et dixit Magister Prior ' Quare,' et respondit, ' Quia est officium opprobrii," et sic raro, vel nunquam, facit clamores, sed bene servat horas suas," &c.

S. B. a. 60. A small scrap of writing sent by an apparitor to the archdeacon :—

" Quis diversi generosi de mea . . . . . sde forni- cacione vicio corrigendi . . . . requiro quod instruere me velitis apparitorem vestrum ad citandum ipsos viciosos," &c.

S. B. a. 132. A fragment of the prior's private note-book :—

"Fratres jurant ultra modum, ut dicitur.

"Tres in infirmaria habent pueros (qy.) in cameris suis, ut dicitur.

"It. Juvenes fratres habent vestimenta inordinata."

S. B. a. 125. A sheet of paper folded to make sixteen narrow pages.

Upon this are written the names of those monks of Ch. Ch. who were on the rota for duty on certain Sundays and festivals. The same names occur among those of the monks dispersed at the Dissolution.

Matters connected with excommunications and ecclesiastical censures can be found by the references A. 3, A. 6, S. 414, S. 417, S. 419, S.B. a. 9, 10, 15, 28, 64, 157.

Disputes, Archbishops' and Priors'.

C. 1,292. At a time when the monks of Ch. Ch. were proceeding against their Abp. Theobald in the court of Rome, some malicious persons spread a report that they had personally ill-treated their opponent, who on his part generously contradicts the calumny. Addressing the prior and convent, he writes, "Monachi "Cant. ecclesie, specialiter nobis a deo commisso, ap-"pellationem quandam quasi contra nos aliquando "fecisse dicuntur, cujus appellationis occasione, rei "geste sinistri interpretes, aut ob odium monachorum, "vel potius ob nostri favorem, tanquam per mendacia "nostram captantes gratiam, publice eos infamare "conati sunt, asserentes illos in nostram necem con-"spirasse, manus in nos injecisse, et alia in hunc mo-"dum plura egisse. Quorum maledicorum assertiones, "utpote quibus nullum inest veritatis vestigium, nos "zelo Dei repellentes, prefati conventus monachos, non "solum a predictis, verumtamen ab omni infamie nota, "immunes esse erga nos veritatis verbo attestamur ; "quemadmodum et erga omnes prelatos suos semper "fuisse dinoscuntur," &c. The archbishop solemnly anathematises anyone who after this disclaimer shall spread the idle tale.

C. 1,284. A notice from Urban III. to Abp. Baldwin. He requires that the Archbishop shall not, pendente lite, molest the convent of Ch. Ch., who have sent their prior and three monks to Rome to seek the Pope's protection against the Archbishop. This MS. passed under the eye of Gervase, and was copied by him. (Script. X., Col. 1,319).

A. 26. John of Anagni bears witness that he first heard of, and then saw, the coercion which the monks suffered at the time when they made their compact with Abp. Baldwin, and therefore "auctoritate quam fungi-"mur statuimus Apostolica, quod neque concordia sic "facta, neque compromissio violenter extorta, neque "scriptum sic conceptum, valere debeat, aut aliquid . . . . monachis in posterum prejudicium afferre." (Gervase of Canterbury, Col. 1,324, Scriptores X.)

H. 103, 1184-92. In the quarrel between Abp. Baldwin and the convent, arising from the foundation of a college of canons at Hackington, the Bishop of Bath and his fellows forbid, by the Pope's authority, the celebration of divine offices in the chapel, and they give notice that on a day they shall cause the chapel to be destroyed.

H. 102. The same commissioners declare the erection of a chapel at Hackington to be illegal and "funditus "destruendam judicavimus . . . . nos in executione "sui mandati procedere precipit, predictum locum "maledictum, et prophanum, apostolica condempna-"verat auctoritas, et suspensos . . . . illos qui . . . . "in capella illa divina celebrare presumpserint decre-"verat."

L. 138, 1200. In the dispute between Abp. Hubert and the convent concerning Lambeth College, Bishop Hugh of Lincoln and his fellows, Eustace of Ely and Abbot Sampson of Bury, announce to the convent that that are delegated by the Pope to arbitrate in the quarrel; they therefore cite the Prior and Convent to appear by a properly authorised proctor on the morrow of St. Michael.

L. 175. Another notice in all respects similar to the last.

L. 135. A second and more peremptory summons, the first having been disregarded.

L. 136, 1200. Memorandum declaring the consent of the Archbishop, and of the prior and convent of Christ Church, to accept the award, whatever it may be, of the arbitrators appointed by the Pope.

L. 130, 1200. The award of the arbitrators, corroborated by their seals, and further authenticated by the seals of thirteen other dignitaries. The terms of the arbitration have often been printed, and it is not necessary to say

more than that the Archbishop is allowed to build a church, but not on the old foundations of that destroyed by Papal authority; that he is permitted to institute from 12 to 20 Premonstratensian canons, who are to be supported by an income derived from the Archbishop's churches or private possessions.

L. 129, A. 5, L. 131, and L. 132 are all repetitions of the above-mentioned award.

L. 133. Abp. Hubert, in presenting the award to the Pope, makes light of the fears of the convent "timentes, "ut reor, ubi non erat timor." He declares that he believes both parties in the dispute were actuated by a desire to do what was right, "studiis quidem duce-"bamus dissimilibus et diversis, sed zelo non dissimili."

L. 134, 1200. Letters sent by the arbitrators to the Pope, asking for a confirmation of their award, a copy of which accompanied this letter.

L. 137. A transcript of the Lambeth award, with the confirmation by Innocent III. This is endorsed, "Scrip-"tum est in tercio quaterno quarti libri registrorum "Dni. Innocencii Pape III."

A. 168. The process of the prior and convent of Canterbury against Abp. Edmund. This report to the Pope (Gregory IX.) is sent by three abbots whom he appointed to arbitrate between the parties. The Pope's commission is first recited, and in it is contained a statement of the oppressions which the convent assert they have endured at the Abp.'s hands. The arbitrators are required to conclude a peace if it be in any way possible, but if they cannot succeed the case is to be remitted to Rome. The parties were cited to appear on a certain day, but the defendant disregarded the summons and another day was fixed, but before that day prohibitory letters came from the King, asserting that the cause was one which might well be heard in a secular court. On the day of the hearing the defendant pleaded the King's letters, and the arbitrators took time for considering the point ; ultimately the monks, fearing the King, withdrew from the prosecution. The Pope nevertheless ordered the judges to proceed, and again the King forbade them, but this time he showed characteristic signs of yielding, and requested that they would, at all events, wait until the Legate, who was "in "jannis," should arrive. When Otho the Legate did come, in June 1237, he entirely disregarded the King's prohibition, and appointed a day for the Abp. to appear at Rome.

C. 34, 1237. A composition made between Abp. Edmund and the convent of Ch. Ch. The document gives the details of the causes of complaint which the convent alleged against the Abp., and among other matters they accuse him of detaining a sum of twenty-two thousand marks which was assigned to them as damages, by Abp. Stephen, at the time of the removal of the general interdict. The remainder of the deed sets forth the conditions of the composition, which was executed in the form of a bipartite indenture, the present MS. being the prior's half.

C. 36, 1238. Abp. Edmund, acknowledging that neither he nor his successors can claim any right to seize the temporalities of the priory of Ch. Ch. when the office of prior is vacant, promises that he will not attempt to do so.

C. 205, 1247. "Placita de Juratis et assisa apud "Cant. in octabis Sci. Johannis Bapt. coram H. de "Batonia et sociis suis, justiciariis itinerantibus, Anno "Regni Regis H. fil. Regis Johis. xxxii."

Several rolls of parchment containing the writs, precedents, and arguments ex parte the Prior of Canterbury, who was plaintiff, Archbishop Boniface being defendant. The plaintiff's precedents go back to the time of the Conquest, and his arguments to a more remote. date ; thus—"A prima fundacione ecclesie Xpi. Cant. dotata "fuit ecclesia possessionibus suis cum omnimodis liber-"tatibus et liberis consuetudinibus quibus communiter "utebantur Archiepiscopi et Monachi per tempora lon-"gissima, dividentes singulis annis, per eorum ministros, "fructus de possessionibus . . . provenientes, ad "sustentacionem Archiepiscopi et Monachorum. Et "cum tediosum videretur quolibet anno tales facere "divisiones, tandem, de consensu cujusdam Archi-"episcopi et monachorum, ... divise fuerunt pos-"sessiones, ne in posterum inter eos oriri videretur "contencio," &c. Among the precedents are cases in which Archbishop hanged delinquents on his own gallows. A writ addressed to the Sheriff of Kent reads :—"H. dei gra., &c. Vicecomiti Kancie, &c., precipimus "tibi, sicut alias precepimus, quod distringas Bonifacium "Archiepiscopum Cant. per terras et catalla sua," &c.

C. 39 and A 7, 1258. Composition made between Abp. Boniface and the convent. These are two copies of the same deed, each occupying a whole skin of parchment. The composition takes the form of a bipartite indenture, one part of which, with a duplicate, remained in the hands of the Prior of Ch. Ch.

C. 38, 1258. Abp. Boniface informs his bailiffs and agents that he has made a composition with the convent, and that, therefore, they are to allow the tenants and servants of the priory to enjoy their rights without farther molestation, "juribus integre et plenarie uti "permittatis absque ullo impedimento."

A. 31. Not earlier than 1290. "Damna illata Priori "per Ballivios Archiepiscopi."

The composition made with the Abp., and the instructions which he sent to his bailiffs, did not put an end to the oppressions of which the convent complained, and hence this long roll, which sets forth—

1. The composition.
2. A notice to the bailiffs that in defiance of right they have levied amerciaments which belonged to the priory, and given them to the Abp.
3. Two schedules, enumerating the particulars of the excesses of which the prior and convent complain.

E. 176, 1365. A large finely written deed, by which Archbishop Simon Islip restores to the priory of Ch. Ch. the churches of Eastry and Monkton, which his predecessors Baldwin and Hubert had taken as a part of the Archbishop's share of the property belonging to the church of Canterbury. The initial letter and head-line of this MS. are embellished by a pen-and-ink drawing representing a Rustic on foot blowing a horn whilst following a half-bred greyhound, who pursues a hare, the Rustic carrying a leveret suspended from a pole over his shoulder.

Dissolution of Monasteries.

Only a few notices of the great reform are to be found in the Chart. Ant., but those which relate to this subject are enumerated below.

O. 125, O. 126, 1519. Two deeds by which in one case the master and brothers of the Maison Dieu of Ospringe, and in the other the prior and convent of Christ Church, the over-lords, convey their respective interests in the Maison Dieu to the College of St. John the Evangelist in the University of Cambridge.

These documents are not strictly connected with the great Dissolution, but they point to a failure in religious zeal, which first allowed these small foundations to die out, and afterwards permitted the larger houses to be forcibly suppressed almost without opposition.

O. 161, 5 April 1540. A valuation of all the manors and possessions of the former monastery of Christ Church, assigned at the Dissolution, 5th April, 1540, to the Cathedral Church of Canterbury, except certain lands acquired by Sir Christopher Hales.

O. 189. "The King's patent for paying pensions to the "expelled monks of the late priory of Christ Church, "Canterbury." This paper refers to three only of those who received pensions, the Prior Goldwell, J. Elphe, and Nicholas Clement; the others, forty-seven in number, to whom either pensions or offices in the new foundation were assigned, must have been provided for in another similar deed.

S. B. b. 140. Is an undated, carelessly written inventory of a large quantity of articles of plate. The character is that of the middle of the 16th century, and the plate, although there is no title to declare it, evidently belonged to Christ Church.

The various items are catalogued in terms which show that the writer was a stranger who had no previous knowledge of the several articles. He does not write, as a monastic officer would have done, "Three cups "of Simon Islip," or "A covered cup, with a foot, of John "Morton;" but "ix potts grete and small, in silver "dishes v dos. and xi dishes mccxviii unc."

There are two exceptions to this ignorance of the names of the pieces of plate; one cup is called "the "Langton pott," and a piece, possibly a dish decorated with engraved figures, is designated "the ix wordeys," (the nine worthies). That the stranger was also an appraiser is shown by the fact that every piece of plate has its weight set down, and at the end, after a statement of the total weights of "white plate" and "gilt plate," a memorandum values the former at 3s. per ounce, and the latter at 3s. 8d.

The summa totalis of the weights is written, "Sm. iiii lb. i unc." (4,000 pounds and one ounce of silver).

S. B. b. 139. Is a similar list, in an earlier handwriting, entitled "Jocalia in officio celerarii;" but even in this document the writer gives names to only one or two of the articles, as "Cyphus de murra ex dono W.

"Hankyn vicarii de Bleen," and "6 olle S. Islep." The weights of the several pieces are here given, but no prices are annexed. It is remarkable that here as in the previous catalogue the silver dishes amount to five dozen and some odd dishes.

It is probable that the first of these inventories is the draft made by the appraiser at the time when the monastery passed from the hands of the prior into the keeping of the King.

C. 190, 1557. A grant from Philip and Mary to Cardinal Pole of that house and premises in the Mint yard of the late priory of Ch. Ch., which was formerly held by the almoner of the monastery.

The initial letter of this large deed occupies one sixth of the whole area of the parchment; it is executed with the pen without colours, and contains full length portraits of the King and Queen, wearing their regalia, and sitting under a cloth of estate.

The seal, in brown wax, is 6 inches in diameter. It represents on one side the royal pair sitting in state; on the other they are seen riding about in a field, wearing the every-day dress of the period. In this reverse of the seal the artist has attempted to produce a picturesque effect by the employment of artifices in perspective and fore-shortening, the statuesque stiffness usually found in seals being discarded.

D. 106, 1553. Lease from the King, advised by the Court of Augmentations, of certain lands lately belonging to the dissolved religious house known as the Domus Dei in Dover.

N. 16. "Valor annualis possessionum, &c., nuper "Priori et Conventui Sce. Trinitatis Norwicensis perti-"nentium." A parchment document accompanied by many sheets of returns written upon paper. Temp. Edw. VI.

R. 68, 1604. Copy of the deed of re-endowment by James I. of the collegiate church of Ripon, which has since become the cathedral church of the diocese. The annual sum assigned to the new cathedral is 347l., an amount larger by a hundred pounds than the endowment as reported by Collier (Eccl. Hist.).

Domestic Economy.

C. 1293, 13th cent. Nineteen rules, being the surviving part of a set of twenty-seven, compiled for the regulation of an archbishop's household. These rules of "Hosebondrie" relate both to domestic and to rural economy. One specimen of each kind is here given:—

"¶. La vinte-deusime reule vous aprent de defendre les diners, e les sopers, hors de sale.

"Defendez les diners, e les sopers, hors de sale, en "muscetes, e en chambres; kar de ceo surt mut de "wast, e nul honur a seinur ne a dame.

"¶. La vintequartime reule vous aprent les deus reules de vendre, e de batre nostre ble.

"Tenez deus reules endreit de vente, e de batre de ble, ke is ne soit ble vendu ke la forre ne vous remaigne a estrainer vos faudes de berbiz lb jur, e a compost dedenz la curt, e fees certien ke le estrein issi retenu vous vaudera tuz jurs la meite del ble vendu. De autre part ne suffree, en nule manere, ke lem bate aveine, en nul liu, devont noel, ne a p(ro)vendre, ne a vente, einz soit tut a achat si vus poez; e apres le noel, kaunt lem commence a semer aveine, fetes batre vostre aveine, o tel forre, batu si freschement, cuntrevaudra, si un poi soit medle de foin, trestut fein, e durra greinure force a vos bests, e vigur a travailer. E bien poez entendre, ke si vous volez aveine vendre, dunc la porrez vous mieus vendre e plus rendra kaunt, a force covent, ke chescun la eit a semer."

Minute directions are given for calculating the length of time during which the Abp.'s household can be entertained at the different manors without impoverishing them. Before the programme is settled for the season, the writer directs that attention be paid to the quantity of fish, flesh, and grain which may be looked for at each manor, allowance being made for the kind of weather which has prevailed during the preceding months.

The last rule reads, "Je lo ke a deus sesuns del au "facez vos grons achas; ceo est vos vins, e vostre cife, "e vostre garderobe, a la feste de Seint Botulf [June "17] ceo ke vous despenderez en Lindeseie, e Norfolk, "e en le val de Beauvere, e en cel pais de Kaversham, "e en cel de Suthamtone de Wincestre, e Sumarsete; a "Bristowe vos robes akatez a Seint Jue [probably SS. "Simon and Jude, Oct. 28.]"

C. 184, 1340. The prior borrows 120l. from Master Bernard Sistre, Archdeacon of Canterbury, giving this promissory note as security.

C. 165, 1221. A parchment containing an account of sundry payments which did not fall within the department of either of the monastic officers. It might be entitled "Miscellaneous Expenses for the Year 1221." Some of the items are available as evidence of customs, &c., for example:—

" Pro xvi doliis vini emptis ante Natale per manum " Willi. Wenton monachi, cum vectura, xxii. lib. xv " sol.

" In vino in refectorio nostro die computacionis " nostre xvi sol.

" Pro lignis trahendis ad Opus Honorii, ad ignem " suum, monachi apud Stm. Jacobum.

" Mattheo Goseballe, Cirurgico, pro infirmitate prioris " xiii sol. iiiid.

" Elemosinario pro Anniversario regis Ricardi anno " preterito, xx sol.

" Pro sotularibus Willelmi Clerici, et Andree, nepo- " tum Sci. Thome, reparandis contra Natalem." Many other items in this account which refer to the " kinsmen " of St. Thomas " are noticed under that title.

" Portitori brevium pro Osberto monacho defuncto " viiid.

" Alexandro Minutori pro fratribus minuendis iiii " sol. de iiii terminis.

" Pro quadam domicula paranda ad opus Simonis " Aurifabri ad faciendum novum sigillum, iiii sol. id.

" Hugoni de Gerunde ii sol. ad amovendam Cam- " panam Sci. Thome, et alibi suspendendam.

" In libris nostris emendandis.

" Pro habito monachico filii H. de Cobeham et Willi. " consanguinei Sci. Thome, lv sol.

" Portitori rotuli pro Willo. priore, xi sol. iiiid.

" Pro eodem rotulo faciendo, ii sol. xd.

" Priori eunti Oxoniam ad concilium ad expensam " suam, vii lib. xviii sol. iiiid.

" Pro speciebus in die Sci. Dunstani ad cenam, xiii " sol. vid.

" Magistro Willo. Curteis, in translatione Sci. Thome " ad pannos emendandos, xl sol.

" Pro parcamento, xv sol.

" Pro duobus equis ad stabulum prioris emptis de " Widone monacho, ii marc.

" It. Pro speciebus et medecinis ad opus infirmorum " per manum Roberti speciarii, x lib. xi sol. ob.

" Pro metallo empto ad novum sigillum, v sol."

C. 245. " Expensæ factæ circa constructionem Cam- " panilis Angelici."

The central tower of Canterbury Cathedral, named, from an image which formerly surmounted it, the " Angel Steeple," was rebuilt at the end of the 15th century. This MS. records the amount of the outlay during nearly three years, extending from Easter 1494 to Michaelmas 1496. 1,650 quarters of lime were consumed, each quarter costing 8d.; 1,132 tons of Caen stone, purchased for 530l. 8s. 10½d.; and 480,000 bricks were used, costing 3s. 4d. the thousand. The total expense for the whole period amounted to 1,035l. 16s. 3½d., in addition to which the monastery provided out of its stores, lead, nails, ashlar, and ironwork, besides furnishing carts for sand and other materials " que vehebantur caroctis monasterii."

S. B. c. 112. Early 15th cent. Thomas Herne, the chamberlain of Ch. Ch., lays down precise rules to be observed by his successors in the office of chamberlain.

There is scarcely a page in the three volumes of " Scrap Books " but contains some bill for work done and materials furnished, or some memorandum of money paid out by a monastic officer.

The maniple buys a pair of soles at one place and a barrel of salmon at another; the agent goes from fair to fair in the autumn, and purchases sheep and oxen wholesale, to salt down at Martinmas for winter store.

The lawyer's bill of costs, the bill of Master Benet, the apothecary, the horse-doctor's bill, are here, with builders' bills in very large numbers.

A very quaint series of small payments is to be found in the cook's memoranda of petty sums laid out in sundries. One week of these memoranda begins, " Die " Dominica, Fellyngs 2d., Blak podynge 2d. Item in " cena, Trypys 2d. Summa 3d." It will be noticed that here, and the same may be said of almost all cases where there is any calculation, the total is wrongly added. The Roman numerals did not lend themselves freely to the purposes of mediæval arithmeticians.

More important and more formal than the above-mentioned bills are the statements of account prepared by the office-bearers of the monastery for the annual audit. The specimens of complete returns which are preserved belong to the departments of,—

1. The chamberlain, who superintended the clothing and lodging of the brethren.

2. The sacristan, whose duties, summed up in the words " sonitus et hornatus," consisted in announcing the services of the church and providing for their proper celebration.

3. The berthonarius, who had charge of the receipts and issues of grain after it had come to the granaries at Ch. Ch.

The returns made by the treasurers, the custos maneriorum and the almoner are numerous, but less complete than those last-mentioned.

The serjeants and bailiffs at the manors and farms of the priory also sent their accounts of receipts and payments, together with an inventory of the live and dead stock which still remained on hand. Examples of this kind of account exist by hundreds, and range from the end of the 13th to the 16th centuries.

X. 17. A condensed statement, for one year, of the reports of the several officers of the monastery, written, in double column, upon one long narrow membrane. At the head is placed the "Assisa saccarii," or market values for the current year of several agricultural products. Probably rents were accepted either in money or in the shape of produce, this table serving to show the relative quantities of either which the tenants were bound to pay:—

"Assisa saccarii"
Frumentum	xid.
Ordeum	xxviiid.
Avena	xid.
Probenda	xxxd.
Pise	iii sol.
Pensa casei	x sol.
Stoppa mellis	xviiid."

Dover, St. Martin's.

The MSS. from D. 38 to D. 102 relate to an eighty-years-long dispute, in which the convent of Ch. Ch. was engaged with the priory of St. Martin, Dover.

The house at Dover was founded by Abp. Theobald as a cell of the convent of Canterbury. He provided that the Prior of Dover should always be a Canterbury monk, and that novices of the Dover convent should make their profession in the church of Canterbury.

It is clear, from the wording of the foundation deed, that the Abp. intended that the subjection of Dover should be due to the *Church* of Canterbury, and its head the Abp., and not to the *Convent* of Canterbury, with its head the Prior, " justum enim est ut qui Cantuar. ec- " clesie rector et dispositor est, plenam disponendi in " omnibus auctoritatem in Doveronsi ecclesia . . . . " obtineat."

The Prior of Canterbury, backed by a Bull of Honorius III. (1271), claimed from the Dover monastery the submission which even the Dover monks owned was due to the Church of Canterbury. At first the men of St. Martin's were disposed to be obedient, but after a time, being tired of dependence, they appealed against the claims of Ch. Ch. The dispute continued until the year 1350, when, owing to the good offices of Abp. Islip, a composition was entered into by the parties, Canterbury withdrawing all claims to supremacy, and Dover agreeing to pay an annual tribute of five pounds.

Dover Castle.

D. 103, 1227. Fragments of a charter of Hen. III., exempting the county of Kent from all liability to furnish "farragium" to the garrison of Dover Castle.

A. 32, 1261. Abp. Boniface, hearing that certain knights and esquires belonging to Dover Castle have assaulted some tenants of Ch. Ch., despoiling them of their goods, directs the official of the archdeacon to proceed against the delinquents by ecclesiastical censures.

E. 171 and E. 173. Stephen de Pencestre, Constable of Dover Castle, the commander of the garrison at the time of the excesses complained of by Abp. Boniface, restores the horses, waggons, and fodder, which were the goods whose loss had roused the Abp.

Dover Maison Dieu.

D. 104, 1277. A copy made at Rome of a Bull of Nicholas III., by which new privileges are granted, and established ones confirmed, to the Domus Dei of Dover. The instrument names in detail all the privileges, and the sources of the income which the house is to enjoy, and provides that the rule of canons regular of St. Augustine shall be observed in the convent, which is to be immediately under Papal protection.

Eastry.

The manor of Eastry with a share of the tithes belonged to the almonry of Ch. Ch. The convent and the rector of Eastry, not being able to agree upon any

equitable division of the tithes, appealed to the law.
Many of the MSS. in this group are contributed by the
suite which ensued.

E. 167. Abp. Theobald grants the tithes of Eastry to
the almonry.

E. 168 to E. 170. Papers in the suit "Anselm Rector
" of Eastry versus Prior of Ch. Ch."

E. 171 and E. 173. Amends made to Ch. Ch. by the
constable of Dover Castle for trespasses committed in
the manor of Eastry. The first of these deeds is curi-
ously dated,—"anno post mortem Simonis de Appulia
" Exoniensis Episcopi primo." (This bishop died in
1223.)

E. 175, 1365. The convent and the rector of Eastry
agree about their respective shares of a part of the tithes
of Eastry.

E. 176, 1365. Abp. Islip by his deputy, whom he
constitutes " ad hoc organum vocis nostri," restores to
the almonry the church of Eastry, which Abp. Hubert
had appropriated to his own use. In this deed the convent is said to have been so reduced by this and other
spoliations that " fere deficerent, non habentes quod
" manducarent, seu unde alia eis incumbentia support-
" arent."

E. 177, 1366. The King's licence allowing Ch. Ch. to
hold the church of Eastry.

E. 178, 1365. The Prior of Ch. Ch. quotes E. 176, and
writes that, " lest gratuitously yielding so much should
" seem derogatory to the dignity of the Abp.," he gives
in exchange for the church of Eastry, the patronage of the
churches of St. Dunstan and of All Hallows, Bread Street
in the city of London, the King's licence being obtained.

E. 179. Abp. Langham confirms the restoration of
Eastry to the convent, and provides for the payment of
a competent stipend to the vicar.

E 186, 1200. A document belonging to the early
part of the contention between the archbishops and the
convent arising from the appropriation of the church of
Eastry.
This parchment is signed in autograph by Abp. Hubert
and Galfridus Prior of Ch. Ch.

E. 174, 1348. "Terra inventa, et mensurata sub
" periculo maris in hundredo de Eastry et Cornilo."
This roll, 7 feet long by 7 inches wide, gives a great
many examples of the ancient names of fields, and also
of tenants in possession at the time.

E. 184, 1445. A rentale of the manor of Eastry.

E. 184a. " Rotulus de redditibus et consuetudinibus
" manerii de Estreya, de novo compositus sed ab antiquo
" rotulo abstractus."
The land is divided into "sullings," and the rents are
payable either in money or produce, at the option of the
tenant.

E, 188. A long survey of the acreage of the manor,
with the names of some tenants. On the back is a
memorandum of prices of produce and labour.

Faversham.

F. 89. Copy (late 16th cent.) of the foundation deed
of Faversham Abbey, as perused and confirmed by
Edw. IV. The charters recited in this inspeximus
were granted by Edw. III., Stephen (2 charters), John
(2 charters), Hen. III., Matilda Stephen's Queen, and W.
Earl Bolon., and Warrenne.

F. 83. Copies (late 13th cent.) of charters granted to
Faversham Abbey by several Kings, from Stephen to
Edw. I.

In dorso. 1. Copy of inspeximus (1338) of charters of
Stephen and Henry III.

2. Copy of two charters of protection, Hen. III.

3. Mem. of the acquittal of John Smat of North
Darenth, charged with assault and riot.

4. The process against about 40 Kentish men who,
headed by " Joh. Perys factor rotarum," were attached
by the sheriff in 1362 " ad respondendos Regi de diversis
" transgressionibus."

F. 87. Peter Abbot of Cluny to Abp. Theobald. "No-
" tum volumus fieri . . . quod nos dedimus et concessi-
" mus Stephano Regi Angliæ et M. uxori sue Regine, Cla-
" rem baldum qui fuit prior monachorum de Berm. et
" oumeo xii. monachos ejusdem cenobii, ad construendam
" abbaciam suam quam apud Faversham fundare jam
" inceperunt. Preteres absolvo ipsum priorem Clarem-
" baldum et prescriptos monachos ab omni obedientia
" . . . . quam mihi seu ecclesie Cluniacensi antehac
" promiserunt et debebant, sive ecclesie de Cantuari.,
" ut Deo serviant apud Faversham, ita videlicet libere,
" ut neo Abbas Cluniacensis vel Prior de Cant. pre-
" sumant quicquam in Abbatia de Faversham calump-
" niare . . . .," &c.

F. 81. P. Prior of " St. Mary of Charity " [Fleury] to
Abp. Theobald.
He has granted " Rege Stephano et uxore ejus Matilde
" Regina pio expetentibus desiderio, ab omni obedientia
" . . . quam nobis et ecclesie nostre de Caritate, nec-
" non Abbati Petro et Cluniacensi ecclesie debuerant
" . . . . Clarembaldum et xii. monachos . . . . ab-
" solvimus ex parte tam predicti Petri quam nostra,"
&c.

F. 88. Inspeximus by several abbots of certain
charters which grant and confirm to St. Augustine's
Abbey the church of Faversham, with some others.
These churches were the causes of many disputes.
Thorne gives all the papers bearing on this point (Script.
X.).

F. 85. c., 1200. Copies of four charters relating to the
same subject as the last. These are certified to be
authentic by John Card. Soc. Marie in Via lata. A certain carelessness in the composition of the certificate and
a looseness in the handwriting give the idea that the
paragraph was written off by the cardinal's own hand,
without a previous draft. The stiffness of manner and
precision of letter, characteristics of professional scribes,
are both wanting in this certificate, which, moreover,
differs in style from the copies of charters to which it
is appended.

Fordwich.

As will appear from the following charters, the Abbot
of St. Augustine was lord of the soil of Fordwich, but
inasmuch as that the town was a member of the Cinque
Ports, the inhabitants had the right of self-government
to a considerable extent.

F. 46. A narrow roll of two membranes, headed,
" Iste sunt consuetudines quibus Major et Communitas
" de Fordwyco ab antiquo utebantur et adhuc utuntur."
Several paragraphs follow relating to the holding of
the " Hundred Court," with the limits of its jurisdiction.
Then the rights and the duties of the corporation are
defined, and the method by which they are to deal with
evil-doers is prescribed, and, lastly, the procedure in
cases of judicial combat within the borough is settled as
follows :—
" Si aliquis probator extraneus aliquem hominem de
" libertatibus appellaverit de aliqua felonia . . . . dictus
probator in dictam libertatem ingredietur cum toto
apparatu suo, prout dicto probatori decet, et cum venerit
in dictam villam ductus erit ad aquam currentem voca-
tam ' Stour,' et in illa aqua stabit usque ad umbilicum
cum apparatu suo ad modum probatoris prout dictum
est, et paratus ad appellationem probandam; et dictus
liber homo sic appellatus veniet in uno batello cum III
postein eadem aqua ad oppositum dicti probatoris, indu-
tus cum uno indumento vocato ' Storre,' cum uno instrumento vocato ' Ore ' de longitudine III ulnarum, et
ille batellus affirmabitur ad caiam cum una corda, et
in diota aqua cum dicto probatore pugnabit quousque
duellum inter eos finiatur."
On the back are written some laws for regulating the
never very friendly, relations between the Mayor and
Jurats and the Seneschal of the Abbot of St. Augustine's.

F. 47. Copies of eight charters relating to Fordwich
and granted to St. Augustine's Abbey.

1. Grant of the town of Fordwich from Edward the
Confessor to St. Augustine's. This short charter is in
English.

2. Grant by the same King of sac and soc and other
liberties. English and Latin.

3 and 4. Two similar grants by William the Conqueror.

5. Odo Bishop of Bayeux gives all his rights in Fordwich to St. Augustine's.
" Ego Odo Episc. Baioc. et Kanc. comes omnes domos
quas in villa de Fordwyco habeo, et omnes consuetudines mei juris ad ipsam villam pertinentes, pro anima
mea . . . . ecclesie Sci. Augustini in perpetuum pos-
sidendas concedo."

6. A confirmation of 5 by William I.

7. A writ of William I. re-granting to St. Augustine's
the town of Fordwich " quem tenet Hamo Vicecomes."
The writ is directed to Abp. Lanfranc, the Bp. of Con-
tances, Count of Eu, and H. de Montfort, " aliisque
" proceribus regni."
The town had fallen into the hands of the sheriff after
the flight of the timid Abbot Egelsin.

8. The sheriff's surrender of the town in obedience to
the King's writ.
The Sheriff Hamo writes, " Hanc donationem meam
" per psalterium Sci. Augustini, et per cultellum meum,
" super principale altare ejusdem ecclesie manibus
" meis misi."

In dorso is a list of the customs which the abbot was empowered to levy upon imports at Fordwich Quay. They are declared to be the same as those which the Prior of Ch. Ch. collected at Sandwich, and may therefore be found printed in "Boys' History of Sandwich."

German Ships Captured by English Cruisers, *temp.* Hen. IV.

About the time of the accession of Henry IV. cruisers belonging to England, coming out of Calais, sank and captured some ships owned by merchants enrolled in the confederacy of the Hanseatic League. This league, backed by the powerful co-operation of the Teutonic knights, was strong enough to demand compensation and restitution from the King of England, treating with him as one sovereign power with another. English merchants trading to the Baltic lost their ships, which were seized by way of reprisal, and when the question of compensation was raised they put in their counter-claims.

The documents contained in this group furnish materials from which a history of the dispute might be compiled.

It will be noticed that two separate negotiations are recorded here, the same ambassadors being appointed on each occasion, the first in 1405, the other in 1407.

M. 299, 13 May 1405. Short instructions given to the ambassadors who were deputed to mediate between the King of England on the one part, and the Master-General of the Teutonic order on the other.

The ambassadors are instructed to arrange a time and place where they may meet the representatives of the other side, for the purpose of receiving evidence of damage done to the Germans, and of producing evidence of injuries received by Englishmen.

M. 302, 8 Oct. 1405. Confirmation by Henry IV. of a treaty entered into between W. Esturmy, Knight, John Kyngton, clerk, and Will. Brampton, citizen of London, on the part of the English, and Brothers Conrad de Lichtenstein, grand commander, Wernher de Dettinge, commander in Elbing, and Arnold de Hecken, treasurer, proctors of the magnificent and potent Lord Conrad de Inngingen, Master-General of the Teutonic order, on the part of the Germans. The composition, which is recited at length, arranges for the settlement of existing differences, and so far provides for the future as to form a foundation for a general treaty of commerce. The original deed is dated "in castro "Marienbergenai in Prusia, 8 Oct. 1405," the confirmation in 1407.

M. 306, 15 Dec. 1405. Original composition made between the ambassadors of Henry IV. and Hen. de Vredeland, Tideric Casveld, Simon Clovesteen, and Joh. Sotebotter, representatives of the merchants of Lubeck, Bremen, Hamburg, Stralsund, and Greifswald. This is a preliminary treaty, in which the parties agree to receive evidence up to the first day of May following.

M. 308, 28 April 1406. The pro-consuls and consuls of Riga give notice to all whom it may concern, that Ludovic Sthocker, their fellow-citizen, has formally complained that in the previous month he, being in a ship, one of three, making for Flanders, was captured by the English, and two casks of suet (tallow), "duo vasa "cepi (sevi)," his personal property, were taken from him. He has appointed Albert Sthokman, who is already engaged to act for other sufferers, to be his proctor for the purpose of demanding and receiving compensation.

M. 303. A certificate, under the municipal seal of Dorpat (Civitas Tharbetensis),

In this document the city officers set forth in detail the several packages of merchandise which were lost when the ships Engelbert Bonyt and Reyman Boyten were destroyed by the English. Every merchant who sent his venture in these ships distinguished it by a mark. In most cases this mark has the form of a tall cross with shrouds, and sometimes a flag, but although the elements of the several marks are the same, the marks themselves, owing to variations in the combination of the elements, are all different. These merchants' marks are tricked in the margin of the remonstrance, each one opposite to the description of the package which it distinguished.

M. 201. Many fragments of parchment and damaged sheets of paper, containing claims for compensation, and arguments propounded by both sides. The injured condition of these documents makes it impossible to piece together the various portions of evidence into a continuous story.

M. 305, 3 June 1407. A letter from the "Nuncii "Consulares civitatum de Hansa," assembled at Lubeck.

They complain that the English ambassadors are unnecessarily hindering a proposed conference at Dordrecht.

M. 387, 12 June 1407. A letter, in French, written by John Earl of Somerset and Constable of Calais to the English ambassadors. He says that the German remonstrance contains a sentence which he thus quotes:—"Item dantar plures querele contra capitaneum Cales, "Michaelum Scot de Cales, Will. Hornby de eadem, et "quendam Byschop de eadem, et alios ejusdem ville, "ad summam viii. M. nobil."

The captain writes that he is prepared with a sufficient answer to the charge, as he will show at the meeting which is to take place at Dordrecht on the first day of August.

M. 281, 2 July 1407. The King, confessing that the first embassy had failed in its purpose, by this instrument re-appoints the same ambassadors, instructing them to re-open the question of mutual compensation.

K. 8. The Consular Nuncii of the cities of Pruce, assembled at Marienburg, send this notice to the Mayor of Hull, demanding that he shall deliver up certain monies to Godekyn Tydeman, their agent. The money in question was received for some corn which one T. Sutbury, a Hull mariner, had taken from a German ship, and the Nuncii had ascertained that the sum was still in Hull in an unbroken sum.

X. 9, 1404. A certificate, in French, under the seal of the Mayor of Newcastle-upon-Tyne. It testifies that merchandise belonging to a certain merchant of Berwick has been seized in a Baltic port, and that the owners are therefore entitled to compensation.

Y. 56, 1407. A similar certificate, written in Latin, given by the Mayor of York. This document makes claims identical with those in X 9, on behalf of a person of the same name, who, however, is said in this case to be a citizen of York.

Hereford.

H. 113, 1131. Bull of protection and confirmation of privileges granted by Innocent II. to Bp. Robert and the Church of Hereford:

"Decernimus igitur, ut nulli omnino hominum liceat prefatam ecclesiam temere perturbare, aut ejus possessiones auferre, vel ablatas retinere, minuere, vel aliquibus vexationibus fatigare, sed omnia integra conservetur eorum pro quorum gubernatione et sustentatione concessa sunt usibus omnimodis profutura."

This parchment bears the monogram of the Pope, and the (apparently autograph) signatures of seven cardinals.

H. 118, 1598. A notarial instrument by which the dean and chapter appeal against the bishop's right to visit the church.

There are some rolls of accounts kept by the claviger of the church. He records the amounts received, and the sources whence they were derived, adding in each account the manner in which the money was distributed among the canons actually in residence.

Hospitals.

R. 18, 1306. On the death of one Simon, rector of Reculver an inquisition is ordered to inquire into the status of the benefice. The church is reported to be worth 200 marks a year, but it is encumbered with a pension of 20l. assigned by Abp. Lanfranc to the hospitals of Northgate and Harbledown.

This inquisition was made by order of W. de Testa and W. Geraldi, administrators of the diocese, sede vacante. It will be remembered that the see was vacant in 1306, not by the death of an Archbishop, but by the suspension of Robert Winchelsey, who, having offended the King, was outlawed by him and suspended by the Pope.

H. 145, 1355. Copy of a deed by which Abp. Islip confers a permanent endowment upon the hospitals of Northgate and Harbledown.

The income of the hospitals had hitherto consisted of 20l. paid annually by the rectors of Reculver, and a further sum given by the Abps. at their pleasure. In this grant the donor speaks of the uncertainty attaching to the latter source of income, and he recognises the disadvantage under which the poor of the hospitals lay from having to solicit a new grant from every fresh Archbishop; beside which, he says that it often happened that when the see was vacant, and the temporalities in the hands of the King, the hospitals lost their means of living for a long time together.

To remedy this state of affairs, Abp. Islip gave for ever 140l. out of the revenues of the church of Reculver, in addition to the 20l. already coming from that source,

The church had long before been assigned, by Papal authority, to the maintenance of the table of the Abps., and therefore Abp. Simon was able, at all events during his life, to alienate the income. The original of this deed is in the muniment chest of the master of the hospitals.

R. 19, 1355. Confirmation by the Prior and convent of Ch. Ch. of Abp. Simon's grant.

Indulgences.

A. 13, 1297. Abp. Winchelsey's grant of forty days' indulgence to worshippers in the chapel of our Lady in the infirmary of the monks of Canterbury.

A. 33, 1274. "Omnibus Christi fidelibus presentes " litteras, &c. . . . frater R(obertus Kilwardby) mise- " ratione divina Cant. Archiep . . . . , &c. Ut fidelium " Christi devotionem allectivis indulgentiarum muneri- " bus ad caritatis ct devotionis opera propencius excite- " mus, de omnipotentis Dei misericordia, beate Marie " Virginis, et Sci. Thome martyris, ac et omnium sanc- " torum, meritis confidentes, omnibus vere penitentibus " et peccato sua dimittentibus, qui ad tumbam bone " memorie Ade de Chilindenne, quondam prioris " ecclesie nostre Cantuar. pro ejusdem anima et omnium " fidelium defunctorum oraverint, viginti dies de " injuncta sibi penitentia misericorditer sibi relaxamus," &c.

C. 167, 1274. Anianus Bp. of Bangor grants twenty days' indulgence to all who pray for the soul of the above-mentioned Adam Chillenden. In this case it is not necessary that the tomb should be visited.

C. 170, 1296. John (Monmouth) Bp. of Landaff grants twenty days' indulgence to all, but especially to those of his own diocese, who shall hear the divine office in the new chapel of the Prior of Canterbury.

C. 182, 1320. A similar grant by Henry Bp. of St. David's.

C. 226, 1291. Hugh Bp. of the Church of the Nativity at Bethlehem grants forty days' indulgence to those who properly visit the prior's new chapel near the infirmary.

H. 113, 1276. A similar grant by Bp. T. Cantelupe of Hereford.

Inventories.

S. B. c. 12, 1313. "Inventarium bonorum Thome " Romayne defuncti, factum per executores dicti de- " functi."

The deceased was a person of consequence, he had a private chapel containing furniture worth 13*l.* 13*s.* 4*d.*, he also wore a gown furred with minever, and hence it is that the items in the inventory are rich and costly.

At the time of his death the Bishop of Winchester owed Romayne four score pounds; the Prior of St. Mary, Southwark, and the Abbot of Westminster, were also debtors to the estate. It is likely that he was a London citizen, for a shop is mentioned, the weights and utensils in which are valued at twenty shillings.

S. B. b. 215, c. 1331. A fragment of a draft memo- randum by which the treasurers of Ch. Ch., as receivers of the estate of the late Prior Henry of Eastry, are debited with considerable sums of money.

The whole amount received, consisting of florens, ready-money, tallies, and obligations, was 358*l.* 5*s.* 3½*d.* The florens are distinguished as, " florens de Flo- " rentia," each worth 3*s.* 4*d.* ; 2, florens de la mas . . . ., each 5*s.* 10*d.* ; and, 3, florens de agno.

C. 238, 1338. A schedule of valuables drawn up upon the appointment of a new prior.

It will be noticed that each important piece of plate is distinguished by the name of the person who gave it to the monastery.

S. B. c. 63, 1339. Inventory of the stock on the manor of Chartham. There are no prices annexed to the articles here enumerated.

A. 37, 1349. Inventory and valuation of the goods belonging to Abp. Stratford at the time of his death.

The sum total of the appraisement was 6,509*l.* 14*s.* 4*d.* ; of this 1,907*l.* 14*s.* 8*d.* was the value of the books, jewels, plate, and chapel furniture.

The debts of the deceased amounted to 5,925*l.* 13*s.* 4*d.*

The details of the valuation are not given, but each department, as hall, stable, chapel, &c., has the price of its contents annexed to it.

The funeral expenses were calculated at 782*l.* 4*s.* 2½*d.*

A. 34, c. 1303. Three pieces of parchment showing a debtor and creditor account of the estate of the late Abp. Winchelsey. The total assets amounted to 4,232*l.* 15*s.* 0½*d.*, and the funeral cost 459*l.* 8*s.* 7½*d.*

C. 236 and C. 230, c. 1350. Two inventories of the stock, on the several manors belonging to Ch. Ch., which died in " the murrain." These MSS. are peti-

tions addressed to the Bp. of Rochester by the monks of Ch. Ch. They plead the state of poverty into which they have fallen in consequence of the great pestilences affecting man and beast, and they pray that the bishop will give them the church of Westerham, to help them to maintain their traditional hospitality.

The schedules are appended as arguments intended to touch the bishop's heart.

The summa of the losses of animals is thus stated :—

" Boum 257, pretium bovis 15*s.*

Vaccarum cum exitu 511, pretium vacce cum exitu 10*s.*

Ovium 4,585, pretium ovis 18 pence.

Total money loss 792*l.* 12*s.* 6*d.*"

At the same time 1,212 acres of land, formerly profit- able, are said to be inundated by the sea, apparently from want of labourers to maintain the sea walls.

C. 166, c. 1411. "Ornamenta ecclesie Xpi. Cant., et " jocalia, quedam nova, adquisita, et quedam antiqua, " reparata, tempore Thome Chyllendenne prioris."

Three membranes written on both sides, containing a list of the matters mentioned in the title, and also a minute account of all repairs and restorations, as well within the precincts of the monastery as in the outlying manors, done in the time and under the auspices of Prior Thomas Chillenden.

This MS. records the almost total renovation of the monastery and all its possessions.

S. B. b. 68, 1396. An account of all the expenses in- curred in the time of Prior Chillenden for the re- edification of Canterbury College, Oxford. This account extends over two years, and comprises the smallest details. A complete description is here given of the cost of labour and materials required for the construc- tion of a large edifice at the beginning of the 15th century.

S. B. a 126. "M*d* de bonis et catallis ecclesie de " Westwell." A defaced churchwarden's inventory. The date is about 1490.

S. B. a. 191, 1440. An inventory of jewels given in pledge by Prior John Salisbury to Cristina Overton.

These jewels were articles of great value, brooches, cups, spoons with gilded lions for knops, two pairs of coral beads, the " paters " being gilt, washing basins of Paris work, &c.

S. B. b. 32, 1451. Schedule of fixtures attached to a lease.

S. B. b. 40, 1458. Inventory of stock on the farm at Lydd Court. 300 ewes were worth 14 pence each, 100 muttons fifteen pence, 6 boars a shilling each, and 167 lambs each 10 pence.

S. B. c. 110, 15th century. A priced inventory of stock. The lease of which the MS. is a part demises for a term of years, not only the land, but all the store " quyk and dede."

S. B. c. 109, c. 1470. Inventory attached to a lease of the manor of Chartham.

S. B. c. 21, c. 1480. Store on the farm at Bocking. The amount of corn in the granary is said to be " scored " on the door posts."

S. B. b. 166. "The Goods of Thomas Sendall dis- " treyned for rent of the corn-mell at Bokkyng a°. regni Hen. VII*mi*. primo." Household goods, tools of trade, and a pig, all priced.

S. B. c. 143. The inventory of the goodys of Elyn Lightwhite appraised the 18th November . . . . Henry VII.

A long list of furniture, plate, clothes, &c. of a well- to-do person.

O. 134, O. 135, O. 136. Three inventories of books, plate, and household stuff belonging to Canterbury College, Oxford. These all belong to the latter part of the 15th cent., and each was written when a new warden took over the goods from his predecessor.

S. B. b. 91, 1493. An inventory of plate pledged :—

" ffirst a chayre of golde with a crosse wheryn are v perilles and v othir stonys recepta in vigilia Sci. Bene- dicti post festum translationis Sci. Thome A. H. VIII., ix°=xxxs. xd.

" Itm. 1 Agnus Dei with Seint Anthony crosse the belle hangyng theron, xxxiiis.

" It. A rounde owche with iiii perillys & 1 ruby in the myddest, vis. xd. ob.

" Itm. 1 poyr of Bedes of corall with xv gawdens silver and gilt, xs.

" It. Two gemellys of golde oon in another . . . . vs. iiid."

There are 15 items in all.

S. B. a. 188, 1493. "Inventory of the stuffs sent by
"my Lord Prior for his use at the Almonry at Monk-
"ton."

Monkton church belonged to the almonry of the convent, and the parsonage-house, parts of which remain to
this day, was a pleasant country retreat for the prior,
who therefore sent a few articles of comfortable furniture
for his own use.

"A payer of vestyments of baudekyn, the orfresse
"blewe with flower-de-lyse of gold. In the chamber. A
"payer of fustenys, a pilowe of downe, covered with
"lynyn cloth, and a tacell of whyt sylke. A qwylt
"with five lebards. A coverlett with 1 lyon, bordered
"with clowdys. Two cochons, wherof on with a lyon, the
"othyr of red say. Two curteins of blew buckram.
"One covering to a bed of bord Alexandyr, colourys
"yalow and greene, lynyd with blew buccram. A
"basene with an ewer of latten, with can(dle)styk
"dobilnosyd."

S. B. b. 96. Inventarium rerum repertarum in domo
ubi R. Welborne manebat.

A curious inventory of household stuff, arms, and
stores.

"A brestplat, a gorget of stele, fower standardys with
"two gossetts of mayl, three salettys, three billys, one
"bak stele, two pykyd stafys, one bowe, one bad sadyll.

" In the cellar. Two stondys full of ale each of them
"conteyning 13 galons, a kylderkyn of bere half full,
"50 salt fyschys, with two lyngys, a lytyle vessell
"with verjouse, one vessell with bren (brine) and four
"peces of beff therin. A bushyll of colys, seven
"conyakynnys, four stone morters," &c.

S. B. b. 139, 15th cent. A roughly drawn inventory
of the plate in the office of the cellarer of Ch. Ch., written
by an officer of the monastery, who enters the articles a
"six pots S. Islep, two pots H. Chychele," &c.

S. B. b. 140. A similar inventory of plate, with the
weights and prices of the several articles.

S. B. c. 23, probably 1559. A list of costly vestments belonging to Ch. Ch., more than half of which are
placed under a sub-title, "Ornaments given by the late
"Lord Cardynall Poole."

One silver mitre, said to be "defaced," is reported to
weigh 97 ounces.

It is probable that this inventory was made when
Abp. Parker succeeded Cardinal Pole.

Ireland.

By gift of Hervey Mountmorris, the convent of Ch.
Ch. came into possession of lands and ecclesiastical
estates in Ireland.

In the 13th century all the Irish possessions of Ch.
Ch. were made over to the convent of Tinterne, or de
Voto, in the diocese of Ferns.

I. 228. "Littere Johannis Regis, de protectione, et
"de rebus nostris in Hybernia in manum suam
"capiendis."

I. 231, 1245. "Cyrographum inter nos et Abbatem
"et Conventum de Voto in Hibernia, de dimissione
"omnium terrarum nostrarum ibidem, pro nomine
"firme, postea nomine juris perpetui, pro x marcis
"annuatim solvendis in cathedrali ecclesia Batonie ad
"festum Sci. Michaelis."

I. 236. Contemporary copy of the last.

I. 235, July 1245. "Transcriptum carte Abbatis de
"Voto de terra ei vendita in Hibernia, et obligatio ejus
"de annuo redditu x marcarum, et de aliis conditioni-
"bus infra scriptis servandis."

The original gift of the land to Ch. Ch. by Harvey
Mountmorris is quoted in this document. It was
difficult to collect rent from land at such a distance
from home, and the Kings of England required that
persons drawing money from Ireland should either reside in person or provide substitutes who might perform
military service. Under these circumstances it is not
wonderful that the Canterbury monastery should prefer
a certain annual payment, however small, to a larger
but troublesome and uncertain income.

I. 232, 13th cent. The Abbot and convent of Tynterne or de Voto acknowledge that although they have
bought all the Irish farms and town lots (prædia urbana)
belonging to Ch. Ch., yet that they have no claim to the
land at Thamagre, which is the property of Geoffrey St.
John.

I. 234, 1245. Bond by which the monks of Tynterne
undertake, in consideration of the conveyance to them
of the Irish lands belonging to Ch. Ch., to pay an annual
rent of 10 marks, to satisfy all episcopal and archidia-
conal demands, and to supply certain churches with
efficient priests; especially they undertake to provide
that masses shall be said in the church of Brendanus

Banarwe for the late Herveius de Monte Mauricio, a
benefactor of Ch. Ch.

I. 238, 1257. The Prior of Ch. Ch., having appointed
the Abbot of Tynterne to be his proctor for transacting
Irish business, receives this document, which guarantees
him against all claims for fees.

I. 237, 1255. At the instance of Abp. Boniface the
Abbot de Voto adds three marks to the ten in which he
is bound to the Prior of Ch. Ch.

I. 233, 1245. An act of chapter, by which the convent
of Ch. Ch. undertake that the monies received from the
Abbot de Voto in the diocese of Ferns shall be expended
in the purchase of lands and rents, and in no other
manner.

X. 8, 1380. Extract, in French, from an ordinance of
Richard II. which forbids absentees to receive rents or
profits from Irish property.

I. 245. The ordinance of Richard II., founded upon
one of Edw. III., providing that all who owned rents or
lands in Ireland should either there reside, or send a
sufficient number of persons to represent them in the
defence of the country. An exception is made in favour
of ecclesiastical revenues, and the Prior of Ch. Ch. is
permitted to receive, for the term of his life, 13 marks
from the Abbot de Voto.

I. 242 and I. 244. Paper copies of the last.

I. 247, 1422. The King's permission to Prior John
Wodnesborough, allowing him to receive 13 marks
yearly as long as he lives from the abbey of Tynterne,
"aliquibus statutis .... contra absentes a dicta terra
"nostra Hibernia in contrarium factis non obstanti-
"bus."

I. 251, 1428. A similar grant to Prior W. Molash.

I. 250, 1454. A similar grant to Prior Goldstone I.

I. 249, 1432. Inspeximus of a record in the Exchequer
which contains the result of an inquisition made in the
reign of Henry IV., by which it was shown that the
Prior of Canterbury received rents from Irish property
and was an absentee, "contra formam cujusdam ordina-
"tionis .... per Ricardum nuper Regem Anglie
"secundum."

I. 241, 13th cent. A document which shows that, in
addition to an annual rent of 10 marks, the Abbot de
Voto paid, for the transfer to him of the Irish possessions of Ch. Ch., a premium of 625 marks.

I. 239, 1191 to 1206. Demise by Galfridus, Prior of
Ch. Ch., of the ville of Fychard in Ireland to Richard of
London, and his heirs, for an annual rent of 4 marks.

I. 242, 13th cent. Final concord between the Bp.
of Ferns, and the convent of Ch. Ch. By this deed it
is decided that the Bp. shall have the manor of Fychered
and the convent, the churches of Banewe, Kylcogan,
Kylmor, Kinture, and Tagmagre, both parties disclaim-
ing all suits for the future.

I. 243, 1308. R. Bp. of Ferns writes to the Prior of
Ch. Ch., saying that he finds in old writings that when
the English first came to Ireland they seized lands and
churches, some of which, belonging to the church of
Ferns, were given to the Canterbury convent. He finds,
too, that after many suits a composition was entered
into by the Bp. and the convent, by which the convent
resigned to the Bp. all rights in the manor of Fychard.
In the teeth of this composition, a man has now come
to Ferns, saying that, in right of his wife, he is heir to
one Richard of London, to whom the manor was devised
long before ; he brings with him a writing supporting
his claim, sealed with a seal which in no way resembles
that which the Bp. has seen attached to writings emanating from Ch. Ch. He, in consequence of these events,
wishes to know if the muniment-room of Canterbury
contains any evidence relating to the subject, and he
asks the prior to attach to his answer an impression of
the small old seal of the convent, if such a thing exist.

I. 248, 1430. Statement of account between the Prior
of Ch. Ch. and the attorney whom he employs to receive
the 13 marks which are paid by the Abbot de Voto.

I. 240. A Bp. of Emily in the 13th cent. writes to the
Prior of Ch. Ch. to say that David his treasurer, whom
the prior once hospitably entertained, has served a notice
upon the prior and brothers of St. John's in Kilkenny,
thus complying with a request made by the Prior of Ch.
Ch. In a postscript the Bishop says that before he goes
to Ireland "tumbam beati Thome martiris per Dei
"gratiam visitare intendimus."

In the volume of Ch. Ch. letters are two from James
Sherlok, who farmed, under the Prior of Ch. Ch., some
quitrents or other manorial dues in Ireland. Dating
from Waterford in the middle of the 15th cent., he complains that one Talbot has come over, claiming the farm
of one of the manors by virtue of an alleged bargain
made between himself and the Prior of Ch. Ch. Sher-

look requests that letters and parcels intended for him may be sent to a certain merchant in Bristow, who will forward them.

Jubilee.

M. 350, 1520. A packet containg four letters relating to a jubilee which Abp. Warham proposed, if the Pope's sanction could be obtained, to celebrate at Canterbury. The year 1520 was the three hundredth anniversary of the translation, and the three hundred and fiftieth of the martyrdom, of the patron saint of Canterbury.

Three of these letters are written from Rome by the Archbishop's proctor (probably Dr. Grig), and the fourth is from Bedyll, the Archbishop's secretary.

The Pope was plied with arguments and presents, Cardinal Campeggio was privately retained as an advocate, and the Cardinal " Quatuor Sanctorum," in return for valuable gifts, assisted Dr. Grig with his advice.

In spite of arguments and bribes the Papal licence was refused, except upon terms too exorbitant to allow the jubilee to be a pecuniary success.

The Pope (Leo X.) proposed that one half of all the oblations made at the festival should be given towards the building of St. Peter's; to this the Abp. consented provided that, first, the preliminary expenses, including bribes, incurred by him should be deducted from the gross receipts; secondly, that the jubilee should be continued for a whole year; thirdly, that this one permission should be perennial, and that the festival should be celebrated every fiftieth year without any fresh licence.

As there is no record of the actual celebration of this jubilee, it is probable that the negotiations came to nothing; and that six silver goblets for the Cardinal of the Quattro Santi, and a gold cup with a large sum of money for the Pope, were all unprofitably expended.

Great stress was laid upon the fact that a jubilee had been regularly held every fifty years, and that it was established by prescription; hence the Abp. was advised to find some men, noblemen if possible, who, being over sixty-five years of age, might of their own personal knowledge testify to the celebration of a jubilee in 1470.

The appendix to " Somner's Canterbury " contains these letters, but they are not very correctly transcribed.

The vol. of Ch. Ch. letters contains one from Joh. Giglis, made Bishop of Worcester in 1474, who, in writing to the Prior of Ch. Ch., mentions a jubilee in progress at Canterbury at the date of his letter.

Ch. Ch. Letters 54. A very curious story of two incontinent priests, who after living as laymen for a year, went to a general " pardon " at Canterbury, and repenting, assumed their priests' " array." The letter which communicates these facts is not dated, but it is probable that the " pardon " alluded to was the jubilee celebrated at Canterbury in 1470.

Letters Apostolic.

M. 340. Adrian IV. to Abp. Theobald. "Ex injuncto " nobis a Deo summi pontificatus officio attentam cogi- " mus sollicitudinem gerere, et modis omnibus provi- " dere, ne, tempore nostri apostolatus, Ecclesie Dei " rerum suarum detrimentum incurrere debeant, vel " jacturam . . . . Pervenit autem ad nos quod laici " quidam, in cimiterio ecclesie Sce. Marie de Arcubus " intra Londoniam, duas domos ausu temerario con- " struere presumpserunt . . . . fraternitati tue per " apostolica scripta mandamus, quatenus . . . . ipsas " domos, ... omni occasione et dilatione postposita, " auctoritate nostra facias amoveri."

P. 60. Alexander III. to Abp. Richard.

He advises him to entrust the keeping of his seal to a monk of his own church.

C. 51. Alexander III. to Alan Prior of Ch. Ch. and his convent. After saying that above all clergy he was bound to protect those who professed the regular religious life, "eapropter dilecti filii, officio suscepte " ministrationis inducti, et vestris precibus inclinati, " presentibus vobis litteris indulgemus, ut a solutione " decimarum de ortis vestris, de feno, de herbis pascuo- " rum, et de minutis aliis, ita sitis amodo liberi sicut a " quadraginta retro annis noscimini sine interruptione " fuisse, &c."

A. 191, 1203. The Abp. of Canterbury, having ordained a deacon without a title, is required to provide him with a benefice. The Pope argues " cum, secundum aposto- " lum, qui altari servit vivere debeat de altare, et qui " ad onus eligitur repelli non debeat a mercede; patet " a simili, ut clerici vivere debeant de patrimonio Jhu. " Xpi., cujus obsequio deputantur, sicut ipsa nominis

" ratio persuadet, cum enim a cleros (κληρος) appellan- " tur, quia in sui ordinatione vel assumantur in here- " ditatem domini, vel assecuntur hereditatem in ipso, " ut vere possint psallere cum propheta, ' Dominus pars " ' hereditatis mee,' &c."

A. 187, 1206. Innocent III. to King John. The King is requested to promote the election of Reginald the sub-prior of Ch. Ch., who after having been chosen Archbishop by the monks of Canterbury was rejected by them. See under the head " Abps., Election of."

M. 343, circ. 1282. Martin IV. appoints Gifred de Vezano collector in England, Scotland, and Ireland of the subsidy in aid of the Holy Land, giving him authority to arrange for the commutation of vows " tam " crucesignatorum quam aliorum."

Letters, Archbishops'.

C. 218. From Abp. Theobald to Elwin son of Leofstan.

" T. Dei gratia Cantuariensis ecclesie humilis minis- " ter Eilwino Leofstani filio, et R. fratri ejus, et " Johanni filio Radulfi, et omnibus tenentibus de " ecclesia Xpi. Cant. . . . . Mandamus vobis et precipi- " mus, quod in justicia, et sub tuicione Dni. Jeremie " Prioris Cantuar. sitis, et ei, sicut nobis, diligenter " obediatis. Priori vero firmiter, et per obedientiam, " injungimus, ut pro vobis sit, et vos, pro posse suo, in " omnibus justiciam teneat et faciat. Illud eciam " mandando precipimus ne quis de ecclesiis vel terris, " aut hominibus, clericis videlicet et laicis, seu rebus " aliis ad monachos Cantuar. pertinentibus, nisi quem " Prior . . . . ad hoc statuerit, se in aliquo intromittat. " Valete in Xpo. et estote obedientes per omnia."

A. 189 and A. 192 are two collections of letters written by Abp. Winchelsey to the Prior of Cant.

A. 189 c., Aldington, 2 Nov. 1294. The Archbishop calls upon the prior to justify the sentences of suspension and excommunication which he has laid upon various rectors and vicars, during the vacancy of the see.

A. 189 a., July 1296. The Bps. of Albano and Palestrina, writing from Rome, request Abp. Winchelsey to allow W. de Langton, the elect and confirmed of Coventry, to be consecrated abroad, urging that he was likely to be detained in their service for a long time.

A. 189 b., South Malling, 7 Aug. 1296. Abp. Winchelsey's reply to the writers of the last letter. The Archbishop evidently wishes to postpone his answer; he says he must first consult his chapter, which, " propter " distanciam longam, et vie aspere ac montuose discri- " men," he cannot do immediately. He requires also to discuss the matter " cum concilio nostro, undique " nunc, ut morie est, in instanti tempore autumpnali, " disperso." Meanwhile he promises that the delay shall not work to the disadvantage of the new prelate.

A. 193 c., Charing, 14 June 1297. The Abp. to the Prior of Canterbury.

He complains that the priory of Ch. Ch. is languishing through decrease in the number of monks; the diminution has gone so far that, there being only thirty brethren on the foundation, the services in the church are " attenuated." He reminds the prior that " sapiencie " doctrina testat, in multitudine populi sit dignitas " Regis, et in paucitate plebis ignominia principis."

A. 193 e., Slindon, 15-21 Sept. 1298. Abp. Winchelsey to the Prior of Ch. Ch.

Whilst taking steps to fill up the numbers of his convent, the prior is advised to be cautious in the selection of his recruits. The writer draws a parallel between the assumption of the religious habit and the sacrifice prescribed by the Mosaic law; comparing the novice making his profession to the victim of the Jewish altar. Hence he argues that an unblemished body is as essential as an honest conversation. He prescribes that candidates for admission shall be " bone vite secundum " judicium humanum, et honesti in corpore, sicut decet " ministros tam celebris ecclesie pollere undique hones- " tate."

A postscript, " Vobis quasdam litteras pridie nobis " directas per Dom. Rob. de Bardelby (recepimus), " quarum tenore inspecto, faciatis quod vobis visum " fuerit expedire."

A. 193 r., Oxford, 9 Jan. 1299. The Archbishop reproves the Bishop of Ely, who, disregarding a laudable custom, has failed to provide a benefice for a clerk whom the Archbishop nominated at the time of the Bishop's consecration.

A. 189 s., 11 Sept. 1299. Abp. Winchelsey, dating from " Wylughton in Lindeseya distante a Lincoln, " versus provinciam Eboracensem, per duodecem leucas," boasts that he has carried his cross erect through the northern province. Willoughton in Lindsey is, however, nearer 12 miles than 12 leagues distant from Lincoln.

A. 189 e. A letter from a member of the Abp.'s household to a friend, doubtless the Prior of Ch. Ch. The writer tells the person whom he addresses that a cup which he sent to be given to "my Lord" is too paltry for the purpose, especially when it is known that he has never given one before. He has consulted two well-wishers of the giver of the cup, who agree in opinion with the writer, and therefore, out of friendship, they have concocted an excuse, which will give time for the purchase of a richer gift, telling my Lord that a messenger brought the cup as far as Meopham, but was afraid to carry it any further. When this story was told to my Lord, he laughed, and graciously received the letter which had been sent with the cup, this latter being kept out of sight.

A. 193 h., Stebonhethe, [Stepney] 29 March 1303. Abp. Winchelsey to the Prior of Ch. Ch. "Inhibemus vobis ne " adversariis ecclesie nostre, monachis de Sco. Augustino, " vel eorum ministris, aut aliis quibuscunque ipsorum " nomine, oleum sanctum, crisma, vel aliud quod- " ·cunque spirituale, liberatis, ne omnino nobis, et vobis, " ac ecclesie nostre, adversantibus in hiis, vel in aliis, " ad eorum relevamen eis aliqualiter suffragetur. Valete " semper in Xpo."

A. 193 b., Wingham, 21 Nov. 1304. Abp. Winchelsey to the prior. The King has required the Abp. to direct his clergy to perform pious offices for the soul of John, late Earl of Warrenne, "consanguinei regis." Complying with the King's command, the Abp. requests the prior to cause the proper prayers and masses to be recited in his church.

A. 193 s., Lamhegh [Lambeth], 1 March 1305. Abp. to prior.

Abp. Winchelsey, having heard that the Abp. of York is about to return to his province in state, his cross being carried before him, requires the prior to use his whole strength to prevent this intrusion. The northern Abp. had been over sea, and landing at Dover must necessarily pass through Canterbury.

S. B. a. 181, 1305. A quasi private letter from the Abp. to the prior. He thanks the prior for some information which he has given, and says that he need not take the trouble to come to London to the Parliament, for that no business would be transacted except the consideration in the Privy Council (in secretiori regis concilio) of certain articuli touching the state of the realm.

K. 1., Mandate, Pictavie, 28 Jan. 1308. Return, 24 Feb. 1308. A return made by Henry Bp. of Winchester to a mandate of Abp. Winchelsey.

The Abp. had written to the Bp. of Winchester requesting him to officiate at the coronation of Edw. II., because he foresaw "non absque cordis angustia" that he should be prevented from taking the duty upon himself. The Bishop, having crowned the King, certifies the Archbishop, "Hujus igitur auctoritate mandati et com- " missionis vestre, die dominica, videlicet v. Kln Marcii, " Anno Dni. supradicto, excellentissimo principi et do- " mino nostro Edwardo dei gratia Regi Anglie illustri " unccionis gratiam, et coronacionis munus, impen- " dimus vice vestra. In cujus rei," &c.

C. 1294. A roll of four letters sewn together. These were sent by Abp. Walter Raynold to Prior Henry of Eastry. Three are occupied with subjects connected with the discipline of the convent, and are noticed under the head "Discipline." The fourth contains a request that the prior will provide a proper study to which the "Reader" of the convent may retire. Having heard that the prior is about to fit up eighteen now "diversoria" in the cloister, the Bp. judges that one of these will suit the "Lector," who hitherto has gone into the infirmary to prepare his readings; the letter mentions as one recommendation of the new arrangement "ut debiles et infirmi absque strepitu popu- " lari secrecius conquiescant."

A. 193 d., 1314. Gilbert Bp. of London, as leading suffragan of the province, summons the Bp. of Hereford to take part in a consecration at Canterbury. The method of procedure was, that the Abp. summoned the Bp. of London, and the duty of calling all the other suffragans fell upon him. The Bp. of Hereford, bringing this citation in his hand, came to Canterbury, and hence it happens that this collection contains the document, which, a priori, would be looked for at Hereford.

Letters, Priors'.

M. 364, circ. 1240. A roll, composed of eighteen slips of parchment, which is entered in the catalogue "Priors' " letters." This title is misleading, inasmuch as that

the documents are citations, inhibitions, and other law papers, with which the prior is connected only so far as that one or other party in the several suits has sought "tuitionem ecclesie Cantuariensis."

S. B. a. 45, 1331-38. This is a letter from Prior Oxenden to Edw. III., in which the writer asks the King to excuse him from attending the Parliament at York. He writes, "Testis est michi qui abscondita " cordis novit, quod in eo precipue letarer quo vestra " regia magestas felicibus incrementis succresceret, et " regni gubernacula salubriter exerceret, at quia ad " instans parliamentum vestrum . . . . adversa vale- " tudine . . . . impeditus personaliter venire non valeo, " quod grave gero et moleste, ... absenciam meam " excusatam . . . . dignetur habere vestra regia mag- " nitudo . . . . In eo qui dat regibus regnare vestra " valeat semper celsitudo."

London.

The MSS. in this group, more than 120 in number, may all be classed as title-deeds, but since they allude to old customs, and to sites which can still be identified in the modern city, they are here noticed, whilst other title-deeds, referring to places of less historical interest, are passed over.

L. 19. A short charter of Henry II., empowering the Canterbury convent to hold their lands and men in London as securely as they did in the time of the late King Henry.

L. 1. An early lease, circ. 1130, containing four lines and a half of writing. The tenant covenants to pay a rent of 12s., to build on the premises, and to rebuild if, " quod absit," the houses should be destroyed by fire.

L. 2, middle of 12th cent. A priest named Ælgar has given to the convent of Canterbury his church in London, from which the convent are to receive five shillings yearly, and in return for the gift they promise to adopt him into their fraternity whenever it shall please him to forsake the world.

The church given on these terms is bestowed by the convent upon Holye the son of Ælgar the priest, on condition that he shall pay the yearly five shillings, and with the further understanding that at the death of Elias the church shall pass to his next of kin for ever, " si tamen ecclesia dignus fuerit."

L. 4. Gift of a vicarage in St. Mary Bothage to John son of Rohesia and nephew of St. Thomas.

L. 71. A certificate of Abp. Theobald, testifying that Peter the priest of Bothage de London has given his church of St. Mary Bothage, "que sui patrimonii esse " dinoscitur," to the prior and convent of Canterbury, paying to the prior five shillings annually by two equal instalments.

L. 73. Abp. Stephen Langton gives the church of St. Dunstan to the convent of Canterbury, the revenues to be expended upon the repairs of the church of the monastery.

L. 9 and L. 120 refer to this church.

L. 32. A grant to Ch. Ch. by Abp. S. Langton of land which he had exacted from Reginald de Cornhill who had administered the revenues of the see during the time of the Abp.'s exile. "Terram cum domibus " quam R. de C. dedit nobis ot successoribus nostris " in perpetuum pro excessibus quos fecit in Archie- " piscopatum Cantuar. tempore exilii nostri, quando " curam ac custodiam ejusdem archiepiscopatus habuit " ex parte Dni. Regis."

L. 17, 12th cent. Gift by Ralph de Cornhull of a rent of 5s. to the church of Saint Trinity [i.e. Ch. Ch.], Canterbury.

L. 69. Charter of Henry III. conferring upon the monks of Ch. Ch., in respect of their London property, the same privileges as they enjoyed "tempore regis " Henrici avi mei."

L. 393, L. 397, and L. 398, 1313. Three instruments relating to the election of Gilbert de Segrave to fill the vacancy caused by the death of Ralph Baldok, late Bp. of London.

L. 77, 1278. Composition made between the Bishop and Dean of London and the Prior of Ch. Ch. concerning jurisdiction during the vacancy of the See of London.

L. 80, circ. 1225. "Carta prioris & conventus de " Lesnes quod non cedat nobis in prejudicium quod " capellani habeant in Londonia."

The convent of Lesnes had a house and an oratory in the parish of St. Michael Paternosterchurch, (otherwise styled in Riola, a name which is now corrupted into Royal) and the convent of Canterbury, the patrons of the church, required this guarantee before they allowed the

3 K 4

house of Leanes to introduce their chaplains into the oratory.

L. 82. Roger le Duc, as founder of a chantry in All Saints' Bread Street, undertakes that the parish church shall suffer no injury from his new foundation.

L. 94 to L. 110. These are all confirmations by the wardens of the Mercers' Company (custodes misterie mercerie) of appointments to the office of "Magister Col-" legii in ecclesia Sci. Michaelis in Riola." The earliest date is 1424, the latest 1482. The seal displaying the "Maidenhead," the cognisance of the mercers, is attached to all these documents.

M. 391, 1424. Explains what this college was, and how the mercers came to be patrons. The preamble of this deed runs, " Cum Johes. Coven-" tre, Johes. Carpenter, et Willelmus Grove, executores " testamenti Ricardi Whitynton nuper civis et mercerii, " London; in honore Sci. Spiritus, et beate Virginis " Marie, Collegium perpetuum ac quinque capellanis, " unde unus erit magister, ac certis aliis clericis et " choristis obsequia divina cotidie in ecclesia Sci. " Michaelis de Paternostercherche in Riola que ad " nostrum patronatum existit, pro salubri statu Dni. " regis nunc dum vixerit, et anime sue cum migraverit " .... fundaverunt, erexerunt," &c.

M. 340, 1428. A presentation to the vicarage of the above-named church. This dignity was sometimes combined in one person with the office of Master of Whityngton College.

L. 101, 1434. Certificate under the seal of the Mayor of London, extending over two entire membranes, which attests the authenticity of a number of deeds by which endowments were conferred upon the college in the church of St. Michael " in Riola."

L. 99, 1430. A certificate under the seal of the Mayor of London concerning an assize of novel disseisin or " frisce forcie tenta coram vicecomitibus civitatis Lon-" don," in which the bone of contention was a rent of 6s. 8d. in St. Laurence Pountney.

L. 93, 1405, and 110, 1573. Two similar certificates.

L. 119. Extracts from the pleas rolls of the Hustings Court of London. These extracts relate to the enrolment of title-deeds, the earliest of the originals belonging to the year 1279, and the copies to the 15th cent.

L. 127, circ. 1450. Inventory of fixtures, &c. handed over to an incoming tenant of " the vawts of the King's " Head in Chepe." This house belonged to the convent of Canterbury, and the brethren visiting London sometimes charge, among their expenses, small sums laid out in this tavern.

One item in the inventory is " an iron to hang with " busshes upon the sign."

L. 109, 1521. A composition relating to a brewhouse, formerly called " the Pott on the Hoop," but at the date of the composition " the Pewter Pott," in the parish of St. Andrew.

L. 31, 1566. A bargain, in which the dean and chapter are concerned, relating to the land upon which the Royal Exchange was afterwards built.

Manors.

C. 155, circ. 1300. This MS. is very beautifully written on a parchment roll 18 feet long, the head being protected by a leathern flap lined with silk.

It is entitled, " Redditus assisus omnium maneriorum " Ecclesie Xpi. Cantuar." Under the name of each manor are set out the rents, whether in money, labour, or produce, with the terms at which they severally become due.

For example, under the title "Monkton" are first shown the money rents, payable at twelve different times in each year; then follow these items :—

De Cotmannis ad duos terminos xs.
De terra Turk fabri apud Brokeshond xiiis. iiiid.
De novo kydello iis. (probably a kettle-net on the shore).
De alio kydello vid.
De Johanne Noldan vid.
Item de Stongrunde iiis. ixd.
Summa xxxfi. xxiiis. iiid. ob.
Ꮯ Vomeres xii. Ꮯ Esperduz ferri i. Ꮯ Agni xxxiii. Ꮯ De quolibet messuagio i gallum et unam gallinam qui modo amuntat ad DLX. Ꮯ Ova M̃D. scilicet de qualibet domo v ova.

C. 158, circ. 1400. A long parchment roll having the title, " Donationes et adquisitiones maneriorum cum " ecclesiis totius prioratus ecclesie Xpi. Cantuar. con-" cesse et confirmate ut inferius patet." This MS. schedules all the gifts of real estate made to the church, together with the donors' names and the dates of the benefactions.

The series begins in the year five hundred fourscore and seventeen, being the thirty-fifth of Ethelbert, who " dedit Augustino palatium suum, in quo fundata est " ecclesia Cantuar. et in nomine Sci. Salvatoris dedicata " est;" the last acquisition is the manor of Selgrave which Prior Chillenden purchased in 1400 from the widow of Ralph Spickernell. The title and the several heads are rubricated, and on the back is the signature, " Thomas Goldstone monachus ecclesie Xpi. Cantuarie," written by the same hand as the body of the deed.

C. 184, 1392. A receipt for a sum of 58l. 6s. 8d., being part payment of a larger sum of 83l. 6s. 8d. paid by the Prior of Ch. Ch. to Eliz. Spigarnell. This money was probably paid for the manor of Selgrave.

C. 157. The draft from which C. 158 was copied.

C. 156. The full notes from which the draft C. 157 was condensed. This contains many particulars which were omitted in the copies; thus after recording the gift of Walworth in 1051 this MS. further explains, " Predictam villam Edmundus rex dedit cuidam jocula-" tori suo nomine Hitardo. Tempore tandem regis " Edmundi, (Edwardi. ?), idem Hitardus volens limina " Apostolorum Rome (adire), venit ad ecclesiam Xpi. in " Dorobernia, et, per consensum et concessionem ejus-" dem regis Edwardi, dedit eandem villam eidem " ecclesie; cartam quoque ejusdem terre posuit super " altare Xpi., que carta habetur adhuc in eadem " ecclesia."

Arabic numerals are here used to express the dates.

C. 160, 1438. A long roll of eight sheets of paper entitled—
" Annuus valor omnium maneriorum, domorum, " terrarum, ot tenementorum, venerabilium et religios-" orum Prioris et Conventus ecclesie Xpi. Cantuar. tam " in Comitatu Kancie, quam in diversis aliis Comitatibus " Anglie, a festo Sci. Michaelis anno regni regis Henrici " Sexti xxime. usque idem festum extunc proxime " sequens .... per unum annum integrum."

This survey displays the names of the manors, &c. in the left-hand margin, and opposite to each is written the annual rent, if the property were let out to farm; or the various items of revenue in labour, money, or produce, if the convent retained the property in their own hands.

The gross receipts amounted to 2,107l. 8s. 3¼d. and ¾ of a farthing, equal in terms of marks to 3,175 marks 21 pence and ¾ of a farthing.

The expenses were 1,132l. 4s. 10d., leaving a net profit of 984l. 0s. 10¾d.

This erroneous result was arrived at by the scribe after several failures and consequent erasures, the results of long computations in Roman numerals.

C. 161, 1540. " Nuper Monasterium Ecclesie Xpi. in " Civitate Cantuaria."
" Supervisus sive breve extentum .... terrarum, " tenementorum, et aliarum possessionum, tam tempo-" ralium quam spiritualium, dicto nuper monasterio " tempore dissolutionis ejusdem, viz. 5to die Aprilis " Anno regni regis H. 8vi, 31mo. pertinentium sive spec-" tantium, diversis pratis nuper per dominum regem " Xtofero Hales militi datis et concessis tantummodo " exceptis. Captus per Joh. Wylde supervisorem et " auditorem ibidem mense Junii Anno regne regis " predicti 32do."

After the title there follows a complete schedule of the several possessions, to each of which the gross and net value are annexed.

The manors, &c. belonging to St. Augustines' Abbey are included in the schedule.

C. 162, early 18th cent. A paper headed "Dean and " Chapter."
" The names of the several mannors and the severall " courts to the same belonging and the severall officers " yearly chosen at the court leets."

Monasteries and Individuals in Society with Christ Church.

A. 25, circ. 1175. The Abp. of Lyons provides a continental refuge for the Abps. of Canterbury.
" Guischardus dei gratia Lugduniensis Archiepisco-" pus, &c. Notum sit universitati vestre nos conces-" sisse venerabili patri nostro Ricardo Cant. Archi-" episcopo et .... successoribus suis .... terram " de Quinciaco cum omnibus pertinenciis suis, et do-" mum in claustro nostro emptam ab Episcopo Mori-" anensi Guillelmo [Bp. of Maurienne, 1160–76] et " Buri nepote ipsius. Ipse autem dominus Cant. " Archiepiscopus singulis annis faciet servitium refec-" torii honorifice diebus quatuor incipiens a quinto die " Natalis Domini. Postquam vero beatus Martir Thomas " Cantuar. translatus fuerit, quarti diei servitium in diem

" translationis ejus transferetur. Et si forte dominus
" Cantuar. in terra de Quinciaco Castrum firmaverit, erit
" canonicis, et militibus, et hominibus eorum ad refu-
" gium sine incommoditate ipsius Archiepiscopi . . . .
" Anniversarium suum et in ecclesia nostra concessimus
" annuatim faciendum, et ipse similiter nostrum in
" ecclesia Cantuar. Pro defunctis ecclesie sue faciemus
" annuatim servitium in conventu nostro infra xx dies
" post festum Sci. Michaelis, et ecclesia Cantuar. simi-
" liter faciet pro nostris."

B. 390, circ. 1200. A letter from the Abbot of St.
Bertin to the Prior of Canterbury.

The letter forms the prelude to a solemn compact by
which the two houses bind themselves to the performance of acts of mutual charity.

" Decernimus igitur, si vobis placuerit, ut monachi
" ecclesie vestre talem habeant societatem, scilicet ut
" nomina eorum scribantur in martirologio nostro, et
" quisquis sacerdos ecclesie nostre dicat pro defuncto
" vestro tres missas speciales, et memoriam faciat pro
" eo specialem in missa sua usque ad xxx dies. Canta-
" buntur eciam pro eo due misse speciales, et duo
" officia in conventu, et ' Verba Mea ' xxx diebus. Qui
" vero inferioris ordinis fuerint, singuli cantabunt psal-
" mos constitutos. Pronunciato et obitu defunctorum
" vestrorum, exibit conventus a capitulo in ecclesiam
" cantando ' Verba Mea ' pulsatis interim signis."

" Dabitur et pro singulis defunctis vestris prebenda
" unius monachi per vii dies. Cum vero fratres vestri
" ad nos venerint, de licencia abbatis et conventus
" vestri, habeant nobiscum sicut unus ex nobis quamdiu
" vobis placuerit ut nobiscum moram faciant. Verum-
" tamen secreta capituli nostri, quia a sanctis patribus
" nostris prohibitum sub intimatione anathematis, ne-
" mini possumus, vel audemus concedere."

E. 191, 1336. A mortuary roll, to which are subscribed the "Tituli" of several monasteries.

(See a paper by Mr. J. G. Nichols, "Archæol. Journal,"
Norwich. Vol.)

This MS. is written upon three membranes, neatly
joined, with paste, forming a roll of 7 feet in length.
It contains 127 lines of manuscript, beside the grandly
illuminated initial word, which occupies the first line.
The central space of the capital letter at the head of
the document is filled in with a full-length portrait of
the deceased, John Hotham, Bp. of Ely. He is dressed
in alb, dalmatic, and chasuble; on his head is a low
broad mitre, and in his left hand an ornamental pastoral
staff.

The composition takes the form of a notice addressed
by the Prior of the Cathedral Church of Ely to all
Christian people, announcing the death of the bishop of
his diocese :—

" Onus carnis deposuit . . . . desolati filii plangimus
" patrem piissimum, oves pastorem optimum, monachi
" abbatem dignissimum, clerici presulem serenissimum,
" plebs prelatum, et navicula Petri gubernatorem pru-
" dentissimum, filii denique patrem qui nos fovit et aluit
" quemadmodum gallina congregat pullos suos sub alas.
" Grex pusillus pastorem plangimus qui nos de ore
" leonis, et a luporum rapacitate liberavit."

The rest of the MS. is filled with an enumeration of
the virtues of the deceased, composed in the same
turgid style. The public offices which the bishop had
filled are described, and the Old Testament is ransacked
to find parallels to his surpassing qualities.

Lastly, the prayers of the faithful are asked for one
who, with all his virtues, was yet a sinner, " nam sep-
" cies in die cadit justus, et nemo mundus a sorde, nec
" infans quidem unius diei." Giving the keynote to
the monasteries whose tituli are to follow, the writer
adds a prayer, " Creator omium rerum faciat nos seip-
" sum revelata facie contemplari. Anima dni. Johan-
" nis de Hotham quondam Epi. Eliensis, et anime
" omnium fideluim defunctorum, per misericordiam
" Dei, requiescant in pace. Amen. Nostri defuncti
" sint vobis in pace juncti."

After this follow the suffrages of twenty-five monasteries, of various orders, to each of which this roll was
carried. An example will show the formula used by
all :—

" Titulus ecclesie Sce. Marie et Sci. Benedicti Rameseie.
Anima dni. Johis. Epi. Eliens., et anime omnium fidelium defunctorum, per misericordiam Dei, requiescant
in pace. Amen. Oramus pro vestris, orate pro nostris."

These last words are sometimes exchanged for the
verse "Vestris nostra damus, pro nostris vestra roga-
" mus."

C. 165, 1221. In this long memorandum of monastic
expenses several items refer to the custom of giving
notice of deaths to associated monasteries.

" It. Portitori rotuli pro Willelmo Priore xi sol. iiiid."
" Pro eodem rotulo faciendo ii sol. xd."

Several examples show that the death of a single
monk was announced by a " breve," the rotulus being
reserved for prelates.

" It. Portitori brevis pro Honorio monacho viiid.," is
one example out of many.

B. 394, 1497. A note, sent with a "rotulus," by the
Abbot of St. Bertin, announcing the death of the late
abbot, and claiming the usual spiritual good offices.

The note ends with a mention of the rotulus, which
the bearer carried from one monastery to another, and a
hint that a dated titulus was expected. " Diem vero qua
" dictus presentium lator ad vos venerit pro premissis
" in rotulo nostro annotetis, ac eidem nuncio cum per
" vos transierit, pietatis intuitu et amore nostri, victus
" necessarios, sicut vobis et vestris in casu consimili
" nos velletis esse facturos, humaniter ministretis."

Corrodies.

The custom of granting rations of food and drink from
the kitchen of the monastery, in exchange for benefactions, is illustrated by several documents in this collection.

C. 177, 1175–77. This is taken as a typical example.
During the incumbency of Prior Benedict, John Cal-
deron gave to the convent property in Canterbury, in
return for which the convent ensured to Mahalt, his wife,
a daily supply of food, and an annual gift of clothing
from the stores of the monastery. "Nos autem con-
" cessimus Mahalt uxori Johannis, quamdiu vixerit, sin-
" gulis diebus unum panem qualem monachi habent, et
" unum pleinpein, et unum transversam, et tres galones
" cerevisie monachorum, et unum ferculum generale,
" aut duo, sicut unus de monachis in die habuerit. Con-
" cessimus eciam eidem Mahalt unam pelliciam, et unas
" bottas, singulis annis quibus monachi eas habuerint,
" quamdiu ipsa vixerit, post obitum vero dicte Mahalt
" nullus heredum . . . . aliquis poterit clamare," &c.

L. 251. Odo, the prior, grants to W. Fitz-Archibald
and Agnes his wife, and their sons, society with the
Chapter of Canterbury. Also two corrodies in the
cellar for themselves and two men, if they come once
or twice a year to visit the shrines of the saints in the
church. In consideration of these favours, William
gives to the prior and convent an acre and a half of
land, for which they are bound to pay a quitrent of 16
pence.

F. 12. Similar privileges are granted to W. de Eines-
ford, a benefactor.

The Kings of England, by usurpation, or as an acknowledgment of obligations which the monks owed for
protection or toleration, had come to claim the right of
having two corrodies or daily allowances set down to
their credit in the kitchen of Ch. Ch., an annual money
payment sometimes superseding the daily delivery of
food.

C. 89, 1337. Edward III. undertakes that the gift
of these two corrodies " non trahantur in consuetudinem,
" nec eorundem Prioris et Conventus, aut successorum
" suorum, seu domus sue, cedant in prejudicium."

C. 95, 1398. Shows that the warranty of Edw. III.
had not much relieved the monks, for here is an acknowledgment by Richard II. that the two corrodies,
one valued at 20 marks in money, and the other being
the maintenance of one man, had been duly drawn down
to the day of the date ; the names even of the holders
of the corrodies are given both in the time of the grandfather and the grandson. In order to give effectual
relief to the monastery he agrees to forego the patronage
of the corrodies, if the convent will engage on their
part to observe the anniversary of Anne his first wife,
and after his own death will for ever keep the two
festivals of St. Edmund the King—the day, that is, of
the death, and that of the translation—as a commemoration of Richard himself, making mention of his name.

Norwich.

N. 26, 1302. Inspeximus by Henry Prior of Ch. Ch.
of a deed of Abp. Peckham. When Abp. Peckham, in
1281, made a visitation of Norwich Cathedral, the bishop
requested him to inspect and confirm the charters belonging to the church. The Abp., having inspected these
charters, caused copies to be made on three rolls, and
these he confirmed by affixing his seal twenty years
after. Prior Henry caused this copy of Abp. Peckham's
inspeximus to be made, apparently intending by attaching his seal to still further confirm the charters, but
from some cause the seal was not affixed, and the confirmation remained at Canterbury instead of going to
Norwich, which was its first destination.

The charters recited are,—

1. Bp. Herbert Losing's foundation deed, endowing the cathedral which he had built.

2. A confirmation of the same by Paschal II.

3. Confirmation by Abp. Anselm, who records that before the date of his deed both William II. and Henry I. had given charters of protection and approval. Anselm's deed is signed by twelve bishops and nine abbots.

4. Charter of Abp. Thomas of Canterbury, granting and confirming to the church of Holy Trinity, Norwich, the church of St. Giles, in the eastern part of the same city.

5. Bp. W. Ralee's gift of the church of Banburg [Bawburgh].

6. Bp. John (of Oxford) gives the church of St. Margaret de Lenna (Lynn).

7. Gift of the church of St. German, by the same Bp. John.

8. Charter of Bp. Eborhard, who bestows upon the church of Norwich all his rights in the churches of Becham, Hempsted, and Plumsted, together with several parcels of tithes and services.

9. Bp. Eborhard confirms to the church of Norwich all the privileges and possessions which it has rightfully acquired. The bishop's bailiffs have harassed the convent by trespassing, and he believes that these injuries arose from the ignorance of the bailiffs of what were the bounds of the possessions of the convent; to avoid a repetition of the offences he enumerates all the manors, &c. to which the convent can lay claim.

Among the benefactors he mentions Henry I. and Stephen, who bestowed "homines" as freely as they did tithes and acres.

10. A Bishop John bestows the church of Hundringham [Hindringham] upon the cellarer's office in the monastery.

After these recitals is copied Abp. Peckham's confirmation, and this is followed by that of Prior Henry, with the date 1302.

N. 4, 1330. Composition between Norwich and Canterbury, concerning jurisdiction, sede Norwic. vacante.

N. 5. A duplicate of the last.

N. 6. Abp. Mepham's confirmation of the same.

N. 8. Confirmation of the same by the Bp. of Norwich.

N. 27. Abp. Mepham's exemplification and confirmation of the same.

N. 24, 13th cent. A certificate, sub manu publica, concerning the charters by which the Augustinian priory of Thorney held its possessions and privileges.

N. 1, 1249. Certificate by the Prior of Canterbury, affirming that he has inspected a deed of Bp. Walter (Suffeild) of Norwich, which itself was an inspeximus of a charter of Thomas, formerly Bp.

The charter endows the office of the cellarer in the Norwich monastery with various parcels of tithes. A second charter endows the hospital of St. Paul in Norwich.

N. 3, 1283. Small expenses, chiefly for repairs about the court of the Norwich monastery.

N. 7, 1316. Confirmation by the Abp. and the Prior of Canterbury of the ordination of a chantry of four priests which Bp. John Salmon of Norwich had founded in the chapel of St. John the Evangelist, at the western end of the cathedral church.

The church of Westhale was appropriated to the chantry by way of endowment. Beneath the chapel was a crypt, concerning which the founder provides, "in carnario autem subtus dictam capellam Sci. Johannis, ossa humana in civitate Norwici humata, "de licencia Sacriste qui pro tempore fuerit (hiatus), "custodiam (hiatus . . . .) ad resurrectionem generalem honestius conservertur, a carnibus integre "denudata, reponi volumus et observari."

N. 26, 1396. A decree of the Cardinal Cosmatus (tit. Sco. Crucis in Jerusalem, afterwards Innocent VII.), the judge deputed by the Pope to arbitrate in a dispute between the Bp. of Norwich and the convent of Holy Trinity.

N. 10, 1398. A gift, by Henry Bp. of Norwich, of the church of Holm-by-the-sea to the monastery of Lilleshall, Salop. The abbot and convent begged the profits of the church, of which they wore the patrons, alleging that their House, situated on a great high road, was impoverished by the practice of necessary hospitality.

N. 9, 1370–1407. Ten pieces of parchment, each of which contains several copies of certificates of orders conferred under the direction of Henry Spencer, Bp. of Norwich. In many cases the orders were conferred by foreign bishops, acting as suffragans for the bishop of the diocese.

Johannes Smerniensis Archiepiscopus, and Thomas Aladensis Episcopus, are the outlandish prelates who assisted Bishop Henry; and on one occasion Simon Sudbury, then Bp. of London and afterwards Abp. of Canterbury, undertook the duty.

N. 12, 1479. A certificate, under the seal of the bailiffs of Great Yarmouth, testifying that in a suit of frisse forcie Thomas Bosome Prior of Norwich recovered from Robert Swolle an annual rent of 13s. 4d., with arrears and costs.

N. 11, 1454. Inventory of goods in the priory of Lenn Episcopi, taken at the accession of a new prior. The articles are the very homely movables of a small convent.

N. 14, 15, 1500. Sede Norwyc. vacante. The Norwich convent nominate three monks, from whom one is to be chosen by the Prior of Canterbury to act as commissary of the Norwich diocese.

N. 16, temp. Henry VIII. and Edw. VI. A parchment roll entitled, "Valor annualis possessionum . . . . "nuper Priori et Conventui Sce. Trinitatis Norwic. pertinentium." Also several sheets of paper, once fastened together, containing a schedule of the lands, &c. possessed by the Cathedral Church of Norwich, temp. Edwardi VI[ti].

N. 17, 1602. "Dr. Suclyng's discharge for the tenth "due 45 Eliz."

A statement on parchment of the amounts received by Edw. Brown, the collector of a tenth levied upon all ecclesiastical benefices in the diocese of Norwich.

N. 55, 1556. A statement of accounts, made by the collector of rents belonging to the Cathedral Church of Norwich.

Oxford.

These papers chiefly relate to Canterbury College, founded in 1362 by Abp. Islip.

O. 127, 1362. Licence granted by Edward III. to Abp. Simon Islip, authorising him to found a college in Oxford, and to endow it with lands, statute, &c. non obstante.

The King mentions the great pestilence in words which show that after twelve years it had not quite ceased, "Desiderantes incrementum salubre cleri nostri, propter multiplicationem doctrine salutaris que jam per "presentem epidemiam noscitur plurimum deficisse."

O. 128, 1363. Grant and confirmation by William de Islip of the manor of Wodeford in Northants, "custodi "et clericis Aule collegiate Cantuarie in universitate "Oxon. noviter fundate."

O. 129, 1363. A confirmation under the seal of Abp. Islip of the gift of Woodford by W. de Islip.

Alluding to the pestilence he writes, "Quia per sapi- "enciam, sic non absque sudore et laboribus adquisitam, "reguntur regna, et in justicia consonanter ecclesia "militans germinat, et sua diffundit tentoria; nos "Simon, &c., ad hec sepius revolventes intima cordis "nostri, ac considerantes veros in omni sciencia doctos "et expertos in epidemiis presertim plurimum deficisse, "paucissimosque, propter defectum exhibitionis, ad "presens insistere studio litterarum," &c.

O. 130, 1372. Rough draft, on paper, of a confirmation by Abp. W. Wittelsey, of Abp. Islip's appropriation of the church of Pagham to Cant. Coll., Oxon.

P. 22, 1372. The deed of which O. 130 is the draft, executed by the Abp. and bearing his seal.

O. 131, 1373. Licence in mortmain granted by Edward III., permitting certain benefactors to bestow lands on Cant. Coll.

The Abbot of Abingdon is allowed to give a messuage and three shillings of rent. The Prior of St. Fridewyde six messuages and six tofts. W. Dinant and John de Bolton a messuage. Thomas of Gloucester a messuage. The Abbess of Godstow a messuage. The Master and scholars of Baylolhalle a messuage.

O. 133, 1399. A charter of Henry IV. confirming two charters of Richard II., the first of which is in turn a confirmation of the licence of Edward III. (O. 132).

O. 140, 1393. Cant. Coll. having become indebted to T. Tyrwhit, the Master of Balyolhall, in the sum of hundred marks, has settled upon the creditor an annual rent of 26s. 8d., to be received out of the manor of Newington, Oxon, in return for which the creditor discharges the college from present payment of the principal sum.

S. B. b. 68, 1396 and 1397. "Compotus Dni. Willelmi "Chert, custodis Collegii Cant. Oxon. de opere novo."

This is the warden's statement of all the expenses, given in great detail, incurred by Prior Chillenden on account of the reconstruction of the college. It is written upon a folio sheet of paper, folded so as to accommodate four columns of items. Every day's work

DEAN AND CHAPTER OF CANTERBURY. is charged: freestone for the gate, commoner Heading-ton stone for the walls, Stonesfield slates for the roof, and lime for the pargetting, all bought in small quantities as the work demanded, are recorded with the price of each article; even twenty pence given, "ex curialitate," to the masons under the name of glove money (pro cirotecis) are charged in the bill.

S. B. b. 141, 1473. Annual statement of account made by the Warden of Cant. Coll. A much decayed paper recording the ordinary receipts and expenses of the Coll. From some of the items, which are plainly sums received for rent of rooms, it appears that other monasteries beside Christ Church, Canterbury, retained chambers to be occupied by their students, who, whilst enjoying the advantages offered by the teaching of the University, would still be restrained by the rule of St. Benedict. The following are examples :—

("Reddit compotum) de xs. receptis pro camera Wyof " ton, viiis. receptis de Evysham, vs. de Roff., vs. de " fratre de Batell, xs. de Coventre chambyr." One of the Ch. Ch. letters relates that the Peterborough under-graduates, being disorderly, were expelled from this college, and went to Gloster Coll.; then that they were again received at Cant. Coll., whence, as a punishment for renewed disorders, they were sent home to their own monastery.

O. 139, 1371. A document which shows that even before the foundation of Cant. Coll. the Black Monks had made provision for the education of their brethren at the university, without permitting any relaxation of monastic discipline.

By this deed the Prior and convent of Canterbury convey to the Abbot and convent of Westminster, a house which they have hitherto owned " in communi manso nigrorum monachorum . . . . in Stokewelle-" strete . . . . in suburbio Oxonie."

The grant has annexed to it this condition, that if at any time the scholars belonging to Ch. Ch., Cant., should be expelled by law from the college which they inhabited at the time of this grant, then, that the Abbot of West-minster should resign this tenement in the Benedictine manse, and restore it to the convent of Canterbury.

O. 134, O. 135, O. 136, O. 137. Inventories of the goods of Canterbury Coll. in the years 1443, 1459, 1510, 1514 respectively. All the movables of the college are here recorded under the heads,—

1. Libri inventi in librario, et in studiis custodis et aliorum fratrum.
2. Libri juris canonici et civilis inventi in librario.
3. Libri philosophie in librario.
4. Libri reperti in cubiculis fratrum.
5. Reperta in capella.
6. Reperta in cubiculo custodis.
7. Reperta in promptuario.
8. Reperta in coquina.

O. 141, 1500. Prior Goldstone, vicegerent of the Abp. sede vacante, appoints W. Broke, Vice-Warden of All Souls' Coll., Oxon. The nomination had lapsed to the Abp., and Prior Goldstone, as his representative, made the appointment.

O. 131, early 16th cent. "Secundum et ultimum " scrutinium " in the election of a Warden of All Souls'. In this paper each of 23 fellows, in an autograph for-mula, nominates two persons, one a jurist, the other a graduate in arts, thus :—

"Ego W. Broke, juris Canonici Doctor, nomino pro officio custodis hos duos viros, Magistrum Robertum Kent sacre theologie Doctorem, et Magistrum Thomam Love in Jure Baccalaureum."

S. B. b. 187, 1504. A statement of the manner in which Abp. Morton's legacies were applied for the ad-vancement of learning. Many of the halls in which recipients of the Abp.'s bounty resided are now forgotten. " Aula Angularis, Aula do Hynksey, Locus de la New " Yn, Aula Trinitatis, Aula de Aulburne, Hospicium " Novum, Aula Laurencii " would all be difficult to find, except perhaps that " Aula de Aulburne " might be identified in Merton Street. The account ends with the statement that there had been expended in one year, . " pro exhibitionibus scolasticorum, ... ultra exhi-" bitiones duorum confratrum nostrorum domo nostra " Cant. studientium," 60l. 14s.

Payments on account of Proceedings in the Roman Curia.

B. 205, 1275. Prior Ringmere sends money and a gold ornament as a fee to his proctor at Rome.

S. B. c. 9, 1277. John of Battle, formerly proctor of Ch. Ch. at the Pontifical court, having incurred debts in Italy, has left them to be defrayed by the new proctor,

Robert Poucyn. Poucyn went from one creditor to another, accompanied by a notary and other witnesses, in whose presence he paid the money, the notary record-ing the payment on this parchment.

Angelo Girardi is paid 1 mark four shillings and four pence for fodder and wine.

Clara vidua pauper Jacobi, 20s. for wine.

Saltimbene Raynieri, pulletarius, two marks and 10 shillings for poultry and candles.

Blaisius Girardi receives money for hay and wine.

Robertus Anglicus is paid 21s., for which the conside-ration is not recorded.

Pelegrinus " Marescalcus " is paid for shoeing horses.

Jacobus de Viterbo for grain.

Robertus Nicholaus of Orvieto, tabernarius, for wine.

These payments were made at Viterbo, and the amounts are calculated twice in each case, first in Tour-nois, grossi and parvi, and then in marks and shillings sterling.

P. 55, 1273. Raymundus de Nogeriis, the collector, having calculated that the possessions of Ch. Ch. are worth 1,340 marks a year, accepts 138 marks as the Pope's tenth, and for that sum he gives this receipt.

P. 56, 1280. Rob. de Celeseye, proctor at Rome for the convent of Ch. Ch., has incurred a debt of 250 marks, having borrowed that sum from certain merchants of Pistoja, and he gives a bond to secure the amount with interest. The bond was lodged with Andreas de Gan-dulfis, a Papal official, who binds himself by the two in-struments which are copied on this parchment to restore the bond when the money is paid.

P. 57, 1285. A certificate written by a notary, who testifies that he heard R. de Celeseye say, in the church at Tibur, that, if he had money to pay his debts and to carry him on his journey, he would go home at once. This is endorsed, " Protestacio R. de Celeseye, sub " manu publica, quod si habuit pecuniam in presenti " reddere debita a curia recederet." R. de Celeseye was a monk of Ch. Ch. and an advocate for Prior Ringmere.

P. 58, 1286. Receipt given to R. de Celeseye by the butcher Nicholas of Viterbo, to whom he has paid a bill of 15s. 9d., and 20 florins for borrowed money.

P. 59, 1286. A similar receipt for 17s. 4d. on account of money paid to Ficus de Penisio, who describes him-self as " pullarius curiam Romanam sequens."

C. 1,286. A notarial certificate, having the force of a bond, by which R. de Celeseye promises to repay 50 marks which he has borrowed from certain Italian mer-chants.

C. 227, 1296. Notary's certificate testifying that the Prior of Ch. Ch. has paid to Osbert of Florence a sum of 800 marks which he had borrowed from Osbert and the guild to which he belonged, for the purpose of helping the business of the convent at the Roman Court.

A. 190, 1297. Abp. Winchelsey undertakes to repay to the convent 1,744 marks which he borrowed from them to meet the expenses at Rome consequent upon his election.

C. 224, 1289. Receipt given to the prior by Philip de Pomonte and Nicholas de Sco. Victorio, his proctors at Rome, for the amount of their salaries due at the date.

C. 1,289, 1278. The collectors in England of the Pope's tenth acknowledge that they have received from the Prior of Canterbury, 500l. which they had lodged with him for safe keeping.

K. 10, 1300. In a similar transaction the prior, when the money was demanded, proved that he had paid cer-tain portions of the amount to the sub-collectors, and the balance to the Italian merchants who were autho-rised to receive it.

M. 343, 1282. Letter of instructions from Martin IV. to G. de Vezano, his collector in England, Ireland, and Scotland. He gives him authority to commute personal service in the Holy Land for a money payment, and he authorises him to employ ecclesiastical censures against all those who, having promised, neglect to pay.

C. 223, 1278. Receipts given to the prior for payments connected with the Pope's tenth.

Payments, Sundry.

C. 184, 1339. Promissory note given by the Prior of Ch. Ch. to the Archdeacon of Canterbury, from whom he had borrowed 120l. to defray necessary expenses.

C. 219, 1223. Receipt from Abp. Stephen Langton for a sum of 300 marks which he received from the monastery of Ch. Ch. in payment of two sums of 200 and 100 marks borrowed from him by the convent.

Primacy.

A. 1, 1072. The accord entered into by the Abps. of Canterbury and York concerning the supremacy of the former see. This parchment is attested by the signatures of the King, the Queen, Hubert the legate, thirteen bishops, and eleven abbots, and for further corroboration the King's Great Seal is affixed to the lower end of the instrument. The seal in this case is not suspended in the usual manner by strings, but is attached, or as it is termed ' appliqué,' to the membrane itself. A circular piece as large as a sixpence was cut out of the parchment; then, two pieces of wax having been softened, one was applied to each side of the membrane, touching and adhering to each other at the hole; after this, the seal being impressed on one side and the counterseal on the other, the wax spread out into a flat surface on either side of the parchment.

The document is written in a clear, clerkly hand upon fine parchment, the body of the deed and the signatures being all executed by one pen.

This composition; and the MS. itself, have been known to historians from very early times, and in all cases where it is quoted the attesting bishops and abbots are reported to be in number thirteen and eleven respectively.

Now we find that there is another MS. (A. 2.) a duplicate of A. 1; and this, which the historians appear never to have inspected, is the deed actually executed by the royal and dignified personages whose names are subscribed to A. 1.

Here the signatures all appear to be in autograph; even the bold cross of the King and the more delicate one of the Queen seem to have been traced by the royal hands, the pen of Lanfranc being employed to verify them by the words "signum uuilelmi regis," and "signum Mathildis regine," respectively.

The contracting parties and the subscribing witnesses, who in this case are only four in number, affixed their signatures in the following order:—

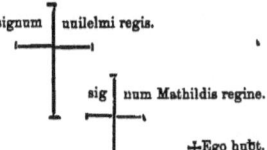

signum | uuilelmi regis.

sig | num Mathildis regine.

✝Ego hubt. sce. romane eccle. lector et dom. Alexandri papo legat. subscripsi.

✝Ego lanfranc⁹ dorobernensis Archieps. subscripsi.   ✝Ego Thomas eboracensis Archieps concedo.

✝Ego uualchelin⁹ uuentan⁹ epɜ. subscripsi.   ✝Ego remigius dorcaces trensis epɜ. subscripsi.

✝Ego erfastus tetfortensis eps. subscripsi.

✝Ego uul stanus uuigornensis eps subscripsi.

There is so much variety of character in the penmanship of these signatures that it is impossible to resist the conclusion that each of them is the work of the person whose name it expresses, except that of Erfastus, whose tremulous hand was only able to delineate his cross. An examination of the bold, square, upstanding autograph of the Bp. of Worcester tempts one to believe, that as his certainly expresses the transparent and firm character of the writer, so the other witnesses may have furnished in their signatures some materials for estimating their moral qualities.

One clause, "Ventilata est autem hec causa prius apud "Uuentanam civitatem, in Pascali solemnitate, in "capella regia que sita est in Castello; postea in villa "regia que vocatur Vuindisor, ubi et finem accepit, "in presentia Regis, Episcoporum, Abbatum diver- "sorum ordinum, qui congregati erant apud curiam in "festivitate Pentecostes," which occurs at the end of A. 1, is not found in A. 2.

As this clause is a note rather than a part of the contract, neither of the contracting parties being in any way affected by it, there is no reason why the clerk should not have added it when, after the signatures had been subscribed to A 2, the original, he made the copy A. 1, which was plainly intended for public exhibition.

A. 24, late 13th century. A parchment (15 inches by 9), entitled "Infrascripta dicunt Prior et Capitulum "ecclesie Xpi. Cantuar. pro jure et libertate ejusdem "ecclesie, videlicet."

After which follow six paragraphs of arguments showing why the Abp. of Canterbury, as patriarch and primate, not as Archbishop, may lawfully carry his cross erect throughout Britain, whilst the Abp. of York may only do so in his own province.

This MS., belonging to the time of Edward I., is connected with those which follow.

A. 189, 1299. A letter from Abp. Winchelsey to the prior at Canterbury, dated from Lincolnshire.

He writes, "Exposito seriosius domino Regi apud "Kaerlaverok in Scociam per nos, viarum et aquarum "discriminibus et periculis variis fatigatos, papali "nuncio nobis injuncto, per Eboracensem provinciam, "et juxta civitatem ipsam, precedente nos sancte crucis "vexillo erecto, die Sabati ante acceptionem litterarum "vestrarum, Dei gratia, in provinciam nostram absque "impedimento venimus incolumes et robusti sine "dampno," &c.

A. 193, 1305. A letter from Abp. Winchelsey to the prior at Canterbury.

The Abp., hearing that the Abp. of York is coming over from the continent, warns the prior that there will be an attempt to carry the cross, and possibly to confer benediction, both of which are to be prevented by the

prior and his deputies, "alioquin omnia loca ipsa per "que erecta cruce transitum fecerit, seu moram, suppo- "natis ecclesiastico interdicto. Inhibeatis et, seu inhi- "beri faciatis, omnibus subditis nostris, sub pena ex- "communicationis, ne se ad ejus benedictionem taliter "incedentis inclinent, seu tali transitu vel mora cam- "panas pulsare sustineant, aut ipsius presumptionibus "faveant quovis modo, presumptores in contrarium per "quascunque censuras ecclesiasticas compescendo. Ne "saltem loca jurisdictionis vestre videatur in nostri "prejudicium libere et pacifice transire, et nos per "dissimulationem hujus videamur ipsius injurie con- "sentire," &c.

Y. 57, 1109. A letter from Abp. Anselm to certain suffragans, warning them to take their cue from him in the matter of Thomas II. Abp. of York.

"Mando et precipio vobis, per sanctam obedientiam "quam ecclesie Cant. et michi debetis, ut, secundum "quod·in subjectis litteris quas Thome Electo Ebor. "destinavi scriptum est, vos erga ipsum Thomam "omnimodo teneatis.

"Anselmus Arch. Cant. et totius Britannie primas "loquor loquens . . . . tibi interdico atque precipio ne "te de aliqua cura pastorali ullo modo presumas inter- "mittere, donec a rebellione quam contra ecclesiam "Cant. incepisti recedas, et subjectionem quam ante- "cessores tui, Tomae videlicet et Gerardus . . . . "antiqua consuetudine professi sunt," &c.

R. 47, circ. 1180. "Transcriptum privilegii Alex. (III.) "Pape de subjectione Roffensis ecclesie." The Pope, addressing Prior Alan, confirms the authority which Canterbury always exercised over the daughter church of Rochester. "Sed omnem subjectionem et reveren- "tiam vobis et Archiepiscopo vestro, tam in dispositione "rerum ipsius ecclesie, quam in substitutione Episcopi, "et in aliis inconcusse futuris decernimus temporibus "conservandas," &c.

A. 41. Professions of obedience made by abbots. Eleven small slips of parchment, containing professions of obedience to the Abp. made in the 12th century by various Kentish abbots at the time of their consecration. "Ego frater Honricus Sancte Radegundis Abbas electus "profiteor sancte Cantuar. ecclesie ejusque vicariis "canonicam obedientiam" is an example.

Of two endorsements on the profession of an Abbot of Boxley, one reads, "Hoc in Anno (1150) venit Henricus "Comes Andagavensium et Dux Northmannorum in "Angliam"; and the other gives an account of the consecration as Abp. of York of Roger Archdeacon of Canterbury, by Abp. Theobald; the Abp. Elect having been preferred to priest's orders a few days before in the infirmary chapel at Canterbury.

C. 118 and C. 119. Original professions of obedience made by suffragan bishops to the Archbishop at the time of their consecration.

The series of these professions begins in the days of Lanfranc, and extends to those of Abp. Peckham at the end of the 13th century.

There are 160 slips of parchment, representing as many consecrations, upon each of which a suffragan promises canonical obedience to the primate.

In early days these compositions were diffuse in style, the phraseology varying with the taste of the writer, but as time went on, a short, business-like formula was adopted excluding all irrelevant matter.

The consecration of Ralph of Chichester, which took place in 1091, after the death of Lanfranc and before the consecration of Anselm, was performed by Thomas I., Abp. of York, as is shown by the profession made at the time.

" Ego Radulfus Sce. Cicestrensis Ecclesie nunc ordi-
" nandus Episcopus, subjectionem, et reverentiam, et
" obedientiam a sanctis patribus constitutam, secundum
" precepta canonum, Sancte Cantuar. ecclesie et ejus
" rectoribus, in presentia Domini Archiepiscopi Thome,
" perpetuo exhibiturum promitto, et super sanctum
" altare propria manu firmo."

The early Welsh bishops accepted Anselm's supremacy without scruple, and styled him "totius Britannie " primas." The profession of Urban of Llandaff is an example of this.

On the back of the profession made by Rob[t]. (de Chesney) of Lincoln is a memorandum relating the particulars of Abp. Theobald's return from St. Audoen to England, at a time when he thought that his presence might mitigate the troubles of church and people.

During the primacy of Boniface the reservation " salvo " ordine meo" is constantly inserted, and at the same period the date of the consecration is usually written on the back of the profession, with a memorandum of the day on which the profession was made. In consequence of the Abp.'s long absence from England, consecration and profession were often separated by some distance of time.

In one case there is a note explaining the absence of some suffragans from the ceremony of a consecration, " quatuor vero Episcopi Walenses non potuerunt venire " nec mittere propter guerram."

Endorsed on the profession of John Bp. of Winton (1282), a foreigner, is this note, " Iste non fuit electus sed " a sede apostolica datus et in curia Romana consecratus."

C. 117. A long roll of contemporary copies of professions of obedience made to Abps. of Canterbury, from the time of Lanfranc to that of Theobald.

The originals of many of these copies are still in the Chartæ Antiquæ.

On the back of this roll are several paragraphs reporting the consecrations of Welsh and Irish bishops by early Abps. of Canterbury.

One example will show the style of the memoranda and the animus which prompted the writers :—

" Anno DCCCCLXIII[o] electione facta regum Morgan-
" nuc Owain, videlicet, et Idwathlann Cadel Chenevin,
" filiorum Morgan Hen, Roderi et Grifud filiorum Elis-
" ses, et totius cleri, et populi Morgannuc, infra ostium
" Tarader in Gui, et ostium Tewi, et dati sibi baculo
" in regali curia a summo rege Anglorum Æthelredo, et
" a Metropolitano Cantuariensis ecclesie, Ælurico archi-
" episcopo, Blederi Episcopus Llandavii consecratus est.
" Et ab eodem Archiepiscopo, Tamerin Episcopus Sci.
" Davit, et successor ejus Elnod nepos, Cantuarie con-
" secrati sunt." The enumeration of Welsh bishops ends with Urban of "Clamorgan" or "Llandaff," whose original profession is mentioned above, and is also copied on the face of this roll.

C. 120. A roll of eight membranes, which at one time was even longer than at present. It contains copies of a general charter of patronage given by Abp. Becket to the monastery of his church, with a confirmation of the same by Gregory VIII., and, lastly, copies of a number of cautionary letters, guarantees from suffragan bishops consecrated out of Canterbury that such consecrations, being celebrated by the special licence of the convent of Ch. Ch., shall not at any time be quoted as precedents to the injury of the convent.

C. 105 to 114, and C. 125 to 143. These are the original " cautiones," copies of which fill the last-mentioned roll.

Mixed with these are a few "littere excusatorie," apologies sent by suffragans who, having been summoned to assist at consecrations, were unable to attend.

D. 108. Bernard of St. David's, a Norman by birth (1115 to 1147), after taking the oath of canonical obedience to the Abp. of Canterbury, and after receiving consecration from his hand, began to claim for his church metropolitical jurisdiction in Wales.

The MS. D. 108, 1145–7, is a long report sent by Nigel of Ely to Eugenius III., formally charging the Bishop of St. David's with an intention of withdrawing from his subjection to Canterbury.

C. 134, C. 136, and C. 137. The same form, word for word, as the last, and addressed to the Pope by Rob. Bathon, R. Exon, and R. Hereford respectively.

D. 107. A letter to the same Pope on the same subject, written by Henry of Blois, Bp. of Winchester. The form in this case varies from the others which precede it.

Priors, Election of.

C. 1,300, 1339. Abp. Stratford's declaration and confirmation of the election of Robert Hathbrand to be prior of Ch. Ch.

C. 1,302, 1390. Abp. Courtney's declaration and confirmation of the election of Prior Thomas Chillenden.

Procurations, Papal.

In 1374 Gregory the XI., with the approbation of the Kings of England and France, sent commissioners to Bruges with authority to act as mediators between the monarchs. The Nuntii were three in number, to each of whom a daily stipend of florins of gold was assigned, and at the end of the mission they made a demand upon the clergy of England for the amount which had become due.

On August 19 the Nuntii sent a notice (P. 51) to the Prior of Canterbury demanding of him as vicegerent of the Archbishop, sede vacante, a sum of 4,416 florins, being the total amount earned by a hundred and twenty days of official duty.

The Prior in a very submissive letter (Ch. Ch. letters 21) protested that the money could not be collected within the allotted time of thirty days. The letter appears to have procured a respite, and active measures were taken by the Prior to satisfy the demand by a rate of an obolus in the mark on all ecclesiastical incomes. Among the Chartæ Antiquæ are returns made by the responsible officers of the dioceses of London, Salisbury, Worcester, and St. David's, giving a list of the benefices, and the sum at which each was assessed.

Ch. Ch. letters 22. A letter of remonstrance sent by Simon Sudbury, then Bp. of London, to Ralph Kesteven, the collector of the procurations.

An exactly similar demand was again made upon the Prior, during the same vacancy of the see, by Pileus Abp. of Ravenna, who by virtue of apostolic letters from the same Pope, dated September 1373, demanded 1,200 florins as payment for a hundred days of service in some way rendered to the English Church.

Again a prolongation of the days of payment was asked for, and apparently obtained, for in January and February of the next year the returns were still coming in from Salisbury, Worcester, and Rochester.

An income tax of a farthing in the pound was levied to satisfy this demand.

The MSS. bearing upon this subject will be found in the catalogue by the references P. 50 to 70.

C. 1,273, 1373. The Cardinal of Cluny, having been deputed to mediate between John de Montfort and Charles of Blois, in order to bring about a satisfactory settlement of the affairs of Brittany, came over to England and charged the expenses of his journey upon the clergy of England. In this MS. Edward III. warns Abp. William that he is not to submit to the extortion, and he promises that he will back the clergy if they resist the claims of the Nuntio, whose ecclesiastical censures must necessarily be harmless where the cause is so unjust.

The people of England, as the King justly writes, were not in any way concerned in the war of the Breton succession.

Proctors.

There are here large numbers of powers of attorney by which ecclesiastical corporations and individuals appointed proctors to represent them. The affairs entrusted to these proctors are usually matters of small importance, but in a few cases they conducted greater concerns.

C. 180. A person is deputed to sit and vote in the Council of Vienne as the representative of the convent of Canterbury.

During the panic which followed the great pestilence of 1348 the clergy of a number of Kentish rural deaneries appointed in each deanery a proctor to take charge of their interests, which were endangered by the confusion consequent upon the deaths of a large proportion of incumbents and of payers of tithes.

Ports, Cinque.

R. 38. Three membranes stitched together, entitled, "Ces sont les usages usez en la vill de Romene de "temps dount memoire ne court."

This MS., which is written in a character belonging to the latter part of the 14th cent., appears to be identical with one in the library of St. Cath. Coll., Cambridge, which is described by Mr. Riley in the Fourth Report of the Hist. MSS. Commission.

The Cambridge MS., containing other matter in addition to the "customs of the town of Romney," is longer than the present document, which ends with the paragraph marked 11a. in Mr. Riley's report.

B. 381 1435. A half share in a boat bestowed in pious uses.

"Thom. Flory capellanus qui scripsit testamentum "cujusdam Thome Perys affirmavit in verbo sacerdotis "coram majore et alteris, quod medietas cujusdam batelli, "vocati ' Seynte Mary Boot,' que nuper fuit W. Lyon, in "custodia dicti Thomas Perys ut unius executorum testamenti dicti Willelmi, deliberaretur Johanni Croucher "alio executori, et ut dictus Johannes disponeret dictam "medietatem batelli supradicti in pios usus pro anima "dicti Willelmi, secundum discretionem suam."

The half share was sold for forty shillings, from which six and eightpence were given to the vicar, the balance being expended on the fabric of the church.

E. 1,246, 1401. A writ of Henry IV., directing his justices, &c., to protect the Cinque Ports in the exercise of those rights which they enjoyed in the days of Henry II., "tempore Regis Henrici proavi Regis Ed-"wardi filii regis Henrici."

Especially the King requires that the inland manor of Bekesbourne shall be reckoned a member of the capital port of Hastings, and that John Cobham, Chivaler, and John Doget, shall be entitled to privileges as barons of the Cinque Ports.

Among the privileges specified is one which John Doget, who was a citizen of London, would especially prize, "de propriis vinis suis de quibus negociantur, "quieti sint de recta prisa nostra, videlicet de uno dolio "vini ante malum, et alio post malum."

The writ also concedes "quod habeant infangenethef, "et quod sint wrecfry, et wittefry, et lestagefry, et "louecopfry, et quod habeant utfangenethef in terris "suis .... eodem modo quo Archiepiscopi, Episcopi, "Abbates, Comites, et Barones habent in maneriis suis "in Comitatu Kancie."

Roman Court, Suits in.

The "Index of Subjects" which is kept in the drawers with the Chart. Ant., contains under the head "Roman "Court" references to a large number of documents referring to suits in and appeals to the Curia.

The matters treated of have no material or historical importance, but the series shows the method of procedure, and the costly difficulties which obstructed the suitors.

It is evident that the convent of Ch. Ch. retained a watchful advocate on the spot, who whenever apostolic letters were granted took care to get letters of warranty and indemnity for Ch. Ch., if there were the remotest chance that the interests of the convent would be affected.

M. 342. A form of oath, written upon parchment, in a hand of the 15th cent. "Ye shall no thing sue or "procure to be sued in the Court of Rome, nor in noon "other place beyond the see, any thing that may be "hurting or prejudiciall to the King oure sovreigne, or "his corowne, nor to any of his subjettis ; nor anything "doo or attempt, that is or may be contrarie to the "lawes of his lande. Ye shall stedfastly and faithfully "abyde his trew liegeman," &c.

C. 187, 1486. A petition on paper, presented to Innocent VIII. by Prior William Sellyng in person.

It appears that the prior was employed by the new King to transact some business with the Pope, possibly to obtain an expression of his approbation of the revolutionary changes which had just been made in the English state. He describes himself in this autograph petition as, "Ad serenitatem vestram, per devotissi-"mum ejusdem et Sancte Romane ecclesie filium Henri-"cum septimum, Anglie regem illustrem, pro praestanda "serenitati vestre et sede apostolica debita obedientia, "orator destinatus."

After this introduction he asks two favours, to each of which the Pope expresses his assent by writing, apparently with his own hand, his "Fiat" opposite to the petition.

In the same hand is added a date "Dat Rome ap^d. "Stmpetrum Pridie Jd. Junii Anno Tercio."

In different parts of the sheet are scrawled a number of signatures in the form of monograms, which doubtless express the concurrence of as many Papal officials.

Rebellions and Civil Commotions.

C. 245, 1213. A narrow slip of parchment, containing a guarantee that King John shall be compelled to adhere to a "pactum" by which he has undertaken to restore the ancient privileges of the church.

This instrument was executed by twelve of the great barons of the realm, and it still bears their seals in a more or less mutilated state.

The "pactum" alluded to is evidently that which the King signed at Dover, 3 May 1213, whereby he undertook to satisfy the prelates "de restitutione ablatorum," under the penalty of losing his patronage of vacant churches, a penalty especially insisted on in this guarantee (Wendover, Ed: Coxe iii. 248). "Viris venerabili-"bus et amicis in Xpos sic) dilectis, Priori et Monachis "ecclesie Soe. Trinitatis Cantuar, G. fil. Petri Comes "Essex Justiciarius, R. Comes Bolon., R. Comes Cestrie, "W. Comes Warrenne, W. Marescallus Comes Pem-"brochie, W. Comes Arundell, W. Comes de Ferrariis, "Will. Briwer, Rob. de Ros, Gillebertus filius R. ejus-"dem, Rogerus de Mortuo Mari, et Petrus filius "Herberti, salutem, et debitam reverentiam. Sciatis "quod bona fide studebimus quod Dns. noster Johannes "rex Anglie pactum et securitatem vobis et aliis, tam "clericis quam laicis, negotium quod inter ecclesiam "Anglicanam et ipsum regem versatum est contingen-"tibus,. firmiter observabit, secundum formam pacis ei "a domino Papa transmissam, et ab eo acceptam. Et "si forte, quod Deus avertat, rex ipse, vel aliquis alius "ex parte sua, contravenerit, nos pro ecclesia contra "violatores securitatis et pacis mandatis apostolicis in-"herebimus, et ipse perpetuo vacantium ecclesiarum "custodiam amittet. Preterea promittimus quod si "quid omissum est, vel minus plene factum, circa hoc "negotium in hoc scripto, propter accelerationem ad-"ventus vestri in Anglia, id cum noveritis secundum "predictam formam perficietur. Et in hujus rei testi-"monium has litteras nostras patentes vobis transmit-"timus. Valete in Domino. Hec autem omnia, sicut "supradicta sunt, firmiter nos observaturos noveritis, "nos de mandato domini regis, tactis sacrosanctis "Ewangeliis, spontanea voluntate, corporali juramento "firmasse. Iterum bene valete."

This MS. is endorsed by the hand of Prior Henry of Eastry :—" Promissio Comitum et Baronum multorum "sub sigillis suis, quod facient regem Johannem firmiter "tenere pactum quod fecit de pace et securitate nobis "et nostris."

M. 247, 1216. A notice addressed by Peter, Bp. of Winchester, the Abbot of Reading, and Pandulph the legate to the Abp. of Cant. and all his suffragans, announcing that they have received apostolical letters commanding them to proceed by way of ecclesiastical censure against the barons who are in arms against the King. The Abp. and the Bps. are required to publish the sentence against the barons on all Sundays and festivals, the penalties of suspension, deposition, and excommunication being threatened against any who are disobedient.

With a few verbal variations this document is given in Wendover, Ed. Coxe iii. 336.

K. 2, 1262, 3, and 4. This MS., consisting of a larger and a smaller piece of parchment, contains contemporary copies of six documents which narrate the history of the dispute between Henry III. and his barons up to the 12th May 1264, two days before the battle of Lewes.

1. The award of Louis IX., acting as arbitrator between the parties, 22nd Jan. 1263.

2. The letter of Urban IV. absolving the King from the oath by which he had sworn to observe the provisions of Oxford. The Pope, employing a bold metaphor, asserts that "Egressus Sathanae a facie Domini, et mit-"tens ventum validum a regione de Styge, regnum "Anglie concussit acriter, ollamque indignationis in "ipso succendit." 1st Sept. 1262.

At the foot of this are written the names of several royalist partisans :—W. de Breuse, J. de Baylol, H. de Perci, R. le fil. Petri, Jacobus de Aldithele, H. de la Fuche, W. de Clifford, and Rob. de Nevile.

The remaining three documents, written upon the smaller piece of parchment which is sewn to the larger,

are to be found under the date in the "Eulogium
"Temporum."

They are:—

1. The barons' address to the King. This was sent
by Earl Simon and G. de Clare on behalf of the confederates.

2. The King's answer of defiance to the barons. Lewes,
12th May.

3. The King of the Romans and Prince Edward to
the Barons, and especially to S. de Montfort and G. de
Clare, whom they charge with aggravated treason,
Even in this last challenge an offer of a safe-conduct is
made to the leaders if they will submit their grievances
to the decision of the courts. Lewes, 12th (possibly 13th)
May.

Probably an agent on the spot sent these copies to the
convent at Canterbury in order to keep the brethren
well informed of the course of contemporary politics.
On a vacant space some scribe of the period has written,
"Bestus es Symon Barjona," an indication of the
tendency of the writer's opinions.

K. 11, 1311. A roll of four membranes, entitled,
"Ceux sunt les noveles ordenaunces faites a Lundres,
"lan du Regne nostre seignur le rei Edward filz le rei
"Edward quynt, et par mesme le rei confirmes, et de
"sa graunt seal eusealles. Et, desouz mesme le seal,
"les dites ordenaunces et le confermement sunt en la
"tresorie de ceste eglise en garde."

This is a contemporary copy of all the documents relating to the reforms imposed upon Edward II. by the
clergy and the adherents of the Earl of Lancaster. The
whole series is included, beginning with the King's
consent to the appointment of ordainers in 1309, and
ending with the forty-two ordinances which, it is here
stated, were proclaimed in the churchyard of St. Paul's,
London, on the 27th Sept. 1311, by Simon, Bishop of
Salisbury.

Two forms are given for the coronation oath: one,
which is in Latin, is to be used if the King be "literate;"
the other, in French, to be taken by an "illiterate"
King.

If the clause in the title, which declares that the original instrument under the King's seal is "in the
"treasury of this church," refer to Canterbury, it is at
the present time no longer true.

S. B. c. 72. A copy of a grant of manorial rights made
by Henry V. to Sir John Phelip. The manors in question are stated to have been the property "Henrici
"Lescrop Chivaler domini de Masham," upon whose
attainder they fell to the Crown.

The grant was dated "Southampton, 6th August,"
no year being mentioned, but as it is well known that
the King was at Southampton in Aug. 1415, when Lord
Scrope's conspiracy was detected, it is to be inferred
that the grant was made to Phelip immediately after
the manors were forfeited by Scrope.

By this grant reversions of other manors were given
to Phelip after the death of Sir Thomas Erpingham, and
again of others upon the death of Joanna the Queen
Dowager, whom the King styles his "mater karissima."

M. 239, 1448. Confession of a felon lying in the gaol
of the Prior of Canterbury, taken by Roger Twhisden
the prior's bailiff.

This so-called confession consists of evidence volun-
teered by the felon, charging a neighbour of his in the
Isle of Thanet with having used treasonable language.

The substance of this paper goes to prove that at this
time the people, becoming unsettled by the childlessness
of the Queen and exasperated by the disasters in France,
were beginning to speak disparagingly of the government and of the King himself.

The inculpated man is reported to have said that
"the Kyng is none abyll to bere the flourisleys nor
"the schyp in his nobyl.—Oure Quene was none abyl
"to be Quene of Inglond, but and he were a pere of or
"a lord of this ream (he really was a farm-labourer)
"he woulde be on of thaym that shuld helpe to putte
"her a doun, for because that seke bereth no child, and
"because that we have no pryns in this land."

Behind this silly accusation there lay two others of a
more tangible kind.

The witness deposes concerning his neighbour that
whenever he got "a brode peny he paryd it wyth his
"knyf, and puttit it into a cuppe," and that on
several occasions had taken sacks of wool by night and
carried them to a creek in the marsh where he sold them
to the "Frenshmen of Depe."

M. 309, 7th July 1450. The King's proclamation of
pardon, offered to John Mortymer and all his followers
without exception.

Special letters of personal pardon are offered, without
fine or fee, to all who shall apply for them. The proclamation states that the possession of one of these
letters by a pardoned rebel would save him from future
persecution.

M. 295, July 1450. Proclamation for the apprehension
of John Cade, "callyng himself Captain of Kent." The
lower corner of this MS. is torn off, and with it the day
of the date, which, however, it is clear was later than
the 7th of July, when the foregoing pardon was offered.

Cade is accused of having used magical books; of
having "rerod upp the Divell in the semblaunce of a
"blak dogge in his chaumbre where he was loggyd at
"Derteford"; of having, whilst living with one Thomas
Dagre in Sussex, killed a woman who was with child.

Politically, he is charged with having been "yeres
"afore sworne to the Frensh partie"; with being now
a "tale-teller," falsely saying that the King's late
pardon was a snare; with desiring to enrich himself
and bring himself to high estate; but there is no hint
that he was a Yorkist partisan.

Finally, again a pardon is offered to those who have
followed Cade, calling him Mortimer. These pardons,
like the first, are to be granted to each person severally,
and no one is to be allowed to plead the amnesty unless
he have a written letter of forgiveness in his possession.

S. B. a. 90, 1483. Richard Knechebole of Mersham,
in the first year of Richard III., informs the Prior of
Ch. Ch. that Will. Lambarde and Stephen Harry have
for some time "ben sculkynge in wodes by day, and
"lying in wayte to robbe the Kynge's lyege people";
that John Edwards having been robbed, the posse of
the district assembled in Bokhanghar wood and captured
the robbers, who were thrown into prison to await
orders from the prior.

The thieves at the time of their arrest were armed
with "a payre of Brecontyns, a swerde, and a stafte of
"heasel," and these weapons offensive and defensive
remained in Knatchbull's hands.

C. 242, circ. 1536. These are two precepts issued by
the Prior of Canterbury, who calls upon his tenants at
Hollingbourne and Chartham to serve the King in arms.
The formula is the same in both cases, the names only
being charged. "The Kyngs grace, for the repression
"of his rebellion in Yorkshire (Lincolnshire), hath
"dyrected hys letters, dated Wyndsore the 28th of the
"moneth of September, to the Pryour of Christchurch
"in Canterbury, that he shall furnysh lx able persones
"to be at Northampton . . . . Wherefore the seide
"pryour according to his allegiaunce . . . . dothe
"send this berar to you, being substancyall tenaunts,
" . . . . soo that ye fayle nott to be at Christchurch at
"Canterbury on Friday nexte comyng at ix of the
"clock before noone, as ye will answere at your perill"
&c.

"To the tenaunts and fermours of the manero of
"Chartham (Hollingbourne)." Signed in autograph,
"Be Thomas Por. of Oryst ya Churche att Cant'bury."
This levy appears to have been made for the suppres-
sion of the "Pilgrimage of Grace."

Rochester.

R. 70 a., circ. 1200. The case submitted to certain
arbitrators by the monks of Rochester appealing against
the acts of their Bishop, Gilbert Glanvil.

In this statement of grievances the monks begin with
a history of their church, extending from the time of
Lanfranc and Gundulph to the date of this petition;
especially they record of each successive Bishop
whether he were a friend of the monks or a despoiler—
in their own words, "custos, vel predo,"

Bp. Gilbert had intruded clerks into the benefices of
the monastery, and had appropriated their revenues for
the purpose of endowing a hospital at Strood.

This MS. is one of the curiosities of the Canterbury
Collection, being the subject of an interesting story.
Many years ago a minor canon, walking in his garden,
heard a great clamour in the air; looking up he saw
some jackdaws disputing for a piece of something which
seemed to them fit for nest-building. In the heat of
their quarrel they dropped the object for which they
contended, and the minor canon picked up, not as the
story goes ("Edinburgh Review," xcvii, 195) a Saxon
charter, but this very MS., which he kept safely as
long as he lived. At his death the parchment passed
into the hands of the Rev. Fredk. Rouch, who retained
it until this present year, when, seeing that the Dean
and Chapter preserved their MSS. with reverent care,
he returned it to their custody.

The incident is thus explained. When the muniments
were catalogued in 1806 small store was set by those

which possessed only a literary value, and these were put aside in some tower chamber, to which the jackdaws through a window. It is unnecessary to say that no MSS. now remain in half-forgotten chambers, or that jackdaws do not now build with "Saxon charters."

R. 70, circ. 1200. A memorandum in which the convent of Rochester continue the complaints begun in R. 70 a., this MS. having reference chiefly to the building and endowing of the hospital.

R. 47, circ. 1179. "Transcriptum privilegii Alex-" andri Papæ" III.

A copy of a letter from Alexander III. to Prior Alan of Ch. Ch., confirming in very vague terms the supremacy which Canterbury had exercised over Rochester from the time of Lanfranc.

R. 48, 1243. A composition made between the Prior of Canterbury and the monks of Rochester. This is a preliminary agreement, by which the Prior of Ch. Ch. binds himself to produce the charters upon which he founds his claims to exercise jurisdiction over the Rochester convent.

R. 50, 1276. Inspeximus by the Prior of Canterbury of a charter of Abp. Theobald, dated 1155, which corroborates an earlier charter of Bp. Gundulph, given to the monks of Rochester.

Gundulph's charter, which is recited in full, was dated 1091, and in it the Bishop enumerated and confirmed all the acquisitions of the church of Rochester, commemorating at the same time the names of those by whose munificence the church had been enriched.

Subsidies and Taxes.

Taxes, tenths, fifteenths, duties on wool, subsidies in aid of the Holy Land, are indicated in the Chart. Ant. by many documents ranging from the 13th to the 15th centuries. These are chiefly demands for or acknowledgments of payments, made by the collectors, and they may be found by the references in the *Index of Subjects* under the head "Subsidies and Taxes."

One, more important than the rest, is :—

A. 120, 1534. Taxation of the diocese of Canterbury on account of a tenth, granted to the King by Convocation in 1529, and payable within five years.

This is a paper book in a parchment cover, authenticated by the seal of Abp. Cranmer. Twelve pages are occupied by the Act of Convocation, the remainder of the book being filled by the details of the taxation as it was levied upon the religious houses and ecclesiastical benefices of the diocese.

Saxon charters.

In the library of the Dean and Chapter is a volume which from the time of Mr. Kemble, who superintended its arrangement, has been known as the "Book of " Saxon Charters," or more shortly, "The Charter " Book." In this are contained twenty-two MSS. of præ-Norman date, nearly all of which are original grants from Kings and other great men of their day. The Chart. Ant. also comprise a few similar MSS. which for some reason Mr. Kemble rejected from the Charter Book. It is to be noticed that at the time of the arrangement of the muniments in 1806 these Saxon charters had not been selected from the Chart. Ant., and that, therefore, each one bears a letter and number corresponding to its place in the catalogue made at that time.

The MSS. contained in the Charter Book are,—

M. 363, A.D. 742, Codex diplomat. 88. This is endorsed in a 10th century character "Libertates ecclesie " Xpi Ethelbaldi regis Merciorum et Cuthberti archi-" episcopi."

M. 340, A.D. 788, Cod. dip. 153. " Privilegium Offæ regis Merciorum."

C. 69, A.D. 790, Cod. dip. 159. Endorsed, "Offa rex Merciorum dedit Atholardo " Archiepo. et ecclesie X' xc tributaria terre, lx vero ad " emendationem ecclesie, xxx autem ad indumentum " fratrum." The charter in the Cod. dip. is copied, not from this original, but from a register and a Lambeth MS.

C. 1, A.D. 803. Declaratio Athchoardi Dorobernensis Archiepiscopi de privilegiis ecclesie. This MS. is not noticed in the Cod. dip., but it is given by Thorpe and Wilkins, and the publication of the Palæographical Society contains a photograph of it.

C. 2, A.D. 803. A copy of the last. Contemporary endorsement, "Actum est in celebri " loco qui vocatur Cloveshof anno ab incarnatione Xpi. " dccciii, indictione x, die iii Id. Octobris."

C. 1,278, A.D. 812, Cod. dip. 199.
12th century endorsement, "Commutatio terrarum " inter Kenulf regis et Wulafred Archiepiscopum."

14th century endorsement, "Carta Ceonulphi regis de " Suordlinge quam dedit Vulfrede Archiepiscopo." Published by the Palæographical Society.

C. 1,279, A.D. 845, Cod. dip. 224.
12th century endorsement, "Rex Egbertus dedit " Werehorne Edrico."

M. 369, circ. 860, Cod. dip. 293. " Privilegium Ealheri."

C. 1,280, A.D. 840, Cod. dip. 243. " Privilegium Berchtwulfi regis Merciorum — An-" glicè."

M. 14, A.D. 863, Cod. dip. 288. " Privilegium Ethelbearhti regis West Saxonum et " Cantuariorum." Endorsed, "Merse ham."

12th century endorsement, "Rex Ethelberhtus dedit " Merseham Ethelredo ministro suo."

F. 150, A.D. 898, Cod. dip. 324.
12th century endorsement, "Ælfredus rex dedit Si-" gilmo terram in Farnlege—Latine."

C. 1,282, A.D. 900, Cod. dip. 328.
Title on fly-leaf, "Petitio cujusdam ad Edweardum " regem West Saxonum—Anglo-Saxonice."

A title-deed composed in a narrative form; it begins, " Leof ie the cythe hu hit wæs ymb thæt lond æt Funtial " tha ðf hida," &c.

E. 206, A.D. 937, Cod. dip. 369. " Privilegium Æthelstani regis Anglie."

This is a grant conferring land at Topsham, near Exeter.

Contemporary endorsement, "Toppeshammes boc."

T. 37, A.D. 670 (erroneous), Cod. dip. 370.
A grant from the same of the same land. Mr. Kemble, who obtained his copy from a modern transcript in the Lansdowne MSS., not having seen this original, describes this as a faulty copy of the last.

S. 261, A.D. 1023, Cod. dip. 737.
12th century endorsement, "Privilegium Cnuti regis " Anglorum de donacione Sandwici, et consuetudinum " ejus, et corono capitis sui."

S. 260, A.D. 1203.
A contemporary translation of the last into English.

S. 259. A copy of Cnut's grant.

R. 14, A.D. 949, Cod. dip. 425.
Charter of Eadred giving Reculver to Ch. Ch., Cant. A duplicate of this is in the MSS. Cott., both that and this being accepted, on the faith of the attestation clause, as in the hand writing of St. Dunstan.

B. 1, A.D. 972, Cod. dip. 704.
Contemporary endorsement, "Ethelred cing (ge)uthe " Ædrices cuythe and his lafe in to Xps. circce thæt his " Boccing tempore Ælrici Archiepiscopi — scriptum " Anglice."

C. 1,281, A.D. 1049, Cod. dip. 787.
Privilegium Eadwardi regis et Confessoris.

B. 2, A.D. 997, Cod. dip. 699. " Testamentum Ætherici—Anglo-Saxonice." This is the will confirmed by Ethelred in B. 1.

A. 207, Cod. dip. 790. Title on fly-leaf. " Cyrographum Godwini Comitis. Anglice." A dispute between St. Augustine's and Leofwine, priest of St. Mildred's. This deed is almost defaced by ancient mildew. Thorpe, Dipl. Ang. 349.

C. 70, 12th century endorsement, "Thurstan dedit " familie ecclesie Xi. Wimbisc. Anglice." Thorpe. Dipl. Ang. 577.

R. 17, 12th century endorsement, "Egelnothus Cant. " Archiepiscopus tradidit L acras de terra Raculfensis " ecclesie duobus hominibus suis ex consensu Decani " ejusdem ecclesie." Cod. dip. 754.

The following MSS. are not in the Charter Book :—

R. 51, Charter 1059, Inspex. 1227. Inspeximus by the Bp. of Evreux and the Abbot of St. Audoen of a charter of Edward the Confessor, by which he gave Ottery to the church of Rouen. Cod. dip. 810.

The copy of Eadward's charter is as nearly a facsimile as the scribe of 1227 could make it.

H. 68, A.D. 1015, Cod. dip. 722. Will of Æthelstan, son of Ethelred II.

This Æthelstan gave Hollingbourne to Christ Church, which fact accounts for the finding of a contemporary copy of his will in the Chart. Ant.

C. 194, A.D. 1006. Cod. dip. 715.
Charter of Ethelred II. conferring privileges upon the church of Canterbury.

H. 130, A.D. 889. A conveyance by which Suithulf, Bp. of Rochester, demises half a plough-land at Haddun to Biorhtwulf. The deed in Latin, the boundaries in English.

After the proem, which is identical with that of Codex
dip. 309, follows the grant,—" Ego Suithuulf Epis. et
" tha higan æt Hrofes cestre dabunt Biorhtuulfo pres-
" byteri aliquam partem terræ in provincio [sic.] Cant.
" in regione que vocatur Haddun id est dimidiam aratri
" pro ejus placabili pecunia," &c.
The deed is very coarsely written and bears the date
889, at which time Suithulf was Bp. of Rochester ; but
on the back is a very beautifully engrossed endorsement,
which professes to be a confirmation of the demise by
King Eadgar and Abp. Dunstan, who lived a hundred
years after Suithulf.
It is difficult to imagine any circumstances which
could require a simple purchase of a small plot of land
to be confirmed by all the magnates of the realm after
the lapse of a whole century.
The endorsement is in these words:—" +Eadgar
" cyninge of his agenre handa sealde thas boc leofrice
" on thara gewitnesse the her benithan standath, Dun-
" stan Arepis. Athelwold Epis. Oswald Epis. Ælfhere
" dux. Ællfwine presbyter ejus. Wulfstan Min(ister),
" Osgar Abbas, Ealdred Min., Eadelm Min., Wulfheh
" Min., Leofstan Min., Ælfheh Min., Wulfsige Min.,
" Byrhtrie Min., Wulfsige Min., Leofric Min."
Endorsement contemporary with the deed, " Haddun
booc."
C. 3. A charter of Edward the Confessor, written in
English, and granting sac and soc, toll and team, &c. to
Ch. Ch., Cant.
C. 4. A similar charter, also in English, given by
William I.
In the invocation at the foot of the charter the King
alludes to his predecessor. " For than thingan the ic
" habbe thas gerihta Xpe. for givene minre saule to
" ecore alyssodnesse, eal swa Eadward King mi mai ær
" dyde," &c.
C. 48. A similar charter of Will. II. written first in
Latin and then in English. This parchment is much
defaced, and the name of the King is lost, but the
clause—" forgeven minre sawle to alyssednesse ealswa
" Eadword King, and min fæder (dyden)"—in the
English portion, and a corresponding form in the Latin
half, show to whom the charter is to be attributed.
C. 9. A similar charter granted by Henry I., " H. thurgh
" godes gefu . . . . kining gret ealle . . . . the Raulf.
" Arcebishop and se hyred æt Xpescircean on Cant-
" wareberig habbath land inne freondlice, and ic kythe
" cow thæt ic hæbbe heom geunnon, thæt hi byon ælc
" thare lande wurthe, the hi hæfdon on Eadwardes
" Kynges dæge mines mæges, and on Willelmes Kynges
" dæge mines fæder . . . .," &c.
C. 41. An inspeximus of a charter of Stephen, written
in English; he refers to the days of Edward his kinsman, of William his grandfather, and " Henrices
" Kinges dæge mines cames."
C. 20, C. 14. Similar charters of Henry II.

Sandwich.

S. 262. A copy of Cnut's charter, by which he
granted the town of Sandwich to the table of the monks
of Ch. Ch., offering at the same time the golden crown
from his head at the altar of the church. The original
charter is in the *Charter Book*, and is 737 of the Codex
dip.
S. 246. " Odo gratia Dei Baiocensis Epis. Lanfranco
" Archiepo et Hamoni Vicecomiti &c. Sciatis omnes
" quia Ego Odo Baioc. Epis. et Cancio Comes, omnes
" domos quas in villa de Sandwich habeo et omnes con-
" suetudines mei juris ad ipsam villam pertinentes, pro
" anima mea et pro anima dni. mei Willelmi regis
" Anglorum ecclesie Xpi. Cantuar. in perpetuum possi-
" dendas concedo."
S. 264. Henry II. grants to the monks of Holy Trinity,
Cant., all the rights in Sandwich which they had in the
reign of his grandfather, as ascertained by an inquest of
twelve men of Dover and twelve of Sandwich.
The privileges conferred by Henry I. are to be seen in
the copy S. 274.—2.
S. 274. 15th cent. copies of two documents referring
to Sandwich.
1, 1282. H. Prior of Ch. Ch. grants to A(ileanora),
consort of King E., all the rights, with certain specified
exceptions, which the convent possesses in Sandwich.
2, 1127. Record of an inquisition taken at Sandwich,
by the oaths of " xxix maturi, sapientes, senes," to ascertain the rights possessed in Sandwich by the convent of
Cant.
S. 269. 13th cent. A composition made between the
Prior of Ch. Ch., and the men of Sandwich, before S. de
Pencestre, Warden of the Cinque Ports.

5.

S. 281, 13th cent. A deed of gift by which David del
Kai and Agnes his wife convey to the convent of Ch.
Ch., in pure and perpetual alms, all their land at
the quay in Sandwich " præter furnum nostrum, quem
" contulimus conventui de Einesham."
S. 269, circ. 1200. A letter from H. de Castello, Archdeacon of Cant., to Abp. Hubert, concerning the
patronage of St. Peter's, Sandwich, and other matters
in that town.
The Abbot of St. Augustine's had in Abp. Richard's
time made a corrupt bargain with the vicar of St.
Peter's, to whom he gave a pension " unius Bisancii," in
consideration of which he was allowed to intrude some
of his monks into the church. It is mentioned that
Herbert Pauper, a former archdeacon, had conferred
(contulit) the church upon the " Provost of Sandwich,"
but that he, preferring a secular life, derived no advantage
from the gift.
S. 263, 1240. A letter to Henry III. from the barons
of Sandwich.
The writers say that they could not give the King an
earlier answer. " Cum pares et combarones nostri in Nor-
" mannie, Pictavie, Gasconie, Ybernie, et Scotie partibus,
" et alibi, pro suis mercandiis promovendis, fuerunt
" absentes," but now having consulted " significamus
" quod nos sumus fideles homines vestri, et de vobis
" terras et libertates nostras tenemus per servitium
" quinque navium, quos vobis invenire debemus semel in
" anno, ad summonitionem vestram, per quindecem
" dies continuos cum sumptibus nostris. Ita tamen in
" qualibet nave sint viginti homines, more maritimo
" armati, et unus rector. Si vero dicte quinque naves
" et homines, ut dictum est, in vestro servitio perstete-
" rint ultra quindecem dies, vos eosdem homines cum
" denariis vestris sustentabitis quamdiu vobis placuerit
" eorundem servitium quod. . . ." &c.
S. 268 and S. 278 are parchment rolls recording
business done in the Hundred Court of Sandwich, in the
years 1281 and 1284 respectively.
S. 266, S. 267, and S. 279.—1286, 7, 8, and 9. These
are annual statements of account rendered by the collector of Sandwich, acting on behalf of the convent of
Ch. Ch. The receipts are given in a gross sum without
details; the expenses consist of small amounts laid out
in building materials and labour. A few entries show
that the connexion of the town with the Cinque Ports
involved the payment of small fees to officers and messengers despatched to the central port of the confederation. Among the items belonging to this class is one
which hints at a tragedy with a thread of interwoven
comedy. " In nuncio portando ad Ballivum apud-
" Romenæ de Barbitonsore occiso."
S. 282, 1276, S. 277, 1278, and S. 266, 1289, are
accounts similar to the above.
S. 280. The report of the collector of the King's
customs at Sandwich.
The dues recorded were levied upon wool fells and
woollen cloth, both imports and exports ; also there
were collected " subsidium iiis. de dolio vini, et xiid. de
" libra."
The MS. is not dated, but the King's 7th year is
mentioned, and the writing belongs to the reign of
Henry IV.
S. 275. Recepta quarundam navium de Baiona in portu
de Sandwyco Anno Dni. MCCLXXI.
After the title follow eight paragraphs, each of which
is occupied by a statement of the duties collected from
some ship trading from Bayonne, with the names of the
adventurers whose ventures were the subjects of taxation.
" It. de nave ' Sci. Leonis' de Baon de qua rector vocatur
Domingus.
De eodem rectore 11s. 1d. de cera, cepo, et seym.
It. de Johanne Veyre iis. iiiid. de cera.
It. de Vincentiano iiiis. vid. de cera et racemis.
It. de Domingocento iiiis. iiid. ob, de cera, ficis, et
racemis.
It. de Vincentiano iiiis. vid. de cera, ficis, racemis, et
de seym.
It. de Gonsalvo iiiis. viiid. de cera, ficis, et racemis.
It. de Pedriano iiiis. viiid. de ficis, racemis, et de datis.
Summa xxixs. viiid. ob.
Inde in retrodono xviiid."
At the foot are eight entries of one line each, under
the title :—
" Recepta Navium applicantium in portu de Sandwyco
cum vinis cartatis tempore vendangii anno supradicto
videlicet :—
" De Willo. de Gomband de Oleron mercatore xxxs.
de vinis.
" It. de Johe de Fereres et Petro de Lyges merca-
toribus xxixs. iiid. de vinis.

3 M

"It. Johe. de Yspania xxiijs. do vinis," &c., &c.
S. 266, S. 283, S. 284. The quay at Sandwich, which
belonged to the monks of Canterbury, was therefore
known as "Monken Key," sometimes as the "Manor of
"Monkynkey"; the officer who presided over its affairs
was called the Custos, and he was bound to render an
annual account of all money which he received and
expended in the exercise of his office.

The references above given indicate three of these
yearly statements, and record the financial condition of
the quay for the years between 1385 and 1392. From
these papers it appears that the chief part of the revenue
was derived from fees paid for the use of the crane on
the wharf; thus 2d. was charged for lifting a cask of
wine, a millstone cost 6d., a pipe of wine 1d., whilst for
21 barrels of salmon 14d. was paid, "videlicet pro tribus
"barrellis 2d."

Cellars and warehouses were attached to the quay,
the rents of which, upon weekly hirings, were received
and accounted for by the custos.

Thomas Elys, the munificent merchant of Sandwich,
is here mentioned in connexion with dealings in
wine. "Item computat solutos Johanni Cundy, pro
"fyggis et reisenys emptis anno regni regis Ricardi
"secundi xiiᵒ, xs. Et in ii doliis vini extrahendis extra
"selarium Thome Elys ad ponendis in carecta Dni.
"Thesaurarii xvid. Et in i dolio vini cariando a
"selario predicti Thome Elys usque Monkenkeye,
"iiiid. Et in ii doliis et i pipe vini adponendis in
"carecta Dni. Prioris xvid. Et in expensis Dni. Hen-
"rici Cranebrok Thesaurarii, et carectarii ibidem,
"die Mercurii proximo post festum Sci. Clementis,
"iis. viiid. Et in vino empto pro eiis eodem die xvd.
"Et in uno dolio vini altera vice cariando a taberna
"predicti Thome usque ad cranagio, in omnibus cos-
"tagiis, una cum conducto unius batelli pro eodem,
"ixd. Et de xd. solutis pro una lagena vini rubii
"empta pro predicto Dno. H. Cranebok," &c.

S. 253, 1563. Chirograph by which the Dean and
Chapter of Canterbury convey a house in Sandwich,
called St. Thomas House, to Roger Manwood, who covenants to found a grammar school upon the premises.

Songs.

S. B. b. 34 and b. 185. These are two MS. songs,
believed to be unedited, and, from the place in which
they are found, to be the composition of monks of Ch.
Ch. They are written by different hands, and appear
to belong to the 15th cent.:—

> "I pray you come kyss me
> My lytle prety mopse
> I pray come kyss me.
>
> Alas good man most now be kyst
> Ye shall not now ye may me trust
> Wherefore go where as ye best lust
> For I wys ye shalnot kyss me.
>
> I wys swete hart yff that ye
> Had askyd a greter thyng of mee
> So onkynd to you I wolde not have bo
> Where(fore) I pray you come kyss me."

Eight more stanzas follow, perhaps even less rhyth-
mical than those given. The last verse brings the dispute to a comfortable conclusion, as has been usual in
amorous songs from the time of "Donec gratus eram
"tibi" to the present day.

> "I now se well that ye are kynd
> Wherefore ye shall now know my mynde
> And as you owne ye shall me fynde
> At all times redy to kyss thee.
>   Finis.   J. Wolstan."

The second song has more merit, and scans fairly:—

> "I will not flee
> To love that hart that lovyth me.
>
> That hart my hart hath in suche grace
> Yᵗ of too harts one hart make wee
> Yᵗ nart hath brought my hart in case
> To love yᵗ hart yᵗ lovyth me.
>
> For one that lyke unto yᵗ hart
> Nev' was nor ys nor nev' shall be,
> Nor nev' lyk cause set ys apart,
> To love yᵗ hart yᵗ lovyth me.
>
> Whych cause gyvyth cause to me and myne
> To serve yᵗ hart of suscrente,
> And styll to syng yᵗ later lyne,
> To (?) love yᵗ hart yᵗ lovyth mee.

> What ev' I say, what ev' I syng,
> What ev' I do, yᵗ hart shall se,
> Yᵗ I shall serve with hart lovyng,
> Yᵗ lovyng hart yᵗ lovyth me.
> Thys knot thus knyt who shall untwyne,
> Since we ' kynyt it do agre,
> To lose nor ffye but both enclyne,
> To love yᵗ hart yᵗ lovyth me.
>
> Farwell of harts yᵉ hart most fyne,
> Farwell dere hart hartly to the,
> And kepe yis hart of meyne for thyne,
> As hart for hart for lovyng me."

Tonbridge.

A. 28, 1258. A composition between Abp. Boniface
and Richard de Clare, Earl of Gloucester, settling the
terms upon which the Earl should hold the manors of
Tonbridge, Hadlow, &c., under the Abp.

Some reservations are introduced establishing the
rights of the convent of Ch. Ch., sede vacante.

This, the prior's part of a tripartite indenture, occupies a whole skin of parchment, and presents an interesting picture of the Abp.'s installation banquet, with
the great feudal lord acting as honorary servitor and
accepting perquisites instead of wages.

"Anno regis Henrici filii regis Johannis quadra-
"gesimo secundo .... convenit inter Bonifacium
"Archiepiscopum Cantuariensem ex una parte, et
"Ricardum de Clare Comitem Glou. et Hereford exal-
"tera, de consuetudinibus et serviciis que predictus
"Archepus. exigebat a predicto comite de tenementis
"que de eo tenet in Tunebreg, &c. .... et unde pre-
"dictus Archiepiscopus exigebat a prefato comite quod
"faceret ei homagium, servicium feodorum quatuor
"militum, sectam ad curiam ipsius Archiepi. pro pre-
"dictis maneriis .... et quod foret superior Senes-
"callus ipsius Archiepi. et successorum suorum ad
"magnum festum eorum, quando contigerit Archiepis-
"copum Cant. intronizari; et scilicet quod esset
"superior Pincerna ipsius Archiepiscopi et successorum
"suorum ad predictum festum, et quod faceret ei
"sectam ad curiam ipsius Archiepi. de Otteford pro
"predicto manerio de Bradstede .... Ita tamen quod
"ratione vel occasione hujus presentis conventionis
"inite in hac parte Priori et Conventui ecclesie Xpi.
"Cant .... nullum prejudicium fiat.
"Et inter predictum comitem ex una parte querentem,
"et predictum Archiepiscopum de hoc quod predictus
"comes exigebat habere, pro servicio senescallie pre-
"dicte, in quolibet festo intronizationis Archiepi.
"Cant., septem robas competentes de scarlet, triginta
"sextaria vini, quinquaginta libras cere ad luminarium
"suum proprium, liberationem feni et avenarum ad
"quatuorviginti equos per duas noctes, et scilicet quid-
"quid remanebit in lardario, festo consummato, post
"compotum receptum, et discos, et salsaria que assi-
"debit coram Archiepo. ad primum ferculum in festo
"predicto. Et pro servicio pincinarie predicte septem
"robas competentes de scarlet &c. .... et in crastino
"festi, compoto recepto, universa dolia evacuata, et ea
"que potata fuerint usque subtus barram, et prehenda-
"tionem ad proximum manerium Archiepiscopi per
"quatuor partes Cantie, ubicunque voluerit, per tres
"dies ad custus ipsius Archiepiscopi, ad sanguinem
"minuendum si voluerit, et cupam quam servist coram
"Archiepo." &c.

F. 32, 1280. "Perambulatio leucate de Thonebregg
"facta coram Dno. Stepho. de Pencestre, Dno. Johe. de
"Cobeham, et Dno. Salomone de Rofecestre, justiciariis
"regis itinerantibus, apud Thonebregg Anno Regis
"Edwardi filii regis Henrici octavo, per sacramentum
"subscriptorum," &c. A parchment record of the
boundaries, knights' fees, and tenants.

Vernacular Tongue, MSS. in the.

A series—unfortunately not without large gaps—of
specimens of our vernacular tongue, from the 8th century to the 16th, may be collected from the Chart.
Ant.

The earliest examples are to be found in the Charter
Book, and as most of the documents therein contained
are reproduced in the Codex Dip., it is not necessary to
do more than to indicate the references under the heading Saxon Charters in this report by which their place
in Mr. Kemble's work can be found.

S. 260. The translation of Cnut's Latin grant is not
in the Cod. Dip., but it may be as well to say that the

Latin original and the literal English translation, which are side by side in the *Charter Book*, afford a good opportunity for comparing the construction of the two languages.

H. 68, Cod. Dip. 722. The will of Æthelstan, the son of Ethelred II., is in its portfolio among the Chart. Ant. and not in the *Charter Book*. Mr. Kemble obtained a copy from some other source, and as this MS. is not referred to in his places, it is liable to be overlooked. This will is made interesting by the familiar style of the language, and the homely character of the Ætheling's bequests; he died young, and distributed his not very magnificent personal possessions among his friends.

C. 3, C. 4, C. 48, C. 9, C. 41, C. 20, and C. 14, all of which are English charters granted by successive Kings from Eadward to Henry II., are not known to have been printed.

M. 251. A burlesque conveyance in English rhyme, dated in the reign of an Edward, but furnishing no indication as to which King of the name is meant.

There are three endorsements :—
1. " A Saxon deed," 16th cent.
2. " The straungest deed that I ever sawe, 5 Oct. 1620."
3. " Given me by Mr. Vincent Denne, 1656." This is in Somner's handwriting.

The deed itself is written in an affected hand, as follows :—

" That wyte alle that nowthe beth
That this writ yhareth and yseth
That ich William the clockere Roberdes sone
That was wyle Muleward yne Duntone
Habbe ygive and ygranted
By thisse chartre confermed
Symon the mareschal and Crystine his wyvo
The wyle that eny man is alive
That thridde dol of a burgage
That me well by heritage
In the barth of Duntone
Alrenuxt the vorsede Symone
Habbe and halde wythhute doute
The wyle the sonne geth aboute

      .   .   .   .   .

Thys writ was ygive at Candelmasse
In the suxe and twentythe more ne lasse
The date of Edward houre Kynghe
God him gyve god endingge."

Deeds such as this have before now been included among " *Saxon* " charters, and the 16th cent. endorser thought that this was a *Saxon* deed; at all events it is plain that it is an *English* one, even if it be Saxon, and it affords a good argument for those who believe that Alfred wrote advisedly when he used the name *English* and not *Saxon* to designate his own tongue.

M. 309 and M. 295. Two proclamations dated 1450 which refer to Cade's rebellion; they afford good examples of courtly English of their date.

I. 205. Depositions of witnesses, not dated, but belonging to the middle of the 15th century. The witnesses were Kentishmen.

" It ys to undyrstande that Jon Dounholm, a man of
" lxx wyntryn of age and more, seyt ther to that on
" hys holydom . . . . ne ther was nevyr yssue out of
" that dych to that othyr syde . . . . but when an
" ootyr made an yssue goyng yn and out by twyxte the
" two waterys, but for eny such yssue that same Jon
" Dounholm at alle tyme know verryli of trowthe that
" thylke ooterysway was on the priory's grund," &c.

M. 347, 1475. A contract to supply cloth by a Salisbury clothier.

S. 297, 1481. Evidence of old men living near Whitstable.

C. 1,235, 1500. Pleadings and depositions, 15 feet in length, relating to a riot in Canterbury. The mayor, who led the riotous citizens, was indicted at the instance of the prior, who was aggrieved. Depositions, pleas, and rejoinders are all in the English of the time.

T. 31, 16th century. A bill by which it was proposed to sanction or compel the building of a permanent bridge between the Isle of Thanet and the mainland. This specimen is later than the last, but still the English has a construction not now in ordinary use. " The " fery is so swered up with wose, &c., that now no fery " . . . . may be there, but only at high spring floods," &o.

M. 352. A fair copy, in the author's own handwriting, of a draft preface in English to Somner's A. S. Dictionary. Somner often consulted the Chart. Ant., and it is very probable that whilst so occupied he dropped

this fair copy among the ancient documents. It is written with laborious neatness, but in the published book is superseded by a Latin preface of greater length.

Visitations.

A. 9, 1284. A letter sent by Abp. Peckham to the Prior and Chapter of Canterbury, which the writer desires them to preserve among their archives, to be used as evidence if it should ever be required.

The Abp. had been making a tour of visitations through the diocese of Wales, where he had been dutifully received until he came to St. David's. At that place the Bishop at first refused to submit to his authority; claiming for himself a modified metropolitan jurisdiction, he consented to accept the writer as Archbishop, but rejected him in the character of Primate.

The Abp. appealed to ancient precedent, refused to entertain the subtle distinction between an archbishop and a primate, and finally, recalling the circumstances of the Bishop's own consecration, when he professed obedience to the Abp. of Canterbury as his metropolitan, he induced him to withdraw his opposition.

Foreseeing that this victory in a fairly-fought field would settle the question of supremacy for ever, the Abp. caused this letter to be written with scrupulous formality, so that it might be available as evidence if ever, in days to come, a Welsh bishop should refuse allegiance to the Canterbury church.

M. 390, 1293. Two parchments which relate the process of an abortive attempt made by the commissary of the convent of Canterbury to visit the parish church of Maidstone, sede vacante.

F. 29, 1294. Memorandum of a visitation made at the church of Feyrfield by the commissary of the convent of Canterbury, sede vacante.

The visitation revealed a lamentable state of affairs :
" —Ibi unus Antiphonarius nullius usus nec alicujus
" valoris, et una legenda nullius valoris. Deficit ibi
" Psalterium, et manuale, et processionale, et ordinale,
" et collectarium, et martilogium. Parietes cancelli
" debiles sunt, quia pleni sunt foraminum. Cemeterium
" est dedicatum et non ecclesia, eo quod est de ligno et
" plastrura terræ. Rector nullum bonum facit in paro-
" chia, et vendidit isto anno omnes fructus. Capellanus
" habet porcionem suam ita exilem, quod non potest
" vivere, nec se honeste sustinere ibidem. Simon
" Capellanus notatur de quadam Natekina, et constat
" melius quod sit verum quam falsum. Clericus
" ecclesie uxoratus est."

This MS. rightly reports that the see was vacant on Trinity Sunday 1294, for although Abp. Winchelsey had been elected, he was detained in Rome, awaiting confirmation, until the autumn of that year.

A. 197, 1334. A parchment endorsed, " Instrumen-
" tum non abbreviatum super processu visitacionis
" Dni. J. Archiepiscopi, in quo instrumento continetur
" modus prefectionis Dni. R(icardi Oxenden) per dictum
" Archiepiscopum judicialiter approbatum." Abp. Stratford made this visitation of the chapter for the purpose of keeping his right alive, and the pretended scrutiny into the legality of the prior's right to hold his office was a mere formal act.

W. 170, 1498. Roger Church, " decretorum doctor " and commissary of Canterbury, notifies to the Prior and convent of Worcester that, by authority of Abp. Morton, he intends to visit their church, the See of Worcester being vacant.

A. 21, 1534. The King directs all dukes, earls, ... and constables to protect and assist the Abp. and his commissary during a visitation which he intends to make throughout his province.

H. 118, 1598. The Dean and Chapter of Hereford protest against their Bishop's claim of a right to visit them.

Wills.

B. 2, A.D. 997. " Testamentum Ætherici," who gave Booking to Ch. Ch. Cod. dip. 699.

C. 70. " Testamentum Thurstani."

H. 68, 1015. Will of Æthelstan Ætheling. He gave Hollingbourne to Ch. Ch.

His swords, drinchorn, and silver-plated trumpet are bequeathed to his friends, and certain parcels of land which he formerly (wrongfully ?) took are restored to the original owners.

W. 223, 1494. Contemporary copy of a mandate from Alexander VI. to the Abbots of St. Augustine, of Westminster, and of St. Albans, requiring them to promote the provisions of a Bull of which he subjoins a copy.

3 M 2

By this latter instrument the jurisdiction of the Abp. of Cant., and during the vacancy of the see, of the Prior of Ch. Ch., in matters touching the probate of wills is settled and confirmed.

W. 209, 1294. Probate copy of the will of Richard de Suthchurch (Essex) Militis. He directs that seven quarters of wheat shall be distributed to the poor on the day of his funeral, on the eighth day after, and at his month's mind. For the space of a month five poor women, in commemoration of the five joys of the Virgin, are to receive a white loaf with appropriate drink (compnaginm). He gives liberal legacies to his workmen and friends, to one of whom he bequeaths " viginti marcas " cum palfredo bayo."

W. 218, 1313. Copy and probate of the will of Abp. Winchelsey.

His books and many rich vestments were given to his cathedral church, and each of his servants, down to his barber who had followed him to Bordeaux during his persecution, was rewarded by a legacy.

A. 14, 1327. Original will of Abp. Walter Raynold.

He bequeaths to his church vestments and hangings embroidered with raised figures representing the martyrdom of St. Thomas of Canterbury; also a precious pontifical ring, set with a sapphire surrounded by emeralds, which once belonged to St. Wulstan. To the shrine of St. Thomas he leaves a ring set with a sapphire engraved with the figure of a lion. He leaves to the shrine of St. Edmund at Pontigny a ruby ring; this he directs shall be suspended to the feretory by a silken lace. To the churches of Worcester, New Windsor, St. Thomas de Acon in London, Wimbledon, Sawbridgeworth, St. Katherine by the Tower, and Walsingham, he bequeaths ornaments and altar furniture. His books are to be distributed among his clerks, but a Bible in three volumes is left to the Prior and convent of Canterbury. To John of Eltham, the King's brother, he gives " unum gladium de guerra cum apparatu de " argento deaurato cum zona & coopertura de serico " rubeo " ; to the Queen Dowager a gold clasp; and to the Bishop of Ely, the superintendent of his executors, a ring with a fine square sapphire.

W. 231, 1337. The will of W. de Turvill, Canon of Lichfield.

He leaves 300 marks to the fabric of his church, namely, for the new work in the choir, and for the lengthening of the Lady Chapel. A hundred pounds are assigned to the succentor and vicars of the cathedral for their encouragement in divine offices, a cup to the dean, and a sum of money to each of the testator's " con-canons."

Many churches and two orders of friars are among the legatees, and a hundred pounds are directed to be expended in masses.

W. 219, 1348. Copy of the will of Abp. John Stratford.

The bequests are such as are usually found in the wills of churchmen of exalted rank : pennies to the poor, fifty masses by fifty priests, relics, and vestments to his cathedral, legacies to his relations, and in addition many sums of money assigned to the repairs of specified bridges, the testator's birthplace and his former diocese of Winchester not being forgotten in this particular.

The Abp.'s best new mitre was left to the convent of Ch. Ch., upon condition that it should never be alienated. It might be lent to succeeding archbishops, providing that the borrower deposited sufficient security ; or even it might be broken up, if out of the materials some good and enduring thing were made for the use of the monastery.

S. B. c. 24, 1366. Copy of the will of W. Edyndon, Bp. of Winchester.

This MS. is much torn, the bottom of the sheet being entirely lost, but the part which remains is fairly legible.

W. 210, 1377. The will of Alice, widow of Alan de Thorlethorp, citizen of York. The property specified consists of veils, hooded tunics, and other trifling articles of dress. The testatrix ordains that her body shall be buried in the minster church of York, " et " non aliter, videlicet, coram ymagine crucifixi, ubi " filius meus Dns. Henricus divina celebrare consuevit."

W. 220, 1398. Copy of the will of John Bukyngham, Bp. of Lincoln.

His chief bequest concerns the foundation of Bukyngham's Chantry.

The will was executed at Canterbury " in quodam " manso vulgariter *Meistr Omers* nuncupato." [As to this name, see Willis in Archaeol. Cant. vii. 96–9.]

W. 221, 1421. Probate and copy of the will of John Kent, of the parish of St. Werburg in Hoo. The testator was a yeoman, who left to 40 priests, to be nominated by his exors., ten shillings (or threepence to each) for celebrating three masses, " unam de Trinitate, " aliam de Sca Maria, et terciam de requiem."

He left also ten marks " ad le gyff hale (gift-ale) " Sce. Werburge sustentand."

W. 212, 1428. The will of Robert Clifford Armiger of Welle and Garrington (in Littlebourne). This instrument is drawn in the shape of a bipartite indenture, one part remaining in the custody of the Prior and convent of Ch. Ch., so that the will was irrevocable. The provisions of the deed are so favourable to the monastery that it is probable that this was given as security for performance of a contract, or for payment of a debt.

W. 213, 1437. The will of Hen. Gerard, chaplain.

The whole of the small personal estate is directed to be expended in pious works for the benefit of the testator's soul. He directs that his missal shall be given to some priest, who at his death shall bequeath it to another with the same condition, " ut sic vicissim, " succedente tempore, ab unoquoque sacerdote, pro " tempore suo, predictum missale habente, pro anima " mea specialius exoretur."

W. 222, 1348. One of Abp. Stratford's exors. renounces his office, and by this deed, executed by the Prior and convent of Ch. Ch., is totally exonerated.

W. 214, 1453. The will of Dame Joan Brenchley.

The property, one manor excepted, is assigned to pious uses, especially to the endowment of a chantry in the church of Bixley, but the residual estate is to be employed in almsdeeds.

W. 215, 1456. The will of Thomas Doncastre, citizen of York.

W. 216, 1459. The will of Anne " sometyme the wif " of John Martyn Justice, late the wif of Thomas " Burges, made at Gravene the viii day of Aprill the " xxxvi yer of the reigne of Kyng Harry the VI{th}."

The property, consisting of estates lying in the neighbourhood of Faversham, is left to the sons of the deceased as tenants in tail. She directs that the rents of one estate shall be allowed to accumulate for three years, and that the total sum thus obtained shall be employed for the benefit of her soul.

W. 217, 1655. Will of Mrs. Margaret Bargrave of Canterbury. W. Somner was appointed sole executor, and it is probable that this document strayed from among his private papers into the Chart. Ant.

Wine given by the Kings of France.

F. 90, 1179. The original grant by Louis VII.

Louis VII. in 1179 gave to the convent of Ch. Ch. an annual allowance of a hundred modii of wine as a propitiatory offering to St. Thomas, at whose shrine he had just offered his devotions for the purpose of obtaining the saint's interposition in favour of his son, who was dangerously ill. That the gift was made in anticipation of, and not in gratitude for, his son's recovery is proved by the date—" Que omnia, ut perpetuam stabi-" litatem obtineant, sigilli nostri auctoritate, ac regii " nominis karactere subtus annotato, presentem cartam " precepimus communiri. Actum Cantuarie Anno ab " incarnatione Domini MCLXXIX. Astantibus," &c.

The great seal of the King, the " character " of his name, and the autograph signature of Hugo the Chancellor, give authority to this instrument.

F. 91. A duplicate of the above.

F. 92, 1180. Philippe II. in the first year of his reign granted to the convent of Ch. Ch. this confirmation of his father's gift of wine. Neither this confirmation nor Louis VII.'s charter makes any mention of the illness from which Philippe was suffering when his father made his pilgrimage. By the terms of these charters the monks were allowed to claim the hundred muids of wine, at the time of the vintage, in the castle of Poissy, and free passage clear of all toll and custom was granted *as far as it lay in the King's power*.

To this document are attached the great seal, the royal monogram, and the signature of the same Hugo the Chancellor.

F. 94, 1189. A short additional charter of Philip Augustus.

He prescribes that the wine shall be measured by the standard of Paris, and that the vineyards of Triel shall supply it. Alluding to the part he was about to take in the third crusade, the King commands the Provost of Poissy to deliver the wine to the Canterbury monks even if after three years he shall not have returned *from an expedition which he is about to undertake.*

F. 99, 1235. Charter of Louis IX. (executed vacante cancellaria, but bearing the king's seal and monogram) by which the grant of wine is confirmed in the terms of the original gift.

F. 100 and F. 101, 1244 and 1263. Two deeds of inspeximus certifying to the existence and authenticity of the last charter.

F. 146, 1478. Charter of confirmation given by Louis XI.

F. 145, 1478–80. Another confirmation by Louis XI. Beside renewing the gift, this king consents that the wine shall be delivered in Gascony and the Bordelais; the reason assigned for this concession being that the country round Poissy was ruined and the vines destroyed.

The *mui* had apparently ceased to be a standard measure, and it is therefore, to avoid ambiguity, declared that three muis make two pipes, and that these two pipes are one tonneau. We learn elsewhere in these MSS. that the mui contained 16 gallons.

The convent at one time possessed three other original charters referring to this subject, namely, a second of Saint Louis, one of Philippe IV., and one of Charles IV. These have disappeared, recitals only remaining preserved in certificates of inspeximus, whilst the duplicate of the charter of Philip Augustus, seal and all, was sold not long ago in a London auction-room, and is probably at present in some private collection.

Affixed to F. 145 by a parchment lace, the point of junction being rendered inviolable by the impression of the King's secretum, are four documents signed by great officers of state, whose concurrence seems to have been required to make the King's grant operative. It would appear that in the time of Louis XI. many intermediate officials interposed themselves between the royal donor and the distant receiver of a favour.

F. 125, F. 126, F. 157, 1479. Three instruments signed by Johan le Grant, Lieutenant-General of the Seneschal of the Boulonnais. These documents recite the charter of Louis XI., and promise the co-operation of the Seneschal, whose seal in fine red wax is attached.

F. 138. Permission, under the seal of Henry II., to import the French wine.

F. 93. A similar grant of Richard I.

F. 95. A similar grant of John.

F. 148. A similar grant of Edward IV.

F. 149, 1514. Copies of all the charters relating to the wine which the convent possessed in 1514, certified by Nicholas Lytlington, official of the Archdeacon of Canterbury.

F. 100, F. 108, F. 110, F. 112, F. 113, F. 147. Copies of some of the above-mentioned charters, and of three others now lost.

F. ·114. A humble petition from Prior Goldstone, addressed to the King of France.

The prior writes that the delivery of the wine has been discontinued for many years owing to the long wars of the time; peace being re-established, he asks that the wine may be sent as it formerly was.

F. 128. A similar petition written on fine parchment. In the book of Ch. Ch. letters there is a draft of a petition to the French King in the handwriting of Prior Sellyng, Goldstone's successor, wherein the anxiety of the writer is plainly expressed in the erasures and interlineations by which he elaborated the style of his composition. The same volume (No. 11), contains a letter which alludes to the King's goodwill in the matter of the wine, and reports that in a conversation on the subject he asked if the messenger "had any tokyn of " Saint Thomas . . . . made as he mygth wer hit on " hys hatt in worshypping of S[t] Thomas, the whiche " wer to him a gret p. . . . (hiatus)."

F. 134. Free pass for the wine through the manor of Andeley, given under the seal of Walter Abp. of Rouen.

F. 122. A duplicate of the last.

A great number of free passes similar to these are among the MSS. of this group. These were given by French lords whose lands lay upon the roads leading from the vineyards to the coast, at the time when, according to the original arrangement, the wine was received at Poissy and embarked at Rouen or Witsand.

F. 104 to F. 107, 1288 to 1300. Reckonings, made by the resident agent of the convent, of the several parcels of wine received from the different growers at Triel. From these it appears that at the time of the vintage each tenant belonging to the district contributed a quantity of wine or grape juice, small or large in pro-

portion to his holding. We learn, from allusions in these papers, that the sum of these contributions seldom amounted to a hundred muids; in this case the prior appears to have been a loser, unless the King by special grace furnished the quantity which was lacking from his own stores. One item will show the manner of keeping these accounts:—"It. Annote le Plaiter iii " sest. de sa vingne de la Fosse."

F. 59, circ. 1300. Letters written from Triel to the prior at Canterbury. From these we gather that at the date Rob. de Lonjumeau (de Longojumello), a native of the district, was the prior's resident agent; that inspectors from Canterbury were sometimes sent over to check his proceedings; and that he was considered to be on the staff of the priory, receiving with the other *bearded* servitors his periodical gifts of livery cloth, the quantity of which it may be seen did not always give him satisfaction.

In addition to the wine derived from the King's gift, the convent produced some on a small estate of their own at St. Brice; the agent who superintended the collection of the wine at Triel also managed the cultivation of the vineyard at St. Brice.

F. 96 and F. 97. Two certificates in which Peter Bishop of Paris testifies that Richolda, widow of Guido Groolai, has given to the convent of Canterbury five quarterii of vineyard at St. Brice.

York.

The portfolio lettered Y. contains some parchments of the 14th cent. relating to disputes between the canons of York and the college of vicars choral (College of St. William) in the cathedral church; also some legal instruments connected with the endowments of this corporation.

Among the Chart Ant. are many MSS. which cannot be collected into groups, the subjects of which they treat being mentioned only in one or two places; but since many of these are illustrative of social and ecclesiastical life in the Middle Ages, they demand just so much notice as will make known the fact of their existence. Some examples of these miscellaneous MSS. will bring to a close this report of the examination of the Canterbury Chartæ Antiquæ: the registers, the volumes of *Ch. Ch. letters*, and to a great extent the three volumes known as the *Scrap Books*, being still undescribed, will follow in another report.

Miscellaneous.

A. 149, 1307. A notarial act certifying to the restoration of Abp. Winchelsey after his suspension by Clement V.

A. 10, 1285. Rob. de Stangrave, having been convicted of breaking into the Abp's park at Malling, called Le Plessit, binds himself with three sureties to make atonement.

X. 6, 1338. The Prior of Ch. Ch. declines to take part in a provincial chapter of English Benedictines; pleading that he, with his horses, his familia, and all his posse, have been summoned by the King to repair to one of the sea-side manors belonging to the convent, there to assist in repelling a foreign enemy, who has already carried fire and slaughter to several places where he has landed. The MS. is nevertheless dated from Canterbury.

S. 395, 1366. The prior, summoned to a Benedictine chapter at Northampton, refuses, for various reasons, to be present.

H. 122, H. 123. Two instruments, by the first of which Abp. Theobald gives a life interest in the tithes of Hellege [Eleigh] to Peter Scriptor his secretary, and by the second the prior and convent confirm the gift.

K. 12, 1329. A copy in Somner's hand of the patent of Edw. III. creating the eldest son of the King, qui pro tempore fuerit, Duke of Cornwall.

C. 279, 1223. The convent of Canterbury agree that, in consideration of a payment of forty marks, the body of W. de Clifford may be buried within the monastery of Cliffe.

C. 40, C. 85, C. 104. Short documents which refer to a custom of presenting a palfrey to each newly elected Prior of Ch. Ch.

B. 255. R[d] afts Symon gives to the convent two deer annually, which are to be delivered at Bocking.

D. 20. An expiatory offering made by W. de Tracy, one of the murderers of Abp. Becket.

This is the original instrument, fortified by the seal of the donor, who by it conveyed to the convent of Ch. Ch. the manor of Doccombe in Devonshire, "pro amore " Dei, et salute anime mee et predecessorum meorum, " ot amore beati Thome Archiepiscopi et martiris, " memorie venerande."

A. 42. A roll of six membranes, containing short lives of Popes and Archbishops of Canterbury.

The series of Popes extends from St. Peter, "princeps " Apostolorum anno incarnationis dominice, secundum " ewangelium xl°, secundum vero Dyonisium xvii^m," to John XII. in 955.

Of the Abps., St. Augustine is the first, and St. Dunstan the last.

Occasional notices of remarkable phenomena and political occurrences are inserted among the bio-graphies.

The original work seems to have been written by a contemporary admirer of St. Dunstan, concerning whom many marvellous stories are here recorded ; the present copy, judging from the character in which it is written, was probably made in the latter half of the 13th cent. The reverse of the parchment, which the historian left blank, has been used for recording memoranda.

1. A long catalogue of privileges granted to Ch. Ch. by many Popes and a few Abps.

2. A fragment of early British history, beginning :— " Post Belinum Trojanum Silvius genuit Brutum," &c.

3. A 13th cent. record of the great folkmote held upon Ponnenden Heath in 1072, under the presidency of Abp. Lanfranc.

The history of this meeting is well known, so that it will only be necessary to say that this memorandum relates how " ex precepto regis ad instanciam Archiepis- " copi, jussum est totum comitatum absque mora " considere, et omnes Francigenas, et precipue Anglos " in antiquis legibus et consuetudinibus peritos, con- " venire ad diraclonandas libertates et consuetudines " quas ecclesia Xpi in terras et privilegiis habeat, atque " in regias terras habere debeat."

Backed by public opinion, as expressed at this gather-ing, Lanfranc recovered for his church all the lands which Bp. Odo and other " proceres regni " had taken from it, and all the privileges which had been suppressed during the time of confusion following the Conquest. The memorandum ends abruptly, leaving the story half told.

Title-deeds.—A very large proportion of the Chart. Ant. are title-deeds, gifts of land or rents, and con-voyances of purchased property.

The Great Catalogue, having been compiled with an eye to this class of documents only, gives all possible information about any particular deed which may be sought for.

M. 344, late 13th cent. A MS. of three membranes, partly written on both sides, containing a list of the knights' fees in Kent, with the names of the tenants and overlords.

C. 168, 1279. A bond, under the seal of the Abbot of Arbroath (Abirbroth), securing the payment of 100 shillings on condition that the Prior and convent of Canterbury should feed " in perpetuum, qualibet die " Martis, tres-decem pauperes, competenter, ex parte " Dni. Alexandri Dei gratia regis Scottorum illustris, " in honorem Dei, et beate Virginis et, Sci. Thome " Martyris."

Printed in facsimile in vol. ii. of the National MSS. of Scotland.

C. 246. A long roll of many membranes, undated, but probably belonging to the 14th cent., containing a detailed description of the pictures which embellish the windows of the aisles of the choir of Canterbury Cathe-dral. To the description of each subject is added a verse illustrating the symbolism.

Example :—

" In medio. Tres reges equitantes—Balaam.
Orietur stella ex Jacob et exsurget homo de Israel.
Yunias, et Jerusalem.

Ambulabant gentes in lumine tuo, &c.
In medio. Herodes et Magi—Christus ot Gentes.
Qui sequuntur me non ambulant in tenebras.
Stella Magos duxit, et eos ab Herode reduxit.
Sic Sathanam gentes fugiunt te Xpo. sequentes.
Pharao, et Moyses cum populo exiens ab Egypto.
. Exit ab crumpna populus ducente columpna."

This MS. is printed in Somner's " Antiquities of Can-terbury," and also in " Gostling's Canterbury Walk."

C. 1,303, 1445. The prior's certificate of a miracle performed at the shrine of St. Thomas.

This certificate tells the story of a congenital cripple who, coming from Aberdeen, visited various shrines without obtaining relief, but to whom an offering at the feretory of St. Thomas brought a complete cure ; so complete was it that after a space of time, during which he visited the "Holy Blood of Wyls-nack," he returned to Canterbury rejoicing, and on foot, (prospere et pedester). Printed in Vol. II. of " Materials for the History of Abp. Becket.

S.B. a. 93. Six inquisitions, taken before the coroner for Essex, on view of the bodies of as many persons who met with violent deaths. They belong to the reign of Edw. III., and include cases of wilful murder, accidental drowning, and manslaughter in an affray. The custom at the time, as here demonstrated, was to compel the finder of the bodies to procure three sureties, and the four nearest neighbours of the deceased to find sureties also, assuming that these, or some of them, must know more about the death than anyone else. In two cases of murder, one victim was shot to death with arrows, and the other knocked down with a gisarme.

C. 167, 13th cent. H. Fitz Winoth gives land to the convent of Ch. Ch., directing that the income shall be spent in mending the books of the library.

H. 88, H. 91, H. 94. Three deeds by which Abp. Theobald gives, and Stephen and Boniface confirm, the church of Halstow to Ch. Ch., Cant. The two latter Abps. recite and approve a limitation of the gift by Abp. Hubert, who assigned the profits of the benefice to the purchasing of books for the library.

S. B. a. 226. Cruce signati. " Hec sunt nomina cruce " signatorum in Archidiaconatu Cornubie." This is the title of a small piece of parchment, upon which is written a list of the recruits furnished to the third crusade by the several deaneries of the Archdeaconry of Cornwall. The volunteers were 43 in number, and their ranks included a tailor, a smith, a shoemaker, two chaplains, a gamekeeper (Gualterus do foresta), a mer-chant, a miller, two tanners, and two women, uxor Portejoie and Hawis de Trevisac.

Presentations to benefices, institutions, and inquisi-tions to ascertain the status of vacant benefices are here in great number.

Acta, inhibitions, and other proceedings in ecclesias-tical courts occur in every division of the Chartæ Antiquæ.

C. 71. A bundle of nine writs, each bearing the seal of Henry II., and many of them tested by " Tom. Canc." These are short grants to Ch. Ch. of free warren and other privileges.

C. 92, &c. MS. relating to fairs and markets which were granted as valuable concessions to the convent of Canterbury. The first charter is one by which Richard II., moved by respect for the church in which the body of his father was buried, granted four fairs in every year to the prior and convent. These were held within the cemetery gate, and the practice has only been dis-continued in our own day. In addition to the fairs held within the precincts of the convent, others were granted, by royal charter, for the convenience of manors at a distance from Canterbury. A copy of the charter by which the city of Rouen held a weekly market is among these papers. Leases of standing-ground for booths, some not very ancient, are abun-dantly found in the collection.

S. B. b. 232. A printed pamphlet, 1642, " The King's " Majesties Charge to all the Judges of England."

J. B. SHEPPARD.

THE CATHOLIC CHAPTER OF LONDON, SPANISH PLACE, MANCHESTER SQUARE.

The papers of which a catalogue is here given form a portion of the collections belonging to the Catholic Chapter of the London district, and are now in the custody of the Very Rev. Provost Hunt, Spanish Place. In addition to these here specified, a very large number of documents not here enumerated are to be found in the same depository, having reference, however, to matters of a private nature; in compliance with the terms of the Commission, of these no notice has been taken in the following pages. The papers are carefully preserved, and are for the most part bound in volumes. The whole series of original letters is well worthy of a more detailed description.

I have to express my grateful thanks to Provost Hunt for the facilities offered me in my examination of these papers.

A volume in folio, of 210 pages, consisting of original letters and papers :—
1. Letters of Mr. Cortess, of the Roman College, to Mr. More, agent in Rome, chiefly on the affairs of the college, A.D. 1623, 1624, pp. 1–68.
2. Records about the Archpriest Birket, A.D. 1612–1614, pp. 69–83.
3. Treatise on the ecclesiastical jurisdiction of Richard Smith, Bishop of Chalcedon, A.D. 1624, pp. 86–121.
4. Original letters and papers concerning the proceedings of the said bishop, A.D. 1624, pp. 122–210.

A volume in folio of 302 pages :—
1. Original bulls and other papers on the jurisdiction, &c. of the Bishop of Chalcedon, with answers to various objections concerning the same. They extend from 1611 to 1636.
2. Original letters and papers by Robert Pett, George Salvin, Thomas Polton, Anthony Champney, George Lea, R. Varnam, E. Bennett, Fr. More, Thomas More, R. Orontes, Thomas Broome, John Kennion, Tho. Worthington, W. Casse, John Aynsworth, Rob. Clerc, William Rayner, William Stanley, and Fr. August. de S. Juan.

A volume in folio, paged from p. 211 to p. 761 :—
1. Papers respecting the obligations and privileges of Regular orders, together with answers to objections concerning the same. Imperfect at end.
2. Various letters, papers, &c., in Latin, English, French, and Italian, by and concerning Mary Percy, daughter of the Earl of Northumberland, abbess of the convent of the Benedictine Nuns at Brussels, and the nuns of the same convent. To two of them are appended 27 signatures of nuns.

A volume in folio, of 495 pages. The more important documents are the following :—
Letter from Robert Lambton to his brother, 10 Jan. 1612.
Printed address to the Catholics of England, 6 Oct. 1636.
Papers connected with the proceedings of Sir Richard Aston at the Court of Spain, 1624.
Letter of R. Orontes to Tho. More, 5 Jan. 1612.
Letters and papers respecting the Spanish match.
Letters of T. Swinnerton, 6 Sept. 1608, Tho. Worthington, 1 March 1613, and Benjamin Carrier to Card. Bellarmin, 10 Jan. 1614.
Attestations given to pilgrims.
List of the names of the more eminent English priests in and out of England.
Extracts from the rental of the English College at Rome, A.D. 1575.
Letter from Mr. Ratcliffe, of Yorkshire, to the Pope, 4 Sept. 1612.
Letter from Dr. Matthew Kellison, 19 Oct. 1632.
Lists of names of Catholic doctors and priests.
Lists of secular and regular priests in Essex and Hampshire, in 1633.
List of divines, metaphysicians, philosophers, and convictors in one of the English colleges on the Continent.
Orders issued by Cardinal Morone for the English College at Rome, with several others issued by the Congregation de Propaganda Fide.
Letters by Tho. Martin, Lond., 10 June 1611, and by F. More, Florence, 4 Sept. 1610.
Epitaphs upon Cardinal Alan, Owen Lewis, and Rob. Persons.
Notice of Edw. Latham, S. J. and Ch. Elmer, with various letters and papers of Edw. Latham, T. Fitzherbert, and Tho. Dingley.

List of English students who passed from the College of S. Omer to that of Valladolid, A.D. 1616–21.
Petition to the Pope by Ralph Jackson, Master of the Savoy.
Various papers connected with and transmitted to the Congregation de Propaganda Fide concerning the Bishop of Calcedon, in 1631. Many have original signatures appended.

A volume in folio of 353 pages :—
A history of the visitation of Douai College in 1612, in which is given an account of the buildings of the same, its constitutions and rules, of the duties of the president and other officers, of the scholars and convictors, and of its receipts and expenses. It consists of seven chapters.
Visitation of the same, 4 Dec. 1626, with various papers connected therewith in 1626 and 1627.

A volume in folio, paged from 463 to 765. It consists of a collection of various letters and papers relating to Dr. Ric. Smith, Bishop of Chalcedon, in 1626 and the following years.

A volume in folio of 329 pages. The more important of its contents are the following papers :—
Regulations by the Cardinals Borghese and Farnese respecting the students of the English College at Rome, A.D. 1600.
Letter from Dr. Bishop to Pope Paul V.
Letter from George Conyers, 24 Sept. 1624.
Letter from Cardinal Pole, 30 Nov. 1554 (Quirini v. 1, 129.)
Letters of John Aynsworth, Rob. Heath, John Wray, John Farmerye, Nic. Sanderson, Roger Parker, and Matthew Kellison.
List of "gentlemen that sickened and died upon the "sudden infection" at Oxford in July, 1577.
Dr. Gage's journal of the chief events of his life from his birth in 1621 to 1677.
Declaration for the Council of Kilkenny.
Letter of Stephen Barnes, 30 Sept. 1629.
Bulls, briefs, and other instruments connected with the Legatine mission of Cardinal Pole into England.
Catalogue of the vicars general, and archdeacons appointed by the Bishop of Chalcedon, in 1625.
Lists (in several forms) of controversial writers on matters of faith in England from 1560 to 1593, with historical and critical remarks.
Extracts from Stowe's Chronicle, translated into Latin.
Compendium Studiorum Thomæ Stapletoni ad an. 1598.

A volume in folio of 287 pages containing miscellaneous papers, of which the following are the more important :—
Letters written by Gio. Bapt. Vives, Wm. Stanney, Cuthbert Crawford, F. Bonaventura (Anglus), Edmund Thornell, the Poor Clares of S. Omer, Tho. More, John Bossevile, Peter Fitton, Wm. Isham, Lewis Vaughan, Matthew Kellison, Card. Blanchetti, Anthony Champney, James Bennett, Wm. Ward, Cuthbert Trollope, and R. Bluett.
Interspersed with the above are various documents of a miscellaneous nature respecting Catholic affairs, chiefly between 1600 and 1630.

A volume in folio, paged from 536 to 759. The more important of its contents are the following :—
Letters written by Geo. Salvin, Geo. Bircked, Rob. Dormer, Edw. Farington, Tho. Brome, Fr. Augustinus de S. Joanne, [Father White], R. Orontes, Rob. Pett, Laurence Kellam, Anthony Champney, Wm. Bishope, W. Little, Anthony Dormer, Wm. Rayner, Francis More, Valentine Lane, Ro. Clapham, Jo. Ratcliffe, and Jo. Bapt. Fabiano.
Various papers, many of which relate to the affairs of the Bishop of Chalcedon, are interspersed throughout this volume.

A thin folio volume marked Lib. A., consisting of the following papers, irregularly numbered :—
1. De beatis tribus juvenibus Anglo-Saxonibus in diocesi Constantiensi.
2. A genealogical table of the English royal families, illustrative of Dolman's treatise upon that subject, A.D. 1593.
3. Chronological lists of English saints.
4. Translations into Latin of various letters and papers of the time of King Henry VIII.

A volume in folio, paged 158–462. It consists for the most part of papers connected with Dr. Ric. Smith, Bishop of Chalcedon, the more valuable of which are :—
Letters of Richard Blount, Rudisend Barlow, Gregory Muskett, W. East, Ch. Lovel, Lord Ward, Geo. Woolley, John Hall, Charles Scott, Geo. Fortiscue, Tho. Arundel,

3 M 4

and . . . Laborne. It contains also a list of the Catholic secular and regular clergy in Sussex and Lincoln in 1633.

A volume in folio, paged 288-519. The more important of its contents are the following:—

Letters written by Th. Gre . . ., Tho. Rooke, H. Strong, David Chambers, Ric. Jonson, Pe. Fitton, Nic. Vincent, G. Muscott, W. Price, F. Carpenter, Marg. Knight, Edw. Coffyn, S.J., Valentine Lane, . . . Nelson, . . . Vives, Mary Pool, prioress of the English Canonesses Regular of Bruges, Matthew Kellison, M. East, Rob. Pett, Ric. Brough, Jo. Ratclif, Benj. Norton, and . . . Mullenax.

List of Catholic clergy in the counties of Lancaster, Durham, Northumberland, Westmoreland and Cumberland.

List of regulars admitted and professed in England.

List of seculars and regulars imprisoned in London, with the name of the prison in which each was confined.

List of seculars and regulars out of prison in England.

List of seculars and regulars in Lancashire, Norfolk, Berkshire, and Somerset.

List of priests (13 in number) who were delivered from prison through the intercession of the Spanish Ambassador, and permitted to go with him into Belgium, in 1613.

List of several of the more important Catholic priests in and out of England.

Various anonymous letters and many documents connected with the Congregation De Propaganda Fide occur throughout this volume.

A folio the paging of which runs from 330 to 635:—

Various letters and papers connected with the history of Cardinal Alan (among which are letters from the Earl of Westmoreland, Lord Dacre, and the Bishop of S. Asaph), together with the oration delivered in 1594 at the English College at Rome upon his death.

Authenticated extract from the register of the University of Douay, 1632.

Speech by Queen Elizabeth, 10 Aug. 1564, in S. Mary's Church, Cambridge, (signed by Ric. Jonson), with the questions to be then disputed in philosophy, medicine, theology, and civil law.

Various bulls, Papal briefs, and other instruments (some printed) upon English affairs.

Letter of Gregory Panzani, Lond., 28 Nov. 1635.

Information exhibited by Rob. Winter in 1629 to the Archbishop of Malines.

A paper upon the invasion of England by the King of Spain, written in the time of Queen Elisabeth.

Various documents connected with the history of the English College at Rome.

Two papers on the English Jesuitesses, more especially Mrs. Ward and Mrs. Mary Allcock.

History of the life and martyrdom of John Nelson, Tho. Sherwood, and Everard Hanse, with the letter written to his brother by Ever. Hanse the day before his death.

A volume in folio, paged 325-533:—

Letters and papers written by Geo. Salvin, Tho. More, Rob. Pett, Anthony Champney, Francis Hore, Ric. Smith, Hierom Heth, Matthew Kellison, Griffith Floid, Rob. Dormer, Owen Lewis, E. Farington, R. Orontes, Rob. Clerc, Benj. Norton, Geo. Lea, Tho. Brome, Dr. Bishop, F. Augustinus de S. Joanne, [Fr. White], Jo. Mush, John Nelson, and Tho. Martin.

A volume in folio, of which the paging runs from 209 to 436:—

Letters and papers connected with the history of Edmund Campion, S.J. with collections for his biography by Ambrose Corbington (who died at Rome in 1648) and Tho. Fitzherbert.

Letters and papers connected with the history of the Bishop of Chalcedon.

Discourse by F. Thomas Courtnay upon the affairs of England about 1650, during the exile of Charles II.

A folio containing 575 pages, in which, among many papers of a private nature, occur :—

Documents on the foundation and history of the English College at Rome.

On the affairs of the Bishop of Chalcedon.

On the state of the English College at Madrid.

On the state of the English College at Douay.

Letters to and from the Court of King James II. at S. Germains.

Among the writers are Lord Melfort, the Duke of Tyronnell, J. Caryll, and J. Betham.

Descriptive list of the Catholic clergy in various parts of England in 1692.

Papers on the foundation and history of the English College at Lisbon.

A thick volume in folio containing a history of the reign of Queen Elizabeth, civil and religious, by Anthony Champney. It is entirely in the handwriting of the author, and is corrected throughout by him. As far as I am aware, this volume has never been used for historical purposes by any recent writer, and appears to be worthy of a careful examination.

A large bundle of miscellaneous papers, of which the following are the most worthy of notice :—

1. "The brief of certain examinations taken before the Lord Bishop of London and some other of H.M. Commissioners Ecclesiastical, in the presence of Tho. Mottreshed, notary public," 22 March 1613, to 29 March 1614, as to having heard Mass at the Spanish Ambassador's house. 3 pp.

2. The first and second "examination of Peter Wilkinson, servant to John Morrell, linendraper, taken by the Lord Archbishop of Canterbury," 1 Dec. 1606. 2 pp.

3. "The examination of Tho. Morrowe, taken 2 June 1603, before the Bishop of London." 1 p.

4. "The examination of Francis Richardson, taken 2 June, before the Bishop of London." 1 p.

5. . . . to Dr. Carier, at Liege, dated at Colloin, 5 Feb. 1614.

6. "Articles against John Clark, recusant," signed by Francis Palmer. 2 pp.

7. "The examination of John Roberts, of Cransvenight, co. Merioneth," taken before the Bishop of London and others, 2 Dec. 1607. 3 pp.

8. "The examination of Tho. Garnet, a prisoner in the Gatehouse," before the Bishop of London, 17 Nov. 1607. 3 pp.

9. Further examination of the same, 7 and 8 April 1608. 4 pp.

10. "The examination of John Kitchyn, of the age of 20 years," examined by the Bishop of London, 21 June 1603. 3 pp.

11. "The examination of Geo. Blackwell, archpriest, taken before the Archbishop of Canterbury and Mr. Dean of Westminster," 1 and 2 July 1607. 4 pp.

12. Letters to Dr. Carier, Dean of Canterbury, from—
David Drummond, 10 Sept. 1613.
Joannes Copperus, 23 Dec. 1613.
———————, 27 Jan. 1614.
———————, 3 Feb. 1614.
———————, 10 Feb. 1614.
Ferdinandus archiepiscopus Coloniensis, 14 Feb. 1614.
Franciscus Florentinus, 15 April 1614.
J. Cardinalis Perronius, prid Paresceves, 1614.
Leo. Ronetrye, 9, Sept. 1613.

13. Dean Carier to the Archbishop of Canterbury; Draft. 3 pp.

14. "Articles proposed unto the priests in Wisbeach, 14 Aug. 1616, by the Bishops of Ely and Rochester." Endd., "To Mr. Pemberton." 2 pp.

15. [Tho. More] to Mr. John Nelson, [1621]. 2 pp.

16. "Answers of John Wentworth, of the parish of St. Giles in the Fields, gent.," Nov. 1637. 3 pp.

17. Relation by Richard Broughton of a book written in English by John King, late Protestant Bishop of London, as to his conversion to the Catholic faith, 30 Jan. 1623. 3 pp.

18. "Wm. Lloyd's speech, who after sentence of death died in Brecknock prison before execution, at which time if he had lived he had designed to have spoken." 3 pp.

19. "John Floyd's speech and manner of execution at Cardiff, July 22, 1679."

20. "The relation of a conference before His Majesty, and the Earl of Rochester, Lord High Treasurer, concerning the Real Presence and Transubstantiation, Nov. 30, 1686." 14 pp.

21. Warning to Geo. Turner, M.D., of Fetter Lane, as to his appearance before the Privy Council by virtue of his bond of 500l., Lambeth, 27 Nov. 1596. 2 pp.

22. "A true relation of such things as passed at the cruel martyrdom of the Rev. Father Hugh Greene, otherwise called Ferdinand Brooke, aged 57, at Dorchester, on Friday, 19 Aug. 1642," dated "from Dorchester June 20, 1643." 10 pp.

23. Six letters by Oliver Plunket to Captain Pulton, originals.

24. "The history of the Roman College." 19 pp.

25. "List of the original letters concerning the English College at Lisbon for the secular clergy." 2 pp.

26. Letter from W. Allen to F. Chasee [sic], prior of the English Carthusians, dated Cambray, 10 Aug. 1577. 13 pp.

27. "De Jure episcopali revmi. episcopi Chalcedonensis in Catholicos in Anglia et Scotia existentes," in 15 chapters.

28. Letter [from J. Sergeant ?] without date or address. 4 pp.

29. Retractation of J. Sergeant, Paris, 9 July 1675, with several papers connected with the same. 4 pp.

30. J. Sergeant's narrative as to his behaviour and usage. Wanting pp. 1-4. Endd., "A fair transcription of my narrative," pp. 23.

31. Bull of Pope Alex. VII. of 20 July.1660, with documents connected with the same.

32. "Subscriptions [without date] against Mr. Blackloe's writings, by the English secular priests of Douay." Injured by rats.

33. Letter from G. Muscott, add. "for my Master," 3 April 1640. 3 pp.

34. The same to the Bishop of Chalcedon, Nov. 19, [1641]. 3 pp.

35. The same to the same, Sept. 13 [1641]. 3 pp.

36. "Censure of Sorbonne upon F. Barnes," 30 May 1627. 2 pp.

37. Address by the Welsh Catholic clergy to Gregorio Panzani on his mission to England. Broadside.

38. "The three lay gentlemen's letter to my Lord Bishop" of Chalcedon, [25 Nov. 1627.] 4pp.

39. "The bishop's [holograph] answer to the three gentlemen." 3 pp.

40. "Dr. Champney's letter to pray for the King Charles I.," London, Nov. 30, 1638. 2 pp.

41. Certificate to the fact of Sir Tobie Matthew, Knight, having been heard to say Mass, Holy well or S. Venefrid's well, 8 Aug. 1631. 2 pp.

42. Notarial instrument attesting the fact of Sir. T. Matthew having said Mass about 5 Oct. 1620.

42*. "A narration of the establishing of the monastery of Bethlem, the first English house of the order of the Immaculate Conception of our B. Lady, in the suburbs of S. Anthony at Paris." 4 pp.

43. History of the foundation of the convents of English Benedictinesses at Brussels, Ghent, Cambray, and Bullen or Pontoise. In Dodd's hand. 2 pp.

44. History of the foundation of "the monastery of Grace-Dieu, of the English Benedictine Dames of Pontoise in the diocese of Rouen," to 10 Dec. 1718. 4 pp.

45. Letter from M. Tempest to her nephew M. Tempest, at Douay, giving an account of the English Benedictinesses at Paris, Aug. 15, 1718. 4 pp.

46. An enlarged "account of the Benedictines in Paris," by Bridget More, sent to Mr. Tempest. 20 pp.

47. History of the Benedictinesses of Dunkirk and Ypres, in Dodd's hand. 1 p.

48. Account, by Augustina Humberstone, of the convent of Augustinianesses at Louvaire, 5 Oct. 1718. Pr. in Archæologia, xxxvi. 74. 4 pp.

49. An account of the Poor Clares at Dunkirk. 7 pp.

50. Letter from John Colleton to Bishop Francis de Castro on the foundation of Lisbon College, Lond., 28 Sept. 1632. 2 pp.

51. "The history of the college at Rhemes," 12 pp.

52. "The beginning and progress of the monastery called Our B. Lady of Syon, Channonesses Regulier of the order of S. Austin, established in Paris A.D. 1634. 6 pp.

53. Birkead, archpriest, to F. Persons, 19 Oct. 1609. 2 pp.

54. T. Carr to . . . . upon the affairs of the Bishop of Chalcedon. 11 pp.

55. Tho. Blackloe to . . . . [address torn off], Paris, 25 Nov. 3 pp.

56. G. Muscott [to the Bishop of Chalcedon ?], Feb. 16. 3 pp.

57. Tho. Albius to the Pope. 12 pp.

58. Calvert, Lord Baltimore [to the Bishop of Chalcedon], 21 July 1642. 4 pp.

59. Dr. Leyburn [to the same], 14 Feb. 1638. 4 pp.

60. "Dr. Leyburn's character." 4 pp.

61. . . . . to . . . . on the affairs of the English College at Rome. 4 pp.

62. On the faculties of missioners into England. Injured by damp. 4 pp.

63. Notes concerning the English Chapter, in the hand of the Bishop of Chalcedon. 4 pp.

64. F. Blunt to the Bishop of Chalcedon, 7 June 1628. In the bishop's hand. 2 pp.

65. Lord Montague to the General of the Jesuits, 6 Aug. 1628. 4 pp.

66. "Status Catholicæ religionis in Anglia, 1632." 4 pp.

5.

67. "Instrumentum publicationis Bullæ sc Brevium D. Episcopi Chalcedonensis, 27 Junii 1632." 3 pp.

68. "The Chapter vindicated; collected from a MS. written before 1680, perhaps about 1670." 26 pp.

69. Wm. Watson on the ecclesiastical condition of France. 2 pp.

70. "Summarium informationis [Joannis Bennetti] de Congregatione Thomæ Worthington in Anglia." 2 pp.

71. "Copy of a letter [by M. K., i.e. Matthew Kellison] to Mr. Preston, alias Widrington," 6 June 1614. Endd., R. Widdrington, Monk. 2 pp.

72. "A copy of His Majesty's letter to the L. Archbishop of Canterbury in the behalf of a Popish priest," Tho. Green, alias Houghton, O.S.B., for some years past a prisoner in the Clink. Westm., 25 Jan. 1622. 2 pp.

73. Robert Jones to [Mr. Birkhead, the archpriest], "Bristow," 26 Sept. 4 pp.

74. "A copy of my letter to Sir John Wintoure, 11 April 1646." Endd., "My Lord Clanricarde writte this copie with his own hand, and sent it me." Loghreagh, 11 April 1646. 4 pp.

75. "A copy of Mr. Colleton's letter to His Majesty." 2 pp.

76. "Mr. Birkhead, archpriest, to Father P[ersons ?], 8 Jan. 1610. 2 pp.

77. Notes respecting the family and personal history of John Calvin; notarial copy, attested at Geneva 24 May 1612. 4 pp.

78. Two letters from Tho. Blacklow to Edward Farington, 2 and 16 Oct. [1627]. 3 pp. and 5 pp.

79. Instructions for Tho. White on going to Rome. Endd. "Mr. Blacklows when he went to Rome." 4 pp.

80. "The secret article made in the French marriage, 1624." "About Spanish and French match." 2 pp.

81. "Articles proposed by the Christian King," twelve in number, as to the exercise of the Catholic faith in England on the French match. 4 pp.

82. "Epistola encyclica de concordia Cleri cum Regularibus," embodying several other documents, 1635. 8 pp.

83. Another paper on the same subject. 2 pp.

84. The Bishop of Chalcedon to the English lay Catholics on the same subject, 16 Oct. 1627. 7 pp. and 8 pp.

85. Letters testimonial by John Colleton, Dean of the Chapter, to the fact of the kindness shown by the Queen of England towards English Catholics, Lond., 20 May 1635. 2 pp.

86. On the introduction of religious congregations or societies into England. 3 pp.

87. Letter for a vicar general, by Richard Bishop of Chalcedon, London, 6 Oct. 1629. 2 pp.

88. . . . . to "M. Antoine Perron, à Paris," 24 April 1633. 2 pp.

89. . . . . to . . . ., Lond., 12 Aug. 1660. 2 pp.

90. Mr. Lancaster to Mr. Geo. Gage, Lisbon, 23 Nov. 1637. 3 pp.

91. G[eorge] G[age] to Mr. Lancaster, 3 Oct. 1649. 2 pp.

92. Dr. Geo. Leyburne to . . . Douay, 23 June 1657. 3 pp.

93. Promise by Dr. Leyburne concerning Tho. White. 2 pp.

94. "The Yorkshire priests' rejection of Mr. Blacloe's books." 2 pp.

95. Dr. Francis Gage to . . . ., Rome, Feb. 20, 1661. 4 pp.

96. Dr. Edward Daniel to the Bishop of Chalcedon, Douay, 26 July. 2 pp.

97. Card. Barberini to Dr. Gage, Rome, 27 June 1679. 3 pp.

98. "Casus; an liceat Catholicis in Anglia uti jure patronatus," Paris, 18 kal. Dec. 1671. 3 pp.

99. Account of the condemnation of Mr. Southworth, 26 June 1654, with his speech at the place of execution. 2 pp.

100. On the oath of the students of the English College at Rome. Endd "Navarri Sententia."—"Cardinal Alan." 7 pp.

101. The Bishop of Chalcedon to Dr. John Lancaster, of Lisbon, 25 Oct. 1649. 2 pp.

102. Dr. Tho. White as to the meaning of the submission of his writings, 2 July 1657. 1 p.

103. Rules and orders of Arras College, Paris. 2 papers. 6 pp.

104. Attestation by Dr. Wright, of Antwerp, "concerning the Bishop of Spalatro his reconciliation to the Church, 1622." 2 pp.

105. "Instructions for Mr. D. Bishop and Mr. D Smith, my procurators in the conference to be had with D. Worthington." 4 pp.

106. W. C. [Mr. Cotton?] to Dr. Carier, 6 Dec. 1613, s.v. 3 pp.
107. Sir T. Lake to Dr. Carier, 1 Nov. 1613 2 pp.
108. W. Turnbull to the same, 3 Dec. 1613. 2 pp.
109. Isaac Casaubon to the same, 10 cal. Sept. 1613. 4 pp.
110. The Nuncio Apostolic to the same, 6 Sept. 1613. 4 pp.
111. Dr. Carier to Mr. Croft, 8 Sept. 1613.' 2 pp.
112. The Nuncio Apostolic to Dr. Carier, 13 Sept. 1613. 3 pp.
113. Card. Du Perron to the same, kal. Oct. 1613. 2 pp.
114. Joannes Copperus to the same, 14 Oct. 1613. 2 pp.
115. The same to the same, 21 Oct. 1613. 2 pp.
116. Cardinal Caietan to Geo. Blacwell, Rome, March 1598, with a copy of the instructions mentioned in the document.
117. Codicil to the will of Dean John Perrott, 10 Oct. 1710.

Various separate papers respecting the ecclesiastical affairs of the English Catholics. The principal are the following :—

Diploma of the Bishop of Chalcedon, confirming the erection of the English Chapter and enumerating its members, Paris, Jan. 8, 1645. Attested copy.

Narratio historica, ea summatim complectens quæ ab initio regni Elizabethæ ad religionem et jurisdictionem in Clero Anglicano ad præsentem annum 1621 declarandum spectare videntur. Auctore Joanne Bennetto, Sacerdote Anglo. Two copies.

Declaration of allegiance to His Majesty, made by the Dean and Chapter of the Catholic English clergy, 1662.

Profession of obedience of English Catholics

Petition and profession of allegiance of English Catholics, presented to King Charles II.

Notes of the English Chapter, copied from an old book in S. John's Chapel, Norwich, 25 pp.

List of the Chapter and Vicars General, 1649.

Letter of Archbishop Peter Talbot to the Roman Inquisition on the affairs of Blackloe and others, 1677.

Compendium Historicum Ecclesiæ in Anglia ab anno 500, maximæ Cleri Anglicani. The second book. About 00 pp. in small 4to In the handwriting of Dodd. It extends to A.D. 1707.

Remarks on the late review of the book of Jansenius, called Augustinus. 40 pp.

Fragment of a Latin dissertation on the Bishop of Chalcedon, and the legitimate institution of the Chapter.

List of subscriptions to the clergy fund, 1630.

The faculty of Angers to the Dean and Chapter, in commendation of their envoy, Dr. Gildon, 1644.

Various letters and papers on the proposed substitution of a provost in place of the Chapter, 1640.

The appointment by the Bishop of Chalcedon of Dr. Geo. Leyburn to a vacant canonry at the request of the Chapter, Paris, Sept. 1649.

Various letters and papers respecting Dr. Leyburn.

Papers respecting the Colleges of Lisbon and Rome.

True relation, by Anne Willoughby, an eye-witness, of the martyrdom of Hugh Green, alias Ferdinand Brook, on Friday, Aug. 19, 1642.

The entertainment of the English Ambassador at Lisbon, 1630.

Inventory of the plate, linen, ornaments, and other utensils belonging to the Queen's Chapel, with acknowledgment of receipt by Lionel Sheldon from Dr. Thomas Godden, treasurer of the said chapel, 13 May 1663.

Abbot Montague's deposition of a conference held at his lodgings in Paris between Sergeant and Dr. Peter Talbot, in 1676.

Sergeant's disclaimer of any antecedent acquaintance with Oates's Plot, 1679.

Sergeant's defence of his theological works, in a letter to Mr. Mettam.

Cardinal Paolucci to the Vicars Apostolic and the clergy of Great Britain, in commendation of their orthodoxy, 11 Feb. 1611.

Bull of Pope Clement XVIII. in favour of the Discalced Carmelites, 1604.

Letters and papers by and concerning Preston and Green, 1621, &c., with the King's pardon of Preston, 1623.

Relation of the several dependancies of the Colleges of Douay, Lisbon, and Paris upon the Chapter, about 1690.

Letter of William Harte Danby, at Lisbon, to Mr. John Hammon, on the commencement and prospects of the college at Lisbon, 1634.

Deed of gift by Edward Bennett to Lisbon College and to priests in North Wales.

Cardinal Farnese to the Archpriest Blackwell, explaining the injunction of Pope Clement VIII.

Report on the visitation of the English Seminary at Paris.

Exemplar protestationis quam 13 Sacerdotes Angli exhibuerunt Reginæ Elizabethæ, 31 Jan. 1602.

Letter from Paris to Rome (signature and address obliterated) on an apostacy in Scotland in 1623.

Pieces (various) concerning the Bishop of Chalcedon and Rudesind Barlow.

Bull of Pope Innocent VIII., 1633. Plantata.

Instructions for the English Archdeacons, 1623.

Propositions on the power of deposing and absolving.

Fragment of a dialogue on the condition and position of the English Catholic clergy, about 1667. About 20 pp.

Memorial to Cardinal Borghese (Protector of the English College at Rome) on the affairs of England, Lond., 1601. Unsigned.

Extracts from four letters by William Watson and others.

Letters of the Provincial of England as to union with the Benedictines, 7 March 1628.

Letter to Cardinal [Barberini?] in defence of Dr. Champney, against a certain agent named Michael in S. Laurence's church.

Extract from a letter by Dr. Thomas Worthington to Mr. Fitlherbert, 2 May 1611.

Memorial, in Italian, respecting the oath demanded from certain priests in England.

Bull by Pope Gregory XV., appointing William Bishop to the see of Chalcedon, 23 March 1623.

Appointment of Edward Bennett as Vicar General, 30 Aug. 1623.

Letter from Philip, Archbishop of Philippi, Vicar Apostolic in Holland, to the Bishop of Chalcedon, Utrecht, 26 July 1628.

"A brief answer to the chiefest objections which some regulars make against demanding of the Bishop of Chalcedon his approbation." 6 pp. folio.

An argument in behalf of the Bishop of Chalcedon. 40 pp., 4to.

Summary of the arguments in favour of the Chapter, with answers to objections, apparently in Sergeant's hand.

Nomina presbyterorum in Anglia qui Episcopos cupiunt.

Another list, seemingly of later date, classed according to districts.

Epistola Episcopi Chalcedonensis ad Summum Pontificem, Paris, 30 May 1632.

Stephen Gough to Bishop Smith, explaining the design of the ecclesiastical congregation which he had established, and asking for associates.

Letters from certain of the Chapter to their brethren and to the Bishop, 13 Nov. 1649.

Letter from John Warham to Bishop Smith.

English translation of the declaration of Cardinal Mellini. Much defaced.

Letters between William Herbert and J. H. Hasselwood, 4 Sept. 1653.

Copy by Father Persons of letters of Cardinal Cajetan, Protector of England, to the president and visitors of the College of Douay, Sept. 1599.

Correspondence between .... Blackfan and William Newman, Madrid, 1622.

Letters patent of Louis XIII. for the establishment of the English ecclesiastical community at the College De Tournay, Dec. 1642.

The superiors of the College of Douay to the clergy, asking for assistance, 14 Aug. 1621.

Two letters from the Archpriest George Blackwell, the former dated Nov. 4, the latter 7 July 1607, from the Gatehouse.

The conditions of the marriage between the Prince of Wales and the Infanta of Spain ; from the Spanish.

Letter from Gregory XV. to the Prince of Wales, April 1623, with the reply of the Prince to the Nuncio who brought it.

The answer of the Prince to the Pope's letter.

F. R. Cavandolz (?) to .... on the reception which the Prince met with in Spain. London, 8 April 1623.

Warrant by King James to certain of his Council to grant pardon and dispensation to Catholics to use their religion.

The Keeper of the Great Seal of England to the judges, Westm. 12 Aug. 1622.

Two letters to Bishop Smith, the former dated Lond., 7 Sept. 1631, the latter without date or signature.

Letter of William Carr (at Rome) to Bishop Smith, 29 June 1641.

Acknowledgment by Card. Barberini of the receipt of a letter from Mark Harrington, Rome, 16 April 1656.

Card. Barberini to Edward Courtenay, rector of the English College at Rome, 29 Dec. 1688.

The principal end contemplated by Arras College in Paris, 28 April 1612.

Account of Chelsea "College of Controversies," designed by Dean Sutcliffe.

Letter of the Bishop of Ossory to the Bishop of Chalcedon, 6 Dec. 1628.

Various papers and letters respecting the acts of the Bishop and the Dean and Chapter.

Letters patent of the Bishop of Chalcedon for Geo. Gage as Vicar General, and Ric. Maurice, Archdeacon of Oxford, Bucks and Berks, Paris, 9 June 1649.

Two letters, probably by Sergeant, 12 Aug. 1656, and 30 Aug. [1690 ?]

The Internuncio at Brussels to Dr. Ellis, 28 Aug. 1660.

Packet of about 20 letters, chiefly to Mr. Metam, probably in 1649, 1650.

Five letters from R. Clark to Wm. Herbert, F. Hoard, &c. No year or place.

Letter of the Provincial of the Recollets, Douay, 8 April 1661.

About 45 letters from Dr. Gage, agent of the Chapter at Rome, to John Holland, secretary, 1659-1661.

Letter from P. Fitton to Mark Harrington, Florence, Sept. 1656.

Letter from Card. Capponi to the subdean, 1656.

Letter from Geo. Leyburn, 13 Dec. 1657.

Four letters from the Nuncio at Paris, 1659, 1660.

Letters from the Internuncio at Brussels to the Chapter, and to John Holland, 1660.

Draft of a memorial to the Pope, 1661.

Letters to and from . . . ,Lesley, at Rome, 1668.

Holt's account of his agency at Rome, 1667-1669.

Short narrative (anonymous) of several agencies at Rome.

Letters from and to the Internuncio at Brussels.

Letter from the Cardinal Protector constituting the Internuncio Ordinary of England, 1667.

Letter from Peter Peterson to Geo. Leyburn.

Letter in reply from Geo. Leyburn to his rev. brethren, 25 June 1667.

Papers concerning the English College at Lisbon, and of the grant made to the same by the Queen Dowager, 1672, 1685.

A true narrative of the imprisonment and trial of David Lewis, dated Uske Prison, April 24, 1679. 12 pp. folio.

Account of the death of Mr. Philip Evans and Mr. John Lloyd at Cardiff, 22 July 1679. 3 pp.

Letters patent of Mark Harrington, subdean, appointing Tho. Barker to be Archdeacon of Somersetshire, &c., 8 May 1657.

Letters patent for Christopher Banks to be Vicar General of Yorkshire and the northern counties, 4 July 1667.

Letters patent for John Leyburn to be a canon, 4 March 1668.

Chronological account of the establishment of the Benedictine Nuns at Brussels, from 1598 to 1718.

Abbess Mary Knatchbull's account of the establishment of the Benedictine Dames at Ghent.

A volume in large folio, consisting of 492 pages closely written in a minute hand by the author, the Rev. Hugh Tootle, alias Dodd, to which he has prefixed the following title :—

"An historical and critical dictionary, comprising the lives of the most eminent Catholicks from the year 1500 to 1688 ; being a complete history of the clergy, regulars, and laymen of that persuasion, who for the two last centuries have distinguished themselves at home or abroad by their piety, learning, or military ability ; particularly of their writers, with a distinct account of their works and those of their adversaries, and explanatory notes, clearing many obscure parts of the English Church history ; the lives of the bishops and clergy deprived upon the Reformation ; those that deserted the Church of Rome, those that were temporisers during the struggle of the two parties ; with an account of those that suffered on the score of religion, or for attempts against the Government, affording many particulars relating to their lives, trials, and execution. Together with the foundation of all the colleges and monasteries abroad, the date of their establishment, and founders' lives, of both sexes ; besides a full and distinct account of the breach with Rome, the divorce, supremacy, dissolution of monasteries, and seeds of the Reformation under Henry VIII., its confused state under Edward VI., opposition it met with under Queen Mary, and last hand put to it by Queen Elizabeth ; the various

fortunes of the Catholic cause during the reigns of King James I., King Charles I. and II., and King James II. supported by a curious collection of original papers and letters never before made publick, and carried on with due regard to the parties and passions which divide mankind."

As might be expected, this work has much in common with Dodd's Church History, published in three volumes folio in 1737. His name nowhere appears in the present compilation. Prefixed are "The author's apologetic preface," "A catalogue of the books, &c. made use of by the author," and six commendatory letters addressed to the author by foreign ecclesiastics in the years 1718 and 1719. The present volume extends no further than the end of the biographies beginning with the letter L.

The following are the more important of the original authorities referred to above and quoted in the present volume. Their value is considerably enhanced by the fact that since these transcripts were made by Dodd several of the originals, then at Douai in the English College, have perished in the first French Revolution :—

1. A proclamation for banishing the English out of the town of Douai, 1578.

2. A petition of the English College at Douai to the magistrates . . . upon the above order, 1578.

3. The Bishop of Chalcedon's approbation of the regulars' faculties, 1627.

4. Mr. Smith's account of Lord Castlehaven.

5. Grant to Dr. Wm. Allen and the English College at Douai by Pope Gregory XIII., A.D. 1575.

6. Indult by Pope Gregory XIII. to Dr. Allen, Dr. Lewis, and Dr. Stapleton, 1578.

7. Brief of Pope Sixtus V. to Card. Allen for the government of the English College at Douai, 1587.

8. Letter of Card. Guise to Dr. Allen, 25 April 1578.

9. Letter of the magistrates of Douai in favour of the English College on its removal to Rheims, 23 April 1578.

10. Dr. Allen's letter to Dr. Vendeville, counsellor to the King of Spain and Bishop of Tournay, 27 July 1578.

11. J. B. Campeggio, Bishop of Majorca, to Card. Allen, 6 Nov., Dec. 1582.

12. Order of King James I. to the Lord Keeper in favour of his Catholic subjects.

13. Letter written by order of the Pope's Nuncio in Paris to the Bishop of Chalcedon, 5 Mar. 1629.

14. Card. Allen to Dr. Richard Barrett, rector of the English College at Douai, 30 Oct. 1588.

15. Card. Caietan, Protector of England, to Dr. Richard Barrett, March 7, 1598.

16. "A common letter of Abbot Mountague, &c. to Dr. Leyburn, concerning Mr. Tho. White."

17. "The secret article of the marriage between England and France in 1624."

18. "Subscription of several clergymen against Mr. White's doctrine."

19. The Lord Keeper's letter to the judges, London, 12 Aug. 1622.

20. Bull for the consecration of Dr. Bishop as Bishop of Chalcedon, 1622.

21. Pope Urban VIII. to Queen Henrietta Maria on her marriage with Charles I.

22. M. de Cararolet (?), almoner to the Spanish Ambassador in London, to Dr. Kellison, president of the English College at Douai, concerning the reception of Prince Charles at the Court of Spain, 8 April 1623.

23. F. Rudisind Barlow, president of the English Benedictines at Douai, to Dr. Wm. Bishop, Bishop of Chalcedon, 15 June 1623.

24. F. Leander de S. Martino, prior of the English Benedictines at Douai, to the same, Aug. 1623.

25. F. Joseph de S. Martino, Provincial of the Benedictines of the province of Canterbury, to the same, 26 Oct. 1623.

26. Don Carlo Colanno, Ambassador of Spain in England, to Card. Mellino, 2 June 1624.

27. "The security agreed of for the quiet of Catholics, 1623."

28. John Colleton to King James I. concerning Dr. Kellison's book.

29. The conditions of the marriage between the Prince of Wales and the Infanta of Spain.

30. Dr. A. Champney, Dean of the Chapter, to the clergy, missioners, &c., concerning prayers for the King, 1636.

31. A discourse between King James II. and Sir Edward Hales, at S. German's, concerning the Test, 2 June 1693.

32. A speech of Andrew Bromich, designed to be his last at the place of execution.

33. Letter of Mr. Birkett, the archpriest, on his death-bed, to the superiors of the Jesuits, 3 April 1614.

34. W. Trumbul to Dr. Carrier Brussels, 1613.

35. The Papal Nuncio at Liege to Dr. Carrier, 6 Sept. 1613.

36. Isaac Casaubon to Dr. Carrier, 10 kal. Sept. 1613.

37. Sir T. Lake to Dr. Carrier, 1 Nov. 1613.

38. Card. Du Perron to Dr. Carrier, 1 Oct. 1613.

39. The Papal Nuncio to Dr. Carrier, 13 Sept. 1613.

40. Dr. Carrier to the Archbishop of Canterbury, 25 May 1614.

41. Dr. Carrier to Mr. C[onstable?], 3 Sept. 1613.

42. Card. du Perron to Dr. Carrier, 1614.

43. Ferdinand, Archbishop and Elector of Cologne, to Dr. Carrier, 14 Feb. 1614.

44. Franciscus Florentinus, rector of the Jesuit's College at Liege, to Dr. Carrier, 15 April 1614.

45. An English Capuchin in Cologne to Dr. Carrier, 5 Feb. 1614.

46. Six letters from F. J. Copper, rector of the Jesuits' College in Cologne, to Dr. Carrier, Oct. and Dec. 1613, and Jan. and Feb. 1614.

47. F. John Blackfan, prefect of the English Mission in Spain, to Mr. Wm. Newman, 7 Aug. 1621.

48. Wm. Newman's answer to the above, 14 Aug. 1621.

49. F. Blacfan's reply to the above, 21 Aug. 1621.

50. Wm. Newman's answer to the preceding letter, 28 Aug. 1621.

51. Testimonial letter in favour of Queen Henrietta Maria, by the Dean and Chapter, 20 May 1635.

52. Pope Innocent XI. to King James II., 16 Aug. 1687.

53. King James II. in answer to the above, 29 Sept. 1687.

54. Pope Innocent XI. in reply, 22 Nov. 1687.

55. King James II. in answer, 22 Dec. 1687.

56. Pope Innocent XI. in reply, 14 Feb. 1688.

57. Information of John Colleton, vice-archpriest, concerning regulars.

58. Mr. Birkett, archpriest, to F. Persons, 8 Jan. 1610.

59. Cardinal Howard to Alex. Hoult, 10 April 1680.

60. J. S[ergeant] to Dr. Godden, 17 April 1679. (Extract.)

61. Card. Barberini to Dr. Francis Gage, 27 June 1679.

62. Resolution by the theologians of Paris on the question, Whether it is lawful for the Catholics in England to use the right of patronage? 1671.

63. James II. to Pope Innocent XI., 19 March 168$\frac{6}{7}$.

64. Pierre Louis de Ruite on the presentation by the King of England to bishopricks in England, Ireland and Scotland, 16 Oct. 1688.

65. Geo. Leyburn's letter on Mr. White's submission, 23 June 1657.

66. The Earl of Westmorland and Lord Dacre to Dr Wm. Allen, 5 March 1583.

67. Petition of the students of the English College at Rome to Lewis Owen.

68. Brief of Gregory XV. for the erection of the English College at Lisbon, 22 Sept. 1622.

69. Instrument for the erection of the English Chapter by Wm. Bishop, Bishop of Chalcedon, 10 Sept. 1623.

70. Protestation of allegiance of thirteen priests to Queen Elizabeth, 31 Jan. 1602.

71. Mr. Peter Fitton's letter concerning the administration of the English College at Rome, 3 July 1623.

72. The decree of the Congregation de Propaganda Fide upon the preceding epistle, 17 April 1624.

73. Tho. Goldwell, Bishop of S. Asaph, to Dr. Wm. Allen, Rome, 17 April 1581.

74. "A short politic discourse concerning the attempts " of the Kings of Spain and Scotland in relation to the " Crown of England," towards the end of the reign of Queen Elizabeth.

75. A letter testimonial of Dr. Owen Lewis, Bishop of Cossano, relating to Mary Queen of Scots, 6 kal. Mar. 1590.

76. Sir F. Englefield to Dr. Allen, president of the English College at Rheims. Madrid, 4 Sept. 1581.

77. Dr. Owen Lewis to Dr. Allen, Rome, 10 March 1579.

78. Account of Antonius de Dominis, Archbishop of Spalatro, by Dr. John Wright, 13 June 1622.

79. Wm. Singleton to Fr. Ffloyd at Lisbon, 7 April 1609.

80. Protestation by Card. Allen and Owen Lewis, Bishop of Cassano, Rome, prid. non. Maii, 1591.

81. Memorial to Pope Paul V. by Dr. Wm. Harrison, archpriest, and his twelve assistants London, 20 Dec. 1619.

82. Breve Papæ Gregorii XIV. ad Cardinalem Alanum, Rome, 18 Sept. 1591.

83. Breve Gregorii Papæ XIII. in favorem Collegii Rhemensis Anglorum.

84. Supplication of several priests in Newgate prison to Pope Paul V.

85. Brief of Pope Gregory XIII. in favour of the exiled English nobles, Rome, 15 April 1575.

86. Decree against certain books of Roger Widrington, 16 March 1614.

87. Extract from the records of the English College at Douai on the visitation of 1626.

87a. Cardinal Cajetan, Protector, to Dr. Worthington, id. Sept. 1599. (Extract.)

88. Dr. Maurice Clenock on the origin of the disturbances of the English College at Rome.

89. Dr. Cesar Clement to Dr. Kellison, 26 June 1616. (Extract.)

90. F. Joseph Creswell to Dr. Worthington, Madrid, 30 Aug. (Extract.)

91. Extract from the decrees of the Congregation de Propaganda Fide. 6 Oct. 1695, and 25 Sept. 1696.

92. Declaration of several English clergymen against the oath of supremacy, 1 June 1679.

93. Form of a license for taking degrees, granted by Dr. Hyde.

94. Form of matriculation in the Academy of Douai.

95. Order of Cardinal Barberini, Protector, against the undue exercise of faculties in England, 7 Dec. 1669.

96. Dr. Tho. Godden to a friend in Paris on the oath of allegiance, 13 May 1674.

97. Testimonial of Cardinal Bandini to Peter Fitton, 4 May 1624.

98. Patent by Cardinal Barberini to Dr. Francis Gage for the presidentship of Douai College. Rome, 25 June 1676.

99. State of the controversy between the University of Douai and the English College.

100. Letters testimonial in favour of Gregorio Panzani, Rome, 1 May 1634.

101. King James II. to Pope Innocent XI., Windsor, 16 June 1687.

102. "Certain heads set down in writing by some Catholic gentlemen and presented to Gregorio Panzani, 16 May 1635." (Extracts.)

103. Gregorio Panzani to John Jennings, provincial of the English Franciscans, 2 cal. Feb. 1634.

104. King James I. to the Archbishop of Canterbury, Jan. 25, 1622.

105. The Cardinal of Lorraine to Dr. Kellison.

106. Dr. Kellison to King James I.

107. Agreement between the English secular clergy and the Benedictines, &c.

108. Gregorio Panzani to F. Ric. Blond [Blount], provincial of the English Jesuits, 28 Nov. 1635.

109. F. Richard Blond to Gregorio Panzani, 4 Dec. 1635.

110. The same to the same, 16 Jan. 1635.

111. The same (general notification), 25 Nov. 1635.

112. Pope Urban VIII. in favour of Gregorio Panzani, 10 Oct. 1634.

A volume in large folio, consisting of 210 pages, closely written in a minute hand by Dodd, containing an Appendix of Documents illustrative of the Biographical Dictionary mentioned above.

The more important papers are the following, all of which are stated to have been transcribed by Dodd from the originals preserved in Douai College, or elsewhere, when he wrote.

Of these the more important are the following :—

1. F. Robert Persons to Edw. and John Bennett, 20 Sept., 18 Oct. 1597.

2. The same to Mr. Salvin [Birket], 23 Aug. 1608.

3. The same to the same, 21 Aug. 1608.

4. The same to the same, 5 July 1608.

5. The same to the same, 12 Oct. 1608.

6. The same to the same, 13 Sept. 1608.

7. The same to the same, 4 Sept. 1608.

8. The same to Mr. Chamberlain [Birkhead], 18 May 1608.

9. The same to Geo. Salvin, 26 Nov. 1608.

10. The same to the same, 4 Oct. 1608.

11. The same to Matthew Kellison, 26 April 1608.

12. The same to Geo. Salvin, 31 May 1608.

13. The same to the same, 2 May 1609.
14. The same to the same, 6 June 1609.
15. The same to the same, 14 March 1609.
16. The same to the same, 4 July 1609.
17. The same to the same, 15 Sept. 160⁹
18. The same to the same, 16 Sept. 1609.
19. The same to the same, 25 July 1609.
20. The same to the same, 4 July 1609.
21. The same to the same, 14 Feb. 1609.
22. The same to the same, 6 June 1609.·
23. The same to the same, 30 Oct. 1609.
24. The same to the same, 6 Mar. 1610.
25. The same to the same, 20 Mar. 1610.
26. The same to the same, 7 April 1610.
27. T. Swinnerton [Thomas Fitzherbert], agent for
the English secular clergy in Rome, to Mr. Chamberlain, 18 May 1608.
28. The same to Geo. Salvin, 31 May 1608.
29. The same to the same, 15 June 1608.
30. The same to the same, 21 June 1608.
31. The same to Dr. Worthington, 2 Aug. 1608.
32. The same to Geo. Salvin, 23 Aug. 1608.
33. The same to Dr. Worthington, 6 Sept. 1608.
34. The same to Geo. Salvin, 4 Oct. 1608.
35. The same to the same. 11 Oct. 1608.
36. The same to Dr. Worthington. 7 Mar. 1609.
37. The same to Geo. Birkhead, Archpriest of England, 23 May 1609.
38. The same to Geo. Salvin, 27 June 1609.
39. The same to Dr. Worthington, 22 Aug. 1609.
40. The same to Geo. Salvin, 19 Sept. 1609.
41. The same to the same, 31 Oct. 1609.
42. The same to the same, 21 Nov. 1609.
43. The same to the same, 6 Feb. 1610.
44. The same to the same, 18 June 1610.
Appended are the following lists :—
1. Remarkable occurrences from 1501 to 1702.
2. English colleges and convents abroad, with the
date of their foundation, 1559-1692.
3. English cardinals.
4. Presidents of Douai College, 1594-1714.
5. Archpriests, 1613-1622.
6. Deans of the Chapter, 1635-1676.
7. Bishops who opposed the Reformation.
8. Deans, archdeacons, and chancellors.
9. Heads and fellows of colleges, prebendaries, &c.
10. Lists of persons executed on account of the King's
spiritual supremacy ; for plots, real or pretended ; for
receiving orders abroad ; for being reconciled to the
Church of Rome ; for entertaining or assisting priests
convicted ; and of persons condemned to die on the aforesaid accounts, but who were either pardoned or died in
prison ; 1535-1681.
11. Lists of Catholic officers and gentlemen, volunteers, who lost their lives in defence of the King's cause
during the Civil War.
12. List of Catholics to whom King Charles II. committed himself upon his retreat to Boscobel, 3 Sept. 1661.
13. List of eminent secular priests who entered into
religious orders.
14. List of papers quoted in the three volumes of the
Biographical Dictionary.
A volume in folio, consisting of 320 pp., containing
original letters and papers, of which the more important
are the following :—
Report to the Cardinals of the Congregation of the
Holy Office respecting the cause of the English Benedictines, A.D. 1608, p. 1.
Various papers respecting the same subject, Valadolid, 18 Sept. 1603, p. 7.
Testimonial respecting John Crouder a priest of the
English College of Valadolid, signed by about 20 priests
and scholars, p. 13.
Various papers respecting the proceedings of George
Birkhead, archpriest, in 1609, p. 17.
Two original letters on the same subject, 22 and 30
March 1609, p. 23.
Dr. Wm. Singleton to Father Floyd, at Lisbon, 9 April
1609, p. 27.
Dr. Birkhead, archpriest, to Richard Smith, his agent
at Rome, 2 May 1609, p. 32.
Letter, without signature and address, on the affairs
of Douay College, 6 May 1609, p. 34.
Cardinal Blanchetti to Geo. Birkhed, 6 May 1609,
p. 36.
Joseph Creswell to Dr. Smith at Rome, 9 May, 1609,
p. 38.
Edward Farington to Dr. Smith, 10 May 1609,
p. 40.
William Denton to Richard Baker, 14 May 1609,
p. 42.

George Salvine to Richard Baker, 16 May 1609,
p. 44.
—— to ——, 17 May, p. 47.
—— to Richard Baker, 5 June 1609, p. 49.
Fragment of a letter, without address or signature,
endd. 10 June 1609, p. 51.
J. Rs. [Mush ?] to Richard Smith, 19 June 1609,
p. 53.
Ed. Farington to D. S. [24 June 1609], p. 55.
Geo. Salvine to Richard Smith, 25 June 1609, p. 57.
William Denton to the same, 18 June, p. 59.
George Salvin to the same, 4 July 1609, p. 63.
The same to the same, 9 July 1609, p. 65.
The same to the same, 6 July 1609, p. 67.
Anthony Viscount Montacute to the same, þrid.
nonas Julii 1609, p. 71.
—— to the same, 11 July, p. 73.
Ed. Farington to the same, 12 July 1609, p. 75.
George Salvine to the same, two letters, 18 June and
20 July 1609, pp. 77, 79.
J. Bosevile to the same, 26 July 1609, p. 81.
George Salvine to the same, three letters, July 30 and
Aug. 2, 1609, pp. 83, 85, 87.
Anthony Viscount Montacute to the same, 4 nonas
Aug. 1609, p. 91.
Anthony Champney to the same, 2 Aug. 1609, p. 93.
Indulgences granted by Pope Paul V. at the instance
of the Lady Lucretia Lingani Gattinari, Countess of
Castro. &c., 10 Sept. 1609, p. 97.
Dr. Bagshaw to Mr. Moore, 4 Aug. 1609, p. 101.
·Dr. Bishop to ——, p. 107.
George Salvine to ——, 9 Aug. 1609, p. 111.
Matthew Holmes to Dr. Richard Smith, 9 Aug. 1609,
p. 113,
Anthony Champney to the same, 14 Aug. 1609,
p. 119.
George Salvine to Richard Baker, 18 Aug. 1609,
p. 121.
B. N. to ——, 28 Aug. 1609, p. 125.
G. West to " Mr. Ben." 4 Sept. 1610, p. 127.
W. Denton to Mr. Baker, 4 Sept. 1609, p. 129.
E. Farington to Tho. West, two letters, 10 Sept.
1609, pp. 133 and 135.
Geo. Salvine to Richard Baker, two letters, 17 Sept.
1609, and 20 Aug. 1609, pp. 137 and 141.
Wm. Bishop and five others to Cardinal Bianchetto,
21 Sept. 1609, p. 145.
Tho. More to Dr. Richard Smith, 23 Sept. 1609,
p. 149.
Several letters of George Salvin to Richard Baker, in
October 1609, p. 151.
Extract from a letter of Father Walpole, 15 Oct.,
from Madrid, p. 179.
W. W. to Mr. Ireland, p. 181.
A. M. to ——, 24 June, p. 183.
Owen Lewis to F. Thomas Moore, p. 187.
Dr. Smith to the Pope, Jan. 1610 and Oct. 1609,
p. 197.
Jo. Bennett to Richard Baker, 19 Oct. 1609,
p. 201.
Anthony Champney to Dr. Smith, 16 Oct. 1609,
p. 204.
George Salvine to Richard Baker, 30 Oct. 1609,
p. 206.
Tho. More to the same, 31 Oct. 1609, p. 208.
Jo. Mush and seven others to Geo. Birkhed, 2 Nov.
1609, p. 211.
[W.] Denton to Mr. Baker, 10 Nov. 1609, p. 213.
Ed. Farington to Dr. Smith, two letters, 12 Nov.
1609, pp. 217 and 219.
Geo. Salvine to Mr. Richard Baker, 14 Nov. 1609,·
p. 221.
The same to Dr. Smith, 24 Nov. 1609, p. 223.
John Redman to the same, 24 Nov. 1609, p. 225.
Dr. Matthew Kellison to the same, 28 Nov. 1609,
p. 227.
Geo. Salvine to Richard Baker, 22 Dec. 1609, p. 229.
Robert Pett to Tho. More, 20 Dec. 1610, p. 233.
Anthony Champney to ——, 22 Dec. 1609, p. 235.
Geo. Salvine to Richard Baker, two letters, 2 Dec.
1609, pp. 237 and 239.
G. West to ——, 1 Dec. 1609, p. 241.
Anthony Champney to Dr. Smith, two letters, 10 Dec.
1609 and 25 Jan. 1610, pp. 243 and 245.
George Salvin to Richard Baker, 18 Jan. 1610, p. 247.
Fran. More to Tho. More, 21 Jan. 1610, p. 251.
Geo. Salvine to Richard Baker, 8 Jan. 1610, p. 253.
John Redman to Richard Smith, 8 Jan. 1610,
·257.
Geo. Salvine to Richard Baker, 5 Jan. 1610, p. 259.

Hierome Heth and P. Ramirez to Dr. Smith, 24 Jan. 1610, p. 261.

Hierome Heth to the same, 20 Feb. 1610, p. 263.

The same and Peter Ramirez to Tho. Heath, 5 Feb. 1610, p. 265.

F. Augustin de S. Juan to Dr. Smith, 3 Mar. 1610, p. 269.

Anthony Champney to Dr. Smith, two letters, 9 and 15 Mar. 1610, pp. 271 and 275.

Balthazar Northe to the same, 13 Mar., p. 273.

Matthew Kellison to the same, 31 Mar. 1610, p. 277.

Geo. Salvine to the same, three letters, April 3 and 11, pp. 279, 283, and 287.

F. Augustin de S. Juan to the same, Passion Sunday 1610, p. 291.

Geo. Salvine to the same, two letters, 23 April and 4 May 1610, pp. 293 and 301.

Ed. Farington and [William] Denton to the same, 2 May [1610], p. 297.

Morgan Clenock and five others to the Pope, 1 June 1610, p. 305.

Geo. Salvine to Richard Baker, two letters, June 10, July 2, 1610, pp. 309 and 315.

Tho. Allen to ——, 3 Dec. 1610, p. 313.

Anthony Champney to Dr. Smith, 6 July 1610, p. 319.

—— to Tho. More, 18 July 1610, p. 322.

Gabriel de S. Maria to Dr. Smith, 22 July 1610, p. 323.

JOSEPH STEVENSON.

PAPERS in the CUSTODY of the RIGHT REV. DR. MANNING, ARCHBISHOP of WESTMINSTER.

The papers described in the following Catalogue form a portion of the extensive series of documents connected with the Catholic affairs of England, which are at this time in the custody of His Grace the Archbishop of Westminster. Although coming from various sources, a large proportion of them naturally has reference to the ecclesiastical affairs of the London District. The portion here catalogued forms about one-half of the entire collection, exclusive of such documents as, from their subject matter, are of a private character.

I have to acknowledge with gratitude my thanks to His Grace for the liberal access which he afforded me to his valuable collection.

A volume in folio, marked E.F. containing original letters and papers, of which the more important are the following :—

1. Extracts from the letters of the Archpriest and others relating to the English persecution, 30 May, 8 June, 1 June, 1611, and from memorials of 4 June and 20 Sept. 1612, p. 1.

2. The Nuncio in France to Wm. [Bishop] Bishop of Chalcedon, Paris, Ides July, 1623, p. 13.

3. [Wm. Bishop] Bishop of Chalcedon, to Cardinal Ubaldini, Lond., 10 Sept. 1623, p. 21.

4. The same to Card. Mellini, Lond., Ides Sept. 1623, p. 23.

5. The same to the Card. S. Susanna, Lond., Ides Sept. 1623, p. 25.

6. The same to Card. Bandini, Lond., 16 Sept. 1623, p. 27.

7. The same to Card. Ludovisi, Lond., 28 Mar. 1624, p. 29.

8. The same to the Pope, Lond., 15 Sept. 1623, p. 31.

9. The same to P. de Berulle, 17 Sept., 1623, p. 33.

10. [Lord Montague] to Dr. Bishop, 1 Aug. 1623, p. 35.

11. Extract from the letters of the Bishop of Chalcedon, 5 Dec. 1623, p. 37.

12. Brief of Pope Gregory XV. to the same, 23 Mar. 1623, p. 39.

13. The Bishop of Chalcedon to the Pope, Lond., 15 Jan. 1624, p. 43.

14. The same to Card. Ludovisi, Lond., 19 Feb. 1624, p. 45.

15. The same to Card. Farnese, Lond. 22 Feb., p. 47.

16. The same to the Pope, Lond., 22 March 1624, p. 49.

17. The English Clergy to the same, Lond., 12 Mar. 1624, p. 49*.

18. The Bishop of Chalcedon to Card. Barbarini, Lond., 1 April 1624, p. 51.

18. Card. Farneso to the Bishop of Chalcedon, Parma, 16 June 1624, p. 53.

19. Instructions for Tho. Rant, agent of the English Clergy in the Court of Rome, p. 57.

20. The Bishop of Chalcedon to F. Rant, 14 Sept. 1623, p. 61.

21. The same to the same, [25 Sept. 1623] p. 63.

22. The same to the same, 25 Nov. 1623, p. 67.

23. The same to the same, 18 Dec. 1623, p. 71.

24. The same to Tho. Harpur and five others, Lond., 29 Dec. 1623, p. 73.

25. The same to Tho. Rant, 29 Dec. 1623, p. 73*.

26. The same to the same, 15 Jan. 1624, p. 75.

27. The same to the same, 27 Jan. 1624, p. 77.

28. The same to the same, 12 Feb. 1624, p. 79.

29. The same to the same, 6 Feb. 1624, p. 81.

30. The same to the same, 22 Feb. [1624], p. 85.

31. The same to the same, 5 March 1624, p. 87.

32. The same to the same, 12 March 1624.

33. Wm. Parker [i.e. Tho. Rant] to the same, 26 March 1624, p. 93.

34. The Bishop of Chalcedon to the same, 2 April 1624, p. 95.

35. Narrative of the life, sickness, and death of Wm. Bishop, Bishop of Chalcedon, p. 97.

36. Letter by a Secular priest to a Regular, 27 April 1627, p. 103.

37. Letters of the Bishop of Chalcedon, 7 Feb. 1627, p. 107.

38. Portion of a treatise on the question between the Bishop of Chalcedon and the Regulars, p. 109.

39. Various papers concerning the same question, 1628, 1629, p. 121.

40. The Marquis of Winchester to the Bishop of Chalcedon, p. 141.

41. "The advice of a nobleman, 16 Aug. 1629," p. 143.

42. F. Leonard, Capuchin, to the Bishop of Chalcedon, 24 July 1630, p. 145.

43. Various papers touching the episcopal authority of the same bishop, pp. 149, 183, 199.

44. Certain heads offered by some of the Catholic nobility of England to Gregorio Panzani, 15 May 1635, p. 165.

45. The Lay Catholics of England against "A Declaration" set forth in their name, p. 175.

46. Dr. Bavent to his brother, 8 Sept. 1611, p. 251.

47. Pope Clement VIII. to Anthony [Browne] Viscount Montague, 5 Feb. 1603. Orig. on vellum. p. 255.

48. The same to the same, confirming certain privileges, 13 Feb. 1603, p. 257.

49. Three letters, viz., to the Cardinals of the Sacred Office, to Fr. Card. Barbarini, and to Card. Magalotti, in 1627, pp. 263, 289.

50. "A true judgment by T. M., a Catholic gentleman, of a certain letter sent by a few lay Catholics to the Bishop of Chalcedon," p. 265.

51. Anthony Maria [Browne] Viscount Montague, to Dr. Kellison, " a lecto meo," 8 Feb. 1627, p. 267.

52. " Don David forbid the house by my Lord Montague]," 1 Feb. 1627, p. 269.

53. Statement by Anthony Maria [Browne, Viscount] Montague, respecting a letter burnt by him, 31 Dec. 1627, p. 271.

54. The same to the Bishop of Chalcedon, Lond., 27 Nov. 1627, p. 273.

55. The Lord Arundell to Viscount Montague, 29 Nov. 1627, p. 273.

56. The Viscount Montague to [Muzio Vitelleeci] General of the Jesuits, 8 Id. Aug. 1628, pp. 275, 319.

57. Pope Alexander VII., conferring certain privileges on the Chapel of Francis Brown, Viscount Montague, Rome, 13 Jan. 1660, p. 280.

58. David [Preston] monk and dean of Monte Cassino, to the Viscount Montague, Lond., 8 cal. Feb. 1628, p. 281.

59. The Viscount Montague to the above-mentioned David, 30 Jan. 1628, p. 283.

60. The same to Fr. Cardinal Barberini, Lond. 4 non. Aug. 1628, p. 285.

61. The same to the Cardinals of the Holy Office, Lond. 4 non. Aug. 1628, p. 287.

62. The same to [Cardinal Barberini ?] 26 Oct. 1628, p. 307.

63. The same to the Pope, London, festival of St. James, 1629. Holograph. p. 323.

64. The same to the same, Lond., 5 cal. Aug. 1628, p. 325.

65. Answer of the same " to the first and last paragraphs of the letter of a nameless author covered " under the letters A. B., and under the title of a " Reverend Priest, written A.D. 1628," p. 329.

A volume in folio, in blue paper boards, lettered " Miscellanea, I., II., III.. Dr., Poynter." The more important of its contents are the following, all of which are originals or contemporary copies.

1. "Relatio status religionis Catholicæ in Anglia, ex "variis litteris tam reverendissimi archipresbyteri "quam aliorum." The first of these refers to the dispatch to Durham of the Princess Arabella, from a letter dated 17 March, 17 pp.

2. "Relatio brevis de præsenti statu Missionis in "Anglia," 1700, 16 pp.

3. Various memorials and other documents connected with the history of the Catholic faith in England, p. 37.

4. Extracts "ex Apologia hierarchiæ Ecclesiæ Angli-"canæ," p. 45.

5. "Thoughts concerning a Procurator at Rome for "the Bishops and Clergy of England, 1696, p. 57.

6. Instructions for Dr. Witham in 1700, p. 73.

7. Instructions for Father Martin concerning the English Mission, A.D. 1718, Ital., p. 77.

8. Respecting F. Hall, a Franciscan missionary in Warwickshire, in 1735, Ital., p. 81.

9. Letter of John Bishop of Thespis to the Congregation of the Propaganda, 6 May 1718, p. 85.

10. On the condition of the Catholics in England, July 1718, Ital., p. 97.

11. Representation to the Pope as to the distressed condition of the English Catholics, p. 107.

12. "The business which remains to be done" for the alleviation of the Catholics in England in 1688, p. 115.

14. Decretum concordiæ super negotia Angliæ, 29 Maii 1695, p. 119.

14. Proceedings before the Cardinals, 5 Sept. 1685, p. 127.

15. Memorialia pro formandis Brevibus porrigenda Card. Albano, p. 131.

16. Brevis informatio circa statum Cleri Secularis in Missione Anglicana, 1737, p. 139.

17. Decreta Congregationis de Propaganda Fide super rebus Angliæ, 25 Sept. 1696, p. 143.

18. Pastoralis Epistola quatuor Episcoporum Catholicorum ad Catholicos laicos Angliæ, A.D. 1688, p. 147.

19. Cardinal Howard to the Pope, 11 June 1694, Ital., p. 155.

20. Quædam observanda spectantia ad regimen Ecclesiæ Anglicanæ, A.D. 1695, p. 159.

21. On the case of the order of the Benedictines in England, p. 163.

22. Measures suggested on the persecution of the Catholics in England in 1717, p. 177.

23. Credential letters for Rev. Geo. Witham, going to Rome, 20 Oct. 1694, p. 187.

24. A paper on the ecclesiastical affairs of England, presented to Card. Albani, 12 Aug. 1695, Ital., p. 189.

25. Agreement between the Vicars Apostolic of England and the Benedictines, 1695, p. 193.

26. Brief of Pope Innocent XII., in favor of the Vicars Apostolic of England, 5 Oct. 1696, p. 197.

27. Report by the Vicars Apostolic in England upon the state of their Missions, 25 Nov. 1734, p. 201.

28. Extract from a letter from England, 29 July 1736, Ital., p. 213.

29. Letter from J. S. Bishop of Thespis to Card. Picus de Mirandola, 15 July 1740, p. 233.

30. Considerations in favor of the Secular Clergy in England, Ital., p. 235.

31. Lections, &c. for Nocturns and Mass on the Feast of St. Augustine, 26 May, p. 239.

32. John, Bishop of Thespis, and another to [the Congregation de Propaganda Fide], 3 Nov. 1735, p. 243.

33. Case submitted to the consideration of the Rota, with opinion thereupon, p. 253.

34. John, Bishop of Thespis, to [the Congregation de Propaganda Fide], 29 April 1730, p. 275.

35. Faculties of Card. Fr. Barberini as head of the English Mission, p. 289.

36. Various papers connected with the Roman Agency of Lorenzo Mayes, p. 293.

37. Report upon the difficulties of the English Mission, submitted to the Congregation de Propaganda Fide in May 1714, after the Bishop's letters of July 1713, p. 321.

38. Particulars respecting the abbot Strickland, doctor of the Sorbonne, Ital., p. 323.

39. Supplica by the Agent of the English Clergy for a search to be made at Rome as to the boundaries of the Parish of Acton, alias Ackaton, near Sudbury, co. Suffolk, p. 329.

40. George, bishop of Marcopolis, Vicar Apostolic in England, to the Cardinal Protector, 28 Mar. 1718, p. 341.

41. Supplica by Dr. Witham, Vicar Apostolic, to be permitted to read heretical books, p. 347.

42. Augustin Lewellin, Provincial of Canterbury, to the Rev. the President residing at Paris, p. 392

A volume in folio, in blue paper boards, lettered "Miscellanea II." (bound up with vol. I.)

The more important papers are the following:—

1. . . . . to King James II., Ital., p. 3.

2. Decrees of the Congregation de Propaganda Fide, 6 Oct. 1695, p. 7.

3. King James II. to Pope Innocent XII., S. Germ., 8 December 1694, p. 11.

4. Bishop Gifford to Mr. Mayes, 3 Aug. 1722, p. 15.

5. Paul Savage, missioner, to Cardinal Howard, Seville, 20 Jan. 1693, p. 23.

6. "Papers concerning the state of our Colleges, and of the Mission," p. 24.

7. List of 31 persons who have left the College of Douai from 1730 to 1735, p. 74.

8. The Duc de Villars "to the Queen," 19 July 1709, Fr., p. 93.

9. Papers relating to Bishop Gordon's Agency, p. 119.

Part III. of the same collection:—

1. The Pope to Henry Howard, secular priest, elect of Utica, 2 Oct. 1720, p. 1.

2. The same to the same, 30 Sept. 1720, p. 3.

3. Pope Gregory XIV. to Card. Allen, 18 Sept. 1591, p. 7.

4. Rules to be observed by the Congregation of Religious Women at Hammersmith, p. 75.

5. Petition to Pope Innocent XII. by George Heneage respecting the saying of Mass in his domestic chapel at Heinstone, co. Lincoln, p. 91.

6. Memorial to the Pope respecting the ecclesiastical affairs of England, 1691, p. 99.

7. Bishop Giffard to the Pope, 5 Dec. 1720, p. 103.

8. Various letters by the Vicars Apostolic of England to Pope Innocent XII. on English affairs, p. 105.

9. Petition of Bishop James Smith, Vicar Apostolic of the Northern District, for licence to change certain festivals, p. 137, p. 139.

10. Various letters, petitions, memorials, and other documents connected with the history of the English Mission, p. 141.

11. Catalogue of papers connected with English Catholics from 1637 to 1672, Ital., p. 183.

12. Report upon the state of the Catholic religion in England, presented to Pope Urban VIII., by Gregorio Panzani, on his return from that kingdom in 1637, Ital., p. 189.

A volume in folio, marked G. H., consisting of the following papers, either originals or contemporaneous copies:—

1. Attestation, by John Colleton and 24 others, as to the excellent conduct of the Benedictine Monks in England, London, 20 July 1614, Lat., p. 1.

2. Jo. Harvey to "le pero Bartin, superieur de S. Luys," 26 Dec. [1623], p. 3.

3. "Copia institutionis Decani et Capitali Chalce-"donensis," Lond., 10 Sept. 1623, Lat., p. 7.

4. "Copia institutionis Vicarii Generalis," &c. Joannis Colletoni, Lond., 30 Aug. 1623, Lat., p. 11.

5. "A copy of the letter by which an archdeacon [Ric. Smith] is constituted, Lond., 22 Aug. 1623, Lat., p. 13.

6. Copies of the addresses of various letters sent to Wm. Bishop of Chalcedon, in 1623, 1624 and 1627, Lat., p. 15.

7. Various letters written by Dean Colleton, the Vicars General, and other members of the English Chapter to the following:—

    1. To the Pope, Lond., S. George's Day, 1624, p. 21.

    2. To the same, 15 April, 1624, p. 23.

    3. To Card. Barberini, 21 April 1624, p. 25.

    4. To Card. Bandini, 16 April 1624, p. 27.

    5. To the Congregation de Propaganda Fide, 21 April 1624, p. 29. (Another copy at p. 47.)

    6. To the Pope, 22 April 1624, p. 31. (Another copy at p. 43.)

    7. To Card. Millini, 21 Oct. 1624, p. 35.

    8. To Mgr. Berullo, 1 Sept. 1624, p. 37.

    9. To the Pope, 1 Sept. 1624, p. 39.

    10. To the same, 21 Oct. 1624, p. 41.

    11. To the same, 15 Feb. 1624, p. 49.

    12. To the same, 22 July 1624, p. 53.

    13. To Card. Barberini (two letters), 22 July 1624, pp. 53, 54.

    14. To the Card. S. Susannæ, 22 July 1624, p. 54.

15. To Card. Farnese, 22 July 1624, p. 55.
16. To D. Vives, 22 July 1624, p. 55.
17. To the Pope, 3 June 1624, p. 57.
8. Card. Millini to Colleton, Rome, 6 July 1624, Ital.,
p. 59.
9. The same to the same, Rome, 21 Sept. 1624, Ital.,
p. 60. (Another copy at p. 141.)
10. " Instrumentum confirmationis Capituli cleri Anglicani," 10 Mar. 1624, Lat., p. 63.
11. Dean Colleton and eleven others to the Pope, 26
Feb. 1629, p. 65.
12. Petition of the English Secular Clergy to the
Pope, p. 69.
13. I. N. [Geo. Gage] to Mr. Blackloe, 28 Aug. 1629,
p. 73.
14. John Colleton and four others to [Card. Barberini ?], Lond., 16 Nov. 1627, p. 75.
15. John Colleton to the Congregation [de Propaganda
Fide ?], Lond., 16 Nov. 1632, p. 77.
16. The same to the Pope, Lond., 26 Feb. 1632, Lat.,
p. 85.
17. The same to the Congregation [de Propaganda
Fide], 2 March 1632, p. 93.
18. [Ant. Champney] to Card. Barberini, Lond., 7
June 1637, p. 97.
19. John Colleton to the Pope, Lond., 28 Sept. 1632,
p. 99.
20. The same to the Congregation de Propaganda
Fide, Lond., 1 Jul. 1632, p. 103.
21. The same to the Pope, Lond., 20 May 1632,
p. 107.
22. The same to the same, Lond., 22 May 1632,
p. 111.
23. The same to [the Congregation de Propaganda
Fide ?], Lond., 10 Feb. 1634, p. 115.
24. The same to Card. Barberini, Lond., 4 cal. Ap.
1635, p. 119.
25. John Jackson, Vicar General, and three others,
to the Congregation [de Propaganda Fide ?], Lond.,
8 Dec. 1636, p. 121.
26. The same and two others to Card. Barberini,
p. 123.
27. John Colleton and five others to the Office of the
S. Inquisition, Lond., prid. non. Maii 1628, p. 125.
28. John Colleton to the Pope, London, 6 July 1631,
p. 133.
29. The same and four others to the Holy Office,
London, 16 Nov. 1627, p. 137.
30. R. Fitton to Blackloe, 27 Sept. [1627], p. 145. 24,
31. John Colleton to Card. Ludovisi, 15 Ap. 16
p. 149.
32. Extract from the letters of Anth. Champney,
15 Aug. 1624, p. 151.
33. Dr. Wm. Bishop to Mr. Bennet, 2 March 1623,
p. 153.
34. John Colleton and others to the Pope, Lond.,
15 Feb. 1624, p. 155.
35. Card. Ludovisi to the Bishop of Chalcedon, Rome,
16 Mar. 1614, p. 157.
36. Jo. Smith [alias Colleton] to Mr. Rant, 25 Sept.
1623, p. 159.
37. John Colleton to the Pope, London, 22 Nov. 1624,
p. 161.
38. The same to Card. Ludovisi, Lond., 1 Sept. 1624,
p. 165.
39. The same to Francis Ingoli [Secretary of the
Propaganda], Lond., 1 Sept. 1624, p. 167.
40. The same to the same, Lond., 3 June 1624,
p. 169.
41. The same to the Pope, Lond., 26 May 1625,
p. 171.
42. The same to [Card. Barberini ?], Lond., 26 May
1625, p. 173.
43. The same to the Congregation de Propaganda
Fide, Lond., 26 May 1625, p. 175.
44. Anth. Champney to Tho. Rant, 13 and 15 Dec.
1623, p. 177.
45. Arthur Pits to the same, 7 Nov. 1623, p. 181.
46. Anth. Champney to the same, Douai, 10 Nov.
1623, p. 183.
47. The same to the same, 13 Oct. 1623, p. 185.
48. Card. Ludovisi to the Bishop of Chalcedon and to
the Vicars-General and Archdeacons of England, 20
Jan. 1624, p. 187.
49. John Colleton and others to Card. Bandini, Lond.,
18 Sept. 1623, p. 189.
50. [The same ?] to Card. Magalotti, [5 Sept. 1625],
p. 191.
51. The Bishop of Chalcedon to the Congregation of
the Holy Office, [15 Jan. 1624], p. 195.
52. [G. Gage] to John Fitton, 19 March 1640, p. 199.

53. The same to the same, 1 May 1640, p. 203.
54. The same to the same, 8 May 1640, p. 205.
55. Reasons against the appointment of a Provost,
p. 209.
56. Anth. Champney to [Mr. Fitton ?], 17 April 1640,
p. 211.
57. The same to the same, 1 May 1640, p. 213.
58. The same to the same, 11 Sept. 1640, with a P.S.
by G. G[age], p. 215.
59. The same to the same, 14 Aug. 1640, p. 217.
60. The same to the same, 3 April 1640, p. 219.
61. " Mr. Fitton's petition for confirmation of the
" Chapter," p. 221.
62. Petition of the Canons and Dean of the English
Chapter to the Pope, with instructions to Mr. Fitton,
p. 223.
63. Instructions for the Archdeacons in visiting their
provinces, p. 227.
64. Letter containing reasons for the validity of the
English Chapter, p. 229.
A volume in folio, consisting of 358 pp., containing
original papers or contemporaneous copies, of which
the more important are the following :
1. " Concerning Mr. More's Tre Luoghi di Monti,"
Rome, 21 Mar. 1625, Lat., p. 1.
2. Notarial copy of the last will of Thomas More,
priest, son of Thomas More, of Barnburgh, co. York,
5 Jan. 1617, attested at Antwerp, in the presence of
Hen. Clifford and Ric. Parry, Lat., p. 13.
3. Appointment by John Colleton, Dean, and the
Chapter, of Tho. More, Archdeacon, to act as their
agent in the Court of Rome, London, 28 May 1624,
Lat., p. 40.
4. Tho. More to Tho. Rant, [17 Sept. 1623], p. 41.
5. Paper concerning the bequest by Seth Olando
[Holland], Englishman, of certain land [near Rome] to
Richard Bishop of Worcester ; two copies, Ital., p. 45.
6. Appointment by Ric. Smyth, Bishop of Chalcedon,
of James Skinner, priest, to act as his agent in the
Court of Rome, Paris, 9 Sept. 1646, Lat., p. 61.
7. Appointment, by John Colleton, Dean, and others
of the Chapter, of Tho. More, Archdeacon of Hertford
and Northampton, to act as their agent in the Court of
Rome, London, 3 October 1624, Lat., p. 70.
8. Appointment, by Matt. Kellison, D.D., President
of the Engl. College at Douai, of Peter Fitton, priest, to
act as his agent in the Court of Rome, 2 Oct. 1634, Lat.,
p. 75.
9. " Mr. [Laurence] Plantin's procuration " by Peter
Fitton, Florence, 19 Jan. 1655, Lat., p. 81.
10. Appointment, by the Bishop of Chalcedon, of Peter
Bedulph, alias Fitton, priest, to act as his agent in the
Court of Rome, London, 10 July 1631, Lat., p. 85.
11. Appointment by Matthew Kellison, D.D., of Tho.
More, " ex nobili stemmate gloriosi Thomæ Mori pro-
" gnatum, hæredem, et pronepotem," (who had been for
many years employed by the archpriests Geo. Birched
and Wm. Harrison as their agent at Rome) to act as his
agent in obtaining a Bishop for the Church of England,
Douai, 4 July 1624, Lat., p. 87.
12. Reasons for the appointment of a Bishop in England [1655], p. 89.
13. " Mr. [Laurence] Plantin's Instructions and Ne-
" gociations " concerning the said appointment, various
papers, p. 93.
14. " Mr. [Francis] Gage's Negociation " on the same
subject, p. 129.
15. Letters from W. Hyde respecting the appointment of a Provost, 1640, p. 169.
16. " An Act against Delinquents," ordered to be
printed 13 July 1659, Printed, p. 179.
17. Papers connected with the appointment of Francis
Gage, S.T.D., Archdeacon of Essex, to act as agent of
the English clergy at Rome, 1659, 1660, Lat., p. 189.
18. Petition of the English secular clergy to the Pope
upon the death of Richard Bishop of Chalcedon, Lat.,
p. 213.
19. Abstract of the penal laws against the Catholics
in England, from 1558, Lat., pp. 215, 303.
20. Abstract of the Relation given by the agent of
the English clergy in Rome on the condition of the
Catholic Church in England [in 1632], Ital., p. 227.
21. Petition to the Pope for the appointment of a
Bishop in England, written in the reply made after the
death of the Bishop of Chalcedon, Lat., p. 231.
22. Reasons by the English clergy for the appointment of a Bishop in England, Lat., pp. 249, 253, 257,
259, 261, 263, 299, 315, 317, 321, 325.
23. List of the members of the Catholic Chapter,
arranged under Vicars-General, Archdeacons, and
Canons of the Chapter, p. 355.

24. Humphry Ellis and the English Chapter to Pope Clement IX., congratulatory on his accession, London, 26 Aug. 1667, Lat., p. 356.

A volume in 4to. consisting of 87 leaves; it is entitled, " De quindecim gloriosis Angliæ martyribus brevis historia, ab Henrico Stilo, Benedictino, ex Anglico sermone in Latinum translata et meliori ordine collocata."

Dedicated Dno. Petro Carpentario, abbati B. Mariæ de Laude.

Index eorum quæ in hac historia continentur.

Præfatio ad lectorem; fol. 4.

Bulla Pii V. de Reginæ Elizabethæ excommunicatione; 10.

Vita et martyrium Cuthberti Mayni, sacerdotis; 13.
———————— Joannis Nelsoni, sacerdotis; 16.
———————— Thomæ Shirvodi, laici; 20.
———————— Everardi Hansii, sacerdotis, et obiter de tribus laicis, Guilielmo scilicet Greeno, Humfrido et Guilielmo Goughis, Christi confessoribus; 21.

Vita et martyrium P. Edmundi Campiani, S. J. presbyteri; 26.

Epistola ejusdem ad Generalem ejus Rectorem; 39.

Amici in laudem ejusdem P. Campiani carmina; 42.

Vita et martyrium Rodolfi Sheruini, sacerdotis; 44.

Epistola ejusdem ad amicos; 50.

Alia ejusdem ad avunculum, Joannem Woodwardum; 51.

Apprehensio et martyrium Alexandri Briani, sacerdotis; 53.

Epistola ejusdem ad R. P. Societatis Jesu, 56.

Examinatio, condemnatio, et martyrium Joannis Payne, sacerdotis; 60.

De septem Sacerdotum post condemnationem examine; 67.

Martyrium Thomæ Fondi [Pondi], sacerdotis; 71.
———————— Joannis Sherti, sacerdotis; 73.
———————— Roberti Jonsoni, sacerdotis; 75.
———————— Guilielmi Filloci, sacerdotis; 77.
———————— Lucæ Kirbei, sacerdotis; 79.

Martyria Laurentii Richardsoni, alias Jonsoni, et Thomæ Cotami, sacerdotum; 82.

The MS. is in a hand of the end of the reign of Queen Elizabeth.

A bundle of original letters and papers addressed, in 1622, to the Rev. John Bennett, Agent at Rome for the English Catholics. The writers are the following:—

W. Kellison, Jan. 11, 12, Mar. 1, Oct. 5, 14.
John Strong, Jan. 25.
Tho. More, Mar. 18.
Fra. He., Mar. 23.
Ant. Champney, Ap. 20, May 11, June 1, 9, Sept. 28.
Jo. Duckett, May 11.
Thomas Fitzherbert, May 22.
Hugo Cavellus, May 14.
Aug. de Raconis, July 4.
. . . . Archdeacon of Cambria, July 16.
Wm. Bishop, July 28, Aug. 25, Sept. 7, Oct. 3. 10, 20, 26, 30, Nov. 15, 18.
Jo. Eaton, July 31, Aug. 31.
Jo. Kenett, Aug. 15, Oct. 4.
W. Farrar, Aug. 25, Sept. 14, 24, 28, 30, Oct. 5, 14, 21, 26, Nov. 2, 9.
C. Clement, Sept. 10.
Oliver Almond, Sept. 10.
J. Barker, Sept. 10.
Edward Bennett, Sept. 14.
A. Pits, Sept. 26.
Wm. Newman, Oct. 8.
Jo. Hervey, Oct. 10, 19.
R. Smith, Oct. 20.
E. Hewes, Oct. 20.
Jo. Heynes, Nov. 25.

A volume in folio, marked 8, pp. 356, consisting of various letters and papers, of which the following are the most important:—

1. Persons's dedication to his answer to Coke's Reports, original holograph draft, with numerous corrections, p. 1.

2. Statement by the Archpriest, George Blackwell, sent to the Office of the Inquisition, concerning certain excesses in England prejudicial to the Catholic religion, A.D. 1601., Lat., p. 49.

3. Corrected original draft of the above, p. 60.

4. On the appointment of an Archpresbyter for the English Catholics, in 1598, Lat., p. 86.

5. Tertia denunciatio quorandam locorum ex quodam scandaloso libro, " Ymportant considerations which " ought to move all true and sownd Catholikes"— " newly imprinted, 1601," p. 133.

5.

6. " Denunciatio alterius scripti seditiosi, seu libelli " famosi, mense Sept. 1601," Lat., p. 149.

7. Another copy of No. 5.

8. Loci quidam decerpti ex quodam libro Anglice conscripto, Lat., p. 173.

9. Another copy of No. 5.

10. Extracts from certain depositions respecting the Priests who left Rome in Sept. 1597, Lat., p. 208.

11. Another copy of No. 2, p. 173.

12. Quæ concernunt D. Jacobum Labornum, armigerum, qui martyrizatus est Lancæstriæ paulo ante Pascha, 1583, p. 223.

13. The same paper in English, p. 225.

14. Account of the festivities at Rouen when the French king received the order of the Garter in 1596, Ital., p. 227.

15. Letter from Sir F. Englefield to Roger Baines [1596], p. 229.

16. Judgment of Sir F. Englefield upon the book upon the English succession, written under the name of Dolman [1596], Lat., p. 230.

17. A clause of a letter of Sir Francis Englefield's to Mr. Thomas Hesket, 27 Jan.

18. On certain Jesuit Fathers in England, p. 236.

19. G. Markham to his brother Robert Markham, at Rome. Florence, 30 Jan., p. 237.

20. Richard Couling to F. Robert Persons, 13 Feb. 1596, Lat., with a PS. in Engl., p. 238.

21. Petitions from the Students of the English College at Rome, to the Cardinal Protector, Lat., p. 239.

22. Richard Couling to Joseph Creswell, Rome, 10 Mar. 1596, Lat., p. 240.

23. Sir Fr. Englefield to Roger Baines [27 Jan. 1596], Engl., p. 242.

24. Henry Bell to F. Holt, 13 Mar. 1596, p. 244.

25. F. Mush to F. Garnet, 15 March 1596, p. 246.

26. Samuel Whartone to F. Edward Howard and F. Richard Dowlinge, 15 March 1596, p. 248.

27. R. Barret [to F. Persons?], Rome, 10 Ap. 1596.

28. Richard Couling to Osmon Tesimond, 8 Ap. 1596, Lat., p. 256.

29. William Gifford, dean of Lille, to . . . [13 Ap. 1596], Lat., p. 258.

30. Richard Couling to Rob. Persons, 8 Ap. 1596, Lat., p. 262.

31. Ro. Williams to the High Treasurer of England and the Earl of Essex, [1593?], p. 264.

32. Complaint of Charles Earl of Westmorland, Timothy Moket, Charles Broun, Ric. Gage, Charles Paget, Wm. Tresom, Ralph Ligon, John Pauncefot, and John Stonor, against Hugh Owen and others. Brussels, 28 May 1596, Lat., p. 266.

33. Dr. Thornell, canon of Vicenza, to . . . . . about Marsham, Hauser, and Bodley, lately released from the Holy Office in Rome, Ital., p. 270.

34. " Memoriale Tempestii mense Junii 1596, datum Cardinali Toleto; ex litteris Giffordii," p. 272.

35. Sir F. Englefield to Roger Bayns, Madrid, 24 Feb. 1596, p. 276.

36. F. Jos. Creswell to the Cardinal S. George, Madrid, 24 May 1596, Ital., p. 280.

37. The same [to the same], Madrid, 17 May 1596, Ital., p. 284.

38. The same to Silvius Antonianus, Madrid, 5 kal. Jun. 1596, Lat., p. 288. " Nunquam fuit tradita."

39. The same to the Pope, Madrid, 20 April 1596, Ital., p. 292. " Non fù mai data.".

40. The same to the same, Madrid, kal. June 1596, Lat., p. 294. " Nunquam tradita."

41. Henry Tichburn to Rob. Persons, Rome, Engl. Coll., 15 June 1596, Lat., p. 296.

42. Dr. Gifford to one of the Scholars of the English College at Rome, Brussels, 19 Sept. 1596, Lat., p. 298.

43. Edmund Thornell to the inmates of the English College at Rome, Venice, 21 Oct. 1596, Lat., p. 302.

44. Fra Diego de Ypes to F. Rob. Persons, 9 Oct. 1596, Span., p. 306.

45. Dr. R. Barrett to F. Rob. Persons, or F. Jos. Cresswell, Rome, 26 Sept. 1596, p. 310.

46. The Priests and Scholars of the English College at Rome to the Cardinal Protector, 1 Oct. 1595 [1596?], Lat., p. 314.

47. Laurence Webbe and six others, D.D. to the Pope, Donai, prid. Id. Nov. 1596, Lat., p. 316.

48. The President and Doctors of the College of Donai to Dr. R. Barrett or F. Alfonso Agazari, 1596, Lat., p. 318.

49. King Philip III. to the General of the Society of Jesus. S. Lorenzo, 10 Oct. 1596, Span., p. 320.

50. Letters testimonial of the English clergy and nobles exiled for the faith, and resident in Belgium, in

3 O

favor of the English Jesuits, Nov. 1596, Notarial attestations, 12 and 13 Dec. 1596, Lat., p. 322.
51. F. Holte [F] to . . . . Rome, 7 Nov. 1596, Ital., p. 330.
52. F. Yo[unger] to Dr. Gifford, 12 Nov. 1596, p. 334.
53. Zenobius Pulesius [Dr. Gifford F] to [Edward Tempest F], 12 Nov. 1596, Lat., p. 336.
54. Dean Gifford to Edw. Tempest and Edw. Bennett, Lille, Nov. 1596, Lat., p. 338.
55. Zenobius Pulesius [Dr. Gifford F] to Edw. Tempest, 22 Nov. 1596, Lat., p. 342.
56. Brief of the Apostolic Nuncio respecting the management of the English residencies in Lisbon and S. Lucar, Madrid, 29 Nov. 1596, Lat., p. 344.
57. Attestation by Wm. Persoy, Wm. Stanley, and six others, English residents in Flanders, exiles for the faith, in favor of the English Jesuits, Brussels, 20 Dec. 1596, Lat., p. 348.
58. Letter to the same effect by the convent of the English Augustinian nuns of Louvaine, signed by Margaret (Clement, abbess, [1596,] Lat., p. 352.
59. Letter to the same effect by " Ludovicus Husius, " presbyter Anglus, quondam B. M. Ill. Cardinalis " [Alani] capellanus," London., 3 non. Dec. 1596, Lat., 356.

A volume in folio, beginning with p. 303, and ending with p. 543. It consists of letters and papers, (originals or contemporary copies) of the year 1612, of which the more important are the following :
1. Rom. Sava [Edw. Bennett] to the Rev. Tho. Moore [Agent for the English Catholic Clergy at Rome], 3 May 1612, p. 303.
2. Rat. [F. Mushe] to Geo. Weste Moore [the same], York, 4 May 1612, p. 305.
3. Ro. Clap[ham] to Geo. Weste [the same], 5 May 1612, p. 307.
4. [D. Anth. Champney] to [the same], 5 May 1612, p. 309.
5. Wm. Rayner to the same, 13 May 1612, p. 311.
6. R. Sava to the same, 13 May 1612, p. 313.
7. Dr. Anth. Champney to the same, 17 May 1612, p. 317.
8. Geo. Salv. to the same, 20 May 1612, p. 319.
9. The same to the same, 9 May 1612, p. 321.
10. The same to the same, 19 May 1612, p. 323.
11. The same to the same, 20 May 1612, p. 327.
12. Fr. August. de S. Juan [F. White] to the same, Douai, 21 May 1612.
13. Wm. Howarde [to the same F], Douai, 26 May 1612.
14. Rob. Pett to the same, Brussels, 26 May 1612, p. 337.
15. Dr. Anth. Champney to the same, 6 June 1612, with a P.S. by " Orontes," p. 339.
16. D. Wm. Byshope to the same, Paris, 4 June 1612, p. 341.
17. B. N. Geo. Weste to [the same F], 6 June 1612, with P.S. of 10 June, p. 343.
18. Rob. Clive to [the same ?], Brussels, 9 June 1612, p. 345.
19. Rat. to G. St. [the same F], 19 June 1612, p. 347.
20. Rob. Pett to the same, Brussels, 16 June 1612, p. 349.
21. Anth. Champney to the same, 19 June 1612, p. 351.
22. R. Cla. to Mr. Geo. Weste, Esquire [the same F], Pater Noster Row, 20 June 1612, with a P.S. of 5 July, p. 353.
23. Ri. Sava to the same, 20 June 1612, p. 355.
24. Hierom Heth to the same, Brussels, 20 June 1612, p. 357.
25. R. Pett to the same, Brussels, 23 June 1612, p. 359.
26. Fragment of a letter of 1 July 1612, p. 361.
27. Anth. Champney to the same, Sorbonne, 3 July 1612, p. 363.
28. Lease by Jachimo van de Spire to John Lampson of a chamber in his house, 1 July 1612, Ital., p. 365.
29. Dedication to James I. of the Latin version of Brerely's Apology, printed at Paris, in 4to., 1615, with 28 lines of Latin poetry in MS. appended, p. 369.
30. Geo. Salv. to Tho. Moore, 3 July 1612, p. 373.
31. T. Browne to Mr. West [the same ?], London, 6 July [1612], p. 375.
32. Rob. Pett to the same, Brussels, 7 July 1612, p. 377.
33. Jerome Heth to the same, 8 July [1612], Lat., p. 379.
34. . . . . . . to Geo. West [the same F], 9 July 1612, p. 381.
35. Geo. Salv. to the same, 15 July [1612], p. 385.

36. Rich. Sara to Tho. West [the same], 17 July [1612], p. 387.
37. Tho. Hethe [F] to the same, London, 19 July [1612], p. 391.
38. Anth. Champney to the same, Sorbonne, 17 July 1612, p. 393.
39. Robert Pett to the same, Brussels, 21 July 1612, p. 395.
40. The same to the same, Brussels, 28 July 1612 p. 397.
.41. R. Orontes [the Bishop of Chalcedon] to the same 31 July 1612, p. 399.
42. Geo. Salv. to the same, 3 Aug. 1612, (with a long P.S.), p. 401.
43. Rob. Pett to the same, Brussels, 4 Aug. 1612, p. 405.
44. —— [B. N.] to Geo. West [the same F], 5 Aug. 1612, p. 407.
45. John Colleton to the same, p. 411.
46. Anth. Champney to the same, 14 Aug. 1612, p. 417.
47. —— [B. N.] to Geo. Weste [the same], 16 Aug. 1612, p. 418.
48. Rob. Pett to the same, Brussels, 18 Aug. 1612, p. 422.
49. R. Orontes [Bishop of Chalcedon] to the same, 28 Aug. [1612], p. 424.
50. Anth. Champneys [to the same], Sorbonne, 28 Aug. 1612, p. 426.
51. Rob. Pett to the same, Brussels, 1 Sept. 1612, p. 428.
52. Wm. Rayner to the same, 29 Sept. [1612], p. 430.
53. [John Nelson] to the same, [2 Sept. 1612], p. 432.
54. Ric. Sava to the same, 5 Sept. 1612, p. 434.
55 Geo. Salv. to Geo. West [the same], 7 Sept. 1612, p. 436.
56. Geo. Salvin to the same, 10 Sept. 1612, p. 438.
57. Anth. Champney to the same, 11 Sept. 1612, p. 440.
58. [B. N.] to Geo. Weste [the same], 20 Sept. 1612, p. 444.
59. Geo. Salv. [to the same], 21 Sept. 1612, p. 448.
60. Wm. Byshope to the same, 25 Sept. [1612], p. 450.
61. Anth. Champney to the same, 25 Sept. 1612, p. 454.
62. Rob. Pett to the same, Brussels, 30 Sept. 1612, p. 456.
63. Ric. Sava to the same, 1 Oct. [1612], p. 458.
64. Geo. Salv. to the same, 1 Oct. 1612, p. 460.
65. Fr. Agostino de S. Juan [F. White] to Wm. West [the same F], Douai, 4 Oct. 1612, p. 463.
66. Geo. Wilson [Sal.] to Anth. Champney, 5 Oct. 1612, p. 465.
67. Rob. Pett to Tho. Moore, Brussels, 6 Oct. 1612, p. 467.
68. The same to the same, Brussels, 8 Oct. 1612, p. 469.
69. Anth. Champney to the same, Sorbonne, 9 Oct. 1612, p. 471.
70. R. Orontes [Bishop of Chalcedon] to the same, " From Cossé, six leagues from Poitiers," 15 Oct. [1612], p. 437.
71. Ratcliff to Geo. West [the same], 17 Oct. 1612, p. 475.
72. [B. N.] to the same, 19 Oct. 1612, p. 497.
73. N. [John Nelson] to the same, 20 Oct. [1612], p. 481.
74. F. Aug. de S. Juan [White] to the same, 23 Oct. 1612, p. 485.
75. Anth. Champney [to the same], 23 Oct. 1612, p. 487.
76. Geo. Sal. to the same, 24 Oct. 1612, p. 489.
77. R. Clapham to Geo. West [the same], 26 Oct. 1612.
78. Rob. Pett to the same, 31 Nov. 1612, p. 495.
79. Ric. Sav. to Tho. West [the same], 1 Nov. 1612, p. 497.
80. L. G. Salv. to the same, 5 Nov. 1612, p. 499.
81. Anth. Champney to the same, 6 Nov. 1612, p. 501.
82. [John Nelson] to the same, 9 Nov. 1612.
83. Rob. Pett to the same, Brussels, 10 Nov. 1612, p. 505.
84. Geo. Salv. to the same, 10 Nov. 1612, p. 507.
85. Rob. Clere to the same, Brussels, 17 Nov. 1612, p. 509.
86. Tho. Rant to the same, 20 Nov. [1612], p. 511.
87. Wm. Byshope to the same, Paris, 21 Nov. [1612], p. 513.
88. Anth. Champneys to the same, 21 and 22 Nov. 1612, p. 517.
89. Geo. Salv. to the same, 23 Nov. 1612, p. 521.

90. Griffin Floid to the same, London, 25 Nov. 1612, Ital., p. 523.

91. Anth. Champneys to the same, 4 Dec. 1612, p. 525.

92. Rob. Pett to the same, Brussels, 1 Dec. 1612, p. 527.

93. Geo. Salv. to the same, 6 Dec. 1612, p. 529.

94. Wm. Sta. to Geo. West [the same], p. 531.

95. Rob. Pett to the same, Brussels, 13 Dec. 1612, p. 533.

96. Anth. Champney to the same, 18 Dec. 1612, p. 525.

97. Tho. Browne to the same, 19 Dec. [1612], p. 537.

98. Tho. Mayne to the same, Brussels, 15 Nov. 1612, p. 539.

99. Rob. Pett to the same, Brussels, 28 Dec. 1612, p. 543.

A bundle of original letters and papers addressed to the Rev. Thomas More, Agent at Rome, for the English Catholics. They relate to the year 1613, and consist of 388 pages. The writers are the following :—

Anth. Champney, Jan. 1, 12, 15, 29, Feb. 12, 26, Mar. 12, 26, Ap. 9, 23, May 8, 9, 20, June 5, 18, July 2, 16, 30, Aug. 13, 27, Sept. 10, 14, 19, 24, Oct. 5, 22, 25, Nov. 14, 19, Dec. 3, 16, 17, 31.

Rob. Pett, Jan. 5, 19, Feb. 1, 16, 23, Mar. 2, 16, 23, April 6, May 4, 18, June 22, 29, July 20, Aug. 17, 30, Sept. 14, Oct. 12, 26, Nov. 9.

Geo. Salv[in], Jan. 10, Feb. 2, Mar. 1, 25, April 2, 20, May 2, 9, June 7, 10, July 2, 26, Aug. 23, Sept. 5, 7, 25, Oct. 20, Nov. 7, 15, 20, Dec. 3, 13.

Wm. Rayner, Jan. 15, May 7, July 2, 31, Aug. 27, Sept. 24, Oct. 22, Nov. 20.

Wm. Byshope, Jan. 15, Feb. 12, Mar.12, Ap. 9, May 6, June 4, July 2, 30, Aug. 27, Sept. 22, Nov. 5, Oct. 8, Dec. 17, 31.

B. N., Jan. 31, Feb. 21, Ap. 24, June 30, Sept. 10, Oct. 2, Nov. 17.

R. Orontes, Feb. 3, July 2, Sept. 9.

. . . . Johnson, Feb. 12.

J. N[elson], Mar. 1, Ap. 12, 20, Nov. 25, Dec. 6, 18, 26.

R. Clapham, Mar. 1, June 2, Aug. 24, Oct. 22, Nov. 21, Dec. 31.

J. Smith [Colleton], Mar. 2.

R. Sar, Mar. 3, Ap. 26, Aug. 24, Sept. 17, Nov. 1, 17, 30.

Tho. White, Mar. 27, Ap. 17.

Simon Stock, Mar. 31.

Hierom Heth, July 31.

Leander de S. Martino, Ap. 10, May 14, July 1.

Rob. Clerc [Pett], Ap. 21, June 1, 7, July 13, Aug. 3, Sept. 29, Oct. 12, Nov. 23, Dec. 7.

Ben., July 2.

Th. Law, May 17.

Matt. Kellison, May 20, Sept. 9, Oct. 8, Nov. 26, Dec. 31.

[Harrison ?] June . . .

John Melling, June 22.

Richard Robinson, June 24, Nov. 4.

. . . . . Colleton, Aug. 9, Oct. 17.

Augustino de S. Juan, Aug. 24.

Cristofer Saukill, Sept. 15.

John Fixer, Oct. 11, Dec. 11.

Tho. Longworth, Dec. 18.

Griffith Floid, Dec. 31.

A bundle of original letters and papers addressed to the Rev. Thomas More, Agent in Rome for the English Catholics. They relate to the year 1615, and consist of 212 pp. The writers are the following :—

Jo. Bosevile, Jan. . . . . .

John Freer, Jan. 2, Mar. 27, May 26, June 19, Sept. 11.

Wm. Ward, Jan. 2, July 29, Aug. 25, Sept. 22, Nov. 1, 30, Dec. 28.

Louis Vaughan, Jan. 3, 10, 18, 22, 31, Feb. 7, 14, 28, Mar. 21, 26, Ap. 18, 25, May 9, July 18, 29, Aug. 8, Sept. 12, Oct. 3, 24, Nov. 21, Dec. 19.

Rob. Clerc, Jan. 10, 24, Feb. 7, 21, Mar. 7, 20, Ap. 1, 18, May 8, 16, 30, June 18, 27, July 12, 25, Aug. 3, 23, Sept. 5, 19, Oct. 2, 17, 21, Nov. 12, 28, Dec. 12.

Francis More, Jan. 12, 23, Feb. 7, 28, Mar. 13, 29, Ap. 5, 25, May 2, 16, June 7, 20, July 4, 20, 25, Aug. 1, 7, 29, Sept. 5, 12, 26, Oct. 5, 26, Nov. 8, 14, 20, Dec. 5, 8, 18.

Wm. Rayner, Jan. 13, May 6, 19, July 14, Aug. 25, Sept. 12, Nov. 3, Dec. 1, 29.

Anth. Champney, Jan. 13, 23, Feb. 10, 14, 24, Mar. 10, 24, Ap. 7, 21, May 6, 19, June 2, 16, July 2, 14, 28,

Aug. 11, 25, 28, Sept. 8, 14, 22, Oct. 15, Nov. 3, 14, Dec. 1, 10, 29.

Geffrey Pole, Jan. 15, Sept. 13.

Wm. Byshop, Jan. 15, Feb. 10, 24, Mar. 27, Ap. 5, 22, July 14, Aug. 25, Dec. 29.

Matt. Kellison, Jan. 29, 31, Feb. 11, Mar. 4, Ap. 6, 19, June 2, July 21, 26, Sept. 8, 30, Oct. 28, Nov. 15, 16, Dec. 19.

Jerome Heth, Feb. . . .

E. Bolton, Feb. 22.

Ric. Salle, Mar. 2, June 9, Oct. 30.

G. Floyd, Mar. 18.

J. Lelio, Mar. 22, 23.

Morgan Clenock, Mar. 23.

Edward Bennett, Mar. 23.

John Bennett, Mar. 23.

Jo. Smithe, Mar. 25, July 11.

Rio. Brough, Mar. . . .

Wm. Harris, Mar. . . .

Cuthbert Trollopp, Mar. . . .

Will. Conningsbey, April 1.

R. Orontes, Ap. 21, Sept. 18.

Sava, Ap. 29.

R. Clapham, May 1, Nov. 19.

Griffith Floyde, May 9, June . . .

F. Nelson, May 10.

De Lene, May 10.

Edw. White, June 20.

John Shores [?], Aug. 14.

Ed. Collecke, Sept. 1.

Wm. Paston, Sept. 14, Nov. 12.

Tho. Lancaster, Sept. 15.

Aug. de S. John, Sept. 21.

John Frere, Oct. 9, Nov. 9, Dec. 4, 17.

Wm. Harison, Oct. 26.

James Clayton, Nov. 2.

Modestus Stephanus, Nov. 28.

Tho. More, Dec. 22.

Henry Paruishe, Dec. 26.

A volume in folio marked A. B., containing a miscellaneous collection of papers, of which the more important are the following :—

1. Brief of Pope Clement VIII., to George Blacwell, the English Archpriest, 5 Oct. 1602.

2. The English Agent at Rome to the Congregation of the Propaganda.

3. Card. Farnese to Geo. Blacwell, 10 Feb. 1607.

4. Dispensation by Card. Barberini to Rob. Blundeston to receive a Doctor's degree, 24 Nov. 1627.

5. Dispensation by the same to the same, 16 Dec. 1607, with various papers connected with the taking of the Doctor's degree by English priests.

6. On the origin of the disputes in the English College at Rome in 1594, from an information given to Card. Baronius.

7. Card. Cajetan to Doctors Percy and Worthington, 7 Mar. 1598.

8. Brief of Pope Clement VIII. to Geo. Blackwell and others, 17 Aug. 1601.

9. F. Persons to the Archpriest Birkett, 21 June 1608.

10. Wm. Birkett to the Cardinals Blanchetti and Farnese, 6 Dec. 1610.

11. The same to Mr. More, English Agent at Rome, 6 Oct. 1610.

12. Dr. Worthington to Dr. Champneys, 27 Dec. 1612.

13. Card. Blanchetti to Birkett, 26 Feb. 1610.

14. Geo. Birkett to the Pope, 5 Feb. 1610.

15. The same to the same, 23 Feb. 1610.

16. Edward Weston to the Cardinals . . . 15 Feb. 1610.

17. Geo. Birkett to the Cardinal Protector of England, 23 Feb. 1610.

18. The same to the Pope, 27 Aug. 1611.

19. The same to Card. Borghese, 26 July 1613.

20. The same to the Pope, 23 Aug. 1713.

21. Wm. Bishop and Anth. Champney to Cardinal Farnese, 4 June 1613.

22. Geo. Birchet to Card. Millini, 20 April 1613.

23. The same to Card. Farnese, 15 May 1613.

24. Doctors Bishop, Champney, Smith and Rayner, to Card. Farnese, 31 July [1613].

25. The same to Card. Borghese, 30 July 1613.

26. Wm. Bishop to Card. Farnese, 14 Jan. 1614.

27. Geo. Birched to the Pope, 27 Mar. 1614.

28. The same to Card. Farnese, 28 Mar. 1614.

29. Dr. Bishop and others to Card. Borghese, 9 cal. Ap. 1614.

30. John Colleton to Card. Farnese, 10 Ap. 1614.

31. Dr. Bishop and others to Card Borghese, 3 June 1614.

32. The same to Card. Millini, 1 July [1614].
33. Jo. Boswell and others to Card. Farnese, 1 Sept. 1614.
34. The same to Card. Millini, 1 Sept. 1614.
35. Geo. Birched to the Pope, 20 Oct. 1613.
36. Dr. Jo. Bennett to Card. Farnese, 4 kal. Sept.
37. Ric. Broughton to Card. Farnese, kal. Jul. 1613.
38. Geo. Birched to the Pope, 3 Dec. 1613.
39. Articles exhibited by Bishop to the Papal Nuncio in Belgium, 16 Ap. 1612.
40. . . . . . to the Pope, 1610.
41. Extracts from the letters of the Archpriest, 15 Dec. 1612, 5 Jan. 1612, 9 Jan. 1612.
42. Dr. Bishop and others to Card. Farnese, 17 May 1612.
43. Doctors Bishop, Smith, Champney, and others, to Cardinals Borghese and Millini, 15 Jan. 1613, 23 Oct. 1612.
44. The same to the General of the Jesuits and others, Oct. 1615, Jan. 1616, Mar. 1616, May 1616, Aug. 1616, June 1610, April 1614, June 1613.
45. Geo. Birched, Archpriest, to Father Jones, Provincial of the Jesuits in England, 3 letters.
46. Father Persons to the Archpriest, Easter even, 1610.
47. The Duchess of Feria to her nephew, Madrid, 3 July 1610.
48. The Archpriest Harrison to the Nuncio Apostolic in Belgium, 8 Mar. 1616.
49. The Archpriest Birched to the Superior of the Jesuits. "Ex lecto meo non. Aprilis."
50. The same to the Priests in England, "pridie ante " mortem, 5 Ap. 1614."
51. The same to Cardinals Bellarmin and Farnese, 1612 and 1613.
52. Matthew Kellison to Card. Farnese, 5 Dec. 1616.
53. Letters to the Pope from Ric. Smith, Edw. Bennett, and Wm. Stanney, 1610, 1611.
54. Letter of 13 Priests, imprisoned in London, to Pope Paul V.
55. The Archpriest Birched to Card. Millini, Vice-Protector of England, 15 July 1612.
56. The same to Card. Bellarmin, 15 July 1612.
57. The same and others to Pope Paul V., July 1, Aug. 1611.
58. Letters from the Priests in Sussex, Lancaster, Wales, Oxford, York, and London to the same, 1610, 1611.
59. Roger Caduallader, shortly before his martyrdom, to John Bennett.
60. The Archpriest Birched to . . . 3 July 1612.
61. Tho. Martin, Priest, a prisoner in London, to Card. Mellini, 1612.
62. The Archpriest Birched and others on the despatch of the Procurator to Rome, 5 Feb. 1609.
63. Letters to the Pope in recommendation of the Rev. Thomas More, agent of the English Clergy.
64. Letters of the Archpriest to the Orator of the King of Spain at Rome, to the Cardinals of the Congregation of the Sacred Office, Card. Farnese, Protector of England, Card. Aldobrandini, J. B. Vives, and Card. Bollarmin, Jan. Feb. 1612.
65. Edw. Bennett to Card. Farnese, cal. Junii 1611.
66. Letter from a Priest, imprisoned (for the second time) in London, 1 Dec. 1611, taken to Rome, 10 Mar. 1612.
67. The Archpriest Birched to the Pope, 16 Nov. 1612.
68. Concerning certain books written by Roger Widdrington and Father Persons.
69. Letter to the Pope concerning Lewis Vaughan, an English Priest.
70. Various letters and papers concerning the establishment of the Episcopate in England.
71. "Nomina sæcularium sacerdotum in Anglia (numero 115) qui valde expedire judicant ut ipsis præficiantur Episcopi; cum nominibus eorum quos tanto muneri idoneos censent."
A large bundle containing letters and papers to and from various individuals connected with the English Court at St. Germains, from 1689 to 1717, among which are several relative to the campaign in Flanders in 1692.
A bundle in 4to. containing 15 fasciculi of a Compendious History of the Church of England from 1500, and of "Memoirs of the English Orthodox Clergy" since the same date; both in the handwriting of Dodd, the historian.
A packet of original letters to and from the Rev. Alban Butler, Bishops Stonor, Tho. Talbot, and Challoner, Mr. Brockholes, W. Green, John Hornyhold, and H. Tich. Blount, from 1748 to 1777.

A thick folio volume, unpaged, consisting of the letters and papers, manuscript and printed, of the Rev. Dr. Robert Gradwell, Rector of the English College at Rome, and Coadjutor of the London district, being for the most part his correspondence with the Very Rev. Wm. Poynter, Bishop of Halia, from 1817 to 1828.
A thick folio volume, unpaged, consisting of the journals of Dr. Gradwell, from his arrival at Rome, Monday, 2 Nov. 1817 to 21 March 1825, with various illustrative papers.
A volume in folio, unpaged, consisting of the journals of Dr. Gradwell, from Friday, 15 April 1825 to his arrival in London, 23 Aug. 1828, with several papers connected with the history of the students in the English College.
A volume in folio, unpaged, with the title "Diarium " illarum rerum quæ Duaci an. 1575, a festo Omnium " Sanctorum in Anglorum Seminario evenerunt." The entries, many of which are exceedingly curious, extend to 8 Aug. 1593.
At the end occur copies of the following letters:—
Dr. Ric. Barrett, president of Douay, to Card. Caietan, Apostolic Legate. Dat. Rheims, 6 Jan. 1590.
Card. Caietan, in answer to the above. Dat. Paris, 6 Feb. 1570.
Dr. Barrett to the Cardinal, Rheims, 31 March 1590.
Cardinal Caietan, in reply, Paris, 4 April 1590.
Dr. Edmund Gennings to Dr. Barrett, Abbeville, 17 April 1590.
A volume in folio, extending from pp. 401 to 648, consisting of miscellaneous letters and papers, of which the more important are the following:—
1. Morgan Clenock to the Archpriest, in favour of Lewis Vaughan, 2 papers.
2. Papers concerning the English Agency at Rome.
3. Remarks concerning the new Martyrology for England, Scotland, and Ireland, published about 1630.
4. The English Catholics to the King of France, asking for his intercession.
5. Papers concerning the Archpriest Blackloe and Bishop Smith.
6. Status Angliæ, ultimo Januarii 1635.
7. Observanda pro clariori notitia status religionis Catholicæ in Anglia, 1635.
8. List of the Protestant Bishops in England in 1635.
9. Instructions for the Agent at Rome on various matters connected with the condition of England in 1635.
10. Status cleri regni Hiberniæ, 1638.
11. Lord Digby's speech in favor of Lord Strafford.
12. Letters of the Privy Council of England for disarming Catholics, 20 Jan. and 28 Feb. 1612.
13. Various papers concerning the Visitation of Douay College, Nov. and Dec. 1612.
14. Thomas Tunstall's account "of the manner of " F. Walpoules giving of the exercise to one of the " scholars," Engl., with a Latin translation.
15. New rules issued in Douay College, Nov. 1612.
A volume in 4to. consisting of 87 pp. containing " A Catalogue of the several treatises written by J. " S[erjeant] for Catholic Faith, with the names of the " Protestant authors he refuted, most of which were of " the greatest fame for learning, and highest dignity " for place; and the issue of the particular contests " and the final upshot of the whole controversy." Prefixed is a dedication to the Right Hon. my Lord Perth. The treatise is dated, at the end, Paris, 3 Sept. 1700. From the corrections and additions with which it abounds, this would appear to be the author's copy.
A bundle of papers respecting the history of Douay College.
1. A general account of the present state of the college, 1 Feb. 1672.
2. A similar paper, May 1670.
3. A similar paper, 1 Jan. 1673.
4. Clement VIII. to Geo. Blackwell, 5 Oct. 1602.
5. Extract from the first Douay Diary concerning the College.
6. Letter from the President of Douay to the Nuncio Apostolic of Belgium respecting the College, and other matters, 26 Oct. 1622.
7. "The manner of F. Walpole's giving the exercise " to one of the scholars," signed Thomas Tunstall.
8. History of the foundation and estate of Douay College, May 1666.
9. Names of those students of Douay who have taken the oath appointed by the Propaganda at Rome in 1627, 1628, and 1629.

JOSEPH STEVENSON.

UNIVERSITY COLLEGE, OXFORD.

The various ancient documents, now in the possession of this College, are mentioned in the order in which they were brought to my notice by Mr. E. J. Payne.—

The oldest Computi, or Bursars' Accounts, of the College, that are now known to exist, are the following :—

"Compotus Magistri Roberti Bower, Socii ac Pro-
" curatoris Collegii Magistri Willelmi de Dunelmo,
" Mickel Universite Hall vulgariter nuncupati, a Festo
" Sancti Michaelis Archangeli, anno regni Regis
" Ricardi, Secundi post Conquæstum, quinto, usque ad
" idem Festum anno revoluto." We here see it styled
" The College of William de Durham, commonly called
" Mickel (Great) University Hall " (A.D 1382, 3).

The following places in Oxford are named in this Account-roll as paying rents to the College, the Latin notes against them, as to the locality, being in a hand of the 17th century :—Maydenhall (in St. Peter's in the East); Olyfaunthalle, or Elephant Hall (in St. Mildred's Parish); Shield Hall (St. Mildred's); St. Thomas' Hall (St. Mildred's); University Hall (or the Lesser University Hall) in Schools Street (St. Mary's Parish); Brasenose Hall (St. Mary's); Hamptone Hall (St. Mildred's); St. Edward's Hall (St. Mary's); Stantone Hall (St. Mary's); Crowdale Hall (St. Peter's in the East); Lodelow Hall (St Peter's in the East); Holwey's House and garden (opposite All Saints'); John Baret's House (St. Mary's); tenement of John Brasier (St. Peter's in the East); the garden beyond the Castle (St. Thomas' Parish); Canterbury College (St. Edward the King); tenement of Richard Merser (St. George's); the shop of Pyry; tenement of William Sanders; tenement of Robert Westby (All Saints'); tenement of John Wyndesore; tenement of John Shethor—Waginarii—(St. Martin's Parish); tenement of Richard Cornewayle (All Saints' Parish); added to which are, rents from Holdernesse, (in the county of York). Against the "shop of Pyry" is a Latin note to this effect—" Perhaps at the corner of " Carfax—but query." In another hand, " A false con- " jecture." (Who shall decide?) The mention of Brase- nose Hall, at this early date, will not escape the reader's notice.

Among the chambers which then paid rent are,—" The " principal Chamber. The chamber next to it. The " chamber under it. The chamber above the kitchen- " garden (erbarium), near the hall. The chamber " above the kitchen garden, in the other pleasure " garden (disporto). The chamber with the hall. The " chamber opposite the well. The chamber next to it."

Payments are made,—" To the Canon of St. Frides- " wyde, the proctor of the Abbey of Abyndone, the " proctor of Osneye, the proctor of St. Peter's in the " East." Then follow payments for commons and battels of the Fellows. Among these payments also are those,—" For the paving of Stantone Hall," " For " the paving of the Hostel (Hospitii);" in the latter being the items, " To ten boys working the sand for two days " 5s. 2d." " Ale for the workmen 12d."

The following are the "foreign," or outdoor, "ex- penses" for the year,—" Expenses of Master John " Midylton and Master Robert Gower, going to " London, and while there, on the Octaves of St. Hillary, " with their servant M.J., and Robert Westby with " his servant. First at Tettisworthe, drink 1½d., horse- " bread 1½d. At Wycumbe, staying there the night, " for bread 1d., ale 2d., eggs 2d., wine 5d., fire 2d., " candles ½d., bed 1d., hay for three horses 3d., oats 6d., " shoeing ½d. On the morrow, at Woxebrigge [Ux- " bridge], for bread 1d., ale 1d., wine 2½d., meat 4d., " horse-bread 3d. At London, the same day, before " supper, for drink 2d., for supper 11d., hay for three " horses 3d., oats 6d. The second day at London, " for breakfast 4d., supper 11d., oats for three horses 3d., " straw 1d. The third day at London, for dinner 5d., " supper 7d., oats 3d., horse-bread 1½d. The fourth " day at London, for breakfast 2d., drink 1½d., supper " 9d., oats 3d. The fifth day at London, for breakfast, " in bread 1d., drink 2d., meat 3d., fire 1d.; for supper, " in bread 1d., drink 3d., meat 2d., fire 2d., beds 2d., " candle ½d., oats 3d. The sixth day at London, for " dinner 14d. At night, for beds 1d., fire 1d., candle ½d., " oats 3d. The seventh day at London, for dinner 12d., " beds 2d., drink 2d., fire 1d., candle 1½d., oats 3d. The " eighth day at London, at dinner, for bread 1½d., meat " 4d., fire 2d. At night, bread 1½d., drink 2d., meat 2d., " beds 2d., fire 2d., candle ½d., oats 3d. The ninth " day at London, for bread 1½d., drink 2d., meat 4d., " fire 1d. At supper, bread 1½d., drink 2d., fire 1d., " beds 2d., candle ½d., horse-bread 2d. The tenth day " at London, at dinner, bread 1½d., drink 2d., meat 3d., " fire 1d. At supper, bread 1d., drink 2d., meat 3d.,

" fire 1d., bed 2d., candle ½d., oats 3d. The eleventh " day at London, for breakfast 4½d. At dinner, for " bread 1d., drink 2d., meat 5d., fire 2d., horse-bread ½d., " pay for three horses nine days and nights 5s. On the " same day, after breakfast, the expenses of Master " Robert Gower from London to Oxford.—At Woxe- " brigge [Uxbridge] staying the night, bread ½d., drink " 1d., meat 3d., fire ½d., bed 1d., hay 1d., oats 1½d., " horse-bread ½d. At Wycumbe, for dinner, drink 1d., " meat 2d., horse-bread 1d. At Tettusworthe, drink ½d., " horse-bread ½d. I also paid to our attorney in the " Common Bench [Pleas] 6s. 8d. For wine given to " Ed. Gifford and Alan Couper 10d. For a copy of " the plea 13d. For wine given to David Hanmer 11d. " For hire of one horse 20d." On the above journey the servants, if they accompanied the Fellows on the road, must have walked, if they did not ride behind their masters. In the year 1383, David Hanmer, a Ser- jeant-at-law, (who was treated with drink, as stated in the Account) became a Justiciar of the King's Bench. His daughter, Margaret, was the wife of Owen Glyndowr.

The next Computus is for the 6th and 7th year of the same reign, (A.D. 1383, 4,) being the Account of Master John Taylor, Fellow and Proctor. In it repairs of the " White Hall " within the College, are mentioned. The " women who drew out the straw " (for the thatch) were paid 5d. " Red lead (cerussa) for the tilers 1d." Moss 6½d. (for binding the clay walls). Red earth 4d. Mending the lock of the hall door 2d.; that of the buttery 1d. Under the repairs of Stanton Hall, the "stable" is mentioned. " For ale for the cleansers of the latrine " (cloacariis) 1d."

The next Computus is for the 7th and 8th year of the same reign (A.D. 1384, 5); being the Account of Master Richard Gysborn. Among the Expenses are,—" For gifts " for having counsel, in wine and breakfast, and one writ " and other matters 32s. 11½d." " For wine given to " the men of Abyndone, in the chamber of Gower 12d. " To a kinsman of Belknap, (probably Robert Belknap, " the then Chief Justice of the Common Pleas) 8d." The manciple and cook, the barber, and the laun- dress, receive pay. The rent received for the " White " Hall " (within the College) this year, is 12s.

The next Computus is for the 8th year of the same reign (A.D. 1385, 6); being the Account of Master John Pokelyngton (who was afterwards Master of the College). Among the sums expended are,—" For Taylor and " Gower going to the last Parliament, at London 30s. " For wine for Charltone and his wife 2s. 4d. For " spices (dessert) 11d. For wine for Burley, and other " necessaries 19d." (not improbably, Sir Simon Burley, who was afterwards beheaded). " For mending a " chalice 4d. For parchment for the register 4d. For " parchment for the roll 4d." As in the preceding year, the repairs of the Halls belonging to the College were carried on upon a large scale, those of Shield Hall more particularly. The walls of the College itself were repaired with straw; used, no doubt, for mixing with the clay.

The next is the Computus for the 9th year of Richard the Second (A.D. 1386, 7), but it is much mutilated at the beginning. From the accounts for their commons, it would seem that the Fellows were then but three in number. Among the "Expenses," are,—" For wine given to the Chancellor [of the " University] at the time of the Account 8d. For " pears 2d. For moos (moss) and stones 12d. Paid " John Leper 3s. 4d. Paid Edmund Keenyan 3s. 4d. " For wine given to Charltone and his kinsman 3s. 8d. " For spices given to the same 7d. For mosse, and " mending a roller (tribulæ) 5½d. For lattes [laths] " and pynnys 3s. 4d. To John Glasyer, for making " windows for our Chapel, and other work, 6s. 5d." (This is the earliest mention of the College Chapel in these accounts). " For a mortar, and the pestle " thereof 4s. 4d." Under the repairs of Drowdal Hall, a " board for the well " (tabula gurgitis) is mentioned, price 2½d. " For soudyr (solder), and the making " thereof 20d." " Red earth," as being used for buildings, repeatedly occurs. The students in the College who paid rent for their rooms, were William Multone and Richard Pester.

The next Account now existing, is the Computus of Master Robert Gower, for the 11th year of Richard the Second (A.D. 1388, 9). Wyntyrtone has a room this year, in succession, apparently, to Multone; while persons named "Plymtone" and "Stapyltone" also pay for rooms. Four Fellows are now receiving commons and battels. Among the "Expenses" are " Wine and " pears for the Chancellor 7d. To a writer (scriptori) " 2s. For binding the quires (ligaturæ quaternorum) 5d. " For one rake for the garden 6d. For a wheel of the

"spit (? *verticulo catostæ*) —. For a carpenter working
"at the hen-house (*domum gallinarum*) 12*d*."

The next Computus, now existing, is that of John
Marshall, for the 14th year of the same reign (A.D.
1391, 2). Among the items are,—" Paid a certain Friar
"for bringing back a book to the College 18*d*. For
"wine for the Chancellor, at the time of the Account
"10*d*. For wine and a breakfast given to Sir Robert
"Charltone 30*d*. For gloves given to his men 2*s*. 5*d*.
"For wine at the time when Master Robert Gower
"entered upon (*intravit*) the 'Sententiæ,' 2*s*. 4*d*. For
"mending 2 *bankqwers* (coverings of the benches for
"the banquet, or dessert) 4*d*. To a boy for mending
"the well (*fontis*), 2*d*. To boys for cleansing the am-
"bulatory (*spatiatorium*) 4*d*."

The next Computus is that of Thomas Foston, for
the 15th year of the same reign (A.D. 1392, 3). Four
Fellows were now in residence.—"For straw for the
"wall between our College and Little University Hall
"18*d*" (probably the "White Hall," which lately formed
part of the College buildings). "For wine, when the
"servant of Sir Robert Scharelton (Charlton) supped
"with Master John Taylyor 4*d*. For trees for the
"pleasure-garden (*disporto*) 12*d*. For mending the
"Chapel vestments 21*d*." The expenses for building
the wall between the College and Little University Hall
are then added. Then,—"For carrying away the old
'wall between our pleasure-garden and the pleasure-
"garden of Lodlow Hall. For one vestment before
"the altar in our Chapel 22*d*. For candles in the
"Chapel 12*d*. For *torchys* 16*d*." Under the head of
Hampton Hall:—"To James Sthaytchare (Thatcher),
"for 7 days, 2*s*. 4*d*. To his wife, as many days 14*d*."

The next now existing is the Computus of John
Fayt, for the years 1399, 1400. New College pays
a rent, for Maydynhalle. The number of Fellows has
now increased to six : the chambers in the College inhabited by those not Fellows, have also increased in
number ; one of them is held, at a rent of 13*s*. 4*d*., by
John, a monk of Furness. Master Henry Crumpe pays
20*d*. to this College, his name having occurred about
ten years before ; he was originally an opponent of
Wyclif, but afterwards became his strong supporter.

The next is a Computus of John Fayt, 2nd year of
Henry the Fourth (A.D. 1400, 1). A number of payments first occur here for various Schools in Oxford.—
"For the Lower Schools 4*s*. For one Upper School
"2*s*. 6*d*. For another School 20¼*d*. Petyngtone owes
"for his Schools 20*d*."

The Computus, or Account, of Thomas Heth, for the
3rd year of Henry the Fourth (A.D. 1401, 2), is the
next. Three of the Schools before-named are here
called "The three Schools in Schools Street." "Ex-
"penses in the Library 17*s*. 11*d*."

The next Account is, apparently, for the year 1406,
but without the name of the Procurator, or Bursar, or
the year, being mentioned. After this date, the accounts
of expenditure are almost wholly omitted, reference
being evidently intended to be made to other rolls or
papers, which have probably long since perished.
Among the rents received in this reign appears one
(40*s*.) for the "Little University Hall, in High Street,"
the former "White Hall," probably. Some, if not many,
of these latter Computi, which, in general, are nothing
but long rent-rolls, have the signature of the Chancellor
of the University, as Visitor *ex officio*, in the reigns of
Henry the Fifth and Henry the Sixth. The preceding
Computi are all in Latin.

A somewhat mutilated roll of parchment, in Latin,
bearing date 1423, intituled (tr.):—" Memorandum as
"to the things, vessels, and other instruments, belong-
"ing as well to the buttery as the kitchen of the College
"of William of Durham in Oxford ; delivered into the
"custody of Thomas Benwell, Procurator, and of
"Thomas Talbot, cook, of the same College, A.D.
"1423." The following are some extracts :—" In the
"buttery, a piece of silver, with a coverele to the same ;
"14 silver spoons, 9 with long handles (*stert*), and
"5 with shorter, 12 having the founder's arms . . .
"2 wooden tables, one gallon, and one *pynt*. One pipe
"(*pipa*) for keeping the cloths, closed with a key. One
"cask for *vordjuse* (verjuice), another for lentils, and
"one other for *uysell* (? vinegar). A cloth for the high
"table, one wanting . . . A chest for keeping
"cloths ; and another which stood in the Chapel, with
"a cover. Two table-cloths for the high table, one for
"principal days. Four hand-napkins, for placing after
"dinner, two of the best cloth, for principal days . .
". . Memorandum, that Master John Castell lost
"one spoon, price —." "Instruments of the kitchen"
follow ; and then "In the office of the Procurator—
"There are in the keeping of Thomas Benwell, the

"Procurator—First, one good bushel, sealed with the
"Chancellor's seal. One barrow, with a wheel : 2
"rollers ; 2 mattocks ; one sieve ; three benches, one
"long, another shorter, and the third, in the kitchen,
"very short. One pair of balances, with weights, for
"gold. One spit for birds, made of *voyer*."

The following are some items from an English description of the furniture in the Master's Lodge, at a
later date :—" The Colledge stuffe in hospitio Magistri,
"A.D. 1587°, anno regni Elizabethæ 29°, Maii 12°."
"In the haule below, a backe and side bench of wayns-
"cott . . . A court cupboorde . . . A waynscott
"portall. 2 waynscott windowes with cubboordes. In
"the upper haule . . . Hangings of greene say. In
"the little chamber. A bedsteede corded. Hanginges
"of greene and red saye. A curtayne in the window.
"A vallaunce of red velvet, about the bedsteede. In
"the gallerie. A joyned table, with 3 formes. Mattes
"in the flowre. Mappe—Orbis nova divisio in 4[er]
"partes, secundum neotericos (A new division of the
"globe into four parts, according to the moderns).
"A Mapp of the Low Countreyes. A mapp of Spayne.
"The mapp of the Worlde by Ortelius. Mercator's
"mapp of Europe. A mapp of Italye. . . . The
"pictures of the 7 Liberall Sciences. A mappe of the
"sege of Malta. In the studie . . . In the wayn-
"scote chamber . . . A bed-stedde. A truccle bed."
"Hanginges of Dornix [Damask of Tournay], etc."

There are a considerable number of ancient deeds in
the possession of this College, dating from the time of
Henry the Third, if not an earlier date. Several of
them are in a mutilated, and almost illegible, condition,
owing apparently to the action of fire at some remote
period : but most, if not all, of them, have been transcribed into a series of eleven quarto volumes, compiled
about the close of the 17th century, and beginning of the
18th, by William Smith, for many years Senior Fellow
of the College, and afterwards Rector of Melsonby, in
Yorkshire. He was the author also of a book, now of
considerable rarity, intituled,—" The Annals of Uni-
"versity College, proving William of Durham the true
"Founder : and answering all their arguments who
"ascribe it to King Alfred," printed at Newcastle-upon-
Tyne, in 1727. These volumes, still kept in the Muniment-room, are a striking monument of the writer's
industry.

One of the earliest deeds, followed by a series relating to the same property, is an indenture (in Latin)
beautifully written, and perfect, whereby William le
Orfoure (Goldsmith), of Oxford, conveys to Philip de
Wormenhale and Alice, his wife, his messuage, situate
in the parish of All Saints in Oxford, containing one
hall with three sollars [or sun-rooms] and two cellars,
and one brewhouse, for the lives of them and of either
of them, at a yearly rent of 34*s*. 4*d*. Dated at Oxford,
on the Saturday next before the Decollation of St. John
the Baptist, in the 24th year of the reign of King Edward
the First (A.D. 1296.) "Witnesses, Philip de Owe,
"Mayor of Oxford, Thomas de Henxe and Ralph de
"Stoke, bailiffs, Henry Oweyn, John de Ow, Nicholas
"Orfeure, Thomas de Mowy, Andrew de Pyrye, Robert
"de Wormenhale, Richard Especer, William de
"Hedindon, and others."

There is another still earlier deed, somewhat mutilated by fire, date about 1240 ; whereby Henry Segrim
and Matilda, his wife, convey to Andrew Achart,
parson of Spersholt, a tenement lying near the land of
William Knyt, in Kiboldestret, in the Parish of St. John,
in Oxford, for a yearly rent of 4 shillings, he having
already given 2 marks and a quarter of wheat. "Wit-
"nesses, Hugh Fulvus and Thomas Granger, then
"Provosts, Richard Bodi', Richard Curteis, Pentecoste,
"William Crompe, Hugh Fitz-Philip, William Knyt,
"William Clerk, and others." This deed is beautifully
written. The two oblong seals are in fine condition ;
one, in green wax, representing, apparently, a French
lily, has the legend " S. Henrici Segrim ;" the other,
also in green wax, represents a rose, with the legend
" S. Maltilde,"—" the seal of Maltilda." The person
calling himself " Pentecoste," without any other name,
was probably a Jew.

A deed dated the 20th of February, in the 8th year
of King Henry the VIIth, being a Composition between the King and " his humble oratours and daily
"bedemen, John Rokesburgh, Clerk," Master of the
College, and the Fellows thereof—witnessing that the
King, " of his bounteous grace, and for the tender
"zeal, love, and charitable affection, that his good
♥ grace beareth and bath unto the soul of Dame Anne
"late Countess Warrewyke deceased, whom God
"pardon and assoile, of his most blessed and charitable
"almes, for divers great considerations moving his

" noble Grace," had given 40l. sterling to the said
" Master, to be distributed, " for the health and wele of
" the soul " of the said Countess, in manner following :
—"The said Maister and Fellows shall kepe or do to
" be kept within the said College yerely, during the
" term of four score yeers" then next ensuing, " a
" solempne *Dirige* by note on that day that it
" fortuned the said noble Countesse to decease on;
" that is to say, yerely on the day of Seint Mighell
" the Archangell, and a solempne Mass of *Requiem*
" to be kept and devoutly songe there on the morowe
" for the soul of the same noble Countesse ; and that
" the Maistor of the said College . . . shall sing
" the said Masse, if he be disposed so to do, or else the
" said Maister . . . shall commaund and do some
" other discreet and virtuous preste and Fellowe of the
" said College in his sted in that behalve, and that as
" wel the said Maister or ony other Felowe, that shalle
" so synge the said high Masse in his stede, as all
" other Felowes of the same Colleg, tho which shall
" be disposed to sing Masse there that day, shall de-
" voutly remembre in his Masse these words in his
" Secund *Memento*, after the receyvinge of Cristis
" body—'Ihesu, Fili David, miserere animæ famulæ
" ' tuæ, Annæ nuper Comitissæ Warrewyke,' and that
" every poure scoler of the tenne poure scolers
" founded by the charitable almes of the College,
" shulle say, devoutly knelynge on their knees, bitwene
" thelevacion and the reception of the most glorious
" and blessed body of Criste—'Ihesu, Fili' [etc., as
" above] ; for the whiche yeroly Obits, Masses, praiers,
" and godly observaunces, so in fourme above said
" solemply and devoutly to be observed, stablished,
" and kept, the said Maister and his successours,
" Maisters of the said College for tho tyme beynge,
" shulle dispose and distribute, or cause to be disposed
" and distributed, yerely, every yare, duringe the
" terme of four score yeres above said, for the soule of
" the sayde noble Countesse, tenne shillings in maner
" and fourme ensuynge ; that is to wyte, to the saide
" Maister of the said Colege for the tyme beynge, xiid.,
" to every Folowe of the same Colege vid., and to
" every of the said ten poure scolers iiiid. ; and overe
" and beside this, the said Maister and Felowes, for
" them and their successours, by common assent and
" aggreement, receyve and grauntene by those presents
" the soule of the said good Lady to be partener and
" partable amonge the soules of other noble benefac-
" tours of the said place of there Masses, praiers, [the
" following words down to ' graces,' have a line
" through them] indulgences, bulles, remissions,
" graces, and suffrages of Cristis Holy Chirche, tho
" whiche shalbe ministered, said, or done, by the said
" Maister and Felowes within the said Colege duringe
" allo the said terme. To the whiche Diriges, Masses,
" prayers, observances, and godly suffrages of Cristis
" holy Chirche, feithfully, fermely, and inviolably, to
" be kept and observed in manere and fourme above-
" said, the said Maister and Felowes, and their suc-
" cessours, bynden them in their consciences before
" Almighty God by these presentes, during allo the
" terme aforesaid." The College have thereto set their
seal, and the King has commanded his to be set thereto.
H.R. (the letters running one into the other) is added
at the foot.

The above-named Anne, Countess of Warwick, was
Anne (Beauchamp), widow of Richard Neville, Earl
of Warwick, known in history as " the Kingmaker,"
who was slain at the Battle of Barnet in 1471.

The Admission Books and Registers of the College,
now known to exist, are comparatively few in number,
dating from only the close of the 17th century.

It is with much pleasure that I acknowledge my
obligations to C. J. Faulkner, Esqre., Fellow, Tutor, and
Bursar, of the College, for the facilities he afforded me
in examining the contents of the Muniment-room under
his charge. I also owe my best thanks to E. J. Payne,
Esqre., Fellow of the College, for many marks of kind
attention which I received from him, and for the readiness with which, with the view of aiding me in the inspection of these documents, he placed both his personal
services and his rooms at my disposal.

And further, before concluding my Report on the
records of University College, I gladly avail myself of
this opportunity of acknowledging how greatly I have
been indebted to the Revd. Claude Delaval Cobham,
B.C.L., M.A., a member of the College; for the friendly
spirit and energy shown by him, on several occasions, in
doing his utmost to ensure and facilitate my inspection of the archives of several of the Colleges in this
University.

HENRY THOMAS RILEY.

WADHAM COLLEGE, OXFORD.

By the courtesy of the Revd. Dr. Griffiths, the Warden,
to whom I have the pleasure of here expressing my
obligations, I am enabled to give an account of what
may be called "the archives" of this College. They
will be found to be but very limited in number ; owing
mainly to the fact that the House itself,—though it has
well held its own since it was founded,—is but of comparatively recent foundation.—

The Admission Book of the Wardens, Fellows, and
Scholars, of the College, is a large volume, half bound,
with paper leaves, about 300 in number, and coming
down from the earliest days of the College to the present
time.

The first written page, with 1610 entered in the margin,
commences with an account, in Latin, of the laying of
the foundation of the College, formally attested by a
Notary Public, and preceded by the title of the book ;
the following is a translation of it, with which I have
been kindly favoured by the Warden :—"Book of Wad-
" ham College, as to admissions of Wardens, Fellows,
" Scholars, and others, to the said College. In the
" name of God, Amen. By the present public instru-
" ment let it appear evidently unto all, and be known,
" that on Tuesday, to wit, the last day of July, be-
" tween the hours of eight and eleven before noon on
" that day, and in the eighth year of the reign of our
" Lord, James, by the grace of God, of England,
" France, and Ireland, King, defender of the Faith, &c.
" and over Scotland the forty-fourth, the ' Te Deum
" 'laudamus' having been first solemnly sung with
" voices and instruments, and an elegant oration having
" then been made by the Worshipful George Ryves,
" Doctor of Divinity, and Warden of the College of
" Saint Mary Winton in Oxford; in the eastern part
" of this College of Wadham, that is, in the Chapel or
" Church, to the honour of God, the Father, the Son, and
" the Holy Ghost, by the sacred hands of the Worship-
" ful John King, Doctor of Divinity, Vice-Chancellor
" of this benign University of Oxford and Dean of
" Christ Church, and the Worshipful Richard Kilbey,
" Rector of Lincoln College, George Ryves, Warden of
" the College of Saint Mary Winton in Oxford, John
" Spenser, President of Corpus Christi College, and
" John Williams, Principal of Jesus College, Doctors of
" Divinity, in the names of the distinguished gentle-
" man, Nicholas Wadham, Esquire, lately deceased, and
" of Dorothy, his relict, were laid the foundations, or
" rather was laid the chief foundation stone, of this re-
" nowned College of Wadham, so for future ages in the
" perpetual course of time from henceforth to be called.
" Which things being so done, had, and performed,
" to the honour of God, the Father, the Son, and the
" Holy Ghost, there was had another performance of
" vocal and instrumental music." Followed by the
attestation of Thomas Frenche, M.A., Notary Public.
Dorothy Wadham, the Foundress, was not present at
this ceremonial.

The next two pages are occupied with the formal pro-
ceedings on the admission of Robert Wright, Doctor
of Divinity, nominated by the Foundress to be the first
Warden, 20th April 1613. On the five following pages
is recorded the admission of the first Fellows, Scholars,
Chaplains, Clerks, and Servants, on the same 20th of
April, all having been nominated in like manner by the
Foundress.

On the 2nd of September in the same year (p. 9), upon
the resignation of Dr. Wright, John Flemyng was appointed Warden by the Foundress.

The Founder and Foundress residing at Merifield in
Somerset, there was at this period a great influx of
persons born in that country. Robert Blake, afterwards
the celebrated Admiral under the Commonwealth, a
native of Bridgwater, was a Commoner of this College ;
but not being on the foundation, his name does not
appear in the volume under notice. William Blake,
of Bridgwater, probably his brother, was admitted
a Scholar, it is here stated (p. 19), on the 30th of June
1620. Unlike the Admiral, he was an adherent of the
royal cause.

P. 20, Tobias Venner, born at Bridgwater, aged 16, is
admitted a Scholar, 30 June 1622 : probably a son of
Tobias Venner, who practised as a physician for many
years at Bridgwater and elsewhere in Somerset, and
died in 1660, aged 83. The physician wrote in dispraise
of the Bath waters, taken internally ; and is still remembered in literature by his "Via recta ad Vitam longam,"
a treatise on the right mode of living to ensure a long
life.

On p. 41 are recorded two Orders of the Committee for the Reformation of the University. By the first, dated 3 March 1648, Dr. Pitt was removed from the office of Warden. but no mention was made of Wilkins. By the second, dated 7 April 1648, John Wilkins was appointed Warden, in the place of Dr. Pitt, so removed. The two Orders together constitute the procedure whereby John Wilkins, of Magdalen Hall, (the mathematician, afterwards Bishop of Chester), was substituted as Warden for Dr. Pitt. The second Order begins as follows :—" April 7, 1648. Att the Committee " of Lords and Commons for the Reformation of the " Universitie of Oxon. Whereas it appeares to this " Committee, and accordingly was resolved, that Dr. " Pitt was guiltie of high contempt and denyall of au- " thoritie of Parliament, and for an effectuall remedie " thereof it was alsoe resolved, that the said Dr. Pitt be " removed from being Warden of Wadham College " in the Universitie of Oxford, and that John Wilkins, " Master of Arts, be Warden of the said College." At the foot it is stated that this is a true copy of the decree, attested by Thomas Fulkes, Notary Public ; who, instead of the Notary's usual device of a knot, or a wreath, or tho like, has this motto.—"Est Deus, occultos qui vetat " esse dolos." In the margin is signed " Joh. Wilkins, " Gardiañ," in the Notary's hand. On the 3rd of October following, six new Fellows were elected by the Parliamentary Visitors.

In p. 48 is the admission of Gilbert Ironside as Scholar, born at " Steepleton in Com. Dorset ; " admitted 9th July 1651. He was probably son of the Prebendary of York of that name, who was made Bishop of Bristol in 1660, and died in 1671. He was afterwards Warden of the College, and himself became Bishop of Bristol in 1689. On the 25th of September 1652 is entered the admission of Thomas Spratt as Scholar, born at Tallaton, in the county of Devon: he afterwards became Bishop of Rochester.

In p. 76 is entered the admission of Thomas Dunster as a Scholar, 24th September 1675, aged 18, born at Ilminster, in the County of Somerset. He became Warden in 1689.

In p. 79 are the admissions, as Scholars, on the 28th of September 1677, of Humphrey Hody, born at Odcombe, in Somerset, Robert Doyley, born at Southrop, in the County and Diocese of Gloucester, and Thomas Creech, born at Blandford in the County of Dorset, aged 16. Hody was afterwards a celebrated Divine, and Creech is still remembered as the translator of Lucretius, whose example he unfortunately followed in committing the act of self-destruction. Robert Doyley, not improbably, was a member of the same family as Sir William D'Oyley, often mentioned by Pepys in his Diary.

At page 85, under 29th September 1683, one " John " Sagittario," born at Blandford Forum, in the county of Dorset, is admitted a Scholar. The name is spelt " Sagittary," on his admission as a Fellow in 1690.

The admissions, which are limited to those of members on the foundation, stop short at page 102, the year 1694, and are continued at page 121, from 1738 to the present time. The entries for the intervening years are lost, and the cause of this singular hiatus seems to be now unknown.

The earliest Register of the Acts of the College is a paper book, in old leather binding, in good condition ; the entries beginning in 1610.

On the first fly-leaf is the following entry :—" Dec. 22º " año Dñi 1618. Wee the Warden and Fellowes of " Wadham College decree that our trustie Manciple " John Williams, for his diligent and faithfull service to " our College, (for which he was much respected by our " honourable Foundresse during her life, and deserveth " to be well esteemed of us), shall have weekely of every " Fellow-commoner ld., of every other Commoner ob. " qu. (½d.) and of every Batteller ob. (½d.), for his better " incouragement to continewe his carefull and honest " paines. Provided that this grant, made to the said " John Williams, extende to no other man which shall " succeede him ; nor to him any longer then he shall " continewe in his mancipleshippe. William Smythe, " Warden," and the then Fellows.

Page 4, (tr). " On the 12th day of December, 1614, let- " ters were sent to the College, written by Mr. John " Arnolde, signifying the liberality of the most honour- " able Foundress, who with full hand poured forth [ef- " fundebat] 60 pounds to her College ; of which the " following is a faithful copy :—" Good Mr. Doctor. I " have sollicited your sute for your Company unto my " mistris, and I have prevayled so farre with her, as " that she hath sent you, to discharge the carryadge " and settlinge of your bookes, with the makings of your

" seales, fifty poundes ; and withall because yt is the " first Christmas that hath byn kept in Wadham Col- " ledge, my Mrs. hath sent you likewise tenn poundes, " which must be spent this Christmas in Gawdyes " from her, as a token of her remembrance unto the " whole Company ; these monyes are sent by me in " gould, and my mistrisse refers the managinge of yt " unto your self, and the acquayntinge of your Com- " pany with yt. And so with my best remembrance to " your self, and my kynde love to all my good freindes, " I leave you to,God, remayninge alwayes to the uttmost " of my power, your faithfull freind, John Arnolde."

Page 5, the Foundress says, in a postscript to a Letter, dated in 1614. " I would have prayers and fasting dayes " dewlye observed in the house, not allowing any in " theyre chambres to breake it, or elsewhere within the " Colledge."

P. 13. In a Letter dated May 23d, 1616, she says :— " often hearing from you doth greatly revive my minde, " being mine only joy, to understand of all your well- " fares, and that there is unity amongst you."

P. 19.—" I Dorothe Wadham, of Edge, in the county " of Devon, widdow, do decree and ordaine, that the " time of supping, and the disputations that have been " after supper, may be at any howers, at the discretion " of the Warden, so farro forth, that the length of the " disputations be not contracted or shortned ; which I " commande be diligently observed, and still continued " for that length of time as is expressed in my " statutes."

Page 20. She gives direction as to her " servant " Arnold's two kinsmen, now Scollers," being elected into the next two Fellowships that shall be void.

Page 44. A.D. 1627, Mr. Harrington, a Fellow, is deprived of all benefits of his fellowship, he having a private income of 40 pounds per annum. In the following page he is ordered to appear before the Visitor, at Westminster, on the 10th of January next.

On the 17th of November 1627, Toby Venner, B.A. and Scholar, is censured (p. 45) for neglect of certain statutes, and contempt in failing to appear. He is afterwards deprived of his scholarship, for persistence in the like conduct.

Page 49. James Harington, for his conduct, is deprived of all emoluments of his Fellowship, for 6 months, 1st Aug. 1629.

Page 100. A long letter from the King preceding, dated 5th January 1642 (3):—" It is unanimously con- " sented and agreed by the Warden and Fellowes the " 14th of January 1642 (3).—That all the plate of this " College shall be lent unto the King, according to his " Majesties request expressed in his letteres above " written, reserving only our Communion plate. Dan : " Escot, Warden, Will: Blake, Sub-warden " and eight other Fellows.

The entries in this volume end in 1690, page 172.

A paper book, folio, bound in parchment, commencing in 1609, and having for its title, in the first written page, " A note of money layde oute about the building of " Wadham College, from the month of April 1610." The accounts end on the 4th of September 1613 ; and the volume; which probably contains a complete account of the whole building expenses, is not quite filled.

In two small wooden boxes are contained a great number of very early deeds, connected with property held by the College at Writtle, near Chelmsford, in the county of Essex. The following is an account of some few of them, which have been selected for notice :—

A parchment deed, in good condition, of the 14th Edward I., with an oblong seal in white wax, representing a lily, or similar flower, but with the legend effaced : its contents, which are remarkable, are as follow :—" Omnibus Christi fidelibus, ad quos præsens " scriptum pervenerit, Salona, quæ fuit uxor Bertrami " de Montepessulano, salutem in Domino. Noverit " universitas vestra, me, per ordinationem et volun- " tatem parentum et amicorum meorum, et per meam " meram voluntatem, in mea ligea potestate, dedisse et " assignasse, pro me et meis quibuscunque assignatis, " nomine consuetudinum prædictorum [?] puerorum " dicti Bertrami, ad eorum promotionem, cum ad ple- " nam ætatem pervenerint ; videlicet, Johanni, filio et " hæredi prædicti Bertrami, duos equos et unum bovem ; " pretii duarum marcarum in toto, et unam vaccam " cum vitulo suo, pretii octo solidorum in toto, et duas " oves matrices et quatuor agnos, pretii quinque soli- " dorum in toto, et unam pelvem et unum lavatorium " [de] cupro, pretii xviii. denariorum in toto, et unam " carectam ferratam, pretii vi. solidorum et viii. dena- " riorum in toto. Et Angueti, filiæ ejusdem Bertrami, " unam vaccam cum vitulo suo, pretii viii. solidorum,

" et ii. vitulos superannuatos, pretii quatuor solido-
" rum in toto, et iii. oves matrices, pretii triuro soli-
" dorum. Et Johannæ, filiæ ejusdem Bertrami, duas
" vaccas, cum vitulis earum, pretii xvi. solidorum in
" toto, et quatuor oves matrices, pretii quatuor soli-
" dorum. Quæ quidem omnia prædicta catalla dicto-
" rum puerorum, Johannis, Agnetis, et Johannæ, in
" custodia mea remanebunt, usque ad eorum plenam
" ætatem, ad commodum et in incrementum dictorum
" puerorum in omnibus. Et si dicta Agnes et Jo-
" hanna, seu altera earum, infra suam plenariam æta-
" tem fuerit maritata, dicta catalla eisdem, seu alteri
" earum sua portio, restituantur. Ego etiam, dicta
" Salona, prædictos pueros in omnibus sibi necessariis
" pro posse, usque ad eorum plenam ætatem, sustinebo;
" promittens eisdem, et alteri eorum, suam portionem
" dictorum catallorum, vel pretii, in fine eorum plenæ
" ætatis, sine fraude et diminutione, restiturem. Et
" si quis vel quæ dictorum puerorum diem clauserit
" extremum antequam ad plenam ætatem attigerit,
" catalla ipsius defuncti, sine alienatione prædicti
" defuncti, pro anima sua, et patris sui, distribuantur
" pauperibus per visum amicorum illorum.—Datum
" apud Writele, die Mercurii in festo Apostolorum
" Philippi et Jacobi, anno regni Regis Edwardi xiiii°.;
" et prædictum scriptum remaneat in custodia fratris
" Algat'."

Tr.:—"To all the faithful of Christ, to whom the
" present writing shall come, Salona, who was the wife
" of Bertram de Montpellier, greeting in the Lord.
" Know all of you that I, by ordinance and wish of my
" parents and friends, and of my own mere will, in
" my lawful power, have given and assigned, for me
" and my assigns whomsoever, in name of customs of
" the aforesaid [?] children of the said Bertram, for
" their promotion, when they shall have reached full
" age; to wit, to John, son and heir of the aforesaid
" Bertram, 2 horses and one ox, value 2 marks in all,
" and one cow with her calf, value 8 shillings in all,
" and 2 ewe sheep and 4 lambs, value 5 shillings in all,
" and one basin and one ewer [of] copper, value 18
" pence in all, and one iron-bound cart, value 6s. 8d. in
" all. And to Agnes, daughter of the same Bertram,
" one cow with her calf, value 8 shillings, and two
" calves over age, value 4 shillings in all, and 3 ewe
" sheep, value 3 shillings. And to Joan, daughter of
" the same Bertram, 2 cows with their calves, value 16
" shillings in all, and 4 ewe sheep, value 4 shillings.
" All which chattels aforesaid of the said children,
" John, Agnes, and Joan; shall remain in my keeping,
" until their full age, to the advantage of, and increase
" for, the said children in all respects. And if the said
" Agnes and Joan, or either of them, shall be married
" before being of full age, the said chattels are to be
" restored to them, or to either one her portion thereof.
" And I, the said Salona, will maintain the children
" aforesaid in all things necessary for them, until their
" full age, to the best of my power; promising to them
" and to either of them, to restore his and her own por-
" tion of the said chattels, or of the value thereof, with-
" out fraud or diminution, at the end when they reach
" full age. And if any one of the said children shall
" die before reaching full age, the chattels of the one
" so dead, without any alienation from the one aforesaid
" so dead, are to be distributed to the poor, for the soul
" of such one and of his or her father, by view of their
" friends. Given at Writele, on Wednesday the feast
" of the Apostles Philip and James, in the year of the
" reign of King Edward the 14th [A.D. 1286]; and the
" writing aforesaid is to remain in the keeping of brother
" Algat'."

A bond (in Latin) on parchment, by John Geffry, of
Fyfede, and Editha, his wife, to Richard de Aleford
and Elena, his wife; the money to be paid in the church
of All Saints, at Writtle, 30 Edward I.

Release, in Latin, on parchment, by Philip le Brun,
of Writele, of a yearly rent of 5½d. out of 6d. and one
clove (uno clavo gariophili): without date, but belonging to the earlier part of the reign of Edward I. It has
an oblong seal, in dark wax, with a fair impression of
two figures upon it.

A small parchment deed, in Latin, the seal lost,
finely written, without date, but probably the reign
of Henry III.; whereby Walter do Brome grants to
Sawalus de Salwede, for his homage and service, the
land which Roger the Gardener [Gardinerius] held of
him, in Bronwede, near Writele, at a yearly rent of
one penny, Sawalus having paid 16s. beforehand. Witnesses, Walter de Bures, Richard de Bures, William
Geryun, Philip Vineter, Roger de Brome, Reginald
Butler [Pincerna], Alexander de Widiford, Alwin de

5.

Widiford, Alured Fitz-Albini, Walter de Aldewic,
" who wrote this deed," and many others.

A parchment deed, in Latin, without date, but probably of the early part of the reign of Edward I.; being
a grant by Walter, son of Walter Tyrel, to Sawallus de
Salwede, of 10 acres in Haningefelde, at a yearly rent of
12d., half a mark having been paid beforehand. Witnesses, Robert de Cloville, William de Haningefeld,
John de Bedenestede, Roger de Haningefeld, Thomas
Parage, Sawallus Fitz-Radulf, John Peverel, Walter de
Brome, and many others. The seal, in white wax, with
a fleur-de-lis and legend, is in fair condition.

A parchment deed, in Latin, being a grant by Roger
Fitz-Radulf, of Writele, to Bertram de Montpellers,
for his homage and service, and 20s. sterling, of 20
pence of yearly rent which he was wont to receive of
William Burel out of 8 daiwerkis [elsewhere written
" daiwirkes," dayworks] of land, which William Pey
held of him near the bounds [merkos] of the market of
Writell, with a payment of two hens, at our Lord's
Nativity; also one bederepe [precaria] at the lord's
victuals, and one dry bederepe in autumn; he paying a
rent of one clove at Easter. Witnesses, Richard Cook,
Eustace de Brome, Henry de Sperkebrige, Geoffrey de
Reinos, Robert lo Waleis, Alexander de More, Robert
de Sokeleston, Geoffrey Ailmer, John Capon, William
Paskedon, and many others. The oblong seal is whole,
with a fair impression; and the deed, without date,
probably belongs to the time of Henry III.

A small parchment deed, in Latin, being a grant by
John, son of William de Legia, to Sewalus, son of
Adam de Crundene, for his homage and service, of 15
acres of land, which he had with Avice, his wife, in
maritago, in the vill of Hanigefelde, being the 10 acres
which Godewine held, and the five which William Fitz-
Muriel held, at a yearly rent of 18d., 9 shillings being
paid beforehand. Witnesses, Alexander the Chaplain,
Alwrod Gavy, William Fitz-Adam, Walter Chaplain,
Richard Chaplain of Writhell, Bartholomew de Firling,
Robert do Moryns, Richard Gay, Richard de Gurnay,
Philip the Clerk, " and many others." The seal is lost;
the deed is without date, and belongs probably to the
latter part of the reign of Henry III.

A small parchment, in Latin, with a very diminutive
red seal, dated at " Hallifeld Regis," the 10th of July,
12 Edward III. It is only remarkable, as being an
acknowledgment by John Mounpellers the younger,
son of John Mounpellers, that he has received 100s. of
John Mounpellers the elder, his brother. It was not
extremely uncommon, in the middle ages, for two
brothers to have the same Christian name.

A small parchment deed, in Latin, whereby Laurence
Waleys, Thomas Albyn, and John Ruddok, of Wrytele,
grant to Richard Stacy and others a croft, called
" Buddescroft," in Writele, for a yearly rent of one
red rose; 8 Richard II. There are two seals attached.

A parchment deed, in Latin, whereby A., Dean of
St. Paul's, and the Chapter, ratify the grant of the
Venerable Lord, William, Bishop of London, to Adam
Fitz-Nicholas of 30 acres which Robert de Moregny
held in the park of Crundene. Witnesses, A., the Dean,.
Peter of Blois, Archdeacon of London, Richard Arch-
deacon of Essex, Richard Archdeacon of Colchester,
Benedict Precentor of London, Robert de Clifford,
Master Roger the Chaplain, Richard the Younger,
Gilbert Banastre, Braund, John de St. Laurence, Henry
de Civitate, William de Poterne, Raoulf de Besançon,
Richard de Chamham. This deed must bear date about
A.D. 1198; as William de St. Mary Church became
Bishop of London in that year, and Peter of Blois,
Archdeacon, is supposed to have died soon after that
date. The seal (of the Dean and Chapter), of large
size, is broken; it represents St. Paul, with one hand
raised, in the act of benediction, and holding an open
book in the other, the people kneeling around. This
deed, which is in good preservation, is most beautifully
written.

HENRY THOMAS RILEY.

MAGDALENE COLLEGE, CAMBRIDGE.

The earliest now existing Register, or Admission
Book, of this College, begins A.D. 1644. It contains,
however, other entries besides admissions, and is styled
within the cover, in an old hand, " College Register,
" No. I." It is a small folio volume of 233 leaves,
bound in old calf, and its title, on the obverse of the
first page, is—"Catalogus Admissorum in Collegium
" Beatæ Mariæ Magdalenæ, apud Cantabrigienses,

3 P

"Anno Domini millesimo sexcentesimo quadragesimo
"quarto." The first entry is (in Latin), that "John
"Gibbon, son of Antony, of Langton, near Wragby,
"gentleman, aged 16 years, was admitted Pensioner
"the 7th day of September 1644, from the school at
"Islington. Tutor, Sir Perinchiefe". [his title as
Bachelor of Arts].
  In the same page occurs (tr.) : "Samuel Moreland.
"son of Thomas Moreland, Priest, was admitted Sizar
"in this College   May in the 19th year of his age; a
"boy of Wickham's College, near Winchester. Tutor,
"Sir Turner." This, no doubt, was the future secretary to Thurloe, and afterwards known as an experimental philosopher; whose mechanical devices at Chelsea
are mentioned by Pepys. Folio 10 b. "1649, June 9°,
"Richard Cumberland, son of Richard Cumberland,
"citizen of London, in his 17th year, of St. Paul's
"school, was admitted Pensioner; his Tutor, Mr.
"Merryweather," afterwards known as the learned and
eminently virtuous Bishop of Peterborough.
  In fol. 12a, we come to the admission of Samuel
Pepys, the Diarist: in the original Latin ;—"Oct. 1.
"1650, Samuel Peapys, filius Johannis Peapys, annos
"natus, —. e schola Paulina, admissus est Sizator, Tu-
"tor]e, Domino Morland." In the margin there is
an insertion, as in his previous admission at Trinity
Hall :—'Memorandum, eum prius admissum fuisse in
"Aula Trin. 21 die Junii ejusdem anni, ut patet ex
"testificatione Magistri Twells, ibidem Socio [sic], dat.
"Mar. 4, 165?; quo die etiam, in ordinem transiit
"Pensionariorum apud nos." Fol. 14 b. "April 28
"1653. Thomas Doughty, son of Robert Doughty,
"Schoolmaster of Wakefield, in the county of York, in
"his 16th year, was admitted a Sizar from the same
"school. Tutor, Mr. Hill." Against this entry there
is a note in pencil, in an old hand,—"Canon of Windsor,
"and preceptor to James the 2d daughters." There
are great numbers of admissions at this time (about
A.D. 1654), from the Grammar School of Berwick-upon-
Tweed. June 28, 1656, is the date of the admission of
Henry Waterland, probably brother of Daniel, the
eminent divine, afterwards Master of this College.
June 13, 1662. Fol. 30 b. (tr.) :—" John Shakespeare,
"son of a butcher of Coventry, in the county of
"Warwick, was admittted Sizar, aged 19, from the
"public School at Warwick; Master Holling being his
"tutor."
  At fol. 57 the subject changes to lists (Nov. 8, 1648)
of the then Fellows of the College, and then of all the
Fellows under the various heads, from the foundation of
the College.
  Under Oct. 17, 1650, in fol. 62, is the following entry
(tr.) :—"John Sadler, Esquire, Master of Arts, and
"one of the Masters in Chancery, was admitted
"Master or Prefect of this College, by virtue of an
"ordinance of Parliament, dated the 19th of September
"in the same year, with letters under the seal of the
"most honourable Lord, James, Earl of Suffolk." The
entry is signed by six of the then Fellows. James, Earl
of Suffolk, was the then owner of Audley End. John
Sadler, who had also been Town Clerk of the City of
London, was ejected in 1660 : a remarkable prophecy
by him will be found noticed under the head of Emmanuel College, in the preceding Report of this Commission. The election of Samuel Morland, previously
mentioned, as a Fellow, is entered in folio 63, Sept'. 24,
1651 ; as also, that of John Peschell, afterwards Master.
In fol. 63 b is entered the election of Robert Sawyer,
as Fellow, afterwards Attorney General, and named by
Pepys in his Diary : elected June 11th, 1652. In fol.
64 a, under April 16, 1653, is entered the election of
Richard Cumberland as Fellow.
  At fol. 87 b, lists begin of the then Scholars of the
College, on the various foundations, and then the dates
of later admissions of Scholars, on the same foundations ;
Samuel Morland being the earliest named, 8 July 1645.
In fol. 92 is the admission of Samuel Pepys, as a
Scholar, upon the Spendluffe foundation. "April 3°,
"1651. Ego, Samuel Pepys, admissus fui in discipulum
"hujus Collegii, pro Magistro Spenluff." The signature
of thePresident, "J. Sadler;" followed, and those of five
Fellows, among them "Sam : Morland," and "Hez :
"Burton;" the latter was afterwards Prebendary of
Norwich, and wrote the Preface to Dr. Cumberland's
Book on "The Laws of Nature." In fol. 94 is the
admission of Samuel Pepys as a Scholar "on the foun-
"dation of John Smith," three Fellows signing;
among them, his Tutor, and acquaintance in after
life, Samuel Morland.
  Some thirty leaves are written upon, beginning at.
the other end of the volume; commencing with lists of

the College plate in 1647. Much is crossed out with
ink, but the following items are still legible.—"A note
"taken of all the plate now in ye College, Apr. 7, 1647.
"In ye Master's hands: Smith eare pot; Sidley can;
"Guevara can; candle-pot, and porringer; 2 wine
"dishes; one litle square salt; a salt with three knops.
"Mr. Dacres, caudle-pot and cup. Can Bray, Colvile
"stoop, Mr. Tallents. Can Trolope, Mr. Lodington.
"Can Cotton, Mr. Hammond. Stoope Greene, eare
"pot Leek, Mr. Turner. Can Ashton, Mr. Merry-
"weather. Stoope Ashton, Dr Dacres. Stoope Knight,
"stoope Bigge, Mr. Percivalle. Left in ye Butler's
"custody,—6 stoopes Coll. Magd., bowle Byley, bowle
"Appleyard, eare pot Haslerig, ear pot Cotton, ear
"pot Cartwright. 3 old salts. One litle square salt,
"new. A double-gilt salt, 4 wine bowles, 22 spoones."
Entries follow, for the 26th of August 1647 and 16th
September 1648. On the other side of the leaf, among
articles in the Butler's custody; October 25, 1649, is entered "Pot Boone;" afterwards crossed out, with a side-
note against it,—"Ye goodman Townsend saith was lost
"before Dr. Rainbow left ye College [in 1650], on the
"Thankgiving day for ye Victory at Dublin." The
names mostly that follow the above articles of plate are
those of the Fellow-commoners, or Noblemen, by whom
they were presented on leaving.
  The next entry of plate is in 1657, and then in 1663.
In the leaves following, at this end of the volume,
various memoranda of College business are interspersed.
At p. 31 from this end is a copy of a letter (in Latin)
sent by the College, October 5, 1667, to Sir Orlando
Bridgeman, Privy Councillor, and Keeper of the Great
Seal, formerly Fellow of this College. Hezekiah Burton, before-mentioned, became his Chaplain. The lists
of the College plate are brought down to February 25th,
1714.
  There are four additional loose leaves in this volume,
containing various memoranda relative to College business; and, among them, the following, relative to Pepys
the Diarist, who seems to have got into trouble here, in
spite of his election successively to two Scholarships.
"Oct. 21, 1653, Mem. ye Peapys and Hind were solemnly
"admonished by myself and Mr. Hill for having been
"scandalously overseene in drink ye night before. This
"was done in ye presence of all ye Fellows then resident,
"in Mr. Hills chamber. John Wood, Registrarius:"
followed by, "September 9th, 1654. Memorandum,
"ye Sir White and Anderson being both taken drunke,
"should have received admonition for it, but being
"contumacious and refusing to come into ye Hall, they
"had both their names forthwith cut out of ye tables,
"and Sir White was finally expelled, though Anderson,
"upon his reading a recantation, had his name put in
"againe. J. Peachelle, Registr." On another leaf is
an inventory of the College goods, in the hands of the
Butler in 1648.
  Audit Book ; a folio volume of about 250 leaves
in old calf binding, in a somewhat tattered condition.
The earliest entry in it, is probably that in the first
page, in reference to payments from Fellow-commoners,
for the purchase of plate :—"Decretum est unanimi
"consensu Magistri et Sociorum, Martii 29° anno 1574,
"ut singuli Pensionarii post hunc diem in sociorum
"[communam] admittendi, solvant Collegio in die
"admissionis, (pro quibus eorum Tutores sponsionem
"faciant,) viginti solidos cum [? ad] poculum
"argenteum, vel aliquid ejusdem generis, compa-
"randum." Signed—Ricardus Howland Pr. . . .,
Gulielmus Bulkeley, Henricus Vaux, Jacobus Brom-
mell. Richard Howland, the Master, or President,
here named was afterwards appointed Master of St. John's
College, August 1577, or thereabouts. On the other
side of the leaf is a list of the Master (Thomas Neville)
and Fellows, in 1582 or 3, Barnaby Gogo, among them,
afterwards Master (in 1604), and son of Barnaby Googe,
now best remembered as translator of "The Kingdom
"of Antichrist," by Naogeorgus. A list of the Masters,
and their subsequent promotions, is given in p. 3.
In p. 4. is entered :—" Mem. in this book are set down
"Audits and Accounts to page 130, the first Audit,
"1575." In the accounts of 1582, there are payments
entered, as made to the "Baylaffe, Schavenger, Laundres,
"Cooke, Butler," and to "the Musitious 2s. 6d." with
"Presents to my Lord Cheife Justice, 20s." In the
next year's account, there are items,—"To the Bedells
"and Musicianes, 6s. 6d. An Audit supper at the last
"Accounts, 4s. 5d. . . . A marche pane [almond cake],—
"Martii 1°, 1582, 10s. A Combination Sermon, 8d."
At fol. 165 entries of elections of Scholars begin, in
the year 1604. In fol. 167a is the admission of Adrian
Scrope as Scholar, 27th November 1613; probably the

royalist of that name, of Codrington, in Lincolnshire, who fought for King Charles at Edgehill, and not the Adrian Scroop, who sat as one of the judges on the trial of Charles, and, on the Restoration, was beheaded. Fol. 178, Sept. 28, 1633, Henry Blow is admitted Scholar; qy. if of the same family as the eminent muscian and and composer, Dr. John Blow, born in 1648.

Fol. 177. 13th November 1633. Election of Thomas Cracherode as a scholar (qy. if an ancestor of C.M. Cracherode, the famous book-collector). Fol. 213b. admissions of Fellows follow, A.D. 1643. At fol. 224b, is entered a Letter from Theophilus (Howard), Earl of Suffolk, to the Master and Fellows; at the close of which is added the following note:—" Memorandum, that againe upon " Saturday 15 Augusti 1635 the said original Letter " (whereof this is a true copy) and the Statutes of y* " Colledge were publickly and audibly read, by Sir " Gale in the chappelle, immediately after common " prayers, before any fellow or scholar went out of chap- " pell; and then and there the Master of the Colledge " (Henry Smyth) exhorted and advised all fellowes " and scholars to the study of divinity, and monished " and required them all to keepe and observe all the " Statutes of the Colledg and University, together " with all the Canons and lawfull ceremonyes used in " the Church of England generally, and to weare " capps in the hall, and cappes and surplices in the " chappell, and to forbeare all hunting or coursing, and " haunting the towne, especially all such houses or " places where wine, ale, beare [sic], or tobacco, is " soulde." The Letter in question, itself bears reference to the due observance of the College Statutes.

At fol. 230a, admissions of Fellows recommence, in the year 1575, that of James Bromell among them, he being named thereto (as denominatione) by the Queen. In fol. 240b is the admission, as a Fellow, of Adrian Scroope, before mentioned, May 22nd 1618. In fol. 242b, the election of Orlando Bridgman (afterwards Lord Keeper), as Fellow, July 7th, 1624. In fol. 235a is the election of George T . . hby, as a Fellow, to fill the next vacancy, 23rd September 1602; and in fol. 256b is this entry:—" Whereas I, George T . . hby, " Fellow of this College, being convented before the " Maister and Fellowes the 27 of February in the yeare " of our Lord 1607, and then convicted of sundry mis- " demeanors tending to the great offence and the dis- " quiet of the whole society, was consented [sentenced] " to lose my commons or dyet from the 27 day afore- " sayed unto Easter next, and admonished to reforme " my disordered life, and to conforme myselfe to a more " quiet and peacable life; I doe by these presence wil- " lingly confesse myselfe guilty of the premisses, tak- " ing it as an especiall favor done unto me by the " sayed society, that they be not. here to my further " disgrace more particularly excited, and I doe ac- " knowledge the sayed censure to be justly imposed " uppon me; and I doe further protest that I am " hartyly sorry for my former disorders, and will en- " deavour hereafter by my honest and peaceable life " to recover the love and good opinion of the whole " society; and if I shall hereafter faile herein, I shall " be contented to forfet my whole estate and interest " in Magdalen College. In wittness whereof, I have " to this my present submission sett my hand, the dayo " and yeare above written. George T . . hby." Written, in an almost illegible hand, by himself, no doubt.

In fol. 257b there is the following entry:—" Memo- " randum, that the third of March 1597, an advowson " of Stanton Parsonage was granted unto our Master, " Mr. Doctor Palmer, (ether for his use or for any " ffrend of his,) by the consent of the company, whose " names are here subscribed. Signed by John Palmer " (Master), Thomas Yates, Barnabe Goche," and six other Fellows.

The second Register Book is a small paper folio, in old calf, of about 800 pages, containing mostly College Accounts, Admissions of Masters, Fellows, Scholars, and College officers, presentations to livings and exhi- bitions, etc.; the admissions of Pensioners and Sizars beginning in 1674. In fol. 9 is the admission as Fellow- commoners, on the same day, of William Herrick, father, and William Herrick, son (aged 20), of Beau- manor in the county of Leicester, July 4th, 1676. On May 30th, 1677 (fol. 12), is the entry of Thomas Herrick, son of the above William, the Elder, as Pensioner. P. 19, the admission of Samuel Morland, son of Sir Samuel Morland, Baronet, previously mentioned. P.51, admission of Richard Cumberland, son of Richard, Bishop of Peterborough, June 16th, 1694, from Stam ard school. P. 55, admission of John, another son of the

Bishop, May 3rd, 1698. The admissions of Scholars in this book come down to 1814, p. 353. At p. 361 begin, " Orders, Conclusions, Concessions, and Memorandum," the first bearing date November 3rd, 1674.—Among them is the following:—" July y* 20th. 1677. Whereas " Dr Duport, Master of y* College, hath freely bestowed " an organ upon us for y* Chappell, these are to declare " y* wee, y* Fellows of y* College, do thankfully accept " of it." Signed by J. Peachell and Gabriel Quadring, (both afterwards Masters of the College,) and nine other Fellows. All traces of this organ have long since been lost. An allowance of 8 pounds yearly was immediately set upart for payment of an organist, but in 1693 this payment to the organist was discontinued. In p. 370, under the date of December 8th, 1679, is the following entry:—" Whereas of late yeares divers vitious and " disorderly customes have by the petulancy and pre- " sumption of some looser schollers been introduced " into this College, tending notoriously to y* idle ex- " pence of time and money; to wit, excesse and quarel- " ling, and all this to y* manifest corruption and de- " bauchery of youth, and so to y* just scandell and " offence not onely of y* present society, but of many " worthy persons formerly members of y* same, and " utterly strangers to such loose and idle manners in " their time: For prevention of y* like enormities for " y* future, and y* mischievous effects consequent there- " upon [ordered] .... That no Sophister or scholler " whatsoever demand for Sophisters cheese above 12d. " of a pensioner, and 8d. of a sizer; and y* no scholler " after, or at, his first admission, offer or yield to pay " more, and y* he pay it in cheese to be equally divided " twixt himself and y* Sophisters, pensioners by y* " selves, and sizers by y* selves, according to former " and even late custome and priviledge. . . . . That " no scholler at his entrance into a' chamber upen his " first comming to y* Colledge, or upon any removall " afterward, do offer to give money or to treat and " intertaine, eyther by eating or drinking, his chamber " fellowes, or any y* keep above or below y* same floors " or staires, or any other schollers in y* Colledge. " And y* no scholler whatsoever dare to demand or " receive any such treat, entertainment, or money, at, " after, or before, any such entrance or removall, as " aforesaid. That no schollers give or receive at any " time any treat or collation upon account of y* foot- " ball play, on or about Michaelmas Day, further then " Colledge beere or ale in y* open hall to quench their " thirsts. And particularly, that y* most vile custome " of drinking and spending money, Sophisters and " Freshmen together, upon y* account of making or " not making a speech at y* foot-ball time, be utterly " left off and extinguished. That neyther y* Froshmon " nor any others dare at all to make any treat or colla- " tion, as aforesaid, for their comrade. who makes y* " speech on Magdalen Day. That no Sizer, who is a " senior in commons, dare to demand or receive groats " or y* worth of one farthing from any his juniors, upon " their coming to y* table, eyther when Freshmen or " Sophemen, nor y* Fellowes Sizers to exact or receive " admission-money, or y* expence of one farthing, from " any, at their coming to wait and serve tables in y* " hall. That no seniors dare to hale or compell any " his juniors, at y* time of y* yeare, eyther in y* Col- " ledge or out of it, to give them cherries, berries, or " any other expence of fruit whatsoever, nor set others " on to do it. That those sottish and even savage " trickes of grubbing, salting, mustarding, and y* like, " rarely used by any but rakehells and dunces, be " utterly disused and abolished." Signed by J. Pea- chell, the then Master (newly appointed), and nine Fellows.

The book, now known as the "Old Book," is a thin folio paper volume, in old embossed calf, formerly closed with a thong and buckle, and consisting of about 500 leaves, many of them left blank. It contains an account of the various foundations of the College, and its foun- dation Charter. In fol. 12 a is the following, apparently, the earliest entry in the book:—1586. This yeere the " trees in the backside, commonly called the 'Grove,' " were soulde unto Harry Flamson, of Cambridge, " baker, for lxii., and that mony by the Maister (Thomas " Nevile) bestowed towards the makinge of a great " lover for the Colledge Hall." The "Grove" still adjoins the Master's grounds; the "lover" has long since disappeared. In fol. 126b is a list of "Money " given to the New Building in the time when Dr. " Duport and Dr. Peachell was [sic] Masters." The second entry of donations is "Sir Robert Sawyer, 50l.;" and the third, "The Honble. Mr. Secretary Pepys,

" 50l." Under money given to the New Building when Dr. Quadring was Master, Pepys is entered as subscribing an additional sum of 10 pounds. This is the building which now contains the Pepysian Library. This volume is mainly devoted to what may be called the private business of the College.

In a folio volume of blank leaves are preserved, loose, a number of letters written to the College, with the sign manual of Queen Elizabeth, in favour of various persons who, at her desire, were to be admitted to the King's Fellowships in the College. These are Jordan Chadwick, to be chosen in the room of Henry Thrustcrosse, 25th November, in the 35th year of her reign; John Bell, in the room of John Dawbney, 1567; George Fludd, in the room of David Roberts, 7th of October, in the 27th year of her reign. The persons earliest named as being elected to these two Fellowships, were John Dawbney, B.A., and Ciprian Valerie, a Spaniard, then a student in the College; the Queen signs a letter, dated the 12th January, in the 2nd year of her reign, stating her desire that these two may be chosen " to " the rowmes of the same, now presentlie voyde." The names of their predecessors are no longer known. There are mandates in favour also of John Payne, 22nd January, in the 39th year of her reign ; William Goldington, 5th of June 1568; David Roberts, M.A., of Christ's College, 23rd of January 1580. These letters of Queen Elizabeth are followed by similar letters sent by James the First and Charles the Second, similarly signed at the head. Dr. Peachall, the Master, was suspended by James the Second, but there is a letter dated 24th of October 1688, with his sign manual at the head and that of " Sunderland " below, restoring the Doctor to office; he died in 1690. The order for deposition is on parchment, dated 7th May 1687, with the Great Seal attached.

In this book are two letters, dated from Clapham (in Surrey), 22nd of July and 6th of August 1703, and written by Mr. Jackson, nephew of Samuel Pepys, to Dr. Quadring, Master of the College, relative to the death of his uncle, and the gift of his library, either to Magdalene College, or to Trinity. (Jackson was to retain possession for his life, and the College did not come into possession of the library until 1724, when it was removed, with the original book-cases, to the College.) He had been a member of the College himself, and in the Second Register, page 36, is the following entry :—
" Johannes Jackson, filius Johannis, de Brampton in
" Comitatu Huntingdoniæ, 15 annos tantum natus, e
" Schola publica Huntingdoniæ admissus Pensionarius.
" Tutore Magistro Millington, Junii 28º 1686."

My best thanks are due to the Master of the College, the Honourable and Revd. Latimer Neville, for the kind interest which he manifested in the inspection of these volumes. To the Revd. Mynors Bright, Senior Fellow, I feel myself under great obligations, for the readiness with which he afforded me every facility for inspecting them, by placing his rooms at my service, and for giving me much useful and interesting information in reference to the early history of his College. I have also to thank Francis Pattrick, Esq., Senior Tutor of the College, for his good offices in obtaining for me the requisite permission to make this inspection.

HENRY THOMAS RILEY.

PEMBROKE COLLEGE, CAMBRIDGE.

(Second Report.)

There is a considerable number of mediæval Manuscripts in the possession of this College; some of which, as we gather from a very interesting communication made to the Cambridge Antiquarian Society in 1860 by Dr. Corrie, the Master of Jesus College, were gifts made to the Society by various Masters and Fellows shortly after the foundation of the College (in 1347); the number having been increased, by subsequent donations, to about 140, in the course of little more than a century after that date.

Dr. Corrie's list of donors is founded upon an ancient Register, to which his attention had been called by Dr. Ainslie, the then Master of the College; but this authority, we find, stops short, as to Manuscripts, (with perhaps a few exceptions, in the latter part of the 15th century, and leaves the sources from which many of the volumes now in the possession of the College, were obtained, unaccounted for. On examination of the books themselves, some of them, it will be found, were the gift of William Smart, Alderman of Ipswich, (in the

time, probably, of Edward the Sixth); while others appear to have been transferred from the Abbey of Bury St. Edmund's, at the period of the Dissolution of the Monasteries. These volumes are now kept in the Muniment-room of the College, being about 230 in number, some in good condition, and some in various stages of decay. They are mostly still in their original oaken boards, some of which are much worm-eaten and are crumbling to dust. With the courteous permission of Dr. Power, the Master of the College, I have recently examined a portion of them; and the most ancient, probably, among them all, is a folio volume of " Eglogæ," or Excerpts, from the Pastorals of St. Gregory, which, from the writing, would appear to belong to the later Saxon times. There is a 17th century Catalogue of these volumes, in the Muniment-room, compiled by Bishop Wren; as also, a later Catalogue, extracted from the former in the year 1799. The following are the names, as there given, of some few of the volumes :— Anselmus de Similitudinibus ; Apparatus Johannis de Aton ; Armachanus [Fitz-Ralph] de Quæstionibus ; many works of Thomas Aquinas; eight treatises of Johannes de Anchona ; Beda De Templo Salamonis, In Lucæ Evangelium, Historia Anglorum ; Borastoni Distinctiones; Bromyard Tractatus ; Burly In Ethica et Politica, and In Politica (cum Ægidio); Collecta Samuelis Presbyteri ; Comeatoris Sermones; Sermones et Alleg. Historiarum; Historia Scholastica: Gaudavensis Quodlibeticum ; Gilberti et Gaufridi Practica ; Glosses on Scripture ; many volumes of, Gorham super Psalterium, super Lucam, super Epistolas Pauli, Distinctiones et Sermones; St. Gregory, several works of; Halesii Quæstiones; Hieronymus, several works of; Holcot Quodlibeticum, and In Sapientiam ; Hugo de St. Victor ; Januensis (John of Genoa, writer of the " Catholicon ") ; Legendæ Sanctorum ; Isidori Etymologia, and Liber Contra Judæos ; Kilwarby Tabula super Originalia; Kricladensis (John of Cricklade) Homiliæ ; Lanthoniensis Harmonia ; Lincolniensis (Grosteste) Compositio, Dicta cum Tabula, de Lingua, de Literas componendi forma; Lombardi Sententiæ ; Lyræ Postillæ ; Media Villa In 3 Sent. and In 4 Sent. ; Petrarchæ Africa ; Papilla Oculi (attributed to John de Burgh); Raymundi Summa; Repindoni Sermones ; Rogeri Compendium ; Rupellæ Summa de Malo ; Scotus super 2 Sentent. ; Stimulus Conscientiæ ; Summa Summarum ; Tholomæi Centiloquium ; Wallensis in Psalterium. In Dr. Corrie's List, a " Polychronica," and a copy of the Chronicle of Martinus (Polonus) are named, and indeed are the only works of that character there mentioned ; whether they still survive, as a part of the collection, I am unable to say. These volumes, many of which are large folios, and some of them very ponderous, are at present in a locality, which wholly forbids the possibility of a leisurely and thorough examination of them : I have little doubt that, under the auspices of the present Master of this ancient and august foundation, they will ere long be submitted to what they plead for, and well deserve, a thorough cleansing and repair. If transferred to the College Library, they would, in my opinion, adorn its shelves, and perhaps be more than equal in value to any like number of volumes that could be selected from its most valuable contents.

There has been lately found in the College, after having been overlooked, perhaps, for several generations, a small folio volume, in embossed calf binding of the 17th century, in which is inserted a collection of Letters, dating from the 15th century downwards, many of which are deserving of notice. The following is a brief account of them :—

A small Letter, on paper, written and signed by Sir John Fastolf Chlr. [Knight] of Caistor, near Yarmouth, in the 15th century, and addressed,— "To my ryght " wel belovyd Cosyns Henry Inglese and Johan Berney " Escuiers."—" Ryght wel belovyd Cosyns. I comand " me to yow and please you to hafe in knoulege that " at whyche tyme ye were delyvered out of pryson " by the moyen of ii prysonners that y delyvered yow, " whyche as ye know well one was Burd Vynollys and " the other Johan de Seint Johan dit Delot, and in lyke " wyse I boughte anothyr prysonner clepyt Johan Villers for the delyveraunce of Mauthye Sqwyer whyche " mater ye knowythe welle. And for as moche as my " wrytynge that makyth mencion of that delyveraunce " of the said Mauthye be not in my warde, y pray you " that ye wolle undre your seelys certyffye me the " tronthe how the said Mauthye was delyveryd by my " noyen. Y have founde a cedule that makyth mencion " of that prysonner, of whyche y sende you a double, " to be better avertysed of the mator. And therfor " as my trust ys yu yow that ye sende me your goda

" remembrance in as goodly haste as ye may. And
" our Lord kepe you. Wryt at Londone, the v day of
" November." Sir John Fastolf, it is almost needless to
remark, took part in the French wars of Henry the
Fifth and Sixth. (In the preceding Report of this Commission, an account is given of a large collection of
Fastolf deeds and papers preserved at Magdalen College, Oxford).

A Letter, in English, signed, "Syr Water Blownt"
(Treasurer of England) 27th November 1464, and
addressed to the Bishop of Norwich, [Walter Hart].
John Pastone has been outlawed, and the Treasurer begs
the Bishop to allow none of his goods to pass out, if
there are any in the Monastery (Priory) of Norwich.

A short Letter, on paper, addressed—" To my ryght
" trusti and wel beloued frend, Johan Paston Sqyer."
" Right trusty and wel belued frend. I comande me
" to you and for certain mater that I have for to do for
" the which ma[ter] . . sende unto you a Squier of
" myne called Elyngham, praying you to gefe hym
" faythful credence of that he shall declare you in
" myne behalfe as for this tyme. God have you in
" hise keping. Writene at Midleton the xviii. day of
" Julle. Yowre frend.. Scales " In a note, written on
the letter, in a hand of the earlier part of last century,
it is suggested that it is the writing of Lord Scales,
afterwards Earl Rivers, brother of Elizabeth Woodvile,
wife of Edward IV., who was beheaded by order of
Richard the Third; he held the title in right of his
wife, Elizabeth, daughter of Thomas, Lord Scales.

A paper Letter, signed "By your older sone Johan
" Pastone," and " Wretyn at Heyleston the Fryday
" byfor Seynt Michelle ;" and addressed—hys ryght
" worshypful . . . dre [? fadre] Johan Pastone, beyng
" [at] the Flete at Londone, be thys del'"—Syr Thomas
Howes will resign the benefice of Mawteby "to a ful
" prestly man of Norwych callyd Sir Thomas Lyndys',
" whom I suppose ye have knolech of." He asks his
father's assent thereto.

A Letter, on paper, signed " Your lovyng Cousin Tho-
" mas Su[rrey]:" Thomas Howard Earl of Surrey, who
commanded against the Scots (A.D. 1513) at Flodden
Field. It is addressed—" To my right worshipfull cousin
" Sir John Paston;" and is endorsed, in an old hand,
" Littera Com : Surrey." It begins " Cousin Pastone,"
and is to thank him for having been so good a master
to the Earl's servant, William May, and for having, at
such a cost, caused him to be duly apparelled. " Wretin
" at Sherif Hoton the vi. day of July, with the hand of
" Your "—as above.

A Letter, on paper, and in English, signed, in large
characters, " Oxynford " (John de Vere, fourth of that
name, Earl of Oxford,) dated the 3rd of April in the 21st
year of Henry VIII. (A.D. 1530): stating that John Parys
of . . . . in the county of Cambridge has done homage
to the Earl for his land in Gildersland in the said county,
and has paid one third part of the relief; the other
two parts being assigned to his wife for jointure.

A receipt in English, signed "Oxinford" (the same
John de Vere), for 10 pounds, received of Philip Parrys,
" fermer " of his lordship, of Saxton, for one half year.
Dated 21st June 18th of Henry VIII (A.D. 1526).

An acquittance, on parchment, and in English, to
Francis Calthorpe, Esquire, of Norwich, and his sureties,
Philip Calthorpe, of Ludham, and Henry Ingless, of
Dylham in the county of Norfolk, for moneys owing
to the late king, Henry the VIth. It is signed at the
top by King Henry, his successor, with also his peculiar
mark, or device, and is addressed to Cuthbert Tunstall,
Keeper of the Records in Chancery. Below, it is signed
" John Myklate " (apparently,) and " John Roper."

Receipt on paper, signed by Sir George Broke, Lord
Cobham, 17th November 29th Henry VIII.

Receipt, on paper, in English (with three of the
crossbar, or portcullis, devices therein, used by King
Henry the Eighth) for 10 pounds, received as a prest
from William Yelverton, Gent., of Rogham, 7th June
34 Henry VIII.

Receipt on paper, in Latin, 20th July 1545, signed
Thomas [Goderich] Elien, (Bishop of Ely).

Receipt 35 Henry VIII., signed by Matthew Parker,
then Prebendary of Ely.

Another receipt, in Latin, by Thomas Goderich,
Bishop of Ely, A.D. 1536.

Receipt, in English, by Anne de Vere, late the wife
of John, Earl of Oxford, for " the sum of ccl. du to me,
" lady and weddowe, Contys of Oxynford." She was
daughter of Thomas Howard, Duke of Norfolk.

An acquittance, signed by John, " Lord Coniers," in
the third year of King Edward the Sixth.

A warrant—" We sende unto yow by the bearers
" hereof the body of Sir Anthony Kingstone, Knight,
" whome the Quene's Majesties pleasure is ye shall see
" kept in salfe warde untill ye shall receyve farther order
" from hence. Whereof we require yow in no wyse to
" fayle. And so fare ye well. From St. James, the xth
" of December 1555, Your loving frendes " (as below).
" Postscript. Ye must suffer the sayd Sir Anthony
" Kingston to have his man to wayte upon hym, and
" his bed, night-gere, and such other thinges as he shall
" have node of." Signed (William Marquess of)
Winchester (H. Fitz Alan Earl of) Arundell. Edward
(Earl of) Derby. John (Russell Earl of) Bedford.
(William Herbert Earl of) Pembroke. W. Howard
(Earl of Effingham). Cuthb. Duresmo (Tunstall, Bishop
of Durham). Thomas Ely (Thirlby, Bishop of Ely).

A warrant, dated 13th December 1555, directing that
the wife of Thomas Kelk, a prisoner, with his creditors
and securities, shall have liberty to visit him in prison.
Signed Arundell, Edward Derby, Thomas Ely, R.
Ryche (Lord Chancellor), William Paget (Lord Paget),
Edward Hastings (afterwards Baron Hastings of Lough-
borough), William Petre.

A receipt, signed by Thomas Sutton, afterwards
founder of the Charter-house, 1575.

A Letter, dated 6th of December 1613, and signed—
" Your very loving assured friend, Chr : Hatton." The
original direction does not appear, but a note states
that it was addressed to " Mr. Paris Esq." The person
in whose favour it was written, was probably Antony
Rudd, Fellow of Trinity College, Cambridge, afterwards
Dean of Gloucester, and Bishop of St. David's. It begins
in the following singular manner, but becomes less frigid
towards the close.—" Sir. Though there be no parti-
" cular desire on my parte, to induce your good favor
" to accept of any request of myne, yet understanding
" your good dispositions to piety and vertue, I have
" presumed you wyll frendly interprete my good mean-
" ynge in commendynge to your favorable and curteous
" regard a Chaplayne of myne, one Mr. Doctor Rudd,
" in whose behalfe I am most earnestly to intreate you
" to confer upon him the parsonage of Hildersham [in
" Cambridgeshire], etc."

A Letter, dated 18th of December 1593, from Sir
Edward Coke to Bassingbourne Gawdy, Esquire, High
Sheriff of Norfolk, in favour of his deputy bailiff.

A notice, dated 10th of July 1595, signed by three
Justices of the Peace for the County of Cambridge,
granting leave to Ferdinando Paris, a (Popish) recusant,
to remove beyond a distance of five miles from his
dwelling, for a limited time ; he to return before the 10th
of September.

A receipt signed by Horatio Palavicine, of Bedbur-
ham (now Babraham), in the County of Cambridge,
for eight shillings; received from "Mr. Fardinandoe
" Parris Esquire" for his manor of Little Lyntone,
" for ayd-silver and castle ward" for one year, due
to her Majesty " as to the Honour of Richmond fee."
Sir Horatio Palavicene, originally an emissary from the
Pope to collect certain moneys, became a convert, and
appropriated them, in the reign of Queen Elizabeth. He
held a command against the Spanish Armada, and was
buried in the church at Babraham. As mentioned in
Walpole's *Anecdotes of Painting*, the following epitaph
was suggested for him :—

" Here lies Horatio Palavicene,
" Who robb'd the Pope to lend the Queen.
" He was a thief. A thief? Thou lyest;
" For why? He robb'd but Antichrist.
" Him death with besom swept from Babram
" Into the bosom of old Abraham.
" But then came Hercules with his club,
" And struck him down to Beelzebub."

He died on the 6th of July 1600, and, on the 7th of
July in the following year, his widow married Oliver
Cromwell, the future Protector's uncle.

A long Letter, dated at Norwich, the 2nd of July 1600,
beginning —" Right honourable and our very good
" lorde,"—though it does not appear to whom it is
addressed. The writing is extremely faint, and almost
illogible; but it is written in favour of the town of North
Walsham, in Norfolk, a great part of which, within the
space of two or three hours, had been burnt to the
ground. It is signed by " William (Redman) Nor-
" wich,"—the Bishop,—Miles Corbet, Bassingbourne
Gawdy, and six others.

A Letter, signed by the principal inhabitants in and
near Beeston next the Sea, in Norfolk, in behalf of
Henry Clifton, a poor man, with " a wife and three
" smale children," whose house and property have been
destroyed by fire, the 4th of October 1609. It is coun-

3 P 3

teraigned by four Justices of the Peace at the Sessions at Norwich, who allow him 53s. 4d.

A Letter addressed to Sir Edward Coke, the eminent lawyer, by John Coke, his fourth son, as follows:— " Holkham. Innumerablie manie are the benefits, deare " Father, which I have received from youre hands, and " this last, not the least, I hope it shallbe the last in " this kind, and if it will please youre Lord: out of " youre fatherlie love, I deserving, if not to release me " of my debts, I hope your Lord: shall see me soe to " husband my estate, that whereas I have offended " youre Lord: by my carelessness, I shall in some " measure give youre Lord: content, (though never " fully satisfie you,) by being carefull and diligent with a " continuall watchfulness never to offend hereafter, and " to assure youre Lord: of this, I will never lett affec- " tion bear away where discretion should rule; but I " will bend all my endeavours and actions to shew " myself an obedient child to soe loving a father. And " here I present unto youre Lord: a true and reall " summ of all my debts which are my particularlie, as " well in the countrie as in London, beseeching you, " deare Father, to forget what is past, if you see " amendment in the time to come. I humblie take my " leave, my wife and all my children, together with " myselfe, remembring our duties to youre Lord: pray- " ing daylie for youre health, with longe life and happie " daies.—Youre obedient sonne, John Coke."

A long Letter, addressed " To his worshippful frende, " Ferdinando Parys, Esquyer, yeve thes," and signed " John Blennerhaysete,"—the words " of Frense in " Norfolk," being added in a hand of the early part of last century: dated Walden, 28th of July 1563. It mainly bears reference to the Duke of Norfolk's right to tithes of corn growing in the park of Walden.

A Letter, formerly addressed, as stated in a hand of the last century, " To our loving Frend, Ferdinando " Paris, Esq., of Lynton;" dated 2nd of April 1595. The Queen requires light horsemen to increase her forces in Ireland; he is therefore required " either " presentlie to make readie a man meete to serve on " horsebacke, armid with a good cuirasse and a head " peece with sleves of mayle, a light horseman's staffe " and a pistoll, with the horse, or geldinge, to be sounde " and sufficient for the service, with all necessaries," or " to pay the sum of 20l. With the original signatures of Jo: Cant. (Archbishop Whitgift), Jo: Puckering, Huns- don, W. Burghley, Essex, Howard (Earl of Effingham), T. Buckhurst, J. Heneage, J. Fortescue, and Ro: Cecyll (second son of Lord Burghley, and afterwards Earl of Salisbury).

A notice, signed " Jo: Cantuar." (Whitgift, Arch- bishop of Canterbury), addressed to William Monox, ordering him to summon Ferdinando Paris, of Lynton, in the county of Cambridge, and Philippe Parys, his son, who are under a bond of 2,000l. " a peece," to appear within 10 days before the Lords of the Privy Council, or before the Archbishop, upon notice to them given, or left " at the howse of one Edw : Sleepe at the sign of the " Three Kings in Fleet Street, within the suburbbs of " London."—"Given at Lambeth, the 29th of July " 1599."

Receipt by Thomas Sutton (Founder of the Charter- house) for 3l. 10s., received from " Fardynando Parys " Esquier " for one quarter's rent of his manor of Had- stock, 4th December in the 15th year of Elizabeth. This and another receipt are in the handwriting of Sutton; the latter being dated the 13th of October in the eleventh year of the same reign, the payment for the manor of Hadstock being there made by Parys for Richard (Cox), Bishop of Ely.

A Letter, signed " Edmund Norwich " (Dr. Edmund Freke, Bishop of Norwich) and addressed, " To Mr. Fer- " dinando Paris Esquier, at Puddinge Norton in Norffolk." —"Having of late received verie sharpe reprehension, " from my Lordes of the Counsaill for my lenitie ex- " tended towardes you and the reste in question for " religion in thiese partes, upon some complaint made " against me for that your libertie, I am hereupon " urged to calle you and the reste to prison, requiringe " you therefore not to faile in your repaire to James " Bradshawes in Norwich, within tenne daies next " after the receipt hereof, there remayninge as before. " And so I bid you well to faire in Christe. Ludham " [in Norfolk] this 13th of March 1581. Your lovinge " friende."

A Letter signed " Your lovinge frend Fra: Walsing- " ham," the Secretary of Queen Elizabeth, and written in his hand; dated 13th of December 1583, and addressed " To my loving frend Mr. Parrys of Litle Linton Es- " quier." He hears that the parsonage of Hyldersham,

in his gift, is like to become vacant, " the incumbent, " thereof, as I heare, beying in suche weake state of " bodie, as he is not lyke to recover : theise are hartily " to pray you, in case God call him awaye, to bestow " on mee the next donation of the sayd benefice." He promises to place there a sufficient man, such as shall be profitable to that parish and the one adjoining.

An order, addressed " To the Farmours of Her Majes- " ties impost of French and Gasconye wynes ; " — directing them not to levy any impost upon a tun of wine, or part thereof, to be imported by " Mr. Bassing- " bourne Gawdie, Esquire," in the port (apparently) of Norwich; dated 20th of December 1585, and signed by William, Lord Burghley.

A Letter, signed, and apparently written, by Richard Bancrofte, afterwards Bishop of London and Arch- bishop of Canterbury. A note, in a hand of the last century, says that it was addressed to his " Worshipfull " good frend, Mr. Paris, Rector of St. Andrew's Hol- " bourne, Treasurer of St. Paul's, and Prebendary of " Bronesbury, in that church." Its object is to request a favour at his hands in behalf of a " very honest man," one Mr. Smith ; as mentioned below.

A summons, signed " Jo : Cantuar," (John Whitgift, Archbishop of Canterbury) at Croydon, 16th of August 1592, " to Ferdinando Paris; of Linton in Com. Canta- " brig. Esquier, at Edwarde Sleepes howsse in Fleet- " street in London ; " (as being a Popish recusant) he is to appear before the Archbishop, either at Lambeth or at Croydon.

A Letter, signed by Sir John Fortescue, Chancellor of the Exchequer and of the Duchy of Lancaster, ad- dressed—" To Mr. Gawdy Esq' High Sheriff of Nor- " ff[olk] ; " dated, London, 21st of February 1593. It is in reference to the tithe corn belonging to the parsonage of Martham, in Norfolk.

A Letter, in the handwriting of Sir Edward Coke, dated 27th of March 1594, and directed, as stated in a hand of last century, to Sir Thomas Knevet. Since coming into the country, he has had a fit or two of the ague, but has now, he hopes, " prevented " it. He adds, " I am very sorry to heare of my good Lady Hickes. I " pray God send her a speedy and perfect recoverye."

A Letter to Ferdinando Paris, Esquire, dated 17th of August, and signed " Your pore frend Tho. Dove." He was Rector of Hayden, and Vicar of Walden, in Essex, and afterwards Bishop of Peterborough (A.D. 1600- 1630). He understands that Mr. Smith [already men- tioned as Dr. Bancroft's nominee] has taken possession of the parsonage of Hildersham, to which Mr. Paris, apparently, intended that the writer should be presented. The only course is for Mr. Paris, as patron, to proceed by " Quare impedit," otherwise, " there is no remedie, " but patience." There are two other letters by the same writer to Ferdinando Paris.

A copy of a letter of complaint, signed " Elizabeth " Southwell," addressed to Sir Basingbourne Gawdy, and dated 22nd of February 1599— [torn away]. The party addressed is entreated " to entertayne a widowes " complaint of the great disturbance (?) of the towne " of Carbrooke, which cannot be reformed without the " assistance of the . . . . . . Justices of the limitt." Among other complaints,—" The pore are growen so " unruly there, that they have left neither hedge, nor " gate, nor stile, unburned. And now they goe to my " woode, and fell and lopp at their pleasure. The . . . " that they have don of late are not to be repeyred with " 20l." She is " also exceedingly wronged by the " malice of one Luke Unger, of Tottington, who very " dishonestly censured me at his pleasure ; . . . . . . " and animateth them that are prone enogh to evill." The writer of the original letter was daughter of Charles Howard, Earl of Nottingham, Admiral of England, and her first husband, Sir Robert Southwell, served as Rear Admiral against the Spanish Armada ; her second husband was Stewart, Earl of Clanricarde, in Ireland.

A warrant, addressed to Ferdinando Parys, from Nonesuche (in Surrey), the 4th of August 1599. A descent is expected by an army of the King of Spain, to destroy her Majesty's navy, or the City of London. A levy is consequently to be made ; and he is to send to " Shordiche " by the 12th of August " two lawnces and " three light horses, furnished, to remaine for the space " of one moneth." Signed, Nottingham. Tho. Egerton, T. Buckhurst, G. Hunsdon, Ro. North, W. Knollys, Ro. Cecyll, J. Fortescu.

A Letter of Archbishop Whitgift, dated 4th of Septem- ber 1599—but to whom addressed is not stated. It is in reference to the confinement of the recusants in the castle of Banburye, and the palace of the Bishop of Ely, in view of the threatened invasion.

A licence, dated 6th March 1600, signed by Martin [Heton] Bishop of Ely, Umphrey Tyndall [Dean of Ely] and John Cotton, granting leave to Philip Paris, of Lynton, a recusant, to travel, on his business, beyond the distance of 5 miles from his dwelling, until the 30th of the same month. There are four other similar licences, from other Justices of the Peace (the Bishop's name again appearing in three), one dated the 16th of November in the year 1600.

A Letter, written by Sir Edward Coke to Sir Basingbourne Gawdy, dated 28th September 1602. Gawdy's father, having lands in Mylesham, had a book of extents, or valuations, made: Sir Edward, having lands there " with my kynde recomendations to you and my good " lady," asks for the loan of it.

A licence, dated the last of April 1608, granted to Philip Paris, a recusant, enabling him to travel on his law business, for the space of six months. Signed, Northampton, E. Worcester, Salisbury, E. Wotton (Baron Wotton of Maherley), E. Bruce (Lord Kinloss and Earl of Elgin), L. Stanhope, J. Herbert.

A Letter, written by Sir Edward Coke, almost illegible from damp. His eldest daughter is to be married on the 13th September next, at his house in Holborn, and he begs for the " presence and companie " of the person whom he addresses, but whose name does not appear. He is aware " that the waie is long, and the jorney " painefull."

A Letter, written by Sir E. Coke to a person not named, dated 31st of August 1602. It begins—" Howe pitifully " your poore countrey menne, and specially the cost- " menne, have bene afflicted by the lose of Dunkirke, " wo all knowe to our grief; and because I knowe some " scruple hath been made what might be justefied (?) in " that case, you shall recieve letters by this bearer from " the Lordes of the Councell for cloring of that scruple."

A Letter, written by Sir Edward Coke, dated—" From " my Chamber in the Inner Temple London, the seconde " of December 1601;" and addressed to a person not named. It is " on behalf of my servant, William Thurle- " bie. Gent., bailiff of my libertie within the countie " of Norffolk." It requests a " generall warrant for " him, for the breakinge upp of all proces and writts " to be executed within my saide libertie . . . . duringe " this yere of your office," as had been always used by all high Sheriffs in the said County. It was no doubt addressed to Basingbourne Gawdy, already frequently mentioned, who was Sheriff of Norfolk about this date.

A Letter from Sir Edward Coke to Sir B. Gawdy, dated 26th of April 1603, requesting him to continue the bearer, Francis Hexham (?) in office as Bailiff of the Hundred of Tunsted.

A Letter, signed " M. Elie " (Martin Heton, Bishop of Ely), to Mr. Paris, of Linton, dated 16th of February 1602. Mr. Paris had already presented the Bishop's kinsman, Dr. Tinlie, to the living of Duxford: the Doctor is now promoted by the Bishop, who desires Mr. Paris to present his Chaplain in like manner. Dr. Tinlie was Fellow of Magdalen College, Oxford; he was collated to the Archdeaconry of Ely, and died in 1616, Vicar of Witham, in Essex, where he was buried.

A licence, granted to Philip Paris (apparently " Parvis ") of Lynton, a " recusant convict," to travel on his affaris for six months; dated 28th of February 1606. Signed, T. Dorset, T. Suffolk, H. Northampton, Salisbury, G. Zouche, and E. Wotton.

The Certificate of the ruynated estate of the . . . ; " town of Eccles (near N. Walsham, Norfolk), 1605," signed, " Jo. Norwich, Will. Paston, W. (?) Scambler." The town (or rather, village), so far as can be gathered, for some part of the document is illegible, had suffered from the ravages of the sea. (The church and about 70 houses were in this year destroyed by the sea.)

A licence, dated the 23rd of May 1600, and signed by certain Justices of the Peace, enabling Ferdinando Parris and Philip, his son, recusants, to travel beyond five miles from their residence, down to the first of August, next to come.

Licence to Philip Paris, a recusant, to travel for six months. Dated " From Salisbury House ye 18 of " October 1607," and signed, " T. Ellesmere, Canc., H. " Northampton, T. Suffolke, Salisbury."

A similar licence, dated 20th of April 1609, to Philip Paris, and signed, " R. Salisbury, T. Suffolke, L. (?) Stan- " hope, J. Herbert."

A Letter of thanks, for presentation of his Chaplain to the living of Hildersham, signed " Sa: Cicestren;" (Dr. Samuel Harsnet, Bishop of Chichester, afterwards Bishop of Norwich, and Archbishop of York.) There is no address on it, or date; but it was written to one of the Paris family, no doubt.

Another licence, granted to Philip Paris Esq", dated 11th of January 1610; signed " R. Salisbury, H. Nor- " thampton, T. Suffolke, Gilb. Shrewsbury, E. Wotton, " F. Stanhope."

Another similar licence, dated 16th of July 1612: signed, " H. Northampton, Suffolke, E. Worcester, E. " Wotton, Jul. Cæsar (Master of the Rolls), Tho : Pain.

Another similar licence, the date torn out: signed " R. Salisbury, H. Northampton, Exeter, Jul. Cæsar."

Two letters of Sir Edward Paston to Sir Edward Knevet, dated 1611 and 1615.

A licence, granted to Philip Paris, and dated the last of November 1613: signed, " H. Northampton, Lenox " (Lodowick Stuart), E. Worcester, Pembroke, T. " Suffolke, E. Wotton."

A long Letter, from Roger Townshend to his sister, Mrs. Catharine Knevet, at Asshwellthorp in Norfolk. It begins " Noble Sister " and is dated from London 21st of December 162 - : as, among other things, it mentions the relief of Breda, it probably belongs to the year 1624, or 25: in the latter year that place was taken by Spinola.

An order of the " Committee of the House of Com- " mons for Examinations," dated 10th of November 1643, and signed by Miles Corbett (afterwards executed for his share in the Great Rebellion, 16th April 1662) ; for the apprehension of William March, Gent., who is to appear before the Committee, in the Inner Court of Wards at Westminster. Addressed to John Hunt, Esq"., Serjeant at Arms, or his deputy.

A warrant, dated at Northampton, the 15th of Apri 1645, stating that Sir William Andrews, Baronet, having had certain goods taken away by the Parliament soldiers, and sold to the inhabitants of Denton in the said county, leave is granted to him to search for such goods, and to buy them back at the prices that had been given for them ; he giving an account of the goods so bought back, and the sums paid. Signed " Edw : Farmer, " Rob: St. John (apparently), Richard Samwell, Ed. " Harby, John Norton, Tho. Pentlow, Phillip Holman."

A Letter, from Sir William Paston, Bart., to Thomas Knevet, Esq", dated " Queen's Street, 30 January 1650." Among his items of news, it is mentioned that Sir Ralph Skipwith, at his first appearance, was committed to the Tower ; 15 knights and gentlemen of quality, and divers others of inferior rank, in Hampshire, were apprehended " uppon the Norffolk account." Lord Chief Justice St. John goes on Tuesday as extraordinary Ambassador to Holland, and the Earl of Pembroke to Spain. An embassy has arrived from the King of France, to congratulate the Commonwealth.

A Letter, written by Mr. (afterwards, Sir) William Dugdale, " From the King's Head in Linne 23° Maii, neero 8 " at night," to either Sir Edward Bishe, or Mr. Edward Bishe, who was Clarenceux King of Arms, in 1646. The place being so distant from his correspondent's house, he cannot be there till " 2 of the clock " tomorrow afternoon, which he wishes to spend with him. On Monday he goes, by Tilney and other places, to Wisbech.—" We " have with us one Mr. Jonas Moore, the surveyor of " all the South Levell, who hath conducted us through- " out our Itinerarie hither, and is to accompany us to " the end of this large tract, till we come towards Lin- " colne. He hath also his sonne with him, a very pretty " youth."—A postscript is added,—" Mr. Ashmole re- " members his service to Mr. Bishe."

A warrant, with the sign manual at the top of King Charles the Second, and signed at the foot by William Morice, Secretary of State, and dated 9th of July 1660; to the effect that Josias Calmady, of Wenbury, in the county of Devon, late tenant of the impropriate Rectory, or tithes of corn and grain, of Wenbury, belonging to the Dean and Canons of Windsor, shall pay the late annual rent reserved out of the same by the Trustees during the vacancy of the said Dean and Canons, and, for the present, 50l. yearly to the minister that shall be settled in the rectory.

A Letter, written by Sir Thomas Browne, the eminent writer and physician, " To Mr. William Dugdale, at his " lodging at y° Seven Stars on y° North side of St. " Paul's Ch. Yard, London." " This was wrote on, or " about, 1660."—The above is written at the foot, in a hand of the earlier part of last century. Sir Thomas speaks of the [fossil] head and bones " of a very great " fish, yet to be seen, found at Hasburgho in Norfolk, " when the cliff fell down, as it is eaten away by the " sea, and this was within a yard of the toppe. Pray at " your opportunity my service to Mr. Ashmole."—In a postscript,—" I understand a second Volume of Mon- " asticon Anglicanum is in the presse, and almost

" finished. I should bee glad to understand whether it
" will bee a distinct piece, or the first also taken into it.
" Your letters will come more safely unto mee, if you
" leave the post unpaid." The words "Norwich —
"·xvii. [1]657" can be faintly traced in the corner.
Sir Thomas Browne was a member of Broadgates Hall,
now Pembroke College, Oxford; his manuscripts are in
the Bodleian Library and the British Museum.

A Letter, "For his much respected friend Mr. Fowler,
" at Wootton, near Northampton, These," from Ralph
Cudworth, " — 25, 1667 [Chr]ist's Coll : Cambridge."
He states that he considers his own signature, as Master
of the College, sufficient on a receipt, without the College Seal; although he once (and that time only) did
gratify Sir William Andrews with setting to a receipt
so signed the College Seal.

" A note of all the moneyes I have received of Sir
" William Andrewes for his daughter Mrs. Anne."
Here follow eight items, making in all 316l., between
1673 and 1676, and then the signature "Mary Beding-
" feild," with an attestation, in Latin, by a notary at
Bruges, in Flanders; stating that she was Prioress of
the English Convent there.

A Letter, addressed, "For my Lady Andrewes, at
" Dounham Hall, to be left with the Post Master of
" Ingerston Essex. By ye way of Lond :" neatly written
by Eliza Blount; without place or date named. The
words—" so ecclesiastical a person " occur in it, and to
them is added a note, in a hand of the earlier part of
last century :—"This ecclesiastical person was Sam¹
" Parker, D.D., whom King James 2d intended [to
" force] on Magdalen Coll. for their President. He
" would have changed his religion for yt of Rome, so
" great was his obsequiousness to ye King; but his wife
" would not part from him. He was made Bishop of
" Oxford in 1686, about this time; this letter was wrote
" on April 9. Consecrated October 1686, and died in
" March 1687 (8)." The writer, both in her own and
her mother's name, condoles with Lady Andrewes on·
Mrs. Parker's troubles.—"Sir Richard Alibone did us
" the favour to cal heer" (he was one of King James's
Judges, and gave judgment against the seven Bishops,
who were sent to the Tower). "Our Sherif has been
" continued in his office this too years, at first a Pro-
" testant, and now a Catholick; the chapel at Here-
" ford was fitted up and open'd to receive them, and
" six or seven preists to officiate, and an excellent ser-
" mon, my cozen Elliot, as hee has heard in London;
" and the Judg told us, for the credit of our country,
" he had not seen a pretier chapel : therefore I hope
" your Ladyship is convinc'd Herefordshire is a more
" Christian place then Essex. . . . . Cozen Tom Blount
" goes on with his study at Oxford. . . . So ecclesi-
" astical a person, methinks, one such wom : [woman]
" as Mrs. Parker has met with, should put a spot upon
" al the rest I am sorry for. Albeit I am sorry for
" him (but what they would have more further, to quit
" his right to her): and I am doublely sorry for your
" Ladiship. May God Almighty supply to you in al,
" is the prayer of your constant servant." The above
is obscure, to say the least of it.

An original certificate, or affirmation,—"By these
" presents I do certify, as I hope for salvation, that I
" never did deliver, nor cause to be delivered, unto Sir
" William Andrews any commission, as is specified in
" his accusation. Witness my hand this 12 June 1679,
" Th : Whitbred." The latter was Provincial of the
Jesuits in England, tried and condemned for conspiring
the death of the King (Charles II.) in the above year.

A written Catalogue of curiosities in Lady Paston's
closet, at Oxnead Hall, Norfolk, temp. Charles II ; consisting almost wholly of shells, china, and precious
stones, with two ostrich eggs, set in silver. The last
item but two is—"A Jack Napes heade," meaning an
ape's head. The value is set against each article, but in
pistoles.

" Route for One Companye of Major Generall Far-
" rington's Regiment from Odiam to Southampton, to
" march the 9th instant.—Alresford,—Winchester,—
" Southampton; whence they are to pass over to the
" Isle of Wight." Signed by Sir Robert Walpole,
when Secretary of War.

It is with much pleasure that I here acknowledge my
obligations to the Rev. J. C. Rust, Fellow and Tutor of
Pembroke College, for the pains he took in giving me
access to the Manuscript Collection in the Muniment-
room, and for affording me every possible facility for a
leisurely examination of the collection of Letters from
which I have so largely quoted. I have also to thank
the Rev. C. E. Searle, Fellow and Senior Tutor, who

has had the good fortune to recall to memory the fact of
the existence of this Collection, for kindly making the
due arrangements for my inspection.

HENRY THOMAS RILEY.

PEMBROK
COLLEGE
CAMBRIDG

CORPORA-
TION OF
RYE.

THE MANUSCRIPTS OF THE CORPORATION OF RYE.

The archives and records in the possession of the
Corporation of Rye, and preserved in their Town-hall,
are very numerous; consisting, to speak in general
terms, of Charters, volumes, memoranda, and deeds of
various descriptions.

The Charters, granted to the town individually, or in
common with the rest of the Cinque Ports, are to be
found described in Jeake's Charters of the Cinque Ports,
Holloway's History and Antiquities of Rye, and the Histories of the County of Kent.

First among the bound volumes, may be named the
" Custumal" of Rye; a thin folio volume of 26 leaves
of vellum, bound in rough calf of the latter part of last
century : the upper corners on one side have been
eaten away by mice, (before rebinding); otherwise it is
in good condition. It is a copy, no doubt, of an older
book, the earliest portion being written in the time of
Mary or Elizabeth. It begins,—"Theis byn the usages
" of the Comynaltye of the towne of Rye, used ther of
" tyme out of minde, which mens myndes cannot think
" the contrarye." The older articles of the code (in
English) are 66 in number, beginning with Eletcions of
the Mayor, and ending with the rules for the attendance
of the Barons of the Cinque Ports, at the Coronation of
the Kings and Queens of England. These are followed,
at page 31, by the—"Boundaries of the towne of Rye";
at p. 33, the—"Decreis of the towne of Rye . . . . the
" xxth daye of August in the fyft and syxth yere of
" Kinge Phillipe and Queene Mary's reigne, in the
" fyrst yere of Alexr Willes Mayraltye." These
" Decrees" are 168 in number : after which there are
three leaves, in modern writing,—"Extracted from the
" Hundred Book 1825."

All the other volumes of an earlier date, with one or
two unimportant exceptions, though of varying sizes,
were uniformly bound in rough calf, about the year
1776; to which date the latest volume in the series
(and so bound) belongs.

The First Volume, labelled "Chamberlains' Account
" book " on the back, begins with the close of the year
1448, and comes down to the sixth year of King Edward
the Fourth, 1466, 7: its contents will be found more fully
detailed in the sequel. After this, there is a hiatus in
the series, which will also be further noticed in a future
column.

The Second Volume of the series, a large paper folio,
bound in rough calf, has similar contents, being Chamberlains' Accounts, but is differently labelled, as, "Hun-
" dred Book," and comprises the years 1489-1494.

The Third Volume, a massive paper folio, begins in
1494, and ends in 1515. It is labelled "Hundred Book,"
similarly to the preceding one, but contains, under each
successive Mayoralty, the Chamberlains' Accounts.

The Fourth Volume comprises the Chamberlains'
Accounts of 1515-1543.

The Fifth 1545-1550.

The Sixth 1551-1564.

The Seventh 1564-1572.

The Eighth 1573-1593.

After this, the volumes form a mixture of Hundred
Court Books, Assembly Books, and Chamberlains'
Account Books, with one or more Churchwardens'
Books, and come down to the year 1776; being in all
38 or 39 in number, the last volume being numbered 39.

Volume 17 in the series is a large folio volume, with
paper leaves, containing Churchwardens' Accounts
from 1515 to 1570. It would probably well repay a
close examination of its voluminous contents; for but
very little use seems to have been made of it (as indeed
of the great bulk of the Corporation records) by the
late Mr. W. Holloway, in his History and Antiquities
(published in 1847) of the Town of Rye.

Volume 18 in the series seems now to be wanting;
—at least it was in vain that I searched for it among
the Corporation books : it seems not unlikely that it
may have been a continuation of the Churchwardens'
Accounts of the Parish.

Volume 19, a small quarto paper volume, in rough calf,
is filled, as to the earlier part, with matter of a most
miscellaneous description, the latter part comprising
minutes of plaints and proceedings in the Hundred
Courts, in the reign of Henry the Seventh, and the
latter part of the reign of Henry the Eighth : it is

labelled "Court Book," and some further account of it will be found below.

The 20th Volume is also a quarto paper Court Book, and comprises the period 1517-1529; its contents being of a similar description to those contained in the latter portion of the preceding volume.

The 21st is a somewhat larger paper volume, in quarto, comprising from 1530 to 1541; being a Court Book, with contents of a similar description to those of the preceding one.

To revert:—The following are some extracts, bearing reference to the contents of Volume 19, the earliest of the so-called " Court Books." It is labelled on the back with the dates 1497-1504; but this gives a very inadequate idea of the real date of all its contents. The first eight leaves of the book are of vellum, containing remarkably fine samples of writing and flourishes, in various hands, such as Court-hand and old English, or modern Gothic, written in the time of Edward the Fourth; together with precedents as to the different modes of addressing (in writing) the various personages of exalted rank, both lay and ecclesiastical. At the foot of the first page is written (certainly but little in harmony with the rest of the context):—" Hæc [sic] sunt " dies in quibus si homo minuerit sanguinem, infra " decem dies morietur; et si comederit carnes aucarum, " infra quadraginta dies morietur;—ultima die Aprilis, " prima die Lunæ Augusti, ultima die Lunæ Decem- " bris."—" These are the days on which if a men lets " blood, he shall die within 10 days thereafter; and if " he eats goose flesh thereon, he shall die within forty " days thereafter;—the last day of April, the first " Monday in August, the last Monday in December." —The second page contains, in English, the oath of the " Duodecenarii," or " Dozen " of Jurors, on the homage. Several forms of address to the King and other personages follow, with various capital letters in ink, beautifully flourished. On folios 4-7 various alphabets, in different styles of writing, are entered, with some scribblings, of the time of Edward the Sixth, on folio 7a. On folios 7b and 8 are copies of several documents, but without date, and at the foot of folio 8a is written,—" Per me, Wil- " lelmum Roberthe, Clericum villæ de Rie, in Comitatu " Sussexiæ, generosum;"—" By me, William Roberthe, " Clerk of the vill of Rie, in the County of Sussex, " gentleman." Part of this folio has been cut off; on the reverse of it is a copy of a bond (in Latin), and defeasance, of William Diggys, " Gentilman," to Babi- lon Graunford, Esquire, of Rye, dated 10th of Novem- ber in the 13th year of King Edward the Fourth [A.D. 1473]. At folio 9 the entries are no longer on vellum, but the rest of the volume is of paper, nearly through- out: the folios consist, for some pages, of deeds in Latin, attested probably before the Mayor and Jurats, temp. Henry the Seventh. At fol. 14 is a transcript of a deed, in Latin, executed by William Longe, of Rye, in the 2nd year of Henry the Sixth. Fol. 15 is left blank; fols. 16, 17 being occupied with a copy of an English deed in reference to the executors of William Wykwyk, late Vicar of Rye: no date is given, but he was Vicar 1478-1510. Fols. 18-21 contain transcripts of other deeds, temp. Henry VII., both Latin [and English. Fols. 22, 23, are blank. Fol. 24 is a fragment of an older book, with different paper and finer writing; beginning with the proceedings (in Latin) of a Court holden at Rye on the third Monday after Pentecost, in the 6th year of Edward the Fourth. The Homage, among other things, presents that—" John Plumbe did " alienate to John Lyght a cottage lying in Alrethe [or " Alreche], with certain lands called 'Pennylondes, " without leave of Court." Fol. 25 contains present- ments by another Homage, entered in another hand. Fols. 26-28 contain, in an earlier hand, Latin forms for duly giving in a Steward's Account. At fol. 29 follows, in the same hand as the three preceding leaves,— " Computus Johannis Pawlyn, Senescalli Hospitii " Domini Roberti de Harynton, a Festo Paschæ anno " regni Regis Henrici, Sexti post Conquæstum, nono, " usque ad Festum Sancti Michaelis Archiepiscopi . . . " videlicet, pro xxiiii. septimanis:"—" Account of " John Pawlyn, Steward of the Household of Sir Robert " de Harynton, from the feast of Easter in the ninth " year of King Henry, the Sixth after the Conquest, " until the Feast of St. Michael the Archbishop [Arch- " angel] . . . namely, for 24 weeks." In it, receipts are named from the bailiffs of Purlok, [Porlock, in Somerset], of Gleston', and of Grantham; expenses of the household, in London or Porlok, are mentioned; of Sir Robert and his people travelling from London to Porlok; and of the new hostel of the same Lord Haryn- ton at P[orlok]. In fol. 29b, a continuation of the same

J.

Account, the following articles are entered (in Latin) as being bought for victuals;—a salmon, a conger, plaice [pectines], eels, a millewall [green, or Scotch, cod], small fish, milk, butter, a calf, a pig, a swan, 2 partridges, at 3 shillings [? pence] each, one quail 2d, 12 plovers 20d.—It may be here remarked that, if a Lord Harington, of the Christian name of " Robert," is here meant, at the beginning of the reign of Henry the Sixth, no such person is to be found in Sir H. Nicolas's Synopsis of the Peerage.—Fols. 30, 31 contain an Assize of bread, in English, probably of the time of Edward IV.; setting forth, in different columns,— " The price of a quarter of whete. The halfpenny whete " looff. The peny whete looff. The halfpeny loof of " all paynes." Several blank leaves then follow, and one leaf with a copy of an indenture (in Latin) of the 9th year of Henry IV., whereby John Bevere, Chaplain of the Chantry of St. Mary at Rye, and William Ship- man, to ferm let to William Marchant all their land in the parish of Idenne, called " Hiltys land," in right of the said Chantry. Fol. 36 contains a copy of ordinances (in Latin) made by the Corporation, in the 20th year of Richard II., against acts of violence, John Badlyng being Mayor; with the scale of fines payable to the town for the offence of drawing blood. Regulations are also added, as to the future price of herrings; and it is ordered that the Common Seal (which will again come under notice) shall be kept in the custody of the Mayor, under the seals of three or four Jurats, chosen thereto. For a pipe of wine, or cider, drunk in a tavern, a duty of 4 pence is to be paid; if drunk out of a tavern, 2 pence. From the same folio we learn that on the 19th of May in the 10th year of Henry IV. [A.D. 1409] Robert Onewyn was Mayor; on the 1st of April in the 11th year of Henry IV. [A.D. 1410] Thomas Longe was Mayor; persons appearing before them, and paying fines for assaults committed. In fol. 37b are entered Ordinances made at a Court of Gestling, holden at Winchilse, on the 16th of February in the 17th year of Edward IV., the "Combarons" of Hast- ings, Rye, and Winchilse, being present. It is there agreed between the three towns, that if any stranger shall be in debt to any Combaron or inhabitant of either of such towns for fish bought, no new "cost" shall " make flisshe" for him, till he shall have paid the old debt. Fol. 38a contains Ordinances, in Latin, of the 3rd year of Henry VI., as to the freedom, brewers, and bakers, Thomas Pers being Mayor. Every brewster's barrel is to hold 26 gallons, and half barrel 13. If ripiers [carriers and retailers of fish in ripes, or baskets] neglect to pay their "Maltodes," or dues, on leaving the town, they are to pay a fine of 4 pence, additional, on their return. Fol. 38a, in the 6th year of Henry VI., John Seguoos appears before Stephen Bever, the Mayor, and the Jurats, and acknowledges that he has " maliciously offended in words" against the Mayor. However, " by grace of the Mayor," he is pardoned, on condition of not doing so again. One William Keele also is pardoned for a similar offence, committed against William Longe, Mayor, in the 9th year of Henry IV. In the same page there is an entry, in English, that, at a Gestillyng holden at Winchilse on the 8th of July 19th Edward IV., it was agreed by the three towns before-mentioned, that—"He that maketh " flisshe for the King in any of the foresaid three " towns," shall not " make flisshe" for any other person, on pain of paying 40 shillings to his town. Fol. 39a contains ordinances (in Latin), made before William Broughton, Mayor, in the 8th year of King Henry VI.; enjoining that certain "Maltodes" shall be paid fort- nightly, under a penalty, and if any one shall curse the collector thereof,—a not uncommon offence probably— he is to pay 3s. 4d. , On loading vessels with billets, a " Maltode " is to be paid of ½d. per thousand; but if the billets are laid on the " Strond " [the ground by the waterside] then one penny.—" If any person has a cow, " ox, horse, beast of burden, or swine, or other irra- " tional animal, going about in the churchyard, he " shall pay each time, towards the fabric of the church, " 3s. 4d." All persons who have dung standing before their house, are to remove it before the Feast of All Saints, under a penalty of 3s. 4d. Fol. 39b,—Thomas Longe being Mayor, in the 9th year of Henry V., it is enacted that all offenders " summoned to the Tower" [Ypres Tower, in Rye, built by William of Ypres, afterwards used as the common gaol], " and not " attending at the hour assigned, are to pay 12 pence." This is followed, on the same page, by minutes, in English, " of a Brotheryeld [Brothergild] holden at " Romene," on the 14th of May, 18th of Edward the Fourth. Fol. 40 contains minutes, in English, of a

3 Q

Brodhelle, holden at Romene, on the 24th of September, in the first year of Richard III., John Wymonde being Mayor [a so-called Mayor of New Romney, but he was speedily displaced]. "At a Cominaltee holden and as-"sembled in the churche yarde of Rye," on the 8th of July, in the 18th year of King Henry the Eighth, it was " agreed that the two boxes of Maltodes of the reve-" newes of the town shalbe no more opened in the Maior's " howsse, but in the Towne halle, at such tyme as hath " be before accustomed."—"And that ther shall no " Mayre have but 4 li. fee for his yere of Mairealtie, " and quarterly at the opening of the box to be paide, " as 'hath bene tofore used ; and that the Mairesse " shall no more be charged to make a dynner the day " of the opening of the boxis, as hath be wount ; nor " shall not have from hensforth vi₫. viii₫. in rewarde " for the same, as hath bene accustomed." Entries of proceedings in various Courts then follow, bound up irregularly together ; the context from folio 45 to 74 commencing at the 30th year of Henry the Eighth ; while folio 75 reverts to a series of Courts commencing at the 13th year of his predecessor, Henry the Seventh.

The First Volume of the series, or Chamberlains' Account book, already alluded to, is a thin paper folio volume, the entries commencing at the close of the year 1448. In this year the town of Rye, for the second time, was burnt by the French, and it is not im-probable that the preceding books of this description may have been then destroyed ; though, on the other hand, (more especially seeing that some at least of the records then in the hands of this Corporation did not perish in the conflagration), it is equally possible that this was the earliest volume in which such accounts were regularly entered and kept. The volume is nearly perfect, and, in general, in good preservation throughout, the entries being wholly in Latin, in the earlier part. The following is a selection from various portions of its contents.—

Pasted on a fly-leaf at the beginning is a copy of a Charter "Pro libertate villæ," granted on the 26th of October in the first year of Henry, "King of England " and France." The "Patent of the Market" follows (in Latin), granted in the sixth year of the same reign. Folio 1 of the volume, as numbered, begins--"Die " Sanctæ Luciæ Virginis, anno regni Regis Henrici " Sexti, Angliæ, vicesimo septimo, per assensum " .et consensum totius communitatis, electus est ad " officium Majoratus villæ de Ria Johannes Sutton, " ad implendum locum Willelmi Broughton, qui die illo " tollebatur a medio ; animæ cujus Deus, pro summa " misericordia sua, propitietur ;" the election of John Sutton, as Mayor, taking place on the same day (13th December) that his predecessor, William Broughton, died. This is followed (fol. 2) by "Maltodes," or rates, paid by fishermen of Rye for fishing with " trammel " nets." An account of "Receipts of the great box of " Maltodes" follows ; added to which is (in Latin),— " But at this time there was nothing in the Ripiers' " box, but afterwards, on the 9th of February, there " was had from this box 9s. 4d." Matthew Clyffe, a fisherman, pays 12½d. for fishing five weeks with " bosenettys."

Among fines for assaults, is the following (tr.) :—"Robert Burne and John Russell, tailor, made " assault upon William Brande, and, as is said, ran after " 'him on the 'Stronde,' with drawn 'aruncudiis' (or " perhaps, armicudiis, some kind of dagger). The said Burne was fined 20 pence." The Strand, at the foot of the town cliff, is still known by that name.

" John Southyn made assault, in presence of the " Mayor, in the market of the town, upon two strangers, " whose names were John Direchyesone, etc., and the " said Southyn made sign of drawing his 'aruncudum' " out of its sheath, notwithstanding the Mayor's pre-" sence." In fol. 5a there is a long list of expenses in-curred by the Mayor upon the "Water-gate" (Porta Aquatica), and upon mending the quay there. Robert Unwyn is paid 55 shillings for 55 days' attendance at Par-liament ; 4 pence also was spent on taking the account of W. Broughton, the late Mayor, "in the Mayor's house, " upon drinking ale there." The Mayor's stipend, or payment, was 13s. 4d. per quarter. The collectors of " the great maltody box" had 2s. ½d. for their fee. " A certain man who carried a letter for a Brodello "— later, a "Brotherhood"—received 4 pence. Amid the Latin there occurs,—"Item, for beryng up of the returne " of the wrytte for the Parlement, 8d." James Sedley was paid 6 pence "for the hire of the boat, and for his " drinking, when he came from the Brodelle ;" 2 pence also was paid for a quart of wine "for the man who " carried the answer to the letter of process on the vill " of Old Romene." Fol. 6a, "Given to the minstrel of

" the Lord de Say 20d." Also, "Paid for repairs of the " ship called 'Dolmanysbarge of Wynchylse' 5s." " Given to the minstrels of our Lord the King, for the " honour of the town 3s. 4d. Also, given and expended " upon another minstrel of the Lord de Say, who is " called 'Nicholas Lambntarme' 2s. 2d." Fol. 6b., " Given to the minstrel of the Duke of Somerset 12d." At this date the names of James Sedley and Richard Shadwell, as influential men of the town, occur. Fol. 7a, on Sunday after the Feast of St. Bartholo-mew, in the 27th year of Henry the Sixth, John Hamonde was chosen Mayor ; among the "Poundages of " Fishermen "(fol. 7 b) 4 pence is received from Simon Froste, "for fishes called 'molettys' (mullets)." Fol. 8b, Thomas Poope (sometimes written "Pope") pays for the sale "of two pipys and two hogge hedys of wine " that he had sold 6d." Fol. 10a. (tr.) "Constitutions " of the vill and port of Rye. The Constitutions, by " use and custom hitherto accustomed, are, from every " stranger, as though from a prisoner taken, payment of " his finance (finantiam) for his ransom, and, when he " has entered the fortresses of the port, for his passage " thence 3s. 4d. ; he having to pay towards the building " of the walls and gates there, what pertains to the " common weal of the town." Among the foreign fishermen who have to pay such "finance," William Abray is charged for "his wares, as coming from " Dieppe," 21s. 8d.—"A certain strife arose between " Robert——and John Sutton ; whereon Sutton, it is " said, struck the said Robert on the breast with his fist, " upon which the said Robert drew a two-handed sword " out of its sheath." "A strife arose," it is also said, " in presence of the Mayor and Jurats, between Robert " Unwyn and John Sowthyn ; whereupon Robert " violently laid his hand upon his 'aruncudium :'—this Robert, as we have seen, was member of Parliament for the place, and both he and Sutton filled the office of Mayor.—"Every person who takes upon himself the " burden and safeguard of watching, and who is found " asleep, has committed a great and grievous offence, " against the constitution of the town ; for that the " burden and safeguard has been entrusted to him by " the Mayor, or some one else in his place, and in " putting such confidence the town has been deceived ; " therefore he is to be placed at the discretion of the " Mayor and Jurats." Hence, Richard Vynde "being " caught sleeping, in that that he lost his arms, he " offended against the said Constitution."

Fol. 12a.—"Expenses upon a certain 'poursevant' " (pursuivant), for that he carried a seal of the arms of " the Lord Duke of Boughkyngham with him ; and in " reverence for the said seal, a pleasant and joyous " countenance was extended to him 2½d. Expended " upon the said 'pursevant' when we had him to supper, " for reverence for the said Duke of Bughkyngham, " and for the honour of the town, in wine and other " victuals 4d. For wine at the Mayor's house, when " the Lieutenant of Dover was at dinner upon the " capon which the Mayor gave him 4d." In fol. 13b, charges appear for repairs during two weeks of the town walls, near the North Gate. Fol. 14a. "Paid the maker of the pellet-powder " (pulveris librillarum) for the old gounnys (guns), for " his labour 3s. Paid for a quart of vinegar to test " the saltpetre 1½d. Given to the minstrels of our " Lord the King 3s. 4d. Paid on giving mulled wine to " Fysshende in Canon's house, when he brought tho " writ of proclamation 1½d. For provender for the " horses of the minstrels of our Lord the King, in the " house of John Bayle 3d. Paid John Bayle for " making a little sack of sheep's leather, and for the " leather for the sack, which sack was provided to " carry sulphur and saltpetre for the pellet-powder, " which the Lord Chamberlain gave 6d. Paid John " Bayle for a certain strainer through which the char-" coal was sifted or cleansed for the pellet-powder.— " Paid Robert Lubard for making the pellets of iron " 6d."

Of fol. 16 half has been cut away with a knife, the preceding leaf being also mutilated, but not imperfect, so far as the context is concerned.

Fol. 18b. Thomas Sprotte and one Robert are fined 20d. "propter verba sesquepidalia [sic] "—long-worded abuse, probably.

Fol. 19b.—"Paid a certain soldier called 'Robert' by " name, to go to Apuldore, to make inquiry whether " the Captain, with his army, who was then near the " windmill there, bent against that town, or not, 8d." —This must have been Jack Cade, 'or one of his party. " Paid to labourers to throw down branches so as to " make a hedge near the sea-shore, on the east side of

" the town, so that the high tide might no longer hurt
" the shore ; the labourer, John Wetherst, being em-
" ployed two days in throwing them down 10d." There
are numerous other items in reference to this "hedge,"
upon which it was intended that sand should accumulate ;
many waggon-loads of branches, with pegs for fixing
them, being carried thither for " backing " it.

Fol. 20a.—" Paid the expenses of the Common Clerk,
" to go to Tenterden, to tell them that one of us and of
" them should go to London, to labour for the saving of
" the franchise of Tenterden 6d." Fol. 20b.—" Paid John
" Warenne of Udemer, for cleansing the horse-pool
" without the North Gate 2s. 2d. Paid for 3 felt caps
" (caleptris) given to Younge of Bristow, and to Lacon
" and Elam, that they might the sooner be friends to
" us and the franchise of Tenderden 2s. 6d. (Tenterden wtas made a member of Rye by Charter dated 1st
Augus 1449.)

Fol. 26b. (29th Henry VI.)—" Received of the wife of
" Yprys for a common fine levied in the Court of our
" Lord [the King], for certain lands of the said Yprys
" within the liberty of Rie etc. 6s. 8d." This was John
Ypres, late a Jurat, to whom the tower of Ypres (still
standing) was sold by the Corporation. Further mention
will be found made of him in the sequel.

Fol. 27a.—" Paid for a capon and 2 ribs of beef (cos-
" tibus bovinis) given to Master Fankes, 18d." Fol. 27b.
" For watching two nights when a ship was being
" looked out for, off the Cambre, with Frenchmen, 15d."
Fol. 29a.—" For fish bought and given to Richard
" Wyderton, Lieutenant to our Warden, and for fish
" bought for the Mayor and the men empanelled, and
" the servants and other expenses on the 13th of May,
" at the time of the sitting held at Wynchilse 16s. 7d."
The nets that in the early part of the book are called
" bosenettys " are now called " bosmys," under the
head of " Maltodes " levied upon the fishermen of Rye.
These appear to have been a class of " trammell " net.
Where a fisherman used hooks (hokys), his " Maltode "
seems to have been increased.

Fol. 32a.—" Paid Babilon Grauntfort for hire of two
" horses to go to London 6s. 8d. This is the first mention of him ; some fifteen years afterwards, he was
Mayor.—" Paid the expenses of John Unwyn, Babilon
" Grauntfort, and two servants, for riding to Canter-
" bury to the installation of the Bishop [John Kemp]
" there, 4 days, 20s." Fol. 32b.—" Paid for a boat going
" to the general Brodelle at Romney, and returning
" 12d. Paid James Sedle, the younger, to go for Janyn,
" the carpenter, to Ewerst 4d. Paid the same Janyn
" for his coming to see ' le Kay ' upon ' le Strond ' [the
" Quay on the Strand] 8d. Given to the minstrels of
" the Lord Chancellor 12d. For Robert Onwyn, the
" Mayor, being at Reding, for Parliament, 28 days, at
" 18d. for each day 42s. Paid the minstrels of the
" Duke of Bokyngham 3s. 4d." He was the then Lord
Warden of the Cinque Ports.

Fol. 36a.—" Paid for 2 loads (libus loodis) of ' rys '
" (twigs) to make the ' Keye ' at the Strond 22d. Paid
" for mending one ' style ' and the ' dyche ' at Bad-
" dyng 2d." Fol. 36b.—" Paid the minstrels of the
" Lord de Bowseir [Bourchier] and the Lord Fenys
" [Fiennes] 2s. Paid for a stock of fish for Richard
" Witherton, Lieutenant of Dover, to be a guest to
" us in the matter of Tenterden, by John Tregoos 3s.
" For the expenses of Richard Wetherton, Lieutenant of
" our Warden, at Rye, at the time of the sitting there ;
" that is, in bread, ale, white and red wine, and sea
" fish, for supper ; and, for dinner, mutton, porkers,
" geese, capons, and chekyns ; and other costs upon the
" men empanelled, and their servants, 47s. 7d."

Fol. 37a.—" Given to the minstrels of the Lord Duke
" of Bukyngham, and their expenses at the tavern 4s.
" Paid Richard Ryps for his being at Parliament at
" Redyng and London 31. 18d." This Ryps, or Rype, had
formerly been the Mayor's attendant, aud soon became
Mayor himself. Fol. 39a.—" Item, on the day of Seynt
" Luke the Ewangelist cam before me, the said John
" [Suttone], Mayre of the seyd towne off Rye, on Davy
" Howell and John Tregoss, and ther in presence cam
" and recorde the eschaunge of ii hors, the ton a grey
" gyldyng, and the tother a lytell lyght bay with a
" whyght sterre in the forhede ; the said Davy havyyng
" the gray gyldyng for the lyght bay hors off the said
" John, and the said John havyng the said bay hors for
" the said gyldyng off the said Davy ; and for the said
" eschaunge made within the said place of Rye the
" said parties well and truly here paid her toll, after
" our lawes and usage, etc."

Fol. 42a. 32, 33, Henry VI.—" Given to the minstrels
" of the Earl of Warwick 3s. 4d. Given to, the min-

" strels of the Duke of yorke 3s. 8d. (Engl.) Item,
" for a present of porpays to the Bastard of Exettre
" 4d. (Engl.) Payd for ii congris and ii turbuttes for
" to send to my Master Lieftenant 3s. 4d." Fol. 42b.
" Item, in expenses of Hexstall and the ffelyship that
" cam with hym, when the theff was hangyd, bothe on
" eve and morowe 6s. 8d." Hexstall was a servant of
the Lieutenant at Dover Castle.—" Item, in expenses of
" Thomas Haymes, John Davy, Thomas Whythede,
" Robert Brekynden, Robert Dimy, Thomas Robyn,
" James Glover, Thomas Kaxton, off the paryssh and
" hundred of Tentyrden, for the enc e makyng off ser-
" teyn stryves and contraversies be twene the sayd
" hundred and parysshe aforsayd and John Sutton,
" Mayro, Jurats, and Comons, off the towne off Rye,
" 6s. 6d." It seems by no means improbable, from
various circumstances, that the above " Thomas
" Kaxton," who appears to have been a shrewd man of
business, and a lawyer, was a brother of William
Caxton, our first printer. The same person, beyond a
doubt, is found, a short time after this, acting as
Town Clerk, and principal man of business, at Lyde
(now Lydd) ; then Bailiff of Lydd ; and, after that, Town
Clerk of Sandwich ; as seen more fully set forth in the
Reports upon the records of Lydd and New Romney
in the present Report.—" Item, in expenses of the Mayre,
" Laurens Dobyll, James Sedley, Alan Bryce, Thomas
" Kynge, and iii servants with hym at Wyttysham, to
" intercomyn off the Composition makyng with the
" Bayle and Jurats of Tenterden 6s. 10½d. Item, gevyn
" to Kaxton for his labour and comyng hedyr, to over
" se the said Composition 12d."

Fol. 43a.—" Item, paid . to Laurens off Borow for
" rydyng up Dover, for to have pardonyng that we
" should not ryde up so many men as the said warant
" comaundhyt 2s. 4d." Fol. 43b.—" Paid to Rychard
" Wattyssone and Thomas Chatte for the voydyng out
" of the gras off the towne dyche 2s. 1d. Item, gevyn
" to the mynstralles off my Lord of Arundall 3s. 4d.
" Item, in expensis off the Lyeftenaunt and his meyne
" [retinue], and theyr hors, fyrst in brede 2s. In
" smaller court lovys [loaves] 16d. For iiii halff
" pynnes of ale 3s. 4d. For bere, half a boune and ii
" pottes 2s. 4d. In good wyne x galones and a potell
" 7s. In swete wyne for vi quartes 21d. For vi rybbys
" of beef 12d. For a legge off ffele 4d. For iii kapons
" 2s. For a lam 16d. For x chekyns 12d. Payd to
" William Wayte for ii lapster 2d. Payd to Petyr for a
" turbut 16d. To the same Petyr for iiii copyll solys 6d.
" Payd to Rychard Baker for viii boote faggis [b bun-
" dles of faggots] 20d. Payd to John Osand for a
" quarter [?] plays [plaice] and vi copyll soles and
" viii bote plays 2s. 9d. Payd to John Sander for
" viii boot ff [?faggis] 20d. Payd to Clays Jordan for
" viii boote ff 20d. Paid to Harry Shape for a tur-
" but 16d. Payd to Pers Stotey for a doerey 10d.
" Egges 3d. For ii galons of kreme 5d. For ii salt
" ffyshe 8d. Paid for spyces to John Yonge 3s. 6d.
" Payd to Thomas Hoget for his labour 12d. For halff
" a busbell off fflour 8d. For a pynt off houy 2d.
" For powder synamon 4d. Payd to Rychard Waryn
" for ii congres 16d. For wayashynge off the vessels,
" and off the napery 11d."

Fol. 44a.—" Gevyn to the mynstralles off my Lorde
" of Exettre 11d. For a quart off Romney at the selying
" the comyssion for the Parlement 3d."

Fol. 45a. On Sunday after the Feast of St. Bartholomew in the 34th year of Henry VI., Richard Rype,
already mentioned, was chosen Mayor. From about
this point, the entries, to a great extent, are in English.
45b.—" Item, receyvede off Syr Thomas Warner is prest,
" for Warner is liberte, beyng behynde in Sutton is
" tyme, beyng Mayre, 6s. 8d." Among the entries of
" Poundage," from the fishermen of Selcote, the name
of " Stephen Aldrych " frequently occurs.

Fol. 48b. 33, 34 Henry VI.—" Gevyn to the Kynges
" mynstralles 3s. 4d. Gevyn to the mynstrellys off my
" Lord Bowsyrs [Bourchier's] in wyne and mony
" 2s. 2d. Gevyn to men off Lede [Lydd], when they
" shewyd her play 6s. 8d."

Fol. 49a.—" Yevyn to the mynistrallys off my Lord
" off Bykyngham 3s. 4d." Under " Expenses off the
" Liefftenaunt," among other items, are the following :—Payd to John Young for powder off synamon, paper, clowys [cloves], maces, safferon, and
rasons off Corens [raisins of Corinth, or currants]
3s. 6d. Paid for ii capons fett [fetchod] at Stone
16d. For a dosser [dorser] off chekyns 12d. To
" Thomas Kyng his wyff for a henne, 4d. Payd to
" Janyn Reyner for ii congour 14d. To Wylliam Way
" for a quarter flagge and a crabb 16d. To John off

CORPORA-
TION OF
RYE

" Brege for viii bote flag' [?] 2s. 1d.   To Toty for a
" dorrey 4d.   For a lytill turbut bought off a mersh-
" man 3d.   For iii skoppys [? scoops] flowre and dl
" (half)— 11d.   For fewell 6d.   Payd to iii turnors off
" brooches [spits] 3d.   Payd to Hoget for his labour off
" makyng pastyes, dyting [arranging] off the dyner and
" sooper 16d.   To Janyn Marchaunt is wyff, for a bundell
" off grasse 1d.   Fol. 49b.—" Payd and allowed to
" John Bayle for expenses off Haxtall his meyne
" [retinue] in mete, drynke, and other cost off Suttone
" is tyme, when the man was hanged 3s.   Yovyng
" [given] to the Kynges messanger, that brosght the
" Kynge's Privy Seale to Rye, for havyng off a ship or
" two ffor to kepe the see 3s. 4d."
     Fol. 51a. 35 Henry VI.   " Babilon Grantfort " is
now named the first on the list of Jurats.—" Also, it is
" accorded, with the assent off the said Mayre, Jurates,
" and commons, that every ale brewer off the said towne
" off Rye shall answer, gader, and pay the Maltode off
" all such ale as thei shall brewe and delyver to the
" hukkester, to the said Maltoters duryng the said yere,
" uppon the payne and [? of] lesynge off the same
" brethyrne, he that doth the contrarie.   Also, the
" same day, it is accorded and ordeyned by the said
" Mayre and Cominaltee, that the bere brewer whiche
" bryngyn here to the said towne off Rye shall paye to
" the said towne for Maltode off every hole bune [or
" bowne, a measure] bere 2d."   The distinction is here
made between the brewing of ale and of " bere," or
sweet-wort and of ale bittered with herbs.
     Fol. 52a. (tr.)—" Jacob the Flemmynyg, of Salcote,
" for assault made upon Sir William Pynke, Chaplain,
" in the Mayor's house, to the shedding of blood, there-
" fore, according to the Constitution (he pays) 7s."
     Fol. 53a.—" Govyne to Thomas Hexstall for my
" Master, Liefftenaunt, viz. viiid., and for hymsylff to be
" owre good meen, that we com not to Dovorre as for
" the resumpcion, and for beryng up off the aliens
" mony for the terme off Mychelmas 16s. 8d.   In ex-
" penses of the comons when they karyed grete stones
" to the kay, in breed and ale, 8d."
     Fol. 54a.—" Paid to John Breknoke, John Attesson,
" and Thomas Breknok, and Thomas Oxenbruge his
" man, for berynge up of the said vi gonnes unto the
" chyrche 6d."   These " gonnes " had been recently
bought of Hankyn Colyne and Hewe Thomas, for
53s. 4d. ; a " gonner " having been brought to assay
them, at the cost of 8d.—" Paid to Martyn off Dovorre,
" when he browght the proclamation under the Kynges
" Prive Signet, with the commaundment off Dovorre,
" as for that no man shuld resseyve devyses nor lyvereis
" in noon maner wyse 8d.   Payd to Moryce Getard
" for beryng uppe to Dovorre off the alienes mony at the
" terme off Easter, and for the retorne havyng up off
" the warant tham [sic] cam for the dymes off the
" chyrch off Rye, the chyrch off Farlegh, and of Pese-
" mersh 2s."   Fol. 54b.   " Payd to John Suttone for the
" expenses off my Lord off Bukyngham mynstralles 8d.
" Payd to the same John for half c off gonn stones 4s."
Among the expenses of entertaining Richard Wyther-
ton, Lieutenant of Dover Castle, are the following payments to the Mayor; who, unless the money was given
to him in repayment of his previous outlay, seems to
have bred poultry on a large scale.—" Payd for iii capons
" to the Mayr 18d.   Paid for xx chekys [chicks] to the
" Mayr 2s.   Paid to the Mayr for iiii gese 16d.   Paid
" for butter, egges, vyngere, and vergeis [verjuice] 9d.
" Paid, Johane Wymond and Bartyne for wasyshyng
" off the vessells, and servyng at tabyll 6d.   Payd to
" Sutton is ost for i turbat, iii bramys (breams), and i
" gongre 2s. 4d."
     Fol. 55a.—" Payd for the makyng off the towne buttes
" 6d.   Gevyne to my Lorde of yorke his mynstralles
" 3s. 4d.   For bred and ale to the said mynstralles, and
" to a part off the commons 4d.   Paid to the mynstralls
" off the Lord Tresorer 2s. 6d."
     Fol. 58b, 36th Henry VI.—" To John Benett to warne
" the constabyll to sett a fyre the bekyng [beacon] 2d.
" Gefyn to Cakston in reward for bryngyng of his
" felychyp [from Tenterden] 12d.   In expenses uppon
" the felyschyp of Tentyrden at here goyng home 9d.
" Gefyn unto the same felychyppe to be well wyllyng
" to come ajene 10s.   Spent at a drynkyng a nother
" tyme 9d."   We have here another allusion to the busy
lawyer of Tenterden.
     Fol. 59a.—" In expenses in bryngyng my Lord Staf-
" ford to Wynchelse 14d.   Item, to Thomas Hoget for
" makyng of a pytte to laye in a gunne be syde the North
" Gate 6d."
     Fol. 61b.—" Gefyn to my Lorde Schruysberye myns-
" trally's 2s. 6d."

     Fol. 64b.—" Recevied of Babilon Grauntforte and
" Richard Rips, as maltode for salt sold, 3s."
     Fol. 66a. (tr.) " Firte, paid the harpers [sitherato-
" ribus] of the Earl of Pembroke 3s. 4d.   The minstrels
" of the Earl of Warwick, their expenses and other
" things ,4s.   Minstrels of the Duke of York, 4s."
     Fol. 67 has been nearly wholly torn out, by the hand of
some one as ignorant as he was mischievously inclined.
     Fol. 68a. (tr.) Paid for a certain foca [classical Latin,
" phoca]," called a " porpaas" 20d.   " Given to John
" Bayle, serjeant to the Lieutenant, when he carried the
" arms of England and of the Cinque Ports before the
" Lieutenant, through the whole of the port 2d."
     Fol. 72a.—" Received of John Downyg, of the vill of
" Taunton, in the county of Somersette, marchaunde,
" for purchase of his freedom, he paying beforehand,
" 6s. 8d.   And afterwards, yearly he is to pay for
" having such freedom 20d., so long as the same John
" shall stand as our Combaron, and retain our letters
" of such freedom under the common seal and the seal
" of our Mayoralty, attesting it, etc."
     Fol. 73b. 38 Henry VI.—" Paid for mending the town
" mace at London, by the hands of the Mayor, 6s.
" Given to Robert Benet on Wednesday (in London)
" that he might be our friend in the Exchequer, 20d.
" Paid for wine in the afternoon in Cheape (in London)
" with Robert Benet 3½d.   Paid for apples that night,
" in the chamber 1d.   Paid on Friday in the early
" morning for drinking wine when we were setting out,
" 1½d.   Paid for our chamber while we were in London,
" 4½d."   There are other items (in Latin) as to this
visit to London, on law matters, all of them of interest.
     Fol. 74a.—" Paid Babilon Grande (sic. Grandefort) for
" his trouble and expense in excusing the town to our
" Lord the Earl of Arundel, 3s. 4d."   Fol. 74b.—" Paid for
" two bolts of ' froggelockers' for the gates of the
" town, 2s. 3d.   Paid Thomas Barbur, alias ' Nether-
' land,' on the day when the men of the Lord Warre-
" wicke entered the town with a strong band, and took
" down the quarter of the man, and buried it in the
" churchyard, 2d."   This is an incident connected with
the Wars of the Roses.
     In fol 75a, (38 Henry VI.) is a list of (tr.),—" Pay-
" ments and expenses incurred in the time of John
" Rounge about the edifices of the north tower, called
" ' Landgate Tower,' from the 3rd day of September to
" the 24th day of October then next ensuing."   These
items extend over six closely written pages.
     Fol. 78b. (tr.)—" Paid the expenses of John Rounge,
" Mayor, Thomas Kyng, Deputy-Bailiff, John Sutton,
" John Hamond, Richard Rips, and John Bayle, Jurats,
" John Clerke, Common Clerk, and William Sutton, at
" Dover, going and returning, on carrying the mens'
" quarters, when the Mayor and Bailiff, with 4 Jurats,
" were sent under the heaviest penalty, and on pain of
" contempt of our Lord the King 19s. 3d.   For expenses
" at Dover, in drinking malmesey there, in the house
" of Estelle, before dinner, 2d."
     Fol. 79a.—" Paid John Neterton for 12 bundles of
" faggots to make a fire this night, for [warning against]
" the Frenchmen 4d.   Paid for the hire of a certain
" vessel called ' a cok,' to carry the Mayor and John
" Swan out and home from the town to the Cambre 12d.
" Given to the minstrels of the Lord de Dakyrs
" [Dacres] in ready money 12d.   Given to the minstrels
" of the Duke of Bukenham, our Warden, in ready
" money 4s.   Paid for theyr expenses the same time
" 2½d."   Fol. 79b.—" Paid John Pampulon for himself
" and his trouble in sailing to the Cambre, to communi-
" cate with the mariners coming from the West, to
" inquire the news as to the Lord the Earl of Warwick,
" 6d.   Paid a certain marinor of Rye, ' Frosie' by
" name, for his trouble in going to Leede (Lydd), to
" inquire what was the great fleet out at sea and sailing
" 8d.   Paid James Sedly for his trouble and expense
" in carrying a letter from the Earls of March and
" Warwicke to the Mayor and Bailiff, that we should
" meet them on the day following, at Canterbury 6d.
" Paid the night following to Morris Gedard for his
" trouble and for hiring a boat, to go to Wynchilse to
" inquire if the Mayor and Bailiff there intended to
" ride to meet the said Earls, as had been written to
" them 4d.   Paid at Melkehous by the Mayor and
" Common Clerk, when they drank a quart of wine
" there 2½d."
     Fol. 80a. (tr.)—" Paid at Maydeston for dinner, in
" company of the Mayor and Bailiff of Wynchylse 8d.
" Expenses of our horses there 3d.   For wine at
" Sedyngburne, for me [the Mayor] and the Common
" Clerk at dinner there 6d.   Expenses of our horses
" there 4d.   Paid one to attend our horses there while

" feeding 1d." (From Sittingbourne they appear to
" have turned southwards, and not gone to Canterbury,
" the Earls probably having passed on, on their road
" westwards.)—" Paid one to lead us on the way between
" Sedyngburne and Leene [probably now Lenham] 1d.
" Paid our expenses for the night there 2d. Paid our
" expenses in breakfasting there, in company with the
" said Mayor and Bailiff 8d. Paid the expenses of our
" horses there, the night and morning, 4½d. Paid for
" our bed there, and it was well worth it, witness, a
" feather bed 1d. Paid one of Leone with his horse, to
" lead us to Fordemylle; for the way between Leene
" aforesaid and Fordemylle was a nuisance (nociva) to
" us, who had never gone by it 2d. Paid at Apuldore
" for a dinner, in company with the Vicar there, and
" the same Mayor and Bailiff, and for a share of
" that of a certain man of the Earl of Warwicke, and
" of Simon Boteyn; seeing that, being in our company,
" they paid nothing, 8d. Expenses of our horses 1½d. At
" Oxney Ferry, for ferryage, or carriage, of our horses,
" 1d. For expenses this night at supper, in the Mayor's
" house, when we came home 4d. Paid then for hire
" of two horses, for the Mayor and the Common Clerk
" 2s. Paid to John Stephen 'laborer,' and to Wibbeley,
" for their labour one day in carrying up stones upon
" the town walls, in order, as being a matter of necessity,
" to be ready for defence of the town 6d. Paid John
" Stephyn of Barlynde for himself and his beasts carry-
" ing 6 cartloads of rocks or stones, to lay on the town
" walls, for defending the town in resisting the. King's
" enemies 9d. Paid the aforesaid John and Wybbeley,
" for their labour half a day in making hurdles in the
" wood, to put on top of the tower over the Water-gate,
" for men to stand there in defending the town 3d.
" Their expenses that time, in the wood and at home 3d.
" Paid John Stephen of Barlynde for carrying the
" hurdles to the town from the wood 3d. Paid the
" same John for mending the bridge of the North Tower
" 3d. Paid to a man of Lede, bearing a letter sent from
" Calice to Dover, and so through the Ports, to warn us
" that the Frenchmen were ready with all haste to enter
" the Ports, while the counties of Kent and Sussex were
" up (sursum) with the Earls of March and Warwicke,
" at Southampton 8d. Paid by the hands of the Mayor,
" for the King's proclamation at London, to be pro-
" claimed at Rye, as to spoilers and other delinquents,
" 20d."

Fol. 83b.—" Paid for 4 bushels of salt, given to John
" Benge, Clerk of the county of Kent, that he may be
" favourable to us, the town, and the hundred of Ten-
" terden, in the way of friendship, in such matters as
" we have to do, 3s. 4d. Paid Babilon Grandeford for
" being for the town at Battle, to excuse the town to
" the Lord de Audeley, 2s."

Fol. 84b. 39, 40 Henry VI.:—" Given to the minstrels
" of the Earl of Warwick, 20d. Paid for the expenses
" of Thomas Grevill and his son at supper in the
" Mayor's house on Saturday, and at dinner on the
" morrow, to labour for us at Tenterden for our yearly
" payment, which was so in arrear, seeing that the same
" Thomas was great with them of Tenterden; so that
" we might be the sooner contented as to our said yearly
" payment 6½d."

Fol. 86b.—" Paid Thomas Oxenbrugge for his trouble
" in going to Romeney, to inquire whether the French-
" men were arrived in the Downes or not, as was
" reported in Romeney Marsh; John Smyth of Wyn-
" chilse then having brought the news with him, as
" having heard it in the said marsh 8d."

Fol. 87b.—" Item, paied to Babilon Grantford, Squier,
" in ful paiement of his wageis, beyng at the Parle-
" ment of Coventre, and for his ridyng up to London
" whan he was sent up to the Kyng and the Lorddis
" for the towne with excuse; what tyme. it was not, as
" it is now, blessed be God of His grace, of amendment,
" and so to continue 10s. 8d."

Fol. 88b. (tr.).—" Paid for 'planke' and timber for the
" bridge called 'Langate' 6d. Paid for a seam of fish
" given to John Scot, with the consent of the town; for
" that the same John, as Controller, expedited our bill
" for the King's grant of all lands and tenements of
" James Hyde, being within the liberties and franchises
" of Rye 9s. Paid Richard Becwelle for the livery of
" the town at the day [iter] of St. Alban's, given in
" 5 red jackets to our neighbours (rubiis jaketteis con-
" vicinis nostris data) 16s. 8d."—soldiers sent to join the
ranks of the Earls of March and Warwick, at the
second Battle of St. Alban's, are probably here
alluded to.—" Paid the expenses of amending the 'hors-
" 'pond,' outside the North Gate 2d."

Fol. 91b.—" Received from Boner, of Wettressam,
" 'spicer and mercer' for 'haukyng' with spices round
" the town, against the Mayor's warning; notwith-
" standing that the same Boner had been often warned
" by the Mayor not to do so, and yet did it; there-
" fore he forfeited and paid 3s. 4d. Received of the
" Bailiffs of Tenterden and their fellows, when in the
" town at dinner, when our Lieutenant was in the
" town, upon the session on the sea-shore, on Friday
" the 2nd of July, as their expenses 3s. 4d.:" a Court
of Admiralty, held on the sea-shore, is alluded to.

Fol. 94a.—" Paid Robert Lumbard for a certain great
" nail called 'aspek' [a spike] for the 'getey' [jetty]
" and mending a certain 'crowe' of iron 3d. Paid to
" Babilon Graundefort for the Coronation [of Edward
" IV.], as is the usage 26s. 8d. Paid the Mayor for
" the Coronation, as has been the usage heretofore
" 26s. 8d."

Fol. 95b. " Given to the minstrels of our Lord the
" King, 6 in number, 6s. 8d. Expenses of the same
" minstrels 7d."

The volume ends with folio 109, the 6th year of King
Edward the Fourth.

In one of the chests, filled with miscellaneous papers
and documents belonging to the Corporation, I found
a fragment of a large folio paper volume containing
Chamberlains' Accounts, for the 14th, 15th, and 16th,
years of Edward the Fourth, filling up a portion of the
hiatus that exists between the volume from which the
preceding extracts were taken, and the Second Volume
in the bound series, the one that now succeeds it; on
the volumes being rebound, in or about the year 1776,
its existence was probably unknown, or, at least, it was
overlooked. Its contents are full of matters of interest,
and the following are some extracts; being translations
from the Latin, except when otherwise mentioned:—

On Sunday after the Feast of St. Bartholomew, being
the 28th of August, in the 14th year of Edward IV.
[A.D. 1474], " by assent and consent of the whole com-
" munity of the town of Rye," Babilon Graunford was
elected Mayor, " in the place from of old accustomed,"
for the following year; the first set of accounts contained in the fragment being for that period:—Among
other elections on the same day,—" John Notyngham,
" alias Sextene, was chosen to the office of collector for
" the box of the Ripiers on the Stroud, by the Mayor,
" Jurats, and commons, there."

The following are among the receipts for the year.—
" Received of the Bailiff of Tenterden for the vill and
"."hundred, 53s. 4d." Tenterden, as already noticed,
had been made a member, or adjunct, of Rye by Henry
the Sixth; to enable it the more easily to bear its
burden, after its impoverishment on being burnt by the
French in 1448. " Received from Babilon Graunford
" for his workshop [opella], in the market, 20d. From
" the same Babilon for his workshop on the Stronde,
" 12d. From the same Babilon for half a year for
" the Ynnyng at the Gutt, 12d."—" Inning " was the
name given to land recovered from the sea: the
" Gutt" was probably the name of the harbour, as it
then existed.—" From John Yongo for his new building
" near to the churchyard 8d." " Received from a
" certain man, a Flemmyng, 'pro bombagio,' 4d."
Entries under this head frequently occur; it probably means " boomage," a fee for removing the
boom, on admission to the harbour.—" Constitutions of
" the town (fines so called) for disturbances of the
" peace. Of Henry Squytte for an assault upon John
" Roby 20d. Of Richard Knygthe, alias Dawncer, for
" an assault 16d. Of John Roby, for an assault upon
" Henry Squytte 20d." Among the payments for this
year (in English):—" Item, payed to Edward Carpenter
" for makyng of stokkis, and for the Kay at Stronde,
" 16d. Payed for a planke for the Kaye, and 2 pecys
" of tymbere to sett the stokkis uppone 4d. Payed to
" Jamys Lowes and to Thomas Keme for fellyng of
" ryse and stakys for the heggis with owte Londe Gate,
" for ther wages, mete, and drynke 14d." " Ryse,"
elsewhere called " frith " in this fragment, consisted of
twigs, or coppice-wood.—" Item, payed for expences of
" the Maier and ii of his brodern [brethren] at Wyn-
" chelse, beyng for Baseleys matter, at Malyn Ver-
" nyngcomes, uppon Sen Kauterync Evyne [Saint
" Katharine's Eve] for a potel of wine 5d. Payed the
" same tyme for ther boote [boat] to bryng them to
" Wynchilse, and (back) ageyne 13d. Payd the same
" tyme when they wer com home, in the Meyres house
" at sopere, 12d. Payde the nexte day after for a
" dyner in Malyns house at Wynchelse, beyng for same
" mater of Robert Basele ther 2s. 10d. Payede for
" brede, drynge, and candel, the whiche the xii men

" had, syttynge uppon the verdyt in the Tower 7d."
—the Ypres Tower is meant.—" Payede to William,
" the Maires manne, for a gawnde [gallon] of wyne
" whan the sayd queste delyvered up ther verdytt
" 8d.   Payed to Richard Sander for a seme [horse-
" load] of fyche, the whiche was sent up to the Erylle
" of Arundelle, the Satirday after xii day 5s. 6d.
". Payed to the players of Romeney, the which played
" in the chirche 16d.   Payed to John Derby for fetynge
" [fetching] of the forsayde fysche 2d."   The following
items are translated from the Latin :—" Paid the Mayor
" for his wages 13s. 4d. ;" for a quarter, namely, his
" wages " at this time being, as for many years before,
53s. 4d. yearly.—" For the expenses in the Mayor's
" house 6s. 8d.";—this was for giving a dinner there,
on the day of the election.—" Given to the poor, on
" opening the boxes 18d.";—these were the boxes
containing the " Maltodes" and the moneys levied
upon the Ripiers.—" Paid John Cowper 'pro bom-
" bagio.   Paid for bread and ale in the church,
" when John Trego and John Estone made their
" account 3d."   In English,—" Payed whanne the
" Mayier and his broderne sate to fyere [affeer, or
" value] the endymente [? assessment], for bred, ale,
" and woode 2½d.   Payed for a dyner whanne the Bayle
" of Tentirdene and his brother ware her to syt uppone
" an enquery for the Kyng 12d.   Payd to Thomas
" Kembe for makyng clene of a goter by for his dore,
" the whiche hurte the stret, for his days wage, mete,
" and drynke 5d.   Payde in John Usandes house for
" expences in brede and drynke, whan the Chaumber-
" laynes, the Common Clerke, and the Sargeaunte, yid to
" gader the endythmentes, at on tyme 3d.   Payde to
" a manne that browthe the letter fro Roger Brent of
" Canterbyry, that the Mayor and certeyn of his bre-
" therne shulde appere before the Kynge at Sandewych
" 9d.   Payde to John Estone for ii bondel of thache-
" rode [thatch-rods], to thache the baryn [barn] the
" whicho the Mayer hathe of the towne 4d.   Payde to
" the thacher and his man for iii dayes labour, met and
" drynke, and wages 2s. 6d.   Payde in expences in
" mete and drynke upon Hewe Banks, what tyme he
" com from Sandewyche with a commycion fro the
" Kyng to take men, at the Mayer's, in mete and
" drynke 17d.   Payede to the boder [summoner] of
" Dovorre, what tyme he come with a writ for the
" shippyng for the Kynges viage 8d.   Payde in ex-
" pences in brede and drynke whanne John Tregoosse
" and John Estone made ther accountes in the chirche
" 2d.   Item, the same tyme whan they had geve ther
" accountes, come home in to the Maires house, in
" brede and wyne spente 16d.   Payede to the Kynges
" menstrellis what tyme they were here 6s. 8d.   Payede
" the same tyme in the Mayers house for ther expences
" in wyne 12½d.   Payede in expences what tyme we
" wor at [T]entyrdene, for to undirstond what ther
" parte shuld be of the benyvolence, spente ther and
" whan we come home, at sopere 8s.   Payde in expences
" for brede and ale what tyme we satte to assesse the
" bonyvolens 5d.   Payde in expences for brede and
" wyne, what tyme the Bayle of Tentirdene and his
" bretherne come hyder to brynge downe the money of
" the benyvolens 2s. 10d.   Payde to the Dewke of
" Clarance mynstrelles what tyme they were here 5s.
" Spente upon them the same tyme in bred and wine
. " 18d.   Payede to ii menne for to set Moreyce abord
" the Bretenne, what tyme men of Wynchilse fet
" [fotched] hym awaye 4d.   Payed to a man that
" brougth a proclamacion fro Dovorre that there no
" man shulde querrelle with othir, for non olde sores,
" and for drynge 9d.   Payede to Richard Wynde for
" his Parlament wages 13s. 4d.   Payede in John At-
" sones house, in expences, what tyme the Bayle of
" Hastynge was here, for to geve the Mayer knowledge
" what tyme the schippis shulde goo in to the Downys
" 11d.   Payede for a seme of ffysche, the whiche was
" sent to my Lord Dakere 10s. 10d.   Payede to the
" Mayer for xii days iiis. iiiid. a day, the whiche was
" grauntide hym by a commone for to go to Londone,
" to the Tresorer of the Kynges house, for the chypynge
" [shipping] to the Kynges vyage 40s.   Payed to a
" purcevant of my Lorde of Arundelle, the whiche was
" sent to speed tydyng of whan the shippis of Frenche-
" men lay here be fore the towne 2s.   Payed to a
" massenger sent by the Kyng, the whiche browte a
" letter to have a [sic] serten mareneres to the se 8d.
" Payed in expences in bred and whyne in the Maiers
" house, what tyme the Mayer and his brethrene sato
" to undirstonde what men wer best to go to the shippis
" 13d.   Payed upon Mary Magdalyn Day to a manne
" the whiche brouthe wrytyng fro the Kynge for to have

" men (for) the shippes 8d.   Payede to iiii wetchemen
" the whiche whichede [watched] for the towne, what
" tyme the Frencheman lay be fore the towne 8d.
" Payede for the carriage of a seme of ffyche [fish], the
" (which) was sent for the towne to my Lord Dakirs,
" and for the bryngyng home of the venysone 3s. 4d.
" Payede to a porcevaunt of the Kynge, the which
" brougth good tydynges 3s. 4d.   Payede for brede
" and wyne what tyme the Shawmeirlaynes [Cham-
" berlains] layde the booke of ther accountes 4d."
On the Sunday after the Feast of St. Bartholomew,
being the 27th of August, in the 15th year of Edward
the Fourth [A.D. 1475], Robert Lumbard was chosen
Mayor.   The following are some extracts from the
Chamberlain's accounts, in this fragment, for the year
of his Mayoralty. (Tr. from the Latin),—" Received
" of Robert Hekke, riper, for his hepe upon Stronde
" 6s. 8d.;" this alludes to the rent paid to the town by
each fisherman for liberty to place his " heap" of fish
upon the ground by the water-side.—" Received, for
" the Constitutions of the town, of Robert Browne
" for an assault upon Stephen Boteler 20d.   Received
" on the 2nd day of July from a vessel with salt, which
" went to Apyldore, and paid for custom 3s. 4d.
" Received of Master Graunfort [the late Mayor] for
" his vessel with salt, at Stronde 6s. 8d.   Received
" rent for the town for the kychene [kitchen] at the
" tower [of Ypres], from John Morkok 12d."—" Me-
" morandum, that on the xth day of Septembre, the
" xvth yere of our Soverayn Lorde Kynge Edwarde
" the iiiith, it was aggreide by for Roberd Lumbard,
" than beyng Mayor of Rye, by fore the Bayle and
" dyverse of there brothern, with othir certen com-
" moners, at the acompte of John Usande and William
" Parnelle, that alle manner of deVtes [debts] by-
" tewyene the towne and Babilone Graunfort, from
" the begynnyng of the worlde unto the day forsayde,
" is clere satisfyed and content." (Tr. from the Latin.)—
" Paid on the first of September to a certain man of my
" Lord Arundelle, who first brought news of the peace
" between our Lord the King and the King of France
" 3s. 4d."   Engl.—" Payd the ix day of Octobre to a
" berewarde [bearward] of my Lorde of Clarance, for
" baytynge of the berys [bears], for a stake to tey [tie]
" them by 2s. 1d.   Payd the xxii day of Octobre to a
" bodere of Dovorre, for bryngynge of the procla-
" macion that non Englischman should by no Gasken
" wyn of non alyene, 8d.   Payede the xx day of
" Novembre in expences in Wanstalles house at soper, ,
" the first nygth, goyng to the Brodhell holdyn at
" Romney, upon the next morow after Sent Edmonde
" the Kyng, ther beyng Robert Lumbard, the Mayer,
" John Suttone, and John Tregoosse, with other iii of
" ther servauntes 12d.   Upone the next morowe after,
" payd for their brekefast 11d.   Paid the same tyme to
" Wanstalle for horse hire 4d.   Paid the same day in
" Morleyes house for Romney [a kind of Malmsey wine,
" from Napoli di Romania] and for other vitel at ther
" dyner 14d.   Payed the same day in oure commyng
" home at Icede [Lydd] in Thomas Yonges house, for
" Malmesey 8d.   Payede in almes to a Fryere, at the
" instaunce and requeste of the Mayer of Wynchilse,
" the same tyme 4d.   Payed the xv day of Decembre in
" expences for wyne uppone Sir Thomas Mongomery,
" when that Lady Margaret [? the Countess of Rich-
" mond] was here 8d.   Payed the iii day of Janyvere
" to one Stainere of Hastyng for berynge a letter to
" the Baly ther, for to make fflache for us, and to be
" carride and had to my Lorde of Arundelle 2d.   Payd
" for wood, bred, and ale, the whiche was hade to the
" Towyre, to the xii men that were upon the queste 5d."
Tr. from the Latin :—" Paid William Parnelle for a
" farthing of broken gold—quadrante auri fracti—2s. 4d.
" Paid Robert Gooche for a horseload of arrows
" 17s. 4d.   Paid to Richard Wynde for his wage when
" about to go to Parliament, from the account of the
" Ripiers 6s. 6d.   Paid or allowed to Richard Wynde,
" as his wage when going to Parliament out of the
" account of the great Maltode, 6d. for washing, and
" 6d. for his clothes—vestiis suis."—" Theese ben the
" expences don a geyne the commynge of the Leve-
" tenent, the whiche shuld a kept the Courte of the
" Amaraltee with us at Rye the iii day of Aprill.
" First payed for ii coddis 12d.   Payed for a turbat 8d.
" For a rombolde of whyttynge 5d.   For a mary of
" gurnardes, and for ii pirlis[?], bowt of John Edirtone
" 2s. 8d.   For a mary of gurnardes bowt of a Pykerde
" 18d.   For ii elys 12d.   For halfe a samone 12d.   For
" brede 2s.   For spyce 10d.   For ii pottes with ale 10d.
" For ii solys 2d.   For a gurnarde, and anothir dorry
" 14d.   Payede to ii sarvauntes that made and dressed

"the sayd mete 10d. Payede the same tyme at dyner,
"for iiii potellis of redde wyne 16d. Payede the same
"tyme for a potelle of Romney 6d. Payde the same
"afternone in expences in brede and wyne spent
"upone the Baly of Tentyrdene and his feleashyp
"2s. 8d. Payede the same tyme for stale brede 4d.
"Payede the same tyme for woode 4d.   To John
"Estone, for fiowre 8d. Payede in expens for brede
"and drynke for the cokis 2½d. Payede for a newe
"garnet [hinge] for the stokkes, the whiche stondyth
"at the Water Gate 4d. Payede to Groche for the
"todirdelle [? other lot] of the arrowys the vi day of
"Apryle, the whiche was by Hyde unpayed 4s." Tr.
from the Latin.—Paid Thomas Fletcher for mending
"the water ' stayir ' 4d. Paid the minstrels of our Lord
"of Arundelle, as assigned by the Mayor and Jurats,
"6s. 8d.; and for expenses in bread and wine in the
"house of Master Graunford, Alderman, 5d." Engl.—
"Payede the xxii day of Aprill, or that we went to·
"Br[o]dehill, in bred, ale, and vitelles, at oure brekefast
"12d. Payede the same daye in expences for mete and
"drynke at Wanstallis howce at Lede [Lydd] outewardes
"10d. Payede the same nyght at Romney in Morleyes
"houce, in mete and drynke for oure sopere 21d. Payed
"the same next day after at oure departyng from the
"Bradhell, at oure brekefast and dynere in the said
"Morleys houce 2s. 1d. Payed the same daye in the
"Brodelhouce to the comyn box 10s. Payede the same
"tyme to the vi li, the whiche was payed to Pemsey by
"alle the hole houce, for oure parte 11s. 5d. Payed to
"the porter of the Brodhell houce the same tyme 2d.
"Payed to Wenstalle the same tyme homewarde for
"mete and drynke, and horse hyre 8d. Payed for
"horce hyre for John Hamond and Harry Bayly, the
"same tyme 8d. Payede the same tyme for ledying of
"the horce home agayne to Lede 8d. Payede to Barn
"ham the same [time] for bryngyng us to the Cambir,
"and home agayn 20d. Payede the same day home
"wardes at Thomas Yonges houce for Romney [wine]
"11d. Payede the same nyght for oure soper, when
"we wer come home, fore mete and drynke, 2s. 5d.
"Payede to my Lorde of Clarance mynystrallis the xi
"daye of Maye 6s. 8d. Payede in expences done upone
"the same mynstrollis, the same day 23d. Payede the
"xxvii day of Maye to the Kynges mynstrelles 10s.
"Payede the iii daye of June in expences for mannys
"mete and horse mete, what tyme the Mayer, the Baly,
"the Vycare, and the Jurattes, rode to Batell, unto my
"Lorde of Arundell 6s. Payede unto John Harte, the
"manne of law, the xv daye of June, for hys fee 6s. 8d.
"Payed the secunde day after the box opynnyng, at the
"rekynnyng of the comyn boke, upon the Maiere, the
"Comyn Clerke, John Sexten, with othyr moe at oure
"brekefaste 6d. Payede the xi day of August to a
"hodere of Dovorre, the whiche brout a bille chargyng
"the Maier and Balifes to do [cause] come be fore the
"Amerale or Leuetenaunt xviii of the most wisest owre
"Combarouns the xxvi day of August 8d. Paid John
"Sexten for his trouble in writing, by the Mayor, 2s."
The following are extracts from the Accounts in the
time of Henry Bayly, Mayor, who was chosen to that
office on Sunday after the Feast of St. Bartholomew in
the 16th year of Edward the Fourth [A.D. 1476]. Tr.—
"Received of Master Herte for making a pair of butts,
"when at supper, and Master Warner was with us 20d.
"Received of Robert Belyngham, Esquire, for his free
"dom, at the Feast of Easter 3s. 4d. Received from one
"Bretenne [Breton] for his vessel laden with salt 3s. 4d.
"Received, for the Constitutions of the town, from
"Gilbert Rudde, when he drew blood with his nails
"from Thomas Aleyne, John Edirton's man, 20d. Re
"ceived for John Knytte, Stephen Butlere, and William
"Poyntore, for playing at dice [decies] 4s. 4d." The
following items, extracted from a long list, bear reference
to a sumptuous dinner given to the Lieutenant of the
Lord Warden.—"Payede to Roberd Lumbardes wife
"for vi chekynnys, 3d. Payede to John Rippis for
"onyonys, clowis, maces, and saforne 3d. Payede to
"John Tolkyne for saforne i d. Payed to Thomas
"Fletcher for goyng to Levysham for pigges, and yet
"he cowde not spede there i d. Payede to Wibeley, for
"tornynge of the broche [spit] the same tyme i d.
"Payede to Master Graunfort for xviii pesonys [? some
"kind of edible] the same tyme, 9d. Payede to the same
"Master Graunfort for a capone the same tyme 12d.
"Payede to the cookes for his labore, and to Revet
"Hatche 20d. Payede in rewarde to the mynstrelles of
"the Kynges modire [Cecily, Duchess of York], vppone
"our Ladyes Evyn the Natyvite 3s. 4d. Payed for the
"expences don and spent uppone the men that laborde
"abowte the fyer, the whiche was at John Cokkes house

"done by Hautis child, the Munday next after the Fest of
"Seynt Edwarde: fiyrst payed to xiii men, the whiche
"watchid for the saide fyere the next nygth after 4s. 4d.
"Payede for ii halfe bounys of bere for the men to
"drynk, what tyme thei labored uppone the saide fyer 2s.
"Payede for candil had at Oxenbriges for the meune
"that weched the same tyme 1½d. Payed for a dyner for
"the Prynces mynstrelles, ther beyng the Mayor, the
"Baily, John Suttone, Robert Acroche [at the Cross],
"with othir more of theire brothern 22d. Gevyn to
"the saide mynstrelles the same tyme, the viii day of
"Novembire 6s. 8d. By the consent of the Mayer and
"his bretherne, gevyn to the pleyers of Lede [Lydd],
"the whiche pleyede here the Sunday after Cristemas
"halidayes, 16d. By the consent of the Mayer and
"his bretherne and commyners, the money that John
"Graunfort payed for his fredoum was gevyn unto hym
"a yen, to be goode frend unto the towne 6s. 8d. Payed
"the Thursday nexte after the Fest of Sent Hillary
"for a capone ordeyned for Master Ancheres suppere,
"by the concent of the Mayer and serten of his bretherne,
"at which sesone he cam not, and for expences at
"sopere the same tyme 12d. Payed to Master Angere
"for Newnden Brige, in party of payment of v marke
"the xxii day of Janyver 6s. 8d. Payed the xxiiiith daye
"of Janyvere in expences for a dyner for Maister John
"Hert, the man of lawe, that tyme beyng here 16d
"Payed to John Tregoosse for a gret rede boke 6s. 8d.
"Payed to Thomas a Bayne for his Parlemente wages,
"the which was left by hynde unpayode in John Suttone
"his tyme 40s. Payed to the pleyers of Wynchilse, the
"whiche pleyed in the churche yerde, uppone the day
"of the Purificacion of oure Laday 10d. Payed to ii
"carpenteres goyng to Romeney to se the jetyes, and
"to take of them exhsumple 10d. Payede for expences
"uppone the Mayer and the Bailif, afor thei yede to
"Wynchilse, ther to meete with the Mayir of Wynchilse
"and the Bayly of Hastynge, what tyme my Lorde of
"Arundello sent downe wrytynge to atache sirtayne
"persones that robbid uppone the see 4d. Payed after
"the Mayer and his bretherne come owte of the Towere
"[of Ypres] from the affyryng [affecring, or assessing]
"of the quest, unto Mastor Graunfortes hous, to a dyner
"ther, with them beyno present Master Robert Oxen
"brige, Squyer, for expences ther in mete and wyne
"2s. 8d. Gevyn in almes, the same tyme as the Maier
"of Wynchilse and the Bailefe of Hastynge dede, to the
"byrryeng [burying] of Slobuscho 3d. Payed the xi
"day of Aprille to John Alys, smygth, for ii hospis
"[hasps] and ii stapiles for tway dores in Towyre 4d.
"Payed unto John Bele the Saturday next after the
"Fest of Ester for goyng to Brede, to fetche Master
"Robert Oxenbruge and his sonne unto the Meyers and
"to the Baylif for sertayne maters of the towne 4d.
"Payede the same day, whan the said Master Robert
"and his sonne was come, at dynere, there beyng
"present the Mayer, Baylyf, and serteyn of there
"brethern, and also Master Hert, for vitel and wyne
"18d. Payod to Master Thomas Oxenbrige for his
"labour commyng to Rye, and for his goode councelle
"the same tyme 3s. 4d. (In Latin.)—Paid the Mayor's
"wife for expenses in her house 6s. 8d."—This was a
charge for a dinner at the Mayor's house, on the day
of his election.—"Given to the poor and to the servants
"there, 21d."—"These ben the expences spent at the
"Brodhille holdyn at Romene, the Tuysday next after
"the Clause of Ester, ther beyng Henry Bayly, thanne
"Mayer, John Graunfort, Bailif, John Suttone, Esquyer,
"Richard Wynde, John Tregoosse, John Usande, John
"Swanne, Comyn Clerke, William Estone, Thomas
"Oxenbrige, Thomas Litherlonde, Thomas Morris,
"Master Graunforte, ii menne, Robert Mayhowe, that
"(was) wayttyng uppone the Mayer, Nicholas Suttone,
"and John Bayly. That tyme payed fyrst owtewardes
"at Lede [Lydd] at Swannes hous and at Thomas
"Yonges, for bred, wyne, bere, and vittelles 2s. 1d.
"Payed at Romene for ouyre sopere the same daye at
"nygth, for brede, wyne, ale, bere, and vitelles 3s.
"Payed for ther beddes and expences in bred and
"wyne for the feleship, the whiche lay not at Morleys
"that nygth, but at other placis in towne, and for wyne
"that the Mair and his feleshe [fellowship] that layo
"at Morleys hade in the morning, or thei yede in to
"the towne 2s. ½d. Payede for their brekefast, or that
"they yede into the Brodehill house 12d. Payed for
"bred and wyne that was spent uppone the Baylife,
"John Tregoosse, Thomas Oxenbrigc, and othir, whil
"a letter was in the makyng in the Brodhil house, tho
"whiche shulde be sent unto my Lorde of Arundello,
"spent the same tymo 7d. Payod first, in the said
"house of the Brodhill, to the box 10s. 6d. Payede tho

" secunde tyme in the saide house 11s. 4d. Payede to
" the Leyntenaunt his costes, as it was allowede by
" every towne ther the same tyme, for ouro parte 12d.
" Payed at Morleys house for a dyner for the Mayer
" and his bretherne, with all the seid feleship, ther
" beyng present Master Hert, for brede, wyne, ale, and
" vitellis 3s. Payede and gevyn there the same tyme to the
" women, the whiche gadderd for ther Pariche churche 4d.
" Payed to Richard, Master Graunfordes man, there, the
" same tyme, for horsemete for his masters hors, spent
" ther and at Lede, and for othir expences that the said
" Richard and John Bele hade leyde owte, in all 9d.
" Payed homewardes at Lede, for brede, wyne, and for
" checonys [chickens], at Swannes hous, for the Mair,
" Balif, and ther feleship 10d. Payede for vii horse hyere
" ther the same tyme 2s. 4d. Payede for brede and bere
" at the Hermytage homewardes 3d. Payede to William
" Barnham for bot byer owtewardes and homewardes
" 2s. Payede to Maister Hert for his labor commyng to
" the said Brodbill 6s. 8d. Payed to the saide Maister
" Hert for his fees, the whiche he hathe yerly of the
" towne 6s. 8d. Payede for brede, alle, and wyne, and
" for vitelles, the whiche was spent in the Maiers house
" uppone the saide feleship byfore reherside, at ther
" brekefast, or thei yede owte unto the saide Brodehille,
" and at sopere when they were come home 4s. 4d.
" Payede and gevyne to the Quenys mynstrelles, the
" seconde day of Mayo 6s. 8d. Payede the same daye
" for ther dyner, for brede, wyne, and fische 16d.
" Payede and gevyne to the Duke of Clarens (mynstrelles)
" the v day of May 6s. 8d. Payed the same tyme for
" ther soper at Maister Graunfortes hous, the Maier
" and the Bailif, with sertayne of ther bretheren ther
" beyng present, for vitel and wyne, 2s. Payede for a
" seme [horse-load] of fyssche, the whiche was sente
" unto Master Tresorer, when he was here at his wal-
" ynge in [?walling-in] the Marshe 10s. Payed to William
" Barnham for carryeng of the saide fisshe unto Master
" Tresorer, beyng in the Mershe, and also for fetchyng
" over the Maier, the Viker, the Bailif, with othere of
" ther broderne, unto the saide Master Tresorer, and
" home ayene 9d. Payed and spent uppone Master
" Warner and John Yonge, what tyme the said Master
" Warner was (here), and gaif the Maier leve to have
" turf uppone his grownde at the Leo, for to make
" the buttes, the whiche stond now without the North
" Gate 8d." The various items for making the butts
are then added. At the 46th page, this fragment,
the writing of which is upon a very stout wire-wove
paper, comes to an end.

Among the earlier documents stowed away in one of
the chests, there is a torn leaf of vellum with writing
on it, of the close of the 15th century ; the following is
a description of a portion of its contents.—A copy of a
mandate, in Latin, by John (Arundel) Bishop of Chichester, dated the 9th of July 1476. in the church of St.
Thomas, at Wynchelse, upon his Visitation, addressed
to Master William Wykwyk, Vicar of Rye. wherein he
says he has been informed that the Parish church of
Rye is "dedicated in honour of the glorious Virgin
" Mary," and that formerly the parishioners had been
bound to make their due oblations on the Feast of the
Nativity of St. Mary [8th of September] as being the
" Feast of the place," but that in modern times it had
come about that they were wholly absent therefrom ;
some of them going abroad, some frequenting the fairs
in neighbouring places, and others fishing for herrings
in remote parts,—" So that divine worship is not then
" observed by them. as it ought to be, and the due
" oblations are withheld, and hardly ever paid ; " considering therefore that their absence cannot be conveniently prevented, and wishing to appeal to their
consciences ; he orders that all the parishioners of Rye,
of either sex, who are admitted to Holy Communion,
shall in future make their oblations upon the Feast of
the Assumption of St. Mary [15th of August], instead of
the Nativity, and that they shall not be considered bound
to offer on the Feast of the Nativity, unless they wish to
do so, from feelings of devoutness. On the other side of
the leaf are the following entries, in Latin,—" A.D. 1483 ;
" on the last day but one of the month of April, it was
" determined by Adam Oxenbrugge, the then Mayor,
" the Jurats, and the whole community of Rye, that as
" holiness becomes the Lord's house [domum Domini
" decet sanctitudo], in future, to the honour of God and
" of the glorious Virgin Mary, the Parish church of
" the said town, with the churchyard, and the manse
" of the vicarage thereof, should be of the same free-
" dom, and with as much liberty, as the other houses of
" the freemen of the town aforesaid, especially as to
" arrests and other matters." A fresh paragraph then

commences, also in Latin, to the following effect :—
" Also, in the year aforesaid, on the 6th day of July,
" King, Richard and Queen Anne, his consort, were
" crowned at Westminster, by the Reverend Father in
" Christ, and Lord, the Lord Thomas Bowrgchier,
" Cardinal, and Archbishop of Canterbury : at which
" Coronation there were chosen to bear the silk canopy
" over the King and Queen aforesaid, for the Barons
" of the town of Rye, Adam Oxenbrugge, and the then
" Mayor thereof, Thomas Bayen, (and) Robert Croche ;
" who, after the said Coronation, on the same day,
" claimed, in right of the town of Rye aforesaid, the
" canopy that had been carried over the King before-
" named ; which canopy they kept in their possession,
" and afterwards carried away with them, with four
" spears and four silver bells, to the town of Rye afore-
" said : giving surety that they, with their companions,
" the Barons there present, would make answer for the
" said canopy at the next Broodehill held. And so at the
" next Broodehill, which was holden at Romene on the
" 22nd day of July following, it was found in the
" books of the Common House there, that the said
" canopy belonged of right to the town of Rye afore-
" said : and so, by common consent of all the Barons
" then and there present, the said canopy was allowed
" to remain in the town of Rye."—Another paragraph
then commences (tr.) :—" The manner of retaining or
" receiving the canopy at the Coronation of the King
" and Queen, as among the towns of the Cinque
" Ports, namely, Hastyng, Wynchelse, Rye, Romene,
" Heethe, Dovorre, and Sandewyche, is this.—When
" the service is done by the Western Ports, namely,
" Hastyng, Wynchelse, and Rye, as to one canopy,
" then the service is to be done by the Eastern Ports,
" namely, Dovorre, Romene, Sandewyche, and Heethe,
" as to the next two canopies that follow : and when-
" ever any such canopy falls to the Western Ports, then
" each town of those Ports is to have the canopy whole,
" with spears and bells, according to a certain series and
" succession : and when any canopy falls to the Eastern
" Ports, then such canopy shall be divided, with the
" spears and bells, at one time between the towns of
" Dovore and Romene, and at another time between
" the towns of Sandewiche and Heethe, as by acts in
" the Broodehille, and the fact of preceding canopies
" remaining in the said towns, more evidently appears ;
" and as, for example, may be seen below. The canopy
" of King Henry V remained with Hastings ; of his
" Queen, Katharine, with Dovorre and Romene ; of King
" Henry VI, with Sandewiche and Heethe ; of his
" Queen, Margaret, with Wynchelse ; of King Edward
" IV, with Dovorre and Romene ; of his Queen, Eliza-
" bet, with Sandwiche and Heethe ; of King Richard
" III, with Rye ; of his Queen, Anne, with Dovorre
" and Romene ; "—the following are added in succes-
" sively later hands ; —" of King Henry VII, with
" Sandwiche and Heethe ; of his Queen, Elizabeth,
" with Hastyng ; of King Henry VIII with Wynchelse ;
" of his Queen (Katharine) with Sandwyche (and)
" Hethe ; of his Queen, Anne, with Dovorre and
" Romeney ; of King Edward VI, with Rye ; of Queen
" Mary the First [Mariæ Primi] with Sandwych and
" Hyeth."

The following parchment and paper writings (other
than volumes) have been selected for description, from
among the numerous miscellaneous documents lying
promiscuously in the various chests at the Town Hall ;
as constituting, to all appearance, the most ancient, now
existing, of the Corporation records of Rye :—

Two tattered leaves of parchment, which, from the
stitch-marks, have evidently formed a Chamberlain's roll
(in Latin) of Maltotes and other charges, the proceeds
of which were due to the Corporation ; with the expenditure thereof. From the writing, it belongs to the
beginning of the 15th century, but it is in so mutilated
a condition that its exact date can only be surmised : it
appears to belong to the Mayoralty of John Makop, in
the 6th year of the reign of Henry IV. The "Receipts"
consist partly of " Rents of Assize," William Walpol,
among others, paying 21d. The next are charges upon
nets and loads of fish ; " flueres," (a kind of net) are
mentioned, and lasts of " sprottes," or sprats. Under
this head also, William Walpol pays 21d., and John
Fynche a like amount, for " the Term of St. Andrew."
Lists of fines are given, for violating the "Constitutions" of the town, by making assaults, in one instance
with a " pollax," in another with a " daggar." Malitotes " general," and those exacted from " Ripiers,"
(retail dealers in fish), with " Malitotes of rents and
forms " from inhabitants " then follow ; more easily,
(this membrane being comparatively perfect) to be

deciphered:—" First, from John Makope (the Mayor)
" 2s. 4½d. From Robert Dyne, for his mill, 2s. 11d.
" From John Wykam 2s. 6d. From Stephen Pawlyn
" 2s. 6d. From Robert Onewyn 3s. 4d."; and other
receipts of smaller amount. The Chamberlains then
account for a moiety of the "Rents ferm collected from
" strangers." Under the head of "Shares of balengers,"
occurs,—" Also, received from William Longe, for
" Frenchmen taken, 13s. 4d. namely, from two balen-
" gers. Also, from John Hayward 4s."
On the reverse of the roll are the items of expenditure for the same year, but almost wholly illegible in
the earlier part. "Payments to officers and counsel
" for the town," are comparatively easy to be deciphered. The Mayor is paid 100s. "for his office,
" according to the ancient custom of the vill." Then—
" To Robert Oxenbrugge, for his stipend, 26s. 8d; to
" the Common Clerk, 40s., and in cloth for his livery
" 15s.; to him for parchment and ink 2s." These rolls
were superseded in the middle of the 15th century,
if not earlier, by the Chamberlains' Books, which have
already come under notice.

A narrow slip of parchment, about two feet in length,
containing a list of the inhabitants of Rye, as assessed
for—"The half Scot, imposed in the time of John
" Langport, Mayor, in the 2nd year of the reign of
" King Henry the Fifth," for the war with France,
no doubt. The Mayor stands first, for 6s. 8d.; John
Shelle and Robert Onewyn, following for like sums:
these, with eleven others, belonging to the Ward without
the Gate. A much poorer class of people, 21 inhabitants
of Nesse Ward, then follow; then 28 inhabitants of
Watermelle Ward, equally poor; the inhabitants of
Market Warde succeed them, more numerous, but not
more wealthy; except that John Standene is assessed
for 6s. 8d.: in another list, under the same Mayoralty,
but apparently for another assessment, it is stated,
under an abbreviated form, "dm. m." that John Stan-
done was " Lord of the Manor" in this Ward.

In some oblong papers, consisting of 10 small leaves
sewed together, there is entered a list of (apparently)
those summoned to a Hundred Court at Rye, holden
before Adam Oxenbrege, Mayor, in the third year of
King Henry the Seventh, the name of Oxenbrege being
run through with a pen, and "W. Barnham" substituted. The list begins with Adam Oxenbrege, and
John Suttone, Esquire. The localities here named are
Paternoster Rowe, Chepe, The Ma[r]ket Place, Olde
Fisshestrete, and Bukeleresbory. Then, in the same
book, in a list of assessments in the Mayoralty of William
Barnham (Mayor 5 years later, in 1493), the localities
named are, Market Warde, Paternoster Warde, Fissher-
strete Warde, Buklersberry Warde,—names. evidently,
mostly derived from London localities. One of the
persons assessed in this last Ward is entered as—"Harry
" that weddid Qaytow Love;" being assessed at a
payment of 4 pence. Other entries are,—" Richard
" Broke, for Grensted Place 3s. 4d." " Geffray the
" Laborere 4d." " John the Tynker 4d., and Cornelis
" Irescheman 4d." William Estone, William Stonaker,
John Suttone, William Pernelle, and Robert Croche,
are each assessed as owning 400l., the largest sum
named. " Robert Joly, the Fetere," owns but 40s.
Among other surnames, Drynker, Pak, Bigman, and
Cutberd, appear. The total value of the property
possessed by the inhabitants is 6,303l. The property of
certain women, is assessed, as to value, in the following
singular form.—" Lumbardes Love 20 li. Richard Wor-
" thies Love 20 li. Marion, Drilandes Love 10 li.
" Balies Lof 80 li. Richard Wynnes Lof 30 li. Richard
" Waytis Love 5 li." Under their payments, assessed at
2 pence in the pound, they appear in each instance as the
" Wedow" of the persons respectively named. The
mention of these poor widows, as " Loves" of their late
husbands, is almost poetry, and this too where we should
least expect it.

Letters Patent, dated in the 5th year of the reign of
King Richard the Second, bearing reference to the
building of the walls round the town of Rye;—of which
walls some fragments still remain. The document
is endorsed, in a hand of the 16th century, — "A
" Charter for building the walles of Rye." It begins—
" Ricardus, Dei gratia etc. Sciatis quod nos, pro eo
" quod dilecti Barones nostri, Major et Communitas
" villæ de la Rye, manuceperunt coram nobis et Can-
" cellaris nostra villam prædictam muro de petra et
" calce infra triennium a data præsentium in locis
" necessariis sufficienter claudere et firmare.—It is
given at length in Holloway's History and Antiquities of
Rye, 1847; but under the very singular impression that
it belongs to the reign of Richard the First. The town

had been plundered and burnt by the French in 1377,
some 4 or 5 years before.

A very long deed (in Latin), stating that the Prior
and Convent of the Order of Friars Heremites of St.
Austin, in Rye, have granted " to the reverend man,
" William Taillour, of Rye," and to Agnes, his wife,
not only the suffrages of their prayers, but have
assigned a brother, a priest professed of their Order and
Convent, for a sum of money by the said William and
Agnes paid, " and for other benefits bestowed, and in
" future to be bestowed ;" which brother shall celebrate
daily at the altar of St. Nicholas in the Parish church of
Rye, for the healthful estate of them and their children,
and for the soul of John, the brother of the said
William; and for ever for the souls of the said William
and Agnes, when they shall depart this life. Touching
the holy [Gospels], the Prior and Convent have made
corporal oath thereon, and executed these presents. In
case of omission or neglect, they are to incur sentence
of the Greater Excommunication. The seal of their
community, and the seal of the office of Prior, are
attached thereto.—" Given at Rye, in our Chapter place,
" on the 18th day of August in the year of our Lord
" 1368. Present, the venerable men, Sir Stephen
" ———, Dean of the Deanery of Hastyngges, Sir
" William de Leycestre, perpetual Vicar of the church
" of Rye, Richard Baddyng, then Mayor, Henry Golde-
" :eve, John Ivory, Laurence Taverner, John Salerne,
" Stephen Andrew, Laurence Curboyl, Stephen Elyot,
" Thomas Kittay, Robert Bernhard, Richard Pak, John
" Otringham." The two seals, vesica-shaped, and each
representing St. Augustin, in the act of benediction,
are in fair preservation.

Jeake, in his Charters of the Cinque Ports, seems to
imply that the Friars Heremites were only settled in
Rye in the 16th year of Henry the Eighth ; the error
has, however, been corrected in Holloway's History and
Antiquities, where it is noticed that the Austin Friars of
Rye are mentioned so far back as the 37th of Edward
the Third (A.D. 1364).

Gift and confirmation (in Latin), by the Mayor and
Barons of Rye to the Prior and Brethren of the Order of
Friars Heremites of St. Austin, of the Convent at Rye,
of all that place called " Le Haltone;" " saving to us a
" competent space near to the foss, for building the
" wall of our town, and a way to go to such wall." In
case the Prior and Convent shall leave the said place,
or be unwilling to inhabit it, it shall be lawful for the
Mayor and Barons to resume the same.—" In witness
" whereof, we have caused our Common Seal to be set.
" Given at Rye, on Thursday, the Feast of the Transla-
" tion of St. Thomas the Martyr, in the second year of
" the reign of Richard, after the Conquest of England,
" the Second." Witnesses, William Batisforde, William
Hoorne, Robert Ore, Robert Echighame, William Golde-
forde, John Edward. This is the counterpart of the
original deed of gift, and to it a very fine impression
of the seal of the Friars Heremites is attached; representing St. Augustin, holding a crozier, with an
upright anchor before him, and people standing below.
The legend is nearly perfect. This deed goes far
towards shewing that the fine remains of their Convent,
still to be seen at Rye, are of a much earlier date than
that of Henry VIII., a date that has been assigned to
them.

A notification (on parchment), in Latin, to Simon
Northew, Rector of the Parish church of Suthese (near
Lewes) in the Diocese of Chichester, and Vicar in
Spirituals in the Archdeaconry of Lewes, by the Arch-
descon of Lewes ; to the effect, that he has inducted John
Bevere, Priest, into the perpetual Chantry of St.
Nicholas and the Blessed Virgin Mary, in the Parish
church of Rye, on the presentation of William Lange
and Thomas Lange, in succession to Sir John Casselake,
deceased. Dated at Wynchelse, the 22nd of February
1418[9]. Henry [Ware], Bishop of Chichester, named
therein, was Bishop for only 2 years and 9 months.
The document is sealed with the oblong seal of the
Deanery of Lewes, of which only a small fragment is
left.

Copy (on parchment) of a letter, in French, dated
19th of November in the 19th year of Richard the
Second (A.D. 1395), and addressed "by your brethren
" and friends the Mayor and Jurats of the vill of Rye"
to their " Combarons" of one of the Cinque Ports, not
named. They entreat them, as they have frequently
done before, that they will compel John Petham to pay
46s. 8d. which he owes to John Hamonn and Walter
Englisshe, and 10s. damages for the unjust withholding
thereof. The copy is, no doubt, of contemporary date
with the original.

5.

3 R

The following is of interest, as having the signature upon it (T. Stanley) of Thomas, Lord Stanley, created Earl of Derby by Henry the Seventh, in 1485; being a release of all claims and rights of action against the Mayor and Barons of the vill of Rye:—" Noverint universi per " præsentes, me, Thomam Stanley, militem, Dominum " Stanley, Seneschallum Hospitii Domini Regis, remi- " sisse, relaxasse, et omnino in perpetuum quietum-cla- " masse, Majori et Baronibus villæ de Rie, unius villarum " Quinque Portuum Domini Regis, et toti communitati " ejusdem villæ, omnimodas actiones et demandas per- " sonales, quas versus ipsos, vel eorum aliquem, habui, " habeo, seu quovis modo habere potero, ratione alicujus " debiti, compoti, conventionis, contractus, aut alter- " ius causæ, rei, vel materiæ cujuscunque, ab origine " mundi usque in diem confectionis præsentium. In " cujus rei testimonium, sigillum meum præsentibus " apposui. Data vicesimo septimo die Aprilis, anno " regni Regis Ricardi, Tertii post Conquæstum, se- " cundo." Of the small seal the impression is entirely effaced. Platted rushes are inserted in the wax. Lord Stanley was at this time the owner of the Ypres Tower, formerly in the possession of John de Ypres and Thomas Stoughton.

A notification, on parchment, in Latin, to Master William Miltone, Dean of Chichester, and Keeper of the Spiritualties of the Bishopric of Chichester, the See being vacant, by the Archdeacon of Lewes; stating that he has inducted John Morejeve, Priest, into the per- petual Chantry of St. Nicholas and the Blessed Virgin Mary, in the church of Rye, on the presentation of William Longe (elsewhere "Lange") and Thomas Longe, of Rye, the true patrons thereof, upon the death of Sir John Bever, the late Chaplain. Dated the 1st of November 1420.

A notification, on parchment, in Latin, dated A.D. 1279, under five seals, by John, perpetual Vicar of Bexele, proctor of Master Richard de Pagelham, Chancellor of Chichester, executor of the testament of Brice de Rye, deceased, James Marchaunt, co-executor thereof, and John Sampson, called "de Yham," John de Oarette, and the said James Marchaunt, as executors of the testament of Elena, formerly the wife of the said Brice; setting forth that the said Brice, in his testa- ment, with the consent of the said Elena, assigned a certain sum of money to purchase a rent for the main- tenance of two priests, to celebrate daily for the souls of the said Brice and Elena in the church of St. Mary at Rye; and that, such having been the desire of the said Brice and Elena, they have assigned one half of the said rent to Robert le Paumere, Clerk, of Pevenese, that he may be admitted to the holy orders of sub- deacon, deacon, and priest, by the venerable Father, the Bishop of Chichester; to the end that he may be one of the priests celebrating in the Chantry aforesaid. " Given at Winchelese." Of the 5 seals, only one, with the impression of a wheel, is left.

Petition on parchment, in Latin, date 1281, addressed by John Bone, son of Henry Bone, of Rye, and heir of Brice de Rye, to S. [Stephen de Berksteed] Bishop of Chichester, setting forth that a Chantry had been founded in the church of Rye by the said Brice and Helena, his wife, for celebrating a mass daily, "in " honour of God, the glorious Virgin, His Mother, and " all Saints," for the souls of the said Brice and Helena; and begging that, at his presentation, the Bishop will admit Robert de Pevenese, who has already been duly admitted to the requisite sacred orders, to officiate therein. His seal being unknown to most persons, that of the Deanery of Hastings has been added thereto. The latter seal is lost; that of John Bone is perfect, representing a hand holding a bird. There is also a counterpart of this petition, both seals of which are lost.

A formal receipt, on parchment, dated the 41st year of Edward III. As it is one of the very few documents here met with, written in French, it is given in full:— " As tous ixeux qui cestes lettres verront ou orront, " Piers de Brewes, Chivaler, Henry Anger, William " Stantione, Clerk, William Olmestede, et Robert Conert, " Chapeleyn, salut en Dieu. Com nous avoms venduz " a William Taillour de la Rye certeyn bois en nostre " Manoir de la Mote en le Counte de Sussexe, sachetz " nous avoir rescen, jour de la faisance de ycestes, de " lavauntdit William Taillour et Thomas, son . filz, " qarante marcs desterlynges, en pertie du paiement " dune somme au quele les ditz William Taillour et " Thomas a nous sont tenus pur la vente du dit bois; " des quex qarante marcs nous sumes pleynement " paies, et les avauntditz William Taillour et Thomas " acquitoms pur cestes presentz. En tesmoignaunce

" de quele chose, a ceste presente escrit nous avoms " mys nos seals. Donez le qatersiame jour de Octobre, " lan du regne nostre Seignour le Roi Edward Tierce " puis la Conquest, qarantisme primere." It is an acquittance by Peter de Brewes, Knight, Henry Anger, William Stantione, Clerk, William Olmestede, and William Conert, Chaplain, to William Taillour, of Rye, and Thomas, his son, for 40 marks, in part payment for wood bought from their Manor of the Mote, in Sussex. Of the five seals, three are left, in a bad con- dition, one a shield, bearing apparently, a lion rampant.

A contemporary copy of a Certificate (of the time proba- bly of Richard II.) given by the Mayor and Barons of Rye; stating that Joan, the wife of William Ive, of Tenterden, and daughter and heir of Stephen Elyot, late of Rye, is of free condition, and born in free and lawful wedlock :— " Omnibus Christi fidelibus, ad quorum notitiam præ- " sentes litteræ pervenerint, Major et Barones villæ de " Rye salutem. Quia nobis supplicaverunt Willelmus " Ive, de Tenterden, et Johanna, ejus uxor, filia et hæres " Stephani Elyot, nuper de Rya, de vera notitia ipsius " Johannæ testimonium perhibere; universitati vestræ " innotescimus per præsentes, quod, in Plena Commu- " nitate tenta die confectionis præsentium in loco com- " stitato, capta ibidem inquisitione coram nobis de " notitia prædicta, omnes ibidem existentes unanimiter " dixerunt præfatam Johannam esse natam et pro- " creatam in villa prædicta, videlicet, de libero et " legitimo thoro; cujus pater et progenitores liberi " fuere, tam corporibus quam catallis, absque contradic- " tione cujuscunque; unde ad ibidem libertatis benefi- " cium per spatium centum annorum honeste conversati " fuere, bonæ famæ ac conversationis illæsæ, prout " nobis et quampluribus Quinque Portus [sic] palam " dinoscitur et testatur. Et ne testimonii diligentia " prædicti in posterum verteretur in dubium, nos, præ- " dicti Major et Barones, assensu totius communitatis " ejusdem, nostrum Commune Sigillum præsentibus lit- " teris nostris fieri fecimus pestentes [sic]. Datum, etc."

Had Joan been of native birth, i.e., the daughter of a native, or born bondman, impediments would not im- probably have been thrown in the way of her heirship.

The following receipt is of interest, as bearing the seal, (in red wax), of Sir Thomas Holland, the first husband of Joan Plantagenet, "the Fair Maid of Kent," who afterwards married the Black Prince, and was mother of Richard the Second. He claimed the title of Wake in right of his wife, who was niece of Thomas, the last Lord Wake. In 1360 he also assumed the title of "Earl of Kent," in right of his wife, as heir of John Plantagenet, tho last Earl of Kent. The writing is so faint as to be almost illegible:—" As toutz y ceux qui " cestes lettres verront ou orront, Thomas de Holand, " Seigneur Wake, salutz. Sachetz nous avoir rescieu " du baillif du manoir de Isdene trent sept soudes et " deux deiners desterlinges, en partie de paiement de " seissaunt seaze soudes et quatre deiners par an de " nostre fee ferme illoeges. Des queux trent sept " soudes et deux deiners nous nous conissons estre bien " paiez, et lavantdit baillif ent quite, pur le terme susdit, " par cestes noz lettres patentes ensaelees de nostre seal. " Escript a Londres, le quart jour de Mai, lan du regne " le roi Edward, Terce puis le Conquest, trentism " tierce." It is simply an acknowledgment that he has received 37s. 2d. out of a sum of 66s. 4d. due from the bailiff of the manor of Isdene [? Iden]; dated at London the 4th of May 1359. The seal is broken; a shield surmounted by, apparently, two tilting helmets, with large plumes.

A parchment document, in Latin, bearing date the 10th of December, in the 8th year of Henry the Fifth; setting forth, in formal language, that there had ap- peared before the Mayor and Barons of the vill of Rye, John atte Wode and Thomas Langele, Jurats of the said vill, Richard Bedyll, John Wayte, and many other trusty persons; who confessed to them that Joan, late the wife of John Baker, of Gestlyng, in their presence said, and requested them to bear witness thereto, that she would rather eat dirt (mallet manducare terram) than ever alienate to any one those lands, rents, and ser- vices, which are called "Hykeman Thomasisland," or the lands called "Whetfletismershe, and "Padyanns- " mershe," or any rents and services to the same belonging; but that the same should remain wholly to the next heirs, namely, John Burgeys and John Yonge. The four small seals of tho persons named are still appended; but that of the Barons of the vill of Rye (their second seal in date, as herein-after noticed,) is greatly mutilated.

A small parchment indenture, in Latin, bearing date the Sunday before the Feast of St. Thomas tho Apostle, in the 9th year of King Henry the Sixth [A.D. 1430], made between William Brouȝghton, Mayor of Rye, the Jurats, and the community thereof, of the one part, and John de Iprys, of the other; and witnessing that the said Mayor, Jurats, and community, in full commonalty, holden in the church of St. Mary of Rye, before the altar of St. Nicholas, on the day aforesaid, granted to the said John a certain tower situate in the said vill, with reasonable way thereto from the King's highway, with horses, carts, and wains, with reasonable ground also on the south side of the tower as far as the Clyf, of the same breadth as the tower, or more; it to be lawful to the said Mayor, Jurats, and community, and their successors, in time of hostilities or war, together with their goods, to enter the said tower, for defence of the vill aforesaid, that is, for as many as may be reasonably admitted therein; saving the easement therein of the said John, his wife, and their domestics. Upon the understanding, also, that, upon view of the Mayor for the time being, and the said John, those who are to be received therein, shall bring with them a sufficiency of victuals for the time they ought there to remain, through the necessities of war. No consideration is mentioned, and of the Common Seal, appended to the grant, only a fragment is left. There is also the counterpart of this deed, with the seal of John de Iprys attached. The tower of Ypres, here mentioned, built by William of Ypres (in the time probably of King Stephen) is still an ornament to the town of Rye.

A grant (in Latin) on parchment, by John Sedley, John Couthene, Richard Canone, and William Wayte, Wardens of the works and light of the church of St. Mary, at Rye, with the assent of William Broughtone, then Mayor, and of the whole community of Rye, in full commonalty, holden on Sunday the 4th of June, in the 19th year of King Henry the Sixth, to John Ypres, Esquire, and Elizabeth, his wife; of a parcel of land and garden, without the North Gate, adjoining a parcel of land and garden of John Sedley, late of William Munte, and another parcel belonging to Thomas Longe; at a yearly rent of one peppercorn at the Feast of Easter. They have thereto set their seals; but as the said seals to many are unknown, they have procured "the Common "Seal of the Barons of the vill of Rye" to be also appended (A.D. 1441). Witnesses, William Broughton, Mayor, Thomas Pope, Bailiff, Thomas Longe, John Graunger, John Suttone, Richard Bayle; John Comptone, Clerk. Three of the five seals (two of them representing the letters H and W) are left; of that of the Barons of Rye only a small fragment remains.

A large deed, in Latin, on parchment, bearing date—April, 30 Henry VI. [A.D. 1452]; whereby John Iprys, of Rye, Esquire, grants to Thomas Stoghtone, of London, Fishmonger, the tower last above mentioned, in the terms therein stated; also, a tenement, with a cellar beneath, near to the town wall; also, two parcels of land in Rye. And further, he, the said John Iprys, and Elizabeth, his wife, have granted to the said Thomas Stoghtone certain parcels of land and garden without the North Gate, near to the parcel of land and garden of John Sedley, late of William Munte, and the land late of William Pashelewe; also, a piece of land and garden, near to the land of John Downe, and that of the Hospital of St. Bartholomew, and near to the lane that leads to Blekewelle from the King's highway to the south, and near to the land of the heirs of Stephen Langporte, to the north; also, a tenement without the North Gate, near to the lane called "Le Pyggelane;" also, another tenement without the North Gate, near to the tenement late of Stephen Slade, and the lands of John Bayle and John Warner; also, a barn in the said vill, near to the lands of John Sowthen, and of Robert Unwyn and John Younge. Witnesses, John Suttone, John Hamound, James Sedley, John Comton, John Bayle, William Wanstal, Richard Rippys, John Younge. The "seal of "arms" of John Iprys, named as being set thereto, is still appended, and in good condition. Of the Common Seal of the vill of Rye, appended at the request of Elizabeth, his wife, only a fragment is left.

A warrant of attorney, in Latin, on parchment, by the said John Iprys, "late of Rye," appointing John Suttone his attorney, to deliver seisin to Thomas Stoghtone of the tower, and other tenements and hereditaments last mentioned. Dated the 20th of April, in the 30th year of King Henry the Sixth. Of the seal of arms of John Iprys, originally appended, only a fragment is left.

Another warrant of attorney, in Latin, whereby the said John Iprys, late of Rye, appoints John Tregooss his attorney to be receiver, in his name, of all moneys arising from all the lands, tenements, rents, and ser-

vices, which John Suttone, Richard Fourde, Richard Canone, and John Younge, lately bought, of his gift and feoffment, according to the form and effect of a certain deed of feoffment between him and them made. Dated the 8th of April, in the 30th year of Henry the Sixth. Of the seal only a fragment is left.

Warrant of attorney, in Latin, on parchment, by Thomas Stoghtone, of London, Fishmonger, to James Hyde, Esquire, authorizing him to receive the rents and ferms due, in Rye and without, from the tenants of the said Thomas; and especially to receive from John Suttone 12s. 4d., which the said Thomas had allowed him out of his rent for repair of the tenement rented by him; and which repairs are not done, as it is said. Dated the 12th of March, in the 32nd year of Henry the Sixth [A.D. 1454]. It not only has the small seal of Thomas Stoghton, (in good condition, representing a mermaid), but is signed by him as well; being also signed "Noreys." From the next deed, it will be seen that Stoghton soon afterwards sold his Rye property to this same James Hyde. The Mermaid Street, and Mermaid Inn, in Rye, not improbably had their name from the arms of this Thomas Stoghtone.

34 Henry VI. Grant (in Latin) by James Hyde of Rye, Esquire, to John Hyde, of Bredbury Esquire, John Passhole, Esquire, and Thomas Wodeward, of Wynchelse, of " a certain tower, situate in the vill of Rye, with a " certain reasonable way to the said tower, with horses, " carts and wains, and with reasonable ground on the " south side of the said tower as far as Le Clyff, being " of the same breadth as the tower, or more;" also, all other his property in Rye; as he bought the same of Thomas Stowghton, Fishmonger, of London. Witnesses, Richard Rype, Mayor, Laurence Dobylle, Deputy, Thomas Pope, Bailiff, John Suttone the elder, James Sedley, John Younge. A diminutive seal is attached, representing, apparently, a hart. On the exterior is written, in an old hand, "For Baddinge." The Tower of Ypres, which Stoghton had already transferred to James Hyde, is the place conveyed by this deed.

Copy of proceedings on parchment, in French, written in the reign of Richard the Second, on a plaint made to " our very dear brethren, Combarons, and friends;" stating that complaint has been made by " our very dear and " well-beloved Combaron, John Salerne, of La Rye;" that Sir William Sherindone, Chaplain, has broken a covenant with him; forasmuch as he had agreed with the said John Salerne, to obtain, between the Feasts of Christmas and Candlemas in the 13th year of King Richard the Second [A.D. 1389-90] two bulls, sealed with lead, from the Court of Rome, from our most Holy Father, the Pope; one to be an indulgence for him and for Agnes, his partner (sa compuigne), and the other a licence to have a Chaplain at his manor-house of La Leghe continually; such bulls to be delivered by the Feast of the Nativity of St. John the Baptist, in return for a certain sum f money, of which the said William had received 2 marks, in part payment; which bulls the said William had not yet delivered, to the complainant's damage, to the amount of 20l. The said John is therefore called upon to prove the same.

On the back of this, a grant has been written in part, (in Latin) by Helewis William, of Winchelse, relict of Robert Willinm, late of Rye, to Robert Stontone, of Rye, of a tenement near to that of the heirs of Simon Broker, and to the land of the heirs of Matthew Turold, and the tenement of Richard Putsterne; this is followed by a copy, in a neat hand, of the Vulgate version of part of the sixth verse of the first Chapter of the Gospel of St. John.

The following is a paper writing, without full date given, but of the reign of Henry the Sixth.—" Be it " opynly knowen to all them that this writing shal see or " here, that for the cause folowyng, among other causes, " the melle callyd 'Goldhopmelle,' which Robert One- " wyne late helde at the lordes wille, after the custume " of maners, was seysed in to the lordes handes, by " cause the said melle was not welle and sufficiently re- " payred, as hit ofte to have bene. Also, for the declara- " cion of the said Robert, be it knowene that he never " hadde in his kepyng the court rolles of Playden, wher- " turght [? where-through] he at any tyme myght have " amended them, or appaired them. Ne he at any tyme " hathe labord to the amendyng or to the appayriug " as forforth [? far] as y understande, or ever cought " knowe or vele by all the wayes and menes of dilygent " examinacion, that y by my discrecion have made " theryn. And as for the sayd rolles, like as they were " delyvered to me by Simon Bate, late my Steward of " Playdone, so they remayne without amendyng or " appairyng. Yeven under the sealle of myne Abbotey,

" the xiii day of August last. By William, Abbot of
" Robertsbregge." Of the seal, impressed on the paper,
only a few small fragments remain. The Cistercian
Abbey of Robertsbridge, near Battle, is meant.

A testimonial, in Latin, on parchment, by the Mayor
and Barons of Rye, stating that John Wikham, the
bearer thereof, " Schipwrite," had dwelt in that community for 20 years, was of honest conversation, good
fame, and unblemished reputation ; wherefore he had
enjoyed the advantages of the freedom for 16 years,
while building the ships of that port; that from his
goods he scotted and lotted, and bore his burden along
with others.—" And lest the diligence of such testimony
" be at a future time turned into matter of doubt, we,
" the said Mayor and Barons, with the assent of the
" same community, have to these our letters patent
" set our Common Seal. Given at Rye, on the 18th
" day of the month of January, in the 15th year of the
" reign of King Richard the Second." (A.D. 1392). As
no seal appears to have been attached, this is probably
only a draught of the testimonial. Below, in a contemporary hand, has been written by some facetious
person, near five centuries ago, the following Leonine
hexameter :—
" Omnibus est notum, quod multum diligo potum."—
Which we may render.—
" All know, I think, I'm very fond of drink."
Followed by another line :—
" Si mea penna valet, melior mea littera fiet."
(" The pen the better, the finer the letter.")
The scribbling is continued with various single
letters (some often repeated) in alphabetical order,
followed by " Es est Amen."
A parchment writing, in French, some parts of which
are faint and illegible :—" Lez comunes, charges de par
" nostre Seignur le Roy, sur lour fay et legeance de
" luy conseiller a sone Parlement tenutz a Westmestre
" a la quinzaine de Seint Hillare, Ian du regne nostre
" dit Seignur le Roy xviie, sur lez articlez comprisez
" en un endenture fuite par entre nostre dit Seignur le
" Roy et sone adversarie de Fraunce, lez queux luz et
" en partie entenduz, sont considerez par tut le comune
" trois pointz, si chargeantz, cestassavoir, homage,
" lige soveraygnete, et resort, dont lez ditz comunes
" unqes ne oseront emprendre de conseilere ni treter
" de si haute et chargeante matiere. Des quex trois
" pointz lez di-z comunes [sont] autrement deschargez
" a causo qe nulle moderacion dicelles est unqore
" fait, ne lez Seignurs ount nullu conissance quele
" moderacon y serra. Dont nostre dit Seignur le Roy
" eiant avis, sibien par lez Seignurs Espirituels et
" Temporels, Chivaleres, Justises, et altres nobles, ent
" duement examinez en ceste present Parlement, con-
" siderantz lestat de son roialme, sont condescenduz,
" que homage serra fait par bon moderacion a faire
" pur ses terrez de Guyen, tout foitz reservez que
" nostre dit Seignur le Roi, sa corone, son roialme, et
" sez legez dEngletere, biens et chateux, ne soient
" chargez ne abaundonez par ascune manere quecon-
" que, a causc dez ditz hommage, soveraignete, resort,
" service, ou titel fait ou a faire par ascune voie.
" Mesque le Roy et sez heirs, son roialme, et sez leges,
" et lour biens et chateux, soient auxi frances come
" ils ont este ene temps dascun de sez nobles progeni-
" tours. Et sont auxi pourveux et asentuz par nostre
" dit Seignur le Roy, lez Seignurs, et [autres] avaunt-
" ditz, qe en cas que lo pees, et lez contractez faitz, ou
" affaire, parentre nostre dit Seignur le Roy et son
" adversarie de France soient enfreintz par la partie
" du dit adversarie, ou ses heirs, par ascun manere que-
" conques, qadonques nostre dit Seignur le Roy et sez
" heirs resorteront a lour primer estat, droit, et title,
" niont countresteaunt les contractes, reles-ou services
" ent faitz ou affaire. Et depuis que nostre tres re-
" doute Seignur le Roi, les Seignurs, et autres avaunditz,
" considerantz si tendrement lestat du dit roialme et
" son poeple, vollant et considerant que lez contractz
" duement [avant, Rolls of Parlt.] especifiez, soient
" por le mieulz, lez Comunes, avaunditz tous jours
" come obeisantz et suantz aibien la volente du Roy
" come de touz lez Seignurs Esprituelcs et Temporels,
" Chivalers [de honour, Rolls of Parlt.] et Justises,
" ent duement examinerez come devant, ciantz con-
" sideracion a lo consentement du nostre dit Seignur
" le Roy, lez Seignurs Esprituelcs et Temporels, Chiva-
" lors [do honour, Rolls of Parlt.], Justices, et autres
" avaunditz consentent, pur bon pees avoir, a les con-
" tractz du peez avaunt especifiez, a le bon avys nostre
" dit Seignur le Roy, lez Seignurs, et altres avaunt-
" ditz ent faitz en cest present Parlement." The whole
of this passage (in reference to the terms of a proposed

peace with France, in January 1394,) is to be found,
but in a totally different dialect, and with some few
variations, in the Rolls of Parliament, Vol. III., pp.
315, 6. It was, no doubt, then looked upon as a communication of considerable importance; and was most
probably sent inclosed in a letter by one of the Burgesses
in Parliament of the place, to his constituents at Rye,
for their information.

A notification, in Latin, of the 19th year of Richard
II [1395]., on parchment, by John, Lord Beaumont [died
A.D. 1396], Constable of Dover Castle, and Warden of
the Cinque Ports, finely written, and with a fragment of
his seal appended; setting forth that he had received
" by the hands of William Tydecumbe, our receiver in
" the castle aforesaid," the moneys underwritten ;
namely, of issues of the land of William Taillour, one
of the executors of William [? John] Taillour 12d. ; of
land of the same John 10d. ; of land of Thomas Lewes
and John Parker 8d. ; of land of Thomas Wellys and
John Parker 8d. ; of land of John Parker and Robert
Parker 8d.; of land of Laurence Courboille 2s. ; of
issues from William Taillour, " late Mayor of the vill
" of La Rye " 8d. ; issues from Laurence Courbaylle (sic),
one of the collectors of the subsidy 6d.; from the
balance [libra] in the port and vill of La Rye 12d. ;
from the issues of John Otringham and William Taillour 6d. ; from the issues of John Fyst 4d. ; from the
issues of John Hog and William Dogyl 4d. ; from the
issues of William Paston Chuddebe 6d. ; from the issues
of Laurence Courboille and William Taillour 6d. ; from
the issues of Peter Bocher 4d. ; from the issues of
Robert Aleyn and John Otryngham 6d. ; from the
issues of Robert Clerk and Robert Byrkenyd 3d. ; from
the issues of William Lymford and William Taillour
2d. ; from the issues of Henry Goldwyne and Benedict
Sely 3d. ; and from the issues again of William Taillour,"
as executor of the testament of William Taillour 5s. 5d.
These " issues " were apparently the sums due from
various persons in Rye who had collected the subsidy
granted to the King : in cases of death the sums due
from them would be levied from their lands. Who
" William Paston Chuddebe " was, it seems impossible
to divine ; perhaps the word " and " is omitted after
" Paston," and the following word should be written
" —Chuddele." William Paston, who was afterwards
a Justiciar of the Court of Common Pleas, was at this
time a youth about 17 years of age.

In the following document, a lease of the 25th year
of King Henry the Sixth, (carefully and distinctly
written in a small hand), we have an excellent sample
of the English language as it was written in business
matters, in the South West of England, in the middle
of the 15th century : it is but rarely that documents of
this description, in English, occur at so early a date.
The seal, representing a bird, apparently, is still preserved, and the writing is remarkably distinct.—" This
" indenture, made betwene Adam Leulorde, upone the
" one partie, and Robert Onwyne, of Rye, in the Shire
" of Sussexe, gentilman, Johan Suttone, of Rye, fissch-
" monger, and Richard Schadwell, of Rye, in the shire
" of Sussexe, housbondeman, upon the othir partie,
" berithe witnesse that þe said Robert, Johan, and Richard,
" let to ferme to the said Robert, Johan, and Richard,
" his maner of Levisham with alle and almaner londes,
" tenementis, rentis, and services, and all þe appur-
" tinences, lyeng within the lordschip of Brede and
" elliswhere within þe shire of Sussexe, to þe saide
" maner in anywise pertenynyng, forthwithe certayne
" greynos, as it foloweth, that is to say, viii quarters
" whete, viii quarters barly, viii quarters benys, and
" viii semys [horse-loads] otys, mesuride by the mesure
" of Rye : To have and holde the said maner, with all
" his appurtenaunces and graynes afore reherside ; to
" the saide Robert, Johan, and Richard, and to þaire
" assignes, fro the feste of Seint Michelle Archangille,
" next to comme aftir the date of þis presents, unto
" the end and terme of v yeer then next sewyng, uppon
" the condicions that folowen, that is to wete : that the
" said Robert, Johan, and Richard, and thaire execu-
" tours and assignes, shul paie yeerly to the saide
" Adam, his heiris and his assignes, xx li. of lawful
" money of Englande at the Festis of Estir and Seint
" Michelle Archangille, by eyrne porcions ; and the
" borne, the gerner, the stable, and shepyn [sheep-pen],
" of þe saide maner roof-thight kepe at þaire owne
" cost duryng þe terme aforsaide : aud ovir that, bere
" and paie to the owners of þe saide lordship and fe
" of Brede þe rentes and fines for sute of courtes dewo
" and custumable tho saide terme during. And the
" saide Adam, his heires or assigns, þe housis afor re-
" hersid in tymbre werk of þe roofis, and wal thight,

" at þair propre costes sufficiently shul repaire and
" mayntene duryng al the sayde terme. And þe saide
" Robert, Johan, and Richard, and þaire executours
" and assignes, bi al the terme aboue saide, shul haue
" sufficient and resonable plow bote, closure bote, and
" fire bote, one þe saide maner growyng, uppone and
" in þe saide maner to ben spent during þe saide terme,
" without any wast doing. And it shal ben leefful to
" þe saide Adam, his heires and assignes, the saide
" maner to entre and issue in alle couenable tymes, to
" cary and drive uppone the landif and weyes of þe
" saide maner, to outtre [carry away] his graynes in
" the saide maner beyng, betwix the Feste of Seint
" Michell Archangille next comynge after þe date of
" þese presents and Nativitie of Seint Johan Baptist
" þan next folowyng. And ouer that, at all tymes
" leefful þe saide maner to entre and issue, carye and
" dryve, for ouraight and reparacion of þe saide maner,
" with the apurtenaunces. And the saide Adam graun-
" tith, for hym, his heires, and assigns, þat it shal ben
" leofful to the saide Robert, Johan, and Richard, þaire
" executours and assignes, the saide maner in al reson-
" able tyme to entre and issue, and over þe saide
" landes and weyes to cary and dryve, to outtre and
" voide thaire þaire graynes and othir goodes, fro þe
" Fest of Seint Michele Archangille next, and at þe ende
" and terme of þe saide y yeere unto þe Fest of Nativitie
" of Seint Johan Baptist þan next folowyng. And
" yef it hap þat any walscot or waterscotte ben sett
" uppone þe landis of þe saide maner duryng þe saide
" terme, þan þe saide Robert, Johan, and Richard, þair
" executours and assignes, shul kepe þe daies of pay-
" ment therof, paieng after the rate, so þat þe saide
" Adam, his heires, and assignes, forfete to þe bailif of
" the Levelle no wanys [wains] : takinge þerfor fulle
" allowance of þe saide Adam, his heires and assignes,
" at þe payment of þaire ferme abouesaide. And yef
" þe saide Adam come with iii hors iii tymes euery
" yeer duryng the saide terme to þe saide maner, than
" þe saide Robert, Johan, and Richarde, þaire heires and
" assigns, shul fynde þe saide iii hors, and one man al
" þe while þat þe saide Adam abidith þere. And in
" cas þe saide Richard discece within þe term of v yeer
" abouesaide, than it shal ben leefful to þo saide Robert
" and Johan, þaire executours and assignes, þe saide maner
" with his appurtenaunces, (the housis aboue named roof
" thight, payments and delyuerance of alle the greynes
" aboue rehercid to þo saide Adam, his heires and as-
" signes, devly made), to þe saide Adam his heires or
" assignes, up to ȝelde [yield] at þe next fest of Seint
" Michel Archangille þan next sewyng, or the saide
" maner to ferme forth holde duryng þe terme in þe
" forme and condicion aboue rehersid. And in the
" ende and terme of þe saide v yeer the saide Robert,
" Johan, and Richard, the saide maner, as in helyng
" [tiling] of þe housis aboue rehersid, and closures, in
" als good state as þay hem receyved, or in betir, forth-
" with þe sume and als muche of euery greyne [grain] as
" is aboue rehersid, to the saide Adam, his heires or
" assignes, up shul delyuer. And in cas þe saide ferme
" of xx li be behynde unpaied [in] partie or in hole at
" any fest aboue saide, þan be it leefful to þe saide
" Adam, his heires and assignes, in al þe aforesaide
" maner, and al his appurtenaunces, to entre and dis-
" treyne, and distresse so take leeffully to bere awey,
" dryve away, and to hem witholde, til þe ferme so
" beyng behynde to þaym fully be satisfied and paied.
" And yef þe saide ferme of xx li be behynde unpaied,
" after any fest of the festis afore rehersid, at whiche it
" ought to ben paied, by thre monthis, and sufficient
" distresse within þe saide maner and appurtenaunces
" to the paiement of þe saide ferme so beyng behynde
" may not be founde, þan be it leefful to þe saide
" Adam, his heires and assignes, to entre into þe saide
" maner, londes, tenementes, rents, and services, with
" al his appurtenaunces, and þayme in þair hole and
" ful estat to kepe ; and þe saide Robert, Johan, and
" Richard, þaire executours and assignes, to put out
" þerof, þese indenturis notwithstanding. And the
" saide Adam and his heires the saide maner, with al
" londes, tenementes, rents, services, and al his appur-
" tenances, to þe saide Robert, Johan, and Richard,
" thaire executours and assignes, uppone and vndir the
" condicione and forme aboue rehersid, agayns al maner
" folk shul warrant, quite, and defende, during the terme
" abouesaide. In witnesse of al the þinges above wre-
" tyne, þe saide Adam to þe parti of þis endenture at
" þe saide Robert, Johan, and Richard, abyding haþ put
" his seel ; to þo oþer partie, to þe saide Adam delyvered
" and abedeng, þe saide Robert, Johan, and Richard,
" hau put þair seellis. The xxiiii day of August in þe

" ȝeere of þe regne of Kynge Harry þe vi[t] after þe
" Conquest of Englande xxv[d]." (A.D. 1447.) This
indenture, having borne but one seal, was the one
delivered to the lessees. It seems to have been one purpose of the deed to guarantee to the lessees the delivery
of a certain amount of seed, upon their entry on the
lands. The use of the Saxon þ (th) in this deed, and of
the mediæval letter ȝ (in mediæval Latin called "jugum,"
and representing probably a guttural " gh,") will not
pass unnoticed.

A Letter, on parchment, in Latin, by Sir John Devereux, Constable of Dover Castle and Warden of the
Cinque Ports, to the authorities of the Cinque Ports,
containing a communication dated the 8th of June in
the 13th year of Richard II. [A.D. 1390], in Latin,
and by writ of the Privy Seal, to the following effect.
—The King has heard that certain merchants and
others, his lieges, have been in the habit of selling
ships of war and other vessels to aliens in friendship
with England ; but that the said aliens "by reason
" of the excessive profits thence arising, have often
" sold the same to the enemies of the realm ; " from
which to it "inestimable losses" have accrued ; therefore, "to resist the preconceived malice of our said
" enemies, by whom we are on every side surrounded,"
as also, for the safety of the fleet of the realm, the
Constable is enjoined, in every place of the Cinque
Ports, to give notice, by proclamation made, that no
owner of any such ship or vessel, under penalty of for-
feiting double the amount, is to sell such ship or vessel
to aliens, or to exchange it for other goods and merchandize. This is apparently the original notice sent to
Rye by Sir John Devereux (who died in 1394), and a
seal appears to have been formerly attached thereto.
This, however, is somewhat doubtful, as, on the other
side of the parchment, in the same hand, is a copy of
another writ of the same King, in Latin, under the Privy
Seal, bearing date the 4th of June in the same year,
directed to the same official ; ordering proclamation to
be made against the exportation abroad of plate, bullion,
or money, either by natives or aliens, without special
leave for the same. Whether it is an original document
or not, the writing on both sides is of the time of
Richard the Second, and it is in a good preservation.

A Letter, in French, addressed by "Thomas of Lancas-
" ter, the King's son" (second son of Henry the Fourth)
in the 6th year of that reign, to the Mayor, Bailiffs,
" habners," shipmasters, and mariners, in the port of
the vill of Rye, as Steward and Admiral of England,
and Lieutenant of Ireland. Having been appointed
by his father his Lieutenant and Admiral on the seas,
he is disposed to commence his voyage on the same by
taking ship at Sandwich on the 20th of April next to
come ; he therefore desires proclamation to be made in
the port, that all persons who have any ships of war
which they may wish " to maintain for any gain by
" war, in his said voyage," must appear before him
with such ships in their best form (manere), at the said
time and place ; and he further gives notice, that whatever profits and gains such persons shall make from the
King's enemies on such voyage, they shall have and
enjoy freely, without impediment or disturbance ; they
in the meantime to be attentive and obedient to him
and his lieutenants in all points, both as to going and
remaining, whether upon the land or upon the sea. This
document is finely written, but the seal, unfortunately,
is lost.

A summons, in Latin, on parchment, dated the 13th
of July, in the 18th year of Richard II., by John de
Beaumont, Constable of Dover Castle, to the Mayor and
Bailiff of Rye, to enjoin 12 of their Combarons, Jurats
as well as others, to be before him at a Court of Schip-
weye " at the usual place," on the Feast of St. Bartholomew the Apostle then next ensuing,—" to do and
" receive what the Court, according to the custom of
" the Ports aforesaid, shall think proper to decree."
The Mayor and Bailiff are also to be there present.

A notice in French, on parchment, the writing almost
illegible, apparently through the action of water, from
the Mayor, Bailiff, and burgesses, of the port of Dover,
to their " Combarons " of Hastings, Wynchelse, Rye,
Romene, Hethe, and Sandwich ; dated the 9th of
September, in the 19th year of Richard the Second.
For great and very weighty matters touching the defence
of the country, a Brodhille is to be holden at Romene
on Thursday next, and they are requested, each of them,
to send two or three of their most substantial Combarons
thereto : a collection of money, apparently, is about to
be made, but for the greater part, the notice does not
admit of being deciphered.

3 R 3

A writ, on paper, in Latin, the seal now torn away, by John de Beaumont, Constable of Dover Castle, and Warden of the Cinque Ports, dated the 17th of January, in the 17th year of Richard the Second. By a former writ, in obedience to the King's letter, he has ordered the Mayor and Bailiff of Rye to seize William Passelewe, of Rye, and Stephen Elyot, at the suit of Agnes Oungesell [indistinct] in a plea of debt; and they have returned that the said Stephen is dead, but that they have arrested the said William. They are therefore safely to conduct the body of the said William, and to have him before the Warden, or his Lieutenant, in the church of St. James at Dover, at the hour of Prime on the Friday next.

A notice, in Latin, on parchment, from John de Beaumont, Constable of Dover Castle, etc., to the Mayors, Bailiffs, and ministers, of the Cinque Ports, dated the 4th of August, in the 17th year of Richard the Second : reciting a copy of a letter received from the King, to the effect that the truce had been prolonged between him and his "adversary of France;" dated the 26th of June in the 16th year of that reign. The Warden also further recites therein a copy that has been sent to him of a "schedule," in which the terms of such truce, in French, are set forth; it having been first made at Lonlyngham on the 18th of June 1389, and having been since from time to time prolonged. If this is the original notice, the "seal of office," formerly attached to it, is lost.

A notice, in Latin, on parchment, by John de Beaumont to the Mayors, Bailiffs, Jurats, and Combarons, of the Cinque Ports; stating that, as he had summoned them to a Court of Schypweye, at the usual place, on Thursday, the morrow of the Purification last past, he now, by precept of the King, defers the same till Monday the Feast of St. Valentine. Dated the 18th of January in the 19th year of Richard II. The "seal of office," if ever attached to the parchment, is lost. At the foot is written "Sharp Capellanus Cantarie Sanctæ Mariæ;" not improbably, this Sharp, Chaplain of the Chantry of St. Mary, conveyed the missive.

A warrant in Latin, dated at Hastyng, the 1st of July 1462, with fragments of a very fine oblong seal attached; whereby Nicholas Calf, Bachelor " in Decretis," Commissary and Sequestrator General within the Archdeaconry of Lewes, empowers Joan Onewyne to administer to the estate of Robert Onewyne, intestate, deceased : his debts first to be paid, and the residue to be distributed for the health of his soul.

Contemporary copy of a notice (in Latin) by John de Beaumont, Constable of Dover Castle, and Warden of the Cinque Ports, stating that the King (Richard II.) is about to summon a Parliament on the quinzaine of St. Hillary next ensuing, in the 17th year of his reign; each of the Ports is to send two of its best and most discreet Barons thereto.

A Letter, on parchment, in French, but so faint as to be almost illegible, dated at Fescamp (in Normandy) the 18th of December 1389 ; signed at the foot " Biau-" fix." with several flourishes, and with a somewhat mutilated seal appended, representing an angel, holding a shield, charged with three mitres. Guillame Beaufels, Seneschal of Fescamp, makes known that he has seen the letters of " the religious person and honest " brother," Pierre de Derac, Bailiff of Fescamp, wherein it is stated that there had come before him Pierre Onsin, Mahieu Gournay, and Philippe le Ronyer, burgesses of the vill of Fescamp; who had said that in the year 1383 they had heard it testified unto Stephen Cely, called " Playdenne," Stephen Willes, and James Hoppe, Englishmen of the vill of La Rye, who were then prisoners there, that Constance de Rodes, who was then " Master of the said English," had deducted from the ransom of the said Cely, or Playdenne, 35 franks of gold, for and in the name of Thomas Goscelin, burgess of the said vill of Fescamp; such sum being due from the said Goscelin to Alart le Fevre (Smyth) of the vill of Rye. Cely having now, no doubt returned home, this would be an official notice, probably through the Mayor of Rye, to Alard Smyth to look to Cely for the 35 franks due to him from Goscelin, and which had been so deducted from the sum due for Cely's ransom.

A bond, in Latin, dated the 17th of April in the 9th year of Henry the Seventh, whereby Cornelius Lucas, of Calais, mariner, Richard Wodelande, of Bekley in the county of Sussex, " yoman," and John Drynker, of Rye, " yoman," acknowledge that they owe 20 pounds to Adam Oxenbregge, " gentilman," collector of the King's customs, in his vill of Rye. The defeasance, on the other side of the parchment slip, in English, is as follows :—
" The condition of this obligacion is such, that if the with-

" inbounden Cornelys and Richard, or oon of theym, their
" factours, attorney, or assigneis, or any of theym,
" brynge or seynde, or cause to be brought or sent, by
" the Fest of the Nativitie of Seynt Johan Baptist within
" wretene, a certificate from the deputie Lieutenaunt,
" Maier, Tresourer, or Comptroller, of the towne of Calais,
" unto the within named Adam Oxenbregge, or to his
" deputie, therin expressyng and makyng mencion that
" the foresaid Cornelius hath well and truelie delyvered
" and dischargod, at the said Calais, and at noon other
" place, all such billettes and other merchandize, as the
" forsaid Richard hath, at herof making, freight within
" a cogshippe of the said Calais, wherof the forsaid
" Cornelis is master, as in a coket therupone made
" openly apperethe, that thanne this present obliga-
" cione to be voide, and of noon effect. Or els to abyde
" in all his full strength and vertue."

The oldest bit of writing probably, (the Charters excepted, which have been described by Mr. Holloway, in his History and Antiquities of Rye), is a fragment of an Office Book, of, apparently, the early part of the 13th century, consisting of one leaf, in small quarto, and part of another. It contains passages from the New Testament, among them, the anointing of Jesus, and His rebuke to Martha ; followed from time to time by the Sequence, in smaller characters, the length of the pauses in chanting being denoted by the longer or shorter spaces between the words, the general gist of which is the praise of the Virgin Mary. The initial letters have been illuminated in various colours, and words are inserted in various places in rubric, none of which can now be deciphered, they having faded from lapse of time. The writing is finely executed, and, from its singular distinctness, bears marks of its comparatively close relationship to Saxon times. This fragment, not improbably, may have formed part of an addition to a Service Book, or a Martyrology, upon which the early Mayors and other officials of the town were sworn.

Rye was plundered and burnt by the French in the year 1377 (when, as we learn from Walsingham's English History, its church bells and the leaden roof of the church were carried off, but were afterwards recovered); and again, to some extent, in 1448. Jeake says, in his Charters of the Cinque Ports, that in the latter year the early records of the town were destroyed, some few fragments only excepted. It certainly is the fact, that the Account books now existing commence in the latter year ; from which we may perhaps conclude that the records of a like nature, preceding them, had come to an untimely end. The " fragments," however, that have survived, belonging to dates prior to 1448, are, as may be judged from the extracts immediately preceding, more in number than, from Jeake's assertion, might have been expected. In addition to them, there are also now existing, in the various chests belonging to the Corporation, (but in a state of entire confusion when I first examined them), a mass of documents under seal, relative to the transfers of property in the town and places in the neighbourhood (Winchelsea in particular), about 150 in number, for more than two centuries, between the reigns of Henry the Third and Henry the Seventh ; which, not improbably, as in the case of Axbridge, in Somerset, Bridport, and other towns, were from time to time deposited, for safe keeping, with the Mayor, or Common Clerk, of the town. The whole of those documents have been subjected by me to a careful examination ; many of them bear marks of having been immersed in water, (on one of the occasions, probably, on which the town was set on fire by the French); but with only one or two exceptions, they admit of being thoroughly deciphered ; and the remaining columns of this notice will be occupied with a description, in the chronological order in which I have since arranged them, of their contents.

Save from one or two early Charters granted to the town, and the few particulars relative to its transactions in connexion with the other towns and members of the Cinque Ports, all traces of the history of Rye, or of its inhabitants, before about the middle of the 15th century, have until now disappeared ; and its at present known list of Mayors, (a printed copy of which has been very obligingly forwarded to me by Mr. G. Slade Butler,) begins no earlier than 1396 ; comprising in all but eleven, whose names have been hitherto known to have survived, down to the year 1448. From the various documents in question, the names of the Mayors of Rye have now been brought again to light, in almost an unbroken succession, down to 1380, from the first institution probably of the office, towards the close of the 13th century, or, at the latest, the beginning of the 14th (A.D. 1304, 5). Its principal inhabitants for two hitherto forgotten centuries are here to be found mentioned; with, in some instances, particulars in reference to their property, avocations, kinship, and connexions by marriage. The early streets and localities of the place (the formal streets, or streets with names, at an early date being evidently but few in number), are here to be traced; Merstrete, Piggeslane, Schierstrete, the Market place, Schyebourglane, the Halton (where the Austin Friary was afterwards built), the Est Stronde, the Nesse, and the North Gate, being those which are thus mentioned. In reference to family history,—one or more individuals appear of the name respectively of Twysden, Sokeling (later Suckling) and Dedes; while there are more numerous notices in reference to the families of Allard, Salerne, Lunaford, Taillour, Onwyn, Tychebourne, and Oxenbregge. In the time of Edward the Second, Paul Fitz-Robert was evidently the great man of the place; where he is not mentioned as being Mayor, his name invariably occurs next to that of the Mayor, in the list of attesting witnesses. Robert and James Marchant were, no doubt, opulent traders residing in the town. Their names occur as attesting witnesses to deeds, through a long series of years, and Robert Marchant was Mayor of the town in the reigns of Edward the First and his two successors, at intervals extending over forty years or more. Among the curious, and now obsolete, surnames that indicate callings or trades, are,—Bloodlettere (the "Leche" of other places), Mustarder, Crabber, Smerekervere (Butter cutter, or retailer), and we find mentioned a Claryoner (player on the clarion). To proceed now with a detailed list of these documents, the contents of which, at least to some extent, must bring ancient Rye to life again before us.—

Dated at Rye, the Wednesday before the Feast of Tyburtius and Valerianus the Martyrs [April 14th] A.G. 1258. Grant (in Latin) by John, son of Edmund Beckett, to Parcel, daughter of Richard Dyer (or ? Webbe, Tytoris), of land between that of Stephen and Luke Koleram, on the east, and that of Robert Makerel, on the west, at a yearly rent of 5 pence at Mid Lent, at the King's Court to be paid; she having paid 13s. 6d. sterling beforehand. Witnesses, John Thorell, John Pharon, Thomas Pharon, Nicholas Blund, John Gregory, Nicholas de la Nesse, Thomas de la Nesse, Henry Slyphe, Laurence Slyphe, Alexander Helis, Reginald Marchont, Luke Koleram, Robert Makerell. A beautifully written little deed, with a fine and perfect impression of the seal, a fleur-de-lis.

Temp. Henry III. Grant (in Latin) by Henry Slipe to Brice Fitz-Nicholas of a messuage near the land late of Richard de Gatheberge, and that late of John Samson, and that of Andrew Colebrond and William le Paumer, for a yearly rent of one halfpenny, a rent-service of 18d. being reserved to the chief lord; the said Brice having given to him a messuage in Rye, which belonged to Nicholas, his father. Witnesses, William Bysaufz, Herbert James, Henry Bochard, John Torel, Clement Paccok, Laurence Slipe, Nicholas Blund, Nicholas de Nesse, Thomas de Nesse, John Gregory, William son of William Bysaflx, Nicholas Joye, Walter Chaplain, "Notary of this writing." Beautifully written; the seal, appended by, apparently, a silk cord, is nearly whole, but much worn. Torel, Slipe, Nicholas, and Thomas de Nesse, Gregory, and Blund, are witnesses to the deed last mentioned.

Temp. Henry III., no date given. Grant (in Latin) by John Buss to Alexander Pac, of a messuage near to land in Rye late belonging to Roger Sage, at a yearly rent of 2s. payable on the day of St. Andrew; half a mark of silver having been paid beforehand. Witnesses, Nicholas Blund, Reginald Alard. Pharon de Port, Alan Carboyl, Richard Hennyng, Adam Stanlere, Thomas Buchard, William Lambyn, Payen Prud, John his son, Alexander Helis, Peter Ardinge, Stephen le Thaylur. Finely written; the seal is lost. Blund and Helis are witnesses to the deed first mentioned.

Probably, *temp.* Henry III. Grant (in Latin) by Roger le Vynch, with the assent of Alice, his wife, to Alexander le Sweyn, with Parnel, his daughter, in free marriage, of a house in Rye, extending from the highway which leads to the mill, on the west, to the land of John le Bode, on the east; for a yearly rent of 3d., payable at Mid Lent. In case the said Alexander shall have no heirs by the said Parnel, the house is to revert to the said Roger and his heirs. Witnesses, Brice de Rye, John Thorel, Herbert de la Nesse, Nicholas White, Thomas Pharone, Andrew Kolebrond, Laurence Slype, Martin Pamere, Richard Long, Laurence le Sweyn, Andrew de Pottepurye, Herbert Galiot. The seal is lost. No day, year, or reign is mentioned, but several of the witnesses occur in the preceding deeds.

A.D. 1283. Grant (in Latin) by Thomas, son and heir of Hamon de Pipeneselle, to Henry, son of William de Pipeneselle, of half and a quarter of an acre of land at Pipeneselle, in the parish of Rye, in the place called "Piristoy," of the tenure of the Lord Abbot of Fiscamp, lying near the great street which leads from the place called "Clivesgache" to the land called "Regges;" to hold to him, his heirs, and assigns, and to convey the same as he may think fit, save to a house of religion, or to Judaism; he rendering yearly at Clivesgache, on the day of St. Michael, one penny sterling; one half mark sterling having been paid beforehand. Witnesses, William de Pipeneselle, Geoffrey "called "Walterman," John, his son, Bartholomew Wytte, William "called Leeman." William [*sic*] his brother, Reginald le Broc, Thomas de Regges, Bartholomew de Helwestro, John Robert, Robert the Chaplain.—"Done "at Rye; and I put the said Henry in full seisin of the "said land, with the appurtenances, at Pipeneselle, on "Sunday after the Feast of St. Margaret the Virgin." The seal is lost.

Saturday after the Feast of St. Lucy the Virgin, 14 Edward I. Grant (in Latin) by Gervase, son of Richard de Pipeneselle, to Henry son of William de Pipeneselle, and his heirs or assigns whomsoever, "a "house of religion, and Judaism, excepted," of 2 acres of the fee of Pipeneselle; for 2 marks of silver paid beforehand. Witnesses, John Thomas, William Wytte, John Geffrey, Wymund ate Grenevalle, Adam ate Halle, William de Pipeneselle, Bartholomew de Helnestre, John Robert, Wymund Robert, Helyas Witte, Robert the Chaplain. The seal is perfect, six sprigs meeting at a centre.

28 Edward I. Agreement (in Latin) by John Lamsyn and Parnel, his wife, by bond to Pharon Johan, of Rye, to pay 5 shillings of silver yearly as rent for a messuage abutting, on the west, on the King's meadow, on the south, on land of the heirs of Henry de Rackele, and on the north, on the tenement of Gunnild Dethue and Joan, her daughter. In case of non-payment, the said Pharon may distrain by whatever judge he pleases, ecclesiastical or secular; and each time they will give to the bailiff or official distraining 2 shillings of silver. Witnesses, Robert Paulyn, Paulin his son, Justin Alard, Henry de la Nesse, Laurence Dyer, Geoffrey Solas, Peter the Clerk. A fragment of one of the two seals is left.

30 Edward I. Grant (in Latin) by Thomas de Sandherst, brother and heir of Simon, of the parish of Promhelle, to Edmund Andrew, of Wynchelse, son of John Andrew, of his tenement, late of Simon, his brother, at Wike, in the parish of Lyde, of the tenure of Dengemersache, belonging to the Lord Abbot of Battle; which his said brother, Simon, bought of Adam Baker of Winchelse; for 6 marks sterling, paid beforehand. Witnesses, Robert Willeame, Henry Thomas, Godring de Wyke, Richard Meydekin, John Hughe, Gervase Andrew, John Manokin, John Yevegod, Richard Trute[?], William Lefchild, Philip the Clerk. A diminutive seal, with the letter H apparently, and a crown, is still attached. Promhelle, now Broomhill, was partly destroyed by an inundation of the sea, in the 15th year of Edward I. The Courts, at a late date called "Brotherhood" Courts, were probably held at this place, in early times.

32 Edward I. Grant (in Latin) by Ralph Ambroys to Stephen, his son, and Isabel, his daughter, of his tenement in Rye, acquired of John Bone, near the land late of Nicholas atte Nesse, and that late of William de Petepirie, and the tenement late of Stephen Provost; they rendering yearly to the heirs of John Bone 12d. on Sunday in Mid Lent, and 10d. on the Day of St. Michael, and to himself and his heirs one halfpenny in silver, at his principal tenement in Rye. Witnesses, Pharon Johan, the Mayor, Paul Fitz-Robert, Justin Alard, Henry ate Nesse, John Ambroys, Stephen Ambroys, Philip Russe, Richard Whyte, John Whyte, Richard Portesmouthe, Richard Beneit, Peter the Clerk. The seal still remains, apparently some animal is represented. This deed contains the earliest mention of a Mayor, under a stated date, A.D. 1304.

32 Edward I. Grant (in Latin) by William, son and heir of John de Kechennore, to Thomas Dyges of a moiety of the land which he acquired of Adam de Boseny, in the parish of Idenne, in a marsh called "Lewedymers," near the land of Ralph Boseny therein; at a yearly rent of 9d., payable at his house at Pesemersse; 40s. having been paid beforehand. Witnesses, William de Lyghe, Edmunde atte Euere, William Robert, Robert de Leghs, Richard de Glesye, Robert de Petlesham, William de Kechenham, William de la

3 R 4

Hamme. The seal is mutilated, and the deed is torn in half.

33 Edward I. Grant (in Latin) by John de Hauecherste, son of Richard, and Thomas Ater Lieghe, son of Hamon, to Richard de Hauecherst, son of Richard, of half an acre of land, situate in a place called " Yngelberdeslond;" in consideration of 10s. sterling. Witnesses, William John of Hauecherst, Adam Thomas, Symon le Brun, Richard Donet, and others. The seal is lost.

33 Edward I. Grant (in Latin) by John, son of Stephen Ricote, and Margery and Emecota, daughters of the late Stephen Webbe (Teytoris), to Thomas Ricard, of the tenement which they formerly held of Samson de Leuelishamme, and of Juliana, wife of Ralph Attewelle, situate in Rye, near to the tenement of La Lee; they rendering to the said Juliana 1½d. at her principal tenement, on the Feast of St. Michael, and ⅞d. on the Feast of St. Andrew the Apostle; and to the said Samson 2½d. at the same times, and suit at his Court of Leuelishamme; 2 marks sterling having been paid beforehand. Witnesses, Samson de Leuelisham, Robert ate Wode, Richard ate Welle, Ralph de Blykewelle, Peter the Clerk. The three seals are perfect; one of them, a star, is the seal of " Eme le Webbe;" the others are the seals of Margery Recote (a fleur de lis), and John Recote (a star). Peter the Clerk is Peter de Hegsthone, mentioned in the following deed.

34 Edward I. Grant (in Latin) by Peter de Hegsthone, Clerk, and Dionysia, his wife, to Adam de Tuysdenne, butcher, and Parnel, his wife, of a tenement which one Henry, the butcher, formerly held of them, " situate near the Market-place of our Lord the King, in " the vill of Rye;" for a yearly rent of 8s. sterling; 40s. having been paid beforehand. Witnesses, Robert Marchaunt, Mayor, Paul Fitz-Robert, Justin Alard, Richard Beneyt, Richard Portesmothe, Pharon Johan, William ate Wyssche, Geoffrey Solat, John atte More, John Pocok, Symon Knockebregge. Part of the small seal of Peter is left. That of the " Community of the " Vill of Rye," appended " at their prayers, in the name " of the said Dionysia," is lost. This Peter is the Clerk who attests (and no doubt wrote) many of these deeds : see under the fifth and later years of the next reign.

Wednesday before the Epiphany, 35 Edward I. A large indented deed of covenant (in Latin), between Richard de Portesmouth the elder and William Broun, of Wolbaldingherst, whereby the former grants to the latter part of his land, with a grove and other appurtenances, in the parish of St. Mary of Rye, " in " Borgh de Colspore ;" one piece of land being called " Ricardstegh," abutting upon Kaneswische, to the east, at one end, and, on the other, on the common way from the high street towards Longewisch, the said grove being to the south ; the other piece of land being in Longewische, between the land of Elias Broun and that of the heirs of Ralph Aterwelle, abutting at one end upon the Hamme, and on the other upon the land called " Kaneslond." Another piece, called " Torclesacre," lies near the land of Samson de Lewleshamme, and that of Ralph Aterwelle, and called " Regge." A fourth piece of land is called " Brabourne," lying between the heath of Elyas Broun and that of the heirs of Richard de Walbandingherst. Land called " Bletteghe " is also mentioned : the consideration being a yearly payment of half a mark of silver, payable at the four terms of the year. Witnesses, William de Leghe, William de Feldemore, Martin de Podlesham, Daniel de Podlesham, Thomas de Podlesham, Stephen de Tyllingham, Richard de Fonte [or Atewelle], Elyas Broun, Alexander Auc. The seal and its thong are lost.

35 Edward I. Grant (in Latin) by John Torel to Richard de Portesmouthe the younger, of a field called " Crockereafeld," in the vill of Pleydenne, near to the land of Ralph ate Euere and that assigned to the works of the church of St. Mary at Rye, and the land called " Stubbeslond ; " for 4 marks sterling paid beforehand. " Done at Playdenne." Witnesses, Robert Marchant, Mayor of Rye, Justin Alard, Richard le Whyte, Geoffrey Solaz, Robert ate Wode, Robert Caderethedom, Robert Vynch, Robert Agave, Peter the Clerk. There are two impressions, both perfect, of John Torel's seal, a ship with one mast ; one of them being appended to a diminutive letter of attorney, tied to the conveyance, empowering John Forale to deliver seisin to Richard of a field called " Crockereslond."

35 Edward I. Grant (in Latin) by John Torel and Alice, his wife, to Peter de Hegsthone, Clerk, and Dionisia, his wife, of their messuage and land in Merstret, in the vill of Rye ; for a payment of 10s. sterling.

" Done and recorded at Rye, on the Sunday after " Easter." Witnesses, Robert Marchaunt, Mayor, Paul Fitz-Robert, Pharon Johan, Geoffrey Solaz, Justin Alard, Richard Portesmouthe, Philip Russel, Richard Blykewelle. John's seal, a ship with one mast, is perfect ; the seal of the Community of the vill of Rye (the older seal), set thereto on behalf of his wife, is much mutilated ; it represents the church, with the Virgin and Child over the porch : the counter-seal represents a galley, with one mast, steered by an oar. This is the earliest instance in which it occurs ; the latest being the close of the reign of Edward III. As to Peter de Hegsthone, see under the preceding year.

Temp. Edward I. Grant (in Latin) by Thomas Panes to Helias le Corvayser (Shoemaker) and Joan, his wife, of a place near to the common way, going to the tenement late of Henry Pichepap, at a yearly rent of one silver penny ; 2 marks having been paid beforehand. Witnesses, Robert Paulin, then Bailiff, James Marchaunt, Richard his brother, Henry de Rackele, then Mayor, Philip Russel, Reginald Paccoke, John Lambert, Robert Smerekervere [Butter-cutter], Richard de Portesmothe, Walter Schipwerste, Walter Belde, Baker, John Pokoc, Robert de Peveness, Chaplain. The seal is lost. The mention thus early of " the Bailiff," and of the Mayor, deserves notice. This is perhaps the earliest deed, containing the name of a Mayor ; as Henry de Rackele was dead, as we have previously seen, in the 28th year of Edward the First [A.D. 1300.] Robert Paulin, the Bailiff, it will be observed, takes precedence of him.

Temp. Edward I. Gift (in Latin) by John, son of the late Geoffrey Pokok, to Peter de Heghtone, Clerk, of his tenement in the parish of Pleydenne, held of the Court of Idenne, at a yearly rent, at such Court, of 7d. ; the sum of 5s. having been paid beforehand. Witnesses, Robert Marchaunt, then Mayor of Rye, Paul Fitz-Robert, Pharaon Johan, Justin Alard, John le Hwyte, Richard de Portesmouthe the elder, Richard his son, John de la More, Alexander Botemount, Clerk. A small seal, with the impression of a star, is appended. The deed is finely written ; it belongs to the 34th or 35th year of this reign ; Peter the Clerk, has been previously mentioned.

Temp. Edward I. Release (in Latin) by Joan Dore, of the vill of Wynchelse, to Robert, called " Brede- " ware," of her right in a messuage, with buildings thereon, in the vill of Rye, which her late husband, Richard ate Welle, and herself, had purchased of Henry le Yonge ; for 40s. paid beforehand. Witnesses, James Marchant, Robert Fitz-Paulin, Robert le Smerekervere, Henry Yvori, John de Clive, Robert Michel, Robert de Arundel, Henry Ambrois, Ralph Ambrois, John Ginnor, William Hamvile. The large seal, in yellow wax, representing a star, is in fair condition. As to the same property, see under the fifth year of the next reign.

Temp. Edward I., early in the reign. Grant (in Latin) by William Tanner, son of Gilbert Tanner, to Marjary, daughter of William du Val, and Isabel and Eleanor, her daughters, of a half acre of land which he bought of Peter Harang, abutting on the way from Tuteshame to Ealding [now Yalding], they rendering yearly to Peter Deacon 2d. ; 14 shillings of silver having been paid beforehand. Witnesses, William de Tutesham, John, his son, William de Ludeneford, William de Orsmulle, Robert de Yleserrae, Walter Roberd, Benedict Bomur, John le Cod, William called " Cod," Thomas de Punpe, William Poteman, Walter his brother. The seal is lost ; and the deed is finely written.

Temp. Edward I. Grant (in Latin) by Baldewyn de Stowe, Knight, lord of Wyltinge, to William, son of Philip ate Hurst, of a piece of land at Chillonde, called " Le Halstede," in the parish of Holintone, on the road from Wyltinge to Hastinge, and abutting on the meadow called " Smalewyche" and that of John de Ore, at a yearly rent of 12d. ; 40s. having been paid beforehand. Witnesses, John de Ore, John de Peplesham, John de Codinges, Gilbert de Senesuges, William Aurey, Henry and Peter de Wyltinge, Roger le Rede. The seal is lost, but the canvas in which it was wrapped, is still appended.

Temp. Edward I. Grant (in Latin) by Henry Poulin and Joan, his wife, to Reginald de Pichole and Alice, his wife, of one acre of land in Colemoree, in the parish of Rye, lying near the lands of the heirs of John Roger and of William de Hechingham, John Eve, and John Valentine, to hold to them and their assigns (Jews and religious excepted) for ever ; at a yearly rent of one clove at the Feast of St. Michael, payable at their principal house ; in consideration of 24s. paid beforehand. Witnesses, Helyas de Brohexe, William Wylte, Geoffrey

Walterman, Henry de Pipenishille, Wymund atte Walle, Goldwin de Bateberwe, William Munte. Written in a very peculiar hand. The seal is lost.

Temp. Edward I. Grant (in Latin) by John Ambroys to William Elys and Margery, his wife, of a third part of the land which William son of Gervays atte Hoche acquired of John, son of Henry Bone, being 7 acres, in Rye; at a yearly rent of 12*d.* sterling. Witnesses, John de Glesham, John de Bechenore, John de Leghe, William Joce, Robert atte Euere, Robert atte Wode, John Vynch. The seal is lost.

Temp. Edward I. Grant (in Latin) endorsed, "Carta " de Winterlonde, juxta Vinchhulles," by John and William, sons and heirs of William Norman, to Hugh, son of Ingelbert Covent, of half an acre, and half a quarter of an acre, of land, in a plain called "Wynter-" londe," near to the land of Geoffrey Storm and a street called "Denestrete," and extending from Nortburne to the King's highway; at a yearly rent of ½*d.*, at the house of the said John, at Gateberg, to be paid; 20*s.* having been paid beforehand.—"And forasmuch as " much challenge there is wont to be as to the doings " of men, unless the tongues of witnesses, or writing, " have force, we have strengthened this charter with " the impress of our seals." Witnesses, Geoffrey Storm, Hugh Wilkine, William Munt, Galding Hore, Luke du Pre, Walter Spud, Nicholas Lambekyn. Luke, his brother, Hugh Faggere, Geoffrey Munt, William Whytte, Henry Koc, Geoffrey Walterman. The seal of John is still attached. This deed belongs to the earlier part of this reign, and is beautifully written.

Temp. Edward I. Grant (in Latin) by William de Pipenecelle, to Henry, his brother, of his right in an acre of land which fell to him, or might fall to him, after the death of William, their father, such acre being in the parish of La Rie, on the road leading therefrom to Pipeneselle, and near to the land of the heirs of Hamon de Pipenselle; to hold to him, his heirs, and assigns, a house of religion excepted, at a yearly rent of one halfpenny; 6 shillings having been paid beforehand. Witnesses, Geoffrey Waltermand, Geoffrey Storme, William Wit, Elias de Brocheye, Elias son of William de Wyk, Hugh de Gaterberge, William Munt, John, his son, Hugh Hulle, John Eve, William the Clerk. The seal is lost. This deed is written in a remarkable hand, and almost illegible. Date about A.D. 1283.

Temp. Edward I. Grant (in Latin) by Henry le Yonge, of Rye, to Richard ate Welle, of Wynchelese, and Joan, his wife, daughter of the late Walter de Bromleghe, of Wynchelese, of a messuage near to the land of John Austyn and the messuages of Pharon Johan and Robert de Arundel, at a yearly rent of 4*s.*; six marks having been paid for this grant. Witnesses, James Marchant, Robert Fitz-Paulin, Stephen called Clerk, John the Baker, Reginald de Rackele, Reginald Joye, Robert le Smerekervere, Paulin de Horne, John le Nore, Wulvin Moghe, Robert Stalle, Robert le Brode, Laurence the Clerk. The seal is lost.

Temp. Edward I. Grant (in Latin) by Richard, son of William de Pypeneselle, to Henry and William, his brothers, of his part of 2 acres of land which fell to them after the death of their father, in the marsh of Gadeberg, near the lands of Hamon and Robert de Pypenesell; extending from Grenewall to the land of Robert Marscot; to him, his heirs, or assigns, houses of religion excepted, at a yearly rent of 2*d.* sterling, at his " capital house of Pypenesell, to be paid ; " 15*s.* sterling having been paid beforehand. Witnesses, Robert and Hamon de Pipenesell, Robert Kneder, Henry Broc, Henry Koc, Geoffrey Storm, William Munt, Geoffrey Walterman, Henry Lade, Robert Kix, Luke Broc, Richard Snow, Robert Marscot. Most beautifully written. The seal is lost. The deed belongs to the early part of the reign of Edward I.

Temp. Edward I. Grant (in Latin) by John Bone, son of Henry Bone, and heir of Brice de Rye, his grandfather, to Richard Goldeloue and Richard de Portesmouthe, of 14 "ymettas" of his land, of the tenure (manor) of Sir William de Echingehame, in the marsh of Gadebergh; 11 of which lie near to the lands of John de Yham and of the heirs of Nicholas Joy, and of Robert called "Michel," John Thomas, and Reginald Paccok; and also near to Botelefcte: the 3 others, "which in " English are called 'Caltesteyles,' lie near to the fleet " (inlet) which is vulgarly called 'Pipenesellesfleyt:' " rendering to the principal lords 6½*d.* on the day of St. Michael, and to him, at his principal house at Rye, one silver penny, " *de fovgesbulo*" [?] : saving always the walls and waterways (wallis et watergangis) to the said land belonging ; the consideration being 33 marks, paid

beforehand. Witnesses, James Marchaunt, Nicholas de Nesse, Laurence the Dyer, Reginald Paccok, John Thomas, Henry Wytte, Henry de Pipeneselle, Reginald de Rackele, Robert the Chaplain. The seal is in fragments.

2 Edward II. Grant (in Latin) by Thomas, son of the late Thomas ate Nesse, to Sarra, his sister, of his right accruing through the death of Nicholas atte Nesse, late uncle to his father, in houses, rents, and lands, in the vill of Rye. Witnesses, Paul Fitz-Robert, Mayor, Justin Alard, James ate Nesse, Henry ate Nesse, Robert Marchaunt, John le Whyte, John ate More, Stephen Vyse [?], Richard Portesmouth, Peter the Clerk. The small seal, in green wax, representing a star, is in good condition.

5 Edward II. Grant (in Latin) by Sarra, daughter of Thomas de la Nesse, to Peter de Hoghton, Clerk, and Dionisia, his wife, of all the houses, rents, and lands, which she had of the gift of her brother, Thomas ate Nesse; for 40*s.* of silver, paid beforehand. Witnesses, Paul Fitz-Robert, Mayor, Justin Alard, Robert Marchaunt, James, his brother, Richard de Portesmouthe, John Paccok, Geoffrey Solaz, William ate Wische, Thomas Farson, John Salerne, John Kittey, Clerk, Alexander Botemond. The seal, a star, is in good preservation. This "Peter the Clerk" has been previously mentioned.

5 Edward II. Grant (in Latin) by John, son and heir of Richard de Webaldingherste, to Richard Portesmouthe, Baron of Rye, of an acre of meadow, of the fee of the Abbot and Convent of Fiscamp, which is called "Westwiasche," lying upon La Hegheforde, in Rye, near to the land of Elyas Broun and of Guncelin ate Hello; also, a part of an acre called "Le Thoun"; also, half an acre of marled land in the plain called "Le Hok;" in consideration of 40*s.* Witnesses, Paul Fitz-Robert, Sampson de Packham, John Thomas, Daniel de Pedlisham, Thomas, his brother, Robert de Pedlisham, Guncelin ate Helle, Elias Broun, Peter the Clerk. The seal is perfect, representing, apparently, a trefoil.

5 Edward II. Grant (in Latin) by Robert, called " Bredeware," to Henry, called "Mentel," of Penecestre, and Isabel, daughter of Richard le Pours, of Battle, of the tenement in Rye which he bought of Joan Dore, of Wynchelse ; for 7 marks sterling paid beforehand. Witnesses, Paul Fitz-Robert, Mayor, Justin Alard, John Ambroys, Robert Marchaunt, James, his brother, John Paccok, Geoffrey Solaz, William ate Wissche, Richard Portesmouthe, John Salerne, Reginald de Rackele, John Thomas, Peter the Clerk. The seal, representing a ship with a single mast, is in good condition. It is tied with a rush, to the deed of Joan Dore, noticed at the close of the preceding reign.

5 Edward II. Agreement (in Latin) between William, son of Philip the Tailor, and William Godman, Tailor, and Juliana, his wife, daughter of the said Philip; whereby the said William agrees to give his tenement which he lately had of Moyses the Corveser (Shoemaker), of Rye, situate between the high street and the tenement of William Maufras; the said William Godman and Juliana giving him the tenement near the Marketplace, which they had received from the said Philip, the father; the said Philip, the father, to live in the first-named tenement for the rest of his life, with the said William and Juliana, who shall keep the house "wahthiht" [? walltight] and "rofthiht" [roof-tight]. Witnesses, Richard de Portesmouthe, Mayor, Paul Fitz-Robert, Robert Marchaunt, James, his brother, Geoffrey Solaz, William ate Wische, Richard Beneyt. The one seal, formerly appended, is lost.

6 Edward II. Grant (in Latin) by John, son and heir of Geoffrey Pocok, to Richard, son of the late Henry Ambroys, of the messuage near to the place belonging to the heirs of Stephen Ambroys, and the tenement of Elena Wodeman ; rendering to the chief lord of the fee 6½*d.* on Sunday in Mid Lent ; for a payment to the grantor of 40*s.* Witnesses, John Paccok, Mayor, Paul Fitz-Robert, Robert Marchaunt, James, his brother, John le Whyte, William ate Wissche, Geoffrey Solaz, John Kyttey, Thomas Pharon. The small seal, a star, is in a perfect state.

6 Edward II. Grant indented (in Latin) by John Munt to Robert Hulle of a piece of meadow, near to the lands of Richard Hulle, William Storm, and Robert Hulle, in exchange for land in the same parish of Rye, near to the land of Walter Mot. The said Robert to find for the said John a way for driving his cattle to his close of Shrobbes, when it is in grass at summer time. Witnesses, John Thomas the elder, Richard, his son, William Thomas, William Storm, William de Gatebergh,

Walter Wymund, Walter Mot. "Given at Gatebergh,
" the Sunday next after St. Peter's Chains." The seal,
of John Munt, a star, is nearly perfect.

7 Edward II. Grant (in Latin) by Ralph "called
" Slegh," of Rye, to William de Hetherst, dyer, and
Isabel, his wife, daughter of Ralph, of a room (domum)
in the east part of his tenement, being 14 (man's) feet
by 18; at a yearly rent of one farthing, within 12 days
of our Lord's Nativity, to be paid, at his principal tenement; 20s. sterling having been paid beforehand. Witnesses, John Paccok, then Mayor, Paul Fitz-Robert,
Elias Muriele, Robert Marchaunt, John Ambroys,
William ate Wische, Geoffrey Solaz, John, son of
Stephen Ambroys, Stephen, his brother, Richard Blykewelle, Laurence Pharon, William Stase, John Blodletere,
Peter the Clerk. The seal, with the impression of an
axe, and the legend" S. Radulfi Sleh " in the margin, is
perfect.

7 Edward II. Grant (in Latin) by Thomas le Bone-
ved and Juliana, his wife, to Ralph Fitz-John and
Christina, his wife, of the half, or south part, of a
tenement which Gymmota Snoth, the mother of Juliana,
bought of John le Blodletere and Margery, his wife;
they rendering to the said John and Margery 3s. yearly,
and having paid 20s. beforehand. Witnesses, John
Paccoke, Mayor, Paul Fitz-Robert, Robert Marchaunt,
William ate Wissche, Geoffrey Solaz, Henry Goldyeve,
Reginald de Rackele, Richard Blykewelle, John Whyte,
John Ambroys, Stephen, his brother, Andrew Colebrond,
Peter the Clerk. One seal, representing a church-
tower, is in fair condition; of the other, a fragment only
is left.

8 Edward II. Grant (in Latin) by Robert Fitz-Peter
and Emma, his wife, daughter of the late Jordan le
Spycer, to Ralph Fitz-John and Christina, his wife, of
a moiety of the tenement which belonged to Gymmota
Snoth, mother of the said Emma; for one silver mark,
paid beforehand. Witnesses, Robert Marchaunt, Mayor,
Paul Fitz-Robert, Elyas Muriele, John Paccok, William
ate Wishe, Geoffrey Solaz, John Kyttey, John Ambroys,
John Salerne, Robert Vincent, Henry Viss, Peter the
Clerk. The seal of Robert (vesica-shaped) is in good
condition; that of the community of the Barons of Rye,
appended on behalf of Emma, is lost.

8 Edward II. Grant (in Latin) by Stephen Skynnere,
to Thomas Pyron, miller, of the messuage in Rye which
he had of Agnes Soake; at a yearly rent of 5s.; the
sum of 40d. being paid for the grant. "Given on Sun-
" day, the Feast of the Apostles Peter and Paul."
Witnesses, Robert Marchand, Mayor, Paul Fitz-Robert,
Elyas Muriele, James Marchand, William ate Wische,
John Paccok, Geoffrey Solaz, Thomas Faron, Thomas
Muriel, John Kyttey, John Ambroys, Robert Vincent,
Reginald de Rackele, Richard Blykewelle, Peter the
Clerk. The seal is lost.

8 Edward II. Grant (in Latin) by Henry Mentel and
Isabel, his wife, to John Kittey the elder, and Martha,
his wife, of a messuage purchased of Robert Bredeware,
abutting on the messuage late of Pharaon Johan and
that of Robert de Arrundel, and the land of John
Austyn; at a yearly rent, to be paid to Henry le Yonge,
of 4 shillings sterling; 3 marks of silver having been
paid beforehand. His own seal has been set thereto,
and that of the Community of Rye, at the request of his
wife. Witnesses, Robert Marchaunt, Mayor, Paul Fitz-
Robert, Geoffrey Solaz, William de la Wische, Reginald
de Rakkelee, William le Taverner, William de Pesemersch, Luke le Salater. The seals are lost.

8 Edward II. Grant (in Latin) by William de Hetherst, dyer, and Isabel, his wife, to Ralph, son of John
Rolf, and Christina, his wife, of the house which they
had of the gift of Ralph Slegh, with part of a chamber
adjoining thereto, bought of Richard, son of the said
Ralph, for a yearly rent of 2½d.; a sum of 20s. being
paid beforehand. Witnesses, Robert Marchant, Mayor,
Paul Fitz-Robert, John Paccok, William de la Wische,
Geoffrey Solaz, J. Ambroys the younger, Robert, son
of Robert Vincent. The seal of William is in good
condition, that of "the Community of Rye, at the
" supplication of the said Christina appended," is lost.

8 Edward II. Release (in Latin) by John, called
"Le Blodletere," and Margery, his wife, as to a house, part of a
messuage bought of Richard le Knyst; which house is
situate near to a place belonging to the works and
lights of the church of St. Mary, which John Elkyn
holds; and near to a curtilage and the principal messuage of Ralph and Christina, and a curtilage of Paul
Fitz-Robert, "belonging to the Hall," to the south; and
of a rent of 6½d. formerly paid by them to the said John;
they paying a yearly rent of 12 pence in the King's

Court in Rye, on Mid·Lent Sunday; as also, 18d. to
the works and lights of the church of St. Mary; and
one halfpenny to the said Richard le Knyst. His own
seal, and, for greater evidence and security, the seal of
the Community of Rye, have been set thereto. Witnesses,
Robert Marchant, Mayor, Paul Fitz-Robert, Geoffrey
Solaz, John Ambroys, William de la Wyssche, James
Marchand, Richard Beneyt, Alexander Botemont, Clerk.
The seal of John (a star) is unbroken, but partly illegible; that of the "Community," appended in behalf of
Margery, is lost.

9 Edward II. Release (in Latin) by Joan Wyse, relict
of Henry Aumbroys, to John Kyttey the elder, of all
her right and claim, in name of dower, in the lands and
tenements which belonged to the said Henry; for one
mark of silver, paid beforehand. Witnesses, Robert
Marchaunt, Mayor, Paul Fitz-Robert, John Marchaunt,
John Ambroys, Geoffrey Solaz, William de la Wische,
Robert Vincent, Richard Beneyt. The oblong seal, a
starred cross, with the legend " S. Johene Wise," is in
fine condition.

9 Edward II. Release (in Latin) by Henry ate Welle,
and Isabel, his wife, daughter of the late Richard
Martyn, to John Kittey the elder, and Martha, his
wife, of 2d. yearly rent for a tenement formerly belonging to John Nasse, opposite to the principal messuage
of the said John Kittey; 2s. being paid beforehand.
Witnesses, Elyas Muriel, Mayor, Paul Fitz-Robert,
Robert and James Marchaunt, John Aumbroys, William
ate Wische, Robert Vincent, Richard Beneyt, Butcher,
William le Taverner, William de Pesemersh. A fragment of one of the two seals is left.

Temp. Edward II. Grant (in Latin) by Stephen Ambroys, to John Kyttey and [Martha], his wife, of the
lands and tenements which came to him after the death
of Henry Ambroys, his father, and Agatha, his wife;
in return for which, they have given him, for life,
sustenance in the Abbey of Cumbwelle. Witnesses,
" Eliseus " Muriele, Mayor, Paulin ate Rye, Robert and
James Marchant, John Ambroys, John le Hwyte, John
Paccok, John Salerne. This deed is mutilated, and the
seal is lost. The next deed is almost exactly similar to
this, except that it is attested under another Mayor,
James Marchant. Muriele was Mayor in the 9th year
of Edward II., James Marchant in the tenth.

Temp. Edward II. Grant (in Latin) by Stephen Ambroys to John Kittey and Martha, his wife, of the lands
and tenements which came to him after the death of
Henry Ambroys, his father, and Agatha, his wife, in the
parish of La Rye; in return for which, they have given
him, for life, sustenance in the Abbey of Cumbwelle.
Witnesses, James Marchaunt, Mayor, Paulin atte Rye,
Robert Marchant, John Ambroys, John le Wyte, John
Paccok, John Salerne. The seal is lost. This deed
belongs to the 10th year of this reign.

10 Edward II. Grant (in Latin) by Richard Beneyt
to John Kyttey and Martha, his wife, of 5½d. yearly
rent, which he was wont to receive from the tenement
between those of Roger le Prest and Henry Juvene, at
Pentecost; for 5s. paid beforehand. Witnesses, James·
Marchaund, Mayor, Paul Fitz-Robert, Robert Marchaund, Elyas Muriel, John Ambrois, John Paccok,
Geoffrey Solaz, Richard Hurst, Thomas Richard, Peter
the Clerk. A small seal, representing a bird on a spray,
is still attached.

11 Edward II. Grant (in Latin) by Robert " called
" Lotekyn," and Joan, his wife, to Richard Kittey and
Beatricia, his wife, of a place of land within the liberties
of the vill of Rye, near to the lane called " Piggeslane,"
and near to the lands of John Cok and of the heirs of
John·de la More; and to that of Thomas de Bonulon;
at a yearly rent of 2 silver pennies, "on St. Giles's Day,
" at the principal messuage which belonged to William
" Pate, at Wynchelese, to the heirs of the said William
" to be paid:" the said Richard and Beatricia having
given a small parcel of land in Rye, in exchange. Witnesses, Paul Fitz-Robert, Mayor, Robert Marchaunt,
James, his brother, Geoffrey Solaz, John Ambroys,
Robert Vincent, Henry Fish, Richard Beneyt, butcher,
Thomas Ricard. Of the two seals one is lost, a portion of the other, representing a cross, with four pellets,
remaining.

12 Edward II. Grant (in Latin) by Reginald de
Brede to William Waryn and Joan, his wife, of a messuage near to the tenement of John Lyteman, and
that of the heirs of Pharon Johan, also "near to a way
" which is pertaining to the visnet there, by my feoff-
" ment," for a yearly payment of 6d., on Sunday in
Mid Lent 3d., and on the day of St. Michael 3d.; 2s. 6d.
having been paid beforehand. Sealed "in the month of
" August." Witnesses, Paul Fitz-Robert, Mayor, Elias

CORPORA-TION OF RYE.

Muriel, Robert Marchaund, James Marchaund, John Ambroys, John Paulyn, John Kyttey, John Paccok, Robert Vincent, William Gaylard, Henry Fys, Richard Blykewelle, Peter the Clerk. A portion only of the seal is left.

14 Edward II. Grant (in Latin) by Alice, daughter of the late Laurence called "Le Deghere" [the Dyer], to John Le Kok, of her moiety in a parcel of land lying in a lane called "Piglane," near to the land of the heirs of John ate Stronde, and that which belonged to Richard Rycote; for a yearly rent of 6 silver pennies, on Sunday in Mid Lent; 12d. sterling having been paid beforehand. "Given on Passion Sunday." Witnesses, Paul Fitz-Robert, Mayor, Robert Marchaund, James Marchaund, John Ambroys, John Paulyn, Robert Vincent, John Kyttey, Thomas Paccok, William Gaylard, Richard Blykewelle, Thomas the Tanner, Peter the Clerk. The seal, a star, is in fine condition.

14 Edward II. Grant (in Latin) by John le Whyte to John Kyttey the elder, and Martha, his wife, of 8 pence yearly rent, which he was wont to receive on the day of St. Michael from the tenement of Henry Dyges, lately belonging to Walter le Clenchere; they rendering to the chief lords, the heirs of—Ambroys, 1½d. yearly; in consideration of 8s. paid beforehand. Witnesses, Paul Fitz-Robert, Mayor, Robert Marchaund, James Marchaund, John Ambroys, John Paulyn, Geoffrey Solaz, John Paccok, Robert Vincent, William Gaylard, Robert Thomas, Richard Blykewelle, Peter the Clerk. This deed is beautifully written; the seal is lost.

14 Edward II. Grant (in Latin) by John le Whyte to John Kyttéy and Martha, his wife, of 6d. yearly rent which they were wont to pay to him for their salt-house (domo salina) on the Est Stronde, in Rye. Witnesses, Paul Fitz-Robert, Mayor, Robert Marchaund, James Marchaund, John Ambroys, John Paulyn, Robert Vincent, William Gaylard, Robert Thomas, Richard Blykewelle, Peter the Clerk. The seal is lost.

14 Edward II. Grant (in Latin) by Richard le Whyte, son of Richard, to John Kyttey and Martha, his wife, of a fourth part of the Windmill in Rye, called "Heghe-"theghe;" for 40s. to him paid beforehand. Witnesses, Paul Fitz-Robert, Mayor, Robert Marchaund, James Marchaund, John Ambroys, John Paulyn, Robert Vincent, William Gaylard, Geoffrey Solaz, John Paccok, Richard Blykewelle, Peter the Clerk. The seal appended is in fragments.

15 Edward II. Grant (in Latin) by William Storm, of Gateberwe, to Robert Hullo and Helena, his wife, of 1½ acres of land, near to the land of William ate Wische, and that of William ate Welle and of William de Gateborwe; at a yearly rent of 2d. Witnesses, Richard Thomas, William Thomas, John Witte, Edmund Witte, William Storm, John Monte, William Gateberwe. "Given at Gateberwe." The seal is lost.

15 Edward II. Grant (in Latin) by Laurence, son and heir of Pharon Johan, to Ralph Fitz-John and Christina, his wife, of a yearly rent of 12d., from the tenement of John le Taverner; in consideration of 10s. paid beforehand. Witnesses, Paul Fitz-Robert, Robert Marchaund, James Marchaund, John Ambroys, John Paulyn, P[eter] the Clerk. The seal is lost, and the deed has apparently suffered from water, or damp.

16 Edward II. Grant (in Latin) by John Scherale and Goda, his wife, daughter of the late John Torel, to Ralph Fitz-John and Christina, his wife, of 7½d. of yearly rent which they were wont to pay from the principal tenement of John Lambeyn, without the gate of the vill of Rye; for half a mark of silver paid beforehand. "Done on Sunday after the Feast "of the Conversion of St. Paul." Witnesses, Paul Fitz-Robert, Mayor, Robert Marchaund, James Marchaund, John Ambroys, John Paulyn, Robert Vincent, John Paccok, John le Whyte, Robert Thomas, Geoffrey Corboyle, William Gaylard, Symon Merseye, Richard Blykewelle, Peter the Clerk. John's seal (a star) is perfect; of that of the Barons of Rye, set thereto for Goda, only a fragment is left.

16 Edward II. Grant (in Latin) by Reginald de Rakele and Matillidis, his wife, to Ralph Fitz-John and Christina, his wife, of a tenement near to that of the heirs of John Pocok, on the Est Stronde, and to that of Thomas Hallere, at a yearly rent of 4d., payable on Sunday in Mid Lent; they having paid 4l. beforehand. On behalf of Matillidis, the seal of the Barons of Rye is set thereto. "Given on Sunday, the morrow of St. George the "Martyr." Witnesses, Paul Fitz-Robert, Mayor, Robert Marchaund, James Marchaund, John Ambroys, John Paulyn, Robert Vincent, John Paccok, Symon Merseye, Peter the Clerk. Reginald's seal (a star) is perfect, that of the Barons is in fragments.

CORPORA-TION OF RYE.

17 Edward II. Grant (in Latin) by Andrew de Potepyrie to Peter de Hegsthone, Clerk, and Dionysia, his wife, of one penny of yearly rent from 2 messuages standing near the principal tenement of Henry le Juvene; for 20d. sterling, paid beforehand. Witnesses, Paul Fitz-Robert, Robert Marchaund, James Marchaund, John Ambroys, John Paulyn, Robert Vincent, Robert Thomas, Richard Blykewell, John Yevegod. The seal is lost. As to the above Peter, see various notices under the preceding extracts, and the deed next mentioned.

17 Edward II. Grant (in Latin) by Andrew Potepirie, of Rye, to Peter the Clerk, and Dionysia, his wife, of 3d. yearly rent, from the tenement which was of John Peitevyn in Potepiriestrete, and now held by Robert Reinccod. Witnesses, John Whyte, Mayor, Paul Fitz-Robert, Robert and James Marchaund, brothers, John Ambroys, John Paulyn, Robert Vincent, John Paccok, Robert Thomas, William Gaylard, Richard Blykewelle. The small seal, representing a star, is nearly perfect. Peter the Clerk, already noticed, and here named, occurs as the final attesting witness of many deeds of this reign, and was no doubt the writer of them; the present deed is apparently in his hand.

18 Edward II. Release (in Latin) by Alexander, son of Elyas Cole, of Rodmersham, to Simon, son of Vitalis de Chiltone, of his claim in 5 roods of land in the parish of Rodmersham, at Sherlyng, in the field called "Northfelde," near to the land of Alan Cole, on the south, and abutting on the land of the Hospital of St. John, on the east and west. "Given at Sherlyng." Witnesses, Walter le Mere, Richard le Mere, John, his brother, Robert Capeleyn, Edmund, his brother, Alan Cole, John Sokolyng, John his son, John, and William, sons of William Sokelyng, John le Gray, William his son. The seal, somewhat broken, has a shield with an indistinct impression.

18 Edward II. Grant (in Latin) by Robert, "called "Archer," of Wynohelese, and Margery, his wife, to Robert, called "Holstok," baker, and Joan, his wife, of their tenement in Rye, acquired of Richard, son and heir of Roger Belde of Rye, at a yearly rent of 6s. 9d.; for 60s. paid beforehand. Witnesses, James Marchaund, Mayor, Paul Fitz-Robert, Robert Marchaund, John Ambroys, John Paulyn, William Gaylard, Geoffrey Courboyle, John Paccok, Richard Blykewelle, Nicholas Wyllos, Matthew Parys, Ralph Ambroys, William Taylor, Peter the Clerk. The seal of Robert Archer, (a star, like a Maltese cross) is perfect, that "of the Community "of the Barons of Rye," set thereto on behalf of his wife, is lost.

19 Edward II. Grant (in Latin) by John Scherale and Goda, his wife, daughter of the late John Torel, to Ralph Fitz-John and Christina, his wife, of 12d. of yearly rent from the tenement of Robert Faron, in the Market-place of Rye, to be received on Sunday in Mid Lent; also of 6d. yearly rent from the tenement of Richard a Grove, "which was at Veyrheuod (? Wear-"head) without the Gate;" for one mark sterling, paid beforehand. Witnesses, James Marchaund, Mayor, Paul Fitz-Robert, Robert Marchaund, John Ambroys, John Paulyn, Robert Vincent, William Gaylard, Geoffrey Corboyle, Robert Thomas, John Snoghel, Nicholas Willes, Thomas Tannero, John Cok, Thomas Hallere, Richard Blykewelle, Peter the Clerk. The seal of John Scherale (a star) is nearly perfect; of that of the Barons of Rye, appended for Goda, a small fragment only is left.

19 Edward II. Sale (in Latin) by John Kyttay, son of John, to Martha, his mother, the widow of the said John, of all his right in a mill called "Heytchy" on Estrond (East Strand). Witnesses, James Marchaund, Mayor, Paul Fitz-Robert, Robert Marchaunt, John Ambroys, John Paccok, Robert Vyncent, William Gayllar, Geoffrey Corboyle, Nicholas Carpenter, Thomas Tanner. The seal is lost.

Temp. Edward II. Grant (in Latin) by Robert Smith (Faber), of Rye, and Joan, his wife, daughter of the late Walter ate Hoche, and Matillidis, daughter of the said Walter, to Thomas Ricard, of all claims which may arise in the parishes of Rye and Idenne, upon the tenures [manors] of Iwherste and La Lee. Witnesses, Sampson de Pageham, William de Leghe, William de Kechenore, John de Gleshamme, Richard de Glesya, Robert de Pedlishamme, Daniel and Thomas de Pedlishamme, Robert de Leghe, Thomas ate Euero, John, his brother, Peter the Clerk. Two of the three seals in green wax, one representing a star, the other flowers, are still attached.

3 Edward III. Grant (in Latin) by Richard, William, Laurence, and Thomas, sons of John Thomas, and brothers and heirs of Robert Thomas, to John de Toulve-

herst, Corveser, and Parnel, his wife, of their right in a moiety of the tenement which the heirs of James ate Halle lately held. Witnesses, Robert Marchand, Mayor, James Marchand, John Paulyn, Paulyn Marchand, John Ambroys, John Whyte, Thomas atte Nesse, Thomas Muriel, Robert Vyncent, Nicholas Paulyn, Stephen Roussel, Symon Merseye, William Gouss, John Portesmouth, Peter the Clerk. The three seals are lost, and the deed is almost illegible from damp.

4 Edward III. Grant (in Latin) by Thomas Dyges to Stephen ate Leghe, tanner, of the moiety of the land which he acquired of William de Kechenore, in the parish of Idenne, in the marsh called "Lenedimerss;" for 20s. paid beforehand. Witnesses, Sir John de Garlethorpe, Chaplain, Warden of the Hospital of St. Bartholomew at Rye, John Paulyn, Robert and James Marchaunt, John Ambroys, Barons of Rye, John de Kechenore, William de Leghe, John de Gleshame, William de Kechenham, John de Oxnebregge, William ate Hope, Robert de Abotteslonde. The impression of the small seal attached (a star) is almost effaced.

4 Edward III. Grant (in Latin) by Juliana, widow of Richard Portesmouthe, to Margery, widow of Thomas Hallere, of her part of the mill lately built by the said Richard, upon the "folisia" (cliff) near to the Nesse; for a payment yearly, during the life of the said Juliana, of 2 seams (horse-loads) "of good wheat and "reasonable corn," so long as the said mill shall remain there; and if the mill be removed, the said Juliana, if she wishes to receive the said rent, shall pay her share of the expenses of such removal thereof. Witnesses, Robert Marchaunt, Mayor, James Marchaunt, John Paulyn, Nicholas, his brother, John Ambroys, Thomas his brother, Robert Vincent, Thomas Muriele, John Portesmouthe, Peter the Clerk. The seal is whole, but the impression is nearly effaced. Peter the Clerk, who drew so many of these deeds, now disappears.

6 Edward III. An indenture (in Latin) testifying that whereas Thomas, son of Richard de Pipenselle, enfeoffed Robert Elis, of Occene, and Joan, his wife, of 2 acres in the New Marsh, at Pypenselle, the said Thomas is bound to defend the same against the lords of the fee, and especially the Abbot of Fiscamp; and the said Robert agrees to pay him, at his house, at Pypenselle, 16¾d. yearly, and to protect the same land, as to walls and "watergangs." Without witnesses. The seal is lost.

6 Edward III. Grant (in Latin) by John, son and heir of John Taverner, to John, son of Robert Stronge, of a third part of a messuage in a lane leading towards Schierstret, near to the tenements of Robert Bernehond and John le Whyte, and the place of John Enggel, for a term of 1,000 years, with reversion to the grantor's heirs; 10s. having been paid. Witnesses, Robert Vincent, Mayor, Robert and James Marchand, John and Thomas Ambroys, John and Nicholas Paulyn, William Gaylard, Stephen Russel, John the Clerk. The impression on the seal (a star) is almost effaced.

7 Edward III. Grant (in Latin) by Walter Ganter (Glover) and Christina, his wife, to John de Kent, Corveser (Shoemaker), of Rye, of the land, and building thereon, which Christina had acquired of John Portesmouth; situate in Rye at "La Haltone," near the tenement of Richard Elis, and Joan, his wife; at a yearly rent of 2s. In the name of Christina, the common seal of the Barons of Rye is set thereto. Witnesses, Robert (? Marchant, or Vincent), then Mayor, James Marchant, John Ambroys, John Pauly[n], Nicholas, his brother, Stephen Russell, John Heued, John Dyges, Laurence Courboille, John the Clerk. The seal of Walter, representing stars and flowers, is nearly perfect, that of the Barons of Rye is lost.

9 Edward III. Grant (in Latin) by John Roger, "Corveser" of Rye, to John de Kent, "Corveser" of the same, of the land which he acquired of Stephen atte Legh, tanner, in the parish of Idenne, in the marsh called "Lenediesmerch;" in consideration of 4 marks sterling, paid beforehand. Witnesses, John Paulyn, Robert Marchant, James Marchant, John Viel, Paul Marchant, John de Kechenore, William Joce, John de Bosne, Richard de Kelfreȝt The seal (a star) is mutilated.

9 Edward III. Grant (in Latin) by Robert Smyth to Ralph Rorlf and Christina, his wife, of 12d. yearly rent from his tenement within the North Gate of Rye. Witnesses, Robert Marchant, Mayor, James Marchant, John Ambroys, John Paulyn, Nicholas Paulyn, John Yevegod, Laurence Corboille, Robert Arnold, John Tanner. A portion of the seal, a cross formed of four palm-branches, is left.

12 Edward III. Grant (in Latin) by Geoffrey, son and heir of John Kyttey, to Martha Kyttey, his mother, of his part of the mill called "Hegheteghe" in the vill of Rye, which he inherited from his father. Witnesses, Richard Paulyn, Mayor, Robert and Paul Marchaunt, John Paulyn, Laurence Courboille, Symon Merseye, John Yevegod, John the Clerk. A portion of the seal, representing, apparently, a stag's head and antlers, surmounted by a cross, is left.

13 Edward III. Indenture (in Latin), whereby John le Tannere, of Rye, grants to Benedict le Whyte and Parnel, his wife, half an acre of land in the parish of Rye, in the "borgh" of Culppore, "of yards of Normandy," which Margery Red formerly held, of the manor of Brede, near to the land of John Bakere, the land of Landewe, and that of John Marchant; at a yearly rent of 3s. 8½d. Witnesses, John Paulyn, Robert Marchaunt, John Ambroys, Paul Marchaunt, Stephen de Pedlisham, Daniel de Pedlisham, Philip de Pedlisham, William de Tillingham, Walter Martin, Walter de Culppore, John Stevene, of Tillingham. There are two seals attached, but the impressions are undecipherable. The counterpart also accompanies it, its one seal lost.

14 Edward III. Indenture of grant (in Latin) by John Tannere to John Marchaunt and Margery, his wife, of half an acre of land in Rye, in the "borgh" of Culppore, which Margery Reed lately held of the manor of Brede; situate near to the land of Benedict le White. the land of Landewe, and the garden of the Hospital of St. Bartholomew; at a yearly rent of 3s. 8½d. Witnesses, John Paulyn, Robert Marchaunt, Stephen de Pedlesham, Daniel de Pedlesham, William Tillyngham, Walter Martyn, Walter Coulppore, and others. The two seals are still appended, one of them broken; they are oblong and concave, and are alike, and, apparently, representing a man with a sword in his left hand.

14 Edward III. Indenture (in Latin) between Richard le White and Thomas Peronel; whereby the former agrees to remove a house near to the Nesse, between the houses of Nicholas Paulyn and Stephen Russel, and to build another, in like form, between the houses of Laurence Courboille and Philip Skynnere: the timber of the house to be as good as that of the former one; but the said Thomas is to find the ironwork. For moving the house, finding the timber, building, and doing the work, down to the covering, the said Thomas is to pay 12s. 6d. The said house is to be removed and completed before Easter following the date thereof—the Feast of St. Hillary, and on such completion the said Thomas is to pay another 12s. 6d. Witnesses, Paul Portesmouthe, Gervase Skalle, John the Clerk. The seal is lost; and the deed is partly illegible, from having been immersed in water.

14 Edward III. Grant (in Latin) by Richard le Whyte to John Mathew, baker, of a place near to the tenements of Edmund Passele and Thomas Barbour, and near to the place of John Paulyn; at a yearly rent of 12 silver pennies. Witnesses, Thomas atte Nesse, Mayor, Robert Marchant, John Paulyn, Paul Marchaunt, Stephen Russell, Laurence Courboille, Robert Arnold, John Diges, John the Clerk. The seal is nearly whole, but with a worn impression, of a man wielding a sword in his left hand, as already mentioned. It probably belonged to John the Clerk, who prepared the deed. It has somewhat of the aspect of being an ancient gem.

14 Edward III. Release (in Latin) by John Kyttey, brother and heir of Richard, who was son and heir of Richard Kyttey, of Robert Quinterel, of the parish of Pleidoune, as to 12 pence of yearly rent for what was the principal tenement of the said Richard, and as to all claim to the said tenement; for a certain sum paid beforehand. Witnesses, Thomas atte Nesse, Mayor, Robert and Paul Marchaunt, John and Nicholas Paulyn, Stephen Russell, Laurence Courboille, Alexander Kyttey, John Dedes, John the Clerk. Faintly written, and mutilated; the seal is perfect, but with a faint impression of the man with the sword, as above mentioned.

15 Edward III. Grant (in Latin) by John de Kent, "Corveser," to Elias atte Halle, of Rye, of all the land which he acquired of John Roger, of Rye, in the parish of Idenne, in the marsh called "Lenediesmersch." Witnesses, Robert Marchaunt, John Paulyn, Stephen Russel, Nicholas Paulyn, John de Kechenore, Reginald de Hope, Walter Joce, Robert ate Euere, Richard a Grene, John the Clerk. Of the seal, in green wax, representing a star, a portion is left.

15 Edward III. Grant (in Latin) by Dionysia, widow of Peter the Clerk, to Nichola, her daughter, wife of John Hony, of her place near to the tenement of John Lambot, and that late of Thomas de Sandwich, and near to the land late of Thomas Muriele. "Given on Sunday "after the Feast of St. Laurence." Witnesses, Thomas

atte Nesse, Mayor, Robert Marchant, John Paulyn, Nicholas Paulyn, Stephen Russel, Paul Marchant, Symon Merseye, John Dyges, John Magfeld, John the Clerk. The oblong seal, with a sort of Maltese cross, is in fair condition. Peter the Clerk has been frequently mentioned, under this and the preceding reigns.

17 Edward III. Grant (in Latin) by Thomas Pokel, of Canterbury, and Alice, his wife, daughter and heir oj Stephen Skynnere, to William Baker, of Apoldro, of the eastern half of a house formerly belonging to the said Stephen, in Rye; with the reversion after the dower of Margery, widow of the said Stephen, being the other half. Witnesses, Robert Marchaunt, Mayor, John and Nicholas Paulyn, John Ambroys, Paul Marchaunt, Laurence Courboille, Stephen Russel, John Dyges, Matthew Baker. The seal of Thomas is mutilated; of that of "the Com- "munity of Rye," appended "at the instance of Alice," only a small fragment is left.

17 Edward III. Grant (in Latin) by Robert Scot and William Sprot, and Agnes, his wife, of a place of land in the same, and Agnes, his wife, of a place of land in the said town, near the tenement of Henry Pasteman there; at a yearly rent of 2s., to be paid to the chief lords of the fee. "Given at Hastynge, on Monday after "the Feast of St. Matthias the Apostle. Witnesses, "Richard Goldwyne, then Bailiff of Hastynge, Robert, "his brother, Richard Thurbarn, John Boneyt, Thomas, "his brother, Ralph Hardyng, John Aloyn." The two seals are lost, and the little deed, which is finely written, is much torn.

18 Edward III. Grant (in Latin) by John de Graf- herst, of Iklesham, to William de Eytone of his lands and tenements in Iklesham and Geslinge. Witnesses, John de Cresay, Richard Thomas, Thomas de Stonlynke, John de Sapertone, Alan de Ferne, John de Rotelonde. A small seal (apparently a star) is appended. No con- sideration is mentioned in this deed, the writing of which is very faint.

21 Edward III. Grant (in Latin) by William Brun to Nicholas Pawlyn, of a yearly rent of 12d. from his tenements at Le Hole. Witnesses, William Paulyn, James Marchaunt, Paul Portesmudthe, Robert Bocher, Peter the Clerk. The writing is partly effaced by damp, and the seal is lost.

23 Edward III. Indenture (in Latin) witnessing that, whereas William de Eytone enfeoffed Sir John de Wardintone, perpetual Vicar of the church of Iklesham, and John de Sapertono, of all his lands and tenements in Iklesham and Gestlyng, it is his will that they shall hold the said tenements for 16 years, at a yearly rent of 100s. sterling. Given at Iklesham. Witnesses, John de Ote, John Cressy, John de Pidintone, William de Lyndherst, Thomas Elys, John de Estwyk. There are two small seals in red wax, with the impressions much worn.

23 Edward III. Release (in Latin) by Parnel, widow of John de Kent, of Rye, to Stephen, son of Stephen Andrew, of Wynchelse, of her right in an acre and a quarter of land which the said Stephen had, of the gift of Joan, widow of Stephen Russel, in the parish of Brede, and in a certain marsh called "Wytflet," abutting on the land called "Cassemarysland," and on lands belonging to John Vynch, the heirs of John Wallere, and the heirs of Richard Thomas. Witnesses, John Wytte, William Hemhamme, John Hemhamme, William Clerk, Henry de Wyke, William de Brosexae. The seal (a star) is somewhat broken.

25 Edward III. Grant (in Latin) by Stephen, son and heir of Stephen Andrew, of Wynchelse, to William Taillour, son of William Taillour, of Rye, of all his lands and tenements in Rye, Wynchelse, and Ihamme. "Done at Wynchelse." Witnesses, Robert Arnald, Mayor of Wynchelse, Paul Portesmothe, Mayor of Rye, Paul Marchaunt, Bailiff of Rye, Vincent Fynch, John Longhe, of Wynchelse, Benedict Sely, Walter Salerne, and Walter Bydynden, of Rye, and Richard Smyth, of Ihamme. The seal is still appended, the impression appearing to be a human face.

25 Edward III. Grant (in Latin) by John de Sapir- tone to Sir John de Wardyngtone, perpetual Vicar of Iklesham, of his interest in the lands, rents, and tene- ments, late of John de Grofherst in Iklesham and Gest- lyng. Witnesses, William de Lyndhurst, William Clerk, Elias Bakere, Robert Bakere, Robert Lideham, Thomas Elys. The seal is lost.

26 Edward III. Letter of attorney (in Latin) of Martha, widow of John Kyttey the elder, appointing Stephen Andrew her attorney to give seisin to William Taylour, son of William Taylour the elder, of all her lands at Pipensell "in the borgh of Gatebergh." Her seal, much worn, is still attached.

26 Edward III. Grant (in Latin) by William Bonho, of Rodemersham, to Richard Tichebourne, of half an acre of land in Rodmersham, in a place called "Longelonde," near to the land of the Hospital of St. John, and the lands of the heirs of John Bonho and of Peter de Chiltone, and the land of the heirs of Alan Colu; also, a parcel of land lying at the Doune, near the land of the heirs of Sir Roger de Hegham. Witnesses, Richard Otte- forde, William Thruleghe, John Sokolynge, Richard atte Court, William de Nordenne, William Hunts. "Given "at Rodmersham, on Sunday after the Feast of the "Invention of the Holy Cross."

26 Edward III. Grant (in Latin) by Robert Dyvet to William Austyn and Agatha, his wife, of the messuage which he had of John Mabyew, in Cherestrete, near the land of the Prior and Convent of Christ Church, Can- terbury, and the messuages of Alexander Pyrmeldo and John Yardherst. "Done at Manenerchero" (indis- tinct). Witnesses, William Cryndhey, William Reynold, William ate Pynne, Richard Mello, Robert Derwold. The seal is nearly whole, with a worn impression or, apparently, the lamb and flag. It seems doubtful to what place this deed relates.

27 Edward III. Grant (in Latin) by John Peytevyn to James Bonjour and Sarra, his wife, of his messuages in Wynchelse, formerly belonging to John Eppelman, at a yearly rent of 10s. Witnesses, Henry Goldsive, Mayor, Benedict Sely, Walter Bydyudenue, William Taillour, Paul Portesmouthe, John Wasshere. A frag- ment of a small and beautiful seal, tied with silk, and apparently charged with three crosses pattees fichees, is appended.

27 Edward III. Release (in Latin) by John, son and heir of Robert Alard, of Wynchelse, to John Peytevyn, of the same, of all his right and claim in all the lands, tenements, services, and rents, with the advowson of half the Chantry of the Chapel of St. Nicholas, in the church of St. Mary at Rye, in the vills of Rye, Pese- mershe, Brede, and Udymere, which came to him, by heirship, after the death of John Ambroys, of Rye. For greater surety, he has procured the seal of the Mayoralty of the vill of Wynchelse to be set thereto. Witnesses, Robert Arnold, then Mayor of the vill of Wynchelse, John Fynch, Vincent Fynch, Benedict Sely, William Taillour, William de Pageham, John de Pageham, John Paulyn of Merle, Walter Soxtayn, John Wylcok, William Joce, Simon Joce, Robert Dymond, Bartholomew Androw, John Estwyk, Clerk. His seal, representing a person standing in a porch, is fairly perfect; of the seal of Wynchelse only a portion is left.

28 Edward III. Grant (in Latin) by William Breke- ston the elder, and Joan, his wife, to John Thomas and Alice, his wife, of a messuage without the gate of Rye, and near to the land of John yevagode, and situate be- tween the tenement of Abraham Cane and that of Henry Penyale, at a yearly rent of 4s. Witnesses, Henry Goldseve, Mayor, William Taillour, Paul Portesmouthe, William Brekeston the younger, Nicholas Smyth, Richard Pak, John Jolyf, John Lad, Clerk. The small seal of William (a kind of trefoil) is perfect; but the seal of the Commonalty of Rye, which was set "for greater "security," is in a mutilated conditon.

28 Edward III. Grant (in Latin) by Peter Mulwod, of the parish of Playdenne, to Richard Pak, of Rye, of the moiety of a place of land, with half the house built thereon, formerly belonging to William Joye; also, 2s. of yearly rent which he was wont to receive of Alice Kytteye, from the principal tenement, formerly belong- ing to Nicholas Joye, situate in the Market-place. Witnesses, Paul Portesmouthe, Mayor, Henry Goldseve, Benedict Cely, John Curboille, Richard Gaillard, Lau- rence Taverner, John Lad, Clerk. The seal is lost.

29 Edward III. Grant (in Latin) by William, "by "God's sufferance," Abbot of the Monastery of Begeham, and the Convent thereof, for the many benefits re- ceived from Walter Lacy and Joan, his wife, "and, as "it is hoped, in future to be received," to them, for their lives, of a yearly payment of 8 marks, at their dwelling-house in Rye to be paid. In case of nonpay- ment within 8 days from any of the terms therein named, power is given to them or their attorney to distrain upon the manor of Teleton, belonging to the Convent. The seal of the Convent, formerly attached, is lost.

31 Edward III. Release (in Latin) by Richard Gayllard to Thomas Bakere and Joan, his wife, of all his right in a windmill in Rye, formerly belonging to Thomas Hallere, situate at the Nesse upon the Falese (Cliff), near the harbour, on the south side. Witnesses, Paul Portesmouth, then Mayor, William Taillour, Bene- dict Cely, John Courboille, Henry Goldseve, Richard Baddyng, John Wasshere. The seal is lost. This is

the first appearance of the name of "Baddyng," afterwards much connected with the history of Rye.

32 Edward III. Grant (in Latin) by Thomas and William Potter, sons and heirs of Walter Potter, to Adam Foughle and Matildis, his wife, of a tenement situate near the tenement of the heirs of John Tanner, and that of Alice Seward. Witnesses, Paul Portesmouthe, Mayor, William Taylour, Benedict Cely, Henry Goldȝeve, John Curboile, Walter Lucy, Ralph Ambroys. The two seals are lost.

32 Edward III. Grant (in Latin) by Thomas Bakere and Joan, his wife, to William Tayllour and Agnes, his wife, of one half of a windmill, formerly of Thomas Hallere, situate on the Falaise (Cliff) at the Nesse, near to the harbour of the sea. Witnesses, Paul Portesmouthe, Mayor, Benedict Cely, Henry Goldȝeve, John Courboille, Walter Lucy, Richard Baddyng, John Lad, Clerk. A large portion of the seal of Thomas is left. The seal of the Commonalty of the vill of Rye, set thereto, "at the instance " of Joan, is lost.

33 Edward III. Grant (in Latin) by Matildis, widow of William Pykevirle, to John Aleyn and Margery, his wife, of her principal tenement in the parish of La Rye, situate on the highway leading from Pleydenne to Rye, on the east, and near the lands of Robert Allard, on the west, and near to the messuage of the heirs of Benedict le Webbe. Witnesses, Paul Portesmouth, Mayor, William Taillour, Bailiff, John Finch, Richard Hogheles, Robert Allard, Thomas Pott, John Lad, Clerk. The seal, in red wax, apparently representing the Virgin and Child, with a penitent kneeling, is nearly perfect.

35 Edward III. Release (in Latin) by John, son of Alan Ussack, to Richard de Tichebourne, of his right in half an acre of land in Rodemersham, in the place called " Sherlyngesfeld," near the lands of John Morys, of the heirs of Peter de Chiltone, and of the Hospital of St. John, and near to the way from Sherlynge to Cokerilstrote. "Given at Rodemersham." Witnesses, Richard de Otteforde, William Bonho, William Thrulegh, Richarde ate Cust, William Huitte, William Neweman. The seal is whole, but the impression very indistinct.

35 Edward III. Grant (in Latin) by Adam Voghel, of Playdoune, to William Taillour, of Rye, and Agnes, his wife, of a tenement acquired of Thomas and William Potter, sons and heirs of Walter Potter, near the tenement of the heirs of John Tanner, and that of Alice Seward. Witnesses, Paul Portesmouthe, Mayor, Benedict Sely, Henry Goldȝeve, John Courboille, John Marchaund. The seal is unbroken, with no impression beyond a dent.

35 Edward III. Grant (in Latin) by Robert, son of Robert Alard, of Yhamme, to Robert de Hethe, of Ydenne, and Alice, his wife, of a messuage in Rye, between the messuage of Matillidis, widow of William de Pigevyrle, and the land of the brethren of the Hospital of St. Bartholemew. Witnesses, Paul Portesmouthe, Mayor, William Pageham, John Paulyn, Richard Kechenore, John Finch, Richard Seward, John Marchaund. Each party has set his seal to this indenture, but only one, with a worn impression, is left.

36 Edward III. Grant (in Latin) by William Taillour to Thomas Horsman and Goda, his wife, of a place near to the tenement of Thomas Douno and John Potyn; at a yearly rent of 4s. Witnesses, Henry Goldȝeve, Mayor, Benedict Cely, Richard Baddynge, John Ivory, Thomas Kittay, John Otringham, Clerk. The seal is whole, but the impression much worn.

37 Edward III. Grant (in Latin) by William Taillour and Agnes, his wife, to Stephen Andrew and Joan, his wife, of a place near the tenements of Stephen Elyot, John Crabber, John Otringham, Robert Spicer, and William Idenne; such place having been acquired of John Shypman, of Hetho; in tail general, at a yearly rent of 6s. 8d. Witnesses, Henry Goldȝevo, Mayor, Benedict Cely, Richard Baddyng, John Salerne, Simon atte Wod, John Otringham. The seal is broken, the impression, a human face, apparently.

37 Edward III. Grant (in Latin) by Thomas Bakere and Joan, his wife, to Richard Wyke, "Tannere," and Alice, his wife, of a piece of land near to the land of Joan South, and the land of William Storm, called "Le Teynton," and abutting on the meadow called "Le Kynggeswische," and the King's highway called "Blekelane;" which land came to the said Joan after the decease of Richard Gailard, her father; at a yearly rent of 2s. Witnesses, Henry Goldȝeve, Mayor, William Taillour, James Dyghes, William Brekestone the elder, William Storm, William Brekestone the younger, Robert the Clerk. The seal of Thomas Bakere is perfect, representing a man on a lion, apparently, blowing a horn, with "IRIDE" above. Of the "seal of the Com-

" munity of the vill of Rye," which, for greater surety, Joan had procured to be appended, only a portion is left.

37 Edward III. Grant (in Latin) by Walter Symoun, of Pesemersch, to Gervaise Symoun and Parnel, his wife, of his piece of land called "Kombys Wyssoh," and of another piece, called "Kombys Tegh," and half an acre called "Kombys Teghe Hyl," and half an acre called "Baldebourne" and "Heggyshole," of the fee of Lodeleghe, Witnesses, John Paulyn, Richard Hethenore, William, his brother, John Wylkoc, Robert de Legh, John Oseborn, John Dyn. "Given at Pesemersch, on " Sunday after the Feast of St. Katharine." A fragment of the seal is left.

37 Edward III. Grant (in Latin) by Robert Quyntrel, of the parish of Playdenne, and Nichola, his wife, to John Jolyf, of Rye, of the lands which they hold of the Court of Brede, called "Pesex, Ploggescroft, La "Wybssche, Brounys, and Le Hok." Witnesses, Richard Pak, of Rye, John Fynho, Stephen Potyn, William ate Grove, Danyel Gybbe. Of the two seals, only a fragment of one remains. There is no consideration mentioned in the deed.

39 Edward III. Grant (in Latin) by John Foghelere (Fowler), of the parish of Pesemersch, to Gervase Simond and Parnel, his wife, of a moiety of a piece of land in the said parish, in a place called "Berlyngbroke," near Baldebourne, adjoining the land of Eggishale. "Given " at Pesemersch." Witnesses, John Paulyn, Walter Symond, William Kenep, Richard de Coumbe, John Anite. The seal is whole, but with a faint impression. It is tied, with a rush, to the preceding deed.

39 Edward III. Grant (in Latin) by William, son of John Matheu, of Rye, to William Taillour and Agnes, his wife, of a tenement near Schytbourglane on the south, the sea-shore on the east, and the King's highway on the west. Witnesses, Thomas Taillour, Mayor, Henry Goldȝeve, Benedict Cely, Richard Baddyng, Stephen Andreu, John Salerne. The seal, broken, represents a dragon, apparently.

40 Edward III. Grant (in Latin) by Thomas Taillour and John Ivory, Wardens of the work and lights of the church of St. Mary at Rye, to John Osbarn and Sarra, his wife, of a place of land lying at the Haltone, near to the tenement formerly of Alexander Kittay, the place formerly of Simon Lukke, and the tenement late of John Yevogod; for a yearly rent of 6d. sterling. In witness whereof, they have obtained the common seal of the vill to be set thereto. Witnesses, Richard Baddyng, Mayor, William Taillour, Henry Goldȝeve, Stephen Andrew, John Crabbar, Robert the Clerk. A fragment of the old town seal is left.

41 Edward III. Grant (in Latin) by Richard Baddyng and Joan, his wife, to William Taylour and Agnes, his wife, of three vacant places, near the messuages of John Wotteghe, Adam Persone, and Henry Kyttey; which came to the said Joan after the death of Walter Bechyndenne and Dame Joan Rossel, her mother; at a yearly rent of 4 pence halfpenny farthing, and one red rose, to be paid at the Nativity of St. John the Baptist. Witnesses, Henry Goldȝeve, Benedict Cely, John Ivory, Stephen Andrew, Stephen Eliot. The seal of Richard is nearly complete, but with the impression almost effaced; of the seal of the Community of Rye, appended on behalf of his wife, a portion is broken away.

41 Edward III. Grant (in Latin) by Robert de Hethe and Alice, his wife, to Roger Geffray, of West Mallyngge, and Margaret, his wife, of a messuage in Rye, situate between the tenement late of William and Matildis Pykfirlle and the land of the Hospital of St. Bartholomew. Witnesses, Richard Pak, Nicholas Smyth, Thomas Stakyndenne, William Brekstone, William Walram. The two seals are in fair preservation; that of Alice being a lozenge intersected by another.

45 Edward III. Grant (in Latin) by Thomas Taillour and Joan, his wife, to John Otringham and Agnes, his wife, of a place which he acquired of Matthew Torold and Juliana, his wife, near to the place of John Otringham, late of Stephen Russel, and his own place, lately belonging to Stephen Polchestre, and to the land late of John Callere; also, another place, near the place late of Alice Raulyn; at a yearly rent of 6s. 8d. His own seal, and, for greater security, the seal of the Commonalty of Rye, is set thereto. Witnesses, John Ivory, Mayor, William Taillour, Laurence Courboille, John Salerne, Robert Bernehand, Stephen Eliot, Robert Bocher, John Crabbarc, Robert the Clerk. The seal of Thomas Taillour is perfect, a shield charged with a crescent, and, apparently, two swords crossed; that of the "Community"—the old seal—is much broken: it is the last instance in which it appears; the matrix (a

fine work of art) was probably lost when the town was plundered, five years after this, by the French.

45 Edward III. Grant by William Taillour, to Thomas Donne and Margery, his wife, of a place of land which Thomas Horsman formerly held of him, situate near to the place [vacant space] of John Potyn ; at a yearly rent of 3s. "Given at Rye, on Sunday, the " Feast of St. Bartholomew the Apostle." Witnesses, John Ivory, Laurence Curboyl, John Salerne, Stephen Eliot, Stephen Andrew, Simon Lonseford, John Otringham, Clerk. The seal, a shield of iron-heater shape, is very similar to that of Thomas Taillour, just described, but with a much worn impression.

45 Edward III. Grant (in Latin) by John Peytevyn, of Wynchelse, to William Passelewe, son of John, of the vill of Rye, and Isabel, his wife, of 2s. out of 7s. of yearly rent which they were wont to pay him, for a tenement formerly of John Callere of Rye, near the tenements of John Vox, Walter Scherman, and Thomas Taillour. Witnesses, William Taylour, Mayor, Thomas Taillour, Bailiff, Laurence Courboille, John Yvori, John Salerne, Laurence Taverner, Symon atte Wode, Robert Bucher. The impression on the seal is the letter E, surmounted by a crown.

46 Edward III. Release (in Latin) by Richard Marchamme and Odierna, his wife, to Stephen Andrew and Joan, his wife, of the piece of land which they had lately of the gift of the said Stephen and Joan, formerly belonging to Richard Shipman, near the tenements of John Crabbare and Robert Spicer, and that of Stephen Eliot. There are no witnesses to this deed ; the seals of Richard Marchamme and of the vill of Rye, appended at the request of Odierna, have disappeared.

46 Edward III. Release (in Latin) by John Crabber and Agnes, his wife, to Stephen Andrew and Joan, his wife, of a piece of land near that of William de Ideune, and that late of Robert Spicer, "Given at Rye, on' " Sunday in Mid Lent." Witnesses, John Ivory, Mayor, William Taillour, Thomas Taillour, Laurence Curboyl, Robert Bernhand, Stephen Elyot, Robert Bochere, Simon de Lonseford, John Otringham. The seal of John Crabber, apparently, two branches of a tree, with a bird, is in fair condition ; the seal "of the Community " of the vill of Rye," procured to be set thereto by Agnes, has disappeared. The deed is still tied, with the original rush, no doubt, to the preceding deed.

46 Edward III. Grant (in Latin) by Stephen Eliot, to Robert Bochere and Benedicta, his wife, of a piece of land in Rye, near to the land of Lenclesham, and the land lately belonging to Robert Bochere the elder ; at a yearly rent of 2s. Witnesses, John Ivory, Mayor, Thomas Taillour, Laurence Courboille, John Wettegh, Simon atte Wode, Robert the Clerk. The seal, originally with a fine impression of a decorated cross and flag, is in fragments.

48 Edward III. Indenture of grant (in Latin) by William Taillour the elder, to John Berlelot and Joan, his wife, of a place between that late of Alice Bowfrount and the highway, and near to the site of his mill, and the land late of William Maghefeld ; at a yearly rent of 22d. "Given at Rye, on Sunday the Octave of " Easter." Witnesses, Thomas Taillour, Mayor, Laurence Curboyl, John Salerne, Simon Lonseford, Stephen Elyot, Robert Bocher, John Otringham, Clerk. The seal is perfect, representing 4 branches of palm or fir meeting in form of a cross.

48 Edward III. Grant (in Latin) by William Taillour the elder, to Stephen de Wye, butcher, and Alice, his wife, of a place near to the selds (open sheds) of Reginald Bocher and Richard Whyte, and to "the " Market-place of our Lord the King," on the north, and the grave-yard of the church of St. Mary, on the south, at a yearly rent of 4s. Witnesses, Thomas Taillour, Mayor, Laurence Curboyl, John Salerne, Simon Lonseford, Robert Bernhand, Stephen Elyot, John Otringham, Clerk. The seal is whole, but the impression on the shield is effaced. Is is tied with a rush to the deed next mentioned.

48 Edward III. Release (in Latin) by Robert Stonehurst to William Taillour the elder, of all his right in a place near to the selds of Reginald Bocher and Richard Whyte, and to the Market-place and the grave-yard of the church of St. Mary. Witnesses, John Salerne, Laurence Curboyl, Reginald Bocher, Robert Bocher, Richard Marchant, John Otringham. The seal, as above, four palm branches meeting in the centre, is in fair condition.

48 Edward III. Release (in Latin) by Thomas Taillour to William Passelew, of his right in a place of land lying in the marsh called "Padihamesmerch,"

which the said William to ferm let to William Taillour, his late father. Not attested ; the seal is lost.

50 Edward III. Grant (in Latin) by William Whyting and Isabel, his wife, daughter and heir of Henry Kittay, to Robert Flemyng and Matildis, his wife, of a place near the land late of John Janeman, and the land of the community called " Le Haltone," and the land of John Osbarne and of the heirs of William Taillour ; at a yearly rent of 4s. On behalf of Isabel, the seal of the Community of the town of Rye has been set thereto. Witnesses, Simon Lonseforde, Mayor, Richard Baddyng, Thomas Taillour, John Salerne, Laurence Curboyl, Stephen Elyot, John Otringham, Clerk. William's seal, the same as that of Thomas Baker, described under the 37th year of this reign, a man blowing a horn, still exists ; that of the town is lost.

1 Richard II. Release (in Latin) by Thomas Taillour, to William, his brother, and Joan, his wife, of his claim in the lands which he had of the gift of William Taylour, his father, in the parish of Idenne ; as also, his share in all lands and tenements similarly received in Sussex and Kent. As his seal is unknown, the seal of the Mayoralty of the vill of Rye is set thereto. Witnesses, Simon Lonseford, Reginald Portysmowthe, Robert Londeneys, of Wynchelsee, Reginald Bocher, Peter Bocher, Richard Whyte, Stephen Elys. The seal of the Mayoralty is in good condition, and this is the first time it appears ; being used in place of the seal of the Community, probably, now lost.

3 Richard II. Grant (in Latin) by John Osbarn to Richard Eldrych and Alice, his wife, of that place which he had acquired of the Wardens of the works and lights of the church of St. Mary at Rye, lying upon La Haltone, at a yearly rent to the said Wardens of 6d. Witnesses, Simon Lonsforde, Mayor, John Salerne, Laurence Courboille, Stephen Elyot, John Crabbare, Robert Bocher, Robert Aleyn, Clerk. The seal is perfect, but with a faint impression ; apparently, a female holding a flower.

4 Richard II. Grant by indenture (in Latin) by John Erby and Juliana, his wife, of Wynchelse, to John Burgoyne, of the same, and Margery, his wife, of a pightlo of a place of land at La Trecherie, below the cliff of the said town, near to the places of Robert Londeneys and Michael Strodman, and towards the Salt Marsh ; at a yearly rent of 12 silver pennies. " Given at Wynchelse, on Sunday after the Feast of " St. Lucy the Virgin." Witnesses, Robert Londeneys, then Mayor, Simon Salerne, Henry Cele, Henry Hokere, Thomas Robinhood, William Hobolyn. The two small seals, in green wax, are still attached.

8 Richard II. Grant (in Latin) by Alard Smythe, of La Rye, to Peter Rede, of Dovorre, of all his lands and property, moveable and immovable. " These being wit- " nesses," then a blank. A fragment only of the seal is left, and no consideration is mentioned. This Alard Smythe is mentioned in the Fescamp document, relative to the ransom of prisoners, before mentioned.

8 Richard II. Grant (in Latin) by Richard Hefdrop and Alice, his wife, to John Eadmund, and Robert and John, his sons, of 1½ acres of land in the parish of Odymere, of the tenure of Brede, lying between the King's highway, called " Coopercsstrete," to the east, and land called " Fysshbeltre," to the west, and near to a place formerly belonging to Lorchon Thomas, to the north. Witnesses, John Monte, Stephen Wytte, John Wymond, Luke Wytte, John Edestone, William Wytte. The two seals are nearly perfect, one with fanciful devices, but indistinct.

8 Richard II. Grant indented (in Latin) by Thomas Taillour, to Robert Holstok and Agatha, his wife, of a place near to the Market of Rye, and near the place held by Thomas Prestone of John atte Wode, and that of Robert Bocher: such place formerly belonging to John Pikestrawe ; "which I recovered by award, " according to the ancient law of the vill"; at a yearly rent of 6s. 8d. Witnesses, Robert Dyn, Mayor, John Marchame, William Bleseworthe, Walter Disscur, Robert Beregrove, Clerk. The seal is almost perfect, with a faint impression of a shield.

9 Richard II. Grant (in Latin) by John Moryng, called " Dragener," to John Bertclot and Robert Beregrove, Clerk, of his lands and tenements, rents and services, in the vill of Rye. Witnesses, John Marchame, Mayor, Stephen Elyot, John Macop, John Corveisor, John Carpenter. The seal, broken, is still attached.

13 Richard II. Grant by indenture (in Latin) by Isabel Batot, of Wynchilse, and John Lamsyn, her son, to William Flecher, of Rye, and Isabel, his wife, of a messuage without the North Gate of Rye, near to the land of Robert Wayte, and the land called " Kyngis-

3 S 4

" wysshe," and the garden of William Hereward; at a yearly rent of 10s. Witnesses, Laurence Lunsford, Mayor, John Baddyng, Bailiff, John Salerne, Stephen Elyot, John Macopo, Richard Tichebourne, John Plumptone, Clerk. The two seals are perfect; one of them, very rude in design, represents a soldier with helmet and shield; the other, apparently, a flower with four petals.

14 Richard II. Release (in Latin) by Matildis de Dene, otherwise called " de Berelynde," of the parish of Badlismere, in Kent, to Richard Tichebourne, of Rye, of all right and claim in the lands late had by her of the gift and grant of John de Hastynge, formerly of Prestone, near Canterbury, as they lie at Berelynde, in the parish of Pesemersshe, " of the tenure of Bromsmythe." Witnesses, Richard de Coumbo, John Hoghet, Walter Sextayn, Simon Sote, John Symonde. " Given at Pese-" mersah." The seal is partly broken; it represents a church with a spire, surmounted by a cross.

14 Richard II. Acknowledgment (in Latin) by William Harry. " Chevaler," and Joan, his wife, formerly wife of Peter Rede, of Dovorre, and executrix of the testament of the said Peter, of the receipt from Joan, widow and executrix of Thomas Tayllour, by the hands of John Gcsebourne the younger, of 25 marks. " Given " on Sunday before the Feast of St. Laurence." Of the two seals appended, a fragment of one only, a shield charged, apparently, with six lilies, is left.

15 Richard II. Grant (in Latin) by Robert Hengxhullo, of Faviresham, and Mabel, his wife, to William Atevante, of Rye, and Margery, his wife, of a piece of land within the liberty of Rye, in a marsh called " Seint " Marie Croft," near to the common land, and the lands of William Blaisworthe, John Salerne, and Joan, relict of Richard Baddyng. The said Robert thereto sets his seal, " and for greater surety in the premises, " I the aforesaid Mabel, of my free will, have caused the " common seal of the Barons of Rye to be set to these " presents, in name of a fine, in testimony of the pre-" mises." Witnesses, John Baddyng, Mayor, Laurence Lunsford, John Bertelot, Robert Dyn, John Plumptone, Clerk. The grantor's seal is whole, though with a very faint impression; of the seal of the Barons—the more recent one, the matrix of which still exists (this being the first time it occurs) with the Virgin and Child,—only a fragment is left. The earlier seal of the " Barons," occurs till the 45th year of the reign of Edward III.

15 Richard II. Obligation (in Latin), whereby William Londoneys, of the parish of St. Margaret, Canterbury (or, perhaps, Kent), William Pylland, of the parish of Boxle, John Waleys, of Boxle, and John Smyth, of Est Mallyng, " mason," of the county of Kent, bind themselves to John Baddyng, of Rye, to the payment of 120l. at the Feast of St. Michael then next ensuing. Three out of the four seals are still attached. The defeasance of this bond, in connexion with some public building, no doubt, is lost.

15 Richard II. Grant (in Latin) by Robert Bocher, son and heir of Peter Bocher, to John Macopo and Alice, his wife, of a vacant place of land, near to the curtilage late of Luke Coupere, and that late of John Randis, and near to the tenement of the heirs of Richard Hwite, and to that of John Prechil; at a yearly rent of 4s. 6d. Witnesses, John Salerne, Mayor, John Baddyng, Laurence Lunsford, John Berttelot, John Plumpton, Clerk. The diminutive seal is perfect, T with a cross above it.

A.D. 1392. Copy of a letter of attorney (in Latin), whereby Ralph Repyndone, Parson of the church of Walesby, in the diocese of Lincoln, appoints John de Ivclich, Clerk, his attorney to receive corporal possession, in the Hospital of St. Bartholomew, at Rye, as set forth in letters patent of Richard, then King of England. " Given in the manor of Wodestoke, on the 9th day of " October." This is evidently a contemporary copy of the original; to which, as the seal of the said Ralph was to many unknown, the seal of " Master Nicholas Slake, " Archdeacon of the church of Welles," was set. To the present document no seal has ever been attached. See under the 19th year of this reign.

16 Richard II. Bond (in Latin) of Richard Bernard, of Rye, to Richard Tychebourne, for 7l. 5s. 4d. A fragment of the seal is left.

16 Richard II. Release (in Latin) by Joan, widow of Thomas Taillour, and Juliana, " daughter and heir of " the said Thomas and Joan," to Robert Parker, of their claim to a piece of land called " Ambroyses-" toune," in the parish of Pleydenne, near to the sea shore on the east, and to the land of Stephen Paulyn, at " Lo " Grene Oke," on the south, the land of Thomas Gold, on the west, " and the land in which Le Gute lies, to the " north." " Given at Pleydenne." Witnesses, Thomas

Bono, Thomas Gold, Thomas Peneherst, Geoffrey and Robert Qwyndrelle. The seal is lost.

16 Richard II. Grant (in Latin) by John Bakere and Agnes, his wife, to John Waryn, of Pleydenne, of the vacant place which they had of the gift and feoffment of Roger Welle, of Kenertone, in the parish of Rye. Witnesses, William Smyth, Geoffrey Quintrelle, John Newestrete, John Elgod, Thomas Forster, John Salesbury. The single small seal is still attached; it represents, apparently, the letter M.

18 Richard II. Grant (in Latin) by William Passhelowe the elder, to William Shypman and Joan, his wife, of a vacant place in the Market, near to the aclds [storehouses or sheds, open at the sides] of Robert Bocher, to the south; which place Robert Mustarder held of him, after it was awarded to him by judgment of the Mayor and Jurats. Witnesses, William Dyn, Mayor, Henry Portour, Bailiff, Richard Tychebourne, Laurence Lounsforde, John Bertelot, John Maffey, Clerk. The seal, representing the letter W, is broken.

19 Richard II. Letter of attorney (in Latin) by Ralph Repyntone, Clerk, official within the King's household, appointing John Dent his attorney, to ask and receive of John Bowetby, of Rye 7l. 13s. 4d., which he had recovered in the King's Court at La Rye. " Given at " Wyndesore, on the 19th day of September." The seal, the impression of which is effaced, has rushes inserted in the wax at the margin. See above under A.D. 1392.

20 Richard II. Release (in Latin) by John Moore and John Mellere, of the parish of Hawekherst, in the county of Kent, to the Mayor and Barons of the vill of La Rye, of all personal actions whatsoever that they may have a right to bring against them. The two seals are lost.

21 Richard II. Grant (in Latin) by Thomas Langelee, of the vill of La Rye, and Joan, his wife, to John Cotiller, vicar of La Rye, and Robert Dysour, of a tenement situate near to those of Henry Nichol, Laurence Lounceford, and the heirs of John Seward; which tenement the said Joan and John Yonge, " Claryoner," her late husband, had of the gift of Laurence Lounceford and Joan, his wife, daughter of John Yvory. Witnesses, John Baddyng, Mayor, Richard Tychebourne, " Lieute-" nant," William Asshe, Bailiff, Laurence Lounceford, William atte Vaute, John Hamon, Jurats, John Maffey, Clerk. The seal of Thomas is still attached; that of " the Community of the Barons of Rye," formerly appended in behalf of his wife, is lost.

21 Richard II. Grant (in Latin) by William Wodeward, of Playdenne, to Robert Edmund, of Rye, and Margaret, his wife, of a place, with the houses built thereon, between the place formerly of Walter Wykham, and afterwards of John Marchame, and the place of Andrew Crokkere, and the land late of John Brok. Witnesses, John Baddynge, Mayor, Robert Dyne, John Langport, Laurence Lunceford, William atte Vaute. The seal is broken, and a fragment only left.

21 Richard II. Grant (in Latin) by Peter Rcade, of Dovorre, son of Peter, to Richard Tychebourne, of Rye, and Joan, his wife, of the lands and tenements in Rye which Peter the elder purchased of Alard Smythe; at a yearly rent of 8s. Witnesses, William atte Vaute, Mayor, William Asshe, Bailiff, John Baddyng, Robert Dyne, John Langeport, John Macop, William Englys. The seal, in red wax, is in fair condition, representing a shield, charged with a fish (probably a dolphin) with waves beneath.

21 Richard II. Letter of attorney (in Latin), whereby Roger Baret appoints John Maffey his attorney, to give seisin to William atte Welle and Richard Chesman, of a tenement situate near to those of the heirs of William Godhewe, of Robert Assendone, and of Robert Dysour, and near the sea-shore, to the south. The seal is whole, but the impression much worn.

22 Richard II. Conveyance (in Latin) by John Radding, Laurence Lounceford, and John Wykham, Wardens of the works of the church of St. Mary in the town of Rye, with the assent of the parishioners, to Robert Dyn, John Langeport, and John Macop, of all lands and tenements, rents and services, belonging to the church, within the liberty of the town, for ever, they appending the seal of their office thereto. Witnesses, William atte Vaute, Mayor, John Hamond, John Bertelot, Walter Englyash, Philip Loonge, William Blayseworthe, John Maffey, Clerk, and others. The seal of the Commonalty of Rye, in almost perfect condition, is still attached; without the galley, as Counterseal, but with a very diminutive impression of a bird, with expanded wings, on the reverse.

22 Richard II. Grant (in Latin) by John Salerno, of Idenne, to Richard Tychebourne, of the vill of La Rye, and Joan, his wife, of 4 acres of land upon the highway leading from Le Hole to Woundenepyrye, and adjoining land of Robert Bocher the elder, called " Wellesfelde." " Given at Le Hole, in the parish of Rye." Witnesses, Robert de Echynghamme, John Chytecroft, William Marchaunt, John As, John Ellertone. The seal is lost.

22 Richard II. Grant (in Latin) by William Kechynore, of the parish of Idenne, and Juliana, his wife, to Richard Tychebourne, of Rye, and Joan, his wife, of a tenement called " Le Hole," and 3 pieces of land and heath belonging thereto, in Rye, which they had of the feoffment of Robert Booher, of Rye. " Given at Le " Hole aforesaid, on the 4th day of October." Witnesses, William atte Vaute, Mayor, John Baddyng, John Chytecroft, John Salerne, William Mot. The two seals are in fair condition ; that of Juliana has the letter J, with a crown above it.

4 Henry IV. Grant (in Latin) by Richard Tychebourne to Robert Onewyn, of his tenement without the North Gate, which he bought of Peter Reede, and of a vacant place bought of William Brekeston, near the lands of John Macop. Witnesses, William Vaute, Mayor, John Langporte, William Longe, John Roberd, Philip Longe, William Shipman, Thomas Longe, Clerk. The seal is lost.

4 Henry IV. Letter of attorney (in Latin) given by John Maffey to Richard Dyn and Robert Bocher, of the vill of La Rye, to deliver to Robert Wevere and Juliana, his wife, daughter of the late Joan Spryner, seisin of the moiety of the lands and tenements which the said John had, together with Richard Wyndesore, of the gift and feoffment of the said Joan; according to the force and effect of a certain feoffment made to the said Robert and Juliana. There is a small seal attached, with the figure of a bird.

6 Henry IV. Grant (in Latin) by Joan, widow of John de Leghe, to John Beegyndone, of the parish of Lyde, of a tenement in Rye, near the vacant place of John Baddyng, late Otrynghames, to the east, and the garden of John Bartelot, to the south, and a place belonging to the said Joan, to the west. Witnesses, John Macope, Mayor, William Vawte, Stephen Wy, John Bartelot, Thomas Longe, Clerk. The seal is lost.

7 Henry IV. Grant (in Latin) by Robert Onewyn to William, Lord of Echyngham, Knight, John de Chitecrofte, and William Longe, of all his lands, rents and tenements, within or without the liberties of the Cinque Ports, in Kent and Sussex, except one virgate in Pesexe. Witnesses, the said William Longe, then Mayor, John Langeporte, Robert Dyne, William Vawte, John Macope, John Robert, Richard de Wermyncham, Clerk. The seal and thong are lost.

7 Henry IV. or V. (qu. which). Grant (in Latin) by Robert Kyng, of Wynchelse, to Walter Yong, Richard Tychebourne, Thomas Longe, and John Colet, of all his rents and services, both within and without the Cinque Ports. " Given at Wynchelse." Witnesses, Vincent Vynch, then Mayor of that place, Robert Fyschelake, Bailiff, John Salerne, John Hewe, Thomas Thondyrre, Robert Burgoyne, Thomas Thondyrre the younger, Alan Kentone, John Barbour. The seal, representing a key and initials, is nearly perfect.

10 Henry IV. A very long indenture (in Latin), as to defeasance of a bond for 100l. given by William Longe, of Rye, to John Salerno, of Idenne ; William Armesty, of Hadle, in Suffolk, and John Avelyn, citizen of London, being likewise bound in a bond for 115l. 12s. to the said William. " Given at Idenno." Witnesses, John Robert, Thomas Longe, Laurence Mersey, William Shipman, Richard de Wermyncham, Clerk. The small seal, with a faint impression of two letters, is still attached.

10 Henry IV. Lease (in Latin) by John Coteler, Clerk, John Botertok, and John Knight " Cowper," to Stephen de Wy, of an acre of land, which they had of the feoffment and gift of William, son and heir of William Bleseworth, the land lying near to that of William Walpol and of William Vawt; and extending lengthwise from the cave [or vault, " antro "] of the vill of Rye, to the land of the said William Vawt, to the north. Witnesses, William Longe, Mayor, John Macope, Robert Dyne, John Langport, John Robert, Laurence Mersey, Richard de Wermyncham, Clerk. Two of the seals are tolerably perfect, the third is lost.

11. Henry IV. Grant (in Latin) by John Salerne, of Idenne, to John Macope, of a parcel of land without the North Gate, near to the land of John Randys, and the lands of John Roper and William Vawt, at a yearly rent of one peppercorn, at the Feast of St. John the Baptist. Witnesses, William Longe, Mayor, John Langport, William Vawt, Philip Longe, Laurence Mersey, Stephen de Wy, Richard de Wermyncham, Clerk. A small seal, with a cross and globe, and I.S., is attached.

11 Henry IV. Grant (in Latin) by Robert Burgoyne, of Wynchelse, to Robert and Roger atte Gate, of all his land and tenements in Wynchelse. " Given at Wyn- " chelse." Witnesses, William Skele, Thomas Yonge, Saunder Bentley, Richard Snaylham, William Nicholle. It has had no seal attached, and being on paper, is probably only a copy of a deed. It is in a mutilated condition.

11 Henry IV. Grant (in Latin) by John Macope and John Langport, Wardens of the church of St. Mary, and of the works thereof, with the assent of the Mayor and community, to Richard Posterfe, of a messuage near the land late of John atte Leagh, now of Robert Onewyn, and lands late of William atte Nesshe and John Bertlot, at a rent of one peppercorn, payable at Easter. Witnesses, William Longe, Mayor, William Vawt, William Shipman, John Robert, Richard de Wermyncham, Clerk. The oblong seal remains, but the device, on a shield under a canopy, will hardly admit of being deciphered.

11 Henry IV. Grant (in Latin) by Peter Hendenne, of Wynchelse, to John Danyelle the elder, and Robert Holdenne, of the same, of all his lands and tenements in the county of Sussex. Given at Wynchelse. Witnesses, Robert atte Gate, Mayor, Robert Fyshlake, Bailiff, John Wottone, William Folde, John Danyelle the younger, Edward Hopyar, John Hopyar. A small seal is attached, in a mutilated state ; a chevron can be distinguished, on a shield.

12 Henry IV. Grant (in Latin) by Joan Tychebourne, widow, to John Coteler, Clerk, John Aas, of the parish of Idenne, and William Brym, of a tenement called " Le Hole," and 18 acres of land and heath thereto pertaining, which, with Richard Tychebourne, her late husband, she had of the feoffment of William Kechynoro and Juliana, his wife. " Given at Le Hole aforesaid." Witnesses, John de Chytecroft, William Marchant, Philip Trody, William Mot, William Passhelew, John Leneham, William Smyth. A seal, representing a cross and circle, is still attached.

12 Henry IV. Letter of attorney (in Latin) by Joan Tychebourne, appointing William Wodewarde and Stephen Wayt, of Saltecote, her attorneys, to deliver seisin to John Coteler, Clerk, John Aas, and William Brym, of the tenement called " Le Hole," and 3 pieces of land and heath, in the parish of La Rye. " Given at " Le Hole," the same date as the preceding. A seal, similar to the preceding one, is attached.

12 Henry IV. Grant (in Latin) by William de Worthe, of the parish of Tenterdenne, to Roger atte Gate, of Wynchelse, and Robert Onewyne, of Rye, of a tenement and 11 acres of arable land, which he purchased of Richard Amery and Thomas, his son, situate on the Denes (Dennas) of Acre and of Hoedene ; also, 30 acres of land inherited from Agnes, his mother in the same parish, on the Dene of Haukeherst, called " Curtland " and " Nederland ;" also, all the lands called " Cornccote," in the tenure [the Court of] of Cornecote. " Given at " Tenterdenne, on the 26th day of March." Witnesses, Stephen Adam, William Godday, John Geffe, John William, John Bate, John do Worthe, Stephen Donett. The seal is lost.

12 Henry IV. Grant (in Latin) by William Acdenne, son of Thomas Acdenne, of the parish of Wystreshamme, in the county of Kent, to Robert Onewin, of the reversion of his lands in the new marsh called " Corboylles- " mersch," near Rye, and also in Seyntemarycrofte, near Rye, as well within the liberty thereof as without, with reversion of all the lands called " Lee," in the parishes of Rye and Pesemersche, formerly belonging to John Paulyn the elder. Witnesses, Thomas Longe, Mayor, John Chytekrofte, John Salerne, Robert Oxenbregge, John Schelle, Laurence Merseye, Thomas Langele, Henry Thorne, Geoffrey Cooke. The seal, a large W, is in a mutilated condition.

13 Henry IV. Bond (in Latin) of William Akeden, of Canterbury, to Robert Onewyn, of Rye, in the sum of 40l., payable within the Octave of St. Michael. His own seal being unknown, he has also procured the seal of the office of the Mayoralty of Rye to be set thereto. The latter seal is lost, the former, apparently representing the letter H, still remains. This is tied with string to the preceding deed.

1 Henry V. Certificate (in Latin) by Stephen Thomme, Clement Treveman, John Wyt, and John Bykynden, " as it is worthy and just with our trusty " neighbour in a trusty cause to certify," that John

Hodynette owes to Reginald Page, their "neighbour,
" of the vill of Redyngge," 61s. 6d. Their four seals
are appended on a thong, one in fair condition, with two
objects resembling love-knots, surmounted by a cross.

3 Henry V. Grant (in Latin) by Nicholas Monyn and
Alice, his wife, of the county of Kent, to John, their
son, of their lands and tenements, rents and services, with the advowson of half the Chantry of St.
Nicholas in the church of St. Mary, at Rye, in the
villa of Wynchelse, Rye, Pesemershe, Brede, and Udymere, which came to Alice after the death of Agnes,
daughter of John Peytevyn, of Wynchelse. Given at
Wynchelse. Witnesses, Roger ate Gate, the Mayor,
Vincent Fynch, Thomas Oxebregge, William Werde,
Stephen Donet. With two small seals, the impressions
partly effaced.

3 Henry V. Power of attorney (in Latin) by Nicholas
Monyn and Alice, his wife, to William Blosmo and
Alan Kyntone, to give seisin to John, their son, of all
the lands, in Wynchelse, Rye, Pesemersh, Brede, Udymere, or elsewhere, which they had conveyed to him,
with the advowson of half the Chantry of St. Nicholas,
as in the preceding. With two small seals, as before.

3 Henry V. Grant (in Latin) by Geoffrey Wodeland,
of the parish of Odymere, to Thomas Wylles, and Alice,
relict of Walter Vynche, of Rye, of land in the parish
of Ikelysham, in the place called "Gregge," which
Robert Herst had of Vincent de Wodelande, for a term
of 12 years: and if they are disturbed in possession
thereof, then they shall take in fee simple the two
pieces of land called "Fogelysham " and "Kokenham."
" Given at Ikelysham, on Sunday after the Feast of
" our Lord's Epiphany." Witnesses, Stephen Echyn-
ton, Robert Tollinstall, Robert Schepherde, Thomas
Schepherde, Simon Bayforde. Of the small seal, representing W., a portion is left.

4 Henry V. Acquittance (in Latin) by William, son
of Thomas Aodenne, of the parish of Wy‡treshamme, of
Robert Onewin, of Rye, for 3l., in part payment of 6l.
The small seal attached, representing W, is perfect.

5 Henry V. Indenture (in Latin), stating that whereas
Thomas Longe and William Schipman had granted
to Richard Londenays, Robert Londenays, and Ralph
Kyrkeby, the tenement which they had lately had, of
the gift and feoffment of Geoffrey Cooke and Agnes, his
wife; yet that it is the will of the said Richard, Robert,
and Ralph, that if the said Geoffrey Cooke, or any one
in his name, shall pay to them, at the Feast of the
Nativity or of St. John the Baptist, next ensuing, 10
shillings, and continued sums of 10 shillings, amounting
in all to a sum of 7 pounds 10 shillings, then the said
deed shall be held as null. Under certain circumstances,
the said Geoffrey is to hold them indemnified against
John Vynhawe, his heirs and assigns. Witnesses,
Robert Onewin, Mayor, John Schelle, John Langport,
John at Wode, Stephen Wy, William Chaloner, Clerk.
The seal, which has a faint impression of a flower, is
broken.

6 Henry V. Grant (in Latin) by Agnes, relict of
Henry Prichett, daughter and heiress of Robert Strode-
man, of Pypesille, to Robert Onwyn, of a tenement in
Pypesille, 4 acres, and one grove adjacent. " Given at
" Pypesille." Witnesses, John Chitecroft, Esquire,
John Wymond the elder, John Brooke, William
Crowche, John Stefene, William Brook, Roger Courteys,
Clerk. The impression of the seal is almost effaced; it
represents, apparently, a sort of decorated cross.

7 Henry V. Grant (in Latin) by John Halle, of Ore,
Esquire, to Henry Dobyll, of Wytreshamme, of the wardship of the lands, and tenements, and person, of Elizabeth, daughter of John Grenewyche, son of Margery Pe-
syndenne, cousin and heir of Joan, sister of Stephen
Paulyn; with the maritage of the said Elizabeth; because the said Joan held lands of him by knight-service
in Potte and Farlegh, in Sussex, on the day of her
death; in return for a certain sum of money paid.
The deed has no witnesses, and the seal is lost.

7 Henry V. Indenture (in Latin), whereby William
Caunvile grants to Robert Onewyn his lands and tenements, with a yearly rent of 55s., a cook and two hens,
which Alice, the late mother of William, received in
the parish of Pesemersh. " Given at Pesemersh, the
" 15th day of March," in the year above-named. The
indenture has no witnesses. The seal, a diminutive
one, with some straggling letters, is perfect.

7 Henry V. Release (in Latin) by John Edstone the
elder, of the parish of Brede, to Robert Onewyn, of
Rye, of his right in a piece of land lying near " Le
" Hole," late of Benedict Andrew. Witnesses, John
Shelle, Mayor, William Longe, Thomas Pere, Stephen

9 Henry V. Grant (in Latin) by John Edstone the
elder, of Brede, to Robert Onewyn, of Rye, of the
lands, tenements, and rents, called "Pypeneselle," in
the parish of Rye, which he had of the gift and feoffment of Robert Webbe. " Given at Pypeneselle." Witnesses, John Wymonde the elder, William Crouche,
John Brokke the elder, John Wymonds the younger,
William Brokke, Richard Brokke, Roger Curteys,
Clerk. The seal is whole, the impression apparently
being the letter I.

1 Henry VI. Bond (in Latin) of John Nevow, of
Rye, to Robert Taylour, of the same, in 4 marks sterling,
payable at the Feast of the Annunciation then next
ensuing. The seal, representing the letter N, is still
attached.

3 Henry VI. Grant (in Latin) by Robert Onewyne
to Henry Dobylle, of Wygtresham, of all those lands
called "Porteamothes landes," containing 10 acres of
marshland " and susannes (fallows)," formerly belonging
to Reginald Portesmowthe, and 15 acres of land in Pes-
mersshe, formerly bought of John Grovere, situate on
the Dene (Dennam) of Esshwydenam, " Given at Pes-
" mersshe, on the last day of September." Witnesses,
John Castwysle, Richard Stewne, William Doraunt, of
Rye, William Wykynge, Thomas Bosne. The seal is
lost.

5 Henry VI. Grant (in Latin) by Thomas Longe to
Simon Remys of a parcel of land, with a cellar beneath,
in the vill of Rye, situate near the land late belonging
to Robert Onewyn, on the east, and the town wall, on the
south, and the little lane leading to the wall, to the
west; at a yearly rent of one penny. Without witnesses; the diminutive seal is still appended, but the
impression is indistinct.

6 Henry VI. Grant (in Latin) by William Batot, of
Wynchelse, and Joan, his wife, to Thomas Longe, of Rye,
of two parcels of land, with one parcel of water lying
between them, in a certain marsh called " Seinte-
" maryescroft," by a certain wall, leading towards
Horlyngdene, and near to the land of the heirs of
Robert Onewyne, and that late of Stephen Wy. Witnesses, Thomas Perys, Mayor, William Broughtone,
Thomas Langle, John Batot, Walter Stoodham. The
small seal, with the impression of the letter I with a
crown, is in fair preservation.

7 Henry VI. Grant (in Latin) by Henry Dobyll, of
Wyghtreshamme, to Joan, widow of Robert Onewyne,
of all the land, called " Portesmowtheslandes," being
10 acres of marsh land, and the " susanne" [fallow]
formerly belonging to Reginald Portesmowthe, in the
parish of Pesemersshe, which he purchased of the said
Robert Onewyne; to her for life, remainder to Robert,
son of the said Robert Onewyne; remainder to Roger
atte Gate, of Wynchelse, if the said Robert shall die
without heirs of his body lawfully begotten. " Given at
" Pesemersshe." Witnesses, Richard Stowne, Richard
Fowgylle, Richard atte Vanne, John Castwysle. The
small seal, in red wax, with the impression of a St.
Andrew's cross, is perfect.

9 Henry VI. Release (in Latin) by John Webbe,
son of Robert Webbe, to Roger at Gate of Wynchelse,
and Robert, son of Robert Taylour, late of Rye, of all
his right and estate in the marsh lands and " susannes,"
which the said Robert Taylour bought of the aforesaid
Robert Webbe, in the parishes of Rye, Udymere, and
the Manor of Brede. " Given at Gatebergh." Witnesses,
Thomas Long, Stephen Langport, Thomas Langley,
William Monte, Thomas Estone, John Wymond,
Thomas Walcok. The seal is mutilated; it represents,
apparently, an animal's head.

10 Henry VI. Grant (in Latin) by Simon Remys to
John Yprys, Esquire, of a tenement, with a cellar
beneath, and a garden, near the land late of Robert
Onewyn, and near the town wall, to the south, and a
lane leading from the high street to the wall, to the
west. Witnesses, William Broughtone, Mayor, Stephen
Bevor, Lieutenant, Thomas Pope, Bailiff, Stephen Langport, Thomas Longe, John Batot, John Gaunther, Richard
Baylly. A small seal, a branch of a tree ending in a
cross, is appended. No consideration is mentioned in
the deed.

16 Henry VI. Demise (in Latin) by Simon Cheyne,
Andrew Wychard, and Robert Pecard, to Richard
Pusterff and Alice, his wife, of a parcel of land, called
" Hetewateris," with a yearly fee-farm rent of 4s.
issuing from a messuage late of Walter Fynche; such
parcel lying near the land of Stephen Bever and
Richard Bayle, and the Chantry land, and the land late
of William Warre; which land and rent they had of

CORPORA-
TION OF
RYE.

the gift and feoffment of William Cheyne and Alianor, his wife, and of John Warenere and Isabel, his wife; at a yearly rent of 12d. Witnesses, Richard Essp[icer], Mayor, Thomas Longe, Thomas Langley, Stephen Bever, John Batot, John Sutton, John Sote. The three seals are left, but the impressions of two are effaced; the third, probably of Andrew Wychard, representing the letter A, surmounted with a crown.

19 Henry VI. Grant (in Latin) by Isabel Hokere to John Cedle, and Joan, his wife, of a tenement and garden without the North Gate, near the garden of Thomas Longe. Witnesses, William Broughton, Mayor, Thomas Pope, Bailiff, Thomas Longe, John Gaunther (Glover), John Suttone, Richard Bayly, John Parys. The small seal, R, with a crown above it, is perfect.

19 Henry VI. Grant by indenture (in Latin) by Simon Cheyne, Andrew Wychard, and Robert Pecard, to John Bayle, of a parcel of land, formerly of John Peylond, near the land of Henry Elyssone, late of William Lyon, and near that late of Richard Alrede, and formerly of Henry Pycott; also, near to land of John Bayle, formerly belonging to Brekstone, and near the stone wall of the town, to the north; the said land having been lately had by them of the gift and feoffment of William Cheyne and Alianor, his wife, and John Warner and Isabel, his wife; at a yearly rent of 4 pence. Witnesses, William Broughton, Mayor, Thomas Pope, Bailiff, Thomas Longe, John Sedley, John Suttone, Richard Bayle, John Comptone, Clerk. The three small seals, in fair condition, are still attached; that probably of Wychard has a capital A; a second, apparently, a flower; and the third is indistinct.

21 Henry VI. Grant (in Latin) by John Sedley to Richard Bayle and John Bayle, of Rye, of a messuage with a garden and croft, without the North Gate, near the road leading to the spring called "Blykewelle," and adjoining the lands of John Parys, and those of the heirs of John Salerne, and of Robert Taylour, and that of John Ypres, and that late of John Seignour; the same messuage having lately belonged to John Munte. Witnesses, William Broughton, Mayor, Thomas Pope, Bailiff, John Suttone, James Sedley, Richard Canon, William Wayte, John Comptone, Clerk. The seal, with the impression of two keys, is still attached.

21 Henry VI. Release (in Latin) by John Sedley to Richard Bayle and John Bayle of all claim to a messuage by the preceding deed granted to them. Some of the witnesses attest, that are named in that deed, and the name of Richard att Wode is added. The seal is appended, as in the other deed. "Given on the Feast of "St. Michael the Archangel." By another deed under seal, attached, the said John appoints James Sedley his attorney to deliver seisin.

21 Henry VI. Indenture of release (in Latin) by Robert Onewyne, otherwise called "Taylour," son of Robert Onewyne, to Richard Putsterffe, of a yearly rent of 2s., for a certain "place of land" in Rye. Witnesses, William Broughton, Mayor, Thomas Pope, Bailiff, John Sedley, John Suttone, Richard Bayle, Richard Canone, John Comptone, Clerk. The seal has the impression of a shield, charged with a chevron, and, apparently 3 mullets. It has the original rush twisted round the thong.

33 Henry VI. Grant (in Latin) by Laurence Dobyll to Thomas Pope, Esquire, of all his goods, live and dead, moveable or immovable, whatsoever and wheresoever; and that this his gift might have full effect, he gave and delivered to the same Thomas, in the name of seisin and possession of all the said goods and chattels, moveable and immovable, one silver spoon. Witnesses, Robert Onwyne, James Sedley, Robert Cocke. The seal is lost.

33 Henry VI. A long deed (in Latin) not attested by witnesses, reciting that whereas Robert Onwyne had, in the 26th year of the same reign, granted to John Fordman, alias Hamond, and Agnes, his wife, his messuage, in Rye, situate near the vacant land belonging to the King, late of Stephen Marchant, and near the town walls and the land of Richard Bailly, at a yearly rent of 2 shillings; he hereby grants to Bartholomew Pollard, William Broune, citizens and grocers of London, and William Wygot, otherwise Somercote, Chaplain, the said rent of 2 shillings, with powers of distress for the same. The seal is lost. This, like various other deeds of this period, was, no doubt, a grant to religious uses.

37 Henry VI. Grant (in Latin), not attested by witnesses, by Robert Onwyne, Esquire, to Robert Dalyngryggc, Esquire, Thomas Brasse, "yoman," and John Brigge, "fyssher," of all his goods and chattels, and all his property, moveable and immovable. No consideration is mentioned, and the seal is lost.

6 Edward IV. Deed indented (in Latin), whereby Babilon Graunford, Esquire, Mayor of the vill of Rye, and the Jurats thereof, with the assent of all the community, grant and confirm to Robert Croche a parcel of land on Le Stronde [the Strand], adjoining the land of William Hille, at a yearly rent of 2 shillings. Witnesses, Richard Fineis [Fiennes] Knight, Lord of Daker, Thomas Echyngham, Knight, Lord of Echyngham, Robert Oxenbrage, Esquire, Thomas Thunder, Mayor of Wynchelse, William Biker, of Brede. This is the counterpart, executed by Robert Croche, and his small seal is still attached. It is endorsed, in an ancient hand "Thys ys the ded of " shoppe of Strond."

24 Edward IV. A deed (in Latin) badly written, whereby Henry Auchier, of Lossenham, in the county of Kent, Esquire, grants to Richard Bayle, son and heir of John Bayle, late of Rye, a yearly rent of 12 pence, arising from a messuage in which the said John lived, "while life was his companion;" such messuage being near the lands of Richard Wynde and William Barneham, and also near to the town walls. The grantee is to pay yearly to the Wardens of the goods of the parish church of St. Mary one penny of lawful English money, to the use of the said church. Witnesses, Adam Oxenbrugge, Mayor, Robert Croche, and Richard Wynde. A small seal, with the impression of, apparently, some animal rampant, is appended.

7 Henry VII. A long deed indented (in Latin), whereby John Floure, of Rye, grants to Richard Brecnoke a parcel of land near the lands late of John Bukherst, now of William Stille and Henry Fletcher; at a yearly rent of 4 pence. Witnesses, William Barnham, Mayor, Stephen Wayte, Thomas Litherlond, John Cheseman, William Estone, Robert Wymond, John Swanne, Common Clerk of the vill of Rye. The seal, of one of the two parties, is apparently intended to represent a shield with a field vert.

7 Henry VII. A deed (in Latin) whereby Edmund Wyble, of Wynchelse, appoints William Estone, of Rye, "Bocher," his attorney to deliver to Adam Oxenbregge, "Gentilman," possession of a tenement of his, in Rye. Part of the small seal, the impression effaced, is still appended.

12 Henry VII. A letter of attorney (in Latin) of Robert Crouche, appointing Henry Stephyne, of Rye, his attorney, to deliver to Clement Adam and John Tylere seisin of the lands and tenements, which, with Thomas Thunder, Richard Davy, of Wynchelsee, and Richard Bergrove, Clerk, Rector of the parish church of Snergate, in the Marsh of Romono,' John Estone, William Bernan, and Alan Crosserd, of Uhorst, in Sussex, deceased, he had had of the gift and feoffment of John Bayle, by deed in the 11th year of Edward the Fourth. The small seal, apparently the letter R, is still appended.

12 Henry VIII. A letter of attorney (in Latin) by the Mayor and Community of the vill of Rye, appointing John Shurley, Esquire, Cofferer of the King's household, and Bailiff of the vill aforesaid, and Nicholas Whyte, their attorneys and proctors, to appear before the King and his Council, and then and there to produce all and all manner of their charters and confirmations thereof, letters patent and close, writs, precepts, ordinances, statutes, acts, and provisions, touching their liberties and privileges, and to claim, prosecute, and defend, the same. A fragment only of the town seal is left.

From the time that the place was plundered by the French in the year 1377, the deeds deposited with the town officials, it will be observed, greatly decreased in number. For some years after that date, but few transfers of lands or houses are recorded; and consequently, the names of the Mayors at this period less frequently come to light than at an earlier date. From the time of Henry the Sixth, the practice of depositing deeds with the officers of the Corporation, gradually fell into disuse. In the great majority of instances, the properties transferred, in the town itself, are only described by their position in reference to the adjoining properties, streets being but rarely mentioned; consequently, the exact locality of them, at the present day, can in but very few instances be identified.

I have, in conclusion, the pleasure of expressing my obligations to C. P. Meryon, Esqre., the Worshipful the Mayor of Rye,—by whose desire, in combination with that of the Town Council, this inspection of the Corporation records has been made,—for his courtesy in placing the whole collection at my disposal for the purposes of inspection, and providing me with every possible facility for a thorough examination of the more

CORPORA-
TION OF
RYE.

ancient portion of them. To G. S. Butler, Esqre., F.S.A., my thanks are also justly due, for the useful informatiou he so readily imparted to me, during my visit, in reference to the past history and antiquities of his native town; a subject which, from his intimate acquaintance with it, he has evidently made peculiarly his own; and upon which a very large amount of additional light, it is hoped, will be found to have been thrown, in the columns of the present Report.

HENRY THOMAS RILEY.

THE CORPORATION OF LYDD, KENT.

By the kind favour of the present Bailiff of Lydd, T. M. Bass, Esq., and owing to the good offices of Henry Stringer, Esq., Town Clerk jointly of New Romney and Lydd, I have had the opportunity of making a lengthened examination of such of the earlier archives of this ancient town as are now known to exist. Broadly speaking, they may be divided into Charters, deeds, and volumes.—

The earliest Charter, probably now no longer in existence, was granted by Edward I., bearing date the 12th of February, in the 18th year of his reign [A.D. 1290], whereby he granted that the Barons of Lyde and Ingemareys [now Dengemarsh], jointly forming a member of the port of Romenhale [Old Romney], should have the same liberties and free customs as the Barons of Romenhale and the other Barons of the Cinque Ports then had; they finding one ship in aid of the service of five ships due from the Barons of Romenhale, as often as summoned to take part in the King's expeditions. This Charter was confirmed by King Edward II.; but his Charter, like the preceding one, probably now no longer exists.

In the Book of Accounts (fol. 142 b), herein-after more fully mentioned, there is an extract, in a hand of the reign of King Henry VI., from Pleas of Juries and Assizes, holden before Hervey de Stanton and other Justiciars Itinerant, at Canterbury, on the Octaves of St. John the Baptist, in the 6th year of the reign of King Edward II. [A.D. 1313], wherein the said Charters are in part recited, and are then allowed in favour of the Barons of Lyde and Ingemareys. To turn now to the Charters that have survived :—

The earliest Charter now existing, in the possession of the Corporation, is a Charter (in Latin) of Inspeximus and Confirmation, dated at Westminster the 12th of July in the 38th year of Edward III. [A.D. 1364]; confirming the said Charter of Edward I. to the Barons of Lyde and Ingemareys, and granted with the object of rectifying any omission by reason of non-user of the privileges therein granted. The seal, of green wax, is much mutilated; but the Charter has a contemporary painting on it of the arms of the Corporation, a church, with a steeple, joined on to the half of a ship of war.

The next are,—a Charter of 1 Richard II., [A.D. 1378] dated 17th February, and similarly confirming that of Edward I. A part of the Great Seal, in green wax, is left.

An Inxpeximus Charter of 13 Richard II., [A.D. 1390] dated 10th of February, confirming a Charter of Edward III., who thereby confirmed a Charter granted to the Cinque Ports in the 26th year of Edward I., 28th of April [A.D. 1298]; and Exemplification thereof, for the men of Lyde and Ingemareys. A fragment of the Great Seal, in green wax, is left.

A Charter of 1 Henry IV., 20th of February [A.D. 1400], confirming the Charter of King Edward I. to the Barons of Lyde and Ingemareys. A fragment of the seal, in green wax, is left.

A Charter of 1 Henry V., 24th of October [A.D. 1413], being a Confirmation of the Great Charter of Edward I. to the Cinque Ports, and extension thereof to the Barons of Lyde and Ingemareys. "Extracted by John Wakeryng " [the then Master of the Rolls] and John Thoralby."

A Charter of 2 Henry V., 18th of January [A.D. 1415], in the same terms as the preceding. Some fragments of the Great Seal, in green wax, are left.

Contemporary copy of a Charter, 4 Edward IV., 25th of March [A.D. 1464], of confirmation to the Barons of the Cinque Ports; reciting the rights of the Cinque Ports in the times of Edward the Confessor and William the Conqueror.

Among the town's papers there is a small, round, black leather box, labelled, erroneously, as containing "An " Inquisition, taken on the death of a man, by the Bailiff " and Jurats of Lydd"; whereas its sole contents are in the shape of a parchment document, dated 1386, bearing reference to a plaint made by the Barons of

Lyde to the Prior of Bilsington (in Kent), in reference to the carrying off of some cattle.

There are several Court-Books, and other business books, still existing, belonging to the 15th, 16th, and 17th, centuries; the entries in which seem to be, in general, of a formal and comparatively uninteresting character. Among them are some leaves of paper, of folio size, which formerly were part of a Register of plaints in Court, for debt and trespass, beginning in the first year of Henry VIII., A.D. 1509. The grounds of action are in each case stated, but in the most succinct form possible.

The town Accounts, (after a few years called the " Chamberlain's Accounts "), begin near the commencement of the reign of Henry VI. : the earlier portion of them, down to the reign of Richard III., being contained in a quarto paper volume of 185 written leaves, bound in limp parchment, (without much attention to the proper chronological sequence of its contents,) if we may form an opinion from the numeration of the pages then added, about the time of James I. The names of the various Common Clerks, by whose hands the entries were successively made, have been found by me, from internal evidence, to be,—William Elis, William Leycroft, Thomas Caxton, Robert Lucas, William Nycolle, and James Bate. From the following summary of its contents, of which, in all, about one sixteenth part has been here extracted, it will be found that they are of singular interest; and of a nature so peculiar and so diversified, as to shew the great importance, in former times, as a member of the Cinque Ports, attached to the town of Lyde and its fishing station of Denge Ness.—In the earlier part of these entries, the gifts recorded as made by the Corporation to men in office, both great and small, must have absorbed a very large proportion of the revenue derived from the " scots," or rates, and taxes under other denominations, which were being continually exacted. Troops of minstrels, attached to the households of the great, and players from the surrounding country, on their own account, were continually visiting the town, receiving largesse and refreshments, bestowed with no sparing hand. The "Boy Bishop," with his companions, came over from New Romney on St. Nicholas' Day each year, (the church of which had St. Nicholas for its patron Saint), and was rewarded with fees and feasting, on an equal scale of liberality. Candles were kept burning in the Common House, on the nights of the Nativity of John the Baptist (Midsummer Day) and St. Peter's Day. Watchfires were lighted upon the shore over and anon, straw, reeds, and wood, being carted thither for the purpose. Men were kept on the watch in the church steeple for days and weeks together, to give first notice of the approach of a foreign foe : early notice of "Frenchmen" being now received from, and now sent to, the other Cinque Port towns. Frequently we read of "cries made," or proclamations, at the church-style, on the necessity of calling in the cattle from the fields, possible marauders being, no doubt, near at hand. Soldiers are quartered upon the town from time to time; broils and "debates" arise in consequence, and, with frank avowal, the bribes are entered in the book which were paid to their officers to get rid of them. The Bailiff and Jurats take refreshment occasionally, while in council, at the Common House, the charges being defrayed out of the town moneys: but, with a commendable simplicity, they are mostly contented with dry bread and a draught of either ale or beer, (a distinction between the two beverages being clearly drawn). Deputations of the Bailiff, Common Clerk, and Jurats, are continually leaving the place, on horseback, for the transaction of the town's business, at London, Dover, Sandwich, or Canterbury; one of such deputations even following Jack Cade to London, with the present of a porpoise; in order, no doubt, to conciliate his favour, in case he should finally get the upper hand. The Lieutenant of Dover Castle sits in session of Court of Admiralty from time to time upon the sea-shore; supper on the one day is duly followed by dinner on the next, and the items of the bill of fare are placed before us. Wrestling-matches appear in these entries; one at Brookland in particular on a Sunday, some members of the Corporation being in attendance, and handsomely rewarding the victor. Proclamations are made against tennis and dice-playing, to induce the youth of the town to turn to bow and arrows, and other manlier recreations. The town guns are continually under repair, or being dragged on sledges to the sea-side, to the Gote (Gut), or to the Ness; indeed, on one occasion the towns-folk turn to making their own gun, and the items of expenditure "Abowte the gunne, the Serpen-

CORPORA-
TION OF
LYDD.

"tyne" appear in long detail. Items also for equipping and provisioning the townships, supplied to the royal navy from time to time, frequently appear. In accordance with the provisions of the "Customall of Lyde," a thief has his ear nailed to a door, to check his lightfingered proclivities. Pleased with the novelty of the sight, and true to the kindly feeling which in those days was evidently its characteristic, the Corporation bestows 8 pence upon "the man who came through with "the dromedary." The incoming Mayor and Jurats were chosen at varying times in the year; though latterly St. Mary Magdalen's Day (22nd of July) seems to have been the time fixed upon for the Bailiff's election. Among contemporary names of the great, those of the Earls of Warwick and Arundel most frequently occur. Humphrey, Duke of Gloucester, Earl Rivers, and the Earl of March, also appear.

In the early part of the volume, there are numerous items as to the building of the "Common House," or place of meeting for the Corporation, a structure built of wood only. Towards the close, however, items appear in reference to the building of a "Court House," a more substantial structure evidently, but now no longer existing. In these times, as indeed down to a recent period, the church tower was surmounted by a steeple; and from some entries in the volume, it would appear that the belfry was a wooden fabric in the churchyard; similar perhaps to the remarkable belfry of that nature still surviving in the neighbouring parish of Brookland. The church bells too are frequently mentioned, and the church organs at times.

To proceed now with extracts of some of the more characteristic passages:—

Apart, and by itself, on the flyleaf of the earliest written portion of the book, there is (in Latin) the following remarkable entry:—"On Thursday, the 17th "of August, in the 7th year of King Henry the Sixth "[1429], came here Joan, the mistress (concubina) of "Thomas Frenshe, Parish Clerk of Lyde, from the side "of Dengemershe, being the wife of William Mardone, "daughter, as she says, of the late Sir John Hille, "Knight, of the county of Somerset, before William "Sharley the elder, Bailiff there, and William Bate "and other Jurats, and other trustworthy persons "[named]; who was examined upon divers matters and "charges: which Joan there made oath upon the Book, "touching the Holy Evangelists of God, that she would "go out of the liberty of the vill of Lyde, and never "enter again the liberty aforesaid, nor approach that "liberty within 7 miles of the same, on pain of perpetual "imprisonment; and so she departed."

Accounts 6, 7, Henry VI. (1428, 9):—These accounts begin, with a Pentameter in Latin:—

"Assit principio Sancta Maria meo." [Here at my outset may Saint Mary be.]—"Given to the players of "Romene, who shewed their play here 13s. 4d. For "bread, wine, and ale, for the players 5s. 5d. For wine "for a valet of the Crown, who brought a letter here 6d. "Given to a herbyiour [harbinger, or billet-master,] of "the Lord Salysbury, that he might prevent the soldiers "from coming hither 8s. 8d. Paid the Vicar, in part "payment for the organs 13s. 4d. Paid by the hands "of the Jurats of Lyde for drink of the Bishop from "Romene, and other men of the same town, who came "here with him, on St. Nicholas Day, 4s. 3d." This was the "Boy Bishop," who, in honour of the festival of St. Nicholas, 6th December, yearly visited this town, from New Romney, down to the reign of Richard III., if not later.—"Paid for 3 wylde malardys given to Derell "Esquire, when he was here, in name of the common-"alty 10½d. For fish given to him 12d. Paid for 2 "heryns (herons) for the Seneschal of Dover, in name "of the commonalty 14d." The accounts were presented by the Jurats to the commonalty this year on a Sunday, and on the same day the Jurats for next year were chosen: most business transactions, in general, take place on a Sunday, almost throughout the book.

7, 8, Henry VI. (1429, 30).—"Received from Simon "Hayton, for a certain rebelliousness in words against "the Jurats 10s." Jo⁻ ⁻Selvyr pays 12d., and Thomas Hykke 5s., for the like offence. The "Common House," or place for Corporation meetings, was being built this year, and this Account is full of the items: it was, evidently, built of wood.—"Paid for bread and ale for the "Jurats and commonalty at the muster 10d." — See what is a continuation, probably, of this Account, (fols. 49 and 153 of the volume) in the sequel.

8, 9, Henry VI. (1430, 1).—"Given to the players of "Romene, who shewed their play here on Sunday after "the Feast of the Nativity of John the Baptist, the "Account day 6s. 8d. For their expenses, and those of

"others with them, in bread, wine, and bere 2s. 8d. Given "to the players of Rokynge [now Ruckinge] shewing "their play here, on Saturday after the Feast of Relics "[third Sunday after the Feast of St. John the Baptist] "6s. 8d. For a candle burning in the Common House, "on the nights of St. John and St. Peter 2d. Paid at "Romene, on the Account day, towards the repair of "Illesbroge 9d." This was a wooden bridge over the river Rother, about a mile from Romney. The channel of the river has been for centuries filled up; and the site of the bridge is now partly a cornfield. Items for its repair repeatedly occur in this book.—"Paid the min-"strels of the Duke of Gloucester, when they came "here, as a courtesy 6s. 8d." This item occurs yearly, down to the time almost of Humphrey's death.—"Paid "Andrew Heyne, for riding to Sandwich, to get a Clerk "there for the Parish of Lyde 2s. 6d." In place probably, of the delinquent, Thomas Frenshe, already mentioned.— "Paid the ship's cook, for his labour 3s. 4d." The ship which the people of Lyde were bound to supply, as their contribution to the King's navy. In every year's account, also, mention is made of payment of the "fifth "penny," which the town had to pay as a member with New Romene, which contributed to the Crown the other four fifth parts of a sum assessed, towards the expenses of the navy.—"Paid the relict of Honywode for the "expenses of the herbyiour [harbinger] of the Lord "Marshal of England 12d. To the relict of John "Thomas, for a swan given to the Seneschal of Dover "3s. 4d. To William Bate, for a bulloke for the ship "18s. Paid for a letter from Dovorre to arrest the "men who came from beyond sea, without leave and "without billets, and for crying the same 5d. Paid "the Vicar on the old debt for the organs 6s. 8d. Given "to Janyn the Pursuivant [le Pursewant] of Sir Elias "Lynot, as a courtesy 21d. For a pair of bellows for "the Common House 3d. Expenses upon the Seneschal "of Dovorre in the house of the relict of John Hony-"wode 8s. 6½d. Fish sent and given to the Lieutenant "of Dovorre, for having his friendship 2s. Rushes for "the Common House, against the Feast of St. John the "Baptist. For 2 heronsewys [heronshaws, or young "herons] sent to the Seneschal of Dovorre 18d. To "William Bate, for cheese bought for him for the ship, "last year 3s. 4d."

9, 10 Henry VI (1431, 2).—"The Jurats of this year "lent Thomas Dygone [probably the person elsewhere "called 'Thomas Box'] 5 marks from the common "purse, when going to the Northsee, and he repaid the "same well and trustily, and paid as increase thereon 7s. "Given as a courtesy to the minstrels of the Lord of "Gloucester, when here on Saturday before the Feast "of St. Margaret.—For making the trendille of wax "6s. 8d." The trendille was probably a wheel, or corona, used in the church, with wax candles on it.—"Expenses "of the Jurats in the house of Thomas Bate 4d. For a "swan from Richard Clement, and for wildefowle, "sent to the Seneschal of Dovorre, for having his "friendship 2s. 5d."—The horse and the man, carrying the swan and "wildefowle," cost 1s.—"Expenditure "by the hands of Stephen Lestell and Robert Williams, "upon the voyage of our Lord the King, coming "from Calais to England, from Thursday before the "Purification of the Blessed Virgin Mary to Tuesday "before the Feast of St. Valentine the Martyr.— "First, for a ship for that voyage 23s. 4d. Pay of "7 sailors 26s. 8d."—The items are continued at further length; the vessel so hired being part of the Lydd's escort. The vessel was hired at Rediuge (a place near Tenterden); William Broker received 1s. for hiring it, and it lay at the Camber; a name which seems then to have been given to the coast extending between Lydd and Winchelsea; (the "Cambor Farm" still exists, near Lydd).—"Spent for bread, wine, and ale, given to the "Bishop of St. Nicholas, from the vill of Romene 5s. 7d. "For one plays [plaice] sent to the wife of Richard "Ildeshalgate by the Jurats 4d. Given to the players "of Romene, on the Eve of the Apostles Peter and "Paul, shewing their play here 6s. 8d."

10, 11 Henry VI. (1432, 3).—"For wine given to John "Shelley, on the day of St. Margaret the Virgin, for "having his counsel 6d. Paid Cokke, the smythe, for "ironware for the Common House 3s. 4d. Expended "upon the Seneschal and Ralph, and their servants, "being here on the Feast of St. Michael the Arch-"angel, for having a verdict upon an inquest of the "Admiralty; first, for meat 23d. For wylde fowle "and one capone 11d. For fish 5d. For bread, ale, "and fuelle, and the horses' dinner 4d. For spices, "the cook, and the wynders [of the spit] 7d. For a "quart of sweet wine 3d. Paid for meat for the Lieu-

CORPOR-
TION OF
LYDD.

" tenant of Dovorre when here at supper, on Corpus
" Christi Day 2s. 4d. Bread 19d. Wine 5s. 8d. Ale
" 2s, Three capons 15d. Spices 6d. Wood, vinegar,
" and milk 5d. Sending the horses of the Lieutenant
" from the Camber to Lyde, and back again 10d."—to
return to Dover by sea.—" For letyr for the horses 4d.
" Paid the cook and the servants, for their trouble 8d.
" Paid the pagis [pages] for watching the Lieutenant's
" horses here, when he was at Wynchelse 20d. Paid
" for 4 herynsewys [heronshaws] sent to the Seneschal
" of Dovorre in the name of the community, and for
" carriage of them 3s. 4d. For the man's trouble, who
" took them 6d. On the Day of Saint Anne, the mother
" of Mary, in the 11th year of King Henry VI., the
" Jurats lent out of the common purse to William Bate,
" of Lyde 9 li; for which sum John Baker and William
" Melele bind themselves, their heirs, and executors,
" and all their goods, wheresoever they may be found,
" to pay the same to the said Jurats, upon a fortnight's
" warning, without any delay."

11, 12 Henry VI. (1433, 4). "Given to the Common
" Serjeant of the vill of Romene, as a courtesy [' curi-
" ' ositate ' is the word generally used in this sense]
" 4d."—Fish, 3 hernesewys, and a swan, are also sent
to the Seneschal of Dovorre, " in the name of the Com-
" monalty."—" Expended on the minstrels of the Duke
" of Gloucester, on the 17th of July 17d. For candles
" burning in the Common House on the night of the
" Nativity of St. John the Baptist 1d."

12, 13 Henry VI. (1434, 5).—" Expenses upon the
" Lord of Crowthorne when here at Lyde, on the day
" of St. Mary Magdalen.—Bread 4d. ' Wine 4s. 1d.
" Moat 11d. 2 capons 14d. Fish ; 2 plaice 6½d. Paid
" Richard Hamone for one plaice 3d. Richard Jan
" for one plaice 2d. For spices 2½d. Powdered ginger
" 2d. For fuel —. Given as a courtesy to the minstrels
" of the Duke of Northfolk, when here on the Feast of
" All Hallows 5s. Paid for the expenses of Thomas
" Wynday and others who were at Romeno on the day
" of St. Nicholas the Bishop, at the Brodhill there 1s.
" For fish given to the Lieutenant, when sitting at
" Romene for the Admiralty 11d. For one potel of
" sweet wine, given to the Lieutenant and Seneschal,
" when they came from Wynchelse 6d."

13, 14 Henry VI. (1435, 6).—" Paid by the hands of
" William Smyth, in the name of all the Jurats, for
" one breakfast [jantaculo] given to the Seneschal of
" Dovorre and the Common Clerk there, for having
" their friendship in a case touching the community
" of Lyde, in the month of August etc. 5s. 4d. Paid
" for the expenses of nine Jurats and the commonalty,
" riding to the Archbishop of Canterbury, for the matter
" of John Dyne, who beat Sir William Loue, late Vicar
" of the church of Lyde, which John was put in the
" stocks 2s. 9d. Paid to William Leycroft, the Common
" Clerk, going to Rome, for his salary for half a year,
" with leave of all the Jurats and the commonalty
" asked and obtained, who began his journey on Mon-
" day after the feast of our Lord's Epiphany 13s. 4d."
—Immediately after this entry, Leycroft being now
absent, the hand changes in which the entries are
made.—" Allowed John Galwey for 4 heronsewys given
" to the Lieutenant 2s. 8d. Paid expenses on the day
" of muster, that is, for 2 days 15d. Paid expenses at
" Wynchelse, for hiring a ship 5s. 4d." Among the
stores for the ship are :—" Butter bought for the ship
" 15½d. One cheese [casu] for the ship 9d. Dishes
" and platris, and one bolle [bowl] for the ship 6d. To
" 2 men working at the ship on Rogation Day 8d. For
" one tabilcloth bought for it 12½d. Paid the herby-
" jour of the Earl of Saresbery, when here 3s. 8d. Paid
" the minstrel of William Warbilton, when he was here
" 6s. 8d. Expended upon the Lieutenant, on St. Barna-
" bas' Day ; first for meat 12d. For chekyns 6d. Bread,
" ale, and fuelle, 18d. 3 potelles of wine 10d. On the
" Tuesday following, for a supper to the Lieutenant ;
" first, for bread 5½d. For ale 18d. Wine 12d. Meat
" 20d. Chekyns 4d. Fish 2d. Spycerie 2½d. Oats 6d.
" Hay and litere 3s. 4d. A table for 3 men 14d. Ex-
" penses incurred by Thomas Wynday : first, a pipe of
" sithir [cider] 9s. Carriage thereof 9d. Half a pipe of
" cider 5s. Bread and ale 1d. Fish 2d. Fuel for tallowing
" the ship 3d. Garleke and onyns 2d. For writing this
" account for the half year 4s. 6d. Paid for expenses
" incurred upon Roger Twissynden, in the matter of
" Nicholas Shallwell 21d."

14, 15 Henry VI. (1436, 7).—" Paid a man for bring-
" ing a letter here from the King, for shipping to watch
" the sea 5d. Paid to John the Pursewant for carrying
" to Dovorre Castle an answer on the matter aforesaid
" 20d. Paid for 2 horns bought for the wachemen

" 3s. 4d. Expended upon Horne, bailiff of the Lord
" Archbishop of Canterbury, when he was here on the
" matter of Shalwell 7d. For a potelle of wine given
" to William Sevaunte Esquire, for having his friend-
" ship 4d. To a man for carrying a letter hither from
" Dovorre Castle, for the King of Portugale ; and for
" expenses upon him, and for 2 cries made for the King
" 6d. Richard Glover paid, by appointment of the
" Jurats, for expenses incurred upon the auditours, the
" croysour [crozier, or cross-bearer], and clerk of the
" kitchen, of the Lord Archbishop of Canterbury, when
" here, 21d. For bread and ale, when the Jurats sat
" on the Rype, to view the mustour 7d. For a letter
" sent here to arrest ships, for crossing over to Flanders
" 5d. The same Richard Glover paid for expenses at
" Canterbury, when there with the Lieutenant of
" Dovorre to excuse this town from the voyage, on
" passing over into Flanders 7s. 6d. Given, as a courtesy,
" to Thomas the Clerk of Wynchilse, when here on the
" day of the dedication of the church, and throughout
" the week 20d. Lent to the fabric [or woodwork] of
" the new belfry 3½i. 6s. 8d."

15, 16 Henry VI. (1437, 8).—" Paid Thomas Wynday
" for 2 lodys of ryse [twigs] bought for the tynyng
" [dividing] of the bassels [butts] 2s. 8d. Paid the ex-
" penses of all the Jurats when they were together,
" when the soldiers made the bate [dispute] with
" Thomas Hugheyne 13d. For a gallon of wine, given
" to the knight [militi] who was in the house of James
" Ayllewyne, at his supper, that we might have his
" friendship 8d. For another gallon of wine, given to
" the knight who was in the house of Thomas Atte
" Bregge, and other expenses upon him 19d. For
" another gallon of wine given to the said knight, and
" to the esquire of the Earl of Warwick, in the house
" of James Ayllewyne 8d. For the pay of the warde-
" men and expenses incurred upon them, when they
" watched for the soldiers aforesaid 2s. 10d. Expenses
" incurred by Thomas Atte Bregge and Richard
" Glovere, when at Wynchilse, for two days, with the
" Earl of Warwyke, to get a discharge for the soldiers,
" that they might pass out of this town 4s. 6d. Given
" to the harbyjour [harbinger, or billet-master] of the
" Lord Earl of Warwyke, coming here from Wynchil-
" see the first time, to make cry here, that no soldier
" was to take anything without well paying for it, and
" to see as to the bate [dispute] that was here between
" the men of this town and the soldiers 6s. 8d. Given
" as a courtesy to the trumpet, the clerk, and the valet,
" of the same harbyjour 3s. Given to the esquire of
" the knight who was in the house of James Ayllewyne,
" that he might pass on to Wynchelse, for the said
" harbyjour to come here 3s. 4d. Given to the said
" harbyjour of the Earl of Warwyke, for his pains,
" when he came here to discharge the soldiers 6s. 8d.
" To the clerk of the herbyjour, as a courtesy, 2s. To
" the valet of the same herbyjour, as a courtesy 8d.
" Expended on the supper of the said herbyjour, the
" same night 5d. For dinner and supper of the herby-
" jour and his servants 20d. For the paper bought for
" making belettes 1d. Paid for peace being made be-
" tween the town of Lyde and the soldiers, and for the
" debate [strife] between this town of Lyde and those
" soldiers, by ordinance of the same Earl and Sir An-
" drew Hogard, Knight 20s. Paid for expenses upon
" the men of Romene, when they shewed here the sporte
" [probably, wrestling] on St. Matthew's Day 14d. Paid
" the Common Clerk of the town of Romene, who
" brought a letter for the rescue of the Castle of
" Gynys [Guynes, near Calais] 6d. For the dinner of
" a man going over to the Ness [Dengeness], to cry
" and shew the same letter to the fishermen there 2d.
" To Robert Glovere, for riding to the Lieutenant at
" Dovorre, for him to excuse the town of Lyde from
" the voyage for the Castle of Gynys 6s. For wine
" given to John Derelle, when he came here for the
" goods of the Vicar of Newechirche, arrested here 6d.
" Expended on the Lieutenant, when here on Wednes-
" day before the Feast of St. Margaret, and for the
" expenses of a Queste [Inquest] before him the same
" day, of 18 men :—For bread 3s. 4d. Ale 2s. 6d. Beer
" [' birra,' as distinguished from ' cervisia '], 2s. 6d.
" Wine 2s. 7d. Meat 2s. 8d. Capons 18d. Spices 9d.
" Fish 2s. 1d. Oats 4s. 10d. Hay 2s. 4d. Paid the
" cook for his trouble 6d. For wood 5d. The turnspit
" 2d. Butter and eggs 4d. Salt, vinegar, and wash-
" ing the cloths, 6d. Paid a woman for cleaning the
" vessels, 2d."

16, 17 Henry VI. (1438, 9).—" Expended upon the
" commonalty of Lyde, and on the men of the town of
" Romene, when here on the morrow of St. Laurence,

"when the fray was at Promhill 3s. 4d. Paid for send-
"ing back a returne to Dovorre Castle of a letter sent
"here for Geoffrey Haeilwode, a poor man 20d. Ex-
"penses upon delivery of grain to the poor at the
"Feast of Christ's Nativity 6d."—Mention is made
of gifts of corn to the poor, yearly, at Easter and
Christmas, almost down to the end of the book—temp.
Richard III. The "minstrels [mimi] of the Duke of
"Gloucester" visited the place twice, according to the
Account of this year, in August and the following July.

17, 18 Henry VI. (1439, 40).—"For samone and salt
"fish that was bought for a Queste of 18 men,
"being at Romene before the Lieutenant of Dovorre
"3s. 2d. For one turbutte and mullettes bought 7d.
"Expenses incurred in obtaining 4 eels given to the
"Lieutenant there, at the same time 14d. For 2 tur-
"buttes given to him there 12d. Given to a certain
"clerk of the Lady of Bukholte, who came here, being
"sent by her to be Parish Clerk 3s. Paid for one
"cunghar [conger] given to the Lady of Ecchingham
"2s. Paid for wine given to the steward of the Arch-
"bishop of Canterbury, when at Lyde, to have
"his friendship 2s. Paid a clerk for warning the poor
"as to the grain to be given and delivered to them at
"Easter 3d. Expenses incurred at Dovorre, upon an
"inquisition there about the alyons who were here;
"the Constable and Common Serjeant being then
"there, 2s. 4d. Paid a man who carried a letter from
"Dovorre for the money of the alyons, 4d. Expenses
"of the Common Serjeant carrying up that money to
"Dovorre 9d. For hire of a horse to Dovorre, when
"the money of the alyons was carried thither 8d."—
After this date, charges for carrying the aliens' money
to Dovorre, repeatedly occur: the object being, no
doubt, that it might not be employed in the purchase
of shipping, or other materials, to the public detriment.
—"For 3 herynsewys [heronshaws] sent and given to
"the Seneschal of Dovorre and Ralph of Le Chekkere
"[the Exchequer], for having their friendship for the
"town 2s. Paid Thomas Jan, for 13 lb, of wax bought
"for the trendylle 8s. 8d. Paid the same Thomas for
"making the said trendylle 2s. 6d. To William Ley-
"croft [Common Clerk] for composing this account 4s."

18, 19 Henry VI. (1440, 1).—"Given to a man who
"was a prisoner, from Wynchilse, passing through all
"the Ports, for the pety raunssone 8d."—a prisoner
collecting the ransom money, which he had engaged
to pay.—"Expended here upon the said prisoner 7d.
"Given to the players of Wytesham, shewing here
"their play, in the month of June 6s. 8d. Given to the
"players here from Romene 6s. 8d. Expenses incurred
"upon the players, in the house of James Ayllewyne
"4s. Paid for one 'alfta' [? cup] for the common
"house, bought of Henry Lucas 15s. For drink for
"the Jurats, when they sat together 5d. Given to the
"players from Herne, shewing their play here 7s.
"Paid for hire of a horse to carry to the Seneschal of
"Dovorre one cowpull of senetys [cygnets] sent to him,
"for having his friendship 8d."

19, 20 Henry VI. (1441, 2).—"Expenses incurred
"upon Wraby, cross-bearer of the Lord Archbishop of
"Canterbury, when here 3s. 4d. Paid to William
"Lestell, going over to Crotay 3s. 4d. Given to a
"man, who brought hither one bucke, sent by the
"Archbishop of Canterbury to the men of Lyde 20d.
"For spices bought for baking the same bucke 6d.
"For the baking of it 4d. Paid to John Fermour for
"a letter from Dovorre Castle, for the expedition to
"Crotey, 4d. Paid the same John for carriage of the
"things to the Camber, of the men who were chosen
"for the expedition to Crotey 8d."

The following is the next Account, on the same leaf
as the preceding one; four years being here omitted,
some of which will be noticed in the sequel:—

24, 25 Henry VI. (1446, 7).—"For red wax for seal-
"ing an acquittance by the men of a ship of Hulle, for
"the town 1d. For the expenses incurred about Ri-
"chard Clitherowe, Esquire, and by the Jurats of this
"town, he being Commissioner of our Lord the King,
"for goods lost in the sea by the Bishop of Chichester
"4d. For wildefowle sent to Neteham, Clerk of
"Dovorre Castle, to have his friendship about the said
"matter of Richard Clitherowe 7d. For the expenses
"of Richard Aleyn and his horse, riding to the said
"castle, to obtain advice that the said Richard Cle-
"therow was not to sit here; and he did not, 8d.
"Paid Stephen Elys an old debt, on the voyage of the
"Lady Isabel, Queen of England 16d."—This debt
must have been owing more than 40 years.—"Paid
"William Melale, late Constable of this town, for a
"letter coming for the Shepway to be held by the

"Duke of Gloucester; which was not held by him, 4d.
"For one cowpull of frankyd swannys sent to our Lord
"the Archbishop of Canterbury, he then being and
"lying at Maydenstone, to have his friendship for the
"whole of the town 8s. Also, paid for ledyng up of
"the same cowpull, and for a nothir cowpull sente to
"hym 4s. 4d. Given to a minstrel of Sir James Say,
"being at Lyde 3s. 4d. Paid for making the buttys
"against the day for play 9s. 2d." The later part of
this Account is entered wholly in English, for the first
time; it being largely occupied with,—"The expenses
"made by the steryng [stirring] of Sir Andrew Aylle-
"wyn aganys the towne." This "Sir Andrew" was
the late Vicar of the town: one of the long items runs
thus :—"Also, the charuge Sir Andrew procuryd that
"William Bette was arestyd in Londone, as we sup-
"pose, for 2 thousand marke, for the Archedekyns
"Officiall eware ther that the Archedekyn of Canter-
"bury ne he knew not therof. The costes and expensis
"at that tyme made for counsell to be had for to have
"the feturs of yrone of his leggys, and for [to] come
"out of prisone, comyth to 40s. And the aside prisone-
"ment [made] grete harme and scathis to the towne."
Another extraordinary item is as follows :—"And also,
"the sayd maynetenours that caused this good soo to be
"spendid awaste, sayn and enformyth the comyns that
"the snorne man toke a false quarell; the whiche
"shulde desire Maistur William Habbenge, and none
"other, for her Vykero. Whereto we say and reporte
"us upon the bille of poticyon putte to oure Lord of
"Canterbury, that we desired a Vicare here resident.
"And nought only him, but if the lawe wolde geve
"hit hym, to the whiche we mygte not say nay by
"right if the lawe wille yeve hit hym."—This does not
seem very intelligible.—"Also we, sworne men, certifie
"you comyners, that this forsaid goode hadde never
"be spendid ne witholde, nade be Sir Andrew and his
"mayntenaunce beyng in this towne. For we reporte
"us to the most parte of you, that we uolde nevyr
"have goo owte of towne therfore, nade we be com-
"pelled ther too, that we moste nedys doo hit."

25-27 Henry VI. (1447-9).—"For expenses incurred
"at London, when William Smyth and Thomas Jan
"were there, and at Croydon, before the Lord Arch-
"bishop of Canterbury, on the 1st of August 23s. 4d.
"Given to the minstrels of the Lord de Say [Constable of
"Dover Castle] as a courtesy, when here at Lyde, 2s.
"For the carriage of one cowpull of swans to Dovorre.
"given to Ralph Toke, Mayor of Dovorre, to have his
"friendship for the town, paying for the horse 8d. For
"the carriage of 2 cowpull of swans, given to Gervase
"Clifton, Lieutenant of Dovorre Castle, to have his
"friendship to the town 4d. For oats given to the
"swans by Richard Aleyn 8d. Paid to John Walter,
"of the parish of Brokeland, for 9 hernesewys sent to
"Ralph Toke, to have his friendship for the persons
"that were indicted, 6s. 8d. Given to the minstrels
"of our Lord the King, as a courtesy 6s. 8d. Delivered
"to the Churchwardens of Lyde, for expenses upon
"the hangyng of the bells 53s. 4d. Paid John Bate
"and Laurence Elys their expenses at London, about
"the bells 9s. 10d. Paid Henry Aleyn for one cowpull
"of fat oygnets, and John Bate the elder for another
"cowpul of cygnets, sent to the Lord Archbishop of
"Canterbury 6s. 8d. Paid the expenses incurred upon
"ledyng up the said 2 copull of cygnets to Lambe-
"hethe, given to the said Archbishop, while there
"5s. 6d. For capons and fish given to Ralph Toke,
"the Marshal, and the Seneschal, of the Castle 3s. 9d.
"Given to minstrels of the Archbishop of Canterbury,
"and of the Lord de Say, as a courtesy 3s. 4d. Deli-
"vered to William Groce, common servant [or serjeant]
"to the town, for riding to Sandwich, to know when the
"men of that town would come to the ship 20d. Paid
"to James Buye for a horse drawing a cart to Sandwich,
"with the harneys, taken thither for the ship 16d.
"Paid the wife of John Ayllewyne for the expenses
"of the minstrels of our Lord the King, when here in
"the month of July, 2s. 3d. Paid for 4 lambs given to
"the Lieutenant of Dovorre, when his ship lay at the
"Broke Ende 3s. 4d. Given to the minstrels of the
"Lord de Say, being here in the Court house [Curia]
"20d. Given to — Yerthe, harbyjour of the King, for
"having his friendship, so that he might not assign
"many soldiers to this place 6s. 8d. Paid Matthew
"Turgis, for bote-hire from Sandwich to Romene—
"bryngyng home of gere of men of this towne, goyng
"in the ship 21d. Paid for wine given to the Lord
"of Powys, here on two occasions 15d. Expenses
"incurred by James Ayllewyne and Henry Alayn,
"riding from Lyde to Appuldre, and from thence

" to Wynchelse, to speak with Erthe, the King's harby-
" jour 2s. 2d."

28 Henry VI. (1450).—" For bread and ale had on
" the Rype, on the day of the muster 5½d. Paid for
" one horse to Dovorre, ledyng up thedir bred and
" flessh, what tyme the Luetenant sent hedir for men
" to kepe the Castell of Dovorre 8d. For a pound of
" candles burning in the Common House, the night of
" St. John the Baptist 2d. Paid at Hethe, ther baytyng
" the Juratys and comyners sent to Dovorre, for to
" kepe the Castelle ther, by the prayer of the Luetenant
" 2s. 8d. Paid at Romene, in drynkyng ther, as they
" come ridyng homeward 4d. For drinking in the
" house of John Saulys the same evening, when they
" came home 8d. Given to 2 men bringing a letter from
" the Captain, at the suit of Henry Lucas 2s. Paid
" John Benet for a horse, on which John Fermour the
" younger, the Constable, rode to Assheforde—for to
" aspye tythynge [tidings] of the Capitayne of the oste
" 4d."—An allusion to Cade's rebellion, the " Captain "
being the name by which he was generally known.—
" Expenses at Assheforde, of the said Constable, at the
" same time 1d. Paid Thomas Buntyng for a cry. on
" the peace between the King of England and the King
" of Scots and the Flemings 1d. For 2 other cries for the
" mustur to be made 2d. Paid a man bringing a letter
" from Dovorre Castle, sent through all the ports, that
" the save-condid [safe-conduct] be not broken 4d.
" Given to a man who brought a letter hither from the
" King 4d. For wine given to Geoffrey Godeloke at
" Romene, being (sent) there by the Jurats and com-
" moners, when Christian was killed by the men of
" Romene 8d. Paid for one purpoys, sent to the Captain
" by the Jurats and commoners 6s. Paid for the hire
" of one horse, ledyng up the said purpoys from Heri-
" etysebam to Londone to the Capitayn 12d. For the
" hire of a horse that John Menewode rode uppon to
" Londone the same tyme, for to helpe to present the
" purpoys to the Capitayn 14d. Paid for an horse
" hire (sic) that Richard Alayn rode uppon from Lyde
" to Londone, with the purpoys 20d. For expenses the
" same time, in ledyng uppe of the purpoys 2s. 8d."—
This anonymous " Captain " to whom the porpoise was
presented, was, no doubt, Jack Cade himself, and he is
so alluded to in the records of Rye ; the desire being
" to have his friendship," in case of his ultimate
success.—" Paid to John Hays, for carrying a letter to
" the Captain, in excuse of his treason 3s. 4d."

28-30 Henry VI. (1450-2).—Among the receipts is one
" For light silver 26s. 8d.," the same as " torch silver "
elsewhere ; money paid for lights burning before the
bodies of the dead in the church.—" Expenses incurred
" by the Constables, Jurats, and commoners, when
" James Godard, William Frost, and William Frode,
" brought hither a commission that the men should
" meet the Duke of Somerseto 17d. Expended in bread
" and wine, when John Passheley, Knight, and Robert
" Horne, were here 20d. Expenses when Gervays
" Cliftone was here at Lyde, coming from Portysmouth
" 18d. Expenses of 20 men, riding to the Duke of
" Somersete, when at Wylmyntone 5s. 5d. Paid a man
" carrying a letter from Dovorre Castle fur Selonde
" and Holonde 5d. Given to two captains who came
" here on a certain Saturday 2s. Expended upon them
" at the same time 2d. Paid John Bate the elder
" for 2 copulls of cygnets, given to the Lieutenant of
" Dovorre Castle, to have his friendship 8s. Given to
" a minstrel of the Archbishop of Canterbury, as a
" courtesy 3s. 4d. Spent on the Day of St. Nicholas in
" the 29th year of King Henry the Sixth, upon the Bishop
" from Romene 5s. 4d. Paid for the hire of 5 horses to
" Braburne, to speak with my Master Gervase Cliftone,
" when there, upon the matter of the Rector of Seynt
" Mary-chirche, in the monthe of January in the 29th
" year 3s. 4d. For wilde fowle given to my Master Ger-
" vase Cliftone, at the same time, to have his friendship
" 16d. For hire of horses to Canterbury, and from thence
" to Osprynge, and from thence to Braburne, to speak
" with our Lieutenant on divers matters of the town, at
" the time when our King came to Canterbury, being
" out two days and a night 16d. In expenses when
" that John Fermour the younger, the Constable, and
" William Groce, were sent up to Canterbury, to
" speke with owre Luetenannt for counsell for to be had,
" for to wete [know] how we shulde be rulyd when
" the Kynges men come hedur for the Vicare; for
" mennys mete and horsemete, the same nyghte 7d.
" In expenses and feys when William Groce [the
" Common Serjeant] was in prison in the Castill of
" Canterbury 6s. 5d. Item, he loste ther his purse, and
" his money therinne 6s. 5d. Item, he loste ther his

" sworde, his daggere, a payre of botys, and a payre of
" sokkys, price of 4s. Item, he payd ther to the maistur
" portere of the Castill, for to gete hym his horse,
" his cloke, and his sporys agayne, 8s. 1d. Paid for
" 6 cadys of sprot rede [dried sprats] yeven to the
" Luetenannt for frenship to be had 6s. 11d. Paid the
" expenses of Milet riding to Folkestone, to enquire
" about the ships which were in the Downys, in the
" month of June in the 29th year 2d. For 2 Myd-
" somerys candles, for the Common House, to stand there
" on the night of the Nativity of St. John the Baptist
" 1d. For 2 fagetys of brome [broom] 1d. For car-
" riage of belet [billets] and brome to the New Gote,
" for to make a wacchefyre there, the Fryday byfore
" Relek Sunday, in the 29th year 2d. For wax bought
" for the trendyll hanging in the church of Lyde, before
" the high cross there 5s. 9d. Paid David for making
" it up 20d. Paid at Shippeway, to the Warden, the
" Duke of Bokyngham, there sitting 53s. 4d. For
" bread and ale given to the players of Romene, in the
" house of Richard Glovere 6d. Paid to 2 captains here
" with the Lord de Redvers, for to be delyvered of the
" sowdeors then beyng here, 6s. 8d. Paid for the horse
" on which William Gros rode to Hethe, and for his
" expenses, when speaking there for the parish priest
" 7d. For a cry made for keeping the wacche and the
" warde on the sea-shore 1d. For another cry to cease
" hall [pilam] playing, and to take to bows 1d. For a
" hundred of wood, had at the firehowse, to make
" wacche ferys there 5d. In expenses made aboute the
" chief herbejowre and aboute Gye, on a Fryday at evyn
" for her [their] soper 8d. And for expensis of 2 horsis
" that nyghte for to have a dyscharge for the sowdears,
" And so they assyngnyd us to be with hem, at Romene
" at her logyng. And so Andrew Newland was sente
" theder for a letter that every sowdeare shulde remeve
" hennys [hence], the whiche expensis bith 4d. And
" when this letter came to Gye, for to do crie this
" mater, then payde in wyne 8d. Item, in expensis
" made by the Constable, Jurates, and commoners,
" in the howse of Jamys Ayllewyne, when Sir Andrew
" Ayllewyne [the late Vicar] was there, and toke his
" leve and wente towardes Romene, 20d. Paid 3 men for
" drawyng of brome for a day, for the wacche [watch-
" fire] 15d. For the carriage of brome to divers places
" on the coast, for the wacche 15d. For expenses
" made at Romene for to enquire of the wacche, and
" where the bekyns shulde be made, 4s. Given the
" King's minstrels, when here in the month of May
" 6s. 8d. Paid, the expenses of the Lieutenant of
" Dovorre Castle, when sitting here in Admiralty, on
" the sea-shore, the 11th of May 4li. 2s. 5d. Given to
" the minstrels of the Duke of Bokyngham, when here
" on the Eve of the Apostles Peter and Paul 6s. 8d.
" Expended upon them 8d." The " Newebygging "
[New Building], a locality in the town, afterwards
frequently alluded to, is first mentioned under this
year.

30, 31 Henry VI. (1452,3).—" For se[r]chyng in the
" 2 Countrys [? for Counties] at Londone, if any
" persone of the towne of Lyde hadde be suyd in the
" Hustynges 16d. Paid Richard Hughelot, tailor, for
" 2 curlewys sent to the Lientenant and to Henxtall
" 15d." Also, a turbot (20d.), and an eel (5d.) and a
conger (12d.), are sent to the Lieutenant,—" to have
" his friendship."—" Given to a certain man at Brok-
" lond, for a courtesy 20d. For wyldefowle given and
" sent to Robert Horne, for having his friendship 9d.
" Given to the minstrels of the Duke of Exeter, when
" here, as a courtesy 3s. 4d. Given to the minstrels
" of the Lord the Earl of Arundel, as a courtesy 3s. 4d.
" Given to the minstrels of our Lord the King, as a
" courtesy, 6s. 8d. Given to a man of Dovorre Castle
" for bringing a letter for a sitting of the Admiralty
" upon the sea-shore 4d. Given to William Groce [the
" Common Serjeant] a gown, value 6s. 8d., to hym
" promysid mony day. Given to James Ayllewyne for
" 1 cappe, to hym promysed the laste yere at the day
" of Counte and of Election, for his labur hadde at
" Canterbury before the Lordys, when the Kyng, owre
" most Saverayne Lord, lay ther at Canterbury, 13s. 4d.
" Memorandum, that awarde was made the day of elec-
" tion by alle the forsayde Jurattes and commoners of
" Lyde, that alle olde dettys beyng by hinde unpayde
" to the Parisshe Clerkys of Lyde, that is for to saye, to
" William Leycroft of the party of Lyde, William
" Brownflette of the parte of Dengemershe, shulle
" well and truly be gaderyd up, and to hem shull be
" payd"—a clerk for each side of the Parish.—" Also
" the same day they have made awarde that the
" forsayde Jurattes of this yere shulle nue augystt

" her bokys and rollis of her quarteragis, and augysto
" [agist, or assess] every persone afteir his havyng
" etc."

31, 32 Henry VI. (1453, 4).—" Payment made by the
" Jurats for the delivery of grain to the poor, against
" the Feast of Easter 6d. For wilde fowle sent to the
" Lieutenant of Dovorre Castle, against the Feast of
" the Nativity of our Lord Jesus Christ 23d." Shortly
after this, 6 molets [mullets], one bace [bass], and
4 herynsewys [heronshaws, or young herons,] are
entered as sent to the Lieutenant " to have his friend-
" ship." " Given to the minstrels of the Archbishop
" of Canterbury, when here at Lyde 2s. Paid for
" expenses about the Lieutenant of Dovorre Castle
" being here at Lyde, on Wednesday the 22nd of May,
" at supper, and on Thursday, the day after, at dinner,
" when he sat here, in Admiralty upon the sea-shore,
" in all 32s. 10½d. Given to the minstrels of our Lord
" the King, when here on Sunday before the Feast of
" our Lord's Ascension 6s. 8d. Expended upon them,
" the same day 3s. 4d. Given to the players of
" Hamme, shewing their play here, on the Day of the
" Translation of St. Thomas of Canterbury, 3s. 4d. For
" bread and drink given to them 11d. Expended on
" the minstrels of the Duke of Excetur, on the 6th of
" July 16d."—8 " cadys of sprot " [barrels of sprats]
are sent as presents to various persons; two of them
" to Gervase Clifton, coming home from Burdeux,
" for 2s. Given to Cok of Sandwich, wrestling at
" Broclond [Brookland] on Sunday before the Feast of
" the Assumption of St. Mary the Virgin, by consent
" of the Jurats and commons of Lyde, who were at the
" said wrestling 3s. 4d."

32, 33 Henry VI. (1454, 5).—" Expended upon a min-
" strel of the Archbishop of Canterbury, in bread and
" wine 5d. Paid and given to him, as a courtesy, the
" same day and time, 3s. 4d. Paid John Swan, car-
" penter, in part payment for the newe rofe [roof] of
" the church 40s. Expended upon a messenger of the
" Lord Archbishop of Canterbury, when here, on
" passing through the Ports, to warn the men thereof
" to be present at the enthroning of the Archbishop
" [Thomas Bourchier] 2d. Given to the minstrels of
" the Lord the King, when here on the 4th of May
" 6s. 8d."—" Paid the expenses of John Locok, Baliff,
" and Richard Barley, Common Serjeant, riding to
" Dovorre, to carry thither the money of the aliens
" dwelling in this town 3s. 4d. Expenses of Richard
" Barley, when he was at Wynchilse, for the fish given
" to the Lieutenant of Dovorre Castle by the men of
" the town of Wynchilse 3s. 4d. Paid for a horn,
" bought for this place 8d. Paid to Laurence Bate,
" for making the buttes 11s. 11d. Expended upon the
" minstrels of the Lord Duke (sic) of Arundille, when
" here, 8d. Expenses of the Lieutenant of Dovorre
" Castle, when he sat here on the sea-shore 37s. 4d.
" For bread and beer given to the players of Romene,
" shewing their play here, on the day of the dedication
" of the church 2s. Given to the same players, as a
" courtesy 10s. Expended on the minstrels of the Duke
" of Exetur 16d. Expended on the players of the town
" of Romene 8d."

33, 34 Henry VI. (1455, 6).—From this point, the
entries are very rarely made in Latin.—" In expensis
" made abowte the mynistrallys of oure Lord the Duke
" of Bokyngham, beyng here abowte the Feste of Seynt
" Bartylmewe last past 2s. 1d. And no peny they
" hadde of yifte [gift] here. Fisshe yevyn to oure
" Lorde the Archebyshop of Canterbury, beyng at
" Appuldre 3s. 4d. For horsehure too tymys, rydyng
" for to speke with the forsaid Archebisshop, comyng
" from Apuldre rydyng to the Castell of Saltwode 22d.
" For 2 cowpull of swannys yevyn to the forsaid Arch-
" bisshop of Canterbury, beyng at the Castell of Salt-
" wode 16s. 8d. In expensis made on Saint Nicholas'
" Day, abowte the Bysshop of Romene 9d. For fisshe
" sente to the Luetenaunt and to Hexstall, on Seint
" Gregory Day, for frenship to be hadde for the
" maysturs of botys [masters of boats] of Lyde 4s. 8d.
" In expensis made the iiiith day of July, beyng here
" Sir Thomas Keryell, the Luetenaunt of the Castill
" of Dovorre, and hir [their] wyvys, seing the play of
" Seint George 18s. 6d. For 4 criys made for the
" Kyng, owre most Soveraine Lord 4d. Yevyn to the
" mynstrels of our Lord the Kyng, beyng here in
" the month of Aprill, 6s. 8d. For gunne powder bou3te
" at Sandewyche 6s. 8d. Expenses made abowte men
" of the cuntrey coming hedir, to withstonde the
" Kynges enemyes comyng uppe on londe, at the Fyre
" howse and at the Brokys Ende, Thursday the 8th day
" of July last past 18s. 10d. In expensis made abowte

5.

" the Kynges messager bryngyng hedir the Kynges
" Privy Seall for men (who) shulde kepe the see, and he
" was here on Seint Jamys Day 2s. For the expenses of
" 2 carpenters settyng up the maste in the stepull, and
" also for her labur 15d. "

34-36 Henry VI. (1456-8).—" Given to a man
" bringing a letter from the Luetenaunt of Dovorre to
" Rye, for shippes to kepe the see, forthwith other
" shippis of Londone and of other places, sent thorowe
" alle the Portys for to withstande the navee of Fraunce,
" beyng then in the North See, 4d. For cariage of ston
" from Romene to Lyde for to make of gunne stonys, on
" Fryday nexte byfore Saint Bartholomew Day 2d.
" To John Further wachyng yn the stepull on Seint
" Laurence Day was xii monthe 2d. To 2 men
" wacchyng in the stepull for a ny3te 4d. Paid for
" gunne stonys [cannon balls of stone] 10s. 4d. Paid in
" expenses made abowte John Grynforde and Thomas
" Hexstall, and for other mo personys beyng here to
" make acorde by twene maisturs of botys of this towne
" and the Portyngalens [Portuguese] 7s. 4d. Paid for
" 2 shidys [sledges] for to draw the gunnys to the
" Nesse 4d. Paid to Thomas Ayllewyne for rydyng to
" Canterbury, for hym and for his man beryng up 2
" letters, on to the Priour of Crechirche [Christchurch],
" and an othur to the Mayre of Canterbury, for men of
" this towne, pylgryms, my3te resorte thedur in pylgri-
" mage 12d. In expenses mad ther, abowte 2 gantylmen
" of the forsayd Priour, goyng with Thomas Ayllewyne
" to speke with the Mayre for the same pilgryms 12d.
" For a quarte of malmesyn, yevyn to the Mayris wyfe,
" 3d. Paid to Robert Uffyntone for stokkyng of the grete
" gunne 3s. 4d. Paid for wode and brome, and for
" cariage therof to the see side, in the monthe of August,
" when enemys were ther 8d. For an horse hure
" ledyng fysshe to John Grynford, sente to hym on
" Shere Thursday, for frendship to be had, 8d. For 2
" cadys of sprot, yevyn to the Luetenaunt of Dovorre,
" for frendship to be hadde, 14d. In expenses made by
" John Saulys and Thomas Ayllewyne the 2de day of
" Juin, abowte a man of counsell makyng 2 lettres,
" and sente to Canterbury, on of hem sente to the Priour
" of Cricherche [Christ Church], and that othur to the
" Mayre of Canterbury, that menne of Lyde, pylgryms,
" my3te goe and come thedur withowte restyng [arrest],
" by Robert Glover 20d. In expenses made abowte the
" same man of counsell 9½d. Expenses made abowte
" the Gunne, the Serpentyne:—Inprimis, paid to the
" gunne makers on Sunday nexte byfore Seint Thomas
" Day of Inde [India, perhaps July 3] 11s. 8d. Paid to
" John Boldyng for byndyng of the grete gunne with
" serpentyne, and for irone aad ther too 18s. Paid to
" John Godfray, bocher, lente to the makyng of the
" gunne 3s. 4d. In expenses made by Richard Barley
" and William the gunne maker, when they wente to
" Wynchilse and to Hastyng for to bye metalle for the
" forsayde serpentyne, 3s. 6d. Paid to William Gros,
" for bras lente to the same gunne 3s. 4d.—Yevyn to
" the mynstrellys of the Duke of Bokyngham, oure
" Wardayn, beyng here the 21 day of May last past
" 6s. 8d. Paid to John Hunte, yevyn to John Cheyne,
" of Romene, for counsell to be had for the mater of
" John Charlys, outlawed, 3s. 4d. For 6 horse hure
" same tyme, ledyng up to Dovorre the same John
" Charlys 3s. 4d. Paid for freshe fysshe and for salte
" yelys [eels], yevyn to oure Lorde the Archebyshop of
" Canterbury, lying at Saltewod in Lenton laste past
" 7s. 10d. Paid to the same Jamys (Ayllewyne) for 2
" horse labour drawyng 2 gunnys to the Nesse 2d. Paid
" to William Growte for di3ting [preparing] of 3
" dyners, and for his labour to Sandwyche fachyng ther
" gunne powdur 2s. Paid in expenses made by the
" Jurattes, and by the Constabull Thomas Bate, on
" Seint Blasis Day laste past, sittyng to gadur for a
" inquyraunce made upon straungers beyng that tyme
" in this towne 2s. 1½d. Yevyn to Martyn of Dovorre
" bryngyng a letter hedur, that no manne shulde take
" no leverey of no lord ne gentylman, the whiche was
" proclaymd here, 4d. Paid to a man, crying that the
" wache [was] to be kepte by the see side, and that no
" man shulde playe at the tenys [tennis] 1d. Given to
" a man of the Luetenaunt, makyng a crie at the see
" ayde 4d. Paid to a man ledyng strawe to the Nue
" Havyn, and for the same strawe, and for the cariage
" therof, for to make a wache fyre ther 6d. Given to a
" man bryngyng a letter comyng from the Luetenaunt
" of Dovorre, isente from the Yerle of Warwyk from
" Caleys, that the Frenshemen wolde come hedur 4d.
" Given to a man makyng a crye to mustur at Romene
" by fore the Yerle of Stafford, in the monthe of Sep-
" tember 1d. Given to anothur makyng a crye that

3 U

" every man of this towne shulde keepe her wache in
" 3 partyes, and also in the stepull, 1d. Payd and yevyn
" to the mynstrellys of oure Lorde the Kyng, beyng
" here on Tuesday the 11 day of October 6s. 8d. Payd
" to 2 carpynters for mete and drynke for a day,
" mendyng the gunnys, the Munday that the Frenshe
" men come on londe at the Nesse 4d. Paid to a masone
" for smale gunne stonys, that is for to say, 29, 2s. 4d."
36 Henry VI. (1458).—The Accounts are now (fol. 53)
no longer entered in the hand of William Leycroft, as
Common Clerk, but in that of Thomas Caxton, who,
though not this year, succeeded him in the following
one. This Caxton, no doubt, was the same person of
that name who is mentioned in the Chamberlain's
Accounts of Rye, shortly before this date, as acting
as a leading law-man for the town of Tenterden, in
its transactions with Rye. After serving some years as
Common Clerk of Lyde, Caxton retired from office,
and ultimately became Bailiff of the town. Mention
is made in Boys's *History of Sandwich* of a Thomas
Caxton, Town Clerk there in 1476; identical with
this person, no doubt. He is mentioned more than
once, as himself writing out these accounts : they are
entered in a fine bold hand, and in general he writes the
word *Ihu* (Jesus) at the top of each page, (a practice
more common in the West of England at this date). It
is clear that for many years he was the most active man
of business in this place, and his evident abilities tend
to confirm the impression that he was nearly related to
William Caxton, our first printer.—" Paid for fysche,
" for Walter Moyle, 2s. 8d."—Moyle was a Judge of the
Common Pleas, residing at Eastwell.—" For fysche for
" Sir Thomas Kyryell 9d. Paid to the mynstralles of
" the Duke of Bukyngham 6s. 8d."—There are several
items here for keeping watch at the " Weyis Ende " ;
among them,—" Paid to Thomas Quykeman for carriage
" of a loode of woode to the Weyis Ende, and carriage
" of a gunne to the Nesse 6d. For bere and sider inne
" the Common House, to the Jurats 4d. Paied to John
" Fermour the yongger, for expenses of James Ayle-
" wyn . . . at Wynchelse to speke with menne of the
" Porter for the shipp that shold go a werre [to war]
" 18d. To John Fermour the elder for fysche to the
" olde Lieutenaunt at Romene 10d. Paid for 2 horse to
" the Nesse for to fetche 4 gunnes there 5d. Paid for
" wrytyng and complyyng the troublis matere of Thomas
" of Aghene to gedir, remembryng the grete wronge and
" undewe vexacion had to the towne of Lyde 3s. 4d."—
There are several entries on this matter, but the charge
against this Thomas of Agen (a place in France, on the
Garonne), connected probably with the quartering of
soldiers here, is involved in obscurity : Caxton, with his
ever ready pen, was probably the person employed to
" write and compile " these troubles : indeed, the use of
these very words almost implies the scholar and man of
business. It seems not unlikely that Caxton may have
been first brought to the notice of the people of Lyde, in
consultation upon this matter.—" Paid in expences of
" Thomas Caxtone and his horse, beyng here 2 dayis
" abowte the townys nethis [needs], on Hoke Monday
" 8d."—This is the earliest mention of Caxton's presence
in the town.—" Paid for fysche yeven to Sir Thomas
" Kyryell, at the entryng in to his office of Lieutenaunt-
" ship of Dovorre, 2s. Paid to John Hunte for horsehire
" to Dovorre and to Caunterbury, for Thomas Bate to
" speke with my Lord of Bukyngham 16d. Paid for a
" cabon by the see 12d :"—a wooden hut for fishermen,
often mentioned afterwards.—" Paid be Thomas Aylewyn
" for 2 horse hyres for myself on the townes nethes
" [needs] to Grenford (at Dover) for councell 16d."—
Caxton is here speaking of himself.—" Paid to a child to
" go to Andrew Bate 1d. Paid for 2 yerdis and half of
" grene clothe for the Common Serjaunt, at 22d. a yerde
" 4s. 7d. Paied to Thomas Caxtone for horse 2 tymys to
" Sir Thomas Kyriell, and onys to Dovor onne the
" townys nethes [needes], to shew the mater of Thomas
" Aghene, 16d. Paid for Kyriells costes, when he went
" to the Lorde of Warwike 5s. 1d. In horsemete for 7
" horses 1 day and 2 nyȝthis, 2s. 5d. Paid in expences-
" of the cariage of the mennys harneys to the see syde,
" that went with the Erle of Warwyke, and expences
" in the bote of bred and bere, 5s. 8d. Paied to 23
" menne that went with the Erle of Warwyk at the
" townes election to the see, every manne 3s. 4d., 3 li.
" 16s. 8d. Paied to Thomas Aylewyne for his wrongfull
" vexacion hadde at Caunterbury, rydyng ther onne the
" townes nethes [needs], for to speke with the Meyre
" of Caunterbury for the shipp that shold go a werre
" [to war], sewyd be Robert Glover, for the grete malice
" that he owid to the towne 16s. Paid to Robert
" Howghe for bryngyng our menne a borde be fore

" the Lorde of Warwykes persone, there havyng grete
" thonkes 6s. 8d."
36-38 Henry VI. (1458-60).—" Paied to Thomas Cax-
" tone, the first day of October, of his wagis 6s. 8d."—
This is the first entry as to Caxton, in his new office of
Common Clerk. He seems to have begun with double
the salary of Leycroft, his predecessor.—" Paied for
" delyvere of Simone Reede unto the howse of Lazaris
" 10s. Paid to expence of 8 men rydyng to Caunter-
" bury to our Lord of Caunterbury, suyng for a Viker
" resident, be a supplicacion 10s. 1d. Paied in expence
" of drynkyng of the Lieustenaunt and othirs, and
" drynkyng of the sworne menne at the Common Howse
" at the muster 20d. Paid in expences at the delyvery
" of poore menne cornis [grain] 8d. Paid to John
" Howlet junior, of olde dette 3s. 4d. Paied in expences
" of my Mayster Moyle, and other, ynne the moneth of
" Octobre, at Thomas Ailwynnes, thenkyng his labour
" that he did for the towne, to the Lord of Caunterbury,
" 6s. 8d. In expences abowte the Steward (of Dover
" Castle) and his wyff, beyng here the 10 day of Juyn,
" at Thomas Ailwynnes, 4s. Paid for 4 cryis at the
" Cherchestyle for the Kynge and the towne 4d. Paied
" to the Kyngges menstrellis the weke before Wytsentyd
" 6s. 8d. Paied to the Duke of Bukenham's menstrelles
" 3s. 4d. Paied to Caxtone for expences at Romene, for
" councell for the matere of John Dane 4d. Paid to
" James Bate for a dayis labour at Waychehows 5d.
" Paid to Harry Colyne for half a day dragging at the
" Goote for the Waycohehous 8d. In expences of diverse
" menne goyng to Dovorre unto the Lord of Warwike,
" for to have goo to the see 13s. 2d. Paid for a horse-
" hire for Richard Knyȝth to Romene, to wete there,
" whan here menne shold ben redy for the Lord of
" Warwyke 6d. For dyggyng of clay, and leying therof
" with ynne the buttes 12d. For digging of turvis
" [turfs], and leying of the same, and diggyng and
" abotyng of the sandbankes 10d. In expences of the
" Kynggis menstrelles for them and there horse 22d.
" Paid for the Crosse to Robert Newis, and other costes,
" forth with horsehire 3li. 10s."—This was perhaps a
market-cross.—" Paid to Thomas Bate the younger, for
" a dayis labour for hym and his manne at the Weyis
" Ende, at the Waychehows, 8d. Paid to Caxton for
" horsehire to Sir Thomas Kyriell, to lede up fysche 4d.
" Paied to Hans Pekilheryng, of olde dette, 12d."—His
name often appears as a resident, and he is also mentioned in the records of Romney.—On Sunday after
the Feast of the Translation of St. Edward in the
38th year—" it was agreed that Thomas Caxtone, the
" Common Clerk, should have a gown each year."
38 Henry VI.—1 Edward IV. (1460-2).—" Paid to
" Caxtone, for his gowne of the towne 6s. 8d. Paid in
" expences of the Lord Reverys [Rivers] messenger,
" which rode thorow the Portes 6d. Paid to Caxtone
" for expences ridyng to Cherryng, to speke with the
" Vikere wheche was yane purpos to a laboryd to a
" bene Vikere here 12d. In expences of the Jurettes
" labouring abowt the sowdiours that shold go up to
" Sandwhiche to the Lorde Reverys 12d. Paid in
" expences of the Vikere of Cherryng, beyng heere the
" Sonday a fore Saint Thomas of Ynd [India] 18d.
" For wyldefowle and fysche yeve to hym 23d. Paid in
" expences of the Baylyff Andrew Bate, William Gros,
" and the Common Serjeaunt, sent be message to the
" Lord Reverys to speke with him 10s. 10d. Paid to
" the cartars for ledyng mennys harneys to Sandwhiche,
" and 3 cariages to the Nesse 11s. 4d. Paid in ex-
" pences of John Fermour and Caxtone ridyng to
" Sandwhiche to the Lord Reverys, and to Gervase
" Clyftone 3s. 8d. Paid in the expences of the Bischop
" of Romene, beyng here onne St. Nicholas Day, at
" Andrew Bate's hows, 7s. 9½d. Paid in expences of
" John Searlis, William Benet, and Caxtone, beyng at
" Romene, with the Jurettes, to comene [commune]
" of our demenyng for the Lordes men of Warrewyk
" 20d. Paid in expences to Thomas Aylewyne, and
" Caxtone, and Trendelherst, and Barle, to London, to
" speke with the Lordes for the towne, the tyme that
" the Lord of Warrewykes men landyd here. And for
" to knowe how we shuld spede and be gydyd, 28s. 8d.
" Paid to Richard Lowys, for waycohyng at Weyis Ende,
" for hym and his horse, 6d. Paid in expences of
" Caxtone to Wynchelse, for councell on a letter of
" proces that came from Laurens Holdernesse 10d.
" Paid for horsehire for John Fermour and Caxtone to
" Sandwhiche 2s. 8d. Paid to John at Wyk for amend-
" yng of a gunne, and the bressyng 20d. Paid for a
" lombe sent Mayster Hornys for Janever 12d. Paid
" for brengyng of a letter from the Lordes of Caleys,
" for Frenshmen, 4d. Yeven to John Clerk, Steward

" of the Lord of Caunterbury, for his cowncell and good
" advise on our charteris and fraunchise 6s. 8d. Paid
" for horse hyre to Caunterbury, for Thomas Aylewyne
" and Caxtone 8d. Paid in expencis of Walter Moyle,
" beyng here ynne Lent 10s. 4d. Paid to Gros for bred
" and half bunne [a measure so called] beers at Nesse,
" the tyme the Frenshmenne roode there 3s. 8d. Paid
" to the Lord of Caunterbury's mynstrelles beyng here
" ynne May 3s. 4d. Paid to the menstrelles of the
" Duke of Bukingham, beyng here ynne May, 3s. 4d.
" Paid in expenses of Vincent Sedele and Caxtone
" ridyng to Canterbury, to speke with Mayster Horn,
" and Fogge for the menne of the Lord of Marchis in
" prysone 6s. 11d."—The " Lord of March " was afterwards Edward the Fourth.—" Paid to Robert Newis in
" fulle paiement of money borrowed at Londone of
" Hamptone for the jurnay of Northampton, above we
" have resseved 22s."—This appears to be interest on
money borrowed for fitting out soldiers who fought under
the Earl of Warwick at the Battle of Northampton, 1460.—
" For horsehire of James Frode and Caxtone to Canter-
" bury, to speke with Rogger Brent, for councelle for
" the towne 2s. Paid for horshire to Romene, when
" menne of werre were in the Cambour 2d. Paid to
" James Base for 1 cariage with vitell to the Nesse 6d.
" For 1 loode strawe to the Nesse 6d. Paid to hym for
" his labour to help set up the bekene at the Weyis
" Ende 3d. Paid in expences of Gros and Caxtone
" ridyng to Grenford, the Monday and Tuysday afore
" Cristemasse, for to comone of the tretis betwix Moyle
" and the towne, and also for Robert Glover, 12d.
" Paid for horshire and expences of Caxtone at Hornys
" with a letter that came from Caleis, for Frenshemen
" 6d. Paid to the jurnay of St. Albonys, in money to
" them that went—to 34 men and 2 strangeris 11li. 10s."
—An item for payment of troops supplied by the town,
who fought under the Earls of March and Warwick, at
the Second Battle of St. Alban's 1461.—Paid to " See-
" fowghill [elsewhere called 'Seefowl'] for wayche
" ynne the steple for 8 days 16d."—He watched a further 6 and 14 days in the steeple.—" Paid for vittelle
" sente to Londone ; to the jurnay of York 3li. 11s 9d."
—For support of the town's contingent, which fought,
under the Earl of March, in the campaign which closed
at Towton, in Yorkshire, 1461.—" For beryng of a letter
" to Rye, for Frenshmenne 8d. ;"—giving notice of the
approach of the French.—" Paid to James Lucas, for
" horsehire for Naysbe is man beryng tithyngges [ti-
" dings] to Sandwichf for Frenshmenne 16d."—Caxton
and others go on two journeys to London, at this period,
in reference to a matter about "Trendleherst."—" Paid
" in expencis at the last Brodhill of Andrew Bate, Gros,
" and Caxtone 16d. Paid for expencces of ledyng up the
" manne to the Kyng, that wasse take with letters
" from the Duke of Somerset 26s. 8d."—The Duke of Somerset was Henry de Beaufort, beheaded in 1463. Many
items are entered as to the " town gunnes " at this date.
" —Paid to William Mellale for wayoche, for horse and
" hymselfe, for 8 nightis with a horse 4s. Paid in ex-
" pences of Barry and his felowshipp, at Cornelius, on
" Holy Rood Day 20d. For gunne wheles, and a whele
" for the bekene 4d. Paid for two cryis for the mus-
" ter 2d. In expences of Jurattes at muster on St.
" Petre's Day 2d." Thomas Caxton is the largest creditor but one of the town at this date, the debt due to
him being 49s. 6d. ; of which, as stated in a note added,
he repaid himself 13s. 4d. on St. Machutus' Day, 15th
November.

A 1, 2, Edward IV. (1462, 3) : the earlier part of this
Account is in Latin.—" Paid the minstrels of the Earl
" of Warwick on the Feast of All Hallows, 3s. 4d. Paid
" the expenses of Thomas Aylewyne, Andrew Bate,
" William Gros, John Fermour, James Frode, Thomas
" Caxtone, and John Kny3t, riding and going to
" London, for one month and more, on the matters be-
" tween the town and Walter Moyle, in the months of
" November and December, at the Parliament, in the
" first year of Edward." The visits to London, by
Caxton and others, on town business, about this period,
are very numerous.—" Paid for a cry for the goodes of
" the karek, 1d."—in allusion to the public sale of goods
from a foreign carack, wrecked on the Ness.—" Paid in
" expences at Canterbury, in drynkyng yeven to diverse
" menne, and expences of Caxtone his horse, and
" Barleis horse 5s. 8d. In expencces at Apoldre for
" vitie [wine] 6s. 7d. Paid for horshire to Westyng-
" hanger with James Frode, to speke with the Unther
" Shereff, 6d. Paid for two cryis, one for tenys pleyers,
" another for the wayoche 2d. Paid for wex [sealing
" wax] for inquisition of the karek lost 1d. Paid to
" William at Wyke for ironworke to the buttes 9d."

The following is an entry at the end of this year's
account.—" Also hit is ordeynyd be the Comon Semble,
" that alle foreneres fischermenne beyng and fyschyng
" here in diverse sesons, wekely resortyng, drying
" her fysche a land, shall pay to the commone scotte of
" here fysche merchaunt, to be taskyd, as for catell, like
" as they use in Wynchelse and Rye."
2, 3, Edward IV. (1463, 4).—" Paid John Wolvyne of
" the debt to the church from the torcheselver, for set-
" tyng of the torchis, woodewerk, ironwerk, and labour of
" W. Benet, 3s. 8d. In expences of John Searlis, Andrew
" Bate, John Hunt, Vincent Searle, Thomas Caxtone,
" and Barle, rydyng to Fristone, to speke with Sir John
" Scotte, for the sowdiours to Caleis, the 2 day of Sep-
" tember, 2s. 8d. Yeven to the Kynges menstrelles at
" Michelmas 3s. 4d. Payd in expensses of the Lord
" Warden's menstrelle 16d. Paid to Vincent Sedele, in
" full payment of dette owyng to hym for lyverey cloth
" to men of Caleis 13s. Paid to the pleyers of Romene
" on Dedication day 6s. 8d. Paied to Thomas Howghe-
" lyne for waycchyng with his hors at Weysend,
" whanne tithyngges of Frenshemen come here 6d.
" For 2.oriis, one to have water at mennys doors, the
" other for men to go to Caleis 2d."—The water at the
doors was to be in readiness, in case of fire.—" Paied to
" the hangmanne for his labour 12d. For his expencces
" 6d. Paid to Martynnys son, for brengyng a letter
" how the feld was broke in the North, and to let [hin-
" der] passage over the see 4d. Paid for bryngyng of
" a letter how the Kyng wold ynne to Scotland, and
" how vitellers sholde follow aftere 4d."—This is in
allusion to the landing of Queen Margaret, and the support she received from Scotland.— " Paiede to Barle
" rydyng with a knyghte to the Erle of Worcester, in
" to the Downys 4d. Paied to the Ly3thelver of [? or]
" torcheselver of olde dette in ful paiement of the same,
" to Vincent Sedele 3s. 6d."
3, 4 Edward IV. (1464, 5).—Among the receipts,
for the first time.—" From strange men fishing here,
" for their scot to the town 23s. 8d. From merchants
" shewing (their wares) in market, beyond the statute
" of the town 14d."—" Paid to Martynne brenggyng a
" maundement for the pees betwix Ingland and Fraunce
" be land 4d. Paid for a cheyne to the stokkis, with a
" lokke, 10d. Paid to a man brenggyng a maundement
" for Flaunders war 4d. In expencces of Caxtone to Wyn-
" chelse, for to speke with Mayster Thunder, uponne
" the procces of Robert Newhous 8d. Paid in expencces of
" the Lord of Warrikes marshalle 10d. Paid in expencces
" of Mayster Thunder and his wyff, beyng here the 11
" day September 6s, 11d. Paid in expencces of Thomas
" Aylewyne, and Thomas Caxtone, and Barle, beyng at
" Brodhylle the 12 day of September, for the sute of
" the Chartres of Portes, 20d. Item, of the comone
" money paied to the orgone maker for the orgonis ;
" whiche the cherche owith to the towne 18s. 8d."
4, 5 Edward IV. (1465, 6).—" Paid in expencces of
" the Baylyff, Thomas Aylewyne, John Kempe, Thomas
" Caxtone, Richard Barle, and Morley, for the maunde-
" ment that come from Dovore, recytyng to have Mar-
" garete Bewe to Londone, at the sute of Walter Moyle,
" and to shew our Wardeyne our compleynt 4li. 2s.
" Paid for wyne to the Sufficane, whan he was here 3d.
" Paid for a porpays sent to Mayster Scott 9s. For
" bryngyng hom of the porpays 6d."
5, 6 Edward IV. (1466, 7).—" Received from William
" Benet and Thomas Caxtone for one gunne, that weighs
" 2 cwt., 3 quarters, 18 lb., at 12s. 4d. the cwt., total
" 36s." The following entry is here made (fol. 76 b) :—
" 22nd day of January Robart Matrasmakere came
" before the Bayly and Jurattes, and confessayd hym
" gylty for brekyn of the Kynges prysone, and ther afore
" the Bayly he hath found surety to kepe the towne
" harmles, Wylliam Gray and John Ivy, and the said
" Robart to kep good rewle pay not a 100s."—" Yevene
" to a manne brengyng tythyngges from the Baylyf of
" Hastyng, how Frenshemen were at the see 4d. Paiede
" to Thomas Bayene (their London agent) for our
" Charter, be Andrewe Bate and Thomas Caxtone, and
" also for his fee 3li. 4d. Paiede to a manne brenggyng
" the pees of the Kyng of Denmark 6d. Paiede for
" gunne powther, fet at Sandewhiche 5s. 4d. Paiede
" for expencces of the pleyers of Hethe, here onne De-
" dication Day 8s. 10d. Yeven to hem, the same tyme
" 6s. 8d. In expencces of the pleyers of Romene shewryng
" here pleay here on Whitsond Monday 3s. Yevene to
" them the same time 6s. 8d. Paiede to 4 waychemen the
" first Sonday at the play of Romene 16d."—The reason
probably is, that they watched on the shore, while
the play was going on.—" Paiede to my Lorde of Caun-
" terbury menstrelle 20d."

6, 7 Edward IV. (1467, 8).— " Memorandum, that
" Harry Bate ys chosyn the debyte of Lyde on Seynt
" All Sowlyn Day " (2nd November). " Paid for a cry to
" have bogges out of the feldis 1d. Paid for a cry to
" shet yn shoppys at Service tyme 1d. Paied by the
" Baylyff to a manne of Dovorre, brengyng the pees be-
" twix Ingland and Breteyne 4d. Paied in expences of
" the Lieutenaunt of Dovorre and his menne, beyng here
" onne Schroff Thersday 9s. 4d. Paied in expences of
" oure bane [bann, or notice] cryars of oure play 20d.
" Paiedo to a manno beyng a nyghte at Caunterbury,
" fetchyng the Abbates Charter, with the surveier 8d.
" Paied to my Lord of Warwykes menstrelle 20d. Paied
" for a baco and ele sent to Mayster Lieftennaunt 3s. 4d.
" For horsbire there to his place in the Weld [Weald]
" 6d. Paied in exspences of William Bate and Caxtone
" to Londone, for to breng relacion of apoyuttement of
" trety betwix the Lord of Batell and the towne
" 18s. 10d."— The Abbot of Battle, " John Newton " by
name, is meant. Caxton's salary is now found increased
from 13s. 4d., to 20s., per quarter ; but in this year, from
the following item, still in Caxton's own writing, we find
that he ceased to hold the office of Common Clerk ; resigning it, not improbably, for more lucrative pursuits :—
" Paied to Robert Lucas, at his comenaunt [? covenant]
" makyng with the Baylyff and Jurattes to be Clerk
" here 5d. Paiede for a porpays sent to Londone to
" Mayster Fogge and Scotte 6s. Yovene to the manne
" that had the dromedary 8d. Paied to Vincent and
" Caxtone for exspences to London for the mater of the
" Abbate of Batelle, brengyng home a bylle of tho
" Abbates mater, and makyng an answere to oure Coun-
" celle 13s. Paied for a boyscholl [bushel, as a standard]
" for the towne 8d. Paied to Caxtone in ful paiement
" of his salery for Midsomer and Michelmesse 40s."—
This is the last item of this description.—" Paied for a
" lokke to the common pound 6d. For two wrastlyng
" colers [collars] 10d. One staff for the Comon Serjaunt
" 2d. Paied to John Blossom to breng message to the
" towne for the porpays 2d."

7, 8 Edward IV. (1468, 9).—The entries,—at least
for the present, are now no longer in Caxton's hand.—
" Paid to Smythys Pot, the carpenter, for makyng of
" the brygge [bridge] to the Won Way (elsewhere
" ' Ven Way ') 2s. 4d." Presents of " cades of sprot "
are mentioned as being sent to Mayster Skot, Syr John
Fogge, Syr John Gylford, Master Gilford, and Mayster
Foggys, followed by these items.—" Payd. for a capone
" to William Wenstell, gevyn to Maister Markham and
" Maister Grenford 6d. Payd for a galune of rede wine
" gevyn unto theym in the townys name at that tyme
" 8d. Payd for there sopere, at that sopere beyng John
" Serlys, Thomas Caxtune, and Robert Lucas, to pray
" the sayd jentylmen to be frendly in our mater, he
" twyxt the Abbot of Batayl and us 7s. 5d. Payd unto
" the Baylyf, that the sayd Baylyf payd to a manne
" wacchyng at Gore Wall 4d." From this Account, it
appears that Lucas's salary was but 6s. 8d. per quarter ;
one-third, only, of that of Caxton, at the time of his retiring from office. Entries follow here of various deeds
executed in the closing years of Edward IV. and the
earlier years of Henry VII. (fols. 82 b—86 b) ; they are
written in the hand of James Bate, the Common Clerk,
hereafter mentioned ; as in the case of entries made by
Caxton, under whom he was probably trained, the word
" Jhu" (Jesu) appears at the top of most of these
pages. In a deed of the 18th of Edward IV., the
" Stremedyke," of Lyde, is mentioned.

Folios 87 a—99 a are occupied with contemporary entries of deeds, beginning in the 7th year of Henry VI.,
and ending in the earlier part of the reign of his successor. The only facts in them worth notice, are ;—
mention of the " public highway leading from West-
" broke, through the rectory, to the church of All
" Saints of Lyde ;" land of " John Schelley, in Lyde ;"
the Court (or Manor) of " Old Langport " there ; the land
there " of the Prior of Bilsyntone ;" " Pigwell Wall ;"
the " Court (or Manor) of New Langport ; the highway
" leading from the church to Hettiswall ;" the street
called " Tryggestrete ;" mention of one Simon Hayton,
of Lyde, and his wife, having the Christian name
of " Mace ;" a locality called " Lambardyswall ;" the
" Watergange, of White Kempe," and " a certain green
" way leading from the Thre Elettes to the Brode-
" water." The entries in fols. 95 b—98 a are in Caxton's
hand. At fol. 98 b, there are three entries, in the hand,
evidently, of Robert Lucas, his successor ; the first of them
being as follows :—" This xiithe day of February, the yere
" and the regne of our Soverayn Lord King Edward
" the iiiithe after the Conquest of Inglond the viithe,
" came Johan Adam of Lyde afore the Baylyfe and

" Jurattes of the for sayd towne, and confesseid opynly,
" without ony cearcion sayd, that one Johan Andrew, of
" Tenet, delyvyryd to the forsayd Johan Adam, at
" dyvers tymys, sum tyme whete, sum tyme bere
" [barley], and other pod ware, for to sow yt uppone
" his propyr landes, unto the great hurte of the sayd
" jentylman."—The entries at the foot of this page and
in fol. 99 a, are again in Caxton's hand.

At folio 99 b, the Corporation Accounts are resumed ;
being a continuation of those for 7 and 8 Edward IV.
(1468, 9).—Among the receipts are the following :—
" Received from Hans Skomakar, for his servant,
" Thomas Skot, for an assault 3s. 4d. From Thomas
" Caxtone, for a breakfast to the Seneschal on St.
" George's Day, 6s. 8d :"—a collection probably made
by Caxton.—" From men of West contray fishing
" here, 3s. 6d. For polmoney [poll money] 3s. 3d.
" Resseyvyd of William Barbour for blod schedyng,
" 6s. 8d."— Among items of expenditure :—" Expences
" on the Day of St. Nicholas, for the Bishop from
" Rumene 5s. 10d. Payd for fyche bouthe at Nesse,
" gyvyn to Sir John Fogge, and Sir John Skot, to
" be brendly [friendly] un to our mater be twyxt the
" Abbot and us, at all tymys of rede 3s. 8d. Delyveryd
" unto John Kemp, the 2nd day of February, rydyng
" with John Searlys and Thom[a]s Caxtone to Lundun, to
" answer the Abbot of Batell, of hys ple takyn uppon
" John Serlys and Thomas Caxtune, for beryng away
" of x mille (thousand) of wytyng at Dyngenesse 26s. 8d.
" Payd Thomas Caxtun beyng for the sayd mater at
" London a monyth 15s. 2d. Payd to the sayd Thomas
" Caxton on Candylmesse Day last was, he coming
" hom to enforme the comynnys of the Abbotes
" vrongful sute, and so goyng up agayn to Lundun
" with hys answere of the benche and the comyns,
" 10s. Payd for the expencys of Sir John Skot, and
" Mayster Hawth, comyng downe to the sayd towne
" of Lyde on Seynt Georgeys Eve last vae, for the
" mater be twyxt us and the Abbot.—Payd to Anneys
" [Agnes] Tutor for bred and ale the eve and the
" sayd day 5s. 2½d. Payd to the sayd Anneys for a
" potel of vyneger 3d. To the same Anneys for half a
" bunne of bere 20d. For woode 6d. For fyach, to
" the sayd Anneys at that tyme, 12d. For fyre in ther
" chamber, and candyll 8d. For 2 baschell and half of
" otys 12½d. For hors breede [bread] 8d. For hay 7d.
" For half hundryd eggs to the sayd Anneys 4d. Payd
" unto the sayd Anneys for her beddyng, her labour,
" and her servaunts, and for the veschyng [washing] of
" the clothys 2s. 2d. For 6 galunys of wyne to Wylliam
" Venstall 4s. For spycyry 18½d. For hors mete 9½d.
" For a gungyr [conger] lowth for the sayd dyner 17d.
" For 4 coddes, and the bryngyng home 2s. 1d. For
" 2 copyll of solys and a pyrle [? brill] 6d. For a snoke
" [?] and a 2 solys 5d. For a cungyr and 4 rode
" lyschys 14d. Payd to Thomas Gros for half bunne of
" bere, i drunk in the Nesse, Syr John Skot and Syr
" John Hawth at that tyme beyng ther, with Jurats of
" Lyde 20d." The following are among the items for a
dinner to " Mayster Grenford, on Seynt Gerge Eve.—
" Payd to Thomas Caxtone for an ele to the forsayd
" dyner 12d. Payd to Mawd Browne for weschyng
" of wescell [vessels] ther 3d. Payd unto the schewars
" of the play of Apuldur 3s. 8d." The usual route
from Lydd to London appears, at this time, to have
been, by horse to Gravesend, and from thence by boat.
—" Payd unto Thomas Caxtone, (allowed) in hys skot,
" to geve the Baylyfe good concell for the plee be
" twyxt William Fermour and John Carlylle, there
" beyng al the forene atornays to ple the sayd ple 20d.
" Payd for the letter, borne to Rye on the 8th day
" of Juin, warnyng theym of the Frenchmen 8d. Payd
" unto Richard Barley for 4 cryes at the chyrcho style
" 4d."—He was Common Serjeant, and Crier as well.
—The end of this Account (after fol. 102 of the present
numeration) is missing, as also the beginning of that
for the next year, but in fol. 184 of the volume, noticed
in the sequel, it appears.

8, 9 Edward IV. (1469, 70) :—the items of expenditure,
however, are given, and written nearly throughout in
Caxton's hand.—" Paid in exspences of John Serles and
" Caxtone rydyng to Caunterbury, metyng with Sir
" William Terell, to see tho Boundes of the frannchis
" of tharchibisshoppe be twix Blakewase and Dengo-
" nesse, unther autentik seale 5s. Paied for horshire for
" Caxtone and Barle, whan they went to London 6s. 8d.
" Paied in exspences of John Serles, Harry Bate, Thomas
" Caxtone, and Laurence Gros, beyng at Londone, the
" Abbates matere, for bootchire to Westminster, while
" they were there 2s. Paied for horshiro for John
" Searlis and Caxtone to Caunterbury, and from thens

" to Gravysende 6s. 8d. For horshire for Harry Bate
" and Lawrense Gros to Gravysende 4s. Paied in ex-
" spences divers tymes at the Cardynalis Hatte, of the
" Sergeauntes of Lawe and menne of Councell, Thomas
" Bayene, oure atturnay, and other, comenyng [com-
" muning] of oure maters 5s. 4d. Paied to Maister
" Catysby, for pletyng [pleading] at the barre divers
" tymes this quarter."—This was John Oatesby, afterwards a Judge, and finally one of the unpopular and unfortunate ministers of Richard III. In November,
Caxton was 20 days in London, in reference to the
" Abbates mater;" and was there again after Easter.—
" Yoven to the servaunt of oure Lorde of Caunterbury
" brengyng a deer to towne from the seid Lord, and in
" exspences 2s. 8d. Paied to Stephen Hoigge, for a
" porpays yevene to the Lord of Caunterbury 6s. Paied
" to Harry Colyne for lodyng of gunnys in the Nesse,
" and for an horse there, there beyng Frenshmen 8d.
" Paied for a letter from my Lord of Warricke to
" thabbot of Battell, be Henry Bate 5d. Paied in ex-
" spences of Serles, Caxtone, Gros, . . . and others,
" havyng a day with the Abbates Councell at Wyncheles
" 4s. 10d. Paied to the whechemen that waytchithe
" Robert Lucas in the Common Hows 2s. 10d."—Here
we have apparently Caxton's successor, as Town Clerk,
under arrest.—" Paied to Richard Barle for beryng of a
" pot of gunnepowder to the Nesse 1d. — Paied
" to the menstrelles of the Lorde of Arundell 3s. 4d.
" Paied to the menstrelles of the Kyngge 3s. 4d, Paied
" to the pleyars of Stone, crying the banes [notice of
" their play] here 3s. 4d. Paied to a manne brengyng
" a letter from Romene, to warne us of the navy of
" Frenshmen 4d. Paied to 2 men for waycohyng in the
" stepyll 12d. Paied to 21 menne, goyng on the viage
" with the Lordes of Clarence and Warwyk 7li. 6s. 8d."
9, 10 Edward IV. (A.D. 1470, 71). This year " William
" Wanstall and Thomas Caxtone were chosen Treasurers
" for the year, and receivers in the common purse."—
" Delivered to Richarde Barley, when he rode for Cales
" [Calais] 5s. 7d. Paid to Caxtone for his spendyng at
" Dovorre for the prisoners in Scotland 19d. Paid to
" Vyncent Sedle for his horsse to Caunterbury, for to
" spere byfore the Kyng 12d. Payde in expences to
" Dovorre of the Baily, Vyncent Sedle, [and] Thomas
" Caxtone, when they fett [fetched] the othe 23d. Payde
" to John Symone, for mendyng of the comyne cheste
" in the cherche 4d. Payd for naylyng of Thomas
" Norys is ere 12d. Paide at Romene. for havyng ther
" letter of record of Dyngenesse, in all expences there,
" 2s. 2d. Paide to Thomas Gros for exapences whenne
" a man came from Maister Skot, to have menne to
" labour with the Kyng 10d. Paide for the mace 5s.
" Paide for menne wachyng by the sea 6d. Payde to a
" manne of Sir John Scotte, bryngyng tydynges fromme
" Lynkkolle [Lincoln] 8d. Paide for bryngyng of the
" grete Proclamacion 4d. Paide to a manne bryngyng
" commaundement that we shulde areste all maner of
" schippis bylongyng to the Yerle of Warwike 4d.
" Paide to a manne of Wyncheles bryngyng the Kynges
" Privy Seale and another letter therewith, for menne
" to there carvell 4d. Payde to a manne bryngyng a
" Privy Seale, how that the Kyng had seed the office
" of Wardenschipp into his handes 4d." The preceding account is written, in a fine hand, by William
Nycolle, the new Common Clerk. A general payment
is mentioned at the end.—" Item, Thomas Caxtone
" hathe receyved in all thynges 55s. 4d." Henry VI.
was temporarily restored to the throne from October
1470 to about April 1471. There is an entry in fol. 109
belonging to this period, (tr. from the Latin)—" On the
" second Sunday after the Feast of St. Michael the
" Archangel, in the — year of the reign of King Henry
" the Sixth;" the clerk was at a loss what year to call
it; it was, correctly, the 49th.

10, 11 Edward IV. (1471, 2); the Interregnum of
Henry being included in that space.—" Paid to Rychard
" Howlett of owlde det, rydyng 2 tymys for heyren-
" sewys [heronshaws] to Apildowre, ayenst the comyng
" of the Kyng 12d. Payd for one crye to have catell
" owte of the feldys 1d. Paid to Wyllyam Barbour
" goynge to the Camber, to knowe whether that menne
" of werre beyng there were cumyng to towne to robbe
" oure nybowrs the alyonys [aliens] 4d. Paid for
" 1 pursse to kepe in the towne his monye 1d. Paid to
" 6 menne goyng to Sandwiche to wayte onne the
" Kynges Cownsell 22s. Paid to Thomas Jekynne for
" carying of 2 hurte menne from the Nesse 4d. Paid
" to Thomas Caxtone for horshire to Gravisende, with
" William Bonet 2s. Paid to Wyllyam Bonett and
" Thomas Caxtone, for that they spended in Londone
" 13s. 4d. Paid to Caxtone his manne bryngyng us

" tydynges that the Kyng was commyng with his oste
" into Kente 2s. Spended upone the Knygth commyng
" from the rode (?) 3d. Paide for a letter sente from-
" Dovorre, warnyng us of the Danys 4d. Spended
" upon wachemenne at the Nesse the same tyme 6d.
" Payde to wachemenne waochyng in the stepyll the
" same tyme 4½d. Spended at Cawnterbury, when
" Thomas Caxton, Thomas Groce, John Kempe, and
" John Puleyn, rode to the Kyng 15s. 6d. Spended at
": Londone, whenne Thomas Caxtone and Harry Bate
" were there with the Kyng 19d. Spended in the
" clirche upon the Bayly and Jurattes, whenne they
" enquired what lyvelod menne have in Lyde 2d."—for
the purpose of assessing a " scot," or income tax.—" Paid
" to John Bakone, goyng to Langer to se what schippes
" that they were, the which rode there 4d. Spendyd
" at the takyng of the manne, the which the Lordes
" sent for to Asschforde 4d. Paid for wachyng of the
" schipmenne 6d. To Vyncent Sedle, for his horsse
" to Folkestone, whenne thye fet gunstonys 6d. To
" Thomas Bate, for 1 peyr of whelys to the gunne 18d.
" Paid to Wyllyam Swanne for his horsse and his childe
" to Syr John Fogge, with Thomas Caxtone, beryng to
" hym a presente, 12d. For one horse and a childe
" [page] to Syr John Scotte, when the sowders wente
" to Sandwich 6d." Fol. 113a., (tr. from the Latin) :—
" On Sunday before the Feast of St. Michael the Arch-
" angel, Thomas Caxtone was chosen Bailiff of the
" town of Lyde for the following year."—
From fol. 113b to fol. 115a several transcripts of deeds
are entered, of the reign of Edward IV. ; mostly written
by James Bate, with " Jhu " at the top of the page. In
fol. 113b is the copy of a will of Alice Kokyred, dated
10th June 1490; she leaves 3s. 4d. for a priest to
celebrate Masses in the church of All Saints at Lyde;
and to Isabel Kokyrhed, her sister, she leaves her best
gown, and her best cow of " browne " colour. In fol.
115a, there is a copy of a deed, whereby, in the 9th year
of Edward IV., Alice Cokeryd (the same person, probably)
and John, her husband, convey to Thomas Caxton,
Simon Bate, and two others, a message in Lyde,
situate between those of Henry Bate and Thomas
Caxtone, with 2 pieces of land in the tenure of the
Court of Aldyngton. It was a secret conveyance to
religious uses, no doubt. In fol. 116a, on the page
reversed, there is an entry of the acknowledgment of a
deed; the deed being dated in the 9th year of Edward
IV., the acknowledgment bearing date the 7th of June
in the first year of King Edward V., a reign extending
little beyond two months. The entry is in the hand of
James Bate.

11, 12 Edward IV. (1472, 3) : Caxton being Bailiff
this year.—" Spended uppone the Bayly and Trazarerys
" [Treasurers] receyvyng the monye of the towne 2d.
" Spended uppone the Stuarde of the Lorde Archebys-
" shop of Caunterbury 2s. Paid to Thomas Caxton for
" writyng and makyng a supplicacion to the Lordes of
" Arundelle and to the Leutenaunte 8d. Spended
" uppone the Admyralle, in alle thynges 59s. Paid to
" John Symone for makyng of fetres [fetters] 2s. 2d.
" For amendyng of the stokkes 4d. Yevyne to the
" mynstrellys of our Lord Wardene 3s. 4d. Spended
" uppon a .manne of his in wyne 2d. Spended at
" Hastynges by the Bayly, and others with hym, 18s. 7d.
" Delyvered to Thomas Caxton and Wyllyam Nycoll,
" rydyng to Sandwich, to speke with tho master of the
" carvell for to ordeyn menne for us 13s. 4d." (This
item has a line run through it.)—" Paid to Laurence
" Groce rydyng to Romene to warn theme of the navye
" of Frenshmenn 8d. Paid to Wyllyam Swanne for his
" childe rydyng to Harry Horne. to warne hym of the
" navy rydyng at Nesse, 4d. Paid in expences of the
" Baily and Thomas Groce beyng (at) London, and 2
" children [pages] with themme 17s. For a proclama-
" cion for to have harnesse to the Nesse, and leve dyse
" pleying [dice playing] 1d. Paid to owld Robert,
" carying a gunne to the Nesse 4d. Spended on the
" Monkes of Batell in wyne 12d. In wyne to the
" Kynges messenger 1½d. Spended uppon Veake, the
" Lorde of Arundell his mann 4d. For one cade sprot
" yeve to hym 12d. For horse to Gravysende for me
" and my child [the Common Clerk and his page] 4s.
" Paid to the servaunte of Romene bryngyng autoryte
" of havyng agayne of oure franchese 8d. Paid to one
" bryngyng a letter from Sandwich for the French
" navye 4d. In expences of the Bailif and John
" Durham at Romene, spekyng with the Lord Matri-
" face [?] 4½d. In exspences of the Bailif and Wyllyam
" Swanne at Cawnterbury, attendyng onne the Lorde
" Matriface 6s. 5d. For reede for waschmen to brenne
" [watchmen to burn] 3d. In exspences onne my

3 U 3

" Lorde of Arundelle his manne, bryngyng a lettre for
" the schip loste at the Wayhisende 8d. Paid to John
" Symon, having of [off] the fetres from the thefe
" 4d. Paid for wyne yevyn to Sir John Culpeper 10d.
" —Expences aboute the theffe.—First, deliveryde to
" Richard Barly for exspences of the theffe 8d. For
" strawe 1d. For wache [watch] to Robart Longe 3d.
" For makyng of the stokkes, to Jamys Maket, 6d.
" For tymbre therto 4d. For yryne werke 16d. To
" John Toyte beryng knowlege to Hastynges 8d. Paid
" to Richard Barle and his felowe, lying in the Comyne
" Howse, and wachyng there every nyghte for one
" weeke 14d. In exspences that weeke for the theffe
" 8d. [The next week.] In exspences of the theffe 6d.
" Paid for one paire of schone [shoes] to his dow{s}ther
" 3d. Paid to Richard Barle for wachyng 11 wekes, 7d.
" one weke, 6s. 5d. Item, yeven to the quest of womenne
" 4d.",— summoned, perhaps, in reference to the
daughter.—"To the hangmanne 8d. Paid to John
" Durham for 2 haltris 3d. To the Duke of Clarens
" his mynstrallys 3s. 4d. Paid to hymme that browgth
" a commawndment for alyens sylvyr 4d." In fols.
121b and 122a is contained an Account, in Caxton's hand,
of expenses incurred upon provisioning and fitting out
the town's ship, upon a first and second " riage :" the
crew seem to have been about 20 in number :—"Item,
" it is owyng to Edwarde Alwey for occupyng of his
" bote, and hurtyng of his cabelyng 6s. 8d."

12, 13 Edward IV. (1473, 4). Among the receipts this
year occurs :—"Item, receyved of Thomas Caxtone,
" chapmanne, ' pro sua contributione,' for his scot,
" 14d."—"Paid for one crye to have catele oute of the
" feldes 1d. Paid for mattes to the Comyne Howse 10d.
" Spended at Londone by the Bayly [and others], beyng
" there to helpe to be dyschargeged [sic] of the mayve
" 15s. 5½d. Yevyne to John Bette, goyng to the Ile of
" Oxney to speke with the queste 12d. Spended at
" Rye be Thomas Caxtone and others 7s. Spended
" upone the Lorde Cardynalle his menne, in all thynges
" 3s. 6d." (Thomas Bourchier, Archbishop of Canterbury, and Cardinal, is meant.) "Paid to Thomas
" Caxtone, advysyng a letter to our Lorde of Cawnter-
" bury for the wrek 4d. Paid to hym copying the said
" Lorde his evydence 8d. Paid to Gilbarde to speke
" with the maister of the Antony 12d. Paid to the
" mynstrallys of the Lorde of Arundelle 20d. Yevyne
" to the Kynges mynstrallys 3s. 4d. To the Duke of
" Clarence his mynstrallys 3s. 4d. To John Bette, carying
" strawe to the Gutte [for watchfires] 6d. Paid for one
" crye to sett water at menne- his dorys 1d. Spended
" by the Baylif, John Kempe, Willyam Nycolle, and
" others, beyng with oure Cardynall, 10s. Paid to a
" manne bryngyng a proclamacion of the Kyng of
" Scottes 4d. Paid for one gurnarde fet [fetched] at
" Rye by J., and yevyn to the Lorde Cardynall his
" menne 8d." The fish now known as the " gurnard,"
could not surely be of such a value.—"For one
" molet yevyne to them 6d. Paid for 3 potellys of
" wyne 9d. For one potelle of bastarde 5s. Unto
" themme onne the Hundred day, for 3 potellys of wyne
" 9d. Delyverid to Thomas Caxtone, rydyng to Os-
" prenge to speke with Sir John Fogge 3s. 4d. Spended
" by the Baylye, Thomas Caxtone (and others) beyng at
" Londone for the queste, and uponne oure dayes menne
" 38s. 6d. Yevyne to Cattysby, oure serjaunt, 3s. 4d.
" Paid for the dyner of the menne of the Mersche 2s. 3d.
" Paid for one crye to have menne in to the Antony
" [the town's ship] 1d. Spended by John Alweye uponne
" the Admyrall 5s." Fols. 126b and 127a are occupied
with the enrolment, (in the hand probably of James
Bate), of a deed in the 15th of Edward IV. In it
mention is made of a piece of land called " Meneland,"
in the "Eastfelde."

At fol. 128a, after a break, the accounts recommence,
in the 17th year of Edward IV. (1478): among the sums
received, one " Thomas Bagot " pays 5s. ; and 25s. 4d.
is received as " Lordshypsylver." On the other side
(128b) is a portion of the account of debts due in the
16th year ; Thomas Caxton "owing for 2 old scots of
" the Lordship of Scotteney, 6s."

Fols. 129, 130, contain various entries, out of place,
in Caxton's hand, belonging to the earlier years of
Edward IV. In Latin, fol. 129a, there is the following
entry :—"Thomas Bocher, and John Etherik, and James
" Hevere, have certified on the day of St. Katharine
" the Virgin, that Henry Bate sold one sow and one
" ewe sheep, not wholesome. Also Henry, servant of
" Henry Bate, says that the sow aforesaid was not
" wholesome. Also, the butchers aforesaid present that
" Andrew Bate follows the craft of a butcher, to the
" nuisance and destruction of the craftsmen there."

Fol. 129b.—"On the 22nd of May, in the 5th year of
" King Edward IV., before the Bailiff and Jurats, Ed-
" mund Smythe, and Isabel, his wife, have made oath
" that they will depart from the town of Lyde, and will
" not again approach the same, unless it be for the sake
" of pilgrimage, or upon a voyage of our Lord the
" King ; nor will they approach within 7 miles of the
" said town. And they further have made oath, that
" they will do no evil or damage, either by act or
" words, to the Bailiff, Jurats aforesaid, or commonalty ;
" but well and trustily will behave themselves, as being
" trusty to our Lord the King, and to his lieges."—"On
" the 18th of October in the 6th year of Edward IV.
" William Benet produced in Court 6 silver spoons,
" valued and appraised at 7s. 9½d. ; of which amount
" 6s. 10d. is due to the said William, and so there
" remains the sum of 11d: [sic] in the hands of the said
" William."—"On the day of St. Clement, in the 6th
" year of Edward IV., Andrew Bate made plaint
" before the Bailiff and Jurats against John Sedele,
" that the said John said of him, Andrew, that he was
" an extortioner, and that (he) had dryven away halff
" Dengemersh. And the said John denied this, and
" said that he did not say so, but that the said Andrew
" shold dryve menne owt of Dengemersh, as menne
" said." From a large amount of evidence subjoined,
it appears that Andrew was possessed of large herds of
cattle, which, to the injury of his neighbours, overran
their lands, and the greater part of Denge Marsh.—
" Thomas Smyth said that he wold not have sold his
" landes at Dengemersh for dowble the selver, yf he
" my{s}th have occupyd in pees. . . And that be the
" catell of Andrew Bate he was grevously hurted, thorow
" whiche he lost yerely his corne, which was cause
" that he sold his londe. Item, the said Andrew drove
" his mare into the mire, whiche was cawse of here
" dethe." The result of these plaints does not appear.
At a Common Assembly, holden on the 9th of June in
the 5th year of Edward IV., it was " ordeigned, that
" alle Westrenmen havynge fyshe at Nesse dreyid, shall
" be distreynnyd be here bodyis to yeve acompte of
" here fyshe. . . and to pay of every 1000 whytyng 2d.,
" and of every 100 lang fysshe [ling], codde, and conger,
" 2d. And of every 20s. fysshe that they sell be londe
" 4d., to the common profet."

From fol. 131a to fol. 153b, the matter belongs mostly
to the reigns of Henry VI. and Edward IV., the leaves
having been misplaced in the binding ; their contents
will be noticed in the sequel.

At fol. 154a, the Account, in the hand of James Bate,
for the 17th year of Edward IV., is continued.—"Paid
" to the Prince his minstrelles 4s. (Prince Edward,
" afterwards Edward V.) To the Quene hir min-
" strellys 16d. To players of Romene 6s. 8d. Paid
" James Bate, in full payment for his wage, and his
" liverey gowne 20s. Paid for 2 warrantes, one for the
" pese of the Kyng of Denmarke, and the other for
" wole and wolfells, shorlyng and morlyng 8d. Paid
" for proclamacions made for tenys playeres, dyse
" players, and koyle players 1d. Paid in expenses of
" the Bailiff, Jurates, and commenys, goyng to Romene,
" to see our Customes 2s. 2d.". The " Custumal " of
Lyde, kept at Romney, is meant.—" Paid John Symon
" for spykes, and settyng onne the feterys of the
" preste [priest] 8d. In expenses of John Ohenew,
" John Ford, and Thomas Conyer, comyng to comene
" [commune] for the benevolens sylver 4d. (Fol. 155.)
" Paid Thomas Caxtone for wrytyng of the customes
" 13s. 4d." This book, " The Customall of Lyde,"
already noticed, still exists ; and further mention of it
will be found in the sequel.

17, 18 Edward IV. (1478, 9).—" Received from Yer-
" yeshgrotes and badde sylver 3s. 8d.":—Irish groats
and clipped money, probably are meant, as being
forfeited by those who circulated them.—" Paid the
" minstrels of our Lord the King 2s. Paid the common
" purse a 5th part for a ayde for preserving our Charter
" 24s. 8d. ;"—Romney probably paying the other four-
fifths. " Paid to a manne of Dovorr portant hither
" of the Acte of Parliament 4d. Paid in expences of
" the Yeryll of Arundellys menne, beyryng a letter for
" wacche for the Flemynges 20d. Paid to the wrasselyng
" 6s. 8d. Paid to bane cryars of Folstone 6s. 8d.":
(players who first cried their play throughout the
neighbourhood, and then acted in the town). " Paid
" in exspens of the sayd bane cryars of Folstone 6s. 8d.
" Paid to John Symone, smythe, for smythyng of the
" federys [fetters] of the preste 2d."

18, 19 Edward IV. (1479, 80).—" Paid for 4 capons,
" given to the Abbot of Batele and four knights, being
" at Lyde upon the matter between the Lord Arch-

" bishop of Canterbury and the Lord Abbot 3s. 2d.
" Paid the minstrels of the Lord the King 20d. Paid
" Robert Grygge for cleansing the Wateryng by the
" Mill 6d. Paid to the ravyne boochar for takyng of
" ravynys [ravens] 22d. Paid to Richard Fullar, bear-
" ing a letter for the peace between our King and the
" King of Spayne 4d. Paid to Goderynges dowghetyr,
" pour mayde, for hosyne and shoys, and other thynges
" 2s. 4d. Paid to the players of Rye, as a reward 12d.
" Paid for a bagge for the scale villa ætius, (of this
" town) 1d. Paid to the Quene is mynstrelles 2s. Paid
" in exspenses at sysyng [assizing] of the busshels,
" and of the Quenea mynstrelles 16d. Paid for 4 pro-
" clamacions atte chirchestyle 4d."

19, 20 Edward IV. (1480, 1):—" In this year died
" William Elys; may God have mercy on his soul (not
" improbably the former Common Clerk of that name).—
" Paid the Common Clerk for parchment, and writing
" the new book. Paid to the players of the Lord of
" Arundelle 12d. Paid the expenses of Gervase Hoorne
" Esquire and Thomas Oxenbregge, when here upon
" the matter of the Abbot of Battle 16d. Paid to the
" minstrels of the Lord of Arundelle 16d. Paid to the
" bane cryars of the town of Romene 6s. 8d. To the
" minstrels of the Lord the King 5s. 5d. To the min-
" strels of the Queen 3s. 4d. To the minstrels of the
" Prince 12d. Paid the expenses of the Bailiff, Vincent
" Sedle, and the commoners, when at Romene, when
" Inbasterys [Ambassadors] of France (? were there) 2s.
" Paid expenses of the men of the town of Romene and
" other men of the Marsh at Lyde, fetchyng home of
" the George 4s. 10d. :"—one of their ships for the royal
navy ; so called, probably, after the Duke of Clarence.—
" Paid to the leperys [lepers], whenne the George was
" fette home fro Hethe 4d. John Catelyne owes for
" his scot 8d."

20, 21 Edward IV. (1481, 2).—" Paid John Teylar
" [Tiler] in taskwork, teylyng the Courtehowse 7s. ;"
—the first mention that occurs, of a Court-house as
distinguished from the former " Common House," of
wood.—" Paid Andrew Bate for 1000 teyle [tiles], half
" a hundred corner and 2 regge [ridge] teylys, for the
" Courte hows 2s. Paid the minstrels of the Lord of
" Arundelle 20d. Paid Thomas Yownge (and) Laurence
" Gros, goyng to Rye and to Wynchylse, to speke with
" the menne of werre, be a letter sent fro Master
" Gervayse Hoorne 2s. 8d. Paid the expenses of the
" Bailiff, Jurats, and commoners, riding to Dovorre,
" Asshford, and Hethe, for the benevolence of the Lord
" the King 20s. Given to the Lieutenant to help us, as
" to the benevolence to the Lord the King 6s. 8d. Paid
" for fish and its carriage to Asshford, given to the
" Lieutenant and the Commissioners there 9s. 2d. Paid
" to my Lady of Yorke ys menstrelles 12d."

21, 22 Edward IV. (1482, 3).—" Paid Thomas Maykyne,
" to kepe Goderyngys doughtyr 3s. 4d." A leaf is
missing (after fol. 165).

22 Edward IV., 1 Richard III. (A.D. 1483, 4).—" Re-
" ceived from men standing in the market-place, this
" year 1s. 6d. From brasyarys standing in the market-
" place 20d. Received from polsylver [poll-silver] this
" year 21s.—Paid James Bate, the Common Clerk, his
" wage 26s. 8d. Paid John Baker for a gunne 3s. 4d.
" Paid in the house of John Aylowyne the expenses of
" the Bishop from the town of Romene, on the feast of
" St. Nicholas 5s. 4d. Paid the expenses of John a
" Forde, of the town of Romene, for tydings of the
" Parliament 2s. Paid the expenses of the Bailiff,
" Thomas Gros, and other men, riding to Rochester, to
" speak with the gentlemen, and comyng home 7s. 4d.
" Paid the minstrels of the Lord Duke of Gloucester,
" Protector and Defender of England 2s. Paid the
" minstrels of the Queen of England 12d. Paid the
" expenses of Thomas Gros, Thomas Yow[n]ge, and
" John Nycolle, riding to Sandwich for certain evidences
" and books, with Thomas Caxtone 11s. 7d. Paid for
" horseir [horse-hire] of 3 horwys 3s."—As already
noticed, Caxton had now removed to Sandwich ; and,
from this item, he would seem to have carried away
some of the Corporation records with him.

1, 2 Richard III. (1484, 5).—" Paid Thomas Berell for
" dekyng [dyking] of the common Wateryng near the
" Mill 5s. Paid the expenses of the Bailiff of Romene
" and John a Forde, coming to the town of Lyde,
" praying that the men would go out to the Marsh to
" the Lord Cardinal, the Archbishop of Canterbury
" [Thomas Bourchier] 8d. Paid for mendyng of
" Wyllyam Aleyne ys jak 3d. Paid to the wacche-
" maste 13s. 4d." Probably a mast erected for a light.—
" Paid for one lb. candylle 1½d. Paid for 2 comene
" scotte bokes to James Bate 3s. 4d. Paid Richard

" Fullar, when he brought hither the commission of
" the Lord King Richard, in the night 8d. Paid John
" Umfray, when he brought hither the letter as to peace
" between King Richard and the King of Scotland, for
" a month, 4d. Paid William Nowell, Cutnose, and
" Watkyne the Furbusher, for their wages 7s. 6d. Paid
" for wylde fowle sent to Rafe Asshetone, Knyghte 18d.
" Paid the expenses of Ralph Asshetone, Knight, the
" Bailiff, and the Jurats, in the house of Thomas Yonge,
" when they made oath to the Lord King Richard
" 32s. 5d. Paid the expenses of Sir Rave Asshdowne
" and Maister Kemp, Commyssioners of (the) Kynge,
" comyng to Lyde to see the monstre, at the houses of
" John Aylwyne and Thomas Yong 17s. 9d. Paid expen-
" ses at the muster of our Lord the King 10d. Paid the
" minstrels of the Lady Anne, Queen of England, and
" their expenses 2s. Paid for a payr of hosyns of
" ruset for Goderynges dowghter 5d. To William
" Aleyne for his jakke, in part payment 2s." Goderynge
was some poor man, whose history we are not told.

2, 3 Richard III. (1485).—" Paid in exspenses of the
" Bailiff, John Aylwyne, William Kempe, and others,
" goyng to Wynchylse, to speke with the Lord Gray for
" menne shold not go a warre 5s. 2½d. Paid for a queyer
" of papyr 3d. Paid the minstrels of the Lady of York
" [Cecily, Duchess of York] 12d. Paid for a kertylcloth
" of Herry Goderynges doughtyr, and for makyng
" therof 3s. 1d. Paid John Playce for brengyng home
" of Wylliam Aleyns jak 20d. Paid to John Bowdyne
" for a forlok of a gunne 4d. To John Bette for caryage
" of a gunne to Nesse 2d. To the minstrels of the Earl
" of Arundelle 12d. Paid to the playres in the hyghe
" strete 5d. Paid to John Bowdone for mendyng of the
" loke of the prisonhows dore, and stapyll therto 2s.
" Paid to John Whyte goyng to Knolle, carrying thither
" a letter to the Lord Cardinal of Canterbury, upon the
" matter as to our Charter 2s." The above, like many
other entries, is in the hand of James Bate, the Common
Clerk : from the peculiar nature of his writing, and his
habit of writing "Jhu" (Jesu) at the head of most pages,
we have fair grounds, as already stated, for supposing
that he had been trained under Thomas Caxton's tutel-
age.—In the latter part of these accounts, it deserves
remark that the expenditure on presents was not nearly
so great as in former years : the sums of money given
to minstrels and players were not so large; and deputations of numerous persons, sent to a considerable
distance, were much less frequent than formerly.

Leaves 176-185 (the end) are inserted without reference to chronological sequence, they belonging to various
dates ; before bringing them under notice, for a moment
we must revert to the previous insertions out of their
chronological order, notice of which has hitherto been
omitted.

Fol. 49 (blank on the reverse) is misplaced, it con-
taining a number of memoranda, in Latin, of 7-9
Henry VI. On Sunday after the Nativity of St. John
the Baptist, 7th Henry VI., Thomas Hykkys produced
as his pledges, Thomas Ikham, harper, and John
Pevenyssey, that he would abide by the award of the
Jurats as to a "rebelliousness in words " against the
Bailiff, Jurats, and commonalty. He afterwards acknowledges it, and pays to the common purse 6s. 8d. ;
All persons appointed by the Bailiff and Jurats, to go to
Romene or elsewhere, on the business of the town, and
refusing, without reasonable cause, are to pay 10s. On
the Day of St. Bartholomew, in the same year, the day
on which Hykkys acknowledged his offence, it was
enacted that so often as he should utter any unbecoming
(inhoneste) words against the Bailiff and Jurats, he should
have a like punishment; and he "consented and agreed
" so to do, in all things." John Selvir was also put upon
similar terms. Persons refusing to pay their quota
towards the stipend of the Parish Clerk of Lyde, are to
be distrained by the Common Serjeant.

Folios 131-153, misplaced—23 Henry VI. (1445)—
the commencement of the Account is wanting, and there
are no fewer than 7 Scots, or taxations, levied for this
year.—" Paid Thomas Love, carpenter, for making the
" gynne for castyng of the belfry — Paid Richard
" Swetyng for mending the Wateryng 16d. Paid
" Thomas Buntyng for keeping the torches of the
" church this year 20d. Paid Stephen Howhe for his
" boat to Farlay, and for his trouble, 2s. 6d. Paid
" Richard Wodeman, carpenter, for making doors for
" the new belfry 26s. 8d. Paid John Greneforde,
" attorney for this town in London 13s. 4d. Paid the
" shyngeler for his labour, 3s. Paid Richard Swetyng
" for carriage of one purpays to the Lord of Scar-
" burghe, Governor of Dover Castle, for having his

" friendship 20d. Paid 2 shyngelers and a boy, mend-
" ing the old rofe of the church 20d." Repairs seem to
have been done this year to the church on an extensive
scale ; and a further account is added, of these expenses,
amounting in all to nearly 30li.—" Received of ly3te
" selvyr [money for candles and torches in the church]
" collected from Lydestrete and from the Newe-
" bygyng, and from the Est Rype 3li. 6s. 8d. The
" like from Dengemershe 6s. 8d. The like on the side of
" Westebroke 6s. 8d. Received from Richard Glovere
" for wool left by legacy for the work of the new
" belfrey, 4d.—Paid the expenses incurred by John
" Sarlis, when he went to Wynchilse to see the ship
" of Sir Thomas Kyryell, that was to be hired for this
" town, 2s. Paid towards the ' sawerys ' [? meaning] 2s.
" 8d." Under another Scot, or taxation :—" Received
" for torches that were burning around the body of
" Thomas atte Bregge 6s. 8d. From money collected
" by men and women on Hokke Day 29s. 11d." The
items of this Account enter largely into the rigging and
equipment of the ship hired by the town, of Sir Thomas
Kyriel, from Wynchelse.—" Paid William Kempe for
" one purpoys given to Master John Fray, Chief Baron
" of our Lord the King, to have his friendship 18d.
" Delivered to Richard Hughelot, mariner, pursere of
" the said ship of the town of Lyde, 6li. 3s. 4d. Paid
" at Appuldore for the breakfast of the men who went
" thither for the ship called ' Le Rugo Cole,' of Bre-
" tagne ; huryd [hired] for the voyage for escorting the
" Lady Margaret, who is to be Queen of England, into
" England 10d. For a cheese bought of John Bate for
" the ship 6d. Paid for 7 potells of bere drunk in the
" Common House 7d. Paid the master of the ship of
" Bretagne 6s. 8d. Paid for shalis [?] of hemp for
" talowyng the said ship 2s. Paid for fresh herrings
" for the ship 15½d. Paid for the carriage of one pipe-
" cotur to the Sergeaunt of Dengemershe, for putting
" in the bread 1d. :"—this was probably a pipe for wine,
sawed in half, for storing the ship's bread. The Account
is followed by one for the outfit of another ship,
similarly sent to escort Queen Margaret to England.
—" Paid John Sarlis the former debt for payment
" made by him at Sandwich for hiring the ship called
" the ' Trinite,' for the town of Lyde, for the voy-
" age on escorting the Lady Margaret, who is to be
" Queen of England, into England 29s. 4d."—Many of
the items are run through with the pen, and a note
says that there was sent to Richard Hughelot, the purser, at Portesmouth 3li. 5s. 8d.—" For a bordclothe for
" the ship, and for a bord, 20d. Paid William Brownflet
" for rygyng [ridging] the house with turfs, situate in
" the churchyard, 3d. Paid Thomas Olberd for bring-
" ing the ship into the Camber from Appuldore 4d.
" Paid for one kildyrkyn of butter, bought for the
" ship, 3s. 6d. Paid for the expenses of the Bretons of
" the ship, here at Lyde 23d. Paid Gydney, owner of
" the ship of the town of Sandwich, in part payment
" for hire 8li."—No doubt, Sir John Gedney, Lord
Mayor of London in 1447 : he elsewhere receives 10li.
on two occasions. The Jurats of the town delivered to
" John Garard the younger, and John William the
" elder, when they went over to the ship lying at Har-
" flete 6li." Under another Scot, or taxation, for this
year,—" They answer for 40s. received from Richard
" Hughelot, mariner, pursere of the said ship, called
" the Trinite, of Sandewich. They answer for 33s. re-
" ceived by them as given to the fabric [wood-work]
" of the new belfry by all the salvers of the takylle of
" the ship from Hulle."

23, 24 Henry VI. (1445, 6) :—" Received of ly3te selvyr
" 30s. this year, which was spent for making of the
" belefiore, and hanging the bells. The gift of William
" Say, Esquire, to the new work of the belfry, 3s. 4d.
" Given to the minstrels of our Lord the King, when
" here last year, 3s. 4d." Lead for the belfry is mentioned among the items of this account, partly paid from
the light-silver ; the lead being bought in London, and
there put on board ship, for Sandwich ; whence it was
again brought,—" 9 sowys of lead," in quantity—by
ship to the Camber.—" Paid the plumbere for helyng
" [covering] the belfry, and for sowdere for the pipys
" 37s. Paid and given to the bereward, as a courtesy
" 12d. Paid Richard Aleyne for horsehire, when he
" rode to Sandwich, to make there the last payment for
" the ship hired for the voyage, on escorting the Queen
" to England 16d. Given to the minstrels of the Duke
" of Gloucester 3s. Expended upon them 4d. Paid the
" expenses at Dover of John Sarlys, Thomas Wynday,
" Stephen Elys, with the Common Serjeant, being there
" before the Lieutenant, sitting in the church of St.
" James ; to speak with him to have his favour as to

" a queste of the Admiralte by 18 men, that it would
" not come thither, as was intended to come 6s. 8d.
Continuation of leaves misplaced.—9. Edward IV.,
(1470). — " Memorandum, that on Seinte Margett
" [Margaret] ys Daye the yore by fore sayde, was
" delyvered to Harry Bate and John Pultone, and there
" felyschypp assigned with them, goyng to the helpe of
" Kyng Edwarde, our Soverayne Lord, with my Lord
" of Warwike 9li. 6s. 8d. Item, to Richarde Valance 8d."
This probably bears reference to the hostilities which
ended in the temporary dethronement of Edward by
Warwick, October 1470—April 1471.—" Memorandum,
" that the 21 daye of January, tho yer of the regne of
" oure Soverayne Lorde Kyng Edwarde the IVthe the
" 9the (1470), byfore the Baily and Jurattes, it was agreed
" by all the maisters of the botes, and comyns, that frome
" that tyme forwarde shulde be kepte contynualle
" wache at the Nesse by the saide maisters and their
" manye [household] every festefull day, both the
" evyne and the daye, and at al other tymys of charge.
" And that, for every maister and moyny a manne.
" And no manne to be assigned to the said wache but
" an oneste indweller. And yf any of the seide mais-
" ters lakke at his wache, and no manne there for hym,
" be he amerced, as oftentymys as he lakketh ther, at
" 12d. ; and every other of the seide maynye at 6d. . .
" . . . . . and that mercement lowyd to goo to the
" reparacion of the gunnys at the seide Nesse. Also,
" every bote maynyo [crew] to have at the seid Nesse
" 4 bowys and all thynges perteynyng sufficiently to
" them, at the leste, and 4 gode byllys [bills] or stavys.
" And what master and moynye that lakketh of the seide
" ordinaunce and wepynes, be they amerced at 12d."
In Latin, it is further stated, in continuation of the
same page, that on the 29th of May in the 10th year of
Edward IV. William Iddryk, of the county of Kent,
labourer, shewed to the Bailiff and Jurats a deed of
pardon for past offences against the King ; which being
shown, on cry made, he was set at liberty.

In fol. 142a, under the 12th year of Edward IV.,
(1473), the " court," or " manor," of " Waborne,"
at Lyde, is named, and a locality called " Hamptounys-
" crosse" [Hampton's Cross]. In fol. 143, 13 Edward
" IV., land of the Fraternity of All Saints at Lyde," is
mentioned, a brotherhood, no doubt, connected with
the parish church of All Saints. In fol. 144b, lands are
mentioned as situate in the parishes of Lyde and Prom-
hyll, between Goryswalle and the sea.

In an Account of (apparently) the 13th of Edward IV.
(1474), Henry Bate being Bailiff, are the following
items :—" Paid to Willyam Growte, for makyng of a
" dyner to the Admyralte, of owlde dette 6d. Spended
" upone the Byschopp of Romene 5s. 4d."—the boy
Bishop, St. Nicholas, being meant.

Account for 13, 14 Edward IV. (1474) ; the whole
written in Thomas Caxton's hand.—" Paid to Thomas
" Caxtone for 2 mesures of assise of pewter ; that one,
" a quart off wine mesure, that other a pynt of ale
" mesure, bow3th be the Standard at Sandwyche 17d.
" Paid for expenses with the Maire there, and other
" officers 14d. Paid to the mynstrelles of the Lord
" Wardeyne this yere 3s. 4d. Paid to the bane cryars
" of Hothe, for reward and expenses, 7s. 10d. Paid to
" the bane cryars of Folkstone, for reward and expenses,
" 8s. 4d. Paid to the Kyngges menstrelles beyng
" here 6s. 8d. Paid this yere for 8 criis at the cherche-
" style 8d. Paid to Thomas Caxtone for wrytyng and
" attendyng for this acomp 3s. 4d. Memorandum, as
" distresses :—For John Edward, for 16d., one mare.
" For John Hamond, for 8d., one lyne, leded. For Roger
" Pellander, for 6d., one axe and one . . ." (illegible).

14, 15 Edward IV. (1475, 6) :—in the latter year, Caxton, as already mentioned, probably removed to Sandwich, as Town Clerk there : we have seen him visiting
that place in the Account of the preceding year. This
Account is apparently in the hand of James Bate, the
Common Clerk. Among " Receipts " are the following
items :—" Received from Andrew Bate, for bones of the
" beffe 20d. Of Andrew Bate, for salt befe 20d. Of
" Stephen Locoke for flour, 10s. Expenses of the Bailiff
" and Andrew Bate riding to Sandwich, to converse with
" the Lord the King, 6s. 6d. Paid John Hystede, Parish
" Clerk, for his harvest 6s. 8d."—an extra fee paid to the
officials in harvest time.—" Paid for wrytyng of a new
" scotte boke, and assesyng of the Parysshe Clerke is
" boke 2s. 4d. Paid to Richard Barlo for riding to
" Apoldre, to speak as to a new clerk, and horshair 12d.
" Paid in expenses atte delivery of the pour pepylle is
" corne 10d. Paid wrytyng of a pese betwyx the Kyng of
" England and Scotland, and in expens of a gentylmanne
" here 16d. Paid to the Kyngges menstrellys 3s. 4d.

"Paid expenses of the Bailiff and Jurats on choosing
"21 men for the ship of Lyde 2s. Paid Robert Admand
"and William Admand for sleyng [slaying] of befe 11d.
"Paid in expenses att sleyng and dyyhtyng [pre-
"paring] of beffe 2½d. Paid John Bette, riding to
"Dovorre, to warn of Frensh flete, 8d. Paid for a
"capone yevyne to John Keryelle 8d. Paid Richard
"atte Gate, master of the ship 7s. 6d. ¹Paid for one
"hundred weight wode and strawe to the weche atte
"see, and caryage, 22d. Paid for 4 stone crusys to the
"shypp 6d. For botyr 8d. For garlyk and oynonys 2d.
"For gret [coarse] salt 1d. For dysshes and tren-
"cherys 2d. For mostard ½d. For fresshe fetelle
"[? victuals] 7d. For papyr [pepper] ½d. For a ladyll
"½d. Paid for heir [hire] of the ketyll 12d. For a
"tubbe to water [soak] fleshe 4d. For 5 pipes of here
"37s. 6d. Paid for makyng of paveys [shields], and
"payntyng of them 14s. For bord to make paveys 8d.
"Paid expenses of Thomas Groce at Sandwich, speak-
"ing with the Lieutenant 6d. Expenses at Canterbury
"of the said Thomas Grose, and horseheir, on speaking
"with our Lord the King and our Warden, 19d. Paid
"Thomas Caxtone for wrytyng of 2 bokes and 2 inden-
"tures, atte 10th penye of the Scotte 4s. Paid to the
"saudiouris [soldiers] that went with John Keryell
"23s. 4d. Paid for 4 capones, yevyne to the Abbate of
"Batell, 3s. 2d. In expenses whenne Thomas Hex-
"stalle, Maire of Dovore, is manne was here to inquere
"for the Frensh flete 4d. Paid for makyng of jakettes
"3s. 10d. Paid for one flycche of bacone to Robert
"Howgh 16d.—There are in arrear John Bregge,
"Thomas Caxtone, and Thomas Bate, in the collection
"of lyvelode, as set forth by the boke :"—the "lyve-
"lode" was probably an income tax, or rate upon
profits earned. John Bregge (or "a Bregge") was one
of the Jurats in the following year.

15, 16 Edward IV. (1476, 7).—"Paid to John Brewar
"and his fellowys breyngyng the shipe to Camer
"[Camber] 6d. Paid John Wolfyn for mendyng of the
"gunnes 10d. Paid to Richard a Gate, atte the comyng
"over of the Kynge, in reward, 4s. 8d."
Fol. 153 probably belongs to the Account for the 7th
and 8th years of Henry VI., fol. 8 in the volume:—
"Paid by the hands of the aforesaid Thomas Jan the
"expenses of the Bishop of St. Nicholas from the town
"of Romene, when here on St. Nicholas' Day, in the
"house of William Turnour, for wylde fowle for him
"and his people 14½d. Paid to a man who brought
"a letter from Dovorre, for arresting the men who
"came from Franco into England without leave 4d.
"Paid the wife of William Turnour, for the men of
"Romene who were here with the Bishop of St. Nicholas
"on St. Nicholas Day 3s. 4d. Paid William Menewode,
"working at the Common House 4½ days, at 5d. per
"day 23d. Paid fur wine given to a lord arrested
"here, who came from beyond sea, 12d. Paid for one
"stokfysbe, oil, oysters, and wine, in the house of John
"Baker, for the Jurats and John Adam, Esquire, and
"James Lowys and others with him, who were to go to
"Dengemersshe, by precept in a letter from Dovorre,
"for receiving and watching the goods of the Scots
"12d:"—a hand is drawn in the margin, to call notice
to this.—"For bread and ale for the Jurats, who chose
"men for the voyage of our Lord the King 3d. Paid
"for 4 poinads of candles for the ship 6d. Paid for
"bread and wine given to the herbyjour of the Lord
"Marchalle of England, in the house of Lynot 16d.
"Paid for a gallon of wine given to the wife of John
"Shelley 8d. Paid William Bate for 3 potells of butter
"for the ship 12d."
The remaining leaves in the volume, folios 176-185,
are bound up promiscuously, and belong to various
dates. Fol. 176 contains various memoranda, in Latin;
one of the 36th year of Henry VI. (1458), to the effect
that Henry Cartare, the run-away apprentice of Thomas
Knyżth (Knight) of Stapylle, had come to an agreement
with his master, before the Bailiff and Jurats of Lyde;
the apprentice being pardoned for all the offences by
him committed "since the world began." In the same
year, one Thomas Charle is accused by certain strangers
of being a Scot by nation, and not a friend of the King;
upon which he is put in prison, and the accusers are to
appear at 9 the next morning. They fail to do so, on
cry made, and he is released. As to a certain maidservant called "Joan Swan," living with Stephen
Hoigge, of Lyde, a dispute arises (in the same year)
between the said Stephen and William Swanne of
Romene. They agree to abide by the arbitration of
Andrew Bate and John at Wyke thereon. Fol. 177 :—
"Also, the sayd day—Seynt Austenya Day the Doctor,
"in the viiith yere of the Kyng that now ys (Edward

"IV.)—thay are agreyd and fully conclude Robert
"Lucas to occupy the sayd service of the Town Clark-
"schyppe the yere than next folowyng, takyng for hys
"hyre 26s. 8d. and gown." An agreement is also made
the same year, with Wylliam Horn, "Vicorye of Lyde;"
that "Robert Lucas, Clark of the sayd paryche, shall
"have of the sayd Vicorye, or of hys debite, every Sun-
"day in the yere a penny, upon thys condicion; that
"the said Robert or a lawfull debyte [deputy], bryng
"hem to hys hows halywatyr."—The meaning of the
following entry (fol. 177b) is not altogether evident; but
it belongs to the year in which Caxton resigned the
Town Clerkship, and was succeeded by Robert Lucas.—
"Memorandum, that the 2d day of October in the 8
"year of the regne of Kyng Edward the IVth, aperyd
"afore the Baylyfe and Jurates of Lyde, in the Com-
"mon Hows, Wylliam Olberd of the sayd towne; and
"there confeseyd that Andrew Bate opynly sayd that
"Thomas Caxtone and Vyncent Sedley scholde have
"spendyd of the townys money 5 markes to bere hym
"sylfe owt for the man that was gydyd owt off our
"fraunchyse in to the foreyne, and so leid up etc; whych
"manne was longyng unto Mayster Alfray of Sowth-
"sexe etc."
Fol. 178b.—Fragment of an Account belonging to 27,
28 Henry VI. (A.D. 1449, 50):—"Paid John Buntyng
"an old debt due to the servant of the Bailiff of Marshe-
"londe, that carts might pass upon the Wall (super
"Wallam) when tho belfry was making, according to a
"promise made to him, 20d."
Fol. 179a. Fragment of an Account without date, but
about A.D. 1490.—"Payed to the power man kepyng
"the power chyld 12d. Payed for a stoyll for the
"clerk 2d. Payed for makyng clene of the dongen
"2d."
Fol. 179b contains an agreement, in Latin, with the
Bailiff, Jurats, and commoners, dated the Day of St.
Edmund the Confessor 1466, for Robert Lucas to be
Parish Clerk, at a salary of 20s. per quarter, together
"with half profit of all the bells, with other profits of
"the same office." Below, in another hand :—"On the
"11th day of January in the 7th year of King Edward
"IV., came John Edryke, William Frode, and John
"Swanne, before the Bailiff and Jurats, and entered
"into recognizances, each for himself in 20 li., to be
"paid to the Bailiff and Jurats, or their successors, at
"the Feast of Easter then next, under the following
"condition, namely ;—if John Edryke shall not covet or
"desire the wife, the daughter, or the maid servant, of
"William Ferdygley, of Lyde, nor yet of any other
"man of the parish of Lyde, then this obligation and
"recognizance shall be held as null ; otherwise it is to
"remain in full force."—Also,—" On the 16th day of
"January in the 7th year of the reign of King Edward
"IV., came one John Andrews, bailiff of the liberty of
"the Abbess [for "Abbot"] of Battle, as supported by
"Andrew Bate, of Lide, and delivered a certain Dis-
"tringas, in the words following :—'Distrain John
"'Serlis, of Lyde, yeman, and Thomas Caxtune, of the
"'same, yeman, by all their lands, etc., and issues, etc.,
"'so that I have their bodies at Westminster on the
"'Octave of St. Hillary, before the Justiciars of our
"'Lord the King, to make answer to John [Newton]
"'Abbot of the Monastery of St. Martin, at Battle, in
"'a plea of trespass.—By the Sheriff of Kent to John
"'Andrewe, bailiff of the liberty of the Abbot of
"'Battle.'" Fol. 181b (partly in Caxton's writing)
contains a long account, in English, of alleged exactions
by Andrew Bate, from "Western men," drying their
whiting on the Nesse, while Caxton is represented as
supporting William Rolfe, in his offer to the Abbot of
Battle, as lord of the manor, of a larger rental for the
manor of Dengemersh, against Bate : "cabons" are
mentioned, evidently the wooden huts of the fishermen
there. Andrew Bate, at this time, seems to have been
"fermour" of Dengemersch; much; it was alleged, to
the detriment of the place.
Fol. 182a, in Caxton's hand, in Latin:—"Memorandum,
"that on the Day of St. Anne, mother of the Virgin, in
"the 5th year of the reign of King Edward IV., came
"before the Bailiff and Jurats of Lyde, Agnes, relict of
"John Hunt, and, after all things being taken into
"account, the town owes the said Agnes for rent of the
"house for the great organs, 13s. 4d.; and further, she
"gave up to the church of Lyde 5s. 10d. of her debt,
"for the souls of John Hunt and of Sir Roger Jelever.
"And the said Jurats granted that the Churchwardens
"should pay the said 13s. 4d. to the said Agnes."—
"On the same day, Alexander Gray, being in prison,
"because he fled to the church for a wound inflicted
"upon Simon Etterik, supposing him dead therefrom;

5.

3 X

" and the same Simon having been hitherto sound for
" the space of 40 days since the wound was inflicted,
" and no action having been brought against the said
" Alexander; was, by award of the Bailiff and Jurats,
" restored to his liberty in the church, and therefore
" acquitted." The following (in Latin), on the same
" folio, is in the hand of James Bate :—" Memorandum,
" on the 17th day of the month of September, at the
" 8th hour at night, in the 2nd year of the reign of
" King Henry VII., there came one John Davy, and
" entered the churchyard of All Saints in Lyde, and
" asked for privilege of church there, and a Coroner;
" and Laurence Gros, Bailiff there, as Coroner, exa-
" mined the said John Davy, for what reason he was
" there ——": it then breaks off. Fol. 182b.—"On the
" 4th day of March, in the 4th year of the reign of King
" Edward IV., Edward Elys and Richard Harry, feoffees
" of Stephen Harry, came, and promised to give 100s.
" and more, of the money received, and to be received,
" from the tenement late of the said Stephen, unto the
" church of Lyde, on condition that the name of the
" said Stephen should every Sunday be published and
" prayed for, among the other Benefactors of the same
" church."

Fol. 184, a, b, is a fragment of the Account for the 8th
and 9th years of Edward IV. (1469, 70): the following
are among the items :—" Received from men standing
" in the market, beyond one day in the week 3s. 4d.
" Received from a Common Scott without polle money
" 19 li. 14s. 10d. Fines for drawing daggers this year
" 3s. 4d. Payd unto Thomas Caxtune for hys hors 2
" tymys to Gravyshende 4s. Payd unto the sayd
" Thomas Caxtune for syttyng with the Baylyfe [John
" Serlys] in court 3s. 4d. Payd unto Vincent Sedlay,
" he drynkyng with Thomas Bayene at Londone, 4d."
Bayene, as already noticed, was the town's London
agent.—" Payd unto Thomas Caxtune goyng to Lun-
" dune, havyng every day 6d. a day; beyng owt 22
" days for the mater betwyxt the Abbot and us, 11s."

On closing these extracts, a few additional remarks, in reference to Thomas Caxton, and his probable
relationship to William Caxton, our first printer, may
perhaps be not out of place.—He left Lyde, as already
noticed, in 1476, to accept office as Common Clerk of
Sandwich. That William Caxton was, by apprenticeship
with Robert Large, Mercer, a member of the Mercers'
Company in London, is a well known fact. Among the
persons who sued for the royal pardon, as having taken
part in the Rebellion known as " Jack Cade's Insurrec-
" tion," appears the name of Hugh Caxton, of Sandwich,
Mercer (Jack Cade's Rebellion, by B. B. Orridge, p. 68).
In the following year, as we learn from Mr. Blades's
Life of Caxton, an order was sent from the Mercers'
Company in London, to some person (not named) at
Sandwich, for gowns for the gentlewomen of the Duchess
of Burgundy; in close proximity to whose Court, at
Bruges, William Caxton was then living. It is only a
surmise, but certainly not an improbable one, that this
order may have been given to Hugh Caxton, of Sandwich; and this, through the intervention, all the more
probably, of William Caxton, if connected with him by
blood. On the other hand, Thomas Caxton's visits to
Sandwich, as entered in this book, are very numerous,
and sometimes prolonged—though certainly in reference
to the town's business—as set forth in various items
between the years 1458 and 1476.

One other circumstance also deserves remark, in reference to this question.— One of William Caxton's
fellow apprentices in London was a " Robert Dedes;"
a person of which surname, as seen in the Report upon
the Records of Rye, was residing in that place in the
reign of Edward III. Supposing, as elsewhere suggested, that William Caxton was a native of Tenterden,
he may not improbably have been influenced in selecting
Robert Large as his master, by a (comparatively) near
neighbour, Robert Dedes, of Rye, a member perhaps
of the same family as the John Dedes of the time of
Edward III.

The Custom Book, Customall, or Custumal, of Lyde,
as transcribed by Thomas Caxton, from the older copy
at Romney, and for which he was paid the sum of 13s.
4d. just before his departure for Sandwich in 1476, has
been previously alluded to.—This identical copy, a
thin quarto volume, of 28 leaves of vellum, still exists
among the archives of the Corporation of Lydd. The
first 13 leaves, containing 75 heads, or chapters, are, to
all appearance, wholly written in Caxton's hand; those
on the remaining 15 belonging to various more recent
dates. With the exception of the first three leaves,
which are slightly mutilated, the volume is in good
condition. On the parchment cover, which is somewhat

torn, and is formed of 2 leaves of an illuminated folio
Service-book of the 14th century, is written, in a hand
of a somewhat more recent date than Caxton's time,
" The Customall of Lydd." There are various names
scribbled on the cover, in later hands, John Bate and
John Bartruppe in the number; but, among them, his
own name does not appear. Among them also, the
adage, " Homo homini lupus "—Man to man is a wolf,
twice appears. A few passages among the more curious
of these Ordinances deserve to be noticed.—

" Also, it is used that whanne a manne fleeth to Holy
" Chirche, the Baylef, as Coroner, shal come to him to
" examyne him [as to] the cause of his fleyng etc. And
" he wylle felony k[n]owlech, be it inrollyd. And thanne
" he shalle abyde in the churche xl dayes, yf he wille,
" and att the ende of the seid xl dayes, he shalle for-
" swere the Kynges londe ther before the Baylif and
" Jurattes, and he shall chose his porte for to passe;
" and if he wille make abjuracion within xl dayes, he
" shalbe except [accopted] therto, and a noon after tho
" abjuracion he shalle take the crosse, and then the
" Baylif shalle do cry, onne the Kynges behalfe, that
" no manne, on forfettour of his lyfe and lyme, do
" him no harme, as long as he is in the Kynge's high-
" way toward his porte. . . . . .

" Also, it is used, if ony be founde cuttyng purses or
" pikeyng purses or other smale thynges, lynyn, wollen,
" or other goodes, of lytille value, within the fraunchise,
" att the sute of the party, [he] be brought in to the high
" strete, and ther his ere naylyd to a post, or to a cart
" whele, and to him shalbe take a knyffe in hand. And
" he shall make fyne to the towne, and after forswere
" the towne, never to come ayene. And he be found
" after, doyng in lyke wise, he thanne to lose his other
" ere. And he be found the thirde tyme, beryng tokyne
" of his ii eris lost, or els other signe by which he is
" knowene a theffe, att sute of party be he jugged
" [judged] to deth."—The "knife in hand" was delivered to him, that he might liberate himself by cutting
off his own ear.—

" Also, it is ordenyd, that the Kynges comone Court
" shalbe hold the Saturday, before the Baylif and
" Jurattes, sittyng in the Comene House, the Kynges
" Jugges; and at ix of the cloke, before the Court
" begynne, the great belle be knellyd a xii strokes, or
" moo, as for warnyng to the Court. . . . . .

" Also, it is used that the market be hold in the high
" strete, both of vetaylle and of all other manner of
" marchaundise brought by strangers; and that no
" manne be sufferde for to sell his ware goyng howse
" by howse."

Among the regulations belonging to a somewhat later
date, it is enacted, apparently in the reign of Henry
VIII., as to " Taverne kepers, or Typpelers," among
other things,—" That none be admitted, but suche as
" shalbe able to have competent lodgings for strangers
" and weyfarynge men, and to have a competent stent of
" fuell wood, mete for suche occupyenge. . . . . .

" Item, that none refuse to sell owte of there dores
" suche wyne, ale, or beare, as thaye use to sell in there
" owne houses, uppon payne of fyne and amercement.

" Item, that none putte sale any kynde of vytells in
" ther howses uppon the Sundayes or holly dayes, in the
" tyme of Devyne Servyce in the churche, uppon payne
" of amercement, except it be to suche strangers as
" shall come at the tyme of Common Prayer, and cannot
" tarry any long whyle, without frawde or culler. . . . .

" Item, that they retayne no man's servantes in there
" howses at unlawfull tymes, nor suffer them at any
" tyme to playe at unlawfull games, or to kepe yll rule
" in there houses, uppon payne of grevous amercement."
Chandlers are enjoined, " that there be no lack of
" candell at any tyme by the space of xxiiii howers
" together, uppon payne of amercement."

Among " Ordynances concernynge everye perticuler
" person," are the following, out of a great number,—
" Item, for avoydynge of commen annoyances, yt is
" orderyd that none shall washe any clothes at any
" commen wells of the towne, nor gyve any horse, geld-
" ynge, mare, or bullock, drynk at the buckett of any
" suche well, uppon payne of iis. for every such offence.

" Item, that none shall mysuse or mysorder the
" common wells called ' Pyggwell,' or ' Kete Well,"
" to the hurt or detrement of the water of sprynges of
" the same well . . . uppon payne of iiis. 4d.

" Item, that every poore man within this towne have
" of his owne in his howse or close, at Michelmas every
" yeare, three lodes of fuell wood, at the least; uppon
" payne of imprisonment, and to be found suspicyous
" of hedge pykynge and wood stelynge.

" Item, it is ordered that no collection or gatheringe
" be used in the church uppon the Sabothe daye, or
" holly dayes, but only for the poore people, uppon
" payne of xxs. for every offence."
In reference to Bakers,—" That there breade be well
" made, holsome, and good paste, and well bake; and
" that thaye bake no muste corne, uppon payne of for-
" fayture of theire breade.
" Item, that there commen kyndes of brede be whyte,
" ravell [whitey-brown], and browne, and no lacke
" hereof at any tyme. And that they gyve vantage to
" every dosen and half dosen, uppon payne of amerce-
" ment;"—the loaf thrown in to make the " baker's
" dozen," or half-dozen, is alluded to.
" Item, that every commen baker have his proper
" marke, to be allowed by the Baylyf, and recorded in
" the towne bookes, uppon payne of amercement."
As to Brewers,—" That thaye refuse not to sell there
" bere to poore folkes by the pynne [? measured up to
" the 'pin'], coppell [small cup], or gallon, for there
" redy monye, nor to any other inhabytant not beynge
" oustomed with them; uppon payne-of amercement. .
" . . . ,
" Item, that there be no lacke of beere at any tyme
" throughe there defaute, uppon payne of amerce-
" ment."
As to Butchers.—" That thaye kyll not (to put- to
" sale) any measely fleshe, nor rotten or unwholsome
" fleshe. And that there fleshe be well kylde and well
" fedde, mete to be allowed in any market, uppon payne
" (of) forfaiture of the same.
" Item, that thay sell not their tallowe owte of the
" towne, yf any chandler in the towne will buy the
" same, uppon payne of fyne.
" Item, that no butcher leave of kylling, or sellinge
" of flesh, before Shroftide."
The entries in this " Oustomall " end with some new
forms of oath in the reign of James the Second.
Among the muniments of the Corporation of Lydd,
there are a number of tattered folio leaves of paper,
with writing in a hand of, apparently, the latter half of
the 17th century; being a copy of a series of curious
memoranda in reference to the early history of the town
and its various manors, drawn up, for some legal purpose, in the earlier part of the reign of Queen Elizabeth.
Some of the information contained in these memoranda
seems to have been derived from recondite sources, in
part, at least, probably now no longer in existence:
extracts of the more important portions are therefore
subjoined :—
" Memorandum, it is to be noted that the Archbishop
" of Canterbury was allways the chief Lord of the towne
" of Lydd, as now the Queene is; and that the Bayliffe,
" Jurats, and Commons, of the same towne by old
" Charters were called,—' Homines Archiepiscopi Can-
" ' tuariensis in Lydd et Dengemarsh,' or ' in Lydd et
" ' Ingemarsh, commorantes;' " which indeed were his
" tenants.
" There is comprehended within the liberties of Lydd,
" 3 Bouroughs, viz., Lydd, Dengemarsh, and Orwell-
" stone (otherwise Orwarstone). The Bourough of Lydd
" is a cirquit, known by marks and bounds, lying wholy
" within the tenure of the Court of Aldington, apper-
" taining to the said Archbishop. The which bonrough
" was called, in Latin, ' Collecta de Lydd,' and in old
" English ' The Cullet of Lydd;' and was divided into
" two Inges and one Verge; as appeareth by an old
" book of the Archbishop of Canterbury called ' The
" ' Black Book,' and bearing no date.
" And afterwards, the service done to the Archbishop
" of Average (a service done by and with beasts and
" cattell), before all time of memory, was charged
" (? changed) and turned to a sum of money; as much
" as the service of Average then came unto, viz.,—
" 7li. 8s. 3d. for (? with) a henne, and 30s. for common
" fine and all proffits of Court, yearly. So that the said
" men or tennants so called, which be Baylif, Jurats,
" and Commons, that be freeholders of Lydd, be Lords
" in mean of the said bourough of Lydd, holding the
" same of the manner of Aldington for the rent and
" common fine abovesaid, and have, apertaining to the
" same, their common called ' the Ripe,' ' Holmstone,'
" and ' Beach.'
" (Note. The inhabitants of Lydd and tennants of the
" Archbishop did not assume unto themselves the name
" of Baylif, Jurats, and Commonalty, of Lydd, till the
" reign of King Henry the Sixt.)
" The Bourough of Orwellstone, otherwise Orwastone,
" is the land on the north and west side of the towne to
" Old Romenye; and is called, as appeareth by old pre-
" cedents of the bounds and Barony of Lydd, ' Inge-

" ' marsh :' and is divided into 3 parts, Westbrook, Or-
" welletone, and Mydley, holden of divers Lords; viz.,
" some part of Orwellstone, as part of Mydley, and the
" Marsh called ' New Lands,' were parcell of the 2
" Inges and one Verge above mentioned. And West-
" brook lyeth within divers Lordships, being mean
" lands to the Archbishop, as Old Longport, New
" Longport, Bletching, and the Vicar of Lydd. The
" residue of Orwellstone is holden of divers Lords,
" as the mannor of Belgare, the mannor of Jacques
" Court, the manor of Warehorne, the Sextre of Christ
" Churche, the Castle of Rochester, the late Chappell of
" Batleghe, the Dean and Chapter of Christ Churche,
" and of no other Lordes.
" The Bourough of Dengemarsh is the land on the
" east and south side of the town, or Ripe, to the sea,
" and is partly holden of the mannor of Aldington, and
" appertaining to the said tennants of the Archbishop
" of Canterbury dwelling in Lydd, and part of the
" mannor of Dengemarsh sometime of the Abbot of
" Battell, and, before that, the Prince; and by King
" William the Conqueror given to the Abbot of Battell;
" that is to say, all the lands lying on the east and south
" side of the water course of Dengemarsh is within the
" lordshipp of the Abbot of Battell, and all the lands
" lying between the Ripe and the water course, and so
" to Polehill, lieth in the Lordshipp of the Archbishop
" of Canterbury; as by the bounds thereof hereafter
" mentioned may plainly appear."
The above entries are followed by—" Orders taken
" for the Ripe, the 26th of September 1574, by the
" Bayliffe, Jurats, and Commons, of Lydd." The commoners, in a code of 28 resolutions, agree thereby to
forego their rights of common on the Ripe, and, in lieu
thereof, to have a flock of sheep there for the general
use of the town; but how this was to be effected, in the
way of division, is not stated. A town shepherd was to
be appointed for keeping the stock, as follows :—" Item,
" it is ordered that yearly, at the Feast of St Mary
" Magdalen, there shall be chosen a shepperd to keep
" and look to the sheep of the towne, by the Bayliffe,
" Jurats, and Commons, as they may accord; which
" shepperd shall yearly make account of the number
" yearly remaining, and of the increase and decay of
" the same. And which shepperd shall yearly put in
" sureties for his dealing."
This is followed by an account of the sheep then given
for the formation of the town flock, to be pastured on
the Ripe.—" The benevolence of sheep given to the
" towne by the Bayliff, Jurats, and Commoners, as
" followeth.—John Heblethwait, Bayliff, notwithstand-
" ing his great loss in sheep last year," gives " 6 ews."
Among others " Thomas Bate, Jurat," gives " 40 ews,"
and " John Bate, Jurat, 10 ews," the total given being
" 392 ews."
The Memoranda then proceed with,—" The bounds of
" the Archbishop's Franchess, somtime so called, or
" the ground which now is called ' Bishoprick;' which
" seemeth to be made by way of pertition between the
" Archbishop and his tenants, and the Barrons of Lydd:"
the boundaries, stated at length, having been " found and
" presented by Andrew Bate and John Bate, tennants to
" the Lord Archbishop, in the 2nd year of King Edward
" IV., 1462." This is followed by—" The bounds of the
" Barrouy, including the Archbishoprike, as it was pre-
" sented in the 2nd year of King Edward IV., 1462,"
such bounds being also given in full.
The following is an extract, in continuation, of the
principal portions of these Memoranda :—
" And it is to be noted that the cirquit of ground
" commonly called the ' Bishoprick,' is, in the antient
" records of the principall Court of Aldington, called
" ' the Denn of Lydd,' whereof came first the name of
" ' ' Denemarsh;' to wit, the marsh lieing under, or by,
" the Den of Lydd; for the same Denn of Lydd is a
" bank ground much higher than all the rest of the
" marshes or grounds adjoyning.
" And the said Denn of Lydd is holden of the Mannor
" of Aldington, by the Barrons of Lydd, for the yearly
" rent of 7li. 8s. 3d., as before is mentioned, and for
" the sum of 30s. yearly in the name of a common fine,
" for not appearing at Aldington Court, and for all
" mannor of proffits of Court, escheats, reliefs, and other
" dutyes.
" The which Denn of Lydd of old time, long sithence,
" was divided into two Inges, or Yeats, called in the
" Latin Records, ' jugum terræ.' And the service that
" in old time was done and had for the said 2 Inges, or
" Yates of land, was called ' averagium,' and was done
" by catell.

"Item, it appeareth in an old antient book of record
" of the Archbishop, called 'the Black Book," which
" is at Lambeth, to be seen in the title called ' Collecta
" ' de Lydd,' that certain tennants of Lydd, to the
" number of 5 or 6 and 40, did hold ' unum jugum terræ
" ' in Lydd ; et debent unum averagium' :—since
" which time the service above mentioned was turned
" into the afore mentiond sum of money . . . . The
" which antient Record above mentioned, being written
" in the said booke of the Archbishop of Canterbyry, is
" of such antienty, that it carryeth not date, neither is
" it mentioned whether before or sithens the Conquest
" that service was used ; but the said Record maketh
" mention that one marsh, lying in Mydley, parcell of
" the lands before mentioned, was the marsh ' which
" ' Bonniface, the Archbishop precedeing, did inclose ;'
" which Bonniface was in the time of King Henry the
" Third.
  " Dengemarsh is within the franchise and liberties of
" Lydd, and is that parcell of ground or cirquit that
" lieth on the east and south side of the Ripe to the
" seasward ; adjoining to the Denn of Lydd, and com-
" monly called ' Dengemarsh ;' which may be the cor-
" ruption of speech, yet the old Records and Charters
" do call it ' Dengemares,' or ' Dengemarsh.' The book
" called ' Doomsday' doth make mention that Promhill,
" Lydd, Orwarestone, alias Orwelstone, and Dengemarsh,
" were members to the towne and port of Romeneye,
" and so were before the Conquest, in the time of King
" Edward the Confessor, and his progenitors ; the which
" members were so allowed by the King's Recorder,
" and by the same towne and port admitted so to
" be ; and were contributors to Romeneye before all
" memory, bearing and paying a proportionable part of
" all their charges till the time of King Edward the
" First, who granted to his barrons of Lydd a Charter,
" to be in all points as free as Romeneye and Hasting,
" with other the Cinque Ports, finding, in aid and
" confederation to Romeneye, one shipp at the trans-
" portation of the King, parcell of five shipps wherewith
" Romeneye is charged. These words ' concessimus
" ' Barronibus nostris,' doth import they were united to
" the liberty of the Five Ports before, or els he would
" not have called [them] ' barrones nostris [nostri],'
" ' his barrons,' or, ' our barrons.' And so it appeareth
" by the Inspections [Inspeximus] of Edward 3rd, which
" reciteth the Charter of King Henry 3rd and King
" John, made ' Hominibus Archiepiscopi Cantuariensis
" ' de Hlyde et Dengemersh.' So by that Charter of
" Edward 1st, they be at a service certain, whereas
" before they were charged at the will of Romeney,
" their head Porte.
  " For it appeareth by an antient Record, written in
" French, which carrieth no date, that Lydd and the
" rest of the members was appointed to 8 shipps, and
" Romeneye 4 ; but I take that Record to be corrupt
" and untrue, as by Doomsday appeareth ; and allso
" the Charter and useage to the contrary. Also, the
" towne of Romeney were wont to charge Lydd and the
" rest of the members with the — penny of all maner of
" charges. But now of late, in the time of King Henry
" the 7th (1490) there was a composition between the
" two townes for 3li. yearly to be paid, the 22 of March,
" in discharge of all duties to that towne, saveing the
" fifth shipp, the fifth penny of the Burgesses' wage to
" Parliament. Yet that is but an exaction ; for the
" Charter of Edward 1st dischargeth them from all other
" charges, saveing of one shipp only. But the composi-
" tion is, in lieu of all charges.
  " King William the Conqueror, after he had conquered
" the realm, the Archbishop of Canterbury, the Barrons
" and gentlemen of Kent, and the Barrons of the Cinque
" Ports, with the whole commons of Kent, resisted the
" King, till he had admitted their laws, liberties, and
" free customs, which before that time they used and
" enjoyed ; which being granted and allowed by the
" King, that shire of Kent had still their custom of
" Gavell kind ; and so did the Cinque Portes, as well in
" Kent as in Sussex ; and allso, the Barrons of the Ports
" had all their liberties and customs confirmed, and the
" Archbishop likewise enjoyd his liberties and priviledges
" appertaining to his See. Amongst the which, the towne
" of Lydd was his towne, and he lord of the same, as
" appertaining to the mannor of Aldington, and is in-
" corporate by the name of ' Homines Archiepiscopi
" ' Cantuariensis in Lydd et Dengemarsh commorantes."
  " And the said King, William the Conqueror, after
" he had erected and founded an Abbey att Battell, gave
" to the Abbot of the same his mannor of Dengemarsh
" in Lydd ; which was a mannor-house, and certain
" demesnes belonging to the same, lying within the

" bourough of Dengemarsh. But all the lands within
" the same bourough did not belong to the said manor,
" but did belong to divers other men and barrons of
" Lydd and Dengemersh, as they yet do belong."
  " Reasons shown in the time of Queen Elizabeth, that
" she hath no right to the Ripe of Lydd.—
  1. " If the Queen have right to the Ripe, then she
" hath right to the whole towne ; for that the same
" standeth upon the Ripe, and over the same.
  2. " If the sea did overflow it, and that it was won
" of the sea, then it must be proved when it was won,
" either by witness, writeings, or chronicles, which
" cannot be shewed, nor proved.
  3. " For the antiquity of the towne and plott, not to
" be lately won from the sea, appeareth by the face and
" view of the antienty of the towne and church, and
" buryall of men cross-legged, and such like monu-
" ments ; and that there hath been a forrest there, great
" trees under the ground do shew : so yet it appeareth
" in the marshes called "the Samp" on the north side
" of the said town.
  4. " Lydd doth appear in the Book of Doomsday,
" before the Conquest, to be a towne, and not sea.
  5. " Lydd is ' Terra continens ' [land joining] unto the
" town of Romenye, and a member therof, and so called
" at this day ; which doth appear to be land sixteen
" hundred years agoe, when the Romains came in ;
" for it was the ' Curia Romanorum,' and so in all
" writeings it is called ' Romaine Hall' ; and then, as
" old chronicles and presedents do shew, the sea in
" time past was from Appledore to Hythe, and then
" Romeneye and Lidd were an island, and inhabited by
" the Romains and Lidd for strength.
  6. " Also, the old records in the Tower and Exchequer
" shew, amongst the townships taxable to the fifteenths
" etc., that Lydd is mentioned to be one, and accounted
" to be in the Hundred of Longport, and in the Lath of
" Shypway.
  7. " So that if there were any deluge to be proved of
" Lydd, by the chronicles, evedences, records, or other-
" wise, it was before land, and then no sea ; and then
" the water going away again, it must be granted that
" this deluge doth not give any title to the Crown.
  8. " And besides, the Queens Highness hath a mannor
" called ' Dengemarsh,' which was part of the possessions
" of the Abby of Battell, and at the time of the Con-
" quest given to the Abby, then being the demesne
" lands of the Crown and revenue ; which mannor is
" between Lydd and the sea."
  Omitting some paragraphs, as of no interest, the
paper continues.—
  12. " They have also a common seale for this purpose
" for selling and letting their land, which time out of
" mind hath been used, besides the common seal of
" the town and the seal of office belonging to the Bay-
" liffe ; and at this time the same grounds be lett to
" farme under the same seal with the Bishops mitre,
" which was the seal granted them by the Archbishop,
" the lord of the towne, at the beginning of their in-
" corporation. And their Corporation was long before
" the Conquest, as appeareth by their Charters, which
" do make mention that they shall be so free, and injoy
" all those liberties and freedoms, which they have
" honorably and freely enjoy'd in the times of King
" William the Conqueror, King Edward the Confessor,
" and their progenitors, Kings of England.
  13. " And further, their common seal affirmeth no
" less ; which carryeth in the shield a church and half
" a shipp, and over the church a scutcheon, having
" therein a cross and foure ramping lyons ; which were
" anexed to their former arms, the church and half
" shipp, in the time of King Siweno (or Swayne) in
" consideration of divers exploits by the Barrons of Lydd,
" done at the arivsall of the Danes, which then attempted
" to arive at Lydd. Note—The Danes [attemp]ting to
" land at Ways End, were slain with great slaughter
" by the Barrons of Lydd, etc.
  14. " And there did remain within 20 years last past
" two hills or round banks by the sea-side, at a place
" called the 'Way's End,' west from the towne, where-
" of one remaineth yet, and the other is worn away by
" the sea ; the which hills were full of dead men's
" bones ; and the common report of old antient men in
" the towne always have been, and it is, that they have
" heard their ancestors say, that they were the bones of
" certain Danes that attempted here to arive.
  " Then joyn all this together, that this ever was land,
" and not known ever by writeings, evidences, records,
" or chronicles, that this land was inned from the sea,
" but ever firm land ; and then the possession ever
" being with the towne, setting, letting, buying and

" selling of houses there standing, a fee farm payd for it,
" a common scale for this purpose; what can be more
" to overthrow the Queen's pretended tytle as of land
" now lately won of the sea, or of any other tytle that
" in any other respect can be made to it?"

From the old pagination on the folios of these memoranda, they are evidently incomplete, some portions of them now being lost.

The above tradition, it may be added, as to the mounds erected over the bones of the Danes on the sea-shore, seems to have been transferred, at a later date, to Hythe. Leland, who visited the latter place in the reign of Henry VIII., makes no mention of it, or of the vast collection of bones in the charnel-house beneath the chancel; which are said (upon no reliable authority) to have been removed thither from the sea-shore.

In concluding this Report, I avail myself of the opportunity of expressing my obligations to my friend Henry Stringer, Esq., the Town Clerk, for the interest he has taken in these researches, and the pains, of which he has not been sparing, to provide me every possible facility for furthering them.

HENRY THOMAS RILEY.

THE MANUSCRIPTS OF THE CORPORATION OF NEW ROMNEY.

(Second Notice.)

Since writing my preceding Report upon the still surviving archives of this ancient town, an ample opportunity has been afforded me, by the united kind offices of my friends H. B. Walker, Esqre., one of the Jurats, and Henry Stringer, Esqre., Town Clerk of the Corporation, to make a thorough examination of the earlier among them; documents which, from their voluminousness, were of necessity but succinctly touched upon in that Report.

The earliest Volume now preserved, as there stated, is a thin mutilated small folio, commencing with a list of such persons, in the various Wards, as were assessed to the Poll-tax, which gave rise to Wat Tyler's Rebellion in 1381; and then continuing with an account of the assessments to Maltote (or rate upon the sale of commodities), and the successive items of Corporation expenditure, in detail, down to the feast of the Annunciation in the 7th year of that reign (A.D. 1384). With one or two slight inaccuracies, (more particularly as to its date), the whole, with of its contents have been printed in that able, but now somewhat rare, book, Boys' *Materials for the History of Sandwich*; and consequently may be looked upon as too patent to the reading public to necessitate any further notice of its contents in this Report, however curious, as indeed they really are.—The following, it must be borne in mind, however lengthy in appearance, are but a few extracts only, though the more interesting passages, it is believed, have in general been selected; about nine tenths probably of each volume, exclusive of the frequently recurring lists of names, being of necessity left unnoticed.

The Second Volume of the Corporation Accounts, may be described as a mutilated volume, which, if we are to trust an old numeration of the 17th century, contained 144 leaves of parchment, folio size, the first seven of which are now lost. A fragment of ancient binding, in white leather, is still hanging about it, and the first five or six leaves are in a very tattered condition. The earlier part of the volume is briefly described in the preceding Report, under the head of—"Fragments of a " folio book, consisting of 23 leaves of parchment," these leaves having been found by me separate from the rest of the volume. The first three pages of this portion are occupied by entries of the reigns of Richard II., Henry IV., and Henry VI.; of which some notice will be taken at the close of the present extracts from the main contents of this volume; its earliest entries commencing at page 4 of the volume in its present state, or the reverse of folio 9 under its old numeration.

7, 8 Richard II. A.D. 1384, 5.—As in the preceding Volume of the town Accounts, the list of "Maltotes," or rates collected from the freemen and inhabitants, begins with Holynbroke Ward, and William Holynbroke (from whose family the Ward, no doubt, had its name) heads the list. The largest sums paid this year are by Stephen Adam 15s. 2d. and William Seford 12s. 1d., in Holynbroke Ward; Seford then being, to all appearance, the head innkeeper in the town; Andrew Colyn 17s., in Butchery Ward; Richard Sprott 20s. 2¼d.

in Hospital Ward; Stephen Spoon 19s. 5d., in Hamersond Ward; and Nicholas Portour 11s. 6½d. in Deme Ward. William Seford again pays 10s. 1d. as being rated, not under a Ward, but as a Vintner. John Newene, (probably so called from keeping the New Inn) pays 9d. in his Ward (Holynbroke) and 5s. as a Vintner. William Ropere pays the highest Maltote loviod, as a Butcher, 14s. 0½d. Of the seven "Hospites," hostelers, or lodging-house keepers, who pay Maltote this year, six are women. The smallest Maltote received from any one is two pence. Among other receipts, (translated from the Latin) is 12d. from Richard Grygory for selling " one porpoise, and 12d. from Stephen Spoon " for 'selling one porpoise." This fish was evidently looked upon as a delicacy in those times, and the above fine was exacted for every porpoise sold without the limits of the town. Daniel Rowe, the former Common Clerk, (who is mentioned in the preceding Report, and in that upon the documents at St. Catharine's College, Cambridge), is frequently named in these accounts, as acting for the town at Dover and other places, and on the occasion of disputes with the town of Lydd, in the present instance. Among the payments this year are the following " entries.—6s. 4d. for the expenses of William Holyn- " broke, William Childe, and William Tyece, on the last " day of May, when they conversed with the Lieutenant " [of Dovur Castle] as to making terms with Lyde. " 100s. given to the Lieutenant the same day. 20s. " given to William Tydecoumbe [Serjeant-at-law] the " same day. 6s. 8d. sent through Robert Essex to " William Tydecombe, to be retained for us, as " counsel, against the men of Lyde. 39s. 10d. expended " upon Simon de Burley, Warden of Dover Castle. " 6s. 8d. expended upon the Lieutenant in the house of " William Holynbroke. 3l. 6s. 8d. expenses of Simon " Clerk, our Bailiff at Great Jernemuth (Yarmouth)." John Frost, at this date, was Common Clerk. Daniel Rowe, the previous Common Clerk, is set down as living in Sharle Ward, in the year preceding this: in the present year his name does not occur among those who pay Maltote, and in the accounts his name no longer appears: he probably died early in 1385.

8, 9 Richard II. A.D. 1385, 6.—William Holyngbroke, though not paying the largest Maltote, heads the list. Among the Receipts:—"8s. of Robert Stonherste, " for contempt committed by him against the com- " munity of Romene. 45s. received from William " Holyngbroke for one cloth of silk. 20d. from Simon " Clerk, for weighing of ' dates.'"

Payments.—"5s. for bread and wine, with the " Lieutenant. 6s. 9d. for the expenses of a supper to " the Lieutenant, in bread, wine, pepper, sephrone " [saffron], and fish. 54s. 8½d. for expenses upon the " Archbishop [William Courtenay] and his household, " at Romene. 6d. for wine bought in the house of " John Newene for the men of Hugh Fastolfe. 3s. 9d. " for making 12 pavises [shields]. 18d. paid for " ' dates ' sent to John de Orleskotte for the keeper of " the Chest, with the Evidences. 3s. 4d. paid as a " reward to the Common Clerk for writing out the " watches upon the sea-coast. 20d. for one dyole " [dial]," for the town balenger, or barge; the minutes of expenses upon fitting it out are very numerous. There are several items also for work upon the Slow, (or Sluice), probably then at the mouth of the harbour.

9, 10 Richard II. A.D. 1386, 7.—Under "Maltotes," William Holyngbroke still heads the list. The Maltotes of the Vintry, or wine trade, have increased in number and amount this year, Richard Mortimer paying 12s., William Seford 6s., and William Holyngbroke 2s. 9d. Adam Joefdi [Thursday] and his partner 6d. The Butchers also, William Ropere at their head, pay large amounts; and about this time, not improbably, the town was at the height of its affluence. Among the receipts.—" Received 6s. 8d. of the men of the town of " Wynchelse, for their share of the costs incurred at " London by John Salerne and John Elys upon a copy " of Magna Charta. Received of William Holyngbroke " 15l. 8s. 1d. for a part of the common balenger (or " barge, which had been recently broken up); also, " 12 pieces of silver money of Spain, received from him " for the same."—"Paid 8s. expenses of jurors incurred " upon the arrest of men of Lyde, at Lyde. 14d. for a " writ to the keeper of Rochester Bridge, for passage " there. 6l. 3s. 4d. the expenses of Simon Lonceford " and John Salerne, riding to London at Michaelmas " to the Parliament. 3l. 6s. 8d., the expenses of John " atte Halle, for 38 days at the same Parliament, he " taking 20d. per day." 131. 6s. 8d. are the " expenses " of the Slowe," or Sluice, this year; some other items being superadded. There are many items also for the

fitting out of the new balenger, or town barge; 3s. being
paid for a kettle (cacabo) for it.

10, 11 Richard II., A.D. 1387-8, William Holyngbroke, of Holyngbroke Ward, heads the list of Maltotes. James Tyece appears in this year for the first
time, in Holyngbroke Ward, as there paying the
very humble sum of 2d. In the preceding year he
paid 2d. as a Vintner; and in this year he also pays 11d.
in High Mill Ward. He afterwards rose, in the town,
to be a man of eminence. The payments of the Vintry
this year are fourfold in number those of the preceding
year, Alice Mortimer paying the highest sum, 10s. 8d.;
probably she was the widow of Richard. William
Ropere still heads the list of Butchers, in the amount of
his Maltote.—"Paid Margery Watts 3s. for hire of one
" room for the rigging, for three quarters of this year.
" 10s. 10d. given to the men of Hythe for their play.
" 23s. 2½d., the expenses of Stephen Adam and William
" Holyngbroke in conferring with the Lord Archbishop.
" 4s. 4d. paid for the expenses incurred in saving a ship
" at the Kenele."

11, 12 Richard II. A.D. 1388, 9. William Holyngbroke is at the head of the list of Maltotes paid: Alice
Mortimer has disappeared from the Vintry; and William Ropere still pays the largest Maltote as a Butcher.
In fol 25 b, (old numeration), under this year, there is
an interpolation, to the following effect (translated):—
" Be it remembered, that John Lewyne was arrested
" for his rebelliousness committed against Symon
" Clerk, Jurat, and the other Jurats, at the dest (? dais),
" on the 11th of December in the 20th year of the
" reign of King Richard the Second, and was bound
" in a penalty of 20s., by pledges, Symon Beaupry and
" James Hikke, if guilty thereof for the future."—
Account of 11, 12 Richard II. continued.—"Received
" 40s. from the executors of John (? Simon) Colrede
" for one anchor which the said Simon took at Romene,
" upon the sands there."—"Paid 11l. 2s. 3d. to John
" Elys, to deliver the same to the Warden of Dover
" Castle, on the promise made to him at the Shepwey.
" 11s. 2d. for fish sent to the lady, the wife of Sir
" John Devros. 7s. 10d. paid for making the bridge of
" Illo;"—a wooden bridge over the Rother : the locality
where this bridge once stood, is still pointed out.—"Paid
" to Nicholas Peintour, mason, and his men, for
" their work upon the Slow (Sluice). Paid 26l. 13s. 4d.
" to Nicholas Whateman, carpenter, for his work
" upon the Slow. Paid 3l. 15s. to Andrew Colyn for
" digging in the Ree. Paid John Louecok 18s. for a
" panel for the Slow."

12, 13 Richard II. A.D. 1389, 90. William Holyngbroke is still the first in the list: Hugh Fletcher pays
the highest Maltote as a Butcher, William Ropere the
next.—"Paid 6s. 8d., by James Tyece and Robert Jeffe,
" for groynynge the bridge of Ille. Paid 3s. 4d. to
" John Salmon, pilotage (lodmanagio) to Scotland (for
" the town balenger). Paid 8d. for a pound of sealing-
" wax (cera gummates). Paid 21½d. for engraving the
" little seal. Paid 11s. 2d. for fish sent to the Arch-
" bishop, being at Saltwode."

On fol. 30 a a transcript is given of a long indenture
bearing date the 21st of Richard II. (1398), and made
between William Porter and Robert Geffe, of the
one part, and Edith, the wife of Andrew Colyn, of
Romene, of the other part. The following localities
are mentioned in it.—A messuage, called " the Salt-
" shoppe," in the Parish of St. Laurence. A messuage in Spytelstrete, in the Parish of St. Laurence. A stall (stallagium) at which the said Andrew
used to stand. An acre of land called " Brettysacre"
in the Parish of Hope All Saints, " near the land
" of the heirs of William Holyngbroke the elder,"
and near the " land of Crawthorne." A messuage
called the " Kayhouse," in the Parish of St. Nicholas,
at Romene. A stall in the Parish of St. Laurence,
at which John Hurtyn, of Hethe, used to stand. Two
acres of land, situate at Bowetonne, in the Parish of
Lyde, near the land of William Septvantz, Knight, and
the land there of James Tiece. A stall in the Parish
of St. Laurence, opposite the market called " the
" Poultry [le Pultrie]." A new barn and a new stall,
in the Spitelstrete, in the Parish of St. Laurence. A
house called " the Henhouse;" the latter, possibly,
may have been a mere fowl-house.

13, 14 Richard II. A.D. 1390, 1: William Holyngbroke, of Holyngbroke Ward, is still named first
among the inhabitants. Three millers are named, serving
under three different masters, as paying Maltote, in
Hope Ward. In the "Vintry," John Lucas, "of the
" Hope" (Hoop) pays 4d.; and he, or another person
so called, pays 22d. as a "Mariner."—"For remunera-

" tion given to a certain messenger, sent to ¿erne-
" mouthe (Yarmouth) for the saving of the liberties of
" Romene there. Paid for capons and cygnets sent
" to the Lord Archbishop of Canterbury, at Saltwode,
" and horses hired for the same, with messengers
" 27s. 10d. Expenses of the Jurats and their horses,
" then riding to the same lord 26s. 8d. Expenses of
" the Slowe (Sluice) and of the bridge of Horne, and
" of repair of the way at Walgate 11s. 8d. For the
" pay of John Pecham, Common Clerk, for the whole
" year, and remuneration given to him, 56s. 8s."

14, 15 Richard II., A.D. 1391, 2. As hitherto,
William Holyngbroke heads the list. The name of
" John Cakstone" appears this year, for the first time; a
man of some means, as paying one of the highest
Maltotes in Holyngbroke Ward. Reference will again
be made to him, at a later date. In Heymelle (High
Mill) Ward, Simon Esdmund pays 10d. for Maltote;
Margery, his wife, is named, but pays nothing. John
Orgoner, (as he has done from the beginning of the book)
pays 12d. for Maltote, in Joce Ward : it was his duty
probably to play the organ in the church of St. Nicholas,
or St. Laurence. Receipts—"16d. for an old debt from
" William Swantone, late Vicar of Romene, for a
" Maltote. 40s. for a fine from John Talbot, Bailiff
" of Romene, paid to the commonalty this year,
" because he offended against it."—"Paid for the
" expenses of 18 best men of the town, riding to the
" Lord Archbishop of Canterbury, to protect the liberty
" of the town, and that the said Lord might not usurp
" it 28s. 4½d. Paid for all costs incurred upon 24
" capons, 24 geese, 24 pullets, sent to the Constable of
" Dover, on holding the Schipwey 31s. 8d. Paid in
" divers expenses upon Edward Dalingregge, Knight,
" when in the town for one night, to ride on the
" morrow to the Schipwey, namely, in wine, capons,
" and pullets, sent to him 6s. 1d." Large sums are
spent this year upon a ship, " hired and arrayed for
" the King's service."—"Expenses upon Henry de
" Horne, when he came to the town of Romene, to
" treat with the commonalty thereof, for the bridge
" called ' Hornysbregge' 3s. 7d. For rent for a sollar
" hired in the house of Henry Roger, for three
" quarters, to put the things belonging to the com-
" monalty there 3s."

15, 16 Richard II., A.D. 1392, 3 : William Holyngbroke is at the head of the list. John Bacheler pays
2s. 2d. for Maltote in Hope Ward, and Salamon Mous
9d. William Robyn pays, as a Mariner, 3s. 1½d. and
2s. 6d. for a trauulers, probably a trawling-net.—"Paid
" for divers expenses at various times upon the Slow,
" and taking down of the bridge of Hornesbregge, and
" Walgate, and other necessary expenses 3l. 11s. 7d."

16, 17 Richard II. A.D. 1393, 4. : William Holyngbroke
heads the list. John Cakestone is here written as
" Kaketone"; his Maltote having declined from 4s. 4d.
to 3s. " John Swetemouth" pays 22d. in Hamersmith
Ward. The occupation of " Hospites," or Hostelers, is
now no longer limited to women, but equally shared by
the two sexes.

At fol. 41 b. an interpolation occurs (in Latin) bearing
date the 12th year of Henry VI. (A.D. 1433) stating that
Melis Vantellicht, of Danske, (Dantsic), master of the
ship " Mary Knygth," which had been wrecked, claimed
certain goods that had been salved, and were in the town
of Romene, and that the Jurats and certain commoners
made composition with him for 7 marks 6 shillings ;
whereupon a release was duly executed by Vantellicht.

16, 17 Richard II. continued.—"They answer for
" fines received, for dung 10s. 10d. and 2s. fines for
" swine. Also 12d. received for one pipekoker (empty
" winecask). And 2s. received for ferm (rent) of the
" Slow" :—this may mean that the revenues of the Slow,
or Sluice, had been recently let on lease.—"Expenses
" of John Elys, being at London various times for the
" making of indentures for the Cinque Ports, as to their
" liberties 4l. 4s. Paid for yarne and a cord for the
" wine 4s. 4d. ; and for making up of the same 15d. :"—
this was for " Wyntredyng and porterage of wine," upon
which town dues, or Maltotes, were raised.—" Paid for
" the desque which stands in the church of St. Nicholas
" 20d." A list of the " Barge stores " is given under
this year. An interpolation (in Latin) at fol. 42 b. states
that on the 9th of June in the 20th year of Richard II.
(1397), " came Symon Spicer of Hethe, into our Chancery,"
before the then Bailiff, Richard Water, (a Notary, and
probably appointed by the Archbishop of Canterbury) .
and the Jurats, as also, before Henry Philpot, Jurat of
Hethe, and John Smalwode, Common Clerk of Hethe,
and entered into a certain bond.

17, 18 Richard II. A.D. 1394, 5. The name of William Holyngbroke disappears for a time, he probably being absent from the town ; the name of Joan Holyngbroke probably his wife, heads the list of inhabitants paying Maltotes. John Cakystone pays a reduced Maltote, of 2s. No fewer than 48 persons pay Maltote under the head of "Vintry" this year. Payments,—" They account " for expenses incurred in gifts to the Lady Beamont, " in the absence of the Warden [John Lord de " Beaumont], he being in Ireland at the time, when the " same lady was delivered of a son ; the same as the " other Barons did at divers times, and on the day on " which the same lady was churched ; on which day " the best [valentiores] men of the town of Romene " were at Dover Castle, at dinner there, 7l. 11s. 6d. " Paid the Lord de Beaumont, on account of the pro- " mise made by the Cinque Ports, and in remuneration " of the officers at Dover Castle, and in other costs " incurred thereon, before the departure of the Lord " de Beaumont for Ireland 11l. 8s. 8d. For expenses " incurred by Jurats sent at different times to Stephen " Betenham, and for victuals bought for the same " Stephen, when he came to Romene, to give his " counsel for maintaining the liberties of Romene " 38s. 10d. For presents given to John Wottone, and " expenses incurred to gain an order of the Lord Arch- " bishop, as to destroying the market, except upon feast " days 23s. 10d. For gifts to, and expenses incurred " upon, John Drakx and William Lente, Serjeants-at- " arms to our Lord the King, coming severally at " different times with letters patent for holding inquest " as to goods coming by wrec upon the sea-coast this " year, 30s. 10d. For the expenses of Stephen Adam, " John Elys, Hugh Fleger, James Tiece, and John " Pecham, riding to Maidestone by appointment of the " Jurats, to know the will of the Lord Archbishop, " what he purposed to do against the liberties of " Romene : and also, upon Master Richard Water, " Notary, coming from Canterbury, for making chal- " lenges (provocationibus) in Romene 52s. 3d. For " expenses upon John Colpeper, for a certain breakfast " 16s. For expenses of John Pecham riding (equi- " tantis) to Ireland for the community, and his remu- " neration for 11 weeks 10l."

18, 19 Richard II., A.D. 1395, 6. Joan Holyngbroke heads the list of Maltotes. John Cakstone pays an increased Maltote of 3s. 10d.—" Paid for gifts given to " the Lord de Bealmont [Beaumont], Warden of the " Cinque Ports, when he arrived from Ireland, and to " the Lady de Bealmont, in the absence of the said " lord, as the other Barons did, for the maintenance of " the liberties of the Cinque Ports this year, 9l. 12s. 6½d. " For divers gifts and expenses this year, in the Jurats " making suit to the Reverend Father, the Lord Arch- " bishop of Canterbury, to put his bailiwick into " the hands of the community of Romene, at ferm " 15l. 14s. 7½d. Paid rent for the chamber for the " Jurats, and forms in the same ; costs of the Slow ; and " stores, and costs of the Schipwey this year 41s. 6d."

19, 20 Richard II. A.D. 1396, 7 ; Joan Holyngbroke is the first in the list, beginning with Holyngbroke Ward : William Clederow, a townsman afterwards of note, appears for the first time. John "Cakton" pays an enlarged Maltote of 4s. ; and a Robert Cakton also appears, paying 4d. " A stranger there dwelling," pays 14d. in "Bocherye" Ward. 8d. is paid for Maltote upon two porpoises, "cut up," or, by retail.—" Received 42s. " for dishes, chargers[parapsidibus],ox-hides, and other " things sold this year." "Spent on buying a new " barge 53l. 6s. 8d. For making, repairing, and mend- " ing, together with divers tools, and carpenters' wages, " as to the said barge 28l. 10s. 4½d. Expenses at Parlia- " ment of John Yon and Robert Geffe, and two grooms, " and four horses, holden on the 19th of February " 106s. 0½d. Expenses incurred upon the Queen's " [Isabel of France] Coronation, by Stephen Adam, " Symon Clerk, John Gardiner, and James Tiece, with " purchase of 3 garnitures [garnementorum] of baudekyn " with 3 hoods of scarlet, and 4 men and 8 horses, going " and returning 12 days, 12l. 19s. 8d. Paid for the " repair and mending of the house of the Slowe [Sluice " house] 9s. 9d." It is found also that 10l. is due to the Hospital of St. John.

20, 21 Richard II., A.D. 1397, 8. The name of William Holyngbroke now reappears: he pays the com- paratively large Maltote of 6s. 8d., there being a note against it, "pro agreamento," by agreement, it being understood, probably, to include all that might have been due in his absence. The name of Joan Holyngbroke follows, with the small Maltote of 9d., John "Cakton" pays 4s., Robert Caktone 2s. 8d., these in Holyngbroke

Ward ; but in Bocherye Ward, a Robert Caktone pays also 14d. In addition to the preceding payment by William Holyngbroke, John Turnour pays a sum of "3s. 9d. " of the Maltote of William Holyngbroke in arrears " from the 19th year." Three men are excused from paying in Joce Ward, "because they are mariners ;" we may perhaps hence conclude, that this Ward was adjacent to the sea-shore. The Hostelers, consisting of five women, are but few in number now ; their lodging-houses probably being gradually superseded by the inns. Under "the Vintry," William Lucas is mentioned as still keeping the "Hope" [Hoop] ; and John You, the Member of Parliament, pays the largest Maltote for im-porting wine.—" Presents sent to the Archbishop and " Lieutenant of the Castle, and gifts to the said Lieu- " tenant and to John Wyttone, and the Clerk of the " Castle, and to John Blakeburne, Serjeant-at-arms to " the King, and to other Serjeants 6l. 5s. 6d." This is followed (fol. 52 b.) by "The Account of Symon Clerk, " Robert Geffe, surveyor of the barge, and John Palmere, " master thereof." In the same page tuns and pipes of wine, perry, [pirotar'], and cider [segear'] are mentioned as being warehoused in the town.—"On the 23rd day " of December, Richard Grygori was sworn to search " all boats coming with fish and herrings to market, " so that no one should sell any fish or herrings from " any boat at market or elsewhere, until all the fish " or herrings in every boat should have been exposed " for sale."

21, 22 Richard II., A.D. 1398, 9: William and Joan Holyngbroke head the list of Maltotes; John "Cakton" pays a Maltote of 4s., but Robert "Cakton" disappears. William Elmet pays 2s. 5d. jointly with "Argent, his " wife." In Joce Ward, against John Organer, the Organist's name, is entered "mortuus est," he is dead. In Mill Ward, Stephen Adam now has a mill, in addition to the Heyemulle (High Mill). In fol. 51 a. is entered (as an interpolation) the formal resignation, (1 Henry IV.) to the twelve Jurats of Romene, of the Mastership of the House, or Hospital, of St. John, by John Wygynton, Master thereof:—" Received 24s. from Roger Coupere, " arrears of his account upon the voyage from Rochel " to Dunkirke, in the time of John Palmere, master of " the ship or barge." Items occasionally occur to shew that the Corporation earned money by freightage on board their ship, or barge, when on foreign service.—" Paid " for a house standing on the Quay of St. Nicholas, " bought of John Tymberden for the community this " year 106s. 8d. Given to John Rone, coming hither " from Flanders to make the Sluice, for his pains 23s. 4d. " and for his expenses the time he stayed here, namely, " for 3 days 20d. In the prosecution for forbidding the " market of Lyde, and other costs and expenses 23s."

22, 23 Richard II., 1 Henry IV., A.D. 1399, 1400. William and Joan Holyngbroke, in Holyngbroke Ward, are at the head of the list of Maltotes. John "Cakton" pays 4s.—" Received at Milford 9l. 13s. 4d. for wages " of men and ships," "Costs upon the Slow ; and of " our Lord the King (Henry IV.), by John Lanceforde, " John Gardiner, and John Talbot, for 10 days, with " purchase of 3 gowns and 3 hoods of scarlet, and " broidyng of 3 sleeves, and making up of the gowns and " hoods, with hire of their horses 9l. 11s. 4d. Costs " incurred upon the pleas holden at Westminster, and " lances and bells 3s. 4d.," for the canopy held over the Sovereign by the Barons of the Cinque Ports.—" For " renewal of the Charters this year, 6l. 12s. 10½d. For " the costs of . . . . and for the costs of Robert Holier " and John May, riding to Sandwich and to London, " and along the sea-coast, to obtain news as to the " arrival of the present King."

1, 2 Henry IV., A.D. 1399, 1400. William and Joan Holyngbroke head the list of Maltotes : John "Cakton" pays 3s. 4d. In a deed interpolated, of the 5th year of this reign, fol. 59 a. mention is made of St. Martin's churchyard.—" Expended upon the barge for 7 weeks, " on a voyage to Newcastle, this year, 8l. 7d. Gifts, " costs, and rewards, given for return of writs, and for " letters of Brodhull, and to the players of Heithe, this " year 35s. 7d. For digging a delve (dam) for the " barge, and strikyng the rigging of the barge, and for " the warden of the same, and to William Brabesone, " for melting the tallow 11s. 7d." The tallow would be used for rubbing the barge, to make it water-tight. " To John Fynch, for paper, wax, oil, and spices, bought " of him, and for pilotage at [? to] Kirkeleye 28s. 1d." Probably Kirkley, or Kirtley, near Lowestoft, is meant : the Bailiff sent from Romney to the Fair at Yarmouth would probably land there.—" For repair of the Common " House this year 9s. 6d." In an interpolation in fol. 60 a. of the sixth year of Henry IV., the Jurats are men-

tioned as "holding session" in the church of St.
Nicholas. Reginald Willes is put upon his good
behaviour for having sold an oar belonging to the
commonalty, and taken possession of the "common
"boat," against the will of the Jurats. In the same
year presentment is made to the Jurats, in the same
church, as to the finding of 250 pounds of wax, near
the sea-shore, The Bailiff of the town takes, "in the
"name of the Lord," (the Archbishop of Canterbury),
88 pounds, the rest being divided among the freemen
and non-freemen who had found it.

Fol. 60 b, further interpolations occur, among them
the following, (tr.):—"Be it remembered, that whereas
"various dissensions and disputes had been mooted
"between the Barons and community of the town of
"Romene of the one part, and many men of the Marsh
"of Romene of the other part, as to certain land
"within the two walls towards Appuldre extending,
"and to the community of the town of Romene per-
"taining; which land the said men of the Marsh of
"Romene have occupied, and do not cease daily to
"occupy, to the no small prejudice and grievance
"of the aforesaid Barons and their heirs; therefore
"the said Barons of Romene, desiring and wishing to
"resist the malevolent designs of the said men of the
"Marsh of Romene, and to prevent their occupation
"of the land aforesaid with their cattle, distrained
"William Keno and Thomas Mersaher, occupying the
"land aforesaid with their sheep; that is to say, on the
"2nd day of May in the 9th year of the reign of Henry
"the Sixth. Wherefore, on the morrow of the said
"day came the aforesaid William Kene to the vill of
"Romene, and put himself upon the favour of the
"Jurats; which Jurats decided that the same William
"should pay 6s. 8d. for occupation of the said land;
"and the aforesaid Jurats to ferm let the same parcel
"to the said William, to have and to hold the same to
"him and his assigns."

Fol. 61a, John Hamone, of Radynge [Reading Gate,
near Tenterden], in the 19th of Richard II., is put upon
terms by the Jurats, sitting in Chancery, not to throw
"lastage or sand" in the haven. John Kenne, in the
20th year of the same reign, "binds himself in Chancory
"before the Jurats," not to speak evil of the Jurats, or
offend against them. In the 21st year, the same John
Kenne is fined for speaking evil of James Tiece, one of
the Jurats. In the same page a transcript is given of
a royal precept to John Wode, of Smethe, the King's
escheator, in reference to markets wrongfully held,
weekly, by the men of the ville of Lyde and Broklande
[Lydd and Brookland], enjoining inquisition to be held
thereon.

Fol. 61 b, (tr.).—"On Tuesday next after Palm Sunday
"in the 14th year of the reign of King Richard II.
"Richard Grigory confessed that he had offended
"against the custom of the town; and out of reverence
"for the Duke of Lancaster, the 100s. in which he had
"been before bound to the community were reduced to
"6 shillings, etc." On the 16th of April in the same
year, John Bode, of Mergate, is bound in future not to
obstruct the entry of sea water into the haven, by throwing sand or anything else therein. Stephen Fere is
fined 5s. for buying 100 mackerel at Widisnesse, for
3 shillings, and afterwards selling them in the market.
Richard Stills is fined 6s. 8d., for buying 200 mackerel
at the "Keye," before sunrise, and selling the same in
market. On the 28th of October in the same year,
Nicholas Hamon acknowledges that he has offended
against the community, by absenting himself from the
town, during the time of the King's service, and pays
6s. 8d. fine.

2, 3 Henry IV., A.D. 1400, 1. William Holyngbroke
(but paying no Maltote) heads Holyngbroke Ward; Joan
Holyngbroke pays 4d. John Talbot, (who was at one
time the Archbishop's Bailiff of the town) pays 13s. 4d.
the highest Maltote levied in the Ward. The Maltote
of John "Caktone" is reduced so low as 18d.—"22l. 12d.
"received this year for freight of 42 tuns of wine of
"La Rochele, brought in the new barge, at 10s. 6d.
"per tun."—"Expended upon victuals for the Arch-
"bishop and Warden of the Cinque Ports, and presents
"given to them this year 9l. Expenses of James Tiece
"riding to Dover, with William atte Vawte, for the dis-
"charge of 3 balengers and 2 barges, demanded by the
"King for the escort of the Queen [Joan of Navarre] to
"Calais 4s. 8d. Gift to, and expenses of, John Bytham,
"Serjeant-at-arms to our Lord the King, coming here
"to stay ships bound for Gascony 7s. 6d. For timber
"and workmen at the Sluice, the latrine, and the delf
"for the new barge 3l. 14s. 6d. Expenses of William
"Cliderowe, sent to London for renewing the Charter,

"as to certain articles mooted between the brethren
"of the Cinque Ports 6s. 8d. To Peter Reade, of Dover,
"Bailiff of Jernemouth [Yarmouth] this year 3l. 6s. 8d.
"To a certain man of Dover, for carrying the said
"money 4d. Expenses of divers men, as well Jurats
"as others, riding to Smallyde at different times, to
"see and buy the new barge, and to pay for the same
"30s. 4d. Paid to the Chapel of Smallyde, at the
"launche of the barge 3s. 4d. For purchase of the
"same vessel 40l. 6s. 8d. For victuals for the same ship,
"and ready money given to the master, on going to
"Rochelle 10l. 9s. 9¼d. Paid James Hakeman, for a
"gonnepouch bought of him, for the voyage to Scot-
"land 5s. Paid John Barone, carpenter, in part pay-
"ment for making the common latrine 9s. 4d. Paid
"John Maffey, for compilation of this account 10s."
The name of the town barge seems to have been the
"Oneswithe," or "Eneswithe;" but on this point the
context, entered in a remarkably small hand, is somewhat confused and doubtful.

3, 4 Henry IV., A.D. 1401, 2. The name of William
Holyngbroke now disappears, and he is probably dead;
Joan, perhaps his widow, heads the list of Maltotes;
John "Cakton" pays an increased Maltote. of 4s.
Among the "Receipts"—"From St. John's House 10l."
"Paid expenses this year in making new gates to the
"sluice of Snergate 16l. 10s. 9s. Victuals and other
"necessaries for the voyage from Bretagne 17l. 10s. 4d.
"For making and digging the new harbour [novum
"portum] 41l. 6s. 6d. For expenses on the Lord Arch-
"bishop, the Lieutenant of Dover, and others coming
"to the town this year 5l. 14s. 5d. At Parliament,
"upon Coronation of the Queen of England, and a 15th
"allowed 18l. 5d. To John Halegood, Master of St.
"John's House, 13s. 4d. in part payment of a debt of
"10l."

4, 5 Henry IV., A.D. 1402, 3. Joan Holyngbroke
still heads the list of Maltotes; John "Caktone" pays
4s. Alice Talbot, probably the widow of John, pays
the largest Maltote in Holyngbroke Ward.—"Received
"6l. 6s. 8d. for our share on our ship escorting [con-
"ducentis] wools. to Flanders, and other profits to the
"same ship pertaining."—"Be it remembered, that
"on the 23rd day of the month of March in the 5th
"year of the reign of King Henry IV., the Jurats of
"Lyde and Dungemareys made account in the church
"of St. Nicholas, at Romene, before the Jurats there,
"of all their outlays and expenses, and the said Jurats
"paid 6l. 1d. as their rated proportion of the said
"expenses; the Jurats of Dungemareys paying 24s.,
"their fifth thereof."

5, 6 Henry IV., A.D. 1403, 4: Joan Holyngbroke
heads the list of Maltotes, paying 6d.; Alice Talbot pays
the very large sum of 16s. 6d.; John "Caktone" paying, as before, 4s. The name of William Caustone
appears almost immediately below his, without a sum
for Maltote being annexed thereto.—"Received 17s. 6d.
"from Richard Cobbe, for rent of the Common House
"at Snergate, from the feast of the Nativity of John the
"Baptist to this day. Also, 5s. received for occupation
"of the Common House at the Keye. Also, 19s. 8d.
"received as a fourth part of wax, found by certain
"men of the town, not freemen, near the sea."—"Paid
"for a boat, bought for the common ship 27s. Spent
"on the pig-house [domo porcorum], and for minor
"expenses 4s. 10½d."—"Be it remembered that John
"Wygynton, on the 12th day of February in the 7th
"year of the reign of King Henry IV., was chosen
"Master of the House of St. John, at Romene, for the
"term of his life; and it was granted him that he
"should have out of that house one corrody of 8d.
"weekly, on the understanding that he lives well and
"honestly. And on the same day, the said John
"acknowledged before the Jurats of the town afore-
"said, that, if he should die holding such office of
"Master, then the said house should have of his goods
"40s. sterling."

6, 7 Henry IV., A.D. 1404, 5: Joan Holyngbroke still
heads the list, but no Maltote is placed against her
name, she being no longer in trade, probably. John
"Cakstone" pays an increased Maltote, of 5s. 7d.;
William Caustone is named, but pays no Maltote.—
"Received 30s. from rebels in the community, for that
"they contradicted the lawful precepts of the Jurats,
"in keeping their watch, and in other matters touching
"the good rule of the town aforesaid. 3s. received
"from William Denys, for hire of the house of the
"community upon the Keye. 10s. from Richard
"Colyn, for letting of the house at Snergate. 7l. 18s.
"received from Thomas Kent, Master of the common
"ship, for freight of 39 tuns of wine from Burdeux.

" 50s. for the share of such ship in one tun of oil,
" taken up at sea, on the same voyage. Also, 15l. 12s.
" freight of 40 tuns of wine, and one tun of oil, the
" goods of merchants ; such merchants having 21 tuns
" as 20, according to the manner of merchants. 12d.
" for certain wood that was found at Gerounde
" [Gironde]. 2s. 6d. received as freight for 3 pipes of
" wine in the said ship from Sandwych to Romene."
—" Paid 50s. 7d. for planks, timber, carriage, and
" workmen, on repair of Illesbrigge, and digging at
" the Sluice ; 7l. 15s. 8d. as promised to our Warden of
" the Cinque Ports." The expenses of the common
ship, in being fitted out for its voyage to Bordeaux,
form a large part of the items this year.

7, 8 Henry IV., A.D. 1405, 6 : the name of Joan
Holyngbroke now disappears; and Stephen Holyngbroke, (paying 18d. for Maltote), in Sharle Wood, is,
for a time, the only representative of this once opulent
family. John " Cakston" pays 5s. 4½d. for Maltote ; and
William Caustone is mentioned, in the same Ward of
Holyngbroke, without a sum there annexed to his name as
a Maltote ; but he pays 3d. under the head of Vintry.—
" Received 8s. 4d. as freight for 5 thousand of bylet in
" the common ship, for Sandwich."—" Paid 6l. 13s. 1d.
" for a new gate this year, made for the Slow,
" 6l. 4s. 10d. for canevas for a new sail to the ship, and
" carriage thereof from London. 4l. 14s. 2d. for wheat,
" bread, cider, meal, fish, salt, firewood, and other
" supplies for the common ship, to Burdeux. 3l. 12s. 2d.
" expenses of John Ivo, John Maffey, William Robyn,
" Alexander Upton, John Wilyam, and others, and in
" presents for having counsel and friendship in the
" trial against John Knyght in the Admiralty Court,
" in the plea of account."

8, 9 Henry IV., A.D. 1406, 7 ; the names of John
Cakstone and William Caustone now disappear. The
former may very possibly have been nearly related to the
Thomas Caxtone, mentioned in an accompanying Report (on the Records of Rye) as a lawyer, first living at
Tenterden ; and then (in the Report upon the Records of
Lydd) as removing to Lydd, and holding the office, first
of Common Clerk there, and afterwards of Bailiff; from
which place he removed, as Common Clerk, to Sandwich, in 1476. Whether the person at present under
notice, John Cakstone, was removed by death, or
whether he left Romney, for some other place, perhaps
Tenterden, there are no grounds for ascertaining. The
name of Causton, is said to have been but a variation of
" Cakstone," or " Caxtone ;" but this seems somewhat
doubtful, as we here have them in juxta-position.—
" Received 3s. 4d. from a certain Portuguese, for retail
" of salt. Received 55s. 3d. collected by Vincent for
" digging the Common Ree [? the bed of the river
" Rother]."—" Paid 14s. 10½d. for a certain present
" made to the Archbishop of Canterbury, to have his
" good assistance in prosecuting our business. 9l. 14s. 3d.
" for the digging of the Ree. 13l. 6s. 8d. to Robert
" Barone, in part payment of 20l. for a certain sluice
" newly made."

9, 10 Henry IV., A.D. 1407, 8. In this year, we miss
the name of William Roper, who has generally paid
the largest Maltote, as a Butcher, during the last 20
years.—" Received 3s. 4d., a free gift of John Hacche,
" Vicar of Romene, that the Jurats in future shall not
" hold their session in his church, while Divine Service
" is being celebrated."—" Paid 5l. 2s. 3d. costs and
" expenses for renewing the General Charter, with the
" clause of Licet. Paid 6s. 8d. for cleansing the
" Market dyke. Paid 3l. 18s. to Thomas Rokyule,
" Master of St. John's House, on the old debt, so that
" nothing is now due."

10, 11 Henry IV., A.D. 1408, 9. Maltote is paid for
" Spitlemelle," or Hospital Mill, in Hospital Ward.
Thomas Mellore pays also 3d. for " Loverotismelle,"
Loverote's Mill, in the same Ward.

An interpolation in fol. 77a states that on the 19th of
January in the 12th year of Henry VI., Richard Glover,
of Lyde, took of Stephen Pocock, Master of the House of
St. John the Baptist, 8½ acres belonging to the Brethren
and Sisters of that house, situate in the Parish of Lyde,
according to the terms of an indenture then made.

10, 11 Henry IV. continued.—" Received 6s. 8d. of
" John Palmere, for one keggyngancre [kedge anchor]
" sold to him."—" 6s. 8d. given to the players of Lyde,
" as a courtesy, for the honour of the town. Paid
" 21s. 8d. to William Clidrowe, for rent of the house
" in which the Jurats hold their sessions, for a year and
" a half, and half a quarter, at 13s. 4d. per annum.
" 5l. for expenses and presents made at London, with
" the other brethren of the Cinque Ports there, for
" maintaining their liberties."

5.

11, 12 Henry IV., A.D. 1409, 10. A person named
" Robert Curthose" pays 2d. for Maltote in Hospital
Ward. —" Received of Thomas Mylet, for letting of
" the house of the community at Snergate 11s. 2d.
" Received 6s. increase upon white salt bought by the
" Jurats for the community. Received 4l. 12d. moneys
" assessed for the digging of the water-course."—" Paid
" 6s. 8d. to Hugh Fleger for 12 cartloads of stones, to
" renew the pavement, near the corner of Simon Leg.
" Paid 15s. 9d. for timber, nails, canvas, cords, and
" other necessaries, for repairing the sluice at Snergate.
" 32s. 11½d. to carpenters and labourers working
" thereat. 52s. 8d. to divers countrymen digging there,
" for cleansing the gates of the sluice. 40s. 8d. for wine
" given to the Lord Archbishop of Canterbury, for
" having his good will. Paid 5s. to divers men,
" labouring in the new Sluice this year. Paid 5l. 10s.
" the expenses of William Clidrowe riding to London
" twice, by order of the Brodhill, to prosecute divers
" business before our Lord the Prince, touching the
" state of the Cinque Ports. Paid 5s. for hire of horses
" and expenses incurred, in carrying our Charters to
" Faversham, for the same cause. Paid 13s. 4d. to Hugh
" Fleger, in name of the heirs of William Holyngbrook,
" for hire of the Common House this year. Paid 20s.
" expenses of William Clidrowe and John Maffey, and
" their servants, with horsehire, to Canterbury, to have
" counsel from Stephen Bettenham on divers pleas
" moved in Court ; and for one dozen of salted eels sent
" him, because he would receive nothing from us.
" Paid 10s. 10d. for repair of our house at Snergate,
" and for wages of the keeper there. Paid 2s. 1½d. for
" drink and fuel at the dent [dais] in the Common
" House."

In fol. 80 b, a Composition, or Agreement, is entered,
in Norman French, signed by the Bailiff and Jurats of
Romene, on the 7th of November 1412 : it seems to be
of so remarkable a nature as to deserve translation ;—
" To all those who this privy letter shall see or hear, the
" Bailiff and Jurats of the town of Romene, greeting in
" our Saviour. We do let you know that, for the especial
" desire and the good will that the masters and mariners
" below named, have to keep and maintain certain
" needful and profitable contracts and appointments
" below written ; there have met and appeared before
" us, on this day, John Palmer, William Robyn, John
" Broclond, Simon Pere, William Wottone, John May-
" dekyn, John Saltero, William Saltere, Thomas Fel-
" diswelle, John Hughelyn, John Lucas, Richard
" Walter, and John Penfelde, all masters and mariners
" of the said town of Romene, John Smythe, William
" Makemete, William Sharlo, Simon Loonge, Simon
" Gerard, Robert William, Richard William, Fraunceys
" Hayne, Henry Maynard, Stephen Losse, Stephen
" atte Wyk, John Skral, Nicholas Galiet, Richard
" Beneyt, Michael Spicer, Nicholas Knyvet, William
" Englye, and Thomas Dygone, all masters and mariners
" of the town of Lyde ; the which say and acknowledge,
" that they do will, and do grant, as well for them-
" selves as for all other masters and mariners, abiding
" in the towns aforesaid, and in the boundaries around,
" that all masters and mariners dwelling on the coast
" of France, from Harfleu as far as Hendrenesce, and
" in the boundaries around, who may be taken by the
" masters and mariners above-named, or by others of
" the said towns of Romene and Lyde, shall be acquitted
" of their ransom or payment, in the manner that
" follows : that is to say, that every master shall be
" acquitted of his ransom, or payment, for six nobles,
" with his expenses, 20 sterlings [pence] for each week,
" for his table ; and every mariner shall be acquitted
" for 3 nobles, with his expenses, 20 sterlings for each
" week, for his table, with half a noble for his safe-
" conduct. And if it happen that a fishing-boat be
" taken on the one coast or the other, all the boat, with
" its nets and tackle, shall be acquitted for 40 pence
" sterling. And so a man of the one coast or the other,
" who is dwelling within the boundaries aforesaid, in
" whatsoever place he may be taken, shall be acquitted
" as to ransom or payment. And if it happen that from
" the one coast or the other there be taken a gentleman
" or a merchant, those who take him might, and may,
" put him to such payment and ransom as shall please
" them, and seem good to them, without in any way
" infringing or weakening the contracts and engage-
" ments above agreed upon. They and every of them,
" to wit, the masters and mariners above-named,
" promising by their faith and by their corporal oath,
" that all the aforesaid contracts and engagements
" shall from henceforth on their part be strictly held,
" kept, and observed, without ever going to the con-

3 Y

" trary thereof. Provided always, that it be so done also
" by those dwelling between the town of Harfleu and
" Hendrenesse unto the masters and mariners between
" the town of Hamptone [Southampton] and the Isle of
" Tanet. In witness of which matter, at the prayer
" of the masters and mariners above named, we, the
" aforesaid Bailiff and Jurats of Romene, to these letters
" have set the seal of our office, the 7th day of Novem-
" ber, in the year of Grace 1412."

In an interpolated entry in the same folio, 80 b, the
two parties, in a case there stated as to be submitted
to arbitration, agree that if either shall contravene the
award, the one shall pay 100s. to the church of St.
Nicholas at Romene, or the other 100s. to the church
of Hope All Saints.

12, 13 Henry IV., A.D. 1410, 1. In this year, the
name of William Caustone reappears in Holyngbroke
Ward, but without a Maltote annexed. The names of
Hugh and William Holyngbroke also appear in this
Ward, with the small Maltotes of 5d. and 4d. annexed,
Hugh paying 3d. also under the head of Vintry. Three
men pay one shilling each for selling a " porpoys" out
of the town this year.—" Received 13s. 4d. from the
" Wardens of the church of St. Laurence for one bell,
" silver-gilt, sold to them. Also, 12s. from the Wardens
" of the church of St. Nicholas, for another bell of the
" same; which bells came to the community at the
" Coronation of Henry IV., King of England, at West-
" minster. Received 38l. 6s. from moneys assessed by
" the community for making the Sluice anew, and
" repairs. Also, 20s. received from John Hache, Vicar
" of Romene, for the same work."—" Paid 21½d. for wine
" given and drunk among the commoners of the town,
" on their petition. 26s. 3d. for fish brought and sent to
" the Lord the Prince, our Warden, at Dover. 13s. 4d.
" for one sturgeon, and its carriage; bought and sent
" to Richard Clyderowe, Esquire. Also, 3l. 16s. 5d.
" expenses of 21 men, Jurats as well as others, with
" hire of horses and servants, when at Dover on the
" morrow of our Lord's Ascension, and there for 3 days
" and 3 nights, on Inquisition made for the King, as
" well in the church of St. James there, as on the sea-
" shore. 6s. for wine given to Sir John Pelham, Knight,
" for divers benefits, by his favour, done to us hereto-
" fore. Also, 9s. 4d. for wine given to Sir John Wake-
" ryngge, Archdeacon of Canterbury, and Sir John
" Prendirgest, and others, coming to the town, to have
" their friendship. 45s. 6d. expenses of victuals with
" the mariners, sent to Sandwich by sea, by command
" of the Lord the Prince. 33l. 6s. 8d. paid to a Hollander
" [Dutchman] in part payment of 100l. for the Sluice.
" Also, 6d. paid to him in the name of Goddisselver
" [God's silver, a hansel]. 10s. 10d. paid to divers
" carpenters and labourers drawing timber to the
" Sluice, near Geffes Saltcote. 13s. 4d. for rent of the
" Common House. 4s. 11d. for counters, coals, rushes,
" and wine, drunk at various times at the session of
" the Jurats and others coming amongst them. Also,
" 7s. 10d. for our part of the service which the Lord
" de Bardolf claims to have of the Cinque Ports at
" Dover. 4s. to James Tiece for hire of a certain
" room, in which certain goods of the community are
" kept."

13 Henry IV., 1 Henry V., A.D. 1412, 3. The name
of William Caustone does not appear this year.—" Re-
" ceived as a gift of Nicholas Middeltone, Chaplain,
" this year, to the Sluice 6s. 8d. Of Hugh Neweman,
" Chaplain, for the same 6s. 8d. Of James Muryell,
" Chaplain, for the same 6s. 8d.; and of Nicholas Oby,
" Chaplain, for the same 6s. 8d."—" Paid to Thomas
" Mayhew, of Sandwich, for his suit before our Lord
" the King, in abridgement of our voyage 16s. 8d.
" Paid to divers men for the walls, for digging, and
" for throwing out the water, both day and night, in
" making the dammes for the site of the Sluice,
" 36l. 6s. 8d. Paid to Brice Shert and to Thomas
" Rokesle for surveying the same work 40s. Paid
" William Thwoyt and his companions, for digging and
" walling, in making the wall around Jeffes Saltcote,
" and for digging opposite the Qwenehalle, and for
" other days' work done by them about the Sluice,
" 5l. 4s. 2½d. For hurdles and stanchons bought for
" the dammes 6s. 2d. Paid for the painting of 23
" pavises [shields], and their renewing or repair
" 7s. 3½d. Paid divers carpenters working at Snergate
" this year 5s. Paid the takers of pigs, and for impound-
" ing them 4s. 11d. Paid Gerard Matthyessone at divers
" times 43l.; in part payment. For woollen cloth, and
" shearing it, and making it up into one gown and
" four hoods, for the said Gerard and his 3 worms n
" 20s. 2d."—This Gerard was probably the " Hollander,"

before mentioned.—" Paid for iron chains for the small
" gates of the Sluice, and to the sawyers sawing boards
" to cover the Sluice, in the name of the said Gerard
" 10s. 11d. For 4 boltes, 2 binders, hooks, and one
" lock with a key, for the turnepyke 3s. 2d. For a
" chain, lock, and key, for the wheel of the Sluice 16d.
" Paid to John Adam for his wages in Parliament, at
" Westminster, 25 days 3l. 2s. 6d., at 2s. 6d. per day."

Among some ordinances, inf. French, at fol. 84 b is
the following :—" Also, that all the dunghelles standing
" on the franchise, in the highway, be removed by
" those who made them, on penalty, at the discretion
" of the Jurats; and that no man put dung in the
" highway from henceforth, under such penalty. Also,
" that no swine shall be allowed to go within the
" franchise, out of keeping; and if there be any such,
" let it forthwith be taken by certain officers of the
" town, thereto assigned and sworn, and put in the
" pound; which pound shall be made at the common
" costs of the town. And that no swine shall be
" delivered up, until its owner shall have paid, for
" each swine, one penny, of which the community
" shall have one half, and the takers the other half."

In the same page, in Latin,—" It was ordained and
" enacted by the Bailiff and Jurats of the town of
" Romene, that all priests [presbiteri], and those who
" commonly frequent taverns, shall be in their houses
" where they ought to pass the night, at nine o'clock
" at the outside, under a penalty of 6s. 8d., to be levied
" from the said delinquents, and applied by the Bailiff
" and the community, in equal parts; and that no taverner
" shall maintain such delinquents, under the penalty
" aforesaid. Also, it was ordained etc., that all cur
" [scuriles] dogs shall be expelled from the town, or
" at least be safely kept, so that they do no harm, under
" a penalty of 20d., within eight days after publication
" of the said enactment, to be levied from those re-
" belling against the same."

The following is from a set of enactments, in French.
bearing date the 5th year of Henry VI., interpolated
in fol. 85 a.—Persons, free of the town, selling wine
within it, are to pay 12d. per pipe, if sold wholesale;
but 2s. if " by way of tappyng." Persons, not freemen,
are in all cases to pay 2 shillings.—" Also, it is ordained,
" that every man selling cider in the said town, shall
" pay 6d. for each pipe."

In fol. 85 b an entry is made, under the 14th year of
Henry IV., with a pen run through it, that, whereas
Dame [Domina] Beatrix Prendergest had exposed a
tun of wine, in a tavern called " Rome," contrary to
the tenor of the mandates before stated, William
Herberd, Chaplain, appeared before the Jurats, and
gave security for 10 marks on her behalf.—" John
" Boturforde, on the Eve of the Annunciation of the
" Blessed Mary, in the first year of the reign of
" Henry V., was arrested and imprisoned, for that he
" broke the seal of the Common Serjeant, when put
" upon his house by precept of the Jurats :" his fine
was 20s.—" On the 8th of August in the first year of
" the reign of King Henry V., John Hughelyn was
" presented, for that he transgressed and offended
" against the statutes of the town, seeing, that he
" cursed and lied to John Palmere, one of the Jurats,
" and also contradicted William Robyn, his twentyman
" [vintenario] and the Jurats, in making watch of the
" said town. On being examined, he acknowledged
" the trespass, and pledged himself in 10l., by favour
" of the Jurats."—" Also, on the 21st day of July, in
" the 2nd year of the reign of King Henry V., Thomas
" Curray was arrested by the Common Serjeant, for
" that he repeatedly refused to come before the Jurats
" of the vill of Romene, to perform the duties of
" Collector of Maltotes of the same town, and he would
" not go there. Therefore the Jurats of the said town
" proceeded to the house of the said Thomas, to arrest
" him, and to make him come to the Common House,
" to make answer why he refused to be arrested. Upon
" which day the same Thomas stood at his door, with
" a certain implement called a ' wefd,' to resist the
" said Jurats, against the usages of the town aforesaid;
" and there he said that he would not go with them to
" prison until after noon on that day. But afterwards,
" when the Jurats had departed, after noon, the said
" Thomas surrendered himself to prison, and voluntarily
" entered the Common House, as a prisoner, and there
" confessed the trespass aforesaid." He was thereupon
fined 20s., and gave surety to the amount of 4l.—" Also,
" on the first day of February in the year above men-
" tioned, William Horewode was arrested and im-
" prisoned in the Common House, for that, whereas
" certain dissensions had arisen between him and John

"Olyversone, and the Jurats of the said town had "wished to make peace, between them, he, the said "William, declared that the said Jurats intended to do "him an injury, to the scandal of the Jurats aforesaid, "and the disgrace of the whole community." His fine was 20d. and he gave surety in 7 marks for his good behaviour.

1, 2 Henry V., A.D. 1413, 4. Under the Wards, now jointly, of Hamersnoth and Colbrond, Bartholomew Bermakere pays 4d.: his occupation, probably, was the "making of beer." John Hughelyn pays a Maltote "upon sprottes" [sprats] of 10d.—"Received 11l. 6s. 8d. "of the goods of John Ive, for a corrody of 26s. from "St. John's House, to the behoof of Joan, daughter of "John Rolfe. Also, 40s. from the same goods to the "use of the community, for the health of the soul of the "said John Ive. Also, 33s. 4d. received from James "Lowys, from the goods of Hugh Tiece, for charity's "sake. Also, 8l. 10s. 6d. received from Thomas Rokyale "for one tun and one pipe of wine belonging to the "community, drunk in the tavern of Cnobette. 3s. 4d. "from John Fastolfe, for an impression of the common "seal to a certain writing of attachment, here in Court "recovered. 20s. from John Mountfort, in name of John "Hughelyn, for divers trespasses, and his bad behaviour "towards the Jurats, against the custom of the town. "35s. from Thomas Milet, at the feast of our Lord's "Nativity, for rent of our house at Snergate for 3 years. "Also, 19½d. moneys collected from divers men riding "and hunting beyond the new Sluice." Paid,—"First, "the costs and expenses of William Cliderow, William "Chance, and James Lowys, being at Westminster this "year, at the King's Coronation, 4l. 14s. 7½d. Given "to the players [histrionibus] in the Hall that day 10s. "And for 3 gowns of scarlet for the same 6l. 18s. Given "by William Cliderowe and James Lowys to the Clerk "of the Rolls, to have his friendship as to allowance of "the 10th and 15th, granted in Parliament 3s. 4d. "Given to the Usher of the Parliament Chamber, at "the same time 8d. Paid for the writing of the Acts of "Parliament 12d. Paid the wages of John Gartone, "being at London for renewal of the Charter, and for "obtaining writs of the 10th and 15th, for 24 days 40s. "Also, for our share of the fine, sealing, writing, and "presents given to the lawyers for having their counsel "on the same case 5l. 13s. 4d. Paid to our Warden, for "one tun and one pipe of wine bought of him 6l. Also, "for drawing the same, and a place for it in the tavern "10s. For wine given to the Lord Archbishop 9s. 4½d. "Expenses of Thomas Milet, at Snergate, for repair of "our houses there for 3 years past 31s. For mending "the Common House upon the Keye, and mending the "latrine; two loads of rys [twigs] and half a quarter of "stanchones for making a hedge to close the way to the "Sluice; and for making the same, canvas, tallow, old "hides, nails, and other small things, bought for the "benefit of the Sluice 16s. 2d. Paid Gerard Mathyessone "in part payment of his contract 22l. 2s. 5d. Expenses "of James Tiece and James Lowys, riding to Cranebrok "to represent to the Lord Archbishop of Canterbury, "that we may have 5 marks to the use of the community "out of the goods of Hugh Tiece 5s. 4d. Paid Hugh "Fleger and James Lowys for Colbrondes tenement, "bought of them for a Common House 16l. Paid certain "people of Olderomene for making a damme there in "the preceding year, at the bridge 3s. 4d. Expenses of "fish sent to the Lieutenant at Dover, that we may have "his friendship in divers causes touching the state of "the Cinque Ports 7s. 1d.

2, 3 Henry V., A.D. 1414, 5. In Sharle (now called "Sherlegh") Ward, one "John atte Sluz" is rated to the Maltote; from which we have some ground for concluding that the Sluice was situate in that Ward. In Hamersnoth and Colbrond Wards, now united," a certain "stranger dwelling in Leggesoore" pays 9d.; " a cer-"tain piper" [quidam fistulator] 2d.; and a certain "cufator" [? cupmaker] 2d. The "Hospites," hostel, or lodging-house, keepers, no longer appear; being super-seded probably by the taverners, or vintners. Against the ten Butchers this year a sum total of 58s. 7d. is placed, with a note that it was entered in that form, because the collectors of the Maltote "had lost the "tallies."—"Received of Thomas Turgis 18d., for one "herthstok [?] sold to him, the property of the Common "House, 6s. from people carrying and riding beyond the "Sluice, in sprottyme"—sprat time.—"Collected 34s. 4d. "upon the Strond, Maltotes from the market."—"Paid "21l. 15s. 9½d. for digging in the port this year. 4s. 1d. "for fish given to the Earl of Arundel, coming to the "town this year; and for wine given to the Archbishop, "coming to the town, to have his influence, and other

"things 11s. 7½d. For carriage of thorns, to make a "close between the land of the commonalty and the "land of James Tiece 2s. 1d. For small expenses, such "as fuel, nails, rushes, and sometimes drink with divers "men coming to the town 7s. 2½d."

Fol. 91 b.—"Richard Wottone was arrested on the "13th day of June in the fourth year of King Henry V., "for that he took his servant, whom the Jurats had "handed over to Simon Pere, to go to Harfleu with "victuals for our Lord the King, and withdrew him from "the ship; in derogation of the estate of the Jurats, and "against the usage of this town."—He was fined 3s. 4d., and had to find surety for his good behaviour.

"Be it remarked, that Walter Harwarstok, on the "13th day of this month of March in the 7th year of "King Henry V., [was arrested], because that, with "opprobrious and crooked words, he had vilified the "venerable Jurat, James Tiece, saying and calling "him a false and perjured man." He was accordingly fined 4 pence, and put upon surety for his good beha-viour.

3, 4 Henry V., A.D. 1415, 6. There are no fewer than 44 entries under the head of "Vintry" this year; the "tavern of Rome" being down for 3s. 4d. A cer-tain "cuphator" [cup maker] is also set down, but there is no Maltote entered against his name.

Interpolation in fol. 92 b.—"Be it remarked, for the "lasting remembrance thereof, that on the 4th day of "June in the 10th year of the reign of King Henry V., "Thomas Bartone, Common Clerk of Romene, has re-"ceived from his masters, Jurats of the town aforesaid, "and from William Pyers, barbour, and Peter Newene, "then Wardens [Chamberlains] of the said town, a small "piece of land lying in his garden, near to his own land "and to a wall belonging to the community, and to land "of James Tiece, and to a lane leading from the High "Street to the churchyard of St. Nicholas, he rendering "yearly to the town 4 pence."

3, 4 Henry V. continued.—"Received from men of "the foreign 22l. 6s. 8d. for divers trespasses and injuries "by them often committed, against the liberty of the "Cinque Ports. 6s. 8d. a gift from Robert Penfeld, to-"wards the work of the new Sluice. 3s. 4d. from John "Lunceford, rent for the common garden at Clo-"brandes."—"Paid 33s. 9d., costs for the Lord de Tal-"bot, to have his favour as to his ships for the voyage, "3l. 2d. for divers costs of the belenger of Richard. "Walter for the same voyage. 3l. 15s. 9d. for repair of the "barge of the said lord, on the same matter. 11l. 6s. 8d. "delivered to John Grymesby, for victuals for 84 men, "on a voyage for our Lord the King this year, towards "Holand, for 15 days. 18s. 6½d. for victuals brought to go "to Calais, to await the arrival of the King from Har-"fiet." There are also a few other items as to men and ships for the campaign this year, (in which occurred the Battle of Agincourt).—"45s. 6d. for divers persons "labouring in wallyng and groynynge, for the strengthen-"ing of the Sluice. 13l. 16s. 8d. paid to the Lord Hum-"frey, Duke of Gloucester, and Warden of the Cinque "Ports, as our share of 100l. granted to him on the day "of his reception at the Shepwey. 28s. in gifts and "rewards to the surveyor of the works (at Dover Castle) "and others to whom it seemed proper, for the common "advantage. 10s. 11d. for victuals for divers good man "and mariners, going to sea against our enemies, who "were then off the coast. 16s. 8d. to John Gartone, to "make prosecution at London, together with Richard "Huntyngdone, of Hastynge, against the men of Jerne-"mouth [Yarmouth], for divers injuries by them against "us purposed or moved. Paid 28s. 4d. to the men of "Hastynge, as our part of the composition made "between the men of this coast and the men of France, "for ransom and payment for prisoners on either side. "26s. 8d. paid to Clement Bridham for taking care of "the Scluse. 3s. 4d. for our share of the payment of the "Common Clerk of the Cinque Ports, for registering the "Acts of the Brodhill. 4s. 7d. for paper, wax, drink "among the Jurats and others, strangers, coming to "the town, and for coal to warm the Jurats and others "in winter time."—"To the church of St. Nicholas of "Romene there are due 40s., moneys borrowed of it."

Fol. 94 a. "The Account of Richard Walter, master of "the ship called 'the Marye' of Romene, as to one voy-"age to Bu[r]deux in the 4th year of the reign of King "Henry V." Among the items appear—"26l. 17s. 6d. "freight of 53 tuns and one pipe stowed in the same "ship on its return." 50s. is the sum paid for freight of merchandize to Burdeux; 5s. is its share of pillage taken on the voyage. This is followed by—"The Account "of John William, master of the same ship, for a "second voyage to Burdeux, in the year above-

" mentioned." 56 tuns of wine are brought on the
voyage home.—" 19s. for table [mensa] sold to divers
" men in the ship, on the voyage aforesaid " ; by these
men passengers probably are meant.

4, 5 Henry V., A.D. 1416, 7. In this year Hamersnoth Ward is not mentioned, but it is probably included under Colbrond Ward. (After folio 95, the pagination and sequence of the folios is wholly incorrect,
the various years having been thrown indiscriminately
together, when the volume was rebound, probably at
the close of the 16th century.)—" Paid the expenses and
" wages of divers mariners of Romene, for safely con-
" ducting our ship to Apuldrefiet, for her second voy-
" age this year to Burdeux, and for reggings and keep-
" ing of the same 22s. 1d. For wine, sievre [cider],"
" and bers, bought for the same voyage 10l. 4s. 10d. For
" the cost of one vessel and four mariners going to
" Calais, for the passage back of our Lord the King 28s.
" For the cost of one boat and mariners, to fish there for
" the King 7s. 2d." Under the 7th year of the same
reign, in the same folio, mention is made of the hire
by the community" of one balenger, vulgarly called
" the Dunstan." In the same folio it is also stated
that on the 15th of December, in the 7th year of the
same reign, Thomas Sthepeneton took of the Jurats a
" house called " the Slowhous " [Sluice House], at Snergate, for 5 years, at a yearly rent of 10s. " in the Common
" Exchequer of Romene to be paid ;" the Jurats duly
to keep the said house in repair.

Two leaves have been cut out here, and they not
improbably contained the Account, now missing, for
5, 6, Henry V.

6, 7 Henry V., A.D. 1418, 9. Hamersnoth Ward reappears in this Account. Under Scharle Ward, a William
Holyngbroke pays one halfpenny, as Maltote.—" Paid
" for cygnets, capons, and geese, given to the Lord
" Archbishop of Canterbury 18s. 6d. For work done
" upon the Market dyk 2s. 4d."

7, 8 Henry V., A.D. 1419, 20. In this year, for the
first time, the Maltote paid by each person is not annexed
to the name : about this time, also, mention of the Wards
of Colbrand, Codde, Deme, and Joce, disappears. Thomas
Stephenstone pays 4s. rent for the Slouesshouse [Sluice
House] for the past year.

An entry, in Latin, at the foot of fol. 100 b. to the
following effect :—" We, the Bailiff and good men, and
" all the commonalty, of the town of Great Jernemouth,
" signify unto you that the attorneys of some towns of
" the Barons of the Cinque Ports, on Sunday next after
" the Feast of St. Michael last past, at the hour of
" Prime, delivered to us another writ under tenor of
" this writ ; upon which an answer such as this was
" given to them, that whereas it is contained in a
" certain Composition between the Barons of the Cinque
" Ports and the citizens of the said town of Jerne-
" mouth, that the same Barons, at the time of the Fair
" of the said town of Jernemouth, for 40 days
" shall have custody of the bread, in such form as
" to have 4 serjeants, one of whom is to carry the
" banner of the kingdom, and another is to sound
" a horn for gathering the people, this year they
" ought not to exercise such office ; seeing that, in
" the year last past, as to exercise of that office, their
" liberty, through their own default, was discontinued ;
" so that, without the special favour of our Lord the
" King for renewing their liberty, as it seems to us,
" they ought not to exercise that office. And seeing
" that that writ requires that we should permit the
" Barons to use and enjoy that office, according to the
" tenor of the Letters and Charter of the Lord the King
" as to their liberties made, it was required of them to
" shew the same ; the which they would not shew, but
" said that they had them not with them. And further,
" it was told them, that if by virtue of that writ they
" ought to enjoy the liberty aforesaid, they must use
" such liberty in the customary manner ; namely, every
" Lord's Day, during the Fair, at the hour of Prime,
" before High Mass is begun there ; whereas, at the
" time when this writ was delivered, the hour of Prime
" had passed, and High Mass was begun, and so they
" had let pass their proper time." These disputes in
reference to the rights and prerogatives of the Bailiffs
of the Cinque Ports at Yarmouth Michaelmas Fair,
as to the assize of bread and other matters, were the
source of frequent discord, probably, for centuries.

8, 9 Henry V., A.D. 1420, 1.—" Received as a Maltote
" from the Porters and Measurers of the Strond 26s. 6d.
" —Paid expenses incurred on preparing the krayer
" [a sort of vessel] of Hethe, and in money delivered
" to the hired man going to sea with the said krayer
" 26l. 10s. 8d. For expenses upon the Lord Archbishop,

" namely, for wine given and [?] other funeral [funerali-
" bus] expenses, at divers times incurred, for the business
" of the town 20s. 11d. To the Barons for the Queen's
" Coronation 6l. 21d. Expenses upon the voyage to
" Crotay, at the feast of Christ's Nativity 3l. 19s. 9d. Ex-
" penses for going to seek the King and Queen at
" Calais 3l. 13s. 10d."

9, 10 Hen. V., A.D. 1421, 2.—" Expenses incurred in
" the repair, or the building, of the Common House
" 45s. 1d. Expenses on the voyage of our Lord the
" King, in crossing over from Sandwich to Calais
" 29l. 10s. 1¼d. Paid to divers strangers and people of
" the Court 2s. 8d."

1, 2 Henry VI., A.D. 1422-4.—" Paid John Onterdel
" for keeping the Scluse this year 22s. 2d. Paid him
" for making a gate for the said Scluse 19s."—Onterdel
not improbably was a Hollander, or Dutchman, from
his name.—Paid to the men of Lyde " when they came
" with their May [a play], and ours, on two occasions, and
" when (they came) to converse with us as to the two
" voyages to Crotay 19s. ½d. Paid for candles, rushes,
" and other things for the Feast of St. John, in the
" Common House 5½d. Paid upon two voyages to
" Crotaye this year 15l. 15s. 10d. Given to the min-
" strels of the Duke of Gloucester 6s. 8d. Paid for
" pullayes and ropes, to the department of the Porterage
" pertaining 2s. 5d. Paid John Horne, for the hire
" of a bushel measure for measuring the salt 10d. Paid
" him for purchase of the said bushel for the common
" use 19d. Paid Thomas Bartone, Clerk of the com-
" munity, in part payment for his labour 20s."

In an interpolated register of a conveyance of a
house in the Parish of St. Laurence, in the 10th year of
Henry VI., apparently of some importance, there is a
covenant to keep it thatched with straw. To the same
house there was also belonging " a lead [unum plumb-
" um] called a forneye, and a great kettle."

Another interpolation, in the same page.—" On the
" 8th day of August, in the 20th year of the reign of
" King Henry VI., John Godynough, not free, was
" arrested, because he had come to the Common House,
" not warned, to hear the common counsel of the said
" town of Romene. And he submitted himself to the
" correction of the Jurats, and was sworn upon his
" oath to be good and trusty to the commons and
" liberties of the said town, and to conceal the common
" counsel."

2, 3 Henry VI., 1424, 5. For this year no list of
Maltotes appears.—" Paid to William Byfeld, tailor, of
" Lyde, from moneys left in the common chest by
" Simon Legge, to the use of his daughter 3l. Paid
" for divers expenses and the hire of ships for the
" voyage of the Lord Duke of Gloucester 6s. 7d."

3, 4 Henry VI., 1425, 6.—" Received of Geoffrey
" Cropwode 2s. 6d. for the common house at Snergate.
" 6s. 8d. of William Whyting, for the barn and garden
" there, belonging to the community. 12d. for the
" cutting up of one porpays."—" Paid for renewing
" the patent of our general Charter, for our share 14s.
" Paid for repair of the Common House which William
" Whyting has to ferm, and for repair of the house
" at the Slough 16s. 6½d. Paid for making a rope,
" namely, a kuble, for the Slough 25s. 10d. For a bell
" for the Common House 5s."

4, 5 Henry VI., 1426, 7. In this and the preceding
year, a William Holyngbroke appears as one of the
Jurats : his name is under Scharle Ward, but no Maltote
is set against it.—" Received 20s. in part payment of
" 40s. for the gate of the Slough [Sluice], sold at Sner-
" gate."—" Given to the men of Wyghtersham, upon the
" showing of their Interlude 6s. 8d. Paid William Love
" for ryes [twigs] for the Rysbank 4s. For new coun-
" ters bought 3d. Paid for the making of a clapyr for
" the little bell in the Common House, and for hanging
" the same 3s. 10d. Paid for red wax, and one matte,
" and other necessaries, for the Common House 6d."

5, 6 Henry VI., A.D. 1437, 8. William Holynbroke,
a Jurat, pays 8d. for Maltote, in Sharle Ward.—" Re-
" ceived 6d. for sponye [spoons] from Robert Merusher.
" 6d. from the relict of Peter Newene, for a labourer
" for one day in the haven. 20s. for the old gate of
" the Sluice, sold to Luke Harnden. 20s. from John
" Bate, for his pasture upon the Salt Marsh. 4s. from
" the same, by the hands of Richard Clytherowe, for
" going beyond the Sluice. 6d. paid by John Harneys,
" in one bushel of white salt, for going beyond the
" Sluice. 20d. from the relict of Stephen Harry, for a
" parcel of land of the community between the Walls."
These " Walls," no doubt, marked the ancient bed of
the Rother, to Old Romney, or to Snergate.—" 5s. 8d.
" received from the Porters on the Strande, for the

" portorage of fish this year. 20d. from John Halle for
" a parcel of land of the community between the Walls.
" 6d. of William Barbour for the like."—" Paid William
" Lokyer for nails and bonds for the common chest 19d.
" Rushes for the Common House 3d. Paid Bartholomew
" Randolfe for saving the gate of the Sluice 8d."

6, 7 Henry VI., A.D. 1428, 9.—" Received 6s. 8d. for
" the tenement of the community at Snargate, let to
" the relict of N. Coppewode. 4d. for croppis, the
" common property, sold at Rokynge. 4d. received for
" a garden of the community let to ferm to Geoffrey
" Poter, near the Keyhouse. 20d. received of Agnes
" Harry, for rent of a parcel of the common land [between
" the Walls]. 8d. received from Richard Bydyndene
" for a certain gold chain, found in the sea this year."—
" Paid for wine and fish given to the Lord Archbishop
" of Canterbury 47s. 8d. Paid for sweet wine drunk in
" the Common House 3d. Paid for rushes and mardylle,
" bought for the Common House 6½d. Paid for the
" expenses of seven Jurats and three servants, riding
" to Dover, and for horses hired, on account of the
" wrekke from Portugal, on mission of the Lieutenant
" 12s. 10d. Paid Henry Tolkyn, glazier, mending the
" glass window in the Common House 13d. Paid for
" two gallons of wine, given to the venerable men
" coming with the Lord of Salesbury 16d. Paid John
" Gardyng, carpenter, for mending the common latrine,
" and for boards and nails for the same 11s. 1½d. Paid
" William Crystemasse, for trying to keep in the swine
" 1d. Paid Robert Skiptone, the Common Clerk, for
" his wages 40s."

7, 8 Henry VI., A.D. 1429, 30.—" Received 2s. from
" three persons who slept in summer, at the time of the
" watch. 4d. from Geoffrey Porter, for the rent of a piece
" of land without the Sluice."—" Paid for making the
" bascelles [butts] at the Barrokes [? sandhills] 20d.
" To the minstrels of the Duke of Gloucester 7s. 8d.
" Given to certain persons, coming from Hyerne with a
" certain play 10s. 8d. Paid to a messenger of the Lord
" of Gloucester, coming with a letter for armed men
" and archers, to be had in Romene and its members
" 3s. 7d. Paid to John Chaplayn, carrying three lances,
" used at the Coronation of the Lord Henry, the King,
" from London to Romene 3s. 4d. Paid for three yards
" of canevas, with a cord, for the said lances 21d. Given
" to the herbegeour [harbinger] of the Lord the King,
" in a gallon of wine 8d. Paid the expenses of Thomas
" Smythe, draper, and Henry Eylwyne, riding to
" Redyng and Sardwich, three times, to obtain ships
" for the voyage of our Lord the King 7s. 1½d. Paid
" for making a wall near the Sluice, in the marsh
" 3s. 8d. Paid Thomas Smythe, drapere, for the pro-
" vender of the horses of an Esquire-at-arms and a
" clerk of the ships of our Lord the King, that we
" might have their friendship 20d. Paid for their
" victuals, with wine given to them 2s. 2d. Given to
" the minstrels of the Lord the King, at his Coronation
" 6s. 8d."

8, 9 Henry VI., A.D. 1430, 1.—" Received 6d. from
" divers men, not free, riding beyond the Sluice.
" Received from the men of Hethe, for divers damages
" done by them to our ships 3s. 4d."—" Paid for expenses
" of the Lord the King, to Calais 18l. 14s. Paid for
" ale and wine consumed in the Common House 12d.
" Given to the play of Rokynge 6s. 8d. For bread,
" wine, and fodder for horses, given to the minstrels
" of the Lord of Gloucester 3s, 2d. Paid for 5 bordes
" 300 the thlattes [thatch-laths], and 1000 tyel prigges
" [tile nails], for repair of the Common House 4s. 2d.
" Paid Robert Skiptone, for our share in entering the
" Acts of the Cinque Ports 3s. 4d. Paid for expenses of
" the men of Lyde, on the day of their account, in the
" house of James Lowys, 2s. 6d. Paid for one molet
" and one gournard [gurnard] bought and given to the
" Lieutenant of Dover Castle, that we might have his
" good friendship 14d. Paid Thomas Smythe, drapere,
" for carrying divers Charters of our Lord the King to
" London, to discharge our foreign lands etc. 6s. 8d."

9, 10 Henry VI., A.D. 1431, 2. In Hope Ward, the
name of " Joan Brekespere " occurs. Only 5 names
appear under the head of " Vintry " this year, William
Whytyng importing 8 pipes of wine, and paying 6s. 4d.
" —Received 20d. in part payment for 2 years' rent of
" the common house at Snargate. 2s. received as a
" certain fine from Thomas Edryk and William Kenc,
" for occupying the common land between the Walls.
" 21d. received on cider this year."—" Paid divers
" expenses upon the men of the Marsh 11l. 2s. 1½d.
" Expenses on the Sloughehowse at Snargate 3s. Paid
" to Simon Grene, for making a cry to bring the com-
" mons together 1d. Paid Thomas Inglond, for bread,

" ale, and cider, consumed in the Common House 9d.
" Paid for one dog of iron, for the Common House 12d.
" Paid 6 men watching on St. Peter's Eve. Paid
" Ralph Herbard for green cloth, bought for the
" exchequer in the Common House 2s. 6d."

10, 11 Henry VI., A.D. 1432, 3. In this year, in
addition to the nine Wards of preceding years, a new
Ward appears.—" Warda Jacobi Tyece," " The Ward
" of James Tyece." He had probably bought a considerable portion of landed property, and had had sufficient influence to have it constituted a Ward.—" Paid
" for wine given to the players of our town 16d. Paid
" for wine, ale, and cider, consumed when surveying
" the haven and the Slow 16d. Paid the expenses of
" Geoffrey Lawther, Lieutenant of Dover Castle 24s. 8d.
" Given to the players of Lede, for their expenses
" 10s. 4d. Paid Roger Wenlok, Common Clerk, his
" wages 32s. 11d. Paid the expenses of the Seneschal
" of Dover Castle, when he received the verdict of the
" 12 Jurats, upon the sea-shore 2s. 6d. Paid for blow-
" ing the horn for gathering the commoners 2d. Paid
" William Byfeld for wine consumed, on shewing the
" play of Lede 16d. Paid Thomas Boltere, Common
" Clerk, for his wages 22s. 8d. Paid for 2 gallons of
" wine, given to the players when they shewed the
" May [in ostensione Maii] 16d."

11, 12 Henry V., A.D. 1433, 4.—" Received 46s. 8d.
" of Richard Stotard, because he did not ride to Jerne-
" mouth [Yarmouth], when he was chosen Bailiff.
" Received 2s. of Thomas Roggere for rent of land
" between the Walls. 3s. 4d. of John Erle for rent of
" land between the Walls. 16d. of Matthew Playdone
" for rent of land between the Walls.—Paid to Thomas
" Hosyer, because he went to Jernemouth in the name
" of Richard Stotard 3l. Paid John Gardener for his
" trouble on the Slowe of Snergate 4s. 5d. Paid Wil-
" liam Whytyng for one sturgyn, given to the Lord
" Archbishop of York 5s. Paid for expenses upon the
" common house at Snergate 14s. 6d."

12, 13 Henry VI., A.D. 1434, 5.—" Received 4l. 6s. 8d.
" of the men of Snergate, for stone sold to them. 3s. 4d.
" of James Bomelond, for pasture of sheep upon the
" Gorse."—" Paid a clerk sent from London that he
" might take the office of Common Clerk 3s. 4d. Paid
" for the expenses of the new wall, and for ryse [twigs]
" and other necessary things 21s. 11½d. For carriage of
" timber from Snergate to Romene 12½d. Paid Thomas
" Boltere, Common Clerk, his stipend for the time he
" stood in office 33s. 4d. Paid 2d. for blowing the com-
" mon horn, on the Day of the Annunciation," the day on
which the accounts for the past year were made out.

13, 14 Henry VI., A.D. 1435, 6. Three persons pay
Maltote on cider this year; 10 pipes in all, at 3d. per
pipe. The " Mill of James Lowys" pays Maltote, other
than the " Eigh mill."—" Paid Robert Wycham for his
" trouble, when he came from Canterbury to make a
" covenant to be Common Clerk 2s. 4d. Paid William
" Holyngbroke for 2 elms bought for the new pynnok
" [drain] 20d." The expenses of making this drain
follow, at considerable length.—" For wine given to the
" Earl of Southfolk 4s. 6d. Paid a man for carrying a
" letter making mention of the capture of Depe 6d.
" Given to the King's herbergeour, at the time of the
" soldiers being here 6s. 8d. For wine given to him 6d.
" Given to John Shelle, when he brought news as to
" a common Brodhille for the voyage of the Duke of
" York 8½d."

14, 15 Henry VI., A.D. 1436, 7. Three persons are
entered as paying for " pasture between the Walls," on
the recovered land, probably, of the bed of the Rother ;
three others pay for pasture " on the Gorse."—" Given
" to John Exsam, Clerk of the ships of our Lord the
" King, at various times, that we might have his friend-
" ship 10s. For repairing the Common House 12d.
" Paid William Ludbrugh for carriage of timber from
" Snergate to the great Sluice 2s. 4d."

15, 16 Henry VI., A.D. 1437, 8. The rent for the
house at Snergate is entered at 5s. William Warmestone
pays 3s. 3d. " for pasture between the Walls, from Illis-
" brege to New Romene. John att Mede for like pasture
" 20d." John Fuller pays 8d. for the rent, for one quarter,
" of the house upon the Strand,"—probably the " Key-
" house " before mentioned.—" Paid for a breakfast
" given to the men of Lyde 14d. Paid John Buxhirst for
" his labour upon pipes and barrels with stores, provided
" for the voyage of the Duke of York 7d. Paid to Rose
" Milhale for spices for the Lieutenant of Dover, an old
" debt 10d."

16, 17 Henry VI., A.D. 1438, 9. In addition to the
rents for the localities last mentioned, Richard Prowde
pays 20d. for pasture between Elsebrege and the

3 Y 3

"Barre;" John Legge pays 2s. for pasture called "the
"Horseho;" Alice Barbour and William Synderford
8d. for a piece of land, called "the Harpe." Also,—
"Received 3s.3d. from William Warmestone, for pasture
"between Elsebregge and the Bruge [Bridge] of Old
"Romene. Also, 10d. from William Worth for one
"kedell in the past year."—"Paid to John Sompter
"for mending two eyes of the cords pertaining to the
"great Slowe 3d. Paid to William Watte, labouring
"2 days upon the stone wall of the common pound 9d.
"Paid to Richard Clitherowe for the support of our
"work done at Rowchester [?] 22s. 4d."
17, 18 Henry VI., A.D. 1439, 40. Under the head of
Vintry, the amount of tuns, butts, pipes, or hogsheads,
imported by each person, is stated. The rent of the
"House upon the Stronde" is entered as that "of the
"Keyhous" this year.—"Paid divers expenses incurred
upon Walter Sheryngtone, and other persons. riding
with him, to survey the new watercourse of the haven
"10s. 10½d. Paid for 11 elmes, bought for bonyng
"[? booming] the harbour, and for laying the same
"7s. 10d. Given to the Common Clerk, who is to be,
"coming from Wynchelse, to make the agreement, 20d.,
"and for wine given at the same time 6d. Given to a
"man coming from Wynchelse, to know whether the
"truce ought to be kept between us and them of Depe
"8d. Given to John Rogger, for carrying to Dover
"the moneys of persons not English born 10d."
The account for 18, 19 Henry VI appears to be
wanting.
19, 20 Henry VI., A.D. 1441, 2. The name of Wil
liam Holyngbroke no longer appears, in Sharle Ward;
and this once important family is, apparently, extinct.
The "Keyhous" or "House on the Stronde" is here
mentioned as "the Common House."—"Received
"Maltotes from strange Ripiers 11d. Received 6s. 8d.
"of William Chenew for allowing sale of the stone
"walls of Colbrandes. Received 11½d. of John Lucas
"and William Feldeswelle and their companions,
"going out to sea to fish for a week."—"Given to
"the men of Wyghtsham, to shew their play upon the
"Crokhill 3s. 4d. For wine given to them 8d. Given
"to the men who played upon the Crokhille 2s. 3d.
"For the expenses of Richard Clytherow, John Chenew,
"William Warmestone, James Lowys, and Stephen
"Bakherst, with their servants, riding to Canterbury,
"to talk with the Seneschal of the Lord Archbishop of
"Canterbury as to the office of Bailiff of Romene 17s. 2d.
"For mending the latrine at the Slough 18d. Given
"to a man, bringing a letter of the Lord Duke of
"Gloucester, to have men at Cxotay 4d. Paid to John
"Joseph, Common Clerk, for his wages, 60s."
The remaining entries in this volume (fols. 140-144)
are of a miscellaneous nature, and belong to various
dates. They are mostly of a wholly formal character,
and do not call for notice. The following extracts have,
however, been selected from the Latin of the original.
On the 30th April, in the 9th year of Henry V.,
appeared before Clement Overton, Bailiff, and the
Jurats, of New Romene,—"John Barwell, Clerk, Rector
"of Old Romene; and confessed that he had offended
"against our Lord the King, and the community
"of Romene, and against the liberties of the fran-
"chise thereof, in that he had procured two writs
"of the King, to vex Henry atte Stone and another,
"before the Chancellor of our Lord the King." He
offered to pay 10l. for the offence, but they pardoned
him the whole thereof, save 20s.—"And then, the said
"Jurats and Bailiff well saw the humility of the said
"John Barwell, and so pardoned him the aforesaid 20s.,"
whereupon, he made corporal oath that he would never
again offend against the liberties of the Cinque Ports.
"On the 12th day of August in the 6th year of the
"reign of King Henry IV., John Mokayt, of Romene,
"was arrested by the Jurats, and imprisoned, for that
"he had wished that all the Jurats of Romene had
"been burnt in the common ship." He confessed his
offence, paid a fine of 6s. 8d., and was put upon surety
as to his future good behaviour. This calamity, which
befell the "Common ship" of the town, does not seem
to be elsewhere noticed.
"On the 26th day of May in the 12th year of Henry
"IV., John Goldhorde was presented by trustworthy
"persons; for that, when the Jurors were at Dover, in
"virtue of a mandate of our Lord the Prince, he said
"that the Jurats aforesaid were looked upon at Dover as
"so many grooms, [garciones]." Upon confessing his
offence, he was fined 6s. 8d., and put upon surety as to
his future good behaviour.
On the 18th of October in the 14th year of King
Henry IV., Hugh Newenton, Chaplain, was arrested

and imprisoned for cursing John Lunceford, one of the
Jurats, and calling him a false thief. On confessing
his offence, he was fined 20s. to the community, and
was ordered to pay 20s. to John Lunceford, and to find
surety for his future good behaviour.
At fol. 143 a. is given a part of the Account of the
Jurats for 23, 24 of Henry VI., A.D. 1445, 6. A Maltote is entered as—"from Bretons this year, for 120
"quarters of salt," but the amount is omitted.—"Paid
"to the minstrels of the Lord of Scerburgh, 12d.
"Paid John Colkyn 10s. for digging in the channel,
"near Saltcote." The last page of this volume (fol.
144 b.) is almost wholly illegible.
The first leaf of the volume, as already mentioned,
contains various miscellaneous entries, mostly of the
22nd year of the reign of Henry VI. It is in a sadly
tattered condition, but the following are a few extracts
from it:—
"Walter Spaldyng, Clerk, Vicar of Romene, born at
"Penbrugge (now Pembridge) in the county of Hereford,
"was admitted to the freedom on the 22nd day of March,
"in the 20th year of the reign of King Henry VI.
"And he ought to pay 8s. 8d., which is wholly pardoned
"him; and he is to pay, for his yearly contribution,
"6d." A pen is run through this entry, and at the
end it is stated, in Latin,—"Because he renounced the
"freedom."
"John Iprys, born at Dursham, was admitted to the
"freedom, on the 12th day of August in the 22nd year
"of the reign of King Henry VI. And he gives for
"his freedom 3s. 4d." Not improbably, this was the
John do Ypres who was so closely connected with the
borough of Rye.
On the obverse of the next leaf, the reverse of which
contains the earliest entries in the volume, (belonging
to 7, 8 Richard II., as already stated), there are some
entries written at the close of that reign, and the
beginning of the reign of Henry IV. One of them is
a copy of a precept made by Nicholas Watte, Bailiff,
and the Jurats, of Romene, to John Lunsforde, as to
delivery of a house and appurtenances; dated "in the
"church of St. Nicholas of Romene, 28th of April,
"in the first year of Henry IV." Another is a copy,
one or two words being illegible, of—"Lestatut de
"Admi[ralte] fait lan du Roy Richard Seconde xv,"
Statute of the Admiralty, made in the 15th year of
King Richard the Second.
The Volume in continuation of the preceding, is a
large folio, originally containing 138 leaves of parchment, in the fragments of a leather cover; the first
leaf now being lost, and the last five or six in a
tattered condition, apparently gnawed by mice. The
preceding volume ends with the Account of 19, 20
Henry VI., and a portion of that of the 23rd and 24th
years of the same reign. The concluding portion of
that volume is evidently lost, as the present, of which
only the first leaf is wanting, begins with the
26, 27 Henry VI., A.D. 1448, 9. Nine Wards only
appear; and comparatively few of the names have the
Maltote set against them. Richard Clederowe, as heretofore, heads Holyngbroke Ward. "Hans Pykylheryng,"
who has the comparatively large Maltote of 3s. 4d.
against his name, appears in Boucherie Ward. Among
the "Advocantes," meaning, persons "avowing" themselves to be freemen of the town, the name of Walter
Moyle is mentioned. He lived at Eastwell, in Kent,
and became Chief Justice of the Common Pleas in
1461. As to sums received:—"They answer for 6s. 8d.
"received in part payment of a greater sum, for the
"of Cayhous [Keyhouse] sold this year. 2½d. received
"from a certain stranger, as Maltote upon oynonys
"[onions] this year. 23s. 6d. received as Maltote from
"strange Ripiers upon the Stronde."—"Paid 4s. 0½d.
"as the cost of Thomas Cowpere and the hire of his
"horse, riding to London for a new Charter. 12d. for
"salmon, bought and given to John Grenford, Senes-
"chal of Dover Castle, to have his friendship. 6s. 8d.
"given to minstrels of our Lord the King this year.
"7s. 6½d. to John Carpenter, of Hastynges, for suit
"made at Yernemouth, and for wine given to Master
"Foxe, Dean of Hastynges, by general assent of the
"Brodhulle. 12d. for making the poleye for the
"porters." There are very numerous entries now of
admissions to the freedom, of persons born in various
parts of England.
Folio 6 is wanting.
27, 28 Henry VI., A.D. 1449, 50. The names of
Gerard Forselle, Richard Lamplow, and John Sellenger,
appear this year in Holyngbroke Ward, with which the
Ward of James Ticce is now united. But one person
pays under the head of "Vintry," and one only for cider.

"They answer for 20s. given to the community by
"Geoffrey Goodlok out of his wages at the Parliament
"holden at Westminster."—"Paid for blowing the
"horn, on Account day, last year 2d. Given to the
"minstrels of the Lord Archbishop and of the Lord
"de Saye, with wine given to them 7s. 6d. For making
"the buttes 8s. 6d. Paid for 3 dozens of poyntes 6d.
"Paid William Martyn, for digging a gutter in the
"wall 10s. Paid William Harneys for his labour,
"digging two days in the Pette [Pit] at Fowelnes 8d.
"Paid for 2 pieces of timber for the bridge at Fowyl-
"nesse 18d." In a deed, transcribed in fol 10 b., dated
17th Henry VI., acres of land in "the Southlesis, in
"the Parish of St. Laurence, in Romene," are mentioned.

28, 29 Henry VI., A.D. 1450, 1. The mention of
the "Ward of James Tiece" now disappears. In the
joint Wards of Hamersmoth and Olbard, the "Rector
"of the Church of St. Mary in the Marsh" appears,
with "the Vicar of Romene" following.—"Paid for
"a certain porpays, with carriage thereof, sent to the
"Lord Archbishop of Canterbury 13s. Given to Alexan-
"der Mosewell, to make inquiry as to the Insurrection
"8d."—Jack Cade's Insurrection is meant.—"For his
"horse-hire at that time 6d. Paid for fuel, all con-
"sumed in the Common House at divers time, and
"straw for the Common House 4½d. Paid Richard
"Brykeynden for a certain cornshovyll 3d. For wine
"given to the men of Lyde, on the night when they
"watched 2s. 2d. Given to a man carrying a quarter
"of a man, to supersede the said quarter 3s. 4d.;" in
other words, they bribed the man to carry onwards his
hideous burden, part of the body of one of the rebels,
and deposit it elsewhere.—"Paid 18d. for a pair of
"boots, as a reward promised to him."—"The com-
"munity owes to John Sellenger, for his wages in
"Parliament at Leicester 4l. 19s."

Fol. 13 b.—"Sir Richard Barker, born at Tykell, in
"the county of York, was received to the freedom of
"the Eve of the Annunciation of the Blessed Virgin
"Mary, in the 30th year of the reign of King
"Henry VI. And he gave 20d. for fine."

In terms of apprenticeship entered in fol. 14 a.,
29th Henry VI., it is provided that the intending
apprentice shall not play at dice or chequer-board; and
that, at the end of his service, his master shall give
him 10s., or a bed of that value.

In fol. 14 b. is a lease for four years, by Andrew
Aylewyne, Clerk, of the rectory-house of Romene, called
Aliens' Pounteney [Pounteney Alienig'], together with
a grange, 2 barns, and a stable, in Spytelstrete, and
formerly called "Bouremannys Bernis" [Boureman's
Barns].

29, 30 Henry VI., A.D. 1451, 2.—"Sampson Duche-
"man" is named under Holyngbroke Ward, Simon
Wygge and Thomas Eadmund in Hospital Ward, and
John Walkot in Sharley Ward.—"Received 4s. for a
"parcel of land between the Walls."—"Paid 18s. 2d. to
"the men of Fordwych for our share of a certain suit
"by them made against the Abbot of St. Augustine's,
"for their liberties. Paid 3s. 8d. for making a
"bekene in the campanile of St. Nicholas. Given to
"Alexander Mosewell, for riding to inquire news as
"to the Duke of York, on his arrival in Kent, with
"his horsehire 6s."

30, 31 Henry VI., A.D. 1452, 3.—"Received of
"Richard Barker, Vicar of Romene, for the salt-pit
"upon the Gorst 4s. Received 2s. 8d. for herrings
"forfeited this year for being sold at night. 3s. 4d. in
"part payment for the house at Snargate, sold this
"year. Expenses of Richard Forde and William
"Copelande, riding to Croydone, to talk with the Lord
"Archbishop, with the hire of the horse of the said
"Richard 13s. 4d. Paid costs and expenses of Robert
"Scras and John Forde, riding to London to com-
"municate with the Lord Archbishop, for the preser-
"vation of our new Charter; with 6s. 8d. given to our
"attorney in the Exchequer, and to the serjeant of the
"Lord Archbishop, with their horse-hire 25s. Also,
"for one fish called a 'dolphyn,' sent to the Lord
"Archbishop, with carriage and expenses 15s. 10d.
"For dinner of the horse of the Archbishop's sur-
"veyor, with wine given to the surveyor 3s. 6d. For
"expenses of the Jurats, surveying the Market dyk,
"with wine given to John Cheynu, when he received
"his money for going to Jernemouth [Yarmouth] 6d.
"For a certain book bought for the Court 4s. 4d."

31, 32 Henry VI., A.D. 1453, 4. In this year the
name of John Lambard first appears; in Hope Ward:
—"Received of the Vicar of Romene for the saltpit
"near his tenement, upon the Gorsse 4s. 6d. Simon

"Colyn, for the Horsho 2s. Thomas Cowpere, for a
"parcel of land, called 'the Harpe' 4d."

Interpolation in folio 20, as to enfeoffment, in the
21st year of Edward IV. of a parcel of land called
"Barrockes," in the Parish of Hope All Saints, in the
fee of the Courts of Lymynge and Cronthorne.

31, 32 Henry VI. continued.—"Received 12d. of
"John Tarselle, a fine for breaking the common
"pounde."—"Paid 5d. for the horses' dinner of the
"minstrels of the Archbishop of Canterbury. In full
"payment to the wife of John Sellenger, for the wages
"of the said John in Parliament at Leicester 40s.
"Paid the expenses of Robert Scras and Richard
"Gardenere, mending the Lowpete of the Gote [Low
"pit of the Gut] 3d."

On a small parchment leaf, inserted:—"On the
"night of the Lord's Day next after the Feast of the
"Nativity of St. John the Baptist, in the 34th year of
"King Henry VI., John Sandys was watching for
"Thomas Edmund, which John was found asleep in
"the market-place of the same town; whereupon the
"same John, on the Tuesday after, was arrested by
"the Common Serjeant, and imprisoned. And he
"made fine to the community, 21d., according to the
"ordinance made as to watching; and by favour of
"the Jurats he was pardoned 8d. On the same day,
"Cornelius Williamson was arrested, because he left
"the watch without leave of his twentyman [vinten-
"arii]; and he paid a fine of 21d., according to the
"ordinance aforesaid; and as security for such fine
"he placed in the hands of the Jurats one brass platter
"and two plates of pewtre, and one sausere; and he had
"15 days to pay it in. On which day came Mariona,
"wife of the same Cornelius, and offered the money
"aforesaid; and by favour of the Jurats she was par-
"doned 10 pence."

32, 33 Henry VI., 1454, 5.—"Paid by John Porter
"for land situate between the Walls, near the harbour
"[' juxta port'] ; that is, from the Horssho to Long-
"brigge, near Cotehelle 2s." Several "forlands" are
also mentioned, as let by the Corporation.—"Paid to
"John Joseph, our Bailiff at Yernemouth 3l. 6s. 8d.
"Paid 13d. for one base [bass, a fish] sent to Haxtall,
"Clerk of Dover Castle, to have his friendship in the
"return of a certain mandate directed to us, to make
"inquisition as to the goods and chattels, lands and
"tenements, which William Tykle had on the day of
"his death. 3s. 6d. given to the messenger of the
"Archbishop [Thomas Bourchier] for the installation
"of the Archbishop; with wine given to him. Also,
"given to Richard Bartone, minstrel of his Lordship
"of Canterbury 20d."

33, 34 Henry VI., 1455, 6; the list of Maltotes is
given, with the inhabitants of the Wards; but the
receipts and expenditure do not appear.

In fol. 28 a. there is an entry (tr.):—"James Frode,
"of Oldromene, and there born, was admitted to the
"freedom of the said vill of Oldromene on the 25th of
"March, in the 35th year of King Henry VI.; and he
"did fealty. On the same day, William, his son, was
"admitted."

34, 35 Henry VI., 1456, 7.—"Joseph Hamon, other-
"wise Cinyare, pays for the Salt-pit opposite the High
"Mill, 5s. yearly. Richard Clederow, for rent of the
"house and garden near the Common House."—"Paid
"13s., given to the players of Lyde, with bread and
"wine given to them. 3s. 4d. for making a certain
"butte at the Barrockes. 3d. for coonteris bought this
"year. 10d. for fish bought and given to Haxtall,
"Clerk of Dover Castle, to have his friendship on a
"certain inquisition and resumption. 5d. for the
"expenses of the Jurats on interview with John Cobbe,
"as to a certain dam, ordered to be made at Stonbreg
"[Stonebridge], by the Jurats of the Marsh, to the
"nuisance of the town. 6s. 8d. for 2 gonnys [guns]
"with six chambers [cum sex cameris], bought for the
"community. 66s. 8d. paid to Robert Scras, as our
"share in a certain suit against the men of Yerne-
"mouth and Norwich, for a trespass this year com-
"mitted against our Bailiffs there, at the time of
"the Fair. 24s. 6d. for bows and arrows bought and
"delivered to certain persons in the town, unstrung,
"together with four bows, being in the Common
"House."

Fol. 32 a.—"John Russell, servant of John West, son
"of William West, of Herryettesham, was arrested on
"Friday next after the Feast of St. Edmund the Bishop,
"in the 37th year, for that he bought 13 hundred of
"herrings of Robert Hoo before sunrise, at Fowle-
"nesse, before it had come to market."

35, 36 Henry VI., 1457, 8. In this year, the name of Richard Clederow (who had been representative in Parliament) no longer heads Holyngbroke Ward ; but for two years he still pays rent for a house and garden, in which he is then succeeded by John Chenewe. — " John Portere pays for the Saltcote 5s. John " Hykke, for the *forland* between Ilysbregge and " Old Romene 2s. John Kynge, for the *forland* be- " tween the Harpe and Ilysbregge 2s."—" Paid to John " Joseph, in part payment of his wages for riding to " London, with the other Barons of the Cinque Ports, " to commune with the Council of our Lord the King, " upon the safe-keeping of the country 20s. For divers " expenses upon Thomas Kyrielle, Gervase Clyftone. " Knights, Robert Horne, Culpeper, and other men of " the country, when the French were at Sandwich " 16s. 10d. Expenses of the Lord the Earl of Stafforde, " when he came to view the country 22s. 2½d. Paid " Thomas Haxtall and John Cobbe, for having their " friendship for delivery of a prisoner 13d." John Cobbe is now the first on the list of "Advocantes," persons claiming to be free, but residing without the precincts ; who made, it would seem, certain payments, and to whom, probably, certain privileges were allowed.

36, 37 Henry VI., A.D. 1458, 9 :—" John Kinge " pays—for the pasture between the Horssho and Illys- " bregge." This " pasture " is identical with the " forland," previously mentioned. — " Paid 4l. for " mending the Slow [Sluice]. Paid 10s. to William " Mayster, the Common Clerk." Fol. 37 a.—" Be it remembered, that on Friday, the " Eve of the Translation of St. Thomas the Martyr, in " the year before-mentioned, Simon Maket was ad- " mitted to the rule and governance of the Hospital of " St. John at Romene, by name of Prior of the said " Hospital, taking for his wages and soap for washing " the vestments of the said hospital, yearly 20s. On " the same day also, John Porter was admitted Sene- " schal of the said hospital, to supervise the lands and " tenements thereof, and to let them to ferm, and to " receive the rents thereof, and to account for the " same, taking for his labour yearly 15s."

37, 38 Henry VI., A.D. 1459, 60. There is nothing to extract, worthy of remark. Fol. 40 a. Interpolations of later date. — " William " Lambarde, born at Canterbury, was admitted to the " freedom of Romene on the 1st day of April, in the " 22nd year of the reign of King Edward IV. ; and " he pays for his fine 3s. 4d." "John Cheyne, Knight, " born at Scherlond, in the Parish of Eastchcrch, in " the Isle of Sheppey, was admitted to the freedom of " Romene on the last day of May, in the 2nd year of " the reign of King Henry VII.: and he gives for " fine 10s., and for his yearly contribution 2s., and to " the fleet of the Lord the King 3s. 4d., and to the " Parliament of the Lord the King 2s. ; and to every " Coronation of the Lord the King 20d." He was son of William Cheyne, Chief Justice of the King's Bench.

38, 39 Henry VI., A.D. 1460, 1. In this year the name of William Hardynge appears in Sbarle Ward ; and a John Zakary in Olbard Ward.—" Paid a man " carrying a letter from the commons to the Marquess " of Salisbury [? Richard Neville, Earl of Warwick] and " the Lord de Fauconberge 2d. Paid John Chenew " and John Joseph, for their trouble about the new " Charter this year 20s."

1, 2 Edward IV., A.D. 1461, 2.—" Remark, that the " men of Old Romene did not pay for their contribution " this year. Whereupon, it was ordered by the com- " munity that they should be distrained for their " contribution, and precept was given to the Common " Serjeant, with others, to distrain for their contribution. " They afterwards came and paid such contribution ; " that is, 20s., and submitted themselves to the com- " munity for their dismissal ; and they were forgiven " on their (good) behaviour."—" Paid Richard Hore for " tiling the Common House, and for his dinner 10d. " Paid for our share of a certain gift of 100 marks to " Richard, Earl of Warwick, our Warden, to have his " friendship in the office of Warden aforesaid, at the " Court of Shepewey 11l. 2s. 3d. Paid to William " Legh, Common Clerk, for his wages 25s."

2, 3 Edward IV., A.D. 1462, 3. The name of John Badmynton, an inhabitant of the town, and a Jurat for a short period, appears this year, for the first time.— " Robert Scras pays for a little garden behind the Com- " mon House 4d. Received of the men of Old Romene " for a certain subsidy granted to the King, for the " defence of the town of Calais 10s."—" Paid to Robert " Clytherow, bringing letters of our Lord the King and

" the Earl of Warwick to have men ready for sea, in " support of his ships 6s. 8d. Paid for wine given to " the Lord de Fawkynbregge 15d. Paid for a breakfast " with the men of Lyde, on the day of their account " 5s. 8d."

3, 4 Edward IV.,[?]A.D. 1463, 4.—" The relict of William " Clytherow pays for rent of the house with a garden, " near the Common House, 4s. yearly. John Haymon, " as rent for the Saltpit and *saltlaynes* yearly 4s." Fol. 50 (tr.) :—" Over King Edward IV., on the day of " his Coronation, the Barons of the Cinque Ports bore a " canopy of cloth of gold upon 4 gilt lances, or spears, " and at each corner of the said canopy a bell hanging, " of silver gilt ; whose due, of right and of honour, it is " to do so ; as in Charters of former kings of England, " and the grant of the said King Edward, and the " customs of the Cinque Ports, more clearly appears. " And the said canopy, lances, and bells, were delivered " by the Barons of the Cinque Ports to the Barons of " Romene and Dovorre, to whom on this occasion they " belonged ; and among them they were divided, " namely, half of the said cloth, and 2 lances, and 2 bells, " to the Barons of the town of Romene, and the other " half of each thereof to the Barons of Dovorre."

3, 4 Edward IV., continued.—" Paid Robert Scras " [serving in Parliament for the town] for moneys ex- " pended upon the Lord Dacres, Comptroller of the " Treasury of the King's household, and others of the " Council of our Lord the King, together with the " Barons of the Cinque Ports, at London, on two occa- " sions, in taking counsel for confirmation of the new " Charter 3s. 6d. For moneys expended on the Ad- " miral this year 13s. 4d. For a small cord for the " bell in the Common House 3s. 4d. Paid to Agnes " Forde for the play of the Interlude of our Lord's " Passion, 6s. 8d. Paid to Thomas Pety, of Dovorre, " Bailiff of Jernemuth this year 66s. 8d." Fol. 51 a. " John Derynge, born at Lymynge, was " admitted to the freedom of Romene, and sworn, on " the 26th of May, in the 4th year of the reign of King " Edward IV. : and he paid for fine 3s. 4d. ; and his " yearly payment to the community there is to be 16d. " And on the same day, John,.his son, was admitted." In fol. 52 a., under the year 1465, a messuage, situate in the Parish of St. Laurence, is mentioned as being " commonly called *Le Soler*,—the Cellar."

4, 5 Edward IV., A.D. 1464, 5.—5, 6 Edward IV., A.D. 1465, 6.—" Laurence Whatman and Augustus Frode " pay for the pasture between Ilysbregge and Old " Romene 2s." " Paid a man, bringing a letter for the " Queen's Coronation 8d. Paid Robert Scras and " Thomas Howlot, for being at the Coronation of our " Lady the Queen, 7 days 35s." Of the following entry, in fol. 56 a., the first part is run through with a pen :—" John Cheynew, born at Romene, " free by birth, was admitted to the franchise and " sworn, on the 17th day of April, in the 6th year of the " reign of Edward IV., King of England.—He is con- " demned [dampnatur] ; because publicly, before the " Jurats and the commonalty, on the day of the Annun- " ciation of the Blessed Virgin Mary, in the 20th year " of the reign of King Edward IV., he refused [refutavit] " his freedom." Fol. 56 b.—" The Testament of John Bukherst, ex- " tracted for the reason written below.—In the name " of God, Amen. On the 10th day of January in the " year of Our Lord 1465, I, John Bukherst, of the " Parish of St. Laurence of Romene, being sound in " mind etc., do make my testament in this manner. " First. I leave my soul to Almighty God, and my body " to be buried in the churchyard of St. John the Baptist " at Romene aforesaid. Also, I leave to the high altar " of St. Laurence, for my tithes and oblations forgotten, " 6 pence. Also, to the light of the Holy Trinity there " 6d. Also, to the light of St. Catharine there 3d. " Also, I leave 4 pence for a wax taper to burn before " the image there of St. Thomas of Dancastre. Also, I " leave to the Prior of the Friars of Rye 6d. Also, I " leave to Alice, my daughter, after the decease of " Rose, my wife, one girdle of *sangueyne*, silver-plated, " one basin and one ewer, and one great platter. Also, " to Isabel, my daughter, one *copbord*, and one basin. " Also I leave to Joan Palmer one red chest, etc." His will, in reference to his lands, is then referred to, and it is given at length in fol. 58 a. He leaves his principal tenements, with 3 acres, near Ilysbrege, to his wife, Rose, for life. The residue is to be disposed of for the health of his soul, and the souls of his parents and benefactors, and all faithful deceased. John Bukherst, it may be added, was a Jurat, and paid Maltote in Butchery Ward ; which we may hence conclude to have been, partly, at least, in the Parish of St. Laurence. St. Thomas of Dancastre, was probably St. Thomas, or Thomas Plantagenet, Earl of Lancaster, who was beheaded in 1321.

6, 7 Edward IV., A.D. 1466, 7.—"Paid the men who " were players from Hethe, this year 6s. 8d. For the " expenses of Thomas Howlot and others, going to " Lyde, to hold a conference with the men there as " to the men of the Marsh; and for wine given to " Caxstone, of Lyde, bringing a message from John " Cobbes 8d. For wine given to the players of Hethe " 22d. Expenses of John Cobbes, Henry Martyne, " and 5 others, viewing the harbour here 2s. 8d." This John Cobbes, or Cobb, was one of the most influential of the "Advocantes," appears this year also, as one of the "Advocantes." In the preceding year "John Fryght" and "John Lytyl- " brother" appear as residents in Bochorye Ward. As to "Caxstone," here named, further mention of him will be found in the sequel.

Fol. 59 a.—"John Hykkys, born at Old Romene, free " by birth, was admitted to the franchise of Old " Romene, and sworn, on the 23rd day of October, in " the 8th year of the reign of Edward IV."

Fol. 60 a.—"William Courthope, born in the Parish " of Lymynge, in the County of Kent, was admitted " to the freedom of Romene, on the 8th day of Fe- " bruary in the 20th year of Edward IV. And he " gives for fine nothing, because he is forgiven by " the Jurats. And he is to pay 12d. for his yearly " contribution."

7, 8 Edward IV., A.D. 1467, 8.—"Paid the expenses " of Richard Brodnex, Richard Lynter, and others, " making scrutiny of the Levell, for the harbour 12d½. " Paid to the players of Lyde, in reward, bread, and " drink, given to them 7s. 11d." The Maltotes now are no longer entered against the names.

8, 9 Edward IV., A.D. 1468, 9.—"John Hamon " pays, for rent of the salt-pit, one seam of white salt." " John Derynge" appears in this and the preceding year as one of the "Advocantes," his name following that of "Master John Bacheler," and each paying 20 pence.—"Paid to a man bringing news about French " ships at sea 8d. For fish given to the Lord Arch- " bishop of Canterbury 15d. Paid the expenses of " John Cobbe, Richard Brodnex, Richard Lynter, and " William Pyrvile, and divers other persons of the " marsh, for levelling and taking the water of the said " marsh by the Fowlnesse, as set forth in particulars " in the paper-book 12s. 2d. Paid the expenses of " Thomas Howlot, John Fraunces, and Thomas Cou- " pers, and others, going to Apuldre, to converse with " William Pyrvile, as to making a harbour 17d. For " carriage of timber for the Gutte from Apuldre to " Romene, and for carrying divers other loads of " timber to the Gutte in this town, as set forth in the " paper 17s. Paid for the labour and table of Richard " French, working with Pyrvile at the East Gutte 20d. " Paid for ringing the bells on the day of election of " the Jurats 1d. Paid William Gregory for sharpynge, " roggynge, and settynge, the bomes 9d.:"—probably booms across the mouth of the haven.

9, 10 Edward IV,. A.D. 1469, 70.—"Paid a man, " bringing a letter as to the French ships, standing " for England 6d. Paid John Cheynew, Thomas " Couper, and others, employed on the voyage of the " Earl of Warwick this year 34s. 10d. [The men of the " Cinque Ports were supporters of the Earl of War- " wick against Edward IV.] Paid William Selver, of " Apuldre, for his labour upon the tree at Bylayngton, " given by John Cobbes for the work of the Gutte " 2s. 4d. Paid men for making scrutiny in the Helmes, " for carrying off the water of the marsh 8d. Paid a man " bringing royal letters to have men at Canterbury to " speak with our Lord the King 6d. Paid for mending " the Market dyke at Randeslowys 3d. Paid the ex- " penses of Robert Scras and John Castlake riding to " Dovorre, for the prisoners in Scotland 3s. 8d. Paid " the expenses of Robert Scras, John Castlake, and " others, and the expenses of their horses, at Canter- " bury, when our Lord the King was there 5s. 8d."

10 Edward IV.—49 Henry VI., A.D. 1470, 1.—"The " Jurats answer for 3l. 6s. 8d. received as their share " from the men of Lyde, of 10l. given for the voyage of " our Lord the King, for conducting back our Lady " the Queen, this year. Received upon the sale of " one dolphin 12d. For a tree sold in the common " garden 2s. 4d."—"Paid for wine given to the men " of the Marsh, on the day of the confirmation of their " liberties 7d. Paid for the Acts of the Parliament " 12d. For laying the bomes, and for the bomes 22d."

Fol. 70 a.—"Robert Stuppeny, born at Ivechyrche, " was admitted to the freedom of Romene, and sworn, " on the 5th of February in the 13th year of the reign " of King Edward IV., and 6s., 8d. was to be his fine, " to be paid on the Feasts of the Annunciation of the " Blessed Mary, of the Nativity of St. John the " Baptist, of St. Michael the Archangel, and our Lord's " Nativity [erroneously, put as the Annunciation] in " equal parts." This is the first mention of a family long resident in Romney. The tomb of Richard Stuppeny is still to be seen in St. Nicholas' church there; he probably was a son of this Robert. In the same page,—"Sir John Greyff, born at Dalketh in " Scotland," is admitted to the freedom.

11, 12 Edward IV., A.D. 1471, 2.—"Expenses about " Geoffrey Horne, at Apuldre, by Robert Scras, Thomas " Coupere, John Fraunces, and others, to ride with " him to our Lord the King 6s. 11½d. Paid to the " minstrels of the Lord Warden 2s. Expenses of " Robert Scras and William Legh, riding to Arundel " with other Barons of the Cinque Ports, to hold " counsel with our Warden, for re-confirming our " freedom 6s. 10½d. Paid a footman [pedestro] of our " Warden 12d. Paid a man bringing venesone from " the Lord Archbishop 4d. Paid a man carrying " a letter from the Lord of Arundell, and from the " Mayor and Jurats of Wynchelse, as to a present to " be given to our Warden 6d. Paid a man for bringing " a letter from the Mayor of Sandwich, as to warning " of the French ships 6d. Paid for bomes, settyng, and " carying 2s. 8d. Paid the Commissioners of our Lord " the King at Asshetisforde [Ashford], as fine for the " whole town 13l. 6s. 8d. For a swan given to them " 3s. 4d. For capons 2s. Paid the expenses of the Lord " of Arundelle, sitting here to make inquisition as " to the men who were at Blakheth [Blackheath] " 47s. 0½d."

12, 13 Edward IV., A.D. 1472, 3. This is the last year in which a list of those paying Maltote is given under their respective Wards.—"For wine given to " Sir John Fogge, Knight 2s. Paid the Common Ser- " jeant for keeping the Gutte and the Helmes 16d."

13, 14 Edward IV., A.D. 1473, 4.—"For reward of " the minstrel of the Earl of Arundel 20d. For the " oxpenses of John Chenew, riding with a porpos to the " Lord Cardinal [Thomas Bourchier] 2s. 7d. Paid for " the expenses of the Lord Arundel, bread 4s. 5d. " Reward given to the trumpetrs and fotemen 16d. " Paid a man bringing a proclamation, as between our " Lord the King and the King of Danemarke 16d. " Paid John Lytylborder for fish given to the Lord of " Norwyche 4d. Paid John Lane for the like 12d. " Paid John Tuder, Bailiff, for a breakfast given at Par- " liament 3s. 6d. Paid Robert Eve for the chambir of " the gonne 10d. Paid the Bailiff of the Marsh [Ma- " rischo] and others, viewing the water of the Level " from the Gotte to the sea 23d. Paid the wages of the " Warden, for this town 22s. Paid for toling the bell " 2d."

Fol. 76 a.—"Sir [Dompnus] Robert Bernyngham, " Prior of the House of St. John the Baptist, of the " town of Romene, born at Bernyngham [now Bern- " ingham] in the county of Suffolk, was admitted to " the franchise of Romene, on the 8th day of October, " in the 20th year of the reign of King Edward IV. " And he was sworn and made free. And the fine was " pardoned him by the Jurats."

14, 15 Edward IV., A.D. 1474, 5.—Many of the following entries bear reference to the Thomas Caxtone who has elsewhere been mentioned in these Reports under the heads of Rye and Lydd. In the Report upon the latter place, it is mentioned that he was Common Clerk there for some years, and that he became Common Clerk of Sandwich in 1476. Caxton seems to have served here temporarily, probably both as Common Clerk and in other capacities.—"Paid Thomas Caxtone " for his wages at the Common Court 4d. For wine " given to Thomas Caxtone 2d. Again, to the said " Thomas, in wine given to him 7d. Paid Thomas " Caxtone for his wages at the Brodhull 2s. For his " table 4d. Paid the minstrels of the Earl of Arundel " 10d. Paid the minstrels of the Duke of Clarence 12d. " Paid for a present to the Bailiff's boy, 8d. Paid " one bringing a mandate from Dover Castle for " proclamation as to Irish groats 4d. Paid in the " house of Richard Randeslow, for proclamation of the " banys [notice of a play to be acted] of Folstone 6d. " Paid to the men of Folstone in the house of Robert " Scrase, for proclamation of the banys 5d. Paid the " men of Folstone on the day of crying the banys 4s. 6d. " Paid wages to the watche 8d. Paid Thomas Caxtone

" his wages for holding the Court 8d. For the table of
" the same Thomas 7d. Paid the same Thomas his
" wages for holding the Court and other expenses 14d.
" Paid in the House to Thomas Caxtone 2d. Paid for
" wine given to Master Moyle for the common Gutte
" 5d. :—(a survey, probably, of the Gote, or Gutte.)—
" Paid to the King's minstrels 3s. 6d. Paid Richard
" Fuller for 5 bushels of oats for the swans 14d.
" Paid Nicholas Morley for oats for the swans 3s. 1d.
" Paid the same Nicholas for 2 cygnets 3s. Paid at a
" breakfast with the Bailiff of Lyde, Thomas Couper,
" and others, at the house of Nicholas Holle 14d. Given
" to the Bailiff's boy 8d. Expended in the house of
" Richard Bandislow, on the departure of the Bailiff
" 2d. Paid Richard Chambro for his wages, and for
" keeping the rabbits 18s. Paid to John Fermour for
" performing the duties [occupatione] of Common Clerk
" 12s. 6d."

15, 16 Edward IV., A.D. 1475, 6.—" Moneys received
" for rabbits this year 14s."—The Account for this year,
it deserves remark, is slightly rubricated.—" Paid for
" mending the Book of Customs in the days of King
" Richard, and for paper 3d. Paid for beer [bera] and
" ale in the Common House, at the time of assessing
" the scot 10d. Paid for expenses upon Thomas Ba-
" gott 7d. Paid for one pottle of wine, given to Feeke, the
" bodar [summoner] of Dover 5d. Paid for expenses at
" Brokland and in Romene, upon Henry Lokke, of Hethe,
" and upon the slaying of the cattle 4d. Paid the men
" who brought the gonne to the Common House from
" the harbour 1d. Paid Richard Fuller for watching
" one night, for himself and his horse 4d. Paid Thomas
" Wilson for himself and his cart and 2 horses, in
" carrying the harness of William Holt and 5 other
" men of his company to Dover, who were to go with
" John Kyriel to sea, in a certain ship called the ' Faul-
" ' cone ' 18d. Paid John Robyne for paper bought at
" Calais 10d. Paid Thomas Usborne for the expenses
" of the men and horses of the Bishop of Norwich, at
" the time of the Absolution of the town 13s. 5d. Paid
" John Herd for expenses of men and horses in his
" house at the time of the Bishop of Norwich 17d. Paid
" Robert Glover for hire of his horse to Chart, at the
" time of the Absolution of the town 6d. Paid William
" Dobille for expenses in his house of men and horses
" at the time of the Bishop of Norwich 4s. Paid John
" Robyn for mending the forms [formularum] of the
" Common House 1d."

Fol. 79 a.—James Goldwell, Bishop of Norwich, born
" at Great Chart, in the county of Kent, was admitted
" to the franchise of Romene, on the 4th of February,
" in the 17th year of King Edward IV., and was sworn.
" And all contribution is forgiven him, and given to
" him, by the Jurats and community of the town, on the
" 21st of December in the   year   of the reign of
" King Edward IV. aforesaid."—" John Goldwell, born
" at Great Chart, in the county of Kent, was admitted
" to the franchise of Romene, on the 13th day of May
" in the 18th year of the reign of King Edward IV.,
" and was sworn. And his contribution is forgiven
" him by the Jurats and community of the town
" aforesaid."

16, 17 Edward IV., A.D. 1476, 7.—" Given as a
" 'reward to John Grygge for writing a certain book of
" covenants [doubtful], and other necessary things
" therein contained 20d. Paid for wine, given to John
" Waterman and another servant of the Lieutenant of
" Dover 3d. Given as a reward to the minstrels of
" Lord Arundell 10d. Given as reward, and expenses,
" of the minstrels of our Lord the King 4s. Paid on
" Monday in the week of Pentecost for two men work-
" ing [laborantibus] at Old Romene, to hear an inquisi-
" tion held between Sir Robert Esone, Chaplain there,
" and Laurence Honer 7d. Paid expenses on Thursday
" in the week of Pentecost upon Master Gervase Hoorne
" and others 7d. Presents and rewards given to the
" men of Lyde, at the time of proclaiming the banns of
" their play 8s. 5d. Paid John Paynet for his watch-
" ing on Tuesday in the week of Pentecost, at time of
" the play 4d." [Two others receive similar pay.]
" Paid for a capon bought of Thomas Goore, given to
" the Lord Cardinal 12d." [Two other capons for the
like purpose 2s. 8d.] " Paid Thomas a Gore for carry-
" ing thorns and fagottes to the Gote 2d. Paid John
" Cheynew for his trouble and expenses in riding to
" speak with the Lord Cardinal, the Archbishop of
" Canterbury 8d. Paid the said John for a capon given
" to the said Lord Cardinal 12d. Given to the
" minstrels of the Lord the Prince 12d. Paid Robert
" Stuppeny in part payment of an old debt of 6s. 8d. on
" a certain lone 19d." [Elesbregge is largely repaired

at this date.]—" Paid Henry Somer, with John Lucas,
" for talowyng the ship in which he sailed, for 2 days.
" taking 3d. per day, 6d."

Fol. 88 b.—" Hamon Lambard, born at Demcherche,
" in the County of Kent, was admitted to the franchise
" of old Romene on the day of the Annunciation of
" the Blessed Virgin Mary, in the 12th year of the
" reign of King Edward IV."

Fol. 89 a.—" On the 3rd day of April in the 18th year
" of the reign of King Edward IV., Gervase Hoorne,
" Esquire, born at Apoldor, in the county of Kent, was
" admitted to' the franchise of Romene, and sworn, and
" made free; and his contribution was forgiven him,
" and was given to him by the Jurats and community
" of the town. On the 21st day of December in the 17th
" [? 18th] year of the reign of King Edward IV., Adam
" Ridley, born at Haltwesell, in the county of Northum-
" berland," was similarly admitted.

17, 18 Edward IV., A.D. 1477, 8.—" Paid William
" Knyght for making seats in the church of St. Lau-
" rence, on the Feast of the Annunciation of the Blessed
" Virgin Mary, in the 17th year 2d."—There is a similar
entry to this in each year, for many years following.—
" Rewards given to the minstrels of our Lady the Queen
" 20d. Paid William Gregory for carrying one load
" of hay from Willyngham to the Gote 4d. For wine
" and fish given to William Hawte, Knight 8d. For
" wine given to the Treasurer of the household of our
" Lord the King 8d. Paid the minstrels of the Lord
" Duke of Gloucester 10d. Paid the minstrels of our
" Lord the King 2s. Paid George Gate for 2 dogges of
" iron for the Gote 2s. 4d. Paid Thomas Wilsone for
" a piece of timber for the bridge over the Market-
" dyke 2d. Paid for bomes for the havyn 16d. Paid for
" fish given to the Coroner of our Lord the King 20d.
" Paid John Grygge, Common Clerk of this town, for
" his wages this year 50s."

18, 19 Edward IV., A.D. 1478, 9.—" Paid by the Jurats
" to William Knyght, Sacrist of the church of St.
" Laurence, for making seats for the Jurats in the said
" church, on the Feast of the Blessed Virgin Mary
" above - mentioned [the Annunciation] 2d. Paid a
" watchman of Dover Castle, bringing a proclamation
" as to Irish groats 8d. Given as a reward to the
" minstrels of Sandwich 20d. Given as a reward to the
" criers of the banns of Folstone 6s. 8d. Expenses
" upon the players of Folstone 2s. 11d. Reward to the
" Queen's minstrels 3s. 10d. Paid expenses of the men
" of Lyde, at the time of proclaiming their banns 8d.
" Reward to the minstrels of the Duke of Gloucester
" 12d. Reward to the men of Lyde, proclaiming their
" banns 6s. 8d. For a bushel of hoppes, given to John
" Brode, Coroner of our Lord the King 12d. Paid to
" William Quikmanne, for watching, at the time of the
" first play of Lyd 4d. Paid John Fermour, for making
" 2 dams in the Crekys upon the Gorse 10s. Paid John
" Lane for fish given to the Bishop of Norwich 16d.
" Paid expenses of the men of Folstone and Lyd, at the
" time of the banns here 3s. Paid Henry Deveniash,
" for watching, at the time of the play of Lyd 4d.
" Paid Richard Fuller, for watching at the time of the
" first play of Lyd 4d. Expenses of the men of Lyd
" in the house of John Castlake, at the time of pro-
" claiming the banns of Lyd and Folstone 12d. Paid
" William Gregory for a porpes and other fish, given to
" the Lord Cardinal, Archbishop of Canterbury 14s."

19, 20 Edward IV., A.D. 1479, 80.—" Paid the minstrels
" of our Lord the Prince 12d. Reward to the minstrels
" of the Lord of Arundell 8d. Paid John Cheynew for
" a capon given to the Bishop of Norwich 20d. Paid
" him for 3 geese given to the said Lord 12d. Paid
" William Lewene for working at the walle near the
" Helmes, for 3 days and a half 17½d. Paid as a reward
" to the Queen's minstrels 3s. 4d. Reward to the min-
" strels of the Duke of Gloucester 12d. Paid William
" Lewene, labouring at the Sewers near the walle, and
" covering up the Market dyke 14½d. Paid William
" Dobell for goslings [ancerulis] sent to the Lord Bishop
" of Norwich 12d. Paid Richard Fuller for working at
" the Common House with the tiler, and for the taking
" down [discoratione] thereof, together with whitel-
" ymyng the same house, for 6 days 2s. 6d."

Fol. 92 b.—" Thomas Otway, born at Effyngham, in
" the county of Sutherey, was admitted to the franchise
" of Romene, on the 23rd day of January, in the 20th
" year of the reign of Edward IV., and was sworn and
" made free; and he gives as his free 4s., and as his
" yearly contribution 12d."—" William Persy, born at
" Shilbotell [near Alnwick] in the county of Northum-
" berland, was admitted to the franchise of Romene, on
" the 23rd day of January in the 20th year of the reign

" of King Edward IV., and was sworn and made free,
" and he gives as his fine 3s. 4d., and as his yearly
" contribution 12d., if he dwell without ; and 12d. to
" the King's fleet, and to the Coronation of our Lord
" the King 12d."
20, 21 Edward IV., A.D. 1480, 1.—" Received for 3
" books 5s. 8d."—" Paid William Gregory for half a
" porpesse 5s. Paid as a reward given to the Queen's
" minstrels 2s. Rewards given to the King's minstrels
" 3s. 4d. Paid a watchman of Dover Castle, making
" proclamation as to malefactors of Denemarke 8d.
" Rewards to the minstrels of our Lord the Prince 2s.
" To the minstrels of the Earl of Arundell 2s. Paid
" expenses of the Ambassadors of the King of France,
" and gentlemen of our Lord the King, on a message
" from the same our Lord the King 13s. 4d. Reward
" given to the minstrels of our Lady, the King's mother
" [Cecily, Duchess of York] 2s. Reward given to the
" minstrels of the Duke of Gloucester 20d. Paid ex-
" penses of the men of Lyd, when here, for the honour
" of this town 4s. 4d. Paid the expenses of the men of
" Lyd, at the time of putting up the image of St. George
" 2s. Paid expenses of divers Jurats and commoners
" being at Canterbury, with the Council of the Lord
" Cardinal Archbishop, as to the Gores 18s. 4d. Paid
" men working to fill up the seler under the Common
" House, by way of covenant 2d."
21, 22 Edward IV., A.D. 1481, 2.—" Paid for fish given
" to the Commissioners of the Lord the King 10s. 3d.
" Paid Thomas Galion for a porpesse given to the Lord
" Cardinal 20s. Paid for a quart of malmsey given to
" the Master Lieutenant of Dover 4d. For fish given
" to the Lord Cardinal at Canterbury 5s."
22, 23 Edward IV., A.D. 1482, 3.—" Received 6d. from
" a certain ship, taking the common ground with coals."
—" Paid for a gallon of wine given to John Aldy, John
" Swanne, and John Honywode 8d. Paid the Common
" Clerk of Sandwich for writing the award between
" Romene and Lyde 4d. Paid Thomas Caxstone and
" Wanstall, of Lyde, in the name of the whole of their
" community, when they brought their contribution
" 3s. 4d. Paid the same Thomas and Wanstalle, as a
" reward 8d. Paid for crying the banns of the town of
" Hethe, as a reward 6s. 8d. Paid the minstrels of our
" Lady the Queen, as a reward 2s. 8d. To the minstrels
" of the Duke of Gloucester 16d. To the minstrels of
" the Lord the Prince 12d. Paid a clerk coming from
" Sandwich to be Common Clerk, as his reward 2s.
" Paid for 2 mullets given as a present to John Scott,
" Knight 11d. Paid the expenses of John Ford and
" other men, going to Dover, to go in a certain ship
" with Parker, called the 'Grete Portyngale' 2s. 4d.
" Paid Nicholas Morley for 2 swans given to the Lord
" Cardinal 8s. Paid the Bailiff's boy for riding with the
" said swans to Knolle 8d. Paid William Perey for
" measuring coals in the Helmys, and for drink at that
" time 3d. Paid the expenses of Jurats and others at
" the time of measuring the Marsh 2s. Paid the expenses
" of John Forde and Gervase Horne, for 2 breakfasts
" given to the Lords and other gentlemen of the House
" of Parliament, on part of our town 20s."
23 Edward IV., 1 Richard III., A.D. 1483, 4.—
" Paid for a pottle of wine and a quart of malmsey
" given to the Mayor of Sandwich and his brethren, as
" we wanted them to be our friends against the men of
" Lyde 10d. Paid the minstrels of our Lord King
" Richard [originally written 'Duke of Gloucester'], as
" a reward 3s 4d. Expended upon them, in the house
" of Thomas Usbarne 8d. Paid to a certain man of the
" Earl of Arundell, bringing a commission as to the
" King's Coronation, as a reward 20s. Paid for a mes-
" sage from Dover Castle, postponing [contradicenti]
" Parliament and the Coronation 20d. Expended upon
" the minstrels of the Lord of Northumberland 5d.
" Paid Laurence Norkyne for hire of his horse to
" Hethe, for Richard Fuller, riding to learn how many
" Barons they chose for the Coronation of the Lord the
" King Edward V. 4d. Paid John Cheynew, riding to
" aid at the Coronation of King Edward V., for 8 days,
" at 2s. per day, 16s. Paid Patrick Gille for one capon,
" which the Jurats gave to Master William Scotte,
" against the Feast of All Saints in the 22nd year 20d.
" Paid 2 minstrels of the Lord Arundell, as a reward 8d.
" Paid William Colstone, for his trouble in coming here
" from Canterbury for the indentures 6s. 8d. Paid the
" expenses of the Bailiff and John a Forde riding to Es-
" shetisforde [Ashford], to communicate with the gentry
" 3s. 8d. Paid Edward Middilton for his trouble, going
" to Maidstone to inquire the news 20d. Paid Vincent
" Fynche, Bailiff, for his wages at the Coronation of King
" Richard, for 8 days, 16s. Paid a servant of Lord

" Arundell, bringing a proclamation to take the gentry
" 20d. Paid Thomas Galione for one hawsere, having in
" length 80 fadome [fathoms] 4s. Paid John Umfrey,
" Common Clerk, for his wages, 50s. Paid as a reward
" to Thomas Ponte, for going to Old Romene, to speak
" with them, that they might find one man 2d. Paid
" a certain minstrel of the Lord Arundel, in the house
" of Richard Randislowe 8d."
Fol. 97 a.—" William Lovelas, born at Wykham, near
" Canterbury, was admitted to the franchise of Romene,
" on the 14th day of June in the first year of the reign
" of King Richard III., and he is to give for his fine,
" paid beforehand, 6s. 8d. And if he remain without
" the liberty of the said town, he shall give, for his
" yearly contribution 20d. He was sworn and made
" free." The surname "Lovelass" is still remembered,
as that of a writer of authority upon "Wills."
1, 2 Richard III., A.D. 1484, 5.—" Received from
" Robert Stuppeny 12d. for fish forfeited at Foulenesse."
—A fruitless attempt, it will be seen, was made to set
up a Mayor for the town, under the momentary auspices
of King Richard, probably.—" Paid for fish bought by
" the Mayor, and given to Ralph Asshdon, Knight,
" 18d. For making a certain silver mace at Canter-
" bury 19s. 7d. For the expenses of John Castelake,
" riding to Canterbury, about the said mace, 9 days,
" 5s. 7d. Reward given to the minstrels of our Lady the
" Queen, and expended upon them 3s. 5d. Expended
" upon George Cheynewe, in the house of Richard
" Randislowe, when he came to communicate with the
" town as to a Mayor 18½d. Paid for one quart of
" malmsey and one quart of reade wyne, given to the
" Mayor of Sandwich and his brethren on the day of
" the Brodell 6d. Paid John Stephynsone, Common
" Clerk of Sandwich, and expended upon him in the
" house of William Dobyll 18d. Paid a watchman of
" Dover Castle, bringing a proclamation as to the Earl
" of Oxford and other gentlemen, as traitors 4d. Paid
" the expenses of John Siltone, in the house of Richard
" Randislowe, when he came to communicate with the
" Mayor, on certain matters of the town 2s. Paid the
" expenses of Adam Tuter, when he brought a Privy
" Seal to depose the Mayor, 18d. For expenses in the
" house of Richard Randislow upon the Bailiff and
" Jurats of this town, and the Bailiff and Jurats of the
" Marsh, when they were in communication that they
" might be one Corporation 17d. For a quart of claret
" wyne given to the Bailiff of the Marsh, on his depar-
" ture 2d. Paid Richard Fridde for making the gonne,
" in part payment, 4d. Expended upon the Mayor and
" Jurats in the house of John Dobyll, when the Mayor
" went to Lyde to converse with the Lord lo Grey 18d."
It is not stated who this simulated Mayor was ; but
according to the earliest Court Book of Rye, "John
" Wymonde" would appear to have been his name.
Fol. 98 a.—" John Rickmanne, born at Lymmynge, in
" the county of Kent, was admitted to the franchise
" of Old Rome[ne], on the 24th of March in the 4th year
" of the reign of King Henry VII."
2 Richard III., 1 Henry VII., A.D. 1485, 6.—" Paid
" Robert Eve for making the markyng-iron for the town
" 4d. Paid Henry Malford, carrying news from the
" Mayor of Rye, as to the Coronation of the present
" King 8d. Paid a certain man, bringing news and a
" letter from the Mayor of Dover, as to the resumption
" of the liberties of the Cinque Ports 4d."
1, 2 Henry VII., A.D. 1486, 7.—" Received 18d. of
" John Watts and Clement Baker, as a fine for playing
" at cards [lusione ad le cardes]. Received 7s. for pas-
" ture upon the Gorse this year."—" Paid the minstrels
" of our Lady the Queen 2s. Paid a waite of Dover
" Castle, bringing a proclamation of war between Charles
" of France and the King of the Romans 4d. Paid as a
" reward to the criers of Lyde, when they cried their
" banns 6s. 8d. Paid their expenses in the house of
" Thomas Bursell 6s. 8d. For 2 horns for the waites 2s.
" Expended on the surveyor of the Lord Chancellor,
" with horsmete 3s. 1d. Paid the expenses of Richard
" Gildford, Knight, [and] of Edward Ponynges, Knight,
" in the house of William Dobyll 2s. 8d. Paid a waite of
" Dover Castle, bringing a mandate as to vagabonds 4d.
" For fish given to the above gentlemen 10d. Paid a
" waite of Dover Castle, bringing a proclamation of
" peace between the King and the Duke of Bretagne, 6d.
" Paid for 2 jakettes, for Henry Robyne and James
" Richard, 2s. 4d."
2, 3 Henry VII., A.D. 1487, 8.—" Received 20d. as a
" fine from John Watte, for playing at cards."—" Paid
" for wine given to the surveyor of the Lord Cardinal,
" in the house of William Dobyll 6d. Paid Richard Ful-
" ler—pro sessione de le Hessestake [?]. Paid for game

" given to the Lord Cardinal 2s. 6d. Paid the expenses of
" William Dobyll and others, riding to Maydistone, to
" the Lord Cardinal, about the havyne 6s. 10d. Paid
" the expenses of certain Jurats and commoners when
" they were at Kildfordmersah, for water there for the
" havyne 17d. Paid the expenses of the men of Lydde,
" when they sealed the indenture, in the house of
" Richard Randislow 3s. 8d. Paid the expenses of the
" men of Lydde, when they were here to communicate
" about the burning of the cabin [cabannia] of the relict
" of William Gregory, in the house of William Dobyll
" 17d. Paid for the seme (horseload) of fish that was
" given to the Lord Cardinal 9s. Paid John Playdene,
" for a capon given to the Lord Cardinal 8d."

3, 4 Henry VII., A.D. 1488, 9.—" Paid the expenses of
" William Wodar, at Apuldore, when he was there with
" Gervase Hoorn, Knight, about the havene 3d. Paid
" the expenses of the Jurats in the houses of William
" Dobill and Thomas Galione, when they surveyed the
" common watercourse in the Holmys 2d. Paid the
" minstrels of the Lord the King, with their expenses
" 2s. 5d. Paid the expenses of the Jurats, when they
" were collecting the capons for the Lord Archbishop 3d.
" Given as a reward to the banners of Apuldore, when
" they cried their banns 3s. 4d. Given to the surveyor
" of the Archbishop 2 molettes, price 14d. Paid the
" relict of Richard Randislowe for wine given to the
" Archbishop, when he was at St. Mary Church 18d.
" Paid William Wode, for a capon given to the Lord
" Archishop 12d."

4, 5 Henry VII., A.D. 1489, 90.—" Received 2s. 8d.
" this year, for the old house near the Keye."—" Paid
" Robert Pundherst, for scouring a watercourse [aquagii]
" near the Vicarage 2d. Expended upon the Bailiff of
" the Marsh, and the Jurats thereof, in the house of
" Thomas Usbarne, when they viewed the watercourse
" for the havyne 3s. 4d."—Several other sums are this
year expended upon the haven.—" Paid the banners
" of the play from Charte, in the house of Thomas
" Usbarne 2s. 10d. Paid for 2 capons given to the Lord
" Archbishop, 2s. For 2 geese given to the same Lord
" 8d. Paid the minstrels of the Earl of Arundel 4d.
" Paid for wine in the house of William Dobill, given
" to a man of Richard Gildforth, Knight, coming for the
" gunnis and cabillis of the week 10d. Expended upon
" the surveor, when he came to measure the land for
" the havyne 8s. 4½d. Paid Thomas Lambard for red
" wax 8d. Paid William Brownyng, the (new) Common
" Clerk, for his stipend 5s. Paid Thomas Galione his
" expenses at Lyde, when he went thither to see the
" original of our play there [ad videndum originalem
" ludi nostri ibidem] 4d."

5, 6 Henry VII., A.D. 1490, 1.—" Paid for putting up
" the kokyngstole 4d. Paid the wardens [gardianis] of
" the play for the loan of vestments 20s. Paid a mes-
" senger who brought a proclamation of the peace
" between our King and the King of Denmarke 4d. Paid
" 2 men watching by the sea-shore 4d. Paid in reward
" given to the minstrels of our Lord the Prince 8d.
" Paid a messenger who brought a commission to have
" archers at the town of Calais 6d. Paid for a potell
" of wine given to the Bailiff of Lyde, when he came
" to inquire about the said archers 5d. Paid Robert
" Eve for mending 5 gunnys 13d. Paid a man who put
" the woman on the cokyngstole 5d. Paid John Elys
" for the jacket [le jaket] 10d. Paid John Wardene
" for the crane that was given to Richard Gildeforth,
" Knight 16d."

6, 7 Henry VII., A.D. 1491, 2.—" Paid John Melalo for
" cloth to make jakettes for the soudyers 10s. 1d. Paid
" John a Lane for the gunstonys 13d. Paid a messenger
" from Dover Castle for a proclamation as to Erisshyens
" [Irish pence] 4d. Paid expenses upon the criers of
" the banns of Wy, in the house of William Dobyll
" 2s. 11d. Paid as a reward to the minstrels of Sande-
" wyche 8d. Paid for digging up the turfis for the
" butts 2d. Paid expenses of William Wodar and
" John Plaideno when they rode to London for artillari
" 4d. Paid Robert Eve for 2 vorlokkes for the 5 gunys
" 5d. Paid Thomas Arnold for his expenses when he
" rode to Dele, to communicate with Master Joseph as
" to the armour and artillari 5d."

Fol. 103 a., a memorandum is entered, in English, that
at the Annunciation in the 8th year of King Henry VII.
leave was given by the Bailiff, Jurats, and commonalty,
of Romene, to Vincent Fynche to bar and inclose a
lane between his tenement in the Parish of St. Martin's
and the lands called " Barrokkes."—William Dobyll
and John Warden have a lease of the Common Marsh of
the town, as a reward for the making of a Goote.

Fol. 103 b., in a grant executed by John Boldistone,
Rector of Ivechurch, 8th of Henry VII., mention is made
of the Market dyke, the common watercourse called
" the Sole," and a lane called " Shoptownelane." In
the same page, John Wilson, born at Norram [now
Norham] in the county of Durham, is admitted to the
freedom.

7, 8 Henry VII., A.D. 1492, 3.—" Received 46s. 8d. of
" the men of Old Romene, towards the voyage for
" escorting our Lord the King this year beyond sea."—
" Paid William Lucas, master of the Antony of Snode-
" land, for prest for himself and 2 mariners in that
" ship 8s. Paid Clement Galyone, master of the
" Trinity of Folkestone, for prest 4s. Paid John Lucas,
" master of the James of Romene, for his prest and that
" of six mariners 16s. Paid a man for bringing pipes
" and other vessels from divers places to the byrehouses
" 2d. Paid for 9 yerdes of blankett for jakettes 6s.
" Paid Cornelius Note for victuals in the Thomas of
" Newhethe 3s. 6d. Paid Thomas Gregory for making
" the jakettes for the mariners, and for claspes 3s. 6d.
" Paid the mariners as a reward, in copper money to
" be divided between them 18d. Paid Richard Fuller
" for bread, eggs, and butter, bought for the ships 6d.
" Paid Thomas Gregory for riding to Apoldore for the
" ship of Thomas a Lye 3d. Paid William Stokes for
" 2 pairs of shoes for the mariners of Snodelande 12d.
" Paid Richard Dunche for himself and his servant,
" watching by night in the ship of Newhede [New
" Hythe] 4d. Paid Robert Bysshop, for watching at
" the bekene, with Henry Howlott 16d. Paid John Tyler
" for carrying 4 lunnes of byere [beer] to Hethe, for the
" ships there 8d. Paid Moses Armynarde for cheese
" for the ships 16d. Paid William Pyxe for his stipend
" this year 50s." This account is about ten times the
ordinary length, and is full of items in reference to
the supply and equipment of shipping, for the King's
service.

8, 9 Henry VII., A.D. 1493, 4.—" Paid the criers of
" the banns of the play of Lyd 6s. 8d. Paid the expenses
" of divers Jurats riding to Master Ponynges at West-
" rynghangre, and spent upon the servants of Master
" Ponynges in the house of Henry Baldwyne at the
" same time 3s. 4d. Expended upon the breakfast for
" the criers of the banns of Lyd 4s. 4d. Paid for 4
" capons given to Master Ponynges 5s. 4d. Paid
" Andrew Clerk for the expenses upon Giles Love,
" coming to the town upon the requisition of the Jurats,
" at the time of the vexation caused by Robert Tory
" 21d. Paid Thomas Frensshe for making up the
" pavyssee, and mending the skrene in the Common
" House 9d. Paid Edward Hexstalle, of Dover, for the
" share of this town in one tun of wine given to Edward
" Ponynges, Knight, by all the Ports 15s. Paid Andrew
" Clerk for the expenses upon Master Ponynges and
" his servants at the Crowne 8s. 11d. Paid William
" Baldwyne of Ivecherche for carriage of the bomes,
" from Ivecherche aforesaid to the havene 16d. Paid
" Thomas Lambarde for watching in the town at the
" time of the play of Lyd 4d. Paid Richard Fuller
" and James Markeby for 4 curlewes sent to Master
" Ponynges 2s. Paid as a reward to the minstrels of
" our Lord the King 2s. Paid Richard Paysshe for wine
" given to the criers of the banns of the play of Rye
" 8d. Paid William Pyx, Common Clerk, for his year's
" wages 50s. Paid Richard Fuller for his labour in
" laying the bomes 2d. Paid Thomas Gregory for
" expenses upon the great surveyor from the house
" of the Lord Cardinal 18d. Paid the expenses of
" Vincent Fynche and others, on departing and re-
" turning from Canterbury, for the prisoner 9d.
" Paid Thomas Gregorye for expenses upon a Friar of
" Rye, at the same time 5d. Paid the same Thomas
" for 2 horses' dinner for 10 days, when they came
" from Canterbury with the prisoner 3s. Paid for
" making the Longbregge 12d. Paid a Friar of Rye
" who came to hear the confession of the prisoner 12d.
" Paid the hakeneyman of Canterbury as a reward for
" his horses, beyond what was agreed 17d. Given to
" the minstrels of our Lady the Queen 12d. Paid Wil-
" liam Swanne for 4 geese given to the Lord Cardinal
" 2s. Given to the minstrels of the Duke of Bedford 8d.
" Paid for beer given to the men of Lyde, who rode
" forth upon the expedition of our Lord the King, when
" our enemies were in the Downes 4d."
At this point, fol. 107, the Accounts of one year are
missing :—(but see the extracts from the succeeding
volume).

10, 11 Henry VII., A.D. 1495. 6.—" Received of Vin-
" cent Fynche for rent of the Salt Marsh and of the
" warenne this year 106s. 8d. Received of John Lau-

" ther, Clerk, for the rent of the House of St. John the
" Baptist 10s. Received 11d. of Richard Dodde, of
" Old Romene, for occupation between the Walls from
" Ilesbregge to Olde Romene."—"Paid the expenses
" of some men helping the carpenters in taking down
" the *bemes* of the Common House 2s. Paid the expenses
" of the Jurats and their servants riding to the Lord
" Cardinal, in Easter week 13s. 3d. Paid John Tuder,
" Bailiff, as a reward given to him for his wages in
" Parliament the past year 6s. 8d.; and be it known
" that the residue of the wages of the said John is
" forgiven by him, to the use and advantage of this
" town.—Given as a reward to the minstrels of the
" Lord Duke of York [afterwards Henry VIII.], Warden
" of the Cinque Ports 3s. 4d. Given to the minstrels
" of the Lord the Prince 3s. 4d. Paid Richard Fuller
" [the Common Serjeant] for working at cleansing the
" High Street and the Market dyke two days 8d. Paid
" a messenger from Dover Castle, bringing a pro-
" clamation against the Scots 6d. Paid a serjeant of
" Dover Castle, bringing a Letter of *myssef* (missive)
" from our Lord the King as to receiving our Lady of
" Spain [Katharine of Aragon] 8d. Paid Moses Army-
" nard for 2 *lodes* of lome for the Common House 4d.
" Paid for the *congrs* given to Master Ponynges 3s."
Capons are mentioned as frequently given to the Cardinal. Robert Stuppene first appears among the Jurats
in this year.

11, 12 Henry VII., A.D. 1496,.7.—"Paid William
" Waryne, of Dover, and others, for our share of one tun
" of wine given to Master Ponynges, and for fish given
" to the Lord Cardinal, and for divers copies of writings
" 18s. Reward given to the minstrels of our Lord 'the
" King 3s. 4d. Paid a serjeant of Dover Castle, bringing
" a mandate for a proclamation as to the Roman groats
" [le Romans grottes] 8d. Paid for a paper common
" book printed [paupiro libro communi impresso] 1d.
" Paid the expenses on the election of a Common Clerk
" 2d. Spent on the Preacher 23d. Paid expenses upon
" the Preacher 23d. Paid Thomas Prenestone, Chaplain,
" the debt for the play, in full payment of his bill
" 6s. 8d. Paid Thomas Gammoll, Chaplain, for the same,
" in full payment of his bill 15s."—Three other like
bills are settled, amounting to 14s.—"Paid Richard
" Fuller for warning upon to players [gamesters] in
" divers places 12d. . Paid John Belle, Common Clerk,
" for his wages from the Feast of our Lord's Nativity
" 12s. 6d. Paid Thomas Gregorie, expenses of the play
" 2s. 8d." There are several items of expenditure for
capons given to the Lord Cardinal (John Morton,
Archbishop of Canterbury).

12, 13 Henry VII., A.D. 1497, 8.—"Paid the serjeant-
" keeper of the beasts of the Lord, Warden of the Ports, as
" a reward 2s. 10d. Paid as a reward to the minstrels of
" our Lady the Queen, and expended upon them 3s 10d.
" Paid John Delle, as a reward for writing the new Cus-
" tumal 3s. 4d. Expended on the minstrels of our Lord
" the Prince 2s. 8d. Paid a minstrel of the Lord Cardinal
" as a reward 12d. Paid a serjeant of Master Ponynges,
" carrying a mandate of our Lord the King as to Peter
" Warbekke 8d. For 2 capons given to the Lord Car-
" dinal 2s. 4d. Paid expenses of mending the haven
" this year 60s. 11¾d."

13, 14 Henry VII., A.D. 1498, 9.—"Received by the
" hands of Peter Wynche from Thomas Doble 4s. for
" the land between the Walles. Received from Robert
" Toby 3s. 4d. for rent of the House of St. John the
" Baptist. Paid the minstrels of the Lord Cardinal and
" the Lord Oxford, as a reward 2s. 3d. The minstrels
" of our Lady the Queen 12d. The minstrels of our Lord
" the King 3s. 4d. Paid a servant of Master Ponynges,
" carrying a mandate for seizing ships when the Duke
" of Suffolke was going to Flanders 8d. Expended
" upon the Vicar of Lydde, when he came to preach in
" the church of St. Nicholas, on the Second Sunday in
" Lent 2s. 4d. Paid Richard Pasche for wine, when he
" went to the town of Rie 9d. Paid Thomas Gregori for
" wine given to the wife of William Scot, in the house
" of Vincent Fynch 8d. Paid in reward upon the
" players [super ludorum] of the Lord Arundell 12d."—
The Latin in which these entries are made, is of the very
worst.

14, 15 Henry VII., A.D. 1499, 1500.—"Received 12d.
" of Robert Stuppene for rent of land between the Walles,
" from Ilesbregge to Olderomene. Received 3s. 4d. from
" William Mugge for rent of land between the Walles,
" near Lynghoke, for 2 years."—"Paid for 6 capons given
" to the Lord Cardinal 5s. 6d. Paid a carpenter for his
" wages upon the High Cross 2s. 8d. Paid expenses
" upon the cry of the banns of the play of Haldene
" 18d. Paid William Hortone for timber for the High

" Cross 6s. 7d. Paid John Holle for 43 feet of *borde* for
" the High Cross 3s. 4d. For 740 tiles for the same
" Cross 3s."

15, 16 Henry VII., A.D. 1500, 1.—"Received 3l. 6s. 8d.
" of Vincent Fynche for rent of the Saltmarsh. Re-
" ceived 8d. of Thomas Hunde for rent of land in the
" Hoppegardyn, for four years. Received of the widow
" of William Swanne for rent of land between the Walls,
" from Ilesbregge as far as the Barre, 2s. 8d.."—"Paid
" John Lane his wages for keeping the *clokke* for one
" quarter 12d. [This clock was in the church of St.
" Laurence]. Paid William Bukherst his wages for the
" *clokke* 4s."

16, 17 Henry VII., A.D. 1501, 2.—"Received 12s.
" in full account for lands belonging to St. John the
" Baptist. Received of Robert, parish clerk of St.
" Laurence, for drawing blood of Thomas Wevill 20d.
" —Paid John Lane as a reward for carrying a parcel
" of the banns of the play of the town of Romene 8d.
" Paid Richard Humfrey for his expenses in riding to
" London, for the *serch* of the *billettes* in the Exchequer
" of our Lord the King there 11s. 8d. Given as a reward
" to a minstrel of Master Ponynges, and paid his
" expenses 18d. Paid Master Blachenden as a reward
" for his trouble in the Exchequer, when Richard
" Humfrey went to search for the fifteenths and tenths,
" in wine given to him 4d."

17, 18 Henry VII., A.D. 1502, 3.—"Paid Richard
" Humfrey for his expenses when he went to Hastynges
" for a certificate of Magna Charta 16d. Paid as a
" reward to the Bailiff and Jurats of Lyd, when they
" came to cry their play 6s. 8d. Spent upon the men
" of Lydde when they came from Hide with the banns
" of their play 14d. Delivered to the Warden of this
" town for the play [pro ludendo], in the way of *lone*
" 20s. 6d. Paid the relict of John Wardene, in full
" payment for the carriage of *gers* from London to
" Romene, for the play 3s. 4d. Paid John Lane for
" his labour in that play 3s. 4d. Reward given to the
" minstrels of the Lord Admiral 3s. 4d."

18, 19 Henry VII., A.D. 1503, 4.—"Received of
" John Bonvassall, Clerk, for the Lane 2d. Paid'the
" Bailiff and Jurats of Hithe, when they came to cry
" the banns of Hythe 6s. 8d." [Large sums were also
spent, at the same time, on their entertainment. These
banns, probably, were slips of parchment, of a descriptive character, distributed to those who were to see the
play.]—"Paid William Wodar for hay, on the occasion
" of the play 12d. Paid him for wine delivered at
" the play 7d."

19, 20 Henry VII., A.D. 1504, 5.—"Paid as a reward
" to the minstrels of the Lord Oxford, with their ex-
" penses 3s. 4d. Paid Thomas Lambard, in full pay-
" ment of the old debt owing to him by the town for
" the play 28s. 3d."

Fol. 117 b. contains the admission of Mighell Bone-
vassall, born at Saint Mary Mount [apud Seynte Mari
de Monte] to the freedom, on the 25th of May in the
21st year of Henry VII. (A.D. 1506). At this point,
the leaves in this volume containing the Accounts for
some years are missing; but are entered, originally
perhaps in duplicate, in the volume next described.

23, 24 Henry VII. A.D., 1508, 9.—"Paid the criers
" of the play of Bedresden this year 3s. 4d. Paid as
" a reward to the minstrels of the Lord the Prince
" 2s. 8d. Paid William Cotyng for his labour in
" *schoeing* [shoeing horses] at divers times 16d. Paid
" Robert Walter and William Bukherst their wage
" for making the *buttes* near the mill 4s." Part of this
Account has been cut out.

24 Henry VII., 1 Henry VIII., A.D. 1509, 10.—
" Received 20s. of Thomas Arnolde for land belonging
" to the House of St. John the Baptist."—"Paid a
" serjeant of Dover Castle, bringing a monition as to
" the *sckenesse* [the plague], against the Coronation of
" our Lady the Queen 8d. Paid as a reward to the
" minstrels of our Lord the King 2s. Paid to the
" *bereward* of our Lord the King, as a reward 16d."

At fol. 119 a., a recognizance in the sum of 40l., by
Richard Stuppene the elder to Thomas Gregori, is
entered; dated the 1st of December, in the 2nd year
of Henry VIII. A pen is run through it, in proof that
it had been satisfied. It was this Richard, probably, who
was buried in St. Nicholas' Church at New Romney;
and at whose tomb the yearly election of Mayor still
takes place.

At the foot of fol. 119 b., is entered the admission of
Richard Stuppene the elder, born at Keneston, to the
freedom, on the 22nd of March in the 3rd year of
Henry VIII.; paying nothing for his fine. He appears

however on the list of Jurats in the preceding year.
Robert Stuppene's name has disappeared.

1, 2 Henry VIII., A.D. 1510, 1.—" Received 5s. of
" Richard Humfrey for timber sold to him from the
" place called the 'Slow.' Received 3s. 10d. of the widow
" of Thomas Lambard for rent of land lying in the
" place called 'Southlese,' and from that place to Ilee-
" bregge. Received 6d. from the same for land in-
" closed in the lane near the place called 'Colver-
" 'lese.' Received 4d. of Richard Humfrey for a parcel
" of land near Perys figo crosse."—" Paid the expenses
" of the Bishop, when he came to bless the High Cross
" 6s. 6½d. Reward given to the minstrels of the Earl
" of Oxford 3s. 1d. Paid the relict of Thomas Lambard,
" in full payment for his expenses at the Coronation
" of our Lord the King and the Queen 2s. 8½d. Paid
" as a reward to a serjeant of our Lord the King,
" called the 'berward' 2½d.

2, 3 Henry VIII., A.D. 1511, 2.—" Received 20d.
" of Richard Richards of Old Romene, for leave given
" to him to make a way to his barn near the church-
" yard of St. John the Baptist."—" Paid William
" Bukhurst for a new cord for the clokke 14d. Paid
" a serjeant of Dover Castle, bringing a commission
" from our Lord the King to hold a muster of the men
" who were to go to Gildreland 8d. Paid as a reward
" to the men of Halden, when they came to cry their
" play 20d. Paid to the men of Brokeland for the
" like 5s. Paid as a reward to the men of Folkestone
" for the like 6s. 8d. Paid John Hakett for his outlay
" upon Master Copledike, when he came to view the
" men who were to go to Gildrelond 2s. 2d. Paid
" Thomas Glover for canvas of gussets, standers, and
" aprons of mayle 12d."

3, 4 Henry VIII., A.D. 1512, 3.—" Paid the expenses
" of a certain priest of Oxford, for a sermon made in
" the church of St. Nicholas in Lent 6d. Paid Clement
" Baker for his expenses for a dinner given to the Lord
" Warden, at London, at the time of Parliament 17s. 4d.
" Paid for half a porpes given to the Lord Cardinal
" 10s. 10d. For half a porpes given to the Lord Admiral
" 10s. 6d. For canvas for the porpes 6d. Expended on
" the Suffragan, when he came to this town 8d. Paid
" Richard Stuppene the elder, for arms bought of him
" 13s. 4d. Paid the expenses of Richard Humfrey,
" riding to Master Scott, to shew him the words used
" by Michel Bonevassell 8d. Paid as a reward to the
" minstrels of the Duke of Bukyngham 2s. 8d. Paid to
" the King's bearward, as a reward 3s. 5d. Paid a man
" bringing a warning from Rye of three ships of the
" King of France 4½d. Paid as a reward to the players
" of St. Mary's 8d. Paid William Bukherst for a
" salette [head-piece] bought of him 3s. 4d. Paid
" Moses Armynard for the [la] wodknyf 2s. 4d. Paid
" a serjeant of Dover Castle, bringing a letter as to
" the excommunication of the King of France 8d.
" Paid George Cobbes, Common Clerk, for his wages
" for one quarter 12s. 6d. Paid Clement Baker for his
" expenses upon Master Roper [? the son-in-law of
" Sir Thomas More], Master Hale, and others, at the
" time of Parliament 4s. 10d."

4, 5 Henry VIII., A.D. 1513, 4.—" Received 16d.
" for the mill called Southmill."—" Paid Henry Holle,
" Joseph Hakkett, Christopher Herfeld, and John
" Buntyng, as a reward for their trouble and expenses
" upon the play 13s. 4d. Paid Henry Robyn for hiring
" 2 men with arms, at Westynghanger 4d. Paid a
" man bringing a mandate from the Queen, as to the
" escape of the maryners and soldiers, without leave
" given 8d. Paid a man bringing a letter from the
" Lord Howard, the Admiral, for watching the bekons
" for the Scottes and Frenchmen 8d. Paid a man bring-
" ing a proclamation that all Frenchmen should wear
" white crosses on the left shoulder 8d. Paid for wine
" given to the Lord Suffragan 4d. Paid William
" Woodar for going to Asshford, to inquire for a clerk
" for this town 8d."

5, 6 Henry VIII., A.D. 1514, 5.— " Received of
" Richard Gybeon for rent of the common land lying
" between the Walles, from a certain place called the
" 'Barre' to Ilysbrege, for two years past 5s. 4d.
" Received 6d. in part payment for blood drawn
" between priests."—" Paid John Adam, the bereward
" of our Lord the King, as a reward 2s. Paid Edward
" Frencham, Clerk, his wages for a quarter 12s. 6d.
" Paid a man bringing a mandate to prepare for the
" Queen of France [the Princess Mary] passing beyond
" sea 8d. Paid Robert Dunney as a reward, when he
" came to view the havyn 2s."

6, 7 Henry VIII., A.D. 1515, 6.—" Paid expenses of
" Master Manwood, when he preached here 15d. Paid

" for wine and fish given to the Lord Suffragan [Domino
" Suffricano] 2s. 2d. Paid a serjeant of our Lady the
" Queen, bringing news of the Princess [de la Princes]
" 3s. 6d."—the birth of the Princess Mary, February
18, 1516, is alluded to:—" Paid as a reward to the
" minstrel of Master Ponynges 12d. (he is called John
" Thoroll in the next book.) Paid the expenses of
" the Bailiff and Jurats of Lyd when they brought
" their contribution, and the fifth part of the payment
" to the Burgess in Parliament, in the house of Thomas
" Glover 5s. 4d. Paid Clement Baker his wages as
" Burgess in Parliament, 17 days at 2s. per day, 34s.
" Paid the executors of the said Clement Baker, for
" one set of brekynders [? brigantines, a light suit of
" mail], being in arrears, and not paid in his life-time
" 10s. Paid John Baker for the crabs and fish given
" to the Lord Cardinal 14d. Paid Richard Stuppeny
" the remainder of his wages as Burgess in Parliament,
" last year 38s. 10d. Paid William Bedell for the molett
" [mullet] given to the Lord Suffragan 10d."

7, 8 Henry VIII., A.D. 1516, 7.—" On the 5th of
" May given to the players of our Lord the King 12d.
" Expended upon Sir Richard Pever, Vicar of Romene
" 6s. 4d. Paid for drinkings of the Combarons in the
" dwelling-house of John Hyxe on the matter of the
" said Richard Pever, the Vicar 5s. Spent at the Crowne
" when the jurors came from Estringhanger, on the
" matter aforesaid 5s. 4d. Paid Robert May, Common
" Clerk of Romene and of the Cinque Ports, for his
" wages this year 50s. Paid for cutting the Mersshe
" walle, which is called 'Lambardes Wall' 3d. Paid
" Thomas Beanqnike for watching Richard Pever, the
" Vicar, when he was in Smallisporte, for his de-
" merits 6d."

8, 9 Henry VIII., A.D. 1517, 8.—" Paid for drinkings
" at the Croun, with the serjeant of the Lord Arch-
" bishop of Canterbury, concerning the Saltmersshe 7d.
" Paid John Alwey for watching Smallesporte, while
" Richard Pever was there in prison for his offences 6d.
" Paid Simon Wodford for one cord to serve for the
" clock, namely, in the church of St. Laurence 12d.
" Paid for drinkings at Master Glover's, with the mes-
" senger of our Lord the King, when he brought news
" concerning the commotion which there was among
" the Apprentices of London 6½d. Paid and given to
" the players of Appoldore, when they cried their banns
" here 32s. 10d. Paid for a dinner at the Crowne,
" while Mistress Rose was here 3s. 8d. Paid the ex-
" penses of our players, as set forth in the Account
" of Christopher Hensfeld 3l. 18s. 5d. Paid Richard
" Ward for his labour on the old havene 19s. 6d. Paid
" Richard Stuppeny the elder, in reference to the old
" havene 37s. 6d. Alms given to the Brothers Obser-
" vant at Canterbury 3s. 4d."

9, 10 Henry VIII. A.D. 1518, 9.—" Received of John
" Bate, Chaplain, (as a fine) for drawing blood of John
" Legat, Chaplain 21d. Received of Richard Lambert for
" drawing blood of John Bate, Chaplain 21d. Received
" of William Tadlows, deputy-bailiff of the Archbishop
" of Canterbury, at Romeno, for the rent of Southe-
" mersshe, otherwise called 'Commenmersshe,' or 'Salt-
" 'mersshe,' from the feast of St. Michael the Archangel
" in the 9th year to the same feast in the year next
" ensuing 3l. 6s. 8d. Received of Hermaone, the
" servant of Richard Stuppeny the elder, when he
" made an assault on Robert Paris, a Jurat 3s. 6d."
—" Paid at the Bordelle for a breakfast, as was the
" wont from of old 4s. Given to the players of Wyn-
" chelay and Rie, as a reward 18d. Given to Doctor
" Scott, who preached here, in drink, 10½d. Paid
" William Bukerst for keeping the clock of St. Lau-
" rence's for a year 4s."

10, 11 Henry VIII., A.D. 1519, 20.—" Paid the
" minstrel of Sir Edward Ponynges 12d. Given to
" a minstrel of the Lady Arundel 16d. Item, paid for
" a bylle sent to the Bayley, conservyng the grounde (of
" the) Spitill 8d. Paid for fish for the Lord Ponynges,
" namely, a baise and 2 elys 3s. 4d. Item, paid for
" borde and for nayle for the Proclamation, 2d."

In fol. 131 b., an entry is made, in English, to the
effect that, on the 13th day of March, in the 12th year
of King Henry VIII., Richard Lambarde, of New
Romeney, appeared before Richard Stuppeny the
elder, and other Jurats, and James a Barrowe, Common Clerk, and acknowledged that he had delivered
to " Richard Gybsone, of Londone, serjeant of the
" armys of our Soverayng Lord the Kyng," certain
tenements situate in the Parishes of St. Nicholas and
St. Laurence in that town ; a marsh called " Newe
" beggyng," a field called " Coulver Leysse," a field

called "Safferon Leysse," and a field called "Chey-
" newes."

11, 12 Henry VIII., A.D. 1520, 1. The entries are
in English.—"Paid to a bodar (messenger) for the
" proclamation conserning the wacche and privy
" serche, and adnullyng of gally halfpence 16d. For
" wyne spent upone the Merahemeu at the beskone,
" 4d. Paid to Turrolde, my Lorde Wardens myn-
" strelle 14d. Paid at Master Stnppenys for drynk-
" yng, when acotte was seysyd [assessed] 3s. 11d.
" Paid in expences at the Crowne upone Staple of
" Hethe, and Adam the barewarde, in rewarde, 3s. 4d."
The ordinary Account is followed by a separate one of
some length, thus headed:—"Costes and expences
" abowte the schyppys, conservyng the transportyng
" of the Kyngs Grace over to Calys, be the space of
" 15 dayes."

12, 13 Henry VIII., A.D. 1521, 2.—"Item, leide out
" in rewarde to the players of Broklond 4s. Item, in
" expenses upon them, att drynkynge 6s. 8d. Item,
" paide uppone Seynt Laurence Day in rewardes to
" the Kynges mynstrelles 12d. Paid in rewarde to the
" Duke of Suffolkes berewarde 2s. 4d. Paid to John
" Mores, Comen Clerk, for his wages for 3 quarters
" 37s. 6d."

The Accounts for the next two years are missing;
there following, at fol. 135, a portion of that for—

15, 16 Henry VIII., A.D. 1524, 5.—"Paid to Edward
" Wodell, for mowing down of the weedes at the comen
" place 1d. Item, in expenses upon my Lord Wardene,
" when he was att ladyng of his tymbre 15d. Geven
" to the cariars of the same tymbre 4d."

16, 17 Henry VIII., A.D. 1525, 6; numerous sums
are received for rent of the town lands this year; two
persons pay rent for a "Salte cote," and the "comen
" grounde" at Snargate is also mentioned.—"In ex-
" penses uppone Hewe Smythe, my Lorde Wardene's
" servant, whenne he sett the felowe out of prysone,
" whiche was laide in for takyng away of the Portyng-
" gal's sailes from Tyers 12d. Gevyne to one that
" went to Seyntmaricherche att that tyme for a crane,
" to be gevyne to my Lord Wardene 2d. Item, paid to
" Mores whenne he went to Londone to Master Gybsone,
" with the bill of arreyment for the play etc. 8s. Paid
" in expenses att William Garrarde, whenne the Lorde
" of Misrewle of Olde Romeney came to towne 40d."

Entry at fol. 137 a.—"Att this daye it is condescended
" by all the comons, that from hensforth Johan Wilsone
" shall be taken as no freeman, onto tyme he hath
" proved hymme self to be anne Englishman."

17, 18 Henry VIII., A.D. 1526, 7. This Account
occupies the last two leaves, folios 137, 8; they are much
mutilated, and, to a great extent, the writing is illegible.—"Paide for William Taberer, the wayts, for his
" bourdyng.—Geven in rewarde to my Lord Cardynalle
" mynstrelles 3s. 3d. In reward to the Kynges players."
The last page is almost wholly illegible, and some
leaves which followed have been cut out.

(Since the preceding account of their contents was
written, the two volumes last described, I am glad to
say, thanks to the attention and liberality of H. B.
Walker, Esqre., have been substantially bound, and
thoroughly repaired.)

The next book in sequence is a small folio paper
volume, bound in limp parchment, with a numeration
in a hand of the 16th century. The first leaf contains
proceedings of the Jurats in the 7th year of King
Henry VII.; after which, it includes assessments of
Maltotes, and Scots for the King's shipping, upon the
inhabitants of New Romene, and Corporation Accounts.

Fols. 2-28 contain only lists of names of the inhabitants, as assessed to Scots for the King's shipping. In
fol. 29 are entered, in Latin,—"Receipts of sums given
" by the youths and other friends of this town, towards
" the shipping, this year;" among the trades are
named tailors, smiths, labourers, shoemakers, and a
salter. "Hanastaeus, servant of John Stokes," gives 6d.

Fol. 22 b.—"Received of John Knechebulle 4s. 1½d."
about the 8th of Henry VII.: this is the first instance
in which the name appears. The surnames of Whateman, Epps, and Wygge, appear in the same page.

In fol. 30 b., 9 Henry VII., there is a long list of fines
for drawing blood. John Cheynewe the younger, and
Laurence Cotard, are each fined 21d. for drawing blood
from the other. William Busse is fined a like sum for
drawing blood from John Souner; also "John Galyone,
" Clerk of St. Martin's 21d., for drawing blood of
" Richard Byssbop."

In fol. 47 is an entry of a louse, 10th Henry VII., for
7 years to Vincent Fynche, "Gentilman," of all the

Salt marsh, with the fresh pasture in the Helmes, and
the fore warren belonging to the Jurats and commons
of Romene. Vincent Fynche and John Tuder were at
this time Burgesses in Parliament for the town.

In fol. 48 b. et seq. is entered the expenditure by the
Corporation in the 9th and 10th years of Henry VII.
(A.D. 1494, 5), which does not appear in the folio parchment volume last noticed. The following are some
extracts:—"Given as a reward to the minstrels of our
" Lady the Queen, and for wine for them 2s. Given as
" a reward to the criers of the banns of the play of
" Brokelond 4s. Paid expenses upon them in the
" house of Henry Baldewyne 3s. 4d. Paid Peter
" Wynche for beer given to the criers 2d. Given as
" a reward to the criers of the banns of the play of
" Hethe 6s. 8d. Paid Henry Robyne for a potell of
" wine given to them 4d. Paid Peter Wynche for beer
" given to them 2d. Paid expenses upon them in the
" house of Henry Baldewyne 4s. Paid as a reward to
" a serjeant of our Lord the Prince, who came with
" the babyone (baboon) 12d. Given as a reward to the
" players of the Prince 10d. Paid John Hakette for
" his labour, in settyng the bones in the havens 4d.
" Paid Richard Bursell for watching in the town, at
" the time of the play of Lyd 4d."

Fol. 50 a., 1st of March 10th. Henry VII., John Cheynewe, Gentilman, and John Holle, give surety for the
good behaviour of the master and mariners of the ship
called the "James" of Romene. In the same month,
John Adam, carpenter, and John Hoveayde, enter into
like surety to keep the peace.

Fol. 50 b. contains an entry as to the freedom.—
" William a Bowe hath granted for his fredom ii
" lambes, or iis. in money, to be payde at the fest of
" Seynt Michell next comyng. John Bursell hath
" granted to lend to the town x shepe by the space of
" iii yere." Similarly, John Playden lends 20 sheep
for 3 years, Henry Baldwyn 6 sheep for 2 years,
Robert Joseph 4 sheep for 3 years, Vincent Fynche
20 sheep for 3 years.

Fol. 52 b., 9 Henry VII.—"Thomas Usbarne the
" elder pays rent for a parcel of land in the Hop-
" gardyn, withdrawn from the common Marsh."

Fol. 58, 8, 9, (apparently) Henry VII.; items which
do not appear in the preceding volume.—"Paid
" Thomas Gregorye for a potell of wine given to the
" criers of the banns of the play of Rye 4d. Reward
" given to the criers of the banns of the play of Rye,
" 4s. Paid Richard Fuller for the heptre [?] at the Long-
" bregge 1d. Paid as a reward to a Friar of Rye for
" confessing the prisoner put to death [ad mortem
" positum] 12d.;" (given before, apparently, but in
another form.) " Paid 2 men watching the prisoner in
" the gaol for 2 nights 8d."

At this point, fols. 60-67 are wanting; fols. 68a-70 a.
contain the account of expenditure, only, of 11, 12
Henry VII., the whole of which is preserved in this
volume last noticed. In fol. 74 a. Richard Knechebulle
" pays 5s. for the freedom, sold to him;" in fol. 75 a,
John Knechebulle pays 4s. 2d., as an " Advocans," or
one claiming the freedom, but dwelling without the
liberties. In fol. 78b., the 14th year of Henry VII.,
Richard Knechbulle, as being an " extravagans," or
freeman living beyond the liberties, agrees to pay to the
Chamberlain 4d. yearly. In fol. 80 a., the same year, the
persons who have in the past year sold cider in the town
(venditores cesaris) are 13 in number. Also, in the
same year,—"Received of Phineas Usbarne the elder,
" for rent of a parcel of land in the Hopgardyne, re-
" covered from the common Marsh 2d. Of William
" Strogulle for rent of a parcel of the King's high-
" way, containing 12 roods, on the north side of
" his messuage, in the Parish of St. Martin's 6d."

Fol. 80 b.—" On the Feast of the Annunciation of the
" Blessed Mary, in the 13th year of the reign of King
" Henry VII., it was enacted that the criers of the banns
" of the play of Romene, commons of that town, should
" carry in their banns, or at least bills of the same, before
" the Feast of St. George next after that date; and that
" those who failed therein, should be imprisoned 40
" days, or else find sureties for delivery of the same."
This entry is in very corrupt Latin.

Fol. 88 a.—14th Henry VII.; succeeding John Bell,
Richard Humfrey is named as the Common Clerk.

In fol. 95 a., 16 Henry VII., is enrolled a sale by
" Thomas Otewey, son of Thomas Otewey," of a tenement, near land called " Lotroches," in Romney.

In fol. 108 a., occurs this hexameter, a scribbling,
temp. Henry VII.—"Dum sumus in mundo, vivamus
" corde jocundo."

CORPORA-
TION OF
NEW
ROMNEY.

In fol. 119 b. a list of names of persons is given, who are presented for " blodwyke " [blodwite], punishment for assault with bloodshed.

Fol. 120 b., on Friday before Christmas Day, in the 20th year of the reign of Henry VII.,—" Thomas Gregori " was sworne uppon his halydom othe, that he had well " and truly delyvered iii letters of processe unto the " Bayleif of Lydde."

In fol. 125 b., 21 Henry VII., John Crosse and Mighell Bonevassulle are bound to keep the peace, on pain of paying 13s. 4d.—" unto overy of the three chirchis;" the three, no doubt, being those of St. Nicholas, St. Laurence, and St. Martin.

Fol. 129.—" On this day (the Annunciation, 21st Henry " VII.) it is aggred and enacted, and for a law for ever " to be kepte, that any servaunt, that is to say, a man " servuant that takith for his wages 40s. by yere, shall " pay yerely to the comyn charge, that is to say, for " Maltehode [Maltote], at what tyme it is gadred, " 4d."

The entries at fol. 136 b., for 20, 21 Henry VII. (A.D. 1505, 6) are not given in the preceding book : the following are some extracts :—" Paid as a reward for crying " the banns of the play of Brokelond 5s. Paid the " expenses of the banns on the same day, in the house " of Edward Wodell 5s. 4½d. Paid as a reward to the " minstrels of the Lord the Prince, and expended on " them 21d. Paid the minstrel of Master Ponynges, as " a reward 12d. Paid the expenses upon the Brothers " Observant in the house of Edward Wodell, when " they camo to preach in the church of St. Nicholas " 6d."

Fol. 142 a., 21, 22 Henry VII. (A.D. 1506, 7).—" Paid, " as a reward, to the minstrels of the Lord the King 2s. " Paid for one shefe and a half of arrowes 3s. 9d. Item, " paide for poyntes for the bregandynes 1d. Paid " William Mugge for eawyng [sewing] of the canvas " uppon the gorgettes of maile and aprons of maile " 8d."

Fol. 144 b. (22, 23 Henry VII.).—" Thomas Musterdyne " pays rent for common land between the Walls, that " is, from Ilesbregge to Longfare, for one year, 4d."

Fol. 146 b.—22, 23 Henry VII. (A.D. 1507, 8).—" Re- " ceived custom for salt in the havyn from a French- " man 20d.—Paid Robert Walker and William Bukherst " their money for making the buttes 4s."

Fol. 148 b.—" The 15th day of Juin the first yere of " the raigne of our Soueraigne Lorde, King Harry the " VIIIth, the Jurats of the towne of Romeney have " electe for burgesis of the Coronacion of our Soveraigne " Lorde Kynge Harri the VIIIth and the Quene, Johan " Holle, Clement Baker, Thomas Lambarde, and Thomas " Glover."

Fol. 149, 23, 24 Henry VII., A.D. 1508. 9.—Among those paying the " general Malctot " this year, is named " Edward at the Cherche stile of Sayute Martyns," paying 4 pence.

The Account of the expenditure of 24 Henry VII.— 1 Henry VIII., fol. 152, does not correspond with that given in the preceding volume : the following are some extracts :—" Paide in expenses uppon the Suffrecan, " whanne he was here, the Tuysday before Ester 16d. " Paid as a reward to the men of Lydde, when they " came to cry their play 6s. 8d. Paid the wages of 4 " burgesses at the Coronation of our Lord the King and " the Queen 4 marks. Paid the minstrels of our Lord " the King, as a reward 2s. 4d. Paid the minstrels of " our Lord the King, Henry VIII. 2s. Paid Thomas " Glover in full, for his wage at the Coronation 2s. 8d." In this year, among the " Contributions dewe by certein " persons to the towne of Romeney," Richard Knacche- bulle is named, as owing 4d.

Fol. 155 b.—" The last day of Marche, the furste yere " of our Soveraigne Lorde Kyng Harri the VIIIth, one " John Hubbard was distrayned for dute perteynyng " to the towne for Maltehote the space of 5 yere, every " yere 6d., summa 2s. 6d., the whiche distresse is 3 " pannys of bras, and a ketylle."

Several of the yearly Accounts now given are almost repetitions of those in the preceding volume.

Fol. 168 b.—" Be it known that the Chamberlain, for " the time being, of the town of Romene, let to Robert " Davy at the Feast of the Annunciation of the Blessed " Mary, in the 3rd year of the reign of King Henry VIII. " common land of the said town ; that is, from the place " called Ilesbregge to Oldromenebregge, for one year, " he to pay 12d."

Fol. 169, 3, 4 Henry VIII., A.D. 1512, 3,—Richard Knachebulle and John Whatmanne are among those making payments this year.

Fol. 170. Peter Johnson, " born at Delfe in the parts " of Holand," is among those admitted to the freedom.

Fol. 178, apparently 4, 5 Henry VIII., A.D. 1513, 4 :— " Paid Master Doctor, that is, the Rector of Wyttyssham, " for his expenses 2s. For tymber pertaining to the " common ditch of the town 12d. Paid Thomas Mown- " soone, as a reward when he came from Asshford to " Romney to serve as Common Clerk to the said town, " he remaining there for 5 days ; for his trouble and " expenses 2s. 8d. Paid for 4 capons given to Master " Ponynges 5s. 4d." In the same year, the Maltote paid for the ' Southmelle' (South Mill) by Simon Wood- ward, is 16d.; that by William Fardyngly for the Hyzemelle (High Mill) is 2s. Retailers are to pay " for every tonne of swett (sweet) wynne 8d., and for " every tonne of Gaskonne wynne 4d." In the same folio (183) a messuage called " Cowpers" is mentioned.

Fol. 187 b., 5 Henry VIII., Robert Apsole, born in the Parish of Myltone, in the county of Kent, is admitted to the freedom.

This volume ends, at fol. 196 b., with some memoranda of the 7th year of Henry VIII.

The next book to be noticed, in chronological sequence, is a quarto paper volume ; being a collection, apparently, of fragments, put together, if we may judge from the numeration of the pages, in the 16th century, and bound in limp parchment: the first 56 leaves of it, as then arranged, being lost. It seems to be partly an Assembly Book, and partly a book of Accounts. At fol. 57 it begins with the first year of Queen Mary, but lower down on the page the entries belong to the first and other years of Elizabeth ; the next page continuing with the " Common Scot " Accounts of the first year of Elizabeth. The name of Agnes Stuppeny appears ; from the comparative amount of her assess- ment (6s. 8d.) a person of some opulence ; John Stup- peny pays but 4d.—" George at Mr. Couchman's," " John that was at Chaundlers," and " the boy at " Mr. Buntynges," are also respectively charged 4d. Three persons are taxed, as living " bytweene the Walles" with this addition.—" Note that these 3 last sommes " were taxed upon inhabitants within the parish of " Olde Romeney. And therefore these were dwellyng " in the Liberty of New Romeney, though in the parish " of Olde Romeney."

At fol. 70 (original pagination) there are entries of persons admitted to the freedom in the 21st year of King Henry VIII. ; on the reverse of which folio is the following curious entry (tr.) :—" On which day (the Feast " of St. John the Baptist, 8th Henry VIII.) the book " called ' Le Pleyboke' was delivered to Henry " Robyn, to keep such book to the use of the town " aforesaid until etc." The Common Clerk who made this entry (in very bad Latin) was Robert May. The question arises whether this was a common Plea Book only, or a Play Book, connected with the Town Play, next mentioned.

On the 14th of December, in the same year, the Jurats and commons—" chose Wardens, to have the play of " Christ's Passion, as from olden time they were wont " to have it, namely, Richard Stuppeny, Christopher " Hensfeld, Robert Paris, John Buntyng, William " Bedell." In the same page it is stated that, on the 5th of October in the following year, Robert Browne, " born in the vill of Hamersmyth, in the county of Mid- " dellsex," was admitted to the franchise. Also, " Upon " which day (date not named) the book called ' Le " Playloke' was delivered from the keeping of Henry " Robyn into the hands of Robert May, Common Clerk " there, safely and securely to be kept to the use and " behoof of the said town."

Fol. 72 :—" On the sixth day of July in the 9th year " of Henry VIII. Richard Bursell the younger sent " to Robert May, Common Clerk, by William Bukherste, " for Le Pleyboke aforesaid, and then and there he " delivered the same to the said William, and so the " book now remains in his hands."

Fol. 72 b. On the 13th of December in the 9th year of the same reign, four persons named,—" then and " ther examyned uppon ther halydome othes, whether " that the halfe cove the whiche was seized at Hithe " by Richard Butler wer good and able fleisshe and " merchandisable ; the whiche affermed it god and " able in the presence aforesaid."

Fol. 73 b., 13th of March, 9 Henry VIII. surety for 40s. is given by John Wilson, of Romene, to James Swanne, of Lydd, for " horsses fleishe " of him bought.

In fol. 75 a. 22 November, 8 Henry VIII. is an account, apparently, of voluntary contributions—" To the provyng " of the dykes of the Havene ;" 5 persons subscribe in the parish of St. Nicholas, and nine in that of St.

Laurence, 13s. 2d. being the sum collected. No other parish is named.

Fol. 80 b. :—On the 18th of December 8 Henry VIII. the Jurats distrained, for the benefit of creditors, the grain of John Haket, lying in the barn of Nicholas Poynet—"as well in grain as in sheaf," of whatsoever kind.—"So much so, that the said John suddenly, and "unforeseen, departed from the town aforesaid to "Sanctuary at Faversham."

At fol. 82 the list of Maltotes collected, is continued from the preceding volume, at 7, 8 Henry VIII. (A.D. 1516, 7.)

At fol. 87 b. are given the receipts for 8, 9 Henry VIII. (A.D. 1517, 8.) Porpoises sold out of town are still subject to a Maltote of one shilling. Deryk, the servant of John Stuppeny, pays 20 pence for an assault.

At fol. 90 are the accounts of expenditure for a year, the date not named, but evidently 7, 8 Henry VIII. A.D. 1516, 7:—"Paid a man bringing a mandate from "the Lord Warden, warning us of the Scottisshe barke "that was upon the sea 8d." Other payments are given, as in the preceding extracts from the folio volume.

Fol. 100 b. 8, 9 Henry VIII., A.D. 1517, 8.—"Payments "made by order of the Brodhill;" some of the entries appear in the Account for this year given in the second folio previously noticed. The following seem to be additional to those there given.—"Given to the col-"lectors of the parish church of Ostringhanger for "torchelight, that is, in the chamber of the Lord Warden "[Sir Edward Poynyngs] 4d. Given to the butler "there 4d. Paid on the 26th day of May to a serjeant "of the Lord Warden, who then brought a mandate to "the Barons of New Romene here, that they ought "not to play the play of the Passion of Christ until they "had had the King's leave etc. 9d."

Fol. 105. On the 24th of January, 9 Henry VIII. John Chilton, of Romene, "Gentilmanne," acknowledges himself indebted to Stephen Buntyng, of Lyde, "Yo-"manne" and to Thomas Waynflete, of the city of Canterbury, "Vyntener."

In fol. 112 some additional accounts are given for 9, 10 Henry VIII., A.D. 1518, 9.—"Paid Richard Thor-"wall as a reward, because he is a minstrel of Sir "Edward Ponynges, Warden, on the last day of May 16d. "Paid Thomas Wainflete 3s. 4d. Expended upon Sir "Master Doctor [Domini Magistri Doctoris] preaching "in the church of St. Nicholas, on the 23rd day of "January."—Paid for repairs to the havens 11s. 1d." Wild fowl and fish are charged for, as being sent to the Lord Warden.

Fol. 115 b. et seq : on the 18th of April, 9 Henry VIII. by common assent of the Jurats and commoners it was enacted, that from thenceforth no more "Maletoltes" should be collected ; but that Scottes and half Scottes should be gathered. To all appearance "Maletoltes" were sums levied upon the sale of commodities; and "Scots" were assessed upon the property of the in-dividual.

Fol. 117 : at the same Assembly it was "established, "condescended and enacted," that, as the inhabitants of Greate Jernemouth had recently decreed that the Bailiffs from the Cinque Ports should reside there full forty days, instead of 3 weeks or a month only, as theretofore, the Bailiff should from thenceforth have an augmentation to his payment, of 40 shillings.

Fol. 117 b., contains an account of the first levy of "Scots." Richard Stuppeny the elder, Jurat, pays the largest sum, 10s. William Woder, Jurat, pays but 8d. —"quia senex et pauper," because old and poor. The smallest Scots, in amount, are 4d.

Fol. 119; on the 30th June, 10 Henry VIII., it was agreed that warning should be given to Richard Lambert, of Romene, to have made at the course called the "Town Dike Watercourse," a gutter, called "a "pynnoke," a foot and a half square, at least. On the —day of July in the same year, John Chilton, Jurat, ask security of his brethren against Henry Houll and Patrick Mores, "laborer," especially "as to the burning "down of his houses." The said Henry was arrested, and called upon to find security.

Fol. 120.—"On Thursday the 10th day in February "Thomas Henry and Leonard Kyrkeby with wordes "of malice assaulted either other, and in so moch "that they went together in handes at Hokkes dore, "where the said Leonard brake the hede of the said "Thomas with a stone, and of him drew blode, ayenst "the peace." They were called upon to find surety to answer to the Hundred, and were bound over, each, in a sum of 40s., to keep the peace; the breaking of the head seems to have had no extra weight as against Leonard Kyrkeby.

5.

Fol. 120 b.; in the 10th Henry VIII. a Recorder appears for the first time, Robert May, the late Town Clerk.

Fol. 122, John Baker owes 3s. "for ferme of the "Havene stremes."

Fol. 123 b., 1st March, 10 Henry VIII. the "Court-"hall" of Romene, is mentioned for the first time.

Fol. 126, a later insertion, 20 August, in the first year of Queen Mary; a meeting of the Jurats is men-tioned as taking place "on Sondaye" in the "Guylede-"halle" of Romney.

Fol. 127 b. Account of expenditure for 10, 11 Henry VIII.; many items being given in addition to those in the folio volume before noticed.—"Gevyne to the banne "criers of Brokelond, in reward and expences 13s. 6d. "Payd to the brynger of the precepte concornynge "the eschape of the rovers of the see 8d. Peydo "to Richard Afforde for halfe porpesse that was sent "unto Mr. Wardene 6s. 8d. Paid to the Duke of "Suffolk berrewarde 15d. Paid to my Lord Wardens "mynstrello 18d. Paid to Henry Robyn for hys "expence goyng to Apuldore Cryke with the pro-"clamacyon 6d."

Fol. 130, 11 Henry VIII.: A "common pond," in the Parish of St. Laurence, in Romene, is mentioned, known as "Trewsole."

Fol. 130 b., 12 Henry VIII. cognizance is taken of an affray between Peter Johnson, "cordoner," and James Twisseler, the former bearing all the costs of the affray.

Fol. 131, in the same year, "Robert Warham, Gentyl-"man," is mentioned as being the Bailiff of Romene; a kinsman, probably, of William Warham, Archbishop of Canterbury, who appointed to that office.

Fol. 133, 13 Henry VIII. John Morrys is named as being Common Clerk.

Fol. 135, in this year among those paying Scot are named, "William Fright, alias Pulter 4d. The tyler 4d. "The sheperde 4d. Servaunts with Mr. Lamberde."

The closing leaves of the volume are occupied with entries of the time of Elizabeth. In fol. 142 b. is an entry of the 24th of February in the 8th year of that reign, with a marginal contemporary note—"4li. yearely "to be payde out of the townes purse towards the "mayntenaunce of a good schoolemaster."—Above it is written, in a like hand "vac.," i.e., "to be omitted ;" immediately below which stands, in a little later hand, "—More pittie." The "good schoolemaster" was to "be appointed for the better edyffyeng, erudicion, and "bryngeing upp, of youthe within the seide towne."

Fol. 144, on the 10th of December 9 Elizabeth, 3 yards of land at Slowe (or Sluice) Gate are lot. The High Street was paved this year, and in the details, the "High Cross" is mentioned.

Fol. 145, in the same year of Elizabeth, an ordinance is made for scouring the Town Ditch; the same to be done by the owners of lands adjoining thereto.

Fol. 145, b. in the same year, an ordinance is made as to such as shall cut the Sea-wall, or the Pynnoke.

Fol. 146, 7th of October in the same year, the Mayor and the Jurats order that there shall be paid yearly 10s. "to the Glayser, for glaseng of [the] churche of "St. Nycholas."

Fol. 148, on the 7th of March, 10 Elizabeth, the Mayor, Jurats, and commoners, agree,—"That all the players, or "the moste part of them, shall enter into sufficient "boundes of 40s. to Mr. Wallishe, at or before the next "daye of rehersalle . . . . with condicion effectually "to prosecute the playe the same; otherwise every "player having . . . shalle presently surrender all "their partes up again into the handes of Arthur Dee; "and so to be no more spoken of, or any more repeti-"tion of rehersall thereof had or made." The above entry seems almost to defy explanation.

Fol. 148 b., on the 9th of June, 10 Elizabeth, William Epps, Mayor, and the Jurats and commons,—"have "agreed, in consideration of the Quenes Majesties ".proclamation concerning the Lotterie, that thei shall "rise out of the townes purse 40s. of good money of "Inglonde, being iiii lottes. And so the posey for "the seid lott to goe and berwytten under the townes "name."—"Also they have agreed that one Snowe, a "pore lame boye, being borne at Romeney, and abiding "at Lydde by the space of 3 or foure yeres, and nowe "ys sente the towne, in consideration to have hyme "seite some occupacion, they have geven out of their "comon purse towardes the same 20s., which ys paid "to the Baylyf of Lydde."

Fol. 149.—"That Mr. Parker shall have authoritie "to devise for the towne, that ys to provide and bey "for Mr. Wyllcok, Counsellour, 4 fatt wethers, and "to be sento London for hyme, towardes the prepara-

4 A

" cion of his redinge dynnere—the charges thereof to
" arise out of the comen purse."

Fol. 149 b., 2nd January 11 Elizabeth, Thomas Sterr,
butcher, is fined 10s.; because he did " highe [raise] his
" price of beffe, contrarye to the order by the seide
" Meyer and Jurstes to hym geven."

Fol. 152, without date, but about 12 Elizabeth:—
" Be yt lykewyse enactyd, that from hensforth ther
" schalbe sold no more stone out of thys towne; for
" whosoever that carryth or sellyth eny out of thys
" towne, schalle forfett totiens quotiens xxs."

Fol. 152 b. James Carrowe is mentioned as being the
Common Clerk in the 12th year of Elizabeth. In a
slip at the end of the book, in a hand of the time,
apparently, of Henry VIII., mention is made of—" The
" commen grownde, the whiche lyeth betwene the
" Wallys to Apuldore ward."

The volume ends at fol. 152; but up to fol. 57 the
leaves are wanting, as already noticed.

                                        HENRY THOMAS RILEY.

THE BOROUGH OF HIGH WYCOMBE, OR CHIPPING WYCOMBE, BUCKS.

The archives of this ancient borough are comparatively few in number, and those few are now in the
hands of the Wycombe Municipal Charity Trustees; to
whose courtesy I am indebted for an opportunity of
examining them. They consist of a single volume, and
a number of deeds, some of them belonging to a very
remote date.—

The volume in question, when in use, was known as
the " Leger-Book" Number 1, a large quarto, in limp
black leather, containing about 230 leaves of parchment,
all filled (with one or two exceptions) with entries of
various dates. The volume, at the beginning, is padded
with seven leaves, and at the end with eleven, of a law
book, in writing of the beginning, probably, of the 14th
contory, with illuminated initial letters in red and blue;
the context, much abbreviated, being apparently a series
of commentaries upon the Pandects of the Emperor
Justinian, with glosses in the margin. Some of these
leaves are perfect; others have been wantonly cut and
slashed with a knife. The writing on the leaves is beautiful, probably by an Italian hand, but very minute: the
subject in general seems to be the inheritance and
division of property.

The volume, most probably in its present (decayed)
binding, was given to the town in the year 1475 by
William Redehode (or Redhood) the then Mayor; as we
learn from an inscription in the first (numbered) folio,
said to be written in Redehode's own hand, of the Latin
of which the following is a translation:—" In the name
" of God, Amen. In the year of our Lord 1475, and in
" the year of the reign of King Edward, after the Con-
" quest the Fourth, the fiftyeenth, I, William Redehode,
" then Mayor of the vill and borough of Wycombe, to
" the honour of God, the Blessed Virgin Mary, and All
" Saints, have given this book [istud librum] to the bur-
" gesses of the said vill and borough, called 'A Register'
" for all the goods, charters, evidences, rents, and
" names of feoffees, of all lands and tenements, with
" their appurtenances, to the Parish Church of Wy-
" combe aforesaid, and to the said Burgesses, pertaining
" or belonging, within the vill aforesaid, etc."

William Redehode was also a citizen, and salter, of
London; and the house in which he dwelt, at High
Wycombe, near the Church, is still pointed out. He
erected in the church a screen, or parclose, with a well-
preserved inscription, which was existing until recently.

On the second of the two parchment fly-leaves at the
beginning is written, in a hand of the 17th century:—
" The first Charter which I read of granted to this
" Borrough, was granted by Kinge Henry the Third,
" father to Kinge Edward the First. James Bigg."—He
was Mayor in 1647.

Fol. 2a contains an award, in English, 18th Henry VII.,
between Gefery Pusey and John Poytefore, and Jone
Pusey and William Pusey, of the one part, and Raffe
Waryne, William Johnson, and Alis, his wife, of the
other part. Various properties in the town are named;
among them, a tenement called " Amyots."

Fol. 3 contains—" An Inventory of the goods of the
" Parish Church of All Saints at Wycombe, made there
" A.D. 1475, in the time of Nicholas Grove, John Porter,
" William Harper, and Thomas Lytylpage the younger,
" Wardens of the church aforesaid: in the first place"
(the preceding is in the Latin, the following in Eng-
lish).—

" A sewte of vestmentes of rede bawdekyne, beryng
" werke damaske branchis of gold, with lyons and
" byrdis of the same. A sewte of staffe berynge werke
" branchis of grene, with levis of golde. A sewte of
" rede velevet, powdyrde with crownes of gold. A
" sewte of blews bawdekyn, berynge werke grene
" branchis with byrdis of golde. A sewte of white
" bawdekyne, powdyrde with byrdis of golde. A sewte
" of white bawdekyne, with damaske-werke. A sewte of
" rede sylke, powderid with white branchis. A sewte
" of blacke for Requiem Mas. A chesapylle of rede
" bawdekyne, powdered with birdis of golde, with an
" awbe [alb] longyng therto. A sewte of grene velewet,
" except the cope, beryng a grene bawdekyne. A
" chesapyll and tenekylle of sylke, beryng branchis of
" blewe purpylle with apys of golde, with apparell
" therto. A sewte of blew sylke, with rayes of golde,
" except the awbys and copis of playne white sylke. A
" white chesapyll, with apparell therto; ii chesapyllis
" of sylke with apparelle therto; ii olde chesapylles of
" sylke; vii pelowis of sylke and of bawdekyne; iii
" pallis of clothe of sylke, powderide with gold; vi
" auter clothis to lye uppone the hye auter. A palle
" for the herses of blacke sylke; a blacke saye clothe
" [perditur, lost.—Note]; another of wollen [perditur,
" lost.—Note]. Item, v longe hoselyng towellis of diaper;
" ii waisshinge towells for the hye auter; a blacke
" frontell for the hye auter, with branchis of grene
" powderid with squierelles of gold. Item, a blewe
" frontell with branchis of grene, powderid with hyndis
" of golde. Item, v corperas cases of diverse clothis of
" sylke, vii corporasais casis of lynnyne. Item, a purse
" of clothe of gold: a purse of clothe of sylke, with the
" reliquis. Item, iii baneris of sylke, with the stavis
" therto, a crosse baner of sylke, with a staffe of copur
" and gylte; a crosse staffe peyntid; iiii banir clothis
" of lynnyne. Item, a canape of purpull sylke, with
" iiii botons gylt; a canape of white clothe; vi py-
" nounse [pennons] of sylke; iii pendauntes of sylke;
" iii lecturne clothis. Item, iiii steynide clothis for
" the hye auter, with iiii curtayns, ii steynid clothis,
" with a frontell counterfeet clothe of gold for the hye
" auter; ii curtayns of purpylle sylke; ii auter clothis
" for Lent, with the curtayns; iii lecturne clothis for
" Lent. A staynid clothe of golde, powderid with
" gold and sylver for the Sepulcur, with a lynnyne
" clothe therto; a Sepulcur of tymber with a stole
" therto. A vayle of white, with a crosse of rede; ii
" canstykkys of latone, to stonde uppone the hye auter;
" ii grete canstykkys of latone, to stonde in the queir.
" A sensare of latone; a shippe of latone; a pyx-box of
" latone, with a box of ivorie. A crismatorie of sylk,
" that weyth xxvii unces. A chalys with a patent of
" sylver and gylt, that weythe xvi unces and i quarter.
" A chalys with a patent of sylver and gylt, that weyth
" xviii unces and i quart. A chalys with a patent of
" sylver and gylt, that weythe xxvii unces and dwt. A
" chalys with a patent of sylver and gylt, that weythe
" xxx unces i quarter. A chalys with a patent of
" sylver, that weythe xii unces and dwt. A sensare
" with cheyns of sylver, that weythe xxxvii unces. A
" sensare with cheynes of sylver, that weythe xxxiiii
" unces' i quarter. Item, ii shippes of sylver, with ii
" sponys of 'sylver, that weyth xx unces, iii quarters,
" and dwt. A crosse of sylver and gylt, that weythe
" lxxiiii unces; a fote of a crosse, with a penacull of
" sylver and gylt, that weythe lxi unces; ii crewettes
" of sylver, that weyne ix unces and quarter; ii besyns
" of sylver, that weyne xxx unces; ii canstykkys of
" sylver, that weyne xlix unces and half unce. Item, a
" pax of sylver and gylt, with v stonys, that weythe
" xv unces; a lytyll box sylver and gylt, that weyth
" 3 unces; a lytyll box of sylver, with dyverse reliquis
" therin; a box of copur and gylt, and enamilde, with
" reliquis therin. A crosse of copur and gylt, another
" crosse of copur and gylt with iiii stonys. A crosse of
" latene; another of tree [wood]: a surplice for the
" quere. Item, ii Mas bokys to the hye auter; ii grete
" Luggeris [Leigers, or Antiphonars] in the queire; iiii
" Portowis [Portifories, or Portehors]; a Responsor,
" with a lytyll Graylle; v Grayles; vi Prossessioneris;
" ii Manuellis; i Dirgeboke; ii Pystyl bokys [Epistle
" books]; a Logent; i Ordinallo; i Martilage [Mar-
" tyrology]; a Cathalicane [Catholicon]; a lantorne;
" an halywater stok of latone; ii lecteruys of tymber;
" ii hoselyng bellys [houseling bells]; iii bellis for the
" bedmanne [bedeman, or summoner]; ii beris [biers]
" with ii coffyns therto. Item, i crowe of irene, weing
" ix li. weight. Item, a sute of clothe of golde tyssu
" of the gyfte of Sir John Stoktone of Londone, with
" alle the sparelle. Item, ii copys of whighte damaske,

" the orferasse [orfrays] of blew damaske, *ex dono*
" *Willelmi Redehode* [the gift of William Redehode].
" Item, ii blac copys of worstede, the orferasse of blew
" worstede, poudered with letters of gold, *ex dono dicti*
" *Willelmi Redehode* [the gift of the said William Rede-
" hode]. Item, a palle of imperiall a—. Item, a Pro-
" cessionary, coveryd with black damaske. Item, ii
" awter clothis of blew worstede, powderyd with flowyrs
" of golde and spangyls of sylver. Item, ii curteynes
" of blew sarsenet, frengyd with sylke. Item, a pyx
" of sylvyr gylt, with a lytyll pece of sylver, weyeng
" xvi unces. Item, ii candystykkes of latene, stondyng
" in Seynt Nicholas chauncelle. Item, a kercheffe of
" plesans, with a bordur of sylke and goldo, *ex dono*
" *Johannis Collarde.* Item, a gowne of purpylle sarsenet
" for Ihesus awter, *ex dono Johannis Oollarde.* Item, a
" cloth of blac worstede for the herse, with a whyte
" crosse imbrowderyd in v placis with the name of
" Jhesus. Item, a canape of launde, with iiii botons
" of nodylle werke, frengyd rounde abowte with rede
" sylke and golde, *ex dono Margeriæ Bontynge* [the gift
" of Margery Bontynge]. Item, a lynnyne cloth, with
" a crosse of blac bokeram, for the roode. Item, a
" towelle to hossyll [administer the Sacrament to] peple,
" conteynyng by estymacion xix yerdes, with blew
" porolles [? tufts] at the ende. Item, a baner cloth of
" blew sylke, chaungeable with a fegure of the Trinite,
" of the yefte of John Collardo. A chales with a patent
" of sylver and gylte, weyeng x unces, of the yefte of
" William Redehode *ad dict_m Capellan Beata Maria*
" [to the said Chapel of St. Mary]." At the end of all
this is written, probably by some zealous spirit in early
Protestant times,—" Vacat," to be left out; in addition
to which, a pen is lightly run through the whole of the
context.

This is followed, in fol. 4b, by a like Inventory, taken
in the year 1503; some of the former items have disappeared, and others are added. Among the latter:—
" A sewte of rede sylke, with sterris and the floure
" de luce. A sewte of blak with flouris of golde
" in the crosse. A cope of greno bawdekyne with
" lyones rampyone of gold. A chéssebylle of grene
" borde alisaundro [a cloth probably resembling sandal-
" wood] with a crosse of saye sylke. Myters of diverse
" sewtes. ii stremers of sylke, one rede, another blewe.
" iii qweyres noted, of the Visttacion of oure Lady,
" iii qweyres of the Transfiguration of Jhesu, and the
" Masse also. Two bokes, on off Seynt Austen's workes,
" another of Seynt Gregories worke. iiii wol stremers
" to goo by the crosse uppone high days."
At fol. 6 is entered.—" Anno 1647 Kinge Charles
" marched through this towne from Casum [Cavers-
" ham] towards Woburne in Bedfordshire;" to which is
added, in another hand,—" Mr. James Big then beinge
" Mayor;" and then to that, by another person, with
somewhat of unction probably—" and aftewards was
" beheaded at Whitehall Gate uppon the 30th day of
" January Anno Domini 1648"—which has elicited
the annexed remark—" To the perpetuall infamy of the
" English nation."
In fol. 7b follows an Inventory of the Church goods
made on the 20th of January 10 Henry VIII. (A.D.
1519), in the presence of Thomas Kare, Mayor. The
last in general resembles the preceding ones: the
" Lyght awltor" is mentioned; the " Bowre aultere;"
the " Resurrection awltre;" " Jesus awltere;" " Saynt
" Clement's awltere." Many " vestments" are mentioned; among them " A vestment of grene dornekke"
[cloth of Tournay], " A stremer of bokerham, image
" of our Lady," " A baner of bokerham of Saynt
" Poule."
This is followed, in fol. ix., by an Inventory (of the
same date) " of the godes, jewellys, and ornamentes
" belongynge to the Chapelle of oure Lady." Among
the items, the following may be noticed:—" A crowne
" for our Lady, silver and gylte, with stonys on the
" border of the same. Another crowne, lesse, wyth
" eyght stonys on the borders of the same. An ouche
" of silver, lyke a bokylle of silver, and gylte. A pair
" corallo bedys with xl stonys, of silvere and gylte, and
" rynge of silver"—a line ran through it, and added
—" Sold to Johan Putt." " A pair of blak bedys, with
" xxi stonys of silver and too ringes of silver"—" The
" rynges wher sold."—" A pair of bedys, rede amber,
" with one peny of silver upone them."—" Ther lakketh
" the peny."—" Another pair bedys of yellow amber,
" with gaudes of jasper stonys. A pair of bedys, ambor
" and glasse, with ii ringes of sylver"—" The rynges
" were solde."—" A pair of blacke gettys [jet] bedys,
" and anothyr of ambur. A chaplet for our Lady, of
" tyssewe. A garment to oure Lady of white, with

" ermyns. A Masseboke, prented. A lytolle Portewas,
" called our Lady Portewas [Portifory] A curten
" clothe, for our Lady lofte. A gyrdylle, one pen-
" dentes with aukament [? tin]: iiii thyrchoys [tur-
" quoises] with a laude [a large bead.]
Fol. x. " Memorandum, delivered into the handis of
" John Standisho the xithe daye of Octobre, in the
" first yere of our Soveraigne Lorde Kynge Edwarde
" the Sixt.—
" Inprimis, ii chalices; which ii chalices were de-
" livered to Simone Watnall, then Mayor. Item, a
" vestment of blewe brannchide damaske, with a redde
" crosse thereupone with all. Item, a vestment of
" redde and blewe dornycke, with a grene crosse
" thereupone. Item, a blacke vestment, with grene
" birdes and flower de luces, and the crosse with
" splaide and gilt of golde. Item, a white vestment
" of dornicke, with a crosse of grene silke, witho
" sterrys [stars] of gold thereupone. Item, a Masse
" booke, with a corporas case, and ii corporasses therein.
" Item, a glasse paxe, ii crewettes. Item, ii alter
" clothis of diaper, and one of playne clothe. Item,
" an alter hanginge of blewe silke, with white flowrys.
" Item, v halfe shetys, with ii kerchevys. Item, a
" yerde and a quarter of tyssu. Item, another pece of
" tissue. Item, a canvas clothe for the aulter."
Fol. x b. " An Inventorie of the Churche goodes that
" be lefte, taken the xxiiii daye of Aprell in the vith
" yere of the reigne of ower Soveraigne Lorde Kinge
" Edwarde the Sixto, in the presents of Mr. George
" Parteferr, then Maior, and his brethren William
" Corwyne, Edwarde Corye, Rowlande Wytnall, and
" Gilys Skidmore, Churchewardens.—"
" Inprimis, a sute of blacke worsted, with R of golde,
" and the lynene that belongith thereto, with one coope
" of the same. Item, an olde sute of white bawdekyne,
" with damaske flowrys, without a coope, havinge ii
" albys. Item, a sute of blewe and grene bawdekyne,
" with hynder of golde, and a coope, with all the
" lynens therto belongynge. Item, a sute of redde
" silke with sterris and the flowredeluce, lackynge all
" the lynen, with ii coopis. Item, a sute of black, with
" flowris of golde on the crosse, with ii lynens therto
" belonginge. Item, a pawle of blewe velvet, with
" flowers of golde. Item, an aulter clothe of blewe
" worstede, with flowris. Item, i olde courteynes of
" sarcenet, of purple colourid. Item, ii courteyns of
" red sarcenet olde. Item, i coope of redde velvet.
" Item, i redde coope of damaske, with flowris. Item,
" iiii albys for chyldren, with ii aulter clothis of
" red damaske. Item, a vestment of red sateene,
" with Saint John Baptist. Item, a vestment of blewe
" damask, with the albe therto belonginge. Item, vii
" towellys of lynen, and ñii litle towels for the aultere.
" Item, vii casis and xi corporas clothis. Item, a vest-
" ment of redde dornecke, wythout lynnen. Item, a
" pilowe of red velvet. Item, a pese of chaungeable
" sarcenet. Item, five aulter clothis of lynnen, one of
" them ys diaper. Item, twoo desk clothis. Item, iii
" olde vestmentes, with ii albys, one of them redde,
" with the crosse of Saint George, and an other grene,
" velvet, and the thirde with flowers redde and grene.
" Item, iiii silke stremers, litle. Item, an olde grene
" aultre clothe. Item, a white coope of damaske,
" wyth images an the orphresyres. Item, v surplesses
" olde, wythe a lynnen courteyne. Item, xi cofers, ii
" candilstickes of lattene, with one chayre. Item, a
" vestment of white fustyane, with the lynnen."
Fol. xi b. The next Inventory is an almost similar
hande; probably following close upon the previous one,
in the reign of Edward VI. " The Inventorye of the
" Churche goodes nowe remainynge to the same.—
" Inprimis, iii chalices with ii patentes. Item, i
" coope of redde velvet, and another of white damaske,
" with flowers of golde. Item, an olde sute of white,
" lackynge a coope, and all the lynnen. Item, ii olde
" deske clothes, and ii grete brasse pottes. Item, i
" crysmatory of latten, i crosse of cooper [copper] part
" gilte. Item, ii sencers of latten, vii candylstickes for
" the aulters. Item, i blewe aulter clothe hanginge of
" satten, abrydged. Item, ii stremers, and ii square
" banners, with iiii poolys therto. Item, ii olde pallys
" [palls] hanginge at the highest aultere. Item, ii
" paintid hanginges for the other ii aulters. Item,
" iii heres [?] for the iii aulters. Item, i vestment of
" reddo velvet, withe the albe to the same. Item, an
" olde white vestment of dornecke, with the albe. Item,
" iii aulter clothes of lynen, olde; with iiii towels and
" ii short towelles. Item, a vayle for Lent season, of
" olde clothe paynted. Item, ii candilstickes to sett
" talowe candelles in. Item, ii crosses of tymber, with

" a crysmatory of tymbere. Item, ii corporas cases,
" with a corporess clothe. Item, a greate Antiphoner
" of parchement, with a Grayll of parchement, and an
" Antiphoner of paper, unbounde, with a Graill of
" paper, unbounde. Item, i Processionall of parche-
" ment, and ii of paper, unbounde. Item, an olde
" manuell, and another manuell of parchement, un-
" bounde. Item, a Masse booke of a small volume, with
" a Ymnalle of paper. Item, an olde Masse booke, with
" ii litle Portuous [Portifories], and iii olde surples.

Fol. xiii. under the head of " Rents belonging to
" the Chamber," a Rouland Lyttelboy is mentioned as
a tenant. The surname " Littlepage " has previously
occurred.

· Numerous entries follow here, in reference to town
charities and bequests for the poor; and various orders
made, in the 17th century, by the Common Council.

Fol. xxi.—" Anno regni Regis Henrici Septimi decimo
" octavo, xiith of November." " Inventory of the
" goods in the Chapel of the Blessed Mary the Virgin
" there, in the time of William Aley and Hamlet
" Taylour, Wardens, delivered before Robert Asche-
" brok, Mayr." The following are among the items
mentioned.—

" ii chalys, one grete dobyll gylde, a nothir parte
" thereof gylde, with a scripture [writing] abowte the
" fote, praying for the sowlys of William Redhode and
" his frendis. A crowne of silver, upon oure Ladyes
" hede, and gylde. A pebe of corall, with ii typpys of
" sylvere. A bedestone of silver, anamelled."

Fol. xxii b, under date 24 March 1657, moneys are
raised for the purpose of renewing the Charter of the
town, by anticipating the rent yearly paid by Jerome
Gray for the old Guildehall: at the head of the page
some royalist has written.—" This is to gaine a Charter
" from Olliver, in the Rumpers time; which Charter
" was burned on the day our most gratious Kinge
" Charles the Second was crowned, whom I pray God
" to send long to reigne." Below are written in the
same hand, the words, apparently, " Rumper's Charter."

Fol. xxiii, a contemporary entry of the 15th of Edward
IV., wherein John Foulmere, of Bekenysfelde, " hus-
" bondmanne," acknowledges a deed before William
Redehode, " then Mayor of the vill of Wycombe."

Fol. xxiv b.—" 1647. Jhon Welson had one [surety],
" and Mr. Pettifer, Alderman, engaged himself that he
" should wait upon the Mayor to church every Sabboath.
" Day, upon payment of 2s. 6d. to be paid of the said
" Mr. Pettifer for every neglect."

Fols. xxvi b. xxvii. William Child, Gentleman, of
Chesham, an attorney in the Court of the Mayor and
Aldermen, (for several specified " misdemeanours," (in
the form of bad expressions, the instances being given),
" slovenly language, malepart caridge, and fanatick
" like deportment," was declared to be no longer an
attorney of that Court.

Fol. xxxi. " 27° die Septembris 1692. Memd^um that
" att a common Councill then mett, it was ordered by
" us whose names are hereunder written, that the
" inscription att the front of the new Almeshouses shal-
" bee cutt out, and an new inscription made in the
" place thereof, in honour of Queene Elizabeth, the Donor
" and Benefactor to this Corporation." Signed by Jo:
Bigg, Mayor, and eight others.

Fol. xxxi b. On the 8th of January 1664 " benge Sab-
" both Day," Samuell Trone, Jeromia Stevens, Nicholas
Noy, John Littleboy, John Cook, George Ball, and Joseph
Steven, " labourrers, and being professed and knowne
" Quakers, having this day assembled themselves to-
" gether, with divers women, at the house of John
" Raunce in this burrough, under pretence of religious
" worshipp, contrary to a late Act of Parliament," were
committed, for 3 months, to the house of correction.
Four of them were, soon after, again committed, for a
repetition of the offence.

Fol. xxxiii. Copy of the will of Edward Cary the
elder ; apparently of the time of Edward IV. ; he mentions a street in the borough of Wycombe, " called
" Fogmore, in the fee of the Abbess of Godstowe."
" Frogmore " was the correct form of the name.

Fol. xxxiii b, (without date given.) " I Thomas Davies
" doe declare that I hold that there lyes noe obligacion
" upon me or any other person from the oath commonly
" called the ' Solemne League and Covenant'; and that
" the same was in itselfe an unlawfull oath, and imposed
" upon the subjects of this realme against the knowne
" lawes and liberties of the kingdoms."

According to the old pagination, after fol. xxxv, seven
folios are missing, having evidently been cut out of the
book.

Fol. xlvib, under A.D. 1665 a tenement at the east
end of the borough, " of old called the ' Hermitage,' and
" of late the ' Snails,'" is mentioned.

Fol. liii.—" An Order for wearing the badges," of
very considerable length. Among other things it is
stated,—" And whereas the poore people of the said
" burrough are growne very numerous, and are likely
" to increase dayly, to the great impoverishment of the
" tradsmen of the said burrough, many of them through
" idleness being able to work, yett will not, because
" they find an easier way of living by collection. And
" unlesse some speedy care be taken to prevent the
" excessive growth of such poore, all or the greatest
" part of the tradsmen of the said burrough in a short
" time are like to come to poverty, and to bee unable
" to maintain themselves and familye by reason of such
" great taxes towards the releiffe of the poor." The
benefit of the " easie rates " when " the poor people wore
" badges," is then adverted to; and it is therefore ordered
by the Mayor and the major part of the " Common
" Councell," that before the Overseers or Churchwardens
give " any releiffe, collection, or money, to any poore
" man or woman of the said burrough, they shall give
" a badge, being the sign of the swan, or the town armes,
" and shall cause him, her, or them, to wear the same
" upon his or her uppermost garment at all times, soo
" as the same may be seen apparently and openly."
In case of refusal, no relief or " collection " is to be
given ; as it is clear that the person refusing can live
without it.

Fols. lxii-lxxiii contain a kind of register of acts of
the Corporation from the time of Edward I.; entered
(from older authorities) in Latin, in a hand of, apparently,
the time of Edward IV. From it we find that Gervais
le Baker was Mayor 3 Edward II., and that in that year
a yearly sum of 14d., was remitted to William Outred,
out of a rent of 2s. 2d. which he paid yearly for the
tenements formerly belonging to Matilda de Burneham.
Also, at the same time, a remission of rent was made to
Edward Haueryngden on a tenement formerly belonging
to the " Assigns of the Chapel of St. Mary," in the street
called " Bynethebrugge."—[Beneath Bridge; this street,
I believe, can no longer be identified]. At the same
date the " lane called ' Croyndoneslane ' " is mentioned;
Crendon Lane of the present day.

On Thursday after Hokke Day, that is, on the Feast
of the Invention of the Holy Cross,—" In a large and full
" court of the vill of Wycombe, it was agreed that the
" butchers of the town should take the skins and hides,
" with the heads," of all cattle and animals killed within
their houses, and shew and expose them at their stalls, bona
fide for public sale; and that if the dealers of the town
should refuse to buy them, they might then be at liberty
to sell them to stranger dealers. The butchers appealed
against this, in favour of stranger dealers being put on
a level, as to purchase, with those of the town ; but this,
it was deemed, would be to the town's prejudice; so it
was refused.

In the 9th year of the same reign, a pightle of land
is granted to Thomas le Warner, tailor, in Frogmore
Street.

In the same year, it was ordered by the Mayor and
Commons, that all weavers working within the town,
shall only give 12d. yearly to the Gildani, for each argoys
[? loom] working. The " Gildani," are frequently named
with the Mayor and Bailiffs about this date; it was their
duty, probably, to regulate the " gilds," or trades, of
which the " Merchants' gild" seems to have been the
chief.

In the 12th of Edward II. Gervais le Baker was again
Mayor. A rivulet is mentioned as running near a
wooden building in Frogmore Street.

Fol. lxiii b. Under the same year, the lane leading to
" Croyndene " is again mentioned. This, no doubt, was
the dene, or valley, where the " croyns," or old ewes,
were harboured in winter. Croydon in Surrey, is named
" Croyndene " in Domesday, and for the same reason,
probably.

Fol. lxv. 20 Edward III. the " Wardens of the work of
" St. Mary's " are mentioned; the Chantry Chapel of
St. Mary probably being, at that time, under repair.
In the 23rd year of the same reign, by his testament,
Matthew, son of Matthew le Fuller, left a tenement in
the High Street, to maintain a lamp to be always burning
before the altar of St. Mary in the church of Wycombe.
At this date, meetings before the Mayor, Bailiffs, and
commons, were known as " Gilds."

Fol. lxviii. (tr.)—" On Tuesday in the 4th week of Lent,
" in the 40th year of the reign of King Edward III., it
" was ordained that every child of a burgess, who at
" the time appears to be the oldest, after the decease of

" his father, on claiming the freedom, shall have the
" same, on paying 10½d., without any further payment;
" namely, to the Mayor 1d., to the clerk ½d., to the under-
" bailiff ½d., to the Gildsmen [Gildanis] 8d., and to the
" Master of St. John's ½d.; he making oath, etc."

Fol. lxviii b. 43rd Edward III., Thomas Gerveys is
named as being Mayor, in June of that year.

Fol. lxix. A locality in Wycombe, called "The Cressoho,"
is named under the year 1368. "Newland Street" is
named under 1378. It deserves remark that (apparently)
a division of land is mentioned as "terra unius fenestri."

Fol. lxx., in the 4th Richard II., a "solar" (or sun-
parlour) at the end of the Gildhall is let to John Deye
for life, at a yearly rent of 3s. 4d.

Fol. lxx b.—"At a view of Frankpledge, holden on
" Thursday before the Feast of our Lord's Ascension,
" comes Richard Donne, Chaplain, and asks of the com-
" monalty that he may have one 'bugittum'; and it is
" granted to him, he paying yearly for the same to the
" vill of Wycombe 2d.; namely, at the house of John
" Knyght in the High Street; in the 4th year of the
" reign of King Richard II." The "bugittum," elsewhere written "buchettum," was probably an oxstall, or
a similar outhouse. About this date, mention of a field
called the "Reye" frequently occurs.

Fol. lxxi. Nicholas Sperlyng is named as being Mayor
on the Eve of our Lord's Nativity 12 Richard II. (A.D.
1388.)

Fol. lxxi b, 13 Richard II., a lane called "Poukelane"
is mentioned, near Newland Street.

Fol. lxxii,.14 Richard II., month of October, John
Petytevyne is named as Mayor.

Fol. lxxii b. 21 Richard II., month of October, Nicholas
Sperlyng is named as Mayor.—" On Thursday in Cœna
" Domini [Our Lord's Supper] in the 21st year of
" the reign of King Richard II., before the Mayor and
" Commons of the town, it was ordained and granted,
" that no person, of whatsoever condition, in the vill
" of Wycombe dwelling, after the 10th hour at night
" should go wandering about the town, except for reason-
" able cause for such wandering. And if any one were
" found wandering about after the said hour, he was to
" be taken by the officers of the town, and imprisoned,
" and kept in prison until delivered by the Mayor, or
" his deputy, and the commons, etc." On same day it
was ordered that no one was to be a "dicer" [aliator]
in the town, on pain of imprisonment.

Fol. lxxiii b, an order is mentioned as being made,
18 Henry VII., "at the Law Day, holden in the Rye," in
other words, held in the open air : William Aley then
being Mayor. On the 13th of March, 1 Edward VI.,
Richard Cary is named as Mayor.

Fol. lxxiv, 10 Henry VIII., a suit is mentioned, relative
to a meadow called "Templesmede," or "Fyscherysmede."

Fol. lxxv b.—"Memorandum, that at the Law Day
" hold at Wycomb in the Yeld Hall, the Thorsday next
" after the Fest of Sent Luke the Avangell' yn the yerre
" of oure Lorde God xiiiic.ᵡ. and x (1490), afforre
" Roger Bramston, then Mayre of the town, yt ys
" orderit be the avys of the sayd Mayrre and hees
" bretherne, and granted be alle the borgess and com-
" monalte, that be dwellyng withyn thay same town,
" that eff there be any borges dwelling withyn the
" same town from this day forthe, were [wear] any
" leffray [livery], sayne [sign], ar [or] conysant [cog-
" nizance], contorare to the Statutes of the lande, shalle
" lees his fredom and xl s. of lawfull monay of Yngland,
" the on hallf to the Mayrre, the tother hallf to the
" Baylyf, for the tym beying; to be levede upon the
" goodes and chatelles be the sam Baylyf of them so
" founde fawte."

Fol. lxxvii b.—"Memorandum, that it is agryed at
" the Lauday in the Rye, the Thursday next after the
" Fest of Sant George, before Roberd Aschobroke,
" Mayre of the towne of Wycombe, with the burgesses,
" with the comunalte of the same Burgh, that the Mille
" callyd the 'Brygemille' schalle have goynge in the
" Rye there one geldyng, to lede with all unto the
" seide mille, payeng yerly unto the Gyldens of the seid
" [Burghe] for the tyme boynge iis.; and as ofte as it
" may happyn' the seide geldyng to be founde lose
" within the saame Rye, be the Gyldan for the tyme
" boynge, to be pounded, and pay at every tyme so
" founde iid.; and for defaute of non payment of the
" seid iis. of yerely rente, it schalbe leffull unto the
" seide Yeldens for the tym beyng to enter and to dis-
" treyn . . . apone any of the godys and catalles of
" the occupation of the seide mylle for the tyme beyng.
" Wyche agreement was graunted the xviith yere of the

" regne of Kynge Harry the VIIth, and the day above-
" seid etc."

Fol. lxxvii. Richard Burch is mentioned as Mayor
" at the Invention of the Holy Cross, 4 Henry VIII.

Fol. lxxvii b :—"That the Thorsday next after the
" Fest of St. Thomas the Martyr, the xxᵗʰ yere of
" Kyng Harry the VII., in the full Gilde Aule, before
" Nicholaus Jerarde, Mayre of the buroogh, and all
" the hole comunyte of the same, that it is orderyd and
" stabely acted, that the Yelde Hall dore shalbe stand-
" ynge opyne freely, whereas ony burgess be committed
" to warde, be the comaundment of the Mayre for the
" tyme beyng; and inspeciall that other burgess may
" have licens to exorte and advise hymme to the
" beste etc." Thomas Frere is named as Mayor in
May 1509. Thomas Pymm, Gentleman, is this year relieved from holding all offices, save that of burgess of
Parliament.

Fol. lxxviii b has "Jhesus Mercy" written at the head
of it, a usage much observed in the documents and
official records of the West of England, at about this date.

Fol. lxxix b., 7 Henry VIII., a place called "Poulys-
" rewe" [Paul's Row] is mentioned, near Coppyndhalle.

Fol. lxxx. a piece of land is mentioned, called "Mil-
" borns," and a meadow called "Trinite Mede," 9th
Henry VIII.

Fol. lxxx b, 10th Henry VIII., Richard Pede and
Thomas Scheresafeld having reviled the Mayor, Thomas
Frere, and cited him before the Court of Arches, it is
agreed at a Court holden of the Mayor, Aldermen, "and
" the more parte of the burgesses," that, if they persist in such course, they shall pay a fine of 40s., and lose
heir freedom, with such other punishment as may be
thought proper.

At fol. lxxxi, same date, a list of the chief burgesses
is given; among them are, John Kelehogge, John
Lytylboy, and Jans Cutt. Orders are made for the due,
or better, keeping of their common pasture called the
" Rye," and for defending their title to the same
against Rowland Messinger, Clerk, the Vicar.

Fol. lxxxi b, 19 Henry VIII., regulations are made as
to the Fair held on the Day of St. Thomas the Martyr, in
the street called "Eatyntowne;" George Peytefere being
Mayor. It is also then enacted,—"That no maner of
" manne nor womanne that shall brew to sale and typ-
" pyll, (shall keep) it with hym or hyre, but send it
" forthe into the towne to the typpollars, for to be sold
" according to the assayer's prysse."

Fol. lxxxii b; in May 32 Henry VIII., William Gravet
is named as Mayor.

Fol. lxxxiv, 20 April, 2 Philip and Mary, Thomas
Pymme is Mayor: Robert Gravet being Mayor in the
5th year of the same reign.

Fol. lxxxv b, 22nd April, 2 Elizabeth, John Sterling is
mentioned as Mayor: on that day, all deeds and conveyances theretofore made by the Corporation, were duly
ratified and confirmed.

Fol. lxxxi b; 26th April, 5 Elizabeth, Rowland Wit-
nall, alias Elys, is named as Mayor; all persons bringing burdens of wood, out of the hedges or elsewhere,
" or any pershes, or other yong trees," into the town in
the daytime, are to be punished with the stocks.

Fol. lxxxvii; 24th April, 6 Elizabeth, William
Twhaytes, Mayor.

Fol. lxxxviii.—"Memorandum, that the xxvth daie of
" November, anno Domini 1576, anno xviiiᵐᵒ. Elizabethæ
" Reginæ, William Fletewoodde, Esquier, Recorder of
" the citie of Londone, did gyve unto the Maire, Bai-
" lyffes, and burgesses, of this burowe one staffe of stele
" ring yrne [iron] parcel gilt and damerskyne, to be
" a staffe of justice for the towne, in perpetuum rei
" memoriam."

Fol. xc.; 30th March 1593 an order was made—"That
" noe manner of hogges and awyne shall goe out of the
" owner's house without his driver or keper, within the
" precincte of this burrough, except the same hogge or
" pigge be were well ringed or pegged, that the sam
" maye not digg or root."

Fol. xci.; an order is made by the Mayor and the
greater part of the "capitall burgesses, and Bayliffes,"
dated this 20th of March, 42 Elizabeth, repealing an
order made in the preceding year: followed by the
respective signatures of the Mayor and other persons
then present; being the earliest instance in the volume
of such signatures being annexed.

Fol. xciv; 21st September 1606, an order was made
that the Bailiffs should from thenceforth keep two
Feasts yearly in the Guildhall for the Mayor and burgesses, on the days on which the "Leetes" are held;
under a penalty of 20s., to be paid by each Bailiff, on
neglect thereof.

Fol. xciv b. The tailors inhabiting within the borough, complaining that they were much oppressed with the number of foreign tailors coming within the liberty, and much impoverished and hindered thereby, an order was made on the 16th of October, 7 James I., that in future such foreign tailors should keep no shop in the town; and in case of contravention of the order, their shop-windows should be shut up by the serjeant of the town; if further resistance were made, they were to be committed to prison.

Fol. ciii b:—"Memorandum, that the 2ᵈ June 1660, "the foure leaves of this booke were now cutt out and "defaced, wherein were entered the corrupt and unjust "orders of Collonel Tobias Bridges against divers mem- "bers of this Common Counsell and burgesses of this "burrough, by order of the Common Counsell of this "burrough. William Davenport."—Accordingly, the four following leaves are missing. In the same folio, by an order of 16th February 1656, we find George Tymberlake elected Bailiff in the room of Thomas Sedgwick, "who was excluded by order." In the preceding year (1655) George Moore is removed from his Aldermanship, for absenting himself from the town; Nicholas Bradshaw being Mayor.

Fol. cxi b, contains a copy of a most remarkable address, presented to King Charles II.:—

"To the King's most excellent Majestie. The most "humble addresse of your Majesties most loyall sub- "jects, the Mayor, Aldermen, Bailiffs, Burgesses, "and other inhabitants of your Majesties Antient Cor- "poracion of Cheppyng Wycombe, in the county of "Buckingham.

"May it please your sacred Majestie. Most of our "late defeated Politicians, disappointed of theire dark "dissignemontes by your Majesties profound wisdome "and divine provision, have endeavoured to disarrange "all loyall adresses either as uselesse and insignificant, "or as discountenanced and unregarded, and that the "glutt of them doth cloy and surfeit rather than satisfie "your Majestie.

"Notwithstanding these slye ejected discouragements, "wee have alwayes detested and rejected them, togeather "with theire now exploded scanty and forsaken abet- "tors; and have ever incerted our loyall selves amongst "the resolute, grave, and deliberate persons; and wee "doe most highly applaud the stout Fidelios, the stre- "nuous, brisk, and valiant youth of this your now much "undeluded nation.

"Wee therefore, your Majesties most dutyfull and "most devoted subjects, entyrely professe that wee "will, to the utmost stresse of our sinewes, to the "latest gaspe of our lives, and the last solitary mite in "our coffers, adhere to your Majestee. And wee be- "seech your Majesties most gratious acceptance of our "most humble and unfeigned thankfullnesse for all "your Majesties most princely purposes, comprized in "your Majesties most gracious declaration; your royall "resolves for frequent Parliaments; your most pious "intentions to perpetuate the Protestant religion "amonge us; your equall government in Church and "State by the laws establisht; and the legall (though "wee hope in God the many years remote and distant) "discent of your royal diadem.

"Many have outstript us in the wing, but none shall "exceed us in theire wishes: wee envye much theire "more early applye, but none shall ever appeare more "faithfull, though many in this have been more "fortunate.

"God preserve your Majestie from all rebellious ma- "chinations. Amen.

"This adresse was delivered to his Majestie, by "Doctor Lluelyn, att Windsore, upon Bartholomew Day "Anno 1681. Mr. Henry Bigg being then Mayor. "Teste Jo: Bigg. T. Clerke."

The "defeated politicians," alluded to in this marvellous composition, were probably Shaftesbury, Algernon Sidney, and Somers.

Fol. cxii b. contains an account of the election, 11 November 1671, of Mr. William Larner, of Bradenham, Clerk, as School-master of the Free School, in place of Mr. Philip Humfrey, deceased. The latter having died very poor, his successor is bound, on his election by the Common Council, to pay to his widow, Katherine, ten pounds in the course of the next two years, "provided he "doe not turne Quaker in the mean time, or otherwise "become a Sectary, and not observe and obey the "Liturgy of the Church of England."

Many of the succeeding folios are devoted wholly to the admissions (complimentary and otherwise) of burgesses, or freemen, during the earlier half of the 18th

century, the Duke of Bridgwater and the Earl of Shelburne in the number.

At fol. cxl entries of the time of Edward IV. are resumed, as follows:—

"Wycombe.—At the Gildhall there holden, on the "14th day of December in the 14th year of the reign of "King Edward, after the Conquest the Fourth, before "Thomas Gate, then Mayor, there being, with the "consent and will of all the burgesses and tenants of "the Chapel of the Blessed Mary the Virgin, it was "there ordained "—(the preceding translated from the Latin)—"that the preyst hired that syngeth or seyth "Mas at oure Lady auter, and all other preistis that "shalle be hired in tyme to come in the Chapell forseid "for ever to sey Mas, and bytwene the offatorie, or "[before] that he wasshe at the lavatorie, he shall turne "hym at the auteris ende, and pray for the good state, "welfare, and prosperite of all the tenauntes, menne "and womenne, bretheryne and sisteris unto the seide "Chapell of Oure Lady and for the good state, welfare, "and prosperite, of all the tenauntes, menne and "womenne, bretheryne and susteris unto the saide "Chapell of Oure Lady, and for the good staat, welfare, "and prosperite, of Wyllym Redehode and Jone his "wyfe, and of Margerie Fyssher, terme of theire lyves, "and for all theire kynred, being alyve. Wich done, "Misereatur etc. Pater noster cum Suffragiis, and a Colet "[Collect] Deus caritatis etc. And after the decees of "the said William Redehode and Jone his wyfe, and of "Margerie Fyssher, to be prayed for with them that "be departed out of this world, it is to be understonde "that when the preist hath prayed for the quicke, than "he stondyng stylle at the auteris ende shall pray for "the sowlis of alle the tenauntes, menne and womenne, "and of alle the sowlis of alle the brethern and susteris "and benefactors of the same Chapell; and in especyell "for the sowlis of Richard Redehode Agnes, and Agnes, "his wyfes, and for the sowlis of alle theire kynrede, "for the sowlis of William Lancastelle, Emma his wyfe, "and for the sowlis of all ther kynred; for the sowlis "of John Covyntre and Jone his wyfe, and of alle the "kynred; for the sowlis of Henry Colleshill and Agnes "his wyfe, and for alle there kynred; for the soule of "Thomas Fyssher and for alle his kynrede; and for alle "Cristene sowlis he shalle say De profundis, with the "Versiclis and Colet Inclina or Fidelium, as in a tabylle "stondyth uppone the same auter opynly it apperyth. "For the whiche dayly prayeris kept, the forsaid Henry "Colleshille Yeve to the towne of Wycombe the re- "version of his house, with the gardyne lying therto, "bytwene the house of the Charnelle, that the preistis "of the Charnelle dwelle in, on the est part, and the "house of Thomas Gate, somtyme Jone Briggewateris, "on the west part, the Kynges hyewey on the south "part; the whiche house the forsaid William Redo- "hode hath repairde and made. Whiche costis and "chargis drawith to the somme of xiiii li. Also, the "forsaid William Redehode willeth and graunteth that "after his decea be delivered to the keperis of Oure "Lady auter, and collectoris of Oure Lady rent, a "chalys, part gylt, with the scripture on the fote— "Orate pro animabus Ricardi Redehode Agnetis uxoris "ejus, Willelmi Redehode et Johanna uxoris ejus, weying "x unces and more of troye weyght; one preist to "synge ther with on the werkedayes. The forsaide "Meyre, burgeys, and tenauntes, wollen and grauntyne "that yf the preist that now is, that seyth Mas at oure "Lady auter, and alle other preistis that shalle be hirede "in tyme to come to syng at the forsaide auter, shal "pray dayly for the forsaid lyvis and sowlis by name. "And yf it so fortune and happe the forsaid lyvis and "soulys to be unprayed for by iii dayes in a month, the "forsaid preist to lese [lose] iiiid. of his wagys to the "reparacion of the same channselle, as ofte tymes as he "and any other, in tyme to come, so dothe foryete the "forsaide lyves and soulis, unprayed for. And yf it so "be that the collectors of Oure Lady rent, the whiche "shalle pay for the wagys of the forsaid preist, rebate "not so moche of his wagys as ofte tymes as defawte is "founde, and acounte theruppone in the rekenyngis "not do, than the chirchemen, to the behovith "[behoof] of the chirche, to receyve the forsaide iiiid. "of the preistis wages, to be payed by the hondis of "the collectors of Oure Lady rents, and they to acounte "uppone the same. Also the tabylle, on the auter, with "names, to be repayrid at alle tymes when it nedith, on "the cost of Oure Lady rent."

Fol. cxl b.—"Also, the day and yeer within written, "before the said Mayor and burgesses, it was granted "to William Redehode and his assigns "—(the above tr. from the Latin)—"to have a part of the watur that cometh

" out of Frogmore, thorow William Estis house, late
" William Petypas, unto the gardyn of the saide William
" Redehode, the whiche gardyn longyth to the place
" that the forsaid William dwellith in, ayenst the west
" side of the chirche of Wycombe, so that the forsaide
" William, or his assignes, make and kepe a brigge in
" Frogmore, over the same watur, ayenst a house
" that longyth to the Chapell of the Holi Trinite in
" Wycombe. This brigge sufficiently made and kept
" the forsaide William and his assignes to have his
" esement and servyse of the forsaid water, without
" lettyng of any persone or personys, by the graunte of
" the forsaid Meyr and burgeys."
Fol. cxli; the following is tr. from the Latin.—" Also,
" at a view of frankpledge holden in the Bye, before
" Richard Cary, Mayor, with the consent of all the bur-
" gesses there, on the 8th of May, in the 17th year of
" the reign of King Edward, after the Conquest the
" Fourth, it was ordained and granted unto William
" Redehode and his assigns, that those two Chaplains,
" called ' Oure Lady Preist,' and the ' Boure Preist,'
" who now are, or for the time being shall be, shall
" have and hold those 2 chambers, with the gardens
" adjoining and their appurtenances, late of Henry
" Colleshille, near to the tenement called ' The Char-
" ' nelle House,' on the north side of the churchyard ;
" to have and to hold the said two chambers, with the
" gardens adjoining, and their appurtenances, to the
" aforesaid Chaplains, so long as they hold and fulfil
" their offices; rendering yearly therefor to the said
" William Redehode and his assigns 13s. 4d. of lawful
" money of England, at the two usual terms of the year,
" namely, the Feasts of St. Michael the Archangel and
" of the Annunciation of the Blessed Virgin Mary ; to
" be paid yearly by the hands of the Collector of the
" rents of the Chapel of the Blessed Virgin Mary, and
" of the renter of the rectory there, etc."
Fol. cxli b.—The Thursday after Midlent Sunday, 20
Henry VII., Nicholas Jerard is mentioned as Mayor.—
" In the Gilde Haule holdene the day above wretyne
" etc., that it is stabylly actide from this forthe that no
" burgesse nor forener make no labour nor desir no man
" to speke before the day of election of the Meyre, for
" no singular desir, but every manne to schewe ther
" voyces at ther owne mynde, without trobyll or un-
" resonabille doynge ther in the tyme of ther election,
" under the payne of every burgess that so offendyth,
" with dewe prove, to lose xx s., and that to be levied of
" his godes to the behove of the Chaumbre the one
" halfe, and the other halfe to the reparacion of the
" Chirche. And every forener so offendyng, to lose
" x s., and to be levied in lyke wyse etc."
Fol cxliv b, A.D. 1612, an inn called " The George " is
mentioned.
Fol. 146 b. Under date 27 May 1615, a list is given
" of the names of the adventurers for Virginia," i.e.,
of persons who ventured sums of money in the Lottery
made on the new settlement there; the largest venture
being that of Robert Kempe, Gent., who subscribes 40s. ;
the smallest sums subscribed being 5s. The Common
Clerk probably made the entry, and does not appear to
have very favourably regarded the speculation, as he
ends the list with " Possibilia spes comitatur."—after
which is entered.—" Memorandum that it is agreed
" amongst the said adventurers that Roberte Gray,
" seargeant, and Edward Randall, Parishe Clarke, shall
" have, eyther of them, the benefitt of a lott of 5s., for
" there paines in collecting of the abovesaid somys of
" money, as well and fully as though they had adven-
" tured there lottes." Many children's names having
been entered, each for a lot, the following is added.—
" It is agreed the parents of the said children shall have
" and take the sommes due to the children, and dis-
" charge the towne."
Fol. 156 b.—" Memorandum, that this 6th day of March
" 1664, Nicholas Wilson gave security to dwell in the
" Burrough, and to follow his only vocation of distilling
" strong waters, and did then assume and undertake not
" to follow any other calling by keeping of a retaile shop,
" or the like ; and then at his admittance did pay a
" fine of 50s. to the towne. Jno. Boulter Clerk."
Fol. 177 b. 22nd September 1681.—" I, John Michell,
" doe hereby declare that I hold that there lyes noe
" obligacion upon mee or any other person, from the
" oath commonly called the ' Solleme League and
" ' Covenant.' And that the same was in itselfe an
" unlawfull oath, and imposed upon the subjectes of this
" kingdome, against the knowne lawes and libertyes of
" this kingdome. John Mitchell."
" Memorundum, that the day and yeare abovesaid the
" above-named Mr. John Mitchell was duely elected

" and sworne Mayor of this Burrough, and did then
" take all the oathes required to bee taken by such a
" magistrate, by the Statute for regulating of Corpora-
" cions made in the 13th yeare of his Majesties reigne.
" Testis, Johannes Bigg,. Comunis Clericus."—The
above declaration, made on taking office, repeatedly
occurs in the latter part of the volume.
Fol. 208 b :—" Memorandum, that in the year 1686 the
" ewe tree now growing in the church yard, was planted
" by John Sharp, keeper of the Bowling Green, who
" hath desired, when hee dyes, to be buryed under it.
" Test. John Bigg, sen'."
The remaining portion of the volume is occupied with
admissions to the freedom ; elections of Mayors, Aldermen, and Bailiffs, in the latter half of the 17th century ;
the oaths to be administered to the several officials ;
and an Index to the contents of the volume. Enough
has been extracted to shew their singularly miscellaneous character; and the utter want of all system and
chronological order in the sequence of these entries.
The latest entries are between 1730 and 1740 ; after
which date they are continued in Ledger No. 2.
There are also a number of early deeds, formerly
belonging to the Corporation, now in the hands of the
Municipal Charity Trustees: the following is some
account of the most ancient among them :—
A small parchment deed, in Latin, the seal lost,
belonging to the reign of Henry III.; whereby the
burgesses of Wicumbe agree, for the love and services
of Adam Fitz-Walder, that they will be his attorneys
to see and prosecute that the grant and promise made
to him by the Abbess and Convent of Godstowe shall be
fulfilled ; namely, to see that a priest shall celebrate in
the church at Wicumbe for the souls of Walder, his
father, and of Alina, his mother, and for his own soul,
and the soul of Agnes, his wife. Also, that the brethren
and sisters of the Hospital of Saint John the Baptist
shall yearly cause to be distributed to the poor, for the
souls aforesaid, bread of 2 quarters of wheat, on the day
of St. Mary in March, between Prime and Tierce.
Witnesses, Hubert, Vicar of Wicumb, Humfrey de Dun,
John de Croendene, Richard de Rouen, Simon Hochede,
Geofrey de Hugendene, and others.
A small parchment deed, in Latin, beautifully written,
the seal lost, temp. Edward I.; whereby Hervey the
Clerk, son of William, son of Horvey, grants to William
Tailor [Scissor] a shop in Wicumb, adjoining the cellar
of Walter de Poderugge, and the shop of Robert the
smith, to hold the same freely, quietly, wholly, well, and
in peace; but not to convey to houses of religion : at a
yearly rent of 9s., at 2 terms in the year. Witnesses,
William Fitz-Walder, Walter de Poderuge, Thomas
Wauder, Simon Tanner, William Menge, William Tabbe,
Richard de Horningel, Richard de Sobintune, John de
Dusteburg, Hugh Smith [Faber], Robert Bordwat, and
others.
A diminutive Latin deed poll, on parchment, seal lost,
apparently of the close of the reign of Henry III. ;
whereby Cecily, widow of William Reyner, grants to
William le Weyte [the Watchman] and Alice, his
wife, a piece of land which she had in name of dower,
and which the said William held of Emma Ruffe ; she
having received 9s. 6d. beforehand. Witnesses, John
de Essewelle, William de Lude, John de Croinde[n],
Nicholas Hochede, John de Pushulle, Thomas de la
Lude, David the Miller, and others.
A parchment deed, in Latin, seal lost, probably of the
early part of the reign of Edward I.; whereby Gervase
de Wycumbe grants to Geoffrey le Mercer, of Hugendene,
and Margery, his wife, a messuage in Wicumbe, between
the messuages late of Roger Pur and Gilbert le Chaloner,
at a yearly rent of 3s.; he having received 40s. of silver
beforehand. Witnesses, William Fitz-Walder, Walter
de Puderuge, Thomas Wauders, Robert de Eschburg,
John de Dusteburge, William Tabbe, Henry Fitz-William,
William Dreuge, Richard de Horningel, Robert de
Horningel, Adam Bil, Hugh Smith, Robert the Baker,
and others.
A small parchment deed, in Latin, seal lost, belonging
probably to the close of the reign of Henry III. ; whereby
Robert le Portere, of Wycumbe, grants to Geoffrey le
Mercer half of a shop, between the shop of Walter Bil
and the tenement which Hugh the Cutler held of Richard
the Saddler ; he paying a yearly rent of 4d. to the
villate of Wicumbe for the same; 20s. of silver having
been paid to him beforehand. Witnesses, William
Wauder, Hervey Fitz-William, Gervase the Draper,
Walter Bil, John de Dusteburg, Walter de Puderuge,
Benedict Bil, John de Horningel, William de Puderuge,
Hugh the Cutler, Gilbert de Haveringedone, and many
others.

A small parchment deed, in Latin, seal lost, of about the same date; whereby Adam le Kareter, [Carter], of Wycomb, grants to Stephen Bolebec a part of his capital messuage in the vill, which lies nearest to the tenement which belonged to Walter de Puderuge; as also, all the wall on the north side thereof; at a yearly rent of 2s. he having received 2 marks of silver beforehand. Witnesses, William Wauder, Thomas Wauder, Hervey Fitz-William, William de Lude, Walter de Puderuge, William his son, Roger le Cuver [Cooper], Thomas de St. Alban's, Peter Kippelune, William Cole, William le Taillur, and others.

A parchment deed, in Latin, the seal lost, finely written, of about the same date; whereby William Wauder grants to Hugh le Taillur a messuage in the vill of Wycumbe, on the fee of the Abbess of Godstowe; between the messuage which Simon de Santredune held, and the messuage which William le Taillur held; at a yearly rent to the Abbess and Convent of Godstowe of 2s. 4d., and to himself of 2d. yearly: the said Hugh also giving a yearly rent of 3s. 2d. to support a Mass, for ever, of the Blessed Virgin Mary in the mother church of that vill; arising from the messuage which Geoffrey de Agmodesham held, lying between the messuage which Hugh Pimme held and that which Turric the Carpenter held; the said Hugh rendering yearly 2d. to William and his heirs. Witnesses, Thomas Wauder, William de Lude, Hervey Fitz-William, Simon de Santredune, John de Ireland, William de Puderuge, William le Taillour, John de Radeneche. Ralph Warner, Richard Warner, Gervase le Ferrun [Ironmonger].

A small parchment deed, in Latin, belonging to the reign of Edward I., the seal lost; whereby Ralph de Croindene, son and heir of John de Croindene, of Wycumbe, grants to God and the Chapel of the Blessed Mary of Wycumbe, for the support of a Chaplain, there serving God and the Blessed Mary for the health of the souls of him and his ancestors, a piece of ground near the churchyard of the church of All Saints, between the tenements of Thomas le Wauder and William le Cotiler. Witnesses, Roger Hutred, Thomas Wauder, William the Goldsmith, Matthew the Fuller, Gilbert de Haveringdoune, John le Casiere, Thomas de Wycumbe, Clerk, and others.

A parchment deed, in Latin, somewhat mutilated, the seal lost, of about the same date; whereby Thomas de la Lude grants to Thomas le Taylur, of Little Marlow, for 20s. of silver paid beforehand, a shop in the borough of Wycumbe, between the shop of Richard Mowerton and that of Ralph Gerveys; at a yearly rent of 8s. of silver; he warranting the same to the said Thomas against all men and women. Witnesses, Thomas Wauder, Roger Utred, William the Goldsmith, William the Draper, Roger the Cordwainer, Richard Mowerten, Ralph Gerveys, John de Bretwelle, Thomas de Wycumbe, Clerk, and many others. This and the preceding deed are, no doubt, in the writing of the said Thomas, the Clerk.

A small parchment deed, in Latin, the seal lost, probably of the earlier part of the reign of Edward I.; whereby Ralph Gerveis, of Wycumbe, grants to Thomas the Tailor [Cissor], of Wycumbe, and Cecily his wife, "for 2 marks of silver of good and lawful money," paid beforehand, a piece of ground [placeam] near to that of William the Goldsmith, and near the tenement of Alice de Ireland; they paying one rose yearly, at the Nativity of St. John the Baptist. Witnesses, Roger Hutred, Mayor of Wycumbe, Walter le Lorimer, Walter Pilfedis, William the Goldsmith, Richard de Mandwelle, John de Bristwelle, Roger de Menholte, and many others.

A parchment deed, in Latin, finely written, the seal lost, of the earlier part of the reign of Edward I.; whereby William, called "le Taylur," son and heir of William le Taylur, of Wycumbe, grants to Thomas le Taylur, of Little Marlow, for one mark of silver, paid beforehand, a shop, situate between that of Richard Mowerton and that of Ralph Gerveys; he rendering 9s. yearly to the chief lords; "that is 4s. 4d. [? 6d.] at the Feast of St. Michael, and 4s. 4d. [? 6d.] at the Feast of St. Mary in March." Witnesses, Thomas Wauder, Nicholas de Kent, William the Goldsmith, Richard de Sandwelle, William the Draper, Roger the Cordwainer, John de Byrchwelle, Richard Mowerton, Ralph Gerveys, Thomas the Clerk, and many others.

A parchment deed, in Latin, seal lost, of the time of Edward I.; whereby Thomas son of John West, of Sandhurst, grants to Ralph, son of John le Bogelere, of Sandhurst, a piece of ground called the "Hethplot," lying between the "garston" of Ralph de Hulle and the lane which leads from the heath towards the house of Henry do Wyfald: he rendering yearly 3 halfpence for the same; 15d. sterling having been paid beforehand. Wit-

nesses, Adam de Benethfeld, Robert Norman, John le Bogelere, Ailward West, Hervey de Ford, John the Miller, Roger Chepman, and others. This deed bears reference, probably, to Sandhurst near Wokingham, in Berkshire.

A large sheet of parchment, in Latin, much mutilated, the seal once appended now lost; being the probate copy of the testament of Thomas Waldere. It begins:—"In "the name of the Father, and the Son, and the Holy "Ghost, Amen. I, Thomas Waldere, of Wycumbe, in "this my last sickness, on the Sunday next after the "Feast of St. Nicholas, A.D. 1291, before Sir John, "perpetual Vicar of Wycumbe, Stephen Agod, John "Bil, John the Clerk, son of Matthew, and others, "seeing and hearing the same, do make my testament "in this manner. First, I give and leave my soul to "Almighty God, and my body to be buried in the "churchyard of the parish church of All Saints of "Wycumbe." He gives to the high altar of that church, for arrears of tythes, 5s. To Sir John the Vicar 2s. To the parish Chaplin 6d. To the second (Chaplain) 6d. To Stephen, Chaplain of St. Mary's 12d. To the 6 Clerks serving in the church aforesaid 12d. To buy torches to be lighted around my body 10s. To buy linen cloth to sew my body in 8d. To buy cloth for the poor on the day of my burial, and for one month after 40s. For the meeting of my neighbours on the day of my burial 13s. 4d. To the Friars Minors of Rading 2s. To the Friars Preachers of Oxford 2s. To the Friars Minors of Oxford 2s. To the Friars of the Order of St. Austin, at Oxford 12d. To the Friars of Mount Carmel at Oxford 12d. To the Nuns of Merlawe, for pittances 2s. To the Hospital of St. John at Wycumbe —— of yearly rent from the tenements which Osbert de Santersdene formerly held 2s.; from the tenement of William Beryar 8d.; and from the tenement of Hugh Eadmund in the Lane 4d. To the Nuns of Merlawe all his right in the tenement and curtilage, formerly of Thomas le Blakiere. To the Abbess and Convent of . . . . for the support of a Chaplain celebrating in the church of Wycumbe, for the souls of his ancestors, and for his soul 4s., that is, from the tenement of Roger . . . 12d., and from the tenement which Roger Cristemasse held 3s. . . . . . . To Agnes, his wife, 3s. of yearly rent for the term of her life, that is, from the tenement of John Gregory 20d., and from the tenement which Robert le Barbur held, between the tenement of William . . . . . and that of Walter de Dusteburwe 16d.; and after the decease of Agnes, to John Gregory and his heirs. Also, to the same Agnes, all his rents within the borough of Wycumbe not otherwise left, for term of her life. Also, to Thomas, son of Geoffrey Clerk, after the decease of Agnes, 3d. of yearly rent, namely, from the shop which Robert le Poltere formerly held 2d., and from the shop of Payen le Casiere 1d. To John son of John de La Rye 3s. of yearly rent, to be received from a croft called the "Pondlond," which John de Bristewelle held of him, in the suburb of Wycumbe. To Thomas, son of Nicholas Walder, 6d. of yearly rent, to be received from the tenement of the said Nicholas, his father. To the heirs of Henry Agod he gives and remits all the rent which he was wont to receive, by the hands of the said Henry, from the tenement formerly belonging to him and Agatha, his wife, for the health of his soul. To Agnes, daughter of Ralph Walder, 6d. of yearly rent from a curtilage formerly of Richard le Mounere. To Thomas Warner 1d. of yearly rent from the curtilage of Roger de Schenholte in Bergerie. He makes his executors Agnes, his wife, John Gregori, and Michael . . . . Endorsed as having been proved in the church of Wycumbe, before the Archdeacon of Buckingham, on Friday after the Feast of St. Lucy the Virgin, A.D. 1290 [? 1291]. This Thomas Waldere was probably the wealthiest man of his time in Wycombe.

A parchment deed, in Latin, the seal lost; being a bond indented, whereby Ralph Rethel, of Wycumbe, acknowledges that he is indebted in one mark yearly to be paid to Matildis, widow of Nicholas le Vineter, of Wycumbe, to be levied from his tenement in Wycumbe, which had belonged to her husband; with power of distress therein. Witnesses, Roger Outred, Richard le Hurlere, Hugh le Casiere, then Bailiffs of the Borough of Wycumbe, William the Goldsmith, Richard de . . . , John de Bristowe, William lo Heyward, Gervaise le Bakers, Geoffrey the Clerk, and others. Given at the Feast of the Exaltation of the Holy Cross, in the year of the reign of King Edward, son of King Henry, 23.

A large parchment deed, in Latin, finely written, the seal lost; whereby William le Drapere of Wycumbe grants to Ralph de Hayles, for 30s. paid beforehand, a tenement there, situate between the tenement which belonged to John le Cluter and that late of Ralph le Viniter, and adjoining, on the north, to the land of the Abbess of Godestowe; he paying 5d. yearly to the chief lords of the fee, and 4d. yearly to the grantor, and the heirs of Alice, his wife. Witnesses, Roger Oughtred, Gervase the Baker, Richard le Hurlere, William le Caysere, Robert Power, Geoffrey de Sandwelle, John de Brightwelle, and others. Given at Wycombe, on the feast of the Annunciation of our Lady, in the year of the reign of King Edward, son of King Henry, 24.

A parchment deed, in Latin, somewhat mutilated, the seal lost; whereby Gervasie, called "le Bakere," of Wycombe, grants to Ralph de la Calenge, for 7 marks sterling paid beforehand, a curtilage at "la Grene" [the Green] in the vill of Wycombe, between the tenements which Gilbert de la Grene and Adam Freysel held; also, a meadow which is called "Lutlemed," which he had had of the gift and feoffment of Richard de la Grene, in Wycombe, lying between the meadow of the Templars and the great meadow formerly belonging to John de la Grene; also, a yearly rent of 12d., from the tenement late held by Adam Freysel at the Grene. Witnesses, John de la Linde [?], John de Esshewelle, Geoffrey de Hugendone, William Neyrunt, Richard le Horlere, John Gregorii, Richard de la Hul, Richard Turri, and others. Given at Wycombe, on Saturday next after the Feast of St. Matthias the Apostle, in the year of the reign of King Edward, son of King Henry, 29.

A parchment deed, in Latin, the seal lost; whereby Adam de Schenholte, brother and heir of Henry de Schenholte, grants to Gervaise, called "le Bakere," of Wycombe, his right in a tenement which his said brother recovered in the King's Court against Richard le Cotiler; situate in the street called "Bynuthebrugge," between the tenement which Walter le Harnere held, of the fee of the Hospital, and the tenement which Benedict le Hennemeis held; at a yearly rent of 12 silver pence. Witnesses, Roger Ouctred, Edmund de Haveringdon, Richard le Archer, then Bailiffs of the borough, Richard le Horlere, John de la Grene, Thomas le Tayllour, Roger the White-tawyer, Robert the Smith, Thomas Andrew, and others. Given at Wycombe, on the 2nd day of May, in the year of the reign of King Edward, son of King Henry, 30.

A parchment deed, in Latin, the seal lost; whereby Richard, called "le Moyner," of Wycombe, grants to James called "le Tayllour," of Wycombe, and to Cecily, his wife, for 4 marks of silver paid beforehand, a shop in Wycombe which he had of the gift and grant of Ralph Gerveys. Witnesses, Roger Ouctred, then Mayor of the borough, Edward de Haveringdone, Richard le Bowyere, then Bailiffs, Gervaise le Bakere, Ralph le Hurlere, John de la Grene, William le Heyward, John Andreu, Richard Onyet, and others. Given at Wycombe, on the 9th day of December, in the year of the reign of King Edward, son of King Henry, 31.

A small parchment deed, in Latin, the seal lost; whereby Agatha, widow of Ralph Gerveys, called "Tropinel," of Wycombe, grants and quitclaims to Thomas le Taillour all her right of dower in the tenement lying between that of William Gerveys, her son, and that of Thomas le Taillour, and extending from the high street to the kitchen which William de Hallynge held, and for some time belonging to Geoffroy de Ireland. Witnesses, Gervase le Baker, William le Heyward, Richard Onyet, Gregory le Barbur, Henry Wade, and others. Given at Wycombe, on the Feast of St. Luke the Evangelist, in the year of the reign of King Edward, son of Edward, 5:—temp. Edward II.

A small parchment deed, in Latin, the seals lost; whereby Richard, son of Thomas Andreu, and Joan, his wife, grant to Adam, son of Matthew le Fullere, a messuage in the borough of Wycumbe, near the tenements which William Goldsmith and Robert Kippelove held, and extending from the High Street to the running water; for a sum of money paid beforehand—the amount not named. Witnesses, William Outred, John Ballard, Gilbert Man, John Benyt, John Geky, and others. Date 23rd January 1 Edward III.

There is also a counterpart of the preceding deed, with but one seal originally, now lost; executed on the same day, but with additional witnesses to those before-named; John Borgeys, William atte Lythe, William atte Welle, "and many others." This, no doubt, was the counterpart executed by the grantee.

A small parchment deed, in Latin, finely written, the seal lost; whereby Ralph de Wydindone grants to Richard Sywat, of Wycombe, a meadow in the Newelond, between the meadow of the said Richard and that of William Bil, also adjoining the meadow of John le

Thrower and the curtilage late of John de Weston. No consideration is mentioned, beyond the clause binding the grantee to do the services, due and accustomed, to the chief lords of the fee. Witnesses, Thomas Gerveys, John de Bradele, Michael le Heyward, William Bil, John Throwere, and others: 5 Edward III.

A parchment deed, in Latin, mutilated, without seal; whereby Nicholas, son of Alexander de Colshulle, of Hugendone, Roger son of John Ranner, and Andrew Scly, of the same place, release and forgive to John le Clerk, Mayor of Wycombe, John le Ferrour, John Goyr, John son of Andrew Batyn, of Wycombe, John de Stonhulle, Richard Bencyt, Richard Perkyn, Robert de Crempeslithe, late Bailiffs and Constables of the borough of Wycombe, John Ballard, of the same, and the whole community of the said borough, all actions, claims, and demands whatsoever. Given at Aillesbury, 6 August 15 Edward III. It is stated there that the parties making the release have thereto set their seals. There is no indication that to the present document any seal was ever set: it is perhaps only a copy.

A small parchment deed, in Latin, the seal lost; whereby Walter le Frere, of Wycombe, grants to the Mayor and community of the borough 6 pence of yearly rent which he used to receive from the tenement which John Bronnstel held in Croyndenclane. No consideration is mentioned. Witnesses, Matthew le Fullere, William Outred, John Ballard, John Matthew, Ralph le Hurler, Thomas the Clerk; 10th June 21 Edward III.

A parchment deed, in Latin, the seal lost; whereby John de Haveryngdoune, of Wycombe, grants to Robert Bencyt and Emma, his wife, a pightle of meadow in the street Bynuthebrugge, running down to the rivulet No consideration is mentioned. Witnesses, John de Sandwelle, Mayor, Geoffrey le Freynche, Richard Andreu, Henry atto Slou [at the Sluice], Simon Pemino; 13 September, 21 Edward III.

A parchment deed, in Latin, the seal lost; whereby the Prior and Convent of Bustelesham [Bisham, Berks.] remit and quitclaim to John atte Done, of Wycombe, all their claims to 2 messuages near the tenements late of Richard Sywat and John Benceyt; and which tenements were left to them by the testament of Adam Mahen. Witnesses, Robert Whelere, Mayor of Wycombe, Richard Sywat, Walter Smythe, John de Taleworthe, Thomas Ballard, and others. Given at Bustelesham, on Saturday after the Feast of the Translation of St. Thomas the Martyr, 33 Edward III.

A parchment deed, in Latin, the seal lost; whereby Robert Beneyt, of Wycombe, grants to Andrew Hyemis, Chaplain, a meadow without the said borough, between the meadow of Richard Preyntiz and that of William atte Dene. Witnesses, Robert Whelere, William atte Dene, Richard Hortone, Thomas Ward, Thomas Ravel, John Jeky, John Ballard, and others. Given at Wycombe, the Sunday before our Lord's Ascension; 36th Edward III.

A somewhat large parchment deed, in Latin, faintly written, the seal lost; whereby John Geyr, of Thunderlee, in the Hundred of Rochforde [in Essex], grants to Thomas Revell, William Frere, Walter Noble, and Richard Huyrthe, of Wycombe, Wardens of the work of the Blessed Mary of Wycombe, a yearly rent of 2s., arising from a tenement in the street of Froggemore, near the tenement late of Gilbert Marchal, between the rivulet and the High Street; and from another tenement in Newlond Street, near the tenements which John de Westone and Agnes de Abyate formerly had. Witnesses, Roger de Estwyk, John Poter, Walter Honesdone, John Osbarne, Gilbert Throwere, and many others. Given at Thunderlee, on Sunday the Feast of St. George the Martyr, 41 Edward III.

A parchment deed, in Latin, somewhat mutilated, the seal lost; whereby John le Smythe, of Bradenham, grants to John Palmere, "irmongere," of Wycumbe, a meadow called "le Passche," lying between the way which leads from Bygery [? indistinct] towards the mill of Thomas atte Lude, and the water running from the sluice of the mill of Philip de Broutone. Witnesses, Thomas Gerveys, Mayor of Wycombe, Thomas Ballard, Richard Jordan, Bailiffs, William atte Dene, Thomas Cornewayle, Giles atte Reye, Nicholas atte Broke. Given at Wycombe, on Monday before the Feast of St. George the Martyr, 44 Edward III.

A parchment deed, indented, in Latin, the seal lost; whereby William Frere, of Wycombe, grants to Thomas Revel, Walter Noble, and Richard Hughete, Wardens of the work of the Blessed Mary of Wycombe, a messuage in Newlond Street, between the meadow of William atte Dene and that late of John Sandwelle;

they paying yearly 6s. 8d. to the grantor and Cecle [sic.]
qy. Cecily or Celia] his wife. Witnesses, William atte
Dene, Mayor of Wycombe, Thomas Ballard and Richard
Jurdan, Bailiffs, Thomas Cornwaile, John Bramptone,
Stephen Kirkeby, Walter Frere, and others. Dated
18th March, 45 Edward III.

A parchment deed, in Latin, mutilated, the seal lost;
whereby Roger Schenholte, of Saunderdone, grants to
William atte Dene, his right and interest in 16 pence of
yearly rent arising from a tenement between one formerly
belonging to William ate Combe, and that of Walter
Sywet; the said William himself having lately acquired
the said tenement of Philip Breghtone [? being torn]
and Alice, his wife. Witnesses, John Ballard, Richard
Kele, Thomas Cornewayle, John Jeky, John Broun
"Diere," and others. Given on Thursday, the Feast of
the Nativity of St. John the Baptist, 46 Edward III.

On parchment, what is probably, the probate copy of
the testament of William atte Coumbe, in Latin, dated
"Tuesday,—A.D. 1354:" whereby he leaves "to the
"Holy Land, 6d.; to the church of Lincoln 6d.; to the
"church of Haveringdoune, for my soul, and the soul of
"Thomas [my uncle], 18d. and one sheep;" to the church
of Bradenham one sheep; to the church of Hugendene
one sheep; and to the church of Wycombe one sheep;
to Sir Roger, Chaplain of the parish, 6d.; to the Sacrist
3d.; to the Clerk, 2d. He leaves to the Wardens of the
church of Wycombe 2s. of yearly rent from the tenement of Richard le Carpenter, formerly of John le
Mareys [Marsh] "to find one torch and the raising
"[levationem] of the body of Christ, in the Chapel of
"the Blessed Mary of Wycombe." To the same Wardens
also 6d. yearly, to be received from a certain shop which
formerly belonged to Matthew le Fullere, near the tenement of W. le Carpenter. Also, to the same Wardens
one penny of rent from the tenement which belonged to
Serche, towards the fabric of the church. To Roger
Rawnor, one quarter of draget [mixed corn]; to Ha-
wise, wife of the same Roger, one black steer; and
to the two daughters of Roger 2 sheep. To his own 3
daughters, 3 sheep. To John, son of John atte Coumbe,
one calf, 2 two-years' sheep, and 2 bushels of draget.
Also 20s. to be spent on the day of his burial, and the
same on his Anniversary days. The residue of his goods
he leaves to be distributed, at the discretion of his executors, for his soul, and the soul of Thomas atte
Coumbe, his uncle; one earthen pot [brec'] excepted;
which he leaves to the house of St. John the Baptist, of
Wycombe. To the high altar of Haveryngdoune he
leaves 2d; to the altar of the Blessed Mary 2d.; and to
the altar of St. Thomas 2d. To the Friars Minors of
Radinge one bushel of wheat, and one bushel of draget;
and to his sister Susanna half a quarter of wheat. "And
"for the execution of this testament, I do make, ordain,
"and appoint, Sir John, Parson of Bradenham, and
"Edith, my wife, to be executors."

A parchment Latin deed indented, in duplicate, the
seals lost in both instances; whereby Walter Noble,
John Bramptone, Richard Brounstel, and Richard
Highete, "Wardens of the work of the Blessed Mary
"of Wycombe," grant to John Reynald and Matildis,
his wife, and Cecily, their daughter, one measuage, with
half an acre of arable land, situate in the borough of
Wycombe, at La Cresche; between the tenement of
John Wydyndone and the land of William Hayward,
for their lives respectively, at a yearly rent of 4s. 4d.;
with power of distress, and a covenant to keep the said
messuage in good repair, "in timbering and in tiling."
Witnesses, Thomas Revel, Mayor, William Prophete and
William Haykyn, Bailiffs, John Jeky, John Barone,
diere, and others. Given at Wycombe, on Wednesday,
the Feast of St. Michael the Archangel, in the 2nd year
of King Richard II. Of the two counterparts, that
executed by the grantors has had four seals, that by
the grantees two.

A parchment deed, in Latin, one of the two seals, in
red wax, nearly whole; whereby Richard Brounstel
and Richard Heygate, of Wycombe, grant to Richard
Peytevyn, Sir Richard Butte, Chaplain, and Nicholas
Sperlynge, a meadow which they had of the gift
and feoffment of John Palmere, which is called the
"Plasshete," in Wycombe, and lies between the King's
highway which leads from Begerye Street to the mill
of Thomas atte Lude on one side, and the water coming
from the sluice of the mill of Philip Broughtone, on
the other. Witnesses, Richard Kele, then Mayor of
Wycombe, John Spycero and Ralph Drynkere, then
Bailiffs, William atte Dene, Richard Sandcwelle, and
others. "Given at Wycombe, on the Sunday before the
"Feast of the Exultation [sic] of the Holy Cross, in

"the 16th year of the reign of King Richard, after the
"Conquest the Second."

A small parchment deed, in Latin, the seal lost, of
the same date; whereby William atte Dene, of Wycombe,
grants to the persons last named, a meadow which he
had, of the gift of Andrew Lyouns, Chaplain; lying
without the borough of Wycombe, near the field late of
Richard Nerynyte. The same witnesses as to the preceding deed, William Depham added.

A large parchment indenture tripartite, in French,
the seals lost, and the deed much mutilated; stating
that there have been disputes between the Mayor and
Commonalty of Wycombe and Ralph Lude, Esquire;
the former claiming 21 shillings of rent from certain
tenements which the said Ralph holds of them in the
said vill; also 2s. 3d. from a meadow similarly held;
they also claim an old rental touching the Mayor and
Commonalty, which the said Ralph has in his possession;
and they complain that he has built on the waste land
belonging to the vill. They have therefore submitted
to the award "of the very noble and very gracious
"Lady, Joan de Bo[hun]e, [?] Countess of Hereford;
who has awarded that the said Ralph shall pay such
rent of 21s. Awards are then made as to the rental of
2s. 3d., suit of Court, and the building on the town waste;
but the greater part of the context is wholly effaced.
As to the old rental claimed, the said Ralph is to have
a copy made thereof, which he shall keep, and shall
deliver the rental itself to the said Mayor and Commonalty; the copy which he retains being sealed with
the common seal. "Given at Westmynstre, the 27th
"day of October, in the 9th year of the reign of King
"Henry, after the Conquest the Fourth." It may be
worth enquiry who this "Countess of Hereford" was;
possibly, a younger daughter and coheir of Humphrey
de Bohun, Earl of Hereford, who died without heir
male in 1372.

A parchment deed, in Latin, indented, the seal lost;
whereby John Cotyngham and Thomas Mortone, Clerk,
grant to John Hampdene, son of Thomas, of Wycombe,
all the lands and tenements in the "foreign" of
Wycombe, called "Toterugge," which they lately had
of the gift and feoffment of the said Thomas, and which
he had of the gift and feoffment of William Clerk, of
Wycombe. Also, they grant the lands and tenements
in Aschendone, which they had of the gift and feoffment
of the said Thomas, to hold in tail general to the said
John Hampdene; remainder, in like manner, to his
sister Joan; remainder to Edmund, lord of Hampdene,
and his heirs for ever. Witnesses, Thomas Merstone,
then Mayor of the vill of Wycombe, Andrew Sperlyng,
Thomas Durem, John Savage, William Clerk, and
others. "Given at Wycombe, on Sunday after the
"Feast of the Apostles Peter and Paul, in the 4th year
"of the reign of King Henry, after the Conquest the
"Fifth." This deed having had but one seal (now
lost), must have been the counterpart, executed by the
grantee. The heralds' books shew that the family of
Hampden, of Wycombe, was a collateral branch of the
family of Hampden, of Hampden, of which John Hampden, the Parliamentary leader of the 17th century, was
a member.

A parchment deed, in Latin, one of the two seals
partly remaining; whereby John Spycere, of Wycombe,
and Alice, his wife, grant to John Shrymptone two
cottages and the garden adjoining, in Croyndene Lane,
between the curtilage late of Roger Ryps and that of
Thomas Aneresdelle, and the one late of Thomas atte
Lude; which cottages they had had of the gift and
feoffment of Richard Pycheron, of Arundelle. Witnesses,
William Clerk, Mayor of Wycombe, Thomas Scarbroke
and William Lytelboy, Bailiffs, Thomas Merstone,
William Potanale, Richard Shrymptone, William
Shrymptone, and others. "Given at Wycombe, on the
"Sunday next before the Feast of St. Luke the Evan-
"gelist, in the 7th year of the reign of King Henry,
"after the Conquest the Fifth."

A large parchment deed, in Latin, the seals lost;
whereby John Benet, Clerk, and William Stockene, of
Wycombe, grant to Andrew Sperlyng, Roger More,
Thomas Merstone, John Covyntre, Thomas Aneresdelle,
William Broughtone, William Potenale, John Chapman, Walter Cery, Richard Huchyndene, John Cotyngham, and William Pycot, a yearly rent of 53s. 4d.; to be
received from a tenement situate between the tenement
of John Welle and that late of John Clerke, and extending from the King's highway to the close of the
rectory of Wycombe; such tenement being called the
"Newe In," and lately had of the gift and feoffment of
John Kele. Witnesses, William Clerke, John Hampdene, John Savage, John Justicar, John Corbrygge,

and others. "Given at Wycombe, on Wednesday "before the Feast of the Nativity of the Blessed Mary, "in the 6th year of the reign of King Henry, after the "Conquest the Fifth."

A parchment writing, in Latin, *temp.* Henry VI., containing copies of two deeds:—by the first, Richard Sandwelle, of Wycombe, grants to John Bryan, citizen of London, John Sandwelle, Thomas Merstone, Richard Merstone, Thomas Squire [Armiger], William Vachell, and John Wodcock, all his lands and tenements in the parish of Wycombe. Witnesses, Nicholas Sperlyng, William Merchaunt, Thomas Comyne, Thomas Andresdell, John Mundy, and others. "Given at Wycombe, on "the Feast of St. Brice the Bishop, in the 3d year of the "reign of King Henry, after the Conquest the Fourth." —By the next deed, on the same parchment, William Fachell [for Vachell] of Coles near Redyng, (probably as one of the two survivors of the preceding feoffees), remits and releases to Thomas Merstone, of Wycombe, (probably the other survivor), all his right in the lands and tenements before mentioned. Witnesses, John Wellesbourne, Mayor of Wycombe, William Lambard, William Smythe, Bailiffs, John Hampdene, William Stoktone, William Broughtone, and others. "Given "at Wycombe, on Tuesday next after the Octaves of "the Purification of the Blessed Mary, in the 5th year "of the reign of King Henry, after the Conquest the "Sixth."

A parchment deed, indented, in Latin, the seal lost; whereby Thomas Merstone, Mayor of Wycombe, John Wellesbourne, John Hampdene, Thomas Anersdelle, John Covyntre, John Wyke, Richard Whyte, burgesses thereof, grant to Roger Bakere a tenement in Crendon Lane, between the garden of John Orede and those of the Abbot of Messendene and Thomas Clerke, and near to the tenement of John Wellesbourne, late of William Halle, and the land of William Northwyke, at a yearly rent of 2s. to the Wardens of the Blessed Mary of Wycombe. Witnesses, Thomas Merstone, Mayor, Thomas Maynolf, William Persone, Bailiffs, John Justycer, Edward Cary, John Blakpol, and others. Executed on Thursday before the Feast of the Apostles Simon and Jude, 19 Henry VI.

In a mutilated Probate copy of the testament of John .... of Wycombe, dated 20th February 1436, of which nearly one half has perished, mention is made of the place of burial in the churchyard there of "Thomas "Sprot, late Vicar of that church;" and a house in the town is named, "called the George:" beyond this, so mutilated is its condition, that, though of great length, nothing else of interest can be gathered from it. A fragment of the seal of the Archdeaconry is still attached: and an endorsement states that the testament was proved before the Official of the Archdeacon of Bucks, on the 18th of April 1437. The testator's sons were named Thomas and Richard, his wife's name was Margery, and he had a daughter named Matildis. He seems to have been a man of opulence; makes bequests to the clergy and towards the building of the Church; and leaves 8s. 4d. for a silver chrismatory for its use, and 12d. to find a lamp to burn in the choir.

A parchment deed, indented, in Latin, somewhat decayed, its two seals, in red wax, surviving, but one without an impression; whereby John Prykke and Richard Redhod, of Wycombe, grant to Agnes, widow of Henry Colshulle, a tenement and curtilage, in Wycombe, between the tenement of the Chantry of the Holy Trinity on the east, and that of Joan Brygwater, on the west, extending from the highway along the churchyard to the land of John Wellesbourne, on the north; to hold to the said Agnes for life; remainder to John, son of Henry Colshulle, above mentioned, remainder to William, his brother, remainder to John Hampdene, Mayor, or the Mayor for the time being, and to John Wyke and Walter Colarde, or other the Wardens of the works of the church of Wycombe; to sell and dispose of the same for the use of the said church, and for the health of the souls of the said Henry Colshulle, his parents and benefactors. Witnesses, John Hampdene, Mayor of Wycombe, Robert Colyn and William Barnard, Bailiffs, Robert Cotyngham, John Blakpolle, John Sadeler, Thomas Croft, and many others. Dated on the Feast of St. Michael, 20 Henry VI. This is probably the earliest instance in which the family of Redhode is mentioned.

A large parchment deed, indented, in Latin, its one seal, in red wax, remaining, representing, apparently, a lily; whereby John Hampdene, Mayor of Wycombe, John Wellesbourne, Thomas Merstone, John Blakpolle, Robert Cotyngham, John Wyke, Walter Colarde, and Edward Cary, grant to Thomas Croft a tenement and

garden in Wycombe, in the street called "Estyntone," between the tenement of Robert Broune and the toft and garden late of William Scheresfelde, and extending to the town ditch; at a yearly rent of 10d. to the Mayor and burgesses, and of 10d. to the Bailiffs, William Frere and John Hamonde; with powers of distress. To the part remaining with the Mayor and burgesses [the present one], Thomas Croft has set his seal. Witnesses, Gewin Le Penne, Juda Wellesbourne, Thomas Hullemede, William Crowe, John Gate, and others. Dated 30th December, 22 Henry VI.

A large parchment deed in Latin, somewhat mutilated, with seal in red wax, three shields thereon, impressions effaced: whereby Thomas Merstone grants to Robert Cotyngham, John Wellesbourne, John Redselle, John Blakpolle, John Martyne, John Sadeler, John Wokyngham, Thomas More, John Merstone, William Trewe, William Redhode, William Corbrygge, Walter Mundy, and Thomas Crofte, a yearly rent of 58s. 4d., arising from a tenement in Wycombe called the "Newynne" and the "Saresenehede" [Saracen's Head], situate in the High Street, between the tenement of Thomas Wheler, Clerk, Vicar of Huchendene, on the east, and the tenement of John Wellesbourne, on the west, and extending to the Rectory close, called the "Bourcheys," to the north; he having had the same, with Andrew Sperlyng and others, all now deceased, of the gift and feoffment of John Benet, Clerk, and William Stoktone, of Wycombe, in a deed of the 8th year of King Henry V. Witnesses, John Hampdene, Walter Colard, John Corbrygge, Richard Redhode, William Haeylbury, and others. Dated on the Feast of the Conception of the Blessed Mary, 24 Henry VI.

A small parchment deed, in Latin, with a seal in brown wax, the impression effaced; whereby Thomas Lettortfort, of the parish of Cookham, Esquire, grants to Robert Cotyngham, John Hampdene, John Blakpolle, Walter Colard, John Wokyngham, William Veer, *alias* Trewe, and John Sadeler, a messuage and garden in Wycombe, in the street called "Estyntone," between the tenement of Agnes 'Bisshope and Crendon Lane. Witnesses, Robert Cotyngham, Mayor of Wycombe, John Scharpe and John Gate, Bailiffs, Thomas Merstone, Richard Redhood, Richard Ernolde, William Frere, Thomas Croft, John Lytelboy, and others. Dated 4th February, 25 Henry VI.

A parchment deed indented, in Latin, the seal lost; between John Hampden, Mayor of Wycombe, Thomas Browne, Richard Cary, Bailiffs, Robert Cotyngham, Walter Colardo, John Corbrygge, John Wyke, Walter Mondy, and William Barre, "com-burgesses" of the same vill, of the one part, and John Blakpolle, of the other; reciting that the latter was seised in his demesne, as of fee, of one messuage, with its appurtenances, in Wycombe, near the bridge, between the tenement late of Stephen Dormere, on the north, and the rivulet running to the mill called "Brygmylle," on the south; and abutting on the highway leading to Merlow on the east; and that the same John and the previous owners of the said messuage had been wont to repair and maintain a latrine, under the roof of that messuage, to the easement of the community of the vill of Wycombe; whereas the said John had now built a new latrine in the middle of the rivulet, near the bridge, he willed and granted thereby that he and his heirs, and all in possession of the said messuage, should in future maintain such latrine newly built, at their own costs and expenses. In case of neglect so to do, power is thereby given to the community to enter the said messuage, and restore the place in question to its former state. Witnesses, Gewin de la Penne, Thomas Geky, William Dormere, Robert Deram, William Schrymptone, and others. Dated 21st May, 27 Henry VI.

A small parchment indenture, in Latin, the seal lost; whereby John Wokyngham and John Sadeler, Wardens of the Chapel of the Blessed Mary of Wycombe, and collectors of the rents thereof, with the assent of all the brethren and tenants of the said Chapel, grant and let to William Redhood a meadow of the Blessed Mary, called "the Plassey," near the moor, by the mill called "Broghtone Mylle," in the foreign of Wycombe, for a term of 80 years, at a yearly rent of 6 pence. Dated 10th October, 27 Henry VI. There are no witnesses to this deed.

A large parchment indenture, in Latin, much mutilated, the seal lost; whereby John Blakpolle, Mayor, John Hampdene, Robert Cotyngham, Walter Colard, John Wokyngham, John Sadeler, William Veer, Walter Mundy, Thomas Croft, John Lytelboy, Robert Ernold, and William Redhood, grant to John Russello, *alias* Carpenter, a messuage between the tenement of Agnes

Bysshop and Crendone Lane, at a yearly rent of 6s. 8d. to the grantors aforesaid, and to John Pymme and John Tytyng, Bailiffs, and the Bailiffs for the time being, 2s. 8d.; with powers of distress. The attestation is torn and illegible. The date is — September, 27 Henry VI.

A parchment deed, in Latin, partly effaced, and the seal lost; whereby Henry Puttenham, Esquire, grants to John Hode the elder, Robert Cotyngham, John Wellesbourne the elder, and John Redeshille the elder, of Wycombe, a piece of meadow in the borough of Wycombe, lying in a street called "Seynt Marie Strete," running from the tenement of the said John Hode to the King's highway, leading to a certain pasture called "the Reye;" and near to a certain moor called "Hor-"synchircheyerde," on the east; which the said Henry had, of the gift and feoffment of Robert Forster and Peter Condray, Esquire, at a yearly rent of 2 ounces of pepper, at Our Lord's Nativity. Witnesses, John Martyne, Mayor, William Buntynge, John Gomme, Bailiffs, John Hampdene, John Blakepolle, and others. Dated 7th April, 28 Henry VI.

A parchment deed, in Latin, somewhat mutilated, the seal lost; whereby John Merstone, son and heir of Thomas Merstone, of Wycombe, remits, releases, and quitclaims, to John Hampdene, John Wellesbourne, Robert Cotyngham, John Blakpolle, Walter Colarde, John Sadeler, William Veer, Barnaby Stokke, Walter Mundy, Thomas Croft, John Lytelboy, Robert Ernold, and William Redhood, all his right to a shop in the market of Wycombe, between the two shops of Thomas Merstone, his father. Witnesses, John Martyne, Mayor, William Bontynge, John Gomme, Thomas Brown, Richard Cary, and others. Dated, the Feast of the Nativity of St. John the Baptist, 29 Henry VI. A fragment of a deed is pasted on to this; which, translated, reads—"writing shall see or hear, Thomas Merstone " has confirmed to John Hampdene, Robert Cotyngham, " Barnabas Stokker, Thomas . . ."

A small parchment indenture, in Latin, mutilated, the seal lost; stating that whereas Thomas More, of Wycombe Magna, Esquire, by his writing obligatory is bound to John Blakpolle, Walter Collard, Walter Mondy, and William Redhode, in a sum of 80 li., to be paid at Whitsuntide next; if by then he shall give good surety for a yearly rent of 6s. 6d. to the Vicar of Wycombe, they will be satisfied therewith ; the same to arise from a tenement opposite the church, in which Thomas Raverdyn dwells ; and to be paid half yearly to John Hampdene and other persons there named. Dated 22nd January, 34 Henry VI.

A parchment deed, in Latin, the seal lost; whereby William Spenser, of Myssenden, grants to John Wellysbourne and John Colshille, a croft and garden adjoining, at Great Kingishille, lying between the common pasture called "Wycombe Hethe," on the east, and a field called "Heyonisfelde" on the west, and near the land called "Blakes," to the north ; also 3 pieces of land in Heyonisfelde [now Higgins-field]. Witnesses, Juda Wellysbourne, Thomas Clerk, Richard Huone, Thomas Tirry, Henry Rouse, and others. " Given at Huchyndene, on " Monday next after the Feast of St. Ursula the Virgin, " in the 32nd year of the reign of King Henry, after " the Conquest the Sixth.

A large parchment indenture, in Latin, much mutilated, the seal lost; whereby John Martyne, Mayor of the vill of Wycombe, John Wellisborne, John Blacpolle, Robert Cotyngham, Walter Collard, John Admer, William Balkburgh, Walter Mondy, William Corbrygge, Barnabas Stokker, and Nicholas Oxenford, burgesses, grant to John Russelle a garden in Estyntone Street, in Wycombe, between the tenement of Thomas Lytylpage and that late of Thomas Croft ; and extending from the King's highway, on the south, to the garden of Barnabas Stokker, on the north; he rendering yearly to the Wardens of the Chapel of St. Mary 12 pence. The said John to build a new tenement in the said garden, near the road, 29 feet of assize in length, and 16 in width. Witnesses, Robert Bardesey, Robert Dureain, Henry Newman, Thomas Gery, Richard Dormer. Dated 20th December 39 Henry VI.

A large parchment deed, much mutilated, the seals lost; whereby Edmund Arnold, citizen and grocer of London, and Katherine, his wife, grant to William Redehode, citizen and salter of London, dwelling in Wycombe, Richard Graunt, citizen and salter of London, and William Colard, of Wycombe, mercer, their tenement called "the Garet," in Wycombe aforesaid, between the tenement of William Pygot, and that of Richard Savage, and near the Market place on the south. Walter Mundy being Mayor and John Sheyffelde [?] and Robert . . . . Bailiffs. Witnesses, John Martyn, Robert . . . .

John Sharpe . . . and others. Dated 4th of March, 5 Edward IV. There are two fragments pasted to this deed ; one of them part of a power of entry and distress ; the other consisting of, apparently, four Latin verses; two of them illegible, the other two apparently :

" Caseus est dignus [correctly, from another source, " Caseus insignie], non est dandus nisi dignis.

" Caseus est carus, sic dixit praesul avarus."

" Cheese is worthy [Fine cheese is] to be given only " to the worthy. Cheese is dear, so said the greedy " prelate."

A parchment deed, in Latin, of the seal a fragment only left; whereby William Colshulle, son and heir of Henry, releases and quitclaims to John Sharpe, William Redehode, Richard Cary, Christopher Waas, William Bontyng the elder, John Pymme, Walter Cary, Laurence Watforde, Edward Cary, William Bontyng the younger, Robert Brampstone, and Ralph Nasshe, his right and title in a tenement and curtilage in Wycombe, between the tenement of the Chantry of the Holy Trinity, on the east, and that late of Joan Bryggewater, on the west; and extending from the King's highway, near the churchyard, on the south, to the land late of John Wellesbourne, on the north. "Given on the 6th day of " April, in the year from the beginning of the reign of " King Henry the Sixth, 49, and in the first year of his " recovery of the royal power." Deeds belonging to this short term, October 1470—April 1471, are of but rare occurrence.

A parchment deed, in Latin, very indistinct, the seal lost ; whereby Richard Cary, the Mayor, William Redehode, and others named, grant to John Sharpe, a tenement and garden in Saint Mary Street, between the garden of John Blacpoll and the tenement of Joan Burrey, and extending from the high street to the meadow of John Pusey; also, a cottage situate in a lane going towards the Eldeyeldehall [Old Guildhall], late belonging to William Body; he rendering yearly to Roger Brampstone and Thomas Peytevere, Bailiffs of Wycombe, and their successors, the two sums of 8 pence and 12 pence. Witnesses, John Penne, Thomas Gery, Richard Dormer, Richard Dyker, John Golofer, and others. Dated 10th of May, 16 Edward IV.

A parchment indenture, in Latin, with seal in brown wax, broken, and with no impression ; whereby Roger Brampstone, Mayor, and Thomas Okebanke and Thomas Watforde, Bailiffs, and Christopher Waas, Richard Cary, William Redehode, Thomas Pymme, John Peytever, John Blappelle, Richard Bernards, Walter Cary, Thomas Broune, and Thomas Baydon, burgesses, grant to Robert Asshbroke a certain messuage in Wycombe, in a street called "Powlesrewe" [Paul's Row], near the bridge, between the tenement late of William Dormer and the rivulet running to the mill called "Bryggmille," to the south, and abutting upon the King's highway leading towards Merlowe ; on condition that he keep in repair a latrine standing in the middle of the rivulet, near the said bridge, to the easement of the community of the vill of Wycombe ; with power of entry and distress, in case of non-repair thereof. Witnesses, John Penne, John Poynant, Thomas Lytilboye, William Frere, John Goodsone, and others. Dated 6th of March, 5 Henry VII.

A parchment indenture, in Latin, the seal lost; whereby William Clerke, Richard More, John Ratlef, and Thomas Sextone, Wardens of the Parish Church of Chepyng Wycombe, with the assent of Robert Aschebroke, Mayor, John Aley, Roger Brampstone, Thomas Pymme, and all other the burgesses, grant to Nicholas Wynshurste a tenement and garden without the borough, in a street called "Frogmore," near the tenement late of John Whyte, on the east and north, and the dam of the mill called "Bardeseys-mylle," and the tenement of William Russelle, on the west and south; at a yearly rent to the said Wardens of 4s., and of 2d. to the Wardens of the Chapel of the Blessed Mary in the church aforesaid ; and also a yearly payment of 22d. to Nicholas Jerarde; with powers of distress. Dated 29th September, . . . VII.

A parchment deed, in Latin, the seal lost; whereby William Colshulle, of Great Missyndene, grants to William Bunse the meadow and 3 pieces of arable land, within the parish of Huchyndene, upon Great Kyfgyshulle; the meadow being called "Curtismede,"and extending from the common, called "Kyngyshulle," to a field there, called "Hugynesfelde." Witnesses,Richard More, John Colsulle, John Nasshe, John Brykhulle, Nicholas Wydmer, and others. Dated at Kyngushulle, 8th October, 20 Henry VII.

The preceding are followed by seven deeds of the time of Henry VIII., three of them in English; four of the reign of Edward VI., all in English : one of the

BOROUGH
OF HIGH
WYCOMBE.

reign of Philip and Mary, in Latin; of which last the following is a description:—

A large parchment deed, the seal lost, but signed "George Peytefere:" by it, George Peytevere, Gentleman, one of the Aldermen of the vill of Chepyng Wicombe, grants and confirms to Thomas Frere, alias Pymme, Gentleman, the then Mayor, William Dormer, Knight, Robert Dormer, his son, Esquire, John Cheyney, of Agmondesham, Esquire, William Chalfount, Gentleman, John Borrell, Christopher Petefere, John Sterlyng, Rowland Wytnall alias Elys, Thomas Boty alias Parkyns, Timothy Pymme, John Pusey, Thomas, son of Robert Pusey, Thomas Bele, Daniel Cary, Thomas Wynch, Nicholas Jerard, son of Nicholas, Richard Lytilboye, William More, son of William, butcher, William Chelfounte, son of Thomas, and George Pymme, a yearly rent of 53s. 4d., arising from a tenement in Wycombe, called "the Antelope," in the High Street there; with power of distress. Dated the 17th of April, in the years of the respective reigns of Philip and Mary 2 and 3.

The documents of Elizabeth's reign are eleven in number; they are of a miscellaneous nature, and, in general, of no interest.

One is a mandate to the Sheriff of Bucks, to summon Jurors in a cause to be tried between John Greneland and Thomas Eles, Complainants, and John Adyssone, Defendant; on another slip, the names of the jurors summoned are given. Three of the documents, in English, are letters of attorney, and a fourth is a deed in amplification of a previous deed, to ensure quiet enjoyment.

In concluding this notice of these Church deeds, all that has been saved, probably, from the wreck of time, to throw some faint light upon the remote history of Chepping Wycombe, it only remains to be remarked, that of the families still dwelling there in the 17th century, those of Pymme and Utred, or Oughtred, appear to have been the oldest: the once powerful family of Waldere, evidently, soon became extinct, so far at least as Wycombe was concerned. William Oughtred, the divine and mathematician, born at Eton in 1573, was not improbably connected with the Wycombe family of that name.

It only remains for me to express my obligations to John Parker, Esqre., Solicitor to the Wycombe Municipal Charity Trustees, for the interest he has taken in my researches, and the facilities he so readily obtained, with the view of enabling me to make a thorough examination of the few surviving records of this ancient town.

HENRY THOMAS RILEY.

CORPORA-
TION OF ST.
ALBAN'S.

THE MANUSCRIPTS OF THE CORPORATION OF ST. ALBAN'S.

The following is an account of the, at present existing, records belonging to the Corporation of St. Alban's; for an opportunity of inspecting which I have much pleasure in acknowledging myself indebted to the courtesy of T. W. Blagg, Esq., the Town Clerk. The books and papers are preserved in the old Corporation chest, at the Town Hall; they are comparatively few in number, and of no great antiquity: many probably have been lost amid the mutations and vicissitudes to which in former ages the place has been subjected; in addition to which, it must be borne in mind, that the town only received its Charter of Incorporation so late as the reign of Edward the Sixth:—

Liber Electionum, or Court Book; a thin paper folio volume, in limp parchment, of about 140 pages. Its earliest entry is the Election of "Mayor, Burgesses, and "Assistants in Common Council," in the 28th year of Queen Elizabeth, A.D. 1586. It contains entries of proceedings in the "Court of the Mayor and Burgesses," sometimes in Latin, but mostly in English. The then existing Companies of the Barbers, Bakers, Shoemakers, "Bruers," and Butchers, are mentioned. The entries are continued to p. 127, the 9th year of James the First. Commencing at the other end of the volume, there are three leaves, containing an account of "corsletts," bills, and "men trayned," in the respective Wards of St Alban's, in the years, apparently, 1563 and 1587. In the latter year, among the arms used for training, "quillivers" (calivers), "muskettes," bills, and "bowes," appear. The back of the volume is braced with a fragment of a manuscript of the 14th century, a Latin treatise on various religious subjects, with glosses, "The Good Shepherd" being in the number. Inclosed in the volume are some loose leaves, of a similar nature

CORPORA-
TION OF
ALBAN'S

to the contents of the volume, but belonging to a later date, the year 1634 to 1639. At the end of the last date follows—" The Oath in the Act made 13 Car. 2nd, for the " well governing and regulateing of Corporations."

The now operating Charter of the town is still preserved. It belongs to the reign of Charles the Second; bearing date the 4th of July 1667, and being a confirmation of the Charters that had preceded it. The Charter, as to its form, is remarkable not only for its drawn and coloured portrait of King Charles the Second at the head of it, but for the fact of its being also accompanied with other pictorial illustrations. At the head of one of the folios is a view of St. Alban's at that date, apparently in Indian ink. Sopwell, the building that succeeded the nunnery there, is seen depicted in its then integrity; a portion only of its ruins now remains; the Clock-tower also is depicted, the Abbey Church, St. Peter's, and St. Stephen's. In the margin of the same leaf, also painted apparently in Indian ink, is a very tall "Royal Oak," containing in its foliage a series of three golden crowns. The Charter of Incorporation granted to the town, bears date the 12th of May, in the 7th year of King Edward the Sixth (A.D. 1553). It has been printed, in the original Latin, in Clutterbuck's *History of Hertfordshire, Vol. 1.*

A Charter granted to the town by Queen Elizabeth, bears date the 7th of February in the second year of her reign (A.D. 1560), and has part of the Great Seal attached to it.

A Charter of King James the First, granted in the 8th year of his reign, ratifies the Charter of Edward the Sixth, so far as it empowers the erection of a Grammar School in the Church: a piece of barbarism formerly enacted within the precincts of its beauteous Lady's Chapel, but now happily put an end to; an attempt being about to be made to restore this adjunct to this Abbey Church to somewhat of its original beauty and integrity.

A Charter of Charles the First, bearing date the 17th of December in the 8th year of that reign (A.D. 1632); it has also a part of the Great Seal attached.

Another Charter of King Charles the First, bearing date the 27th of July in the 16th year of his reign (A.D. 1640).

A Charter of King James the Second, with an engraved portrait of the Sovereign, bearing date the 16th of March, in the first year of his reign (A.D. 1685). After the Revolution of 1688, this Charter was held to be illegal, and null and void. A fragment only of the Great Seal is left.

A Patent, in Latin, bearing date the 24th of March, in the 12th year of Queen Elizabeth (A.D. 1570), whereby at the request of the Lord Keeper of the Great Seal, Sir Nicholas Bacon, "for the relief and sustentation" of the Schoolmaster and the Grammar School, she grants to the Mayor and Burgesses the liberty of licensing two taverns for the sale of wine; they to receive, in behalf of the School, the sums due for such licence. The Great Seal, once attached to the Patent has now gone.

A small quarto paper volume, bound in limp vellum, and endorsed "Poor rates for Abbey Parish, with Over-" seers' Accounts, 1655 to 1672." It is finely written, in general, and in good preservation.

"Constitutions" of the Borough, beautifully written, in English, and bearing date the 18th of September, in the tenth year of King Charles the First, A.D. 1634. The seals are appended by silver cords, and are preserved in cases of boxwood; being those of Thomas Lord Coventry, Lord Keeper, Sir Thomas Richardson, Chief Justice of the King's Bench, and Sir Robert Heath, Chief Justice of the Common Pleas. The document consists of seven large sheets of parchment, and is in good preservation.

An Inventory, in Latin, of the goods and "cattalls" of Richard Rainshaw, Esq., of St. Alban's 1572, founder of what is now known as "Richard Renshaw's Charity," and of which the Corporation are trustees.

A folio paper volume, in limp parchment, with brass clasps, containing minutes of the elections of Mayors and other officers, and meetings of the Mayors and burgesses, from 1640 to 1732. There are no leaves wanting, apparently; but there is no entry between Michaelmas Day 1648, "the 24th year of the reign of our Lord Charles, "by the grace of God, King of England, France, and "Ireland," and the 27th of June 1649. The volume is in good preservation, and, if thoroughly examined, would be found probably to contain much matter of interest.

Among the older deeds belonging to the Corporation, none of which apparently go very far back, is one of the 15th of May in the 4th year of Henry the Seventh

(A.D. 1489) in which mention is made of "Bothelynge-
"stock," "Le Stockhowse," and a lane called "Bothel-
"stret," in the town of St. Alban's.

An Exemplification of the Borough boundaries, in the
reign of Charles the First. The description of the
boundaries is given in English.

The miscellaneous papers and documents, belonging
to the Corporation, of any pretensions to antiquity, are
the following:—

A Letter of Request, on the occasion of a fire at the
town of Nantwich, in Cheshire, in 1583. It is signed
with signatures (copied, not original) of Thomas Bramley
Chancellor, Francis Earl of Bedford, Walter Mildmaye,
Christopher Hatton, Francis Walsingham, and several
others of the Queen's ministers; and states that, as had
been learned from the Earl of Darbye, and "others of
"good credytt," the towne of Nampwiche had lost 800
houses by fire "with the moste parte of the goodes and
"householde stuffe of the inabitantes to a verye greate
"valewe, whereby a greate number of the inhabitantes,
"beinge men of good worth, are, with their wives,
"children, and famylyes, utterly spoyled and undone,
"and the town become desolate, whiche of late was not
"only of good welthe and trade, by reason of the situa-
"tion; but allso of good importance for the service of
"her Majestie and the realme, beinge a thoroughfare
"lyenge convenyently for the receipte of soldiers,
"carryage, and munytion, to be sent into the realme of
"Irelande." The Queen herself, "having contributed
"to a good valewe, hopeth that her lovinge subjectes
"will allso have commyseration of the lamentable estate
"of these poore afflicted inhabitantes, as they wolde
"desire relief of others, upon the like visitation from
"Goddes hande." Collections of money are consequently ordered to be made for their relief.

A long Letter, of two small folio pages of paper,
endorsed, in an old hand, "Proposalls for setting the
"poor to spin in this burrough," and signed "Saint
"Albones this 2 of May 1618. Per me Steven Langley,
"Clothier." The general object of the writer seems to
be, though his mode of expressing himself is less clear
than his writing, to have poor and destitute persons in
the town thoroughly taught the art of spinning. After
much to this purpose, he concludes:—"Lastly ffor the
"advansment of the country by the knowledge of
"curious wosted woll workes and exelent yernes,
"I hould itt good and necessary that there bee 2 or 3
"maides, Dutch or Inglish, of most religiouse parent-
"age, and them sselves of good skill in spinninge and
"of good behaviour: such to bee sought out and kept
"in a rednes in the same house [for teaching the art]:
"which may bee allowed by the maiestrate to goe to
"any gentleman or yeo[man's] house in the country
"that desireth to have them to teach their wife,
"children, or servantes such workes: and soe to retoure
"againe, at theiro tyme lymitted, to the same house: to
"bee apointed likwise to some other that shall desire
"them herein," etc.

In a paper under date the 25th of May in the 26th
year of Queen Elizabeth (A.D. 1584) and signed by John
Clarke, he, as "one of the principall burgesses of the
"borrough of St. Albon's," in consideration of 12 pence to
him paid, promises to pay to John Comport, of the same
town, the sum of 20 shillings, within one month after
the said John Comport shall procure such benevolence
and payment of money to be yearly paid unto the Mayor
of the said borough for the time being, "for and towardes
"the keeping of eyght geldings, mares, or horses,
"within the saide borroughe for the service of hir
"Majestey for post horses and carryedge of the poultry
"for hyr Majesty. So that all straungers and others
"not inhabitaunts within the saide borroughe shalbe
"discharged thereof, and theyre geldings, mares, and
"horses, not to be taken for . . . the service at any
"time."

This paper, the exact meaning of which seems somewhat obscured by the endorsement, is endorsed, in an
old hand,—"The Postmaster's agreement for keeping
"of horses."

A bond, in Latin, with defeasance in English, entered
into by Thomas Ramridge, tailor, of Luton, with Barth.
Lawrence and Richard Whelpley, on the 29th of March,
1587; to the effect that "he shall not at any time here-
"after by himself or his servants, or any other for
"him, use, exercise, or occupye his occupation, that is
"to saye, the occupation of a tayllour within the bor-
"ronge, or . . . . fetche any worke from any inhabi-
"tant of the said borroughe to be wrought elsewhere for
"the same inha [bi] tant, without fraud or covine."
This document deserves remark from the fact, that a
Thomas Ramridge had died Abbot of St. Alban's about

60 years before. If they were members of the same family,
its fortunes, to all appearance, had not improved.

An order, finely written, on paper, and signed by
Richard Newcourt, Deputy Registrar (the laborious
author of the *Repertorium*) "made by the Right Revd.
"Father in God, Henry, by divine permission, Lord
"Bishop of London, on the 12th day of November 1679
"about a seate in the Abbey Church of St. Alban's, etc."
It states that there had been a difference between the
worshipful the Mayor and Aldermen of the town, and
one Mr. Dagnall, an attorney, about a pew or seat in the
Abbey Church, in which he had been formerly seated
by the Churchwardens; which seat and the one adjoining had been recently made into one, one of the Churchwardens dissenting. The Churchwardens, however, had
lately come to an agreement on the matter, and had
placed the Aldermen's wives in the two seats, now laid
into one, and had placed the Schoolmaster's wife, who
had formerly sat in one of the said two seats, "in
"another convenient pew, to her own good likeing."
Further, they would have removed the said Mr. Dagnall
into the uppermost seat, next the Aldermen, and then
were still ready to do so, "if he pleased to accept the
"same." His Lordship, therefore, "being very well
"assured that the said Maior and Aldermen did not
"make er interpose any order about the said seates at
"their Town Court in prejudice to his Lordship's
"ecclesiasticall jurisdiction, as hath been suggested,
"was pleased to approve what has been done therein,
"and . . . to ratify and confirme the laying of the said
"two seates into one, and the placeing of the Alder-
"men's wives in the same."

A Letter, in good preservation, addressed—"To my
"very assuerede and good ffreinde, Mr. Babbe, Maior of
"the Boroughe of St. Albans—Yeave [give] theise." It
is addressed—"Frome Lincolnes Inne the xiiith daye of
"October 1593" and signed "Your very ffreynd allwayes
"to use Robert Spenser." The letter states that "this
"pore woman the wydowe Evans have byn with me,
"I pray youe let her have your favour. She doth
"honestly lyve and use the trade of classes [sic, but qy.
"the meaning] for the gettinge of her lyvinge, and
"have used the towne theise iii or iiii yeres, comynge
"and goyinge for her money," etc. The sand still lies
upon it, with which the ink was dried.

A curious Letter, the address of which is lost, but
otherwise perfect, and written by John Thomas, a native of Bois-le-Duc, in Holland, the then Master of
the Grammar School at St. Alban's, in a neat and
legible hand. His monument is still to be seen in
the Abbey Church; and, from it we learn that he was
a teacher of eminence, who had been a schoolmaster
in France, Belgium, and Ireland, after being driven
out of his native country. The letter seems, from
its earnestness and simplicity, to deserve transcription:—"Right Worshipfull Mr. Maior your humble
"and obedient client, John Thomas Hyloocmius, the
"Schoolmaster of thys free schooles, beyng requested
"of thys bearer, good man Kente, desyre most ernestly
"off your Worship not to take in cvell part thys my
"bold entrepryse to trouble your Worship. Because
"he ys a poore man, I could not in conscience refuse
"hym. Hys request ys that I should helpe to entreat
"your Worship that yon would be so good with hym,
"and wryte, or send, to Mr. Williams, our parson,
"that by your auctoritie and apointement, he myght
"declare in the pulpite unto the people and commende
"the miserable estate off thys poore man, that some
"men may be ordeyned to ghather a collection off the
"wel disposed and devoute people. Thus Right Wor-
"shipfull Mr. Maior, I ernestly desyre you to graunte
"us this charitable deed, wiche the Lord wil see and
"reward in the day of Hys appearaunce. No more,
"but pray your Worship to pardon me that I wryte
"thus negligentlye and unordinately unto your W₁ for
"the man was very hasty, and I scarce was at ease,
"and so cold that I could hardly hold the pen in my
"hand, and he standyng and urgyng me till I had done.
"21 November anno 1583, in my schoole. Joann:
"Thomas Hyloocmius [i.e., of Bois le Duc]." The
writing, in places, shews signs of a hand somewhat
tremulous from cold. The question seems worth suggestion, whether John Thomas, (from his mastery of
the English language, evidently a clever man), may not
have owed his appointment, as the first Master of the
new Grammar School, to Sir Nicholas Bacon, (who is
known to have interested himself in the school); and
have been one of the early instructors of Francis Bacon.
On his monument it is stated, that his scholars were a
company of generous birth "generosa cohors."

A Letter, addressed "To the worshipful and my very "ffrinde Mr. Mayore of St. Albones, and to Mr. Good- "ridge of the Black Bull there Yeve these." It is written at "Lillingston Dayrell this viiith day of De- "cember 1583. Your ffrinde Paule Dayrell." The letter is brief, and is simply in favour of the bearers, his "neyghbors of Thorneborowes," who have had 21 "of "hogges stollen from them." He desires the Mayor's "lawfull favour and furderance unto these bearers for "there expedition," in prosecuting the offenders.

A Letter, dated 12th August 1584, and signed "Your "lovinge frende John Cutts," addressed "To my very "frend Mr. Mayre Yeue [give] these." It is to the following effect:—"Mr. Mayer—Whearoas I was pur- "posed to invyte my good neighbors to the mariage "of my man, and accordinge to the custome used in "such cases; and for that yt fell so out as my Lord "Chancellers comynge unto my howse in Cambridg- "shire hath called me from hence before I was deter- "myned; Mr. Weebb, my good frende, in my absence "in Essex sought meanes, as I undirstande, in good "will to my servaunt, to assaye the liberalytie of "your townsmen towards the helpinge fforwarde of a "poore begynner, which, as I fynde to be more then I "have deserved, so am I desirous to signifye my good "will agayne, that I might not seeme eyther unthank- "full nor indetted to much where I have geven lytle "cause, I praye you all accept of this I send you; "namly a bucke to be mery together such as herein I "have bene beholdinge unto; and withall a drynkinge "penye, partly to discharge your wyne at your feast as "I meane it I shal be beholdinge unto yow. And so I "bide yon hartely farewell." The meaning of this obscurely worded letter seems to be, that he had in- tended to invite the Mayor and Corporation to the marriage of his man-servant, and then make a collec- tion in the man's behalf, he being but a "poor begin- "ner." That, being compelled to be elsewhere, he could not do so; but that his friend, Mr. "Weebb," has made the collection, and with more success than he could have expected. He therefore presents the contributors with a buck for their feast, and a contribution towards the expense of their wine.

A Letter, addressed—"Too my very good ffrynd Mr. "Babb Maior of the town of Seynt Alban's," and signed "Your loving frynd John Brokett." Its date is pro- bably 1584 or 85, and it is as follows:—"Mr. Maior upon "Twesdaye nexte by the grace of God we mynde to "vowe yowr soldears at Nomansland, praying yow "that your 22 qualivers furnished to be ther by six "of the clock in the morning and we do allowe to every "soldiar xiid. the day for his wagis and one pound and "a halfe of powder for the two days and iid. for matche. "And this to be collectyed amongst yow ageynst the "day so as the poore men may be payd and the servise "well performyd. Also I pray yow geve me the "notise of sutche men as you do thynke most fyt for "this poorposse, allwayse remembring that by your "choyse we may have them forthcomming. Yf yow "have a dosin halbertes, I pray yow lett me have them "and I will returne them safe unto yow agayne. And "as I will comend yow to God. Brokethall, this present "Fryday."

Another Letter, on the same subject, addressed "To "my very verie lovinge ffreind Mr. Babbe Maior of "St. Alban's Give theise," and signed "Your loving "frynd John Brokett." It is as follows:—"Mr. Maior "I pray yow yf yow have annye defectes in your "corslattes or your calivers, lett them be presently "amondyd, and yow shalbe sparyd for all the rest, "and shall not be traynyd at all, nor yett amend "anye of them, and besyde your arnyd men shalbe "browght for the only twyse, but your shott [artillery] "must be traynyd four days. Also yow must spare me "four boemen and no more. Thus I will commend "yow to God and geve you notise of the day at some "other tyme as we can be preparyd, but I think yt "will not be above seven days. Broketthall this 2 of "June."

Another Letter on the same subject, written originally by John Brokett, but signed, at a later time and in another ink, by John Cutts; and addressed, "To our very "loving ffrend Mr. Mayor of St. Albones theis."— "Sir For that upon Monday nexte the Sessions is "apoynted at Hertford, and upon the Tuesday follow- "yng is nowe apoyntyd your Session Day at Seynt "Albons for the Libertye, we have apoyntyd upon "Wedensday folowyng being the xvth day of this "instant for our traynyng. Therfor I pray yow apoynt "sitche men as we have allrody traynyd to atend upon "me apoyntyd to be theyr captoyn, as also xv of your

"ablest men armyd with corslettes with theyr pikes. "I take your number of qualivers is xxii, and also we "desiar yow to apoynt me fowr of the ablest bowe men "in all your towne, and they all to be redy in Keye "Field by six of the cloke in the fornone. Thus "mutche I hoope shall be sufficient unto yow to have "all well apoyntyd, as owr trust is in yow. Written "from London this 6 of Juli. Your loving fryndes "John Brokett John Cutts. For the chargis you "know I, shall not need to sett downe, having yowr "number certyn." There are also some other letters by Sir John Brokett, or by Brokett and Cutts, on the same subject.

A Letter, addressed "To my loving frind Mr. Maior "of St. Alban's, and to the rest of his brethren:" it is signed "F. Bedford." (Francis, Earl of Bedford, 1554–85) but the body of the letter is written in another hand. It is dated "From Bedford House the 29 of January" but no year is named. The letter is as follows, the "Lord Keeper" referred to being, no doubt, Sir Nicholas Bacon:—"After my right harty commenda- "cions unto yow. Good Mr. Maior, here is an ould "servaunt of my Lord Keeper's, a good honest man, "hath a sute unto yow, that yt would please yow to "examin one Dorothy Grymes uppon certayne thinges "he shall declare unto yow. And I am to desier yow "that yow would accomplish his request herin, and to "show him your lawfull favour in this matter. And "if yow do him my pleasure herin for my sute, I shall "think myself beholding unto yow. And so do bid yow "right heartely ffarewell. . . . . (Postscript) Yf his "matter be good, I pray yow do what yow can for him, "and not otherwayes."

A Letter, addressed "To our vearie lovinge frend tho "Maior and his bretherne of the towne of Sainte "Albones," signed by Sir John Brokett and John Cutts, already mentioned. "Mr. Maior Knowinge that in all ages "and by her Majestys lawes victuall is to be provided "and killed for the sicke and suche as by the lawe shall "be licenced to eate fleshe in Lente, and for that Roger "Beche, one of your townes men, a butcher, is desirous "of your favour, and hath made meanes to us that we "wolde entreate your good will in the graunting of "him your licence to kill fleshe this Lent according "as he was appointed thereunto the laste yeare. These "are to praie yow the rather for our sakes to graunte "his suite, in which doinge you geve us occasion to "requite the same in anny of your semblable requestes. "And so we presume of your brothers assent herein. "Thus we bidd you hartelie farewell. From Brokett "Hall, this seconde daie of Marche 1583. Yowr "assuryd fryndes John Brokett John Cutts."

A paper writing, containing three folio pages of accounts for training soldiers at St. Alban's in 1585. The items are very numerous; among them the following perhaps deserve notice.—"First payd to Richard "Laurence corporal to the qualivers [calivors] for two "days wagis. . . vs. Item, payd for ii ℔. of powder "and two peeces of matche, alowed to the said Richard "Lawrence for two dayes iis. iiiid. Item, payd to th "drommer for his two dayes wagys iiiis. Item, payd "for wagys to xiii men tranod in corslettes xiiis. "Item, payd to Barnaby Lawrence for makyng of "hoose and dublettes for ii men xiis. vd. Item, paid "to Mr. Peetre for a rapier iiiis. viiid. Item, payd to "the cutlar for mending Mr. Cartar's qualiver viiid. "Item, payd for a fflaxe and a tutcho box, that weare "burned at Nomansland iiiis."—["Flaxo" was pro- bably a "flask" for gunpowdor.]—The account ends with items constituting the "Charges of the settyng up "of the beacon."

In a small bundle of accounts pinned together, and all belonging apparently to the Mayoralty of Mr. Babb, in 1583, is the following: it shews how the Justices and Commissioners, present at the muster, fared:—"The "note of the chargis at the dynnare for the Justices and "Comyssioners, with ther mene, at the muster. Item, "halfe a busshell of oystars xd. For buttore xxd. For "lenge [ling] and grene fyshe, or habberdene iiiis. iiiid. "For boylld veyle and bacone, xxd. For boyled befe "and for ii legges of muttone, iiiis. vid. For veyle "rosted, and lambe, and capons iii, aud on [ono] henne "at xviis. vid. For a pegg [pig] and frosshe somone, "and ii trouttes, and cylcs [eels] in brothe, viiis. iiiid. "For iii rochattes [piper fish] in brothe, for iii had- "dockes, and iii sawltc eyla, iiiis. vid. For quensse "[quince] pyes and aple tarttes, and fegges, and "almons, fruit and chese, vd. Brede and bere xs. vid. "For wyne viii pottles and iii pynttes, wherof viii "pottles and a quart of clarett wyne and a pottle "and a pynt of sacke, ixs. iid. Sume is iii li. viiis. id.

The following is an account for the Sessions Dinner in 1579.—" A not of all the chargis for the Sessions " Dyner kept for the borroughe the xvi day of Decem- " boi anno regni Dominæ Reginæ Elizabethe xxii°. " In primis, for veal, befe, and legges of mutton, xs. " Item, for ii gyese and ii pygges vs. viiid. Item, for " peper, suger, fruites, and other spices to backe the " chinepyes and venison, xs. viiid. Item, for two " couple of ffatt rabbettes iis. Item, for iiii capons to " boyle and roste, vs. Item, for purtreges, wooddcokes, " and larkes, iiiis. Item, for snett to bake the veneson " and other thinges iiiis. Item, for egges to make " whit brothe vid. Item, for warden pyes apele " tartes, iiis. iid. Item, for clarett wyne and sacke, vis. " Item, for flour to bake the pyes, xiid. Item, for wine, " ale, and beare, viis. vid. Item, paid to under cokes " and torn spittes, xvid. Summa lixs. xd."

HENRY THOMAS RILEY.

THE CORPORATION OF SANDWICH.

Upon the occasion of a short visit recently paid by me to the town of Sandwich, by the kind courtesy of the Worshipful the Mayor, R. Joynes Emmerson, Esqre., to whom I am desirous of here expressing my obligations, I was afforded an opportunity of seeing the archives which are preserved in the Town Hall there. So far as my researches extended, I am able to say that they are, for the most part, in fair condition, and that, as compared with those of some other corporate bodies, they seem to have been carefully preserved. The contents of the more ancient among them have already been exhaustively described by the late Mr. W. Boys, a Jurat of the town, in his able and interesting work, *Collections for a History of Sandwich:* such being the case, I felt myself precluded from entering upon anything like a close examination of them, as a detailed description of their contents would only have been a needless repetition of what has been for now nearly a century patent to the public. The following are a few details, relative to the earlier volumes containing the municipal records of the place, both as a town and as a member of the Cinque Ports, which, for the most part, are not to be found in Boys's work.—

The "Custumal" of Sandwich, is a small quarto volume, of 76 leaves of vellum or parchment, bound in the old wooden boards, which have now come loose, and stand in need of repair. Many of the pages are soiled, but nowhere illegible, and it may be said to be in very fair condition throughout. A large portion of the book, which is in Latin, has been translated by Boys in his work, and he has the following remarks upon it in his Preface:—"Part of it was copied from a more " ancient manuscript, written by Adam Champneys in " the year 1301; and was transcribed in the beginning " of Edward the Fourth's reign by John Serles, Town " Clerk of Sandwich, who has interwoven with the " older work many observations and customs of his " own time, and introduced charters and letters patent " of dates subsequent to 1301. So much as was written " by Mr. Serles is in a fair text hand, with very fre- " quent mistakes; but many entries have been made " since his time by different Town Clerks."

The oldest of the Year Books, or Journals of Corporation transactions,—and the oldest volume now in the possession of the Corporation—is the Black Book, or Old Black Book, a large folio volume, with paper leaves, and bound in old embossed leather. Pasted on the inside, at the beginning of the volume, there is the following note, in the hand of Boys, the historian of Sandwich:—"This book originally contained 318 folios, " in which are the following deficiencies, anno 1817. " Folio 1, a small fragment only remaining. Folio 2, " tattered, and a small part gone. Folios 13 and 19 " missing. Folios 71 and 84, tattered. Folios 85, 143, " 144, 145, 158, 159, 270, 271, 317, missing." The entries begin in 1432 *temp.* Henry VI., and end in 1487, 8 (*temp.* Henry VII.), the third mayoralty of William Salmon. It has been borrowed from by Boys, in his work already mentioned; but there is much matter in it, of course, which he has not extracted.

The White Book is the next of the Year Books, a thick folio of originally 378 leaves of paper, and generally in good condition. Boys has inserted, on the first leaf, a paper with the following note:—"Folios missing " in the year 1817, 53, 54, 55, 104, 137, 148, 149, 173, " 187, 188, 291—300, 307, 355, 364, 374, 375, 376, 377." On the first leaf is written, in German text, in a comparatively modern hand,—"The Yeare Booke called

" the White Booke 1488." The first four or five leaves are eaten away somewhat by mildew. Its contents end with the Mayoralty of Roger Manwood in 1526.

The next is, as inscribed on the first leaf, " The Yeare " Book, called the old Red Booke," a thick paper folio volume of 251 leaves, bound in old calf : it has suffered considerably from damp. It begins in 1527, and ends with the Mayoralty of Thomas Mucklewick, in 1551. The binding, of embossed leather, not improbably, was once red, but now it is a deep brown.

The next of the Year Books is the Little Black Book; a smaller folio, of 376 leaves of paper, in fair condition, bound in old black embossed calf. It begins with the Mayoralty of Thomas Menesse in 1552, and ends with that of John Tyson in 1567.

The new Red Book follows, a thick folio, in fair condition, with paper leaves, bound in black embossed calf, now in tatters. It begins in 1568, John Tysar being the Mayor, and ends with the Mayoralty of Richard Porridge, in 1581.

The next is the " Year Book called A and B," a large folio, in good condition, containing 379 leaves, in old black embossed calf. It begins with the Mayoralty of Stephen Rucke, in 1582, and ends with that of William Wood, in 1608. This volume is strengthened on the inside of the binding with part of an ancient Service Book, containing anthems, written in very large characters, with musical notation, and finely illuminated.

The next is the New Black Book, or Book C and D, a large folio, in good condition, containing 441 leaves of paper, bound in embossed leather. It commences in 1608, William Harflete being Mayor, and ends with the Mayoralty of George Wood, in 1642.

Book E and F, containing 445 leaves of paper, in good condition, bound in old rough calf. It begins with the Mayoralty of Henry Forstall, in 1642, and ends, in 1730, with that of Harflete Spratt.

Book G and H, a large folio, in good condition, containing about 460 leaves (the later ones not paginated) bound in old rough calf. It begins with the Mayoralty of Peter Crickett in 1731, and ends with that of Peter Rolfe, in 1828.

An old folio volume, containing about 300 leaves of paper, some in bad condition, bound in what is now in tatters, but was once black embossed leather. It contains records of fines, and other conveyances of property, acknowledgments by married women, to bar dower, records of wills registered, and copies of various other documents. Its earliest entry belongs to the 20th year of Henry the Eighth, (A.D. 1529), and its latest occurs in the Mayoralty of Henry Forstall, in 1642.

In addition to the above, and some other volumes of Corporation Accounts which do not call for notice, there are a considerable number of miscellaneous letters and papers belonging to the Corporation; which, in general, bear marks of having been preserved with care. At some period in, probably, the earlier half of last century, they seem to have been collected, and to some extent, perhaps, assorted, and placed in three portfolios, one of large, and two of smaller, size. On the inside of each of these portfolios there is pasted a summary, or rather, what professes to be a summary, of its contents, in the handwriting of Boys, the historian of Sandwich, previously mentioned. These summaries, so far as they go, appear to be correct; but they are mostly written in so concise and so perfunctory a manner, that, without reference to the document itself, their meaning is not to be easily understood. The following is a brief description of such among these letters and documents, as seem to be the most deserving of notice :—

In the larger portfolio.—

Process of Withernam, issued from Folkestone 1626, two papers.

A Certiorari from Dover Castle, signed by William Brooke, Lord Cobham, Constable of Dover Castle, and Lord Warden of the Cinque Ports, 16th century.

An assessment towards the 15th, in the 34th Edward III., in French, on paper; nine-tenths illegible from damp. A fragment only is left of the impressed seal, that of the Mayoralty of Sandwich.

Return, in Latin, on paper, to the Lord Warden's mandate to distrain John Hubard, holder of the office of King's butler in the port of Sandwich.

A list, in Latin, on paper, of names of the Barons of Sandwich not contained in the certificate of Sir William Morant and others, Collectors of the duties on wools granted to the King, in Kent; writing of the 14th century.

Certificate, in Latin, of the Collectors of Customs in Sandwich in 1367, on paper, and mutilated.

Appointment by the Crown of supervisors of malt and " bere," 4th year of Edward IV. [A.D. 1464, 5]; on paper, in Latin, imperfect.

Mandate by Henry, Prince of Wales, (afterwards Henry VIII.), as Constable of Dover Castle, and Admiral of the Cinque Ports, as to the coin of England. In English, finely written, and nearly perfect.

Copy of a Petition of the Mayor and Jurats of New Romney to William Brooke, Lord Cobham, Lord Warden, as to their right to use process of Withernam against towns in France and Flanders ; in English, on paper, date 1560.

Incorporation of the Shoemakers of Sandwich, in 1562, on parchment, in English, imperfect.

A Composition made between the Cinque Ports and the Lord Warden, William Brooke, Lord Cobham, in 1574, on eight large folio leaves of paper.

Draught of a lease by Roger Manwood to John Paramor, of the Tower house, or turret, which the said Roger holds by the grant or demise of Thomas Smythe of Ostenhanger, Esquire. The tenant is not to meddle, with the game of coneys in the warren there; on paper, 16th century.

Order made by the Lord Warden for restoring the commons of the town of Sandwich, and the parishioners of St. Peter's, to their voices, or votes, for the non-suiting of a cause in Chancery ; and for establishing the companies of Woollendrapers, Linendrapers, Mercers, and Taylors, there ; in English, on parchment, date 1623 ; signed " Theo : Suffolke ; " Theophilus Howard, Earl of Suffolk, the then Lord Warden.

Warrant, (in English, and finely written) for convening the Vintners, Cooks, Innholders, and others, to take licenses, and enter into recognizances.

A list of grievances, submitted by the Cinque Ports to the Lord Warden, Theophilus, Earl of Suffolk, in the 5th year of Charles the First.

Draught of a Petition of the Free Barons, or Free men, of the town of Sandwich to the House of Commons, to be restored to their " voices " in elections; on paper, without date.

Draught of a Petition of the Commons of Sandwich to the Privy Council, to the like effect; on two leaves of paper, without date.

Copy of a return made by the Mayor of Faversham to a writ of Habeas Corpus, from Westminster ; to the effect, " quod non currit in Portubus "—that it does not run in the Ports.

A very long sheet of parchment, containing a list of those who, in these parts, formed an Association for the protection of the person of King William from assassination, in 1696. The signatures, more than 100 in number, bear different dates in June and July in that year.

A Charter, on parchment, much mutilated, and mounted on cotton, as to tronage on wool ; date the 32nd year of Edward the Third ; without a seal.

Confirmation of the Charta Forestæ, 28th Edward the First, only some fragments, stretched on cotton ; without a seal.

Confirmation of Magna Charta, in the 28th year of Edward the First; in fragments, and mounted on cotton; without a seal.

Confirmation of privileges granted to the Cinque Ports, by King Richard the Third ; in fragments, mounted on cloth ; without a seal.

In one of the two smaller portfolios, are the following :—

Remonstrance of the Gentry of Kent, with their signatures, Robert Filmer, John Tufton, Jacob Astley, and others, to the Lord Lieutenant, against Sir John Bancks being nominated for Winchelsea, his " person " and principles being so obnoxious to the whole county." It contains, apparently, the genuine signatures, but has no date, and it is doubtful if it was ever sent.

Letter by Sir W. Trumbull, dated, Whitehall 15th October 1696, in favour of Edward Burrell, who " is de-" signing to stand for a Fellowship in our Colledge," (All Souls, Oxford). Addressed to the then Warden of All Souls.

Letter, signed " E. Winchilsea," with this endorse-" ment, Lady Dowager Winchelsea's Letter to her son-" in-law, Doctor L. W. Finch, concerning his Father, " the Earl of W., Ambassador in Turkey."

Letter, signed " Jo: Tillotson 13th September 1689," in reference to some one to whom the King has just given a Prebend of Canterbury ; " next to his Majestie, " you are greatly obliged to the Earl of Nottingham, " for his zeale and concernement for you." It is " addressed " To the Honorable Leopold Finch Esq", " at Eastwell in Kent."

5.

The Lord Warden's Orders for the reformation of the Government of Sandwich, 1602.

Returns as to corn and malt in the Cinque Ports in 1608, a great number of papers.

Report of the Commissioners for viewing Sandwich Haven in 1559.

Report of Andrian [sic] Andreson, the engineer, thereon.

Petition of the men of Sandwich to the Lord Warden, respecting the Cuts near Retisborough (Richborough); in English, of the 15th century, mutilated.

Report to the Commissioners as to horses, vessels and mariners, in Sandwich, in 1565.

List of vessels employed in fishing at Yarmouth, from Ramsgate ; vessels and number of men belonging to Yarmouth, at Sandwich; several papers.

Statement of the refusal of the inhabitants of Brightlingsea (near Colchester, in Essex), to contribute to the expenses of the Brotherhoods, in 1631, they not having been required to do so since the 10th of Elizabeth [A.D. 1568].

Copy of the Corporation's address to Charles the First, with a list of signatures.

Copy of Articles of Misdemeanor exhibited before the King in Council, against Bartholomew Combe, Mayor of Sandwich, in 1682.

Copies of heads proposed to be inserted on the renewal of the great, or general, Charter of the Cinque Ports.

Claim of privileges, in French, by the Barons of the Cinque Ports, at the Coronation, temp. William and Mary.

Documents as to putting in force the Statutes against Papists, in the year 1715.

Quietus in the Exchequer, given to Sir Edward Ryngeley, holder of the Lestage, in the 8th year of Henry the Eighth ; in Latin, mutilated.

Quietus given to the Lord Warden of the Cinque Ports, in the 19th year of Elizabeth.

A series of papers containing amercements of the Constable of Dover Castle and others, in the reign of Elizabeth.

Memoranda as to Courts of Shepway, holden from the 26th year of Henry the Sixth [A.D. 1447, 8].

Copy of a Writ of Inquisition as to the Privileges of the Cinque Ports, in the 14th of Edward the Fourth ; and Return thereto.

Proceedings of a Generall Brothyrhill, holden at New Romney, on Tuesday " after the close of Easter," in the 6th year of Henry the Seventh : six leaves, the entries in English, in good preservation.

Account of armour in Sandwich, and its members, in 1558.

Report as to the state of the town of Sandwich in 1559.

Paper on the castles and landing-places on the Kentish Coast.

Release by Margarett Udmore [?], in the handwriting of Sir Roger Manwood 1559.

Names of those constituting the Watch at Sandown, without date.

Inquisition as to the number of ships and mariners at Sandwich, in 1561.

Regulations as to the price of Labour, in 1561.

Proceedings of a Court of Guestling, holden at Rye, on the 3rd of January 1597, with the names of those attending there.

Copy of the Lord Warden's patent, 7th of Elizabeth, his right to wreck, and his oath.

The number and families of mariners in Sandwich, without date.

In the other smaller portfolio there is an equal, if not larger, number of documents, mostly belonging to the 16th and 17th centuries. The following are the principal among them :—

An order for mustering the Militia, date 1559.

Letters written by William Brooke, Lord Cobham, Lord Warden of the Cinque Ports, to the Mayors, Bailiffs, and Jurats, of the Cinque Ports, in reference to outrages at sea committed by vessels belonging to those ports, date 1560.

Letter written by the same Lord Warden for the due execution of Exchequer Writs in the Cinque Ports, date 1560.

Advice given by Sir Roger Manwood, as Counsel, to the Corporation of Sandwich, to send to the Secretary of State twelve cushions.

Letter sent by the Corporation of Sandwich to Secretary Cecill, with six arras cushions, " the first work of " the strangers in the town," meaning, probably, settlers from the Low Countries ; they also ask his favour as to their suit for the haven; date 1561.

4 C

Letter from Lord Cobham, the Lord Warden, forbidding the Corporation to meddle with the affairs of the Bailiwick; date 1569.

Letter from the same, commanding the Corporation to displace Thomas Thomsone, a Jurat.

Copy of a Letter written by the Mayor and Jurats to the Lord Warden, in reference to a riot at Sandwich; date 1570.

Copy of a Letter to the Lord Warden, in reference to Burgesses to Parliament.

Order from the Lord Warden, for the apprehension of James Greno, a butcher, charged with the murder of one Cryspe, alias Crippes; date 1570.

An account of the proceedings against the person who killed one Cryppes "a warrener of Mr. Serjeant Love-" laces connyes," in "the Downs,"—a farm lying between Sandwich and the sea: addressed to the Lord Warden by the Mayor and Jurats of Sandwich; date 1570.

Letter to the Mayor and Jurats of Sandwich from the Lord Warden, complaining of them for imprisoning his servant, Gilbert Knowles, date 1570.

Letter from Sir Roger Manwood, on Exchequer Writs.

Letter from Lord Cobham, the Lord Warden, being an order to the Mayor and Jurats to stop all vessels and mariners, and return their numbers; date 1570.

Letter signed by J. Taylor, and addressed to Mr. Fagg: in it he says, among other things,—" It shalbe " very well that you send my lord the benevolence " which the Ports promised my lord at your last being " with his Lordship. It shalbe the cause that his Lord-" ship shalbe the better mindfull of you and of your " suyte." The name of the " Lord " here alluded to does not appear; the Lord Warden probably is meant.

A communication from the Lord Warden as to the Militia, and in reference to certain seditious writings, that had been " lost and dispersed in common places," date 1571.

Letter from Sir Roger Manwood to the Mayor and Jurats, recommending a poor widow to their consideration, date 1571.

Letter from Sir Roger Manwood, on the town's quitrents, date 1571.

Original order from the Privy Council, for securing the owner of a vessel which had " spoiled the Earl of " Worcester"; signed " W. Burghley, R. Leycester, E. Lyncoln, T. Sussex," date 1572.

A similar Letter, ordering the Mayor of Sandwich, Dover, or Feversham, as the case might be, to send up before them one Captain Oliver, accused of piracy, but who said he was acting under the Prince of Orange, in seizing woad going to Rochelle; signed as in the preceding, but " T. Smith " added; date 1572.

Letter to the Mayor of Sandwich :—" After our harty " comendacions—Where Samuel Seth, of your towne, " by his supplicacon exhibited to us, hath complayned " of greate iniurye don unto hym by those of the Bryll, " ye shall understande that we all have a verye good " mynde to releave the said Seth, and others in like " manner wronged in goods or person. And therefore " whatsoever yow maye or canne lawfully devise or " doe for his or theire reliefe, we doe advise yow, and " will yow to doe, assuring yow that yow shall have " the Queenes Majesties lawfull allowance and sup-" portacon of your lawfull doeinges therin, with all " favor. So fare ye well. From the Courte, the 18 " of June 1573. Your loving friends." Signed " T. " Sussex" [Thomas Ratcliffe, Earl of Sussex] and another. A third signature, probably that of Secretary Walsingham, has been cut off.

Letter from the Lord Warden, as to the number of " hackeney horses" to be found in Sandwich, date 1573.

Order from certain County Justices, for the apprehension of Henry Butcher, of Deale, accused of " lewd " behaviour " and other offences; signed " Roger Man-" wood, Edward Boys, Thomas Godwyn," and " Robert " Alcok ;" date 1576.

Letter to the Mayor and Jurats of Sandwich from (Secretary) Francis Walsyngham, concerning certain prisoners taken by Mr. Holstocke, committed to their charge; date 1576.

Commission of Array for levying soldiers to practise archery etc., date 1577.

Copy of a letter from the Privy Council, for enforcing a Sumptuary Law, date 1577.

Letter from the Mayor and Magistrates of Graveling, concerning some persons who had been shipwrecked near Dunkirk: beautifully written, and apparently well expressed as to language, but it has no date.

Letter " to the officers of Sandwich," with his signature, from Lord Burghley, enjoining them to allow of shipping some wheat for Dover, date 1579.

A paper, signed by certain of the County Justices, complaining of exactions, grievous to the farmers and the County; date 1584.

Letter from Lord Cobham, the Lord Warden, enjoining that 12 ships be furnished by this Cinque Ports for the defence of the Narrow Seas; date 1587.

Letter from Sir Thomas Fane, Lieutenant of Dover Castle, for the relief of sundry bakers, date 1591.

Letter from the same to the Mayor of Sandwich, enjoining that 22 " hackneyes " be provided, " for the " use of Mr. Secretary and his trayne," being in number about 200 ; date 1597.

Reference, on a dispute between Dover and Sandwich, respecting their proportion of the expenses of furnishing ships, to certain gentlemen of the county.

Letter from Sir Thomas Fane, as to the duty of watching and guarding the beacons on the coast; date 1597.

Letter from Henry, Lord Cobham, Lord Warden of the Cinque Ports, on the same subject; date 1597.

Letter from Sir Thomas Fane, Lieutenant of Dover Castle, for mustering the Militia; date 1597.

Letter from Henry, Lord Cobham, Lord Warden, ordering payment of arrears of ship-money; date 1598.

Letter as to arbitration, with the aid of witnesses, in the dispute between Dover and Sandwich about shipmoney; date 1598.

Order of the Privy Council for the proclamation of James, King of Scotland, as King of England, 27th March 1603; with about twenty original signatures, the first of which has been cut out.

Copy of a Letter from Henry, Earl of Northampton, Lord Warden, relative to the duties on beer exported; date 1604.

Letter, signed " George Byng," to William Harflete, Mayor of Sandwich, date 1609.

Paper sent by certain County Justices, concerning the plague at Sandwich, and in reference to the temporary removal of the market; also, in terms of expostulation with those to whom it is sent, who, however, are not named ; date 1610.

Various papers relating to the establishment of a Fishery, date 1611.

Letter to the Mayor and Jurats of Sandwich from " the Counsel for Virginia," concerning the settlement of that colony; and papers relative thereto, with the names of the subscribers to the undertaking; date 1610.

Letter from Edward, Lord Zouch, Lord Warden, to the Mayor of Sandwich; among other things, he says that " he has been afflicted with the payne of the gout;" date 1616.

Letter from the same to the Mayor and Jurats, Commonalty and inhabitants, of Sandwich, requiring a subscription for the King and Queen of Bohemia; date 1620.

Letter from the Privy Council, requiring the Corporation of Sandwich to send some fit person to confer with them about the coin, date 1621. Some of the signatures have been cut out.

Letter from John Philipott, Somersett [Herald], offering himself as a Burgess in Parliament for Sandwich ; date 1627.

Letter from Edward Dering, on a matter pending at the Assizes, and the necessity of appearing; date 1630.

Letter from John Philipott, Somersett [Herald], to the Corporation of Sandwich, giving an account of his services; date 1631.

Notices, signed " Dorset " and " Edward Dering," containing orders to Mayors and others to search for a packet of value, " lately miscared," for her Majesty's use, and directed to Mr. Robert Oxwick; date 1631.

Fragment (not easily intelligible) of an order from the Privy Council, dated July 1632.

An order, signed by Edward Master, for payment of Ship-money, at Canterbury, 1st of March 1638 (9).

Letter from John Manwood, offering himself as a Burgess in Parliament for Sandwich; dated from Dover Castle, 29th December 1639.

Letter from Secretary Edward Nicholas to the Mayor of Sandwich, ordering him—" to stop Dr. Tyrrel, an " antient Irish prieste, and one Burck, another Irish " priest, of about 40 years old, and of a middle stature, " who weares a greene cloth sute and a periwigg, and " coming over from France or other parts beyond the " seas, and having the repute of dangerous instru-" mentes . . . . with no good intentions to this " kingdom ;" date 1641.

Letter from Edward Partriche, as to proceedings in Parliament, date 1641.

Copy of papers on propositions made for an Association of certain Counties, 23rd January 1642 (3).

Order, (signed by H. Elsinge, Clerk,) made in Parliament, for choosing a new Town Clerk for Sandwich ; Robert Jager, the late Town Clerk, having been committed to Newgate by the House, for misdemeanour committed by him against the Parliament.

Regulations proposed by the County Justices, to prevent the spread of the plague, date 1644.

Letter from Edward Partheriche, as to a Fast appointed, date 1646.

Letter from John Boys, Deputy Lieutenant of Dover Castle, with injunctions to secure the person of the Duke of York, who is expected to embark in woman's apparel ; date 1648.

Letter written by Algernon Sydney, (without date beyond 16th July, but probably when he was Governor of Dover Castle), as to the town of Sandwich taking no money from his company, when on the march.

Two letters from Thomas Harrison, of the Rainbow, in the Downs, date 1650. He says that Mullett, "that " noted Cavalier, is at present in your harbour, ready " fitted with 5 or 6 guns, pretending to go to New- " castle."

Letter from Edward Brooke, of Magdalen College, Oxford, wherein he declines an invitation to serve the town of Sandwich, "in the great work of the ministry ;" date 1652.

Notice of the Charter of Sandwich having been called in by the Committee for Corporations, signed "Samuel " Blagrave"; date 1652.

Letter signifying encouragements given for sailors ; signed "R. Salwey, Jo: Carew," at Whitehall; date 1652.

Warrant, signed "Oliver," the Lord Protector, enjoining that persons shall be stopped, who attempt to pass the seas without license; date 1654.

Notice of an embargo temporarily laid on shipping ; signed by order of Council, 16th of March, 1655.

Letter from Thomas Kelsey to the Mayor and Jurats of Sandwich, as to differences in the town about performing Divine Service, date 1656.

Letter from Thomas Seymour, Speaker of the House of Commons, enjoining the attendance of Members in the House : without date.

Opinion of "Counsel" (Thomas Loudlaw) as to the jurisdiction of the Cinque Ports at Yarmouth; 13th September 1558.

Letter of William Lockhart, commending the care of sick soldiers, from Dunkirk, date 1658.

The following documents, which did not come under my notice when at Sandwich, have since been named to me by Mr. Dorman.—

Two Grants, bearing date respectively 1295 and 1345.

Sign Manual of King Richard the Third.

The taking of Sanctuary by one guilty of murder, 1487.

Taxation of the Barons of Fordwich, in 1542.

It would be an omission on my part, were I to neglect this opportunity of expressing the obligations I am under to Thomas Dorman, Esqre., a member of the Corporation of Sandwich, for his good offices rendered me on the occasion of my taking these notes; in the way of giving me much useful information in reference to the records and past history of this ancient town.

HENRY THOMAS RILEY.

THE PARISH DOCUMENTS OF HARTLAND, N. DEVON.

(Second Report.)

Since my preceding Report upon the Church books belonging to this Parish, a large collection of additional documents, probably near one hundred in number, have been forwarded to the Commission, for examination, by the Revd. Mr. Chope, the Vicar of the Parish. Upon inspection, many of them have been found to be deeds and papers of the last two centuries, of an ordinary routine character, belonging to the "Governors" and feoffees of the Church lands and goods; while many others are indentures of parish apprenticeship, orders made for rating, bonds and orders made on affiliation and for settlement, parish discharges for paupers, attorneys' bills, and certificates of seisin, belonging to the 17th and 18th centuries. The following is a description of most of those documents which bear an earlier date.—

A Catalogue, or list, of documents, beautifully written, with the following heading :—"The 8th of May 1663; " rec[d] then of the 24 Governors of the Parishe of " Hartland thirtie seaven particulars hereunder written, " as followeth." To these 37, three more are added in a later hand : out of all the items mentioned in it, bonds, leases, and depositions, only five or six seem to have survived.

The only deeds among these surviving documents, with any fair pretensions to antiquity, (one belonging to the reign of Mary excepted), are but three in number, as follow.—A parchment deed, in Latin, bearing date the 30th of October in the 23rd year of Henry VII. [A.D. 1507], clearly written, in good condition, with the parchment thong still appended, but the seal lost. It is a feoffment made by Thomas Knapman, reciting that Thomas Dalyn, of Luttisford, and Robert Rawe, had conveyed, on the 28th of August in the 16th year of King Edward IV., to the said Thomas Knapman, jointly with Philip Besmont, Esquire, John Denys of Orlegh, William Coffyn, Thomas Cutlyff, John Coke the younger, John Leyman, John Clyff, and Thomas Veyle, all now deceased, certain lands and tenements in Yeryche, in the parish of West Putford, in the county of Devon, lands lately held by Isabel Puddyng, in Chepyng Toryton, and a tenement in which Batina, late the wife of Robert Gifford, lately dwelt, with 12 acres and their appurtenances, in Herton, and a tenement near "Her- " ton Mille," which Alice Bagilhole lately held, in the parish of Hertlond. He now gives and demises the same to Laurence Cutlyff, Thomas Docton junior, Laurence Prust of Ilmycote, John Husband, John Veyle, and John Draper; making Hugh Prust and William Blanchard his attorneys to deliver seisin. The witnesses are, Richard Lorymer, Abbot of Hertlond, Louis Pollard, John Prust, Peter Cawode, and others. "Given " at Hertlond," date as above. This deed is chiefly of interest for the names of persons which it contains, Denys, Gifford, Coffyn, and the Abbot. It is endorsed " 12," and is so numbered in the old "Catalogue" previously mentioned.

A lease, on parchment, in Latin, in duplicate ; being the lessee's part and the lessors' counterpart, the two seals of the one, and the one seal of the other, being lost ; whereby the above-named Laurence Cuttelyffe and John Husband, of Gawliche, gentlemen, Feoffees of the lands of the parish church of Stoke St. Nectau the Martyr, of Hartland, in the county of Devon, lease to Richard Chauntrell of Hartland, a tenement called "Cawlehouse," or "Colehouse," in the borough of Harton in the parish aforesaid, for a term of 70 years, at a yearly rent of 2 shillings. Dated the 15th of April, in the 36th year of King Henry VIII. [A.D. 1545]. It is endorsed "15," and is so entered in the old Catalogue previously mentioned.

A parchment deed, indented, in Latin, the two seals lost ; whereby the two Feoffees above-named, in consideration of 40 shillings, give leave to Agnes Bagilbole to rebuild a messuage in the borough of Harton, she paying them a yearly rent of 8 shillings, as also, in their name and behalf, a yearly rent of 9s. 7d. to the chief lord of the premises : remainder, after the decease of, or surrender by, the said Agnes, to William Botteler and Joan, his wife, for their lives, and the life of the longest liver, on the terms before-mentioned. They also appoint Philip Olyver, and William Bagylhole, of Loveland, their attorneys to give seisin and possession. Dated the 3rd of February, in the second year of King Edward VI. [A.D. 1548].

A paper-writing, dated 17th of March 1634 (bearing reference to ship-money, the cause of so many troubles in those times), being a precept of Sir Thomas Drewe, Sheriff of Devon, to the Constables of Hartland, and to William Atkinson, Charles Yeo, and Laurence Deyman, "Collectors by me appoynted for his Majesties " service, for gettinge foorth of shippinge for his Ma- " jesties service." The persons, he states, thereunder named, " doe obstynately and rebelliously refuse to " paye such reasonable sommes of money as hath bene " by me assessed on them for and towards the advance- " ment of his Majesty's service, in gettinge foorth of " shippinge for the better safeguard of his Majesty's " subjects against robbers and pyrates both of sea and " land . . . to the disharringe of his Majesties " lovinge subjectes, and evill example of others who " may thereby take encouragement to adventure the " like rebellious and obstinate refusall." Injunctions are then given to levy the money by distraint on the recusants' goods. Among the nine who have so refused to pay, are named Thomas Cooke, assessed for 3l. 6s. 8d., and John Lapthorne 12 shillings. The surname of

HARTLAND. "Lapthorne," in connexion probably with a member of the same family, will be found mentioned in the further account given of the Portledge documents, in this Report.

In reference to this subject, and the John Lapthorne above-mentioned, the following occurs ;—a diminutive torn letter, sealed, and addressed,—"To my very " cosine Mr. Phillip Elston, at the 6 Clarks Office in " Chancery Lane dd ;" and endorsed in a contemporary hand,—"Mr. Sherriff's discharge of Lapthorne and Fer- " retts ship-mony." It is probably the Sheriff's own writing, and is as follows.—"I woulde have you to for- " beare the levieng of xs. [? xii] upon John Lapthorne, " milner [miller], and six shillinges upon John Ferrett " in Hartland, servante unto Hughe Prist, untill you " receave farther directions from me Tho: Drewe. " This 20th of Marche 1634."

A small paper-writing of the end of Elizabeth's reign ; belonging to the time when the parish provided, not coffins, but shrouds, for the poor, when carried to the grave; headed,—"A note of such shrowdes as weare " delivered." There are eight items, the following three among them.—"Imprimis Riches wife hade iiii " yeardes of creas at xd. per yeard, iiis. iiiid., in threed " id. Prustes daughter had iii yeardes and half of " creas at xd.—iis. xid., in threed id. The oulde man " Ashton had iiii yeardes of creas at xd.—iiis. iiiid., in " threed id." The texture here spoken of is elsewhere written "crease."

A paper, written in a diminutive hand, being an original set of Church Treasurer's Accounts for the year 1638, 9. In the Account itself, the following is the only entry of interest.—"To enquire who was buried in " the church and not paid for. Those that have a " tombestone laid over them are to pay xxs., the rest " viz. viiid., according to an order. Suzan Tooker, " and for putting a stone on her. Thomasine Larimar, " Anne Hardwicke, Nicholas Velly gent., Christopher " Nicholl." On the outside is the following endorse- ment, followed by eleven signatures.—"The second day " of November anno Domini 1639. It is agreed on, " that John Gibbins shall before Christmas next erect " and new build upon the roodloffe in our church, on " both sides of the organs there, so many seates as the " same will conveniently containe ; and the said John " is to have the benefit of the first sitting of the same " for the terme of their lives that shalbe therein re- " spectively placed, and for their only use that shalbe " so placed ; and that the said John shall not no- " minate or place any one in any of the said seates " without the approbation and consent of the 24 gover- " nours of the Parishe church of Hartland or the most " part of them, and each one that shall sit in any of " the said seates, to be erected as aforesaid, is to pay " yearely towardes the reparation of the said Parish " church one penny."

A loose paper, headed,—"The Constable Cookes " accompt for the Militia, for a monthes pay towardes " the payment of the foote souldiers in August 1651." There seems to be no entry of any interest in it.

A loose paper, headed,—"The rate appointed to be " collected for the reparation of the Parish church of " Hartland. Northgather 1634." It gives a list of all the hamlets or districts within the Parish, with all the householders therein, beginning with Abbey Berry, in which Nicholas Luttrell heads the list with xxiis. vid. Blackpoole mill, Martadon, Tichbury, and Blegbery, follow, with some other places. John Lapthorne occurs under Harton Mill, being assessed at ii pence. The divisions for collecting the church moneys, it may be here observed, were styled "Northgather, Westgather," and "Middlegather."

Two loose papers, pinned together, of Churchwardens' Accounts for 1638, 9. Among the items are,—"Paid " Mr. Atkins' man for three wild cats' heads, xiid. " Paid Henry Smeath for a feeches [fitches] head iid. " Paid the doggwhipper vid. Paid Hugh Hollaford for " amending a twest of the vanne [? vane] iiiid. Those " that have a tombestone laid over them are to pay " xxs., the rest vis. viiid., according to an order."

A loose paper, containing an account of John Bond and Richard Hockaday, Churchwardens, from Easter 1639 to Easter 1640; the first item being.—"May 30th. " Laied out at Torrington, at the Officialls Court, being " questioned because perambulations were neglected in " the parishe, in the Rogation weeke, iis. vid." An- other is.—"September 8th. Paid William Shepheard's " wife for meate, drinke, and lodginge, for x Irishe " people, for their supper and breakfast iis. Dec' 19th. " Paid John Hollaford for suitables and neales [nails] for " the poore man's box iiiid. January 6. Paied for ii foxe

" heads iis. January 9. Paid to our xi Irishe people " xiid. March 2. Paied the apparitor for a article " Booke vid. Paid Richard Pearse for xvi^eene gallands " one quarte and one pinte of wine at 12d. ob. the " quarte iiil. viiis. iiid." The various items of wine in this year's Account, (partly tent, at 20d. the quart, and partly inferior wine), amount to the apparently large aggregate, when added together, of 24½ gallons.

Some Churchwardens' miscellaneous Accounts and memoranda, sewed together, belonging to the 13th and 14th years of James the First.

A large mass of loose quires, in perhaps twenty different parts, each containing from 12 to 20 leaves on the average: some in a tattered condition, and some in good preservation. These fragments having been put together by me, and arranged in chronological order, have proved to be portions of what was originally an Account-book of Church expenses, beginning in the year 1597; the original purchase of which, as one of its earliest entries, will be found mentioned in the sequel. The first leaf is detached, and somewhat injured by damp, commencing with the following heading.—"Hart- " land Churche. The Accompte of William Hooper, " William Atkyn of Blegbery, John Seccombe, and " Eychard Yeo, governors of the goodes of the Parish " Churche of Hartland, from the feast of All Sayntes, " in the yeare of our Lorde God one thousand five " hundred nynety and seven untill the same feaste then " nexte followinge, beinge the yeare wherein the said " William Atkyn did the office [of Paymaster], and the " seconde yeare of their office, as followeth."—The book continues down to the year 1706, and contains the yearly accounts of the successive Churchwardens, as well as the Governors. Speaking in general terms, the principal items that occur in it, are minutes of expenditure upon the church bells, which were being repeatedly re-cast or repaired; expenses (at an earlier date) of repairing or renewing the "church armour," consisting of "mus- " quets," pikes, swords, daggers, and corslets; supplies of sacramental wine, which was bought sometimes at hand, and sometimes fetched from Northam, Clovelly, Bideford, or even Launceston ; expenditure for stone or lead, the latter of which was brought from Bristol, and landed either at Northam, or "Clovelley Key ;" expendi- ture for the repeated renewals of the "shindles," or wooden tiles, for the roof of the church, purchases of which were made, some thousands at a time, and a " shindle-house" was appropriated for their storage; and rewards given for the killing of wild-cats, foxes, grays, and fitches. The volume is nearly perfect, there being but few interruptions from the loss of leaves; and its entries amount to several thousands in number : the following are some few extracts from them.—

In the Account for 1597, 8.—"Item, paid for a booke " sent from the Archdeacon, when her Majesties fleete " went to the see iiid. Paid to George Husbande for " three bullett bagges for the three churche musquettes " xiid. Geven to a poore man that had a licence under " the Greate Seale to begg vid. Paid for lace to fasten " the lyninge of the morians belonging to the churche " corslettes, and for priming yrons for the chirche " musquettes iid. Paid to George Pruste for carrieinge " of one of the churche musquettes to Torrington, att " the trayninge, and home again vid. Paid to Roger " Syncombe for mendinge the head of one of the churche " pikes id. Paid [at the Archdeacon's Visitation] for " Peter's farthinges [sometimes written 'farthing' only] " and somner's fee xxd. Paid for a hilt and handle, " and a scabert for a sworde, and for mendinge a dagger " of the church iis. Paid for respite untill Christmas " to make a Register booke in parchment, of those that " are borne, weded [sic], and buried, in this parish iiiid. " Given at Torrington to the souldiers impreste for " Ireland, for their dynner xiid. Paid att Exon for a " corslett furnished, and iii musquettes furnished, " haveinge one dagger [fixed probably, for use as a " bayonet], and for a pike vil. xiiis. Paid for this " accompte booke, boughte att Exon by John Abbatt " and by hym brought home for nothinge iiis. Paid for " a girdle and hanginges for one of the churche armors, " xiid." In the Account for 1598, 9.—"Paied for two " ' Quorum nomina ' iiis. [repeatedly entered afterwards " as ' Coram nomina '] iiiis. Paid for a xi yeardes and a " quarter of dowlesse, at xiiiid. the yeard, to make a " paire of surplex xiiis. id. Paid to John Frier for " keepinge the dogges out of the churche this yeare iis. " Paid the xth of November 1598 for the carriage of " iii men's armor at Torrington, when the souldiers " went into Ireland xiid. Paid for the amendinge of " one of the churche calivers, with a morian, flaske, and " toch box [touch box] and other furniture for the same

RYLAND. " xs. viid."—The " church armor " was carried at this
time to Woolfardisworthie and to Buckland Brewer,
" att the trayning."—" Paid more for the carriage of
" gunpowder, matche, and some parte of the armor
" from Hartland to South Tavistocke, when the soul-
" diers went firste to Plymmouthe iis. vid. Paid att
" Plymmouthe for two swordes for the pyoners id.
" Paid for a blacke bill for the pyoners iis. iiid. Paid
" for a passporte for those that brought home the
" horses from Southe Tavistock, which the souldiers did
" ride, when they went firste to Plymmouth xiid. Paid
" for singinge bookes for the churche, viz., the Psames
" and other godlie bookes in fower and five partes vis."
Account for 1599, 1600,—" Paid to Robert Winter for
" keeping the church yeat [gate] vid. Paid for two
" yeardes of inkle [small tape] id. Paid for a lock to put
" on the post nagg id. [sic in MS., not ' bagg,' mean-
" ing, probably, the post horse]." Account for 1600, 1,
—" Received for two souldiers coates, a olde surplus,
" and a raquett, of the churche goodes, which were
" solde vis. viiid. Paid to Richard Yeo for strappes for
" the Booke of Comon Prayer id. Paid for a booke con-
" taining the Queenes Injunctions, for the parishe vid.
" Paid to her Majesty's Purveior for this parishe xvis.
" vid. Paid for two calivers for the parish, for Ireland
" service xiis."—When the soldiers sett out on this
occasion, it would seem that it was from Barnstaple.—
" Paid to the same Phillipe [Maye] for takeinge out of the
" base of the crosse iis. ;"—a rooting up of the churchyard cross, in all probability, is meant. Account for
1601, 2,—" Geven towards the reedifyinge of a towne
" consumed with fire iiis. iiiid. Paid for a fox head to
" Mr. Coffin's huntsman xiid. Paid to the cutler for a
" chape for a sworde, makenge cleane of the same, and
" mendinge of a flaake viiid. Geven to Mr. Haswill,
" the preacher, for preachinge two tymes in our
" churche vs."—" Peter's farthings " are again paid,
at the Archdeacon's Visitation.—" Given towards the
" relief of Richard Grafton, decaied in her Majesty's
" service vs. Paid for an arminge sword vis. Paid to
" Alice Deyman and Richard Waldon, in goeinge to
" Exon to geve evidence against Radegon Yeo, being
" arraigned for murdering of her childe, at the last
" Assises, towards their expences vis. viiid." From
entries about this time, it would seem to have been
much the custom for poor persons to leave a sheep to
the church, by will. Account for 1602, 3,—" Paid for a
" glassinge bottle [merely meaning, a glass bottle] to
" carry wyne in viiid. Paid for a sandglasse xviiid.
" Paid to William Maye for setting of a litle borde
" by the chauncell dore for the sandglasse to stand on
" iid. Paid to Hugh the Glasier for glasses for the little
" squinches of the tower xd. Paid for the travell and
" expences of Richard Ellacott in comminge to viewe
" one of the church windowes, beinge ruinous viiid."
Account for 1603, 4,—" Paid for the bringing of a letter
" for the collection towards the reliefe of Geneva vid.
" Geven towards the collection for Geneva xiis." Foxes'
heads are very frequently brought in at this time : and
notices of the " church armor " become of less frequent
occurrence.—" Paid to Peter Blagdon by the consent of
" the Churchwardens, for the seatinge of the churche
" xl. xvs. vid. It is agreed by Mr. Abbatt and the reste
" of the xxiiii¹¹ present at this accompt, that the said
" Peter Blagdon shall repay the said xl. xvs. vid. about
" Shrovetide next, or before, if there be occasiou for
" the use of it to be imploied for the church ; and the
" same so required by Mr. Abbatt and Mr. Docton : "—
a singular arrangement, and one hardly advantageous,
it would seem, to Peter Blagdon ; a doubt probably
existed as to the legality of the payment. Account for
1604, 5, " Paid to Richard Yeo for shrowdes for
" those who died at Forswill and others, as it appeareth
" by his bill shewed att this accompt xxviis. iid. Paid
" for a booke of Constitutions and Cannons Ecclesiasti-
" call xvd. Paid for a bottle of glasse xviiid. Paid
" for a tyninge bottle [bottle made of tin] ' xvid.
" For a standing pot of tynne to put wyne in, att
" the tyme of the Communion vis." Account for
1605, 6,—" Paid to William Maye for amending the
" billowes [bellows] and certaine pipes of the organs
" xiid. Geven to Mr. Maye's sonnes for their attend-
" ance in singing in the church xiid. Paid to Steven
" Beare for comminge for the money collected for the
" decaied churches and chapples vid,"—in the North of
England, as we learn from the next account, vis. viiid.
being the sum there named as being collected on two
occasions. Account for 1606, 7,—" Paid for 7 yeardes
" and a half of dowlas to make the clarkes sur-
" plus, at 15d. the yard, xs. iiii½d. Geven towards
" the reedifying of Collompton xvd. Geven to-

wards the building of the steeple of St. Sidwill's HARTLAND.
" neere Exon iiis. iiiid. Geven to the ringers on the
" 5th of August ixs. Paid to Nicholas Cholwill for a
" graies head xiid." In the Account for 1607, 8, occurs
this item, for the first time,—" Paid to the ringers the
" vth of November 1608, vs. ; " also,—" Paid to the
" ringers the 24th of March, viis." [the day on which
King James succeeded to the English Crown.] " Paid for
" the expences of the wardens and questmen, att the
" Bishopes Visitation, viis. iiiid. Geven to the singing
" boyes xiid. Paid for the diall on the church wall
" iiis." Account for 1608, 9,—" Paid for the Com-
" munion table xs. Paid for the carriage thereof from
" Clovelly xiid. Paid for a matt for Mr. Dove to kneel
" on iiid."—Mr. Dove, it may be remarked, was the
amanuensis and accomptant of the parish, and it is in
his handwriting, there is every reason for concluding,
that the present entries are made. — Account for
1609, 10.—" Geven to two poore men, being some tyme
" taken captives by the Turkes, and their toyngues
" cut out viiis. Paid for a new pulpite xxxiiis. iiid.
" For bringing the same pulpit from Bediford xvd.
" For a booke of Bishop Jewell's works, to remayne
" in the church by commandment xxxs. To Henry
" Keyne for bringing the same booke from Exon iiiid.
" Paid for our [the Churchwardens'] passage over the
" water, when we fetcht wyne iiiid.,"—from Northam,
probably. Account for 1612, 3,—" Paid at another
" tyme for expences at Torrington, about the Princes
" [? Charles, Prince of Wales] side money vs." Account
for 1613, 4,—" Receaved of Mr. Docton as a guift
" towards the setting up of the King's armes and Sen-
" tences on the walles in the church iiis. iiiid. Receaved
" from John Blagdon as a guift from the youth of this
" parish towards the casting of the bells iiid. viis. Paid
" to Alse [Alice] Popham for drinke, when the three
" bells were let downe [for recasting] iiid. Paid for
" canvas of Cane [Caen] and silke and thred to make a
" pulpit cloth and cushion xxiid. Paid to Skitch for a
" chaine to tye the booke of Erasmus iiiid. Paid to
" William Meye for worke about the place for the ten
" Commandments to stand iiiid. . Paid to John Lang
" for making the Minister's seate xxxs. Paid to John
" Coleman to hoise out the bells at Barnestable Keye
" iis. When Thomas Cholwill and myself were to
" Barnestaple 3 daies to see the bells cast vis. To
" Philip Nicholl for carrying the bells to Northam
" from Barnestaple in a boate, viis. vid. To Peter
" Peard for a mat to lie in Mr. Dove's seate viiid. To
" Humfrey Skitch for 2 paire of gims [hinges] for Mr.
" Dove's seate xiid. For the Paraphrase of Erasmus xiiis.
" Paid to Tristram Prust for 12 gallons and a quart of
" Canary wine against Easter, at 9[d.] per quart
" 1l. 16s. 9d." Account for 1614, 5,—" Paid to Henry
" Ratcleiffe, for carrying of a lettre to Exon about the
" seate busines iis. Paid to Martyn Snowe for his paines
" in blowing the organ this yeare iis. Paid to Philip
" Can, dogwhipper, for his wages this yeare iis. Paid
" for two Spanish pikes, with their heads xxs. Paid
" to Lawrence Deyman, for his register's fee for
" the recording the order for the seates xs. Paid for
" one pottell of wine against Trinity Sonday xviiid.
" Paid for my expenses at Torrington, when I paid the
" money that was collected for the building of a church
" in the Palsgraves countrey viiid. Geven to a poore
" man, having a breef, by the consent of Mr. Nicholas
" Luttrell iiiis. Paid young Assheton, of Welcombe, for
" killing 4 foxes iiiis." The " Peter's Farthing " still
" appears each yeare, 3s., or 3s. 6d., in amount. Account for
1615, 6 ;—payments of 2 pence for a " fitchewe's head,"
now frequently occur.—" Paid for the lent of a zaw
" to zaw the [gate] postes vid. Paid for a scabbard to
" the church sword xiid." Account for 1617, 8,—" Paid
" a Gloster man who had his house burnt, he having a
" breife to gather the countrey xviiid." Account for
1619, 20,—" Paid towards the following of abusives con-
" cerning the church xxs. For two pints of wine for a
" private Communion iiiid. Paid Mr. Sparke for his
" paines here for two sermons, by the direction of the
" 24tie xs. Paid Mr. Greenwood for his paines for
" two sermons xs. Paid Mr. Badcock for his paines
" for preaching xxs. Paid Mr. Sherwood for his preach-
" ing here the 16th of September xvis. viiid." In
the account for 1622, 3, a charge of 12 pence is made
for one quart of wine " against a wedding ; " on
" which occasions, indeed, the Sacrament seems to
have been usually administered. — " Paid Mr. Isack
" for his paines in preaching here in Mr. Chapman's
" absence xs. Paid John Pearse for ten dozen of rookes
" heads xxd. Gave to Mr. Tobey Sherwood, for two
" sermons vis. Gave to an Irishman that had a

4 C 3

" passe from the Councell. Gave to two other Irish
" gentlewomen that travelled by passe viiid. Paid
" Mr. Ballard for a sermon vs. Paid Mr. Browne's
" expenses when he preacht here iis." Account for
1624, 5,—" Gave to two souldiers, being prest to goe
" in the King's shipps vis. Paid Anderton for two
" Yeo for an houre glasse xd. Paid Justinian
" Yeo for an houre glasse xd. Paid William Maye for
" setting up of the King's name on the pulpit, and for
" mending the north church doore iis. vid. Paid for
" a Service-book to be read Wednesday xiid. Paid
" for the fetching of Sibbelley Briant's seate, when she
" stood excommunicated iis. vid." Account for 1626, 7,
—" Gave to two poore women, prisoners in Turkey
" iiid. Gave to Simon Quance and his partners, that fol-
" lowed and killed a madd mastiff dog xiid." It is perhaps
somewhat remarkable that there are no items for ringing
bells in this account, or the preceding one. Account
for 1628, 9,—" Paid for a Prayer booke for the Fleete
" iiid. Paid to 9 Irish people, with the consent of the
" Constable Prust xiid." Account for 1630, 1,—" Paid
" the ringers at the birth of the young Earle of Bathe
" iis."—probably a son of Edward Bourchier, the then
Earl of Bath ; if so, he must have died before the Earl,
whose title went to his cousin, Henry, in 1636.—" Paid
" Abraham Bond for a post to set the houre glasse on
" xd. Gave to one Robert Burton, a poore scholler, at
" the request of Mr. Churton iis. Paid William Roch
" and his wife and 3 children, which had a passe to
" gather as they were travelling homeward iiid."
Account for 1631, 2,—" Received of Hugh Mitchell, of
" Loveland, for a seate for his sonne William to sit in
" during his father's life, with George Prust, of Luttis-
" ford 2s. Of Mr. Thomas Velley, for a seate for him
" to sit in, either in the former seate behinde the organs,
" or the next seate behinde it 2s. Of Thomas Dallin
" the younger and Thomas Rowe for the seate under
" the roodloffe to sit in respectively, during the lives
" of their fathers, 2s. a peice. Received of John Crang
" to sit with Charles Prust, and to leave the seate he
" now sits in 6d. Paid for an houre glasse 1s. 4d. For
" cariage of the same from Barn[staple] 2d. Paid for
" 9 yards of holland at 10 grostes the yard, to make
" supplesses 1l. 10s. Paid Anderton for a Fraier for
" the Quepne 3d." At this period many items occur
for the relief of " Irish people." Account for 1632, 3,
—" Paid for the Act against cursing and swearing 6d."
4s. 6d. is charged " for diett then," and 6d. " for hors-
" meate," when the Act was sent for, probably to Barnstaple ; about this period the payment of fees for ringing
the bells on certain days, appears to have been discontinued. Account for 1634, 5,—" Paid John Loosemore
" for setting upp 6 Sentences in the church, and on the
" porches, and for playing the organs 1l. Paid John
" Loosemore for a diall for the church 12s. Paid for a
" booke to be read, touching the Gunpowder Treason
" 10d. Paid hym (Richard Deyman) more, which he
" had given to a minister's wife, which had a passe 1s."
Account for 1636, 7,—" Paid for making the clarke's
" surplesse 1s. 2d. Gave to two poore men, the one of
" them having his hand and leg out off, 2s." In the
next year there are several receipts of 5s. from men,
for seats for their wives; for example,—" Received of
" Henry Bagilboll, for his wife to sit in the new seate
" in the south middle rowe, 5s."—" Gave towards the
" redeeming of a captive in Genowaye [?] 1s. 9½d.
" Paid Mr. Incledon [not the regular organist] his
" paines to play the organs 14s. Paid the kitching boy
" to the Abbey, for a graves head, 4d. Gave Mr. Lever-
" land to preach the 7th of October 5s. Paid John
" Couch for a toyte [haassock] for Mr. Churton to kneele
" upon 3d." Some leaves of the book are probably
wanting here, but the original Accounts for 1638–
1640 still exist among these papers, and have been previously noticed. Account for 1640, 1,—" Paid for two
" bookes for the Fast 2s. Paid for a praier for the King
" 6d. Gave to a man who had a collection under the
" Lord Bishop of Exon's hand 2s. 6d." Payments to
the "dogwhipper" come to an end for a time about
the year 1645. Account for 1646, 7,—" Paid for iron
" stuffe about the minister's pue 3s. 4d." Account for
1647, 8,—" Paid for a tit [hassock] for the minister 2d.
" Paid Charles Deyman for preserving of the chalice
" from the troopers 13s. 4d." Account for 1648, 9,—
" Paid William Noy for keeping the dogs out of church,
" 3s. Gave Mr. Scampe for a sermon 6s. 6d." (The
Scampes, it may be observed, were an Ilfracombe family).
—Though it is now the time of the Commonwealth, the
administration of the Sacrament seems to have gone
on as before, in this remote parish. Account for
1649, 50,—" Paid Richard Pearse for wine for a Com-

" munion, the 9th of September, being for 8 quartes
" of Mallago sacke, at 16d. the quarte." Tent wine
is also used. Many Irish people are relieved this
year. Account for 1650, 1,—" Paid for taking down
" the organs 4s." For 1651, 2,—" Spent on the ringers
" when the day of Thanksgiving was 5s." For 1652, 3,—
" Allowed for my paines to ride at Justice Fortescues
" for a warrant to receive in the church rates 1s." In
1653 it is not the Account of the "Governors of the
" goods" of the church, or of the Churchwardens, that
is entered, but "Hartland church. The Accompt of the
" foresaid Anthony Hamlyn of such mony as he hath
" received and paid from the first of November 1653
" untill Easter then next following." Account for
1654, 5,—" Gave Mr. Braddon for two sermons 6s."
Heads of fitchews, foxes, wildcats, and "graies," are
still paid for, on a very large scale. From the Account
for 1655, 6, it appears that Churchwardens were then
again chosen, and gave in their accounts. William
Noy, the dogwhipper, still receives his "fee," of 4 shillings; the next item being,—" Paid William Powell
" for carrying the mony to Mr. Champneys for the
" inhabitants of the valley of Lucerne 2s. 6d." Account
for 1659, 60,— "Paid William Bishop to ride to
" Pourtledge, and for his horse to ride there, to buy
" timber for the church 1s. Paid George Prust for 12
" hedgebores heads 1s." Account for 1660, 1,—" Paid
" the painter for painting the King's armes 2l. ; " somewhat singularly, in the preceding account, the only
charge for ringing the bells is for ringing on the 5th of
November ; the Restoration, to all appearance, was not
then welcomed with a peal.—"Paid Mr. Rogers for
" quartering of four travellers which required [it of]
" us, by the King's orders 8s. 6d."
There is an hiatus in these fragments, from 1663 to
1668. In the account for 1668, 9, William Noy is paid
4 shillings "for doing his office":—" disbursed to the
" foxcatcher in the behalfe of the parishe 9s. 9½d. Paid
" the ringers the 29th of May /68 2s. Paid John Lut-
" trell, gent, for two fox heads 4s." Account for 1669–
70,—" Gave to 4 travellers, to aide them in their way to
" Penzance 1s." For 1670, 1,—" To Master Anthony
" Coffin, for 30 fich heads 2s. 6d. Gave to a woman that
" had a passe, and came from Lundon to goe to Bod-
" mant [Bodmin] 6d. Gave to 12 that came from
" Ireland with a passe, theare houses and goods all
" burnt 1s. For writing to [sic] duplicates of the
" brife to redeeme the Christians out of Turkey 3s."
For 1671, 2,—" Received of Thomas Prust, of Natcot,
" Gent, for that part of the seate that was Blagdon's, in
" which hee now sits, 3s. 4d. Received of Master
" William Lambe for that that did beelonge to Blagdon
" for the swimming [women] ; but hee is not to place in a
" teuet [haasock], but Mistresse Emme Canne is to sit
" theare till hee come to bee an inhabitant 3s. 4d." For
1672, 3,—" Paid to eleven semen 3s. Paid to fower
" semen and his wife [sic] 3s. Master Anthony Coffin
" for 27 fich heds 2s. 3d." For 1675, 6—" Paid to
" Ozias Couch, for doeing out of William Noys office [as
" dog-whipper] 1s." At this point there is another
hiatus, the next Account being that for a part of 1678,
9 ;—" Ozias Couch [who has now succeeded Noy] for
" sweeping the church and whipping the doggs halfe
" yeare 4s." For 1679–80,—" Received of William
" Prust, of Harton, for a seate for his wife, being the
" seacond seate in the souther middle roome above the
" south churche doore 3s." The word "roome," as
meaning a pew, is suggestive. For 1680, 1—" Paid
" William Orchard, minister, for arrears in the yeare
" 1679, for offices don for the parish, according to the
" order of the Honorable Governors of Sutton's Hos-
" pitall [the Charterhouse] 7l. 10s." For 1682, 3,—
" Paid Thomas Simons for a box to kepe the parishe
" accomptes 3s. Paid Edmond Cowle for breaking of
" his ground, and useing of his goods when the bels
" were cast 10s. Paid the bell-founder for castinge of
" the bells 28l." For 1683, 4,—" Received of Richard
" Ellis wife for the second seat in the south middle
" roome 3s. 4d. Received for a heriott upon the death
" of William Luttrell, Gent, for West Staddon 2l. Paid
" for the King's Declaration 6d. Paid for a booke for
" the parson 6d." For 1684, 5,—" Paid for a booke for
" Master Orchard 2s. Paid the ringers the 9th of
" September 6s. Paid eight seamen that had a pas to
" travell to Pensance 1s. Paid to tenn seamen that
" had a pass to travell to Fsmoth 1s. Paid the ringers
" the 19th day of February 7s. Paid the ringers
" the 23rd of Aprill 12s." For 1686, 7,—" Paid for
" beere when the bels were drawne up into the tower
" 3s. 2d." For 1687, 8—" Paid the ringers the 30th of
" January and the 6th of February, 6s."—The bells in

HARTLAND. this year must have been tolled in remembrance of the death of Charles the First on the 30th of January, and rvng for the accession of James the Second on the 6th of February.—For 1688, 9—"Paid the ringers att the " news of the birth of the Prince 4s." [afterwards known in history as the First Pretender]. " Paid the ringers " the fowerth of July for the deliverance of the Bishops " 10s. Paid the ringers the fourteenth of February, " being a day of Thanksgiving 12s. Paid the ringers " upon the news of King William 2s. Paid the ringers " Cronation day 11s." For 1689–90,—" For a new " maund [probably a basket] for the church 7d. Paid " the ringers att the news of the birth of the Prince " 5s. :"—it is singular that this latter item should have been divided between two years; or, possibly, allusion may be made to the birth of one of the children of the Princess Anne. For 1690, 1,—"Paid William Grow- " den which had a pas to travell for the redemtion " of his father in Turkey 3s. Paid to fower seamen " which were taken by the French, and retaken by " the Dutch 3s. Paid to a traveller that had a pas for " a towne in Lincolnshire, which was drowned by " water 3s. Paid the ringers at the returne of the King " 6s." For 1691, 2—"Paid the ringers att the news of " the reduceing of Ireland 8s. Paid the ringers att the " news of the taking of Gallaway [Galway] 4s. Paid " for a booke of the Fast 6d." For 1692, 3—"Paid " the ringers att the overthrow of the French fleet " 10s." For 1693, 4—"Paid Zios (for Ozias) Couch for " sweeping the church, and whipping the dogs 10s." " Paid three men, one carryed a horseback, which " [with] a pas 1s. 6d. Paid the ringers att the news of " the King's return from Flanders 5s." A similar item to this last occurs in the next year's Accounts. At this period, seamen and travellers are being continually relieved by the Churchwardens, sometimes in companies of ten or fifteen at a time. For 1695, 6—" To Thomas " Shutt for two foxes heads 4s. To Richard Harris for " two old foxes heads 10s."—Fitches' heads are now but seldom paid for; but " old foxes " seem to have been largely caught.—" Paid the ringers att the news of " the victory in Flanders 5s. Paid the ringers att the " news of the last victory, att sea 8s." For 1696, 7— " Paid Edmond Woodley for sweeping the church and " whipping the dogs 10s. Paid a man that redeemed " his father from Turkey 5s. Paid one maimed souldier " 1s. Paid the ringers att the news of the comming " home of the King from Flanders 6s." For 1697, 8— " Spent upon Bideford men for singing 6s. Paid the " ringers att the news of the Peace 10s. Paid to " seaven and twenty souldiers that had a pas 2s. 6d." The whole of the Account for 1699, 1700 is wanting. For 1701, 2,—"Paid the ringers when Queen Anne " was crownd 8s." For 1702, 3—"Paid the ringers " at the taking of Vigo 8s." The last in these Ac- counts is for the year 1705, 6; Edmond Woodley is still paid 10 shillings " for his services,"—sweeping the church, and whipping the dogs, most probably, as before stated; a few payments are made for " fitchew's heads," and one traveller only is relieved, but with the com- paratively large sum of 2 shillings. Down to the close of the 17th century, the women had seats, in Hartland .Church, it is evident from these entries, apart from those occupied by the other sex.

Among these papers there is a printed proclamation of King Charles the Second, dated the 10th of August in the 22nd year of his reign, A.D. 1670, for the collec- tion of moneys for redeeming Christian captives in Turkey; in a mutilated condition, accompanied by two folio leaves of paper writing, with this heading,—"Hart- " land, February the 8th 1670 (1). Duplicate of wat " hath bin collected, with theare names, for the redeem- " ing of the poore Cristians out of Turkey." This list, not improbably, included every householder in Hartland at that day; the subscriptions varying from 5 shillings to 2 pence. It is headed with the name of " Thomas " Docton, gen.," who gives 5 shillings, " Mistress " Briget Docton " giving one shilling, " Houmphry " Coffin, gen.," and " Fraunces Coffin, gen.," each con- tribute 6 pence; a like sum being subscribed by " Thomas " Coffin, gen." "Thomas Prust, gen. and his family " contribute 8 shillings; Peter Lapthorne, the miller, of Colehouse, or Colehey, subscribes 2 pence. The sum total gathered may be learned from the receipt, en- closed with the paper,—" Feb : 8th 1671 (1). Received " the sum of nine pounds eight shillings of Richard' " Yeo [at first written ' Yawe'] which was gathered " in Hartland for the redemption of the poore cap- " tives in Turkish slavery. I say received by me Rob : " Simpson D. R."

HENRY THOMAS RILEY.

THE MANUSCRIPTS OF THE TOWNS OF WEYMOUTH AND MELCOMBE REGIS.

[In the possession of the Corporation.]

The Corporation of this borough is still in possession of some of the ancient Charters that were granted by the Sovereigns of England to the town of Melcombe Regis, and some only; any that may have been granted to the town of Weymouth, are either missing, or are no longer in existence. The following is a brief account of the more ancient of the documents and records now remaining in the Corporation's hands.—

A parchment deed (in Latin), imperfect, and decayed, almost to shreds, dated in July 1252; whereby William de Taunton, Prior of the Church of St. Swithun, at Win- chester, and the Convent, grant that their port of Weymouth shall be a free port for ever; and that every one shall be at liberty to moor there, and dispose of his merchandize, paying to them the customs due for the same. The then limits of the borough are given, within which those enjoying the privileges of freemen must reside. Among localities of ancient Weymouth, there are named herein, the "Hope Hus" (Hope House, " Hope" is a place still known in the locality), the Cross, and a well called " The Tunn."

An Inspeximus Charter of King Edward the Second, granted to the town of Melcombe Regis, dated the 22nd of January, in the 11th year of his reign (A.D. 1318). The Charter (in Latin), which is in a somewhat mutilated condition, confirms the one that had been granted by King Edward the First, his father, in the 8th year of his reign [A.D. 1280]; whereby he had conceded to the burgesses of Melcombe all rights which the citizens of London had; and further, the present Charter grants to the burgesses several pieces of vacant land, situate in St. Thomas's Street, St. Mary's Street, and St. Edmund's Street,—all which streets still exist. " Bakerestrete," there mentioned, is now no longer known. The original silk cords, and a fragment of the Great Seal, are still appended to the deed.

A Charter of Inspeximus and Confirmation of the pre- ceding Charter, by King Edward the Third, dated at New Sarum, the 3rd of November, in the second year of his reign [A.D. 1328]; much mutilated, and with only a fragment of the Great Seal left. There is also a duplicate copy of this Charter, in an equally bad condi- tion, the seal entirely gone.

Exemplification, in Latin, made, at the instance of the burgesses of Weymouth, on the 10th of February in the 41st year of Edward the Third [A.D. 1367], of a finding (upon inquisition, at Shirbourne, in the 8th year of Edward the First, before the Justiciars, John de Reygate and others : upon which Inquisition it was found, that the Earl of Gloucester and Hertford claimed certain rights in Wyk, Portland, Weymouth, and Helle- well; the successive holders of such rights having been the Prior of St. Swithun, Almaric [de Valence] Bishop Elect of Winchester, Earl Richard [de Clare], and the (then) present Earl. The seal, which was appended by a thong of parchment, is lost.

A small Charter, in Latin, bearing date the 27th of November, in the 5th year of Henry the Seventh [A.D. 1489], confirming certain measures that had been taken in the reign of Henry the Sixth for lightening the burdens of the town of Melcombe, it having then been recently ravaged by " our adversaries of France and " Normandy." The burgesses are to hold from hence- forth of the Crown at a fee farm rent of 20s. only, for all tenths and fifteenths. This document is in good preser- vation, and part of the seal, on a strip of parchment, is left.

A Charter, bearing date the 10th of November, in the 4th year of Henry the Eighth [A.D. 1512], confirming the one last-mentioned. It is in good condition, but the seal is lost.

An Exemplification, bearing date the 1st of June, in the 13th year of Elizabeth [A.D. 1571] under the Great Seal, of the Act of Parliament for the union of the two Boroughs and Corporations of Weymouth and Melcombe Regis. The document is in good preservation, but the seal is lost.

A Charter, dated the 3rd of July in the 24th year of Elizabeth [A.D. 1582], explanatory of the Mayor's duties in the government of the united Boroughs of Weymouth and Melcombe Regis. A fragment of the Great Seal is left. These are followed by several other Charters, of a later date, belonging to the reigns of Elizabeth, Charles the First, and William and Mary.

In addition to the above Charters, the only other old records now in the Corporation's possession, seem to be two large folio paper volumes, bound in parchment,

4 C 4

The first volume contains about 400 leaves, and its pages are little more than half filled. The first 76 pages contain miscellaneous matter connected with the union of Weymouth and Melcombe Regis, in 1571, and the Oaths of the Officials of the Corporation; after which the volume becomes a Register of proceedings in the Law Courts of the town. The first Court mentioned in the book belongs to the year 1616, and it is thus headed: —" Curia Legalis et Visus Franci plegii, una cum Curia " de Melcombe Regis, infra burgum et villam . . . " ultimo die Septembris, anno Domini 1616." These entries end with the year 1681. At the end of the volume there are a number of leaves, with entries of the Sessions of the peace in the 6th and 7th years of Charles the First, now loose, but originally forming part of the contents of the volume. At the time of the great Rebellion, the last Court named as held under the reign of that King, is headed : —" Villa de Weymouth et Melcombe.—Curia Legalis, cum Visu Franci Plegii, pro " Waymouth, ibidem die Lunæ, nono die Octobris, " anno regni Domini nostri Caroli, Dei gratia, An- " gliæ, Scotiæ, Franciæ, et Hiberniæ, Regis, Fidei " Defensoris, vicesimo quarto, 1648 ;" thus loyally acknowledging his title, while in the hands of his enemies, and within four months of his (so-called) trial and death. The first Court after that date is entered under this title :—" The Court Leete and Law day, with view of " Frankpledge, together with the Court of Melcombe " Regis, within the Borough and Town of Weymouth " and Melcombe Regis, in the County of Dorset, then " held the third day of October, in the yeare of our " Lord 1649." Like the one next described, this volume in some places is decayed and tattered through damp; standing much in need of the repair which, I am glad to learn, while writing these lines, it will shortly receive.

The next is a volume of similar size and appearance; being an Assembly Book, at the Guildhall, of the Mayor, Aldermen, Bailiffs, and capital and principal burgesses, for the Borough and Town of Weymouth and Melcombe Regis; the first entry being of a Court holden on the 9th day of October 1617. At page 26 a list of enrolments of apprenticeship begins, the earliest entry going so far back (copied probably from a preceding volume, now lost,) as 1614. These lists of apprenticeships are continued to the year 1641. A list is also given of the tenants in burgage in 1616. On the Weymouth side, the names of the tenants only are stated, with the amounts due; but in Melcombe, the property then held by each person, arranged according to the streets, is described. Between the years 1645 and 1648 many entries that would have been appropriately made in this volume, are made in the one, for those years, which now forms part of Mr. Sherren's Collection, and from which large extracts will be found in the present Report. The Assembly Book now under notice, ends, at p. 426, with " Minutes of a " Hall," holden on the 10th of April 1695.

I have here to acknowledge, with thanks, the good offices rendered me in many ways, during my prolonged examination of these records, in combination with Mr. Sherren's Collection, by T. B. Groves, Esqre, one of the members of the Common Council of the Borough of Weymouth and Melcombe Regis; owing to whose suggestion (arising from the laudable interest which he takes in the past history of his native town) it is, primarily, that this inspection has been made.

HENRY THOMAS RILEY.

THE MANUSCRIPTS OF THE TOWNS OF WEYMOUTH AND MELCOMBE REGIS.

[Mr. Sherren's Collection.]

With the exception of some early Charters of Melcombe Regis, two or three other documents, and two Minute-books of the 17th century, which are elsewhere described in the present Report, it is most probable that all such of the ancient records of Weymouth and Melcombe Regis as are now in existence, have come into the possession of Mr. James Sherren, of St. Mary's Street, Weymouth; who received permission to remove them, many years ago, as I learn from him, from a stable in which they were then deposited as so much rubbish; and so had the good fortune to rescue them from the housemaid and fire-grate, to whose tender mercies a considerable portion of them had been already consigned. Notwithstanding the extensive havoc that, no doubt, had been already made among them, partly by such agency, and partly by decay, the papers and documents in Mr. Sherren's Collection are some hundreds in

number. The whole having been placed in my hands by Mr. Sherren, most obligingly, for the purpose of a thorough and searching examination, I have selected the following, as being either the most ancient documents, or the most worthy of notice.—

A set of enrolments, on long sheets of parchment, eight in number, of proceedings in the Law Court of the borough of Melcombe Regis, in the 20th and 21st years of the reign of Richard the Second (A.D. 1396–98). Some of the entries in these enrolments (which are all in Latin) throw light upon the manners and usages of the time; and as they are the earliest documents in existence (the Charters excepted) that bear reference to the remote history of the place, I have thought it advisable to quote rather largely from them. Persons, both men and women, are repeatedly fined for brewing " contrary to the assize, for selling ale in cups (in ciphis), " or in vessels without the seal (signo), or for tapping " (tappare) without due supervision." The Bailiffs of the town (Melcombe Regis) are amerced at the first Court, the records of which are preserved, (Monday after the Feast of St. Michael 1396), for not having brought into Court a sword that had been drawn " against the King's " peace;" as also, a " baselard," (a short sword, worn by civilians), that had been drawn by one William Corfe. William Helier [the Tiler] appears at the first Court, and pays 6 pence for Richard London, who had drawn a " daggar," against the peace. This Court ends with the following entry, (tr.) :—" Twelve free men, being sworn, " whose names appear on the schedule sewed hereto, " present that Philip Bat has a step put upon the high- " way near to the door of his tenement, to the nuisance " of those passing by; therefore he is amerced. John " Shudde uses a quart measure that is unfair [minus " justa]; therefore he is amerced." At the next Court, on Tuesday after the Feast of St. Martin the Bishop (11 November), in the 20th year of the same King (1396), the Bailiffs present that John Swan drew blood with his hand from Thomas Deigher [Dyer], against the peace; therefore he is amerced. The accused who fail to appear, are " attached," by their goods, such as horses, cows, or swine, being seized. Thomas Vicory and Emma, his wife, are amerced for not prosecuting their suit against Edith atte See, in a plea of debt. Mention is made in this Court of certain " burgages," (houses or lands held by burgage tenure), that had been first named in the Law Court of " Hokke Term," in the 19th year of the same reign, which now remain in the hands of the King, through default of heirs, and for rent (payable to the King) that had been in arrear thereon. At the next Court, Tuesday after Epiphany, in the 20th year [1397] John Shudde, (whose name frequently appears, as getting into trouble,) is complained of for " breaking the arrest " of one cask of ale, which had been arrested by the Under-bailiffs; " for they had tasted it [tastavere], supposing (rightly) " that the said ale was bad, not good and sound for the " body of man." Richard Moryssh makes plaint against Thomas Walyssh in a plea of trespass; " which Thomas " is a burgess; therefore, according to the custom of the " vill, he remains unattached, until he shall have made " default (in appearing) three times." At the Court holden on Tuesday after St. Matthias [24th February] in the 20th year [1397], Thomas Sterer [? Steersman, or Pilot] is "amerced for drawing, against the peace, a " staff upon Agnes Cappers, his pledge (or surety) being " Hugh Deer." The Bailiffs also present that they " arrested " two trees lying felled in the tenement of William Fyssher, for his rent [burgage-rent], which had been in arrear ten years or more; " which trees Henry " Harbour had carried away from thence, with their " leave; and he (Fyssher) had found as his mainpernors " [or sureties] John Northover and Eustace Kemere " [? Comber, or Kembster] for his paying such rent, " when the other burgesses of the vill pay for their " burgages." The Bailiffs further present that in the lane called " Maydestrete," dung is placed, to the nuisance of the community.—This street is called " Mayden Strete," in other enrolments; and, as " Maiden " Street," it still exists.—" John Joce [Joseph] makes " plaint against John Northovere in a plea of trespass, " which John Northovere is a burgess of the vill, and " does not appear; so, according to the custom of the " vill, he remains non default, and it stands over." On the same day,—" Thomas Sterer, in full Court, finds pledges, " William Smert and Thomas Walyssh, for his good " behaviour (gestura) and that of Cristina, his wife, " under penalty of 20l., towards Agnes Capper and " others, the liege men of the King." At the Law Court holden on Tuesday after the Feast of St. Ambrose the Bishop [4th April], in the 20th year [1397].—" The " Bailiffs present that Cristina, the wife of Thomas

"Sterer, against the peace, drew a rake against Edith
"Ketes; so she is amerced;" a portion of this membrane
is quite illegible. At the Law Court of "Hokke Term,"
holden on the 15th of May, in the 20th year [1397], Henry
Barbour is amerced in the sum of 3 pence, for drawing
blood with his fist from Richard Kete the elder. At
the same Court, Edith Ketys is amerced (in the sum of
3 pence) with five others, for breaking the assize as to
brewing ale, also "for using cups and other false mea-
"sures." Further,—"Twelve free men, being sworn,
"present that the Abbot of Myddelton Abbas [now
"Milton Abbas, in Dorset], the Abbot of Netele [Net-
"ley, near Southampton], the Lady of Beaumond, John
"Syward, John Gonyg, Robert Calch, Nicholas Bayly,
"William Corf, Thomas Cronk, Henry Broune, John
"Bakebere, the Abbot of Abbodesbury, Robert Veel,
"Nicholas Webbe, Thomas Stapilforde, John Cleybury,
"Henry Rykard, William Momford, burgesses, who
"owe suit at this day, make default; therefore they
"are to be amerced; as also, Nicholas Berde. Also, that
"William Heliere had justly (juste, but qy. injuste) raised
"hue and cry against Richard, the Chaplain of Thomas
"Cole (the Mayor), therefore he was amerced 6 pence."
They also presented "that John Swan broke the arrest
"of Thomas Cole, the Mayor of this vill, and of Thomas
"Sterer, the Under-bailiff, as to two leaden measured
"cuves, or vessels, [cupis metretis] and other goods, to
"the value of 40 shillings, arrested in the house of
"Walter Clopton, at the suit of the party complaining
"against him in a plea of debt, such complainant being
"John Shudde." This latter person, himself, is also
presented, "for placing dung in a vacant place oppo-
"site to the Chapel in Melcombe Regis, to the grievous
"damage of the common people walking there." The
existence of this Chapel is mentioned (in Dean Chandler's
Register at Salisbury) about a century before this ;
but there seems to be no other record of it than the
present one, at this date ; from a document at Salisbury
we learn that there was "no place dedicated to God"
in Melcombe Regis in 1428.—The mother church, it
may be here observed, was, and still is, that of Radi-
polo. (The Walter Clopton above mentioned, can
hardly have been the person of that name who was the
Chief Justiciar of the King's Bench, and had formerly
been member of Parliament for the borough: it is just
possible, however, that he may be here alluded to, as
being owner, or lessor, of the house.)—"Robert Clavyle
"was entered anew to be on the assize, and sworn."—
The name of Clavell often appears in the Weymouth
records of a later date.—"Robert Walkelayn, being
"present this day in Court, spontaneously [agrees]
"that he will, before the Feast of the Nativity next to
"come, erect a good and competent house for making
"a mill therein, in Melcombe Regis." Among his six
sureties is "Thomas Cole, of Weymouth," not the then
Mayor of Melcombe, of that name. (Melcombe, it may
be here remarked, is said to have had its name from its
windmill, or mills, and the "combe," or valley, in
which it is situate.) At this Court, a person whose
name is obliterated, is attached in a plea of debt, for
"the arrest of a third part of 30 tuns of red wine."
To this membrane, a small slip of parchment is attached,
containing the panel of the 12 free men, or jurors,
before mentioned, 4 of whom have the name of William,
2 John, 2 Thomas, one each, Eustace, Richard, Robert
and Henry. The next Court is holden on Tuesday after
the Nativity of St. Mary (8th of September) in the 21st
year of Richard the Second [1397]. William Tilie is
fined three pence for drawing a "dagger" upon John
Cokeman. The dagger also was forfeited ; but it was
to be sold back to the said William for 8 pence ; John
Shudde being his surety for payment of both sums.
An "Election of Officers" follows.—"The twelve men
"that were sworn to choose officers for the following
"year, chose for the office of Mayor of the same vill
"Henry Forde, and he was sworn. For the office of
"Bailiffs, Eustace Kemere and John Cokeman ; and
"they were sworn. For the office of Constables of
"the same bailiwick, William Smert and William
"Hellyer ; for the office of Under-bailiffs, Roger Fox
"and Hugh Deer." Precept was given to bring Roger
Conke, servant of Richard Latoner, and to put him on
the Assize. These names of ancient Mayors of Melcombe,
it may be here observed, have been hitherto lost, and
are now for the first time brought to light. The next
Court is holden on Tuesday after the Feast of St.
Michael, in the 21st year [1397]. The twelve jurors,
named in the schedule before alluded to, present that
William Mustart (elsewhere named "Mustard"), Robert
Smythe, Thomas Stapulforde, John Ricard, William
Forde, John Sterer, William Monfort, John Bakere,

John Wedene, Henry Broke, Robert Calche, John Neel,
the Abbot of Netle, the Lady of Frampton, William
Walkelyn, and Nicholas Webbe, burgesses of the vill.
have made default in appearing. They were all fined
3 pence, that sum appearing over the name of each.
The jurors also present that Philip Attewell, Richard
Kete, Edith Cartere, and Thomas Russell, have put
dung on the Quay (la Kaye), at the east end of the tena-
ment of Thomas Russell, "to the nuisance of the whole
"vill."—It may be here remarked, that the noble
family of Russell springs from this part of Dorset.
"They also chose William Bicard and William Helier
"to collect the King's rent this time, and chose Henry
"Clere and Hugh Deer to keep a certain polye [pulley,
"or crane], with a cord, belonging to the Commonalty
"of the same vill, and collect the profits thereof."
The next Court is holden on Tuesday after the Feast of
St. Thomas the Apostle (21st of December); and the
next, and last on this set of rolls, on Tuesday before the
Feast of St. Gregory (12th of March) in the 21st year
of the same reign [1398]. At the latter Court, Richard
Latonere is presented for drawing a "dagger" upon
Richard Kete, against the peace, and order is given to
seize the said knife ; but as the Under-bailiffs are
found to have concealed it (concell'), they themselves are
amerced 2 pence. John de la Wythel drew a "dag-
"gare," against the peace, upon Henry Semero ; and
because the Under-bailiffs did not have it in Court, they
were amerced 4 pence, and ordered to produce the
dagger as well. As to the tenement of Agnes Capper,
which Edward Skynner lately occupied, it remained in
the hands of the King, by reason of the idiotcy of the
said Agnes. Towards the end of this roll, there are
five smaller slips of parchment sewed to it, with entries
in Latin, the contents of one of which are as follow :—
"Melcombe. Payments and expenses incurred by
"Eustace Kemere and William Helier, Bailiffs there,
"from the Feast of St. Michael in the 18th year [1394]
"to the Feast of St. Michael in the 19th year, of the
"reign of King Richard the Second [1395]. First, the
"expenses of William Helier, for going to London for
"the Community, 13s. 4d. The expenses of Robert
"Calche [Member of Parliament], going to Parliament
"for the Commonalty of the town, 13s. 4d. Wages of
"the Steward, 40d. For fowls brought as a present to
"Walter Clopton [the then Chief Justiciar of the
"King's Bench], 2s. 6d. Expenses of Walter Clopton,
"when he came here, all included, 5s. 2d. Expenses
"of the Steward, coming here divers times, and of the
"Bailiffs going to the Sessions and County Court
"holden at Dorchestre, divers times, 18s. 9d. For one
"cord, bought for drawing up wine, 2s. 8d. For two
"bonds of iron bought for the pollee, 8d. Melcombe.
"Moneys received from Eustace Kemero and William
"Heliere on their account, at the Feast of the Nativity
"of St. Mary in the 20th year [1396] ; and delivered to
"Thomas Cole, Mayor of the same vill, 72s. 7½d."
The next document, though brief, is curious, as being
an enrolment, on parchment (in Latin), fastened to the
same roll as the preceding, of proceedings in a Pie-
powder Court ; a document of this nature, of that early
date, being, no doubt, rarely to be met with.—"Melcombe
"Regis. A Court of Pie-powder, holden there on
"Wednesday next after the Feast of St. Leonard (6th
"of November) in the 21st year of the reign of King
"Richard the Second (1397). Henry Marchant is at law
"(ad legem) against William Helyere, for that he did
"not [as had been asserted] make trespass against him
"by striking him with his hand, at Melcombe Regis,
"in a certain spot called the place of William Richard,
"on Tuesday the Feast of St. Leonard in the 21st year
"etc. ; on surety of John Northovere and Eustace
"Kymere. Afterwards the same Henry was amerced,
"because of default in making his law" [establishing
his innocence of the charge, by producing witnesses
to swear as to his innocence]. "William Heliere was
"amerced for making a false plaint against Eustace
"Kymero in a plea of trespass. William Walkelyn
"was at law against William Helyere, for that he did
"not make assault upon him with a certain stone,
"against the peace, on Tuesday the Feast of St Leo-
"nard in the year aforesaid, at Melcombe ; on surety
"of Eustace Kemere and Henry Marchaunt. After-
"wards, the said William Walkelyn was amerced for
"default in making his law against William Helier
"aforesaid. Henry Marchaunt was to keep the peace
"towards William Heliere, and other liege men of our
"Lord the King, on penalty of 40d. . . . . . The
"Bailiffs present that William Helier raised a club
"against Eustace Kymer, Henry Barbere, and William
"Walkelyn, whether justly or not, they know not.

"Therefore, inquisition is to be made." This was a Court probably, in which foreigners, or non-freemen, (who were presumed, as travellers, to come with "dusty "foot") could implead or be impleaded, for debt or damages. A diminutive piece of parchment, attached to the above, contains, in a brief and summary form, proceedings at Courts holden on Tuesday next after Hokke Day [the third Tuesday after Easter Sunday] and Tuesday the Feast of St. Barnabas (11th of June) in the 21st year of the same reign [1398].

The next of the three Law Court Rolls now surviving, begins with Tuesday after the Feast of the Epiphany, in the first year of the reign of Henry the Fourth [1400]. It is in a very mutilated state, and consists of two small sheets of parchment only, with two parchment slips attached. Among other things, Thomas Cole and Wilhelmina, his wife, executors of the will of Henry Frampton, make plaint against Emma Gilbertes, in a plea of debt; and she is accordingly attached, by seizure of one small pot and one cup (in another place described as a mazer, bound with silver,) valued at 13s. 4d. Thomas Wotton makes plaint against John Elys in a plea of debt, his surety being John Jurdan,—a surname, which, as "Jurdeyn," or "Jerdan," frequently occurs in these records, during the 17th century.—In a portion of the roll, partly mutilated and partly illegible, John Abbot is mentioned as the then Mayor. The next Court mentioned is the Law Court of Hokke Term, on Tuesday after the Feast of St. John Port Latin (6th of May), in the first year of Henry the Fourth (1400). Among other things, the twelve jurors present that Roger Fox had found within the vill one barrel of "pych" (pitch); whereupon, the said Roger came into Court, and made fine with the Court for such barrel, in the sum of 2s. Also, that a black horse had come there from strange parts at the last Feast of the Purification of St. Mary, and that cry had been made, and no one claimed it; so it was to remain in the custody of the bailiff until superannuated [quousque superannuat]. The next is the Law Court holden on Tuesday after the Feast of the Nativity of St. Mary (8th of September), in the first year of Henry the Fourth (1400). Among other things, the twelve jurors, being sworn, choose Henry Forde for Mayor, John Benefeld and Eustace Keymer for Bailiffs, and Hugh Deer and Roger Fox for Under-bailiffs. The next is the Law Court holden on Tuesday after the Feast of St. Michael, in the second year of Henry the Fourth (1400). This roll, which contains nothing of interest, ends with three lines of proceedings of a Court of Pie-powder holden on Tuesday before the Feast of St. Nicholas the Bishop (6th of December), in the second year of Henry the Fourth [1400].

The third, and only other, Roll of this description, in Mr. Sherren's Collection, is an enrolment commencing with the 16th of December, in the 34th year of King Henry the Sixth [1455], being from 50 to 60 years later than the preceding ones. Mention is made of a burgage in "Seynthomastrete" (St. Thomas Street, still existing under that name), as being in the hands of the Mayor and Commonalty, for arrears of rent. John Rogger is to make answer to the Mayor and Commonalty for having ceased to keep his watch, as also for not having paid his rent the five preceding years. The next Court is holden on the 21st of January, in the same year of Henry the Sixth [1456]. The tasters [tastatores] of ale present that Geoffrey Samwyse had brewed twice and Alianor Houpere once, and sold ale, against the assize: he is amerced 2 pence, and she one penny.—"Samways," it may be remarked, is a very common name in Weymouth at a much later date.— Precept is also given at this Court to Robert Chapman, to remove a dog of his, that bites and kills sheep, geese, and other poultry, of his neighbours, "to the grievous "nuisance of such neighbours," on pain of paying 3s. 4d. Order is also given to attach John Russell, in a plea of debt by Geoffrey Samwyse. The name of William Gigges occurs here more than once; John Soppe is also another name mentioned. The next Court is holden on the 16th of February, in the 34th year of King Henry the Sixth [1456]. Robert Chapman, owner of the dog before-mentioned, is "at law," now (with four witnesses, or jurors), against Robert Clark, "for that he did not kill one goose of his, with his dog, "value of the goose 40 pence." The Roll ends with a list of various payments made into the King's Exchequer, between the 30th and 35th years of Henry the Sixth, now more than half obliterated.

One of the most ancient documents in Mr. Sherren's Collection is a small parchment deed, in Latin, without date, but belonging either to the reign of Edward the

Third or Richard the Second. The single seal which belonged to it is lost; but it is a deed poll, whereby William Peverel, of Estringestede, (East Ringstead, in Dorset) grants to William Gervays, of Melcombe, and Cristina, his wife, a messuage and curtilage, situate between his own messuage and that of Adam Trate, for 32 shillings of silver, paid to him beforehand. Witnesses, Thomas Slyde, Nicholas Smith (Fabro), Henry Langyro, Henry Bendis, Henry de Ringstede, and many others. The above is the only early deed in the whole collection.

Among these multifarious records there is a portfolio, containing a large assortment of papers, probably near a hundred in number, belonging mostly to the reign of Elizabeth, and some few to that of James the First. On a close examination, however, it has been found that the whole of them, with but comparatively few exceptions, consist either of depositions of witnesses, and of pleadings in private actions, or suits in the local Courts, often about ships and mercantile claims, now of no interest; or else, of papers in connexion with the frequent disputes that took place between Melcombe Regis (with its Mayor) and Weymouth (with its Bailiffs), previous to their union by Act of Parliament, in the 13th year of Elizabeth's reign; but which, in spite of such union, were still for some years continued. By this Act of Union they were united under the name or title of the "Town of Weymouth and Melcombe Regis," with one Mayor and two Bailiffs for the two. William Pytte, (a member of the same family that afterwards gave birth to the great Earl of Chatham, and his even more illustrious son,) was Mayor in 1586, 7, and other years; in these papers his name frequently occurs. Among them there are several Accounts of Roger Keate, the Mayor, on the occasion of his frequent visits to London in 1576, on business of the Corporation; also, one or two other sets of Accounts of nearly the same date. The following are two items selected from the contents of this portfolio :—

The first, a paper writing, in a rather obscure hand, shadows forth the coming of the Spanish Armada, two years later :—"xixth of July 1586 before Mr. Mayor, "Mr. Richard Pytte,'Mr. Magoor [sic]; Nicholas Abra- "ham, of Lyrpole (Liverpool), Merchaunte, and Johan "Lamberte, of the same, shipman, saye that theire "beinge prysoners in Bilboe for the space of xii. "monethes and xx dayes last past, came from thence "about the xxiiii of June, by our accounte [our "reckoning], and duringe the tyme of there being in "Bilboe, did understande by credible reporte that "there was provided and sholde be 700 saillos of "shippes, gallis, galiasses, pynnesses, and pattashes, "and of men to the number of cc and eightie thou- "sande, and by reporte commonlye there had, for "Englande. And further doe saye, that they hard "one Captayne Teretuno of Bilboe reporte to one "Roger Stacye, of Saltasshe, that yf he wolde staye "and goe withe him to Lysshebourne (Lisbon), he "wolde lande him at Waterforde. John LL. Lam- "bert his signe {Nicholas ⎱ ." "Abraham ⎰

A written paper, giving some account of the old records then in the possession of the Corporation.— "Sent up to Mr. Hanam [the Recorder] the 6th of "Februarie 1577. The new and last Charter. The "Statute under seall. The olde Booke. The copy of "the Quo Warranto of Weymouth. A Letter under "the name of Mr. Fleetwood, Recorder [of London]; "John Tomson, Richard Compton. William Watson. "and Fabian Phillips. The copie of Poole Charter, in "Latin and in English. Another Book of notes under "Mr. Raynolds' writing. Sent before this by Nicholas "Ceate.—The copie of the Quo Waranto and Commis- "sion for Melcombe."

Among various loose papers, not contained in the portfolio above-mentioned, is an account of Roger Keate's expenses in 1578, for "Chardges disbursed "about the townes affarres." From this "account" we learn that he left Weymouth, on horseback, on Saturday, the last day of May, and reached London on the 3rd of June. For many days he pays for "bote hire to "and from Greenwich [where the Court then was] 8d. "or 10d." The following are other items in the Account:—"Item, payed for a supper bestowed upon Tal- "bot, the Clarke of the Towre iii s. vi d. Item, payed "for seeinge iii or iiii bundells of recordes at the "Tower iii s. iiii d. For a payre of showes [shoes] "xvi d. Item, payed to my hostes for 42 meales, at "vi d. per meale, xxi s. Item, for my horsemate for "24 daies at gras, at iiii d. per day viii s. Item, for "shoyinge my horse viii d. Item, for wasshinge my

" sherte xii d. Item, for drinckinge in the morninge
" and other times at my hostes [hostess], over and
" above my ordinary tables, by all the tyme above said,
" ii s. x d. Item, given to the ostlers and kepers of my
" horse at grasse viii d. Item, to the maydes of the
" house vi d."

In a portfolio, with clasp, in Mr. Sherren's Collection,
numbered (1), there are probably near a hundred documents, each inclosed in a doubled sheet of blank paper.
The following are selected from them.—

A sheet of paper, with writing in an almost illegible
hand :—" In that the vth day of June 1576, William
" James alias Ledoze, being commanded by Owen Ray-
" noldes, Maior of Weymouth and Melcombe Regis,
" and Mr. Thomas Howard, Esquire, and Barnarde
" Mason, bailiffes and justices of the peace of the
" towne aforesayd, to find suretyes to answer at the
" next Assyses to suche matters as shoulde then be
" layd to his chardge, then answered these wordes
" followinge, vist. :—' I hope to be found a trewer
" ' subjecte then suche as shall say anything to my
" ' chardge.' . Likewise Richard Pit, the older, an-
" swered that the said Ledoyse, alias James, shoulde
" not put in suretyes for the sayd matter, but remayne
" as prisoner. Also the sayd James, in further speache
" to the Mayor aforesaid, sayd that he hadd spoken to
" as good men as he was. Further, the aforesaid
" Richard Pitt affyrmyd that the opynions of the town
" judges beinge offered to the Quene's Majesties' honour-
" able Counsell, was by them tost over the barre, and
" not regarded. These words also he spoke.—Before
" Mr. Mason's comynge, he examined the sayd Ledoys
" in the presence of Thomas Clarke, one of the ser-
" geauntes of the sayd—and Henry Knight. But he
" added farther, that when the Counsell had caste the
" opinion over the barre, no man woulde take the same
" upp, but John Peers."

The subject here in dispute was probably a reference
to Parliament in respect of the quarrels and disputes
that were then going on between Weymouth and Melcombe ; which, by Act of Parliament some five years
before, had been united.

Copy of a " Letter to the Right Honourable Thomas
" Howard, and his Answer;" both written upon the
same sheet.—" So it is (if hit please your Worshippe)
" that the great lamentation of the scoller of Oxforde,
" sithence [since] your Worshippes departure, movethe
" us to wryte to you againe for his deliveraunce and
" settinge at libertye; who now briskelye confesseth
" himselfe to have abused his dewtie towardes God, his
" cuntrye, and your Worshippe, and cannot deny but
" that he himself, with Robert Egerton, contrived that
" licence, even of sett purpose, to gett monye in this
" cuntrye for there better exhibition. Wherefore if hit
" maie please yow to wryte back youre favourable wil-
" lingnes for his delyveraunce, there is no other likeli-
" hoode but that he maie prove an honest man. Mel-
" combe, this xxvth of Januarie, a° Domini, 1580.
" Youres to commande, Henry Rogers, William Pit,
" Rychard Pitt, John Mounsell." The Answer thereto,
written below.—" I hope neyther any off yow all dobte
" off my wyllyngness to gratyfy any off your desyors,
" neyther off any dysposysyon to shoo mercy, but suche
" may be the sequell yn thys cause [case] yf I shod do
" eyther off them, that yow myght repent yow off your
" requeste, and myself be found unable to aunswer my
" doynge. Synce my departure from Melkum, I have
" sene letters dyrected from the Counsayle to apprehend
" all suspysyous parsons [persons] that are unknowen,
" and espesyally such as go dysgysed, wheroff thys
" advertysment they geve : sum go leke maryners,
" sum leke marchants, sum leke scollers, sum leke laks
" [? lackies], sum leke sarvyng men. Therefor, I pray
" contynew not the favor which may turne [to] so dayn-
" gerus a repentance, but fourthwythe to serche hym
" thoroughly yn alle, ynayde off his garmentes, and
" to cause him to shew where Egerton ys, and how he
" may be apprehended, then to geve advertyment
" thereof to sum —, whereby they may fynde menes
" to take hym, though he be yn some other cuntry.
" So yourselves I pray to be more carefull off your
" common wele, then petyfull off a shambles [shame-
" less] forsworn varlot, to yow all so mere a stranger
" as by lekelyhode he may be the worst man levyng.
" Thor ys suche lamentable news from Scotland and
" from the North, as I wylle not commytte ytt to the
" trust off thys paper, grete trobles above ; worke there-
" fore wysely yn thes and other the leke caases [cases]
" which may hapen yn my absence. Your lovyng
" frend, Thos. Howarde." This Thomas Howard was
a younger son of Thomas, Duke of Norfolk, and had

been summoned to Parliament as a Baron by Writ in
1579. He had previously been one of the two Bailiffs of
the town of Weymouth and Melcombe Regis, an office
which might be held by a person not a freeman of the
place.—On the back of these copies is written what
appears to be the Oxford man's information against
Egerton, in writing conspicuous for its badness :—" I
" left him at . . . . a Monday was 3 wyekes; he wilbe
" at Oxford on Shrofe Monday, at one Smalimans, one
" of the bedelles of the Universite, dwelling within
" Est Gate." The copy of the original letter, is thus
addressed.—"To the right Woorshipfulle Master Thomas
" Howarde, Esquier, geve these with speede." The
Oxford student, apparently, had been going about the
country with a forged licence to beg; and was suspected
of being a malignant.

A Letter from the same Lord Thomas Howard to
William Pytt, of Weymouth; of the date probably of
1581. It begins, " Mr. Pyt," and goes on to say that it
is impossible to do anything in Parliament,—" For when
" I should have bestoed chargeable somms off mony
" yn framyng bylls, yn rewardyng them that should
" speke ffavorably yn them, yn gratifying the Speker
" and other men off authoryte, then should I loke for a
" hard passage off the byll, by reson that Syr Chrys-
" topher Hatton's countenance and credit wod worke
" muche agaynst yt, and surely wod overthrow yt,when
" yt should come to her Majesty's hands, and therefore
" would not cast away your money at this time in
" so . . . . affairs. Wors than thys, theis wyked men
" are so ffavoured and petyed, as they had by Parla-
" ment clene overthrone your fformer decre and quyet-
" ness for ever, yff I had not throughly labored all
" my ffrendes, and the Counsayle also, ffor the stopping
" off the same." This seems to be a letter of some importance, as shewing the political intrigues and party-
spirit of the day.

Another Letter from the same, of nearly the same
date, addressed—" To my loving frends of Melcum geve
" this : " —It begins,—" Such hath byn the slender
" delynge, or such hathe byn the yndyrect delyings, off
" sum of Melcum, as the money allredy gathered, I
" dobt me wylle returne small or no benefyt unto the
" toune at all ; therefor provyde no more mony untyll
" the same may be better ymployed. There is one
" Tomson plased yn the Hows by my Lord of Bedford,
" so as yt ys not possyble for me to do my plesure yn
" respect off that I myght have don, yff I had byn yn
" the howse, notwithstandyng they shall want no care-
" full good wyll in my doyngs."

Another Letter, from the same Lord Thomas Howard
to Mr. Pit, endorsed (in pencil) " 10 June 1582." In it
he says,—" I pray, accordyng to your promys, cause the
" fylthe behynd the towne to be rydd agaynst Myd-
" somer, about the tyme, God wyllyng, I wylbe at
" home, to make amends for my long absence;" he
alludes, probably, to the slime and refuse accumulated in
what is known as the " Backwater."

Another Letter, from the same to the same, dated 12th
July 1581. In a postscript, he adds,—" I trust to fynd
" the town clene, and all the annoyance behind the
" towne removed, accordyng to promys."

Another Letter, from the same to the same, dated "Lon-
" don, the 2 of March." He begins by saying—," I res-
" ceyved your letters, Mr. Pyt, the fyrst off Apryll, wher-
" in you leve to my dysoresyon my stay here, and suppose
" that Mr. Tomson can and will do as muche for your
" affairs as occasyon shall requyre. To that I answer
" I thynk hym no enemey to the towne, so know I that
" he neyther ys off suffoyent credyt to do yt, nor
" yet wylle adventure to cross the doyngs off grete
" parsons [persons] ffor to wyn the favor off ten suche
" townes. . . . You wante no enemys, therffore
" I pray dele wysely yn all your actyons, and yn
" orderyng off your market, which no doute had ben
" cauled bak, yff I had not ben here to aunswer yt;
" and yet ys yt not determyned, but at leisure tyme
" the Counsayle wyll common [commune] furder with
" me; but I nothing doute the satysfyng off them yn
" that, and yn all other poynts allso tuching your
" towne, which I wyll tender as yff the holle towne
" were my own, and do hope yff the the Parliament
" prosede to do that which ya not loked ffor. I
" pray you yn any wysse let all the myxsons [dung-
" hills] and annoyances be caryed away byffore the
" spryng do cum." In a postscript is added ". . . .
" I pray desyer him [your brother Rychard] to stay
" the six peses of sayle cloth which I byspake of hym,
" and I pray when any penyworth of good pych and tar
" shall cum, let me have for [four] barrels of fyne tar
" of the bigger band [? brand], and tow [two] of pych.'

In another Letter, date in 1586, addressed by Lord Thomas Howard,—" To my loving ffrende Mr. Wyllyam " Pit, Maior off Weimouth and Melkom Regis, give " these ;" the writer asks of him—" with help of his " brethren and frendes," a loan of 40 pounds for six " weeks, when it shall be repaid with, " a quarter of whete, " for the freendly lone theroff; otherwise I will deliver " good and parfyt whete, at iii s. iiii d. the busshell, to " levy thys 40 pounds ; which mony I wol not for any " thing myss a Fryday night or Saturday morning. I " am yndifferent which off theis two offers be taken, " preying you most hartely I may be freended to have " the mony, what soe ever I give, to serve a present " paiment, and such as I cannot breke, with my credit. " The mache [? sample] ys good for bakers, and such as " make byskey [biscuit] ; for my whete ys very good, " such as I sell to my neyghbours for iiii s. the busshell. " Redy to requyte, do byd you farewell. From Walter- " ston, thys present Wednesday 1586. Your very " loving frend Thomas Howarde." There are also in this collection several other Letters from the same personage, coming down to the year 1593, if not a later date.

The following are extracts from the accounts of a person not named, but Roger Keate, in all probability ; for his expenses in going to London on business of the town.—" I tooke my journey towarde London on Mon- " daie the vith of Februarie 1575(6). Spent as followeth. " The vith, viith, and viiith daies nothing, because Mr. " Howarde paid my charge to London. Inprimis, at " Sarum for mendinge my spurre leathers, and geevin " to the hosteler for pains taken about a medecin for my " horse, ii d. . . . Item, on Fridaie the tenth of " Februarie, in the companie of certain courtiers, and " of Mr. Robert Gregorie, at Westminster, at the Sar- " razin's Head, v s. Item, for 2 paire of shooes, and for " greasinge my bootes, iiii s. iiii d. Item, for a pockett, " because my pocket was all torne with the carriage of " the money, vi d. . . . Item, on Saterdaie the xith " of Februarie to dinner at Westminster, in a certain " courtier's companye, xx d. Item, spent in sundrie " drinkinges in Mr. Gregories companie, and in " companie with Thomas Clementes and Thomas Sam- " wise, ii s. ii d. Item, given to the dorekeeper of the " Counsell Chamber, ii s. vi d. Item, for new stall- " inge my bootes, xvi d. Item, for a new paire of " spurres, because I lost my spurres."—Another some- what similiar account of Roger Keate's has been already given.

There is preserved a long correspondence, in 1569, between Weymouth and Melcombe Regis, about defaults in abiding by the award as to the collection of the " Petty Customs," at the mouth of the river, or har- bour ; which had long been a cause of contention be- tween the two towns. The Bailiffs and officials of Weymouth address those of the other place in civil enough terms, and sign themselves,—" Your friends ;" but the people of Melcombe make answer, among other things,—" The more it semethe unto us, why youe " shoulde so impudently burthen us with youre owne " faulte ;" and sign themselves,—" Your poore op- " pressed neighbours of Melcombe Regis." The above- mentioned papers are copies only of the original correspondence.

A parchment deed (in Latin) of the 35th year of Henry the Eighth (1543), whereby Richard Michell, Mayor, and the Bailiffs, of Melcombe, in consideration of 11s. 4d., paid by William Peros, as of the stipend " of " our priest" [nostri sacerdotis], celebrating in the Chapel of St. Mary, at Melcombe, grant to him a burgage, or parcel of vacant land, on the south side of the said Chapel, between the "perambulatoria" [? cloisters] around the said Chapel, on the north side, and the vacant land now belonging to the town, but formerly to John Blackabere, on the south side ; and extending towards a tree that is called " Le gret Elme " [the great Elm], neare Maidenstrete, on the east side, and towards another tree with a like name, near Seynte Maryestrete, on the west side. The seals both of the Commonalty and the Mayoralty of Melcombe were originally set hereto, but are now lost.

A bill indented, dated the 1st of October and 1st of May, probably in 1571, 2, wherein Owen Rainoldes, Mayor, acknowledges the receipt of 47s. 4d. " towardes his " wayges, expenses, and allowances for being Burges " of the Parliament." After the union of the two towns under one Corporation, there were four burgesses elected for Parliament ; the two highest on the poll being considered to be members for Weymouth, and the next two, members for Melcombe. Owen Rainoldes was one of the members for Melcombe side.

A paper writing, mutilated, and in an almost illegible hand. When deciphered, it is as follows :—" Die Saturni " tertio die Februarii, anno regni Dominæ nostræ Eliza- " bethæ xxx.° [A.D. 1588], apud The Taverne vocat ' The " ' Bores Hedd' . . . die et anno supradictis, Johannes " Broke, de W[eymouth] M[elcombe] Regis, in Comi- " tatu Dorsetiæ, dixit hæc verba, videlicet,—That the " Exemplification for the unitie of the haven of Wey- " mouth M[elcombe] Regis, under the Greate Seale, was " forged by procurement of the townesmen, and that a " priest or person [parson] near the North Battery was " the forger thereof, and had for this purpose xx li. " And that one Henrie Holman, of thile of Portlande, " was witness thereof; in the presence of us . . . . " John Davys de . . . sen." In the early days after the union of the two towns by Act of Parliament, they seem to have been much known under the name of " Weymouth Melcombe Regis," without the interposi- tion of the conjunction " and."

A small paper writing, in a neat and legible hand :— " A note of such thinges as are delivered to John Gun- " drey, Gentleman, this xth daye of Aprill anno Domini " 1591, by Mr. Maior of Weymouth Melcombe Regis. " Imprimis, Mr. Gibbes Direction. Item, Mr. Swaynes " note of the case in the Book of Assize. Item, the " Incorporation of Mayors. Item, the Boundarye, under " seal. Item, the Charter of Edward I., and the copie " thereof. Item, the warrant whereby the distresse was " taken. Item, a note of the discoverye of the title of " Weymouth. Item, the copye of Mr. Watkins pur- " chase of Raddypole. Item, the plot of the boundes. " Item, the Charter exemplified in the Queen's time " for me Jo. Gundrey." The Charter of Edward the First to Melcombe Regis, which was existing at the above date, is now lost.

A Letter, dated 9th of October 1593, and signed " Howard,"—Charles, Lord Howard of Effingham, Lord High Admiral. He has been informed by Thomas Alworthe, of Bristol, merchant, and his own servant, Thomas Ware, that a " carvell," belonging to them, " was caryed away by some lewed maryners," and sold, without the owners' consent : and that those (some persons of those parts) who bought her,—" set her onte " to the sea under commissione of reprisall, naming " her the ' Tabacco pipe,' in which voiage it was ther " good hap to take an Indian prise, laden with hides " and other merchandise." The persons to whom this Letter is addressed, are requested to " arrest" the said carvell and prize, in favour of the rightful owners of the carvell. The Letter is addressed,—" To all officers " of the Admiralty, to all Maiors, Justices of peace, " Bayliffs, and other Her Majesty's officers to whom " it may apertaine." Tobacco had been introduced into England, by Sir W. Raleigh, only about eight years before this mention of the ship, " the Tabacco pipe."

There are various papers respecting the bringing of fresh water into Melcombe Regis from two springs in the common of pasture called " South Downe," in the manors of Sutton Poyntz and Preston ; the water then in use being " something brecheye [? brackish] ;" be- longing to the reign of Elizabeth.

A paper, signed by William Waltham, Mayor [A.D. 1616], and 13 or 14 others, containing,—" The names " of the parsons of Radipole [the mother church of " Melcombe Regis] which have bin from time to time " by the space of three score yeares last paste and up- " wardes; and how they have used to say divine service " in the Chapple of Melcombe Regis in the severall " times wherein they were parsons there." The person first named in the list is " Mr. Simon Bell," who had been sometime " Prior of the Priorye, or Fryerie, of " Melcombe." " Threescore years past, he was parson " of Radipoll, and so' continued during his life."

An autograph Letter, in a fine hand,—" Mr. Mayor; " Theis shal be both to pray and require you to send " all the constables in your towne to the musters at " Dorchester to-morrow by ix of the clock in the morn- " inge, and to place them uppon the tallest and meetest " persons you have there to serve with them. Wherof " expecting that yow will not faile, do bid you fare- " well. Wolveton, this xiiiith of July 1590. Your " freend, George Trenchard." There are also several other communications of a like nature, by the same hand.

A precept of the Justices of the Peace, signed " George " Trencharde, John Willyams, 30 Septr. 1585," to the " Borough of Weymouthe Melcombe Regis," as to the muster, armour, and training. A portion of it is as follows :—" Furthermore, you shall cawse each shott to " bringe with him bulletts, a rolle of matche, and one " pounde and half of powder, and not to showte one

" shott thereof before such tyme as he shall be directed
" to which ende he shall expende the same."

A confession, dated the 3rd of March 1585, by William
Samwayes, to the effect that he had laid hands upon
Ralph Colston, because the said Ralph rescued George
Moone; who had been arrested by authority of the
Bailiffs, William Ledoze and Roger Gyer; before John
Mokette, Mayor. Of interest only, for the occurrence
of the surname of Colston, so well known in connexion
with Bristol.

A paper, indistinctly written, addressed to the Mayor,
Bailiffs, Constables, etc., for the apprehension " of John
" Younge, of the cyttie of Exeter, of the age of 50 yeres
" or upwardes, a surgen by his syence, his apparell black,
" and doth speake French-like"; he being suspected
of felony: date, 5th of January 1582.

A Letter, signed " Chr: Hatton," and directed,—" To
" my very lovinge frend Mr, Tho. Mounshall, Maior of
" Melcombe Regis." He expostulates, at great length,
on part of Her Majesty's Privy Council, on the violent
proceedings of the authorities, in staying certain bushels
of salt belonging to " Robert Bushoppe, a poor man;"
" From the Court at Sunnynghill, the 3 of Sept' 1583."
Pleas (in Latin) in a Court holden at Weymouth 1st
of July 1610, in an action of debt by William Mower
against Samuel Grosse, of Great Yarmouth, in the county
of Norfolk, for his wages, as mastere, for 2 months and
21 days, of the vessel called the "Mayflower," on a
voyage from Plymouth to Middleborough (Middelburgh
in Zealand, in Holland). It seems not improbable that
this was the same vessel that afterwards carried the
Pilgrim Fathers to the coast of Massachusetts in 1620,
where they founded Plymouth Dock, in New England.

A Letter, addressed to the authorities of Weymouth
and Melcombe Regis, signed by Theophilus, Earl of
Suffolk (son of Lord Thomas Howard, previously mentioned), and dated " Audley End July 11th 1626"; asking
them to make a return to him, in accordance with directions in a Letter to him of the Lords of the Council, a
copy of which is enclosed, bearing date the 10th of July
1626. In it they speak of the preparations for an invasion
of England, then being made in Spain and Flanders.
All able men from the age of 16 to threescore are to be
enrolled. He himself (the Earl) is to report generally on
the state of defence of the three Counties of Cambridge,
Suffolk, and Dorset, by the 10th of August next. In a
postscript to the Earl's Letter is added—" To my verie
" loving freends, Mr. Henry Hastings Esquier, Sir
" Tho. Freke, Sir Jo. Browne, and Sir Nath' Napper,
" Deputy Lieutenants for the Countie of Dorset, these be
" delivered." Below, the names of " citties or townes,"
are added; " Cambridge, Ipswich, Edmondsburie, Poole,
" Lyme, Weymouth, and Melcombe," with the amounts
of powder, match, and lead, in those places, respectively, in store; Weymouth having 2½ lasts of powder,
2½ tons of match, and 2½ tons of lead.

A Letter, addressed to the Mayor of Weymouth and
Melcombe Regis, from Dorchester, " the last of Sep-
" tember 1626," and signed by John Browne, Thomas
Freke, and Richard Strodes, three Deputy Lieutenants.
The Mayor is informed that he has at Weymouth the
lieutenants and ensign of Sir Thomas Yorke's Company,
with part of such Company. The intent of the writers
was, that the people of Weymouth should receive the
officers so consigned to them, and therefore the fewer
of the Company had been sent. Their expectation had
been that means would be taken to billet the officers
" in some private house amongst you;" but on the
contrary, " they, being at a common inn, doe finde it
" very chargeable." The authorities are therefore asked
to find the lieutenants 20 silings, and the ensign 13
shillings, per week; the same to be returned out of
their pay, when received from the King.

A letter to the " Right Worshipful the Mayor of Wey-
" mouth and Melcombe Regis," signed " Jhon Wattes,"
without date. He is commanded by " my Lord of Den-
" bighe, Vice-admirall of his Majesties fleete, now
" bound to sea," to write and inclose a note " of such
" men as are pressed, and stand tested for His Majesties
" service;" and have since run away, or are absent.
If found, they are to be sent aboard his Majesty's
ship the Red Lyon. A postscript is added,—" My Lord
" entreatethe youe to remember his service unto Sir
" Thomas Freake, with many thanckes for his present."

A contemporary copy of a Letter from the Lords of the
Council, dated the 28th of October 1629; stating that in
Holland and especially at Amsterdam, as also in France,
more particularly Rochell, and in the " porte towns in
" Britany," there is " a contagious and infectious sick-
" ness, whereof great numbers dayly dye;" and that the
infection has been lately brought into the " Isle of Sylley,

" by a marchant shipp of those portes that lately touched
" there." Directions are therefore given at length, for
staying communication with the infected places.

A small paper, neatly written, with a number of signatures mostly finely written, of the then chief personages of St. Helier's, in the Isle of Jersey; in Norman
French.—" Nous soubssignes, Connestable et principaulx
" do la paroisse de la Trinite, certifions a Monsieur le
" Bailly, et a Messieurs de justice, que nous trouvons
" Abraham Coutaunce et Jeanne, sa femme, bien propre
" et capable pour tenir taverne en la dite paroisse, et
" tenir maison ouverte a tous hostes et gens de bien;
" en soy veiglant, gouvernant, et conduisant, suyvant
" aux ordres de justice. Donne a St Helier, le 27 jour
" du mois de Mars 1633."—" We the undersigned, Con-
" stable and principal persons of the parish of the Trinity,
" do certify to Messire the Bailly and my Lords of jus-
" tice, that we find Abraham Coutaunce and Jean, his
" wife, very proper and capable to keep tavern in the
" said parish, and to keep house open to all guests and
" people of means; watching, governing, and conduct-
" ing themselves, according to the orders of justice.
" Given at St Helier's, the 27th day of the month of
" March, 1633." Among the signatures, ten in number,
the surname " Dumaresque" twice occurs.

A written sheet of paper, the purport of which is as
follows.—" xii. February 1636. A note of the Charters
" sent to London to Mr. Recorder. Exemplification of
" Liberties the 8 Edward I., made 41 Edward 3d. The
" Great Charter. A testimony of divers Charters in
" Winton remaining, granted by Kinge Ethelred.
" Grant of the Prior of St. Swythine's to Weymouth,
" anno 38 regni Regis Henrici 3. Grant of divers
" Libertys anno 11mo Edwardi 2d. Exemplification of a
" Quo Warranto brought in 8 Edward I. Exemplifica-
" tion of the Charters anno 22do Elizabethæ, which
" were granted 41 Edwardi 3d. Confirmation of the
" Charters anno 1mo et 2do Elizabethæ. Exemplifica-
" tion of an Act of Parliament anno 13to Elizabethæ.
" A perpetuity of the fee farme anno 40 Elizabethæ.
" A decree made 23de Elizabethæ. Exemplification of
" an Order 24 Elizabethæ. A decree made sexto Eliza-
" bethæ. A decree 24to and 25to Elizabethæ. Papor.
" —Inquisition 6th Edward 3.—Wanting this 27th of
" January 1639 of the towne writinges.—Inquisition in
" paper. Exemplification of an Act of Parliament, in
" confirmation of the Chartre anno 1 and 2 Elizabethæ.
" —Delivered the 27th of January 1639 unto Mr.
" Francis Gape, [the Town Clerk], 5 ancient Accounts
" of the former Mayors." A pen is run through the
entry as to missing papers, in a darker ink.

A paper writing, stating that William Pease, Gent.,
has been appointed by the Commissioners for the Navy
to see to the impressing and raising of 250 mariners in
the County of Dorset; choice to be made of the best
and most sufficient mariners and seafaring men, " and
" not of such as be loose and unskilfull, and not fit to be
" imployed in soe important a service. From the
" Courte of Whitehall, this 21st of June 1626.' (Signed)
" G. Buckingham, Hollande, E. Conway, Pembroke,
" Carlyle, Carletone, Grandisone, J. Coke, Jul. Cæsar,"
and others. Addressed to "Sir George Trenchard,
" Sir Tho. Freke, Sir Jo. Strangwayes, Sir Jo. Browne,
" the Mayors of Weymouth and Poole, or any of them."

A Letter, addressed,—" To my loving friend Mr.
" Humfrey Jolliff, att the signe of the Black Spread
" Eagle, belynde St. Clement's Church Yard in the
" Strand, at Mr. Gowur's house, London. Give these."—
" Mr. Jolliff. Herewith you shall receive a Court
" Booke kept by Mr. Smale; it is one of the antientes
" that I have in my custody, the rest being locked up
" in the Town chest among antient records; I was
" willing to have sent up my present booke that I now
" keepe, but that I cannot spare the same, for that I
" have every day use thereof. I hope this (though not
" so well kept as could be wished) will serve the turne
" at present, and satisfy of your keeping the Court.
" We hold another Court on Weymouth syde, but that
" holds pleas of causes under 40s., and is by act: only,
" being kept 'de tribus in tres' [three-weekly],
" whereof there is noe question, as I conceive. As for
" wrecks of sea, ffloatsam, jettson, and lagan, I know
" none can give you better information thereon than
" Mr. Mayor, who is now in London. You have also
" many others of our towne there, with whom you
" [can] conferre about that businesse, and who (for
" ought I know to the contrary) are able to make
" affidavit thereof. And thus, with my love remem-
" bered to you, I rest your very loving freind, Fran :
" Gape. Melcomb Regis, 5to Januarii 1638." As
already noticed, Francis Gape was at this time Town

Clerk of Weymouth and Melcombe Regis. Mr. Henry Mitchell was the then Mayor.

A Letter, addressed,—To my loving frendes, the "Maior and his brethren of the town of Melcombe "Regis," "signed F. Bedforde," [Francis; Earl of Bedford], and dated the 3rd of January 1558. He thanks them for giving him the nomination of one of their burgesses to Parliament, and names John Moynes of Bruteporte [Bridport] as such; he excusing them from paying to such member "the ordinary and dayly sty-"pends, heretofore accustomed to be given to the "burgesses for their attendance on your affayres "there."

A Letter, signed "Pembroke," and dated the 11th of May 1569; addressed,—"To my loving frindes, the "Maior, burgesses, and inhabitants of the towne of "Melcombe Regis, in the Countie of Dorset." The Earl hears that they are going to build a wharf, extending six feet within the precincts of the liberties of the town of Weymouth. As Steward of the latter place, for settlement of any dispute that may thence arise, he proposes that each side shall choose a lawyer to peruse their Charters respectively.

The following paper as to the operations of the African pirates on the English coasts, contains some curious particulars. It is written on foolscap in a fine hand, and from the body of papers it is grouped with, appears to belong to the year 1636 :—"From Plymouth "it was advertised that 15 sayle of Turks were upon "this coast, and that divers mischeifs were don by "them, whereof their Lordships were allready adver-"tised by letters from that towne. From Dartmouth. "—That the Dorothy of that port, of 80 tons, was "taken near Silly, abouth a moneth since. That a "collyer of Axmouth comming with culme, was chased "by the Turks, and very hardly escaped. That the "Swann of Topisham was sett upon by two great "Turkes men of warr neer Silley, and were driven to "runn even on shore to save themselves from them. "That divers fishermen were taken in the western "parts, being there a fishing, to the number of 40 "persons. That the Larke of Topisham, of the burden "of 80 tons, having 15 men and a boy in her, was "lately taken by them, and the master slayne. That "the Patience of Topisham was taken 2 dayes after her "setting to sea, towards the Newfoundland.—That the "person that is sent to negotiate these businesses with "the Lords, have a speciall care to represent the danger "the Newfoundland men are like to be in att their "returne about Michaelmas, unlesse some speedy "course be taken for guarding the coasts by severall "ships. That the annoyances we receive is mostly by "the pirates of Sally [Sallee], which is a place of little "strength, and they might easily be kept in if some "few ships were imployed to lye upon ther coast.— "Since this information, a barque of Topisham, called "'The Rosegarden,' coming from Mirretto [?], and "having aboard her neer 100 fardells of white ware "belonging to the merchants of Exon, and a few other "merchants of other places, hath been taken, and the "barque, goods, and seamen, caryed away by them. "It is certainly known that there are five Turks in the "Severne, wher they weekly take either English or "Irish; and that there are a great number of their "ships in the Channell, upon the coast of France and "Biscay. Whereby it is come to passe that our ma-"riners will noe longer goe to sea, nor from port to "port; yea, the fishermen dare not putt to sea, to take "fish for the country. If timely prevention be not "used, the Newfoundland fleet must of necessity suffer "by them in an extraordinary manner. It is therefore "desired that his Majesty be petitioned that some ships "may be imployed to ryde allwayes at the Barr-foot of "Sally, to keep those in which are in the harbour, and "to take those with their prises which shalbe brought "home by them. That a convenyent nomber of nimble "ships may allways be kept upon the Irish and this "coast, which may be victualled here and there, and "not returne to Portsmouth or London to be victualled. "That a commission might be granted to any of his "Majesty's subjects, which would undertake it, to take "Turks and other pirates, and to dispose of them and "their goods at their pleasure, yeilding unto his "Majesty his fifteenes. That in such ships as shalbe "sent to Sally, seamen might be appointed by his "Majesty to be comanders." There are a number of other papers of the year 1636, connected with measures for the suppression of the Turkish pirates, the city of Exeter taking the lead in the movement. The port of Cardiff and its vicinity, it may be added, was their chief place of refuge in these daring attacks.

A parchment writing, with a fragment of the town seal still attached; being probably a duplicate copy of the Petition :—"To the Queen's Majesties most Honnor-"able Privie Counsell. It may please your Honnors "that whereas John Brouke of Waymouth did exibit a "suplycacion to the Queenes Maiestie in the names of "her Highnes tenantes of the sayde toune againste the "Maior and inhabitantes of Meloomb Regis, and being "acompanyed therein by dyvers persons by him pro-"cured of purpose, supposinge that by the shwe [sic] "of a multytude he should the better mayntayne his "antrwe [sic] exclamacions. As allso to coullor his "former contemptes and dysobeydient deallinges sun-"dry tymes committyed againste her Maiestis cawse, "decrees, and orders, made and establyshed for the "better and quyeter government of thys towne and "corporation of Waymouth and Melcomb Regis. And "for that his mysdemenour of the said Brouke maye the "playner apere unto your Honnours, and his aside com-"panye, wee have thought yt convenyent to singnyfye "unto your Honnours the severall names of all the saide "procured persons, as allso with ther adytions here-"under wrytten, wherby shall also apere that some of "the saide persons are none of Her Majesties tenantes "in Waymoth, nor free of the said toune; whose base "and slender credyte wee refer to the judgment of the "honourables and worshipfulls of this sheere [shire]. "And for trwe [sic] testimony hereof wee hereunto set "the sealle of this towne, the xxith of August in the "xxiiiith yere of the regne of our Soveragne Ladie the "Queen's Majestie [1582]." Written below, on a sepa-rate line. "John Brouke, baker, the chef dysturber of "the government of this toune." Below it, in three divisions :—"William Doderell, mercer. John Warde, "maryner. Walter Boyt, tayllor. Nicholas Willms, "tayllor. Laurence Brouke, tayllor. Robart Veake, "maryner. Richard Abot, maryner. Stevin George, "shwmaker. John Willshere, lyterman. Thomas Groyn, "husbondman. Richard Karrantone, shoemaker. Chris-"topher Symons, tayllor, William Mounsell, merchant. "Gilbert Clavell, berebrewer. Richard Jurdayne, "yeman. Nicholas Gardener, tanner.—These ar no "tenantes, nor holdeth any inherytance in the said "toune."

A Letter from Lord Charles Howard, Lord High Admiral, afterwards Earl of Nottingham, chief com-mander against the Spanish Armada :—"After my "verie hartie commendations unto you. Forasmuch as "I am certyfyed that greate quantitie of oade is brought "into sundrie partes and places of Dorsetshire, which "was taken by the Prince of Condye in his passage to "Rochell; wiche cause the French Ambassador heere "dothe very earnestlie folowe to her Majestie and the "Lords of the Councell, by expresse commaundment "from the Kinge his Majestie; wiche beinge of "waighte, and to be considered by the Lorde of the "Councell, I have therefore thought good to will and "require you to make stay of all suche oade with what "convenient speede you maie, after the receite hereof, "untill you heare further orders from me or the Lords "of the Counsell for the same. Thus committinge the "due regarde hereof to your carefull consideration, not "dowtinge of your goode will and redines to accom-"plishe theffecte hereof, I bid you hartilie well to fare. "From the Courte at Grenewiche, this 17 of Februarie, "1585. Your very lovinge frend C. Howard. To my "verie lovinge frende Mr. Frauncis Hawlye Esquier, "Vice-admyralls deputie of Dorset, and to his deputies. "in his absence, gyve these." There is a note written on it—"This letter was delivered to Mr. Mayor and his "brethren the 6 of Marche 1585 ; at whiche time Mr. "Jo. Wells shewed full auctoritee from my Lord "Admirall to him geven for the clarkeshippe and ser-"jantshippe of thadmiraltie." From the following almost contemporary note at the foot, it appears that the Letter is not now perfect; or at least, that the copy of the Letter written in compliance therewith on the opposite leaf of the original Letter, has been torn off:—"In the other side of the same letter, Mr. Francis Hawlye "directed his mynde to John Wells, to this effect, "that he should arrest and make staye of all oade "in Waymouth and Melcombe porte, that hath there "come yn since the cumminge home of shippinge from "Rochele, in condnctinge the Prince of Condye the-"ther. And lykewysse, to arrest and staye all such "oade as Mr. Fenner solde to divers merchauntes in Mel-"combe. And for not obedience, to arrest the per-"sones so not obeyinge." By "oade" is probably meant "wode," or woad, the "Isatis tinctoria;" for-merly much grown in Normandy and Picardy, and used for dyeing blue.

WEYMOUTH AND MELCOMBE REGIS.

A Letter, addressed "To my verie loving frend Mr. "William Pitt, Maior of the towne of Weymouth and "Melcomb Regis." Dated "From my howse in "Barnelmes the xviiith of July 1587. Your verie "loving frend Frs. Walsingham." Robert Gregory, of that town, has charged Frampton, one of his "deputies "for the customes there," with having "caried himself "verie disorderly." The Mayor is requested to examine them on the matter, and certify.

A Letter, addressed,—"To my very goode frende the "Maior of Weimouth and Melcom Regis be these "geven," and signed "Your lovinge frende Winches- "ter," [William Paulet, Marquess of Winchester]; the Lord Lieutenant of the County of Dorset.—"Where of "late there was a pinace of your towne of Weimouth "called 'The Gifte,' bound to the seas in warlicke sort, "which by you was staied. Sithence which time this "berer, Henry Edwardes, one of the company bounde to "sea in the saide vessell, hathe bine with me, and shewid "a license to them graunted from my Lorde Admirall; "these are therefore to will you to suffer the saide "vessell to departe to the seas, with suche victell and "other thinges, as at this present they have provided "for ther jorney. And this my letter shalbe your dis- "charge in that behalfe. Even so I bid you farwell. "Tidworthe the xxxth of Julye 1587."

A Letter, addressed—"To our lovinge frinde George "Trenchard Esquire:"—"After our hartie comenda- "cons. We perceve by your letters directed unto me "the Secretary, that you have made staye of certen "hulkes laden with vittalls and other comodities, which "weare brought into the roade of Portland out of there "course towardes the coaste of Spayne, by three of "her Majesties subjectes shippes that returned out of "the Straights; wherein we doe very well allowe of "your discrete and considerat manner of proceedinges, "and because yt appearethe by the contentes of your "sayde letters that the sale of the corne and other "victualls wherewith the sayde hulkes are partly laden "would greatlie releve the want and scarcitie that is "in that country, wee thincke meete that yf any mer- "chauntes or others may there be founde, that will be "contented to deale in the buyinge of the same at "some reasonable rate and price, you shoulde then "deale and perswade with the sayde straungers to "yelde to the uttringe and sellinge there in the cun- "trye of there sayde corne or othere vittalls, or of "some parte thereof, lettinge them understande that "yt is a matter agreable with cemon custome and the "lawes of nacons, that when any shipps laden with "vittalls happen to come uppon the waste of any coun- "trye where there ys for the tyme wante or scarcitie "of vittalls, whethere yt be voluntarylie or by compul- "sion, the prince of that cuntrye dothe and maye use "the advauntage to cause the same to be solde to his "owne subictes for there own necessary use and pro- "vision, for redie monny; uppon which motion and "perswasions, yf they shalbe contente to sell there "sayde vittalls, then maye you cause the sayde mer- "chauntes or others, whome you shall before have dealt "withall, to buy the same; foreseeinge nevertheles, "that good and readie payments be made unto the "parties, accordinge to the price that maye be agreed "on, leaste otherwise they shoulde have any just occa- "sion to complayne of to her hinderaunce, by the for- "bearaunce of there monny. But yf notwithstandinge "suche travell and indevour as by yow shalbe used "in the matter, yow shall find them unwillinge to "yelde to the sale of there sayde vyttalls here, we "thincke fytt you shoulde suffer them quietlie to de- "parte and hould on ther owne course; for that her "Majestie hathe a speciall care not to utter any ill "usage to the merchauntes of theaste partes, for dyvers "waightie consideracons, and specially in respecte of "the provisions of corne that her subiectes have from "thence in this yeare of scarcity. And soe wee bid "yow farewell. At Greenwich, the seconde of June "1587. Your lovinge frindes Chr. Hatton Can. W. "Burghley. R. Leycester. C. Howarde. Hunsdon. F. "Walsingham. Ant. Asheley. — George Trenchard, "Esqr, Mayor of Weymouth."

A Letter, in reference to the disputes and "contro- "versie betwene the townes of Waymouth and Mel- "combe Regis, about their privileges and franchises." Dated "From Windsor Castle the 20th of September "1586," and addressed "To our verie lovinge freindes, "Thomas Howard, George Trenchard, and John Wil- "liams, Esquires." Signed, "T. Bromley, Canc. W. "Burghley. F. Warwyk. C. Howard. Hunsdon. Jamys "Croft. Chr. Hatton. Frs. Walsingham."

A Letter, mutilated at the beginning, in reference to building a bridge over the haven between Weymouth and Melcombe Regis. A contribution is recommended to be made throughout the County, for the purpose. The Letter, dated "From the Court at Greenwich the "xxiith of May 1592," is addressed "To our very loving "fellows the Justices of the Peace of the County of "Dorset," and is signed, "Jo. Cant.· W. Burghley. "C. Howard. J. Hunsdon. F. Buckehurst. J. Wolley. "A. Ashley."

WEYMOUTH AND MELCOMBE REGIS.

A Letter, addressed "To our very loving ffrend Mr. "William Pitt, Mayor of Weymoth Melcombe Regis. "Yeve theis."—"Mr. Mayor. Theis shalbe both to "pray and require yow (yf your health can so permit) "to meete us this day by two of the clock in the after- "noone at Bolehaies, as allso to warne all theis heere- "under written, or any other ells in your towne that "are skillfull in fortification, that they in like sort "attend us at the tyme and place prefixed; for that "we are to use their judgementes in vewing the daun- "gerous places for landing of thenemy; intending for "the same purpose to lye this night at Melcomb, and "so to travell therehence to mouve along the sea coast "to Lyme. Thus resting your loving ffrendes, we "bidd yow hartely farewell. From Wolveton, this "Towsday morning the xiiith of March 1586. Thomas "Howarde, John Horsey, George Trenchard, John "Willyams." Persons above alluded to,—"Mr. Rich- "ard Pitt, Mr. John Payne, Hewgh Randall, Olyver "Gregory." Wolveton, near Dorchester, was the residence of the Trenchards.

A Letter, addressed,—"To my very loving ffrendes the "Maior of Waymouth and his bretheren."—"After "my very harty comendations—Wheare I am geven to "understand that there are certaine sugers and other "comodyties brought into that port, the precmption "whereof by vertue of Charter (as I am informed) "belongeth to yowe, I have thought good to send this "bearer, my sarvant, Thomas Myddelton, to you; and "hartely to praye youe for my sake, and upon such "reasonable composition with you, for a certaine gaine "upon the hondryth, to graunt unto him your privi- "lege therin, that befor any other he may have the "refusall of all the sayd sugers and other comodyties "thear, as he shall think good to buy, yelding such "payment as betweene the sellers and him may be "agreed upon. Wherein not doubting but youe wyll "respect my request in frindly sort, I bydd yow "hartely farewell. From the Court in Greenwich, this "xiiith February 1586. Your loving frend (signed) "Frs. Walsyngham."

Copy of a Letter of Secretary Walsingham, his sig- nature being imitated in facsimile; with an endorse- ment, in old writing.—"Sir ffr. Walsingham, his "letter to the Lord Chefe Baron, in Michaelmas Terme, "anno xxix°."—"After my very harty commendations "to your Lordship. Whereas I am given to understand "that there is a controversie lately revived by them "of Waymouth against them of Melcombe, which is "presently to be heard in the Exchequer Chamber. "Forasmuch as I am informed that the complaint im- "porteth no other thing then that which hath been "heretofore determined both by decree and by Com- "mission, as well from the Lords of the Counsell as "out of the Court of the Exchequer, and that the "matter is pursued by the common instrumentes to "the breakers thereof, who are noted to be seditious "and apt to raise tumultes, opposing themselves "against all authority, and putting the officers in dan- "ger, which have attempted to suppresse their vio- "lence. I have,therefore thought good to desire your "Lordship to have good consideration of the matter, "that the same being found as it is reported unto me, "th'offenders may be discouraged to work the lyke, by "receaving condigne punishment according to theire "demerites. And so I bid your Lordship hartely fare- "well. From the Court at Richmond, the 15 of No- "vember 1586. Your assured loving frend. Frs: "Walsyngham." In one of the Journals in Mr. Sher- ren's Collection, there is another copy of this letter, with a like imitation of Walsingham's signature. It seems a remarkable fact that the Corporation should become acquainted with the existence of a letter of this nature.

A Letter from Lord C.Howard (afterwards Earl of Not- tingham) addressed,—"To mie verie lovinge freindes "the Mayor and Bayliffes of Weymouth and Melcombe "Regis."—"After mie verie hartie commendations "unto yow. I have received your lettre of the vith "day of this January by this bearer, and am verie well "content that some of the ffysshe shalbe sould for the

" better relief of the towne, at such reasonable price
" which by yow and John Smyth shalbe thought mete.
" For as it doth not appertaine to me, soe will I not
" sett downe any price for that which maie be called
" hereafter in question ; yet doe I thinke, and soe would
" have it knowne, that the towne is to be favoured in
" the price more then any others. I thanke you for
" your newes out of Spaine ; and pray you, as occasion
" of such matters may fale out, to acquaint me there-
" with, whome you shall find myndefull of your good-
" wills therein. Soe fare you hartely well. From the
" Court at Greenwich, this 14 of January 1586(7).
" Your verie lovinge ffreind (signed) C : Howard."

Another Letter ,by the same, addressed,—" To my
" verie lovinge freinde, Wylliam Pytt, Mayor of Wey-
" mouth and Melcombe Regis, and to others of that
" Corporation, give these."—" After my verie hartie
" commendations unto yow. I have received your
" letter of the 18 of Aprill, and marvell not a litell that
" Mr. Hawley would send proces ether to staie the
" goods or to arreast the parties to apeare before him
" at Corfcasstell. Therefore as you have done well in
" permittinge the goods lawfullye bought to pass away
" accordinge to my letters, and wisely in takeinge
" recognizance of the captaine and the companie to
" aunsweare any matters in their late voyages for sup-
" posed piracie, according to his proces ; soe now doe I
" require you to discharge the same recognizance ; for
" that the captaine standeth bound to me in the highe
" Court of the Admeraltie to aunsweare to whatsoever
" may be objected against him or them for any thinge
" done in the same voyage. And as I will not in any
" waye wittingly prejudice your libertees and privi-
" ledges, soe will I not lose the prerogative and right
" incident to myne office, and therefore pray you to
" send up some about the middell of the next terme to
" confer with my counsell therein, and yf they finde
" you to have right in any thihgs touching the Admi-
" raltie, I will not debarr you of your dewe that may
" come thereby. And soe I leave you to the Almighty.
" From the Court at Grenewich, this 26 of Aprill 1587.
" Your very loving freind (signed) C : Howard."

A long Letter, on foolscap, with autograph signature,
as follows : addressed,—" To our loveing freinds the Mayor
" or other cheefe officers of the townes of Waymouth
" and Poole."—" After our hartie comendacions. His
" Majestie [Charles I.] well understanding the ambicion
" and mallice of his declared enemie, the King of
" Spaine, and being certified from all partes what great
" preparations of sea and land forces are in readines
" for the invasion of theise kingdomes, hath by the
" advise of his Councelle, as well of Estate as of Warre,
" taken this royal resolution, not only with a new and
" strong ffleete to carrie the warre as farre as may be
" from our owne coasts, and to assaile the enemio within
" his owne ports, but also to arme and strengthen
" himselfe upon his owne coast, that by God's blessing
" he may repell and frustrate anie attempts which may
" be made against us either from Flanders or from
" Spaine. And considering that the religion, libertie,
" lives, and estates of us all are no lesse engaged herein
" then his Majesties owne safetie and honour, hee doth
" not doubt that all his loveing subjects will shew their
" forwardnes and courage in performing no less (or
" rather more) then upon like occasions hath with great
" alacritie ben don in former tymes. And because theise
" great occasions, besides the whole strength of his
" Majesties navic royall, require a present preparation
" of a considerable nomber of the shipps of his subjects,
" his Majestie, of his royall grace and wisdome, to
" make the burden more easie, hath commaunded a
" proportionable distribution to be made amongst the
" ports of this kingdom, that most helpe may be re-
" quired from the places of power, and that the weaker
" may be charged with so manie shipps onely as by our
" letters shalbe assigned ; and that therein also they
" may be assisted not onely by their membrs, but by
" the inland townes and counties adjoyneing, according
" to such directions as shall be given in that behalfe.
" And now, according to this his Majesties most gratious
" will and pleasure, the towne of Waymouth and Poole,
" with the other sea townes and ports of that parte, is
" appointed to sett out but twoe shipp of 2— tonns in
" burden, which must carrie twelve peeces of ordinance,
" and be fitt in warlike manner with all necessarie
" tackles, sea stores, and munition, and maned with
" — men at least, and victualled for three monethes.
" And because it is conceived that their is not any shipp
" belonging to that porte of that burden and force,
" which may be fitt for this service, there is order
" already given for such shipp to be sent you from

" London, which is to be hired and furnished by your-
" selves in such state as shall be fitt. And if you want
" men, there is likewise order given to the Justises,
" your neighbours, to supplie from the countie a third
" parte of the coplement of your shipps out of such
" able bodies as may be fitt to use musketts. And
" the Justises are also directed to assist and beare a
" part with you in the provision of victualls. And if
" you cannott gett powder and shott in those partes,
" the officers of the ordinance shall see you furnished
" therewith at a moderate charge ; soe as haveing all
" these helpes, and your imployment beeing intended
" no further than our coast, and for defence of the
" kingdome, which cannot be deserted without dangers
" and reproach, we rest assured that, like men of
" courage and zeale to the common cause, you will not
" faile to use such dilligence and expedition in setting
" forth the shipps, that the other portes may not prevent
" [i.e. anticipate] you in coming sooner to the rendes-
" vous at Portsmouthe, whence the whole fleete must
" sette to sea by the end of July, and is not to be re-
" tarded by the neglect of anie, who shall thereby
" incurre his Majesties just offence. And so wee bid
" you hartily fare well. From the Court at Whitehall
" the last of June 1626."—[In another hand]—Post-
scriptum. " You have to observe the proportion of 2
" men to every 8 tonnes, for the manning of your
" shippes." — " Your loveing freinds (signed) Tho.
" Coventrye. Marleburgh. Manchester. Montgomery.
" G. Buckingham. Totnes. Pembroke. Kellie. Grandi-
" son. E. Conwey. D. Carleton. J. Edmondes. Jo. Suck-
" ling. Robt. Naunton, Rich. Weston. J. Coke, Jul.
" Cæsar. Hum. May." There is an endorsement on this
Letter, in a contemporary hand : — " Receaved this
" letter the 12th daye of July, aboute 8th of clocke in
" the eaveninge 1626."

Another and somewhat similar Letter, addressed,—
" To our verie loveing frends, the Mayor, Magistrates,
" and cheefe officers of Waymouth."—" After our hartie
" commendations. Whereas his Majestie hath beene
" advertised from divers good parts, that the King of
" Spaine, both in his remote and neere dominions, doth
" prepare a puissant army by sea and land to invade
" this kingdome, in a most hostile manner, insomuch
" that now very suddenly wee expect an attempt upon
" us, and because we have represented to his Majestie,
" that you, as being next the danger, wil be most con-
" cerned herein, his Majestie, out of his royall and
" tender care of your good, taking into consideration
" the present condition and weaknes of your towne,
" hath thought fitt not only to send you tymely warning
" hereof, but gratiously to authorize and give you leave
" by [the] advice of the Lo. Leiuetennant, or in his
" absence the Deputie Leiuetennants, of your shire,
" and three of the Justises of Peace next adjoyning, to
" fortifie your towne by all those waies and meanes
" which may best secure you from the invasion of the
" enemy. And for that purpose to use this letter as a
" warrant ; not doubting that accordingly you will take
" the assistance of such ingineers and experienced men
" in the warres as may make your towne most defensible ;
" assuring you for the rest that his Majestie hath
" noe intercours herein any way to discharg himself
" from the due care he hath of your safeties, but only
" to incite and stirr you upp ; that in imitation of other
" townes in forraine countries, which have beene drawne
" to the same exigent, and which have made use of the
" same remedies, you would, according to the libertie
" his Majestie doth voucsafe unto you, take the benefitt
" of this his favour for the securing yourselves from
" theise iminent dangers. The further proofe of which
" his Majesties gratious intencion we doubt not but to
" procure unto you, when we shall understand of your
" forwardnes herein. In the meane tyme, if you shall
" discover any considerable number of shippes, or other
" apparent argument of an enimie upon your coasts,
" we doe require and charge you, not only to fyre the
" beacons, and warne the countries adjoyning of your
" danger, but to send as imediate word thereof. And
" so we bidd you farewell. From the Court at White-
" hall, the 7th of July 1626. Your very loving friends
" Marleburgh. Manchester. Totnes. J. Bridgewater.
" E. Conwey. J. Coke."

A Letter, addressed,—" To our verie loving friends,
" the Maior and Aldermen of Waymoth and Melcombe
" Regis, these be delivered." Dated "Blandford, 3e
" Augusti 1626," and signed " Henry Hastings. Tho.
" Freke. John Browne. Nath. Napper." The Lords of
the " Privie Counsell " have abated one of the three
ships first assessed upon the three ports and county of
Dorset, and expect the other two to be " presently sett

" forth." They are requested to meet the undersigned at Dorchester on the Tuesday next, to receive further information on the contents of the letters which they have received. There is a postscript added :—" Wee " further desier you to take notice wee and the muster- " master will be at Weymoth, to vew and see your " trained companies, upon Wednesday the ninth of this " instant August."

These are numerous sets of yearly Accounts of the Mayors of Weymouth and Melcombe Regis in Mr. Sherren's Collection, belonging to the 16th and 17th centuries, mostly in small folio pamphlet form; in addition to which there are several of what may be termed " volumes," recently put in brown paper covers. The following is a brief account of them.—

A large folio volume, of 68 leaves of very stout paper, several of them, towards the close, being left blank. It has formed part of a thicker volume, the first leaf, in old numerals, being numbered 39 ; its character would seem to have been, partly that of a journal, and partly a common-place book, containing forms, precedents, and statutes. It begins with forms of indentures and obligations. At fol. 43, " The Customes of Billinggate, " here written out, of the Guildhall of London, ordered " by the Maior, Aldermen, and Commons," being a translation of the Latin code, a copy of which is to be found in the Liber Albus, belonging to the Corporation of the City of London. The Oaths of various Officials follow ; then, at fol. 49,—" Melcomb Regis. The sub- " sidie paide owt of the said town in anno 1570, as " followyth " :—the sums paid appearing under the heads of " Laundes, Goodes, Denyzins, Allyens, Sessors [? Settlers.]" This list is for Melcombe Regis only, its union with Weymouth having taken place in the following year. Seven persons pay the subsidy in respect of " Lands," Owin Raynoldes (a celebrated Mayor of the place) paying 3l., George Bagge 40s., Margarett Pytte 3l. Seven persons pay in respect of " Goods ; " one Denizen, Jervaise Mocket, " for goods " 20s. ; three Aliens, and three Sessors : hence may be formed an idea of the then extent and resources of Melcombe Regis, (the portion of the present Weymouth that lies east of the haven, and facing the sea.) The book, having originally belonged solely to the town of Melcombe Regis, still contains entries in reference to the exclusive rights of inhabitants of that place : in folio 51 are given, —" Certayne Speciall Articles towchinge the chyeff " and pryncipall poyntes of Melcombe Regis Charter, " gevinge them boath the name and profits of the port, " which the Bayllyfes and inabytaunts of Weymouth " have and do withold from theme." Then follow the Articles, extracted from the Charter granted to Mel- combe Regis in the 8th year of King Edward the First, which probably no longer exists, but which is recited in that of the 11th of Edward the Second, still in the pos- session of the Corporation. This is followed, in folio 52, by " Certayne other manyfeste proufe and sufficient " good evidence, declaringe and aprovinge Melcombe " Regis to ben the port and moreover the creeke as " woll by Statude [sic] lawe of the realme, and by the " graunt of the Charter of Pole, as also by the custumes " and Controlers accompts, geven up to the Exchoquer " in the xxxvi. yere of King Henry the Eyghth." Fol. 52b has " Thearle of Penbrouke his letter to the Maior " and burgh of Melcomb Regis, procured by the Ballys " of Waymouth upon a false informacion." In fol. 53 is a copy of a Letter, addressed probably to the Earl of Pembroke, acknowledging the receipt of his " gentell " letters." At fol. 53b is a copy of a somewhat singular Letter from Robert, Earl of Leicester :—" My Lord of " Leciter his letter for 40 horses." " For asmuche as I " am credibielie informed that within the counties of " Dorcet and Somerced ther be divers and sondrie pas- " tures and other grounds so overpressed and rescevid " with a nombre of smalle nags, as well horses as mares, " contrarie to the Statute in that case provided, as that " thereby the good race and brecde of sufficient service- " able horses and geldinges ys greatlie impayred and " hindered, I have thought good by vertue of myne " office to lysenoe and authorise this berrer, Robart " Gregorie, my servaunte, to by for his reasonable " monye within the said too shyres the nomber of " fortie of the same smalle unlawfull beastes, and them " to transport beyounde the seas, ther to sell againe, or " otherwise to exchaunge for other comodities to his best " behauf and benyfit. And therefore these shalbe to " require yowe and every of yowe, to suffer the said " Gregory quietlie to inbarqe and transport the same " fortie smalle beastes owt of any of hir Majesties " havens within the said twoo counties of Dorcet and

" Somerced, without any your let, staye, or mollestacion, " wherof faylle ye not, as you will answer to the con- " trarie. At the court; the iiiith of June 1571. R. " Lesiter. To all Shryves, Justices, etc." At fol. 56, the union of the towns has now taken place (13th Eliza- beth), and the volume is devoted to entries of the united Corporations:—" Waymouthe and Melcombe Regis. " Constitucyons and orders made and ffully agreed " uppon by the Mayor, Justices, and Allderdmen [sic], " Comon Counsell of the same toune, the viiith daie of " Julie in the xiiith yere of the raigne of our most " gracious and soverain Ladie, Quene Elizabeth, Anno " Domini 1571." Fol. 57b,—" Constytucyons for the " maytenance of the haven, fullie agreed uppon, and " ratyfied." Fol. 58,—" Constytucyons agaynste annoy- " ances of the saide toune fully ratyfyed and establyshed, " the penalties whereof beinge forfayoted ar to be re- " ceyved by the receiver of the same toune, and none " other." Fol. 58b,—" Constitucions agreed uppon for " the tranquilitie and better quietnes of the said towne, " as aforesaid, the second daye of October, anno regni " Reginæ Elizabethæ prædictæ xiii°." These " Con- " stitutions" are signed, in folio 59, " By me Rychard " Pitt, Maior. By me Thomas Hanam, Recorder," fol- lowed by the signatures of all the then principal inhabit- ants of the united towns. At fols. 60, 61, follow copies of various letters written to the Corporation. Fol. 62 et seq., the mode of " Kepinge of Courte," and holding inquisition as to various offences. Fols. 66b, 67, Assess- ments to the Subsidy granted to her Majesty A.D. 1571. Fol. 68,—" The copie of a Letter sent from certayne of the " Queenes Majesties most honourable Privie Counsell to " certayne Commissioners, as may appere uppon the sen- " ister complaynt of thinhabitants of Waymouth, uppon " articles falsly by them aleaged against thinhabitants " of Melcombe." Fol. 72, Answer of John Jeffary and Roger Manwode, the Commissioners (apparently) ap- pointed to arbitrate in the said disputes. Fol. 72 b. " A taxation made for the Townes causes, the xith of " October 1583, in the time of Bartelmew Allyn, Mayor:" 20 shillings is the largest sum assessed, and sixpence the smallest.—Fol. 73 b, " This order was had, made, " and taken, in the Councell Chamber, by the Queen's " Majesties most honorable Privie Councell there as- " sembled, the later ende of June, or 1, 2, or 3 daye of " Julye 1582, et anno Reginæ 24°. That none of Way- " mouth shalbe againe hard at the Counstable [error " for ' Council '] table etc." It is thereby ordered that no petition by the inhabitants of Waymouth is to be heard at the Council table, in favour of John Brooke, of that place, who is in prison for disobeying the enact- ments consequent upon the union of the towns in 1571. From fol. 74 it appears that Brooke was a merchant of Waymouth, imprisoned in the Fleet Prison. One of his offences was " Contemptuous speches of an order " made in the Court of Exchequer, viz., that it is " not worthe a button." Fol. 75,—" A taxation made the " last of Aprill 1584, aboute the bridge to be erected " (between Weymouth and Melcombe Regis)," Bartel- " mews Allyn, Mayor." Fol. 76,—" The names of the " xxiiiti chosen and supplied in the roomes of suche as " were ded, taken in Aprill 1584, in the time of Mr. " Bartelmew Allyn's Mayoraltie." Fol. 76b,—" Con- " stitucions made and agreed uppon for the payment of " suche taxation as well uppon freemen at lardge as " other men, the xxxth daye of December, anno Eli- " zabethæ nunc Reginæ xxvii°." This is signed by " Thomas Howarde, Hewgh Randell, Mayor," the then Bailiffs, and all the chief inhabitants of the town. Fol. 77b,—" Orders and Constitutions made and agreed " uppon, the xiiith dayo of October in the xxxvith yeare " of the reign of our Soveraigne Ladye Elizabeth, the " Quene's Majestie that now is." This is signed by " Robert Morris, Mayor," and the principal officials and men of the town. Fol. 78,—" The Counsells letter for " aucthorisinge certaine Justies at lardge to assiste the " Mayor for the time beinge in executinge justice etc." Fol. 79, copy of a Letter from Francis Walsingham to the Lord Chief Baron. It is to the same effect as the copy already mentioned, and Walsingham's signature here also is facsimiled. Fol. 80,—" A generall taxation, maid " the xxth day of Julye 1591 by these persones heare under " wryten, to be weickly paid from the furste day of June " until thaire be a sufficient some of mony gathered " for fyndinge [founding] of the jeattye on Melcombe " side." One or two copies of letters then follow, the last date being 1594; the volume ending with a trans- lation of the " Statute of Winchester." On the 14th of October 1594 (fol. 81), Richard Swayne succeeds Serjeant Hanham as Recorder ; the latter having been appointed on the union of the towns in 1571.

A book, small folio, paper, imperfect, containing minutes of the proceedings of the Law Court of Weymouth and Melcomb Regis, from 17th January to 1st of October, 18th Elizabeth; there is a presentment by the Jury, in English, at the end, 1st October 1576. The cases themselves seem to be mostly actions for debt.

The next volume, in date, is of a somewhat similar nature, containing proceedings of the Law Courts, with View of Frank Pledge, together with the Manor Court, held at Waymouth, Wareham, Portland, or Portlond, Pimperne Hundred, and Wyke Regis, these being, all of them, royal manors, and the Courts there being held by the stewards of the manors respectively. The entries begin at the 1st of October in the 24th of Elizabeth, and end the 3rd of September in the 25th. As in the preceding volume, the entries are in Latin, but the " Ordinationes " that are occasionally introduced are in English. For example, on the 15th of April, in the 25th year, at a Law Court, or View of Frank Pledge, holden at Waymouth, it is ordered,—" That the boere " and alle brewers and sellers wythin this libertye shall " sell theyre drynk under the renge at iiijd. the gallonde, " and beyng stale att iiijd. the gallonde, and to use just " measures uppone payne for every that make deffalt " to forfeit iis. vid." Also, at the same Court,—" That " every hyghe tenant shall be bounden unto her Majestie " with suretyes for his under tenant, yf he hathe auye, " that he shall dyscharge the parysshe of all such under- " tenants, and of the sequell [family, or wife and chil- " dren], and thatt they shalbe of good governent and " no wood stenlers, upon payne for every hyghe tenant " makyng deffalt, to forfeit vs." There are also con- tained in this volume minutes of the—" Three weeks' " Court," " Curia Dominæ Reginæ de tribus septi- " manis ; " a Court formerly held in pleas of debt under the sum of 40 shillings, from time to time, at the several places whose names are above-mentioned. At a Law Court and Manor Court holden at Waymouth, on the 8th of April, in the 25th year of Elizabeth, the following order was made :—" Hytt ys ordenyd and decreed by " the consent of the Jurators and others, thatt the " Charters and other evydences and wryttynges concern- " yng or belongynge to the towne and the lybertye " of the same, shalbe kepte in the commone cheaste, " accordynge to thauncyent usage of the towne ; as " allso the towne scale. And that nothyne in the sayde " cheast shalbe taken oute, nor the sayd chest openyd, " except there be present xii of the burgesses of the sayd " towne. That none shall suffer theyr pyggos at lardge " in any place wythyn the towne, uppone payne to fforfett " for every foote one peny, and the fyerst [first] to take " to the same. Thet the shambles be taken downe, and " savyd to the use of the towne, or otherwyse. That " they who bryng the butter or cheese to the towne to " sell, shall stande att the markett place, and nott to " goo to the howses, so as the towne maye be generally " servyd. That the ffyshers doo bryngo theyr fyshe " into the markett, that the towne maye be fyrst servyd. " That the buttes maye be newe made." There appear to be many particulars of value among these entries in reference to the royal manor of Portland, in those days ; there are some entries also bearing reference to the town of Wareham.

A thin folio paper volume, containing proceedings of the Court of Waymouth and Melcombe Regis, from the 24th of November in the 27th year of Queen Elizabeth to the 13th of July in the same year ; imperfect, and in a mutilated condition. The proceedings are before Hugh Randall, the Mayor, or his Deputy, and seem to be mostly actions for debt. The minutes are entered partly in English, but mostly in Latin

The next is a thin small folio paper volume, containing proceedings (in Latin) in " The Court of our Lord the " King in the Guildhall, which has been holden time " out of mind " for the town of Waymouth and Mel- combe Regis, beginning on the 9th of September in the 4th year of King James the First, and ending on the 20th of April in the 7th year of the same reign.

The next is a similar volume, in good condition, con- taining proceedings of the same Court, from the 2nd of October in the 2nd year of James the First to the 12th of August in the 4th year of the same reign; the entries are mostly in Latin, but some few in English. Appli- cation is occasionally made by persons who " stand " in dread of their life, or some hurt of their members " to be done unto them," by others.

A similar volume, beginning 21st October in the 4th year of James the First, and ending the 31st January in the 6th year of the same reign. The entries are in Latin, and it is imperfect at the beginning.

A thin volume of a similar nature, imperfect, and con- taining only a few leaves. It begins in July, and ends 5th of September 1609.

A similar book, but on smaller paper, beginning 20th April in the 11th year of James the First, and ending the first of October in the 14th year of the same reign. The contents (in Latin) seem mostly to be actions of debt or trespass, before the Mayor, Aldermen, Bailiffs, burgesses, and community, of the town. In this and the preceding book, the Court is also described as having been holden "time out of mind "—cujus contrarii me- " moria hominum non existit."

A thicker volume, almost perfect, with its old parch- ment cover, the entries beginning on the 29th of March 1625, and ending, the last three or four leaves being much mutilated by damp, on the 1st of May 1627. Among other matters, there is an entry (in Latin) to the effect that Avice Locke, widow, had offended " against form " of the Statute," by selling smaller beer (minorem cervisiam) than at the rate of one ale-quart (unum le alequarte) for one penny.

The next is a similar volume, the entries beginning at the 23rd of December in the 4th year of Charles the First, and ending the 11th of May 1630. As in the preceding volumes, the entries are generally pleas of debt or trespass, in Latin; but in this volume, appren- ticeships are enrolled (in English) as well. At the other end of the volume are a few copies of letters written by or to the Maior, in 1621-3, in reference to matters con- nected with the trade of the town.

A similar small folio volume, the entries beginning on the 6th of September 1631, and ending the 24th of November in the 9th year of Charles the First : there seem to be no entries of apprenticeships in it. Com- mencing at the other end of the volume, are the minutes (in Latin) of a single Piepowder Court, holden at the Guildhall on the 4th of April in the 8th year of Charles the First; the only case apparently being an action of debt by Matthias Cassomar, gentleman, against James Jolly, Knight, " Senciur de Besne," otherwise called. " James Jolly, Seiur de Besne, Knight," for a sum of 265l. After repeated adjournments, judgment is given in favour of the complainant. This is the only entry here of proceedings in a Court of Piepowder, since the 14th century, that has been met with.

The next volume, in date, is a Minute-book of the Corporation, a small folio, in its original stiff parchment binding. Its latest entry belongs to 1649, its earliest apparently being of the 21st of March 1644 ; when Mr. Francis Gape, Town Clerk, seemingly without notice given, but not improbably for political reasons, suddenly abandons his office, and Richard Stovile is elected, by ten votes of the Corporation, against Gilbert Loader, with two. In p. 11, 29th January 1644, " It is ordered " that the Towne Liter [Lighter] shall bee forthwith " trimmed upp, and made fit for service." The fol- lowing entry (p. 8) bears reference to the Parlia- mentarian soldiers then quartered in the town :— " The examination of Martha Gould of Waimouth and " Melcombe Regis, widow, the 10th day of January " 1644 (5), who sayeth that John Barnes, one of Leui- " tenant Colonell Cokers souldiers, on or about Fry- " day last about 6 or 7 of the clocke, at night, brough. " into the Examinant's howse one quarter of a fatt pig " or a porker, and there left it with this Examinant; " which this Examinant did salt, and putt it up in a " tub, and kept untill the constables upon search found " it in her powdering [salting] tub." There are many further examinations entered in reference to this pig. P. 12,—3rd of July 1645, " Concerning the Governor's " proposall about takeing downe the timber of part of " the Chappell. The Maior and Company do humbly " conceive itt that the timber should remaine, and " that it should be covered. And in regard it was spoiled " in the tyme of the seige, the state may bee at two " thirds of the charge for the covering of it, and the " townesmen of Waymouth at the other third, if the " Governor shall thinke it fitt that it be covered againe. " but not otherwise. As touching the building of a " fort at the Looking place—the Maior and Company " now presente doe agree that a rate shall bee made " upon the townsmen for the raising of teune pownds " towards the charge thereof, yf the Governour please " to order the raising of a fort there." P. 15,—" It " is agreed that such liters as there shall bee occasion " of, shall be ympressed for the use of the towne, " by warrant from the Vice-admirall, for the carry- " ing away of the soile which now lies in the streetes " and lanes." An order is afterwards made, that the inhabitants shall collect the "durt" before each person's house, and that the same shall be removed twice a week by horse and cart. Admissions to the freedom frequently occur in the early part of this volume. P. 19,—" Memorandum, at a Hall on Friday the xxth " of September 1645, there was paid in unto Mr. John " Thornton, the Towne Steward, 20 shillings for a fine " paid by the tobacco merchaunt, for a licence to sell " his tobacco here." P. 40, 21st November 1645,— " Mr. Robert Hardy, of Melcombe Regis, apothecary, " on his oath sayeth that on Wednesday last, in the " afternone, he heard Thomas Allin, one of the cun- " stables, say that a company of Cavaleer raskals had " abused him, which spake faire to his face, and abused " him behind his back."--" Roberte Waall of this " towne, merchaunte, on his oath, sayeth that on Wed- " nesday last he, being present on the bridge, heard " Thomas Allin, one of the cunstables, call Mr. George " Churchey, one of the Aldermen of this towne, a drunk- " en malignant knave, and say there was a good " nice fraternity of them." P. 45, 19th December " 1645,—" John Dudle, clerk of the Parish of Melcomb " Regis, is this day promised by the Maior and Com- " pany xl s. for ringing of the bell from Michaelmas " last till Lady Day next, at 4 in the morning and at 8 " at night, and for keeping of the clock according to " the former custome." In p. 48 there is a corrected draught of a Petition to Parliament, the nature of which is to some extent explained by this entry, in p. 49, —" Another Potition to the Standing Committee by the " said Maior, etc. To the Honourable Committee of " the County of Dorsett. The humble Petition of your " Maior, Aldermen, etc. Humbly Shewith, That your " Petitioners being deeply affected with the necessity " of having an able, godly preacher of the word to bee " setled amongst them, and a sufficient mayntenance " for such a minister, doe conceive itt their duty to " present their petition to that end unto youre high " Court of Parliament. Your Petitioners doe therefore " humbly crave your letter unto the Speaker of the " House of Commons in favour of the Petition herewith " tendred unto you. And your Petitioners shall pray, " etc." P. 53, 11th March 1645 (6).—" This day, Captain " John Arthur, Vice-admirall of the County of Dorset, " came before Mr. Thomas Waltham, Mayor and Jus- " tice of Peace and Quorum of this towne, and did " sweare his peace against John Waltham, of Way- " mouth and Melcomb Regis aforesaid, merchaunt. And " the said John Waltham did say that hee would take " away the life of the said Captaine Arthur, and called " him many opprobious [sic] names, viz., rogue, toade, " cowardly slave, severall tymes, and used many other " abusive termes towards the said Captaine Arthur, in " the presence of the said Maior, and swore two oaths, " by the name of God and God's wounds, in the said " Maior's presence. And it appears unto the said " Maior, upon the oath of the said Captaine Arthur and " of Arthur Holman, of Weymouth and Melcomb Regis " aforesaid, merchant, that the said John Waltham " assaulted and strooke the said Captain Arthur within " this towne. Further, the said Arthur Holman testi- " fied upon his oath, that the said John Waltham first " strooke the said Captain Arthur with his fist, and " afterwards strooke him with a sticke in his face, " which brake the skin of his face neere his eye. John " Browne, Esquire, testifieth on his oath, that the said " John Waltham this day said that hee would kill the " said John Arthur, and that hee would make noe " more to kill him than a toade. And the said John " Waltham said unto the said Captaine Arthur that of " this Court, hee would have right upon him." The result was, that Waltham was put upon his recogni- zances in the sum of 80 l. In the same page William Fudge is fined 5 shillings for being drunk, which sum was to be paid to Constable Leonard Hillard, for the use of the poor. P. 56, 20th March 1645,—" It is " ordered and agreed upon, that all the inhabitants of " this towne in the afternoon in every weeke, forthwith " upon the toling of the Hall bell, shall clense ther " gutters before their severall howses, lands, and " grownds, at the same time, and carry away all such " durt and soile unto severall wast places in places void " and convenient in Waymouth," under certain penal- ties there stated. P. 57,—" Mr. John Huney sayeth that " Roger Legg, one of Captaine Henry Culliford's soul- " diers, on Tuesday 16 March, brake up the pound in " the Fryery, and tooke out thence one pigg of the said " John Huneyes, which was impounded by the porters " for annoying the streetes." The " pigga " seem also to have led to other annoyances; p. 57,—" Daniell Windsor, " one of the porters of this towne, on his oath, deposeth " that hee being in the execution of his office in the " ympounding of the piggs of William James for going

" about the streetes of the towne, Wensday last, Mary, " the wife of the said William James, called this depo- " nent base consart and base raskall, and other oppro- " brious names." P. 58,—10th April 1646. John Dudley says on his oath, that Robert Saunders, mariner, had said " that Mr. Ince and Mr. Way, the two ministers, " were knaves both in their preaching, and that the " said Mr. Way did preach plaine Popery; and that he " would justifie to Mr. Ince his face, that he was a " knave in his preaching, and that he would soundly " hoare of it; or used words to the like effect. And " . . . . that the said Robert Saunders said in this " examinant's hearing that hee fought not against tho " Papists for their religion, for twas lawful for every " man to use his conscience, but hee fought against " them as blouddy men; and said that hee would fight " as valiantly against the Presbiterians, as ever hee did " against the Cavaleers." P. 60,—5th May 1646, John Thomas, one of the Corporals of Lieutenant Colonel Coker's Company, arrests a " marriner " and a sailor of Southampton; the former for being drunk, the latter being " well entred in beere; " one of the offenders, ho says, " blasphemously swore " one oath, the other three oaths. The town, it may be here remarked, was at this time in the hands of the Parliamentarian forces, under the command of Colonel Sydenham, and oaths were rigorously counted. P.61,—" John Biere, mariner, on his " oath sayeth that on Wensdaie last, about 7 of the clock " in the eveninge, this deponent was upon the key, " neere the George, where hee heard John Jourdain " say to Mr. Henry Rose, one of the Bailiffes and Jus- " tices of this towne, that hee was a cavaleer, and as bad " as Fabian Hodder, [who was condemned to death, if " not executed, by the Parliamentarians], or worse; " and was a two faced knave. And that [he] heard " Mr. Bailiff says to Jourdain,—that hee, meaning " Mr. Bailiff, would throw downe all againe shortly." Another witness, David Dove, by name, improves upon this, at the next Court (p. 62) and asserts that the said John Jordan [sic] then said,—" Thou art a double-faced " man, and Fabian Hodder is an honester man then " thou; for hee hath stood to what hee hath undertaken, " but thou hast turned on every side." Jourdain ac- knowledges his offence, but is pardoned at the inter- cession of Bailiff Rose. This was on the 8th of May 1646, and on the 15th, Isaac Bolt gives information that he has heard Giles Gregorie, sailor, say in an alehouse kept by Robert Wyer, a sergeant of Captayne Bragg's Company,—" that Thomas Waltham, Waltham's calls, " Maior of this towne, is a traitour." Gregorio is con- sequently put upon his recognizances in the sum of 40l., to appear at the next Sessions of the peace, with two sureties of 20l. each. On the 27th of May in the same year (p. 63), John Waltham, merchant, is accused by Richard Covett of threatening to kill Captain John Arthur [who was a strong Parliamentarian], and calling him " cuckoly rogue," with another bad name. Of Mrs. Pitt it was also alleged that he spoke in as strong terms, as being " an Independant loose woman [by " periphrasis], and that he would have her, and all " other such Independant loose women whipt out of " the towne." In p. 64 it is stated that,—" The said " John Waltham carryed himselfe very saucily before " the said Maier, and sayd that the said Richard Covett " [the witness against him] shuld not write, and bidd goe " about his business, and tooke him by the arme, and " tooke away the Towne Clerke's bookes from him;" the consequence being, that the said witness has here omitted to sign his name, as was usually done. From the following passage (p. 75), the 19th of June 1646, we learn that at this date spirit-drinking, as a help towards getting drunk, had already set in:—James King, servaunte of Richard " Keate, of Waymouth, blacksmith, by his own confession " before Mr. Maier and Mr. Bailiff Leddoze, was drunk " on Saturday last in the afternoone in Waymouth; and " confesseth that hee and one about Osmington drank " a cupp of beere at Dorothy Benfeilds, and from there " the said King, and some others, went to Caseways, " and there drank strong waters, and came home, and " quarrelled, and strooke his master." The father and master [with singular leniency] promise to pay his fine within a fortnight, 5 shillings " for the use of the poore." P. 77,—8 July 1646, " Katheryne Kinde, widow, being " examined on her oath, sayeth that about 3 weekes " sithens [since], she was neere the shopp of Mr. John " Swetman, where Mr. Maddox and others had discourse " about Independentes. And shee heard the said Mr. " Maddockes [sic] say that hee did beleive there would " bee a greater warre then had ben yett, if they did " goe to putt downe Independentes." P. 84,—" Ma- " thewes Day, 21 Septr. 1646. This day Doctour John

" Bond tooke his oath of Recorder of this towne, and
" his oath of supremacye." John Bond, of Lutton, who
was also Member for this town, had been a Fellow of St.
Catharine's Hall, Cambridge, and was at this time
Master of Trinity Hall, in that University. P. 95,—
" George Churchey, of Waymouth and Melcomb Regis,
" humbly sheweth that upon Tuesday the 13th of Oc-
" tober 1646, being market-day in that borough, about
" three of the clocke in the afternoone, as the said Mr.
" Churchey was following his calling, (divers countrey
" cheapemen being then in the towne, who were in-
" debted to him), Mr. Peter Peeke, meeteing him in the
" market-place, told him that hee should forthwith
" quarter in his house 3 souldiers : the said Churchey
" answered him,—' Sir, you know that I pay weekly by
" ' your order six pence unto Daniel Hawk, one of your
" ' souldiers, and that my house being full of children,
" ' I have noe roome to entertaine any.' Mr. Pike [sic]
" then replied,—' Make your composition with these
" ' men,' there being then in company seaven or eight
" souldiers. My answere was, that what he did order
" I would pay. His answer againe was,—' Will you or
" ' will you not ?' Myne againe was, that I would con-
" forme myself as others of the towne did ; whereupon
" he commanded his souldiers to carry me to the Black
" Rodd, which I willingly obeyed, and entered without
" any refusall, and being in the staires of the Hall,
" where prisoners use to bee, I was followed by the
" said Mr. Pike, who straightly charged his keeper to
" clapp mee up a close prisoner ; which I perceiving,
" being at the topp of the staires, I turned myself
" about, and told him he needed not to feare ; I was
" a prisoner, and would use noe indirect way to escape,
" and if hee pleased he might clapp irons on my legge
" (therewith I tendered him my legg, in obedience), hee
" being at the foot of the staires, and myselfe at the
" topp ; whereupon, in a fury, he mountes the staires,
" thundering out these words,—' Dost thou spurne at
" ' mee with thy foot ?' and he takes mee by the cloak,
" and pulls mee over three or foure staires, in much
" danger ; whereupon my speech unto him was, that
" hee would forbeare to assault me in the prison, for
" that I was not under his command, but a prisoner,
" and that I desired the priveledge of a prisoner.
" Whereupon I remained there untill nyne of the clocke
" in the night ; at which tyme he came againe and told
" me, yf I would pay eighteene pence weekely for soul-
" diers lodgeing, I should bee free. My answer was, that
" he well knew I was never backwards to any payment
" in the garrison, and that what hee ordered I was ready
" to obey, as I had formerly answered him ; whereupon
" I was freed. On Monday the 25th of October Lieu-
" tenant Peake sent to mee in the morning 2 souldiers
" to quarter at my house. I told them I did quarter two
" already, at a widowes house, and would soe continue
" to lend them bedding and lodgeing as formerly I did ;
" notwithstanding, a little before night hee sent a ser-
" jeant with 4 souldiers to quarter at my house. I
" asked them who sent them, who told mee it was
" the Leiutenant Colonell. I asked them if hee were at
" home, who answered hee was. Then in obedience to
" his warrant, I presently went over to him to give him
" satisfaction, how my lodgeings in my house were
" disposed of. But by the way, neere the mayne guard,
" Leiutenant Peeke came, in a hasty and colericke
" manner, to meet mee, and told mee I would not obey
" the L. Colonel's warrant. I then told him I was
" goeing to him to acquaint him whom I did quarter,
" and how I had quartered souldiers formerly, and was
" soe contented so to do ; but he answered mee that I
" should have more in my house. I told him I could
" not ; but hee said I should, and gave me many pro-
" voking and urgent termes, insomuch hee said I had
" sworne, and the oath, hee sayeth, was ' by God,' and
" hath soe taken his oath ; which, if it were upon my
" salvation, I doe verily beleive it, there was not any
" such oath sworne, but in this manner I said unto him,
" when hee said they should quarter in my house, I
" said,—' God [sic] Sir, they shall nott,' soe that I did
" not sweare by God, as they falsely do accuse mee for
" swearing. Soe the same Munday night, about seaven
" of the clocke, there came Leiutenant Peeke, Captain
" Harding, 2 serjeants, and many musketeers, with
" matches burneing, and cam into my house in a hostile
" manner, and affrighted my people, and in a speciall
" manner a sicke sonne in a dying condition, and
" brought in the 4 souldiers. I told them I could not
" lodge them in my house, because my beds were all
" full ; but I would lodge the two souldiers, as formerly
" I did, and told them I would spare them an house,
" which had a chimney in it, a locke and key to the

" door, that they might goe and come in and out at
" their pleasure. This would not give them content,
" but I must lodge them in my house, but pay for their
" quarter abroad ; and gave me many provokeing termes.
" Captain Harding told me I was a malignant and a
" Cavaleer, both of them abuseing mee in my owne
" house, and told mee that it was happy for mee I was
" proclaimed a traitour in the King's ruleing tyme, but
" Mr. Peeke would have account of my French journey ;
" and, as I can prove, he hath bin long seeking to
" prove some untruths which should be raised against
" mee, and would know what I have don for the Par-
" liament, which I am ready to render an account of.
" And after a long and troublesome discourse, they
" left the four souldiers in my house, so that the 2
" souldiers I quarter, or lent them bedding, they went
" to their old quarters ; the other two, I preferred to
" give them fower pence betwixt them to pay for their
" lodgeing, soe that at the length they departed in a
" loveing manner, and well contented, and would not
" have any money to pay for their quarters. And soe
" I thought all had ben quiet ; but betwixt 8 and 9
" of the clocke he sent 3 other souldiers ; one of them
" came into the towne not long since, for feare of a presse
" in the country, one Nathaniel Trim ; the other was, as
" I am informed, a Cavalier souldier a little since, his
" name ' John Butcher.' These came with the match
" burning, the other had no musket ; but these three
" would have lodgeing in my house, and knockt at my
" door in such furious manner, as though they would
" break up my doores, and comaunded a candle to go
" to bed. I told them they were best know where they
" should lodge first ; they told me that they would
" lodge in my house. I told them I had sailes ; if they
" would lodge in them, they should, but I had no bed
" then free to lodge them in. But they made as though
" they would have lodged in my sick son's or my
" other sonne's bed : but I kept them out, and still they
" continued in a quarrelling and threatening manner,
" untill they saw my sonnes abed, and then would
" needs see my daughter's lodgeing, which they did ;
" and when they saw all the beds disposed of, then
" they searched the house, and cupboards in the house,
" for bedding ; and in the end gave them a groat, and
" soe they went." P. 97,—23rd October 1646,—" It
" is ordered by the Maior, Bailives, Aldermen, and
" burgesses, that yf any deal boards which are landed
" out of the Hamburger now in the harbour, shall be
" laden in carts to bee carried out of the towne, they
" shall bee presently seised on for the use of the
" towne ; untill further [? notice] bee given. This
" order is given to the porters, for the doeing of this
" same." P. 98,—2nd November 1646. " Reasons
given by the townesmen of Waymouth and Melcomb
Regis for the setling of Mr. Ince in this towne, and
not in Dunhead. Mr. Ince having used his function
of a minister in this towne, as a preacher to the
garrison almost 2 yeares, the townesmen had severall
conferences with him to settle him amongst them as
their pastor ; and the Maior, Aldermen, Bailiffes, and
burgesses, of the towne, at a meeting in the Towne
hall to that purpose, upon a full debate of the busines,
proposed the same solemly to Mr. Ince, who at that
time ingaged himselfe to bee their minister, in case
bee might have a competency of maynetenance ; for
the procurement whereof, the Maior, Aldermen,
Bailiffes, and burgesses, promised their endeavours,
and in pursuance of the same, they sent one of the
Bailiffes and Justices of the towne to London, with a
petition to the Parliament to settle some maynetenance
on the towne for a minister, nothing arising out of
the towne, (being very poore and populous), but what
the people please voluntarily to contribute. And
upon their endevours they obtayned a promise of
100l. per annum to be settled upon this and Radipole,
which is but one pastorall charge. And the townesmen have generally promised to contribute according
to their abilities for the more comfortable subsis-
taunce of the said Mr. Ince, and to provide him a
house fitt for his habitation. Notwithstanding, Mr.
Ince, (as the townesmen are informed), contrary to
their expectations, hath sithence ingaged himselfe to
the parishioners of Dunhead [in Wilts] to bee their
minister ; which is a very small charge of soules in
comparison of this towne ; soe that this populous place,
of knowne consequence, is now left wholy destitute of
any setled teacher. And the townesmen doe further
humbly offer that they conceived Mr. Ince was fixed
to the town, as 'tis a garrison for the Parliament.
And not only the townesmen, but the souldiery and
the parts adjacent, are very much concerned in

" his continuance heere, who have unanimously mani-
" fested their earnest desier of the same, in regard he
" was a great incouragement to the souldiers in the
" late seige against the towne, in his own example and
" instructions unto them ; soe that through Gods good-
" nes hee was very instrumentall in the preservation of
" the place. And the souldiery and the townesmen
" are very much troubled and discontented upon hear-
" inge of his removall." From an entry at the other
end of the volume, we learn that Mr. Ince was troubled
in conscience as to whether he could, under these circumstances, break his promise to the people of Dunhead ; the matter was accordingly referred to the House
of Commons, who again referred the case to certain
members of the Assembly of Divines, nominated for
that purpose. These seem to have been the six persons
next mentioned ; but their decision nowhere appears.—
P. 99, " The persons elected for the Townsmen. Mr.
" Stephen Marshall, Mr. Herbert Palmer, Mr. Obadiah
" Sedgwick, Mr. Ed. Calamy, Doctour Temple, Mr.
" Caudry." (Stephen Marshall was a violent Puritan
preacher of those times, ridiculed in Hudibras ; Herbert
Palmer, a Puritan of exemplary life, who had been
presented by Archbishop Laud to the living of Ashwell,
in Hertfordshire ; he was also President of Queens' College, Cambridge, from 1644 to 1647, when he died, in
his 47th year. Obadiah Sedgwick was a well known
member of the Assembly of Divines. Edmund
Calamy, the Nonconformist, is remembered as one
of the authors of Smectymnus, a treatise against
Episcopacy, written in answer to Bishop Hall. " Doc-
" tour Temple" was probably Peter Temple, a member of the Long Parliament, and one of the judges
of King Charles the First.) P. 104,—" John Milles of
" Kirton, in Devon, sayler, George Lawrence, saylor,
" a Norman, being both newly married, are to find
" security to discharge the towne by Fryday next, or
" else to depart the towne." P. 105, 29th December
1646,—" Mr. John Knight, of Yetminster, came this
" day before Mr. Maior and the Company, and desires
" to bee admitted to sett upp a Grammar Schoole in
" this towne, upon certan termes by him proposed.
" Butt the towne did not admitt of his termes, yett
" were content to admitt him as the only master of the
" Latin tongue ; upon which hee desired one monthes
" respite, to give his answeare to the towne, which was
" graunted unto him accordingly." P. 106,—15th January 1646-(7). " Memorandum, that heeretofore there
" was collected in the church in Melcomb fower
" pounds fower shillings and six pence, for the redeem-
" ing of two captives out of Argeir [Algiers] ; which
" money was delivered over to Mr. George Churchey,
" one of the Overseers of the poore, for the use afore-
" said." P. 107, (same date).—" It is agreed upon and
" soe ordered by a full consent of all now presente, that
" in regard Mr. Edward Buckler hath taken greate
" paynes in his ministry in Melcomb, for which hee
" hath not had any reward, and for that this toune is
" wholy destitute of a pastour, that a Petition shall bee
" presented to the Committee of the County (who
" placed him in Weeke Regis) to take him off thence,
" and to settle him minister of the towne. And that
" in the meane tyme, a dwelling house with thappur-
" tenances be forthwith provided for the said Mr.
" Buckler, fitt for his quality and condition, at the
" townes charge, in case the said Mr. Buckler, at the
" next Hall, shall like of these propositions, and con-
" sent unto them." Mr. Ince, it would appear, had
not complied with their solicitations, and had given
Dunhead the preference. P. 108, 1st February 1646-(7).
William Luke, sonne of Thomasine Luke, widow,
" for playinge yesterday, being the Saboth, . . .
" . . . and disturbing Mr. Buckler, the minister, as he
" was exercising and praying with his parishioners,
" upon his submission, was excused for the present."
In the same page we have " The Aunsweare of Mr.
" Edward Buckler, Clerke. For ordering me an house
" in Melcomb gratis, I doe thanke the towne, and
" lookeing upon it as a favour shall endeavour to
" deserve it. To the townes desire to have mee their
" minister I shall condiscend, with these following pro-
" visos, vizt. That 6 divines (to whom I shall shortly
" addresse myselfe) judge my departure from Weeke
" [Wyke Regis,] and my [remo]vall hither to bee law-
" full and expedient. That the Committee of this
" County, and others concerned in it, and I, doe agree
" upon termes of settlement and maintenance. That
" I bee assured by the towne that what shall faile at
" any time hereafter of the stipend at first allowed mee
" by the Parliament, shall by their contribution be
" made up ; soe that such contribution exceed not 50l.

" per annum. When the town shall satisfy mee in the
" last of these provisoes, I shall, in some competent
" time after their aunsweare received, give them satis-
" faction in the other thing. Feb. 1st, 1646 (7)." On the
5th of February Mr. Buckler's proposition was accepted,
and it was agreed, if necessary, to raise such 50l. by a
rate. P. 120, 4th August 1647. " Francis Reymond, of
" Portland, hollier [tiler], did depose that John Fawne,
" seaman, in his bearing, Munday last, at the sign of
" the Shipp, did say that Captain John Arthur was a
" French dogg, a curre, and a toad." Fawne is therefore bound in his recognizances, to the amount of 20l.,
to appear at the next Sessions of the Peace. Captain
Arthur was Collector of the Customs, and a most
zealous Parliamentarian, as appears from other passages in the book ; he became Mayor in 1649. P. 142,
in January 1648, the Town Clerk is instructed to treat
with Mr. George Thorne, " to exercise his ministry "
within the town for one year. The negotiations therefore
with Mr. Buckler had, no doubt, failed. P. 142. Same
date,—" William Reape was this day chosen Clark of
" the parish, in the place of John Dudly, Clark ; and
" hee is to receive the usuall wages for ringing iiii. and
" viii., sixpence for every knell. And he is to teach
" (according to his owne offer) the poore children to
" write and cipher, without any reward for his paynes
" of those parents who are not able to paye." P. 166—
29th September 1648.—" Whereas this day there was
" driven ashoare 2 great ffishes called ' Campas ' [?Gram-
" pus] within the precincts of this towne, and some
" difference hath arised betweene the Towne and Cap-
" tain Arthur, Vice-Admirall, to whom the same ffishes
" belong, it is agreed betweene them that the towne
" write to Mr. Bond, our Recorder, for the decideing
" of the same ; and in case they belong to the towne,
" that Captain Arthur shall deliver up the same, which
" are now in his possession, unto them, the towne
" allowing him the charge bee shall be att in the interim
" about them." P. 167 (same date).—" Mr. Churchey
" brought into the Halle, and delivered over to the
" Towne, an auncient booke of records of this towne,
" which was lately in the hands of Mr. Francis Gape,"
—who had been recently Town Clerk. The latest date
at this part of the book is on this page, 21st November
1648. The volume has also some entries of miscellaneous memoranda and correspondence, beginning
at the other end, and extending over nine pages. The
correspondence is mostly in reference to grants by
Parliament for the repair of the harbour, which had
fallen into a state of decay, and grants proposed (successively) to Mr. Ince, and to Mr. George Thorne, late
Fellow of Sidney Sussex College, Cambridge. There
is the evidence also given, on the 12th of October 1649,
by two witnesses, 74 and 83 years of age, as to former
Perambulations of the borough on Ascension Day.
The minister of Rodipoll [now Radipole], it is stated,
used at the same time to go on procession, in like
manner, with his parishoners ; at a certain place he
read a chapter in the Bible, and a Psalm, which was
then sung. There are also entered formal proceedings of Law Courts and View of Frankpledge ; and
there are many other passages in the volume of considerable interest, but which will not admit of transcription at the present day, cases of affiliation, more
particularly. Taken altogether, it is a curious record
of the vicissitudes which a place had to submit to, while
held in a state of siege, and submitted to the rigours
and annoyances of Puritan occupation : under such circumstances, espionage, as might be expected, reigned
supreme.

The next volume, in date, is a large paper folio, rather
decayed at the beginning, being the Treasurer's Accounts for 1668-93. On June 8, 1668, there are charges
" fore fagotts for a bone fiere on the King's birth day
" 4s. 6d." In 1669, a person dignified with the name
of " John Locke" was earning money for the Corporation, as master of the town " liter." At this time the
Treasurer was Sir Roger Cuttance. The entries seem
in general to be of an ordinary and uninteresting character. There is the following entry in 1682,—" Paid
" Edward Lake's bill for fireing the guns upon the
" happy newes of His Majesty's safe deliverance for [sic]
" the horrid plotts of Presbiterians lately discovered,
" 6s. 8d." In 1683, September 16th,—" Paid Edward
" Lake's bill . . . for firing the gunne on the 9th in-
" stant, being Thanksgiving Day for His Majestie and
" Royall Highness safe deliverance from the late con-
" spiracy against them." 1685, October 14th,—" To a
" bill of disbursements for the gallows, burning and
" boiling the rebells executed per order at this towne,
" 16l. 4s. 3d.,"—in allusion to the atrocities inflicted

upon the bodies of those who had been engaged in Monmouth's rebellion.

Minutes (in Latin) of the Court of Record, holden at Weymouth and Melcombe Regis, from the 29th of May to the 18th of September 1677; consisting of two leaves only, under a paper cover; with one leaf added, bearing reference to Courts holden in October in the second year of James II. (A.D. 1686).

The latest volume in this Collection is a Minute-book of the Corporation, the last entries in which belong to the year 1724; a thick folio paper volume, in good condition, bound in vellum. Some of the entries in the volume are curious; but in general, they seem to be of too recent a date to call for notice. In p. 42 there is the following entry :—" xxiii° die Junii 1702. On this " present day Marmaduke Rawdon, Captain Lieftenant " of the Royall Regiment of Fusaleirs, under the com- " mand of Major Generall Hara, did voluntaryly take " the oaths of abjuration appointed. (Signed) Marma- " duke Rawdon, Cha : Langrish Mayor, John Pitt Bay- " liff." In p. 68, under date of 22nd August 1704, mention is made of the playing of shuffleboard at an inn, for ale : a recent mention of a game which, at least in this country, is now unknown. In pp. 72, 73, under date of 27th December 1704, one Dr. Griffin is named, " who hath a stago in this town," as being applied to for a recipe for the cure of cramp : a quack doctor, who exhibited his nostrums on a wooden stage. At the beginning of this century, a Dr. Bossy, of the like call- ing, still " had his stage," in London, on Tower Hill.

The Sherren Collection, it may be here noticed, has, to some slight extent, been made use of by the late Mr. George Roberts, in his *Social History of the Southern Counties of England in past Centuries.* (London, 1856.)

Since the preceding Report was written, I have re- ceived information, I am sorry to say, of Mr. Sherren's decease : a man of literary tastes, and much regretted by all who knew him.

HENRY THOMAS RILEY.

THE CORPORATION OF FOLKESTONE.

The following are some transcripts of papers, of the time of Edward the Fourth, in the possession of the Corporation of Folkestone, which have been transmitted for notice, through the Rev. R. C. Jenkins, Rector of Lyminge, by the Worshipful the Mayor of that town : preceded by a brief description of the subject of this correspondence; in which the language is pretty nearly followed of Mr. Jenkins's courteous communication, which accompanied the Letters in question.—

Thomas Banns, or Banes, formerly a monk, having secularized, had become Chaplain to Cecily, Duchess of York, (the widow of Richard, Duke of York, and) the King's mother. Obtaining the influence alike of the King, the Duchess, and the Archbishop of Canterbury, he prevails upon the Mayor of Folkestone to recognize and receive him as Prior of the Benedictine Priory there, to which he seems to have been appointed either by the monks or the Archbishop of Canterbury.

In the meantime, however, Henry Ferrers, brother of the Earl Ferrers, and brother-in-law to John, Lord Clynton, had, as being under the latter's patronage, received the same appointment at his hands. Lord Clynton, we find, also claims a kind of regal authority over " his town and commons of Folkestone;" but the Mayor, probably standing in awe of the still greater authority arrayed on the other side, (however unworthy of such support Banes may, in reality, have been,) pro- bably from the first inclined in that direction.

The first item in the correspondence, is a Letter, in English, from Lord Clynton, to the Mayor, Jurats, and Commons, of Folkestone. In ostensibly bland terms, his Lordship first tries upon the Mayor the powers of persuasion. His letter is written on vellum, in a small hand.—

" John, Lord Clyntone and Say, to oure trusty and " welbeloved the Maire, Jurats, and Commons, of oure " towne of Folkeston, send greting. And forsomuche " as we understand the malicious disposition wille and " entent of Dan Thomas Banns, late pretended Prioure " of oure Priory of Folkestone forsaide, to destourbe " oure trusty and faithful brother, Henry Ferrers, of " his possessions, title, and intresse, of and in the said " Priory, and that that bene appertenyng therto, late " ycvene to oure said brother in your presence.—We " therefor wol and charge yow, and also hertily pray " yow that if the said Dan Thomas Banns, or any other " for hym, come to oure said towne to make any suche

" destourbance or chalonge, that ye and everyche of yow, " with al youre might resiste thair malice and dis- " posicione, and theym to arrest, [and] appeal, and " justifie, after the lawe and custume of our said towne, " at suche tyme as ye shal by oure said brother, his " servauntes, and ministres be ther of . . . ., yeving " in commandement to alle oure servauntos, officers, " and menyall menne, to them . . to be obedient, " assisting, and attendant. And that ye . . . ., as " we shal be youre good lorde. Yeven the xxv day of " May, the yere of the regne of our liege lord King " Edwarde the iiii^the the iii^te." [A.D. 1463.]

A day or two after the receipt of the preceding letter, the Mayor, if not already acquainted with the circum- stances of the case, must have been much perplexed by receiving the following, from a probably still more influential personage, the Duchess of York; (written on paper) :—

" The Kyngys Moder, Duchesse of York.

" Trusty and welbeloved, we grete you welle. And " whereas we understande that it hathe pleased my " lord and son the Kyng, and also our cousin tharche- " bisshope of Caunterbury, entendering the righte of " oure welbeloved Chapellaine, Thomas Banye, to wryte " for hym unto you and othe [r], for to see hym reioyce " such lyvelode as he oughte of righte to have; we " desiro and pray you that, according unto the tenure of " the letters of oure said lord and son, and cousin, " aforesaid, ye put you in devoyr to the performyng of " the same, and withe the more diligence, at oure " especiall contemplacion, as we trust you. And that " no personne vexe, inquiet, nor trouble hym, as we " may for his sak thank you in in [sic] tyme to comme. " Yeven under our signet, in our place at Baynardys " Castelle in Londone, the xxvii day of Maye.

(Addressed) " To our trusty and welbeloved The
                          " Mayre and Jurattes of Folkestone,
                                    " and to everiche of theyme."

(There is a scrawl in the margin, in large characters, which, we may guess, was intended for her signature, " Cecyly.")

A day later, the Mayor receives another Letter from Lord Clynton; who calls upon him to set at nought any instructions upon the matter, save those coming from himself; supported as he is, in spite of King and Duchess, by the Lord Ferrers, the Lord Herbarde [William Herbert, afterwards Earl of Pembroke], and other Lords of the King's Council ; on paper:—

" Righte worshupful Sirs. Y pray yow, as ye love my " worship, profit, and welfare, that for any letters sende " to yow by the King or by my Ladi of Yorke for Dan " Thomas Banns, a yenst the welfare of my brother " Ferrers, that ye suffre not the said Banns in no wise " to entre in to the priorie of Folkestone, but hym utturly " resiste and defende in my title, as my verrai right " and patronage, as fulle and hole as y were there my " self. And y, uppone the peyne of alle my landis and " godis, shal save yow alle harmlees a yenst the King " and, my saide Lady, bi the holp of my Lord Ferrers, " my Lord Herbarde, and othere lordis of the Kinges " Councelle, that knowithe my right and title. And " hit shalle not be longe to, but the King and my Lady " shalle write the contrarie that is wretene for the saide " Banns; for y have spoke withe my lerned councelle of " alle this, and thei sey me, gif ye obey this writinge " that is broughte to yow fro the King and my Lady, " ye shalle breke for ever the liberte and fraunchis of the " Portis for ever, whicho were youre undoing and my " shaame for ever; and that y wolde not, for all my " land. And therefore y charge yow, that ye woll un- " derstand and takithe heed of any writing for any talis " or writinges, for your welfare and my worship, and " alle myne heirs hereafter. And over that, y charge " all my servauntes, that thei be helping towarde yow " to defende and resist the said Banns. And also y " charge yow, as ye wille aunswere to me therefore, that " ye arrest the saide Banns, and alle tho that comme " withe hym, except the Kinges Serjauntes and my Lady " of Yorkes, and tham saufly kepe in prisone, unto tyme " that thoi aunswere to certaine contemptes and tros- " passes doone to me and my Lordship of Folkestone, a " yenst the privilege, and franchis, and liberte, of the " Portis, and not to deliver tham withoute my special " commandement. Yeven at Westminstor, under my " signe manual fore youre surete, the xxviii day of " May.

" And that my bailly theere   Your herty and
" be attendaunt to this com-   faithefulle
" maundement. And also the   John Lord Clyntone
" depute of my said bailly,   and Say,
" for any excuse.   " CLYNTON."

(Addressed) "To tho Maire, Juratis, and alle my good
" communes and servauntes of my
" towne of Folkstone."

Singularly enough, immediately upon this letter
follows another, written (privately probably), to the
Mayor; warning him of the consequences of his too
evident tendency to oppose his Lordship's wishes in
behalf of Ferrers; (on paper):—

"Maire. We mervaile moche of youre disposicione
" towardes us and oure brother Ferrers, withe that
" untrew monke. Thinke not the contrarie, but as law
" wille, thow wilte righte sore repent thi dedis, for thei
" beene nothur vertuous nor lanful, for thou settist my
" commaundement at noughte. And yit thow shalt
" righte wel think y am thi lorde, and so wille be, and
" that thow shalt right wel know, or els the law shal
" faile me. We send a letter late to tho and the
" Jurattis as for my aside brother, and for special
" favour that thow haddist to the saide monke, thow
" kepist the lotter fro tham, and wilt not nor woldist
" suffre tham to know thontent therof. And therefore
" in alle thy governannce and rewle, as to this mater,
" hit is and shal be righte wel understand. And such
" charge as y have yevene myne officer, casa [i.e. in
" case] y charge, we have not a doo therwithe, for
" thoghe thow [will]ist, hit shal right litell availle,
" saf to thyne own hurt. Writtens at Londone in
" hast, the xxix dai of May.
                      " JOHN LORD CLYNTON AND SAY."
(Addressed) "To the Maire of Folkstone."

Immediately after this, recourse is had, on the part
of Ferrers, to legal proceedings, and an appeal to the
Apostolic See: the nature of which is explained by the
following official communication, (on paper,) in Latin;
a close translation of which involved piece of composition, it has been thought as well to subjoin.—

"Officialis Curiæ Cantuariensis, discretis viris, Mor-
" gano Ayssheley et Willelmo Barbour, ac universis
" et singulis rectoribus, vicariis, capellanis [this word
" is repeated], curatis et non curatis, clericis, et literatis
" quibuscunque, per Provinciam Cantuariensem ubilibet
" constitutis, salutem in Auctore salutis. Ex parte
" venerabilis viri, Domini Henrici Ferrers, Prioris
" Prioratus de Flokkestone, Cantuariensis Diœcesis,
" nobis existit intimantum [intimatum], quod idem
" Henricus fuit et est dictum Prioratum canonice
" assecutus, ac ipsum Prioratum, sic assecutum, cum
" suis juribus et pertinentiis universis, per nonnulla
" tempora possedit pacifice et quiete; et, salvis in-
" frascriptis, sic possidet etiam in præsenti; ac pro
" Priore ejusdem Prioratus fuit, et est, communiter
" dictus, tentus, habitus, et reputatus, palam, publice,
" et notorie. Et licet ex parte ejusdem Henrici, Prioris,
" integri status, bonæ famæ, opinionis illæsæ, et con-
" versationis honestæ, ac in possessione præmisorum
" existentis, metuentis tamen, ex quibusdam causis pro-
" babilibus, et verisimilibus co[n]jecturis, sibi circa præ-
" missa grave posse in futurum præjudicium generari,
" (ne quis, in ipsius præjudicium, circa præmissa, vel
" eorum aliquod, quicquam attemptet, seu faciat aliqua-
" liter attemptari,) ad Sacrosanctam Sedem Apostoli-
" cam, et pro tuitione Curiæ Cantuariensis prædictæ,
" palam et publice legitime extiterit provocatum; qui-
" dam [tamen] Frater Thomas Banns, monachum se
" prætendens, in mando apostatando discurrens, notorie
" excommunicatus, atque de crimine pessimo et non
" nominando, (pro quo Schema Omnipotens civitates et
" opida multa destruxit), per eum confessato, ac etiam
" judicialiter convictus, et propterea in hac parte in-
" habilis; qui nichil juris in dicto Prioratu habuit, seu
" habet aliqualiter, vel ad eum; juri, titulo, et pos-
" sessioni, ejusdem Henrici in eodem Prioratu, absque
" causa rationabili seu legitima quacunque, temere se
" opposuit, et opponit; ac dictum Prioratum ad ipsum
" pertinuisse, pertinere, et pertinere debere, ipsumque,
" Thomam, Priorem ejusdem Prioratus fuisse et esse,
" (licet sic non fuerit,) verum, sic publice asseruit et
" prædicavit; ac eundem Henricum, Priorem, dicti
" Prioratus verum et canonicum possessorem, quominus
" jure, titulo, et possessione, sais in dicto Prioratu
" libere uti et gaudere valeat, temere impedivit et
" fecit, sicque impedit et facit; ac sic et alias dictum
" Heuricum, Priorem, in præmissis, et circa ea, per se
" et suos, multipliciter et indebite inquietavit et per-
" turbavit, sicque molestat, inquietat, et perturbat,
" etiam in præsenti; ac sic se ville opponere, prædicare,
" asserere, impedire, facere, molestareque, inquietare
" ac perturbare, sa pius publice comminabatur at com-
" minatur, nititurque, ut asserit et intendit; et ad hoc
" se paravit et parat, villiter [viliter] et injuste, in
" ipsius, Henrici, Prioris prædicti, præjudicium non
" modicum, et gravamen; unde, ex parte ejusdem,

" sentientis ex præmissis gravaminibus indebite præ-
" gravari, ab eisdem ad Sedem Apostolicam, et pro
" tuitione Curiæ Cantuariensis, legitime extitit appel-
" latum. Quocirca vobis, communiter et divisim,
" committimus et mandamus, firmiter injungendo,
" quantocius præfato Fratri Thomæ Banes, cæterisque
" omnibus et singulis quibus jus exigit in hac parte
" inhiberi, auctoritate dictæ Curiæ, inhibeatis; quibus
" nos etiam, tenore præsentium, sic inhibemus; no,
" pendente in dicta Curia nostra Cantuariensi hujusmodi
" tuitoriæ appellationis negotio, quicquam, hac occasione,
" in dictæ partis appellantis præjudicium, attemptent,
" seu faciant aliqualiter attemptari, quominus liberam
" habeat hujusmodi tuitoriæ suæ appellationis prosecu-
" tionem, prout justam. Citetis insuper, seu citari faciatis,
" peremptorie, dictum Fratrem Thomam Banes, quod
" compareat coram nobis, sive alio dictæ Curiæ Præsi-
" denti, in eclesia Beatæ Mariæ de Arcubus, Londoniis,
" proximo die juridico post festum Commemorationis
" Sancti Pauli proximo futurum, in hujusmodi tuitoriæ
" appellationis negatio [negotio] processurus, et procodi
" visurus, facturusque ulterius, et recepturus, quod in
" ea parte justitia suadebit. De diobus vero receptionis
" præsentium, ac citationis et inhibitionis vestrarum
" modoque et forma earundem, necnon quod in præ-
" missis feceritis, nos, vel alium dictæ Curiæ Præsi-
" dentem, ductis [dictis] die et loco, debite certificetis,
" per vestras, seu sic certificet ille vestrum qui prius
" nostrum mandatum fuerit executus, per suas, litteras
" patentes, harum seriem continentes, authentice sigil-
" latas. Datim Londoniis, Kalendis Junii, anno Domini
" millesimo cccclxiii[o]."

"The Official of the Court of Canterbury, to the
" discreet men, Morgan Ayssheley and William Bar-
" bour, and to all and singular the rectors, vicars,
" chaplains, with cure and without cure, clerks, and
" literates whomsoever, throughout the Province of
" Canterbury wheresoever being, health in the Author
" of salvation. On behalf of the venerable man, Dan
" Henry Ferrers, Prior of the Priory of Flokkestone
" [sic], in the Diocese of Canterbury, it is unto us in-
" timated, that the same Henry canonically has held
" and does hold the said Priory, and the same Priory,
" so held, with its rights and all its appurtenances, for
" some time has peacefully and quietly possessed; and,
" save as below written, does so possess even at this
" present; and as Prior of the same Priory has been,
" and is, commonly called, held, had, and reputed,
" openly, publicly, and notoriously. And although, on
" behalf of the same Henry, the Prior, being of sound
" estate, of good fame, of unblemished repute, and of
" honest conversation, and in possession of the premises,
" still fearing, from certain probable causes, and on
" likely conjectures, that grievous prejudice might in
" future unto him be engendered as to the premises,
" (to the end that no one, to his prejudice, should
" attempt aught, or in any way cause aught to be at-
" tempted, as to the premises, or any thereof), appeal
" has openly and publicly lawfully been made to the
" Holy Apostolic See, and for the protection of the Court
" of Canterbury before-mentioned; [still] one Brother
" Thomas Banns, pretending himself to be a monk, wan-
" dering to and fro in the world as an apostate, notoriously
" excommunicated, and [accused] of a crime most foul
" and not to be named,—for which Almighty Provi-
" dence has destroyed many cities and towne—the same
" being by him confessed, and be also judicially con-
" victed thereon, and by reason thereof disqualified
" in this behalf; and one who neither has had, nor has,
" any right whatever in any way in the said Priory,
" or to the same; unto the right, title, and possession,
" of the same Henry in the same Priory, without
" reasonable or lawful cause whatsoever, has rashly
" opposed, and does oppose, himself; and that the said
" Priory unto him has pertained, does pertain, and
" ought to pertain, and that he, Thomas, was and
" is, (though such is not the fact,) true true Prior of
" the same Priory, has so publicly asserted and
" preached; and has rashly hindered and acted, and
" so does hinder and act, as not to let the same Henry,
" the Prior, of the said Priory the true and canonical
" possessor, freely use and enjoy his right, title, and
" possession, in the said Priory; and so and in other
" ways has in manifold manners and unduly disquieted
" and disturbed the said Henry, the Prior, in the
" premises, and about them, by himself and his people,
" and so does molest, disquiet, and disturb, even at
" this present; and has oftentimes publicly threatened,
" and does threaten, that he will so oppose him, preach,
" assert, hinder, do, and molest, disquiet, and disturb,
" and does endeavour, as he does assert and intend;
" and unto the same has prepared and does prepare

CORPORA-
TION OF
FOLKE-
STONE.
—

"himself, vilely and unjustly, to the no small pre-
"judice and grievance of him, Henry, the Prior
"before-mentioned: as to the which, on behalf of
"the same, feeling himself by the before-stated
"grievances to be unduly aggrieved, lawful appeal
"has been made to the Apostolic See, and for pro-
"tection of the Court of Canterbury, against the
"same. Wherefore, unto you, jointly and severally, we
"do entrust and command, strictly enjoining, that,
"so soon as possible, you do, by authority of the said
"Court, inhibit the aforesaid Brother Thomas Banes,
"and all and singular the others whom right demands
"to be inhibited in this behalf; the which we also, by
"tenor of these presents, do so inhibit; that, while
"the matter of this appeal for protection is pending in
"our Court of Canterbury, they shall, on this pretext,
"attempt, or cause in any way to be attempted, aught
"to the prejudice of the said party appealing, that so he
"may not have free prosecution of such his appeal for
"protection, as [is] just. You are to cite also, or cause
"to be cited, peremptorily, the said Brother Thomas
"Banes, that he appear before us, or other President
"of the said Court, in the church of St. Mary le Bow
"[or, at Arches] in London, on the next justice day
"after the feast of the Commemoration of St. Paul
"[30th June] next ensuing, in this business of appeal
"for protection to proceed and see proceedings taken,
"and to do further and receive that which justice in
"that behalf shall suggest. And as to the days of
"receipt of these presents, and of your citation and
"inhibition, and the manner and form of the same, as
"also, what you shall have done in the premises, you
"are, at the said day and place, duly to certify by
"your, or he among you who shall have first executed
"our mandate, is to certify by his, letters patent, con-
"taining the proceedings herein, authentically sealed,
"us or other the President of the said Court. Given
"at London, on the Kalends of June [1st June]. A.D.
"1463."

This is closely followed by a formal Letter, in Latin,
from Lord Clynton, to the Mayor and Bailiffs of
Folkestone, (on paper); a translation of which is here
added—

"Johannes, Dominus de Clyntone et Say, Miles,
"Dominus de Folkestone, quæ est membrum Portus
"Dovorriæ, in Comitatu Kanciæ, unus Custodum
"pacis Domini nostri Regis in Comitatu Kanciæ
"conservandæ, Majori villæ de Folkestone prædictæ,
"et ballivo ipsius Johannis villæ prædictæ, necnon
"in hac parte suo sufficienti deputato, salutem.
"Vobis, et cuilibet vestrum, ex parte Domini nostri
"Regis, ex parte Magni Gardiani Quinque Portuum,
"præcipimus et mandamus, quod capiatis, seu aliquis
"vestrum capiat, Domipuum Thomam Banna, monachum,
"si inventus fuerit in balliva vestra; et eum salvo
"custodiatis, seu aliquis vestrum custodiat, absque
"aliqua contradictione, aut in balliam aut in manucap-
"tionem, ad respondendum tam dicto Domino nostro
"Regi quam præfato Magno Gardiano, de certis
"feloniis, proditionibus, insurrectionibus, transgres-
"sionibus, robbiriis, et routeriis, contra formam Statuti
"inde editi et provisi, infra membrum prædictum
"factis. Et hoc nullatenus omittatis, seu aliquis
"vestrum omittat [written 'amittat'], sub pœna incum-
"bente. Et qualiter hoc præceptum nostrum in execu-
"tionem posuistis, seu aliquis vestrum posuit, nobis
"constari faciatis indilate. Datum sub sigillo nostro,
"quinto die Junii, anno regni Regis Edwardi Quarti
"tertio."

This paper is not addressed: it bears at the foot the
impress of the seal, much defaced, but with a border
of rushes still surrounding it—

"John, Lord Clyntone and Say, Knight, Lord of
"Folkestone, which is a member of the Port of
"D vorre, in the County of Kent, one of the Keepers
"for keeping the peace of our Lord the King in the
"County of Kent, to the Mayor of the vill of Folkestone
"aforesaid, and the Bailiff of the same John in the vill
"aforesaid, as also to his sufficient deputy in this
"behalf, greeting. Unto you, and each of you, on
"behalf of our Lord the King, and on behalf of the
"Great Warden of the Cinque Ports, we do enjoin and
"command, that you take, or that one of you take,
"Dan Thomas Banns, monk, if he be found in your
"bailiwick; and that you safely keep him, or one of
"you safely keep, without any gainsaying, either on
"bail or on mainprise, to make answer as well to our
"said Lord the King, as to the Great Warden afore-
"said, as to certain felonies, treasons, insurrections,
"trespasses, robberies, and riots, against the form of
"the Statute thereon made and provided, within the
"member aforesaid committed. And this you are in

CORPO-
TION OF
FOLK-
STON
—

"no wise to omit, nor is any one of you to omit, on the
"peril attached thereto. And how you have put in
"execution this our precept, or one of you has put
"the same, you are to let us be certified without delay.
"Given under our seal, the 5th day of June, in the
"year of the reign of King Edward the Fourth the
"third."

A Letter from Thomas [Bourchier], Archbishop of
Canterbury, closely follows; strongly encouraging the
Mayor, Jurats, and Commons, of Folkestone, to resist
the demands of Lord Clynton in the said matter, as
having no right or title whatever in reference thereto,
(on paper):—
"T. Archbisshoppe of Canterbury.

"Trusti and welbeloued we grete you wele. And
"forasmuche as we understand by youre letters, late
"directed unto us, that ye have be helping and assist-
"ing unto oure right welbeloued Dan Thomas Banys,
"Priour of Folkestone, according to the Kinges hon-
"ourabil letters, and our writing sent unto you in
"that behalve: whereof we thanke you alle right
"hertly that ye have soo doo, desiring specialy that
"ye wul contynue the same unto hym hereaftere, as
"alle right and good conscience axethe; acertaynynge
"yon that the Lord Clyntone, as the case requirethe,
"oughte nat to have to doo in the matiere on any
"wise, notwithstandinge the saide Lord Clyntone hath
"desired and promysid faithfully unto us by monthe
"to doo and be demeanyd in the matiere as we wul
"have hym. Wherefore we desire and wul, that ye
"feere nat to doo that right requirethe in the matiere,
"as oue truste is in you. And like as youre neigh-
"bour, bringer hereof, canne more largely informe you
"according to oure conceipt in this partie, to whome
"wul ye yeve credence in that behalve. God have
"you in kepinge. Written in oure manoire of
"Lamehithe, the xi daie of June.
(Addressed) "To oure trusti and welbeloued the
"Maire, Jurattes, and Communes, of
"the toune of Folkestone, in the
"Countee of Kent."

The correspondence, so far, apparently, as it has been
preserved, ends with two paper fragments of Letters,
addressed by Lord Clynton to the Mayor and Jurats of
Folkestone; the latter of them directly charging Banes
with most heinous crimes and offences. Their date does
not appear, but they were written after the letters of
the 28th and 29th of May 1463.

". . . . Also, Sirs, y wille and charge yow, that
"ye aunswere the messager [messenger] that bringethe
"the Kinge's letters and my Ladi of Yorkes letters,
"that ye dare not take uppone yow to medle of these
"maters withoute the advice of me and of my councelle;
"bicause hit concernethe myne inheritaunce and also
"my worship, and also the keping of the liberte and
"fraunchis of my towne of Folkestone, where ynne ye
"be dwellers. And,withe this aunswere y doute me not
"ye shal plese the King and my Lady. And there-
"fore, uppone my perille, douteth not of my Lord of
"Caunterbury nor of noone othere, for this mater.
"And y charge yow that this letter be rad openly afore
"the communes of my saide towne, except the mater
"conteyned in this bille."

(Second Paper.) "Also, Sirs, y declare to yow alle
"that the saide Banns is a fals sodomyte, and for opene
"and proved sodomyte stante acursed, and may not
"be assoyled of no Bisshop in England, but of the Pope.
"And yit [that] the saide Banns, by the law of the
"Chirche, most in his owne persone at Rome doo his
"great penaunce therefore, and els to be brand as a
"fals sysmatik, and an herytick to God and alle Holy
"Churche. And alle that eet and drynk withe hym are
"cursed or [i.e. whether] help. And that in resonable
"hast shalle be declarid afore yow of recorde, under
"sufficiant auctorite, selis, and witnesse. And there-
"fore y charge yow to have not a doo withe him, other-
"wise than to kepe hym in prisone, but the King and
"the Lordis is not informed herof, but thei shalle be
"in hast: for alle the writinges that the saide Banns
"can shew for his absolucione of the saam, ben of noone
"effecte nor of auctorite. And Sirs, thoghe the Kinge,
"letters and my Ladi of Yorkes letters come to yow bi a
"fals informacione of the saide Bannes, jit [yet] hit is
"not the Kinges intent nor will to hurt me nor my
"brother for suche a fals man."

Banes succeeded in retaining the office of Prior, until
the year 1493; when, as we learn from Dugdale's
Monasticon, he was removed from office for dilapidating
the property of the house.

HENRY THOMAS RILEY.

THE MANUSCRIPTS OF THE PARISH OF MENDLESHAM, CO. SUFFOLK.

Lying in the middle of Suffolk, and in one of the most fertile districts of the county, Mendlesham retains some of the characteristics which caused John Kirby, author of the " Suffolk Traveller," in the last century, to call it disdainfully " a dirty town." On the other hand, it is fortunate in possessing a noble church, that has been fitly restored within the last few years, a considerable property in land left for charitable uses in the parish by former inhabitants, and an unusually interesting collection of parish documents.

On entering the belfry chamber, which has long been the depository of these records, I found myself surrounded by ancient chests, and piles of rusty armour borne in past times by the trained bandsmen of the town. On turning the three locks and raising the heavy lid of the largest of these chests I found the coffer full of papers,—sheets of papers stitched together (with from four to eight sheets in each stitched set), and an almost countless number of separate pieces of paper covered with writing. The state of these records was remarkable. It seemed that each set of stitched papers had been first crumpled with the hand and then thrown into the huge box. Most of the single sheets bore signs of having been treated in the same rough manner, on being rudely confided to the coffin of settled accounts. With the assistance of Mr. Barnes, a most intelligent churchwarden, who afforded me effectual aid in this part of my work, I straightened out and arranged these crumpled papers according to their dates. On having thus brought the accumulation of records into something like order, I found them to be an incomplete series of accounts, setting forth the particulars of the yearly disbursements of Mendlesham churchwardens, from the time of Mary to the opening years of the eighteenth century; the sets of stitched sheets being the complete bills for their respective years, whilst the loose pieces of paper were the vouchers for the items of the yearly accounts. In the smaller chests of the belfry chamber were found old parish accounts, registers, and a considerable number of deeds and records on parchment. At the vicarage, in the personal custody of the Rev. Edmund Roger Mainwaring White, M.A., who was good enough to afford me every facility for inspecting the archives of his parish, I found other registers, one of which (" A Boake for the Registering of all Mariages, " Births, and Buryalls in the towne of Mendelsham, " made the six and twenty day of November 1653," and closing with the year 1659), deserves especial notice.

The Mendlesham records may therefore be arranged in the following divisions :—(a.) The parish account books and yearly accounts of churchwardens. (b.) The parish registers. (c.) The old deeds of the parish chest.

(a.) The Parish Account Books.

1. The churchwardens' account-book from the year 1541 to 1696, with especial memoranda on its flyleaf and three last leaves, and this title on its opening page, " The Towne Boke of Mendyllsh'm made the yere of " ou' souvrayn lord King Henry VIII'e, xxxii'h of ou' " Lord 1541."

2. The churchwardens' book from 1699 to 1786.

3. The parish book from 1714 to 1793.

4. The yearly accounts of the churchwardens from the time of Mary to the beginning of the eighteenth century.

Extracts from these records.

1541. Md. y' at this xvi'he daye of Januarii y' yere abouesayd Gylbrett Blomefield & y' towne of Mendyllsh'm in y' presens of those persons abouesoyd, & he hatho cowntyd & dyschargyd for hys forme to y' feast of St. Archangell last past.

1544. Md. Wyltur Boymond and Thomas, y' yere abouesed and x. days of January in y' same yere w' Ivon Marfield & Robert Beale haue soulde vnto Gylbart y' gouldsmyth of Ipyswch 1 payre of sensers, 1 payre of chaylis of dubyll gylte, 1 pyxe, a schep as a spone, soulde vnto y' forsayd Gylbyrd aftr iii s. vi d. the ounce, the wyche sume movn'tythe vnto xvi li. and ii s. viii d., by y' consente of Wyll'm Singultn gentyll and Wyllym' Dunckyn y' elder. And a croslyt of plate and gylt w' stones and ii payre of challysysh of paarayl gylt.

1545. Item. Sould the iiii'th daye of February in the yere of o' Lord God . . . a crosse of gylt for xii li. By the churche wardens that is for to, Wyll'm Seman, Robert Aldose, John Goodwyn, wythe assent and consent of all the namys aboue sayd.

5.

—— M'. That the reckynyng was madetho xiiii day of April the 4 yeare of the reigne of o' Souerigne lorde Kyngo Edwarde the VI. betwene the towneshipp of Mendylsham and Wylliam Seman, Robert Aldous, John Goodwynn, chirchewardens. A cleare & draughte of & for all the churche goodes of Mendylsham of them solde & geven before the date aboue wrytten, sauyng they are content yf any can dewly prove any thynge forgotten they are content to slowe it.

Eobardes Schorrardes bylle of a counte for the towne goodes (no date is given in the bill, which appears to have been drawn in the first year of Mary) contains these items :—

Imprimis, payd for caryuge of breeke for the alter, and lyme	v d.
Item, payd for my meate and drynke when I went to Burye to y' visitacion of the byshope	iiii a.
Item, payd for holy breade	iii d.
Item, payd for shortnyng of y' garmonts and for makyng of y' oloth of y' pyxe	
Item, payd for a li. candell on Chrystemasse daye in the mornyng	ii ob.
Item, payd for kord for y' pyxe	i d.
Item, payd for v li. waxe	iii s. ix d.
Item, payd for makyng of it into candelles	viii d.
Item, payd Mr. Viccary for y' lector	viii d.
Item, payd to Blake of Cotten for payntyng of the roode	iii s.
Item, payd to Buxton of Cotton, for settyng together of y' same	iiii d.
Item, payde for y' ii postyle bokes to y' olde viccar	x s.
Item, payd for a masse boke	v s.
& for bryngyng home of them	ii d.
Item, payde to Thom'a Whyghtyng for makyng of y' lector that stonde on the alter	iiii d.

1574. The reconyng of John Seaman and Robert Dunckon, churchewardens :—

Item, pd. to Edmund Pland, scolemaster, for his quarter's wages	xxxiii s. iiii d.
Item, pd. to Edward Turpyn y' alowance of a calfe taken for the quene more then y' quen's price	iii s. viii d.
Item, pd. to the cunstables for the alowance of a wey of chese, & half a reawall of butter taken for the quene, and for carying it to Ypswich	xiii s. ii d.
Item, pd. to Ries wyfe for drink for the ringers wehen they ronge for joy of that day yt the quen's maiestye was crowned	xii d.
Item, pd. to the bell-founder when he did take the bell to make, in earnest	iiii d.
Item, pd. to Willm' Martin for carying of the bell to Bury	viii s. viii d.
Item, for the costs of Jeremy Beale & I when we went to Bury to see the weight of the bell	iii s. xi d.
Item, pd. to the muscion that came to bring the sound of the bell	iii s. viii d.
Item, pd. to Nycolas Embold for carying of the bolts of iron to Bury, & for meat and drinke that he bestowed of y' musicion	

The account contains no less than wenty-four separate entries of money paid for the recasting of this bell, which was a costly business.

1586. A true and fulle reconynge for tho year 1586. Mr. Mylles Docker and John Seaman, church-wardens.

Item, payde to the constables, beynge Thom'a Whytinge & Thom's Walker, tho xxiii daye of Februarye for that they layd oute more than the quenes price for on weight and three qr'ers of cheso & six firkins of butter, & ther charges	xxiis, vi d.
Item, pay to them more for thre combe oates more than the quenes price	x s.
Item, also layd oate for thre pyntes of clarett wyne for the communyon	ix d.
Item, payd for thre pyntes of muskadine for the communion the xiii'th of Apryll	x d.
Item, payd to Mr. Rigges, theight of May for too dozen catcohismyes	iii s. iiii d.

The accounts contain frequent charges for canary (or canarii, as it is usually spelt) as well as claret and

4 F

muscadine, for sacramental use. The allowances to constables for what they had paid in excess of the Queen's price for provisions, furnished to the royal purveyors, are also numerous in the Elizabethan bills; and one is continually coming in the accounts on mention of the trained bands, and allowances to the militiamen. Of the inconveniences and grievances often arising from compulsory service in the trained bands, a good illustration is afforded by the following petition to the Mendlesham churchwardens of some year in Queen Elizabeth's time :—

" These are to certifye the towneshyp of Mendlesham with all that there are diverse poore men within your towne : which were greatlie chargede at the two trayneinges the last somer a Ypswich, desireinge to be restored agayne from pt. of theyre expensis, which we were at if it can be ; and because that you shoulde not thynke but that we have just cause to complayne ; we will put you in remembersunce of the thynge and how the order was ; wher by you myght the better conceyve of vs ; in this behalfe ; we were commanded by the Quene's Maiesties justices at the muster at Melles Grene to be at Ypswich the next Tuesday by eyght of the clok in the forenoone in payne of imprisonement ; therfore bycause the comaundement was so strayght and the tyme of the yeare so whote ; and also to saie the trathe we thought that if we should have gone in the morneinge we shoulde haue byn so wearye, that we thought we shoulde not haue ben able to do our prince seruice ; therfore we wente on the Mondaye at nyghte to our bedds ; and on the Tuesdaye by the said hower as it was appoynted we were called won by one in order, and when we were vewide ouer as the manner was some did serue and other some did not serue ; and they that did scrue had wages and they that did not had nothinge. Wherefore when we were there we would haue ben content to serue byoause we myghte haue hadd wages as the rest that did serue hadd. And yet we that did not serue dust not come awaye byoause we hadd no such commaundement, and so laye from Mondaye at nyght vntill Thursdaye about wone of the cloke ; and then those that did not serue hadd commaundement that they myght departe if they would ; whych some of you can tell how we did stonde disoreation ; but the charges were somwhat tedious vnto some of vs besydes the los of our worke at that tyme of the yere, whych we leaue vnto your meditation. And also at the last trayneinge we that did not serue at the trayneing before were commaunded by the constables to be at Ipswych, as well as they that did serue and so we were. When we cam thither we were called forth to be loke vppon ; then we that did not serue at the trayning before did not serue at this same trayneinge ; which coulde haue byn contented to serue, if it had pleased the muster masters as well as them that did serue. And therefore wee beinge pore men and men of occupation we woude desyre you to consider of the tyme of the yere when these two trayninge were ; the first was made the weeke before Penticost and the last in the begynnige of haruest ; that is when pore mens should haue provided thinges necessario to lyue by after wardes ; those losses and others suche lyke will bringe vs vnto begerie, except you and suche as yon are do considere of vs. And thus if we hadd no neade to complaysne we woulde kepe scilence. Prayeinge to Almightie God that he would of his mercie and goodnes provyde thinges as shalbe profitable both for our soules and bodyes, &c., et sic vale in Christo.

" (Signed) By us John Rudlond als. Mather, John Mathor, Willm. Coper, Bartholomew Knygtes, Henrye Dixon, Francis Dorman, William Coper, Henrie Dixon, Richard Ridnalo, John Beale, Wilfm. Conger, John Manings, Bartholomew Knyghtes, Edm. Goer, senior, Richard Andrew, als. Morgan, John Moor, Fraunois Dorman."

No date.

(b.) The Parish Registers.

1. Register of baptisms, marriages, and deaths from the beginning of the year 1558 to the November of 1653.

2. Register from the November of the year 1653 to the end of 1659.

3. Register from the beginning of the year 1662 to the end of 1712, from which date the series of registers is complete to the present time.

Register No. 2 is noteworthy as commemorating the new practices of a revolutionary period. Instead of the records of baptisms it gives the registrations of births.

It contains also the records of civil marriages before justices of the peace, performed by parishioners of Mendlesham, in accordance with the provisions of the Marriage Act of the Parliament of 1653, during the three years, when no other form of marriage was valid ; as well as the records of marriages celebrated at church in succeeding years, when matrimony could be solemnized by the minister in the parish church, though the civil ceremony in the justice's parlour was still binding and usual.

Extracts from this " Boake for Registering :"—

1653. Thomas Garrod and Ann Bridges being 3 times published were married before Ed. Harvey, Esquyer, the 15th December.

1653. Tho. Garrod and Ann Bridges, maried the 15th of December before Edmund Harvey, Esquyr.

1656. A contract of matrimony betwen John Killet and Sary Cook, was published publickly in the publick assembly, February 8, February 15, February 22, both resedent in Mendlesham.

1656. John Killet and Sary Cook, there marriage was solemnised March the 5th, before the wor'dl Mr. Edmund Fernly, Esquier and justice of the peace.

1656. A contract of matrimony betwene John Esse widower and Mary Beatts single woman was published publickly ons three severall lords dayes in the publicke assembly that is to say Marche the first March the caite and Marche the twenty tow in 1656 both resedent in Mendlesham. John Esse and Mary Beatts there marriage was solemnised April the seconde befor the right worshipfull Mr. Edmund Fernaly, Esq.

1656. Publication of a contract of marriage betwene William Stanard and Mary Juel was performed in the publique meeting place July 5, July 12, July 19, commonly called the church ; both resident in Mendlesham. William Stanard and Mary Juel thir marriage was solemnised July the 23, before the right worshipful Mr. Edmund Ferneley, Esq.

1656. A contract of matrimony betwen John Birds, of Great Thornham, and Margaret Stauerd, of Mendlesham, was published in the market accordinglye, thre severall maket days January 13, January 20, by Henry Nash being then rog and upon February 3, 1656, by me Edmund Cockrill.

1656. John Bird and Margret Stanard, their marriage was solemnised before Mr. Edmund Fernely, Esquire, February 19th, a justice of peace.

1657. John Crosby and Elisebeth Churchman thir marriage was solemnised before Christopher Wragge minister October 15, 1657 in the place commonly called the Church.

1657. Thomas Lockwood and Mary Samant thir marriage was solemnised before Mr. Christopher Wragge minister in the Common Meeting place commonly called the Church. October 13th, 1657.

The book contains (with other evidence of the general confusion of registers of the time, and of the consequent desire of married people to create new testimony of their wedlock, some entries ; of which the following vague record may be given as a specimen :—

1657. Thomas Jordan and Elizabeth Baldry of Westrope ther marriag was solemnized March the 11th 1657 at Rattlesden by Sqr. Browne justice of the pepoe as they informe.

The marriage of John Bird and Margaret Stanerd's marriage, Feb. 3, 1656, is the last instance in the register of lay marriage before a justice of the peace. The subsequent marriages were solemnized by the minister in the public meeting place, commonly called the Church.

On the last page of this register appear the following characteristic notes :—

1. Registerium in intervallo rebellionis ub anno 1653 ad ann. 1660 in quo restaurabatur Carolus Secundus. In quibus facile est conjicere, quod multa sunt omissa, omnia confuse scripta, juxta modum ejusdem ætatis, in quâ sub religionis et reformationis pretexto omnes res ecclesiasticas non tantum defloruore, sed pene extinctæ fuere. Ordo episcopalis sublatus, et presbyteri, qui regis et ecclesiæ partibus adhesere, universim sequestrati, et curis detrusi ; et quod observandum est, in nulla regni parte plures a fidelitate ad rebellionem defecere quam in hisce locis associatis. Wm. Smyth, Vic. D. D.

2. (Written by a second writer against Dr. Smyth's signature)—" Non ministravit in hâc ecclesiâ (de Mendlesham) Gulielmus Smith in intervallo Rebellionis. Teste hoc parvulo registerio.—Chr. Wragge, mortuus est, A.D. 1661 : Nomenque Gul. Smith, in anno 1662, tunc primum invenitur.

MENDLE-
SHAM.

&. Gulielmus Smyth; s· quo observatio super-scripta facta fuit quod rebellionem in hisce locis; non sequestratus, neque a cura detrusus fuit in illis temporibus; quamvis multa amicitia, amor multos, et desiderium vehementissimum pristinæ disciplinæ cum possidere videbantur. O tempora! oh, mores! . Hoc mihi videtur Rich^le Chilton, vicar, 1746.

In the *Parish Register Abstract* (printed by order of the House of Commons, 2 April 1833) this register is described as an "imperfect, 1653-1661."—a description that is somewhat erroneous, as the record, beginning in November 1653, closes at the end of 1659. That Dr. Smyth, vicar of Mendlesham in 1662, did not regard it as a portion of a register that covered the years 1660 and 1661, may be inferred from his words, "registerium " in intervallo rebellionis ab anno 1653 ad 1660." No register for the years '60 and '61 is preserved amongst the Mendlesham archives.

(c.) Old Deeds, Charters, and other Parchments of the Parish Chest:

They comprise—

(1.) 8 Edward III. Conveyance of one acre and half an acre of land in Mikelfeld from Robertus dil Mersach to Katrina Mickelfeld, her heirs and assigns.

(2.) 20 Edward III. Conveyance of a messuage in Mendlesham, lying before the gate of the manor house of Mendlesham, from John Olyve of Mendlesham to Geoffroy Chapman.

(3.) 26 Henry VI. Conveyance of a messuage in Mendlesham from Robert Mannyng, Thomas Goodwene, William Baret, and John Adgoor of Mendlesham to Thomas Dunkon, Johanna his wife, William Starlyng, clerk, and John Swalwe, chaplain, their heirs and assigns.

(4.) 30 Henry VI. Conveyance of a messuage in Mendlesham from William Barret, Thomas Alte, Watyr Peyntour and Richard Taylour to Thomas Alte Watyr de Stonham Parva, Margery his wife, Thomas Crowe of the same place, and John Swale, screvenor.

(5.) 38 Henry VI. Conveyance of a messuage in Mendlesham, from Thomas Dunkon, Johanna his wife, William Starling, clerk, and John Swalwe, clerk, to Robert Tyryngton, Robert Dunch or Booher, and Thomas Aldbous.

(6.) 11 Edward IV. Last will and testament of Robert Oake of Mendlesham.

(7.) 8 Henry VIII. Last will and testament of Henry Jesop of Mendlesham.

(8.) 8 Henry VIII. Conveyance of a messuage near the market place of Mendlesham, from Richard Pyttman and John Airty to Edward Cressent, Richard Stodd, and William Cressent.

(9.) 20 Henry VIII. Final agreement made at Westminster before King's Justices, between William Sengelton and others, plaintiffs, and William Messenger, and Margaret his wife, defendants.

(10.) 30 Henry VIII. Bond by which John Arnold obliges himself, his heirs and assigns, to abide by the award of John Cage of Wolpett, yeoman, John Wage the elder, Thomas Berte of Wederden, tanner, and Lawrence Lynge, appointed to arbitrate in a dispute respecting title to lands, between the said John Arnold of the one part and John Takon and William Takon thairn of the other part.

(11.) 32 Henry VIII. General release and quit-claim by William Duckon, yeoman, of Mendlesham, to Robert Prynne, of the same place, labourer.

(12.) 36 Henry VIII. Conveyance of a messuage in Mendlesham from Andrew Wilkyn, ' groser,' to John Anger of ' Penderyng,' co. Essex.

(13.) 6 Edward VI. Release and quit-claim to William Syngleton, John Gernyshe, gentleman, and William Donken of Mendlesham, by Thomas Knyvett of 'Bokenham,' in respect to all his title and interest, present and future, in certain lands and tenements in Mendlesham called ' Pechers ' and ' Lutts.'

(14.) 6 Edward VI. Copy of record in the rolls of the manor of Mendlesham of the admission of Francis Gascoigne, gentleman, Charles Syngleton, gentleman, Henry Gascoigne, gentleman, William Dunken, John Dunken, senior, Sweyn Eldnys, George Reves, Robert Sheppard, Thomas Blomefield, Richard Randall, Jeremy Hubberd, and Michael Revitt, newly appointed trustees under the will of Henry Jesop. The record describes this copyhold part of Henry Jesop's bequest to the parish:—' Ad hanc curiam, Will'mus Donken, sen., " præsens in curia reddidit in man' d'ñe quinq' acr' et " d'i-terre-v'æt' ten' Luttys ac unu messuagiu variu cu " vi. acr' terr' inclus' ejusdem ter' Luttys cu p'tin quas " Wilts huit per jus accrescendi post mortem Georgii

MENDLE-
SHAM.

" Syngylton et Nicholas Seman quos supvi'xit qniq' " annuatim de p'mista cu p'fato Willimo ad diu'sos " ysus et effectus so'dm ulasan voluntatem Henrici " Jessop seisiti fuerunt."

(15.) 1 Mary. Conveyance of lands and tenements in Mendlesham and Cotton, in consideration of the sum of 40l. from Sir Thomas Knyvett, of Buckenham Castle, co. Norfolk, to the parish of Mendlesham. The agreement for this transfer was made by Sir Edmund Knyvett, father of Sir Thomas, and carried into effect by the latter, after his father's death.

(16.) Hock-mundays, 6 Elizabeth. Agreement between Thomas Knyvett, lord of the manor of Mendlesham, of the one part, and the tenants of the said manor of the other part, for ending controversy respecting the customs of the manor, and defining the rights of the lord and the liabilities of tenants.

(17.) 7 Elizabeth. Release and quit-claim by Edmund Jesope, of Wetheringsett, co. Suffolk, grandson and heir to Henry Jesope, of Mendlesham, in respect to all those lands and tenements, &c. called Pechers, formerly belonging to Henry Jesope and his wife, Johanna Pecher, daughter and heiress of John Pecher, and now in the occupation of Richard Gurnyshe, gen'., John Shurlond, Richard Shepparde, and Charles Seman, of Mendlesham, who have paid Edmund Jesope a sum of money in satisfaction of his claims.

(18.) 20 Elizabeth. New enfeoffment of lands bequeathed in trust for charitable uses in the parish of Mendlesham, by Robert Oake. Old feoffees: Simon Harleston and Barnaby Gybson. New feoffees: Richard Garneys, Thomas Shurlond, John Salmon, Richard Dunckon, William Docker, Robert Dunkon, John Blomefield, Thomas Hubbarde, Thomas Aldowse, Thomas Whiting, Jeremy Beale, senr., Armoas Beale, William Dunkon, Edmund Whiting, John Seman (son of Thomas Seaman), John Whytynge, Swethin Muakam, Thomas Dunnett, Charles Seman, Simon Edgar, and Bryst Bronwyn.

(19.) 34 Elizabeth. Memorandum of the conveyance of a messuage from Richard Amys to Andrew Bardewell, of Melles, co. Suffolk, and of Richard Amys's undertaking to maintain Andrew Bardewell's title to the said messuage.

(20.) 36 Elizabeth. New enfeoffment of the Jesope trust lands and tenements " cum oibus suis p'tinent' in " villa de Mendlesham voc' Pechers que nuper fuerunt " cojusdam Henrici Jesop."

(21.) 5 James I. Conveyance of a messuage in Mendlesham from Peter Pretyman, of Backton, co. Suffolk, to Nicholas Balf of the same place.

(22.) Conveyance in consideration of the sum of 20l. of two parts of a messuage abutting on the Guild Hall (gildam anlam) of Mendlesham, from Nicholas Powhage, husbandman, to Richard Partridge.

(23.) 12 James I. Conveyance of a messuage in Mendlesham to Master Duck.

(24.) 14 James I. Agreement between Thomas Goodwyn, of Little Stonham, co. Suffolk, lord of the manor of Mendlesham, of the one part, and the tenants of the said manor of the other part, for settling controversies respecting the customs of the manor, and fixing the rights and liabilities of the lord and his tenants. The indenture recites the earlier agreement between Sir Thomas Knyvett and the tenants, and states that after purchasing the manor of Sir Thomas, John Eldred, Esquire (from whom Thomas Goodwyn bought the manor) endeavoured to set aside the arrangement made between Sir Thomas and the tenants.

(25.) 14 James I. Inspeximus of the enrolment of the above-named agreement and of proceedings in the Court of Chancery, together with the final decree of the Court, giving effect to the agreement. The great seal of this charter is perfect.

(26.) 14 James I. Inspeximus of the enrolment of the same indenture, with record of proceedings and decree, in the court of the Duchy of Lancaster.

(27.) 15 James I. Conveyance of a messuage in Mendlesham by Peter Duck to John Sheppard, Robert Seaman, and other inhabitants of Mendlesham, in trust, for the residence of a schoolmaster, the maintenance of a grammar school, and the relief of the poor of the town.

(28.) 16 James II. Release and quit-claim by Thomas Partings, of Kettlebar, co. Suffolk, to James Fenn. of Mendlesham, in respect to his title to a messuage called Jacksmans.

(29.) 6 Charles I. Conveyance of a messuage in Mendlesham from Humfrey Bardwell, of Mellis, co. Suffolk, linen-weaver, to Henry Bardwell, of Sahum Comit (Earl's Soham), co. Suffolk.

MENDLE-
SHAM.

(30.) 24 Charles I. Mortgage of a messuage in Mendlesham to John Dunkon and Robert Dunkon by Henry
Bardwell, of Mendlesham, the sum lent to Henry Bardwell on the security being 16l.

(31.) 7 Charles II. Conveyance of messuages and
tenements in Medlesham from John Dunkon and Robert
Dunkon to Edmund Sheppard, Thomas Butts, Robert
Ridnall, and Barnaby Barker, of Mendlesham.

(32.) 26 Charles II. New enfeoffment of the lands
left to the parish for charitable uses.

(31.) Fifteen copies (on parchment) of proceedings
in the court of the manor of Mendlesham; all of them
recording the admission of customary tenants of the
manor.

It has not escaped the reader that a large proportion
of these deeds had no relation to properties bequeathed
to the parish. They were documents belonging to private persons, who consigned them, in accordance with
general usage, to the parish chest for safety. The number of the documents thus confided to the great coffer
and never withdrawn from it by their depositors or their
representatives points to the prevalence of the practice.
Something yet remains to be told in connexion with
this account of the Mendlesham parchments. In the
vestry of the church may be seen a brass plate, on which
the vicar and churchwardens in an early year of the present century engraved brief descriptions of the several
properties held by trustees for the benefit of the parish.
This brass record mentions the lands left to the parish by
its earliest benefactor Robert Cake, who, in the year 1473,
and by a testament drawn in contracted law Latin, bequeathed his property, in the first instance, to pay the
fifteenths of the lord king, "et aliud on² ibidem d'oi
" d'ñi Regs cû accidit v'l acciderit," charged upon the
inhabitants of Mendlesham; the surplus of income, after
the payment of the taxes of the wealthier folk, being all
that he bequeathed for the relief of the poor and sick.
Proper prominence is given on the brazen tablet to the
name of Robert Cake, as a benefactor of the parish.
The same is the case with Peter Duck, who, in the 15th
year of James I., gave Mendlesham property for the
endowment of a school-house. But against three of
the properties, belonging to the parish and described
in brass, no donor's name appears. The plate declares
that the donor of each of these gifts is *unknown*. Mendlesham has long enjoyed such distinction amongst the
parishes of Suffolk by owning property which came to
her from undiscoverable benefactors, that some of the
townsfolk scarcely relished the announcement that my
search of their church documents had explained their che-
rished mystery and falsified their brass tablet. On hearing that the three benefactions, from unknown sources,
were all from the same donor, Henry Jesop, who died
at Mendlesham in an early year of Henry VIII.'s reign,
old inhabitants of the place declared they had never
heard of the name of Jesop in connexion with the parish.
The production of benefactor's will had little effect on
minds disposed to question the genuineness of the discovery, for, though written in English, it was of course
illegible to persons unfamiliar with handwriting of the
sixteenth century.

The last will and testament of Henry Jesop (or
Jesope, as the surname is spelt in some of the Mendles-
ham documents, or Jessop, as it is usually spelt in
Suffolk at the present time).

" In nòie Dei Amen. I Henry Jesop of Mendelys-
" h²m of goode and hoole meende beyng y² xvi daye of
" the monyth of Septembr in y² yeere of owre Lorde
" Gode m'cccoc²xvi² make my testamēt and laste wyll
" in thys forme follryng. First I be qwethe my soule
" to Allmyghty God, to owre Lady Seynt Mary, & to
" alle the seyntes in heuen & my body to be beryed
" in y² chyrch yerde of Mendelysh²m. Item I be
" qweth to y² hiey autyr of y² name chyrch iiii s. Item
" I wyll y² Jone my wyffe haue my tenemēts callyd
" Waters and Fedelers and Peynters to geve & to
" selle aftyr my dyscease. Item I wyll y² my wyfe
" haue my tenemēt callyd Pecher & Lotts terme of
" her lyffe & tyll Mychelmasse aftyr her decease,
" payeng to Dauie Willyā Bedyngfeld of Soynt Ed-
" monds Bery my son xiii s. & iiii d. be yeere. And
" aftyr y² decesse of Jone my wyffe I wylle y² forsayd
" tenemēt callyd Pechers & Lotts remayne to the
" towne of Mendelysh²m to y² fyndyng of a clarke to
" pley att y² organys for a p'petuite. And y' y² chyrch
" revys and too moo of y² towne shall medyll w² all
" and no moo of y² towne paying to Davie Wyllyā
" Bedyngfeld my son be yeere terme of hys lyff xiii s.
" & iiii d. Item I wyll y² Jone my wyffe kepe a
" yeerdsye for me yeerly terme of her lyffe w² in y²
" chyrch of Mendelysh²m and aftyr her decesse I wyll

MENDLE-
SHAM.

" y² towne of Mendelysh²m kepe a sangarede for me &
" my wyffe w² in y² chyrch of Mendelysh²m p'petuall.
" Also I wyll y² Jone my wyffe schalle make no stryppe
" ner waste in fellyng of tymbyr, but for y² rep'acion of
" y² howays & to kepe y² howays suffycyently in repar-
" acon terme of her lyfe. Item I wylle haue a preste
" to synge for me w² in y² chyrch of Mendelysh²m y²
" space of haffe a yeere. Item, I wyll Dauie Wyllyā
" Bedyngfeld my son syng for me in Bery Abbey y²
" space of haffe a yeere. Item I wyll y² Dauie Wyllyā
" my son haue my blake hors my best kandelstyke
" a charger my red bedcloth a payro of blankettes &
" a payre of schetes. Item I wyll y² Jone Jenor haue
" a melche kowe. Item I wyll y² Jo hn Jesop my god-
" son of Mekefeld haue a yeoryng boloke. Item I
" wyll y² my goddowetyr Isbelle Rowe haue a yeeryng
" boloke. Item I wyll y² Thom²s Norfolys chylderen
" haue vi lambys. Item I wyll Isbelle Baker haue a
" yeryng bulloke. Item I be qwethe to y² chyrch of
" Mendelysh²m to y² makyng of y² roofe iii li to be
" takyn of Thom²s Bocher of Needh²m & xx s. of
" Rychard Dryver of Cretyng of my dette. And as I
" shewyd Mas² Vekery of Mendelysh²m, Wyllye Don-
" ken & Wyllyā Mathew yf they & y² chyrch revys
" wold take it of y² forsayd Thom²s & Rychard or ellys
" I geve noon for I wyll nott haue my executors
" trobelyd for y² said iiii li. Item I be qwethe to
" Thom²s Stanton of Ypwychvi s. viii d. Item I wyll
" y² my executors haue x combe whete & iii combe
" malte to my berying & my xxx² day. It I wyll y²
" haue a bulloke & x schepe & a weye of chese to my
" berying & my xxx² day. It all y² resydue of my
" catell & corne & stuffe of howahold on be qwethe I
" wyll y² my wyff haue ytt. It I be qwethe to Symond
" Egger of Mendelysh²m & to Thomas Benett of Meke-
" feld eche of them vi s. viii d. whom I chose & make
" my executors & Syr Thom²s Tyrrell of Gyppyng,
" knyght, sup'vysor of thys my last wylle these wetten-
" esse, Sr Wyllyā Becha, Vekery of Mendelysh²m,
" Wyllyā Donken, Wyllyā Mathew, Wyllyā Bevyll &
" John Norfoll of y² towne forsayd cû aliis.

There is no need to apologise for publishing the
ipsissima verba, of the will, which restores to us so
expressive a word as " sangarede " for a chanted service
and which demonstrates that at least as late as the
earlier decades of the sixteenth century the burials of
wealthy persons were sometimes celebrated in East
Anglia with feasts, lasting for 30 days. But what is
most surprising in the story of this will and its maker
is, that the latter should for a considerable period have
fallen completely out of the knowledge of the people of
the very town that benefitted so largely by his munificence. This fact is the more astonishing, as the
Mendlesham documents prove that Henry Jesop's name
and beneficence must have been familiar to the people
of Mendlesham, at least as late as the first generation
of the seventeenth century. In the seventh year of
Elizabeth, the trustees of his bequests satisfied with
money his grandson Edmund Jesope, in respect to some
title he had or imagined himself to have to the testator's property; just as a few years earlier they had
quieted with payment the claims of Thomas Knyvett of
Bokenham. In the thirty-sixth year of the same Queen,
new trustees were appointed for the lands lately belonging to Henry Jesope, some of whom probably lived to
see Charles I. ascend the throne. And yet at the
beginning of the present century Henry Jesope's name
and acts were so utterly forgotten in the parish, which
retained possession of his legacies, that the vicar and
churchwardens of Mendlesham wrote in brass that his
lands came to the parish from an unknown benefactor.
The discovery of Robert Cake's will also throws light
on the manner in which the taxpayers of Mendlesham
used to divide the income of bequeathed property
amongst themselves, giving little or none of it to the
poor. From the instrument it is clear that Robert
Cake's first purpose was to relieve the tax-payers of his
parish from the burden of King's taxes. The words,
defining the testator's first object, are both comprehensive and precise :—" sd acquietand' soluend' & exone-
" rand' quint' decim' dñi regis et aliud on² ibidem
" dñi Regs cû accidit v'l acciderit soluend' p' villat'
" de Mendlessh²m prout pro inhabitanti²3 in eadem."
It follows from these words that the yeomen and other
tax-payers of the parish, who used to apply the revenues
of the charity to the payment of their dues to the Crown
were guilty of no abuse of charity, but were only acting
in accordance with the donor's will.

JOHN CORDY JEAFFRESON.

THE CHURCH BOOKS OF THE PARISH OF ALWINGTON, NORTH DEVON.

Through the kind offices of J. R. Pine Coffin, Esquire, of Portledge, and by the courtesy of the Reverend — Mules, the Rector of the Parish, I have been favoured with an opportunity of examining the Church Books of Alwington; adjoining to Parkham, the books belonging to which Parish have been the subjects of notice in a previous Report.

The oldest of the Register Books, now surviving, is an oblong folio volume, with leaves of parchment, the writing upon the earlier of which is almost wholly obliterated. The opening leaves of this volume, in its original state, are evidently lost, and, in its present condition, it begins with Baptisms, about A.D. 1550. Further on in the book, some of the leaves are mutilated, and in some the writing is totally effaced. The Baptisms in this volume end in 1654.

The entries of Marriages begin in 1553 or 4 : " were " woded " is the earlier form, " were wedded " later. Couples are never " married " in this volume, or in the succeeding one, with some few exceptions in the latter ; " wedded " being the usual form. The Marriages end in 1654. The entries of Burials begin A.D. 1549, and end in 1642, the book being imperfect at the end. During the period in question, Thomasin, or Thomasia, appears, in this parish, to have been the favourite name for females.

The succeeding volume is a similar oblong folio, but thicker, with leaves of parchment, bound in wooden boards, one side of which is lost. It begins, with Marriages, in February 1654, ending 27th of February 1717. The Baptisms begin 29th of November 1653, ending 25th of December 1716. The Burials begins 29th of November 1653, and end in 1717. The notices in these two volumes, of births and deaths of members of the Coffin family, of Portledge, in this parish, are numerous. The entries are of a very meagre description, and contain nothing that calls for further notice.

A thin paper folio volume, bound in limp vellum, with the following title,—" A book to register the names " of such persons as have died in the Parish of Alwing- " ton, since the First day of August 1678." Its object was, the registering of affidavits as to whether or not the dead had been buried in woollen, in conformity with the Act of Parliament 30 Charles II. (A.D. 1678) ordering to that effect, under a penalty of 5 pounds. In 1767 the affidavits cease, the entries of burials being continued to 1775. From squire to peasant, throughout, all went to the grave in their woollen garb ; the fine, exacted for burial in more costly habiliments, being in no one instance, so far as I observed, submitted to.—

" Odious ! in woollen, 'twould a Saint provoke,"— the fair and frail one to whom this sentiment is imparted by the Poet, had no sympathizers in Alwington.

The earliest now existing Church-Rate Book, is an oblong folio paper volume, bound in leather, and beginning in 1767, the latest entries being in 1824. The volume is little more than half-filled. Though of so recent a date, there are some few entries in it that may perhaps deserve notice.—

The ringers received yearly 7 shillings for ringing the bells on the 5th of November, down to the latter date ; it being (with perhaps a single exception) the only occasion in the year on which any payment to them was made. The people of Alwington seem, at the period in question, to have had but little taste for the chase ; and in their number few genuine sportsmen, probably, were to be found. There are numerous entries for the killing of foxes and their cubs, the tariff being at first two shillings, later three, and then five shillings, per head. The other animals, the slayers of which were similarly subsidized by the Churchwardens, but at lower rates, were martrels, (or martens), greys or badgers, (sometimes written " baggers," sometimes " bagges "), hedgehogs, fetches or fitches (weasels), orteres (otters), jays, hawks, kits or kites, and, at a more recent date, sparrows, crows, magpies, and hoops (bullfinches).

The following are some additional extracts from the volume.—A.D. 1767. " Paid for this book to keep " accounts 8s. 9d." 1768, " Paid him [John Rogers, " the Clerk] for caching the molls [moles] and spreding " ye hills, 1s. 6d." 1776, " Paid the Pariter [Appari- " tor] for a form of Prayer for the Young Princes, 1s." 1778, " To a curten for the pulpett, 2s. 3d." 1779, " To a traveling woman that had a pass signed by the " Mayor of Bideford 6d." Entries of this nature become very numerous towards the close of the century. 1783, " To six tyts [hassocks, elsewhere called " kneeling

" toytes "] for the church, 6s." At the same date also is the following entry,—" Memdum. No hawks, jays, " fitches, or badgers, to be allowed for in future. The " bells being now in good order, it is supposed nothing " but grease will be wanted for the ensuing year, nor is " the Churchwarden to be allowed anything for doing his " office." Only one of the two Churchwardens, annually elected, seems, for some years, to have been the acting Churchwarden. For some years after this date, the sums allowed for the killing of birds and " vermin " are but few in number, but gradually the above order, as to hawks and badgers, came to be disregarded. 1790, " To " Parkham men, for killing a old fixin [vixen] fox, " 2s. 6d." 1792, " To a new pich pipe for the singers, " 5s. 6d." 1803, " To Mr. James Peard for teaching " the singers 6l. 6s. :"—this comparatively liberal payment is soon reduced to one guinea. 1804, " Relieved " 3 children and their mother stranded at Hale, Cornwall 4s. Paid for killing 3 foxes 9s 6d." 1806, " For " new drawing the sun dial 1s. 6d." 1807, " Agreed by " the Parishioners of Alwington, to pay three pence per " dozen for old sparrows, and two pence per dozen for " young do., and one penny per piece for hoops. Provided they are killed in the parish." 1809, " Paid " for one old fox, and 6 young, 7s. 6d. For one out shell, " 9d." 1810, " Mr. Ching for killing two foxes 10s." 1811, " To Edward Bale for fox ale [payment in ale for " killing a fox] 5s. My boys for killing 5 dozen of " sparrows 1s. 0½d." :—to which of the two Churchwardens " My boys " belonged, is not stated. 1816, " Paid " Edward Bale for fox ale 15s." 1822, " Green baize " bag for the bass viol 5s. 9d. William Bailey for playing bass viol 10s. Edward Williams, for playing " flute 10s. N.B. Revd. Mr. Morrison gave a bass viol " cost ——. Mr. Wackeril a flute, cost 1l." The Revd. Mr. Morrison was one of the Churchwardens, for several years.

On the last written leaf is the following entry:— " Memorandum of what has been formerly allowed for " killing sundry vermin and mischievous birds. Fox " each, 5s. Badgers 1s. Hedgehogs 3d. Hawks and " kites 6d. old, 3d. young. Magpies, crows, and jays " 3d. Hoops, each 1d. Sparrows, per dozen 2½d. " Thrushes 1d. Fitchetts, or weasels, 4d." The entries as to sparrows and thrushes have a line run through them, — and the entry noticed is succeeded by the following :—" Memorandum, at a Vestry held Monday " 19th of April 1824 (being Easter Monday). It was " agreed that those who kill foxes or mischievous " birds, as mentioned above, should produce their " account of it at Easter next, when their bills will be " investigated and paid, as the majority of Vestry shall " direct, by subscription. W. W[ackeril] Church " Warden." All this has as much the air of being obsolete, as if it had happened three centuries ago.

HENRY THOMAS RILEY.

THE MANUSCRIPTS OF THE CORPORATION OF DARTMOUTH.

With the sanction of —. Puddicombe, Esq., the Mayor, and the Common Council, of Dartmouth, accorded to me personally in the most courteous terms, I have recently had the opportunity of making a prolonged examination of the ancient records in their possession ; and, by the courtesy of Percy Hockin, Esq. the Town Clerk, to whom I have much pleasure in acknowledging my obligations, every possible facility has been afforded me for doing so.

These records, which, taken altogether, are very numerous, may be divided into four classes ; charters, volumes, deeds, and miscellaneous documents. The miscellaneous documents of a date prior to the reign of Henry the Eighth, are comparatively few in number, and have not been examined by me sufficiently at length to admit of my giving a description of them in the present Report: those of a more recent date, with scarcely an exception, so far as I have examined them, present no feature of either interest or usefulness that calls for notice. The pages of this Report will therefore be limited to a description of the books belonging to the Corporation, and of the contents of a portion of such among the deeds and documents under seal, between the reigns of Henry the Third and Henry the Sixth, as give information in reference to the ancient history of the town, its localities,—some of which have perished out of mind and memory,—its old tenures, and its former officials and inhabitants. The remaining deeds, the town Charters, and the earlier miscellaneous documents, not improbably, will form the subject of a second Report.

The Corporation books, or Registers, are many in number, and, some of them, singularly ponderous; nothing beyond a mere description of them can be attempted in this Report.

The earliest volume is a large paper folio, in its original boards and tattered calf leather, the pages not numbered, but containing about 300 leaves. The cover is lined at the beginning and end with two parchment leaves, illuminated in red and blue, part apparently of a 14th century MS. of the Pandects of Justinian. It is labelled on the outside "Borough Court, 2nd Richard "Second, 1378," but this is a mistake; a few leaves only are lost at the beginning, and the regular entries commence with the 2nd year of the reign of Richard the Third. Leaves 3 to 6, contain musical notation, in a hand of the early part of the 16th century; the words beginning with—" Et exultavit spiritus meus," Luke i. 47. The first Law Court, the proceedings of which are entered in folio 7a, was holden on Monday after the feast of St. Michael, in the 2nd year of Richard the Third. The last entry is the 30th of March in the 21st year of Henry VIII. (A.D. 1530), but one or more leaves are lost at the end. The minutes of the Courts and in the 3rd year of Henry VIII.: and the entries throughout are of a most miscellaneous description, and evidently embody the then current history of the town.

The next Court Book is a large folio, in old limp ornamented calf, containing 222 leaves of paper; its entries commence on Monday after Michaelmas Day, in the 3rd year of Henry VIII., and end at the Feast of St. Matthew in the 29th year of the same reign.

The next volume is a very large folio, in old limp ornamented calf, containing nearly 300 leaves of paper. It begins on Monday after Michaelmas in the 29th year of Henry VIII., and ends with the second year of Philip and Mary, there being some miscellaneous entries also at the end. In the padding of the tattered cover of this volume is inserted, with other matter, a portion of two leaves of a very early printed Latin and English Grammar; "Secunda pars opuscoli."—"Of verbis person-"ales;" only two pages of the Grammar are prefect.

A large folio, bound in calf, with thongs and an ornamented brass buckle; containing about 490 leaves of paper. It begins with the Law Court holden on Monday the 12th of October, in the 3rd and 4th years of Philip and Mary, and the regular entries end in the 9th of Elizabeth. The binding has been strengthened with a fragment of a handsomely illuminated Latin MS. (on legal matters) of the 14th century; the subject appears to be parental authority, and the legal liabilities of the different degrees of relationship.

A large folio, bound in ornamented calf, with a thong, containing 466 leaves of paper. It begins in April, the 9th year of Elizabeth, and its entries end in February, in the 19th year of her reign.

The next volume is a very large folio, bound in calf, and containing 570 leaves of paper; its entries commence in April in the 19th year of Elizabeth, and end in September in the 34th year of her reign.

At this point there seems to be a hiatus of about ten years.

A large folio, bound in limp calf, containing about 550 leaves of paper. Its entries begin in February in the 43rd year of Elizabeth, and end in the 10th year of James the First. The sides are strengthened with fragments of a finely illuminated Service Book, of the 14th century, with musical notation.

The next is a large folio paper volume, in limp calf, containing about 400 leaves. Its entries, beginning at one end, are from the tenth year of Elizabeth to the 43rd year of that reign, being proceedings of the Queen's Water Bailiff at Dartmouth. At the other end, it begins with the Law Courts from the 2nd year of Charles the First, down to the tenth year of the same reign.

A small folio paper volume, bound in limp parchment, containing at one end the Law Courts from the last day of August, in the 11th year of King Charles the First, down to the 24th day of January 1648 (9) fol. 236; to which date they are held in his name. The same Courts are held, under various other denominations, down to the 23rd of July in the same year. There are miscellaneous entries on about 68 pages, beginning at the other end of the volume.

The remaining books seem to be of a miscellaneous character.

A quarto volume, containing about 200 leaves, half of them filled, bound in embossed calf, now in a tattered condition. It contains various Corporation Accounts, beginning in the first year of Henry VIII.; but imme-

diately passes on to the 9th; though, to all appearance, none of its contents are lost. 1547 is the date of the latest account.

A small folio book, of about 300 leaves, bound in embossed calf, has 13 leaves filled with miscellaneous matters, the rest remaining blank. The earliest entry is, "A Constitution for the weekely meetinge of the " Maior and Common Counsell, at the Guildhalle, made " the xiiith daye of December 1604." The latest entry bears date the 17th of August 1676.

A small quarto paper book, in limp parchment, braced with a fragment of a law Manuscript of the 13th century: 55 of the leaves are written upon at one end, the earliest entries apparently, (as to the mode of admission of enfranchised persons), belonging to the reign of Henry VIII., so far as the writing is concerned; the latest of the "Constitutions" here entered belonging to the year 1773. The entries at the other end of the book are of a somewhat similar nature, ranging from the reign of Henry VIII. to 1777. Three-fourths of the volume remain in blank.

A quarto book of Minutes, in limp parchment, containing 146 leaves of paper, being orders made by the Mayor and Common Council. At page 33 is the following order,—"xvⁱᵉ die Julii 1579. Nicholas Jackmarme "is att this tyme appoynted to cause his daughter, "beyng a sike woman, to be forthwith putt one [? out] "his house, and on this side Michaelmas next to pro-"vide some convenient house oute of this towne, or "otherwyse order to be taken that he shall not any "longer keep a common bakehouse." The latest entries are in 1609. The cover, black with dirt and scribbling, is part of a finely illuminated Service-Book, of the 14th century, with musical notation.

A thin quarto paper book, with a paper cover, of about 40 leaves, being inquisitions held by the Coroner, between 1603 and 1624.

A folio volume, of about 300 leaves of paper, in old calf, containing proceedings of the Law Courts and other matters from 1690 to 1699.

A large folio, of 369 leaves of paper, in stiff parchment covers, containing proceedings of the Law Courts from 1699 to 1769.

The early deeds, and documents that may come under that definition, belonging to the Corporation, from the reign of Henry III., and indeed earlier, down to the time of Henry VIII., are very numerous; in part, they seem to have belonged to property transferred to feoffees in the middle ages for the use of the Church: while many others of them, as at Axbridge and other Western towns, and again, at Rye in Sussex, may have been placed in the hands of the Common Clerk for safe custody; and, on being superseded by later deeds, were never claimed. The following is a selection of some of the earlier of these deeds, as throwing more or less light on the inhabitants and localities of the town and its vicinity, at a remote period; some hundreds, probably, being of necessity left unnoticed in this Report. Before entering upon an examination of those documents, it may be not inopportune to remark that the ancient and legal appellation of the town is "Clifton Dartmouth Hardness;" it being an aggregate of what in the middle ages formed three townships, Clifton, on the East by South, Dertemouth, in the middle, and Hardness, on the West; the latter so called probably as being the "ness," or promontory, ending in the "hard," or beach. The mother church of Dartmouth was the church of St. Clement at Townstall, or Tunstall, about a mile inland, on the summit of a steep hill; St. Saviour's, the present church of Dartmouth, was built as a chapel of ease to Townstall, in 1374.

A small parchment deed, in Latin, the seal lost, apparently of the beginning of the reign of Edward I., whereby Richard Fitz-William, William being son of Stephen, grants to Robert Uppehille one messuage, "in " my vill of Dertemue," between the houses of Ernald Scot and William de Wight; at a yearly rent of 15d., payable at 3 terms of the year. For this gift and grant Robert has paid him one bezant (a gold coin of Byzantium). Witnesses, Peter the Chaplain, Thomas Perer, Richard de Sede, Thomas Wombe, Wiot Crispin, Walter Long, William de Wight, Jesse (probably a Jew), "and many others."

A parchment deed, being a grant, in Latin, by Gilbert Fitz-Stephen, Lord of Nortone, to Henry Burde and Isobel, daughter of John de Cruce [Cross], of a piece of land in the burgh of Dertemouth, near the tenement of Edward Wilyson, on the west side of the way going down from the "great street" towards the "falaise," (high cliff); at a yearly rent of 3d., and on condition of his paying 2 suits at his Court at Dartsmouth, at Michael-mas and Hockeday. Witnesses, Philip Burde and others. *Temp.* Edward I. The small seal is much mutilated.

A small parchment deed, in Latin, with a large seal in white wax, representing a flower, probably of the begin-ning of the reign of Edward I.; whereby Richard Fitz-William, William being son of Stephen, grants to Richard, son of Richard de Sede, one messuage in the vill of Hardenesse, before the chapel of St. Clair; at a yearly rent of one pound of wax at the Feast of St. Michael; one besant having been paid beforehand.

A small parchment deed, with a small seal, mutilated, *temp.* Edward I., whereby Gilbert Fitz-Richard, Richard being son of Stephen, grants to William Smith (Fabro) of la Fosse, one messuage in Cliftone of Dertemue, between the way leading from the vill of Dertemue towards the chapel of St. Clair and "my mill-dam "of Dertemue;" he paying a yearly rent of 6 pence, and "such other services as my burgesses of Dertemue "do;" 2s. having been paid beforehand. Witnesses, Henry Burd, and others named.

A small parchment deed, in Latin, with a seal of green wax, representing a knight on horseback, with shield and sword, *temp.* Edward I.; whereby Gilbert Fitz-Richard, Richard being son of Stephen, grants to Thomas Pelliper [Skinner] one garden on the west side of the vill of Cliftone, to hold to him and his assigns, religious houses and Jews excepted, at a yearly rent of 6 pence. Witnesses, John Clobard, Martin le Vois, Walter de Fawy, William Aubin, Thomas de Cruce [Cross], Richard, his brother, William Crispin, "and " many others."

A small parchment deed, *temp.* Edward I., in Latin, whereby Richard Fitz-William, William being son of Stephen, grants to Roger Joie one messuage in his vill of Hardenesse, at a yearly rent of 12d.; the sum also of 12d. being paid beforehand. Witnesses, Thomas Porer, Wiot Crispin, Brian de Virga, Walter Dubeldai, "and others." The seal is lost.

A small parchment deed, in Latin, with seal repre-senting a shield of arms, but indistinct, *temp.* Edward I; dated "At Southwerk near London, on Thursday in the " week of Pentecost, in the year of the reign of King " Edward the 21st" whereby Gilbert Fitz-Richard, Richard being son of Estephen, "Knight, of the county " of Devon," grants to Nicholas de Thoukesburi, Clerk, all his manors of Nortone, Dertemue, Tonstalle, Har-dynesse, and Cliftone Dertemue; to hold of the chief lords of the fee. Witnesses, Richard le Clerk of Suth-werk, Roger le Poleter, Henry Graspeys, Ralph Sparowe, Richard le Tymbermongers, Walter Crowe, Gilbert de Fawy, Robert de Pole, William Hemyng, Thomas Fyna-mur, Robert the Baker, William Man, Ralph Reymard, "and others." This is an important deed in reference to the history of Dartmouth, as Nicholas de Thoukesburi [Tewkesbury] ultimately conveyed the whole of these possessions to Guido de Brienne.

A parchment deed, in Latin, whereby Gilbert Fitz-Richard, Richard being son of Stephen, lord of Nor-tone, grants to Philip Burde, and Constance, his wife, his mill of Hardenesse, with all multure and suit thereof, and with the foss of the said mill and the dam thereto belonging; to hold in tail general, on payment of one rose at the Nativity of John the Baptist; the said Philip having paid 200l. sterling beforehand. Witnesses, Sirs Henry de la Pomeroy, Peter de Fissacre, Hugh le Ferrers, John de Aysselegh, Knights, Robert de Malestone, Ralph de Doddescombe, William de Penellys, Richard de Byneleghe, Gilbert de Fawy, Ralph Renat, Ilary Crok, William Hemmyng, "and " others." "Given at Derthemue, on Sunday after the " Feast of St. Remigius, at the end of the 24th year of " the reign of Edward, son of King Henry." Though stated therein to the contrary, no seal, apparently, has ever been attached; and this may possibly have been a duplicate, not executed.

A parchment deed, being a grant, in Latin, by Gilbert Fitz-Stephen to Thomas Ivone, Chaplain, of one tene-ment in the vill of Dertemue, with a garden, situate in Cliftone, near the tenements of Robert de Slapetone and William le Mouwere; at a yearly rent of 12d., "and such suits of Court, as the other freemen make;" 20s. having been paid beforehand. The seal, with a shield, the impression indistinct, still remains. Of the early part of the reign of Edward I. A few witnesses are named.

A parchment deed, being a grant, in Latin, by Sabina, daughter of Thomas Yvon, Chaplain, to Gilbert de Fawy, of Dertemue, of her tenement in Clyftone in Dertemne, being the most southerly tenement of the

fee of the lord of Nortone; for 15l. paid beforehand. Witnesses, Robert de Pole, William Hemmeng, John Faukes, Gilbert de Pole, William de Hoo, "and others." *Temp.* Edw. I. The seal is lost. The mention of the " daughter of a Chaplain," deserves notice.

A parchment deed, in Latin, whereby Gilbert Fitz-Richard, Richard being son of William, son of Stephen, grants to Adam Cade, for his homage and service, a messuage on the west side of " his fosse of Hardinesse," and part of a garden in the west side of the vill of Har-dinesse, above the road which leads to Tunstealle, at a yearly rent of 6d.; to hold to him, his heirs, and assigns, a house of religion excepted; 6d. having been paid beforehand. Witnesses, William Finamur, Roger Tubbe, then Provost [or Reeve], John Clobard, Martin de Bois, Thomas de Cruche [Cross], Ralph de Harde-nasse, Walter Wite of Hardenasse, John Borberel, William Crispin, "and many others." *Temp.* Edward I.

A parchment deed, in Latin, whereby Nicholas de Theokesbure, lord of Hywiche; grants to Geoffrey Gilbert, of Dertemue, and Isabel, his wife, wardship of the land and heir of John Fitz-John of Wichemor; his father being dead, and the land held by him by knight-service of the said Nicholas; 20 marks having been paid to him beforehand. Witnesses are named. Given at Nortone, on Palm Sunday, in the 9th year of Edward II.

A parchment deed, in Latin, whereby Gilbert Fyz-Estevene, lord of Dertemue, grants to Gilbert de Fawy, of Dertemue, his tenement in Clyftone in Dertemue, " being the last of his fee below the bank, as near on " the south as will allow you to go down to the sea;" rendering yearly 12 pence and 2 suits of Court at Der-temue, as the other free burgesses do, and 2 shillings for relief, when falling due; 83s. 4d. having been paid beforehand. Witnesses are named, John Faukes, and others. Dated the 4th October, 21st Edward I. A seal in brown wax is attached, representing a star, with a bird in its centre.

A parchment deed, in Latin, whereby Richard Fitz-William, William being son of Stephen, grants to John Clobard in " place " (vacant ground) in his vill of Derte-mue, near the shore, which lies nearest to the house of Heming, with a garden between that of Andrew le Scot and that of William Flemyng [Flandrensis]; at a yearly rent of 12d., 2 shillings having been paid beforehand. Witnesses, Richard Farmer, of Tunstalle, William Aubiry, David Gillore then Provost [or Reeve], Gocelin, William Finamur, John Borberel, Thomas de Cruce [Cross], and Richard, his brother, "and many others." A large seal is attached, a flower with expanded petals. *Temp.* Edward I. The family of Fleming here named was the one probably to which belonged Richard le Fleming, Justiciar, in the reigns of Richard I. and John, and which gave its name to Stoke Fleming, and was long connected with Dartmouth.

A parchment deed, finely writen, in Latin, *temp.* Henry III.; whereby Margaret, daughter of Ralph de Saint Lo [Laudo] quit-claims to John, son of John de Silvestone, the whole of her right in all the land of Niweham, in all the land of Penuran, and in all the land of Talskydi, which she had claimed against him in full County Court of Cornwall, by writ of right of the Lord the King; such quit-claim being made in her pure widow-hood; 20 marks being paid beforehand. Witnesses, Robert Fitz-Richard, William Fitz-Richard, Serlo de Penpol, John the Seneschal, Walter de Trenerbin, Geoffrey Fitz-Bernard, Thomas de Pridias, Reginald, and Geoffrey his brother, Odo de Trenerbin, Roger his brother," and others." The seal is lost.

A parchment deed, with a fragment of a large seal, in green wax :—" Omnibus Sanctæ Matris Ecclesiæ filiis, " Willelmus filius Stephani, salutem. Noverit uni-" versitas vestra me, causa Dei, et intuitu pietatis, " dedisse et concessisse Deo et ecclesiæ Sanctæ " Trinitatis de Torre, et Canonicis ibidem Deo servien-" tibus, ecclesiam de Tunistal, cum omnibus pertinentiis " suis, pro salute animæ meæ, et Isabel, uxoris meæ, et " hæredum meorum, et omnium antecessorum et suc-" cessorum nostrorum, et pro anima Willelmi de Ber-" obelse, in liberamque, puram, et perpetuam eleemosy-" nam; Et ut hæc mea donatio rata et inconcussa " permaneat, eam sigilli mei appositione roboravi. " Teste; Domino G. Wintoniensi Episcopo, Willelmo " Briw[ere], Ricardo Heriet, Thoma de Usseburne, " Henrico de Lepumei, Johanne de Torintone, Matthæo " filio Herberti, Ricardo Flandrenai, Widone de Aube-" mare, Willelmo Bavian, Martino Capellano, Radulpho " de Brui, Radulpho de Mora, Reginaldo de Anbemara, et " multis aliis." Tr.—"To all sons of Holy Mother Church, " William Fitz-Stephen, greeting. Know all of you that " I, for the sake of God, and for pious considerations, have

" given and granted to God and the church of the Holy
" Trinity of Torre, and the Canons there serving God,
" the church of Tunistal, with all its appurtenances.
" for the health of my soul, and of Isabel, my wife, and
" my heirs, and all our ancestors and successors, and
" for the soul of William de Bercheles, in free, pure,
" and perpetnal alms. And that this my gift may
" remain ratified and unshaken, I have confirmed it
" with setting thereto my seal. Witnesses, Sir G.
" Bishop of Winchester, William Briwere, Richard
" Heriet, Thomas de Ussebarne, Henry de Lapumel,
" John de Torintone, Matthew Fitz-Herbert, Richard
" Fleming, Wido de Aubemarle, William Bavion, Martin
" the Chaplain, Ralph de Brai, Ralph de More, Regi-
" nald de Aubemarle, and many others." This deed
must have been executed before the death of Godfrey
de Lucy, Bishop of Winchester, who died A.D. 1204.
William Briwere, the Founder of Torre Abbey, for
Præmonstratensian Canons, died before 1226, and
Richard Heriet (like Briwere, a Justiciar), died before
April 6, 1208.

A small parchment deed, with a large portion of the
Bishop's seal attached :—" Universis Sanctæ Matris
" Ecclesiæ filiis, ad quos præsens scriptum pervenerit,
" Willelmus, miseratione divina, Exoniensis Ecclesiæ
" minister humilis, salutem in Domino. Qui cœlum
" terræmque regit, pietatis Suæ miseratione disposuit,
" ut cultum divini nominis ampliantes, intuitu caritatis,
" partem cum Ipso possideant in regno cœlorum, et
" vitam sempiternam: Cum igitur laborantibus in
" vineâ Domini in Sabaoth panem diutinum [? diur-
" num] largiri conveniat, et eorum augmentare facul-
" tates, juri consonum, ac Deo sit acceptum, qui, di-
" vinis orationibus jugiter insistentes, virtutum ac vitæ
" decorantur excellentia, necnon hospitalitatis munera,
" juxta suarum vires facultatum, conferentes, ad se
" confluentibus vultum hylarem prætendant; nos, divinæ
" caritatis intuitu, ecclesiam de Tunestalle, vacantem,
" et ad donationem religiosorum virorum Abbatis et
" Conventus de Torre de jure spectantem, cisdem
" Abbati et Conventui, de consensu Capituli nostri
" Exoniæ, contribuimus et concessimus, in proprios usus
" imperpetuum possidendam, cum omnibus ad eandem
" pertinentibus. Ita tamen, quod eadem ecclesia divi-
" nis imposterum officiis non fraudetur, sed continue
" resideat ibidem capellanus sæcularis, honestus et
" ydoneus, qui se in ecclesia memorata exerceat utiliter
" et honeste : salva sit etiam in omnibus episcopalis et
" Exoniensis Ecclesiæ dignitas. In cujus rei testimo-
" nium, huic scripto sigillum nostrum apponi fecimus."
Tr. :—" To all sons of Holy Mother Church, to whom
" the present writing shall come, William, by divine
" mercy, the humble servant of the Church of Exeter,
" greeting in the Lord. He who rules the heaven and
" the earth, in the mercy of His pity hath so disposed,
" that those augmenting the worship of the divine
" name, for charity's sake, shall possess a share with
" Him in the kingdom of heaven, and everlasting life.
" Since therefore it is proper to give to those who
" labour in the vineyard of the Lord of Sabaoth their
" daily bread, and to increase their means [therein], it
" must be consonant with right, and acceptable to God,
" also to augment the means of those, who, constantly
" devoting themselves to prayer to God, are adorned with
" excellence of virtues and of life, and who, bestowing
" the gifts of hospitality, according to the extent of their
" means, shew a cheerful countenance to those resorting
" to them; we, for the love of God, with the consent
" of our Chapter of Exeter, have contributed and
" have granted the church of Tunestalle, which is
" vacant, and of right belonging to the gift of the
" religious men, the Abbot and Convent of Torre, unto
" the same Abbot and Convent for over to their own
" use to possess the same, with all things unto the same
" pertaining. So, however, that the same church be
" not in futuro defrauded of divine ministrations, but
" that a secular chaplain continually reside there,
" honest and fitting therefor, who shall in the church
" aforesaid usefully and honestly demean himself; and
" that there be saved also in all things the episcopal
" dignity, and that of the Church of Exeter. In witness
" of which matter, to this writing we have caused to be
" set our seal." The bishop who thus granted the
rectory, or great tithes, of Tunstall to the Abbot and
Canons of Torre, in consideration of their placing a
Chaplain therein, was William Briwere, Bishop of Exeter
from A.D. 1224 to 1244. According to some authorities,
he was a cousin to the Justiciar of the same name,
before-mentioned, who founded the Abbey of Torre.

A parchment deed, in Latin, whereby John Aubyn, of
Dertemue, grants to Hillary Crok, of Hardinasse, his

tenement in Clyftone, belonging to Richard Fitz-
Stephen, between the tenement of John de Fonte [At-
well] and that which Thomas Yvo, Chaplain, held ; 10
marks having been paid beforehand. Witnesses, Sir
Peter de Fisacre, then Seneschal, John Faukes, Richard
de Strete, John de Crosse, Philip Rurde, John de
Fonte, Robert de Pole. " Given at Dertemue, on the day
" of the Purification of the Blessed Mary, in the year of
" Grace 1280, and of the reign of King Edward the
" ninth." To this deed are attached the seal of John
Aubyn, a decorated cross, and the most ancient seal
of the Corporation of Dartmouth, in green wax, a galley
with one mast, and sail ; the sole impression of it,
apparently, that the Corporation now possesses.

A parchment deed, in Latin, whereby Geoffrey de
Pole grants to Ralph Crispin and his heirs, 2 " furlings "
of land in Ferncumb, which he held of his father, and
one field of his demesne, on the west side of the way
from Ferncume ; to hold for doing the service of one
eleventh part of a knight's fee. For the grant, Ralph has
given one mark of silver to the said Geoffrey, and to his
mother one mark. Witnesses, Roger Crispin, William
Crispin, Nicholas de Badistone, Roger de Halheville,
and others named. Of the time of Henry III., or prior
thereto. The seal is lost.

A parchment deed, in Latin, whereby William
Fleming [Flandrensis] grants to Gilbert Fitz-Adam,
Adam being son of Sebrith, for his homage and service,
that land in his vill of Cliftone, below the bank, near
the houses of Robert Fitz-Siward and Oliver le
Taverner, and land for making a garden on the south
side of his vill of Cliftone, near the way going to Wel-
flut, next to the garden belonging to Ranulph Godes-
grace ; to hold to him, his heirs and assigns, a house of
religion excepted, at a yearly rent of 2s. ; for 18s. paid to
him beforehand, and to Avice, his spouse, one bezant. He
also gives to the said Gilbert a message and garden
which belonged to Adam Fitz-Sebrith, at a yearly rent
of 18 pence, one barrel of wine being given to him
beforehand. Witnesses, Sir Robert de Mandewil,
Nicholas de Merieth, Gilbert de Hosteswelle, Laurence
Fleming [Flandrensis], William le Chenye, Richard
Chaplain, Geoffrey de Bromlege, Robert de Hundrigge,
Richard de Cumbe, Roger son of Richard Fitz-Sebrith,
Hysaac de Hestinges, Richard de Sege, " and many
" others." A long silken cord is attached, but the seal
is lost. Of the time, probably, of Edward I.

A parchment deed, being a grant, in Latin, by Richard
called " Fitz-Stephen," lord of Nortone, to Ervey Mako-
glad, of a tenement in the vill of Dertemue, at a yearly
rent of 15d., and for making two suits of Court each
year ; half a mark of silver having been paid beforehand.
Witnesses, Sir Peter de Fisacre, John de Cross, Richard
de Strete, William Joie, Robert de Pole, William de
Pole, Nicholas de Cumbe, " and others." Temp.
Henry III. The grantor's seal, a shield, with a faint
impression, is still attached. Another conveyance of
another tenement, the same persons being parties, is
attached, Philip Rurde and Richard Hurtebirs being
additional witnesses.

A parchment deed, being a grant by Adam de
Metheyne, of Tottoneys, to Roger Hurtevile, for his
homage and service, of one house in the vill of Derthemue, between those formerly held by Roger Tubbe
and Andrew le Scot ; he rendering to him yearly one pair
of white gloves at Easter, and to the lord of Derthemue
12 pence ; 21 marks of silver having been paid beforehand. Witnesses, Richard the Tuilor, Provost [or
Reeve] of Derthemue, William Finamur, Bailiff of the
lord of Derthemue, Thomas de Cruce [Cross], Roger
Tubbe, Adam Hovernoth, Helyas de la Hamme, John
Knillevole, Richard White, Ran[dolf] Browse, " and
" many others." Temp. Edward I. A beautifully
written deed ; the seal represents a fleur-de-lys.

A parchment deed, being a grant by Richard de Sege
to Martin Fake of one messuage in the vill of Cliftune,
below the street and way which extend to the sea-shore,
near the house of Roger Cok ; he rendering yearly 2
shillings sterling, at 4 terms of the year, the said Martin
having given to him 4 marks of silver beforehand, and
to Alice, his wife 2s. ; to Beatrix, his daughter 12d. ; to
Walter, his son, one pair of boots ; to Laurence, his son,
one coat [tunicam] ; to Eliota, his daughter 6d. ; and to
Fliria [?], his daughter 6d. Witnesses, Sir Laurence
Fleming, Yssac de Hestinges, Jordan Palmere, Roger
" Roket, Jordan Palmere, John Clobard, and many
others." The deed belongs probably to the earlier half
of the reign of Henry III. ; of the oblong seal, in green
wax, the impression is almost wholly effaced.

A parchment deed, being a grant, in Latin, by Richard
Fitz-Stephen to William de Lehge, son of Nicholas of

Buckfast Bridge [Ponte Bukfestriæ], for his homage and service, of a place to make a quay, six feet in width, lying towards the mill-dam, and extending from the garden of the said William, in Hardinasse; to hold to him, his heirs, and assigns, religious houses and Jews excepted, for a yearly payment of one pound of cummin, within the Octaves of St. Michael; half a sextary of wine having been paid beforehand. Witnesses, Sir W. de Fissacre, Walter de Alebore, W. Hemminge, Richard Hartleby, Robert Sclyming [?], Symon Arthur, Brother Philip de Kyngeswere, " and many others." Temp. Edward I.; a small seal, in green wax, representing apparently a two-headed eagle, is attached.

A parchment deed, in Latin, being a record of a covenant made in the Court of the Lord the King, in a suit moved between Gilbert, son of Richard Fitz-Stephen, claiming the advowson of the church of Tunstalle against the Abbot and Convent of Torre; whereby he quitclaimed all right to the same, for 20 marks sterling. " In witness whereof, the said Gilbert has set his seal " hereto." Witnesses, Robert le Deneys, John de Asselegbe, Knights, Peter Heym, Philip Rurde, William de Aleburn, "and others." " Given at Tunstalle, on " Tuesday before the feast of the Epiphany, A.D. 1294, " in the year of the reign of King Edward the 23rd." The seal is lost.

A small square parchment deed, in Latin, whereby Andrew Burstax, of Poudrame, grants to Geoffrey Gilbert, a " place " of land, with its appurtenances, which Richard de la Schute, tailor, once held of Gilbert Fitz-Stephen, lord of Nortone, the same extending towards the water of Derte; he rendering to the chief lord yearly 12d. and two suits of Court; 40s. having been paid beforehand. Witnesses, Hyllary Croke, William de Hardenesse, John Michel, John Somer, Roger Borberol, Roger Chaplain, [maker] of this work, and many other " suitors"; (Roger the Chaplain was, no doubt, the writer of the deed). Given at Dertemuthe, on Thursday before the Feast of the Nativity of the Blessed Mary, in the year of the reign of King Edward the Younger [Edward II.] the third. The small seal, in green wax, represents two triangles intersecting each other.

A parchment deed, in Latin, being a grant by Walter Wyte to Geoffrey Taben, his son, and Alice de Chedelingtone, his son's wife, for his son's homage and service, of a part of his tenement in Hardinasse, which is situate near the ditch of the burying-ground of St. Clair; the beams of his own house to support the roof of that of his son; at a yearly rent of 4d. sterling, 12d. having been paid beforehand. Witnesses, Richard de Chiwille, then Seneschal, Martin le Boys, John Clobard, William le Bon, William Heming, Adam Cade, William Crispyn, " and " others." A small green seal, representing a flower, is attached. Probably temp. Edward I.

A parchment deed, being an indenture, in Latin, whereby Margaret and Joan, daughters and heirs of Richard Hurteby, of Cliftone of Dertemue, grant, with quitclaim, to Gilbert de Pole, a gutter upon their wall and tenement; right of entry and of removal thereof, in case of necessity, being reserved to themselves; the said Gilbert paying a yearly rent of 6d. sterling. Witnesses, Philip Rurde, Gilbert de Fawy, William Hemmyng, Richard le Baker of Hardenesse, William Joe [? Joie] "and many others." Of the early part of the reign of Edward I. The seals are lost.

A parchment deed, in Latin, being a grant by William de Briteville to Walter, Vicar of Tottoneys, of 2s. of rent which he had in the vill of Tottoneys, from the house in which Robert the Cook formerly dwelt, namely, the two shillings which Rike de Strete was wont to pay, at 2 terms of the year; 20s. having been paid to him beforehand, within the four benches [scanna] of the Guildhall of Tottoneys. Witnesses, John Cuillevale, then Provost [or Reeve], Walter le Bon, Richard de Clautone, Richard White, Robert de Dertemuthe, Thomas de Strete, Walter the Clerk, " and others." A fragment of the seal, in green wax, is left; the deed belongs to the reign of Henry III.

A parchment deed, being a grant, in Latin, by Thomas Longe, of Dertemuthe, to Ralph de Boseham, of a messuage in Cliftune, near the messuage formerly of Roger Koket, at a yearly rent of 6d. sterling; 3 marks having been paid to him beforehand, and 3s. to his wife, Emma. Witnesses, John Clobard, Walter Baket, Thomas de Cross, John de Cross, Martin Bois, Richard de Cross, Symon Wyte, Elyas de la Hamme, William Finamur, " and many others." Of the latter part of the reign probably of Henry III.; the seal is lost.

A parchment deed, in Latin, whereby John Clobard is bound to pay yearly to Richard Fitz-William, William being son of Stephen, as chief lord, one pound of cummin. Temp. Henry III. or Edward I. The seal, in green wax, represents a flower with expanded petals.

A parchment deed, in Latin, whereby Henry le Coggere, son of Brunkelot and Beatrix de Sede, grants to Walter de Plymtone his right in a tenement in Dertemue; for 10 silver marks, paid beforehand. Witnesses, William Gravesend, Bailiff, Walter de Aleburne, John Clobard, Edward Rurde, William Heming, David Heming, and Nicholas Heming, with others named. Temp. Edward I. The seal has the impression of a onemasted ship, probably a cog.

A parchment deed, in Latin, whereby Isabel, relict of Henry de Plymtone, quit-claims to Robert de Pole her right in her tenement in Cliftone in Dertemu[the]: 10 marks sterling having been paid beforehand. Witnesses, Gilbert de Fawwy, William Hemming, William de Pole, William Wylekyn, Martin le Glover, William de Hoo, Walter Choda, " and others. Given at Derte-" muhe, on Tuesday after the Feast of our Lord's Epi-" phany, in the year of the reign of King Edward the " 18th." The oblong seal, in brown wax, is perfect. Two duplicates, with like seals, are attached to it.

A parchment indenture, in Latin, whereby Gilbert Pole, of Clyftone Dertemouth, grants to John Foldhay and Cristina, his wife, and Joan, their daughter, a piece of land in Clyftone Dertemouth near the dam [bedum] of the mill; at a yearly rent of 12d. Witnesses, William Bacoun, Mayor of the burgh of Clyftone Dertemouth, John Gordoun, William Hemyng, and others named. " Given at Clyftone Dortemouth, on Wednesday, the " feast of the Exaltation of the Holy Cross," 19th Edward III. The small seal has an excellent impression of a cock.

A parchment deed, in Latin, being a grant by Roger de Pole to John Smythe and Alice, his wife, of a house in Cliftone Dertemouth, situate opposite " la Pillarie "; and a curtilage on the north side of the way which leads from the Cross towards the west, at the " forde " going to the "Mylpole." Witnesses, Ralph Breuwere, Mayor, and others named. Dated 24th Edward III. The seal is lost.

A small parchment deed, in Latin, whereby Richard Pody, of Hardinasse, grants to Alice, his daughter, his tenement in Hardinasse, between the way leading from Hardinassefiorde towards Tunstalle, and adjoining the sea on the east. Witnesses, Martin ate Schute, William ate Fosse, smith, John Wyte, smith, William Person, Henry Gaberel. " and many others." Dated at Hardynasse, in the 7th year of Edward III: A fragment of the seal, representing a ship, is left. Henry Gaberel was probably a member of the family which gave name to Stoke Gabriel; and possibly they may have been a branch of the Jersey family of Gaborel. The church at Stoke Gabriel being dedicated to St. Gabriel, it seems not improbable that this was their patron Saint.

Grant in Latin, on parchment, by Geoffrey Gilberd to William Wilkyn, of a piece of land which he had of Andrew Burstax, near the water of Derthe [river Dart]; he rendering to the chief lords a yearly rent of 12d. Witnesses, William Edward, William Bacoun, William Hemmyng, Richard Pody, Gilbert the Chaplain, " maker " of this work " (hujus operis confectore: writer of the deed). Dated at Dertemuth, in the 18th year of Edward II.

A parchment deed, in Latin, whereby Gilbert de Pole, of Dertemouthe, grants to Thomas Swete and Joan, his wife, a piece of land in Cliftone Dertemouthe, having the street which is called the "Keye" on the west side, and as much as they can reclaim, as against the sea, on the east side. Witnesses, Henry de Wyteleghe, Mayor of the burgh of Cliftone Dertemouth, William Bacoun, John Gurdone, William Heming, John Cotte, John Haulee, John Scoz, then Bailiff. Dated 18th Edward III. A seal in red wax, with flowers for device. The family of Haule, or Hauley, eminent merchants, was long resident in Dartmouth; their mercantile transactions were so extensive, that they gave rise to the lines, still remembered in connexion with their trade, in this town,—

" Blow the wind high, blow the wind low,
" It bloweth good to Hauley's hoe."

A parchment deed, in Latin, whereby Gilbert Fowy grants to Thomas Taillour, of Dertemouth, a toft of land in Cliftone Dertemuthe, which lies near the high road leading from Beatriglonde towards Bayardscove, and near a toft of the land of the Lord Guy de Bryene, lord of the same vill, on the west side; at a rent of 6d. yearly. Witnesses, William Clerk, Mayor of the vill, John Clerk, William Knollo, William Harry, Roger Polo, Luke Bacon, Bailiff of the vill. Dated on Wednesday before the Feast of Saint Scolastica the Virgin, 50th Edward III. The seal, in red wax, represents a star, with palm branches inserted. Bayardscove is the spot, near the water, now known as "Bear's Cove."

An indenture, in French, being an award by John Bernews and John Prideaux, Esquires, between Philip Howell and John, his wife, of the one part, and John Juyll, son and heir of Alexander Juyll, late of Dertemouthe, of the other part; dated Monday before the Feast of the Assumption, 2nd year of Henry V. Two small seals, of the parties to the award, are attached.

A parchment deed, being a grant, in Latin, by John Slade, of Slade, and Beatrix, his wife, to John Carnargh, Rector of Southpole, of a yearly rent of 13s. 4d. from their lands and tenements in Slade and Goddyshalter [now Goodshelter], for a term of 7 years. Dated at Slade, in the 8th year of Henry V.

A parchment deed, being a grant, in Latin, by William Knolle, of Derthmute, to John Northcote, of Nywetone, and Thomas, his brother, of his lands in Clyftone Derthmute and Hardenasse. Witnesses, John Hauleghe, Mayor, John Clerk, William Henry, Roger Pole, John Knolle, "and many others." Dated 49th Edward III. The seal, a shield in red wax, is in fair condition.

A parchment deed, being a grant, in Latin, by William Rurde to John de Haulee and Elizabet, his wife, and the heirs of their bodies lawfully begotten, of a piece of land in Cliftone Dertemouthe, near the new mill which stands on the fosse, between the key of the said John and Elizabet, on the south, and the "Golet" of the said new mill, on the north, and as much as they can reclaim from the sea, on the east; at a yearly rent of 4d. sterling. Dated 18th Edward III. The seal, in red wax, a shield, charged with two bugles, two stars, and apparently, an arrow, is in fair condition.

A parchment deed, being a grant, in Latin, by William Gardiner to John Northecote, of Nywetone, and John Fotray, of a tenement in the vill of Clyftone Dertemouthe. Dated 46th Edward III. The impression of the seal, in dark wax, is much effaced.

A parchment deed, being a grant, in Latin, by Nicholas Fiz-Estevene, to Joan Taillour, of a piece of land, near the water conduit running to Bozetone [Abovetown], on the north; she rendering to the chief lord one red rose yearly, at the Feast of St. John the Baptist, and to the grantor one halfpenny at the Feast of St. Michael. Dated the 13th of Edward III. The seal, in dark wax, is mutilated, and has the impression of a bird.

A parchment deed, in Latin, whereby Robert Sparowe, of Blanforth Forum, in the county of Dorset, quit-claims to William Stamforth, of Asch . . . his right to 2 shambles in the market of Blanforth Forum. Witnesses, Sir John Popham, Knight, Robert Bourton, Thomas Freman, John Page, of Sarum, Richard Abraham, Thomas Schogge. Dated 14th February, in the 19th year of Henry VI. The impression of the seal, in red wax, is wholly effaced.

A parchment deed, being a quit-claim, in Latin, by Alice, widow of Hugh Pewterer, late of Brydeport, to John Newburgh the elder, John Beatriscombe, William Olyver, Richard Burghe and Joan, his wife, of her right in tenements, cottages, curtilages, and shambles, in Blaneford Forum, and elsewhere. Dated 20th February, 7th Edward IV. The seal is still attached, a fanciful device of a cross, in red wax. "Beatriscombe" (valley of Beatrice) is probably the early form of the name now known as "Battiscombe."

A Latin deed, on parchment, being a grant by Elizabeth Rokley to John Halwell and others, of, among other property, her tenement called "Halles Bakehows," [Hall's Bakehouse] and her close of land lying between Bakone parket [? Bacon market] and the Verobekynn [? Verebek's inn] in Blandford. Dated 14th Edward IV. A small seal, representing, apparently, a horse, is still attached.

A portion of a Latin deed, whereby —— ate Nesse, of Sandwich, conveys to Robert ate Halle, of the parish of Eastri (in Kent), and others, his tenements in the vill of Sandwich. Dated — January in the year — of King Henry —, Thomas Louvyk, then Mayor of Sandwich, John Ricard, William Gaylere, Richard Spycer, and others. A small red seal, with a trade device, is attached. How this deed came here, it seems difficult to surmise.

A parchment indenture, in Latin, whereby Maurice, son and heir of William Coffyn, grants to Alexander Juel, of Derthemowth, half of a tenement in Clyftone Derthemowth Hardenesse, on the north side of the churchyard of the Holy Trinity, and half a close adjoining the highway leading from the church of St. Clement; to hold the same for 30 years, at the yearly rent of one penny. Witnesses, John Foxleghe, Mayor, Richard Harry, Philip Cradeley, John Syneger, William Cross, "barbour, and others." Dated in the 10th year of

King Henry IV. The seal has an initial letter, with rushes platted around it.

A deed, in Latin, whereby Alice Hare, widow of William Hare, of Brideport, quit-claims to Alice, widow of Hugh Pesatrer, of Brideport, her right in a tenement in Blaneford Forum, near a meadow called "Stoke-mede;" and in a cottage in the East town of Blaneford; and in a shamble near the stone cross, erected in the market-place there. Dated in the 36th year of King Henry VI. The seal, in red wax, represents a small flower.

A parchment indenture, in Latin, whereby John Hayward the elder, of Aysberton [Ashburton], grants to Robert Creyer and Thomasia, his wife, a piece of land in Aysberton, lying at Syngmore, near to the water called "Derthe" [Dart], at a yearly rent of 8 pence. Witnesses, William Beke of Devenebye, John Stroyte, John Bowyere, Alexander Weke, William Steel of Aysberton, "and many others." Dated at Aysberton, in the 7th year of Henry V. A diminutive seal is attached, in red wax, with a fanciful device.

A parchment deed, being a release, in Latin, by Ibota, widow of William Knolle, to her son, William, of her right in messuages in Dertemouth, called "Wheteneplace." Dated in the 11th year of Henry IV. A seal in brown wax, is appended, the letter I. with a crown above it.

A parchment deed, in Latin, being a grant by Mark Pole, of Fawy [now Fowey], to Walter Bacheler, of Dertemouth, Merchant, of a tenement near that of John Hauley, Esquire. Witnesses, Tristram Curteys, Stephen Kendale, John Amarle, Thomas Galy, Stephen Jaan, "and others." "Given at Lostwythielle, on Saturday "after the Feast of our Lord's Ascension, in the 5th "year of the reign of King Henry, after the Conquest "the Fifth." The seals of the Mayoralty of Lost-withiel and of the grantor, are attached.

A parchment indenture, in Latin, whereby licence is granted by Matilda Helyer, and Joan Burel, to Robert Mynchone, to join his tenement to their wall, the house called "Poyngnone." Witnesses, John Hawle, Mayor of Dertemouth, Richard Lundone, Bailiff, William Clerk the Younger, Walter Worthi, Richard Harry, "and "others." Dated in the 2nd year of Henry IV.

A parchment deed, being a grant, in Latin, by John Botringan and Joan, to Nicholas Stebbyng: mention is made of the way from Hardenesseforde towards the chapel of St. Clair; the King's highway towards Walffete; and the hill "called Crowetorre." Witnesses William Forster, Mayor, Walter Cok and Thomas Taillour, Bailiffs, John Bruscheford, Robert Bowyer, burgesses, John Gardener, William Lye, Chaplains. Dated in the first year of Edward IV. The seal of John Botringan, in red wax, is twice attached; a shield, charged, apparently, with roses; as also, the seal of the Mayoralty of Dertemouth.

A parchment deed, being a grant, in Latin, by William Langge the younger, to Alisander Juyll, burgess, of a tenement near the churchyard of the Holy Trinity. Witnesses, John Hawle, Mayor, Hugh Westone, Bailiff, and others named. Dated in the 14th year of Richard II. A small seal, in red wax, is attached.

A parchment deed, in Latin, whereby John Clerk, of Dertemouthe, and Joan, his wife, grant to Richard Wole and Joan Burell, for life, a tenement in Hardenasse; the said John and Joan to keep the same in repair, for the lives of the grantees, and to find Richard all his necessary victuals, as often as he is in poverty or bed-ridden, and to pay for him 20s. for his ransom, "if by "reason of war he should be taken upon the sea : and "may it not be so." Witnesses, William Glover, Mayor, Thomas Aysshendene, Bailiff, John Foxley, and others. Dated in the first year of Henry VI. Two small red seals are attached, one with the initial I, the other representing a boar's head.

A parchment deed, being a grant, in Latin, by John Talbot, Knight, brother and heir of Ralph Talbot, to John Speke, Knight, of all his possessions in Dertmouthe Clifton, Dertmouthardnes, Kingeswere, and Baconshayes, in the county of Devon; naming Thurstan Harope and Philip Gronewode his attorneys to deliver seisin. "Given at Salesbury, the 1st day of March, "in the 20th year of the reign of King Henry the "Seventh." Signed "S. John Talbot, Knyght." A small seal is attached, but the impression is almost wholly effaced.

A parchment indenture being a grant, in Latin, by Robert Wymond and Alesia, his wife, to Alexander Chapelayn and Anna, his wife, of a messuage called "La Chapele," in Cliftone Dertemouthe, between the tenement formerly of Stephen Sopere, on the west side, and that which belonged to Richard Swet, on the east. Witnesses, Roger Pole, then Mayor of Cliftone Dertemouthe Hardenasse, John Matheu, Ralph Bevere, John Geyg, John Hag, and others. Dated in the 25th year of Edward III.

A parchment deed, being a grant, in Latin, by Richard Londone to Michael Salmone and Alice, his wife, of a tenement in Clyftone Dertemouthe Hardenasse, situate on the King's highway, near the "Steppys," on the east side. Witnesses, John Walsche, Mayor, Michael Molyner and John Knytth, Bailiffs, and others named. Dated in the 17th year of Henry VI. A small red seal is attached, with a device almost obliterated.

A parchment deed, in Latin, whereby John Raleghe, mariner, of Dertemouth, grants to Robert Pampallone [? part torn away] a tenement in Monkenestrote, within the manor of Northtone, near Hardenasse; he rendering yearly to the Abbot and Convent of Torre 12 pence, and the services due and accustomed for the same. Dated in the 11th year of Richard II. The seal, in red wax, is mutilated. Not improbably this was a member of the family from which Sir Walter Raleigh sprang.

A parchment deed, being a Latin grant by John Horewode, Rector of the parish church of Blaneford Mary, and John Touker, of Chepyngblaneforde, to Walter Resone and Margery, his wife, of Chepyngblaneforde, of a certain tenement, and a rent of 12 pence, in Blaneford Mary aforesaid. Witnesses, Sir Thomas Drwet, Rector of the church of Chepynblansford, Thomas Gogeyn, Henry Storke, Hugh Smythe, John Bekene, " and many others." Dated in the 21st year of Richard II. The seal of John Horewode represents the Virgin and Child; the impression of the other seal is indistinct. The two present Parishes of Blandford St. Mary and Blandford Forum are here meant.

A parchment deed, in Latin, being a grant by Isabel, relict of William Broketone, to John Brusheford, John Yabbecombe, and Nicholas Stebbyng, of all her possessions, by will of her late husband, in Clyftone Dortmouthe Hardenasse. Dated in the 30th year of Henry VI. A very small seal is attached, in red wax, apparently of some beauty, representing a man and woman standing side by side. Allusion to the family of Brookedon will be found made in the notice of Mr. Prideux's document relative to Dartmouth.

A parchment deed, in Latin, being a grant by Thomas de Lytteltone to Henry de Dertemouth and Margaret, his wife, of a messuage in Boghetone [Above-town], in Smythenestrete, near the tenement formerly of Terric Piers, Chaplain. Witnesses, Thomas Asshendene, William Knolle, William Clork, Walter Worthy, John Poldreseek, William Taillour, William Damyet, then Bailiff. Dated 13th of Richard II. The seal, in red wax, has the initial I.

A small parchment deed, in Latin, whereby William de Pralle [now Prawle] and his heirs bind themselves to warrant against all men to Ralph de Godishaltre, for his homage, relief, and service, as much land in Godishaltre [Goodshelter], and as fully, as his predecessors had of the Prior and Convent of Taunton; he rendering yearly 15s. sterling. Witnesses, Walter Bacoune, Sheriff of Devon, Sir Wido Britevill, William de Dockebere, Gilbert Crispin, Wido Crispin, Hugh Crispin, and many others. Of the seal, in red wax, a fragment only is left. Of the time, probably, of Henry VI.

A parchment deed, in Latin, being a grant by Joan, widow of Nicholas Gybbe, to John Harry and Walter Cole, of her tenement in Great Tottene within the gates there, near the Easte Wallys, to the north. Witnesses, William Rowe, Mayor of the vill of Tottene, Richard Tucker, Richard Geffray, Roger Cole, Richard Hoygge, then Provost [or Reeve] " of the burgh of the " vill aforesaid." Dated at Tottene, in the 15th year of Henry VI.

A parchment deed, in Latin, being a grant by Guy de Briene, Knight, lord of Cliftone Dertemouthe Hardenasse, to Thomas Taillour, of Dertemouthe, of a piece of land near the Schute which leads from the shore to the sea; at a yearly rent of 6d. sterling. Dated in the 50th year of Edward III. The seal, representing his arms, in red wax, is mutilated.

A parchment deed, in Latin, being a grant by John More, Thomas Gylle, John Meryfeld, John Cade, and Richard Rake, to Richard Cade, Abbot of Torre, of all the messuages which they had in Tounestalle, of the gift of John, Jeornelle; and which they had in Torre Mohun, of the gift of Richard Crocker and Margery, his wife, and of Richard Wolstone. Witnesses, Otes Gylbert, John Holbeme, and Roger Werthe. Dated in the

35th year of Henry VI. Two of the five seals, in red wax, attached, are mutilated.

Grant, in Latin, a parchment deed, by Benedict Kent to Walter Scugger of a tenement, near the church garden on the south side, for a term of 20 years; on payment of one red rose yearly, at the Feast of the Nativity of John the Baptist. Witnesses, Richard Marke, Mayor of the vill of Dertemouth, Thomas Gale, John Hillyng, John Lambyne, and William Cosyne. Dated in the 17th year of Henry VI. The impression on the seal is effaced.

A parchment deed, in Latin, being a grant by Geoffrey Gilberd, of Dertemuth, and Isabel, his wife, to John Cotta and Constance, his wife, of one piece of land in Clyftone Dertemuthe, near the road descending from the King's highway to the sea, and near the road lying above the falaise [or high cliff], and going down to the sea-shore; at a yearly rent of one silver penny to the chief lords of the fee. Witnesses, William Wylkyn, William Bacon, John Gordon, William Hemmyng, Henry de Wyteleye. Dated in the 17th year of Edward III. Of the two seals, in green wax, one represents a flower, the other a key.

Grant, in Latin, on parchment, by Nicholas Hawley, Esquire, to Thomas Loveney, alias Gater, for his good and laudable service, and his counsel given, and in future to be given, of a tenement and garden in Clyftone Dertemouth; to hold the same for his life, at a yearly rent of one penny. Witnesses, Richard Karswell, Mayor, and others named. Dated in the 19th year of Henry VI. The seal, in red wax, is almost perfect; a shield charged with two bugles, two stars, and an arrow.

A parchment indenture, in Latin, whereby Walter Cole grants half of a tenement in Totteneys to John Gybbe, Chaplain, son of Joan, and the heirs of his body lawfully issuing, and if he die without such heirs of his body, then to John Ward and Margery, his wife, daughter of the said Joan. Witnesses, Richard Tucker, Mayor of the vill of Totteneys, John Petard, John Worthy, Stephen Bealleghe, John Colatone, then Provost [or Reeve] of the burgh of the said vill, " and " many others." Dated in the 22nd year of Henry VI. The seal, in red wax, has a fanciful device, like two or more keys. The mention of "heirs of the body" of the "Chaplain" deserves remark.

A large parchment indenture, in Latin, whereby Joan, widow of Nicholas Stebbyng, grants to Thomas Symond and Katherine, his wife, her palisaded place [palatinm], and garden adjoining, situate in Southtoune Dertmouth, near the highway leading from Daweshill towards Walfotcrosse, on the east, and the hill called "Croterhill," on the west; to hold for 90 years, at a yearly rent of 4 silver pennies. Witnesses, Richard Cade, Mayor, Walter Amadas and Thomas Williams, Bailiffs, Thomas Gale, William Forster, William Hervy, John Fissher, Robert Coode, and many others. Dated in the 16th year of Edward IV.

A parchment deed, in Latin, whereby Hugh Talbot, brother of Ralph, gives to Walter Amadas, and four others named, all his chambers called "The Prestes " Chambyrs," in Clyfton Dertmouth Hardnesse, on the north side of the cemetery of the chapel of St. Saviour [the present church]. Dated in the 12th year of Henry VII. By another deed, attached by a rush to the preceding, Talbot names Nicholas Semer and Robert Savery, his attorneys to deliver seisin and possession thereof; the same date as before. Of the two seals, in red wax, only small fragments remain. The family of Captain Savery, whose name is connected with the earlier annals of the steam engine, belonged to this vicinity.

A small parchment indenture, in Latin, between John Lancetone and Joan, daughter of Robert Perkhay, of the one part, and Joan, widow of William de Chedelyngtone, of the other part; agreeing that the said Joan, widow, shall have dwelling and easement in the house which they had of the gift and feoffment of the said Joan, widow; and that she shall enter therein to dwell, on the Feast of the Apostles Simon and Jude, in the second year of King Edward the Third. Also, she is to have her easement, both in hall, and chamber, and kitchen, so long as she shall live and be without husband; and if she takes a husband, she is to go away with her husband, and abide with him. But if she shall survive her said husband, she is to return to the said tenement, and abide there, as before, all the days of her life. Witnesses, William Edward, Gilbert de Pole, Roger le Taillour, Peter Polymond, Richard Gordone, " and others." " Given at Dertemouthe Suthtone, on " Wednesday, the Feast of the Exaltation of the Holy " Cross, in the year of the King's reign above-men-

4 G 2

" tioned." The seal, in brown wax, is broken, and a fragment only of its impression, a flower, is left.

A small parchment deed, in Latin, with a small seal in green wax, with the impression of two stars and a palm-tree; whereby Robert Gilbard, Chaplain, appoints Robert Hulle his attorney, to put Idonia, widow of William Lorymer, in possession of all his tenements. Dated "at Doulissche [now Dawlish], on Sunday before " the Feast of St. Mary Magdalene, in the 38th year " of the reign of King Edward the Third."

A small parchment indenture, in French, with fragment of a seal, in red wax; made between Walter Hauleghe, "Serjeant at arms of our Lord the King, and " lieutenant of the Admiral," of the one part, and William Knolle, Mayor of the vill of Dertemouth, and William Stybbe, Bailiff of the water of the same vill, of the other part; witnessing that the said Walter has taken as forfeit to our said Lord the King 3 ships of the said vill; namely, the Margaret, of which the said William Knolle and William Croft are owners, the Codser, of which William Jeke and John Haule are owners; and the James, of which John Haule is owner; and has delivered them into the keeping of the said Mayor and Bailiff, until the King shall have ordained at his will thereon; unless indeed they will come to Hamptone [Southampton], with the other ships of the same port. Given at Dertemouthe, the 1st day of September, in the 46th year of King Edward III. These ships were "pressed," probably, for the King's service.

A small parchment deed, in Latin, finely written, with a small seal in red wax; whereby Richard Chiefe, dwelling within the parish of St. Austyne, in Cornwall, quit-claims to William Lambyn, late master of the little balinger, called the "Jonet of Dertemouthe," formerly of Cancalle [in France], all manner of actions, plaints, and demands, from the beginning of the world until the making thereof. Dated at Dertemuth, the 19th of December, in the 14th year of King Henry IV.

A small parchment deed, in Latin, temp. Edward I., whereby Richard Fitz-Stephen, lord of Nortone, grants to Richard de Bridaport, baker, 2½ acres of land lying near the highway from Tonstaylle to Modbyry, for a yearly rent of 5s. and two suits of Court yearly at Nortone, on reasonable summons of eight days. And if the said Richard, his heirs, or assigns, shall be amerced by judgment of his or their peers, they are to be acquitted, at each Court, for 3 pence: 4 shillings having been paid beforehand. Witnesses, Sir Peter de Fissacre, William de Penillis, Robert do Malestone, Gilbert de Fauwy, and others. The seal, in brown wax, is mutilated; apparently, on a shield, a bird with expanded wings.

A small parchment deed, in Latin, whereby Alice Lyttone, "whom John Holeway lately in deed (de facto " tenuit in uxerem) held as wife," acknowledges to have received of the said John 10 marks sterling, one bed, and one gown (tunicam), in full and final payment of all dower or debt whatsoever to which the said John in 'any way to her was bound; and as to which she gives him a full release. In witness whereof, she has procured the seal of the Officiality of Totoneys to be set thereto. Dated at Tavystoche, the 24th of April 1366. The seal of the Official is somewhat mutilated; it represents apparently a font, the cover surmounted by a floriated cross, and two keys on either side of the cross.

A small parchment deed, in Latin, probably temp. Edward I.; whereby William de Praule grants to John de Slade his water called "the Oldewaye," lying below his wood of Praule, called "the Oldewode," with all lets and ducts of water running to the mill of Slade; at a yearly rent of one silver penny, if demanded. Witnesses, Walter de Bath, then Sheriff of Devon, Sir Wido de Bruteville, William de Byckebury, Gilbert Crespyn, Wido de Brione, Roger de Pull, "and many " others." The seal, in brown wax, is perfect, representing a shield with a chevron. Wido de Brione, here named, it may be remarked, was probably father of Guido de Briene, afterwards lord of Dartmouth, and lord of Stokenham, near Prawle.

A parchment deed, in Latin, whereby John de Scherpham grants to John, his son, and Walter de Thorslegh, a messuage and land in Sherpham [on the Dart, near Totnes], with the house, close, and all its appurtenances; the same having descended to him by the death of John Averey. Witnesses, Martin Bodyn, John Martyn, Walter Piers, John Brouse, Stephen Lefte, and others. "Given at Scherpham, on Sunday after the " Feast of the Apostles Peter and Paul," in the 50th year of the reign of King Edward the Third. The seal, in green wax, represents a star, with flowers inserted.

A diminutive parchment deed, in Latin, whereby the Prior of St. Nicholas at Exeter, Collector of the tenth, imposed as a subsidy for the Roman Church, acknowledges the receipt of sums respectively from the churches of Welleburgh, Torrebrwere, Tonstalle, Bradeworth, Hanoke, the pension from the Prior of Tottoneys, the prebend of the Abbot of Torre of Asse Clyft, the temporalities of the Abbot: the same being for the first term of the third year of the said payment. "Given under our seal, at Exeter, the 13th of the " Kalends of December, A.D. 1303." A small seal, in dark wax, is attached, in fine condition, representing the Salutation, with legend to that effect.

A parchment deed, in Latin, being a grant by Nicholas de Theuksbiry to Richard Podi, of a toft in Hardenasse in Nortone; at a yearly rent of 6d. And if the said Richard falls under the mercy of the lord at Nortone, " and may it not be so," he shall be quit of such amercement for one penny. Witnesses, Geoffrey Gilbert, William Wilekyn, William Gore, Nicholas Bealde, and William de Chapel, "and others." Given at Nortone, "on Thursday, the Feast of St. Bartholomew, in " the year of the reign of King Edward [the First] the " 6th." A small seal in brown wax, with his shield of arms, charged with 3 anchors, is attached.

A parchment indenture of covenant, made between John le Noreys and Margery, his wife, and Robert de la Pytte and Isabel, his wife, on division of the fees to the said wives belonging, on the death of their father, Walter de la Spynee: John and Margery are to have the demesne in Northoe; and Robert and Isabel the demesne in Pennenk, and all the land of Holeway, in the Parish of Landbilp, [? Landulph, near Saltash]. Witnesses, John de Ralegh. John le Chalons, Knights, William de Nywecome, William Dryney, Peter de Haydone, and others. "Given at Coletone, on Tuesday " before the Feast of St. Dunstan the Archbishop," in the 8th year of King Edward II. A small fragment only of the seal is left. This John de Ralegh was probably father, or grandfather, of the John, mentioned as living in the reigns of Edward III. and Richard II.

A small parchment deed, in Latin, prior to the preceding, whereby John Heringod, lord of Sampford Spynee [near Tavistock], sells and grants to Henry le Norreys and Master Robert de la Pitte, Clerk, the wardship and maritage of Margery and Isabel, daughters and heirs of Walter de Spynee, for 35 pounds sterling. Witnesses, Sir Gilbert de Cnovile, Sheriff of Devon, Sir John de Asleghe, Knights, William de Nywetone, Robert de Lynham, John de Caletone, and others. " Given at Exeter, on Thursday after the Feast of St. " Leonard," in the 24th year of Edward I. A fragment of the seal, in green wax, representing a horse caparisoned, is left. From the deed previously mentioned, we learn to whom the co-heiresses were married.

An indenture of covenant, on parchment, in Latin, (attached to the two preceding), dated the Feast of Pentecost, in the 53rd year of the reign of King Henry, son of King John, between Henry de Spynee, Knight, and Sir Richard de Hilum, Rector of the church of Heantone; whereby the said Henry grants to the said Rector his tenement of Teyng for a term of 6 years; 22 marks being paid beforehand. Witnesses, Sir Henry de Chambernun, Sir Mauger de St. Albin, Sir John Wig', Knights, Master Oliver de Tracy, Master Adam de Breviel, Ralph le Spicer, Nicholas de Stoke, Clerk, and others. Of the seal, in green wax a fragment only is left. Three other small deeds, relative to the same family, temp. Edward I. are also attached.

A deed of partnership, on parchment, in Latin, between two merchants, whereby Henry Bakleford, merchant, delivers to John Denebaud, of Dertemouth, merchant, 50 pounds sterling, for their common advantage in trading; the said John to account for the same, so often as required by the said Henry: adventure to be made therewith, by common consent, and not otherwise; each unto the counterpart of the indenture left in the other's hands has set his seal. "Given at Derte- " muthe, on Wednesday, the Eve of the Exaltation of " the Holy Cross, in the ninth year of the reign of " King Richard the Second." They then further agree that yearly, at the Feasts of St. George, the Nativity of St. John the Baptist, and St. Michael, the stock, profit (utilitas), and money, shall be ready for view by the said Henry, at Dertemuth, "faithfully then to be paid." And the said John is to find rooms and cellars for the stock aforesaid, but is to receive or reckon nothing for the same.

A parchment deed, to the following effect:—
" Sciant præsentes et futuri, quod ego, Thomas " Wambe, Capellanus, filius et hæres Thomæ Wambe,

" dedi, concessi, et hac præsenti carta mea confirmavi,
" Deo et Ecclesiæ Sancti Salvatoris de Torre, et Canoni-
" cis ibidem Deo servientibus, de Ordine Præmonstra-
" tensium professis, unum mesuagium in Tunstalle,
" cum orto, quod situm est inter ecclesiam Sancti
" Clementis et domum personæ ejusdem villæ ; tenen-
" dum et habendum dictum mesuagium in liberam,
" puram eleemosinam, de me et hæredibus meis, libere,
" quiete, et integre imperpetuum, sicut ego vel pater
" meus unquam prædictum mesuagium tenuimus. Et
" ego vero, prædictus Thomas, et hæredes mei, præ-
" dictum mesuagium dictis Canonicis, cum omnibus
" pertinentiis, contra omnes homines warantizare,
" acquietare, et defendere, tenemur. Ut hæc autem con-
" ventio et concessio, et hujus cartæ confirmatio, rata
" et inconcussa imperpetuum permaneat, eam præsenti
" scripto et sigilli mei impressione roboravi. Hiis tes-
" tibus, Domino Thoma, tunc Archidiacono Tottoniæ,
" Willelmo de Pomeray, Willelmo Flandrensi, Wil-
" lelmo Finamur, Johanne Globard, Willelmo Bon,
" Martino de Bosco, et multis aliis. Datum apud Derte-
" mwe, die Sancti Stephani, anno regni Regis Henrici
" sexto-decimo." Part of a small seal is attached. This
deed is written in a hand of the time of Edward II.,
and is probably forged. There is also a duplicate of it, of
like appearance, in this collection. The following is a
translation of it :—" Know present and to come, that I,
" Thomas Wambe, Chaplain, son and heir of Thomas
" Wambe, have given, granted, and by this my present
" charter have confirmed, to God and the Church of
" Saint Saviour at Torre, and the Canons there serving
" God, of the Order of Præmonstratensians professed,
" one messuage in Tunstalle, with a garden, which is
" situate between the church of Saint Clement and the
" house of the parson of the same vill ; to hold and
" have the said messuage in free [and] pure alms,
" of me and my heirs, freely, quietly, and wholly
" for ever, as I or my father ever held the messuage
" aforesaid. And I, the aforesaid Thomas, and my heirs,
" are bound against all men to warrant, acquit, and
" defend, the said messuage unto the said Canons, with
" all the appurtenances thereof. That this covenant
" and grant, and the confirmation of this charter, may
" remain ratified and unshaken for ever, I have cor-
" roborated it by this present writing, and the impress
" of my seal. These being witnesses, Sir Thomas, then
" Archdeacon of Tottoneys, William de Pomeray,
" William Fleming, William Finamur, John Globard,
" William Bon, Martin de Bois, and many others.
" Given at Dertemue, on the day of St. Stephen, in the
" year of the reign of King Henry the sixteenth."
The family of Bon, or Le Bon [The Good], which in
those days would be pronounced " Boon," not improbably
gave its name to the locality in Dartmouth, now known
as " Mount Boon."

A parchment deed, in French, made between William
Parecombe and John Elys, of Nywetone Abbot, stating
that whereas the said William is bound and obliged to
the said John in 20 pounds, to be paid at the Michaelmas then next ensuing, the said John still willeth and
granteth, that if John Skynner, of Nywetone, chooses
for himself two men, and abides by their award, and
that of two other men chosen on part of him, John Elys,
of Nywetone, and Joan, his wife, and William Knolle
and Isabel, his wife, and acts as they shall award upon
a claim which the said John Skynner has against the
said John and Joan, William and Isabel, as to certain
lands and tenements which belonged to one John Muryel
in Nyweton ; then the said writing obligatory shall be
held as null ; but if otherwise, it shall stand in force.
" Given on Wednesday after the Feast of St. Gregory
" the Pope, in the year of the reign of our Lord Richard,
" the Second after the Conquest, the third." A diminutive seal, with the letter O, within a thong, is
attached.

A Latin deed, on parchment, whereby John Speke,
Knight, remits unto Walter Amadas, Robert Holond,
Thomas Newman, John Holond, and John Hyllinge,
his right and interest in one tenement in Cliftone Dart-
mouth Hardness, situate between the sea, on the east
side, and the tenement pertaining to the chapel of St.
Saviour, on the west, the palisaded place of John Row,
on the north, and the churchyard of St. Saviour, on the
south. Witnesses, William Hokemore the younger,
Richard Hakewyll, William Bond, " and many others."
Dated the 8th of April, in the first year of Henry VIII.
The seal is lost.

By another like deed, Sir John Speke conveys to the
same parties his interest in two tenements and a vacant
piece of ground, one of them being the tenement previously mentioned. No rental, or consideration, is men-

tioned in either deed, and the conveyance was probably
to religious uses. The latter deed bears date the 4th of
May, in the first year of Henry VIII. The seal is lost.

A paper writing, to the following effect :—" In Dart-
" mouth, the 11th of February 1642.—Reseved by me,
" leftennente generalle of the westrene forces 2 peses
" of brasse ordinance of the Corporation of Dartmothe,
" said takene from the castell, wayinge bothe two
" thousand foore hundred eightye sixe pound. And as
" foor the foresayd gunns, I promise to restore the
" sayme, ore give satisfaction. Witness my hand, the
" yeare and daye above writtene, W. Ruthven." The
writing is better than the spelling. Indorsed, " Collonel
" Ruthyen Receipt for the 2 brasse gunns, which are
" now a[t] Helsone Castell."

A map of the time of Charles I., neatly executed, with
boundaries in various colours ; with this title :—" The
" description of the lands that are set out unto the
" Corporation of Dartmouth, being the first lott of the
" second quarter of the Barronie of Rathconrath, in
" the countie of Westmeath."—" By a scale of 40
" perches to an inch." The acreage of each of the
localities is given, and the following are the localities
by name, each given with boundaries : Gibbstowne, ½
this towne forfeited ; Lurgan ; Ardbrennan ; Red Bogg ;
Rathcarrah ; Ardbrenan ; Lenamore ; Cappahinam ;
Cleoneaghard ; Lockerstowne ; Firrahfin ; Part of Togherstowne ; Part of Ballina Carrow ; Conerij ; Reedy
Bog ; Part of Croghold ; Ballrath ; Ballyferrath ;
Nicholstowne ; Oldtowne ; Churchtowne ; Monenstowne
Doonedonnells. Other localities, without the boundaries,
are, Tobbericormeick ; Ballencurr ; Killare ; Cloonow-
namore ; part of Togherstowne ; Enewestowne ; part of
Croghold ; Milltowne ; Barretstowne ; Corra ; part of
Ballina Carrow ; Logh ; Loghan ; Balliglass ; the Bar-
ronie of Moyassell and Magherideervan.

There are also among the Corporation documents a
considerable number of early deeds bearing reference
to Exeter ; they are mixed indiscriminately with the
others, and it seems difficult to say how they could have
reached this locality ; deposited perhaps for safe keeping.
The following is a notice of a portion of them :—

A parchment deed, in Latin, whereby Sarra Hog,
widow of John le Qeu [the Cook], grants to Philip
Loucook, citizen of Exeter, her two selds in the fore
part of her tenement, without the West Gate of the city
of Exeter, situate between the porch of her tenement,
on the east, and the cellar which the said Philip had of
her, on the west ; at a yearly rent, after the end of a
term of 29 years, of 60 shillings. Witnesses, Richard
de Chessebethe, then Seneschal of Sir Hugh de Courtenay, Walter de Hoghetone, Henry Sely, deghere [dyer],
John Laurentz, deghere, Elias de Keminestone, John de
Nymet the elder, Roger de Ohamptone, " and others."
Given at Exeter, on Tuesday, the Feast of St. Michael
the Archangel, in the year of King Edward [the Second]
son of Edward, the 17th. By another deed, attached
thereto, she conveys to the same Philip, all her cellar,
with 2 sollars, and one herbary to the same cellar
annexed, situate without the West Gate of the city of
Exeter, between her selds, and extending from the great
bridge of Exeter, on the south, to her own tenement, on
the north ; at a yearly rent, after a term of 29 years, of
100 shillings sterling. The witnesses and the date are
the same as in the other deed. One seal is lost ; of the
other, in brown wax, part of the impression, a star,
remains.

A parchment deed, in Latin, beautifully written ; temp.
Henry III. or Edward I., with an oblong seal, represent-
ing, apparently a tulip ; whereby Jordan, son of Nicholas
Gorel, grants to Henry Tropenel a tenement without the
West Gate of Exeter ; 20s. having been paid to him
beforehand within the four benches [quatuor scanna] of
the Guildhall. Witnesses, Hillary Blund, then Mayor,
Geoffrey Strange, Hugh de Langedone, Roger Fitz-
Henry, Walter La Chawe, Martin Rof, John Pudding,
Roger Siden, Richard Walrond, John Hastement, John
Champeneys, John Banberi, " and others."

A small parchment deed, in Latin, with a large seal,
in white wax, a fleur-de-lys, with legend, dated 29th
Henry III. ; whereby Joan, who was daughter of Dende-
nay Trenchard, grants to Henry Hog all her land in
Smithenestrete, between the land of Richard Lyricoo
and that of Gunnild, daughter of the said Dendenay, at
a yearly rent of 12d. For the grant he has given
her a new gown [tunicam] of " bluet." Witnesses,
Martin Rof, Mayor of Exeter, John de Okestune and
Thomas Rof, then Provosts [or Reeves], Sir Thomas,
Chaplain of St Mary the Great, Roger, Chaplain of St.
Maban, William Palmar, Robert Peytevin, William Hog

4 G 3

Thomas Picher, William de Sampford, Stephen Hog, Clerk, " and many others."

A parchment deed, in Latin, temp. Henry III. or Edward I., whereby Felicia, late the wife of Henry Hog, grants to Hugh Martyn, weaver, her tenement in the city of Exeter in Smiþenestrete, near to "the street " which leads to the Arches of St. John's," and to the seld of John Pycot, at a yearly rent of 11s.; 4s. having been paid beforehand. Witnesses, Martin Durling, Mayor, Richard Alayn, Nicholas de Lane [Venolla], Hugh Facun, John Roke, John de Fentone, John de Okistone, Walter de Okistone, John de Coletone, John Gascoyne. A seal in white wax, iron-heater shaped, with impression of a bird, is appended.

A small parchment deed, in Latin, whereby Nicholas Pocok confirms to Henry Hog the grant which Joan, his wife, daughter of Daudeney Trenchard, made to the said Henry of 5 shillings of rent from the tenement late of Alured Irish, situate in Smithene Street, between the tenement of Paulin Taverner and that of Peter de Culmstoke, extending from such street to Priests' street; 8s. having been paid beforehand. Witnesses, Martin Rof, Mayor of Exeter, Walter de Moltone and Robert Sp[ar]owe, Provosts [or Reeves], Peter de Culmstoke, John Irish, Robert de Culmstoke, Martin Derling, Adam Hemery, Richard Roget, John Baubi, Clerk, " and " others." Temp. Henry III. The seal is lost.

A Latin deed, on parchment, exquisitely written in modern Gothic, the seal lost, whereby Roger le Poer grants to Jordan Pichot his part of the tenement between the land of Randulf Hilbert and the land of Richard Chardenache, without the South Gate of the city of Exeter, on the way as you go to Thopasham, at a yearly rent of 2 shillings; to hold to him, his heirs and assigns, a religious house excepted. Witnesses, Master Peter Wimund, Hillary Blund, Mayor of Exeter, Roger Belebuche and Gilbert Blund, Provosts [or Reeves] of Exeter, Thomas Rof, William Bulle, " and " many others." Temp. Edward I.

A like Latin deed, in the same hand, whereby Roger Giffard grants to Jordan Pichot the other part of the same tenement; with the like witnesses, Martin Rof added. An oblong seal in green wax is appended, with a kite-shaped shield, apparently charged with three shuttles.

A grant, in Latin, on parchment, by Geoffrey Fitz-John to Henry Tropinel, of his land in the South Street of the city of Exeter, near the land of Jordan Fitz-Philip, and that of Clarembald and of Richard of Poictiers, to hold to him and his heirs and assigns, a house of religion excepted; at a yearly rent of half a mark of silver, and, to the Nuns of Polslo, one mark of silver, who are, for the same, to acquit the said tenement as against the Monks of St. Nicholas; 16 marks having been paid beforehand within the 4 benches of the Guildhall of Exeter. Witnesses, Master Serlo, Dean of the Chapter of St. Peter of Exeter, Illary Blund, Mayor, Roger Delebuche and Gilbert Blund, Provosts [or Reeves], John Cha[m]pernun, John Turebert, John Puddyng, Walter La Chowe, Nicholas Gervase, Geoffrey Taverner, John Clerk, Walter Clerk, and others named. An oblong seal, in green wax, representing a priest in the act of benediction. Temp. Henry III. or Edward I.

A parchment indenture, in Latin, whereby John le Keu, and Sarra, his wife, grant to William de Cry-ditone, citizen of Exeter, a tenement in Smethene street in Exeter, near the tenement late of John Gas-coyng; in exchange for a tenement and curtilage situate in the Prebend of La Hoghes, near Exeter, ex-tending longthwise from the Great Park of la Hoghes to the street called "Kouwykstret." Witnesses, Philip Louekoke, Mayor, Martin le Keu, of Bryddeforde, Thomas le Spicer, John de Roydevers, Richard de Wottone, Seneschal, John Bolle, Roger Bolle, John Gilberd. "Given at Exeter, on Monday after the Feast " of the Assumption of the Blessed Mary, in the year " of the reign of King Edward [the Second], son of " King Edward, the 13th." A small seal is attached.

An indenture, on parchment, in Latin, whereby Peter Soth, citizen of Exeter, grants to John le Keu [the Cook] and Sarra, his wife, a tenement and curtilage situate in the Prebend of La Heghes, and extending along the King's highway leading from Exeter towards Ide, to the park of the lord of La Heghes, called the " Sothparc," at a yearly rent of 4s. 6d. Witnesses, Walter Jugement [or, perhaps, " Ingement "], then Seneschal of Heghes, William Austyn, Thomas Codilep, Roger Holle, Thomas Ladde, Walter le Hurt. "Given " at Exeter, on Wednesday after the Feast of St. Martin " in Winter, in the year of the reign of King Edward " [the Second], son of King Edward, the 7th." The

seal, in green wax, is whole, representing what is in-tended for a flower.

An indenture, on parchment, in Latin, whereby Wil-liam Coffyn and Maurice, his son, " of the County of " Devon," being bound to Alexander Juyll, of Derthe-mouthe in 30l. sterling by statute staple, yet if the same Maurice shall fulfil his covenant as to a moiety of a tenement in Clyfton Derthemouthe Hardenysse, and a moiety of a tenement and close in the demesne of Nortone, the said statute shall be held as of no effect. Witnesses, William Wilaforde, Mayor of the city of Exeter, Richard Larkstoke, Thomas Estone, John Pollow, Henry Mayow, Seneschal of the said city, and others. Dated at Exeter, 2nd of August in the 10th year of Henry IV.

HENRY THOMAS RILEY.

THE HISTORICAL MANUSCRIPTS BELONGING TO THE CORPORATION OF FORDWICH IN KENT.

The town of Fordwich, which at the present day is a small village, was in the Middle Ages a place of some commercial activity. As a member of the port of Sand-wich, it was entitled to all the privileges which belonged to the Cinque Ports, and in addition, it possessed some peculiar liberties granted by royal charter.

The Abbot of St. Augustine's in Canterbury was lord of the manor, and claimed certain customs upon all im-ports; whilst the mayor and jurats had a monopoly of the common quay at which these imports were necessarily landed.

In consequence of this divided jurisdiction, frequent disputes arose between the corporation and their officers on the one hand, and the bailiff of St. Augustine's, the abbot's resident representative, on the other.

Although the town has shrunk to a village, and the imports have ceased to arrive at the quay, the corpora-tion is by no means extinct. It still owns a town hall of 16th century date; and such privileges as the changed times have left to it are zealously guarded by the public-spirited mayor, and by the jurats, who are selected from the gentry of the neighbourhood. It is to the en-lightened conservatism of the present mayor, H. Cooper Esq., that the corporation owes its dignity and respecta-bility; and the writer of this report begs to acknowledge the courteous kindness which he received from Mr. Cooper during his examination of the contents of the muniment chest in the town hall.

The great bulk of the records contain abbreviated reports of causes determined in the mayor's court. These extend from the 15th to the 17th century, and chronicle small trespasses punished by correspondingly small penalties.

There are, however, two volumes which are worthy of a detailed notice.

The first, a leather-bound book, containing sixty parch-ment leaves of quarto size, appears to have been put together in the 17th century. It contains the Custamale of the port, and various other matters which seemed at the time when the volume was bound to deserve preser-vation.

The second, a paper book in a parchment cover, contains the inventory of the church plate of Fordwich and the churchwardens' accounts for the first half of the 16th century.

The Leather-bound Book.

The oaths of the mayor, of the treasurer, of a jurat, and of a freeman, occupy many pages here and there throughout the volume.

The formula in which these oaths were administered varied with political changes. By the most modern example a freeman is required to swear that he will be " from this day forth to the day of your death a true " freeman of the Lord Protector and his successors, and " the state of this town of Fordwich."

A page is devoted to a description in French of the boundaries of the franchise.

This is written in a hand of the 15th century, and is probably a copy of an original, more ancient survey. To ensure to the commonalty of the town full command of both banks of the river, which was the highway of the town and the source of its prosperity, it is declared that the boundary lies back from the water's edge " si longe-" ment come un home, estaunt en une batell al plein " meer, purra jetier un axe de vii li, appelle 'Taperaxe,' " sur la terr." This rough-and-ready means of measure-ment is prescribed for the determination of limits by the bye-laws of other members of the Cinque Ports.

The passing of regulations for controlling the fishery in the public river seems to have occupied a good deal of the attention of the municipal council, whose utmost vigilance hardly restrained the encroaching monks of St. Augustine's, who looked to this river for the furnishing of their table on meagre days.

At some time in the 15th century an arrangement was made by which the monastery was allowed to have the produce of one weir out of three which were annually erected, as in the present day, at the commencement of the fishing season.

Very jealous of her neighbour Sandwich, the town enacted severely protectionist laws in respect of the use of the common quay with its crane.

As a means of avoiding law-suits the mayor appointed every year four freemen to act as arbitrators, who after hearing both sides in any case of trespass should make an award which was to be held as binding upon the parties. Any person who refused to accept their decision, or who attempted to carry the cause to another court, forfeited a hundred shillings, or went to prison for a year.

The prison, a filthy hole about 9 feet square, still exists, and these alternative penalties prove how great has been the decrease in the value of money since the time when a fine of five pounds was considered to be a penalty as heavy as a year's detention in such a den as Fordwich gaol.

Besides these miscellaneous matters the volume contains a Kalendar, Gospels for the administrations of oaths, and the Custumal of the town.

The Kalendar, of 15th century date, is written upon vellum, and has the two first and the two last pages finely illuminated in ultramarine and vermilion; the intermediate pages, apparently filled in by another hand, are less ornamental. The months are divided into kalends, nones, and ides, and the Saints' days are written in a firm black letter.

The 29th of December was at one time marked as the winter festival of St. Thomas the Martyr, but some Protestant town clerk has roughly erased the name, which, however, can still be deciphered.

The Gospels, a portion selected from each Evangelist, are written on four pages of vellum, the first line of the page being rubricated and the initial capital nicely illuminated.

The Gospels chosen are the 2nd chap. of St. Matthew, a part of the 1st chap. of St. Mark, a part of the 17th chap. of St. Luke, and the first 14 verses of the 16th chap. of St. John. These are in English, and follow Tyndal's second version. To make an oath binding upon the conscience of a witness it was not necessary that it should be sworn upon the entire book of the Gospels; a portion, as in this case, selected from each was considered to be, according to the vulgar saying, "enough to swear by."

The Custumale, which appears to belong to the end of the 15th century, occupies 73 pages of the book, and is divided into 31 clauses, each of which has an illuminated initial letter, other letters here and there upon the page being capriciously spotted with red.

The first clause contains a copy of a charter of Henry II., granting to the men of Fordwich freedom from toll and other liberties. A general clause at the end confirms all the privileges which the town enjoyed " tempore " regis Edwardi, Willelmi primi, et secundi, et Henri " cisvi mei."

The second prescribes the forms which were to be observed at the election of a mayor.

The third, the oath of a mayor.

The fourth treats of the election of jurats.

The fifth requires that all weights and measures shall be justified by the new mayor.

The sixth regulates the trade of brewing.

The seventh treats " de poena percutientium et " cultellos trahentium."

The eighth declares the rules which govern the hundred court.

The ninth prescribes the manner in which lands may be bequeathed.

The tenth explains " quomodo proximiores de san- " guine habebunt primam emptionem terræ."

The eleventh disposes of " rem furtivam " found in innocent hands.

The twelfth regulates the appropriation of waifs and strays.

The thirteenth explains " quomodo et quot modis " possunt esse liberi et liberæ."

The fourteenth, " quomodo debent terræ et tenementa " infancium infra ætatem custodiri."

The fifteenth recites a charter of Edward III. " de " statu orphanorum."

The sixteenth treats " de Withernamo capiendo," explaining that by this term is meant reprisal upon the men of any town which, after a formal request from the mayor of Fordwich, has failed to administer justice in a cause in which a Fordwich man is plaintiff.

The seventeenth claims that all freemen shall have a right to share in the profits of mercantile ventures.

The eighteenth treats " de recognitionibus finium."

The nineteenth gives to the mayor the right of administering to the estates of intestates.

The twentieth provides for the punishment of misdemeanants. If the offender be a foreigner, not a man of Fordwich, keeping out of the limits of the franchise, the mayor may apply for assistance to the warden of the Ports.

The twenty-first admits that the mayor is bound to protect merchants resorting to the town.

The twenty-second declares that the King's seneschal or clerk of the market may not lawfully exercise his functions within the liberties. A charter of a King Edward is quoted to confirm this claim.

The twenty-third defines the liberties which the Abbot of St. Augustine's possesses in Fordwich.

1. He has his prison, from which if a felon escape the fault shall lie at the door of the abbot.

2. He has his bailiff.

3. He is entitled to certain fines, and forfeitures of the goods of felons and fugitives, &c.

The twenty-fourth gives the form of oath by which the abbot's bailiff is to bind himself.

The twenty-fifth explains the regulations, and the extent of the jurisdiction, to which the mayor's court can lay claim.

The twenty-sixth continues the same subject.

The twenty-seventh regulates the holding of the hundred court, over which the abbot's bailiff presides; " cujus serviens nomine ' Cachepol '" shall give three days' notice to parties who are required to appear.

The twenty-eighth treats of the ways in which arrears of rent may be recovered.

The twenty-ninth explains how certain maritime disputes may be settled by arbitration.

The thirtieth defines what felonies may be dealt with in the hundred court, and what must be sent to the court of Shipway. This clause shows that the Fordwich court might lawfully inflict capital punishment, and that this sentence was, as in other Cinque Ports, carried out by drowning. " Et omnes qui condempnati sunt in " illo casu, vel in alio aliquo casu, usque ad mortem, de- " bent duci a predicta curia Dni. Abbatis, per Stouram " usque ad quendam locum vocatum ' Thefeswelle,' et ibi " manda sue sub tibiis debent ligari, videlicet ' Knebont,' " et vivi festinanter depelli et emergi (demergi). Et hoc " fiat per ipsum qui sequitur;" the prosecutor being made the executioner.

The thirty-first is an inspeximus by Edward III., of an inspeximus by Edward II. of a charter of Edward I., who confirmed to the Cinque Ports certain liberties which they enjoyed in the 44th year of Henry III.

The Churchwardens Accounts.

The paper book of churchwardens' accounts has upon the fly-leaf a statement of the lands belonging to Fordwich Church in 1548.

The rents yielded by these lands, here set down at 2l. 3s. 5d. a year, appear to have been employed in maintaining the services and repairing the fabric of the church, and they are quite distinct from the stipend of the priest.

On the second page is a statement similar to the last, but written a generation earlier; here a tenant named Ralph Hoggyn an occupier, there his tenement is in the possession of the " heyres " of Ralph Hoggyn.

On pages 3 and 4 is an inventory of the plate and vestments belonging to the church in 1501. The articles herein enumerated suggest a church sufficiently, but not superabundantly supplied with the means of carrying on the services.

The " londys apperteyning to the cross-light " are next specified; the income from these sources, amounting to an annual 3s. 10d. was applied to the maintenance of the lamp which burned before the rood.

Then follows a record of the " weights of the chalisses " in the churche of Fordwich," the sum total amounting to 44¾ ounces.

The remainder of the book is filled with the yearly statements of account made by successive churchwardens, and extending from Michaelmas 1510 to February 1540.

The receipts in these debtor and creditor accounts consist of the rents paid for church lands, with, in some

CORPORA-
TION OF
FORDWICH.

years, small additions derived from extraordinary sources. One illiterate churchwarden debits himself with a sum of 4s. 1d. on account of " mony gadyrryed in the church," and at another time 6s. was received for honey made by the church bees.

The payments represent the expenses which the churchwardens incurred in the performance of their office ; for example :—

" It., payd at the vysitacion, viiid.
It., payd for wassbyng the church clothys, xiid.
It., payd unto Mast. Parson for obetts, 4s. 11d.
It., payd unto the wax chawndeler for all manner of lyghts, as hit a perith in his boke, 11d.
It., payd unto the ryngers at the feast of Corpus Xpi, 4d.
Mem⁴., received of Colyar vli. of new wax for owre Lady lyght, Saynt Anny's lyght, and Saynt Margarett's lyght. Payd for strekyng of the same lyghts, viid. For the wrethyng (writing) of thys accompt, 3d."

The last M.S. in the muniment chest is a begging commission, of 15th century date. This parchment professes to be a permit from the King, allowing the widow of Syr John Holte to travel the country for the purpose of asking alms from the charitable and patriotic.

" Henry by the grace of God, &c., to all his well beloved Archbyshopps .... and to all curetes of holy churche, also to all schyrefes, mayros, and baylyves and manciples, &c. Forasmuch as our well beloved servaunt Elizabeth Holte was the weyfe of Syr John Holte, Knyth, the wych longe tyme continued in our werres, and by fortune of the seyde werres was ytake prisoner in the partes of Normandy and yput in the Castell of the Mount of St Mychell, and there was ysette to the fenaunce 1140 marks, the seyde John and Elizabeth not of power to paye the seyde summes, alle her londys and tenements, for the payment of the seyde summes and fynaunce, leyden to mortgage ben to the perpetuall ondoynge of the foreseyde John and Elizabeth. And wythin 15 dayes of the payment of the seyde fynaunce the foreseyde John dyed at Roone, and as soon as the seyde Elizabeth come to Ynglond sche was arestyd and grevysly afexyd for divers dettys " &c.

The commission goes on to say that the " Abp. of " Canterbury, and the Bps. of Winton and Wyrcester, " have offered to such as shall refresch the forseyde " Elizabeth with theyre almes " indulgence amounting in all to " thirteen skor dayes," to which the Bishop of Bath has added forty dayes more. It is not unlikely that the bearer of this roving commission was an impostor, whose credentials some keen-witted mayor of Fordwich impounded ; if this were not so then the poor woman must have died at Fordwich, leaving her commission in the hands of the corporation.

The muniments of Fordwich are kept in a strong chest, standing in an airy, dry town hall. They are in good condition and well cared for.

J. B. SHEPPARD.

EARL OF
ABERDEEN.

THE MANUSCRIPTS OF THE EARL OF ABERDEEN AT
HADDO HOUSE.

These consist of an extensive series of charters connected with the baronies of Haddo, Kellie, Methlic, and other neighbouring lands in the parishes of Tarves, Methlic, Fyvie, and Deer, and those relating to the barony of Auchtercoull in the upper district of Aberdeenshire.

There is also a collection of political letters addressed by contemporary statesmen to the first Earl of Aberdeen, while Lord Chancellor of Scotland, and a volume of accounts which contains the details of his Lordship's expenditure during the same period.

In the library is a household book of King James the Fifth of Scotland, containing an account of the Royal expenditure for the year from September 1538 to September 1539.

Among the charters (many of which have suffered from the effects of damp) are a considerable number possessing points of historical interest. Of these I noted the following.

Charter by John de Berclay de Menteth Lord of Petmacaldore to William de Camera Lord of Auchnawys of all his lands of Methlayk in the shire of Aberdeen, to be held of the King in capite, sealed with his seal, and in further evidence with the seal of his dearest father William de Fodringhay, Knight. Witnesses Alexander Bishop of Ross, Master William of Dyngwale, Dean of Ross, Hugh Fraser, Alexander of Chesholme, Hugh of Moines, and many others. [Circa 1380.]

Charter of Robert III. King of Scotland to his Esquire David of Fonlarton, for his faithful service, of the lands of the two Methelaykis, which were unrighteously possessed by William of Melgedrum, and which came into the King's hands by the verdict of an assize which sat in the Royal presence at Kyncardyn in the Mernis on the 11th of December 1375. To be held by the said David and his heirs, whom failing by John of Fonlartoun son natural of the said David and his heirs, whom failing by Geoffrey son natural of the said David and his heirs, whom all failing by the assignees of the said David ; rendering to the King and his heirs Kings of Scotland one shilling of silver at the chief messuage of the lands on the feast of Pentecost yearly. Witnesses William and John Bishops of St. Andrews and Dunkeld, John the King's eldest son, Earl of Carryk and stewart of Scotland, Robert Earl of Fyf and Menteth his son, William Earl of Douglas and Marr, Sir James of Lyndesay the King's nephew and Sir Alexander of Lyndesay the King's kinsman, at Perth. 12th Dec. 1401.

Charter by Simon de Ettale chantor of the cathedral church of Aberdeen, nephew and heir of the late Sir William Lang, canon of said church, with consent of William of Ettale burgess of Aberdeen, his brother to Thomas Kynidy, constable of Aberdeen, of all his lands of Argeth lying " in Scolocaria de Elone " within the shiro of Aberdeen. To be held of the bishop of St. Andrews for the time. Dated at Aberdeen, 26 January 1415. Witnesses Gilbert Bishop of Aberdeen, chancellor of Scotland, Thomas of Tyningham, Archdeacon of Aberdeen, John of Tulach, rector of Logi in Buchan, William of Cadiow and Andrew Taillefer.

The " Scolocaria " of Ellen referred to in the above charter consisted (as appears by an inquest in 1387 called by the bishop of St. Andrews) of church lands held from the bishop by certain tenants called Scolocs or Scologs—under burden of providing for the parish church of Ellon, four clerks with copes and surplices, able to read and sing sufficiently—one part of the lands being bound to find a house for the scholars, another to furnish 24 wax candles for the park or perk before the high altar, and another being bound to find a smithy at Ellon.

Charter of confirmation by James I. King of Scotland, confirming a charter of his cousin John Stewart formerly Earl of Buchan to David de Wintoun of the lands of Andyt in the earldom of Buchan, to be held by the said David and Janet of Keth his spouse and their heirs male, whom failing by Ingeram de Wyntoun cousin of the said David and the heirs male of his body, whom all failing by his nearest heirs male bearing the name and arms of Wyntoun. Dated at Stirling, 2nd January 1411. Witnesses Malcolm Flemyng, Lord of Bygure, Alexander Seton, Lord of Gordon, and others. The charter of confirmation is dated at Edinburgh, 17th September 1423.

Charter of confirmation by James I. King of Scotland, to William Coutis, of the lands of Uchteroonle on the resignation of Alicia and Edina Lummysden. To be held of the King by the said William and after his death by Alexander of Coutis, his brother and the heirs male of his body, whom failing by John of Coutis, cousin of the said Alexander and his heirs male, whom all failing by Alexander of Coutis, brother of the said John and his heirs male of the body, whom all failing to the lawful heirs of the said Alexander of Coutis, brother of the said William. Dated at Edinburgh, 30th January 1433.

Charter by William Fonlartone de Aberewane to James Gordon, of an annual of ten marks out of the lands of Haddauch. Dated at Aberdeen [   ] July 1467.

Charter by the said William Fonlartone to the said James Gordon, of the lands of Haldauche and the Shadow half of Mekill Methlike, excepting one croft of the said lands called " le Crystyis Croft," dated 22nd June 1469. The lands of Aberawane in Strathern are conveyed as warrandice lands.

Letters of procuratory by William Fonlertoun, of Methlyk, for resigning into the King's hand his lands of Hawdauch of Methlyk, with half of Mekle Methlyk. The procurators are George Earl of Huntley, David Guthery of that ilk, John Ogistoun of Crag, Alexander Lesly of Balcomy, David Crechtoun of Cranstoune, James Schaw of Saulchy, Duncan Sancher of Murcroft. Dated at Aberdeen, 16th December 1471.

Instrument of resignation by Alexander Lesly of Wardoris, in the hands of George Lesly of that ilk, as superior, of the lands of Middil Knokynblewis, Brekoch, Drummeis, and Glassach, to Patrick Gordon of Methlek. Dated 5th Sept. 1480, within the Chapel of the Blessed Virgin Mary of Garioch. Witnesses, Alexander Lummysden, rector of Fliak, Patrick Lesly of Balquhanc, Robert Daumahoy, Patrick Strathachin, Thomas

Lesly, Sir Andrew Ingrame, Robert Stevinsone, Andrew Thomson, chaplains, and David Lesly, the Mair of Lesly, with others.

Charter by David Annande of Ouchterellone to Patrick Gordon of Methlick, of his lands of the park of Kellie, with the lands of Owirhil. Dated at Aberdeen, 12th February 1482. Witnesses, Sir James Ogilvy of Deskfurd, Robert Blindsell, Provost of Aberdeen, Alexander Menzies, John Culan, John Colisono, Donald Bannerman, and Sir Robert Weir, notary.

Precept of Sasine by Malcolm Drummond of Megour, in favour of an honourable man, Alexander Gordon, of the five merk lands of Andait, dated at Edinburgh, 28th June 1510. Witnesses, John Lord Drummond, David Drummond of Cowquhalzie, Master William Toncht, Alexander Gordon of Bodwin, Master James Smythland, and John Drummond of Muthil.

Instrument of Sasine on charter by James Redhench of Tullichiddel, in favour of the chancellor, prebendaries, and regents of the new college in the University of Aberdeen, for a yearly service to be said for him and for other pious and meritorious works, of his four merk land of Culliny, and his one merk land of Andate, lying in the shire of Aberdeen. Dated 20th August 1511.

Precept of Sasine, by Melchior Cullane of Knawane, son and heir of the late Jaspar Cullane of Knawane, burgess of Aberdeen, to George Craufurd of Federat, for giving sasine of the lands of Knawane, lying in the barony of Kelly, to Thomas Menzies, of Pitfodellis, Provost of Aberdeen. Dated at Aberdeen, 14th April 1539.

Decreet arbitral, by Robert Innes of Invermerky, James Gordoun of Haddow, John Keith of Ludquharne for the part of Robert Master of Erskine, William Strathauchin, of Glenkindie, his tenant of the lands of Auchnagatt, within the barony of Kelly, Patrik Chene of Essilmonth, Maister James Wauthaun, parsoun of Une, and Maister Alexander Ogilvy of the Glassach for the part of ane noble man Gilbert Gray of Scheves, and ane honourable man George Gordoun of Geicht, his oure lord, in ane action debateable of landymeris betuix the lands of Sauquhat pertenand to the said Master of Erskyne, and the lands of Auchnagatt perteining to the said William Strathauchin on the tane part, and the lands of Guiltors pertaining to the said Gilbert Gray, and to the said George Gordoun as Baron of Scheves, together with ane Reverend father in God Robert Abbot of Kinloss, overseman chosen by the said parties. Signed at the Hill of Kalmafillie by the said arbiters "bandis our handis" 18th April 1540, before witnesses, the Lord Erskyn [   ] Chene of Strathloch, John Gordon of Longar, Robert Innes of Moniecabok, Duncan Gordon in Knaven, Thomas Annand in Ochterellon, Alexander Buchan of Auchmacoy, and Master Peter Galbraith, notary public.

The decreet ran that "the rycht meithis and merchis " is and salbe in all tyme cuming betuix the saidis " landis of Auchnagatt, Saulquhat, and Quyltas, " begynnand at the west in the myddis of the resk " betuix the propir landis of the said George on the " west part, and the landis of Auchnagatt on the est " part, as is proppit be us in the myddis of the said " resk, and fra that command eist to ane how hoill at " the fute of the hill of Kilmafillie crocit be us, and " fra that ascendand up the hill carne be carno as we " haif proppit to the heid of the said hill, and sua the " hold of hill as the wynd and wedder devydes to ane " carne quhilk we haif callit this day the Commoun " Carne, and fra that discendand carne be carne to " the Halymanis Seit, and fra that linealie carne be " carne as is crossit and pottit be us to the feild " stane."

Charter by John Master of Erskine, with consent of Lord Erskine, his father, of the lands of Mains of Kellie, and others to James Gordon of Haddoch, paying 6l. 30s. 4d. Scots to the Abbot and Convent of Lundores. Dated at Stirling, 19th October 1553.

License by James Gordon of Sauchoke to his son Robert Gordon, of Sauchok, to "annalie and wadset the " toun and lands callit Murdois Hill alias Halymannis " Seat," lying within the Barony of Kellic. Dated at Kellie, 11th March 1578.

Discharge and receipt by James Gordon of Haddoch to Alexander Chalmers of Cults, for the title deeds of the lands of Little Methlik. The deeds are enumerated, and the first is a charter by umquhile William Chalmer of Fyndone to Thomas Chalmer his son of the Thain— of Little Meythlik, dated in the year of God 1400. The discharge is dated at Aberdeen, 1st April 1598.

5.

The political letters to which I have referred were addressed to Lord Aberdeen by Sir George Mackenzie of Tarbet, Lord Clerk Register; William Marquis of Queensberry; James Earl of Perth; Sir William Paterson, Clerk to the Privy Council; John Bishop of Edinburgh; Patrick Earl of Strathmore; George Marquis of Huntly; James Earl of Arran; Sir Andrew Forrester, Under Secretary of State; Charles Earl of Middleton; Cromwell Lockhart of Lee; George Earl of Linlithgow; Sir John Cochrane of Ochiltree; Kenneth Earl of Seaforth; Sir George Mackenzie, Lord Advocate; William Duke of Hamilton; the Provost and Magistrates of Aberdeen; George Earl Marischal; Sir John Grahame of Claverhouse; Elizabeth Duchess of Lauderdale; Alexander Archbishop of St. Andrews; the Lord Maitland, Lord Justice Clerk.

These letters were printed for the Spalding Club in the year 1851, and it is thus unnecessary for me to enter on a detailed description of them in this place. Those of Grahame of Claverhouse may be referred to as touching on many points of interest, besides furnishing specimens of the corrupt orthography of this great general. In the first, dated 1st March 1683, written on a journey through Lanarkshire to England, he says, "I found " Clidesdeall full of layn [lies]; such as my Lord Huntlys " gitting a regiment, but that my lord Deuk Hamilton " and Atholl opposed it strongly in Councell; and that " the King was either dead or daying, at least quyt " deaf; and many other lays."

Somewhat later in the same year he gave an account of his dealings with the people of Galloway which thus concludes, "and it may be nou saiffy said that Galouay " is not only as peacable, but as regular as any pairt of " the contry on this seyd Tey. And the rebelles ar " reduced without blood, and the contry brought to " obedience and conformity to the Church Government " without severity or extortion; feu heritors being " fyned, and that but gently; and under that non is or " ar to be fyned, but two or three in a parish; and the " authority of the church is restored in that contry, and " the ministers in saifty."

On the 9th of June 1683 he writes from Stirling to urge that the sentence of hanging should be carried out against a man who had been "actually in the rebellion " and continued in that state for four years." After stating his reasons he adds, "I am as sorry to see a " man day [die], even a whiguo, as any of them selfs; " but when on days [one dies] for his owen faults, and " may sawe a hundred to fall in the lyk, I have no " scrupull."

The volume of accounts to which I have referred contains the entries of moneys received and expended by John Gordone upon the accompt of the Earle of Aberdein Lord High Chancellor of Scotland from 10th May 1682 to 21st November 1684.

Many of the disbursements throw light on the social arrangements of the period, and I selected the following as specimens:

The first show that the Lord Chancellor enjoyed the sports of hawking, hunting, and horse racing. On 17th July 1682 there is paid to "the man that brought the " hauks," 23l. 10s. (Scots); then " for hoods, bells, and " uthir things, 5s. 4s."; for "ane halk glove, 12s."; for " ane halk leuer, 1l. 16s."; for "halk meat, 2s."; for " two pair of bells and three hoods, 4l. 14s."; " To my " Lord going to tho hauking, 5l. 16s."; " To my Lord " goeing to hunting per receipt, 12l. 14s."; "To Patrik " Logan for goeing north with hauks, 32l."; " To my " Lord going to Leith to his race per account, 8l. 8s."; " for weighing the men att Leith that rade, 1l. 8s."; " To the man that ran the night before the race, " 18s."; "Item to the tuo grooms drink money att " winning the race at Leith, 8l. 8s."; "Item to the " Edinburgh officers with the cup, 14l."; "Item to the " Smith boy plaitt the running horse feet, 14s."

Payments occur for books by well known writers. " To Sir Jo. Dalrymples man with Stairs decisions, " 2l. 18s."; "Sir James Turners man with a book, " 1l. 9s."; " To my Lord Glendoyicks man for Acts of " Parliament, 1l. 9s."; " For Grotius de jure belli et " pacis, 2l. 18s." Frequent entries appear of douceurs given to the servants of friends who sent presents to the Lord Chancellor. Thus "To my Lord Lithgows " man for plums, 1l. 4s." " To Waithries man for mor- " foulls, 1l. 8d."; "To Sir John Dalrymples man with " apricocks, 1l. 9s."; " To my Lord Lithgoues man " with portrigos, 14s."; " To Gights gardener with " plums, 14s."; " To Lady Errols man with pears, 14s."; " Drink money to Sir John Whitfuirds man with fruit, " 2l. 18."; " To Lord Doans man with a deir, 2l. 18s."; " To Sir George Lockharts man with a horse, 2l. 16s.";

H

" To Sir Patrick Humes man with a deir, 2l. 18s."; " To my Lord Kinnairds man with a goose, 14s."; " To Sir William Purves man with a sword, 1l. 10s."; " To Lord Crawfurds man with sparrow grasse, 1l. 8s."; " To my Lord Oxfurds man with a dog, 14s."; " To the " Marquis of Douglas man with Sullen goose, 14s."; " Item to Macleods man with haucks, 14l."; " To my " Lord Dumfermlings man with fruit, 1l. 8s."; To my " Lord Blairs man with wild fowl, 14s."; " To the " Captain of Clan Ronalds man with a hauk, 5l. 16s."; " To my Lord Lorns man with a deir, 2l. 16s."; " To " my Lord Monteiths man with a deir, 4l. 4s."; " To " my Lord Lithgows man with eils, 14s."; " Item to " his man with peatches, 8s."; " To my Lord Wintons " man with pears, 1l. 8s."; " Item to my Lady Huntlys " man with a deir, 1l. 8s."; " Item to my Lord Strath- " mores man with English hounds, 4l. 6s."; " Item to " the minister of Curries man with ane English hound, " 1l. 9s."; " Item to Huntlys fouler with pouts, 2l. 2s."; " To Errols man with a tersel off falcon, 2l. 18s."; " To " Glenbuckets man with dogs, 7s."

The entries of the Lord Chancellor's personal outlays form not the least curious part of the accounts. They relate to articles of dress and travelling expenses, payments to the poor, attendance at court and in the country, family expenses, and other outlays of a miscellaneous character.

" Gloves to my lord " cost, 2l. 18s.; " To my Lord " himself goeing to Cranstoune, 17l. 8s."; " for helping " my lords shoe, 1s."; " To my Lord on Sunday, " 1l. 8s."; " for a pock to my Lords hatt, 7s. 10d."; " To a cobbler for dressing my Lords boots, 14s." " To " my Lord goeing to Landerdales burial per receipt, " 9l. 16s."; " To my lord goeing to churoh per account, " 1l. 9s."; " To my Lord off pocket money per account, " 21l. 2s. 6d."; The following payments at London are in sterling money. " Item to Dumfermlings man to trim " my lord, 5s."; " for two fyne shirts and a poynt gravat, " 10l. 15s."; " Item for a castor hatt to my Lord, 1l."; " To William Lockhart for a fyne pirie wig, 5l. 5s."; " for takeing a coatch over water to Windsor, 1s."; " To the King, Queen, and Dukes footmen, 3l. 4s. 6d."; " For a hackney chair to my Lord, five days, 17s. 6d."; " For my Lord lodgeing five nights att Windsor, " 17s. 6d."; " Item for my lords expenses comeing up " to London, 10l." The total expenses incurred in travelling to London from Edinburgh, staying there a fortnight, and returning to Edinburgh, amounted to, 150l. 17s. 11d.

The outlays for a journey from Edinburgh to Aberdeenshire included the following : " Drink money at " Abbotshall, 13l." (Scots.) " Drink money at Cupar, " 11l. 12s." " To the poor at Abbotshall and Cupar, " 14s."; " For a boat to my Lord himselfe, 5l. 18s."; " To Claiverhous man to guid the horse weill, 14s.; " The poore at Dundie, 10s."; " To my lord himself at " Glames, 11l. 12s."; " To the poor at Glames, 12s."; " To the musitioners at Kinaird, 2l. 18s."; " Drink " money at Fetteresso, 1l. 9s." " To the porter there, " 1l. 9s." " To the man keeps the Calsay port, 1l. 8s."; " To the drummer at Aberdeen, 2l. 18s."; " In Mrs. " Burnetts for drink and accomodation 35l. 9s. 8d."; " For lime and seck ther in the morneing, 3l."; " For " five horses post from Burntisland to Aberdeen, 35l."; " To my lord upon Sunday at Skein, 1l. 8s."; " Drink " money at Glenfarquhar, 11l. 12s."

On a journey to Gordon Castle there was paid " for " drink money at Craig of Boyne, 8l. 14s."; " To a " musitioner ther, 1l. 9s."; " To the poor at Cullen of " Boyn, 7s."; " To maisoons at Wrights at the Booge, " 5l. 16s."; " For drink money at the Booge, 17l. 8s."; " To the two footmen to drink by the way, 7s."; " To " the trumpeter at Invereugie, 2l. 18s."; " To Meldrums " trumpeter, 2l. 18s." The following sums were disbursed at Aberdeen on a return journey from Kellie to Edinburgh :—" To a sutor for mending a malle, 1s."; " Drink money to the drummers of Aberdeen, 8l. 14s."; " For our laueing in Aberdeen att night, 6l. 14s."; " Drink money to Widow Burnets tapster, 2l. 18s."; " Drink money to fiddlers, 1l. 9s."; " To a poor body at " Athroes, 9s."; " To my Lord Athols pypers, 1l. 8s."

Among the miscellaneous disbursements are the following :—" To one Johnston, a poet, by order, 5l. 16s."; " To a poor scholler, by order, 14s."; " To a poor sea- " man, by order, 1l. 9s."; " Drink money for a pouny to " my Lord Hadd, 5l. 10s."; " My Lord Haddo to pay " for clubs, 1l. 16s."; " To ane distracted wyfe called " Johnston, 14s."; " To a poor gentlearman, by my Lords " order, 1l. 9s."; " To a man keips the bouling grein, " 14s."; " To the beddels that keips my Ladys scatt, " 2l. 18s."; " To my Ladys receipts for house furnish-

" ing, from the 15th of January to the 4th of June " 1683, 1,946l. 17s. 4d." " Item to the clerk and beddels " quhen Katherin was baptised, 13l." " To the beddels " of the Abay church, 1l. 9s."

It appears to me that the whole record ought to be printed.

JOHN STUART.

THE MANUSCRIPTS OF THE EARL OF LAUDERDALE, AT THIRLESTANE CASTLE.

This collection comprises the title-deeds of the family estates from the seventeenth century—and an extensive series of ancient charters relating to lands in different parts of the kingdom, which became vested in the family for a time by marriage or other causes, and have since been disposed of.

Of all these there is a full and careful inventory, in nine folio volumes, to which I have referred in preparing my report.

But besides the documents still remaining in the charter-room, there was a great mass of charters and papers relating to the barony of Thirlestane and other lands of the Maitlands of Thirlestane, dating from the 12th century, which were almost wholly destroyed by being buried in the ground at Balcarres for safety after the battle of Dunbar in the year 1650.

Inventories of these had fortunately been prepared by John, first Earl of Lauderdale, and after the Restoration the Scottish Parliament, at the instance of his son the second Earl (afterwards Duke) of Lauderdale, passed an Act wherein it was stated that the inventories in question were written by the late Earl himself; " and " seing it is notour that the said Earle was ane under- " standing nobleman of eminent and unquestionable " integritie, so that it cannot be doubted but that the " whole writs contained in the saids inventars wer " extant when he made and wrote the inventars of the " same with his aine hand," the Parliament ordained the inventories to have as great force and effect as if the original titles had been preserved.

All these inventories being engrossed ad longum in the Act of Parliament, the vast store of materials for family history and topography which they contain is still available. (Acts of the Parliaments of Scotland, vol. vii., p. 134.)

The papers of a public nature still at Thirlestane are described under the following head of the inventory.

" Public papers, which were in the custody of Charles " Earl of Lauderdale at the time of his death, still kept " by the family, tho' they are now of no consequence."

Part I. Containing copies of the King's letters and commissions to the Treasury anent the revenue and excise and customs, with lists of pensions and warrants for payment thereof, and many other such public writs.

Part V. Papers anent disarming the country anno 1678, with lists of people's names in many different parishes in the West Country who carried arms; depositions concerning arms, and accounts of arms brought in out of these parishes.

Part VI. Memorials, proposals, and other memorandums anent reducing the Highlanders to obedience to the laws; also letters anent the fishing company and other public business.

Part VII. Proclamations anent Conventicles, Bonds and other Writs relative thereto. Proclamation against owning King James VII., &c.

Part VIII. Lists of persons to be gratified by forfeitures, 1679. Warrants for seizing Lord Bargany and setting him at liberty again. Accounts of money laid out in repairing Stirling and Blacknoss Castles and Palace of Holyrood House. Report by the Lord Treasurer on the condition of the Castle of Edinburgh.

Part X. Old accounts of the rents of the Castle of Edinburgh payable to the Duke of Lauderdale as Governor thereof, and received by Sir William Sharp for him.

The following gift is connected with the public services of the Duke of Lauderdale :—

Gift under the Privy Seal of King Charles II. in favour of John Earl (afterwards Duke) of Lauderdale, of the teinds of the parish of Cranshaws and lands of Swinton, and of all the moveable estate belonging to John Swinton of that ilk at the time of his forfeiture; narrating the good and faithful service of the said Earl and his father and grandfather Chancellor of Scotland, and others his predecessors, to the King and his father and grandfather and other Royal progenitors, not only in great trust affairs and offices of State, as those of Chancellor, Privy Seal, Secretary, wherein persons of that family had often been employed, but also in other employments and negotiations both at home and abroad; and in special calling to mind that with great zeal and affection the said Earl did adhere to the King in the hardest and worst of times in advancing his service and opposing the usurpers, he did in the end resolve to sacrifice and devote his life and fortune to His Majesty's service, and in the year 1650 did accompany the King in his expedition to Scotland, and constantly waited on him till he was taken at Worcester, and after that time being imprisoned, sequestrated, robbed, and dispossessed and forfeited of all his estate, which was disposed of by the cruel usurpers; he was transported divers times from prison to prison, and with much patience, cheerfulness, and courage, past and endured in his person and estate all the degrees, kinds, and extremities of misery which could be expected from a cruel and implacable enemy to loyalty and faithfulness, and death itself in resolution and expectation which was unavoidable would have followed if God had not wonderfully restored the King; and the King being most willing to acknowledge and reward the said services, and considering that a great part of the said Earl's estate was possessed for many years by John Swinton sometime of that ilk, therefore he grants, &c. Dated 25 May 1661.

The following series of early titles of the lands of Hatton and others in the county of Edinburgh comprises many of considerable interest. The lands became vested in the family of Lauderdale in the year 1652, by marriage, but were sold in the end of last century.

They are described as "Antient titles found in the "Charter Chest of Halton, which do not connect with "the Title Deeds of the family, and only kept for "antiquity."

Ratification by Henry de Sinclair to Gilbert de Hunter of an alienation made to him by William de Byseth, pupil to the said Henry de Sinclair, of his lands of Meldon and Kidston. 1326.

Resignation by Richard Browne in the hands of King Robert III. of his lands of Borrowmore in the shire of Edinburgh. 27th March 1375.

Charter by Robert, Steward of Scotland, to William de Ledele, of his lands of Lochtillock, in the barony of Ratho.

Resignation by Thomas de Elphingston in the hands of William Laird of Seton, of an annual rent of 5 merks Scots out of the barony of Enernet, in the constabulary of Hadington. 5th February 1384.

Tack between John de Mareff, Laird of Egglisface, and John de Nudre, whereby John de Mareff lets to the said John de Nudre the lands of Westerage of Eglisface for 40 merks sterling for 13 years. 20th June 1392.

Precept of sasine on a charter by William Earl of Douglas to Sir William Borthwick of that ilk of the lands of Nainthorn and others. 15th May 1449.

Gift by King Robert II. to Alan de Lawedre of 10l. sterling yearly during the King's pleasure, as the said Alan's salary for being Justiciary Clerk upon the south side of the Water of Forth. 14th January 1373.

Commission or order under the Privy Seal of Robert II., King of Scots (in consequence of a decreet of Council), to Alan de Lawedre, Constable of the Castle of Temptallon, to make the said castle free to Robert Earl of Fyfe and Monteith, King Robert's son. Dated 7th January 1389.

Charter of alienation by William de Moravia, son and heir of David de Moravia, to Alan de Lawdre, of the lands of Dallincathe, lying in the lordship of Symondtoun, barony of Kyle, and shire of Ayr, with right of tenandry, to be held of the overlord of Symontoun, blench, conform to the tenor of the charter of the late Sir David de Lyndissay, Knight, Lord of Symontown, to the foresaid David de Moravia. About 1375.

Confirmation of the preceding charter by James de Lyndissay, Lord of Crawford and Symontoun. No date.

Renunciation by Osanna de Boyes, daughter and heir of Walter de Boyes, of a plea which she had against Alan de Lawdre anent the said lands, and of all right she had thereto in his favour.

Obligement by Fergus de Erth to Alan de Lawedre, whereby he obliged him to grant charters of the lands of Wormistoun [Urmorastoun], in the regality of Lauder, to the said Alan, and to warrant the same against all men and women; the said lands being sold by Richard de Erth, son to the said Fergus. Dated on the Feast of St. Peter ad Vincula, 1366.

Obligement by Andrew Hebroun, or Trabroun, lord of the same, to Alan de Lawedre, owning the receipt

from Alan of 5l. 6s. 8d. sterling to pay his creditor, and obliging himself that neither he nor any other in his name should take penny or pennyworth out of his lands of Newbigging and Burngreyns till Alan should be satisfied of his said sum. 24th October 1384.

Resignation by William de Welston in the hands of Alan de Lawdre, Lord of Haltoun, his superior, of the lands of Ayrealand, in the barony of Ratho. Dated St. Valentine's Day, 1402.

Precept by Robert II., when Steward of Scotland, for infefting Malcolm, the son of John, the son of Niel of Carrick, in the lands of Whitelaid, in the barony of Leggertwood, as heir, served to the said John, his father. Dated 6th April 1359.

Discharge by Thomas Cissoris to Alan de Lawdre of 22 merks sterling, contained in his obligation. 5th March 1361.

Obligation by Hew Campbell, son to Andrew Campbell, Laird of Lowden, to Alan Lawdre, of Halton, for 6l. 13s. 4d. sterling, as the relief of his lands. Dated 26th May 1394.

Tack by John Kingysse, Laird of Kingysside, to Alan de Lawdre of his lands of Kingysside, in the constabulary of Lawdre, for 10 years, for 26s. 8d. yearly. Dated 8th June 1387.

Confirmation by Robert King of Scots to John of Halton, of the town and lands of Halton. Dated at Scone, 11th June 1374.

Procuratory by John of Haltoun to Adam de Glendenellbyne and William Elphingston, for resigning his lands of Haltoun in the King's hands, superior thereof. Dated at Kinkell, 13th July 1377.

Precept by the said John to William of Elphingstoun, his baillie of Halton, for giving sasine to Sir Alan Lawdre and Elizabeth his spouse, of the town and lands of Haltoun. Dated at Kinkell, 15th July 1377.

Charter of the said lands by the said John to the said Sir Alan, bearing to be on payment of a sum of money. Without date.

Precept out of the Chancery of King Robert II. for giving sasine to Alan of Lawdre and Elizabeth his spouse, of the town and lands of Haltoun. Dated at Kindroch, 26th July 1377.

A charter of resignation by the King to the said Alan and his spouse is dated at Kindroch, on the same day as the last.

Charter by John Elder, of Craigy, and Margaret his spouse, discharging to Alan Lawdre, of Haltoun, an annual rent of 6l. 0s. 4d., formerly due to him out of the lands of Halton, with a ratification by Margaret, spouse of the said John. Dated at Craigy, 12th March 1396.

Titles of Norton:—

Charter of confirmation by Robert, Steward of Scotland, confirming a charter by Richard, called Mercator, to Finlaw, son of Henry and Helen his spouse. Without date.

Charter of confirmation by Robert, Steward of Scotland, to Finlaw, son of Henry, of two carrucates of land in Norton, formerly belonging to Ibuks and Annaks, of Nortoun, to be held blench.

Charter of confirmation by Robert, Steward of Scotland, to Alan of Lawdre and his spouse, of the said two carrucates, on the resignation of the said Finlaw. A charter by the said Robert, as King of Scotland, confirming the above charter, was granted on 10th March and 2nd year of his reign.

Charter of confirmation by Robert King of Scots of a charter by Hew Earl of Eglingtoun, to Alan of Lawdre and his spouse. Dated 10th March and 2nd year of the King's reign.

Titles of Ratho:—

Charter of confirmation by Alexander King of Scots, confirming a donation by Henry de Bonne, Earl of Hereford, to William Noble, of two carrucates of land in Ratho. 28th April, no year.

Charter of confirmation by Robert King of Scots to Patrick Noble, of the lands of Westhall of Ratho, for performance of the services used in the time of Alexander King of Scots. Dated at Dundee, 15th October, and 11th year of the King's reign.

Charter of confirmation by John King of Scots to the said Patrick Noble, on the resignation of Thomas Noble, his father, in which the said Patrick is freed from thirlage to the mill of Ratho, which lands were acquired by the predecessors of the said Thomas Noble from Henry Earl of Hereford and Constable of England. Dated at Traquair, 6th December 1394.

Deed of wadset by Thomas Orippay, of Platt and Scotstown, of the lands of Westhall and Northraw of Ratho and Platt, and of the lands of Scotstown, within

the barony of Abercorn, wadsetting the said lands to
Alan of Lawdre, and obliging him not to set the said
lands without the consent of the said Alan, under a
penalty of 200l., one half of which (if exigible) is to go
for building the church of St. Andrews, the other to
Alan himself. Dated at Edinburgh, 10th December
1375.

Charter of alienation by Thomas Cripnay of Scotatown
of the said lands of Platt and others, to Alan of Lawdre,
and that in consideration of the sum of 120l. sterling
paid to him ; to be held blench for payment of a silver
penny in the church of Ratho in time of High Mass,
and to be holden of his superior, ward. The precept
of sasine thereon is dated 16th July 1379.

Charter of approbation and ratification by Egidia
Lindsay, spouse to unquhile Hew of Eglingtoun, in her
widowhood, confirming to Alan of Lawdre all alienations
and assedations made or to be made by Thomas Cripnay
to Alan of Lawdre, heritably or otherways, for all the
days of her lifetime, of the lands of Westhall and
Northraw of Ratho, reserving to her the annual rent
of 4 merks 6 shillings payable furth thereof. Sealed
at North Berwick, with the seal of William Lindsay of
Byres, her brother, 11th December 1377.

Charter by the said Egidia, and James Douglas of
Dalkeith, her second husband, is in the same terms, and
is without date.

Charter in the same terms by Elizabeth of Elingtoun,
daughter and heir to Hew of Eglingtoun, in her lawful
widowhood, with consent of her friends, is without
date.

Charter in the like terms by John of Eglingtoun,
nephew and heir of the said Hew of Eglingtoun, confirming the foresaid alienations to Alan of Lawdre.
Sealed by himself and Alexander Ramsay of Dalhousie,
his kinsman. No date.

Obligation by Alexander of Montgomery, laird of
Conyton, obliging him to give to Alan Lauder his
charter of blench farm of the lands of Platt, Westhall,
Northraw, and two ploughlands of Nortoun when required, he delivering to the said Alexander the resignation of Thomas Cripnay. No date.

Another charter by Alexander of Montgomery to the
said Alan, is sealed by himself and Alexander Ramsay
of Dalhousie. No date.

Disposition by the said Alexander to the said Alan of
four merks and eight shillings exigible out of the lands
of Platt and Westhall, for a sum paid by the said Alan
for relieving his lands of Boningtoun from James
Douglas of Dalkeith and Egidia Lindsay his spouse.
No date.

Discharge of said annual rent by the said James
Douglas, whereby he had a liferent right from his said
spouse. Dated 7th May 1379.

Discharge by the said Alexander to the said Alan of
20l. sterling as the price of the annual rent before discharged, which he says is for losing his lands of Boning-
ton. Dated at Tamtallon, 23rd February 1385.

Charter of confirmation by Patrick Cripney, grandson of Thomas Cripney, ratifying all former charters
by his grandfather to Alan of Lawdre, of the lands of
Platt and others. Sealed in the Monastery of New-
battle, 10th June 1401.

General confirmation by Robert King of Scots to the
said Alan Lauder, ratifying all charters and evidents
made to him for whatever cause or way throughout the
kingdom of Scotland. Dated at Edinburgh, 15th July
and 13th year of the King's reign [1402].

Licence by James King of Scots to William Lauder of
Halton, to re-edify his house at Halton, and to appoint
porters and others officers thereat. Signed by the King
himself, and dated at Stirling, 12th October, in the 2nd
year of the King's reign.

Writs of the constabulary of Dundee, and of various
lands in the neighbourhood of Dundee.

Charter by John King of Scots to Alexander Scrym-
sheur, proceeding on the verdict of an inquest finding
that the constable of the Castle of Dundee had been in
possession of the lands pertaining thereto, and was
in use to receive the duties thereof, therefore granting
to the said Alexander the said office of constabulary
and privileges thereof. Dated 11th July, 9th year of the
King's reign.

Charter by the said John King of Scots to the said
Alexander Scrimsheur of the lands called Campus
Superior prope vill. de Donde ex parte boreali cum
illis acris in Campo Occidentali . . . et Constabularia
Castri de Donde . . . pro homagio et servitio nobis et
successoribus nostris faciendis. Et portando vexillum
nostrum in exercitu nostro. Dated 20th June and
10th year of the King's reign.

Precept by Robert Bruce Comes de Carrik unus de
Custodibus regni Scotiæ, narrating that Alexander
Scrimsheur de dono domini Willelmi Wallays infeo-
datus et sasitus est de Constabularia Castri de Donde
et de quibus [dam] dictæ villæ de Donde adjacentibus
aliis terris; therefore commanding the Sheriff and
Baillies of Forfar as follows, " Vobis nomine Joannis
" Comyn filii concustodis regni Scotiæ nostræ et nostro
" mandamus præcipimus, Quatenus ipsum in eodem
" statu in dictis terris et constabularia ponatis et
" manuteneatis in omnibus sicut easdem tenuit dono
" dicti Willelmi antiq. custodis dicti regni." 5th December 1303.

Precept by Robert King of Scots for infofting Nicolas
Scrimzeour in Maram de Donde, 13th August 1328.

Charter by Robert King of Scots to Nicol Scrimzeour
of the office of constabulary of Dundee, with the perti-
ments, and a hundred shilling land of the dominical
lands of Dundee. The reddendo is carrying the King's
standard in his army for all other burdens, &c. Dated
10th February 1317.

Charter by the said Robert King of Scots to the said
Nichol Scrimzeour of the said office of standard-bearer,
and of the lands of Hillfield, South Bordland, and Mary-
field, with the pertinents, in the barony of Inverkeithing,
which lands pertained to Roger Mowbray, who was
forfeited. The reddendo is " Inveniendo nobis et here-
" dibus nostris dictum Nicholaus et heredes sui in officio
" supradicto duos homines sufficientes armatos ad
" vexilla nostra portanda in exercitu nostro pro quibus
" nos et heredes nostri inveniemus equos. Dated
at Aberdeen, 12th March 1323.

Warrant under the Quarter Seal of King James V.,
directed to the Lyon and the Heralds and Pursevants,
and commanding the Treasurer to make payment to
James Scrimzeour, constable of Dundee, of the bygone
fees and duties due to him for carrying the King's
banner : Narrating that by reason of his office of bannerman, and his infeftment of the same, the said James
was entitled to have, at " the time of bearing our said
" banner, twa grathit horse for bering of the same, or
" els fourty pund strieveling, to furnish him in horse
" and harness according to his office." Dated 3rd
September 1528.

Old writs of Bulzeon and Katermaylen, formerly belonging to the family of Dudhope.

Confirmation by Laurence de Karramund to Rodul-
phus de Donde, of a donation by the son of William
Chaunturel, to Rodulph of Kethermalyn, of the tenement of Molgund. Without date.

Instrument of resignation ad remanentiam by Margaret Mortimer, relict of Robert Ross of Tarbet, of her
fourth part of the lands of Katermalyn in the hands of
John Scrimzeour of Dudhope. Dated 7th April 1447.

Precept of clare constat by James Cramond of
Aldbar, for infefting John Scrimzeour of Dudhope in
the lands of Bulzeon, alias Katermalyn, and mill
thereof, lying in the barony of Melgund and shire of
Forfar. Dated 24th February 1553.

Old titles of Stradichty and others belonging to the
family of Dudhope.

Sasine, dated 14th April 1425, in favour of Thomas
Clerk, burgess of Dundee, of the lands of Kirktoun, of
Strathdighty, in the regality of Kirrymuir, on precept
by William Douglas, Earl of Angus.

Bond by the Earl of Angus, whereby he obliged himself to receive James Scrimzeour, his cousin, to be his
tenant in the said lands. Dated 20th January 1444.

Assignation by the said Thomas Clark to John Scrimzeour, son of James Scrimzeur of Dudhope, of the foresaid lands. Dated 6th March 1450.

Charter by David King of Scots, in favour of Alexander
Scrymseour of Dundee, of the lands of Ferdell, in the
shire of Perth. Dated 14th March, and the 29th year of
the King's reign.

Charter by Alexander King of Scots, in favour of
Gillacop McGilchriest, of the five penny land of Fench-
ran, &c., in Errigaythel. 1st August and 26th year of
the King's reign.

Precept by Alexander de Ile, Earl of Ross, Lord of
the Isles and barony of Kincardine, for infefting Sir
John Scrimzeour of Dudhope in the lands of Faslada-
waoh, Balmaquyn, Acharny, and mill thereof. Dated
10th October 1444.

Gifts and mortifications of lands, tenements, acres,
and annual rents lying about the town of Dundee, by
many of the burgesses of Dundee, the family of Dudhope,
and others, to the chaplainries within the church of
Dundee, called St. James's, St. Stephen's, St. Michael's,
St. Mary's, and St. Salvator's. Presentations to said
chaplainries, and other old charters and sasines of

burghal tenements in Dundee not connected with the said chaplainries.

Charter by Robert King of Scots, in favour of Gilbert de Glastre, whom failing, to Alexander Scrimseour of Dundee, of the lands and castle of Glacestre, in Argyllshire. 3rd May 1374.

The following old charters escaped the general destruction of the Lauderdale titles. They are mostly grants to the Abbey of Dryburgh, and have been printed in the chartulary of Dryburgh :—

Carta resignationis per Joannem de Maxwel, militem dominum de Carlaverok in favorem Alexandri Mateland de tota terra de Pencateland jacente in vicecomitatu de Edynburgh. Circa 1343.

Carta per Robertum de Maxwell dominum de Carlaverok, Deo et Beatæ Mariæ et Monasterio de Dryburgh, de tota illa terra cum pertinent. jacen. in villa et territorio de West Pencaitland super resignatione Joannis Mautalont domini de Thrillystane. Circa 1400.

Carta per Joannem Maxwel de Pencatland militem Deo et Ecclesiæ Sanctæ Mariæ de Dryburgh de Patronatu Ecclesiæ de Pencaitland. Circa 1343.

Charter by John Mautalant, Lord of Thirlstane, son of Robert Mautulant, to the Monastery of Dryburgh, of the lands of Snawdoun.

Donatio per Ricardum de Morvil Beatæ Mariæ et Sancto Leonardo et Infirmis fratribus Hospitalis de Louuerd de terra ubi Hospitalis de Louuerd sita est. Circa 1170.

Donatio per Willelmum de Abirnithy militem to the Monastery of Dryburgh de Molendino de Ulkistoun in villa de Louedre. A.D. 1273.

The following relate to the Priory of Haddington :—

Notarial instrument containing commission by the Convent of the Abbey of Haddington to Elizabeth Hepburn, prioress thereof, to feu, rent, or set in tack the lands belonging to the monastery. Dated 25th May 1559.

Charter of alienation by the said Elizabeth, prioress foresaid, to William Maitland, younger, of Lethington, Principal Secretary of State to Mary Queen of Scotland, of the dominical lands of the Monastery of Haddington, the lands of Muirtoun, Westhopes, Easthopes, Woodend, Newlands, Rindslaw, Snawdoun, Carfrae, and Little Newton, all in the constabulary of Haddington, for payment of certain quantities of victual and sums of money. Dated 6th December 1563.

JOHN STUART.

THE MANUSCRIPTS OF THE MARQUIS OF AILSA.

The Lordship of Galloway, although it may be considered to have been part of Scotland in the twelfth century, yet continued in possession of its peculiar Celtic laws and customs for more than two centuries afterwards.

In the reign of King William the Lion, the great territories of the Lords of Galloway suffered a division, whereby the country of Carrick which formed part of them was assigned to Duncan, grandson of Fergus, Lord of Carrick, who became Earl of Carrick.

Of this ancient stock it would seem that the family of Kennedy, now represented by Lord Ailsa, was originally a branch.

The first of them appearing in record is Gilbert of Carrick, whose son Duncan of Carrick, in the time of William the Lion, granted to the nuns of St. Mary, of North Berwick, the patronage of the church of Kirkbride, in Carrick.

Shortly after this Niel, Earl of Carrick, granted to Roland, of Carrick, probably the grandson of the above Duncan, a charter, which is the first of a series, all illustrative of points of clan polity.

By this deed the Earl granted and confirmed to Roland of Carrick and his heirs the right of being head of their kin in all pleas relating to Kenkenoll, and the office of Baillie, and the leadership of the men of the country under the Earl. This charter was confirmed by King Alexander III., at Stirling, in the year 1276. These documents are found in the Register of the Great Seal. The first original charter of this series now at Culzean is one by King Robert III., dated 28th January 1405, whereby he confirmed to James Kennedy, son of Sir Gilbert Kennedy, Knight, the right of being head of his kin, and the leadership of the men of the country, as in the earlier grants.

On the 3rd August 1455, King James II. confirmed to Gilbert Kennedy, of Dunure, the same privileges, but with some remarkable variations of expression. He

constituted "dictum Gilbertum et heredes suos caput " progenei et consanguineorum ac amicorum de lez " Makmaykains et de Werichsach tam in Calumpniis " quam in aliis articulis negociorum ad supradictum " officium spectantibus cum conduccione et gubernacione " dicti primogenei et hominum, ac armorum ostensione " et serviciis de lez Kynchaldiis ac cum devoriis [etc.] " adeo libere sicut aliquis capitaneus seu caput dicti " progenei dictum officium . . . . tenuit seu pos- " sedit."

On 23rd October 1454, James II. granted a charter to John Kennedy, son and apparent heir of Gilbert Kennedy, of Dunure, of the said offices, on the resignation of the said Gilbert. There is a substitution of the brothers of John in succession, and a reservation of Gilbert's liferent. "Reservata tamen administracione dictorum " officiorum cum pertinenciis predicto Gilberto Ken- " nedy, pro toto tempore vite sue."

Besides this peculiar and indeed unique class of documents, the collection at Culzean comprises an extensive and valuable series of family muniments, especially useful for the history of the district, but furnishing also illustrations of national history and policy.

Of these I noted the following :—Copy of a remission by King Robert I. to Gilbert of Carryk, Knight, for the surrender of the Castle of Lochdoune to the English, by Arthur, his son-in-law, and for the delivery of Cristofer Seton, the king's son-in-law, "sibi impositi licet minus " juste, ut verius intelloximus." The remission, which is undated, is recorded in the Register of the Great Seal.

Charter by King David II. to John de Kennedy, of the lands, tenements, and possessions belonging to or acquired by him, and confirming the same to him, dated 18th January 1357.

Charter by Marjory de Montgomery, cousin and heir of Christian de Montgomery, to John Kennedy, of the lands of Cassillis, in the earldom of Carrick, dated 27th August 1363, with her seal, and also with the common seals of the Monastery of Crossragwell, and the burgh of Ar, and the seals of Thomas Flemyng, Earl of Wygton, and Sir Duncan Wallays, Knight, taen sheriff of Ayr. Witnesses, John Abbot, of Paisley, Robert Abbot, of Kilwyning, and others. Charter by King David II., dated 27th August 1363, confirming the last charter.

Charter by Malcolm, son of Rolland of Carrick, to John Kennedy, of Dunure, of the twopenny land called Freuchane and Kenechane, in the parish of Keucchanel Munterduffy, in the Earldom of Carrick. The charter is without date, and is witnessed by John Stewart, Earl of Carric, Sir Nicolas, Abbot of Crossragwell, Gilbert Kennedy, John, son of Henry, John, son of Alexander, Adam, son of Thomas, and others.

Charter by Thomas Fleming, heir of Malcolm, Earl of Wigton, deceased, to Sir Gilbert Kennedy, Knight, son and heir of John Kennedy of Dunure, of the town of Kyrkyntolach. Witnessed by Sir Duncan Wallace, Nicolas of Knocdolian, Adam of Foulerton, William of Conyngham, the son, Knights, Gilbert Kennedy, John, son of Henry, Adam, son of Thomas, and others.

Charter by King Robert II., to John Kennedy, of Dunure, of the half of the barony of Dalrymple, on the resignation of Malcolm, son of Gilcrist, son of Adam de Dalrymple. Dated 30th March 1371.

Copy of deed of Foundation by John Kennedy, of Dunure, of a chapel in honor of St. Mary Virgin, near the cemetery of the parish church of Maybole, for a priest and three chaplains to celebrate divine service for the weal of himself, Mary his wife, and their children, conveying various lands and annual rents. Dated at Dounouur, by 29th November 1371.

Gift of King Robert II., to John Kennedy, of Dunure, of the relief due and payable from the lands which belonged to the deceased Arthur de Dalrymple. Dated 4th May 1375.

Charter by King Robert II. to John Kennedy of Dunure, of all the property acquired by him in time bygone, and confirming the same to him. Dated 13th November 1381.

Letter by John Kennedy, of Dunure, ordaining the senior priest of the chapel founded by him at Maybole, to be the provost of the same, with right of government. Dated 1st March 1383.

Charter by Malcolm Fleming, of Biggar, to Sir Gilbert Kennedy, son of John Kennedy, of Dunure, and Agnes Maxwell, his wife, and a series of heirs, of the forty shilling land of Kirkintulach, and ratifying charter by the said John Kennedy, of Dunure, to the said Sir Gilbert, and the heirs therein mentioned. Dated 27th January 1384.

4 H 3

Charter by King Robert II. to the chaplain, celebrating divine service in the chapel of St. Mary of Maybole, founded by John Kennedy, of Dunure, of the ten pound land of Nether Glennop, in the earldom of Carrick, which had formerly been given by the ancestor of the said John to the abbot and canons of Bangor, " et que nos contingunt racione forisfacture eorundem " ad pacem et fidem Regis Angliæ existencium de " presenti." Dated at Kilwinning, 17th September 1385.

Charter by John the Stewart of Scotland and Earl of Carrick, ratifying the last charter. Dated at Dundonald, 13th February 1385.

Bull of Pope Clement VII., in favour of Thomas Hay, clerk of the diocese of St. Andrew's, dispensing with the defect of his birth,—he being the son of a bishop descended from an honourable family of barons, his mother also being of an honourable race,—declaring him capable of promotion to the office of the priesthood at the lawful age, and to hold benefices, and if one of them should be in a church where his father is beneficed, yet if the same is canonically conferred on him, he shall be allowed, in the presence or absence of his said father, to celebrate in a free and lawful manner masses and other divine offices, provided he do not succeed in this benefice to his father, nor be joined with him in the ministry of the altar. Dated at St. Peter's, 14th of the calends of November, and the ninth year of the Pope's Pontificate (1387), directed " Reverendo in " Christo Patri et Domino Domino Jacobo Episcopo " Rossensi domino suo observando, Scoto, in Scocia."

Indenture dated at Stirling, 8th November 1408, between Robert Duke of Albany, and Sir Gilbert Kennedy, of Dunoir, whereby, in reference to a deed of settlement made by the said Sir Gilbert of his lands of Dunoir and others on a series of heirs, of which the said governor grants " that he na his ayris salnocht " mak reuocatione of the said joynt feftment, na talyo " na mak impediment, na distroublance tharein in time " to cum be na way ; For the quhilk consent and gude " will the said Schyr Giibert has made his duelling " and speciale retenew with our said lords the governor, " and with his leuchfull ayris, in pece and in were, at " at his gudely power, for al the terme of his lyfe before " al uther dedelike personis, his allegiance aucht to " the king snerly out tane."

Charter by John Macgillilan, son and heir of Ingelram Mcugillilan, to Fergus Kennedy, of Bomunyn, of the half of the upper barony of Glastyncher, commonly called Dalecarn, with his seal and the common seal of the Abbey of Crossraguall. At Corsereguall, 18th March 1415. Witnesses, Alexander Kennedy, of Ardstenchere, John Cathkert of that ilk, Sir John of Hamiltoun, lord de le Rosa, Knight, John Kennedy, of Dalsask, Alexander of Hamiltoun, and Alan of Cathkert, with others.

Instrument dated 2nd July 1444, setting forth that in presence of James, Bishop of St. Andrew's, appeared Sir John Kennedy, Lord of Blaacharne, Knight, and John Kennedy, his son and apparent heir, who became men for the term of ten years to Gilbert Kennedy, Lord of Dunnure, who was also present and received the oath of homage and fealty of the said Sir John and his son,—their fealty to the King and their feudal superiors being excepted. The said Gilbert was to pay yearly to the said Sir John 20 merks, besides other 10 merks for his homage and service, and because the said sum of 10 merks seemed for the time to be too small, the Bishop of St. Andrews bound himself to pay to him twc marks in addition. The transaction took place at Cascyllis, near the great garden thereof, in presence of Sir Henry Wardlaw, Lord of Terry, Knight, Robert of Mure, Esquire and George Martyne, citizen of St. Andrews.

James Kennedy, Bishop of St. Andrews, was brother of Gilbert Kennedy, who was created Lord Kennedy about ten years after.

Bond of manrent by Gilbert Kennedy, son of Alexander Kennedy, of Ardstyncher, to Gilbert Kennedy of Dunure, for the lands of arensene. Dated 23rd March 1447, with his seal of arms. Witnesses, Edward of Maxwel, son to Lord Maxwel, Andrew Agnew, of Salchare, Rychard Singlar, Patrick Agnew, and William of Twynam. At Calmanale, 23rd April 1447.

Charter by King James II. to Gilbert Kennedy, of Dunure, of the keeping of the Castle of Lochdoun and lands called the Pennyland belonging thereto, on the resignation of John Kennedy of Coyf. Dated 17th May 1450.

Charter by Finlaus Asenan dominus de Caruchan to Gilbert Kennedy, son of the deceased Alexander Kennedy, of Ardstyncher, of the lands of Oasgangill, in the parish of Girvan, on the resignation of William Mackenzel, 23rd July 1450. Reddendo, a pair of gloves on the feast of the translation of St. Cuthbert at the church of Girvan. Dated at Kyrodine. Witnesses, Colin Mac Alyssunder de Daltussen, Maurice McCharry, John Murdochson, Maurice McGilroe, Martine Mclurg, John of Achynell, Malcolm Assenane, with others.

Charter of King James II. to Gilbert Kennedy of Dunure, declaring him and his heirs male chief of his name, and conferring on him the office of Baillie of Carrick, on his own resignation. Dated 13th February 1450.

Another Charter by the King of the same tenor, on a like resignation. Dated 25th May 1451.

Charter by Gilbert Kennedy, of Dunure, in favour of a chaplain for celebrating divine service in the collegiate church of Maybole, for the weal of himself, Catherine Maxwell, his wife, and their children, of the lands of Larginlane, and others. Dated 18th May 1451.

Charter of James Earl of Douglas to Mark Haliburton, his kinsman and secretary, of the lands of Glengenate, and others, in the barony of Trabeath and earldom of Carrick, on the resignation of John Auchinleck of that ilk. Dated 28th March 1453, at Douglas. Witnesses, Hugh Earl of Ormond, James Lord Balvany, James Lord of Hamylton, Andrew Ker of Auldtonburn, and others.

Obligation by James Earl of Douglas to the said Mark Haliburton, narrating the above grant, and stating that if he should happen to be troubled in his possession of the said lands by Margaret, the Earl's wife, or his heirs, the earl shall be bonnd to provide him in a ten pound land of equal value in Lothian, Clydesdale, or Galloway. Dated 28th March 1454, at Douglas, and sealed and signed by the Earl, " James erl Dowglaas."

Resignation by Gilbert Kennedy, of Dunure, of the office of Baillie of Carrick and others in the King's hands, for infeftment to be given to John Kennedy, his son and apparent heir. Dated 12th October, 1454.

Charter following thereon by King James II. Dated 15th November 1454.

Charter by King James II. to James Stewart, of Anchterhouse, his brother, of the half of the barony of Trabeath in Carrick, which had come into the King's hand through the forfeiture of Mark de Haliburton. Dated 19th April 1457.

Charter by King James II. to Marion Countess of Angus, of the above lands on the resignation of the said James Stewart. Dated 20th March 1457.

Discharge by Thomas Dundnf of that ilk to Morris McCharry, for the sum of 50 gold nobles, paid by the said Maurice to the said Thomas and his heirs, with Janet Dunduf of the four merkland of Gallachan. Dated 21st June 1462.

Charter by William, prior of Whithorn, to Gilbert Kennedy, son of the deceased Alexander Kennedy of Ardstynchar, and Margaret Cunningham, wife of the said Gilbert Kennedy, in the twenty-five shilling land of Craigneil, on the resignation of Robert Shanks. Dated 9th August 1464.

Charter by Thomas Kennedy, of Carslo, heritable coroner of the earldom of Carrick, to Thomas Kennedy, of Craigfyn, his son, of the office of coroner of the earldom of Carrick, with the fees thereof, to be held of the King. Witnesses, Mr. John Law, chaplain, John Chalmer, Alderman of Ayr, and James Preston, notary. Dated 20th May, 1513.

Charter by John Earl of Ross and Lord of the Isles, to his native esquire John Davidson, son and heir of Gilbert Davidson, of the teinds of Greenan in the earldom of Carrick. Dated Killuinan, 2nd April, 1475.

Obligation by Donald de Ilay, of Glins and Dunivaig, principall councillor of John, Earl of Ross, and Lord of the Isles, to warrant and defend the last charter. Dated at Irvine, 8th October 1475.

Charter by John de Ilay to John Davidson, his native esquire, son of the late Gilbert Davidson, of the lands of Greenan. Dated at Islay 20th August 1476. Witnesses, Rolland Macican of Dowart, Donald Balloch, of Denovan, Hector Maclean of Cullachboy, Nigel Macbryde, Archdean of Sodor, and Sir James Werk, priest.

Procuratory by John Lord Kennedy to John Dundas of that ilk to appear in presence of King James IV., and resign the office of Baillie of Carrick for new infeftment to David Kennedy, his oldest son and apparent heir. Dated 3rd July 1489.

Definitive sentence by John Sproull, vicar of Carmunnock, Commissary of Mr. Martin Reid, official of Glasgow, in the cause of bastardy moved before him at the instance of William Mundwell, son and apparent heir of John Mundwell, of Cark, and the late Katherine Kennedy, his wife, sister of the late David Kennedy, of Craigneil, against John Kennedy, of Cragneil, a minor, son of the said David, procreate between him and Bessete Reid, his wife. The plea was that John Kennedy is illegitimate, and had been begotten in incest, in respect it was known that David and Besseta were, before being contracted in marriage, related within the fourth degree, and their marriage was not solemnized in the face of the church, and therefore William Mundwell ought to succeed to the goods of David, being only son of Catherine Kennedy, his sister, procreated between her and John Mundwell, her husband. The official absolved John from the imputation of bastardy, whereupon instruments were taken : in the metropolitan church of Glasgow, on 13th August 1511. Witnesses, Sir John Hawick and Sir Martin Reid, chaplains, Mr. James Neilson, vicar of Colmonell, Mr. Walter Curry, and Mr. James Houston.

Commission by David, Bishop of Galloway, and commendator of the Abbey of Tongland, with consent of the chapter of Whithorn, constituting Gilbert, Earl of Cassilis, Baillie over all the lands of the Bishop of Galloway, and also conferring on his lordship the office of captain and keeper of the Manor Place, and Loch of Inch, in the Rinnis of Galloway, " for the part that he has kepit to " our Souerane lord in his les age, and tomy lord Gouer- " nour his tutour and protectour." Dated at Whithorn, 25th March 1516.

Decreet at the instance of Gilbert, Earl of Cassilis, against John Dunduff of that ilk, in the Baillie Court of Carrick, holden at the Broomhill beside Maybole, by Fergus Dalrymple, and Edward Waugh, baillies of Carrick, relative to the teinds of Dunduff. Dated 31st October 1533.

Instrument on the institution of Thomas Hay, Abbot of Glenluce, into the abbacy thereof, bearing that Sir John Mill, procurator for the abbot, passed to the personal presence of Mr. David Gibson, priest and canon of the metropolitan church of Glasgow, and presented to him a Bull of Pope Pius IV. in favour of the said abbot, dated, at St. Peter's at Rome, 15th of the calends of May, 1560, requiring him to put the same to execution, which he having received and read, thereafter passed to the Abbey of Glenluce, and to the principal gate thereof, knocked three or four several times and demanded admission into the choir, was refused access by Cuthbert Kirkpatrick, servant to John Gordon of Lochinvar, who had forcibly occupied the abbey and expelled the monks therefrom, the said David then read and published the Bull to all having interest, and gave canonical institution of the abbacy to Sir John Mill as procurator foresaid, by delivering to him a cap and a book in token of his possession and government, and thereafter he passed to the church of the Abbey, and in presence of the parishioners therein assembled, again published the said Bull, when Sir David Bullock, prior, Sir John Galbraith, sub-prior, Sir John Anderson, vicar, and Sir Andrew Langlands, Sir Alexander Cairns, and Sir William Halkerton, monks, then chapterly convened, unanimously admitted and received the said Thomas Hay for their abbot and superior. Whereupon the said David Gibson protested that the Bull was duly published, and institution given in terms thereof. Witnesses, Andrew Agnew, sheriff of Wigton, David Kennedy of Baltersan, Hugh Kennedy of Cascreoch, James Kennedy of Ochterlour, and Archibald Kennedy of Synones. Dated at the Abbey of Glenluce on the feast of St. Michael, 1560.

Instrument dated at Glenluce, 17th November 1561, whereby it is shown that John Gordon of Lochinvar removed himself and his servants from the Abbey and delivered up the same to Gilbert, Earl of Cassilis, heritable Baillie thereof, by delivery of the key to the Earl, and that in terms of a decreet arbitral by James Commendator of Pittenweem, ratified by the said Earl, the said Abbot, and the said John Gordon, at Holyroodhouse, on the 4th November 1561.

Instrument on the institution of Mr. Allan Stewart, Abbot of Crossragwell into the abbacy thereof, bearing his compearance in the abbey, holding in his hands a deed of gift by Queen Mary, and relative letters by John, Archbishop of St. Andrews, Primate of Scotland, and papal legate, conferring on him the said abbacy. Whereupon he received institution and possession thereof, and was received and admitted into the Church by Sir Michael Dewar, the superior, and the monks. Witnesses, Allan Stewart and John Stewart, sons of the laird of Galrig, Allan Stewart in Braidly, and Patrick Wooplay. Dated at Crossragwell, 16th December 1565.

Licence by King James VI. and the Privy Council of Scotland to John, Earl of Cassilis, permitting him to go out of the Kingdom into the parts of France, Germany, and the low countries, and to remain there for five years. Dated at Newmarket, 24th January 1619.

A series of 13 letters from Queen Mary of Scotland to the Earl of Cassilis are arranged in a volume by themselves.

The first is dated Edinburgh, 29th May 1562. In it she states that, with the advice of her lords, she and her good sister, the Queen of England, are to meet at some place near the borders of both realms, " to the " end we may be sic familiarite intertean the peace " and incres farder amytie betwix us," requiring the Earl to be ready to attend her by the 15th of July next, at Edinburgh, well furnished for a stay of two or three months, and because her whole train will be clad in dule, he and his company are to be after that sort.

Precept ordaining a letter to pass under the Privy Seal, granting a tack of the Abbey of Crossragnel to Gilbert Earl of Cassilis for 13 years, renewable till the full end of 19 years, for payment of the sum therein specified. Dated 10th February 1565.

Letter from the Queen, Edinburgh, 16th March 1565. —" Be reion this trowblis laitlyo occurrit hais tane sum " staye quhairthrow sik forcis and assemleis as wo " requueyrit ar nocht at this present necessar, yet " newirtheles we pray yow to addres yourself, accom- " paneit with your substantius houshald and kynnis- " men, and sik baronnis as ye ken ar voilland to forder " our enterprysis, to cowm to ws with all possible " diligence, and at meiting ye sall knaw forder off " owr mynd and intentioun."

The Queen writing from Carlisle, 20th May 1568. " Forsamekle as I for the saalftie of my bodie findand " na suir acces nor place within my realme to retire " me at this tyme, as ye may knaw I was constraixmit " to leve the samen and to pas to this cuntry of Ing- " land, quhair I assur you I have bene rycht weill res- " sauit and honorablie accompaigned and traicted. I " have deliberit to pas fortherward in France to pray " the King, my guid broder, to support and help me to " delyuer and releue my Realme of sic Rebellions " troublis and oppressionis that now regnis within thó " samin, and to depart farth of this toun the xxiv. day " of this instant moneth. Thairfore, I pray yow effec- " tuuslie traist cusing, that ye in the menetyme hald " yourself constant in my seruice, and aduerteiss your " freindis and neighbouris . . . to serue me quhan the " occasiounsall offer, as ye have done trewly afore this " tyme, speciallie at the last battal whair (as I am ad- " werteist) ye have done richt weill your devoir, ye " beiand on your featis whilk sall nocht be forgot be " me in tyme coming. With the help of God I houp " to returne agaon about the xv. day of August nixt " with gud company for the effect foresaid, God will- " ing. This I beleve ye will do, as my traist is and " wes aye in yow, and for to mak ane end of my bill I " will commit yow to the protectiuon of the Eternal " God, at Carleil, the xx. of Maij 1568."

[On the back.] I pray you, my lord, excuss this stamp because the queno has na uther at this time.

Another letter from the Queen is dated from Carlisle, 25th May 1568. " We have ressauit your writting tho " xxv. of this instant, and thairby understand your " constancie quhilk is weill provin to us, and mon " never be forgot sa lang as we leve. . . . We are " heir honorable ressauit and in vero gud hop schortlie " to writt to yow sic thinges that salbe to your confort " and our weill, for we dont nocht to be put in our " awin place agane, with the grace of God, the help of " guid freindis heir, your L., and our loving subjectis " assistance very schortlie, als sone ye will beging to " have some experience. In the mene tyme ye may " weill assure yourself thair sal na eardlie pleasour " confort as quhill we help to releve our trublis freindis. " Pray and you to exercise your wit to entertene and " confort them, quham ye find bear us gude mynd and " do that ye can to winn sic freindis as ye find is " nochtnotable offendaris to ws quhais fauoris we " desyre nocht."

On 6th July 1568, the Queen writes from Carlisle. Refers to her recent communications and his continued fidelity, " nocht doubting bot ye will contienew firme and " stable in the samyn, and yet being, thankis to God, in " gud health and weelfair, we thocht expedient be this " present to assure you of the samyn. Praying you that " ye latt, my lord Murrayo, ressauc nane of our mailles " in thai pairtes nor nane of his. Bot that ye uptak " and ressane the samyn, bestowing it on soldatis to do

" ws service quhair ye have a do with thame sicklyk, as
" we haif written to the Laird of Lochinwer and utheris
" in the cuntrey. My Lord Flemyng arrivit yesterdaye
" to us fra Loundoun quha is boun in Scotland, to whom
" ye sall gif credeit, and will schaw yow af our pro-
" ceedingis at mair lenth and apply, nor we think it
" expedient to wreit at this tyme. Feir nocht quhat
" contrarious tydingis be schawin yow of us for, God
" willing, our trew and faythfull subjectis will gett re-
" lief be France and Spanye, suppois Ingland will
" nocht assist us to the destructioun of our Enemys
" and your honor and confort." The following words
are in the Queen's own hand, " Your mest assured
frind."

The next is dated Bowtoun, 23rd October 1568.
" We haif understand your gud mynd and seruice
" declarit to us . . . be Lord Boyde. . . . Ye sall wytt
" that at this conference quhilk hes bene in York be-
" twix our Commissioneris and thais of the Quen,
" our Gud Sisteris, quhair our rebellis hes beene hard,
" and found nathing to thair advantage, our affaires
" (thankis to God) ar proceidit in gud maner and weill
" advanced, and the Quene, our gud sister, in the
" meanetyme hes desyrit ws to send sum of our lordis
" towartis hir, as in lyk maner of the said is reabellis
" wil be thair. Quhairfor we haif send up our traist
" counsalouris the Bischop of Ross, my lord Hereis,
" and the Abbot of Kilwynning at quhais returning
we luik to haif ane gud resolutioun, and as we 'ar ad-
" wertised of the futherance thairof in the same manner
" sall mak yow participant of the samyn."

She renews her promise to reward his good service,
and with reference " to sic ane mater as he presently
" desires," she adds, " considerand the estaite we are
" presentlie in coould nocht fulfill your haill desyre in
" effect as ye requyrit as vnvalabill for your proffeitt,
" quhairof we haif communicat with the said beirar at
" mair lenth. . . Praying yow to continue in keiping
" the cuntrey and our faythfull subjectis (so far as ye
" may) in gud peace and quyetnes till our obedience."

The following addition is in the Queen's own hand :—
" Ye schal be assureid that I schal be als kerful off your
" weil and off your hous as you schal wusche me, as I
" schai heir by your awn man waum tu I hef spoknll
" my mynd. Your richt gud Cusignes."

The next is dated Bowtoun, 6th December 1568.
" Forsamekill as we ar aduertist that our Commis-
" sioneris for dyuers resonabill caussis hes brokin the
" negociacioun of our affaires, quhilk wes afoir our
" Sister the Quene of England, and hes tane up the
" mater fra her swa we persaif na gud mennis to be haid
" thairby, heirfor seing our rebellis continewis in the
" destructioun thai may do to us, our faithful subjectis,
" and realme, with intentioun to do war fra this furth,
" nor in tymes bypast gif thai be sufferit, we praye
" yow that ye be in reddines with your haill freindis
" and force in substantious maner to prevene the tyme
" with the saidis rebellis, and tak the first advantage
" may be gotten of thame, nocht only to stop thair waye
" in hame cuming gif it uar possible, bot presentlieg if
" ye can apprehend ony of the principallis of thame in
" handis quha ar at hame lyk as thai haif of ouris that
" na mair tyme be lost. We haif nocht as yitt gotten
" advertisment heirof be our saidis commissioneris bot
" swa sone we gett the samyn ye salbe participant, God
" willing, Quhome mott preserve you."

" Bowtoune, 5th January 1568. We haif ressauit your
" lettir fra your servitor Sanders Eclis, quha hes
" schawin us of twa horsis ye haif send us standing in
" Dumfries, because as yitt we ar nocht resolut that thai
" sould cum heir. Thanking yow werraye hertlic thair-
" of and hes desyrit the said Sanders to retene the
" said horsis with himselff in Dumfreis till we get uthir
" newes from the Court of Ingland, and that for ane x.
" or xii. dayeis to the effect we maye then knaw quhat
" salbe done with the same. Quhairfor ye sall excus
" him of his long tary. We haif na uthir newes to
" wryt to yow than thais we haif writtin with the laird
" of Skeldoun quhilkis, as thai occur yo salbe advertisit
" of the samen."

The next letter is dated Tutbery, 10th February 1568.
In it the Queen refers to the Earl's faithful constancy
and " now specially seing the resolucion of our affaires
" and proceiding thairof ar sa neir apperantlie to tak
" gud effect. Prayis yow that ye will persoweir in
" setting forward all that quhilk may redound to the
" weilfair and aduancement of our authoritie. And
" albeit we wryt nocht sa amplie and sa oft to owery
" ane of yow as we wald do, for dyuers discommoditeis,
" and cheiflie becaus our lettres are commonly tane be
" the waye, yett be nocht discouragit nor skar nocht

" thairat giff we wryt to thame only of quhome ye may
" understand our desyre woill aneuch, and think nocht
" that we leif for that to esteme eworie man in his awin
" dogrie. Bot considering our commoditie that we
" maye nocht writt to all ye sall excuse us thairin,
" Quhairfor we haif despeschit our lovit servitour, the
" Lard of Gartly, present beirar heirof, towarts all thais
" with quhome he may communicat to schaw yow our
" mynd mair amplie nor we can wryte quhome ye sall
" credreit and sicklyke our traist Cusigne and Coun-
" salour, the Duke of Chastelherault, being retournit in
" our realme, will declair and mak mair manifest unto
" yow our will and intentioun."

The following is an addition by the Queen herself,
" ie vous prie en labsance do mi lord boyd que ie
" retiens pour vn temps pour mon seruise suporter et
" meintenir son fils et seruiteurs en leur actions mi
" lord heris vous informera de lestat de mes affayres
" ie vous prie aussi vser de son bon conseil comme
" celui qui scet lestast des choses issi."

Writing from Tutbery, 7th April 1569, the Queen
wonders at not having heard this long time of advertisements furth of Scotland. " Now presentlie we
" have ressauit the double of certane articlis quhilk
" the Quene our Gud sister hes send to us, delyerit
" to hir be Mr. Johne Wod, contening the headis of
" certane commowning betuix the Duke of Chestelher-
" ault and utheris in his name with the Erle of
" Murraye at Glasgow, the xiii day of Marche last wes
" quhairin thair is dyveris headis contenit nocht onlie
" prejudice to us, bot also to thair awin honour,
" dewitie, and promesses sa oft tymes maid and con-
" fermiit to us as to thair Soverane, quhilk makis us
" on na wayis to beleif bott the same ar invented be
" our robellis as dyuers utheris has bene of befoir, to
" caus us take ane ewill opinioun of our faythful sub-
" jectis, quhilk we will nocht do unto the tyme we be
" surely aduertisit, nocht doubting that ye will remane
" in lykmaner constant towart us " and let her know
' at least of his own part in all proceedings, " for (praysit
" be God) we ar in hoip of ane gud succes and ex-
" peditioun in our causes throw the gud intertenement
" and confortabill writingis that we haif ressauit fra
" the Quene our gud sister, as also be sic assured
" aduertisementis and lettres that we haif presentlie
" gottin of France, quhilk the present berar our Ser-
" vitour will mak knawin to yow, quhome ye sall
" credeit." Referring [etc.].

The Queen's next letter is dated Wingfield, 4th June
1569. " Forsamekill as in tyme by past we haif ewer
" aduertesit yow be our lettres of our proceidingis with
" the Quene of England, our gud sister, nocht as amply
" as we wold haif done be ressone of the discommoditie
" of passage hes bene betuix thir realemes, bot at the
" leist of the gud opinioun we hade of the resolutioun
" thairof, and now our traiste cousigne and counsalour
" my Lord Boyd, ane of our Commissioneris, towardis
" our said sister being returnit fra hir and hir counsale
" we haif depeschit him with thir presentis in our
" realme to declair unto yow at lenth the treuth and
" gud estait of our affaires and our mynd in all thingis,
" Quhilk becaus of his sufficiency we wold nocht wryt
" amply. Bot referring the same to him [etc.]"

The last of the Queen's letters is dated from Shefeild
6th May 1571. In it she understands that amid all the
revolts of the subjects he has borne a good mind towards her " yet partlie for feir of los of his gudis and
" partlie be the crafty persuasionis of our enymeis ye
" haif bene constranit ether to concur with oure aduer-
" sares, or ellis to ly by and abstrack your forces from
" the ayde and supporte of our Lieutenamentis," &c.
Yet she will not impute his assistance to her rebellis
in evil part, but still esteem him a dutiful subject in his
heart, and because her intent is to support him and
encourage him to profess openlie his obedience to her as
his natural Sovereign. She for that cause has given
chargo to the Bishop of Galloway to declare to him her
good mind and will, " quha as ane faithful Commissioner
" hes weil done his devoir in treating with the Quene
" our gud sister for our restitutioun and releif of yow
" our gud subjectis and seing ther is no occasioun nocht-
" withstanding this new dolay to be disparit of the
" obtening of ane finall end of our lang swtis at oure said
" gud sisteris hand we will yow in tymes to cum to
" declair yourself sic as heir efter ye wald have us your
" frend for ever." She asks him to assist her said cousin
with aid and arms, and has assigned out of her thirds as
much yearly as will make his bishoprick of Galloway
free of all pensions during his lifetime, praying that he
would make payment of as much as should be assigned
to him out of the abbeys of Glenluce and Crossragall of

the thirds thereof which would be allowed by the Queen's Collectors [etc.].

In the charter room is a cabinet, in the drawers of which is an unarranged collection of papers, among which are a good many family letters of the 17th century. Several of these are from the Duchess of Hamilton, in one of which, dated 15th September 1659, to the Earl of Cassilis, she informs him that "When my Lord went " first to the Generall [Monck] he was pleased to give " him a fortnight's tyme to advise whether he would sign " the engagement or not upon his perell that he should " come to Dalkeith at the fortnight's end. At which " tyme the Generall took such paines to perswade him " to syne that paper, which would free him from the " troble of imprisonment, but he refusing that, all the " favour he could obtain was one week more, and that " on Monday next he should render himself prisoner to " the Governor of Douglas Castle."

Letter from A. Brodie dated Edinburgh, 3 July 1650, " to the Earls of Cassilis and Lothian and remanent " Commissioners which attended the King's Majesty in " Holland," announcing that yesterday the Parliament " did ratify the Treatie and declared the King's con-" cessions satisfactory, and have this day solemnly by " proclamation admitted him to the exercise of his " Government, but that no approbation nor exoneration " to his Lordship or themselves had been taken." " Ther hath been much debat anent persons, but the " Parliament hath so obstinatlie adheard to ther own " determination that we could scarce obtain any credit " at ther hands."

Among the letters I noticed one from Charles, King of France (1570); one from the Hague in April 1650, from " Amalie P. Orange," various letters from " George " Fletcher " in 1682, which refer throughout to public events of the time. In the same collection is an extensive series of estate accounts and rentals from 1640, downwards.

Plenary Indulgence by Pope Benedict XIV. to Thomas Kennedy, a Scotch baronet, granting to him and all his kindred by blood or marriage unto the third degree inclusive, as also to 50 persons to be named by him at his pleasure, a plenary Indulgence at the point of death, provided they being then truly penitent, and having confessed and partaken of the Holy Communion,—or in so far as they may not have been able to do that—being at least contrite in spirit, and shall have invoked (if not with the mouth at least in the heart) the most holy name of Jesus. On one of the margins of the illuminated parchment on which the Indulgence is engrossed, is written " nemina personarum," with room for 50 names. These, however, are not filled in. The Indulgence is sealed and signed by " Joseph Livizzani, Secr."

JOHN STUART.

THE MANUSCRIPTS OF THE MARQUIS OF BUTE AT MOUNTSTUART.

The letters in question were not accessible at the time of my previous inspection of Lord Bute's papers.

The first series, consisting of a miscellaneous Scotch correspondence, ranges in date from 1683 to 1763, and has been arranged chronologically in a volume.

The earliest in date were addressed to Sir James Stewart, heritable Sheriff of Bute, who was created first Earl of Bute in 1703.

They begin with a letter dated 31st July 1683 from the Earl of Aberdeen, Lord Chancellor of Scotland, on the condition and temper of the Shire of Argyll and the behaviour and inclinations of the people towards His Majesty's service, approving of the Sheriff's diligence in obtaining information. Others in the same year are from the Duke of Queensberry, Earl of Perth, and Sir George McKenzie.

In one, signed " Raith," from Edinburgh, in July 1690, the writer says he is glad to hear that the Sheriff neither had nor designs to have any meddling with any people that make it their work to disturb the government and so the peace of the country.

Sir James Stewart was married in the same year 1663 to Agnes, eldest daughter of Sir George Mackenzie, of Rosehaugh. On 28th November 1692 Elizabeth Mackenzie, a younger sister of Lady Stewart, writes to her " Dear Sister," the Sheriff's wife, the first of a series of letters of a domestic nature.

On 6th March 1691 the Earl of Linlithgow writes from Linlithgow Palace a letter expressive of his great friendship for the Sheriff, and touching the state of the country he adds, " I have good grounds to believe that

5.

" we shall have no disturbance in this Island this en-" sewing season."

There are several letters from the Duke of Hamilton in 1692-3. In one of them, from London, in February, after referring to the state of political parties, he says, " But I hope in God my actions shall sho me to be a " trew hearted Scotesman, who will make it his endea-" vours to recomend himself noe otherways but by " persewing the trew interest of my cuntrie."

One from the Duke, dated Hamilton, 10th October 1700, begins, " Good honest Sherife ! I have received " your obliging letter this day, and your good friend " and mine, the Prior of Blantyre, is present at the " writting of this."

The " Prior " thus referred to was Lord Blantyre, whose ecclesiastical title was founded on the grant by King James VI. to his ancestor of the Priory of Blantyre.

Referring to the elections, the Duke says, " If you " have regard for anything that can preserve your " contrie and whats most valuable to itt, you must " now make noe further hesitation in coming in to con-" tribute to the good of itt. This will grow delay " [daily] more and more plain to you, and if you neg-" lect this opportunity, I may boldly say you neaver " can have such a one heerafter to shew yourself a " triew hearted Scotesman. Now the question will be " whither wee shall be a free people or slaves, and " dependant on others, without a power of extricating " ourselves heerafter. Theres nather time to be lost " nor any further roome for ruminating upon this " mater. It's now or never that whats valewable to " Scotland must be head or lost. When my lord Blan-" tyre sees you, I am sure he will second you."

The Duke again writes from Holyrood House on 2nd November 1700 :—" I think I should have added nothing " to what I wrott last to you from Hamilton, and " trusted to my lord Blanter to send it to you. I hope " its come safe long or now ; but I must now tell " you if you are not willing to see yourself and contrie " destroyed, I hope you'l come to prevent it, for tho' I " her there was a preliminary votte this day in relation " to my Bro. Box Election, which after two days strug-" ling came to be votted. They carried itt but by " one, when all the forces were most chapterly con-" vened, soe you see how much you have to answer for " by your absence . . . . if you dont come in now when " it may doe soe much good, both you and all thes that " follow that cours must be counted the authors of all " our futtre and present miseries, which I hope you'l " prevent in soe far as depends on you."

Lord Haddo writes from Edinburgh on 30th January 1701 to " My dear sweet and most affectional comerad," on various subjects, and among others, on the state of political parties. " I hear of noe treaty nore accomo-" dation betwixt the Dukes. There cannot as yet be " any certain account anent the parliament of England, " only it is generally believed that the Tory party will " prevail. I have been much taken up since you went " from this in the Duke of Gordon's affair, and I am " sure you'l be glad to know that my lord Argyle this " week has sisted his process for this Session of Parlia-" ment against the Duke. This I judge he has done, " because of some letters from Court in favour of the " Duke."

One from the Earl of Antrim (sent by Mr. Alexr. McDonnell) is dated Dunluce, 25th August 1701. In it he thanks the Sheriff " for the many services and kind-" nesses done him and his Bro. San., for which and " other your favours done to my name in that country. " I return you many thanks."

In a letter from the Duke of Hamilton, dated Holy-rood House, 9th September 1702, his Grace writes :— " My good freind Sherife ! Since I had soe good ano " occasion as by this present Bearer, I would not omitt " telling you that sometyme agoe I had a letter from " Lord Blantyre acquainting me that her Majesty was " desirous that the Marquise of Tweddall, E. of Tulli-" bardin, and I should come and wait upon her, and " yesterday I receaved ane other lettor from the High " Treasurer of England consorning what my Lord " Blantyre had written by her Majestys Command : " noe now we are preparing ourselves to goe to court, " and we intend to be there against the time her M. " returns from the Bath. The Treasurer tells me her " M. Royal inclinations are to take such measures as " shall be most proper and advisable to preserve her " ancient Kingdom in peace, and to compose all the " divisions and animosities of her subjects there, so it " would appear that at present ther are healing mea-" sures in view.

4 I

" I write this also to tell you, my dear friend, that I
" hope you'l not oppose my good honest Robin, for he
" thinks himself sure you are not avers to him, and I
" am convinced it is soe."

Lord Haddo, writing from Kelly, 14th August 1702,
refers to political news, the accounts of the Duke of
Queensberry's illness and of his recovery,—of his arrival
and good reception at Court, and the Queen's approbation of his behaviour as to the Abjuration.

The Earl of Mar writes from London on 17th November 1705 with offers of service. On 6th May 1708
his Lordship again writes that he has represented to
the Queen the good service of the Sheriff, and announces her order for the liberation of the Sheriff's
brother and Lord Balmerino.

Various letters from the Earl of Glasgow in 1711 are
on family affairs, as are others from the Earl of Montrose and Campbell of Ardkinglas in 1712.

On 5th July 1715 Lord Belhaven writes that he has
delayed to answer the Sheriff's letters, on account of
the pain which it cost him to send the disagreeable
news of " our worthy and good friend being dismissed
" from all the employments he had from the King, and
" which is most crewell of all was forced from the
" Prince his master extremely contrary to his inclina-
" tion ; nor could the view of the most horrible conse-
" quences that might have followed upon the Princes
" refusal to parte with him, have obliged him to agree
" to it, had it not been at the Dukes own and repeated
" and earnest desire, he having offered three times to
" resign it upon his knee before the Prince could be
" persuaded to accept of it. The afflicted condition of
" the best of princes and kindest of masters would
" have without doubt given you the utmost pain, as it
" did to every body that had the happiness of knowing
" him, but, dr. Bute, we have this comfort still, that
" millions regret his misfortune, and non dare hold up
" their face and own they had a hand in it, and where
" he had one friend before I doe assure you he has
" now ten . . . . The crime laid to his charge is that
" he dissuaded the Prince from accepting the Regency
" in the terms the King proposed, which is very false."

Then follow notices of the new appointments.

There are letters from William Stewart, Provost of
Edinburgh in 1716 ; Colonel Erskine, Edinburgh, 1716 ;
Earl of Buchan, Edinburgh, 1717 ; Viscount Garnock,
1717 ; and John Bishop of Edinburgh, from Greenhall,
1722.

There is a series of letters from John Duke of Argyll
and his brother, the Earl of Islay, commencing in 1712.

On 9th August 1714 Lord Islay writes from Duding-
ston :—" I had the pleasure to receive your letter yes-
" terday. It has been the greatest satisfaction to me
" these two years, while my enemies have prevailed,
" to find him most my friend whom I most wished to
" be so. I had sent you word of the Queens illness
" when first I heard of it, but that not knowing then
" what might happen, it was my opinion that your
" Lordship should be quiet at home, and not ruin your
" familie for uncertainties. My Brother and I indeed
" were in a different case, for condemned persons run
" no risque in making their escape, whatever the
" danger may be in attempting it to one capable of a
" pardon ; but fate has now otherwise determined
" affairs, and I hope we shall soon have it in our power
" to do our duty in justice both to our friends and
" enemies. I go for London this day, to endeavour to
" be there when the King comes . . . . There is all
" the appearance in the world that there will not be
" any disturbance either here or in England."

On 22nd September Lord Islay writes from the same
place :—" I am at last arrived in order to be a spec-
" tator of our famous election. . . . Our Brethren are
" so strongly corrupted, that having disserved them
" and the Country is now the only title to their favour."

Lord Islay writes many letters subscribed " Your
" Slave," full of familiar banter, but with many references to politics.

On 1st January 1716 the Duke of Argyll (to whose
sister Lord Bute was married) writes, and refers to an
attempt of the Earl of Sunderland, " who seems at
" present to have more power than I'm afraid is con-
" sistent with the welfare of the King and Country,
" designs to try if he can hurt me by calling me to
" account in Parliament. My cause I know to be good,
" but that does not prevent its being necessary to have
" my friends present, so I must beg, my dear Lord,
" that you will not fail to be here by the meeting of
" the Parliament."

Lord Islay writes from London on 19th October :—
" I can give you in two words a notion of the many

" various reports that are always a going about my
" Brother and me. We happen to have got pretty
" forward in the world for our ages, and that joyned
" with some foundation of interest at home makes us
" always observe the posture of affairs so as to endea-
" vour to withstand the open attempts of our enemies,
" and to avoid the little artifices of many who pretend
" to be our friends. For this end we always judge for
" ourselves without any prejudice of any side farther
" than honour and interest joined oblige us. This
" makes a man who would willingly lead us blindly
" into all his measures, say we are never to be pleased,
" intractable, &c. Another whose interest it is to have
" plunged in the extremity of his party (and conse-
" quently their slaves) say we are not steady to our
" party, that he does not know where to have us, &c.
" All little under favorites, fearing their trade would
" cease by persons of distinction or interest having the
" reins entirely in their hands, continually insinuate
" that we are dangerous, if we have too much power,—
" that its better to make creatures, and give them
" credit, interest, and power, than support those who
" by having interest of their own are more independent,
" &c. Thus Politics is a continual petty war and
" gamb, and as at all other games, we will sometimes
" win and sometimes loose, and he that plays best and
" has the best stock has the best chance. In the main
" I think we have been pretty lucky, considering the
" constant attempt of many sorts of people to oppress
" us. I assure you, my dear Lord, if we happen to
" succeed it shall be of service to you ; if otherwise,
" we shall take care in time that it shall be so too."

Lord Islay again writes from London, Saturday,
17 J : . . . . :—" Pray keep our folks from talking of
" my brother and me by way of commending us in
" tender points and to strangers who make very ill uses
" of such discoveries. It is enough that we can main-
" tain an interest with some of both sides without
" giving up anything we must and ought to maintain,
" and if I can save myself or my friends by being
" thought a Mahometan by a Turk, I'l never decline
" it.—Your Slave."

On 4th April 1722 the Duke of Argyll writes from
London :—" I send you enclosed the letter I received
" from Lord Sunderland yesterday morning, and today
" the King commanded me to acquaint you with the
" contents of it. I have a reason why I would not have
" as yet known who you are to succeed, but only that
" you are in the Bedchamber. There is one thing good
" in this, that the payment is very exact, which can be
" said of few offices at present."

On 27th March [no year] the Duchess of Argyll
writes to Lady Bute :—" I hope this will find dear Lady
" Bute perfectly recovered. I cant condole with you
" that this child was not a son. You having 2 fine
" ones already have reason to be satisfyed, and he that
" has had the small pox may be reckoned as good as 2 ;
" so mortal as that distemper has been this year in town
" never was known." Others from her Grace are dated
in 1712 and 1714.

On 29th November 1715 Sir John Shaw writes from
Greenock :—" My Lord Duke is very well and my Lord
" Islay in a fair way of recovery. I saw his wounds
" dressed on Saturday, which look't so well that I hope
" in a little time he will be able to sign the just sen-
" tence against those who desired to have broke the
" arm of justice, tho' I am convinced the dog that gave
" the wound fell upon the spot. I have now nothing
" new to tell you, but only that upon Saturday last one
" of Marr's Lieutenants deserted, and came in to his
" Grace, who gives one account that they are busie on-
" trenching themselves in Perth, and there's mighty
" divisions among them, so that I am hopeful if Marr
" does not hang himself the poor people that he has so
" much imposed upon will take care of him."

Col. Middleton writes from Stirling on 19th November 1715 :—" Sunday last we engaged the rebells after
" having laid on our arms all night a little beyond
" Dumblain. They advanced in vast numbers and
" much better order than anybody expected, and attackt
" us. They pressed our left wing so hard that they
" gave way in great confusion, and thinking that wee
" on the right had undergon the same fate, runn all
" straight to Stirlin with the loss of about 300 men
" and some officers killed and wounded and taken
" prisoners. Coll. Lamam and Capt. Chicely prisoners.
" Capt. Arnul and six or seven other officers killed.
" L⁴ Forfar mortally wounded, the joint of his knee
" shot of so that its a miracle if he recovers. My Lord
" Duke and his Brother were with us on the right, con-
" sisting of Portmores, Evans, and Stairs dragoons,

" Forfar, Wightman, Montague, and some regiments
" of foot, whose fate happened to be much better for
" ourselves and for his Majesties service. Wee defeated
" them entirely and pursued them about 2 miles ; took
" 14 colours and standards, 4 pieces of cannon, and
" a great deal of their ammunition and baggage.
" Among their killed are Strathmore, Auchterhouse,
" Captain of Clanronald, Fraserdale, and many others.
" Panmure mortally wounded ; Marshal slightly
" wounded, but escaped ; Barrowfield, Logy, Achter-
" tyre, Monboddo, and many other gentlemen prisoners.
" Lord Islay is wounded in his arm and his side, but
" very hearty, and in a mighty good way, and I hope
" out of all danger ; the Duke perfectly well. We
" reckon we have lost nearly 400 men and about 18 [?]
" officers ; have killed, wounded, and taken of the
" rebels above 1200."
Lord Islay, writing on 26th November 1715 from
Stirling, says :—" As for our men, tho' we cannot yet
" dismiss, yet I hope in two or three days we shall be
" at some certainty and that we may dismiss them all
" as we hear the Rebells have done theirs except the
" clans whom they keep in garrison at Perth."
Ad. Campbell, from Fanab, Glenfalloch, on 14th
November 1715, writes :—" I came here last night from
" Strathfillan. I came to the end of Loch Dochart earlie
" in a morning, and the shouldiers being cold made great
" fires on the first loun we came to. This made them
" towards Lochtay believe that all above them was
" burnt. There were fyrie crosses sent everie where,
" and the E. B., who was at Drummond at that time
" with the E. Mar and the chief men of that partie, was
" in a werie great confusion. I am told there's a de-
" tachment of 2,000 men ordered against us. We must
" be much on our guard, being within a nights march
" of them."
Three days later the same writer says :—" There's
" one returned last night whom I sent to the E. Mars
" armie for intelligence, who hapned to be there at the
" time of the battle. He tells that the McDonalds,
" McLeans, and what men the E. Breadalbine had there
" were on the right of Mars armie, and that the battle
" was begun by them ; that their opposite fled at the
" first fire towards Stirling, and that they made some
" slaughter in the pursuit. He sayes that much about
" ye time the rest of the E. Mars armie fled at the first
" fire and fled towards the water of Alan wher ther
" were a great many killed and drowned. Among
" them who ran away were Locheil, Apin, Huntly, Sea-
" forth, the Athol men, and a great many more. He
" says E. Mar fled among the first . . . . The most of
" the comon souldiers are fled home. He says he mett
" Appin and Locheil returning with a few men to
" Ardoch, where the rest were. He did see the Captain
" of Clanranald dead who was killed at the first fire."
Lord Islay writes from Invarary on 9th October 1715 :—
" I can very easily imagine, from the variety of diffi-
" culties I meet with here, that you cannot possibly
" have things ready as you would desire. These High-
" landers are a most unaccountable pack of—— I dont
" know what to call them . . . . I hardly believe the
" Clans will spend their time so ill as to molest us here
" while to be sure L⁴ Mar presses them hard to joyn
" him. I have had no news from the Christian part
" of the Country fresher than what I had at Stirling.
" We had a letter yesterday from the Highlander I
" have been tampering with this long time, and he
" assures us he will joyn my Brother with his fellow
" cherubims this week. I do really incline to believe
" he will. I am thinking your people will be as good,
" if not better, than any for the Sea Expedition, being
" both Seamen and having no relations among the Bar-
" barians in these parts. I would not have you by any
" means hurry yourself in coming here before you have
" settled all you have to do."
From Stirling Lord Islay writes on 31st December
1715. Enclosing a proxy for signature he adds :—" It
" seems they have something to do at the beginning of
" the Parliament, for my Lord Townshend wrote to me
" very pressingly about proxies. He tells me that the
" King approves of my opinion in relation to the Clans,
" so that I hope they'l be pretty well handled. The
" Rebels have all declared for some days that the
" Pretender is landed, and is to be at Perth tonight.
" My Lord Mar and some others went as it were to
" meet him from Perth some days ago, so that we take
" it for granted that either the one is come into Scot-
" land or the other is gone out."
In a letter from Lord Glasgow, 1st Oct. [no year], he
says :—" To be free with you I mightily want one
" hour's conference with you anent this affair of the

" Union which I make no accompt of ; for you know
" the last appearance I made against that damned Ab-
" juration, though the Union served for an argument
" above board, that was not the impulse or reason
" in my heart why I opposed so much the Abju-
" ration, and now, though England should grant never
" so fair Articles and terms of Union, I am fully deter-
" mined through God's strength never to make nor
" medle directly or indirectly with their German Royal
" family."
A long letter, apparently from Lord Breadalbane, but
without date or place (except April 28), is mainly occupied with the Elections. He begins by complaining of
his feeble health. " I am as to public affaires of the
" same opinion as when we parted, it having been in
" the politicks an old fault in me, and a very great
" one, not to be changeable as to my opinion." He
wishes to be advised if such of the nobility as are suspected (though not accused) for treason or treasonable
practices will be sustained, altho' set at liberty before
the time of Election ; " whereof I doubt (supposing that
" to be one of the designs for securing them), unless
" they be vindicat of that suspicion before they vote,
" and next, if they be not set at liberty, the question is,
" if the proxies of these prisoners be valid, altho'
" qualified according to law. These points I would be
" cleared in, and I wish to have a draught of the proxy
" and the diet of Election when and where. . . . .
" Be pleased to let me know by what manner I am to
" serve the Earle of Weems and the Earle of Northesk,
" otherwise than by my own vot, for I judge them to
" be very worthie persons and good country men. I
" wish to know who were my friends in Council, and
" how our young Lord Ila behaved. As for me and
" neighbour Duke Atholl, who continues very ill, what
" is past in Council is no secret. Cause write it be way
" of journall. I have ordered my agent Colin Kirk to
" receive your commands by word or write. I am not
" sure if your brother be prisoner or to be sent to Lon-
" don as it is reported, or what is his crymes." The
following sentences are written in a feeble hand, different
from that used in the previous part of the letter :—" I
" askt my old friend if the wealth he so confidently
" asserted should heap upon us be still in his head,
" to which he gave but a doubtful answer, but said,
" altho' that should not hold, yet we should have
" better, which is an Amen Government, and that I
" should not be put in the Castle of Edinburgh without
" a known cause. I pray you ask him which is the
" easiest, that or the Tower. I am not in the least sur-
" prized with what has or will befall us. My d. Lord,
" adieu."
A series of original letters addressed by Lady Mary
Wortley Montagu to her sister the Countess of Mar,
arranged in a volume. They are 42 in number, and a
pencil marking informs us that of these 28 have been
printed, but in several cases with passages omitted and
expressions altered. This remark would seem to refer
to the earlier editions of Lady Mary's letters, as in that
of 1861 by Mr. Thomas there appear nine of the remaining 14 of the present collection said to remain unprinted, viz., Nos. 7, 13, 14, 15, 36, 38, 39, 47, and 50 of
the letters to Lady Mar, printed in his first volume.
They have been printed, however, from copies and not
from the original letters.
In the first of the unprinted letters Lady Mary writes :
—" I am heartily sorry (Dear Sister), without any affec-
" tation for any uneasyness that you suffer, let the cause
" be what it will, and wish it was in my power to give
" you some more essential mark of than unavailing
" pity, but I am not so fortunate, and till a fit occasion
" of disposing of some superfluous diamonds, I shall
" remain in this sinfull seacole Town, and all that re-
" mains for me to do is to shew my willingness (at least)
" to divert you, is to send you faithful accounts of what
" passes among your acquaintance in this part of the
" world . . . . For my own part I have some cot-
" teries where art and pleasure reign, and I should not
" fail to amuse myself tolerably enough, but for the
" damn'd quality of growing older and older every day,
" and my present joys are made imperfect by fears of
" the future."
One of which the first page is noted as having been
printed p. 167, but of which other seven pages remain
unprinted, thus concludes :—" The Duchess of Kingston
" grunts on as usual, and I fear will put us in black
" Bombazine soon, which is a real greif to me. My
" dear Aunt Cheyne makes all the money she can of
" Lady Francesee, and I fear will carry on those politics
" to the last point, though the girl is such a fool, 'tis
" no great matter. I am going within this half hour

" to call her to Court. The most diverting story about
" Town at present is in relation to Edgecombe [and
" Miss Tichbourne], though your not knowing the
" people concerned as well as I do, will, I fear, hinder
" you from being so much entertained by it."

In one dated "Rome, Feb. 14, N.S.," Lady Mary
says :—" The letter you sent to Venice never came to
" my hands, and this which I received yesterday is
" the first I have had from you. I am now in a place
" where I hear you spoke of with a great deal of regard
" and remembered with a real esteem."

In another, "Mr. Baily is dismissed the Treasury
" and consoled with a pension of equal value ;" and
after referring to her acquaintance and Rodrique,
says that the best thing would be a general Act for
divorcing all the people of England.

At the end is a letter from the Earl of Bute to Lady
Mary, dated Mountstuart, Dec. 31, 1740. announcing
that Lady Bute had been delivered of a son on the previous night.

A letter to Lady Mar, apparently from Lady Gower,
states that the Duchess Dowager of Kingston wished to
get the guardianship of her grandson, but the Duke at
14 had confirmed those appointed by his grandfather's
will.

JOHN STUART.

THE MANUSCRIPTS OF LORD KINNAIRD AT ROSSIE PRIORY.

The collection here comprises large masses of charters
relating to the lands of Kinnaird, in the Carse of
Gowrie, a barony from which the family represented by
Lord Kinnaird drew their name, as also to the lands of
Inchture and others which subsequently became vested
in the family by marriage. There are likewise various
charters relating to the barony of Cowbin in the shire
of Murray, which, as well as Skelbol in that of Sutherland, were acquired by the marriage of Thomas of
Kinnaird with Egidia heiress of Walter Murray of
Cowbin in the early part of the fifteenth century, and
belonged to the family of Kinnaird for a time after that
event.

The three earliest charters of the series were delivered
up to Sir Patrick Thriepland on his purchase of the
barony of Kinnaird many years ago, as appears from a
memorandum among the papers. By the first of these
charters King William the Lion conferred on *Radulphus
dictus Rufus* the barony of Kinnaird. The second was
granted by Richard son of Radulphus to Isabel his
sister ; and the third was a deed confirming the last,
granted by Radulphus de Kinnaird to Richard son of
Isabel.

Radulphus de Kynard, said to have been the grandson
of the last-named Radulphus, swore fealty to King
Edward I. at Kincardine in the Mearns on 4th August
1296.

The oldest charter now remaining in the collection is
one by Raigenaldus de Kynnard, *dominus particularis*
de Inchtur, by which he confirmed to his cousin Andrew
de Muncur of that ilk, the lands of Muncur in the shire
of Perth, as held by the said Andrew and his predecessors " pront per veredicum proborum et discretorum
" patrie sum veraciter informatus." The lands were
held blench, with the singular reddendo by the vassal
of a chaplet of roses yearly to be presented at the Law
of Inchtur, on the feast of St. Margaret Queen, " cum
" oris osculo utriusque nostrorum in signum pacis et
" concordis," with a pair of white gloves. The charter
is without date, but, besides the granter's seal, is authenticated with the seals of Patrick Gray Lord of Brox-
mouth, Andrew Gray Lord of Fowlis, and Andrew
Gray " ejus filius naturalis femoris "—men who flourished
in the end of the fourteenth and early part of the
subsequent century.

The next in date is a Procuratory by Alan of Kynarde
of that ilk to his son and heir apparent Thomas of
Kynnarde, for giving seisin to John Abbot of Scone, of
certain lands in the barony of Kynnarde, dated at
Scone, 28th April 1478 : the witnesses being Silvester
Rettre of that ilk ; William Hay of Lynplum, Knight ;
Edmund Hay ; Mr. Henry Cramby, Vicar of Kyns-
pindy ; Sir James Flemyng, Vicar of Collace ; David
Brioss of Petdenys ; Mr. Walter Small ; William Peblis ;
Thomas Grinlaw ; John Cramby ; and Sir John of
Kynninmonth, Chaplain, and others.

Charter dated 10th May 1476, under the Great Seal
of King James III., confirming a charter by Alan de
Kynard of Cowbin, with consent of Egidia de Moravia

his mother, and his other relatives and friends, to his
brother-german Thomas of Kynnard, and his heirs male,
of the lands of Cowbin, Dalpotty, Esterbin, Myreton,
and Aikenheade, in the shire of Forres, of date 1st
September 1465, and witnessed by John Scrimgeour,
Constable of Dundee ; James Matelande of Quenysbery ;
William Kynnard of Kynninmonde ; John Scrimgeour,
son of the late Nicholas Scrimgeour, burgess of Dundee ;
and others.

Reversion by James Ogilvy of Inchmertyn to Thomas
Kinnaird of Skelbo, relative to a right of annual rent
out of the lands of Kynnard, granted by Alan Kynard
of that ilk, father of the said Thomas, to David Ogilvy
of Inchmertyn, on payment of 120 merks on the high
altar of the Parish Kirk of Perth. Dated at Inchmertyn,
6th January 1506.

Indenture dated at Kynard, 4th March 1511, between
Thomas Kynard of Skelbo and Andrew Kynard of that
ilk, touching the gift of the marriage of the late Thomas
Spalding, burgess of Dundee,

Letters of Manrent by Rore Murray of Spangdale to
Thomas Kynnard of that ilk. Murray to be his man
and servant, and to ride and gang with him all the days
of his life, excepting his allegiance to the King and the
Bishop of Caithness, " becaus at the said Thomas has
" given me a competent fe tharfor in liferent for all the
" days of my life, to do to him my best service I kan
" within the boundis of Sutherland, and farther within
" the sheriffdom of Inverness upon the said Thomas
" expensis, unless I have a lawful excuse." Dated at
Dornoch, 10th June 1512. Witnesses, John of Kynnard ; Alexander Urquhart ; Walter Kynnard of Culbin ;
David Mudy, burgess of Dornoch ; and John Murray.

Of miscellaneous charters, I noted the following as
of historical interest.—Charter by Alexander Erwyne,
Lord of the Forest of Drum, to John Bel, for his good
service, of various oxengates of land in the barony of
Inchture. Dated at Aberdeen, 18th November 1416.
Witnesses, Alexander de Seton, Lord of Gordon ; Sir
Walter Lyndesay, Sir Alexander of Forbes, Knights ;
William of Chalmers ; and William Cryne, with many
others.

Charter by Walter Haliburton of that ilk and Bal-
ligirnach, to Andrew de Muncur, lord of that ilk, of
the lands called Threplande and Mireflat of Muncurr,
held blench on payment of a mark at the Castle thereof
at the feast of Pentecost yearly if asked, Dated at Balli-
girnach, on the feast of St. John Baptist, 1422. Witnesses, Andrew Gray of Fowlis ; Sir Walter of Bikerton ;
David de Ogilbi, and others.

Charter by Dungallus Makdowal, lord of the fourth
part of the lands of Yhester, to his consanguineus
Eustace Maxwell, lord of the third part of Strachardill,
of his fourth part of the barony of Telyn in the shire
of Forfar, and his fourth part of the barony of Pulgawy
in the earldom of Gowry, in excambion for his fourth
part of the barony of Yhester, and the fourth part of
the baronies of Dunkemlaw and Moram, and lands of
Giffardgate within the constabulary of Hadynton and
sheriffdom of Lothian, along with the fourth part of a
pound of cumin payable yearly out of a croft near the
town of Forfar by John de Grabat and his heirs to the
said Eustace. Dated at Dundee, 15th August 1427.
Witnesses, John de Strathawan, Vicar of the Collegiate
Church of Bothanis, and Thomas Melligane, priests ; Mr.
John Idill, notary public ; Robert de Ledhous, burgess
of Dundee ; and Henry de Strathawane, with others.

Charter of Confirmation of the preceding charter
under the Great Seal of James II. 1441.

Instrument dated 23rd November 1448, narrating the
settlement by Andrew Lord Gray and Sir Andrew
Ogilvy of Inchmartine, Knights, as arbiters in a dispute
between John Buttergask, son and heir-apparent of
Richard Buttergask of that ilk, and Thomas Bell, farmer,
relating to a Templeland belonging to the Hospital of
St. Germains, lying in Inchture. The land is to remain
with Thomas, who is to pay 20 merks to John upon the
altar of St. Katherine Virgin, in the Parish Church of
Inchture. Witnesses, Gilbert Monorgund of that ilk ;
Thomas Fife, Chaplain ; Robert Kynnard, Esquire ; and
others.

Charter by Sir Walter Stewart, Knight, of Strathowyn,
to Margaret Strilynge his spouse, for her many good
services, and for her life, the lands of Pitkass Morynche
Thomebetht, Auchdregeno, and others in the lordship
of Strathowyn and shire of Banff, rendering service at
head courts at Drummyn when required. Dated at
Drummyn, 4th Dec. 1479.

Notarial Instrument dated 9th June 1483, at the
instance of David Ogilvy of Inchmertyne, setting forth
his readiness to perform to John Muncreff of that ilk,

then being present, all the obligations undertaken by him touching the marriage to be contracted between John Muncreff, son and heir of the said John, and Egidia, daughter of the said David, and in special to deliver to the said John, on the feast of the Nativity of John Baptist ensuing, the sum of 100*l*. Scots; and if he had hitherto been negligent in the performance to the said John of Muncreff of what was right under the said contract, he was now to be bound to the performance thereof to the satisfaction of James of Muncreff, uncle of the said John Muncreff of that ilk, and Robert Donyng, burgess of Perth. Done within the parish church of the burgh of Perth, at the altar of St. Monan, in presence of Laurence Lord Oliphant; Alexander Blayr of Balthiok, and James Oliphant of Arquholze; Andrew Charteris of Cuthilgurdy; Mr. Alexander Murray, Canon of the Collegiate Church of Abernethy; Thomas Blayr, son and apparent heir of the late Alexander Blayr; David Lyndissay of Lekowy; John Oliphant of Dron; Mr. James Fentoune, Rector of the Parish Church of Dupleyne; and William of Abbircrommy, with many others.

Charter by William Bishop of Aberdeen, Chancellor of the University of Aberdeen, and Conservator and Preceptor of the House of St. Germans, to Walter Bell and Elizabeth Small his wife, of certain Templelands in Inchtur, reserving the liferent of Ranald Bell, father of the said Walter, to be held of the Bishop as Preceptor foresaid. Dated at Edinburgh, 10th June 1506. Witnesses, Sir John Elphynstoun of that ilk, Knight; John Kynnarde of Inchstur; David Monorgund of that ilk; John Charteris, son and heir-apparent of Thomas Charteris of Kynfawnis, Andrew Elphinstoun of Selmys; and Alexander of Waristoun, with others.

Instrument of possession to Agnes Bell, as heir of Walter Bell, in Inchtare, in three Templelands of Inchtare, on a precept by William Bishop of Aberdeen, Chancellor of the University thereof, and Master of the Hospital of St. Germans in Lothian. Dated 4th August 1510.

Charter by Gilbert Monorgund to Andrew Moncur of that ilk, of the lands of Adeland rede land and the 9 riggis, 11 riggis, 14 riggis, and thrislehome lying in the barony of Langforgund. Dated at Perth, 16th September 1519. Witnesses, Mr. Robert Monorgund, Rector of Banchry; John Mason; Michael Anderson, burgess of Dundee; William Fife; and Robert Seres, junior, notary public.

Among the miscellaneous papers are the following:—

Commission by the noblemen, gentlemen, and heritors of Perthshire, appointing George Kinnaird of Rossie, and Mr. John Nairne of Mukersie, to meet General Monck at Edinburgh, to treat about the affairs of the county. Dated 10th October 1659.

The "dowbell" of a Letter, dated Perth, October 26th 1659, addressed to General Monck by a correspondent, whose signature has been torn off), on the position of public affairs—and especially of affairs in the county of Perth—enclosing a paper of 15 queries or suggestions for the General's consideration, as to the best methods of securing the peace and welfare of the country. The tenor of these may be gathered from a few of them:—

1. If your Lordship march away and give up all the garrisons to the owners of them: that caire may be taken that they be not byssed be the gentleman that ye know of, for ther is some that hes relations to him.

2. That your Lordship may send to gett intelligence what he is presentlie doeing in respect that we have some suspect and surmises that he is making preparation for some mischief to us, and your Lordship's interest, and some of his militarie freinds in our shyre hes been with him this fortnight.

3. Iff he should ryse he and all his people being armed and we nott; what is best and sall be the best to prevent this?

4. Iff he should ryse, that ane fitt persone may be thought upon by your Lordship to command us, and that there may be soe many Inglish officers and Scots noblemen and gentlemen benorth Tay thought upon by your Lordship that ye may trust too, for to regulat affairs in your absence, and to be readie upon ane call either to oppose him or to assist your Lordship as may fall out.

6. In all thir former respects that your Lordship may not leave this countrie desolat and comfortless, having all ther hopes upon your Lordship, and the justnes of your intentions and straightnes of your wayis, but to take in all faithfull and honest men, who will spend to the last drop of their blood with you for the freedome of the people, you being their stock and hopes, whairupon they rely should be overthrowen, then all their

freinds and weill wishers are ruined and destroyed without being in ane capacitie to helpe themselves.

Commission (to which are attached the signatures of many of the nobility in Perthshire) to Sir George Kinnaird, as commissioner for the county, to repair to General Monck at Berwick and treat with him on matters concerning it. Dated 3rd December 1659.

Letter from the Countess of Strathmore to the Laird of Balthayock, without date, but apparently about 1594. It is in the following terms:—

Trayst freynde. Efter my hartlie commendatiounis, this salbe to aduertis yow that his Majestie is cum to Sanct Johnstoun and is of mynde to pas to the North apone the rebellis. Thairfoir I pray yow to be heir the morne be awcht houris with your freindis and seruandis bodin to pass with his Majestie, as ye wod the weill of my husband, the caus of quhais dyat at your cuming ye salbe aduortisit. Remitting the rest thairto I commit yow to God. Off Glamis this Setterday, Be

Your gud freinde,
Euphame Douglas.

To the richt Hon^bl. the Laird
off Balthayok.

JOHN STUART.

THE MANUSCRIPTS OF LORD WHARNCLIFFE.

The papers belonging to Lord Wharncliffe, in the hands of his agent at Dundee are of greater value and more general interest than the portion of them in the Charter room at Belmont already reported on. They consist for the most part of charters and other documents relating to portions of his Lordship's lands, but in the light which they threw on several families of note at an early time, and their illustrations of ancient modes of tenure, they have an interest not often possessed by formal deeds of investiture.

One series of these relates to the lands of Cupermaculty in Perthshire, lying within the Regality of the Abbot of Dunfermline, which, as we find from the register of the Abbey, were granted to the church of Dunfermline, along with the church of the Holy Trinity of Dunkeld, by Adam, Bishop of Caithness, and Malcolm the Fodrth, King of the Scots, in perpetual alms for the weal of the soul of David King of Scotland.

A document in the same register shows that a claim having been made on the part of the Crown for a certain sum from the Abbot on account of his neglect to give suit for the lands of Cupermacultin, Fordoni, and others, in the court of the Sheriff of Perth, an inquest was held before Alexander Cumyn, Earl of Buchan, Justiciary of Scotland, through various baronies, whether suit was owing from the said lands or not, and after careful enquiry, Sir Gilbert of Hay, Knight, who had been present at the inquest thereafter, in "pleno Colloquio domini regis," at Holyrood, on the 14th of January 1255, pronounced the verdict of the baronies to be that they had seen the men of the lands come to the said court, but never as suitors: whereupon the King "in pleno colloquio predicto per commune" "consilium magnatum suorum ibidem existencium," altogether freed the Abbot from suit for the said lands in time coming.

The lands in the year 1282 were confirmed by the Abbot of Dunfermline to Malcolm de Ferenderach, in suchwise as they had been previously possessed by John de Ferenderach, and from this family they passed into the possession of Sir James Fraser, of Ferenderach. In his time the charters in Lord Wharncliffe's collection begin, the first being a charter by John, Abbot of Dunfermlyn to Sir Richard Comyn, Knight, of the lands of Cupermaculty, with an annual rent of 5 merks of Sterlings, out of the lands of Fordwy, which lands and annual rent belonged to Sir James Fraser, Knight, and were resigned by him in the Monastery of Dunfermlyn, on the 2nd day of November 1394, in presence of Unfredus Conynghame, Knight, and of Sir William Rede and Alan de Lyn, monks thereof, as well as of William de Lyndesay, Richard Comyn, and Richard Ayson, Esquires. Dated at the Monastery of Dunfermlyn on said day, in presence of Walter Bishop of St. Andrew's, Master Duncan Petyt, Archdeacon of Glasgow, Chancellor of Scotland, Master John of Caron, Rector of the Church of Rathon, and noblemen Sir Walter Olyfaunt and Sir John of Ramesay, of Kernoc, Knights. The charter contains the following clause:— "Sciatis autem dictus Ricardus et heredes sui habebit " et habebunt forisfactam vaccam vacce et ovis de " hominibus suis legiis infra dictis terris de Cuper-

"maculty et de Forduy manentibus, et nos autem "habemus forisfacta vaccam et ovem excedencia."

Charter by John, Abbot of Dunfermlyn, narrating the resignation by Sir Richard Cumyn, Knight, made at Dunfermline on the 20th of February 1403, in presence of Laurence, Abbot of Inchcolm, Sir Thomas Mungale, Prior of Dunfermlyn, Sir William Reston, Sacrist of Dunfermlyn, and Richard de Mungale, monks, Mr. Andrew de Trebrain, Elemosinar General of our Lord the King, and of his having consequently granted to the said Sir Richard Cumyn, Knight, the said lands of Cupermaculty and annual rent of 5 merks out of Fordewy in liferent, and after his death to David Cumyne, his son natural, and Cristian, daughter of Malice Dawson, his wife, and the survivor of them and their heirs male, lawfully begotten; whom failing, to John Cumyne, son natural of the said Sir Richard, and the heirs male of his body, lawfully begotten; whom failing, to return to the said monastery, in pure and perpetual alms, for the weal of Sir Richard's own soul, and the souls of his predecessors. Dated · at Dunfermlyn, 20 February 1403; witnesses, Laurence, Abbot of Inchcolm, Sir Archibald Stewart, Knight, Mr. Andrew of Trebrown, Elemosinar General of our Lord the King, Sir Walter Bell, Rector of the Church of Kyngorn, Malice Dawson Andrew Endswane, William Dolar, Esquires, Thomas Twyn, Notary Public, and others.

The lands continued in the possession of the Cumings down to the beginning of the seventeenth century. On 3rd April 1601 they were resigned by John Cuming into the hands of Queen Anne as Superior. This took place in the Queen's Chamber at Holyrood, in presence of Mr. John Elphinstone and Mr. John Kennedie, apparent of Baltersave, the King's servants, John Ker and Thomas Rutherford, servants of Lord Roxburgh, with others. The charter which followed thereon is dated at Dalkeith, 10th May 1601, and is signed by the King and Queen, being sealed with the Queen's Seal.

On 13th June 1606, John Cuming of Cowtie, and John Cuming, son and heir of the late Archibald Cuming, brother-german of the said John, conveyed the lands to James Halyburton, of Petcur, and Margaret Serymgeour, his spouse. The charter is dated at Cupar in Argus, before witnesses, Patrick Butter, of Gormok, Mr. Alexander Wedderburn, of Kingany, Alexander Ramsay, Burgess of Dundee, and John Blair, Apparent of Balgillo.

Another series of early charters relate to the lands of Newtyle, Kilpurny, Balcraig, and others.

The first is a charter by Robert, King of Scots, to William Olifaunt, Knight, of the lands of Newtyle and Kynprony, in the shire of Forfar, to be held in free barony with all the liege and native men of the said lands, performing the fourth part of a knight's service in the King's army. Dated at Newbotyll, 21st Decr. 1317.

A notarial copy of this charter made at the instance of Sir John Olyfaunt, Knight, Lord of Aberdalgy, on 2nd October 1438, in the house of the Carmelite Brethren, of Tulylum, near Perth, in presence of Brother Laurence Pentland, Prior thereof, John Were, Brother of said house, Sir David Anderson, Chaplain, and Andrew Murray, Esquire.

Charter by David II., King of Scots, narrating that Walter Olyfant, having resigned the lands of Newtyle and Kynprony, "in pleno consilio nostro," at Perth, on 20th January 1364, the King, therefore, now confirmed them to the said Walter and Elizabeth, his spouse, the King's sister, rendering for the said lands a pair of silver spurs on the feast of All Saints at Halton of Newtyle yearly, in name of Blench Farm, with three suits at the King's Court at Forfar. Dated at Edinburgh, 28th February 1364.

A similar charter by the King of same date confirming to the said Walter and his said spouse the lands of Ochtertyre and Balcraig, on the resignation of the said Walter, the reddendo being three broad arrows on the feast of St. Martin yearly, at Ochtertyre in name of Blench Farm, with three suits at the King's Courts at Forfar.

Cognition at the Myre of Newtyll betwixt the lands of Newtyle and Ochtertyre, belonging to John Lord Oliphant, and the lands of Migill, belonging to John, Earl of Crawford, before Andrew Lord Gray, Sheriff of Forfar. Dated 24th September 1508.

Charter by Robert King of Scots, on the resignation by Niel, of Carrick, in the King's hands of the lands of Uchtertyre which had belonged to John Comyn, granting them to Sir William Oliphant, Knight, for the service of thee archers in the King's army, and Scottish service used and wont. Dated at Scone, 20th March 1326. (20th year.)

Testimonial of David Guthre of Kyncaldrum, Sheriff depute of Forfar, that in virtue of the King's brieve he had given sasine at the Chemys of the third part of Ochtertyre and Mill, to William Hakate, of the third part lands of Octertyre Balcraig and Mill. Sealed with the seal of the Sheriff of Forfar, 7 December 1457.

Writ, dated 13 November 1524, setting forth that within the Consistory, in St. Giles College church, of Edinburgh, in presence of Mr. Thomas Cowtis, perpetual vicar of Cargyll, and official of St. Andrew's, within the archdeanery of Lothian, appeared Elizabeth Aytoun, spouse of John Halket of Pitfirren, and there apart from her husband, resigned her third part of Ochtertyr and Balcraig in favour of Robert Marser, in Mekilhour, in presence of Thomas Marjoribanks, Philip Dernly, father, and others. A fine seal of the official remains at this writ.

Precept of Sasine, by George Archdeacon of St. Andrew's, and perpetual Commendator of Dunfermline, for infefting George Blair, son and heir of the late David Blair of Pethy, and his heirs, whom failing, John Ogilbe, son and heir apparent of James Ogilbe, of Cukistone, and his heirs, whom failing, the nearest heirs of Marjorie Durye, mother of the said George and John, in the lands of Bennathy. The cause of granting is said to be "in augmentationem ecclesie veteris ruinose et in "magna parte delapse, tociusque nostri monasterii "reparacionem decorem et policiam. Dated at Dunfermline, 11 March 1538.

Precept of Sasine, dated 1 July 1543, by the said George, for infefting John Ogilvy, son and apparent heir of James Ogilvy, of Cukistoun, in the lands of Bennathy. The precept has the signature of the Commendator and 20 monks.

Charter by Patrick Haldane, of Wester Keillour, to his son and apparent heir, Silvester Haldayne, of the lands of Wester Keillour, dated at Perth, 4 April 1492. Witnesses, James Rattray, Vicar of Cullace, James Muncur of Balluny, Robert Small in Foderynnis, and others.

Charter by John Abbot of Lundores and convent thereof, to Janet Blair, relict of Archibald Anderson, of Bournemouth, in liferent, and George Blair of Gairdoun, brother of the said Janet, in fee of the lands of Balman. Besides the reddendo, of money, the vassals were bound to provide sufficient carriages for conveying the Abbot's goods bought in the market at Cupar in Augus to the water of Tay, near Lundores, as they had been in use to do. They were also to ride with the Abbot's men in the army of the King, or at any rate to find a sufficient horse with his attendant on foot, to bear the Abbot's carriages, with his men, against invaders of the realm in time of war, whenever it might be necessary. They were also to give lodging to the Abbot's servants, with his cattle bought beyond the Mounth, and provide them in all necessaries at their own proper charges. Signed at Lundores on 13th April 1542 by John the Abbot, James Carstairs, sub-prior, and 18 monks.

Instrument of Sasine, dated 28 May 1500, on the Sheriff's precept narrating the King's brieve for giving sasine to John Lord Oliphant, of the lands of Kilpurny and others. The Mair is desired to take security for two silver pennies " besnd the duplicacion of the blanche " farme of the lands of Twrings and Drummy, and of " ii. pundis gynger for the dowblyne of blanche ferme " of the landis of Gallowraw forsaidis, and of sex bred " harrow heddis for the dowblyne of the blanch ferme " of the twa pairt of the said lands of Ochtertyre and " Bawcraig, and of twa par of quhyt spurris for the " dowblyne of the blenche ferme of the landis of Newtyl " and Kynpurni, and for the sessing oxin and uthers ye " dw efter the tenor, forme, and effect of our Souerane " lordis breiff." Witnesses, David Maxwell, Esquire, and others.

Retour of the service at Edinburgh on 2nd May 1566, of Laurence Lord Oliphant, as heir of Laurence his father, in the lands and baronies of Aberdagy and Duplyne:—the lands and barony of Gask; Newtyle, Kilpurny; parts of Auchtertyre and Balcraig, Turingis, and Drymme; lands and barony of Galray in Forfarshire; lands and barony of Glensaucht in Kincardineshire, and lands of Muirhouse and Nakitcorss in Edinburghshire.

The blench duties due for these lands to the Crown were various and curious, and may be referred to as specimens of the somewhat jocular tenures then prevalent.

For the lands of Aberdagy and Duplyne there was due "unam merulam sive speculum " at Aberdagy, on the feast of St. Peter and Vincula yearly.

For Gask, a chaplet of white roses at the manor of Gask on the feast of St. John Baptist.

For Newtyld, a pair of spurs on the feast of All Saints.

For Auchtertyre and Baucraig, three broad arrows at Martinmas.

For Turing and Drymme, a silver penny at Christmas.

For Galray, a pound of ginger, at Pasch.

For Glensaucht, " a chaplet of mastick," at the manor of Kincardine, on the feast of SS. Peter and Paul.

For Muirhouse and Nakitcorss, a tersel of falcon at the Castle of Edinburgh.

The lands of Muirhouse were first conferred on Sir William Olifaunt by King Robert Bruce, whose charter bears that it was granted " in escambium pro quadam " pecia terre quam Joannes de Balliole cepit infra " clausuram parci de Kyncardin in le Merenis et quam " terram dicto parce volumus remanere."

Sir William Olifaunt, after having submitted to King Edward I. in the year 1297, afterwards threw in his lot with the national party. Being in command of the Castle of Stirling, he was besieged in it, in the year 1304, by King Edward in person, and the garrison having capitulated in the month of July in that year, Sir William was carried to London, where he was detained in captivity for four years, when he was released by Edward II.

From King Robert he received grants of various lands, besides those enumerated in the charters now reported on.

Besides the large masses of documents out of which the above were selected, there is a MSS. volume, entitled "Court Book of the Baronies of Newtyle, Keillours, " Cowty, and Bendochie," begun September 1725, when Patrick Grant of Bonhard, Baillie, held his court at the mill of Newtyle, and at which Mr. Charles Rattray, of Gelliebanks, produced a letter of bailliary and chamberlainry, granted by Anne Countess of Bute, in his favour. The courts seem ordinarily to have been held at Haltoun and Newtyle, and the proceedings illustrate the condition of agriculture in the district, and in some measure bear on points of social economy.

In a court held on 8th November 1725, certain Acts were passed and recorded, with a direction that they should be read over once or twice in the year, when the tenants should be convened in greatest number. The Acts had the following heads :—

1. Act anent commodties.

2. Act anent planting and cutting of trees and breaking of enclosures.

3. Act anent the milnes and farm meall.

4. Act anent the moss.

5. Act anent breaking of enclosures.

6. Act anent vagrant persons. The tenants were prohibited from admitting any person into their grasshouses who have not a visible way of living, and are not of good fame, and bring not a sufficient testimony of their good behaviour.

7. Act anent good neighbourhood. The tenants in use to have common herds for sheep and cattle are not to take on them to separate their flocks, or refuse to join in the common charge of keeping herds, and that they have their respective proportions of grass, meal, and teathing of their own field, according to their proper shares, under the penalty of ten pounds toties quoties.

8. Act anent the meadow.

9. Act anent sward ground.

10. Act anent smyddies.

11. Act anent stipends.

12. Act anent biggins.

13. Act anent the tenants—attending courts, &c.

14. Act anent sowing of pease.

15. Act anent complaints and assessments.

16. Act anent the disposal of corns.

17. Act anent millars.

At the court which followed this one, other Acts of a like nature were passed, and bear to have been made at the instance of the Countess of Bute, " and sanctioned " by the tenants of Roschaugh's Estate in Perth and " Forfar."

One of the additional Acts thus enacted is against public-houses and offices not authorised, and provides " That none presume to set up an alehouse, brew or " vend ale or any other liquors, neither set up smiddies " or exercise the smith's craft, nor set up malt barns, " or make malt, but by the special allowance or appro- " bation of the master; and when any persons are so " authorized and appointed to exerce these different " trades, that all the inhabitants of the Barony be ob- " liged, as their occasions require, to employ them; and

" the brewers, smiths, and maltmen of the Barony shall " be preferred to all others; they in their respective " offices giving due service, attendance, and work, to " those of the barony who employ them. The penalty " of the possessors or tenants not employing them shall " be 40s. Scots, and the penalty of the brewers, smiths, " and maltmen not doing faithfully thier parts shall be " 10l. Scots, besides the damages."

Others are " For encouraging the enclosing of " grounds," and " For encouraging and regulating the " spinning of yarn."

JOHN STUART.

MUNIMENTS OF SIR JOHN BETHUNE, BARONET, AT KILCONQUHAR IN THE COUNTY OF FIFE.

Sir John Bethune is paternally a Lindsay, and has taken the surname of Bethune in terms of an entail of the estate of Kilconquhar made by a former proprietor of the Bethune family. Sir John is the chief of the Lindsays of Wormiston in the county of Fife; and as such, he is the male representative of the Lords Lindsay of the Byres, and of the Lindsays Earls of Lindsay, who have all figured prominently in the history of Scotland, along with their great chiefs the Earls of Crawford.

Sir John Bethune is in possession of a large collection of muniments relating to the families of Lindsay and Bethune, but the greater mass of them do not fall within the scope of the Commission, not being documents of an historical character. There are, however, a number of early charters and letters which require to be reported on, and these are here arranged in three divisions :—1. Charters: 2. Letters: and, 3. Miscellaneous Papers.

Several of the charters quoted or referred to are very ancient, dating from the latter half of the twelfth century, and have some additional historical value from the presence of certain names attesting the respective deeds. One charter, unfortunately not well authenticated, purports to have been granted to a certain Venerus in the year 1165. Four charters are given in full; three of these are in Latin and belong to the 12th century; the fourth is in the Scotch dialect and was granted in the year 1456.

The second division embraces a number of letters of the seventeenth century addressed chiefly to Patrick Lindsay of Wormiston, then commissary of St. Andrews, from three successive archbishops of that see, James Sharp, Alexander Burnet, and Arthur Ross. Three letters of the unfortunate archbishop first mentioned are given entire, one of which is an affectionate address to his former parishioners at Crail on the eve of his elevation to the see of St. Andrews; another, written four years prior to his murder on Magus-moor, comments on the Act of Fife with relation to the suppression of conventicles.

The few miscellaneous papers given, embrace an interesting document of a rare kind, being the copy, in all probability contemporary, of a Brieve issued at Dumbarton in 1310 by King Robert the Bruce, ordering an investigation to be made of the dues and privileges of the Constable of Crail, an office which had long pertained to the family of Spens of Wormieston, with the return thereto; an order of Charles I. releasing Mr. John Lyndesay from prison, and a certificate anent the same matter a few days later from the first Marquis of Montrose; also a warrant and grant of liberty to Patrick Lyndesay by Colin, third Earl of Balcarras.

I.—Charters.

1. Document indorsed " Copie of the chartour grantit " be King William of the lands of Wolmerstoun." The charter (according to this copy) bore the date of 1165, the first year of the reign of William I. (the Lion). The boundaries of the lands of Wormieston are minutely described, and the grantee is one Venerus, who is to hold the lands therein mentioned in fee and heritage immediately of the Crown, for the yearly payment to King William and his heirs of two pennies under the name of blench farm at Pentecost, if asked. In this copy the names of the attesting witnesses are not given. This charter is not sufficiently authenticated, although it is referred to, without suspicion of its genuineness, in an inventory of the charters, &c. of Wormieston prepared in the year 1662.

2. Charter by King William I. (the Lion), in favour of Robert of Gaugingrey of the lands of Gaugingrey. [Granted between the years 1189–1192.]

"Willelmus Dei gratia Rex Scottorum, omnibus probis hominibus tocius terre sue, clericis et laicis salutem : Sciant presentes et futuri me dedisse et concessisse et hac carta mea confirmasse Roberto filio Henrici Pincerne, Gasgingrei, per easdem diuisas per quas Archenbald, Abbas de Dunfermelin, cum probis hominibus meis et per preceptum meum terram illam ei perambulauit : Tenendam sibi et heredibus suis, de me et heredibus meis, in feudo et hereditate, in terris et pratis et pascuis, et cum communi pastura de mora de Kellin, libere et quiete : Faciendo inde forinsecum seruicium, tantum, scilicet quantum pertinet ad dimidiam carucatam terre in Kellin shire : Concessi eciam predicto Roberto et heredibus suis ut quieti sint de multur : dn domo sua propria ad molendinum meum de Kellina Set uolo quod homines sui dent multuram : Testibus, Hugone cancellario meo, Henrico Abbate de Aberbrothoc, Roberto de Londonia, Johanne de Hasting, Bernardo de Haudene, Dunecano de Lascelles, Herberto Maroscallo, Herberto de Camera : Apud Kingorn."

3. Charter by King William I. (the Lion) in favour of William of Glasgingrey of the lands of Glasgingrey. [Granted subsequent to the preceding charter, between the years 1189–1192.]

This grant is the same, almost in language, as the preceding one to Robert, father of the grantee herein mentioned. The attesting witnesses are "Hugo can-
"cellarius meus, Robertus de Londonia, Robertus de
"Quinci, Willelmus de Lindesia, Willelmus de Haia,
"Henricus Biset, Willelmus Giffarde, Walterus Mur·
"dahe," and the charter is dated "Apud Strivelin
"(Stirling) xxviii die Augusti."

4. Charter by Alexander III. in favour of Sir Nicholas Hay of the lands of Glasgyngrey, proceeding upon the resignation thereof in the King's hands by Ada of Glasgyngrey, one of the heirs portioners of the deceased William of Glasgyngrey. Dated 4th October 1282.

"Alexander Dei gratia Rex Scottorum, omnibus probis hominibus tocius terre sue, clericis et laicis, salutem. Cum Eda de Glasgyngrey, filia quondam Willelmi de Glasgyngrey, die dominica proxima ante festum beate Margarete virginis, anno Domini M° CC° octogesimo secundo, in capella nostra de Clony, nobis per fustum et baculum resignauerit totam terciam partem terre de Glasgyngrey quam ipsa Eda de nobis iure hereditario tenuit, tanquam vna heredum predicti quondam Willelmi de Glasgyngrey, ad infeodandum Nicolaum de Haya, militem, de eadem terra cum pertinenciis : Sciatis nos ad instanciam predictorum Ede et Nicholai ac amicorum suorum eundem Nicholaum de dicta tercia parte terra de Glasgyngrey dictis die, loco et anno infeodasse, et homagium suum inde recepisse : Tenendam et habendam de nobis et heredibus nostris eidem Nicholao et heredibus suis in feodo et hereditate, in terris, pratis, et pascuis, et cum communi pastura de mora de Kellyne quanta pertinet ad dictam tertiam partem terre prenominate, libere, integre et quiete : faciendo inde nobis forinsecum seruicium quantum pertinet ad tantam terram in Kellynacyre : Concessimus etiam predicto Nicholao et heredibus suis vt quieti sint de multura de domo sua propria ad molendinum de Kellyn : Set volumus quod homines eorum dent multuram, secundum quod in carta felicis recordacionis domini Willelmi Regis, aui nostri carissimi, plenius est expressum : Testibus, Jacobo Senescallo Scocio, Willelmo de Sancto Claro, Roberto de Cambrune, Symone Fraser, Patricio de Graham, et Ricardo Fraser, Apud Newbotyll, quarto die Octobris anno regni nostri tricesimo quarto."

[Part of the great seal is still appended to this charter.]

5. Charter by Gilbert of Caskyngray in favour of Nicholas de Hay, Lord of Errol, of his land of Caskyngray. [Before 1293.]

"Omnibus hanc cartam visuris uel audituris, Gilbertus de Ca-kyngray filius et heres Laurencii et Ellote de Caskyngray, eternam in Domino salutem : Noueritis me dedisse, concessisse, et hac presenti carta mea confirmasse domino Nicholao de Haya, domino de Errolle, totam terram meam de Caskyngray, cum omni iure et redditibus quod et quos hactenus habui in eadem terra, ac quod et quos ego uel heredes mei habere aliquo casu poterimus in posterum in terra predicta : Tenendam et habendam dicto domino Nicholao et heredibus suis de domino Rege, adeo libere et quiete, bene et pacifice, sicut ego et antecessores mei prefatam terram tenuimus aut tenere potuimus : faciendo inde debita ex consueta seruicia que ego et antecessores mei facere solebamus et tenebamur : Ita quod nec ego uel heredes mei nec aliquis per nos, aliquid iuris uel clamii de cetero in dicta terra uel eius redditibus habere uel exigere

poterimus. In cuius rei testimonium sigilla domini Johannis Dei gratia prioris Sancti Andree et domini Radulphi de Lascelles presenti carte apponi procuraui et in simul sigillum meum apposui : Hiis testibus antedicto dompno priore, domino Johanne archidiacono Sancti Andree, dominis Radulpho de Lascelles et Hugone de Haya, militibus, Willelmo de Abirorumby, Adam Marescallo, Rogero filio Nicholai, et aliis."

6. An infeftment by resignation of Robert de Trumbley in favour of Laurence Laird of Wolmerstoun, Constable of Crail, of the lands of Torbreg, with 28 acres of land in the tenement of Wolmerstoun, under two great seals.

This infeftment is referred to in the Wormiestoun inventory of 1662, and was probably made about the year 1300.

7. An indenture made betwixt Thomas Hay of Balcomie and Laurence of Wolmerstoun, for the decision of the way betwixt Balcomie and Wolmerstoun. Dated 1326, and referred to in the inventory ut supra.

8. A contract, written on parchment, betwixt Thomas Hay of Balcomie and Laurence of Wolmerstoun anent the lands of Stewartflat. Dated 1326, and referred to in the inventory ut supra.

9. An instrument of sasine "past upon ane precept "out of the Chancellarie," whereby Isobel of Wolmerstoun is infeft in three fifth parts of the lands of Wolmerstoun. Dated 1386, and referred to in the above inventory.

10. A bond, written on parchment, given by John Weymis, laird of Kincaldrum, to Annas of Wolmerstoun of forty pounds money.

Dated 4th August 13[--], and referred to in the inventory.

11. An inventory of Annas of Wolmerstoun made by her for her lifetime to Duncane Spens of all her lands lying within the barony of Wolmerstoun. Dated 17th June 1390, and referred to in the inventory of 1662.

12. An instrument annulling the sasine taken by John Weymis of Rires, knight, of the lands of Wolmerstoun and Brodlayis, made by Annas of Wolmerstoun. Dated 31st July 1394, and referred to in the inventory.

13. Charter by William de Hay, Lord of Errol and Constable of Scotland, with consent of Gilbert his eldest son and heir, of all the lands of Castyngray in the shire of Fife which the granter held in chief of the Crown : To be held by the foresaid Nicholas and the lawful heirs male of his body, whom failing to revert to the said William Lord of Errol and his heirs, of the granter and his heirs, in fee and heritage for ever, as freely, fully, &c. as they had been held by the said William de Hay or any of his predecessors, the said Nicholas and his heirs rendering the customary forinsic service to the Crown, and to the said William and his heirs the service due and wont, viz' "wardam, releuium, humagium et "seruicium," the frank tenement of the lands being reserved by William de Hay for himself during his lifetime.

Given under the seal of the said William and his son Gilbert at Farvy, 17th February 1431. The witnesses are Alexander de Seton de Gordon, Andrew Stewart, Alexander de Irwyne, John de Ogyston of that ilk, and many others.

14. Letters by William Earl of Errol, confirming an inquest declaring Gilbert Hay to be the nearest and lawful heir of his father Nicholas Hay of Castyngray, in the lands of Castyngray. Dated 14th December 1456.

"Tyll all and sindry to quhais knawlage thir presentes lettres salcum, Williame Erle of Erole, lorde the Haia and constabile of Scotlande, gretyng in Gode : Sen it is neidful and meritabile to ber leile witnessing to suthfastnes, and specealy in the thingis quhilkis ar declaryt and done in jugement, Then it is that befor vs attendand in jugement in our curt haldin at Slanys, the dai of the date of thir makyne of thir presentes lettres, comperit personaly our cusing Gilbert the Haia, son and air till quhillum our eeme, Nicholl the Haia, and askit ande requeryt vs to grant hym ane inquest of that our curt of quhat landis and annuale rentis, with the pertynance, the said Nychol the Haia deyt last vest and saisit as of fee, in dow fourme ; And we herrande and considerande his resonable desire and request, gert call to that inquest thir personis vnderwrytyne, that is to say, Rycharde the Wans, Williame Rode off Coliston, Dauid Haia of Essindy, Williame the Wans, Symon Banerman, James Berclay, John of Moncreffe, Thomas of Lask, Thom Gray, Slanys paraywant, Alexander Haia, Dauid Rede, John of Murref, Williame Modane, Alane Gray, and George off Fentone. The quhilkis, the gret ath sworne, said at the said Nichol the Haia, vmquhill fader to the said Gilbert deyt last vest and asisit as of fee of the landis of Castingray and of Fudy, with thar pertynance, liand in our barony of Errol, within the schirefdome of Fife, and at the foresaid Gilbert the Hais is lauchful and nerrast air of the said Nichol vmquhil his fader, off the said landis with the pertynance, and at he is nocht yheit of lauchfull age, bot he sall be of perfite and lauchful age at the fest of the Invencion of the Halicroice, callit Beltane, next to cum, efter the date of thir presentes lettres, and at the said landis with the pertynance ar now worth be yher xxv lib., and thai war worth in tyme of pese xx lib.; and at thai ar haldin of vs be seruice of ward and relief, mantrent and seruice; and at thai ar now in the said Gilbertis handis be saising giffin be vs till hym a yher syne and mair, nochtwithstanding his nonage; the quhilk saisine and possessione now as than quhen he sal be of lauchfull age, and than as now, we approve, ratifiis and confermys be the tenour of thir presentes lettres. To the quhilkis, in witnes of veritee, and of the foresaid thingis, our seele, togidder with the seole of Richarde the Wans, for hym, and procurit be al thaim at was apon the inquest for thaim all as is appensit, at Slanys, the xiiij. dai of December, yhe yhere of God a thousand four hundreth fiftee and sax : Witnes, maister Johne Lummysdene, persoune of Sanctmodois, Schir Alexander Banerman and Schir Thomas Broune, chaplanes, with othiris diuers."

II.—Letters.

(1). Letters from James Sharp, Archbishop of St. Andrews.

15. "Edinburgh, Apryll 29, 1661.

" Mistress,

" This is to pay my thanks for your kyndnes to my wife, of the constancy wherof she and I upon all occasions have cause to be sensible: I must part with her for a time now as formerly, of which she will acquaint your ladyship : and therfor shall leave her upon your hand. If I can be of any use to yow or yours wherever my lot shall be cast, I hope yow will doe me the right as not to doubt of my readines, and good will. I have engaged to my lord thesaurer that no new order come from above in behalf of John Boswell; and if no motion come from thence, my lord resolves to take his hazard with what can be done for him here. It may be beleeved that I will preferr your sones interest in that busines to any other, and wherin I can contribute to the furthering of it, I will not be wanting. Remember my service to the Laird your sone and his ladye, to your daughter, your sone George. All mercy and peace attend yow all.

I am, Mistress,
Your assured freind to serve yow,
JA. SHARP.

" I had wreat a particular letter to your sone, but that I have no time. The letter my wife is to give to him he may be pleased to communicat to the elders of the Session."

Dorso.—" For his much Honored the Ladye Wormiestoun."

JS

16. [Written from London in May 1661.]

" Honored and dearly beloved in the Lord:

" James Moncreif can acquaint yow that I am commandit to make a journey for London. It was in my heart and desire to have seen yow befor my going, but I could not. It hath been, I confess, to your disadvantage and my greif that I have been so often parted from yow; and albeit now my interest in yow is not such as it hath been, yet I shall ever think myself obliged to be concerned in the wele of the parish, and contribute what I can towards it. That yow have not been prowydit of a minister befor this can not in reason be imputed to me, who have no other designe but that yow may have a pious faythfull man fitted for the Lord's work amongst yow, to which purpose I have spoke to my Lord Thesaurer who assures that he will come over, and by your own consent present one, whose ministrie may have success amongst yow. My heart's desires on your behalf are continually with the great Sheaphcard of the flock, that he would prowyde for yow a pastor after his own heart who may make up the wants of my ministrie amongst yow, which is the greatest blissing I can wish unto yow; and till it be the Lord's good pleasure so to order, my prayer to the Lord, and my exhortation is to yow, that yow may be helped to watch over the people over whom yow are sett, and by your example and care keep them in the

fear of God and obedience and love of the ordinances of Jesus Christ. The only wise and good God prowyd for yow, bliss, guyd and prosper yow ! To His grace and tender mercies yow are commendit by
Your most loving faythfull friend
to serve yow,
JA. SHARP."

Dorso.—" For his much Honored Patrick Lyndsay of Wormiestoun, to be communicated to the elders of the Session of Craill."

17. " Edinburgh, January 14 [16]75.

" Honll Sir,

" The Act of Fyfe in the contryving and presenting of which yow had a cheef hand, when read at the Council board, was very pleasing to all, but in regaird of some defects, was committed to the further consideration of my Lord Chancellor and others; which after beeng reported to the Council with the amendements, did pass at a full meeting without contradiction, and I beleeve is by my Lord Chancellor transmitted to the 4 meetings in the severall presbytries. The Council, —finding the band did not mention the ingaging to live orderly in obedience to the lawes, meaning nothing but the lawes which doe forbid disorderly baptisms & marriages, and expresly injoyn the keeping of the respective parish churches, the neglect wherof is the cause of conventicling and must lead to irreligion, and atheism,—have therfor resolved to adde that clause in the band, which is expected will not be scrupled by any heretour in Fyfe : for it is more eligible to give way to conventicles then to allow or connyve at withdrawing from the church, and publick meetings for God's worship. And in regard that vagrant preachers and intercommuned ministers are the cheef incendiaries, and give lyfe and boldnes to these disorders, it was judged necessary that [a] clause be addit also, which relates to the not harbouring of these persons, and endeavouring they may be apprehendit. The fynes of delinquents belonging to the King, the Lords of the Thesauray could not be induced to allow they should be imployed for the defraying of the charge mentioned in the Act; and that wheras 20 dayes provision is ordered to be levyed for the militia of Angus who are to march to the west country, 14 dayes only are ordered for Fyfe, and so much for the militia of the Lowthians, who besyds must goe upon duty. The commission for lovying of the money and the 4 captains are also past the Council, but I hope we shall obtain some allowance off the fynes for incouragement of the captains and other officers. This account I give yow, Sir, of the summe and reasons of these alterations of that Act which are judged to be necessary, and will be made the patern according to which other shyres where disorders are to be rectifyed must expect termes, else by force they will be impeled to the greater cost. Fyfe has done itself and my Lord Chancellor much right by the late actings at Cowper upon reasons I shall make appear to yow at meeting; and in my opinion a ready and cheerfull obedience to the Council's orders at this tyme without stiking, will prevent the detriment and dishonour which else must come upon Fyfe; and your care to have all done as it ought, is beseeched by,
Sir,
Your assured freind and servant,
SCT. ANDREWS."

Dorso.—" For the Honll. the Laird of Wormieston, Commissar of St. Andrews."

18. Fourteen other letters of less interest than those above given in full, from Archbishop Sharpe to the Laird of Wormieston, then Commissary of Saint Andrews.

19. A letter from Alexander Burnet, Sharpe's successor in the archbishopric of St. Andrews, to the Laird of Wormieston, dated 1681.

20. Three letters, all written in 1686, from Arthur Ross, Burnet's successor in the archbishopric of St. Andrews, and the last holder of the See before the Revolution, to the Laird of Wormieston.

21. A letter from Sir Alexander Areskine, dated at London, January 23, 1711, in which the writer acknowledges to the Laird of Wormieston the receipt of a letter from Dr. Arbuthnot inclosed in one from the Laird to himself, and says, " I have spoke to him, " and wee shall both concur in any thing that can be " serviceable to the Doctor." He also refers to a report, which he considers credible, that the Queen had that morning requested the Duke of Argyll to assume the duties of Ambassador and of Commander of her Forces in Spain. The Duke had that day at dinner intimated to the Earl of Mar that he would accept the offer. He further writes :—" The news in the coffee hous this

" day is that the D. of Marlborough will goe over
" Captain Generall, as formerly, to Flanders."

III.—Miscellaneous Papers.

22. Brieve of King Robert I., with return thereto,
setting forth the dues and privileges of the Constabular
of Craill, 1310 :—Robertus Dei gracia rex Scotorum,
justiciaro suo ex parte boreali aque de Forth, vel eius
locum tenentibus seu tenenti, salutem: Monstrauit
nobis Laurencius de Wenmerstoun euidencias quas
habet de custodia constablarie nostre de Karale de
temporibus antiquis, quod quidem officium eidem
Laurencio in feodo et hereditate ex mera voluntate
nostra concedimus in perpetuum et confirmamus.
Quare vobis mandamus et firmiter precipimus, quatinus
per probos homines et fideles et burgenses, per quos
rei veritas melius sciri poterit et dinosci, diligentem
et fidelem recognicionem fieri faciatis super comoditatibus, feodis, et iuribus pertinentibus ad officium dicte
constabularie nostre : et etiam quid dictus Laurencius
nomine officii predicti faciet. Et quid per dictam
recognicionem inueneritis deinceps in eadem forma
firmiter custodiri faciatis. Datum apud Dumbrettane
quinto die Marcii, anno regni nostri quarto. Teste
meipso. . . . . .
Recognicio facta apud Cuprum in Fyffe de mandato
eiusdem domini nostri Regis, coram Willelmo de Strabrok et Henrico de Prestoun locum tenentibus nobilis
viri Domini Roberti de Keth, Justiciarii ab aqua de
Forth usque Orknay ad festum Sancti Dionisii Martiris,
anno gracie millesimo tricentesimo duodecimo, per
fideliores et meliores patrie subscriptos, juratos videlicet:
Dominos Dauid de Wemys, Alexandrum de Dambyrtoun,
Johannem de Haya de Achnawchtane, Malisium de
Douery, Johannem de Dündemor, Willelmum de Monte
Alto, Willelmum Suard, Milites; Thomam de Balkasky,
Walterum de Karale, Johannem de Abircrumby, Hen-
ricum de Aynstrother, Bartholomeum de Kyldunchane,
Hernœum de Strathanry, Walterum Scot, Thomam Bell,
Johannem dictum Goddysmane, burgenses Sancti Andree;
Willelmum Boner, Willelmum Comyn, burgenses de
Kyngorne; Willelmum Brawncho, Johannem filium
Josue, burgenses de Innerkethyne; Radulfum dictum
Yung, Henricum Herward, Willelmum filium Mariorie,
Gilbertum filium Johannis, Laurencium de Petolly,
Mauricium de Pottergat, Adam filium Johannis, burgenses de Karale: super comoditatibus, feodys, et uiribus
pertinentibus constablariis de Karal, de iure et antiqua
consuetudine. Qui iurati dicunt, quod constablarius
de Karal qui pro tempore fuerit de iure capiet de una
batella per diem viginti albos pisces pro denario: et sic
singulis in circuitu equaliter diuidendo. Et habebit per
annum ad duo tempora capiendi allecia, sex milia pro
denariis suis ad precium domini regis: et de qualibet
batella veniente ad villam de Karale cum morellis,
vnum morellum ad electionem constabillarii pro uno
denario. Insuper habebit de bracinis, videlicet, de
qualibet braciatrice que seruisiam vendit vnam lagenam
cum dimidia pro vno denario quotiens omnes bracinant
et vendunt; exceptis hospitularüis. Ac predicti iurati
dicunt quod est officium constabularii de Karale qui
pro tempore fuerit, quod debet de iure habere custodiam
castri de Karale, et precipere ianitori ad recipiendum
omnimodos homines attachiatos et omnes districtos
captos pro comodo domini nostri Regis, et leuare omnes
firmas domini nostri regis infra baroniam de Karale et
easdem super warandis expendere. Ac habet recipere
preceptum domini nostri Regis super fractura sue
proüidencie et ad videndum quod custos moris et
warandie faciat officium suum, ut ad recipiendum omnes
sectas presentatas castro de Karale, tam de purgacione
baronie quam de nequicia, quas predictas sectas con-
stabularius vicecomiti presentabit; et omnes alias sectas
sibi presentatas quecunque aut vndecunque sint, ita
in eisdem potest testificare; et omnimoda plegia sibi
inuenta, si que fuerint, presentabit vicecomiti de Fyffe
qui pro tempore fuerit; et capiet per annum de domino
nostro Rege quadraginta solidos pro feodo suo. Ac
asciatis me Willelmum de Strabrok et Henricum de
Prestoun socium meum sigilla nostra predicte recogni-
cioni dedisse, dicto die et loco, habentes . . . . . .
[MSS. torn] . . . Regis in warandio. Datum et cet."

23. " Charles R.

"These are to require all and euery one whom it
may concerne, that forthwith upon sightthereof, yo" sett
at libertie Mr. John Lindsay of Wormestoune out of
yo' custodie and prison, wheeof yo" are not to fayle, as
yo" will be answer⁶ˡᵉ at yo' highest perille. Given under

our hand and signett at Newcastle the 30th day of July
1646.

By his Majesties command,

LANRICK."

24. There is a certificate to the same effect from James
first Marquis of Montrose, as follows :—

" Thes are to show that I had not, nor hes anay thing
to charge Mr. Joⁿ Lindsay, younger, of Wilmerstoun
withall, and knowes nothing bot that he should be sett
at libertie according to my several desyirs to that effect.
Given under my hand at Old Montrose, Agust the 9th,
1646.

MONTROSE."

25. Warrant and grant of liberty to Patrick Lindsay
of Wormieston, from Colin Earl of Belcarres.

" Wee Coline Earle of Balcarres, shirreff principall
of Fyfe, one of his Majesties privie Counsill, and haveing
power and warrand from his Majesties high commissioner
to dispence with such heritors in Fyfe as is infirme and
sickly from goeing to the hoast. Therffor, being certainlie
informed of the inabilitie and sicknees of Patrick Lyndsay
of Wormestoune, I doe heirby declair that he is in
saiftie and friedom to stay at home, and shall not
heirefter be troubled, quarrelled, nor fyned for the same
being absent from his Majestie's said hoast at the present
expedition, and that for the causes above exprest. In
witnes q'off we have subscrybed thir presents with our
hand. Att Kirkaldie the twentie thrid day of May jᵐ viᶜ
and eightie fyve [1685] yeirs.

BALCARRAS."

Having given at length in this Report the more
important and interesting of the Charters and Letters,
and as the remainder are not numerous, and the terms
of them fully stated, I do not think it is necessary to
suggest that any separate Calendar of them should be
prepared.

WILLIAM FRASER.

Edinburgh, 32, Castle Street,
18th July 1874.

THE MANUSCRIPTS OF SIR WILLIAM FORBES, BART.,
OF CRAIGIEVAR, AT FINTRAY HOUSE.

The barony of Coule and Ohelo formed part of the
great possessions of the powerful family of the Ostiarii
or Durwards, the last male representative of which
died towards the end of the 13th century, leaving three
daughters, who carried their large estates into other
families.

The lands of Coule and Onele next belonged to the
Earls of Fife, and the earliest of the charters in this
collection is an extract of a charter by King Robert II.
to his son Robert Earl of Fife and Menteith, of the
barony of Coul and Onele, which belonged to Isabella
Countess of Fife, daughter of Duncan Earl of Fife, and
who in her widowhood resigned the said barony at the
Monastery of Dunfermline on the day of granting the
said charter. Dated at Dunfermline, 12 August 1389.

About a century after this time the barony became
vested in Patrick, third son of James second Lord
Forbes, and ancestor of the present owner. This appears by the next charter in point of date being one by
King James III. to his esquire Patrick Forbes of the
barony of Onele, vis., the lands of Coule, Kincragy,
and Le Cors, to be held of the King for the annual payment of 21l. and 3 marts, or for each mart 15s., and
also to the Bishop of Aberdeen for second tithes due
from these lands, 46s. 8d. Dated at Edinburgh, 10th
October 1482. Witnesses, Alexander Duke of Albany,
Earl of March, Mar, and Garuiach, Lord of Annandale
and Man, Guardian of the East and West Marches, and
Admiral of the Kingdom; John Bishop of Glasgow, the
King's Chancellor; James Bishop of Dunkeld; John
Earl of Athol and James Earl of Buchan, the King's
uncles; David Earl of Craufurd; John Lord Kennedy,
William Lord Borthwick; Mr. Archibald Quhitlaw;
Archdeacon of Lothian, the King's Secretary; Patrick
Lech, Canon of Glasgow and Clerk of Register.

David, as son of Patrick Forbes, had a charter under
the Great Seal from King James IV. of the lands of
Kincragy and Le Cores on the resignation of Patrick,
and reserving his lifferent. The charter narrates that
Patrick Forbes of Fotherbiras holds these lands of the
King, for payment of the specified feu duty and second
tithes, and that he is at present at the King's summons
to hear the said lands decerned to belong to the Crown,
but that the King annuls said summons and action and
all their consequences, and on account of good service

done to his father and himself by the said Patrick, the great expenses of infeftment in said lands under his father, and certain sums of money paid into his Treasury, grants this charter to the said David, which is dated at Edinburgh 30 April 1506.

By another charter, dated at Edinburgh 11 January 1510, King James IV. granted to David Forbes, son natural of Patrick Forbes, and Elizabeth Panitere the wife of the said David, the lands of Onele, Corse Kincragy, and others, reserving the liferent of Patrick, who had resigned the lands of Coule into the hands of the King, who had otherwise disposed of them, which lands are thereby united and incorporated into a free barony to be called the barony of Onele. This David enjoyed in his day the warlike soubriquet of "David Trail the Axe."

The lands of Corse came by succession to be vested in Patrick Forbes, Bishop of Aberdeen, who died in 1635, and in his son, Dr. John Forbes, Professor of Divinity in King's College, Aberdeen, who died in 1648.

The lands of Craigievar, which for upwards of two centuries belonged to a family of the name of Mortimer, were acquired in the year 1610 from John Mortimer by William Forbes, the bishop's brother, whose son William was in the year 1630 created a baronet of Nova Scotia.

Among the writs of Craigievar the oldest is a charter by King James II. to Edmund Mortimere of the lands of Craigievar and others, on his own resignation, dated at Aberdeen 12 November 1457. Witnesses, George, Bishop of Brechin, Chancellor; Patrick Lord Glammis; James Lord Forbes; Mr. James Stewart, Dean of Moray, the King's Treasurer; Thomas Waus, Dean of Glasgow, his Secretary; and Ninian Spot, Canon of Dunkeld, his Comptroller of Accounts.

The instrument of resignation is dated within the lodging of John Fyff, in Aberdeen, on 12 November 1457, and sets forth that Edmund Mortimer on bended knees resigned his said lands into the hands of George Bishop of Brechin and Chancellor of Scotland, as having authority of the King to that effect. The witnesses were William, Thoyne of Caldor; Sir Alexander Yong, Canon of Aberdeen; and Alexander Forbes of Petelegocht.

The lands of Wester Fowlis and Easter Leochel, which were added to his estate by Sir John Forbes in 1675, originally belonged to the Monastery of Monymusk. They came into the possession of the Earls of Huntly, and by a charter dated at Huntly 21 March 1554, they were conveyed by George Earl of Huntly to George Gordon of Beldorney. The witnesses to this charter are George Lord Gordon, Alexander Seton, younger, of Meldrum, John Gordon of Dunmeyth, William Con, Patrick Maitland, Alexander Meldrum, James Stevin, and others. It was confirmed by David Prior of Monymusk and John Elphinston of Invernochty, his assistant and successor, and by the King. When the lands became vested in Sir John Forbes, the grant in his favour was confirmed by the Bishop and Chapter of Dunblane as representing the Prior of Monymusk.

The lands of Wester Corse for a time belonged to the family of Pantoun of Pitmedden. By decreet of the Lords of Council and Session, on a summons raised by David Forbes, tenementer of the lands of Easter Corse, against John Pantoun, for his "wrangwiss ryving" "furth" of the common between their properties, it is decerned that the disputed ground is to remain common to both.

The lands thereafter belonged to the Frasers of Stonywood (ancestors of the Lords Fraser), from whom they passed to the Urrys of Pitfichie (a family from which Sir John Hurry, who served on both sides in the civil strifes of the time of Charles I., was sprung), and at last were bought by William Forbes of Corse. Among the papers are titles of these different families, as well as of the Skenes of Wester Corss, who were superiors of the lands; and selections from the whole have been printed by the Spalding Club, in their Collections on the History of the Shires of Aberdeen and Banff.

A prominent feature of the collections at Fintray House is the correspondence of Sir Andrew Mitchell of Thainston. This gentleman, who studied at Edinburgh under Maclaurin, was for a time the representative of the county of Aberdeen in Parliament, and afterwards acted as British Ambassador at the Court of Fredrick the Great, from 1753 till his death at Berlin in 1771, where he acquired distinction on account of his diplomatic ability.

Sir Andrew Mitchell at his death without issue left his property, including his papers, to Sir Arthur Forbes, Bart., of Craigievar and Fintray. In the year 1810 a portion of Sir Andrew's political papers were acquired

from Sir William Forbes, the son of Sir Arthur, by the Trustees of the British Museum, and are now arranged in that noble repository. A memoir of Sir Andrew Mitchell, by Mr. Andrew Bisset, barrister, of Lincoln's Inn, was published in the year 1850, in which, use is made of the collection in the Museum, and of the papers still left at Fintray House.

Among the letters is a series from Dr. Maclaurin to Mitchell (then Mr. Andrew Mitchell) in London. In November 1735, the Professor writes that he has got a wife, "whom I think agreable but is tender, and a "diverting boy. I have a girl too since Tuesday last, "but I have not the least acquaintance with her as "yet." "A new theorem or problem is still one of "my greatest ragouts, and I study rather more than "formerly, because I am more at home and less ex-"posed to idle company." He concludes with some of the "town's talk" of Edinburgh, both in civil and ecclesiastical matters.

In a letter dated in May 1736 he gives an account of the General Assembly, before which Principal Campbell had been called: "He is obstinate, and will not "own his expressions exceptionable in any degree. "His oratio academica in the committee was found to "contain exceptionable expressions by seven majority. "The minority indeed only voted a delay. I must is -"like that discourse, but yet we wish him to get of for "the sake of liberty. He explains by self-love to be "delighting in the glory of God."

One in April 1737 relates to several telescopes sent to London by Mr. Short. "I have not as yet done with "receiving letters from the country about the eclipse, "tho some of them signify little. I am to draw up my "account without delay now." Others relate to matters about the clergy of Edinburgh, his Fluxions, the Philosophical Society of Edinburgh, his books and mathematical subjects.

A series of letters from Mr. Robert Dundas of Arniston, on the politics of Edinburgh and Aberdeen, and general subjects, range in date from 1752 to 1755. In one of 1 November 1755, he writes, " I have obliged " the Duke of Newcastle, though in my life I never did " anything with greater reluctance." In another dated February 1752, he refers to a report "that Mr. Mit-"chell had been the means of stopping H. H" [Henry "Home] letter to be our judge, by saying to the Eng. "M. that his family was disaffected in so far as his "father was in the rebellion of 1715." He gives the opportunity of contradicting it.

Several letters to Mr. Mitchell from Lord Deskford, 1752-5.

In one of March 22, 1752, he refers to Mr. Mitchell's employment abroad, his supposed connexion with the letter of appointment of Lord Kames as a judge. " Your crime is having some share of the Duke of New-"castle and Mr. Pelham's favour, without depending "upon those who call themselves the Scotch ministry "for it." He goes on to speak of the difficulty of Mr. Mitchell's election for the county of Aberdeen, with the whole weight of the Scotch ministry against him, and discusses local politics.

Letter in October 1752, from Lord Aberdour, at Leyden, about the law classes there.

Five papers relating to Miss Villiers Pitt, 1752.

Two news letters from Earl Granard, at Spa, September 1753.

Drafts of letters and papers on public affairs, by Mr. Mitchell, 1752, 1753.

Memoranda by him of arguments to be used, Brussels, 1752 and 1753, with regard to negotiations. Heads of conversations with the Marquis de Botta; hints concerning the trade with Flanders; a description of the ceremonial at opening the Conference, 1739, &c.

A series from Mr. Burnett of Kenmay (who became his secretary after his mission to Berlin), extends from 1742 to 1747, and in one of them is an account of his proceedings in the late rebellion.

There are six letters from Principal Blackwell, one of which relates to the publication of his "Memoirs of "the Court of Augustus."

A series from the Earl of Findlater, 1752-55, are principally on the politics of the day. Another set from the Earl of Morton, 1749-1752, relate to Mr. Mitchell's election for the county of Aberdeen; Lord Lauderdale's incivility to Lord Morton, his neighbour; and his attempts to vindicate Mr. Mitchell in the matter of the judgeship of Lord Kames, and politics.

Letters from Mr. Robert Wallace, Edinburgh, in one of which, dated 4 February 1752, are remarks as to the election of Mr. David Hume as successor to Mr. Ruddiman as librarian in the Advocates' Library.

Two news letters from Earl Granard, dated Spa, September 1755.

Papers by President Munchausen, 1757. Various "Memoires" and "Precis d'une Conference,"relating to the treaty with the Duke of Brunswick.

Drafts and copies of letters by Mitchell from Breslau in 1759 to Lord Holdernesse, the Duke of Newcastle, and Mr. Pitt. In one to the letter (on 8th January) he assures him of his satisfaction that the Prussian Majesty is so highly pleased with the measures pursued by the King's Ministers and with the fair, candid, and honest manner in which they have behaved to him. "If any- "thing could add to the joy I felt on this occasion, it "was to hear His Prussian Majesty make the parallel "between his former ally and his present, and the com- "parison between the behaviour of the French and "English Ministers. But amidst general applause it "would be unjust to conceal from you the very par- "ticular and distinguished approbation with which that "monarch has been pleased to honour your conduct; "the Prussian Ministers at London having transmitted "to their master an account of what you said in the "House of Commons when it was proposed to address "the King not to deliver up Louisbourg to the French "by any subsequent treaty of peace. The King of "Prussia admired the firmness of your behaviour in "replying instantly in the manner you did, and said "the declaration you made on that occasion was like a "great statesman; and he, honest man, he concluded "with these words ' enfin ce'toit un coup de maitre.' " In a letter to the Duke of Newcastle, of January 1759, he begs him to ask the Order of the Bath for him from the King. In one of 5 May 1759 to Earl Holdernosse, he says, " His P[russian] M[ajesty] surpasses, if pos- "sible, his usual activity, vigilance, and application, "and as he is resolved to continue on the defensive as "long as possible, I flatter myself all will go well." On 20th May 1759 he writes to Mr. Pitt that the K[ing] of P[russia] had expressed his warmest wishes for peace. "He asked me, ' But can your ministers "' make a peace—are things yet in that situation ? ' "I answered, ' I was sure they wished for peace,' and "says he, ' I hope I shall not be forgot.' My reply "was prevented by the King's adding immediately, "' No! I am in no danger. Mr. Pitt is an honest man, "' and firm; my interests are safe in his hands.'"

Writing from Forgau to Earl Holdernesse on 22 October 1759 ("but not sent," as is marked in the draft), he gives an account of the battle of Cunners- dorff, fought on the 12th of August, of the situation of the Prussian army, and a good deal of detail.

A long letter from the King of Prussia to Mr. Mit- chell, signed "Frederic," and dated Berlin, 19 Aug. 1756.

Relation by Comte Tottleben of the fighting between 26 September and 18 October 1760.

Letters dated Wilsdruff, Dec. 1759, from Mr. Mit- choll to the Duke of Newcastle and Mr. Pitt, are marked "Private," and give an account of the progress of events, and his conversations with the Prussian King. Many drafts of letters to the Duke of Newcastle and others during conferences at Brussels, 1752-3.

A mass of duplicates of despatches from Lord Hol- dernesse to Mr. Mitchell, 1757.

A mass of communications from President Mun- chausen, dated from Hanover, 1756-1764.

Several letters from General de Schmettau, Hanover February 1757.

Drafts of letters from Mr. Mitchell to the Secretary of State, Berlin, 1756. Many of them are marked "Secret."

Letter from the Duke of Brunswick to Sir Andrew Mitchell, with extracts from a letter of King Frederick regarding Sir Andrew. Dated Brunswick, 24 February 1757.

Copies of letters from the Duke of Newcastle to Mr. Mitchell, 1752-3.

Returns and other papers relating to grievances in trade between England and Flanders, 1714 and 1738.

A bundle of papers, conventions, and others for the campaign of 1748.

Resultat of the conferences between the Earl of Chesterfield and Mr. Trevor, and the deputies of their high mightinesses, March 1745. Treaties with various Powers. Abridgement of the treaty of 1495, between Henry VII. of England and Philip Archduke of Burgundy.

. Plan for reducing the English history to general heads, and for the better connecting of these facts.

A series of papers consisting of propositions, resolu- tions, answers, and commissions at the Conference, May 1752.

State of the negotiations at Brussels, January 1754. Letters between the King and Prince of Prussia, July 1757. A short recapitulation of the matters which gave rise to the conferences at Antwerp in 1737-38-39, with observations thereon. Copies of papers by the Secretary of State submitted to the King relative to the resolutions of the States General of October 1738.

Eight letters from " H. Warrender" (1740-55), (one to Mr. Mitchell at Brussels in 1752), with political news and gossip.

Memoranda of journies by Mr. Mitchell in Holland and Flanders 1730-31, and in France and Italy 1731-32.

Notes of a visit by Mr. Mitchell to Rome in 1733; descriptions of the Vatican library, galleries of paint- ings and statuary. Notes of a journey through Italy in 1734.

A volume containing notes of the letters written from day to day from 1742 to 1745, by Mr. Mitchell, while Under Secretary of State for Scotland, to the Lord Advocate, Mr. Solicitor Dundas, Lord George Hay, Lord Justice Clerk, Sir John Cope, Lord Rollo, and many other correspondents. Letter from Mr. A. Burnett to Sir Arthur Forbes, dated Berlin, 29 July 1771, announcing the death of Sir Andrew Mitchell.

Book of accounts of the Rev. William Mitchell, one of the ministers of Edinburgh, 1695-1727. This gentle- man was father of Sir Andrew Mitchell.

General Wade's reports on the state of the Clans and the Highlands, 1724.

Description of the hills, glens, and passes in the counties of Aberdeen, Angus, Mearns, and Banff, and the disposition of troops for the protection of the country, 1747; with notes of the various routes by which stolen cattle are driven to the South.

Memorial concerning a cross-road from Inverlochy, by Ruthven of Badenoch, and through Braemar to Aber- deen, with descriptions of the Grampian range, of the Castle of Kindrochit, and of the Castle at Braemar built in 1628, by John Erskine Earl of Mar; and a notice of the Earl's rising in 1715.

Memorial anent the thieving and depredations in the Highlands of Scotland and Countries bordering thereon.

Memorandum anent the true state of the Highlands, as to their Chieftainries, Followings, and Depredations before the late Rebellion.

In the library at Fintray House is the original MS. Diary of Dr. John Forbes, ranging in date from 1624 to 1647. This learned man was celebrated among his contemporaries for his deep piety and great humility. He wrote various works on ecclesiastical subjects, which were collected in two folio volumes printed at Amster- dam in 1703. To this work the editor has prefixed a Life of the Author, with selections from the diary translated into Latin.

Dr. Forbes had more than his share of the troubles incident to the times in which he lived, and the diary, which he has styled " Spiritual Exercises," contains many reflections on the difficulties which surrounded him, and many affecting prayers for guidance in straits where he was led by his intense love of peace on the one side impelling him to submit to the Covenant, and his scrupulous adherence to principle on the other, which prevailed, and led to his deprivation from the office of professor of divinity at King's College, Aber- deen, and his banishment to a foreign country.

While the diary is mainly occupied with devotional thoughts and prayers, there are occasional entries which illustrate the state of the country, and furnish details of public events.

In 1636 he records that " some unrighteous and cruel " limmers Highland men cam under silence of night, " and violently spoyled the houses of some of my " tenants in Corse, as they hade beene doeing to many " others our neighbours, for a long space of tyme be- " fore, uncontrolled, and by some also encouradeged " by connivence and correspondence, as is well knowen " in Scotland. I bearing therof, and beholding how " small appearance was of humano help, and remem- " bring that in the tymes of my ancestors, since me- " morie of man, the lyke hade not been practised upon " that land, which God now hade given to me by " heritable succession; I said the lyke indeed hath not " been accustomed against my forbeers, and it seemeth " that theise robbers doe take advantage through dis- " esteem of me, as being a schoolman, wenithdraw " from that pairt by reasoun of my spirituall calling,

" and being unaccustomed with such medlies ; but I
" serve the same God whom my ancestors served, and
" I hope in his mercy, that he will shew me the way
" whereby theise robbers shall repent themselves of this
" wicked attempt. In the meantyme they were spread-
" ing abroad menacing speeches, boasting to set for my
" person if I compleened to the Secret Counsell, or
" essayed any course against them, or refused to buy
" their peace, as many others had done by paying to
" them blackmail. I finding myself in this assault and
" difficultie, I trusted not in any other means which I
" used, but I did sett myself to seeke God by humble
" prayers and supplications." Fol. 48.

Again, two years later, he writes : " Also finding
" myself yet compassed with dyvers afflictions by the
" good hand of my heavenly father, upon myself, my
" wife, my daughter, and my estait, and my reputation,
" and upon my friends ; and remembring how fear-
" fully I have been threatened and reproached and
" troubled both by my countrymen, subscryvers of the
" late Covenant, boasting to take my life and my estate
" and my good name from me all at once, and to bury
" them all in ignominie, and also by the savadge High-
" landmen who took captive one of my tenants, being
" my cousin also, and thretned to kill him except they
" got in hast a very greit ransom." Fol. 58.

In this year, 1638, he prepared " A peacable Warning
" to the Subjects in Scotland," which in his diary he
says was done at the request of the Marquis of Huntly,
and his intention in which he thus describes : " I con-
" sidering that it became me not to stryve for words
" wherat they took exception, and which they did inter-
" pret as reproachfull against them, altho' my constant
" intention was lovingly to warne them, I resolved with
" the advyse of some brethren, to publish that warn-
" ing in print, removing out of it all hastie words, and
" craving pardon for anything that was amiss, thus to
" declare to all men my Christian and peaceable dispo-
" sition. Heirby they seemed to be somewhat ap-
" peased, but yet some of them doe continew threatning
" me, if so they may drive me by humane terrour to
" approve and goe their way, which truely my con-
" science suffereth me not to do." Fol. 59.

In 1640 he was summoned to appear before the General
Assembly held in July of that year at Aberdeen. In
his diary he records his daily preparation by prayers,
and the subjects on which he was questioned. Thus :
" Upon the 30th day of Julie 1640, in the morning
" early, revolving what had passed yesterday, I found
" that in my words before the Assembly there were
" some which I should rather not have spoken, and
" that I hade omitted some words which hade been very
" convenient to be spoken ; and fearing lest any offence
" have arisen therby in the mynds of my brethren,
" and fearing desertion, I prayed and wept unto God
" for mercy, and that he would remeid and remove all
" offences given by me to any, or taken by any at me,
" that day or at any tyme, and to be with my heart and
" with my mouth, and to grant me mercy and grace
" in his sight, and convenient mercy and favour in
" the eyes of all with whome I have to doe ; and I
" was comforted in God ; to him be glorie for ever.
" Amen."

" Upon the first of August 1640 I compeared before
" the Committee of the Generall Assemblie, and being
" questioned upon many things, I found God's mercifull
" presence so evidently with me, as notwithstanding of
" my scruples concerning the Covenant, and of my
" wreittings, yet they were pleased with me. Also they
" tooke in good part my answeris to other questions
" upon the 4th and 5th dayes of the same moneth.
" Now all the dayes of the General Assemblie I prayed
" every day with groans and tears unto God to be with
" me, and give me a comfortable outgett and a blessed
" event, and to forgive all my sinnes ; and the Lord
" heard me. Praised be the Lord."

The case was continued for farther consideration in
Edinburgh, and at a later time a sentence of deprivation
was passed against Dr. Forbes for declining to take the
Covenant, and he was compelled to take refuge in Hol-
land. He returned to Scotland in 1647, and died at his
Castle of Corse in the following year.

The diary extends to 179 folios.

There is also in the library the Court Book of the
lands and barony of Fintray from 1711 to 1724. The
Courts were held at Haltoun of Fintray.

JOHN STUART.

This collection is drawn from three sources.

The first and largest part of it consists of charters
and papers relating to the barony of Allardice in Kincardineshire, which from a very early period belonged
to the family of Allardice of that ilk, now represented
by Mrs. Allardice.

The second series is connected with the Earls of
Airth and Menteith, and the claims to the dormant title
which have been made in the House of Lords by the
late Mr. Barclay-Allardice, and by Mrs. Barclay-Allardice, his daughter, arising through the marriage, in
1662, of Sir John Allardice of that ilk with Mary, one
of two sisters of William last Earl of Menteithe and
Airth.

A third set of papers relate to the family of Barclay
of Ury, in Kincardineshire, through the marriage of
the heiress of the family of Allardice with Robert Barclay of Ury in 1776.

Among the ancient writs of the barony of Allardice
are many of considerable interest, especially as illustrating tenures, and processes of Scottish law relating
to land.

Of these I selected the following for description :—

Extract from the Books of Council and Session of a
charter by William King of Scots (1165–1214) to Walter,
son of Walter the Scot (Scotti) of Alredies, to be held by
the service of one archer with horse and habergeon, and
performing common service, as much as pertains to 13
oxgates of land as the charter of his father bears. Witnesses, Hugh the King's Chancellor, G[ilbert] Abbot
of Aberbrothock, Earl Duncan, Justiciar, Robert de
Quinci, Robert of London, Philip of Mowbray, William of Hay, John of Hastinges, Yvo of Vipont, Walter
urdac, Roger of Lakern, Thomas son of Tankard.
Mated at Stirling, 16th of October [no year]. The
original charter was registered in the Books of Council
and Session on 20th August, 1703.

Charter by John of Allyrdis of that ilk, confirming
to John called Harwer, for his good services to his
father and also to himself, all his lands of Ardgrane,
with their pertinents, in Buchan in the shire of Aberdeen, which had been previously granted by his father
to the said John Harwer and his heirs, and also to one
assignee to whom he might desire to assign the said
land. Reddendo a pair of gilt spurs in name of blench
farm yearly at the feast of the Annunciation of the
Blessed Virgin Mary, if asked, and performing to our
lord the King, and to other lords of the fee, the services exigible from such a land. Sealed with the seal
of the granter, and in farther testimony with the seal of
a noble man, Alexander of Straton, of that ilk, at Aberdeen, 1 September, 1376. Witnesses, John Frasser,
Philip of Abirbuthnot, William Lassellis, Thomas of
Rate, Alexander Bannerman, Alan Fauconer, burgess
of Monrose, Thomas Spryng, burgess of Aberdeen, and
many others.

Instrument dated 20 February, 1458, within the
church of St. Giles, at Edinburgh, on the refusal of
the Bishop of Brechin, Chancellor of Scotland, to allow
to be repledged the goods and lands of Thomas Allirdes
of that ilk, which had been recognosced, according to
the request then made by him to said Bishop, Chancellor aforesaid. Witnesses, William Murray de la Gask,
Sir Robert Crechtoun of Sanchar, William Murray of
Tyermam, and Mr. Alexander of Carsteris, rector of
Keth, with many others.

Notarial instrument dated 12 March, 1458, setting
forth that in presence of the King, James the Second,
by the grace of God King of Scots, and his Council
and the prelates and nobles of the kingdom in great
number in the Town House of the burgh of Perth, appeared Thomas Allirdes of that ilk, and there desired
that his lands of Allirdes, with their pertinents, in the
shire of Kincardyn, his lands of Ochterlese and Polglassy and Ardgrane, with their pertinents, in the shire
of Aberdeen, and his goods, now for certain causes
recognosced in the King's hands, might be given to him
to borch, offering himself ready for his said lands and
goods to do whatever by the law and custom of the
kingdom ought to be done. Upon which the said
Sovereign Lord, by delivery of a staff which he held in
his hands, gave the same to him in broch, in presence of
Thomas Bishop of Dunkeld, Ninian Elect confirmed of
Whithorn, Malise Earl of Mentethe, William Earl Marischal, James Lord Levingstoun, Great Chamberlain
of Scotland, Patrick le Grahame, Patrick Lord of
Glamys, Robert Levingstoun of Drumry, and John

Ogilby of Luntrethyn, Knights, with many others. The notary is John de Atheray, Treasurer of Dunkeld, Clerk of the King's Council.

Notarial instrument dated 2 May 1459, within the Court House of the burgh of Aberdene, at a court held by Walter Lyndesay of Bewfurd, sheriff of the said burgh, setting forth the compearance of Thomas Allirdes of that ilk, accused of the spoliation of David Dempstar of Achterless his lands of Balglassy in the barony of Achterles, and the unjust detention of the rents thereof for the space of twelve years last by-past, for the amount of which he was found liable in re-payment, in a certain session held in Edinburgh, as appeared by a decreet thereof under the testimony of the Great Seal ; the said Thomas alleging that the said spoliation, rents unjustly detained, and the said decreet itself were false, offering himself ready to prove that at the time of making of the said decreet there was no session held at Edinburgh or in any part of Scotland, and alleging also that he is now in the King's ward "ob quam rem namos et bona sua " injuste abstulerant." He therefore protested solemnly " quod quicquid prefatam materiam concernens quo- " nismodo in dicta curia deliberatum seu indicatum " esset in prejudicium vel detrimentum hereditatis sue " minime verteretur." These things were so done at 11 o'clock before noon : on which day, at two hours after-noon, within the chamber of Alexander of Douglas, sheriff depute of Aberdene, the said Thomas earnestly asked of the said Walter, the sheriff, a copy of a certain letter or precept, written on parchment and sealed with the King's seal, touching the execution of the foresaid decreet of said session, which had been presented to the sheriff in court ; which sheriff answering him said that he declined to give a copy of the said precept until the King and his Council should first be consulted. The witnesses to the first act were noble and potent men, William Earl of Erole, Lord of Hay, William Earl Marischal, Lord of Keith, Alexander of Irwin, Laird of Drum, William Hay of Ure, David Aberbuthnot of that ilk, and Alexander of Strathachyn of Dulyewarde. The witnesses to the second act were David Lyndesay of Forest, Philip Lyndesay, Robert of Rossy, John of Tulche, David Allirdes, and Alexander Glone, with others.

Notarial instrument dated 24 January 1470, on the presentation by Thomas Allardes of that ilk to venerable and noble men, councillors of the King, of a schedule or paper relating to a sum of money claimed by John Dempstare as rents of the lands of Polglassy, with the pertinents, recognosced and unjustly given to broch to the said John, the said Thomas asserting that he was the possessor of the same. Of which schedule the tenor follows :—

" Soŭeran lord, and nobilis of our soneran lordis counsale. I, Thomas Allirdes of that ilk, protestis that I enter nocht in pley here at this tyme anent the sum-mondis made apone me be Jhone Dempstare and till his instance, for I understand at the mater aucht nocht to resort nor procede here at present tyme befor your lordschipis, be thir rasonis folonand. In the first the sumoundis war not signet nor selit be the summoundare as it aucht to be of resoune as wes actit in the last Par-liament. Secundly, this questioune movit apone me be Jhone Dempstare my perti hes beynne reconist befor in his faderis tyme and mynne, and lattin to borgh to him be wrang informatioun and parcialite of the bischop Schoriswode, chancellare for the tyme, he beand his familiar man, and syne thairoftir it was reformit in a counsale generale in King James the Secundis tyme, your progenitour, quhame God assoilze, and lattin me to borgh, and sa was I restorit to my possessioune agane and tuk sesinge be Jhone Skrimgeour Masare that levis yit, throu comand of the King ; and, my lordes, I under-stand that it is agane the comoune law and consuetud that ony mater or questioune decidit and decretit be a generale counsale or Parliament, sould resort or remane to be determinit in a laware court, and this caus neulingis movit upon me throw meyneis be Jhonne Dempstare, dependis upon my fee and heritage of the samyn landis of Polglassy, the quhilkis I was restorit to as said is be the King, as my documentis beris witness ; and alsua, my lordis, thir landis of Polglassy ar to me proppir fee and heritage thir twenti yeris and ma sen synne and befor as my perti beris witnes, and als the said Jhonne Dempstare clamis thame in fee and heritage til him, and tharefor he folowis me of twenti yeris malis in his faderis tyme, his brotheris and in his awine tyme, and thus we clame thame fee and heritage for us baith, and sa thai ar fee and heritage till [ane] of us apone law but drede ; and, my lordis, sen thai ar fee and heritage, I beseik your lordshipis at the reverence of al I may be

deferrit to my juge ordinar, and to keip sic law and con-suetude to me and my sympilnes as ye do till utheris our soueran lordis lieges, and gif your lordschippis dois utherwais herein I protest it turne me to na prejudice and my said fee and heritage." After the reading of which schedule to the said lords, the said Thomas of Allirdes ut supra. These things were done at Strineline about two o'clock afternoon on the day before specified, in presence of Reverend Fathers in Christ Andrew Bishop of Glasgow, William Bishop of Orknay, Andrew Lord Avandale, Chancellor of Scotland, Colin Earl of Argyle, James Lord Hammiltoune, and Alexander Lord Glammys, with many others.

Notarial transumpt dated 28 May 1474, within the Court House of Aberdeen, before a noble man, Walter Lindesay, sheriff depute of Aberdeen, then sitting in judgment, setting forth that John Allerdes of that ilk compeared and craved that a brieve of our sove-reign lord for serving him heir to his father Thomas in two parts of the lands of Uchtirless, with the pursal-butis and their pertinents, should be copied and tran-sumed, which desire was granted and the brieve en-grossed, in presence of honorable men, Alexander Forbes of Petslegow, Knight, Alexander Fraser of Durris, and Duncan Forbes, Esquires, and many others.

Charter by King James III. under the Great Seal in favour of George Meldroum, son and heir-apparent of William Meldroum of Fyvy and Elisabeth Innes, his spouse, of the lands of Petkary, in the shire of Kincar-dine, on the resignation of the said William. Dated at Edinburgh, 10 March 1482.

Charter by Alexander Irvin of Drum to John Al-lardes of that ilk, of his lands of Fulzemond, in the barony of Auchindoir, in warrandice of two parts of the lands of Ardgrane, in the earldom of Buchan, sold by him and his son by a charter of same date. Dated at Aberdeen, 24 November 1485. Witnesses, Mr. Adam Gordone, rector of Kinkell and chantor of Murray, Robert Aberbuthnot of that ilk, Alexander Menzeis, Alexander Burnet of Leis, Alexander Irvin of Belteis, David Allirdes, Sir John Arveling, and Sir Robert Leis, chaplains and notaries, with others.

Notarial instrument, dated 26 June 1490, setting forth that, in presence of a notary and witnesses, ap-peared a prudent woman, Joneta Betsoun, wife of James Allerdes '' et fide media manualiter obligata est hono- '' rabili viro Johanni Allardes de eodem ac domino de '' Ochterless forma subsequenti, vis', si contingat pre- '' fatum Jacobum sponsum suum de hac vita antea '' eam decedere, quod abhinc non duceret alium virum '' in sponsam suum, nec de bonis eo tempore prolibus '' inter prefatam Jacobum et Jonetam genitis pertinen- '' tibus, ullatenus in fraudem et damnum earundem '' disponeret absque prefati domini de Allirdes consilio '' et consensu. Et si contrarium fecerit quod absit '' assedacio terrarum de Cuschne per prefatam domi- '' num dictis Jacobo et Jonete et eorum diucius viventi '' facta sine mora expiraret." These things were done at Cuschne at eight o'clock in the evening, in presence of Archibald Rate of Drumtocty, and John Malwyn, ap-parent of Hervistoune.

Notarial instrument, dated 12 June 1493, setting forth the compearance of honorable men, Sir John Rutherfurde of Terlane, Knight, and Robert Blinsele, burgess of Aberdeen, who produced the seal of a noble man, Alexander Irwyn of Drum, and by his authority affixed the same to a contract of marriage, written on parchment, entered into between the said Alexander Irwyn and Alexander his son and apparent heir on the one part, and John Allirdes of that ilk and Janet his daughter and heir-apparent on the other part. Done within the lodging of the said Robert in the burgh of Aberdeen, in presence of Gilbert Ketht, son of the laird of Invergy, Mr. Alexander Gordon, vicar of [ ]linge, Thomas Prat, John Kintor, John Gordon, William Cuminge, and Mr. Alexander Massy, notary, with others.

Notarial instrument, dated 5 November 1495, shewing that, in presence of a notary and witnesses, " compeared " James Allirdes, et fideliter promisit ad faciendum " servicium fidelitatemque servandam in omnibus ut " decet honorabili viro Johanni Allirdes de eodem ac " domino de Ochtirles heredibusque suis pro toto suo " tempore vitæ, cum ad dictum servicium debite pre- " monitus fuerit. Et si, quod absit, dictum contingat " Jacobum in contrarium devenire viz., si notabilem " defectum in servicio suo faceret, ipso ad hoc compe- " tenter abdoc ut prefertur premonito. Tunc in instanti " ac sine mora assedacio terrarum de Cuschne dicto " Jacobo et uxori sue facta prout in literis desuper

" confectis plenius continetur penitus expiraret."
These things were done in the Hall of Allirdes at two
o'clock afternoon, in presence of discreet men, Sir
Andrew Valentyn and Sir Robert Blaklawis, chaplains.

Notarial instrument dated 13th November 1500,
shewing that in presence of William Bishop of Brechin,
then sitting in judgment, appeared James Richardson,
chaplain, procurator of John Allerdes of that ilk, and
produced certain letters of reversion by Alexander
Irwyn, apparent of Drum, and Jonat Allirdes his spouse,
of the two parts of the lands and barony of Ouchterles,
sealed with their seals and dated 13 December 1499,
and after presenting and reading thereof, the said procurator " ab honorabili domicella Joneta Allirdess
" sponsa Alexandri Irwyne, filii et apparentis heredis
" honorabili viri Alexandri Irvin de Drum inquisivit
" si ad sigillacionem dictarum literarum reversionis
" libere et voluntarie pro parte sua consentiebat. Que
" quidem Joneta non vi auit metu ducta [etc.] Sigillum
" suum proprium in manum tenens intra cujus circum-
" ferentiam tria folia de le holyne cum undis [   ]
" sculpta erat in absencia sponsi antedicti tactis Sacro
" Sancti dei Evangeliis in manibus dicti episcopi jura-
" mentum prestitit corporale quod ad dictarum litera-
" rum sigillacionem liberrime incoacta et ex propria
" voluntate motuque consensit." These things were so
done in the choir of the parish church of Montrose at
eleven o'clock before noon, in presence of Mr. George
Meldrum, chantor of Brechin, Sir David Ochterlowny,
vicar of Monheky, Alexander Grahame, William Murell,
John Grahame, William Allirdes, and Mr. John
Nauchty, notary.

Notarial instrument, dated 15 June 1512, setting
forth that John Allardes of that ilk, having compeared
" plegium sive le borghe in manu Thome Bissato mari
" feodatarii Regii, vicecomitatus de Aberdene pouuit,
" quo de jure arrestaret novam culturam formatam in
" Drowmdewane et blada sive grana in eadem crescencia
" non Remouenda ac veractum vulgo le fauche infra
" eandem non laboranda una cum edificiis constructis
" in dictis terris de Dronmedewane prope Blakfurd non
" fungend. Pro injusta occupacione earundem terrarum
" donec per leges titulo juris cujus sint discuciantur.
" Quia ipsas dictus Johannis Allerdes sibi allegabat
" pertinere et partem esse sue partis baronie de Ouch-
" tirless. Et ut sibi Inwino Garden Regis auctoritate
" inhiberet ne ipsas terras occupet usque in profinitum
" tempus legale. Et ut eandem arrestam sibi intimaret
" non obstantibus ipsis arrestamentis iteratis vicibus.
" In pretaxatis alias affiris minime valentibus." These
things were done on the lands of Drowmdewane at
twelve o'clock noon, in presence of George Meldrum of
Five, Sir Gilbert Hay of Ardendracht, Knight, Walter
Barclay of Tolly, George Abercromby of Petmethane,
Robert Gordon of Bealle, Patrick Stewart of Latheris,
Robert Allerdess, Mr. Alexander Ogilvy in Glashalche
Magnus de Monte alto, son and apparent heir of John
Mowat of Loscragy, Andrew Crage of Cragisfyntray,
Thomas Meldrum of that ilk, James Crafurd of Fethe-
ray, James Bissate, and Mr. Andrew Patrickson, notary,
with many others.

Licence under the Privy Seal of James V., dated
Edinburgh, 22 March 1516, permitting John Allardes
of that ilk to sell annalie or wedsett his landis and
barony of Allirdes, in the Sheriffdom of Kincardine.

Notarial instrument, dated 5 September 1522, setting
forth that on that day John Allirdes of that ilk, and John
his lawful son and heir, compeared at the Market Cross
of Aberdeen, and there by proclamation thrice repeated
by the mouth of David Herine, one of the officers of
the said burgh, at the command of the said John, the
father and son warned a noble man, Alexander Irwein,
of Forglind, son and heir of Sir Alexander Irwein
of Drum, and Janet Allirdes, his wife, spouse of the
said Alexander Irwein, of Forglin, to appear in the
church of St. Nicholas of Aberdeen, on Monday the 3rd
of November next, to receive the sum of 1,200 merks,
due for the redemption of two parts of the barony of
Ochterles, in terms of letters of reversion.

Tack by John Abbot of Lundores, and Convent of the
same, to Gilbert Keith of Troup and Isobel Forbes his
spouse, and to William Keith their son, for 19 years, of
the lands called Scottistoune, together with Marcorye
and the officiar land of the same within the barony of
Witatonis and sheriffdom of Kincardine. Dated at
Lundores, 24 July 1532. Signed by the abbot, sub-
prior, and 23 monks.

Charter by James V. to John Allirdes of that ilk of
the lands of Allirdes, with the principal messuage, and
mains lands of Little Barres and Leys, lying in the
shire of Kincardine, and also the two parts of the lands

and barony of Ochterles, containing two parts of the
lands and barony of Ochterles, two lie parsantis, one
part of the lands of Ordley, Thomastoune, Smailburne,
Quysneis, Knokleith and mill thereof, two parts of the
lands of Bonkillis, Bakyhill Langschaubrae, Logyal-
toun, Fischerford, Reidhill, and Hessiewellis, with the
manor thereof; also all the lands of Blakfurd, Bad-
dinskeith, and Innercherny, in the shire of Aberdeen;
resigned by the said John, and now united into one
whole and free barony, to be called the barony of
Allirdes, ordaining the manor-house of Allirdes built
and building, to be the principal messuage of the said
barony. Dated at St. Andrews, 28 May 1540.

Instrument on the resignation into the King's hands
by John Allardes of his lands of Allirdes, dated 28
May 1540, on which the above charter proceeds :—" Acta
" erant infra Monasterium Sancti Andree in Palacio
" Serenissimi Principis nostri Jacobi Quinti Scotorum
" regis hora quarta pomeridiana, Presentibus ibidem
" Reverendissimo in Christo Patre et domino David
" miseracione divina titulo Sancti Stephani in Celio
" Monte Cardinali presbytero, Sancti andree Archi-
" episcopo Tocius Scocie primate legato nato Ecclesie
" Cathedralis Mirapiciensis in Gallia administratoro
" generali, Monasterii de Aberbrothok Commendatario
" perpetuo, nobilibus et potentibus dominis Johanne
" domino de Innermeith, Thoma Erskin do Breichen
" milite et S. D. N. Regis Secretario, et Henrico Kempt
" de Thomastoun testibus," &c.

Inquest held at Aberdeen, 9th January 1553, serving
John Allardes as heir of James Allardes, his uncle, who
fell under the royal banner at Pinkie, in the lands of
Balgowny in the barony of Frendraught and shire of
Aberdeen, held blench of William Crichton of Frendraught, and that in virtue of a General Act in favour of
the heirs of those falling in said battle.

Testament dative and inventar of the goods of
Robert Allardes, apparent of that ilk, at the time of his
death in Edinburgh, 26 December 1587, given up by
Captain Andrew Stewart, as tutor dative, to Elizabeth
Allardes, only lawful daughter of the deceased.

Summons raised against John Allardes and his tenants
by Margaret Erskine, Lady Petcarie and Banffe, under
certain obligations in a contract between her and John
Allardes of that ilk, dated 31 December 1587, and a
copy thereof, which is entitled, " Copie for John Allardes
" apperand of that ilk as executor and universall intro-
" metter to the maist venemous pestiferous serpent,
" Margartt Erskyne, Lady Makterey, 4 of August
" 1597."

A contract dated 22 July 1592, between John Allardes
of that ilk and his tenants, Thomas Strathauchin in
Leyis and Robert Falconer in Classindrum, on the one
part, and Barbara Forbes, Lady Petcarrie on the other.
" The said lady is God-willing to come and meitt at
" ane speciall week day at the kirk of Arbuthnot, betwixt
" nine and twelf horis afoir none, betwixt the date of thir
" presentis and the twantie fyrst day of August nixto-
" cum, and thair sall acknawledge and confess the
" wrange done unto the laird of Allardes in this last
" fact committit at the Moss of Monymont, and sall
" promas in all tymes cuminge interteinament of guid
" freyndschip and concord without braik of hir pert,
" craving the lyik concord and freyndschip to be ex-
" tendit to hir on his part in all tymes cumminge, with
" promeis also that scho sall caus her twa brethir
" Robert Forbes, prior of Monymusk, and Abraham
" Forbes in Blaktoun, accumpanie hir to the said kirk
" and acknawledge the sameyn giff scho may obteine
" thame thairto, quhais compeirance to the said kirk
" salbe signefeit be the said Barbara to the said John
" Allardes sex dayes off befoir the said day."

A large mass consisting of upwards of a hundred
unarranged papers of the sixteenth and seventeenth
centuries, many of them receipts for payment of teinds
of the lands of Scotstown to the provost and masters of the New College of St. Andrews; vouchers and
discharges of loans; law papers; contracts of marriage; contracts with neighbouring proprietors; submissions and relative decreets, and old inventories of
title deeds.

Among the papers relating to the Earldom of Menteith are the following :—

Charter by William Earl of Menteith to Agnes Gray,
his future spouse, of the barony of Kinpont, dated
30 March 1612.

Procuratory of resignation in favour of John Lord
Kinpont and Lady Mary Keith proceeding on their
contract of marriage, dated 11 April 1632.

Letter from the Earl of Airthe to James Livingston
of Beill, one of His Majesty's Bedchamber, dated Edin-

burgh, 17 September 1639 :—"Richt worthie and loveing
" freind, the reasone that I have beine so long in wret-
" ting to His Majestie wes that I resolved to be silent
" until I micht have something of importance to vrett,
" and altho I know His Majestie is advertised by many
" daylie of the procedure of this assemblie, yet he hath
" hade no shorter relatione then that which I send heir-
" with, whairfor I intreate yow to delyver this tother
" letter to His Majestie and desyre ane answer, for I have
" sende this berar expressely for it, and His Majestie's
" effaires doe requyre that the answer may be returned
" with diligence. I have send yow herein ane little
" scroll which containeth the most materiall things
" which ar doone in this assemblie : it is only for your
" awin wee, and therfor efter yow have redd it, burne
" it, and I hope His Majestie will do so with my lettor,
" and the paper within it. I had send you that money
" long er this, bot that Williame Gray hath beene this
" thrie weekes in Angous and wilbe heir the morrow,
" and I assure yow he shall immediately send ane
" warrand to his factor thair to pay yow, and I shall
" dispatch it with ane man of my awin, for altho' His
" Majestie be owing me far greater soumes, yet I shall
" never for such ane triffle as is owing me have such
" ane base thocht as to seeke allowance of such ane
" soume ; therefore expect it, and lett not this berar nor
" any living know that there is anything of this kynde
" betwix yow and me. Now I must intreate that as
" yow love the goode of His Majestie's effaires, and as
" yow doe respect me in particular, to hasten bak this
" berar, and intreate His Majestie to vrett the answer
" to my letter, and I beseech yow to inclose His Ma-
" jestie's letter within one of your awin to me. So
" wishing yow all happiness, I shall ever rest your
" treulie affectionat freind to serve yow. " AIRTHE."

Charter by King Charles I. in favour of John Lord
Graham of Kinpont and Lady Mary Keith his spouse,
eldest daughter of the Earl Marischal, and William
their eldest son, of the lands of Kilbryde. Dated 8 January 1644.

Note of Lady Mary Graham's contract of marriage
with Sir John Allardes of that ilk. Dated 26 September 1662.

Memorandum and queries for the Laird of Allardyce,
1694 :—" The Laird of Allardyce being the eldest sister
" son to the deceast Earl of Monteith, and Graham
" of Gartmore the youngest sister's son, and so they
" both the nearest of kin to the Earl in blood, and who
" can succeed to him, and the late Marquess of Mon-
" tross having, as is informed, impetrate a disposition
" from the Earl of his whole estate, and which dispo-
" sition was got by threatening even to the hazard of
" the Earles life, which can be proven, and the Lady
" Marquess, mother to this Marquiss, who is under
" tutorie with severall others without warrand by ex-
" hibitione, has with some of the friends gone to the
" house of one Brown, where the Earles charter chest
" was lyeing, and carrying the papers away under
" silence of night without inventareing or sealling up
" the samen by warrand of Councill, Session, or other
" magistrate, to the prejudice of the nearest of kin who
" have interest as appearand heirs, and had lykeways
" particular dispositions from the Earle in his ain
" time to severall interests which were in the charter
" chest among the other papers which they medled
" with : Queritur, If this will not be a ryott, and if a
" bill may not be drawn to the Councill at the ap-
" pearand heirs instance for sequestrating and inven-
" tarying the saids writes and taking the oathes of the
" Lady Marques [   ] the tutor and others pre-
" sent, and to find and declare it to be a ryott."

Then follow questions on the subject of teinds, and
on a point arising out of the marriage of Anna, sister
to the Laird of Allardes, to the Laird of Brackley.

Information for the Earl of Montoith, 1696.

Answers for the Marquis of Montrose to the claim
given in by the Laird of Allardes, 8 July 1709.

Ane Inventorie of the Evidents of Kinpont.

Official extract of the Airth patent, 1790.

The following papers are from that part of the collection which relates to the Barclays of Ury :—

Extract, dated 17 April 1626, of contract dated 12
April 1624, and registered in the Sheriff Court books
of Kincardine between William Earl Marischal and
certain inhabitants of the town of Stonehaven, containing obligation by him to grant to them feus of their
tonements ; and with provisions for maintenance of
bridges and causewnys, the election of magistrates, &c.

Contract of marriage between the Laird of Allardes
and Elizabeth Barclay, 1690.

Extract, dated 28 August 1733 from the Sheriff
Court books of Kincardine, of disposition and right to
the shore dues, and customs of two mercats for upholding the pier of Stonhyve, by William Earl Marischal,
dated 10 May 1697.

Copy of a letter sent by Barclay of Ury to the Earl
of Marr :—

" Ury, 12th of $\frac{4}{mo.}$ 1713.

" Respected frind,
" Had I the honour of thy acquaintance as much
as I have of my very good frind thy brother Grange,
I should not put thee to the trouble of this apologie,
but hopes thou will excuse what I cannot help, and not
take it amiss that I become thy humble suiter in behalf
of myselfe and my friends in this nation. Our caice is,
wee cannot with freedom take the benefite of the solemn
affirmation formerly granted to our friends in England,
and now under consideration of the House of Commons
to be renued and extended to us, without it be made
easier and more agreeable to the simple and plain precept of our Lord and Saviour Jesus Christ. I begg of
thee, with all the earnestness I can, that if it come your
length, thou wold become our advocate for ane amendment so as to make it effectual, to us, thy friends in
the Ancient Kingdom, as well as thousands of our
brethren in England under the same difficultys with us,
wee always being willing to be subjected, upon the
breach of our simple affirmation to the same penalties
by law inflicted upon perjurie. The befriending us in
this will be a work of great charity, and I hope will
draw donn upon thee and thy family those blessings
bestowed upon such as helps to relive the oppressed for
conscience sake. I know I need not use it as an argument to so great a man that it wold put ane infinite
obligation upon all receiving benefits by it, and in
particular thy true friend R. Barclay."

A draught is preserved of a similar letter to the
Earl of Argyll of the same date.

In a list of manuscripts lent by Robert Barclay
Allardice of Ury to John Barclay of Alton in Hampshire, 9th month 1826 (but now among the papers) are,
the following entries :—" 3 & 4. Two little pocket diaries
" of R. Barclay, the apologist, in his own hand. A
" Journal, imperfect. A Quaker's notion of the divine
" light in a letter to a friend by R. B."

A Genealogy of the Barons of the Mearns unto the
year of God 1578 :—Straiton of Lauriston, Strachan of
Thornton, Graham of Morphie, Barclay of Mathers,
Ramsay of Balmain, Wood of Balbegno, Ogston of
Kirklands of Fettercairn, Lindsay of Broadland, Leslie
of Pitnamoon, Douglas of Glenbervie, Falconer of
Halkerton, Middleton of Killhill, Rait of Hallgreen,
Lundy of Benholm, Lyall of Balmaliddy, Hay of Ury,
Straton of Craigie, Strachan of Monboddo, Falconer of
Balandroe, Moncur of Slains, Fraser of Durris, Tulloch
of Cragnastoune, Melvill of Herviston, Arbuthnot of
that ilk, Irvine of Drum, Barclay of Johnston, Barclay
of Balmakuan, Douglas of Bridgefoord, Ogilvie of
Barras.

A genealogical account of the Barclays of Ury (a
modern copy).

Notes of various members of the family of Barclay
(some of them American), 1659-1774.

JOHN STUART.

THE MANUSCRIPTS OF A. D. R. BAILLIE COCHRANE,
Esq., of Lamingtoune, M.P.

The ancient and knightly family of Baillie have been
in possession of the barony of Lamingtoune, in the
upper ward of Lanarkshire, for many centuries. Its
members have on various occasions occupied a prominent position in national affairs, and have intermarried
with many of the noble and powerful families of Scotland. The records, however, which at one time remained to witness the varied fortunes and growing importance of the family, have been dispersed, and the
charter chest, to which Mr. Baillie Cochrane gave me
ready access, contains only fragments of the earlier
series of charters with the usual progress of title deeds
of later date.

Nisbet, the writer on Scotch heraldry, in the early part
of last century, examined the charter chests at Lamingtoune, where he saw a charter by King David II., dated
27 January 1368, confirming to Sir William Baillie,
Knight, the barony of Lambistoun, and these lands

A. D. R.
BAILLIE
COCHRANE,
Esq.

still belong to Mr. Baillie Cochrane, the descendant of the grantee.

The only papers of historical interest which I noticed among the masses of business documents, relate to a portion of the estate, in the neighbourhood of the town of Lanark, which was held by the tenure of baking certain wafers of bread for the King when he happened to reside at Lanark.

The earliest document of the series is a charter by Murdach, Duke of Albany, to John Ker, burgess of Lanark, of all and whole the lands called Wafralandis, with their pertinents in the territory of the burgh of Lanark, between the burgh and the parish church. The reddendo is thus expressed : " Faciendo domino nostro " regi, et heredibus suis dictus Johannes et heredes " sui pro dictis terris cum pertinenciis pisturam wafra- " rum dicti domini nostri regis quociens ipsum domi- " num regem apud Lanark contigerit residere." Dated at Stirling, 30 November 1422. Witnesses, William, Bishop of Glasgow, Chancellor of Scotland ; Alexander Stewart, of Kinclevin, the Regent's son ; Archibald of Cunningham, sheriff of Stirling ; Alan of Otterburn, secretary, and others.

Charter by John Ker, burgess of Lanark, Lord of Vaufreisfiat, and John Dobysoun, burgess of Lanark, of the four acres belonging to him in the territory of the burgh of Lanark. Paying to him therefor within the parish church of Lanark, on the feast of the Nativity, a penny Scots, in name of blench farm. Dated in the granter's manor at Lanark, 5 December 1429, before witnesses (who also witnessed the giving of seisin to the said John Dobysoun by the said John of Vaufreflat, the Lord Superior) ; Sir Robert Tyningham, chaplain ; William Ker, the granter's son, William Clerksoun, Baillie of the burgh of Lanark for the time, and others.

Instrument of sasine, dated 13 October 1471, in favour of William Doby, chaplain, as lawful heir of John Doby, Vicar of Stow, who died seised in four acres of Wafraflat. Sasine was given by William Ker, burgess of Lanark, and Lord of Wafraflat.

Instrument dated 21 August 1489, containing sentence by John Quhitlawe, Licentiate in Degrees, Canon of Dunkeld, and rector of the parish church of Pennycoko, commissary of William, Archbishop of St. Andrews, in favour of Sir William Doby, in a unit at the instance of Thomas Carr, laic, against him, touching their rights in four acres of Uafraflat, moved before the official of Glasgow.

There are many masses of titles relating to the lands of Waufraflat, Hyndford, Boathaugh, Hyndshaw, Lamington, Bonnington, Coblehaugh, and other lands.

JOHN STUART.

A. J. W. H.
K. Er-
SKINE, Esq.

REPORT on the MANUSCRIPTS of AUGUSTUS JOHN WILLIAM HENRY KENNEDY ERSKINE, Esquire, of DUN, in the County of FORFAR, by WILLIAM FRASER, Edinburgh.

The lands and barony of Dun have been possessed by the family of Erskine for upwards of five centuries. Sir Robert Erskine of Erskine, ancestor of the Lords Erskine and Earls of Mar, was proprietor of the barony of Dun, in the reign of King David the Second. In the following reign, he resigned the barony to his eldest son Sir Thomas Erskine, knight, who obtained from King Robert the Second a Charter of the barony dated on the 8th of November 1376. After his acquisition of Dun, Sir Thomas Erskine was designated Lord of Dun, as appears from a Charter granted by him to Adam Forster, burgess of Edinburgh, of the lands of Carcary in the barony of Dun, dated 28th April 1385. [Original Charter at Kinnaird.]

Sir Thomas Erskine of Dun resigned the barony of Dun in favour of his second son, Sir John Erskine, who obtained from King Robert the Third a Charter of the barony dated 25th October 1392. Under the designation of John of Erskine, Knight, Lord of Dun, Sir John granted a Charter of the lands of Carcary to Walter of Ogilvy, dated 18th March 1400. That Sir John Erskine was the direct ancestor of the family of Erskine of Dun, which is the oldest existing branch of the historical house of Erskine.

In the course of the long-continued descent of the line of Dun, there have been several members of the family who have taken an active and prominent part in the civil and ecclesiastical business of Scotland.

Four of the Erskines of Dun fell in the fatal Field of Flodden in the year 1513, namely, John then Laird

of Dun, Thomas his brother, Sir John his eldest son ; and Alexander another son. Although the house of Dun, like other baronial houses in Scotland, was much weakened by that disastrous battle, the Erskines of Dun in the immediately succeeding generations, had a wonderful vitality. In the year 1588 four generations of the family were all living and in manhood at the same time, the superintendent, his eldest surviving son Sir Robert, John of Logy, son of Sir Robert, and John of Nathrow, who was the son of John of Logy. It is remarkable that these four Erskine Lairds all in the direct line of succession to each other, successively died in each of the four following years. The Superintendent died in 1589, his son Sir Robert in 1590, his grandson John in 1591, and his great grandson, also John, in 1592. [Obits of the Lairds of Dun.]

A. J. W. H.
K. Er-
SKINE, Esq.

At the same time that these four Lairds were living upon the estate, there were five ladies, the wives or the widows of Lairds, who also derived their livings from the estate. These were heavy burdens to bear, even although they only continued for a short time ; and in a contract of marriage of one of the family in the year 1591, special reference is made to the embarrassment of the estate through life-rents, terces, and other burdens.

John Erskine of Dun, early joined the ranks of the Reformers, and he became the friend and follower of John Knox, who refers to him in his History as being " marvelouslie illuminated." In the year 1556, after his arrival from Geneva, Knox visited Erskine at his place of Dun, where he remained a month, daily exercising in doctrine, and where the principal in that country resorted to him. Knox afterwards made a second visit to Dun ; and he records that teaching there in greater liberty, his hearers required that he should administer to them the sacrament of the " Lord's Table," and that the greater part of the gentlemen of the Mearns were partakers.

Being active in the overthrowing of the old and establishing the new form of faith, and being possessed of great learning and business capacity, John Erskine was appointed to the office of Superintendent of Angus and Mearns. He was elected moderator of four general assemblies between the years 1564 and 1566 ; and in all his prominent and responsible positions, he carried himself with such moderation as to merit the approval of his Sovereign, and the principal parties both in the Church and State.

From the family papers now reported on, it appears that the Superintendent was born in the year 1509, and that he survived till the year 1589. He thus lived in the time of five Sovereigns and of seven Regents of Scotland. He was too young to take part in business during the reign of the two first of these Sovereigns, but of the other three he was the correspondent. The letters to him from these Sovereigns and Regents are quoted in the present Report.

When his father fell at Flodden in the year 1513, the Superintendent was left a child of less than five years old. He was fortunate in having for his guardian his uncle, Sir Thomas Erskine of Brechin, Secretary to King James the Fifth. Sir Thomas was careful to give his nephew the advantage of a liberal education, both at home and abroad, of which he derived the benefit in the prominent positions which he afterwards occupied. His mother, Margaret Ruthven, dowager Countess of Buchan, appears also to have been very dutiful to her son during his minority.

Previous to the Reformation, John Erskine was on friendly relations with Cardinal Betoun, who in the year 1544, earnestly asked his advice and assistance, which were also solicited by several noblemen and ecclesiastics of high rank. [Nos. 1, 13, and 14 infra.] In one of these letters it is remarked that King James the Sixth had as good an opinion of Erskine as of any subject in Scotland.

It is also worthy of notice that the family of Erskine was, at the beginning of the 16th century, on terms of intimate friendship with the families of Melville and Paniter, both of which are prominent in the period of the Scottish Reformation. Not only was there the most intimate relation between John Erskine, afterwards the Superintendent, and the lay members of the family of Paniter, which was one of the most influential in Montrose, and to which David Paniter the Commendator of Cambuskenneth was related, but it appears from an early Charter that Erskine, while yet a boy, was on close terms with the Commendator himself ; and in a paper referred to in this Report, the Abbot enters into an indenture with Sir Thomas Erskine, which shows the close intimacy that had existed between

A. J. W. H.
K. kd-
SKINE, Esq.

Paniter and the immediate ancestors of the Superintendent (No. 53).

A still more decided influence appears to have been
exerted upon young Erskine by his connexion with the
family of Melville. The lands of Baldovy seem at
one time to have formed part of the estates of the family
of Erskine of Dun : and Richard Melville, father of
Andrew Melville the Reformer, appears as one of John
Erskine's Curators in the year 1526. The youth of
Erskine was thus passed amidst impressions from both
sides of the religious movement in Scotland ; and it may
be that in this way was generated in him that spirit of
moderation which made him to be respected by all
the parties of the State.

Archbishop Spottiswoode in his History records a very
flattering opinion of Erskine. He says that he governed
the portion of the country committed to his " superin-
" tendence with great authority, till his death, giving
" no way to the innovations introduced, nor suffering
" them to take place within the bounds of his charge,
" while he lived. A baron he was of good rank, wise,
" learned, liberal, and of good courage ; who for divers
" resemblances, may well be said to have been another
" Ambrose. He left behind him a numerous posterity,
" and of himself and of his virtues a memory that shall
" never be forgotten."

As the father of Archbishop Spottiswoode was one of
the co-superintendents along with Erskine, the Archbishop must have derived from his father his knowledge
of the character of Erskine, and he was thus enabled
to pronounce his eulogium on the best authority.

Although the superintendent Erskine is best known
and most prominent in history in his official capacity,
he was occasionally called on to act in a civil and
military as well as an ecclesiastical character. In the
years 1578 and 1579, while he was superintendent, he
was required by King James the Sixth to recover the
fortress of Redcastle near Arbroath, an ancient strong-
hold dating from the time of King William the Lion ;
and Erskine was required to keep the castle in his own
hands. [Nos. 66, 67, and 69.]

In his own letter to the King he says,—" In the weires
" we had with Ingland, quhen the Inglismen possessit
" Dondie, Bruchtie Craig, and the firth thair, I defendit
" the countrie at my power from thair invasiones at the
" desyr of the Queinis grace Regent and Duck of Chatil-
" roy thane Goüernour. I biggit ane forth in Montrois,
" tuik vp ane gret number of men of weir for a lang
" tyme, and furnisit all of my awin guidis, sua that the
" sowmes debursit be me exceidit tuentie thousand
" merkis." [No 16 infra.]

About ten years after his appointment as Superintendent, his own parsonage of Dun become vacant.
King James the Sixth presented Mr. James Erskine,
who is not designated. He was probably one of the
younger sons of the Superintendent of that name.
James Erskine studied under the learned Melancthon.
Amongst the Dun Papers there is preserved the Act of
admission by the Superintendent of James Erskine into
the parsonage of Dun. A copy of the Act is here given
as a specimen of the form observed in such cases by the
Reformed Church :—" Jhone Erskeine the seruand of
" Jesus Christ, Superintendent of Angwss &c., unto
" the Congregation of God within the paroche of Dwn,
" and to all vtheris quhais knowlege thir presentis sall
" to cum, üischis euerlesting health in Christ our Lord.
" Forsamekle as the personage of Dwn lyand within
" the Dioce of Sanctandrois and Sheriffdome of Forfar
" is vacand throw the deceias of vmquhill Dame Ewfame
" Leslie last Prioresse of Elcho, quhilk personage sum-
" tyme pertenit to the priorie of Elcho, and now our
" soueraine Lord hes pesentit vnto ws he his Grace
" letters of presentation Mr. James Erskeine to be
" admitted to the ministrie of the Kirk and to the gift
" and possessioun of the personage foirsaid, We according
" to the Commissioun of the Kirk gewn vnto ws and vnto
" his hienes directioun, hes takin triall of the said Mr.
" James conuersatioun and doctrine, and hes found him
" sufficientlie qualifeit to instruct that congregatioun
" in the trew word of God and way of Salvatioun, and
" therebye conuenient to enter in the ministrie to be
" profitable in the samyn, he resoun quhairof we haue
" admittit him to the cair. and charge of the said
" congregatioun : and hes gewin him for his honest
" sustentatioun the said personage, with all teinds, frutis,
" manss, gleib and vtheris pertinentis thairof whatsum-
" ever, during all the days of his lyfe, conform to the
" said presentatioun alanerlie, and nay vther wais :
" Quhairfoir in the name of the eternall God, and vnder
" the paine of inobedience, we requeir yow and ilk ane
" of yow ministeris and redaris of the Kirkis of

" Strakathro' respectiue, as ye sal be requirit heirvpone,
" to pas to the said Kirk of Dwn, and vtheris placis
" necessar, thair to giff the said Mr. James lawchfull
" institutioun in the said personage, and als to put him
" in reall possessioun of the samyn, with all that pertenis
" thairto, be placing him in the pulpit of the said Kirk,
" and be deliuerance of the buik of God callit the Bible
" in his handis : and requeir all the gentillmen and
" inhabitantis of the said parochioun to intend and
" obey to him as to the lawchful pastour of thair sawles,
" with sic reuerence as becums thame to do of the law
" of God, as at mair lenth is conteinit in the saidis
" letters of presentatioun of the dait at Edinburgh the
" 21st day of September 1570 ; prouiding that the said
" Maister James mak residence at the said paroche Kirk
" and exeout his office faythfullie thairat to the comfort
" of the floke gewin in his cwir, and continew in honest
" and godlie conuersatioun, swa that nay sklaunder
" arryss be him to the euangell ; and in caice that be
" decreit of the generall assemblie of the Kirk (to the
" jugement quhairof he sal be alweiss subiect) he be
" found aither negligent in doctrine or sklandrous in
" lyfe, or for guid caus worthie and meit to be trans-
" portit to ane vther place and charge, this present
" admissioun, with all that sall happin to follow thair-
" upone, to be null ; and sum vther qualifeit persone to
" be presentit to the said personage of new, eftir the
" forme and tennour of the saidis letters of presenta-
" tioun in all pointis. In witnes of the quhilk thing to
" thir our letters of admissioun subscriuit with our hand,
" the seale of our office is affixit at Dwn the 29th day of
" September 1570.

(L.S.)   (signed) JHONE ERSKINE."

Five years afterwards the parsonage became vacant by
the death of Mr. James Erskine ; King James the Sixth
and the Regent Mortoun presented John Erskine of Dun
to the parsonage. Being Superintendent of the district,
Erskine could not admit himself, and the presentation
was addressed to Mr. John Wynram, Superintendent of
Fife. It narrates the qualification, literature, and good
conversation of John Erskine, and of "his long travels
" in the Ministrie within the Kirk of God." In
Wynram's letter of admission of Erskine, after referring
to the presentation, he states that " according to the
" desire quhairof, knowine by large experience, the suffi-
" cient qualification, the godly literature and gude
" conversation of the said John Erskine, together with
" his great labours and diligent travel sustained in the
" Ministrie of the Kirk of God within this realm," he
admits him to the charge.

A family occupying such a prominent position for so
many centuries as the Erskines of Dun, necessarily
accumulated many munimeuts connected with their
landed estates, and also in reference to the public business of Scotland, in which they took a leading part.
The Charters, correspondence and miscellaneous papers
of the Erskines of Dun appear to have been preserved
from any accident of fire, and they have now a considerable collection, including several documents of historical
interest. The charters of the landed estates now and
formerly belonging to the Barony of Dun are both
numerous and ancient, but they do not require any
special notice : The collection of other papers, however,
has formerly attracted the notice of historians. Thomas
Innes, the learned author of the critical essay on the
History of Scotland, extracted valuable information
from the Dun Papers. Bishop Keith also found them
of service in his History of the Church of Scotland
which was published in the year 1735. More recently
the Council of the Spalding Club made a still larger use
of them by including a selection of the Dun Papers in
the fourth volume of their MISCELLANY printed in the
year 1849. Although the present Report is written
from the Original Papers which are in my own custody,
the selection of them which was printed by the Spalding
Club has also been referred to for convenience.[*]

In addition to the Dun Papers proper, there is now
in the Charter Room at Dun a separate collection which
formerly belonged to the Biddells of Haining in the
county of Selkirk. Mr. John Riddell of Haining was
sheriff of that county, in the reign of King Charles the
Second. Commissions were granted to Sheriff Riddell
and others on the Scotch and English sides of the
Borders for the suppression of theft, and also for the
punishment of those who frequented conventicles and
neglected their parish churches, and other ecclesiastical
irregularities.

A. J. VI.
K h-
SKINE, Esq.

* Since this Report was written, the whole Papers have been returned
to Dun.

Through the marriage of David Erskine of Dun, who became a Lord of Session and Justiciary under the title of Lord Dun, with Magdalen Riddell, daughter of Sheriff John Riddell, the papers of Riddell of Haining were transferred to the Dun repositories.

A short notice of the Papers of the Riddells of Haining is given in the present Report in a separate section.

The entire Report is arranged under the following divisions:—

   I. Correspondence of the Erskines of Dun from the year 1544.
   II. Royal warrants and Commissions, and Miscellaneous Papers of the Erskines of Dun from the year 1474.
   III. Correspondence of the Family of Riddell of Hainidg in the shire of Selkirk, now at Dun, from the year 1674.
   IV. Royal Commissions and relative Papers connected with the Scottish Borders from the year 1619.

I.—Correspondence of the Erskines of Dun from the year 1544.

. 1. Original letter of Cardinal Beton to John Erskine of Dun, St. Andrew's, 25th October [1544]. The Cardinal refers to a diet to be held by the Regent Arran at Edinburgh, at which he has no doubt Erskine will be present, on the 1st of November then next, expresses his confidence in his inclination to serve the governor, and assures him that his good will and the "gret wais "and solistatioun maid with mony your gret freyndis "to do the sammin," should come to the higher honour of him and his house and friends, which the writer would "procure and fortifie," as he had more fully stated in a letter to Dun's cousin Sir Thomas Erskine of Brechin, Knight. The Cardinal requests the Laird of Dun to be present at St. Andrew's on Wednesday with his friends and servants, so that they might all set off together on Thursday towards the Lord Governour.

(Signed by the Cardinal.)
"To the rycht honorable and our rycht trast cousin "the Lard of Dvn."

2. Mary Queen Dowager of Scotland to the Laird of Dun. Stirling Castle, 11th January [1547-8].

The Queen Dowager thanks the laird of Dun for his service in defence of the common weal of the realm and of her "derrest dochter," praying he will continue in the same. She assures him that she should soon obtain such support for the relief of the country from the trouble that was instant, as should comfort him and honourable men like him for having proved true to their native realm; and she thinks herself "addettit "till do onto him sic pleshir" as might be conform to his good deserving.

Signed by the Regent "La bien vostre MARIE R."
"To our traist friend the larde of Dvn."

The signature alone is holograph of the Queen Dowager.

3. Mary, Queen Dowager of Scotland to the Laird of Dun. Stirling, 12th March [1547-8].

With reference to information she had obtained regarding the purposed sailing of some ships from Montrose with victual, contrary to the "commone weill," the Queen Regent charged the Laird of Dun to seize and escheat to the Crown any ships in the port of Montrose with such a purpose.

The Regent subscribes herself "La bien vostre "MARIE R."
(Indorsed) "To oure weillbelouit and traist freind "the Lard of Dvne and provest of Montross."

4. Mary, Queen Dowager of Scotland to the Laird of Dun. Edinburgh, 29th August 1549.

From this letter it appears that the Laird of Dun had desired artillery and men for the fort [in Montrose], and that a company of men had been sent there under Captain Beauchastell. This company had not been received, and Erskine, who appears to have considered the appointment of a captain as trespass on his own right apparently as constable of the constabulary of Montrose, had written on this matter to the Queen Regent. She denies any intention of taking from him any of his "heretage," states the necessity of soldiers having over them a captain who was no stranger, and declares it to be her "mind" that these forces should be used by his command and "avise." The letter closes thus in a postscript: "Als it is nocht best that "sic thing suld be done, considering we haue writing "so mekill guid of your part to the King, or that now "ony thing suld be schawin of you in the contrar."

The Regent subscribes "La bien vostre MARIE R."

5. James, Earl of Murray, Regent of Scotland, to the Comptroller. Edinburgh, 2nd November 1567.

The Regent orders the Comptroller not to "mell or "intromet," with any thirds of benefices assigned to the ministers for their stipends, of the '66 crop, either of silver or victuals, but to suffer the ministers or their collectors to use them at their pleasure, and he commands the comptroller to restore to the ministers any victuals with which he may have intromitted.

Holograph signature, "JAMES, Regent."

6. Official letter of Adam Erskine, commendator of Cambuskenneth to the Laird of Dun, younger, requesting him to urge his father [John Erskine, Superintendent of Angus and Mearns], to be present on the 15th of June 1579, at the castle of Stirling, at the court summoned to inquire into the "passening" [poisoning] of the Earl of Athole. Lady Athole and other of Athole's friends were to be present. The Earl of Mar seems to have been interested in the trial and the attendance of his kinsmen is anxiously desired. "I dout nocht bot "ȝe will do thairin as ȝe tendir the Kingis estait, and "my Lord of Mar's weill and honour, for thair is "sindrie gret materis to be intrettit at the said day, "the quhilkes giff thay be weill handillit at this tyme, "it sall put my Loird to the gretter rest." Dated at Stirling Castle, 10th June 1579.

7. David, Earl of Cranford, to his "rycht traist "cousing Robert Erskin off Dun younger." Cairny, 13th August 1579. The Earl wishes Erskine to present to the King letters of horning with their executions, which he had obtained against John Lyoun younger of Cossonis. The Earl states that Lyoun was dependent on him for his living, holding of him a wadset under redemption, and that he never could obtain the small yearly duty Lyoun owed him. Lyoun had conspired with the Master of Glammis to murder the Earl of Cranford in his bed, and so the Earl for this ingratitude was "mowit "to persew him by ordour off law."

8. John Hepburn, Minster of Brechin, "to the richt "honorabil Lord off Dun, Superintendent off Angus "and Mernis." Brechin, 23rd March [1579].

The writer refers to a synodal convention to be held by the Superintendent at Montrose on the 23rd March. He had summoned James Stirling, "citiner," of Brechin, to appear before that court; and he mentions the summons of Walter Grym, whose crimes "the rider "and comissioner's" would show him at length. He excuses his own non-attendance, owing to impediments which prevent his sitting, standing or riding.

9. The Reverend Thomas Smeton, "at the command "of the brethren send in comission," writes from St. Andrews, 30th July 1580, to John Erskine, the Superintendent, concerning the proceedings in the General Assembly, and "sute in court thir many dayes by-"past." He fears their matters in council will not have the issue they desire, nor will it be according to "the necessitie of this horrible confusion, quhilk is "lyk to wraik the kirk of God in this countree," while he regrets the absence of Erskine through weakness and disease of body, he requests him, from time to time to "let them understand his godlie counsell and "iudgement concernyng the vphold of thir ruynous "wallis of afflicted Herusalem."

10. James Scrimgeour, Constable of Dundee, to John Erskine, the Superintendent. 18th January 1580.

This is a letter of presentation, whereby the constable nominates and presents Robert Gray, lawful son to Patrick Gray of Ballegerno, to the "altarage that "was superstitioualie erectit in the honour of Saint "Margaret Quene, situat within the kirk of Dundc, "quhairof the nominatioun and presentatioun of ane "competent persone thairto pertenis heretablie to me "in patronage, and to confer and gif collacioun and "institucioun thairapone belangis vnto you as bischop "and superintendent of the samyn." The presentee is described as a scholar of good "ingine," able to increase in literature and sciences civil and divine. The various annual rents constituting the endowment, and the lands and tenements from which they are derived, are specified; and the whole endowment, extending to eight pounds six pennies of annual rent, besides a piece of burgage land, is "to be liftit and vptakin yeirlie, "vsit and disponit be the said Robert during his liftime "to support his buirding and expensis at grammar "scoles and scholes of vniuersiteis in his minoritie, and "to by his bukis to help his stwdie, to the fine that he "may cum to perfectioun of knawlage to maintene the "religioun and set furth the gospell of Jesus Christ." The writer then requests Erskine to give Robert Gray formal collation and institution upon the said altarage, &c.

11. King James VI. "to our richt traist freind the "Laird of Dun, ane of our ordinarie counsallours, or in "cace of his indispositioun and inabilitie to travell, to "his sonne Robert Erskin younger, of Dwn." Haly-rudehous, 1st March 1580.

"Richt traist freind and counsallour we greit yow hartly weill. This haynous disobedience and rebellioun in James Gray and certaine of his complices be the withhalding of the house of Reidcastell in manefest contempt of our charge direct to him to render and delyner the same to the officiar executour thairof vnder the paine of treasoun, hes movit ws to tak sic ordour with it as may remove the exemple thairof fra any other subiect that we sall happin to charge with the lyke; and to that effect to direct our commissioun to yow our trustie freind and servand to persewe and aseege the said house with fyre, sworde, and all other kynde of wearelyke, ingynes for the recoverie thairof furth of their handis, conteyning ane command and charge to all and sundrie our liegis within the shirriffdome of Forfar, to meit yow in the maist substancious and fensible maner, ready to pas fordwair with yow to that effect. Quhilk we will earnestlie desyre yow earnestlie to put executioun in all pointis as ye will do ws speciall plesyr and gude seruice. Thus we commit yow to God."

(Signed)   JAMES R.

12. King James VI. to the provost and bailies of the burgh of Dundee. Halyrudehouse, xii March 1580. This letter is of the same tenor as that to the Laird of Dun of the 1st March, and the King desires them to conform in all points to the Commission he had directed to the Laird of Dun younger.

Signed by the King, JAMES R.

13. John, Earl of Montrose [Lord High Treasurer], and Sir John Maitland [Secretary of State], to the Laird of Dun. Edinburgh, 18th November 1584.

Dun is addressed as "my lord and father." They had shown his letter to the King, who approved of it all except the "conuenying off the mynistre to gidder "quhill obediens be farst to his Maiesteis statutis." His Majesty sends him a commission for the ministry of Angus and Mearns, with a bond to be subscribed by the ministry within his jurisdiction similar to that which had been subscribed in the Edinburgh district. "His Maiestey hess that guid oppynioun off yow that "he will be layth to sie any seditioun provyit or "mynistrat in your boundis, for His Maiestey is aluayiss "weill myndit to you in your particular, giff that the "cause be not in your self, for truly His Hiness hess "alss guid oppynioun off yow at this present alss he "hess off any subiect in Scotland."

14. "P. Sanct Androe" [Patrick Adamson, Titular Archbishop of St. Andrews], to the Superintendent, who is throughout addressed as "my Lord" and as "your Lordship." The letter is dated from St. Andrews, 22nd January 1584, in answer to a letter from the "lord of Dune," and states that the King's commission for Dun had come with letters to the Archbishop himself, and had been directed to Mr. James Melvin in Arbroath. The Superintendent would learn His Majesty's intention with regard to the diocese of Dunkeld on coming to Dunkeld, and he should take order as before for the parts of the diocese of St. Andrews lying within Angus and Mearns. He wishes him to do in the dioeese of St. Andrews as he did in Brechin.

15. "The brethren wpoun the exercise of Montross "Brechin and Mernis," write to the Superintendent from Montrose, 29th January 1584, regarding the Convention which had met at Montrose on the previous day. The convention was thought to have less grace through his Lordship's absence. Two obligations had been presented by Mr. Henry Duncan, one of which, "want-"ing the condition," was thought hard to agree to. There was some appearance of danger if the said subscriptions were not presented to the King before the 1st of February. His lordship's care of the brethren is referred to with confidence, and some ministers are named out of each exercise to wait on him.

16. Letter to King James VI. from John Erskine Superintendent of Angus and Mearns:—

[This letter is probably the draft of the principal letter which had been sent to the King. The draft bears an indoration to the effect that it is "ane wretting send to "the Kingis Grace." It bears no date but it was probably written about the year 1587 or 1588, as the writer asks the King to enjoy his possession but for one year, as he hopes by that time to be delivered from the

bondage of corruption. He died in the year 1589. The letter gives a summary of the labours of the Superintendent, under his own hand. It has not been known till I lately found it at Dun, and it is now given entire.]

"Pleis your Maiestie to consider that I am your graces subiect and a barrone of your graces realme, and that ane of the maist ancient of yeiris. I haif bene ane faithfull seruand to your hynes nobill predicessouris and to your graces self wnto this day. I haif euer bein obedient to your Maiesties lawes, ordinances and proclamationes. I haif vsit me sua that my nychtbouris complenit nocht on me. I wes neuer accusit for cryme befoir your graces iustice. I tuik neuer remissioune for ony offence, in respect of the quhilk your Maiestie aucht the mair to regaird me. Farther, I neuer spairit my trawellis, my bodye nor guidis, in seruing of my priuce and for the commoune welth. Of sum thinges thairof I will putt your grace in remembrance. In the weires we had with Ingland quhen the Inglis men possessit Dondie, Bruchtie Craig and the forth thair, I defendit the countre at my power fra thair invasiones, at the desyr of the queinis grace regent, and Duck of Chatilroy thane gouernour. a biggit ane forth in Montroia, tuik vp ane gret number of men of weir for a lang time and furnisit all of my awin guidis, sua that the sowmes debursit be me exceidit tuentie thousand merkis as the comptis buir, and yet may be sein. Efter this at the queinis grace regent desyr, and estaittis of parliament, I passit to France in comissioune with the Lordis that wes directit for the marryage of the queinis grace your maiesties mother. My oxpensais thair wos gret, as thy that wos in company dois knawe. Efter this, knawing how necessar it wes a brig to be vpone the Noir watter, at the desyr of thame that had the gouernment and recompens promisit me, I byggit that brige, and warit gret sowmes thairvpone, as thy that luikis on the werk may consider. The queinis grace regent, and the counsall willing to recompance my gret costis, referrit to my self quhat accident or vther thing I wald desyr for recompence, I beand leth to pres thame dreffe tyme. Than at the last in the queinis grace tyme your maiesties mother, wes assignit to me (whill farther mycht be had) this pensioune that I haif nowe of the Kirk, quhilk wes na recompance to me, for the same haif I spendit yeirlie in the cause of the Kirk and now presentlie in vsing and fulfilling the office that I haif of your grace and the Kirk. I haif possessit it thir mony yeiris past, and now to tak it fra me cane nocht be without my gret displesour to sie my guid seruice sua ingratlie recompensit. Heirfoir I maist humble beseik your grace that I may bruik my possessioune bot for a yeir, hoiping or that tyme be passit I sal be delyuerit fra the bondage of corruption. Your Maiesties guid ansuer I desyr.

Your m. humbill and obedient subiect

JHONE ERSKYN.

17. King James VI. to the Laird of Dun [Robert son of the Superintendent]. Stirling, 17 August, 1590. We give entire this peculiar and plain-speaking letter:—

"Traist freind we greit yow weill. It is heavalie lamentit to ws vpoun the behalff of our louit Grissell Forrester relict of vmquhile Samuell Erskyne your sone, that albeit we promitit to grant and dispone in fauour and for the support of hir and hir barne, your oy the escheit of hir said vmquhile husband fallin in our handis for the allegit putting of violent handis in his awin persoun, yit ye have be contrauentioun of ws and our thesawrer, vnder pretence and promeis to apply the said escheit to the vse and behuiff of hir and hir barne, purchest our gift thairvpoun and be vertew of the samin not onle mellit and intrometit with the haill cornes, guidis, and geir belanging to your said sone and his spous: Bot secluidit and put hir maist schamefulle and vnnaturaly frome the possessioun and profeit of that rowme belanging to him and hir in coniunct festment, quhilk we think verrey strange and a mater sua inconscionable in your persoun, being in the rank and estimatioun of a barroun in the contrey, and of sa godle and honorable ane hous, as we have not hard of the lyke. We wald be glaid that as all guid persounes regraites and pieties the cais of this semple and young gentill woman, wraikit and redactit in mesary, as appeires, be your vngodle and vnnaturall dealing, sa ye wald remord your awin conscience, and baith for the accomplischement of our promeis maid first to dispone the said gift to hir and hir barne, and your awin honour and naturall dewatie, ye will tak sic ordour as sche may be restoirit to the guides, cornes, and vtheres intrometit with be yow, as said is, or ony vtheres vnder yow be vertew of that escheit, and to the possessioun of that sowme belanging to hir in coniunct festment, sua that we heir na forther occasioun of complent thairannent howsaouir ye pretend rycht

A. J. W. H.
K. Er.
SKINE, Esq.

thairto bo the said gift of escheit. Vtherwais to assuir your selff that we will querrel and call the samin in questioun, and challango yow of your dewtie and promeis thairannent as the caus mereites. Sua leuking for your ansuer with the beirar to the effect, in cais of your refuissell of this our godle requesit abone writtin, we may put remeid thairto, We commit yow to God. Of Striuling the xvii day of August 1590. JAMES R.

Indorsed : "To our traist freind the Larde of Dwn."

18. James VI. of Scotland, and afterwards I. of England, to the ministers of the Presbytery of Mearns. Holyroodhouse, 4th April 1603.

The King commands Mr. Alexander Forbes, minister of Fetterkairne, a member of the Mearns Presbytery, to accompany him to London, on the occasion of the death of Queen Elizabeth with other ministers similarly called, and to bring back to Scotland directions to the General Assembly regarding the preservation of the peace and unity of the Kirk. He asks the Presbytery to appoint one of their number to serve at Fettercairne in Forbes's absence.

Signed by the King, JAMES R.

19. James Halyburtoune of Pitcur, writes to the Laird of Edzell, October 30, 1608, mentioning that the Laird of Dun was much troubled by the Bishop of St. Andrew (George Gladstaines), for not producing the original sasine of Logy Montrose. He asks this writ from Edzell. Then "we sall immediatlie be at ane "waif point with the bischip."

20. Henrie Erskine to his brother the Laird of Dun, Edinburgh, 16th July 1625. Mentions that he had consulted with Mr. George Flesher, advocate, anent the laird's "Patent of a Baronet." When in England he had been promised by Sir William Alexander that a patent should be kept for the Laird of Dun in a "good rowme." It would cost 3,000 marks, and the writer thinks that his brother should insist on being placed next those who have already obtained patents.

21. Letter from the Privy Council of Scotland to the Laird of Dun, dated Haliruidhouse, 24th August 1626, requesting him to continue in the sheriffship of Forfar till the next commission day, when it was hoped the horning against the Laird of Bonnytoun sheriff-elect would be "purged," and he would be able to enter on the office. Signed by George Viscount Dupplin, Chancellor, and Thomas, Earl of Melros, as Lord Privy Seal.

22. Letter from the Privy Council of Scotland to the Laird of Dun, dated from Holyruidhouse, 31st August 1627. They had written him before concerning the war His Majesty had undertaken against France, asking what number of men he could furnish for the service. He had sent no answer worthy to be returned to His Majesty. "Thairfor these are of new to requesit and "desyre yow to send in to the burgh of Edinburgh "betuixt and the 20th day of September nixt suche "number of personnis as yow may furnishe in this "mater, and thair delyver thame to the erle of Mor"toun and his officers, who will be thair readie to "attend and ressave thame ; and that they be personns "of good vigour and abilitie of bodie and not of these "who are in the commoun rolls for the service of the "King of Denmark."

Signed by the Chancellor, the Earls of Wintoun, Linlithgow, and Haddington.

23. Lady Marie Erskine, daughter of John, Earl of Mar, and Countess Marischall, to William Delgardno, in Chreobie. Her cousin, the Laird of Denmark's service, had accepted the post of captain in the King of Denmark's service, and was to levy 300 men in Scotland. He asks Delgardno to "try out" in the bounds whereof he had chargo, "for all sort of men that ye think fitting to "want and that ar meit to go to the warres." Dated at Canongait (Edinburgh), 21st March 1627.

24–32. Nine letters from Patrick Maule, of Panmure, afterwards Earl of Panmure, the favourite attendant of King Charles the First, all addressed to his nephew, Alexander Erskine, Laird of Dun.

24 (1.) First letter, dated 8th May 1631.

Among other things he writes :—" My lord of Mor"tone can mak noe excouse for his unwillingnesse to giue "way to yow for transporting of victuall, but that he "was not in Scotland ; and these that war their, was "mor able too judge of the plantie which was in the "kingdome then hee could . . . . .
"I wnderstand in lyk maner by the Aduocat that the "lord of Spyine hathe past a renunsiatione in my "fauours of my landes of the Baroni of Dunie, which "I tak for kindlie from him, not that I think they war "in much danger . . . . . . For that bussines "which youe left with me anent the making of salt in

" Ireland, I haue mou'd his Majestie theirin. Wher"wpone I find soe maney questiones and doutes aryse "that I can not ansuer them, soe that I fear it must "lay wntill my hom-coming."

25 (2.) Second letter, dated 10th March 1633. Chiefly reates to the King's intended visit to Scotland. After stating his unwillingness to bestow his daughter on the laird of Bonnytoun, owing to the youth of his daughter, the large number of children the laird already had, although yet a young man, and the incumbrances on his estate, he writes :—" For yow being in Edinbrough "at His Majesties being their I know not what to "aduyse. I beliue uerely there wilbe few gentle-man "of qualetie in the kingdome but wilbe their, and yett "I know it must be chargeable to these that comes. "As for a place to serue in during His Majesties being. "their : befor this all places was apointed, and if they "war not, I can not imagine aney place that hade bein "fitting for youe wnlesse it hade bein a meater-hous"hold, and that number hath bein full abone this tow "yearis. For the rest of the placis I know non that "is fitting for a gentill-man of qualetie. My lord "Mortone is to be at home about the end of this month, "and if their be aney place that youe haue a mynd too, "I persuad my-self bee wilbe willing to giue you con"tentment in it, for hee and my Lord Traquar hath "the disposing of all places."

26 (3.) Third letter, dated 16th December 1635. Concerning the writer's claim to Balmaledy and other lands. He adds, " I have not forgotin Gilderoy, but "cannot make the King to apprehend it as I would."

27 (4.) Fourth letter, dated 1st November 1636. The King and the Earl of Traquair had gone to Newmarket.

28 (5.) Fifth letter, dated 12th January 1636-7. Mentions Maule's having procured a letter from His Majesty to the town of Montrose, in favour of James Guthrie, which he sends with His Majesty's letter to the town. "It is a thing uerey wnfiting for him to doe, for hee "hath noe pouer to apoint there clark." Maule accuses Erskine of being " sloe in wreiting " to him.

29 (6.) Sixth letter, dated 22nd November 1637. Maule writes :—" As to your wish that I should be "cairfull to doe all the good I can in this present "bussiness of the church, be confidant I shall neuer "be wanting therin to the utermost of my pouar, and "beliue me I haue not bein eidle with my best inde"nouris to giue his majestie the true informationse "with as much aduantage to thise that hath apeer'd "in this bussines as posiblie I could, soe that I hope "(if they bee discreete, and stand to there ground, "and not brak amongse them selfis) that the bussines "shall haue a good euent."

30 (7.) Seventh letter, dated 23rd February 1638. Maule thanks his nephew for the interest he had taken in bringing about Jeane's marriage [probably the marriage of Maule's daughter to the Earl of Northesk]. "For the church affair I can adde no thing to "what I haue wreatin in my former letters to youo "which I hope will com saufiid to your hands. I pray "God all things may be . . . quieted. For the "presedant I assure y . . . . hath (soe farr as I can "learne) . . . . self uerey well, and I beliue if . . . . . "would haue takin hold of his . . . . . the countrio should haue gotine contentment. But what conclusions was takine and send home with Traquair, I am persuadit was resolued befor euer tho presedant cam heere. Befor the reseat of your letter I hard of your being in Edinbrogh at the tym of the tumolt in Brechin, which I was uerey glade to heere, and am uerey well plesed in resauing the assurance thereof from your-self, for I should be sorie that youe should doe that at which their might be iust grounds of exseptiones, for a man should carie him-self soe, that their may not be notish takine of his behaiuour forther then his good wishes to the bussines.

" For the pricis of uictuall heere : the barly, pease, beones, and oits is uerey deere, for good barly is at fourtie shilline starling the querter, beanes at that sam rait, oites at aughteine and tuantie shilline the querter. I haue procured from his Majestie a warant to the Lord Treasurer for giuing leesance to me for the transporting of fiftie challders of uictuall, which I haue heer-with send youe tho coppie, and withall I haue wreatin this letter my self to him theiranent, for if youe find that their is aney good theirin to bo done, cause deliuer the warand with my letter, if otherwyse keepe them both untill I sie youe."

31 (8.) Eighth letter, dated 2nd February 1639. Maule in this letter says :—" Tho unsertintie of de-"liuerie of letters make me that I dar not wreit freele.

A. J. W. H.
K. Er.
SKINE, Esq.

4 L 3

"His Majestie coming to York the first of Aprill is
"com to your knowledg befor this, where their is to
"be a powerfull armie; how or wher it shalbe im-
"ployed is not to be knowne. I shall pray for pace,
"but I fear if his Majestie be forsed to soe much
"trouble and charge both to him-self and the wholl
"keengdome, that the couenanters shall not gate so
"much of their will as they exspect. I am sure they
"might haue made faire condisiones, both for church
"and kingdome, if it hade bein takin in tyme; but
"what they can doe now God knowes. I must hope
"the best, for I am confidant, all good men will
"indeuour to seek pace."

32 (9.) Ninth letter, dated 11th April 1640, with a
postscript of the 24th. Maule says that "bussines
"comes to that height," that there was no safety in
writing as all letters were intercepted. He entreats his
nephew, although he does not hope to persuade him to
abandon the course he had taken "to carrie himself
"with that temper and discratione that their may not
"be cause to tak greater exception at him then at
"others that is ingadged as he is." He beseeches him
to say nothing disrespectful to the King's person, as
that might "preiudge" him and do no good to the
"busines." "Remember that Kings hath long ears."

"The Erll of Montrois ureat a letter to me since my
coming. I acquented His Majestie with what he ureat
to me and shewed His Majestie the latter he ureat to
Mr. Routhen his ouncle and returned him His Majesties
answer theirto which I [   ] hee ureat to him, and
uithall he promesid to mak my excuse, for not wreiting, for I could say nothing bott what I had spokin
to Mr. Routhen, soe if that my excuse for not wreiting
bee mead it is enough, but if it bee not, Mr. Routhen
did me the mor wrong, for I should be loith to negliok
that dueti which his respect to me hath euer merited.
Therefore I pray you lett him know what I haue
wreatin."

33. Copy letter from King Charles I. 18th June
[1640]. "Trustie and weill belouit, greyt you weill.
"Hawing fullie vnderstood of your constant affectione
"to our seruice and sufferingis for the same we giue
"you hartie thankis; and as heirtofor we haue wrettine,
"we will not be wnmyndfull therof, but our subjectis
"whuo have offendit ws, hawing at this tyme giwin
"ws satisfactione excepting of that we proponit to
"them, we thocht it fitt to acquent you therewith to
"the end you doe not proceid in anie thing tuiching
"hostilitie; but that you sattill your tyme in ane
"peaceabill way; and so we bid you hartilie farweill.
"At Birkis from our camp, the 18 day of Juni." [No
address.]

34. Holograph order by David Leslie, Lieutenant-
General of the forces in Scotland, desiring all officers
and soldiers under his command, and all others to suffer
the laird of Dun with his servants to pass and repass to
Edinburgh without let or molestation. Given at Multers,
6th April 1649.

35. The same to his "loving comerad Colonell
"Keithe." Perth, October 8, 1649. "Yours of the
"eight of this . . . . is come this evining to my
"hands schoing me of your returne into the countrie
"and desire to be excepted as others of your conditione
"with assurrance of securrity for bygones. My advice
"is that yee present your self to the committie of
"esteits quho did sett out acts for those of your con-
"ditione that did come into the countrie againe, who
"I belive will be easily satisfied and desire no more
"of yow then securritie for the peace of the countrie
"in times coming." He then asks Keith to visit him
on his way from Edinburgh . . . "I wish you will
"consider quhat seruice yee ar doing to God or your
"prince, and that ye wold remember the last warning
"quher God was plased with ane handfull to beate
"suche ane gallant armie and yeet to spare yow, thus
"desiring your favourable constructione of him quho
"honores your persone, take quhat course you will."

36. Lord Spynie and Ogilvey and Robert Beattie to
David Erskine. Intimating that Erskine's father had
died on Tuesday night. Would allow none to write
home concerning his sickness. He was buried on
Thursday night in St. Martin's Church, accompanied
by the greater part of the nobility and all the gentry
of Scotland then in London. "He ows about ane
"hundereth and twente ponds sterling hier, and if
"wee had not ingadged for the payment thairof his
"corps had bein arrested."

37. Letter signed by the following Lords:— Mar,
Eglintoune, Balmerino, Linlithgow, Kilsyth, Northeek,
and by Alex. Erskine, Lyon [King of Arms], Hugh
Paterson, Geo. Lockhart, Ja. Murray, John Carnegy,

Alexander McKenzie, Al. Cuming, and Ja. Murray, but
unaddressed. [Probably to one of the Scottish bishops.
He is addressed as "My Lord."] London, March 21st,
1712–13.

"The enemies of the Church of England here, who
"are much alarm'd at any countenance that is shown
"to the Episcopal party in Scotland, and who are in-
"defatigable in their endeavours to keep us still under
"the hatches, have no other game left . . . but to
"represent us all, both clergy and laity, as enemies
"to the present Government." These avowed that the
Episcopal clergy would not take the oaths or pray for
the Queen. The latter accusation was true of many.
While these rumours are spread, they continue, "it is
"impossible that we can succeed in our weak endea-
"vours for the church. It cannot be expected that
"the Queen will grant her protection to those that will
"not so much as pray for her; it is what her ministry
"cannot have the face to ask of her."
Their friends in England thought it absolutely necessary in order to counteract these reports, that the
Scottish Episcopal clergy should send up an address
testifying their affection to Her Majesty's person and
government. His lordship's assistance is prayed for.
No time was to be lost; Parliament would assemble the
following week, and their enemies were prepared for a
violent attack. The clergy should pray for the Queen
and send up the address speedily.

38. Captain James Erskine, M.P., to his brother Lord
Dun. London, March 27th, 1715.
Regarding a petition against his election on the
ground of his having been carried by an unlawful
council at Montrose and by bribery at Brechin. He
asks his brother for 30l. as "thes things cannot be don
"without money." The petition would be brought
before the bar of the House of Commons, "wher litle
"justice is to be expected, but only interest determines,
"for though your not named in the petition youl be
"brought in for bribery."

39. John, Fourth Marquis of Tweeddale, Secretary
of State, to Lord Dun, pressing him to reconsider his
resignation of the office of Commissioner of the Court
of Justiciary. Whitehall, 23rd June 1744.

40. Archibald, Third Duke of Argyll, to Lord Dun,
apparently on the same matter as in the preceding
letter. London, February 19th, 1744–5.

41. John, Marquis of Tweeddale, Secretary of State
to Lord Dun, appointing Lord Drumore as his successor
in the above office, and continuing to Lord Dun a salary
of .100l. Whitehall, 7 March 1744–5.

42. "To the Right Honourable the Lords of Councill
"and Session, the humble address of the Lord Dun, one
"of their number," intimating his resolve to resign his
office. Copy, 1753.

43. The Lords of the Court of Session to Lord Dun,
regretting his resolution to resign connexion with them.
Edinburgh, 25 July 1753.

44. Holograph letter from Archibald Duke of Argyll
to Lord Dun on his resignation. Edinburgh, 17 August
1753.

II. Royal warrants and commissions and miscellaneous papers of the Erskines of Dun from the
year 1474.

45. Discharge by John of Chawmer " Maister of Sainct
"Germanss* and persoun of Abirluthnochth" in favour
of " an honourable squyar" John of Erskyn of Dun, of
100 merks scotts as full payment of the teind sheaves
of the Kirk of Abirluthnocht for the year 1473. Dated
31 July 1474.

46. Factory by John of Chawmer pensioner of Saynt
Germanss, appointing " an honourable squyar" John of
Erskine of Dun to receive for him from Sir Patrick
Pyot the sum of 46 merks due to the said John of Chaw-
mer for the teind sheaves of the towns of the Bernys
and the Ecclesmaldie in the parish of Abirluthnot.
Dated 2nd August 1475.

47. Notarial certificate by Walter Clerk, priest in the
diocese of Brechin, relating that John Erskin of Dun
had appeared on the lands of umquhile Walter Ogstoun
of Pertht, and had there given satisfaction to several
tenants and servitors of the said Walter for felony committed by John Erskine and others against them, and
for oppression of them and destruction of their grain
and other goods ; and that these tenants, &c., quit-claimed
the said offenders for ever. 9 July 1490.

48. Lease by Alexander Maull of Hadderwick of half
his lands of Haderveik and others in the shire of Forfar,

A. J. W. H.
K. Eso.
SKINE, Esq

to John of Erskine of Dun for 19 years, for 40s. yearly. 3 March 1491.

49. Remission by King James IV. to John Erskine younger of Dun. Dundee 13 February, 1501.

The king pardons the premeditated felony committed by John Erskine younger of Dun against Walter Ogilvy, William Nudry and others in the burgh of Montrose, and also remits all crimes and offences, and frees him from all action to which he might be liable for any crimes committed by him previous to the date of the present remission, excepting treason, homicide &c.; provided he gave satisfaction to those who had been aggrieved, that in future no just cause of complaint should be found against him; and further the king inhibited all persons on pain of death or loss of limb from inflicting any injury on the said John Erskine for his past transgressions.

50. Inventory of the personal estate and testament of John Erskine of Dun who died at Flodden. Dated 15 August, 1513. Confirmed 19 August, 1513.

"Inventarium omnium bonorum Johannis Erskyn de Dwn factum ibidem per seipsum xv° die mensis Augusti anno domini m° v° xiii° coram hiis testibus, dominis Georgeo Foulartoun vicario de Dwn, Johanne Willok, Johanne Ettail, capellanis, et magistro Johanne Nauchti notario publico cum diuersis aliis."

His estate is thus divided (1.) Goods in the diocese of St. Andrews: (2.) Debts due to him in that diocese: (3.) Goods in the diocese of Brechin: (4.) Debts due to him in that diocese: (5.) His debts to others. The whole estate after the deduction of all his debts amounted to 170l. 19s. 10d.

The value of farm-stock and of the various kinds of grain in Scotland at this time may be ascertained from this inventory. The "utensilia et domicilia" are estimated in a lump at 40l. Four work-horses are valued at 26s. 8d., 41 ploughing oxen at 20s. a piece: 28 cows at 16s.; 18 calves at 2s., one bull at 1l. 13s.; score and four sheep at 30d. each. Oats which appear to have been sown on this estate in greater quantity than any other grain, are valued at 40d. per boll; barley at 8s.; wheat at 10s.; peas at vis. 8d.

By his testament, which is appended to the inventory of his estate, John Erskine nominated Katherine Monypenny his spouse and Mr. Thomas Erskine his son to be his executors. The inventory and testament were made a few weeks before the battle of Flodden.

51. Inventory of the personal estate of Sir John Erskine younger of Dun, Knight, father of the Superintendent, and who also died at Flodden, dated 15 February, 1513 and confirmed by the commissary of Saint Andrews on 3 April 1516.

There is a considerable difference in the valuation of the stock &c. in this inventory from that of Sir John's father. The oats are valued at 4s., barley at 6s. 8d., peas at 6s. 8d. There is still more difference in the horses, one of which is valued at 4l. 13s. 4d. and other two at 40s.

One item of debt is "servis metentibus grana in " awtumno vi lb."

Dame Margaret Ruthven is named in the confirmation as the relict of Sir John Erskine.

The inventory was made a few months after the knight was killed at Flodden.

52. Letter by John Duke of Albany Governor of Scotland under king James the Fifth, to the laird of Dun and his tutors to come to the governor at Edinburgh to give him their counsel and assistance with regard to the intended invasion of Scotland by her " aid enemys of Ingland." This invasion the governor means to resist. The party summoned were to " pre- " termit nocht the furnissing of their part of men of " were to the bordouris" under the order contained in a separate letter. Dated at Edinburgh, 17 September [1514].

53. Indenture dated at Edinburgh, 1 April 1517, between "ane venerable fader in God" Patrick Abbot of Cambuskenneth and secretary to the king on the one part, and Mr. [afterwards Sir] Thomas Erskine tutor to John Erskine of Dun, for himself and as procurator to Katrine Monypenny his mother on the other part. By this indenture Patrick Pantar is to receive repayment of 120 merks which he had paid to the bishop of Caithness, king's treasurer, for John Erskine, while he " differis" two other sumes also due by the said um- quhile John Erskine, one of 250 merks, the other of 50 pounds, "in hope and traist of the said Master " Thomas, Katrine, te frendis and har alliances gude " bering kindnes and behaving towart the said vener- " able fader, his kynnismen," &c. These sums, however, were to be paid in event of any unkindness being ex-

hibited to the Abbot. The second contracting party were to be ready to "gang in all honest materis and " querrellis agains all parties exceptand the king, " gouernoure and Erll of Huntly," in defence of the Abbot.

The indenture is subscribed " Patricius Panitar Abbas :" de Cambuskenneth Secretarius" and T. Erskyne. The seal of Panitar is affixed, but only a fragment remains.

54. Notarial instrument narrating that on the 10th October, 1521, James Stewart of Reland, sheriff depute of Banff, appeared before several witnesses in the market place of Banff and made a declaration as to certain amerciaments to which the "tenentes husbandi et " inhabitores" of Knokorth &c., had become liable through their absence from the courts assigned to them for the "wapinschawing." These fines were, " 35 vaccas " et ly zong oxin, et 23 ly stottis et steris," all which were valued at 40l. scots, and were offered to the tenants, &c., for payment of the said sum or on sufficient caution for the payment by a certain day. None of them, however, appearing, the cattle were taken posses- sion of according to order of law by the said James Stewart.

55. Contract of marriage, dated at Dundee, 20 Decem- ber 1522, by which it is agreed betwixt David Earl of Craufurd on the one part, and John Erskyn of Dun with consent of James Stewart of Ryland, and Mr. Thomas Erskyne of Haltoun, his tutors, on the other part, in manner following:—The said John Erskyn is to marry and have to wife Elizabeth Lindsay daughter of the earl of Craufurd whenever he should arrive at the perfect age of 14 years : two days before the marriage Lord Craufurd was to pay over 700 merks for the redemption of Erskine's lands; and among other things it is advised by Erskine's tutors that on his coming to the age of 14 years and entering on the possession of his lands, he shall bestow on his sister Katerine a year's profit of the whole of his lands for her marriage. This duplicate of the contract is signed by the Earl of Craw- ford.

56. Notarial instrument narrating that James Lear- month of Darsy, provost of St. Andrews, and James Beinstoun of Lammyclaithame appeared in the presence of George Atkinson notary public on the 4th June 1526 : that the deceased Edward bishop of Caithness had at his death given the patronages of three chaplainries to David Learmonth of Clatto, father of the foresaid James Lear- month, present contractor; these chaplainries to "be fund- " it for the guid and veill and honour of vmquhill Eduard " bischop and his saull heill that is grewit in the paroch " Kirk of the cete of Sanctandris, and inlikwyiss for the " guid and veill of the saull and honour of vmquhill ane " reuerend fader in God Jhone bischoip of Orkney last " deceissit, grawit in the college of Sanct Saluatour " foundit within the said ciete and for louabill suffrage for " to be done for the saidis Reuerendis faderis saullis in " all tymis to cum, at places foresaid, according to thair " honour and bredhedia veill ;" that hereby the said James Learmonth founds a chaplainry in the college of " our " Salvatour" for the purpose above mentioned, and for the sum of 100l. scots transfers the patronage of the same to James Beinstoun; and that James Beinstoun binds himself to find caution to Gawane bishop of Aberdeen, or failing him to James Loarmonth, that he will, as ex- ecutor of John bishop of Orkney, complete the three foundations and dispone the money according to the will of the founder, " on the paines of cursing."

57. Licuse under the signature of King James V. to John Erskin of Dun, Thomas Erskin, son of Sir Thomas Erskin of Brechin, Knight, Secretary to the King, and John Lamby of Duncany, to travel into France, Italy, or any other parts beyond sea, to remain abroad for two years for the doing of their lawful business; and to take or have transmitted to them such gold, &c., as they may require. They were to suffer no "skaith" by acts or prosecutions of any kind during their absence. Dated at Stirling, 16 April, in the 29th year of the reign (1542).

58. Similar license for 3 years to John Erskin, elder, franktenementer of Dun, Thomas Erskin son of Sir Thomas Erskine of Brechin, John Erskin fiar of Dun, and William Erskin parson of Donchquhale. Edinburgh, 10 May (1542).

59. Commission by King James V. to (Sir Thomas Erskine) his Secretary, and David Lindesay of Adzell, to order his lieges and tenants of the Earldom of Craufurd, Dun, Brechin, Adzell and Montrose, who were unfit for war, to furnish able persons to join the host as their substitutes; and this notwithstanding former proclama- tions of the King and his commission to the Sheriff of Forfar. Dated at Edinburgh, 19 October 1542.

A. J. W. H. K. Erskine, Esq.

60. License by Queen Mary under the signature of the Regent Arran to John Erskyne of Dun to travel abroad for five years. St. Andrews, 12 March 1545–6.

61. Lease of the Abbey of Scone for nineteen years to John Erskine of Dun, and grant to his lady in liferent, of the lands of Blaknes, Driburgh, and Blagartno, by Patrik bishop of Moray and Commendator of Scone. Perth, 13 February 1546–7.

62. Lease of the fruits of the parsonage and vicarage of Arbuthnot for three years by Sir Vilzem Rynd parson of Arbuthnott, and Robert Erskin dean of Aberdeen, in favour of John Erskin of Dun, for 300 merks yearly. Brechin, 23 April 1552.

63. Letter of Mary Queen of Scots, dispensing with the attendance of John Erskin of Dun and his servant at the raid to be convened in Edinburgh to pass with the regent to the burgh of Jedburgh. Edinburgh, 26 October [1552]. Subscribed by James Duke of Chatelherault as Governor.

64. "At Aberdene quinto Januarii 1558. The Counsall gevin be the denye and cheptour of Aberdene to my lord bischope of Aberdene thair ordinar at his lordschippis desyr for reformatioun to be maid and stancheing of hereseis pullelant within the diocie of Aberdene, and the ordour prescrui(t) to be obseruit to the sammyn effect." Three pages folio.

This important document has been long known to historians and is printed in the Introduction to Bishop Keith's History of Scotland, p. xiv., edition 1734.

65. Letter by Francis and Mary King and Queen of Scotland, &c., given under the Royal signet at Sanctandrois, the 22d February [1559], narrating that, "Forsa-" mekle as the lordis of our secrete counsale havand " consideratioun that the blak freris place of Montroiss " wes first ane hospitale for the povirs of that toune, " and that the saidis freris being sturdy beggaris vnder " colour of almess and moyoun of courte for the tyme, " spulzet the poor thairof, intrusand thame selfis thairin, " and takand the haill place and rentis thairof to thame; " and sen it hes plesit God of his grite mercy to open " thair ipocrasie and maist justlie to caus thame be " eiectit thairfra, it becumis the saidis lordis of thair " dewitie, bayth towardis God and man, to restoir the " poore of the said toun to the said hospitalitie as to " their ald and maist[richtfull] possessioun."

Therefore the lords appoint the said Blackfriars Place with all its lands, &c. to be distributed to the poor of Montrose; and order a hospital to be erected thereupon "according as tyme and expensis of the superexcressens " giff ony beis will suffer" for the entertainment of the poor. The lords also being persuaded of his "fayth, " conscience, and pietie towarte the poore" constitute John Erskyn of Dun general factor, intromittor, and uplifter, and distributer of the fruits of the hospital, keeper and "conseruare" of the "excrescence gyff ony beis," disposer of the same for the erection of a hospital, principal master, "admittare, imputtare and owtputtare" of the "poore and nedy thairin" at his discretion. All persons in debt to the institution are commanded to make immediate payment on pain of horning and imprisonment in the castle of Dumbertane during their Majesties pleasure.

66. Letter by King James VI., dated from the Castle of Stirling, 14 May [1579], to John Erskine Laird of Dun and his son Robert or either of them: commanding the safe conduct of those who were in the house of Reidcastell, especially of John Stewart brother to James Lord Innermeith, into the King's presence; and that the Erskines should make an inventory of Lord Innermeith's goods, now pertaining to his "faderless bairnes" and should retain possession of them until further notice from the King and Counsel. Subscribed by the King, the Earl of Leuenax and Robert Commendator of Dunfermline.

67. Letter, dated from the Castle of Stirling, 26 September 1579, enjoining the Laird of Dun elder, to surrender the house of Reidcastell to John Stewart, on obtaining sufficient caution from him for the charges he had been subject to while keeper of the Castle. The alleged ground of this delivery is, that John Stewart had deadly enemies in that district ready to pursue him, and that such a residence would conduce to his better safety. Subscribed by the King and the Commendator of Dunfermline.

68. License by King James VI., to his "weilbelouit " counsallour" John Erskine of Dun and the persons with him in company, to eat flesh as oft as they please from the 13th February following the issue of the order to the 26th March: and this notwithstanding the recent royal proclamation or other inhibitions. Holyroodhouse, 10 February 1580. Subscribed by the King and by the Earls of Argyll and Montrose.

A. J. W. H. K. Erskine, Esq.

69. Letter by King James VI., commanding John Erskine younger of Dun, immediately "to surrender the house of Reidcastell and its plenishing into the hands of James Lord Innermaith." Subscribed by the King at Holyroodhouse 14 March 1580.

70. Licence by King James VI. to John Erskin of Dun " his bairnis, freindis, men, tennentis, seruandis and " propir dependaris" to remain at home from "the rayd " appointit toward Strineling for persute of certane oure " rebellis and tratouris quhilkis surprisit oure toun and " castell of Strineling and fortifiit and withheld the " sammyn agains ws and oure auctoritie laitlie in the " moneth of Aprile instant." Subscribed by the King at Edinburgh, 25th April 1584.

71. Extract of decree of the Lords of Council, dated at Halyruid house, 16th November 1584.

Narrates that Patrick Lord Drummond, Robert Drummond of Carnock, David sometime commendator of Dryburgh, and Robert Erskin fiar of Dun, by their obligation, dated the 3rd, and registered in the books of secret council the 20th December 1583, had become bound as sureties for Adam (Erskine) sometime commendator of Cambuskenneth, that he should leave the realms of Scotland, England and Ireland within thirty days after the date of the obligation, "wind and wedder serving," that he should remain beyond seas during the time mentioned in the royal license, and during his absence behave himself as a dutiful subject to his Sovereign Lord, "and suld do, attempt nor practize nathing in " hurte or preiudice of his hienes estate and trew " religioun presentlie preicheit and be the law establissed " within this realme," under the pain of 10,000*l.* scots. But in contempt of this obligation and decree the commendator remained in the realm of England, and was there residing at the date of this decree, and in the interval had practised, attempted, devised, and committed sundry crimes of treason and "lese maiestie," of which he was convicted in Parliament. The cautioners refused to pay the sums stated in their obligation, and this decreet was consequently obtained to compel Robert Erskine to pay his part of the sum, for which he had become bound, and which amounted to 2,500*l.*

72. "Ane Licence to you L(ordship) for eating of flech," [Dorso], subscribed at Haliruidhouse 25th February 1584 by King James VI., James Stewart Earl of Arran, and John Lord Thyrlstane, as follows:

"We vnderstanding that our weilbelouit clerk Johnne Erskyne of Dwn is past the age of lxxvj yeiris, and that he is seikle and subiect to diuer's infirmities and diseasis: Thairfor be the tennour heirof with auise of the Lordis of our secrete counsell gevis and grantis Licence to him to eit flesh as oft as he sall think expedient on the forbiddin dayis in the oulk, to wot, Woddinisday, Fryday, and Satterday, and in the tyme of Lentroun, during all the dayis of his lyftyme . . ."

73. Summons in name of King James VI. from the Lords of Exchequer, dated at Stirling 9th September 1588, raised at the instance of John Erskine of Dun, superintendent of Angus and Mearns, against the Abbot of Arbroath, the Bishop of Brechin, the Abbot of Cupar, and others, for the payment of his stipend for the year 1585. The stipend consisted of money and victuals as follows:—

	lb.	*s.*	*d.*
From the siluere third of Arbroath	170	4	2¾
" third of Cupar -	52	16	6¾
Charterhouss - - -	22	0	10
From the Jedburgh and Restennete	25	6	8
Third of the preceptory of Maisondow - - - - -	13	6	8
Thomas Knox's annavele in Brechin - - - - -	0	0	12
From the third of Edwie parsonage - - - - -	27	2	2¾
From the prices of the victualls of Kinnell - - - -	26	13	4
Summa -	337	11	6¼

The Victuals are:—

		Chalders	Bolls	Firlots	Pecks
Arbroath Abbacy	"fayte"	4	12¾	0	0
"	beer	6	14	3	1¾
"	beer	5	8	0	0
Brechin	"fayte"	0	3¾	0	0
	beer	5	2¾	0	0
	meill	3	2	0	0

74. Grant under the privy seal of King James VI., dated 1 November 1587, to John Eskine, of his stipend

as superintendent out of the thirds of certain benefices [as in No. 73]. The preamble runs thus :—

" Wit ye ws, Considering the lang, ernest, and fructfull travellis tane and bestowit be oure louit Johne Erskyn of Dwn superintendent of Angus and Mernis, in the suppressing of superstitioun, papistrie and idolatrie, and avancement and propagatioun of the evangell of Jesus Christ the tyme of the reformatioun of the religioun, and in his ydent, and faithfull perseuerance in the samin contenuallie sensyne to the grit glorie of God, and singular conforte of all oure subiectis within the boundis of Angus and Mernis now flurisheing aboundantlie in the preiching of the trew word of God and rycht administratioun of the sacramentis be the grace of God and industrie of the said Laird of Dun," &c.

75. Commission by King James VI., and the Lords of the Privy Council to John Earl of Mar, and such of his friends and servants as he should nominate. Dated Edinburgh, 13 November 1610.

Narrates that the King and Council had been informed that David Blenhois in the Leyis of Dun, Thomas Stone there, George Kirk, John Kirk, and Gilbert Campbell, all in Logy, and one called " Irishe James, ane vagabound," " vpon some godles, wicked, and detestable " opinioun and apprehension of thair awne had con- " sultit, conferrit, resolued and concludit to haif the " lyvis of   Erskine of Dwne and   Erskin his " brather, tua young boyis, the eldest of thame not past " ten yeiris of age, and that onther be poysoun, witche- " craft or some vther diuilishe, vnhappy and detestable " practizes, and had had sundrie meetingis and con- " ferenceis anent the forme, maner, meanes, and possi- " bilityis of the execution of their vnhappy resolution, " and they do await some fitt tyme and occasioun when " and whair thay sall execute the same." Power is given to Mar, and those to be appointed by him to seize these persons and examine them, taking their depositions in different chambers or prisons, and causing them, if necessary, to be put to the torture.

76. Contract between Alexander Erskine and James Blair, son of Sir John Blair of Balgillo, Knight, whereby the former, for the love and favor which he bears to the said James Blair, assigns to the latter his right under a patent granted to him by Alexander Lord Spynie, Colonel, to levy 300 soldiers to go to Germany for the service of the King of Denmark, and the sum of 900 dollars, each being worth 58s., besides 160 dollars already paid to the officers, to furnish him with 100 of the men, and obtain a new patent from Lord Spynie, while James Blair consents to pay 500 merks Scots, for any skaith that might be sustained by the other contracting party. Dundee, 29 March 1627.

77. Temperance Bond, Dundee, 5 July 1627. The parties to this contract, which is attested by four witnesses, are Alexander Erskine of Dun, and Sir Jhone Blair of Balgillo. They bound themselves to drink nothing, except in their own dwellings, till the 1st of May 1628, under the penalty of 500 merks Scots, for the first "failzie and brack," and of 100 merks for every succeeding one, and for security agreed to register the contract. The reason alleged for this agreement is that the "access [i.e. excess] of drinking is prohibit bothe " be the Law of God and Man," and that they were " willing to giue guid exampill to vtheris be their lyff' " and conversacioun to abstain from the lyke abuse."

78. Order by King Charles I., dated at Whitehall, 30 March 1631, to his Treasurers, &c. in Scotland, to allow Alexander Erskein of Dunne to transport 80 chalders of wheat, barley, and oats, from Scotland to any port in His Majesty's dominions.

79. Grant under the Privy Seal of King Charles I. at Oxford, January 31, 1643–4, of a pension of 200l. yearly to Sir Alexander Erskine of Dun, Knight, for the services of himself and his predecessors to the King and his progenitors.

80. Signature superscribed by King Charles II., containing a Ratification of the foregoing grant, dated 5 March 166?.

81. Extract from the records of Parliament held at Edinburgh on the 23 December 1669, of an Act in favor of David Erskine of Dun containing the establishment of a yearly fair to be held on the Muir of Dun on the second Wednesday after Whitsunday, for " buying and " selling of horse, nolt, sheip, meill, malt, and all sort " of grane, cloath, lining and woollon, and all sort of • " merchant commodities." The usual customs are granted to David Erskine and his heirs.

82. Valuation of the firs in the parks about Kildrummy, the principal castle of the Earl of Mar, in the Earldom of Mar and Garioch, 22 April 1704.

5.

The trees are valued from 24s. to 8s. each, and the whole number 13,151 deducting 2s. " for workmanship " on each, is set down as worth 7,523l. 12s.

Nine papers relating to the history of the Erskines of Dun, vizt. :

83. " A brief historical account of the Erskines of " Dun." Contains the life of Sir Robert Erskine, Scottish hero of King David's time.

84. Notes relating to the family of Dun, 1376–1646.

85. " Erskine of Dun." From Sir Thomas Erskine, immediate ancestor of this branch of the Erskines to David Erskine, 9th baron of Dun. [1668.]

86. Copy MSS. on some of the early Erskines.

87. " The obeits of the lardis and ladeis of Dwn efter " the yeir of God 1500."

88. " The obitis of the lairdis and ladeis of Dwne." [1504–1613.]

89. Copy of the " obitis of the lairdis and ladeis of " Dwne," from 1504 continued to the year 1698.

90. Memorial to John Erskine of Dun, containing copies of the " obitis," &c.

91. " The death of the lairdis and ladeis of Dun fra " the yeir of God 1504, vnto yeir of God 1580."

III.—Correspondence of the Family of Riddell of Haining, now at Dun, from the year 1674.

92. Thomas Denton, one of the English Commissioners on the borders to Sir James Johnson, Knight, Westraw, near Langholme, Carlisle, 20 December 1674. Knowing Johnston's " seale " for suppressing theft and rapine on the borders, he wishes to let him know when the English Commissioners " are about to act anything " considerablly in that affair." There was to be a " Gaol delivery " at Carlisle on the 27th January. The gaol was full of thieves, while there were others out on bond. He wishes Johnston or any other of the Scottish Commissioners to be present ; their presence would be a terror to the thieves and an encouragement to the English Commissioners to prosecute. There had been shortly before this a small gaol-delivery at Morpeth preparatory to " a greater purposed execution " there the following spring.

93. The Earl of Carlisle [address wanting]. Noward, 1st November 1676. Sends to the Scottish Commissioners a list of persons of " evil fame and dissolute lives," who had disturbed the peace of the Borders. Many were reputed to have gone to Ireland, and were ready to return on the least opportunity. He wishes their return to be prevented, and any vessel coming from Ireland into Portpatrick or any other Scotch port to be watched. There was to be a gaol-delivery at Morpeth after Christmas.

The list referred to in the Earl's letter contains 33 names, chiefly Armstrongs and Elliots. Some of the worthies have peculiar appellatives, " Black James," " Great Simon," " Long John," " The Bastard," " Patty," " Little Arthur," &c.

94. Petition of the Commissioners of Justiciary for the Scottish Borders to the Duke of Lauderdaill, his Majesty's High Commissioner for the Kingdom of Scotland. Kelso, 31st May 1678.

The Commissioners complain that all their " waike " paynes and endevours " for suppressing the thefts, robberies, and misdemeanors of the Borders were hindered by suspensions of sentences and forfeitures granted to criminals and their cautioners by the Lords of Council, &c., who were misinformed by favourers of these malefactors, and followed their false information without consulting the Commissioners or the donator of these fines and forfeitures. They crave " that no sus- " pentione be granted of any sentences pronounced be " the Commissioners of justiciarie, or of any bands " granted be cautioners for fellones without consigna- " tione of the soume chairged for, or at least untill two " or three of the Commissioners and the donator to the " gift of the fynes be first hard to object against the " reasones of suspentione. Without which the Com- " missioners thair paynes and traivells and the interest " of that court will be rendered rediculus."

This petition is signed by Sir William Scott, of Harden, and other four Scotts, James Murray, of Hangingshaw, John Rutherford, of Edgerstoun, John Ker, and others.

95. Letter from James Duke of Buccleuch and Monmouth to John Riddell, Laird of Hanneing, Scotland. Whitehall, 1st October 1678.

" Sir,—I am informed that Adam Elliott, in Mosspeebles, on of my tenents, haueing been induced to become surety for the good behaviour of some persones under the penalties of considerable soumes of money to the Commissioners of the Border, it seems they

4 M

haue thought fitt to descerne him lyable to the payment of these summs, and I understand that yow haue a gift from the King of the fynes imposed by these Commissioners, therefore I most interpose with you, in behalfe of that man, that yow would show him all the kindness yow can, for whatever pairt yow shall exact of that fine most impair of my rents, seeing it shall not onely incapacitat him to continow in his farme, bot lykewayes to pay his bygone rests. Therefore I hope I shall not need to trouble yow nor my selfe any furder. but does expect that yow will endeavour by your returne to this to putt ane obligatione upon,

Sir, your friend and servant,
                    BUCCLEUCH AND MONMOUTH."

96. A. Forrester, Secretary to John Duke of Lauderdale, to the Laird of Haining. Whitehall, 26th November 1678. Had received and delivered Hayning's letter to the Duke of Monmouth. He says, "I am told that " ther is none who thinks himselfe more concerned " than his Grace is, to suppresse the thefts and depre-" dations about the Borders."

97. The Scottish Commissioners to the English Commissioners. Kelso, 21st March 1678-9. Anent the desire of the English Commissioners that the fine imposed on Christopher Jameson should be mitigated. The Scottish Commissioners answer that they considered it their duty to adhere to their judgment.

98. Patrick Maxwell, of Kirkconnell, one of the Commissioners on the Scottish Borders, to the Laird of Hayning. 24th May 1679. He was every day expecting his servant from Ireland to give him the deputy of Ireland's pleasure when to receive Irving and Armstrong at Portpatrick.

99. Petition [1681]. "To His Royall Highness and " the Lords of his Majesties most Honourable privie " Councell. The humble petition of the Commissioners " of the Borders :—
   " Sheweth,
   " That your petitioners have ever been willing to " serve the King their Soveraigne and Master in keep-" ing the Borders of both kingdomes quiet and peace-" able upon their own expenses. But of late some " notorious theeves having abstracted themselves from " underlying the law, have disappointed all the methods " that are ordinar for quieting the borders by offering " to suspend and reduce our sentances, whereby they " escape justice, and we are brought to such great ex-" penses that we will not hereafter be able to bestow " either the attendance or monney that such tedious " processes will requyre. And as it is oure interest to " be verie careful to be exact justiciares in that place. " So it is the interest of the King and both the king-" domes that the good old formes of the Borders be not " altered. Nor wer they ever in so good a condition as " they are now. notwithstanding even of these broken " times.
       " May it' therefore please youre Royall Highness
       " and your Lordships to discharge anie reduc-
       " tiones, suspensiones, or advocationes before any
       " judicatorie whatsoever, which shall encouradge
       " and oblidge us to distribute impartiall justice,
       " and in which if wee faile, wee are still lyable
       " to His Sacred Majestie from whom wee deryve
       " our commission."

100. William, Marquis (afterwards Duke) of Queensberry, Lord High Treasurer, and Lord Drummond, to the Sheriff Principal of Selkirk and his deputes. Edinburgh, 13th April 1683. Requires all judges and magistrates to send in a true and exact account of all fines that had been imposed by them on heritors for "Phana-" tick irregularities and disorders" since the last royal indemnity after Bothwell-bridge: also the names and qualities of the persons fined, their crimes, what fines were paid, and what remained unpaid.

101. Colin McKenzie to the Laird of Haining, Sheriff of Selkirk. Jedburgh, 8th October 1684. By command of the Lords of the Privy Council he orders the sheriff to cite all the heritors, ministers, elders, and readers within the shire of Forrest and Selkirk to compear before their lordships at Jedburgh on the 14th of the same month : the ministers to bring with them complete lists of all "irregular persones whither baptizers of " their children or withdrawers from ther parish " churches."

102. Janet Brodie, Lady Torwoodlie [who signs "Your " affectionat sister"] to the Laird of Haining. Torwoodlie, 8th October 1684. Her infirmities had prevented her attendance at church for five years. She states that it is her principle, and was her practice, to go to church without any scruple when she had health. She encloses a "testimonie" to the same effect from the

minister, elders, and clerk of session at Stow, dated 7th September 1684.

103. James Earl of Perth, chancellor, to the Laird of Drumelzier. Edinburgh, 14th May 1685. The High Commissioner and Privy Council strictly require Drumelzier to call together all the heritors, freeholders, and their followers in the shires of Selkrig and Peebles, sufficiently armed and with 20 days' provision, conform to a recent proclamation of the King, and to rendezvous them in a convenient place, there to remain till they should receive orders from Colonel Graham of Claverhouse, or whoever should be appointed by the Council. William Hay encloses the above letter to Sheriff Riddel, requesting him to summon the heritors, &c. of Selkrigshire to be at Selkrig at 12 o'clock on the 20th.

104. Order from James Earl of Perth, chancellor, to the Laird of Haining, to apprehend James Nicol in Buckcleuch, and keep him or send him to Lieutenant Graham, to be by him sent in with a good guard. 26th January 1665.

105. Colin McKenzie, Clerk of the Privy Council, to the magistrates of Selkirk. 13th September 1688. Enclosing extract from the Acts of the Privy Council, authorising the magistrates of royal burghs to remain in office, in accordance with a royal letter of the 29th August, suspending for the time the election of all such municipal officers.

106. The same to the same. 22nd October 1688. Giving a peremptory command of the Privy Council to the magistrates to buy in all the gunpowder in their burgh, and to seize all powder in suspected places.

107. David Fyffe to Mr. Andrew Riddell at Bath. Edinburgh, May 14, 1706. Describes his return from accompanying Riddell and the Earl of Traquair towards Bath. "After we parted from you, we came to Shop, " wher we dined, and was not thrifty there, and with a " great deal of difficulty I perswaded the Laird and " brother to goe and see Lowther House; wher, in-" deed, we saw a finer house than any in our antient " kingdome, and that roome, done by Varro, defeats the " gallery at Versailles. Ther is a great deal of fine " rooms, and pictures of value, besides fine statues, and " a stable of fine horses and brood as any in England." The rest of the letter is for the most part occupied with a relation of the drinking exploits of the party.

Besides these letters there are many others in reference to the same subject of the Borders, and also letters on professional matters from the celebrated Dr. Archibald Pitcairn who practised in Edinburgh.

IV. Royal Commissions and relative Papers connected with the Scottish Borders, from the year 1619.

108. Royal Proclamation, commanding all Scotsmen to send in their complaints against the inhabitants of the English borders before the 12th November, for the meeting of the Commissioners of Scotland and England at Newcastle on the 29th November 1619.

109. Printed bond by the Committee of Estates of Parliament to Violet Douglas, Lady Riddell, elder, for 2,400l. scots, advanced by her for the armies sent to England and Ireland. Edinburgh, 24th December 1644.

110. Articles of agreement concluded between the English and Scottish Commissioners of the Borders, chiefly relating to the transferring of prisoners to their proper court of jurisdiction. Morpeth, 5th October, 1665.

111. Extract ratification of the preceding articles at Morpeth by the Lords of the Scotch Privy Council. Edinburgh, 21st December 1665.

112. Royal Commission under the signature of the Lords of the Scottish Council, appointing William Earl of Roxburgh and others Commissioners of the Scottish Borders, with certain powers. 8th January 1669.

113. Additional articles of agreement to those concluded at Morpeth in 1665, between the Commissioners of the Borders of England and Scotland. One article orders constables in Bedlingtonshire, Norhamshire and Ilandshire, &c., in England, and all on the Scottish Borders, to search suspected places. Another orders any person who received again any of his goods that were stolen should inform the Commissioners as to how he came by them. Subscribed by the Earl of Carlisle, Lord Morpeth, and others. Carlisle, 29th August 1674.

114. Decree of the Privy Council anent the procedure of the Commissioners of the Scottish Borders, in apprehending and imprisoning Robert Broune and Christopher Jamesone, Englishmen. Edinburgh, 6th September 1677;

A. J. W. H.
K. ER-
SKINE, ESQ.

115. Copy Instructions, under the signature of Lord Chancellor Rothes, as authorised by the Lords of the Privy Council, to Adam Urquhart of Meldram, justice of the peace for the shires of Berwick, Roxburgh, Selkirk and Peebles. He is directed to summon together all the justices in these shires, and the members of this convention are empowered to appoint whatever constable they deem expedient. He is to use diligent endeavours to inform himself of any intended conventicles, to dissipate those meetings with the assistance of the people around, to imprison persons found at or retiring from them, and to act against these conventicles, with any commander of the King's forces who might be at hand. He is to seize "vagrant ministers" or who preach without allowance of there ordinaryes." He is to cite before him men or women who shall be at conventicles, or are guilty of illegal marriages or baptisms, and who have resided forty days within his jurisdiction. The woman is always to be fined according to the husband's quality. If the criminals be cited personally and do not compear, they are to be "unlawed" in 50l. scots, "toties quoties as frequently as you can." He is desired to apprehend any who contemptuously disobey the discipline and censure of the church, and imprison them till they find security for their obedience: and this at the request of the parish minister. He is to put in force the 1st Act, 3 Sess. 1 Parl. ch. 3. He is to apply to his own use the whole fines of those who are not landed, in other cases one half was to go to the commissioners, the other half to the King. Dated 8 May 1679.

116. Extract Commission of the Privy Council to Adam Urquhart, renewing his commission of 4 March 1680, by which he and those to be appointed by him, were empowered to proceed against conventicles in the shires of Berwick, Roxburgh, and Selkirk. The utmost diligence was to be used in obtaining lists of the rebel heritors, and of their resetters and correspondents, and sheriffs, baillies, burgh magistrates, parish ministers, &c., were to be compelled to give evidence against them on pain of imprisonment. Urquhart is thanked for his service in prosecuting his former commissions, and this renewal is made on the ground that an interruption in the prosecution had provoked the old disorders. Edinburgh, 27 January 1681.

117. Extract Act of Privy Council, Edinburgh, 21st July 1681, in favour of Adam Urquhart of Meldram as Sheriff in these parts, containing decreet against James Murray of Philiphaugh, sheriff principal of Selkirk, and William Murray his depute, for abetting conventiclers. It is narrated that Adam Urquhart of Meldram, John Riddell of Hayning, William Elliot of Dunlairbyre, George Pringle of Blindlie, and Hary Ker of Gradane, were commissioned to Act as justices in the shires of Selkirk, Roxburgh, and Peebles, against conventicles and such disorders, but that their attempts had been materially frustrated by the two Murrays of Philiphaugh, who had designed to hinder the execution of the laws against some who were "notour ringleaders," by citing such persons before them, pronouncing sentence against them, and receiving pretended bonds for their fines. An instance is given of the way in which the Murrays frustrated the attempts of the justices specially commissioned. Hearing of a court to be held by them at Selkirk, Murray and his depute appeared at the Tolbooth on the appointed day with two justices who are called "pretended," and ordered the persons summoned, to be present at his court on the following Thursday. The special justices went to hold their court in the Tolbooth, when Murray and his depute informed them that they had sent the accused home, and fines were accordingly imposed on the absentees. Murray held his court. The justices held their second meeting on the day to which they had adjourned, the accused appeared, pleading that they had been already fined by the sheriff. The sheriff himself acted as their procurator, and "proposed frivolous and disingenuous defences " . . . and he behaved himselfe in that manner that " he gives great encouragement to disorderly persons," even asserting that the Privy Council had no power to grant such commission. It is complained of the sheriff's grand uncle, John Murray of Ashistiell, that he had himself confessed that, after his appearance before the Privy Council, he had received "Mr. Thomas Wilkie " a vagrant preacher, entertained him in his house all " night, and recepte rebells and vagrant preachers upon " all occasions." John Stoddart of Williamhoe who had been fined several times, was countenanced by the sheriff. "The most frequent and considerable conven- "ticles," in the shire were held in the parish where Murray resided and near his house. Since the Act of Indemnity was issued he had conversed with and enter-

tained conventiclers, especially William Stoddart in Cams, Mr. Alexander Lennox and Mr. Thomas Wilkie, "va- " grant intercommuned persons," while his depute had entertained such "notorious traitors" as Mr. John Welsh, John Caile, William Stoddart, Turnbull of Standhill, Alexander called Captain Home, while they were " in actuall rebellion in the toune of Selkirk," and conversed and drank with them when they had seized the arms, drums, &c., of the militia. Sentence against the sheriff is deferred till next council day, but meanwhile he is ordered to pay 2 rixdollars to each witness adduced against him in this process. William Murray is ordered to be conveyed to Edinburgh and committed to the Tolbooth till his trial. The complaining justices are approved and thanked for their diligent and faithful prosecution of the trust committed to them.

A. J. W. H.
K. ER-
SKINE, ESQ.

118. Precept of poynding issued by sheriff Murray against various persons in the parish of Yarrow for attending conventicles. We give a few of the names and fines:—

	£
Robert Baptie in Ladhope, five conventicles	125
Andro Tod in Catslackknow, two conventicles	50
Francis Hardie in Dewchar, one conventicle	25
John Murray in Lewinshope, six conventicles	150
John Gilles younger in Philiphaugh, one conventicle	22

The total number of persons is 32, and the sum of their fines 2,128l. scots. Dated 26th March 1681.

119. A list of the leaders of the militia in the west of Roxburghshire as it was rectified in June 1682.

Buccleuch, 21 horse : Laird of Cavers, 3 horse : Glaidstaines in Cavers, 1 horse, &c. The whole number of horse is 50.

120. Information for the commissioners of the borders 1681. Showing that the lords of session have no legal right to suspend or reduce the sentences of the commissioners. It is an independent tribunal with criminal jurisdiction. "When causes have depended long before " the lords of the session, the lords themselves being " obliged to judge by the border laws and customes, " and so they must send commissions to the commis- " sioners of the borders to try what these are; and so " at last the commissioners of the borders will be still " the onlie judges."

121. Commission by King Charles the Second and the Privy Council to the sheriffs of Selkirkshire, Sir Francis Scott of Thirlstone, James Murray of Deuchar, Riddell of Hayning, and others, to proceed against those who were "debauched with schismaticall and seditious prin- " cipalls," especially against those who had "either " been arte and part of the contriving, affixing, spread- " ing, and publishing the late traiterous and bloody " declaration." It is complained that the rebels had " of late erected themselves under a mock forme of " government " and had declared war, from which His Majesty infers that these "inhumane monsters" con- sider it "not only lawful but a duty upon them to kill " us." Dated 30th December 1684.

122. A list of the chief recusants in the parish of Ettrick. Undated.

123. List of articles to be voted upon at the general convention of the burghs at Edinburgh on 3rd July, 1688. Sent by the town council of Edinburgh to the magistrates and council of the burgh of Selkirk.

124. Memorandum of interrogatories to be put to the persons imprisoned, as ordered by Her Majesty's letter, in relation to the invasion or practices against the government. The last of the 13 interrogatories is : "If " they know that Mr. Charles Fleeming and Boyn " younger have come lately from France: If they have " seen them or what informations they brought thither." No date.

125. Five papers relating to a contract made in 1671 between King Charles II. and the Laird of Hayning as to the rearing of a breed of horses in Scotland. The speculation was not a paying one for Hayning. Hayning laid out his lands for the purpose mentioned, but he never received the promised horses from the King, who in lieu thereof presented him with the Border fines. Hayning in 1682 petitioned to be discharged from the agreement.

126. "Memoriall to the Queens most excellent Majes- " tie concerning the restraining the importation of Irish " corns and cattell into Scotland, the preventing many " frauds in the Tobacco trade, the preventing the expor- " tation of wool and preserving the salmond fishing " from the Mule of Galloway to the port of Inverloohie."

In addition to the papers above specified there are portions of three volumes, two of them stitched in leaves, another partly bound in parchment, containing the proceedings by the commissioners of the Scottish Borders, under the commissions before mentioned. One of these volumes contains a record of the proceedings from July 1674 to June 1675, and occupies in all about 80 pages folio; the other volume contains a similar record of proceedings from March 1676 to May 1679 and occupies in all 202 pages. The third volume or minute book contains a briefer note of the proceedings.

Besides these three formal volumes there are many detached papers connected with the proceedings of the commissioners. These latter chiefly relate to actions against persons who were guilty of the crimes of stealing cattle and sheep which was long a special characteristic on both sides of the Borders, of making counterfeit coin, &c. and show the constant attempts, sometimes made it appears with enthusiastic vigour and corresponding severity, to suppress by the arm of law that form of crime by which so many lawless depredators supported themselves and which was a constant sore in the government of both England and Scotland.

WILLIAM FRASER.

Edinburgh, 32 Castle Street,
23 March 1874.

THE MANUSCRIPTS OF WILLIAM COSMO GORDON, ESQUIRE, AT FYVIE CASTLE.

The name Formartin is now applied to one of the five districts into which the county of Aberdeen is divided. At an early period of our history it was a thanage, and formed part of the demesne lands of the Crown, of which the Castle of Fyvie was the chief messuage. It continued to be the property of the Crown till towards the end of the fourteenth century, when the barony was conferred by King Robert II. on his eldest son, the Stewart of Scotland, afterwards King Robert III., who soon resigned it to his cousin, Sir James Lyndesay.

In 1296 Edward I. halted at Fyvie Castle on his route from Kintore to Banff, and about a century later the wife of Sir James Lyndesay was besieged in the castle by her nephew, Robert de Keith, son of the Marischall, as related in Wyntounis Cronykil.

" A thousand and thre hundyr yero
    Nynty and five, or thare-by nere,
    Robert the Keth, a mychty man
    Be lynage, and apperand than
    For to be a lord of mycht
    Of mony lands of rycht richt
    In Fermartine at Fivy
    Assegit his awnt, a gud lady,
    That tyme the Lord of Craufurdis wyf
    (That led in al hir tyme gud lif),
    Schir James de Lyndesay than hir lord,
    Movit agane hym in discord,
    For his mesownys first gert he
    Fra thare werke removit be;
    And quha that Wattyr broucht fra the barn
    He gert thaim oft wytht his ost spurn.
    Thus he demanyt that lady
    Wythin the castil of Fivy."

Sir James Lyndesay on hearing of this assembled about 400 men and 'crossed the Mounth to raise the siege. He was met, however, at the Kirk of Bourty by Sir Robert Keith, who had the worst of the day, and lost 50 of his men. So that—

" Fra thine he past noucht til Fivy
    For til assege that gud lady."

B. ix., c. xvi.

From the charters at Fyvie it appears that the barony of Fermartyne came from Sir James Lyndesay to Sir Henry Preston in the following way. Sir Henry, who, as well as Sir James, were engaged in the doughty fight of Otterburn, would seem to have there captured the English Knight, Sir Ralph Percy. And a charter by King Robert II. in favour of Preston, on the resignation of Sir James Lyndesay, His Majesty's brother-in-law, narrates that it was for the ransom of Percy, the right to which he probably surrendered to the King.

Sir James Lyndesay left two daughters, who, notwithstanding of the King's grant, still retained certain rights in the barony. Margaret, the eldest, was married to Thomas Colville, of Oxenham, and Eufemia, the second, was married to Sir John Herys, of Trareglys, Knight.

An agreement between Margaret, the eldest daughter, and Sir Henry Preston relative to the surrender by her of her part of the lordship and barony of Fermartyn, viz., the castle and burgh of Fyvie, is dated within the sacristy of St. Nicholas Church at Aberdeen, 4 February

1403, and engrosses a charter in his favour by Thomas Colville and the said Margaret, dated 12 June 1397.

A charter by King Robert III., dated 1 September 1405, confirms a like deed of surrender by Sir John Herys and Eufemia, his wife, by which they conveyed to Sir Henry Preston and Elizabeth, his spouse, their part of the lordship and barony of Fermartyn, viz., of the castle and burgh of Fyvie, with tolls and burgh rents. This charter, with a few of the older Fyvie charters, is printed in the Topographical Collections of the Spalding Club (vol. I., p. 499, et seq.).

Sir Henry Preston died about 1433, having probably built one of the towers of the Castle, which has always been known as "the Preston Tower." He appears to have left two daughters, one of whom, Mariotade Preston, was married to John of Forbes, son of Sir Alexander of Forbes, Knight. She was a widow in 1420, when on the 6th of July of that year, she, as daughter and one of the heirs of Sir Henry Preston, Knight, of Formartyn, granted a charter to the said John Forbes in marriage of one half of the barony of Fermartyn.

Alexander of Meldrum, who in 1438 appears as dominus de Fyvy, is believed to have acquired his part of Fermartyn by marriage with another daughter of Sir Henry Preston.

A charter by King James IV. to George Meldrum, son and heir apparent of William Meldrum, of Fyvie, granting to him the lands and barony of Fermartyn, is dated 30 January 1502.

By an instrument dated at the Chapel of St. Michael the Archangel, at Fetkarry, on 2 October 1511, Alexander, eldest son of the said George, resigned his right of succession to his younger brothers, William and George, on account of a bodily infirmity of ten years standing.

George Meldrum was infeft in the lands and barony of Fyvy, alias Formerthin, on 12 March 1577.

Towards the end of the 16th century they passed into the hands of Alexander, son of George, Lord Seton, who, after having had various dignities and offices conferred on him by James VI., was created Earl of Dunfermline in 1606.

Among the papers at Fyvie is a commission to him (dated 13 December 1604) as Lord Fyvie, appointing him to the office of Lord High Chancellor of Scotland; also "Commission for creating Lords Home, Drum- "mond, and Fyvie Earls of Home, Perthe, and Dun- "fermling," dated 11 February 1605. "The creation "parfyted, 4 March 1605." This refers to "Carta "erectionis Comitatus de Dunfermline," 4 March 1605-6.

There is also a Royal gift dated 6 April 1611, granting to him the keeping of the palice, park, and yairds of Halyroodhouse, "Palacii nostri de Halyroodhouse ac "roboraŕii sive saltus ad idem spectan. hortorum po- "mariorum viridariorum hortulorum pratorum," &c. This grant followed on the death of George, Earl of Dunbar, and gave Lord Dunfermline power to appoint officers under him "pro custodia, nec non et hortulanos "olitores ac alios servos qui colent laborent ac in re- "paratione et policia custodiant omnes hortos viridarios "tum borealia tum australia ac parvum hortum intra "dictam palatium," with 20l. of money and one chalder and four bolls of barley, as the fee for keeping the said North Garden; 33l. 6s. 8d. of money, and one chalder and ten bolls of barley for keeping the south garden, with fourteen bolls of barley for keeping the small garden, besides 66l. for keeping the said palace and its pertinents—" et integram deuoriam commodi- "tatum et proficuum que ipse acquirere seu facere "possit de dicta saltu nostro de Halyrudhouse."

Lord Dunfermline greatly embellished the noble pile of Fyvie Castle, having added to it the "Seton Tower," and by various other works harmonised the two earlier Preston and Meldrum towers with his own addition.

He was succeeded in the year 1622 by his son Charles, second Earl of Dunfermline. This peer was engaged in various political missions in the stirring times of Charles I. and Charles II. The title became extinct in the person of his son James, the fourth Earl, who fought under the Viscount Dundee at the battle of Killie-crankie. He was forfeited in 1690, and died at St. Germains in 1694. The barony of Fyvie was then purchased by William, Earl of Aberdeen, by whom it was given to a younger son, the ancestor of its present owner.

There are many State Papers in the collection here, principally of the period of the second Lord Dunfermline. Of these I noted—

Safe-conduct by Charles I. to Charles Earl of Dun-fermline, John Lord Loudon, Sir William Douglas, of

Cavers, Sir Patrick Hepburn, of Wauchton, John Smith, Mr. Alexander Wedderburn, Mr. Alexander Henrieston, and Mr. Archibald Johnston, commissioners from Scotland, to attend the conference at Ripon on Thursday, 1 October, under the sign manual and privy seal, and dated at York, 28 September 1640.

Instructions by King Charles I. to ———, containing proposals to the Parliament of Scotland for the pacification of the kingdom, and interceding for the Earl of Traquair and the absentees, and stating his intention of being present in the Parliament in person under the sign manual, and dated Whythall, 16 June 1641.

Copy order of Lords and Commons in Parliament assembled sent to the General Assembly of the Church of Scotland at St. Andrews, relating to their petition to the King and their desire to avoid a civil war, dated 21 July 1642.

Instructions of King Charles I. to Charles Earl of Dunfermline as Commissioner to the General Assembly of the Kirk held at St. Andrews, under the sign manual, and dated at Leicester, 23 July 1642.

Letter from King Charles I. to Charles Earl of Dunfermline, Commissioner to the General Assembly at St. Andrews, requiring him to make known to the Assembly His Majesty's answer to a petition of the two Houses of Parliament in England, and the reply of the two Houses of Parliament, wherein they had refused His Majesty's propositions for reconciling differences, under the sign manual, and dated at Beverley, 26 July 1642.

Copy letter from Charles Earl of Dunfermline, Commissioner to the General Assembly of the Kirk at St. Andrew's, to Charles I., intimating the Assembly's appointment of Lord Maitland (afterwards Duke of Lauderdale) as bearer of their answer to the Parliment's declaration, and of their supplication to His Majesty, dated St. Andrews, 5 August 1642.

Letter from Charles I. to Charles Earl of Dunfermline, commissioner as aforesaid, in answer to his Lordship's letter of the 2nd August, under the sign manual, and dated York, 7 August 1642.

Copy letter from Charles Earl of Dunfermline to Charles I., professing his sincerity in His Majesty's cause, and hinting that some others had more zeal than prudence, dated 30 January 1643.

Letter from King Charles I. to Charles Earl of Dunfermline requiring him to assemble his friends, vassals, and dependants, and make known to them His Majesty's willingness to maintain the established government, ecclesiastical and civil, in contradiction to the seditious pamphlets then scattered by His Majesty's enemies, under the sign manual, and dated at Oxford, 21 April 1643.

Copy letter from Charles I. addressed to the Speaker of the House of Lords *pro tempore*, to be communicated to the two Houses of Parliament at Westminster, and to the Commissioners for the Parliament for Scotland, wherein the King proposes to disband his army, dismantle his garrisons, and return to the two Houses of Parliament, they giving their faith for the preservation of his honour, person, and estate, and his adherents being allowed to return to their homes unmolested in their persons or properties, and also that an Act of Oblivion and free pardon should be passed, under the sign manual, and dated at Oxford, 23 March 1645.

Salvus conductus sub signo manuali Caroli I. in favorem Joannis Butler, ducis, equitum, a principio belli inservientis venia impetrata in Galliam alias transmarinas regiones proficiscendi, datum atque signatum in Aula Novi Castri super Tiniam 14 Januarii 1646.

Copy obligation by Charles I. under the sign manual, to confer on Charles Earl of Dunfermline, Gentleman of his Bedchamber, the place of Lord Privy Seal of Scotland, on the removal or death of the Earl of Roxburgh, dated Newcastle, 10 December 1646; with form of gift and admission to that office, and also of gift of the Principal Shoriffship of Aberdeenshire.

Gift by Charles I. to the said Earl of the office of Keeper of the Privy Seal of Scotland, vacant by the death of Robert Earl of Roxburgh.

Warrant of King Charles I. addressed to the Treasurer of Scotland, for a yearly pension of 1,000l. in favour of Charles Earl of Dunfermline, one of the Lords of the Bedchamber. Dated Newcastle, 16 January 1647.

A true copy of His Majesty's Message to the Houses of Parliament by the Earl of Dunfermline, in regard to his leaving Holdenby unwillingly (June 1647).

Extract Act of the Committee of Estates, setting forth the great losses which Charles Earl of Dunfermline and his tenants on his estates in Aberdeenshire and Morayshire had sustained, and recommending to Parliament that he should be relieved from all public burdens until

he should be reimbursed; and also that he should be paid the value of 800 bolls of meal furnished by his tenants of Fyvie for the use of the Earl of Argyle's army in 1645, with the interest of the same. Dated Edinburgh, 26 February 1650.

Copy Paper presented to Charles II. at Breda by the Commissioners of the Estates of Scotland, containing the demands, under three heads, for a settlement of differences, preparatory to his restoration, dated 4 April 1650; with a Paper from the King in answer, desiring to know whether the Paper of the Commissioners, contained all their demands, and a further Paper by the Commissioners stating that it did so, and that upon his agreeing to these demands they had warrant immediately to invite him to his ancient kingdom of Scotland. Dated 14 April 1650.

Draft Concessions by the King to the demands of the Commissioners contained in the Paper last noted, with His Majesty's demands under eight heads, upon receiving security for the fulfilment of which the King professed his willingness to agree to the demands of the Commissioners. (Without date.)

Amended copy of the last paper.

Observations by the Commissioners on the King's demands.

Extract Act of Committee of Estates, whereby upon hearing the Commissioner for the Shire and Boroughs of Fife upon the controverted horses of the present levy, the Committee exempted the Boroughs from the levy, and decerned the Shire to afford 280 horses. Dated Perth, 15 October 1650.

Requisition addressed to the Earls of Dunfermline and Callander from the Committee of Estates, summoning them to attend a meeting at [   ], in the Isle of Bute, on the 8th of October next 1651. (Signed) Loudon, Tullibardin, Glencairn, Lothian, Wemyss, Linlithgow, Argyll, A. Blackhall, James Menteith, and others. With a letter from the Earl of Callander to the Earl of Dunfermline stating his inability to attend. Dated Revin, 4 October 1651.

Copy Letter from Charles II. to the Earl of Middleton, Commissioner to the Parliament of Scotland, desiring that a dispute between Charles Earl of Dunfermline and Alexander Livingstone regarding the possession of a certain estate should be determined by the Lords of Council and Session, and that the Parliament should not interfere therein; under the sign manual, and countersigned by the Earl of Lauderdale. Dated Whythall, 10 June 1661.

Copy Injunction to the Sheriff Principal of Aberdeenshire to enforce the Act against Conventicles and to levy the fines incurred. Signed by the Earl of Rothes, 6 March 1667.

Letter from R. Maitland (afterwards fourth Earl of Lauderdale and translator of Virgil) to James Earl of Dunfermline regarding his absence from the host, regretting that he dare not solicit the Lords on his behalf, but promising to mention the matter to his father, and, in conclusion, advising him to be in town next session. Dated Edinburgh, 7 July 1680.

Letter from George Adamson to James Earl of Dunfermline, with newsletters and gazettes, and alluding to Mr. Spence's confession and the Primate's hopeless illness. Dated 23 August 1684.

Among some miscellaneous papers I noted the following:—

Presentation by James VI. to William Dunbar, minister of Dyke and Moy, to the united parsonages and vicarages of Dyke and Moy, now vacant by the decease of umquhile George Bishop of Moray, the vicarage of Dyke by the forfaltour or barratrie of Mr. John Leslie, sometime Bishop of Ross, and for not confession of his fault conform to our Act of Parliament, and the parsonage of Moy by decease of umquhile Mr. William Sutherland, and the vicarage of Moy by deprivation of John Dunbar, last possessor of the said benefices. It is dated at Dalkeith, 6 May 1592, and given under the privy seal. The presentation is addressed to the Presbytery of Forres, who were to admit William Dunbar without any new or special presentation or collation, to give him their collation and provision thereupon in respect of his qualification and actually serving in the ministry.

Among the charters are a few of early date, not directly connected with the barony of Fyvy, which seem worthy of note.

Ordinance touching a dispute between Thomas de Melgdrum, Lord of Achyneve, and John of [   ], about the lands of Culter, on the Dee, which had been submitted to the determination of Sir James of Lyndesay, Lord of Crawford; dated in the lodging of the

4 M 3

said Sir James at Perth, 1 April 1387; in presence of William of Lyndesay, Lord of Byris, Sir Gylbert of Graham, Sir George of Lesley, Sir John of Maxwel, Sir William of Newbygyng, and Sir Robert of Levyngstoun, knights.

Grant [dated probably A.D. 1362], by William, of Meldrum, Lord of Auchneef and Petkary, of various annual rents to the altar of St. Laurence and St. Ninian, in the church of St. Nicholas of Aberdeen, for a chaplain to serve thereat, and to find a sufficient light and other ornaments for the said altar, as well as bread and wine. The subjects granted were to be vested for these purposes in the alderman and four baillies of Aberdeen, and the guardians of the church work of St. Nicholas, who might distrain the tenants of the granter on either side of the Mounth, "tanquam pro debito " divino vel ipsorum proprio debito secundum leges et " consuetudines burgorum sic quod non oporteat " ipsos ad hoc alicujus officiarii Regis licentiam petere " vel habere." Sealed with the seals of William of Meldrum, the granter, of the Bishop of Aberdeen, and of the burgh of Aberdeen. Witnesses, Sir William of Keith, Knight, and Marischal of Scotland, Sir Alexander of Fraser, Knight, Sheriff of Aberdeen, Thomas Mercer, Alderman of Aberdeen, William of Leth, and John Crab, burgesses of Aberdeen.

Charter by Sir Alexander, Lord of Seton Guardian of the House of St. John of Jerusalem of Torfechyn, narrating that by the evils of the wars in Scotland Walter Grethened, burgess of Aberdeen, lately his tenant in fee and heritage of the lands of Ochtyrelon, in Buchan, had been reduced to such poverty that for his relief and subsistence he had been compelled to sell these lands, without the said Sir Alexander's consent, to William of Melgdrum, son of the late John, of Melgdrum, and that it would be more for his advantage to have the said William than the said Walter for his tenant, therefore confirming to him the said lands, he making the customary returns, and giving suit at three head courts at Little Harthill, in the Garuyach. Dated at Aberdeen, on Monday after the feast of St. Mary Virgin, 1345.

Grant by William Meldrum, Lord of Fyvie, to the altar of St. Ninian, within the church of St Nicholas of Aberdeen, at Aberdeen, 17 August 1490.

Presentation by Andrew Meldrum of Fyvy, Patron, of the chaplainry of St. Ninian, vacant by the decease Mr. Alexander Allardes last chaplain, in favour of Andrew King, clerk and burgess of Aberdeen, at Aberdeen, 10 October 1593.

Register of the rights of the chaplainry of St. Ninian, presented by Andrew King, chaplain to Alexander Lord Fyvy, patron.

JOHN STUART.

THE MANUSCRIPTS of the Family of HOME of RENTON, in the County of BERWICK, now in the possession of Miss MARY ELEANOR STIRLING of Renton.

The family of Home of Renton, is descended from the Homes of Wedderburn, a distinguished branch of the great border house of the Earls of Home. The first who acquired the estate of Renton was Patrick Home, second son of Alexander Home of Manderston, a younger son of Wedderburn. Patrick Home married Janet Ellem, daughter and heiress of David Ellem of Renton and Butterdean, of an ancient family in the county of Berwick. Renton then became the territorial designation of Patrick Home and his descendants. The eldest son of the marriage of Patrick Home and Janet Ellem was Alexander Home of Renton, who held the office of sheriff-principal of Berwickshire from the year 1616 to 1621. In his official capacity he was very rigorous in the punishment of witches; and in a letter from his son, dated in 1624, and addressed to his kinsman Sir Patrick Home of Polwarth who then held the office of sheriff, it is stated that Alexander Home burned seven or eight witches at Coldingham. In the present collection are two letters from King James the Sixth of Scotland, then First of England, to the same Alexander Home regarding the affairs of Sir George Home, Earl of Dunbar. (Nos. 28 and 29.)

The son and successor of the rigorous sheriff was Sir John Home, who became Lord Renton as a lord of session. He held a prominent place among the Scotchmen of his time. According to Wodrow the historian, he was one of the greatest zealots for episcopacy in Scotland; and his own petition to King Charles II. (No. 37 of this Report), bears evidence of his close

attachment to the house of Stuart. He claims to
have been the first in Scotland who took up arms in defence of King Charles I., and not only did he spend his entire fortune in the Royal cause, but he was even forced to flee the country in a destitute condition. His loyalty, however, received ample compensation on the restoration of King Charles II. He was knighted, created a privy councillor, and on the 4th June 1663, nominated a lord of session and justice clerk. Lord Renton died in 1671, leaving two sons by his wife Margaret Stewart, daughter of John Stewart, commendator of Coldingham, son of Francis, Earl of Bothwell, whose father John Stewart was also commendator of Coldingham, and a natural son of King James the Fifth. The eldest son of Lord Renton was Sir Alexander Home, of Coldingham. His grandson, Sir John Home, who died in January 1788, was the last of his line. The second son of Lord Renton was Sir Patrick Home of Renton, who was created a baronet of Nova Scotia in 1632. His son, Sir John Home, claimed the title of Earl of Dunbar, as heir-male of George the first Earl. His son Sir James, the third baronet, who died in 1785, is said to have been the last of his line.

Henry Home of Kames, who, under the designation of Lord Kames, was celebrated both as a judge and as the author of several learned works, was descended from the Homes of Renton.

Owing to the connexion of the owners of Renton with the ancient priory of Coldingham, the collection of family papers contains several documents of interest relating to that religious house. The collection also embraces a number of early documents, containing interesting notices of men conspicuous in the annals of their country. Among these are Andrew Forman, Bishop of Moray, Henry Balnaves of Halhill, James Kirkcaldy of Grange, Robert Logan of Restalrig, and Sir George Home, afterwards Earl of Dunbar, the favourite minister of King James the Sixth. Andrew Forman, one of the foremost Scottish statesmen and diplomatists of his day, is witness to several deeds executed at the priory of Coldingham in 1509, one on the 11th June and another on the 12th July, and in these various writs the name of Henrison, clerk of the Justiciary, appears beside that of Forman. We may suppose that these two politicians resided in the priory of Coldingham, or in that district for several weeks, and that the object of their visit was somehow connected with the administration of the Church lands. A Thomas Forman, Esquire, probably an ancestor of the famous ecclesiastic, witnessed a notarial instrument relating to the forestry of Coldingham, dated in 1410, and fully described in the present report. Several of the charters introduce to us James Kirkcaldy of Grange, the Treasurer of Scotland, in the act of despoiling the Abbey of Coldingham of its lands of Press or Pressis, and enriching with them his brother, George Kirkcaldy (vide No. 15, etc.). We find the Protestant leader Henry Balnaves, so highly eulogised by Knox, in the company of Kirkcaldy, at the Monastery of Coldingham, in March 1539.

From the present papers it appears that Robert Logan was alive on the 31st August 1605 (No. 26.). In 1603 he still enjoys the favour of King James VI., but the charter No. 26, dated 31st August 1605, by which Logan alienates his lands of Flemington to the Earl of Dunbar, King James's favourite, at once suggests from the nature of the transfer that suspicion had been directed against him as being intimately connected with the Gowrie conspiracy. Logan's signature to this deed lacks its former firmness, and it may be conjectured that James was only prevented by compassion for his age and feebleness from subjecting Logan himself to that trial which was carried out in 1608 against his fellow conspirators, when the bones of the deceased laird of Restalrig were produced in court. It is worthy of notice that George Sprot, a notary, who was afterwards executed for concealment of the Gowrie conspiracy, appears as a witness to this charter of 1605; and we have also the name of James Bowir, perhaps the same person who was servitor to Logan, and his accomplice, although he is here designated "parson of Auchincraw." The narrative in the charter by King James VI. in favour of George, Earl of Dunbar, indicates by its peculiarly bombastic style, that the King himself may have assisted in the composition of the glowing eulogy.

ANCIENT CHARTERS.

1, Charter by William de Rydale in favour of John de Rayntoun, burgess of Southberwick, of two oxgates of land in Nether Aytoun in the tenement of Flemyngtoun, which are called Baxterlande, with free " bresing " butcheris," and other privileges. To be held of the said William de Rydale and his heirs for an annual payment to him of six silver pennies, and to the Lord of Coldingham through him of 18 silver pennies, at fixed and usual terms. To this charter was affixed the seal (now lost) of the granter, and, as his was little known, those of the " religiosus vir," Sir Adam de Ponte Fracto, prior of Coldingham, Sir Henry de Prandirgest, Knight, and John, son of Walter, then Sheriff of Berwick and steward of the aforesaid priory, were also appended. The charter is dated at Aytoun, 5th July 1325.

2. Charter by William Riddell in favour of John de Reyntoun, burgess of Southberwick, of an oxgate of land in Nether Aytoun within the tenement of Flamingtoun, called the land of Margaret Aire. To be held of the said William Riddell for yearly payment to him and his heirs of three silver pennies, and to the lord of Coldingham through him of nine silver pennies, at fixed and usual terms. The seals of the same persons bear to have been appended to this charter as to the preceding charter, and the charter is dated at Aitoun, the Wednesday immediately preceding the feast of Saint Michael the Archangel [September 29] 1325.

3. Notarial instrument narrating that on the 12th February 1410 Gilbert de Lummysden appeared before the court held at Renton by John de Aclyfe, prior of Coldingham, who sat as judge, and there on behalf of Mariot, his spouse, as forester of the barony of Coldingham, claimed from the said lord prior all the stipends or emoluments due to the foressid office, to be declared by an assize : that the prior, admitting the reasonableness of his petition, forthwith instructed his bailiff, Alexander of Home, to summon an assize of " good and " elderly men " to his court : that the bailiff accordingly selected and summoned James of Qwhytlaw, Patrick Broun, Patrick Sleyth, William of Rayntoun, John of Paxtons, Robert of Fenwick, Richard Blakberd, and 12 others therein named, who, having sworn a great oath and been fully advised, found that John the Forester received the underwritten :—

Food and drink for himself and his man, and forage for their horses when they came to the prior's house.

Item, they found the forester to be keeper of " wrak " and wayffe " within the said lordship, and entitled to receive from the said wrak and wayfe 12 pennies for every pound, reserving the balance for the use of, and for disposal by, the lord prior.

Item, if any ship or boat should land in the harbour or elsewhere in the lordship, laden with grain, salt, coals, or any such freight, and should sell thereof, the forester was to receive for his own use a boll before and a boll behind the mast.

Item, for anchorage of a ship, 12 pence, and of a boat 4 pence.

Item, a threave of oats from every husband-land of the farms of the lord prior, the husband-lands of the town of Coldingham only excepted.

Item, from every waggon of goods, 4 pence.

Item, from every " tractus equinus " [horse load], 1 penny.

Item, from every " quercus quadratus " drawn by oxen, 4 pence.

Item, wood hens due according to custom.

Item, John the Forester received at Christmas a suit of clothes fit to be worn by gentlemen (roba generosis apta).

These and all other dues hitherto enjoyed by John the Forester were to be similarly enjoyed by his foresaid son, Gilbert, until another charter was produced ; but the jury declared that they did not know whether these emoluments were due by law or from use and wont. They had only seen that such things had been usually allowed. In consequence of this decreet the present notarial instrument was prepared at Renton in presence of Sir William Drake, monk, sacristan of Coldingham ; Sir John Broun, vicar of Eddrem ; Sir Richard of Spot, chaplain ; Patrick of Home, Robert de Blackwod, Thomas Forman, John de Lummysden, Thomas de Lummysden, David of Home, esquires, and many others.

4. Precept of sasine by John, commendator of Coldingham, for infefting John Logan, son of John Logan of Lastalrig (Restalrig) as heir of his father in the lands of Flemyntone. 6th August 1495.

5. Instrument of resignation by John Lumsden into the hands of John, prior of Coldingham, of his six husband-lands in the town of Rentoun in favour of Alexander Ellem and Christian Lumsden, his spouse. Dated 11th June 1509. This instrument was signed in the choir of the monastery of Coldingham, and the two

witnesses attesting are, the famous Andrew Forman, here designated "Andrew, Bishop of Moray, Commen- " dator of Pettinweym, and of Cottingham in England," and Mr. James Harrison " clerk of the general Justiciary " of our supreme Lord the King." These two persons are also witnesses to the subsequent sasine of the 19th June, and to a charter of the 26th July by John prior of Coldingham in favour of the above Alexander Ellem and Christian Lumsden.

6. Notarial instrument of resignation, narrating that on the 10th August 1512, John Lummisden of Coldingham personally compeared before Lord Alexander, Archbishop of St. Andrew's, perpetual commendator of the monastery of Dumfermline and of the priory of Coldingham, and on bended knees (flexis genibus sedens) resigned into the hands of the said Alexander as lord superior thereof the third part of a carucate of land in the town and territory of Coldingham in favor of Alexander Ellem, spouse of Cristiane Lummisden, daughter of the said John Lummisden. Done in the royal palace adjoining the monastery of the Holy Cross in Coldingham.

7. Lease by Adam prior of Coldingham, with consent of the chapter thereof, narrating that for great sums of money received by them from Alexander Ellem in Rantoun, for payment of their tax to the King and for redeeming them from great debts due by them for the " weill " of the abbey, and for great sums of money payed by him for the utility of their place and abbey, and " convertiu in the common weill," utility, and profit of the same, they set to the said Alexander Ellem and his heirs, for 19 years, the lands of Rantoun, for 16 merks and 4 shillings yearly; reserving to themselves the "thirle multure" thereof, &c. Dated 2 October, 1535.

8. Commission by Pope Paul III. to Richard Lausoun, archdeacon of the cathedral church of Sodor, and John Guilliermi, provost of the collegiate church of Seytoun in the diocese of St. Andrews, to inquire into the preceding grant of the lands and town of Renton, and, if satisfied with the agreement, to approve and confirm it. Dated 15 March, 1535.

9. Proclamation by Richard Lausoun, archdeacon of the cathedral church of Sodor, and John Guilliermi, licentiate in laws, provost of the collegiate church of Seytoun in the diocese of St. Andrews, to all rectors, vicars, &c. in Scotland, in obedience to an order from Pope Paul III., requiring an inquest to be made with reference to the grant of the lands of Renton to Alexander Ellem, and commanding all who had, or considered themselves to have, an interest in these lands, to be present at the court for hearing such matters to be held on the chapel or aisle of St. Thomas in the church of St. Giles, Edinburgh, on the 21st July following. Dated at St. Giles', 13 July, 1536.

The seals of Richard Lausoun, and of the provost of Seytoun, are appended. The seal of the provost is a ship on the sea. Circumscription, "S. Johannis Willi. " Prepositi de Seto."

10. Letter of confirmation by the said Archdeacon Lauson, provost Guilliermi, and the lord dean of Restalrig, of the grant of the lands of Renton in favour of Alexander Ellem. Made at St. Giles', Edinburgh, 21st July 1536.

11. Papal rescript by Cardinal Antonius, commissioning the archdeacon of the church of Glasgow, the dean of Restalrig, and the provost of Seytoun, to inquire into the grant of the lands of Pressis made by the prior of Coldingham to George Kirkcaldy, brother-german of James Kirkcaldy of Grange, and, if satisfied with the agreement, to approve and confirm it. Given at St. Peter's, Rome, 4th nones of September, 5th year of Pope Paul III. [1539].

The charter here referred to was given by the chapter to Kirkcaldy on 9th January, 1538.

12. Charter by Adam, prior, and the chapter of the monastery of Coldingham, in favour of Robert Logane, son and heir apparent of Robert Logane of Restalrig, of the lands of Flemyngtoun in the barony of Coldingham, which had been resigned by Robert Logane, elder, in favour of his son, the life-rent of the lands being reserved by Robert Logane, elder ; and a third part after his decease in favour of Elizabeth Hume, his spouse. The charter is dated at the monastery of Coldingham, 4th March 1539. Two of the witnesses are James Kirkcaldy of Grange, Lord Treasurer of Scotland, and Mr. Henry Balnaves of Halhill.

13. Letters of confirmation by John Leddar, archdeacon of the church of Glasgow, John Guilliermi, provost of Seytoun, and the lord dean of Restalrig, in obedience to letters from Cardinal Anthony, of a grant

of the lands of Pressis by Adam, prior of Coldingham, in favour of George Kirkcaldy. The lands to be held for payment of six merks yearly to the prior of Coldingham. Done in the collegiate church of St. Giles', Edinburgh, on 25th August 1541.

14. Charter by George Kirkcaldy, brother-german of James Kirkcaldy of Grange, in favour of Alexander Hume, brother-german of umquhile David Hume of Wedderburne, of the lands of Pressis in the barony of Coldingham; to be held of the granter and his heirs from the prior and convent of Coldingham for paying yearly to the prior of Coldingham the sum of six merks. Dated at Edinburgh, 10th January 1542. Two of the witnesses are Henry Balnavis, of Hallhill, and John Kirkcaldy, brother-german of the granter.

15. Notarial instrument, narrating that on January 23rd, 1542, the sub-prior and convent appeared for the chapter of the monastery of Coldingham, and in the chapter-house exposed and declared how they had given a charter of the lands of Pressis to George Kirkcaldy on January 9 1538, that the grant was made in obedience to the "supplicatio litterarum Serenissimi quondam "domini nostri Regis (cuius anime propicietur Deus)," and through fear of the Prince; and that, nevertheless they confirm the grant by George Kirkcaldy to Alexander Home (No. 14 supra) on account of the numerous favours, aids, &c. which the latter had bestowed on the monastery.

A confirmation of the grant was given on the same day, signed by John, commendator, &c. No mention is made in it of the ground of the gift.

16. Precept from Queen Mary to Gawin, Archbishop of Glasgow, enjoining him to issue a proper charter of confirmation under the great seal of the grant of the lands of Pressis in favour of Alexander Hume [as in 14 supra].

The precept reserves to the Crown "devotorum preces "et orationum suffragia de eisdem perprius visitata et "consueta." Dated at Edinburgh, 19th March 1542.

17. Charter by John, commendator, and the convent of Coldingham in favour of Alexander Hume, in Hielawis, and Barbara Hume, his spouse, of the four merk lands of Hielawis, &c., for aids, &c., often given by him to the said monastery, and especially for a certain sufficient sum of money paid by him "gratanter "et integre" for the repairing of the monastery when it was razed and burned by "our ancient enemies of "England." To be held for rendering certain sums of money therein specified, with 12 capons and 4 "pultre "foulis." Dated at the monastery of Coldingham, 8th April 1547.

18. Charter by Robert Logane, of Restalrig, and Margaret Suytoun, his spouse, in favour of James and William Auchincraw, of the 10 merk lands of Flemyngtoun. [Margaret Seton signs with her own hand.] Part of her seal remains, three crescents within the royal treasure. Edinburgh, 10th December 1547.

19. Ancient copy charter by George, archdeacon of St. Andrews and commendator of Dunfermline, in favour of Archibald Edmestoun, of the lands of Wolmet, in the lordship of Musselburgh and shire of Edinburgh. Dated at the monastery of Dunfermline, 10th December 1555.

20. Instrument of sasine in favour of Robert Logane, son and heir of umquhile Robert Logane, of Restalrig, of the lands of Flemyngtoun in the barony of Coldingham. Dated at Fastcastell, 5th May 1576.

21. Charter by Robert Logane, of Restalrig, in favour of David Ellem of Rantoun, of certain lands in the barony of Coldingham. Dated at Fastcastell, 29th October 1577.

22. Charter by John, commendator of Coldingham, and James Durhame, of Duntarvie, his administrator, with the consent of King James VI., Francis Earl of Bothwell, and others, in favour of Sir George Home of Pryoursknow, Knight, and familiar servitor to King James, of the lands of Horsley, &c., in the barony of Coldingham and shire of Berwick. To be held for payment yearly to the commendator of Coldingham of 20l. Scots. There are attached six seals, including those of the King and the Earl of Bothwell. Dated at Kelso and Holyroodhouse, 30th January 1590.

23. Contemporary office copy under the hand of Sir John Skene, clerk, register, of a charter by King James the Sixth in favour of Robert Logane of Restalrig, of the mains, mills, and fortress of Fastcastle, the lands of Flemingtoun, and others, which he and his ancestors had formerly held of the prior of Coldingham: but which were now annexed to the Crown to be held by yearly payment to the King of 30s. Dated at Stirling, 22nd August 1598.

24. Charter of confirmation by King James the VI. in favour of Robert Logan of Restalrig, of the lands and barony of Restalrig, which he had resigned into the hands of the King for new infeftment, erecting them into one entire and free barony called the barony of Restalrig: also containing a novodamus. Dated at Holyrood House, 5th April 1603.

An instrument of sasine, proceeding on a precept in the preceding charter, was executed at the manor of Restalrig, 1st November 1603.

25. Charter by Robert Logan of Restalrig, with consent of Marioun Ker, his spouse, in favour of George Earl of Dunbar, in fulfilment of a contract formerly agreed upon between the granter and grantee of the whole lands of Flemyngtoun in the barony of Coldingham, to be held for payment to the Crown of the sum of 36s. yearly. Dated 30th and 31st August 1605. Among the witnesses are George Sprot, notary, and James Bowir parson of Auchincraw. "Mareoin Ker" signs with her own hand.

26. Precept from the Crown, proceeding on a charter of novodamus by King James the VI., to George Earl of Dunbar, Lord Home of Berwick, &c., of the lands of Greenelaw, Reidpeth, Fowlden, Edingtoun, Pincartouns, Lochend, Fastcastell, Flemyngtoun, &c., and erecting the same of new into one free earldom, lordship, and barony to be called the earldom of Dunbar. Dated at Whitehall and Perth, 1st and 9th July 1606.

The following preamble precedes the grant:—

"Inasmuch as we, revolving frequently in our memory "the faithful, most profitable, lengthened, and most "pleasing obediencies and services rendered to us by our "most faithful and beloved Kinsman and familiar coun- "sellor George Earl of Dunbar, Lord Home of Berwick, "high treasurer of our realm of Scotland, and Chancellor "of the Exchequer in England, who having in his earliest "youth really dedicated and firmly bestowed all the cares "and thoughts of his body and soul, his whole life even "to us, and to our safety, service, and most noble will, "has continued to this day with the same constancy and "perfect fidelity in this his most noble purpose of deserv- "ing well of us." In this strain King James proceeds to narrate that, while the country, as distracted by factions among the nobles and the people and the royal person was even endangered, Sir George Home remained a watchful and faithful minister, despising all the allurements that were wont to destroy and enervate the courtiers of Kings, and his nerves of wisdom and industry were kindled by the highest care and a sort of divine providence, so that he was able to detect the dangers that hung over the King and to avert them. The less upright lords fearing his prudence, fidelity, and industry, a large force of rebels was collected by them, and the King not being able to furnish a force sufficiently strong to cope with them, Sir George Home retired from Court, unwilling to expose the King to danger, and escaped with difficulty. He was, however, when the storm had blown past, again restored to Court, and to his former offices, which he fulfilled with even greater faithfulness and care, and he accompanied his Majesty on affairs of the greatest moment into Norway and Denmark. [Here he especially recommends Home's "summa prudentia et "rara taciturnitas," which we may suppose Home exercised in manner specially pleasing to James in the marriage expedition of 1589, here obviously referred to.]

The King gives him the credit of having successfully and alone fully discovered and combated the rebellious schemes of Bothwell; praises his management of the Treasury of Scotland; speaks of his energetic endeavours by home and foreign diplomacy to pave the way of James to the English throne, so that on Queen Elizabeth's death his accession was attained without shedding of blood.

ROYAL AND OTHER LETTERS.

27. Letter of gift by King James the Sixth to Sir George Home of Spot, of the ward, nonentries, &c. of all the lands, tenements, &c. which belonged to David Ellem of Renton, and to Jonet, his daughter, and Patrick Home, her spouse, within the barony of Coldingham. 1580.

28. King James the Sixth to Alexander Home of Renton, Palace of Whitehall, 28th May 1612. Subscribed by King James the Sixth, and also by Alexander, Master of Elphinstone, as treasurer.

Relates that direction had been given to Alexander Home, by a former special warrant from the King, to intromit with the rents, duties, &c. not uplifted before the death of the Earl of Dunbar. He is commanded to deliver the sums he had collected to the agent of the

Earl of Suffolk, Chamberlain of the King, who would employ the sums to defray the debts of the deceased Earl. The King had written to his Session and Council in Scotland to expede a special Act in favour of Alexander Home, liberating him from the burden of all arrestments which might be taken out against him by the creditors of the deceased Earl. The letter is superscribed by the King.

29. King James the Sixth to Alexander Home of Renton and George Nicolsone. The "Mannour of "Theobaldes," 16th July 1612.

Authorises Home and Nicolsone to "thresh out" whatever corns still remained in their custody, belonging to the late Earl of Dunbar. This letter is subscribed by the King, and it shows to what minute and commonplace subjects his Majesty occasionally directed his attention.

30. Copy letter of King James VI. to the Lords of the Scottish Council. Newmarket, 15th December 1616.

Explains the grounds of his purposed visit to his "native and antient kingdome of Scotlande."

31. Warrant by King Charles I. in favour of John Home of Renton. Whitehall, 13th February 1641.

Orders his general, and all other officers and ministers of justice whom it might concern, to permit John Home with his family to pass safely to his residence in Scotland.

A special clause intimates his high displeasure if "the said Jhone Hoome of Rentone should anywayes "suffer ether in his persone or estaite by reasone of his "affectione to our service during the tyme of these "laite disorders." Superscribed by the King.

32. Warrant by King Charles II. in favour of John Sibald, servant to the Laird of Renton. The Court at Stirling, 6th June 1651.

Orders his magistrates and other officers and soldiers to permit John Sibald to pass at Anstruther or any other convenient place on the coast of Fife for Lothian and the Merse. Superscribed by the King.

33. Letter by King Charles II., countersigned by the Earl of Lauderdaill, to the Earl of Glencairne, Chancellor, and the president and senators of the College of Justice. Whitehall, 4th June 1663. Copy.

The King has resolved to keep Sir Robert Murray at the Court, although he had formerly nominated him a senator of the College of Justice. He appoints John Home of Renton in his stead.

34. The Earl of Lauderdaill to his much honoured cousin the Laird of Renton. Windsor Castle, 20th July 1657.

Commissions to the Laird of Renton to sell part of the Earl's lands to satisfy his Lordship's creditors.

35. The same to the same. Windsor Castle, 13th August 1657.

On the Earl of Lauderdaill's affairs.

36. The Earl of Lauderdaill to the Lord Justice Clerk (Sir John Home). Whitehall, 26th July 1664.

On business not specified.

37. Draft Petition of Sir John Home of Renton to King Charles II. [Date torn away.]

Narrates "That whereas your Maiestie by your letter "to your late Commissioner the Earle of Middleton, of "the date the 2d of January 1661, was gratiously pleased "to take particular notice of the petitioner's singuler "heavy sufferings in the yeares 1639, 1640, 1641, "amounting to eight thousand pounds sterling; and "that for his ready obedience to your Royall father's "speciall commands, and that your said father of blessed "memory had ingaged his Royall word for satisfaction "of the same, which your Maiestie conceived yourselfe "bound to make good, and accordingly required your "said commissioner, as he tendered your Maiesties "owne, but more particularly your dearest father's "honnour, to endeavour that your Parliament might "take some effectuall course for the petitioner's pay- "ment of the aforesaid sume; and yet notwithstanding "thereof, declared your Royall intention to imploy the "ffynes for releife of your good subiects who had beene "great sufferers, and that the petiiioner had the "honnour to be the first, who to the hazard of his life "and sequestration and ruine of his Estate and fortune, "did publickly assert the Royall interest and did firmely "and constantly adhere to your Maiestie and your Royall "father dureing the whole tracke and tyme of the late "troubles, whereby and by the calamities of the late "usurpations, his family is reduced to a low and ruined "condition, except your Maiestie in your Royall wisdom "and princely bountie shall provide remeid for the "same."

5.

The petitioner then prays the King to save his family from perishing, and to appoint the payment from fines or otherwise of the foresaid sum, and of 2,000 pounds lost in the troubles of the years 1650 and 1651.

38. William Somervell to Mr. John Chisholme, "Minister of the Gospell for present att Rentoune." Edinburgh, 23 September [16]97.

Chiefly on the articles of peace agreed upon between France and England. "The newes of the peace has put "allmost all other newes out of date. It will not be "proclaimed till one of the articles be interchanged, "and then wee shall have another merry day of it as we "had upon Saturday last. It is thought if anything be "done for the French protestants it is done by private "comouneings, and there is no doubt bot, if ther shall "happen to be good and firme freendship betwixt the "two Kings, our King will procure at last the French "King's favour towards them."

The letter also narrates: "The letters gives account "only of one passage remarkable: that the French King "should have said that he never did beleeve that the "Czar of Muscovy wes in Holland till that he heard that "the King of Ingland had payed him a visite, and then "he made no furder doubt of it,—which is the first time "that ever he wes heard name the P[rince] of O[range] "King. It is said that the Czar is to have 500 officers "from the K[ing] of Great Brittain, and that he is not "to come to London. The King had him at dinner, and "with quhich the Czar wes so well pleased as to the "customee, maners, and service at the King's table that "he invited himselfe again to dine with the King which "was very well takone."

MISCELLANEOUS PAPERS.

39. Copy inquest made at Langton in presence of John Cokburne of Chapelclench, and Adam Anderson in Langformacus, sheriffs-depute of Berwick, of the value of the lands of the barons and free-tenants temporal, held of her Majesty the Queen and situated in the aforesaid shire. Dated 26th February 1554.

40. Petition to the Lord Protector entitled "Ane "trew schedull of the past of the long and great suf- "ferings of the bordering shyre of Berwick." [No date, but written during the Protectorate, and after 1653.]

The complaint bears that the shire had been maintaining all its former imports notwithstanding the loss of Berwick, and the lands of the Earl of March in East Lothian; and that the sufferings of the county during the late troubles had been singular. It had long been the centre of war; the whole Scots armies had been there many days during 1639 and 1640, and extreme impoverishment had followed their entertainment; while this was made worse by the destruction of the corns, wood, etc. Likewise, their sufferings had been great by reason of the army raised towards the close of 1643 having been quartered there during the greater part of the winter, and they had also suffered from the levy of 1644 under the Earl of Callendar. In 1648 they had suffered long and heavily from the English army, from the broken condition of the Scots army, and from the garrisons at Berwick and Home Castle; and lastly, they had suffered from the entry of the English army in 1650-1, till it was restrained by the care of the officers. Also, the late pretended roll of valuations could never be respected, in that shire at least, for several reasons, which are given at length in the petition.

41. Draft copy petition by Sir John Home of Renton to King Charles II., sent to [very probably the Earl of Lauderdale]. Sir John Home narrates that for his loyalty to the King, during the years 1639-1641, by commission from the committee that had assumed the government, his rents had been uplifted, his house, plundered, his plantings and woods cut down and sold, and his whole stock disposed of, to the value of 8,000l. He was banished with his wife and many young children and rendered destitute; he was obliged to leave the country or starve; and during this time he had burdened his estate to the amount of 1,500l., chiefly spent in his Majesty's service. In 1648-1651 he had lost, by the English, corn, stock, household stuff, &c., to the sum of 4,000l. Petitions his Majesty to reimburse him of all his losses, according to his Majesty's proclamation of 1638.

42. Paper, 7 pages folio, entitled "Answeris for the "crafts of Edinburgh to the paper entituled The Petitione "of the provest, baillies, and councell of Edinburgh." This petition had accused the crafts of being seditious.

43. "Memorial for lybelling a summons or precept "at the instance of Sir Robert Home of Renton, Baronet,

4 N

MISS M. B.
STIRLING. " against Captain Christopher Pomphray of Berrie-
" haughs and his tennants and cottars." January 24th,
1721.

Narrates that an assault had been made on Sir Robert's
attorneys while attempting to collect the old custom
of the office of Forestry. The curious perquisite was,
one wood or reek hen out of each dwelling-house that
kindled fire and had reek within the barony of Coldingham, and particularly of nine reek hens yearly out of
the lands and estate of Berriehaughs. Captain Pomphray armed himself against the collectors of the obnoxious tax with " swords, pistols, guns, ... and
" did in a masterfull and outragious way obstruct, &c."
the pursuer and his officers.

WILLIAM FRASER.

Edinburgh, 32, Castle Street,
23rd July 1874.

MR. AND
MRS.
MAXWELL
WITHAM. The MANUSCRIPTS of MRS. DOROTHY MARY MAXWELL
WITHAM of KIRKCONNELL, and her husband,
ROBERT MAXWELL WITHAM, ESQUIRE.

The family of Maxwell of Kirkconnell is very ancient,
and traces its origin to Aymer de Maxwell, second son
of Sir Herbert Maxwell of Maxwell and Carlaverock,
and brother of Sir Herbert Maxwell, first Lord Maxwell
and ancestor of the long line of peers now represented
by the Lord Herries. The estate of Kirkconnell, in the
Stewartry of Kirkcudbright (not to be confounded with
the former parish of that name in the Stewartry of
Annandale, immortalized by the pathetic story of fair
Ellen Irving of " Kirkconnell Lee "), came into the
possession of this younger branch of the Maxwells by
the marriage of the Aymer de Maxwell just mentioned
to Janet of Kirkconnell of that ilk, the representative
of an ancient family which is supposed to have owned
that estate from about the middle of the eleventh
century. The date of this marriage cannot be definitely
ascertained : but Aymer de Maxwell and Janet his
spouse obtained from King James the Second a charter
of the lands of Kirkconnell on the 20th March 1456;
and it is probable that the event took place about the
year 1430. The family of Kirkconnell was unfailing in
its support of the parent Maxwells, Lords Maxwell and
Earls of Nithsdale, and was engaged in many of the
bloody border feuds. During the four centuries of
possession of these lands by the family of Maxwell, of
Kirkconnell, in direct descent from Aymer its founder,
several of its representatives and cadets attained distinction, not only in the military sphere, but in the more
peaceable pursuits of literature and science. A prominent cadet of this house was William Maxwell, a
younger son of the Laird of Kirkconnell, who, after
serving in the household of Mary of Guise, joined a Scottish regiment in the service of the French King. His
grandson, James Maxwell, M.A., wrote an autobiography,
and several works on religion and the history of the
Church. A distinguished member of this house in
modern times was James Maxwell, who was infefted in
the lands of Kirkconnell in 1734. Like many others of
the same family which remained steadfast, not without
much persecution, to the Catholic Church, he received
his education at the College of Douay, and as a confidential officer of Prince Charles, took part in the insurrection
of 1745. After the battle of Culloden he escaped to
France, and in the interval which elapsed previous to his
return to Scotland in 1750 he composed a " Narrative of
" Charles Prince of Wales' Expedition to Scotland in
" the Year 1745," which possesses not only historical
value as a record of the observations of one who knew
intimately the secret workings of the Pretender's Council, and the military events of the period, but the additional interest of being composed with " a remarkable
" degree of precision and taste." This treatise was
published by the Maitland Club in 1841. His second
son, William Maxwell (born in 1760), while studying in
the medical schools of France, came under the influence
of the revolutionary ideas then current in that country,
and, as one of the National Guards, attended in arms
at the execution of Louis XVI. in 1793. It is related of
him that he dipped his handkerchief in the blood of the
executed king; and his impulsiveness gained him the
appellation of " Dagger Maxwell." On his return to
Scotland he settled in Dumfries, and in the peaceful
profession of physician attained a very high reputation
in his native country. He was the friend of Robert
Burns, the Scottish poet, and attended him with
peculiar care during his last illness at Dumfries. After
the poet's death he exerted himself with the utmost

zeal to excite sympathy in the public mind for his
destitute widow and children. He died at Edinburgh
in 1834. The last male representative of the name and
family of Maxwell was James Maxwell, who died in
1827, and whose only child and heiress, Dorothy Mary
Maxwell, married in 1844 her cousin Robert Shawe
James Witham, now called Robert Maxwell Witham
of Kirkconnell, eldest surviving son of William Witham
of Gray's Inn, London.

For further particulars as to this family I would refer
to " The Book of Carlaverock, vol. i. pp. 600, 601,
(Edinburgh, 1873), where a complete pedigree is given,
with notices of the more important individuals.

From the present report a few of the documents
which might have been worthy of a place were omitted,
as they have already been published by me in " The
" Book of Carlaverock," vol. ii., pp. 431, 434, 435.

On the 11th July 1448, a notarial instrument of perambulation of the marches of Lesser Aird, Greater
Aird, and Kirkconnell, as fixed by an assize before
Alexander Mur, the justiciar of Annandale, was obtained
by William Abbot of Sweetheart and Amer de Maxwell
of Kirkconnell ; the assize consisting of 21 " good and
" true men," among whom are two Gledstanis. In 1456
King James the second granted the charter of the lands
of Kirkconnell already referred to; and an instrument
of sasine, of the 13th November 1461, narrates that the
same Amer de Maxwell, founder of this line, had
disposed of the lands of Keltown, in the shire of Dumfries, to George Nelsoun of Maidenpap. The only interest that attaches to this last writ arises from the
presence of certain names as attesting witnesses :—John
Panter, who appears as burgess of Dumfries, although
we know this family to have been connected with Forfarshire, and the two thoroughly Celtic names of
McIlauch, and McMolane,considered respectable enough
burgesses, even at this early period, to find a place in
the same parchment with the Lord Maxwell. There
are other writs of this comparatively early period, but
none of them possess any historical interest.

The present report contains notices of, I. A collection
of letters from royal and noble personages; II. A
manuscript volume of King James the Second, certified
by Queen Mary of Modena in 1702; and, III. Two
registers of the Scots College of Douay.

None of these papers have any direct connection
with the family of Kirkconnell, and have been acquired
by purchase or otherwise. Special interest attaches
itself to the authentic original of the Douay Register,
and to its little companion based on it and containing
additions. It is to be hoped that some day the former
may find some patron generous enough to lay its entire
and valuable details before the public. It might also
be well if the interesting, though less valuable, volume
of King James the Second were made public in its
entirety.

I.—Collection of Letters from Royal and Noble Personages.

1. Letter of King Henry VIII. of England, indorsed
as follows :—" To the right excellent, right highe and
" mightie prynce, our most derest brother and nephew
" the King of Scottis."

"Right excellent, right high and mighty prince,
our most dereste brother and nephieu, we recommende vs
vnto youe in our most hertie and affectuous maner (by
this berer your familyar seruitour Dauid Wood) we
haue not only receyued your most louing and kinde
lres declaring howmoche ye tendre and regarde the
conseruation and mayntenance of good amytie betwene
vs roted and grounded as well in proximitie of blood
(as in the good offices, actes, and doyngis showed on
our partie) whiche ye to our greate comforte affirme
and confesso to be dayllly more and more in your consideracion and remembraunce (but also two caste of faire
and good haukes whiche presented in your name and
sent from youe) we take in most thankfull parte, and
gyve vnto youe our most hertie thankis for the same.
Taking greate comforte and consolacion to perceyve
and vndrestande by your said lres and the credence
committed to your said familiar seruitour Dauid Wood
(which we haue redde and considered) and also send
vnto youe with thise our lres answer vnto the same
(that ye like a good and vertnous prince) haue so moche
to herte and mynde the good rule and ordre vppon the
borders, with redresse and reformacion of suche at-
temptatis as haue ben commytted and don in the
same. Not doubting but if ye for your partie as we
intende for our (doo effectually persiste and contynue
in so good and vertuouse purpose and intente) not only

our realmes and subgiettis shall lyve quyetly and peasably without occasion of breche, but also we their heddes and gouernours shall soo encrease and augment our syncere love and affeccion (as it shalbe to the indissoluble assuraunce of good peax and amytie to the inestimable benefite, wealth, and comoditie of vs, our realmes and subgiettis hereafter).

"Right excellent, right high and mightie prynce, our most dereste brother and nephieu, the blessed Trynytie haue you in his gouernaunce. Geven vnder our signet at Yorke Place besides Westmester the xith day of Decembre.

"Your lovying brother and vncle,
"HENRY R."

[The signature is King Henry's.]

2. "Answers made by the Kingis highnes to suche articles of credence as were exhibite in writing from his derest brother and good nephiew the King of Scottis by his famylier seruant Dauid Wodd."

This paper, which occupies 3½ pages folio, is signed "Henry R." It is apparently the paper mentioned *supra* in the King's letter.

In answer to the first three articles of the proposal of King James V. communicated by David Wood, King Henry states his readiness to have the "mysorders" of the borders removed, and that he, to "thintent that "the trouthe may be knowen whither any suche enor-"mytics haue ben committed on this side as in the "said articles of credence be alleged," had charged the wardens of his borders upon "a day of true" when they should examine the troubles and take measures accordingly; and prays the king of Scotland to give a similar charge to his wardens.

In answer to the fourth article, which had expressed King James's hope for the "conseruacion of the peax," and fear least some sinister report should deprive him of King Henry's trust, the King of England declares himself to be "a prince of most franke (syncere) "and playne dealing, and without colour, compasse, "or pretence," who esteemed all other princes to be the same, above all his "derest brother and "nephew," &c.

In answer to the last article, in which King James purposes sending particulars concerning "certayn ovirtures" of marriage made to him "as wel on the "Frenche Kingis as also on thempers behalfe" in order to obtain Henry's advice, the English King expresses his readiness to give such counsel "as he shall "thinke most highly to conduce to the honour, suretie, "and commoditie, of his said good brother's persoun, "and the wealtho and benefite also of that his realme."

3. Eighteen Articles of Instruction to the Postulate of Ross, Scottish Ambassador to France, under the signature of the Earl of Arran, "James G."—James Governor of Scotland. The paper is indorsed "Arti-"culis to the postulat Ros, ambassadour towart "Fraunce," and under this, in a different hand, is added "resavit in Parise the xxvij day of Maii 1547." The ambassador was David Pantar, then bishop-elect of Ross, and for years the representative of Scotland at the Court of France.

The first "article" lays a basis for the others. The most Christian King is desired to keep the "article of "comprehensioun of our souerane lady her realme and "subiectis contenit in the last treate of peax takin "betuix ye maist cristin Kingis fader [Francis I.] ", . . . & ye King of Ingland that last decessit "[Henry VIII.]," so that Scotland might "brouk" a perfect peace with England similar to that possessed by France.

The subsequent "articles" narrate various violations of the "comprehensioun" on the part of England, in particular the capture of the Johnstouns by an English force, and the seizure of Lord Maxwell's House of Langhop, afterwards occupied by a garrison of English, and the starting-point of daily incursions which the Governor and Council predict in "proces of tyme sall "grow to plane conquest." In the event of a treaty not being agreed upon by France and England, France is desired to send money and arms to Scotland; and, should the French King decide to land an army in England, the Scottish forces would co-operate from the North. King Henry is also desired to secure the favour of Denmark and the Emperor.

The last "item" brings forward a common Catholic allegiance as a bond of union between France and England. The ambassador is desired to show the King that the absolution sent by Francis I., his father, to the "slayaris" of Cardinal Betun was insufficient, and to

desire him to send to the Pope for a wider absolution "conforme to this memoriall."

4. Letter in French dated "Paris ce vij^e Auril 1587," shortly after the execution of Mary Queen of Scots, written by Ja. Archeuesque de Glasgo [James Bethune, then ambassador from Scotland at the Court of France], and the rest of the Council established for the administration of her dowry in France. Addressed "Au Roy "Descosse" [James VI]. The execution of Mary is spoken of as a deed "inhuman et detestable," worthy of the vengeance of God, and which had touched the hearts of all good Frenchmen, so that tears and regrets were universal. Part of the Queen's dowry yet remained, which might be applied to the clearance of her debts in France and England; and in this matter they waited upon the pleasure of the King.

5. Letter of date 22 September 1615, to King James I. by Lord Nor . . . , on the assault which he states Lord Willoughby made on him in a church or churchyard. It is gallant, vigorous, and well-written.

6. Receipt, dated at Leith, 29 September 1655, by Geo. Bilton, acknowledging the payment of 300l. sterling, the second moiety of a fine of 600l. imposed by the Protector on Lord Duffus. The original fine was 1,500l., but by an ordinance of 6th April 1655, by which many fines were suspended, that of Lord Duffus was reduced. The receipt is a printed form.

7. Letter, dated Edinburgh 14 May 1661, from Sir William, shortly afterwards Lord Bellenden, to a "noble "Lord." It principally relates to the action of the Lords and Parliament. ". . . . If those now in com-"petition with me have performed equally that duetie "that all of ws pettie officers of State ought to his "Majestie, I leave your Lordship to judge . . . . . "I shall patientlie suffer my confynement till his "Majestyes pleasour be knowin, being necessitat not "to appear in Parliament or at the Articles butt with "losse of my honour which is no less dear to me then "it ought to be, and I hope will admit of something "of tendernes in your consideration. Yesterday ther "was ane new Act brought in to the Parliament after "the accustomed maner, by surpryze . . . . At "present it seemes that that precious clerk, who "assumes to himself the glory of all the great things "done for his Majestie, is never satisfyed but in "taynting the honor of his conntrie without exception : "and when he is pleased to extend himselff on that "subject, nothing butt gall and wornwood is destilled "from his pen . . . . Some have not obtayning a "present positive answer from my Lord Treasurer for "passing of ther grants in the Exchequer are resolved "to pass them in Parliament. Why such voluntarie "Acts from the King should be made bynding to his "Majestyes prejudice, or to speak it more plainely to "the absolut ruin of his Majesties Revenues, I nather "doe nor can be brought to understand. What his "Majesty hath given more then what he had to give, "will be clearlie represented after the sitting of the "Exchequer ather by Earle Crawfurd or myself."

8. Letter from the Earl of Linlithgow to a Lord, whose name is not mentioned, dated Linlithgow, May 7th 1664, states that Mr. Robert Fleiming, a "fanatick" minister, had sailed that day for Rotterdam with consolatory letters and money (the collections had been not inconsiderable) for the banished ministers in Holland, from which his lordship feared that disturbances might arise to the "peace of this kirk and kingdome." It is suggested that Sir William Davidson or his deputes should be ordered to secure and search the ship on her arrival at Rotterdam, or, if Fleiming had gone to land before his lordship's order arrived, that a watchful eye should be kept upon him.

9. Letter written from Lerwick, 2nd December, by Col. William Sinclair to the "Earl of Lauderdaill, his "Majesties Cheiff Secretarie of Steat for the kingdome "of Scotland." Complaining of abuses done in Shetland, and mainly of the abuse done to the King himself in the wrecking of a richly laden vessel named the Carmerland, that had been cast away near Lerwick the winter before he came, out of which, as he had been credibly informed, 24 bags of gold had been taken, each of which contained 1,800 ducats, besides other valuables. The prize was to be sent to Leith. The letter is indorsed 1665.

10. The Earl of Caithness writes from Edinburgh, October 23, 1668, to the Earl of Lauderdale, concerning the "mutuall persuts betwixt the shyre of Caithness "and Sutherland :" complaining of groundless calumnies vented against himself and the shire of Caithness; and enclosing a "remitione" which he wishes passed, hoping

that then his difficulties may be removed. On the back is the date 1668.

11. Letter from Henry Welkie, Dortreck [Dort] $\frac{14}{24}$ August 1668, to [the Earl of Lauderdale]. Narrating that the conservitour and commissioners from the burghs of Scotland, observing that the trade of Scotland had removed from Zeeland and Flanders to the province of Holland, had fixed on Dort as a fitting place for the staple, and were then discussing the several articles with the magistrates of that city.

12. A. Ramsay, provost of Edinburgh, writes from this city to the Earl of Lauderdale concerning their former privileges with France, on the 8th January 1669, at the request of the merchants there, to the end that by his lordship's mediation the heavy impost of 50 " solz " per ton might be removed, now that a treaty of commerce was being made between that country and England.

13. Sir Alexander Fraser, physician to King Charles II., writes as follows to the Lord High Commissioner of Scotland, from " Whythall," 23 July [16]70 :—

" May it please your G[race]. This place affords " no newes. The best and I am sure the most well- " come to your Grace and kingdom, is the recovery " of his R.H. Feauer, coughe, and all other symptomes " are evanished, good appetit to his meat, longs to " hunt, abhominats all noxious temptations and *im-* " *pedimenta sanitatis.* The Duk of Bugingham, with " the Lord Buckurst, Sir Ch. Sidly, Mr. Stanly, James " Porter, and 4 seruants sets out Moonday at night, " without traine, coach, or any thing of greatnes : his " aboad fortnight only. They discourse variously of " his journy, and because I know not, I will say " nothing of it. His Ma. in good health : dined this " day at Sir Tho. Ingrams. Hunts Monday. All are " going to their country houses. The exchequer shoot " up for a month. I hope by the next to hear of your " G[race's] seaff arrivall and of all your company. " And so, with the tender of my duty to your G. and " all the noble company, I remeane

" Your G.—— most humble obedient servant,
" S. A. FRASER."

14. Paris, 3 April 1661. Andrew Lord Rutherford [here " Roterfoort "], afterwards killed in Africa, to Lord ——— : writes—" We are informed that all the " cloathing or other merchandise bocht heir for our " King's coronation doe pay great customes in France, " and are confisqueit in England." He is trying to " get some thing past at an easie rate " for his corre- " spondent. " I will be forced to ruin your Lordship " with two laced bands. For boottops, you may carry " as the mode is heir, woven of whyt silk with whyt " silk stockins, and a ruban past round about them. " This is the great mode heir which cometh from " England."

15. Edinburgh, 7 September 1661. Earl of Glencairn and Sir John Gilmour to [the Earl of Lauderdale], on a vacancy on the bench.

16. Kellie, 14 October 1661. The Earl of Kellie to Lord ———. Had been during the previous week sworn a member of the Secret Council. The Earl of Tweed- dale's enlargement had been discussed for two days : it had been pressed by the Earl of Rothes, and opposed by " very considerable persons in the Counsel."

17. Dublin, 2 December 1663. Sir Arthur Forbess to the Earl of Lauderdale.

18. Edinburgh, 2 February 1664. Sir Archibald Primrose to Lord ———, with the Acts of the Scotch Parliament.

19. Edinburgh, September 17, 1664. Sir John Gilmour to Lord ———, recommending Mr. John Lockhart for the vacancy in the Session.

20. 17 February 1667. The English Commissioners of Trade to the Scotch Commissioners, requesting a list of the names, burdens, and ports of all prize ships and foreign-built ships belonging to Scotland; also a list of their own Scottish-built ships.

21. Edinburgh, 6 May 1669. General Robert Mont- gomery to the Earl of Lauderdale, concerning his pension.

22. Edinburgh, 1 July 1669. Mr. Thomas Hay to Lord ———.

23. July 31 (no year), John Lord Rothes to ———.

24. Leith, 11 September (no year). Anne Countess of Balcarres to Lord ———.

II.—MS. Volume of King James the Second, certified by Queen Mary of Modena in 1702.

25. MS. copy of a work by King James II., post octavo size, bound in red morocco, entitled " A collec-

" tion of several of his late Maiesties papers of devotion, " copied exactly out of the original manuscripts left by " his Majesty in his own handwriting." The collec- tion embraces 172 pages, and has the following certificate of authentication on the last page, holograph of Mary of Modena, widow of King James II. :—

" This is a trew copy of the original papers, which are now in my hands, and which, when the King my son and I make no mor use of them, are to be deposited in the Scotts' Colledge of Paris, ther to be preserved with the rest of the King of ever blessed memory his original papers, conforme to his Maiesty's intention.
" MARIA R.

" St. Germains, Jan. 27, 1702."

To this note of the widowed Queen is appended another, signed " L. Ineso " [Lewis Innes, her Majesty's almoner]. The note states " that three short papers " written in his said late Majesty of ever blessed " memory his own hand were added to the collection " of the originall papers and pasted to the last of " them by the Queen's order, at St. Germans, this " 5 December 1703, by me, L. Inese." These articles are not copied into this volume.

The volume also contains a table of contents, and to this Innes has added another note, specifying the con- tents of the three articles added on the 5th December 1703.

The articles in the entire volume are 35 in number. The last five are written in French; all the others are in English.

Most of the articles are of a devotional nature; a few are controversial, as those entitled " Advice to Con- " verts " and " Motives of Conversion." One paper of the former class (No. 17) entitled " Wishes to dy and to " be with Christ," appears to be the latest written by the King; it is dated July 31, 1700, only six weeks before his Majesty's decease. Another paper (No. 15) contains his " Distribution of time." He resolves to rise at seven in the morning, or half an hour later, and never to be more than eight hours in bed. In a special prayer composed by himself he prays that the Prince of Orange " may repent his past life." He praises the Trappists in various articles; traces his conversion to his first visit to them, and in a special paper (No. 12) on the edification, &c. he had received at La Trappe, he speaks of his visits to that monastery as a necessity for his spiritual life.

Innes's description of the papers added by him in 1703 to the original collection is as follows :—

" The 1st paper is the beginning of the project of a letter designed for the Pr*** of Den.

" The 2d is the project of a letter from one English Catholic to another upon the publication of his Majesties Declaration for liberty of Conscience.

" The 3 discourses of the danger of being praised even by good men, and tho' what is said of us be true."

[It is probable that this copy of " the Collection, &c." of King James II. is unique. If the original was transmitted, as Mary of Modena's note would lead us to expect, to the Scots College at Paris, it is un- doubtedly lost. The fate of the MSS. of James placed in that institution is given in the prefatory notice to the " Memoires de Jacques II.," published at Paris in 1824. During the ravages of the French Revolution they were transferred to St. Omer as a temporary resting-place before their final removal to England; but through fear of their discovery, and apprehension of serious results therefrom to her husband, the wife of a Frenchman to whom they had been intrusted at first mutilated and afterwards destroyed them. If these papers, however, were not deposited in the Scots College, but retained in the family of Stuart, they may yet exist in the Stuart Papers removed from Rome in 1810 and placed in the library of Carlton House. These Stuart Papers are now at Windsor Castle.]

III.—Two Registers of the Scots College of Douay.

26. I. The first of these registers is a folio volume. It is known in the Kirkconnell Library as the " Larger " Register of Douay," to distinguish it from another register to be afterwards mentioned, which is called the " Smaller Register of Douay."

It contains,—

1. The names of the various alumni of the Scots College, which was successively established at Pont-à- Mousson, Douay, and Louvain, commencing with the entries of students under Father Creichton at Pont-à- Mousson in 1581, and continuing till the close of the year 1772. A short account is given of the character and fortune of each student. Each preceptor added in

his turn whatever news he heard of any former pupil of the college.

2. In addition to the lists of alumni, there are in the volume a number of unbound sheets of paper which contain various historical fragments by the early preceptors of the college, relating to the foundation and history of this institution, with accounts of its revenue and benefactors, and other matters historical and financial relative to the college.

The register is incomplete, as appears from the paging, which is not continuous.

II. In addition to the Douay register now mentioned, there is another volume of octavo size, called the "Smaller Douay Register," which contains a list of the alumni of the Scots College from the year 1581 to the year 1742. This list has been abstracted chronologically from the larger register, as is evidenced by the latter so far as it now exists. The names of the pupils show that they were connected with many distinguished Scotch families, and a number of them are extracted for this purpose. It is also remarkable that the first and second names at the beginning of the list are those of Bruce and Wallace, which may be considered as good Scottish names at the foundation of the Scots College at Pont-à-Mousson.

Of the number of students in the first list, from 1581 to 1592, fully one-half entered upon an ecclesiastical life; a majority remained upon the Continent, not a few having, subsequently to leaving Pont-à-Mousson, entered the Society of Jesus; a large number, however, returned to Scotland, and became, to use the expression of the register, "boni operarii." The fate of several is not recorded, probably because unknown to the writer. We may therefore suppose that these did not adopt a clerical life. Seven became teachers in colleges and elsewhere; two followed the profession of law; one became a physician, and another a merchant; two, Robert Bruce and James Leslie, followed the life of the Court; James Myrton, "aliquamdin bonus operarius, post lapsum in Angliam ivit," and was living there in 1598. Two are mentioned as having married. The Bruce and Wallace names are thus entered :—

1581. Guilielmus Bruce nepos magistri Henrici Keir
1581 : Professor legum in Germania.
1581. Mr. Guilielmus Vallace Edinburgensis magister Creytton a Lugtoun est nunc monachus in prouincia Limonicensi, factus sacerdos Mussipontani.

The second list is thus headed :—"Alumni Scoti Duacenees à 1593 et Lovanienses à 1595 ab eodem P. Gul'. Creytton descripti Julio 1598 dum seminarii curam deponeret."

The first entry here (of 1593) is :—

Mr. David Law ex Calviniano Catholicus factus ad seminarium, Mussiponti admissus et iterum Duaci unde sacerdos missus 1594 ad missionem Scoticam, in itinere ab Anglis captus, post incarcerationis annum cum dimidio, rediit Lovanium ut inde Romam iret ad societatem, sed remissus fuit mense Junii 1598 ad missionem Scoticam ad experimentum antequam reciperetur in societatem.

The second entry is Mr. Wm. Barclay, lawful son of the Laird de Tolye, who also studied successively at the three universities of Mussipontum, Douay, and Louvain, and having completed theology (absoluta theologia) was sent to Paris in June 1598, where he became professor of humanity.

Some of the residents at Douay boarded at their own expense; of others (and this is a more frequent notice) it is mentioned that after a long term at Douay or Louvain they withdrew to another field, in order to relieve the former seminary of the burden of their maintenance. In this list, and among those who maintained themselves, are found two names of scions of the noble Scotch families of Huntly and Angus :—

1594. Gulielmus Gordon, frater Comitis Huntlaei vixit in seminario sub legibus seminarii sed propriis expensis factus Franciscanus non perseveravit. Gulielmus Gordon parvulus puer precedentis famulus dimissus est post annum cum dimidio, pro seminario non aptus.

1596. Franciscus Douglas frater Comitis Angusiani in Seminario Lovaniensi suis expensis vivens, ex calviniano factus est catholicus, ivit Romam ubi philosophiam absolvit hoc anno 1598.

A large number of the entries here are of Protestants (Calviniani) who had ibecome Catholics. Some of them are spoken of as "vir maturi." Nor were all Catholics when they entered the college, as the following shows :—

Mr. Alex' Seton Calvinianus juvenis modestus et boni ingenii. Agitur de ejus conversione de qua est bona spes.

Robert Strachan, another "Calvinianus," was admitted the same year confessedly "pro tentanda ejus conversione."

The next division embraces a few names of pupils under the "procuratorship" of George Elphingston, from 1598 to 1603. Among other names we have Andrew Crichton, who having become a secular priest in Scotland was seized in August 1610, "et patrem Patri-" cium Andersonum prodere voluit."

T next division is thus headed :—Joannes Libion suscipiens 1° April 1606, vicariam curam seminarii Scotorum Lovaniensis ex mandato R. P. Gulielmi Veranneman Rectoris collegii Societatis invenit in Seminario sequentes alumnos. Cetori 23 admissi fuerunt tempore Joannis Libion a 1mo Aprilis 1606 usque 15 Xbris 1608.

The first entry is a comparatively long one concerning Mr. Rogerius Lyndesius, son of the Baron of Mains, who became an active member of the Scottish Mission, and died in 1666 "in opinione Sanctitatis." He was seized in Scotland in 1610, and "confessed much con-" cerning Father Patrick Anderson."

There are four of the name of Macbrec: Patrick, Alexander, James, who suffered imprisonment and was condemned to death in the time of Cromwell; and John, who entered in 1607 among the "figuristae," became noted in Germany, and was one of the deputies appointed to escort from France Maria Gonzaga, who was afterwards crowned Queen of Poland in July 1646. He is described as "magno in pretio habitus ab omnibus " aulicis ob ingenium vastum, omniumque linguarum " peritiam."

1612. William Christie laboured as a member of the Society in Austria for about 20 years. He was Rector of the Scottish Seminary at Rome for three years, and obtained a similar post at Douay in 1650.

1620. 15 May. Robert Maxwell (known at Douay as Jacobus Lindsayus), son of Maxwell, Laird of Conheeth, was dismissed in 1623. [A number are mentioned as having different names at Louvain. Some were dismissed on account of sickness; others, such as Gilbert Seton (entered 6 June 1620) "ob moras insolentes," and yet others because "inepti ad studia."]

Entries under Father Charles Malapert :—

1620, 31st Oct. Patrick Gray (there known as Forbes), 14 years of age, brother of Lord Gray. He died in Germany.

Henry Seton, natural brother of the Laird of Munie.
John Seton, brother of ditto. Died in misery at Paris.
Sebastian Carider, 16 years, son of Sir William Carider, long in the service of his most Catholic Majesty.

In 1626 some of the students died of the plague, and others were dismissed on this ground. Among the dry, curt notes we come upon such a kindly notice as this, "Rogerius angelice hic obiit peste."

1621. Edward Maxwell (there called Gramius), entered at 13, brother of Robert Maxwell above-mentioned.

From 1623, pupils admitted by Father Lambertus Lobetius :—

1625. John Seton, son of the Chamberlain of Fife; became Superior of the Scottish Seminary at Madrid.

1627, 7th October. Was entered Adam Gordon of Cult as a student of poetry. In 1631 he returned to Scotland, but in 1646 he crossed to Rome, and ultimately became Rector of Douay, April 1668.

On the same day entered David Abercromby of Petelpie as a student of composition. On account of his health he departed in June 1631. In 1640 he became tutor to the second son of the Earl of Winton, and some years later devoted himself to medicine in London.

Father James Bonfrerius succeeded Lobetius in September 1628.

28th July 1629. Frederick Maxwell, son of Lord Herries, who afterwards became a member of the Society, and died as Rector of the Scotch Seminary at Madrid in November 1632.

Bonfrerius was succeeded by Father Barnard Robinoy in October 1631.

Among others entered in 1632 was Alexander Maxwell, son of Lady Gribton, who about that time resided in Paris; and John Gordon, a nephew of the Baron of Cluny.

John Robæus first succeeded Robinoy in September 1632.

6 January 1633. Was entered Robert Francis Irainus of Aberdeen, 19 years of age. He became a presbyter of St. Bernard, and subsequently a Capuchin, and lived at Somerset House, London, till the death of the Queen in 1671.

Robæus died 13 March 1633, and was succeeded by Father Hypolitus Curiæus.

Father William Leslie succeeded as rector in 1634.

4 N 3

MR. AND
MRS.
MAXWELL
WITHAM.

29 October 1634. James Brown, son of John of Lochiel, entered at 15 years of age. Was at the college of the Jesuits in Paris in 1642. After teaching humanity, giving three courses in philosophy, and haranguing for a year, he returned to govern the college in June 1668.

After two other rectors, Thomas Robæus was called to govern the college, 26 September 1640.

15 October 1640. " Dñus Alexander Iruinus exul " jam a 16 annis è Scotiâ cum uxore Marioria Menzies ob " invictam in fide Catholica constantiam propter quam " in patria, ubi domus ejus semper habita est pro domo " Societatis, totidem ante exilium annis insudita passus " est, adhuc licet fundo satis opulentus bonis tamen " suis ob exilium et temporum angustias frui non " potest." Irvine brought his two sons to the college, Robert Francis and Alexander, the former of whom subsequently studied at Madrid and Rome.

10 September 1643. Walter Forbes, son of James Forbes of Blacktown and Magdalen Fraser, daughter of Sir Alex. Fraser of Philorth. His record is this : "uxorem duxit, et hæreticus factus est."

[There are other entries even more terse : e.q., "uxorem " duxit et obiit."]

His brother Arthur, 6 years younger and only 12, entered the same day.

2nd October. " Joannes de Burgen, 18 annos : filius " unicus illustris Domini Octaviani de Burgen Scoto- " flandri et dominæ de Zoninghem . . dimissus ut " lubricus et inconstans postquam jam 2ᵈᵉ aufugisset."

1644, 10 March. John Forbes, son of Duncan Forbes of Campbell [? Camphill], 17 years of age, afterwards studied a year at Madrid, and returning to Scotland reverted to the Protestant faith. " Est jam 1671, prætor " capitalis, permanetque singulario nostrorum et Ca- " tholicorum amicus."

On the 25th was entered James Forbes, son of John Forbes of Corsinday.

Father Robert Gall succeeded Robæus in September 1646.

1647, 17 January. John Ogilvie, 16 years, was a son of Sir John Ogilvie of Craig (son of James sixth Lord of Airly), who was imprisoned for his faith in Edinburgh Castle. He became a member of the Society, and died as a student at Douay.

James Iruinus, son of Sir Alex. Irvine of Drum.

1649, 28 April. Archibald and James Semple, brothers of Lord Semple. James afterwards went to Madrid.

James Douglas, son of Lord Mordington, 11 years of age.

Robert Gall was succeeded by Father William Christie in May 1650.

Gall died and was succeeded by Father James Anderson in May 1653.

Father William Christie succeeded Anderson in 1656.

1656. Alexander Iruinus, son of Alexander Irvine of Belty.

1657, 7th March. " Henricus Lindsaius, hic Andreas " Graius æt. 12, ad figuristas, filius unicus Comitis " Craufordiæ et Margaretæ Gramiæ Comitis Montethii " filiæ. Dimissus quia illegitimus." The college was not always so strict.

1657, 31 August. Francis Crichton, son of Viscount Frendraught. Became a soldier, leaving the college of his own accord.

1658. Robert Seton, younger son of the Earl of Winton. At his death in 1673 he left 30,000 merks Scots to the Scotch College of Douay.

1662. Robert Fordesius (Fordyce) who was twice rector of Douay, and was also procurator of the Mission at Paris.

1663. Alexander Irvine, son of Sir Alexander Irvine of Drum.

1665. James Sempil, son of Lord Sempil, 10 years of age.

1666. Christopher Iruin (19) left through sickness; afterwards sent to Rome by his father, Sir Christopher Iruin.

Father Adam Laurence Gordon succeeded Christie in March 1666.

1667. James Douglas, son of Lord Mordington, 16 years.

William his brother, 14 years.

Francis, 12 years.

Father James Brown succeeded Father Gordon in 1668.

1668. Herbert Maxwell, 15 years of age, son of Maxwell of Kirkconnell. " Egregius filius Societatis ultra 34 " annos : in aula Jacobi Regis missionarius."

1670. Robert Semple, eldest son of Lord Semple, 15 years of age.

1670. Thomas Preston, grandson of General Preston, Viscount Taragh in Ireland, &c. " Multum debet Col- " legio nec spes est solutionis."

1670. Sir Edward Widrington, 15 years, was drowned 7th April 1672.

Father Thomas Robæus succeeded Father Brown in 1671.

1672. William Skeen, son of the Baron of Skeen.

1675, 25 May. " Georgius Setonus primogenitus " Joannis Baronis de Garleton equitis aurati et Chris- " tinæ Hume filiæ Baronis de Renton, 10 annos. Parisiis " adductus a R. P. Alexandro Conæo."

Father G. Inglis succeeded Robæus in 1676.

Father Thomas Paterson succeeded Inglis in 1680.

1681. Charles Gordon, 11, and Patrick Gordon, 9, sons of Charles Lord Aboyne.

1685. William Hay, brother of Lord Kinnoul.

1685, " 18 Septembris. Alexander McKenzie, hic " White, filius et frater Comitis Seaforthii : postea fidem " deseruit factusque est colonellus pro rege Gulielmo " 3ᵉ."

1685. George Gordon, brother of Charles (see 1681), 10 years. Joined the Society.

John, his brother, 8 years.

1689. Adam Urquhart, son of Urquhart of Meldrum, and grandson of Lord Huntly. Entered the Society.

1689, 18 May. " Carolus Fleming, frater Comitis " Wigtonii [he was afterwards Earl]. Fidelis valde " religioni Catholicæ et regi suo semper perstitit."

1691. Frederick Howard, son of the Duke of Norfolk. Went to the English College at Andomar in 1693.

1691. James and William Maxwell, sons of James Maxwell of Kirkconnel.

1692. Thomas Drummond, son of the Duke of Melfort. William, his brother, 6 years, became Archpriest of St. Eustachius in Rome, and Canon of St. Paul's, Liege.

1693. John and Charles Drummond, 14 and 12 years, sons of Lord Perth.

1694. Andrew, son of Lord Melfort.

1694, 18 July. Robertus Dumbar. Rediit in Scotiam valetudinarius Septembris 2ᵉ 1699.

1695, 21 Januarii. Joannes Grant aliter Le Grand ex patre Petro Grant de Caron et — Dumbar. Sept- embri 1696 abiit ad tyrocinium Romanum.

1695, " 20 Septembris. Joannes Grant, 10 annis, ex " Joanne de Ballendalloch. 22 Novembris 1702 abiit " insalutato hospite."

1698, 18 Aprilis. " Georgius Seton, 12 annis, ex patre " Georgio de Garleton, post philosophiam in Scotiam " rediit."

1698. James Grierson, son of Sir Robert Grierson of Lag. He left on the 29th June 1700.

1700. Reginald and Philip, brothers of Thomas, William, and Andrew Drummond.

1714, July. " Andreas Seaton, 16 annos, frater Georgii " et Joannis ex Garleton : ivit in Hispaniam ubi factus " est miles."

1723, " 2 Novembris. Alexander Stanislaus Grant " desertis Benedictinis Scotis, Wirsburgensibus, et " Anglis, Parisiensibus, at tandem militia etiam Hol- " landia rediit ad monasterium suum Wirsburgense. " Hic per aliquot menses fuit antequam Benedictinus " fieret inter Anglos."

1732. Reginald McKenzie, son of the Marquis of Seaforth, 7 years of age.

Nicholas, his brother, entered in 1735.

1734. James Dalzell, 7 years, nephew of Lord Carn- wath.

The last entry in this book is that of John Nairne, 24 August 1742. The register occupies altogether 60 pages. The latter portion embraces fewer representa- tives of Scotch families ; the most frequent name in this part is that of Maxwell, which represents the families of Terraughty, Kirkconnell, Munches, Orchardtown, &c.

The list of names is continued in the larger register to the year 1772, but very few of the names recorded after the year at which the smaller record ends are Scotch.

WILLIAM FRASER.

Edinburgh, 32, Castle Street,
4th August 1874.

THE MANUSCRIPTS OF THE ROYAL BURGH OF PERTH.

In the very dawn of our national history we discover a community gathered together on the fertile and central banks of the Tay at Perth, which in later times, through royal favour and general policy, came to be endowed with the rights and franchises of a King's burgh.

Among the papers of the Corporation is a series of Royal Charters, which are recited and confirmed in a charter of King James VI. to the burgh, dated at Holyrood House, 15 November 1600.

The earliest of these, by King William the Lion, contained no words of incorporation, but conferred many exclusive privileges on the burgesses of Perth, which extended over the sheriffdom. A charter by King Robert I. conferred on the burgesses the rights of guildry and of merchandise in all places within the sheriffdom of Perth, with certain prohibitions and rights of pre-emption. Other charters confirming and amplifying the burghal privileges were granted by David II., Robert II., Robert III., James II., and James V.

The earliest volume of the Burgh Register contains the Acts of Council from 1543 to 1684. In it are copies of deeds and ordinances of various dates, some of which contain points of historical interest. Among these are "Discharge Robert Bruce of Clakmannan to the burgh " of Perth," "Remission to the burgh of Perth by " Laurance Lord Oliphant of Abirdalgie, Knight, for " the douno casting of the hous of Duplyne, and of the " spoilzeatioun of it and of Abirdalgie," "Remission " by King James V. to the town of Perth for burning " of the house of Craigie," "Decreit in favouris of the " burgh of Perth pronuncit be the borrowis for the " prioritie of place of Dundie," "Bakband be Elizabeth " Gray, Countes of Huntlie, with consent of Alexander " Erle of Huntlie, to the burgh of Perth, anent a li- " cence upon their comoun wallis in the Speygait," " Indentour of the bowt of Balhousie," " Indentour " betwix the hous of Ruthven, the Laird of Balhousie, " and the toune of Perth anent the uphaulding of Lowis " Wark," " Indentouris betwix the Aldermen, Counsall, " and Communitie of the burgh of Perth and Robert " Kinglassie, tuiching the gild herbar and the com- " moun calsayes."

There is also recorded in this volume a missive to the burgh of Perth from King James I. (superscribed Jacobus Scotorum Rex), announcing that he has, "thankit " be God, maid appoyntment of our delywerance with " the excellent King of Ingland, and for neidfull dis- " penss that we man mak on our passage, and for pay- " ment that we sould mak quhair we ar awand in " London, we have writtin to our aime of Albanie to " send us of our awin gudis to pay our debtis and mak " our costis as worschip weeld, and gif he help us not " as we haif prayed him and chargied, necessitie com- " pellis us to pray yow till help us with sum pairt of " dispenss at this tyme. Quhairfoir speciallie we pray " yow and requyris that ye gif us or len us a certain " portioun of your propir gudis as ye ar disposed. " Quhilk we sal gar be allowit to you in your earest " custome quhat euir it be, and send us this good with " ane honest burges of your awin, quhilk sall hawe saif " conduyeit as the berare of this lettres sall doe you " witt. To the quhilk ye give firme credence in oure " name, and gif ye can not find to refresh us in this " mister we doe you to witt that it is oure will, and we " chairge yow ye put no merchandise to the see that " aw us custom under all payne that may follow in tyme " to cum till ye hawe licence and commandement of us. " Wreitten at Londoun, the aught day of August, under " with the ring of the [ ]."

Obligation by James I., King of Scots, to relieve the four burghs of Edinburgh, Perth, Dundee, and Aberdeen of the sum of fifty thousand marks, for payment of which they had become bound to Henry King of England for the liberation of the said King James. Dated Durham, 26 March 1424.

In 1544 there is recorded a list of the ornaments of Our Lady Altar, within the parish kirk of the burgh :— " Imprimis, ane chesable of blak ueluet with the pe- " roris of blue ueluet, stole and fannoune of bird Alex- " ander. Alb, amyt, and belt. Ane chesable of auld " claitht of gold with the peroris, stole, and fannoune " of bird Alexander. Alb, amyt, and belt. Ane chesable " of grene dammess . . . . . samyn, parouris of burd " Alexander, and the belt, alb, and amit. Ane chesable " of . . . . Ane uthir auld chesable of quhite silk, and " the thrid chesable of auld . . . . Ane stole and fan- " none. Ane new pront mess buke, ane auld. Ane " buke of . . . . . mes buke of prent. Three pair of " towellis witht thre frontellis. Ane pend of . . . . with " ane frontell thairat of reid dammess. Ane pend of " pirne sating under the tabernakle . . . . . Three " coddis of auld pirne silk. Ane corporale with ane " cass ; four gret chandillaris for the precatis, and four " for the herss ; four precatis. Ane crewet. Ane pig for " wyne. [Ane hingand] chandillar of brass ; ane uthir " of trene work. Ane vaie pend at the alter. Ane " [siluer chandillar] gilt. Twa new torches and tua ald. " Ane spoon of siluer ; and . . . . chandillaris in Johne " Smetonis hand, as yit one deliuerit."

The poynt of precedency between the burghs of Perth and Dundee was long contested, and after appearing to be settled it was opened up again. In the volume now referred to, a decreet in favour of the claims of Perth is recorded, and in a later one is entered a missive from James VI., addressed to the Earl Marischal, on the same subject :—"We greit you weill. It is oure will, " and we command you, that ye place the commissioners " of our burgh of Perth in the secund place, and nixt " the commissioners of our braght of Edinburght the " haill tyme of this Parliament, and in tyme cuming " that thai may have the prioritie, first rank, place, " and wote, befor the commissionaris of Dundie, ac- " cording to thair . . . . . . and decreet of our haill " burrowis gewin thairanent, as ye will answer to us " [&c.]. Subscryuit with our hand at Holyrudhous, " the penult day of Maii 1594."

Minute of the Convention of Burghs held at Perth, 21 June 1582, settling the above question of priority in favour of Perth over Dundee, to which the signatures of all the commissioners are attached.

JOHN STUART.

CIRCULAR OF THE SECRETARY OF THE COMMISSION.

HISTORICAL MANUSCRIPTS COMMISSION.

Rolls House, Chancery Lane.

Her Majesty has been pleased to appoint under Her Sign Manual certain Commissioners to ascertain what MSS. are extant in the collections of private persons and in institutions, which are calculated to throw light upon subjects connected with the Civil, Ecclesiastical, Literary, or Scientific history of this country. A copy of the Commission is inclosed, which will best explain the object Her Majesty has in view.

The Commissioners think it probable that you may feel an interest in this object, and be willing to assist in the attainment of it, and with that view they desire me to lay before you an outline of the course which they propose to follow.

If any nobleman or gentleman express his willingness to submit any paper or collection of papers within his possession or power to the examination of the Commissioners, they will cause an inspection to be made by some competent person, upon the information derived from whom the Commissioners will make a private report to the owner on the general nature of the papers in his collection, such report will not be made public without the owner's consent, but a copy of it will be deposited and preserved in the Public Record Office, to which no person will be allowed to have access without the consent of the owner of the papers reported on.

Where the papers are not mere insulated documents, but form a collection which appears to be of Literary or Historical value, a chronological list or brief calendar will be drawn up, and a copy thereof presented to the owner, and to no other person without his consent, but the original of such calendar will be deposited for preservation in the Public Record Office, to which no person will be allowed to have access without the consent of the owner of such collection.

The Commissioners will also, if so requested, give their advice as to the best means of repairing and preserving any papers or MSS. which may be in a state of decay, and are of Historical or Literary value.

To avoid any possible apprehension that the examination of papers by the Commissioners may extend to or include any title deeds or legal documents, I have to call your attention to the fact that nothing of a private character or relating to the titles of existing owners is to be divulged, and to assure you that positive instructions will be given to every person who examines the MSS. that if in the course of his examination any title deeds or other documents of a private character chance to come before him, they are to be instantly put aside, and are not to be reported on or calendared under any pretence whatever.

The object of the Commission is solely the discovery of unknown Historical and Literary materials, and in all their proceedings the Commissioners will direct their attention to that object exclusively.

In no instance will any MSS. be removed from the owner's residence without his request or consent, but if for convenience any MSS. be intrusted to the Commissioners, they will be deposited in the Public Record Office, and be treated with the same care as if they formed part of the Public Muniments, and will be returned to the owner at any time specified by him.

The costs of inspections, reports, and calendars, and the conveyance of documents, will be defrayed at the public expense without any charge to owners.

The Commissioners will feel much obliged if you will communicate to them the names of any gentlemen who may be able and willing to assist in obtaining the objects for which this Commission has been issued.

I have the honour to be,
Your obedient servant,
JOHN ROMILLY,
Secretary.

LONDON:
Printed by GEORGE E. EYRE and WILLIAM SPOTTISWOODE
Printers to the Queen's most Excellent Majesty.
For Her Majesty's Stationery Office.

www.ingramcontent.com/pod-product-compliance
Lightning Source LLC
Chambersburg PA
CBHW021929110726
47901CB00003B/763